P9-APO-598

The Norton Anthology of World Masterpieces

FOURTH CONTINENTAL EDITION

VOLUME 2

P·489
P·653

Uniform with this volume,
and also under the General Editorship of
Maynard Mack

THE ONE-VOLUME EDITION OF

The Norton Anthology
of World Masterpieces

FOURTH CONTINENTAL EDITION

THE TWO-VOLUME EDITION OF

The Norton Anthology
of World Masterpieces

FOURTH EDITION

VOLUME 1

Literature of Western Culture through the Renaissance

VOLUME 2

Literature of Western Culture since the Renaissance

A COMPANION VOLUME

Masterpieces of the Orient
Edited by G. L. Anderson
Available in Enlarged and Shorter Editions

Gineura Saari
Fall '86

The Norton Anthology
of World Masterpieces

FOURTH CONTINENTAL EDITION

Maynard Mack, *General Editor*
Yale University

Bernard M. W. Knox
Center for Hellenic Studies

John C. McGalliard
The University of Iowa

P. M. Pasinetti
University of California, Los Angeles

Howard E. Hugo
Late of the University of California, Berkeley

René Wellek
Yale University

Kenneth Douglas
Late of Yale University

Sarah Lawall
University of Massachusetts, Amherst

VOLUME 2
Literature of Western Culture since the Renaissance

W·W· NORTON & COMPANY· NEW YORK · LONDON

Copyright © 1980, 1979, 1974, 1966, 1965, 1962, 1956 by W. W. Norton & Company, Inc. Printed in the United States of America.

All Rights Reserved

BOOK DESIGN BY JOHN WOODLOCK

Since this page cannot legibly accommodate all the copyright notices, pages 1635 and 1636 constitute an extension of the copyright page.

Library of Congress Cataloging in Publication Data

Mack, Maynard, 1909–   ed.
  The Norton anthology of world masterpieces: Fourth continental edition.

  Third ed. published in 1974 under title: The continental edition of world masterpieces.
  Includes index.
  CONTENTS: v.1. Continental literature through the Renaissance.—v.2. Continental literature since the Renaissance.
    1. Literature—Translations into English.
    2. English literature—Translations from foreign languages. I. Title.
PN6019.M2 1980b   808.8   79–23506

ISBN 0-393-95090-5

4 5 6 7 8 9 0

Contents

PREFACE TO THE FOURTH EDITION   xi

Masterpieces of Neoclassicism

INTRODUCTION   1

LIVES, WRITINGS, AND CRITICISM   15

JEAN-BAPTISTE POQUELIN MOLIÈRE
(1622–1673)
     Tartuffe, or The Imposter   19

JEAN RACINE (1639–1699)
     Phaedra   80

FRANÇOIS, DUC DE LA ROCHEFOUCAULD
(1613–1680)
     Maxims   124

JEAN DE LA FONTAINE (1621–1695)
     Fables   128

FRANÇOIS-MARIE AROUET DE VOLTAIRE
(1694–1778)
     Candide, or Optimism   133

DENIS DIDEROT (1713–1784)
     Rameau's Nephew   210

Masterpieces of Romanticism

INTRODUCTION   239

LIVES, WRITINGS, AND CRITICISM   266

JEAN-JACQUES ROUSSEAU (1712–1778)
  Confessions   273

JOHANN WOLFGANG VON GOETHE
  (1749–1832)
    Faust
      Prologue in Heaven   283
      The First Part of the Tragedy   286

FRANÇOIS RENÉ DE CHATEAUBRIAND
  (1768–1848)
    René   371

ERNST THEODOR AMADEUS HOFFMANN
  (1776–1822)
    A New Year's Eve Adventure   393

HEINRICH HEINE (1797–1856)
  The Rose, the Lily, the Sun, and the Dove   416
  A Spruce Is Standing Lonely   417
  A Young Man Loves a Maiden   417
  Loreley   417
  My Beauty, My Love, You Have Bound Me   418
  The Silesian Weavers   418
  The Asra   419
  Babylonian Sorrows   420
  How Slowly Time, the Loathsome Snail   421
  The Migratory Rats   421
  At Parting   423
  Morphine   423

ALEXANDER SERGEYEVICH PUSHKIN
  (1799–1837)
    Eugene Onegin
      Canto I   424
      Canto II   444

VICTOR-MARIE HUGO (1802–1885)
  Reverie   459
  Tomorrow, at Daybreak   460
  Memory of the Night of the Fourth   460
  Et nox facta est   462
  Sowing Season. Evening   468

GEORG BÜCHNER (1813–1837)
Woyzeck   469

MIKHAIL YURIEVICH LERMONTOV
(1814–1841)
Princess Mary   492

Masterpieces of Nineteenth-Century Realism and Naturalism

INTRODUCTION   557

LIVES, WRITINGS, AND CRITICISM   587

GUSTAVE FLAUBERT (1821–1880)
Madame Bovary   591

FYODOR DOSTOEVSKY (1821–1881)
Notes from Underground   846

LEO TOLSTOY (1828–1910)
The Death of Iván Ilyich   934

HENRIK IBSEN (1828–1906)
Hedda Gabler   981

ANTON CHEKHOV (1860–1904)
The Cherry Orchard   1042

Masterpieces of the Modern Age

INTRODUCTION   1089

LIVES, WRITINGS, AND CRITICISM   1135

CHARLES BAUDELAIRE (1821–1867)
Flowers of Evil
Correspondences   1151
Former Life   1151
Beauty   1152
Jewels   1152
Her Hair   1153
I Adore You as Much . . .   1154
Invitation to the Voyage   1154
Song of Autumn I   1156
Heautontimoroumenos   1156
Spleen ("Old Pluvius, month of rains")   1157

Spleen ("I have more memories") 1157
Spleen ("I'm like the king of a rain-country") 1158
Spleen ("When the low heavy sky weighs like a lid") 1159
To a Passer-By 1159
Meditation 1160
Paris Spleen
The Stranger 1160
The Double Room 1161
The Bad Glazier 1162
L'Invitation au voyage 1164
Windows 1166

STÉPHANE MALLARMÉ (1842–1898)
Tired of the Bitter Repose 1167
Sea Breeze 1167
Another Fan 1168
The Afternoon of a Faun: Eclogue 1169
Saint 1172
Sonnet ("This virgin, beautiful and lively day") 1173
The Tomb of Edgar Poe 1173
The Tomb of Edgar Poe (transl. by Mallarmé) 1174
All the Soul Indrawn . . . 1174
A Lace Curtain . . . 1175

ARTHUR RIMBAUD (1854–1891)
The Seekers of Lice 1176
Les chercheuses de poux 1176
Lice-Hunters (transl. by Ezra Pound) 1177
The Lice-Hunters (transl. by Robert Lowell) 1178
The Drunken Boat 1178
A Season in Hell
Night of Hell 1182
Morning 1184
Farewell 1184
The Illuminations
III. Tale 1186
XI. Morning of Drunkenness 1187
XIV. The Bridges 1187
XXIII. Flowers 1188
XXV. Seascape 1188
XXIX. Barbarian 1188

AUGUST STRINDBERG (1849–1912)
The Ghost Sonata 1189

LUIGI PIRANDELLO (1867–1936)
Henry IV 1215

MARCEL PROUST (1871–1951)
Remembrance of Things Past
Swann's Way: Overture   1259

SIDONIE-GABRIELLE COLETTE (1873–1954)
The Cat   1302

THOMAS MANN (1875–1955)
Tonio Kröger   1371

RAINER MARIA RILKE (1875–1926)
Duino Elegy III   1417

FRANZ KAFKA (1883–1924)
The Metamorphosis   1422

ISAK DINESEN (1885–1962)
Sorrow-Acre   1462

ANNA AKHMATOVA (1889–1966)
Requiem   1488

ANDRÉ BRETON (1896–1966) and
PAUL ÉLUARD (1895–1952)
The Immaculate Conception
Intra-Uterine Life   1495

BERTOLT BRECHT (1898–1956)
Mother Courage and Her Children   1497

VLADIMIR NABOKOV (1899–1977)
Cloud, Castle, Lake   1556

BENJAMIN PÉRET (1899–1959)
A Life Full of Interest   1563

ISAAC BASHEVIS SINGER (1904–
The Gentleman from Cracow   1567

JEAN-PAUL SARTRE (1905–1980)
No Exit   1581

ALBERT CAMUS (1913–1960)
The Renegade   1614

A NOTE ON TRANSLATION   1627

COPYRIGHT NOTICES   1635

INDEX   1637

Preface to the Fourth Edition

The Continental Edition of *The Norton Anthology of World Masterpieces* is an anthology of Western literature containing only writings from the ancient and the modern foreign languages. It reaches in time from Homer and the Old Testament writers to Vladimir Nabokov and Isaac Singer, and the literatures represented in it include Greek, Latin, Hebrew, Gaelic, French, German, Italian, Spanish, Russian, Norwegian, Swedish, and Yiddish.

This fourth edition is, we think, the best to date. Notable additions to the selections from the ancient world, the middle ages, the romantics, and the moderns combine with the introduction of important new authors and several brilliant new translations to make the volumes now before you an immensely flexible, practical, and attractive instrument for teaching the literature of continental Europe.

Our representation of the twentieth century has been particularly enriched. In this edition no fewer than seven modern writers appear for the first time: Colette (a short novel); Isak Dinesen (a short story); Anna Akhmatova (a lyric sequence); André Breton and Paul Éluard (a collaborative surrealist prose poem); Vladimir Nabokov (a short story); and Benjamin Péret (a short story). The Romantic period has also been rethought, with the former scattering of lyric poems by diverse authors giving way to more substantial selections from Heine and Hugo, and with the addition of three new authors: E. T. A. Hoffman (a tale), Mikhail Lermontov (a short story), and Georg Büchner (a play). In the earlier periods we have been able to find space for substantial enlargements of existing selections as well as for several previously unrepresented writers—for example, nine medieval lyric poets who wrote in Latin (including Boethius, Abélard, St. Thomas Aquinas, and the anonymous bards of the Carmina Burana), together with another exciting medieval poet who wrote in French: François Villon.

We have also made a handful of substitutions. The replacement of Euripides' *The Trojan Women* by his *Hippolytus* permits in-

teresting crossweavings when Racine's *Phaedra* is reached. Ibsen's
Hedda Gabler, replacing his *The Wild Duck*, invites some fascinating comparisons not only with Euripides' and Racine's Phaedra
but (for those with an eye to representative cultural symbols) with
Emma Bovary and Mother Courage. The long opening chapter of
Proust's *Remembrance of Things Past*, which we have substituted
for his account of the soiree at the Marquise de Saint-Euverte's,
offers a more concise entry into the author's themes and methods.
Mann's *Tonio Kröger* replaces his *Felix Krull* because it comments
so poignantly on the deep cleavage between life and art, action and
contemplation, which characterizes modern culture generally;
Brecht's *Mother Courage and Her Children*, because it shows that
seminal modern playwright working on the largest of canvasses; and
Sartre's *No Exit*, welcomed back after an absence of one edition,
because it offers so powerful a metaphor for the modern condition.
For the teacher who thrives on experiment and exploration, as most
of us do, these exchanges are transparent gains.

To the selections from authors already represented, we have been
able to add in this edition substantial new portions of the *Odyssey*
and the *Aeneid*, several further chapters from *Don Quixote*, and
poems by Hugo and Heine. Further, the representations of the
Symbolist poets Baudelaire and Rimbaud have been augmented
not only by further poems by these authors but by the inclusion
of Stéphane Mallarmé.

The treatment of lyric poets and lyric poetry has also undergone
some rethinking. Though there is no wholly satisfactory way of
confronting this problem, as our Note on Translation explains
(p.1627), we have been unwilling to banish the genre altogether,
since that would exclude it from what is often the last as well as
the first college-level course in literature that many students take.
This time, accordingly, we have largely abandoned our former brief
samplings from many writers, choosing instead to represent a select
few in some depth: Catullus, Ovid, Petrarch, Heine, Hugo,
Baudelaire, Rimbaud, and Mallarmé. The translations vary widely
in aim and method, some being in verse and others line for line
in prose, but all are reasonably accurate in conveying the images
and structure of the originals even if not the prosody or over-all
effect. Teachers interested in discussing the art of verse translation
in class will find, besides the familiar Note referred to above, two
interesting opportunities in the text: Rimbaud's "Les Chercheuses
de poux" is accompanied by three English versions, a closely accurate one by Wallace Fowlie and freer ones by Ezra Pound and
Robert Lowell, while Mallarmé's "The Tomb of Edgar Poe" is
given not only in Roger Fry's but in Mallarmé's own English.

Finally, our translations. We have always been vigilant about these, as our long-time users know, and have tried with each successive edition to make improvements. We believe we have succeeded in doing so again. A long consideration of the two great modern verse translations of the *Iliad* has persuaded us to give our vote in this edition to Robert Fitzgerald, whose unmatched *Odyssey* we have already used for several years. With less reluctance but some regret, we have also let go Dryden's elegant rendering of Lucretius in favor of Rolfe Humphries' version, unquestionably more comfortable for a twentieth-century eye and ear. Allan Mandelbaum's fine *Aeneid*, winner of the National Book Award, has replaced C. Day Lewis's on somewhat similar grounds, and Joseph Sheed's *Confessions* of St. Augustine brings a vernacular lucidity where Elizabethan grandeur reigned before. We welcome also to this category Walter Arndt's witty, vigorous *Eugene Onegin*. In Chekhov, where the tone of idiomatic conversation is so crucial to the author's effect, Avrahm Yarmolinsky's finely modulated English diction has given way to Eugene Bristow's no less sensitive American style. And the standard Leishman-Spender translation of Rilke's *Duino Elegies* has been replaced by a new, more American and rhythmically more vital translation by David Young. To all our translators new and old, not forgetting Rex Warner for our new *Hippolytus*, Galway Kinnell for our version of Villon's *Testament*, Robert M. Adams for Machiavelli, Vladimir Nabokov for Lermontov, and Ralph Manheim for our *Mother Courage and Her Children*, we offer hearty thanks, and to their publishers as well.

In conclusion, we welcome a new colleague, Professor Sarah Lawall of the Comparative Literature department of the University of Massachusetts, Amherst, to our collegium of editors. The revisions in the current Introduction to the Modern World, and the texts, notes, introductions, and bibliographies for the authors and works newly added are all hers, and we look forward to her further collaboration in editions yet to come. We also welcome the contribution of Alexander Gelley, University of California, Irvine, who selected and introduced the Heine poems. We must, unhappily, at this same time record the grievous losses of Kenneth Douglas by accidental death, and Howard E. Hugo, taken from us prematurely by illness. Kenneth and Howard were among the original seven editors of this anthology, and by their judicious choices they probably brought more recalcitrant students to an appreciation of neoclassic, romantic, and modern world writing than any other anthologists in history. We applaud their work and honor their memory. *Si monumentum requiris, circumspice.*

The Editors

The Norton Anthology
of World Masterpieces

FOURTH CONTINENTAL EDITION

VOLUME 2

Masterpieces of Neoclassicism

EDITED BY
HOWARD E. HUGO
Late of the University of California, Berkeley

FROM MOLIÈRE TO DIDEROT

Words such as "Reformation" and "Renaissance" are rich in connotations of drastic alteration, rebirth, and revolt—the new arising from the old and the old interpreted with sudden vigor and apparent heterodoxy. Not so are the names given at the time or by posterity to the last half of the seventeenth century and the first half of the eighteenth: the "neoclassical" period, the "Age of Reason," the "Enlightenment," the "Century of Light." Here are terms indicative of relative quiescence, the triumph of consolidation and harmony over innovation and disorder. There is some truth in these phrases, but not the whole truth.

While men have never ceased to invigorate their thought by returning to the masterpieces of Greece and Rome, the special task of the Renaissance—to bring back to life a world bypassed or partly forgotten—seemed finished by the end of the seventeenth century. The "Quarrel of the Ancients and the Moderns" (to be referred to again later on) was fought with an acerbity that happily cost nobody's blood. Was modern man inferior, equal, or possibly superior to his glorious classical ancestors? Whatever their answer, the participants in the "Quarrel" recognized continuity with the great minds of classical antiquity. Similarly the religious strife occasioned by Protestant attacks on the institution of the Roman Catholic Church lost its acrimony. Conflicts henceforward were likely to be between nations, not sects, and to concern politics and the balance of

1

power instead of the individual's private relation to God. True, Louis XIV's revocation of the Edict of Nantes in 1685 upsets any easy picture of the gradual emergence of religious toleration, for the "Sun King" thereby denied to Protestants the right to practice their own variety of Christianity. Yet the French Regency repented that monarch's action some thirty years later, and in 1689 the English Toleration Acts set a broad pattern slowly emulated by most European commonwealths.

Political and economic wars, on the other hand, abounded: struggles about Spanish, Austrian, Polish, and Bavarian successions; various Silesian engagements; the war between Peter the Great and Charles XII of Sweden; ancillary combats in the New World and in the recently colonized East. Nationalistic marches and countermarches fill the years we now consider. The punctilio and formal splendor portrayed in Chapter 3 of Voltaire's *Candide* (in this volume) is that author's ironical commentary on his own best of all possible worlds from the point of view of man's organized inhumanity to man. Certainly it cannot be said that peace elected the Enlightenment as the moment to proclaim "olives of endless age." Yet fortunately the horrible slaughter of the Thirty Years' War (1618-1648) was not soon repeated. Europe had almost two hundred years from the start of that catastrophe before undergoing devastation on a similar scale. Then the battles of Napoleon's *Grande Armée* and his opponents involved hundreds, not merely tens, of thousands.

Classical Greece viewed its gods as residing serenely on Mount Olympus. Neoclassicism produced a pantheon of monarchs who enacted comparable roles within a more human, but also more elegant, environment. The modern state had arisen from its feudal antecedents; and kings, both absolute and enlightened, tended more and more to symbolize the aspirations of the countries they headed. At first glance the age seems to be dominated by the lengthening shadows of its rulers. What other epoch, for instance, could boast three political personalities of the order of Peter and Catherine of Russia, and Frederick II of Prussia—all called "the Great"? Add to them Maria Theresa of Austria and the Holy Roman Empire, with her forty-year reign; the radiant figure of Louis XIV; and the less spectacular but equally important English monarchs—Anne and her Hanoverian descendants, the first three Georges.

Nevertheless, the growth of certain theories about kingship made the condition of royalty less secure. Simpler medieval and Renaissance assumptions had invested earthly rulers with divine rights (even if the problem of Church and State, pope and emperor, persisted). When for example the English under Cromwell executed Charles I—to the horror of many contemporary Europeans—John Milton, in his *Tenure of Kings and Magistrates* (1649), attempted to justify the regicide by invoking precedents, history, common sense, and Holy Scripture. A true king, said Milton, enjoys his office by "the eminence of his wisdom and integrity." A tyrant, in contradistinction, "reigns only for himself and his faction." But his arguments for and against monarchy were slowly superseded by the notion that men live together by virtue of a social contract—the theme of such disparate thinkers as Hobbes, Locke, Rousseau, and many of the French *philosophes*. At the start of the eighteenth century a monarch, acting *in loco parentis*, was still generally considered necessary for the state, particularly if the royal prerogatives were circumscribed by custom or constitution. The age of neoclassicism and the Enlightenment accepted its rulers, but in good rationalist fashion attempted to define their station and duties within an orderly civil society. Future generations were to find more radical and violent solutions. Chapter 26 of *Candide* is strangely prophetic of the shape of things to come. Here the six indigent and dispossessed kings convening at the Carnival of Venice are portrayed as ultimately inferior to the commoner, Candide, who joins them: "Who is this fellow who is able to give a hundred times as much as any of us, and who gives it?"

These are broad cultural and political characteristics of the age. When we turn from them to the contributions of the philosophers of the period, generalization becomes more difficult: Descartes, Spinoza, Locke, Leibnitz, Berkeley, Hume, La Mettrie, D'Alembert, Holbach— what common denominator will reconcile such differing minds? Yet most thinkers manifested

two tendencies. First, they challenged traditional Christianity and classical philosophy by posing questions of a complex and problematic nature and thus helped to bring about what Paul Hazard has called a crisis in European thought. And second, they stressed that man's mind alone is the sole judge of the readings we make of the universe, of God, and of man; they assumed, as almost no earlier philosophers had done, that the cosmos conforms to what human experience and our judgments and abstractions seem to prove. They were, in short, *rationalists*, although many of them would be surprised at being so labeled.

In England, Sir Francis Bacon had earlier laid down a program for new scientific studies, although for him these were but dimly ascertained. Induction was to be the tool whereby we would derive "axioms from the senses and particulars, rising by a gradual and unbroken ascent, so that it [i.e., the inductive method] arrives at the most general axioms last of all. This is the true way, but as yet untried." (*Novum organum*, 1620). His comment may seem relevant chiefly to the growth of the physical sciences, as indeed it was. Nevertheless, it also helped to determine the cast of thought in the subsequent century.

Descartes' *Discourse of Method* (*Discours de la méthode*, 1637) indicated that he was no Baconian worshiper of induction; yet he insisted on starting from one certain "truth" of observation—"I think, therefore I am" —in building up a philosophical system. Perhaps most important,

Descartes sharpened the distinction between mind and matter, spirit and body. After him philosophers tended to fall into one camp or the other: either asserting, as "idealists" (like Berkeley), that all reality is ultimately mind and spirit; or, as materialists (like Hobbes and many of the more extreme French *philosophes*), that reality is finally reduced to the world of matter. But whatever their beliefs, they all held one belief in common. To these thinkers the universe made *rational* sense; it possessed a discernible pattern; it moved according to fixed scientific and mathematical laws. And here the early scientists came to the aid of their more abstract-minded colleagues, with Newton making the greatest contribution; for it was he who synthesized the scientific work done from Copernicus to his own day, to produce a plausible and orderly picture of the material universe, the "Newtonian world-machine." At least one writer included in this portion of the anthology — Voltaire —wrote with full conviction of its existence.

TYPES OF NEOCLASSICISM— MOLIÈRE AND RACINE

Seventeenth-century religious conflicts created a strongly centralized Catholic France, particularly after the revocation of the Edict of Nantes in 1685, which effectively ended French Protestantism. The emergence of a strongly centralized Catholic France may be viewed in one aspect as a triumph of the Counter Reformation—the various efforts taken by the Roman Catholic Church, in the face of the Protestant Reformation, to strengthen doctrine and dogma. Yet this monolithic new commonwealth had secular antecedents. Under Louis XIV Versailles and Paris were soon felt to be what Rome had been under Augustus Caesar, and the line from Greece and Rome to France was asserted to be direct and unbroken. Racine and Molière wrote in a milieu that united Renaissance and Counter Reformation. Whatever the precise ingredients may have been, seventeenth-century French neoclassicism emerges as a combination of these cultural forces, one religious and the other secular. Stated in other terms, two conceptions of the human condition were in opposition—man in a state of grace and man in a state of nature.

Even the famous "Quarrel of the Ancients and the Moderns," mentioned earlier, was symptomatic of the tension between these antithetical outlooks. The Renaissance had extolled classical, pagan antiquity and made it the model for human conduct and aspiration. But now the possibility gained credence that modern man might *excel* the Greeks and Romans and not merely emulate them in an effort to regain a lost golden age. Hence the birth of the idea of progress in history—a concept relatively new to mankind, and one hard to reconcile with the Christian notion of man's fall from his pristine felicity. The "Moderns" were those who insisted that modern culture could equal or surpass that of the classical period; the "Ancients," those who joined literary modesty to something very like a Christian sense of imperfection. Yet while one side felt itself to be an inglorious heir and the other a superior son, *all* were convinced that they were neoclassic, a happy synthesis of the ancient and modern.

MOLIÈRE

Within this cultural environment of neoclassicism, France's two greatest dramatists, one in the comic and one in the tragic vein, wrote their plays. Molière, the comic dramatist, leaned heavily toward the pole of the natural, rational, and humanistic. His concern is not with metaphysics or with an eventual state of eternal salvation. He portrays man as a product of the social order. As Sainte-Beuve long ago pointed out, Molière's characters are untouched by any thought of Christian grace. Only one of his plays, the famous *Tartuffe* (1664), is concerned with a near-religious theme, and even this work is preoccupied more with an analysis of mundane hypocrisy than with the assessment of true belief. Each of Molière's plays is actually an *exemplum* and a critical study of the failure to conform to an ideal of urbanity, solid pragmatism, worldly common sense, good taste, and moderation—all the secular virtues of antiquity and Louis XIV's new state. Both Tartuffe and Orgon are ludicrous, for each fails to meet these criteria of behavior. Tartuffe is a rogue and a scoundrel, a hypocrite whose apparent religiosity and asceticism are eventually unmasked. Orgon is a dupe, in whom Molière satirizes

the solid, middle-class citizen. Orgon's false values impel him to give his daughter a "good" marriage against her wishes, disinherit his son, sign over his property to Tartuffe, and himself be tricked by a fashionable rascal who uses pretended piety as an excuse for financial gain and amatory satisfaction.

Voltaire's description of true comedy as "the speaking picture of the follies and foibles of a nation" can readily be applied to Molière's plays. Actually Voltaire had the Greek comic playwright Aristophanes in mind; to compare Molière with Aristophanes is to see once more how close was the bond between neoclassicism and classical antiquity. Aristophanes' panorama of Athenian citizens displays the same infinite variety as Molière's collection taken from the Parisian scene. Stock characters were easily drawn from two societies where social stratification was menaced by a rising commercialism, and the resulting *parvenu* became material for the satirist's pen. Finally the problems of the day—political, religious, educational, ethical—served as subject matter for both Aristophanes and Molière. From the Greek playwright through the Latin authors Plautus and Terence and later the creators of the Italian Renaissance *commedia dell' arte*, the tradition of classical comedy moves to Molière. The topical issues may no longer interest us—arranged marriages, the excessive refinement of precious fops, and so on—but the classical vision of man in society rather than man the individual, the ideals of universality and rationality, these transcend the local and the temporary.

RACINE

When we move from the racy, realistic prose of comedy to Racine's lofty language of tragedy, more comprehension of the age and its conventions is required. It has always been difficult for the English reader, accustomed to the apparent looseness and gusto of Shakespearean drama, to savor the French playwright's decorous elegance. We are puzzled by the careful control and compression insisted on through adherence to the unities of time, place, and action; by the intrusion of long, distracted monologues, the alternating debatelike interchange between characters, and the operalike duets, and by the circumlocution of the vocabulary.

Racine's model for *Phaedra* (*Phèdre*, 1677) was the *Hippolytus* of Euripides. Racine assures us in his preface that he has retained all that is suitable from the Greek tragedy—and added to it ingredients which make it more pertinent to the audience of his own time. In Euripides' drama the protagonist is not Phaedra but Hippolytus, depicted as a follower of Artemis (Diana) and thus bound by vows of rigid chastity. This condition leads him into *hubris* (overweening human pride) toward Aphrodite (Venus) and thus brings Nemesis (judgment) upon him —all according to the conventional Greek view of life. Phaedra appears in only two scenes, never face to face with Hippolytus; and her death occurs halfway through the play. No doubt the more

thoughtful, discerning members of Euripides' audience caught a note of his own skepticism about the dubious ethics of the gods; but the action of the drama is satisfying on a human level alone, since the cause of Hippolytus' downfall is the pride implicit in his excessive, vehement denial of Phaedra. For the story of Theseus, Racine was indebted also to Plutarch's life of Theseus; and possibly, although he denied it, to the *Phaedra* (alternatively entitled *Hippolytus*) of the Roman Stoic Seneca. In Seneca's play Hippolytus is portrayed as a Stoic philosopher; Phaedra, not Hippolytus, suffers the wrath of Venus; and while he remains technically the protagonist, Phaedra is the focal figure, with her shameless love mixed with guilt. No divinities enter Seneca's declamatory, rhetorical drama, and Venus is the mere personification of passion.

Like his Greek predecessor and like Milton in *Samson Agonistes*, Racine deals with one terrible day—the culmination of previous events and states of feeling—and his technique is in keeping also with the tenets of French classical drama. He concentrates not on the pale Hippolytus, who even in Euripides' drama seems more a passive instrument of two rival goddesses than an active protagonist, but rather on the tormented, passion-racked Phaedra. She becomes a Greek woman with a Christian conscience, for the peculiar remorse Racine has his heroine exhibit when once she is aware of her illicit love is an emotion that was unknown to the ancient world.[1] Within her soul the fundamental conflict is between one overwhelming passion and the restraining power of reason. Her tragic flaw, to use the Aristotelian phrase, is her abnegation of rational responsibility for her moral conduct. The entire play is a slow unfolding, rather than a record of the development, of this fatal weakness. Only the most insensitive reader could be unaffected by Racine's skillfully conveyed, intricate psychological analysis—the cognizance of forces deep within the well of the unconscious that imperil the tenuously held supremacy of the intellect—and by the tone of majestic, dignified sadness.

TYPES OF NEOCLASSICISM— LA ROCHEFOUCAULD, LA FONTAINE

The word *moraliste* which describes these two authors is difficult to translate into English. Naturally "moralist" is the cognate, but for us the word has overtones of someone preaching a definite moral code and employing didactic persuasion. This description does not quite fit the *moraliste*. From Montaigne and Pascal to Gide, Camus, and Sartre, French literature has abounded with writers employing all the traditional literary forms—as well as diaries, notebooks, fables, essays, and aphorisms—to present a total "morality" and outlook on life, a commentary based on observations about the given elements, the *données*, of human nature. Generally the *moraliste* says, "This is the way human nature is"—not, "This is the way human nature should be." Satire is occasionally the mode of expression, but seldom evoked with any burning desire to correct man's vices and foibles. The animal universe of La Fontaine is emblematic of our own, where silly geese, clever foxes, pretentious frogs, and lazy grasshoppers sketch the rich varieties of human foolishness. But even here the human comedy seems more to be observed and savored than censured. To exercise the intellect in an acute dissection of motives and conduct is an end in itself.

LA ROCHEFOUCAULD

La Rochefoucauld's *Maxims* (from which we have excerpted nearly sixty from more than three hundred) shocked his contemporaries when first they appeared in 1665. The modern reader, insulated against shock by his post-Freudian worldliness, may do well to ponder *Maxim* 384: "We ought never to be

(margin, handwritten: "post-Freudian worldliness"?)

1. So intense is her self-recrimination that some critics have attributed it to Racine's Jansenist background. The Jansenist order was a group within the Catholic Church concerned chiefly with the Augustinian concept of predistination and Divine Election. This preoccupation, as well as their general austerity and asceticism, links the Jansenists to Calvinism and the Puritan movement in England. The order was bitterly opposed by the Jesuits, and the Jansenist center at Port-Royal was destroyed in 1709-1710. Like the heroine of Euripides' tragedy, Racine's Phaedra implies that the gods have brought about her destruction. It is also possible to interpret her assertion in Jansenist-Christian terms as referring to a fall from grace.

surprised, save that we can still be surprised." The social milieu and the course of La Rochefoucauld's career offer some explanation for the mood of acerbity and bitter reflectiveness, even downright cynicism, in these pithy statements. When he was a young man, La Rochefoucauld's family and the class to which he belonged still enjoyed real power and prestige. But the age of Richelieu and later the reign of Louis XIV witnessed a steady decline of both these factors. What privileges the nobility entertained were increasingly the gift of monarchs and ministers whose concern was the consolidation of royal prerogatives. Moreover, failure and defeat marked La Rochefoucauld's active life, both politically and militarily. His castle was burned in the wars of the *Fronde*, a natural son was killed in battle, near-blindness for himself came as the result of a wound. Poverty and the infidelity of several mistresses scarcely contributed to produce in him a vision of life as bliss, and in his *Memoirs* (1662) can be traced a pattern of deepening disillusionment. Yet such data only partially explain the cast of La Rochefoucauld's mind, which had a genius like Newton's for reducing complex phenomena to a single simple (and also over-simple) principle.

La Rochefoucauld, indeed, accomplished for the domain of human nature what Machiavelli had achieved for statecraft some centuries earlier, and accomplished it with such apparent stark simplicity of phrasing that we are often dazzled. *Maxim* 218

is a good example. "Hypocrisy is the tribute that vice pays to virtue" ("L'hypocrisie est un hommage que le vice rend à la vertu"). Here four abstractions, carefully balanced in pairs, occur within barely twice as many words. Vice and virtue we are accustomed to consider in opposition, but hypocrisy coupled with homage or tribute startles the mind, so that the relation between vice and virtue takes on new dimensions.

One other characteristic of La Rochefoucauld's commentaries is the generality of his expression. A major tenet of neoclassical criticism, Continental and English, was the asserted superiority of the universal statement over the particular, the generic class over the individual. Hence the *Maxims*, delivered in a tone of assurance that twentieth-century man with his dubieties might well covet, deliberately aim at the typical rather than at the unique. Sainte-Beuve aptly described La Rochefoucauld as "the polished misanthrope, insinuating and smiling," and while the tender-minded may be appalled at the aphorist's ruthless dissection of love, honor, friendship, and the like, they will be hard pressed to phrase a rebuttal with such precision combined with such grandeur of generality.

LA FONTAINE

La Fontaine's *Fables* describe a more genial world than that of his cynical contemporary. They too, especially in the abstract statements that conclude most of the little tales in verse, have all of mankind as their concern, and their association with children's literature is more apparent than real. Though La Fontaine shrewdly dedicated the first six books of *Fables* to France's most important child, the six-year-old son of Louis XIV, obviously his talking animals are far removed from the inanities of Donald Duck and his friends, and from those conversing beasts in today's comic strips ostensibly created to delight the juvenile reader. His pungent tags—e.g., "Every flatterer lives at the expense of the person who listens to him" ("Chaque flatteur vit au dépens de celui qui l'écoute") —are not the sort of observations that bring chortles to the nursery. The timeless appeal of his tales, full of anecdotal skill and psychological subtlety, is better summed up in Alexander Pope's neoclassical dictum: "True wit is Nature to advantage dressed,/ What oft was thought, but ne'er so well expressed:/ Something whose truth convinced at sight we find. . . ." La Fontaine's borrowings from Aesop, Phaedrus, and other minor Greek and Latin fabulists may also be thus explained. They are in keeping with the aesthetics of an age that felt its chief artistic merit to lie in perpetuating and renewing the classical tradition. Perhaps the highest compliment paid to these *Fables* is the remark of the critic who submitted that if the world were suddenly shattered, the next day (if man were permitted to reconstruct its animalian content) the birds and beasts would behave precisely as they are made to do by La Fontaine.

As modern readers and hence heirs willy-nilly to romanticism and the cultural tradition of the last one hundred and fifty years, we may feel that these two seventeenth-century writers are excessively objective and impersonal. We are accustomed to veiled autobiography in literature, where the "I" of the artist is never far from his creation. Romantic affinities for the peculiarities of each individual have blunted our appreciation of the grandeur of generality, where human nature is viewed as a totality, permanent and unchanging, and the task of the man of letters is to treat mankind in its public rather than its private context. La Rochefoucauld's and La Fontaine's minds, critical and decorous, chary of enthusiasm and aristocratically scornful of democratic friendliness (today's "togetherness"), may strike us as chilly. They speak with a *courage de tête* (literally, "courage of the head") and a surety we often attribute to intellectual arrogance. Finally, they lack the solemnity that our own Age of Anxiety too often confuses with profundity. They are witty and seemingly casual. Their grace, ease, and apparent simplicity deceive us. It is good to remember Horace Walpole's remark, "The world is a comedy to those that think, a tragedy to those who feel." With them, as with Voltaire, the rapid play of mind over human experience should not obscure an underlying seriousness of intention.

TOWARD THE EN-
LIGHTENMENT

In our day, or within the last twenty-five years, we have become accustomed to seeing our own cultural milieu, and that of our immediate predecessors, defined only in terms which are deprecatory, negative, or cynical —for example, "the Jazz Age," "the Lost Generation," "the Age of Anxiety," or "the Age of Longing." Hence, we are not well equipped to appreciate the eighteenth century, when for the first time in history men announced to each other and to posterity that theirs was an Age of Reason, an *Enlightenment*. Voltaire, in his *Last Remarks on the "Pensées of M. Pascal*, exclaimed with joy, "What a light has burst over Europe within the last few years! It first illuminated all the princes of the North; it has even come into the universities. It is the light of common sense!" Crane Brinton epitomizes the movement in *Ideas and Men* (1950) when he speaks of "the belief that all human beings can attain here on this earth a state of perfection hitherto in the West thought to be possible only for Christians in a state of grace, and for them only after death."

Traditional Christianity had been securely moored by a pair of anchors: *faith* ("the substance of things hoped for, and the evidence of things not seen") and *reason*. The two elements were always linked in an unstable combination. To watch the progress of thought in the seventeenth century is to see the latter gradually usurp the position of the former. Biblical exegesis had succeeded in weakening the concept of the biblical God of miracles. Of what practical use were the records of an obscure Hebrew tribe for the "modern" man who trusted in his subjective rational capabilities, and for whom the wonders of the orderly universe were disclosed daily by contemporary scientists and philosophers? Reason, rapidly assuming a state of near-deification, could show men how to control themselves and their environment. Furthermore this same environment—nature —began to seem increasingly benign as man explored its previously concealed workings.

Deism became the most satisfying metaphysical position for most intellectuals. Taking their departure from the traditional arguments of "first cause" and "design" which were used to demonstrate the existence of God, they could conceive of a Supreme Being—*Monsieur l'Être*, a French wit said—who was an impersonal cosmic clockmaker, the prime mover of Newton's vast mechanical machine, remote and abstract. In short, one now invented a God to whom one could not pray and from whom one could not expect forgiveness. (Voltaire once wrote an article describing the fallacy of prayer, finding the act impious, superfluous, and ineffective.) The doctrinal handbook of the Middle Ages had been the *Summa theologica* of St. Thomas Aquinas; the Century of Light was to produce its *Encyclopedia* (*Encyclopédie*), a joint effort published from 1751 to 1776 by the leading French *philosophes*, edited by Diderot, and designed to popularize and disseminate the new doctrines.

Deism attempted to reconcile Christianity with "modern" rationalism. In one sense this was nothing new. We must remember that from the very start, Christian thinkers—St. Paul and the early Church fathers—faced the task of amalgamating Hebraic ideas about a revealed Messiah, the Son of God, with Greek rationalist philosophy. Many centuries later it was inevitable that for intellectuals imbued with scientific attitudes, the revelatory aspects of Christianity—invoking that same God who spoke to Pascal—would retreat before more analytical approaches. The period when modern philosophy was formed can be placed between Galileo (1564–1642) and Leibnitz (1646–1716). While differences between interim thinkers such as Hobbes, Spinoza, and Descartes may seem to be more paramount than similarities, these men were unanimous in their rejection of medieval logic and in their insistence that the axioms of the new mathematical physics were consonant with the authentic workings of the universe. The omniscience and activity of God has to conform with the same laws He had established, and there could be no room for divine caprice and arbitrary conduct. The critical climate of the age is succinctly revealed in Alexander Pope's epitaph intended for Sir Isaac Newton's tomb in Westminster Abbey. "Nature and Nature's Laws lay hid in Night:/ God said, *Let Newton be!* and all was Light."

Hence Deistic thinkers constructed or adumbrated complicated philosophic abstractions such as the Great Chain of Being, plenitude, and the principle of sufficient reason. Gott-

fried Wilhelm Leibnitz, himself a respectable figure in the history of philosophy, was responsible for much of the dissemination of the new doctrine, mostly through the writings of his more superficial disciples. Leibnitz's hypothesis of "many possible worlds"—which in less capable hands became a theory of "the best of all possible worlds"—ran somewhat as follows. God considered an infinite number of possible worlds before the Creation; but His final decision was to make a world where good predominates over evil. A cosmos *without* evil would actually not have been as "good" as one where evil is a minor ingredient, since many "goods" are related to certain evils. (For example, by definition the existence of free will implies the possibility of sin, for there must be an alternative upon which to exercise the power of free choice. God therefore invented the forbidden apple, and Adam's fall ensued.) According to this view, the world contains a preponderance of good over evil in the long run, and the evil it does possess is no argument against God's benevolence. Reduced to finite, human terms, this philosophical outlook became known as *Optimism*. The student must be careful not to confuse it with our everyday use of the word.

VOLTAIRE
AND THE
ENLIGHTENMENT

The younger Voltaire began as an Optimist and embraced these ideas in his early *Discourse in Verse on Mankind* (*Discours en vers sur l'homme,* 1738). For a time it may have appeared to him, particularly since he participated in the writing of the *Encyclopédie*, that he and his fellow philosophers were leading the rest of humanity toward a revival of the golden age on earth by dint of unaided "reason." But the course of Voltaire's own life and the pattern of his intellectual development brought about inevitable disillusion.

Tragedy has been described as a pattern in which theory is destroyed by a fact. For Voltaire and many of his contemporaries, the stubborn fact that threatened to destroy the theories of the Century of Light was the Lisbon earthquake of November 1, 1755, when an estimated thirty to fifty thousand persons perished—ironically on All Saints' Day, when the churches were crowded. It was the greatest natural catastrophe in Western Europe since Pompeii disappeared under Vesuvius' lava. In 1756 Voltaire wrote his first bitter rebuttal of the Optimists, the *Poem on the Disaster of Lisbon* (*Poème sur le désastre de Lisbonne*). He revaluated the self-satisfied cosmic acceptance of these philosophers as complacent, negative fatalism. For him it was "an insult to the sadness of our existence"—we who are "Tormented atoms on this pile of mud/ Swallowed up by death, the mere playthings of Fate." Voltaire's concluding line in the poem expresses his *respect* for God and his *love* for humanity.

The major work that grew out of Voltaire's disgust with Optimistic metaphysics was *Candide*. Written with incredible speed in 1758 (he claimed in three days) and out of white-hot indignation, it was published in 1759 and ran to some forty editions within twenty years. Like Dante, Voltaire immortalized his enemies. Pangloss, Candide's mentor, is a caricature of the Optimistic philosophers Christian Wolf(f) and Leibnitz. Jean-Jacques Rousseau, Voltaire's intellectual enemy (he once remarked, "If Rousseau is dead, it's one scoundrel the less"), flattered himself into believing that the portrait was of him. But Voltaire's satiric concern with individual thinkers was peripheral, and the truth is that his main target was a system, a way of looking at the world. Here he joins the company of great French *moralistes* we have earlier discussed. The framework for *Candide* is one that was popular with seventeenth- and eighteenth-century writers—the exotic romance, the travel story. The romancer could use such a story to satisfy the age's desire for vicarious voyaging and knowledge of distant, strange lands. The satirist could use it to indulge in contemporary and often dangerous criticism without fear of persecution. The philosopher could use it to reinforce the rationalists' conviction that all men are basically alike—children of "reason."

But we must not ignore the subtle ingredient added by Voltaire, the element that gives the book its distinctive flavor. This is Voltaire's *parody* of his literary models. The tale is a satire, almost a burlesque, of the romance, the adventure story, and the pedagogical novel. Did a novel ever contain more ridiculous improbabilities? Within a rigid formal structure (ten chapters in the Old World, ten in the New World, and the last ten back in Europe and Asia Minor) we are presented with dozens of recognition scenes, most of them accompanied by appropriate flashbacks as the once-lost character tells his tale to the wondering Candide. "I am consoled by one thing," says the ingenuous young man. "We see that we often meet people we thought we should never meet again." The recognition device is an excellent way to impose a design upon what otherwise would be a series of loosely linked adventures. It is also Voltaire's ironical commentary on storybook life in comparison with our own sorry existence, where the lost stay lost and the dead remain dead. Several of the major "deaths" in the story fortunately turn out to be not permanent; but half of Lisbon, two entire armies, the inhabitants of one ship and two castles, and miscellaneous llamas, monkeys, and sheep are summarily dispatched. A dim view of this best of all possible worlds!

In a later tale, *The Simple Fellow* (*L'Ingénu*, 1767), Voltaire has a priest tell the wandering Huron hero that God must have great designs for him, since He moves the young man about so freely. To this the Indian retorts that more likely the devil plans his itinerary. Candide never descends to such pessimism, even when at last he recovers his beloved Cunégonde, now a haggard washerwoman on the shores of the Bosphorus. Perhaps it is the vision of Eldorado that saves Candide (and Voltaire) from complete despair. For a brief time the hero is allowed to dwell in a never-never land, a composite of all the utopian dreams of the Enlightenment.

The nineteenth-century writer Flaubert said that *Candide* was a book that made you want to gnash your teeth. Flaubert also commented that the conclusion of *Candide*, with its admonition to work, may be "serene and stupid, like life itself." Yet the garden must be cultivated. In a letter written in 1759, Voltaire remarked, "I have read a great deal; I have found nothing but uncertainties, lies, fanaticisms, and I am just about in the same certainty concerning our existence as I was when I was a suckling babe; I much prefer to plant, to sow, to build, and above all to be free." Voltaire seems to say that the answer is neither a complacent acceptance of existence —Optimism—nor an equally fatuous condemnation—pessimism —but rather an intermediate path which may be called *meliorism*.

DIDEROT AND THE END OF NEOCLASSICISM

Naturally no single author, even less a single work, can merit the fame of "ending" a cultural epoch. Yet so far as a single work may mark finis to an age, Diderot's *Rameau's Nephew* (*Le Neveu de Rameau*, written sometime during the 1760's and early 1770's) marks finis to at least those attitudes associated with the eighteenth century in popular thought: restraint, reasonableness, and *bon goût* (good taste) as personal ideals; formal order in the arts and a high sense of measure and proportion; respect for the past and the classical tradition; concern for man in society and general human nature rather than for the individual with his unique personality. Add to these the general sentiment shared by the writers we have been considering: that man may be merely *rationis capax*—a creature *capable* of reason—rather than rational; yet this is the primary attribute of the human condition.

Through his impertinent, parasitic, nay-saying musician, Diderot brings all such criteria into question; and the critical response to this erosion of classical values demonstrates the efficacy of his book. Carlyle praised what he held to be Diderot's exaltation of the superior man over the average. Baudelaire singled out the writer's "Satanism." Karl Voss discovered a proto-Nietzsche. Maurice Barrès took the *Nephew* to be proof that the Enlightenment had died well before the end of the eighteenth century. John Morley called Rameau's dissolute nephew a "squalid and tattered Satan," "a Mephistopheles out at elbow, a Lucifer in low waters; yet always diabolic, with the bright fire of the pit in his eyes." For Karl Marx the young beggar showed Diderot's awareness of a disintegrating socio-economic situation and the eternal class struggle. Hegel found in him the embodiment of a dialectical turning point in world history. Shaw and Freud read into him

their own interpretations of the human personality. This formidable barrage of names may intimidate the reader rather than encourage him, and in many cases the critics have found more in the little work than may legitimately be located there. Let us consider a few points which, however, justify their variant responses.

The dialogue form—popular with Greek and Roman satirists and taken over by neoclassic writers—enabled Diderot to convey shocking sentiments through the mouth of the impudent nephew. Yet the presence of the conservative "Myself"—who acts as "straight man"—also freed Diderot from any imputation that Rameau's attitudes were necessarily his. Indeed, as in many of the Socratic dialogues, it is difficult to say what the author's position *is*. We know from Diderot's life that his volatile and tempestuous personality carried him from idea to idea, and consistency of outlook was alien to his temperament. He also once stated that to make a convincing literary character, the counterpoint most needed was that of "extreme and opposite feelings in his soul." Thus "He" and "Myself," ostensibly protagonist and antagonist, perhaps form one composite figure—namely Diderot. At the same time the dichotomies are real: moralist-amoralist, bourgeois-bohemian, abstract philosopher-creative artist, idealist-cynic, social man–anarchist, teacher-buffoon.

The *Nephew* belongs to an old literary tradition of parasitical vagabondage and self-proclaimed roguery. But his antecedents and predecessors—which include the "vice" or "ruffler" in late medieval plays, the Arlecchino (Harlequin) of Italian *commedia dell' arte*, the picaresque hero in seventeenth- and eighteenth-century novels, and even Diogenes, the father of all cynics, for whom Diderot had a professed admiration—practiced their vagrant lives within certain social frameworks and conventions to which they implicitly adhered. Not so the musician. His negativism seems to admit no values. For him even egotism dissolves in self-denigration, as we see from the pantomiming and play-acting. In the course of an apparently random conversation, this itinerant artist genially touches on a range of topics of whose scope the casual reader may remain unaware, so deft is Diderot's artistry. Indeed, the haphazard progression of ideas and sentiments within the piece

is as unclassical as the ideas adopted. Both in spirit and in method we seem closer to the Romantic revolt than to the world extending in time from Molière to Diderot. Society, he tells us, is a fraud, and so he can cynically enjoy being a "happy brigand" among "wealthy brigands." Human nature resembles animal nature, where each species devours the other. If the Nephew plays the hypocrite, at least he is forthright and no mean dissembler like his fellows. His vices are "natural," and he derides any attempt to suppress them by rational means: reason's standards are unobtainable. The late Albert Camus, who singled out *Rameau's Nephew* as an eighteenth-century literary landmark, might aptly have applied to it one of his favorite *bons mots*: not the Cartesian "Cogito, ergo sum" ("I think, therefore I am"), but "Je me révolte, donc nous sommes" ("I rebel, therefore we are").

LIVES, WRITINGS, AND CRITICISM
Biographical and critical works are listed only if they are available in English.

JEAN-BAPTISTE POQUELIN MOLIÈRE

LIFE. Born in Paris in 1622 as Jean-Baptiste Poquelin. His father was upholsterer to the king. Molière attended the Jesuit school at Clermont and later studied under the famous "libertine" and Epicurean philosopher Gassendi. At about the age of twenty-five he joined the Illustrious Theater (*Illustre Théâtre*), a company of traveling players formed by the Béjart family. From 1646 to 1658 Molière and his troupe toured the provinces, playing mostly short pieces after the fashion of the Italian *commedia dell' arte*. In 1658 the players were ordered to perform before Louis XIV in Paris, and soon after their initial success they became the Troupe de Monsieur, enjoying royal patronage. Despite the intrigues of rival companies, particularly that of the

Hôtel de Bourgogne, Molière's prestige increased; and when his theater of the Petit Bourbon was demolished, the king gave him the Palais-Royal theater in 1661. Molière married Armande Béjart in 1662—an unfortunate match, since his enemies spread the scandal that she was his daughter by a former mistress, Madeleine Béjart, although in reality the women were sisters. *Tartuffe*, a study in religious hypocrisy, first produced in 1664, embroiled the playwright with certain groups in the Church. The king was forced to ban it, but Molière succeeded in having the play published and reperformed by 1669. In 1673, although ailing, the author-actor insisted on playing the lead role in his *Imaginary Invalid*, and he died a few hours after a performance on February 17, 1673. The

Church refused him burial; but Louis XIV interceded at the pleas of his widow, and a compromise was effected.

CHIEF WRITINGS. Molière's first great success was *The High-Brow Ladies* (*Les Précieuses ridicules*, 1659), a satire on the intellectual pretensions of Parisian fashionable society. Approximately two dozen comedies can be definitely identified as his own. Among these are *The School for Husbands* (*L'École des maris*, 1661); *Don Juan* (1665)—a treatment of the legendary hero; *The Misanthrope* (*Le Misanthrope*, 1666); *Tartuffe* (1664-1669); *The Miser* (*L'Avare*, 1668); *The Bourgeois Gentleman* (*Le Bourgeois Gentilhomme*, 1670); *The Wise Ladies* (*Les Femmes savantes*, 1672); and his last play, *The Imaginary Invalid* (*Le Malade imaginaire*, 1673). *The Bourgeois Gentleman* was first performed at Chambord on November 14, 1670, and in Paris on November 29. Molière played the part of M. Jourdain. It is actually entitled a "comedy-ballet"; the court composer Lully (Lulli) wrote the incidental music for the play and sang the role of the Mufti. The part of Lucile was taken by Molière's wife.

BIOGRAPHY AND CRITICISM. Karl Mantzius, *Molière* (1908), is a good factual account of the author's life. C. H. C. Wright, *French Classicism* (1920), offers a brief survey of the period; Martin Turnell, *The Classical Moment* (1947), includes studies of Molière, Racine, and Corneille; W. G. Moore, *Molière: A New Criticism* (1950), is a recent study in English, as are J. D. Hubert, *Molière and the Comedy of Intellect* (1962) and D. B. Wyndham Lewis, *Molière: The Comic Mask* (1959). Recommended also are the chapter on Molière in E. Auerbach, *Mimesis* (1953); L. Grossman, *Men and Masks: A Study of Molière* (1963); and R. McBride, *The Sceptical Vision of Molière* (1977).

JEAN RACINE

LIFE. Born in 1639 in the Valois district, eighty miles from Paris. His father was a government official. Racine attended the College de Beauvais, and from 1655 to 1659 studied at the Jansenist center of Port-Royal, when that institution was at its peak. (Pascal wrote his *Provincial Letters*, the *Provinciales*, dealing with Port-Royal, in 1656 and 1657.) Racine came to Paris in 1660, encouraged by a friend, the poet La Fontaine. His early plays were failures, and he went into seclusion at Uzès, in Provence—for an interval of retirement similar to Milton's Horton period. He returned to Paris early in 1663, received the patronage of the court and the nobility, and soon came to be one of the leading playwrights, along with Molière and Corneille. He left Paris in 1677, officially to write history; married Catherine de Romanet (after earlier liaisons with two of his actresses); and returned to Port-Royal—a move indicative of his increasing piety and interest in religious spec-

ulation. (Most of his seven children became nuns or priests.) He led the life of the affluent country gentleman, interrupted by occasional trips to Paris and by missions as historiographer on Louis XIV's campaigns during the period from 1678 to 1693. Racine died in 1699 and was buried at Port-Royal. His body was exhumed when the place was destroyed in 1711, and he was placed next to Pascal at the church of St. Étienne-du-Mont in Paris.

CHIEF WRITINGS. Racine's plays, twelve in all, consist of an early comedy, *The Suitors* (*Les Plaideurs*, 1668), based on Aristophanes; two tragedies, *The Thebaid* (*La Thébaïde*, 1664), and *Alexander the Great* (*Alexander le Grand*, 1665), both imitative of Corneille; seven "profane" or secular tragedies; and two biblical dramas. His first major writing was *Andromache* (*Andromaque*, 1667), and this play enjoyed a success almost as great as that of the famous *Cid* of Corneille. *Britannicus* followed in 1669, *Bérénice* in 1670, *Mithridates* (*Mithridate*) in 1673—three tragedies whose sources were classical historians: Tacitus, Suetonius, and Plutarch. *Bajazet* (1672), marked an excursion into oriental *decor*; it is perhaps the most contemporary of Racine's plays, since despite the exotic locale, the plot—according to Racine—came from an adventure that had taken place only thirty years before. Both *Iphegenia* (*Iphigénie*, 1674), and *Phaedra* (*Phèdre*, 1677), were modeled on plays by Euripides. The latter was performed at the Hôtel de Bourgogne, the theater used by Molière's rivals; and it was after the play's success that Racine went into semiretirement. Twelve years later, at the request of Mme. de Maintenon, Racine wrote his first biblical drama, *Esther* (1689); this, like *Athalia* (*Athalie*, 1691), dealt with Old Testament material, and both plays were designed for performance at Mme. de Maintenon's school for girls at Saint-Cyr.

BIOGRAPHY AND CRITICISM. An excellent biography of the playwright, A. F. B. Clark, *Racine* (1939), may be supplemented by M. Duclaux, *The Life of Racine* (1925); K. Vossler, *Racine* (1926). C. H. C. Wright, *French Classicism* (1920), and Martin Turnell, *The Classical Moment* (1947), are recommended for background material. A recent and interesting study of Racine's plays is V. Orgel, *A New View of the Plays of Racine* (1948); a valuable edition of *Phèdre* has been prepared by R. C. Knight (1943); and translations by Lacy Lockert of several of Racine's plays—including *Phèdre*—in rhymed alexandrine couplets were published in 1936. E. Auerbach's chapter on Racine in *Mimesis* (1953) is excellent; and there is also G. Brereton, *Jean Racine: A Critical Biography* (1951); K. Wheatley, *Racine and English Classicism* (1956); M. Bowra, *The Simplicity of Racine* (1956); and the chapters on Racine in W. Sypher, *Four Stages of Renaissance Style* (1955) and in F. Fergusson, *The Idea of a Theater* (1949). More recently, there is B. Weinberg, *The Art of Jean Racine* (1963); P. France, *Racine's Rhetoric* (1965); O. de Mourgues, *Racine: Or, The Triumph of Relevance* (1967); a series of essays about Racine edited by R. C. Knight (1969); P. H. Nurse, *Classical Voices* (1971), with a chapter on Racine; M. Turnell, *Jean Racine: Dramatist* (1972); and G. Pocock, *Corneille and Racine* (1973).

FRANÇOIS, DUC DE LA ROCHEFOUCAULD

LIFE. Born on September 15, 1613, in Paris as Prince de Marcillac, La Rochefoucauld later received the title of Duke. He had an early army career. At 16 (in 1629), the year he married, he came to court. Through Mme. de Chevreuse he became attached to Anne of Austria, Louis XIII's wife, whose escape to Brussels he once tried to effect. He spent eight days in the Bastille, and was then exiled to his family estates after eight years of intriguing at Court. When Anne became regent, La Rochefoucauld opposed her advisor, Mazarin. La Rochefoucauld fought on the side of the Prince de Condé in the two outbreaks during Louis XIV's minority: the *Fronde of the Parlement* (1648–1649), and the *Fronde of the Princes* (1650–1653), and was wounded in 1652. He spent the remainder of his life as close friend to Mme. de Sablé, Mme. de La Fayette, and Mme. de Sévigné, whose salons were intellectual centers in Paris. He died March 17, 1680 —legend has it in the arms of the theologian Bossuet.

CHIEF WRITINGS. His *Maxims* were first published anonymously in 1665; the last augmented edition appeared in 1678. La Rochefoucauld's *Memoirs* (1662) are chiefly concerned with his experiences as a *Frondeur*.

BIOGRAPHY AND CRITICISM: E. Gosse, *Three French Moralists* (1918); H. A. Grubbs, *The Originality of La Rochefoucauld's Maxims* (1929); M. Bishop, *The Life and Adventures of La Rochefoucauld* (1951); Sister M. F. Zeller, *New Aspects of La Rochefoucauld's Style* (1954); and W. G. Moore, *La Rochefoucauld* (1969).

JEAN DE LA FONTAINE

LIFE. Born July 8, 1621, at Château-Thierry in Compiègne, where his father was chief huntsman and forester on the royal preserves. At one time La Fontaine briefly considered entering holy orders; he studied law, was admitted to the bar, but never practised. He married Marie Héricart when he was 26 (in 1647); they were separated in 1649. An indolent life in the provinces was succeeded after 1656 by an equally pleasant existence in Paris, where he was the favorite of various elegant ladies: the dowager Duchesse d'Orléans, Mme. de la Sablière (at whose residence he lived for many years), Mme. d'Hervart. Nicolas Fouquet, Superintendent of Finance (1653-1661) under Louis XIV, became his patron. When Fouquet

fell, denounced by Colbert and others for his dubious financial operations, La Fontaine readily found other benefactors to guarantee him a life devoid of monetary worries. Molière, Racine, and Boileau were his close friends. He became a member of the French Academy in 1684; La Fontaine was on the side of the "Ancients" in the famous literary quarrel between the Ancients and the Moderns. Epicurean and skeptic, by temperament inclined toward neither philosophy nor religion, he increased his Christian devotions after a serious illness in 1692. He died April 13, 1695.

CHIEF WRITINGS. The *Fables*, published in twelve books (1668, 1678–1679, 1694) were his masterpiece. Other works included *Stories and Tales in Verse* (1664), mainly imitations from Ariosto and Boccaccio.

BIOGRAPHY AND CRITICISM. F. Hamel, *La Fontaine* (1912); P. A. Wadsworth, *Young La Fontaine* (1952); M. Sutherland, *La Fontaine* (1953); M. Guiton, *La Fontaine: Poet and Counterpoet* (1961).

FRANÇOIS-MARIE AROUET DE VOLTAIRE

LIFE. Born on November 21, 1694, in Paris, as François-Marie Arouet. His father was a minor treasury official, originally from Poitou. Voltaire attended a Jesuit school and later undertook and abandoned the study of law. He spent eleven months in the Bastille (1717–1718), imprisoned by *lettre de cachet*, for writing satiric verses about the aristocracy. By 1718 he was using the name Voltaire. Literary and social success soon followed; speculations in the Compagnie des Indes made him wealthy by 1726. That same year the Chevalier de Rohan had him beaten and again sent to the Bastille, and 1726–1729 saw him in exile, mostly in England. From 1734 to 1749 he pursued philosophical, historical, and scientific studies, and became the companion of Mme. du Châtelet on her estate at Cirey. His election to the French Academy took place in 1746. From 1750 to 1753 he stayed with Frederick the Great of Prussia, at Potsdam, after Louis XV had failed to give him sufficient patronage. That unstable alliance broke in 1753. Soon after, Voltaire bought adjacent property in France and Switzerland, and settled first at his château, Les Délices, just outside Geneva, and then at nearby Ferney, on French soil. It was from there that he, as the foremost representative of the Enlightenment, directed his campaigns against intolerance and injustice. He made a triumphant return to Paris in 1778, and died there on May 30.

CHIEF WRITINGS. Voltaire's first serious work was a tragedy on Greek lines, *Oedipus* (*Oedipe*, 1715). His epic, *The Henriad* (*La Henriade*)—in praise of the tolerance of Henry IV—was published in 1728. His stay in England produced the *Letters on the English* (*Lettres sur les Anglais*, 1733); but before that, in 1731, appeared the *History* of *Charles XII* (*Histoire de Charles XII*) of Sweden—perhaps the first "modern" history. *Zadig* (1748), was his first famous philosophical tale, and *Candide* (1759), marked the summit of his achievement in this genre. Another major historical enterprise was *The Century of Louis XIV* (*Le Siècle de Louis XIV*, 1751). His *Philosophical Dictionary* (*Dictionnaire philosophique*, 1764) may be considered most typical both of Voltaire and of the Encyclopedists. In quantity, Voltaire's correspondence is almost unequaled, since he wrote to virtually every important intellectual, social, and political figure of his age.

BIOGRAPHY AND CRITICISM. Good biographies and studies of Voltaire are H. N. Brailsford, *Voltaire* (1935); R. Aldington, *Voltaire* (1934); G. Brandes, *The Life of Voltaire* (undated); and N. Torrey, *The Spirit of Voltaire* (1938). The best edition of *Candide*—to which this editor is greatly indebted—is by A. Morize, 1913. Also recommended are more recent studies: I. O. Wade, *Voltaire and "Candide"* (1959); P. Gay, *Voltaire's Politics: The Poet as Realist* (1961): two articles by W. Bottiglia in *Publications of the Modern Language Association*, "Candide's Garden," LXVI (September, 1951); N. Mitford, *Voltaire in Love* (1957); "The Eldorado Episode in *Candide*," LXXIII (September, 1958); T. Besterman, *Voltaire* (1969); and J. Hearsey, *Voltaire* (1976).

DENIS DIDEROT

LIFE. Born on October 5, 1713, in Langres, the eldest son of a master-cutler. He attended a Jesuit school, was tonsured at twelve, and almost entered that order. Diderot went to college in Paris, and gradually shifted toward secularism. In 1743 he married his former mistress, Antoinette Champion, against his father's wishes. He met Rousseau in 1743. He frequented the salons and cafés attended by the intellectuals, and made a living by translating and similar literary hack-work. He was appointed chief editor

(January 21, 1746) of the projected *Encyclopedia*. Volume I appeared on July 1, 1751, and the same year Diderot was elected to the Berlin Academy. From 1751 to 1757 the seven volumes of the *Encyclopedia* were published, but increasing opposition made each volume successively more difficult to print. The Attorney General banned the work in 1759; Rome condemned it the same year. Ten more volumes were secretly published in 1765, and a four-volume supplement in 1776. Diderot's friendship with Sophie Volland commenced in 1756. Catherine II of Russia bought his library in 1767 (with the author acting as custodian until his death). He went to Russia as her guest in 1773, returning to Paris in 1774. He met Voltaire in 1778, when that writer made his triumphant return to Paris to die there. Diderot died July 30, 1784.

CHIEF WRITINGS. His first important work was *The Indiscreet Jewels* (1748), a bawdy satire. A short novel, *The Nun* (1770)—anticlerical and pornographic—was published posthumously in 1796. Two plays were performed in 1757 and 1758: *The Natural Son* and *The Father of the Family*. *Rameau's Nephew* (written in the 1760's, possibly concluded in the early 1770's) appeared first in Goethe's German translation (1805). Not until 1891 was there any edition based on the original manuscript. *Discussion Between D'Alembert and Diderot*, *D'Alembert's Dream*, *Continuation of the Discussion*, etc. (all written 1769, published in 1830), are dialogues like the *Nephew*. *The Paradox about the Comedian* (1773, published 1830) concerns the art of acting. *A Treatise on Beauty* (1750) and the *Essay on Painting* (1765), along with the posthumously printed *Salons*, establish Diderot as one of the first modern critics of the fine arts.

BIOGRAPHY AND CRITICISM. J. Morley, *Diderot and the Encyclopedists* (1897); E. M. Steel, *Diderot's Imagery* (1941); A. Vartanian, *Diderot and Descartes* (1953); R. Wellek, *A History of Modern Criticism* (*1750–1950*) (1955); L. G. Crocker, *The Embattled Philosopher* (1954); A. M. Wilson, *Diderot* (1957); J. Lough, *Essays on the Encyclopédie of Diderot and D'Alembert* (1968).

JEAN-BAPTISTE POQUELIN MOLIÈRE
(1622–1673)

Tartuffe or The Imposter (Le Tartuffe ou L'Imposteur) *

Preface

Here is a comedy that has excited a good deal of discussion and that has been under attack for a long time; and the persons who are mocked by it have made it plain that they are more powerful in France than all whom my plays have satirized up to this time. Noblemen, ladies of fashion, cuckolds, and doctors all kindly consented to their presentation,[1] which they themselves seemed to enjoy along with everyone else; but hypocrites do not understand banter: they became angry at once, and found it strange that I was bold enough to represent their actions and to care to describe a profession shared by so many good men. This is a crime for which they cannot forgive me, and they have taken up arms against my comedy in a terrible rage. They were careful not to attack it at the point that had wounded them: they are too crafty for that and too clever to reveal their true character. In keeping with their lofty custom, they have used the cause of God to mask their private interests; and *Tartuffe*, they say, is a play that offends piety: it is filled with abominations from beginning to end, and nowhere is there a line that does not deserve to be burned. Every syllable is wicked, the very gestures are criminal, and the slightest glance, turn of the head, or step from right to left conceals mysteries that they are able to explain to my disadvantage. In vain did I submit the play to the criticism of my friends and the scrutiny of the public: all the corrections I could make, the judgment of the king and queen who saw the play,[2] the approval of great princes and ministers of state who honored it with their presence. the opinion of good men who found it worthwhile, all this did not help. They will not let go of their prey, and every day of the week they have pious zealots abusing me in public and damning me out of charity.

I would care very little about all they might say except that their devices make enemies of men whom I respect and gain the support of genuinely good men, whose faith they know and who, because of

* Molière's *Tartuffe* translated by Richard Wilbur.

The first version of *Tartuffe* was performed in 1664 and the second in 1667. The third and final version was published in March, 1669, accompanied by this preface. When a second edition of the third version was printed in June, 1669, Molière added his three petitions to Louis XIV; they follow the preface.

1. a reference to some of Molière's earlier plays, such as *Les Précieuses ridicules* and *L'Ecole des femmes*.

2. Louis XIV was married to Marie Thérèse of Austria.

the warmth of their piety, readily accept the impressions that others present to them. And it is this which forces me to defend myself. Especially to the truly devout do I wish to vindicate my play, and I beg of them with all my heart not to condemn it before seeing it, to rid themselves of preconceptions, and not aid the cause of men dishonored by their actions.

If one takes the trouble to examine my comedy in good faith, he will surely see that my intentions are innocent throughout, and tend in no way to make fun of what men revere; that I have presented the subject with all the precautions that its delicacy imposes; and that I have used all the art and skill that I could to distinguish clearly the character of the hypocrite from that of the truly devout man. For that purpose I used two whole acts to prepare the appearance of my scoundrel. Never is there a moment's doubt about his character; he is known at once from the qualities I have given him; and from one end of the play to the other, he does not say a word, he does not perform an action which does not depict to the audience the character of a wicked man, and which does not bring out in sharp relief the character of the truly good man which I oppose to it.

I know full well that by way of reply, these gentlemen try to insinuate that it is not the role of the theater to speak of these matters; but with their permission, I ask them on what do they base this fine doctrine. It is a proposition they advance as no more than a supposition, for which they offer not a shred of proof; and surely it would not be difficult to show them that comedy, for the ancients, had its origin in religion and constituted a part of its ceremonies; that our neighbors, the Spaniards, have hardly a single holiday celebration in which a comedy is not a part; and that even here in France, it owes its birth to the efforts of a religious brotherhood who still own the Hôtel de Bourgogne, where the most important mystery plays of our faith were presented[3]; that you can still find comedies printed in gothic letters under the name of a·learned doctor of the Sorbonne[4]; and without going so far, in our own day the religious dramas of Pierre Corneille[5] have been performed to the admiration of all France.

If the function of comedy is to correct men's vices, I do not see why any should be exempt. Such a condition in our society would be much more dangerous than the thing itself; and we have seen that the theater is admirably suited to provide correction. The most forceful lines of a serious moral statement are usually less powerful than

---

3. a reference to the *Confrérie de la Passion et Résurrection de Notre-Seigneur* (the Fraternity of the Passion and Resurrection of Our Saviour), founded in 1402. The Hôtel de Bourgogne was a rival theater of Molière.

4. probably Maitre Jehan Michel, a medical doctor who wrote mystery plays.

5. Pierre Corneille (1606–1684) and Racine were France's two greatest writers of classic tragedy. The two dramas Molière doubtlessly had in mind were *Polyeucte* (1643) and *Théodore, vierge et martyre* (1645).

those of satire; and nothing will reform most men better than the depiction of their faults. It is a vigorous blow to vices to expose them to public laughter. Criticism is taken lightly, but men will not tolerate satire. They are quite willing to be mean, but they never like to be ridiculed.

I have been attacked for having placed words of piety in the mouth of my impostor. Could I avoid doing so in order to represent properly the character of a hypocrite? It seemed to me sufficient to reveal the criminal motives which make him speak as he does, and I have eliminated all ceremonial phrases, which nonetheless he would not have been found using incorrectly. Yet some say that in the fourth act he sets forth a vicious morality; but is not this a morality which everyone has heard again and again? Does my comedy say anything new here? And is there any fear that ideas so thoroughly detested by everyone can make an impression on men's minds; that I make them dangerous by presenting them in the theater; that they acquire authority from the lips of a scoundrel? There is not the slightest suggestion of any of this; and one must either approve the comedy of *Tartuffe* or condemn all comedies in general.

This has indeed been done in a furious way for some time now, and never was the theater so much abused.[6] I cannot deny that there were Church Fathers who condemned comedy; but neither will it be denied me that there were some who looked on it somewhat more favorably. Thus authority, on which censure is supposed to depend, is destroyed by this disagreement; and the only conclusion that can be drawn from this difference of opinion among men enlightened by the same wisdom is that they viewed comedy in different ways, and that some considered it in its purity, while others regarded it in its corruption and confused it with all those wretched performances which have been rightly called performances of filth.

And in fact, since we should talk about things rather than words, and since most misunderstanding comes from including contrary notions in the same word, we need only to remove the veil of ambiguity and look at comedy in itself to see if it warrants condemnation. It will surely be recognized that as it is nothing more than a clever poem which corrects men's faults by means of agreeable lessons, it cannot be condemned without injustice. And if we listened to the voice of ancient times on this matter, it would tell us that its most famous philosophers have praised comedy—they who professed so austere a wisdom and who ceaselessly denounced the vices of their times. It would tell us that Aristotle spent his evenings at the theater[7] and took the trouble to reduce the art of making comedies to

6. Molière had in mind Nicole's two attacks on the theater: *Visionnaires* (1666) and *Traité de Comédie*, the Prince de Conti's *Traité de Comédie* (1666).

7. a reference to Aristotle's *Poetics* (composed between 335 and 322 B.C., the year of his death).

rules. It would tell us that some of its greatest and most honored men· took pride in writing comedies themselves[8]; and that others did not disdain to recite them in public; that Greece expressed its admiration for this art by means of handsome prizes and magnificent theaters to honor it; and finally, that in Rome this same art also received extraordinary honors; I do not speak of Rome run riot under the license of the emperors, but of disciplined Rome, governed by the wisdom of the consuls, and in the age of the full vigor of Roman dignity.

I admit that there have been times when comedy became corrupt. And what do men not corrupt every day? There is nothing so innocent that men cannot turn it to crime; nothing so beneficial that its values cannot be reversed; nothing so good in itself that it cannot be put to bad uses. Medical knowledge benefits mankind and is revered as one of our most wonderful possessions; and yet there was a time when it fell into discredit, and was often used to poison men. Philosophy is a gift of Heaven; it has been given to us to bring us to the knowledge of a God by contemplating the wonders of nature; and yet we know that often it has been turned away from its function and has been used openly in support of impiety. Even the holiest of things are not immune from human corruption, and every day we see scoundrels who use and abuse piety, and wickedly make it serve the greatest of crimes. But this does not prevent one from making the necessary distinctions. We do not confuse in the same false inference the goodness of things that are corrupted with the wickedness of the corrupt. The function of an art is always distinguished from its misuse; and as medicine is not forbidden because it was banned in Rome,[9] nor philosophy because it was publicly condemned in Athens,[10] we should not suppress comedy simply because it has been condemned at certain times. This censure was justified then for reasons which no longer apply today; it was limited to what was then seen; and we should not seize on these limits, apply them more rigidly than is necessary, and include in our condemnation the innocent along with the guilty. The comedy that this censure attacked is in no way the comedy that we want to defend. We must be careful not to confuse the one with the other. There may be two persons whose morals may be completely different. They may have no resemblance to one another except in their names, and it would be a terrible injustice to want to condemn Olympia, who is a good woman, because there is also an Olympia who is lewd. Such procedures would make for great confusion everywhere. Everything under the sun

---

8. The Roman consul and general responsible for the final destruction of Carthage in 146 B.C., Scipio Africanus Minor (*ca.* 185-129 B.C.), collaborated with the writer of comedies, Terence (Publius Terentius Afer, *ca.* 195 or 185 -*ca.* 159 B.C.).

9. Pliny the Elder says that the Romans expelled their doctors at the same time that the Greeks did theirs.

10. an allusion to Socrates' condemnation to death.

would be condemned; now since this rigor is not applied to the countless instances of abuse we see every day, the same should hold for comedy, and those plays should be approved in which instruction and virtue reign supreme.

I know there are some so delicate that they cannot tolerate a comedy, who say that the most decent are the most dangerous, that the passions they present are all the more moving because they are virtuous, and that men's feelings are stirred by these presentations. I do not see what great crime it is to be affected by the sight of a generous passion; and this utter insensitivity to which they would lead us is indeed a high degree of virtue! I wonder if so great a perfection resides within the strength of human nature, and I wonder if it is not better to try to correct and moderate men's passions than to try to suppress them altogether. I grant that there are places better to visit than the theater; and if we want to condemn every single thing that does not bear directly on God and our salvation, it is right that comedy be included, and I should willingly grant that it be condemned along with everything else. But if we admit, as is in fact true, that the exercise of piety will permit interruptions, and that men need amusement, I maintain that there is none more innocent than comedy. I have dwelled too long on this matter. Let me finish with the words of a great prince on the comedy, *Tartuffe*.[11]

Eight days after it had been banned, a play called *Scaramouche the Hermit*[12] was performed before the court; and the king, on his way out, said to this great prince: "I should really like to know why the persons who make so much noise about Molière's comedy do not say a word about *Scaramouche*." To which the prince replied, "It is because the comedy of *Scaramouche* makes fun of Heaven and religion, which these gentlemen do not care about at all, but that of Molière makes fun of *them*, and that is what they cannot bear."

THE AUTHOR

First Petition[13]

(presented to the King on the comedy of Tartuffe)

Sire,

As the duty of comedy is to correct men by amusing them, I be-

11. One of Molière's benefactors who liked the play was the Prince de Condé; de Condé had *Tartuffe* read to him and also privately performed for him.

12. A troupe of Italian comedians had just performed the licentious farce, where a hermit dressed as a monk makes love to a married woman, announcing that *questo e per mortificar la carne* ("this is to mortify the flesh").

13. The first of the three *petitions* or *placets* to Louis XIV concerning the play. On May 12, 1664, *Tartuffe*—or at least the first three acts roughly as they now stand—was performed at Versailles. A cabal unfavorable to Molière, including the Archbishop of Paris, Hardouin de Péréfixe, Queen-Mother Anne of Austria, certain influential courtiers, and the Brotherhood or Company of the Holy Sacrament (formed in 1627 to enforce morality), arranged that the play be banned and Molière censured.

lieved that in my occupation I could do nothing better than attack the vices of my age by making them ridiculous; and as hypocrisy is undoubtedly one of the most common, most improper, and most dangerous, I thought, Sire, that I would perform a service for all good men of your kingdom if I wrote a comedy which denounced hypocrites and placed in proper view all of the contrived poses of these incredibly virtuous men, all of the concealed villainies of these counterfeit believers who would trap others with a fraudulent piety and a pretended virtue.

I have written this comedy, Sire, with all the care and caution that the delicacy of the subject demands; and so as to maintain all the more properly the admiration and respect due to truly devout men, I have delineated my character as sharply as I could; I have left no room for doubt; I have removed all that might confuse good with evil, and have used for this painting only the specific colors and essential lines that make one instantly recognize a true and brazen hypocrite.

Nevertheless, all my precautions have been to no avail. Others have taken advantage of the delicacy of your feelings on religious matters, and they have been able to deceive you on the only side of your character which lies open to deception: your respect for holy things. By underhanded means, the Tartuffes have skillfully gained Your Majesty's favor, and the models have succeeded in eliminating the copy, no matter how innocent it may have been and no matter what resemblance was found between them.

Although the suppression of this work was a serious blow for me, my misfortune was nonetheless softened by the way in which Your Majesty explained his attitude on the matter; and I believed, Sire, that Your Majesty removed any cause I had for complaint, as you were kind enough to declare that you found nothing in this comedy that you would forbid me to present in public.

Yet, despite this glorious declaration of the greatest and most enlightened king in the world, despite the approval of the Papal Legate[14] and of most of our churchmen, all of whom, at private readings of my work, agreed with the views of Your Majesty, despite all this, a book has appeared by a certain priest[15] which boldly contradicts all of these noble judgments. Your Majesty expressed himself in vain, and the Papal Legate and churchmen gave their opinion to no avail: sight unseen, my comedy is diabolical, and so is my brain; I am a devil garbed in flesh and disguised as a man,[16] a libertine, a disbeliever who deserves a punishment that will set an example. It is not

14. Cardinal Legate Chigi, nephew to Pope Alexander VII, heard a reading of *Tartuffe* at Fontainebleau on August 4, 1664.

15. Pierre Roullé, the curate of St.

Barthélémy, who wrote a scathing attack on the play and sent his book to the king.

16. Molière took some of these phrases from Roullé.

enough that fire expiate my crime in public, for that would be letting me off too easily: the generous piety of this good man will not stop there; he will not allow me to find any mercy in the sight of God; he demands that I be damned, and that will settle the matter.

This book, Sire, was presented to Your Majesty; and I am sure that you see for yourself how unpleasant it is for me to be exposed daily to the insults of these gentlemen, what harm these abuses will do my reputation if they must be tolerated, and finally, how important it is for me to clear myself of these false charges and let the public know that my comedy is nothing more than what they want it to be. I will not ask, Sire, for what I need for the sake of my reputation and the innocence of my work: enlightened kings such as you do not need to be told what is wished of them; like God, they see what we need and know better than we what they should give us. It is enough for me to place my interests in Your Majesty's hands, and I respectfully await whatever you may care to command.

(*August, 1664*)

Second Petition[17]

(*presented to the King in his camp before the city of Lille, in Flanders*)

Sire,

It is bold indeed for me to ask a favor of a great monarch in the midst of his glorious victories; but in my present situation, Sire, where will I find protection anywhere but where I seek it, and to whom can I appeal against the authority of the power that crushes me,[18] if not to the source of power and authority, the just dispenser of absolute law, the sovereign judge and master of all?

My comedy, Sire, has not enjoyed the kindnesses of Your Majesty. All to no avail, I produced it under the title of *The Hypocrite* and disguised the principal character as a man of the world; in vain I gave him a little hat, long hair, a wide collar, a sword, and lace clothing,[19] softened the action and carefully eliminated all that I thought might provide even the shadow of grounds for discontent on the part of the famous models of the portrait I wished to present; nothing did any good. The conspiracy of opposition revived even at mere conjecture of what the play would be like. They found a way

17. On August 5, 1667, *Tartuffe* was performed at the Palais-Royal. The opposition—headed by the First President of Parliament—brought in the police, and the play was stopped. Since Louis was campaigning in Flanders, friends of Molière brought the second *placet* to Lille. Louis had always been favorable toward the playwright; in August, 1665, Molière's company, the *Troupe de Mon-* sieur (nominally sponsored by Louis's brother Philippe, Duc d'Orléans) had become the *Troupe du Roi.*

18. President de Lanvignon, in charge of the Paris police.

19. There is evidence that in 1664 *Tartuffe* played his role dressed in a cassock, thus allying him more directly to the clergy.

of persuading those who in all other matters plainly insist that they are not to be deceived. No sooner did my comedy appear than it was struck down by the very power which should impose respect; and all that I could do to save myself from the fury of this tempest was to say that Your Majesty had given me permission to present the play and I did not think it was necessary to ask this permission of others, since only Your Majesty could have refused it.

I have no doubt, Sire, that the men whom I depict in my comedy will employ every means possible to influence Your Majesty, and will use, as they have used already, those truly good men who are all the more easily deceived because they judge of others by themselves.[20] They know how to display all of their aims in the most favorable light; yet, no matter how pious they may seem, it is surely not the interests of God which stir them; they have proven this often enough in the comedies they have allowed to be performed hundreds of times without making the least objection. Those plays attacked only piety and religion, for which they care very little; but this play attacks and makes fun of them, and that is what they cannot bear. They will never forgive me for unmasking their hypocrisy in the eyes of everyone. And I am sure that they will not neglect to tell Your Majesty that people are shocked by my comedy. But the simple truth, Sire, is that all Paris is shocked only by its ban, that the most scrupulous persons have found its presentation worthwhile, and men are astounded that individuals of such known integrity should show so great a deference to people whom everyone should abominate and who are so clearly opposed to the true piety which they profess.

I respectfully await the judgment that Your Majesty will deign to pronounce; but it is certain, Sire, that I need not think of writing comedies if the Tartuffes are triumphant, if they thereby seize the right to persecute me more than ever, and find fault with even the most innocent lines that flow from my pen.

Let your goodness, Sire, give me protection against their envenomed rage, and allow me, at your return from so glorious a campaign, to relieve Your Majesty from the fatigue of his conquests, give him innocent pleasures after such noble accomplishments, and make the monarch laugh who makes all Europe tremble!

(*August, 1667*)

---

20. Molière apparently did not know that de Lanvignon had been affiliated with the Company of the Holy Sacrament for the previous ten years.

Third Petition

(*presented to the King*)

Sire,

A very honest doctor[21] whose patient I have the honor to be, promises and will legally contract to make me live another thirty years if I can obtain a favor for him from Your Majesty. I told him of his promise that I do not deserve so much, and that I should be glad to help him if he will merely agree not to kill me. This favor, Sire, is a post of canon at your royal chapel of Vincennes, made vacant by death.

May I dare to ask for this favor from Your Majesty on the very day of the glorious resurrection of *Tartuffe*, brought back to life by your goodness? By this first favor I have been reconciled with the devout, and the second will reconcile me with the doctors.[22] Undoubtedly this would be too much grace for me at one time, but perhaps it would not be too much for Your Majesty, and I await your answer to my petition with respectful hope.

(*February*, 1669)

21. a physician friend, M. de Mauvillain, who helped Molière with some of the medical details of *Le Malade imaginaire*.

22. Doctors are ridiculed to varying degrees in earlier plays of Molière: *Dom Juan*, *L'Amour médecin*, and *Le Médecin malgré lui*.

Characters†

MME PERNELLE, *Orgon's mother*

ORGON, *Elmire's husband*

ELMIRE, *Orgon's wife*

DAMIS, *Orgon's son, Elmire's stepson*

MARIANE, *Orgon's daughter, Elmire's stepdaughter, in love with Valère*

† The name Tartuffe has been traced back to an older word associated with liar or charlatan: *truffer*, "to deceive" or "to cheat". Then there was also the Italian actor, Tartufo, physically deformed and truffle-shaped. Most of the other names are typical of this genre of court-comedy and possess rather elegant connotations of pastoral and *bergerie*.

Dorine would be a *demoiselle de compagne* and not a mere maid; that is, a female companion to Mariane of roughly the same social status. This in part accounts for the liberties she takes in conversation with Orgon, Madame Pernelle, and others. Her name is short for Théodorine.

VALERE, *in love with Mariane*
CLEANTE, *Orgon's brother-in-law*
TARTUFFE, *a hypocrite*
DORINE, *Mariane's lady's-maid*
M. LOYAL, *a bailiff*
A POLICE OFFICER
FLIPOTE, *Mme Pernelle's maid*

The SCENE *throughout: Orgon's house in Paris*

Act I

SCENE 1. *Madame Pernelle and Flipote, her maid, Elmire,*
Mariane, Dorine, Damis, Cleante

MADAME PERNELLE. Come, come, Flipote; it's time I left this place.
ELMIRE. I can't keep up, you walk at such a pace.
MADAME PERNELLE. Don't trouble, child; no need to show me out.
  It's not your manners I'm concerned about.
ELMIRE. We merely pay you the respect we owe. 5
  But, Mother, why this hurry? Must you go?
MADAME PERNELLE. I must. This house appals me. No one in it
  Will pay attention for a single minute.
  I offer good advice, but you won't hear it.
  Children, I take my leave much vexed in spirit. 10
  You all break in and chatter on and on.
  It's like a madhouse with the keeper gone.
DORINE. If . . .
MADAME PERNELLE. Girl, you talk too much, and I'm afraid
  You're far too saucy for a lady's-maid.
  You push in everywhere and have your say. 15
DAMIS. But . . .
MADAME PERNELLE. You, boy, grow more foolish every day.
  To think my grandson should be such a dunce!
  I've said a hundred times, if I've said it once,
  That if you keep the course on which you've started,
  You'll leave your worthy father broken-hearted. 20
MARIANE. I think . . .
MADAME PERNELLE.   And you, his sister, seem so pure,
  So shy, so innocent, and so demure.
  But you know what they say about still waters.
  I pity parents with secretive daughters.
ELMIRE. Now, Mother . . .

---

12. *Madhouse:* in the original, *la cour du roi Pétaud*, the Court of King Pétaud where all are masters; a house of misrule.

MADAME PERNELLE.   And as for you, child, let me add
   That your behavior is extremely bad,   25
   And a poor example for these children, too.
   Their dear, dead mother did far better than you.
   You're much too free with money, and I'm distressed
   To see you so elaborately dressed.   30
   When it's one's husband that one aims to please,
   One has no need of costly fripperies.
CLEANTE. Oh, Madam, really . . .
MADAME PERNELLE.   You are her Brother, Sir,
   And I respect and love you; yet if I were
   My son, this lady's good and pious spouse,   35
   I wouldn't make you welcome in my house.
   You're full of worldly counsels which, I fear,
   Aren't suitable for decent folk to hear.
   I've spoken bluntly, Sir; but it behooves us
   Not to mince words when righteous fervor moves us.   40
DAMIS. Your man Tartuffe is full of holy speeches . . .
MADAME PERNELLE. And practises precisely what he preaches.
   He's a fine man, and should be listened to.
   I will not hear him mocked by fools like you.
DAMIS. Good God! Do you expect me to submit   45
   To the tyranny of that carping hypocrite?
   Must we forgo all joys and satisfactions
   Because that bigot censures all our actions?
DORINE. To hear him talk—and he talks all the time—
   There's nothing one can do that's not a crime.   50
   He rails at everything, your dear Tartuffe.
MADAME PERNELLE. Whatever he reproves deserves reproof.
   He's out to save your souls, and all of you
   Must love him, as my son would have you do.
DAMIS. Ah no, Grandmother, I could never take   55
   To such a rascal, even for my father's sake.
   That's how I feel, and I shall not dissemble.
   His every action makes me seethe and tremble,
   With helpless anger, and I have no doubt
   That he and I will shortly have it out.   60
DORINE. Surely it is a shame and a disgrace
   To see this man usurp the master's place—
   To see this beggar who, when first he came,
   Had not a shoe or shoestring to his name
   So far forget himself that he behaves   65
   As if the house were his, and we his slaves.
MADAME PERNELLE. Well, mark my words, your souls would fare
        far better

If you obeyed his precepts to the letter.

DORINE. You see him as a saint. I'm far less awed;
   In fact, I see right through him. He's a fraud.   70

MADAME PERNELLE. Nonsense!

DORINE.   His man Laurent's the same, or
      worse;
   I'd not trust either with a penny purse.

MADAME PERNELLE. I can't say what his servant's morals may be;
   His own great goodness I can guarantee.
   You all regard him with distaste and fear   75
   Because he tells you what you're loath to hear,
   Condemns your sins, points out your moral flaws,
   And humbly strives to further Heaven's cause.

DORINE. If sin is all that bothers him, why is it
   He's so upset when folk drop in to visit?   80
   Is Heaven so outraged by a social call
   That he must prophesy against us all?
   I'll tell you what I think: if you ask me,
   He's jealous of my mistress' company.

MADAME PERNELLE. Rubbish! [*To* ELMIRE] He's not alone, child,
      in complaining   85
   Of all of your promiscuous entertaining.
   Why, the whole neighborhood's upset, I know,
   By all these carriages that come and go,
   With crowds of guests parading in and out
   And noisy servants loitering about.   90
   In all of this, I'm sure there's nothing vicious;
   But why give people cause to be suspicious?

CLEANTE. They need no cause; they'll talk in any case.
   Madam, this world would be a joyless place
   If, fearing what malicious tongues might say,   95
   We locked our doors and turned our friends away.
   And even if one did so dreary a thing,
   D' you think those tongues would cease their chattering?
   One can't fight slander; it's a losing battle;
   Let us instead ignore their tittle-tattle.   100
   Let's strive to live by conscience' clear decrees,
   And let the gossips gossip as they please.

DORINE. If there is talk against us, I know the source:
   It's Daphne and her little husband, of course.
   Those who have greatest cause for guilt and shame   105
   Are quickest to besmirch a neighbor's name.
   When there's a chance for libel, they never miss it;
   When something can be made to seem illicit
   They're off at once to spread the joyous news,

Adding to fact what fantasies they choose. 110
By talking up their neighbor's indiscretions
They seek to camouflage their own transgressions,
Hoping that others' innocent affairs
Will lend a hue of innocence to theirs,
Or that their own black guilt will come to seem 115
Part of a general shady color-scheme.

MADAME PERNELLE. All that is quite irrelevant. I doubt
That anyone's more virtuous and devout
Than dear Orante; and I'm informed that she
Condemns your mode of life most vehemently. 120

DORINE. Oh, yes, she's strict, devout, and has no taint
Of worldliness; in short, she seems a saint.
But it was time which taught her that disguise;
She's thus because she can't be otherwise.
So long as her attractions could enthrall, 125
She flounced and flirted and enjoyed it all,
But now that they're no longer what they were
She quits a world which fast is quitting her,
And wears a veil of virtue to conceal
Her bankrupt beauty and her lost appeal. 130
That's what becomes of old coquettes today:
Distressed when all their lovers fall away,
They see no recourse but to play the prude,
And so confer a style on solitude.
Thereafter, they're severe with everyone, 135
Condemning all our actions, pardoning none,
And claiming to be pure, austere, and zealous
When, if the truth were known, they're merely jealous,
And cannot bear to see another know
The pleasures time has forced them to forgo. 140

MADAME PERNELLE. [*Initially to* ELMIRE] That sort of talk
        is what you like to hear;
Therefore you'd have us all keep still, my dear,
While Madam rattles on the livelong day.
Nevertheless, I mean to have my say.
I tell you that you're blest to have Tartuffe 145
Dwelling, as my son's guest, beneath this roof;
That Heaven has sent him to forestall its wrath
By leading you, once more, to the true path;
That all he reprehends is reprehensible,
And that you'd better heed him, and be sensible. 150
These visits, balls, and parties in which you revel

141. *That sort of talk:* in the original, a reference to a collection of novels about chivalry found in *La Bibliothèque bleue* (*The Blue Library*), written for children.

Are nothing but inventions of the Devil.
One never hears a word that's edifying:
Nothing but chaff and foolishness and lying,
As well as vicious gossip in which one's neighbor   155
Is cut to bits with épée, foil, and saber.
People of sense are driven half-insane
At such affairs, where noise and folly reign
And reputations perish thick and fast.
As a wise preacher said on Sunday last,   160
Parties are Towers of Babylon, because
The guests all babble on with never a pause;
And then he told a story which, I think . . .
     [*To* CLEANTE] I heard that laugh, Sir, and I saw that wink!
Go find your silly friends and laugh some more!   165
Enough; I'm going; don't show me to the door.
I leave this household much dismayed and vexed;
I cannot say when I shall see you next.
     [*Slapping* FLIPOTE]Wake up, don't stand there gaping into
     space!
I'll slap some sense into that stupid face.   170
Move, move, you slut.

SCENE 2. *Cléante, Dorine*

CLEANTE.   I think I'll stay behind;
I want no further pieces of her mind.
How that old lady . . .
DORINE.   Oh, what wouldn't she say
If she could hear you speak of her that way!
She'd thank you for the *lady*, but I'm sure   5
She'd find the *old* a little premature.
CLEANTE. My, what a scene she made, and what a din!
And how this man Tartuffe has taken her in!
DORINE. Yes, but her son is even worse deceived;
His folly must be seen to be believed.   10
In the late troubles, he played an able part
And served his king with wise and loyal heart,
But he's quite lost his senses since he fell
Beneath Tartuffe's infatuating spell.
He calls him brother, and loves him as his life,   15
Preferring him to mother, child, or wife.
In him and him alone will he confide;
He's made him his confessor and his guide;

---

161. *Towers of Babylon:* i.e. Tower
of Babel. Mme. Pernelle's malapropism
is the cause of Cléante's laughter.
    11. *the late troubles:* a series of polit-
ical disturbances during the minority of
Louis XIV. Specifically these consisted

of the *Fronde* ("opposition") of the
Parlement (1648-1649) and the *Fronde*
of the Princes (1650-1653). Orgon is
depicted as supporting Louis XIV in
these outbreaks and their resolution.

He pets and pampers him with love more tender
Than any pretty maiden could engender,   20
Gives him the place of honor when they dine,
Delights to see him gorging like a swine,
Stuffs him with dainties till his guts distend,
And when he belches, cries "God bless you, friend!"
In short, he's mad; he worships him; he dotes;   25
His deeds he marvels at, his words, he quotes,
Thinking each act a miracle, each word
Oracular as those that Moses heard.
Tartuffe, much pleased to find so easy a victim,
Has in a hundred ways beguiled and tricked him,   30
Milked him of money, and with his permission
Established here a sort of Inquisition.
Even Laurent, his lackey, dares to give
Us arrogant advice on how to live;
He sermonizes us in thundering tones   35
And confiscates our ribbons and colognes.
Last week he tore a kerchief into pieces
Because he found it pressed in a *Life of Jesus:*
He said it was a sin to juxtapose
Unholy vanities and holy prose.   40

SCENE 3. *Elmire, Mariane, Damis, Cléante, Dorine*

ELMIRE. [To CLEANTE] You did well not to follow; she stood in
        the door
    And said *verbatim* all she'd said before.
    I saw my husband coming. I think I'd best
    Go upstairs now, and take a little rest.
CLEANTE. I'll wait and greet him here; then I must go.   5
    I've really only time to say hello.
DAMIS. Sound him about my sister's wedding, please.
    I think Tartuffe's against it, and that he's
    Been urging Father to withdraw his blessing.
    As you well know, I'd find that most distressing.   10
    Unless my sister and Valère can marry,
    My hopes to wed his sister will miscarry,
    And I'm determined . . .
DORINE.   He's coming.

SCENE 4. *Orgon, Cléante, Dorine*

ORGON.   Ah, Brother, good-day.
CLEANTE. Well, welcome back. I'm sorry I can't stay.

---

37. Laurent's act is more salacious than the translation might suggest.

How was the country? Blooming, I trust, and green?
ORGON. Excuse me, Brother; just one moment.
    [*To* DORINE]   Dorine ...
    [*To* CLEANTE] To put my mind at rest, I always learn   5
The household news the moment I return.
    [*To* DORINE] Has all been well, these two days I've been gone?
How are the family? What's been going on?
DORINE. Your wife, two days ago, had a bad fever,
    And a fierce headache which refused to leave her.   10
ORGON. Ah. And Tartuffe?
DORINE.   Tartuffe? Why, he's round and red,
    Bursting with health, and excellently fed.
ORGON. Poor fellow!
DORINE.   That night, the mistress was unable
    To take a single bite at the dinner-table.
    Her headache-pains, she said, were simply hellish.   15
ORGON. Ah. And Tartuffe?
DORINE.   He ate his meal with relish,
    And zealously devoured in her presence
    A leg of mutton and a brace of pheasants.
ORGON. Poor fellow!
DORINE.   Well, the pains continued strong,
    And so she tossed and tossed the whole night long,   20
    Now icy-cold, now burning like a flame.
    We sat beside her bed till morning came.
ORGON. Ah. And Tartuffe?
DORINE.   Why, having eaten, he rose
    And sought his room, already in a doze,
    Got into his warm bed, and snored away   25
    In perfect peace until the break of day.
ORGON. Poor fellow!
DORINE.   After much ado, we talked her
    Into dispatching someone for the doctor.
    He bled her, and the fever quickly fell.
ORGON. Ah. And Tartuffe?
DORINE.   He bore it very well.   30
    To keep his cheerfulness at any cost,
    And make up for the blood *Madame* had lost,
    He drank, at lunch, four beakers full of port.
ORGON. Poor fellow!
DORINE.   Both are doing well, in short.
    I'll go and tell *Madame* that you've expressed   35
    Keen sympathy and anxious interest.

SCENE 5. *Orgon, Cléante*

CLEANTE. That girl was laughing in your face, and though
    I've no wish to offend you, even so

I'm bound to say that she had some excuse.
How can you possibly be such a goose?
Are you so dazed by this man's hocus-pocus   5
That all the world, save him, is out of focus?
You've given him clothing, shelter, food, and care;
Why must you also . . .

ORGON.   Brother, stop right there.
  You do not know the man of whom you speak.

CLEANTE. I grant you that. But my judgment's not so weak   10
  That I can't tell, by his effect on others . . .

ORGON. Ah, when you meet him, you two will be like brothers!
  There's been no loftier soul since time began.
  He is a man who . . . a man who . . . an excellent man.
  To keep his precepts is to be reborn,   15
  And view this dunghill of a world with scorn.
  Yes, thanks to him I'm a changed man indeed.
  Under his tutelage my soul's been freed
  From earthly loves, and every human tie:
  My mother, children, brother, and wife could die,   20
  And I'd not feel a single moment's pain.

CLEANTE. That's a fine sentiment, Brother; most humane.

ORGON. Oh, had you seen Tartuffe as I first knew him,
  Your heart, like mine, would have surrendered to him.
  He used to come into our church each day   25
  And humbly kneel nearby, and start to pray.
  He'd draw the eyes of everybody there
  By the deep fervor of his heartfelt prayer;
  He'd sigh and weep, and sometimes with a sound
  Of rapture he would bend and kiss the ground;   30
  And when I rose to go, he'd run before
  To offer me holy-water at the door.
  His serving-man, no less devout than he,
  Informed me of his master's poverty;
  I gave him gifts, but in his humbleness   35
  He'd beg me every time to give him less.
  "Oh, that's too much," he'd cry, "too much by twice!
  I don't deserve it. The half, Sir, would suffice."
  And when I wouldn't take it back, he'd share
  Half of it with the poor, right then and there.   40
  At length, Heaven prompted me to take him in
  To dwell with us, and free our souls from sin.
  He guides our lives, and to protect my honor
  Stays by my wife, and keeps an eye upon her;
  He tells me whom she sees, and all she does,   45
  And seems more jealous than I ever was!
  And how austere he is! Why, he can detect
  A moral sin where you would least suspect;

In smallest trifles, he's extremely strict.
Last week, his conscience was severely pricked   50
Because, while praying, he had caught a flea
And killed it, so he felt, too wrathfully.

CLEANTE. Good God, man! Have you lost your common sense—
Or is this all some joke at my expense?
How can you stand there and in all sobriety . . .   55

ORGON. Brother, your language savors of impiety.
Too much free-thinking's made your faith unsteady,
And as I've warned you many times already,
'Twill get you into trouble before you're through.

CLEANTE. So I've been told before by dupes like you: 60
Being blind, you'd have all others blind as well;
The clear-eyed man you call an infidel,
And he who sees through humbug and pretense
Is charged, by you, with want of reverence.
Spare me your warnings, Brother; I have no fear   65
Of speaking out, for you and Heaven to hear,
Against affected zeal and pious knavery.
There's true and false in piety, as in bravery,
And just as those whose courage shines the most
In battle, are the least inclined to boast,   70
So those whose hearts are truly pure and lowly
Don't make a flashy show of being holy.
There's a vast difference, so it seems to me,
Between true piety and hypocrisy:
How do you fail to see it, may I ask?   75
Is not a face quite different from a mask?
Cannot sincerity and cunning art,
Realty and semblance, be told apart?
Are scarecrows just like men, and do you hold
That a false coin is just as good as gold?   80
Ah, Brother, man's a strangely fashioned creature
Who seldom is content to follow Nature,
But recklessly pursues his inclination
Beyond the narrow bounds of moderation,
And often, by transgressing Reason's laws,   85
Perverts, a lofty aim or noble cause.
A passing observation, but it applies.

ORGON. I see, dear Brother, that you're profoundly wise;
You harbor all the insight of the age.
You are our one clear mind, our only sage,   90

50-52. *Last week . . . wrathfully:* In the *Golden Legend* (*Legenda santorum*), a popular collection of the lives of the saints written in the thirteenth century, it is said of St. Marcarius the Elder (d. 390) that he dwelt naked in the desert for six months, a penance he felt appropriate for having killed a flea.

The era's oracle, its Cato too,
And all mankind are fools compared to you.
CLEANTE. Brother, I don't pretend to be a sage,
Nor have I all the wisdom of the age.
There's just one insight I would dare to claim: 95
I know that true and false are not the same;
And just as there is nothing I more revere
Than a soul whose faith is steadfast and sincere,
Nothing that I more cherish and admire
Than honest zeal and true religious fire, 100
So there is nothing that I find more base
Than specious piety's dishonest face—
Than these bold mountebanks, these histrios
Whose impious mummeries and hollow shows
Exploit our love of Heaven, and make a jest 105
Of all that men think holiest and best;
These calculating souls who offer prayers
Not to their Maker, but as public wares,
And seek to buy respect and reputation
With lifted eyes and sighs of exaltation; 110
These charlatans, I say, whose pilgrim souls
Proceed, by way of Heaven, toward earthly goals,
Who weep and pray and swindle and extort,
Who preach the monkish life, but haunt the court,
Who make their zeal the partner of their vice— 115
Such men are vengeful, sly, and cold as ice,
And when there is an enemy to defame
They cloak their spite in fair religion's name,
Their private spleen and malice being made
To seem a high and virtuous crusade, 120
Until, to mankind's reverent applause,
They crucify their foe in Heaven's cause.
Such knaves are all too common; yet, for the wise,
True piety isn't hard to recognize,
And, happily, these present times provide us 125
With bright examples to instruct and guide us.
Consider Ariston and Périandre;
Look at Oronte, Alcidamas, Clitandre;
Their virtue is acknowledged; who could doubt it?
But you won't hear them beat the drum about it. 130
They're never ostentatious, never vain,
And their religion's moderate and humane;
It's not their way to criticize and chide:

127-128. *Ariston . . . Clitandre:* vaguely Greek and Roman names derived
from the elegant literature of the day;
not names of actual persons.

They think censoriousness a mark of pride,
And therefore, letting others preach and rave,   135
They show, by deeds, how Christians should behave.
They think no evil of their fellow man,
But judge of him as kindly as they can.
They don't intrigue and wangle and conspire;
To lead a good life is their one desire;   140
The sinner wakes no rancorous hate in them;
It is the sin alone which they condemn;
Nor do they try to show a fiercer zeal
For Heaven's cause than Heaven itself could feel.
These men I honor, these men I advocate   145
As models for us all to emulate.
Your man is not their sort at all, I fear:
And, while your praise of him is quite sincere,
I think that you've been dreadfully deluded.

ORGON. Now then, dear Brother, is your speech concluded?   150
CLEANTE. Why, yes.
ORGON.   Your servant, Sir.   [*He turns to go.*]
CLEANTE.   No, Brother; wait.
There's one more matter. You agreed of late
That young Valère might have your daughter's hand.
ORGON. I did.
CLEANTE.   And set the date, I understand.
ORGON. Quite so.
CLEANTE.   You've now postponed it; is that true?   155
ORGON. No doubt.
CLEANTE.   The match no longer pleases you?
ORGON. Who knows?
CLEANTE.   D'you mean to go back on your word?
ORGON. I won't say that.
CLEANTE.   Has anything occurred
Which might entitle you to break your pledge?
ORGON. Perhaps.
CLEANTE.   Why must you hem, and haw, and hedge?
The boy asked me to sound you in this affair . . .   160
ORGON. It's been a pleasure.
CLEANTE.   But what shall I tell Valère?
ORGON. Whatever you like.
CLEANTE.   But what have you decided?
What are your plans?
ORGON.   I plan, Sir, to be guided
By Heaven's will.
CLEANTE.   Come, Brother, don't talk rot.   165
You've given Valère your word; will you keep it, or not?

ORGON. Good day.
CLEANTE.   This looks like poor Valère's undoing;
  I'll go and warn him that there's trouble brewing.

Act II

SCENE 1. *Orgon, Mariane*

ORGON. Mariane.
MARIANE.   Yes, Father?
ORGON.   A word with you; come here.
MARIANE. What are you looking for?
ORGON. [*Peering into a small closet*] Eavesdroppers, dear.
  I'm making sure we shan't be overheard.
  Someone in there could catch our every word.
  Ah, good, we're safe. Now, Mariane, my child,   5
  You're a sweet girl who's tractable and mild,
  Whom I hold dear, and think most highly of.
MARIANE. I'm deeply grateful, Father, for your love.
ORGON. That's well said, Daughter; and you can repay me
  If, in all things, you'll cheerfully obey me.   10
MARIANE. To please you, Sir, is what delights me best.
ORGON. Good, good. Now, what d'you think of Tartuffe, our guest?
MARIANE. I, Sir?
ORGON.   Yes. Weigh your answer; think it through.
MARIANE. Oh, dear. I'll say whatever you wish me to.
ORGON. That's wisely said, my Daughter. Say of him, then,   15
  That he's the very worthiest of men,
  And that you're fond of him, and would rejoice
  In being his wife, if that should be my choice.
  Well?
MARIANE. What
ORGON.   What's that?
MARIANE.   I . . .
ORGON.   Well?
MARIANE.   Forgive me, pray.
ORGON. Did you not hear me?
MARIANE.   Of *whom*, Sir, must I say   20
  That I am fond of him, and would rejoice
  In being his wife, if that should be your choice?
ORGON. Why, of Tartuffe.
MARIANE.   But, Father, that's false, you know.
  Why would you have me say what isn't so?
ORGON. Because I am resolved it shall be true.   25
  That it's my wish should be enough for you.
MARIANE. You can't mean, Father . . .

ORGON.   Yes, Tartuffe shall be
Allied by marriage to this family,
And he's to be your husband, is that clear?
It's a father's privilege . . .

SCENE 2. *Dorine, Orgon, Mariane*

ORGON. [To DORINE]   What are you doing in here?
Is curiosity so fierce a passion
With you, that you must eavesdrop in this fashion?
DORINE. There's lately been a rumor going about—
Based on some hunch or chance remark, no doubt—   5
That you mean Mariane to wed Tartuffe.
I've laughed it off, of course, as just a spoof.
ORGON. You find it so incredible?
DORINE.   Yes, I do.
I won't accept that story, even from you.
ORGON. Well, you'll believe it when the thing is done.   10
DORINE. Yes, yes, of course. Go on and have your fun.
ORGON. I've never been more serious in my life.
DORINE. Ha!
ORGON.   Daughter, I mean it; you're to be his wife.
DORINE. No, don't believe your father; it's all a hoax.
ORGON. See here, young woman . . .
DORINE.   Come, Sir, no more jokes;
You can't fool us.   15
ORGON.   How dare you talk that way?
DORINE. All right, then: we believe you, sad to say.
But how a man like you, who looks so wise
And wears a moustache of such splendid size,
Can be so foolish as to . . .
ORGON.   Silence, please!   20
My girl, you take too many liberties.
I'm master here, as you must not forget.
DORINE. Do let's discuss this calmly; don't be upset.
You can't be serious, Sir, about this plan.
What should that bigot want with Mariane?   25
Praying and fasting ought to keep him busy.
And then, in terms of wealth and rank, what is he?
Why should a man of property like you
Pick out a beggar son-in-law?
ORGON.   That will do.
Speak of his poverty with reverence.   30

29. *Allied by marriage:* This assertion
is important and more than a mere device in the plot of the play. The second
placet or petition insists that Tartuffe be
costumed as a layman, and Orgon's plan
for him to marry again asserts Tartuffe's
position in the laity. In the 1664 version
of the play Tartuffe had been dressed in
a cassock suggestive of the priesthood,
and Molière was now anxious to avoid
any suggestion of this kind.

His is a pure and saintly indigence
Which far transcends all worldly pride and pelf.
He lost his fortune, as he says himself,
Because he cared for Heaven alone, and so
Was careless of his interests here below. 35
I mean to get him out of his present straits
And help him to recover his estates—
Which, in his part of the world, have no small fame.
Poor though he is, he's a gentleman just the same.

DORINE. Yes, so he tells us; and, Sir, it seems to me 40
Such pride goes very ill with piety.
A man whose spirit spurns this dungy earth
Ought not to brag of lands and noble birth;
Such worldly arrogance will hardly square
With meek devotion and the life of prayer. 45
. . . But this approach, I see, has drawn a blank;
Let's speak, then, of his person, not his rank.
Doesn't it seem to you a trifle grim
To give a girl like her to a man like him?
When two are so ill-suited, can't you see 50
What the sad consequence is bound to be?
A young girl's virtue is imperilled, Sir,
When such a marriage is imposed on her;
For if one's bridegroom isn't to one's taste,
It's hardly an inducement to be chaste, 55
And many a man with horns upon his brow
Has made his wife the thing that she is now.
It's hard to be a faithful wife, in short,
To certain husbands of a certain sort,
And he who gives his daughter to a man she hates 60
Must answer for her sins at Heaven's gates.
Think, Sir, before you play so risky a role.

ORGON. This servant-girl presumes to save my soul!

DORINE. You would do well to ponder what I've said.

ORGON. Daughter, we'll disregard this dunderhead. 65
Just trust your father's judgment. Oh, I'm aware
That I once promised you to young Valère;
But now I hear he gambles, which greatly shocks me;
What's more, I've doubts about his orthodoxy.
His visits to church, I note, are very few. 70

DORINE. Would you have him go at the same hours as you,
And kneel nearby, to be sure of being seen?

ORGON. I can dispense with such remarks, Dorine.
[*To* MARIANE] Tartuffe, however, is sure of Heaven's blessing.
And that's the only treasure worth possessing. 75
This match will bring you joys beyond all measure;
Your cup will overflow with every pleasure;

You two will interchange your faithful loves
Like two sweet cherubs, or two turtle-doves.
No harsh word shall be heard, no frown be seen,   80
And he shall make you happy as a queen.

DORINE. And she'll make him a cuckold, just wait and see.

ORGON. What language!

DORINE.   Oh, he's a man of destiny;
He's *made* for horns, and what the stars demand
Your daughter's virtue surely can't withstand.   85

ORGON. Don't interrupt me further. Why can't you learn
That certain things are none of your concern?

DORINE. It's for your own sake that I interfere.

[*She repeatedly interrupts* ORGON *just as he is turning to speak to his daughter.*]

ORGON. Most kind of you. Now, hold your tongue, d'you hear?

DORINE. If I didn't love you . . .

ORGON.   Spare me your affection.   90

DORINE. I'll love you, Sir, in spite of your objection.

ORGON. Blast!

DORINE.   I can't bear, Sir, for your honor's sake,
To let you make this ludicrous mistake.

ORGON. You mean to go on talking?

DORINE.   If I didn't protest
This sinful marriage, my conscience couldn't rest.   95

ORGON. If you don't hold your tongue, you little shrew . . .

DORINE. What, lost your temper? A pious man like you?

ORGON. Yes! Yes! You talk and talk. I'm maddened by it.
Once and for all, I tell you to be quiet.

DORINE. Well, I'll be quiet. But I'll be thinking hard.   100

ORGON. Think all you like, but you had better guard
That saucy tongue of yours, or I'll . . .

[*Turning back to* MARIANE]   Now, child,
I've weighed this matter fully.

DORINE. [*Aside*]   It drives me wild
That I can't speak.

[ORGON *turns his head, and she is silent.*]

ORGON.   Tartuffe is no young dandy,
But, still, his person . . .

DORINE. [*Aside*]   Is as sweet as candy.   105

ORGON. Is such that, even if you shouldn't care
For his other merits . . .

[*He turns and stands facing* DORINE, *arms crossed.*]

DORINE. [*Aside*]   They'll make a lovely pair.
If I were she, no man would marry me
Against my inclination, and go scot-free.

He'd learn, before the wedding-day was over,   110
How readily a wife can find a lover.

ORGON. [*To* DORINE] It seems you treat my orders as a joke.

DORINE. Why, what's the matter? 'Twas not to you I spoke.

ORGON. What *were* you doing?

DORINE.   Talking to myself, that's all.

ORGON. Ah! [*Aside*] One more bit of impudence and gall,   115
And I shall give her a good slap in the face.

     [*He puts himself in position to slap her;* DORINE, *whenever
     he glances at her, stands immobile and silent.*]

Daughter, you shall accept, and with good grace,
The husband I've selected . . . Your wedding-day . . .

[*To* DORINE] Why don't you talk to yourself?

DORINE.   I've nothing to say.

ORGON. Come, just one word.

DORINE.   No thank you, Sir. I pass.   120

ORGON. Come, speak; I'm waiting.

DORINE.   I'd not be such an ass.

ORGON. [*Turning to* MARIANE] In short, dear Daughter, I mean
     to be obeyed,
And you must bow to the sound choice I've made.

DORINE. [*Moving away*] I'd not wed such a monster, even in jest.
     [ORGON *attempts to slap her, but misses.*]

ORGON. Daughter, that maid of yours is a thorough pest;   125
She makes me sinfully annoyed and nettled.
I can't speak further; my nerves are too unsettled.
She's so upset me by her insolent talk,
I'll calm myself by going for a walk.

SCENE 3. *Dorine, Mariane*

DORINE. [*Returning*] Well, have you lost your tongue, girl? Must
     I play
Your part, and say the lines you ought to say?
Faced with a fate so hideous and absurd,
Can you not utter one dissenting word?

MARIANE. What good would it do? A father's power is great.   5

DORINE. Resist him now, or it will be too late.

MARIANE. But . . .

DORINE.   Tell him one cannot love at a father's whim;
That you shall marry for yourself, not him;
That since it's you who are to be the bride,
It's you, not he, who must be satisfied;   10
And that if his Tartuffe is so sublime,
He's free to marry him at any time.

MARIANE. I've bowed so long to Father's strict control,

I couldn't oppose him now, to save my soul.   14

DORINE. Come, come, Mariane. Do listen to reason, won't you?
  Valère has asked your hand. Do you love him, or don't you?

MARIANE. Oh, how unjust of you! What can you mean
  By asking such a question, dear Dorine?
  You know the depth of my affection for him;
  I've told you a hundred times how I adore him.   20

DORINE. I don't believe in everything I hear;
  Who knows if your professions were sincere?

MARIANE. They were, Dorine, and you do me wrong to doubt it,
  Heaven knows that I've been all too frank about it.

DORINE. You love him, then?

MARIANE.   Oh, more than I can express.   25

DORINE. And he, I take it, cares for you no less?

MARIANE. I think so.

DORINE.   And you both, with equal fire,
  Burn to be married?

MARIANE.   That is our one desire.

DORINE. What of Tartuffe, then? What of your father's plan?

MARIANE. I'll kill myself, if I'm forced to wed that man.   30

DORINE. I hadn't thought of that recourse. How splendid!
  Just die, and all your troubles will be ended!
  A fine solution. Oh, it maddens me
  To hear you talk in that self-pitying key.

MARIANE. Dorine, how harsh you are! It's most unfair.   35
  You have no sympathy for my despair.

DORINE. I've none at all for people who talk drivel
  And, faced with difficulties, whine and snivel.

MARIANE. No doubt I'm timid, but it would be wrong . . .

DORINE. True love requires a heart that's firm and strong.   40

MARIANE. I'm strong in my affection for Valère,
  But coping with my father is his affair.

DORINE. But if your father's brain has grown so cracked
  Over his dear Tartuffe that he can retract
  His blessing, though your wedding-day was named,   45
  It's surely not Valère who's to be blamed.

MARIANE. If I defied my father, as you suggest,
  Would it not seem unmaidenly, at best?
  Shall I defend my love at the expense
  Of brazenness and disobedience?   50
  Shall I parade my heart's desires, and flaunt . . .

DORINE. No. I ask nothing of you. Clearly you want
  To be Madame Tartuffe, and I feel bound
  Not to oppose a wish so very sound.
  What right have I to criticize the match?   55

Indeed, my dear, the man's a brilliant catch.
Monsieur Tartuffe! Now, there's a man of weight!
Yes, yes, Monsieur Tartuffe, I'm bound to state,
Is quite a person; that's not to be denied;
'Twill be no little thing to be his bride.   60
The world already rings with his renown;
He's a great noble—in his native town;
His ears are red, he has a pink complexion,
And all in all, he'll suit you to perfection.

MARIANE. Dear God!

DORINE.   Oh, how triumphant you will feel   65
At having caught a husband so ideal!

MARIANE. Oh, do stop teasing, and use your cleverness
To get me out of this appalling mess.
Advise me, and I'll do whatever you say.

DORINE. Ah, no, a dutiful daughter must obey   70
Her father, even if he weds her to an ape.
You've a bright future; why struggle to escape?
Tartuffe will take you back where his family lives,
To a small town aswarm with relatives—
Uncles and cousins whom you'll be charmed to meet.   75
You'll be received at once by the elite,
Calling upon the bailiff's wife, no less—
Even, perhaps, upon the mayoress,
Who'll sit you down in the *best* kitchen chair.
Then, once a year, you'll dance at the village fair   80
To the drone of bagpipes—two of them, in fact—
And see a puppet-show, or an animal act.
Your husband . . .

MARIANE.   Oh, you turn my blood to ice!
Stop torturing me, and give me your advice.

DORINE. [*Threatening to go*] Your servant, Madam.

MARIANE.   Dorine, I
beg of you . . .   85

DORINE. No, you deserve it; this marriage must go through.

MARIANE. Dorine!

DORINE.   No.

MARIANE.   Not Tartuffe! You know I think him . . .

77. *bailiff:* a high-ranking official in the judiciary, not simply a sheriff's deputy as today.

78. *mayoress:* the wife of a tax collector (*élu*), an important official controlling imports, elected by the Estates General.

79. *the best chair:* In elegant society of Molière's day, there was a hierarchy of seats and the use of each was determined by rank. The seats descended from *fauteuils, chaises, perroquets, tabourets,* to *pliants.* Thus Mariane would get the lowest seat in the room.

82. *puppet-show . . . act:* in the original, *fagotin,* literally a monkey dressed up in a man's clothing.

DORINE. Tartuffe's your cup of tea, and you shall drink him.

MARIANE. I've always told you everything, and relied . . .

DORINE. No. You deserve to be tartuffified.   90

MARIANE. Well, since you mock me and refuse to care,
   I'll henceforth seek my solace in despair:
   Despair shall be my counsellor and friend,
   And help me bring my sorrows to an end. [*She starts to leave.*]

DORINE. There now, come back; my anger has subsided.   95
   You do deserve some pity, I've decided.

MARIANE. Dorine, if Father makes me undergo
   This dreadful martyrdom, I'll die, I know.

DORINE. Don't fret; it won't be difficult to discover
   Some plan of action . . . But here's Valère, your lover.   100

SCENE 4. *Valère, Mariane, Dorine*

VALERE. Madam, I've just received some wondrous news
   Regarding which I'd like to hear your views.

MARIANE. What news?

VALERE.   You're marrying Tartuffe.

MARIANE.   I find
   That Father does have such a match in mind.

VALERE. Your father, Madam . . .

MARIANE.   . . . has just this minute said
   That it's Tartuffe he wishes me to wed.   5

VALERE. Can he be serious?

MARIANE.   Oh, indeed he can;
   He's clearly set his heart upon the plan.

VALERE. And what position do you propose to take,
   Madam?

MARIANE.   Why—I don't know.

VALERE.   For heaven's sake—   10
   You don't know?

MARIANE.   No.

VALERE.   Well, well!

MARIANE.   Advise me, do.

VALERE. Marry the man. That's my advice to you.

MARIANE. That's your advice?

VALERE.   Yes.

MARIANE.   Truly?

VALERE.   Oh, absolutely.
   You couldn't choose more wisely, more astutely.

MARIANE. Thanks for this counsel; I'll follow it, of course.   15

VALERE. Do, do; I'm sure 'twill cost you no remorse.

MARIANE. To give it didn't cause your heart to break.

VALERE. I gave it, Madam, only for your sake.

MARIANE. And it's for your sake that I take it, Sir.

DORINE. [*Withdrawing to the rear of the stage*]
    Let's see which fool will prove the stubborner.   20

VALERE. So! I am nothing to you, and it was flat
    Deception when you . . .

MARIANE.   Please, enough of that.
    You've told me plainly that I should agree
    To wed the man my father's chosen for me,
    And since you've deigned to counsel me so wisely,   25
    I promise, Sir, to do as you advise me.

VALERE. Ah, no, 'twas not by me that you were swayed.
    No, your decision was already made;
    Though now, to save appearances, you protest
    That you're betraying me at my behest.   30

MARIANE. Just as you say.

VALERE.   Quite so. And I now see
    That you were never truly in love with me.

MARIANE. Alas, you're free to think so if you choose.

VALERE. I choose to think so, and here's a bit of news:
    You've spurned my hand, but I know where to turn   35
    For kinder treatment, as you shall quickly learn.

MARIANE. I'm sure you do. Your noble qualities
    Inspire affection . . .

VALERE.   Forget my qualities, please.
    They don't inspire you overmuch, I find.
    But there's another lady I have in mind   40
    Whose sweet and generous nature will not scorn
    To compensate me for the loss I've borne.

MARIANE. I'm no great loss, and I'm sure that you'll transfer
    Your heart quite painlessly from me to her.

VALERE. I'll do my best to take it in my stride.   45
    The pain I feel at being cast aside
    Time and forgetfulness may put an end to.
    Or if I can't forget, I shall pretend to.
    No self-respecting person is expected
    To go on loving once he's been rejected.   50

MARIANE. Now, that's a fine, high-minded sentiment.

VALERE. One to which any sane man would assent.
    Would you prefer it if I pined away
    In hopeless passion till my dying day?
    Am I to yield you to a rival's arms   55
    And not console myself with other charms?

MARIANE. Go then; console yourself; don't hesitate.
    I wish you to; indeed, I cannot wait.

VALERE. You wish me to?

MARIANE.   Yes.

VALERE.   That's the final straw.

Madam, farewell. Your wish shall be my law.   60

[*He starts to leave, and then returns: this repeatedly.*]

MARIANE. Splendid.

VALERE. [*Coming back again*]

This breach, remember, is of your
making; It's you who've driven me to the step I'm taking.

MARIANE. Of course.

VALERE. [*Coming back again*] Remember, too, that I am merely
Following your example.

MARIANE.   I see that clearly.

VALERE. Enough. I'll go and do your bidding, then.   65

MARIANE. Good.

VALERE. [*Coming back again*] You shall never see my face again.

MARIANE. Excellent.

VALERE. [*Walking to the door, then turning about*]
                         Yes?

MARIANE.   What?

VALERE.   What's that? What did you
say?

MARIANE. Nothing. You're dreaming.

VALERE.   Ah. Well, I'm on my way.
Farewell, *Madame.*   [*He moves slowly away.*]

MARIANE.   Farewell.

DORINE. [*To MARIANE*]   If you ask me,
Both of you are as mad as mad can be.   70
Do stop this nonsense, now. I've only let you
Squabble so long to see where it would get you.
Whoa there, Monsieur Valère!

[*She goes and seizes VALERE by the arm; he makes a great
show of resistance.*]

VALERE.   What's this, Dorine?

DORINE. Come here.

VALERE.   No, no, my heart's too full of spleen.
Don't hold me back; her wish must be obeyed.   75

DORINE. Stop!

VALERE.   It's too late now; my decision's made.

DORINE. Oh, pooh!

MARIANE. [*Aside*]   He hates the sight of me, that's plain.
I'll go, and so deliver him from pain.

DORINE. [*Leaving VALERE, running after MARIANE*]
And now *you* run away! Come back.

MARIANE.   No, no.
Nothing you say will keep me here. Let go!   80

VALERE. [*Aside*] She cannot bear my presence, I perceive.
To spare her further torment, I shall leave.

DORINE. [*Leaving* MARIANE, *running after* VALERE]
　Again! You'll not escape, Sir; don't you try it.
　Come here, you two. Stop fussing and be quiet.
　　[*She takes* VALERE *by the hand, then* MARIANE, *and draws
　　them together.*]
VALERE. [*To* DORINE] What do you want of me?　　　　　85
MARIANE. [*To* DORINE] What is the point of this?
DORINE. We're going to have a little armistice.
　[*To* VALERE] Now, weren't you silly to get so overheated?
VALERE. Didn't you see how badly I was treated?
DORINE. [*To* MARIANE] Aren't you a simpleton, to have lost your head?
MARIANE. Didn't you hear the hateful things he said?　　90
DORINE. [*To* VALERE] You're both great fools. Her sole desire, Valère,
　Is to be yours in marriage. To that I'll swear.
　[*To* MARIANE] He loves you only, and he wants no wife
　But you, Mariane. On that I'll stake my life.　　　95
MARIANE. [*To* VALERE] Then why you advised me so, I cannot see.
VALERE. [*To* MARIANE] On such a question, why ask advice of *me*?
DORINE. Oh, you're impossible. Give me your hands, you two.
　[*To* VALERE] Yours first.
VALERE. [*Giving* DORINE *his hand*] But why?
DORINE. [*To* MARIANE]　And now a hand from you.
MARIANE. [*Also giving* DORINE *her hand*]
　What are you doing?
DORINE.　　　　　　　There: a perfect fit.　　　　100
　You suit each other better than you'll admit.
　　[VALERE *and* MARIANE *hold hands for some time without
　　looking at each other.*]
VALERE. [*Turning toward* MARIANE]
　Ah, come, don't be so haughty. Give a man
　A look of kindness, won't you, Mariane?
　　[MARIANE *turns toward* VALERE *and smiles.*]
DORINE. I tell you, lovers are completely mad!
VALERE. [*To* MARIANE] Now come, confess that you were very bad
　To hurt my feelings as you did just now.　　　　　105
　I have a just complaint, you must allow.
MARIANE. *You* must allow that you were most unpleasant . . .
DORINE. Let's table that discussion for the present;
　Your father has a plan which must be stopped.　　　110
MARIANE. Advise us, then; what means must we adopt?
DORINE. We'll use all manner of means, and all at once.
　[*To* MARIANE] Your father's addled; he's acting like a dunce.
　Therefore you'd better humor the old fossil.
　Pretend to yield to him, be sweet and docile,　　　115
　And then postpone, as often as necessary,

The day on which you have agreed to marry.
You'll thus gain time, and time will turn the trick.
Sometimes, for instance, you'll be taken sick,
And that will seem good reason for delay;   120
Or some bad omen will make you change the day—
You'll dream of muddy water, or you'll pass
A dead man's hearse, or break a looking-glass.
If all else fails, no man can marry you
Unless you take his ring and say "I do."   125
But now, let's separate. If they should find
Us talking here, our plot might be divined.
[*To* VALERE]Go to your friends, and tell them what's occurred,
And have them urge her father to keep his word.
Meanwhile, we'll stir her brother into action,   130
And get Elmire, as well, to join our faction.
Good-bye.

VALERE. [*To* MARIANE] Though each of us will do his best,
It's your true heart on which my hopes shall rest.

MARIANE. [*To* VALERE] Regardless of what Father may decide,
None but Valère shall claim me as his bride.   135

VALERE. Oh, how those words content me! Come what will . . .

DORINE. Oh, lovers, lovers! Their tongues are never still.
Be off, now.

VALERE. [*Turning to go, then turning back.*]
                    One last word . . .

DORINE.   No time to chat:
You leave by this door; and you leave by that.
        [DORINE *pushes them, by the shoulders, toward opposing
        doors.*]

Act III

SCENE 1. *Damis, Dorine*

DAMIS. May lightning strike me even as I speak,
May all men call me cowardly and weak,
If any fear or scruple holds me back
From settling things, at once, with that great quack!

DORINE. Now, don't give way to violent emotion.   5
Your father's merely talked about this notion,
And words and deeds are far from being one.
Much that is talked about is never done.

DAMIS. No, I must stop that scoundrel's machinations;
I'll go and tell him off; I'm out of patience.   10

130. *Elmire:* Orgon's second wife.

DORINE. Do calm down and be practical. I had rather
My mistress dealt with him—and with your father.
She has some influence with Tartuffe, I've noted.
He hangs upon her words, seems most devoted,
And may, indeed, be smitten by her charm. 15
Pray Heaven it's true! 'Twould do our cause no harm.
She sent for him, just now, to sound him out
On this affair you're so incensed about;
She'll find out where he stands, and tell him, too,
What dreadful strife and trouble will ensue 20
If he lends countenance to your father's plan.
I couldn't get in to see him, but his man
Says that he's almost finished with his prayers.
Go, now. I'll catch him when he comes downstairs.

DAMIS. I want to hear this conference, and I will. 25

DORINE. No, they must be alone.

DAMIS.   Oh, I'll keep still.

DORINE. Not you. I know your temper. You'd start a brawl,
And shout and stamp your foot and spoil it all.
Go on.

DAMIS.   I won't; I have a perfect right . . . 30

DORINE. Lord, you're a nuisance! He's coming; get out of sight.
[DAMIS *conceals himself in a closet at the rear of the stage.*]

SCENE 2. *Tartuffe, Dorine*

TARTUFFE. [*Observing* DORINE, *and calling to his manservant off-stage*] Hang up my hair-shirt, put my scourge in place,
And pray, Laurent, for Heaven's perpetual grace.
I'm going to the prison now, to share
My last few coins with the poor wretches there.

DORINE. [*Aside*] Dear God, what affectation! What a fake! 5

TARTUFFE. You wished to see me?

DORINE.   Yes . . .

TARTUFFE. [*Taking a handkerchief from his pocket*]
                                  For mercy's sake,
Please take this handkerchief, before you speak.

DORINE. What?

TARTUFFE.   Cover that bosom, girl. The flesh is weak,
And unclean thoughts are difficult to control.
Such sights as that can undermine the soul. 10

DORINE. Your soul, it seems, has very poor defenses,

8. *Cover that bosom:* The Brotherhood of the Holy Sacrament (*cf.* note 13, p. 23) practiced almsgiving to prisoners and kept a careful, censorious check on female wearing apparel if they deemed it lascivious. Thus, Molière's audience would have identified Tartuffe as sympathetic—hypocritically—to the aims of the organization.

And flesh makes quite an impact on your senses.
It's strange that you're so easily excited;
My own desires are not so soon ignited,
And if I saw you naked as a beast,   15
Not all your hide would tempt me in the least.

TARTUFFE. Girl, speak more modestly; unless you do,
  I shall be forced to take my leave of you.

DORINE. Oh, no, it's I who must be on my way;
  I've just one little message to convey.   20
  Madame is coming down, and begs you, Sir,
  To wait and have a word or two with her.

TARTUFFE. Gladly.

DORINE. [*Aside*]   *That* had a softening effect!
  I think my guess about him was correct.

TARTUFFE. Will she be long?

DORINE.   No: that's her step I hear.   25
  Ah, here she is, and I shall disappear.

SCENE 3. *Elmire, Tartuffe*

TARTUFFE. May Heaven, whose infinite goodness we adore,
  Preserve your body and soul forevermore,
  And bless your days, and answer thus the plea
  Of one who is its humblest votary.

ELMIRE. I thank you for that pious wish. But please,   5
  Do take a chair and let's be more at ease.
    [*They sit down.*]

TARTUFFE. I trust that you are once more well and strong?

ELMIRE. Oh, yes: the fever didn't last for long.

TARTUFFE. My prayers are too unworthy, I am sure,
  To have gained from Heaven this most gracious cure;   10
  But lately, Madam, my every supplication
  Has had for object your recuperation.

ELMIRE. You shouldn't have troubled so. I don't deserve it.

TARTUFFE. Your health is priceless, Madam, and to preserve it
  I'd gladly give my own, in all sincerity.   15

ELMIRE. Sir, you outdo us all in Christian charity.
  You've been most kind. I count myself your debtor.

TARTUFFE. 'Twas nothing, Madam. I long to serve you better.

ELMIRE. There's a private matter I'm anxious to discuss.
  I'm glad there's no one here to hinder us.   20

TARTUFFE. I too am glad; it floods my heart with bliss
  To find myself alone with you like this.
  For just this chance I've prayed with all my power—
  But prayed in vain, until this happy hour.

ELMIRE. This won't take long, Sir, and I hope you'll be   25

Entirely frank and unconstrained with me.
TARTUFFE. Indeed, there's nothing I had rather do
Than bare my inmost heart and soul to you.
First, let me say that what remarks I've made
About the constant visits you are paid   30
Were prompted not by any mean emotion,
But rather by a pure and deep devotion,
A fervent zeal . . .
ELMIRE.   No need for explanation.
Your sole concern, I'm sure, was my salvation.
TARTUFFE. [*Taking* ELMIRE'*s hand and pressing her fingertips*]
Quite so; and such great fervor do I feel . . .   35
ELMIRE. Ooh! Please! You're pinching!
TARTUFFE.   'Twas from excess of zeal.
I never meant to cause you pain, I swear.
I'd rather . . .   [*He places his hand on* ELMIRE'*s knee.*]
ELMIRE.   What can your hand be doing there?
TARTUFFE. Feeling your gown: what soft, fine-woven stuff!
ELMIRE. Please, I'm extremely ticklish. That's enough.   40
     [*She draws her chair away;* TARTUFFE *pulls his after her.*]
TARTUFFE. [*Fondling the lace collar of her gown*]
My, my, what lovely lacework on your dress!
The workmanship's miraculous, no less.
I've not seen anything to equal it.
ELMIRE. Yes, quite. But let's talk business for a bit.
They say my husband means to break his word   45
And give his daughter to you, Sir. Had you heard?
TARTUFFE. He did once mention it. But I confess
I dream of quite a different happiness.
It's elsewhere, Madam, that my eyes discern
The promise of that bliss for which I yearn.   50
ELMIRE. I see: you care for nothing here below.
TARTUFFE. Ah, well—my heart's not made of stone, you know.
ELMIRE. All your desires mount heavenward, I'm sure,
In scorn of all that's earthly and impure.
TARTUFFE. A love of heavenly beauty does not preclude   55
A proper love for earthly pulchritude;
Our senses are quite rightly captivated
By perfect works our Maker has created.
Some glory clings to all that Heaven has made;
In you, all Heaven's marvels are displayed.   60
On that fair face, such beauties have been lavished,
The eyes are dazzled and the heart is ravished;
How could I look on you, O flawless creature,
And not adore the Author of all Nature,

Feeling a love both passionate and pure   65
For you, his triumph of self-portraiture?
At first, I trembled lest that love should be
A subtle snare that Hell had laid for me;
I vowed to flee the sight of you, eschewing
A rapture that might prove my soul's undoing;   70
But soon, fair being, I became aware
That my deep passion could be made to square
With rectitude, and with my bounden duty,
I thereupon surrendered to your beauty.
It is, I know, presumptuous on my part   75
To bring you this poor offering of my heart,
And it is not my merit, Heaven knows,
But your compassion on which my hopes repose.
You are my peace, my solace, my salvation;
On you depends my bliss—or desolation;   80
I bide your judgment and, as you think best,
I shall be either miserable or blest.

ELMIRE. Your declaration is most gallant, Sir,
But don't you think it's out of character?
You'd have done better to restrain your passion   85
And think before you spoke in such a fashion.
It ill becomes a pious man like you . . .

TARTUFFE. I may be pious, but I'm human too:
With your celestial charms before his eyes,
A man has not the power to be wise.   90
I know such words sound strangely, coming from me,
But I'm no angel, nor was meant to be,
And if you blame my passion, you must needs
Reproach as well the charms on which it feeds.
Your loveliness I had no sooner seen   95
Than you became my soul's unrivalled queen;
Before your seraph glance, divinely sweet,
My heart's defenses crumbled in defeat,
And nothing fasting, prayer, or tears might do
Could stay my spirit from adoring you.   100
My eyes, my sighs have told you in the past
What now my lips make bold to say at last,
And if, in your great goodness, you will deign
To look upon your slave, and ease his pain,—
If, in compassion for my soul's distress,   105
You'll stoop to comfort my unworthiness,
I'll raise to you, in thanks for that sweet manna,
An endless hymn, an infinite hosanna.
With me, of course, there need be no anxiety,

No fear of scandal or of notoriety. 110
These young court gallants, whom all the ladies fancy,
Are vain in speech, in action rash and chancy;
When they succeed in love, the world soon knows it;
No favor's granted them but they disclose it
And by the looseness of their tongues profane 115
The very altar where their hearts have lain.
Men of my sort, however, love discreetly,
And one may trust our reticence completely.
My keen concern for my good name insures
The absolute security of yours; 120
In short, I offer you, my dear Elmire,
Love without scandal, pleasure without fear.

ELMIRE. I've heard your well-turned speeches to the end,
And what you urge I clearly apprehend.
Aren't you afraid that I may take a notion 125
To tell my husband of your warm devotion,
And that, supposing he were duly told,
His feelings toward you might grow rather cold?

TARTUFFE. I know, dear lady, that your exceeding charity
Will lead your heart to pardon my temerity; 130
That you'll excuse my violent affection
As human weakness, human imperfection;
And that—O fairest!—you will bear in mind
That I'm but flesh and blood, and am not blind.

ELMIRE. Some women might do otherwise, perhaps, 135
But I shall be discreet about your lapse;
I'll tell my husband nothing of what's occurred
If, in return, you'll give your solemn word
To advocate as forcefully as you can
The marriage of Valère and Mariane, 140
Renouncing all desire to dispossess
Another of his rightful happiness,
And . . .

SCENE 4. *Damis, Elmire, Tartuffe*

DAMIS. [*Emerging from the closet where he has been hiding*]
          No! We'll not hush up this vile affair;
I heard it all inside that closet there,
Where Heaven, in order to confound the pride
Of this great rascal, prompted me to hide.
Ah, now I have my long-awaited chance 5
To punish his deceit and arrogance,
And give my father clear and shocking proof
Of the black character of his dear Tartuffe.

ELMIRE. Ah no, Damis; I'll be content if he
    Will study to deserve my leniency.   10
    I've promised silence—don't make me break my word;
    To make a scandal would be too absurd.
    Good wives laugh off such trifles, and forget them;
    Why should they tell their husbands, and upset them?
DAMIS. You have your reasons for taking such a course,   15
    And I have reasons, too, of equal force.
    To spare him now would be insanely wrong.
    I've swallowed my just wrath for far too long
    And watched this insolent bigot bringing strife
    And bitterness into our family life.   20
    Too long he's meddled in my father's affairs,
    Thwarting my marriage-hopes, and poor Valère's.
    It's high time that my father was undeceived,
    And now I've proof that can't be disbelieved—
    Proof that was furnished me by Heaven above.   25
    It's too good not to take advantage of.
    This is my chance, and I deserve to lose it
    If, for one moment, I hesitate to use it.
ELMIRE. Damis . . .
DAMIS.   No, I must do what I think right.
    Madam, my heart is bursting with delight,   30
    And, say whatever you will, I'll not consent
    To lose the sweet revenge on which I'm bent.
    I'll settle matters without more ado;
    And here, most opportunely, is my cue.

SCENE 5. *Orgon, Damis, Tartuffe, Elmire*

DAMIS. Father, I'm glad you've joined us. Let us advise you
    Of some fresh news which doubtless will surprise you.
    You've just now been repaid with interest
    For all your loving-kindness to our guest.
    He's proved his warm and grateful feelings toward you;   5
    It's with a pair of horns he would reward you.
    Yes, I surprised him with your wife, and heard
    His whole adulterous offer, every word.
    She, with her all too gentle disposition,
    Would not have told you of his proposition;   10
    But I shall not make terms with brazen lechery,
    And feel that not to tell you would be treachery.

---

34. My cue: In the original stage directions, Tartuffe now reads silently from his breviary—in the Roman Catholic Church, the book containing the Divine Office for each day, which those in holy orders are required to recite.

ELMIRE. And I hold that one's husband's peace of mind
   Should not be spoilt by tattle of this kind.
   One's honor doesn't require it: to be proficient   15
   In keeping men at bay is quite sufficient.
   These are my sentiments, and I wish, Damis,
   That you had heeded me and held your peace.

SCENE 6. *Orgon, Damis, Tartuffe*

ORGON. Can it be true, this dreadful thing I hear?
TARTUFFE. Yes, Brother, I'm a wicked man, I fear:
   A wretched sinner, all depraved and twisted,
   The greatest villain that has ever existed.
   My life's one heap of crimes, which grows each minute;   5
   There's naught but foulness and corruption in it;
   And I perceive that Heaven, outraged by me,
   Has chosen this occasion to mortify me.
   Charge me with any deed you wish to name;
   I'll not defend myself, but take the blame.   10
   Believe what you are told, and drive Tartuffe
   Like some base criminal from beneath your roof;
   Yes, drive me hence, and with a parting curse:
   I shan't protest, for I deserve far worse.
ORGON. [*To* DAMIS] Ah, you deceitful boy, how dare you try   15
   To stain his purity with so foul a lie?
DAMIS. What! Are you taken in by such a bluff?
   Did you not hear . . . ?
ORGON.   Enough, you rogue, enough!
TARTUFFE. Ah, Brother, let him speak: you're being unjust.
   Believe his story; the boy deserves your trust.   20
   Why, after all, should you have faith in me?
   How can you know what I might do, or be?
   Is it on my good actions that you base
   Your favor? Do you trust my pious face?
   Ah, no, don't be deceived by hollow shows;   25
   I'm far, alas, from being what men suppose;
   Though the world takes me for a man of worth,
   I'm truly the most worthless man on earth.
      [*To* DAMIS]
   Yes, my dear son, speak out now: call me the chief
   Of sinners, a wretch, a murderer, a thief;   30
   Load me with all the names men most abhor;
   I'll not complain; I've earned them all, and more;
   I'll kneel here while you pour them on my head
   As a just punishment for the life I've led.

ORGON. [*To* TARTUFFE] This is too much, dear Brother.
   [*To* DAMIS]   Have you no heart?
DAMIS. Are you so hoodwinked by this rascal's art . . . ?   35
ORGON. Be still, you monster.
   [*To* TARTUFFE]   Brother, I pray you, rise.
   [*To* DAMIS] Villain!
DAMIS.   But . . .
ORGON.   Silence!
DAMIS.   Can't you realize . . . ?
ORGON. Just one word more, and I'll tear you limb from limb.
TARTUFFE. In God's name, Brother, don't be harsh with him.   40
   I'd rather far be tortured at the stake
   Than see him bear one scratch for my poor sake.
ORGON. [*To* DAMIS] Ingrate!
TARTUFFE   If I must beg you, on bended knee,
   To pardon him . . .
ORGON. [*Falling to his knees, addressing Tartuffe*]
                  Such goodness cannot be!
   [*To* DAMIS] *Now, there's* true charity!
DAMIS.   What, you . . . ?
ORGON. Villain, be still!   45
   I know your motives; I know you wish him ill:
   Yes, all of you—wife, children, servants, all—
   Conspire against him and desire his fall,
   Employing every shameful trick you can
   To alienate me from this saintly man.   50
   Ah, but the more you seek to drive him away,
   The more I'll do to keep him. Without delay,
   I'll spite this household and confound its pride
   By giving him my daughter as his bride.
DAMIS. You're going to force her to accept his hand?   55
ORGON. Yes, and this very night, d'you understand?
   I shall defy you all, and make it clear
   That I'm the one who gives the orders here.
   Come, wretch, kneel down and clasp his blessed feet,
   And ask his pardon for your black deceit.   60
DAMIS. I ask that swindler's pardon? Why, I'd rather . . .
ORGON. So! You insult him, and defy your father!
   A stick! A stick! [*To* TARTUFFE] No, no—release me, do.
   [*To* DAMIS.] Out of my house this minute! Be off with you,
   And never dare set foot in it again.   65
DAMIS. Well, I shall go, but . . .
ORGON.   Well, go quickly, then.
   I disinherit you; an empty purse
   Is all you'll get from me—except my curse!

SCENE 7. *Orgon, Tartuffe*

ORGON. How he blasphemed your goodness! What a son!

TARTUFFE. Forgive him, Lord, as I've already done.
[*To* ORGON] You can't know how it hurts when someone tries
To blacken me in my dear Brother's eyes.

ORGON. Ahh!

TARTUFFE.   The mere thought of such ingratitude   5
Plunges my soul into so dark a mood . . .
Such horror grips my heart . . . I gasp for breath,
And cannot speak, and feel myself near death.

ORGON. [*He runs, in tears, to the door through which he has just
      driven his son.*]
You blackguard! Why did I spare you? Why did I not
Break you in little pieces on the spot?   10
Compose yourself, and don't be hurt, dear friend.

TARTUFFE. These scenes, these dreadful quarrels, have got to end.
I've much upset your household, and I perceive
That the best thing will be for me to leave.

ORGON. What are you saying!

TARTUFFE.   They're all against me here;
They'd have you think me false and insincere.   15

ORGON. Ah, what of that? Have I ceased believing in you?

TARTUFFE. Their adverse talk will certainly continue,
And charges which you now repudiate
You may find credible at a later date.   20

ORGON. No, Brother, never.

TARTUFFE.   Brother, a wife can sway
Her husband's mind in many a subtle way.

ORGON. No, no.

TARTUFFE.   To leave at once is the solution;
Thus only can I end their persecution.

ORGON. No, no, I'll not allow it; you shall remain.   25

TARTUFFE. Ah, well; 'twill mean much martyrdom and pain,
But if you wish it . . .

ORGON.   Ah!

TARTUFFE.   Enough; so be it.
But one thing must be settled, as I see it.
For your dear honor, and for our friendship's sake,
There's one precaution I feel bound to take.   30
I shall avoid your wife, and keep away . . .

ORGON. No, you shall not, whatever they may say.
It pleases me to vex them, and for spite
I'd have them see you with her day and night.
What's more, I'm going to drive them to despair   35

By making you my only son and heir;
This very day, I'll give to you alone
Clear deed and title to everything I own.
A dear, good friend and son-in-law-to-be
Is more than wife, or child, or kin to me. 40
Will you accept my offer, dearest son?

TARTUFFE. In all things, let the will of Heaven be done.

ORGON. Poor fellow! Come, we'll go draw up the deed.
Then let them burst with disappointed greed!

Act IV

SCENE 1. *Cléante, Tartuffe*

CLÉANTE. Yes, all the town's discussing it, and truly,
Their comments do not flatter you unduly.
I'm glad we've met, Sir, and I'll give my view
Of this sad matter in a word or two.
As for who's guilty, that I shan't discuss; 5
Let's say it was Damis who caused the fuss;
Assuming, then, that you have been ill-used
By young Damis, and groundlessly accused,
Ought not a Christian to forgive, and ought
He not to stifle every vengeful thought? 10
Should you stand by and watch a father make
His only son an exile for your sake?
Again I tell you frankly, be advised:
The whole town, high and low, is scandalized;
This quarrel must be mended, and my advice is 15
Not to push matters to a further crisis.
No, sacrifice your wrath to God above,
And help Damis regain his father's love.

TARTUFFE. Alas, for my part I should take great joy
In doing so. I've nothing against the boy. 20
I pardon all, I harbor no resentment;
To serve him would afford me much contentment.
But Heaven's interest will not have it so:
If he comes back, then I shall have to go.
After his conduct—so extreme, so vicious— 25
Our further intercourse would look suspicious.
God knows what people would think! Why, they'd describe
My goodness to him as a sort of bribe;
They'd say that out of guilt I made pretense
Of loving-kindness and benevolence— 30
That, fearing my accuser's tongue, I strove

To buy his silence with a show of love.

CLÉANTE. Your reasoning is badly warped and stretched,
And these excuses, Sir, are most far-fetched.
Why put yourself in charge of Heaven's cause?   35
Does Heaven need our help to enforce its laws?
Leave vengeance to the Lord Sir; while we live,
Our duty's not to punish, but forgive;
And what the Lord commands, we should obey
Without regard to what the world may say.   40
What! Shall the fear of being misunderstood
Prevent our doing what is right and good?
No, no: let's simply do what Heaven ordains,
And let no other thoughts perplex our brains.

TARTUFFE. Again, Sir, let me say that I've forgiven   45
Damis, and thus obeyed the laws of Heaven;
But I am not commanded by the Bible
To live with one who smears my name with libel.

CLÉANTE. Were you commanded, Sir, to indulge the whim
Of poor Orgon, and to encourage him   50
In suddenly transferring to your name
A large estate to which you have no claim?

TARTUFFE. 'Twould never occur to those who know me best
To think I acted from self-interest.
The treasures of this world I quite despise;   55
Their specious glitter does not charm my eyes;
And if I have resigned myself to taking
The gift which my dear Brother insists on making,
I do so only, as he well understands,
Lest so much wealth fall into wicked hands,   60
Lest those to whom it might descend in time
Turn it to purposes of sin and crime,
And not, as I shall do, make use of it
For Heaven's glory and mankind's benefit.

CLÉANTE. Forget these trumped-up fears. Your argument   65
Is one the rightful heir might well resent;
It *is* a moral burden to inherit
Such wealth, but give Damis a chance to bear it.
And would it not be worse to be accused
Of swindling, than to see that wealth misused?   70
I'm shocked that you allowed Orgon to broach
This matter, and that you feel no self-reproach;
Does true religion teach that lawful heirs
May freely be deprived of what is theirs?
And if the Lord has told you in your heart   75
That you and young Damis must dwell apart,

Would it not be the decent thing to beat
A generous and honorable retreat,
Rather than let the son of the house be sent,
For your convenience, into banishment?   80
Sir, if you wish to prove the honesty
Of your intentions . . .

TARTUFFE.   Sir, it is a half past three.
I've certain pious duties to attend to,
· And hope my prompt departure won't offend you.
CLÉANTE. [*Alone*] Damn.

SCENE 2. *Elmire, Mariane, Cléante, Dorine*

DORINE. Stay, Sir, and help Mariane, for Heaven's sake!
She's suffering so, I fear her heart will break.
Her father's plan to marry her off tonight
Has put the poor child in a desperate plight.
I hear him coming. Let's stand together, now,   5
And see if we can't change his mind, somehow,
About this match we all deplore and fear.

SCENE 3. *Orgon, Elmire, Mariane, Cléante, Dorine*

ORGON. Hah! Glad to find you all assembled here.
[*To* MARIANE] This contract, child, contains your happiness,
And what it says I think your heart can guess.
MARIANE. [*Falling to her knees*]
Sir, by that Heaven which sees me here distressed,
And by whatever else can move your breast,   5
Do not employ a father's power, I pray you,
To crush my heart and force it to obey you,
Nor by your harsh commands oppress me so
That I'll begrudge the duty which I owe—
And do not so embitter and enslave me   10
That I shall hate the very life you gave me.
If my sweet hopes must perish, if you refuse
To give me to the one I've dared to choose,
Spare me at least—I beg you, I implore—
The pain of wedding one whom I abhor;   15
And do not, by a heartless use of force,
Drive me to contemplate some desperate course.
ORGON. [*Feeling himself touched by her*]
Be firm, my soul. No human weakness, now.
MARIANE. I don't resent your love for him. Allow
Your heart free rein, Sir; give him your property,   20
And if that's not enough, take mine from me;
He's welcome to my money; take it, do,

But don't, I pray, include my person too.
Spare me, I beg you; and let me end the tale
Of my sad days behind a convent veil.   25

ORGON. A convent! Hah! When crossed in their amours,
All lovesick girls have the same thought as yours.
Get up! The more you loathe the man, and dread him,
The more ennobling it will be to wed him.
Marry Tartuffe, and mortify your flesh!   30
Enough; don't start that whimpering afresh.

DORINE. But why . . . ?

ORGON.   Be still, there. Speak when you're spoken to.
Not one more bit of impudence out of you.

CLÉANTE. If I may offer a word of counsel here . . .

ORGON. Brother, in counselling you have no peer;   35
All your advice is forceful, sound, and clever;
I don't propose to follow it, however.

ELMIRE. [*To* ORGON] I am amazed, and don't know what to say;
Your blindness simply takes my breath away.
You are indeed bewitched, to take no warning   40
From our account of what occurred this morning.

ORGON. Madam, I know a few plain facts, and one
Is that you're partial to my rascal son;
Hence, when he sought to make Tartuffe the victim
Of a base lie, you dared not contradict him.   45
Ah, but you underplayed your part, my pet;
You should have looked more angry, more upset.

ELMIRE. When men make overtures, must we reply
With righteous anger and a battle-cry?
Must we turn back their amorous advances   50
With sharp reproaches and with fiery glances?
Myself, I find such offers merely amusing,
And make no scenes and fusses in refusing;
My taste is for good-natured rectitude,
And I dislike the savage sort of prude   55
Who guards her virtue with her teeth and claws,
And tears men's eyes out for the slightest cause:
The Lord preserve me from such honor as that,
Which bites and scratches like an alley-cat!
I've found that a polite and cool rebuff   60
Discourages a lover quite enough.

ORGON. I know the facts, and I shall not be shaken.

ELMIRE. I marvel at your power to be mistaken.
Would it, I wonder, carry weight with you
If I could *show* you that our tale was true?   65

ORGON. Show me?

ELMIRE.   Yes.
ORGON.   Rot.
ELMIRE.   Come, what if I found a way
 To make you see the facts as plain as day?
ORGON. Nonsense.
ELMIRE.   Do answer me; don't be absurd.
 I'm not now asking you to trust our word.
 Suppose that from some hiding-place in here   70
 You learned the whole sad truth by eye and ear—
 What would you say of your good friend, after that?
ORGON. Why, I'd say . . . nothing, by Jehoshaphat!
 It can't be true.
ELMIRE.   You've been too long deceived,
 And I'm quite tired of being disbelieved.   75
 Come now: let's put my statements to the test,
 And you shall see the truth made manifest.
ORGON. I'll take that challenge. Now do your uttermost.
 We'll see how you make good your empty boast.
ELMIRE. [*To* DORINE] Send him to me.
DORINE.   He's crafty; it may be hard
 To catch the cunning scoundrel off his guard.   80
ELMIRE. No, amorous men are gullible. Their conceit
 So blinds them that they're never hard to cheat.
 Have him come down. [*To* CLEANTE *&* MARIANE] Please leave us,
  for a bit.

SCENE 4. *Elmire, Orgon*

ELMIRE. Pull up this table, and get under it.
ORGON. What?
ELMIRE.   It's essential that you be well-hidden.
ORGON. Why there?
ELMIRE.   Oh, Heavens! Just do as you are bidden.
 I have my plans; we'll soon see how they fare.
 Under the table, now; and once you're there,   5
 Take care that you are neither seen nor heard.
ORGON. Well, I'll indulge you, since I gave my word
 To see you through this infantile charade.
ELMIRE. Once it is over, you'll be glad we played.
  [*To her husband, who is now under the table*]
 I'm going to act quite strangely, now, and you   10
 Must not be shocked at anything I do.
 Whatever I may say, you must excuse
 As part of that deceit I'm forced to use.
 I shall employ sweet speeches in the task
 Of making that impostor drop his mask;   15

I'll give encouragement to his bold desires,
And furnish fuel to his amorous fires.
Since it's for your sake, and for his destruction,
That I shall seem to yield to his seduction,
I'll gladly stop whenever you decide   20
That all your doubts are fully satisfied.
I'll count on you, as soon as you have seen
What sort of man he is, to intervene,
And not expose me to his odious lust
One moment longer than you feel you must.   25
Remember: you're to save me from my plight
Whenever . . . He's coming! Hush! Keep out of sight!

SCENE 5. *Tartuffe, Elmire, Orgon*

TARTUFFE. You wish to have a word with me, I'm told.
ELMIRE. Yes, I've a little secret to unfold.
Before I speak, however, it would be wise
To close that door, and look about for spies.
    [TARTUFFE *goes to the door, closes it, and returns.*]
The very last thing that must happen now   5
Is a repetition of this morning's row.
I've never been so badly caught off guard.
Oh, how I feared for you! You saw how hard
I tried to make that troublesome Damis
Control his dreadful temper, and hold his peace.   10
In my confusion, I didn't have the sense
Simply to contradict his evidence;
But as it happened, that was for the best,
And all has worked out in our interest.
This storm has only bettered your position;   15
My husband doesn't have the least suspicion,
And now, in mockery of those who do,
He bids me be continually with you.
And that is why, quite fearless of reproof,
I now can be alone with my Tartuffe,   20
And why my heart—perhaps too quick to yield—
Feels free to let its passion be revealed.
TARTUFFE. Madam, your words confuse me. Not long ago,
You spoke in quite a different style, you know.
ELMIRE. Ah, Sir, if that refusal made you smart,   25
It's little that you know of woman's heart,
Or what that heart is trying to convey
When it resists in such a feeble way!
Always, at first, our modesty prevents
The frank avowal of tender sentiments: 30

However high the passion which inflames us,
Still, to confess its power somehow shames us.
Thus we reluct, at first, yet in a tone
Which tells you that our heart is overthrown,
That what our lips deny, our pulse confesses,   35
And that, in time, all noes will turn to yesses.
I fear my words are all too frank and free,
And a poor proof of woman's modesty;
But since I'm started, tell me, if you will—
Would I have tried to make Damis be still,   40
Would I have listened, calm and unoffended,
Until your lengthy offer of love was ended,
And been so very mild in my reaction,
Had your sweet words not given me satisfaction?
And when I tried to force you to undo   45
The marriage-plans my husband has in view,
What did my urgent pleading signify
If not that I admired you, and that I
Deplored the thought that someone else might own
Part of a heart I wished for mine alone?   50

TARTUFFE. Madam, no happiness is so complete
As when, from lips we love, come words so sweet;
Their nectar floods my every sense, and drains
In honeyed rivulets through all my veins.
To please you is my joy, my only goal;   55
Your love is the restorer of my soul;
And yet I must beg leave, now, to confess
Some lingering doubts as to my happiness.
Might this not be a trick? Might not the catch
Be that you wish me to break off the match   60
With Mariane, and so have feigned to love me?
I shan't quite trust your fond opinion of me
Until the feelings you've expressed so sweetly
Are demonstrated somewhat more concretely,
And you have shown, by certain kind concessions,   65
That I may put my faith in your professions.

ELMIRE. [*She coughs, to warn her husband.*] Why be in such a
        hurry? Must my heart
Exhaust its bounty at the very start?
To make that sweet admission cost me dear,
But you'll not be content, it would appear,   70
Unless my store of favors is disbursed
To the last farthing, and at the very first.

TARTUFFE. The less we merit, the less we dare to hope,
And with our doubts, mere words can never cope.

We trust no promised bliss till we receive it;   75
Not till a joy is ours can we believe it.
I, who so little merit your esteem,
Can't credit this fulfillment of my dream,
And shan't believe it, Madam, until I savor
Some palpable assurance of your favor.   80

ELMIRE. My, how tyrannical your love can be,
And how it flusters and perplexes me!
How furiously you take one's heart in hand,
And make your every wish a fierce command!
Come, must you hound and harry me to death?   85
Will you not give me time to catch my breath?
Can it be right to press me with such force,
Give me no quarter, show me no remorse,
And take advantage, by your stern insistence,
Of the fond feelings which weaken my resistance?   90

TARTUFFE. Well, if you look with favor upon my love,
Why, then, begrudge me some clear proof thereof?

ELMIRE. But how can I consent without offense
To Heaven, toward which you feel such reverence?

TARTUFFE. If Heaven is all that holds you back, don't worry.   95
I can remove that hindrance in a hurry.
Nothing of that sort need obstruct our path.

ELMIRE. Must one not be afraid of Heaven's wrath?

TARTUFFE. Madam, forget such fears, and be my pupil,
And I shall teach you how to conquer scruple.   100
Some joys, it's true, are wrong in Heaven's eyes;
Yet Heaven is not averse to compromise;
There is a science, lately formulated,
Whereby one's conscience may be liberated,
And any wrongful act you care to mention   105
May be redeemed by purity of intention.
I'll teach you, Madam, the secrets of that science;
Meanwhile, just place on me your full reliance.
Assuage my keen desires, and feel no dread:
The sin, if any, shall be on my head.   110

[ELMIRE *coughs, this time more loudly.*]
You've a bad cough.

ELMIRE.   Yes, yes. It's bad indeed.

TARTUFFE. [*Producing a little paper bag*]
A bit of licorice may be what you need.

ELMIRE. No, I've a stubborn cold, it seems. I'm sure it
Will take much more than licorice to cure it.

---

104. *Whereby . . . liberated:* Molière appended his own footnote to this line: "It is a scoundrel who speaks."

TARTUFFE. How aggravating.

ELMIRE.   Oh, more than I can say.   115

TARTUFFE. If you're still troubled, think of things this way:
  No one shall know our joys, save us alone,
  And there's no evil till the act is known;
  It's scandal, Madam, which makes it an offense,
  And it's no sin to sin in confidence.   120

ELMÍRE. [*Having coughed once more*]
  Well, clearly I must do as you require,
  And yield to your importunate desire.
  It is apparent, now, that nothing less
  Will satisfy you, and so I acquiesce.
  To go so far is much against my will;   125
  I'm vexed that it should come to this; but still,
  Since you are so determined on it, since you
  Will not allow mere language to convince you,
  And since you ask for concrete evidence, I
  See nothing for it, now, but to comply.   130
  If this is sinful, if I'm wrong to do it,
  So much the worse for him who drove me to it.
  The fault can surely not be charged to me.

TARTUFFE. Madam, the fault is mine, if fault there be,
  And . . .

ELMIRE.   Open the door a little, and peek out;   135
  I wouldn't want my husband poking about.

TARTUFFE. Why worry about the man? Each day he grows
  More gullible; one can lead him by the nose.
  To find us here would fill him with delight,
  And if he saw the worst, he'd doubt his sight.   140

ELMIRE. Nevertheless, do step out for a minute
  Into the hall, and see that no one's in it.

SCENE 6. *Orgon, Elmire*

ORGON. [*Coming out from under the table*]
  That man's a perfect monster, I must admit!
  I'm simply stunned. I can't get over it.

ELMIRE. What, coming out so soon? How premature!
  Get back in hiding, and wait until you're sure.
  Stay till the end, and be convinced completely;   5
  We mustn't stop till things are proved concretely.

ORGON. Hell never harbored anything so vicious!

ELMIRE. Tut, don't be hasty. Try to be judicious.
  Wait, and be certain that there's no mistake.
  No jumping to conclusions, for Heaven's sake!   10
    [*She places* ORGON *behind her, as* TARTUFFE *re-enters.*]

SCENE 7. *Tartuffe, Elmire, Orgon*

TARTUFFE. [*Not seeing* ORGON]
Madam, all things have worked out to perfection;
I've given the neighboring rooms a full inspection;
No one's about; and now I may at last . . .
ORGON. [*Intercepting him*] Hold on, my passionate fellow, not so
fast!
I should advise a little more restraint.   5
Well, so you thought you'd fool me, my dear saint!
How soon you wearied of the saintly life—
Wedding my daughter, and coveting my wife!
I've long suspected you, and had a feeling
That soon I'd catch you at your double-dealing.   10
Just now, you've given me evidence galore;
It's quite enough; I have no wish for more.
ELMIRE. [*To* TARTUFFE] I'm sorry to have treated you so slyly,
But circumstances forced me to be wily.
TARTUFFE. Brother, you can't think . . .
ORGON.   No more talk from you;
Just leave this household, without more ado.   15
TARTUFFE. What I intended . . .
ORGON.   That seems fairly clear.
Spare me your falsehoods and get out of here.
TARTUFFE. No, I'm the master, and you're the one to go!
This house belongs to me, I'll have you know,
And I shall show you that you can't hurt *me*   20
By this contemptible conspiracy,
That those who cross me know not what they do,
And that I've means to expose and punish you,
Avenge offended Heaven, and make you grieve   25
That ever you dared order me to leave.

SCENE 8. *Elmire, Orgon*

ELMIRE. What was the point of all that angry chatter?
ORGON. Dear God, I'm worried. This is no laughing matter.
ELMIRE. How so?
ORGON.   I fear I understood his drift.
I'm much disturbed about that deed of gift.
ELMIRE. You gave him . . . ?
ORGON.   Yes, it's all been drawn and signed.
But one thing more is weighing on my mind.   6
ELMIRE. What's that?
ORGON.   I'll tell you; but first let's see if there's
A certain strong-box in his room upstairs.

Act V

SCENE 1. *Orgon, Cléante*

CLÉANTE. Where are you going so fast?

ORGON.   God knows!

CLÉANTE.   Then wait;
  Let's have a conference, and deliberate
  On how this situation's to be met.

ORGON. That strong-box has me utterly upset;
  This is the worst of many, many shocks.   5

CLÉANTE. Is there some fearful mystery in that box?

ORGON. My poor friend Argas brought that box to me
  With his own hands, in utmost secrecy;
  'Twas on the very morning of his flight..
  It's full of papers which, if they came to light,   10
  Would ruin him—or such is my impression.

CLÉANTE. Then why did you let it out of your possession?

ORGON. Those papers vexed my conscience, and it seemed best
  To ask the counsel of my pious guest.
  The cunning scoundrel got me to agree   15
  To leave the strong-box in his custody,
  So that, in case of an investigation,
  I could employ a slight equivocation
  And swear I didn't have it, and thereby,
  At no expense to conscience, tell a lie.   20

CLÉANTE. It looks to me as if you're out on a limb.
  Trusting him with that box, and offering him
  That deed of gift, were actions of a kind
  Which scarcely indicate a prudent mind.
  With two such weapons, he has the upper hand,   25
  And since you're vulnerable, as matters stand,
  You erred once more in bringing him to bay.
  You should have acted in some subtler way.

ORGON. Just think of it: behind that fervent face,
  A heart so wicked, and a soul so base!   30
  I took him in, a hungry beggar, and then . . .
  Enough, by God! I'm through with pious men:
  Henceforth I'll hate the whole false brotherhood,
  And persecute them worse than Satan could.

CLÉANTE. Ah, there you go—extravagant as ever!   35
  Why can you not be rational? You never
  Manage to take the middle course, it seems,
  But jump, instead, between absurd extremes.
  You've recognized your recent grave mistake

In falling victim to a pious fake;   40
Now, to correct that error, must you embrace
An even greater error in its place,
And judge our worthy neighbors as a whole
By what you've learned of one corrupted soul?
Come, just because one rascal made you swallow   45
A show of zeal which turned out to be hollow,
Shall you conclude that all men are deceivers,
And that, today, there are no true believers?
Let atheists make that foolish inference;
Learn to distinguish virtue from pretense,   50
Be cautious in bestowing admiration,
And cultivate a sober moderation.
Don't humor fraud, but also don't asperse
True piety; the latter fault is worse,
And it is best to err, if err one must,   55
As you have done, upon the side of trust.

SCENE 2. *Damis, Orgon, Cléante*

DAMIS. Father, I hear that scoundrel's uttered threats
Against you; that he pridefully forgets
How, in his need, he was befriended by you,
And means to use your gifts to crucify you.
ORGON. It's true, my boy. I'm too distressed for tears.   5
DAMIS. Leave it to me, Sir; let me trim his ears.
Faced with such insolence, we must not waver.
I shall rejoice in doing you the favor
Of cutting short his life, and your distress.
CLÉANTE. What a display of young hotheadedness!   10
Do learn to moderate your fits of rage.
In this just kingdom, this enlightened age,
One does not settle things by violence.

SCENE 3. *Madame Pernelle, Mariane, Elmire, Dorine, Damis, Orgon, Cléante*

MADAME PERNELLE. I hear strange tales of very strange events.
ORGON. Yes, strange events which these two eyes beheld.
The man's ingratitude is unparalleled.
I save a wretched pauper from starvation,
House him, and treat him like a blood relation,   5
Shower him every day with my largesse,
Give him my daughter, and all that I possess;
And meanwhile the unconscionable knave
Tries to induce my wife to misbehave;
And not content with such extreme rascality,   10

Now threatens me with my own liberality,
And aims, by taking base advantage of
The gifts I gave him out of Christian love,
To drive me from my house, a ruined man,
And make me end a pauper, as he began.   15

DORINE. Poor fellow!

MADAME PERNELLE.   No, my son, I'll never bring
Myself to think him guilty of such a thing.

ORGON. How's that?

MADAME PERNELLE.   The righteous always were maligned.

ORGON. Speak clearly, Mother. Say what's on your mind.

MADAME PERNELLE. I mean that I can smell a rat, my dear.
You know how everybody hates him, here.   20

ORGON. That has no bearing on the case at all.

MADAME PERNELLE. I told you a hundred times, when you were
      small,
That virtue in this world is hated ever;
Malicious men may die, but malice never.   25

ORGON. No doubt that's true, but how does it apply?

MADAME PERNELLE. They've turned you against him by a clever lie.

ORGON. I've told you, I was there and saw it done.

MADAME PERNELLE. Ah, slanderers will stop at nothing, Son.

ORGON. Mother, I'll lose my temper . . . For the last time,   30
I tell you I was witness to the crime.

MADAME PERNELLE. The tongues of spite are busy night and noon,
And to their venom no man is immune.

ORGON. You're talking nonsense. Can't you realize
I saw it; saw it; saw it with my eyes?   35
Saw, do you understand me? Must I shout it
Into your ears before you'll cease to doubt it?

MADAME PERNELLE. Appearances can deceive, my son. Dear me,
We cannot always judge by what we see.

ORGON. Drat! Drat!

MADAME PERNELLE.   One often interprets things awry;   40
Good can seem evil to a suspicious eye.

ORGON. Was I to see his pawing at Elmire
As an act of charity?

MADAME PERNELLE.   Till his guilt is clear,
A man deserves the benefit of the doubt.
You should have waited, to see how things turned out.   45

ORGON. Great God in Heaven, what more proof did I need?
Was I to sit there, watching, until he'd . . .
You drive me to the brink of impropriety.

MADAME PERNELLE. No, no, a man of such surpassing piety

Could not do such a thing. You cannot shake me.   50
I don't believe it, and you shall not make me.

ORGON. You vex me so that, if you weren't my mother,
I'd say to you . . . some dreadful thing or other.

DORINE. It's your turn now, Sir, not to be listened to;
You'd not trust us, and now she won't trust you.   55

CLÉANTE. My friends, we're wasting time which should be spent
In facing up to our predicament.
I fear that scoundrel's threats weren't made in sport.

DAMIS. Do you think he'd have the nerve to go to court?

ELMIRE. I'm sure he won't: they'd find it all too crude   60
A case of swindling and ingratitude.

CLÉANTE. Don't be too sure. He won't be at a loss
To give his claims a high and righteous gloss;
And clever rogues with far less valid cause
Have trapped their victims in a web of laws.   65
I say again that to antagonize
A man so strongly armed was most unwise.

ORGON. I know it; but the man's appalling cheek
Outraged me so, I couldn't control my pique.

CLÉANTE. I wish to Heaven that we could devise   70
Some truce between you, or some compromise.

ELMIRE. If I had known what cards he held, I'd not
Have roused his anger by my little plot.

ORGON. [*To* DORINE, *as* M. LOYAL *enters*] What is that fellow
looking for? Who is he?
Go talk to him—and tell him that I'm busy.   75

SCENE 4. *Monsieur Loyal, Madame Pernelle, Orgon, Damis,
Mariane, Dorine, Elmire, Cléante*

MONSIEUR LOYAL. Good day, dear sister. Kindly let me see
Your master.

DORINE.   He's involved with company,
And cannot be disturbed just now, I fear.

MONSIEUR LOYAL. I hate to intrude; but what has brought me here
Will not disturb your master, in any event.   5
Indeed, my news will make him most content.

DORINE. Your name?

MONSIEUR LOYAL.   Just say that I bring greetings from
Monsieur Tartuffe, on whose behalf I've come.

DORINE. [*To* ORGON] Sir, he's a very gracious man, and bears
A message from Tartuffe, which, he declares,   10
Will make you most content.

CLÉANTE.   Upon my word,
I think this man had best be seen, and heard.

ORGON. Perhaps he has some settlement to suggest.
How shall I treat him? What manner would be best?

CLÉANTE. Control your anger, and if he should mention   15
Some fair adjustment, give him your full attention.

MONSIEUR LOYAL. Good health to you, good Sir. May Heaven confound
Your enemies, and may your joys abound.

ORGON. [*Aside, to* CLEANTE] A gentle salutation: it confirms
My guess that he is here to offer terms.   20

MONSIEUR LOYAL. I've always held your family most dear;
I served your father, Sir, for many a year.

ORGON. Sir, I must ask your pardon; to my shame,
I cannot now recall your face or name.

MONSIEUR LOYAL. Loyal's my name; I come from Normandy,   25
And I'm a bailiff, in all modesty.
For forty years, praise God, it's been my boast
To serve with honor in that vital post,
And I am here, Sir, if you will permit
The liberty, to serve you with this writ . . .   30

ORGON. To—*what?*

MONSIEUR LOYAL.   Now, please, Sir, let us have no friction:
It's nothing but an order of eviction.
You are to move your goods and family out
And make way for new occupants, without
Deferment or delay, and give the keys . . .   35

ORGON. I? Leave this house?

MONSIEUR LOYAL.   Why yes, Sir, if you please.
This house, Sir, from the cellar to the roof,
Belongs now to the good Monsieur Tartuffe,
And he is lord and master of your estate
By virtue of a deed of present date,   40
Drawn in due form, with clearest legal phrasing . . .

DAMIS. Your insolence is utterly amazing!

MONSIEUR LOYAL. Young man, my business here is not with you,
But with your wise and temperate father, who,
Like every worthy citizen, stands in awe   45
Of justice, and would never obstruct the law.

ORGON. But . . .

MONSIEUR LOYAL. Not for a million, Sir, would you rebel
Against authority; I know that well.
You'll not make trouble, Sir, or interfere
With the execution of my duties here.   50

DAMIS. Someone may execute a smart tattoo

On that black jacket of yours, before you're through.
MONSIEUR LOYAL. Sir, bid your son be silent. I'd much regret
Having to mention such a nasty threat
Of violence, in writing my report.   55
DORINE. [*Aside*] This man Loyal's a most disloyal sort!
MONSIEUR LOYAL. I love all men of upright character,
And when I agreed to serve these papers, Sir,
It was your feelings that I had in mind.
I couldn't bear to see the case assigned   60
To someone else, who might esteem you less
And so subject you to unpleasantness.
ORGON. What's more unpleasant than telling a man to leave
His house and home?
MONSIEUR LOYAL.   You'd like a short reprieve?
If you desire it, Sir, I shall not press you,   65
But wait until tomorrow to dispossess you.
Splendid. I'll come and spend the night here, then,
Most quietly, with half a score of men.
For form's sake, you might bring me, just before
You go to bed, the keys to the front door.   70
My men, I promise, will be on their best
Behavior, and will not disturb your rest.
But bright and early, Sir, you must be quick
And move out all your furniture, every stick:
The men I've chosen are both young and strong,   75
And with their help it shouldn't take you long.
In short, I'll make things pleasant and convenient,
And since I'm being so extremely lenient,
Please show me, Sir, a like consideration,
And give me your entire cooperation.   80
ORGON. [*Aside*] I may be all but bankrupt, but I vow
I'd give a hundred louis, here and now,
Just for the pleasure of landing one good clout
Right on the end of that complacent snout.
CLÉANTE. Careful; don't make things worse.
DAMIS.   My bootsole itches
To give that beggar a good kick in the breeches.   85
DORINE. Monsieur Loyal, I'd love to hear the whack
Of a stout stick across your fine broad back.
MONSIEUR LOYAL. Take care: a woman too may go to jail if
She uses threatening language to a bailiff.   90
CLÉANTE. Enough, enough, Sir. This must not go on.
Give me that paper, please, and then begone.

---

52. *black jacket:* in the original, *just-aucorps à longues basques,* a close-fitting, long black coat with skirts, the customary dress of a bailiff.

MONSIEUR LOYAL. Well, *au revoir*. God give you all good cheer!
ORGON. May God confound you, and him who sent you here!

SCENE 5. *Orgon, Cléante, Mariane, Elmire, Madame Pernelle,*
Dorine, Damis

ORGON. Now, Mother, was I right or not? This writ
    Should change your notion of Tartuffe a bit.
    Do you perceive his villainy at last?
MADAME PERNELLE. I'm thunderstruck. I'm utterly aghast.
DORINE. Oh, come, be fair. You mustn't take offense   5
    At this new proof of his benevolence.
    He's acting out of selfless love, I know.
    Material things enslave the soul, and so
    He kindly has arranged your liberation
    From all that might endanger your salvation.   10
ORGON. Will you not ever hold your tongue, you dunce?
CLÉANTE. Come, you must take some action, and at once.
ELMIRE. Go tell the world of the low trick he's tried.
    The deed of gift is surely nullified
    By such behavior, and public rage will not   15
    Permit the wretch to carry out his plot.

SCENE 6. *Valère, Orgon, Cléante, Elmire, Mariane, Madame*
Pernelle, Damis, Dorine

VALERE. Sir, though I hate to bring you more bad news,
    Such is the danger that I cannot choose.
    A friend who is extremely close to me
    And knows my interest in your family
    Has, for my sake, presumed to violate   5
    The secrecy that's due to things of state,
    And sends me word that you are in a plight
    From which your one salvation lies in flight.
    That scoundrel who's imposed upon you so
    Denounced you to the King an hour ago   10
    And, as supporting evidence, displayed
    The strong-box of a certain renegade
    Whose secret papers, so he testified,
    You had disloyally agreed to hide.
    I don't know just what charges may be pressed,   15
    But there's a warrant out for your arrest;
    Tartuffe has been instructed, furthermore,
    To guide the arresting officer to your door.
CLÉANTE. He's clearly done this to facilitate
    His seizure of your house and your estate.   20

ORGON. That man, I must say, is a vicious beast!
VALÈRE. You can't afford to delay, Sir, in the least.
  My carriage is outside, to take you hence;
  This thousand louis should cover all expense.
  Let's lose no time, or you shall be undone;   25
  The sole defense, in this case, is to run.
  I shall go with you all the way, and place you
  In a safe refuge to which they'll never trace you.
ORGON. Alas, dear boy, I wish that I could show you
  My gratitude for everything I owe you.   30
  But now is not the time; I pray the Lord
  That I may live to give you your reward.
  Farewell, my dears; be careful . . .
CLÉANTE.   Brother, hurry.
  We shall take care of things; you needn't worry.

SCENE 7. *The Officer, Tartuffe, Valère, Orgon, Elmire, Mariane,*
    Madame Pernelle, Dorine, Cléante, Damis

TARTUFFE. Gently, Sir, Gently; stay right where you are.
  No need for haste; your lodging isn't far.
  You're off to prison, by order of the Prince.
ORGON. This is the crowning blow, you wretch; and since
  It means my total ruin and defeat,   5
  Your villainy is now at last complete.
TARTUFFE. You needn't try to provoke me; it's no use.
  Those who serve Heaven must expect abuse.
CLÉANTE. You are indeed most patient, sweet, and blameless.
DORINE. How he exploits the name of Heaven! It's shameless.   10
TARTUFFE. Your taunts and mockeries are all for naught;
  To do my duty is my only thought.
MARIANE. Your love of duty is most meritorious,
  And what you've done is little short of glorious.
TARTUFFE. All deeds are glorious, Madam, which obey   15
  The sovereign prince who sent me here today.
ORGON. I rescued you when you were destitute;
  Have you forgotten that, you thankless brute?
TARTUFFE. No, no, I well remember everything;
  But my first duty is to serve my King.   20
  That obligation is so paramount
  That other claims, beside it, do not count;
  And for it I would sacrifice my wife,
  My family, my friend, or my own life.
ELMIRE. Hypocrite!
DORINE.   All that we most revere, he uses   25
  To cloak his plots and camouflage his ruses.

CLEANTE. If it is true that you are animated
  By pure and loyal zeal, as you have stated,
  Why was this zeal not roused until you'd sought
  To make Orgon a cuckold, and been caught?   30
  Why weren't you moved to give your evidence
  Until your outraged host had driven you hence?
  I shan't say that the gift of all his treasure
  Ought to have damped your zeal in any measure;
  But if he is a traitor, as you declare,   35
  How could you condescend to be his heir?
TARTUFFE. [*To the* OFFICER] Sir, spare me all this clamor; it's grow-
    ing shrill.
  Please carry out your orders, if you will.
OFFICER. Yes, I've delayed too long, Sir. Thank you kindly.
  You're just the proper person to remind me.   40
  Come, you are off to join the other boarders
  In the King's prison, according to his orders.
TARTUFFE. Who? I, Sir?
OFFICER.   Yes.
TARTUFFE.   To prison? This can't be true!
OFFICER. I owe an explanation, but not to you.
  [*To* ORGON] Sir, all is well; rest easy, and be grateful.   45
  We serve a Prince to whom all sham is hateful,
  A Prince who sees into our inmost hearts,
  And can't be fooled by any trickster's arts.
  His royal soul, though generous and human,
  Views all things with discernment and acumen;   50
  His sovereign reason is not lightly swayed,
  And all his judgments are discreetly weighed.
  He honors righteous men of every kind,
  And yet his zeal for virtue is not blind,
  Nor does his love of piety numb his wits   55
  And make him tolerant of hypocrites.
  'Twas hardly likely that this man could cozen
  A King who's foiled such liars by the dozen.
  With one keen glance, the King perceived the whole
  Perverseness and corruption of his soul,   60
  And thus high Heaven's justice was displayed:
  Betraying you, the rogue stood self-betrayed.
  The King soon recognized Tartuffe as one
  Notorious by another name, who'd done
  So many vicious crimes that one could fill   65

---

39. *police officer:* in the original, *un
exempt.* He would actually have been a
gentleman from the king's personal body-
guard with the rank of lieutenant-colonel
or "master of the camp."

Ten volumes with them, and be writing still.
But to be brief: our sovereign was appalled
By this man's treachery toward you, which he called
The last, worst villainy of a vile career,
And bade me follow the impostor here   70
To see how gross his impudence could be,
And force him to restore your property.
Your private papers, by the King's command,
I hereby seize and give into your hand.
The King, by royal order, invalidates   75
The deed which gave this rascal your estates,
And pardons, furthermore, your grave offense
In harboring an exile's documents.
By these decrees, our Prince rewards you for
Your loyal deeds in the late civil war,   80
And shows how heartfelt is his satisfaction
In recompensing any worthy action,
How much he prizes merit, and how he makes
More of men's virtues than of their mistakes.

DORINE. Heaven be praised!

MADAME PERNELLE.   I breathe again, at last. 85

ELMIRE. We're safe.

MARIANE.   I can't believe the danger's past.

ORGON. [*To* TARTUFFE]. Well, traitor, now you see ...

CLÉANTE. Ah, brother, please,
    Let's not descend to such indignities.
    Leave the poor wretch to his unhappy fate,
    And don't say anything to aggravate   90
    His present woes; but rather hope that he
    Will soon embrace an honest piety,
    And mend his ways, and by a true repentance
    Move our just King to moderate his sentence.
    Meanwhile, go kneel before your sovereign's throne   95
    And thank him for the mercies he has shown.

ORGON. Well said: let's go at once and, gladly kneeling,
    Express the gratitude which all are feeling.
    Then, when that first great duty has been done,
    We'll turn with pleasure to a second one,   100
    And give Valère, whose love has proven so true,
    The wedded happiness which is his due.

80. *late civil war:* a reference to Orgon's role in supporting the king during the Fronde (see note 11, p. 32).

JEAN RACINE
(1639–1699)

Phaedra (Phèdre) *

Preface †

Behold another tragedy whose theme is borrowed from Euripides! Although I have followed a rather different path than did this author for the course of the action, I have not failed to embellish my play with everything that seemed to me to be striking in his. While I took from him only the simple idea of the character of Phaedra, I might say that I owe to him perhaps the most logical elements of his stagecraft. I am not at all surprised that this character has had such a happy success since the days of Euripides, and that moreover it has been so successful in our own century, since the character has all the qualities required by Aristotle for the tragic hero that are proper for the raising of pity and terror. In all truth, Phaedra is neither completely guilty nor completely innocent. She is plunged by her fate, and by the anger of the gods, into an illegitimate passion for which she feels horror from the very start. She makes every attempt to surmount it. . . .

I have even taken care to make her a little less repellent than she is in classical tragedy, where she herself resolves to accuse Hippolytus. I believed that calumny was too low and too black to put in the mouth of a princess who otherwise showed such noble and virtuous feelings. This baseness seemed to me more fitting for a nurse, who could possess more servile inclinations, and who nevertheless only delivered this false accusation to save the life and honor of her mistress. . . .

Hippolytus, in Euripides and in Seneca, is accused of having in effect seduced his stepmother. . . . But here he is merely accused of planning to do it. I wished to spare Theseus a confusion in his character which might have made him less appealing to the audience.

Concerning the character of Hippolytus, I have noticed that among the Ancients Euripides was blamed for representing him as a philosopher free from any imperfection. The result was that the

---

* Translated by Robert Lowell. The original play was written in rhymed hexameter (or Alexandrine) couplets; Lowell's version is in pentameter (or Heroic) couplets, the verse form of Pope's "The Rape of the Lock" and "An Essay on Man," but Lowell observes that his couplet is "run on, avoids inversion and alliteration, and loosens its rhythm with shifted accents and occasional extra syllables. . . ."

† From the Preface published with the first edition in March, 1677. Translated by Howard E. Hugo.

death of the young prince caused more indignation than pity. I thought I should give him some weakness which would make him slightly culpable in his relations with his father, without however, robbing him of the magnanimity with which he spares Phaedra's honor, and let himself be charged without implicating her. I term "weakness" that passion that he bears for Aricia, in spite of himself: she who is the daughter and the sister of his father's mortal enemies. . . .

To conclude, I do not yet dare state that this play is my best tragedy. . . . What I can affirm is that I have never written one where virtue is brought more to light than in this. The slightest errors are severely punished here. The mere idea of crime is regarded with as much horror as the crime itself. . . . Passions are only revealed to the eyes to show all the disorder that they cause; and vice here is painted in colors so that one may recognize it and hate its hideousness. . . . This is what the first tragic poets always maintained. Their theater was a school where virtue was no less well taught than in the schools of philosophy. . . .

Characters

THESEUS (THÉSÉE), *son of Ægeus and king of Athens*

PHAEDRA (PHÈDRE), *wife of Theseus and daughter of Minos and Pasiphaë*

HIPPOLYTUS (HIPPOLYTE), *son of Theseus and Antiope, queen of the Amazons*

THERAMENES (THÉRAMÈNE), *tu-tor of Theseus*

ARICIA (ARICIE), *princess of the blood royal of Athens*

OENONE, *Phaedra's nurse and confidante*

ISMENE (ISMENE), *Aricia's confidante*

PANOPE, *Phaedra's lady in waiting*

GUARDS

The SCENE *is laid at Troezen, a town in the Peloponnesus, on the south shore of the Saronic Gulf, opposite Athens.*

Act 1

SCENE I. *Hippolytus, Theramenes*

HIPPOLYTUS. No, no, my friend, we're off! Six months have passed
    since Father heard the ocean howl and cast
    his galley on the Aegean's skull-white froth.
    Listen! The blank sea calls us—off, off, off!
    I'll follow Father to the fountainhead   5
    and marsh of hell. We're off. Alive or dead,
    I'll find him.
THERAMENES.   Where, my lord? I've sent a host of veteran sea-
    men up and down the coast;

each village, creek and cove from here to Crete   10
has been ransacked and questioned by my fleet;
my flagship skirted Hades' rapids, furled
sail there a day, and scoured the underworld.
Have you fresh news? New hopes? One even doubts
if noble Theseus wants his whereabouts   15
discovered. Does he need helpers to share
the plunder of his latest love affair;
a shipload of spectators and his son
to watch him ruin his last Amazon—
some creature, taller than a man, whose tanned   20
and single bosom slithers from his hand,
when he leaps to crush her like a waterfall
of honeysuckle?

lovely images...

HIPPOLYTUS.   You are cynical,
my friend. Your insinuations wrong a king,
sick as myself of his philandering.
His heart is Phaedra's and no rivals dare   25
to challenge Phaedra's sole possession there.
I sail to find my father. The command
of duty calls me from this stifling land.

THERAMENES. This stifling land? Is that how you deride
this gentle province where you used to ride   30
the bridle-paths, pursuing happiness?
You cured your orphaned childhood's loneliness
and found a peace here you preferred to all
the blaze of Athens' brawling protocol.
A rage for exploits blinds you. Your disease is boredom.   35

HIPPOLYTUS. Friend, this kingdom lost its peace,
when Father left my mother for defiled
bull-serviced Pasiphaë's child. The child
of homicidal Minos is our queen!

THERAMENES. Yes, Phaedra reigns and rules here. I have seen   40
you crouch before her outbursts like a cur.
When she first met you, she refused to stir
until your father drove you out of court.
The news is better now; our friends report
the queen is dying. Will you cross the seas,   45
desert your party and abandon Greece?

11. *Hades' rapids:* The river Acheron in Epirus was thought to flow into the Underworld.
18. *Amazon:* that tribe of Greek women who spent their time in warfare and hunting.
20. *single bosom:* a reference to the legend that the Amazons cut off the right breast in order to draw their bows further.
45. *queen:* i.e., Phaedra, daughter of Minos of Crete and of Pasiphaë, sister to Circe. Enamored of a white bull sent by Poseidon, Pasiphaë consequently gave birth to the Minotaur, the Cretan monster later slain by Theseus. Thus Phaedra was half-sister to the Minotaur.

Why flee from Phaedra? Phaedra fears the night
less than she fears the day that strives to light
the universal ennui of her eye—
this dying woman, who desires to die!   50
HIPPOLYTUS. No, I despise her Cretan vanity,
hysteria and idle cruelty.
I fear Aricia; she alone survives
the blood-feud that destroyed her brothers' lives.
THERAMENES. Prince, Prince, forgive my laughter. Must you fly 55
beyond the limits of the world and die,
floating in flotsam, friendless, far from help,
and clubbed to death by Tartars in the kelp?
Why arm the shrinking violet with a knife?
Do you hate Aricia, and fear for your life,   60
Prince?
HIPPOLYTUS. If I hated her, I'd trust myself and stay.
THERAMENES. Shall I explain you to yourself?
Prince, you have ceased to be that hard-mouthed, proud
and pure Hippolytus, who scorned the crowd
of common lovers once and rose above   65
your wayward father by despising love.
Now you justify your father, and you feel
love's poison running through you, now you kneel
and breathe the heavy incense, and a god
possesses you and revels in your blood!   70
Are you in love?
HIPPOLYTUS.   Theramenes, when I call
and cry for help, you push me to the wall.
Why do you plague me, and try to make me fear
the qualities you taught me to revere?
I sucked in prudence with my mother's milk.   75
Antiope, no harlot draped in silk,
first hardened me. I was my mother's son
and not my father's. When the Amazon,
my mother, was dethroned, my mind approved
her lessons more than ever. I still loved   80
her bristling chastity. Later, you told
stories about my father's deeds that made me hold

53-54. *survives . . . lives:* According
to one legend, Aegeus, father of Theseus,
was the adopted son of Pandion. Pallas,
Pandion's second son, had in turn fifty
sons. These were the Pallantids and all
brothers to Aricia; Theseus killed them
because they threatened his own kingship
of Athens.
76. *Antiope:* an Amazon, and sister
to Hippolyta, the queen of the Amazons.

Antiope was beloved by Theseus, who
carried her off to Athens. The Amazons
then invaded Attica (Athens) in an effort to recover Antiope, but they were
defeated in battle and Hippolyta lost her
life. Antiope's son by Theseus was Hippolytus.
81. *chastity:* The Amazons were traditionally scornful of love.

back judgment—how he stood for Hercules,
a second Hercules who cleared the Cretan seas
of pirates, throttled Scirron, Cercyon,   85
Procrustes, Sinnis, and the giant man
of Epidaurus writhing in his gore.
He pierced the maze and killed the Minotaur.
Other things turned my stomach: that long list
of women, all refusing to resist.   90
Helen, caught up with all her honeyed flesh
from Sparta; Periboea, young and fresh,
already tired of Salinis. A hundred more,
their names forgotten by my father—whore
and virgin, child and mother, all deceived,   95
if their protestations can be believed!
Ariadne declaiming to the rocks,
her sister, Phaedra, kidnapped. Phaedra locks
the gate at last! You know how often I
would weary, fall to nodding and deny   100
the possiblity of hearing the whole
ignoble, dull, insipid boast unroll.
And now I too must fall. The gods have made me creep.
How can I be in love? I have no specious heap
of honors, friend. No mastered monsters drape   105
my shoulders—Theseus' excuse to rape
at will. Suppose I chose a woman. Why
choose an orphan? Aricia is eternally
cut off from marriage, lest she breed
successors to her fierce brothers, and seed   110
the land with treason. Father only grants
her life on one condition. This—he wants
no bridal torch to burn for her. Unwooed
and childless, she must answer for the blood
her brothers shed. How can I marry her,   115
gaily subvert our kingdom's character,
and sail on the high seas of love?

THERAMENES.   You'll prove
nothing by reason, for you are in love.
Theseus' injustice to Aricia throws
her in the light; your eyes he wished to close   120

---

91. *Helen:* famed as the most beautiful of women, daughter of Zeus and Leda, sister of Castor and Pollux, later the wife of Menelaus of Sparta. When still a young girl, she was abducted by Theseus and Pirithoüs (king of the Lapiths in Thessaly). Her brothers rescued her and brought her back home to Leda and Leda's husband, Tyndareus.

92. *Periboea:* mother of Ajax.
93. *Salinis:* Salamis, island in the Gulf of Aegina on the eastern shore of Greece, off which the Greeks later defeated the Persians in a naval battle, 480 B.C.
97. *Ariadne:* Phaedra's sister, deserted by Theseus after she rescued him from the Minotaur.

are open. She dazzles you. Her pitiful
seclusion makes her doubly terrible.
Does this innocent passion freeze your blood?
There's sweetness in it. Is your only good
the dismal famine of your chastity? 125
You shun your father's path? Where would you be,
Prince, if Antiope had never burned
chastely for Theseus? Love, my lord, has turned
the head of Hercules, and thousands—fired
the forge of Vulcan! All your uninspired, 130
cold moralizing is nothing, Prince. You have changed!
Now no one sees you riding, half-deranged
along the sand-bars, where you drove your horse
and foaming chariot with all your force,
tilting and staggering upright through the surf— 135
far from their usual course across the turf.
The woods are quiet . . . How your eyes hang down!
You often murmur and forget to frown.
All's out, Prince. You're in love; you burn. Flames, flames,
Prince! A dissimulated sickness maims 140
The youthful quickness of your daring. Does
lovely Aricia haunt you?
HIPPOLYTUS.   Friend, spare us.
I sail to find my father.
THERAMENES.   Will you see.
Phaedra before you go?
HIPPOLYTUS.   I mean to be
here when she comes. Go, tell her. I will do 145
my duty. Wait, I see her nurse. What new
troubles torment her?

SCENE II. *Hippolytus, Theramenes, Oenone*

OENONE.   Who has griefs like mine,
my lord? I cannot help the queen in her decline.
Although I sit beside her day and night,
she shuts her eyes and withers in my sight. 150
An eternal tumult roisters through her head,
panics her sleep, and drags her from her bed.
Just now she fled me at the prime
of day to see the sun for the last time.
She's coming.
HIPPOLYTUS.   So! I'll steal away. My flight 155
removes a hateful object from her sight.

127. *Antiope:* Hippolytus' mother.

SCENE III. *Phaedra, Oenone*

PHAEDRA. Dearest, we'll go no further. I must rest.
I'll sit here. My emotions shake my breast,
the sunlight throws black bars across my eyes.
My knees give. If I fall, why should I rise,   160
Nurse?
OENONE.   Heaven help us! Let me comfort you.
PHAEDRA. Tear off these gross, official rings, undo
these royal veils. They drag me to the ground.
Why have you frilled me, laced me, crowned me, and wound
my hair in turrets? All your skill torments   165
and chokes me. I am crushed by ornaments.
Everything hurts me, and drags me to my knees!
OENONE. Now this, now that, Madam. You never cease
commanding us, then cancelling your commands.
You feel your strength return, summon all hands   170
to dress you like a bride, then say you choke!
We open all the windows, fetch a cloak,
rush you outdoors. It's no use, you decide
that sunlight kills you, and only want to hide.
PHAEDRA. I feel the heavens' royal radiance cool   175
and fail, as if it feared my terrible
shame has destroyed its right to shine on men.
I'll never look upon the sun again.
OENONE. Renunciation or renunciation!
Now you slander the source of your creation.   180
Why do you run to death and tear your hair?
PHAEDRA. Oh God, take me to some sunless forest lair . . .
There hoof-beats raise a dust-cloud, and my eye
follows a horseman outlined on the sky!
OENONE. What's this, my lady?
PHAEDRA.   I have lost my mind.   185
Where am I? Oh forget my words! I find
I've lost the habit now of talking sense.
My face is red and guilty—evidence
of treason! I've betrayed my darkest fears,
Nurse, and my eyes, despite me, fill with tears.   190
OENONE. Lady, if you must weep, weep for your silence
that filled your days and mine with violence.
Ah, deaf to argument and numb to care,
you have no mercy. Spare me, spare
yourself. Your blood is like polluted water,   195

---

178. *sun:* i.e., Helios, the sun-god,   184. *horseman:* Phaedra is thinking of
father of Pasiphaë, Phaedra's mother.   Hippolytus.

fouling a mind desiring its own slaughter.
The sun has died and shadows filled the skies
thrice now, since you have closed your eyes;
the day has broken through the night's content
thrice now, since you have tasted nourishment. **200**
Is your salvation from your terrified
conscience this passive, servile suicide?
Lady, your madness harms the gods who gave
you life, betrays your husband. Who will save
your children? Your downfall will orphan them, **205**
deprive them of their kingdom, and condemn
their lives and future to the discipline
of one who abhors you and all your kin,
a tyrant suckled by an amazon,
Hippolytus . . .

PHAEDRA.   Oh God!

OENONE.   You still hate someone; **210**
thank heaven for that, Madam!

PHAEDRA.   You spoke his name!

OENONE. Hippolytus, Hippolytus! There's hope
in hatred, Lady. Give your anger rope.
I love your anger. If the winds of love
and fury stir you, you will live. Above **215**
your children towers this foreigner, this child
of Scythian cannibals, now wild
to ruin the kingdom, master Greece, and choke
the children of the gods beneath his yoke.
Why dawdle? Why deliberate at length? **220**
Oh, gather up your dissipated strength.

PHAEDRA. I've lived too long.

OENONE.   Always, always agonized!
Is your conscience still stunned and paralyzed?
Do you think you have washed your hands in blood?

PHAEDRA. Thank God, my hands are clean still. Would to God **225**
my heart were innocent!

OENONE.   Your heart, your heart!
What have you done that tears your soul apart?

PHAEDRA. I've said too much. Oenone, let me die;
by dying I shall escape blasphemy.

OENONE. Search for another hand to close your eyes. **230**
Oh cruel Queen, I see that you despise
my sorrow and devotion. I'll die first,

---

205. *children:* Phaedra's sons, Acamas
and Demophöon.

217. *Scythian cannibals:* Scythia, the
home of the Amazons, was for the ancient Greeks associated with barbarians.

and end the anguish of this service cursed
by your perversity. A thousand roads
always lie open to the killing gods.   235
I'll choose the nearest. Lady, tell me how
Oenone's love has failed you. Will you allow
your nurse to die, your nurse, who gave up all—
nation, parents, children, to serve in thrall.
I saved you from your mother, King Minos' wife!   240
Will your death pay me for giving up my life?

PHAEDRA. What I could tell you, I have told you. Nurse,
only my silence saves me from the curse
of heaven.

OENONE.   How could you tell me anything
worse than watching you dying?

PHAEDRA.   I would bring   245
my life and rank dishonor. What can I say
to save myself, or put off death a day.

OENONE. Ah Lady, I implore you by my tears
and by your suffering body. Heaven hears,
and knows the truth already. Let me see.   250

PHAEDRA. Stand up.

OENONE.   Your hesitation's killing me!

PHAEDRA. What can I tell you? How the gods reprove me!

OENONE. Speak!

PHAEDRA.   On Venus, murdering Venus! love
gored Pasiphaë with the bull.

OENONE.   Forget
your mother! When she died, she paid her debt.   255

PHAEDRA. Oh Ariadne, oh my Sister, lost
for love of Theseus on that rocky coast.

OENONE. Lady, what nervous languor makes you rave
against your family; they are in the grave.

PHAEDRA. Remorseless Aphrodite drives me. I,   260
my race's last and worst love-victim, die.

OENONE. Are you in love?

PHAEDRA.   I am insane with love!

OENONE.   Who is he?

PHAEDRA. I'll tell you. Nothing love can do could
equal . . . Nurse, I am in love. The shame
kills me. I love the . . . Do not ask his name.   265

OENONE. Who?

PHAEDRA.   Nurse, you know my old loathing for the son
of Theseus and the barbarous amazon?

---

257. *rocky coast:* Theseus abandoned
Ariadne on the island of Naxos, off the
southern coast of Greece in the Aegean
Sea.

OENONE. Hippolytus! My God, oh my God!

PHAEDRA. You,
not I, have named him.

OENONE. What can you do,
but die? Your words have turned my blood to ice. 270
Oh righteous heavens, must the blasphemies
of Pasiphaë fall upon her daughter?
Her Furies strike us down across the water.
Why did we come here?

PHAEDRA. My evil comes from farther off. In May, 275
in brilliant Athens, on my marriage day,
I turned aside for shelter from the smile
of Theseus. Death was frowning in an aisle—
Hippolytus! I saw his face, turned white!
My lost and dazzled eyes saw only night, 280
capricious burnings flickered through my bleak
abandoned flesh. I could not breathe or speak
I faced my flaming executioner,
Aphrodite, my mother's murderer!
I tried to calm her wrath by flowers and praise, 285
I built her a temple, fretted months and days
on decoration. I even hoped to find
symbols and stays for my distracted mind,
searching the guts of sacrificial steers.
Yet when my erring passions, mutineers 290
to virtue, offered incense at the shrine
of love, I failed to silence the malign
Goddess, Alas, my hungry open mouth,
thirsting with adoration, tasted drouth—
Venus resigned her altar to my new lord— 295
and even while I was praying, I adored
Hippolytus above the sacred flame,
now offered to his name I could not name.
I fled him, yet he stormed me in disguise,
and seemed to watch me from his father's eyes. 300
I even turned against myself, screwed up
my slack courage to fury, and would not stop
shrieking and raging, till half-dead with love
and the hatred of a stepmother, I drove
Hippolytus in exile from the rest 305
and strenuous wardship of his father's breast.
Then I could breathe, Oenone; he was gone;
my lazy, nerveless days meandered on
through dreams and daydreams, like a stately carriage
touring the level landscape of my marriage. 310

Yet nothing worked. My husband sent me here
to Troezen, far from Athens; once again the dear
face shattered me; I saw Hippolytus
each day, and felt my ancient, venomous
passion tear my body limb from limb;   315
naked Venus was clawing down her victim.
What could I do? Each moment, terrified
by loose diseased emotions, now I cried
for death to save my glory and expel
my gloomy frenzy from this world, my hell.   320
And yet your tears and words bewildered me,
and so endangered my tranquillity,
at last I spoke. Nurse, I shall not repent,
if you will leave me the passive content
of dry silence and solitude.   325

SCENE IV. *Phaedra, Oenone, Panope*

PANOPE. My heart breaks. Would to God, I could refuse
 to tell your majesty my evil news.
 The King is dead! Listen, the heavens ring
 with shouts and lamentations for the King.
PHAEDRA. The King is dead? What's this?
PANOPE.   In vain   330
 you beg the gods to send him back again.
 Hippolytus has heard the true report,
 he is already heading for the port.
PHAEDRA. Oh God!
PANOPE.   They've heard in Athens. Everyone
 is joining factions—some salute your son,   335
 others are calling for Hippolytus;
 they want him to reform and harden us—
 even Aricia claims the loyalty
 of a fanatical minority.
 The Prince's captains have recalled their men.   340
 His flag is up and now he sails again
 for Athens. Queen, if he appear there now,
 he'll drag the people with him!
OENONE.   Stop, allow
 the Queen a little respite for her grief.
 She hears you, and will act for our relief.   345

SCENE V. *Phaedra, Oenone*

OENONE. I'd given up persuading you to live;
 death was your refuge, only death could give

you peace and save your troubled glory. I
myself desired to follow you, and die.
But this catastrophe prescribes new laws: 350
the king is dead, and for the king who was,
fate offers you his kingdom. You have a son;
he should be king! If you abandon
him, he'll be a slave. The gods, his ancestors,
will curse and drive you on your fatal course. 355
Live! Who'll condemn you if you love and woo
the Prince? Your stepson is no kin to you,
now that your royal husband's death has cut
and freed you from the throttling marriage-knot.
Do not torment the Prince with persecution, 360
and give a leader to the revolution;
no, win his friendship, bind him to your side.
Give him this city and its countryside.
He will renounce the walls of Athens, piled
stone on stone by Minerva for your child. 365
Stand with Hippolytus, annihilate
Aricia's faction, and possess the state!
PHAEDRA. So be it! Your superior force has won.
I will live if compassion for my son,
devotion to the Prince, and love of power 370
can give me courage in this fearful hour.

Act 2

SCENE I. *Aricia, Ismene*

ARICIA. What's this? The Prince has sent a messenger?
The Prince begs me to wait and meet him here?
The Prince begs! Goose, you've lost your feeble wits!
ISMENE. Lady, be calm. These are the benefits
of Theseus' death: first Prince Hippolytus 5
comes courting favors; soon the populous
cities of Greece will follow—they will eat
out of your hand, Princess, and kiss your feet.
ARICIA. This felon's hand, this slave's! My dear, your news
is only frivolous gossip, I refuse 10
to hope.
ISMENE.   Ah Princess, the just powers of hell
have struck. Theseus has joined your brothers!
ARICIA.   Tell
me how he died.

365. *Minerva:* the Greek Goddess Athene, patroness of Athens.

> hey, I'm wondering: who decides when a Greek
or | Roman hero dies? Wouldn't the
creator of U Theseus get pissed
if Racine just randomly knocked off Theseus

ISMENE.   Princess, fearful [tales] what about facts?
are circulating. Sailors saw his sails,
his infamous black sails, spin round and round   15
in Charybdis' whirlpool; all hands were drowned.
Yet others say on better evidence
that Theseus and Pirithoüs passed the dense
darkness of hell to rape Persephone.
Pirithoüs was murdered by the hound;   20
Theseus, still living, was buried in the ground.
ARICIA. This is an old wives' tale. Only the dead
enter the underworld, and see the bed
of Queen Persephone. What brought him there?
ISMENE. Princess, the King is dead—dead! Everywhere   25
men know and mourn. Already our worshipping
townsmen acclaim Hippolytus for their king;
in her great palace, Phaedra, the self-styled
regent, rages and trembles for her child.
ARICIA. What makes you think the puritanical   30
son of Theseus is human. Will he recall
my sentence and relent?
ISMENE.   I know he will.
ARICIA. You know nothing about him. He would kill
a woman, rather than be kind to one.
That wolf-cub of a fighting amazon   35
hates me above all women. He would walk
from here to hell, rather than hear me talk.
ISMENE. Do you know Hippolytus? Listen to me.
His famous, blasphemous frigidity,
what is it, when you've seen him close at hand?   40
I've watched him like a hawk, and seen him stand
shaking beside you—all his reputation
for hating womenkind bears no relation
to what I saw. He couldn't take his eyes
off you! His eyes speak what his tongue denies.   45
ARICIA. I can't believe you. Your story's absurd!
How greedily I listen to each word!
Ismene, you know me, you know how my heart
was reared on death, and always set apart
from what it cherished—can this plaything of   50
the gods and furies feel the peace of love?

---

16. *Charybdis:* in mythology, the destroying daughter of Poseidon and Gaea who lived beneath a large rock bearing her name, on the Sicilian side of the narrows between Sicily and Italy, and opposite Scylla—the cave at these same straits where the goddess-monster Scylla lived.

18-19. *Pirithoüs . . . Persephone:* Theseus went with Pirithoüs, king of the Lapiths, to Hades to help him steal Persephone. Hercules freed Theseus, whom Pluto had imprisoned, but could not free Pirithoüs, who was later killed.

What sights I've seen, Ismene! "Heads will roll,"
my brothers told me, "we will rule." I, the sole
survivor of those fabulous kings, who tilled
the soil of Greece, have seen my brothers killed,   55
six brothers murdered! In a single hour,
the tyrant, Theseus, lopped them in their flower.
The monster spared my life, and yet decreed
the torments of this childless life I lead
in exile, where no Greek can look on me;   60
my forced, perpetual virginity
preserves his crown; no son shall bear my name
or blow my brothers' ashes into flame.
Ismene, you know how well his tyranny
favors my temperament and strengthens me   65
to guard the honor of my reputation;
his rigor fortified my inclination.
How could I test his son's civilities?
I'd never even seen him with my eyes!
I'd never seen him. I'd restrained my eye,   70
that giddy nerve, from dwelling thoughtlessly
upon his outward grace and beauty—on mere
embellishments of nature, a veneer
the Prince himself despises and ignores.
My heart loves nobler virtues, and adores   75
in him his father's hard intelligence.
He has his father's daring and a sense
of honor his father lacks. Let me confess,
I love him for his lofty haughtiness
never submitted to a woman's yoke.   80
How could Phaedra's splendid marriage provoke
my jealousy? Have I so little pride,
I'd snatch at a rake's heart, a heart denied
to none—all riddled, opened up to let
thousands pass in like water through a net?   85
To carry sorrows to a heart, alone
untouched by passion, inflexible as stone,
to fasten my dominion on a force
as nervous as a never-harnessed horse—
this stirs me, this enflames me. Devilish Zeus   90
is easier mastered than Hippolytus;
heaven's love-infatuated emperor
confers less glory on his conqueror!
Ismene, I'm afraid. Why should I boast?
His very virtues I admire most   95
threaten to rise and throw me from the brink

of hope. What girlish folly made me think
Hippolytus could love Aricia?
ISMENE.   Here
he is. He loves you, Princess. Have no fear.

SCENE II. *Aricia, Ismene, Hippolytus*

HIPPOLYTUS. Princess, before   100
I leave here, I must tell you what's in store
for you in Greece. Alas, my father's dead.
The fierce forebodings that disquieted
my peace are true. Death, only death, could hide
his valor from this world he pacified.   105
The homicidal Fates will not release
the comrade, friend and peer of Hercules.
Princess, I trust your hate will not resent
honors whose justice is self-evident.
A single hope alleviates my grief,   110
Princess, I hope to offer you relief.
I now revoke a law whose cruelty
has pained my conscience. Princess, you are free
to marry. Oh enjoy this province, whose
honest, unhesitating subjects choose   115
Hippolytus for king. Live free as air,
here, free as I am, much more free!
ARICIA.   I dare
not hope. You are too gracious. Can you free
Aricia from your father's stern decree?
HIPPOLYTUS. Princess, the Athenian people, torn in two   120
between myself and Phaedra's son, want you.
ARICIA. Want me, my Lord!
HIPPOLYTUS.   I've no illusions. Lame
Athenian precedents condemn my claim,
because my mother was a foreigner
But what is that? If my only rival were   125
my younger brother, his minority
would clear my legal disability.
However, a better claim than his or mine
now favors you, ennobled by the line
of great Erectheus. Your direct descent   130
sets you before my father; he was only lent

---

124. *foreigner:* In Euripides' time, Athenian law made the son of an Athenian and a non-Greek woman illegitimate. Hippolytus' mother was Antiope the Amazon. Yet in Racine, and in Euripides, it is not made clear why Phaedra's childen do not suffer from the same liability.
130. *Erectheus:* son of Hephaestus and Gaea, brought up secretly by Athene in her temple. He subsequently became king of Athens, where he introduced her cult.

this kingdom by adoption. Once the common
Athenian, dazed by Theseus' superhuman
energies, had no longing to exhume
the rights that rushed your brothers to their doom.   135
Now Athens calls you home; the ancient feud
too long has stained the sacred olive wood;
blood festers in the furrows of our soil
to blight its fruits and scorch the farmer's toil.
This province suits me; let the vines of Crete   140
offer my brother a secure retreat.
The rest is yours. All Attica is yours;
I go to win you what your right assures.

ARICIA. Am I awake, my lord? Your sayings seem
like weird phantasmagoria in a dream.   145
How can your sparkling promises be true?
Some god, my lord, some god, has entered you!
How justly you are worshiped in this town;
oh how the truth surpasses your renown!
You wish to endow me with your heritage!   150
I only hoped you would not hate me. This rage
your father felt, how can you put it by
and treat me kindly?

HIPPOLYTUS.   Princess, is my eye
blind to beauty? Am I a bear, a bull, a boar,
some abortion fathered by the Minotaur?   155
Some one-eyed Cyclops, able to resist
Aricia's loveliness and still exist?
How can a man stand up against your grace?

ARICIA. My lord, my lord!

HIPPOLYTUS.   I cannot hide my face,
Princess! I'm driven. Why does my violence   160
so silence reason and intelligence?
Must I be still, and let my adoration
simmer away in silent resignation?
Princess, I've lost all power to restrain
myself. You see a madman, whose insane   165
pride hated love, and hoped to sit ashore,
watching the galleys founder in the war;
I was Diana's liegeman, dressed in steel.
I hoped to trample love beneath my heel—

156. *Cyclops:* one-eyed giants possessing vast strength, generally thought by
the Greeks to dwell in Sicily, where they
lived in a lawless and cannibalistic
fashion.

168-170. *Diana's liegeman ... flaming*

Venus: In the original play by Euripides,
even more is made of Hippolytus worshipping Artemis (Diana), to the exclusion of Aphrodite (Venus), and the
latter goddess' jealousy brings about his
destruction.

why is it sometimes Venus, & sometimes Aphrodite? Is it the latter Greek?

alas, the flaming Venus burns me down,   170
I am the last dependent on her crown.
What left me charred and writhing in her clutch?
A single moment and a single touch.
Six months now, bounding like a wounded stag,
I've tried to shake this poisoned dart, and drag   175
myself to safety from your eyes that blind
when present, and when absent leave behind
volleys of burning arrows in my mind.
Ah Princess, shall I dive into the sea,
or steal the wings of Icarus to flee   180
love's Midas' touch that turns my world to gold?
Your image drives me stumbling through the cold,
floods my deserted forest caves with light,
darkens the day and dazzles through my night.
I'm grafted to your side by all I see;   185
all things unite us and imprison me.
I have no courage for the Spartan exercise
that trained my hand and steeled my energies.
Where are my horses? I forget their names.
My triumphs with my chariot at the games   190
no longer give me strength to mount a horse.
The ocean drives me shuddering from its shores.
Does such a savage conquest make you blush?
My boorish gestures, headlong cries that rush
at you like formless monsters from the sea?   195
Ah, Princess, hear me! Your serenity
must pardon the distortions of a weak
and new-born lover, forced by you to speak
love's foreign language, words that snarl and yelp . . .
I never could have spoken without your help.   200

SCENE III. *Aricia, Ismene, Hippolytus, Theramenes*

THERAMENES. I announce the Queen. She comes hurriedly,
    looking for you.
HIPPOLYTUS.   For me!
THERAMENES. Don't ask me why;
    she insisted. I promised I'd prevail
    on you to speak with her before you sail.   205
HIPPOLYTUS. What can she want to hear? What can I say?

---

180. *Icarus:* son of Daedalus. With his father he escaped from Minos of Crete by means of wings made from feathers and wax. Despite Daedalus' warnings, Icarus flew too high; the sun melted the wax, and he fell into the sea.

181. *Midas:* King of Phrygia, to whom the god Dionysus granted the wish that all he touched might be changed to gold.

ARICIA. Wait for her, here! You cannot turn away.
Forget her malice. Hating her will serve
no purpose. Wait for her! Her tears deserve
your pity.

HIPPOLYTUS.   You're going, Princess? And I must go   210
to Athens, far from you. How shall I know
if you accept my love?

ARICIA.   My lord, pursue
your gracious promise. Do what you must do,
make Athens tributary to my rule.
Nothing you offer is unacceptable;   215
yet this empire, so great, so glorious,
is the least precious of your gifts to us. [the Royal "we"?]

SCENE IV. *Hippolytus, Theramenes*

HIPPOLYTUS. We're ready. Wait, the Queen's here. I need you.
You must interrupt this tedious interview.
Hurry down to the ship, then rush back, pale   220
And breathless. Say the wind's up and we must sail.

SCENE V. *Hippolytus, Oenone, Phaedra*

PHAEDRA. He's here! Why does he scowl and look away
from me? What shall I do? What shall I say?

OENONE. Speak for your son, he has no other patron.

PHAEDRA. Why are you so impatient to be gone   225
from us, my lord? Stay! we will weep together.
Pity my son; he too has lost his father.
My own death's near. Rebellion, sick with wrongs,
now like a sea-beast, lifts its slimey prongs,
its muck, its jelly. You alone now stand   230
to save the state. Who else can understand
a mother? I forget. You will not hear
me! An enemy deserves no pity. I fear
your anger. Must my son, your brother, Prince,
be punished for his cruel mother's sins?   235

HIPPOLYTUS. I've no such thoughts.

PHAEDRA.   I persecuted you
blindly, and now you have good reason to
return my impudence. How could you find
the motivation of this heart and mind
that scourged and tortured you, till you began   240
to lose the calm composure of a man,
and dwindle to a harsh and sullen boy,
a thing of ice, unable to enjoy
the charms of any civilized resource

except the heavy friendship of your horse,   245
that whirled you far from women, court and throne,
to course the savage woods for wolves alone?
You have good reason, yet if pain's a measure,
no one has less deserved your stern displeasure.
My lord, no one has more deserved compassion.   250

HIPPOLYTUS. Lady, I understand a mother's passion,
a mother jealous for her children's rights.
How can she spare a first wife's son? Long nights
of plotting, devious ways of quarrelling—
a madhouse! What else can remarriage bring?   255
Another would have shown equal hostility,
pushed her advantage more outrageously.

PHAEDRA. My lord, if you had known how far my love
and yearning have exalted me above
this usual weakness . . . Our afflicting kinship   260
is ending . . .

HIPPOLYTUS.   Madame, the precious minutes slip
by, I fatigue you. Fight against your fears.
Perhaps Poseidon has listened to our tears,
perhaps your husband's still alive. He hears
us, he is surging home—only a short   265
day's cruise conceals him, as he scuds for port.

PHAEDRA. That's folly, my lord. Who has twice visited
black Hades and the river of the dead
and returned? No, the poisonous Acheron
never lets go. Theseus drifts on and on,   270
a gutted galley on that clotted waste—
he woos, he wins Persephone, the chaste . . .
What am I saying? Theseus is not dead.
He lives in you. He speaks, he's taller by a head,
I see him, touch him, and my heart—a reef . . .   275
Ah Prince, I wander. Love betrays my grief . . .

HIPPOLYTUS. No, no, my father lives. Lady, the blind
furies release him; in your loyal mind,
love's fullness holds him, and he cannot die.

PHAEDRA. I hunger for Theseus. Always in my eye   280
he wanders, not as he appeared in hell,
lascivious eulogist of any belle
he found there, from the lowest to the Queen;
no, faithful, airy, just a little mean
through virtue, charming all, yet young and new,   285
as we would paint a god—as I now see you!
Your valiant shyness would have graced his speech,

---

263. *Poseidon:* Neptune, god of the sea, son of Cronus and Rhea.

he would have had your stature, eyes, and reach,
Prince, when he flashed across our Cretan waters,
the loved enslaver of King Minos' daughters.   200
Where were you? How could he conscript the flower
of Athens' youth against my father's power,
and ignore you? You were too young, they say;
you should have voyaged as a stowaway.
No dawdling bypath would have saved our bull,   295
when your just vengeance thundered through its skull.
There, light of foot, and certain of your goal,
you would have struck my brother's monstrous soul,
and pierced our maze's slow meanders, led
by Ariadne and her subtle thread.   300
By Ariadne? Prince I would have fought
for precedence; my every flaming thought,
love-quickened, would have shot you through the dark,
straight as an arrow to your quaking mark.
Could I have waited, panting, perishing,   305
entrusting your survival to a string,
like Ariadne, when she skulked behind,
there at the portal, to bemuse her mind
among the solemn cloisters of the porch?
No, Phaedra would have snatched your burning torch,   310
and lunged before you, reeling like a priest
of Dionysus to distract the beast.
I would have reached the final corridor
a lap before you, and killed the Minotaur!
Lost in the labyrinth, and at your side,   315
would it have mattered, if I lived or died?

HIPPOLYTUS. What are you saying, Madam? You forget
my father is your husband!

PHAEDRA.   I have let
you see my grief for Theseus! How could I
forget my honor and my majesty,
Prince?

HIPPOLYTUS. Madame, forgive me! My foolish youth   320
conjectured hideous untruths from your truth.
I cannot face my insolence. Farewell . . .

PHAEDRA. You monster! You understood me too well!
Why do you hang there, speechless, petrified,
polite! My mind whirls. What have I to hide?   325
Phaedra in all her madness stands before you.
I love you! Fool, I love you, I adore you!
Do not imagine that my mind approved
my first defection, Prince, or that I loved

your youth light-heartedly, and fed my treason 330
with cowardly compliance, till I lost my reason.
I wished to hate you, but the gods corrupt
us; though I never suffered their abrupt
seductions, shattering advances, I
too bear their sensual lightnings in my thigh. 335
I too am dying. I have felt the heat
that drove my mother through the fields of Crete,
the bride of Mınos, dying for the full
magnetic April thunders of the bull.
I struggled with my sickness, but I found 340
no grace or magic to preserve my sound
intelligence and honor from this lust,
plowing my body with its horny thrust.
At first I fled you, and when this fell short
of safety, Prince, I exiled you from court. 345
Alas, my violence to resist you made
my face inhuman, hateful. I was afraid
to kiss my husband lest I love his son.
I made you fear me (this was easily done);
you loathed me more, I ached for you no less. 350
Misfortune magnified your loveliness.
I grew so wrung and wasted, men mistook
me for the Sibyl. If you could bear to look
your eyes would tell you. Do you believe my passion
is voluntary? That my obscene confession 355
is some dark trick, some oily artifice?
I came to beg you not to sacrifice
my son, already uncertain of his life.
Ridiculous, mad embassy, for a wife
who loves her stepson! Prince, I only spoke 360
about myself! Avenge yourself, invoke
your father; a worse monster threatens you
than any Theseus ever fought and slew.
The wife of Theseus loves Hippolytus!
See, Prince! Look, this monster, ravenous 365
for her execution, will not flinch.
I want your sword's spasmodic final inch.

OENONE. Madam, put down this weapon. Your distress
attracts the people. Fly these witnesses.
Hurry! Stop kneeling! What a time to pray! 370

---

353. *Sibyl*: originally the daughter of
Dardanus and Neso, who had prophetic
powers. Later the name was used about
many old women who could foretell the
future. Apollo granted the Cumaean
Sibyl a lifetime of a thousand years, but
not lasting youth.

SCENE VI. *Theramenes, Hippolytus*

THERAMENES. Is this Phaedra, fleeing, or rather dragged away
  sobbing? Where is your sword? Who tore
  this empty scabbard from your belt?

HIPPOLYTUS.   No more!
  Oh let me get away! I face disaster.
  Horrors unnerve me. Help! I cannot master   375
  my terror. Phaedra . . . No, I won't expose
  her. No! Something I do not dare disclose . . .

THERAMENES. Our ship is ready, but before you leave,
  listen! Prince, what we never would believe
  has happened: Athens has voted for your brother.   380
  The citizens have made him king. His mother
  is regent.

HIPPOLYTUS. Phaedra is in power!

THERAMENES. An envoy sent from Athens came this hour
  to place the scepter in her hands. Her son
  is king.

HIPPOLYTUS. Almighty gods, you know "this woman!"   385
  Is it her spotless virtue you reward?

[handwritten: hmm. Just a hint of sarcasm]

THERAMENES. I've heard a rumor. Someone swam aboard
  a ship off Epirus. He claims the King
  is still alive. I've searched. I know the thing
  is nonsense.

HIPPOLYTUS.   Search! Nothing must be neglected.   390
  If the king's dead, I'll rouse the disaffected
  people, crown Aricia, and place our lands,
  our people, and our lives in worthy hands.

Act 3

SCENE I. *Phaedra, Oenone*

PHAEDRA. Why do my people rush to crown me queen?
  Who can even want to see me? They have seen
  my downfall. Will their praise deliver me?
  Oh, bury me at the bottom of the sea!
  Nurse, I have said too much! Led on by you,   5
  I've said what no one should have listened to.
  He listened. How could he pretend my drift
  was hidden? Something held him, and made him shift
  his ground . . . He only wanted to depart
  and hide, while I was pouring out my heart.   10
  Oh how his blushing multiplied my shame!
  Why did you hold me back! You are to blame,

[handwritten: how easy that war to proclaim]

Oenone. But for you, I would have killed
myself. Would he have stood there, iron-willed
and merciless, while I fell upon his sword?   15
He would have snatched it, held me, and restored
my life. No! No!

OENONE.   Control yourself! No peace
comes from surrendering to your disease,
Madam. Oh daughter of the kings of Crete,
why are you weeping and fawning at the feet   20
of this barbarian, less afraid of fate
than of a woman? You must rule the state.

PHAEDRA. Can I, who have no courage to restrain
the insurrection of my passions, reign?
Will the Athenians trust their sovereignty   25
to me? Love's despotism is crushing me,
I am ruined.

OENONE.   Fly!

PHAEDRA.   How can I leave him?

OENONE. Lady, you have already banished him.
Can't you take flight?

PHAEDRA.   The time for flight has passed.
He knows me now. I rushed beyond the last   30
limits of modesty, when I confessed.
Hope was no longer blasting through my breast;
I was resigned to hopelessness and death,
and gasping out my last innocent breath,
Oenone, when you forced me back to life.   35
You thought I was no longer Theseus' wife,
and let me feel that I was free to love.

OENONE. I would have done anything to remove
your danger. Whether I'm guilty or innocent
is all the same to me. Your punishment   40
should fall on one who tried to kill you, not
on poor Oenone. Lady, you must plot
and sacrifice this monster, whose unjust
abhorence left you dying in the dust.
Oh humble him, undo him, oh despise   45
him! Lady, you must see him with my eyes.

PHAEDRA. Oenone, he was nourished in the woods;
he is all shyness and ungracious moods
because the forests left him half-inhuman.
He's never heard love spoken by a woman!   50
We've gone too far. Oenone, we're unwise;
perhaps the young man's silence was surprise.

OENONE. His mother, the amazon, was never moved
by men.

PHAEDRA.   The boy exists. She must have loved!

OENONE. He has a sullen hatred for our sex.   55

PHAEDRA. Oh, all the better; rivals will not vex
  my chances. Your advice is out of season;
  now you must serve my frenzy, not my reason!
  You tell me love has never touched his heart;
  we'll look, we'll find an undefended part.   60
  He's turned his bronze prows seaward; look, the wind
  already blows like a trumpeter behind
  his bulging canvas! The Acropolis
  of Athens and its empire shall be his!
  Hurry, Oenone, hunt the young man down,   65
  blind him with dazzling visions of the crown.
  Go tell him I relinquish my command,
  I only want the guidance of his hand. *Is that all she can*
  Let him assume these powers that weary me, *do? Bribe him?*
  he will instruct my son in sovereignty.   70
  Perhaps he will adopt my son, and be
  the son and mother's one divinity!
  Oenone, rush to him, use every means
  to bend and win him; if he fears the Queen's
  too proud, he'll listen to ~~her~~ slave. Plead, groan,   75
  insist, say I am giving him my throne . . .
  No, say I'm dying! *his*

SCENE II. *Phaedra*

PHAEDRA.   Implacable Aphrodite, now you see
  the depths to which your tireless cruelty
  has driven Phaedra—here is my bosom;
  every thrust and arrow has struck home!   80
  Oh Goddess, if you hunger for renown,
  rise now, and shoot a worthier victim down!
  Conquer the barbarous Hippolytus,
  who mocks the graces and the power of Venus,
  and gazes on your godhead with disgust.   85
  Avenge me, Venus! See, my cause is just,
  my cause is yours. Oh bend him to my will! . . .
  You're back, Oenone? Does he hate me still?

SCENE III. *Phaedra, Oenone*

OENONE. Your love is folly, dash it from your soul,
  gather your scattered pride and self-control,   90
  Madam! I've seen the royal ship arrive.
  Theseus is back, Theseus is still alive!
  Thousands of voices thunder from the docks.
  People are waving flags and climbing rocks.

While I was looking for Hippolytus . . .   95
PHAEDRA. My husband's living! Must you trouble us
  by talking? What am I living for?
  He lives, Oenone, let me hear no more
  about it.
OENONE.   Why?
PHAEDRA.   I told you, but my fears
  were stilled, alas, and smothered by your tears.   100
  Had I died this morning, I might have faced
  the gods. I heeded you and die disgraced!
OENONE. You are disgraced! *You are a disgrace!*
PHAEDRA.   Oh Gods of wrath,
  how far I've travelled on my dangerous path!
  I go to meet my husband; at his side   105
  will stand Hippolytus. How shall I hide
  my thick adulterous passion for this youth,
  who has rejected me, and knows the truth?
  Will the stern Prince stand smiling and approve
  the labored histrionics of my love   110
  for Theseus, see my lips, still languishing
  for his, betray his father and his King?
  Will he not draw his sword and strike me dead?
  Suppose he spares me? What if nothing's said?
  Am I a gorgon, or Circe, or the infidel   115
  Medea, stifled by the flames of hell,
  yet rising like Aphrodite from the sea,
  refreshed and radiant with indecency?
  Can I kiss Theseus with dissembled poise?
  I think each stone and pillar has a voice.   120
  The very dust rises to disabuse
  my husband—to defame me and accuse!
  Oenone, I want to die. Death will give
  me freedom; oh it's nothing not to live;
  death to the unhappy's no catastrophe!   125
  I fear the name that must live after me,
  and crush my son until the end of time.
  Is his inheritance his mother's crime,
  his right to curse me, when my pollution stains

115-116. *gorgon . . . Medea:* The Gor-
gons were three sisters, the most famed
being Medusa; they were frightful in
appearance, with snakes in their hair,
large mouths and irregular teeth, and
flaming eyes; they were winged, and had
claws. Circe, Pasiphaë's sister, was a
magician who lived on the island of
Aeaea. Her chief feat was changing Odysseus' men into swine. Medea, at one time
beloved by Jason when he was questing
for the Golden Fleece, had a notably
bloodthirsty career: she strewed her
brother's limbs on the sea, killed Jason's
uncle by persuading his daughters to cut
him up in small pieces and boil them in a
cauldron, killed Jason's second wife with
a poisoned bridal robe, and murdered the
two children she had had by Jason.

the blood of heaven bubbling in his veins?   130
The day will come, alas, the day will come,
when nothing will be left to save him from
the voices of despair. If he should live
he'll flee his subjects like a fugitive.

OENONE. He has my pity. Who has ever built   135
firmer foundations to expose her guilt?
But why expose your son? Is your contribution
for his defense to serve the prosecution?
Suppose you kill yourself? The world will say
you fled your outraged husband in dismay.   140
Could there be stronger evidence and proof
than Phaedra crushed beneath the horse's hoof   *Hippolytus*
of blasphemous self-destruction to convince
the crowds who'll dance attendance on the Prince?
The crowds will mob your children when they hear   145
their defamation by a foreigner!
Wouldn't you rather see earth bury us?
Tell me, do you still love Hippolytus?

PHAEDRA. I see him as a beast, who'd murder us.

OENONE. Madam, let the positions be reversed!   150
You fear the Prince; you must accuse him first.
Who'll dare assert your story is untrue,
if all the evidence shall speak for you:
your present grief, your past despair of mind,
the Prince's sword so luckily left behind?   *ah...*   155
Do you think Theseus will oppose his son's
second exile? He has consented once!

PHAEDRA. How dare I take this murderous, plunging course?

OENONE. I tremble, Lady, I too feel remorse.
If death could rescue you from infamy,   160
Madam, I too would follow you and die.
Help me by being silent. I will speak
in such a way the King will only seek
a bloodless exile to assert his rights.
A father is still a father when he smites,   165
You shudder at this evil sacrifice,
but nothing's evil or too high a price
to save your menaced honor from defeat.
Ah Minos, Minos, you defended Crete
by killing young men? Help us! If the cost   170
for saving Phaedra is a holocaust
of virtue, Minos, you must sanctify
our undertaking, or watch your daughter die.
I see the King.

PHAEDRA.   I see Hippolytus!   *human —*
                                                differen) Images

SCENE IV. *Phaedra, Theseus, Hippolytus, Oenone*

THESEUS. Fate's heard me, Phaedra, and removed the bar   175
that kept me from your arms.
PHAEDRA.   Theseus, stop where you are!
Your raptures and endearments are profane.
Your arm must never comfort me again.
You have been wronged, the gods who spared your life   180
have used your absence to disgrace your wife,
unworthy now to please you or come near.
My only refuge is to disappear.

SCENE V. *Theseus, Hippolytus*

THESEUS. What a strange welcome! This bewilders me.
My son, what's happened?
HIPPOLYTUS.   Phaedra holds the key.   185
Ask Phaedra. If you love me, let me leave
this kingdom. I'm determined to achieve
some action that will show my strength. I fear
Phaedra. I am afraid of living here,
THESEUS. My son, you want to leave me?
HIPPOLYTUS.   I never sought   190
her grace or favor. Your decision brought
her here from Athens. Your desires prevailed
against my judgment, Father, when you sailed
leaving Phaedra and Aricia in my care.
I've done my duty, now I must prepare   195
for sterner actions, I must test my skill
on monsters far more dangerous to kill
than any wolf or eagle in this wood.
Release me, I too must prove my manhood.
Oh Father, you were hardly half my age,   200
when herds of giants writhed before your rage—
you were already famous as the scourge
of insolence. Our people saw you purge
the pirates from the shores of Greece and Thrace,
the harmless merchantman was free to race   205
the winds, and weary Hercules could pause
from slaughter, knowing you upheld his cause.
The world revered you. I am still unknown;
even my mother's deeds surpass my own.
Some tyrants have escaped you; let me meet   210
with them and throw their bodies at your feet.

I'll drag them from their wolf-holes; if I die,
my death will show I struggled worthily.
Oh, Father, raise me from oblivion;
my deeds shall tell the universe I am your son.   215

THESEUS. What do I see? Oh gods, what horror drives
my queen and children fleeing for their lives
before me? If so little warmth remains,
oh why did you release me from my chains?
Why am I hated, and so little loved?   220
I had a friend, just one. His folly moved
me till I aided his conspiracy
to ravish Queen Persephone.
The gods, tormented by our blasphemous
designs, befogged our minds and blinded us—   225
we invaded Epirus instead of hell.
There a diseased and subtle tyrant fell
upon us as we slept, and while I stood
by, helpless, monsters crazed for human blood
consumed Pirithoüs. I myself was chained   230
fast in a death-deep dungeon. I remained
six months there, then the gods had pity,
and put me in possession of the city.
I killed the tyrant; now his body feasts
the famished, pampered bellies of his beasts.   235
At last, I voyaged home, cast anchor, furled
my sails. When I was rushing to my world—
what am I saying? When my heart and soul
were mine again, unable to control
themselves for longing—who receives me? All run   240
and shun me, as if I were a skeleton.
Now I myself begin to feel the fear
I inspire. I wish I were a prisoner
again or dead. Speak! Phaedra says my home
was outraged. Who betrayed me? Someone come   245
and tell me. I have fought for Greece. Will Greece,
sustained by Theseus, give my enemies
asylum in my household? Tell me why
I've no avenger? Is my son a spy?
You will not answer. I must know my fate.   250
Suspicion chokes me, while I hesitate
and stand here pleading. Wait, let no one stir.
Phaedra shall tell me what has troubled her.

221. *a friend:* Pirithoüs.
226. *Epirus:* a district in western Greece, on the Ionian Sea.

SCENE VI. *Hippolytus*

HIPPOLYTUS. What now? His anger turns my blood to ice.
Will Phaedra, always uncertain, sacrifice   255
herself? What will she tell the King? How hot
the air's becoming here! I feel the rot
of love seeping like poison through this house.
I feel the pollution. I cannot rouse
my former loyalties. When I try to gather   260
the necessary strength to face my father,
my mind spins with some dark presentiment . . .
How can such terror touch the innocent?
I LOVE ARICIA! Father, I confess
my treason to you is my happiness!   265
I LOVE ARICIA! Will this bring you joy,
our love you have no power to destroy?

Act 4

SCENE I. *Theseus, Oenone*

THESEUS. What's this, you tell me he dishonors me,
and has assaulted Phaedra's chastity?
Oh heavy fortune, I no longer know
who loves me, who I am, or where I go.
Who has ever seen such disloyalty   5
after such love? Such sly audacity!
His youth made no impression on her soul,
so he fell back on force to reach his goal!
I recognize this perjured sword; I gave
him this myself to teach him to be brave!   10
Oh Zeus, are blood-ties no impediment?
Phaedra tried to save him from punishment!
Why did her silence spare this parricide?
OENONE. She hoped to spare a trusting father's pride.
She felt so sickened by your son's attempt,   15
his hot eyes leering at her with contempt,
she had no wish to live. She read out her will
to me, then lifted up her arm to kill
herself. I struck the sword out of her hand.
Fainting, she babbled the secret she had planned   20
to bury with her in the grave. My ears
unwillingly interpreted her tears.
THESEUS. Oh traitor! I know why he seemed to blanch
and toss with terror like an aspen branch
when Phaedra saw him. Now I know why he stood   25
back, then embraced me so coldly he froze my blood.

Was Athens the first stage for his obscene
attentions? Did he dare attack the Queen
before our marriage?

OENONE.   Remember her disgust
and hate then? She already feared his lust.   30

THESEUS. And when I sailed, this started up again?

OENONE. I've hidden nothing. Do you want your pain
redoubled? Phaedra calls me. Let me go,
and save her. I have told you what I know.

SCENE II. *Theseus, Hippolytus*

THESEUS. My son returns! Oh God, reserved and cool,   35
dressed in a casual freedom that could fool
the sharpest. Is it right his brows should blaze
and dazzle me with virtue's sacred rays?
Are there not signs? Should not ADULTERER
in looping scarlet script be branded there?

HIPPOLYTUS. What cares becloud your kingly countenance,
Father! What is this irritated glance?
Tell me! Are you afraid to trust your son?

THESEUS. How dare you stand here? May the great Zeus stone
me, if I let my fondness and your birth   45
protect you! Is my strength which rid the earth
of brigands paralysed? Am I so sick
and senile, any coward with a stick
can strike me? Am I a schoolboy's target? Oh God,
am I food for vultures? Some carrion you must prod   50
and poke to see if it's alive or dead?
Your hands are moist and itching for my bed,
Coward! Wasn't begetting you enough
dishonor to destroy me? Must I snuff
your perjured life, my own son's life, and stain   55
a thousand glories? Let the gods restrain
my fury! Fly! live hated and alone—
there are places where my name may be unknown.
Go, find them, follow your disastrous star
through filth; if I discover where you are,   60
I'll add another body to the hill
of vermin I've extinguished by my skill.
Fly from me, let the grieving storm-winds bear
your contagion from me. You corrupt the air.
I call upon Poseidon. Help me, Lord   65
of Ocean, help your servant! Once my sword
heaped crucified assassins on your shore
and let them burn like beacons. God, you swore

my first request would be fulfilled. My first!
I never made it. Even through the worst   70
torments of Epirus I held my peace;
no threat or torture brought me to my knees
beseeching favors; even then I knew
some greater project was reserved for you!
Poseidon, now I kneel. Avenge me, dash   75
my incestuous son against your rocks, and wash
his dishonor from my household; wave on wave
of roaring nothingness shall be his grave.

HIPPOLYTUS. Phaedra accuses me of lawless love!
Phaedra! My heart stops, I can hardly move   80
my lips and answer. I have no defense,
if you condemn me without evidence.

THESEUS. Oh coward, you were counting on the Queen
to hide your brutal insolence and screen
your outrage with her weakness! You forgot   85
something. You dropped your sword and spoiled your plot.
You should have kept it. Surely you had time
to kill the only witness to your crime!

HIPPOLYTUS. Why do I stand this, and forbear to clear
away these lies, and let the truth appear?   90
I could so easily. Where would you be,
if I spoke out? Respect my loyalty,
Father, respect your own intelligence.
Examine me. What am I? My defense
is my whole life. When have I wavered, when   95
have I pursued the vices of young men?
Father, you have no scaffolding to rig
your charges on. Small crimes precede the big.
Phaedra accused me of attempting rape!
Am I some Proteus, who can change his shape?   100
Nature despises such disparities.
Vice, like virtue, advances by degrees.
Bred by Antiope to manly arms,
I hate the fever of this lust that warms
the loins and rots the spirit. I was taught   105
uprightness by Theramenes. I fought
with wolves, tamed horses, gave my soul to sport,
and shunned the joys of women and the court.
I dislike praise, but those who know me best
grant me one virtue—it's that I detest   110
the very crimes of which I am accused.

100 *Proteus:* an old man of the ocean, keeper of Poseidon's seals, capable of assuming any form he wished.

How often you yourself have been amused
and puzzled by my love of purity,
pushed to the point of crudeness. By the sea
and in the forest, I have filled my heart
with freedom, far from women.

THESEUS.   When this part
was dropped, could only Phaedra violate
the cold abyss of your immaculate
reptilian soul. How could this funeral urn
contain a heart, a living heart, or burn
for any woman but my wife?

HIPPOLYTUS.   Ah no!
Father, I too have seen my passions blow
into a tempest. Why should I conceal
my true offense? I feel, Father, I feel
what other young men feel. I love, I love
Aricia. Father, I love the sister of
your worst enemies. I worship her!
I only feel and breathe and live for her!

THESEUS. You love Aricia? God! No, this is meant
to blind my eyes and throw me off the scent.

HIPPOLYTUS. Father, for six months I have done my worst
to kill this passion. You shall be the first
to know . . . You frown still. Nothing can remove
your dark obsession. Father, what will prove
my innocence? I swear by earth and sky,
and nature's solemn, shining majesty . . .

THESEUS. Oaths and religion are the common cant
of all betrayers. If you wish to taunt
me, find a better prop than blasphemy.

HIPPOLYTUS. All's blasphemy to eyes that cannot see.
Could even Phaedra bear me such ill will?

THESEUS. Phaedra, Phaedra! Name her again, I'll kill
you! My hand's already on my sword.

HIPPOLYTUS.   Explain
my terms of exile. What do you ordain?

THESEUS. Sail out across the ocean. Everywhere
on earth and under heaven is too near.

HIPPOLYTUS. Who'll take me in? Oh who will pity me,
and give me bread, if you abandon me?

THESEUS. You'll find fitting companions. Look for friends
who honor everything that most offends.
Pimps and jackals who praise adultery

---

116. *women:* In Euripides' play, much
is made of Hippolytus' allegiance to Ar-   temis (Diana), the "queen and huntress,
chaste and fair."

and incest will protect your purity!

HIPPOLYTUS. Adultery! Is it your privilege
to fling this word in my teeth? I've reached the edge
of madness . . . No, I'll say no more. Compare   155
my breeding with Phaedra's. Think and beware . . .
She had a mother . . . No, I must not speak.

THESEUS. You devil, you'll attack the queen still weak
from your assault. How can you stand and face
your father? Must I drive you from this place   160
with my own hand. Run off, or I will flog
you with the flat of my sword like a dog!

SCENE III. *Theseus*

THESEUS. You go to your inevitable fate,
Child—by the river immortals venerate.
Poseidon gave his word. You cannot fly: 165
death and the gods march on invisibly.
I loved you once; despite your perfidy,
my bowels writhe inside me. Must you die?
Yes; I am in too deep now to draw back.
What son has placed his father on such a rack?   170
What father groans for such a monstrous birth?
Oh gods, your thunder throws me to the earth.

SCENE IV. *Theseus, Phaedra*

PHAEDRA. Theseus, I heard the deluge of your voice,
and stand here trembling. If there's time for choice,
hold back your hand, still bloodless; spare your race! 175
I supplicate you, I kneel here for grace.
Oh, Theseus, Theseus, will you drench the earth
with your own blood? His virtue, youth and birth
cry out for him. Is he already slain
by you for me—spare me this incestuous pain!   180

THESEUS. Phaedra, my son's blood has not touched my hand;
and yet I'll be avenged. On sea and land,
spirits, the swift of foot, shall track him down
Poseidon owes me this. Why do you frown?

PHAEDRA. Poseidon owes you this? What have you done   185
in anger?

THESEUS.   What! You wish to help my son?
No, stir my anger, back me to the hilt,
call for blacker colors to paint his guilt.
Lash, strike and drive me on! You cannot guess

164. *river:* the Styx, the chief river in
Hades and sacred to the gods themselves,
so that their most binding oath was by
the Styx. If such an oath were broken,
the god would lie as one dead for a year.

the nerve and fury of his wickedness.
Phaedra, he slandered your sincerity,
he told me your accusation was a lie.
He swore he loved Aricia, he wants to wed
Aricia. . . .

PHAEDRA.   What, my lord!

THESEUS.   That's what he said.
Of course, I scorn his shallow artifice.
Help me, Poseidon, hear me, sacrifice
my son. I seek the altar. Come! Let us both
kneel down and beg the gods to keep their oath.

SCENE V. *Phaedra*

PHAEDRA. My husband's gone, still rumbling his own name
and fame. He has no inkling of the flame
his words have started. If he hadn't spoken,
I might have . . . I was on my feet, I'd broken
loose from Oenone, and had just begun
to say I know not what to save his son.
Who knows how far I would have gone? Remorse,
longing and anguish shook me with such force,
I might have told the truth and suffered death,
before this revelation stopped my breath:
Hippolytus is not insensible,
only insensible to me! His dull
heart chases shadows. He is glad to rest
upon Aricia's adolescent breast!
Oh thin abstraction! When I saw his firm
repugnance spurn my passion like a worm,
I thought he had some magic to withstand
the lure of any woman in the land,
and now I see a schoolgirl leads the boy,
as simply as her puppy or a toy.
Was I about to perish for this sham,
this panting hypocrite? Perhaps I am
the only woman that he could refuse!

SCENE VI. *Phaedra, Oenone*

PHAEDRA. Oenone, dearest, have you heard the news?

OENONE. No, I know nothing, but I am afraid.
How can I follow you? You have betrayed
your life and children. What have you revealed,
Madam?

PHAEDRA.   I have a rival in the field,
Oenone.

OENONE.   What?

PHAEDRA.   Oenone, he's in love—
this howling monster, able to disprove
my beauty, mock my passion, scorn each prayer,
and face me like a tiger in its lair—   230
he's tamed, the beast is harnessed to a cart;
Aricia's found an entrance to his heart.

OENONE. Aricia?

PHAEDRA.   Nurse, my last calamity
has come. This is the bottom of the sea,
All that preceded this had little force—   235
the flames of lust, the horrors of remorse,
the prim refusal by my grim young master,
were only feeble hints of this disaster.
They love each other! Passion blinded me.
I let them blind me, let them meet and see   240
each other freely! Was such bounty wrong?
Oenone, you have known this all along,
you must have seen their meetings, watched them sneak
off to their forest, playing hide-and-seek!
Alas, such rendezvous are no offence: 245
innocent nature smiles of innocence,
for them each natural impulse was allowed,
each day was summer and without a cloud.
Oenone, nature hated me. I fled
its light, as if a price were on my head.   250
I shut my eyes and hungered for my end.
Death was the only God my vows could bend.
And even while my desolation served
me gall and tears, I knew I was observed;
I never had security or leisure   255
for honest weeping, but must steal this pleasure.
Oh hideous pomp; a monarch only wears
the robes of majesty to hide her tears!

OENONE. How can their folly help them? They will never
enjoy its fruit.   260

PHAEDRA.   Ugh, they will love forever—
even while I am talking, they embrace,
they scorn me, they are laughing in my face!
In the teeth of exile, I hear them swear
they will be true forever, everywhere.
Oenone, have pity on my jealous rage;   265
I'll kill this happiness that jeers at age.
I'll summon Theseus; hate shall answer hate!
I'll drive my husband to annihilate
Aricia—let no trivial punishment,

her instant death, or bloodless banishment . . .   270
What am I saying? Have I lost my mind?
I am jealous, and call my husband! Bind
me, gag me; I am frothing with desire.
My husband is alive, and I'm on fire!
For whom? Hippolytus. When I have said   275
his name, blood fills my eyes, my heart stops dead.
Imposture, incest, murder! I have passed
the limits of damnation; now at last,
my lover's lifeblood is my single good.
Nothing else cools my murderous thirst for blood.   280
Yet I live on! I live, looked down upon
by my progenitor, the sacred sun,
by Zeus, by Europa, by the universe
of gods and stars, my ancestors. They curse
their daughter. Let me die. In the great night   285
of Hades, I'll find shelter from their sight.
What am I saying? I've no place to turn:
Minos, my father, holds the judge's urn.
The gods have placed damnation in his hands,
the shades in Hades follow his commands.   290
Will he not shake and curse his fatal star
that brings his daughter trembling to his bar?
His child by Pasiphaë forced to tell
a thousand sins unclassified in hell?
Father, when you interpret what I speak,   295
I fear your fortitude will be too weak
to hold the urn. I see you fumbling for
new punishments for crimes unknown before.
You'll be your own child's executioner!
You cannot kill me; look, my murderer   300
is Venus, who destroyed our family;
Father, she has already murdered me.
I killed myself—and what is worse I wasted
my life for pleasures I have never tasted.
My lover flees me still, and my last gasp   305
is for the fleeting flesh I failed to clasp.
OENONE. Madam, Madam, cast off this groundless terror!
Is love now an unprecedented error?
You love! What then! You love! Accept your fate.
You're not the first to sail into this strait.   310

283. *Europa:* Carried off by Zeus in
the form of a bull, Europa conceived
three children by him, of whom one was
Minos, Phaedra's father.
288. *judge's urn:* After his death,
Minos of Crete became, along with his
brother Rhadamanthus, one of the judges
of souls in the Underworld. The urn held
the lots which determined to what abode
in the Underworld the souls of the dead
were to be sent.

Will chaos overturn the earth and Jove,
because a mortal woman is in love?
Such accidents are easy, all too common.
A woman must submit to being woman.
You curse a failure in the source of things. 315
Venus has feasted on the hearts of kings;
even the gods, man's judges, feel desire,
Zeus learned to live with his adulterous fire.

PHAEDRA. Must I still listen and drink your poisoned breath?
My death's redoubled on the edge of death. 320
I'd fled Hippolytus and I was free
till your entreaties stabbed and blinded me,
and dragged me howling to the pit of lust.
Oenone, I was learning to be just.
You fed my malice. Attacking the young Prince 325
was not enough; you clothed him with my sins.
You wished to kill him; he is dying now,
because of you, and Theseus' brutal vow.
You watch my torture; I'm the last ungorged
scrap rooting in this trap your plots have forged. 330
What binds you to me? Leave me, go, and die,
may your punishment be to terrify
all those who ruin princes by their lies,
hints, acquiescence, filth, and blasphemies—
panders who grease the grooves of inclination, 335
and lure our willing bodies from salvation.
Go die, go frighten false flatterers, the worst
friends the gods can give to kings they've cursed!

OENONE. I have given all and left all for her service,
almighty gods! I have been paid my price! 340

Act 5

SCENE I. *Hippolytus, Aricia*

ARICIA. Take a stand, speak the truth, if you respect
your father's glory and your life. Protect
yourself! I'm nothing to you. You consent
without a struggle to your banishment.
If you are weary of Aricia, go; 5
at least do something to prevent the blow
that dooms your honor and existence—both
at a stroke! Your father must recall his oath;
there is time still, but if the truth's concealed,
you offer your accuser a free field. 10
Speak to your father!

HIPPOLYTUS.   I've already said

what's lawful. Shall I point to his soiled bed,
tell Athens how his marriage was foresworn,
make Theseus curse the day that he was born?
My aching heart recoils. I only want   15
God and Aricia for my confidants.
See how I love you; love makes me confide
in you this horror I have tried to hide
from my own heart. My faith must not be broken;
forget, if possible, what I have spoken.   20
Ah Princess, if even a whisper slips
past you, it will perjure your pure lips
God's justice is committed to the cause
of those who love him, and uphold his laws;
sooner or later, heaven itself will rise   25
in wrath and punish Phaedra's blasphemies.
I must not. If I rip away her mask,
I'll kill my father. Give me what I ask.
Do this! Then throw away your chains; it's right
for you to follow me, and share my flight.   30
Fly from this prison; here the vices seethe
and simmer, virtue has no air to breathe.
In the confusion of my exile, none
will even notice that Aricia's gone.
Banished and broken, Princess, I am still   35
a force in Greece. Your guards obey my will,
powerful intercessors wish us well:
our neighbors, Argos' citadel
is armed, and in Mycenae our allies
will shelter us, if lying Phaedra tries   40
to hurry us from our paternal throne,
and steal our sacred titles for her son.
The gods are ours, they urge us to attack.
Why do you tremble, falter and hold back?
Your interests drive me to this sacrifice.   45
While I'm on fire, your blood has changed to ice.
Princess, is exile more than you can face?
ARICIA. Exile with you, my lord? What sweeter place
is under heaven? Standing at your side,
I'd let the universe and heaven slide.   50
You're my one love, my king, but can I hope
for peace and honor, Prince, if I elope
unmarried? This . . . I wasn't questioning
the decency of flying from the King.
Is he my father? Only an abject   55

38. *Argos:* chief city in Argolis, in the northeastern Peloponnesus.
39. *Mycenae:* also in Argolis, and center of the Mycenaean civilization, with close Cretan connections.

spirit honors tyrants with respect.
You say you love me. Prince, I am afraid.
HIPPOLYTUS. Aricia, you shall never be betrayed;
accept me! Let our love be sanctified,
then flee from your oppressor as my bride.   60
Bear witness, oh you gods, our love released
by danger, needs no temple or a priest.
It's faith, not ceremonial, that saves.
Here at the city gates, among these graves
the resting places of my ancient line,   65
there stands a sacred temple and a shrine.
Here, where no mortal ever swore in vain,
here in these shadows, where eternal pain
is ready to engulf the perjurer;
here heaven's scepter quivers to confer   70
its final sanction; here, my Love, we'll kneel,
and pray the gods to consecrate and seal
our love. Zeus, the father of the world will stand
here as your father and bestow your hand.
Only the pure shall be our witnesses: 75
Hera, the guarantor of marriages,
Demeter and the virgin Artemis.
ARICIA. The King is coming. Fly. I'll stay and meet
his anger here and cover your retreat.
Hurry. Be off, send me some friend to guide   80
my timid footsteps, husband, to your side.

SCENE II. *Theseus, Ismene, Aricia*

THESEUS. Oh God, illuminate my troubled mind.
Show me the answer I have failed to find.
ARICIA. Go, Ismene, be ready to escape.

SCENE III. *Theseus, Aricia*

THESEUS. Princess, you are disturbed. You twist your cape   85
and blush. The Prince was talking to you. Why
is he running?
ARICIA.   We've said our last goodbye,
my lord.
THESEUS.   I see the beauty of your eyes
moves even my son, and you have gained a prize
no woman hoped for.
ARICIA.   He hasn't taken on   90
your hatred for me, though he is your son.

76. *Hera . . . Demeter:* Hera was Zeus's wife, hence queen of the gods. She was closely associated with marriage. Demeter, the daughter of Cronus and Rhea, mother of Persephone, was also associated with marriage and fertility.

THESEUS. l follow. I can hear the oaths he swore.
  He knelt, he wept. He has done this before
  and worse. You are deceived.

ARICIA.   Deceived, my lord?

THESEUS. Princess, are you so rich? Can you afford   95
  to hunger for this lover that my queen
  rejected? Your betrayer loves my wife.

ARICIA. How can you bear to blacken his pure life?
  Is kingship only for the blind and strong,
  unable to distinguish right from wrong?   100
  What insolent prerogative obscures
  a light that shines in every eye but yours?
  You have betrayed him to his enemies.
  What more, my lord? Repent your blasphemies.
  Are you not fearful lest the gods so loathe   105
  and hate you they will gratify your oath?
  Fear God, my lord, fear God. How many times
  he grants men's wishes to expose their crimes.

THESEUS. Love blinds you, Princess, and beclouds your reason.
  Your outburst cannot cover up his treason.   110
  My trust's in witnesses that cannot lie.
  I have seen Phaedra's tears. She tried to die.

ARICIA. Take care, your Highness. When your killing hand
  drove all the thieves and reptiles from the land,
  you missed one monster, one was left alive,   115
  one.... No, I must not name her, Sire, or strive
  to save your helpless son; he wants to spare
  your reputation. Let me go. I dare
  not stay here. If I stayed I'd be too weak
  to keep my promise. I'd be forced to speak.   120

SCENE V. *Theseus*

THESEUS. What was she saying? I must try to reach
  the meaning of her interrupted speech.
  Is it a pitfall? A conspiracy?
  Are they plotting together to torture me?
  Why did I let the rash, wild girl depart?   125
  What is this whisper crying in my heart?
  A secret pity fills my soul with pain.
  I must question Oenone once again.
  My guards summon Oenone to the throne.
  Quick, bring her. I must talk with her alone.   130

SCENE V. *Theseus, Panope*

PANOPE. The Queen's deranged, your Highness. Some accursed
  madness is driving her; some fury stalks

behind her back, possesses her, and talks
its evil through her, and blasphemes the world.
She cursed Oenone. Now Oenone's hurled   135
herself into the ocean Sire, and drowned.
Why did she do it? No reason can be found.
THESEUS. Oenone's drowned?
PANOPE.   Her death has brought no peace.
The cries of Phaedra's troubled soul increase.
Now driven by some sinister unrest,   140
she snatches up her children to her breast,
pets them and weeps, till something makes her scoff
at her affection and she drives them off.
Her glance is drunken and irregular,
she looks through us and wonders who we are;   145
thrice she has started letters to you, Sire,
thrice tossed the shredded fragments in the fire.
Oh call her to you. Help her!
THESEUS. The nurse is drowned? Phaedra wishes to die?
Oh gods! Summon my son. Let him defend   150
himself, tell him I'm ready to attend.
I want him!
      [*Exit* PANOPE.]
               Neptune, hear me, spare my son!
My vengeance was too hastily begun.
Oh why was I so eager to believe
Oenone's accusation? The gods deceive   155
the victims they are ready to destroy!

SCENE VI. *Theseus, Theramenes*

THESEUS. Here is Theramenes. Where is my boy,
my first-born? He was yours to guard and keep.
Where is he? Answer me. What's this? You weep?
THERAMENES. Oh, tardy, futile grief, his blood is shed.   160
My lord, your son, Hippolytus, is dead.
THESEUS. Oh gods, have mercy!
THERAMENES.   I saw him die. The most
lovely and innocent of men is lost.
THESEUS. He's dead? The gods have hurried him away
and killed him? . . . just as I began to pray . . .   165
What sudden thunderbolt has struck him down?
THERAMENES. We'd started out, and hardly left the town.
He held the reins; a few feet to his rear,
a single, silent guard held up a spear.
He followed the Mycenae highroad, deep   170
in thought, reins dangling, as if half asleep;
his famous horses, only he could hold,

trudged on with lowered heads, and sometimes rolled
their dull eyes slowly—they seemed to have caught
their master's melancholy, and aped his thought.   175
Then all at once winds struck us like a fist,
we heard a sudden roaring through the mist;
from underground a voice in agony
answered the prolonged groaning of the sea.
We shook, the horses' manes rose on their heads,   180
and now against a sky of blacks and reds,
we saw the flat waves hump into a mountain
of green-white water rising like a fountain,
as it reached land and crashed with a last roar
to shatter like a galley on the shore.   185
Out of its fragments rose a monster, half
dragon, half bull; a mouth that seemed to laugh   *Europa & Zeus*
drooled venom on its dirty yellow scales
and python belly forking to three tails.
The shore was shaken like a tuning fork,   190
ships bounced on the stung sea like bits of cork,
the earth moved, and the sun spun round and round,
a sulphur-colored venom swept the ground.
We fled; each felt his useless courage falter,
and sought asylum at a nearby altar.   195
Only the Prince remained; he wheeled about,
and hurled a javelin through the monster's snout.
Each kept advancing. Flung from the Prince's arm,
dart after dart struck where the blood was warm.
The monster in its death-throes felt defeat,   200
and bounded howling to the horses' feet.
There its stretched gullet and its armor broke,
and drenched the chariot with blood and smoke,
and then the horses, terror-struck, stampeded.
Their master's whip and shouting went unheeded,   205
they dragged his breathless body to the spray.
Their red mouths bit the bloody surf, men say
Poseidon stood beside them, that the god
was stabbing at their bellies with a goad.
Their terror drove them crashing on a cliff,   210
the chariot crashed in two, they ran as if
the Furies screamed and crackled in their manes,
their fallen hero tangled in the reins,
jounced on the rocks behind them. The sweet light
of heaven never will expunge this sight: 215
the horses that Hippolytus had tamed,

212. *Furies:* Roman name *(Furiae)* for the Greek Erinyes—the three winged goddesses of vengeance, with snakes for hair, named Alecto, Tisiphone, and Megaera.

now dragged him headlong, and their mad hooves maimed
his face past recognition. When he tried
to call them, calling only terrified;
faster and ever faster moved their feet,   220
his body was a piece of bloody meat.
The cliffs and ocean trembled to our shout,
at last their panic failed, they turned about,
and stopped not far from where those hallowed graves,
the Prince's fathers, overlook the waves.   225
I ran on breathless, guards were at my back,
my master's blood had left a generous track.
The stones were red, each thistle in the mud
was stuck with bits of hair and skin and blood.
I came upon him, called; he stretched his right   230
hand to me, blinked his eyes, then closed them tight.
"I die," he whispered, "it's the gods' desire.
Friend, stand between Aricia and my sire—
some day enlightened, softened, disabused,
he will lament his son, falsely accused;   235
then when at last he wishes to appease
my soul, he'll treat my lover well, release
and honor Aricia. . . ." On this word, he died.
Only a broken body testified
he'd lived and loved once. On the sand now lies   240
something his father will not recognize.
THESEUS. My son, my son! Alas, I stand alone
before the gods. I never can atone.
THERAMENES. Meanwhile, Aricia, rushing down the path,
approached us. She was fleeing from your wrath,   245
my lord, and wished to make Hippolytus
her husband in God's eyes. Then nearing us,
she saw the signs of struggle in the waste,
she saw (oh what a sight) her love defaced,
her young love lying lifeless on the sand.   250
At first she hardly seemed to understand;
while staring at the body in the grass,
she kept on asking where her lover was.
At last the black and fearful truth broke through
her desolation! She seemed to curse the blue   255
and murdering ocean as she caught his head
up in her lap; then fainting lay half dead,
until Ismene somehow summoned back her breath,
restored the child to life—or rather death.
I come, great King, to urge my final task,   260
your dying son's last outcry was to ask
mercy for poor Aricia, for his bride.
Now Phaedra comes. She killed him. She has lied.

SCENE VII. *Theseus, Phaedra, Panope*

THESEUS. Ah Phaedra, you have won. He's dead. A man
was killed. Were you watching? His horses ran 265
him down, and tore his body limb from limb.
Poseidon struck him, Theseus murdered him.
I served you! Tell me why Oenone died?
Was it to save you? Is her suicide
A proof of your truth? No, since he's dead, I must 270
accept your evidence, just or unjust.
I must believe my faith has been abused;
you have accused him; he shall stand accused.
He's friendless even in the world below.
There the shades fear him! Am I forced to know 275
the truth? Truth cannot bring my son to life.
If fathers murder, shall I kill my wife
too? Leave me, Phaedra. Far from you, exiled
from Greece, I will lament my murdered child.
I am a murdered gladiator, whirled 280
in black circles. I want to leave the world;
my whole life rises to increase my guilt—
all those dazzled, dazzling eyes, my glory built
on killing killers. Less known, less magnified,
I might escape, and find a place to hide. 285
Stand back, Poseidon. I know the gods are hard
to please. I pleased you. This is my reward:
I killed my son. I killed him! Only a god
spares enemies, and wants his servants' blood!

PHAEDRA. No, Theseus, I must disobey your prayer. 290
Listen to me. I'm dying. I declare
Hippolytus was innocent.

THESEUS. Ah Phaedra, on your evidence, I sent
him to his death. Do you ask me to forgive
my son's assassin? Can I let you live? 295

PHAEDRA. My time's too short, your highness. It was I,
who lusted for your son with my hot eye.
The flames of Aphrodite maddened me;
I loathed myself, and yearned outrageously
like a starved wolf to fall upon the sheep. 300
I wished to hold him to me in my sleep
and dreamt I had him. Then Oenone's tears,
troubled my mind; she played upon my fears,
until her pleading forced me to declare
I loved your son. He scorned me. In despair, 305
I plotted with my nurse, and our conspiracy
made you believe your son assaulted me.
Oenone's punished; fleeing from my wrath,

she drowned herself, and found a too easy path
to death and hell. Perhaps you wonder why   310
I still survive her, and refuse to die?
Theseus, I stand before you to absolve
your noble son. Sire, only this resolve
upheld me, and made me throw down my knife.
I've chosen a slower way to end my life—   315
Medea's poison; chills already dart
along my boiling veins and squeeze my heart.
A cold composure I have never known
gives me a moment's poise. I stand alone
and seem to see my outraged husband fade   320
and waver into death's dissolving shade.
My eyes at last give up their light, and see
the day they've soiled resume its purity.

PANOPE. She's dead, my lord.

THESEUS.   Would God, all memory
of her and me had died with her! Now I   325
must live. This knowledge that has come too late
must give me strength and help me expiate
my sacrilegious vow. Let's go, I'll pay
my son the honors he has earned today.
His father's tears shall mingle with his blood.   330
My love that did my son so little good
asks mercy from his spirit. I declare
Aricia is my daughter and my heir.

324-325. *Would . . . her:* The performances of the *Comédie Française* traditionally end with this line, the remainder being regarded as anticlimactic.

FRANÇOIS, DUC DE LA ROCHEFOUCAULD
(1613–1680)
Maxims*

5. The continuance of our passions no more depends on us than
does the continuance of our lives.

6. Passion often makes a fool out of the ablest of men, and renders ability to the silliest.

9. The passions show an unfair and personal bias, which makes
them dangerous to follow; and one should beware of them, even
when they seem the most reasonable.

---

* First published 1665; last augmented
edition 1678. Translated by Howard E.
Hugo. La Rochefoucauld published five
editions during his lifetime (1665, 1666,
1671, 1675, 1678), in the process of
which he added new maxims and rewrote
some of the earlier ones.

14. Men are apt not only to forget kindness and injuries; they even hate those who have benefited them, and cease to hate those who have wronged them. Diligence in rewarding good and punishing evil seems to them a bondage to which they will scarcely submit.

17. The modesty of happy persons comes from the peace of mind which good fortune lends to their spirits.

19. We all have strength enough to bear the misfortunes of others.

22. Philosophy easily triumphs over past and future evils; but present evils triumph over philosophy.

25. It requires greater virtue to bear good fortune than bad.

26. Neither the sun nor death can be looked at steadily.

38. We make our promises according to our hopes, and keep them according to our fears.

43. Man often believes he leads, when indeed he is being led; and while his mind directs him toward one goal, his heart drags him unconsciously toward another.

49. We are never as happy or as unhappy as we imagine ourselves to be.

64. Truth does not accomplish as much good in the world, as its counterfeits work evil.

72. If you judge love by most of its results, it seems more akin to hate than to friendship.

76. With true loves as with ghosts: everyone speaks of them, but few have seen them. *hey, what about Petrarch & Laura ?*

78. For most of mankind, love of justice is nothing more than the fear of suffering injustice.

93. The old love to give good advice, to console themselves for no longer being in a condition to give bad examples.

98. Each speaks well of his heart, and no one dares speak so well about his mind.

102. The head is forever fooled by the heart.

119. We are so accustomed to disguising ourselves from others, that we end by disguising ourselves from ourselves.

123. We would scarcely ever enjoy ourselves, if we never flattered ourselves.

132. It is easier to be wise for others than to be wise about oneself.

136. There are those who would never have been in love, had they never heard about love.

149. To refuse praise means that you want to be praised twice.

155. Some disgusting persons possess virtue, and others also exist who are pleasing with all their blemishes.

169. Although sloth and timidity impel us toward our duty, often our virtue gets all the credit.

174. We would do better to employ our intelligence in coping with present misfortunes, than in foreseeing those which might happen to us.

185. Evil, like good, has its own heroes.

190. Only great men can possess great faults.

195. What often prohibits us from abandonment to a single vice is that we own many more.

210. As we grow old, we become sillier and wiser.

218. Hypocrisy is a tribute that vice pays to virtue.

235. We easily console ourselves when our friends suffer disgrace, if the occasion serves to bring out our affection for them.

259. The pleasure of love is in loving; and we are happier in our own passion than in the passion we inspire.

298. For most of mankind, gratitude is no more than a secret wish to receive even greater benefits.

303. No matter how many nice things they say about us, we never learn anything new.

304. We often pardon those who bore us; we can never forgive those whom we bore.

308. Moderation has been made a virtue in order to curb the ambition of the great, and also to console those who are mediocre in either fortune or merit.

310. Sometimes occasions occur in life from whence you have to be slightly mad in order to extricate yourself.

326. Ridicule hurts our honor more than does dishonor itself.

327. We admit our small failings only in order to persuade others that we have no greater ones.

354. Certain defects, when placed in a good setting, shine more brilliantly than virtue itself.

384. We ought never to be surprised, save that we can still be surprised.

391. Fate never seems so blind as she does to those she has not favored.

392. One should cope with luck as one does with health: enjoy it when things go well, be patient when things go badly, and never take recourse to extreme remedies except in the last resort.

409. We would often be ashamed of our finest acts, if the world were aware of the motives behind them.

417. In love, first cured is best cured.

422. All the passions cause us to make mistakes, but love causes us to make the most ridiculous ones.

428. We easily forgive our friends those faults that personally do not touch us.

429. Women in love forgive major indiscretions more easily than they do small infidelities.

439. We would scarcely wish zealously for things, if we really understood the things we wanted.

442. We try to ennoble those faults which we do not wish to correct.

445. Weakness, rather than virtue, is vice's adversary.

453. In major affairs, we should strive less to create situations than to profit from those already present.

458. Our enemies come closer in their judgments about us than we ever do about ourselves.

464. There exist extremes of well-being and misery that go beyond our sensibility and imagination.

496. Quarrels would not last long, if the wrong were only on one side.

499. Ordinarily one pays no attention to a woman's first love-affair until she has had a second.

15. In the misfortunes of our best friends, we always find something not displeasing.[1]

---

1. *In . . . displeasing*: from Barbin's *Supplementary Maxims* (1693).

JEAN DE LA FONTAINE
(1621–1695) *little baby...*

Fables*

The Grasshopper and the Ant[a]

Until fall, a grasshopper
    Chose to chirr;
With starvation as foe
When northeasters would blow,
And not even a gnat's residue   5
Or caterpillar's to chew,
She chirred a recurrent chant
Of want beside an ant,
Begging it to rescue her
With some seeds it could spare   10
Till the following year's fell.
"By August you shall have them all,
Interest and principal."
Share one's seeds? Now what is worse
For any ant to do?   15
Ours asked, "When fair, what brought you through?"
—"I sang for those who might pass by chance—
Night and day, an't you please."
—"Sang, you say? You have put me at ease.
A singer! Excellent. Now dance."   20

The Fox and the Crow[b]

On his airy perch among the branches
    Master Crow was holding cheese in his beak.
Master Fox, whose pose suggested fragrances,
    Said in language which of course I cannot speak,
        "Aha, superb Sir Ebony, well met.   5
How black! who else boasts your metallic jet!
        If your warbling were unique,
        Rest assured, as you are sleek,
One would say that our wood had hatched nightingales."

* The original title: *Aesop's Fables Rendered into Verse by M. de La Fontaine.* Aesop, a slave of Samos, reputedly lived in the sixth century B.C., although his actual existence is doubtful. But fables were early collected under his name. The English translation is by Marianne Moore.

a. Book I, No. 1; Aesop No. 134. (Aesop, a slave of Samos, reputedly lived in the 6th century B.C., although his actual existence is doubtful. But fables were early collected under his name.)

b. Book I, No. 2; Aesop, No. 204. Cf. also Phaedrus (Latin fabulist, first century A.D.), I, 13.

All aglow, Master Crow tried to run a few scales,   10
       Risking trills and intervals,
Dropping the prize as his huge beak sang false.
The fox pounced on the cheese and remarked, "My dear sir,
       Learn that every flatterer
      Lives at the flattered listener's cost: 15
A lesson worth more than the cheese that you lost."
       The tardy learner, smarting under ridicule,
Swore he'd learned his last lesson as somebody's fool.

The Frog Who Would Be an Ox[c]

      That great ox, built just right!
      Eying the beast, although at best
A mere egg's height or less, the frog mustered might
And spread out and swelled and expanded his chest
      To approximate the ox, his despair;   5
      Then said to another frog, "Compare:
I'm his size. See, now I need not defer."
"Still small."—"Now?"—"By no means."—"Now I am
                not outclassed."
"Not nearly large enough." The poor envier
      Burst; overtested at last.   10
Our world is full of mentalities quite as crude:
The man of trade must house himself so kings would stare;
      Each small prince's deputies are everywhere.
      Each marquis has pages—a multitude.

The Town Rat and the Country Rat[d]

    In this ancient parable,
    Town rat proffered country rat
    A fashionable meal
    As a change from this and that,

    Where on a rug from Turkey,   5
    A feast for two was ready.
    Fond fancy alone could see
    The pair's joint ecstasy.

    Fine food made each's plate replete—
    More dainties there than greed could paint,   10
    But as they were about to eat,
    Noises were heard; the pair felt faint.

c. Book I, No. 3; Aesop No. 420;   *d.* Book I, No. 9; Aesop, No. 301; Horace, *Satires*, II. 6.
Phaedrus, I, 24.

At the door, sniff and smell.
What was scratching steadily?
Both frightened ill, half fell,   15
Then fled confusedly.

When they had dared to reappear,
In seclusion with relief,
The city rat resumed, "My dear,
Come now, divide the beef."   20

—"I have dined," the field rat said;
"Be my guest, pray, a day hence,
Though you'll not find, I am afraid,
Similar magnificence.

Yet I'm never in danger: I've supped,   25
Carefree from year to year;
And so farewell. What is good cheer
Which death threats can disrupt?"

The Wolf and the Lamb*

Force has the best of any argument:
    Soon proved by the story which I present.

    A thirsty lamb was drinking where
    A brook ran crystal clear.
Up came a wolf who had been lured there   5
   By hunger, since it was a spot where prey might be.
"Soiling it, intrepid transgressor?" the wolf growled,
      "Leaving me to drink what you fouled?
Such impropriety involves a penalty."
—"Bear with me," the lamb said, "your Majesty.   10
    I've not trespassed anywhere.
    I'm twenty feet from where you were;
    Am here, where what you can't drink went
       In its descent;
    And to be mathematical,   15
How have I possibly by what I have done
    Polluted water of your own?"
—"You stirred the mud." Bloodthirsty minds are small.
"And the past year as well, I know you slandered me."
—"How?" the lamb asked. "I, unweaned, born recently—   20
    This very year? I still require home care."
      —"Your brother then, you've one somewhere."
   —"But I have none."—"It was some relative then;

*. Book I, No. 10; Phaedrus. I, 1.

All of you sheep are unfair;
　　You, your shepherds, and the dogs they train.　25
I have a debt to myself to discharge."
　　Dragged down a wooded gully,
　　The small was eaten by the large
　　Unconditionally.

The Oak and the Reed*f*

　　The oak said to the reed, "You grow
Too unprotectedly. Nature has been unfair;
A tiny wren alights, and you are bending low;
　　If a fitful breath of air
　　Should freshen till ripples show,　5
　　You heed her and lower your head;
Whereas my parasol makes welcome shade each day
And like the Caucasus need never sway,
　　However it is buffeted.
Your so-called hurricanes are too faint to fear.　10
Would that you'd been born beneath this towering tent I've made,
　　Which could afford you ample shade;
　　Your hazards would not be severe:
　　I'd shield you when the lightning played;
　　But grow you will, time and again,　15
On the misty fringe of the wind's domain.
I perceive that you are grievously oppressed."
The rush said, "Bless you for fearing that I might be distressed;
　　It is you alone whom the winds should alarm.
I bend and do not break. You've seemed consistently　20
　　Impervious to harm—
　　Erect when blasts rushed to and fro;
As for the end, who can foresee how things will go?"
Relentless wind was on them instantly—
　　A fury of destruction　25
Which the North had nursed in some haunt known to none.
　　The bulrush bent, but not the tree.
　　Confusion rose to a roar,
　　Until the hurricane threw prone
That thing of kingly height whose head had all but touched
　　　　　　　　　　　　　　　God's throne—　30
Who had shot his root to the threshold of Death's door.

The Dairymaid and Her Milk-Pot*g*

Perrette's milk-pot fitted her head-mat just right—
　　Neatly quilted to grip the pot tight.

---

f. Book I, No. 22; Aesop, Nos. 143　　*g.* Book VII, No. 10. Source is Bona-
and 180.　　　　　　　　　　　　　venture des Périers, *Novella* 14.

Then she set off to market and surely walked well,
In her short muslin dress that encouraged long strides,
Since to make better time she wore shoes with low heel   5
    And had tucked up her skirt at the sides.
     Like summer attire her head had grown light,
      Thinking of what she'd have bought by night.
In exchange for the milk, since supposing it gone,
She'd buy ten times ten eggs and three hens could be set.   10
Taking care all hatched out, she'd not lose more than one
    And said, "Then there'll be pullets to sell.
I'll raise them at home; it is quite within reason,
     Since shrewd Master Fox will be doing well
If I can't shortly buy a young pig and grow bacon.   15
The one I had bought would be almost half grown;
He'd need next to no feed—almost nothing at all;
When he's sold I'll have funds—good hard cash to count on.
Then with room at the barn for some stock in the stall,
I could buy cow and calf if the pig had sold high;   20
If I'd not had a loss, I'd add sheep by and by."
Perrette skipped for joy as she dreamt of what she'd bought.
The crock crashed. Farewell, cow, calf, fat pig, eggs not
          hatched out.
The mistress of wealth grieved to forfeit forever
     The profits that were mounting.   25
     How ask her husband to forgive her
     Lest he beat her as was fitting?
     And thus ended the farce we have watched:
     Don't count your chickens before they are hatched.

     Whom does a daydream not entrance?   30
     Have castles in air no romance?
Picrochole, Pyrrhus, Perrette—a fool's or wisdom's mirth—
     Every hearth can give them birth.
Each of us loves a daydream—the fondest think on earth,
Illusion has a charm to which our minds succumb;   35
     Since it captures whatever has worth.
     All hearts are ours, we pluck each plum.
When alone, I tower so tall that the bravest shiver.
I crush and see Persian emperors suffer.
     I am a king, an idol.   40
My head is diademed with gems that rain:
Then the king's deep problems by some unjust reversal,
     Are Jean de La Fontaine's again.

---

32. *Picrochole . . . Perrette:* names
that belong to the seventeenth-century
tradition of the pastoral (*bergerie*),
where elegant aristocrats played at being shepherds and shepherdesses.

FRANÇOIS-MARIE AROUET DE VOLTAIRE
(1694–1778)
Candide, or Optimism*

*translated from the German of Doctor Ralph with the additions
which were found in the Doctor's pocket when he died at Minden in
the Year of Our Lord 1759*

CHAPTER 1
How Candide Was Brought up in a Fine Castle and How He Was Driven Therefrom

There lived in Westphalia,[1] in the castle of the Baron of Thunder-Ten-Tronckh, a young man on whom nature had bestowed the perfection of gentle manners. His features admirably expressed his soul, he combined an honest mind with great simplicity of heart; and I think it was for this reason that they called him Candide. The old servants of the house suspected that he was the son of the Baron's sister by a respectable, honest gentleman of the neighborhood, whom she had refused to marry because he could prove only seventy-one quarterings,[2] the rest of his family tree having been lost in the passage of time.

The Baron was one of the most mighty lords of Westphalia, for his castle had a door and windows. His great hall was even hung with a tapestry. The dogs of his courtyard made up a hunting pack on occasion, with the stableboys as huntsmen; the village priest was his grand almoner. They all called him "My Lord," and laughed at his stories.

The Baroness, who weighed in the neighborhood of three hundred and fifty pounds, was greatly respected for that reason, and did the honors of the house with a dignity which rendered her even more imposing. Her daughter Cunégonde,[3] aged seventeen, was a ruddy-cheeked girl, fresh, plump, and desirable. The Baron's son seemed in every way worthy of his father. The tutor Pangloss was the oracle of the household, and little Candide listened to his lectures with all the good faith of his age and character.

Pangloss gave instruction in metaphysico-theologico-cosmoloonigology.[4] He proved admirably that there cannot possibly be an effect

---

* Translated with notes by Robert M. Adams.

1. Westphalia is a province of western Germany, near Holland and the lower Rhineland. Flat, boggy, and drab, it is noted chiefly for its excellent ham. In a letter to his niece, written during his German expedition of 1750, Voltaire described the "vast, sad, sterile, detestable countryside of Westphalia."

2. Quarterings are genealogical divisions of one's family tree. Seventy-one of them is a grotesque number to have, representing something over 2,000 years

of uninterrupted nobility.

3. Cunégonde gets her odd name from Kunigunda, wife to Emperor Henry II, who walked barefoot and blindfolded on red-hot irons to prove her chastity; Pangloss gets his name from Greek words meaning all-tongue.

4. The "looney" I have buried in this burlesque word corresponds to a buried *nigaud*—"booby" in the French. Christian Wolff, disciple of Leibniz, invented and popularized the word "cosmology."

without a cause and that in this best of all possible worlds[5] the Baron's castle was the best of all castles and his wife the best of all possible Baronesses.

—It is clear, said he, that things cannot be otherwise than they are, for since everything is made to serve an end, everything necessarily serves the best end. Observe: noses were made to support spectacles, hence we have spectacles. Legs, as anyone can plainly see, were made to be breeched, and so we have breeches. Stones were made to be shaped and to build castles with; thus My Lord has a fine castle, for the greatest Baron in the province should have the finest house; and since pigs were made to be eaten, we eat pork all year round.[6] Consequently, those who say everything is well are uttering mere stupidities; they should say everything is for the best.

Candide listened attentively and believed implicitly; for he found Miss Cunégonde exceedingly pretty, though he never had the courage to tell her so. He decided that after the happiness of being born Baron of Thunder-Ten-Tronckh, the second order of happiness was to be Miss Cunégonde; the third was seeing her every day, and the fourth was listening to Master Pangloss, the greatest philosopher in the province and consequently in the entire world.

One day, while Cunégonde was walking near the castle in the little woods that they called a park, she saw Dr. Pangloss in the underbrush; he was giving a lesson in experimental physics to her mother's maid, a very attractive and obedient brunette. As Miss Cunégonde had a natural bent for the sciences, she watched breathlessly the repeated experiments which were going on; she saw clearly the doctor's sufficient reason, observed both cause and effect, and returned to the house in a distracted and pensive frame of mind, yearning for knowledge and dreaming that she might be the sufficient reason of young Candide—who might also be hers.

As she was returning to the castle, she met Candide, and blushed; Candide blushed too. She greeted him in a faltering tone of voice; and Candide talked to her without knowing what he was saying. Next day, as everyone was rising from the dinner table, Cunégonde and Candide found themselves behind a screen; Cunégonde dropped her handkerchief, Candide picked it up; she held his hand quite innocently, he kissed her hand quite innocently

---

5. These catch phrases, echoed by popularizers of Leibniz, make reference to the determinism of his system, its linking of cause with effect, and its optimism. As his correspondence indicates, Voltaire habitually thought of Leibniz's philosophy (which, having been published in definitive form as early as 1710, had been in the air for a long time) in terms of these catch phrases.
6. The argument from design supposes that everything in this world exists for a specific reason; Voltaire objects not to the argument as a whole, but to the abuse of it. He grants, for example, that noses were made to smell and stomachs to digest but denies that feet were made to put shoes on or stones to be cut up into building blocks. His full view finds expression in the article or, "causes finales" in the *Philosophical Dictionary*

with remarkable vivacity and emotion; their lips met, their eyes lit up, their knees trembled, their hands wandered. The Baron of Thunder-Ten-Tronckh passed by the screen and, taking note of this cause and this effect, drove Candide out of the castle by kicking him vigorously on the backside. Cunégonde fainted; as soon as she recovered, the Baroness slapped her face; and everything was confusion in the most beautiful and agreeable of all possible castles.

CHAPTER 2
What Happened to Candide Among the Bulgars[7]

Candide, ejected from the earthly paradise, wandered for a long time without knowing where he was going, weeping, raising his eyes to heaven, and gazing back frequently on the most beautiful of castles which contained the most beautiful of Baron's daughters. He slept without eating, in a furrow of a plowed field, while the snow drifted over him; next morning, numb with cold, he dragged himself into the neighboring village, which was called Waldberghoff-trarbk-dikdorff; he was penniless, famished, and exhausted. At the door of a tavern he paused forlornly. Two men dressed in blue[8] took note of him:

—Look, chum, said one of them, there's a likely young fellow of just about the right size.

They approached Candide and invited him very politely to dine with them.

—Gentlemen, Candide replied with charming modesty, I'm honored by your invitation, but I really don't have enough money to pay my share.

—My dear sir, said one of the blues, people of your appearance and your merit don't have to pay; aren't you five feet five inches tall?

—Yes, gentlemen, that is indeed my stature, said he, making a bow.

—Then, sir, you must be seated at once; not only will we pay your bill this time, we will never allow a man like you to be short of money; for men were made only to render one another mutual aid.

—You are quite right, said Candide; it is just as Dr. Pangloss always told me, and I see clearly that everything is for the best.

They beg him to accept a couple of crowns, he takes them, and offers an I.O.U.; they won't hear of it, and all sit down at table

7. Voltaire chose this name to represent the Prussian troops of Frederick the Great because he wanted to make an insinuation of pederasty against both the soldiers and their master. *Cf.* French *bougre*, English "bugger."

8. The recruiting officers of Frederick the Great, much feared in eighteenth-century Europe, wore blue uniforms. Frederick had a passion for sorting out his soldiers by size; several of his regiments would accept only six-footers.

together.

—Don't you love dearly . . . ?

—I do indeed, says he, I dearly love Miss Cunégonde.

—No, no, says one of the gentlemen, we are asking if you don't love dearly the King of the Bulgars.

—Not in the least, says he, I never laid eyes on him.

—What's that you say? He's the most charming of kings, and we must drink his health.

—Oh, gladly, gentlemen; and he drinks.

—That will do, they tell him; you are now the bulwark, the support, the defender, the hero of the Bulgars; your fortune is made and your future assured.

Promptly they slip irons on his legs and lead him to the regiment. There they cause him to right face, left face, present arms, order arms, aim, fire, doubletime, and they give him thirty strokes of the rod. Next day he does the drill a little less awkwardly and gets only twenty strokes; the third day, they give him only ten, and he is regarded by his comrades as a prodigy.

Candide, quite thunderstruck, did not yet understand very clearly how he was a hero. One fine spring morning he took it into his head to go for a walk, stepping straight out as if it were a privilege of the human race, as of animals in general, to use his legs as he chose.[9] He had scarcely covered two leagues when four other heroes, each six feet tall, overtook him, bound him, and threw him into a dungeon. At the court-martial they asked which he preferred, to be flogged thirty-six times by the entire regiment or to receive summarily a dozen bullets in the brain. In vain did he argue that the human will is free and insist that he preferred neither alternative; he had to choose; by virtue of the divine gift called "liberty" he decided to run the gauntlet thirty-six times, and actually endured two floggings. The regiment was composed of two thousand men. That made four thousand strokes, which laid open every muscle and nerve from his nape to his butt. As they were preparing for the third beating, Candide, who could endure no more, begged as a special favor that they would have the goodness to smash his head. His plea was granted; they bandaged his eyes and made him kneel down. The King of the Bulgars, passing by at this moment, was told of the culprit's crime; and as this king had a rare genius, he understood, from everything they told him of Candide, that this was a

---

9. This episode was suggested by the experience of a Frenchman named Courtilz, who had deserted from the Prussian army and been bastionadoed for it. Voltaire intervened with Frederick to gain his release. But it also reflects the story that Wolff, Leibniz's disciple, got into trouble with Frederick's father when someone reported that his doctrine denying free will had encouraged several soldiers to desert. "The argument of the grenadier," who was said to have pleaded pre-established harmony to justify his desertion, so infuriated the king that he had Wolff expelled from the country.

young metaphysician, extremely ignorant of the ways of the world, so he granted his royal pardon, with a generosity which will be praised in every newspaper in every age. A worthy surgeon cured Candide in three weeks with the ointments described by Dioscorides.[1] He already had a bit of skin back and was able to walk when the King of the Bulgars went to war with the King of the Abares.[2]

CHAPTER 3

How Candide Escaped from the Bulgars, and What Became of Him

Nothing could have been so fine, so brisk, so brilliant, so well-drilled as the two armies. The trumpets, the fifes, the oboes, the drums, and the cannon produced such a harmony as was never heard in hell. First the cannons battered down about six thousand men on each side; then volleys of musket fire removed from the best of worlds about nine or ten thousand rascals who were cluttering up its surface. The bayonet was a sufficient reason for the demise of several thousand others. Total casualties might well amount to thirty thousand men or so. Candide, who was trembling like a philosopher, hid himself as best he could while this heroic butchery was going on.

Finally, while the two kings in their respective camps celebrated the victory by having *Te Deums* sung, Candide undertook to do his reasoning of cause and effect somewhere else. Passing by mounds of the dead and dying, he came to a nearby village which had been burnt to the ground. It was an Abare village, which the Bulgars had burned, in strict accordance with the laws of war. Here old men, stunned from beatings, watched the last agonies of their butchered wives, who still clutched their infants to their bleeding breasts; there, disemboweled girls, who had first satisfied the natural needs of various heroes, breathed their last; others, half-scorched in the flames, begged for their death stroke. Scattered brains and severed limbs littered the ground.

Candide fled as fast as he could to another village; this one belonged to the Bulgars, and the heroes of the Abare cause had given it the same treatment. Climbing over ruins and stumbling over corpses, Candide finally made his way out of the war area, carrying

1. Dioscorides' treatise on *materia medica*, dating from the first century A.D., was not the most up to date.

2. The name "Abares" actually designates a tribe of semicivilized Scythians, who might be supposed at war with the Bulgars; allegorically, the Abares are the French, who opposed the Prussians in the conflict known to hindsight history as the Seven Years' War (1756–1763). For Voltaire, at the moment of writing *Candide*, it was simply the current war. One notes that according to the title page of 1761, "Doctor Ralph," the dummy author of *Candide,* himself perished at the battle of Minden (Westphalia) in 1759.

a little food in his knapsack and never ceasing to dream of Miss Cunégonde. His supplies gave out when he reached Holland; but having heard that everyone in that country was rich and a Christian, he felt confident of being treated as well as he had been in the castle of the Baron before he was kicked out for the love of Miss Cunégonde.

He asked alms of several grave personages, who all told him that if he continued to beg, he would be shut up in a house of correction and set to hard labor.

Finally he approached a man who had just been talking to a large crowd for an hour on end; the topic was charity. Looking doubtfully at him, the orator demanded:

—What are you doing here? Are you here to serve the good cause?

—There is no effect without a cause, said Candide modestly; all events are linked by the chain of necessity and arranged for the best. I had to be driven away from Miss Cunégonde, I had to run the gauntlet, I have to beg my bread until I can earn it; none of this could have happened otherwise.

—Look here, friend, said the orator, do you think the Pope is Antichrist?[3]

—I haven't considered the matter, said Candide; but whether he is or not, I'm in need of bread.

—You don't deserve any, said the other; away with you, you rascal, you rogue, never come near me as long as you live.

Meanwhile, the orator's wife had put her head out of the window, and, seeing a man who was not sure the Pope was Antichrist, emptied over his head a pot full of ——— Scandalous! The excesses into which women are led by religious zeal!

A man who had never been baptized, a good Anabaptist[4] named Jacques, saw this cruel and heartless treatment being inflicted on one of his fellow creatures, a featherless biped possessing a soul[5]; he took Candide home with him, washed him off, gave him bread and beer, presented him with two florins, and even undertook to give him a job in his Persian-rug factory—for these items are widely manufactured in Holland. Candide, in an ecstasy of gratitude, cried out:

—Master Pangloss was right indeed when he told me everything

3. Voltaire is satirizing extreme Protestant sects that have sometimes seemed to make hatred of Rome the sum and substance of their creed.
4. Holland, as the home of religious liberty, had offered asylum to the Anabaptists, whose radical views on property and religious discipline had made them unpopular during the sixteenth century. Granted tolerance, they settled down into respectable burghers. Since this behavior confirmed some of Voltaire's major theses, he had a high opinion of contemporary Anabaptists.
5. Plato's famous minimal definition of a man, which he corrected by the addition of a soul to distinguish man from a plucked chicken. The point is that the Anabaptist sympathizes with men simply because they are human.

is for the best in this world; for I am touched by your kindness far more than by the harshness of that black-coated gentleman and his wife.

Next day, while taking a stroll about town, he met a beggar who was covered with pustules, his eyes were sunken, the end of his nose rotted off, his mouth twisted, his teeth black, he had a croaking voice and a hacking cough, and spat a tooth every time he tried to speak.

CHAPTER 4

How Candide Met His Old Philosophy Tutor, Doctor Pangloss, and What Came of It

Candide, more touched by compassion even than by horror, gave this ghastly beggar the two florins that he himself had received from his honest Anabaptist friend Jacques. The phantom stared at him, burst into tears, and fell on his neck. Candide drew back in terror.

—Alas, said one wretch to the other, don't you recognize your dear Pangloss any more?

—What are you saying? You, my dear master! you, in this horrible condition? What misfortune has befallen you? Why are you no longer in the most beautiful of castles? What has happened to Miss Cunégonde, that pearl among young ladies, that masterpiece of Nature?

—I am perishing, said Pangloss.

—Candide promptly led him into the Anabaptist's stable, where he gave him a crust of bread, and when he had recovered: —Well, said he, Cunégonde?

—Dead, said the other.

Candide fainted. His friend brought him around with a bit of sour vinegar which happened to be in the stable. Candide opened his eyes.

—Cunégonde, dead! Ah, best of worlds, what's become of you now? But how did she die? It wasn't of grief at seeing me kicked out of her noble father's elegant castle?

—Not at all, said Pangloss; she was disemboweled by the Bulgar soldiers, after having been raped to the absolute limit of human endurance; they smashed the Baron's head when he tried to defend her, cut the Baroness to bits, and treated my poor pupil exactly like his sister.[6] As for the castle, not one stone was left on another, not a shed, not a sheep, not a duck, not a tree; but we had the satisfaction of revenge, for the Abares did exactly the same thing to a

---

6. The theme of homosexuality which attaches to Cunégonde's brother seems to have no general satiric point, but its presence is unmistakable. See Chapters 14, 15, and 28.

nearby barony belonging to a Bulgar nobleman.

At this tale Candide fainted again; but having returned to his senses and said everything appropriate to the occasion, he asked about the cause and effect, the sufficient reason, which had reduced Pangloss to his present pitiful state.

—Alas, said he, it was love; love, the consolation of the human race, the preservative of the universe, the soul of all sensitive beings, love, gentle love.

—Unhappy man, said Candide, I too have had some experience of this love, the sovereign of hearts, the soul of our souls; and it never got me anything but a single kiss and twenty kicks in the rear. How could this lovely cause produce in you such a disgusting effect?

Pangloss replied as follows: —My dear Candide! you knew Paquette, that pretty maidservant to our august Baroness. In her arms I tasted the delights of paradise, which directly caused these torments of hell, from which I am now suffering. She was infected with the disease, and has perhaps died of it. Paquette received this present from an erudite Franciscan, who took the pains to trace it back to its source; for he had it from an elderly countess, who picked it up from a captain of cavalry, who acquired it from a marquise, who caught it from a page, who had received it from a Jesuit, who during his novitiate got it directly from one of the companions of Christopher Columbus.[7] As for me, I shall not give it to anyone, for I am a dying man.

—Oh, Pangloss, cried Candide, that's a very strange genealogy. Isn't the devil at the root of the whole thing?

—Not at all, replied that great man; it's an indispensable part of the best of worlds, a necessary ingredient; if Columbus had not caught, on an American island, this sickness which attacks the source of generation and sometimes prevents generation entirely— which thus strikes at and defeats the greatest end of Nature herself —we should have neither chocolate nor cochineal. It must also be noted that until the present time this malady, like religious controversy, has been wholly confined to the continent of Europe. Turks, Indians, Persians, Chinese, Siamese, and Japanese know nothing of it as yet; but there is a sufficient reason for which they in turn will make its acquaintance in a couple of centuries. Meanwhile, it has made splendid progress among us, especially among those big armies of honest, well-trained mercenaries who decide the destinies of nations. You can be sure that when thirty thousand men fight a pitched battle against the same number of the enemy, there will be about twenty thousand with the pox on either side.

7. Syphilis was the first contribution of the New World to the happiness of the Old. Voltaire's information comes from Astruc, *Traité des maladies vénériennes* (1734).

—Remarkable indeed, said Candide, but we must see about curing you.

—And how can I do that, said Pangloss, seeing I don't have a cent to my name? There's not a doctor in the whole world who will let your blood or give you an enema without demanding a fee. If you can't pay yourself, you must find someone to pay for you.

These last words decided Candide; he hastened to implore the help of his charitable Anabaptist, Jacques, and painted such a moving picture of his friend's wretched state that the good man did not hesitate to take in Pangloss and have him cured at his own expense. In the course of the cure, Pangloss lost only an eye and an ear. Since he wrote a fine hand and knew arithmetic, the Anabaptist made him his bookkeeper. At the end of two months, being obliged to go to Lisbon on business, he took his two philosophers on the boat with him. Pangloss still maintained that everything was for the best, but Jacques didn't agree with him.

—It must be, said he, that men have corrupted Nature, for they are not born wolves, yet that is what they become. God gave them neither twenty-four-pound cannon nor bayonets, yet they have manufactured both in order to destroy themselves. Bankruptcies have the same effect, and so does the justice which seizes the goods of bankrupts in order to prevent the creditors from getting them.[8]

—It was all indispensable, replied the one-eyed doctor, since private misfortunes make for public welfare, and therefore the more private misfortunes there are, the better everything is.

While he was reasoning, the air grew dark, the winds blew from all directions, and the vessel was attacked by a horrible tempest within sight of Lisbon harbor.

CHAPTER 5
Tempest, Shipwreck, Earthquake, and What Happened to Doctor Pangloss, Candide, and the Anabaptist, Jacques

Half of the passengers, weakened by the frightful anguish of seasickness and the distress of tossing about on stormy waters, were incapable of noticing their danger. The other half shrieked aloud and fell to their prayers, the sails were ripped to shreds, the masts snapped, the vessel opened at the seams. Everyone worked who could stir, nobody listened for orders or issued them. The Anabaptist was lending a hand in the after part of the ship when a frantic sailor struck him and knocked him to the deck; but just at that moment, the sailor lurched so violently that he fell head first over the side, where he hung, clutching a fragment of the broken mast.

8. Voltaire had suffered losses from various bankruptcy proceedings, which lend a personal edge to his satire here, besides diverting its point a bit.

The good Jacques ran to his aid, and helped him to climb back on board, but in the process was himself thrown into the sea under the very eyes of the sailor, who allowed him to drown without even glancing at him. Candide rushed to the rail, and saw his benefactor rise for a moment to the surface, then sink forever. He wanted to dive to his rescue; but the philosopher Pangloss prevented him by proving that the bay of Lisbon had been formed expressly for this Anabaptist to drown in. While he was proving the point *a priori*, the vessel opened up and everyone perished except for Pangloss, Candide, and the brutal sailor who had caused the virtuous Anabaptist to drown; this rascal swam easily to shore, while Pangloss and Candide drifted there on a plank.

When they had recovered a bit of energy, they set out for Lisbon; they still had a little money with which they hoped to stave off hunger after escaping the storm.

Scarcely had they set foot in the town, still bewailing the loss of their benefactor, when they felt the earth quake underfoot; the sea was lashed to a froth, burst into the port, and smashed all the vessels lying at anchor there. Whirlwinds of fire and ash swirled through the streets and public squares; houses crumbled, roofs came crashing down on foundations, foundations split; thirty thousand inhabitants of every age and either sex were crushed in the ruins.[9] The sailor whistled through his teeth, and said with an oath:

—There'll be something to pick up here.

—What can be the sufficient reason of this phenomenon? asked Pangloss.

—The Last Judgment is here, cried Candide.

But the sailor ran directly into the middle of the ruins, heedless of danger in his eagerness for gain; he found some money, laid violent hands on it, got drunk, and, having slept off his wine, bought the favors of the first streetwalker he could find amid the ruins of smashed houses, amid corpses and suffering victims on every hand. Pangloss however tugged at his sleeve.

—My friend, said he, this is not good form at all; your behavior falls short of that required by the universal reason; it's untimely, to say the least.

—Bloody hell, said the other, I'm a sailor, born in Batavia; I've been four times to Japan and stamped four times on the crucifix[1]; get out of here with your universal reason.

9. The great Lisbon earthquake and fire occurred on November 1, 1755; between thirty and forty thousand deaths resulted.
1. The Japanese, originally receptive to foreign visitors, grew fearful that priests and proselytizers were merely advance agents of empire, and expelled both the Portuguese and Spanish early in the seventeenth century. Only the Dutch were allowed to retain a small foothold, under humiliating conditions, of which the notion of stamping on the crucifix is symbolic. It was never what Voltaire suggests here, an actual requirement for entering the country.

Some falling stonework had struck Candide; he lay prostrate in the street, covered with rubble, and calling to Pangloss: —For pity's sake bring me a little wine and oil; I'm dying.

—This earthquake is nothing novel, Pangloss replied; the city of Lima, in South America, underwent much the same sort of tremor, last year; same causes, same effects; there is surely a vein of sulphur under the earth's surface reaching from Lima to Lisbon.

—Nothing is more probable, said Candide; but, for God's sake, a little oil and wine.

—What do you mean, probable? replied the philosopher; I regard the case as proved.

Candide fainted and Pangloss brought him some water from a nearby fountain.

Next day, as they wandered amid the ruins, they found a little food which restored some of their strength. Then they fell to work like the others, bringing relief to those of the inhabitants who had escaped death. Some of the citizens whom they rescued gave them a dinner as good as was possible under the circumstances; it is true that the meal was a melancholy one, and the guests watered their bread with tears; but Pangloss consoled them by proving that things could not possibly be otherwise.

—For, said he, all this is for the best, since if there is a volcano at Lisbon, it cannot be somewhere else, since it is unthinkable that things should not be where they are, since everything is well.

A little man in black, an officer of the Inquisition,[2] who was sitting beside him, politely took up the question, and said: —It would seem that the gentleman does not believe in original sin, since if everything is for the best, man has not fallen and is not liable to eternal punishment.

—I most humbly beg pardon of your excellency, Pangloss answered, even more politely, but the fall of man and the curse of original sin entered necessarily into the best of all possible worlds.

—Then you do not believe in free will? said the officer.

—Your excellency must excuse me, said Pangloss; free will agrees very well with absolute necessity, for it was necessary that we should be free, since a will which is determined . . .

Pangloss was in the middle of his sentence, when the officer nodded significantly to the attendant who was pouring him a glass of port, or Oporto, wine.

2. Specifically, a *familier* or *poursuivant*, an undercover agent with powers of arrest.

CHAPTER 6
How They Made a Fine Auto-da-Fé to Prevent Earthquakes, and How Candide Was Whipped

After the earthquake had wiped out three quarters of Lisbon, the learned men of the land could find no more effective way of averting total destruction than to give the people a fine auto-da-fé[3]; the University of Coimbra had established that the spectacle of several persons being roasted over a slow fire with full ceremonial rites is an infallible specific against earthquakes.

In consequence, the authorities had rounded up a Biscayan convicted of marrying a woman who had stood godmother to his child, and two Portuguese who while eating a chicken had set aside a bit of bacon used for seasoning.[4] After dinner, men came with ropes to tie up Doctor Pangloss and his disciple Candide, one for talking and the other for listening with an air of approval; both were taken separately to a set of remarkably cool apartments, where the glare of the sun is never bothersome; eight days later they were both dressed in *san-benitos* and crowned with paper mitres[5]; Candide's mitre and *san-benito* were decorated with inverted flames and with devils who had neither tails nor claws; but Pangloss's devils had both tails and claws, and his flames stood upright. Wearing these costumes, they marched in a procession, and listened to a very touching sermon, followed by a beautiful concert of plainsong. Candide was flogged in cadence to the music; the Biscayan and the two men who had avoided bacon were burned, and Pangloss was hanged, though hanging is not customary. On the same day there was another earthquake, causing frightful damage.[6]

Candide, stunned, stupefied, despairing, bleeding, trembling, said to himself: —If this is the best of all possible worlds, what are the others like? The flogging is not so bad, I was flogged by the Bulgars. But oh my dear Pangloss, greatest of philosophers, was it necessary for me to watch you being hanged, for no reason that I can see? Oh my dear Anabaptist, best of men, was it necessary that you should be drowned in the port? Oh Miss Cunégonde, pearl of young ladies, was it necessary that you should have your belly slit open?

He was being led away, barely able to stand, lectured, lashed, ab-

---

3. Literally, "act of faith," a public ceremony of repentance and humiliation. Such an auto-da-fé was actually held in Lisbon, June 20, 1756.
4. The Biscayan's fault lay in marrying someone within the forbidden bounds of relationship, an act of spiritual incest. The men who declined pork or bacon were understood to be crypto-

Jews.
5. The cone-shaped paper cap (intended to resemble a bishop's mitre) and flowing yellow cape were customary garb for those pleading before the Inquisition.
6. In fact, the second quake occurred December 21, 1755.

solved, and blessed, when an old woman approached and said,
—My son, be of good cheer and follow me.

CHAPTER 7

How an Old Woman Took Care of Candide, and How
He Regained What He Loved

Candide was of very bad cheer, but he followed the old woman
to a shanty; she gave him a jar of ointment to rub himself, left him
food and drink; she showed him a tidy little bed; next to it was a
suit of clothing.

—Eat, drink, sleep, she said; and may Our Lady of Atocha, Our
Lord St. Anthony of Padua, and Our Lord St. James of Compostela
watch over you. I will be back tomorrow.

Candide, still completely astonished by everything he had seen
and suffered, and even more by the old woman's kindness, offered
to kiss her hand.

—It's not *my* hand you should be kissing, said she. I'll be back
tomorrow; rub yourself with the ointment, eat and sleep.

In spite of his many sufferings, Candide ate and slept. Next day
the old woman returned bringing breakfast; she looked at his back
and rubbed it herself with another ointment; she came back with
lunch; and then she returned in the evening, bringing supper. Next
day she repeated the same routine.

—Who are you? Candide asked continually. Who told you to be
so kind to me? How can I ever repay you?

The good woman answered not a word; she returned in the evening, and without food.

—Come with me, says she, and don't speak a word.

Taking him by the hand, she walks out into the countryside with
him for about a quarter of a mile; they reach an isolated house,
quite surrounded by gardens and ditches. The old woman knocks at
a little gate, it opens. She takes Candide up a secret stairway to a
gilded room furnished with a fine brocaded sofa; there she leaves
him, closes the door, disappears. Candide stood as if entranced; his
life, which had seemed like a nightmare so far, was now starting to
look like a delightful dream.

Soon the old woman returned; on her feeble shoulder leaned a
trembling woman, of a splendid figure, glittering in diamonds, and
veiled.

—Remove the veil, said the old woman to Candide.

The young man stepped timidly forward, and lifted the veil.
What an event! What a surprise! Could it be Miss Cunégonde?
Yes, it really was! She herself! His knees give way, speech fails him,
he falls at her feet, Cunégonde collapses on the sofa. The old

woman plies them with brandy, they return to their senses, they exchange words. At first they could utter only broken phrases, questions and answers at cross purposes, sighs, tears, exclamations. The old woman warned them not to make too much noise, and left them alone.

—Then it's really you, said Candide, you're alive, I've found you again in Portugal. Then you never were raped? You never had your belly ripped open, as the philosopher Pangloss assured me?

—Oh yes, said the lovely Cunégonde, but one doesn't always die of these two accidents.

—But your father and mother were murdered then?

—All too true, said Cunégonde, in tears.

—And your brother?

—Killed too.

—And why are you in Portugal? and how did you know I was here? and by what device did you have me brought to this house?

—I shall tell you everything, the lady replied; but first you must tell me what has happened to you since that first innocent kiss we exchanged and the kicking you got because of it.

Candide obeyed her with profound respect; and though he was overcome, though his voice was weak and hesitant, though he still had twinges of pain from his beating, he described as simply as possible everything that had happened to him since the time of their separation. Cunégonde lifted her eyes to heaven; she wept at the death of the good Anabaptist and at that of Pangloss; after which she told the following story to Candide, who listened to every word while he gazed on her with hungry eyes.

CHAPTER 8
Cunégonde's Story

—I was in my bed and fast asleep when heaven chose to send the Bulgars into our castle of Thunder-Ten-Tronckh. They butchered my father and brother, and hacked my mother to bits. An enormous Bulgar, six feet tall, seeing that I had swooned from horror at the scene, set about raping me; at that I recovered my senses, I screamed and scratched, bit and fought, I tried to tear the eyes out of that big Bulgar—not realizing that everything which had happened in my father's castle was a mere matter of routine. The brute then stabbed me with a knife on my left thigh, where I still bear the scar.

—What a pity! I should very much like to see it, said the simple Candide.

—You shall, said Cunégonde; but shall I go on?

—Please do, said Candide.

So she took up the thread of her tale: —A Bulgar captain appeared, he saw me covered with blood and the soldier too intent to get up. Shocked by the monster's failure to come to attention, the captain killed him on my body. He then had my wound dressed, and took me off to his quarters, as a prisoner of war. I laundered his few shirts and did his cooking; he found me attractive, I confess it, and I won't deny that he was a handsome fellow, with a smooth, white skin; apart from that, however, little wit, little philosophical training; it was evident that he had not been brought up by Doctor Pangloss. After three months, he had lost all his money and grown sick of me; so he sold me to a jew named Don Issachar, who traded in Holland and Portugal, and who was mad after women. This jew developed a mighty passion for my person, but he got nowhere with it; I held him off better than I had done with the Bulgar soldier; for though a person of honor may be raped once, her virtue is only strengthened by the experience. In order to keep me hidden, the jew brought me to his country house, which you see here. Till then I had thought there was nothing on earth so beautiful as the castle of Thunder-Ten-Tronckh; I was now undeceived.

—One day the Grand Inquisitor took notice of me at mass; he ogled me a good deal, and made known that he must talk to me on a matter of secret business. I was taken to his palace; I told him of my rank; he pointed out that it was beneath my dignity to belong to an Israelite. A suggestion was then conveyed to Don Issachar that he should turn me over to My Lord the Inquisitor. Don Issachar, who is court banker and a man of standing, refused out of hand. The inquisitor threatened him with an auto-da-fé. Finally my jew, fearing for his life, struck a bargain by which the house and I would belong to both of them as joint tenants; the jew would get Mondays, Wednesdays, and the Sabbath, the inquisitor would get the other days of the week. That has been the arrangement for six months now. There have been quarrels; sometimes it has not been clear whether the night from Saturday to Sunday belonged to the old or the new dispensation. For my part, I have so far been able to hold both of them off; and that, I think, is why they are both still in love with me.

—Finally, in order to avert further divine punishment by earthquake, and to terrify Don Issachar, My Lord the Inquisitor chose to celebrate an auto-da-fé. He did me the honor of inviting me to attend. I had an excellent seat; the ladies were served with refreshments between the mass and the execution. To tell you the truth, I was horrified to see them burn alive those two jews and that decent Biscayan who had married his child's godmother; but what was my surprise, my terror, my grief, when I saw, huddled in a *san-benito* and wearing a mitre, someone who looked like Pangloss! I rubbed my eyes, I watched his every move, I saw him hanged; and I fell back in a swoon. Scarcely had I come to my senses again, when I saw you stripped for the lash; that was the peak of my horror, consternation, grief, and despair. I may tell you, by the way, that your skin is even whiter and more delicate than that of my Bulgar captain. Seeing you, then, redoubled the torments which were already overwhelming me. I shrieked aloud, I wanted to call out, 'Let him go, you brutes!' but my voice died within me, and my cries would have been useless. When you had been thoroughly thrashed: 'How can it be,' I asked myself, 'that agreeable Candide and wise Pangloss have come to Lisbon, one to receive a hundred whiplashes, the other to be hanged by order of My Lord the Inquisitor, whose mistress I am? Pangloss must have deceived me cruelly when he told me that all is for the best in this world.'

—Frantic, exhausted, half out of my senses, and ready to die of weakness, I felt as if my mind were choked with the massacre of my father, my mother, my brother, with the arrogance of that ugly Bulgar soldier, with the knife slash he inflicted on me, my slavery, my cookery, my Bulgar captain, my nasty Don Issachar, my abominable inquisitor, with the hanging of Doctor Pangloss, with that great plainsong *miserere* which they sang while they flogged you—and above all, my mind was full of the kiss which I gave you behind the screen, on the day I saw you for the last time. I praised God, who had brought you back to me after so many trials. I asked my old woman to look out for you, and to bring you here as soon as she could. She did just as I asked; I have had the indescribable joy of seeing you again, hearing you and talking with you once more. But you must be frightfully hungry; I am, myself; let us begin with a dinner.

So then and there they sat down to table; and after dinner, they adjourned to that fine brocaded sofa, which has already been mentioned; and there they were when the eminent Don Issachar, one of the masters of the house, appeared. It was the day of the Sabbath; he was arriving to assert his rights and express his tender passion.

CHAPTER 9
What Happened to Cunégonde, Candide, the Grand Inquisitor, and a Jew

This Issachar was the most choleric Hebrew seen in Israel since the Babylonian captivity.

—What's this, says he, you bitch of a Christian, you're not satisfied with the Grand Inquisitor? Do I have to share you with this rascal, too?

So saying, he drew a long dagger, with which he always went

armed, and, supposing his opponent defenceless, flung himself on Candide. But our good Westphalian had received from the old woman, along with his suit of clothes, a fine sword. Out it came, and though his manners were of the gentlest, in short order he laid the Israelite stiff and cold on the floor, at the feet of the lovely Cunégonde.

—Holy Virgin! she cried. What will become of me now? A man killed in my house! If the police find out, we're done for.

—If Pangloss had not been hanged, said Candide, he would give us good advice in this hour of need, for he was a great philosopher. Lacking him, let's ask the old woman.

She was a sensible body, and was just starting to give her opinion of the situation, when another little door opened. It was just one o'clock in the morning, Sunday morning. This day belonged to the inquisitor. In he came, and found the whipped Candide with a sword in his hand, a corpse at his feet, Cunégonde in terror, and an old woman giving them both good advice.

Here now is what passed through Candide's mind in this instant of time; this is how he reasoned: —If this holy man calls for help, he will certainly have me burned, and perhaps Cunégonde as well; he has already had me whipped without mercy; he is my rival; I have already killed once; why hesitate?

It was a quick, clear chain of reasoning; without giving the inquisitor time to recover from his surprise, he ran him through, and laid him beside the jew.

—Here you've done it again, said Cunégonde; there's no hope for us now. We'll be excommunicated, our last hour has come. How is it that you, who were born so gentle, could kill in two minutes a jew and a prelate?

—My dear girl, replied Candide, when a man is in love, jealous, and just whipped by the Inquisition, he is no longer himself.

The old woman now spoke up and said:—There are three Andalusian steeds in the stable, with their saddles and bridles; our brave Candide must get them ready: my lady has some gold coin and diamonds; let's take to horse at once, though I can only ride on one buttock; we will go to Cadiz. The weather is as fine as can be, and it is pleasant to travel in the cool of the evening.

Promptly, Candide saddled the three horses. Cunégonde, the old woman, and he covered thirty miles without a stop. While they were fleeing, the Holy Brotherhood[7] came to investigate the house; they buried the inquisitor in a fine church, and threw Issachar on the dunghill.

Candide, Cunégonde, and the old woman were already in the lit-

7. A semireligious order with police powers, very active in eighteenth-century Spain.

tle town of Avacena, in the middle of the Sierra Morena; and there, as they sat in a country inn, they had this conversation.

CHAPTER 10

In Deep Distress, Candide, Cunégonde, and the Old Woman Reach Cadiz; They Put to Sea

—Who then could have robbed me of my gold and diamonds? said Cunégonde, in tears. How shall we live? what shall we do? where shall I find other inquisitors and jews to give me some more?

—Ah, said the old woman, I strongly suspect that reverend Franciscan friar who shared the inn with us yesterday at Badajoz. God save me from judging him unfairly! But he came into our room twice, and he left long before us.

—Alas, said Candide, the good Pangloss often proved to me that the fruits of the earth are a common heritage of all, to which each man has equal right. On these principles, the Franciscan should at least have left us enough to finish our journey. You have nothing at all, my dear Cunégonde?

—Not a maravedi, said she.

—What to do? said Candide.

—We'll sell one of the horses, said the old woman; I'll ride on the croup behind my mistress, though only on one buttock, and so we will get to Cadiz.

There was in the same inn a Benedictine prior; he bought the horse cheap. Candide, Cunégonde, and the old woman passed through Lucena, Chillas, and Lebrixa, and finally reached Cadiz. There a fleet was being fitted out and an army assembled, to reason with the Jesuit fathers in Paraguay, who were accused of fomenting among their flock a revolt against the kings of Spain and Portugal near the town of St. Sacrement.[8] Candide, having served in the Bulgar army, performed the Bulgar manual of arms before the general of the little army with such grace, swiftness, dexterity, fire, and agility, that they gave him a company of infantry to command. So here he is, a captain; and off he sails with Miss Cunégonde, the old woman, two valets, and the two Andalusian steeds which had belonged to My Lord the Grand Inquisitor of Portugal.

Throughout the crossing, they spent a great deal of time reasoning about the philosophy of poor Pangloss.

—We are destined, in the end, for another universe, said Candide; no doubt that is the one where everything is well. For in

8. Actually, Colonia del Sacramento. Voltaire took great interest in the Jesuit role in Paraguay, which he has much oversimplified and largely misrepresented here in the interests of his satire. In 1750 they did, however, offer armed resistance to an agreement made between Spain and Portugal. They were subdued and expelled in 1769.

this one, it must be admitted, there is some reason to grieve over our physical and moral state.

—I love you with all my heart, said Cunégonde; but my soul is still harrowed by thoughts of what I have seen and suffered.

—All will be well, replied Candide; the sea of this new world is already better than those of Europe, calmer and with steadier winds. Surely it is the New World which is the best of all possible worlds.

—God grant it, said Cunégonde; but I have been so horribly unhappy in the world so far, that my heart is almost dead to hope.

—You pity yourselves, the old woman told them; but you have had no such misfortunes as mine.

Cunégonde nearly broke out laughing; she found the old woman comic in pretending to be more unhappy than she.

—Ah, you poor old thing, said she, unless you've been raped by two Bulgars, been stabbed twice in the belly, seen two of your castles destroyed, witnessed the murder of two of your mothers and two of your fathers, and watched two of your lovers being whipped in an auto-da-fé, I do not see how you can have had it worse than me. Besides, I was born a baroness, with seventy-two quarterings, and I have worked in a scullery.

—My lady, replied the old woman, you do not know my birth and rank; and if I showed you my rear end, you would not talk as you do, you might even speak with less assurance.

These words inspired great curiosity in Candide and Cunégonde, which the old woman satisfied with this story.

CHAPTER 11
The Old Woman's Story

—My eyes were not always bloodshot and red-rimmed, my nose did not always touch my chin, and I was not born a servant. I am in fact the daughter of Pope Urban the Tenth and the Princess of Palestrina.[9] Till the age of fourteen, I lived in a palace so splendid that all the castles of all your German barons would not have served it as a stable; a single one of my dresses was worth more than all the assembled magnificence of Westphalia. I grew in beauty, in charm, in talent, surrounded by pleasures, dignities, and glowing visions of the future. Already I was inspiring the young men to love; my breast was formed—and what a breast! white, firm, with the shape of the Venus de Medici; and what eyes! what lashes, what black brows! What fire flashed from my glances and outshone the glitter

---

9. Voltaire left behind a comment on this passage, a note first published in 1829: "Note the extreme discretion of the author; hitherto there has never been a pope named Urban X; he avoided attributing a bastard to a known pope. What circumspection! what an exquisite conscience!"

of the stars, as the local poets used to tell me! The women who helped me dress and undress fell into ecstasies, whether they looked at me from in front or behind; and all the men wanted to be in their place.

—I was engaged to the ruling prince of Massa-Carrara; and what a prince he was! as handsome as I, softness and charm compounded, brilliantly witty, and madly in love with me. I loved him in return as one loves for the first time, with a devotion approaching idolatry. The wedding preparations had been made, with a splendor and magnificence never heard of before; nothing but celebrations, masks, and comic operas, uninterruptedly; and all Italy composed in my honor sonnets of which not one was even passable. I had almost attained the very peak of bliss, when an old marquise who had been the mistress of my prince invited him to her house for a cup of chocolate. He died in less than two hours, amid horrifying convulsions. But that was only a trifle. My mother, in complete despair (though less afflicted than I), wished to escape for a while the oppressive atmosphere of grief. She owned a handsome property near Gaeta.[1] We embarked on a papal galley gilded like the altar of St. Peter's in Rome. Suddenly a pirate ship from Salé swept down and boarded us. Our soldiers defended themselves as papal troops usually do; falling on their knees and throwing down their arms, they begged of the corsair absolution *in articulo mortis*.[2]

—They were promptly stripped as naked as monkeys, and so was my mother, and so were our maids of honor, and so was I too. It's a very remarkable thing, the energy these gentlemen put into stripping people. But what surprised me even more was that they stuck their fingers in a place where we women usually admit only a syringe. This ceremony seemed a bit odd to me, as foreign usages always do when one hasn't traveled. They only wanted to see if we didn't have some diamonds hidden there; and I soon learned that it's a custom of long standing among the genteel folk who swarm the seas. I learned that my lords the very religious knights of Malta never overlook this ceremony when they capture Turks, whether male or female; it's one of those international laws which have never been questioned.

—I won't try to explain how painful it is for a young princess to be carried off into slavery in Morocco with her mother. You can imagine everything we had to suffer on the pirate ship. My mother was still very beautiful; our maids of honor, our mere chambermaids, were more charming than anything one could find in all Africa. As for myself, I was ravishing, I was loveliness and grace su-

---

1. About halfway between Rome and Naples.
2. Literally, when at the point of death.

Absolution from a corsair in the act o murdering one is of very dubious valid ity.

preme, and I was a virgin. I did not remain so for long; the flower which had been kept for the handsome prince of Massa-Carrara was plucked by the corsair captain; he was an abominable negro, who thought he was doing me a great favor. My Lady the Princess of Palestrina and I must have been strong indeed to bear what we did during our journey to Morocco. But on with my story; these are such common matters that they are not worth describing.

—Morocco was knee deep in blood when we arrived. Of the fifty sons of the emperor Muley-Ismael,[3] each had his faction, which produced in effect fifty civil wars, of blacks against blacks, of blacks against browns, halfbreeds against halfbreeds; throughout the length and breadth of the empire, nothing but one continual carnage.

—Scarcely had we stepped ashore, when some negroes of a faction hostile to my captor arrived to take charge of his plunder. After the diamonds and gold, we women were the most prized possessions. I was now witness of a struggle such as you never see in the temperate climate of Europe. Northern people don't have hot blood; they don't feel the absolute fury for women which is common in Africa. Europeans seem to have milk in their veins; it is vitriol or liquid fire which pulses through these people around Mount Atlas. The fight for possession of us raged with the fury of the lions, tigers, and poisonous vipers of that land. A Moor snatched my mother by the right arm, the first mate held her by the left; a Moorish soldier grabbed one leg, one of our pirates the other. In a moment's time almost all our girls were being dragged four different ways. My captain held me behind him while with his scimitar he killed everyone who braved his fury. At last I saw all our Italian women, including my mother, torn to pieces, cut to bits, murdered by the monsters who were fighting over them. My captive companions, their captors, soldiers, sailors, blacks, browns, whites, mulattoes, and at last my captain, all were killed, and I remained half dead on a mountain of corpses. Similar scenes were occurring, as is well known, for more than three hundred leagues around, without anyone skimping on the five prayers a day decreed by Mohammed.

—With great pain, I untangled myself from this vast heap of bleeding bodies, and dragged myself under a great orange tree by a neighboring brook, where I collapsed, from terror, exhaustion, horror, despair, and hunger. Shortly, my weary mind surrendered to a sleep which was more of a swoon than a rest. I was in this state of weakness and languor, between life and death, when I felt myself

---

3. Having reigned for more than fifty years, a potent and ruthless sultan of Morocco, he died in 1727 and left his kingdom in much the condition described.

touched by something which moved over my body. Opening my eyes, I saw a white man, rather attractive, who was groaning and saying under his breath: '*O che sciagura d'essere senza coglioni!*'[4]

CHAPTER 12

The Old Woman's Story Continued

—Amazed and delighted to hear my native tongue, and no less surprised by what this man was saying, I told him that there were worse evils than those he was complaining of. In a few words, I described to him the horrors I had undergone, and then fainted again. He carried me to a nearby house, put me to bed, gave me something to eat, served me, flattered me, comforted me, told me he had never seen anyone so lovely, and added that he had never before regretted so much the loss of what nobody could give him back.

'I was born at Naples, he told me, where they caponize two or three thousand children every year; some die of it, others acquire a voice more beautiful than any woman's, still others go on to become governors of kingdoms.[5] The operation was a great success with me, and I became court musician to the Princess of Palestrina . . .'

'Of my mother,' I exclaimed.

'Of your mother,' cried he, bursting into tears; 'then you must be the princess whom I raised till she was six, and who already gave promise of becoming as beautiful as you are now!'

'I am that very princess; my mother lies dead, not a hundred yards from here, buried under a pile of corpses.'

—I told him my adventures, he told me his: that he had been sent by a Christian power to the King of Morocco, to conclude a treaty granting him gunpowder, cannon, and ships with which to liquidate the traders of the other Christian powers.

'My mission is concluded,' said this honest eunuch; 'I shall take ship at Ceuta and bring you back to Italy. *Ma che sciagura d'essere senza coglioni!*'

—I thanked him with tears of gratitude, and instead of returning me to Italy, he took me to Algiers and sold me to the dey of that country. Hardly had the sale taken place, when that plague which has made the rounds of Africa, Asia, and Europe broke out in full fury at Algiers. You have seen earthquakes; but tell me, young lady, have you ever had the plague?

—Never, replied the baroness.

—If you had had it, said the old woman, you would agree that it is far worse than an earthquake. It is very frequent in Africa, and I

---

4. "Oh what a misfortune to have no testicles!"
5. The castrate Farinelli (1705–1782), originally a singer, came to exercise considerable political influence on the Kings of Spain, Philip V and Ferdinand VI.

had it. Imagine, if you will, the situation of a pope's daughter, fifteen years old, who in three months' time had experienced poverty, slavery, had been raped almost every day, had seen her mother quartered, had suffered from famine and war, and who now was dying of pestilence in Algiers. As a matter of fact, I did not die; but the eunuch and the dey and nearly the entire seraglio of Algiers perished.

—When the first horrors of this ghastly plague had passed, the slaves of the dey were sold. A merchant bought me and took me to Tunis; there he sold me to another merchant, who resold me at Tripoli; from Tripoli I was sold to Alexandria, from Alexandria resold to Smyrna, from Smyrna to Constantinople. I ended by belonging to an aga of janizaries, who was shortly ordered to defend Azov against the besieging Russians.[6]

—The aga, who was a gallant soldier, took his whole seraglio with him, and established us in a little fort amid the Maeotian marshes,[7] guarded by two black eunuchs and twenty soldiers. Our side killed a prodigious number of Russians, but they paid us back nicely. Azov was put to fire and sword without respect for age or sex; only our little fort continued to resist, and the enemy determined to starve us out. The twenty janizaries had sworn never to surrender. Reduced to the last extremities of hunger, they were forced to eat our two eunuchs, lest they violate their oaths. After several more days, they decided to eat the women too.

—We had an imam,[8] very pious and sympathetic, who delivered an excellent sermon, persuading them not to kill us altogether.

'Just cut off a single rumpsteak from each of these ladies,' he said, 'and you'll have a fine meal. Then if you should need another, you can come back in a few days and have as much again; heaven will bless your charitable action, and you will be saved.'

—His eloquence was splendid, and he persuaded them. We underwent this horrible operation. The imam treated us all with the ointment that they use on newly circumcised children. We were at the point of death.

—Scarcely had the janizaries finished the meal for which we furnished the materials, when the Russians appeared in flat-bottomed boats; not a janizary escaped. The Russians paid no attention to the state we were in; but there are French physicians everywhere, and one of them, who knew his trade, took care of us. He cured us, and I shall remember all my life that when my wounds were healed, he made me a proposition. For the rest, he counselled us simply to

6. Azov, near the mouth of the Don, was besieged by the Russians under Peter the Great in 1695–1696. The janizaries were an élite corps of the Ottoman armies.

7. The Roman name of the so-called Sea of Azov, a shallow swampy lake near the town.

8. In effect, a chaplain.

have patience, assuring us that the same thing had happened in several other sieges, and that it was according to the laws of war.

—As soon as my companions could walk, we were herded off to Moscow. In the division of booty, I fell to a boyar who made me work in his garden, and gave me twenty whiplashes a day; but when he was broken on the wheel after about two years, with thirty other boyars, over some little court intrigue,[9] I seized the occasion; I ran away; I crossed all Russia; I was for a long time a chambermaid in Riga, then at Rostock, Vismara, Leipzig, Cassel, Utrecht, Leyden, The Hague, Rotterdam; I grew old in misery and shame, having only half a backside and remembering always that I was the daughter of a Pope; a hundred times I wanted to kill myself, but always I loved life more. This ridiculous weakness is perhaps one of our worst instincts; is anything more stupid than choosing to carry a burden that really one wants to cast on the ground? to hold existence in horror, and yet to cling to it? to fondle the serpent which devours us till it has eaten out our heart?

—In the countries through which I have been forced to wander, in the taverns where I have had to work, I have seen a vast number of people who hated their existence; but I never saw more than a dozen who deliberately put an end to their own misery: three negroes, four Englishmen, four Genevans, and a German professor named Robeck.[1] My last post was as servant to the jew Don Issachar; he attached me to your service, my lovely one; and I attached myself to your destiny, till I have become more concerned with your fate than with my own. I would not even have mentioned my own misfortunes, if you had not irked me a bit, and if it weren't the custom, on shipboard, to pass the time with stories. In a word, my lady, I have had some experience of the world, I know it; why not try this diversion? Ask every passenger on this ship to tell you his story, and if you find a single one who has not often cursed the day of his birth, who has not often told himself that he is the most miserable of men, then you may throw me overboard head first.

9. Voltaire had in mind an ineffectual conspiracy against Peter the Great known as the "revolt of the strelitz" or musketeers, which took place in 1698. Though easily put down, it provoked from the emperor a massive and atrocious program of reprisals.
1. Johann Robeck (1672–1739) published a treatise advocating suicide and showed his conviction by drowning himself. But he waited till he was 67 before putting his theory to the test. For a larger view of the issue, see L. G. Crocker, "The Discussion of Suicide in the 18th Century," *Journal of the History of Ideas*, XIII, 47–72 (1952).

CHAPTER 13
*How Candide Was Forced to Leave the Lovely
Cunégonde and the Old Woman*

Having heard out the old woman's story, the lovely Cunégonde paid her the respects which were appropriate to a person of her rank and merit. She took up the wager as well, and got all the passengers, one after another, to tell her their adventures. She and Candide had to agree that the old woman had been right.

—It's certainly too bad, said Candide, that the wise Pangloss was hanged, contrary to the custom of autos-da-fé; he would have admirable things to say of the physical evil and moral evil which cover land and sea, and I might feel within me the impulse to dare to raise several polite objections.

As the passengers recited their stories, the boat made steady progress, and presently landed at Buenos Aires. Cunégonde, Captain Candide, and the old woman went to call on the governor, Don Fernando d'Ibaraa y Figueroa y Mascarenes y Lampourdos y Souza. This nobleman had the pride appropriate to a man with so many names. He addressed everyone with the most aristocratic disdain, pointing his nose so loftily, raising his voice so mercilessly, lording it so splendidly, and assuming so arrogant a pose, that everyone who met him wanted to kick him. He loved women to the point of fury; and Cunégonde seemed to him the most beautiful creature he had ever seen. The first thing he did was to ask directly if she were the captain's wife. His manner of asking this question disturbed Candide; he did not dare say she was his wife, because in fact she was not; he did not dare say she was his sister, because she wasn't that either; and though this polite lie was once common enough among the ancients,[2] and sometimes serves moderns very well, he was too pure of heart to tell a lie.

—Miss Cunégonde, said he, is betrothed to me, and we humbly beg your excellency to perform the ceremony for us.

Don Fernando d'Ibaraa y Figueroa y Mascarenes y Lampourdos y Souza twirled his moustache, smiled sardonically, and ordered Captain Candide to go drill his company. Candide obeyed. Left alone with My Lady Cunégonde, the governor declared his passion, and protested that he would marry her tomorrow, in church or in any other manner, as it pleased her charming self. Cunégonde asked for a quarter-hour to collect herself, consult the old woman, and make up her mind.

The old woman said to Cunégonde: —My lady, you have

2. Voltaire has in mind Abraham's adventures with Sarah (Genesis xii) and Isaac's with Rebecca (Genesis xxvi).

seventy-two quarterings and not one penny; if you wish, you may be the wife of the greatest lord in South America, who has a really handsome moustache; are you going to insist on your absolute fidelity? You have already been raped by the Bulgars; a jew and an inquisitor have enjoyed your favors; miseries entitle one to privileges. I assure you that in your position I would make no scruple of marrying My Lord the Governor, and making the fortune of Captain Candide.

While the old woman was talking with all the prudence of age and experience, there came into the harbor a small ship bearing an alcalde and some alguazils.[3] This is what had happened.

As the old woman had very shrewdly guessed, it was a long-sleeved Franciscan who stole Cunégonde's gold and jewels in the town of Badajoz, when she and Candide were in flight. The monk tried to sell some of the gems to a jeweler, who recognized them as belonging to the Grand Inquisitor. Before he was hanged, the Franciscan confessed that he had stolen them, indicating who his victims were and where they were going. The flight of Cunégonde and Candide was already known. They were traced to Cadiz, and a vessel was hastily dispatched in pursuit of them. This vessel was now in the port of Buenos Aires. The rumor spread that an alcalde was aboard, in pursuit of the murderers of My Lord the Grand Inquisitor. The shrewd old woman saw at once what was to be done.

—You cannot escape, she told Cunégonde, and you have nothing to fear. You are not the one who killed my lord, and, besides, the governor, who is in love with you, won't let you be mistreated. Sit tight.

And then she ran straight to Candide: —Get out of town, she said, or you'll be burned within the hour.

There was not a moment to lose; but how to leave Cunégonde, and where to go?

CHAPTER 14

How Candide and Cacambo Were Received by the Jesuits of Paraguay

Candide had brought from Cadiz a valet of the type one often finds in the provinces of Spain and in the colonies. He was one quarter Spanish, son of a halfbreed in the Tucuman[4]; he had been choirboy, sacristan, sailor, monk, merchant, soldier, and lackey. His name was Cacambo, and he was very fond of his master because his

3. Police officers.
4. A city and province of Argentina, to the northwest of Buenos Aires, just at the juncture of the Andes and the Grand Chaco.

master was a very good man. In hot haste he saddled the two Andalusian steeds.

—Hurry, master, do as the old woman says; let's get going and leave this town without a backward look.

Candide wept: —O my beloved Cunégonde! must I leave you now, just when the governor is about to marry us! Cunégonde, brought from so far, what will ever become of you?

—She'll become what she can, said Cacambo; women can always find something to do with themselves; God sees to it; let's get going.

—Where are you taking me? where are we going? what will we do without Cunégonde? said Candide.

—By Saint James of Compostela, said Cacambo, you were going to make war against the Jesuits, now we'll go make war for them. I know the roads pretty well, I'll bring you to their country, they will be delighted to have a captain who knows the Bulgar drill; you'll make a prodigious fortune. If you don't get your rights in one world, you will find them in another. And isn't it pleasant to see new things and do new things?

—Then you've already been in Paraguay? said Candide.

—Indeed I have, replied Cacambo; I was cook in the College of the Assumption, and I know the government of Los Padres[5] as I know the streets of Cadiz. It's an admirable thing, this government. The kingdom is more than three hundred leagues across; it is divided into thirty provinces. Los Padres own everything in it, and the people nothing; it's a masterpiece of reason and justice. I myself know nothing so wonderful as Los Padres, who in this hemisphere make war on the kings of Spain and Portugal, but in Europe hear their confessions; who kill Spaniards here, and in Madrid send them to heaven; that really tickles me; let's get moving, you're going to be the happiest of men. Won't Los Padres be delighted when they learn they have a captain who knows the Bulgar drill!

As soon as they reached the first barricade, Cacambo told the frontier guard that a captain wished to speak with My Lord the Commander. A Paraguayan officer ran to inform headquarters by laying the news at the feet of the commander. Candide and Cacambo were first disarmed and deprived of their Andalusian horses. They were then placed between two files of soldiers; the commander was at the end, his three-cornered hat on his head, his cassock drawn up, a sword at his side, and a pike in his hand. He nods, and twenty-four soldiers surround the newcomers. A sergeant then informs them that they must wait, that the commander cannot talk to them, since the reverend father provincial has forbidden all

5. The Jesuit fathers. R. B. Cunningham-Grahame has written an account of the Jesuits in Paraguay 1607–1767, under the title *A Vanished Arcadia*.

Spaniards from speaking, except in his presence, and from remaining more than three hours in the country.[6]

—And where is the reverend father provincial? says Cacambo.

—He is reviewing his troops after having said mass, the sergeant replies, and you'll only be able to kiss his spurs in three hours.

—But, says Cacambo, my master the captain, who, like me, is dying from hunger, is not Spanish at all, he is German; can't we have some breakfast while waiting for his reverence?

The sergeant promptly went off to report this speech to the commander.

—God be praised, said this worthy; since he is German, I can talk to him; bring him into my bower.

Candide was immediately led into a leafy nook surrounded by a handsome colonnade of green and gold marble and trellises amid which sported parrots, birds of paradise,[7] humming birds, guinea fowl, and all the rarest species of birds. An excellent breakfast was prepared in golden vessels; and while the Paraguayans ate corn out of wooden bowls in the open fields under the glare of the sun, the reverend father commander entered into his bower.

He was a very handsome young man, with an open face, rather blonde in coloring, with ruddy complexion, arched eyebrows, liquid eyes, pink ears, bright red lips, and an air of pride, but a pride somehow different from that of a Spaniard or a Jesuit. Their confiscated weapons were restored to Candide and Cacambo, as well as their Andalusian horses; Cacambo fed them oats alongside the bower, always keeping an eye on them for fear of an ambush.

First Candide kissed the hem of the commander's cassock, then they sat down at the table.

—So you are German? said the Jesuit, speaking in that language.

—Yes, your reverence, said Candide.

As they spoke these words, both men looked at one another with great surprise, and another emotion which they could not control.

—From what part of Germany do you come? said the Jesuit.

—From the nasty province of Westphalia, said Candide; I was born in the castle of Thunder-Ten-Tronckh.

—Merciful heavens! cries the commander. Is it possible?

—What a miracle! exclaims Candide.

---

6. In fact, the Jesuits, who had organized their Indian parishes into villages under a system of tribal communism, did their best to discourage contact with the outside world.

7. In this passage and several later ones, Voltaire uses in conjunction two words, both of which mean humming bird. The French system of classifying humming birds, based on the work of the celebrated Buffon, distinguishes *oiseaux-mouches* with straight bills from *colibris* with curved bills. This distinction is wholly fallacious. Humming birds have all manner of shaped bills, and the division of species must be made on other grounds entirely. At the expense of ornithological accuracy, I have therefore introduced birds of paradise to get the requisite sense of glitter and sheen.

—Can it be you? asks the commander.

—It's impossible, says Candide.

They both fall back in their chairs, they embrace they shed streams of tears.

—What, can it be you, reverend father! you, the brother of the lovely Cunégonde! you, who were killed by the Bulgars! you, the son of My Lord the Baron! you, a Jesuit in Paraguay! It's a mad world, indeed it is. Oh, Pangloss! Pangloss! how happy you would be, if you hadn't been hanged.

The commander dismissed his negro slaves and the Paraguayans who served his drink in crystal goblets. He thanked God and Saint Ignatius a thousand times, he clasped Candide in his arms, their faces were bathed in tears.

—You would be even more astonished, even more delighted, even more beside yourself, said Candide, if I told you that My Lady Cunégonde, your sister, who you thought was disemboweled, is enjoying good health.

—Where?

—Not far from here, in the house of the governor of Buenos Aires; and to think that I came to make war on you!

Each word they spoke in this long conversation added another miracle. Their souls danced on their tongues, hung eagerly at their ears, glittered in their eyes. As they were Germans, they sat a long time at table, waiting for the reverend father provincial; and the commander spoke in these terms to his dear Candide.

CHAPTER 15

How Candide Killed the Brother of His Dear Cunégonde

—All my life long I shall remember the horrible day when I saw my father and mother murdered and my sister raped. When the Bulgars left, that adorable sister of mine was nowhere to be found; so they loaded a cart with my mother, my father, myself, two serving girls, and three little murdered boys, to carry us all off for burial in a Jesuit chapel some two leagues from our ancestral castle. A Jesuit sprinkled us with holy water; it was horribly salty, and a few drops got into my eyes; the father noticed that my lid made a little tremor; putting his hand on my heart, he felt it beat; I was rescued, and at the end of three weeks was as good as new. You know, my dear Candide, that I was a very pretty boy; I became even more so; the reverend father Croust,[8] superior of the abbey, conceived a most tender friendship for me; he accepted me as a novice, and shortly after, I was sent to Rome. The Father General had need of

8. It is the name of a Jesuit rector at Colmar with whom Voltaire had quarreled in 1754.

a resupply of young German Jesuits. The rulers of Paraguay accept as few Spanish Jesuits as they can; they prefer foreigners, whom they think they can control better. I was judged fit, by the Father General, to labor in this vineyard. So we set off, a Pole, a Tyrolean, and myself. Upon our arrival, I was honored with the posts of sub-deacon and lieutenant; today I am a colonel and a priest. We are giving a vigorous reception to the King of Spain's men; I assure you they will be excommunicated as well as trounced on the battlefield. Providence has sent you to help us. But is it really true that my dear sister, Cunégonde, is in the neighborhood, with the governor of Buenos Aires?

Candide reassured him with a solemn oath that nothing could be more true. Their tears began to flow again.

The baron could not weary of embracing Candide; he called him his brother, his savior.

—Ah, my dear Candide, said he, maybe together we will be able to enter the town as conquerors, and be united with my sister Cunégonde.

—That is all I desire, said Candide; I was expecting to marry her, and I still hope to.

—You insolent dog, replied the baron, you would have the effrontery to marry my sister, who has seventy-two quarterings! It's a piece of presumption for you even to mention such a crazy project in my presence.

Candide, terrified by this speech, answered: —Most reverend father, all the quarterings in the world don't affect this case; I have rescued your sister out of the arms of a jew and an inquisitor; she has many obligations to me, she wants to marry me. Master Pangloss always taught me that men are equal; and I shall certainly marry her.

—We'll see about that, you scoundrel, said the Jesuit baron of Thunder-Ten-Tronckh; and so saying, he gave him a blow across the face with the flat of his sword. Candide immediately drew his own sword and thrust it up to the hilt in the baron's belly; but as he drew it forth all dripping, he began to weep.

—Alas, dear God! said he, I have killed my old master, my friend, my brother-in-law; I am the best man in the world, and here are three men I've killed already, and two of the three were priests.

Cacambo, who was standing guard at the entry of the bower, came running.

—We can do nothing but sell our lives dearly, said his master; someone will certainly come; we must die fighting.

Cacambo, who had been in similar scrapes before, did not lose his head; he took the Jesuit's cassock, which the commander had been wearing, and put it on Candide; he stuck the dead man's square hat on Candide's head, and forced him onto horseback. Everything was done in the wink of an eye.

—Let's ride, master; everyone will take you for a Jesuit on his way to deliver orders; and we will have passed the frontier before anyone can come after us.

Even as he was pronouncing these words, he charged off, crying in Spanish: —Way, make way for the reverend father colonel!

CHAPTER 16
What Happened to the Two Travelers with Two Girls, Two Monkeys, and the Savages Named Biglugs

Candide and his valet were over the frontier before anyone in the camp knew of the death of the German Jesuit. Foresighted Cacambo had taken care to fill his satchel with bread, chocolate, ham, fruit, and several bottles of wine. They pushed their Andalusian horses forward into unknown country, where there were no roads. Finally a broad prairie divided by several streams opened before them. Our two travelers turned their horses loose to graze; Cacambo suggested that they eat too, and promptly set the example. But Candide said: —How can you expect me to eat ham when I have killed the son of My Lord the Baron, and am now condemned never to see the lovely Cunégonde for the rest of my life? Why should I drag out my miserable days, since I must exist far from her in in the depths of despair and remorse? And what will the *Journal de Trévoux* say of all this?[9]

Though he talked this way, he did not neglect the food. Night fell. The two wanderers heard a few weak cries which seemed to be voiced by women. They could not tell whether the cries expressed grief or joy; but they leaped at once to their feet, with that uneasy suspicion which one always feels in an unknown country. The outcry arose from two girls, completely naked, who were running swiftly along the edge of the meadow, pursued by two monkeys who snapped at their buttocks. Candide was moved to pity; he had learned marksmanship with the Bulgars, and could have knocked a nut off a bush without touching the leaves. He raised his Spanish rifle, fired twice, and killed the two monkeys.

—God be praised, my dear Cacambo! I've saved these two poor creatures from great danger. Though I committed a sin in killing an inquisitor and a Jesuit, I've redeemed myself by saving the lives of two girls. Perhaps they are two ladies of rank, and this good deed may gain us special advantages in the country.

He had more to say, but his mouth shut suddenly when he

9. A journal published by the Jesuit order, founded in 1701 and consistently hostile to Voltaire.

saw the girls embracing the monkeys tenderly, weeping over their bodies, and filling the air with lamentations.

—I wasn't looking for quite so much generosity of spirit, said he to Cacambo; the latter replied: —You've really fixed things this time, master; you've killed the two lovers of these young ladies.

—Their lovers! Impossible! You must be joking, Cacambo; how can I believe you?

—My dear master, Cacambo replied, you're always astonished by everything. Why do you think it so strange that in some countries monkeys succeed in obtaining the good graces of women? They are one quarter human, just as I am one quarter Spanish.

—Alas, Candide replied, I do remember now hearing Master Pangloss say that such things used to happen, and that from these mixtures there arose pans, fauns, and satyrs, and that these creatures had appeared to various grand figures of antiquity; but I took all that for fables.

—You should be convinced now, said Cacambo; it's true, and you see how people make mistakes who haven't received a measure of education. But what I fear is that these girls may get us into real trouble.

These sensible reflections led Candide to leave the field and to hide in a wood. There he dined with Cacambo; and there both of them, having duly cursed the inquisitor of Portugal, the governor of Buenos Aires, and the baron, went to sleep on a bed of moss. When they woke up, they found themselves unable to move; the reason was that during the night the Biglugs,[1] natives of the country, to whom the girls had complained of them, had tied them down with cords of bark. They were surrounded by fifty naked Biglugs, armed with arrows, clubs, and stone axes. Some were boiling a caldron of water, others were preparing spits, and all cried out: —It's a Jesuit, a Jesuit! We'll be revenged and have a good meal; let's eat some Jesuit, eat some Jesuit!

—I told you, my dear master, said Cacambo sadly, I said those two girls would play us a dirty trick.

Candide, noting the caldron and spits, cried out: —We are surely going to be roasted or boiled. Ah, what would Master Pangloss say if he could see these men in a state of nature? All is for the best, I agree; but I must say it seems hard to have lost Miss Cunégonde and to be stuck on a spit by the Biglugs.

Cacambo did not lose his head.

—Don't give up hope, said he to the disconsolate Candide; I

1. Voltaire's name is "Oreillons" from Spanish "Orejones," a name mentioned in Garcilaso de Vega's *Historia General del Perú* (1609), on which Voltaire drew for many of the details in his picture of South America. See Richard A. Brooks, "Voltaire and Garcilaso de Vega" in *Studies in Voltaire and the 18th Century*, XXX, 189-204.

understand a little of the jargon these people speak, and I'm going to talk to them.

—Don't forget to remind them, said Candide, of the frightful inhumanity of eating their fellow men, and that Christian ethics forbid it.

—Gentlemen, said Cacambo, you have a mind to eat a Jesuit today? An excellent idea; nothing is more proper than to treat one's enemies so. Indeed, the law of nature teaches us to kill our neighbor, and that's how men behave the whole world over. Though we Europeans don't exercise our right to eat our neighbors, the reason is simply that we find it easy to get a good meal elsewhere; but you don't have our resources, and we certainly agree that it's better to eat your enemies than to let the crows and vultures have the fruit of your victory. But, gentlemen, you wouldn't want to eat your friends. You think you will be spitting a Jesuit, and it's your defender, the enemy of your enemies, whom you will be roasting. For my part, I was born in your country; the gentleman whom you see is my master, and far from being a Jesuit, he has just killed a Jesuit, the robe he is wearing was stripped from him; that's why you have taken a dislike to him. To prove that I am telling the truth, take his robe and bring it to the nearest frontier of the kingdom of Los Padres; find out for yourselves if my master didn't kill a Jesuit officer. It won't take long; if you find that I have lied, you can still eat us. But if I've told the truth, you know too well the principles of public justice, customs, and laws, not to spare our lives.

The Biglugs found this discourse perfectly reasonable; they appointed chiefs to go posthaste and find out the truth; the two messengers performed their task like men of sense, and quickly returned bringing good news. The Biglugs untied their two prisoners, treated them with great politeness, offered them girls, gave them refreshments, and led them back to the border of their state, crying joyously: —He isn't a Jesuit, he isn't a Jesuit!

Candide could not weary of exclaiming over his preservation.

—What a people! he said. What men! what customs! If I had not had the good luck to run a sword through the body of Miss Cunégonde's brother, I would have been eaten on the spot! But, after all, it seems that uncorrupted nature is good, since these folk, instead of eating me, showed me a thousand kindnesses as soon as they knew I was not a Jesuit.

CHAPTER 17

Arrival of Candide and His Servant at the
Country of Eldorado,[2] and What They Saw There

When they were out of the land of the Biglugs, Cacambo said to Candide: —You see that this hemisphere is no better than the other; take my advice, and let's get back to Europe as soon as possible.

—How to get back, asked Candide, and where to go? If I go to my own land, the Bulgars and Abares are murdering everyone in sight; if I go to Portugal, they'll burn me alive; if we stay here, we risk being skewered any day. But how can I ever leave that part of the world where Miss Cunégonde lives?

—Let's go toward Cayenne, said Cacambo, we shall find some Frenchmen there, for they go all over the world; they can help us; perhaps God will take pity on us.

To get to Cayenne was not easy; they knew more or less which way to go, but mountains, rivers, cliffs, robbers, and savages obstructed the way everywhere. Their horses died of weariness; their food was eaten; they subsisted for one whole month on wild fruits, and at last they found themselves by a little river fringed with coconut trees, which gave them both life and hope.

Cacambo, who was as full of good advice as the old woman, said to Candide: —We can go no further, we've walked ourselves out; I see an abandoned canoe on the bank, let's fill it with coconuts, get into the boat, and float with the current; a river always leads to some inhabited spot or other. If we don't find anything pleasant, at least we may find something new.

—Let's go, said Candide, and let Providence be our guide.

They floated some leagues between banks sometimes flowery, sometimes sandy, now steep, now level. The river widened steadily; finally it disappeared into a chasm of frightful rocks that rose high into the heavens.[3] The two travelers had the audacity to float with the current into this chasm. The river, narrowly confined, drove them onward with horrible speed and a fearful roar. After twenty-four hours, they saw daylight once more; but their canoe was smashed on the snags. They had to drag themselves from rock to rock for an entire league; at last they emerged to an immense horizon, ringed with remote mountains. The countryside was tended for pleasure as well as profit; everywhere the useful was joined to the agreeable. The roads were covered, or rather decorated, with ele-

2. The myth of this land of gold somewhere in Central or South America had been widespread since the sixteenth century.

3. This journey down an underground river is probably adapted from a similar episode in the story of Sinbad the Sailor.

gantly shaped carriages made of a glittering material, carrying men and women of singular beauty, and drawn by great red sheep which were faster than the finest horses of Andalusia, Tetuan, and Mequinez.

—Here now, said Candide, is a country that's better than Westphalia.

Along with Cacambo, he climbed out of the river at the first village he could see. Some children of the town, dressed in rags of gold brocade, were playing quoits at the village gate; our two men from the other world paused to watch them; their quoits were rather large, yellow, red, and green, and they glittered with a singular luster. On a whim, the travelers picked up several; they were of gold, emeralds, and rubies, and the least of them would have been the greatest ornament of the Great Mogul's throne.

—Surely, said Cacambo, these quoit players are the children of the king of the country.

The village schoolmaster appeared at that moment, to call them back to school.

—And there, said Candide, is the tutor of the royal household.

The little rascals quickly gave up their game, leaving on the ground their quoits and playthings. Candide picked them up, ran to the schoolmaster, and presented them to him humbly, giving him to understand by sign language that their royal highnesses had forgotten their gold and jewels. With a smile, the schoolmaster tossed them to the ground, glanced quickly but with great surprise at Candide's face, and went his way.

The travelers did not fail to pick up the gold, rubies, and emeralds.

—Where in the world are we? cried Candide. The children of this land must be well trained, since they are taught contempt for gold and jewels.

Cacambo was as much surprised as Candide. At last they came to the finest house of the village; it was built like a European palace. A crowd of people surrounded the door, and even more were in the entry; delightful music was heard, and a delicious aroma of cooking filled the air. Cacambo went up to the door, listened, and reported that they were talking Peruvian; that was his native language, for every reader must know that Cacambo was born in Tucuman, in a village where they talk that language exclusively.

—I'll act as interpreter, he told Candide; it's an hotel, let's go in.

Promptly two boys and two girls of the staff, dressed in cloth of gold, and wearing ribbons in their hair, invited them to sit at the host's table. The meal consisted of four soups, each one garnished with a brace of parakeets, a boiled condor which weighed two hundred pounds, two roast monkeys of an excellent flavor, three hundred birds of paradise in one dish and six hundred humming birds in another, exquisite stews, delicious pastries, the whole thing served up in plates of what looked like rock crystal. The boys and girls of the staff poured them various beverages made from sugar cane.

The diners were for the most part merchants and travelers, all extremely polite, who questioned Cacambo with the most discreet circumspection, and answered his questions very directly.

When the meal was over, Cacambo as well as Candide supposed he could settle his bill handsomely by tossing onto the table two of those big pieces of gold which they had picked up; but the host and hostess burst out laughing, and for a long time nearly split their sides. Finally they subsided.

—Gentlemen, said the host, we see clearly that you're foreigners; we don't meet many of you here. Please excuse our laughing when you offered us in payment a couple of pebbles from the roadside. No doubt you don't have any of our local currency, but you don't need it to eat here. All the hotels established for the promotion of commerce are maintained by the state. You have had meager entertainment here, for we are only a poor town; but everywhere else you will be given the sort of welcome you deserve.

Cacambo translated for Candide all the host's explanations, and Candide listened to them with the same admiration and astonishment that his friend Cacambo showed in reporting them.

—What is this country, then, said they to one another, unknown to the rest of the world, and where nature itself is so different from our own? This probably is the country where everything is for the best; for it's absolutely necessary that such a country should exist somewhere. And whatever Master Pangloss said of the matter, I have often had occasion to notice that things went badly in Westphalia.

CHAPTER 18
What They Saw in the Land of Eldorado

Cacambo revealed his curiosity to the host, and the host told him: —I am an ignorant man and content to remain so; but we have here an old man, retired from the court, who is the most knowing person in the kingdom, and the most talkative.

Thereupon he brought Cacambo to the old man's house. Candide now played second fiddle, and acted as servant to his own valet. They entered an austere little house, for the door was merely of silver and the paneling of the rooms was only gold, though so tastefully wrought that the finest paneling would not surpass it. If the truth must be told, the lobby was only decorated with rubies and emeralds; but the patterns in which they were arranged atoned for the extreme simplicity.

The old man received the two strangers on a sofa stuffed with bird-of-paradise feathers, and offered them several drinks in diamond carafes; then he satisfied their curiosity in these terms.

—I am a hundred and seventy-two years old, and I heard from my late father, who was liveryman to the king, about the astonishing revolutions in Peru which he had seen. Our land here was formerly part of the kingdom of the Incas, who rashly left it in order to conquer another part of the world, and who were ultimately destroyed by the Spaniards. The wisest princes of their house were those who had never left their native valley; they decreed, with the consent of the nation, that henceforth no inhabitant of our little kingdom should ever leave it; and this rule is what has preserved our innocence and our happiness. The Spaniards heard vague rumors about this land, they called it El Dorado; and an English knight named Raleigh[4] even came somewhere close to it about a hundred years ago; but as we are surrounded by unscalable mountains and precipices, we have managed so far to remain hidden from the rapacity of the European nations, who have an inconceivable rage for the pebbles and mud of our land, and who, in order to get some, would butcher us all to the last man.

The conversation was a long one; it turned on the form of the government, the national customs, on women, public shows, the arts. At last Candide, whose taste always ran to metaphysics, told Cacambo to ask if the country had any religion.

The old man grew a bit red.

—How's that? he said. Can you have any doubt of it? Do you suppose we are altogether thankless scoundrels?

Cacambo asked meekly what was the religion of Eldorado. The old man flushed again.

—Can there be two religions? he asked. I suppose our religion is the same as everyone's, we worship God from morning to evening.

—Then you worship a single deity? said Cacambo, who acted throughout as interpreter of the questions of Candide.

—It's obvious, said the old man, that there aren't two or three or four of them. I must say the people of your world ask very remarkable questions.

Candide could not weary of putting questions to this good old man; he wanted to know how the people of Eldorado prayed to God.

—We don't pray to him at all, said the good and respectable

---

4. *The Discovery of Guiana,* published in 1595, described Sir Walter Raleigh's infatuation with the myth of Eldorado and served to spread the story still further.

sage; we have nothing to ask him for, since everything we need has already been granted; we thank God continually.

Candide was interested in seeing the priests; he had Cacambo ask where they were. The old gentleman smiled.

—My friends, said he, we are all priests; the king and all the heads of household sing formal psalms of thanksgiving every morning, and five or six thousand voices accompany them.

—What! you have no monks to teach, argue, govern, intrigue, and burn at the stake everyone who disagrees with them?

—We should have to be mad, said the old man; here we are all of the same mind, and we don't understand what you're up to with your monks.

Candide was overjoyed at all these speeches, and said to himself: —This is very different from Westphalia and the castle of My Lord the Baron; if our friend Pangloss had seen Eldorado, he wouldn't have called the castle of Thunder-Ten-Tronckh the finest thing on earth; to know the world one must travel.

After this long conversation, the old gentleman ordered a carriage with six sheep made ready, and gave the two travelers twelve of his servants for their journey to the court.

—Excuse me, said he, if old age deprives me of the honor of accompanying you. The king will receive you after a style which will not altogether displease you, and you will doubtless make allowance for the customs of the country if there are any you do not like.

Candide and Cacambo climbed into the coach; the six sheep flew like the wind, and in less than four hours they reached the king's palace at the edge of the capital. The entryway was two hundred and twenty feet high and a hundred wide; it is impossible to describe all the materials of which it was made. But you can imagine how much finer it was than those pebbles and sand which we call gold and jewels.

Twenty beautiful girls of the guard detail welcomed Candide and Cacambo as they stepped from the carriage, took them to the baths, and dressed them in robes woven of humming-bird feathers; then the high officials of the crown, both male and female, led them to the royal chamber between two long lines, each of a thousand musicians, as is customary. As they approached the throne room, Cacambo asked an officer what was the proper method of greeting his majesty: if one fell to one's knees or on one's belly; if one put one's hands on one's head or on one's rear; if one licked up the dust of the earth—in a word, what was the proper form?[5]

—The ceremony, said the officer, is to embrace the king and kiss him on both cheeks.

5. Candide's questions are probably derived from those of Gulliver on a similar occasion; see *Gulliver's Travels*, Book IV.

Candide and Cacambo fell on the neck of his majesty, who received them with all the dignity imaginable, and asked them politely to dine.

In the interim, they were taken about to see the city, the public buildings rising to the clouds, the public markets and arcades, the fountains of pure water and of rose water, those of sugar cane liquors which flowed perpetually in the great plazas paved with a sort of stone which gave off odors of gillyflower and rose petals. Candide asked to see the supreme court and the hall of parliament; they told him there was no such thing, that lawsuits were unknown. He asked if there were prisons, and was told there were not. What surprised him more, and gave him most pleasure, was the palace of sciences, in which he saw a gallery two thousand paces long, entirely filled with mathematical and physical instruments.

Having passed the whole afternoon seeing only a thousandth part of the city, they returned to the king's palace. Candide sat down to dinner with his majesty, his own valet Cacambo, and several ladies. Never was better food served, and never did a host preside more jovially than his majesty. Cacambo explained the king's witty sayings to Candide, and even when translated they still seemed witty. Of all the things which astonished Candide, this was not, in his eyes, the least astonishing.

They passed a month in this refuge. Candide never tired of saying to Cacambo: —It's true, my friend, I'll say it again, the castle where I was born does not compare with the land where we now are; but Miss Cunégonde is not here, and you doubtless have a mistress somewhere in Europe. If we stay here, we shall be just like everybody else, whereas if we go back to our own world, taking with us just a dozen sheep loaded with Eldorado pebbles, we shall be richer than all the kings put together, we shall have no more inquisitors to fear, and we shall easily be able to retake Miss Cunégonde.

This harangue pleased Cacambo; wandering is such pleasure, it gives a man such prestige at home to be able to talk of what he has seen abroad, that the two happy men resolved to be so no longer, but to take their leave of his majesty.

—You are making a foolish mistake, the king told them; I know very well that my kingdom is nothing much; but when you are pretty comfortable somewhere, you had better stay there. Of course I have no right to keep strangers against their will, that sort of tyranny is not in keeping with our laws or our customs; all men are free; depart when you will, but the way out is very difficult. You cannot possibly go up the river by which you miraculously came; it runs too swiftly through its underground caves. The mountains which surround my land are ten thousand feet high, and steep as walls; each one is more than ten leagues across; the only way down is over precipices. But since you really must go, I shall order my engineers to make a machine which can carry you conveniently. When we take you over the mountains, nobody will be able to go with you, for my subjects have sworn never to leave their refuge, and they are too sensible to break their vows. Other than that, ask of me what you please.

—We only request of your majesty, Cacambo said, a few sheep loaded with provisions, some pebbles, and some of the mud of your country.

The king laughed.

—I simply can't understand, said he, the passion you Europeans have for our yellow mud; but take all you want, and much good may it do you.

He promptly gave orders to his technicians to make a machine for lifting these two extraordinary men out of his kingdom. Three thousand good physicists worked at the problem; the machine was ready in two weeks' time, and cost no more than twenty million pounds sterling, in the money of the country. Cacambo and Candide were placed in the machine; there were two great sheep, saddled and bridled to serve them as steeds when they had cleared the mountains, twenty pack sheep with provisions, thirty which carried presents consisting of the rarities of the country, and fifty loaded with gold, jewels, and diamonds. The king bade tender farewell to the two vagabonds.

It made a fine spectacle, their departure, and the ingenious way in which they were hoisted with their sheep up to the top of the mountains. The technicians bade them good-bye after bringing them to safety, and Candide had now no other desire and no other object than to go and present his sheep to Miss Cunégonde.

—We have, said he, enough to pay off the governor of Buenos Aires—if, indeed, a price can be placed on Miss Cunégonde. Let us go to Cayenne, take ship there, and then see what kingdom we can find to buy up.

CHAPTER 19
What Happened to Them at Surinam, and How Candide Got to Know Martin

The first day was pleasant enough for our travelers. They were encouraged by the idea of possessing more treasures than Asia, Europe, and Africa could bring together. Candide, in transports, carved the name of Cunégonde on the trees. On the second day two of their sheep bogged down in a swamp and were lost with their loads; two other sheep died of fatigue a few days later; seven or eight others starved to death in a desert; still others fell, a little after, from precipices. Finally, after a hundred days' march, they had only two sheep left. Candide told Cacambo: —My friend, you see how the riches of this world are fleeting; the only solid things are virtue and the joy of seeing Miss Cunégonde again.

—I agree, said Cacambo, but we still have two sheep, laden with more treasure than the king of Spain will ever have; and I see in the distance a town which I suspect is Surinam; it belongs to the Dutch. We are at the end of our trials and on the threshold of our happiness.

As they drew near the town, they discovered a negro stretched on the ground with only half his clothes left, that is, a pair of blue drawers; the poor fellow was also missing his left leg and his right hand.

—Good Lord, said Candide in Dutch, what are you doing in that horrible condition, my friend?

—I am waiting for my master, Mr. Vanderdendur,[6] the famous merchant, answered the negro.

—Is Mr. Vanderdendur, Candide asked, the man who treated you this way?

—Yes, sir, said the negro, that's how things are around here. Twice a year we get a pair of linen drawers to wear. If we catch a finger in the sugar mill where we work, they cut off our hand; if we try to run away, they cut off our leg: I have undergone both these experiences. This is the price of the sugar you eat in Europe. And yet, when my mother sold me for ten Patagonian crowns on the coast of Guinea, she said to me: 'My dear child, bless our witch doctors, reverence them always, they will make your life happy; you have the honor of being a slave to our white masters, and in this way you are making the fortune of your father and mother.' Alas! I don't know if I made their fortunes, but they certainly did not make mine. The dogs, monkeys, and parrots are a thousand times less unhappy than we are. The Dutch witch doctors who converted me tell me every Sunday that we are all sons of Adam, black and white alike. I am no genealogist; but if these preachers are right, we must all be remote cousins; and you must admit no one could treat his own flesh and blood in a more horrible fashion.

—Oh Pangloss! cried Candide, you had no notion of these abominations! I'm through, I must give up your optimism after all.

—What's optimism? said Cacambo.

—Alas, said Candide, it is a mania for saying things are well

---

6. A name perhaps intended to suggest VanDuren, a Dutch bookseller with whom Voltaire had quarreled. In particular, the incident of gradually raising one's price recalls VanDuren, to whom Voltaire had successively offered 1,000, 1,500, 2,000, and 3,000 florins for the return of the manuscript of Frederick the Great's *Anti-Machiavel.*

when one is in hell.

And he shed bitter tears as he looked at his negro, and he was still weeping as he entered Surinam.

The first thing they asked was if there was not some vessel in port which could be sent to Buenos Aires. The man they asked was a Spanish merchant who undertook to make an honest bargain with them. They arranged to meet in a cafe; Candide and the faithful Cacambo, with their two sheep, went there to meet with him.

Candide, who always said exactly what was in his heart, told the Spaniard of his adventures, and confessed that he wanted to recapture Miss Cunégonde.

—I shall take good care *not* to send you to Buenos Aires, said the merchant; I should be hanged, and so would you. The lovely Cunégonde is his lordship's favorite mistress.

This was a thunderstroke for Candide; he wept for a long time; finally he drew Cacambo aside.

—Here, my friend, said he, is what you must do. Each one of us has in his pockets five or six millions' worth of diamonds; you are cleverer than I; go get Miss Cunégonde in Buenos Aires. If the governor makes a fuss, give him a million; if that doesn't convince him, give him two millions; you never killed an inquisitor, nobody will suspect you. I'll fit out another boat and go wait for you in Venice. That is a free country, where one need have no fear either of Bulgars or Abares or jews or inquisitors.

Cacambo approved of this wise decision. He was in despair at leaving a good master who had become a bosom friend; but the pleasure of serving him overcame the grief of leaving him. They embraced, and shed a few tears; Candide urged him not to forget the good old woman. Cacambo departed that very same day; he was a very good fellow, that Cacambo.

Candide remained for some time in Surinam, waiting for another merchant to take him to Italy, along with the two sheep which were left him. He hired servants and bought everything necessary for the long voyage; finally Mr. Vanderdendur, master of a big ship, came calling.

—How much will you charge, Candide asked this man, to take me to Venice—myself, my servants, my luggage, and those two sheep over there?

The merchant set a price of ten thousand piastres; Candide did not blink an eye.

—Oh ho, said the prudent Vanderdendur to himself, this stranger pays out ten thousand piastres at once, he must be pretty well fixed.

Then, returning a moment later, he made known that he could not set sail under twenty thousand.

—All right, you shall have them, said Candide.

—Whew, said the merchant softly to himself, this man gives twenty thousand piastres as easily as ten.

He came back again to say he could not go to Venice for less than thirty thousand piastres.

—All right, thirty then, said Candide.

—Ah ha, said the Dutch merchant, again speaking to himself; so thirty thousand piastres mean nothing to this man; no doubt the two sheep are loaded with immense treasures; let's say no more; we'll pick up the thirty thousand piastres first, and then we'll see.

Candide sold two little diamonds, the least of which was worth more than all the money demanded by the merchant. He paid him in advance. The two sheep were taken aboard. Candide followed in a little boat, to board the vessel at its anchorage. The merchant bides his time, sets sail, and makes his escape with a favoring wind. Candide, aghast and stupified, soon loses him from view.

—Alas, he cries, now there is a trick worthy of the old world!

He returns to shore sunk in misery; for he had lost riches enough to make the fortunes of twenty monarchs.

Now he rushes to the house of the Dutch magistrate, and, being a bit disturbed, he knocks loudly at the door; goes in, tells the story of what happened, and shouts a bit louder than is customary. The judge begins by fining him ten thousand piastres for making such a racket; then he listens patiently to the story, promises to look into the matter as soon as the merchant comes back, and charges another ten thousand piastres as the costs of the hearing.

This legal proceeding completed the despair of Candide. In fact he had experienced miseries a thousand times more painful, but the coldness of the judge, and that of the merchant who had robbed him, roused his bile and plunged him into a black melancholy. The malice of men rose up before his spirit in all its ugliness, and his mind dwelt only on gloomy thoughts. Finally, when a French vessel was ready to leave for Bordeaux, since he had no more diamond-laden sheep to transport, he took a cabin at a fair price, and made it known in the town that he would pay passage and keep, plus two thousand piastres, to any honest man who wanted to make the journey with him, on condition that this man must be the most disgusted with his own condition and the most unhappy man in the province.

This drew such a crowd of applicants as a fleet could not have held. Candide wanted to choose among the leading candidates, so he picked out about twenty who seemed companionable enough, and of whom each pretended to be more miserable than all the others. He brought them together at his inn and gave them a dinner, on condition that each would swear to tell truthfully his entire history. He would select as his companion the most truly miserable and rightly discontented man, and among the others he would distribute various gifts.

The meeting lasted till four in the morning. Candide, as he listened to all the stories, remembered what the old woman had told him on the trip to Buenos Aires, and of the wager she had made, that there was nobody on the boat who had not undergone great misfortunes. At every story that was told him, he thought of Pangloss.

—That Pangloss, he said, would be hard put to prove his system. I wish he was here. Certainly if everything goes well, it is in Eldorado and not in the rest of the world.

At last he decided in favor of a poor scholar who had worked ten years for the booksellers of Amsterdam. He decided that there was no trade in the world with which one should be more disgusted.

This scholar, who was in fact a good man, had been robbed by his wife, beaten by his son, and deserted by his daughter, who had got herself abducted by a Portuguese. He had just been fired from the little job on which he existed; and the preachers of Surinam were persecuting him because they took him for a Socinian.[7] The others, it is true, were at least as unhappy as he, but Candide hoped the scholar would prove more amusing on the voyage. All his rivals declared that Candide was doing them a great injustice, but he pacified them with a hundred piastres apiece.

CHAPTER 20
What Happened to Candide and Martin at Sea

The old scholar, whose name was Martin, now set sail with Candide for Bordeaux. Both men had seen and suffered much; and even if the vessel had been sailing from Surinam to Japan via the Cape of Good Hope, they would have been able to keep themselves amused with instances of moral evil and physical evil during the entire trip.

However, Candide had one great advantage over Martin, that he still hoped to see Miss Cunégonde again, and Martin had nothing to hope for; besides, he had gold and diamonds, and though he had lost a hundred big red sheep loaded with the greatest treasures of the earth, though he had always at his heart a memory of the Dutch merchant's villainy, yet, when he thought of the wealth that remained in his hands, and when he talked of Cunégonde, especially just after a good dinner, he still inclined to the system of Pangloss.

7. A follower of Faustus and Laelius Socinus, sixteenth-century Polish theologians, who proposed a form of "rational" Christianity which exalted the rational conscience and minimized such mysteries as the trinity. The Socinians, by a special irony, were vigorous optimists.

—But what about you, Monsieur Martin, he asked the scholar, what do you think of all that? What is your idea of moral evil and physical evil?

—Sir, answered Martin, those priests accused me of being a Socinian, but the truth is that I am a Manichee.[8]

—You're joking, said Candide; there aren't any more Manichees in the world.

—There's me, said Martin; I don't know what to do about it, but I can't think otherwise.

—You must be possessed of the devil, said Candide.

—He's mixed up with so many things of this world, said Martin, that he may be in me as well as elsewhere; but I assure you, as I survey this globe, or globule, I think that God has abandoned it to some evil spirit—all of it except Eldorado. I have scarcely seen one town which did not wish to destroy its neighboring town, no family which did not wish to exterminate some other family. Everywhere the weak loathe the powerful, before whom they cringe, and the powerful treat them like brute cattle, to be sold for their meat and fleece. A million regimented assassins roam Europe from one end to the other, plying the trades of murder and robbery in an organized way for a living, because there is no more honest form of work for them; and in the cities which seem to enjoy peace and where the arts are flourishing, men are devoured by more envy, cares, and anxieties than a whole town experiences when it's under siege. Private griefs are worse even than public trials. In a word, I have seen so much and suffered so much, that I am a Manichee.

—Still there is some good, said Candide.

—That may be, said Martin, but I don't know it.

In the middle of this discussion, the rumble of cannon was heard. From minute to minute the noise grew louder. Everyone reached for his spyglass. At a distance of some three miles they saw two vessels fighting; the wind brought both of them so close to the French vessel that they had a pleasantly comfortable seat to watch the fight. Presently one of the vessels caught the other with a broadside so low and so square as to send it to the bottom. Candide and Martin saw clearly a hundred men on the deck of the sinking ship; they all raised their hands to heaven, uttering fearful shrieks; and in a moment everything was swallowed up.

—Well, said Martin, that is how men treat one another.

8. Mani, a Persian mage and philosopher of the third century A.D., taught (probably under the influence of traditions stemming from Zoroaster and the worshippers of the sun god Mithra) that the earth is a field of dispute between two almost equal powers, one of light and one of darkness, both of which must be propitiated. Saint Augustine was much exercised by the heresy, to which he was at one time himself addicted, and Voltaire came to some knowledge of it through the encyclopedic learning of the seventeenth century scholar Pierre Bayle.

—It is true, said Candide, there's something devilish in this business.

As they chatted, he noticed something of a striking red color floating near the sunken vessel. They sent out a boat to investigate; it was one of his sheep. Candide was more joyful to recover this one sheep than he had been afflicted to lose a hundred of them, all loaded with big Eldorado diamonds.

The French captain soon learned that the captain of the victorious vessel was Spanish and that of the sunken vessel was a Dutch pirate. It was the same man who had robbed Candide. The enormous riches which this rascal had stolen were sunk beside him in the sea, and nothing was saved but a single sheep.

—You see, said Candide to Martin, crime is punished sometimes; this scoundrel of a Dutch merchant has met the fate he deserved.

—Yes, said Martin; but did the passengers aboard his ship have to perish too? God punished the scoundrel, and the devil drowned the others.

Meanwhile the French and Spanish vessels continued on their journey, and Candide continued his talks with Martin. They disputed for fifteen days in a row, and at the end of that time were just as much in agreement as at the beginning. But at least they were talking, they exchanged their ideas, they consoled one another. Candide caressed his sheep.

—Since I have found you again, said he, I may well rediscover Miss Cunégonde.

CHAPTER 21

*Candide and Martin Approach the Coast of France:
They Reason Together*

At last the coast of France came in view.

—Have you ever been in France, Monsieur Martin? asked Candide.

—Yes, said Martin, I have visited several provinces. There are some where half the inhabitants are crazy, others where they are too sly, still others where they are quite gentle and stupid, some where they venture on wit; in all of them the principal occupation is lovemaking, the second is slander, and the third stupid talk.

—But, Monsieur Martin, were you ever in Paris?

—Yes, I've been in Paris; it contains specimens of all these types, it is a chaos, a mob, in which everyone is seeking pleasure and where hardly anyone finds it, at least from what I have seen. I did not live there for long; as I arrived, I was robbed of everything I possessed by thieves at the fair of St. Germain; I myself was taken for a thief, and spent eight days in jail, after which I took a proofreader's job to earn enough money to return on foot to Holland. I knew the writing gang, the intriguing gang, the gang with fits and convulsions.[9] They say there are some very civilized people in that town; I'd like to think so.

—I myself have no desire to visit France, said Candide; you no doubt realize that when one has spent a month in Eldorado, there is nothing else on earth one wants to see, except Miss Cunégonde. I am going to wait for her at Venice; we will cross France simply to get to Italy; wouldn't you like to come with me?

—Gladly, said Martin; they say Venice is good only for the Venetian nobles, but that on the other hand they treat foreigners very well when they have plenty of money. I don't have any; you do, so I'll follow you anywhere.

—By the way, said Candide, do you believe the earth was originally all ocean, as they assure us in that big book belonging to the ship's captain?[1]

—I don't believe that stuff, said Martin, nor any of the dreams which people have been peddling for some time now.

—But why, then, was this world formed at all? asked Candide.

—To drive us mad, answered Martin.

—Aren't you astonished, Candide went on, at the love which those two girls showed for the monkeys in the land of the Biglugs that I told you about?

—Not at all, said Martin, I see nothing strange in these sentiments; I have seen so many extraordinary things that nothing seems extraordinary any more.

—Do you believe, asked Candide, that men have always massacred one another as they do today? That they have always been liars, traitors, ingrates, thieves, weaklings, sneaks, cowards, backbiters, gluttons, drunkards, misers, climbers, killers, calumniators, sensualists, fanatics, hypocrites, and fools?

—Do you believe, said Martin, that hawks have always eaten pigeons when they could get them?

—Of course, said Candide.

—Well, said Martin, if hawks have always had the same character, why do you suppose that men have changed?

—Oh, said Candide, there's a great deal of difference, because freedom of the will . . .

As they were disputing in this manner, they reached Bordeaux.

9. The Jansenists, a sect of strict Catholics, became notorious for spiritual ecstasies. Their public displays reached a height during the 1720's, and Voltaire described them in *Le Siècle de Louis XIV* (chap. 37), as well as in the article on "Convulsions" in the *Philosophical Dictionary*.
1. The Bible. Voltaire is straining at a dark passage in Genesis 1.

CHAPTER 22

What Happened in France to Candide and Martin

Candide paused in Bordeaux only long enough to sell a couple of Dorado pebbles and to fit himself out with a fine two-seater carriage, for he could no longer do without his philosopher Martin; only he was very unhappy to part with his sheep, which he left to the academy of science in Bordeaux. They proposed, as the theme of that year's prize contest, the discovery of why the wool of the sheep was red; and the prize was awarded to a northern scholar who demonstrated[2] by A plus B minus C divided by Z that the sheep ought to be red and die of sheep rot.

But all the travelers with whom Candide talked in the roadside inns told him: —We are going to Paris.

This general consensus finally inspired in him too a desire to see the capital; it was not much out of his road to Venice.

He entered through the Faubourg Saint-Marceau,[3] and thought he was in the meanest village of Westphalia.

Scarcely was Candide in his hotel, when he came down with a mild illness caused by exhaustion. As he was wearing an enormous diamond ring, and people had noticed among his luggage a tremendously heavy safe, he soon found at his bedside two doctors whom he had not called, several intimate friends who never left him alone, and two pious ladies who helped to warm his broth. Martin said: —I remember that I too was ill on my first trip to Paris; I was very poor; and as I had neither friends, pious ladies, nor doctors, I got well.

However, as a result of medicines and bleedings, Candide's illness became serious. A resident of the neighborhood came to ask him politely to fill out a ticket, to be delivered to the porter of the other world.[4] Candide wanted nothing to do with it. The pious ladies assured him it was a new fashion; Candide replied that he wasn't a man of fashion. Martin wanted to throw the resident out the window. The cleric swore that without the ticket they wouldn't bury Candide. Martin swore that he would bury the cleric if he continued to be a nuisance. The quarrel grew heated; Martin took him by the shoulders and threw him bodily out the door; all of which caused a great scandal, from which developed a legal case.

2. The satire is pointed at Maupertuis Le Lapon, philosopher and mathematician, whom Voltaire had accused of trying to adduce mathematical proofs of the existence of God and whose algebraic formulae were easily ridiculed. 3. A district on the left bank, notably grubby in the eighteenth century. " 'As I entered [Paris] through the Faubourg Saint-Marceau, I saw nothing but dirty stinking little streets, ugly black houses, a general air of squalor and poverty, beggars, carters, menders of clothes, sellers of herb-drinks and old hats,' J.-J. Rousseau, *Confessions*, Book IV." 4. In the middle of the eighteenth century, it became customary to require persons who were grievously ill to sign *billets de confession*, without which they could not be given absolution, admitted to the last sacraments, or buried in consecrated ground.

Candide got better; and during his convalescence he had very good company in to dine. They played cards for money; and Candide was quite surprised that none of the aces were ever dealt to him, and Martin was not surprised at all.

Among those who did the honors of the town for Candide there was a little abbé from Perigord, one of those busy fellows, always bright, always useful, assured, obsequious, and obliging, who waylay passing strangers, tell them the scandal of the town, and offer them pleasures at any price they want to pay. This fellow first took Candide and Martin to the theatre. A new tragedy was being played. Candide found himself seated next to a group of wits. That did not keep him from shedding a few tears in the course of some perfectly played scenes. One of the commentators beside him remarked during the intermission: —You are quite mistaken to weep, this actress is very bad indeed; the actor who plays with her is even worse; and the play is even worse than the actors in it. The author knows not a word of Arabic, though the action takes place in Arabia; and besides, he is a man who doesn't believe in innate ideas.[5] Tomorrow I will show you twenty pamphlets written against him.[6]

—Tell me, sir, said Candide to the abbé, how many plays are there for performance in France?

—Five or six thousand, replied the other.

—That's a lot, said Candide; how many of them are any good?

—Fifteen or sixteen, was the answer.

—That's a lot, said Martin.

Candide was very pleased with an actress who took the part of Queen Elizabeth in a rather dull tragedy[7] that still gets played from time to time.

—I like this actress very much, he said to Martin, she bears a slight resemblance to Miss Cunégonde; I should like to meet her.

The abbé from Perigord offered to introduce him. Candide, raised in Germany, asked what was the protocol, how one behaved in France with queens of England.

—You must distinguish, said the abbé; in the provinces, you take them to an inn; at Paris they are respected while still attractive, and thrown on the dunghill when they are dead.[8]

—Queens on the dunghill! said Candide.

—Yes indeed, said Martin, the abbé is right; I was in Paris when

5. Descartes proposed certain ideas as innate, Voltaire followed Locke in categorically denying innate ideas. The point is simply that in faction fights all the issues get muddled together.
6. Here begins a long passage interpolated by Voltaire in 1761; it ends on p. 186.
7. *Le Comte d'Essex* by Thomas Corneille.
8. Voltaire engaged in a long and vigorous campaign against the rule that actors and actresses could not be buried in consecrated ground. The superstition probably arose from a feeling that by assuming false identities they denied their own souls.

Miss Monime herself[9] passed, as they say, from this life to the other; she was refused what these folk call 'the honors of burial,' that is, the right to rot with all the beggars of the district in a dirty cemetery; she was buried all alone by her troupe at the corner of the Rue de Bourgogne; this must have been very disagreeable to her, for she had a noble character.

—That was extremely rude, said Candide.

—What do you expect? said Martin; that is how these folk are. Imagine all the contradictions, all the incompatibilities you can, and you will see them in the government, the courts, the churches, and the plays of this crazy nation.

—Is it true that they are always laughing in Paris? asked Candide.

—Yes, said the abbé, but with a kind of rage too; when people complain of things, they do so amid explosions of laughter; they even laugh as they perform the most detestable actions.

—Who was that fat swine, said Candide, who spoke so nastily about the play over which I was weeping, and the actors who gave me so much pleasure?

—He is a living illness, answered the abbé, who makes a business of slandering all the plays and books; he hates the successful ones, as eunuchs hate successful lovers; he's one of those literary snakes who live on filth and venom; he's a folliculator . . .

—What's this word *folliculator*? asked Candide.

—It's a folio filler, said the abbé, a Fréron.[1]

It was after this fashion that Candide, Martin, and the abbé from Perigord chatted on the stairway as they watched the crowd leaving the theatre.

—Although I'm in a great hurry to see Miss Cunégonde again, said Candide, I would very much like to dine with Miss Clairon,[2] for she seemed to me admirable.

The abbé was not the man to approach Miss Clairon, who saw only good company.

—She has an engagement tonight, he said; but I shall have the honor of introducing you to a lady of quality, and there you will get to know Paris as if you had lived here four years.

Candide, who was curious by nature, allowed himself to be brought to the lady's house, in the depths of the Faubourg St.-

9. Adrienne Lecouvreur (1690–1730), so called because she made her debut as Monime in Racine's *Mithridate*. Voltaire had assisted at her secret midnight funeral and wrote an indignant poem about it.
1. A successful and popular journalist, who had attacked several of Voltaire's plays, including *Tancrède*. Voltaire had a fine story that the devil attended the first night of *Tancrède* disguised as

Fréron: when a lady in the balcony wept at the play's pathos, her tear dropped on the devil's nose; he thought it was holy water and shook it off—psha! psha! G. Desnoiresterres, *Voltaire et Jean-Jacques Rousseau*, pp. 3–4.
2. Actually Claire Leris (1723–1803). She had played the lead role in *Tancrède* and was for many years a leading figure on the Paris stage.

Honoré; they were playing faro[3]; twelve melancholy punters held in their hands a little sheaf of cards, blank summaries of their bad luck. Silence reigned supreme, the punters were pallid, the banker uneasy; and the lady of the house, seated beside the pitiless banker, watched with the eyes of a lynx for the various illegal redoublings and bets at long odds which the players tried to signal by folding the corners of their cards; she had them unfolded with a determination which was severe but polite, and concealed her anger lest she lose her customers. The lady caused herself to be known as the Marquise of Parolignac.[4] Her daughter, fifteen years old, sat among the punters and tipped off her mother with a wink to the sharp practices of these unhappy players when they tried to recoup their losses. The abbé from Perigord, Candide, and Martin came in; nobody arose or greeted them or looked at them; all were lost in the study of their cards.

—My Lady the Baroness of Thunder-Ten-Tronckh was more civil, thought Candide.

However, the abbé whispered in the ear of the marquise, who, half rising, honored Candide with a gracious smile and Martin with a truly noble nod; she gave a seat and dealt a hand of cards to Candide, who lost fifty thousand francs in two turns; after which they had a very merry supper. Everyone was amazed that Candide was not upset over his losses; the lackeys, talking together in their usual lackey language, said: —He must be some English milord.

The supper was like most Parisian suppers: first silence, then an indistinguishable rush of words; then jokes, mostly insipid, false news, bad logic, a little politics, a great deal of malice. They even talked of new books.

—Have you seen the new novel by Dr. Gauchat, the theologian?[5] asked the abbé from Perigord.

—Oh yes, answered one of the guests; but I couldn't finish it. We have a horde of impudent scribblers nowadays, but all of them put together don't match the impudence of this Gauchat, this doctor of theology. I have been so struck by the enormous number of detestable books which are swamping us that I have taken up punting at faro.

—And the *Collected Essays* of Archdeacon T——[6] asked the abbé, what do you think of them?

3. A game of cards, about which it is necessary to know only that a number of punters play against a banker or dealer. The pack is dealt out two cards at a time, and each player may bet on any card as much as he pleases. The sharp practices of the punters consist essentially of tricks for increasing their winnings without corresponding risks.
4. A *paroli* is an illegal redoubling of one's bet; her name therefore implies a title grounded in cardsharping.
5. He had written against Voltaire, and Voltaire suspected him (wrongly) of having committed a novel, *L'Oracle des nouveaux philosophes*.
6. His name was Trublet, and he had said, among other disagreeable things, that Voltaire's epic poem, the *Henriade*, made him yawn and that Voltaire's genius was "the perfection of mediocrity."

—Ah, said Madame de Parolignac, what a frightful bore he is! He takes such pains to tell you what everyone knows; he discourses so learnedly on matters which aren't worth a casual remark! He plunders, and not even wittily, the wit of other people! He spoils what he plunders, he's disgusting! But he'll never disgust me again; a couple of pages of the archdeacon have been enough for me.

There was at table a man of learning and taste, who supported the marquise on this point. They talked next of tragedies; the lady asked why there were tragedies which played well enough but which were wholly unreadable. The man of taste explained very clearly how a play could have a certain interest and yet little merit otherwise; he showed succinctly that it was not enough to conduct a couple of intrigues, such as one can find in any novel, and which never fail to excite the spectator's interest; but that one must be new without being grotesque, frequently touch the sublime but never depart from the natural; that one must know the human heart and give it words; that one must be a great poet without allowing any character in the play to sound like a poet; and that one must know the language perfectly, speak it purely, and maintain a continual harmony without ever sacrificing sense to mere sound.

—Whoever, he added, does not observe all these rules may write one or two tragedies which succeed in the theatre, but he will never be ranked among the good writers; there are very few good tragedies; some are idylls in well-written, well-rhymed dialogue, others are political arguments which put the audience to sleep, or revolting pomposities; still others are the fantasies of enthusiasts, barbarous in style, incoherent in logic, full of long speeches to the gods because the author does not know how to address men, full of false maxims and emphatic commonplaces.

Candide listened attentively to this speech and conceived a high opinion of the speaker; and as the marquise had placed him by her side, he turned to ask her who was this man who spoke so well.

—He is a scholar, said the lady, who never plays cards and whom the abbé sometimes brings to my house for supper; he knows all about tragedies and books, and has himself written a tragedy that was hissed from the stage and a book, the only copy of which ever seen outside his publisher's office was dedicated to me.

—What a great man, said Candide, he's Pangloss all over.

Then, turning to him, he said: —Sir, you doubtless think everything is for the best in the physical as well as the moral universe, and that nothing could be otherwise than as it is?

—Not at all, sir, replied the scholar, I believe nothing of the sort. I find that everything goes wrong in our world; that nobody knows his place in society or his duty, what he's doing or what he ought to be doing, and that outside of mealtimes, which are cheerful and congenial enough, all the rest of the day is spent in useless quarrels, as of Jansenists against Molinists,[7] parliament-men against church-men, literary men against literary men, courtiers against courtiers, financiers against the plebs, wives against husbands, relatives against relatives—it's one unending warfare.

Candide answered: —I have seen worse; but a wise man, who has since had the misfortune to be hanged, taught me that everything was marvelously well arranged. Troubles are just the shadows in a beautiful picture.

—Your hanged philosopher was joking, said Martin; the shadows are horrible ugly blots.

—It is human beings who make the blots, said Candide, and they can't do otherwise.

—Then it isn't their fault, said Martin.

Most of the faro players, who understood this sort of talk not at all, kept on drinking; Martin disputed with the scholar, and Candide told part of his story to the lady of the house.

After supper, the marquise brought Candide into her room and sat him down on a divan.

—Well, she said to him, are you still madly in love with Miss Cunégonde of Thunder-Ten-Tronckh?

—Yes, ma'am, replied Candide. The marquise turned upon him a tender smile.

—You answer like a young man of Westphalia, said she; a Frenchman would have told me: 'It is true that I have been in love with Miss Cunégonde; but since seeing you, madame, I fear that I love her no longer.'

—Alas, ma'am, said Candide, I will answer any way you want.

—Your passion for her, said the marquise, began when you picked up her handkerchief; I prefer that you should pick up my garter.

—Gladly, said Candide, and picked it up.

—But I also want you to put it back on, said the lady; and Candide put it on again.

—Look you now, said the lady, you are a foreigner; my Paris lovers I sometimes cause to languish for two weeks or so, but to you I surrender the very first night, because we must render the honors of the country to a young man from Westphalia.

The beauty, who had seen two enormous diamonds on the two hands of her young friend, praised them so sincerely that from the fingers of Candide they passed over to the fingers of the marquise.

As he returned home with his Perigord abbé, Candide felt

---

7. The Jansenists (from Corneille Jansen, 1585–1638) were a relatively strict party of religious reform; the Molinists (from Luis Molina) were the party of the Jesuits. Their central issue of controversy was the relative importance of divine grace and human will to the salvation of man.

some remorse at having been unfaithful to Miss Cunégonde; the abbé sympathized with his grief; he had only a small share in the fifty thousand francs which Candide lost at cards, and in the proceeds of the two diamonds which had been half-given, half-extorted. His scheme was to profit, as much as he could, from the advantage of knowing Candide. He spoke at length of Cunégonde, and Candide told him that he would beg forgiveness for his beloved for his infidelity when he met her at Venice.

The Perigordian overflowed with politeness and unction, taking a tender interest in everything Candide said, everything he did, and everything he wanted to do.[8]

—Well, sir, said he, so you have an assignation at Venice?

—Yes indeed, sir, I do, said Candide; it is absolutely imperative that I go there to find Miss Cunégonde.

And then, carried away by the pleasure of talking about his love, he recounted, as he often did, a part of his adventures with that illustrious lady of Westphalia.

—I suppose, said the abbé, that Miss Cunégonde has a fine wit and writes charming letters.

—I never received a single letter from her, said Candide; for, as you can imagine, after being driven out of the castle for love of her, I couldn't write; shortly I learned that she was dead; then I rediscovered her; then I lost her again, and I have now sent, to a place more than twentyfive hundred leagues from here, a special agent whose return I am expecting.

The abbé listened carefully, and looked a bit dreamy. He soon took his leave of the two strangers, after embracing them tenderly. Next day Candide, when he woke up, received a letter, to the following effect:

—Dear sir, my very dear lover, I have been lying sick in this town for a week, I have just learned that you are here. I would fly to your arms if I could move. I heard that you had passed through Bordeaux; that was where I left the faithful Cacambo and the old woman, who are soon to follow me here. The governor of Buenos Aires took everything, but left me your heart. Come; your presence will either return me to life or cause me to die of joy.

8. Here ends the long passage interpolated by Voltaire in 1761, which began on p. 181. In the original version the transition was managed as follows. After the "commentator's" speech, ending: —Tomorrow I will show you twenty pamphlets written against him. —Sir, said the abbé from Perigord, do you notice that young person over there with the attractive face and the delicate figure? She would only cost you ten thousand francs a month, and for fifty thousand crowns of diamonds . . .

—I could spare her only a day or or two, replied Candide, because I have an urgent appointment at Venice.

Next night after supper, the sly Perigordian overflowed with politeness and assiduity.

—Well, sir, said he, so you have an assignation at Venice?

This charming letter, coming so unexpectedly, filled Candide with inexpressible delight, while the illness of his dear Cunégonde covered him with grief. Torn between these two feelings, he took gold and diamonds, and had himself brought, with Martin, to the hotel where Miss Cunégonde was lodging. Trembling with emotion, he enters the room; his heart thumps, his voice breaks. He tries to open the curtains of the bed, he asks to have some lights.

—Absolutely forbidden, says the serving girl; light will be the death of her.

And abruptly she pulls shut the curtain.

—My dear Cunégonde, says Candide in tears, how are you feeling? If you can't see me, won't you at least speak to me?

—She can't talk, says the servant.

But then she draws forth from the bed a plump hand, over which Candide weeps a long time, and which he fills with diamonds, meanwhile leaving a bag of gold on the chair.

Amid his transports, there arrives a bailiff followed by the abbé from Perigord and a strong-arm squad.

—These here are the suspicious foreigners? says the officer; and he has them seized and orders his bullies to drag them off to jail.

—They don't treat visitors like this in Eldorado, says Candide.

—I am more a Manichee than ever, says Martin.

—But, please sir, where are you taking us? says Candide.

—To the lowest hole in the dungeons, says the bailiff.

Martin, having regained his self-possession, decided that the lady who pretended to be Cunégonde was a cheat, the abbé from Perigord was another cheat who had imposed on Candide's innocence, and the bailiff still another cheat, of whom it would be easy to get rid.

Rather than submit to the forms of justice, Candide, enlightened by Martin's advice and eager for his own part to see the real Cunégonde again, offered the bailiff three little diamonds worth about three thousand pistoles apiece.

—Ah, my dear sir! cried the man with the ivory staff, even if you have committed every crime imaginable, you are the most honest man in the world. Three diamonds! each one worth three thousand pistoles! My dear sir! I would gladly die for you, rather than take you to jail. All foreigners get arrested here; but let me manage it; I have a brother at Dieppe in Normandy; I'll take you to him; and if you have a bit of a diamond to give him, he'll take care of you, just like me.

—And why do they arrest all foreigners? asked Candide.

The abbé from Perigord spoke up and said: —It's because a beggar from Atrebatum[9] listened to some stupidities; that made him commit a parricide, not like the one of May, 1610, but like the one of December, 1594, much on the order of several other crimes committed in other years and other months by other beggars who had listened to stupidities.

The bailiff then explained what it was all about.[1]

—Foh! what beasts! cried Candide. What! monstrous behavior of this sort from a people who sing and dance? As soon as I can, let me get out of this country, where the monkeys provoke the tigers. In my own country I've lived with bears; only in Eldorado are there proper men. In the name of God, sir bailiff, get me to Venice where I can wait for Miss Cunégonde.

—I can only get you to Lower Normandy, said the guardsman.

He had the irons removed at once, said there had been a mistake, dismissed his gang, and took Candide and Martin to Dieppe, where he left them with his brother. There was a little Dutch ship at anchor. The Norman, changed by three more diamonds into the most helpful of men, put Candide and his people aboard the vessel, which was bound for Portsmouth in England. It wasn't on the way to Venice, but Candide felt like a man just let out of hell; and he hoped to get back on the road to Venice at the first possible occasion.

CHAPTER 23

Candide and Martin Pass the Shores of England; What They See There

—Ah, Pangloss! Pangloss! Ah, Martin! Martin! Ah, my darling Cunégonde! What is this world of ours? sighed Candide on the Dutch vessel.

—Something crazy, something abominable, Martin replied.

—You have been in England; are people as crazy there as in France?

—It's a different sort of crazy, said Martin. You know that these two nations have been at war over a few acres of snow near Canada, and that they are spending on this fine struggle more than Canada itself is worth.[2] As for telling you if there are more people

9. The Latin name for the district of Artois, from which came Robert-François Damiens, who tried to stab Louis XV in 1757. The assassination failed, like that of Châtel, who tried to kill Henri Quatre in 1594, but unlike that of Ravaillac, who succeeded in killing him in 1610.

1. The point, in fact, is not too clear since arresting foreigners is an indirect way at best to guard against home-grown fanatics, and the position of the abbé from Perigord in the whole transaction remains confused. Has he called in the officer just to get rid of Candide? If so, why is he sardonic about the very suspicions he is trying to foster? Candide's reaction is to the notion that Frenchmen should be capable of political assassination at all; it seems excessive.

2. The wars of the French and English over Canada dragged intermittently through the eighteenth century till the

in one country or the other who need a strait jacket, that is a judgment too fine for my understanding; I know only that the people we are going to visit are eaten up with melancholy.

As they chatted thus, the vessel touched at Portsmouth. A multitude of people covered the shore, watching closely a rather bulky man who was kneeling, his eyes blindfolded, on the deck of a man-of-war. Four soldiers, stationed directly in front of this man, fired three bullets apiece into his brain, as peaceably as you would want; and the whole assemblage went home, in great satisfaction.[3]

—What's all this about? asked Candide. What devil is everywhere at work?

He asked who was that big man who had just been killed with so much ceremony.

—It was an admiral, they told him.

—And why kill this admiral?

—The reason, they told him, is that he didn't kill enough people; he gave battle to a French admiral, and it was found that he didn't get close enough to him.

—But, said Candide, the French admiral was just as far from the English admiral as the English admiral was from the French admiral.

—That's perfectly true, came the answer; but in this country it is useful from time to time to kill one admiral in order to encourage the others.

Candide was so stunned and shocked at what he saw and heard, that he would not even set foot ashore; he arranged with the Dutch merchant (without even caring if he was robbed, as at Surinam) to be taken forthwith to Venice.

The merchant was ready in two days; they coasted along France, they passed within sight of Lisbon, and Candide quivered. They entered the straits, crossed the Mediterranean, and finally landed at Venice.

—God be praised, said Candide, embracing Martin; here I shall recover the lovely Cunégonde. I trust Cacambo as I would myself. All is well, all goes well, all goes as well as possible.

CHAPTER 24

About Paquette and Brother Giroflée

As soon as he was in Venice, he had a search made for Cacambo in all the inns, all the cafés, all the stews—and found no trace of

peace of Paris sealed England's conquest (1763). Voltaire thought the French should concentrate on developing Louisiana where the Jesuit influence was less marked.
3. Candide has witnessed the execution

of Admiral John Byng, defeated off Minorca by the French fleet under Galisonnière and executed by firing squad on March 14, 1757. Voltaire had intervened to avert the execution.

him. Every day he sent to investigate the vessels and coastal traders; no news of Cacambo.

—How's this? said he to Martin. I have had time to go from Surinam to Bordeaux, from Bordeaux to Paris, from Paris to Dieppe, from Dieppe to Portsmouth, to skirt Portugal and Spain, cross the Mediterranean, and spend several months at Venice—and the lovely Cunégonde has not come yet! In her place, I have met only that impersonator and that abbé from Perigord. Cunégonde is dead, without a doubt; and nothing remains for me too but death. Oh, it would have been better to stay in the earthly paradise of Eldorado than to return to this accursed Europe. How right you are, my dear Martin; all is but illusion and disaster.

He fell into a black melancholy, and refused to attend the fashionable operas or take part in the other diversions of the carnival season; not a single lady tempted him in the slightest. Martin told him: —You're a real simpleton if you think a half-breed valet with five or six millions in his pockets will go to the end of the world to get your mistress and bring her to Venice for you. If he finds her, he'll take her for himself; if he doesn't, he'll take another. I advise you to forget about your servant Cacambo and your mistress Cunégonde.

Martin was not very comforting. Candide's melancholy increased, and Martin never wearied of showing him that there is little virtue and little happiness on this earth, except perhaps in Eldorado, where nobody can go.

While they were discussing this important matter and still waiting for Cunégonde, Candide noticed in St. Mark's Square a young Theatine [4] monk who had given his arm to a girl. The Theatine seemed fresh, plump, and flourishing; his eyes were bright, his manner cocky, his glance brilliant, his step proud. The girl was very pretty, and singing aloud; she glanced lovingly at her Theatine, and from time to time pinched his plump cheeks.

—At least you must admit, said Candide to Martin, that these people are happy. Until now I have not found in the whole inhabited earth, except Eldorado, anything but miserable people. But this girl and this monk, I'd be willing to bet, are very happy creatures.

—I'll bet they aren't, said Martin.

—We have only to ask them to dinner, said Candide, and we'll find out if I'm wrong.

Promptly he approached them, made his compliments, and invited them to his inn for a meal of macaroni, Lombardy partridges, and caviar, washed down with wine from Montepulciano, Cyprus,

---

4. A Catholic order founded in 1524 by Cardinal Cajetan and G. P. Caraffa, later Pope Paul IV.

and Samos, and some Lacrima Christi. The girl blushed but the Theatine accepted gladly, and the girl followed him, watching Candide with an expression of surprise and confusion, darkened by several tears. Scarcely had she entered the room when she said to Candide: —What, can it be that Master Candide no longer knows Paquette?

At these words Candide, who had not yet looked carefully at her because he was preoccupied with Cunégonde, said to her: —Ah, my poor child! so you are the one who put Doctor Pangloss in the fine fix where I last saw him.

—Alas, sir, I was the one, said Paquette; I see you know all about it. I heard of the horrible misfortunes which befell the whole household of My Lady the Baroness and the lovely Cunégonde. I swear to you that my own fate has been just as unhappy. I was perfectly innocent when you knew me. A Franciscan, who was my confessor, easily seduced me. The consequences were frightful; shortly after My Lord the Baron had driven you out with great kicks on the backside, I too was forced to leave the castle. If a famous doctor had not taken pity on me, I would have died. Out of gratitude, I became for some time the mistress of this doctor. His wife, who was jealous to the point of frenzy, beat me mercilessly every day; she was a gorgon. The doctor was the ugliest of men, and I the most miserable creature on earth, being continually beaten for a man I did not love. You will understand, sir, how dangerous it is for a nagging woman to be married to a doctor. This man, enraged by his wife's ways, one day gave her as a cold cure a medicine so potent that in two hours' time she died amid horrible convulsions. Her relatives brought suit against the bereaved husband; he fled the country, and I was put in prison. My innocence would never have saved me if I had not been rather pretty. The judge set me free on condition that he should become the doctor's successor. I was shortly replaced in this post by another girl, dismissed without any payment, and obliged to continue this abominable trade which you men find so pleasant and which for us is nothing but a bottomless pit of misery. I went to ply the trade in Venice. Ah, my dear sir, if you could imagine what it is like to have to caress indiscriminately an old merchant, a lawyer, a monk, a gondolier, an abbé; to be subjected to every sort of insult and outrage; to be reduced, time and again, to borrowing a skirt in order to go have it lifted by some disgusting man; to be robbed by this fellow of what one has gained from that; to be shaken down by the police, and to have before one only the prospect of a hideous old age, a hospital, and a dunghill, you will conclude that I am one of the most miserable creatures in the world.

Thus Paquette poured forth her heart to the good Candide in a hotel room, while Martin sat listening nearby. At last he said to Candide: —You see, I've already won half my bet.

Brother Giroflée[5] had remained in the dining room, and was having a drink before dinner.

—But how's this? said Candide to Paquette. You looked so happy, so joyous, when I met you; you were singing, you caressed the Theatine with such a natural air of delight; you seemed to me just as happy as you now say you are miserable.

—Ah, sir, replied Paquette, that's another one of the miseries of this business; yesterday I was robbed and beaten by an officer, and today I have to seem in good humor in order to please a monk.

Candide wanted no more; he conceded that Martin was right. They sat down to table with Paquette and the Theatine; the meal was amusing enough, and when it was over, the company spoke out among themselves with some frankness.

—Father, said Candide to the monk, you seem to me a man whom all the world might envy; the flower of health glows in your cheek, your features radiate pleasure; you have a pretty girl for your diversion, and you seem very happy with your life as a Theatine.

—Upon my word, sir, said Brother Giroflée, I wish that all the Theatines were at the bottom of the sea. A hundred times I have been tempted to set fire to my convent, and go turn Turk. My parents forced me, when I was fifteen years old, to put on this detestable robe, so they could leave more money to a cursed older brother of mine, may God confound him! Jealousy, faction, and fury spring up, by natural law, within the walls of convents. It is true, I have preached a few bad sermons which earned me a little money, half of which the prior stole from me; the remainder serves to keep me in girls. But when I have to go back to the monastery at night, I'm ready to smash my head against the walls of my cell; and all my fellow monks are in the same fix.

Martin turned to Candide and said with his customary coolness: —Well, haven't I won the whole bet?

Candide gave two thousand piastres to Paquette and a thousand to Brother Giroflée.

—I assure you, said he, that with that they will be happy.

—I don't believe so, said Martin; your piastres may make them even more unhappy than they were before.

—That may be, said Candide; but one thing comforts me, I note that people often turn up whom one never expected to see again; it may well be that, having rediscovered my red sheep and Paquette, I will also rediscover Cunégonde.

---

5. His name means "gillyflower," and Paquette means "daisy." They are lilies of the field who spin not, neither do they reap.

—I hope, said Martin, that she will some day make you happy; but I very much doubt it.

—You're a hard man, said Candide.

—I've lived, said Martin.

—But look at these gondoliers, said Candide; aren't they always singing?

—You don't see them at home, said Martin, with their wives and squalling children. The doge has his troubles, the gondoliers theirs. It's true that on the whole one is better off as a gondolier than as a doge; but the difference is so slight, I don't suppose it's worth the trouble of discussing.

—There's a lot of talk here, said Candide, of this Senator Pococurante,[6] who has a fine palace on the Brenta and is hospitable to foreigners. They say he is a man who has never known a moment's grief.

—I'd like to see such a rare specimen, said Martin.

Candide promptly sent to Lord Pococurante, asking permission to call on him tomorrow.

CHAPTER 25
Visit to Lord Pococurante, Venetian Nobleman

Candide and Martin took a gondola on the Brenta, and soon reached the palace of the noble Pococurante. The gardens were large and filled with beautiful marble statues; the palace was handsomely designed. The master of the house, sixty years old and very rich, received his two inquisitive visitors perfectly politely, but with very little warmth; Candide was disconcerted and Martin not at all displeased.

First two pretty and neatly dressed girls served chocolate, which they whipped to a froth. Candide could not forbear praising their beauty, their grace, their skill.

—They are pretty good creatures, said Pococurante; I sometimes have them into my bed, for I'm tired of the ladies of the town, with their stupid tricks, quarrels, jealousies, fits of ill humor and petty pride, and all the sonnets one has to make or order for them; but, after all, these two girls are starting to bore me too.

After lunch, Candide strolled through a long gallery, and was amazed at the beauty of the pictures. He asked who was the painter of the two finest.

—They are by Raphael, said the senator; I bought them for a lot of money, out of vanity, some years ago; people say they're the finest in Italy, but they don't please me at all; the colors have all turned brown, the figures aren't well modeled and don't stand out

6. His name means "small care."

enough, the draperies bear no resemblance to real cloth. In a word, whatever people may say, I don't find in them a real imitation of nature. I like a picture only when I can see in it a touch of nature itself, and there are none of this sort. I have many paintings, but I no longer look at them.

As they waited for dinner, Pococurante ordered a concerto performed. Candide found the music delightful.

—That noise? said Pococurante. It may amuse you for half an hour, but if it goes on any longer, it tires everybody though no one dares to admit it. Music today is only the art of performing difficult pieces, and what is merely difficult cannot please for long. Perhaps I should prefer the opera, if they had not found ways to make it revolting and monstrous. Anyone who likes bad tragedies set to music is welcome to them; in these performances the scenes serve only to introduce, inappropriately, two or three ridiculous songs designed to show off the actress's sound box. Anyone who wants to, or who can, is welcome to swoon with pleasure at the sight of a castrate wriggling through the role of Caesar or Cato, and strutting awkwardly about the stage. For my part, I have long since given up these paltry trifles which are called the glory of modern Italy, and for which monarchs pay such ruinous prices.

Candide argued a bit, but timidly; Martin was entirely of a mind with the senator.

They sat down to dinner, and after an excellent meal adjourned to the library. Candide, seeing a copy of Homer [7] in a splendid binding, complimented the noble lord on his good taste.

—That is an author, said he, who was the special delight of great Pangloss, the best philosopher in all Germany.

—He's no special delight of mine, said Pococurante coldly. I was once made to believe that I took pleasure in reading him; but that constant recital of fights which are all alike, those gods who are always interfering but never decisively, that Helen who is the cause of the war and then scarcely takes any part in the story, that Troy which is always under siege and never taken—all that bores me to tears. I have sometimes asked scholars if reading it bored them as much as it bores me; everyone who answered frankly told me the book dropped from his hands like lead, but that they had to have it in their libraries as a monument of antiquity, like those old rusty coins which can't be used in real trade.

—Your Excellence doesn't hold the same opinion of Virgil? said Candide.

7. Since the mid-sixteenth century, when Julius Caesar Scaliger established the dogma, it had been customary to prefer Virgil to Homer. Voltaire's youthful judgments, as delivered in the *Essai sur la poésie épique* (1728), are here summarized with minor revisions—upward for Ariosto, downward for Milton.

—I concede, said Pococurante, that the second, fourth, and sixth books of his *Aeneid* are fine; but as for his pious Aeneas, and strong Cloanthes, and faithful Achates, and little Ascanius, and that imbecile King Latinus, and middle-class Amata, and insipid Lavinia, I don't suppose there was ever anything so cold and unpleasant. I prefer Tasso and those sleepwalkers' stories of Ariosto.

—Dare I ask, sir, said Candide, if you don't get great enjoyment from reading Horace?

—There are some maxims there, said Pococurante, from which a man of the world can profit, and which, because they are formed into vigorous couplets, are more easily remembered; but I care very little for his trip to Brindisi, his description of a bad dinner, or his account of a quibblers' squabble between some fellow Pupilus, whose words he says *were full of pus*, and another whose words *were full of vinegar*.[8] I feel nothing but extreme disgust at his verses against old women and witches; and I can't see what's so great in his telling his friend Maecenas that if he is raised by him to the ranks of lyric poets, he will strike the stars with his lofty forehead. Fools admire everything in a well-known author. I read only for my own pleasure; I like only what is in my style.

Candide, who had been trained never to judge for himself, was much astonished by what he heard; and Martin found Pococurante's way of thinking quite rational.

—Oh, here is a copy of Cicero, said Candide. Now this great man I suppose you're never tired of reading.

—I never read him at all, replied the Venetian. What do I care whether he pleaded for Rabirius or Cluentius? As a judge, I have my hands full of lawsuits. I might like his philosophical works better, but when I saw that he had doubts about everything, I concluded that I knew as much as he did, and that I needed no help to be ignorant.

—Ah, here are eighty volumes of collected papers from a scientific academy, cried Martin; maybe there is something good in them.

—There would be indeed, said Pococurante, if one of these silly authors had merely discovered a new way of making pins; but in all those volumes there is nothing but empty systems, not a single useful discovery.

—What a lot of stage plays I see over there, said Candide, some in Italian, some in Spanish and French.

—Yes, said the senator, three thousand of them, and not three dozen good ones. As for those collections of sermons, which all to-

---

8. The reference is to Horace, *Satires* I. vii; Pococurante, with gentlemanly negligence, has corrupted Rupilius to Pupilus. Horace's poems against witches are *Epodes* V, VIII, XII; the one about striking the stars with his lofty forehead is *Odes* I.i.

gether are not worth a page of Seneca, and all these heavy volumes of theology, you may be sure I never open them, nor does anybody else.

Martin noticed some shelves full of English books.

—I suppose, said he, that a republican must delight in most of these books written in the land of liberty.

—Yes, replied Pococurante, it's a fine thing to write as you think; it is mankind's privilege. In all our Italy, people write only what they do not think; men who inhabit the land of the Caesars and Antonines dare not have an idea without the permission of a Dominican. I would rejoice in the freedom that breathes through English genius, if partisan passions did not corrupt all that is good in that precious freedom.

Candide, noting a Milton, asked if he did not consider this author a great man.

—Who? said Pococurante. That barbarian who made a long commentary on the first chapter of Genesis in ten books of crabbed verse? That clumsy imitator of the Greeks, who disfigures creation itself, and while Moses represents the eternal being as creating the world with a word, has the messiah take a big compass out of a heavenly cupboard in order to design his work? You expect me to admire the man who spoiled Tasso's hell and devil? who disguises Lucifer now as a toad, now as a pigmy? who makes him rehash the same arguments a hundred times over? who makes him argue theology? and who, taking seriously Ariosto's comic story of the invention of firearms, has the devils shooting off cannon in heaven? Neither I nor anyone else in Italy has been able to enjoy these gloomy extravagances. The marriage of Sin and Death, and the monster that Sin gives birth to, will nauseate any man whose taste is at all refined; and his long description of a hospital is good only for a gravedigger. This obscure, extravagant, and disgusting poem was despised at its birth; I treat it today as it was treated in its own country by its contemporaries. Anyhow, I say what I think, and care very little whether other people agree with me.

Candide was a little cast down by this speech; he respected Homer, and had a little affection for Milton.

—Alas, he said under his breath to Martin, I'm afraid this man will have a supreme contempt for our German poets.

—No harm in that, said Martin.

—Oh what a superior man, said Candide, still speaking softly, what a great genïus this Pococurante must be! Nothing can please him.

Having thus looked over all the books, they went down into the garden. Candide praised its many beauties.

—I know nothing in such bad taste, said the master of the house;

we have nothing but trifles here; tomorrow I am going to have one set out on a nobler design.

When the two visitors had taken leave of his excellency: —Well now, said Candide to Martin, you must agree that this was the happiest of all men, for he is superior to everything he possesses.

—Don't you see, said Martin, that he is disgusted with everything he possesses? Plato said, a long time ago, that the best stomachs are not those which refuse all food.

—But, said Candide, isn't there pleasure in criticizing everything, in seeing faults where other people think they see beauties?

—That is to say, Martin replied, that there's pleasure in having no pleasure?

—Oh well, said Candide, then I am the only happy man . . . or will be, when I see Miss Cunégonde again.

—It's always a good thing to have hope, said Martin.

But the days and the weeks slipped past; Cacambo did not come back, and Candide was so buried in his grief, that he did not even notice that Paquette and Brother Giroflée had neglected to come and thank him.

CHAPTER 26

About a Supper that Candide and Martin Had with Six Strangers, and Who They Were

One evening when Candide, accompanied by Martin, was about to sit down for dinner with the strangers staying in his hotel, a man with a soot-colored face came up behind him, took him by the arm, and said: —Be ready to leave with us, don't miss out.

He turned and saw Cacambo. Only the sight of Cunégonde could have astonished and pleased him more. He nearly went mad with joy. He embraced his dear friend.

—Cunégonde is here, no doubt? Where is she? Bring me to her, let me die of joy in her presence.

—Cunégonde is not here at all, said Cacambo, she is at Constantinople.

—Good Heavens, at Constantinople! but if she were in China, I must fly there, let's go.

—We will leave after supper, said Cacambo; I can tell you no more; I am a slave, my owner is looking for me, I must go wait on him at table; mum's the word; eat your supper and be prepared.

Candide, torn between joy and grief, delighted to have seen his faithful agent again, astonished to find him a slave, full of the idea of recovering his mistress, his heart in a turmoil, his mind in a whirl, sat down to eat with Martin, who was watching all these events coolly, and with six strangers who had come to pass the carnival season at Venice.

Cacambo, who was pouring wine for one of the strangers, leaned respectfully over his master at the end of the meal, and said to him: —Sire, Your Majesty may leave when he pleases, the vessel is ready.

Having said these words, he exited. The diners looked at one another in silent amazement, when another servant, approaching his master, said to him: —Sire, Your Majesty's litter is at Padua, and the bark awaits you.

The master nodded, and the servant vanished. All the diners looked at one another again, and the general amazement redoubled. A third servant, approaching a third stranger, said to him: —Sire, take my word for it, Your Majesty must stay here no longer; I shall get everything ready.

Then he too disappeared.

Candide and Martin had no doubt, now, that it was a carnival masquerade. A fourth servant spoke to a fourth master: —Your majesty will leave when he pleases—and went out like the others. A fifth followed suit. But the sixth servant spoke differently to the sixth stranger, who sat next to Candide. He said: —My word, sire, they'll give no more credit to Your Majesty, nor to me either; we could very well spend the night in the lockup, you and I. I've got to look out for myself, so good-bye to you.

When all the servants had left, the six strangers, Candide, and Martin remained under a pall of silence. Finally Candide broke it.

—Gentlemen, said he, here's a funny kind of joke. Why are you all royalty? I assure you that Martin and I aren't.

Cacambo's master spoke up gravely then, and said in Italian: —This is no joke, my name is Achmet the Third.[9] I was grand sultan for several years; then, as I had dethroned my brother, my nephew dethroned me. My viziers had their throats cut; I was allowed to end my days in the old seraglio. My nephew, the Grand Sultan Mahmoud, sometimes lets me travel for my health; and I have come to spend the carnival season at Venice.

A young man who sat next to Achmet spoke after him, and said: —My name is Ivan; I was once emperor of all the Russias.[1] I was dethroned while still in my cradle; my father and mother were locked up, and I was raised in prison; I sometimes have permission to travel, though always under guard, and I have come to spend the carnival season at Venice.

The third said: —I am Charles Edward, king of England[2]; my

9. His dates are 1673–1736; he was deposed in 1730.
1. Ivan VI reigned from his birth in 1740 till 1756, then was confined in the Schlusselberg, and executed in 1764.

2. This is the Young Pretender (1720–1788), known to his supporters as Bonnie Prince Charlie. The defeat so theatrically described took place at Culloden, April 16, 1746.

father yielded me his rights to the kingdom, and I fought to uphold them; but they tore out the hearts of eight hundred of my partisans, and flung them in their faces. I have been in prison; now I am going to Rome, to visit the king, my father, dethroned like me and my grandfather; and I have come to pass the carnival season at Venice.

The fourth king then spoke up, and said: —I am a king of the Poles[3]; the luck of war has deprived me of my hereditary estates; my father suffered the same losses; I submit to Providence like Sultan Achmet, Emperor Ivan, and King Charles Edward, to whom I hope heaven grants long lives; and I have come to pass the carnival season at Venice.

The fifth said: —I too am a king of the Poles[4]; I lost my kingdom twice, but Providence gave me another state, in which I have been able to do more good than all the Sarmatian kings ever managed to do on the banks of the Vistula. I too have submitted to Providence, and I have come to pass the carnival season at Venice.

It remained for the sixth monarch to speak.

—Gentlemen, said he, I am no such great lord as you, but I have in fact been a king like any other. I am Theodore; I was elected king of Corsica.[5] People used to call me *Your Majesty*, and now they barely call me *Sir*; I used to coin currency, and now I don't have a cent; I used to have two secretaries of state, and now I scarcely have a valet; I have sat on a throne, and for a long time in London I was in jail, on the straw; and I may well be treated the same way here, though I have come, like your majesties, to pass the carnival season at Venice.

The five other kings listened to his story with noble compassion. Each one of them gave twenty sequins to King Theodore, so that he might buy a suit and some shirts; Candide gave him a diamond worth two thousand sequins.

—Who in the world, said the five kings, is this private citizen who is in a position to give a hundred times as much as any of us, and who actually gives it?[6]

3. Augustus III (1696–1763), Elector of Saxony and King of Poland, dethroned by Frederick the Great in 1756.

4. Stanislas Leczinski (1677–1766), father-in-law of Louis XV, who abdicated the throne of Poland in 1736, was made Duke of Lorraine and in that capacity befriended Voltaire.

5. Theodore von Neuhof (1690–1756), an authentic Westphalian, an adventurer and a soldier of fortune, who in 1736 was (for about eight months) the elected king of Corsica. He spent time in an Amsterdam as well as a London debtor's prison.

6. A late correction of Voltaire's makes this passage read: —Who is this man who is in a position to give a hundred times as much as any of us, and who actually gives it? Are you a king too, sir?

—No, gentlemen, and I have no desire to be.

But this reading, though Voltaire's on good authority, produces a conflict with Candide's previous remark: —Why are you all royalty? I assure you that Martin and I aren't.

Thus, it has seemed better for literary reasons to follow an earlier reading. Voltaire was very conscious of his situation as a man richer than many princes; in 1758 he had money

Just as they were rising from dinner, there arrived at the same establishment four most serene highnesses, who had also lost their kingdoms through the luck of war, and who came to spend the rest of the carnival season at Venice. But Candide never bothered even to look at these newcomers because he was only concerned to go find his dear Cunégonde at Constantinople.

CHAPTER 27
Candide's Trip to Constantinople

Faithful Cacambo had already arranged with the Turkish captain who was returning Sultan Achmet to Constantinople to make room for Candide and Martin on board. Both men boarded ship after prostrating themselves before his miserable highness. On the way, Candide said to Martin: —Six dethroned kings that we had dinner with! and yet among those six there was one on whom I had to bestow charity! Perhaps there are other princes even more unfortunate. I myself have only lost a hundred sheep, and now I am flying to the arms of Cunégonde. My dear Martin, once again Pangloss is proved right, all is for the best.

—I hope so, said Martin.

—But, said Candide, that was a most unlikely experience we had at Venice. Nobody ever saw, or heard tell of, six dethroned kings eating together at an inn.

—It is no more extraordinary, said Martin, than most of the things that have happened to us. Kings are frequently dethroned; and as for the honor we had from dining with them, that's a trifle which doesn't deserve our notice.[7]

Scarcely was Candide on board than he fell on the neck of his former servant, his friend Cacambo.

—Well! said he, what is Cunégonde doing? Is she still a marvel of beauty? Does she still love me? How is her health? No doubt you have bought her a palace at Constantinople.

—My dear master, answered Cacambo, Cunégonde is washing dishes on the shores of the Propontis, in the house of a prince who has very few dishes to wash; she is a slave in the house of a onetime king named Ragotski,[8] to whom the Great Turk allows three crowns a day in his exile; but, what is worse than all this, she has lost all her beauty and become horribly ugly.

---

on loan to no fewer than three highnesses, Charles Eugene, Duke of Wurtemburg; Charles Theodore, Elector Palatine; and the Duke of Saxe-Gotha.
7. Another late change adds the following question: —What does it matter whom you dine with as long as you fare well at table?
I have omitted it, again on literary grounds (the observation is too heavy and commonplace), despite its superior claim to a position in the text.
8. Francis Leopold Rakoczy (1676–1735) who was briefly king of Transylvania in the early eighteenth century. After 1720 he was interned in Turkey.

—Ah, beautiful or ugly, said Candide, I am an honest man, and my duty is to love her forever. But how can she be reduced to this wretched state with the five or six millions that you had?

—All right, said Cacambo, didn't I have to give two millions to Señor don Fernando d'Ibaraa y Figueroa y Mascarenes y Lampourdos y Souza, governor of Buenos Aires, for his permission to carry off Miss Cunégonde? And didn't a pirate cleverly strip us of the rest? And didn't this pirate carry us off to Cape Matapan, to Melos, Nicaria, Samos, Petra, to the Dardanelles, Marmora, Scutari? Cunégonde and the old woman are working for the prince I told you about, and I am the slave of the dethroned sultan.

—What a lot of fearful calamities linked one to the other, said Candide. But after all, I still have a few diamonds, I shall easily deliver Cunégonde. What a pity that she's become so ugly!

Then, turning toward Martin, he asked: —Who in your opinion is more to be pitied, the Emperor Achmet, the Emperor Ivan, King Charles Edward, or myself?

—I have no idea, said Martin; I would have to enter your hearts in order to tell.

—Ah, said Candide, if Pangloss were here, he would know and he would tell us.

—I can't imagine, said Martin, what scales your Pangloss would use to weigh out the miseries of men and value their griefs. All I will venture is that the earth holds millions of men who deserve our pity a hundred times more than King Charles Edward, Emperor Ivan, or Sultan Achmet.

—You may well be right, said Candide.

In a few days they arrived at the Black Sea canal. Candide began by repurchasing Cacambo at an exorbitant price; then, without losing an instant, he flung himself and his companions into a galley to go search out Cunégonde on the shores of Propontis, however ugly she might be.

There were in the chain gang two convicts who bent clumsily to the oar, and on whose bare shoulders the Levantine[9] captain delivered from time to time a few lashes with a bullwhip. Candide naturally noticed them more than the other galley slaves, and out of pity came closer to them. Certain features of their disfigured faces seemed to him to bear a slight resemblance to Pangloss and to that wretched Jesuit, that baron, that brother of Miss Cunégonde. The notion stirred and saddened him. He looked at them more closely.

—To tell you the truth, he said to Cacambo, if I hadn't seen Master Pangloss hanged, and if I hadn't been so miserable as to murder the baron, I should think they were rowing in this very galley.

9. From the eastern Mediterranean.

At the names of 'baron' and 'Pangloss' the two convicts gave a great cry, sat still on their bench, and dropped their oars. The Levantine captain came running, and the bullwhip lashes redoubled.

—Stop, stop, captain, cried Candide. I'll give you as much money as you want.

—What, can it be Candide? cried one of the convicts.

—What, can it be Candide? cried the other.

—Is this a dream? said Candide. Am I awake or asleep? Am I in this galley? Is that My Lord the Baron, whom I killed? Is that Master Pangloss, whom I saw hanged?

—It is indeed, they replied.

—What, is that the great philosopher? said Martin.

—Now, sir, Mr. Levantine Captain, said Candide, how much money do you want for the ransom of My Lord Thunder-Ten-Tronckh, one of the first barons of the empire, and Master Pangloss, the deepest metaphysician in all Germany?

—Dog of a Christian, replied the Levantine captain, since these two dogs of Christian convicts are barons and metaphysicians, which is no doubt a great honor in their country, you will give me fifty thousand sequins for them.

—You shall have them, sir, take me back to Constantinople and you shall be paid on the spot. Or no, take me to Miss Cunégonde.

The Levantine captain, at Candide's first word, had turned his bow toward the town, and he had them rowed there as swiftly as a bird cleaves the air.

A hundred times Candide embraced the baron and Pangloss.

—And how does it happen I didn't kill you, my dear baron? and my dear Pangloss, how can you be alive after being hanged? and why are you both rowing in the galleys of Turkey?

—Is it really true that my dear sister is in this country? asked the baron.

—Yes, answered Cacambo.

—And do I really see again my dear Candide? cried Pangloss.

Candide introduced Martin and Cacambo. They all embraced; they all talked at once. The galley flew, already they were back in port. A jew was called, and Candide sold him for fifty thousand sequins a diamond worth a hundred thousand, while he protested by Abraham that he could not possibly give more for it. Candide immediately ransomed the baron and Pangloss. The latter threw himself at the feet of his liberator, and bathed them with tears; the former thanked him with a nod, and promised to repay this bit of money at the first opportunity.

—But is it really possible that my sister is in Turkey? said he.

—Nothing is more possible, replied Cacambo, since she is a dish-washer in the house of a prince of Transylvania.

At once two more jews were called; Candide sold some more diamonds; and they all departed in another galley to the rescue of Cunégonde.

CHAPTER 28
What Happened to Candide, Cunégonde, Pangloss, Martin, &c.

—Let me beg your pardon once more, said Candide to the baron, pardon me, reverend father, for having run you through the body with my sword.

—Don't mention it, replied the baron. I was a little too hasty myself, I confess it; but since you want to know the misfortune which brought me to the galleys, I'll tell you. After being cured of my wound by the brother who was apothecary to the college, I was attacked and abducted by a Spanish raiding party; they jailed me in Buenos Aires at the time when my sister had just left. I asked to be sent to Rome, to the father general. Instead, I was named to serve as almoner in Constantinople, under the French ambassador. I had not been a week on this job when I chanced one evening on a very handsome young ichoglan.[1] The evening was hot; the young man wanted to take a swim; I seized the occasion, and went with him. I did not know that it is a capital offense for a Christian to be found naked with a young Moslem. A cadi sentenced me to receive a hundred blows with a cane on the soles of my feet, and then to be sent to the galleys. I don't suppose there was ever such a horrible miscarriage of justice. But I would like to know why my sister is in the kitchen of a Transylvanian king exiled among Turks.

—But how about you, my dear Pangloss, said Candide; how is it possible that we have met again?

—It is true, said Pangloss, that you saw me hanged; in the normal course of things, I should have been burned, but you recall that a cloudburst occurred just as they were about to roast me. So much rain fell that they despaired of lighting the fire; thus I was hanged, for lack of anything better to do with me. A surgeon bought my body, carried me off to his house, and dissected me. First he made a cross-shaped incision in me, from the navel to the clavicle. No one could have been worse hanged than I was. In fact, the executioner of the high ceremonials of the Holy Inquisition, who was a subdeacon, burned people marvelously well, but he was not in the way of hanging them. The rope was wet, and tightened badly; it caught on a knot; in short, I was still breathing. The cross-

1. A page to the sultan.

shaped incision made me scream so loudly that the surgeon fell over backwards; he thought he was dissecting the devil, fled in an agony of fear, and fell downstairs in his flight. His wife ran in, at the noise, from a nearby room; she found me stretched out on the table with my cross-shaped incision, was even more frightened than her husband, fled, and fell over him. When they had recovered a little, I heard her say to him: 'My dear, what were you thinking of, trying to dissect a heretic? Don't you know those people are always possessed of the devil? I'm going to get the priest and have him exorcised.' At these words, I shuddered, and collected my last remaining energies to cry: 'Have mercy on me!' At last the Portuguese barber[2] took courage; he sewed me up again; his wife even nursed me; in two weeks I was up and about. The barber found me a job and made me lackey to a Knight of Malta who was going to Venice; and when this master could no longer pay me, I took service under a Venetian merchant, whom I followed to Constantinople.

—One day it occurred to me to enter a mosque; no one was there but an old imam and a very attractive young worshipper who was saying her prayers. Her bosom was completely bare; and between her two breasts she had a lovely bouquet of tulips, roses, anemones, buttercups, hyacinths, and primroses. She dropped her bouquet, I picked it up, and returned it to her with the most respectful attentions. I was so long getting it back in place that the imam grew angry, and, seeing that I was a Christian, he called the guard. They took me before the cadi, who sentenced me to receive a hundred blows with a cane on the soles of my feet, and then to be sent to the galleys. I was chained to the same galley and precisely the same bench as My Lord the Baron. There were in this galley four young fellows from Marseilles, five Neapolitan priests, and two Corfu monks, who assured us that these things happen every day. My Lord the Baron asserted that he had suffered a greater injustice than I; I, on the other hand, proposed that it was much more permissible to replace a bouquet in a bosom than to be found naked with an ichoglan. We were arguing the point continually, and getting twenty lashes a day with the bullwhip, when the chain of events within this universe brought you to our galley, and you ransomed us.

—Well, my dear Pangloss, Candide said to him, now that you have been hanged, dissected, beaten to a pulp, and sentenced to the galleys, do you still think everything is for the best in this world?

—I am still of my first opinion, replied Pangloss; for after all I am a philosopher, and it would not be right for me to recant since Leibniz could not possibly be wrong, and besides pre-established harmony is the finest notion in the world, like the plenum and subtle matter.[3]

2. The two callings of barber and surgeon, since they both involved sharp instruments, were interchangeable in the early days of medicine.

CHAPTER 29

How Candide Found Cunégonde and the Old Woman Again

While Candide, the baron, Pangloss, Martin, and Cacambo were telling one another their stories, while they were disputing over the contingent or non-contingent events of this universe, while they were arguing over effects and causes, over moral evil and physical evil, over liberty and necessity, and over the consolations available to one in a Turkish galley, they arrived at the shores of Propontis and the house of the prince of Transylvania. The first sight to meet their eyes was Cunégonde and the old woman, who were hanging out towels on lines to dry.

The baron paled at what he saw. The tender lover Candide, seeing his lovely Cunégonde with her skin weathered, her eyes bloodshot, her breasts fallen, her cheeks seamed, her arms red and scaly, recoiled three steps in horror, and then advanced only out of politeness. She embraced Candide and her brother; everyone embraced the old woman; Candide ransomed them both.

There was a little farm in the neighborhood; the old woman suggested that Candide occupy it until some better fate should befall the group. Cunégonde did not know she was ugly, no one had told her; she reminded Candide of his promises in so firm a tone that the good Candide did not dare to refuse her. So he went to tell the baron that he was going to marry his sister.

—Never will I endure, said the baron, such baseness on her part, such insolence on yours; this shame at least I will not put up with; why, my sister's children would not be able to enter the Chapters in Germany.[4] No, my sister will never marry anyone but a baron of the empire.

Cunégonde threw herself at his feet, and bathed them with her tears; he was inflexible.

—You absolute idiot, Candide told him, I rescued you from the galleys, I paid your ransom, I paid your sister's; she was washing dishes, she is ugly, I am good enough to make her my wife, and you still presume to oppose it! If I followed my impulses, I would kill you all over again.

—You may kill me again, said the baron, but you will not marry my sister while I am alive.

3. Rigorous determinism requires that there be no empty spaces in the universe, so wherever it seems empty, one posits the existence of the "plenum." "Subtle matter" describes the soul, the mind, and all spiritual agencies—which can, therefore, be supposed subject to the influence and control of the great world machine, which is, of course, visibly material. Both are concepts needed to round out the system of optimistic determinism.
4. Knightly assemblies.

CHAPTER 30
Conclusion

At heart, Candide had no real wish to marry Cunégonde; but the baron's extreme impertinence decided him in favor of the marriage, and Cunégonde was so eager for it that he could not back out. He consulted Pangloss, Martin, and the faithful Cacambo. Pangloss drew up a fine treatise, in which he proved that the baron had no right over his sister and that she could, according to all the laws of the empire, marry Candide morganatically.[5] Martin said they should throw the baron into the sea. Cacambo thought they should send him back to the Levantine captain to finish his time in the galleys, and then send him to the father general in Rome by the first vessel. This seemed the best idea; the old woman approved, and nothing was said to his sister; the plan was executed, at modest expense, and they had the double pleasure of snaring a Jesuit and punishing the pride of a German baron.

It is quite natural to suppose that after so many misfortunes, Candide, married to his mistress, and living with the philosopher Pangloss, the philosopher Martin, the prudent Cacambo, and the old woman—having, besides, brought back so many diamonds from the land of the ancient Incas—must have led the most agreeable life in the world. But he was so cheated by the jews[6] that nothing was left but his little farm; his wife, growing every day more ugly, became sour-tempered and insupportable; the old woman was ailing and even more ill-humored than Cunégonde. Cacambo, who worked in the garden and went into Constantinople to sell vegetables, was worn out with toil, and cursed his fate. Pangloss was in despair at being unable to shine in some German university. As for Martin, he was firmly persuaded that things are just as bad wherever you are; he endured in patience. Candide, Martin, and Pangloss sometimes argued over metaphysics and morals. Before the windows of the farmhouse they often watched the passage of boats bearing effendis, pashas, and cadis into exile on Lemnos, Mytilene, and Erzeroum; they saw other cadis, other pashas, other effendis coming, to take the place of the exiles and to be exiled in their turn. They saw various heads, neatly impaled, to be set up at the Sublime Porte.[7] These sights gave fresh impetus to their discussions; and

5. A morganatic marriage confers no rights on the partner of lower rank or on the offspring. Pangloss always uses more language than anyone else to achieve fewer results.
6. Voltaire's anti-Semitism, derived from various unhappy experiences with Jewish financiers, is not the most at-

tractive aspect of his personality.
7. The gate of the sultan's palace is often used by extension to describe his government as a whole. But it was in fact a real gate where the heads of traitors and public enemies were gruesomely exposed.

when they were not arguing, the boredom was so fierce that one day the old woman ventured to say: —I should like to know which is worse, being raped a hundred times by negro pirates, having a buttock cut off, running the gauntlet in the Bulgar army, being flogged and hanged in an auto-da-fé, being dissected and rowing in the galleys—experiencing, in a word, all the miseries through which we have passed—or else just sitting here and doing nothing?

—It's a hard question, said Candide.

These words gave rise to new reflections, and Martin in particular concluded that man was bound to live either in convulsions of misery or in the lethargy of boredom. Candide did not agree, but expressed no positive opinion. Pangloss asserted that he had always suffered horribly; but having once declared that everything was marvelously well, he continued to repeat the opinion and didn't believe a word of it.

One thing served to confirm Martin in his detestable opinions, to make Candide hesitate more than ever, and to embarrass Pangloss. It was the arrival one day at their farm of Paquette and Brother Giroflée, who were in the last stages of misery. They had quickly run through their three thousand piastres, had split up, made up, quarreled, been jailed, escaped, and finally Brother Giroflée had turned Turk. Paquette continued to ply her trade everywhere, and no longer made any money at it.

—I told you, said Martin to Candide, that your gifts would soon be squandered and would only render them more unhappy. You have spent millions of piastres, you and Cacambo, and you are no more happy than Brother Giroflée and Paquette.

—Ah ha, said Pangloss to Paquette, so destiny has brought you back in our midst, my poor girl! Do you realize you cost me the end of my nose, one eye, and an ear? And look at you now! eh! what a world it is, after all!

This new adventure caused them to philosophize more than ever.

There was in the neighborhood a very famous dervish, who was said to be the best philosopher in Turkey; they went to ask his advice. Pangloss was spokesman, and he said: —Master, we have come to ask you to tell us why such a strange animal as man was created.

—What are you getting into? answered the dervish. Is it any of your business?

—But, reverend father, said Candide, there's a horrible lot of evil on the face of the earth.

—What does it matter, said the dervish, whether there's good or evil? When his highness sends a ship to Egypt, does he worry whether the mice on board are comfortable or not?

—What shall we do then? asked Pangloss.

—Hold your tongue, said the dervish.

—I had hoped, said Pangloss, to reason a while with you concerning effects and causes, the best of possible worlds, the origin of evil, the nature of the soul, and pre-established harmony.

At these words, the dervish slammed the door in their faces.

During this interview, word was spreading that at Constantinople they had just strangled two viziers of the divan,[8] as well as the mufti, and impaled several of their friends. This catastrophe made a great and general sensation for several hours. Pangloss, Candide, and Martin, as they returned to their little farm, passed a good old man who was enjoying the cool of the day at his doorstep under a grove of orange trees. Pangloss, who was as inquisitive as he was explanatory, asked the name of the mufti who had been strangled.

—I know nothing of it, said the good man, and I have never cared to know the name of a single mufti or vizier. I am completely ignorant of the episode you are discussing. I presume that in general those who meddle in public business sometimes perish miserably, and that they deserve their fate; but I never listen to the news from Constantinople; I am satisfied with sending the fruits of my garden to be sold there.

Having spoken these words, he asked the strangers into his house; his two daughters and two sons offered them various sherbets which they had made themselves, Turkish cream flavored with candied citron, orange, lemon, lime, pineapple, pistachio, and mocha coffee uncontaminated by the inferior coffee of Batavia and the East Indies. After which the two daughters of this good Moslem perfumed the beards of Candide, Pangloss, and Martin.

—You must possess, Candide said to the Turk, an enormous and splendid property?

I have only twenty acres, replied the Turk; I cultivate them with my children, and the work keeps us from three great evils, boredom, vice, and poverty.

Candide, as he walked back to his farm, meditated deeply over the words of the Turk. He said to Pangloss and Martin: —This good old man seems to have found himself a fate preferable to that of the six kings with whom we had the honor of dining.

—Great place, said Pangloss, is very perilous in the judgment of all the philosophers; for, after all, Eglon, king of the Moabites, was murdered by Ehud; Absalom was hung up by the hair and pierced with three darts; King Nadab, son of Jeroboam, was killed by Baasha; King Elah by Zimri; Ahaziah by Jehu; Athaliah by Jehoiada; and Kings Jehoiakim, Jeconiah, and Zedekiah were enslaved. You know how death came to Croesus, Astyages, Darius, Dionysius of Syracuse, Pyrrhus, Perseus, Hannibal, Jugurtha, Ariovistus, Caesar, Pompey, Nero, Otho, Vitellius, Domitian, Rich-

8. Intimate advisers of the sultan.

ard II of England, Edward II, Henry VI, Richard III, Mary Stuart, Charles I, the three Henrys of France, and the Emperor Henry IV? You know . . .

—I know also, said Candide, that we must cultivate our garden.

—You are perfectly right, said Pangloss; for when man was put into the garden of Eden, he was put there *ut operaretur eum,* so that he should work it; this proves that man was not born to take his ease.

—Let's work without speculating, said Martin; it's the only way of rendering life bearable.

The whole little group entered into this laudable scheme; each one began to exercise his talents. The little plot yielded fine crops. Cunégonde was, to tell the truth, remarkably ugly; but she became an excellent pastry cook. Paquette took up embroidery; the old woman did the laundry. Everyone, down even to Brother Giroflée, did something useful; he became a very adequate carpenter, and even an honest man; and Pangloss sometimes used to say to Candide: —All events are linked together in the best of possible worlds; for, after all, if you had not been driven from a fine castle by being kicked in the backside for love of Miss Cunégonde, if you hadn't been sent before the Inquisition, if you hadn't traveled across America on foot, if you hadn't given a good sword thrust to the baron, if you hadn't lost all your sheep from the good land of Eldorado, you wouldn't be sitting here eating candied citron and pistachios.

—That is very well put, said Candide, but we must cultivate our garden.

DENIS DIDEROT
(1713–1784)
Rameau's Nephew (Le Neveu de Rameau)*

Vertumnis, quotquot sunt, natus iniquis.—HORACE[1]

Rain or shine, it is my regular habit every day about five to go and take a walk around the Palais-Royal.[2] I can be seen, all by myself, dreaming on D'Argenson's bench.[3] I discuss with myself questions of politics, love, taste, or philosophy. I let my mind rove wantonly, give it free rein to follow any idea, wise or mad, that may come uppermost; I chase it as do our young libertines along Foy's Walk,[4] when they are on the track of a courtesan whose mien is giddy and face smiling, whose nose turns up. The youth drops one and picks up another, pursuing all and clinging to none: my ideas are my trollops.

If the weather is too cold or rainy, I take shelter in the Regency Café,[5] where I entertain myself by watching chess being played. Paris is the world center, and this café is the Paris center, for the finest skill at this game. It is there that one sees the clash of the profound Legal, the subtle Philidor, the staunch Mayot;[6] that one sees the most surprising strokes and that one hears the stupidest remarks. For although one may be a wit and a great chess player, like Legal, one may also be a great chess player and a fool, like Foubert[7] and Mayot.

One day I was there after dinner, looking hard, saying little, and listening the least amount possible, when I was accosted by one of the oddest characters in this country, where God has not stinted us. The fellow[8] is a compound of elevation and abjectness, of good

* From *Romeau's Nephew and Other Works* by Denis Diderot, translated by Jacques Barzun & Ralph Bowen. Uupublished during his life, Diderot's work has a strange history. After his death in 1784, Catherine the Great bought his books and some of his manuscripts, including *Rameau's Nephew*. A second manuscript copy somehow reached Germany around 1800; Schiller read it, and Goethe translated it in 1805. This and other versions reached nineteenth-century readers, but imperfectly; and 1950 saw the first complete critical edition. Diderot probably wrote the dialogue during the 1760's and early 1770's. The editor has abridged the present version.

1. *Vertumnis . . . iniquis:* "Born beneath all the changeful stars there are."
2. *Palais-Royal:* palace north of the Louvre.
3. *D'Argenson's bench:* René-Louis, Marquis D'Argenson (1694–1757), one-time Minister of Foreign Affairs who devoted his old age to philosophy.

His "bench" was a favorite spot for Diderot.
4. *Foy's Walk:* This, and Argenson's Walk, marked the east-west boundaries of the gardens surrounding the *Palais*. *Foy's Café* was in the Palais-Royal, *galérie Montpensier*, and existed until 1863. Foy's Walk was noted for its attractive perambulating courtesans.
5. *Regency Café:* on the square of the *Palais-Royal*.
6. *Legal . . . Philidor . . . Mayot:* friends of Diderot, the first two noted chess-players.
7. *Foubert:* a surgeon.
8. *fellow:* Jean-Philipe Rameau (1683–1764), leading French composer and musical theorist, had a nephew, Jean-François Rameau: baptized 1716, married 1757, mentioned in police archives (1748) as having "a scarcely sociable character . . . insulted the directors of the Opera." Since he was a beggar, his death was unrecorded.

sense and lunacy. The ideas of decency and depravity must be strangely scrambled in his head, for he shows without ostentation the good qualities that nature has bestowed upon him, just as he does the bad ones without shame. Apart from this, he is endowed with a strong constitution, a special warmth of imagination, and an unusual power of lung. If you ever meet him and are not put off by his originality, you will either stuff your fingers into your ears or run away. Lord, what lungs!

He has no greater opposite than himself. Sometimes he is thin and wan like a patient in the last stages of consumption; you could count his teeth through his skin; he looks as if he had been days without food or had just come out of a Trappist monastery.[9] The next month, he is sleek and fat as if he ate regularly at a banker's or had shut himself up in a Bernardine convent.[10] Today his linen is filthy, his clothes torn to rags, he is virtually barefoot, and he hangs his head furtively; one is tempted to hail him and toss him a coin. Tomorrow he is powdered, curled, well dressed; he holds his head high, shows himself off—you would almost take him for a man of quality. He lives from day to day, sad or cheerful according to luck. His first care on arising in the morning is to ascertain where he will dine; after dinner he ponders supper. Night brings its own worries—whether to return on foot to the garret where he sleeps (unless the landlady has taken back the key from impatience at receiving no rent); or whether to repair to a suburban tavern and await the dawn over a crust of bread and a mug of beer. When he hasn't as much as sixpence in his pocket, as sometimes happens, he falls back on a cab-driving friend of his, or the coachman of a noble lord, who gives him a shakedown in a stable, alongside the horses. The next morning he still has bits of his mattress in his hair. If the weather is mild, he perambulates all night up and down the Cours-la-reine[11] or the Champs-Elysées.[12] Daybreak sees him back in town, all dressed from yesterday for today and from today perhaps for the remainder of the week.

I have no great esteem for such eccentrics. Some people take them on as regular acquaintances or even friends. But for my part it is only once a year that I stop and fall in with them, largely because their character stands out from the rest and breaks that tedious uniformity which our education, our social conventions, and our customary good manners have brought about. If such a character makes his appearance in some circle, he is like a grain of yeast that ferments and restores to each of us a part of his native individuality.

---

9. *Trappist monastery:* order of monks famed for their austerity.

10. *Bernardine convent:* Cistercian monks, reformed by St. Bernard of Clairvaux. In eighteenth-century France, their order was associated with good living.

11. *Cours-la-reine:* a popular eighteenth-century promenade along the Seine.

12. *Champs-Elysées:* By 1770, this now-famous boulevard was just starting to become popular.

He shakes and stirs us up, makes us praise or blame, smokes out the truth, discloses the worthy and unmasks the rascals. It is then that the sensible man keeps his ears open and sorts out his company.

I knew my man from quite a while back. He used to frequent a house to which his talent had given him entrée. There was an only daughter; he swore to the father and mother that he would marry her. They shrugged it off, laughed in his face, told him he was crazy. But I lived to see it happen. He asked me for a little money, which I gave him. He had somehow made his way into a few good families, where he could always dine provided he would not speak without asking permission first. He kept quiet and ate with fury. He was remarkable to see under that restraint. If he had the inclination to break the treaty and open his mouth, at the first word all the guests would shout "Why Rameau!" Then rage would blaze in his eyes and he fell to eating with greater fury still. You wanted to know his name and now you know it. He is the nephew of the famous musician who delivered us from the plainsong of Lully[13] that we had intoned for over a century, and who wrote so much visionary gibberish and apocalyptic truth about the theory of music —writings that neither he nor anyone else ever understood. We have from him a number of operas in which one finds harmony, snatches of song, disconnected ideas, clatter, flights, triumphal processions, spears, apotheoses, murmurings, endless victories, and dance tunes that will last for all time. Having eliminated "the Florentine"[14] in public favor, he will be eliminated by the Italian virtuosos—as he himself foresaw with grief, rancor, and depression of spirits. For no one, not even a pretty woman who wakes up to find a pimple on her nose, feels so vexed as an author who threatens to survive his own reputation—witness Marivaux[15] and the younger Crébillon.[16]

He accosts me: Ha ha! So there you are, master Philosopher! And what are you up to among all these idlers? Do you waste your time, too, pushing wood? (That is the contemptuous way of describing chess and checkers.)

MYSELF. No, but when I have nothing better to do, I enjoy watching those who push well.

HE. In that case you don't enjoy yourself very often. Apart from Legal and Philidor, the others don't know what they're doing.

13. *Lully:* Jean-Baptiste Lully (1632–1687), appointed chamber composer and conductor to Louis XIV in 1653. Lully wrote ballet scores for many of Molière's plays, including *The Bourgeois Gentleman*; he is best known for his operas and instrumental and keyboard suites.

14. *"the Florentine":* i.e., Lully, born in Italy.

15. *Marivaux:* Pierre de Marivaux (1688–1763), dramatist whose comedies are famous for their light wit and badinage.

16. *Crébillon:* Prosper Crébillon (1674–1762), dramatist—although "the younger" suggests his son Claude (1707–77), author of suggestive tales.

MYSELF. What of M. de Bissy?[17]

HE. Oh that one is to chess what Mlle. Clairon[18] is to acting: they know about their respective playing all that can be *learned*.

MYSELF. I see you're hard to please. You forgive nothing but sublime genius.

HE. True: in chess, checkers, poetry, eloquence, music and other nonsense of that kind, what's the use of mediocrity?

MYSELF. Not much use, I admit. But it takes a crowd to cultivate the game before one man of genius emerges. He is one out of many. But let it go. It's an age since I've seen you. I don't think about you very much when I don't see you but I'm always glad when I do. What have you been doing?

HE. What you and I and the rest do, namely, good and evil, and also nothing. And then I was hungry and I ate when I had the chance. After eating I was thirsty and I have occasionally drunk. Meanwhile my beard grew and when grown I had it shaved.

MYSELF. There you did wrong. A beard is all you lack to be a sage.

HE. Right you are. My forehead is broad and wrinkled; I have a glowing eye, a beaky nose, spacious cheeks, thick black brows, a clean-cut mouth, curved-out lips and a square jaw. Cover this ample chin with a flowing beard and I assure you it would look splendid in bronze or marble.

MYSELF. Side by side with Caesar, Marcus Aurelius, and Socrates.

HE. No. I should like it better between Diogenes[19] and Phryne.[20] I am as cheeky as the one and often visit the sisters of the other.

MYSELF. And you are still in good health?

HE. Usually, yes, but not so well today.

MYSELF. How is that? You have a paunch like Silenus[21] and a face like——

HE. A face like its counterpart. That's because the spleen which is wasting my dear uncle seems to fatten his dear nephew.

MYSELF. Speaking of the uncle, do you ever see him?

HE. I see him pass in the street.

MYSELF. Doesn't he do anything for you?

HE. If he ever has done anything for anybody, it must be without knowing it. He is a philosopher after a fashion: he thinks of no one but himself; the rest of the universe doesn't matter a tinker's dam to him. His wife, his daughter, may die as soon as they please. Provided the parish bells that toll for them continue to sound the intervals of the twelfth and the seventeenth, all will be well. It's lucky for him and that's what I envy especially in men of genius.

---

17. *Bissy:* Claude Henri de Bissy (1721–1810), playwright, member of the French Academy; admired by Diderot.

18. *Mlle. Clairon:* an actress who, like Bissy, was noted for her restraint and control.

19. *Diogenes:* blunt-spoken Cynic philosopher of Athens (ca. 412–323 B.C.).

20. *Phryne:* Athenian courtesan.

21. *Silenus:* fat god of wine and fertility.

They are good for only one thing—apart from that, zero. They don't know what it is to be citizens, fathers, mothers, cousins, friends. Between you and me, one should try to be like them in every way, but without multiplying the breed. The world needs men, but men of genius, no; I say, no! No need of them. They are the ones who change the face of the earth. Even in small things stupidity is so common and powerful that it is not changed without fracas. What results is partly the reformer's vision, partly the old status quo —whence two gospels, a parti-colored world. The wisdom of the monk Rabelais[22] is the true wisdom for his own peace of mind and other people's too: to do one's duty, more or less, always speak well of the father superior, and let the world wag. It must be all right since the majority is content with it. If I knew history, I could prove to you that evil has always come here below through a few men of genius; but I don't know any history because I don't know anything at all. The devil take me if I've ever learnt a single thing and if, having learnt nothing, I am worse off. One day I was at table with one of the King's Ministers who has brains enough for ten. Well, he showed us as plain as two and two make four that nothing is more useful to the nations of the earth than lies, nothing more harmful than the truth. I don't quite recall his proof but it followed very clearly that men of genius are poisonous and that if at birth a child bore the mark of this dangerous gift of nature, he should be either smothered or thrown to the dogs.

MYSELF. And yet those people who are so down on genius all pretend to have some.

HE. I'm sure they think so inside, but they don't dare admit it.

MYSELF. From modesty! So you developed from then on an undying hatred of genius?

HE. Which I'll never get over.

MYSELF. But I remember the time when you were in despair at the thought of being a common man. You'll never be happy if the pros and cons weigh with you equally. You should make up your mind and stick to it. I agree with you that men of genius are usually odd, or—as the saying goes, "great wits are sure to madness near allied";[23] but that doesn't change the truth that ages without genius are despised. Men will continue to honor the nations where genius thrived. Sooner or later they put up statues to them and call them benefactors of the race. With all due respect to the sublime minister you were quoting. I believe that although a lie may serve for a while, it is harmful in the long run; and, contrariwise, truth necessarily is best in the long run, even though it may do harm at the

22. *Rabelais:* François Rabelais (ca. (1490–1553), author of *Gargantua and Pantagruel*. The sentiments are those of Friar John, who accompanies first the father, then the son, in their exploits.
23. "*great wits . . . allied*": Cf. Dryden, *Absalom and Achitophel*, line 163.

moment. From which I incline to think that the man of genius who denounces a common error or who establishes a general truth always deserves our veneration. Such a man may fall a victim to prejudice or existing law; but there are two kinds of laws—those based on equity, which are universally true, and those based on whim, which owe their force only to blindness or local necessity. These last cast odium on their violator for only a brief moment, an odium which time casts back upon the judges and the peoples who carried out the law. Which of the two, Socrates or the judge who made him drink hemlock, is today the dishonored man?

HE. A great comfort to Socrates! Was he any the less convicted? any the less put to death? Was he less of an agitator? In violating a bad law, did he not encourage fools to despise the good ones? Wasn't he in any case a queer and troublesome citizen? A while ago you yourself were not far from marking down the man of genius too!

MYSELF. Listen, my dear fellow. A society should not tolerate any bad laws, and if it had only good ones it would never find itself persecuting men of genius. I never said that genius went with evil nor evil with genius. A fool is more often a knave than a genius is. And even if the latter is difficult to get on with, irritating and irritable—add wicked, if you like—what do you infer from it?

HE. That he should be drowned.

MYSELF. Gently, dear fellow. Look and tell me—I shan't take your uncle as an example. He is a hard man, brutal, inhuman, miserly, a bad father, bad husband, and bad uncle. And it is by no means sure that he is a genius who has advanced his art to such a point that ten years from now we shall still discuss his works. Take Racine instead—there was a genius, and his reputation as a man was none too good. Take Voltaire——

HE. Don't press the point too far: I am a man to argue with you.

MYSELF. Well, which would you prefer—that he should have been a good soul, at one with his ledger, like Briasson,[24] or with his yardstick, like Barbier;[25] legitimately getting his wife with child annually—a good husband, good father, good uncle, good neighbor, fair trader and nothing more; or that he should have been deceitful, disloyal, ambitious, envious, and mean, but also the creator of *Andromaque, Britannicus, Iphigénie, Phèdre,* and *Athalie*?[26]

HE. For himself I daresay it would have been better to be the former.

MYSELF. That is infinitely truer than you think.

HE. There you go, you fellows! If we say anything good, it's like lunatics or people possessed—by accident. It's only people like you

24. *Briasson:* Antoine-Claude Briasson, printer and publisher, associated with Diderot in the *Encyclopedia.*

25. *Barbier:* a shopkeeper who sold silk, gold, and silver.

26. *Andromaque . . . Athalie:* plays by Racine.

who really know what they're saying. I tell you, Master Philosopher, I know what I say and know it as well as you know what you say.

MYSELF. Let's find out: why better for Racine?

HE. Because all those mighty works of his did not bring him in twenty thousand francs, and if he had been a good silk merchant of rue St. Denis or St. Honoré, a good grocer or apothecary in a large way of business, he would have amassed a huge fortune, in the course of doing which there is no pleasure he would have failed to enjoy. From time to time he would have given a dollar to a poor buffoon like me and I would have made him laugh, besides procuring for him an occasional young girl to distract him a little from eternally living with his wife. We would have eaten excellent meals at his table, played high, drunk excellent wines, coffee, liqueurs; we would have had delightful picnics—you can see I knew perfectly well what I was saying—you laugh, but let me finish—it would have been better for those around him.

MYSELF. Unquestionably. Provided he hadn't used unworthily the riches acquired in legitimate trade, and had kept from his house all the gamblers, parasites, sycophants, idlers, and debauchees, as well as ordered his shopboys to beat up the officious gentlemen who would help husbands to a little distraction from habitually living with their wives.

HE. Beat up, my good sir, beat up! No one is beaten up in a well-ordered city. The profession is respectable; many people, even persons of title, are in it. And what in hell do you think money is for, if not to have good board, good company, pretty women, every kind of pleasure and every sort of amusement? I'd rather be a beggar than own a fortune without these enjoyments. But to come back to Racine. The fellow was of use only to people he didn't know, at a time when he had ceased to live.

MYSELF. Granted. But compare the good and the evil. A thousand years from now he will draw tears, will be admired by men all over the earth, will inspire compassion, human kindness, love. People will wonder who he was, from what country, and France will be envied. As against this, he brought suffering on a few persons who are dead and in whom we take no interest. We have nothing more to fear from his vices or his errors. It would no doubt have been preferable if nature had bestowed upon him the virtues of a good man as well as the talents of a great one. He is a tree which has stunted a few trees in his vicinage and blighted the plants growing at his feet; but his topmost branch reached the sky and his boughs spread afar. He has afforded shade to those past, present, and future who come to rest close to his majestic trunk. He bore fruit of exquisite savor and that will not perish. Again, it would be desirable if Voltaire had the sweetness of Duclos,[27] the ingenuousness of Abbé Trublet,[28] the rectitude of Abbé d'Olivet;[29] but as that cannot be, consider the really interesting side of the problem; forget for a moment the point we occupy in time and space, and project your vision into centuries to come, into the most remote places, and nations yet unborn. Think of the welfare of our species and, supposing that we ourselves are not generous enough, let us thank nature for knowing her business better than we. If you throw cold water on Greuze's[30] head, you will extinguish his talent together with his vanity. If you make Voltaire less restive under criticism, he will not delve into the soul of Merope[31] and will no longer move you.

HE. But if nature is as powerful as she is wise, why not make them as good as they are great?

MYSELF. Don't you see that if you argue this way you upset the general order of things? If everything here below were excellent, nothing would be excellent.

HE. You are right. The important point is that you and I should exist, and that we should be you and I. Outside of that, let everything carry on as it may. The best order, for me, is that in which I had to exist—and a fig for the most perfect world if I am not of it. I'd rather *be*—and be even a silly logic-chopper—than not be at all.

MYSELF. There is nobody who thinks otherwise and yet who fails to attack the scheme of things, blind to the fact that in doing so he repudiates his own existence.

HE. True enough.

MYSELF. So let's accept things as they are, find out their worth and their cost, and forget whatever we do not know well enough to assess it. It perhaps is neither good nor bad, but only necessary, as so many good people think.

HE. I don't follow all that you're preaching to me. Apparently it's philosophy and I tell you I will have no truck with it. All I know is that I'd be quite well pleased to be somebody else, on the chance of being a genius, a great man. I have to admit it. Something tells me I'd like it. I have never heard any genius praised without its making me secretly furious. I am full of envy. When I hear something discreditable about their private lives, I listen with pleasure: it brings me closer to them; makes me bear my mediocrity more easily. I say to myself: to be sure, you would never have been

---

27. *Duclos:* Charles Duclos (1704–1772), noted for his elegant language and vulgar behavior.

28. *Trublet:* Nicolas-Joseph-Charles Trublet (1697–1770), satirized by both Voltaire and Diderot for the subtlety beneath his apparent friendliness. Elsewhere Diderot described Trublet as "an animal with much wit."

29. *Olivet:* Pierre Jean Thoulier Olivet (1682–1768), whom Diderot and his friends attacked for his hypocrisy.

30. *Greuze's:* Jean Baptiste Greuze (1725–1805), portrait painter who painted according to Diderot's esthetic theories, known for his excessive vanity.

31. *Merope:* tragedy (1743) by Voltaire.

able to write *Mohammed*,[32] but then neither would you have praised Maupeou.[33] So I have been and I still am vexed at being mediocre. Yes, it's true, I am both mediocre and vexed. I have never heard the overture to *Les Indes Galantes*,[34] nor the singing of "*Profonds abîmes du Ténare, Nuit, éternelle nuit*,"[35] without thinking painfully: these are things I shall never be author of. I was obviously jealous of my uncle, and if at his death were found some grand pieces for harpsichord, I would not hesitate to remain myself and be him too.

MYSELF. If that's all that's troubling you, it isn't worth it.

HE. It's nothing, just a passing shadow.

[Then he started to sing the overture of *Les Indes Galantes* and the air "*Profonds abîmes*," adding:]

The whatever-it-is inside me speaks and says to me: "Rameau; you'd give a great deal to have composed those two pieces; if you had done two, you would surely have done two more; and after a certain number you would be played and sung everywhere. You would walk about with head erect, your mind would bear witness to your own merit. Other people would point you out and say— 'That's the man who wrote those lovely gavottes.' "[36] [And he sang the gavottes. Then with the appearance of a man deeply moved by a rush of happiness, he added with a moist eye, while rubbing his hands together:] "You would have a comfortable house" [measuring its breadth with his arms], "a good bed" [he made as if to recline carelessly on it], "good wine" [tasting it with a smack of tongue against palate], "a good carriage and pair" [raising his foot to climb in], "pretty women" [whom he seized by the breast and gazed at voluptuously]. "A hundred loungers would come and flatter you daily." [He thought he saw them around him—Palissot,[37] Poinsinet,[38] the Frérons father and son,[39] La Porte.[40] He heard them, preened himself, agreed with what they said, smiled at them, ignored them, despised them, sent them off, recalled them—then continued:] "Thus you would be told at breakfast that you are a

32. *Mohammed:* play by Voltaire (1742), a strong attack on religious fanaticism.

33. *Maupeou:* René Nicolas de Maupeou (1714–1792), chancellor of France from 1768–1774, dissolved the *parlements* in 1771. The popularity of Voltaire's satirical *History of the Parlement of Paris,* written just previous to this event, helped prepare public opinion for Maupeou's *coup d'état,* which Voltaire favored. Obviously the nephew did not.

34. *Les Indes Galantes:* ballet by Rameau, 1735.

35. *"Profonds . . . nuit":* "Deep abysses of Tenares, Night, eternal night." Song from Rameau's opera, *Castor and Pollux* (1737).

36. *gavottes:* The gavotte was originally a peasant dance, later introduced into the court of Louis XIV.

37. *Palissot:* Charles Palissot de Montenoi (1730–1814), bad writer and plagiarist, ridiculed by Diderot.

38. *Poinsinet:* Antoine-Henri Poinsinet (1734–1769), another fraudulent writer.

39. *Frérons father and son:* Elie-Catherine Fréron (1719–1776) and his son Stanislaus-Louis-Marie (born 1754), literary enemies of Diderot. The elder Fréron was also strongly disliked by Voltaire.

40. *La Porte:* Abbé Joseph Delaporte (1718–1779), who attempted to mediate in the Diderot-Fréron quarrel.

great man, you would read in *Three Centuries of French Literature*[41]
that you are a great man, by nightfall you would be convinced that
you are a great man, and that great man, Rameau the Nephew,
would fall asleep to the soft hum of praise buzzing in his ears. Even
while asleep, he would look sated, his chest would rise and fall
with bliss, he would snore like a great man."

[In saying this, he collapsed softly on the bench, closed his eyes
and imitated the blissful sleep he was imagining. Having enjoyed
this felicity of restfulness for a few moments, he awoke, stretched,
yawned, rubbed his eyes and looked about him for the dull flatterers
who might linger.]

MYSELF. You think, then, that a happy mortal snores in his sleep?

HE. Think so! When I, poor wretch, am back in my garret for the
night and I have stuck myself within covers, I am shriveled up, my
chest is tight and my breath uneasy—it is a sort of feeble plaint that
can hardly be heard; whereas a financier makes the whole house resound and astonishes the entire street. But what grieves me today
is not that I sleep meanly and snore wretchedly.

MYSELF. That's sad enough.

HE. What's happened to me is far worse.

MYSELF. What is it?

HE. You've always taken an interest in me because I'm a good
fellow whom you despise at bottom but who amuses you——

MYSELF. I don't deny it.

HE. —so I'm going to tell you.

[Before he begins he gives a mighty sigh and puts both his hands
to his head; then he recovers his composure and says:] "You know
that I am an ignoramus, a fool, a lunatic, a lazy, impudent, greedy
good-for-nothing—what we Burgundians call a ne'er-do-well—a
blackguard, in short."

MYSELF. What a eulogy!

HE. Gospel truth from beginning to end, not a word out of place.
Let's not argue about it, please; no one knows me better than I and
I haven't said all I know.

MYSELF. I don't mean to annoy you: I accept everything you say.

HE. Well, I used to live with people who had taken a liking to me
precisely because I had all these qualities to a rare degree.

MYSELF. Strange! Until now I had thought that one hid them
from oneself, or that one forgave oneself while condemning them in
others.

HE. Hide them from oneself! Who can? You may be sure that
when Palissot is alone and reflects upon himself he tells himself
different. In tête-à-tête with his colleague he and the other confess

41. *Three Centuries of French Litera-* Sabatier de Castres, wherein Diderot was
ture: pretentious work (1772) edited by treated in negative terms.

that they're a pair of prize scoundrels. Despise defects in others!
My people were fairer than to do that and my character was a
pleasure to them. I was treated like a king. They missed every
moment I was away from them. I was their dear Rameau, pretty
Rameau, *their* Rameau—the jester, the buffoon, the lazy dog, the
saucy rogue, the great greedy boob. Not one of these epithets went
without a smile, a chuck under the chin, a pat on the back, a cuff, a
kick. At table it was a choice morsel tossed to me; elsewhere a liberty
I could take with no consequence—for I am truly a person of no
consequence. Anyone can do what he pleases with me, about me, in
front of me. I never get on my high horse. Ah, the little gratuities
that came my way! What a consummate ass I am to have lost all
that! I have lost it all because once, once in my life, I showed common sense. I promise you, never again!

MYSELF. What was it all about?

HE. A piece of incredible folly, unimaginable, unforgivable.

MYSELF. But what kind of folly was it?

HE. Rameau, Rameau, you weren't taken on for your folly, the
folly of possessing a little good taste, a little wit, a little sense.
Rameau, my friend, this will teach you to stay the way God made
you, the way your patrons wanted you. Failing which, they seized
you by the shoulder and showed you the door. They said: "Faker,
beat it and don't come back. It wants to be sensible, does it? Beat it!
Good sense, we have more of that than we know what to do with."
You went, biting your fingernails: it's your tongue you should have
bitten off first. You thought of that too late and here you are, in
the gutter, penniless, and nowhere to go. You were being fed like
a fatted calf, and now you're back at the slop shop; well-housed,
and now you'll be lucky to have your garret back. You had a bed;
now the loose straw awaits you between the coachman of M. de
Soubise[42] and Robbé[43] the grubstreet hack. Instead of sweet silent
sleep, as you had it, one ear will be filled with the neighing and
stamping of horses, the other with the far worse noise of a thousand
harsh verses. Wretch, idiot, lunatic at the mercy of a million
damnable fiends!

MYSELF. But is there no way to regain your passport? Did you
commit so unpardonable a crime? Were I in your place, I'd go
back to my patrons: you must be more indispensable than you think.

HE. Oh, I'm convinced that without me around to make them
laugh, they're bored stiff.

MYSELF. That's why I'd go back. I wouldn't give them time to

---

42. *Soubise:* owner of the largest
stables in Paris, which were favored by
vagabonds for shelter.

43. *Robbé:* Pierre-Honoré Robbé de
Beauveset (1712–1792), author of a poem
about smallpox.

get used to my absence, or to take up some decent amusement. Who knows what might come of it!

HE. That's not what I'm afraid of: it couldn't happen.

MYSELF. Well then, some other genius may take your place.

HE. With difficulty.

MYSELF. Granted. Just the same, I'd go back as you are—my face fallen, my eyes wandering, unbuttoned and unkempt—in the really tragic attire in which you are. I'd throw myself at the feet of the goddess, glue my face to the ground, and without once getting up, I'd say in a weak sobbing voice: "Forgive, my lady, forgive! I am a wretch, a monster, the victim of a momentary lapse, for you know very well I am not subject to suffering from common sense. I promise it will never happen again."

[What is amusing is that while I was saying this, he was acting it out in pantomime. He was prostrate at my feet, his face on the ground, and seemed to be clutching in both his hands the tip of a slipper. He was crying and sobbing out words: "I swear it, my dear Queen, I promise, never will I do it again, never, never, never." Then, suddenly jumping up, he said in a perfectly sober, serious way:]

HE. You're right, of course. I can see it's the better way. She is kind. M. Vieillard[44] says she is very kind, and I know somewhat that she is. But still, to go and humiliate myself before the little bitch, to cry mercy at the feet of a second-rate actress who is invariably hissed off the stage! I, Rameau, son of M. Rameau, apothecary of Dijon, a man of substance who has never crooked the knee to anyone, I, Rameau, the nephew of him who is called the great Rameau, him who can be seen pacing the Palais-Royal upright and with arms akimbo ever since M. Carmontelle[45] depicted him bent and with his hands behind his back! I who have composed keyboard works that no one plays but which may be the only works of today posterity will like, I (in short) would go and—no, my dear sir, impossible! [And putting his right hand on his heart he added:] I feel something here which swells in pride and says to me: "Rameau, you will do no such thing. A certain dignity attaches to the nature of man that nothing must destroy. It stirs in protest at the most unexpected times, yes, unexpected, for there are days when I could be as vile as required without its costing me anything. On those days, for a penny I'd kiss the arse of the little Hus."

MYSELF. But see here, she's pretty, kind, plump, and white-skinned, and that's an act of humility that even a prouder man than you could condescend to.

---

44. *She . . . Vieillard:* Rameau refers to an actress, Adelaide Hus, mistress of a banker named Bertin. Vieillard also became her lover, replacing Bertin; and the story became a comic scandal in Paris.

45. *Carmontelle:* His sketch of Rameau was then famous.

HE. Let's be clear about this—there's kissing and kissing, literal and metaphorical. Consult that old Bergier[46] who kisses the arse of the Duchess de La Marck,[47] both literally and metaphorically—a case in which the two species disgust me equally.

MYSELF. If my suggestion does not seem expedient to you, then at least be courageous enough to be poor.

HE. It's very hard to be poor while there are so many wealthy fools to sponge on. And then contempt for oneself—that's unbearable! . . .*

MYSELF. Why resort to these vile little tricks?

HE. Why vile, if I may ask? They are part of my profession. There's nothing degrading in acting like everybody else. I did not invent these tricks. And I should be a clumsy oaf not to make use of them. I know well enough that if you apply to my case certain general principles of morals which they all talk about and never put into practice, it will turn out that white is black and black is white. But, Master Philosopher, it is with universal morality just as with universal grammar: there are exceptions in each language that you learned people call—what is it you call them?

MYSELF. Idioms?

HE. That's what I mean. Well, each profession makes exceptions to universal morality and those I'd like to call *trade idioms*.

MYSELF. I follow you. Fontenelle[48] speaks and writes well even though his style is full of French idioms.

HE. Likewise the sovereign, the minister, the financier, the judge, the soldier, the writer, the lawyer, the public prosecutor, the merchant, the banker, the workman, the singing teacher, the dancing master, are very respectable people even though their conduct deviates in several ways from absolute good behavior and is full of moral idioms. The older the profession the more the idioms; the worse the times become, the more the idioms multiply. A man is worth what his trade is worth; in the end they're equal; hence people make the trade go for as much as they can.

MYSELF. What appears clearest in all this tangle is that there are no honest trades and no honest men in them.

HE. Have it your own way. But as a compensation there are but few gougers outside their own shops. The world would get on pretty well if it weren't for a number of people who are called industrious, reliable, conscientious followers of duty, strict. Or what amounts to

46. *Bergier:* Nicolas-Sylvestre Bergier (1718–1790), theologian disliked by Diderot.

47. *Duchess de La Marck:* Marie de Noailles (born 1719), strongly devotional and opposed to Diderot and the *philosophes*.

* In the passage deleted by the editor, Rameau satirizes the young daughter of a middle-class family. He also pantomimes a violinist and a keyboard performer—the "vile little tricks" referred to in the following passage.

48. *Fontenelle:* Bernard le Bouvier de Fontenelle (1657–1757), author of *The Plurality of the Worlds* (1686)—an elegant piece of scientific popularization.

the same thing: ever in their shops practicing their trades from morn till night and doing nothing else. Result is: they're the only ones to get rich and full of reputation.

MYSELF. By sheer strength of idiom!

HE. Exactly. I see you understand. Now an idiom that is common to all trades—as there are some common to all nations and no less common than folly—is to try to get as many customers as possible. The common folly is to think that the largest tradesman is the best. Those are two exceptions to universal ethics one can do nothing about. Call it credit or "good will," it is nothing in itself but it's worth a great deal in public opinion. Don't they say: "A good name is worth a money belt?" Yet plenty of people have a good name who have no money belt, and I notice that nowadays the money insures the name. The great thing is to have both and that is precisely what I am after when I employ what you call my vile tricks. I give lessons and give them the right way—that's the absolute rule. I make people believe that I have more pupils than there are hours in the day—that's my idiom.

MYSELF. And you really give good lessons?

HE. Yes, or not bad, passable. The ground bass theory of the dear uncle has simplified everything. Formerly I swindled my pupil, yes, undoubtedly swindled. Nowadays I earn my feet at least as much as my colleagues.

MYSELF. Did you formerly swindle without qualms?

HE. Without qualms. They say, when one thief robs another the Devil laughs. My pupils' parents were fat with ill-gotten gains. They were courtiers, tax collectors, wholesalers, bankers, stockbrokers. I merely helped them—I and some others in their employ —to make restitution. In Nature all species live off one another; in society all classes do the same. We square things up with one another without benefit of the law. La Deschamps[49] some time since, and now la Guimard,[50] avenges the King upon his tax collector; after which the dressmaker, the jeweler, the upholsterer, the lace-maker, the confidence man, the lady's maid, the cook, and the saddler avenge the tax collector upon la Deschamps. Amid all this no one but the idiot or the loafer is taken advantage of without levying tribute on anybody else—and it serves him right. You can infer from this that the exceptions to universal ethics, or moral idioms, about which people make so much fuss under the name of mutual depredations, don't amount to anything, really. When all is said and done the only thing that matters is to see straight.

MYSELF. I admire you for that.

---

49. *La Deschamps:* Anne Marie Pagès (1730–1775?), famous courtesan who sold her town house in Paris to pay off huge debts, and entered the money-lending business.

50. *la Guimard:* another prostitute or courtesan whose career was similar.

HE. And think of poverty! The voice of conscience and honor is pretty feeble when the guts cry out. Isn't it enough that if I ever get rich I shall be bound to make restitution? I am prepared to do this in every conceivable way—through gorging, through gambling, through guzzling, and through wenching.

MYSELF. But I'm afraid you will never get rich.

HE. I suspect it too.

MYSELF. Suppose it did work out, what then?

HE. I would act like all beggars on horseback. I'd be the most insolent ruffian ever seen. I'd remember every last thing they made me go through and pay them back with slings and arrows. I love bossing people and I will boss them. I love being praised and they will praise me. I'll have the whole troop of Villemorien's[51] boot-lickers on salary, and I'll say to them what's been said to me: "Come on, dogs, entertain me." And they will. "I want decent people pulled to pieces." And they will be—if any can be found. Then too, we'll have women, and when drunk we'll thee-and-thou one another. We will drink and make up tales and develop all sorts of whims and vices. It will be delightful. We'll prove that Voltaire has no genius; that Buffon[52] is always up on stilts like the turgid declaimer he is; that Montesquieu[53] was only a wit. We'll tell D'Alembert[54] to stick to his ciphering and we'll kick behind and before all the little stoics like you who despise us from sour grapes, whose modesty is the prop of pride, and whose good conduct springs from lack of means. Ah, what music you'll hear from us!

MYSELF. Knowing what worthy use you would make of wealth, I see how deplorable it is that you are poor. You would certainly be doing honor to human nature, good to your compatriots and credit to yourself.

HE. I almost think you're making fun of me, Master Philosopher. But you don't even suspect with whom you're tangling; you don't seem to know that at this very moment I represent the most important part of Town and Court. The well-to-do of every description have either said or not said to themselves the words I've just confided to you; the fact remains that the life I would lead in their position is precisely theirs. That's where you fellows are behind the times. You think everybody aims at the same happiness. What an idea! Your conception presupposes a sentimental turn of mind which is not ours, an unusual spirit, a special taste. You call your quirks virtue, or philosophy. But virtue and philosophy are not made

---

51. *Villemorien's:* Philippe-Charles Legendre de Villemorien, wealthy land-owner.

52. *Buffon:* Georges Louis Leclerc Buffon (1707–1788), naturalist and author of a famous *Natural History.*

53. *Montesquieu:* Charles de Secondat, Baron de Montesquieu (1689–1755), po-

litical philosopher; author of the satirical *Persian Letters* (1721) and *The Spirit of the Laws* (1748), a study of comparative government.

54. *D'Alembert:* Jean le Rond D'Alembert (1717–1783); philosopher, mathematician, and co-editor of the *Encyclopedia* with Diderot.

for everybody. The few who can, have it; the few who can, keep it. Just imagine the universe philosophical and wise, and tell me if it would not be devilishly dull. Listen! I say hurrah for wisdom and philosophy—the wisdom of Solomon: to drink good wines, gorge on choice food, tumble pretty women, sleep in downy beds—outside of that, all is vanity.

MYSELF. What! And fighting for your country?

HE. Vanity! There are no countries left. All I see from pole to pole is tyrants and slaves.

MYSELF. What of helping your friends?

HE. Vanity! No one has any friends. And even if one had, should one risk making them ungrateful? Look close and you'll see that's all you get for being helpful. Gratitude is a burden and burdens are to be shuffled off.

MYSELF. To hold a position in society and discharge its duties?

HE. Vanity! What difference whether you hold a position or not, provided you have means, since you only seek a position in order to get wealth. Discharge one's duties—what does that bring you?—jealousy, worries, persecution. Is that the way to get on? Nonsense! Pay court, pay court, know the right people, flatter their tastes and fall in with their whims, serve their vices and second their misdeeds—there's the secret.

MYSELF. Watch over the education of one's children?

HE. Vanity! That's a tutor's business.

MYSELF. But if a tutor, imbued with your principles, neglects his duty, who will pay the penalty?

HE. Not I anyhow. Possibly, some day, my daughter's husband or my son's wife.

MYSELF. But suppose that either or both plunge into vice and debauchery?

HE. Then that is part of their social position.

MYSELF. If they disgrace themselves?

HE. It's impossible to disgrace yourself, no matter what you do, if you are rich.

MYSELF. Ruin themselves, then?

HE. Too bad for them.

MYSELF. It seems to me that if you overlook the conduct of your wife, your children and your servants, you might easily overlook your own affairs.

HE. Not so, if you will permit me: it is sometimes difficult to procure money, hence one uses a prudent foresight.

MYSELF. You will pay little attention to your wife?

HE. None, an it please you. The best behavior toward one's dearer half, I think, is to do what suits her. Do you suppose company would be tolerable if everyone minded his own business?

MYSELF. Why not? I'm never so happy in the evening as when I'm pleased with my forenoon.

HE. Me too.

MYSELF. What makes society people so choosey about their entertainment is that they are utterly idle.

HE. Don't you believe it: they are always on the go.

MYSELF. They never tire themselves and so can never feel refreshed.

HE. Don't you believe it: they are constantly weary.

MYSELF. Pleasure is always their business, never a desire.

HE. All the better: desires are ever nagging.

MYSELF. They wear everything out. Their soul gets dull, boredom masters them. Whoever should take their life at the height of their load of plenty would be doing them a good turn. For they know of pleasure only that portion which soonest loses its zest. I am far from despising sensual pleasures. I have a palate too and it is tickled by a delicate wine or dish; I have eyes and a heart and I like to look at a pretty woman, like to feel the curve of her breast under my hand, press her lips to mine, drink bliss from her eyes and die of ecstasy in her arms. Sometimes a gay party with my friends, even if it becomes a little rowdy, is not displeasing to me. But I must confess that I find it infinitely sweeter to succor the unfortunate, to disentangle a bad business, to give helpful advice, to read some pleasant book, to take a walk with a man or woman who is dear to me, to spend a few instructive hours with my children, to write a page of good prose, to carry out my duties, or to tell her whom I love something tender and true which brings her arms about my neck.

I know of certain deeds which I would give all I possess to have done. Voltaire's *Mohammed* is a sublime work, but I would rather have rehabilitated the Calas family.[55] A man I know left home for Cartagena;[56] he was a younger son in a country where primogeniture is the law. While abroad he learns that his elder brother, a spoiled child, has ruined his father and mother, driven them out of the castle, and left them to languish in some provincial town. What does the younger son do, who after the harsh treatment meted out by his parents had gone to seek his fortune far away? He sends them help. He winds up his affairs, comes back rich, restores his parents to their home, marries off his sisters. Ah, my dear Rameau, that man looked upon this period as the happiest in his life. He had

---

55. *Calas family:* In 1762, Jean Calas —a Protestant living in Toulouse—was accused of hanging his son, who wished to leave the Protestant faith. The senior Calas was tortured on the wheel; the trial was a judiciary sham, and Voltaire tried to get the trial reviewed. Jean Calas was officially exonerated on March 9, 1765.

56. *Cartagena:* Spanish port on the Mediterranean.

tears in his eyes as he spoke of it and as I tell you this, I feel my heart dilate with gladness and my tongue falter with emotion.

HE. Queer people, you are!

MYSELF. And you are people to be pitied, unless you can see that one can rise above one's fate and make oneself independent of misfortune by actions such as I have described.

HE. That's a kind of happiness I would find it hard to become familiar with, it is so rarely found. Then according to you, people should be decent?

MYSELF. To be happy?—Certainly.

HE. Yet I see a quantity of decent people unhappy and a quantity of people happy without being decent.

MYSELF. So it seems to you.

HE. Wasn't it because I acted sensibly and frankly for one instant that tonight I don't know where to find a meal?

MYSELF. Not at all: it's because you have not always been sensible and frank; because you did not learn soon enough that the first step is to secure the means of life apart from servitude.

HE. Apart or not, my way is surely the easiest.

MYSELF. And the least assured and the least decent.

HE. But the most consistent with my nature, which is idle, stupid, and crooked.

MYSELF. Granted.

HE. Since I can secure my well-being with the aid of vices natural to me, that I have acquired without labor and that I retain without effort, vices congenial to the habits of my countrymen, agreeable to the tastes of my protectors, and closer to their little needs than any virtues could be—for virtues would annoy them all day long like so many accusations—in view of all this, it would be strange indeed for me to bedevil myself like a damned soul and turn myself into what I am not; to acquire a character alien to mine, with laudable traits, no doubt (I won't argue), but difficult to maintain and make use of. It would do me no good, perhaps worse than no good, by implying a satire of the rich people in whose company paupers like me must find their livelihood.

Virtue is praised, but hated. People run away from it, for it is ice-cold and in this world you must keep your feet warm. Besides, I would grow bad-humored, infallibly. For note how often devout people are harsh, touchy, unsociable. The reason is that they have compelled themselves to do an unnatural thing. They're in pain, and people in pain make others suffer. That's not the life for me, nor for my patrons. I must be gay, easy, jolly, droll, entertaining. Virtue earns respect and respect is inconvenient; virtue is bound to be admired, and admiration is no fun. I deal with people who are bored and I have to make them laugh. Now what is laughable is absurdity and folly. I must consequently be absurd and a fool. Even had nature not made me such, the quickest way would be to put on the appearance. Fortunately, I don't need to be a hypocrite; there are enough of them around, not counting those who deceive themselves. The Chevalier Morlière[57] who snaps his hatbrim on his ear, sniffs the air and looks at every passer-by over his shoulder; who drags the longest sword next to his thigh and has an insult ready for anyone unarmed; in short, who defies every man on principle, what is he really up to? He does what he can to persuade himself that he is a man of spirit, though he's a coward. Tweak his nose and he will take it mildly. If you want to make him pipe down, just raise your voice, lift your cane, or let your foot contact his buttocks. Full of surprise at finding himself a coward, he will ask you who told you of it, how you knew. Himself did not suspect it the moment before. His long and habitual aping of bravery had fooled him; so much mimicry had ended by seeming real.

And what of that woman who mortifies her flesh, who visits prisons, who attends all meetings organized for charity, who walks with lowered lids and would not dare look a man in the eye; who is continually on guard against the temptations of the senses—does any of this keep her heart from burning, her breast from sighing, her flaming desires from obsessing her? Her imagination at night rehearses the scenes of the *Portier des Chartrains* and the postures of Aretino.[58] What then happens to her? What does her maid think when she has to get up in her shift and fly to the aid of her mistress who is suffocating? Justine, you can go back to bed, it isn't you your mistress is calling for in her fever.

And if friend Rameau himself should ever show indifference to wealth, women, good cheer, and idleness, if he should begin to stoicize, what would he be? A hypocrite. Rameau must stay what he is—a scoundrel in luck among well-heeled scoundrels; not a holier-than-thou character nor even a virtuous man eating his dry crust alone or near some other beggar. To cut it short, I want none of your kind of happiness, none of the satisfactions of a few visionaries like yourself.

MYSELF. I can see, my dear fellow, that you don't know what I refer to and that you are apparently not made to find out.

HE. Thank God for that! It would only make me starve to death, die of boredom, and croak with remorse.

---

57. *Morlière:* Jacques Rochette de la Morlière (1719–1785), elegant gentleman whose scandalous life forced him to resign from the *Musketeers*, and who at one point was chief *claqueur* (leader of applause) at the theater, served several jail sentences.

58. *Portier . . . Aretino:* referring to one of Diderot's own books, published first at Rome, then at Frankfurt (1748) —anonymously, due to its pornographic content; and to Pietro Aretino (1492–1556?), sixteen of whose sonnets, illustrated by Julio Romano, became pornographic classics.

MYSELF. That being so, the one piece of advice I can give you is to hurry back into the place whence you so carelessly got kicked out.

HE. You want me to do that which you do not object to when it's literal, but which is a little repugnant to you when metaphorical?

MYSELF. That's my advice.

HE. Well—apart from the metaphor, which repels me now and may not repel me later——

MYSELF. How odd you are!

HE. Not in the least. I'm perfectly ready to be abject, but not under duress. I'm willing to lower my dignity—you're laughing!

MYSELF. Certainly. Your dignity makes me laugh.

HE. To each man his own kind. I'm willing to forget mine, but at my pleasure, not on somebody else's order. Shall it be said that at the word "Crawl!" I am to crawl? That's the worm's natural gait and it is mine too, when we are left alone, but we turn and rear, both of us, when stepped on. I was stepped on and mean to rear off. And then you have no idea what a shambles that house is. Imagine a melancholy crotchety individual, a prey to vapors, wrapped up in two or three layers of dressing gown, who likes himself but dislikes everything else; who can hardly be made to smile by one's utmost contortions of body and mind, who looks with a lackluster eye on the lively twistings of my face and the even livelier ones of my intellect. For between ourselves, compared to me the ugly Benedictine so famous at court for his grimacing is, all boasting aside, nothing but a wooden Indian. I badger myself in vain to reach the sublimest lunacy—it's no use. Will he laugh or won't he? That's what I have to keep asking myself in the midst of my exertions. You can guess what harm so much uncertainty does to talent. My hypochondriac with his head swallowed up in a nightcap down to his eyes looks like an immovable idol with a string tied to its chin and running down beneath his chair. You wait for the string to be pulled but it is never pulled; or if the jaw drops it is only to let out some chilling word, from which you learn that you have not been understood and that your apish tricks have been wasted. That word is the answer to a question you put four days ago. The word spoken, the mastoid muscle contracts and the jaw clamps. . . .*

MYSELF. What have you read?

HE. I keep rereading Theophrastus,[59] La Bruyère and Molière.

MYSELF. Excellent books.

HE. They're even better than people think, but who knows how to read them?

---

* At this point the Nephew describes how to flatter a stupid, obese, and wealthy girl.

59. *Theophrastus:* Greek author (ca. 372–287 B.C.), whose *Characters* were imitated by La Bruyère.

MYSELF. Everybody according to his capacity.

HE. I should say almost no one. Can you tell me what they look for in them?

MYSELF. Instruction mixed with entertainment.

HE. But what kind of instruction: that's the point!

MYSELF. The knowledge of one's duty, the love of virtue and the hatred of vice.

HE. Now what I find there is a compendium of what to do and what not to say. When I read *The Miser*, I say to myself: "Be as miserly as you like, but don't talk like the miser." When I read *Tartuffe*,[60] I say: "Be a hypocrite if you choose, but don't talk like one. Keep any useful vices, but don't acquire the tone and air which would make you ridiculous. Now to avoid these one must know what they are, and the authors mentioned have give us excellent portraits. I am myself and I remain such, but I act and speak just as I ought to. Far from despising the moralists, I find profit in them, particularly those who depict morals in action. Vice offends men only from time to time; but the symptoms of vice offend day and night. It is surely better to be arrogant than to look it. The arrogant character insults you only now and then; the arrogant look insults you continually. And by the way, don't suppose that I am the only reader of my kind. My sole merit is to have accomplished systematically, through good judgment and right reason, what most other people do by instinct. Hence their reading does not make them better than I, and they remain ridiculous despite their efforts; whereas I am such only when I choose, and so surpass them by far. The same skill which saves me from ridicule on certain occasions, enables me at other times to incur it with high art. I recall whatever others have said, whatever I have read, and I add to all this my original contribution, which is surprisingly abundant.

MYSELF. It was wise of you to impart these mysteries to me, else I would have thought you self-contradictory.

HE. I'm nothing of the kind, for if it is necessary to avoid ridicule once, it is fortunately just as necessary to incur it a hundred times. There is no fitter role in high society than that of fool. For a long time the King had an appointed fool. At no time was there an appointed sage. I am Bertin's[61] fool and that of many others—yours, possibly, this minute; or maybe you are mine. A real sage would want no fool; hence he who has a fool is no sage; and if no sage, must be a fool. And were he the King himself; he may be his own fool's fool. In any event, remember that in a subject as variable as manners and morals nothing is absolutely, essentially, universally true or false—unless it be that one must be whatever self-interest

---

60. *Miser . . . Tartuffe:* plays by Molière, 1668 and 1664–1669.

61. *Bertin's:* Louis-Auguste Bertin de Blagny, a pedant disliked by Diderot.

requires, good or bad, wise or foolish, decent or ridiculous, honest or vicious. If virtue by chance led to fortune, I should have been as virtuous—or virtuous-seeming—as the next man. I was bidden to be ridiculous and I made myself so. As to vice, nature alone took care of that; though when I say vicious I am merely using your language. For if we really thrashed things out, we might find ourselves each calling virtue what the other calls vice and t'other way round. . . .*

MYSELF. Enough of your naughtiness, will you! Let's talk of something else. I've had a question on the tip of my tongue since we started chatting.

HE. Why have you held it back so long?

MYSELF. I was afraid to be inquisitive.

HE. After what I've told you, I can't imagine what secret I could withhold from you.

MYSELF. You are in no doubt about the opinion I have of you?

HE. No doubt at all. You think me most abject and contemptible. And so I am in my own eyes—sometimes. Not often. I congratulate myself on my vices more often than blame myself. But your contempt does not vary.

MYSELF. Just so. But then why show yourself to me in all your turpitude?

HE. First, because you know a good deal of it to start with, and I stand to gain more than I lose by confessing the rest.

MYSELF. How is that, tell me?

HE. If there's one realm in which it is essential to be sublime, it is in wickedness. You spit on ordinary scum, but you can't deny a kind of respect to a great criminal: his courage amazes, his ferocity overawes. People especially admire integrity of character.

MYSELF. But this admirable integrity, you haven't reached it yet. I find you now and again weak in principle. You don't seem to know if your wickedness comes from nature or from study, nor whether you have pursued your studies far enough. . . .†

HE. . . . Gold, gold is everything; and everything, without gold, is nothing. Therefore, instead of having my son's head stuffed with grand maxims which he would have to forget under pain of being a pauper, this is what I do whenever I have a gold piece—not often, to be sure: I plant myself in front of him, draw the piece from my pocket, show it to him with admiring looks, raise my eyes to heaven, kiss the gold in front of him, and to show him still more forcibly the importance of the sacred coin, I stammer out the names and point out with the finger all the things one can buy with it—a beau-

---

* Here the Nephew describes a dinner party and other occasions where he excels in the role of a parasite.
† Here a technical discussion about contemporary music is deleted, as well as a scene where the Nephew parodies certain popular singers of the day. Through *Rameau's Nephew*, Diderot is able to criticize musical tendencies which he deplored.

tiful gown, a beautiful hat, a good cake; next I put the coin in my pocket, parade before him proudly, pull up my coat tails and strike my waistcoat where the money lies. Thus do I make him understand that it is from that coin I draw the self-assurance he beholds.

MYSELF. Nothing could be better. But what if some day, being deeply persuaded of the value of money, he should . . .

HE. I follow you! One must shut one's eyes to that. There is no principle of conduct wholly without drawbacks. At the worst, one goes through a bad half hour, then all is over.

MYSELF. Yet in spite of your wise and courageous views, I continue to think it would be a good thing to make him a musician. I know of no better way to approach the rich, to serve their vices, and to turn one's own to advantage.

HE. True. But I have projects for even quicker and surer success. Ah, if I only had a daughter! But no man can do as he likes, he must take what he gets and do the best he can with it. For which purpose one must not, like most fathers, stupidly give children who are destined to live in Paris the education of ancient Sparta. One might as well plot their ruin. If the native training is bad, the fault lies with the manners and customs of my country, and not with me. No matter who is responsible, I want my child happy, or what amounts to the same thing, honored, rich, powerful. I know the easiest ways to accomplish this, and I mean to teach them to my son early in life. If you wise men blame me, the majority (and success itself) will absolve me. He will have gold—it's I who tell you so, I guarantee it—and if he has a great deal, he will lack nothing, not even your admiration and respect.

MYSELF. You might be wrong about those.

HE. If so, he can do without, like many other people.

[There was in all he said much that one thinks to oneself, and acts on, but that one never says. This was in fact the chief difference between my man and the rest of us. He admitted his vices, which are also ours: he was no hypocrite. Neither more nor less destestable than other men, he was franker than they, more logical, and thus often profound in his depravity. I was appalled to think of what his child would become under such a tutor. It was clear that if he was brought up on a system so exactly framed on our actual behavior, he would go far—unless he was prematurely cut off on the way.]

HE. Never you fear! The important thing that a good father must do is not so much to give his child vices that will bring him wealth and foolish traits that will make him a favorite of the great—everybody does as much: not systematically like me, but by casual precept and example. No, what is more difficult is to teach him the golden art by which he can avert disgrace, shame, and the penalties of the law. These last are dissonances in the harmony of society, which one must know how to use, prepare, and resolve. Nothing is duller than a progression of common chords. One wants some contrast, which breaks up the clear white light and makes it iridescent.

MYSELF. Very good. Your comparison brings me back from morals to music. I digressed in spite of myself, for to speak frankly, I prefer you as musician rather than as moralist.

HE. And yet I am only second-rate in music, whereas I am a superior moralist.

MYSELF. I doubt this; but even if it were so, I am an honest man and your principles do not suit me.

HE. So much the worse for you. Oh, if I only had your talent!

MYSELF. Leave my talent alone; let's go back to yours.

HE. If I could express myself as you do! But my vocabulary is a damned mongrel—half literary and well-bred, half guttersnipe.

MYSELF. Don't think I speak well. I can only tell the truth and, as you know, that doesn't always go down.

HE. It's not for telling the truth that I envy you your gifts. Just the opposite—it's to tell lies. If I only knew how to throw together a book, how to turn a dedication, intoxicate some fool with praises and make my way among women!

MYSELF. As for all that, you know much more about it than I do; I am not even fit to be your pupil.

HE. Oh, what abilities you are letting go to waste, not even suspecting what they're worth!

MYSELF. I reap whatever I sow, no more, no less.

HE. If that were true, you wouldn't be wearing these coarse clothes —linen coat, woollen stockings, thick-soled shoes and superannuated wig.

MYSELF. Granted. One must be terribly clumsy if one isn't rich after sticking at nothing to acquire wealth. But there are people like me, you see, who don't consider wealth the most important thing in the world—queer people.

HE. Very queer. No one is born that way. It's an acquired idea; it's unnatural.

MYSELF. For man?

HE. For man. Everything that lives, man included, seeks its wellbeing at the expense of whoever withholds it. I'm sure that if I let my little savage grow up without saying a word to him, he would of his own accord want to be richly dressed, magnificently fed, liked by men and loved by women, and concentrate on himself all the goods of life.

MYSELF. If your little savage were left to himself and to his native blindness, he would in time join the infant's reasoning to the grown man's passions—he would strangle his father and sleep with his mother.

HE. Which only proves the need of a good education. There's no argument. But what is a good education if it is not one that leads to all the enjoyments without trouble or danger?

MYSELF. I am almost with you there, but let's not go into it.

HE. Why not?

MYSELF. Because I think we are only superficially in agreement, and if we look into the question of troubles and dangers, we shall no longer be at one.

HE. And what's the harm of that?

MYSELF. Let it go, I say. What I know on the subject I shan't be able to teach you. You will have an easier time teaching me what you know about music, of which I am ignorant. Dear Rameau, let us talk music; and tell me how it is that with your remarkable power for understanding, remembering and rendering the most beautiful works of the great masters, with your contagious enthusiasm for them and for conveying them, you have never done anything that amounts to anything. . . .*

HE. From tumble to tumble I had fallen you know where. I lived there like a rat in a cheese. I left, and now we'll have to squeeze the guts again, go back to the gesture of the finger and the gaping mouth. Nothing is stable in this world. Today at the top of the heap, tomorrow at the bottom. Accursed circumstance guides us and does it very badly.

[Then drinking what was left in one of the bottles and addressing his neighbor, he said: "Sir, a pinch of snuff, for kindness' sake. You have a mighty handsome snuffbox. You are not a musician? No? So much the better for you, for they're all poor buggers, a pitiable lot. Fate has decreed that I should be one, while in Montmartre[62] there may be in a windmill, a miller or a miller's helper who has never heard anything but the click of the ratchet but who would have found the most enchanting melodies. To the mill, Rameau! To the mill, that's the place for you!"]

MYSELF. Whatever a man tries, Nature destined him for that.

HE. Then she makes some very odd blunders. I can't for myself see from those heights where everything comes to the same thing— the man who prunes a tree with his shears and the slug that eats off the leaves being just two insects each doing his duty. You go and perch on the epicycle of Mercury,[63] and like Réaumur,[64] who classifies the flies into seamstresses, surveyors, and reapers, you classify mankind into carpenters, builders, roofers, dancers, and singers: that's your affair, I shan't meddle with it. I am in this

---

* Here several pages are deleted, where the Nephew deplores his own lack of genius, his own artistic mediocrity—"to be called Rameau is extremely embarrassing"—and describes his life as an itinerant musician.

62. *Montmartre:* in Diderot's time, still a rural area on the right bank of the Seine, later to be famous as a center of Bohemian life.

63. *perch . . . Mercury:* image used by Montaigne to criticize those who pretend to superior knowledge. The idea of the epicycle, which attempted to explain the discrepancies between observed planetary motion and Ptolemaic astronomical theory, was derided by eighteenth-century *philosophes.*

64. *Réaumur:* R.-A. F. de Réaumur, celebrated physicist and naturalist.

world and here I stay. But if it is natural to be hungry—I always come back to hunger, for it's with me an ever-present sensation—I find that it is no part of good order to be sometimes without food. What a hell of an economy! Some men replete with everything while others, whose stomachs are not less importunate, whose hunger is just as recurrent, have nothing to bite on. The worst of it is the constrained posture in which need holds you. The needy man doesn't walk like the rest, he skips, twists, cringes, crawls. He spends his life choosing and performing positions.

MYSELF. What kind of "positions"?

HE. Go ask Noverre the choreographer.[65] The world numbers more positions than his art can reproduce.

MYSELF. So you too, if I may use your expression—or rather that of Montaigne—are perched on the epicycle of Mercury and considering the different pantomimes of humankind.

HE. No, I tell you, no. I am far too clumsy to rise so high. I yield to the cranes their foggy realms. I crawl on the earth, look about me, and take my positions. Or else I entertain myself watching others take theirs. I am good at pantomime, as you shall see.

[Thereupon he begins to smile, to ape a man admiring, a man imploring, a man complying. His right foot forward, the left behind, his back arched, head erect, his glance riveted as if on another's, openmouthed, his arms are stretched out toward some object. He waits for a command, receives it, flies like an arrow, returns. The order has been carried out; he is giving a report. Attentive, nothing escapes him. He picks up what is dropped, places pillow or stool under feet, holds a salver, brings a chair, opens a door, shuts a window, draws curtains, gazes at master and mistress. He is motionless, arm hanging, legs parallel; he listens and tries to read faces.] Then he says: "There you have my pantomime; it's about the same as the flatterer's, the courtier's, the footman's, and the beggar's."

This man's vagaries, like the tales of Abbé Galiani[66] and the extravaganzas of Rabelais, have often plunged me in deep reverie. Those are three storehouses from which I have drawn some absurd masks that I have then projected on the faces of the gravest figures. I seem to see Pantaloon[67] in a prelate, a satyr in a presiding judge, a porker in a friar, an ostrich in a king's minister, and a goose in his under secretary.

MYSELF. According to you [I went on], there are innumerable beggars in this world, for I hardly know anyone who doesn't use at least a few of your dance steps.

---

65. *choreographer*: Jean-George Noverre (1727–1810), ballet-master at the *Opéra-Comique* from 1753 to 1756.

66. *Galiani*: Abbé Ferdinand Galiani (1728–1787), statesman, man-of-letters, economist; one of Diderot's best friends;

part of the circle of *philosophes* that included Diderot, Grimm, D'Holbach, Helvétius, etc.

67. *Pantaloon*: stock figure of the aged pedant, selfish and libidinous.

HE. You are right. In the whole country only one man walks—the King. Everybody else takes a position.

MYSELF. The King? Even about him there might be something more to say. Don't you suppose that from time to time he finds near him a little foot, a little nose, a little curl that makes him perform a bit of pantomime? Whoever stands in need of another is needy and takes a position. The King takes a position before his mistress and before God: he dances his pantomime steps. The minister trips it too, as courtier, flatterer, footman and beggar before his king. The crowd of self-seekers dance all your positions in a hundred ways, each viler than the next, in front of the minister. The noble Abbé, in furred cape and cloak, dances attendance once a week at least before the official who appoints to benefices. Really, what you call the beggar's pantomime is what makes the world go round. Every man has his Bertin and his little Hus.

HE. It's very consoling to me.

[While I spoke he mimicked in killing fashion the positions of the figures I enumerated. For the little Abbé, for example, he held his hat under his arm and his breviary in the left hand. With the right he lifted the train of his cloak, stepping forward with his head a little to one side, eyes lowered, and giving the very image of the hypocrite. I thought I was seeing the author of *The Refutation*[68] petitioning the Bishop of Orleans. When he came to the courtiers and self-seekers, he crawled like a worm—the image of Bouret[69] before the Auditor-General.]

MYSELF. Your performance is unsurpassable [said I]. But there is one human being who is exempted from the pantomime. That is the philosopher who has nothing and asks for nothing.

HE. And where does the creature hide? If he has nothing, he must be suffering; if he asks for nothing, he will get nothing—and so will always suffer.

MYSELF. No. Diogenes made fun of his wants.

HE. But a man needs clothes.

MYSELF. He went naked.

HE. Wasn't it ever cold in Athens?

MYSELF. Not so often as here.

HE. But people had to eat.

MYSELF. No doubt.

HE. At whose expense?

MYSELF. At Nature's. Whom does the savage beg from? The earth, the animals and fishes, the trees and plants and roots and streams.

HE. An inferior menu.

---

68. *The Refutation*: Abbé Gabriel Gauchat (1709–1774) attacked the doctrines of Diderot and the *philosophes* in nineteen volumes.

69. *Bouret*: possibly alluding to a role played by the celebrated comedian, Claude-Antoine Bouret (d. 1783), whom Diderot admired.

MYSELF. But abundant.

HE. And badly served.

MYSELF. Yet it's the one whose leavings appear on all our tables.

HE. You have to admit that our cooks, pastrymen, confectioners, and caterers add a little of their own. If your Diogenes stuck to his austere diet, his organs must have been exceedingly docile.

MYSELF. You are wrong. The Cynic's costume was that of our monks and equally virtuous. The Cynics were the Carmelites and Cordeliers[70] of Athens.

HE. I've caught you then! Diogenes must have danced a pantomime, if not in front of Pericles,[71] at least in front of Lais and Phryne?[72]

MYSELF. Wrong again. The others paid dear the same courtesan who gave herself to him for pleasure.

HE. What if the courtesan was busy and the Cynic in haste?

MYSELF. He went back to his tub and did without.

HE. Do you advise me to do the same?

MYSELF. I'll stake my life it is better than to crawl, eat dirt and prostitute yourself.

HE. But I want a good bed, good food, warm clothes in winter, cool in summer, plenty of rest, money, and other things that I would rather owe to kindness than earn by toil.

MYSELF. That is because you are a lazy, greedy lout, a coward and a rotting soul.

HE. I believe I told you so myself.

MYSELF. The good things of life have their worth, no doubt, but you overlook the price of what you give up for them. You dance, you have danced, and you will keep on dancing the vilest pantomime.

HE. True enough. But it's cost me little and it won't cost me anything more. For which reason I should be quite wrong to take up another position, which would cause me trouble and which I could not hold. But from what you tell me I see that my poor dear little wife was a kind of philosopher. She had the courage of a lion. Sometimes we had no bread and no money and had already sold all our clothes. I would throw myself across the foot of the bed and rack my wits to find someone who would lend us a fiver that I'd never repay. She, gay as a lark, would sing and accompany herself at the clavier. She had the throat of a nightingale; I'm sorry you never heard her. When I took part in some musical evening I took her with me and on the way I would say: "Come, my lady, get yourself admired, display your talents and your charms, overwhelm, captivate." She would sing, overwhelm, captivate. Alas! I lost her, the

---

70. *Carmelites and Cordeliers:* Roman Catholic mendicant orders.
71. *Pericles:* Athenian statesman (495?–429 B.C.).
72. *Lais and Phryne:* courtesans.

poor thing. Besides her talents, she had a tiny mouth the width of a finger, a row of pearls for teeth, and then eyes, feet, a skin, cheeks, breasts, legs like a doe, thighs and buttocks for a sculptor. Sooner or later she would have had a chief tax collector at least. Her walk, her rump, ye gods, what a rump!"

[At once he imitated his wife's walk, taking little steps, perking his nose up in the air, flirting with a fan, swinging his hips. It was the caricature of our little coquettes, laughable and true. Then resuming his speech, he said: "I used to take her everywhere—to the Tuileries, the Palais-Royal, the Boulevards. She could not possibly have stayed with me. When she went across the street in the morning, hatless and in her smock, you would have stopped just to look at her and you could have held her waist with both thumbs and forefingers without squeezing her. Those who followed her and watched her trot along on her little feet or who gauged that rich rump outlined in her thin petticoats would hasten their pace. She let them come up then turned on them two big dark and glowing eyes that stopped them in their tracks. For the right side of the medal fully matched the reverse. But alas! I lost her and all my hopes of fortune went with her. I had taken her for no other reason, I had told her my plans. She was too intelligent not to see that they were assured of success and too sound of judgment not to agree with their aim."

[At which he began to sob and choke as he said: "No, no, I never shall get over it. Ever since, I've taken minor orders and wear a skullcap."]

MYSELF. From grief?

HE. If you like. But really in order to carry my soup plate upon my head. . . . But let's see what time it is, because I am going to the Opera.

MYSELF. What's on the program?

HE. Dauvergne's *Les Troqueurs*.[73] The music has some fine things in it. Too bad he wasn't the first to write them. Among the dead there are always a few to annoy the living. Can't be helped. *Quisque suos patimur manes*.[74] But it's half past five; I hear the bell ringing vespers for me and Abbé Canaye.[75] Farewell, Master Philosopher, isn't it true that I am ever the same?

MYSELF. Alas! Yes, unfortunately.

HE. Here's hoping this ill fortune lasts me another forty years. He laughs best who laughs last.

73. *Dauvergne's "Les Troqueurs":* The *Barterers*, opera by Antoine Dauvergne (1713–1797), mediocre operatic composer who tried to unite the French and Italian styles.

74. *Quisque . . . manes:* from Virgil (*Aeneid,* VI, 743): "Each of us has to endure his own misdeeds"—i.e., live down the past.

75. *Canaye:* Abbé Canaye (1694–1782), lover of the opera. Diderot points out that the bell at the *Palais-Royal* rings at 5:30 to announce the opening of the theater, at the same time that the vesper chimes are rung.

Masterpieces of
Romanticism

EDITED BY

HOWARD E. HUGO

Late of the University of California, Berkeley

FROM ROUSSEAU TO PUSHKIN

Only a little less than a hundred years separate Rousseau's completion of his *Confessions* (1770) from Pushkin's *Eugene Onegin* (1830). Though there are broader chronological stretches in other sections of this anthology, one may venture to say that few periods offer more radical shifts in man's entire outlook than do these years. In fact one measure of the works we have selected is the awareness their authors show (often more implicit than explicit) of such mutations.

"Everything goes to the people and deserts the kings, even literary themes, which descend from royal misfortunes to private misfortunes, from Priam to Birotteau"—so lamented the Goncourt brothers in 1866. From Homer's great monarch of Troy to Balzac's perfume manufacturer in Paris in the 1830's there is a vast movement, not only in time but also in the human spirit—a movement from the heroic hero that still interested Shakespeare and Racine to the unheroic hero of the nineteenth-century bourgeoisie. The dates 1775, 1789, 1830, and 1848 (all falling within the confines of this portion of the anthology) mark years of revolution when middle-class protests against the *status quo* emerged with various degrees of violence. Only one major monarch—Charles I of England—was deposed in the seventeenth century. By contrast, the reader will recall having met six kings in Chapter 26 of *Candide*, all impoverished and in exile. The nineteenth century was to see political alterations unanticipated by political theorists, as "the divinity [that]

239

doth hedge a king" was examined with rational suspicion, and monarchical and aristocratic powers were curtailed or abolished. The firing of "the shot heard round the world" at Concord (1775) and the fall of the Bastille (1789) mark dramatic moments which made actual the abstract political thought of eighteenth-century philosophers (with their paper constitutions, social contracts, declarations of the rights of man, and plans for perpetual peace). By 1850, it seemed to many political liberals that the bourgeoisie was politically and socially canonized. Continental revolutions in 1830 and 1848 and legislative reforms in England (chiefly in 1832) may have disappointed a few radicals by their compromises; but on the whole, the ascendancy of the middle class was guaranteed.

The change just outlined was "horizontal," cutting across national boundaries. The Enlightenment had set the goal, for the rational man, of being a "citizen of the world"; later eighteenth-century thought and nineteenth-century Romanticism moved from such universality toward the phenomenon known as nationalism. Rousseau's claim for personal uniqueness was expanded to apply to the individuality of the *Volk*, the nation, or the race. Nationalism was curiously intertwined with political liberalism from the French Revolution on. At times "vertical" national interests even superseded more generous ideas of man's brotherhood and the abolition of world-wide tyranny. The Year One, announced in

Paris in September, 1792, was intended to inaugurate a new egalitarian millenium for the *entire* human race; yet twelve years later Napoleon was crowned Emperor of the French. The amalgam of political liberalism and nationalism was not rare: many thinkers, the Italian liberal Mazzini, for example, regarded nationalism as a necessary stage before man reached true awareness of humanity as a whole. From 1815 to 1853 the comparative absence of all warfare save colonial engagements seemed to display the relative harmlessness of nationalism. We have had the dubious advantage of another hundred years of history, to watch it flourishing in its full horror.

Political upheavals in this period had their counterpart in the Industrial Revolution, which indeed accentuated notions of "class" and "nation" and began the transformation of most of Western Europe from an agrarian to a primarily industrial culture. The Reformation had earlier underscored the dignity and necessity of individual labor, and had indicated a connection between spiritual and material prudence and enterprise. With the growth of wealth, industry, manufacturing, and colonies came a need for more comprehensive theories. Adam Smith's *Wealth of Nations* (1776) set the pattern for subsequent economic speculation and practice: the laissez-faire state, permitting free trade, free markets, and free competition, in keeping with what Smith termed the "obvious and simple system of natural liberty." The advocacy of economic liberalism places Smith and his followers squarely within the tradition of middle-class liberalism, broadly defined. The modern reader should note Smith's assumption that economic individualism, without any form of government regulation, will result in public benefit and ultimate harmony. This difference in viewpoint distinguishes the early liberal from his spiritual descendants, who enlarged, rather than circumscribed, the scope of governmental function.

The Industrial Revolution was made possible by the technological innovations of applied science. One thinks of the steam engine perfected by James Watt toward the end of the eighteenth century; George Stephenson's locomotive, built in 1814; the telegraph, in 1844, and so on. What theology had been to the Middle Ages, science was to become to the nineteenth century. To the already established abstract field of mathematics were slowly added the more empirical studies of astronomy, physics, geology, and chemistry. Shortly after 1800, biology became a recognized area of study, as scientists dealt more and more systematically with the organic as well as the inorganic. When Auguste Comte expounded his "Positive philosophy" in the 1820's, and spoke of the need of an additional "life science" (sociology), the definition of the scientific disciplines seemed complete. Comte divided human history into "religious-superstitious," philosoph-

ical," and "scientific-positivistic" periods, and announced that the world was now enjoying the last of the three.

The trends we have just discussed inevitably gave rise to countertrends. The rise of the bourgeoisie and of democratic egalitarianism had opponents—not only defenders of privilege, and those who could say with Talleyrand, "No man not alive before 1789 knows the sweetness of life," but also those who anticipated the horrible potentialities implicit in "the revolt of the masses," later described by Ortega y Gasset. The "liberating" impulses of early nineteenth-century nationalism too frequently evolved into aggressive national pride or, worse, into rampant racism. The exponents of a free mercantile economy, assuming without justification that man's individual actions will naturally produce economic harmony, inspired economists like Karl Marx to correct the balance by elaborating theories according to which the independent capitalist would disappear altogether in the inexorable class struggle that (in Marx's view) he was helping to create. Finally, the faith in progress and the future which science apparently underwrote—the belief that man was destined to be biologically, materially, and morally better—was from its inception queried by those who feared the sin of pride, whether defined in Christian or in classical terms, and by those who resented the displacement of absolute truth by the relative, pragmatic truths which science asserted.

If some common direction is sought beneath these manifold tendencies, it may be found in the rise of secularity and in what the historian Lecky called "a declining sense of the miraculous." Medieval man knew that he lived in God's world, and Christianity had permeated every aspect of daily living. Whether the Reformation came as a symptom or a cause of weakened faith, the existence in the West of several hundred churches in 1700, in comparison with one Church in 1300, indicated doubts and questionings where once had been absolute doctrinal certainty. Politics and economics were increasingly shorn of theocratic presuppositions; and by the time of the Age of Reason, religious truth itself had to pass the tests of empirical and rational inquiry. Naturally there were individual thinkers, and even mass movements, who protested the departure from Christian orthodoxy; but, in general, during the first half of the nineteenth century, Christianity for the intellectual was absorbed into what Comte called vaguely "a religion of humanity." (Christianity for the average man often was summed up in a remark attributed to Lord Melbourne: "No man has more respect for the Christian religion than I have, but really, when it comes to intruding it into private life. . . .")

In 1859, Darwin published his *Origin of Species*. At first hailed with delight by many critics—for did not evolution make progress as *real* as the law of gravitation, and even coincide with ideas of Christian teleolo-gy?—Darwin's book was soon attacked by churchmen for destroying certain fundamentalist theses, and the fight between religion and science began in earnest. More important, as the century moved on, certain deeper minds were disturbed by the new conceptions of a universe from which mind and spirit seemed excluded, where chance determined change, where "survival of the fittest" and "natural selection" suggested that might and force won over right, and where moral laws were illusory fictions. Herbert Spencer's remark—"Nature's discipline is a little cruel that it may be very kind"—was then regarded either as small comfort or as downright erroneous. It is within this climate of opinion that romanticism ends and realism begins.

ROMANTICISM— SENTIMENT AND NATURE

The preceding remarks range far ahead of the first works in this section. Let us return briefly to the mid-eighteenth century, when, in the period of transition from the Enlightenment to romanticism, certain philosophical, political, and cultural presuppositions at one time thought to be eternally true were discussed, then criticized, then finally abandoned. Once again we are faced with the fact that men very radically change their opinions within a relatively short span of history. Out of the mass of attitudes and ideas, we abstract two which seem particularly significant: the change in the concept of nature and the growing importance attributed to the sentiments, feelings, emotions, passions.

Frederick the Great, onetime patron of Voltaire, described *Candide* as "Job in modern dress," and it is good to remember that the Book of Job ends in mystery. In *Candide* the same mystery is posed en route, although the work itself ends with acceptance. Why does evil exist in the universe? Why does the good man suffer? What is the relation of God to mankind? Does the cosmos run according to some rational scheme comprehensible to the human mind? Eighteenth-century science and mathematics had seemed to confirm the mechanistic view that all parts of nature were intelligible. Yet an increasing number of dark spots on the once illuminated intellectual horizon puzzled and confused later thinkers. Nature was to remain the comforting talisman for romanticism that it had been for the Age of Reason, but we shall see that "nature" came to be redefined. The romantics were as anxious as their classical and neoclassical forbears to fathom the riddle of man in his world, but henceforth it was felt that perhaps the heart—the emotions—and not the head held the key to ultimate comprehension of the universe. To understand this change, we must examine the growing cult of sentiment in the eighteenth century.

It would be foolish to imagine that at a certain moment people stopped thinking and began feeling. The Enlightenment had made much of the "moral sense," and the early decades of the eighteenth century had enjoyed an honest tear with innumerable sentimental novels and plays. But on the whole the deliberate exploitation of the emotions had been held suspect; and if ultimate values—laws about the cosmos, the arts, society, and so on—were at stake, those areas of the psyche which related to the feelings were conceived to be irrelevant. Spinoza, in *Of Human Bondage, or The Power of the Affections* (1667) said, "In so far as men are subject to passions, they cannot be said to agree in nature." The idiosyncrasy resulting from adherence to personal emotion rather than to the generally accepted principles of reason was not considered ideal material for literature in a period unusually dedicated to ideas of universality, social man, communication between minds, and conformity to classical norms. Then, for reasons that are still not clear, philosophical introspection, reverie, the melancholy heart became fashionable. The brooding, solitary daydreamer came into his own, with varieties of "spleen," "the blue devils," *Weltschmerz* ("world sorrow"), *le mal du siècle* ("the sickness of the century"). Rousseau's *Confessions* (1781-1788), filled with this kind of passionate unrest, were hailed by a reading public already assured of the primacy of the emotions.

I am commencing [said Rousseau] an undertaking, hitherto without precedent, and which will never find an imitator. I desire to set before my fellow-men the likeness of a man in all the truth of nature, and that man is myself. Myself alone! I know the feelings of my heart, and I know men. I am not made like any of those I have seen; I venture to believe that I am not made like any of those who are in existence.

From the objective norms that were the delight of the Age of Reason, we turn to the subjective, innate, indefinable, and *unique* core of each individual. The "man of feeling" (the phrase forms the title of a popular novel by the Scottish writer, Henry MacKenzie, published in 1771) replaced the elegant conversationalist of the salon, coffee house, and boudoir. And his feelings were mostly mournful. Earlier eighteenth-century sentimental literature had displayed *both* pleasurable and painful experiences, enriched by laughter and tears. The romantics endeavored to show that sensibility was not equated with happiness, and romantic literature in general is rarely comical or amusing. Pushkin does occasionally smile wryly, but after the manner of Byron, whom he so admired: "And if I laugh at any mortal thing, 'Tis that I may not weep." In Rousseau's novel, *Julie ou La Nouvelle Héloïse* (*Julia, or The New Héloïse*, 1761), the young hero Saint-Preux exclaims poignantly, "For me there is only a single way to be happy, but there are millions of ways to be miserable."

For the romantics, the so-called "tender passion"—love—gained pre-eminence among all the feelings. The modern colloquial usage of "romantic" with connotations of moon-June-spoon is in part a legacy from

that period. With the exception of Racine's *Phèdre*, the preceding section of this anthology contains, significantly, no literature dealing with love. Candide voyages from continent to continent to find his elusive Cunégonde, but her chief virtue—physical indestructibility—scarcely qualifies her for the role of a *romantic* heroine. The eighteenth century —despite its finesse, social decorum, and elegance—abounds with works displaying the relations between the sexes as surprisingly lusty and earthy, or as a kind of psychological game with possession the assumed goal of the male partner. Against such amorous franchise the romantics rebelled. We shall watch Faust and Margaret, among other heroes and heroines, asserting that love is a genuine spiritual entity and a condition eagerly to be coveted—not for purposes of physical satisfaction but because unhappy as the condition may be, life is meaningless unless we exist in that state of morose delight.

Even as the age brought a revaluation of the less ratiocinative, more intuitive processes of the psyche, it also brought new colorings to the concept of nature. From classical antiquity through most of the eighteenth century, the word *nature* had meant the totality of existence, the entire cosmos—animate and inanimate—with its laws and activity, and when it meant anything less than this, it had usually meant the whole nature of man—common human nature. But in the cult of nature inspired by the romantic movement, the term came to mean something much more limited: the physical world apart from man's achievements—that is, the landscape and countryside, the sea and mountains. In a sense this idealization of nature was no innovation. The Hebraic-Christian tradition had begun with a garden. Pagan antiquity in Greece and Rome had produced pastorals and bucolics, in which the vision of the simple life in close proximity to animals and the land was portrayed. But the cleavage that Rousseau and his heirs now felt to exist between the individual and his environment led to a redefinition of "nature." Neoclassical society, polished and polite, had been essentially urban, although the philosopher-gentleman could enjoy the country as a respite from strenuous city life with its Court and Parliament, salons and coffee houses, wit and conversation. The formal garden—like Voltaire's at Ferney, with two head gardeners and twenty laborers—may be taken as a symbol of what was held to be a happy compromise between the country's annoying miscellaneousness and civilized mankind's love of order. As Dr. Johnson, Voltaire's contemporary, put it: "Sir, they who are content to live in the country are fit for it."

In the passage above from Rousseau, he stated that he is psychologically unique and like no other man past or present. From this sense of acute individuality, it is only a short step to a feeling of being alien and misunderstood. If our insensitive contemporaries reject us, we can always find comfort in the great sympathetic soul of nature —nature who "never did betray/The heart that loved her."

The heroes of later eighteenth-century literature move out from the confines of city and drawing room to the seas and forests. By the early nineteenth century the new hero has become stereotyped and hostility to organized society a cliché. If any member of society gained the romantic's approbation, it was generally the simple rustic who—like the innocent child—was close to nature and therefore morally purer than his sophisticated fellows. Primitivism long had interested the rationalist thinkers, and the untutored mind afforded the *philosophes* fascinating material for their studies of general mankind, although for this purpose distant, exotic savages (Voltaire's *Oreillons*, for instance) were more pleasing and more conveniently remote than the local peasantry. Later eighteenth-century expansions of this concept marked a shift from mere interest in the Noble Savage to positive approval. Serious doubts were raised as to the validity of urbanity and cultivation and about the notion of progress itself. Perhaps the unspoiled savage partook of a Golden Age where hearts rather than purses were gold, where there was no *mine* or *thine*, no artificial legislation, no social hierarchy. Though Rousseau's "natural man" drew a shout of derision from Voltaire, who saw men once more getting down on all fours in abdication of their rational-human capabilities, Voltaire was fighting a rearguard action, and the success of a work he ridiculed proved it. Few literary productions have attained the popularity of the Ossian poems (1760-1763), ostensibly translated by James Macpherson. *Fingal* and *Temora*, two "epics" in the group, depicted early Scottish-Celtic-"Erse" days in an elegiac, melancholy tone. What critics seemed most to admire was the *goodness* of all the characters. The poems of Ossian, for example, were among the favorite reading of a most unprimitive figure—Napoleon. That Macpherson's work was later proved a forgery in no way diminished his incredible influence. Twenty-five years afterward, Bernardin de Saint-Pierre published *Paul and Virginia* (*Paul et Virginie*, 1788), in which the life of decadent Europe was contrasted unfavorably with life on an unspoiled, Eden-like island. "Here there is merely wooden furniture, but there you find serene faces and hearts of gold."

France had been the Continental fortress of the Age of Reason, as our selection of readings in the preceding section of the anthology indicates. The headquarters of the new ideology moved to the "misty" north and Germany. That country demonstrated conscious romantic symptoms during the 1770's with its "Storm and Stress" (*Sturm und Drang*) movement in literature —led by a coterie of young writers fired by naturalistic, anti-French, anticlassical feeling. In their twenties, they were impregnated with notions about

"genius" that should transcend any fettering rules and standards, convinced of the primacy of the passions over the meddling intellect, desirous of writing simple folk poetry stemming directly from the heart of the race, anxious to identify the spirit of man with the spirit of the new "nature," and, finally, eager to use literature as a vehicle in the search for philosophic truth— the pursuit of the Absolute, the underlying reality of existence. This was one of the first *avant-garde* groups. Among those who contributed to the "Storm and Stress" movement was Johann Wolfgang von Goethe. His *Faust*, Part I, begun during these years, is an illustration of the fully developed romantic mood.

ROMANTICISM AND THE
METAPHYSICAL QUEST—
GOETHE'S FAUST

Goethe, speaking of *Faust* to his friend and amanuensis Eckermann, once commented, "I think that I have given them a bone to pick." Seldom in Western literature has a work been so provocative to its audience; yet many a critic has sunk deep in the morass of intellectualism when attempting to explicate the play. The average reader will find *Faust* difficult going. He will be aware that there is more to it than meets the eye, although perhaps his feeling of disquietude will overbalance any pleasure the reading has afforded. If he is honest with himself, however, he will be forced to one conclusion upon completing *Faust*: he has been in the

to do nothing is worse than death

Faust

presence of one of the greatest of the world's masterpieces. Such an experience *should* lead to healthy confusion, since the reader—with the artist—has just taken a plunge into the unknown.

The first part of *Faust* was published by Goethe in 1808. Many years had gone into its creation. His so-called *Ur-Faust* ("early" or "primitive" *Faust*) was written between 1770 and 1775, and *Faust, a Fragment,* appeared in 1790. Behind Goethe's extensive labors lay the whole legend of the Renaissance scholar, Dr. Faustus, who quested after universal knowledge by means of white magic—that is, orthodox science—and the more terrible instrument of black magic. A real Johannes Faustus lived from 1480 to 1540. His adventures, much embroidered, were related by Johannes Spies twenty-seven years later, and these became the subject for innumerable puppet shows and popular folk-dramas throughout the seventeenth and eighteenth centuries in Germany. Hence from childhood on, the Faust myth was familiar to Goethe; and from the time he was twenty until he died at eighty-two, the theme never left his imagination. To trace the slow genesis of *Faust*, Part I, and later *Faust*, Part II (the sequel published posthumously in 1833), is fascinating to the scholar, but dull for the student. The important fact to be grasped is simple. Once again, as in Greek tragedy and Racine's *Phèdre*, we have the playwright using traditional, legendary, even mythical material.

The "Prologue in Heaven" Benedetto Croce has called "the jest of a great artist . . . deliberately archaic, and slightly in the style of Voltaire." We should not be misled by its cosmic humor and high irony. It must be read with care, for the key to subsequent events is found in the dialogue between God and Mephistopheles. The paean of the Archangels in praise of the wonderful universe is succeeded by the nay-sayer's insouciant remarks. Like Satan in the Book of Job (the opening scene is obviously modeled on Job 1:6-12 and 2:1-6) Goethe's devil has just returned "from going to and fro in the earth, and from walking up and down on it." What he has seen has only increased his contempt for that silly grasshopper, man. The angels may place man a little lower than themselves. Mephistopheles finds restless mankind scarcely an improvement over primordial chaos. Already we note that Mephistopheles' quarrel is not with man or with Faust; his challenge is leveled at God and His fitness as a creator!

Then follows the *first* wager, which is between God and a fallen divinity. Faust is discontented, says Mephistopheles. That beautiful gift of reason has induced nothing but fatal curiosity. His bewilderment, answers God, is temporary; and He turns Faust over to this most cynical of devils for the rest of his life. No holds are barred for Mephistopheles. He is given *carte blanche* to lure Faust in any fashion. The cryptic language

Fragonard Boucher Watteau

may obscure the real issue for the reader. Here is no simple temptation to be naughty. Mephistopheles' aim is to undermine Faust's whole *moral* sense, the awareness that values of good and evil do exist despite man's difficulties in defining them. A being of searchings and questionings, living a life of constant aspiration toward goals but dimly seen—this, as described by God, is the being He has created in His own image. We shall see shortly how the terms of the *second* pact between man and devil are an attempt on Mephistopheles' part to stop this vital activity, thus implicitly defeating God's description of life as an eternal Becoming.

Such a vitalistic and dynamic interpretation of the human condition is the essence of romantic philosophy. Christianity had posited a state of grace, and Christian thought is the history of attempts to determine how erring man might finally enjoy eternal bliss. The Enlightenment, ignoring the mystery of faith implicit in Christian doctrine, had expanded the element of reason to be an end in itself. Romanticism, suddenly aware of dynamic (even irrational) principles underlying both man and nature, took striving—tentative progression and development, and pure endeavor—and made it the defining quality of mankind. In the second part of *Faust* (about which we shall speak briefly later on), Goethe has a chorus of angels proclaim, "Should a man strive with all his heart/ Heaven can foil the devil." The paradox of *Faust*

is that of a man finally redeemed by a God whose reality Faust doubts. Goethe has written a modern *Divine Comedy* paralleling Dante's, but it is "divine comedy" of the profoundest irony.

Following the prologue we move from heaven to earth—a shift in background reminiscent of the epic. The setting of the opening of the play is traditional: "a high-vaulted narrow *Gothic* room." It reminds us of Goethe's role in the "Storm and Stress" group, the young writers of Germany who were anxious to rescue the native scene, and also the Middle Ages, and also Shakespeare (their idol), from the undervaluations of the Enlightenment—by which they meant France and French neoclassicism. The late C. S. Lewis, in *The Screwtape Letters* (1942), pointed out how "the long, dull, monstrous years of middle-aged prosperity or middle-aged adversity are excellent campaigning weapons" for the devil, and Goethe's Heinrich Faust is in the full maturity of worldly success. He owns everything—and nothing. He as polymath has investigated the entire field of human knowledge to find a chaos of relativism. A simple three-meal-a-day life is impossible for him. He cherishes a passion for the Absolute which his pedantic assistant Wagner cannot comprehend. Black magic yields little save despair. Death is one road to possession of final truth, but a childhood memory of naïve faith averts suicide. At this critical stage Mephistopheles enters (first in the guise of a poodle, and we remember that the Greek root of the word *cynic* means "dog"). The real action of the play begins.

The Prince of Darkness is a gentleman, and the devil soon abandons his earlier disguises for the elegant costume of the polished gallant and wit. He had minced no words when he said previously, "I am the Spirit which always denies" ("*Ich bin der Geist der stets verneint*"). Now he offers *his* wager to Faust. Their pact is a corollary of the one we witnessed in Heaven. An interesting point, however, is that Faust frames the terms. We have already indicated that God's picture of Mephistopheles does not coincide with the devil's view of himself. The relation of the tempter to Faust presents us with an additional facet to his character, for Mephistopheles never really understands the nature of his companion's problem. *If* Mephistopheles can destroy Faust's sense of aspiration, *if* Faust can say of any single moment in time that *this* is complete fulfillment of desire—then the devil wins, and God and man are defeated. Such repose and satiety would represent an end to striving. It would also—and here is the subtle touch—mean a cessation of Faust's moral awareness. By the achievement of a final "good" on earth, the whole conception of good and evil as being in a state of development would be denied. Faust examines existence in terms of a question that only modern man could conceive; certainly it was unknown to the Greeks with their feeling for

limitation. Is a life of tireless movement toward an undefined goal worth living? And the devil (orthodox conservative and traditionalist that he is) can hardly be expected to grasp such a radical query.

The varieties of pleasure that the devil parades before the hero are proffered in an effort to supply *the* moment of complete satisfaction, and thus obfuscate Faust's values. Mephistopheles almost wins with Margaret (Gretchen). But love is more complicated than mere sex, and Faust's love comes to mean the acme of human aspiration. From love he learns to break through the bonds of his individual ego and to see his state in humanity. Margaret's tragedy enhances rather than diminishes Faust's moral sensibility, and Mephistopheles is a puzzled, disappointed sensualist when he takes Faust back to Gretchen's dungeon for the last poignant scene in the play. It is essential that the reader comprehend how much the author stresses the nature of Faust's affection, how love is raised to the level of a high philosophical concept. Stendhal showed only his lack of perception when he remarked: "Goethe gives Faust the Devil for a friend; and with this powerful ally, Faust does what we have all done at the age of twenty—he seduces a seamstress."

Even before the first part of *Faust* was published, Goethe thought of writing a second drama where the hero would turn from individual to social concerns. From approximately 1800 to 1831 Goethe worked on

Faust, Part II, a play designed principally to be read. To read it is, in the words of one critic, "a pilgrimage from which few have returned safe and sound." Few works in modern times present us with such a conglomeration of shifting symbols, and we move from mystery to mystery, carried forward by Goethe's incomparable verse and brilliant ideas. A "Classical Walpurgis Night" synthesizes ancient Greece and the Gothic north. Goethe returns to the older Faust legend to have his aging protagonist marry Helen of Troy, now a widow after the death of Menelaus. Their union begets Euphorion (the spirit of new humanity; it is said that Goethe had Byron in mind as his model). Faust also undertakes a military career to save a shaky kingdom from falling. The ultimate activity pursued by Faust consists in reclaiming land from the sea, and he sees the vision of a new, happy community composed of industrious mankind. *This* is at last the consummate moment for him, and Mephistopheles—a nearly exhausted tempter—wins the wager in a dubious victory. But Faust's satisfaction is potential rather than actual: the vision lies in the indeterminate future for which he strives. The angels rescue Faust's soul from the forces of evil and bear him in triumph to heaven. Goethe's God seems to say that Faust's errors are necessary imperfections of man's growth. Imperfections in time are perfections in eternity. Faust's has been a "good" life. The final lines of the great drama, declaimed by the *Chorus Mysticus*

in heaven, sum up the author's profound affirmation of existence.

> All that is past of us
> Was but reflected;
> All that was lost in us
> Here is corrected;
> All indescribables
> Here we descry;
> Eternal Womanhead
> Leads us on high.
> [*Das Ewig-Weibliche/
> Zieht uns hinan*]

CHATEAUBRIAND AND THE ROMANTIC HERO

While a royalist exile in England, Chateaubriand conceived of a plan to write an apology for Christianity, wherein certain fictional tales would serve as *exempla* to illustrate the efficacy of true belief. He had flirted with philosophical skepticism in his youth. The statement he made about his conversion is interesting: "My conviction came from the heart; I wept and I believed." Anxious to return to France, he was unsure about the reception such an ambitious work, *The Genius of Christianity* (*Le Génie du Christianisme*), would obtain. He produced *Atala* (1801) as a trial balloon, and the results were highly gratifying. A rapid sequence of events in 1802 displays the changing temper of the times. On April 8 Napoleon signed a Concordat with the pope, restoring the Church to France after ten years of enforced secularism. On April 14 *The Genius of Christianity* was published, including both *Atala* and *René*. On April 18 a *Te Deum* was sung in Notre Dame

Cathedral in Paris, with all the ancient splendor of the *ancien régime*, to celebrate peace between Church and State. That fantastic creation of the Revolution, the Goddess of Reason, was dethroned; and the Madonna returned to supplant her. Thus a changing religious mood contributed to ensure the triumph of Chateaubriand's book. His decision in 1805 to reprint *Atala* and *René* apart from the larger work shows that his impressive arguments in the *Genius* had been brushed aside by the common reader who preferred imaginative enjoyment to moral edification. This is the impression one receives from three contemporaries. "I read *René,* and I shuddered," said Sainte-Beuve. George Sand, leading female novelist who preferred a male *nom de plume,* behaved true-to-form when she commented, "It seemed that René was myself." Maurice de Guérin confided to his *Journal,* "This reading [of *René*] soaked my soul like rain from a storm." *René* came to be for the youth of France in the 1810's and 1820's what Goethe's *Werther* (1774) had been for readers across the Rhine a generation earlier. In each case social and philosophical dislocations had produced a state of mind such that a single book articulated sentiments dimly felt. With *René* the eternal theme of moral man in immoral society received a new local habitation and a name.

Behind the creation of this *novella* lay Chateaubriand's grander plan, and *René* is best comprehended if the author's ideas—sometimes barely implicit in the story—are sketched. *The Genius of Christianity* starts with an attack on the *Encyclopédie*—"that tower of Babel of science and reason." Chateaubriand then takes recourse to history. Christianity is *better* because it represents an emotional increase over all prior faiths, and even Adam's fall was caused by his sterile intellectualism before he succumbed to the temptation. Chateaubriand's digressions deal less with the intelligent design of the circumambient universe often celebrated by the Deists than with its aesthetic charms and beauty. "The Christian God is poetically superior to ancient Jupiter," he declares—a declaration that must have been surprising to theologians in Rome, Geneva, and Canterbury; and also both Testaments are more moving *qua* literature than the classics of Greece and Rome. Theologians had always emphasized that man's sojourn on earth was but a temporary phase. Chateaubriand reverts to their idea and reaffirms the role of the Christian pilgrim-voyager, faced with salvation or damnation, whose emotional intensity is an improvement on pagan intellect. Gothic architecture, ecclesiastical ruins and tombs, remind the Christian of his dim mortality; the aspiration of the church spire pointing toward heaven displays a yearning for divinity that the more "horizontal" dimensions of Greek temples can never possess. Finally, in a chapter entitled *About the Vagueness of the Passions* ("Du Vague des Passions"), he cites the contribution that Christianity has made in canonizing the emotion of love, and lists famous lovers, all postdating the birth of Christ. For him progress meant not mere intellectual aggrandizement, the progress of the *philosophes*. "The more that people advance in civilization, the more increases this condition of the *vagueness* of the passions." Christian love, an aspect of such "vagueness," meant a salutary synthesis of *eros* and *agape*, profane and sacred love, in Chateaubriand's mind. Thus *René* is in part an *exemplum*, in which the incestuous feelings of brother and sister clash with Amelia's Christian decision to enter a convent, and René is made to feel the full horror of his illicit passion. Yet the resulting unalleviated melancholy exalts him as a hero of sensibility above crasser fellow men. Here lay René's appeal to the readers who discovered in him a paradigm for their own conditions.

Romantic themes abound in the novel: the hero's childhood is unhappy in that he is misunderstood by others; nature responds like a violin to his fluctuating moods, incestuous love tragically distinguishes him from his happier but duller contemporaries. Most romantic of all, perhaps, are his voyages. Candide, that epitome of the rationalist in search of a better world, travels extensively, and the eighteenth century fairly swarms with accounts of young men who take the Grand Tour to fill out their education and acquaint themselves with the ways of polite society. But the romantic voyage

which frames René's lugubrious narrative adds a new element. Here the hero moves from civilization and the company of insensitive fellow beings toward an unknown, exotic, mysterious terrain, where there is always the promise—though rarely the fulfillment—that the jaded soul will discover peace. Thus we gradually arrive at those curious romantic voyages of the imagination, quests we normally associate with the world of dreams: Hoffmann's *Tales*, Coleridge's *Ancient Mariner*, Melville's *Moby Dick*—works that look ahead to Rimbaud's *Drunken Ship* (*Bateau ivre*) and the bizarre universe of Franz Kafka with that castle forever out of reach. "Anywhere out of this world," cried Baudelaire in a dialogue he undertook with his soul (from *The Spleen of Paris*, 1869). "Life is a hospital where every invalid wants to exchange his bed for someone else's."

THE TALES OF E. T. A. HOFFMANN

Gothic stories of supernatural horror are not a Romantic invention. They were already popular in the eighteenth century, when novels such as Horace Walpole's *The Castle of Otranto* (1764) and Mathew Gregory Lewis's *The Monk* (1796) sent delicious shivers up many spines, while the literary works and fairy tales of still earlier centuries abound in ghosts, demons, and magic. But in the tales of E. T. A. Hoffmann the horrific is not merely sensational. It is shaped and colored by his introspective grasp of his own obsessions and terrors, the stuff of the irrational mind. Devils, phantom doubles (or *Doppelgänger*), and other supernatural apparitions take shape not from religious or literary tradition but from the artist's own subjectivity, expressing the forces of the subconscious.

Hoffmann was a highly emotional and sensitive man who, however well he may have served as manager of various artistic ensembles and as a civil servant, went through life "with his skin off," spontaneous and touchy. In his writings, too, the tone often shifts suddenly between worldly irony and passionate abandon. His fictional alter egos, including Erasmus Spikher in *A New Year's Eve Adventure* (1815) and Johannes Kreisler, a conductor who was the persona for Hoffman's music criticism, resemble him in their quirkiness and vulnerability, buffeted as they are by the force of their own passions and the disdain of bourgeois society.

Hoffmann's stories are abundantly furnished with details from their author's life. In *A New Year's Eve Adventure* he is behind not only Erasmus Spikher but the Travelling Enthusiast of the frame story—like Hoffmann a musician—and the "editor" whose comments provide yet another frame. Both Julia and Giulietta—the latter name is an Italian version of the former—are fantasy-projections of a young girl named Julia Marc with whom Hoffmann had recently been fervently in love; she, like the fictional Julia, was to marry a solid citizen, while Hoffmann, like Spikher, was to return to his own calm, stolid wife. Even Peter Schlemihl, who

makes a brief appearance in the wine cellar, has autobiographical meaning, for he is the creation of Hoffmann's friend Adalbert von Chamisso; the Spikher story is in fact a dark variation on Chamisso's tale of Schlemihl's adventures. (Appropriately, Chamisso was among the first to know Hoffmann's story, as he was part of the small circle of friends to whom Hoffmann read it shortly after New Year's Day, 1814.) It is no wonder that when several Hoffmann tales, including *A New Year's Eve Adventure*, were dramatized in 1851 by Barbier and Carré, Hoffmann himself was made the hero of all the adventures.

But Hoffmann's achievement goes beyond fictionalized autobiography. By fusing his own experiences and feelings with elements of the supernatural and grotesque he sought to create a literature of fully Romantic sensibility, one that could express the workings not only of the rational but the irrational mind. The real Julia Marc was no cold sophisticate like the fictional Julia, no *femme fatale* like Giulietta, but a teenaged victim of circumstances. The qualities of her fictional counterparts owe little to her but much to fantasies which, Freud has argued, men build out of their relations with their mothers and project onto the other women in their lives. Like Freud, too, Hoffmann was deeply interested in dreams, and indeed the Spikher story has something of the shape and tone of a nightmare: the vain effort to flee a monstrous threat, Dapertutto's magical comings and goings, the phantom double, even the story's inconclusive end (as if the dreamer had awakened), all follow a dream-logic familiar to us.

The controlled irrationality of Hoffmann's stories has inspired writers as diverse as Dostoevsky, Baudelaire, and Edgar Allan Poe, and even musicians such as Robert Schumann (who named a set of fantastic piano pieces *Kreisleriana*) and Hector Berlioz, whose *Fantastic Symphony: Episode in the Life of an Artist* is like a Hoffmannesque tale in music. But Hoffmann was by no means universally admired; Goethe, for one, thought his a sick talent. In a way, Goethe and Hoffmann define two extremes of the Romantic view, and the contrast is especially vivid if one compares *Faust* with *A New Year's Eve Adventure*. Both turn on the same motif, a pact between a man and the devil, but to opposite ends. The bargain in *Faust*, between a scholar of powerful intellect and a debonair, witty devil he knows how to control, is a symbol of human energy and aspiration; that between the hapless Erasmus Spikher and the loathsome, red-cloaked fiend Dapertutto symbolizes human weakness and sensuality. Faust ultimately wins and is carried up to heaven, but Spikher is lost before he ever meets his devil, in thrall to his uncontrollable and finally murderous infatuation with Giulietta, able only by a great effort of will to step back from the blackest depravity, and thereafter doomed to a life of hopeless, lonely wandering. Goethe's is not only the more optimistic but of course the greater work, but Hoffmann's frenzied pessimism may often speak more directly to modern readers.

HEINRICH HEINE AND THE ROMANTIC LYRIC

For many readers of poetry, especially non-Germans, Heine has come to represent the epitome of the German Romantic spirit, but he is probably better viewed as a transitional figure for whom Romanticism was an inheritance on which he drew but to which he did not significantly add. To say this is not to diminish his stature but to indicate where his contribution to the literary tradition may be located. In surveying his own career, near the time of his death Heine wrote, ". . . with me the old poetic school of the Germans came to an end, while at the same time I inaugurated the new school, that of modern German lyric poetry."

One feature that places Heine beyond the German Romantics (that is, figures like Frederick Hölderlin, Novalis, the Schlegel brothers, and Clemens Brentano) is that he could view the massive and kaleidoscopic achievement of Goethe's career with admiration but also a certain distance, no longer feeling that he had to work under the Olympian poet's shadow. Heine did share with many of the Romantics a sense that the primary source of the lyric impulse came from *Volkspoesie* (the popular and mythic traditions of a racial or national group as transmitted through folk songs and tales). It was Gottfried Herder, Gothe's friend, who first made this material widely available through collections of folk songs made between 1778 and 1789. Subsequently two poets of the Romantic generation proper, Achim von Arnim and Brentano, made a second major collection of folk poetry, *The Child's Horn of Plenty (Des Knaben Wunderhorn,* 1806–1808). The blend of folkish diction, apparent artlessness, and direct emotional appeal found in these collections soon created a poetic idiom as pervasive and susceptible to stereotype as the Elizabethan sonnet. It supplied the basic idiom of German poetry for at least a century. (It is worth noting, though, that Gothe was already able to evoke this strain in the early 1770s in such poems as Gretchen's ballad of the King of Thule and her song at the spinning wheel, which formed part of the *Urfaust,* or first fragmentary version of *Faust, Part I.*)

The Book of Songs (1827) spread Heine's reputation throughout Europe and the world. It typified for many readers the immediacy, simplicity, and pathos of the German *lied* (literally "song" but also short lyric poem). The extensive use of Heine texts for art songs in the nineteenth century tended to accentuate the Romantic and sentimental side of his literary achievement. (Thus the first and third poems in our selection are part of Schumann's famous song cycle *Dichterliebe* "A Poet's Love," 1840.) The overwhelming popularity of Heine's early poetry bred not only a swarm of imitators but also strong negative reactions, responses which have continued into this century and have significantly colored his literary reputation. Since in many ways Heine fulfilled the image of a self-absorbed, alternately moody and naively spontaneous songster, the more calculated, witty, and acerbic tones of his poetry were overlooked by one part of his public (the less critical readers who "caught Heine" as one catches the measles, as one of his critics mocked), or else resented by another, more conservative group. These saw Heine as a dissolute cosmopolitan (his residence in Paris for the second half of his life seemed to confirm this) who had fed on the pure strain of the folk tradition but profaned it through his sophistication and irony. Few major poets have known such great popularity together with such a persistent and variously motivated chorus of detractors.

The appeal of Heine's love poems lies in their combination of wit and erotic suggestion. Though the theme of unfulfilled love is one of the legacies of the folk tradition, Heine gave it a wry, bittersweet turn that is reminiscent of Petrarchan poetry and of such pointed, self-conscious lyrics as Goethe's late cycle of poems, the *West-östlicher Divan* (1819). A poem like the "Loreley," however, strikes a rare balance between the haunting, inexplicable force of a mythic subject and a modern mood of nostalgia and sentimental abandon.

A good part of Heine's output after his removal to Paris in 1831 consisted of reportage and commentary on a wide range of cultural and political topics. This journalism was essential for his financial support, but Heine brought to it an alert intelligence and a brilliant style that made this part of his work almost as popular as his poetry. While in no sense an original political thinker, Heine had been from his early years strongly interested in political issues. The brief Napoleonic rule of his native Düsseldorf during his childhood imbued him with a heroic ideal that made him particularly critical of the greed and complacency of the Restoration and bourgeois culture which followed (an attitude not unlike that of his near-contemporary Stendhal). This attitude, together with a Voltairian sense of outrage over social injustice, made him a particularly astute commentator of French conditions during the reign of Louis-Phillipe (1830–1848).

In the early part of his Paris residence Heine was drawn to the socialist principles of St.-Simonism, and during the 1840s he became friendly with Karl Marx and the communist circles active in Paris. His assessment of their aims was positive but not unreserved, as a careful reading of that remarkable fable "The Migratory Rats" reveals. At one level it represents a scathing portrayal of the bourgeois order, the fat rats who stay at home but become cowed and terrified by the threatened takeover of the have-nots. The poet's advice to these cowardly burghers is given directly in the last four stanzas. But the undeniable needs of the hungry rats does not make their demeanor or methods in the least attractive. Their bestiality and the narrowness of their "soup-logic" not only frighten the social establishment in the poem but clearly revolt the poet too.

In a political text of the same period as this poem (1854)

Heine reiterates a view already expressed earlier, namely that the "future belongs to the Communists. . . ." (It should be remembered, though, that at this period communism was in no sense a unified movement with a consistent ideology and tended to overlap with many socialist groupings.) But he adds that this prophecy is made "in a tone of worry and extreme trepidation. . . . Truly, it is only with fear and trembling that I think of the times when these ominous destroyers of images will gain power; they will shatter with their calloused hands all those marble monuments of beauty so dear to my heart; they will annihilate all those pastimes and trifles of fancy that the poet so loves. . . ." While the satiric thrust of a poem like "The Migratory Rats" anticipates in many ways the strategy of a Bertolt Brecht, it is clear from pronouncements like these that Heine was far from ready to associate himself with a proletarian future.

Much of the poetry that Heine wrote during the last eight years of his life while confined to his bed by a wasting spinal disease represents a type of expressivity that is very different from the Romantic ideal of a spontaneous expression of feeling. There is no doubt that these poems derive from the poet's personal and anguished experience. Yet in contrast to the characteristic Romantic lyric, there is no effort here to elevate the inward, subjective essence of the poet and associate it with natural elements or transcendent spiritual forces. On the contrary, the poet's voice, or persona, is unalterably bound to the mundane. It employs a language that is colloquial and particularized and does not shirk from exposing the self's frailty and even indignity—a stance to be found in much modern poetry since at least T. S. Eliot.

Heine once characterized these late poems to a friend who visited him in his sick room in these terms: ". . . beautiful, aren't they? terribly beautiful! It is like a plaint from a grave, a cry in the night from someone buried alive, or else from a corpse, or even from the grave itself. Yes, German poetry has never yet heard such strains, and could not have, since no poet has yet been in such a situation. . . ." What rescues these works from sentimentality and self-pity is first of all a grim but by no means embittered humor, a humor that betokens an undiminished acuity of observation; and then a fierce, unchastened questioning spirit, motivated not only by his own suffering but by a larger sense of inequality and injustice in the world. In this sense these valedictory poems written from the "mattress grave" (as Heine termed it), such as our selections "Babylonian Sorrows" and "How slowly Time, that loathsome snail," reveal a continuity with the social and political attitudes of his earlier years.

RUSSIAN ROMANTICISM—
PUSHKIN'S EUGENE ONEGIN

It has long been a critical commonplace to say that all the currents of the eighteenth century meet in Pushkin, and all the rivers of the nineteenth flow from him. *Eugene Onegin* is acknowledged his masterpiece, the novel in verse that took him eight years to complete (1823–1830), with a few minor touches added in 1831). The initial idea came from Byron's immensely popular *Beppo*, his *Childe Harold*, and chiefly his *Don Juan* (1819–1824). From the latter Pushkin derived the notion of a long narrative poem in regular stanzaic patterns—fourteen lines of iambic tetrameter, with carefully alternating masculine and feminine endings; a subject taken from contemporary life in society—a departure from some of Pushkin's earlier works, with their exotic historical or geographical milieus; and a tone mixing wit with seriousness, irony with lyricism. Byronic too is the hero: handsome, debonair, elegant, a "child of his century" in his frequent fits of melancholy and ennui, and his overriding contempt for the feelings of others, which then fill him—as satanic dandy and fallen angel— with remorse and self-recrimination. The poem abounds in the same sort of digressions of which Byron was so fond—humorous, serious, lyrical, occasionally polemical. Even certain epic machinery is burlesqued and parodied (just as Byron opens Canto III of *Don Juan* with the invocation "Hail, Muse! *et caetera*"). But Pushkin's plot is far tighter, despite his admission that when he began he had no definite plan for the poem's conclusion, and there is a definite deepening of the emotions through the eight cantos. The young St. Petersburg dandy, rake, and cynic comes to know the meaning of tragedy when we arrive at what Prince D. S. Mirsky has called "the unhappy, suggestively muffled ending." The moral stature attained by Tatyana in her final rejection of Onegin (she remains the virtuous wife despite the realization of her love for him) molds her into a most un-Byronic heroine. Yet, as noted earlier, both Don Juan and Onegin share a quality of mind caught up in two of Byron's lines: "And if I laugh at any mortal thing,/ 'Tis that I may not weep." This is *Romantic irony*, or at least one aspect of that attitude: not verbal irony, where a statement means something different from what it seems to say, but the irony resulting from the individual's compartmentalizing his personality, so that the "thinking ego" watches the "feeling ego" with objectivity; and the human being, split between actor and spectator, experiences a desire to plunge into life coupled with an equally strong urge to stand apart from it. We have mentioned Horace Walpole's aphorism in another context: "The world is a comedy to those that think, a tragedy to those who feel." It is almost as if certain Romantics had discovered that the same person could do both, and would consequently be doomed to remain in a state of unstable equilibrium.

Eugene Onegin is best understood if the reader is also cognizant of a larger cultural trend in Russian literature, the dichotomy between Slavophiles and Westerners. Onegin is a Europeanized aristocrat—typically from St. Petersburg, a "French" city, and not from Moscow—infected by Western intellectualism and skepticism, and a prototype for the "useless hero" who appears in so many Russian novels in the nineteenth century. Tatyana, on the other hand, was acclaimed by Dostoevsky, in a famous *Address on Pushkin* (1880), to be the embodiment of all the Russian and Slavophile virtues, untainted by Western decadence and spiritual corruption, existing in harmonious rapport with her environment. This pattern of East versus West was to be repeated with variations by most of the major Russian writers until the Revolution in 1917, and it is testimony to Pushkin's genius that he was one of the first to seize upon its larger implications.

VICTOR HUGO AND FRENCH ROMANTIC POETRY

Chateaubriand said that he started the Romantic school in France with *René*. At about the same time, Mme de Staël introduced German literature to French readers, and the "new" romantic mood received further encouragement. Yet not until the 1820s and 1830s did certain configurations of thought and feeling that we associate with full-blown romanticism emerge in the generation that included Victor Hugo, born in 1802. Possibly this cultural lag is to be attributed to political history, and to the turbulent times after the French revolution that included a Republic, Directorate, Napoleonic Empire, foreign wars, and two Restoration kings. Furthermore, cultural changes do not happen overnight. The early French Romantics were still influenced by the example of their own "classical" tradition, a disciplined, noble, and idealizing literature stemming from the period of Racine and La Fontaine. In a country where one of the first poets to write in the modern tongue also published a *Defense and Illustration of the French Language* (Joachim Du Bellay, 1549), it is not surprising that both progressive and conservative forces should come to blows over questions of style—which they literally did during the tumultuous opening days of Victor Hugo's revolutionary play of 1830, *Hernani.*

Classical French poetry aimed at nobility and universality of tone and image; individuality and originality were not particularly prized. Classical verse aimed at a subtly varied but essentially regular harmony based chiefly on the alexandrine, a 12-syllable line with a pause or caesura after the sixth syllable. (French meter is based on syllable count, unlike English stressed poetry; the alexandrine is the traditional line, much as iambic pentameter is the traditional English meter.) The rhyme scheme is extremely sophisticated, with rhymes called "weak," "sufficient," or "rich" according to the number of syllables they reached back into the line, and an interesting balance of types was expected inside a poem. Probably the best example of supple yet regular classical meter is to be found in La Fontaine, (see pp. 128–132). Rules of poetry became elabo-

rately and rigidly codified during the eighteenth century, however, and poetic "nobility" often appeared merely as pompous and artificial elegance. The Romantics refused to be bound by these rules, or by the traditional genres held up for imitation. They wrote odes and ballads, or long stanzaic poems experimenting with verse lengths for effect as Hugo does in a diamond-shaped poem, "The Djinns." Hugo is also famous for having "dislocated" the two-part alexandrine to give it a triple rhythm (the "Romantic trimeter"), and for creating long passages of enjambed verse (*Et nox facta est*) in which the sense of individual lines gives way to a whole impression. Verse forms were now subordinated to the poetic imagination instead of dictating its limits, as had too often happened in the neoclassical period.

Hugo's visionary imagination ("Reverie") and universalizing tendency ("Sowing Season: Evening") are important in his poetry, but he also writes topical verse about specific events. Influenced by the vogue for the historical novelist Walter Scott (1771–1832), and by the popularity of the "anticlassical" Shakespeare (*Othello, Hamlet,* and *Romeo and Juliet* were presented in English in the late 1820s to enthusiastic Parisian audiences), he was ready to reject the constraints of preceding tradition. Hence his preface to the play *Cromwell* in 1827 became a manifesto for Romantic drama and summarized many of the beliefs of the new literature. Nature, truth to life, and freedom of the imagination would dominate. There was no limit on subject matter. In place of noble diction and imagery, ordinary words and situations—even the ugly and the grotesque—were admitted. Genres would be mixed and rules broken in the search for realism and authenticity. The poet would express heart and soul rather than mere intellect, and look to the Middle Ages and Shakespeare rather than to Greece and Rome for examples.

Because of its length, *Cromwell* was published but not performed, and the preface was better known and more influential than the play. On February 25, 1830, the example of Romantic drama heralded ·by the preface finally appeared: Hugo's *Hernani*, a melodrama of love, jealousy, heroism, and revenge set in Spain. The official censors had demanded certain changes, but allowed the play to appear "so that the public may see just how far astray the human mind can go, once freed from rules and propriety." Audiences came prepared to hoot or applaud, depending on whether they were "classics" or "romantics," and the play's first week was a time of constant tumult with shouting and fistfights between enraged partisans of both sides. Classical proprieties were shocked by the humor mixed with tragedy, and even more by the triple suicide on stage at the end of the play. Audiences used to noble thoughts in rolling alexandrines were offended to hear Don Ruy Gomez called a "stupid old man," or King Carlos complain about the size of a broomcloset.

While such revolutionary changes were easier to execute in plays and novels, Hugo's poetry also expresses a concreteness and specificity lacking in much earlier verse. His series of attacks on Napoleon III, whose *coup d'état* in 1851 sent the poet into twenty years of exile, produced poems like the "Memory of the Night of the Fourth" ("Souvenir de la nuit du 4") where the bereaved grandmother's grief and the poet's indignation are conveyed in a series of homely details. The description in "Tomorrow, at Dawn" ("Demain, dès l'aube") is more purified, and only at the end does the reader realize that the poet is describing a day-long journey to visit the tomb of his drowned daughter, but the details of landscape, seaport, grave, and time of day are nonetheless specific to a particular setting and situation. While these scenes never discover the fascination with objective detail shown by the realists and naturalists, and are clearly colored by a governing emotion, they show a French Romantic imagination that is less preoccupied by a quest for the absolute than its German neighbor, an imagination that moves toward a sense of history and the particular event—history interpreted, of course, by the visionary poet.

Hugo's late poetry is devoted to this larger sense of history, a grandiose vision that covers the range of human history in *The Legend of the Centuries* (*La Légende des siècles*) and all creation in *The End of Satan* (*La Fin de Satan*) and *God* (*Dieu*). Here he combines many themes dear to the Romantic poet: the poet as prophet, magus, or seer, interpreting the universe to the reader; the heroic rebel, a satanic figure striving to throw off limitations; human progress and salvation through liberty and an ultimate reconciliation of opposites. The scope is truly Biblical, and also recalls Milton's *Paradise Lost* in its picture of Satan as the rebellious archangel. The style reinforces an epic grandeur: Lucifer, thrown out of heaven, falls for thousands of years through an infinite, darkening space as the stars go out around him, yet his own immensity is enhanced by the fact that he blows upon the last star as if it were a coal, trying frantically to keep it ablaze. The star in turn spews lava and sulphur, resenting like Lucifer the extinction of its light. Satan's enormous pride and independence were sympathetic to Romantic poets, who saw themselves as perpetual revolutionaries against authoritarian regimes (even though their worship of the "great man" led regularly—as with Napoleon— to dictatorship) and the stodgy comfort of bourgeois society. This sympathy takes on startling dimensions for a Biblical epic when Jesus, in the second book of *The End of Satan*, appears as a divinely good but finally ineffective figure, and when one learns that ultimate salvation will come only through Liberty, the child of God and a plume from Lucifer's wing. Hugo did not try to portray this future (as Goethe did briefly at the end of *Faust*), and perhaps it cannot be described since it includes the rebellious spirit and thus perpetual change. Yet the emphasis on change, individual

liberty, and superhuman will returns us to central Romantic themes, and unites Hugo's vision, though in a more optimistic vein, to the melancholy sensitivities of Chateaubriand and Lermontov.

GEORG BÜCHNER—WOYZECK

Though written in 1836, four years after Goethe's death, *Woyzeck* is not in any sense Romantic. The young Goethe and his contemporaries had extended the range of tragedy to encompass middle-class characters, often alter-egos of themselves; later, Goethe and Friedrich Schiller (1759–1805) had turned to heroic tragedy, in which idealized figures strive for victory in or beyond the world. Georg Büchner, a scientist and an admiring reader of Shakespeare, would accept neither a subjective nor an idealized literature. He sought to render human nature as it really is, and with the naturalists who were soon to dominate European fiction and drama he demanded that art be lifelike, that its characters and situations might conceivably exist in the real world —"Nothing else matters; we then have no need to ask whether [the art work] is beautiful or ugly." *Woyzeck* is the most striking embodiment of his aesthetic.

The most sympathetic and fully developed characters, Woyzeck and Marie, are not only desperately poor but constantly exploited by those better off than themselves, for *Woyzeck* is a drama of radical social consciousness, the earliest in a powerful tradition. The sharp, economical, sometimes obscene prose Büchner's characters speak concedes nothing to literary convention or indeed the conventions of social decorum, and looks ahead to Brecht. His protagonists' faithfully drawn, sordid humanity anticipates Ibsen and Zola; their fatalistic acceptance of a world they cannot change makes them ancestors of the existential heroes of Sartre and Camus. Büchner's social and economic views have echoes in Marx, and other qualities of his work herald the theaters of expressionism, cruelty, and the absurd. It is as if Büchner had been writing not for his century but for ours. When it was first acted in 1913, the centenary of the author's birth, *Woyzeck* seemed almost contemporary, and in some respects it still does.

But Büchner was indeed of his time, and his plays and letters show an incisive understanding of the established political, social, and literary orders, against all of which he was in revolt. When a university student, he formed a radical secret society that sought to foment a peasant revolution, and his first published work was an anonymous pamphlet explaining to the peasants their oppression by the highborn and wealthy, who were shown to be using the government as a tool of that oppression; this argument anticipates that of the *Communist Manifesto* thirteen years later. No revolution took place, but Büchner's knowing, unsentimental sympathy with the lowliest of his fellow creatures were decisive for his literary work. The poor appear in all of his plays, even briefly in the elegant comedy *Leonce and Lena* (1836), and

take center stage in *Woyzeck*, whose story could not have seemed fit for literary treatment except to a Büchner. *Woyzeck*'s subject and style also reflect distaste for Schiller's heroic dramas, whose characters Büchner described as "marionettes with sky-blue noses and affected pathos." Their ennobled motives and heightened speech were to him a falsification for which *Woyzeck* can be seen as a corrective.

Büchner's quest for dramatic truth led him to use history and contemporary events as sources. His first play, *Danton's Death* (1835), is a historical drama set in the darkest days of the Reign of Terror that followed the French Revolution, and about one-sixth of the dialogue is quoted or slightly paraphrased from historical sources. The prose fragment *Lenz* (1836), though in some respects fictional, is about a poet named Reinhold Lenz who had been Goethe's contemporary and whose artistic views agreed with Büchner's own. There was even a real Woyzeck, a barber and former soldier who in 1824 murdered his mistress and was hanged for it, though later exonerated as mentally unbalanced; the doctor, seemingly a grotesque parody, is quite closely modelled on one of Büchner's professors of medicine. *Woyzeck*, like *Danton's Death*, adopts bits of dialogue as well as characters and situations from published sources.

But like Shakespeare, who also borrowed freely from his sources, Büchner turned these raw materials to other than purely documentary use. Woyzeck matches his real-life model in many externals, but his relations with Marie, his intelligence, and his social awareness are supplied by Büchner. Marie is a far more attractive character in every way than the actual barber's mistress, who was a widow of forty-six, and she has her own rudimentary sense of social injustice. And the society within which they move, whatever its sources in the world the author knew, is more than a slice of rather seamy nineteenth-century life; it is a gallery of timeless, nightmarish grotesques, among whom poor mad Woyzeck and promiscuous Marie can be seen as victims deserving Büchner's and our compassion.

Büchner's dramatic structure also has its roots in Shakespeare's practice. Scenes flash by, some playing barely half a minute; settings change disjunctively; our normal sense of time is apparently suspended; tone shifts from the colloquial to high seriousness to folksong to parody to the obscene, between scenes and within them. But Büchner's dramaturgy is more compressed than Shakespeare's. *Danton's Death* is half as long as *Hamlet*; *Woyzeck*, with over twenty-five scene changes, runs little longer than the first act of *King Lear*, and its choppiness and pace remind us less of a stage play than of a movie. Within the narrow frame Büchner has room not only for a complex and fully developed dramatic action but for scenes, as in Shakespeare, which contribute to context, tone, and mood but are wholly outside the plot. Such digressions, which Büchner uses to engage us more intensely with his characters and

their plight, were turned to very different purposes a century later in Brecht's *Mother Courage and Her Children*.

Though now accepted as a masterpiece, *Woyzeck* presents us with large and insoluble textual problems. Büchner's short life was cut off by sudden illness before the play, which his letters indicate was clear in his mind, was set down in a full draft. His last effort breaks off before Marie's murder, and we cannot be certain which later scenes should be included, which omitted, their order, or even how the play should end. Generations of editors have tried to piece together reading and acting versions from the four drafts, all of which are fragmentary, often contradictory, and nearly illegible. (The first editor misread *Woyzeck* as *Wozzeck*, an error which even today has not been wholly suppressed.)

How should the play end? There is a sketch in the first draft showing Woyzeck standing mute under arrest while a policeman chortles over the murder; perhaps Büchner meant his Woyzeck, like the original, to stand trial and go to the gallows. No trial scene survives, however, and most versions end with Woyzeck drowning in the pond at the end of scene 26, a tidy but not wholly satisfactory conclusion. The famous opera by Alban Berg (1925), using Büchner's text for the most part, concludes with scene 27—the children running to look at Marie's corpse—which has the Büchner touch. The Austrian playwright Hugo von Hofmannsthal even wrote a closing scene, meant for the 1913 premiere but never used, in which the doctor conducts the inquest on Marie's and Woyzeck's deaths. Our translation ends open-endedly with Woyzeck's arrest and thus, one might say, makes Büchner an accidental predecessor of yet another modern dramatic school, the theater of improvisation and chance. We may end the play as we like. Indeed, the characters and their milieu are so sharply drawn that we can supply a trial scene from our imaginations, and like Hofmannsthal infer with some confidence what each witness would say.

LERMONTOV AND THE LATER ROMANTIC HERO

Forty years after Chateaubriand's *René*, it was no longer possible to create the same kind of Romantic hero without mockery. The figure of the pure, melancholy and doomed youth had become a pose, used chiefly by young men trying to make an impression. Lermontov had read Chateaubriand, Byron, and Benjamin Constant (whose *Adolphe*, in 1816, gave the Romantic hero new depths of psychological realism), and in his own land Pushkin, whose *Eugene Onegin* is in many ways a precursor of Pechorin, the protagonist of *A Hero of Our Time* (*Geroi nashogo vremeni*, 1840). This novel contains both a parody version in Grushnitsky, and in Pechorin a new, more complicated version of the Romantic hero. The latter is an essentially moral man whose subtlety and cynicism make him, according to the author, "a portrait composed of all the vices of our generation in the fullness of their development." He retains elements of the tradi-

tional hero—unhappy love, frustrated idealism, alienation from society, an urge for constant travel—but all are filtered through a twisted life and dogged self-analysis that are far from René's experience and indeed make it seem almost passive. Pechorin illustrates what happens when the Romantic genius is forced to live as part of a corrupt age; his degeneration reflects the limited possibilities available for the creative personality, and becomes a criticism of his time.

Although Lermontov wrote poems and plays, he is best known in English translation for *A Hero of Our Time*, a novel composed of five separate tales that together relate the story of Grigoriy Pechorin, a Russian officer on duty in the Caucasus. The focus moves gradually inward: at the beginning, the narrator only hears about a certain Pechorin who has kidnapped and caused the death of the Circassian girl Bela, and who refuses to recognize his old sergeant's claim to friendship; the last three stories, however, come from Pechorin's own journal, left by chance in the narrator's hands. Pechorin seen from outside is the corrupt member of a privileged military class: spoiled, cold, cynical, opportunistic, and totally destructive in his relationship with others. The Pechorin of the journal is the same, but the character seen from inside becomes much more complex and less easily evaluated. He is cold but also passionate, brutal but elegant, ruthless and domineering but sensitive, cynical but idealistic, opportunistic but honest, brimming with energy that never seems to find a goal. Desperately intelligent, he is quickly able to size up other people and is scornful of a society whose pretenses are so easily revealed. This intelligence, which he uses to manipulate other people, is also turned on himself, cynically questioning his own motives and emotions. "Yet it pleases me that I am capable of weeping. It may have been due, however, to upset nerves . . . and to an empty stomach."

Pechorin is a hero of sensibility, like René, but he is also overlaid with a kind of intellectualism that the earlier hero does not have. Like René, Pechorin is in tune with nature, which often seems to reflect his moods. A realist, however, he draws no spiritual sustenance from nature: it is alien materiality, rather than an earthly sign of religious truths. If there is an order in the stars, he says in "The Fatalist," it is not one that we can know. Pechorin, again like René, pursues the ideal love: not, however, with a single star-crossed passion but in a series of unhappy affairs with different women that reveals little meeting of souls and leaves his partners dead, brokenhearted, or betrayed, inevitably the worse for having met him. Even Pechorin's capacity for love is called into question, and by himself. He loves all women rather than any one of them; he is incapable of friendship; he seeks love but is afraid of any lasting union, driven on by a peculiar boredom (the *ennui* of Onegin, or later of Baudelaire) that sets in as soon as he has accomplished his immediate aim. Pechorin's travels too are not the typically Romantic

voyage to an exotic country from which he can look back at his own civilization, but the wanderings of a military officer exiled to the provinces: adventures in the spas, forts, and small towns of the Russian countryside. Appearing between Byron's *Don Juan* (1819–24) and Flaubert's *Madame Bovary* (1856), Pechorin shares their quest for the perfect love and prefigures Emma's frustration inside a petty, demeaning society. Finally, however, Pechorin is no pure and noble soul, misunderstood by vulgar society, although he is able to use this Byronic pose to great effect with Princess Mary. Whatever essential nobility he has is cracked and flawed by self-love, by his passion to control and dominate others, and by a destructive cruelty that even he himself does not quite understand.

Yet Pechorin is still a hero, even in the ironic and limiting sense of the title. If he is a composite of the vices of his generation, still he is the most interesting and full personality in the book and, suggests the author, even those whom he has harmed "possibly will find some justification" for him upon reading the self-accusatory journal of which "Princess Mary" is a part. Fatalistic, brave, impulsive but controlled, a cynical idealist in perpetual search of a challenge worthy of him, Pechorin's combination of passion and intellect touches the extremes of human existence. He is a later incarnation of the Romantic hero, no longer isolated from society but a part of it: alienated, but stifled and to some extent shaped by a petty society whose "hero" or exponent he has become.

LIVES, WRITINGS, AND CRITICISM

Biographical and critical works are listed only if they are available in English.

JEAN-JACQUES ROUSSEAU

LIFE. Born on June 28, 1712, in Geneva, son of a watchmaker. Unhappy as an engraver's apprentice, he left home while still in his teens, and for a time lived with Mme. de Warens—the first of many female protectors. He led a peripatetic existence and held many positions: as music teacher, secretary, footman, government official under the king of Sardinia, clerk in the Bureau of Taxes in Paris (where he settled in 1745). There he lived with Thérèse le Vasseur, with whom he had five children (all deposited at an orphanage). In 1756 Mme. d'Épinay invited him to live on her estate at Montmorency. Official criticism of his books several times forced Rousseau, like Voltaire, to leave France for Switzerland; in 1766 he traveled to England as guest of the philosopher David Hume. He was permitted to return to Paris in 1770 on condition that he write nothing against government or religion. Rousseau died on July 3, 1778, at Ermenonville. His body was brought to the Pantheon in Paris in 1794, during the Revolution.

CHIEF WRITINGS. His writings fall into four categories: Works involving music: *On Modern Music* (*Dissertation sur la musique moderne*, 1743); *Letter on French Music* (*Lettre sur la musique française*, 1752); *Musical Dictionary* (*Dictionnaire de musique*, 1767); and an opera, *The Village Soothsayer* (*Le Devin du village*, 1752). Political writings: *Concerning the Origin of Inequality among Men* (*Discours sur l'origine et les fondements de l'inégalité parmi les hommes*, 1754) and *The Social Contract* (*Le Contrat social*, 1762). A book, nominally a novel, on education: *Emile* (1762). Autobiographical productions: a novel, *Julie, or the New Heloise* (*Julie, ou La Nouvelle Héloïse*, 1761); the *Confessions*, composed between 1765 and 1770, published in 1781–1788; and *Musings of a Solitary Stroller* (*Les Rêveries du promeneur solitaire*), composed between 1776 and 1778, published in 1782.

BIOGRAPHY AND CRITICISM. J. Morley, *Rousseau* (1873, revised 1886); F. Macdonald, *Rousseau* (1906); I. Babbitt, *Rousseau and Romanticism* (1919); M. B. Ellis, *Julie: A Synthesis of Rousseau's Thought* (1949); E. Cassirer, "Rousseau," in *Rousseau, Kant, Goethe* (1945); H. Höffding, *Rousseau and His Philosophy* (1930); Frances Winwar, *Jean-Jacques Rousseau: Conscience of a Era* (1961); F. C. Green, *Jean-Jacques Rousseau: A Critical Study of His Life and Writings* (1955). Excellent is the series of essays about the author in *Yale French Studies*, No. 28 (1962). There are also J. Guéhenno, *Jean-*

Jacques Rousseau (1966); W. and A. Durant, *Rousseau and Revolution* (1968); J. McManners, *The Social Contract and Rousseau's Revolt against Society* (1968); W. Blanchard, *Rousseau and the Spirit of Revolt* (1968); M. Einaudi, *The Early Rousseau* (1968).

JOHANN WOLFGANG VON GOETHE

LIFE. Born on August 28, 1749, in Frankfurt-am-Main, Germany. From 1765 to 1768 Goethe attended Leipzig University, then the center of French culture in Germany. It was at the end of that time that he met Suzanna von Klettenberg, eminent Pietist and mystic, who interested him in the theosophy of the period. At the University of Strassburg, in 1770–1771, he made the acquaintance of Gottfried Herder, leader of the new German literary movement later called the "Storm and Stress" (*Sturm und Drang*) movement. Herder showed the young writer the importance of Shakespeare (as opposed to the French neoclassic authors) and interested him in folk songs and in the need for an indigenous German literature. On a series of trips to Switzerland he began his scientific and philosophical studies. In 1775 Goethe moved to Weimar, and there his long friendship with the reigning duke, Karl August, began. He also received the first of several government appointments which guaranteed him financial independence. From 1786 to 1788 he took his famous Italian trip. He met the author Schiller in 1794, and their fruitful relationship was terminated only by the latter's death in 1805. Goethe married Christiane Vulpius in 1806 and subsequently legitimitized the son they had had some twelve years earlier. In 1808 occurred his meeting with Napoleon, an encounter mutually impressive; and four years later he met Beethoven. From 1823 to 1832 he was in the daily company of Johann Peter Eckermann, who was thus able to record, in his *Conversations with Goethe* (*Gespräche mit Goethe*, 1836–1848), all the commentary and criticism that Goethe's long life had accumulated. Goethe's presence made Weimar a cultural mecca for twenty years, and during that period there was scarcely a prominent European intellectual who did not come there to pay his respects. He died on March 22, 1832.

CHIEF WRITINGS. Goethe's earliest verse is in the rococo tradition of French and German eighteenth-century poetry. It was not until he was influenced by Herder—and until his many love affairs took on a more serious cast—that he achieved writing of high stature. His first great play, *Götz von Berlichingen*, 1773, was a product of his Shakespeare studies and his enthusiasm for the preromantic

"Storm and Stress" movement. About the same time, he started the first of many sketches for *Faust*, Part I. *The Sorrows of Young Werther* (*Die Leiden des jungen Werthers*), the short novel that inflamed the youth of Europe as did no other book before or after, was published in 1774. Goethe's increasing interest in classical literature led to the creation of such plays as *Iphigenia* (*Iphigenie auf Tauris*, 1787), and *Torquato Tasso* (1790) and the epic-idyll *Hermann and Dorothea* (*Hermann und Dorothea*, 1798). His two largest novels were *Wilhelm Meister's Apprenticeship* (*Wilhelm Meisters Lehrjahre*, 1795–1796), and *Wilhelm Meister's Travels* (*Wilhelm Meisters Wanderjahre*, 1821). *Faust*, Part I, appeared in 1808; *Faust*, Part II, completed in 1831, was published in 1833. Goethe's fame as a lyric poet rests on the many volumes of verse he wrote, from his first *Poems* (*Gedichte*, 1771) through the *Roman Elegies* (*Romische Elegien*, 1795); *Ballads* (*Balladen*, 1798); the enigmatic *West-East Divan* (*Westöstlicher Diwan*, 1819); and the last great *Marienbad Elegies* (*Marienbad Elegien*, 1823). His scientific writings fill several volumes. Most of Goethe's critical commentary is found in the penetrating *Truth and Poetry* (*Dichtung und Wahrheit*, 1811–1833).

BIOGRAPHY AND CRITICISM. Biographies and general studies of Goethe include A. Bielschowsky, *Life of Goethe* (1905–1908); K. Viëtor, *Goethe the Poet*(1949); E. Ludwig, *Goethe*(1928); B. Fairley, *A Study of Goethe* (1948); T. Mann, *Essays of Three Decades* (1947), and introduction to *The Permanent Goethe* (1948); A. Schweitzer, *Goethe* (1949); E. M. Wilkinson and L. A. Willoughby, *Goethe, Poet and Thinker* (1962); H. Hatfield, *Goethe* (1963); B. Croce, *Goethe* (1923); W. H. Bruford, *Culture and Society in Classical Weimar* (1962). For *Faust*, consult D. J. Enright, *Commentary on Goethe's Faust* (1949); F. M. Stawell and G. L. Dickinson, *Goethe and Faust* (1928); E. M. Butler, *The Myth of the Magus* (1948) and *The Fortunes of Faust* (1952); S. Atkins, *Goethe's Faust: A Literary Analysis* (1958); P. M. Palmer and R. P. More, *Sources of the Faust Tradition* (1910); G. Santayana, "Goethe," in *Three Philosophical Poets* (1910); A. Gillies, *Goethe's Faust: An Interpretation* (1957); R. Peacock, *Goethe's Major Plays* (1959); E. Mason, *Goethe's Faust* (1967); G. Lukacs, *Goethe and His Age* (1969).

FRANÇOIS RENÉ DE CHATEAUBRIAND

LIFE. Born September 4, 1768, at Combourg, St. Malo, Brittany, to a noble family allied to both the Spanish and English ruling houses. Chateaubriand obtained a lieutenant's commission in the army, just before the Revolution in 1789. In 1791 he spent five months in North America, returning in January, 1792. He married Céleste Buisson de la Vigne. He joined the royalist, counter-Revolutionary forces, and was wounded at the battle of Valmy (1792). Chateaubriand left (May, 1793) for exile in England, where he lived as a teacher and translator. His mother died in 1798; Chateaubriand, hitherto mildly skeptical, became an ardent Catholic ("I wept and I believed"). He returned to France in 1800. The success of *The Genius of Christianity* (1802) was in part responsible for Napoleon's appointing him to two diplomatic posts, one to the Vatican. He resigned after the execution of the Duc D'Enghien, traveled extensively in Italy, Greece, and the Holy Land (1806–1807), then retired to his country estate at Aulnay. He was appointed by Louis XVIII as Minister of the Interior (1815). In 1818 he became the lover of Mme. de Recamier, who was but one of his many mistresses. He was appointed ambassador to Berlin in 1821, to London in 1822 and Foreign Minister in 1823; Charles X made him ambassador to Rome in 1828. He retired from politics when the Bourbons fell in 1830. His last years were spent writing and traveling. Chateaubriand died July 4, 1848.

CHIEF WRITINGS. *The Essay on Revolutions* was his first work: it was politically ambiguous, and at times anticlerical. *Atala* (1801) was a pilot study intended to test the future reception of *The Genius of Christianity* (1802), into which it was incorporated—the book that included *René* and *The Martyrs*. (The latter was an epic treating the early persecution of the Christians under Domitian). *An Itinerary from Paris to Jerusalem* (1811) described his travels; *Memoirs from Beyond the Grave* (published 1849–1850) was his autobiography.

BIOGRAPHY AND CRITICISM. A. Maurois, *Chateaubriand* (1938); J. Evans, *Chateaubriand* (1939); T. C. Walker, *Chateaubriand's Nature Scenery* (1946).

E.T.A. HOFFMANN

LIFE AND WRITINGS. Ernst Theodor Wilhelm Hoffmann was born in Königsberg, Prussia, in what is now northeastern Germany, on January 24, 1776. His father was a lawyer and judge as well as a talented musician, and the son too would later be all three. However, the parents divorced in 1778 and Hoffmann was brought up in the household of his mother, who was mentally unstable and who had gathered about her various eccentric relations none of whom had much understanding of or sympathy with the boy's sensitivity. An uncle instructed him in conventional subjects and music, and at twelve Hoffmann could draw and compose.

His formal education included three years studying law at the University of Königsberg, from which he graduated at nineteen. (In those days a baccalaureate was neither required nor expected of a law student.) After practicing law for a few years in Königsberg, Hoffmann decided to enter the Prussian civil service, and in 1799 he passed the qualifying examinations with honors. He was assigned to a post as assessor in the Prussian-controlled Polish town of Pozen, but in 1802, after offending several important civil and military officials there with his caricatures, he was sent to the dreary town of Plozk. Two years later he was rescued through the intervention of a school friend, Theodor Hippel, and reassigned to Warsaw. Hoffmann's government career had been checkered but was undoubtedly promising, as he was not only intelligent but hard-working.

His energy and industry can be measured by the fact that while capably performing his official duties, Hoffmann also pursued careers in several arts and, further, an eventful private life. He wrote operas, incidental music for plays (his *The Cross on the Baltic* is generally considered the first truly Romantic music) and instrumental works in profusion; he worked in the theater as music director, manager, and even set designer; he read extensively in the new German Romantics; and, in Warsaw, he not only conducted the Music Academy's orchestra but supervised the reconstruction of the Academy's main building and even painted some murals in it. Since coming of age he had engaged in passionate affairs with women, one of them married, until in Plozk he married Maria Thekla Michaelina Rorer, a Polish woman with no artistic pretensions but of a calm and forgiving disposition—on which Hoffmann, in his thirties still attractive to women and also given to bouts of heavy drinking, was rather too often to presume.

Despite these many artistic projects it was his government salary which supported Hoffmann, his wife, and their baby daughter. In 1806, when Napoleon defeated Prussia, German bureaucrats were replaced wholesale by Frenchmen, leaving Hoffmann without a job. His wife and child were sent to live with relatives in Posen while he went to Berlin, the Prussian capital, to earn whatever living he could. He nearly starved. His friend Hippel managed to keep Hoxmann alive by finding him musical and theatrical work, and in 1808 he was appointed music director of the theater in Bamberg, where he was joined by his wife (a cholera epidemic having carried off their daughter). There he eked out an existence for several years, managing the theater, composing, giving music lessons, painting portraits, and writing—his first tale, "Ritter Glück" (1809), and his first music criticism were published then. He also conceived a one-sided passion for a sixteen-year-old music student, Julia Marc.

In 1812 this precarious situation fell apart. The theater had gone bankrupt, and Bamberg was too small a city to support even so prodigious a freelancer as Hoffmann, while he was not yet able to earn much by his writing. Moreover, he had been forbidden by the Marcs to see Julia again after a drunken tussle with her fiancé, a Hamburg banker whom she married in December (and with whom she was to be desperately unhappy). Then, in 1813, came a reversal of fortune. A legacy from an uncle gave Hoffmann a measure of financial security, increased by his appointment that year as operatic conductor in Dresden and Leipzig and by the immediate success of his first story collection, *Fancy-Flights in the Manner of Callot* (1814). At about this time Hoffmann adopted as his own the middle name of the great Austrian composer Wolfgang Amadeus Mozart (1756–91), in homage and perhaps also ironically: Mozart had died young and destitute after failing to sustain his great early popularity. But the name brought Hoffmann good luck. Through Hippel he was recalled to Berlin in 1814, immediately after Napoleon's defeat, and in 1816 he was appointed a judge and administrator of the Prussian Appellate Court.

In Hoffmann's last years he was a celebrity. He published three novels and two more collections of tales, *Night Pieces* (1817) and *The Serapion Brothers* (1819–21), as well as much music criticism under the pen name of "Johannes Kreisler, conductor." After his opera UNDINE (1816) was performed in Berlin Hoffmann wrote no more music, but his tales have been adapted for operas and ballets by other composers as diverse as Offenbach, Delibes, Tchaikovsky, and Hindemith. Those happy years were not many, however, as his earlier deprivations and excesses had weakened his health, and he died of a nervous disorder on January 25, 1822.

BIOGRAPHY AND CRITICISM. Brief biographical and critical accounts are included in the two currently available books of his tales in English, *Tales of E. T. A. Hoffmann* (1969), ed. and trans. by Leonard J. Kent and Elizabeth C. Knight, and *The Best Tales of Hoffmann* (1967), ed. by E. F. Bleiler. Other stories include H. W. Hewett-Thayer, *Hoffman: Author of the Tales* (1948).

HEINRICH HEINE

LIFE. Born December 13, 1797, in Dusseldorf, then occupied by the French. He was brought up by a warm-hearted but impractical father and an enlightened, "Rousseauian" mother. After the failure of his father's business in 1819 he became financially dependent on his uncle Salomon, a rich banker in Hamburg. This relationship both sustained and plagued him for the rest of his life. Heine fell in love successively with two daughters of Salomon, his cousins Amalie and Therese, but was rejected by each. Salomon launched him in a business, which failed, and then financed his studies, intended to prepare him for the law. At Bonn Heine attended A. W. Schlegel's lectures on literature and was stimulated to write poetry. He transferred to Gottingen, from whence he was expelled for challenging an anti-Semite to a duel. In Berlin in 1821 he heard Hegel's lectures at the University, and became a member of the literary salon of Rahel and Varnhagen von Ense. Heine received a law degree in 1825 and then officially converted to Lutheranism as a necessary condition for obtaining any government position. But he failed to make a career either in the law or in university teaching and in the late 1820s turned increasingly to a career as a writer. Disgusted by German nationalism and the increasing Jewish pogroms, at the same time fired by the promise of the July Revolution of 1830 in France, he left in 1831 for exile in Paris. He served there as the correspondent of German newspapers. Political affiliations with the Young German group (Borne, Herwegh, Gutzkow, Grabbe) placed Heine on the Prussian proscription list. A nostalgic trip to Germany (1843–1844) heightened his disillusionment with his homeland. From 1834 he lived with Eugenie Mirat ("Mathilde"), an uneducated French shopgirl to whom Heine remained passionately attached to the end of his life. They were married in 1841. From 1848 he was bedridden with spinal paralysis. His financial condition remained precarious and the modest pension that his uncle had left him at his death in 1844 was continued only on the condition that Heine suppress a large part of the memoirs on which he was at work. To the end he remained lucid, receiving friends in his sickroom, intensely occupied with his literary work. He died February 17, 1856.

CHIEF WRITINGS. Heine's first poems appeared in 1821, but *The Book of Songs* (1827) brought him fame as a lyric poet. Heine experimented with two Byronic dramas: *Almansor* and *Ratcliff* (1823); one unfinished novel, *The Rabbi of Bacherach*. *Travel Sketches* (1826–1831) included *The Trip Through the Harz*. His best critical writings are to be found in his *Salons* (1834–1840) and *The Romantic School* (1833). *New Poems* (1844), *Atta Troll*, a long narrative tale in verse (1847); *Romanzero* (1851) and the posthumous *Last Poems* constitute the remainder of his writing. *Lutezia* (1854), a collection he made of articles written between 1840 and 1843 on French political conditions.

BIOGRAPHY AND CRITICISM. M. Arnold, "Heine," in *Essays in Criticism* (1865); A. Vallentin, *Poet in Exile* (1934); L. Untermeyer, *Heine* (1937); M. Brod, *Heine* (1956); E. M. Butler, *Heine* (1956); W. Rose, *Heine* (1956); B. Fairley, *Heine* (1950); S. S. Prawer, *Heine* (1960), and *Heine the Tragic Satirist* (1961); L. Hofrichter, *Heinrich Heine*, translated by B. Fairley (1965). Meno Spann, *Heine* (1966); A. I. Sandor. *The Exile of Gods: Interpretation of a Theme and a Technique in the Work of Heinrich Heine* (1967); Jeffrey L. Sammons, *Heinrich Heine, The Elusive Poet* (1969).

ALEXANDER PUSHKIN

LIFE. Born at Moscow, June 6, 1799 (May 26, Old Style). Pushkin was a member of an old boyar family; his maternal great-grandfather was an Abys-

sinian general ennobled by Peter the Great. He entered the *Lyceum* (at Tzarkoe Selo, near St. Petersburg) in 1811. Upon finishing his schooling (in 1817) he was attached to the Ministry of Foreign Affairs, in a nominal position enabling him to lead the life of a dandy and man of fashion. Suspected of political liberalism, he was exiled (in 1820) to southern Russia to aid in the administration of newly founded colonies. He made his first trip to the Caucasus; in 1823 he was transferred to Odessa. Suspected of atheistic tendencies and dismissed from the service (1824), Pushkin was ordered to stay on the family estate at Mikhailovskoye, near Pskov—an exile which fortunately saved him from a more active involvement in the ill-fated Decembrist Revolution (1825). Pardoned by the new Tsar, Nicholas I, he was allowed to return to Moscow. He married Natalie Goncharov (1831), and was reappointed to the Foreign Service in 1832. Pushkin was fatally wounded in a duel with Baron George Heckeren d'Anthes. He died February 10, 1837 (January 29, Old Style).

CHIEF WRITINGS. Pushkin was an avid reader of Byron, whose work many of his pieces resemble. Early tales include *The Captive of the Caucasus* and *The Fountain of Bakhchisarai* (1822); a long poem, *The Gypsies* (1824). He wrote a Shakespearean drama, *Boris Godunov* (1825, published 1831), and the narrative poem *Poltava* (1829); he began his *History of Pugachev's Revolt in 1773* in 1834; he completed his one long novel, *The Captain's Daughter*, in 1836. His most famous short story is *The Queen of Spades* (1833). Pushkin completed *Eugene Onegin* in 1830 (it was published in 1833). This and *The Queen of Spades* were made into operas by Tchaikovsky, *Boris Godunov* by Moussorgsky, *Ruslan and Ludmilla* by Glinka, *The Golden Cockerel* by Rimsky-Korsakov.

BIOGRAPHY AND CRITICISM. Walter Arndt. *Pushkin Threefold: Narrative. Lyric, Polemic and Ribold Verse* (1972); John Bayley, *Pushkin: A Comparative Commentary* (1971); B. L. Brasol, *The Mighty Three* (1934); J. Lavrin, *Pushkin and Russian Literature* (1947); David Magarshack, *Pushkin*; D. S. Mirsky, *Pushkin* (1926); Vladimir Nabokov, *Eugene Onegin in Verse, 4 vols.* (1964), this is the most complete and reliable explication of *Eugene Onegin*; Henri Troyat, *Pushkin* (1970); S. H. Cross and E. J. Simmons, *Pushkin* (1937).

VICTOR HUGO

LIFE AND WRITINGS. Victor Hugo was born on February 26, 1802, at Besançon, the third son of a Napoleonic officer (who later became a general) and a Royalist mother. When he was two years old the family moved to Paris, which Hugo always considered his childhood home. The marriage was not happy and the parents were often separated; the children stayed chiefly with their mother. The family traveled a good deal, and Hugo's education was irregular except in 1812–14 when he studied Latin literature intensively. After his mother's death in

1821, Hugo was reconciled with his father and came to admire Napoleon as a symbol of heroism.

In 1816, he began writing poetry and verse tragedies, and discovered his literary ambitions: "I want to be Chateaubriand or nothing." He studied law from 1818 to 1821, and was a founding editor of the short-lived journal, *The Literary Conservative* (1819–21). He wrote articles and criticism under various names, and began a novel. In 1822 a royal pension of 1000 francs for *Odes and Diverse Poetry* (*Odes et poésies diverses*) enabled him to marry Adèle Foucher. The next year he became an editor of *The French Muse* (1823–24), for which he wrote poetry, literary criticism, and (despite his lack of religious training in childhood) essays on religious topics; he also published a fantastic novel, *Han of Iceland* (*Han d' Islande*) that showed the influence of Walter Scott.

With *Odes and Ballads* (*Odes et ballades*, 1826), Hugo began the series of poems, novels, and plays that made him the leading figure among the young Romantics. The preface - to *Cromwell* (1827) defined Romantic drama and served as a manifesto; *Hernani* (1830), and the battles among factions in the opening-night audience, was its demonstration. *The Hunchback of Notre Dame* (*Notre Dame de Paris*) appeared in 1842, a year after Hugo had finally been elected (on the fifth try) to the French Academy.

In 1833 Hugo met Juliette Drouet, who became the first of his many mistresses and remained faithful to him for fifty years, traveling with him, copying his works for the publisher, and keepiig him company in exile. His favorite daughter Léopoldine drowned in 1843. Hugo was a royalist at this time, and was made a peer in 1845. However, he was interested in politics, and was elected to the Constitutional Assembly after the 1848 revolution. When President Louis Napoléon (nephew of Napoléon I's brother) seized power in 1851, later proclaiming himself Emperor of the French as Napoléon III, Hugo fled the country and stayed in exile on the English Channel island of Guernsey until 1870. Here he wrote bitter attacks on "Napoléon the Little," and refused amnesty in 1859: "When liberty returns to France, I shall return."

During his years of exile Hugo wrote major poems: *The Punishments* (*Les Châtiments*, 1853), *Contemplations* (*Les Contemplations*, 1856, an immediate success and best-seller), *The Legend of the Centuries* (*La Légende des siècles*, 1859), and the first part of *The End of Satan* (*La Fin de Satan*, 1854). There were also novels: Les Misérables (1862) and *Toilers of the Sea* (*Travailleurs de la mer*, 1866). He returned to Paris in 1871, during the Franco-Prussian war and the seige of Paris, where he again

entered politics and was elected deputy in the provisional government after the fall of France. Except for a brief return to Guernsey in 1872–73, Hugo remained in Paris where he was honored as a national figure and elected senator in 1876. He died on May 22, 1885, and was buried in the Pantheon after an enormous state funeral in which his own casket was, at his request, that of a pauper.

BIOGRAPHY AND CRITICISM. Matthew Josephson, *Victor Hugo, a Realistic Biography* (1942); Elliott M. Grant, *The Career of Victor Hugo* (1945); André Maurois, *Olympio; the Life of Victor Hugo* (1954, transl. Gerard Hopkins 1956); M. Easton, *Artists and Writers in Paris: The Bohemian Idea, 1803–1867* (1965); André Maurois, *Victor Hugo and His World* (1965, transl. Oliver Bernard 1966); Richard B. Grant, *The Perilous Quest* (1968); Charles Affron, *A Stage for Poets: Studies in the Theatre of Hugo and Musset* (1971), Noel B. Gerson, *Victor Hugo: A Tumultuous Life* (1971, pen name for Samuel Edwards); John P. Houston, *Victor Hugo* (1975); Joanna Richardson, *Victor Hugo* (1976).

GEORG BÜCHNER

LIFE AND WRITINGS. Georg Büchner was born in October 17, 1813, near Darmstadt, the capital of the German duchy of Hesse. His father, a physician, had served with the armies of Napoleon and retained some French sympathies; his mother's interest in literature, and in German folksong, were likewise to influence her son's life and work. At eighteen Büchner was sent to the University of Strasbourg to study medicine, and his two years there were the happiest of his life. His vocation for scientific work was strong, and he also became engaged to Minna Jaegele, a daughter in the family with which he boarded.

To complete his advanced training in Hesse, a requirement if he was to practice there, Büchner reluctantly left Strasbourg in 1833 and enrolled at the University of Giessen. He was soon appalled by the political repression of the intellectuals—all publications were censored, all opposition spied on, all universities closely watched for radicals—and by the plight of the peasants, heavily taxed to pay the new ruler's debts and starving after a poor harvest. Early in 1834 he formed a secret radical group, the Society of the Rights of Man, to foment a revolution in which all the oppressed, middle-and lower-class alike, were to join against the misusers of wealth and power. To test the peasants' ripeness for revolution he wrote and had distributed among them a pamphlet, *The Hessian Courier*, which in its social and economic analysis is a clear forerunner of *The Communist Manifesto* (1847). The peasants, however, handed the pamphlets over to the police, and suddenly Büchner and his fellows were in great danger. Many were arrested and given long jail sentences, and in July 1835 a warrant was issued against Büchner himself. It was too late: in March he had escaped to Strasbourg, and he was to spend the rest of his short life in exile.

In the previous two months, to raise money for his escape, he had written his first play, *Danton's Death*, and in Strasbourg he translated two Victor Hugo dramas for the same purpose; all were published later in the year, his only literary works to be known before his death. Since his imaginative writings could not support him or make possible a marriage with Minna, he turned to work on a scientific thesis on the nervous system of the barbel fish. The Strasbourg Natural History Society elected him to membership and published his thesis, and when he sent a copy to the newly founded University of Zürich he was awarded a Ph.D. *in absentia* without having to undergo the oral examination. He was shortly invited to come there to teach.

Büchner traveled to Switzerland in the autumn of 1836, bringing with him a new play, *Leonce and Lena*, which he had written to win a prize for new German comedies but submitted too late; a fictional vignette, *Lenz*, with an historical protagonist, Goethe's contemporary, poet and dramatist Reinhold Lenz (1751–92), whose aesthetic had much in common with Büchner's own; and, evidently, drafts of two new plays, *Woyzeck* and a lost drama about the Renaissance Italian satirist Pietro Aretino. After a successful trial lecture at the University he began in November a lecture course in comparative anatomy. He also revised *Leonce and Lena* and worked on the two other plays, and early in 1837 told Minna that all three were almost ready for publication. But suddenly he fell ill with typhus, and after three weeks of fever and pain he died on February 19, 1837.

Büchner's literary reputation is largely posthumous; though *Danton's Death* was published during his lifetime, *Leonce and Lena* did not appear until 1850, *Woyzeck* until 1879, and all three in corrupt and bowdlerized editions. Stage productions were even slower in coming: *Leonce and Lena* in an amateur production in 1895, *Danton's Death* by a small Berlin company in 1902, and *Woyzeck* in Munich in 1913. Since the publication of Bergemann's critical edition in 1922, reconstructing Büchner's originals as far as possible (the manuscripts for all but *Woyzeck* having been lost, and the latter not only fragmentary but almost illegible), his works have taken their places in the repertory as classics of the German theater. The two best contemporary translations, by Carl Richard Mueller (1963) and Victor Price (1971), are based on Bergemann's acting edition, but Mueller incorporates additional material from the drafts, ending his version with Woyzeck's arrest, while Price ends with Woyzeck's death. Mueller includes the three plays, *Lenz*, and *The Hessian Courier*, Price only the plays. A new critical edition by Werner Lehmann began to appear in 1967, but no English translations based on Lehmann have yet been published.

BIOGRAPHY AND CRITICISM. The best studies in English are Herbert Lindenberger, *Georg Büchner* (1964), and Maurice B. Benn, *The Drama of Revolt* (1976). The former quotes from the Bergemann edition in English, the latter from Lehmann in German.

MIKHAIL LERMONTOV

LIFE. Mikhail Yuryevich Lermontov was born on October 3, 1814, in Moscow. His father was a retired military officer and small landowner; his mother, the only child of a rich aristocratic family, was of fragile health and died in 1817. Lermontov's grandmother disliked her son-in-law intensely and, using her wealth and political connections, forced him to relinquish the child to her at her country estate at Tarkhany, in the Penza district. Lermontov was torn between these two relatives, both of whom he loved, until the father's death in 1831.

The young Lermontov was spoiled by his devoted grandmother but received a complete aristocratic education, learning German, French, and English from native tutors. He also suffered from childhood illnesses that left him somewhat stoop-shouldered, and necessitated several trips to the Caucasus for his health. Lermontov attended a noblemen's pension school in Moscow from 1828 to 1830, where he keenly felt the scorn of the other students for his own position as poor relation, but he also was privately tutored by the poet Merzlyakov and began to write poetry. From 1832 to 1834 he studied at the Guards' School in St. Petersburg, after which he received an officer's commission in the Life Guard Hussars Regiment, stationed outside St. Petersburg. Lermontov entered into the social life of the capital, acquiring a reputation as a ladies' man, writing dramas, and beginning a novel. In 1837, however, his indignant poem on the death of the poet Alexander Pushkin was taken as an attack on the throne, and Tsar Nicholas I had him imprisoned, demoted, and transferred to a dragoon regiment in the Caucasus.

In May 1837 Lermontov, exhausted by the trip and troubled by rheumatism, took a leave from his regiment to visit the health spa at Pyatigorsk. Here he sketched and painted, and in the fall traveled extensively throughout the region on the way to rejoin his regiment. In 1838, due to his grandmother's efforts, he was transferred back to St. Petersburg and ultimately to his old regiment. Lermontov hoped at this point to quit military service and devote himself to writing, but his grandmother, on whom he was dependent, opposed this decision. He continued to publish poetry and prose, however, including stories that later became chapters of *A Hero of Our Time*, and to associate with the young intelligentsia of the "Circle of Sixteen," a liberal group disliked by the Tsar's police. In 1840, Lermontov was again ordered into exile by the Tsar, ostensibly because of a duel with the son of the French ambassador, but more likely for his rebellious nature and insolent attitude—among other things, he was supposed to have insulted the Tsar's daughters at a ball. Sent to the Caucasian front, he distinguished himself in the battles against mountain tribes but was refused promotions by the Tsar. On the way back to the front after an abruptly cancelled leave in Saint Petersburg, he stopped at Pyatigorsk with a friend and arranged to go on sick leave there; his incessant teasing of a vain colleague led to another duel on July 15,

1841, and Lermontov, not quite twenty-seven years old, was shot through the heart.

CHIEF WRITINGS. *A Hero of Our Time* (*Geroi nashogo vremeni*, 1840, first transl. 1854). "Moscow" (translation of "Sashka" in *Russian Songs and Lyrics*, transl. John Pollen, 1917), *A Sheaf From Lermontov*, transl. J. J. Robbins (1923), *Three Russian Poets*, transl. VI. Nabokov (1944). *The Demon and Other Poems*, transl. Eugene Kayden (1965), *Selected Poetry*, transl. L'Ami and Welikotny (1967), *A Lermontov Reader* transl. Guy Daniels (1967).

BIOGRAPHY AND CRITICISM. Anna Heifetz, comp., *Lermontov in English: a list of works by and about the poet* (1942); Janko Lavrin, *Lermontov* (1959); John Mersereau, Jr., *Mikhail Lermontov* (1962); C.E. L'Ami and Alexander Welikotny, *Michael Lermontov; biography and translation* (1967); Laurence Kelly, *Lermontov: Tragedy in the Caucasus* (1978).

JEAN-JACQUES ROUSSEAU
(1712–1778)

Confessions*

Part I
BOOK I

[The Years 1712–1719.] I am commencing an undertaking, hitherto without precedent, and which will never find an imitator. I desire to set before my fellows the likeness of a man in all the truth of nature, and that man myself.

Myself alone! I know the feelings of my heart, and I know men. I am not made like any of those I have seen; I venture to believe that I am not made like any of those who are in existence. If I am not better, at least I am different. Whether Nature has acted rightly or wrongly in destroying the mould in which she cast me, can only be decided after I have been read.

Let the trumpet of the Day of Judgment sound when it will, I will present myself before the Sovereign Judge with this book in my hand. I will say boldly: "This is what I have done, what I have thought, what I was. I have told the good and the bad with equal frankness. I have neither omitted anything bad, nor interpolated anything good. If I have occasionally made use of some immaterial embellishments, this has only been in order to fill a gap caused by lack of memory. I may have assumed the truth of that which I knew might have been true, never of that which I knew to be false. I have shown myself as I was: mean and contemptible, good, high-minded and sublime, according as I was one or the other. I have unveiled my inmost self even as Thou hast seen it, O Eternal Being. Gather round me the countless host of my fellow-men; let them hear my confessions, lament for my unworthiness, and blush for my imperfections. Then let each of them in turn reveal, with the same frankness, the secrets of his heart at the foot of the Throne, and say, if he dare, 'I was better than that man!' " . . .

I felt before I thought: this is the common lot of humanity. I experienced it more than others. I do not know what I did until I was five or six years old. I do not know how I learned to read; I only remember my earliest reading, and the effect it had upon me; from that time I date my uninterrupted self-consciousness. My mother

* Completed in 1770; published in 1781–1788. The selections reprinted here are from *The Confessions of Jean-Jacques Rousseau*.

had left some romances behind her, which my father and I began to read after supper. At first it was only a question of practising me in reading by the aid of amusing books; but soon the interest became so lively, that we used to read in turns without stopping, and spent whole nights in this occupation. We were unable to leave off until the volume was finished. Sometimes, my father, hearing the swallows begin to twitter in the early morning, would say, quite ashamed, "Let us go to bed; I am more of a child than yourself."

In a short time I acquired, by this dangerous method, not only extreme facility in reading and understanding what I read, but a knowledge of the passions that was unique in a child of my age. I had no idea of things in themselves, although all the feelings of actual life were already known to me. I had conceived nothing, but felt everything. These confused emotions which I felt one after the other, certainly did not warp the reasoning powers which I did not as yet possess; but they shaped them in me of a peculiar stamp, and gave me odd and romantic notions of human life, of which experience and reflection have never been able wholly to cure me. . . . .

How could I become wicked, when I had nothing but examples of gentleness before my eyes, and none around me but the best people in the world? My father, my aunt, my nurse, my relations, our friends, our neighbours, all who surrounded me, did not, it is true, obey me, but they loved me; and I loved them in return. My wishes were so little excited and so little opposed, that it did not occur to me to have any. I can swear that, until I served under a master, I never knew what a fancy was. Except during the time I spent in reading or writing in my father's company, or when my nurse took me for a walk, I was always with my aunt, sitting or standing by her side, watching her at her embroidery or listening to her singing; and I was content. Her cheerfulness, her gentleness and her pleasant face have stamped so deep and lively an impression on my mind that I can still see her manner, look, and attitude; I remember her affectionate language: I could describe what clothes she wore and how her head was dressed, not forgetting the two little curls of black hair on her temples, which she wore in accordance with the fashion of the time.

I am convinced that it is to her I owe the taste, or rather passion, for music, which only became fully developed in me a long time afterwards. She knew a prodigious number of tunes and songs which she used to sing in a very thin, gentle voice. This excellent woman's cheerfulness of soul banished dreaminess and melancholy from herself and all around her. The attraction which her singing possessed for me was so great, that not only have several of her songs always remained in my memory, but even now, when I have lost her, and as I grew older, many of them, totally forgotten since the days of my

childhood, return to my mind with inexpressible charm. Would anyone believe that I, an old dotard, eaten up by cares and troubles,
sometime find myself weeping like a child, when I mumble one of
those little airs in a voice already broken and trembling?

. . . I have spent my life in idle longing, without saying a word,
in the presence of those whom I loved most. Too bashful to declare
my taste, I at least satisfied it in situations which had reference to
it and kept up the idea of it. To lie at the feet of an imperious
mistress, to obey her commands, to ask her forgiveness—this was
for me a sweet enjoyment; and, the more my lively imagination
heated my blood, the more I presented the appearance of a bashful
lover. It may be easily imagined that this manner of making love
does not lead to very speedy results, and is not very dangerous to
the virtue of those who are its object. For this reason I have rarely
possessed, but have none the less enjoyed myself in my own way
—that is to say, in imagination. Thus it has happened that my
senses, in harmony with my timid disposition and my romantic
spirit, have kept my sentiments pure and my morals blameless,
owing to the very tastes which, combined with a little more impudence, might have plunged me into the most brutal sensuality. . . .

I am a man of very strong passions, and, while I am stirred
by them, nothing can equal my impetuosity; I forget all discretion,
all feelings of respect, fear and decency; I am cynical, impudent,
violent and fearless; no feeling of shame keeps me back, no danger
frightens me; with the exception of the single object which occupies
my thoughts, the universe is nothing to me. But all this lasts only
for a moment, and the following moment plunges me into complete
annihilation. In my calmer moments I am indolence and timidity
itself; everything frightens and discourages me; a fly, buzzing past,
alarms me; a word which I have to say, a gesture which I have to
make, terrifies my idleness; fear and shame overpower me to such
an extent that I would gladly hide myself from the sight of my
fellow-creatures. If I have to act, I do not know what to do; if
I have to speak, I do not know what to say; if anyone looks at me,
I am put out of countenance. When I am strongly moved I sometimes know how to find the right words, but in ordinary conversation
I can find absolutely nothing, and my condition is unbearable for
the simple reason that I am obliged to speak.

Add to this, that none of my prevailing tastes centre in things
that can be bought. I want nothing but unadulterated pleasures,
and money poisons all. For instance, I am fond of the pleasures
of the table; but, as I cannot endure either the constraint of good
society or the drunkenness of the tavern, I can only enjoy them
with a friend; alone, I cannot do so, for my imagination then
occupies itself with other things, and eating affords me no pleasure.

If my heated blood longs for women, my excited heart longs still more for affection. Women who could be bought for money would lose for me all their charms; I even doubt whether it would be in me to make use of them. I find it the same with all pleasures within my reach; unless they cost me nothing, I find them insipid. I only love those enjoyments which belong to no one but the first man who knows how to enjoy them.

. . . I worship freedom; I abhor restraint, trouble, dependence. As long as the money in my purse lasts, it assures my independence; it relieves me of the trouble of finding expedients to replenish it, a necessity which always inspired me with dread; but the fear of seeing it exhausted makes me hoard it carefully. The money which a man possesses is the instrument of freedom; that which we eagerly pursue is the instrument of slavery. Therefore I hold fast to that which I have, and desire nothing.

My disinterestedness is, therefore, nothing but idleness; the pleasure of possession is not worth the trouble of acquisition. In like manner, my extravagance is nothing but idleness; when the opportunity of spending agreeably presents itself, it cannot be too profitably employed. Money tempts me less than things, because between money and the possession of the desired object there is always an intermediary, whereas between the thing itself and the enjoyment of it there is none. If I see the thing, it tempts me; if I only see the means of gaining possession of it, it does not. For this reason I have committed thefts, and even now I sometimes pilfer trifles which tempt me, and which I prefer to take rather than to ask for; but neither when a child nor a grown-up man do I ever remember to have robbed anyone of a farthing, except on one occasion, fifteen years ago, when I stole seven *livres* ten *sous*. . . .

BOOK II

[The Years 1728–1731.] . . . I have drawn the great moral lesson, perhaps the only one of any practical value, to avoid those situations of life which bring our duties into conflict with our interests, and which show us our own advantage in the misfortunes of others; for it is certain that, in such situations, however sincere our love of virtue, we must, sooner or later, inevitably grow weak without perceiving it, and become unjust and wicked in act, without having ceased to be just and good in our hearts.

This principle, deeply imprinted on the bottom of my heart, which, although somewhat late, in practice guided my whole conduct, is one of those which have caused me to appear a very strange and foolish creature in the eyes of the world, and, above all, amongst my acquaintances. I have been reproached with wanting to pose as an original, and different from others. In reality, I have never troubled about acting like other people or differently from them. I sincerely desired to do what was right. I withdrew, as far as it lay in my power, from situations which opposed my interests to those of others, and might, consequently, inspire me with a secret, though involuntary, desire of injuring them.

. . . I loved too sincerely, too completely, I venture to say, to be able to be happy easily. Never have passions been at once more lively and purer than mine; never has love been tenderer, truer, more disinterested. I would have sacrificed my happiness a thousand times for that of the person whom I loved; her reputation was dearer to me than my life, and I would never have wished to endanger her repose for a single moment for all the pleasures of enjoyment. This feeling has made me employ such carefulness, such secrecy, and such precaution in my undertakings, that none of them have ever been successful. My want of success with women has always been caused by my excessive love for them. . . .

BOOK III

[The Years 1731–1732.] . . . I only felt the full strength of my attachment when I no longer saw her.[1] When I saw her, I was only content; but, during her absence, my restlessness became painful. The need of living with her caused me outbreaks of tenderness which often ended in tears. I shall never forget how, on the day of a great festival, while she was at vespers, I went for a walk outside the town, my heart full of her image and a burning desire to spend my life with her. I had sense enough to see that at present this was impossible, and that the happiness which I enjoyed so deeply could only be short. This gave to my reflections a tinge of melancholy, about which, however, there was nothing gloomy, and which was tempered by flattering hopes. The sound of the bells, which always singularly affects me, the song of the birds, the beauty of the daylight, the enchanting landscape, the scattered country dwellings in which my fancy placed our common home—all these produced upon me an impression so vivid, tender, melancholy and touching, that I saw myself transported, as it were, in ecstasy, into that happy time and place, wherein my heart, possessing all the happiness it could desire, tasted it with inexpressible rapture, without even a thought of sensual pleasure. I never remember to have plunged into the future with greater force and illusion than on that occasion; and what has struck me most in the recollection of this dream after it had been realised, is that I have found things again exactly as I had imagined them. If ever the dream of a man awake resembled a prophetic vision, it was assuredly that dream of mine. I was only deceived in the imaginary duration; for the days, the years, and our whole life were

1. Rousseau refers here to Mme. de Warens, whom he also calls "mamma."

spent in serene and undisturbed tranquillity, whereas in reality it lasted only for a moment. Alas! my most lasting happiness belongs to a dream, the fulfilment of which was almost immediately followed by the awakening. . . .

Two things, almost incompatible, are united in me in a manner which I am unable to understand: a very ardent temperament, lively and tumultuous passions, and, at the same time, slowly developed and confused ideas, which never present themselves until it is too late. One might say that my heart and my mind do not belong to the same person. Feeling takes possession of my soul more rapidly than a flash of lightning; but, instead of illuminating, inflames and dazzles me. I feel everything and see nothing. I am carried away by my passions, but stupid; in order to think, I must be cool. The astonishing thing is that, notwithstanding, I exhibit tolerably sound judgment, penetration, even finesse, if I am not hurried; with sufficient leisure I can compose excellent impromptus; but I have never said or done anything worthy of notice on the spur of the moment. I could carry on a very clever conversation through the post, as the Spaniards are said to carry on a game of chess. When I read of that Duke of Savoy, who turned round on his journey, in order to cry, "At your throat, Parisian huckster," I said, "There you have myself!"

This sluggishness of thought, combined with such liveliness of feeling, not only enters into my conversation, but I feel it even when alone and at work. My ideas arrange themselves in my head with almost incredible difficulty; they circulate in it with uncertain sound, and ferment till they excite and heat me, and make my heart beat fast; and, in the midst of this excitement, I see nothing clearly and am unable to write a single word—I am obliged to wait. Imperceptibly this great agitation subsides, the confusion clears up, everything takes its proper place, but slowly, and only after a period of long and confused agitation. . . .

BOOK IV

[The Years 1731–1732.] . . . I returned, not to Nyon, but to Lausanne. I wanted to sate myself with the sight of this beautiful lake, which is there seen in its greatest extent. Few of the secret motives which have determined me to act have been more rational. Things seen at a distance are rarely powerful enough to make me act. The uncertainty of the future has always made me look upon plans, which need considerable time to carry them out, as decoys for fools. I indulge in hopes like others, provided it costs me nothing to support them; but if they require continued attention, I have done with it. The least trifling pleasure which is within my reach tempts me more than the joys of Paradise. However, I make an exception of the pleasure which is followed by pain; this has no temptation for me, because I love only pure enjoyments, and these a man never has when he knows that he is preparing for himself repentance and regret. . . .

Why is it that, having found so many good people in my youth, I find so few in my later years? Is their race extinct? No; but the class in which I am obliged to look for them now, is no longer the same as that in which I found them. Among the people, where great passions only speak at intervals, the sentiments of nature make themselves more frequently heard; in the higher ranks they are absolutely stifled, and, under the mask of sentiment, it is only interest or vanity that speaks.

. . . Whenever I approach the Canton of Vaud, I am conscious of an impression in which the remembrance of Madame de Warens, who was born there, of my father who lived there, of Mademoiselle de Vulson who enjoyed the first fruits of my youthful love, of several pleasure trips which I made there when a child and, I believe, some other exciting cause, more mysterious and more powerful than all this, is combined. When the burning desire of this happy and peaceful life, which flees from me and for which I was born, inflames my imagination, it is always the Canton of Vaud, near the lake, in the midst of enchanting scenery, to which it draws me. I feel that I must have an orchard on the shore of this lake and no other, that I must have a loyal friend, a loving wife, a cow, and a little boat. I shall never enjoy perfect happiness on earth until I have all that. I laugh at the simplicity with which I have several times visited this country merely in search of this imaginary happiness. I was always surprised to find its inhabitants, especially the women, of quite a different character from that which I expected. How contradictory it appeared to me! The country and its inhabitants have never seemed to me made for each other.

During this journey to Vévay, walking along the beautiful shore, I abandoned myself to the sweetest melancholy. My heart eagerly flung itself into a thousand innocent raptures; I was filled with emotion, I sighed and wept like a child. How often have I stopped to weep to my heart's content, and, sitting on a large stone, amused myself with looking at my tears falling into the water! . . .

How greatly did the entrance into Paris belie the idea I had formed of it! The external decorations of Turin, the beauty of its streets, the symmetry and regularity of the houses, had made me look for something quite different in Paris. I had imagined to myself a city of most imposing aspect, as beautiful as it was large, where nothing was to be seen but splendid streets and palaces of gold and marble. Entering by the suburb of St. Marceau, I saw nothing but dirty and stinking little streets, ugly black houses, a general air of slovenliness and poverty, beggars, carters, menders of old clothes, criers of decoctions and old hats. All this, from the outset, struck me so forcibly, that all the real magnificence I have since seen in Paris has been unable to destroy this first impression, and I have always retained a secret dislike against residence in this capital. I may say that the whole time, during which I afterwards lived there, was employed solely in trying to find means to enable me to live away from it.

Such is the fruit of a too lively imagination, which exaggerates beyond human exaggeration, and is always ready to see more than it has been told to expect. I had heard Paris so much praised, that I had represented it to myself as the ancient Babylon, where, if I had ever visited it, I should, perhaps, have found as much to take off from the picture which I had drawn of it. The same thing happened to me at the Opera, whither I hastened to go the day after my arrival. The same thing happened to me later at Versailles; and again, when I saw the sea for the first time; and the same thing will always happen to me, when I see anything which has been too loudly announced; for it is impossible for men, and difficult for Nature herself, to surpass the exuberance of my imagination.

. . . The sight of the country, a succession of pleasant views, the open air, a good appetite, the sound health which walking gives me, the free life of the inns, the absence of all that makes me conscious of my dependent position, of all that reminds me of my condition— all this sets my soul free, gives me greater boldness of thought, throws me, so to speak, into the immensity of things, so that I can combine, select, and appropriate them at pleasure, without fear or restraint. I dispose of Nature in its entirety as its lord and master; my heart, roaming from object to object, mingles and identifies itself with those which soothe it, wraps itself up in charming fancies, and is intoxicated with delicious sensations. If, in order to render them permanent, I amuse myself by describing them by myself, what vigorous outlines, what fresh colouring, what power of expression I give them!

. . . At night I lay in the open air, and, stretched on the ground or on a bench, slept as calmly as upon a bed of roses. I remember, especially, that I spent a delightful night outside the city, on a road which ran by the side of the Rhône or Saône, I do not remember which. Raised gardens, with terraces, bordered the other side of the road. It had been very hot during the day; the evening was delightful; the dew moistened the parched grass; the night was calm, without a breath of wind; the air was fresh, without being cold; the sun, having gone down, had left in the sky red vapours, the reflection of which cast a rose-red tint upon the water; the trees on the terraces were full of nightingales answering one another. I walked on in a kind of ecstasy, abandoning my heart and senses to the enjoyment of all, only regretting, with a sigh, that I was obliged to enjoy it alone. Absorbed in my delightful reverie, I continued my walk late into the night, without noticing that I was tired. At last, I noticed it. I threw myself with a feeling of delight upon the shelf of a sort of niche or false door let into a terrace wall; the canopy of my bed was formed by the tops of trees; a nightingale was perched just over my head, and lulled me to sleep with his song; my slumbers were sweet, my awaking was still sweeter. . . .

In relating my journeys, as in making them, I do not know how to stop. My heart beat with joy when I drew near to my dear mamma, but I walked no faster. I like to walk at my ease, and to stop when I like. A wandering life is what I want. To walk through a beautiful country in fine weather, without being obliged to hurry, and with a pleasant prospect at the end, is of all kinds of life the one most suited to my taste. My idea of a beautiful country is already known. No flat country, however beautiful, has ever seemed so to my eyes. I must have mountain torrents, rocks, firs, dark forests, mountains, steep roads to climb or descend, precipices at my side to frighten me. . . .

BOOK V

[The Years 1732–1736.] . . . It is sometimes said that the sword wears out the scabbard. That is my history. My passions have made me live, and my passions have killed me. What passions? will be asked. Trifles, the most childish things in the world, which, however, excited me as much as if the possession of Helen or the throne of the universe had been at stake. In the first place—women. When I possessed one, my senses were calm; my heart, never. The needs of love devoured me in the midst of enjoyment; I had a tender mother, a dear friend; but I needed a mistress. I imagined one in her place; I represented her to myself in a thousand forms, in order to deceive myself. If I had thought that I held mamma in my arms when I embraced her, these embraces would have been no less lively, but all my desires would have been extinguished; I should have sobbed from affection, but I should never have felt any enjoyment. Enjoyment! Does this ever fall to the lot of man? If I had ever, a single time in my life, tasted all the delights of love in their fulness, I do not believe that my frail existence could have endured it; I should have died on the spot.

Thus I was burning with love, without an object; and it is this state, perhaps, that is most exhausting. I was restless, tormented by the hopeless condition of poor mamma's affairs, and her imprudent conduct, which were bound to ruin her completely at no distant date. My cruel imagination, which always anticipates misfortunes, exhibited this particular one to me continually, in all its extent and in all its results. I already saw myself compelled by want to separate from her to whom I had devoted my life, and without whom I could not enjoy it. Thus my soul was ever in a state of agitation; I was devoured alternately by desires and fears. . . .

BOOK VI

[The Year 1736.] . . . At this period commences the brief happiness of my life; here approach the peaceful, but rapid moments which have given me the right to say, *I have lived*. Precious and regretted moments! begin again for me your delightful course; and, if it be possible, pass more slowly in succession through my memory, than you did in your fugitive reality. What can I do, to prolong, as I should like, this touching and simple narrative, to repeat the same things over and over again, without wearying my readers by such repetition, any more than I was wearied of them myself, when I recommenced the life again and again? If all this consisted of facts, actions, and words, I could describe, and in a manner, give an idea of them; but how is it possible to describe what was neither said nor done, nor even thought, but enjoyed and felt, without being able to assign any other reason for my happiness than this simple feeling? I got up at sunrise, and was happy; I walked, and was happy; I saw mamma, and was happy; I left her, and was happy; I roamed the forests and hills, I wandered in the valleys, I read, I did nothing, I worked in the garden, I picked the fruit, I helped in the work of the house, and happiness followed me everywhere— happiness, which could not be referred to any definite object, but dwelt entirely within myself, and which never left me for a single instant. . . .

I should much like to know, whether the same childish ideas ever enter the hearts of other men as sometimes enter mine. In the midst of my studies, in the course of a life as blameless as a man could have led, the fear of hell still frequently troubled me. I asked myself: "In what state am I? If I were to die this moment, should I be damned?" According to my Jansenists, there was no doubt about the matter; but, according to my conscience, I thought differently. Always fearful, and a prey to cruel uncertainty, I had recourse to the most laughable expedients to escape from it, for which I would unhesitatingly have anyone locked up as a madman if I saw him doing as I did. One day, while musing upon this melancholy subject, I mechanically amused myself by throwing stones against the trunks of trees with my usual good aim, that is to say, without hardly hitting one. While engaged in this useful exercise, it occurred to me to draw a prognostic from it to calm my anxiety. I said to myself: "I will throw this stone at the tree opposite; if I hit it, I am saved; if I miss it, I am damned." While speaking, I threw my stone with a trembling hand and a terrible palpitation of the heart, but with so successful an aim that it hit the tree right in the middle, which, to tell the truth, was no very difficult feat, for I had been careful to choose a tree with a thick trunk close at hand. From that time I have never had any doubt about my salvation! When I recall this characteristic incident, I do not know whether to laugh or cry at myself. You great men, who are most certainly laughing, may congratulate yourselves; but do not mock my wretchedness, for I swear to you that I feel it deeply. . . .

JOHANN WOLFGANG VON GOETHE

(1749–1832)

Faust*

*Prologue in Heaven*ᵃ

The LORD. The HEAVENLY HOSTS. MEPHISTOPHELESᵇ *following*.

[*The* THREE ARCHANGELS *step forward*.]

RAPHAEL. The chanting sun, as ever, rivals
 The chanting of his brother spheres
 And marches round his destined circuit—
 A march that thunders in our ears.
 His aspect cheers the Hosts of Heaven   5
 Though what his essence none can say;
 These inconceivable creations
 Keep the high state of their first day.

GABRIEL. And swift, with inconceivable swiftness,
 The earth's full splendour rolls around,   10
 Celestial radiance alternating
 With a dread night too deep to sound;
 The sea against the rocks' deep bases
 Comes foaming up in far-flung force,
 And rock and sea go whirling onward   15
 In the swift spheres' eternal course.

MICHAEL. And storms in rivalry are raging
 From sea to land, from land to sea,
 In frenzy forge the world a girdle
 From which no inmost part is free.   20
 The blight of lightning flaming yonder
 Marks where the thunder-bolt will play;
 And yet Thine envoys, Lord, revere

---

* From Goethe's *Faust*, translated by Louis MacNeice. Part I was first published in 1808. Goethe's Dedication and the Prologue at the Theater have not been included, since neither is part of the play itself. All of Part I, except for a few minor omissions made by the translator (indicated in the footnotes), is reprinted here.

a. probably written in 1798. The scene is patterned on Job 1:6–12 and 2:1–6.

b. The origin of the name is still debatable. It may come from Hebrew, Persian, or Greek, with such meanings as "destroyer-liar," "no friend of Faust," "no friend of light."

The gentle movement of Thy day.

CHOIR OF ANGELS. Thine aspect cheers the Hosts of Heaven   25
Though what Thine essence none can say,
And all Thy loftiest creations
Keep the high state of their first day.

[*Enter* MEPHISTOPHELES.]

MEPHISTOPHELES. Since you, O Lord, once more approach and ask
If business down with us be light or heavy—   30
And in the past you've usually welcomed me—
That's why you see me also at your levee.
Excuse me, I can't manage lofty words—
Not though your whole court jeer and find me low;
My pathos certainly would make you laugh   35
Had you not left off laughing long ago.
Your suns and worlds mean nothing much to me;
How men torment themselves, that's all I see.
The little god of the world, one can't reshape, reshade him;
He is as strange to-day as that first day you made him.   40
His life would be not so bad, not quite,
Had you not granted him a gleam of Heaven's light;
He calls it Reason, uses it not the least
Except to be more beastly than any beast.
He seems to me—if your Honour does not mind—   45
Like a grasshopper—the long-legged kind—
That's always in flight and leaps as it flies along
And then in the grass strikes up its same old song.
I could only wish he confined himself to the grass!
He thrusts his nose into every filth, alas.   50

LORD. Mephistopheles, have you no other news?
Do you always come here to accuse?
Is nothing ever right in your eyes on earth?

MEPHISTOPHELES. No, Lord! I find things there as downright bad
as ever.
I am sorry for men's days of dread and dearth;   55
Poor things, *my* wish to plague 'em isn't fervent.

LORD. Do you know Faust?

MEPHISTOPHELES.   The Doctor?

LORD.   Aye, my servant.

MEPHISTOPHELES. Indeed! He serves you oddly enough, I think.   60
The fool has no earthly habits in meat and drink.
The ferment in him drives him wide and far,
That he is mad he too has almost guessed;
He demands of heaven each fairest star

---

58. *Doctor:* i.e., doctor of philosophy.   stopheles shifts from *du* to *ihr*, indicat-
60. *you:* In the German text, Mephi-   ing his lack of respect for God.

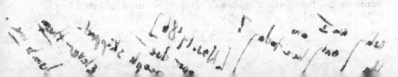

And of earth each highest joy and best,   65
  And all that is new and all that is far
  Can bring no calm to the deep-sea swell of his breast.
LORD. Now he may serve me only gropingly,
  Soon I shall lead him into the light.
  The gardener knows when the sapling first turns green   70
  That flowers and fruit will make the future bright.
MEPHISTOPHELES. What do you wager? You will lose him yet,
  Provided *you* give *me* permission
  To steer him gently the course I set.
LORD. So long as he walks the earth alive,   75
  So long you may try what enters your head;
  Men make mistakes as long as they strive.
MEPHISTOPHELES. I thank you for that; as regards the dead,
  The dead have never taken my fancy.
  I favour cheeks that are full and rosy-red;   80
  No corpse is welcome to my house;
  I work as the cat does with the mouse.
LORD. Very well; you have my permission.
  Divert this soul from its primal source
  And carry it, if you can seize it,   85
  Down with you upon your course—
  And stand ashamed when you must needs admit:
  A good man with his groping intuitions
  Still knows the path that is true and fit.
MEPHISTOPHELES. All right—but it won't last for long.   90
  I'm not afraid my bet will turn out wrong.
  And, if my aim prove true and strong,
  Allow me to triumph wholeheartedly.
  Dust shall he eat—and greedily—
  Like my cousin the Snake renowned in tale and song.   95
LORD. That too you are free to give a trial;
  I have never hated the likes of you.
  Of all the spirits of denial
  The joker is the last that I eschew.
  Man finds relaxation too attractive—   100
  Too fond too soon of unconditional rest;
  Which is why I am pleased to give him a companion
  Who lures and thrusts and must, as devil, be active.
  But ye, true sons of Heaven, it is your duty
  To take your joy in the living wealth of beauty.   105
  The changing Essence which ever works and lives
  Wall you around with love, serene, secure!
  And that which floats in flickering appearance

95. *Snake:* the serpent in Genesis, who tempted Adam and Eve.

Fix ye it firm in thoughts that must endure.

CHOIR OF ANGELS. Thine aspect cheers the Hosts of Heaven   110
    Though what Thine essence none can say,
    And all Thy loftiest creations
    Keep the high state of their first day.
       [*Heaven closes.*]

MEPHISTOPHELES. [*Alone*] I like to see the Old One now and then
    And try to keep relations on the level.   115
    It's really decent of so great a person
    To talk so humanely even to the Devil.

The First Part of the Tragedy

NIGHT

In a high-vaulted narrow Gothic room FAUST, *restless, in a chair at his desk.*

FAUST. Here stand I, ach, Philosophy
    Behind me and Law and Medicine too
    And, to my cost, Theology—
    All these I have sweated through and through
    And now you see me a poor fool   5
    As wise as when I entered school!
    They call me Master, they call me Doctor,
    Ten years now I have dragged my college
    Along by the nose through zig and zag
    Through up and down and round and round   10
    And this is all that I have found—
    The impossibility of knowledge!
    It is this that burns away my heart;
    Of course I am cleverer than the quacks,
    Than master and doctor, than clerk and priest,   15
    I suffer no scruple or doubt in the least,
    I have no qualms about devil or burning,
    Which is just why all joy is torn from me,
    I cannot presume to make use of my learning,
    I cannot presume I could open my mind   20
    To proselytize and improve mankind.

    Besides, I have neither goods nor gold,
    Neither reputation nor rank in the world;
    No dog would choose to continue so!
    Which is why I have given myself to Magic   25
    To see if the Spirit may grant me to know
    Through its force and its voice full many a secret,

May spare the sour sweat that I used to pour out
In talking of what I know nothing about,
May grant me to learn what it is that girds
The world together in its inmost being,
That the seeing its whole germination, the seeing
Its workings, may end my traffic in words.

O couldst thou, light of the full moon,
Look now thy last upon my pain,
Thou for whom I have sat belated
So many midnights here and waited
Till, over books and papers, thou
Didst shine, sad friend, upon my brow!
O could I but walk to and fro
On mountain heights in thy dear glow
Or float with spirits round mountain eyries
Or weave through fields thy glances glean
And freed from all miasmal theories
Bathe in thy dew and wash me clean!

Oh! Am I still stuck in this jail?
This God-damned dreary hole in the wall
Where even the lovely light of heaven
Breaks wanly through the painted panes!
Cooped up among these heaps of books
Gnawed by worms, coated with dust,
Round which to the top of the Gothic vault
A smoke-stained paper forms a crust.
Retorts and canisters lie pell-mell
And pyramids of instruments,
The junk of centuries, dense and mat—
Your world, man! World? They call it that!

And yet you ask why your poor heart
Cramped in your breast should feel such fear,
Why an unspecified misery
Should throw your life so out of gear?
Instead of the living natural world
For which God made all men his sons
You hold a reeking mouldering court
Among assorted skeletons.

Away! There is a world outside!
And this one book of mystic art
Which Nostradamus wrote himself,

30
35
40
45
50
55
60
65

68. *Nostradamus:* Latin name of the French astrologer and physician Michel de Notredame, born in 1503. His col-lection of rhymed prophecies, *The Centuries,* appeared in 1555.

Is this not adequate guard and guide?
By this you can tell the course of the stars,   70
By this, once Nature gives the word,
The soul begins to stir and dawn,
A spirit by a spirit heard.
In vain your barren studies here
Construe the signs of sanctity.   75
You Spirits, you are hovering near;
If you can hear me, answer me!

    [*He opens the book and perceives the sign of the Macrocosm.*[a]]

Ha! What a river of wonder at this vision
Bursts upon all my senses in one flood!
And I feel young, the holy joy of life   80
Glows new, flows fresh, through nerve and blood!
Was it a god designed this hieroglyph to calm
The storm which but now raged inside me,
To pour upon my heart such balm,
And by some secret urge to guide me   85
Where all the powers of Nature stand unveiled around me?
Am I a God? It grows so light!
And through the clear-cut symbol on this page
My soul comes face to face with all creating Nature.
At last I understand the dictum of the sage: 90
'The spiritual world is always open,
Your mind is closed, your heart is dead;
Rise, young man, and plunge undaunted
Your earthly breast in the morning red.'

    [*He contemplates the sign.*]

Into one Whole how all things blend,   95
Function and live within each other!
Passing gold buckets to each other
How heavenly powers ascend, descend!
The odour of grace upon their wings,
They thrust from heaven through earthly things   100
And as all sing so *the* All sings!

What a fine show! Aye, but only a show!
Infinite Nature, where can I tap thy veins?
Where are thy breasts, those well-springs of all life
On which hang heaven and earth,   105
Towards which my dry breast strains?
They well up, they give drink, but I feel drought and dearth.

---

[a]. literally, "the great world"; the universe as a whole.

[*He turns the pages and perceives the sign of the* EARTH
SPIRIT.]

How differently this new sign works upon me!
Thy sign, thou Spirit of the Earth, 'tis thine
And thou art nearer to me.   110
At once I feel my powers unfurled,
At once I glow as from new wine
And feel inspired to venture into the world,
To cope with the fortunes of earth benign or malign,
To enter the ring with the storm, to grapple and clinch,   115
To enter the jaws of the shipwreck and never flinch.
Over me comes a mist,
The moon muffles her light,
The lamp goes dark.
The air goes damp. Red beams flash   120
Around my head. There blows
A kind of a shudder down from the vault
And seizes on me.
It is thou must be hovering round me, come at my prayers!
Spirit, unveil thyself!   125
My heart, oh my heart, how it tears!
And how each and all of my senses
Seem burrowing upwards towards new light, new breath!
I feel my heart has surrendered, I have no more defences.
Come then! Come! Even if it prove my death!   130
    [*He seizes the book and solemnly pronounces the sign of the*
    EARTH SPIRIT. *There is a flash of red flame and the* SPIRIT
    appears in it.]
SPIRIT. Who calls upon me?
FAUST. Appalling vision!
SPIRIT. You have long been sucking at my sphere,
    Now by main force you have drawn me here
    And now—   135
FAUST. No! Not to be endured!
SPIRIT. With prayers and with pantings you have procured
    The sight of my face and the sound of my voice—
    Now I am here. What a pitiable shivering
    Seizes the Superman. Where is the call of your soul?   140
    Where the breast which created a world in itself
    And carried and fostered it, swelling up, joyfully quivering,
    Raising itself to a level with Us, the Spirits?
    Where are you, Faust, whose voice rang out to me,

109. *Spirit of the Earth:* The Mac- figure seems to be a symbol for the
rocosm represented the ordered, har- energy of terrestrial nature—neither
monious universe in its totality; this good nor bad, merely powerful.

Who with every nerve so thrust yourself upon me? 145
Are you the thing that at a whiff of my breath
Trembles throughout its living frame,
A poor worm crawling off, askance, askew?

FAUST. Shall I yield to Thee, Thou shape of flame?
I am Faust, I can hold my own with Thee. 150

SPIRIT. In the floods of life, in the storm of work,
In ebb and flow,
In warp and weft,
Cradle and grave,
An eternal sea, 155
A changing patchwork,
A glowing life,
At the whirring loom of Time I weave
The living clothes of the Deity.

FAUST. Thou who dost rove the wide world round, 160
Busy Spirit, how near I feel to Thee!

SPIRIT. You are like that Spirit which you can grasp,
Not me!

    [*The* SPIRIT *vanishes.*]

FAUST. Not Thee!
Whom then?
I who am Godhead's image, 165
Am I not even like Thee!

    [*A knocking on the door.*]

Death! I know who that is. My assistant!
So ends my happiest, fairest hour.
The crawling pedant must interrupt 170
My visions at their fullest flower!

    [WAGNER *enters in dressing-gown and nightcap, a lamp in
his hand.*]

WAGNER. Excuse me but I heard your voice declaiming—
A passage doubtless from those old Greek plays.
That is an art from which I would gladly profit,
It has its advantages nowadays. 175
And I've often heard folks say it's true
A preacher can learn something from an actor.

FAUST. Yes, when the preacher is an actor too;
Which is a not uncommon factor.

WAGNER. Ah, when your study binds up your whole existence 180
And you scarcely can see the world on a holiday
Or through a spyglass—and always from a distance—
How can your rhetoric make it walk your way?

FAUST. Unless you feel it, you cannot gallop it down,
Unless it thrust up from your soul 185

Forcing the hearts of all your audience
With a primal joy beyond control.
Sit there for ever with scissors and paste!
Gather men's leavings for a rehash
And blow up a little paltry flicker   190
Out of your own little heap of ash!
It will win you claps from apes and toddlers—
Supposing your palate welcome such—
But heart can never awaken a spark in heart
Unless your own heart keep in touch.   195

WAGNER. However, it is the delivery wins all ears
And I know that I am still far, too far, in arrears.

FAUST. Win your effects by honest means,
Eschew the cap and bells of the fool!
True insight and true sense will make   200
Their point without the rhetoric school
And, given a thought that must be heard,
Is there such need to chase a word?
Yes, your so glittering purple patches
In which you make cat's cradles of humanity   205
Are like the foggy wind which whispers in the autumn
Through barren leaves—a fruitless vanity.

WAGNER. Ah God, we know that art
Is long and short our life!
Often enough my analytical labours   210
Pester both brain and heart.
How hard it is to attain the means
By which one climbs to the fountain head;
Before a poor devil can reach the halfway house,
Like as not he is dead.   215

FAUST. Your manuscript, is that your holy well
A draught of which for ever quenches thirst?
You have achieved no true refreshment
Unless you can tap your own soul first.

WAGNER. Excuse me—it is considerable gratification   220
To transport oneself into the spirit of times past,
To observe what a wise man thought before our days
And how we now have brought his ideas to consummation.

FAUST. Oh yes, consummated in heaven!
There is a book, my friend, and its seals are seven—   225
The times that have been put on the shelf.
Your so-called spirit of such times
Is at bottom merely the spirit of the gentry
In whom each time reflects itself,

225. *its seals are seven:* See Revelation 5:1.

And at that it often makes one weep   230
And at the first glance run away,
A lumber-room and a rubbish heap,
At best an heroic puppet play
With excellent pragmatical Buts and Yets
Such as are suitable to marionettes.   235

WAGNER. And yet the world! The heart and spirit of men!
We all would wish to understand the same.

FAUST. Yes, what is known as understanding—
But who dare call the child by his real name?
The few who have known anything about it,   240
Whose hearts unwisely overbrimmed and spake,
Who showed the mob their feelings and their visions,
Have ended on the cross or at the stake.
My friend, I beg you, the night is now far gone;
We must break off for this occasion.   245

WAGNER. I'd have been happy sitting on and on
To continue such a learned conversation.
To-morrow however, as it is Easter Day,
I shall put you some further questions if I may.
Having given myself to knowledge heart and soul   250
I have a good share of it, now I would like the whole.
    [*Exit* WAGNER.]

FAUST. [*Alone*] To think this head should still bring hope to
        birth
Sticking like glue to hackneyed rags and tags,
Delving with greedy hand for treasure
And glad when it finds an earthworm in the earth!   255

That such a human voice should here intrude
Where spiritual fulness only now enclosed me!
And yet, my God, you poorest of all the sons
Of earth, this time you have earned my gratitude.
For you have snatched me away from that despair   260
Which was ripe and ready to destroy my mind;
Beside that gigantic vision I could not find
My normal self; only a dwarf was there.

I, image of the Godhead, who deemed myself but now
On the brink of the mirror of eternal truth and seeing   265
My rapturous fill of the blaze of clearest Heaven,
Having stripped off my earthly being;
I, more than an angel, I whose boundless urge
To flow through Nature's veins and in the act of creation
To revel it like the gods—what a divination,   270

What an act of daring—and what an expiation!
One thundering word has swept me over the verge.

To boast myself thine equal I do not dare.
Granted I owned the power to draw thee down,
I lacked the power to hold thee there.   275
In that blest moment I felt myself,
Felt myself so small, so great;
Cruelly thou didst thrust me back
Into man's uncertain fate.
Who will teach me? What must I shun?   280
Or must I go where that impulse drives?
Alas, our very actions like our sufferings
Put a brake upon our lives.
Upon the highest concepts of the mind
There grows an alien and more alien mould;   285
When we have reached what in this world is good
That which is better is labelled a fraud, a blind.
What gave us life, feelings of highest worth,
Go dead amidst the madding crowds of earth.

Where once Imagination on daring wing
Reached out to the Eternal, full of hope,   290
Now, that the eddies of time have shipwrecked chance on chance,
She is contented with a narrow scope.
Care makes her nest forthwith in the heart's deep places,
And there contrives her secret sorrows,   295
Rocks herself restlessly, destroying rest and joy;
And always she is putting on new faces,
Will appear as your home, as those that you love within it,
As fire or water, poison or steel;
You tremble at every blow that you do not feel   300
And what you never lose you must weep for every minute.

I am not like the gods—that I too deeply feel—
No, I am like the worm that burrows through the dust
Which, as it keeps itself alive in the dust,
Is annulled and buried by some casual heel.   305

Is it not dust that on a thousand shelves
Narrows this high wall round me so?
The junk that with its thousandfold tawdriness
In this moth world keeps me so low?
Shall I find here what I require?   310
Read maybe in a thousand books how men
Have in the general run tortured themselves,

With but a lucky one now and then?
Why do you grin at me, you hollow skull?
To point out that your brain was once, like mine, confused   315
And looked for the easy day but in the difficult dusk,
Lusting for truth was led astray and abused?
You instruments, I know you are mocking me
With cog and crank and cylinder.
I stood at the door, you were to be the key;   320
A key with intricate wards—but the bolt declines to stir.
Mysterious in the light of day
Nature lets none unveil her; if she refuse
To make some revelation to your spirit
You cannot force her with levers and with screws.   325
You ancient gear I have never used, it is only
Because my father used you that I retain you.
You ancient scroll, you have been turning black
Since first the dim lamp smoked upon this desk to stain you.
Far better to have squandered the little I have   330
Than loaded with that little to stay sweating here.
Whatever legacy your fathers left you,
To own it you must earn it dear.
The thing that you fail to use is a load of lead;
The moment can only use what the moment itself has bred.   335

But why do my eyes fasten upon that spot?
Is that little bottle a magnet to my sight?
Why do I feel of a sudden this lovely illumination
As when the moon flows round us in a dark wood at night?

Bottle, unique little bottle, I salute you   340
As now I devoutly lift you down. In you
I honour human invention and human skill.
You, the quintessence of all sweet narcotics,
The extract of all rare and deadly powers,
I am your master—show me your good will!   345
I look on you, my sorrow is mitigated,
I hold you and my struggles are abated,
The flood-tide of my spirit ebbs away, away.
The mirroring waters glitter at my feet,
I am escorted forth on the high seas,   350
Allured towards new shores by a new day.
A fiery chariot floats on nimble wings
Down to me and I feel myself upbuoyed
To blaze a new trail through the upper air

326–327. *gear . . . father:* Later we find that Faust's father was a doctor of medicine.

Into new spheres of energy unalloyed.   355
Oh this high life, this heavenly rapture! Do *you*
Merit this, you, a moment ago a worm?
Merit it? Aye—only turn your back on the sun
Which enchants the earth, turn your back and be firm!
And brace yourself to tear asunder the gates   360
Which everyone longs to shuffle past if he can;
Now is the time to act and acting prove
That God's height need not lower the merit of Man;
Nor tremble at that dark pit in which our fancy
Condemns itself to torments of its own framing,   365
But struggle on and upwards to that passage
At the narrow mouth of which all hell is flaming.
Be calm and take this step, though you should fall
Beyond it into nothing—nothing at all.

And you, you loving-cup of shining crystal—   370
I have not given a thought to you for years—
Down you come now out of your ancient chest!
You glittered at my ancestors' junketings
Enlivening the serious guest
When with you in his hand he proceeded to toast his neigh-
     bour—   375
But to-day no neighbour will take you from my hand.
Here is a juice that makes one drunk in a wink;
It fills you full, you cup, with its brown flood.
It was I who made this, I who had it drawn;
So let my whole soul now make my last drink   380
A high and gala greeting, a toast to the dawn!
     [*He raises the cup to his mouth. There is an outburst of
     bells and choirs.*]
CHORUS OF ANGELS. Christ is arisen!
                    Joy to mortality
                    Whom its own fatally
                    Earth-bound mortality   385
                    Bound in a prison.
FAUST. What a deep booming, what a ringing tone
    Pulls back the cup from my lips—and with such power!
    So soon are you announcing, you deep bells,
    Easter Day's first festive hour?   390
    You choirs, do you raise so soon the solacing hymn
    That once round the night of the grave rang out from the
        seraphim

381. *dawn:* See l. 248.   an old medieval Easter hymn, freely
382. *Christ is arisen!:* first line of   adapted by Goethe.

As man's new covenant and dower?

CHORUS OF WOMEN. With balm and with spices
'Twas we laid him out,   395
We who tended him,
Faithful, devout;
We wound him in linen,
Made all clean where he lay,
Alas—to discover   400
Christ gone away.

CHORUS OF ANGELS. Christ is arisen!
The loving one! Blest
After enduring the
Grievous, the curing, the   405
Chastening test.

FAUST. You heavenly music, strong as you are kind,
Why do you search me out in the dust?
Better ring forth where men have open hearts!
I hear your message, my faith it is that lags behind;   410
And miracle is the favourite child of faith.
Those spheres whence peals the gospel of forgiving,
Those are beyond what I can dare,
And yet, so used am I from childhood to this sound,
It even now summons me back to living.   415
Once I could feel the kiss of heavenly love
Rain down through the calm and solemn Sabbath air,
Could find a prophecy in the full-toned bell,
A spasm of happiness in a prayer.
An ineffably sweet longing bound me   420
To quest at random through field and wood
Where among countless burning tears
I felt a world rise up around me.
This hymn announced the lively games of youth, the lovely
Freedom of Spring's own festival;   425
Now with its childlike feelings memory holds me back
From the last and gravest step of all.
But you, sweet songs of heaven, keep sounding forth!
My tears well up, I belong once more to earth.

CHORUS OF DISCIPLES. Now has the Buried One,   430
Lowliness ended,
Living in lordliness,
Lordly ascended;
He in the zest of birth

394–401. *With balm . . . away:*
Goethe makes free use of the New
Testament here. None of the Evange-
lists says that Christ was laid in the
tomb by women. According to Mark
and Luke, they came on the third day
intending to anoint the body, but He
was gone from the tomb.

435

Near to creating light;
We on the breast of earth
Still in frustrating night!
He left us, his own ones,
Pining upon this spot,
Ah, and lamenting,   440
Master, thy lot.

CHORUS OF ANGELS.   Christ is arisen
From the womb of decay!
Burst from your prison,
Rejoice in the day!   445
Praising him actively,
Practising charity,
Giving alms brotherly,
Preaching him wanderingly,
Promising sanctity,   450
You have your Master near,
You have him here!

EASTER HOLIDAY

Holidaymakers of all kinds come out through the city gate.[a]

FIRST STUDENT. Lord, these strapping wenches they go a lick!
Hurry up, brother, we must give 'em an escort.
My programme for to-day is a strong ale,
A pipe of shag and a girl who's got up chic.

FIRST GIRL. Look! Will you look at the handsome boys!   5
Really and truly its degrading;
They could walk out with the best of us
And they have to run round scullery-maiding!

SECOND STUDENT. Hold on, hold on! There are two coming up behind
With a very pretty taste in dress;   10
One of those girls is a neighbour of mine,
She appeals to me, I must confess.
You see how quietly they go
And yet in the end they'll be taking *us* in tow.

BEGGAR. [*Singing*] Good gentlemen and lovely ladies,   15
Rosy of cheek and neat of dress,
Be kind enough to look upon me
And see and comfort my distress.
Leave me not here a hopeless busker!

---

a. It has been shown that Goethe had Frankfurt-am-Main in mind for this scene, and the "gate" referred to is the Sachsenhausen Tor, or Affenthor. The translator omits a few lines here which include other local references—to a hunting lodge, or *Forsthaus*, two miles southwest of the gate; to an inn called the Gerbermühle on the Main River; and to a village, probably Oberrad.

Only the giver can be gay.   20
A day when all the town rejoices,
Make it for me a harvest day.

FIRST BURGHER. I know nothing better on Sundays or on holidays
Than to have a chat about war and warlike pother
When far away, in Turkey say,   25
The peoples are socking one another.
One stands at the window, drinks one's half of mild,
And sees the painted ships glide down the waterways;
Then in the evening one goes happily home
And blesses peace and peaceful days.   30

SECOND BURGHER. Yes indeed, neighbour! That is all right with me.
They can break heads if they like it so
And churn up everything topsyturvy.
But at home let us keep the status quo.

OLD WOMAN. Eh, but how smart they look! Pretty young things!   35
Whoever saw you should adore you!
But not so haughty! It's all right—
Tell me your wish and I can get it for you.

FIRST GIRL. Come, Agatha! Such witches I avoid
In public places—it's much wiser really;   40
It's true, she helped me on St. Andrew's night
To see my future sweetheart clearly.

SECOND GIRL. Yes, mine she showed me in a crystal,
A soldier type with dashing chaps behind him;
I look around, I seek him everywhere
And yet—and yet I never find him.   45

SOLDIERS. [*Singing*] Castles with towering
                        Walls to maintain them,
                        Girls who have suitors
                        But to disdain them,
                        Would I could gain them!   50
                        Bold is the venture,
                        Lordly the pay.

                        Hark to the trumpets!
                        They may be crying
                        Summons to gladness,   55
                        Summons to dying.
                        Life is a storming!
                        Life is a splendour!
                        Maidens and castles   60
                        Have to surrender.

41. *St. Andrew's night:* Actually, St. Andrew's eve, November 29. This was the traditional time for young girls to consult fortunetellers about their future lovers or husbands.

whoops!. went to see The Front Page instead ('86)

> Bold is the venture,
> Lordly the pay;
> Later the soldiers
> Go marching away. 65

[FAUST *and* WAGNER *are now walking off on the road to the village.*]

FAUST. River and brook are freed from ice
By the lovely enlivening glance of spring
And hope grows green throughout the dale;
Ancient winter, weakening,
Has fallen back on the rugged mountains 70
And launches thence his "Parthian shafts"
Which are merely impotent showers of hail
Streaking over the greening mead;
But the sun who tolerates nothing white
Amidst all this shaping and stirring of seed, 75
Wants to enliven the world with colour
And, flowers being lacking, in their lieu
Takes colourful crowds to mend the view.
Turn round and look back from this rise
Towards the town. From the gloomy gate 80
Look, can you see them surging forth—
A harlequin-coloured crowd in fête!
Sunning themselves with one accord
In homage to the risen Lord
For they themselves to-day have risen: 85
Out of the dismal room in the slum,
Out of each shop and factory prison,
Out of the stuffiness of the garret,
Out of the squash of the narrow streets,
Out of the churches' reverend night— 90
One and all have been raised to light.
Look, only look, how quickly the gardens
And fields are sprinkled with the throng,
How the river all its length and breadth
Bears so many pleasure-boats along, 95
And almost sinking from its load
How this last dinghy moves away.
Even on the furthest mountain tracks
Gay rags continue to look gay.
Already I hear the hum of the village, 100
Here is the plain man's real heaven—
Great and small in a riot of fun;
Here I'm a man—and dare be one.

WAGNER. Doctor, to take a walk with you

Is a profit and a privilege for me   105
But I wouldn't lose my way alone round here,
Sworn foe that I am of all vulgarity.
This fiddling, screaming, skittle-playing,
Are sounds I loathe beyond all measure;
They run amuck as if the devil were in them   110
And call it music, call it pleasure.
[*They have now reached the village.*]

OLD PEASANT. Doctor, it is most good of you
    Not to look down on us to-day
    And, pillar of learning that you are,
    To mill around with folk at play.   115
    So take this most particular jug
    Which we have filled for you at the tap,
    This is a pledge and I pray aloud
    That it quench your thirst and more mayhap:
    As many drops as this can give,   120
    So many days extra may you live.

FAUST. Thank you for such a reviving beer
    And now—good health to all men here.
        [*The people collect round him.*]

OLD PEASANT. Of a truth, Doctor, you have done rightly
    To appear on this day when all are glad,   125
    Seeing how in times past you proved
    Our own good friend when days were bad.
    Many a man stands here alive
    Whom your father found in the grip
    Of a raging fever and tore him thence   130
    When he put paid to the pestilence.
    You too—you were a youngster then—
    Where any was ill you went your round,
    Right many a corpse left home feet first
    But you came out of it safe and sound,   135
    From many a gruelling trial—Aye,
    The helper got help from the Helper on high.

CROWD. Health to the trusty man. We pray
    He may live to help us many a day.

FAUST. Kneel to the One on high, our friend   140
    Who teaches us helpers, who help can send.
        [FAUST *and* WAGNER *leave the* CROWD *and move on.*]

WAGNER. You great man, how your heart must leap
    To be so honoured by the masses!
    How happy is he who has such talents

---

129. *your father:* See l. 327 in the preceding scene. The old German Faust legend made Faust's father a peasant; but Nostradamus (see note to l. 68 in the preceding scene) and Paracelsus (1493–1541), two physician-astrologers closely linked to the Faust myth, were famous for their plague-curing remedies.

And from them such a crop can reap!   145
The father points you out to his boy,
They all ask questions, run and jostle,
The fiddles and the dancers pause
And, as you pass, they stand in rows
And caps go hurtling in the sky;   150
They almost kneel to you as though
The eucharist were passing by.

the ceremony of the Last Supper — the offering of the bread [flesh] & the wine [blood]

FAUST. Only a few steps more up to that stone!
Here, after our walk, we will take a rest.
Here I have often sat, thoughtful, alone,   155
Torturing myself with prayer and fast.
Rich in hope and firm in faith,
With tears and sighs to seven times seven
I thought I could end that epidemic
And force the hand of the Lord of Heaven.   160
But now the crowd's applause sounds to me like derision.
O could you only read in my inmost heart
How little father and son
Merited their great reputation!
My father was a worthy man who worked in the dark,   165
Who in good faith but on his own wise
Brooded on Nature and her holy circles
With laborious whimsicalities; *intense*
Who used to collect the connoisseurs
Into the kitchen and locked inside   170
Its black walls pour together divers
Ingredients of countless recipes;
Such was our medicine, the patients died
And no one counted the survivors.
And thus we with our hellish powders   175
Raged more perniciously than the plague
Throughout this district—valley and town.
Myself I have given the poison to thousands;
They drooped away, *I* must live on to sample
The brazen murderers' renown.   180
WAGNER. How can you let that weigh so heavily?
Does not a good man do enough
If he works at the art that he has received
Conscientiously and scrupulously?
As a young man you honour your father,   185
What he can teach, you take with a will;
As a man you widen the range of knowledge
And your son's range may be wider still.
FAUST. Happy the man who swamped in this sea of Error
Still hopes to struggle up through the watery wall;   190
What we don't know is exactly what we need

And what we know fulfils no need at all.
But let us not with such sad thoughts
Make this good hour an hour undone!
Look how the cottages on the green   195
Shine in the glow of the evening sun!
He backs away, gives way, the day is overspent,
He hurries off to foster life elsewhere.
Would I could press on his trail, on his trail for ever—
Alas that I have no wings to raise me into the air!   200
Then I should see in an everlasting sunset
The quiet world before my feet unfold,
All of its peaks on fire, all of its vales becalmed,
And the silver brook dispersed in streams of gold.
Not the wild peaks with all their chasms   205
Could interrupt my godlike flight;
Already the bays of the sea that the sun has warmed
Unfurl upon my marvelling sight.
But in the end the sungod seems to sink away,
Yet the new impulse sets me again in motion,   210
I hasten on to drink his eternal light,
With night behind me and before me day,
Above me heaven and below me ocean.
A beautiful dream—yet the sun leaves me behind.
Alas, it is not so easy for earthly wing   215
To fly on level terms with the wings of the mind.
Yet born with each of us is the instinct
That struggles upwards and away
When over our heads, lost in the blue,
The lark pours out her vibrant lay;   220
When over rugged pine-clad ranges
The eagle hangs on outspread wings
And over lake and over plain
We see the homeward-struggling crane.

WAGNER. I myself have often had moments of fancifulness   225
But I never experienced yet an urge like this.
Woods and fields need only a quick look
And I shall never envy the bird its pinions.
How differently the joys of the mind's dominions
Draw us from page to page, from book to book.   230
That's what makes winter nights lovely and snug—
The blissful life that warms you through your body—
And, ah, should you unroll a worthwhile manuscript,
You bring all heaven down into your study.

FAUST. You are only conscious of one impulse. Never   235
Seek an acquaintance with the other.
Two souls, alas, cohabit in my breast,
A contract one of them desires to sever.

The one like a rough lover clings
To the world with the tentacles of its senses;   240
The other lifts itself to Elysian Fields
Out of the mist on powerful wings.
Oh, if there be spirits in the air,
Princes that weave their way between heaven and earth,
Come down to me from the golden atmosphere   245
And carry me off to a new and colourful life.
Aye, if I only had a magic mantle
On which I could fly abroad, a-voyaging,
I would not barter it for the costliest raiment,
Not even for the mantle of a king.   250

WAGNER. Do not invoke the notorious host
Deployed in streams upon the wind,
Preparing danger in a thousand forms
From every quarter for mankind.
Thrusting upon you from the North   255
Come fanged spirits with arrow tongues;
From the lands of morning they come parching
To feed themselves upon your lungs;
The South despatches from the desert
Incendiary hordes against your brain   260
And the West a swarm which first refreshes,
Then drowns both you and field and plain.
They are glad to listen, adepts at doing harm,
Glad to obey and so throw dust in our eyes;
They make believe that they are sent from heaven   265
And lisp like angels, telling lies.
But let us move! The world has already gone grey,
The air is beginning to cool and the mist to fall.
It's in the evening one really values home—
But why do you look so astonished, standing there, staring that
    way?   270
What's there to see in the dusk that's worth the trouble?

FAUST. The black dog, do you mark him ranging through corn and
    stubble?

WAGNER. I noticed him long ago; he struck me as nothing much.

FAUST. Have a good look at the brute. What do you take him for?

WAGNER. For a poodle who, as is the way of such,   275
Is trailing his master, worrying out the scent.

FAUST. But don't you perceive how in wide spirals around us
He is getting nearer and nearer of set intent?
And, unless I'm wrong, a running fire
Eddies behind him in his wake.   280

WAGNER. I can see nothing but a black poodle;
It must be your eyes have caused this mistake.

FAUST. He is casting, it seems to me, fine nooses of magic

About our feet as a snare.

WAGNER. *I* see him leaping round us uncertainly, timidly,   285
  Finding instead of his master two strangers there.

FAUST. The circle narrows; now he is near.

WAGNER. Just a dog, you see; no phantoms here.
  He growls and hesitates, grovels on the green
  And wags his tail. Pure dog routine.

FAUST. Heel, sir, heel! Come, fellow, come!   290

WAGNER. He is a real poodle noodle.
  Stand still and he'll sit up and beg;
  Speak to him and he's all over you;
  Lose something and he'll fetch it quick,
  He'll jump in the water after your stick.   295

FAUST. I think you're right, I cannot find a trace
  Of a spirit here; it is all a matter of training.

WAGNER. If a dog is well brought up, a wise man even
  Can come to be fond of him in such a case.
  Yes, he fully deserves your name upon his collar,   300
  He whom the students have found so apt a scholar.

FAUST'S STUDY

He enters with the poodle.

FAUST. I have forsaken field and meadow
    Which night has laid in a deep bed,
    Night that wakes our better soul
    With a holy and foreboding dread.
    Now wild desires are wrapped in sleep   5
    And all the deeds that burn and break,
    The love of Man is waking now,
    The love of God begins to wake.

Poodle! Quiet! Don't run hither and thither!
Leave my threshold! Why are you snuffling there?
Lie down behind the stove and rest.   10
Here's a cushion; it's my best.
Out of doors on the mountain paths
You kept us amused by running riot;
But as my protégé at home
You'll only be welcome if you're quiet.   15

    Ah, when in our narrow cell
    The lamp once more imparts good cheer,
    Then in our bosom—in the heart
    That knows itself—then things grow clear.   20
    Reason once more begins to speak
    And the blooms of hope once more to spread;
    One hankers for the brooks of life,
    Ah, and for life's fountain head.

Don't growl, you poodle! That animal sound   25
Is not in tune with the holy music
By which my soul is girdled round.
We are used to human beings who jeer
At what they do not understand,
Who grouse at the good and the beautiful   30
Which often causes them much ado;
But must a dog snarl at it too?

But, ah, already, for all my good intentions
I feel contentment ebbing away in my breast.
Why must the stream so soon run dry   35
And we be left once more athirst?
I have experienced this so often;
Yet this defect has its compensation,
We learn to prize the supernatural
And hanker after revelation,   40
Which burns most bright and wins assent
Most in the New Testament.
I feel impelled to open the master text
And this once, with true dedication,
Take the sacred original   45
And make in my mother tongue my own translation.
    [*He opens a Bible.*]
It is written: In the beginning was the Word.
Here I am stuck at once. Who will help me on?
I am unable to grant the Word such merit,
I must translate it differently   50
If I am truly illumined by the spirit.
It is written: In the beginning was the Mind.
But why should my pen scour
So quickly ahead? Consider that first line well.
Is it the Mind that effects and creates all things?   55
It *should* read: In the beginning was the Power.
Yet, even as I am changing what I have writ,
Something warns me not to abide by it.
The spirit prompts me, I see in a flash what I need,
And write: In the beginning was the Deed!   60

Dog! If we two are to share this room,
Leave off your baying,
Leave off your barking!
I can't have such a fellow staying
Around me causing all this bother.   65
One of us or the other

---

43. *master text:* i.e., the Greek.   **47.** *In the beginning . . . Word:* John 1:1.

Will have to leave the cell.
Well?
I don't really like to eject you so
But the door is open, you may go.   70

But what? What do I see?
Can this really happen naturally?
Is it a fact or is it a fraud?
My dog is growing so long and broad!
He raises himself mightily,   75
That is not a dog's anatomy!
What a phantom have I brought to my house!
He already looks like a river horse *a mare*
With fiery eyes and frightful jaws—
Aha! But I can give you pause!   80
For such a hybrid out of hell
Solomon's Key is a good spell.
    [SPIRITS *are heard in the passage.*]
SPIRITS. Captured within there is one of us!
Wait without, follow him none of us!
Like a fox in a snare   85
An old hell-cat's trembling there.
But on the alert!
Fly against and athwart,
To starboard and port,
And he's out with a spurt!   90
If help you can take him,
Do not forsake him!
For often, to earn it, he
Helped our fraternity.
FAUST. First, to confront the beast,   95
Be the Spell of the Four released:
    Salamander shall glow,
    Undine shall coil,
    Sylph shall vanish
    And gnome shall toil.   100
One without sense
Of the elements,
Of their force
And proper course,
The spirits would never   105
Own him for master.
    Vanish in flames,
    Salamander!

82. Solomon's Key: the *Clavicula Salomonis*, a standard work used by magicians for conjuring; in many medieval legends, Solomon was noted as a great magician.

96. *Spell of the Four:* Salamanders were spirits of fire; undines, of water; sylphs, of air; and gnomes, of earth.

Commingle in babble of streams,
Undine!   110
Shine meteor-like and majestic,
Sylph!
Bring help domestic,
Lubber-fiend! Lubber-fiend!
Step out of him and make an end!   115
None of the Four
Is the creature's core.
He lies quite quiet and grins at me,
I have not yet worked him injury.
To exercise you   120
I'll have to chastise you.
Are you, rapscallion,
A displaced devil?
This sign can level
Each dark battalion;   125
Look at this sign!
He swells up already with bristling spine.
You outcast! Heed it—
This name! Can you read it?
The unbegotten one,   130
Unpronounceable,
Poured throughout Paradise,
Heinously wounded one?
Behind the stove, bound by my spells,
Look, like an elephant it swells,   135
Filling up all the space and more,
It threatens to melt away in mist.
Down from the ceiling! Down before—!
Down at your master's feet! Desist!
You see, I have not proved a liar;   140
I can burn you up with holy fire!
Do not await
The triply glowing light!
Do not await
My strongest brand of necromancy!   145

[*The mist subsides and* MEPHISTOPHELES *comes forward from behind the stove, dressed like a travelling scholar.*]

MEPHISTOPHELES. What is the noise about? What might the gentle-
    man fancy?
FAUST. So that is what the poodle had inside him!
    A travelling scholar? That casus makes me laugh.
MEPHISTOPHELES. My compliments to the learned gentleman.
    You have put me a sweat—not half!   150

143. *triply glowing light:* perhaps   gent rays.
the Trinity, or a triangle with diver-

FAUST. What is your name?

MEPHISTOPHELES. The question strikes me as petty
For one who holds the Word in such low repute,
Who, far withdrawn from all mere surface,
Aims only at the Essential Root.   155

FAUST. With you, you gentry, what is essential
The name more often than not supplies,
As is indeed only too patent
When they call you Fly-God, Corrupter, Father of Lies.
All right, who are you then?   160

MEPHISTOPHELES. A part of that Power
Which always wills evil, always procures good.

FAUST. What do you mean by this conundrum?

MEPHISTOPHELES. I am the Spirit which always denies. p-290
And quite rightly; whatever has a beginning   165
Deserves to have an undoing;
It would be better if nothing began at all.
Thus everything that you call
Sin, destruction, Evil in short,
Is my own element, my resort.   170

FAUST. You call yourself a part, yet you stand before me whole?

MEPHISTOPHELES. This is the unassuming truth.
Whereas mankind, that little world of fools,
Commonly takes itself for a whole—
I am a part of the Part which in the beginning was all,   175
A part of the darkness which gave birth to light,
To that haughty light which is struggling now to usurp
The ancient rank and realm of its mother Night,
And yet has no success, try as it will,
Being bound and clamped by bodies still.   180
It streams from bodies, bodies it beautifies,
A body clogs it when it would run,
And so, I hope, it won't be long
Till, bodies and all, it is undone.

FAUST. Ah, now I know your honourable profession!   185
You cannot destroy on a large scale,
So you are trying it on a small.

MEPHISTOPHELES. And, candidly, not getting far at all.
That which stands over against the Nothing,
The Something, I mean this awkward world,   190
For all my endeavours up to date
I have failed to get it under foot
With waves, with storms, with earthquakes, fire—

---

153. *Word:* See l. 47 in this scene.
159. *Fly-God:* an almost literal translation of the name of the Philistine deity Beelzebub.
176. *darkness:* Mephistopheles here

speaks as the Prince of Darkness, the rôle in Christianity acquired by the devil from the Persian Manichaean deity Ahriman.

Sea and land after all stay put.
And this damned stuff, the brood of beasts and men, 195
There is no coming to grips with them;
I've already buried heaps of them!
And always new blood, fresh blood, circulates again.
So it goes on, it's enough to drive one crazy.
A thousand embryos extricate themselves 200
From air, from water and from earth
In wet and dry and hot and cold.
Had I not made a corner in fire
I should find myself without a berth.

FAUST. So you when faced with the ever stirring, 205
The creative force, the beneficent,
Counter with your cold devil's fist
Spitefully clenched but impotent.
You curious son of Chaos, why
Not turn your hand to something else? 210

MEPHISTOPHELES. We will give it our serious attention—
But more on that subject by and by.
Might I for this time take my leave?

FAUST. Why you ask I cannot see.
I have already made your acquaintance; 215
When you feel like it, call on me.
Here is the window, here is the door—
And a chimney too—if it comes to that.

MEPHISTOPHELES. I must confess; there's a slight impediment
That stops me making my exit pat, 220
The pentagram upon your threshold—

FAUST. So the witch's foot is giving you trouble?
Then tell me, since you're worried by that spell,
How did you ever enter, child of Hell?
How was a spirit like you betrayed? 225

MEPHISTOPHELES. You study that sign! It's not well made;
One of its corners, do you see,
The outside one's not quite intact.

FAUST. A happy accident in fact!
Which means you're in my custody? 230
I did not intend to set a gin.

MEPHISTOPHELES. The dog—he noticed nothing, jumping in;
The case has now turned round about
And I, the devil, can't get out.

FAUST. Then why not leave there by the window? 235

MEPHISTOPHELES. It is a law for devils and phantoms all:
By the way that we slip in by the same we must take our
    leave.

---

221. *pentagram:* a magic five-pointed star designed to keep away evil spirits, principally the female incubus or witch.
222. *witch's foot:* the pentagram.

One's free in the first, in the second one's a thrall.

FAUST. So Hell itself has its regulations?
   That's excellent; a contract in that case   240
   Could be made with you, you gentry—and definite?

MEPHISTOPHELES. What we promise, you will enjoy with no reserva-
      tions,
   Nothing will be nipped off from it.
   But all this needs a little explaining
   And will keep till our next heart-to-heart;   245
   But now I beg and doubly beg you:
   Let me, just for now, depart.

FAUST. But wait yet a minute and consent
   To tell me first some news of moment.

MEPHISTOPHELES. Let me go now! I'll soon be back   250
   To be questioned to your heart's content.

FAUST. It was not I laid a trap for you,
   You thrust your own head in the noose.
   A devil in the hand's worth two in hell!
   The second time he'll be longer loose.   255

MEPHISTOPHELES. If you so wish it, I'm prepared
   To keep you company and stay;
   Provided that by my arts the time
   Be to your betterment whiled away.

FAUST. I am in favour, carry on—   260
   But let your art be a pleasing one.

MEPHISTOPHELES. My friend, your senses will have more
   Gratification in this hour
   Than in a year's monotony.
   What the delicate spirits sing to you   265
   And the beauties that they bring to you
   Are no empty, idle wizardry.
   You'll have your sense of smell delighted,
   Your palate in due course excited,
   Your feelings rapt enchantingly.   270
   Preparation? There's no need,
   We are all here. Strike up! Proceed!
      [*The* SPIRITS *sing*.]

SPIRITS. Vanish, you darkling
      Arches above him,
      That a more witching   275
      Blue and enriching
      Sky may look in!
      If only the darkling
      Clouds were unravelled!
      Small stars are sparkling,   280
      Suns are more gently
      Shining within!

Spiritual beauty
Of the children of Heaven
Swaying and bowing   285
Floats in the air,
Leanings and longings
Follow them there;
And ribbons of raiment
The breezes have caught   290
Cover the country,
Cover the arbour
Where, drowning in thought,
Lovers exchange their
Pledges for life.   295
Arbour on arbour!
Creepers run rife!
Grapes in great wreathing
Clusters are poured into
Vats that are seething,   300
Wines that are foaming
Pour out in rivulets
Rippling and roaming
Through crystalline stones,
Leaving the sight of   305
The highlands behind them,
Widening to lakes
Amid the delight of
Green-growing foothills.
And the winged creatures   310
Sipping their ecstasy,
Sunwards they fly,
Fly to discover
The glittering islands
Which bob on the wave-tops   315
Deceiving the eye.
There we can hear
Huzzaing in chorus,
A landscape of dancers
Extending before us,   320
All in the open,
Free as the air.
Some of them climbing
Over the peaks,
Some of them swimming   325
Over the lakes,
Or floating in space—
All towards existence,
All towards the distance

Of stars that will love them,   330
The blessing of grace.

MEPHISTOPHELES. He is asleep. That's fine, you airy, dainty young-
    sters
You have sung him a real cradle song.
For this performance I am in your debt.
You are not yet the man to hold the devil for long.   335
Play round him with your sweet dream trickeries
And sink him in a sea of untruth!
But to break the spell upon this threshold
What I need now is a rat's tooth.
And I needn't bother to wave a wand,   340
I can hear one rustling already, he'll soon respond.
The lord of rats, the lord of mice,
Of flies, frogs, bugs and lice,
Commands you to come out of that
And gnaw away this threshold, rat,   345
While he takes oil and gives it a few—
So there you come hopping? Quick on your cue!
Now get on the job! The obstructing point
Is on the edge and right in front.
One bite more and the work's done.   350
Now, Faust, till we meet again, dream on!

FAUST. [*Waking*] Am I defrauded then once more?
Does the throng of spirits vanish away like fog
To prove that the devil appeared to me in a dream
But what escaped was only a dog?   355

FAUST'S STUDY

The same room. Later.

FAUST. Who's knocking? Come in! *Now* who wants to annoy me?
MEPHISTOPHELES. [*Outside door*] It's I.
FAUST.   Come in!
MEPHISTOPHELES. [*Outside door*]
                          You must say 'Come in' three times.
FAUST. Come in then!   5
MEPHISTOPHELES. [*Entering*] Thank you; you overjoy me.
We two, I hope, we shall be good friends;
To chase those megrims of yours away
I am here like a fine young squire to-day,
In a suit of scarlet trimmed with gold
And a little cape of stiff brocade,   10
With a cock's feather in my hat
And at my side a long sharp blade,

9. *a fine young squire:* In the popular
plays based on the Faust legend, the
devil often appeared as a monk when
the play catered to a Protestant audience, and as a cavalier when the
audience was predominantly Catholic.

And the most succinct advice I can give
Is that you dress up just like me, 15
So that uninhibited and free
You may find out what it means to live.

FAUST. The pain of earth's constricted life, I fancy,
Will pierce me still, whatever my attire;
I am too old for mere amusement, 20
Too young to be without desire.
How can the world dispel my doubt?
You must do without, you must do without!
That is the everlasting song
Which rings in every ear, which rings, 25
And which to us our whole life long
Every hour hoarsely sings.
I wake in the morning only to feel appalled,
My eyes with bitter tears could run
To see the day which in its course 30
Will not fulfil a wish for me, not one;
The day which whittles away with obstinate carping
All pleasures—even those of anticipation,
Which makes a thousand grimaces to obstruct
My heart when it is stirring in creation. 35
And again, when night comes down, in anguish
I must stretch out upon my bed
And again no rest is granted me,
For wild dreams fill my mind with dread.
The God who dwells within my bosom 40
Can make my inmost soul react;
The God who sways my every power
Is powerless with external fact.
And so existence weighs upon my breast
And I long for death and life—life I detest. 45

MEPHISTOPHELES. Yet death is never a wholly welcome guest.

FAUST. O happy is he whom death in the dazzle of victory
Crowns with the bloody laurel in the battling swirl!
Or he whom after the mad and breakneck dance
He comes upon in the arms of a girl! 50
O to have sunk away, delighted, deleted,
Before the Spirit of the Earth, before his might!

MEPHISTOPHELES. Yet I know someone who failed to drink
A brown juice on a certain night.

FAUST. Your hobby is espionage—is it not? 55

MEPHISTOPHELES. Oh I'm not omniscient—but I know a lot.

FAUST. Whereas that tumult in my soul
Was stilled by sweet familiar chimes
Which cozened the child that yet was in me
With echoes of more happy times, 60

I now curse all things that encompass
The soul with lures and jugglery
And bind it in this dungeon of grief
With trickery and flattery.
Cursed in advance be the high opinion   65
That serves our spirit for a cloak!
Cursed be the dazzle of appearance
Which bows our senses to its yoke!
Cursed be the lying dreams of glory,
The illusion that our name survives!   70
Cursed be the flattering things we own,
Servants and ploughs, children and wives!
Cursed be Mammon when with his treasures
He makes us play the adventurous man
Or when for our luxurious pleasures   75
He duly spreads the soft divan!
A curse on the balsam of the grape!
A curse on the love that rides for a fall!
A curse on hope! A curse on faith!
And a curse on patience most of all!   80

　　　　[*The invisible* SPIRITS *sing again.*]

SPIRITS. 　　　　Woe! Woe!
　　　　　　　　You have destroyed it,
　　　　　　　　The beautiful world;
　　　　　　　　By your violent hand
　　　　　　　　'Tis downward hurled!   85
　　　　　　　　A half-god has dashed it asunder!
　　　　　　　　From under
　　　　　　　　We bear off the rubble to nowhere
　　　　　　　　And ponder
　　　　　　　　Sadly the beauty departed.   90
　　　　　　　　Magnipotent
　　　　　　　　One among men,
　　　　　　　　Magnificent
　　　　　　　　Build it again,
　　　　　　　　Build it again in your breast!   95
　　　　　　　　Let a new course of life
　　　　　　　　Begin
　　　　　　　　With vision abounding
　　　　　　　　And new songs resounding
　　　　　　　　To welcome it in!   100

MEPHISTOPHELES. These are the juniors
　　　　　　　　Of my faction.
　　　　　　　　Hear how precociously they counsel

---

73. *Mammon:* the Aramaic word for "riches," used in the New Testament; medieval writers interpreted the word as a proper noun, the name of the devil, as representing covetousness or avarice.

Pleasure and action.
Out and away   105
From your lonely day
Which dries your senses and your juices
Their melody seduces.

Stop playing with your grief which battens
Like a vulture on your life, your mind!   110
The worst of company would make you feel
That you are a man among mankind.
Not that it's really my proposition
To shove you among the common men:
Though I'm not one of the Upper Ten,   115
If you would like a coalition
With me for your career through life,
I am quite ready to fit in,
I'm yours before you can say knife.
I am your comrade;   120
If you so crave,
I am your servant, I am your slave.

FAUST. And what have I to undertake in return?

MEPHISTOPHELES. Oh it's early days to discuss what that is.

FAUST. No, no, the devil is an egoist   125
And ready to do nothing gratis
Which is to benefit a stranger.
Tell me your terms and don't prevaricate!
A servant like you in the house is a danger.

MEPHISTOPHELES. I will bind myself to your service in this
world,
To be at your beck and never rest nor slack;
When we meet again on the other side,
In the same coin you shall pay me back.

FAUST. The other side gives me little trouble;
First batter this present world to rubble,   135
Then the other may rise—if that's the plan.
This earth is where my springs of joy have started,
And this sun shines on me when broken-hearted;
If I can first from them be parted,
Then let happen what will and can!   140
I wish to hear no more about it—
Whether there too men hate and love
Or whether in those spheres too, in the future,
There is a Below or an Above.

MEPHISTOPHELES. With such an outlook you can risk it.   145
Sign on the line! In these next days you will get
Ravishing samples of my arts;
I am giving you what never man saw yet.

FAUST. Poor devil, can *you* give anything ever?
  Was a human spirit in its high endeavour   150
  Even once understood by one of your breed?
  Have you got food which fails to feed?
  Or red gold which, never at rest,
  Like mercury runs away through the hand?
  A game at which one never wins?   155
  A girl who, even when on my breast,
  Pledges herself to my neighbour with her eyes?
  The divine and lovely delight of honour
  Which falls like a falling star and dies?
  Show me the fruits which, before they are plucked, decay   160
  And the trees which day after day renew their green!

MEPHISTOPHELES. Such a commission doesn't alarm me,
  I have such treasures to purvey.
  But, my good friend, the time draws on when we
  Should be glad to feast at our ease on something good.   165

FAUST. If ever I stretch myself on a bed of ease,
  Then I am finished! Is that understood?
  If ever your flatteries can coax me
  To be pleased with myself, if ever you cast
  A spell of pleasure that can hoax me—   170
  Then let *that* day be my last!
  That's my wager!

MEPHISTOPHELES. Done!

FAUST. Let's shake!
  If ever I say to the passing moment   175
  'Linger a while! Thou art so fair!'
  Then you may cast me into fetters,
  I will gladly perish then and there!
  Then you may set the death-bell tolling,
  Then from my service you are free,   180
  The clock may stop, its hand may fall,
  And that be the end of time for me!

MEPHISTOPHELES. Think what you're saying, we shall not forget it.

FAUST. And you are fully within your rights;
  I have made no mad or outrageous claim.   185
  If I stay as I am, I am a slave—
  Whether yours or another's, it's all the same.

MEPHISTOPHELES. I shall this very day at the College Banquet
  Enter your service with no more ado,
  But just one point—As a life-and-death insurance   190
  I must trouble you for a line or two.

FAUST. So you, you pedant, you too like things in writing?
  Have you never known a man? Or a man's word? Never?

188. *College Banquet:* actually the *Doctorschmaus,* or dinner given by a successful candidate for a Ph.D. degree.

Is it not enough that my word of mouth
Puts all my days in bond for ever? 195
Does not the world rage on in all its streams
And shall a promise hamper *me*?
Yet this illusion reigns within our hearts
And from it who would be gladly free?
Happy the man who can inwardly keep his word; 200
Whatever the cost, he will not be loath to pay!
But a parchment, duly inscribed and sealed,
Is a bogey from which all wince away.
The word dies on the tip of the pen
And wax and leather lord it then. 205
What do you, evil spirit, require?
Bronze, marble, parchment, paper?
Quill or chisel or pencil of slate?
You may choose whichever you desire.

MEPHISTOPHELES. How can you so exaggerate 210
With such a hectic rhetoric?
Any little snippet is quite good—
And you sign it with one little drop of blood.

FAUST. If that is enough and is some use,
One may as well pander to your fad. 215

MEPHISTOPHELES. Blood is a very special juice.

FAUST. Only do not fear that I shall break this contract.
What I promise is nothing more
Than what all my powers are striving for.
I have puffed myself up too much, it is only 220
Your sort that really fits my case.
The great Earth Spirit has despised me
And Nature shuts the door in my face.
The thread of thoughts is snapped asunder,
I have long loathed knowledge in all its fashions. 225
In the depths of sensuality
Let us now quench our glowing passions!
And at once make ready every wonder
Of unpenetrated sorcery!
Let us cast ourselves into the torrent of time, 230
Into the whirl of eventfulness,
Where disappointment and success,
Pleasure and pain may chop and change
As chop and change they will and can;
It is restless action makes the man. 235

MEPHISTOPHELES. No limit is fixed for you, no bound;
If you'd like to nibble at everything

213. *blood:* This method of con-
firming an agreement with the devil is
older than the Faust legend—in which
it always appears—and is partly a
parody of the rôle of blood in the Christian Sacrament.

Or to seize upon something flying round—
Well, may you have a run for your money!
But seize your chance and don't be funny!   240

FAUST. I've told you, it is no question of happiness.
The most painful joy, enamoured hate, enlivening
Disgust—I devote myself to all excess.
My breast, now cured of its appetite for knowledge,
From now is open to all and every smart,   245
And what is allotted to the whole of mankind
That will I sample in my inmost heart,
Grasping the highest and lowest with my spirit,
Piling men's weal and woe upon my neck,
To extend myself to embrace all human selves   250
And to founder in the end, like them, a wreck.

MEPHISTOPHELES. O believe *me*, who have been chewing
These iron rations many a thousand year,
No human being can digest
This stuff, from the cradle to the bier.   255
This universe—believe a devil—
Was made for no one but a god!
He exists in eternal light
But *us* he has brought into the darkness
While *your* sole portion is day and night.   260

FAUST. I will all the same!

MEPHISTOPHELES.   That's very nice.
There's only one thing I find wrong;
Time is short, art is long.
You could do with a little artistic advice.   265
Confederate with one of the poets
And let him flog his imagination
To heap all virtues on your head,
A head with such a reputation:
Lion's bravery,   270
Stag's velocity,
Fire of Italy,
Northern tenacity.
Let *him* find out the secret art
Of combining craft with a noble heart   275
And of being in love like a young man,
Hotly, but working to a plan.
Such a person—*I'd* like to meet him;
'Mr. Microcosm' is how I'd greet him.

FAUST. What am I then if fate must bar   280
My efforts to reach that crown of humanity
After which all my senses strive?

---

279. *Mr. Microcosm:* i.e., man viewed as the epitome of the universe.

MEPHISTOPHELES. You are in the end . . . what you are.
　You can put on full-bottomed wigs with a million locks,
　You can put on stilts instead of your socks,　285
　You remain for ever what you are.
FAUST. I feel my endeavours have not been worth a pin
　When I raked together the treasures of the human mind,
　If at the end I but sit down to find
　No new force welling up within.　290
　I have not a hair's breadth more of height,
　I am no nearer the Infinite.
MEPHISTOPHELES. My very good sir, you look at things
　Just in the way that people do;
　We must be cleverer than that　295
　Or the joys of life will escape from you.
　Hell! You have surely hands and feet,
　Also a head and you-know-what;
　The pleasures I gather on the wing,
　Are they less mine? Of course they're not!　300
　Suppose I can afford six stallions,
　I can add that horse-power to my score
　And dash along and be a proper man
　As if my legs were twenty-four.
　So good-bye to thinking! On your toes!　305
　The world's before us. Quick! Here goes!
　I tell you, a chap who's intellectual
　Is like a beast on a blasted heath
　Driven in circles by a demon
　While a fine green meadow lies round beneath.　310
FAUST. How do we start?
MEPHISTOPHELES.　　　　　　We just say go—and skip.
　But please get ready for this pleasure trip.
　　[*Exit* FAUST.]
　Only look down on knowledge and reason,
　The highest gifts that men can prize,　315
　Only allow the spirit of lies
　To confirm you in magic and illusion,
　And then I have you body and soul.
　Fate has given this man a spirit
　Which is always pressing onwards, beyond control,　320
　And whose mad striving overleaps
　All joys of the earth between pole and pole.
　Him shall I drag through the wilds of life
　And through the flats of meaninglessness,
　I shall make him flounder and gape and stick　325
　And to tease his insatiableness
　Hang meat and drink in the air before his watering lips;
　In vain he will pray to slake his inner thirst,

And even had he not sold himself to the devil
He would be equally accursed.[a]   330
    [*Re-enter* FAUST.]
FAUST. And now, where are we going?
MEPHISTOPHELES.   Wherever you please.
  The small world, then the great for us.
  With what pleasure and what profit
  You will roister through the syllabus!   335
FAUST. But I, with this long beard of mine,
  I lack the easy social touch,
  I know the experiment is doomed;
  Out in the world I never could fit in much.
  I feel so small in company   340
  I'll be embarrassed constantly.
MEPHISTOPHELES. My friend, it will solve itself, any such mis
      giving;
  Just trust yourself and you'll learn the art of living.
FAUST. Well, then, how do we leave home?
  Where are your grooms? Your coach and horses?   345
MEPHISTOPHELES. We merely spread this mantle wide,
  It will bear us off on airy courses.
  But do not on this noble voyage
  Cumber yourself with heavy baggage.
  A little inflammable gas which I'll prepare   350
  Will lift us quickly into the air.
  If we travel light we shall cleave the sky like a knife.
  Congratulations on your new course of life![b]

THE WITCH'S KITCHEN[c]

Every sort of witch prop. A large cauldron hangs over the fire.
MONKEYS *sit around it, seen through the fumes.*

MEPHISTOPHELES. Look, what a pretty species of monkey!
  She is the kitchen-maid, he is the flunkey.
  It seems your mistress isn't at home?
MONKEYS. Out at a rout!
        Out and about!
        By the chimney spout!   5
MEPHISTOPHELES. How long does she keep it up at night?
MONKEYS. As long as we warm our paws at this fire.

---

a. Between Faust's exit and entrance, the translator omits a scene in which Mephistopheles cynically interviews one of Faust's students.

350. *gas:* indicative of Goethe's scientific interests. The first hydrogen balloon was sent aloft in Paris in 1783, and several letters by Goethe refer to this new experiment.

b. The translator omits the next scene, in Auerbach's Cellar, where Faust and Mephistopheles join a group of genial drinking companions and Mephistopheles performs the trick—traditional in early Faust stories—of making wine flow from the table.

c. Certain transpositions have been made in this scene. [Translator's note.]

MEPHISTOPHELES. How do you like these delicate animals?

FAUST. I never saw such an outré sight.   10

I find it nauseating, this crazy witchcraft!
Do you promise me that I shall improve
In this cesspit of insanity?
Do I need advice from an old hag?
And can this filthy brew remove   15
Thirty years from my age? O vanity,
If you know nothing better than this!
My hope has already vanished away.
Surely Nature, surely a noble spirit
Has brought some better balm to the light of day?   20

MEPHISTOPHELES. My friend, you once more talk to the point.

There is also a natural means of rejuvenation;
But that is written in another book
And is a chapter that needs some explanation.

FAUST. I want to know it.   25

MEPHISTOPHELES.   Right. There is a means requires

No money, no physician, and no witch:
Away with you this moment back to the land,
And there begin to dig and ditch,
Confine yourself, confine your mind,   30
In a narrow round, ever repeating,
Let your diet be of the simplest kind,
Live with the beasts like a beast and do not think it cheating
To use your own manure to insure your crops are weighty!
Believe me, that is the best means   35
To keep you young till you are eighty.

FAUST. I am not used to it, I cannot change   *come on: do a*

My nature and take the spade in hand.   *Thoreau!*
The narrow life is not my style at all.

MEPHISTOPHELES. Then it's a job for the witch to arrange.   40

FAUST. The hag—but why do we need just her?
Can you yourself not brew the drink?

MEPHISTOPHELES. A pretty pastime! I'd prefer
To build a thousand bridges in that time.
It is not only art and science   45
That this work needs but patience too.
A quiet spirit is busy at it for years
And time but fortifies the subtle brew.
And the most wonderful ingredients
Go into it—you couldn't fake it!   50

---

11. *crazy witchcraft:* In composing this scene, Goethe may have had in mind certain paintings by the Flemish artists David Teniers the Younger (1610–1690) and Pieter Breughel the Younger (1564?–1638).

44. *bridges:* The folk legend existed that the devil built bridges at the request of men. As a reward, he caught either the first or the thirteenth soul to cross each new bridge.

The devil taught it her, I admit;
The devil, however, cannot make it.
Tell me, you monkeys, you damned puppets,
What are you doing with that great globe?

HE-MONKEY. This is the world: 55
        It rises and falls
        And rolls every minute;
        It rings like glass—
        But how soon it breaks!
        And there's nothing in it.   60
        It glitters here
        And here still more:
        I am alive!
        O my son, my dear,
        Keep away, keep away!   65
        You are bound to die!
        The shards are sharp,
        It was made of clay.

[FAUST *has meanwhile been gazing in a mirror.*]

FAUST. What do I see in this magic mirror?
What a heavenly image to appear!   70
O Love, lend me the swiftest of your wings
And waft me away into her sphere!
But, alas, when I do not keep this distance,
If to go nearer I but dare
I can see her only as if there were mist in the air—   75
The fairest image of a woman!
But can Woman be so fair?
In that shape in the mirror must I see the quintessence
Of all the heavens—reclining there?
Can such a thing be found on earth?   80

MEPHISTOPHELES. Naturally, when a God works six days like a black
And at the end of it slaps himself on the back,
Something should come of it of some worth.
For this occasion look your fill.
I can smell you out a sweetheart as good as this,   85
And happy the man who has the luck
To bear her home to wedded bliss.

[*The* WITCH *enters down the chimney—violently.*]

WITCH. What goes on here?
        Who are you two?
        What d'you want here?
        Who has sneaked through?   90
        May the fever of fire
        Harrow your marrow!

MEPHISTOPHELES. Don't you know me, you bag of bones? You
    monster, you!

Don't you know your lord and master? 95
What prevents me striking you
And your monkey spirits, smashing you up like plaster?
Has my red doublet no more claim to fame?
Can you not recognize the cock's feather?
Have I concealed my countenance? 100
Must I myself announce my name?

WITCH. My lord, excuse this rude reception.
It is only I miss your cloven foot.
And where is your usual brace of ravens?

MEPHISTOPHELES. I'll forgive you this once, as an exception; 105
Admittedly some time has pass't
Since we two saw each other last.
Culture too, which is licking the whole world level,
Has latterly even reached the devil.
The Nordic spook no longer commands a sale; 110
Where can you see horns, claws or tail?
And as regards the foot, which is my *sine qua non*,
It would prejudice me in the social sphere;
Accordingly, as many young men have done,
I have worn false calves this many a year. 115

WITCH. Really and truly I'm knocked flat
To see Lord Satan here again!

MEPHISTOPHELES. Woman, you must not call me that!

WITCH. Why! What harm is there in the name?

MEPHISTOPHELES. Satan has long been a myth without sense or
sinew; 120
Not that it helps humanity all the same,
They are quit of the Evil One but the evil ones continue.
You may call me the Noble Baron, that should do;
I am a cavalier among other cavaliers,
You needn't doubt my blood is blue— 125
[*He makes an indecent gesture.*]

WITCH. Ha! Ha! Always true to type!
You still have the humour of a guttersnipe!

MEPHISTOPHELES. Observe my technique, my friend—not a single
hitch;
This is the way to get round a witch.

WITCH. Now tell me, gentlemen, what do you want? 130

MEPHISTOPHELES. A good glass of your well-known juice.
And please let us have your oldest vintage;
When it's been kept it's twice the use.

WITCH. Delighted! Why, there's some here on the shelf—
I now and then take a nip myself— 135
And, besides, this bottle no longer stinks;

---

104. *brace of ravens:* Perhaps Goethe was thinking of the Norse god Odin, who owned two such birds: Hugin (Thought) and Munin (Memory).

You're welcome while I've a drop to give.
[*Aside*] But, if this man is unprepared when he drinks,
You very well know he has not an hour to live.

MEPHISTOPHELES. He's a good friend and it should set him up;   140
I'd gladly grant him the best of your kitchen,
So draw your circle and do your witching
And give the man a decent cup.
    [*The* WITCH *begins her conjuration.*]

FAUST. But, tell me, how will this mend my status?
These lunatic gestures, this absurd apparatus,   145
This most distasteful conjuring trick—
I've known it all, it makes me sick.

MEPHISTOPHELES. Pooh, that's just fooling, get it in focus,
And don't be such a prig for goodness' sake!
As a doctor she must do her hocus-pocus   150
So that when you have drunk your medicine it will take.

WITCH. The lofty power
        That is wisdom's dower,
        Concealed from great and clever,
        Don't use your brain   155
        And that's your gain—
        No trouble whatsoever.

FAUST. What nonsense is she saying to us?
My head is splitting; I've the sensation
Of listening to a hundred thousand   160
Idiots giving a mass recitation.

MEPHISTOPHELES. Enough, enough, you excellent Sibyl!
Give us your drink and fill the cup
Full to the brim and don't delay!
This draught will do my friend no injury;   165
He is a man of more than one degree
And has drunk plenty in his day.
    [*The* WITCH *gives* FAUST *the cup.*]
Now lower it quickly. Bottoms up!
And your heart will begin to glow and perk.
Now out of the circle! You mustn't rest.   170

WITCH. I hope the little drink will work.

MEPHISTOPHELES. [*To* WITCH] And you, if there's anything you
        want, all right;
Just mention it to me on Walpurgis Night.
[*To* FAUST] Come now, follow me instantly!
You've got to perspire, it's necessary,   175
That the drug may pervade you inside and out.

---

173. *Walpurgis Night:* the eve of   supposed to assemble on the Brocken,
May Day (May 1), when witches are   a peak in the Harz Mountains.

I can teach you later to value lordly leisure
And you soon will learn with intensest pleasure
How Cupid stirs within and bounds about.

FAUST. Just one more look, one quick look, in the mirror!   180
That woman was too fair to be true.

MEPHISTOPHELES. No, no! The paragon of womanhood
Will soon be revealed in the flesh to you.
[*Aside*] With a drink like this in you, take care—
You'll soon see Helens everywhere.   185

                    IN THE STREET

FAUST *accosts* GRETCHEN *as she passes.*

FAUST. My pretty young lady, might I venture
To offer you my arm and my escort too?

GRETCHEN. I'm not a young lady nor am I pretty
And I can get home without help from you.
[*She releases herself and goes off.*]

FAUST. By Heaven, she's beautiful, this child!   5
I have never seen her parallel.
So decorous, so virtuous,
And just a little pert as well.
The light of her cheek, her lip so red,
I shall remember till I'm dead!   10
The way that she cast down her eye
Is stamped on my heart as with a die;
And the way that she got rid of me
Was a most ravishing thing to see!
[*Enter* MEPHISTOPHELES.]
Listen to me! Get me that girl!   15

MEPHISTOPHELES. Which one?

FAUST.   The one that just went past.

MEPHISTOPHELES. She? She was coming from her priest,
Absolved from her sins one and all;
I'd crept up near the confessional.
An innocent thing. Innocent? Yes!   20
At church with nothing to confess!
Over that girl I have no power.

FAUST. Yet she's fourteen if she's an hour.

MEPHISTOPHELES. Why, you're talking like Randy Dick   25
Who covets every lovely flower
And all the favours, all the laurels,
He fancies are for him to pick;

185. *Helens:* Faust marries Helen of Troy in the second part of *Faust.*
25. *Randy Dick:* in the original German, "Hans Liederlich"—i.e., a profligate, since *liederlich* means "careless" or "dissolute."

But it doesn't always work out like that.

FAUST. My dear Professor of Ancient Morals,　　　　　30
Spare me your trite morality!
I tell you straight—and hear me right—
Unless this object of delight
Lies in my arms this very night,
At midnight we part company.　　　　　　　　　　　35

MEPHISTOPHELES. Haven't you heard: more haste less speed?
A fortnight is the least I need
Even to work up an occasion.

FAUST. If I had only seven hours clear,
I should not need the devil here　　　　　　　　　　40
To bring *this* quest to consummation.

MEPHISTOPHELES. It's almost French, your line of talk;
I only ask you not to worry.
Why make your conquest in a hurry?
The pleasure is less by a long chalk　　　　　　　　45
Than when you first by hook and by crook
Have squeezed your doll and moulded her,
Using all manner of poppycock
That foreign novels keep in stock.

FAUST. I am keen enough without all that.　　　　　　50

MEPHISTOPHELES. Now, joking apart and without aspersion,
You cannot expect, I tell you flat,
This beautiful child in quick reversion.
Immune to all direct attack—
We must lay our plots behind her back.　　　　　　55

FAUST. Get me something of my angel's!
Carry me to her place of rest!
Get me a garter of my love's!
Get me a kerchief from her breast!

MEPHISTOPHELES. That you may see the diligent fashion　　60
In which I shall abet your passion,
We won't let a moment waste away,
I will take you to her room to-day.

FAUST. And shall I see her? Have her?

MEPHISTOPHELES.　　　　　　　　No!　　　　　　65
She will be visiting a neighbour.
But you in the meanwhile, quite alone,
Can stay in her aura in her room
And feast your fill on joys to come.

FAUST. Can we go now?　　　　　　　　　　　　　　70

MEPHISTOPHELES.　　　　It is still too soon.

---

30. *Professor:* in the original German, Herr Magister Lobesan ("Master Worshipful")—stuffed shirt, or academic prig.

FAUST Then a present for her! Get me one!
    [*Exit* FAUST.]
MEPHISTOPHELES. Presents already? Fine. A certain hit!
  I know plenty of pretty places
  And of long-buried jewel-cases;   *75*
  I must take stock of them a bit.

GRETCHEN'S ROOM

GRETCHEN. [*Alone, doing her hair*] I'd give a lot to be able to say
  Who the gentleman was to-day.
  He cut a fine figure certainly
  And is sprung from nobility;
  His face showed that—Besides, you see,   *5*
  He'd otherwise not have behaved so forwardly.
    [*She goes out; then* MEPHISTOPHELES *and* FAUST *enter.*]
MEPHISTOPHELES. Come in—very quietly—Only come in!
FAUST. [*After a silence*] I ask you: please leave me alone!
MEPHISTOPHELES. Not all girls keep their room so clean.
FAUST. [*Looking around*] Welcome, sweet gleaming of the
    gloaming   *10*
  That through this sanctuary falls aslope!
  Seize on my heart, sweet fever of love
  That lives and languishes on the dews of hope!
  What a feeling of quiet breathes around me,
  Of order, of contentedness!   *15*
  What fulness in this poverty,
  And in this cell what blessedness!

  Here I could while away hour after hour.
  It was here, O Nature, that your fleeting dreams
  Brought this born angel to full flower.   *20*
  Here lay the child and the warm life
  Filled and grew in her gentle breast,
  And here the pure and holy threads
  Wove a shape of the heavenliest.

  And you! What brought you here to-day?   *25*
  Why do I feel this deep dismay?
  What do you want here? Why is your heart so sore?
  Unhappy Faust! You are Faust no more.

  Is this an enchanted atmosphere?
  To have her at once was all my aim,
  Yet I feel my will dissolve in a lovesick dream.
  Are we the sport of every current of air?

And were she this moment to walk in,
You would pay for this outrage, how you would pay!
The big man, now, alas, so small,   35
Would lie at her feet melted away.

MEPHISTOPHELES. Quick! I can see her coming below.

FAUST. Out, yes out! I'll never come back!

MEPHISTOPHELES. Here is a casket, it's middling heavy,
I picked it up in a place I know.   40
Only put it at once here in the cupboard,
I swear she won't believe her eyes;
I put some nice little trinkets in it
In order to win a different prize.
Still child is child and a game's a game.   45

FAUST. I don't know; shall I?

MEPHISTOPHELES.   You ask? For shame!
Do you perhaps intend to keep the spoil?
Then I advise Your Lustfulness
To save these hours that are so precious   50
And save me any further toil.
I hope you aren't avaricious.
After scratching my head so much and twisting my hands—
        [*He puts the casket in the cupboard.*]
Now quick! We depart!
In order to sway the dear young thing   55
To meet the dearest wish of your heart;
And *you* assume
A look that belongs to the lecture room,
As if Physics and Metaphysics too
Stood grey as life in front of you!   60
Come on!
        [*They go out; then* GRETCHEN *reappears.*]

GRETCHEN. It is so sultry, so fusty here,
And it's not even so warm outside.
I feel as if I don't know what—
I wish my mother would appear.   65
I'm trembling all over from top to toe—
I'm a silly girl to get frightened so.
        [*She sings as she undresses.*]
    There was a king in Thule
    Was faithful to the grave,

---

68. *Thule:* the fabled *ultima Thule*
of Latin literature—those distant lands
just beyond the reach of every explorer.
In Roman times, the phrase probably
denoted the Shetland Islands. Goethe
wrote this ballad in 1774; it was published and set to music in 1782. The
poem also served as the inspiration for
the slow movement of Mendelssohn's
Italian Symphony.

To whom his dying lady 70
A golden winecup gave.

He drained it at every banquet—
A treasure none could buy;
Whenever he filled and drank it
The tears o'erflowed his eye. 75

And when his days were numbered
He numbered land and pelf; *?*
He left his heir his kingdom,
The cup he kept himself.

He sat at the royal table 80
With his knights of high degree
In the lofty hall of his fathers
In the castle on the sea.

There stood the old man drinking
The last of the living glow, 85
Then threw the sacred winecup
Into the waves below.

He saw it fall and falter
And founder in the main;
His eyelids fell, thereafter 90
He never drank again.

[*She opens the cupboard to put away her clothes and sees
the casket.*]

How did this lovely casket get in here?
I locked the cupboard, I'm quite sure.
But what can be in it? It's very queer.
Perhaps someone left it here in pawn 95
And my mother gave him a loan on it.
Here's a little key tied on with tape—
I've a good mind to open it.
What is all this? My God! But see!
I have never come across such things. 100
Jewels—that would suit a countess
At a really grand festivity.
To whom can these splendid things belong?

[*She tries on the jewels and looks in the looking-glass.*]

If only the ear-rings belonged to me!
They make one look quite differently. 105
What is the use of looks and youth?
That's all very well and fine in truth

But people leave it all alone,
They praise you and pity you in one;
Gold is their sole   110
Concern and goal.
Alas for us who have none!

A WALK

Elsewhere and later. MEPHISTOPHELES *joins* FAUST.

MEPHISTOPHELES. By every despised love! By the elements of hell!
I wish I knew something worse to provide a curse as well!
FAUST. What's the trouble? What's biting you?
I never saw such a face in my life.
MEPHISTOPHELES. I would sell myself to the devil this minute   5
If only I weren't a devil too.
FAUST. What is it? Are you mad? Or sick?
It suits you to rage like a lunatic!
MEPHISTOPHELES. Imagine! The jewels that Gretchen got,
A priest has gone and scooped the lot!   10
Her mother got wind of it and she
At once had the horrors secretly.
That woman has a nose beyond compare,
She's always snuffling in the Book of Prayer,
And can tell by how each object smells   15
If it is sacred or something else;
So the scent of the jewels tells her clear
There's nothing very blessed here.
'My child,' she cries, 'unrighteous wealth
Invests the soul, infects the health.   20
We'll dedicate it to the Virgin
And *she'll* make heavenly manna burgeon!'
Gretchen's face, you could see it fall;
She thought: 'It's a gift-horse after all,
And he *can't* be lacking in sanctity   25
Who brought it here so handsomely!'
The mother had a priest along
And had hardly started up her song
Before he thought things looked all right
And said: 'Very proper and above board!   30
Self-control is its own reward.
The Church has an excellent appetite,
She has swallowed whole countries and the question
Has never arisen of indigestion.
Only the Church, my dears, can take   35
Ill-gotten goods without stomach-ache!'

FAUST. That is a custom the world through,
　A Jew and a king observe it too.
MEPHISTOPHELES. So brooch, ring, chain he swipes at speed
　As if they were merely chicken-feed,　　　　　　　　　40
　Thanks them no more and no less for the casket
　Than for a pound of nuts in a basket,
　Promises Heaven will provide
　And leaves them extremely edified.
FAUST. And Gretchen?　　　　　　　　　　　　　45
MEPHISTOPHELES.　　　　　Sits and worries there,
　Doesn't know what to do and doesn't care,
　Thinks day and night on gold and gem,
　Still more on the man who presented them.
FAUST. My sweetheart's grief distresses me.　　　　50
　Get her more jewels instantly!
　The first lot barely deserved the name.
MEPHISTOPHELES. So the gentleman thinks it all a nursery game!
FAUST. Do what I tell you and get it right;
　Don't let her neighbour out of your sight.　　　55
　And don't be a sloppy devil; contrive
　A new set of jewels. Look alive!
　　　　[*Exit* FAUST.]
MEPHISTOPHELES. Yes, my dear sir, with all my heart.
　This is the way that a fool in love
　Puffs away to amuse his lady　　　　　　　　60
　Sun and moon and the stars above.

MARTHA'S HOUSE

MARTHA. [*Alone*] My dear husband, God forgive him,
　His behaviour has *not* been without a flaw!
　Careers away out into the world
　And leaves me alone to sleep on straw.
　And yet I never trod on his toes,　　　　　　5
　I loved him with all my heart, God knows.　　　[*Sobs.*]
　Perhaps he is even dead—O fate!
　If I'd only a death certificate!
　　　　[GRETCHEN *enters.*]
GRETCHEN. Frau Martha!
MARTHA.　　　　　　　Gretelchen! What's up?　　　10
GRETCHEN. My legs are sinking under me,
　I've just discovered in my cupboard
　Another casket—of ebony,
　And things inside it, such a store,
　Far richer than the lot before.　　　　　　15
MARTHA. You mustn't mention it to your mother;

She'd take it straight to the priest—like the other.

GRETCHEN. But only look! Just look at this!

MARTHA. O you lucky little Miss!

GRETCHEN. I daren't appear in the street, I'm afraid,   20
  Or in church either, thus arrayed.

MARTHA. Just you visit me often here
  And put on the jewels secretly!
  Walk up and down for an hour in front of my glass
  And that will be fun for you and me;   25
  And then an occasion may offer, a holiday,
  Where one can let them be seen in a gradual way;
  A necklace to start with, then a pearl ear-ring; your mother
  Most likely won't see; if she does one can think up something
     or other.

GRETCHEN. But who brought these two cases, who could it be?   30
  It doesn't seem quite right to me.
     [*Knocking.*]
  My God! My mother? Is that her?

MARTHA. It is a stranger. Come in, sir!
     [*Enter* MEPHISTOPHELES.]

MEPHISTOPHELES. I have made so free as to walk straight in;
  The ladies will pardon me? May I begin   35
  By inquiring for a Frau Martha Schwerdtlein?

MARTHA. That's me. What might the gentleman want?

MEPHISTOPHELES. [*Aside to* MARTHA] Now I know who you are,
     that's enough for me;
  You have very distinguished company.
  Forgive my bursting in so soon;   40
  I will call again in the afternoon.

MARTHA. Imagine, child, in the name of Piety!
  The gentleman takes you for society.

GRETCHEN. I'm a poor young thing, not at all refined;
  My God, the gentleman is too kind.   45
  These jewels and ornaments aren't my own.

MEPHISTOPHELES. Oh, it's not the jewellery alone;
  She has a presence, a look so keen—
  How delighted I am that I may remain.

MARTHA. What is your news? I cannot wait—   50

MEPHISTOPHELES. I wish I'd a better tale to relate.
  I trust this will not earn me a beating:
  Your husband is dead and sends his greeting.

MARTHA. Dead? The good soul? Oh why! Oh why!
  My husband is dead! Oh I shall die!   55

GRETCHEN. Oh don't, dear woman, despair so.

---

36. *Schwerdtlein:* literally. "little sword." Her husband is a soldier.

MEPHISTOPHELES. Listen to my tale of woe!

GRETCHEN. Now, while I live, may I never love;
    Such a loss would bring me to my grave.

MEPHISTOPHELES. Joy must have grief, grief must have joy.   60

MARTHA. How was his end? Oh tell it me.

MEPHISTOPHELES. He lies buried in Padua
    At the church of Holy Anthony,
    In properly consecrated ground
    Where he sleeps for ever cool and sound.   65

MARTHA. Have you nothing else for me? Is that all?

MEPHISTOPHELES. Yes, a request; it's heavy and fat.
    You must have three hundred masses said for his soul.
    My pockets are empty apart from that.

MARTHA. What! Not a trinket? Not a token?   70
    What every prentice keeps at the bottom of his bag
    And saves it up as a souvenir
    And would sooner starve and sooner beg—

MEPHISTOPHELES. Madam, you make me quite heart-broken.
    But, really and truly, he didn't squander his money.   75
    And, besides, he repented his mistakes,
    Yes, and lamented still more his unlucky breaks.

GRETCHEN. Alas that men should be so unlucky!
    Be assured I shall often pray that he may find rest above.

MEPHISTOPHELES. *You* deserve to be taken straight to the altar;   80
    You are a child a man could love.

GRETCHEN. No, no, it's not yet time for that.

MEPHISTOPHELES. Then, if not a husband, a lover will do.
    It's one of the greatest gifts of Heaven
    To hold in one's arms a thing like you.   85

GRETCHEN. That is not the custom of our race.

MEPHISTOPHELES. Custom or not, it's what takes place.

MARTHA. But tell me!

MEPHISTOPHELES.   His deathbed, where I stood,
    Was something better than a dungheap—
    Half-rotten straw; however, he died like a Christian   90
    And found he had still a great many debts to make good.
    How thoroughly, he cried, I must hate myself
    To leave my job and my wife like that on the shelf!
    When I remember it, I die!
    If only she would forgive me here below!   95

MARTHA. Good man! I have forgiven him long ago.

MEPHISTOPHELES. All the same, God knows, she was more at fault
      than I.

63. *Anthony:* Mephistopheles' lie acquires added irony from the fact that this is one of Padua's most famous churches, its basilica holding the bones of St. Anthony.

MARTHA. That's a lie! To think he lied at the point of death!

MEPHISTOPHELES. He certainly fibbed a bit with his last breath,   100
  If I'm half a judge of the situation.
  I had no need, said he, to gape for recreation;
  First getting children, then getting bread to feed 'em—
  And bread in the widest sense, you know—
  And I couldn't even eat my share in peace.   105

MARTHA. So all my love, my loyalty, went for naught,
  My toiling and moiling without cease!

MEPHISTOPHELES. Not at all; he gave it profoundest thought.
  When I left Malta—that was how he began—
  I prayed for my wife and children like one demented   110
  And Heaven heard me and consented
  To let us capture a Turkish merchantman,
  With a treasure for the Sultan himself on board.
  Well, bravery got its due reward
  And I myself, as was only fit,   115
  I got a decent cut of it.

MARTHA. Eh! Eh! How? Where? Has he perhaps buried it?

MEPHISTOPHELES. Who knows where the four winds now have
      carried it?
  As he lounged round Naples, quite unknown,
  A pretty lady made him her friend,   120
  She was so fond of him, so devoted,
  He wore her colours at his blessed end.

MARTHA. The crook! The robber of his children!
  Could no misery, no poverty,
  Check the scandalous life he led!   125

MEPHISTOPHELES. You see! That is just why he's dead.
  However, if I were placed like you,
  I would mourn him modestly for a year
  While looking round for someone new.

MARTHA. Ah God! My first one was so dear,   130
  His like in this world will be hard to discover.
  There could hardly be a more sweet little fool than mine.
  It was only he was too fond of playing the rover,
  And of foreign women and foreign wine,
  And of the God-damned gaming-table.   135

MEPHISTOPHELES. Now, now, he might have still got by
  If he on his part had been able
  To follow your suit and wink an eye.
  With that proviso, I swear, I too
  Would give an engagement ring to you.   140

MARTHA. The gentleman is pleased to be witty.

MEPHISTOPHELES. [*Aside*] I had better go while the going's good;

She'd hold the devil to his word, she would!
And how is it with *your* heart, my pretty?
GRETCHEN. What does the gentleman mean?   145
MEPHISTOPHELES. [*Aside*]   Good, innocent child!
Farewell, ladies!
GRETCHEN.   Farewell!
MARTHA.   O quickly! Tell me;
I'd like to have the evidence filed   150
Where, how and when my treasure died and was buried.
I have always liked things orderly and decent
And to read of his death in the weeklies would be pleasant.
MEPHISTOPHELES. Yes, Madam, when two witnesses are agreed,
The truth, as we all know, is guaranteed;   155
And I have a friend, an excellent sort,
I'll get him to swear you this in court.
I'll bring him here.
MARTHA.   O yes! Please do!
MEPHISTOPHELES. And the young lady will be here too?   160
He's an honest lad. He's been around,
His politeness to ladies is profound.
GRETCHEN. I'll be all blushes in his presence.
MEPHISTOPHELES. No king on earth should so affect you.
MARTHA. Behind the house there—in my garden—   165
This evening—both of you—we'll expect you.

IN THE STREET

FAUST. How is it? Going ahead? Will it soon come right?
MEPHISTOPHELES. Excellent! Do I find you all on fire?
Gretchen is yours before many days expire.
You will see her at Martha's, her neighbour's house to-night
And that's a woman with a special vocation,
As it were, for the bawd-cum-gipsy occupation.   5
FAUST. Good!
MEPHISTOPHELES. But there is something *we* must do.
FAUST. One good turn deserves another. True.
MEPHISTOPHELES. It only means the legal attesting   10
That her husband's played-out limbs are resting
At Padua in consecrated ground.
FAUST. Very smart! I suppose we begin by going to Padua!
MEPHISTOPHELES. There's no need for that. What a simple lad
      you are!
Only bear witness and don't ask questions.   15
FAUST. The scheme's at an end if you have no better suggestions.
MEPHISTOPHELES. Oh there you go! What sanctity!
Is this the first time in your life

You have committed perjury?
God and the world and all that moves therein,   20
Man and the way his emotions and thoughts take place,
Have you not given downright definitions
Of these with an iron breast and a brazen face?
And if you will only look below the surface,
You must confess you knew as much of these   25
As you know to-day of Herr Schwerdtlein's late decease.

FAUST. You are and remain a sophist and a liar.

MEPHISTOPHELES. Quite so—if that is as deep as you'll inquire.
Won't you to-morrow on your honour
Befool poor Gretchen and swear before her   30
That all your soul is set upon her?

FAUST. And from my heart.

MEPHISTOPHELES.   That's nice of you!
And your talk of eternal faith and love,
Of one single passion enthroned above   35
All others—will that be heartfelt too?

FAUST. Stop! It will! If I have feeling, if I
Feel this emotion, this commotion,
And can find no name to call it by;
If then I sweep the world with all my senses casting   40
Around for words and all the highest titles
And call this flame which burns my vitals
Endless, everlasting, everlasting,
Is that a devilish game of lies?

MEPHISTOPHELES. I'm right all the same.   45

FAUST.   Listen! Mark this well,
I beg you, and spare me talking till I'm hoarse:
The man who *will* be right, provided he has a tongue,
Why, he'll be right of course.
But come, I'm tired of listening to your voice;   50
You're right, the more so since I have no choice.

MARTHA'S GARDEN

They are walking in pairs: MARTHA *with* MEPHISTOPHELES,
GRETCHEN *on* FAUST'S *arm*.

GRETCHEN. The gentleman's only indulging me, I feel,
And condescending, to put me to shame.
You travellers are all the same,
You put up with things out of sheer good will.
I know too well that my poor conversation   5
Can't entertain a person of your station.

FAUST. One glance from you, one word, entertains me more

Than all this world's wisdom and lore.
[*He kisses her hand.*]

GRETCHEN. Don't go to such inconvenience! How could you kiss
    my hand?
It is so ugly, it is so rough.   10
I have had to work at Heaven knows what!
My mother's exacting, true enough.
    [*They pass on.*]

MARTHA. And you, sir, do you always move round like this?

MEPHISTOPHELES. Oh, business and duty keep us up to the min-
    ute!
With what regret one often leaves a place   15
And yet one cannot ever linger in it.

MARTHA. That may go in one's salad days—
To rush all over the world at random;
But the evil time comes on apace
And to drag oneself to the grave a lonely bachelor   20
Is never much good in any case.

MEPHISTOPHELES. The prospect alarms me at a distant glance.

MARTHA. Then, worthy sir, be wise while you have the chance.
    [*They pass on.*]

GRETCHEN. Yes, out of sight, out of mind!
You are polite to your finger-ends   25
But you have lots of clever friends
Who must leave *me* so far behind.

FAUST. Believe me, dearest, what the world calls clever
More often is vanity and narrowness.

GRETCHEN.   What?   30

FAUST. Alas that simplicity, that innocence,
Cannot assess itself and its sacred value ever!
That humility, lowliness, the highest gifts
That living Nature has shared out to men—

GRETCHEN. Only think of *me* one little minute,   35
I shall have time enough to think of you again.

FAUST. You are much alone, I suppose?

GRETCHEN. Yes, our household's only small
But it needs running after all.
We have no maid; I must cook and sweep and knit   40
And sew and be always on the run,
And my mother looks into every detail—
Each single one.
Not that she has such need to keep expenses down;
We could spread ourselves more than some others do;   45
My father left us a decent property,

14. *business:* Mephistopheles speaks as a traveling salesman.

A little house with a garden outside town.
However, my days at the present are pretty quiet;
My brother's in the army,
My little sister is dead. 50
The child indeed had worn me to a thread;
Still, all that trouble, I'd have it again, I'd try it,
I loved her so.

FAUST. An angel, if she was like you!

GRETCHEN. I brought her up, she was very fond of me. 55
She was born after my father died,
We gave my mother up for lost,
Her life was at such a low, low tide,
And she only got better slowly, bit by bit;
The poor little creature, she could not even 60
Think for a minute of suckling it;
And so I brought her up quite alone
On milk and water; so she became my own.
On my own arm, on my own knee,
She smiled and kicked, grew fair to see. 65

FAUST. You felt, I am sure, the purest happiness.

GRETCHEN. Yes; and—be sure—many an hour of distress.
The little one's cradle stood at night
Beside my bed; she could hardly stir
But I was awake, 70
Now having to give her milk, now into my bed with her,
Now, if she went on crying, try to stop her
By getting up and dandling her up and down the room,
And then first thing in the morning stand at the copper;
Then off to the market and attend to the range, 75
And so on day after day, never a change.
Living like that, one can't always feel one's best;
But food tastes better for it, so does rest.

[*They pass on.*]

MARTHA. No, the poor women don't come out of it well,
A *vieux garçon* is a hard nut to crack. 80

MEPHISTOPHELES. It only rests with you and your like
To put me on a better tack.

MARTHA. Tell me, sir: have you never met someone you fancy?
Has your heart been nowhere involved among the girls?

MEPHISTOPHELES. The proverb says: A man's own fireside 85
And a good wife are gold and pearls.

MARTHA. I mean, have you never felt any inclination?

MEPHISTOPHELES. I've generally been received with all consideration.

MARTHA. What I wanted to say: has your heart never been serious?

MEPHISTOPHELES. To make a joke to a woman is always precarious.

MARTHA. Oh you don't understand me!

MEPHISTOPHELES.   Now *that* I really mind!
But I do understand—that you are very kind.
[*They pass on.*]

FAUST. You knew me again, you little angel,
As soon as you saw me enter the garden?   95

GRETCHEN. Didn't you see me cast down my eyes?

FAUST. And the liberty that I took you pardon?
The impudence that reared its head
When you lately left the cathedral door.

GRETCHEN. I was upset; it had never happened before;   100
No one could ever say anything bad of me—
Oh can he, I thought, have seen in my behaviour
Any cheekiness, any impropriety?
The idea, it seemed, had come to you pat:
'I can treat this woman just like that'.   105
I must admit I did not know what it was
In my heart that began to make me change my view,
But indeed I was angry with myself because
I could not be angrier with you.

FAUST. Sweet love!   110

GRETCHEN.   Wait a moment!
[*She plucks a flower and starts picking off the petals.*]

FAUST.   What is that? A bouquet?

GRETCHEN. No, only a game.

FAUST.   A what?

GRETCHEN.   You will laugh at me. Go away!   115
[GRETCHEN *murmurs.*]

FAUST. What are you murmuring?

GRETCHEN.   Loves me—Loves me not—

FAUST. You flower from Heaven's garden plot!

GRETCHEN. Loves me—Not—Loves me—Not—
Loves me!   120

FAUST.   Yes, child. What this flower has told you
Regard it as God's oracle. He loves you!
Do you know the meaning of that? He loves you!
[*He takes her hands.*]

GRETCHEN. Oh I feel so strange.

FAUST. Don't shudder. Let this look,   125
Let this clasp of the hand tell you
What mouth can never express:
To give oneself up utterly and feel
A rapture which must be everlasting.

Everlasting! Its end would be despair.   130
No; no end! No end!
> [*She breaks away from him and runs off. After a moment's thought he follows her.*]

MARTHA. [*Approaching*] The night's coming on.
MEPHISTOPHELES.   Yes—and we must go.
MARTHA. I would ask you to remain here longer
But this is a terrible place, you know.   135
It's as if no one were able to shape at
Any vocation or recreation
But must have his neighbour's comings and goings to gape at
And, whatever one does, the talk is unleashed, unfurled.
And our little couple?   140
MEPHISTOPHELES.   Carefree birds of summer!
Flown to the summerhouse.
MARTHA.   He seems to like her.
MEPHISTOPHELES. And vice versa. That is the way of the world.

A SUMMERHOUSE

GRETCHEN *runs in and hides behind the door.*

GRETCHEN. He comes!
FAUST. [*Entering*]   You rogue! Teasing me so!
I've caught you!
> [*He kisses her.*]

GRETCHEN.   Dearest! I love you so!
> [MEPHISTOPHELES *knocks.*]

FAUST. Who's there?   5
MEPHISTOPHELES.   A friend.
FAUST.   A brute!
MEPHISTOPHELES.   It is time to part, you know.
MARTHA. [*Joining them*] Yes, it is late, sir.
FAUST.   May I not see you home?   10
GRETCHEN. My mother would—Farewell!
FAUST.   I must go then?
Farewell!
MARTHA.   Adieu!
GRETCHEN.   Let us soon meet again!   15
> [FAUST *and* MEPHISTOPHELES *leave.*]

Dear God! A man of such a kind,
What things must go on in his mind!
I can only blush when he talks to me;
Whatever he says, I must agree.
Poor silly child, i cannot see   20
What it is he finds in me.

FOREST AND CAVERN

FAUST. [*Alone*] Exalted Spirit, you gave me, gave me all
    I prayed for. Aye, and it is not in vain
    That you have turned your face in fire upon me.
    You gave me glorious Nature for my kingdom
    With power to feel her and enjoy her. Nor   5
    Is it a mere cold wondering glance you grant me
    But you allow me to gaze into her depths
    Even as into the bosom of a friend.
    Aye, you parade the ranks of living things
    Before me and you teach me to know my brothers   10
    In the quiet copse, in the water, in the air.
    And when the storm growls and snarls in the forest
    And the giant pine falls headlong, bearing away
    And crushing its neighbours, bough and bole and all,
    With whose dull fall the hollow hill resounds,   15
    Then do you carry me off to a sheltered cave
    And show me myself, and wonders of my own breast
    Unveil themselves in their deep mystery.
    And now that the clear moon rises on my eyes
    To soften things, now floating up before me   20
    From walls of rocks and from the dripping covert
    Come silver forms of the past which soothe and temper
    The dour delight I find in contemplation.

    That nothing perfect falls to men, oh now
    I feel that true. In addition to the rapture   25
    Which brings me near and nearer to the gods
    You gave me that companion whom already
    I cannot do without, though cold and brazen
    He lowers me in my own eyes and with
    One whispered word can turn your gifts to nothing.   30
    He is always busily fanning in my breast
    A fire of longing for that lovely image.
    So do I stagger from desire to enjoyment
    And in enjoyment languish for desire.
        [MEPHISTOPHELES *enters.*]
MEPHISTOPHELES. Haven't you yet had enough of this kind of
    life?   35
    How can it still appeal to you?
    It is all very well to try it once,
    Then one should switch to something new.
FAUST. I wish you had something else to do
    On my better days than come plaguing me.   40
MEPHISTOPHELES. Now, now! I'd gladly leave you alone;

You needn't suggest it seriously.
So rude and farouche and mad a friend
Would certainly be little loss.
One has one's hands full without end!   45
One can never read in the gentleman's face
What he likes or what should be left alone.

FAUST. That is exactly the right tone!
He must be thanked for causing me ennui.

MEPHISTOPHELES. Poor son of earth, what sort of life   50
Would you have led were it not for me?
The flim-flams of imagination,
I have cured you of those for many a day.
But for me, this terrestrial ball
Would already have seen you flounce away.   55
Why behave as an owl behaves
Moping in rocky clefts and caves?
Why do you nourish yourself like a toad that sips
From moss that oozes, stone that drips?
A pretty pastime to contrive!   60
The doctor in you is still alive.

FAUST. Do you comprehend what a new and vital power
This wandering in the wilderness has given me?
Aye, with even an inkling of such joy,
You would be devil enough to grudge it me.   65

MEPHISTOPHELES. A supernatural gratification!
To lie on the mountain tops in the dark and dew
Rapturously embracing earth and heaven,
Swelling yourself to a godhead, ferreting through
The marrow of the earth with divination,   70
To feel in your breast the whole six days of creation,
To enjoy I know not what in arrogant might
And then, with the Old Adam discarded quite,
To overflow into all things in ecstasy;
After all which your lofty intuition   75
    [*He makes a gesture.*]
Will end—hm—unmentionably.

FAUST. Shame on you!

MEPHISTOPHELES.   Am I to blame?
You have the right to be moral and cry shame!
One must not mention to the modest ear   80
What the modest heart is ever agog to hear.
And, in a word, you are welcome to the pleasure
Of lying to yourself in measure;
But this deception will not last.

61. *doctor:* i.e., the doctor of philosophy.

Already overdriven again, 85
If this goes on you must collapse,
Mad or tormented or aghast.
Enough of this! Back there your love is sitting
And all her world seems sad and small;
You are never absent from her mind, *what a bummer.* 90
Her love for you is more than all.
At first your passion came overflowing
Like a brook that the melted snows have bolstered high;
You have poured your passion into her heart
And now your brook once more is dry. 95
I think, instead of lording it here above
In the woods, the great man might think fit
In view of that poor ninny's love
To make her some return for it.
She finds the time wretchedly long; 100
She stands at the window, watches the clouds
As over the old town walls they roll away.
'If I had the wings of a dove'—so runs her song
Half the night and all the day.
Now she is cheerful, mostly low, 105
Now has spent all her tears,
Now calm again, it appears,
But always loves you so.

FAUST. You snake! You snake!

MEPHISTOPHELES. [*Aside*] Ha! It begins to take! 110

FAUST. You outcast! Take yourself away
And do not name that lovely woman.
Do not bring back the desire for her sweet body
Upon my senses that are half astray.

MEPHISTOPHELES. Where's this to end? She thinks you have run
off, 115
And so you have—about half and half.

FAUST. I am still near her, though far removed,
Her image must be always in my head;
I already envy the body of the Lord
When her lips rest upon the holy bread. 120

MEPHISTOPHELES. Very well, my friend. I have often envied you
Those two young roes that are twins, I mean her two—

FAUST. Pimp! Get away!

MEPHISTOPHELES.   Fine! So you scold? I must laugh.
The God who created girl and boy 125
Knew very well the high vocation
Which facilitates their joy.
But come, this is a fine excuse for gloom!

You should take the road to your sweetheart's room,
Rather than that to death, you know. 130

FAUST. What is the joy of heaven in her arms?
Even when I catch fire upon her breast
Do I not always sense her woe?
Am I not the runaway? The man without a home?
The monster restless and purposeless 135
Who roared like a waterfall from rock to rock in foam
Greedily raging towards the precipice?
And she on the bank in childlike innocence
In a little hut on the little alpine plot
And all her little household world 140
Concentrated in that spot.
And I, the loathed of God,
I was not satisfied
To seize and crush to powder
The rocks on the river side! 145
Her too, her peace, I must undermine as well!
This was the sacrifice I owed to Hell!
Help, Devil, to shorten my time of torment!
What must be, must be; hasten it!
Let her fate hurtle down with mine, 150
Let us go together to the pit!

MEPHISTOPHELES. How it glows again, how it boils again!
Go in and comfort her, my foolish friend!
When such a blockhead sees no outlet
He thinks at once it is the end. 155
Long live the man who does not flinch!
But you've a devil in you, somewhere there.
I know of nothing on earth more unattractive
Than your devil who feels despair.

GRETCHEN'S ROOM

GRETCHEN *is alone, singing at the spinning-wheel.*

GRETCHEN. My peace is gone,
My heart is sore,
I shall find it never
And never more.

He has left my room 5
An empty tomb,
He has gone and all
My world is gall.

My poor head

Is all astray,
My poor mind
Fallen away.   10

My peace is gone,
My heart is sore,
I shall find it never   15
And never more.

'Tis he that I look through
The window to see,
He that I open
The door for—he!   20

His gait, his figure,
So grand, so high!
The smile of his mouth,
The power of his eye,

And the magic stream   25
Of his words—what bliss!
The clasp of his hand
And, ah, his kiss!

My peace is gone,
My heart is sore,
I shall find it never   30
And never more.

My heart's desire
Is so strong, so vast;
Ah, could I seize him   35
And hold him fast

And kiss him for ever
Night and day—
And on his kisses
Pass away!   40

MARTHA'S GARDEN

GRETCHEN. Promise me, Heinrich!

FAUST.   If I can!

GRETCHEN. Tell me: how do you stand in regard to religion?
  You are indeed a good, good man
  But I think you give it scant attention.   5

FAUST. Leave that, my child! You feel what I feel for you;

---

1. *Heinrich:* i.e., Faust. In the   Johann (John). Goethe changed it to
legend, Faust's first name was generally   Heinrich (Henry).

For those I love I would give my life and none
Will I deprive of his sentiments and his church.
GRETCHEN. That is not right; one must believe thereon.
FAUST. Must one?
GRETCHEN.   If only I had some influence!
Nor do you honour the holy sacraments.
FAUST. I honour them.
GRETCHEN.   Yes, but not with any zest.
When were you last at mass, when were you last confessed?
Do you believe in God?
FAUST.   My darling, who dare say:
I believe in God?
Ask professor or priest,
Their answers will make an odd
Mockery of you.
GRETCHEN.   You don't believe, you mean?
FAUST. Do not misunderstand me, my love, my queen!
Who can name him?
Admit on the spot:
I believe in him?
And who can dare
To perceive and declare:
I believe in him not?
The All-Embracing One,
All-Upholding One,
Does he not embrace, uphold,
You, me, Himself?
Does not the Heaven vault itself above us?
Is not the earth established fast below?
And with their friendly glances do not
Eternal stars rise over us?
Do not my eyes look into yours,
And all things thrust
Into your head, into your heart,
And weave in everlasting mystery
Invisibly, visibly, around you?
Fill your heart with *this*, great as it is,
And when this feeling grants you perfect bliss,
Then call it what you will—
Happiness! Heart! Love! God!
I have no name for it!
Feeling is all;
Name is mere sound and reek
Clouding Heaven's light.
GRETCHEN. That sounds quite good and right;

And much as the priest might speak,
Only not word for word.

FAUST. It is what all hearts have heard
In all the places heavenly day can reach,
Each in his own speech;
Why not I in mine?

GRETCHEN. I could almost accept it, you make it sound so fine,
Still there is something in it that shouldn't be;
For you have no Christianity.

FAUST. Dear child!

GRETCHEN.   It has long been a grief to me
To see you in such company.

FAUST. You mean?

GRETCHEN.   The man who goes about with you,
I hate him in my soul, right through and through.
And nothing has given my heart
In my whole life so keen a smart
As that man's face, so dire, so grim.

FAUST. Dear poppet, don't be afraid of him!

GRETCHEN. My blood is troubled by his presence.
All other people, I wish them well;
But much as I may long to see you,
He gives me a horror I cannot tell,
And I think he's a man too none can trust.
God forgive me if I'm unjust.

FAUST. Such queer fish too must have room to swim.

GRETCHEN. I wouldn't live with the like of him!
Whenever that man comes to the door,
He looks in so sarcastically,
Half angrily,
One can see he feels no sympathy;
It is written on his face so clear
There is not a soul he can hold dear.
I feel so cosy in your arms,
So warm and free from all restraint,
And his presence ties me up inside.

FAUST. You angel, with your wild alarms!

GRETCHEN. It makes me feel so ill, so faint,
That, if he merely happens to join us,
I even think I have no more love for you.
Besides, when he's there, I could never pray,
And that is eating my heart away;
You, Heinrich, you must feel it too.

FAUST. You suffer from an antipathy.

GRETCHEN. Now I must go.

FAUST.   Oh, can I never rest
  One little hour hanging upon your breast,
  Pressing both breast on breast and soul on soul?
GRETCHEN. Ah, if I only slept alone!   100
  I'd gladly leave the door unlatched for you to-night;
  My mother, however, sleeps so light
  And if she found us there, I own
  I should fall dead upon the spot.
FAUST. You angel, there is no fear of that.   105
  Here's a little flask. Three drops are all
  It needs—in her drink—to cover nature
  In a deep sleep, a gentle pall.
GRETCHEN. What would I not do for your sake! *YIKES*
  I hope it will do her no injury.   110
FAUST. My love, do you think that of me?
GRETCHEN. Dearest, I've only to look at you
  And I do not know what drives me to meet your will
  I have already done so much for you
  That little more is left me to fulfil.   115
     [*She goes out—and* MEPHISTOPHELES *enters.*]
MEPHISTOPHELES. The monkey! Is she gone?
FAUST.   Have you been spying again?
MEPHISTOPHELES. I have taken pretty good note of it,
  The doctor has been catechised—
  And much, I hope, to his benefit;   120
  The girls are really keen to be advised
  If a man belongs to the old simple-and-pious school.
  'If he stand that', they think, 'he'll stand *our* rule.'
FAUST. You, you monster, cannot see
  How this true and loving soul   125
  For whom faith is her whole
  Being and the only road
  To beatitude, must feel a holy horror
  Having to count her beloved lost for good.
MEPHISTOPHELES. You supersensual, sensual buck,   130
  Led by the nose by the girl you court!
FAUST. O you abortion of fire and muck!
MEPHISTOPHELES. And she also has skill in physiognomy;
  In my presence she feels she doesn't know what,
  She reads some hidden sense behind my little mask,   135
  She feels that I am assuredly a genius—
  Maybe the devil if she dared to ask.
  Now: to-night—
FAUST.   What is to-night to you?
MEPHISTOPHELES. I have my pleasure in it too.   140

ominous

AT THE WELL

GRETCHEN *and* LIESCHEN *with pitchers.*

LIESCHEN. Haven't you heard about Barbara? Not what's passed?
GRETCHEN. Not a word. I go out very little.
LIESCHEN. It's true, Sibylla told me to-day:
    She has made a fool of herself at last.
    So much for her fine airs!   5
GRETCHEN.   Why?
LIESCHEN.   It stinks!
    <u>Now she feeds two when she eats and drinks.</u>
GRETCHEN. Ah!
LIESCHEN. Yes; she has got her deserts in the end.   10
    What a time she's been hanging on her friend!
    Going the rounds
    To the dances and the amusement grounds,
    She had to be always the first in the line,
    He was always standing her cakes and wine;   15
    She thought her looks so mighty fine,
    She was so brazen she didn't waver
    To take the presents that he gave her.
    Such cuddlings and such carryings on—
    But now the pretty flower is gone.   20
GRETCHEN. Poor thing!
LIESCHEN.   Is that the way you feel?
    When we were at the spinning-wheel
    And mother kept us upstairs at night,
    She was below with her heart's delight;
    On the bench or in the shady alley   25
    They never had long enough to dally.
    But now she must grovel in the dirt,
    Do penance in church in a <u>hair shirt.</u>
GRETCHEN. But surely he will marry her.   30
LIESCHEN. He'd be a fool! A smart young chap
    Has plenty of other casks to tap.
    Besides he's gone.
GRETCHEN.   That's not right.
LIESCHEN. If she hooks him she won't get off light!   35
    The boys will tear her wreath in half
    And we shall strew her door with chaff.
        [LIESCHEN *goes off.*]

---

3. *Sibylla:* a friend of Gretchen's; not to be confused with the "Sibyl" named in l. 162 of the scene in the witch's kitchen.

37. *chaff:* in contrast to the bridal bouquet. In Germany this treatment was reserved for girls who had "fallen."

GRETCHEN. [*Going home*] What scorn I used to pour upon her
   When a poor maiden lost her honour!
   My tongue could never find a name   40
   Bad enough for another's shame!
   I thought it black and I blackened it,
   It was never black enough to fit,
   And I blessed myself and acted proud—
   And now I too am under a cloud.   45
   Yet, God! What drove me to this pass,
   It was all so good, so dear, alas!

RAMPARTS

*In a niche in the wall is an image of the Mater Dolorosa.[a] In
front of it* GRETCHEN *is putting fresh flowers in the pots.*

GRETCHEN.   Mary, bow down,
        Beneath thy woeful crown,
        Thy gracious face on me undone!

        The sword in thy heart,
        Smart upon smart,   5
        Thou lookest up to thy dear son;

        Sending up sighs
        To the Father which rise
        For his grief and for thine own.

        Who can gauge   10
        What torments rage
        Through the whole of me and how—
        How my poor heart is troubled in me,
        How fears and longings undermine me?
        Only thou knowest, only thou!   15

        Wherever I may go,
        What woe, what woe, what woe
        Is growing beneath my heart!
        Alas, I am hardly alone,
        I moan, I moan, I moan   20
        And my heart falls apart.

        The flower-pots in my window
        I watered with tears, ah me,
        When in the early morning
        I picked these flowers for thee.   25

a. literally, "sorrowful mother"; i.e., the Virgin Mary.

Not sooner in my bedroom
The sun's first rays were shed
Than I in deepest sorrow
Sat waking on my bed.

Save me from shame and death in one!
Ah, bow down
Thou of the woeful crown,
Thy gracious face on me undone.

NIGHT SCENE AT GRETCHEN'S DOOR

VALENTINE. When I was at some drinking bout
  Where big talk tends to blossom out,
  And my companions raised their voice
  To praise the maidens of their choice
  And drowned their praises in their drink,   5
  Then I would sit and never blink,
  Propped on my elbow listening
  To all their brags and blustering.
  Then smiling I would stroke my beard
  And raise the bumper in my hand   10
  And say: 'Each fellow to his taste!
  But is there one in all the land
  To hold a candle to my own
  Dear sister, Gretchen? No, there's none!'
  Hear! Hear! Kling! Kling! It went around;   15
  Some cried: 'His judgment is quite sound,
  She is the pearl of womanhood!'
  That shut those boasters up for good.
  And now! It would make one tear one's hair
  And run up walls in one's despair!   20
  Each filthy fellow in the place
  Can sneer and jeer at my disgrace!
  And I, like a man who's deep in debt,
  Every chance word must make me sweat.
  I could smash their heads for them if I tried—   25
  I could not tell them that they lied.
      [FAUST *and* MEPHISTOPHELES *enter.*]
VALENTINE. Who comes there, slinking? Who comes there?
  If I mistake not, they're a pair.
  If it's he, I'll scrag him on the spot;
  He'll be dead before he knows what's what!   30
FAUST. How from the window of the sacristy there
  The undying lamp sends up its little flicker

Which glimmers sideways weak and weaker
And round it presses the dark air.
My heart too feels its night, its noose.   35

MEPHISTOPHELES. And I feel like a tom-cat on the loose,
Brushing along the fire escape
And round the walls, a stealthy shape;
Moreover I feel quite virtuous,
Just a bit burglarious, a bit lecherous.   40
You see, I'm already haunted to the marrow
By the glorious Walpurgis Night.
It returns to us the day after to-morrow,
Then one knows why one's awake all right.

FAUST. I'd like some ornament, some ring,   45
For my dear mistress. I feel sad
To visit her without anything.

MEPHISTOPHELES. It's really nothing to regret—
That you needn't pay for what you get.
Now that the stars are gems on heaven's brocade,   50
You shall hear a real masterpiece.
I will sing her a moral serenade
That her folly may increase.
        [*He sings to the guitar.*]

MEPHISTOPHELES.   Catherine, my dear,
                  What? Waiting here   55
                  At your lover's door
                  When the stars of the night are fading?
                  Oh don't begin!
                  When he lifts the pin,
                  A maid goes in—   60
                  But she won't come out a maiden.

                  So think aright!
                  Grant him delight
                  And it's good night,
                  You poor, poor things—Don't linger!   65
                  A girl who's wise
                  Will hide her prize
                  From robber's eyes—
                  Unless she's a ring on her finger.
        [VALENTINE *comes forward.*]

VALENTINE. Damn you! Who're you seducing here?   70
    You damned pied piper! You magician!
    First to the devil with your guitar!

54–69. *Catherine . . . finger:* adapted by Goethe from Shakespeare's *Hamlet*,
Act IV, Scene 5.

Then to the devil with the musician!

MEPHISTOPHELES. The guitar is finished. Look, it's broken in two.

VALENTINE. Now then, to break your heads for you!   75

MEPHISTOPHELES. Doctor! Courage! All you can muster!

Stick by me and do as I say!

Quick now, draw your feather duster!

I'll parry his blows, so thrust away!

VALENTINE. Then parry that!   80

MEPHISTOPHELES.   Why not, why not?

VALENTINE. And that!

MEPHISTOPHELES.   Of course.

VALENTINE.   Is he the devil or what?

What's this? My hand's already lamed.   85

MEPHISTOPHELES. Strike, you!

VALENTINE.   Oh!

[VALENTINE *falls*.]

MEPHISTOPHELES.   Now the lout is tamed!

But we must go! Vanish in the wink of an eye!

They're already raising a murderous hue and cry.   90

MARTHA. [At *the window*] Come out! Come out!

GRETCHEN. [At *the window*]   Bring a light!

MARTHA. [As *before*] There's a row and a scuffle, they're having a
fight.

MAN. Here's one on the ground; he's dead.

MARTHA. [*Coming out*] The murderers, have they gone?   95

GRETCHEN. [*Coming out*] Who's here?

MAN.   Your mother's son.

GRETCHEN. O God! What pain! O God!

VALENTINE. I am dying—that's soon said

And sooner done, no doubt.

Why do you women stand howling and wailing?   100

Come round and hear me out.

[*They all gather round him*.]

Look, my Gretchen, you're young still,

You have not yet sufficient skill,

You bungle things a bit.

Here is a tip—you need no more—   105

Since you are once for all a whore,

Then make a job of it!

GRETCHEN. My brother? O God! Is it I you blame!

VALENTINE. Leave our Lord God out of the game!

What is done I'm afraid is done,   110

As one starts one must carry on.

You began with one man on the sly,

There will be more of them by and by,
And when a dozen have done with you
The whole town will have you too.   115

When Shame is born, she first appears
In this world in secrecy,
And the veil of night is drawn so tight
Over her head and ears;
Yes, people would kill her and forget her.   120
But she grows still more and more
And brazenly roams from door to door
And yet her appearance grows no better.
The more her face creates dismay,
The more she seeks the light of day.   125

Indeed I see the time draw on
When all good people in this town
Will turn aside from you, you tart,
As from a corpse in the plague cart.
Then your heart will sink within you,   130
When they look you in the eye!
It's good-bye to your golden chains!
And church-going and mass—good-bye!
No nice lace collars any more
To make you proud on the dancing floor!   135
No, in some dark and filthy nook
You'll hide with beggars and crippled folk
And, if God pardon you, he may;
You are cursed on earth till your dying day.

MARTHA. Commend your soul to the mercy of God!   140
Will you add slander to your load?

VALENTINE. If I could get at your withered body,
You bawd, you sinner born and hardened!
Then I should hope that all my sins
And in full measure might be pardoned.   145

GRETCHEN. My brother! O hell's misery!

VALENTINE. I tell you: let your weeping be.
When you and your honour came to part,
It was you that stabbed me to the heart.
I go to God through the sleep of death,   150
A soldier—brave to his last breath.
        [*He dies.*]

CATHEDRAL

Organ and anthem. GRETCHEN *in the congregation. An* EVIL
SPIRIT *whispers to her over her shoulder.*

EVIL SPIRIT. How different it all was
Gretchen, when you came here
All innocent to the altar,
Out of the worn-out little book
Lisping your prayers,   5
Half a child's game,
Half God in the heart!
Gretchen!
How is your head?
And your heart—   10
What are its crimes?
Do you pray for your mother's soul, who thanks to you
And your sleeping draught overslept into a long, long
        pain?
And whose blood stains your threshold?
Yes, and already under your heart   15
Does it not grow and quicken
And torture itself and you
With its foreboding presence?

GRETCHEN. Alas! Alas!
If I could get rid of the thoughts   20
Which course through my head hither and thither
Despite me!

CHOIR.   Dies irae, dies illa
                       Solvet saeclum in favilla.

[*The organ plays.*]

EVIL SPIRIT. Agony seizes you!   25
The trumpet sounds!
The graves tremble
And your heart
From its ashen rest
To fiery torment   30
Comes up recreated
Trembling too!

GRETCHEN. Oh to escape from here!
I feel as if the organ
Were stifling me,   35
And the music dissolving
My heart in its depths.

CHOIR.   Judex ergo cum sedebit,
                       Quidquid latet adparebit,

23–24. *Dies . . . favilla:* Day of
wrath, that day that dissolves the world
into ashes. (The choir is singing the
famous thirteenth-century hymn by
Thomas Celano.)

38–40. *Judex . . . remanebit:* When
the judge shall be seated, what is hidden
shall appear, nothing shall remain un-
avenged.

                    Nil inultum remanebit.   40

GRETCHEN.   I cannot breathe!
             The pillars of the walls
             Are round my throat!
             The vaulted roof
             Chokes me!—Air!   45

EVIL SPIRIT. Hide yourself! Nor sin nor shame
             Remains hidden.
             Air? Light?
             Woe to you!

CHOIR.   Quid sum miser tunc dicturus?   50
                     Quem patronum rogaturus?
                     Cum vix justus sit securus.

EVIL SPIRIT. The blessed turn
             Their faces from you.
             The pure shudder   55
             To reach out their hands to you.
             Woe!

CHOIR.   Quid sum miser tunc dicturus?

GRETCHEN.   Neighbour! Help! Your smelling bottle!
             [*She faints.*]

WALPURGIS NIGHT

FAUST *and* MEPHISTOPHELES *making their way through the Hartz Mountains.*

MEPHISTOPHELES. A broomstick—don't you long for such a con-
             veyance?
    I'd find the coarsest he-goat some assistance.
    Taking this road, our goal is still in the distance.
FAUST. No, so long as my legs are not in abeyance,
    I can make do with this knotted stick.
    What is the use of going too quick?   5
    To creep along each labyrinthine valley,
    Then climb this scarp, downwards from which
    The bubbling spring makes its eternal sally,
    This is the spice that makes such journeys rich.
    Already the spring is weaving through the birches,   10
    Even the pine already feels the spring;
    Should not our bodies too give it some purchase?
MEPHISTOPHELES. Candidly—I don't feel a thing.
    In my body all is winter,
    I would prefer a route through frost and snow.   15
    How sadly the imperfect disc

50–52. *Quid . . . securus:* What whom shall I appeal when scarcely the
shall I say in my wretchedness? To righteous man is safe?

Of the red moon rises with belated glow
And the light it gives is bad, at every step
One runs into some rock or tree!   20
Permit me to ask a will o' the wisp.
I see one there, he's burning heartily.
Ahoy, my friend! Might I call on you to help us?
Why do you blaze away there to no purpose?
Be so good as to light us along our road.   25

WILL O' THE WISP. I only hope my sense of your mightiness
Will control my natural flightiness;
A zigzag course is our accustomed mode.

MEPHISTOPHELES. Ha! Ha! So it's men you want to imitate.
In the name of the Devil you go straight   30
Or I'll blow out your flickering, dickering light!

WILL O' THE WISP. You're the head of the house, I can see that all
    right,
You are welcome to use me at your convenience.
But remember, the mountain is magic-mad to-day
And, if a will o' the wisp is to show you the way,   35
You too must show a little lenience.

FAUST, MEPHISTOPHELES, WILL O' THE WISP. [*Singing successively*]
            Into realms of dreams and witchcraft
            We, it seems, have found an ingress.
            Lead us well and show your woodcraft,
            That we may make rapid progress   40
            Through these wide and desert spaces.

            Trees on trees—how each one races,
            Pushing past—how each one hastens!
            And the crags that make obeisance!
            And the rocks with long-nosed faces—   45
            Hear them snorting, hear them blowing!

            Through the stones and lawns are flowing
            Brook and brooklet, downward hustling.
            Is that song—or is it rustling?
            Sweet, sad notes of love—a relic—   50
            Voices from those days angelic?
            Thus we hope, we love—how vainly!
            Echo like an ancient rumour
            Calls again, yes, calls back plainly.

            Now—Tu-whit!—we near the purlieu   55
            Of—Tu-whoo!—owl, jay and curlew;
            Are they all in waking humour?

21. *will o' the wisp:* the Jack o' ⸍ folklore, this was thought of as leading
lantern, or ignis fatuus. In German ⸜ travelers to their destruction.

In the bushes are those lizards—
Straggling legs and bloated gizzards?
And the roots like snakes around us   60
Coil from crag and sandy cranny,
Stretch their mad and strange antennae
Grasping at us to confound us;
Stretch from gnarled and living timber
Towards the passer-by their limber   65
Polyp-suckers!
        And in legions
Through these mossy, heathy regions
Mice, all colours, come cavorting!
And above, a serried cohort,   70
Fly the glow-worms as our escort—
More confusing than escorting.

Tell me what our real case is!
Are we stuck or are we going?
Rocks and trees, they all seem flying   75
Round and round and making faces,
And the will o' the wisps are blowing
Up so big and multiplying.

MEPHISTOPHELES. Hold my coat-tails, hold on tight!
Standing on this central height   80
Marvelling see how far and wide
Mammon lights the peaks inside.

FAUST. How strangely through the mountain hollows
A sad light gleams as of morning-red
And like a hound upon the scent   85
Probes the gorges' deepest bed!
Here fumes arise, there vapours float,
Here veils of mist catch sudden fire
Which creeps along, a flimsy thread,
Then fountains up, a towering spire.   90
Here a whole stretch it winds its way
With a hundred veins throughout the glen,
And here in the narrow neck of the pass
Is suddenly one strand again.
There, near by, are dancing sparks   95
Sprinkled around like golden sand.
But look! The conflagration climbs
The crags' full height, hand over hand.

MEPHISTOPHELES. Does not Sir Mammon light his palace

---

82. *Mammon:* See the note to l. 73, p. 314. Mammon is portrayed as leading a group of fallen angels in digging out gold and gems from the ground of Hell, presumably for Satan's palace in Milton's *Paradise Lost*, Book I, ll.. 678 ff.

In splendid style for this occasion? 100
You are lucky to have seen it;
Already I sense the noisy guests' invasion.

FAUST. How the Wind Hag rages through the air!
What blows she rains upon the nape of my neck!

MEPHISTOPHELES. You must clamp yourself to the ancient ribs of
the rock 105
Or she'll hurl you into this gorge, to find your grave down there.
A mist is thickening the night.
Hark to the crashing of the trees!
The owls are flying off in fright.
And the ever-green palaces— 110
Hark to their pillars sundering!
Branches moaning and breaking!
Tree-trunks mightily thundering!
Roots creaking and yawning!
Tree upon tree in appalling 115
Confusion crashing and falling,
And through the wreckage on the scarps
The winds are hissing and howling.
Do you hear those voices in the air?
Far-off voices? Voices near? 120
Aye, the whole length of the mountain side
The witch-song streams in a crazy tide.

WITCHES. [*In chorus*]. The witches enter the Brocken scene,
The stubble is yellow, the corn is green.
There assembles the mighty horde, 125
Urian sits aloft as lord.
So we go—over stock and stone—
Farting witch on stinking goat.

A VOICE. But ~~ancient Baubo~~ comes alone,
She rides on a mother sow—take note. 130

CHORUS. So honour to whom honour is due!
Let Mother Baubo head the queue!
A strapping sow and Mother on top
And we'll come after, neck and crop.

The way is broad, the way is long, 135
How is this for a crazy throng?
The pitchfork pricks, the broomstick pokes,
The mother bursts and the child chokes.

VOICE FROM ABOVE. Come along, come along, from Felsensee!
VOICES FROM BELOW. We'd like to mount with you straight away.
We wash ourselves clean behind and before 141

126. *Urian:* a name for the devil.   nurse of Demeter, noted for her ob-
129. *Baubo:* In Greek mythology, the   scenity and ~~bestiality~~.

But we are barren for evermore.

CHORUS. The wind is silent, the star's in flight,
    The sad moon hides herself from sight.
    The soughing of the magic choir   145
    Scatters a thousand sparks of fire.

VOICE FROM BELOW. Wait! Wait!

VOICE FROM ABOVE. Who calls there from the cleft in the rock?

VOICE FROM BELOW. Don't leave me behind! Don't leave me
        behind!
    Three hundred years I've been struggling up   150
    And I can never reach the top;
    I want to be with my own kind.

CHORUS. Ride on a broom or ride on a stick,
    Ride on a fork or a goat—but quick!
    Who cannot to-night achieve the climb   155
    Is lost and damned till the end of time.

HALF-WITCH. So long, so long, I've been on the trot;
    How far ahead the rest have got!
    At home I have neither peace nor cheer
    And yet I do not find it here.   160

CHORUS. Their ointment makes the witches hale,
    A rag will make a decent sail
    And any trough a ship for flight;
    You'll never fly, if not to-night.
    Once at the peak, you circle round   165
    And then you sweep along the ground
    And cover the heath far and wide—
    Witchhood in swarms on every side.
      [*The* WITCHES *land.*]

MEPHISTOPHELES. What a push and a crush and a rush and a
        clatter!
    How they sizzle and whisk, how they babble and batter!   170
    Kindle and sparkle and blaze and stink!
    A true witch-element, I think.
    Only stick to me or we shall be swept apart!
    Where are you?

FAUST.   Here!   175

MEPHISTOPHELES.   What! Carried so far already!
    I must show myself the master on this ground.
    Room! Here comes Voland! Room, sweet rabble! Steady!
    Here, Doctor, catch hold of me. Let's make one bound
    Out of this milling crowd and so get clear.
    Even for the likes of me it's *too* mad here.   180

---

178. *Voland:* one of Mephistopheles' names for himself. *Voland,* or *Valand,* is an old German word for "evil fiend."

There's something yonder casting a peculiar glare,
Something attracts me towards those bushes.
Come with me! We will slip in there.

FAUST. You spirit of contradiction! Go on though! I'll follow.   185
You have shown yourself a clever fellow. Quite!
We visit the Brocken on Walpurgis Night
To shut ourselves away in this lonely hollow!

MEPHISTOPHELES. Only look—what motley flames!
It's a little club for fun and games   190
One's not alone with a few, you know.

FAUST. I'd rather be above there though.
Already there's fire and whorls of smoke.
The Prince of Evil is drawing the folk;
Many a riddle must there be solved.   195

MEPHISTOPHELES. And many a new one too evolved.
Let the great world, if it likes, run riot;
We will set up here in quiet.
It is a custom of old date
To make one's own small worlds within the great.   200
I see young witches here, bare to the buff,
And old ones dressed—wisely enough.
If only for my sake, do come on;
It's little trouble and great fun.
I hear some music being let loose too.   205
What a damned clack! It's what one must get used to.
Come along! Come along! You have no choice.
I'll lead the way and sponsor you
And you'll be obliged to me anew.
What do you say? This milieu isn't small.   210
Just look! You can see no end to it at all.
A hundred fires are blazing in a row;
They dance and gossip and cook and drink and court—
Tell me where there is better sport!

FAUST. Do you intend, to introduce us here,   215
To play the devil or the sorcerer?

MEPHISTOPHELES. I am quite accustomed to go incognito
But one wears one's orders on gala days, you know.
I have no garter for identification
But my cloven foot has here some reputation.   220
See that snail? Creeping up slow and steady?
Her sensitive feelers have already
Sensed out something odd in me.
Here I could *not* hide my identity.

187. *Walpurgis Night:* the eve of
May Day (May 1).

219. *garter:* i.e., he has no decoration
of nobility, such as the Order of the
Garter.

The order of the Bath
The order of the Thistle

"Honi soit qui mal y pense"

But come! Let us go the round of the fires   225
And I'll play go-between to your desires.

COSTER-WITCH. Gentlemen, don't pass me by!
Don't miss your opportunity!
Inspect my wares with careful eye;
I have a great variety.   230
And yet there is nothing on my stall
Whose like on earth you could not find,
That in its time has done no small
Harm to the world and to mankind.
No dagger which has not drunk of blood,   235
No goblet which has not poured its hot and searing
Poison into some healthy frame,
No gewgaw which has not ruined some endearing
Woman, no sword which has not been used to hack
A bond in two and stab a partner in the back.   240

MEPHISTOPHELES. Auntie! You are behind the times.
Past and done with! Past and done!
You must go in for novelties!
You'll lose our custom if you've none.

FAUST. I mustn't go crazy unawares!   245
This is a fair to end all fairs.

MEPHISTOPHELES. The whole crowd's forcing its way above;
You find you're shoved though you may think you shove.

FAUST. Who then is that?

MEPHISTOPHELES.   Look well at Madam;   250
That's Lilith.

FAUST.   Who?

MEPHISTOPHELES.   First wife of Adam.
Be on your guard against her lovely hair,
That shining ornament which has no match;
Any young man whom those fair toils can catch,   255
She will not quickly loose him from her snare.

FAUST. Look, an old and a young one, there they sit.
They have already frisked a bit.

MEPHISTOPHELES. No rest to-night for 'em, not a chance.   260
They're starting again. Come on! Let's join the dance.

[FAUST *dances with a* YOUNG WITCH.]

FAUST.   A lovely dream once came to me
In which I saw an apple tree,

---

227. *Coster-Witch:* The original, *Trödelhexe,* literally means "a witch (dealing in) old rags and clothes."

251. *Lilith:* According to an old rabbinical legend, Adam's first wife (the "female" mentioned in Genesis 1:27) was Lilith. After Eve was created, Lilith became a ghost who seduced men and inflicted evil upon children.

On which two lovely apples shine,
They beckon me, I start to climb.   265

YOUNG WITCH. Those little fruit you long for so
Just as in Eden long ago.
Joy runs through me, through and through;
My garden bears its apples too.

[FAUST *breaks away from the dance*.]

MEPHISTOPHELES. Why did you let that lovely maiden go   270
Who danced with you and so sweetly sang?

FAUST. Ugh, in the middle of it there sprang
Out of her mouth a little red mouse.

MEPHISTOPHELES. Why complain? That's nothing out of the way;
You should be thankful it wasn't grey.   275
In an hour of love! What a senseless grouse!

FAUST. And then I saw—

MEPHISTOPHELES.   What?

FAUST.   Mephisto, look over there!
Do you see a girl in the distance, pale and fair?   280
Who drags herself, only slowly, from the place?
And seems to walk with fetters on her feet?
I must tell you that I think I see
Something of dear Gretchen in her face.

MEPHISTOPHELES. That can do no good! Let it alone! Beware!   285
It is a lifeless phantom, an image of air.
It is a bad thing to behold;
Its cold look makes the blood of man run cold,
One turns to stone almost upon the spot;
You have heard of Medusa, have you not?   290

FAUST. Indeed, they are the eyes of one who is dead,
Unclosed by loving hands, left open, void.
That is the breast which Gretchen offered me,
And that is the sweet body I enjoyed.

MEPHISTOPHELES. That is mere magic, you gullible fool! She
can   295
Appear in the shape of his love to every man.

FAUST. What ravishment! What pain! Oh stay!
That look! I cannot turn away!
How strange that that adorable neck
In one red thread should be arrayed   300
As thin as the back of a knife-blade.

MEPHISTOPHELES. You are quite correct! I see it too.
She can also carry her head under her arm,

290. *Medusa:* the Gorgon, with hair made of serpents, whose glance turned men to stone. She was finally killed by Perseus, and her head was given to Athene.

Perseus has cut it off for her.
Always this love of things untrue![a]   305

[A CHOIR *is heard, pianissimo.*]

CHOIR. Drifting cloud and gauzy mist
Brighten and dissever.
Breeze on the leaf and wind in the reeds
And all is gone for ever.

DREARY DAY—OPEN COUNTRY

FAUST. In misery! In despair! Long on the earth a wretched wanderer, now a prisoner! A criminal cooped in a dungeon for horrible torments, that dear and luckless creature! To end so! So! Perfidious, worthless spirit—and this you have kept from me!
Stand, Just stand there! Roll your devilish eyes spitefully round in your head! Stand and brave me with your unbearable presence! A prisoner! In irremediable misery! Abandoned to evil spirits, to judging, unfeeling man! And I in the meantime—you lull me with stale diversions, you hide her worsening plight from me, you abandon her to perdition!

MEPHISTOPHELES. She is not the first.

FAUST. Dog! Loathsome monster! Change him, Thou eternal Spirit! Change this serpent back to his shape of a dog, in which he often delighted to trot before me at night—to roll about at the feet of the harmless wanderer and, as he tripped, to sink his teeth in his shoulders. Change him back to his fancy-shape that he may crouch in the sand on his belly before me, that I may trample over his vileness!
Not the first, you say! O the pity of it! What human soul can grasp that more than one creature has sunk to the depth of this misery, that the first did not pay off the guilt of all the rest, writhing and racked in death before the eyes of the Ever-Pardoning! It pierces me to my marrow and core, the torment of this one girl—and you grin calmly at the fate of thousands!

MEPHISTOPHELES. Now we're already back at our wits' end—the point where your human intelligence snaps. Why do you enter our company, if you can't carry it through? So you want to fly— and have no head for heights? Did we force ourselves on you— or you on us?

FAUST. Do not bare at me so those greedy fangs of yours! You sicken me! O great and glorious Spirit, Thou who didst deign to appear to me, Thou who knowest my heart and my soul, why fetter me to this odious partner who grazes on mischief and laps up destruction?

[a.] The Walpurgis Night's Dream, which is always cut from performances of *Faust*, is omitted. It occurs between l. 305 and l. 306 of our text.

MEPHISTOPHELES. Have you finished?

FAUST. Save her! Or woe to you! The most withering curse upon you for thousands of years!

MEPHISTOPHELES. I cannot undo the avenger's bonds, his bolts I cannot open. Save her! Who was it plunged her into ruin? I or you?

[FAUST *looks wildly around.*]

MEPHISTOPHELES. Are you snatching at the thunder? Luckily, that is forbidden you wretched mortals. To smash to pieces his innocent critic, that is the way the tyrant relieves himself when in difficulties.

FAUST. Bring me to her! She shall be free!

MEPHISTOPHELES. And what of the risk you will run? Let me tell you; the town is still tainted with blood-guilt from your hand. Over the site of the murder there float avenging spirits who await the returning murderer.

FAUST. That too from *you?* Murder and death of a world on your monstrous head! Take me to her, I tell you; set her free!

MEPHISTOPHELES. I will take you, and what I *can* do—listen! Am I omnipotent in heaven and earth? I will cast a cloud on the gaoler's senses; do you get hold of the keys and carry her out with your own human hands. I meanwhile wait, my magic horses are ready, I carry you off. That much I can manage.

FAUST. Away! Away!

NIGHT

FAUST *and* MEPHISTOPHELES *fly past on black horses.*

FAUST. What do they weave round the Gallows Rock?

MEPHISTOPHELES. Can't tell what they're cooking and hatching.

FAUST. Floating up, floating down, bending, descending.

MEPHISTOPHELES. A witch corporation.

FAUST. Black mass, black water.   5

MEPHISTOPHELES. Come on! Come on!

DUNGEON

FAUST *with a bunch of keys and a lamp, in front of an iron door.*

FAUST. A long unwonted trembling seizes me,
The woe of all mankind seizes me fast.
It is here she lives, behind these dripping walls,
Her crime was but a dream too good to last!
And *you*, Faust, waver at the door?   5
You fear to see your love once more?
Go in at once—or her hope of life is past.

---

1. *Gallows Rock:* the masonry supporting a gallows.

[*He tries the key.* GRETCHEN *starts singing inside.*]

GRETCHEN. My mother, the whore,
    Who took my life!
    My father, the rogue,   10
    Who ate my flesh!
    My little sister
    My bones did lay
    In a cool, cool glen;
    And there I turned to a pretty little wren;   15
    Fly away! Fly away!
    [FAUST *opens the lock.*]

FAUST. She does not suspect that her lover is listening—
  To the chains clanking, the straw rustling.
    [*He enters.*]

GRETCHEN. Oh! They come! O death! It's hard! Hard!

FAUST. Quiet! I come to set you free.   20
    [*She throws herself at his feet.*]

GRETCHEN. If you are human, feel my misery.

FAUST. Do not cry out—you will wake the guard.
    [*He takes hold of the chains to unlock them.*]

GRETCHEN. [*On her knees*] Who has given you this power,
  Hangman, so to grieve me?
  To fetch me at this midnight hour!   25
  Have pity! O reprieve me!
  Will to-morrow not serve when the bells are rung?
    [*She gets up.*]
  I am still so young, I am still so young!
  Is my death so near?
  I was pretty too, that was what brought me here. 30
  My lover was by, he's far to-day;
  My wreath lies torn, my flowers have been thrown away.
  Don't seize on me so violently!
  What have I done to you? Let me be!
  Let me not vainly beg and implore;   35
  You know I have never seen you before.

FAUST. Can I survive this misery?

GRETCHEN. I am now completely in your power.
  Only let me first suckle my child.
  This night I cherished it, hour by hour;   40
  To torture me they took it away
  And now I murdered it, so they say.
  And I shall never be happy again.
  People make ballads about me—the heartless crew!
  An old story ends like this—   45
  Must mine too?

[FAUST *throws himself on the ground*.]

FAUST. Look! At your feet a lover lies
　　To loose you from your miseries.

　　　　[GRETCHEN *throws herself beside him*.]

GRETCHEN. O, let us call on the saints on bended knee!
　　Beneath these steps—but see—　　　　　　　　50
　　Beneath this sill
　　The cauldron of Hell!
　　And within,
　　The Evil One in his fury
　　Raising a din!　　　　　　　　　　　　　55

FAUST. Gretchen! Gretchen!

GRETCHEN. That was my lover's voice!

　　　　[*She springs up: the chains fall off*.]

　　I heard him calling. Where can he be?
　　No one shall stop me. I am free!
　　Quick! My arms round his neck!　　　　　　60
　　And lie upon his bosom! Quick!
　　He called 'Gretchen!' He stood at the door.
　　Through the whole of Hell's racket and roar,
　　Through the threats and jeers and from far beyond
　　I heard that voice so sweet, so fond.　　　65

FAUST. It is I!

GRETCHEN.　　　It's you? Oh say so once again!

　　　　[*She clasps him*.]

　　It is! It is! Where now is all my pain?
　　And where the anguish of my captivity?
　　It's you; you have come to rescue me!　　70
　　I am saved!
　　The street is back with me straight away
　　Where I saw you that first day,
　　And the happy garden too
　　Where Martha and I awaited you.　　　　75

FAUST. Come! Come!

GRETCHEN.　　　　Oh stay with me, oh do!
　　Where *you* stay, I would like to, too.

FAUST. Hurry!
　　If you don't,　　　　　　　　　　　　80
　　The penalty will be sore.

GRETCHEN. What! Can you kiss no more?
　　So short an absence, dear, as this
　　And you've forgotten how to kiss!
　　Why do I feel so afraid, clasping your neck?　85
　　In the old days your words, your looks,
　　Were a heavenly flood I could not check

And you kissed me as if you would smother me—
Kiss me now!
Or I'll kiss you!
    [*She kisses him.*]
Oh your lips are cold as stone!
And dumb!
What has become
Of your love?
Who has robbed me of my own?   95
    [*She turns away from him.*]

FAUST. Come! Follow me, my love! Be bold!
I will cherish you after a thousandfold.
Only follow me now! That is all I ask of you.

GRETCHEN. And is it you then? Really? Is it true?

FAUST. It is! But come!   100

GRETCHEN.   You are undoing each chain,
You take me to your arms again.
How comes it you are not afraid of me?
Do you know, my love, *whom* you are setting free?

FAUST. Come! The deep night is passing by and beyond.   105

GRETCHEN. My mother, I have murdered her;
I drowned my child in the pond.
Was it not a gift to you and me?
To you too—You! Are you what you seem?
Give me your hand! It is not a dream!   110
Your dear hand—but, oh, it's wet!
Wipe it off! I think
There is blood on it.
Oh God! What have you done?
Put up your sword,
I beg you to.   115

FAUST. Let what is gone be gone!
You are killing me.

GRETCHEN. No! *You* must live on!
I will tell you about the graves—   120
You must get them put right
At morning light;
Give the best place to my mother,
The one next door to my brother,
Me a shade to the side—   125
A gap, but not too wide.
And the little one on my right breast.
No one else shall share my rest.
When it was you, when I could clasp you,
That was a sweet, a lovely day!   130

But I no longer can attain it,
I feel I must use force to grasp you,
As if you were thrusting me away.
And yet it's you and you look so kind, so just.

FAUST. If you feel it's I, then come with me! You must! 135

GRETCHEN. Outside there?

FAUST. Into the air!

GRETCHEN.   If the grave is there
And death on the watch, then come!
Hence to the final rest of the tomb 140
And not a step beyond—
You are going now? O Heinrich, if *I* could too!

FAUST. You can! The door is open. Only respond!

GRETCHEN. I dare not go out; for me there is no more hope.
They are lying in wait for me; what use is flight? 145
To have to beg, it is so pitiable
And that with a conscience black as night!
So pitiable to tramp through foreign lands—
And in the end I must fall into their hands!

FAUST. I shall stay by you. 150

GRETCHEN. Be quick! Be quick!
Save your poor child!
Go! Straight up the path—
Along by the brook—
Over the bridge— 155
Into the wood—
Left where the plank is—
In the pond!
Catch hold of it quickly!
It's trying to rise, 160
It's kicking still!
Save it! Save it!

FAUST. Collect yourself!
One step—just one—and you arc free.

GRETCHEN. If only we were past the hill! 165
There sits my mother on a stone—
My brain goes cold and dead—
There sits my mother on a stone—
And wags and wags her head.
No sign, no nod, her head is such a weight 170
She'll wake no more, she slept so late.
She slept that we might sport and play.
What a time that was of holiday!

FAUST. If prayer and argument are no resource,
I will risk saving you by force. 175

GRETCHEN. No! I will have no violence! Let me go!
　　Don't seize me in that murderous grip!
　　I have done everything else for you, you know.
FAUST. My love! My love! The day is dawning!
GRETCHEN. Day! Yes, it's growing day! The last day breaks on
　　　　me!　　　　　　　　　　　　　　　　　　　　　180
　　My wedding day it was to be!
　　Tell no one you had been before with Gretchen.
　　Alas for my garland!
　　There's no more chance!
　　We shall meet again—　　　　　　　　　　　　　185
　　But not at the dance.
　　The people are thronging—but silently;
　　Street and square
　　Cannot hold them there.
　　The bell tolls—it tolls for *me*.　　　　　　　　190
　　How they seize me, bind me, like a slave!
　　Already I'm swept away to the block.
　　Already there jabs at every neck,
　　The sharp blade which jabs at mine.
　　The world lies mute as the grave.　　　　　　　195
FAUST. I wish I had never been born!
　　　　[MEPHISTOPHELES *appears outside.*]
MEPHISTOPHELES. Away! Or you are lost.
　　Futile wavering! Waiting and prating!
　　My horses are shivering,
　　The dawn's at the door.　　　　　　　　　　　200
GRETCHEN. What rises up from the floor?
　　It's he! Send him away! It's he!
　　What does he want in the holy place?
　　It is I he wants!
FAUST.　　　　　　　　You shall live!　　　　　　205
GRETCHEN. Judgment of God! I have given myself to Thee!
MEPHISTOPHELES. [*To* FAUST] Come! Or I'll leave you both in the
　　　　lurch.
GRETCHEN. O Father, save me! I am Thine!
　　You angels! Hosts of the Heavenly Church,
　　Guard me, stand round in serried line!　　　　210
　　Heinrich! I shudder to look at you.
MEPHISTOPHELES. She is condemned!
VOICE FROM ABOVE.　　　　　　　Redeemed!
MEPHISTOPHELES. Follow me!
　　　　[*He vanishes with* FAUST.]
VOICE [*From within, dying away*] Heinrich! Heinrich!　　215

FRANÇOIS RENÉ DE CHATEAUBRIAND
(1768–1848)

René*

On arriving among the Natchez René[1] was obliged to take a wife in order to conform to the Indian customs; but he did not live with her. His melancholy nature drew him constantly away into the depths of the woods. There he would spend entire days in solitude, a savage among the savages. Aside from Chactas, his foster father, and Father Souël, a missionary at Fort Rosalie, he had given up all fellowship with men. These two elders had acquired a powerful influence over his heart, Chactas, through his kindly indulgence, and Father Souël, on the contrary, through his extreme severity. Since the beaver hunt, when the blind sachem[2] had told his adventures to René, the young man had consistently refused to talk about his own. And yet both Chactas and the missionary keenly desired to know what sorrow had driven this well-born European to the strange decision of retiring into the wildernesses of Louisiana. René had always claimed that he would not tell his story because it was too insignificant, limited as it was to his thoughts and feelings. "As for the circumstance which induced me to leave for America," he added, "that must forever be buried in oblivion."

Thus several years[3] went by, and the two elders were unable to draw his secret from him. One day, however, he received a letter from Europe, through the Office of Foreign Missions, which so increased his sadness that he felt he had to flee even from his old friends. Now more than ever they exhorted him to open his heart to them. And so great was their tact, so gentle their manner, and so deep the respect they commanded, that he finally felt obliged to yield. He therefore set a day to tell them, not the adventures of his life, for he had never had any, but the innermost feelings of his soul.

On the twenty-first day of the month the Indians call the "moon of flowers," René went to the cabin of Chactas. Giving his arm to the sachem, he led him to a spot under a sassafras tree on the bank of the Meschacebe.[4] Soon afterwards Father Souël arrived at the meeting place. Day was breaking. Off on the plain, some distance

---

* Translated by Irving Putter. *René* was included in Chateaubriand's *Genius of Christianity* (1802), a long work designed to illustrate its subtitle: *The Poetic and Moral Beauties of Christianity*. Atala, also in the volume, had appeared a year earlier, partly to test the public's reception.

1. *René:* He appears in *Atala* as the melancholy youth who has fled Europe for Louisiana in 1725, and to whom the Indian sage tells the sad tale of his love for Atala.

2. *sachem:* chief.

3. *several years:* René, killed in 1730, tells his story sometime between 1728 and 1730.

4. *Meschacebe:* Mississippi.

away, the Natchez village could be seen with its grove of mulberry trees and its cabins which looked like beehives. The French colony and Fort Rosalie were visible on the river bank at the right. Tents, half-built houses, fortresses just begun, hosts of negroes clearing tracts of land, groups of white men and Indians, all offered a striking contrast of social and primitive ways in this limited space. Towards the east, in the background of this setting, the sun was just beginning to show behind the jagged peaks of the Appalachians, which stood forth like azure symbols against the golden reaches of the sky. In the west, the Meschacebe rolled its waves in majestic stillness, forming for the picture a border of indescribable grandeur.

For some time the young man and the missionary stood marveling at this splendid scene and pitying the sachem who could no longer enjoy it. Then Father Souël and Chactas sat down on the grass at the foot of the tree. René took his place between them, hesitated a moment, and then began speaking in the following manner.

As I open my story, I cannot stifle a feeling of shame. The peace in your hearts, respected elders, and the calm of nature all about me make me blush for the disorder and turmoil of my soul.

How you will pity me! How wretched my perpetual anxieties will seem to you! You who have passed through all the hardships of life, what will you think of a young man with neither strength nor moral courage, who finds the source of his torments within himself, and can hardly lament any misfortunes save those he has brought on himself? Alas! Do not condemn him too severely; he has already been harshly punished!

I cost my mother[5] her life as I came into this world and had to be drawn from her womb with an instrument. My father gave his blessing to my brother because he saw in him his elder son; as for me, I was soon abandoned to strange hands and brought up far from my father's roof.

I was spirited in temper and erratic by nature. As I alternated turbulence and joy with silence and sadness, I would gather my young friends around me, then leave them suddenly and go off to sit by myself watching the swift clouds or listening to the rain falling among the leaves.

Each autumn I would return to the family château,[6] off in the midst of the forests, near a lake in a remote province.

I was timid and inhibited in my father's presence, and found freedom and contentment only with my sister Amelia.[7] We were

---

5. *mother:* Actually Chateaubriand's mother died in 1798, when he was thirty.
6. *château:* The author's home was a

castle at Combourg, on the sea near St. Malo in Brittany.
7. *Amelia:* closely modeled on Chateaubriand's sister Lucile, born in 1764.

closely bound together by our tender affinities in mood and taste; my sister was only slightly older than I. We loved to climb the hillside together or go sailing on the lake or wander through the woods under the falling leaves, and even now memories of those rambles fill my soul with delight. O illusions of childhood and homeland, can your sweetness ever fade away?

Sometimes we strolled in silence hearkening to the muffled rumbling of the autumn or the crackling of the dry leaves trailing sadly under our feet. In our innocent games we ran after the swallow in the meadows or the rainbow on the storm-swept hills. At other times we would whisper poetry inspired in us by the spectacle of nature. In my youth I courted the Muses. Nothing is more poetic than a heart of sixteen in all the pristine freshness of its passions. The morning of life is like the morning of the day, pure, picturesque, and harmonious.

On Sundays and holidays I often stood in the deep woods as the sound of the distant bell drifted through the trees, calling from the temple to the man of the fields. Leaning against the trunk of an elm, I would listen in rapt silence to the devout tolling. Each tremor of the resounding bronze would waft into my guileless soul the innocence of country ways, the calm of solitude, the beauty of religion, and the cherished melancholy of memories out of my early childhood! Oh! What churlish heart has never started at the sound of the bells in his birthplace, those bells which trembled with joy over his cradle, which rang out the dawn of his life, which signaled his first heartbeat, announcing to all surrounding places the reverent gladness of his father, the ineffable anguish and supreme joy of his mother! All is embraced in that magical revery which engulfs us at the sound of our native bell—faith, family, homeland, the cradle and the grave, the past and the future.

True enough, Amelia and I enjoyed these solemn, tender thoughts far more than did others, for in the depths of our heart we both had a strain of sadness, given us by God or our mother.

Meanwhile my father was attacked by a disease which brought him to his grave in a short time. He passed away in my arms, and I learned to know death from the lips of the very person who had given me life. The impression was profound; it is vivid still. It was the first time that the immortality of the soul was clearly present before my eyes. I could not believe that this lifeless body was the creator of my thought; I felt it had to come from some other source, and, in my religious sorrow, close akin to joy, I hoped one day to join the spirit of my father.

Another circumstance fixed this lofty idea even more firmly in my mind. My father's features had taken on a sublime quality in his coffin. Why should this astonishing mystery not be an indication of our immortality? Could not all-knowing death have stamped the secrets of another universe on the brow of its victim? And why could the tomb not have some great vision of eternity?

Overcome with grief Amelia had withdrawn to the seclusion of a tower from which she could hear the chanting of the priests in the funeral procession and the death knell reverberating under the vaults of the Gothic château.

I accompanied my father to his last abode, and the earth closed over his remains. Eternity and oblivion pressed down on him with all their weight, and that very evening the indifferent passer-by trod over his grave. Aside from his daughter and son, it was already as though he had never existed.

Then I had to leave the family shelter, which my brother had inherited. Amelia and I went to live with some aged relatives.

Pausing before the deceptive paths of life, I considered them one by one, but dared not set out along any of them. Amelia would frequently speak of the joy of the religious life, adding that I was the only bond still holding her to the outside world; and her eyes would fix themselves upon me sadly.

With my heart stirred by these devout talks, I would often make by way toward a monastery close by my new dwelling. Once I was even tempted to retire within its walls forever. Happy are they who reach the end of their travels without ever leaving the harbor and have never, as have I, dragged their barren days out over the face of the earth!

In our endless agitation we Europeans are obliged to erect lonely retreats for ourselves. The greater the turmoil and din in our hearts, the more we are drawn to calmness and silence. These shelters in my country are always open to the sad and weak. Often they are hidden in little valleys, which seem to harbor in their bosom a vague feeling of sorrow and a hope for a future refuge. Sometimes, too, they are found in high places where the religious soul, like some mountain plant, seems to rise toward heaven, offering up its perfumes.

I can still see the majestic mingling of waters and forests around that ancient abbey, where I hoped to shelter my life from the whims of fate; I still wander at eventide in those reverberating, solitary cloisters. When the moon cast its wan light on the pillars of the arcades and outlined their shadow on the opposite wall, I would stop to contemplate the cross marking the burial ground and the tall grass growing among the tombstones. O men who once lived far removed from the world and have passed from the silence of life to the silence of death, how your tombs filled my soul with disgust for this earth!

Whether it was my natural instability or a dislike of the monastic life, I do not know, but I changed my plans and decided to go abroad. As I bade my sister farewell, she clasped me in her arms in an almost joyful gesture, as though she were happy to see me leave, and I could not repress a bitter thought about the inconstancy of human affections.

Nevertheless, I set forth all alone and full of spirit on the stormy ocean of the world, though I knew neither its safe ports nor its perilous reefs. First I visited peoples[8] who exist no more. I went and sat among the ruins of Rome and Greece, those countries of virile and brilliant memory, where palaces are buried in the dust and royal mausoleums hidden beneath the brambles. O power of nature and weakness of man! A blade of grass will pierce through the hardest marble of these tombs, while their weight can never be lifted by all these mighty dead!

Sometimes a tall column rose up solitary in a waste land, as a great thought may spring from a soul ravaged by time and sorrow.

I meditated on these monuments at every hour and through all the incidents of the day. Sometimes, I watched the same sun which had shone down on the foundation of these cities now setting majestically over their ruins; soon afterwards, the moon rose between crumbling funeral urns into a cloudless sky, bathing the tombs in pallid light. Often in the faint, dream-wafting rays of that planet, I thought I saw the Spirit of Memory sitting pensive by my side.

But I grew weary of searching through graveyards, where too often I stirred up only the dust of a crime-ridden past.

I was anxious to see if living races had more virtue and less suffering to offer than those which had vanished. One day, as I was walking in a large city, I passed through a secluded and deserted courtyard behind a palace. There I noticed a statue pointing to a spot made famous by a certain sacrifice. I was struck by the stillness of the surroundings; only the wind moaned weakly around the tragic marble. Workmen were lying about indifferently at the foot of the statue or whistled as they hewed out stones. I asked them what the monument meant; some knew little indeed, while the others were totally oblivious of the catastrophe it commemorated. Nothing could indicate so vividly the true import of human events and the vanity of our existence. What has become of those figures whose fame was so widespread? Time has taken a step and the face of the earth has been made over.

In my travels I especially sought out artists and those inspired poets whose lyres glorify the gods and the joy of peoples who honor their laws, their religion, and their dead. These singers come of a

---

8. *I visited peoples*: Chateaubriand's own romantic voyaging came after the publication of *René*.

divine race and possess the only sure power which heaven has granted earth. Their life is at once innocent and sublime. They speak like immortals or little children. They explain the laws of the universe and cannot themselves understand the most elementary concerns of life. They have marvelous intuitions of death and die with no consciousness of it, like new-born infants.

On the mountain peaks of Caledonia, the last bard[9] ever heard in those wildernesses sang me poems which had once consoled a hero in his old age. We were sitting on four stones overgrown with moss; at our feet ran a brook, and in the distance the roebuck strayed among the ruins of a tower, while from the seas the wind whistled in over the waste land of Cona. The Christian faith, itself a daughter of the lofty mountains, has now placed crosses over the monuments of Morven heroes and plucked the harp of David on the banks of the very stream where once the harp of Ossian sighed. Loving peace even as the divinities of Selma loved war, it now shepherds flocks where Fingal once joined battle and has strewn angels of peace amongst clouds once occupied by murderous phantoms.

Ancient, lovely Italy offered me its host of masterworks. With what reverent and poetic awe I wandered through those vast edifices consecrated to religion by the arts! What a labyrinth of columns! What a sequence of arches and vaults! How beautiful are the echoes circling round those domes like the rolling of waves in the ocean, like the murmur of winds in the forest or the voice of God in his temple! The architect seems to build the poet's thoughts and make them accessible to the senses.

And yet with all my effort what had I learned until then? I had discovered nothing stable among the ancients and nothing beautiful among the moderns. The past and present are imperfect statues —one, quite disfigured, drawn from the ruins of the ages, and the other still devoid of its future perfection.

But, my old friends, you who have lived so long in the wilderness, you especially will be surprised that I have not once spoken of the glories of nature in this story of my travels.

One day I climbed to the summit of Etna, that great volcano burning in the middle of an island. Above me, I saw the sun rising in the vast reaches of the horizon, while at my feet Sicily shrank to a point and the sea retreated into the distant spaces. In this vertical view of the picture the rivers seemed little more than lines traced on a map. But while on one side I observed this sight, on the

9. *last bard:* All references in this paragraph are to MacPherson's *Poems of Ossian* (1760–1763), which Chateaubriand knew in the Letourneur translation. MacPherson claimed to have discovered Gaelic (Erse) poems, including an epic *Fingal*, by a third-century blind bard Ossian, which MacPherson published in English translation. Though spurious, their popularity was immense throughout Europe. Caledonia here is Scotland; Cona and Morven are in that country; Selma is northern Ireland (near modern Belfast), where the fighting in *Fingal* takes place.

other my eye plunged into the depths of Etna's crater, whose bowels I saw blazing between billows of black smoke.

A young man full of passion, sitting at the mouth of a volcano and weeping over mortal men whose dwellings he could barely distinguish far off below him—O revered elders! Such a creature is doubtless worthy only of your pity! But think what you may, such a picture reveals my character and my whole being. Just so, throughout my life, I have had before my eyes an immense creation which I could barely discern, while a chasm yawned at my side.

As he uttered these last words René grew silent and soon sank into revery. Father Souël looked at him in surprise, while the blind and aged sachem, not hearing the young man's voice any more, did not know what to make of this silence.

René had fixed his eyes on a group of Indians gaily passing through the plain. Suddenly his countenance softened, and tears fell from his eyes.

"Happy Indians," he exclaimed, "oh, why can I not enjoy the peace which always goes with you! While my fruitless wanderings led me through so many lands, you, sitting quietly under your oaks, let the days slip by without counting them. Your needs were your only guide, and, far better than I, you have reached wisdom's goal through your play and your sleep—like children. Your soul may sometimes have been touched by the melancholy of extreme happiness, but you emerged soon enough from this fleeting sadness, and your eyes rose toward heaven, tenderly seeking the mysterious presence which takes pity on the poor Indian."

Here René's voice broke again, and the young man bowed his head. Chactas held his hands out in the shadows, and, touching his son's arm, he exclaimed, deeply moved, "My son! My dear son!" The ring of his voice drew René from his revery, and, blushing at his weakness, he begged his father to forgive him.

Then the aged Indian spoke thus: "My young friend, a heart such as yours cannot be placid; but you must try to temper your character, which has already brought you so much grief. Do not be surprised that you suffer more than others from the experiences of life; a great soul necessarily holds more sorrow than a little one. Go on with your story. You have taken us through part of Europe; now tell us about your own country. As you know, I have seen France and am deeply attached to it. I would like to hear of the great chief who has now passed on, and whose magnificent cabin[10] I once visited. My child, I live only for the past. An old man with his memories is like a decrepit oak in our woods; no longer able to

10. *great chief . . . cabin:* Louis XIV and Versailles.

adorn itself with its own foliage, it is obliged to cover its nakedness with foreign plants which have taken root on its ancient boughs."

Calmed by these words, René once more took up the story of his heart.

Alas, father, I cannot tell you about that great century, for I saw only the end of it as a child; it had already drawn to a close when I returned to my land. Never has a more astonishing, nor a more sudden change taken place in a people. From the loftiness of genius, from respect for religion and dignity in manners everything suddenly degenerated to cleverness and godlessness and corruption.

So it had been useless indeed to try to find something in my own country to calm this anxiety, this burning desire which pursues me everywhere. Studying the world had taught me nothing, and yet I had lost the freshness of innocence.

By her strange behavior, my sister seemed bent on increasing my gloom. She had left Paris a few days before my arrival, and when I wrote that I expected to join her, she hastened to dissuade me, claiming she did not know where her business might take her. How sadly I reflected on human affection. It cools in our presence and vanishes in our absence; in adversity it grows weak and in good fortune weaker still.

Soon I found myself lonelier in my native land than I had been on foreign soil. I was tempted to plunge for a time into a totally new environment which I could not understand and which did not understand me. My heart was not yet wasted by any kind of passion, and I sought to find someone to whom I could become attached. But I soon discovered that I was giving more of myself than I was receiving of others. It was neither lofty language nor deep feeling which the world asked of me. I was simply reducing my being to the level of society. Everywhere I was taken for an impractical dreamer. Ashamed of the role I was playing and increasingly repulsed by men and things, I finally decided to retire to some smaller community where I could live completely by myself.

At first I was happy enough in this secluded, independent life. Unknown by everyone, I could mingle with the crowd—that vast desert of men! Often I would sit in some lonely church, where I could spend hour after hour in meditation. I saw poor women prostrating themselves before the Almighty or sinners kneeling at the seat of penitence. None emerged from this retreat without a more serene expression, and the muffled noises drifting in from outside seemed like waves of passion or storms of the world subsiding at the foot of the Lord's temple. Mighty God, who from Thy solitude couldst see my tears falling in that holy shelter, Thou knowest how many times I threw myself at Thy feet, imploring Thee to relieve me of the weight of my existence or make over the old man within me! Ah, who has never felt a need of regeneration, of growing young in the waters of the spring and refreshing his soul in the fountain of life? Who does not sometimes feel himself crushed by the burden of his own corruption and incapable of anything great or noble or just!

When night had closed in I would start back to my retreat, pausing on the bridges to watch the sunset. As the great star kindled the mists of the city, it seemed to swing slowly in a golden fluid like the pendulum of some clock of the ages. Then I retired with the night through a labyrinth of solitary streets. As I passed lights shining in the dwellings of men, I imagined myself among the scenes of sorrow and joy which they revealed, and I reflected that under all those roofs sheltering so many people, I had not a single friend. In the midst of these thoughts, the hour began tolling in measured cadence from the tower of the Gothic cathedral, and its message was taken up from church to church in a wide range of tones and distances. Alas!! Every hour in society lays open a grave and draws fresh tears.

But this life, which at first was so delightful, soon became intolerable. I grew weary of constantly repeating the same scenes and the same thoughts, and I began to search my soul to discover what I really sought. I did not know; but suddenly it occurred to me that I might be happy in the woods. Immediately I resolved to adopt a country exile where I could spend the rest of my days, for, though scarcely begun, my life had already consumed centuries.

I adopted this plan with the ardor typical of all my projects and left at once to retire into seclusion in some rustic cabin, just as previously I had left to travel around the world.

People accuse me of being unpredictable in my tastes, of being unable for long to cherish any single illusion. They consider me the victim of an imagination which plunges toward the end of all pleasures as though it suffered from their duration. They accuse me of forever overreaching the goal I can achieve. Alas! I am only in search of some unknown good, whose intuition pursues me relentlessly. Am I to blame if everywhere I find limitations, if all that is finite I consider worthless? And yet, I feel that I love the monotony in the feelings of life, and, if I were still! foolish enough to believe in happiness, I would seek it in an orderly existence.

Total solitude and the spectacle of nature soon brought me to a state almost impossible to describe. Practically bereft of relatives and friends on earth, and never having been in love, I was furiously driven by an excess of life. Sometimes I blushed suddenly and felt torrents of burning lava surging through my heart. Sometimes I would cry out involuntarily, and the night was disturbed both by my dreams and by sleepless cares. I felt I needed something to fill the vast emptiness of my existence. I went down into the valley and up on the mountain, calling, with all the strength of my desire, for the ideal creature of some future passion. I embraced her in the winds and thought I heard her in the river's moaning. Everything became this vision of my imagination—the stars in the skies and the very principle of life in the universe.

Nevertheless, this state of calm and anxiety, of poverty and wealth was not wholly without charm. One day I amused myself by stripping the leaves from a willow branch, one by one, and throwing them into the stream, attaching a thought to each leaf as the current carried it off. A king in fear of losing his crown in a sudden revolution does not feel sharper pangs of anguish than did I, as I watched each peril threatening the remains of my bough. O frailty of mortal man! O childishness of the human heart, which never grows old! How infantile our haughty reason can become! And yet how many men attach their existence to such petty things as my willow leaves!

How can I describe the host of fleeting sensations I felt in my rambles? The echoes of passion in the emptiness of a lonely heart are like the murmurings of wind and water in the silence of the wilderness—they offer their joy, but cannot be portrayed.

Autumn came upon me in the midst of this uncertainty, and I welcomed the stormy months with exhilaration. Sometimes I wished I were one of those warriors who wander amongst winds, clouds, and phantoms, while at other times I was envious even of the shepherd's lot, as I watched him warming his hands by the humble brushwood fire he had built in a corner of the woods. I listened to his melancholy airs and remembered that in every land the natural song of man is sad, even when it renders happiness. Our heart is a defective instrument, a lyre with several chords missing, which forces us to express our joyful moods in notes meant for lamentation.

During the day I roamed the great heath with its forests in the distance. How little I needed to wander off in revery—a dry leaf blown before me by the wind, a cabin with smoke drifting up through the bare tree tops, the moss trembling in the north wind on the trunk of an oak, an isolated rock, or a lonely pond where the withered reed whispered . . . The solitary steeple far off in the valley often drew my attention. Many times, too, my eyes followed birds of passage as they flew overhead. I imagined the unknown shores and distant climes for which they were bound—and how I would have loved to be on their wings! A deep intuition tormented me; I felt that I was no more than a traveler myself, but a voice from heaven seemed to be telling me, "Man, the season for thy migration is not yet come; wait for the wind of death to spring up, then wilt thou spread thy wings and fly toward those unexplored realms for which thy heart longs."

Rise swiftly, coveted storms, coming to bear me off to the spaces of another life! This was my plea, as I plunged ahead with great strides, my face all aflame and the wind whistling through my hair, feeling neither rain nor frost, bewitched, tormented, and virtually possessed by the demon of my heart.

At night, when the fierce wind shook my hut and the rain fell in torrents on my roof, as I looked out through my window and saw the moon furrowing the thick clouds like a pallid vessel plough-ing through the waves, it seemed to me that life grew so strong in the depths of my heart that I had the power to create worlds. Ah, if only I could have shared with someone else the delight I felt! O Lord, if only Thou hadst given me a woman after my heart's desire, if Thou hadst drawn from my side an Eve, as Thou didst once for our first father, and brought her to me by the hand . . . Heavenly beauty! I would have knelt down before you, and then, clasping you in my arms, I would have begged the Eternal Being to grant you the rest of my life!

Alas! I was alone, alone in the world! A mysterious apathy gradu-ally took hold of my body. My aversion for life, which I had felt as a child, was returning with renewed intensity. Soon my heart sup-plied no more nourishment for my thought, and I was aware of my existence only in a deep sense of weariness.

For some time I struggled against my malady, but only half-heartedly, with no firm will to conquer it. Finally, unable to find any cure for this strange wound of my heart, which was nowhere and everywhere, I resolved to give up my life.[11]

Priest of the Almighty, now listening to my story, forgive this poor creature whom Heaven had almost stripped of his reason. I was imbued with faith, and I reasoned like a sinner; my heart loved God, and my mind knew Him not. My actions, my words, my feel-ings, my thoughts were nothing but contradictions, enigmas, and lies. But does man always know what he wishes, and is he always sure of what he thinks?

Affection, society, and seclusion, everything was slipping away from me at once. I had tried everything, and everything had proved disastrous. Rejected by the world and abandoned by Amelia, what had I left now that solitude had failed me? It was the last support which I had hoped could save me, and now I felt it too giving way and dropping into the abyss!

Having decided to rid myself of life's burden, I now resolved to use the full consciousness of my mind in committing this desperate

11. *resolved . . . life:* In his *Memories from Beyond the Grave,* Chateaubriand mentions he once tried suicide as a youth, but the gun failed to fire.

act. Nothing made it necessary to take action quickly. I did not set a definite time for my death, so that I might savor the final moments of my existence in long, full draughts and gather all my strength, like the men of antiquity, to feel my soul escaping.

I felt obliged, however, to make arrangements about my worldly goods and had to write to Amelia. A few complaints escaped me concerning her neglect, and doubtless I let her sense the tenderness which overcome my heart as I wrote. Nevertheless, I thought I had succeeded in concealing my secret; but my sister was accustomed to reading into the recesses of my heart, and she guessed it at once. She was alarmed at the restrained tone of my letter and at my questions about business matters, which had never before concerned me. Instead of answering she came to see me at once with no advance warning.

To realize how bitter my sorrow was later to be and how delighted I was now to see Amelia again, you must understand that she was the only person in the world I had ever loved, and all my feelings converged in her with the sweetness of my childhood memories. And so I welcomed Amelia with a kind of ecstasy in my heart. It had been so long since I had found someone who could understand me and to whom I could reveal my soul!

Throwing herself in my arms, Amelia said to me: "How ungrateful! You want to die and your sister is still alive! You doubt her heart! Don't explain and don't apologize, I know everything; I guessed your intention as though I had been with you. Do you suppose I can be misled, I who watched the first stirrings of your heart? So this is your unhappy character, your dislikes and injustices! Swear to me, while I press you to my heart, swear that this is the last time you will give in to your foolishness; make an oath never to try to take your life again."

As she uttered these words, Amelia looked at me compassionately, tenderly, covering my brow with kisses; she was almost a mother, she was something more tender. Alas! Once again my heart opened out to life's every joy. Like a child, I had only to be consoled, and I quickly surrendered to Amelia's influence. She insisted on a solemn oath, and I readily swore it, not suspecting that I could ever again be unhappy.

Thus we spent more than a month getting used to the delight of being together again. When, instead of finding myself alone in the morning, I heard my sister's voice, I felt a thrill of joy and contentment. Amelia had received some divine attribute from nature. Her soul had the same innocent grace as her body; her feelings were surpassingly gentle, and in her manner there was nothing but softness and a certain dreamy quality. It seemed as though her heart, her thought, and her voice were all sighing in harmony. From her womanly side came her shyness and love, while her purity and melody were angelic.

But the time had come when I was to atone for all my erratic ways. In my madness I had gone so far as to hope some calamity would strike me, so that I might at least have some real reason for suffering—it was a terrible wish, which God in His anger has granted all too well!

O my friends, what am I about to reveal to you! See how these tears flow from my eyes. Can I even . . . Only a few days ago nothing could have torn this secret from me . . . But now, it is all over!

Still, O revered elders, let this story be buried in silence forever; remember that it was meant to be told only under this tree in the wilderness.

Winter was drawing to a close, when I became aware that Amelia was losing her health and repose, even as she was beginning to restore them to me. She was growing thin, her eyes became hollow, her manner listless, and her voice unsteady. People or solitude, my absence or presence, night or day—everything frightened her. Involuntary sighs would die on her lips. Sometimes long distances would not tire her out, and at other times she could barely move about. She would take up her work and set it down, open a book and find it impossible to read, begin a sentence and not finish it, and then she would suddenly burst into tears and go off to pray.

I tried vainly to discover her secret. When I pressed her in my arms and questioned her, she smilingly answered that she was like myself—she did not know what was wrong with her.

Thus three months went by, and each day her state grew worse. The source of her tears seemed to be a mysterious correspondence she was having, for she appeared calmer or more disturbed according to the letters she received. Finally one morning as the time for breakfast had passed, I went up to her rooms. I knocked, but received no answer. I pushed the door ajar; no one was in the room. On the mantel there was an envelope addressed to me. Snatching it up with trembling fingers, I tore it open and read this letter, which will remain with me forever to discourage any possible feeling of joy.

To RENÉ:

"My brother, Heaven bears me witness that I would give up my life a thousand times to spare you one moment's grief. But miserable as I am, I can do nothing to make you happy. Forgive me, then, for stealing away from you as though I were guilty. I could never have resisted your pleas, and yet I had to leave. . . . Lord, have pity on me!

"You know, René, that the religious life has always attracted me. Now the time has come to heed Heaven's call. Only why have I waited so long? God is punishing me for it. It was for you alone that I remained in the world . . . But forgive me; I am upset by the sadness of having to leave you.

"Dear brother, it is only now that I feel the full need of those retreats which I have heard you condemn so often. There are certain sorrows which separate us from men forever; were it not for such shelters, what would become of some unfortunate women! . . . I am convinced that you, too, would find rest in these religious havens, for the world has nothing to offer which is worthy of you.

"I shall not remind you of your oath; I know how reliable your word is. You have sworn it, and you will go on living for my sake. Is there anything more pitiful than thinking constantly of suicide? For a man of your character it is easy to die. Believe me, it is far more difficult to live.

"But, my brother, you must give up this solitude at once; it is not good for you. Try to find some kind of occupation. I realize that you bitterly despise the usual necessity of 'becoming established' in France. But you must not scorn all the experience and wisdom of our fathers. Dear René, it is better to resemble ordinary men a little more and be a little less miserable.

"Perhaps you will find relief from your cares in marriage. A wife and children would take up your days. And what woman would not try to make you happy! The ardor of your soul, the beauty of your thought, your noble, passionate air, that proud and tender expression in your eyes, everything would assure you of her love and loyalty. Ah, how joyfully she would clasp you in her arms and press you to her heart! How her eyes and her thoughts would always be fixed on you to shield you from the slightest pain! In your presence she would become all love and innocence; you would feel that you had found a sister again.

"I am leaving for the convent of B——. It is a cloister built by the edge of the sea and wholly suited to the state of my soul. At night, from within my cell, I shall hear the murmur of the waves as they lap against the convent walls. I shall dream of those walks we once took through the woods, when we fancied we heard the sound of the sea in the tops of the waving pines. Beloved childhood friend, will I ever see you again? Though hardly older than you, I once rocked you in your cradle. Many times we used to sleep together. Ah, if we might one day be together again in the same tomb! But no, I must sleep alone beneath the icy marble of that sanctuary where girls who have never known love rest in eternal peace.

"I do not know whether you will succeed in reading these lines, blurred as they are by my tears. After all, sweet friend, a little sooner or a little later, would we not have had to part? Need I speak of

the uncertainty and emptiness of life? You remember young M——
whose ship was lost off the island of Mauritius.[12] When you received his last letter a few months after his death, his earthly remains
did not even exist any more, and just when you began to mourn for
him in Europe, others in the Indies were ending their mourning.
What can man be, then, when his memory perishes so quickly!
When some of his friends learn of his death, others are already
consoled! Tell me, dear, beloved René, will my memory, too, vanish
so quickly from your heart? O my brother, I tear myself away from
you in earthly time only that we may not be parted in eternity.

AMELIA

"P.S. I am enclosing the deed of my worldly goods. I hope you
will not reject this token of my affection."

Had lightning struck at my feet I could not have been seized by
greater panic. What secret was Amelia hiding from me? Who was
forcing her into the religious life so suddenly? And had she reconciled me to life through her tender affection only to abandon me
now so abruptly? Oh, why had she come back to turn me aside from
my plan? A feeling of pity had brought her back to me, but now,
tired of her disagreeable duty, she was impatiently leaving me to
my misery, though I had no one but her in all the world. People
imagine they have done something wonderful when they have kept
a man from death! Such were my sad reflections. Then, examining
my own feelings, I said, "Ungrateful Amelia, if you were in my
place, if, like myself, you were lost in the void of your existence,
ah, you would not be forsaken by your bother!"

And yet, as I reread the letter, I felt in its tone something so sad,
so tender, that my heart melted completely. Suddenly I had a
thought which gave me hope. It occurred to me that Amelia might
have fallen in love with a man, and dared not admit it. This suspicion seemed to explain her melancholy, her mysterious correspondence, and the passionate tone pervading her letter. I wrote to
her at once, begging her to open her heart to me. Her answer was
not long in coming, but revealed nothing about her secret. She
wrote only that she had obtained dispensation from the novitiate
and was about to pronounce her vows.

I was exasperated by Amelia's stubbornness, by the enigma of
her words, and her lack of confidence in my affection. After hesitating a little about what I would do next, I decided to go to B——
to attempt one last effort to win back my sister. On my way I had
to pass through the region where I was brought up. When I caught
sight of the woods where I had spent the only happy moments of

12. *Mauritius:* in the Indian Ocean.

my life I could not hold back my tears, and I found it impossible to resist the temptation of bidding them a last farewell.[13]

My elder brother had sold the family heritage, and the new owner did not live on the estate. I went up to the château through a long lane of pines. Walking across the deserted courtyard I stopped to gaze at the closed or partly broken windows, the thistle growing at the foot of the walls, the leaves strewn over the threshold of the doors, and that lonely stone stairway where so often I had seen my father and his faithful servants. The steps were already covered with moss, and yellow stock grew between the loose, shaky stones. A new caretaker brusquely opened the doors for me. When I hesitated in crossing the threshold, the fellow exclaimed: "Well, are you going to do what that strange woman did who was here a few days ago? She fainted as she was about to come in, and I had to carry her back to her carriage." It was easy enough for me to recognize the "strange woman" who, like myself, had come back to this spot to find memories and tears!

Drying my eyes with a handkerchief I entered the dwelling of my ancestors. I paced through the resounding halls where nothing could be heard but the beat of my footsteps. The chambers were barely lit by a faint glimmer filtering in through the closed shutters. First I went to see the room where my mother had given her life to bring me into the world, then the room to which my father used to retire, after that the one where I had slept in my cradle, and finally the one where my sister had received my first confessions into the bosom of her love. Everywhere the rooms were neglected, and spiders spun their webs in the abandoned beds. I left the château abruptly and strode quickly away, never daring to turn my head. How sweet, but how fleeting, are those moments spent together by brothers and sisters in their younger years under the wing of their aged parents! The family of man endures but a day, and then God's breath scatters it away like smoke. The son barely knows the father or the father the son, the brother the sister or the sister the brother! The oak sees its acorns take root all around it; it is not so with the children of men!

Arriving at B—— I was taken to the convent, where I asked for an opportunity to speak with my sister. I was told she could not see anybody. I wrote to her, and she replied that, as she was about to be consecrated to God,[14] she was not permitted to turn her thought to the world, and if I loved her, I would avoid burdening her with my sorrow. To this she added: "However, if you plan to appear at

---

13. *farewell:* Chateaubriand saw the old château at Combourg in 1791, just before he left for America, and revisited it once more in 1801.

14. *consecrated to God:* Chateau-briand's sister Lucile never entered a convent, but was briefly married when she was 32 to a man over twice her age. She died at the age of 40.

the altar on the day of my profession, be pleased to serve as my father. It is the only role worthy of your courage, and the only fitting one for our affection and my peace of mind."

This cold determination resisting my burning affection threw me into a violent rage. There were times when I was about to return where I had come from; then, again, I wanted to stay for the sole purpose of disturbing the sacrifice. Hell even goaded me on with the thought of stabbing myself in the church and mingling my last sighs with the vows tearing my sister away from me. The mother superior of the convent sent word that a bench had been prepared for me in the sanctuary and invited me to attend the ceremony, which was to take place the very next day.

At daybreak I heard the first sound of the bells . . . About ten o'clock I dragged myself to the convent in a deathlike stupor. Nothing can ever again be tragic to a man who has witnessed such a spectacle, nor can anything ever again be painful for one who has lived through it. The church was filled with a huge throng. I was led to the bench in the sanctuary, and immediately I fell on my knees, practically unconscious of where I was or what I intended to do. The priest was already at the altar. Suddenly the mysterious grille swung open and Amelia came forward resplendent in all the finery of the world. So beautiful was she, so divinely radiant her countenance, that she brought a gasp of surprise and admiration from the onlookers. Overcome by the glorious sorrow of her saintly figure and crushed by the grandeur of religion, I saw all my plans of violence crumbling. My strength left me. I felt myself bound by an all-powerful hand, and, instead of blasphemy and threats, I could find in my heart only profound adoration and sighs of humility.

Amelia took her place beneath a canopy, and the sacrifice began by the light of torches amid flowers and aromas which lent their charm to this great renunciation. At the offertory the priest put off all his ornaments, keeping only a linen tunic; then, mounting the pulpit, he described in a simple, moving discourse the joy of the virgin who is consecrated to the Lord. As he pronounced the words, "She appeared like the incense consumed in the fire," deep calm and heavenly fragrances seemed to spread through the audience. It was as if the mystic dove had spread its wings to offer its shelter, while angels seemed to hover over the altar and fly back toward heaven with crowns and perfumes.

Ending his discourse, the priest donned his vestments once more and went on with the sacrifice. Sustained by two young sisters, Amelia knelt down on the bottom step of the altar. Then someone came to get me in order that I might fulfill my role as a father. At the sound of my faltering steps in the sanctuary Amelia was about to collapse. I was placed beside the priest for I was to offer him the scissors. At that moment once again I suddenly felt my passion flame up within me. I was about to burst out in fury, when Amelia recovered her courage and darted such a sad and reproachful glance at me that I was transfixed. Religion was triumphant. Taking advantage of my confusion, Amelia boldly brought her head forward; under the holy blades her magnificent tresses fell in every direction. Her worldly ornaments were replaced by a long muslin robe, which sacrificed none of her appeal. The cares of her brow vanished under a linen headband, and the mysterious veil, that two-fold symbol of virginity and religion, was placed on her shorn head. Never had she appeared so beautiful. The penitent's eye was fixed on the dust of the world, while her soul was already in heaven.

However, Amelia had not yet pronounced her vows, and in order to die for the world she had to pass through the tomb. She therefore lay down on the marble slab, and over her was spread a pall, while a torch burned at each of the four corners. With his stole round his neck and his book in his hand, the priest began the service for the dead. The young virgins took it up. O joys of religion, you are powerful indeed, but oh, how terrible! I was obliged to kneel beside this mournful sight. Suddenly a confused murmur emerged from under the shroud, and as I leaned over, my ears were struck by these dreadful words, audible only to myself: "Merciful God, let me never again rise from this deathbed, and may Thy blessings be lavished on my brother, who has never shared my forbidden passion!"[15]

With these words escaping from the bier the horrible truth suddenly grew clear, and I lost control of my senses. Falling across the death sheet I pressed my sister in my arms and cried out: "Chaste spouse of Christ, receive this last embrace through the chill of death and the depths of eternity which already have parted you from your brother!"

This impulse, this cry, and these tears disturbed the ceremony. The priest interrupted himself, the sisters shut the grille, the crowd pushed forward toward the altar, and I was carried away unconscious. Surely I was not grateful to those who revived me! Opening my eyes, I learned that the sacrifice had been consummated, and my sister had been taken with a violent fever. She sent word begging me not to try to see her again. O misery of my life—a sister fearing to talk to her brother, and a brother afraid of having his sister hear his voice! I left the convent as though it were the place of atonement which prepares us in flames for the blessed life, and where all has been lost, as it is in hell—save hope.

15. *forbidden passion:* Some scholars have tried to demonstrate that Amelia's incestuous love had a basis in Chateaubriand's reciprocated affection for his sister Lucile. It is perhaps safest to recall that incest became a popular romantic theme: in Gothic novels, Goethe's *Wilhelm Meister*, Shelley's *Cenci*, Byron's *Manfred*, etc.

There is strength in our soul to sustain us in our own misfortunes, but to become the involuntary cause of someone else's misfortune is completely unbearable. Now that I understood my sister's grief, I imagined how she must have suffered. Several things which I had been unable to understand now became clear—the joy tinged with sadness which my sister had felt when I was leaving on my travels, the efforts she made to avoid me when I had returned, and at the same time, the weakness which kept her from entering a convent for so long. In her sorrow she must have tried to convince herself that she could yet be cured! As for the secret correspondence which had so deceived me—that was apparently made up of her plans to retire from the world and her arrangements for dispensation from the novitiate, as well as the transfer of her property to me.

O my friends, now I knew what it meant to shed tears for grief which was far from imaginary! My emotions, which had been vague for so long, now seized avidly upon this, its first prey. I even felt a kind of unexpected satisfaction in the fullness of my anguish, and I became aware, with a sense of hidden joy, that sorrow is not a feeling which consumes itself like pleasure.

I had wanted to withdraw from the world before receiving the Almighty's command—that was a great crime. God had sent me Amelia both to save and to punish me. Thus does every guilty thought and forbidden act bring on disorder and sorrow. Amelia had begged me to continue living, and I owed it to her not to aggravate her woes. Besides—how strange it seems!—now that my sorrows were real, I no longer wished to die. My grief had become an immediate concern occupying my every moment, so thoroughly is my heart molded of weariness and misery!

And so I suddenly settled on another plan of action; I determined to leave Europe and go to America.[16] At that very time, in the port of B——, they were fitting out a fleet of ships bound for Louisiana. I made arrangements with one of the captains, wrote to Amelia about my plan, and prepared to leave.

My sister had been at the gates of death, but God had reserved for her the supreme crown of virgins and chose not to call her to Him so soon. Her trials on earth were prolonged. Coming down once again into life's painful path she went courageously forward as a heroine in the face of affliction; bent under the cross she saw in her struggles the certainty of triumph and overwhelming glory in her overwhelming woe.

The sale to my brother of what little property I still had, the long preparations of the convoy, and unfavorable winds, all held me in

---

16. *America:* Chateaubriand spent some five months in America (1791– 1792), though it is doubtful whether he saw the "Meschacebe."

port a long time. Each morning I would go for news of Amelia, and always I returned with new reasons for weeping and admiring.

I wandered endlessly about the convent at the edge of the sea. Often I would notice, in a little grilled window overlooking the deserted beach, a nun sitting in a pensive attitude. She was meditating as she gazed out over the broad ocean, where some vessel could be seen sailing toward the ends of the earth. Several times, in the moonlight, I again saw the nun at the bars of the same window. With the star of night shining down upon her, she was contemplating the sea, listening, it seemed, to the sound of the waves breaking sadly on the lonely shores.

I can still hear the bell in the silence of the night calling the sisters to vigils and prayer. As it tolled in slow rhythm and the virgins moved silently toward the altar of the Almighty, I hastened to the convent. There, alone at the foot of the walls, I would listen in reverent rapture to the last strains of the hymns, as they blended beneath the temple vaults with the gentle murmur of the waves.

I do not know why all these things, which should have intensified my anguish, served instead to soften its sting. My tears were less bitter when I shed them out there on those rocks in the wind. My very grief, which was so rare, bore within itself some remedy; for there is joy in the uncommon, even if it is an uncommon calamity. This almost gave me hope that my sister too might become less miserable.

A letter I received from her before my departure seemed to confirm this feeling. Amelia pitied me tenderly for my sorrow, and assured me that time was healing her wound. "I have not given up hoping for happiness," she wrote. "The very immensity of my sacrifice calms me somewhat, now that it is all over. The simplicity of my companions, the purity of their vows, the regularity of their life, everything spreads its healing balm over my days. When I hear the storms raging and the sea bird beating its wings at my window, I, poor dove of heaven, reflect on my joy in finding a shelter from the tempest. Here is the holy mountain, the lofty summit where we hear the last faint murmurs of the earth and the opening harmonies of heaven. It is here that religion gently beguiles a tender soul. For the most violent passion it substitutes a kind of burning chastity in which lover and virgin are at one. It purifies every sigh, it makes the ephemeral flame inviolate, and it blends its divine calm and innocence with the remains of confusion and worldly joy in a heart seeking rest and a life seeking solitude."

I do not know what heaven still holds in store for me, or whether it meant to warn me that everywhere my steps would be harried by storms. The order was given for our fleet to set sail; as the sun began sinking, several vessels had already weighed anchor. I made arrangements to spend the last night on shore writing my farewell letter to Amelia. Around midnight, as my attention was absorbed in my thoughts and tears moistened my paper, my ear was suddenly drawn to the wailing of the winds. As I listened, cannon shots of alarm could be heard through the storm, together with the knell tolling in the convent. I plunged out to the shore where all was deserted and nothing could be heard but the roar of the surf. I sat down on a rock. On one side I could see the vast expanse of shimmering waves, and on the other the somber walls of the convent vaguely reaching up and fading away in the skies. A dim light shone out from the grilled window. O my Amelia! Was it you, on your knees at the foot of the cross, praying to the God of Tempests to spare your unhappy brother? Storm on the waves, and calm in your retreat; men shattered on the reefs before an unshakeable haven; infinity on the other side of a cell wall; the tossing lights of ships, and the motionless beacon of the convent; the uncertain lot of the seaman, and the vestal's vision in a single day of all the days of her life; and yet, O Amelia, a soul such as yours, stormy as the ocean; a catastrophe more dreadful than the mariner's—this whole picture is still deeply engraved in my memory.

Sun of this new sky, now witness to my tears, echoes of American shores repeating these accents, it was on the morrow of that terrible night that I leaned over the ship's stern and watched my native land disappearing forever! Long I stood there and gazed for the last time at the trees of my country swaying on the shore and the height of the convent sinking over the horizon.

As René came to the end of his story he drew a sheet of paper from his breast and gave it to Father Souël; then, throwing himself into the arms of Chactas and stifling his sobs, he waited as the missionary read through the letter.

It came from the mother superior of B——, and described the last hours in the life of Sister Amelia of Mercy, who had died a victim of her zeal and charity, while caring for companions stricken by a contagious disease. The entire community was inconsolable, and Amelia was regarded as a saint. The mother superior added that in her thirty years as head of the house she had never seen a sister so gentle and calm in disposition and none so happy to be relieved of the world's tribulations.

Chactas clasped René in his arms; the old man was weeping. "My child," he said to his son, "how I wish Father Aubry[17] were here. He could draw from the depths of his heart a strange calm which could pacify storms and yet seemed akin to them. He was

---

17. *Father Aubry:* the missionary in *Atala*, who shelters the two Indian lov- ers. It is Aubry who with Chactas buries Atala, after she commits suicide.

the moon on a stormy night. The moving clouds are powerless to carry it along in their flight; pure and unperturbed, it advances serenely above them. Alas, as for me, everything disturbs me and carries me away!"

Until now Father Souël had listened to René's story with a severe countenance and without uttering a word. Although inwardly warm-hearted, he presented to the world an inflexible character. It was the sachem's tenderness which made him break his silence.

"Nothing," he began, "nothing in your story deserves the pity you are now being shown. I see a young man infatuated with illusions, satisfied with nothing, withdrawn from the burdens of society, and wrapped up in idle dreams. A man is not superior, sir, because he sees the world in a dismal light. Only those of limited vision can hate men and life. Look a little farther and you will soon be convinced that all those griefs about which you complain are absolutely nothing. Why, what a shame not to be able to think of the only real misfortune in your life without having to blush! All the purity, all the virtue and faith, and all the crowns of a saint can scarcely make the very idea of your troubles tolerable. Your sister has atoned for her sin, but if I must speak frankly, I fear that through some terrible justice, that confession, emerging from the depths of the tomb, has in turn stirred up your own soul. What do you do all alone in the woods using up your days and neglecting all your duties? You will tell me that saints have retired to the wilderness. Yes, but they were there weeping and subduing their passions, while you seem to be wasting your time inflaming your own. Presumptuous youth, you thought man sufficient unto himself. Know now that solitude is bad for the man who does not live with God. It increases the soul's power while robbing it at the same time of every opportunity to find expression. Whoever has been endowed with talent must devote it to serving his fellow men, for if he does not make use of it, he is first punished by an inner misery, and sooner or later Heaven visits on him a fearful retribution."

Disturbed and humiliated by these words, René raised his head from the bosom of Chactas. The blind sachem began to smile, and this smile of the lips, unrelated as it was to the expression in his eyes, seemed to possess some mysterious, heavenly quality. "My son," said the old man who had once loved Atala, "he speaks severely to both of us; he is reprimanding the old man and the young, and he is right. Yes, you must give up this strange life, which holds nothing but care. Happiness can be found only in the common paths.

"One day the Meschacebe, while yet rather close to its source, grew weary of being only a limpid stream. It called for snows from the mountains, waters from the rivers, and rains from the tempests, and it overran its banks and laid waste its lovely forests. At first the haughty stream applauded its own power. But soon, seeing how everything grew barren along its path and how it now flowed abandoned in its solitude with its waters always troubled, it longed once again for the humble bed which nature had prepared for it, and it pined for the birds and the flowers, the trees and the streams which were once its modest companions along its peaceful course."

Chactas grew silent, and off in the reeds of the Meschacebe the flamingo's call could be heard announcing a storm for the middle of the day. The three friends started back toward their cabins. René walked silently between the missionary, who was praying, and the blind sachem, who kept feeling his way. It is said that, encouraged by the two elders, René returned to his wife, but still found no happiness. Soon afterwards, along with Chactas and Father Souël, he perished in the massacres of the French and Natchez in Louisiana. They still point out a rock where he would go off and sit in the setting sun.

E. T. A. HOFFMANN
(1776–1822)
A New Year's Eve Adventure*

Foreword by the Editor[1]

The Traveling Enthusiast, from whose journals we are presenting another "fancy-flight in the manner of Jacques Callot,"[2] has apparently not separated the events of his inner life from those of the outside world; in fact we cannot determine where one ends and the other begins. But even if you cannot see this boundary very clearly, dear reader, the Geisterseher[3] may beckon you to his side, and before you are even aware of it, you will be in a strange magical realm where figures of fantasy step right into your own life, and are as cordial with you as your oldest friends. I beg of you—take them as such, go along with their remarkable doings, yield to the shudders and thrills that they produce, since the more you go along with them, the better they can operate. What more can I do for the Traveling Enthusiast who has encountered so much strangeness and madness, everywhere and at all times, but especially on New Year's Eve in Berlin?

* Written in 1814, published in 1816 in *Fancy-Flights in the Manner of Jacques Callot* (see note 1).
1. Hoffman himself.
2. A French seventeenth-century painter and engraver, popular with the Romantics for his fantastic, grotesque scenes.
3. Seer, medium.

My Beloved

I had a feeling of death in my heart—ice-cold death—and the sensation branched out like sharp, growing icicles into nerves that were already boiling with heat. I ran like a madman—no hat, no coat—out into the lightless stormy winter night. The weather vanes were grinding and creaking in the wind, as if Time's eternal gearwork were audibly rotating and the old year were being rolled away like a heavy weight, and ponderously pushed into a gloom-filled abyss.

You must surely know that on this season, Christmas and New Year's, even though it's so fine and pleasant for all of you, I am always driven out of my peaceful cell onto a raging, lashing sea. Christmas! Holidays that have a rosy glow for me. I can hardly wait for it, I look forward to it so much. I am a better, finer man than the rest of the year, and there isn't a single gloomy, misanthropic thought in my mind. Once again I am a boy, shouting with joy. The faces of the angels laugh to me from the gilded fretwork decorations in the shops decorated for Christmas, and the awesome tones of the church organ penetrate the noisy bustle of the streets, as if coming from afar, with "Unto us a child is born." But after the holidays everything becomes colorless again, and the glow dies away and disappears into drab darkness.

Every year more and more flowers drop away withered, their buds eternally sealed; there is no spring sun that can bring the warmth of new life into old dried-out branches. I know this well enough, but the Enemy never stops maliciously rubbing it in as the year draws to an end. I hear a mocking whisper: "Look what you have lost this year; so many worthwhile things that you'll never see again. But all this makes you wiser, less tied to trivial pleasures, more serious and solid—even though you don't enjoy yourself very much."

Every New Year's Eve the Devil keeps a special treat for me. He knows just the right moment to jam his claw into my heart, keeping up a fine mockery while he licks the blood that wells out. And there is always someone around to help him, just as yesterday the Justizrat[4] came to his aid. He (the Justizrat) holds a big celebration every New Year's Eve, and likes to give everyone something special as a New Year's present. Only he is so clumsy and bumbling about it, for all his pains, that what was meant to give pleasure usually turns into a mess that is half slapstick and half torture.

I walked into his front hall, and the Justizrat came running to meet me, holding me back for a moment from the Holy of Holies out of which the odors of tea and expensive perfumes were pouring. He looked especially pleased with himself. He smirked at me in a very strange way and said, "My dear friend, there's something nice waiting for you in the next room. Nothing like it for a New Year's

4. Counsellor, prosecutor.

surprise. But don't be afraid!"

I felt that sinking feeling in my heart. Something was wrong, I knew, and I suddenly began to feel depressed and edgy. Then the doors were opened. I took up my courage and stepped forward, marched in, and among the women sitting on the sofa I saw *her*.

Yes, it was she. She herself. I hadn't seen her for years, and yet in one lightning flash the happiest moments of my life came back to me, and gone was the pain that had resulted from being separated from her.

What marvellous chance brought her here? What miracle introduced her into the Justizrat's circle—I didn't even know that he knew her. But I didn't think of any of these questions; all I knew was that she was mine again.

I must have stood there as if halted magically in midmotion. The Justizrat kept nudging me and muttering, "Mmmm? Mmmm? How about it?"

I started to walk again, mechanically, but I saw only her, and it was all that I could do to force out, "My God, my God, it's Julia!" I was practically at the tea table before she even noticed me, but then she stood up and said coldly, "I'm so delighted to see you here. You are looking well." And with that she sat down again and asked the woman sitting next to her on the sofa, "Is there going to be anything interesting at the theatre the next few weeks?"

You see a miraculously beautiful flower, glowing with beauty, filling the air with scent, hinting at even more hidden beauty. You hurry over to it, but the moment that you bend down to look into its chalice, the glistening petals are pushed aside and out pops a smooth, cold, slimy, little lizard that tries to cut you down with its glare.

That's just what happened to me. Like a perfect oaf I made a bow to the ladies, and since spite and idiocy often go together, as I stepped back I knocked a cup of hot tea out of the Justizrat's hand —he was standing right behind me—and all over his beautifully pleated jacket. The company roared at the Justizrat's mishap, and even more at me. In short, everything was going along smoothly enough for a madhouse, but I just gave up.

Julia, however, hadn't laughed, and as I looked at her again I thought for a moment that a gleam of our wonderful past came through to me, a fragment of our former life of love and poetry. At this point someone in the next room began to improvise on the piano, and the company began to show signs of life. I heard that this was someone I did not know, a great pianist named Berger, who played divinely, and that you had to listen to him.

"Will you stop making that noise with the teaspoons, Minchen," bawled the Justizrat, and with a coyly contorted hand and a languorous "Eh bien!"[5] he beckoned the ladies to the door, to

5. Well, then.

approach the virtuoso. Julia arose too and walked slowly into the next room.

There was something strange about her whole figure, I thought. Somehow she seemed larger, more developed, almost lush. Her blouse was cut low, only half covering her breasts, shoulders, and neck; her sleeves were puffed, and reached only to her elbows; and her hair was parted at the forehead and pulled back into plaits—all of which gave her an antique look, much like one of the young women in Mieris's[6] paintings. Somehow it seemed to me as if I had seen her like this before. She had taken off her gloves, and ornate bracelets on her wrist helped carry through the complete identity of her dress with the past and awaken more vividly dark memories.

She turned toward me before she went into the music room, and for an instant her angel-like, normally pleasant face seemed strained into a sneer. An uncomfortable, unpleasant feeling arose in me, like a cramp running through my nervous system.

"Oh, he plays divinely," lisped a girl, apparently inspired by the sweet tea, and I don't know how it happened, but Julia's arm was in mine, and I led her, or rather she led me, into the next room. Berger was raising the wildest hurricanes, and like a roaring surf his mighty chords rose and fell. It did me good.

Then Julia was standing beside me, and said more softly and more sweetly than before, "I wish you were sitting at the piano, singing softly about pleasures and hopes that have been lost." The Enemy had left me, and in just the name, "Julia!" I wanted to proclaim the bliss that filled me. But the crowd pushed between us and we were separated. Now she was obviously avoiding me, but I was lucky enough to touch her clothing and close enough to breathe in her perfume, and the springtime of the past arose in a hundred shining colors.

Berger let the hurricane blow itself out, the skies became clear, and pretty little melodies, like the golden clouds of dawn, hovered in pianissimo. Well-earned applause broke out when he finished, and the guests began to move around the room. It came about that I found myself facing Julia again. The spirit rose more mightily in me. I wanted to seize her and embrace her, but a bustling servant crowded between us with a platter of drinks, calling in a very offensive way, "Help yourself, please, help yourself."

The tray was filled with cups of steaming punch, but in the very middle was a huge cut-crystal goblet, also apparently filled with punch. How did that get there, among all the ordinary punch cups? He knows—the Enemy that I'm gradually coming to understand. Like Clemens in Tieck's "Oktavian"[7] he walks about making a

6. Several members of the Mieris family were painters; perhaps Hoffmann is referring to the eldest, Frans van Mieris (1635–1681), famous for his portraits.

7. The reference is to *Emperor Octavi-* *anus, a Comedy* by Johann Ludwig Tieck (1773–1853), and to the old pilgrim Clemens who is a leading character in it.

pleasant squiggle with one foot, and is very fond of red capes and feathers. Julia picked up this sparkling, beautifully cut goblet and offered it to me, saying, "Are you still willing to take a glass from my hand?" "Julia, Julia," I sighed.

As I took the glass, my fingers brushed against hers, and electric sensations ran through me. I drank and drank, and it seemed to me that little flickering blue flames licked around the goblet and my lip. Then the goblet was empty, and I really don't know myself how it happened, but I was now sitting on an ottoman in a small room lit only by an alabaster lamp, and Julia was sitting beside me, demure and innocent-looking as ever. Berger had started to play again, the andante from Mozart's sublime E-flat Symphony, and on the swan's wings of song my sunlike love soared high. Yes, it was Julia, Julia herself, as pretty as an angel and as demure; our talk a longing lament of love, more looks than words, her hand resting in mine.

"I will never let you go," I was saying. "Your love is the spark that glows in me, kindling a higher life in art and poetry. Without you, without your love, everything is dead and lifeless. Didn't you come here so that you could be mine forever?"

At this very moment there tottered into the room a spindle-shanked cretin, eyes a-pop like a frog's, who said, in a mixture of croak and cackle, "Where the Devil is my wife?"

Julia stood up and said to me in a distant, cold voice, "Shall we go back to the party? My husband is looking for me. You've been very amusing again, darling, as overemotional as ever; but you should watch how much you drink."

The spindle-legged monkey reached for her hand and she followed him into the living room with a laugh.

"Lost forever," I screamed aloud.

"Oh, yes; codille, darling," bleated an animal playing ombre.[8]

I ran out into the stormy night.

In the Beer Cellar

Promenading up and down under the linden trees can be a fine thing, but not on a New Year's Eve when it is bitter cold and snow is falling. Bareheaded and without a coat I finally felt the cold when icy shivers began to interrupt my feverishness. I trudged over the Opern Bridge, past the Castle, over the Schleusen Bridge, past the Mint.[9] I was on Jaegerstrasse close to Thiermann's shop. Friendly lights were burning inside. I was about to go in, since I was freezing and I needed a good drink of something strong, when a merry group came bursting out, babbling loudly about fine oysters and good Eilfer wine. One of them—I could see by the lantern

8. A three-handed card game. To declare *codille* is to win without needing to play out the hand.
9. Landmarks of central Berlin.

light that he was a very impressive-looking officer in the uhlans—
was shouting, "You know, he was right, that fellow who cursed
them out in Mainz last year for not bringing out the Eilfer, he was
right!" They all laughed uproariously.

Without thinking, I continued a little farther, then stopped in
front of a beer cellar out of which a single light was shining.
Wasn't it Shakespeare's Henry V who once felt so tired and discouraged that he "remembered the poor creature, small beer?"[10]
Indeed, the same thing was happening to me. My tongue was practically cracking with thirst for a bottle of good English beer. I hastened down into the cellar.

"Yes, sir?" said the owner of the beer cellar, touching his cap
amiably as he came toward me.

I asked for a bottle of good English beer and a pipe of good
tobacco, and soon found myself sublimely immersed in fleshly comforts which even the Devil had to respect enough to leave me alone.
Ah, Justizrat! If you had seen me descend from your bright living
room to a gloomy beer cellar, you would have turned away from me
in contempt and muttered, "It's not surprising that a fellow like
that can ruin a first-class jacket."

I must have looked very odd to the others in the beer cellar, since
I had no hat or coat. The waiter was just about to say something
about it when there was a bang on the window, and a voice shouted
down, "Open up! Open up! It's me!"

The tavern keeper went outside and came right back carrying two
torches high; following him came a very tall, slender stranger who
forgot to lower his head as he came through the low doorway and
received a good knock. A black beretlike cap, though, kept him
from serious injury. The stranger sidled along the wall in a very
peculiar manner, and sat down opposite me, while lights were
placed upon the table. You could characterize him briefly as pleasant but unhappy. He called for beer and a pipe somewhat grumpily,
and then with a few puffs, created such a fog bank that we seemed
to be swimming in a cloud. His face had something so individual
and attractive about it that I liked him despite his dark moroseness.
He had a full head of black hair, parted in the middle and hanging
down in small locks on both sides of his head, so that he looked like
someone out of a Rubens picture.[11] When he threw off his heavy
cloak, I could see that he was wearing a black tunic with lots of
lacing, and it struck me as very odd that he had slippers pulled on
over his boots. I became aware of this when he knocked out his
pipe on his foot after about five minutes of smoking.

We didn't converse right away, for the stranger was preoccupied

10. Refers to 2 Henry IV, II.ii.10–11,
where Prince Hal confesses an unroyal
preference for weak beer over wine.

11. The hair style is Flemish seventeenth-century, as in the paintings of
Peter Paul Rubens (1577–1640).

with some strange plants which he took out of a little botanical case and started to examine closely. I indicated my astonishment at the plants and asked him, since they seemed freshly gathered, whether he had been at the botanical garden or Boucher the florist's. He smiled in a strange way, and replied slowly, "Botany does not seem to be your specialty, or else you would not have asked such a . . ." he hesitated and I supplied in a low voice, "foolish . . ." " . . . question," he finished, waving aside my assertion. "If you were a botanist, you would have seen at a glance that these are alpine flora and that they are from Chimborazo."[12] He said the last part very softly, and you can guess that I felt a little strange. This reply prevented further questions, but I kept having the feeling more and more strongly that I knew him—perhaps not "physically" but "mentally."

At this point there came another rapping at the window. The tavern keeper opened the door and a voice called in, "Be so good as to cover your mirrors."

"Aha!" said the host, "General Suvarov is late tonight," and he threw a cloth covering over the mirror. A short, dried-up-looking fellow came tumbling in with frantic, clumsy haste. He was engulfed in a cloak of peculiar brownish color, which bubbled and flapped around him as he bounced across the room toward us, so that in the dim light it looked as if a series of forms were dissolving and emerging from one another, as in Ensler's magic lantern show.[13] He rubbed his hands together inside his overlong sleeves and cried, "Cold! Cold! It's so cold! Altogether different in Italy." Finally he took a seat between me and the tall man and said, "Horrible smoke . . . tobacco on tobacco . . . I wish I had a pipeful."

In my pocket I had a small steel tobacco box, polished like a mirror; I reached it out to the little man. He took one look at it, and thrust out both hands, shoving it away, crying, "Take that damned mirror away." His voice was filled with horror, and as I stared at him with amazement I saw that he had become a different person. He had burst into the beer cellar with a pleasant, youthful face, but now a deathly pale, shrivelled, terrified old man's face glared at me with holow eyes. I turned in horror to the tall man. I was almost ready to shout, "For God's sake, look at him!" when I saw that the tall stranger was not paying any attention, but was completely engrossed in his plants from Chimborazo. At that moment the little man called, "Northern wine!" in a very affected manner.

After a time the conversation became more lively again. I wasn't quite at ease with the little man, but the tall man had the ability of

12. A mountain in Ecuador.
13. A popular entertainment of the time. The lantern projected painted transparencies, often telling a story; a new slide was inserted before the old one was removed.

offering deep and fascinating insights upon seemingly insignificant things, although at times he seemed to struggle to express himself and groped for words, and at times used words improperly, which often gave his statements an air of droll originality. In this way, by appealing to me more and more, he offset the bad impression created by the little man.

The little man seemed to be driven by springs, for he slid back and forth on his chair and waved his hands about in perpetual gesticulations, and a shudder, like icewater down my back, ran through me when I saw very clearly that he had two different faces, the pleasant young man's and the unlovely demonic old man's. For the most part he turned his old man's face upon the tall man, who sat impervious and quiet, in contrast to the perpetual motion of the small man in brown, although it was not as unpleasant as when it had looked at me for the first time.—In the masquerade of life our true inner essence often shines out beyond our mask when we meet a similar person, and it so happened that we three strange beings in a beer cellar looked at one another and knew what we were. Our conversation ran along morbid lines, in the sardonic humor that emerges only when you are wounded, almost to the point of death.

"There are hidden hooks and snares there, too," said the tall man.

"Oh, God," I joined in, "the Devil has set so many hooks for us everywhere, walls, arbors, hedge roses, and so on, and as we brush past them we leave something of our true self caught there. It seems to me, gentlemen, that all of us lose something this way, just as right now I have no hat or coat. They are both hanging on a hook at the Justizrat's, as you may know."

Both the tall and the short man visibly winced, as if they had been unexpectedly struck. The little man looked at me with hatred from his old man's face, leaped up on his chair and fussily adjusted the cloth that hung over the mirror, while the tall man made a point of pinching the candle wicks. The conversation limped along, and in its course a fine young artist named Philipp was mentioned, together with a portrait of a princess painted with intense love and longing, which she must have inspired in him. "More than just a likeness, a true image," said the tall man. "So completely true," I said, "that you could almost say it was stolen from a mirror."

The little man leaped up in a frenzy, and transfixing me with his flaming eyes, showing his old man's face, he screamed, "That's idiotic, crazy—who can steal your reflection? Who? Perhaps you think the Devil can? He would break the glass with his clumsy claws and the girl's fine white hands would be slashed and bloody. Erkhhhh. Show me a reflection, a stolen reflection, and I'll leap a thousand yards for you, you stupid fool!"

The tall man got up, strode over to the little man, and said in a contemptuous voice, "Don't make such a nuisance of yourself, my friend, or I'll throw you out and you'll be as miserable as your own reflection."

"Ha, ha, ha," laughed the little man with furious scorn. "You think so? Do you think so? You miserable dog, I at least still have my shadow, I still have my shadow!" And he leaped out of his chair and rushed out of the cellar. I could hear his nasty neighing laughter outside, and his shouts of "I still have my shadow!"

The tall man, as if completely crushed, sank back into his chair as pale as death. He took his head in both his hands and sighed deeply and groaned. "What's wrong?" I asked sympathetically. "Sir," he replied somewhat incoherently, "that nasty little fellow— followed me here, even in this tavern, where I used to be alone— nobody around, except once in a while an earth-elemental[14] would dive under the table for bread crumbs—he's made me miserable— there's no getting it back—I've lost . . . I've lost . . . my . . . oh, I can't go on . . ." and he leaped up and dashed out into the street.

He happened to pass the lights, and I saw that—he cast no shadow! I was delighted, for I recognized him and knew all about him. I ran out after him. "Peter Schlemihl, Peter Schlemihl,"[15] I shouted. But he had kicked off his slippers, and I saw him striding away beyond the police tower, disappearing into the night.

I was about to return to the cellar, but the owner slammed the door in my face, proclaiming loudly, "From guests like these the Good Lord deliver me!"

Manifestations

Herr Mathieu is a good friend of mine and his porter keeps his eyes open. He opened the door for me right away when I came to the Golden Eagle and pulled at the bell. I explained matters: that I had been to a party, had left my hat and coat behind, that my house key was in my coat pocket, and that I had no chance of waking my deaf landlady. He was a goodhearted fellow (the porter) and found a room for me, set lights about in it, and wished me a good night. A beautiful wide mirror, however, was covered, and though I don't know why I did it, I pulled off the cloth and set both my candles on the table in front of the mirror. When I looked in, I was so pale and tired-looking that I could hardly recognize myself. Then it seemed to me that from the remote background of the reflection there came floating a dark form, which as I focused

14. Or earth spirit.
15. The hero of the famous story *Peter Schlemihl's Wonderful History* (1814), by Adalbert von Chamisso (1781–1838). Schlemihl exchanged his shadow for an inexhaustible purse, then refused to buy it back with his soul though its absence brought him contempt and fear. He then obtained seven-league boots and traveled all over the world, wearing slippers over the boots whenever he needed to walk at a normal pace. His avocation, and Chamisso's profession, was botany.

my attention upon it, took on the features of a beautiful woman—
Julia—shining with a magic radiance. I said very softly, "Julia,
Julia!"

At this I heard a groaning and moaning which seemed to come
from behind the drawn curtains of a canopy bed which stood in the
farthest corner of the room. I listened closely. The groaning grew
louder, seemingly more painful. The image of Julia had disappeared,
and resolutely I seized a candle, ripped the curtains of the bed
apart, and looked in. How can I describe my feelings to you when I
saw before me the little man whom I had met at the beer cellar,
asleep on the bed, youthful features dominant (though contorted
with pain), muttering in his sleep, "Giuletta, Giuletta!" The name
enraged me. I was no longer fearful, but seized the little man and
gave him a good shake, shouting, "Heigh, my friend! What are you
doing in my room? Wake up and get the Devil out of here!"

The little man blinked his eyes open and looked at me darkly.
"That was really a bad dream," he said. "I must thank you for
waking me." He spoke softly, almost murmured. I don't know why
but he looked different to me: the pain which he obviously felt
aroused my sympathy, and instead of being angry I felt very sorry for
him. It didn't take much conversation to learn that the porter had
inadvertently given me the room which had already been assigned
to the little man, and that it was I who had intruded, disturbing his
sleep.

"Sir," said the little man. "I must have seemed like an utter lunatic to you in the beer cellar. Blame my behavior on this: every now
and then, I must confess, a mad spirit seizes control of me and
makes me lose all concept of what is right and proper. Perhaps the
same thing has happened to you at times?"

"Oh, God, yes," I replied dejectedly. "Just this evening, when I
saw Julia again."

"Julia!" crackled the little man in an unpleasant tone. His face
suddenly aged and his features twitched. "Let me alone. And please
be good enough to cover the mirror again," he said, looking sadly at
his pillow.

"Sir," I said. "The name of my eternally lost love seems to
awaken strange memories in you; so much so that your face has
changed from its usual pleasant appearance. Still, I have hopes of
spending the night here quietly with you, so I am going to cover
the mirror and go to bed."

He raised himself to a sitting position, looking at me with his
pleasant young face, and seized my hand, saying, while pressing it
gently, "Sleep well, my friend. I see that we are companions in
misery. Julia . . . Giuletta. . . . Well, if it must be, it must be. I
cannot help it; I must tell you my deepest secret, and then you will
hate and despise me."

He slowly climbed out of bed, wrapped himself in a generous white robe, and crept slowly, almost like a ghost, to the great mirror and stood in front of it. Ah—Brightly and clearly the mirror reflected the two lighted candles, the furniture, me—but the little man was not there! He stood, head bowed toward it, in front of the mirror, but he cast no reflection! Turning to me, deep despair on his face, he pressed my hands and said, "Now you know the depths of my misery. Schlemihl, a goodhearted fellow, is to be envied, compared to me. He was irresponsible for a moment and sold his shadow. But—I—I gave my reflection to her . . . to her!"

Sobbing deeply, hands pressed over his eyes, the little man turned to the bed and threw himself on it. I simply stood in astonishment, with suspicion, contempt, disgust, sympathy, and pity all intermingled, for and against the little man. But while I was standing there, he began to snore so melodiously that it was contagious, and I couldn't resist the narcotic power of his tones. I quickly covered the mirror again, put out the candles, threw myself upon the bed like the little man, and immediately fell asleep.

It must have been early morning when a light awakened me, and I opened my eyes to see the little man, still in his white dressing gown, nightcap on his head, back turned to me, sitting at the table busily writing by the light of the two candles. There was a weird look about him, and I felt the chill of the supernatural. I fell into a waking-dream then, and was back at the Justizrat's again, sitting beside Julia on the ottoman. But the whole party seemed to be only a comic candy display in the window of Fuchs, Weide and Schoch (or somewhere similar) for Christmas, and the Justizrat was a splendid gumdrop with a coat made of pleated notepaper. Trees and rosebushes rose higher and higher about us, and Julia stood up, handing me the crystal goblet, out of which blue flames licked. Someone tugged at my arm and there was the little brown man, his old man's face on, whispering loudly to me, "Don't drink it, don't drink it. Look at her closely. Haven't you seen her and been warned against her in Brueghel and Callot and Rembrandt?"[16]

I looked at Julia with horror, and indeed, with her pleated dress and ruffled sleeves and strange coiffure, she did look like one of the alluring young women, surrounded by demonic monsters, from the work of those masters.

"What are you afraid of?" said Julia. "I have you and your reflection, once and for all." I seized the goblet, but the little man leaped to my shoulder in the form of a squirrel, and waved his tail through the blue flames, chattering, "Don't drink it, don't drink it." At this point the sugar figures in the display came alive and moved their hands and feet ludicrously. The Justizrat ran up to me and called

16. It is unclear which characters in pictures by these celebrated seventeenth- century artists Hoffmann means.

out in a thin little voice, "Why all the uproar, my friend? Why all the commotion? All you have to do is get to your feet; for quite a while I've been watching you stride away over tables and chairs."

The little man had completely disappeared. Julia no longer held the goblet in her hand. "Why wouldn't you drink?" she asked. "Wasn't the flame streaming out of the goblet simply the kisses you once got from me?"

I wanted to take her in my arms, but Schlemihl stepped between us and said, "This is Mina, who married my servant, Rascal." He stepped on a couple of the candy figures, who made groaning noises. They started to multiply enormously, hundreds and thousands of them, and they swarmed all over me, buzzing like a hive of bees. The gumdrop Justizrat, who had continued to climb, had swung up as far as my neckcloth, which he kept pulling tighter and tighter. "Justizrat, you confounded gumdrop," I screamed out loud, and startled myself out of sleep. It was bright day, already eleven o'clock.

I was just thinking to myself that the whole adventure with the little brown man had only been an exceptionally vivid dream, when the waiter who brought in my breakfast told me that the stranger who had shared his room with me had left early, and presented his compliments. Upon the table where I had seen the weird little man sitting and writing I found a fresh manuscript, whose content I am sharing with you, since it is unquestionably the remarkable story of the little man in brown. It is as follows.

THE STORY OF THE LOST REFLECTION

Things finally worked out so that Erasmus Spikher was able to fulfill the wish that he had cherished all his life. He climbed into the coach with high spirits and a well-filled knapsack. He was leaving his home in the North and journeying to the beautiful land of Italy. His devoted wife was weeping copiously, and she lifted little Rasmus (after carefully wiping his mouth and nose) into the coach to kiss his father goodbye.

"Farewell, Erasmus Spikher," said his wife, sobbing. "I will keep your house well for you. Think of me often, remain true to me, and do not lose your hat if you fall asleep near the window, as you always do." Spikher promised.

In the beautiful city of Florence Spikher found some fellow Germans, young men filled with high spirits and *joie de vivre*,[17] who spent their time revelling in the sensual delights which Italy so well affords. He impressed them as a good fellow and he was often invited to social occasions since he had the talent of supplying soberness to the mad abandon about him, and gave the party a highly individual touch.

17. Enjoyment of life.

One evening in the grove of a splendid fragrant public garden, the young men (Erasmus could be included here, since he was only twenty-seven) gathered for an exceptionally merry feast. Each of the men, except Spikher, brought along a girl. The men were dressed in the picturesque old Germanic costume, and the women wore bright dresses, each styled differently, often fantastically, so that they seemed like wonderful mobile flowers. Every now and then one of the girls would sing an Italian love song, accompanied by the plaintive notes of mandolins, and the men would respond with a lusty German chorus or round, as glasses filled with fine Syracuse wine clinked. Yes, indeed, Italy is the land of love.

The evening breezes sighed with passion, oranges and jasmine breathed out perfume through the grove, and it all formed a part in the banter and play which the girls (delightfully merry as only Italian women can be) began. Wilder and noisier grew the fun. Friedrich, the most excited of all, leaped to his feet, one arm around his mistress, waving high a glass of sparkling Syracuse wine with the other, and shouted, "You wonderful women of Italy! Where can true, blissful love be found except with you? You are love incarnate! But you, Erasmus," he continued, turning to Spikher, "You don't seem to understand this. You've violated your promise, propriety and the custom. You didn't bring a girl with you, and you have been sitting here moodily, so quiet and self-concerned that if you hadn't been drinking and singing with us I'd believe you were suffering an attack of melancholy."

"Friedrich," replied Erasmus, "I have to confess that I cannot enjoy myself like that. You know that I have a wife at home, and I love her. If I took up with a girl for even one night it would be betraying my wife. For you young bachelors it's different, but I have a family."

The young men laughed uproariously, for when Erasmus announced his family obligations his pleasant young face became very grave, and he really looked very strange. Friedrich's mistress, when Spikher's words had been translated for her (for the two men had spoken German), turned very seriously to Erasmus, and said, half-threateningly, finger raised, "Cold-blooded, heartless German —watch out, you haven't seen Giuletta yet."

At that very instant a rustling noise indicated that someone was approaching, and out of the dark night into the area lighted by the candles strode a remarkably beautiful girl. Her white dress, which only half-hid her bosom, shoulders, and neck, fell in rich broad folds; her sleeves, puffed and full, came only to her elbows; her thick hair, parted in the front, fell in braids at the back. Golden chains around her throat, rich bracelets upon her wrists, completed her antique costume. She looked exactly if she were a woman from Mieris or Rembrandt walking about. "Giuletta," shrieked the girls in astonishment and delight.

Giuletta, who was by far the most beautiful of all the women present, asked in a sweet, pleasant voice, "Good Germans, may I join you? I'll sit with that gentlemen over there. He doesn't have a girl, and he doesn't seem to be having a very good time, either." She turned very graciously to Erasmus, and sat down upon the empty seat beside him—empty because everyone thought Erasmus would bring a girl along, too. The girls whispered to each other, "Isn't Giuletta beautiful tonight," and the young men said, "How about Erasmus? Was he joking with us? He's got the best-looking girl of all!"

As for Erasmus, at the first glance he cast at Giuletta, he was so aroused that he didn't even know what powerful passions were working in him. As she came close to him, a strange force seized him and crushed his breast so that he couldn't even breathe. Eyes fixed in a rigid stare at her, mouth agape, he sat there not able to utter a syllable, while all the others were commenting upon Giuletta's charm and beauty.

Giuletta took a full goblet, and standing up, handed it with a friendly smile to Erasmus. He seized the goblet, touching her soft fingers, and as he drank, fire seemed to stream through his veins. Then Giuletta asked him in a bantering way, "Am I to be your girl friend?" Erasmus threw himself wildly upon the ground in front of her, pressed her hands to his breast, and cried in maudlin tones, "Yes, yes, yes! You goddess! I've always been in love with you. I've seen you in my dreams, you are my fortune, my happiness, my higher life!"

The others all thought the wine had gone to Erasmus's head, since they had never seen him like this before; he seemed to be a different man.

"You are my life! I don't care if I am destroyed, as long as it's with you," Erasmus shouted. "You set me on fire!" But Giuletta just took him gently in her arms. He became quieter again, and took his seat beside her. And once again the gaiety which had been interrupted by Erasmus and Giuletta began with songs and laughter. Giuletta sang, and it was as if the tones of her beautiful voice aroused in everyone sensations of pleasure never felt before but only suspected to exist. Her full but clear voice conveyed a secret ardor which inflamed them all. The young men clasped their mistresses more closely, and passion leaped from eye to eye.

Dawn was breaking with a rosy shimmer when Giuletta said that she had to leave. Erasmus got ready to accompany her home, but she refused but gave him the address at which he could find her in the future. During the chorus which the men sang to end the party, Giuletta disappeared from the grove and was seen walking through a distant *allée*,[18] preceded by two linkmen. Erasmus did not dare follow her.

The young men left arm in arm with their mistresses, full of high spirits, and Erasmus, greatly disturbed and internally shattered by the torments of love, followed, preceded by his boy with a torch. After leaving his friends, he was passing down the distant street which led to his dwelling, and his servant had just knocked out the torch against the stucco of the house, when a strange figure mysteriously appeared in the spraying sparks in front of Erasmus. It was a tall, thin, dried-out-looking man with a Roman nose that came to a sharp point, glowing eyes, mouth contorted into a sneer, wrapped in a flame-red cloak with brightly polished steel buttons. He laughed and called out in an unpleasant yelping voice, "Ho, ho, you look as if you came out of a picture book with that cloak, slit doublet, and plumed hat. You show a real sense of humor, Signor Erasmus Spikher, but aren't you afraid of being laughed at on the streets? Signor, signor, crawl quietly back into your parchment binding."

"What the Devil is my clothing to you?" said Erasmus with anger, and shoving the red-clad stranger aside, he was about to pass by when the stranger called after him, "Don't be in such a hurry. You won't get to Giuletta that way."

"What are you saying about Giuletta?" cried Erasmus wildly. He tried to seize the red-clad man by the breast, but he turned and disappeared so rapidly that Erasmus couldn't even see where he went, and Erasmus was left standing in astonishment, in his hand a steel button that had been ripped from the stranger's cloak.

"That's the Miracle Doctor Dapertutto. What did he want?" asked Erasmus's servant. But Erasmus was seized with horror, and without replying, hastened home.

When, some time later, Erasmus called on Giuletta, she received him in a very gracious and friendly manner, yet to Erasmus's fiery passion she opposed a mild indifference. Only once in a while did her eyes flash, whereupon Erasmus would feel shudders pass through him, from his innermost being, when she regarded him with an enigmatic stare. She never told him that she loved him, but her whole attitude and behavior led him to think so, and he found himself more and more deeply entangled with her. He seldom saw his old friends, however, for Giuletta took him into other circles.

Once Erasmus met Friedrich at a time when Erasmus was depressed, thinking about his native land and his home. Friedrich said, "Don't you know, Spikher, that you are moving in a very dangerous circle of acquaintances? You must realize by now that the beautiful Giuletta is one of the craftiest courtesans on earth. There are all sorts of strange stories going around about her, and they put

18. Avenue. *linkmen*: Torchbearers.

her in a very peculiar light. I can see from you that she can exercise an irresistible power over men when she wants to. You have changed completely and are totally under her spell. You don't think of your wife and family any more."

Erasmus covered his face with his hands and sobbed, crying out his wife's name. Friedrich saw that a difficult internal battle had begun in Spikher. "Erasmus," he said, "let us get out of here immediately."

"Yes, Friedrich," said Erasmus heavily. "You are right. I don't know why I am suddenly overcome by such dark horrible foreboding—I must leave right away, today."

The two friends hastened along the street, but directly across from them came Signor Dapertutto, who laughed in Erasmus's face, and cried nasally, "Hurry, hurry; a little faster. Giuletta is waiting, her heart is full of longing, and her eyes are full of tears. Make haste. Make haste."

Erasmus stood as if struck by lightning.

"This scoundrel," said Friedrich, "this charlatan—I cannot stand him. He is always in and out of Giuletta's, and he sells her his magical potions."

"What!" cried Erasmus. "That disgusting creature visits Giuletta, Giuletta?"

"Where have you been so long? Everything is waiting for you. Didn't you think of me at all," breathed a soft voice from the balcony. It was Giuletta, in front of whose house the two friends, without noticing it, had stopped. With a leap Erasmus was in the house.

"He is gone, and cannot be saved," said Friedrich to himself, and walked slowly away.

Never before had Giuletta been more amiable. She wore the same clothing that she had worn when she first met Erasmus, and beauty, charm, and youth shone from her. Erasmus completely forgot his conversation with Friedrich, and now more than ever his irresistible passion seized him. This was the first time that Giuletta showed without reservation her deepest love for him. She seemed to see only him, and to live for him only. At a villa which Giuletta had rented for the summer, a festival was being celebrated, and they went there. Among the company was a young Italian with a brutal ugly face and even worse manners, who kept paying court to Giuletta and arousing Erasmus's jealousy. Fuming with rage, Erasmus left the company and paced up and down in a side path of the garden. Giuletta came looking for him. "What is wrong with you? Aren't you mine alone?" she asked. She embraced him and planted a kiss upon his lips. Sparks of passion flew through Erasmus, and in a passion he crushed her to himself, crying, "No, I will not leave you, no matter how low I fall." Giuletta smiled strangely at these words, and cast at him that peculiar oblique glance which never failed to arouse a chilly feeling in him.

They returned to the company, and the unpleasant young Italian now took over Erasmus's role. Obviously enraged with jealousy, he made all sorts of pointed insults against Germans, particularly Spikher. Finally Spikher could bear it no longer, and he strode up to the Italian and said, "That's enough of your insults, unless you'd like to get thrown into the pond and try your hand at swimming." In an instant a dagger gleamed in the Italian's hand, but Erasmus dodged, seized him by the throat, threw him to the ground, and shattered his neck with a kick. The Italian gasped out his life on the spot.

Pandemonium broke loose around Erasmus. He lost consciousness, but felt himself being lifted and carried away. When he awoke later, as if from a deep enchantment, he lay at Giuletta's feet in a small room, while she, head bowed over him, held him in both her arms.

"You bad, bad German," she finally said, softly and mildly. "If you knew how frightened you've made me! You've come very close to disaster, but I've managed to save you. You are no longer safe in Florence, though, or even Italy. You must leave, and you must leave me, and I love you so much."

The thought of leaving Giuletta threw Erasmus into pain and sorrow. "Let me stay here," he cried. "I'm willing to die. Dying is better than living without you."

But suddenly it seemed to him as if a soft, distant voice was calling his name painfully. It was the voice of his wife at home. Erasmus was stricken dumb. Strangely enough, Giuletta asked him, "Are you thinking of your wife? Ah, Eramus, you will forget me only too soon!"

"If I could only remain yours forever and ever," said Erasmus. They were standing directly in front of the beautiful wide mirror, which was set in the wall, and on the sides of it tapers were burning brightly. More firmly, more closely, Giuletta pressed Erasmus to her, while she murmured softly in his ear, "Leave me your reflection, my beloved; it will be mine and will remain with me forever."

"Giuletta," cried Erasmus in amazement. "What do you mean? My reflection?" He looked in the mirror, which showed him himself and Giuletta in sweet, close embrace. "How can you keep my reflection? It is part of me. It springs out to meet me from every clear body of water or polished surface."

"Aren't you willing to give me even this dream of your ego? Even though you say you want to be mine, body and soul? Won't you even give me this trivial thing, so that after you leave, it can accompany me in the loveless, pleasureless life that is left to me?"

Hot tears started from Giuletta's beautiful dark eyes.

At this point Erasmus, mad with pain and passion, cried, "Do I have to leave? If I have to, my reflection will be yours forever and a day. No power—not even the Devil—can take it away from you until you own me, body and soul."

Giuletta's kisses burned like fire on his mouth as he said this, and then she released him and stretched out her arms longingly to the mirror. Erasmus saw his image step forward independent of his movements, glide into Giuletta's arms, and disappear with her in a strange vapor. Then Erasmus heard all sorts of hideous voices bleating and laughing in demoniac scorn, and, seized with a spasm of terror, he sank to the floor. But his horror and fear aroused him, and in thick dense darkness he stumbled out the door and down the steps. In front of the house he was seized and lifted into a carriage, which rolled away with him rapidly.

"Things have changed somewhat, it seems," said a man in German, who had taken a seat beside him. "Nevertheless, everything will be all right if you give yourself over to me completely. Dear Giuletta has done her share, and has recommended you to me. You are a fine, pleasant young man and you have a strong inclination to pleasant pranks and jokes—which please Giuletta and me nicely. That was a real nice German kick in the neck. Did you see how Amoroso's tongue protruded—purple and swollen—it was a fine sight and the strangling noises and groans—ha, ha, ha." The man's voice was so repellent in its mockery, his chatter so gruesomely unpleasant, that his words felt like dagger blows in Erasmus's chest.

"Whoever you are," he said, "don't say any more about it. I regret it bitterly."

"Regret? Regret?" replied the unknown man. "I'll be bound that you probably regret knowing Giuletta and winning her love."

"Ah, Giuletta, Giuletta!" sighed Spikher.

"Now," said the man, "you are being childish. Everything will run smoothly. It is horrible that you have to leave her, I know, but if you were to remain here, I could keep your enemies' daggers away from you, and even the authorities."

The thought of being able to stay with Giuletta appealed strongly to Erasmus. "How, how can that be?"

"I know a magical way to strike your enemies with blindness, in short, that you will always appear to them with a different face, and they will never recognize you again. Since it is getting on toward daylight, perhaps you will be good enough to look long and attentively into any mirror. I shall then perform certain operations upon your reflection, without damaging it in the least, and you will be hidden and can live forever with Giuletta. As happy as can be; no danger at all."

"Oh God," screamed Erasmus.

"Why call upon God, my most worthy friend," asked the stranger with a sneer.

"I—I have . . ." began Erasmus.

"Left your reflection behind—with Giuletta—" interrupted the other. "Fine. Bravissimo, my dear sir. And now you course through floods and forests, cities and towns, until you find your wife and little Rasmus, and become a paterfamilias[19] again. No reflection, of course—though this really shouldn't bother your wife since she has you physically. Even though Giuletta will eternally own your dream-ego."

A torch procession of singers drew near at this moment, and the light the torches cast into the carriage revealed to Erasmus the sneering visage of Dr. Dapertutto. Erasmus leaped out of the carriage and ran toward the procession, for he had recognized Friedrich's resounding bass voice among the singers. It was his friends returning from a party in the countryside. Erasmus breathlessly told Friedrich everything that had happened, only withholding mention of the loss of his reflection. Friedrich hurried with him into the city, and arrangements were made so rapidly that when dawn broke, Erasmus, mounted on a fast horse, had already left Florence far behind.

Spikher set down in his manuscript the many adventures that befell him upon his journey. Among the most remarkable is the incident which first caused him to appreciate the loss of his reflection. He had stopped over in a large town, since his tired horse needed a rest, and he had sat down without thinking at a well-filled inn table, not noticing that a fine clear mirror hung before him. A devil of a waiter, who stood behind his chair, noticed that the chair seemed to be empty in the reflection and did not show the person who was sitting in it. He shared his observation with Erasmus's neighbor, who in turn called it to the attention of his. A murmuring and whispering thereupon ran all around the table, and the guests first stared at Erasmus, then at the mirror. Erasmus, however, was unaware that the disturbance concerned him, until a grave gentleman stood up, took Erasmus to the mirror, looked in, and then turning to the company, cried out loudly, "'Struth. He's not there. He doesn't reflect."

"What? No reflection? He's not in the mirror?" everyone cried in confusion. "He's a *mauvais sujet*, a *homo nefas*.[20] Kick him out the door!"

Raging and filled with shame, Erasmus fled to his room, but he had hardly gotten there when he was informed by the police that he must either appear with full, complete, impeccably accurate reflection before the magistrate within one hour or leave the town.

19. Head of his household.　　　　20. A knave, a criminal.

He rushed away, followed by the idle mob, tormented by street urchins, who called after him, "There he goes. He sold his reflection to the Devil. There he goes!" Finally he escaped. And from then on, under the pretext of having a phobia against mirrors, he insisted on having them covered. For this reason he was nicknamed General Suvarov, since Suvarov[21] acted the same way.

When he finally reached his home city and his house, his wife and child received him with joy, and he began to think that calm, peaceful domesticity would heal the pain of his lost reflection. One day, however, it happened that Spikher, who had now put Guiletta completely out of his mind, was playing with little Rasmus. Rasmus's little hands were covered with soot from the stove, and he dragged his fingers across his father's face. "Daddy! I've turned you black. Look, look!" cried the child, and before Spikher could prevent it or avoid it, the little boy held a mirror in front of him, looking into it at the same time. The child dropped the mirror with a scream of terror and ran away to his room.

Spikher's wife soon came to him, astonishment and terror plainly on her face. "What has Rasmus told me—" she began. "Perhaps that I don't have a reflection, dear," interrupted Spikher with a forced smile, and he feverishly tried to prove that the story was too foolish to believe, that one could not lose a reflection, but if one did, since a mirror image was only an illusion, it didn't matter much, that staring into a mirror led to vanity, and pseudo-philosophical nonsense about the reflection dividing the ego into truth and dream. While he was declaiming, his wife removed the covering from a mirror that hung in the room and looked into it. She fell to the floor as if struck by lightning. Spikher lifted her up, but when she regained consciousness, she pushed him away with horror. "Leave me, get away from me, you demon! You're not my husband. No! You are a demon from Hell, who wants to destroy my chance of heaven, who wants to corrupt me. Away! Leave me alone! You have no power over me, damned spirit!"

Her voice screamed through the room, through the halls; the domestics fled the house in terror, and in rage and despair Erasmus rushed out of the house. Madly he ran through the empty walks of the town park. Giuletta's form seemed to arise in front of him, angelic in beauty, and he cried aloud, "Is this your revenge, Giuletta, because I abandoned you and left you nothing but my reflection in a mirror? Giuletta, I will be yours, body and soul. I sacrificed you for her, Giuletta, and now she has rejected me. Giuletta, let me be yours—body, life, and soul!"

"That can be done quite easily, *caro signore*,"[22] said Dr. Dapertutto, who was suddenly standing beside him, clad in scarlet cloak

21. Or Suvarov (1729–1800), who led a Russian army to victories over the Turks and the French.

22. My dear sir.

with polished steel buttons. These were words of comfort to Erasmus, and he paid no heed to Dapertutto's sneering, unpleasant face. Erasmus stopped and asked in despair, "How can I find her again? She is eternally lost to me."

"On the contrary," answered Dapertutto, "she is not far from here, and she longs for your true self, honored sir; you yourself have had the insight to see that a reflection is nothing but a worthless illusion. And as soon as she has the real you—body, life, and soul —she will return your reflection, smooth and undamaged, with the utmost gratitude."

"Take me to her, take me to her," cried Erasmus. "Where is she?"

"A certain trivial matter must come first," replied Dapertutto, "before you can see her and redeem your reflection. You are not entirely free to dispose of your worthy self, since you are tied by certain bonds which have to be dissolved first. Your worthy wife. Your promising little son."

"What do you mean?" cried Erasmus wildly.

"This bond," continued Dapertutto, "can be dissolved incontrovertibly, easily, and humanely. You may remember from your Florentine days that I have the knack of preparing wonder-working medications. I have a splendid household aid here at hand. Those who stand in the way of you and your beloved Giuletta—let them have the benefit of a couple of drops, and they will sink down quietly, no pain, no embarrassment. It is what they call dying, and death is said to be bitter; but don't bitter almonds taste very nice? The death in this little bottle has only that kind of bitterness. Immediately after the happy collapse, your worthy family will exude a pleasant odor of almonds. Take it, honored sir."

He handed a small phial to Erasmus.

"I should poison my wife and child?" shrieked Erasmus.

"Who spoke of poison?" continued the red-clad man, very calmly. "It's just a delicious household remedy. It's true that I have other ways of regaining your freedom for you, but for you I would like the process to be natural, humane, if you know what I mean. I really feel strongly about it. Take it and have courage, my friend."

Erasmus found the phial in his hand, he knew not how.

Without thinking, he ran home, to his room. His wife had spent the whole night amid a thousand fears and torments, asserting continually that the person who had returned was not her husband but a spirit from Hell who had assumed her husband's form. As a result, the moment Erasmus set foot in the house, everyone ran. Only little Rasmus had the courage to approach him and ask in childish fashion why he had not brought his reflection back with him, since Mother was dying of grief because of it. Erasmus stared wildly at the little boy, Dapertutto's phial in his hand. His son's pet dove was on his shoulder, and it so happened that the dove pecked at the stopper of the phial, dropped its head, and toppled over, dead. Erasmus was overcome with horror.

"Betrayer," he shouted. "You cannot make me do it!"

He threw the phial out through the open window, and it shattered upon the concrete pavement of the court. A luscious odor of almonds rose in the air and spread into the room, while little Rasmus ran away in terror.

Erasmus spent the whole day in torment until midnight. More and more vividly each moment the image of Giuletta rose in his mind. On one occasion, in the past, her necklace of red berries (which Italian women wear like pearls) had broken, and while Erasmus was picking up the berries he concealed one and kept it faithfully, because it had been on Giuletta's neck. At this point he took out the berry and fixed his gaze upon it, focusing his thought on his lost love. It seemed to him that a magical aroma emerged from the berry, the scene which used to surround Giuletta.

"Ah, Giuletta, if I could only see you one more time, and then go down in shame and disgrace . . ."

He had hardly spoken, when a soft rustling came along the walk outside. He heard footsteps—there was a knock on the door. Fear and hope stopped his breath. He opened the door, and in walked Giuletta, as remarkably beautiful and charming as ever. Mad with desire, Erasmus seized her in his arms.

"I am here, beloved," she whispered softly, gently. "See how well I have preserved your reflection?"

She took the cloth down from the mirror on the wall, and Erasmus saw his image nestled in embrace with Giuletta, independent of him, not following his movements. He shook with terror.

"Giuletta," he cried, "must you drive me mad? Give me my reflection and take me—body, life, soul!"

"There is still something between us, dear Erasmus," said Giuletta. "You know what it is. Hasn't Dapertutto told you?"

"For God's sake, Giuletta," cried Erasmus. "If that is the only way I can become yours, I would rather die."

"You don't have to do it the way Dapertutto suggested," said Giuletta. "It is really a shame that a vow and a priest's blessing can do so much, but you must loose the bond that ties you or else you can never be entirely mine. There is a better way than the one that Dapertutto proposed."

"What is it?" asked Spikher eagerly. Giuletta placed her arm around his neck, and leaning her head upon his breast whispered up softly, "You just write your name, Erasmus Spikher, upon a little slip of paper, under only a few words: 'I give to my good friend Dr. Dapertutto power over my wife and over my child, so that he can govern and dispose of them according to his will, and dissolve the bond which ties me, because I, from this day, with body and immortal soul, wish to belong to Giuletta, whom I have chosen as wife, and to whom I will bind myself eternally with a special vow.' "

Erasmus shivered and twitched with pain. Fiery kisses burned upon his lips, and he found the little piece of paper which Giuletta had given to him in his hand. Gigantic, Dapertutto suddenly stood behind Giuletta and handed Erasmus a steel pen. A vein on Erasmus's left hand burst open and blood spurted out.

"Dit it, dip it, write. write," said the red-clad figure harshly.

"Write, write, my eternal, my only lover," whispered Giuletta.

He had filled the pen with his blood and started to write when the door suddenly opened and a white figure entered. With staring eyes fixed on Erasmus, it called painfully and leadenly, "Erasmus, Erasmus! What are you doing? For the sake of our Savior, don't do this horrible deed."

Erasmus recognized his wife in the warning figure, and threw the pen and paper far from him.

Sparks and flashes shot out of Giuletta's eyes; her face was horribly distorted; her body seemed to glow with rage.

"Away from me, demon; you can have no part of my soul. In the name of the Savior, begone. Snake—Hell glows through you," cried Erasmus, and with a violent blow he knocked back Giuletta, who was trying to embrace him again. A screaming and howling broke loose, and a rustling, as of raven feathers. Giuletta and Dapertutto disappeared in a thick stinking smoke, which as it poured out of the walls put out the lights.

Dawn finally came, and Erasmus went to his wife. He found her calm and restrained. Little Rasmus sat very cheerfully upon her bed. She held out her hand to her exhausted husband and said, "I now know everything that happened to you in Italy, and I pity you with all my heart. The power of the Enemy is great. He is given to ill-doing and he could not resist the desire to make away with your reflection and use it to his own purposes. Look into the mirror again, husband."

Erasmus, trembling, looked into the mirror, completely dejected. It remained blank and clear; no other Erasmus Spikher looked back at him.

"It is just as well that the mirror does not reflect you," said his wife, "for you look very foolish, Erasmus. But you must recognize that if you do not have a reflection, you will be laughed at, and you cannot be the proper father for a family; your wife and children cannot respect you. Rasmus is already laughing at you and next will paint a mustache on you with soot, since you cannot see it.

"Go out into the world again, and see if you can track down your reflection, away from the Devil. When you have it back, you will be very welcome here. Kiss me" (Erasmus did) "and now—goodbye. Send little Rasmus new stockings every once in a while, for he keeps sliding on his knees and needs quite a few pairs. If you get to Nuremberg, you can also send him a painted soldier and a spice cake, like a devoted father. Farewell, dear Erasmus."

His wife turned upon her other side and went back to sleep. Spikher lifted up little Rasmus and hugged him to his breast. But since Rasmus cried quite a bit, Spikher set him down again, and went into the wide world. He struck upon a certain Peter Schlemihl, who had sold his shadow; they planned to travel together, so that Erasmus Spikher could provide the necessary shadow and Peter Schlemihl could reflect properly in a mirror. But nothing came of it.

The end of the story of the lost reflection.

Postscript by the Traveling Enthusiast

What is it that looks out of that mirror there? Is it really I? Julia, Giuletta—divine image, demon from Hell; delights and torments; longing and despair. You can see, my dear Theodore Amadeus Hoffmann, that a strange dark power manifests itself in my life all too often, steals the best dreams away from sleep, pushing strange forms into my life. I am completely saturated with the manifestations of this New Year's Eve, and I more than half believe that the Justizrat is a gumdrop, that his tea was a candy display for Christmas or New Year's, that the good Julia was a picture of a siren by Rembrandt or Callot—who betrayed the unfortunate Spikher to get his alter ego, his reflection in the mirror. Forgive me. . . .

HEINRICH HEINE
(1797–1856)

The Rose, the Lily, the Sun and the Dove[a]

> The rose, the lily, the sun and the dove,
> I loved them all once in the rapture of love.
> I love them no more, for my sole delight
> Is a maiden so slight, so bright and so white,
> Who, being herself the source of love,   5
> Is rose and lily and sun and dove.

a. Written in 1822–1823. Translated by P.G.L. Webb.

A Spruce Is Standing Lonely[a]

A spruce is standing lonely
in the North on a barren height.
He drowses; ice and snowflakes
wrap him in a blanket of white.

He dreams about a palm tree   5
in a distant, eastern land,
that languishes lonely and silent
upon the scorching sand.

A Young Man Loves a Maiden[b]

A young man loves a maiden
Whose heart for another sighed;
This other loves another
Who then becomes his bride.

The maiden takes the first man   5
Who happens to come her way
Just out of spite and anger;
The youth is left in dismay.

It is an old old story
And yet it's always new;   10
And to whomever it happens
't will break his heart in two.

Loreley[c]

I do not know what haunts me,
What saddened my mind all day;
An age-old tale confounds me,
A spell I cannot allay.

a. Written 1822–1823. Translated by Max Knight and Joseph Fabry.
b. Written 1822–1823. Translated by Ernst Feise.
c. Written 1823–1824. Translated by Ernst Feise. The Loreley was a siren of the river Rhine who was believed to have lured many boatsmen to their destruction. As set to music by Silcher in 1837, this has become one of the most popular of German songs.

The air is cool and in twilight   5
The Rhine's dark waters flow;
The peak of the mountain in highlight
Reflects the evening glow.

There sits a lovely maiden
Above, so wondrous fair,   10
With shining jewels laden,
She combs her golden hair.

It falls through her comb in a shower,
And over the valley rings
A song of mysterious power   15
That lovely maiden sings.

The boatman in his small skiff is
Seized by turbulent love,
No longer he marks where the cliff is,
He looks to the mountain above.   20

I think the waves must fling him
Against the reefs nearby,
And that did with her singing
The lovely Loreley.

My Beauty, My Love, You Have Bound Me [a]

My beauty, my love, you have bound me
As only you can do.
Wrap your arms and legs around me,
And your agile body too.

And now in mighty embraces   5
Entwining and holding on
The most beautiful serpent faces
The happiest Laocoon.

The Silesian Weavers [b]

In gloomy eyes there wells no tear.
Grinding their teeth, they are sitting here:

a. Written in 1823. Translated by Meno Spann.

8. A Greek mythological figure, best known through an ancient statue which shows him entangled in a desperate struggle with two monstrous serpents.

b. Written in 1844. Translated by Aaron Kramer. Silesia was a province of the kingdom of Prussia in northeast Germany, and is now divided between Poland and Czechoslovakia.

This poem was occasioned by violent uprisings of weavers protesting intolerable working conditions in the province of Silesia during June, 1844.

"Germany, your shroud's on our loom;
And in it we weave the threefold doom.
    We weave; we weave.   5

"Doomed be the God who was deaf to our prayer
In Winter's cold and hunger's despair.
All in vain we hoped and bided;
He only mocked us, hoaxed, derided—
    We weave; we weave.   10

"Doomed be the king, the rich man's king,
Who would not be moved by our suffering,
Who tore the last coin out of our hands,
And let us be shot by his blood-thirsty bands—
    We weave; we weave.   15

"Doomed be the fatherland, false name,
Where nothing thrives but disgrace and shame,
Where flowers are crushed before they unfold,
Where the worm is quickened by rot and mold—
    We weave; we weave.   20

"The loom is creaking, the shuttle flies;
Nor night nor day do we close our eyes.
Old Germany, your shroud's on our loom,
And in it we weave the threefold doom;
    We weave; we weave!"   25

The Asra [a]

Daily went the Sultan's beauteous
Daughter walking for her pleasure
In the evening at the fountain
Where the splashing waters whiten.

Daily stood the youthful bondsman   5
In the evening at the fountain
Where the splashing waters whiten,
Daily he grew pale and paler.

Then one evening stepped the princess
Up to him with sudden questions: 10
"You must tell me what your name is,
What your country is, your kinfolk."

---

11. *the king*: Friedrich Wilhelm IV
(1795–1861). Heine's poem is prophetic:
in 1848 the king, though not deposed,
was forced by revolution to grant a constitution to Prussia.
   a. Written in 1846. Translated by Ernst
Feise.

And the bondsman said: "Mohamet
Is my name, I am from Yemen,
And my kinsmen are the Asra,   15
They who die when love befalls them."

Babylonian Sorrows [a]

Death calls me—Sweet, it might be good
If I could leave you in some wood,
Some forest where the firs are high,
Where vultures nest, and wild wolves cry,
And the savage sow, with dreadful roar,   5
Calls to her mate, the great blonde boar.

Death calls—still better would it be
To leave you on the open sea,
My wife—my child—it would be kind,
Although the maniac Northpole wind   10
Lashes the waves there, and out of the deep
The monstrous things that lay asleep,
The shark and crocodile, arise
With open jaws and murderous eyes—
Believe me, Mathild, my wife, my child,   15
Not half so fearful is the wild,
Avenging sea, or the sulking wood,
As this our present neighborhood!
Fierce though the wolf and the vulture be,
The shark, and other beasts of the sea: 20
There are monsters of far less virtue and pity
In Paris, the world's bright capital-city,
City of Loveliness, laughter and revels,
The Hell of angels, Paradise of devils—
To think that you'll be left behind   25
In Paris, is driving me out of my mind!
Black flies are buzzing around my bed;
They seat themselves on top of my head,
On my nose and brow. That pesky race—
There's more than one with a human face,   30
But some of them are especially odd:
They've elephant-trunks like the Hindu god . . .
Inside my brain there's a tumult and cracking;
In think it is a box they're packing,
And my reason journeys off—ah woe!—   35
Before it is time for me to go.

a. Written in 1853–1854. Translated by Aaron Kramer.

How Slowly Time, the Loathsome Snail[a]

How slowly Time, the loathsome snail,
Keeps crawling in its slimy trace!
But I, meanwhile, quite motionless,
Must bide here in this selfsame place.

No ray of sun, no gleam of hope   5
Will fall into my darkened room;
I know I'll trade this baneful cell
For nothing but the churchyard tomb.

Perhaps I have died long ago;
And only spooks may be those vain   10
Phantasms, pageants, which at night
In wild array storm through my brain.

Or afterwalkers they could be,
Old pagan gods, an ilk of Hell;
They love to choose their rousting place   15
In a dead poet's empty skull.—

Then sometimes would seek to record
At dawn the poet's mummied hand
Those awesome lurid orgia
Of specters in nocturnal band.   20

The Migratory Rats[b]

There are two kinds of rat,
The hungry and the fat;
The fat ones happily stay at home,
But the hungry ones set out to roam.

They wander thousands of miles,   5
They have no domiciles;
Straight on they move in a furious run,
They cannot be stopped by rain or sun.

No mountains they cannot skim,
No lakes too broad for their swim!   10
Many get drowned or break their necks,
But those who survive pass over the wrecks.

a. Written 1853–1854. Translated by Ernst Feise. From the cycle of poems, *To Lazarus*, named for the man whom Christ raised from the dead (John 1–44).

19. *orgia*: Orgies.
b. Published posthumously. Translated by Ernst Feise.

These queer peculiar louts
Grow whiskers above their snouts;
As radical egalitarians they wear   15
In ratty fashion close-cropped their hair.

This fierce and radical squad
Knows no eternal God;
Unbaptized they leave their numerous broods,
They keep their women as common goods.   20

A sensuous mob, they think
Only of food and drink;
They ignore, since food is their only goal,
The immortality of the soul.

For such a brutal rat   25
Fears neither hell nor cat;
No goods, nor money they ever acquire,
To redivide the world they desire.

Approaching I see the foe
Of wandering rats, oh woe!   30
They come, already they are at our heels,
Their number is legion, I hear their squeals.

Oh woe! now we are lost!
At our portal their awful host!
The council and mayor shake their heads,   35
They despair of warding off those reds.

The burghers take up arms,
The blackfrocks ring the alarms;
The palladium of public morality,
Property, is in jeopardy.   40

No ringing of bells, no priestly pleas,
No wise and august council decrees,
Not even cannons of wildest gage
Will help you, my children, against their rage.

No help you will find in verbal trick   45
Of worn political rhetoric;
You can't catch rats with syllogisms,
They nimbly jump your finest sophisms.

Soup-logic only and reason-dumplings
Will silence their hungry stomach rumblings,   50

Or arguments of soup donations
Together with Göttingen sausage quotations.

A silent codfish in butter fat
Will satisfy such a radical rat
Much better than any Mirabeau   55
And all the orations since Cicero.

At Parting[a]

Vain worldly yearnings in my breast
Are dead and leave me unobsessed.
Hatred of evils, stilled, no more
Perturbs me—no, nor sorrow for
My own or others' pain-drawn breath.   5
Within me lives yet only death.
The curtain falls, the play now ends;
And, yawning, my dear German friends,
My public, wend their homeward way.
They're far from stupid, I must say.   10
They're dining gaily, quaffing beer,
With songs and laughter, pleasant cheer.
Right was Pelides, famous prince,
Who said in Homer's book long since:
A Philistine, the silliest bore   15
In Stuttgart on the Neckar shore,
Alive, has happiness far more
Than I, dead hero, in the host
Of Hades now the foremost ghost.

Morphine[b]

Great is the likeness of those beauteous two,
The youthful brothers, though the one appears
Much paler than the other, also much
More stern, yes, I might almost say much more
Aristocratic than that one who clasped me   5

52. *Göttingen*: Prussian university city, also a center of commerce.

55. *Mirabeau*: Honoré Gabriel Riqueti Mirabeau (1749–1791), French statesman and famous orator.

56. *since Cicero*: Who died in 43 B.C. For centuries his writings on rhetoric and his collected speeches were guides for public speakers.

a. Published posthumously. Translated by Dwight Durling.

16. *Stuttgart . . . Neckar*: The capital of the kingdom of Baden-Württemberg, whose denizens remain stock figures of fun in Germany today as dull and materialistic.

b. Published posthumously. Translated by Ernst Feise.

Tenderly in his arm—How sweetly gentle
Was then his smile, his glance so full of bliss!
Thus it would happen that his wreath of poppies,
His head encircling, grazed my forehead also
And with strange fragrance banished all the pain   10
Out of my soul—Yet such a kind reprieve
It lasts but a short while, because completely
Restored can I be only when his brother,
The stern and pallid one, inverts his torch.—
Oh, sleep is good, death better—to be sure,   15
The best of all were not to have been born.

14. *inverts his torch*: That is, snuffs it out.

ALEXANDER PUSHKIN
(1799–1837)
Eugene Onegin*

Chapter One

He is in haste to live and hies himself to feel—K. VYAZEMSKY†

1

"Now that he is in grave condition,
My uncle, decorous old prune,
Has earned himself my recognition;
What could have been more opportune?
May his idea inspire others;   5
But what a bore, I ask you, brothers,
To tend a patient night and day
And venture not a step away:
Is there hypocrisy more glaring
Than to amuse one all but dead,   10
Shake up the pillow for his head,
Dose him with melancholy bearing,
And think behind a stifled cough,
'When will the Devil haul you off?' "

2

Thus a young good-for-nothing muses,   15
As in the dust his coach wheels spin,

* Chapters I and II, translated by Walter Arndt. Pushkin completed his verse-novel in 1830, made subsequent revisions until its publication in 1833.
† *Vyazemsky*: Pushkin's friend: poet, critic, satirist.

By a decree of sovereign Zeus's
The extant heir to all his kin.
Friends of Ruslan and of Lyudmila!
Allow me, with no cautious feeler   20
Or foreword, to present at once
The hero of my new romance:
Onegin, a dear friend of mine,
Born where Nevá flows, and where you,
I daresay, gentle reader, too   25
Were born, or once were wont to shine;
There I myself once used to be:
The North, though, disagrees with me.

3

Fresh from a blameless state career,
His father lived on IOU's,   30
He used to give three balls a year,
Until he had no more to lose,
Fate treated young Onegin gently:
Madame first watched him competently,
From her *Monsieur* received the child;   35
The boy was likable, though wild.
Monsieur, a poor *abbé* from Paris,
To spare the youngster undue strain,
Would teach him in a playful vein,
With moral strictures rarely harass,   40
Reprove him mildly for each lark,
And walk him in the Summer Park.

4

But when young manhood's stormy morrow
Broke in due course for young Eugene,
The age of hope and tender sorrow,   45
Monsieur was driven from the scene.
This left Eugene in free possession;
Clad in a London dandy's fashion,
With hair style of the latest cast,
He joined Society at last.   50
In writing and in conversation
His French was perfect, all allowed;

---

17. *Zeus*: the king of the Greek gods.
19. *Ruslan and Lyudmila*: characters in Pushkin's first narrative poem, published 1830.
24. *Néva*: river at Leningrad (formerly St. Petersburg) connecting Lake Ladoga with the Gulf of Finland.
28. *The North*: I.e., St. Petersburg,
"where Néva flows." Pushkin wrote these lines in exile in southern Russia.
34–7. *Madame . . . abbé*: Eugene is raised first by a French governess, then a male tutor, then a priest.
42. *Summer Park*: Summer Palace of Peter the Great, later a public garden.

He danced Mazurkas well and bowed
Without constraint or affectation.
Enough! Society's verdict ran: 55
A bright and very nice young man.

5

Since we pick up our education
In bits and pieces here and there,
To earn a brilliant reputation
With us, thank God, is no affair.   60
It was conceded he had learning
(By judges ruthless and discerning),
Though of a somewhat bookish drift;
For he possessed the happy gift
Of unaffected conversation: 65
To skim one topic here, one there,
Keep silent with an expert's air
In too exacting disputation,
And with a flash of sudden quips
Charm tender smiles to tender lips.   70

6

The Latin vogue has now receded,
And I must own that, not to brag,
He had what knowledge may be needed
To puzzle out a Latin tag,
Flaunt Juvenal in a discussion,   75
Add "Vale" to a note in Russian;
Of the Aeneid, too, he knew,
With some mistakes, a line or two.
To burrow in the dusty pages
Of Clio's chronologic waste   80
Was not to our hero's taste;
But anecdotes of bygone ages,
From Romulus to days just past,
To these his memory clung fast.

7

To hold life cheap for Sound, he never   85
Experienced the sacred curse:
Do what we would, he took forever
Iambic for trochaic verse.

---

53. *Mazurkas*: lively Polish dance in triple time, resembling a polka.
75. *Juvenal*: Decimus Junius Juvenalis (ca. A.D. 60–130), Roman satirical poet.
76. *Vale*: Latin, "farewell."
80. *Clio*: The muse of history.
83. *Romulus*: legendary founder of Rome, eighth century B.C.
85. *Sound*: Poetry.
88. *iambic . . . trochaic*: metrical feet consisting respectively of an unaccented syllable and an accented one (˘ ´), and an accented syllable and an unaccented one (´ ˘).

Homer, Theocritus disdaining,
From Adam Smith he sought his training   90
And was no mean economist;
That is, he could present the gist
Of how states prosper and stay healthy
Without the benefit of gold,
The secret being that, all told,   95
The *basic staples* make them wealthy.
His father failed to understand,
And mortgaged the ancestral land.

8

Eugene's attainments were far vaster
Than I can take the time to show,   100
But where he really was a master,
Where he knew all there is to know,
What early meant in equal measure
His toil, his torment, and his pleasure,
What occupied at every phase   105
The leisured languor of his days,
Was the pursuit of that Fair Passion
Which Ovid sang, and for its sake
Was doomed to drain, in mutinous ache,
His glittering life's remaining ration   110
'Mid dear Moldavia's cloddish loam,
Far from his dear Italian home.

(9)[a]

un acteur
a poseur

10

He learnt so early how to languish,
To reassure, compel belief,
Dissemble hope, feign jealous anguish,   115
Appear morose or sunk in grief,
To seem now proud and now obedient,
Cool or attentive, as expedient!
How dull he could be, with intent,
How passionately eloquent,   120
How casual-warm a letter-sender!
One goal in mind, one seeking most
How utterly he was engrossed!

89. *Theocritus*: Greek pastoral poet in the third century B.C., author of the *Idylls*.

90. *Adam Smith*: Scottish philosopher and economist (1723–1790), author of *The Wealth of Nations* (1776).

108. *Ovid*: Publius Ovidius Naso (43 B.C.–A.D. 18), author of *The Art of Love*, *Metamorphoses*, and much amatory verse; he spent his last years in exile in Moldavia on the Black Sea.

a. Stanzas with two numbers occur because either Pushkin or the Russian censor made deletions. Missing lines are also to be thus explained.

How swift his glance was and how tender,
Bold-shy, and when the time was here,   125
Aglitter with obedient tear!

11

Forever new and interesting,
He scared with ready-made despair,
Amazed the innocent with jesting,
With flattery amused the fair,   130
Seized the chance instant of compliance
To sway ingenuous youth's defiance
By ardor or astute finesse,
Lure the spontaneous caress,
Implore, nay, force a declaration,   135
Ambush the first-note of the heart,
Flush Love from cover, and then dart
To fix a secret assignation . . .
And after that, to educate
His prey in private tête-à-tête!   140

12

How soon he even set aflutter
Inveterate flirts' well-seasoned hearts!
What ruthless scandal could he utter,
Once he resolved with poisoned darts
To bring about a rival's ruin!   145
What snares he laid for his undoing!
Yet you, blithe husbands, by Fate's whim
Remain on friendly terms with him:
Him of all men the shrewd spouse fawns on,
Post-graduate of Faublas' old school,   150
And the most skeptical old fool
And the bombastic ass with horns on,
Contented ever with his life,
Himself, his dinner, and his wife.

[margin handwritten note:] bubbles & cuckolds

(13, 14)

15

The social notes are brought in gently,   155
While he is rising, or before.
What—invitations? Evidently,
Three for a single night, what's more.
A ball here, there a children's party;

---

150. *Faublas*: Faublas was the hero of the novel *The Adventures of Faublas* (1798), by Jean Baptiste Louvet de Cou-
vray (1760–1797). His "adventures" are mainly amatory.

Which will he skip to, our young hearty? ₁₆₀
Which take up first now, let us see . . .
No matter—he can do all three.
Meanwhile there's boulevard parading:
Eugene, in faultless morning trim
And *Bolivar* with ample brim, ₁₆₅
Drives out and joins the promenading,
Till the repeater's watchful peal
Recalls him to the midday meal.

16

Nightfall; the sleigh receives him. Listen:
He's off with shouts of "way—away!" ₁₇₀
His beaver collar starts to glisten
With hoarfrost dusting silver-gray.
On to Talon's, pace unabating,
Kaverin will no doubt be waiting.
He enters: corks begin to fly, ₁₇₅
The Comet's vintage gushes high,
Here roast beef oozes bloody juices,
And near that flower of French cuisine,
The truffle, youth's delight, is seen
The deathless pie Strasbourg produces, ₁₈₀
Mid Limburger's aroma bold
And the pineapple's luscious gold.

17

Their thirst for yet more goblets clamors
To douse the sizzling cutlet grease,
But the repeater's jingling hammers ₁₈₅
Bid them to the new ballet piece.
The stage's arbiter exacting,
Who to the charming queens of acting
His fervent, fickle worship brings
Established freeman of the wings, ₁₉₀
Eugene, of course, must not be missing
Where everyone without *faux pas*
Is free to cheer an *entrechat*,

165. *Bolivar*: the reference is to Simón Bolívar (1783–1830), leader of the revolution of Venezuela against Spain, later dictator of Chile. Bolívar's portraits indicate he favored broad-brimmed headgear.

173. *Talon*: Well-known restaurateur. [Pushkin's note.]

174. *Kaverin*: dandy, sport, man-about-town, and friend of Pushkin, to whom the poet wrote several affectionate poems.

176. *Comet*: A champagne of 1811, also the year of a comet.

180. *pie*: possibly made of goose-liver, for which Strasbourg—the capiital of Alsace—is famous.

181. *Limburger*: known for its odor; a product of the Belgian and Dutch provinces bearing the same name.

185. *repeater*: Pocket watch.

193. *entrechat*: a ballet step, where the feet are struck or crossed while the dancer is in the air.

Jeer Cleopatra, Phèdre, with hissing,
Call out Moïna (in a word,   195
Make sure that he is seen and heard).

18

Ah, Fairyland! In former season
He who was Satire's sovereign keen,
He shone there, Freedom's friend, Fonvízin,
And the deft mimicker, Khyazhnín   200
There Ozeróv in national audits
Took tribute free of tears and plaudits
With young Semyónova to share;
Corneille's majestic muse was there
By our Katénin newly rendered;   205
There did the mordant Shakhovskoy
His riotous comedies deploy,
There to Didelot were laurels tendered,
There, in the backdrops' shady maze,
I whiled away my youthful days.   210

19

My goddesses! Speak, have you vanished?
Oh, hearken to my plaintive call:
Are you the same? Did others banish
And oust, but not replace you all?
Will once again your music capture,   215
The inspired soaring me enrapture
Of our own Terpsichore?
Or will the listless eye not see
On tedious stage familiar faces,
Scan with distraught binoculars   220
An alien world bereft of stars;
Cool witness to those heady graces,
Shall I be yawning at the cast
And mutely hanker for the past?

20

The house is full, the boxes gleaming,   225
Orchestra, pit, all is astir,

195. *Moïna*: heroine in the play *Fin-gal* by Ozeróv, based on James Mac-Pherson's spurious epic of that name (cf. the notes to *René*).
199. *Fonvízin*: writer of comedies during the reign of Catherine the Great.
200. *Knyazhnín*: minor dramatist of the same period.
203. *Semyónova*: popular actress (1786–1849).
205. *Katénin*: translator of plays by Corneille and Racine.
206. *Shakhovskóy*: a prince, and patron of the theater.
208. *Didelot*: French ballet-master in St. Petersburg.
217. *Terpsichore*: Muse of the dance.

Impatient clapping from the teeming
Gallery—then the curtain's whir.
There stands ashimmer, half ethereal,
Obedient to the imperial   230
Musician's wand, amid her corps
Of nymphs, Istómina—to the floor
Touching one foot, the other shaping
A slow-drawn circle, then—surprise—
A sudden leap, and away she flies   235
Like down from Aeol's lip escaping,
Bends and unbends to rapid beat
And twirling trills her tiny feet.

21

Applause all round. Onegin enters,
Walks over toes along his row.   240
His double spyglass swoops and centers
On box-seat belles he does not know.
All tiers his scrutiny embraces,
He saw it all: the gowns and faces
Seemed clearly to offend his sight;   245
He traded bows on left and right
With gentlemen, at length conceded
An absent gaze at the ballet,
Then with a yawn he turned away.
And spoke: "In all things change is needed;   250
On me ballets have lost their hold;
Didelot himself now leaves me cold."

22

While yet the cupids, devils, monkeys
Behind the footlights prance and swoop;
While yet the tired tribe of flunkies   255
Sleep on their furs around the stoop;
While yet they have not finished clapping,
Nose-blowing, coughing, hissing, tapping;
While yet the lanterns everywhere
Inside and outside shed their glare;   260
While yet chilled horses yank the tether
And harness-weary champ the bit,
And coachmen round the fires sit,
And, cursing, beat their palms together:
Onegin has already gone   265
To put his evening costume on.

232. *Istomina*: a dancer who died in
1848.

236. *Aeol*: Aeolus, Greek god of the
winds.

23

Oh, will it be within my powers
To conjure up the private den
Where Fashion's acolyte spent hours
To dress, undress, and dress again?   270
What London makes for cultured whimsy
Of novelties polite and flimsy,
And ships upon the Baltic brine
To us for tallow and for pine,
All that Parisian modish passion   275
And earnest industry collect
To tempt the taste of the elect
With comfort and caress of fashion,
Adorned the boudoir of our green
Philosopher at age eighteen.   280

24

Bronze-work and china on the table
An ambered hookah from Stambul,
Spirits in crystal bottles, able
To soothe the brow with scented cool;
Steel files and little combs unending,   285
And scissors straight and scissors bending,
And brushes—recollection fails—
For hair and teeth and fingernails.
Rousseau—please pardon this digression—
Could not conceive how solemn Grimm   290
Dared clean his nails in front of *him*,
Great bard of silver-tongued obsession.
Our champion of Man's liberties
Here surely was too hard to please!

25

One can be capable and moral   295
With manicure upon one's mind:
Why vainly chide one's age and quarrel?
Custom is lord of all mankind.
Chadáyev-like, Eugene was zealous,
Forestalling censure by the jealous,   300
To shun the least sartorial flaws—
A *swell*, as the expression was.
He used to squander many an hour
Before the mirrors in his room,

---

282. *Stambul*: Istanbul, Constantinople.
290. *Grimm*: Friedrich Melchior, Baron Grimm (1723–1807), friend of Rousseau, Diderot, D'Alembert, etc.
293. *champion*: i.e., Rousseau.
299. *Chadáyev*: An elegant friend of Pushkin's.

Until he issued forth abloom 305
Like playful Venus from her bower,
When in a man's disguise arrayed,
The goddess joins a masquerade.

26

Now that this modish apparition
Has drawn your casual interest, 310
With the discerning world's permission,
I might describe how he was dressed;
I'd do it not without compunction;
Still, to describe is my true function—
But *pantalons*, *gilet* and *frack*— 315
With such words Russian has no truck,
For as it is, I keep inviting
Your censure for the way I use
Outlandish words of many hues
To deck my humble style of writing, 320
Although I used to draw upon
The Academic Lexicon.

27

But never mind this—we must hurry,
For while extraneous themes I broach,
Onegin in a headlong flurry 325
Drives to the ball by hired coach;
Along the housefronts past him speeding,
Down streets aslumber, fast receding,
The double carriage lanterns bright
Shed their exhilarating light 330
And brush the snow with rainbow flutters;
With sparkling lampions, row on row,
The splendid mansion stands aglow;
In shadow-play across the shutters
Flit profile heads of demoiselles 335
And fashionably well-groomed swells.

28

Now he has reached the frontal fareway,
Flashed past the stately doorman, and,
Pausing atop the marble stairway
To touch his hair up with his hand, 340
He enters. The great hall is swarming,

---

315. *pantalons, gilet and frack*: Trousers, waistcoat and dinner jacket, the elements of formal dress. The first two
words are French; the third, German.

322. *Academy Lexicon*: the French
Academy's conservative dictionary of
correct French vocabularly, begun in the
seventeenth century and not yet finished.

The band benumbered by its own storming,
In hum and hubbub, tightly pent,
The crowd's on the Mazurka bent;
Spurs ring, sparks glint from guardsmen's shoulders, 345
Belles' shapely feet and ankles sleek
Whirl by, and in their passing wreak
Much flaming havoc on beholders,
And fiddle music skirls and drowns
Sharp gibes of wives in modish gowns. 350

29

When ardent dreams and dissipations
Were with me still, I worshiped balls:
No safer place for declarations,
Or to deliver tender scrawls.
Beware, you estimable spouses, 355
Look to the honor of your houses!
I wish you well, and so here goes
An earnest word from one who knows . . .
And you, Mamas of daughters, leaven
Your wits and shelter well your pets, 360
Keep straight and polished your lorgnettes!
Or else . . . or else, oh, gracious Heaven!
Such sound advice comes to my tongue
Because I haven't sinned so long.

30

I burnt so much of life's brief candle 365
In levity I now regret!
Still, balls—but for the moral scandal
They breed, I should adore them yet.
I thrill to ardent youth's outpouring,
The crush and blaze, the spirit's soaring, 370
Those beauties artfully arrayed;
I love their feet—though I'm afraid
Throughout our land you won't discover
Three pairs of shapely female feet.
Ah—one I long could not delete 375
From memory . . . and still they hover,
Burnt-out and sad as I may be,
About my dreams and trouble me.

31

When, where, what wildernesses threading
Will you forget them, luckless clown? 380
Dear little feet, where are you treading

The wildflowers of a vernal down?
Fine-bred in climes of Orient mildness,
On snowfields of our boreal wildness
You never left the faintest trace;   385
No, the voluptuous embrace
Of swelling carpets did you treasure.
Has it been long I ceased to rue
My home, my freedom over you,
Forgot my greed for fame and pleasure?   390
Youth's happy years have waned, alas—
Like your light footprints in the grass.

32

The breast of Dian, I adore it,
And Flora's cheek to me is sweet!
And yet I would not barter for it   395
Terpsichore's enchanting feet.
For they, the captive gaze ensnaring
With pledge of bliss beyond comparing,
Unbridle with their token charm
Desires' wayward, wanton swarm.   400
These, friend Elvina, I admire—
By tablecovers half concealed,
In springtime on an emerald field,
In winter, propped before a fire,
When over gleaming floors they flee   405
Or stand on boulders by the sea.

33

I watched the sea when storm was boding,
And, jealous, saw the waves compete,
With uproar each the other goading,
To curl in love about her feet!   410
Then of their kiss how I was aching
With my own lips to be partaking!
Ah—never, even in the blaze
Of early youth's tumultuous days,
Was I so racked with the desire   415
A kiss on maiden lips to claim,
On cheeks on which the roses flame,
On breasts astir with sultry fire;
No, never passion's gusts have wrought
A like destruction in my thought!   420

393. *Dian*: Or Diana, Latin goddess of the hunt. *Flora*: Latin goddess of flowers.

401. *Elvina*: Certain critics have suggested that Pushkin used the name as a conventional device; and in his lyrics, "Elvina" may represent three different females. Here she may be Maria Rajevsky, whom the poet knew when he was exiled to the Caucasus in 1820.

34

I recollect one more such passion—
At times, in daydreams full of balm,
I hold glad hands out, stirrup-fashion—
And feel a foot cupped in my palm;
And still from these bewitching touches   425
Imagination seethes, clutches
The withered heart with fire again
Once more in love, once more in pain! . . .
But silence now—the garrulous lyre
Has praised those haughty ones enough;   430
In vain the odes which they inspire,
In vain the transports which they scoff!
Their speeches and their glances sweet
At last deceive you . . . like their feet.

35

But what about Onegin? Nodding,   435
He's driven homeward from the ball,
While drumbeats have long since been prodding
To life the strenuous capital.
The peddler struts, the merchant dresses,
The cabman to the market presses,   440
With jars the nimble milkmaids go,
Their footsteps crunching in the snow.
The cheerful morning sounds and hustles
Begin, shops open, stacks have puffed
Tall trunks of slate-blue smoke aloft;   445
The baker, punctual German, bustles
White-capped behind his service hatch
And more than once has worked the latch.

36

But, worn-out by the ballroom's clamor,
And making midnight out of dawn,   450
The child of luxury and glamour
Sleeps tight, in blissful shade withdrawn.
At noon or so he wakes—already
Booked up till next dawn, in a steady
Motley routine of ceaseless play: 455
Tomorrow will be like Today.
In youth's bloom, free of prohibition,
With brilliant conquests to his name,
Each day a feast, his life a game,
Was he content with his condition?   460
Or was he hearty and inane
Amid carousals—but in vain?

37

Yes—feeling early cooled within him;
He came to loathe that worldly grind;
Proud beauties could no longer win him   465
And uncontested rule his mind;
Constant inconstancy turns dreary;
Of friends and friendship he grew weary:
One can't forever and again
Chase with a bottle of champagne   470
Beefsteak and Strasbourg liver pasty
And scatter insults all around
When senses swim and temples pound:
And so, although by temper hasty,
Our lad at length was overfed   475
With taunts and duels, sword and lead.

38

A malady to whose causation
We have, alas, as yet no clues,
Known as the Spleen to Albion's nation,
In our parlance just: the Blues—   480
With this disease he was infected;
He never, thank the Lord, projected
To put a bullet through his brain;
But life-at-large now seemed inane;
Wry, gloomy, with Childe Harold vying,   485
He seemed to languish in *salons*,
No worldly gossip, no *Boston*,
Nor tender glance, nor wanton sighing,
Henceforward seemed to touch a string;
He ceased to notice anything.   490

(39, 40, 41)

42

O weird and wondrous lionesses!
It's you he first of all forswore;
And high-life manners, one confesses,
These days are really quite a bore.
Although at times some well-born charmers   495
Talk Say and Bentham at us farmers,
Their conversation on the whole

479. *Albion's nation*: England.

485. *Childe Harold*: Byron's disenchanted hero in the poem by the same name (1812–1818).

487. *Boston*: a game of cards resembling whist, in which the technical terms refer to the British siege of Boston at the start of the American Revolution.

496. *Say . . . Bentham*: Jean-Baptiste Say (1767–1832), French economist who popularized the ideas of Adam Smith; Jeremy Bentham (1748–1832), founder of the Utilitarian philosophy.

Is hard to bear, however droll.
And what is worse, they are so stainless,
So lofty, so intelligent,   500
So piously benevolent,
So preternaturally swainless,
So circumspect and epicene,
Their very sight brings on the Spleen.

43

And you, too, beauteous young sirens,   505
Whose forward cabs begin to cruise,
As night advances, the environs
Of Petersburg's great avenues,
Desist! Eugene has had his measure.
Apostate from the whirl of pleasure,   510
He has retired to his den
And with a yawn reached for his pen.
He tried to write—from such tenacious
Endeavor, though, his mind recoiled;
And so the paper stayed unsoiled,   515
And he stayed out of that vivacious
Fraternity I don't condemn
Because, you see, I'm one of them.

44

Next, still to indolence a victim,
His vacant soul to languor prone,   520
A laudable desire pricked him
To make what others thought his own.
In scores of books, arrayed on shelving,
He read and read—in vain all delving:
Here length, there raving or pretense,   525
This one lacked candor, that one sense;
All had, each in its way, miscarried;
That which was old, was obsolete,
And what was new, with old replete;
Like first his women, he now buried   530
His books, and veiled their huddled shape
On dusty shelf with mourning crape.

45

Of worldly bustle and unreason
I'd shed the burden, as had he,
And we became good friends that season.   535
His features fascinated me,
His bent for dreamy meditation,

His strangeness, free of affectation,
His frigidly dissecting mind.
He was embittered, I maligned; 540
We both had drunk from Passion's chalice:
In either, life had numbed all zest;
Extinct the glow in either breast;
For both, too, lay in wait the malice
Of reckless fortune and of man, 545
When first our lease of life began.

46

He who has lived and thought can never
Look on mankind without disdain;
He who has felt is haunted ever
By days that will not come again; 550
No more for him enchantment's semblance,
On him the serpent of remembrance
Feeds, and remorse corrodes his heart.
All this is likely to impart
An added charm to conversation. 555
At first, indeed, Onegin's tongue
Used to abash me; but ere long
I liked his acid derogation,
His humor, half shot-through with gall,
Grim epigrams' malicious drawl. 560

47

How oft in summer by the river,
When a diffuse translucent glow
Sets the nocturnal sky ashiver—
Nevá's gay mirror loath to throw
The moon back, Dian's pallid semblance— 565
How often, sunken in remembrance
Of bygone ardors, bygone love,
Did we, still moved, but now above
Past hazard, ramble there and quiver
With the night's balm in mute delight! 570
As some fair dream from prison night
The sleeping convict may deliver
To verdant forests—fancy-lorn
We reveled there at life's young morn.

48

His soul in rueful agitation, 575
Stood leaning on the granite shelf
Onegin, lost in meditation,

As once a bard described himself.
And all is calm save for the trailing
Calls of a lonely watchman hailing   580
Another, and the distant sound
Of cabs that over pavements pound;
A lonely boat, its paddles weaving,
Was on the slumbering river borne;
And wayward singing, and a horn   585
Charmed our ears, the silence cleaving . . .
Yet, 'mid nocturnal reveling
Torquato's octaves sweeter sing!

49

O waters of the Adriatic,
O Brenta! I shall see you, know   590
Your witching voice and be ecstatic
With inspiration's quickened flow!
To Phoebus' children consecrated,
By Albion's haughty lyre translated
It was my own and sang through me.   595
The nights of golden Italy,
On their delights I shall be gloating
At will; with a Venetian girl,
Her tongue now silent, now apurl,
In secret gondola be floating;   600
And in her arms my lips will strain
For Petrarch's and for love's refrain.

50

When strikes my liberation's hour?
It's time, it's time—I bid it hail;
I pace the shore, the sky I scour   605
And beckon to each passing sail.
Storm-canopied, wave-tossed in motion
On boundless highroads of the ocean,
When do I win unbounded reach?
It's time to leave the tedious beach   610
That damps my spirit, to be flying
Where torrid southern blazes char

---

578. *a bard*: A. N. Muravyov; Pushkin draws on Muravyov's poem, "To the
Goddess of the Neva."

588. *Torquato's octaves*: The eight-
line stanza (Ottava rima) of the poetry
of Torquato Tasso (1544–1595).

590. *Brenta*: river near Venice, emptying into the Adriatic.

593. *Phoebus' children*: i.e., poets.

594. *Albion's haughty lyre*: e.g., Byron's *Childe Harold*.

602. *Petrarch's . . . refrain*: Refers to
the Italian sonnets which Francesco Pe-
trarca (1304–1374), first and greatest of
the Italian humanists, wrote to Laura.

603. *liberation*: Refers again to Pushkin's southern exile.

My own, my native Africa,
There of dank Russia to be sighing,
Where once I loved, where now I weep,   615
And where my heart is buried deep.

51

My friend Onegin had decided
With me on foreign sights to gaze;
However, Destiny divided
For a long season our ways.   620
His father's days just then had ended,
And promptly on Eugene descended
The moneylenders' hungry breed;
Each with his story and his deed.
Eugene, who hated litigation,   625
Accepting graciously his fate,
Made over the defunct estate
With no great sense of deprivation;
Perhaps he had an inkling, too,
That his old uncle's death was due.   630

52

And as he had anticipated,
His uncle's steward soon sent news
That the old man was quite prostrated
And wished to say his last adieus.
In answer to the grievous tiding,   635
By rapid stage Eugene came riding
Posthaste to honor his behest;
Prepared, in view of the bequest,
For boredom, sights, and simulation,
And stifling yawns well in advance   640
(With this I opened my romance):
But when he reached his destination,
His uncle lay on his last berth,
Due to be rendered unto earth.

53

He found the manor full of mourners,   645
Connections dear and not so dear,
Who had converged there from all corners,
All funeral fans, it would appear.

---

613. *Africa*: Pushkin's maternal great-grandfather may have been Hannibal, son of an Ethiopian king, brought to Constantinople as a hostage and taken by the Russian envoy to Russia; there he became a favorite of Peter the Great, who stood godfather to him, ennobled him, and married him off to one of the court ladies.

They laid to rest the late lamented,
Then, dined and wined and well-contented,   650
The priest and guests left one by one,
Gravely, as from a job well done.
There was Eugene, a landed squire,
Of forests, waters, mills galore
The sovereign lord—he who before   655
Had been a scamp and outlaw dire—
And pleased to see his life's stale plot
Exchanged for—well, no matter what.

54

Two days the solitary meadows
Retained for him their novel look,   660
The leafy groves with cooling shadows
And the sedately murmuring brook;
Next day he did not take the trouble
To glance at coppice, hill and stubble,
Then they brought on a sleepy mood,   665
And he was ready to conclude.
"Spleen" does not spare the landed gentry,
It needs no palaces or streets,
No cards or balls or rhymed conceits.
Spleen hovered near him like a sentry   670
And haunted all his waking life
Like a shadow, or a faithful wife.

55

I'm made to live in some still shire,
I thrive in rural quietude:
'Mid silence, bolder is the lyre,   675
More vivid the creative mood.
On simple pastimes bent, I wander
By the deserted lakeside yonder,
Dolce far niente is my code;
And each succeeding dawn can bode   680
But carefree hours sweetly wasted:
I read a little, sleep a lot
And chase the phantom Glory not.
In years gone by, have I not tasted
In leisure and in shade like this   685
My most unclouded days of bliss?

56

The countryside, love, flowers, leisure,
Green fields—I love their very name;

679. *dolce far niente*: Sweet idleness.

And here, I note once more with pleasure,   690
Eugene and I are not the same.
I say this lest some sneering reader,
Or any God-forsaken breeder
Of heinous libels should appear,
Profess to see my portrait here   695
And circulate the wicked fable
That I walk in my hero's dress,
Like Byron, bard of haughtiness,
As though we were by now unable
On any subject to intone
A song, but on ourselves alone.   700

57

All poets—while I'm on these subjects—
Are given to daydreaming love;
My soul, too, harbored charming objects
Whom I at times have daydreamed of,
And kept an image of their features;   705
The Muse breathed life into these creatures,
Then I could safely serenade
Both my ideal, the mountain maid,
And the Salgir's fair slaves admire.
These days I often listen to   710
A certain question, friends, from you:
"For whom, then, languishes your lyre?
Among the maiden's jealous throng,
To whom do you inscribe your song?"

58

"Whose gazes, kindling inspiration,   715
Have recompensed from melting eyes
Your meditative incantation?
Whom did your verse immortalize?"
Why, nobody, my friends, I swear it!
Love's mindless anguish, should I bear it   720
Once more with no reward at all?
Blest he who in its throes could fall
Into a rhyming fit, thus double
Parnassus' sacred frenzy, sing,
In Petrarch's footsteps following,   725
And not just ease the heart's deep trouble

708. *mountain maid*: heroine of Pushkin's narrative, Byronic poem, *The Caucasian Prisoner*, written with similar
works (*The Gypsies, The Brother Robbers*) between 1820 and 1824.

709. *Salgir's fair slaves*: The Salgir is
a river in the Crimea, setting for two
narrative poems by Pushkin, *The Prisoner of the Caucasus* and *The Fountain
of Bakhchiserai*. The "fair slaves" are
the heroines of the poems.

724. *Parnassus:* Mountain where the
nine muses dwelt.

But earn a famous name to boot:
While I, in love, was deaf and mute.

59

The Muse appeared, past Love's intrusion,
It cleared the mind in darkness bound,   730
And free once more, I seek the fusion
Of feeling, dream, and magic sound.
I write—no heartache stays my finders,
The wayward pen no longer lingers
To trace near verse left incomplete   735
Vignettes of female heads and feet;
Those ashes will not be rekindled;
I grieve still, but I weep no more;
Soon, soon all marks the tempest wore
Into my soul will quite have dwindled: 740
And then—why then I'll write a song
Some five-and-twenty cantos long.

60

I've thought about the hero's label
And on what lines the plot should run;
Meanwhile, it seems, my present fable   745
Has grown as far as Chapter One.
I have gone over it severely,
And contradictions there are clearly
Galore, but I will let them go,
Pay censorship its due, and throw   750
Imagination's newborn baby,
My labor's fruit with all its flaws
To the reviewers' greedy jaws;
To the Nevá, then, child, and maybe
You'll earn me the rewards of fame: 755
Distorted judgments, noise, and blame!

Chapter Two

O rus! . . . —HORACE*

1

The manor where Onegin fretted
Was so enchanting a retreat,
No simple soul would have regretted
Exile so pastoral and sweet:
The squire's mansion lay secluded   5

* "O Russia!" Also a pun on *Horace*.

Against a hill, no wind intruded,
Close-by a steam flowed; and away
There stretched a shimmering array
Of meads and cornfields gold-brocaded,
And hamlets winked; across the grass   10
A wandering herd would slowly pass;
Umbrageous arbors densely shaded
A park, far-rambling and unkempt,
Where pensive dryads sheltered dreamt.

2

The mansion had been built for leisure,   15
As stately houses ought to be,
Hewn to the calm and rugged measure
Of our astute antiquity.
Room after room with lofty ceiling
A tapestried *salon*, revealing   20
Ancestral portraits hung in file
And stoves of many-colored tile.
All this has now been superseded,
Exactly why, I never learned;
But where Onegin was concerned,   25
In any case it went unheeded,
Because he yawned with equal gloom
In any style of drawing room.

3

For his own use Eugene selected
The room where till his late demise   30
The laird had cursed his cook, inspected
The same old view, and swatted flies.
Couch, cupboards, table, all betoken
A simple taste; the floor is oaken,
Nowhere the faintest trace of ink,   35
The cupboards, opened to a chink,
Show batteries of homemade brandy
Some demijohns of applejack,
A twenty-year-old almanac
And an account book lying handy.   40
The busy squire had had no mind
For books of any other kind.

4

Bored in his lordly isolation,
Just to relieve the daily norm,
Eugene at first found occupation   45

446 · *Alexander Pushkin*

In bold agrarian reform.
The backwood wiseacre commuted
The harsh *corvée* had instituted
A quitrent system in its stead;
The serf called blessings on his head.   50
But his more thrifty neighbor, highly
Incensed, swelled in his nook and fought
The wicked and expensive thought;
Another only snickered slyly,
And one and all they set him down   55
As a subversive kind of clown.

5

At first the neighbors started calling;
But when he kept by the back stoop,
Their visits artfully forestalling,
A Cossack cob (to fly the coop   60
When rumbles of a homely coach
First warned him of a guest's approach),
Such conduct struck them as ill bred,
And all the County cut him dead.
"Our neighbor is uncouth; he's crazy;   65
A freemason; he only drinks
Red wine in tumblers; never thinks
To kiss a lady's hand—too lazy;
It's 'yes' and 'no,' no 'ma'am' or 'sir,'"
In this indictment all concur.   70

6

Just at this time the County sighted
One more young landlord, come to seek
His nearby manor, who invited
An equally severe critique.
Vladimir Lensky, in the flower   75
Of youthful looks and lyric power,
And impregnated to the core
With Göttingen and Kantian lore.
From German mists the poet-errant
Brought Teuton wisdom's clouded brew,   80
Dreams of libertarian hue,

48. *corvée*: Payment of rent in physical labor.
49. *quitrent*: rent paid by a freeholder in lieu of services which he might otherwise be found to perform.
60. *Cossack cob*: Cavalry horse.
67. *Red wine*: i.e., a man of foreign tastes. A "good" Russian would drink vodka.
78. *Göttingen*: university (founded 1737) popular with "Westernized" Russians in the early nineteenth century. Immanual Kant (1724–1804), professor at Königsberg, was one of the most influential philosophers of the late eighteenth century.

A spirit fiery, though aberrant,
Relentlessly impassioned speech,
And raven locks of shoulder reach.

7

Not yet by worldly traffic hardened   85
Or by its chill corruption seared,
His soul still knew how to be ardent,
By maidens charmed, by friendship cheered.
Dear ignoramus in the science
Of life, hope was his fond reliance;   90
Across his mind the world still drew
Its web of glitter and ado;
With rosy dreams he would belittle
His spirit's dubious surmise;
The goal of life was to his eyes   95
A species of alluring riddle;
On it he exercised his mind
And nameless marvels there divined.

8

He was assured, by Fate's designing,
A kindred soul must join his own,   100
Who, inconsolably repining,
Daily awaited him alone;
That loyal friends and benefactors
Yearned for the blood of his detractors
And would not flinch from ball and chain   105
To keep his honor free from stain;
That Destiny for us selected
Of dedicated friends a group,
And that the same immortal troupe
Would in bright splendor undeflected   110
One day illume us with its glow
And on the world its bliss bestow.

9

Compassion, noble indignation,
High impulses' ingenuous urge,
Ambition's joyous agitation   115
Stirred in his soul an early surge;
Instinct with Goethe's, Schiller's fire,
He roamed creation with his lyre,
And in their poetry's domains

117. *Schiller*: Friedrich Schiller (1759–1805), close friend of Goethe in Weimar: dramatist, poet, historian, philosopher.

The blood was fired in his veins. 120
Nor, lucky fellow, did he ever
Put the exalted Muse to shame:
From his proud harp there never came
Ought but exalted feelings, never
Worse than a dreamy maiden's plea 125
Or praise of grave simplicity.

10

Of love he sang, love's service choosing,
And limpid was his simple tune
As ever artless maiden's musing,
As babes aslumber, as the Moon 130
In heaven's tranquil regions shining,
Goddess of secrets and sweet pining;
He sang of partings, mists afar,
Of sorrow, of *je ne sais quoi*:
Romantic roses, distant islands 135
He used to sing of, where for years
He poured a generous toll of tears
Into the soothing lap of silence;
He mourned the wilt of life's young green
When he had almost turned eighteen. 140

11

Eugene alone could prize his talents
In those provincial backwoods dim,
The parties of the neighboring gallants
Did not for long appeal to him;
He shunned their stolid congregations. 145
Their sagely trivial conversations
Of haylofts filled and wine laid in,
Of cattle, kennel, kith and kin
Were hardly such as to inspire
Or captivate with worldly wit, 150
With depth of feeling, exquisite
Discernment, or poetic fire;
But their dear wives' colloquial tone
Was far less highbrow than their own.

12

The well-to-do "half-Russian neighbor," 155
Good-looking, too, became fair game;
Much ingenuity and labor
Was spent by many a scheming dame

---

134. *je ne sais quoi*: I know not what [French].

To hook him for her darling daughter,
As settled rural custom taught her.   160
They always work in something light
About the bachelor's dreary plight
The moment he appears, and fluting
Him in where Dunya pours his cup,
They hiss to her: "Dunya, sit up!"   165
And then they even bring her lute in,
On which, ye gods, she starts to strum:
"Into my golden chamber come!"

13

However, Lensky, far from begging
To wear the matrimonial bond,   170
Instead looked warmly to Onegin
For closer ties of friendship fond.
They met—none more unlike created,
Like wave and cliff absurdly mated,
Like ice and flame, or verse and prose.   175
Their alien ways at first impose
Constraint, but soon each finds the other's
Society a pleasant need;
They meet for daily rides; indeed
They soon are closer than two brothers.   180
Thus friends are made (I'm guilty, too)
For lack of anything to do.

14

Today, among us would-be heroes
Such friendship, too, is dead, one shelves
All sentiment; we count as zeroes   185
All other men except ourselves.
The world's Napoleons bemuse us:
Mankind, we think, is there to use as
So many million biped tools,
And feelings are for cranks and fools.   190
Eugene, endowed with more perception
Than many, knew and felt contempt
For men at large, but did exempt
A few (no rule without exception):
Their feelings, as beyond reproof,   195
He honored—though himself aloof.

15

The poet's fiery effusions
Eugene met with a smiling glance,
The judgments riddled with delusions,

And the habitual look of trance— 200
All this to him seemed strange and novel;
But he was careful not to cavil,
Or check the flow with caustic curb,
And mused: Who am I to disturb
This state of blissful, brief infection? 205
Its days are numbered without me;
And in the meantime, let him be
And glory in the world's perfection;
We must forgive Youth's fever sweet
Youthful delirium, youthful heat. 210

16
All subjects led to disputations
Between them and engendered thought;
The covenants of ancient nations,
The varied fruits that learning brought;
And Good and Evil, time-worn errors, 215
The great Beyond's mysterious terrors,
And Destiny and Life in turn
Engaged their serious concern.
Meantimes the poet, with the fulgence
Of his own phrases all ablaze, 220
Read fragments from the northern lays,
The while Onegin with indulgence,
Though he but little understood,
Took in intently what he could.

17
More often, though, our friends debated 225
The passions in their wilderness;
From their harsh sway now liberated,
Onegin could not but confess
To some regretful animation:
Blest he who knew their agitation 230
And issued from it scarred but free,
Who never knew them, twice blest he,
And who could slake desire with parting,
Hate with abuse—what if he tends
To yawn alike at wife and friends, 235
With jealous anguish never smarting,
And his ancestral ducats guards
From the insidious deuce of cards.

18
When we have rallied to the standard
Of a well-tempered quietude, 240

221. *northern lays*: The Germanic mythic sagas.

And blazing passions have been rendered
Absurd, their afterglow subdued,
Their lawless gusts and their belated
Last echoes finally abated—
Not without cost at peace again,   245
We like to listen now and then
To alien passion's rage and seething,
And feel it wrench at our heart;
We play the battered veteran's part
Who strains to listen, barely breathing,   250
To exploits of heroic youth,
Forgotten in his humble booth.

19

For its part, ardent youth gives warning
Of what it feels, and can't deceive;
Aversion, love, rejoicing, mourning;   255
They all are worn upon the sleeve.
Onegin, invalid of passion,
Would listen with a grave expression
As Lensky, eager to impart
What moved him, opened wide his heart.   260
His inmost hoard of artless feeling
Did he confidingly unveil;
His youthful love's ingenuous tale
Onegin was not long unsealing;
A most affecting story, true,   265
To us, however, far from new.

20

He loved—ah, such a love is never
These days to humble mortal known;
With such a love is no one ever
Cursed but the poet's heart alone;   270
With but a sole desire swooning
One dream's relentless importuning,
A single ever-present grief.
Not sobering distance brought relief,
Not numbling years of separation   275
Not riotous pleasure, learning's balm,
No alien beauty's perfumed arm,
Nor yet the Muse's consolation
Had any power to control
The virgin fire in his soul.   280

21

A stripling yet, his Olga fired
The heart untouched by amorous flames,

By him she wanted to be squired,
With him to share her girlish games;
In sheltered groves, across the heather,   285
They used to sport and roam together,
Predestined for the marriage bond
By parents and by neighbors fond.
In her retreat, in peaceful shadow
She blossomed in her parents' view,   290
In charming innocence she grew
Like the shy lily of the meadow,
Unknown in her secluded lea
To butterfly and bumblebee.

22

It was the poet who had fired   295
Her untried passion's maiden dream,
It was her image which inspired
His plaintive reed-pipe's maiden theme.
Farewell, O golden time of frolic!
In sylvan groves the melancholic   300
Found in secluded silence boon
And worshiped Night, and Stars, and Moon—
The moon, celestial luminary,
To whom we, too, our toll have paid
Of many a twilight promenade   305
And weeping, hidden heartache's parry . . .
But lately we have seen in her
But one more lantern's tarnished blur.

23

Demure, obedient ever, seeming
Like poet's life in artlessness,   310
Like sunny morning ever beaming,
Delightful as young love's caress,
With eyes of blue like Heaven's inlets,
A tender smile and flaxen ringlets,
Light grace of movement, voice, and build,   315
Thus Olga . . . novels, though, are filled
With faithful portraits of her features,
You look them up, they're nice—indeed,
I liked the type once, I concede,
But got fed up with the dear creatures.   320
Straight to her elder sister then,
Dear reader, let me turn my pen.

24

Tatyana was her name . . . I grovel
That with such humble name I dare
To consecrate a tender novel.   325
And yet, I ask you, is it fair
To sneer at it? It's full-toned, pleasant,
What if it's fragrant with a peasant
Antiqueness, if it does recall
The servant quarters? We must all   330
Confess, in names we have forsaken
Good taste—and elsewhere, too, it's weak
(Of verse I will not even speak);
Enlightenment just hasn't taken
In our case, for ever since   335
All we have learnt is how to mince.

25

So I repeat her name—Tatyana.
Not by a fresh and rosy hue
Nor by her beauty could she garner
The glances that her sister drew.   340
To wistful silence given, timid
Like deer-fawn at the woodland's limit,
Born in their midst, she seemed to be
A stranger to her family,
Unable to make up to father   345
Or mother; though herself a child,
In children's games and capers wild
She never wished to join, but rather
By her own window she was prone
To muse in silence and alone.   350

26

Imagination, which she relished,
From cradle days her dearest friend,
Wrapped her in fancies that embellished
Her rustic life's unhurried trend.
The delicately nurtured finger   355
Spurned needlework, nor would she linger,
Bent to embroidery hoops, to fine
Dull linen with a silk design.
A child at play before her forum
Of docile dolls (proof of the will   360
To dominate) learns by this drill

What makes the world go round—decorum,
And labors gravely to transfer
To them what Mama just taught her.

27

But Tanya showed no inclination   365
To play with dolls when she was small,
Review with them in conversation
The gowns and gossip of the mall,
And childish mischief was not for her;
She rather thrilled to tales of horror,   370
Which of a somber winter night
Filled her with shuddering delight.
Again, when Nanny used to summon
All Olga's playmates, and had drawn
The girls around her on the lawn   375
To play a tag-game, it was common
To see her spurn the fun and noise,
A stranger to their giddy joys.

28

Upon her balcony at dawning
She liked to bide the break of day,   380
When on the heavens' pallid awning
There fades the starry roundelay,
When earth's faith rim is set to glowing,
Aurora's herald breeze is blowing
And step by step the world turns light.   385
In wintertime, when darkling night
The hemisphere for longer covers,
And sunk in idle quietude,
Beneath a hazied moon subdued,
The languid Orient longer hovers—   390
Roused at accustomed time, she might
Begin the day by candlelight.

29

But novels, which she early favored,
Replaced for her all other treats;
With rapturous delight she savored   395
Rousseau's and Richardson's conceits.
Her honest father, tough old-fashioned,
Last century's child, grew not impassioned

---

384. *Aurora*: Goddess of the dawn.
396. *Rousseau . . . Richardson*: for
the former, cf. notes in this volume;
Samuel Richardson (1689–1761) was an
English author of epistolary novels: *Pamela* (1740–1741), *Clarissa Harlowe*
(1747–1748).

About the harm that books might breed;
He, who was never known to read,   400
Regarded them as empty thrillers
And never thought to bring to light
Which secret volume dreamt at night
Beneath his little daughter's pillows.
His wife, at that, herself had been   405
Long since a slave to Richardson.

30

The reason for her firm devotion
Was not the books she hadn't read,
Nor that from Lovelace her emotion
Had turned to Grandison instead.   410
But years ago her cousin Nancy,
A Moscow princess, caught her fancy
With many lectures in his praise.
All this was part of the sad phase
When she had, much against her feeling,   415
Accepted Larin, while she pined
For quite another, to her mind
Incomparably more appealing:
This Grandison was fond of cards,
A fop, and sergeant of the Guards.   420

31

In dress she was quite like her idol,
Stylish and exquisitely nice;
But presently they set her bridal
And never asked for her advice.
On purpose to appease her sorrow,   425
The wise young husband on the morrow
Left for the country, where her gloom,
Thrown as she was on God knows whom,
At first was measureless and tearful,
The marriage almost came to grief;   430
Then by and by she found relief
In management and grew quite cheerful.
Habit is Heaven's own redress;
It takes the place of happiness.

32

Thus habit soothed the grief that chafed her,   435
The ache that nothing could appease;

---

409. *Lovelace*: seducer of Clarissa.
410. *Grandison*: priggish hero of Richardson's *The History of Sir Charles*

Grandison.
420. *Guards*: élite regiment attached
to the ruling monarch.

Then a great insight was vouchsafed her
That put her finally at ease:
Between the daily work and leisure
She soon contrived to take the measure   440
Of her good spouse and seize the reins;
This put an end to all her pains.
She went about her daily labors,
She labeled pickled-mushroom crocks,
She kept accounts, she shore off locks,   445
Took Sabbath baths like all her neighbors,
Struck at the housemaids when so moved,
And never asked if he approved.

33

In girlhood days she had been keener
To pledge her friends in tender scrawl,   450
Address Praskovya as Paulina
And speak with a melodious drawl;
Tight hourglass corsets she affected,
Her "n"'s were expertly ejected
A *la française* and through the nose;   455
But country life wore out this pose;
The corsets, albums, Nancy's gushing,
A sheaf of poems from the heart,
Receded in her mind; the smart
Pauline reverted back to Russian;   460
She even set herself to mend
Her robe and mobcap in the end.

34

Her honest husband loved her dearly,
In her affairs he did not probe,
In all things trusted her sincerely,   465
And came to dinner in his robe.
His life maintained an even tenor:
Twilight might gather at the manor
Of neighbors a familiar troupe;
A friendly and informal group   470
Who grumbled, aired the latest scandals,
Enjoyed a laugh at this or that;
The shadows lengthened while they sat,
And Olga went to light the candles,
For supper is about to start,   475
And then comes bed. The guests depart.

---

445. *shore off locks*: Serfs designated
by their masters for army service had a
forelock shaved off.

451. *Praskovya . . . Pauline*: She preferred French to Russian names.

455. *A la française*: As in French—
nasally.

35

Their peaceful life was firmly grounded
In the dear ways of yesteryear,
And Russian *bliny* fair abounded
When the fat Shrovetide spread its cheer.   480
Two weeks a year they gave to fasting,
Were fond of games and fortune-casting,
Of roundelay and carrousel;
At Trinity, when peasants tell
Their beads and nod at morning prayer,   485
They dropped three years upon the toll
Of lovage due a dear one's soul;
Their *kvas* they needed like fresh air,
And at their table guests were served
In order as their rank deserved.   490

36

So they grew old like other mortals.
At last a final mansion drew
Asunder its sepulchral portals
Before the husband, wreathed anew.
Near dinnertime he died contented,   495
By friends and neighbors much lamented,
By children, wife, and all his clan
More truly mourned than many a man.
He was a simple, kindly *barin*,
And where his earthly remnant rests,   500
A graven headstone thus attests:
"A humble sinner, Dmitri Larin,
God's servitor and brigadier,
Found peace beneath this marble here."

37

To his ancestral hall returning,   505
Vladimir Lensky sought the plot
Of his old neighbor's last sojourning
And sighed in tribute to his lot.
And long he mourned for the departed:
"Poor Yorick!" quoth he, heavyhearted,   510
"To think he nursed me in his day,
And on his lap I used to play

---

479. *bliny*: Rolled pancake filled with cream cheese.
480. *Shrovetide*: Sunday through Tuesday preceding Ash Wednesday. Shrove Tuesday was once called "pancake day."
484. *Trinity*: Trinity Sunday, the eighth Sunday after Easter.

487. *lovage*: a medicinal herb.
488. *kvass*: a sour Russian beer, brewed from rye.
510. *"Poor Yorick!"*: Hamlet's address to the skull of the clown who once carried him about (V, i, 172 ff).

With his Ochákov decoration!
He destined Olga's hand for me,
And often wondered, would he see   515
That day? . . ." In wistful agitation
He then and there indulged the urge
To pen for him a graveside dirge.

38

There, too, in sorrowful remembrance
He hailed with epitaphs and tears   520
His parents' venerable remnants . . .
Alas—in furrows of the years
By an unfathomed dispensation
The seed of every generation
Strikes hurried root, and fruits, and fails,   525
And new seed rises in its trails . . .
Thus our own giddy wave goes rolling,
Swells high, and tosses foam, and raves,
And sweeps us to our forebears' graves.
Our own bell, friends, is tolling, tolling,   530
Our children's seed will come of age
And swiftly crowd us off the stage.

39

Meanwhile drink deeply of life's essence,
Life's heady draught, enjoy it, friends!
I've learnt its disenchanting lessons,   535
Nor will it grieve me when it ends;
No ghosts can pry my lids asunder;
Only at times a distant wonder
Has power yet to stir my heart;
It would be bitter if my part   540
On this brief stage would not leave on it
The faintest trace. I live and write
Not for applause; my dismal plight,
Let it but fuel the blazing sonnet,
One note that like a faithful friend   545
Bespeaks my name beyond the end.

40

And then, who knows, that single trophy,
By Fate preserved, some heart will sway;
On Lethe's sleepy stream the strophe

---

513. *Ochákov decoration*: medal awarded by Catherine the Great, after the capture of Ochakov (on the Black Sea) from the Turks in 1788.

549. *Lethe*: i.e., oblivion (from the river in Hades of which the dead must drink).

I wrought will not be borne away;   550
Perhaps (sweet solace to the singer!)
Some oaf unborn will point his finger
At my famed likeness and declare:
There was a poet now for fair!
To thee my humble thanks I render,   555
Heir of Aonia's placid strains,
And thee, whose memory retains
My fleeting rhymes, whose hand is tender
And not without indulgence strays
To the old codger's plaster bays!*   560

556. *Aonia*: That part of Greece where the muses' sacred fountains rose.
560. *bays*: figuratively, the poet's laurel wreath.

* Six more cantos complete *Eugene Onegin*. Tatyana falls in love with Onegin and writes him a letter stating her affection. The gloomy hero informs her of his fraternal love for her but says that he could only make her miserable. Meanwhile Lensky courts Olga. At her name-day ball, Onegin dances with Olga and arouses the jealousy of Lensky (Canto V), who is unaware of Tatyana's love for Onegin. Lensky challenges Onegin to a pistol duel and is killed (Canto VI). Onegin leaves the village; Olga marries and departs. Tatyana visits Onegin's empty house, reads his volumes of Byron, and at last understands his melancholy. She and her mother move to Moscow to enjoy the social life (Canto VII).

Several years later, Onegin (now twenty-six) attends a ball in Moscow; he inquires of a prince about a beautiful woman, Tatyana, to discover it is the prince's wife. Onegin calls upon her, and now realizes he loves Tatyana. On his last visit to her—when he finds her reading the last of his several unanswered letters—he falls at her feet, but she rejects him. They once might have been happy, she tells him, but now she will remain faithful to her husband.

VICTOR HUGO
(1802–1885) *

Reverie [a]

Lo giorno se n' andava, e l'aer bruno
Toglieva gli animai che sono 'n terra,
Dalle fatiche loro.

DANTE [§]

Oh, leave me! It's time for the horizon to
Hide in smoke a rough forehead under a circle of mist,
Time for the giant star to grow red and fade away.
Alone the great yellowing wood makes gold the hill:
You might say in these days of autumn's decline   5
The sun and rain turned the forest to rust.

* All selections translated by Mary Ann Caws.
a. Poem dated September 5, 1828, and published in *Les Orientales* (1829).
§ "Day was departing, and the dark air was taking the creatures on earth from their labors." Dante, *Inferno*, Canto II, 1–3: the end of Dante's first day in Hell.
3. *giant star*: The sun.

Oh! Who will suddenly bring to life,
Appearing over there—while I alone dream at the window
And the shadow darkens in the corridor deep—
Some Moorish village, in its dazzle unique   10
Like the rocket splayed out in a sheaf
Piercing this fog with arrows of gold.

Oh spirits, let it come to inspire and to quicken,
My songs darkened again like an autumn sky,
Its magic reflection cast in my eyes,   15
Lengthily, subsiding in stifled sounds,
Notching the thousand towers of its fairy palaces
In the horizon of violet, in haze and in mist.

Tomorrow, At Daybreak[a]

Tomorrow, at daybreak, when the countryside whitens
I shall set out. You wait for me, I know.
I shall go through the forest, shall go by the mountain:
I cannot stay far from you any more.

I shall walk, eyes fixed upon my thoughts,   5
Seeing nothing outside me, hearing no sound,
Alone, unrecognized, my back bent, hands clasped,
Sorrowing, and day for me will be as night.

I shall not look on the gold of evening falling
Nor on the sails descending distant towards Harfleur,   10
And when I come, shall lay upon your grave
A bouquet of green holly and of flowering briar.

Memory of the Night of the Fourth[b]

The child had been struck by two bullets in the head.
The dwelling was clean and modest, peaceful and good.
Above a picture, a blessed branch, and in the room

10. *Moorish village*: Belonging to a Moslem culture in northern Africa, and used as a symbol of oriental splendor.

13. *spirits*: Genies, magical beings in oriental tales.

a. Written on September 4, 1847, the anniversary of the death by drowning four years earlier of Hugo's beloved daughter, Léopoldine, who had recently married. Published in *Les Contemplations* (1856).

1–4. The dawn setting, the feeling of fond impatience, and the use of the familiar form of you (*tu*) all suggest that Hugo is beginning a traditional love poem.

10. *Harfleur*: City near the north coast of France, where Léopoldine was buried.

12. Evergreen plants (symbols of immortality), one growing in the woods and the other on the mountains.

b. Written Dec. 2, 1852. On December 4, 1851, soldiers of Louis Napoléon Bonaparte (who had overthrown the French Republic two days before) marched through Paris shooting at will to discourage any opposition from the populace. Published in *Les Châtiments* (1853).

3. A palm branch hung above a religious picture.

An old grandmother—weeping.
We undressed him in silence. His pale mouth open,
Death was clouding over his vivid eye
His arms hanging down seemed a cry for help.
In his pocket, a boxwood spinning-top.
You could have put your fingers in the slash of his wounds.
Have you ever seen blackberries bleeding in the hedges?
His skull was split open like a log.
The old woman watched them undress him.
Saying: "How white he is! bring the lamp closer.
Oh God! How his poor hair sticks to his forehead!"
And when it was over, took him on her knees.
The night was mournful; you could hear shots
In the street where others were being killed.
"We have to bury the child," some of us said.
And we took a white sheet from the walnut chest.
Then the grandmother carried him to the hearth
As if to warm his stiffened limbs.
Alas! what death touches with its cold hands
Can no longer be warmed at the hearths of this world.
She bent her head over and removed his stockings
And her old hands clasped the dead child's feet.
"Isn't this enough to break your heart,"
She cried. "Sir, he was scarcely eight!
His teachers—for he went to school—were pleased with him.
If I had a letter to send, Sir,
It was he who wrote it. Are they going
To start killing children now? Oh then
They are really villains! Look,
This morning he was playing right here by the window!
Can you imagine their killing my little one, can you?
Just walking in the street, and they shot at him.
He was gentle and kind, Sir, just like little Jesus.
As for me, I'm old and it would be easy for me to go;
How could it have hurt Mr. Bonaparte
To have killed me instead of my child!"
She stopped speaking, sobs stifling her,
Then said, and everyone was weeping around her:
"What will become of me now I'm all alone?
Why don't you tell me that?
Alas! I had nothing else left from his mother.
Why did they kill him! Someone has to explain.
The child didn't shout 'Long live the Republic!' "
We kept quiet, standing there solemn, hats off,
Trembling before this inconsolable grief.

5
10
15
20
25
30
35
40
45

29–30. She cannot write, and is proud of her grandson's education.

Ah mother, you don't understand politics.
Monsieur Napoleon, that's his real name,   50
Is poor and a prince; loves palaces;
Likes to have horses, valets, money
For his gaming, his table, his bedroom,
His hunts, and he maintains
Family, church and society,   55
He wants Saint-Cloud, rose-carpeted in summer,
So prefects and mayors can respect him.
That's why it has to be this way: old grandmothers
With their poor gray fingers shaking with age
Must sew in winding-sheets children of seven.   60

Et nox facta est [a]

I

He had been falling in the abyss some four thousand years.

Never had he yet managed to grasp a peak,
Nor lift even once his towering forehead.
He sank deeper in the dark and the mist, aghast,
Alone, and behind him, in the eternal nights,   5
His wing feathers fell more slowly still.

He fell dumbfounded, grim, and silent,
Sad, his mouth open and his feet towards the heavens,
The horror of the chasm imprinted on his livid face.
He cried: "Death!" his fists stretched out in the empty dark. 10
Later this word was man and was named Cain.

He was falling. A rock struck his hand quite suddenly;
He held on to it, as a dead man holds on to his tomb,
And stopped. Someone, from on high, cried out to him: "Fall!
The suns will go out around you, accursed!"   15
And the voice was lost in the immensity of horror.
And pale, he looked toward the eternal dawn.
The suns were far off, but shone still.

---

50. Louis Napoléon rose to power by emphasizing his relationship to Emperor Napoléon I (the "great" Napoléon); he crowned himself Napoléon III and did not wish to be called by the family name of Bonaparte.
56. *Saint-Cloud*: The summer residence of French rulers.
a. Written in 1854 as the first part of "Outside Earth" (*Hors de la terre*), in *The End of Satan* (*La Fin de Satan*),

an epic poem continued in 1860 but never completed. The Latin title, "And There Was Night," suggests the Biblical "And there was light" (Genesis 1:3).
1. *he*: Satan, formerly the rebellious archangel Lucifer, thrown out of heaven by God. (Revelation 12:7–9 and Isaiah 14:12)
11. *Cain*: The first murderer, Son of Adam and brother of Abel, the victim (Genesis 4:1–15).

Satan raised his head and spoke, his arms in the air:
"You lie!" This word was later the soul of Judas.   20

Like the gods of bronze erect upon their pilasters,
He waited a thousand years, eyes fixed upon the stars.
The suns were far off, but were still shining.
The thunder then rumbled in the skies unhearing, cold.
Satan laughed, and spat towards the thunder.   25
Filled by the visionary shadow, the immensity
Shivered. This spitting out was later Barabbas.

A passing breath made him fall lower still.

II

The fall of the damned one began once more.—Terrible,
Somber, and pierced with holes luminous as a sieve,   30
The sky full of suns withdrew, brightness
Trembled, and in the night the great fallen one,
Naked, sinister, and pulled by the weight of his crime,
Fell, and his head wedging the abyss apart.
Lower! Lower, and still lower! Everything presently   35
Fled from him; no obstacle to seize in passing,
No mountain, no crumbling rock, no stone,
Nothing, shadow! and from fright he closed his eyes.

And when they opened, three suns only
Shone, and shadow had eaten away the firmament.   40
All the other suns had perished.

III

A rock
Emerged from blackest mist like some arm approaching.
He grasped it, and his feet touched summits.

Then the dreadful being called Never
Dreamed. His forehead sank between his guilty hands.   45
The three suns, far off, like three great eyes,
Watched him, and he watched them not.
Space resembled our earthly plains,
At evening, when the horizon sinking, retreating,
Blackens under the white eyes of the ghostly twilight.   50
Long rays entwined the feet of the great exile.
Behind him his shadow filled the infinite.
The peaks of chaos mingled in themselves.

20. *Judas*: Judas Iscariot, the apostle who betrayed Christ (Matthew 26:47–50, 27:35).

27. *Barabbas*: The condemned criminal who was freed instead of Christ (Mark 15:6–15). In Hugo, a strong figure who recognizes the horror of that choice, and in whom the power of Adam rises anew.

In an instant he felt some horrendous growth of wings;
He felt himself become a monster, and that the angel in him 55
Was dying, and the rebel then knew regret.
He let his shoulder, so bright before,
Quiver in the hideous cold of membraned wing,
And folding his arms with his head lifted high,
This bandit, as if grown greater through affront, 60
Alone in these depths that only ruin inhabits,
Looked steadily at the shadow's cave.
The noiseless darkness grew in the nothingness.
Obscure opacity closed off the gaping sky;
And making beyond the last promontory 65
A triple crack in the black pane,
The three suns mingled their three lights.
You would have thought them three wheels of a chariot of fire,
Broken after some battle in the high firmament.
Like prows, the mountains from the mist emerged. 70
"So," cried Satan, "so be it! still I can see!
He shall have the blue sky, the black sky is mine.
Does he think I will come weeping to his door?
I hate him. Three suns suffice. What do I care?
I hate the day, the blueness, fragrance and the light." 75

Suddenly he shivered; there remained only one.

IV

The abyss was fading. Nothing kept its shape.
Darkness seemed to swell its giant wave.
Something nameless and submerged, something
That is no longer, takes its leave, falls silent; 80
And no one could have said, in this deep horror,
If this frightful remnant of a mystery or a world,
Like the vague mist where the dream takes flight,
Was called shipwreck or was called night;
And the archangel felt himself become a phantom. 85
He shouted: "Hell!" This word later made Sodom.

And the voice repeated slowly on his forehead:
"Accursed! all about you the stars will go dark."

And already the sun was only a star.

V

And all disappeared slowly under a veil. 90
Then the archangel quaked; Satan learned to shiver.

---

86. *Sodom*: Biblical city, with Go-
morrah a symbol of corruption and decadence. Both were destroyed by God
(Genesis 18:20–19:28).

Toward the star trembling livid on the horizon
He hurled himself, leaping from peak to peak.
Then, although with horror at the wings of a beast,
Although it was the clothing of emprisonment,   95
Like a bird going from bush to bush,
Horrendous he took his flight from mount to mount,
And this convict began running in his cell.

He ran, he flew, he shouted: "Star of gold! Brother!
Wait for me! I'm running! Don't go out yet!   100
Don't leave me alone!"

      Thus the monster
Crossed the first lakes of the dead immensity,
Former chaos, emptied and already stagnant,
And into the lugubrious depths he plunged.

Now the star was only a spark.   105

He went down further in universal shadow,
Sank further, cast himself wallowing in the night,
Climbed the filthy mountains, their damp gleaming front,
Whose base is unsteady in the cesspool deeps,
And trembling stared before him.

       The spark   110
Was only a red dot in the depth of the dark abyss.

VI

As between two battlements the archer leans
On the wall, when twilight has reached his keep,
Wild he leaned from the mountain top,
And upon the star, hoping to arouse its flame,   115
He started to blow as upon some ember.
And anguish caused his fierce nostrils to swell.
The breath rushing from his chest
Is now upon earth and called hurricane.

With this breath a great noise stirred the shadow, an ocean   120
No being dwells in and no fires illumine.
The mountains found nearby took their flight,
The monstrous chaos full of fright arose
And began to shriek: Jehovah Jehovah!
The infinite opened, rent apart like a cloth,   125

---

99. *Brother*: Satan's original name, Lucifer, means Light-bearer.
112. *battlements*: Indentations opened in the top of the wall of a medieval tower or keep, through which defenders could shoot back.

But nothing moved in the lugubrious star;
And the damned one, crying: "Don't go out yet! I'll go on!
I'll get there!" resumed again his desperate flight.
And the glaciers mingled with the nights resembling them
Turned on their backs like frightened beasts,   130
And the black tornadoes and the hideous chasms
Bent in terror, while above them,
Flying toward the star like some arrow to the goal,
There passed, wild and haggard, this terrible supplicant.

And ever since it has seen this frightening flight,   135
This bitter abyss, aghast like a fleeing man
Retains forever the horror and the craze,
So monstrous was it to see, in the shadow immense,
Opening his atrocious wing far from the heavens,
This bat flying from his eternal prison!   140

VII

He flew for ten thousand years.

                       For ten thousand years,
Stretching forth his livid neck and his frenzied hands,
He flew without finding a peak on which to rest.
The star seemed sometimes to fade and to go out,
And the horror of the tomb caused the angel to shiver;   145
Then a pale brightness, vague, strange, uncertain,
Reappeared: and in joy, he cried: "Onward!"
Around him hovered the north wind birds.
He was flying. The infinite never ceases to start again.
His flight circled immense in that sea.   150
The night watched his horrible talons fleeing.
As a cloud feels its whirlwinds fall,
He felt his strength crumble in the chasm.
The winter murmured: tremble! and the shadow said: suffer!

Finally he perceived a black peak far off   155
Which a fearsome reflection in the shadow inflamed.
Satan, like a swimmer in his effort supreme,
Stretched out his wing, with claws and bald, and specter-pale,
Panting, broken, tired, and smoking with sweat,
He sank down on the edge of the abrupt descent.   160

VIII

There was the sun dying in the abyss.

---

160. *descent*: Literally, *escarpment*, the steep wall before a fortification or cliff.

The star, in the deepest fog had no air to revive it,
Grew cold, dim, and was slowly destroyed.
Its sinister round was seen in the night;
And in this somber silence its fiery ulcers were seen   165
Subsiding under a leprosy of dark.
Coal of a world put out! torch blown out by God!
Its crevices still showed a trace of fire,
As if the soul could be seen through holes in the skull.
At the center there quivered and flickered a flame   170
Now and then licking the outermost edge,
And from each crater flashes came
Shivering like flaming swords,
And fading noiselessly as dreams.
The star was almost black. The archangel was tired   175
Beyond voice or breath, a pity to see.
And the star in death throes under his savage glance,
Was dying, doing battle. With its somber apertures
Into the cold darkness it spewed now and again
Burning streams, crimson lumps, and smoking hills,   180
Rocks foaming with initial brightness:
As if this giant of life and light
Engulfed by the mist where all is fading,
Had refused to die without insulting the night
And spitting its lava in the shadow's face.   185
About it time and space and number,
Form, and noise expired, making
The forbidding and black oneness of void.
Then the specter Nothing raised its head from the abyss.

Suddenly, from the heart of the star, a jet of sulphur   190
Sharp, clamorous like one dying in delirium,
Burst sudden, shining, splendid with surprise,
And lighting from far a thousand deathly forms,
Massive, pierced to the shadow's depths
The monstrous porches of endless deep.   195
Night and immensity formed
Their angels. Satan, wild and out of breath,
His vision dazzled and full of this flashing,
Beat with his wing, opened his hands and then shivered
And cried: "Despair! see it growing pale!"   200

The archangel understood, as does the mast in its sinking,
That he was the drowned man of the shadows' flood;
He furled once more his wing with its granite nails,
And wrung his hands. And the star went out.

189. *Nothing*: Satan.

IX

Now, near the skies, at chasm's edge where nothing changes,   205
One feather escaped from the archangel's wing
Remained and quivered, pure and white.
The angel on whose forehead the dazzling dawn is born
Saw and grasped it, observing the sublime sky:
"Lord, must it too fall into the abyss?"   210
God turned about, absorbed in being and in Life,
And said "Do not discard what has not fallen."

Black caves of the past, porches of time passed
With no date and no radiance, somber, unmeasured,
Cycles previous to man, chaos, heavens,   215
World terrible and rich in prodigious beings,
Oh fearful fog where the preadamites
Appeared, standing in limitless shadow.
Who could fathom you, oh chasms, oh unknown times.
The thinker barefoot like the poor,   220
Through respect for the One unseen, the sage,
Digs in the depths of origin and age,
Fathoms and seeks beyond the colossi, further
Than the facts witnessed by the present sky,
Reaches with pale visage suspected things,   225
And finds, lifting the darkness of years
And the layers of days, worlds, voids,
Gigantic centuries dead beneath giants of centuries.
And thus the wise man dreams in the deep of the night
His face illumined by glints of the abyss.   230

Sowing Season.   Evening.[a]

It is the moment of twilight.
Seated under a portal, I admire
This end of day illuminating
The last hours of labor.

In the fields bathed by night,   5
Deeply moved, I gaze on the rags
Of an old man scattering fistfuls
Of future harvest in the furrows.

---

212. In the second part of *The End of Satan*, "Satan's Feather" (*La plume de Satan*), the feather is brought to life by a divine glance, and becomes the female spirit Liberty. She wins God's permission to plunge into Hell in an attempt to redeem her father (Part III), and in Part IV the repentant archangel is released and recreated as Lucifer.

215. *Cycles previous to man*: Earlier periods from the creation of Adam.

221. *One*: God, *sage*: Literally, *magus*, one of the three Wise Men; here, the poet as seer.

223. *colossi*: Giants of preadamic time.

a. Written August 23, 1865, and published in *Chansons des rues et des bois* (1865).

Tall, his dark silhouette
Towers above the deep ploughing.   10
The fruitfulness of fleeing days
Forms visibly his belief.

He walks along the endless plain,
Going, coming, casting seeds afar,
Opens his hand once more and begins afresh,   15
And, a hidden witness, I meditate

While unfolding its veils
The shadow where sound mixes in
Seems to stretch up to the very stars
The august gesture of his sowing.   20

GEORG BÜCHNER

(1813–1837)

Woyzeck*

Characters

WOYZECK	CHARLATAN
MARIE	OLD MAN WITH BARREL-ORGAN
CAPTAIN	JEW
DOCTOR	INNKEEPER
DRUM MAJOR	APPRENTICES
SERGEANT	KATHY
ANDRES	KARL THE TOWN IDIOT
MARGRET	GRANDMOTHER
PROPRIETOR OF THE BOOTH	POLICEMAN

SOLDIERS, STUDENTS, YOUNG MEN *and* GIRLS, CHILDREN, JUDGE, COURT CLERK, PEOPLE

Scene I—At the CAPTAIN'S.

THE CAPTAIN *in a chair.* WOYZECK *shaving him.*

CAPTAIN. Not so fast, Woyzeck, not so fast! One thing at a time! You're making me dizzy. What am I to do with the ten extra minutes that you'll finish early today? Just think, Woyzeck: you still have thirty beautiful years to live! Thirty years! That makes three hundred and sixty months! And days! Hours! Minutes!

* Written in 1837; published in 1879. Translated by Carl Richard Mueller.

What do you think you'll do with all that horrible stretch of time? Have you ever thought about it, Woyzeck?

WOYZECK. Yes, sir, Captain.

CAPTAIN. It frightens me when I think about the world . . . when I think about eternity. Busyness, Woyzeck, busyness! There's the eternal: that's eternal, that is eternal. That you can understand. But then again it's not eternal. It's only a moment. A mere moment. Woyzeck, it makes me shudder when I think that the earth turns itself about in a single day! What a waste of time! Where will it all end? Woyzeck, I can't even look at a mill wheel any more without becoming melancholy.

WOYZECK. Yes, sir, Captain.

CAPTAIN. Woyzeck, you always seem so exasperated! A good man isn't like that. A good man with a good conscience, that is. Well, say something, Woyzeck! What's the weather like today?

WOYZECK. Bad, Captain, sir, bad: wind!

CAPTAIN. I feel it already. Sounds like a real storm out there. A wind like that has the same effect on me as a mouse. [*Cunningly.*] I think it must be something out of the north-south.

WOYZECK. Yes, sir, Captain.

CAPTAIN. Ha! Ha! Ha! North-south! Ha! Ha! Ha! Oh, he's a stupid one! Horribly stupid! [*Moved.*] Woyzeck, you're a good man. but [*With dignity.*] Woyzeck, you have no morality! Morality, that's when you have morals, you understand. It's a good word. You have a child without the blessings of the Church, just like our Right Reverend Garrison Chaplain says: "Without the blessings of the Church." It's not *my* phrase.

WOYZECK. Captain, sir, the good Lord's not going to look at a poor worm just because they said Amen over it before they went at it. The Lord said: "Suffer little children to come unto me."

CAPTAIN. What's that you said? What kind of strange answer's that? You're confusing me with your answers!

WOYZECK. It's us poor people that . . . You see, Captain, sir . . . Money, money! Whoever hasn't got money . . . Well, who's got morals when he's bringing something like me into the world? We're flesh and blood, too. Our kind is miserable only once: in this world and in the next. I think if we ever got to Heaven we'd have to help with the thunder.

CAPTAIN. Woyzeck, you have no virtue! You're not a virtuous human being! Flesh and blood? Whenever I rest at the window, when it's finished raining, and my eyes follow the white stockings along as they hurry across the street . . . Damnation, Woyzeck, I know what love is, too, then! I'm made of flesh and blood, too. But, Woyzeck: Virtue! Virtue! How was I to get rid of the time? I always say to myself: "You're a virtuous man [*Moved*], a good man, a good man."

WOYZECK. Yes, Captain, sir: Virtue. I haven't got much of that. You see, us common people, we haven't got virtue. That's the way it's got to be. But if I could be a gentleman, and if I could have a hat and a watch and a cane, and if I could talk refined, I'd want to be virtuous, all right. There must be something beautiful in virtue, Captain, sir. But I'm just a poor good-for-nothing!

CAPTAIN. Good, Woyzeck. You're a good man, a good man. But you think too much. It eats at you. You always seem so exasperated. Our discussion has affected me deeply. You can go now. And don't run so! Slowly! Nice and slowly down the street!

Scene II—An open field. The town in the distance.

WOYZECK *and* ANDRES *cut twigs from the bushes.* ANDRES *whistles.*

WOYZECK. Andres? You know this place is cursed? Look at that light streak over there on the grass. There where the toadstools grow up. That's where the head rolls every night. One time somebody picked it up. He thought it was a hedgehog. Three days and three nights and he was in a box [*Low.*] Andres, it was the Freemasons, don't you see, it was the Freemasons!

ANDRES. [*Sings.*]
       Two little rabbits sat on a lawn
        Eating, oh, eating the green green grass . . .

WOYZECK. Quiet! Can you hear it, Andres? Can you hear it? Something moving!

ANDRES. [*Sings.*]
        Eating, oh, eating the green green grass
        Till all the grass was gone.[1]

WOYZECK. It's moving behind me! Under me! [*Stamps on the ground.*] Listen! Hollow! It's all hollow down there! It's the Freemasons!

ANDRES. I'm afraid.

WOYZECK. Strange how still it is. You almost want to hold your breath. Andres!

ANDRES. What?

WOYZECK. Say something! [*Looks about fixedly*]. Andres! How bright it is! It's all glowing over the town! A fire's sailing around the sky and a noise coming down like trumpets. It's coming closer! Let's get out of here! Don't look back! [*Drags him into the bushes.*]

ANDRES. [*After a pause.*] Woyzeck? Do you still hear it?

WOYZECK. It's quiet now. So quiet. Like the world's dead.

ANDRES. Listen! I can hear the drums inside. We've got to go!

---

1. This and the other songs in the play are authentic German songs Büchner knew, and should be sung to tunes of a popular or folk-like character.

Scene III—The town.

MARIE *with her* CHILD *at the window.* MARGRET. *The Retreat passes,* THE DRUM MAJOR *at its head.*

MARIE. [*Rocking the child in her arms.*] Ho, boy! Da-da-da-da! Can you hear? They're coming! There!

MARGRET. What a man! Built like a tree!

MARIE. He walks like a lion. [THE DRUM MAJOR *salutes* MARIE.]

MARGRET. Oh, what a look he threw you, neighbor! We're not used to such things from you.

MARIE. [*Sings.*]
        Soldiers, oh, you pretty lads . . .

MARGRET. Your eyes are still shining.

MARIE. And if they are? Take *your* eyes to the Jew's and let him clean them for you. Maybe he can shine them so you can sell them for a pair of buttons!

MARGRET. Look who's talking! Just look who's talking! If it isn't the Virgin herself! I'm a respectable person. But you! Everyone knows you could stare your way through seven layers of leather pants!

MARIE. Slut! [*Slams the window shut.*] Come, boy! What's it to them, anyway! Even if you are just a poor whore's baby, your dishonorable little face still makes your mother happy! [*Sings.*]
        I have my trouble and bother
        But, baby dear, where is your father?
        Why should I worry and fight
        I'll hold you and sing through the night:
        Heio popeio, my baby, my dove
        What do I want now with love?
[*A knock at the window.*] Who's there? Is it you, Franz? Come in!

WOYZECK. Can't. There's roll call.

MARIE. Did you cut wood for the Captain?

WOYZECK. Yes, Marie.

MARIE. What is it, Franz? You look so troubled.

WOYZECK. Marie, it happened again, only there was more. Isn't it written: "And there arose a smoke out of the pit, as the smoke of a great furance"?[2]

MARIE. Oh, Franz!

WOYZECK. Shh! Quiet! I've got it! The Freemasons! There was a terrible noise in the sky and everything was on fire! I'm on the trail of something, something big. It followed me all the way to the town. Something that I can't put my hands on, or understand. Something that drives us mad. What'll come of it all?

MARIE. Franz!

---

2. From Revelations 9:2. Woyzeck's hallucinations are linked with the vision of St. John the Divine foretelling the end of the world and the Last Judgment.

WOYZECK. Don't you see? Look around you! Everything hard and fixed, so gloomy. What's moving back there? When God goes, everything goes. I've got to get back.

MARIE. And the child?

WOYZECK. My God, the boy!—Tonight at the fair! I've saved something again. [*He leaves.*]

MARIE. That man! Seeing things like that! He'll go mad if he keeps thinking that way! He frightened me! It's so gloomy here. Why are you so quiet, boy? Are you afraid? It's growing so dark. As if we were going blind. Only that street lamp shining in from outside. [*Sings.*]

> And what if your cradle is bad
> Sleep tight, my lovey, my lad.

I can't stand it! It makes me shiver! [*She goes out.*]

Scene IV—*Fair booths. Lights. People.*

OLD MAN *with a* CHILD, WOYZECK, MARIE, CHARLATAN, WIFE, DRUM MAJOR, *and* SERGEANT.

OLD MAN. [*Sings while* THE CHILD *dances to the barrel-organ.*]
> There's nothing on this earth will last,
> Our lives are as the fields of grass,
> Soon all is past, is past.

WOYZECK. Ho! Hip-hop there, boy! Hip-hop! Poor man, old man! Pool child, young child! Trouble and happiness!

MARIE. My God, when fools still have their senses, then we're all fools. Oh, what a mad world! What a beautiful world!

[*They go over to* THE CHARLATAN *who stands in front of a booth, his* WIFE *in trousers, and a monkey in costume.*]

CHARLATAN. Gentlemen, gentlemen! You see here before you a creature as God created it! But it is nothing this way! Absolutely nothing! But now look at what Art can do. It walks upright. Wears coat and pants. And even carries a saber. This monkey here is a regular soldier. So what if he *isn't* much different! So what if he *is* still on the bottom rung of the human ladder! Here there, take a bow! That's the way! Now you're a baron, at least. Give us a kiss! [*The monkey trumpets.*] This little customer's musical, too. And, gentlemen, in here you will see the astronomical horse and the little lovebirds. Favorites of all the crowned heads of Europe. They'll tell you anything: how old you are, how many children you have, what your ailments are. The performance is about to begin. And at the beginning. The beginning of the beginning!

WOYZECK. You know, I had a little dog once who kept sniffing around the rim of a big hat, and I thought I'd be good to him and make it easier for him and sat him on top of it. And all the people stood around and clapped.

GENTLEMEN. Oh, grotesque! How really grotesque!

WOYZECK. Don't you believe in God either? It's an honest fact I don't believe in God.—You call that grotesque? I like what's grotesque. See that? That grotesque enough for you?—[*To* MARIE.] *You want to go in?*

MARIE. Sure. That must be nice in there. Look at the tassels on him! And his wife's got pants on! [*They go inside.*]

DRUM MAJOR. Wait a minute! Did you see her? What a piece!

SERGEANT. Hell, she could whelp a couple regiments of cavalry!

DRUM MAJOR. And breed drum majors!

SERGEANT. Look at the way she carries that head! You'd think all that black hair would pull her down like a weight. And those eyes!

DRUM MAJOR. Like looking down a well . . . or up a chimney. Come on, let's go after her!

Scene V—Interior of the brightly lighted booth.

MARIE, WOYZECK, PROPRIETOR OF THE BOOTH, SERGEANT, *and* DRUM MAJOR.

MARIE. All these lights!

WOYZECK. Sure, Marie. Black cats with fiery eyes.

PROPRIETOR OF THE BOOTH. [*Bringing forward a horse.*] Show your talent! Show your brute reason! Put human society to shame! Gentlemen, this animal you see here, with a tail on its torso, and standing on its four hoofs, is a member of all the learnèd societies—as well as a professor at our university where he teaches students how to ride and fight. But that requires simple intelligence. Now think with your double reason! What do you do when you think with your double reason? Is there a jackass in this learnèd assembly? [*The nag shakes its head.*] How's that for double reasoning? That's physiognomy for you. This is no dumb animal. This is a person! A human being! But still an animal. A beast. [*The nag conducts itself indecently.*] That's right, put society to shame. As you can see, this animal is still in a state of Nature. Not ideal Nature, of course! Take a lesson from him! But ask your doctor first, it may prove highly dangerous! What we have been told by this: Man must be natural! You are created of dust, sand, and dung. Why must you be more than dust, sand, and dung? Look there at his reason. He can figure even if he can't count it off on his fingers. And why? Because he cannot express himself, can't explain. A metamorphosed human being. Tell the gentlemen what time it is! Which of you ladies and gentlemen has a watch? A watch?

SERGEANT. A watch? [*He pulls a watch imposingly and measured from his pocket.*] There you are, my good man!

MARIE. I want to see this. [*She clambers down to the first row of seats;* THE SERGEANT *helps her.*]

DRUM MAJOR. What a piece!

Scene VI—MARIE'S *room.*

MARIE *with her* CHILD.

MARIE. [*Sitting, her* CHILD *on her lap, a piece of mirror in her hand.*] He told Franz to get the hell out, so what could he do! [*Looks at herself in the mirror.*] Look how the stones shine! What kind are they, I wonder? What kind did he say they were? Sleep, boy! Close your eyes! Tight! Stay that way now. Don't move or he'll get you. [*Sings.*]

> Hurry, lady, close up tight
> A gypsy lad is out tonight
> And he will take you by the hand
> And lead you into gypsyland.

[*Continues to look at herself in the mirror.*] They must be gold! I wonder how they'll look on me at the dance? Our kind's got only a little corner in the world and a piece of broken mirror. But my mouth is just as red as any of the fine ladies with their mirrors from top to bottom, and their handsome gentlemen that kiss their hands for them! I'm just a poor common piece! [THE CHILD *sits up.*] Quiet, boy! Close your eyes! There's the sandman! Look at him run across the wall! [*She flashes with the mirror.*] Eyes tight! Or he'll look into them and make you blind!

WOYZECK *enters behind her. She jumps up, her hands at her ears.*

WOYZECK. What's that?

MARIE. Nothing.

WOYZECK. There's something shiny in your hands.

MARIE. An earring. I found it.

WOYZECK. I never have luck like that! Two at a time!

MARIE. Am I human or not?

WOYZECK. I'm sorry, Marie.—Look at the boy asleep. Lift his arm, the chair's hurting him. Look at the shiny drops on his forehead. Everything under the sun works! We even sweat in our sleep. Us poor people! Here's some money again, Marie. My pay and something from the Captain.

MARIE. God bless you, Franz.

WOYZECK. I've got to get back. Tonight, Marie! I'll see you tonight! [*He goes off.*]

MARIE. [*Alone, after a pause.*] I *am* bad, I *am*! I could run myself through with a knife! Oh, what a life, what a life! We'll all end up in hell, anyway, in the end: man, woman, and child!

Scene VII—At the DOCTOR's.

THE DOCTOR and WOYZECK.

DOCTOR. I don't believe it, Woyzeck! And a man of your word!

WOYZECK. What's that, Doctor, sir?

DOCTOR. I saw it all, Woyzeck. You pissed on the street! You were pissing on the wall like a dog! And here I'm giving you three groschen[3] a day plus board! That's terrible, Woyzeck! The world's becoming a terrible place, a terrible place!

WOYZECK. But, Doctor, sir, when Nature . . .

DOCTOR. When Nature? When Nature? What has Nature to do with it? Did I or did I not prove to you that the *musculus constrictor vesicae*[4] is controlled by your will? Nature? Woyzeck, man is free! In Mankind alone we see glorified the individual's will to freedom! And you couldn't hold your water! [*Shakes his head, places his hands behind the small of his back, and walks back and forth.*] Have you eaten your peas today. Woyzek? Nothing but peas! *Cruciferae!*[5] Remember that! There's going to be a revolution in science! I'm going to blow it skyhigh! *Urea Oxygen.* Ammonium hydrochloratem hyperoxidic.[6] Woyzeck, couldn't you just *try* to piss again? Go in the other room there and make another try.

WOYZECK. Doctor, sir, I can't.

DOCTOR. [*Disturbed.*] But you could piss on the wall. I have it here in black and white. Our contract is right here! I saw it. I saw it with these very eyes. I had just stuck my head out the window, opening it to let in the rays of the sun, so as to execute the process of sneezing. [*Going toward him.*] No, Woyzeck, I'm not going to vex myself. Vexation is unhealthy. Unscientific. I'm calm now, completely calm. My pulse is beating at its accustomed sixty, and I am speaking to you in utmost cold-bloodedness. Why should I vex myself over a man, God forbid! A man! Now if he were a Proteus,[7] it would be worth the vexation. But, Woyzeck, you really shouldn't have pissed on the wall.

WOYZECK. You see, Doctor, sir, sometimes a person's got a certain kind of character, like when he's made a certain way. But with Nature it's not the same, you see. With Nature [*He snaps his fingers*], it's like *that!* How should I explain, it's like——

DOCTOR. Woyzeck, you're philosophizing again.

WOYZECK. [*Confidingly.*] Doctor, sir, did you see anything with double nature? Like when the sun stops at noon, and it's like the world was going up in fire? That's when I hear a terrible voice saying things to me!

3. A few pennies.
4. The sphincter muscle of the bladder.
5. Another kind of herb.
6. Urea is the main chemical component of urine, and itself is composed largely of ammonia. However, the expressions here are mostly meaningless jargon.
7. Sea god who could assume different shapes at will.

DOCTOR. Woyzeck, you have an *aberratio!*

WOYZECK. [*Places his finger at his nose.*] It's in the toadstools, Doctor, sir, that's where it is. Did you ever see the shapes the toadstools make when they grow up out of the earth? If only somebody could read what they say!

DOCTOR. Woyzeck, you have a most beautiful *aberratio mentalis partialis*[8] of a secondary order! And so wonderfully developed! Woyzeck, your salary is increased! *Idée fixe*[9] of a secondary order, and with a generally national state. You go about your business normally? Still shaving the Captain?

WOYZECK. Yes, sir.

DOCTOR. You eat your peas?

WOYZECK. Just as always, Doctor, sir. My wife gets the money for the household.

DOCTOR. Still in the army?

WOYZECK. Yes, sir, Doctor.

DOCTOR. You're an interesting case. Patient Woyzeck, you're to have an increase in salary. So behave yourself! Let's feel the pulse. Ah yes.

Scene VIII—MARIE'S room.

DRUM MAJOR *and* MARIE.

DRUM MAJOR. Marie!

MARIE. [*Looking at him, with expression.*] Go on, show me how you march!—Chest broad as a bull's and a beard like a lion! There's not another man in the world like that! And there's not a prouder woman than me!

DRUM MAJOR. Wait till Sunday when I wear my helmet with the plume and my white gloves! Damn, that'll be a sight for you! The Prince always says: "My God, there goes a real man!"

MARIE. [*Scoffing.*] Ha! [*Goes toward him.*] A man?

DRUM MAJOR. You're not such a bad piece yourself! Hell, we'll plot a whole brood of drum majors! Right? [*He puts his arm around her.*]

MARIE. [*Annoyed.*] Let go!

DRUM MAJOR. Bitch!

MARIE. [*Fiercely.*] You just touch me!

DRUM MAJOR. There's devils in your eyes.

MARIE. Let there be, for all I care! What's the difference!

Scene IX—Street.

CAPTAIN *and* DOCTOR. THE CAPTAIN *comes panting along the street, stops; pants, looks about.*

CAPTAIN. Ho, Doctor, don't run so fast! Don't paddle the air so

---

8. A kind of insanity.   9. A delusional obsession.

with your stick! You're only courting death that way! A good man with a good conscience never walks as fast as that. A good man . . . [*He catches him by the coat.*] Doctor, permit me to save a human life!

DOCTOR. I'm in a hurry, Captain, I'm in a hurry!

CAPTAIN. Doctor, I'm so melancholy. I have such fantasies. I start to cry every time I see my coat hanging on the wall.

DOCTOR. Hm! Bloated, fat, thick neck: apoplectic constitution. Yes, Captain, you'll be having *apoplexia cerebria*[10] any time now. Of course you could have it on only one side. In which case you'll be paralyzed down that one side. Or if things go really well you'll be mentally disabled so that you can vegetate away for the rest of your days. You may look forward to something approximately like that within the next four weeks! And, furthermore, I can assure you that you give promise of being a most interesting case. And if it is God's will that only one half of your tongue become paralyzed, then we will conduct the most immortal of experiments.

CAPTAIN. Doctor, you mustn't scare me that way! People are said to have died of fright. Of pure, sheer fright. I can see them now with lemons in their hands. But they'll say: "He was a good man, a good man." You devil's coffinnail-maker!

DOCTOR. [*Extending his hat toward him.*] Do you know who this is, Captain! This is Sir Hollowhead, my most honorable Captain Drilltheirassesoff!

CAPTAIN. [*Makes a series of folds in his sleeve.*] And do you know who this is, Doctor? This is Sir Manifold, my dear devil's coffin-nail-maker! Ha! Ha! Ha! But no harm meant! I'm a good man, but I can play, too, when I want to, Doctor, when I want to . . .

WOYZECK *comes toward them and tries to pass in a hurry.*

CAPTAIN. Ho! Woyzeck! Where are you off to in such a hurry? Stay awhile, Woyzeck! Running through the world like an open razor, you're liable to cut someone. He runs as if he had to shave a castrated regiment and would be hung before he discovered and cut the longest hair that wasn't there. But on the subject of long beards . . . What was it I wanted to say? Woyzeck, why was I thinking about beards?

DOCTOR. The wearing of long beards on the chin, remarks Pliny,[11] is a habit of which soldiers must be broken——

CAPTAIN. [*Continues.*] Ah, yes, this thing about beards! Tell me, Woyzeck, have you found any long hairs from beards in your soup bowl lately? Ho, I don't think he understands! A hair from a human face, from the beard of an engineer, a sergeant, a . . . a

10. A stroke.
11. The Elder (23–70), Roman scholar of natural science, history, military tactics, and other disciplines.

drum major? Well, Woyzeck? But then he's got a good wife. It's not the same as with the others.

WOYZECK. Yes, sir, Captain! What was it you wanted to say to me, Captain, sir?

CAPTAIN. What a face he's making! Well, maybe not in his soup, but if he hurries home around the corner I'll wager he might still find one on a certain pair of lips. A pair of lips, Woyzeck. I know what love is, too, Woyzeck. Look at him, he's white as chalk!

WOYZECK. Captain, sir, I'm just a poor devil. And there's nothing else I've got in the world but her. Captain, sir, if you're just making a fool of me . . .

CAPTAIN. A fool? Me? Making a fool of you, Woyzeck?

DOCTOR. Your pulse, Woyzeck, your pulse! Short, hard, skipping, irregular.

WOYZECK. Captain, sir, the earth's hot as coals in hell. But I'm cold as ice, cold as ice. Hell is cold. I'll bet you. I don't believe it! God! God! I don't believe it!

CAPTAIN. Look here, you, how would you . . . how'd you like a pair of bullets in your skull? You keep stabbing at me with those eyes of yours, and I'm only trying to help. Because you're a good man, Woyzeck, a good man.

DOCTOR. Facial muscles rigid, taut, occasionally twitches. Condition strained, excitable.

WOYZECK. I'm going. Anything's possible. The bitch! Anything's possible.—The weather's nice, Captain, sir. Look, a beautiful, hard, gray sky. You'd almost like to pound a nail in up there and hang yourself on it. And only because of that little dash between Yes and Yes again . . . and No. Captain, sir: Yes and No: did No make Yes or Yes make No? I must think about that.

[*He goes off with long strides, slowly at first, then faster and faster.*]

DOCTOR. [*Shouting after him.*] Phenomenon! Woyzeck, you get a raise!

CAPTAIN. I get so dizzy around such people. Look at him go! Long-legged rascals like him step out like a shadow running away from its own spider. But short ones only dawdle along. The long-legged ones are the lighting, the short ones the thunder. Haha . . . Grotesque! Grotesque!

Scene X—MARIE's *room.*

WOYZECK *and* MARIE.

WOYZECK. [*Looks fixedly at her and shakes his head.*] Hm! I don't see it! I don't see it! My God, why can't I see it, why can't I take it in my fists!

MARIE. [*Frightened.*] Franz, what is it?—You're raving, Franz.

WOYZECK. A sin so swollen and big—it stinks to smoke the angels out of Heaven! You have a red mouth, Marie! No blisters on it? Marie, you're beautiful as sin. How can mortal sin be so beautiful?

MARIE. Franz, it's your fever making you talk this way!

WOYZECK. Damn you! Is this where he stood? Like this? Like this?

MARIE. While the day's long and the world's old a lot of people can stand in one spot, one right after the other.—Why are you looking at me so strange, Franz! I'm afraid!

WOYZECK. It's a nice street for walking, uh? You could walk corns on your feet! It's nice walking on the street, going around in society.

MARIE. Society?

WOYZECK. A lot of people pass through this street here, don't they! And you talk to them—to whoever you want—but that's not my business!—Why wasn't it me!

MARIE. You expect me to tell people to keep off the streets—and take their mouths with them when they leave?

WOYZECK. And don't you ever leave your lips at home, they're too beautiful, it would be a sin! But then I guess the wasps like to light on them, uh?

MARIE. And what wasp stung you! You're like a cow chased by hornets!

WOYZECK. I saw him!

MARIE. You can see a lot with two eyes while the sun shines!

WOYZECK. Whore! [*He goes after her.*]

MARIE. Don't you touch me, Franz! I'd rather have a knife in my body than your hands touch me. When I looked at him, my father didn't dare lay a hand on me from the time I was ten.

WOYZECK. Whore! No, it should show on you! Something! Every man's a chasm. It makes you dizzy when you look down in. It's got to show! And she looks like innocence itself. So, innocence, there's a spot on you. But I can't prove it—can't prove it! Who can prove it?   [*He goes off.*]

Scene XI—*The guardhouse.*

WOYZECK *and* ANDRES.

ANDRES. [*Sings.*]

> Our hostess she has a pretty maid
> She sits in her garden night and day
> She sits within her garden . . .

WOYZECK. Andres!

ANDRES. Hm?

WOYZECK. Nice weather.

ANDRES. Sunday weather.—They're playing music tonight outside the town. All the whores are already there. The men stinking and sweating. Wonderful, uh?

WOYZECK. [*Restlessly.*] They're dancing, Andres, they're dancing!

ANDRES. Sure. So what? [*Sings.*]

> She sits within her garden
> But when the bells have tollèd
> Then she waits at her garden gate
> Or so the soldiers say.

WOYZECK. Andres, I can't keep quiet.

ANDRES. You're a fool!

WOYZECK. I've got to go out there. It keeps turning and turning in my head. They're dancing, dancing! Will she have hot hands, Andres? God damn her, Andres! God damn her!

ANDRES. What do you want?

WOYZECK. I've got to go out there. I've got to see them.

ANDRES. Aren't you ever satisfied? What's all this for a whore?

WOYZECK. I've got to get out of here! I can't stand the heat!

Scene XII—The inn.

The windows are open. Dancing. Benches in front of the inn.

APPRENTICES.

FIRST APPRENTICE. [*Sings.*]

This shirt I've got on, it is not mine
> And my soul it stinketh of brandywine . . .

SECOND APPRENTICE. Brother, let me be a real friend and knock a hole in your nature! Forward! I'll knock a hole in his nature! Hell, I'm as good a man as he is; I'll kill every flea on his body!

FIRST APPRENTICE. My soul, my soul stinketh of brandywine!—And even money passeth into decay! Forget me not, but the world's a beautiful place! Brother, my saddness could fill a barrel with tears! I wish our noses were two bottles so we could pour them down one another's throats.

THE OTHERS. [*In chours.*]

> A hunter from the Rhine
> Once rode through a forest so fine
> Hallei-hallo, he called to me
> From high on a meadow, open and free
> A hunter's life for me.

WOYZECK *stands at the window.* MARIE *and* THE DRUM MAJOR *dance past without noticing him.*

WOYZECK. Both of them! God damn her!

MARIE. [*Dancing past.*] Don't stop! Don't stop!

WOYZECK. [*Seats himself on the bench, trembling, as he looks from there through the window.*] Listen! Listen! Ha, roll on each other, roll and turn! Don't stop, don't stop, she says!

IDIOT. Pah! It stinks!

WOYZECK. Yes, it stinks! Her cheeks are red, red, why should she stink already? Karl, what is it you smell?

IDIOT. I smell, I smell blood.

WOYZECK. Blood? Why are all things red that I look at now? Why are they all rolling in a sea of blood, one on top of the other, tumbling, tumbling! Ha, the sea is red!—Don't stop! Don't stop! [*He starts up passionately, then sinks down again onto the bench.*] Don't stop! Don't stop! [*Beating his hands together.*] Turn and roll and roll and turn! God, blow out the sun and let them roll on each other in their lechery! Man and woman and man and beast! They'll do it in the light of the sun! They'll do it in the palm of your hand like flies! Whore! That whore's red as coals, red as coals! Don't stop! Don't stop! [*Jumps up.*] Watch how the bastard takes hold of her! Touching her body! He's holding her now, holding her . . . the way I held her once. [*He slumps down in a stupor.*]

FIRST APPRENTICE. [*Preaching from a table.*] I say unto you, forget not the wanderer who standeth leaning against the stream of time, and who giveth himself answer with the wisdom of God, and saith: What is Man? What is Man? Yea, verily I say unto you: How should the farmer, the cooper, the shoemaker, the doctor, live, had not God created Man for their use? How should the tailor live, had not God planted in Man the sense of shame? How should the soldier live, had not God endowed Man with the need to slaughter himself? And therefore doubt ye not, for all things are lovely and sweet! Yet the world with all its things is an evil place, and even money passeth into decay. In conclusion, my belovèd brethren, let us piss once more upon the Cross so that somewhere a Jew will die!

Amid the general shouting and laughing WOYZECK *wakens.* PEOPLE *are leaving the inn.*

ANDRES. What are you doing there?

WOYZECK. What time is it?

ANDRES. Ten.

WOYZECK. Is that all it is? I think it should go faster—I want to think about it before night.

ANDRES. Why?

WOYZECK. So it'd be over.

ANDRES. What?

WOYZECK. The fun.

ANDRES. What are you sitting here by the door for?

WOYZECK. Because it feels good, and because I know—a lot of people sit by doors, but they don't know—they don't know till they're dragged out of the door feet first.

ANDRES. Come with me!

WOYZECK. It feels good here like this—and even better if I laid myself down . . .

ANDRES. There's blood on your head.

WOYZECK. *In* my head, maybe.—If they all knew what time it was they'd strip themselves naked and put on a silk shirt and let the carpenter make their bed of wood shavings.

ANDRES. He's drunk.   [*Goes off with the others.*]

WOYZECK. The world is out of order! Why did the street-lamp cleaner forget to wipe my eyes—everything's dark. Devil damn you, God! I lay in my own way: jump over myself. Where's my shadow gone? There's no safety in the kennels any more. Shine the moon through my legs again to see if my shadow's here. *Sings.*]

> Eating, oh, eating the green green grass
> Eating, oh, eating the green green grass
> Till all the grass was go-o-one.

What's that lying over there? Shining like that? It's making me look. How it sparkles. I've got to have it.   [*He rushes off.*]

Scene XIII—*An open field.*

WOYZECK.

WOYZECK. Don't stop! Don't stop! Hishh! Hashh! That's how the fiddles and pipes go.—Don't stop! Don't stop!—Stop your playing! What's that talking down there! [*He stretches out on the ground.*] What? What are you saying? What? Louder! Louder! Stab? Stab the goat-bitch dead? Stab? Stab her? The goat-bitch dead? Should I? Must I? Do I hear it there, too? Does the wind say so, too? Won't it ever stop, ever stop? Stab her! Stab her! Dead! Dead!   *schizophrania?*

Scene XIV—*A room in the barracks. Night.*

ANDRES *and* WOYZECK *in a bed.*

WOYZECK. [*Softly.*] Andres! [ANDRES *murmurs in his sleep. Shakes* ANDRES.] Andres! Hey, Andres!

ANDRES. Mmmmm! What do you want?

WOYZECK. I can't sleep! When I close my eyes everything turns and turns. I hear voices in the fiddles: Don't stop! Don't stop! And then the walls start to talk. Can't you hear it?

ANDRES. Sure. Let them dance! I'm tired. God bless us all, Amen.

WOYZECK. It's always saying: Stab! Stab! And then when I close my eyes it keeps shining there, a big, broad knife, on a table by a window in a narrow, dark street, and an old man sitting behind it. And the knife is always in front of my eyes.

ANDRES. Go to sleep, you fool!

WOYZECK. Andres! There's something outside. In the ground. They're always pointing to it. Don't you hear them now, listen, now, knocking on the walls? Somebody must have seen me out the window. Don't you hear? I hear it all day long. Don't stop. Stab! Stab the——

ANDRES. Lay down. You ought to go to the hospital. They'll give you a schnapps with a powder in it. I'll cut your fever.

WOYZECK. Don't stop! Don't stop!

ANDRES. Go to sleep!   [*He goes back to sleep.*]

Scene XV—THE DOCTOR'S *courtyard.*

STUDENTS *and* WOYZECK *below,* THE DOCTOR *in the attic window.*

DOCTOR. Gentlemen, I find myself on the roof like David when he beheld Bathsheba.[12] But all I see are the Parisian panties of the girls' boarding school drying in the garden. Gentlemen, we are concerned with the weighty question of the relationship of the subject to the object. If, for example, we were to take one of those innumerable things in which we see the highest manifestation of the self-affirmation of the Godhead, and examine its relationship to space, to the earth, and to the planetary constellations . . . Gentlemen, if we were to take this cat and toss it out the window: how would this object conduct itself in conformity with its own instincts towards its *centrum gravitationis*? Well, Woyzeck? [*Roars.*] Woyzeck!

WOYZECK. [*Picks up the cat.*] Doctor, sir, she's biting me!

DOCTOR. Damn, why do you handle the beast so tenderly! It's not your grandmother! [*He descends.*]

WOYZECK. Doctor, I'm shaking.

DOCTOR. [*Utterly delighted.*]. Excellent, Woyzeck, excellent! [*Rubs his hands, takes the cat.*] What's this, gentlemen? The new species of rabbit louse! A beautiful species . . . [*He pulls out a magnifying glass; the cat runs off.*] Animals, gentlemen, simply have no scientific instincts. But in its place you may see something else. Now, observe: for three months this man has eaten nothing but peas. Notice the effect. Feel how irregularly his pulse beats! And look at his eyes!

WOYZECK. Doctor, sir, everything's going dark! [*He sits down.*]

DOCTOR. Courage, Woyzeck! A few more days and then it will all be over with. Feel, gentlemen, feel! [*They fumble over his temples, pulse, and chest.*]

12. As in II Samuel 11:2–5. Bathsheba was the beautiful wife of another man; King David saw her bathing, and she adulterously bore his son Solomon, in turn to become King of the Hebrews.

DOCTOR. Apropos, Woyzeck, wiggle your ears for the gentlemen! I've meant to show you this before. He uses only two muscles. Let's go, let's go! You stupid animal, shall I wiggle them for you? Trying to run out on us like the cat? There you are, gentlemen! Here you see an example of the transition into a donkey: frequently the result of being raised by women and of a persistent usage of the Germanic language. How much hair has your mother pulled out recently for sentimental remembrances of you? It's become so thin these last few days. It's the peas, gentlemen, the peas!

Scene XVI—*The inn.*

WOYZECK *and* THE SERGEANT.

WOYZECK. [*Sings.*]

> Oh, daughter, my daughter
> And didn't you know
> That sleeping with coachmen
> Would bring you low?

What is it that our Good Lord God cannot do? What? He cannot make what is done undone. Ha! Ha! Ha!—But that's the way it is, and that's the way it should be. But to make things better is to make things better. And a respectable man loves his life, and a man who loves his life has no courage, and a virtuous man has no courage. A man with courage is a dirty dog.

SERGEANT. [*With dignity.*] You're forgetting yourself in the presence of a brave man.

WOYZECK. I wasn't talking about anybody, I wasn't talking about anything, not like the Frenchmen do when they talk, but it was good of you.—But a man with courage is a dirty dog.

SERGEANT. Damn you! You broken mustache cup! You watch or I'll see you drink a pot of your own piss and swallow your own razor!

WOYZECK. Sir, you do yourself an injustice! Was it you I talked about? Did I say *you* had courage? Don't torment me, sir! My name is science. Every week for my scientific career I get half a guilder. You mustn't cut me in two or I'll go hungry. I'm a *Spinosa pericyclia;*[13] I have a Latin behind. I am a living skeleton. All Mankind studies me.—What is Man? Bones! Dust, sand, dung. What is Nature? Dust, sand, dung. But poor, stupid Man, stupid Man! We must be friends. If only you had no courage there would be no science. Only Nature, no amputation, no articulation. What is this? Woyzeck's arm, flesh, bones, veins. What is this? Dung. Why is it rooted in dung? Must I cut off my arm?

---

13. *Spinosa* means prickly or thorny, *Pericyclia* is a layer of cells within the root. Modern botany knows no such species.

No, Man is selfish, he beats, shouts, stabs his own kind. [*He sobs.*] We must be friends. I wish our noses were two bottles that we could pour down each other's throats. What a beautiful place the world is! Friend! My friend! The world! [*Moved.*] Look! The sun coming through the clouds—like God emptying His bedpan on the world. [*He cries.*]

Scene XVII—*The barracks yard.*

WOYZECK *and* ANDRES.

WOYZECK. What have you heard?

ANDRES. He's still inside with a friend.

WOYZECK. He said something.

ANDRES. How do you know? Why do I have to be the one to tell you? Well, he laughed and then he said she was some piece. And then something or other about her thighs—and that she was hot as a red poker.

WOYZECK. [*Quite coldly.*] So, he said that? What was that I dreamed about last night? About a knife? What stupid dreams we get!

ANDRES. Hey, friend! Where you off to?

WOYZECK. Get some wine for the Captain. Andres, you know something? There aren't many girls like she was.

ANDRES. Like who was?

WOYZECK. Nothing. I'll see you.   [*Goes off.*]

Scene XVIII—*The inn.*

DRUM MAJOR, WOYZECK, *and* PEOPLE.

DRUM MAJOR. I'm a man! [*He pounds his chest.*] A man, you hear? Anybody say different? Anybody who's not as crocked as the Lord God Himself better keep off. I'll screw his nose up his own ass! I'll . . . [*To* WOYZECK.] You there, get drunk! I wish the world was schnapps, schnapps! You better start drinking! [WOYZECK *whistles.*] Son-of-a-bitch, you want me to pull your tongue out and wrap it around your middle? [*They wrestle;* WOYZECK *loses.*] You want I should leave enough wind in you for a good lady's fart? Uh! [*Exhausted and trembling,* WOYZECK *seats himself on the bench.*] The son-of-a-bitch can whistle himself blue in the face for all I care. [*Sings.*]

> Brandy's all my life, my life
> Brandy gives me courage!

A MAN. He sure got more than he asked for.

ANOTHER. He's bleeding.

WOYZECK. One thing after another.

Scene XIX—*Pawnbroker's shop.*

WOYZECK *and* THE JEW.

WOYZECK. The pistol costs too much.

JEW. So you want it or not? Make up your mind.

WOYZECK. How much was the knife?

JEW. It's straight and sharp. What do you want it for? To cut your throat? So what's the matter? You get it as cheap here as anywhere else. You'll die cheap enough, but not for nothing. What's the matter? It'll be a cheap death.

WOYZECK. This'll cut more than bread.

JEW. Two groschen.

WOYZECK. There! [*He goes out.*]

JEW. There, he says! Like it was nothing! And it's real money!— Dog!

Scene XX—MARIE'S *room.*

THE IDIOT, THE CHILD, *and* MARIE.

IDIOT. [*Lying down, telling fairy tales on his fingers.*] This one has the golden crown. He's the Lord King. Tomorrow I'll bring the Lady Queen her child. Bloodsausage says: Come, Liversausage . . .

MARIE. [*Paging through her Bible.*] "And no guile is found in his mouth." Lord God, Lord God! Don't look at me! [*Paging further.*] "And the Scribes and Pharisees brought unto him a woman taken in adultery, and set her in the midst . . . And Jesus said unto her: Neither do I condemn thee; go, and sin no more." [*Striking hands together.*] Lord God! Lord God! I can't. Lord God, give me only so much strength that I may pray. [THE CHILD *presses himself close to her.*] The child is a sword in my heart. [*To* THE IDIOT.] Karl!—I've strutted it in the light of the sun, like the whore I am—my sin, my sin! [THE IDIOT *takes* THE CHILD *and grows quiet.*] Franz hasn't come. Not yesterday. Not today. It's getting hot in here! [*She opens the window and reads further.*] "And stood at his feet weeping, and began to wash his feet with tears, and did wipe them with the hairs of her head, and anointed them with ointment"[14] [*Striking her breast.*] Everything dead! Saviour Saviour! If only I might anoint Your feet!

Scene XXI—*An open field.*

WOYZECK.

WOYZECK. [*Buries the knife in a hole.*] Thou shalt not kill. Lay here! I can't stay here! [*He rushes off.*]

14. From Luke 7:37–8. Jesus forgave the woman her sins.

Scene XXII—*The barracks.*

ANDRES. WOYZECK *rummages through his belongings.*

WOYZECK. Andres, this jacket's not part of the uniform, but you can use it, Andres.

ANDRES. [*Replies numbly to almost everything with.*] Sure.

WOYZECK. The cross is my sister's. And the ring.

ANDRES. Sure.

WOYZECK. I've got a Holy Picture, too: two hearts—they're real gold. I found it in my mother's Bible, and it said:

> O Lord with wounded head so sore
> So may my heart be evermore.

My mother only feels now when the sun shines on her hands . . . that doesn't matter.

ANDRES. Sure.

WOYZECK. [*Pulls out a paper.*] Friedrich Johann Franz Woyzeck. Soldier. Rifleman, Second Regiment, Second Battalion, Fourth Company. Born: the Feast of the Annunciation, twentieth of July. Today I'm thirty years old, seven months and twelve days.

ANDRES. Go to the hospital, Franz. Poor guy, you've got to drink some schnapps with a powder in it. It'll kill the fever.

WOYZECK. You know, Andres—when the carpenter puts those boards together, nobody knows who it's made for.

Scene XXIII—*The Street.*

MARIE *with little* GIRLS *in front of the house door.*
GRANDMOTHER. *Later* WOYZECK.

GIRLS. [*Singing.*]

> The sun shone bright on Candlemas Day[15]
> And the corn was all in bloom
> And they marched along the meadow way
> They marched by two and two.
> The pipers marched ahead
> The fiddlers followed through
> And their socks were scarlet red . . .

FIRST CHILD. I don't like that one.

SECOND CHILD. Why do you always want to be different?

FIRST CHILD. You sing for us, Marie!

MARIE. I can't.

SECOND CHILD. Why?

MARIE. Because.

SECOND CHILD. But *why* because?

THIRD CHILD. Grandmother, *you* tell us a story!

GRANDMOTHER. All right, you little crab apples!—Once upon a time there was a poor little girl who had no father and no mother.

15. February 2.

Everyone was dead, and there was no one left in the whole wide world. Everyone was dead. And the little girl went out and looked for someone night and day. And because there was no one left on the earth, she wanted to go to Heaven. And the moon looked down so friendly at her. And when she finally got to the moon, it was a piece of rotten wood. And so she went to the sun, and it was a faded sunflower. And when she got to the stars, they were little golden flies, stuck up there as if they were caught in a spider's web. And when she wanted to go back to earth, the earth was an upside-down pot. And she was all alone. And she sat down there and she cried. And she sits there to this day, all, all alone.

WOYZECK. [*Appears.*] Marie!

MARIE. [*Startled.*] What!

WOYZECK. Let's go. It's getting time.

MARIE. Where to?

WOYZECK. How should I know?

Scene XXIV—*A pond by the edge of the woods.*

MARIE *and* WOYZECK.

MARIE. Then the town must be out that way. It's so dark.

WOYZECK. You can't go yet. Come, sit down.

MARIE. But I've got to get back.

WOYZECK. You don't want to run your feet sore.

MARIE. What's happened to you?

WOYZECK. You know how long it's been, Marie?

MARIE. Two years from Pentecost.[16]

WOYZECK. You know how much longer it'll last?

MARIE. I've got to get back. Supper's not made yet.

WOYZECK. Are you freezing, Marie? And still you're so warm. Your lips are hot as coals! Hot as coals, the hot breath of a whore! And still I'd give up Heaven just to kiss them again. Are you freezing? When you're cold through, you won't freeze any more. The morning dew won't freeze you.

MARIE. What are you talking about?

WOYZECK. Nothing. [*Silence.*]

MARIE. Look how red the moon is! It's rising.

WOYZECK. Like a knife washed in blood.

MARIE. What are you going to do? Franz, you're so pale. [*He raises the knife.*]

MARIE. Franz! Stop! For Heaven's sake! Help me! Help me!

WOYZECK. [*Stabbing madly.*] There! There! Why can't you die? There! There! Ha, she's still shivering! Still not dead? Still not dead? Still shivering? [*Stabbing at her again.*] Are you dead? Dead! Dead! [*He drops the knife and runs away.*]

16. Church holiday seven Sundays after Easter.

Two MEN *approach.*

FIRST MAN. Wait!

SECOND MAN. You hear something? Shh! Over there!

FIRST MAN. Whhh! There! What a sound!

SECOND MAN. It's the water, it's calling. It's a long time since anyone drowned here. Let's go! I don't like hearing such sounds!

FIRST MAN. Whhh! There it is again! Like a person, dying!

SECOND MAN. It's uncanny! So foggy, nothing but gray mist as far as you can see—and the hum of beetles like broken bells. Let's get out of here!

FIRST MAN. No, it's too clear, it's too loud! Let's go up this way! Come on! [*They hurry on.*]

Scene XXV—*The inn.*

WOYZECK, KATHY, INNKEEPER, IDIOT, *and* PEOPLE.

WOYZECK. Dance! Everybody! Don't stop! Sweat and stink! He'll get you all in the end! [*Sings.*]

> Oh, daughter, my daughter
> And didn't you know
> That sleeping with coachmen
> Would bring you low?

[*He dances.*] Ho, Kathy! Sit down! I'm so hot, so hot! [*Takes off his coat.*] That's the way it is: the devil takes one and lets the other get away. Kathy, you're hot as coals! Why, tell me why? Kathy, you'll be cold one day, too. Be reasonable.—Can't you sing something?

KATHY. [*Sings.*]

> That Swabian land[17] I cannot bear
> And dresses long I will not wear
> For dresses long and pointed shoes
> Are clothes a chambermaid never should choose.

WOYZECK. No shoes, no shoes! We can get to hell without shoes.

KATHY. [*Sings.*]

> To such and like I'll not be prone
> Take back your gold and sleep alone.

WOYZECK. Sure, sure! What do I want to get all bloody for?

KATHY. Then what's that on your hand?

WOYZECK. Me? Me?

KATHY. Red! It's blood! [PEOPLE *gather round him.*]

WOYZECK. Blood? Blood?

INNKEEPER. Blood!

WOYZECK. I think I cut myself. Here, on my right hand.

INNKEEPER. Then why is there blood on your elbow?

WOYZECK. I wiped it off.

INNKEEPER. Your right hand and you wiped it on your right elbow?

17. Region of southwest Germany.

You're a smart one!

IDIOT. And then the Giant said: "I smell, I smell the flesh of Man." Pew, it stinks already!

WOYZECK. What do you want from me? Is it your business? Out of my way or the first one who . . . Damn you? Do I look like I murdered somebody? Do I look like a murderer? What are you looking at? Look at yourselves! Look! Out of my way!

[*He runs off.*]

Scene XXVI—*At the pond.*

WOYZECK, *alone.*

WOYZECK. The knife! Where's the knife? I left it here. It'll give me away! Closer! And closer! What is this place? What's that noise? Something's moving! It's quiet now.—It's got to be here, close to her. Marie? Ha, Marie! Quiet. Everything's quiet! Why are you so pale, Marie? Why are you wearing those red beads around your neck? Who was it gave you that necklace for sinning with him? Your sins made you black, Marie, they made you black! Did I make you so pale? Why is your hair uncombed? Did you forget to twist your braids today? The knife, the knife! I've got it! There! [*He runs toward the water.*] There, into the water! [*He throws the knife into the water.*] It dives like a stone into the black water. No, it's not out far enough for when they swim! [*He wades into the pond and throws it out farther.*] There! Now! But in the summer when they dive for mussels? Ha, it'll get rusty, who'll ever notice it! Why didn't I break it first! Am I still bloody? I've got to wash myself. There, there's a spot, and there's another . . . [*He goes farther out into the water.*]

Scene XXVII—*The street.*

CHILDREN.

FIRST CHILD. Let's go find Marie!

SECOND CHILD. What happened?

FIRST CHILD. Don't you know? Everybody's out there. They found a body!

SECOND CHILD. Where?

FIRST CHILD. By the pond, out in the woods.

SECOND CHILD. Hurry, so we can still see something. Before they bring it back. [*They rush off.*]

Scene XXVIII—*In front of* MARIE's *house.*

IDIOT, CHILD, *and* WOYZECK.

IDIOT. [*Holding* THE CHILD *on his knee,* points to WOYZECK *as he enters.*] Looky there, he fell in the water, he fell in the water, he fell in the water!

WOYZECK. Boy! Christian!

IDIOT. [*Looks at him fixedly.*] He fell in the water.

WOYZECK. [*Wanting to embrace* THE CHILD *tenderly, but it turns from him and screams.*] My God! My God!

IDIOT. He fell in the water.

WOYZECK. I'll buy you a horsey, Christian. There, there. [THE CHILD *pulls away. To the* IDIOT.] Here, buy the boy a horsey! [THE IDIOT *stares at him.*] Hop! Hop! Hip-hop, horsey!

IDIOT. [*Shouting joyously.*] Hop! Hop! Hip-hop, horsey! Hip-hop, horsey!

He runs off with THE CHILD. WOYZECK *is alone.*

Scene XXIX—The morgue.

JUDGE, COURT CLERK, POLICEMAN, CAPTAIN, DOCTOR, DRUM MAJOR, SERGEANT, IDIOT, *and others.* WOYZECK.

POLICEMAN. What a murder! A good, genuine, beautiful murder! Beautiful a murder as you could hope for! It's been a long time since we had one like this!

WOYZECK *stands in their midst, dumbly looking at the body of* MARIE; *he is bound, the dogmatic atheist, tall, haggard, timid, good-natured, scientific.*

MIKHAIL LERMONTOV

(1814–1841)

Princess Mary*

May 11th

Yesterday, I arrived in Pyatigorsk[1] and rented lodgings on the outskirts of the town, at its highest point, at the foot of Mount Mashuk: when there is a thunderstorm, the clouds will descend down to my roof. At five this morning, when I opened the window, my room was filled with the perfume of flowers growing in the modest front garden. The branches of cherry trees in bloom look into my window, and the wind occasionally strews my desk with their white petals. The view on three sides is marvelous: to the west, the five-peaked Besh Tau looms blue like "the last thunder-

---

* "Princess Mary," from *A Hero of Our Time*, is the second story in Pechorin's journal, which is published by the traveler-narrator who had earlier met him and Maxim Maximich. The translation is by Vladimir Nabokov.

1. A health resort in the northern Caucasus, a mountain range between the Black and Caspian seas. Pyahgorsk is known for its hot sulphur springs. Pechorin has arrived here for rest and relaxation after military service against neighboring mountain tribes.

cloud of a tempest dispersed"; to the north, Mount Mashuk rises like a shaggy Persian fur cap and closes off all that part of the horizon; to the east, the outlook is gayer; right below me, lies the vari-colored, neat, brand-new little town, the medicinal springs babble, and so does the multilingual crowd; and, beyond the town, amphi-theatrical mountains pile up, ever bluer and mistier, while on the edge of the horizon there stretches a silver range of snowy summits, beginning with Mount Kazbek, and ending with the bicephalous Mount Elbruz. It is gay to live in such country! A kind of joyful feeling permeates all my veins. The air is pure and fresh, like the kiss of a child, the sun is bright, the sky is blue—what more, it seems, could one wish? Who, here, needs passions, desires, regrets? However, it is time. I shall go to the Elizabeth Spring: there, I am told, the entire spa society gathers in the morning.

. . . .[2]

Upon descending into the center of town, I followed the boule-vard where I came across several melancholy groups that were slowly going uphill. These were mostly families of landowners from the steppe provinces: this could be inferred immediately from the worn-out, old-fashioned frock coats of the husbands and the elabo-rate attires of the wives and daughters. Obviously they had already taken stock of all the young men at the waters for they looked at me with tender curiosity. The St. Petersburg[3] cut of my military surtout[4] misled them, but soon, recognizing the epaulets of a mere army officer,[5] they turned away in disgust.

The wives of the local officials, the hostesses of the waters, so to speak, were more favorably disposed; they have lorgnettes, they pay less attention to uniforms, they are used to encountering in the Caucasus, an ardent heart under a numbered army button, and a cultivated mind under a white army cap. These ladies are very charming, and remain charming for a long time! Every year, their admirers are replaced by new ones, and here, perhaps, lies the secret of their indefatigable amiability. As I climbed the narrow path leading to the Elizabeth Spring, I overtook a bunch of men, some civilian, some military, who, as I afterwards learned, make up a special class of people among those hoping for the action of the waters. They drink—but not water, they walk little, they flirt only in passing, they gamble and complain of ennui. They are dandies: as they dip their wicker-encased glasses into the well of sulphurous water, they assume academic poses: the civilians wear pale-blue neckerchiefs, the military men allow ruffles to show above their coat-collars. They profess a profound contempt for provincial houses and sigh after the capitals' aristocratic salons where they are not admitted.

2. Indicated the passage of time: no-thing is left out.

3. The royal capital and center of fashion, now Leningrad.

4. Coat.

5. Pechorin has been demoted to the army from the more fashionable Guards.

At last, there was the well. Near it, on the terrace, a small red-roofed structure was built to house the bath, and a little further, there was the gallery where one walked when it rained. Several wounded officers sat on a bench, their crutches drawn up, looking pale and sad. Several ladies walked briskly back and forth on the terrace awaiting the action of the waters. Among them there were two or three pretty faces. In the avenues of vines that cover the slope of Mount Mashuk, one could glimpse now and then the variegated bonnets of ladies partial to shared isolation, since I would always notice, near such a bonnet, either a military cap or one of those round civilian hats that are so ugly. On a steep cliff where the pavilion termed The Aeolian Harp[6] is built, the lovers of scenery perched and trained a telescope on Mount Elbruz: among them were two tutors with their charges, who had come to have their scrofula[7] treated.

I had stopped out of breath on the edge of the hill and, leaning against the corner of the bathhouse, had begun to survey the picturesque landscape, when suddenly I heard a familiar voice behind me:

"Pechorin! Have you been here long?"

I turned around: it was Grushnitski! We embraced. I had made his acquaintance in a detachment on active duty. He had been wounded by a bullet in the leg and had left for the waters about a week before me.

Grushnitski is a cadet. He has been in the service only one year; he wears, following a peculiar kind of foppishness, a soldier's thick coat.[8] He has a soldier's St. George's Cross.[9] He is well built, swarthy and black-haired; judging by his appearance, one might give him twenty-five years of age, although he is hardly twenty-one. He throws his head back when he speaks, and keeps twirling his mustache with his left hand since he uses his right for leaning on his crutch. His speech is rapid and ornate; he is one of those people who, for every occasion in life, have ready-made pompous phrases, whom unadorned beauty does not move, and who solemnly drape themselves in extraordinary emotions, exalted passions, and exceptional sufferings. To produce an effect is rapture to them; romantic provincial ladies go crazy over them. With age they become either peaceful landowners, or drunkards; sometimes, both. Their souls often possess many good qualities, but not an ounce of poetry. Grushnitski's passion was to declaim; he bombarded you with words as soon as the talk transcended the circle of everyday notions: I have never been able to argue with him. He does not answer your objections, he does not listen to you. The moment you stop, he

---

6. A kind of wind harp (named after the Greek Aeolus, god of winds), whose strings, stretched across an open box, sounded in the wind.

7. Diseased tissues associated with tuberculosis and glandular disorder.

8. The plain soldier's coat suggests that Grushnitsky has been demoted from officer rank, for mysterious and romantic reasons.

9. A medal given for bravery in battle.

launches upon a long tirade apparently having some connection with what you have said, but actually being only a continuation of his own discourse.

He is fairly witty; his epigrams are frequently amusing, but they are neither to the point nor venomous; he will never kill anyone with a single word; he does not know people and their vulnerable spots, since all his life he has been occupied with his own self. His object is to become the hero of a novel. So often has he tried to convince others that he is a being not made for this world and doomed to suffer in secret, that he has almost succeeded in convincing himself of it. That is why he wears, so proudly, that thick soldier's coat of his. I have seen through him, and that is why he dislikes me, although outwardly we are on the friendliest of terms. Grushnitski has the reputation of an exceptionally brave man. I have seen him in action: he brandishes his sword, he yells, he rushes forward with closed eyes. Somehow, this is not Russian courage!

I don't like him either: I feel that one day we shall meet on a narrow path, and one of us will fare ill.

His coming to the Caucasus is likewise a consequence of his fanatic romanticism. I am sure that on the eve of his departure from the family country seat, he told some pretty neighbor, with a gloomy air, that he was going to the Caucasus not merely to serve there, but that he was seeking death because . . . and here, probably, he would cover his eyes with his hand and continue thus: "No, you must not know this! Your pure soul would shudder! And what for? What am I to you? Would you understand me? . . ." and so forth.

He told me himself that the reason which impelled him to join the K. regiment would remain an eternal secret between him and heaven.

Yet during those moments when he casts off the tragic cloak, Grushnitski is quite pleasant and amusing. I am curious to see him with women: that is when, I suppose, he really tries hard!

We met like old chums. I began to question him about life at the spa and its noteworthy people.

"Our life here is rather prosaic," he said with a sigh. "Those who drink the waters in the morning are insipid like all invalids, and those who drink wine in the evening are unbearable like all healthy people. Feminine society exists, but there is little comfort therein: these ladies play whist,[10] dress badly and speak dreadful French![11] From Moscow this year, there is only Princess Ligovskoy with her daughter, but I am not acquainted with them. My soldier's coat is like a seal of rejection. The sympathy that it arouses is as painful as charity."

10. A card game, forerunner of bridge.
11. French was preferred to Russian as the language of polite and elegant society.

At that moment, two ladies walked past us in the direction of the well: one was elderly, the other young and graceful. Their bonnets prevented me from getting a good look at their faces, but they were dressed according to the strict rules of the best taste: there was nothing superfluous. The younger one wore a pearl-gray dress closed at the throat, a light silk fichu[12] twined around her supple neck, shoes, *couleur puce*,[13] so pleasingly constricted at the ankle her spare little foot, that even one uninitiated into the mysteries of beauty would have certainly uttered an exclamation, if only of surprise. Her light, yet noble, gait had something virginal about it that escaped definition, but was comprehensible to the gaze. As she walked past us, there emanated from her the ineffable fragrance which breathes sometimes from a beloved woman's letter.

"That's Princess Ligovskoy," said Grushnitski, "and with her is her daughter, Mary, as she calls her after the English fashion.[14] They have been here only three days."

"And yet you already know her name?"

"Yes, I happened to hear it," he answered flushing. "I confess, I do not wish to meet them. Those proud aristocrats look upon us army men as savages. And what do they care whether or not there is a mind under a numbered regimental cap and a heart under a thick army coat?"

"Poor coat," I said with a smile. "And who is the gentleman going up to them and so helpfully offering them tumblers?"[15]

"Oh, that's the Moscow dandy Raevich. He is a gamester: it can be seen at once by the huge, golden watch chain that winds across his sky-blue waistcoat. And what a thick walking stick—like Robinson Crusoe's; and his beard and haircut *à la moujik*[16] are also characteristic."

"You are embittered against the whole of humanity?"

"And there is a good reason for that."

"Oh, really?"

At this point the ladies moved away from the well and came level with us. Grushnitski had time to assume a dramatic attitude with the help of his crutch, and loudly answered me in French:

"*Mon cher, je hais les hommes pour ne pas les mepriser, car autrement la vie serait une farce trop dégoûtante.*"[17]

The pretty young princess turned her head and bestowed a long curious glance upon the orator. The expression of this glance was very indefinite, but it was not derisive, a fact on which I inwardly congratulated him with all my heart.

"This Princess Mary is extremely pretty," I said to him. "She has such velvety eyes—yes, velvety is the word for them. I advise you to

---

12. A light triangular scarf, worn over the shoulders.
13. A brownish purple.
14. That is, instead of the Russian Marya.

15. Glasses of mineral water.
16. Peasant-style; i.e. short.
17. "My good fellow, I hate men so as not to despise them, for otherwise life would be too disgusting a farce."

appropriate this term when you speak of her eyes: the upper and lower lashes are so long, that the pupils do not reflect the rays of the sun. I like this kind of lusterless eyes: they are so soft, they seem to stroke you. However, this seems to be the only nice thing about her face. And her teeth, are they white? This is very important! Pity she did not smile at your pompous phrase."

"You talk of a pretty woman as of an English horse," said Grushnitski with indignation.

"*Mon cher,*" I answered trying to copy his manner, "*je méprise les femmes pour ne pas les aimer, car autrement la vie serait un mélodrame trop ridicule.*"[18]

I turned and walked away from him. For about half an hour, I strolled along the viny avenues, the limestone ledges, and the bushes hanging between them. It was getting hot, and I decided to hurry home. When passing the sulphurous spring, I stopped at the covered walk to draw a deep breath in its shade, and this provided me with the opportunity to witness a rather curious scene. This is how the actors were placed. The elderly princess and the Moscow dandy sat on a bench in the covered walk, and both seemed to be engrossed in serious conversation. The young princess, probably having finished her last glass of water, strolled pensively near the well. Grushnitski stood right beside it; there was no one else on the terrace.

I drew closer and hid behind a corner of the walk. At this moment, Grushnitski dropped his glass upon the sand and tried hard to bend down in order to pick it up. His injured leg hampered him. Poor fellow! How he exerted himself while leaning on his crutch, but all in vain. His expressive face reflected real pain.

Princess Mary saw it all even better than I. Lighter than a little bird, she skipped up to him, bent down, picked up the glass, and handed it to him with a movement full of inexpressible charm. Then she blushed dreadfully, glanced back at the covered walk, but having convinced herself that her mamma had seen nothing, appeared at once to regain her composure. When Grushnitski opened his mouth to thank her, she was already far away. A minute later, she left the gallery with her mother and the dandy, but as she passed by Grushnitski, she assumed a most formal and dignified air, she did not even turn her head, did not even take notice of the passionate glance with which he followed her for a long time until she reached the bottom of the hill and disappeared beyond the young lindens of the boulevard. Presently, however, her bonnet could be glimpsed crossing the street; she hurried through the gate of one of the best houses in Pyatigorsk. Her mother walked in after her, and at the gate gave Raevich a parting nod.

Only then did the poor passionate cadet notice my presence.

18. "My good fellow, I despise women so as not to love them, for otherwise life would be too foolish a melodrama."

"Did you see?" he said firmly gripping me by the hand. "A very angel!"

"Why?" I asked, with an air of the most genuine naïveté.

"Didn't you see?"

"I did: she picked up your glass. Had an attendant been around, he would have done the same thing, and with even more alacrity since he would be hoping for a tip. However, one can quite understand that she felt sorry for you: you made such an awful face when you shifted your weight onto your wounded leg."

"And you did not feel at all touched looking at her at the moment her soul shone in her face?"

"No."

I lied, but I wanted to infuriate him. Contradiction is, with me, an innate passion; my entire life has been nothing but a chain of sad and frustrating contradictions to heart or reason. The presence of an enthusiast envelops me with midwinter frost, and I think that frequent commerce with an inert phlegmatic individual would have made of me a passionate dreamer. I further confess that a nasty but familiar sensation, at that moment, skimmed over my heart. This sensation was envy: I boldly say "envy" because I am used to being frank with myself in everything, and it is doubtful if there can be found a young man who, upon meeting a pretty woman who has riveted his idle attention and has suddenly given obvious preference to another man equally unknown to her, it is doubtful, let me repeat, that there can be found a young man (provided, of course, that he has lived in the *grand monde*[19] and is accustomed to indulge his vanity), who would not be unpleasantly struck by this.

In silence, Grushnitski and I descended the hill and walked along the boulevard past the windows of the house into which our charmer had vanished. She was sitting at the window. Grushnitski jerked me by the arm, and threw upon her one of those blurrily tender glances which have so little effect upon women. I trained my lorgnette[20] on her and noticed that his glance made her smile, and that my insolent lorgnette angered her in no uncertain way. And how, indeed, does a Caucasian army officer dare to train his quizzing-glass on a young princess from Moscow?

May 13th

This morning my doctor friend called on me: his surname is Werner, but he is Russian. Why should this be surprising? I used to know an Ivanov who was German.

Werner is a remarkable man in many respects. He is a sceptic and a materialist, like almost all medical men, but he is also a poet, and this I mean seriously. He is a poet in all his actions, and frequently in his utterings, although in all his life he never wrote two lines of verse. He has studied all the live strings of the human heart

---

19. High society.   20. Eyeglasses with a short handle.

in the same way as one studies the veines of a dead body, but he has never learned how to put his knowledge to profit: thus sometimes an excellent anatomist may not know how to cure a fever. Ordinarily, Werner made unobtrusive fun of his patients, but once I saw him cry over a dying soldier. He was poor; he dreamt of becoming a millionaire but would never have taken one additional step for the sake of money. He told me once that he would rather do a favor for an enemy than for a friend, because in the latter case it would mean selling charity, whereas hatred only grows in proportion to an enemy's generosity. He had a caustic tongue: under the label of his epigram, many a kindly man acquired the reputation of a vulgarian and a fool. His competitors, envious resort doctors, once spread the rumor that he drew cartoons of his patients—the patients became infuriated—and almost all refused to be treated by him. His friends, that is to say, all the really decent people serving in the Caucasus, tried in vain to restore his fallen credit.

His appearance was of the kind that, at first glance, impresses one unfavorably but attracts one later, when the eye has learned to decipher in irregular features the imprint of a dependable and lofty soul. Examples are known of women falling madly in love with such people and of not exchanging their ugly exterior for the beauty of the freshest and rosiest Endymions.[21] Women must be given their due: they have a flair for spiritual beauty. This may be why men like Werner are so passionately fond of women.

Werner was of small stature, thin and frail like a child. One of his legs was shorter than the other, as in the case of Byron;[22] in proportion to his body, his head seemed enormous; he cropped his hair; the bumps of his skull, thus revealed, would have amazed a phrenologist[23] by their bizarre interplay of contradictory inclinations. His small black eyes, never at rest, tried to penetrate your mind. His dress revealed taste and tidiness; his lean, wiry, small hands sported light-yellow gloves. His frock coat, neckcloth and waistcoat were always black. The younger men dubbed him Mephistopheles. He pretended to resent this nickname, but, in point of fact, it flattered his vanity. We soon came to understand each other and became pals—for I am not capable of true friendship. One of the two friends is always the slave of the other, although, often, neither of the two admits this to himself. I can be nobody's slave, while to assume command in such cases is tiresome work because it has to be combined with deceit. I, moreover, am supplied with lackeys and money. We became pals in the following way: I first met Werner in the town of S——, among a numerous and noisy group of young men. Toward the end of the evening, the conversation took a philosophic and metaphysical turn; convictions were dis-

<hr />

21. In Greek myth, a handsome youth with whom the moon goddess Selene fell in love.

22. George Gordon, Lord Byron (1788–1824), the English Romantic poet, who was lame.

23. One who claims to read personality from the skull's conformation.

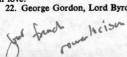

cussed; everyone was convinced of something or other.

"As for me, I am convinced of only one thing," said the doctor.

"Of what?" I asked, wishing to learn the opinion of this man who up to now had been silent.

"Of the fact," he answered, "that, sooner or later, one fine morning, I shall die."

"I'm better off than you," I said. "I've one more conviction besides yours, namely that one miserable evening I had the misfortune to be born."

Everybody found that we were talking nonsense, but, really, not one of them said anything more intelligent than that. Henceforth, we distinguished each other in the crowd. We would often see each other and discuss, together, with great seriousness, abstract matters, until we noticed that we were gulling each other. Then, after looking meaningly into each other's eyes, we began to laugh as Roman augurs did, according to Cicero,[24] and having had our fill of mirth, we would separate well-content with our evening.

I was lying on the divan, with eyes directed at the ceiling and hands clasped under my head, when Werner entered my room. He sat down in an armchair, placed his cane in a corner, yawned, and declared that it was getting hot out of doors. I answered that the flies were bothering me, and we both fell silent.

"Observe, my dear doctor," said I, "that without fools, the world would be a very dull place . . . Consider: here we are, two intelligent people; we know beforehand that one can argue endlessly about anything, and therefore we do not argue; we know almost all the secret thoughts of each other; one word is a whole story for us; we see the kernel of our every emotion through a triple shell. Sad things seem to us funny, funny things seem to us melancholy, and generally we are, to tell the truth, rather indifferent to everything except our own selves. Thus, between us there can be no exchange of feelings and thoughts: we know everything about each other that we wish to know, and we do not wish to know anything more. There remains only one solution: telling the news. So tell me some piece of news."

Tired by my long speech, I closed my eyes and yawned.

He answered, after a moment's thought: "Nevertheless, your drivel contains an idea."

"Two ideas," I answered.

"Tell me one, and I'll tell you the other."

"All right, you start!" said I, continuing to examine the ceiling and inwardly smiling.

"You'd like to learn some details about some resort guest, and I

24. Cicero (*On Divination*, Bk. II, Ch. 24) reports that the Roman Stoic Cato wondered how augurs, those who read omens, could look at each other without laughing.

have already an inkling as to the subject of your concern, because
there have already been inquiries about you in that quarter."

"Doctor! It is definitely impossible for us to converse: we read in
each other's souls." ?

"Now, the other idea. . . ."

"Here is the other idea: I wanted to make you relate something
or other—in the first place, because to listen is less fatiguing; in the
second place, because a listener cannot give himself away; in the
third place, because one can discover another's secret; and in the
fourth place, because such intelligent people as you prefer an audience to a storyteller. Now, to business! What did the old Princess
Ligovskoy say to you about me?"

"You are quite sure that it was the old princess and not the
young one?"

"I'm absolutely sure."

"Why?"

"Because the young princess asked about Grushnitski."

"You've a great talent for putting two and two together. The
young princess said she was sure that that young man in the soldier's coat had been degraded to the ranks for a duel."

"I hope you left her under this pleasant delusion."

"Naturally."

"We have the beginning of a plot!" I cried in delight. "The
denouement of this comedy will be our concern. Fate is obviously
taking care of my not being bored."

"I have a presentiment," said the doctor, "that poor Grushnitski
is going to be your victim. . . ."

"Go on with your story, doctor."

"The old princess said that your face was familiar to her. I
observed to her that no doubt she had met you in Petersburg, at
some fashionable reception. I told her your name. The name was
known to her. I believe your escapade caused a big sensation there.
The old princess started to tell of your exploits, adding her own
remarks to what was probably society gossip. Her daughter listened
with curiosity. In her imagination, you became the hero of a novel
in the latest fashion. I did not contradict the old lady, though I was
aware she was talking nonsense."

"My worthy friend!" said I, extending my hand to him. The
doctor shook it with feeling, and continued:

"If you wish, I'll introduce you. . . ."

"Mercy!" said I, raising my hands. "Does one introduce heroes?
They never meet their beloved other than in the act of saving her
from certain death."

"And so you really intend to flirt with the young princess?"

"On the contrary, quite on the contrary! Doctor, at last I
triumph: you do not understand me! This, however, saddens me,

upper class
people

doctor," I went on, after a moment of silence. "I never disclose my secrets myself, but I am awfully fond of having them divined, because that way I can always repudiate them if necessary. But come, you must describe to me the mamma and the daughter. What sort of people are they?"

"Well, in the first place, the mother is a woman of forty-five," answered Werner. "Her digestion is excellent, but there is something wrong with her blood; there are red blotches on her cheeks. She has spent the latter half of her life in Moscow, and there, in retirement, has grown fat. She likes risqué anecdotes and sometimes, when her daughter is not in the room, says improper things herself. She announced to me that her daughter was as innocent as a dove. What do I care? I was on the point of replying that she need not worry, I would not tell anybody. The mother is being treated for rheumatism, and what the daughter's complaint is, goodness knows. I told them both to drink two glasses of oxysulphuric water daily, and take a diluted bath twice a week. The old princess, it seems, is not used to command; she has great respect for the intelligence and the knowledge of her daughter, who has read Byron in English[25] and knows algebra. It seems that in Moscow young ladies have taken to higher education, and, by Jove, it's a good thing! Our men, generally speaking, are so boorish that to coquet with them must be unbearable for any intelligent woman. The old princess is very fond of young men; the young princess looks at them with a certain contempt—a Moscow habit! In Moscow, all they enjoy is the company of forty-year-old wags."

"And you, doctor, have you been in Moscow?"

"Yes, I had a fair amount of practice there."

"Go on with your story."

"Well, I seem to have told you everything . . . Oh yes! One more thing: the young princess seems fond of discussing sentiments, passions, and so forth. She spent one winter in Petersburg, and did not like it, especially the society there: probably she was given a cool reception."

"You saw no one at their house today?"

"On the contrary, there was one adjutant, one stiff-looking guardsman, and a lady who has recently arrived, a relative of the princess by marriage, a very pretty woman but a very sick one, it seems . . . Didn't you chance to meet her at the well? She's of medium height, a blonde, with regular features, her complexion is consumptive,[26] and she has a little black mole on her right cheek. Her face struck me by its expressiveness."

"A little mole!" I muttered through my teeth. "Really?"

The doctor looked at me and said solemnly, placing his hand on

25. Most Russians then read foreign works in French translation.

26. Tubercular, i.e. flushed.

my heart: "She is someone you know! . . ." My heart, indeed, was beating faster than usual.

"It is now your turn to triumph," I said, "but I rely on you; you will not betray me. I have not seen her yet, but I am sure that I recognize, from your depiction, a certain woman whom I loved in the old days. Don't tell her a word about me; should she ask, give a bad account of me."

"As you please!" said Werner with a shrug.

When he left, a dreadful sadness constrained my heart. Was it fate that was bringing us together again in the Caucasus, or had she come here on purpose, knowing she would meet me? And how would we meet? And, anyway, was it she? Presentiments never deceive me. There is no man in the world over whom the past gains such power as it does over me. Every reminder of a past sorrow or joy painfully strikes my soul and extracts from it the same old sounds . . . I am stupidly made, I forget nothing . . . nothing!

After dinner, around six, I went out onto the boulevard: there was a crowd there; the princess sat with her daughter on a bench, surrounded by young men who vied in paying attention to them. I sat down on another bench some way off, stopped two officers of the D. regiment whom I knew, and began telling them something; apparently, it was amusing, because they began laughing like mad. Curiosity attracted to me some of those who surrounded the young princess; little by little, they all abandoned her and joined my group. I never ceased talking; my stories were clever to the point of stupidity, my raillery, directed at the freaks who passed by, was wicked to the point of frenzy. I went on entertaining my audience till sunset. Several times, the young princess and her mother passed by me, arm in arm, accompanied by a little old man with a limp; several times her glance, falling upon me, expressed vexation while striving to express indifference.

"What has he been telling you?" she inquired of one of the young men who returned to her out of politeness. "Surely, a very entertaining story . . . his exploits in battles?" She said this rather loudly and probably with the intention of pin-pricking me. "Aha," I thought, "you are angry in earnest, my dear princess; just wait, there is more to come!"

Grushnitski watched her like a beast of prey and never took his eyes off her: I bet that tomorrow he will beg somebody to introduce him to her mother. She will be very pleased, because she is bored.

May 16th

During the last two days, my affairs have advanced tremendously. The young princess definitely hates me: people have already reported to me two or three epigrams aimed at me, fairly caustic, but at the same time very flattering. She finds it awfully strange that I, who am used to high society and am on such intimate terms with her Petersburg female cousins and aunts, do not try to make her acquaintance. Every day, we run into each other at the well or on the boulevard; I do my best to lure away her admirers, brilliant adjutants, pallid Moscovites and others—and almost always, I succeed. I have always hated to entertain guests at my house. Now, my place is full every day; people dine, sup, play cards, and, alas, my champagne triumphs over the power of her magnetic young eyes!

Yesterday, I saw her in Chelahov's store: she was bargaining for a wonderful Persian rug. The young princess kept begging her mamma not to be stingy; that rug would be such an adornment for her dressing room! I offered forty roubles more and outbid her; for this I was rewarded by a glance in which glittered the most exquisite rage. About dinner time, I purposely ordered my Circassian horse to be covered with that rug and led past her windows. Werner was with them at the time, and told me that the effect of that scene was most dramatic. The young princess wants to preach a crusade against me: I have even noticed that already two adjutants in her presence greet me very drily, although they dine at my house every day.

Grushnitski has assumed a mysterious air: he walks with his hands behind his back and does not seem to recognize anybody; his leg has suddenly got well, he hardly limps at all. He has found the occasion to enter into conversation with the old princess and to pay a compliment to her daughter. The latter is apparently none too choosy, for since then she has been acknowledging his salute with the prettiest of smiles.

"You are sure you do not wish to make the acquaintance of the Ligovskoys?" he said to me yesterday.

"Quite sure."

"Oh come! Theirs is the pleasantest house at the spa! All the best society here. . . ."

"My friend, I am dreadfully sick of the best society which is not here. And you . . . do you go there?"

"Not yet. I have talked to the young princess a couple of times, and more. It is kind of embarrassing to fish for an invitation, you know, though it is done here . . . It would have been another matter, if I wore epaulets. . . ."

"Oh come! You are much more intriguing this way! You simply don't know how to take advantage of your lucky situation. In the eyes of any sentimental young lady, your soldier's coat is bound to make a hero of you, a martyr."

Grushnitski smiled smugly.

"What nonsense!" he said.

"I'm sure," I went on, "that the young princess is already in love with you."

He blushed to the ears, and puffed out his chest.

O vanity! you are the lever by means of which Archimedes[27] wished to lift the earth!

"You always joke!" he said, feigning to be cross. "In the first place, she knows me so little as yet."

"Women love only those whom they do not know."

"But I have no pretension whatever to make her fond of me, I simply want to gain access to a pleasant house, and it would have been quite absurd if I had any hopes . . . Now you people, for example, are another matter; you St. Petersburg lady-killers, you have only to look . . . and women melt . . . By the way, Pechorin, do you know what the young princess said about you?"

"Really? Has she already started to speak to you about me?"

"Wait—there is nothing to be glad about. The other day I entered into conversation with her at the well, by chance. Her third word was: 'Who is that gentleman with that unpleasant oppressive gaze? He was with you when . . .' She blushed and did not want to name the day, remembering her charming gesture. 'You don't have to mention the day,' I replied to her, 'it will always remain in my memory.' Pechorin, my friend! I do not congratulate you; you are on her black list. And this, indeed, is regrettable because my Mary is a very charming girl!"

It should be noted that Grushnitski is one of those people who, when speaking of a woman whom they hardly know, call her *my Mary, my Sophie,* if she had the fortune to catch their fancy.

I assumed a serious air and replied to him:

"Yes, she is not bad . . . But beware, Grushnitski! Russian young ladies, for the most part, nourish themselves on platonic love, without admixing to it any thought of marriage: now, platonic love is the most troublesome kind. The young princess seems to be one of those women who want to be amused: if she is bored in your presence for two minutes together, you are irretrievably lost. Your silence must excite her curiosity, your talk should never entirely satisy it; you must disturb her every minute. She will disregard convention, publicly, a dozen times for your sake, and will call it a sacrifice, and, in order to reward herself for it, she will begin to torment you, and after that she will simply say that she cannot stand you. Unless you gain some ascendency over her, even her first kiss will not entitle you to a second: she will have her fill of flirting with you, and in two years or so she will marry a monster out of submissiveness to her mother, and will start persuading herself that she is miserable, that she loved only one man, meaning you, but that Heaven had not wished to unite her with him because he wore a soldier's coat,

27. Greek mathematician and inventor (287–212 B.C.). In explaining the principle of the lever, he is supposed to have said "Give me a place to stand and I will move the world."

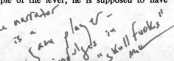

the narrator is a same player – indulges in "skull fucks" me

although under that thick gray coat there beat a passionate and noble heart. . . ."

Grushnitski hit the table with his fist and started to pace up and down the room.

I inwardly roared with laughter, and even smiled once or twice, but fortunately he did not notice.

It is clear that he is in love, for he has become even more credulous than before: there even appeared on his finger, a nielloed, silver ring[28] of local production. It looked suspicious to me. I began to examine it, and what would you think? . . . The name *Mary* was engraved in minuscule letters on the inside, and next to it was the day of the month when she picked up the famous glass. I concealed my discovery. I do not wish to force a confession from him, I want him to choose me for a confidant himself—and it is then that I shall enjoy myself! . . .

Today, I rose late; when I reached the well, there was already nobody there. It was getting hot; furry white clouds were rapidly scudding from the snowy mountains with the promise of a thunderstorm; the top of Mount Mashuk smoked like an extinguished torch; around it there coiled and slithered, like snakes, gray shreds of cloud, which had been delayed in their surge and seemed to have caught in its thorny brush. The air was pervaded with electricity. I plunged into a viny avenue that led to a grotto; I was sad. I kept thinking of that young woman with the little birthmark on her cheek of whom the doctor had been talking. Why was she here? And was it she? And why did I think it was she? And why was I even so sure of it? Were there not many women with little moles on their cheeks! Meditating in this fashion, I came close to the grotto. As I looked in, I saw in the cool shade of its vault, on a stone bench, a seated woman, wearing a straw hat, a black shawl wrapped around her shoulders, her head sunken on her breast: the hat screened her face. I was on the point of turning back, so as not to disturb her revery, when she looked up at me.

"Vera!" I cried involuntarily.

She started and grew pale.

"I knew that you were here," she said.

I sat down near her and took her hand. A long-forgotten thrill ran through my veins at the sound of that dear voice: she looked into my eyes with her deep and calm eyes; they expressed distrust and something akin to reproachfulness.

"We have not seen each other for a long time," I said.

"Yes, a long time, and we have both changed in many ways!"

"So this means that you do not love me any more? . . ."

28. A ring whose incised design is filled with *niello*, a black alloy.

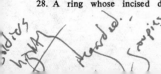

"I am married! . . ." she said.

"Again? Several years ago, however, the same reason existed, and yet. . . ."

She snatched her hand out of mine. And her cheeks flamed.

"Perhaps you love your second husband. . . ."

She did not answer and turned away.

"Or is he very jealous?"

Silence.

"Well? He is young, handsome, he is, in particular, rich, no doubt, and you are afraid . . ." I glanced at her and was shocked: her face expressed profound despair, tears sparkled in her eyes.

"Tell me," she whispered at last, "do you find it very amusing to torture me? I ought to hate you. Ever since we have known each other, you gave me nothing but sufferings . . ." Her voice trembled; she leaned toward me to lay her head on my breast.

"Perhaps," I thought, "this is exactly why you loved me: one forgets joys, one never forgets sorrows. . . ."

I embraced her warmly, and thus we remained for a long time. At last our lips came close together and merged in an ardent rapturous kiss; her hands were as cold as ice, her brow was burning. Between us, started one of those conversations which have no sense on paper, which cannot be repeated and which one cannot even retain in one's mind: the meaning of sounds replaces and enhances the meaning of words, as in the Italian opera.

She definitely does not wish that I meet her husband, that little old gentleman with the limp whom I glimpsed on the boulevard: she married him for the sake of her son. He is rich and suffers from rheumatism. I did not allow myself a single jibe at him: she respects him as a father—and will deceive him as a husband. What a bizarre thing, the human heart in general, and a woman's heart in particular!

Vera's husband, Semyon Vasilievich G——v, is a distant relation of Princess Ligovskoy. He lives near her: Vera often visits the old princess. I gave her my word that I would get acquainted with the Ligovskoys and court the young princess in order to divert attention from Vera. In this way, my plans have not been upset in the least, and I shall have a merry time. . . .

Merry time! Yes, I have already passed that stage of the soul's life when one seeks only happiness, when the heart feels the need to love someone strongly and passionately. At present, all I wish is to be loved, and that by very few: it even seems to me that I would be content with one permanent attachment, a pitiful habit of the heart!

One thing has always struck me as strange: I never became the slave of the women I loved; on the contrary, I have always gained unconquerable power over their will and heart, with no effort at all.

Why is it so? Is it because I never treasured anything too much, while they incessantly feared to let me slip out of their hands? Or is it the magnetic influence of a strong organism? Or did I simply never succeed in encountering a woman with a stubborn will of her own?

I must admit that, indeed, I never cared for women with wills of their own; it is not their department. *sexist bastard*

True, I remember now—once, only once did I love a strong-willed woman, whom I could never conquer. We parted enemies—but even so, perhaps, had our meeting occurred five years later, we would have parted differently.

Vera is ill, very ill, although she will not admit it: I fear she may have consumption, or that disease which is called *fièvre lente*,[29] a completely non-Russian disease for which there is no name in our language.

The thunderstorm caught us in the grotto and detained us there for an extra half hour. She did not make me swear that I would be true to her, did not ask if I had loved other women since we had parted. She entrusted herself to me again with the same unconcern as before—and I will not deceive her. She is the only woman on earth whom I could not bear to deceive. I know that we shall soon part again—perhaps, forever; that each of us will go his separate way, graveward. But her memory will remain inviolable in my soul: I have always repeated this to her, and she believes me, although she says she does not. *he assumes a hell of a lot ...*

At last, we separated: for a long time, I followed her with my gaze until her hat disappeared behind the shrubs and cliffs. My heart painfully contracted as after the first parting. Oh, how that feeling gladdened me! Could it be that youth with its beneficial storms wants to return to me again, or is it merely its farewell glance—a last gift to its memory? And yet it's absurd to think that in appearance I am still a boy: my face is pale but still fresh-complexioned, my limbs are supple and svelte, my thick hair curls, my eyes sparkle, my blood is ebullient.

When I returned home, I got on my horse and galloped out into the steppe. I love to gallop on a spirited horse through tall grass, against the wind of the wilderness; avidly do I swallow the redolent air and direct my gaze into the blue remoteness, trying to distinguish the nebulous outlines of objects that become, every minute, clearer and clearer. Whatever sorrow may burden my heart, whatever anxiety may oppress my mind, everything is dispersed in a moment: the soul feels easy, bodily fatigue vanquishes mental worry. There is no feminine gaze that I would not forget at the sight of mountains covered with vegetation, and illumined by the southern sun, at the sight of the blue sky, or at the sound of a torrent that falls from

29. A low continuous fever that accompanies lung disease.

crag to crag.

I think that the Cossacks[30] yawning on the top of their watch-
towers, upon seeing me galloping without need or goal, were for a
long time tormented by this riddle, for I am sure they must have
taken me for a Circassian because of my dress. Indeed, I have been
told that when riding in Circassian garb, I look more like a Kabardan than many a Kabardan.[31] And, in point of fact, as regards that
noble battle garb, I am an absolute dandy: not one bit of superfluous braid; costly arms in plain setting; the fur of the cap neither
too long nor too short; leggings and boots fitted with utmost exactitude; a white *beshmet;*[32] a dark-brown *cherkeska.*[33] I have studied, for a long time, the mountain peoples' style of riding: there is
no better way of flattering my vanity than to acknowledge my skill
in riding a horse in the Caucasian fashion. I keep four horses: one
for myself, three for pals, so as not to feel dull while ranging the
fields alone: they take my horses with alacrity, and never ride with
me. It was already six in the evening, when I remembered that it
was time to dine. My horse was worn out; I came out onto the road
which led from Pyatigorsk to the German settlement where the spa
society frequently went for picnics. The road ran winding among
bushes, and descending into small ravines where noisy creeks flowed
under the shelter of tall grasses; all around rose an amphitheatre of
blue masses—Besh Tau, Snake Mountain, Iron Mountain and Bald
Mountain. Upon descending into one of these ravines, called *balkas*
in the local dialect, I stopped to water my horse. At that moment,
there appeared on the road a noisy and resplendent cavalcade, the
ladies in black or light-blue riding habits, and the gentlemen in
costumes representing a mixture of Circassian and Nizhni-Nov-
gorodah:[34] Grushnitski rode in front with Princess Mary.

Ladies at Caucasian spas still believe in the possibility of Circassian attacks in broad daylight: presumably, this is why Grushnitski
had hung a sword and a brace of pistols onto his soldier's coat. He
was rather absurd in this heroic attire. A tall shrub hid me from
them, but through its foliage I could see everything and could guess
from the expressions on their faces that the conversation was sentimental. Finally, they drew close to the declivity; Grushnitski took
the princess' horse by the bridle, and then I heard the end of their
conversation: [*bridle*]

"And you wish to remain for the rest of your life in the Caucasus?" the princess was saying.

"What is Russia to me?" answered her companion, "a country

---

30. Russian soldiers, originally from
the Ukraine and forming their own independent communities; at this time, a
privileged military class.

31. The name of two tribes in the
Caucasus mountains.

32. A belted cotton or silk smock
worn over the shirt.

33. A long tunic worn over the beshmet.

34. Nizhny-Novgorod is a large city in
Russia, now renamed Gorkiy.

where thousands of people will look on me with contempt because they are richer than I am—whereas here—here this thick soldier's coat has not prevented me from making your acquaintance. . . ."

"On the contrary . . ." said the princess, blushing.

Grushnitski's face portrayed pleasure. He went on:

"My life here will flow by noisily, unnoticeably, and rapidly under the bullets of the savages, and if God would send me, every year, one radiant feminine glance, one glance similar to the one. . . .

At this point they came level with me; I struck my horse with my riding crop and rode out from behind the bush. . . .

"*Mon Dieu, un Circassien! . . .*"[35] cried the princess in terror.

In order to dissuade her completely, I answered in French, bowing slightly:

"*Ne craignez rien, madame—je ne suis pas plus dangereux que votre cavalier.*"[36]

She was embarrassed—but why? Because of her mistake, or because my answer seemed insolent to her? I would have liked my second supposition to be the correct one. Grushnitski cast a look of displeasure at me.

Late this evening, that is to say around eleven, I went for a stroll in the linden avenue of the boulevard. The town was asleep: only in some windows lights could be glimpsed. On three sides, there loomed the black crest of cliffs, offshoots of Mount Mashuk, on the summit of which an ominous little cloud was lying. The moon was rising in the east; afar glittered the silvery rim of snow-covered mountains. The cries of the sentries alternated with the sound of the hot springs, which had been given free flow for the night. At times, the sonorous stamp of a horse was heard in the street, accompanied by the creaking of a Nogay[37] wagon and a mournful Tatar song. I sat down on a bench and became lost in thought. I felt the need of pouring out my thoughts in friendly talk—but with whom? What was Vera doing now, I wondered. I would have paid dearly to press her hand at that moment.

Suddenly, I heard quick irregular steps—Grushnitski, no doubt. So it was!

"Where do you come from?"

"From Princess Ligovskoy," he said very importantly. "How Mary can sing!"

"Do you know what?" I said to him, "I bet she does not know that you are a cadet; she thinks you have been degraded to the ranks."

"Perhaps! What do I care?" he said absently.

"Oh, I just happened to mention it."

35. "My God, a Circassian!"

36. "Don't be afraid, madame—I am no more dangerous than your companion."

37. Reference to the Nogay steppes, in southern Russia and the eastern Caucasus, and their inhabitants.

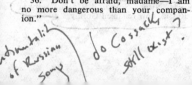

"Do you know, you made her dreadfully angry today? She found it an unheard-of insolence. I had a lot of trouble convincing her that you are too well brought up and that you know the *grand monde* too well to have had any intention of insulting her: she says that you have an impudent gaze and that, no doubt, you have the highest opinion of yourself."

"She is not mistaken . . . Perhaps you would like to stand up for her?"

"I regret that I do not have that right yet. . . ."

"Oh, oh!" I thought, "I see he already has hopes."

"Well, so much the worse for you," Grushnitski continued, "it would be difficult for you to make their acquaintance now; and that's a pity! It is one of the most pleasant houses that I know of."

I smiled inwardly.

"The most pleasant house for me is now my own," I said yawning, and got up to go.

"But first confess, you repent?"

"What nonsense! If I choose, I shall be at the old princess's house tomorrow evening. . . ."

"We shall see. . . ."

"And even, to oblige you, I shall flirt with the young princess. . . ."

"Yes, if she is willing to speak to you. . . ."

"I shall only wait for the moment when your conversation begins to bore her . . . Good-by."

"And I shall go roaming; I could never fall asleep now . . . Look, let's better go to the restaurant, there is gambling there . . . tonight I require strong sensations. . . ."

"I wish you bad luck."

I went home.

May 21st

Almost a week has passed, and I still have not made the acquaintance of the Ligovskoys. I am waiting for a convenient occasion. Grushnitski, like a shadow, follows the young princess everywhere; their conversations are endless: when will he begin to bore her at last? Her mother does not pay any attention to this because he is not an "eligible" young man. That's the logic of mothers for you! I have observed two or three tender glances—an end must be put to it.

Yesterday, Vera appeared for the first time at the well. Since our meeting in the grotto, she has not been out of the house. We dipped our glasses simultaneously and, bending, she said to me in a whisper:

"You don't want to get acquainted with the Ligovskoys? It's the only place where we could see each other."

A reproach! How dull! But I have deserved it. . . .

Apropos, tomorrow there is a subscription dance[38] in the ball-room of the restaurant, and I am going to dance the mazurka with the young princess.

May 22nd

The restaurant's ballroom was transformed into that of the Club of the Nobility. By nine o'clock, everybody had arrived. The old princess and her daughter were among the last to appear: many ladies looked at her with envy and ill will because Princess Mary dresses with taste. Those ladies who regard themselves as the aristo-crats of the place concealed their envy and attached themselves to her. What can you do? Where there is feminine society, there will appear at once a higher and a lower circle. Outside the window, in a crowd of people, stood Grushnitski, pressing his face to the window-pane and never taking his eyes off his goddess: as she passed by, she gave him a hardly perceptible nod. He beamed like the sun. The dancing began with a polonaise;[39] then the band began a waltz. Spurs tinkled, coat tails flew up and whirled.

I stood behind a stout lady: her head was crowned with pink plumes; the luxuriance of her dress recalled the times of farth-ingales,[40] and the variegation of her rough skin, the happy era of black taffeta patches.[41] The largest wart on her neck was con-cealed by the clasp of a necklace. She was saying to her dancing partner, a captain of dragoons:

"That young Princess Ligovskoy is an intolerable little thing! Fancy, she bumped into me and never apologized, but in addition turned around and looked at me through her lorgnette . . . *C'est impayable!*[42] . . . And what is she so proud of? She ought to be taught a lesson. . . ."

"No trouble in getting that done," answered the obliging captain, and went into the next room.

I immediately went up to the young princess and engaged her for the waltz, taking advantage of the easy local customs which allow one to dance with ladies to whom one has not been introduced.

She could hardly force herself not to smile and not to hide her triumph: she managed, however, rather soon to assume a com-pletely indifferent and even severe air. She nonchalantly dropped her hand on my shoulder, slightly inclined her pretty head to one side—and off we went. I do not know a waist more voluptuous and supple! Her fresh breath touched my face; sometimes a curl that

38. A dance in which dancers sign up individually for each dance with a pro-spective partner. *Mazurka*: fashionable, lively Polish dance in triple time, resem-bling the polka.

39. A march-like dance consisting chiefly in a promenade of couples.

40. Broad hoopskirts.

41. Small cut-out pieces of silk, worn on the skin as beauty spots and to cover blemishes.

42. "It's unbelievable!"

had become separated in the whirl of the waltz from its fellows, would brush my burning cheek. I made three turns (she waltzes amazingly well). She was out of breath, her eyes were dim, her half-opened lips could hardly murmur the obligatory "Merci, monsieur."

After several moments of silence, I said to her, assuming a most submissive air:

"I hear, princess, that despite my being completely unknown to you, I have already had the misfortune to earn your displeasure . . . that you've found me insolent . . . Can this be true?"

"And now you would like to confirm me in this opinion?" she replied with an ironic little grimace, which incidentally was very becoming to her mobile features.

"If I had the insolence to offend you in any way, then allow me to have the still greater insolence to beg your pardon. And truly, I would wish very much to prove to you that you are mistaken about me."

"You will find this rather difficult."

"Why so?"

"Because you do not come to our house, and these balls will probably not take place very often."

"This means," I thought, "that their door is closed to me forever."

"Do you know, princess," I said with some vexation, "one should never turn down a repentant criminal: out of sheer despair he may become twice as criminal as before, and then. . . ."

Laughter and whispering among the people around us made me turn and interrupt my sentence. A few steps away from me stood a group of men, and among them was the Captain of Dragoons who had declared hostile intentions against the charming young princess. He was particularly satisfied with something; he rubbed his hands, he laughed and exchanged winks with his companions. Suddenly out of their midst emerged a person in a dresscoat, with a long mustache and a florid face and directed his unsteady steps straight toward the young princess: he was drunk. Having come to a stop in front of the disconcerted princess, and clasping his hands behind his back, he fixed her with his bleary, gray eyes and uttered in a hoarse, treble voice:

"Permetay[43] . . . oh, what's the use of that! . . . I simply engage you for the mazurka. . . ."

"What do you want?" she uttered in a trembling voice, as she cast around her an imploring glance. Alas! her mother was far away, and in her vicinity she could see none of the gentlemen she knew.

---

43. *Permettez,* French for "Permit me": he begins by garbling the polite form of address.

One adjutant, I think, witnessed it all, but hid behind the crowd so as not to be involved in a row.

"Well?" said the drunk, winking at the Captain of Dragoons, who was encouraging him with signs, "don't you want to? Here I am again requesting the honor of engaging you *pour mazurque*[44] ... You think, perhaps, that I am drunk? That does not matter! One is much freer that way, I can assure you."

I saw that she was about to swoon from fear and indignation.

I went up to the drunk, took him rather firmly by the arm and looking steadily into his eyes, asked him to go away, because, I added, the princess had long ago promised to dance the mazurka with me.

"Well, nothing to be done! ... Some other time!" he said with a laugh, and went off to join his abashed companions, who immediately led him away into the other room.

I was rewarded by a deep, wonderful glance.

The princess went up to her mother and told her everything: the latter sought me out in the crowd and thanked me. She informed me that she used to know my mother and was on friendly terms with half a dozen of my aunts.

"I do not know how it happened that we have not met before now," she added, "but you must admit that you alone are to blame for this; you shun everybody: I have never seen anything like it. I hope that the atmosphere of my drawing room will dissipate your spleen[45] ... Am I right?"

I said to her one of those phrases which everyone should have in store for such occasions.

The quadrilles[46] dragged on for a terribly long time.

At last, the mazurka resounded from the upper balcony. The young princess and I seated ourselves.

Never once did I allude either to the tipsy man, or to my former behavior, or to Grushnitski. The impression that the unpleasant scene had made upon her gradually dissipated. Her pretty face bloomed, she joked very charmingly, her conversation was witty, without any pretention to wit, it was lively and free; her observations were sometimes profound. I gave her to understand, by means of a very involved sentence, that I had long been attracted to her. She inclined her young head and colored slightly.

"You're a bizarre person!" she presently said, raising upon me her velvety eyes and laughing in a constrained way.

"I did not wish to make your acquaintance," I continued, "because you were surrounded by too dense a crowd of admirers, and I was afraid of getting completely lost in it."

---

44. For the mazurka.
45. Melancholy boredom.

46. A square dance of French origin, danced by four couples.

"Your fears were unfounded: all of them are most dull. . . ."

"All! Are you sure you mean all?"

She looked at me intently, as if trying to recall something, then she slightly blushed again, and finally uttered resolutely: "*all!*"

"Including even my friend Grushnitski?"

"Why, is he your friend?" she said, revealing some doubt.

"Yes."

"He does not enter, of course, into the category of dull people."

"Rather the category of unfortunate ones," I said laughing.

"Of course! You find it funny? I wish you were in his place."

"Well, I used to be a cadet myself and indeed it was the very best time of my life!"

"But is he a cadet? . . ." she said quickly, and then added: "I thought that. . . ."

"What is it you thought?"

"Nothing! . . . Who is that lady?"

Here the conversation took another direction, and did not return to that subject anymore.

The mazurka came to an end, and we parted—until our next meeting. The ladies left. I went to have supper and ran into Werner.

"Aha!" he said, "so that's the way you are! Didn't you intend not to make the princess's acquaintance in any other way than by saving her from certain death?"

"I did better," I answered him, "I saved her from fainting at a ball. . . ."

"How's that? Tell me. . . ."

"No, try and guess—you, who can guess all things in the world!"

May 23rd

Around seven tonight, I was out strolling on the boulevard. Grushnitski, on seeing me in the distance, came up to me: a kind of absurd exaltation shone in his eyes. He gripped my hand and said in a tragic voice:

"I thank you, Pechorin . . . You understand me?"

"No; but whatever it is, it is not worth gratitude," I answered, having indeed no charitable action on my conscience.

"But what about last night? You can't have forgotten? . . . Mary told me everything. . . ."

"Do you two have everything in common now? Even gratitude?"

"Look," said Grushnitski very importantly, "please do not make fun of my love, if you wish to remain my pal . . . You see, I love her to distraction. And I think, I hope, that she loves me too . . . I have a favor to ask of you. You are going to visit them tonight: promise me to observe everything. I know you are experienced in these matters, you know women better than I do . . . Women! Women! Who will understand them? Their smiles contradict their glances, their words promise and lure, while the sound of their voices drives us away. One minute they comprehend and divine our most secret thought, and the next, they do not understand the clearest hints. Take the young princess, for instance, yesterday her eyes blazed with passion when they rested upon me, today they are dull and cold. . . ."

"This, perhaps, is due to the effect of the waters," I answered.

"You see in everything the nasty side . . . you materialist," he added contemptuously. "Let us switch, however, to another matter." And pleased with this poor pun, he cheered up.

Around half past eight, we went together to the princess's house. Walking past Vera's windows, I saw her at the window. We threw each other a fleeting glance. She entered the Ligovskoys' drawing room soon after us. The old princess introduced me to her as to a relation of hers. Tea was being served; there were many visitors; the conversation was general. I endeavored to ingratiate myself with the old princess; I jested, I made her laugh heartily several times: the young princess also wanted to laugh more than once, but she restrained herself so as not to depart from the role she had assumed. She finds that a languorous air suits her, and perhaps she does not err. Grushnitski was apparently very glad that my gaiety did not infect her.

After tea, we all went into the music room.

"Are you pleased with my obedience, Vera?" I said as I passed her.

She threw me a glance full of love and gratitude. I am now used to those glances, but there was a time when they made my bliss. The old princess had her daughter sit down at the piano: everyone was asking her to sing something. I kept silent and, taking advantage of the hubbub, I drew away toward a window with Vera, who wanted to tell me something very important for both of us. It turned out to be nonsense.

Meanwhile, my indifference was annoying to the young princess, as I could conjecture by a single angry, blazing glance . . . Oh, I understand wonderfully that kind of conversation, mute but expressive, brief but forcible! . . .

She started to sing: her voice is not bad, but she sings poorly. I did not listen, however. In compensation, Grushnitski, with his elbows on the piano, facing her, devoured her with his eyes and every minute kept saying under his breath: *"Charmant! Délicieux!"*[47]

"Listen," Vera was saying to me, "I do not want you to meet my husband, but you must, without fail, please the old princess. It is

---

47. "Charming! Delicious!"

easy for you; you can achieve anything you want. We shall see each other only here. . . ."

"Only here? . . ."

She colored and went on: "You know that I am your slave; I never was able to resist you . . . and for this I shall be punished. You will cease to love me. I wish, at least, to save my reputation . . . not for my own sake: you know that very well! Oh, I beseech you, do not torment me as before with empty doubts and feigned coldness. I shall die soon, perhaps. I feel myself getting weaker every day . . . and, in spite of that, I cannot think of a future life, I think only of you . . . You men do not understand the delights of a glance, of a handshake . . . while I, I swear to you, I, when listening to your voice, I experience such deep, strange bliss that the most ardent kisses could not replace it."

Meanwhile Princess Mary had stopped singing. A murmur of praise sounded around her. I went up to her after all the other guests and said something to her about her voice, rather casually.

She made a grimace, protruding her lower lip and curtsied in a very mocking manner.

"It is all the more flattering to me," she said, "since you did not listen to me at all; but then, perhaps, you do not like music?"

"On the contrary . . . particularly after dinner."

"Grushnitski is right in saying that you have most prosaic tastes . . . And I see that you like music in a gastronomic way."

"You are wrong again. I am far from being a gourmet: my digestion is exceedingly bad. But music after dinner puts one to sleep, and sleep after dinner is good for one's health. Consequently, I like music from a medical point of view. In the evening, on the contrary, it irritates my nerves too much; my mood becomes either too melancholy, or too gay. Both are exhausting, when there is no positive cause to be sad or to be joyful, and, moreover, melancholy at a social gathering is absurd, while immoderate gaiety is improper. . . ."

She did not hear me out, moved away, sat down next to Grushnitski, and there started between them some kind of sentimental conversation. The young princess, it seemed, replied rather absently and irrelevantly to his wise pronouncements, though she tried to show that she listened to him with attention, for now and then he would glance at her with surprise, trying to guess the reason for the inward agitation that expressed itself now and then in her restless glance.

But I have found you out, my dear princess. Beware! You want to repay me in my own coin, to prick my vanity—you will not succeed. And if you declare war on me, I shall be merciless.

In the course of the evening, I tried several times, on purpose, to join their conversation, but she countered my remarks rather drily, and, with feigned annoyance, I finally moved away. The young princess triumphed; Grushnitski, likewise. Have your triumph, my friends, hurry—you won't triumph long! What is to be done? I have a presentiment . . . Whenever I become acquainted with a woman, I always guess without fail, whether she will fall in love with me or not.

I spent the rest of the evening at Vera's side and talked of old times to my heart's content. What does she love me for so much— I really don't know; particularly since she is the only woman who has completely understood me with all my petty weaknesses and wicked passions. Can evil possibly be so attractive?

Grushnitski and I left together: when we got outside, he put his arm through mine and said after a long silence:

"Well, what do you think?"

"That you are a fool," I wanted to answer, but restrained myself, and merely shrugged my shoulders.

May 29th

During all these days, I never once departed from my system. The young princess begins to like my conversation. I told her some of the strange occurrences in my life, and she begins to see in me an extraordinary person. I laugh at everything in the world, especially at feelings: this is beginning to frighten her. In my presence she does not dare to launch upon sentimental debates with Grushnitski, and has several times already replied to his sallies with a mocking smile; but every time that Grushnitski comes up to her, I assume a humble air and leave them alone together. The first time she was glad of it or tried to make it seem so; the second time she became cross with me; the third time she became cross with Grushnitski.

"You have very little vanity!" she said to me yesterday. "Why do you think that I have more fun with Grushnitski?"

I answered that I was sacrificing to a pal's happiness, my own pleasure.

"And mine," she added.

I looked at her intently and assumed a serious air. After this, I did not say another word to her all day. In the evening, she was pensive, this morning, at the well, she was more pensive still. When I went up to her, she was absently listening to Grushnitski, who, it seems, was being rhapsodical about nature; but as soon as she saw me, she began to laugh (very much *mal à propos*),[48] pretending not to notice me. I walked off some distance and stealthily watched her: she turned away from her interlocutor and yawned twice. Decidedly, Grushnitski has begun to bore her. I shall not speak to her for two more days.

48. Inappropriately.

June 3rd

I often wonder, why I do so stubbornly try to gain the love of a little maiden whom I do not wish to seduce, and whom I shall never marry? Why this feminine coquetry? Vera loves me more than Princess Mary will ever love anyone: if she had seemed to me to be an unconquerable belle, then perhaps I might have been fascinated by the difficulty of the enterprise.

But it is nothing of the sort! Consequently, this is not that restless need for love that torments us in the first years of youth, and drives us from one woman to another, until we find one who cannot abide us: and here begins our constancy—that true, infinite passion, which can be mathematically expressed by means of a line falling from a given point into space: the secret of that infinity lies solely in the impossibility of reaching a goal, that is to say, reaching the end.

Why then do I take all this trouble? Because I envy Grushnitski? Poor thing! He has not earned it at all. Or is it the outcome of that nasty but unconquerable feeling which urges us to destroy the sweet delusions of a fellow man, in order to have the petty satisfaction of saying to him, when he asks in despair, what is it he should believe:

"My friend, the same thing happened to me, and still, you see, I dine, I sup, I sleep in perfect peace, and hope to be able to die without cries and tears."

And then again . . . there is boundless delight in the possession of a young, barely unfolded soul! It is like a flower whose best fragrance emanates to meet the first ray of the sun. It should be plucked that very minute and after inhaling one's fill of it, one should throw it away on the road: perchance, someone will pick it up! I feel in myself this insatiable avidity, which engulfs everything met on the way. I look upon the sufferings and joys of others only in relation to myself as on the food sustaining the strength of my soul. I am no longer capable myself of frenzy under the influence of passion: ambition with me has been suppressed by circumstances, but it has manifested itself in another form, since ambition is nothing else than thirst for power, and my main pleasure—which is to subjugate to my will all that surrounds me, and to excite the emotions of love, devotion, and fear in relation to me—is it not the main sign and greatest triumph of power? To be to somebody the cause of sufferings and joys, without having any positive right to it—is this not the sweetest possible nourishment for our pride? And what is happiness? Sated pride. If I considered myself to be better and more powerful than anyone in the world, I would be happy; if everybody loved me, I would find in myself infinite sources of love. Evil begets evil: the first ache gives us an idea of the pleasure of tormenting another. The idea of evil cannot enter a person's head without his wanting to apply it to reality: ideas are organic creations. Someone has said that their very birth endows them with a form, and this form is action; he in whose head more ideas have been born is more active than others. This is why a genius chained to an office desk must die or go mad, exactly as a powerfully built man, whose life is sedentary and whose behavior is virtuous, dies of apoplexy.

The passions are nothing else but ideas in their first phase of development; they are an attribute of the youth of the heart; and he is a fool who thinks he will be agitated by them all his life. Many a calm river begins as a turbulent waterfall, yet none hurtles and foams all the way to the sea. But that calm is often the sign of great, though concealed, strength; the plenitude and depth of feelings and thoughts does not tolerate frantic surgings; the soul, while experiencing pain or pleasure, gives itself a strict account of everything and becomes convinced that so it must be; it knows that without storms, a constantly torrid sun will wither it; it becomes penetrated with its own life, it fondles and punishes itself, as if it were a beloved child. Only in this supreme state of self-knowledge can a man evaluate divine justice.

On re-reading this page, I notice that I have strayed far from my subject . . . But what does it matter? . . . I write this journal for myself and, consequently, anything that I may toss into it will become, in time, for me, a precious memory.

. . .

Grushnitski came and threw himself on my neck: he had been promoted to an officer's rank. We had some champagne. Dr. Werner dropped in soon after him.

"I do not congratulate you," he said to Grushnitski.

"Why?"

"Because a soldier's coat is very becoming to you, and you must admit that an infantry army officer's uniform, made in this watering place, will not give you any glamor. You see, up to now you were an exception, while now you will come under the general rule."

"Talk on, talk on, doctor! You will not prevent me from being delighted. He does not know," added Grushnitski, whispering into my ear: "what hopes these epaulets give me . . . Ah . . . epaulets, epaulets! Your little stars are guiding stars. No! I'm entirely happy now."

"Are you coming with us for that walk to The Hollow?" I asked him.

"I? For nothing in the world shall I show myself to the young princess till my uniform is ready."

"Do you wish me to announce the glad news to her?"

"No, please do not tell her . . . I want to surprise her. . . ."

"By the way, tell me, how are you getting on with her?"

He lost countenance and grew pensive: he wanted to boast and lie, but he was ashamed to do so, and yet it would have been mortifying to admit the truth.

"What do you think, does she love you?"

"Love me? Come, Pechorin, what notions you do have! . . . How could this happen so fast? . . . Even if she does love me, a decent woman would not tell. . . ."

"Fine! And probably, according to you, a decent man should also keep silent about his passion?"

"Ah, my good fellow! There is a way of doing things; there is much that is not said, but guessed. . . ."

"That's true . . . However, the love that is read in the eyes does not bind a woman to anything, whereas words . . . Take care, Grushnitski, she is fooling you."

"She? . . ." he answered, raising his eyes to Heaven and smiling complacently: "I pity you, Pechorin!"

He left.

In the evening, a numerous party set out on foot for The Hollow.

In the opinion of local scientists, that "hollow" is nothing else than an extinguished crater: it is situated on a slope of Mount Mashuk, less than a mile from town. To it leads a narrow trail, among bushes and cliffs. As we went up the mountain, I offered the young princess my arm, and she never abandoned it during the entire walk.

Our conversation began with gossip: I passed in review our acquaintances, both present and absent: first, I brought out their comic traits, and then their evil ones. My bile began to stir. I started in jest and finished in frank waspishness. At first it amused her, then frightened her.

"You are a dangerous man!" she said to me. "I would sooner find myself in a wood under a murderer's knife than be the victim of your sharp tongue . . . I ask you seriously, when it occurs to you to talk badly about me, better take a knife and cut my throat: I don't think you will find it very difficult."

"Do I look like a murderer?"

"You are worse. . . ."

I thought a moment, and then said, assuming a deeply touched air:

"Yes, such was my lot since my very childhood! Everybody read in my face the signs of bad inclinations which were not there, but they were supposed to be there—and so they came into existence. I was modest—they accused me of being crafty: I became secretive. I felt deeply good and evil—nobody caressed me, everybody offended me: I became rancorous. I was gloomy—other children were merry and talkative. I felt myself superior to them—but was considered inferior: I became envious. I was ready to love the whole world—none understood me: and I learned to hate. My colorless youth was spent in a struggle with myself and with the world. Fearing mockery, I buried my best feelings at the bottom of my heart: there they died. I spoke the truth—I was not believed: I began to deceive. When I got to know well the fashionable world and the mechanism of society, I became skilled in the science of life, and saw how others were happy without that skill, enjoying, at no cost to themselves, all those advantages which I so indefatigably pursued. And then in my breast despair was born—not that despair which is cured with the pistol's muzzle, but cold, helpless despair, concealed under amiability and a good-natured smile. I became a moral cripple. One half of my soul did not exist; it had withered away, it had evaporated, it had died. I cut it off and threw it away—while the other half stirred and lived, at the service of everybody. And this nobody noticed, because nobody knew that its dead half had ever existed; but now you have aroused its memory in me, and I have read to you its epitaph. To many people, all epitaphs, in general, seem ridiculous, but not so to me; especially when I recall what lies beneath them. However, I do not ask you to share my views; if my outburst seems to you ridiculous, please, laugh: I warn you, that it will not distress me in any way."

At that moment, I met her eyes: tears dance in them; her arm, leaning on mine, trembled, her cheeks glowed; she was sorry for me! Compassion—an emotion to which all women so easily submit— had sunk its claws into her inexperienced heart. During the whole walk she was absent-minded, did not coquet with anyone—and that is a great sign!

We reached The Hollow: the ladies left their escorts, but she did not abandon my arm. The witicisms of the local dandies did not amuse her; the steepness of the precipice near which she stood did not frighten her, while the other young ladies squealed and closed their eyes.

On my way back, I did not renew our melancholy conversation, but to my trivial questions and jokes she replied briefly and absently.

"Have you ever loved?" I asked her at last.

She glanced at me intently, shook her head and again became lost in thought: it was evident that she wanted to say something, but she did not know how to begin. Her breast heaved . . . What would you—a muslin sleeve is little protection, and an electric spark ran from my wrist to hers. Almost all passions start thus; and we often deceive ourselves greatly in thinking that a woman loves us for our physical or moral qualities. Of course, they prepare and incline their hearts for the reception of the sacred fire: nonetheless, it is the first contact that decides the matter.

"Don't you think I was very amiable today?" said the young princess to me, with a forced smile when we returned from the excursion.

We parted.

She is displeased with herself; she accuses herself of having treated me coldly . . . Oh, this is the first, the main triumph!

Tomorrow she will want to recompense me. I know it all by heart —that is what is so boring.

June 4th

Today, I saw Vera. She has exhausted me with her jealousy. The young princess, it seems, took it into her head to confide the secrets of the heart to Vera: not a very fortunate choice, one must admit!

"I can guess to what it all tends," Vera kept saying to me. "Better tell me now, plainly, that you love her."

"But if I don't?"

"Then why pursue her, disturb her, excite her imagination? Oh, I know you well! Listen, if you want me to believe you, then come next week to Kislovodsk:[49] we are going there after tomorrow. The Ligovskoys remain here for a little while longer. Rent an apartment near by. We shall be living in the big house near the spring, on the mezzanine floor, Princess Ligovskoy will be on the first floor, and next door, there is a house belonging to the same proprietor, which is not yet occupied . . . Will you come?"

I promised, and on the same day sent a messenger to rent those lodgings.

Grushnitski came to see me at six in the evening, and announced that his uniform would be ready on the morrow, just in time for the ball.

"At last I shall dance with her the whole evening . . . What a chance to talk!" he added.

"When is that ball?"

"Why, tomorrow! Didn't you know? A big festival. And the local authorities have undertaken to arrange it. . . ."

"Let's go for a walk on the boulevard."

"Not for anything, in this horrid coat. . . ."

"What, have you ceased liking it?"

I went alone and upon meeting Princess Mary, asked her to dance the mazurka with me. She seemed surprised and pleased.

"I thought you danced only out of necessity, as last time," she said, smiling very prettily.

It seems she does not notice at all Grushnitski's absence.

"Tomorrow you will be agreeably surprised," I said to her.

"What will that be?"

"It's a secret . . . You will discover it for yourself at the ball."

I finished the evening at the old princess's: there were no visitors except Vera and a very entertaining old gentleman. I was in high spirits, I improvised all kinds of extraordinary stories: the young princess sat opposite me and listened to my tosh with such deep, tense, even tender attention that I felt ashamed of myself. What

49. Another spa, forty miles west of Pyatigorsk.

had become of her vivacity, her coquetry, her whims, her arrogant mien, scornful smile, abstracted gaze?

Vera noticed it all: deep melancholy expressed itself on her sickly face: she sat in shadow, near the window, sunk in an ample arm-chair . . . I felt sorry for her.

Then I related the whole dramatic story of our acquaintanceship, of our love—naturally, concealing it under invented names.

So vividly did I picture my tenderness, my anxiety, my transports, in such an advantageous light did I present her actions, her charac-ter, that, willy-nilly, she had to forgive me my flirtation with the princess.

She got up, came over to us, became animated . . . and only at two in the morning did we remember that the doctor's order was to go to bed at eleven.

June 5th

Half an hour before the ball, Grushnitski appeared before me in the full splendor of an infantry army officer's uniform. To the third button, he had attached a bronze chainlet from which hung a double lorgnette; epaulets of incredible size were turned upward like the wings of a cupid; his boots squeaked; in his left hand, he held a pair of brown kid gloves and his cap, and with his right he kept fluffing up, every moment, his shock of hair, which was waved in small curls. Self-satisfaction and, at the same time, a certain lack of assurance were expressed in his countenance: his festive exterior, his proud gait, would have made me burst out laughing, had that been in accordance with my plans.

He threw his cap and gloves onto the table and began to pull down the skirts of his coat and to preen himself before the mirror: a huge black neckcloth that was wound over a tremendously high stiffener, the bristles of which propped up his chin, showed half an inch above his collar. He thought this was not enough; he pulled it up, till it reached his ears. This laborious task—for the collar of his uniform was very tight and uncomfortable—caused the blood to rush to his face.

"I'm told you have been flirting terribly with my princess these days?" he said rather casually, and without looking at me.

"It's not for us, oafs, to drink tea!" I answered him, repeating the favorite saying of one of the most dashing rakes of the past, of whom Pushkin once sang.[50]

"Tell me, how does the coat fit me? Oh, that confounded Jew! . . .[51] How it cuts me under the arms! . . . Have you got any per-fume?"

---

50. Strong liquor, not tea, is the drink of dashing hussars (Russian military of-ficers) like Pavel Kaverin, friend of the poet Alexander Pushkin. See *Eugene Onegin*, chapter 1, line 174 and note.

51. Tailor, a profession followed by many Jews in Russia where the careers open to them were limited.

"Good gracious, do you need any more? You simply reek of rose pomade, as it is."

"No matter. Give it here."

He poured out half of the vial between neck and neckcloth, onto his pocket handkerchief, and upon his sleeves.

"Are you going to dance?" he asked.

"I don't think so."

"I'm afraid that I shall have to begin the mazurka with the princess, and I hardly know one figure of it."

"Have you asked her for the mazurka?"

"Not yet. . . ."

"Look out, you might be forestalled. . . ."

"That's right!" he said, clapping a hand to his forehead. "Goodby . . . I'm going to wait for her at the entrance door." He seized his cap and ran off.

Half an hour later, I also set out. The streets were dark and deserted; around the club, or tavern—whichever you choose to call it—the crowd was dense; the windows shone; the sounds of the military band were brought to me by the evening breeze. I walked slowly; I felt sad . . . "Is it possible," I thought, "that my only function on earth is to ruin other people's hopes? Ever since I have lived and acted, fate has always seemed to bring me in at the denouement of other people's dramas, as if none could either die or despair without me! I am the indispensable persona in the fifth act; involuntarily, I play the miserable part of the executioner or the traitor. What could be fate's purpose in this? Might it not be that it had designated me to become the author of bourgeois tragedies and family novels, or the collaborator of some purveyor of stories for the "Library for Reading"?[52] How should one know? How many people, in the beginning of life, think they will finish it as Alexander the Great or Lord Byron,[53] and instead, retain for the whole of their existence, the rank of titulary counsellor?[54]

Upon coming into the ballroom, I hid in the crowd of men and began to make my observations. Grushnitski stood next to the young princess and was saying something to her with great animation: she listened to him absent-mindedly, kept glancing this way and that, putting her fan to her lips. Her face expressed impatience, her eyes sought around for someone: I softly approached from behind, in order to overhear their conversation.

"You torment me, princess," Grushnitski was saying. "You have

52. A magazine (1834–48) that published translations of foreign fiction as well as local work, and in which Lermontov himself published "Ashik-Kerib: a Turkish tale."

53. Alexander the Great (356–323 B.C.) was king of Macedon and conqueror of most of Asia; Lord Byron added to his renown by joining the Greek struggle for independence from Turkey, and dying at Missolonghi in northern Greece.

54. The Russian civil service contained 14 levels, ranging down from the first (Chancellor); a titulary counsellor ranked ninth.

changed tremendously since I last saw you. . . ."

"You too have changed," she answered, casting upon him a swift glance, in which he failed to discern secret mockery.

"I? I have changed? . . . Oh, never! You know that it is impossible! He who has once seen you, will carry with him, forever, your divine image."

"Stop, please. . . ."

"Why then will you not listen now to what only recently, and so often, you listened with favor?"

"Because I do not like repetition," she answered laughing.

"Oh, I've made a bitter mistake! . . . I thought, in my folly, that at least these epaulets would give me the right to hope . . . No, it would have been better for me had I remained all my life in that miserable soldier's coat to which, maybe, I owed your attention."

"Indeed, that coat suited you much better. . . ."

At this point I came up and bowed to the young princess: she blushed slightly and said quickly:

"An I not right, Monsieur Pechorin, that the gray soldier's coat was much more becoming to Monsieur Grushnitski?"

"I disagree with you," I replied. "In this uniform, he looks even more youthful."

Grushnitski could not bear this blow: like all youths, he professes to be an old man; he thinks that deep traces of passions replace the imprint of years. He cast on me a furious glance, stamped his foot and walked away.

"Now confess," I said to the young princess, "that despite his having always been very absurd, still, quite recently, you thought him interesting . . . in his gray coat?"

She dropped her eyes and did not answer.

All evening Grushnitski pursued the young princess, either dancing with her or being her *vis-à-vis*;[55] he devoured her with his eyes, sighed and pestered her with entreaties and reproaches. After the third quadrille, she already detested him.

"I did not expect this of you," he said, coming up to me and taking me by the arm.

"What, exactly?"

"You are dancing the mazurka with her, aren't you?" he asked in a solemn voice. "She confessed to me. . . ."

"Well, what of it? Is it a secret?"

"Naturally . . . I should have expected this from a frivolous girl, from a flirt . . . But I'll have my revenge!"

"Blame your soldier's coat or your officer's epaulets, but why blame her? Is it her fault that you no longer appeal to her?"

"Why then give me hopes?"

"Why then did you hope? I can understand people who desire

55. Opposite in the dance.

something and strive for it; but who wants to hope?"

"You have won your bet, though not quite," he said with a wrathful smile.

The mazurka began. Grushnitski kept choosing nobody but the princess, the other men chose her continuously: it was obviously a conspiracy against me. So much the better. She wants to talk to me, they prevent her—she will want it twice as much.

Once or twice, I pressed her hand: the second time, she snatched it away, without saying a word.

"I shall sleep badly tonight," she said to me, when the mazurka was over.

"It's Grushnitski's fault."

"Oh no!" And her face became so pensive, so sad, that I promised myself to kiss her hand, without fail, that evening.

People began to leave. As I handed the princess into her carriage, I rapidly pressed her small hand to my lips. It was dark, and no one could see it.

I re-entered the ballroom, well-content with myself.

At a long table, young men were having supper, and among them was Grushnitski. When I came in, they all fell silent: evidently, they had been talking about me. Many are ill-disposed toward me since the last ball, especially the Captain of Dragoons, and now, it seems, an inimical gang is actually being organized against me, under the leadership of Grushnitski. He had such a proud and courageous air.

I am very glad; I love my enemies, although not in a Christian sense: they amuse me, they quicken my pulses. To be always on the lookout, to intercept every glance, to catch the meaning of every word, to guess intentions, to thwart plots, to pretend to be fooled, and suddenly, with one push, to upset the entire enormous and elaborate structure of cunning and scheming—that is what I call life.

During the supper Grushnitski kept whispering and exchanging winks with the Captain of Dragoons.

June 6th

This morning, Vera left for Kislovodsk with her husband. I met their coach as I was on my way to Princess Ligovskoy. Vera nodded to me: there was reproach in her glance.

Whose fault is it? Why does she not want to give me the chance to see her alone? Love, like fire, goes out without fuel. Perchance jealousy will accomplish what my entreaties could not.

I stayed at the princess's an hour by the clock. Mary did not appear; she was ill. In the evening she was not on the boulevard. The newly organized gang, armed with lorgnettes, has assumed a truly threatening appearance. I am glad that the pirincess is ill: they might have done something insolent in regard to her. Grushnitski's hair was all awry and he looked desperate: I think he is really distressed. His vanity, in particular, is injured; but, oddly enough, there are people who are ludicrous even in their despair!

On coming home, I noticed a lack of something. *I have not seen her! She is ill!* Can it be that I have really fallen in love? . . . What nonsense!

June 7th

At eleven in the morning—the hour at which the old Princess Ligovskoy is usually sweating it out in the Ermolov bathhouse—I was walking past her house. The young princess was sitting pensively at the window. When she saw me, she rose abruptly.

I entered the vestibule, none of the servants were there, and without being announced, taking advantage of the local customs, I made my way into the drawing room.

A dull pallor was spread over the princess's pretty face. She stood at the piano, leaning with one hand on the back of an armchair: that hand trembled ever so slightly. I quietly went up to her and said:

"You are angry with me?"

She raised upon me a languid, deep gaze and shook her head; her lips wanted to utter something, and could not; her eyes filled with tears; she sank into the armchair and covered her face with her hand.

"What is the matter with you?" I said, taking her hand.

"You do not respect me! . . . Oh, leave me alone!"

I made a few steps . . . She straightened herself up in her chair; her eyes glittered.

I stopped, with my hand on the door handle, and said:

"Forgive me, princess, I have acted like a madman . . . This will not happen again: I will see to it . . . Why must you know what, up to now, has been taking place in my soul? You will never learn it, and so much the better for you. Adieu."

As I went out, I believe I heard her crying. You have one?

Till evening, I roamed on foot about the outskirts of Mount Mashuk, got terribly tired and, on coming home, threw myself on my bed in utter exhaustion.

Werner dropped in.

"Is it true," he asked, "that you are going to marry the young Princess Ligovskoy?"

"Why?"

"The whole town says so; all my patients are preoccupied with this important news: that's the kind of people patients are; they know everything!"

"Grushnitski's tricks," I thought to myself.

"In order to prove to you, doctor, that these rumors are false, let me inform you in secret that tomorrow I am moving to Kislovodsk."

"And the Ligovskoys, too?"

"No; they remain here for another week."

"So you are not marrying her?"

"Doctor, doctor! Look at me: do I resemble a fiancé, or anything of the kind?"

"I do not say it . . . But you know there are cases," he added with a cunning smile, "in which an honorable man is obliged to marry, and there are mammas who do not at least avert such cases. Therefore, I advise you as a pal to be more careful. Here at the spa the atmosphere is most dangerous: I have seen so many fine, young men, worthy of a better lot, who have gone straight from here to the altar. Would you believe it, there has even been an attempt to have me marry! Namely, on the part of a provincial mamma whose daughter was very pale. I had had the misfortune to tell her that her daughter's face would regain its color after marriage. Then, with tears of gratitude, she offered me her daughter's hand and their entire fortune—fifty serfs, I believe.[56] But I answered that I was incapable of marriage."

Werner left, fully convinced that he had put me on my guard.

From his words, I note that various nasty rumors have already been spread in town about the young princess and me. Grushnitski will have to pay for this!

June 10th

I have been here, in Kislovodsk, three days already. Every day I see Vera at the well and at the promenade. In the morning, upon awakening, I sit down by the window and train my lorgnette on her balcony: she is already long since dressed and awaits the prearranged signal: we meet, as if by chance, in the garden, which descends from our houses to the well. The vivifying mountain air has brought back her color and strength. It is not for nothing that Narzan[57] is termed "The Fountain of Mightiness." The local inhabitants maintain that the air of Kislovodsk disposes one romantically, that here comes the denouement of all the love affairs that ever were started at the foot of Mount Mashuk. And, indeed, everything here breathes seclusion; everything here is mysterious— the dense canopies of linden avenues that bend over the torrent which, as it noisily and foamily falls from ledge to ledge, cuts for itself a path between the verdant mountains; and the gorges filled with gloom and silence that branch out from here in all directions; and the freshness of the aromatic air, laden with the emanations of

56. Serfs were peasants bound to the land. A land-owner possessing 50 serfs was not very rich.
57. The local mineral water.

tall southern grasses and white acacias; and the constant deliciously somniferous babble of cool brooks which, meeting at the far end of the valley, join in a friendly race and, at last, fall into the Podkumok River. On this side the gorge widens and turns into a green glen; a dusty road meanders through it. Every time I look at it, I keep imagining that a close carriage comes there, and from the window of the carriage, there peers out a rosy little face. Many coaches have, by now, passed on that road, but never that one. The suburb beyond the fort has grown populous: in the restaurant, built on a bluff a few steps from my dwelling, lights begin to flicker in the evenings through a double row of poplars; noise and the clinking of glasses resound there till late at night.

Nowhere is there consumed so much Kahetian wine and mineral water as here.

> To mix these two pursuits, a lot of men
> Are eager—I'm not one of them.[58]

Grushnitski with his gang, every day, carouses at the tavern, and hardly nods to me.

He arrived only yesterday, and has already managed to quarrel with three old men who wanted to take their baths before him: definitely—misfortunes develop in him a martial spirit.

June 11th

They have come at last. I was sitting by the window when I heard the rattle of their coach: my heart quivered . . . What is it then? Could it be that I am in love? . . . I am so stupidly made that this could be expected from me.

I have dined at their house. The old princess looks at me very tenderly and does not leave her daughter's side . . . That's bad! On the other hand, Vera is jealous of the young princess—this is a nice state of things I have brought about! What will not a woman do in order to vex a rival? I remember one woman who fell in love with me, because I was in love with another. There is nothing more paradoxical than a woman's mind: it is difficult to convince women of anything; you have to bring them to a point where they will convince their own selves. The sequence of proofs by means of which they overcome their prejudices, is very original: to learn their dialectic, one must overturn in one's mind all the school rules of logic. Here, for instance, is the normal method:

That man loves me; but I am married: consequently, I must not love him.

Now for the feminine method:

---

58. Quoted from Griboedov's comedy, *Woe from Wit* (1833), where it refers to work and play.

I must not love him for I am married; but he loves me—conse-quently. . . .

Here come several dots, for reason does not say anything more, and what speaks mainly, is the tongue, the eyes, and in their wake, the heart, if the latter exists.

What if these notes should ever fall under a women's eyes? "Slander!" she will cry with indignation.

Ever since poets have been writing and women reading them (for which they should receive the deepest gratitude), they have been called angels so many times, that in the simplicity of their souls, they have actually believed this compliment, forgetting that the same poets dubbed Nero a demigod, for money.

It is not I who should speak of women with such spite—I, who love nothing in the world save them—I, who have always been ready to sacrifice to them peace of mind, ambition, life. But then, it is not in a fit of annoyance and offended vanity that I try to tear from them that magic veil, through which only an experienced gaze penetrates. No, all that I am saying about them is only a result of

> The mind's cold observations,
> The mournful comments of the heart.[59]

Women ought to desire that all men know them as well as I do, because I love them a hundred times better, ever since I stopped fearing them and comprehended their little weaknesses.

Apropos, the other day Werner compared women to the enchanted forest of which Tasso tells in his "Jerusalem Liberated":[60] "Only come near," said Werner: "and mercy, what horrors will come flying at you from every side: Duty, Pride, Propriety, Public Opinion, Mockery, Scorn . . . All you have to do is not look and walk straight on: little by little, the monsters disappear and before you there opens a serene and sunny meadow, in the midst of which, green myrtle blooms. On the other hand, woe to you if, at the first steps, your heart fails you and you look back!"

June 12th

This evening has been rich in events. Within two miles of Kislovodsk, in a canyon through which flows the Podkumok River, there is a cliff, called The Ring. This is a gateway formed by nature; it rises from a high hill, and through it the setting sun throws its last flaming glance on the world. A large cavalcade set out thither to view the sunset through that window of stone. None of us, to say the truth, was thinking of sunsets. I was riding by the young princess's side: on our way home, the Podkumok River had to be forded. The shallowest mountain streams are dangerous, especially

59. The concluding lines of Pushkin's verse preface to *Eugene Onegin*.

60. Epic poem by the Italian poet Torquato Tasso (1544–1595).

because their bottom is an absolute kaleidoscope: every day it changes from the pressure of the waves. Where yesterday there was a stone, today there is a hole. I took the princess's horse by the bridle and led it down into the water, which was no more than knee-deep: we started to advance slowly in an oblique direction against the current. It is well-known that when fording rapid streams, one should not look at the water, for otherwise one immediately gets dizzy. I forgot to warn Princess Mary of this.

We were already in midstream, where the current was swiftest, when she suddenly swayed in her saddle. "I feel faint!" she said in a weak voice. I quickly bent toward her and wound my arm around her supple waist.

"Look up!" I whispered to her. "It is nothing, only don't be afraid; I'm with you."

She felt better; she wanted to free herself from my arm, but I wound it still tighter around her tender, soft body; my cheek almost touched her cheek; flame emanated from it.

"What are you doing to me? . . . Good God! . . ."

I paid no attention to her tremor and confusion, and my lips touched her tender cheek; she gave a start but said nothing. We were riding behind: nobody saw. When we got out onto the bank, everybody started off at a trot. The young princess held her horse in; I stayed by her. It could be seen that my silence worried her, but I swore not to say a word—out of curiosity. I wanted to see how she would extricate herself from this embarrassing situation.

"Either you despise me, or love me very much!" she said at last, in a voice in which there were tears. "Perhaps you want to laugh at me, to trouble my soul, and then leave me . . . It would be so base, so mean, that the mere supposition . . . Oh no! Isn't it true," she added in a tone of tender trust, "isn't it true that there is nothing in me that would preclude respect? Your insolent action . . . I must, I must forgive it you, because I allowed it . . . Answer, do speak, I want to hear your voice! . . ."

In the last words, there was such feminine impatience that I could not help smiling. Fortunately, it was beginning to get dark . . . I did not answer anything.

"You are silent?" she went on. "Perhaps you wish me to be the first to say that I love you."

I was silent.

"Do you wish it?" she went on, quickly turning toward me. In the determination of her gaze and voice, there was something frightening.

"What for?" I answered shrugging my shoulders.

She gave her horse a cut of the whip and set off at all speed along the narrow dangerous road. It happened so fast, that I hardly managed to overtake her, and when I did, she had already joined the rest of the party. All the way home she talked and laughed incessantly. In her movements there was something feverish; not once did she glance at me. Everybody noticed this unusual gaiety. And the old princess inwardly rejoiced, as she looked at her daughter; yet her daughter was merely having a nervous fit. She will spend a sleepless night and will weep. This thought gives me boundless delight: there are moments when I understand the vampire . . .[61] And to think that I am reputed to be a jolly good fellow and try to earn that appellation!

Having dismounted, the ladies went to the old princess's. I was excited and galloped off into the mountains to dissipate the thoughts that crowded in my head. The dewy evening breathed delicious coolness. The moon was rising from behind the dark summits. Every step of my unshod horse produced a hollow echo in the silence of the gorges. At the cascade, I watered my steed, avidly inhaled, a couple of times, the fresh air of the southern night, and started back. I rode through the suburb. The lights were beginning to go out in the windows; the sentries on the rampart of the fort, and the Cossacks in outlying pickets, exchanged long-drawn calls.

In one of the houses of the suburb, which stood on the edge of a ravine, I noticed an extraordinary illumination: at times there resounded discordant talk and cries, indicating that an officers' banquet was in progress. I dismounted and stole up to the window: an improperly closed shutter allowed me to see the revelers and to make out their words. They were speaking about me.

The Captain of Dragoons, flushed with wine, struck the table with his fist, demanding attention.

"Gentlemen!" he said, "this is really impossible! Pechorin must be taught a lesson! These fledglings from Petersburg always give themselves airs, till you hit them on the nose! He thinks that he alone has lived in the world of fashion, just because he always has clean gloves and well-polished boots."

"And what an arrogant smile! Yet I'm sure he is a coward—yes, a coward!"

"I think so too," said Grushnitski. "He likes to jest his way out. I once said to him such things, for which another would have hacked me to pieces then and there, but Pechorin gave it all a humorous interpretation. I, naturally, did not call him out, because it was up to him. Moreover, I did not want to get entangled. . . ."

"Grushnitski is mad at him because he took away the young princess from him," said someone.

"What a notion! As a matter of fact, I did flirt slightly with her, but gave it up at once, because I do not want to marry, and it is not

61. The vampire feeds upon human suffering. Stories of vampires were popular in Romantic literature; Lermontov may also be referring to a tale, "The Vampyre," then attributed to Byron.

in my rules to compromise a young girl."

"Yes, I assure you that he is a first-rate coward—that is to say, Pechorin, and not Grushnitski. Oh, Grushnitski is a capital fellow, and moreover, he is a true friend of mine!" said the Captain of Dragoons. "Gentlemen! Nobody here stands up for him? Nobody? All the better! Would you like to test his courage? You might find it entertaining."

"We would like to; but how?"

"Well, listen, Grushnitski is particularly angry with him—he gets the main part! He will pick some kind of silly quarrel with him and challenge Pechorin to a duel . . . Now wait a bit, here comes the point . . . He will challenge him to a duel—good! All this—the challenge, the preparations, the conditions—will be as solemn and terrible as possible—I shall see to that. I shall be your second, my poor friend! Good! But now, here is the hitch: we shall not put any balls into the pistols. I here answer for it that Pechorin will funk it —I shall have them face each other at six paces distance, by Jove! Do you agree, gentlemen?"

"A capital plan! We agree! Why not?" sounded from all sides.

"And you, Grushnitski?"

In a tremor of eagerness, I awaited Grushnitski's reply. Cold fury possessed me at the thought that, had it not been for chance, I might have become the laughing stock of those fools. If Grushnitski had refused, I would have thrown myself upon his neck. But after a short silence, he rose from his chair, offered his hand to the captain and said very pompously: "All right, I agree."

It would be difficult to describe the delight of the whole honorable company.

I returned home, agitated by two different emotions. The first was sadness. "What do they all hate me for?" I thought. "What for? Have I offended anybody? No. Could it be that I belong to the number of those people whose appearance alone is sufficient to produce ill will?" And I felt a venomous rancor gradually filling my soul. "Take care, Mr. Grushnitski!" I kept saying, as I paced to and fro in my room, "I am not to be trifled with like this. You may have to pay dearly for the approval of your stupid cronies. I am not a plaything for you!"

I did not sleep all night. By morning, I was as yellow as a wild orange.

In the morning, I met the young princess at the well.

"Are you ill?" she said, looking at me intently.

"I did not sleep all night."

"Nor did I . . . I accused you . . . perhaps, wrongly? But explain your behavior, I may forgive you everything."

"Everything?"

"Everything . . . Only tell me the truth . . . and hurry . . . I have thought a lot, trying to explain, to justify your conduct: perhaps, you are afraid of obstacles on the part of my family . . . It does not matter. When they hear if it . . . (her voice trembled) my entreaties will convince them . . . Or is it your own situation . . . But I want you to know that I can sacrifice anything for the one I love . . . Oh, answer quick . . . have pity . . . You do not despise me, do you?"

She grasped my hand.

The old princess was walking in front of us with Vera's husband, and did not see anything, but we might have been seen by the promenading patients, of all inquisitive people the most inquisitive gossipers, and I quickly freed my hand from her passionate graps.

"I shall tell you the whole truth," I replied to the princess, "I shall neither justify myself, nor explain my actions. I do not love you."

Her lips paled slightly.

"Leave me," she said almost inaudibly.

I shrugged my shoulders, turned, and walked away.

June 14th

I sometimes despise myself . . . Is this not why I despise others? . . . I have become incapable of noble impulses. I am afraid of appearing laughable to myself. Another man in my place would offer the young princess *son coeur et sa fortune*;[62] but over me the word "marry" has some kind of magic power. However much I may love a woman, if she only lets me feel that I must marry her—farewell to love! My heart turns to stone, and nothing can warm it again. I am ready to make any sacrifice except this one. I may set my life upon a card twenty times, and even my honor—but I will not sell my freedom. Why do I treasure it so? What good is it to me? What do I prepare myself for? What do I expect from the future? . . . Indeed, nothing whatever. It is a kind of innate fear, an ineffable presentiment. Aren't there people who have an unaccountable fear of spiders, cockroaches, mice? Shall I confess? When I was still a child, an old woman told my fortune to my mother. She predicted of me "death from a wicked wife." It made a deep impression upon me then: in my soul was born an insuperable aversion to marriage. Yet something tells me that her prediction will come true, at least, I shall do my best to have it come true as late as possible.

June 15th

Yesterday there arrived here the conjurer Apfelbaum. On the door of the restaurant, there appeared a long *affiche*,[63] informing the esteemed public that the above-named, wonderful conjurer,

---

62. His heart and his fortune.   63. Poster.

acrobat, chemist, and optician, would have the honor to give a superb performance at eight tonight, in the reception hall of the Club of the Nobility (in other words, the restaurant); admission two roubles, fifty.

Everybody intends to go to see the wonderful conjurer: even Princess Ligovskoy, despite the fact that her daughter is ill, took a ticket for herself.

Today after dinner, I passed under Vera's windows. She was sitting on the balcony alone. A billet fell at my feet:

"Tonight, around half past nine, come to me by the main staircase. My husband has gone to Pyatigorsk and will return only tomorrow morning. My footmen and maidservants will not be in the house: I have distributed tickets to all of them, as well as to the princess's servants. I await you. Come without fail."

"Aha!" I thought, "at last I am having my way after all."

At eight, I went to see the conjurer. The spectators assembled shortly before nine: the performance began. In the back rows of chairs, I recognized the lackeys and the maids of Vera and the princess. Everybody was here. Grushnitski sat in the front row, with his lorgnette. The conjurer turned to him every time he needed a pocket handkerchief, a watch, a ring, and so forth.

Grushnitski does not greet me since some time ago, and tonight, once or twice, he glanced at me rather insolently. All this shall be remembered when the time comes to settle our accounts.

Shortly before ten, I rose and left.

It was pitch dark outside. Heavy, cold clouds lay on the summits of the surrounding mountains; only now and then a dying breeze soughed in the crests of the poplars around the restaurant. There was a crowd of people outside the windows. I descended the hill and, turning into the gateway, accelerated my pace. Suddenly it seemed to me that someone was walking behind me. I stopped and looked about me. Nothing could be distinguished in the darkness; however, I took the precaution to go around the house as if I were taking a stroll. As I passed under the windows of the young princess, I again heard steps behind me. A man wrapped up in a military cloak ran past me. This alarmed me: however, I stole up to the porch and swiftly ran up the dark stairs. The door opened, a small hand grasped my hand.

"No one saw you?" said Vera in a whisper, pressing herself to me.

"No one."

"Now do you believe that I love you? Oh! For a long time I wavered, for a long time I was tormented . . . But you made of me all you want."

Her heart was beating violently, her hands were as cold as ice. There began the reproaches of jealousy, plaints: she demanded of me that I confess to her all, saying she would bear, with submission, my unfaithfulness, since all she desired was my happiness. I did not quite believe this, but I calmed her with vows, promises, and so forth.

"So you are not going to marry Mary? You don't love her? And she thinks . . . do you know, she is madly in love with you, the poor thing!"

. . . .

. . . .

Around two o'clock in the morning, I opened the window and, having tied two shawls together, let myself down from the upper balcony to the lower one, holding onto a pillar. In the young princess's room, a light was still burning. Something urged me toward that window. The curtain was not completely drawn, and I could cast a curious glance into the interior of the room. Mary was sitting on her bed, her hands folded in her lap; her abundant hair was gathered under a night cap fringed with lace; a large crimson kerchief covered her slender white shoulders; her small feet hid in variegated Persian slippers. She sat motionless, her head sunk onto her breast; before her, on a little table, a book was opened, but her eyes, motionless and full of ineffable sadness, seemed, for a hundredth time, to skim over the same page, while her thoughts were far away

At this moment, somebody stirred behind a bush. I jumped down from the balcony onto the turf. An invisible hand seized me by the shoulder.

"Aha!" said a rough voice, "you're caught! . . . I'll teach you to visit young princesses at night! . . ."

"Hold him tight!" cried somebody else, springing from behind a corner.

They were Grushnitski and the Captain of Dragoons.

I struck the latter upon the head with my fist, knocked him down, and dashed into the shrubbery. All the paths of the garden which covered the sloping round in front of our houses were known to me.

"Thieves! Help!" they cried. A gun shot rang out; a smoking wad fell almost at my feet.

A minute later, I was already in my room; I undressed and lay down. Hardly had my valet locked the door, than Grushnitski and the captain began to knock.

"Pechorin! Are you asleep? Are you there?" the captain cried.

"I am asleep," I answered crossly.

"Get up! . . . Thieves . . . Circassians . . ."

"I have a cold," I answered, "I'm afraid to catch a chill."

They left. I should not have answered them: they would have gone on looking for me in the garden for another hour. In the meantime, the alarm became terrific. A Cossack came, at full speed, from the fort. There was a universal stir: they started to look for Circassians in every bush—and, naturally, found nothing. But many people, probably, remained firmly convinced that, had the garrison revealed more courage and promptness, at least a score of pillagers would have remained lying about.

June 16th

This morning, at the well, there was nothing but talk about the night raid of the Circassians. Having drunk the prescribed number of glasses of the Narzan water, and having walked the length of the long linden avenue ten times or so, I met Vera's husband, who had just arrived from Pyatigorsk. He took my arm, and we went to the restaurant to have lunch. He was terribly anxious about his wife. "How frightened she was last night," he kept saying, "and to think it should have happened precisely during my absence." We sat down to lunch near a door which led to the corner room, where a dozen young people were assembled, including Grushnitski. For a second time, destiny provided me with the chance to overhear a conversation, which was to decide his fate. He could not see me and, consequently, I could not suspect him of a deliberate purpose; but this only increased his guilt in my eyes.

"Could it have really been the Circassians?" someone said. "Did anybody see them?"

"I shall tell you the whole story," answered Grushnitski, "but please do not give me away. This is how it was. Last night, a man, whom I shall not name to you, came to me and told me that shortly before ten he saw someone steal into the house where the Ligovskoys live. I should mention to you that the old princess was here, and the young princess was at home. So he and I betook ourselves under their windows to waylay the lucky fellow."

I must confess that I was alarmed, although my interlocutor was very busy with his luncheon. He might have heard things that would be disagreeable to him, if Grushnitski had inadvertently guessed the truth; but being blinded by jealousy, the latter did not suspect it.

"Well, you see," Grushnitski went on, "we set out, taking a gun with us, loaded with a blank cartridge—just to frighten him. Till two o'clock, we waited in the garden. Finally—God knows where he appeared from, certainly not from the window, because it was never opened, but presumably he came out through the glass door which is behind the pillar—finally, as I say, we saw someone come down from the balcony . . . How do you like the princess's behavior, eh? Well, I must say, those Moscow misses are something! After that, what would you believe? We wanted to seize him, but he freed himself and, like a hare, dashed into the bushes. It was than I took a shot at him."

A murmur of incredulity resounded around Grushnitski.

"You do not believe me?" he continued. "I give you my honest and honorable word that all this is the very truth, and in proof, if you wish it, I shall name the gentleman."

"Tell us, tell us who he is!" resounded from all sides.

"Pechorin," answered Grushnitski.

At this moment, he raised his eyes—I was standing in the door opposite him—he flushed dreadfully. I went up to him and said slowly and distinctly:

"I regret very much that I entered after you had already given your word of honor in support of the vilest slander. My presence would have saved you from extra knavery."

Grushnitski jumped up from his seat and was about to flare up.

"I beg you," I continued, in the same tone of voice, "I beg you to retract your words at once: you know very well that it is an invention. I do not think that a woman's indifference to your brilliant qualities merits so awful a vengeance. Think well. By affirming your opinion, you lose your right to the name of a gentleman, and you risk your life."

Grushnitski stood before me, with lowered eyes, in violent agitation. But the struggle between conscience and vanity did not last long. The Captain of Dragoons, who was sitting next to him, nudged him with his elbow: he started and quickly replied to me, without raising his eyes:

"Sir, when I say something, I mean it, and am ready to repeat it. I am not afraid of your threats, and am prepared for anything."

"This last you have already proved," I answered coldly and, taking the Captain of Dragoons by the arm, I left the room.

"What is it you want?" asked the captain.

"You are a friend of Grushnitski and will probably be his second?"

The captain bowed with great importance.

"You have guessed," he answered. "I am even obliged to be his second, because the insult inflicted upon him refers also to me. I was with him last night," he added, straightening his stooping shoulders.

"Ah! So it was you that I hit so awkwardly on the head?"

He turned yellow, turned blue; concealed malevolence was expressed in his face.

"I shall have the honor to send you my second today," I added with a very polite bow, pretending not to pay any attention to his rage.

On the porch of the restaurant, I came across Vera's husband. Apparently, he had been waiting for me.

He grasped my hand with an emotion resembling enthusiasm.

"Noble young man," he said with tears in his eyes, "I heard it all. What a scoundrel! What lack of gratitude! Who will want to admit them into a decent house after that! Thank God I have no daughters! But you will be rewarded by her for whom you risk your life. You may rely on my discretion for the time being," he went on, "I have been young myself, and have served in the military service: I know one should not interfere in these matters. Good-by."

Poor thing! He rejoices he has no daughters.

I went straight to Werner, found him at home and told him everything—my relations with Vera and with the young princess, and the conversation I had overheard, from which I had learned the intention those gentlemen had of making a fool of me by forcing me to fight a duel with pistols loaded with blanks. But now the matter was going beyond a joke: they, probably, had not expected such an outcome.

The doctor agreed to be my second; I gave him some instructions concerning the terms of the duel. He was to insist on the affair remaining as secret as possible because, although I am ready to brave death any time, I am not at all disposed to ruin, forever, my future career in this world.

After this I went home. An hour later, the doctor returned from his expedition.

"There is, indeed, a plot against you," he said. "I found at Grushnitski's the Captain of Dragoons and yet another gentleman, whose name I do not remember. For a moment I stopped in the vestibule to take off my rubbers. They were making a lot of noise and arguing. 'For nothing in the world shall I agree," Grushnitski was saying. 'He insulted me in public: before that, things were entirely different.' 'What business is this of yours?' answered the captain. "I take everything upon myself. I was a second in five duels, and you may be sure I know how to arrange it. I have planned it all. Only please do not interfere. It won't do any harm to scare the fellow. But why expose oneself to danger if one can avoid it? . . .' At this moment, I entered. They were suddenly silent. Our negotiations lasted a considerable time. Finally, we decided the matter in the following way: within three miles from here there is a desolate gorge; they will drive there tomorrow at four in the morning, and we shall set out half an hour after them; you will shoot at each other at six paces—Grushnitski himself demanded this. The one who is killed is to be put down to the Circassians. Now, here are my suspicions: they, that is to say the seconds, have apparently altered somewhat their former plan and want to load, with a bullet, only Grushnitski's pistol. This slightly resembles murder, but in time of war, and especially Asiatic war, trickery is allowed. However, Grushnitski seems to be a little nobler than his companions. What do you think, should we show them that we have found them out?"

"Not for anything on earth, doctor! Rest assured, I shall not fall in their trap."

"What then do you want to do?"

"That's my secret."

"See that you don't get caught . . . Remember, the distance is six paces!"

"Doctor, I expect you tomorrow at four: the horses will be ready . . . Good-by."

Till evening I remained at home, locked up in my room. A footman came with an invitation from the old princess—I had him told that I was ill.

. . .

Two o'clock in the morning . . . Sleep does not come . . . Yet I ought to have some sleep so that my hand does not shake tomorrow. Anyway, it would be difficult to miss at six paces. Ah, Mr. Grushnitski! Your mystification will not come off . . . We shall exchange parts: it is now I who will search your pale face for signs of secret fear. Why did you designate yourself those fatal six paces? you think that I shall present my forehead to you without arguing . . . But we shall cast lots . . . and then . . . then . . . what if his luck outweighs mine? What if my star at last betrays me? . . . It would hardly be strange, it has so long served my whims faithfully. There is no more constancy in heaven than there is on earth.

Well, what of it? If I am to die, I'll die! The loss to the world will not be large and, anyway, I myself am sufficiently bored. I am like a man who yawns at a ball and does not drive home to sleep, only because his carriage is not yet there. But now the carriage is ready . . . good-by! . . .

I scan my whole past in memory and involuntarily wonder: why did I live, for what purpose was I born? . . . And yet that purpose must have existed, and my destination must have been a lofty one, for I feel, in my soul, boundless strength. But I did not divine that destination, I became enticed by the lure of hollow and thankless passions. From their crucible, I emerged as hard and cold as iron, but lost forever the ardor of noble yearnings—the best blossom of life. And since then, how many times I have played the part of an axe in the hands of fate! As an executioner's tool, I would fall upon the head of doomed victims, often without malice, always without regret. My love brought happiness to none, because I never gave up anything for the sake of those whom I loved. I loved for myself, for my proper pleasure; I merely satisfied a bizarre need of my heart, avidly consuming their sentiments, their tenderness, their joys and sufferings—and never could I have my fill. Thus a man, tormented by hunger and fatigue, goes to sleep and sees before him rich viands and sparkling wines; he devours with delight the airy gifts of fancy, and he seems to feel relief; but as soon as he awakes—the vision vanishes. He is left with redoubled hunger and despair!

And, perhaps tomorrow, I shall die! . . . And there will not remain, on earth, a single creature that would have understood me completely. Some deem me worse, others better than I actually am. Some will say he was a good fellow; others will say he was a scoundrel. Both this and that will be false. After this, is it worth the trouble to live? And yet one lives—out of curiosity. One keeps expecting something new . . . Absurd and vexatious!

It is now a month and a half already that I have been in the fort of N——. Maksim Maksimich is out hunting. I am alone, I am sitting at the window. Gray clouds have shut off the mountains to their base: through the mist, the sun looks like a yellow blur. It is cold: the wind whistles and shakes the shutters . . . How dull! . . . I am going to continue my journal, which has been interrupted by so many strange events.

I read over the last page: how funny!—I expected to die: it was impossible. I had not yet drained the cup of sufferings, and I now feel that I still have many years to live.

How clearly and sharply the past has crystallized in my memory! Time has not erased one line, one shade!

I remember that, during the night before the duel, I did not sleep one minute. I could not write long. a secret restlessness had taken possession of me. For an hour or so, I paced the room, then I sat down and opened a novel by Walter Scott which lay on my table: it was *The Scottish Puritans*.[64] At first I read with an effort, but then I lost myself in it, carried away by the magic fantasy. Could it be that, in the next world, the Scottish bard is not paid for every glad minute that his book gives?

Dawn came at last. My nerves had quieted down. I looked at myself in the mirror: a dull pallor was spread over my face, which bore the traces of painful insomnia; but the eyes, although surrounded by brown shadows, glittered proudly and inflexibly. I was satisfied with myself.

After having ordered the horses to be saddled, I dressed and ran down to the bathhouse. As I immersed myself in the cold ebullience of Narzan water, I felt the forces of my body and soul return. I emerged from the bath, refreshed and braced up, as if I were about to go to a ball. Try to say after this that the soul is not dependent on the body!

Upon returning home, I found the doctor there. He wore gray riding breeches, a Caucasian overcoat and a Circassian cap. I burst out laughing at the sight of his small figure under that huge shaggy cap: his face is anything but that of a warrior, and on this occasion

64. Title of the French translation of *Old Mortality*, by the Scottish novelist Walter Scott (1771–1832).

it looked longer than ever.

"Why are you so sad, doctor?" I said to him. "Haven't you seen people off on their way to the next world with the greatest indifference, a hundred times before? You should imagine that I have bilious fever. I may get well, and again, I may die; both are in the natural order of things. Try to see in me a patient afflicted with an illness that is still unknown to you—and then your curiosity will be roused to the highest pitch. By watching me you can now make several important physiological observations. Isn't the expectation of violent death, after all, a genuine illness?"

This thought impressed the doctor and he cheered up.

We got on our horses. Werner clutched at the bridle with both hands, and we set off. In a twinkle we had galloped past the fort by way of the suburb, and entered the gorge along which the road wound, half-choked with tall grasses, and constantly crossed and recrossed by a loud brook, which had to be forded, to the great dismay of the doctor, for every time his horse stopped in the water.

I do not remember a bluer and fresher morning. The sun had just appeared from behind the green summits, and the merging of the first warmth of its rays with the waning coolness of the night pervaded all one's senses with a kind of delicious languor. The glad beam of the young day had not yet penetrated into the gorge; it gilded only the tops of the cliffs that hung on both sides above us. The dense-foliaged bushes, growing in the deep crevices, asperged[65] us with a silver rain at the least breath of wind. I remember that on this occasion, more than ever before, I was in love with nature. How curiously I examined every dewdrop that trembled upon a broad vine leaf and reflected a million iridescent rays! How avidly my gaze tried to penetrate into the hazy distance! There, the road was becoming narrower, the cliffs were growing bluer and more awesome, and finally, they seemed to blend in an impenetrable wall. We rode in silence.

"Have you made your will?" Werner suddenly asked.

"No."

"And what if you are killed?"

"My heirs will turn up of themselves."

"Do you mean you have not got any friends to whom you would wish to send a last farewell?"

I shook my head.

"Do you mean there is not one woman in the world to whom you would want to leave something in remembrance?"

"Do you want me, doctor," I answered him, "to open my soul to you? . . . You see, I have outlived those years when people die uttering the name of their beloved and bequeathing a tuft of pomaded

65. Sprinkled.

or unpomaded hair to a friend. When I think of near and possible death, I am thinking of myself only: some people don't do even that. Friends who, tomorrow, will forget me or, worse, will saddle me with goodness knows what fictions; women who, while embracing another, will laugh at me so as not to make him jealous of a dead man—what do I care for them all! Out of life's storm I carried only a few ideas—and not one feeling. For a long time now, I have been living not with the heart, but with the head. I weigh and analyze my own passions and actions with stern curiosity, but without participation. Within me there are two persons: one of them lives in the full sense of the word, the other cogitates and judges him. The first will, perhaps, in an hour's time, take leave of you and the world forever, while the other . . . what about the other? . . . Look, doctor, do you see on that cliff on the right, three black figures? These are our adversaries, I believe."

We set off at a trot.

In the bushes at the foot of the cliff, three horses were tied. We tied our horses there too, and clambered up a narrow path to a flat ledge, where Grushnitski was awaiting us with the Captain of Dragoons and his other second, whose name and patronymic were Ivan Ignatievich. I never learned his surname.

"We have been expecting you for a long time," the Captain of Dragoons said with an ironic smile.

I took out my watch and showed it to him.

He apologized, saying that his was fast.

For several moments there was an awkward silence: at last, the doctor broke it by addressing himself to Grushnitski:

"It seems to me," he said, "that both parties having shown their readiness to fight, and having thus satisfied the demands of honor, you might, gentlemen, talk matters over and close the affair amicably."

"I'm willing," I said.

The captain gave Grushnitski a wink, and he, thinking that I was scared, assumed a proud air, although up to then a dull pallor had been spread over his cheeks. For the first time since we had come, he raised his eyes to look at me; but in his glance there was some kind of perturbation betraying an inner struggle.

"Explain your terms," he said, "and whatever I can do for you, you may be assured. . . ."

"Here are my terms: this very day you will publicly retract your slander and will apologize to me."

"Sir, I am amazed that you dare offer such things to me!"

"What else could I offer you?"

"We shall fight."

I shrugged my shoulders.

"As you please; but consider—one of us will certainly be killed."

"My wish is that it may be you."

"And I'm convinced of the opposite."

He lost countenance, colored, then burst into forced laughter.

The captain took his arm and led him aside: for a long time, they whispered together. I had arrived in a fairly peaceable state of mind, but all this was beginning to annoy me.

The doctor came up to me.

"Listen," he said with obvious anxiety, "you must have forgotten about their plot? I do not know how to load a pistol, but in the present case . . . You are a strange fellow! Tell them that you are aware of their intention, and they will not dare . . . What is the sense of this? They'll bring you down like a bird."

"Please don't worry, doctor, and wait a bit . . . I shall arrange everything in such a way that on their side there will be no advantage whatever. Let them "hugger-mugger" a little." ʲ

"Gentlemen! This is becoming tiresome," I said in a loud voice. "If we are to fight, let us fight: you had plenty of time to talk it over yesterday."

"We are ready," answered the captain. "To your places, gentlemen! Doctor, have the kindness to measure off six paces."

"To your places!" repeated Ivan Ignatievich, in a squeaky voice.

"Allow me!" I said. "There is one further condition. Since we are going to fight to the death, we should do everything possible to keep the matter secret and to avoid our seconds being held responsible. Do you agree?"

"We completely agree."

"Well, this is what I thought up. Do you see at the summit of that sheer cliff on the right, a narrow bit of flat ground? There is a drop of about three hundred feet or more from there; below, there are sharp rocks. Each of us will take his stand on the very edge of the shelf, and in this way even a light wound will be fatal. This must be in keeping with your desire for you stipulated yourself, a distance of six paces. The one who is wounded will inevitably topple down and will be dashed to pieces; the doctor will take out the bullet, and then it should be very easy to ascribe this sudden death to an unfortunate leap. We shall draw lots to decide who is to shoot first. Let me inform you, in conclusion, that otherwise I will not fight."

"Have it your way!" said the captain after glancing meaningly at Grushnitski, who nodded in sign of consent. His face kept changing every minute. I had placed him in an awkward position. Had he fought under ordinary conditions, he might have aimed at my leg, wounded me lightly and satisfied, in this way, his thirst for revenge, without burdening his conscience too heavily. But now he had either to discharge his pistol into the air, or become a murderer, or lastly, abandon his vile plan and expose himself to equal danger with me. At this moment, I would not have wished to be in his place. He led the captain aside and began to say something to him with great heat. I saw his livid lips tremble, but the captain turned away from him with a contemptuous smile. "You're a fool!" he said to Grushnitski, rather loudly, "you do not understand anything! Let us go, gentlemen!"

A narrow trail led up the precipice between the bushes; broken rocks formed the precarious steps of this natural staircase: holding onto bushes, we started to climb up. Grushnitski was in front, behind him were his seconds, and after them came the doctor and I.

"I am amazed at you," said the doctor, giving my hand a strong squeeze. "Let me feel your pulse! . . . Oho! it's feverish! . . . But nothing shows in your face . . . Only your eyes shine brighter than usual."

Suddenly, small stones noisily rolled down to our feet. What was it? Grushnitski had stumbled. The branch which he had grasped broke and he would have slid down on his back, had not his seconds supported him.

"Take care!" I cried to him. "Don't fall beforehand: it's a bad omen. Remember Julius Caesar!"[66]

Presently we reached the top of the jutting cliff: its flat surface was covered with fine sand, as if made especially for a duel. All around, melting in the golden mist of the morning, mountain summits teemed like an innumerable herd, and to the south Mount Elbruz raised its white mass, the last link in the chain of icy crests among which wispy clouds, which had blown from the east, were already roaming. I went to the edge of the natural platform and looked down: my head almost began to turn. Down below it was dark and cold as in the tomb; mossgrown jags of rocks, cast down by storm and time, were awaiting their prey.

The platform on which we were to fight presented an almost regular triangle. Six paces were measured off from the jutting angle and it was decided that he who would have to face first his foe's fire, should stand at the very apex, with his back to the chasm. If he were not killed, the principles were to change places.

I decided to give Grushnitski every advantage; I wished to test him. A spark of magnanimity might awaken in his soul—and then everything would turn out for the best; but vanity and weakness of character were to triumph! . . . I wished to give myself the full right to show him no quarter, if fate spared me. Who has not concluded similar agreements with his conscience?

"Spin the coin, doctor!" said the captain.

The doctor took out of his pocket a silver coin and held it up.

---

66. Caesar's assassination was foreshadowed by several omens.

"Tails!" cried Grushnitski hurriedly, like a man who has been suddenly awakened by a friendly nudge.

"Heads!" I said.

The coin soared up and fell with a tinkle; everyone rushed toward it.

"You're lucky," I said to Grushnitski, "you are to fire first! But remember that if you do not kill me, I shall not miss—I give you my word of honor."

He colored; he was ashamed to kill an unarmed man. I was looking at him intently; for a moment it seemed to me that he would throw himself at my feet, begging for forgiveness, but who could own having such a villainous design? . . . Only one resource remained to him—to fire in the air. I was sure he would fire in the air! Only one thing could interfere with it: the thought that I should demand another duel.

"It is time!" the doctor whispered to me, pulling my sleeve. "If you do not tell them now that we know their intentions, all is lost. Look, he is already loading . . . If you do not say anything, I myself shall. . . ."

"Not for anything in the world, doctor!" I replied, holding him back by the arm. "You would spoil everything. You gave me your word not to interfere . . . What does it matter to you? Perhaps, I wish to be killed. . . ."

He glanced at me with surprise.

"Oh, that's different! . . . Only do not bring complaints against me in the next world."

In the meantime, the captain had loaded his pistols; he handed one to Grushnitski, whispering something to him with a smile; the other he handed to me.

I took my stand at the apex of the platform, bracing my left foot firmly against the rock and leaning forward a little, so as not to fall backward in the case of a light wound.

Grushnitski stationed himself opposite me and at a given signal began to raise his pistol. His knees shook. He was aiming straight at my forehead.

Ineffable fury flared up in my breast.

Suddenly, he lowered the muzzle of his pistol and, going as white as a sheet, turned toward his second:

"I can't," he said in a hollow voice.

"Coward!" answered the captain.

The shot rang out. The bullet grazed my knee. Involuntarily, I took several steps forward so as to get away, as soon as possible, from the brink.

"Well, friend Grushjitski, it's a pity you've missed!" said the captain. "Now it's your turn, take your stand! Embrace me first: we shall not see each other again!" They embraced; the captain could hardly keep himself from laughing. "Have no fear," he added, with a sly glance at Grushnitski. "All's nonsense on earth! . . . Nature is a ninny, fate is a henny,[67] and life is a penny!"

After this tragic phrase, delivered with appropriate dignity, he withdrew to his place. Ivan Ignatievich, with tears, likewise embraced Grushnitski, and now he was left alone facing me. To this day I try to explain to myself what kind of feeling was boiling in my breast. It was the irritation of injured vanity, and contempt, and wrath which arose at the thought that this man, now looking at me with such confidence and such calm insolence, had tried, two minutes before, without exposing himself to any danger, to kill me like a dog, for if I had been wounded in the leg a little more severely, I would have certainly fallen off the cliff.

For several moments, I kept looking intently into his face, striving to discern the slightest trace of repentance. But it seemed to me that he was withholding a smile.

"I advise you to say your prayers before dying," I then said to him.

"Do not worry about my soul more than you do about your own. One thing I ask of you: shoot quickly."

"And you do not retract your slander? You do not ask my pardon? Think well: does not your conscience say something to you?"

"Mr. Pechorin!" cried the Captain of Dragoons, "you are not here to hear confession, allow me to tell you . . . Let us finish quickly, otherwise somebody may come driving through the gorge and see us."

"All right. Doctor, come over to me."

The doctor came. Poor doctor! He was paler than Grushnitski had been ten minutes before.

I spaced on purpose the following words, pronouncing them loudly and distinctly, the way a death sentence is pronounced:

"Doctor, these gentlemen, no doubt in their hurry, forgot to place a bullet in my pistol. Please, load it again—and properly!"

"This cannot be!" the captain was shouting, "it cannot be! I loaded both pistols: perhaps, the ball rolled out of yours . . . That is not my fault! And you have no right to reload . . . no right whatsoever. It is utterly against the rules; I shall not permit it. . . ."

"All right!" I said to the captain. "If so, you and I will have a duel on the same conditions."

He faltered.

Grushnitski stood, his head sunk on his breast, embarrassed and gloomy.

"Leave them alone!" he finally said to the captain who wanted to snatch my pistol out of the doctor's hands. "You know very well

67. **Whore.**

yourself that they are right."

In vain did the captain make various signs to him. Grushnitski would not even look.

Meanwhile, the doctor had loaded the pistol, and now handed it to me.

Upon seeing this, the captain spat and stamped his foot.

"Brother, you *are* a fool!" he said. "A vulgar fool! . . . Since you've relied upon me, you should obey me in everything . . . Serve you right! Perish like a fly . . ." He turned away and, as he walked off, he muttered: "And still it is utterly against the rules."

Grushnitski!" I said. "There is still time: retract your slander and I shall forgive you everything. You did not succeed in fooling me, and my self-esteem is satisfied. Remember, we were friends once. . . ."

His face blazed, his eyes glittered.

"Shoot!" he answered. "I despise myself and hate you. If you do not kill me, I shall cut your throat in a dark alley. There is no room in this world for the two of us . . ."

I fired. . . .

When the smoke dispersed, Grushnitski was not on the ledge. Only dust in a light column still revolved on the brink of the precipice.

All cried out in one voice.

"*Finita la commedia!*"[68] I said to the doctor.

He did not answer and turned away in horror.

I shrugged my shoulders and bowed to Grushnitski's second as I took leave of them.

On my way down the trail, I noticed, among the crevices of the cliffs, Grushnitski's blood-stained body. Involuntrily, I shut my eyes.

I untied my horse and set out for home at a walk: a stone lay on my heart. The sun seemed to me without luster; its ray did not warm me.

Before reaching the suburb, I turned off to the right, down the gorge. The sight of a human being would have been burdensome to me. I wanted to be alone. With slack reins, my head sunk on my breast, I rode a long while; at last, I found myself in a spot that was completely unknown to me. I turned my horse around and began to look for the road; the sun was already setting when I reached Kislovodsk, exhausted, on an exhausted horse.

My valet told me that Werner had called, and handed me two notes: one from Werner himself, the other . . . from Vera.

I unsealed the first one; it contained the following message:

"Everything has been arranged as well as possible; the body has been brought back in a disfigured condition, the bullet has been

---

68 "The comedy is ended": tradi-   end of a stage performance.
tional Italian phrase used to mark the

extracted from the breast. Everybody believes that his death had been caused by an accident; only the commandant, to whom your quarrel was probably known, shook his head, but said nothing. There are no proofs against you whatsoever, and you can sleep in peace . . . if you can . . . Good-by."

For a long time, I could not make myself open the second note . . . What could she tell me? . . . A heavy presentiment agitated my soul.

Here it is, this letter, whose every word is indelibly graven in my memory:

"I write to you with the complete certitude that we shall never see each other again. Several years ago, when parting with you, I thought the same; but Heaven chose to try me a second time. I did not withstand this trial: my weak heart submitted again to the familiar voice. You will not despise me for this, will you? This letter is going to be both a farewell and a confession: I feel obliged to tell you all that has accumulated in my heart ever since it loved you. I shall not blame you—you treated me as any other man would have done; you loved me as your property, as a source of joys, agitations and sorrows, which mutually replaced one another and without which life would have been dull and monotonous. This I understood from the first; but you were unhappy, and I sacrificed myself, hoping that some day you would appreciate my sacrifice, that some day you would understand my deep tenderness, not depending on any circumstances. Since then much time has passed. I penetrated into all the secrets of your soul . . . and realized that my hope had been a vain one. It made me bitterly sad! But my love had grown one with my soul; it became darker, but did not go out.

"We part forever; yet you may be sure that I shall never love another: my soul has spent upon you all its treasures, its tears and hopes. She, who has loved you once, cannot look without a certain contempt on other men, not because you are better than they—oh, no!—but because there is something special about your nature, peculiar to you alone, something proud and mysterious. In your voice, whatever you may be saying, there is unconquerable power. None is able to desire so incessantly to be loved; in none is evil so attractive; the gaze of none promises so much bliss; none knows better to use his advantages; and none can be so genuinely unhappy as you, because none tries so hard to convince himself of the contrary.

"I must now explain to you the reason for my hurried departure: it will seem to you of little importance, since it concerns me alone.

"This morning, my husband came into my room and related your quarrel with Grushnitski. Evidently, I looked terribly upset, for he looked long and intently into my eyes. I nearly fainted at the thought that you must fight today and that I was the cause of it: it seemed to me that I would go mad . . . But now that I can reason, I feel sure that your life will be spared: it is impossible that you should die without me, impossible! My husband paced the room for a long time. I do not know what he was saying to me, I do not remember what I answered him . . . No doubt, I told him that I loved you . . . I only remember that toward the end of our conversation, he insulted me with a dreadful word and went out. I heard him order the coach to be got ready . . . I have now been sitting at the window for three hours, awaiting your return . . . But you are alive, you cannot die! . . . The coach is almost ready . . . Farewell, farewell . . . I perish—but what does it matter? If I could be sure that you will always remember me—I don't say love me—no, only remember . . . Farewell . . . Somebody is coming . . . I must hide this letter. . . .

"You do not love Mary, do you? You will not marry her? Listen, you must make this sacrifice to me: for you I have lost everything in the world. . . ."

Like a madman, I rushed out onto the porch, jumped on my Circassian horse which was being promenaded in the yard, and galloped off, at full speed on the road to Pyatigorsk. Unmercifully I urged my exhausted steed, which, snorting and all covered with foam, carried me swiftly along the stony road.

The sun had already hidden in a black cloud that rested on the ridge of the western mountains; it had become dark and damp in the gorge. The Podkumok River roared dully and monotonously as it made its way over stones. I galloped on, breathless with impatience. The thought of arriving in Pyatigorsk too late to find her, beat like a hammer on my heart. To see her for one minute, one more minute, say good-by to her, press her hand . . . I prayed, cursed, wept, laughed . . . No, nothing can express my anxiety, my despair! Faced by the possibility of losing Vera forever, I felt that she had become dearer to me than anything in the world—dearer than life, honor, happiness! God knows what strange, mad plans swarmed in my head . . . And meanwhile I continued to gallop, urging my horse mercilessly. And presently, I began to notice that my steed was breathing more heavily; once or twice he had already stumbled on level ground. Three miles remained to Essentuki, a Cossack settlement where I might be able to change horses.

Everything would have been saved had my horse's strength lasted for another ten minutes! But suddenly, as we emerged from a small ravine at the end of the defile where there was a sharp turn, he crashed onto the ground. I nimbly jumped off, tried to make him get up, tagged at the bridle—in vain. A hardily audible moan escaped through his clenched teeth; a few minutes later he was dead. I remained alone in the steppe, my last hope gone; I tried to proceed on foot—my legs gave way under me. Worn out by the agitations of the day and by insomnia, I fell on the wet grass and began crying like a child.

And for a long time, I lay motionless and cried bitterly, not attempting to hold back the tears and sobs. I thought my chest would burst; all my firmness, all my coolness vanished like smoke; my soul wilted, my reason was mute and if, at that moment, anyone had seen me, he would have turned away in contempt.

When the night dew and the mountain breeze had cooled my burning head, and my thoughts had regained their usual order, I realized that to pursue perished happiness was useless and senseless. What was it that I still needed? To see her! What for? Was not everything ended between us? One bitter farewell kiss would not enrich my memories, and after it, we would only find it harder to part.

Yet it pleases me that I am capable of weeping. It may have been due, however, to upset nerves, to a sleepless night, to a couple of minutes spent facing the muzzle of a pistol, and to an empty stomach.

Everything is for the best! The new torment produced in me, to use military parlance, a fortunate diverson. Tears are wholesome, and then, probably, if I had not gone for that ride, and had not been compelled to walk ten miles home, that night, too, sleep would not have come to close my eyes.

I returned to Kislovodsk at five in the morning, threw myself on my bed and slept the sleep of Napoleon after Waterloo.[69]

When I awoke it was already dark outside. I seated myself at the open window, unbuttoned my Caucasian overcoat, and the mountain breeze cooled my breast, which had not yet been appeased by the heavy sleep of exhaustion. Far away, beyond the river, through the tops of the dense limes sheltering it, there flickered lights in the buildings of the fort and of the suburb. Around the house, all was quiet. The princess's house was in darkness.

The doctor came in; his brow was furrowed; contrary to his custom, he did not give me his hand.

"Where do you come from, doctor?"

"From the Princess Ligovskoy. Her daughter is ill—a nervous breakdown . . . However, that is not the matter, but this: the authorities are suspicious, and, although nothing can be proved positively, I would nevertheless advise you to be more careful. The princess told me today that she knows you fought a duel over her daughter. She learned it all from that little old man—what's his name? He witnessed your clash with Grushnitski at the restaurant. I came to warn you. Good-by. I suppose we shan't see each other again: you will be transferred somewhere."

---

69. The battle in which he had been decisively defeated, and after which he was exiled for life.

On the threshold, he stopped. He would have liked to shake my hand, and had I displayed to him the slightest desire for it, he would have thrown himself on my neck; but I remained as cold as stone—and he left.

That's the human being for you! They are all like that: they know beforehand all the bad sides of an action. They help you, they advise you, they even approve of it, perceiving the impossibility of a different course—and afterwards they wash their hands of it, and turn away indignantly from him who had the courage to take upon himself the entire burden of responsibility. They are all like that, even the kindest, even the most intelligent ones.

On the following morning, upon receiving from the higher authorities the order to proceed to the fort of N——, I called on the old princess to say good-by.

She was surprised when, to her question, whether I had not anything particularly important to tell her, I answered that I wished her happiness and so forth.

"As to me, I must talk to you very seriously."

I sat down in silence.

It was obvious she did not know how to begin. Her face turned purple, her plump fingers drummed upon the table; at last, she began thus, in a haulting voice:

"Listen, Monsieur Pechorin, I believe you are a gentleman."

I bowed.

"I am even convinced of it," she went on, "although your behavior is somewhat ambiguous; but you may have reasons which I do not know, and it is those reasons that you now must confide to me. You have defended my daughter from slander; you fought a duel for her—consequently, risked your life. Do not reply. I know you will not admit it, because Grushnitski is dead." (She crossed herself.) "God will forgive him, and He will forgive you, too, I hope! . . . That does not concern me . . . I dare not condemn you, since my daughter, though innocently, was the cause of it. She told me everything—I think, everything. You declared your love to her . . . she confessed her love to you." (Here the princess sighed heavily.) "But she is ill, and I am certain that it is no ordinary illness! A secret sorrow is killing her; she does not admit it, but I am certain that you are its cause . . . Listen, you may think, perhaps, that I am looking for rank, for huge riches. Undeceive yourself! I seek only my daughter's happiness. Your present situation is not enviable, but it can improve: you are a man of means. My daughter loves you; she has been brought up in such a way that she will make her husband's happiness. I am rich, she is my only child . . . Tell me, what holds you back? . . . You see, I should not have been saying all this to you, but I rely on your heart, on your honor . . . Remember, I have but one daughter . . . one. . . ."

She began to cry.

"Princess," I said, "it is impossible for me to answer you. Allow me to talk to your daughter alone."

"Never!" she exclaimed, rising from her chair in great agitation.

"As you please," I answered, preparing to go.

She lapsed into thought, made me a sign to wait, and left the room.

Five minutes passed; my heart was beating violently, but my thoughts were clam, my head cool. No matter how hard I searched my breast for one spark of love for the charming Mary, my efforts were in vain.

Presently the door opened, and she came in. Good Lord! How she had altered since I saw her last—and had that been so very long ago?

On reaching the middle of the room, she swayed; I jumped up, gave her my arm and led her to an armchair.

I stood facing her. For a long time we were silent. Her great eyes, filled with ineffable sadness, seemed to seek in my eyes something resembling hope; her pale lips vainly tried to smile; her delicate hands, folded in her lap, were so thin and diaphanous, that I felt sorry for her.

"Princess," I said, "you know that I laughed at you? You must despise me."

A feverish rosiness appeared on her cheeks.

I went on: "Consequently, you cannot love me. . . ."

She turned away, rested her elbow on a table, covered her eyes with her hand, and it seemed to me that tears glistened in them.

"Oh God!" she uttered almost inaudibly.

This was becoming unbearable: another minute, and I would have fallen at her feet.

"So you see for yourself," I said, in as firm a voice as I could and with a strained smile, "you see for yourself that I cannot marry you. Even if you wished it now, you would soon regret it. My talk with your mother obliged me to have it out with you, so frankly and so roughly. I hope she is under a delusion: it will be easy for you to undeceive her. You see, I am playing, in your eyes, a most miserable and odious part, and even this I admit—this is all I'm able to do for you. However unfavorable the opinion you may have of me, I submit to it. You see, I am base in regard to you. Am I not right that even if you loved me, from this moment on you despise me?"

She turned to me as pale as marble; only her eyes glittered marvelously.

"I hate you," she said.

I thanked her, bowed respectfully and left.

An hour later, an express *troika*[70] was rushing me away from Kis-

70. A three-horse carriage.

lovodsk. A few miles before reaching Essentuki, I recognized, by the roadside, the carcass of my gallant steed. The saddle had been removed, probably by some passing Cossack and, instead of the saddle, there were two ravens perched on the dead beast's back. I sighed and turned away.

And now here, in this dull fort, I often scan the past in thought, and wonder why I had not wanted to tread that path, which fate had opened for me, where quiet joys and peace of mind awaited me? No, I would not have got used to such an existence! I am like a sailor born and bred on the deck of a pirate brig. His soul is used to storms and battles, and, when cast out on the shore, he feels bored and oppressed, no matter how the shady grove lures him, no matter how the peaceful sun shines on him. All day long he haunts the sand of the shore, hearkens to the monotonous murmur of the surf and peers into the misty distance. Will there not appear there, glimpsed on the pale line separating the blue main from the gray cloudlets, the longed-for sail, at first like the wing of a sea gull, but gradually separating itself from the foam of the breakers and, at a smooth clip, nearing the desolate quay?

Masterpieces of Nineteenth-Century Realism and Naturalism

EDITED BY
RENÉ WELLEK
Sterling Professor of Comparative Literature, Yale University

As was indicated in the preceding introduction, the nineteenth century is the century of greatest change in the history of Western civilization. The upheavals following the French Revolution broke up the old order of Europe. The Holy Roman Empire and the Papal States were dissolved. Nationalism, nourished by the political and social aspirations of the middle classes, grew by leaps and bounds. "Liberty" became the main political slogan of the century. In different countries and different decades it meant different things: here liberation from the rule of the foreigner, there the emancipation of the serf; here the removal of economic restrictions on trade and manufacturing, there the introduction of a constitution, free speech, parliamentary institutions. Almost all over Europe, the middle classes established their effective rule, though monarchs often remained in more or less nominal power. Two large European countries, Germany and Italy, achieved their centuries-old dreams of political unification. The predominance of France, still marked at the beginning of the century, was broken, and England—or rather Great Britain—ruled the sea throughout the century. The smaller European nations, especially in the Balkans, began to emancipate themselves from foreign rule.

These major political changes were caused by, and in their turn caused, great social and economic changes. The Industrial Revolution which had begun in England in the eighteenth century spread over the Continent and transformed living conditions radically. The enormous increase in the speed and availability of transportation due to the development of railroads and

557

steamships, the greatly increased urbanization following from the establishment of industries, changed the whole pattern of human life in most countries, and made possible, within a century, an unprecedented increase in the population (as much as threefold in most European countries), which was also fostered by the advances of medicine and hygiene. The increase of widespread wealth and prosperity is, in spite of the wretched living conditions and other hardships of the early factory workers, an undeniable fact. The barriers between the social classes diminished appreciably almost everywhere: both the social and the political power of the aristocracy declined. The industrial laborer began to be felt as a political force.

These social and economic changes were closely bound up with shifts in the prevailing outlooks and philosophies. Technological innovation is impossible without the discoveries of science. The scientific outlook, hitherto dominant only in a comparatively limited area, spread widely and permeated almost all fields of human thought and endeavor. It raised enormous hopes for the future betterment of man's condition on earth, especially when Darwin's evolutionary theories fortified the earlier, vaguer faith in unlimited progress. "Liberty," "science," "progress," "evolution" are the concepts which define the mental atmosphere of the nineteenth century.

But tendencies hostile to these were by no means absent. Feudal or Catholic conservatism succeeded, especially in Austria-Hungary, in Russia, and in much of the south of Europe, in preserving old regimes, and the philosophies of a conservative and religious society were reformulated in modern terms. At the same time, in England the very assumptions of the new industrial middle-class society were powerfully attacked by writers such as Carlyle and Ruskin who recommended a return to medieval forms of social co-operation and handicraft. The industrial civilization of the nineteenth century was also opposed by the fierce individualism of many artists and thinkers who were unhappy in the ugly commercial "Philistine" society of the age. The writings of Nietzsche, toward the end of the century, and the whole movement of "art for art's sake," which asserted the independence of the artist from society, are the most obvious symptoms of this revolt. The free-enterprise system and the liberalism of the ruling middle classes also early clashed with the rising proletariat, which was won over to diverse forms of socialism, preaching a new collectivism with the stress on equality. Socialism could have Christian or romantic motivations, or it could become "scientific" and revolutionary, as Marx's brand of socialism (a certain stage of which he called "communism") claimed to be.

While up through the eighteenth century religion was, at least in name, a major force in European civilization, in the nineteenth century there was a marked decrease in its influence on both the intellectual leaders and the masses. Local intense revivals of religious consciousness, such as the Oxford Movement in England, did occur, and the traditional religious institutions were preserved everywhere, but the impact of science on religion was such that many tenets of the old faiths crumbled. The discoveries of astronomy, geology, evolutionary biology, archaeology, and biblical criticism forced, almost everywhere, a restatement of the old creeds. Religion, especially in the Protestant countries, was frequently confined to an inner feeling of religiosity or to a system of morality which preserved the ancient Christian virtues. During the early nineteenth century, in Germany, Hegel and his predecessors and followers tried to interpret the world in spiritual terms outside the bounds of traditional religion. There were many attempts even late in the century to restate this view, but the methods and discoveries of science seemed to invalidate it, and various formulas which took science as their base in building new lay religions of hope in humanity gained popularity. French Positivism, English utilitarianism, the evolutionism of Herbert Spencer, are some of the best-known examples. Meanwhile, for the first time in history, at least in Europe, profoundly pessimistic and atheistic philosophies arose, of which Schopenhauer's was the most subtle, while a purely physical materialism was the most widespread. Thus the whole gamut of views of the universe was represented during the century in new and impressive formulations.

The plastic arts did not show a similar vitality. For a long time, in most countries, painting and architecture floundered in a sterile eclecticism, in a bewildering variety of historical masquerades in which the neo-Gothic style was replaced by the neo-Renaissance and that by the neo-Baroque and other decorative revivals of past forms. Only in France, painting, with the impressionists, found a new style which was genuinely original. In music the highly romantic art of Richard Wagner attracted most attention, but the individual national schools either continued in their tradition, like Italian opera (Verdi) or founded an idiom of their own, often based on a revival of folklore, as in Russia (Tchaikovsky), Poland (Chopin), Bohemia (Dvořák), and Norway (Grieg).

But literature was the most representative and the most widely influential art of the nineteenth century. It found new forms and methods and expressed the social and intellectual situation of the time most fully and memorably.

After the great wave of the international romantic movement had spent its force in the fourth decade of the nineteenth century, European literature moved in the direction of what is usually called *realism*. Realism was not a coherent general movement which established itself unchallenged for a long period of time, as classicism had succeeded in doing during the eighteenth century. There were many authors in the nineteenth century who continued to practice a substantially romantic art (Tennyson and Hugo, for example); there were even movements which upheld a definitely romantic "escapist," antirealist program, such as that of the Pre-Raphaelites in England or the Parnassians in France. But, with whatever exceptions and reservations, in retrospect the nineteenth century appears as the period of the great realistic writers: Flaubert in France, Dostoevsky and Tolstoy in Russia, Dickens in England, James in America, Ibsen in Norway.

What is meant by realism? The term, in literary use (there is a much older philosophical use), apparently dates back to the Germans at the turn of the century—to Schiller and the Schlegels. It cropped up in France as early as 1826 but became a commonly accepted literary and artistic slogan only in the 1850's. (A review called *Réalisme* began publication in 1856, and a critic, Champfleury, published a volume of critical articles with the title *Le Réalisme* in the following year.) Since then the word has been bandied about, discussed, analyzed, and abused as all slogans are. It is frequently confused with naturalism, an ancient philosophical term for materialism, epicureanism, or any secularism. As a specifically literary term, it crystallized only in France. In French, as in English, naturalist means, of course, simply student of nature, and the analogy between the writer and the naturalist, specifically the botanist and

zoologist, was ready at hand. Emile Zola, in the Preface to a new edition of his early novel, *Thérèse Raquin* (1866), proclaimed the naturalist creed most boldly. His book, he claims, is "an analytical labor on two living bodies like that of a surgeon on corpses." He proudly counts himself among the group of "naturalist writers."

The program of the groups of writers and critics who used these terms can be easily summarized. The realists wanted a truthful representation in literature of reality—that is, of contemporary life and manners. They thought of their method as inductive, observational, and hence "objective." The personality of the author was to be suppressed, or was at least to recede into the background, since reality was to be seen "as it is." The naturalistic program, as formulated by Zola, was substantially the same except that Zola put greater stress on the analogies to science, considering the procedure of the novelist as identical with that of the experimenting scientist. He also more definitely and exclusively embraced the philosophy of scientific materialism, with its deterministic implications, its stress on heredity and environment, while the older realists were not always so clear in drawing the philosophical consequences. These French theories were anticipated, paralleled, or imitated all over the world of Western literature. In Germany, the movement called Young Germany, with which Heine was associated, had propounded a substantially antiromantic realistic program as early as the thirties, but versions of the French theories definitely triumphed there only in the 1880's. In Russia, as early as the forties, the most prominent critic of the time, Vissarion Belinsky, praised the "natural" school of Russian fiction, which described contemporary Russia with fidelity. Italy also, from the late seventies on, produced an analogous movement, which called itself *verismo*. The English-speaking countries were the last to adopt the critical programs and slogans of the Continent: George Moore and George Gissing brought the French theories to England in the late eighties, and in the United States William Dean Howells began his campaign for realism in 1886, when he became editor of *Harper's Magazine*. Realistic and naturalistic theories of literature have since been widely accepted in spite of many twentieth-century criticisms and the whole general trend of twentieth-century literature. Especially in the United States, the contemporary novel is usually considered naturalistic and judged by standards of nature and truth. The officially promoted doctrine in Russia is called "socialist Realism."

The slogans "realism" and "naturalism" were thus new in the nineteenth century. They served as effective formulas directed against the romantic creed. Truth, contemporaneity, and objectivity were the obvious counterparts of romantic imagination, of romantic historicism and its glorification of the past, and of romantic subjectivity, the exaltation of the ego and the individual. But, of course, the emphasis on truth and objectiv-

ity was not really new: these qualities had been demanded by many older, classical theories of imitation, and in the eighteenth century there were great writers such as Diderot who wanted a literal "imitation of life" even on the stage.

The practice of realism, it could be argued, is very old indeed. There are realistic scenes in the *Odyssey*, and there is plenty of realism in ancient comedy and satire, in medieval stories (fabliaux) like some of Chaucer's and Boccaccio's, in many Elizabethan plays, in the Spanish rogue novels, in the English eighteenth-century novel beginning with Defoe, and so on almost ad infinitum. But while it would be easy to find in early literature anticipations of almost every single element of modern realism, still the systematic description of contemporary society, with a serious purpose, often even with a tragic tone as well, and with sympathy for heroes drawn from the middle and lower classes, was a real innovation of the nineteenth century.

It is usually rash to explain a literary movement in social and political terms. But the new realistic art surely has something to do with the triumph of the middle classes in France after the July revolution in 1830, and in England after the passage of the Reform Bill in 1832, and with the increasing influence of the middle classes in almost every country. Russia is somewhat of an exception as no large middle class could develop there during the nineteenth century. An absolute feudal regime continued in power and the special character of most of Russian literature must be due to this distinction, but even in Russia there emerged an "intelligentsia" (the term comes from Russia) which was open to Western ideas and was highly critical of the czarist regime and its official "ideology." But while much nineteenth-century literature reflects the triumph of the middle classes, it would be an error to think of the great realistic writers as spokesmen or mouthpieces of the society they described. Balzac was politically a Catholic monarchist who applauded the Bourbon restoration after the fall of Napoleon, but he had an extraordinary imaginative insight into the processes leading to the victory of the middle classes. Flaubert despised the middle-class society of the Third Empire with an intense hatred and the pride of a self-conscious artist. Dickens became increasingly critical of the middle classes and the assumptions of industrial civilization. Dostoevsky, though he took part in a conspiracy against the Russian government early in his life and spent ten years in exile in Siberia, became the propounder of an extremely conservative nationalistic and religious creed which was definitely directed against the revolutionary forces in Russia. Tolstoy, himself a count and a landowner, was violent in his criticism of the czarist regime, especially later in his life, but he cannot be described as friendly to the middle classes, to the aims of the democratic movements in Western Europe, or to the science of the time. Ibsen's political attitude is that of a proud individualist who condemns the "compact majority"

and its tyranny. Possibly all art is critical of its society, but in the nineteenth century this criticism became much more explicit, as social and political issues became much more urgent or, at least, were regarded as more urgent by the writing groups. To a far greater degree than in earlier centuries, writers felt their isolation from society, viewed the structure and problems of the prevailing order as debatable and reformable, and in spite of all demands for objectivity became, in many cases, social propagandists and reformers in their own right.

The program of realism, while defensible enough as a reaction against romanticism, raises critical questions which were not answered theoretically by its defenders. What is meant by "truth" of representation? Photographic copying? This seems the implication of many famous pronouncements. "A novel is a mirror walking along the road," said Stendhal as early as 1830. But such statements can hardly be taken literally. All art must select and represent; it cannot be and has never been a simple transcript of reality. What such analogies are intended to convey is rather a claim for an all-inclusiveness of subject matter, a protest against the exclusion of themes which before were considered "low," "sordid," or "trivial" (like the puddles along the road the mirror walks). Chekhov formulated this protest with the usual parallel between the scientist and the writer: "To a chemist nothing on earth is unclean. A writer must be as objective as a chemist; he must abandon the subjective line: he must know that dungheaps play a very respectable part in a landscape, and that evil passions are as inherent in life as good ones." Thus the "truth" of realistic art includes the sordid, the low, the disgusting, and the evil; and, the implication is, the subject is treated objectively, without interference and falsification by the artist's personality and his own desires. But in practice, while the realistic artist succeeded in expanding the themes of art, he could not fulfill the demand for total objectivity. Works of art are written by human beings and inevitably express their personalities and their points of view. As Conrad admitted, "even the most artful of writers will give himself (and his morality) away in about every third sentence." Objectivity, in the sense which Zola had in mind when he proposed a scientific method in the writing of novels and conceived of the novelist as a sociologist collecting human documents, is impossible in practice. When it has been attempted, it has led only to bad art, to dullness and the display of inert materials, to the confusion between the art of the novel and reporting, "documentation." The demand for "objectivity" can be understood only as a demand for a specific method of narration, in which the author does not interfere explicitly, in his own name, and as a rejection of personal themes of introspection and reverie.

The realistic program, while it has made innumerable new subjects available to art, also implies a narrowing of its themes and methods—a condemnation of the fantastic, the historical, the remote, the idealized, the "unsullied," the idyllic. Realism professes to present us with a "slice of life." But one should recognize that it is an artistic method and convention like any other. Romantic art could, without offending its readers, use coincidences, improbabilities, and even impossibilities, which were not, theoretically at least, tolerated in realistic art. Ibsen, for instance, avoided many older conventions of the stage: asides, soliloquies, eavesdropping, sudden unmotivated appearances of new characters, and so on; but his dramas have their own marked conventions, which seem today almost as "unnatural" as those of the romantics. Realistic theories of literature cannot be upheld in their literal sense; objective and impersonal truth is unobtainable, at least in art, since all art is a "making," a creating of a world of symbols which differs radically from the world which we call reality. The value of realism lies in its negation of the conventions of romanticism, its expansion of the themes of art, and its new demonstration (never forgotten by artists) that literature has to deal also with its time and society and has, at its best, an insight into reality (not only social reality) which is not necessarily identical with that of science. Many of the great writers make us "realize" the world of their time, evoke an imaginative picture of it which seems truer and will last longer than that of historians and sociologists. But this achievement is due to their imagination and their art, or craft, two requisites which realistic theory tended to forget or minimize.

When we observe the actual practice of the great realistic

writers of the nineteenth century, we notice a sharp contradiction between theory and practice, and an independent evolution of the art of the novel which is obscured for us if we pay too much attention to the theories and slogans of the time, even those that the authors themselves propounded. Flaubert, the high priest of a cult of "art for art's sake," the most consistent advocate of absolute objectivity, was actually, at least in a good half of his work, a writer of romantic fantasies of blood and gold, flesh and jewels. There is some truth in his saying that Madame Bovary is himself, for in the drab story of a provincial adulteress he castigated his own romanticism and romantic dreams.

So too with Dostoevsky. Although some of his settings resemble those of the "grime novel," he is actually a writer of high tragedy, of a drama of ideas in which ordinary reality is transformed into a symbol of the spiritual world. His technique is closely associated with Balzac's (it is significant that his first publication was a translation of Balzac's *Eugénie Grandet*) and thus with many devices of the sensational melodramatic novel of French romanticism. Tolstoy's art is more concretely real than that of any of the other great masters mentioned, yet he is, at the same time, the most personal and even literally autobiographical author in the history of the novel—a writer, besides, who knows nothing of detachment toward social and religious problems, but frankly preaches his own very peculiar religion. And if we turn to Ibsen,

we find essentially the same situation. Ibsen began as a writer of historical and fantastic dramas and slowly returned to a style which is fundamentally symbolist. All his later plays are organized by symbols, from the duck of *The Wild Duck* (1884) to the white horses in *Rosmersholm* (1886) and the tower in *The Master Builder* (1892). Even Zola, the propounder of the most scientific theory, was in practice a novelist who used the most extreme devices of melodrama and symbolism. In *Germinal* (1885), his novel of mining, the mine is the central symbol, alive as an animal, heaving, breathing. It would be an odd reader who could find literal truth in the final catastrophe of the cave-in or even in such "naturalistic" scenes as a dance where the beer oozes from the nostrils of the drinkers.

One could assert, in short, that all the great realists were at bottom romanticists, but it is probably wiser to conclude that they were simply artists who created worlds of imagination and knew (at least instinctively) that in art one can say something about reality only through symbols. The attempts at documentary art, at mere reporting and transcribing, are today forgotten.

FLAUBERT, MADAME BOVARY

Flaubert's novel, *Madame Bovary* (1856), is deservedly considered the showpiece of French realism. It would be impossible to find a novel, certainly before Flaubert, in which humble persons in a humble setting are treated with such seriousness, restraint, verisimilitude, and imaginative clarity. At first sight, *Madame Bovary* is a solidly documented and clearly visualized account of life in a village of the French province of Normandy sometime in the forties of the last century. We meet a whole spectrum of social types found in such a time and place: the doctor (actually a "health officer" with a lower degree), a pharmacist, a storekeeper, a notary and his clerk, a tax collector, a woman innkeeper and her stableboy, the priest and his sacristan, a neighboring landowner, and a farmer. We are told the story of a young peasant woman brought up in a convent, who marries a dull man and commits adultery first with a ruthless philanderer and then with a spineless younger man. Overwhelmed by debts concealed from her unsuspecting husband, faced by sudden demands for repayment, disillusioned in love, rebuffed by everybody who might help her, she commits suicide by poisoning herself with arsenic. Nothing seems simpler and more ordinary, and the manner of telling seems completely objective, detached, impersonal. A case is presented which is observed with almost scientific curiosity. The descriptions are obviously accurate, sometimes based on expert knowledge; the clubfoot operation and the effects of arsenic poisoning agree with medical evidence. The setting—the topography of the two villages, the interior of the houses, the inn, the pharmacy, the city of Rouen, the cathedral there, the river landscape, and the particular things and sounds—imprints itself vividly on our memory. Every detail serves its purpose of characterization—from the absurd cap of the schoolboy Charles to the mirror and the crucifix in the deathbed scene; from the sound of Binet's lathe turning out napkin rings to the tap of the stableboy's wooden leg. "The technique of *Madame Bovary* has become the model of all novels" (Albert Thibaudet).

But surely the book could not have kept its grip on modern readers if it were only a superbly accurate description of provincial life in France (as the added subtitle, *Mœurs de province*, suggests). The book transcends its time and place if one thinks of Emma Bovary as the type of the unfulfilled dreamer, as the failed and foiled romanticist, as a female Don Quixote, corrupted by sentimental reading, caught in a trap of circumstance, pitiful and to be pitied in her horrible self-inflicted death.

This central theme has, however, remained ambiguous. What attracted and shocked readers was the uncertainty about the author's attitude toward Emma, particularly at the time of publication when readers were accustomed to being told clearly by addresses and comments what they were to think of the actions and morals of the characters of a novel. *Madame Bovary*, at publication, caused a scandal. The review (*Revue de Paris*) in which it was published serially and the author were hauled into court for immorality and blasphemy and the prosecutor described the book as an incitement to adultery and atheism. In his rebuttal, the defense counsel argued that the novel is rather a highly moral work in which adultery is punished even excessively. Flaubert was acquitted but neither the prosecutor nor the defending attorney interpreted the book correctly. It is neither a salacious novel nor a didactic tract. Some parts of the book are frankly satirical (and thus far from purely objective): The gross village priest who cannot even understand the distress of Emma is flanked by the fussy, shallow, pseudoscientific, enlightened, "progressive" pharmacist Homais. Though they argue and quarrel they are finally reduced to a common level when they eat and snore at the wake next to Emma's corpse. The rightly famous scene of the country fair satirizes and parodies the pompous rhetoric of the officials extolling the glories of agriculture, counterpointing it to the equally platitudinous love talk of Rodolphe and the lowing of the cattle in an amalgam which reduces men and women to a common level of animality. Even Emma is not spared: Her sentimental religiosity, her taste for luxury, her financial improvidence are diagnosed as disguised eroticism. She would not have minded if Rodolphe had drawn a pistol against her husband. In her desperate search for escape she asks Léon to steal for her. In the last attempt to get money she is ready to sell herself. She is indifferent to her child, deceitful even in small matters. Her longing for sensual satisfaction becomes, in the scenes with Léon in the hotel at Rouen, frantic and corrupt. The author weighed the scales against her: She married an excessively stupid and insensitive man; she met two callous lovers; she is tricked by a merciless usurer; she is utterly alone at last. When Charles meeting Rodolphe after her death and after he had discovered her infidelities tells him, ineptly, awkwardly: "It was the fault of destiny," the author expressly approves of this saying. The novel conveys a sense of inexorable determinism, of the vanity of dreaming, of the impossibility of escape from one's nature and station. It conveys a sense of despair, of man's and woman's alienation in an incomprehensible universe but also a hatred for all the stupidity, mediocrity and baseness of people there and everywhere. (Flaubert called them "bourgeois," but included the proletarian masses in his contempt). Emma is pitied because she has, at least, a spark of discontent, the yearning to escape the cage of her existence. But baseness triumphs and the book ends with a sudden change to the present tense: "Homais has just received the cross of the Legion of Honor."

This sense of the inexorable, the fatal, the inescapable is secured also by the precision and firmness of Flaubert's style and the carefully planned architectonics of his composition. If we mean by style the systematic exploitation of the syntactical and lexical possibilities of a language we must class Flaubert with the great stylists: the exact descriptive epithet, the one right word (*le mot juste*) even when he uses the most trivial cliché or the most recondite scientific term coheres with the skillful modulations and rhythms of the sentences, the organization of the paragraphs and the divisions of the sections which are grouped around a series of pictorial scenes: the schoolroom, the rustic wedding, the ball, the visit to the priest, the country fair, the ride in the woods, the clubfoot operation, the opera, the cathedral, the cab ride, the deathbed, to mention only the most memorable.

Madame Bovary is constantly cited as an example for the handling of narrative perspective. The story begins in the schoolroom ostensibly told by a schoolfellow (the word "we" is used in the first pages); it shifts then to the narration of an omniscient author and, off and on, narrows to the point of view of Emma. Much is seen only through her eyes, but one cannot say that the author identifies with her or enters her mind sympathetically. He keeps his distance and on occasion conveys his own opinion. He is not averse even to moral judgments: He speaks of Emma's hardhearted and tightfisted peasant nature (p. 529), he refers to her corruption (p. 622), and Rodolphe is several times condemned for his brutality and cynicism (pp. 575, 620, 708). In the description of extreme unction (p. 719) the author pronounces solemnly his forgiveness (which he suggests would be also God's) for her coveting all worldly goods, her greediness "for the warm breeze and scents of love," and even her sensuality and lust. But mostly Flaubert depicts the scenes by simple description or reproduction of speech or imagined silent reflections. Things and people become at times symbolic even in

an obtrusive way: the wedding bouquet, the plate of boiled beef, and the apparition of the blind beggar who turns up conveniently at the hour of Emma's death. Much is said about her which she could not have observed herself. The famous saying "Madame Bovary c'est moi" cannot be traced back to an earlier date than 1909 when it is reported on distant hearsay in René Descharmes, *Flaubert avant 1857* (p. 103). There are dozens of passages in the letters during the composition of *Madame Bovary* which express Flaubert's distaste for the "vulgarity of his subject," "the fetid smell of the milieu," and his opinion of Emma Bovary as "a woman of false poetry and false sentiments." Usually he defends his choice of theme as a "prodigious *tour de force*," as "an act of crude will power," as "a deliberate made-up thing" though we suspect him sometimes of exaggerating his efforts in order to impress his correspondent in Paris, a facile and prolific novelist and poetess, Louise Colet.

Still, the saying "Madame Bovary c'est moi" has been widely quoted and accepted because it contains a kernel of truth. In Emma, Flaubert combats his own vices of daydreaming, romanticism, exoticism, of which he thought he could cure himself by writing this antiromantic book. But the identification with Emma distracts us from noticing Flaubert's deepseated sympathies with the slowwitted, abused, but honest and loving Charles who rightly opens and closes the book and for the other good people: Emma's father, the farmer Rouault, kind and distressed by all he could not foresee; Justin, the pharmacist's apprentice adoring Emma from afar, praying on her grave; the clubfoot stableboy tortured and exploited for a dream of medical reputation; poor neglected Berthe sent to the cotton mill; the old peasant woman at the fair who for fifty-four years of service got a medal worth twenty-five francs; and even the blind beggar with his horrible skin disease. Moreover, there is the admirable Dr. Lavrière who appears fleetingly like an apparition from a saner, loftier world of good sense and professional devotion. Thus it seems unjust of Martin Turnell to say that the novel is "an onslaught on the whole basis of human feeling and on all spiritual and moral values."

In Flaubert's mind, the novel was also an assertion of the redeeming power of art. His long struggle with its composition, which took him more than five years of grinding drudgery: five days in which he had written a single page, five or six pages in a week, twenty-five pages in six weeks, thirteen pages in seven weeks, a whole night spent in hunting for the right adjective; the ruthless pruning to which he subjected his enormous manuscript, eliminating many fine touches, similes, metaphors, and descriptions of elusive mental states (as a study of the manuscripts has shown) were to him a victory of art over reality, a passionate search for Beauty, which he knew to be an illusion. But one wonders whether the conflict of Flaubert's scientific detachment and cruel observation with the intense adoration of beauty, the thirst for calcu-

lated purity and structure, for "style" as perfection, can be resolved. He tried to achieve this synthesis in *Madame Bovary*. Watching this struggle between heterogeneous elements, and even opposites, should explain some of the fascination of the book.

An explanation of the plot and the stage business is needed to understand properly the performance in *Madame Bovary* of the opera *Lucia di Lammermoor*, which occurs on pages 642–48 of this text. The French libretto by Alp. Royer and Gust. Vaez[1] (published in Brussels in 1839) must be consulted, as it differs greatly from the original Italian libretto by Salvatore Cammarano and resembles only distantly the novel by Walter Scott. The story is one of family hatred: Edgar, the owner of the castle of Ravenswood in the Scottish Highlands, has been expelled by Lord Henry Ashton who had killed his father. He is in hiding as an outlaw. He loves and is loved clandestinely by Lucy, Lord Henry's sister. The opera opens with a hunting scene on the grounds of Ravenswood castle where Henry, his forester called Gilbert (Normanno in the Italian), and other followers comb the grounds for traces of a mysterious stranger whom they suspect to be the outcast Edgar. They are joined by Lord Arthur who is a suitor for Lucy's hand and is favored by her brother as he can save him from financial ruin. Arthur declares his love for Lucy (no such scene is in the Italian). Lucy in the next scene prepares to meet Edgar in a secluded spot; she gives a purse to Gilbert whom she believes to be

1. A pseudonym of J. N. G. Van Niewenhuysen.

her friend though Gilbert is actually scheming with Lord Henry against her. (The scene is not in the Italian original.) Then Lucy is left alone and sings a cavatina beginning: "Que n'avons-nous des ailes." Edgar appears then, played by Lagardy, a fictional tenor. He tells of his hatred for Lucy's brother because of the death of his father. He had sworn vengeance but is ready to forget it in his love for her. Edgar has to leave on a mission to France but in parting the lovers pledge their troth and exchange rings. The stretto contains the words, "Une fleur pour ma tombe," "donne une larme à l'exilé," phrases alluded to in Flaubert's account.

Charles is so obtuse that he thinks that Edgar is torturing Lucy, and Emma has to tell him that he is her lover. Charles protests that he heard him vowing vengeance on her family. He had heard him saying: "J'ai juré vengeance et guerre." Charles has also heard Lord Arthur say, "J'aime Lucie et m'en crois aimé," and has seen Lord Arthur going off with her father arm in arm. But Charles obviously takes her brother Henry for her father.

The second act begins with Gilbert telling his master Henry that he slipped Lucy's ring from the sleeping Edgar, had made a copy and will produce it in order to convince Lucy of Edgar's faithlessness. Charles mistakes the false ring which is shown Lucy for a love gift sent by Edgar. The business with the ring replaced an analogous deception with forged letters in the Italian libretto. Lucy appears dressed for

the wedding with Lord Arthur, unhappily, resisting and imploring, reminding Emma of her own wedding day and the contrast with her false joy soon turned to bitterness. Brandishing a sword Edgar suddenly returns voicing his indignation. There follows a sextet (Lucy, Henry, Edgar, Raimondo the minister, Arthur, Gilbert) which suggests to Emma her desire to flee and to be carried off as Edgar wants to carry off Lucy. But the marriage contract has been signed and Edgar curses her. The third act does not interest Emma any more as Léon has appeared in the interval. She does not care for the scene between Lord Henry and his retainer (called here "servant") Gilbert who introduces a disguised stranger, Edgar of course. The duet between Henry Lord Ashton and Edgar reaffirms their mutual hatred. The mad scene follows. Lucy flees the marriage chamber; she has stabbed her husband and gone mad. She dreams of Edgar and dies. The great aria which was considered the climax of coloratura singing was lost on Emma absorbed in Léon.

One must assume that Flaubert had the French libretto in front of him or remembered its wordings and stage business accurately.[2] A modern reader who knows the Italian libretto from recordings may be puzzled by the discrepancies, and ascribe to Flaubert's imagination or confused memory what is actually an accurate description of the French version.

DOSTOEVSKY, NOTES FROM UNDERGROUND

Dostoevsky, like every great writer, can be approached in dif-

2. Flaubert had seen the opera first in Rouen in 1840 and again in Constantinople in November 1850.

ferent ways and read on different levels. We can try to understand him as a religious philosopher, a political commentator, a psychologist, and a novelist, and if we know much about his fascinating and varied life, we can interpret his works as biographical.

The biographical interpretation is the one that has been pushed furthest. The lurid crimes of Dostoevsky's characters (such as the rape of a young girl) have been ascribed to him, and all his novels have been studied as if they constituted a great personal confession. Dostoevsky certainly did use many of his experiences in his books (as every writer does): he several times described the feelings of a man facing a firing squad as he himself faced it on December 22, 1849, only to be reprieved at the last moment. His writings also reflect his years in Siberia: four years working in a loghouse, in chains, as he describes it in an oddly impersonal book, *Memoirs from the House of the Dead* (1862), and six more years as a common soldier on the borders of Mongolia, in a small, remote provincial town. Similarly, he used the experience of his disease (epilepsy), ascribing great spiritual significance to the ecstatic rapture preceding the actual seizure. He assigned his disease to both his most angelic "good" man, the "Idiot," Prince Myshkin, and his most diabolical, inhuman figure, the cold-blooded unsexed murderer of the old Karamazov, the flunky Smerdyakov. Dostoevsky also used something of his experiences in Germany, where in the 1860's he succumbed to a passion for gambling which he over-

came only much later, during his second marriage. The short novel *The Gambler* (1866) gives an especially vivid account of this life and its moods.

There are other autobiographical elements in Dostoevsky's works, but it seems a gross misunderstanding of his methods and the procedures of art in general to conclude from his writings (as Thomas Mann has done) that he was a "saint and criminal" in one. Dostoevsky, after all, was an extremely hard worker who wrote and rewrote some twenty volumes. He was a novelist who employed the methods of the French sensational novel; he was constantly on the lookout for the most striking occurrences —the most shocking crimes and the most horrible disasters and scandals—because only in such fictional situations could he exalt his characters to their highest pitch, bringing out the clash of ideas and temperaments, revealing the deepest layers of their souls. But these fictions cannot be taken as literal transcripts of reality and actual experience.

Whole books have been written to explain Dostoevsky's religious philosophy and conception of man. The Russian philosopher Berdayev concludes his excellent study by saying, "So great is the value of Dostoevsky that to have produced him is by itself sufficient justification for the existence of the Russian people in the world." But there is no need for such extravagance. Dostoevsky's philosophy of religion is rather a personal version of extreme mystical Christianity, and assumes flesh and blood only in the context of the novels. Reduced to the bare bones of abstract propositions, it amounts to saying that man is fallen but is free to choose between evil and Christ. And choosing Christ means taking upon oneself the burden of humanity in love and pity, since "everybody is guilty for all and before all." Hence in Dostoevsky there is tremendous stress on personal freedom of choice, and his affirmation of the worth of every individual is combined, paradoxically, with an equal insistence on the substantial identity of all men, their equality before God, the bond of love which unites them.

Dostoevsky also develops a philosophy of history, with practical political implications, based upon this point of view. According to him, the West is in complete decay; only Russia has preserved Christianity in its original form. The West is either Catholic—and Catholicism is condemned by Dostoevsky as an attempt to force salvation by magic and authority—or bourgeois, and hence materialistic and fallen away from Christ; or socialist, and socialism is to Dostoevsky identical with atheism, as it dreams of a utopia in which man would not be free to choose even at the expense of suffering. Dostoevsky—who himself had belonged to a revolutionary group and come into contact with Russian revolutionaries abroad—had an extraordinary insight into the mentality of the Russian underground. In *The Possessed* (1871-1872) he gave a lurid satiric picture of these would-be saviors of Russia and mankind. But while he was afraid of the revolution, Dostoevsky himself hoped and prophesied that Russia would save Europe from the dangers of commu-

nism, as Russia alone was the uncorrupted Christian land. Put in terms of political propositions (as Dostoevsky himself preached them in his journal, *The Diary of a Writer*, 1876-1881), what he propounds is a conservative Russian nationalism with messianic hopes for Russian Christianity. It is hard to imagine a political creed more remote from present-day realities.

When translated into abstractions, Dostoevsky's psychology is as unimpressive as his political theory. It is merely a derivative of theories propounded by German writers about the unconscious, the role of dreams, the ambivalence of human feelings. What makes it electric in the novels is his ability to dramatize it in scenes of sudden revulsions, in characters who in today's terminology would be called split personalities, in people twisted by isolation, lust, humiliation, and resentment. The dreams of Raskolnikov may be interpreted according to Freudian psychology, but to the reader without any knowledge of science they are comprehensible in their place in the novel and function as warnings and anticipations.

Dostoevsky is first of all an artist—a novelist who succeeded in using his ideas (many old and venerable, many new and fantastic) and psychological insights for the writing of stories of absorbing interest. As an artist, Dostoevsky treated the novel like a drama, constructing it in large, vivid scenes which end with a scandal or a crime or some act of violence, filling it with unforgettable "stagelike" figures torn by great passions and swayed by great ideas. Then he set this world in an environment of St. Petersburg slums, or of towns, monasteries, and country houses, all so vividly realized that we forget how the setting, the figures, and the ideas melt together into one cosmos of the imagination only remotely and obliquely related to any reality of nineteenth-century Russia. We take part in a great drama of pride and humility, good and evil, in a huge allegory of man's search for God and himself. We understand and share in this world because it is not merely Russia in the nineteenth century, where people could hardly have talked and behaved as Dostoevsky's people do, but a myth of humanity, universalized as all art is.

Notes from Underground (1864) precedes the four great novels, *Crime and Punishment* (1866), *The Idiot* (1868), *The Possessed*, and *The Brothers Karamazov* (1880). The *Notes* can be viewed as a prologue, an introduction to the cycle of the four great novels, an anticipation of the mature Dostoevsky's method and thought. Though it cannot compare in dramatic power and scope with these, the story has its own peculiar and original artistry. It is made up of two parts, at first glance seemingly independent: the monologue of the Underground man and the confession which he makes about himself, called "À Propos of the Wet Snow." The monologue, though it includes no action, is dramatic—a long address to an imaginary hostile reader, whom the Underground man ridicules, defies, jeers at, but also flatters. The confession is an autobiographical reminiscence of the Underground man. It de-

scribes events which occurred long before the delivery of the monologue, but it functions as a confirmation in concrete terms of the self-portrait drawn in the monologue and as an explanation of the isolation of the hero.

The narrative of the confession is a comic variation on the old theme of the rescue of a fallen woman from vice, a seesaw series of humiliations permitting Dostoevsky to display all the cruelty of his probing psychology. The hero, out of spite and craving for human company, forces himself into the company of former schoolfellows and is shamefully humiliated by them. He reasserts his ego (as he cannot revenge himself on them) in the company of a humble prostitute by impressing her with florid and moving speeches, which he knows to be insincere, about her horrible future. Ironically, he converts her, but when she comes to him and surprises him in a degrading scene with his servant, he humiliates her again. When, even then, she understands and forgives and thus shows her moral superiority, he crowns his spite by deliberately misunderstanding her and forcing money on her. She is the moral victor and the Underground man returns to his hideout to jeer at humanity. It is hard not to feel that we are shown a tortured and twisted soul almost too despicable to elicit our compassion.

Still it would be a complete misunderstanding of Dostoevsky's story to take the philosophy expounded jeeringly in the long monologue of the first part merely as the irrational railings of a sick soul. The Underground man, though abject and spiteful, represents not only a specific Russian type of the time —the intellectual divorced from the soil and his nation—but also modern humanity, even Everyman, and, strangely enough, even the author, who through the mouth of this despicable character, as through a mask, expresses his boldest and most intimate convictions. In spite of all the exaggerated pathos, wild paradox, and jeering irony used by the speaker, his self-criticism and his criticism of society and history must be taken seriously and interpreted patiently if we are to extract the meaning accepted by Dostoevsky.

The Underground man is the hyperconscious man who examines himself as if in a mirror, and sees himself with pitiless candor. His very self-consciousness cripples his will and poisons his feelings. He cannot escape from his ego; he knows that he has acted badly toward the girl but at the same time he cannot help acting as he does. He knows that he is alone, that there is no bridge from him to humanity, that the world is hostile to him, and that he is being humiliated by everybody he meets. But though he resents the humiliation, he cannot help courting it, provoking it, and liking it in his perverse manner. He understands (and knows from his own experience) that man is not good but enjoys evil and destruction.

His self-criticism widens, then, into a criticism of the assumptions of modern civilization, of nineteenth-century optimism about human nature and progress, of utilitarianism, and of all kinds of utopias. It is possible to identify definite allusions to a contemporary novel by a radical socialist and revolutionary, Chernyshevsky, entitled *What Shall We Do?* (1863), but we do not need to know the exact target of Dostoevsky's satire to recognize what he attacks: the view that man is good, that he always seeks his enlightened self-interest, that science propounds immutable truths, and that a paradise on earth will be just around the corner once society is reformed along scientific lines. In a series of vivid symbols these assumptions are represented, parodied, exposed. Science says that "twice two makes four" but the Underground man laughs that "twice two makes five is sometimes a very charming thing too." Science means to him (and to Dostoevsky) the victory of the doctrine of fatality, of iron necessity, of determinism, and thus finally of death. Man would become an "organ-stop," a "piano-key," if deterministic science were valid.

Equally disastrous are the implications of the social philosophy of liberalism and of socialism (which Dostoevsky considers its necessary consequence). Man, in this view, need only follow his enlightened self-interest, need only be rational, and he will become noble and good and the earth will be a place of prosperity and peace. But the Underground man knows that this conception of man is entirely false. What if mankind does not follow, and never will follow, its own enlightened self-interest, is consciously and purposely irrational, even bloodthirsty and evil? History seems to the Underground man to speak a clear language: ". . . civilization has made mankind if not more bloodthirsty, at least more vilely, more loathsomely bloodthirsty." Man wills the irrational and evil because he does not want to become an organ-stop, a piano key, because he wants to be left with the freedom to choose between good and evil. This freedom of choice, even at the expense of chaos and destruction, is what makes him man.

Actually, man loves something other than his well-being and happiness, loves even suffering and pain, because he is a man and not an animal inhabiting some great organized rational "ant-heap." The ant-heap, the hen house, the block of tenements, and finally the Crystal Palace (then the newest wonder of architecture, a great hall of iron and glass erected for the Universal Exhibition in London) are the images used by the Underground man to represent his hated utopia. The heroine of *What Shall We Do?* had dreamed of a building, made of cast iron and glass and placed in the middle of a beautiful garden where there would be eternal spring and summer, eternal joy. Dostoevsky had recognized there the utopian dream of Fourier, the French socialist whom he had admired in his youth and whose ideals he had come to hate with a fierce revulsion. But we must realize that the Underground man, and Dostoevsky, despises this "ant heap," this perfectly organized society of robots, in the name of something higher, in the name of freedom. Dostoevsky does not believe that man can achieve freedom and happiness at the same time; he thinks that man can buy happiness only at the expense of freedom, and all utopian schemes seem to him devices to lure man into the yoke of slavery. This freedom is, of course, not political freedom but freedom of choice, indeterminism, even caprice and willfulness, in the paradoxical formulation of the Underground man.

There are hints at a positive solution only in the one section (Section X), which was mutilated by the censor. A letter by Dostoevsky to his brother about the "swine of a censor who let through the passages where I jeered at everything and blasphemed ostensibly" refers to the fact that he "suppressed everything where I drew the conclusion that faith in Christ is needed." In Section XI of the present text (and Dostoevsky never restored the suppressed passages) the Underground man says merely, "I am lying because I know myself that it is not underground that is better, but something different, quite different, for which I am thirsting, but which I cannot find!" This "something . . . quite different" all the other writings of Dostoevsky show to be the voluntary following of Christ even at the expense of suffering and pain.

In a paradoxical form, through the mouth of one of his vilest characters, Dostoevsky reveals in the story his view of man and history—of the evil in man's nature and of the blood and tragedy in history—and his criticism of the optimistic, utilitarian, utopian, progressive view of man which was spreading to Russia from the West during the nineteenth century and which found its most devoted adherents in the Russian revolutionaries. Preoccupied with criticism, Dostoevsky does not here suggest any positive remedy. But if we understand the *Notes* we can understand how Raskolnikov, the murderer out of intellect in *Crime and Punishment*, can find salvation at last, and how Dmitri, the guilty-guiltless parricide of *The Brothers Karamazov*, can sing his hymn to joy in the Siberian mines. We can even understand the legend of the Great Inquisitor told by Ivan Karamazov, in which we meet the same criticism of a utopia (this time that of Catholicism) and the same exaltation of human freedom even at the price of suffering.

TOLSTOY, *THE DEATH OF IVÁN ILYICH*

Tolstoy excited the interest of the West mainly as a public figure: a count owning large estates who decided to give up his wealth and live like a simple Russian peasant—to dress in a blouse, to eat peasant food, and even to plow the fields and make shoes with his own hands. Tragically, this renunciation involved him in a conflict with his wife and family; at the age of eighty-two he left his home and died in a stationmaster's house (at Astápovo, in 1910). By then he had become the leader of a religious cult, the propounder of a new religion. It was, in substance, a highly simplified primitive Christianity which he put into a few moral commands (such as, "Do not resist evil") and from which he drew, with radical consistency, a complete condemnation of modern civilization: the state, courts and law, war, patriotism, marriage, modern art and literature, science and medicine. In debating this Christian anarchism people have tended to forget that Tolstoy established his command of the public ear as a novelist, or they have exaggerated the contrast between the early worldly novelist and the later prophet.

In his youth, Tolstoy served as a Russian artillery officer in the little wars against the mountain tribes of the Caucasus and in the Crimean War against the English and French. His reputation in Russia was at first based on his war stories. In 1862 he married and settled down on his estate, Yásnaya Polyána, where he wrote his enormous novel *War and Peace* (1865-1869). The book made him famous in Russia but was not translated into English until long afterward. Superficially, *War and Peace* is a historical novel about the Napoleonic invasion of Russia in 1812, a huge swarming epic of a nation's resistance to the foreigner. Tolstoy himself interprets history in general as a struggle of anonymous collective forces which are moved by unknown irrational impulses, waves of communal feeling. Heroes, great men, are actually not heroes but merely insignificant puppets; the best general is the one who does nothing to prevent the unknown course of Providence. But *War and Peace* is not only an impressive and vivid panorama of historical events but also the profound story—centered in two main characters, Pierre Bezúkhov and Prince Andrey Bolkónsky—of a search for the meaning of life. Andrey finds the meaning of life in love and forgiveness of his enemies. Pierre, at the end of a long groping struggle, an education by suffering, finds it in an acceptance of ordinary existence, its duties and pleasures, the family, the continuity of the race.

Tolstoy's next long novel, *Anna Karénina* (1875-1877), resumes this second thread of *War and Peace*. It is a novel of contemporary manners, a narrative of adultery and suicide. But this vivid story, told with incomparable concrete imagination, is counterpointed and framed by a second story, that of Levin, another seeker after the meaning of life, a figure who represents the author as Pierre did in the earlier book; the work ends with a promise of solution, with the ideal of a life in which we should "remember God." Thus *Anna Karénina* also anticipates the approaching crisis in Tolstoy's life. When it came, with the sudden revulsion he describes in *A Confession* (1879), he condemned his earlier books and spent the next years in writing pamphlets and tracts expounding his religion. Later, he returned to the writing of fiction, now regarded entirely as a means of presenting his creed. The earlier novels seemed to him unclear in their message, overdetailed in their method. Hence Tolstoy tried to simplify his art; he wrote plays with a thesis, stories which are like fables or parables, and one long, rather inferior novel, *The Resurrection* (1899), his most savage satire on Russian and modern institutions.

But surely if we look back on all of Tolstoy's work, we must recognize its complete continuity. From the very beginning Tolstoy was a Rousseauist. As early as 1851, when he was in the Caucasus, his diary announced his intention of founding a new, simplified religion. Even as a young man on his estate he had lived quite simply, like a peasant, except for occasional sprees and debauches. He had been horrified by war from the very beginning, though he admired the heroism of the individual soldier and had remnants of patriotic feeling. All his books concern the same theme, the good life, and they all say that the good life lies outside of civilization, near to the soil, in simplicity and humility, in love of one's neighbor. Power, the lust for power, luxury, are always evil.

As a novelist Tolstoy is rooted in the tradition of the older realism. He read and knew the English writers of the eighteenth century, and also Thackeray and Trollope. He did not care for the recent French writers (he was strong in his disapproval of Flaubert) except for Maupassant, who struck him as truthful and useful in his struggle against hypocrisy. Tolstoy's long novels are loosely plotted, though they have large over-all designs. They work by little scenes vividly visualized, by an accumulation of exact detail. Each character is drawn by means of repeated emphasis on certain physical traits, like Pierre's shortsightedness and his hairy, clumsy hands, or Princess Marya's luminous eyes, the red patches on her face, and her shuffling gait. This concretely realized surface, however, everywhere recedes into depths: to the depiction of disease, delirium, and death and to glimpses into eternity. In *War and Peace* the blue sky is the recurrent symbol for the metaphysical relationships of man. Tolstoy is so robust, has his feet so firmly on the ground, presents what he sees with such clarity and objectivity, that one can be easily deluded into considering his dominating quality to be physical, sensual, antithetical to Dostoevsky's spirituality. The contrasts between the two greatest Russian novelists are indeed obvious. While Tolstoy's method can be called epic, Dostoevsky's is dramatic; while Tolstoy's view of man is Rousseauistic, Dostoevsky stresses the fall of man; while Tolstoy rejects history and status, Dostoevsky appeals to the past and wants a hierarchical society, and so on. But these profound differences should not obscure one basic similarity: the deep spirituality of both, their rejection of the basic materialism and the conception of truth propounded by modern science and theorists of realism.

The Death of Iván Ilyich (1886) belongs to the period after Tolstoy's religious conversion when he slowly returned to fiction writing. It represents a happy medium between the early and late manner of Tolstoy. Its story and moral are simple and obvious, as always with Tolstoy (in contrast to Dostoevsky). And it says what almost all of his works are intended to convey—that man is leading the wrong kind of life, that he should return to essentials, to "nature." In *The Death of Iván Ilyich* Tolstoy combines a savage satire on the futility and hypocrisy of conventional life with a powerful symbolic presentation

of man's isolation in the struggle with death and of man's hope for a final resurrection. Iván Ilyich is a Russian judge, an official, but he is also the average man of the prosperous middle classes of his time and ours, and he is also Everyman confronted with disease and dying and death. He is an ordinary person, neither virtuous nor particularly vicious, a "go-getter" in his profession, a "family man," as marriages go, who has children but has drifted apart from his wife. Through his disease, which comes about by a trivial accident in the trivial business of fixing a curtain, Iván Ilyich is slowly awakened to self-consciousness and a realization of the falsity of his life and ambitions. The isolation which disease imposes upon him, the wall of hypocrisy erected around him by his family and his doctors, his suffering and pain, drive him slowly to the recognition of *It*, to a knowledge, not merely theoretical but proved on his pulses, of his own mortality. At first he would like simply to return to his former pleasant and normal life—even in the last days of his illness, knowing he must die, he screams in his agony, "I won't!"—but at the end, struggling in the black sack into which he is being pushed, he sees the light at the bottom. " 'Death is finished,' he said to himself. 'It is no more!' "

All the people around him are egotists and hypocrites: his wife, who can remember only how she suffered during his agony; his daughter, who thinks only of the delay in her marriage; his colleagues, who speculate only about the room his death will make for promotions in the court; the doctors, who think only of the name of the disease and not of the patient; all except his shy and frightened son, Vásya, and the servant Gerásim. Gerásim is a healthy peasant lad, assistant to the butler, but because he is near to nature, he is free from hypocrisy, helps his master to be comfortable, and even mentions death, while all the others conceal the truth from him. The doctors, especially, are shown as mere specialists, inhuman and selfish. The first doctor is like a judge, like Iván himself when he sat in court, summing up and cutting off further questions of the patient (or is it the prisoner?). The satire at points appears ineffectively harsh in its violence, but it will not seem exceptional to those who know the older Tolstoy's general attitude toward courts, medicine, marriage, and even modern literature. The cult of art is jeered at, in small touches, only incidentally; it belongs, according to Tolstoy, to the falsities of modern civilization, alongside marriage (which merely hides bestial sensuality), and science (which merely hides rapacity and ignorance).

The story is deliberately deprived of any element of suspense, not only by the announcement contained in the title but by the technique of the cutback. We first hear of Iván Ilyich's death and see the reaction of the widow and friends, and only then listen to the story of his life. The detail, as always in Tolstoy, is superbly concrete and realistic: he does not shy away from the smell of disease, the physical necessity of using a commode, or the sound of screaming. He can employ the creaking of a hassock as a recurrent motif to point up the comedy of hypocrisy played by the widow and her visitor. He can seriously and tragically use the humble image of a black sack or the illusion of the movement of a train.

But all this naturalistic detail serves the one purpose of making us realize, as Iván Ilyich realizes, that not only Caius is mortal but you and I also, and that the life of most of us civilized people is a great lie because it disguises and ignores its dark background, the metaphysical abyss, the reality of Death. While the presentation of *The Death of Iván Ilyich* approaches, at moments, the tone of a legend or fable ("Iván Ilyich's life had been most simple and most ordinary and therefore most terrible"), Tolstoy in this story manages to stay within the concrete situation of our society and to combine the aesthetic method of realism with the universalizing power of symbolic art.

IBSEN, *HEDDA GABLER*

Ibsen's plays can be viewed as the culmination point of the *bourgeois* drama which has flourished fitfully, in France and Germany particularly, since the eighteenth century, when Diderot advocated and wrote plays about the middle classes, their "conditions" and problems. But his works can also be seen as the fountainhead of much modern drama—of the plays of Shaw and Galsworthy, who discuss social problems, and of Maeterlinck and Chekhov, who have learned from the later "symbolist" Ibsen. After a long period of incubation and experimentation with romantic and historical themes, Ibsen wrote a series of "problem" plays, beginning with *The Pillars of Society* (1877), which in their time created a furor by their fearless criticism of the nineteenth-century social scene: the subjection of women, hypocrisy, hereditary disease, seamy politics, and corrupt journalism. He wrote these plays using naturalistic modes of presentation: ordinary colloquial speech, a simple setting in a drawing room or study, a natural way of introducing or dismissing characters. Ibsen had learned from the "well-made" Parisian play (typified by those of Scribe) how to confine his action to one climactic situation and how gradually to uncover the past by retrogressive exposition. But he went far beyond it in technical skill and intellectual honesty.

The success of Ibsen's problem plays was international. But we must not forget that he was a Norwegian, the first writer of his small nation (its population at that time was less than two million) to win a reputation outside of Norway. Ibsen more than anyone else widened the scope of world literature beyond the confines of the great modern nations, which had entered its community roughly in this order: Italy, Spain, France, England, Germany, Russia. Since the time of Ibsen, the other small nations have begun to play their part in the concert of European literature. Paradoxically, however, Ibsen rejected his own land. He had dreamed of becoming a great national poet, but in 1864 he left his country for voluntary exile in Italy, Germany, and Austria. In exile, he wrote the plays depicting Norwegian society—a stuffy, provincial middle class, redeemed, in Ibsen's eyes, by single upright, even fiery, individuals of initiative and courage.

Ibsen could hardly have survived his time if he had been merely a painter of society, a dialectician of social issues, and a magnificent technician of the theater. Many of his discussions are now dated. We smile at some of the doings in *A Doll's House* (1879) and *Ghosts* (1881). His stagecraft is not unusual, even on Broadway. But Ibsen stays with us because he has more to offer—because he was an artist who managed to create, at his best, works of poetry which, under their mask of sardonic humor, express his dream of humanity reborn by intelligence and self-sacrifice.

Hedda Gabler (1890) surprised and puzzled the large audience all over Europe that Ibsen had won in the 1880's. The play shows nothing of Ibsen's reforming zeal: no general theme emerges which could be used in spreading progressive ideas such as the emancipation of women dramatized in *A Doll's House* (1879), nor is the play an example of Ibsen's peculiar technique of retrospective revelation exhibited in *Rosmersholm* (1886). At first glance it seems mainly a study of a complex, exceptional, and even unique woman. Henry James, reviewing the first English performance, saw it as the picture of "a state of nerves as well as of soul, a state of temper, of health, of chagrin, of despair." Undoubtedly, Hedda is the central figure of the play, but she is no conventional heroine. She behaves atrociously to everyone with whom she comes in contact, and her moral sense is thoroughly defective: she is perverse, ego-tistical, sadistic, callous, even evil and demonic, truly a *femme fatale*. Still, this impression, while not mistaken, ignores an-other side of her personality and her situation. The play is, after all, a tragedy (though there are comic touches) and we are to feel pity and terror. Hedda is not simply evil and perverse. We must imagine her as distin-guished, well-bred, proud, beau-tiful, and even grand in her de-fiance of her surroundings and in the final gesture of her suicide. Not for nothing have great ac-tresses excelled in this role. We must pity her as a tortured, tormented creature caught in a web of circumstance, as a victim, in spite of her lashings-out to dominate and control the fate of those around her.

We are carefully prepared to understand her heritage. She is General Gabler's daughter. Ibsen tells us himself (in a letter to Count Moritz Prozor, 4 Decem-ber 1890) that "I intended to in-dicate thereby that as a personal-ity she is to be regarded rather as her father's daughter than as her husband's wife." She has inher-ited an aristocratic view of life. Her father's portrait hangs in her apartment. His pistols tell of the code of honor and the ready es-cape they offer in a self-inflicted death. Hedda lives in Norway, in the nineteenth century, in a stuffy, provincial, middle-class society, and is acutely, even mor-bidly afraid of scandal. She has, to her own regret, rejected the advances of Eilert, theatrically threatening him with her father's

pistol. She envies Thea for the boldness with which she deserted her husband to follow Eilert. She admires Eilert for his es-capades, which she romanticizes with the recurrent metaphor of his returning with "vine-leaves in his hair." But she cannot break out of the narrow confines of her society. She is not an emancipated woman.

When she is almost thirty, in reduced circumstances, she ac-cepts a suitable husband, Jörgen Tesman. The marriage of con-venience turns out to be a ghastly error for which she can-not forgive herself: Tesman is an amiable bore absorbed in his research into the "Domestic In-dustries of Brabant during the Middle Ages." His expectations of a professorship in his home town turn out to be uncertain. He has gone into debt, even to his guileless old aunt, in renting an expensive house and, supreme humiliation for her, Hedda is with child by him. The dream of luxury, of becoming a hostess, of keeping thoroughbred horses, is shattered the very first day after their return from the prolonged honeymoon which for Tesman was also a trip to rummage around in archives. Hedda is deeply stirred by the return of Eilert, her first suitor. She seems vaguely to think of a new rela-tionship, at least, by spoiling his friendship with Thea. She plays with the attentions of Judge Brack. But everything quickly comes to nought: she is trapped in her marriage, unable and un-willing to become unfaithful to her husband; she is deeply dis-appointed by Eilert's ugly death, saying, "Everything I touch seems destined to turn into something mean and farcical." She fears the scandal which will follow when her role in Eilert's suicide is discovered and she is called before the police; she can avoid it only by coming under the power of Judge Brack, who is prepared to blackmail her with his knowledge of the circumstances. Her plot to destroy Thea and Eilert's brainchild is frustrated by Thea's having preserved notes and drafts which Thea eagerly starts to reconstruct with the help of Tesman. Still, while Hedda is in a terrible *impasse*, her suicide remains a shock, an abrupt, even absurd deed, eliciting the final line from the commonsensical Judge Brack: "Good God—people don't do things like that!" But we must assume that Hedda had pondered suicide long before: the pistol she gave to Eilert implies an unspoken suicide pact. He bungled it; she does it the right way, dying in beauty, shot in the temple and not in the abdomen.

The play is not, however, simply a character study, though Hedda is an extraordinarily complex, contradictory, subtle woman whose portrait, at least on the stage, could not be easily paralleled before Ibsen. It is also an extremely effective, swiftly moving play of action, deftly plotted in its clashes and climaxes. At the end of Act I Hedda seems to have won. The Tesmans, husband and aunt, are put in their place. Thea is lured into making confidences. The scene in Act II in which Hedda appeals to Eilert's pride in his independence and induces him

to join in Judge Brack's party is a superb display of Hedda's power and skill. Act II ends with Eilert going off and the two women left alone in their tense though suppressed antagonism. Act III ends with Hedda alone, burning the precious manuscript about the "forces that will shape our civilization and the direction in which that civilization may develop," an obvious contrast to Tesman's research into an irrelevant past. (Ibsen himself always believed in progress, in a utopia he called "the Third Empire.")

The action is compressed into about thirty-six hours and located in a house where only the moving of furniture (the piano into the back room) or the change of light or costumes indicates the passing of time. Tesman is something of a fool. He is totally unaware of Hedda's inner turmoil, he obtusely misunderstands allusions to her pregnancy, he comically encourages the advances of Judge Brack, he complacently settles down to the task of assembling the fragments of Eilert's manuscript, recognizing that "putting other people's papers into order is rather my specialty." Though he seems amiably domestic in his love for his aunts, proud of having won Hedda, ambitious to provide an elegant home for her, his behavior is by no means above reproach. He envies and fears Eilert, gloats over his bad reputation, surreptitiously brings home the lost manuscript, conceals its recovery from Thea; when Hedda tells of its being burned, he is at first shocked, reacting comically with the legal phrase about "appropriating lost property," but is then easily persuaded to accept it when Hedda tells him that she did it for his sake and completely won over when she reveals her pregnancy. After Eilert's death he feels, however, some guilt and tries to make up by helping in the reconstruction of the manuscript, now that his rival no longer threatens his career. Tesman is given strong speech mannerisms: the frequent use of "what?" which Hedda, commenting at the end on the progress of the work on the manuscript, imitates sarcastically, and the use of "fancy that." His last inappropriate words, "She's shot herself! Shot herself in the head! Fancy that!", lend a grotesque touch to the tragic end. Aunt Juliana belongs with him: she is a fussy, kindly person, proud of her nephew, awed by his new wife, eager to help with the expected baby, but also easily consoled after the death of her sister: "There's always some poor invalid who needs care and attention."

Judge Brack is a "man of the world," a sensualist who hardly conceals his desire to make Hedda his mistress, by blackmail if necessary, and is dismayed when she escapes his clutches: in his easy-going philosophy "people usually learn to accept the inevitable."

The other pair, Eilert Loevborg and Thea Elvsted, are sharply contrasted. Thea had the courage to leave her husband; she is devoted to Eilert and seems to have cured him of his addiction to drink but fears that he cannot

resist a new temptation. Eilert tells Hedda unkindly that Thea is "stupid," and there is some truth to that, inasmuch as she is so easily taken in by Hedda. Her quick settling down to work on the manuscript after Eilert's death suggests some obtuseness, though we must, presumably, excuse it as a theatrical foreshortening.

Eilert, we must assume, is some kind of genius. His book, we have to take on trust, is an important work. We are told that he had squandered an inheritance, had engaged in orgies, and had regaled Hedda with tales of his exploits before she chased him with her pistol. When he comes back to town, ostensibly reformed, dressed conventionally, he immediately starts courting Hedda again. Stung by her contempt for his abstinence, he rushes off to Brack's party, which degenerates into a disgraceful brawl in a house of ill fame. His relapse and the loss of the manuscript destroy his self-esteem and hope for any future. He accepts Hedda's pistol but dies an ignominious, ugly death. We see Eilert mainly reflected in Hedda's imagination as a figure of pagan freedom who, she thinks, has done something noble, beautiful, and courageous in "rising from the feast of life so early." She dies in beauty as she wanted Eilert to die.

This aesthetic suicide must seem to us a supremely futile gesture of revolt. Ibsen always admired the great rebels, the fighters for freedom, but *Hedda Gabler* will appear almost a parodic version of his persistent theme: the individual against society, defying it and escaping it in death.

CHEKHOV, *THE CHERRY ORCHARD*

Chekhov differs sharply from the two giants of Russian literature. His work is of smaller scope. With the exception of an immature, forgotten novel and a travel book, he never wrote anything but short stories and plays. He belongs, furthermore, to a very different moral and spiritual atmosphere. Chekhov had studied medicine, and practiced it for a time. He shared the scientific outlook of his age and had too skeptical a mind to believe in Christianity or in any metaphysical system. He confessed that an intelligent believer was a puzzle to him. His attitude toward his materials and characters is detached, "objective." He is thus much more in the stream of Western realism than either Tolstoy or Dostoevsky, and his affinities with Maupassant (to whom he is related also in technical matters) are obvious. But extended reading of Chekhov does convey an impression of his view of life. There is implied in his stories a philosophy of kindness and humanity, a sense of the unexplainable mystery of life, a sense, especially, of man's utter loneliness in this universe and among his fellow men. Chekhov's pessimism has nothing of the defiance of the universe or the horror at it which we meet in other writers with similar attitudes; it is somehow merely sad, pathetic, and yet also comforting and comfortable.

The Russia depicted in Chekhov's stories and plays is of a later period than that presented by Tolstoy and Dostoevsky. It seems to be nearing its end; there is a sense of decadence and frustration which heralds the approach of the catastrophe. The aristocracy still keeps up a beautiful front, but is losing its fight without much resistance, resignedly. Officialdom is stupid and venal. The Church is backward and narrow-minded. The intelligentsia are hopelessly ineffectual, futile, lost in the provinces or absorbed in their egos. The peasants live subject to the lowest degradations of poverty and drink, apparently rather aggravated than improved since the much-heralded emancipation of the serfs in 1861. There seems no hope for society except in a gradual spread of enlightenment, good sense, and hygiene, for Chekhov is skeptical of the revolution and revolutionaries as well as of Tolstoy's followers.

The plays of Chekhov seem to go furthest in the direction of naturalism, the depiction of a "slice of life" on stage. Compared to Ibsen's plays they seem plotless; they could be described as a succession of little scenes, composed like a mosaic or like the dots on an impressionist painting. The characters often do not engage in the usual dialogue; they speak often in little soliloquies, hardly justified by the situation and they often do not listen to the words of their ostensible partners. They seem alone even in a crowd. Human communication seems difficult and even impossible. There is no clear message, no zeal for social reform; life seems to flow quietly, even sluggishly, until interrupted by some desperate outbreak or even a pistol shot.

Chekhov's last play, *The Cherry Orchard* (composed in 1903, first performed at the Moscow Art Theatre on January 17, 1904) differs, however, from this pattern in several respects. It has a strongly articulated central theme: the loss of the orchard, and it has a composition which roughly follows the traditional scheme of a well-made play. Arrival and departure from the very same room, the nursery, frame the two other acts: the outdoor idyll of Act II and the dance in Act III. Act III is the turning point of the action: Lopakhin appears and announces, somewhat shame-facedly, that he has bought the estate. The orchard was lost from the very beginning—there is no real struggle to prevent its sale—but still the news of Lopakhin's purchase is a surprise as he had no intention of buying it but did so only when during the auction sale a rival seemed to have a chance of acquiring it. A leading action runs its course, and many—one may even argue, too many—subplots crisscross each other: the shy and awkward love affair of the student Trofimov and the gay daughter Anya; the love triangle among the three dependents, Yepikhodov, the unlucky clerk, Dunyasha, the silly chambermaid, and Yasha, the conceited and insolent footman. Varya, the practical, spinsterish stepdaughter, has her troubles with Lopakhin, and Simeonov-Pishchik is beset by the same financial problems as

the owners of the orchard and is rescued by the discovery of some white clay on his estate. The German governess Sharlotta drifts around alluding to her obscure origins and past. There are undeveloped references to events preceding the action on stage: the lover in Paris, the drowned boy Grishá, but there is no revelation of the past as in Ibsen, no mystery, no intrigue.

While the events on the stage follow each other naturally, though hardly always in a logical, causal order, a symbolic device is used conspicuously: In Act II after a pause, "suddenly a sound is heard far off in the distance, as if coming from the sky: It is the sound of a string breaking that dies away sadly." It occurs again at the very end of the play followed by "the sound of an ax striking a tree far away in the orchard." An attempt is made to explain this sound at its first occurrence as a bucket's fall in a far away pit, or as the cries of a heron or an eagle owl, but the effect is weird and even supernatural; it establishes an ominous mood. Even the orchard carries more than its obvious meaning: It is white, drowned in blossoms when the party arrives in the spring; it is bare and desolate in the autumn when the axes are heard cutting it down. "From every leaf and every trunk, generations of human beings are gazing down at you," declaims Trofimov, defining his feeling for the orchard as a symbol of repression and serfdom. For Lyubov Ranevskaya it is an image of her lost innocence and of the happier past, while Lopakhin sees it only as an investment. It seems to draw together the meaning of the play.

But what is this meaning? Can we even decide whether it is a tragedy or a comedy? It has been commonly seen as the tragedy of the downfall of the Russian aristocracy (or more correctly, the landed gentry) victimized by the newly rich, upstart peasantry. One could see the play as depicting the defeat of a group of feckless people at the hand of a ruthless "developer" who destroys nature and natural beauty for profit. Or one can see it as prophesying, through the mouth of the student Trofimov, the approaching end of feudal Russia and the coming happier future. Soviet interpretations and performances lean that way.

Surely none of these interpretations can withstand inspection of the actual text of the play. They all run counter to Chekhov's professed intentions. He called the play a comedy. In a letter of September 15, 1903, he declared expressly that the play "has not turned out as drama but as comedy, in places even a farce" and a few days later (September 21, 1903) he wrote that "the whole play is gay and frivolous." Chekhov did not like the staging of the play at the Moscow Art Theatre and complained of its tearful tone and its slow pace. He objected that "they obstinately call my play a drama in playbill and newspaper advertisements" while he had called it a comedy (April 10, 1904).

No doubt, there are many comical and even farcical characters and scenes in the play. Charlotta with her dog eating nuts, her card tricks, her ventriloquism, her disappearing acts, is a clownish figure. Gaev, the landowner, though "suave and elegant," is a windbag obsessed by his passion for billiards, constantly popping candy into his mouth, telling the waiters in a restaurant about the "decadents" in Paris. Yepikhodov, the clerk, carries a revolver and, threatening suicide, asks foolishly whether you have read Buckle (the English historian) and complains of his ill-luck: a spider on his chest, a cockroach in his drink. Simeonov-Pishchik empties a whole bottle of pills, eats a gallon and a half of cucumbers, quotes Nietzsche supposedly recommending the forging of banknotes and, fat as he is, puffs and prances at the dance ordering the "cavaliers aux genoux." Even the serious characters are put into ludicrous predicaments: Trofimov falls down the stairs; Lopakhin, coming to announce the purchase of the estate, is almost hit with a stick by Varya (and was hit in the original version). Lopakhin, teasing his intended Varya, "moos like a cow." The ball with the Jewish orchestra, the hunting for the galoshes, and the champagne drinking by Yasha in the last act have all a touch of absurdity. The grand speeches, Gaev's addresses to the bookcase and to nature or Trofimov's about "mankind going forward" and "All Russia is our orchard," are undercut by the contrast between the sentiment and the character: Gaev is callous and shallow, the "eternal student" Trofimov never did a stitch of work. He is properly ridiculed and insulted by Lyuboy for his scant beard and his silly professions of being "above love." One can sympathize with Chekhov's irritation at the pervading gloom imposed by the Moscow production.

Still, I believe, we cannot, in spite of the author, completely dismiss the genuine pathos of the central situation and of the central figure, Lyubov Ranevskaya. Whatever one may say about her recklessness in financial matters and her guilt in relation to her lover in France, we must feel her deep attachment to the house and the orchard, to the past and her lost innocence, clearly and unhumorously expressed in the first act on her arrival, again and again at the impending sale of the estate, and finally at the parting from her house: "Oh, my beautiful orchard—my dear sweet orchard! . . . My life, my youth, my happiness, goodbye!" That Gaev, before the final parting, seems to have overcome the sense of loss and even looks forward to his job in the bank and that Lyubov acknowledges that her nerves are better and that she sleeps well testifies to the indestructible spirit of brother and sister, but cannot minimize the sense of loss, the pathos of parting, the nostalgia for happier times. Nor is the conception of Lopakhin simple. Chekhov emphasized, in a letter to Konstantin Stanislavsky who was to play the part, that "Lopakhin is a decent person in the full sense of the word,

and his bearing must be that of a completely dignified and intelligent man." He is not, he says, a profiteering peasant (*kulachok*, October 30, 1903). He admires Lyubov and thinks of her with gratitude. He senses the beauty of the poppies in his fields. Even the scene of the abortive encounter with Varya at the end has its quiet pathos in spite of all its awkwardness and the comic touches such as the reference to the broken thermometer. Firs, the old valet, aged eighty-six, may be grotesque in his deafness and his nostalgia for the good old days of serfdom, but the very last scene when we see him abandoned in the locked-up house surely concludes the play on a note of desolation and even despair.

Chekhov, we must conclude, achieved a highly original and even paradoxical blend of comedy and tragedy or rather of farce and pathos. The play gives a social picture firmly set in a specific historical time: the dissolution of the landed gentry, the rise of the peasant, the encroachment of the city; but it does not propound an obvious social thesis. Chekhov, in his tolerance and tenderness, in his distrust of ideologies and heroics, extends his sympathy to all his characters (with the exception of the crudely ambitious valet Yasha). The glow of his humanity, untrammeled by time and place, keeps *The Cherry Orchard* alive in quite different social and political conditions, as it has the universalizing power of great art.

LIVES, WRITINGS, AND CRITICISM
Biographical and critical works are listed only if they are available in English.

GUSTAVE FLAUBERT

LIFE. Born at Rouen, Normandy, on December 12, 1821, to the chief surgeon of the Hôtel Dieu. Flaubert was extremely precocious: by the age of sixteen he was writing stories in the romantic taste, which were published only after his death. In 1840 he went to Paris to study law (he had received his baccalaureate from the local *lycée*), but he failed in his examinations, and in 1843 suffered a sudden nervous breakdown which kept him at home. In 1846 he moved to Croisset, just outside of Rouen on the Seine, where he made his home for the rest of his life, devoting himself to writing. The same year, in Paris, Flaubert met Louise Colet, a minor poetess and lady about town, who became his mistress. In 1849-1851 he visited the Levant, traveling extensively in Greece, Syria, and Egypt. After his return he settled down to the writing of *Madame Bovary*, which took him five full years. *Madame Bovary* was a great popular success. An attempt was made to suppress it, however, and a lawsuit ensued, charging Flaubert with immorality. In 1857 he was acquitted of this charge. The remainder of his life was uneventful. He made occasional trips to Paris, and one trip, in 1860, to Tunisia to see the ruins of Carthage in preparation for the writing of his novel *Salammbô*. Flaubert died at Croisset on May 8, 1880.

CHIEF WRITINGS. *Madame Bovary* (1856); *Salammbô* (1862); *The Sentimental Education* (*L'Éducation sentimentale,* 1869); *The Temptation of St. Anthony* (*La Tentation de Saint Antoine,* 1874); *Three Tales* (*Trois Contes,* 1877), including "A Simple Heart" ("Un Coeur simple"); *Bouvard and Pécuchet* (*Bouvard et Pécuchet,* a posthumous novel, unfinished, 1881).

BIOGRAPHY AND CRITICISM. Erich Auerbach, "In the Hôtel de la Mole," in *Mimesis: The Representation of Reality in Western Literature,* translated by Willard Trask (1953); Benjamin F. Bart, *Flaubert* (1967); *Madame Bovary and the Critics,* edited by Benjamin F. Bart (1966); Victor Brombert, *The Novels of Flaubert* (1966); *Gustave Flaubert: Madame Bovary. Backgrounds and Sources: Essays in Criticism,* edited by Paul de Man (1965); Raymond D. Giraud, *The Unheroic Hero in the Novels of Stendhal, Balzac, and Flaubert* (1957); *Flaubert: A Collection of Critical Essays,* edited by Raymond D. Giraud (1964); Alison Fairlie, *Flaubert: Madam Bovary* (1962); Henry James, "Gustave Flaubert," in *Notes on Novelists* (1914);

Harry Levin, "Flaubert," in *The Gates of Horn: A Study of Five French Realists* (1963); Percy Lubbock, chapters 5 and 6 in *The Craft of Fiction* (1921); Maurice Nadau, *The Greatness of Flaubert,* translated by Barbara Bray (1972); Georges Poulet, "Flaubert," in *The Metamorphoses of the Circle,* translated by Carley Dawson and Eliott Coleman (1967); Philip Spencer, *Flaubert: A Biography* (1952); Enid Starkie, *Flaubert: The Making of the Master* (1967); Francis Steegmuller, *Flaubert and Madame Bovary* (1939, new ed. 1950); Margaret G. Tillett, *On Reading Flaubert* (1961); Anthony Thorlby, *Gustave Flaubert and the Art of Realism* (1957); Martin Turnell, "Flaubert," in *The Novel in France* (1951).

FYODOR DOSTOEVSKY

LIFE. Fyodor Mikhailovich Dostoevsky, born in Moscow on October 30, 1821. His father was a staff doctor at the Hospital for the Poor. Later he acquired an estate and serfs. In 1839 he was killed by one of his peasants in a quarrel. Dostoevsky was sent to the Military Engineering Academy in St. Petersburg, from which he graduated in 1843. He became a civil servant, a draftsman in the St. Petersburg Engineering Corps, but resigned soon because he feared that he would be transferred to the provinces when his writing was discovered. His first novel, *Poor People* (1846), proved a great success with the critics; his second, *The Double* (1846), which followed immediately, was a failure.

Subsequently, Dostoevsky became involved in the Petrashevsky circle, a secret society of antigovernment and socialist tendencies. He was arrested on April 23, 1849, and condemned to be shot. On December 22 he was led to public execution, but he was reprieved at the last moment and sent to penal servitude in Siberia (near Omsk), where he worked for four years in a stockade, wearing fetters, completely cut off from communications with Russia. On his release in February, 1854, he was assigned as a common soldier to Semipalatinsk, a small town near the Mongolian frontier. There he received several promotions (eventually becoming an ensign); his rank of nobility, forfeited by his sentence, was restored; and he married the widow of a customs official. In July, 1859, Dostoevsky was permitted to return to Russia, and finally, in December, 1859, to St. Petersburg—after ten years of his life had been spent in Siberia.

In the last year of his exile, Dostoevsky had resumed writing, and in 1861, shortly after his return, he founded a review, *Time (Vremya)*. This was suppressed in 1863, though Dostoevsky had changed his political opinions and was now strongly nationalist and conservative in outlook. He made his first trip to France and England in 1862, and traveled in Europe again in 1863 and 1865, in order to follow a young woman friend, Apollinaria Suslova, and to indulge in gambling. After his wife's death in 1864, and another unsuccessful journalistic venture, *The Epoch (Epokha)*, 1864-1865, Dostoevsky was for a time almost crushed by gambling debts, emotional entanglements, and frequent epileptic seizures. He barely managed to return from Germany in 1865. In the winter of 1866 he wrote *Crime and Punishment*, and before he had finished it, dictated a shorter novel, *The Gambler*, to meet a deadline. He married his secretary, Anna Grigoryevna Snitkina, early in 1867 and left Russia with her to avoid his creditors. For years they wandered over Germany, Italy, and Switzerland, frequently in abject poverty. Their first child died. In 1871, when the initial chapters of *The Possessed* proved a popular success, Dostoevsky returned to St. Petersburg. He became the editor of a weekly, *The Citizen (Grazhdanin)*, for a short time and then published a periodical written by himself, *The Diary of a Writer* (1876-1881), which won great acclaim. Honors and some prosperity came to him. At a Pushkin anniversary celebrated in Moscow in 1880 he gave the main speech. But soon after his return to St. Petersburg he died, on January 28, 1881, not yet sixty years old.

CHIEF WRITINGS. *Memoirs from the House of the Dead* (1862); *Notes from Underground* (1864); *Crime and Punishment* (1866); *The Idiot* (1869); *The Possessed* (1871-1872); *The Raw Youth* (1875); *The Brothers Karamazov* (1880).

BIOGRAPHY AND CRITICISM. Monroe C. Beardsley, "Dostoyevsky's Metaphor of the 'Underground,'" *Journal of the History of Ideas*, III (June, 1942), 265-290; Maurice Beebe and Christopher Newton, "Dostoevsky in English: A Checklist of Criticism and Translations" in *Modern Fiction Studies* IV (1958); Nikolay N. Berdayev, *Dostoievsky: An Interpretation* (1934, new ed. 1957); R. P. Blackmur, "Studies in Dostoevsky," in *Eleven Essays in the European Novel* (1964); E. H. Carr, *Dostoevsky, 1821-1881: A New Biography* (1931); Richard Curle, *Characters of Dostoevsky: Studies from Four Novels* (1950); *Fyodor Dostoevsky: Notes from Underground*, edited by Robert G. Durgy, translated by Serge Shishkoff, criticism and analysis (1969); Donald Fanger, *Dostoevsky*

and Romantic Realism (1965); Joseph Frank, "Nihilism and *Notes from Underground*," in *Sewanee Review* LXIX (1961); Sigmund Freud, "Dostoievski and Parricide," in *Partisan Review* XIV (1945), 530-44; Vyacheslav Ivanov, *Freedom and the Tragic Life: A Study in Dostoevsky* (1952); Robert L. Jackson, *The Underground Man in Russian Literature* (1958), and *Dostoevsky's Quest for Form* (1966); Janko Lavrin, *Dostoevski: A Study* (1947); David Magarshack, *Dostoevsky* (1962); Konstantin Mochulsky, *Dostoevsky: Life and Work*, translated by Michael Minihan (1967); Middleton Murry, *Fyodor Dostoevsky: A Critical Study* (1916); Richard Peace, *Dostoevsky: An Examination of the Major Novels* (1971); Ernest J. Simmons, *Dostoevski, The Making of a Novelist* (1940); George Steiner, *Tolstoy or Dostoevsky* (1959); Victor Terras, *The Young Dostoevsky, 1846-1849* (1969); Edward Wasiolek, *Dostoevsky: The Major Fiction* (1964); *Dostoevsky: A Collection of Critical Essays*, edited by René Wellek (1962); Avrahm Yarmolinsky, *Dostoevsky: A Study in His Ideology* (1921), and *Dostoevsky: A Life* (1934); L. A. Zander, *Dostoevsky*, translated by Natalie Duddington (1948); Stefan Zweig, *Three Masters: Balzac, Dickens, Dostoevsky* (1930).

LEO TOLSTOY

LIFE. Born at Yásnaya Polyána, his mother's estate near Tula (about 130 miles south of Moscow), on August 28, 1828. His father was a retired lieutenant colonel; one of his ancestors, the first count, had served Peter the Great as an ambassador. His mother's father was a Russian general in chief. Tolstoy lost both parents early in his life and was brought up by aunts. He went to the University of Kazan between 1844 and 1847, drifted along aimlessly for a few years more, and in 1851 became a cadet in the Caucasus. As an artillery officer he saw action in the wars with the mountain tribes and again, in 1854-1855, during the Crimean War against the French and English. Tolstoy had written fictional reminiscences of his childhood while he was in the Caucasus, and during the Crimean War he wrote war stories which established his literary reputation. For some years he lived on his estate, where he founded and himself taught an extremely "progressive" school for peasant children. He made two trips to western Europe, in 1857 and in 1860-1861. In 1862 he married the daughter of a physician, Sonya Bers, who bore him thirteen children. In the first years of his married life, between 1863 and 1869, he wrote *War and Peace*, and between 1873 and 1877 composed *Anna Karénina*. After this, a religious crisis came over him, which he described in 1879 in *A Confession.* The next years were devoted to the writing of tracts— attacks on orthodoxy, the government, and the cult of art, and elaborations of his own religious creed. Only slowly did Tolstoy return to the writing of fiction. His longest later book was *The Resurrection.* In 1901 Tolstoy was excommunicated. A disagreement with his wife about the nature of the good life and about financial matters sharpened into a conflict over his last will, which finally led to a complete break: he left home in the company of a doctor friend. He caught cold on the train journey south and died in the house of the stationmaster of Astápovo, on November 20, 1910.

CHIEF WRITINGS. *The Cossacks* (1863); *War and Peace* (1865-1869); *Anna Karénina* (1875-1877); *A Confession* (1879); *The Death of Iván Ilyich* (1886); *The Power of Darkness* (1886); *The Kreutzer Sonata* (1889); *Master and Man* (1895); *What Is Art?* (1897); *The Resurrection* (1899); *Hadji Murad* (1896-1904).

BIOGRAPHY AND CRITICISM. John Bayley, *Tolstoy and the Novel* (1962); Isaiah Berlin, *The Hedgehog and the Fox: An Essay on Tolstoy's View of History* (1953); R. F. Christian, *Tolstoy's "War and Peace": A Study* (1962), and *Tolstoy: A Critical Introduction* (1969); Maxim Gorky, *Reminiscences of Tolstoy* (1921); Janko Lavrin, *Tolstoy* (1946); Derrick Leon, *Tolstoy: His Life and Work* (1944); Georg Lukács, "Tolstoy," in *Studies in European Realism,* translated by E. Bone (1950); Thomas Mann, "Goethe and Tolstoy," in *Essays of Three Decades,* translated by H. T. Lowe-Porter (1947); *Tolstoy: A Collection of Critical Essays,* edited by Ralph E. Matlaw (1967); Aylmer Maude, *The Life of Tolstoy* (2 vols, 1908–1910); D. S. Merezhkovsky, *Tolstoy as Man and Artist* (1902); Renato Poggioli, "A Portrait of Tolstoy as Alceste," in *The Phoenix and the Spider* (1957); Philip Rahv, "The Death of Ivan Ilyich and Joseph K." and "Tolstoy: The Green Twig and the Black Trunk," in *Image and Idea* (1949); Theodore Redpath, *Tolstoy* (1960); Ernest J. Simmons, *Leo Tolstoy* (1946), and *An Introduction to Tolstoy's Writings* (1968); Logan Speirs, *Tolstoy and Chekhov* (1971); George Steiner, *Tolstoy or Dostoevsky* (1959); Stefan Zweig, *Adepts in Self-Portraiture* (*Casanova, Stendhal, Tolstoy*), translated by E. and C. Paul (1952).

HENRIK IBSEN

LIFE. Born at Skien, in Norway, on March 20, 1828. His family had sunk into poverty and finally complete bankruptcy. In 1844, at the age of sixteen, Ibsen was sent to Grimstad, another small coastal town, as an apothecary's apprentice. There he lived in almost complete isolation and cut himself off from his family, except for his sister Hedvig. In 1850 he managed to get to Oslo (then Christiana) and to enroll at the university. But he never passed his examinations and in the following year left for Bergen, where he had acquired the position of playwright and assistant stage manager at the newly founded Norwegian Theater. Ibsen supplied the small theater with several historical and romantic plays. In 1857 he was appointed artistic director at the Møllergate Theater in Christiana, and a year later he married Susannah Thoresen. *Love's Comedy* (1862) was his first major success on the stage. Ibsen was then deeply affected by Scandinavianism, the movement for the solidarity of the Northern nations, and when in 1864 Norway refused to do anything to support Denmark in her war with Prussia and Austria over Schleswig-Holstein, he was so disgusted with his country that he left it for what he thought would be permanent exile. After that, Ibsen led a life of wandering. He lived in Rome, in Dresden, in Munich, and in smaller summer resorts, and during this time wrote all his later plays. *The Wild Duck* was written in Gossensass, in the Austrian Alps, in 1884. He paid a visit to Norway in 1885, but returned again to Germany. Only in 1891, when he was sixty-three, did Ibsen return to Christiana for good. He was then famous and widely honored, but lived a very retired life. In 1900 he suffered a stroke which made him a complete invalid for the last years of his life. He died on May 23, 1906, at Christiana.

CHIEF WRITINGS. (All of the works listed are plays.) *A Doll's House* (1879); *Ghosts* (1881); *An Enemy of the People* (1882); *The Wild Duck* (1884); *Rosmersholm* (1886); *The Lady from the Sea* (1888); *Hedda Gabler* (1890); *The Master Builder* (1892).

BIOGRAPHY AND CRITICISM. Eric Bentley, "Wagner and Ibsen: A Contrast," in *The Playwright as Thinker* (1946), and "Ibsen, Pro and Con," in *In Search of Theater* (1959); *Contemporary Approaches to Ibsen,* edited by Alex Bolckmans (1966); Muriel C. Bradbrook, *Ibsen: The Norwegian* (1948); Robert Brustein, "Henrik Ibsen," in *The Theater of Revolt* (1964); Brian W. Downs, *Ibsen: The Intellectual Background* (1946), and *A Study of Six Plays by Ibsen* (1950); *Ibsen: A Collection of Critical Essays,* edited by Rolf Fjelds (1965); Hans Heiberg, *Ibsen: A Portrait of the Artist,* translated by Joan Tate (1969); Orley I. Holtan, *Mythic Patterns in Ibsen's Last Plays* (1970); Theodore Jorgenson, *Henrik Ibsen: A Study in Art and Personality* (1945); G. Wilson Knight, *Ibsen* (1962); Halvdan Koht, *Life of Ibsen*, translated by E. Haugen and N. E. Santiello (2 vols., 1971); Janko Lavrin, *Ibsen: An Approach* (1950); F. L. Lucas, *The Drama of Ibsen and Strindberg* (1962); James W. McFarlane, *Ibsen and the Temper of Norwegian Literature* (1960), and *Discussions of Henrik Ibsen* (1962), and *Henrik Ibsen: A Critical Anthology* (1970); Michael Meyer, *Ibsen: A Biography* (1971); Kenneth Muir, *Last Periods of Shakespeare, Racine, Ibsen* (1961); John Northam, *Ibsen's Dramatic Method: A Study of the Prose Dramas* (1953); George Bernard Shaw, *The Quintessence of Ibsenism* (1891, 3rd enl. ed., 1913); Peter F. D. Tennant, *Ibsen's Dramatic Technique* (1948); Maurice J. Valency, *The Flower and the Castle: An Introduction to Modern Drama* (1963); Hermann J. Weigand, *The Modern Ibsen* (1925); Raymond Williams, *Modern Tragedy* (1966); A. E. Zucker, *Henrik Ibsen: The Master Builder* (1927).

ANTON CHEKHOV

LIFE. Anton Pavlovich Chekhov, born on January 17, 1860, at Taganrog, a small town on the Sea of Azov. His father was a grocer and haberdasher; his grandfather, a serf who had bought his freedom. Chekhov's father went bankrupt in 1876, and the family moved to Moscow, leaving Anton to finish school in his home town. After his graduation in 1879, he followed his family to Moscow, where he studied medicine. In order to earn additional money for his family and himself, he started to write humorous sketches and stories for magazines. In 1884 he became a doctor and published his first collection of stories, *Tales of Melpomene*. In the same year he had his first hemorrhage. All the rest of his life he struggled against tuberculosis. His first play, *Ivanov*, was performed in 1887. Three years later, he undertook an arduous journey through Siberia to the island of Sakhalin (north of Japan) and back by boat through the Suez Canal. He saw there the Russian penal settlements and wrote a moving account of his trip in *Sakhalin Island* (1892). In 1898 his play *The Sea Gull* was a great success at the Moscow Art Theater. The next year he moved to Yalta, in the Crimea, and in 1901 married the actress Olga Knipper. He died on July 2, 1904, at Badenweiler in the Black Forest.

CHIEF WRITINGS. Chekhov's stories, which first appeared in scattered magazines, have been collected in many variously titled volumes. The plays were performed in this order: *Ivanov* (1887); *The Sea Gull* (1896); *Uncle Vanya* (1899); *The Three Sisters* (1901); *The Cherry Orchard* (1904); they have been translated by Constance Garnett, 2 vols., 1924.

BIOGRAPHY AND CRITICISM. W. H. Bruford, *Chekhov and His Russia* (1948) and *Anton Chekhov* (1957); Korney Chukovsky, *Chekhov the Man*, trans. by Pauline Rose (1945); Thomas Adam Eekman, *A. Čechov, 1860-1960. Some Essays* (1960); Oliver Elton, "Chekhov" in *Essays and Addresses* (1939); Francis Fergusson, "Ghosts and The Cherry Orchard," in *The Idea of a Theater* (1949); Anna Heifetz (Sherman), *Chekhov in English: A List of Works by and about Him*, ed. by A. Yarmolinsky (1949); Ronald Hingley, *Chekhov, A Biographical and Critical Study* (1950); *Chekhov: A Collection of Critical Essays*, edited by Robert L. Jackson (1967); David Magarshack, *Chekhov the Dramatist* (1952), and *Chekhov: A Life* (1952); Leon Shestov, *Chekhov and Other Essays*, edited by Sidney Monas (1966); Ernest J. Simmons, *Chekhov: A Biography* (1962); Logan Speirs, *Tolstoy and Chekhov* (1971); L. J. Styan, *Chekhov in Performance: A Commentary on the Major Plays* (1971); Maurice Valency, *The Breaking Spring: The Plays of Anton Chekhov* (1966).

GUSTAVE FLAUBERT
(1821–1880)
Madame Bovary*

[*Editor's Note*. An explanation of the plot and the stage business is needed to understand properly the performance in *Madame Bovary* of the opera *Lucia di Lammermoor*, which occurs on pages 910-16 of this text. The French libretto by Alp. Royer and Gust. Vaez[1] (published in Brussels in 1839) must be consulted, as it differs greatly from the original Italian libretto by Salvatore Cammarano and resembles only distantly the novel by Walter Scott. The story is one of family hatred: Edgar, the owner of the castle of Ravenswood in the Scottish Highlands, has been expelled by Lord Henry Ashton who had killed his father. He is in hiding as an outlaw. He loves and is loved clandestinely by Lucy, Lord Henry's sister. The opera opens with a hunting scene on the grounds of Ravenswood castle where Henry, his forester called Gilbert (Normanno in the Italian), and other followers comb the grounds for traces of a mysterious stranger whom they suspect to be the outcast Edgar. They are joined by Lord Arthur who is a suitor for Lucy's hand and is favored by her brother as he can save him from financial ruin. Arthur declares his love for Lucy (no such scene is in the Italian). Lucy in the next scene prepares to meet Edgar in a secluded spot; she gives a purse to Gilbert whom she believes to be her friend though Gilbert is actually scheming with Lord Henry against her. (The scene is not in the Italian original.) Then Lucy is left alone and sings a cavatina beginning: "Que n'avons-nous des ailes." Edgar appears then, played by Lagardy, a fictional tenor. He tells of his hatred for Lucy's brother because of the death of his father. He had sworn vengeance but is ready to forget it in his love for her. Edgar has to leave on a mission to France but in parting the lovers pledge their troth and exchange rings. The stretto contains the words, "Une fleur pour ma tombe," "donne une larme à l'exilé," phrases alluded to in Flaubert's account.

Charles is so obtuse that he thinks that Edgar is torturing Lucy, and Emma has to tell him that he is her lover. Charles protests that he heard him vowing vengeance on her family. He had heard him saying: "J'ai juré vengeance et guerre." Charles has also heard Lord Arthur say, "J'aime Lucie et m'en crois aimé," and has seen Lord Arthur going off with her father arm in arm. But Charles obviously takes her brother Henry for her father.

The second act begins with Gilbert telling his master Henry that he slipped Lucy's ring from the sleeping Edgar, had made a copy and will produce it in order to convince Lucy of Edgar's faithlessness. Charles mistakes the false ring which is shown Lucy for a love gift sent by Edgar. The business with the rings replaced an analogous deception with forged letters in the Italian libretto. Lucy appears dressed for the wedding with Lord Arthur, unhappily resisting and imploring, reminding Emma of her own wedding day

---

*A substantially new translation by Paul De Man.

1. A pseudonym of J. N. G. Van Niewenhuysen.

and the contrast with her false joy soon turned to bitterness. Brandishing a sword Edgar suddenly returns voicing his indignation. There follows a sextet (Lucy, Henry, Edgar, Raimondo the minister, Arthur, Gilbert) which suggests to Emma her desire to flee and to be carried off as Edgar wants to carry off Lucy. But the marriage contract has been signed and Edgar curses her. The third act does not interest Emma any more as Léon has appeared in the interval. She does not care for the scene between Lord Henry and his retainer (called here "servant") Gilbert who introduces a disguised stranger, Edgar of course. The duet between Henry Lord Ashton and Edgar reaffirms their mutual hatred. The mad scene follows. Lucy flees the marriage chamber; she has stabbed her husband and gone mad. She dreams of Edgar and dies. The great aria which was considered the climax of coloratura singing was lost on Emma absorbed in Léon.

One must asume that Flaubert had the French libretto in front of him or remembered its wordings and stage business accurately.[2] A modern reader who knows the Italian libretto from recordings may be puzzled by the discrepancies, and ascribe to Flaubert's imagination or confused memory what is actually an accurate description of the French version.—R.W.]

Part One

I

We were in class when the headmaster came in, followed by a new boy, not wearing the school uniform, and a school servant carrying a large desk. Those who had been asleep woke up, and every one rose as if just surprised at his work.

The headmaster made a sign to us to sit down. Then, turning to the teacher, he said to him in a low voice:

"Monsieur Roger, here is a pupil whom I recommend to your care; he'll be in the second. If his work and conduct are satisfactory, he will go into one of the upper classes, as becomes his age."

The new boy, standing in the corner behind the door so that he could hardly be seen, was a country lad of about fifteen, and taller than any of us. His hair was cut square on his forehead like a village choir boy; he looked reliable, but very ill at ease. Although he was not broad-shouldered, his short jacket of green cloth with black buttons must have been tight about the armholes, and showed at the opening of the cuffs red wrists accustomed to being bare. His legs, in blue stockings, looked out from beneath yellowish trousers, drawn tight by suspenders. He wore stout, ill-cleaned, hob-nailed boots.

We began reciting the lesson. He listened with all his ears, as attentive as if at a sermon, not daring even to cross his legs or lean on his elbow; and when at two o'clock the bell rang, the master was obliged to tell him to fall into line with the rest of us.

2. Flaubert had seen the opera first in Rouen in 1840 and again in Constantinople in November 1850.

When we came back to work, we were in the habit of throwing our caps on the ground so as to have our hands more free; we used from the door to toss them under the desk, so that they hit against the wall and made a lot of dust: it was the fad of the moment.

But, whether he had not noticed the trick, or did not dare to attempt it, the new boy was still holding his cap on his knees even after prayers were over. It was one of those head-gears of composite order, in which we can find traces of the bear- and the coonskin, the shako, the bowler, and the cotton nightcap; one of those poor things, in fine, whose dumb ugliness has depths of expression, like an imbecile's face. Ovoid and stiffened with whalebone, it began with three circular strips; then came in succession lozenges of velvet and rabbit fur separated by a red band; after that a sort of bag that ended in a cardboard polygon covered with complicated braiding, from which hung, at the end of a long thin cord, small twisted gold threads in the manner of a tassel. The cap was new; its peak shone.

"Rise," said the master.

He stood up; his cap fell. The whole class began to laugh. He stooped to pick it up. A neighbour knocked it down again with his elbow; he picked it up once more.

"Get rid of your helmet," said the master, who liked to joke.

There was a burst of laughter from the boys, which so thoroughly put the poor lad out of countenance that he did not know whether to keep his cap in his hand, leave it on the ground, or put it on his head. He sat down again and placed it on his knee.

"Rise," repeated the master, "and tell me your name."

The new boy articulated in a stammering voice an unintelligible name.

"Again!"

The same sputtering of syllables was heard, drowned by the tittering of the class.

"Louder!" cried the master; "louder!"

The new boy then took a supreme resolution, opened an inordinately large mouth, and shouted at the top of his voice as if calling some one, the word "Charbovari."

A hubbub broke out, rose in *crescendo* with bursts of shrill voices (they yelled, barked, stamped, repeated "Charbovari! Charbovari!"), then died away into single notes, growing quieter only with great difficulty, and now and again suddenly recommencing along the line of a seat from where rose here and there, like a damp cracker going off, a stifled laugh.

However, amid a rain of penalties, order was gradually reestablished in the class; and the master having succeeded in catching the name of "Charles Bovary," having had it dictated to him, spelt out, and re-read, at once ordered the poor devil to go and sit down on the punishment form at the foot of the master's desk. He got up, but before going hesitated.

"What are you looking for?" asked the master.

"My c-c-c-cap," said the new boy shyly, casting troubled looks round him.

"Five hundred verses for all the class!" shouted in a furious voice, stopped, like the *Quos ego*,[1] a fresh outburst. "Silence!" continued the master indignantly, wiping his brow with his handkerchief, which he had just taken from his cap. As to you, Bovary, you will conjugate '*ridiculus sum*' twenty times." Then, in a gentler tone, "Come, you'll find your cap again; it hasn't been stolen."

Quiet was restored. Heads bent over desks, and the new boy remained for two hours in an exemplary attitude, although from time to time some paper pellet flipped from the tip of a pen came bang in his face. But he wiped his face with one hand and continued motionless, his eyes lowered.

In the evening, at study hall, he pulled out his sleeveguards from his desk, arranged his small belongings, and carefully ruled his paper. We saw him working conscientiously, looking up every word in the dictionary, and taking the greatest pains. Thanks, no doubt, to the willingness he showed, he had not to go down to the class below. But though he knew his rules passably, he lacked all elegance in composition. It was the curé of his village who had taught him his first Latin; his parents, from motives of economy, having sent him to school as late as possible.

His father, Monsieur Charles Denis Bartolomé Bovary, retired assistant-surgeon-major, compromised about 1812 in certain conscription scandals, and forced at this time to leave the service, had taken advantage of his fine figure to get hold of a dowry of sixty thousand francs in the person of a hosier's daughter who had fallen in love with his good looks. He was a fine man, a great talker, making his spurs ring as he walked, wearing whiskers that ran into his moustache, his fingers always garnished with rings; he dressed in loud colours, had the dash of a military man with the easy go of a commercial traveller. Once married, he lived for three or four years on his wife's fortune, dining well, rising late, smoking long porcelain pipes, not coming in at night till after the theatre, and haunting cafés. The father-in-law died, leaving little; he was indignant at this, tried his hand at the textile business, lost some money in it, then retired to the country, where he thought he would make the land pay off. But, as he knew no more about farming than calico, as he rode his horses instead of sending them to plough, drank his cider in bottle instead of selling it in cask, ate the finest poultry in his farmyard, and greased his hunting-boots with the fat of his pigs, he was not long in finding out that he would do better

1. Neptune becalming the winds in the *Aeneid* (I.135)

to give up all speculation.

For two hundred francs[2] a year he managed to rent on the border of the provinces of Caux and Picardy, a kind of place half farm, half private house; and here, soured, eaten up with regrets, cursing his luck, jealous of every one, he shut himself up at the age of forty-five, sick of men, he said, and determined to live in peace.

His wife had adored him once on a time; she had loved him with a thousand servilities that had only estranged him the more. Lively once, expansive and affectionate, in growing older she had become (after the fashion of wine that, exposed to air, turns to vinegar) ill-tempered, grumbling, irritable. She had suffered so much without complaint at first, when she had seen him going after all the village harlots, and when a score of bad houses sent him back to her at night, weary, stinking drunk. Then her pride revolted. After that she was silent, burying her anger in a dumb stoicism that she maintained till her death. She was constantly going about looking after business matters. She called on the lawyers, the judges, remembered when notes fell due, got them renewed, and at home ironed, sewed, washed, looked after the workmen, paid the accounts, while he, troubling himself about nothing, eternally besotted in a sleepy sulkiness from which he only roused himself to say nasty things to her, sat smoking by the fire and spitting into the cinders.

When she had a child, it had to be sent out to nurse. When he came home, the lad was spoilt as if he were a prince. His mother stuffed him with jam; his father let him run about barefoot, and, playing the philosopher, even said he might as well go about quite naked like the young of animals. As opposed to the maternal ideas, he had a certain virile idea of childhood on which he sought to mould his son, wishing him to be brought up hardily, like a Spartan, to give him a strong constitution. He sent him to bed without any fire, taught him to drink off large draughts of rum and to jeer at religious processions. But, peaceable by nature, the boy responded poorly to his attempts. His mother always kept him near her; she cut out cardboard pictures for him, told him tales, entertained him with monologues full of melancholy gaiety, chatting and fondling in endless baby-talk. In her life's isolation she transferred on the child's head all her scattered, broken little vanities. She dreamed of high station; she already saw him, tall, handsome, clever, settled as an engineer or in the law. She taught him to read, and even on an old piano she had taught him two or three sentimental ballads. But to all this Monsieur Bovary, caring little for arts and letters, said "It was not worth while. Would they ever have the

2. It is very difficult to transpose monetary values from 1840 into present-day figures, since relationships between the actual value of the franc, the cost of living, and the relative cost of specific items (such as rent, real estate, etc.) have undergone fundamental changes. One would not be too far off the mark by reading present-day dollars for Flaubert's francs; that would show Madame Bovary destroyed, at the end of the book, by an 8,000-dollar debt.

means to send him to a public school, to buy him a practice, or start him in business? Besides, with brashness a man can always make his way in the world." Madame Bovary bit her lips, and the child knocked about the village.

He followed the farm laborers, drove away with clods of earth the ravens that were flying about. He ate blackberries along the hedges, minded the geese with a long switch, went hay-making during harvest, ran about in the woods, played hopscotch under the church porch on rainy days, and at great fêtes begged the beadle to let him toll the bells, that he might hang all his weight on the long rope and feel himself borne upward by it in its swing.

So he grew like an oak; he was strong of hand, ruddy of complexion.

When he was twelve years old his mother had her own way; he began his lessons. The curé took him in hand; but the lessons were so short and irregular that they could not be of much use. They were given at spare moments in the sacristy, standing up, hurriedly, between a baptism and a burial; or else the curé, if he had not to go out, sent for his pupil after the *Angelus*. They went up to his room and settled down; the flies and moths fluttered round the candle. It was close, the child fell asleep, and the good man, beginning to doze with his hands on his stomach, was soon snoring with his mouth wide open. On other occasions, when Monsieur le Curé, on his way back after administering the holy oil to some sick person in the neighborhood, caught sight of Charles playing about the fields, he called him, lectured him for a quarter of an hour, and took advantage of the occasion to make him conjugate his verb at the foot of a tree. The rain interrupted them or an acquaintance passed. All the same he was always pleased with him, and even said the "young man" had a very good memory.

Charles could not go on like this. Madame Bovary took strong steps. Ashamed, or rather tired out, Monsieur Bovary gave in without a struggle, and they waited one year longer, so that the child could take his first communion.

Six months more passed, and the year after Charles was finally sent to school at Rouen. His father took him there towards the end of October, at the time of the St. Romain fair.

It would now be impossible for any of us to remember any thing about him. He was a youth of even temperament, who played in playtime, worked in school-hours, was attentive in class, slept well in the dormitory, and ate well in the refectory. He had for guardian a hardware merchant in the Rue Ganterie, who took him out once a month on Sundays after his shop was shut, sent him for a walk on the quay to look at the boats, and then brought him back to college at seven o'clock before supper. Every Thursday evening he wrote a long letter to his mother with red ink and three wax seals; then he went over his history note-books, or read an old volume of "Anarch-asis"[3] that was lying about the study. When he went for walks he talked to the servant, who, like himself, came from the country.

By dint of hard work he kept always about the middle of the class; once even he got an honor mark in natural history. But at the end of his third year his parents withdrew him from the school to make him study medicine, convinced that he could make it to the bachelor's degree by himself.

His mother chose a room for him on the fourth floor of a dyer's she knew, overlooking the Eau-de-Robec.[4] She made arrangements for his board, got him furniture, table and two chairs, sent home for an old cherry-tree bedstead, and bought besides a small cast-iron stove with the supply of wood that was to warm her poor child. Then at the end of a week she departed, after a thousand injunctions to be good now that he was going to be left to himself.

The course list that he read on the notice-board stunned him: lectures on anatomy, lectures on pathology, lectures on physiology, lectures on pharmacy, lectures on botany and clinical medicine, and therapeutics, without counting hygiene and materia medica—all names of whose etymologies he was ignorant, and that were to him as so many doors to sanctuaries filled with magnificent darkness.

He understood nothing of it all; it was all very well to listen—he did not follow. Still he worked; he had bound note-books, he attended all the courses, never missed a single lecture. He did his little daily task like a mill-horse, who goes round and round with his eyes bandaged, not knowing what work it is grinding out.

To spare him expense his mother sent him every week by the carrier a piece of veal baked in the oven, with which he lunched when he came back from the hospital, while he sat kicking his feet against the wall. After this he had to run off to lectures, to the operation-room, to the hospital, and return to his home at the other end of the town. In the evening, after the poor dinner of his landlord, he went back to his room and set to work again in his wet clothes, that smoked as he sat in front of the hot stove.

On the fine summer evenings, at the time when the close streets are empty, when the servants are playing shuttle-cock at the doors, he opened his window and leaned out. The river, that makes of this quarter of Rouen a wretched little Venice, flowed beneath him, between the bridges and the railings, yellow, violet, or blue. Working men, kneeling on the banks, washed their bare arms in the water. On poles projecting from the attics, skeins of cotton were drying in the air. Opposite, beyond the roofs, spread the pure sky

---

3. *Voyage du jeune Anarchasis en Grèce* (1788) was a popular account of ancient Greece, by Jean-Jacques Barthélemy (1716–1795).

4. Small river, now covered up, that flows through the poorest neighborhood of Rouen, used as a sewer by the factories that border it, thus suggesting Flaubert's description as *"une ignoble petite Venise."*

with the red sun setting. How pleasant it must be at home! How fresh under the beech-tree! And he expanded his nostrils to breathe in the sweet odours of the country which did not reach him.

He grew thin, his figure became taller, his face took a saddened look that made it almost interesting.

Passively, through indifference, he abandoned all the resolutions he had made. Once he missed a lecture; the next day all the lectures; and, enjoying his idleness, little by little he gave up work altogether.

He got into the habit of going to the cafés, and had a passion for dominoes. To shut himself up every evening in the dirty public room, to push about on marble tables the small sheep-bones with black dots, seemed to him a fine proof of his freedom, which raised him in his own esteem. It was beginning to see life, the sweetness of stolen pleasures; and when he entered, he put his hand on the door-handle with a joy almost sensual. Then many things compressed within him expanded; he learned by heart student songs and sang them at gatherings, became enthusiastic about Béranger,[5] learnt how to make punch, and, finally how to make love.

Thanks to these preparatory labors, he failed completely in his examination for his degree of *officier de santé*.[6] He was expected home the same night to celebrate his success.

He started on foot, stopped at the beginning of the village, sent for his mother, and told her all. She excused him, threw the blame of his failure on the injustice of the examiners, encouraged him a little, and took upon herself to set matters straight. It was only five years later that Monsieur Bovary knew the truth; it was old then, and he accepted it. Moreover, he could not believe that a man born of him could be a fool.

So Charles set to work again and crammed for his examination, ceaselessly learning all the old questions by heart. He passed pretty well. What a happy day for his mother! They gave a grand dinner.

Where should he go to practise? To Tostes, where there was only one old doctor. For a long time Madame Bovary had been on the look-out for his death, and the old fellow had barely been packed off when Charles was installed, opposite his place, as his successor.

But it was not everything to have brought up a son, to have had him taught medicine, and discovered Tostes, where he could practise it; he must have a wife. She found him one—the widow of a bailiff at Dieppe, who was forty-five and had an income of twelve

5. Pierre-Jean de Béranger (1780–1857) was an extremely popular writer of songs often exalting the glories of the empire of Napoleon I.

6. The degree of Officier de Santé, instituted during the Revolution, was a kind of second-class medical degree, well below the doctorate. The student was allowed to attend a medical school without having passed the equivalence of the *baccalauréat*. He could only practice in the department in which the diploma had been conferred (Bovary is thus tied down to the vicinity of Rouen) and was not allowed to perform major operations except in the presence of a full-fledged doctor. The diploma was suppressed in 1892.

hundred francs.

Though she was ugly, as dry as a bone, her face with as many pimples as the spring has buds, Madame Dubuc had no lack of suitors. To attain her ends Madame Bovary had to oust them all, and she even succeeded in very cleverly baffling the intrigues of a pork-butcher backed up by the priests.

Charles had seen in marriage the advent of an easier life, thinking he would be more free to do as he liked with himself and his money. But his wife was master; he had to say this and not say that in company, to fast every Friday, dress as she liked, harass at her bidding those patients who did not pay. She opened his letters, watched his comings and goings, and listened at the partition-wall when women came to consult him in his surgery.

She had to have her chocolate every morning, attentions without end. She constantly complained of her nerves, her chest, her liver. The noise of footsteps made her ill; when people went away, solitude became odious to her; if they came back, it was doubtless to see her die. When Charles returned in the evening, she stretched forth two long thin arms from beneath the sheets, put them round his neck, and having made him sit down on the edge of the bed, began to talk to him of her troubles: he was neglecting her, he loved another. She had been warned she would be unhappy; and she ended by asking him for a dose of medicine and a little more love.

II

One night towards eleven o'clock they were awakened by the noise of a horse pulling up outside their door. The maid opened the garret-window and parleyed for some time with a man in the street below. He came for the doctor, had a letter for him. Nastasie came downstairs shivering and undid the locks and bolts one after the other. The man left his horse, and, following the servant, suddenly came in behind her. He pulled out from his wool cap with grey topknots a letter wrapped up in a rag and presented it gingerly to Charles, who rested on his elbow on the pillow to read it. Nastasie, standing near the bed, held the light. Madame in modesty had turned to the wall and showed only her back.

This letter, sealed with a small seal in blue wax, begged Monsieur Bovary to come immediately to the farm of the Bertaux to set a broken leg. Now from Tostes to the Bertaux was a good fifteen miles across country by way of Longueville and Saint-Victor. It was a dark night; Madame Bovary junior was afraid of accidents for her husband. So it was decided the stable-boy should go on first; Charles would start three hours later when the moon rose. A boy was to be sent to meet him, in order to show him the way to the farm and open the gates for him.

Towards four o'clock in the morning, Charles, well wrapped up in his cloak, set out for the Bertaux. Still sleepy from the warmth of his bed, he let himself be lulled by the quiet trot of his horse. When it stopped of its own accord in front of those holes surrounded with thorns that are dug on the margin of furrows, Charles awoke with a start, suddenly remembered the broken leg, and tried to call to mind all the fractures he knew. The rain had stopped, day was breaking, and on the branches of the leafless trees birds roosted motionless, their little feathers bristling in the cold morning wind. The flat country stretched as far as eye could see, and the tufts of trees around the farms seemed, at long intervals, like dark violet stains on the vast grey surface, fading on the horizon into the gloom of the sky. Charles from time to time opened his eyes but his mind grew weary, and sleep coming upon him, he soon fell into a doze wherein his recent sensations blending with memories, he became conscious of a double self, at once student and married man, lying in his bed as but now, and crossing the operation theatre as of old. The warm smell of poultices mingled in his brain with the fresh odour of dew; he heard the iron rings rattling along the curtain-rods of the bed and saw his wife sleeping . . . As he passed Vassonville he came upon a boy sitting on the grass at the edge of a ditch.

"Are you the doctor?" asked the child.

And on Charles's answer he took his wooden shoes in his hands and ran on in front of him.

The *officier de santé,* riding along, gathered from his guide's talk that Monsieur Rouault must be one of the well-to-do farmers. He had broken his leg the evening before on his way home from a Twelfth-night feast at a neighbor's. His wife had been dead for two years. There was only his daughter, who helped him to keep house, with him.

The ruts were becoming deeper; they were approaching the Bertaux. The little farmboy, slipping through a hole in the hedge, disappeared; then he came back to the end of a courtyard to open the gate. The horse slipped on the wet grass; Charles had to stoop to pass under the branches. The watchdogs in their kennels barked, dragging at their chains. As he entered the Bertaux the horse took fright and stumbled.

It was a substantial-looking farm. In the stables, over the top of the open doors, one could see great cart-horses quietly feeding from new racks. Right along the outbuildings extended a large dunghill, smoking at the top, while amidst fowls and turkeys five or six peacocks, the luxury of Cauchois farmyards, were foraging around. The sheepfold was long, the barn high, with walls smooth as a hand. Under the cart-shed were two large carts and four ploughs, with their whips, shafts and harnesses complete, whose fleeces of blue wool were getting soiled by the fine dust that fell from the graneries. The courtyard sloped upwards, planted with trees set out symmetrically, and the chattering noise of a flock of geese was heard near the pond.

A young woman in a blue merino dress with three flounces came to the threshold of the door to receive Monsieur Bovary; she led him to the kitchen, where a large fire was blazing. The servants' breakfast was boiling beside it in small pots of all sizes. Some damp clothes were drying inside the chimney-corner. The shovel, tongs, and the nozzle of the bellows, all of colossal size, shone like polished steel, while along the walls hung many pots and pans in which the clear flame of the hearth, mingling with the first rays of the sun coming in through the window, was mirrored fitfully.

Charles went up to the first floor to see the patient. He found him in his bed, sweating under his bed-clothes, having thrown his cotton nightcap right away from him. He was a fat little man of fifty, with white skin and blue eyes, the fore part of his head bald, and he wore ear-rings. By his side on a chair stood a large decanter of brandy, from which he poured himself out a little from time to time to keep up his spirits; but as soon as he caught sight of the doctor his elation subsided, and instead of swearing, as he had been doing for the last twelve hours, he began to groan feebly.

The fracture was a simple one, without any kind of complication. Charles could not have hoped for an easier case. Then calling to mind the devices of his masters at the bedside of patients, he comforted the sufferer with all sorts of kindly remarks, those caresses of the surgeon that are like the oil they put on scalpels. In order to make some splints a bundle of laths was brought up from the carthouse. Charles selected one, cut it into two pieces and planed it with a fragment of windowpane, while the servant tore up sheets to make bandages, and Mademoiselle Emma tried to sew some pads. As she was a long time before she found her workcase, her father grew impatient; she did not answer, but as she sewed she pricked her fingers, which she then put to her mouth to suck them.

Charles was surprised at the whiteness of her nails. They were shiny, delicate at the tips, more polished than the ivory of Dieppe, and almond-shaped. Yet her hand was not beautiful, perhaps not white enough, and a little hard at the knuckles; besides, it was too long, with no soft inflections in the outlines. Her real beauty was in her eyes. Although brown, they seemed black because of the lashes, and her look came at you frankly, with a candid boldness.

The bandaging over, the doctor was invited by Monsieur Rouault himself to have a bite before he left.

Charles went down into the room on the ground-floor. Knives and forks and silver goblets were laid for two on a little table at the foot of a huge bed that had a canopy of printed cotton with figures representing Turks. There was an odor of iris-root and damp sheets that escaped from a large oak chest opposite the window. On the floor in corners were sacks of flour stuck upright in rows. These were the overflow from the neighboring granary, to which three stone steps led. By way of decoration for the apartment, hanging to a nail in the middle of the wall, whose green paint scaled off from the effects of the saltpeter, was a crayon head of Minerva in a gold frame, underneath which was written in Gothic letters "To my dear Papa."

First they spoke of the patient, then of the weather, of the great cold, of the wolves that infested the fields at night. Mademoiselle Rouault did not at all like the country, especially now that she had to look after the farm almost alone. As the room was chilly, she shivered as she ate. This showed something of her full lips, that she had a habit of biting when silent.

Her neck stood out from a white turned-down collar. Her hair, whose two black folds seemed each of a single piece, so smooth were they, was parted in the middle by a delicate line that curved slightly with the curve of the head; and, just showing the tip of the ear, it was joined behind in a thick chignon, with a wavy movement at the temples that the country doctor saw now for the first time in his life. The upper part of her cheek was rose-coloured. Like a man, she wore a tortoise-shell eyeglass thrust between two buttons of her blouse.

When Charles, after bidding farewell to old Rouault, returned to the room before leaving, he found her standing, her forehead against the window, looking into the garden, where the beanpoles had been knocked down by the wind. She turned around. "Are you looking for something?" she asked.

"My riding crop, if you please," he answered.

He began rummaging on the bed, behind the doors, under the chairs. It had fallen to the ground, between the sacks and the wall. Mademoiselle Emma saw it, and bent over the flour sacks. Charles out of politeness made a dash also, and as he stretched out his arm, at the same moment felt his breast brush against the back of the young girl bending beneath him. She drew herself up, scarlet, and looked at him over her shoulder as she handed him his riding crop.

Instead of returning to the Bertaux in three days as he had promised, he went back the very next day, then regularly twice a week, without counting the visits he paid now and then as if by accident.

Everything, moreover, went well; the patient progressed favorably; and when, at the end of forty-six days, old Rouault was seen trying to walk alone in his "den," Monsieur Bovary began to be looked upon as a man of great capacity. Old Rouault said that he could not have been cured better by the first doctor of Yvetot, or even of Rouen.

As to Charles, he did not stay to ask himself why it was a pleasure to him to go to the Bertaux. Had he done so, he would, no doubt have attributed his zeal to the importance of the case, or perhaps to the money he hoped to make by it. Was it for this, however, that his visits to the farm formed a delightful exception to the barren occupations of his life? On these days he rose early, set off at a gallop, urging on his horse, then got down to wipe his boots in the grass and put on black gloves before entering. He liked seeing himself enter the courtyard, and noticing the gate turn against his shoulder, the cock crow on the wall, the farmboys run to meet him. He liked the granary and the stables; he liked old Rouault, who pressed his hand and called him his saviour; he liked the small wooden shoes of Mademoiselle Emma on the scoured flags of the kitchen—her high heels made her a little taller; and when she walked in front of him, the wooden soles springing up quickly struck with a sharp sound against the leather of her boots.

She always reconducted him to the first step of the porch. When his horse had not yet been brought round she stayed there. They had said "Good-bye"; there was no more talking. The open air wrapped her round, playing with the soft down on the back of her neck, or blew to and fro on her hips her apron-strings, that fluttered like streamers. Once, during a thaw, the bark of the trees in the yard was oozing, the snow melted on the roofs of the buildings; she stood on the threshold, went to fetch her sunshade and opened it. The parasol, made of an iridescent silk that let the sunlight sift through, colored the white skin of her face with shifting reflections. Beneath it, she smiled at the gentle warmth; drops of water fell one by one on the taut silk.

During the first period of Charles's visits to the Bertaux, the younger Madame Bovary never failed to inquire after the invalid, and she had even chosen in the book that she kept on a system of double entry a clean blank page for Monsieur Rouault. But when she heard he had a daughter, she began to make inquiries, and she learnt that Mademoiselle Rouault, brought up at the Ursuline Convent, had received what is called "a good education"; and so knew dancing, geography, drawing, how to embroider and play the piano. That was the last straw.

"So that's why he looks so beaming when he goes to see her," she thought. "That's why he puts on his new waistcoat regardless of the rain. Ah! that woman! that woman!"

And she detested her instinctively. At first she solaced herself by allusions that Charles did not understand, then by casual observations that he let pass for fear of a storm, finally by open apostrophes to which he knew no reply.—Why did he go back to the Bertaux now that Monsieur Rouault was cured and that the bill was still unpaid? Ah! it was because a certain person was there, some one who knew how to talk, to embroider, to be witty. So that was what he liked; he wanted city girls! And she went on:

"Imagine old Rouault's daughter being taken for a city girl! The grandfather was a shepherd and a cousin of theirs barely escaped being sentenced for nearly killing someone in a brawl. Hardly a reason to put on airs, or showing herself in church dressed in silk, like a countess. If it hadn't been for the colza crop last year, the old fellow would have been hard put paying his arrears."

For very weariness Charles left off going to the Bertaux. Héloïse made him swear, his hand on the prayer-book, that he would go there no more, after much sobbing and many kisses, in a great outburst of love. He obeyed then, but the strength of his desire protested against the servility of his conduct; and he thought, with a kind of naïve hypocrisy, that this interdict to see her gave him a sort of right to love her. And then the widow was thin; she had long teeth; wore in all weathers a little black shawl, the edge of which hung down between her shoulder-blades; her bony figure was sheathed in her clothes as if they were a scabbard; they were too short, and displayed her ankles with the laces of her large boots crossed over grey stockings.

Charles's mother came to see them from time to time, but after a few days the daughter-in-law seemed to put her own edge on her, and then, like two knives, they scarified him with their reflections and observations. It was wrong of him to eat so much. Why did he always offer a free drink to everyone who came along? How stubborn of him not to put on flannel underwear!

In the spring it came about that a notary at Ingouville, who managed the widow Dubuc's property, one fine day vanished, taking with him all the money in his office. Héloïse, it is true, still owned, besides a share in a boat valued at six thousand francs, her house in the Rue St. François; and yet, with all this fortune that had been so trumpeted abroad, nothing, excepting perhaps a little furniture and a few clothes, had appeared in the household. The matter had to be gone into. The house at Dieppe was found to be eaten up with mortgages to its foundations; what she had placed with the notary God only knew, and her share in the boat did not exceed three thousand francs. She had lied, the good lady! In his exasperation, Monsieur Bovary the elder, smashing a chair on the stone floor, accused his wife of having caused the misfortune of their son by harnessing him to such a harridan, whose harness wasn't worth her hide. They came to Tostes. Explanations followed. There were scenes. Héloïse in tears, throwing her arms about her husband, conjured him to defend her from his parents. Charles tried to speak up for her. They grew angry and left the house.

But "the blow had struck home." A week after, as she was hanging up some washing in her yard, she was seized with a spitting of blood, and the next day, while Charles had his back turned and was closing the window curtains, she said, "O God!" gave a sigh and fainted. She was dead! What a surprise!

When all was over at the cemetery Charles went home. He

found no one downstairs; he went up to the first floor to their room, saw her dress still hanging at the foot of the alcove; then leaning against the writing-table, he stayed until the evening, buried in a sorrowful reverie. She had loved him after all!

III

One morning old Rouault brought Charles the money for setting his leg—seventy-five francs in forty-sou pieces, and a turkey. He had heard of his loss, and consoled him as well as he could.

"I know what it is," said he, clapping him on the shoulder; "I've been through it. When I lost my poor wife, I went into the field to be alone. I fell at the foot of a tree; I cried; I called on God; I talked nonsense to Him. I wanted to be like the moles that I saw on the branches, their insides swarming with maggots, in short, dead, and an end of it. And when I thought that there were others at that very moment, with their wives in their arms, I struck great blows on the earth with my stick. I almost went out of my mind, to the point of not eating; the very idea of going to a café disgusted me—you wouldn't believe it. Well, very slowly, one day following another, a spring on a winter, and an autumn after a summer, this wore away, piece by piece, crumb by crumb; it passed away, it is gone, I should say it has sunk; for something always remains inside, as we would say—a weight here, at one's heart. But since it is the lot of all of us, one must not give way altogether, and, because others have died, want to die too. You must pull yourself together, Monsieur Bovary. It will pass away. Come and see us; my daughter thinks of you time and again, you know, and she says you are forgetting her. Spring will soon be here. We'll have you shoot a rabbit in the field to help you get over your sorrows."

Charles followed his advice. He went back to the Bertaux. He found all as he had left it, that is to say, as it was five months ago. The pear trees were already in blossom, and Farmer Rouault, on his legs again, came and went, making the farm more lively.

Thinking it his duty to heap the greatest attention upon the doctor because of his sad situation, he begged him not to take his hat off, spoke to him in whispers as if he had been ill, and even pretended to be angry because nothing lighter had been prepared for him than for the others, such as a little custard or stewed pears. He told stories. Charles found himself laughing, but the remembrance of his wife suddenly coming back to him depressed him. Coffee was brought in; he thought no more about her.

He thought less of her as he grew accustomed to living alone. The new delight of independence soon made his loneliness bearable. He could now change his meal-times, go in or out without explanation, and when he was very tired stretch himself at full length on his bed. So he nursed and coddled himself and accepted the consolations that were offered him. On the other hand, the death of his wife had not served him ill in his business, since for a month people had been saying, "The poor young man! what a loss!" His name had been talked about, his practice had increased; and, moreover, he could go to the Bertaux just as he liked. He had an aimless hope, and a vague happiness; he thought himself better looking as he brushed his whiskers before the looking-glass.

One day he got there about three o'clock. Everybody was in the fields. He went into the kitchen, but did not at once catch sight of Emma; the outside shutters were closed. Through the chinks of the wood the sun sent across the flooring long fine rays that were broken at the corners of the furniture and trembled along the ceiling. Some flies on the table were crawling up the glasses that had been used, and buzzing as they drowned themselves in the dregs of the cider. The daylight that came in by the chimney made velvet of the soot at the back of the fireplace, and touched with blue the cold cinders. Between the window and the hearth Emma was sewing; she wore no scarf; he could see small drops of perspiration on her bare shoulders.

After the fashion of country folks she asked him to have something to drink. He said no; she insisted, and at last laughingly offered to have a glass of liqueur with him. So she went to fetch a bottle of curaçoa from the cupboard, reached down two small glasses, filled one to the brim, poured scarcely anything into the other, and, after having clinked glasses, carried hers to her mouth. As it was almost empty she bent back to drink, her head thrown back, her lips pouting, her neck straining. She laughed at getting none, while with the tip of her tongue passing between her small teeth she licked drop by drop the bottom of her glass.

She sat down again and took up her work, a white cotton stocking she was darning. She worked with her head bent down; she did not speak, nor did Charles. The air coming in under the door blew a little dust over the stone floor; he watched it drift along, and heard nothing but the throbbing in his head and the faint clucking of a hen that had laid an egg in the yard. Emma from time to time cooled her cheeks with the palms of her hands, and cooled these again on the knobs of the huge fire-dogs.

She complained of suffering since the beginning of the spring from giddiness; she asked if sea-baths would do her any good; she began talking of her convent, Charles of his school; words came to them. They went up into her bed-room. She showed him her old music-books, the little prizes she had won, and the oak-leaf crowns, left at the bottom of a cupboard. She spoke to him, too, of her mother, of the country, and even showed him the bed in the garden where, on the first Friday of every month, she gathered flowers to put on her mother's tomb. But their gardener understood nothing about it; servants were so careless. She would have dearly liked, if only for the winter, to live in town, although the length of the fine days made the country perhaps even more wearisome in the summer. And, according to what she was saying, her voice was clear, sharp, or, suddenly all languor, lingering out in modulations that ended almost in murmurs as she spoke to herself, now joyous, opening big naïve eyes, then with her eyelids half closed, her look full of boredom, her thoughts wandering.

Going home at night, Charles went over her words one by one, trying to recall them, to fill out their sense, that he might piece out the life she had lived before he knew her. But he never saw her in his thoughts other than he had seen her the first time, or as he had just left her. Then he asked himself what would become of her—if she would be married, and to whom? Alas! old Rouault was rich, and she!—so beautiful! But Emma's face always rose before his eyes, and a monotone, like the humming of a top, sounded in his ears, "If you should marry after all! if you should marry!" At night he could not sleep; his throat was parched; he was thirsty. He got up to drink from the water-bottle and opened the window. The night was covered with stars, a warm wind blowing in the distance; the dogs were barking. He turned his head towards the Bertaux.

Thinking that, after all, he had nothing to lose, Charles promised himself to ask her in marriage at the earliest opportunity, but each time the fear of not finding the right words sealed his lips.

Old Rouault would not have been sorry to be rid of his daughter, who was of no use to him in the house. In his heart he excused her, thinking her too clever for farming, a calling under the ban of Heaven, since one never saw a millionaire in it. Far from having made a fortune, the old man was losing every year; for if he was good at bargaining and enjoyed the dodges of the trade, he was the poorest of growers or farm managers. He did not willingly take his hands out of his pockets, and did not spare expense for his own comforts, liking to eat and to sleep well, and never to suffer from the cold. He liked old cider, underdone legs of mutton, brandied coffee well beaten up. He took his meals in the kitchen, alone, opposite the fire on a little table brought to him already laid as on the stage.

When, therefore, he perceived that Charles's cheeks grew flushed if near his daughter, which meant that he would propose one of these days, he mulled over the entire matter beforehand. He certainly thought him somewhat weak, not quite the son-in-law he would have liked, but he was said to be well-behaved, prudent with his money as well as learned, and no doubt would not make too many difficulties about the dowry. Now, as old Rouault would soon be forced to sell twenty-two acres of his land as he owed a good deal to the mason, to the harnessmaker, and as the shaft of the cider-press wanted renewing, "If he asks for her," he said to himself, "I'll give her to him."

In the early fall Charles went to spend three days at the Bertaux. The last had passed like the others in procrastinating from hour to hour. Old Rouault was seeing him off; they were walking along a dirt road full of ruts; they were about to part. This was the time. Charles gave himself as far as to the corner of the hedge, and at last, when past it . . .

"Monsieur Rouault," he murmured, "I should like to say something to you."

They stopped. Charles was silent.

"Well, tell me your story. Don't I know all about it?" said old Rouault, laughing softly.

"Monsieur Rouault—Monsieur Rouault," stammered Charles.

"I ask nothing better," the farmer went on. "Although, no doubt, the little one agrees with me, still we must ask her opinion. So you get off—I'll go back home. If it is 'yes,' you needn't return because of all the people around, and besides it would upset her too much. But so that you may not be biting your fingernails with impatience, I'll open wide the outer shutter of the window against the wall; you can see it from the back by leaning over the hedge."

And he went off.

Charles fastened his horse to a tree; he ran into the road and waited. Half-an-hour passed, then he counted nineteen minutes by his watch. Suddenly a noise was heard against the wall; the shutter had been thrown back; the hook was still quivering.

The next day by nine o'clock he was at the farm. Emma blushed as he entered, and she gave a little forced laugh to hide her embarrassment. Old Rouault embraced his future son-in-law. The discussion of money matters was put off; moreover, there was plenty of time before them, as the marriage could not decently take place till Charles was out of mourning, that is to say, about the spring of the next year.

The winter passed waiting for this. Mademoiselle Rouault was busy with her trousseau. Part of it was ordered at Rouen, and she made herself slips and nightcaps after fashionplates that she borrowed. When Charles visited the farmer, the preparations for the wedding were talked over; they wondered in what room they should have dinner; they dreamed of the number of dishes that would be wanted, and what should be the entrées.

Emma would, on the contrary, have preferred to have a midnight wedding with torches, but old Rouault could not understand such an idea. So there was a wedding at which forty-three persons were present, at which they remained sixteen hours at table, began again the next day, and even carried a little into the following days.

IV

The guests arrived early in carriages, in one-horse chaises, two-wheeled cars, old open gigs, vans with leather curtains, and the young people from the nearer villages in carts, in which they stood up in rows, holding on to the sides so as not to fall, going at a trot and well shaken up. Some came from a distance of thirty miles, from Goderville, from Normanville, and from Cany. All the relatives of both families had been invited, old quarrels had been patched up and near-forgotten acquaintances written to for the occasion.

From time to time one heard the crack of a whip behind the hedge; then the gates opened, a chaise entered. Galloping up to the foot of the steps, it stopped short and emptied its load. They got down from all sides, rubbing knees and stretching arms. The ladies, wearing bonnets, had on dresses in the town fashion, gold watch chains, pelerines with the ends tucked into belts, or little coloured scarfs fastened down behind with a pin, and that left the back of the neck bare. The boys, dressed like their papas, seemed uncomfortable in their new clothes (many that day were wearing their first pair of boots), and by their sides, speaking never a word, wearing the white dress of their first communion lengthened for the occasion, were some big girls of fourteen or sixteen, cousins or elder sisters no doubt, scarlet, bewildered, their hair greasy with rose-pomade, and very much afraid of dirtying their gloves. As there were not enough stable-boys to unharness all the carriages, the gentlemen turned up their sleeves and set about it themselves. According to their different social positions they wore tail-coats, overcoats, shooting-jackets, cutaway-coats: fine tail-coats, redolent of family respectability, that only came out of the wardrobe on state occasions; overcoats with long tails flapping in the wind and round capes and pockets like sacks; shooting-jackets of coarse cloth, generally worn with a cap with a brass-bound peak; very short cutaway-coats with two small buttons in the back, close together like a pair of eyes, and the tails of which seemed cut out of one piece by a carpenter's hatchet. Some, too (but these, you may be sure, would sit at the bottom of the table), wore their best smocks—that is to say, with collars turned down to the shoulders, the back gathered into small plaits and the waist fastened very low down with a stitched belt.

And the shirts stood out from the chests like armour breastplates! Everyone had just had his hair cut; ears stood out from the heads; they had been close-shaven; a few, even, who had had to get up before daybreak, and not been able to see to shave, had diagonal gashes under their noses or cuts the size of a three-franc piece along the jaws, which the fresh air had enflamed during the trip, so that the great white beaming faces were mottled here and there with red spots.

The mairie was a mile and a half from the farm, and they went there on foot, returning in the same way after the ceremony in the church. The procession, first united like one long coloured scarf that undulated across the fields, along the narrow path winding amid the green wheat, soon lengthened out, and broke up into different groups that loitered to talk. The fiddler walked in front with his violin, gay with ribbons at its pegs. Then came the married pair, the relatives, the friends, all following pell-mell; the children stayed behind amusing themselves plucking the bell-flowers from oat-ears, or playing amongst themselves unseen. Emma's dress, too long, trailed a little on the ground; from time to time she stopped to pull it up, and then delicately, with her gloved hands, she picked off the coarse grass and the thistles, while Charles, empty handed, waited till she had finished. Old Rouault, with a new silk hat and the cuffs of his black coat covering his hands up to the nails, gave his arm to Madame Bovary senior. As to Monsieur Bovary senior, who, heartily despising all these people, had come simply in a frock-coat of military cut with one row of buttons—he was exchanging barroom banter with a blond young farmgirl. She bowed, blushed, and did not know what to say. The other wedding guests talked business or played tricks behind each other's backs, egging each other on in advance for the fun that was to come. Those who listened could always catch the squeaking of the fiddler, who went on playing across the fields. When he saw that the rest were far behind he stopped to take breath, slowly rosined his bow, so that the strings should squeak all the louder, then set off again, by turns lowering and raising the neck of his violin, the better to mark time for himself. The noise of the instrument drove away the little birds from afar.

The table was laid under the cart-shed. On it were four roasts of beef, six chicken fricassées, stewed veal, three legs of mutton, and in the middle a fine roast sucking-pig, flanked by four pork sausages with sorrel. At the corners were decanters of brandy. Sweet bottled-cider frothed round the corks, and all the glasses had been filled to the brim with wine beforehand. Large dishes of yellow cream, that trembled with the least shake of the table, had designed on their smooth surface the initials of the newly wedded pair in nonpareil arabesques. A confectioner of Yvetot had been entrusted with the pies and candies. As he had only just started out in the neighborhood, he had taken a lot of trouble, and at dessert he himself brought in a wedding cake that provoked loud cries of wonderment. At its base there was a square of blue cardboard, representing a temple with porticoes, colonnades, and stucco statuettes all round, and in the niches constellations of gilt paper stars; then on the second level was a dungeon of Savoy cake, surrounded by many fortifications in candied angelica, almonds, raisins, and quarters of oranges; and finally, on the upper platform a green field with rocks set in lakes of jam, nutshell boats, and a small Cupid balancing himself in a chocolate swing whose two uprights ended in real roses for balls at the top.

Until night they ate. When any of them were too tired of sitting, they went out for a stroll in the yard, or for a game of darts in the granary, and then returned to table. Some towards the end went to sleep and snored. But with the coffee every one woke up. Then they began songs, showed off tricks, raised heavy weights, competed to see who could pass his head under his arm while keeping a thumb on the table, tried lifting carts on their shoulders, made bawdy jokes, kissed the women. At night when they left, the horses, stuffed up to the nostrils with oats, could hardly be got into the shafts; they kicked, reared, the harness broke, their masters laughed or swore; and all night in the light of the moon along country roads there were runaway carts at full gallop plunging into the ditches, jumping over yard after yard of stones, clambering up the hills, with women leaning out from the tilt to catch hold of the reins.

Those who stayed at the Bertaux spent the night drinking in the kitchen. The children had fallen asleep under the seats.

The bride had begged her father to be spared the usual marriage pleasantries. However, a fishmonger, one of their cousins (who had brought a pair of soles for his wedding present), began to squirt water from his mouth through the keyhole, when old Rouault came up just in time to stop him, and explain to him that the distinguished position of his son-in-law would not allow of such liberties. The cousin was not easily convinced. In his heart he accused old Rouault of being proud, and he joined four or five other guests in a corner, who, through mere chance, had been served the poorer cuts of meat several times over and also considered themselves ill-treated. They were whispering about their host, hoping with covered hints that he would ruin himself.

Madame Bovary, senior, had not opened her mouth all day. She had been consulted neither as to the dress of her daughter-in-law nor as to the arrangement of the feast; she went to bed early. Her husband, instead of following her, sent to Saint-Victor for some cigars, and smoked till daybreak, drinking kirsch-punch, a mixture unknown to the company that added even more to the consideration in which he was held.

Charles, who was anything but quick-witted, did not shine at the wedding. He answered feebly to the puns, *doubles entendres,* compliments, and the customary pleasantries that were dutifully aimed at him as soon as the soup appeared.

The next day, on the other hand, he seemed another man. It was he who might rather have been taken for the virgin of the evening before, whilst the bride gave no sign that revealed anything. The shrewdest did not know what to make of it, and they looked at her when she passed near them with an unbounded concentration of mind. But Charles concealed nothing. He called her "my wife," addressed her by the familiar "tu," asked for her of everyone, looked for her everywhere, and often he dragged her into the yards, where he could be seen from far between the trees, putting his arm round her waist, and walking half-bending over her, ruffling the collar of her blouse with his head.

Two days after the wedding the married pair left. Charles, on account of his patients, could not be away longer. Old Rouault had them driven back in his cart, and himself accompanied them as far as Vassonville. Here he embraced his daughter for the last time, got down, and went his way. When he had gone about a hundred paces he stopped, and as he saw the cart disappearing, its wheels turning in the dust, he gave a deep sigh. Then he remembered his wedding, the old times, the first pregnancy of his wife; he, too, had been very happy the day when he had taken her from her father to his home, and had carried her off riding pillion, trotting through the snow, for it was near Christmas-time, and the country was all white. She held him by one arm, her basket hanging from the other; the wind blew the long lace of her Cauchois headdress so that it sometimes flapped across his mouth, and when he turned his head he saw near him, on his shoulder, her little rosy face, smiling silently under the gold bands of her cap. To warm her hands she put them from time to time in his breast. How long ago it all was! Their son would have been thirty by now. Then he looked back and saw nothing on the road. He felt dreary as an empty house; and tender memories mingling with sad thoughts in his brain, addled by the fumes of the feast, he felt inclined for a moment to take a turn towards the church. As he was afraid, however, that this sight would make him even sadder, he went right away home.

Monsieur and Madame Charles arrived at Tostes about six o'clock. The neighbors came to the windows to see their doctor's new wife.

The old servant presented herself, curtsied to her, apologised for not having dinner ready, and suggested that madame, in the meantime, should look over her house.

V

The brick front was just in a line with the street, or rather the road. Behind the door hung a cloak with a small collar, a bridle, and a black leather cap, and on the floor, in a corner, were a pair of leggings, still covered with dry mud. On the right was the one room that was both dining and sitting room. A canary-yellow paper, relieved at the top by a garland of pale flowers, was puckered everywhere over the badly-stretched canvas; white calico curtains with a red border hung crossways the length of the window; and on the narrow mantelpiece a clock with a head of Hippocrates shone resplendent between two plate candlesticks under oval shades. On the other side of the passage was Charles's consulting-room, a little room about six paces wide, with a table, three chairs, and an office-chair. Volumes of the "Dictionary of Medical Science," uncut, but the binding rather the worse for the successive sales through which they had gone, occupied almost alone the six shelves of a pinewood bookcase. The smell of sauces penetrated through the walls when he saw patients, just as in the kitchen one could hear the people coughing in the consulting-room and recounting their whole histories. Then, opening on the yard, where the stable was, came a large dilapidated room with a stove, now used as a wood-house, cellar, and pantry, full of old rubbish, of empty casks, discarded garden tools, and a mass of dusty things whose use it was impossible to guess.

The garden, longer than wide, ran between two mud walls covered with espaliered apricot trees, to a thorn hedge that separated it from the field. In the middle was a slate sundial on a brick pedestal; four flower-beds with eglantines surrounded symmetrically the more useful vegetable garden. Right at the bottom, under the spruce bushes, a plaster priest was reading his breviary.

Emma went upstairs. The first room was not furnished, but in the second, the conjugal bedroom, was a mahogany bedstead in an alcove with red drapery. A shell-box adorned the chest of drawers, and on the secretary near the window a bouquet of orange blossoms tied with white satin ribbons stood in a bottle. It was a bride's bouquet: the other one's. She looked at it. Charles noticed; he took the bouquet, carried it to the attic, while Emma seated in an armchair (they were putting her things down around her) thought of her bridal flowers packed up in a bandbox, and wondered, dreaming, what would be done with them if she were to die.

During the first days she kept busy thinking about changes in the house. She took the shades off the candlesticks, had new wall-paper put up, the staircase repainted, and seats made in the garden round the sundial; she even inquired how she could get a basin with a jet fountain and fishes. Finally her husband, knowing that she liked to drive out, picked up a second-hand dogcart, which, with new lamps and a splashboard in striped leather, looked almost like a tilbury.

He was happy then, and without a care in the world. A meal together, a walk in the evening on the highroad, a gesture of her hands over her hair, the sight of her straw hat hanging from the window-fastener, and many other things of which he had never suspected how pleasant they could be, now made up the endless round of his happiness. In bed, in the morning, by her side, on the pillow, he watched the sunlight sinking into the down on her fair cheek, half hidden by the ribbons of her nightcap. Seen thus closely, her eyes looked to him enlarged, especially when, on waking up, she opened and shut her eyelids rapidly many times. Black in the shade, dark blue in broad daylight, they had, as it were, depths of successive colors that, more opaque in the center, grew more transparent towards the surface of the eye. His own eyes lost themselves in these depths and he could see himself mirrored in miniature, down to his shoulders, with his scarf round his head and the top of his shirt open. He rose. She came to the window to see him off, and stayed leaning on the sill between two pots of geranium, clad in her dressing-gown hanging loosely about her. Charles, in the street, buckled his spurs, his foot on the mounting stone, while she talked to him from above, picking with her mouth some scrap of flower or leaf that she blew out at him and which, eddying, floating, described semicircles in the air like a bird, caught before it reached the ground in the ill-groomed mane of the old white mare standing motionless at the door. Charles from horseback threw her a kiss; she answered with a nod; she shut the window, and he set off. And then, along the endless dusty ribbon of the highroad, along the deep lanes that the trees bent over as in arbours, along paths where the wheat reached to the knees, with the sun on his back and the morning air in his nostrils, his heart full of the joys of the past night, his mind at rest, his flesh at ease, he went on, re-chewing his happiness, like those who after dinner taste again the truffles which they are digesting.

Until now what good had he had of his life? His time at school, when he remained shut up within the high walls, alone, in the midst of companions richer than he or cleverer at their work, who laughed at his accent, who jeered at his clothes, and whose mothers came to the school with cakes in their muffs? Later on, when he studied medicine, and never had his purse full enough to take out dancing some little work-girl who would have become his mistress? Afterwards, he had lived fourteen months with the widow, whose feet in bed were cold as icicles. But now he had for life this beautiful woman whom he adored. For him the universe did not extend beyond the silky circumference of her petticoat. He reproached himself for not loving her enough; he wanted to see her again, turned back quickly, ran up the stairs with a beating heart. Emma, in her room, was dressing; he came up on tiptoe, kissed her back; she cried out in surprise.

He could not keep from constantly touching her comb, her rings, her scarf; sometimes he gave her great sounding kisses with all his mouth on her cheeks, or else little kisses in a row all along her bare arm from the tip of her fingers up to her shoulder, and she put him away half-smiling, half-annoyed, as one does with a clinging child.

Before marriage she thought herself in love; but since the happiness that should have followed failed to come, she must, she thought, have been mistaken. And Emma tried to find out what one meant exactly in life by the words *bliss, passion, ecstasy,* that had seemed to her so beautiful in books.

VI

She had read "Paul and Virginia,"[7] and she had dreamed of the little bamboo-house, the negro Domingo, the dog Fidèle, but above all of the sweet friendship of some dear little brother, who seeks red fruit for you on trees taller than steeples, or who runs barefoot over the sand, bringing you a bird's nest.

When she was thirteen, her father himself took her to town to

---

7. *Paul et Virginie* (1784) is a story of the sentimental and tragic love of two young people on the tropical island of Ile de France (today, Mauritius). It was the most popular work of Bernardin de Saint-Pierre (1737–1814).

place her in the convent. They stopped at an inn in the St. Gervais quarter, where, at their supper, they used painted plates that set forth the story of Mademoiselle de la Vallière.[8] The explanatory legends, chipped here and there by the scratching of knives, all glorified religion, the tendernesses of the heart, and the pomps of court.

Far from being bored at first at the convent, she took pleasure in the society of the good sisters, who, to amuse her, took her to the chapel, which one entered from the refectory by a long corridor. She played very little during recreation hours, knew her catechism well, and it was she who always answered the Vicar's difficult questions. Living thus, without ever leaving the warm atmosphere of the class-rooms, and amid these pale-faced women wearing rosaries with brass crosses, she was softly lulled by the mystic languor exhaled in the perfumes of the altar, the freshness of the holy water, and the lights of the tapers. Instead of following mass, she looked at the pious vignettes with their azure borders in her book, and she loved the sick lamb, the sacred heart pierced with sharp arrows, or the poor Jesus sinking beneath the cross he carried. She tried, by way of mortification, to eat nothing a whole day. She puzzled her head to find some vow to fulfil.

When she went to confession, she invented little sins in order that she might stay there longer, kneeling in the shadow, her hands joined, her face against the grating beneath the whispering of the priest. The comparisons of betrothed, husband, celestial lover, and eternal marriage, that recur in sermons, stirred within her soul depths of unexpected sweetness.

In the evening, before prayers, there was some religious reading in the study. On week-nights it was some abstract of sacred history or the Lectures of the Abbé Frayssinous,[9] and on Sundays passages from the "Génie du Christianisme,"[10] as a recreation. How she listened at first to the sonorous lamentations of romantic melancholy re-echoing through the world and eternity! If her childhood had been spent in the shops of a busy city section, she might perhaps have opened her heart to those lyrical invasions of Nature, which usually come to us only through translation in books. But she knew the country too well; she knew the lowing of cattle, the milking, the ploughs. Accustomed to the quieter aspects of life, she turned instead to its tumultuous parts. She loved the sea only for the sake of its storms, and the green only when it was scattered among ruins. She had to gain some personal profit from things and she rejected as

8. One of Louis XIV's mistresses, whose mythologized character is familiar to all readers of Alexandre Dumas's *Le Vicomte de Bragelonne* (a sequel to *The Three Musketeers*).

9. Denis de Frayssinous (1765–1841) was a popular preacher who wrote a *Défense du Christianisme* (1825). Under Louis XVIII he became a bishop and minister of ecclesiastical affairs.

10. *Le Génie du Christianisme* (1802) by François-René de Chateaubriand (1768–1848) was an enormously influential book celebrating the truths and beauties of Roman Catholicism, just before Napoleon's concordat with Rome.

useless whatever did not contribute to the immediate satisfaction of her heart's desires—being of a temperament more sentimental than artistic, looking for emotions, not landscapes.

At the convent there was an old maid who came for a week each month to mend the linen. Patronised by the clergy, because she belonged to an ancient family of noblemen ruined by the Revolution, she dined in the refectory at the table of the good sisters, and after the meal chatted with them for a while before going back to her work. The girls often slipped out from the study to go and see her. She knew by heart the love-songs of the last century, and sang them in a low voice as she stitched away. She told stories, gave them news, ran their errands in the town, and on the sly lent the big girls some of the novels, that she always carried in the pockets of her apron, and of which the lady herself swallowed long chapters in the intervals of her work. They were all about love, lovers, sweethearts, persecuted ladies fainting in lonely pavilions, postilions killed at every relay, horses ridden to death on every page, sombre forests, heart-aches, vows, sobs, tears and kisses, little boatrides by moonlight, nightingales in shady groves, gentlemen brave as lions, gentle as lambs, virtuous as no one ever was, always well dressed, and weeping like fountains. For six months, then, a fifteen year old Emma dirtied her hands with the greasy dust of old lending libraries. With Walter Scott, later on, she fell in love with historical events, dreamed of guardrooms, old oak chests and minstrels. She would have liked to live in some old manor-house, like those long-waisted chatelaines who, in the shade of pointed arches, spent their days leaning on the stone, chin in hand, watching a white-plumed knight galloping on his black horse from the distant fields. At this time she had a cult for Mary Stuart and enthusiastic veneration for illustrious or unhappy women. Joan of Arc, Héloïse,[11] Agnès Sorel,[12] the beautiful Ferronière, and Clémence Isaure stood out to her like comets in the dark immensity of history, where also were seen, lost in shadow, and all unconnected, St. Louis[13] with his oak, the dying Bayard,[14] some cruelties of Louis XI,[15] a little of St. Bartholomew's,[16] the plume of the Béarnais, and always the remembrance of

11. Héloise was famous for her love affair with the philosopher Abelard (1101–1164).

12. Agnès Sorel (1422–1450) was a mistress of Charles VII, rumored to have been poisoned by the future Louis XI; "la belle Ferronière" (died in 1540) was one of François I's mistresses, wife of the lawyer Le Ferron who is said to have contracted syphilis for the mere satisfaction of passing it on to the king; Clémence Isaure is a half-fictional lady from Toulouse (fourteenth century), popularized in a novel by Florian as an incarnation of the mystical poetry of the troubadours.

13. St. Louis was King of France, Louis IX (1215–1270). He led the seventh and eighth crusades. He was can-

onized in 1297. According to tradition he dispensed justice under an oak tree at Vincennes (near Paris).

14. Bayard (Pierre du Terrail, seigneur de, 1473–1524) was one of the most famous French captains, distinguishing himself by feats of bravery during the wars of Francis I. He was killed in 1524. Dying, he chided the connétable de Bourbon for his treason in a famous speech.

15. Louis XI was born in 1421 and was king from 1461 to 1483. He ruthlessly suppressed the rebellious noblemen.

16. St. Bartholomew was the massacre of the Protestants ordered by Catherine de Medici in the night of August 23, 1572.

the painted plates glorifying Louis XIV.

In the music-class, the ballads she sang were all about little angels with golden wings, madonnas, lagunes, gondoliers; harmless-sounding compositions that, in spite of the inanity of the style and the vagueness of the melody, enabled one to catch a glimpse of the tantalizing phantasmagoria of sentimental realities. Some of her companions brought keepsakes given them as new year's gifts to the convent. These had to be hidden; it was quite an undertaking; they were read in the dormitory. Delicately handling the beautiful satin bindings, Emma looked with dazzled eyes at the names of the unknown authors, who had signed their verses for the most part as counts or viscounts.

She trembled as she blew back the thin transparent paper over the engraving and saw it folded in two and fall gently against the page. Here behind the balustrade of a balcony was a young man in a short cloak, holding in his arms a young girl in a white dress who was wearing an alms-bag at her belt; or there were nameless portraits of English ladies with fair curls, who looked at you from under their round straw hats with their large clear eyes. Some could be seen lounging in their carriages, gliding through parks, a grey-hound bounding along ahead of the equipage, driven at a trot by two small postilions in white breeches. Others, dreaming on sofas with an open letter, gazed at the moon through a slightly open window half draped by a black curtain. The innocent ones, a tear on their cheeks, were kissing doves through the bars of a Gothic cage, or, smiling, their heads on one side, were plucking the leaves of a marguerite with their taper fingers, that curved at the tips like peaked shoes. And you, too, were there, Sultans with long pipes reclining beneath arbours in the arms of Bayadères; Giaours, curved swords, fezzes; and you especially, pale landscapes of dith-yrambic lands, that often show us at once palm-trees and firs, tigers on the right, a lion to the left, Tartar minarets on the hori-zon, Roman ruins in the foreground with some kneeling camels besides; the whole framed by a very neat virgin forest, and with a great perpendicular sunbeam trembling in the water, where, sharply edged on a steel-grey background, white swans are swimming here and there.

And the shade of the oil lamp fastened to the wall above Emma's head lighted up all these pictures of the world, that passed before her one by one in the silence of the dormitory, and to the distant noise of some belated carriage still rolling down the Boulevards.

When her mother died she cried much the first few days. She had a funeral picture made with the hair of the deceased, and, in a letter sent to the Bertaux full of sad reflections on life, she asked to be buried later on in the same grave. The old man thought she must be ill, and came to see her. Emma was secretly pleased that she had reached at a first attempt the rare ideal of delicate lives, never attained by mediocre hearts. She let herself meander along with Lamartine, listened to harps on lakes, to all the songs of dying swans, to the falling ·of the leaves, the pure virgins ascending to heaven, and the voice of the Eternal discoursing down the valleys. She soon grew tired but wouldn't admit it, continued from habit first, then out of vanity, and at last was surprised to feel herself consoled, and with no more sadness at heart than wrinkles on her brow.

The good nuns, who had been so sure of her vocation, perceived with great astonishment that Mademoiselle Rouault seemed to be slipping from them. They had indeed been so lavish to her of prayers, retreats, novenas, and sermons, they had so often preached the respect due to saints and martyrs, and given so much good advice as to the modesty of the body and the salvation of her soul, that she did as tightly reigned horses: she pulled up short and the bit slipped from her teeth. This nature, positive in the midst of its enthusiasms, that had loved the church for the sake of the flowers, and music for the words of the songs, and literature for the passions it excites, rebelled against the mysteries of faith as it had rebelled against discipline, as something alien to her constitution. When her father took her from school, no one was sorry to see her go. The Lady Superior even thought that she had of late been less than reverent toward the community.

Emma, at home once more, first took pleasure in ruling over servants, then grew disgusted with the country and missed her convent. When Charles came to the Bertaux for the first time, she thought herself quite disillusioned, with nothing more to learn, and nothing more to feel.

But the uneasiness of her new position, or perhaps the disturbance caused by the presence of this man, had sufficed to make her believe that she at last felt that wondrous passion which, till then, like a great bird with rose-coloured wings, hung in the splendor of poetic skies;—and now she could not think that the calm in which she lived was the happiness of her dreams.

VII

She thought, sometimes, that, after all, this was the happiest time of her life: the honeymoon, as people called it. To taste the full sweetness of it, it would no doubt have been necessary to fly to those lands with sonorous names where the days after marriage are full of the most suave laziness! In post-chaises behind blue silken curtains, one rides slowly up steep roads, listening to the song of the postilion re-echoed by the mountains, along with the bells of goats and the muffled sound of a waterfall. At sunset on the shores of gulfs one breathes in the perfume of lemon-trees; then in the evening on the villa-terraces above, one looks hand in hand at the stars, making plans for the future. It seemed to her that certain places on earth must bring happiness, as a plant peculiar to the soil, and that cannot thrive elsewhere. Why could not she lean over balconies in Swiss châlets, or enshrine her melancholy in a Scotch cottage, with a husband dressed in a black velvet coat with long tails, and thin shoes, a pointed hat and frills?

Perhaps she would have liked to confide all these things to some one. But how tell an undefinable uneasiness, changing as the clouds, unstable as the winds? Words failed her and, by the same token, the opportunity, the courage.

If Charles had but wished it, if he had guessed, if his look had but once met her thought, it seemed to her that a sudden bounty would have come from her heart, as the fruit falls from a tree when shaken by a hand. But as the intimacy of their life became deeper, the greater became the gulf that kept them apart.

Charles's conversation was commonplace as a street pavement, and every one's ideas trooped through it in their everyday garb, without exciting emotion, laughter, or thought. He had never had the curiosity, he said, while he lived at Rouen, to go to the theatre to see the actors from Paris. He could neither swim, nor fence, nor shoot, and one day he could not explain some term of horsemanship to her that she had come across in a novel.

A man, on the contrary, should he not know everything, excel in manifold activities, initiate you into the energies of passion, the refinements of life, all mysteries? But this one taught nothing, knew nothing, wished nothing. He thought her happy; and she resented this easy calm, this serene heaviness, the very happiness she gave him.

Sometimes she would draw; and it was great amusement to Charles to stand there bolt upright and watch her bend over her paper, with eyes half-closed the better to see her work, or rolling, between her fingers, little bread-pellets. As to the piano, the more quickly her fingers glided over it the more he wondered. She struck the notes with aplomb, and ran from top to bottom of the keyboard without a break. Thus shaken up, the old instrument, whose strings buzzed, could be heard at the other end of the village when the window was open, and often the bailiff's clerk, passing along the highroad bareheaded and in slippers, stopped to listen, his sheet of paper in his hand.

Emma, on the other hand, knew how to look after her house. She sent the patients' accounts in well-phrased letters that had no suggestion of a bill. When they had a neighbor to dinner on Sundays, she managed to have some tasty dish, knew how to pile the plums in pyramids on vine-leaves, how to serve jam turned out on a plate, and even spoke of buying finger bowls for dessert. From all this much consideration was extended to Bovary.

Charles finished by rising in his own esteem for possessing such a wife. He showed with pride in the sitting-room two small pencil sketches by her that he had had framed in very large frames, and hung up against the wall-paper by long green cords. People returning from mass saw him standing on his doorstep, wearing beautiful carpet slippers.

He came home late—at ten o'clock, at midnight sometimes. Then he asked for something to eat, and as the servant had gone to bed, Emma waited on him. He took off his coat to dine more at his ease. He told her, one after the other, the people he had met, the villages where he had been, the prescriptions he had written, and, well pleased with himself, he finished the remainder of the boiled beef, peeled the crust of his cheese, munched an apple, finished the wine, and then went to bed, lay on his back and snored.

As he had been for a long time accustomed to wear nightcaps, his handkerchief would not keep down over his ears, so that his hair in the morning was all dishevelled and whitened with the feathers of the pillow, whose strings came untied during the night. He always wore thick boots that had two long creases over the instep running obliquely towards the ankle, while the upper part continued in a straight line as if stretched on a wooden foot. He said that this was quite good enough for someone who lived in the country.

His mother approved of his thrift, for she came to see him as before, after there had been some violent row at her place; and yet the elder Madame Bovary seemed prejudiced against her daughter-in-law. She thought she was living above her means; the wood, sugar and candles vanished as in a large establishment, and the amount of stovewood used in the kitchen would have been enough for twenty-five courses. She straightened the linen chests, and taught her to keep an eye on the butcher when he brought the meat. Emma had to accept these lessons lavished upon her, and the words "daughter" and "mother" were exchanged all day long, accompanied by little quiverings of the lips, each one uttering sweet words in a voice trembling with anger.

In Madame Dubuc's time the old woman felt that she was still the favourite; but now the love of Charles for Emma seemed to her a desertion from her tenderness, an encroachment upon what was hers, and she watched her son's happiness in sad silence, as a ruined man looks through the windows at people dining in his old house. She recalled to him as remembrances her troubles and her sacrifices, and, comparing these with Emma's casual ways, came to the conclusion that it was not reasonable to adore her so exclusively.

Charles knew not what to answer: he respected his mother, and he loved his wife infinitely; he considered the judgment of the one infallible, and yet he thought the conduct of the other irreproachable. When Madame Bovary had gone, he tried timidly and in the same terms to hazard one or two of the more anodyne observations he had heard from his mamma. Emma proved to him with a word that he was mistaken, and sent him off to his patients.

And yet, in accord with theories she believed right, she wanted to experience love with him. By moonlight in the garden she recited all the passionate rhymes she knew by heart, and, sighing, sang to him many melancholy adagios; but she found herself as calm after this as before, and Charles seemed neither more amorous, nor more moved.

When she had thus for a while struck the flint on her heart without getting a spark, incapable, moreover, of understanding what she did not experience or of believing anything that did not take on a conventional form, she persuaded herself without difficulty that Charles's passion was no longer very ardent. His outbursts became regular; he embraced her at certain fixed times. It was one habit among other habits, like a familiar dessert after the monotony of dinner.

A gamekeeper, whom the doctor had cured of a lung infection, had given madame a little Italian greyhound; she took her out walking, for she went out sometimes in order to be alone for a moment, and not to see before her eyes the eternal garden and the dusty road.

She went as far as the beeches of Banneville, near the deserted pavilion which forms an angle on the field side of the wall. Amidst the grass of the ditches grow long reeds with sharp-edged leaves that cut you.

She began by looking round her to see if nothing had changed since she had last been there. She found again in the same places the foxgloves and wallflowers, the beds of nettles growing round the big stones, and the patches of lichen along the three windows, whose shutters, always closed, were rotting away on their rusty iron bars. Her thoughts, aimless at first, wandered at random, like her greyhound, who ran round and round in the fields, yelping after the yellow butterflies, chasing the field-mice, or nibbling the poppies on the edge of a wheatfield. Then gradually her ideas took definite shape, and, sitting on the grass that she dug up with little pricks of her sunshade, Emma repeated to herself:—Why, for Heaven's sake, did I marry?

She asked herself if by some other chance combination it would not have been possible to meet another man; and she tried to imagine what would have been these unrealised events, this different life, this unknown husband. All, surely, could not be like this one. He might have been handsome, witty, distinguished, attractive, like, no doubt, the men her old companions of the convent had married. What were they doing now? In town, among the crowded streets, the buzzing theatres and the lights of the ball-room, they were living lives where the heart expands and the senses blossom out. As for her, her life was cold as a garret facing north, and ennui, the silent spider, was weaving its web in the darkness, in every corner of her heart. She recalled graduation day, when she mounted the platform to receive her little wreaths. With her hair in long plaits, in her white frock and open prunella shoes she had a pretty way, and when she went back to her seat, the gentlemen bent over to congratulate her; the courtyard was full of carriages; farewells were called to her through their windows; the music-master with his violin-case bowed in passing by. How far off all this! How far away!

She called Djali,[17] took her between her knees, and smoothed the long, delicate head, saying, "Come, kiss your mistress, you who are free of cares."

Then noting the melancholy face of the graceful animal, who yawned slowly, she softened, and comparing her to herself, spoke to her aloud as to somebody in pain whom one is consoling.

Occasionally there came gusts of wind, breezes from the sea rolling in one sweep over the whole plateau of the Caux country, which brought to these fields a salt freshness. The rushes, close to the ground, whistled; the branches of the beech trees trembled in a swift rustling, while their crowns, ceaselessly swaying, kept up a deep murmur. Emma drew her shawl round her shoulders and rose.

In the avenue a green light dimmed by the leaves lit up the short moss that crackled softly beneath her feet. The sun was setting; the sky showed red between the branches, and the trunks of the trees, uniform, and planted in a straight line, seemed a brown colonnade standing out against a background of gold. A fear took hold of her; she called Djali, and hurriedly returned to Tostes by the highroad, threw herself into an armchair, and for the rest of the evening did not speak.

But towards the end of September something extraordinary befell her: she was invited by the Marquis d'Andervilliers to Vaubyessard.

Secretary of State under the Restoration, the Marquis, anxious to re-enter political life, had long since been preparing for his candidature to the Chamber of Deputies. In the winter he distributed a great deal of firewood, and in the Conseil Général always enthusiastically demanded new roads for his arrondissement. During the height of the Summer heat he had suffered from an abcess in the mouth, which Charles had cured as if by miracle by giving a timely

17. Djali is the name of the little she-goat in Hugo's *Notre Dame de Paris*.

little touch with the lancet. The steward sent to Tostes to pay for the operation reported in the evening that he had seen some superb cherries in the doctor's little garden. Now cherry-trees did not thrive at Vaubyessard; the Marquis asked Bovary for some offshoots. He made it his business to thank him personally and, on that occasion, saw Emma. He thought she had a pretty figure, and that she did not greet him like a peasant; so that he did not think he was going beyond the bounds of condescension, nor, on the other hand, making a mistake, in inviting the young couple.

One Wednesday at three o'clock, Monsieur and Madame Bovary, seated in their dog-cart, set out for Vaubyessard, with a great trunk strapped on behind and a hat-box in front on the apron. Besides these Charles held a carton between his knees.

They arrived at nightfall, just as the lamps in the park were being lit to show the way for the carriages.

VIII

The château, a modern building in Italian style, with two projecting wings and three flights of steps, lay at the foot of an immense lawn, on which some cows were grazing among clumps of large trees set out at regular intervals, while large beds of arbutus, rhododendron, syringas and snowballs bulged out their irregular clusters of green along the curve of the gravel path. A river flowed under a bridge; through the mist one could distinguish buildings with thatched roofs scattered over the field bordered by two gently-sloping well-timbered hillocks, and in the background amid the trees rose in two parallel lines the coach-houses and stables, all that was left of the ruined old château.

Charles's dog-cart pulled up before the middle flight of steps; servants appeared; the Marquis came forward, and offering his arm to the doctor's wife, conducted her to the vestibule.

It was paved with marble slabs and seemed very lofty; the sound of footsteps and that of voices re-echoed through it as in a church. Opposite rose a straight staircase, and on the left a gallery overlooking the garden led to the billiard room, from where the click of the ivory balls could be heard immediately upon entering. As she crossed it to go to the drawing-room, Emma saw standing round the table men with grave faces, their chins resting on high cravats. They all wore orders, and smiled silently as they made their strokes. On the dark wainscoting of the walls large gold frames bore at the bottom names written in black letters. She read: "Jean-Antoine d'Andervilliers d'Yverbonville, Count de la Vaubyessard and Baron de la Fresnaye, killed at the battle of Coutras[18] on the 20th of October 1587." And on another: "Jean-Antoine-Henry-Guy d'Andervilliers de la Vaubyessard, Admiral of France and Chevalier of

18. Battle of Coutras (in the Gironde) was won by Henri de Navarre against the Duke de Joyeuse (1587).

the Order of St. Michael, wounded at the battle of the Hougue-Saint-Vaast on the 29th of May 1692; died at Vaubyessard on the 23rd of January 1693." One could hardly make out the next ones, for the light of the lamps lowered over the green cloth threw a dim shadow round the room. Burnishing the horizontal pictures, it broke up in delicate lines among the cracks in the varnish, and from all these great black squares framed in gold stood out here and there some lighter portion of the painting—a pale brow, two eyes that looked at you, wigs resting on the powdered shoulder of red coats, or the buckle of a garter above a well-rounded calf.

The Marquis opened the drawing-room door; one of the ladies (the Marquise herself) came to meet Emma. She made her sit down by her on an ottoman, and began talking to her as amicably as if she had known her a long time. She was a woman of about forty, with fine shoulders, a hook nose, a drawling voice, and on this evening she wore over her brown hair a simple guipure fichu that fell in a point at the back. A blond young woman sat by her side in a high-backed chair, and gentlemen with flowers in their button-holes were talking to ladies round the fire.

At seven dinner was served. The men, who were in the majority, sat down at the first table in the vestibule; the ladies at the second in the dining-room with the Marquis and Marquise.

Emma, on entering, felt herself wrapped round as by a warm breeze, a blending of the perfume of flowers and of the fine linen, of the fumes of the roasts and the odour of the truffles. The candles in the candelabra threw their lights on the silver dish covers; the cut crystal, covered with a fine mist of steam, reflected pale rays of light; bouquets were placed in a row the whole length of the table; and in the large-bordered plates each napkin, arranged after the fashion of a bishop's mitre, held between its two gaping folds a small oval-shaped roll. The red claws of lobsters hung over the dishes; rich fruit in woven baskets was piled up on moss; the quails were dressed in their own plumage, smoke was rising; and in silk stockings, knee-breeches, white cravat, and frilled shirt, the steward, grave as a judge, passed between the shoulders of the guests, offering ready-carved dishes and, with a flick of the spoon, landed on one's plate the piece one had chosen. On the large porcelain stove inlaid with copper baguettes the statue of a woman, draped to the chin, gazed motionless on the crowded room.

Madame Bovary noticed that many ladies had not put their gloves in their glasses.[19]

At the upper end of the table, alone amongst all these women,

19. The ladies in the provinces, unlike their Paris counterparts, did not drink wine at public dinner parties, and signi-fied their intention by putting their gloves in their wine-glasses. The fact that they fail to do so suggests to Emma the high degree of sophistication of the company.

bent over his full plate, and his napkin tied round his neck like a child, an old man sat eating, letting drops of gravy drip from his mouth. His eyes were bloodshot, and he wore his hair in a little queue tied with a black ribbon. He was the Marquis's father-in-law, the old Duke de Laverdière, once on a time favourite of the Count d'Artois, in the days of the Marquis de Conflans' hunting-parties at le Vaudreuil, and had been, it was said, the lover of Queen Marie Antoinette, between Monsieur de Coigny and Monsieur de Lauzun. He had lived a life of loud dissipation, full of duels, bets, elopements; he had squandered his fortune and frightened all his family. A servant behind his chair shouted in his ear, in reply to his mutterings, the names of the dishes that he pointed to, and constantly Emma's eyes turned involuntarily to this old man with hanging lips, as to something extraordinary. He had lived at court and slept in the bed of queens!

Iced champagne was poured out. Emma shivered all over as she felt its cold in her mouth. She had never seen pomegranates nor tasted pineapples. Even the powdered sugar seemed to her whiter and finer than elsewhere.

The ladies afterwards retired to their rooms to prepare for the ball.

Emma made her toilette with the fastidious care of an actress on her début. She did her hair according to the directions of the hairdresser, and put on the barege dress spread out upon the bed. Charles's trousers were tight across the belly.

"My trouser-straps will be rather awkward for dancing," he said.

"Dancing?" repeated Emma.

"Yes!"

"Why, you must be mad! They would make fun of you; stay in your place, as it becomes a doctor."

Charles was silent. He walked up and down waiting for Emma to finish dressing.

He saw her from behind in the mirror between two lights. Her black eyes seemed blacker than ever. Her hair, gently undulating towards the ears, shone with a blue lustre; a rose in her chignon trembled on its mobile stalk, with artificial dewdrops on the tip of the leaves. She wore a gown of pale saffron trimmed with three bouquets of pompon roses mixed with green.

Charles came and kissed her on her shoulder.

"Don't touch me!" she cried; "I'll be all rumpled."

One could hear the flourish of the violin and the notes of a horn. She went downstairs restraining herself from running.

Dancing had begun. Guests were arriving and crowding the room. She sat down on a bench near the door.

The quadrille over, the floor was occupied by groups of talking men and by servants in livery bearing large trays. Along the line of seated women painted fans were fluttering, bouquets half-hid smiling faces, and gold-stoppered scent-bottles were turned in half-clenched hands, with white gloves outlining the nail and tightening on the flesh at the wrists. Lace trimmings, diamond brooches, medallion bracelets trembled on blouses, gleamed on breasts, clinked on bare arms. The hair, well smoothed over the temples and knotted at the nape, bore crowns, or bunches, or sprays of myosotis, jasmine, pomegranate blossoms, wheat-sprays and corn-flowers. Calmly seated in their places, mothers with forbidding countenances were wearing red turbans.

Emma's heart beat rather faster when, her partner holding her by the tips of the fingers, she took her place in a line with the dancers, and waited for the first note to start. But her emotion soon vanished, and, swaying to the rhythm of the orchestra, she glided forward with slight movements of the neck. A smile rose to her lips at certain delicate phrases of the violin, that sometimes played alone while the other instruments were silent; one could hear the clear clink of the louis d'or that were being thrown down upon the card-tables in the next room; then all struck in again, the trumpet uttered its sonorous note, feet marked time, skirts swelled and rustled, hands touched and parted; the same eyes that had been lowered returned to gaze at you again.

A few men (some fifteen or so), of twenty-five to forty, scattered here and there among the dancers or talking at the doorways, distinguished themselves from the crowd by a certain family-air, whatever their differences in age, dress, or countenance.

Their clothes, better made, seemed of finer cloth, and their hair, brought forward in curls towards the temples, glossy with more delicate pomades. They had the complexion of wealth,—that clear complexion that is heightened by the pallor of porcelain, the shimmer of satin, the veneer of old furniture, and that a well-ordered diet of exquisite food maintains at its best. Their necks moved easily in their low cravats, their long whiskers fell over their turned-down collars, they wiped their lips upon handkerchiefs with embroidered initials that gave forth a subtle perfume. Those who were beginning to grow old had an air of youth, while there was something mature in the faces of the young. Their indifferent eyes had the appeased expression of daily-satiated passions, and through all their gentleness of manner pierced that peculiar brutality that stems from a steady command over half-tame things, for the exercise of one's strength and the amusement of one's vanity—the handling of thoroughbred horses and the society of loose women.

A few steps from Emma a gentleman in a blue coat was talking of Italy with a pale young woman wearing a parure of pearls. They were praising the width of the columns of St. Peter's, Tivoli,

Vesuvius, Castellamare,[20] and the Cascine,[21] the roses of Genoa, the Coliseum by moonlight. With her other ear Emma was listening to a conversation full of words she did not understand. A circle gathered round a very young man who the week before had beaten "Miss Arabella," and "Romulus," and won two thousand louis jumping a ditch in England. One complained that his racehorses were growing fat; another of the printers' errors that had disfigured the name of his horse.

The atmosphere of the ball was heavy; the lamps were growing dim. Guests were flocking to the billiard-room. A servant got upon a chair and broke the window-panes. At the crash of the glass Madame Bovary turned her head and saw in the garden the faces of peasants pressed against the window looking in at them. Then the memory of the Bertaux came back to her. She saw the farm again, the muddy pond, her father in his apron under the apple-trees, and she saw herself again as formerly, skimming with her finger the cream off the milk-pans in the dairy. But in the splendor of the present hour her past life, so distinct until then, faded away completely, and she almost doubted having lived it. She was there; beyond the ball was only shadow overspreading all the rest. She was eating a maraschino ice that she held with her left hand in a silver-gilt cup, her eyes half-closed, and the spoon between her teeth.

A lady near her dropped her fan. A gentleman was passing.

"Would you be good enough," said the lady, "to pick up my fan that has fallen behind the sofa?"

The gentleman bowed, and as he moved to stretch out his arm, Emma saw the hand of the young woman throw something white, folded in a triangle, into his hat. The gentleman picking up the fan, respectfully offered it to the lady; she thanked him with a nod and breathed in the smell of her bouquet.

After supper, consisting of plenty of Spanish and Rhine wines, bisque and almond-cream soups, Trafalgar puddings and all sorts of cold meats with jellies that trembled in the dishes, the carriages began to leave one after the other. Raising the corners of the muslin curtain, one could see the light of their lanterns glimmering through the darkness. The seats began to empty, some card-players were still left; the musicians were cooling the tips of their fingers on their tongues. Charles was half asleep, his back propped against a door.

At three o'clock the cotillion began. Emma did not know how to waltz. Every one was waltzing, Mademoiselle d'Andervilliers herself and the Marquis; only the guests staying at the castle were still there, about a dozen persons.

One of the waltzers, however, who was addressed as Viscount, and whose low cut waistcoat seemed moulded to his chest, came a

20. Castellamare, a port south of Naples.　　21. Cascine, a park near Florence.

second time to ask Madame Bovary to dance, assuring her that he would guide her, and that she would get through it very well.

They began slowly, then increased in speed. They turned; all around them was turning, the lamps, the furniture, the wainscoting, the floor, like a disc on a pivot. On passing near the doors the train of Emma's dress caught against his trousers. Their legs intertwined; he looked down at her; she raised her eyes to his. A torpor seized her and she stopped. They started again, at an even faster pace; the Viscount, sweeping her along, disappeared with her to the end of the gallery, where, panting, she almost fell, and for a moment rested her head upon his breast. And then, still turning, but more slowly, he guided her back to her seat. She leaned back against the wall and covered her eyes with her hands.

When she opened them again, in the middle of the drawing-room three waltzers were kneeling before a lady sitting on a stool. She chose the Viscount, and the violin struck up once more.

Every one looked at them. They kept passing by, she with rigid body, her chin bent down, and he always in the same pose, his figure curved, his elbow rounded, his chin thrown forward. That woman knew how to waltz! They kept it up a long time, and tired out all the others.

Then they talked a few moments longer, and after the good-nights, or rather good-mornings, the guests of the château retired to bed.

Charles dragged himself up by the banister. His knees were giving way under him. For five consecutive hours, he had stood bolt upright at the card-tables, watching them play whist, without understanding anything about it, and it was with a deep sigh of relief that he pulled off his boots.

Emma threw a shawl over her shoulders, opened the window, and leant out.

The night was dark; some drops of rain were falling. She breathed in the damp wind that refreshed her eyelids. The music of the ball was still echoing in her ears, and she tried to keep herself awake in order to prolong the illusion of this luxurious life that she would soon have to give up.

Day began to break. She looked long at the windows of the château, trying to guess which were the rooms of all those she had noticed the evening before. She would have wanted to know their lives, to penetrate into them, to blend with them.

But she was shivering with cold. She undressed, and cowered down between the sheets against Charles, who was asleep.

There were a great many people to luncheon. The meal lasted ten minutes; to the doctor's astonishment, no liqueurs were served. Next, Mademoiselle d'Andervilliers collected some rolls in a small basket to take them to the swans on the ornamental waters, and they went for a walk in the hothouses, where strange plants, bristling with hairs, rose in pyramids under hanging vases from where fell, as from overfilled nests of serpents, long green cords interlacing. The orangery, at the other end, led by a covered way to the tenant houses of the château. The Marquis, to amuse the young woman, took her to see the stables. Above the basket-shaped racks porcelain slabs bore the names of the horses in black letters. Each animal in its stall whisked its tail when any one came near and clicked his tongue. The boards of the harness-room shone like the flooring of a drawing-room. The carriage harness was piled up in the middle against two twisted columns, and the bits, the whips, the spurs, the curbs, were lined up in a row all along the wall.

Charles, meanwhile, went to ask a groom to harness his horse. The dog-cart was brought to the foot of the steps, and all the parcels being crammed in, the Bovarys paid their respects to the Marquis and the Marquise and set out again for Tostes.

Emma watched the turning wheels in silence. Charles, on the extreme edge of the seat, held the reins with his arms spread far apart, and the little horse ambled along in the shafts that were too big for him. The loose reins hanging over his crupper were wet with foam, and the box fastened behind bumped regularly against the cart.

They were on the heights of Thibourville when suddenly some horsemen with cigars between their lips passed, laughing. Emma thought she recognised the Viscount, turned back, and caught on the horizon only the movement of the heads rising or falling with the unequal cadence of the trot or gallop.

A mile farther on they had to stop to mend with some string the traces that had broken.

But Charles, giving a last look to the harness, saw something on the ground between his horse's legs, and he picked up a cigar-case with a green silk border and a crest in the centre like the door of a carriage.

"There are even two cigars in it," said he; "they'll do for this evening after dinner."

"Since when do you smoke?" she asked.

"Sometimes, when I get a chance."

He put his find in his pocket and whipped up the nag.

When they reached home the dinner was not ready. Madame lost her temper. Nastasie answered rudely.

"Leave the room!" said Emma. "You are being insolent. I'll dismiss you."

For dinner there was onion soup and a piece of veal with sorrel. Charles, seated opposite Emma, rubbed his hands gleefully.

"How good it is to be at home again!"

Nastasie could be heard crying. He was rather fond of the poor girl. She had formerly, during the wearisome time of his widowhood, kept him company many an evening. She had been his first patient, his oldest acquaintance in the place.

"Have you dismissed her for good?" he asked at last.

"Yes. Who is to prevent me?" she replied.

Then they warmed themselves in the kitchen while their room was being made ready. Charles began to smoke. He smoked with lips protruded, spitting every moment, drawing back at every puff.

"You'll make yourself ill," she said scornfully.

He put down his cigar and ran to swallow a glass of cold water at the pump. Seizing the cigar case, Emma threw it quickly to the back of the cupboard.

The next day was a long one. She walked about her little garden, up and down the same walks, stopping before the beds, before the fruit tree, before the plaster priest, looking with amazement at all these things of the past that she knew so well. How far off the ball seemed already! What was it that thus set so far asunder the morning of the day before yesterday and the evening of to-day? Her journey to Vaubyessard had made a gap in her life, like the huge crevasses that a thunderstorm will sometimes carve in the mountains, in the course of a single night. Still she was resigned. She devoutly put away in her drawers her beautiful dress, down to the satin shoes whose soles were yellowed with the slippery wax of the dancing floor. Her heart resembled them: in its contact with wealth, something had rubbed off on it that could not be removed.

The memory of this ball, then, became an occupation for Emma. Whenever Wednesday came round she said to herself as she awoke, "Ah! I was there a week—a fortnight—three weeks ago." And little by little the faces grew confused in her remembrance. She forgot the tune of the quadrilles; she no longer saw the liveries and the guest-houses so distinctly; some of the details faded but the wistful feeling remained with her.

IX

Often when Charles was out she took from the cupboard, between the folds of the linen where she had left it, the green silk cigar-case.

She looked at it, opened it, and even smelt the odour of the lining, a mixture of verbena and tobacco. Whose was it? . . . The Viscount's? Perhaps it was a present from his mistress. It had been embroidered on some rosewood frame, a pretty piece of furniture, hidden from all eyes, that had occupied many hours, and over which had fallen the soft curls of the pensive worker. A breath of love had passed over the stitches on the canvas; each prick of the

needle had fixed there a hope or a memory, and all those inter-
woven threads of silk were but the continued extension of the same
silent passion. And then one morning the Viscount had taken it
away with him. Of what had they spoken when it lay upon the wide-
mantelled chimneys between flower-vases and Pompadour clocks?
She was at Tostes; he was at Paris now, far away! What was this
Paris like? What a boundless name! She repeated it in a low voice,
for the mere pleasure of it; it rang in her ears like a great cathedral
bell; it shone before her eyes, even on the labels of her jars of
pomade.

At night, when the carts passed under her windows, carrying fish
to Paris to the tune of "la Marjolaine," she awoke, and listened to
the noise of the iron-bound wheels, which, as they gained the country road, was soon deadened by the earth. "They will be there tomorrow!" she said to herself.

And she followed them in thought up and down the hills, crossing villages, gliding along the highroads by the light of the stars. At
the end of some indefinite distance there was always a confused
spot, into which her dream died.

She bought a plan of Paris, and with the tip of her finger on the
map she walked about the capital. She went up the boulevards,
stopping at every turn, between the lines of the streets, in front of
the white squares that represented the houses. At last she would
close the lids of her weary eyes, and see in the darkness the gas jets
flaring in the wind and the steps of carriages lowered noisily in
front of the theatre-entrances.

She subscribed to "La Corbeille," a ladies' magazine, and the
"Sylphe des Salons." She devoured, without skipping a word, all the
accounts of first nights, races, and soirées, took an interest in the
début of a singer, in the opening of a new shop. She knew the latest
fashions, the addresses of the best tailors, the days of the Bois
and the Opera. In Eugène Sue[22] she studied descriptions of furniture; she read Balzac and George Sand,[23] seeking in them imaginary
satisfaction for her own desires. She even brought her book to the
table, and turned over the pages while Charles ate and talked to
her. The memory of the Viscount always cropped up in everything
she read. She made comparisons between him and the fictional
characters in her books. But the circle of which he was the centre
gradually widened round him, and the aureole that he bore, fading
from his form and extending beyond his image, lit up her other
dreams.

Paris, more vague than the ocean, glimmered before Emma's eyes
with a silvery glow. The many lives that stirred amid this tumult

22. Eugène Sue (1804–1857) a popular novelist, extremely successful at that
period, both as a writer and as a fashionable dandy.

23. George Sand (pseudonym of Aurore
Dupín), prolific woman novelist (1803–
1876).

were, however, divided into parts, classed as distinct pictures. Emma perceived only two or three that hid from her all the rest, and in themselves represented all humanity. The world of ambassadors moved over polished floors in drawing-rooms lined with mirrors, round oval tables covered with velvet and gold-fringed cloths. There were dresses with trains, deep mysteries, anguish hidden beneath smiles. Then came the society of the duchesses; all were pale; all got up at four o'clock; the women, poor angels, wore English point on their petticoats; and the men, their talents hidden under a frivolous appearance, rode horses to death at pleasure parties, spent the summer season at Baden, and ended up, on reaching their forties, by marrying heiresses. In the private rooms of restaurants, where one dines after midnight by the light of wax candles, the colorful crowd of writers and actresses held sway. They were prodigal as kings, full of ambitious ideals and fantastic frenzies. They lived far above all others, among the storms that rage between heaven and earth, partaking of the sublime. As for the rest of the world, it was lost, with no particular place, and as if non-existent. Anyway, the nearer things were the more her thoughts turned away from them. All her immediate surroundings, the wearisome countryside, the petty-bourgeois stupidity, the mediocrity of existence seemed to her the exception, an exception in which she had been caught by a stroke of fate, while beyond stretched as far as eye could see an immense land of joys and passions. In her wistfulness, she confused the sensuous pleasures of luxury with the delights of the heart, elegance of manners with delicacy of sentiment. Did not love, like Indian plants, need a special soil, a special temperature? Sighs by moonlight, long embraces, tears flowing over yielded hands, all the passions of the flesh and the languors of tenderness seemed to her inseparable from the balconies of great castles where life flows idly by, from boudoirs with silken curtains and thick carpets, well-filled flower-stands, a bed on a raised daïs, and from the flashing of precious stones and the golden braids of liveries.

The boy from the post-office who came to groom the mare every morning passed through the passage with his heavy wooden shoes; there were holes in his apron; his feet were bare in his slippers. And this was the groom in knee-breeches with whom she had to be content! His work done, he did not come back again all day, for Charles on his return put up his horse himself, unsaddled it and put on the halter, while the maid brought a bundle of straw and threw it as best she could into the manger.

To replace Nastasie (who finally left Tostes shedding torrents of tears) Emma hired a young girl of fourteen, an orphan with a sweet face. She forbade her wearing cotton caps, taught her to address her in the third person, to bring a glass of water on a plate, to knock before coming into a room, to iron, starch, and to dress her; she wanted to make a lady's-maid of her. The new servant obeyed without a murmur, so as not to be dismissed; and as madame usually left the key in the sideboard, Félicité every evening took a small supply of sugar that she ate alone in her bed after she had said her prayers.

Sometimes in the afternoon she went across the road to chat with the coachmen. Madame stayed upstairs.

She wore an open dressing-gown, that showed under the shawl-shaped collar a pleated blouse with three gold buttons. Her belt was a corded girdle with great tassels, and her small wine-red slippers had a large knot of ribbon that fell over her instep. She had bought herself a blotter, writing-case, pen-holder, and envelopes although she had no one to write to; she dusted her shelf, looked at herself in the mirror, picked up a book, and then, dreaming between the lines, let it drop on her knees. She longed to travel or to go back to her convent. She wanted to die, but she also wanted to live in Paris.

Charles trotted over the country-roads in snow and rain. He ate omelettes on farmhouse tables, poked his arm into damp beds, received the tepid spurt of blood-letting in his face, listened to death-rattles, examined basins, turned over a good deal of dirty linen; but every evening he found a blazing fire, his dinner ready, easy-chairs, and a well-dressed woman, charming and so freshly scented that it was impossible to say where the perfume came from; it might have been her skin that communicated its fragrance to her blouse.

She delighted him by numerous attentions; now it was some new way of arranging paper sconces for the candles, a flounce that she altered on her gown, or an extraordinary name for some very simple dish that the servant had spoilt, but that Charles swallowed with pleasure to the last mouthful. At Rouen she saw some ladies who wore a bundle of charms hanging from their watch-chains; she bought some. She wanted for her mantelpiece two large blue glass vases, and some time after an ivory nécessaire with a silver-gilt thimble. The less Charles understood these refinements the more they seduced him. They added something to the pleasure of the senses and to the comfort of his fireside. It was like a golden dust sanding all along the narrow path of his life.

He was well, looked well; his reputation was firmly established. The country-folk loved him because he was not proud. He petted the children, never went to the public-house, and, moreover, his good behavior inspired confidence. He was specially successful with heavy colds and chest ailments. Being much afraid of killing his patients, Charles, in fact, only prescribed sedatives, from time to time an emetic, a footbath, or leeches. It was not that he was afraid of surgery; he bled people copiously like horses, and for the pulling of teeth the strength of his grasp was second to no one.

Finally, to keep up with the times, he subscribed to "La Ruche Médicale," a new journal whose prospectus had been sent him. He read it a little after dinner, but in about five minutes, the warmth of the room added to the effect of his dinner sent him to sleep; and he sat there, his chin on his two hands and his hair spreading like a mane to the foot of the lamp. Emma looked at him and shrugged her shoulders. Why at least, was not her husband one of those silently determined men who work at their books all night, and at last, when at sixty the age of rhumatism was upon them, wear a string of medals on their ill-fitting black coat? She would have wished this name of Bovary, which was hers, to be illustrious, to see it displayed at the booksellers', repeated in the newspapers, known to all France. But Charles had no ambition. An Yvetot doctor whom he had lately met in consultation had somewhat humiliated him at the very bedside of the patient, before the assembled relatives. When, in the evening, Charles told this incident Emma inveighed loudly against his colleague. Charles was much touched. He kissed her forehead with a tear in his eyes. But she was angered with shame; she felt a wild desire to strike him; she went to open the window in the passage and breathed in the fresh air to calm herself.

"What a man! what a man!" she said in a low voice, biting her lips.

She was becoming more irritated with him. As he grew older his manner grew coarser; at dessert he cut the corks of the empty bottles; after eating he cleaned his teeth with his tongue; in eating his soup he made a gurgling noise with every spoonful; and, as he was getting fatter, the puffed-out cheeks seemed to push the eyes, always small, up to the temples.

Sometimes Emma tucked the red borders of his undervest into his waistcoat, rearranged his cravat, and threw away the faded gloves he was going to put on; and this was not, as he fancied, for his sake; it was for herself, by an expansion of selfishness, of nervous irritation. At other times, she told him what she had been reading, some passage in a novel, a new play, or an anecdote from high society found in a newspaper story; for, after all, Charles was someone to talk to, an ever-open ear, an ever-ready approbation. She even confided many a thing to her greyhound! She would have done so to the logs in the fireplace or to the pendulum of the clock.

All the while, however, she was waiting in her heart for something to happen. Like shipwrecked sailors, she turned despairing eyes upon the solitude of her life, seeking afar some white sail in the mists of the horizon. She did not know what this act of fortune would be, what wind would bring it, towards what shore it would drive her, if it would be a rowboat or an ocean liner with three decks, carrying anguish or laden to the gunwales with bliss. But each morning, as she awoke, she hoped it would come that day; she listened to every sound, sprang up with a start, wondered that it did not come; then at sunset, always more saddened, she longed for the next day.

Spring came round. With the first warm weather, when the pear-trees began to blossom, she had fainting-spells.

From the beginning of July she counted off on her fingers how many weeks there were to October, thinking that perhaps the Marquis d'Andervilliers would give another ball at Vaubyessard. But all September passed without letters or visits.

After the shock of this disappointment her heart once more remained empty, and then the same series of identical days recommenced.

So now they would keep following one another, always the same, immovable, and bringing nothing new. Other lives, however flat, had at least the chance of some event. One adventure sometimes brought with it infinite consequences and the scene changed. But nothing happened to her; God had willed it so! The future was a dark corridor, with its door at the end shut tight.

She gave up music. What was the good of playing? Who would hear her? Since she could never, in a velvet gown with short sleeves, striking with her light fingers the ivory keys of an Erard concert piano, feel the murmur of ecstasy envelop her like a breeze, it was not worth while boring herself with practising. Her drawing cardboard and her embroidery she left in the cupboard. What was the use? What was the use? Sewing irritated her.

"I have read everything," she said to herself.

And she sat there, letting the tongs grow red-hot or looking at the rain falling.

How sad she was on Sundays when vespers sounded! She listened with dull attention to each stroke of the cracked bell. A cat slowly walking over some roof put up his back in the pale rays of the sun. The wind on the highroad blew up clouds of dust. A dog sometimes howled in the distance; and the bell, keeping time, continued at regular intervals its monotonous ringing that died away over the fields.

Then the people came out from church. The women had waxed their wooden shoes, the farmers wore new smocks, and with the little bareheaded children skipping along in front of them, all were going home. And till nightfall, five or six men, always the same, stayed playing at corks in front of the large door of the inn.

The winter was severe. Every morning, the windows were covered with rime, and the light that shone through them, dim as through ground-glass, sometimes did not change the whole day long. At four o'clock the lamp had to be lighted.

On fine days she went down into the garden. The dew had left a silver lace on the cabbages with long transparent threads spreading from one to the other. No birds were to be heard; everything seemed asleep, the fruit tree covered with straw, and the vine, like a great sick serpent under the coping of the wall, along which, on drawing near, one saw the many-footed woodlice crawling. Under the spruce by the hedgerow, the curé in the three-cornered hat reading his breviary had lost his right foot, and the very plaster, scaling off with the frost, had left white scabs on his face.

Then she went up again, shut her door, put on coals, and fainting with the heat of the hearth, felt her boredom weigh more heavily than ever. She would have liked to go down and talk to the maid, but a sense of shame restrained her.

Every day at the same time the schoolmaster in a black skull-cap opened the shutters of his house, and the village policeman, wearing his sword over his blouse, passed by. Night and morning the post-horses, three by three, crossed the street to water at the pond. From time to time the bell of a café would tinkle, and when it was windy one could hear the little brass basins that served as signs for the hairdresser's shop creaking on their two rods. The shop was decorated with an old engraving of a fashion-plate stuck against a window-pane and with the wax bust of a woman with yellow hair. He, too, the hairdresser, lamented his wasted calling, his hopeless future, and dreaming of some shop in a big town—at Rouen, for example, overlooking the harbour, near the theatre—he walked up and down all day from the mairie to the church, sombre and waiting for customers. When Madame Bovary looked up, she always saw him there, like a sentinel on duty, with his skull-cap over his ears and his woolen jacket.

Sometimes in the afternoon outside the window of her room, the head of a man appeared, a swarthy head with black whiskers, smiling slowly, with a broad, gentle smile that showed his white teeth. A waltz began, and on the barrel-organ, in a little drawing-room, dancers the size of a finger, women in pink turbans, Tyrolians in jackets, monkeys in frock-coats, gentlemen in knee breeches, turned and turned between the armchairs, the sofas and the tables, reflected in small pieces of mirror that strips of paper held together at the corners. The man turned the handle, looking to the right, to the left and up at the windows. Now and again, while he shot out a long squirt of brown saliva against the milestone, he lifted his instrument with his knee, to relieve his shoulder from the pressure of the hard straps; and now, doleful and drawling, or merry and hurried, the music issued forth from the box, droning through a curtain of pink taffeta underneath an ornate brass grill. They were airs played in other places at the theatres, sung in drawing-rooms, danced to at night under lighted lustres, echoes of the world that reached even to Emma. Endless sarabands ran through her head, and, like an Oriental dancing-girl on the flowers of a carpet, her thoughts leapt with the notes, swung from dream to dream, from sadness to sadness. When the man had caught some pennies in his cap he drew down an old cover of blue cloth, hitched his organ on to his back, and went off with a heavy tread. She watched him going.

But it was above all the meal-times that were unbearable to her, in this small room on the ground-floor, with its smoking stove, its creaking door, the walls that sweated, the damp pavement; all the bitterness of life seemed served up on her plate, and with the smoke of the boiled beef there rose from her secret soul waves of nauseous disgust. Charles was a slow eater; she played with a few nuts, or, leaning on her elbow, amused herself drawing lines along the oil-cloth table-cover with the point of her knife.

She now let everybody in her household go its own way, and the elder Madame Bovary, when she came to spend part of Lent at Tostes, was much surprised at the change. She who was formerly so careful, so dainty, now spent whole days without dressing, wore grey cotton stockings, and used tallow candles to light the house. She kept saying they must be economical since they were not rich, adding that she was very contented, very happy, that Tostes pleased her very much, and other such statements that left her mother-in-law speechless. Besides, Emma no longer seemed inclined to follow her advice; on one occasion, when Madame Bovary had thought fit to maintain that masters ought to keep an eye on the religion of their servants, she had answered with a look so angry and a smile so cold that the old lady preferred to let the matter drop.

Emma was growing difficult, capricious. She ordered dishes for herself, then she did not touch them; one day drank only pure milk, and the next cups of tea by the dozen. Often she persisted in not going out, then, stifling, threw open the windows and put on light dresses. After she had well scolded her maid she gave her presents or sent her out to see neighbors. She sometimes threw beggars all the silver in her purse, although she was by no means tender-hearted or easily accessible to the feelings of others; like most country-bred people, she always retained in her soul something of the horny hardness of the paternal hands.

Towards the end of February old Rouault, in memory of his cure, personally brought a superb turkey to his son-in-law, and stayed three days at Tostes. Charles being with his patients, Emma kept him company. He smoked in the room, spat on the andirons, talked farming, calves, cows, poultry, and municipal council, so that when he left she closed the door on him with a feeling of satisfaction that surprised even herself. Moreover she no longer concealed her contempt for anything or anybody, and at times expressed singular opinions, finding fault with whatever others approved, and approving things perverse and immoral, all of which left her husband wide-eyed.

Would this misery last for ever? Would she never escape from it? Yet she was the equal of all the women who were living happily. She had seen duchesses at Vaubyessard with clumsier waists and commoner ways, and she hated the divine injustice of God. She leant her head against the walls to weep; she longed for lives of adventure, for masked balls, for shameless pleasures that were bound, she thought, to initiate her to ecstacies she had not yet experienced.

She grew pale and suffered from palpitations of the heart. Charles prescribed valerian drops and camphor baths. Everything that was tried only seemed to irritate her the more.

On certain days she chattered with feverish profusion, and this overexcitement was suddenly followed by a state of torpor, in which she remained without speaking, without moving. What then revived her was to pour a bottle of eau-de-cologne over her arms.

As she was constantly complaining about Tostes, Charles fancied that her illness was no doubt due to some local cause, and, struck by this idea, he began to think seriously of setting up practice elsewhere.

From that moment she drank vinegar to lose weight, contracted a sharp little cough, and lost all appetite.

It cost Charles much to give up Tostes after living there four years, just when he was beginning to get somewhere. Yet if it must be! He took her to Rouen to see his old master. It was a nervous condition; she needed a change of air.

After some looking around, Charles discovered that the doctor of a considerable market-town in the arrondissement of Neufchâtel, a former Polish refugee, had vanished a week earlier. Then he wrote to the local pharmacist to ask the size of the population, the distance from the nearest doctor, how much his predecessor had earned in a year, and so forth; and the answer being satisfactory, he made up his mind to move towards the spring, if Emma's health did not improve.

One day when, in view of her departure, she was tidying a drawer, something pricked her finger. It was a wire of her wedding-bouquet. The orange blossoms were yellow with dust and the silver-bordered satin ribbons frayed at the edges. She threw it into the fire. It flared up more quickly than dry straw. Then it was like a red bush in the cinders, slowly shrinking away. She watched it burn. The little pasteboard berries burst, the wire twisted, the gold lace melted; and the shrivelled paper petals, fluttering like black butterflies at the back of the stove, at last flew up the chimney.

When they left Tostes in the month of March, Madame Bovary was pregnant.

Part Two

I

Yonville-l'Abbaye (named after an old Capuchin abbey of which not even the ruins remain), is a market-town some twenty miles from Rouen, between the Abbeville and Beauvais roads. It lies at the foot of a valley watered by the Rieule, a little river that runs into the Andelle after turning three water-mills near its mouth; it contains a few trout and, on Sundays, the village boys entertain themselves by fishing.

Leaving the main road at la Boissière, one reaches the height of les Leux from where the valley comes into view. The river that runs through it has divided the area into two very distinct regions: on the left are pastures, while the right consists of tilled land. The meadow stretches under a bulge of low hills to join at the back with the pasture land of the Bray country, while on the eastern side, the plain, gently rising, broadens out, showing as far as the eye can reach its blond wheatfields. The water, flowing through the grass, divides with a white line the color of the meadows from that of the ploughed fields, and the country is like a great unfolded mantle with a green velvet cape bordered with a fringe of silver.

On the horizon rise the oaks of the forest of Argueil, with the steeps of the Saint-Jean hills scarred from top to bottom with red irregular lines; they are rain-tracks, and these brick-tones standing out in narrow streaks against the grey colour of the mountain are due to the high iron content of the springs that flow beyond in the neighboring country.

These are the confines of Normandy, Picardy, and the Ile-de-France, a mongrel land whose language, like its landscape, is without accent or character. The worst Neufchâtel cheeses in the arrondissement are made here; and, on the other hand, farming is costly because so much manure is needed to enrich this brittle soil, full of sand and stones.

Up to 1835 no practicable road for getting to Yonville existed, but about this time a cross-road was cut, joining the Abbeville to the Amiens highway; it is occasionally used by the Rouen teamsters on their way to Flanders. Yonville-l'Abbaye has remained stationary in spite of its "new outlet." Instead of improving the soil they persist in keeping up the pasture lands, however depreciated they may be in value, and the lazy village, growing away from the plain, has naturally spread riverwards. It is seen from afar sprawling along the banks like a cowherd taking a nap by the side of the river.

At the foot of the hill beyond the bridge begins a roadway, planted with young aspens that leads in a straight line to the first houses in the place. These, fenced in by hedges, are in the middle of courtyards full of straggling buildings, wine-presses, cart-sheds, and distilleries scattered under thick trees, with ladders, poles, or scythes hooked over the branches. The thatched roofs, like fur caps drawn over eyes, reach down over about a third of the low windows, whose coarse convex glasses have bull's eyes in the middle, like the bottom of a bottle. A meagre pear-tree may be found leaning against some plaster wall crossed by black beams, and one enters the ground-floors through a door with a small swing-gate that keeps out the chicks when they pilfer, on the threshold, crumbs of bread steeped in cider. Gradually the courtyards grow narrower, the houses closer together, and the fences disappear; a bundle of ferns swings under a window from the end of a broomstick; there is a blacksmith's forge and then a wheelwright's, with two or three new carts outside that partly block the way. Then across an open space appears a white house at the end of a round lawn ornamented by a Cupid, his finger on his lips. Two cast-iron jars flank the high porch, copper signs gleam on the door. It is the notary's house, the finest in the place.

The church is on the other side of the street, twenty paces farther down, at the entrance of the square. The little graveyard that surrounds it, closed in by a breast-high wall, is so full of graves that the old stones, level with the ground, form a continuous pavement, on which the grass has, by itself, marked out regular green squares. The church was rebuilt during the last years of the reign of Charles X.[24] The wooden roof is beginning to rot from the top, and here and there black hollows appear in the blue paint. Over the door, where the organ should be, is a gallery for the men, with a spiral staircase that reverberates under the weight of their wooden shoes.

The daylight coming through the plain glass windows falls obliquely upon the pews perpendicular to the walls, here and there adorned with a straw mat inscribed, in large letters, with the name of some parishioner. Further on, where the nave grows narrow, the confessional faces a small Madonna, clothed in satin, wearing a tulle veil sprinkled with silver stars and with cheeks stained red like an idol of the Sandwich Islands;[25] finally, a painted copy entitled "The Holy Family, a gift from the Minister of the Interior," flanked

---

24. Charles X (1757–1836), son of Louis XV, was the last Bourbon king; he was expelled by the July Revolution (1830).

25. Sandwich Islands is the old name for Hawaii. They were named after John Montagu, fourth Earl of Sandwich (1718–1792) who served as first Lord of Admiralty when the islands were discovered.

by four candlesticks, crowns the main altar and rounds off the view. The choir stalls, of pine wood, have been left unpainted.

The market, that is to say, a tiled roof supported by some twenty posts, occupies by itself about half the public square of Yonville. The town hall, constructed "after the designs of a Paris architect," is a sort of Greek temple that forms the corner next to the pharmacy. On the ground-floor are three Ionic columns and on the first floor a gallery with arched windows, while the crowning frieze is occupied by a Gallic cock, resting one foot upon the Charter[26] and holding in the other the scales of Justice.

But what catches the eye most of all is Mr. Homais' pharmacy, right across from the Lion d'Or. In the evening especially its lamp is lit up and the red and green jars that embellish his shop-front cast their colored reflection far across the street; beyond them, as in a Bengal light, the silhouette of the pharmacist can be seen leaning over his desk. His house is plastered from top to bottom with inscriptions written in longhand, in round, in lower case: "Vichy, Seltzer and Barrège waters, depurative gum drops, Raspail patent medicine, Arabian racahout, Darcet lozenges, Regnault ointment, trusses, baths, laxative chocolate, etc." And the signboard, which stretches all the breadth of the shop, bears in gold letters "Homais, Pharmacist." Then at the back of the shop, behind the great scales fixed to the counter, the word "Laboratory" appears on a scroll above a glass door on which, about half-way up, the word Homais is once more repeated in gold letters on a black ground.

Beyond this there is nothing to see at Yonville. The street (the only one) a gunshot long and flanked by a few shops on either side stops short at the turn of the high road. Turning right and following the foot of the Saint-Jean hills one soon reaches the graveyard.

At the time of the cholera epidemic, a piece of wall was pulled down and three acres of land purchased in order to make more room, but the new area is almost deserted; the tombs, as heretofore, continue to crowd together towards the gate. The keeper, who is at once gravedigger and church sexton (thus making a double profit out of the parish corpses), has taken advantage of the unused plot of ground to plant potatoes. From year to year, however, his small field grows smaller, and when there is an epidemic, he does not know whether to rejoice at the deaths or regret the added graves.

"You feed on the dead, Lestiboudois!" the curé told him one day.

This grim remark made him reflect; it checked him for some time; but to this day he carries on the cultivation of his little tubers, and even maintains stoutly that they grow naturally.

Since the events about to be narrated, nothing in fact has changed at Yonville. The tin tricolour flag still swings at the top of

26. The *Charte constitutionelle de la France*, basis of the French constitution after the Revolution, bestowed in 1814 by Louis XVIII and revised in 1830, after the downfall of Charles X.

the church-steeple; the two streamers at the novelty store still flutter in the wind; the spongy white lumps, the pharmacist's foetuses, rot more and more in their cloudy alcohol, and above the big door of the inn the old golden lion, faded by rain, still shows passers-by its poodle mane.

On the evening when the Bovarys were to arrive at Yonville, the widow Lefrançois, the landlady of this inn, was so busy that she sweated great drops as she moved her saucepans around. To-morrow was market-day. The meat had to be cut beforehand, the chickens drawn, the soup and coffee made. Moreover, she had the boarders' meal to see to, and that of the doctor, his wife, and their maid; the billiard-room was echoing with bursts of laughter; three millers in the small parlour were calling for brandy; the wood was blazing, the charcoal crackling, and on the long kitchen-table, amid the quarters of raw mutton, rose piles of plates that rattled with the shaking of the block on which spinach was being chopped. From the poultry-yard was heard the screaming of the chickens whom the servant was chasing in order to wring their necks.

A slightly pockmarked man in green leather slippers, and wearing a velvet cap with a gold tassel, was warming his back at the chimney. His face expressed nothing but self-satisfaction, and he appeared as calmly established in life as the gold-finch suspended over his head in its wicker cage: he was the pharmacist.

"Artémise!" shouted the innkeeper, "chop some wood, fill the water bottles, bring some brandy, hurry up! If only I knew what dessert to offer the guests you are expecting! Good heavens! Those furniture-movers are beginning their racket in the billiard-room again; and their van has been left before the front door! The 'Hirondelle' might crash into it when it draws up. Call Polyte and tell him to put it away . . . Imagine, Monsieur Homais, that since morning they have had about fifteen games, and drunk eight pots of cider! . . . Why they'll tear my billiard-cloth to pieces!" she went on, looking at them from a distance, her strainer in her hand.

"That wouldn't be much of a loss," replied Monsieur Homais. "You would buy another."

"Another billiard-table!" exclaimed the widow.

"Since that one is coming to pieces, Madame Lefrançois. I tell you again you are doing yourself harm, much harm! And besides, players now want narrow pockets and heavy cues. They don't play the way they used to, everything is changed! One must keep pace with the times! Just look at Tellier!"

The hostess grew red with anger. The pharmacist added:

"You may say what you like; his table is better than yours; and if one were to think, for example, of getting up a patriotic tournament for Polish independence or for the victims of the Lyon floods . . ."[27]

"It isn't beggars like him that'll frighten us," interrupted the landlady, shrugging her fat shoulders. "Come, come, Monsieur Homais; as long as the 'Lion d'Or' exists people will come to it. We are no fly-by-nights, we have feathered our nest! While one of these days you'll find the 'Café Français' closed with a fine poster on the shutters. Change my billiard-table!" she went on, speaking to herself, "the table that comes in so handy for folding the washing, and on which, in the hunting season, I have slept six visitors! . . . But what can be keeping the slowpoke of a Hivert?"

"Are you waiting for him to serve your gentlemen's dinner?"

"Wait for him! And what about Monsieur Binet? As the clock strikes six you'll see him come in, for he hasn't his equal under the sun for punctuality. He must always have his seat in the small parlour. He'd rather die than eat anywhere else. And he is finicky! and particular about his cider! Not like monsieur Léon; he sometimes comes at seven, or even half-past, and he doesn't so much as look at what he eats. Such a nice young man! Never speaks a cross word!"

"Well, you see, there's a great difference between an educated man and a former army man who is now a tax-collector."

Six o'clock struck. Binet came in.

He was dressed in a blue frock-coat falling in a straight line round his thin body, and his leather cap, with its lappets knotted over the top of his head with string, showed under the turned-up peak a bald forehead, flattened by the constant wearing of a helmet. He wore a black cloth vest, a hair collar, grey trousers, and, all the year round, well-blacked boots, that had two parallel swellings where the big toes protruded. Not a hair stood out from the regular line of fair whiskers, which, encircling his jaws, framed like a garden border his long, wan face, with smallish eyes and a hooked nose. Clever at all games of cards, a good hunter, and writing a fine hand, he had at home a lathe, and amused himself by turning napkin-rings, with which he crammed his house, jealous as an artist and selfish as a bourgeois.

He went to the small parlour, but the three millers had to be got out first, and during the whole time necessary for resetting the table, Binet remained silent in his place near the stove. Then he shut the door and took off his cap as usual.

"Politeness will not wear out his tongue," said the pharmacist, as soon as he was alone with the hostess.

"He never talks more," she replied. "Last week I had two travel-

27. The allusion dates the action of the novel as taking place in 1840; during the winter of 1840, the Rhône overflowed with catastrophic results. At the same time, Louis Philippe was under steady attack for his failure to offer sufficient assistance to the victims of the repression that followed the insurrection of Warsaw (1831).

ling salesmen here selling cloth, really a cheerful pair, who spent the night telling jokes. They made me weep with laughter but he, he stood there mute as a fish, never opened his mouth."

"Yes," said the pharmacist, "no imagination, no wit, nothing that makes a man shine in society."

"Yet they say he is a man of means," objected the landlady.

"Of means?" replied the pharmacist. "He? In his own line, perhaps," he added in a calmer tone. And he went on:

"Now, that a businessman with numerous connections, a lawyer, a doctor, a pharmacist, should be thus absent-minded, that they should become whimsical or even peevish, I can understand; such cases are cited in history. But at least it is because they are thinking of something. How often hasn't it happened to me, for instance, to look on my desk for my pen when I had to write out a label, merely to discover, at last, that I had put it behind my ear?"

Madame Lefrançois just then went to the door to see if the "Hirondelle" was not coming. She started. A man dressed in black suddenly came into the kitchen. By the last gleam of the twilight one could see that he was red-faced and powerfully built.

"What can I do for you, Monsieur le curé?" asked the hostess, as she reached down a copper candlestick from the row of candles. "Will you have something to drink? A thimbleful of *Cassis*? A glass of wine?"

The priest declined very politely. He had come for his umbrella, that he had forgotten the other day at the Ernemont convent, and after asking Madame Lefrançois to have it sent to him at the rectory in the evening, he left for the church; the Angelus was ringing.

When the pharmacist no longer heard the noise of his boots along the square, he confessed that he had found the priest's behaviour just now very unbecoming. This refusal to take any refreshment seemed to him the most odious hypocrisy; all priests tippled on the sly, and were trying to bring back the days of the tithe.

The landlady took up the defence of her curé.

"Besides, he could double up four men like you over his knee. Last year he helped our people to bring in the hay, he carried as many as six bales at once, he is so strong."

"Bravo!" said the pharmacist. "Now just send your daughters to confess to such vigorous fellows! I, if I were the Government, I'd have the priests bled once a month. Yes, Madame Lefrançois, every month—a good phlebotomy, in the interests of the police and morals."

"Be quiet, Monsieur Homais. You are a godless man! You have no religion."

The chemist replied:

"I have a religion, my religion, and I even have more than all these others with their mummeries and their juggling. I adore God, on the contrary. I believe in the Supreme Being, in a Creator, whatever he may be. I care little who has placed us here below to fulfill our duties as citizens and parents; but I don't need to go to church to kiss silver plates, and fatten, out of my pocket, a lot of good-for-nothings who live better than we do. For one can know him as well in a wood, in a field, or even contemplating the ethereal heavens like the ancients. My God is the God of Socrates, of Franklin, of Voltaire, and of Béranger! I support the *Profession de Foi du Vicaire savoyard*[28] and the immortal principles of '89! And I can't admit of an old boy of a God who takes walks in his garden with a cane in his hand, who lodges his friends in the belly of whales, dies uttering a cry, and rises again at the end of three days; things absurd in themselves, and completely opposed, moreover, to all physical laws, which proves to us, by the way, that priests have always wallowed in squalid ignorance, and tried to drag whole nations down after them."

He stopped, looked around as if expecting to find an audience, for in his enthusiasm the pharmacist had for a moment fancied himself in the midst of the town council. But the landlady no longer heard him; she was listening to a distant rolling. One could distinguish the noise of a carriage mingled with the clattering of loose horseshoes that beat against the ground, and at last the "Hirondelle" stopped at the door.

It was a yellow box on two large wheels, that, reaching to the tilt, prevented travellers from seeing the road and dirtied their shoulders. The small panes of narrow windows rattled in their frames when the coach was closed, and retained here and there patches of mud amid the old layers of dust, that not even storms of rain had altogether washed away. It was drawn by three horses, the first a leader, and when it came down-hill its lower side jolted against the ground.

Some of the inhabitants of Yonville came out into the square; they all spoke at once, asking for news, for explanations of the delay, for their orders. Hivert did not know whom to answer first. He ran the errands in town for the entire village. He went to the shops and brought back rolls of leather for the shoemaker, old iron for the farrier, a barrel of herrings for his mistress, hats from the hat-shop and wigs from the hairdresser, and all along the road on his return journey he distributed his parcels, throwing them over fences as he stood upright on his seat and shouted at the top of his voice, while his horses went their own way.

An accident had delayed him. Madame Bovary's greyhound had escaped across the field. They had whistled for him a quarter of an

28. *Profession du Foi du Vicaire savoy-ard* (1762) is Rousseau's declaration of faith in God, a religion of his heart, coupled with a criticism of revealed re-ligion. It is included in Book IV of his pedagogic treatise *Émile* but was fre-quently reprinted as an independent pamphlet.

hour; Hivert had even gone back a mile and a half expecting every moment to catch sight of her; but they had been forced to resume the journey. Emma had wept, grown angry; she had accused Charles of this misfortune. Monsieur Lheureux, a draper, who happened to be in the coach with her, had tried to console her by a number of examples of lost dogs recognising their masters at the end of long years. He had been told of one, he said, who had come back to Paris from Constantinople. Another had gone one hundred and fifty miles in a straight line, and swum four rivers; and his own father had owned a poodle, which, after twelve years of absence, had all of a sudden jumped on his back in the street as he was going to dine in town.

II

Emma got out first, then Félicité, Monsieur Lheureux, and a nurse, and they had to wake up Charles in his corner, where he had slept soundly since night set in.

Homais introduced himself; he offered his homages to madame and his respects to monsieur; said he was charmed to have been able to render them some slight service, and added cordially that he had taken the liberty to join them at dinner, his wife being away.

When Madame Bovary entered the kitchen she went up to the fireplace. With two fingertips she caught her dress at the knee, and having thus pulled it up to her ankle, held out her black-booted foot to the fire above the revolving leg of mutton. The flame lit up the whole of her, casting its harsh light over the pattern of her gown, the fine pores of her fair skin, and even her eyelids, when she blinked from time to time. A great red glow passed over her with the wind, blowing through the half-open door.

On the other side of the fireplace, a fair-haired young man watched her in silence.

As he was frequently bored at Yonville, where he was a clerk at Maître Guilleumin, the notary, Monsieur Léon Dupuis (the second of the *Lion d'Or*'s daily customers) often delayed his dinner-hour in the hope that some traveller might come to the inn, with whom he could chat in the evening. On the days when his work was done early, he had, for want of something else to do, to come punctually, and endure from soup to cheese a *tête-à-tête* with Binet. It was therefore with delight that he accepted the hostess's suggestion that he should dine in company with the newcomers, and they passed into the large parlour where Madame Lefrançois, hoping to make an impression, had had the table laid for four.

Homais asked to be allowed to keep on his skull-cap, for fear of catching cold; then, turning to his neighbor:

"Madame is no doubt a little fatigued; one gets so frightfully shaken up in our *Hirondelle*."

"That is true," replied Emma; "but moving about always amuses me. I like a change."

"It is so tedious," sighed the clerk, "to be always riveted to the same places."

"If you were like me," said Charles, "constantly obliged to be in the saddle" . . .

"But," Léon went on, addressing himself to Madame Bovary, "nothing, it seems to me, is more pleasant—when one can," he added.

"Moreover," said the pharmacist, "the practice of medicine is not very hard work in our part of the world, for the state of our roads allows us the use of gigs, and generally, as the farmers are well off, they pay pretty well. We have, medically speaking, besides the ordinary cases of enteritis, bronchitis, bilious affections, &c., now and then a few intermittent fevers at harvest-time; but on the whole, little of a serious nature, nothing special to note, unless it be a great deal of scrofula, due, no doubt, to the deplorable hygienic conditions of our peasant dwellings. Ah! you will find many prejudices to combat, Monsieur Bovary, much obstinacy of routine, with which all the efforts of your science will daily come into collision; for people still have recourse to novenas, to relics, to the priest, rather than come straight to the doctor or the pharmacist. The climate, however, is truly not too bad, and we even have a few nonagenarians in our parish. The thermometer (I have made some observations) falls in winter to 4 degrees, and in the hottest season rises to 25 or 30 degrees Centigrade at the outside, which gives us 24 degrees Réaumur as the maximum, or otherwise stated 54 degrees Fahrenheit (English scale), not more. And, as a matter of fact, we are sheltered from the north winds by the forest of Argueil on the one side, from the west winds by the Saint Jean hills on the other; and this heat, moreover, which, on account of the watery vapours given off by the river and the considerable number of cattle in the fields, which, as you know, exhale much ammonia, that is to say, nitrogen, hydrogen, and oxygen (no, nitrogen and hydrogen alone), and which sucking up the humus from the soil, mixing together all those different emanations, unites them into a single bundle, so to speak, and combining with the electricity diffused through the atmosphere, when there is any, might in the long-run, as in tropical countries, engender poisonous fumes,—this heat, I say, finds itself perfectly tempered on the side from where it comes, or rather from where it ought to come, that is the south side, by the south-eastern winds, which, having cooled themselves in crossing the Seine, reach us sometimes all at once like blasts from Russia!"

"Do you at least have some walks in the neighborhood?" continued Madame Bovary, speaking to the young man.

"Oh, very few," he answered. "There is a place they call La Pâture, on the top of the hill, on the edge of the forest. Sometimes, on Sundays, I go and stay there with a book, watching the sunset."

"I think there is nothing so beautiful as sunsets," she resumed; "but especially by the seashore."

"Oh, I love the sea!" said Monsieur Léon.

"And doesn't it seem to you," continued Madame Bovary, "that the mind travels more freely on this limitless expanse, of which the contemplation elevates the soul, gives ideas of the infinite, the ideal?"

"It is the same with mountainous landscapes," continued Léon. "A cousin of mine who travelled in Switzerland last year told me that one could not picture to oneself the poetry of the lakes, the charm of the waterfalls, the gigantic effect of the glaciers. One sees pines of incredible size across torrents, cottages suspended over precipices, and, a thousand feet below one, whole valleys when the clouds open. Such spectacles must stir to enthusiasm, incline to prayer, to ecstasy; and I no longer wonder why a celebrated musician, in order to stimulate his imagination, was in the habit of playing the piano before some imposing view."

"Do you play?" she asked.

"No, but I am very fond of music," he replied.

"Ah! don't you listen to him, Madame Bovary," interrupted Homais, bending over his plate. "That's sheer modesty. Why, my friend, the other day in your room you were singing 'L'Ange Gardien[29] to perfection. I heard you from the laboratory. You articulated with the skill of an actor."

Léon rented a small room at the pharmacist's, on the second floor overlooking the Square. He blushed at the compliment of his landlord, who had already turned to the doctor, and was enumerating to him, one after the other, all the principal inhabitants of Yonville. He was telling anecdotes, giving information; no one knew just how wealthy the notary was and there were, of course, the Tuvaches who put up a considerable front.

Emma continued, "And what music do you prefer?"

"Oh, German music; that which makes you dream."

"Have you been to the opera?"

"Not yet; but I shall go next year, when I'll be living in Paris to get a law degree."

"As I had the honour of putting it to your husband," said the pharmacist, "with regard to this poor Yanoda who has run away, you will find yourself, thanks to his extravagance, in the possession of one of the most comfortable houses of Yonville. Its greatest convenience for a doctor is a door giving on the Walk, where one

29. A sentimental romance written by Mme. Pauline Duchambre, author of several such songs that appeared in the keepsakes.

can go in and out unseen. Moreover, it contains everything that is useful in a household—a laundry, kitchen with pantry, sitting-room, fruit bins, etc. He was a gay dog, who didn't care what he spent. At the end of the garden, by the side of the water, he had an arbour built just for the purpose of drinking beer in summer; and if madame is fond of gardening she will be able . . . "

"My wife doesn't care to," said Charles; "although she has been advised to take exercise, she prefers always sitting in her room reading."

"Just like me," replied Léon. "And indeed, what is better than to sit by one's fireside in the evening with a book, while the wind beats against the window and the lamp is burning? . . ."

"What, indeed?" she said, fixing her large black eyes wide open upon him.

"One thinks of nothing," he continued; "the hours slip by. Without having to move, we walk through the countries of our imagination, and your thought, blending with the fiction, toys with the details, follows the outline of the adventures. It mingles with the characters, and it seems you are living their lives, that your own heart beats in their breast."

"That is true! that is true!" she said.

"Has it ever happened to you," Léon went on, "to discover some vague idea of one's own in a book, some dim image that comes back to you from afar, and as the fullest expression of your own slightest sentiment?"

"I have experienced it," she replied.

"That is why," he said, "I especially love the poets. I think verse more tender than prose, and that it makes one weep more easily."

"Still in the long-run it is tiring," continued Emma, "and now, on the contrary, I have come to love stories that rush breath-lessly along, that frighten one. I detest commonplace heroes and moderate feelings, as one finds them in nature."

"You are right," observed the clerk, "since these works fail to touch the heart, they miss, it seems to me, the true end of art. It is so sweet, amid all the disenchantments of life, to be able to dwell in thought upon noble characters, pure affections, and pictures of happiness. For myself, living here far from the world, this is my one distraction. But there is so little to do in Yonville!"

"Like Tostes, no doubt," replied Emma; "and so I always sub-scribed to a lending library."

"If madame will do me the honor of making use of it," said the pharmacist, who had just caught the last words, "I have at her disposal a library composed of the best authors, Voltaire, Rousseau, Delille,[30] Walter Scott, the 'Echo des Feuilletons'; and in addition I

---

30. Jacques Delille (1738–1813) wrote idyllic descriptive poems; *Les Jardins* (1782) is best known.

receive various periodicals, among them the 'Fanal de Rouen' daily, being privileged to act as its correspondent for the districts of Buchy, Forges, Neufchâtel, Yonville, and vicinity.''

They had been at the table for two hours and a half, for Artémise, the maid, listlessly dragged her slippered feet over the tile-floor, brought in the plates one by one, forgot everything, understood nothing and constantly left the door of the billiard-room half open, so that the handle kept beating against the wall with its hooks.

Unconsciously, Léon, while talking, had placed his foot on one of the bars of the chair on which Madame Bovery was sitting. She wore a small blue silk necktie, which held upright, stiff as a ruff, a pleated batiste collar, and with the movements of her head the lower part of her face gently sunk into the linen or rose from it. Thus side by side, while Charles and the pharmacist chatted, they entered into one of those vague conversations where the hazard of all that is said brings you back to the fixed centre of a common sympathy. The Paris theatres, titles of novels, new quadrilles, and the world they did not know; Tostes, where she had lived, and Yonville, where they were; they examined all, talked of everything till the end of dinner.

When coffee was served Félicité left to prepare the room in the new house, and the guests soon rose from the table. Madame Lefrançois was asleep near the cinders, while the stable-boy, lantern in hand, was waiting to show Monsieur and Madame Bovary the way home. Bits of straw stuck in his red hair, and his left leg had a limp. When he had taken in his other hand the curé's umbrella, they started.

The town was asleep; the pillars of the market threw great shadows; the earth was all grey as on a summer's night.

But as the doctor's house was only some fifty paces from the inn, they had to say good-night almost immediately, and the company dispersed.

As soon as she entered the hallway, Emma felt the cold of the plaster fall about her shoulders like damp linen. The walls were new and the wooden stairs creaked. In their bedroom, on the first floor, a whitish light passed through the curtainless windows. She could catch glimpses of tree-tops, and beyond, the fields, half-drowned in the fog that lay like smoke over the course of the river. In the middle of the room, pell-mell, were scattered drawers, bottles, curtain-rods, gilt poles, with mattresses on the chairs and basins on the floor—the two men who had brought the furniture had left everything about carelessly.

This was the fourth time that she had slept in a strange place. The first was the day she went to the convent; the second, of her arrival at Tostes; the third, at Vaubyessard; and this was the fourth; and it so happened that each one had marked in her life a new beginning. She did not believe that things could remain the same in different places, and since the portion of her life that lay behind her had been bad, no doubt that which remained to be lived would be better.

III

The next day, as she was getting up, she saw the clerk on the Place. She had on a dressing-gown. He looked up and bowed. She nodded quickly and reclosed the window.

Léon waited all day for six o'clock in the evening to come, but on going to the inn, he found only Monsieur Binet already seated at the table.

The dinner of the evening before had been a considerable event for him; he had never till then talked for two hours consecutively to a "lady." How then had he been able to express, and in such language, so many things that he could not have said so well before? He was usually shy, and maintained that reserve which partakes at once of modesty and dissimulation. At Yonville, his manners were generally admired. He listened to the opinions of the older people, and seemed to have moderate political views, a rare thing for a young man. Then he had some accomplishments; he painted in water-colours, could read music, and readily talked literature after dinner when he did not play cards. Monsieur Homais respected him for his education; Madame Homais liked him for his good-nature, for he often took the little Homais into the garden—little brats who were always dirty, very much spoilt, and somewhat slow-moving, like their mother. They were looked after by the maid and by Justin, the pharmacist's apprentice, a second cousin of Monsieur Homais, who had been taken into the house out of charity and was also being put to work as a servant.

The druggist proved the best of neighbors. He advised Madame Bovary as to the tradespeople, sent expressly for his own cider merchant, tasted the wine himself, and saw that the casks were properly placed in the cellar; he explained how to stock up cheaply on butter, and made an arrangement with Lestiboudois, the sacristan, who, besides his ecclesiastical and funereal functions, looked after the main gardens at Yonville by the hour or the year, according to the wishes of the customers.

The need of looking after others was not the only thing that urged the pharmacist to such obsequious cordiality; there was a plan underneath it all.

He had infringed the law of the 19th Ventôse, year xi., article 1,[31] which forbade all persons not having a diploma to practise medicine; so that, after certain anonymous denunciations, Homais had

---

31. Ventôse ("windy") was the sixth month of the calendar established by the French Republic (from February 19 to March 20). The government of the Republic made the new year begin on September 22, 1792; thus the Year xi is 1801, and the 19th Ventôse March 10.

been summoned to Rouen to see the royal prosecutor in his private office; the magistrate receiving him standing up, ermine on shoulder and cap on head. It was in the morning, before the court opened. In the corridors one heard the heavy boots of the gendarmes walking past, and like a far-off noise great locks that were shut. The druggist's ears tingled as if he were about to have a stroke; he saw the depths of dungeons, his family in tears, his shop sold, all the jars dispersed; and he was obliged to enter a café and take a glass of rum and soda water to recover his spirits.

Little by little the memory of this reprimand grew fainter, and he continued, as heretofore, to give anodyne consultations in his back-parlour. But the mayor resented it, his colleagues were jealous, he had everything and everyone to fear; gaining over Monsieur Bovary by his attentions was to earn his gratitude, and prevent his speaking out later on, should he notice anything. So every morning Homais brought him the paper, and often in the afternoon left his shop for a few moments to have a chat with the Doctor.

Charles was depressed: he had no patients. He remained seated for hours without speaking, went into his consulting-room to sleep, or watched his wife sewing. Then for diversion he tried to work as a handyman around the house; he even tried to decorate the attic with some paint that had been left behind by the painters. But money matters worried him. He had spent so much for repairs at Tostes, for madame's toilette, and for the moving, that the whole dowry, over three thousand écus, had slipped away in two years. Then how many things had been spoilt or lost during their move from Tostes to Yonville, without counting the plaster curé, who, thrown out of the carriage by a particularly severe jolt, had broken in a thousand pieces on the pavement of Quincampoix!

A more positive worry came to distract him, namely, the pregnancy of his wife. As the time of birth approached he cherished her more. It was another bond of the flesh between them, and, as it were, a continued sentiment of a more complex union. When he caught sight of her indolent walk or watched her figure filling out over her uncorseted hips, when he had the opportunity to look at her undisturbed taking tired poses in her armchair, then his happiness knew no bounds; he got up, embraced her, passed his hands over her face, called her little mamma, wanted to make her dance, and, half-laughing, half-crying, uttered all kinds of caressing pleasantries that came into his head. The idea of having begotten a child delighted him. Now he wanted nothing more. He knew all there was to know of human life and sat down to enjoy it serenely, his elbows planted on the table as for a good meal.

Emma at first felt a great astonishment; then was anxious to be delivered that she might know what it felt like to be a mother. But not being able to spend as much as she would have liked on a suspended cradle with rose silk curtains, and embroidered caps, in a fit of bitterness she gave up looking for the layette altogether and had it all made by a village seamstress, without choosing or discussing anything.

Thus she did not amuse herself with those preparations that stimulate the tenderness of mothers, and so her affection was perhaps impaired from the start.

As Charles, however, spoke of the baby at every meal, she soon began to think of him more steadily.

She hoped for a son; he would be strong and dark; she would call him George; and this idea of having a male child was like an expected revenge for all her impotence in the past. A man, at least, is free; he can explore all passions and all countries, overcome obstacles, taste of the most distant pleasures. But a woman is always hampered. Being inert as well as pliable, she has against her the weakness of the flesh and the inequity of the law. Like the veil held to her hat by a ribbon, her will flutters in every breeze; she is always drawn by some desire, restrained by some rule of conduct.

She gave birth on a Sunday at about six o'clock, as the sun was rising.

"It is a girl!" said Charles.

She turned her head away and fainted.

Madame Homais, as well as Madame Lefrançois of the Lion d'Or, almost immediately came running in to embrace her. The pharmacist, as a man of discretion, only offered a few provisional felicitations through the half-opened door. He asked to see the child, and thought it well made.

During her recovery, she spent much time seeking a name for her daughter. First she went over all names that have Italian endings, such as Clara, Louisa, Amanda, Atala; she liked Galsuinde pretty well, and Yseult or Léocadie still better. Charles wanted the child to be called after her mother; Emma opposed this. They ran over the calendar from end to end, and then consulted outsiders.

"Monsieur Léon," said the chemist, "with whom I was talking about it the other day, wonders why you do not choose Madeleine. It is very much in fashion just now."

But Monsieur Bovary's mother protested loudly against this name of a sinner. As to Monsieur Homais, he had a preference for all names that recalled some great man, an illustrious fact, or a generous idea, and it was in accordance with this system that he had baptized his four children. Thus Napoleon represented glory and Franklin liberty; Irma was perhaps a concession to romanticism, but Athalie[32] was a homage to the greatest masterpiece of the French stage. For his philosophical convictions did not interfere with his

---

32. *Athalie* is a tragedy by Jean Racine (1639–1699) written in 1691 for the pupils of Saint-Cyr. Racine had abandoned the regular stage after a spiritual crisis and wrote two sacred tragedies *Esther* and *Athalie* for the young girls of Saint-Cyr.

artistic tastes; in him the thinker did not stifle the man of sentiment; he could make distinctions, make allowances for imagination
and fanaticism. In this tragedy, for example, he found fault with
the ideas, but admired the style; he detested the conception, but
applauded all the details, and loathed the characters while he grew
enthusiastic over their dialogue. When he read the fine passages he
was transported, but when he thought that the Catholics would use
it to their advantage, he was disconsolate; and in this confusion of
sentiments in which he was involved he would have liked both to
crown Racine with both his hands and take him to task for a good
quarter of an hour.

At last Emma remembered that at the château of Vaubyessard
she had heard the Marquise call a young lady Berthe; from that
moment this name was chosen; and as old Rouault could not come,
Monsieur Homais was requested to be godfather. His gifts were all
products from his establishment, to wit: six boxes of jujubes, a
whole jar of racahout, three cakes of marsh-mallow paste, and six
sticks of sugar-candy that he had come across in a cupboard. On the
evening of the ceremony there was a grand dinner; the curé was
present; there was much excitement. Towards liqueur time, Monsieur
Homais began singing "Le Dieu des bonnes gens."[33] Monsieur Léon
sang a barcarolle, and the elder Madame Bovary, who was godmother, a romance of the time of the Empire; finally, M. Bovary,
senior, insisted on having the child brought down, and began bap-
tizing it with a glass of champagne that he poured over its head.
This mockery of the first of the sacraments aroused the indignation
of the Abbé Bournisien; Father Bovary replied by a quotation from
"La Guerre des Dieux";[34] the curé wanted to leave; the ladies implored, Homais interfered; they succeeded in making the priest sit
down again, and he quietly went on with the half-finished coffee in
his saucer.

Monsieur Bovary père stayed at Yonville a month, dazzling the
natives by a superb soldier's cap with silver tassels that he wore in
the morning when he smoked his pipe in the square. Being also in
the habit of drinking a good deal of brandy, he often sent the
servant to the Lion d'Or to buy him a bottle, which was put down
to his son's account, and to perfume his handkerchiefs he used up
his daughter-in-law's whole supply of eau-de-cologne.

The latter did not at all dislike his company. He had knocked
about the world, he talked about Berlin, Vienna, and Strasbourg, of
his soldier times, of his mistresses, of the brilliant dinner-parties he
had attended; then he was amiable, and sometimes even, either on
the stairs or in the garden, would catch her by the waist, exclaiming:

---

33. "Le Dieu des Bonnes Gens" is a
deistic song by Béranger (see p. 757, n.5).
34. "La Guerre des Dieux" ("The War
of the Gods") is a satirical poem by
Evarite-Désiré Deforge (later Viscount
de Parny, 1753–1814) published in 1799.
It ridicules the Christian religion.

"Charles, you better watch out!"

Then the elder Madame Bovary became alarmed for her son's happiness, and fearing that her husband might in the long run have an immoral influence upon the ideas of the young woman, she speeded up their departure. Perhaps she had more serious reasons for uneasiness. Monsieur Bovary was the man to stop at nothing.

One day Emma was suddenly seized with the desire to see her little girl, who had been put to nurse with the carpenter's wife, and, without looking at the calendar to see whether the six weeks of the Virgin[35] were yet passed, she set out for the Rollets' house, situated at the extreme end of the village, between the highroad and the fields.

It was mid-day, the shutters of the houses were closed, and the slate roofs that glittered beneath the fierce light of the blue sky seemed to strike sparks from the crest of their gables. A heavy wind was blowing; Emma felt weak as she walked; the stones of the pavement hurt her; she was doubtful whether she would not go home again, or enter somewhere to rest.

At that moment Monsieur Léon came out from a neighboring door with a bundle of papers under his arm. He came to greet her, and stood in the shade in front of Lheureux's shop under the projecting grey awning.

Madame Bovary said she was going to see her baby, but that she was getting tired.

"If . . ." said Léon, not daring to go on.

"Have you any business to attend to?" she asked.

And on the clerk's negative answer, she begged him to accompany her. That same evening this was known in Yonville, and Madame Tuvache, the mayor's wife, declared in the presence of her maid that Madame Bovary was jeopardizing her good name.

To get to the nurse's it was necessary to turn to the left on leaving the street, as if heading for the cemetery, and to follow between little houses and yards a small path bordered with privet hedges. They were in bloom, and so were the speedwells, eglantines, thistles, and the sweetbriar that sprang up from the thickets. Through openings in the hedges one could see into the huts, some pig on a dung-heap, or tethered cows rubbing their horns against the trunk of trees. The two, side by side, walked slowly, she leaning upon him, and he restraining his pace, which he regulated by hers; in front of them flies were buzzing in the warm air.

They recognised the house by an old walnut-tree which shaded it. Low and covered with brown tiles, there hung outside it, beneath the attic-window, a string of onions. Faggots upright against a thorn fence surrounded a bed of lettuces, a few square feet of lavender,

---

35. Originally the six weeks that separate Christmas from Purification (Feb. 2nd); in those days, the normal period of confinement for a woman after childbirth.

and sweet peas strung on sticks. Dirty water was running here and there on the grass, and all round were several indefinite rags, knitted stockings, a red flannel undershirt, and a large sheet of coarse linen spread over the hedge. At the noise of the gate the wet nurse appeared with a baby she was suckling on one arm. With her other hand she was pulling along a poor puny little boy, his face covered with a scrofulous rash, the son of a Rouen hosier, whom his parents, too taken up with their business, left in the country.

"Go in," she said; "your baby is there asleep."

The room on the ground-floor, the only one in the dwelling, had at its farther end, against the wall, a large bed without curtains, while a kneading-trough took up the side by the window, one pane of which was mended with a piece of blue paper. In the corner behind the door, shining hob-nailed shoes stood in a row under the slab of the washstand, near a bottle of oil with a feather stuck in its mouth; a Mathieu Laensberg[36] lay on the dusty mantelpiece amid gunflints, candle-ends, and bits of tinder. Finally, the last extravagance in the room was a picture representing Fame blowing her trumpets, cut out, no doubt, from some perfumer's prospectus and nailed to the wall with six wooden shoe-pegs.

Emma's child was asleep in a wicker-cradle. She took it up in the wrapping that enveloped it and began singing softly as she rocked it to and fro.

Léon walked up and down the room; it seemed strange to him to see this beautiful woman in her silk dress in the midst of all this poverty. Madame Bovary blushed; he turned away, thinking perhaps there had been an impertinent look in his eyes. Then she put back the little girl, who had just thrown up over her collar. The nurse at once came to dry her, protesting that it wouldn't show.

"You should see some of the other tricks she plays on me," she said. "I always seem to be sponging her off. If you would have the goodness to order Camus, the grocer, to let me have a little soap; it would really be more convenient for you, as I needn't trouble you then."

"All right, all right!" said Emma. "Good-bye, Madame Rollet."

And she went out, wiping her shoes at the door.

The woman accompanied her to the end of the garden, complaining all the time of the trouble she had getting up nights.

"I'm so worn out sometimes that I drop asleep on my chair. You could at least give me a pound of ground coffee; that'd last me a month, and I'd take it in the morning with some milk."

After having submitted to her thanks, Madame Bovary left. She had gone a little way down the path when, at the sound of wooden shoes, she turned round. It was the nurse.

---

36. A farmer's almanac, begun in 1635   in farms and country houses.
by Mathieu Laensberg. frequently found

"What is it?"

Then the peasant woman, taking her aside behind an elm tree, began talking to her of her husband, who with his trade and six francs a year that the captain . . .

"Hurry up with your story," said Emma.

"Well," the nurse went on, heaving sighs between each word, "I'm afraid he'll be put out seeing me have coffee alone, you know men . . ."

"But I just told you you'll get some," Emma repeated; "I will give you some. Leave me alone!"

"Oh, my dear lady! you see, his wounds give him terrible cramps in the chest. He even says that cider weakens him."

"Do make haste, Mère Rollet!"

"Well," the latter continued, making a curtsey, "if it weren't asking too much," and she curtsied once more, "if you would"— and her eyes begged—"a jar of brandy," she said at last, "and I'd rub your little one's feet with it; they're as tender as your tongue."

Once they were rid of the nurse, Emma again took Monsieur Léon's arm. She walked fast for some time, then more slowly, and looking straight in front of her, her eyes rested on the shoulder of the young man, whose frock-coat had a black-velvet collar. His brown hair fell over it, straight and carefully combed. She noticed his nails, which were longer than one wore them in Yonville. It was one of the clerk's chief concerns to trim them, and for this purpose he kept a special knife in his writing-desk.

They returned to Yonville by the water-side. In the warm season the bank, wider than at other times, showed to their foot the garden walls from where a few steps led to the river. It flowed noiselessly, swift, and cold to the eye; long, thin grasses huddled together in it as the current drove them, and spread themselves upon the limpid water like streaming hair. Sometimes at the top of the reeds or on the leaf of a water-lily an insect with fine legs crawled or rested. The sun pierced with a ray the small blue bubbles of the waves that broke successively on the bank; branchless old willows mirrored their grey barks in the water; beyond, all around, the meadows seemed empty. It was the dinner-hour at the farms, and the young woman and her companion heard nothing as they walked but the fall of their steps on the earth of the path, the words they spoke, and the sound of Emma's dress rustling round her.

The walls of the gardens, crested with pieces of broken bottle, were heated like the glass roof of a hothouse. Wallflowers had sprung up between the bricks, and with the tip of her open parasol Madame Bovary, as she passed, made some of their faded flowers crumble into yellow dust, or else a spray of overhanging honeysuckle and clematis would catch in the fringe of the parasol and scrape for a moment over the silk.

They were talking of a troupe of Spanish dancers who were expected shortly at the Rouen theatre.

"Are you going?" she asked.

"If I can," he answered.

Had they nothing else to say to one another? Yet their eyes were full of more serious speech, and while they forced themselves to find trivial phrases, they felt the same languor stealing over them both; it was like the deep, continuous murmur of the soul dominating that of their voices. Surprised with wonder at this strange sweetness, they did not think of speaking of the sensation or of seeking its cause. Future joys arc like tropical shores; like a fragrant breeze, they extend their innate softness to the immense inland world of past experience, and we are lulled by this intoxication into forgetting the unseen horizons beyond.

In one place the ground had been trodden down by the cattle; they had to step on large green stones put here and there in the mud. She often stopped a moment to look where to place her foot, and tottering on the stone that shook, her arms outspread, her form bent forward with a look of indecision, she would laugh, afraid of falling into the puddles of water.

When they arrived in front of her garden, Madame Bovary opened the little gate, ran up the steps and disappeared.

Léon returned to his office. His employer was away; he just glanced at the briefs, then cut himself a pen, and finally took up his hat and went out.

He went to La Pâture at the top of the Argueil hills at the beginning of the forest; he stretched out under the pines and watched the sky through his fingers.

"How bored I am!" he said to himself, "how bored I am!"

He thought he was to be pitied for living in this village, with Homais for a friend and Monsieur Guillaumin for master. The latter, entirely absorbed by his business, wearing gold-rimmed spectacles and red whiskers over a white cravat, understood nothing of mental refinements, although he affected a stiff English manner, which in the beginning had impressed the clerk.

As for Madame Homais, she was the best wife in Normandy, gentle as a sheep, loving her children, her father, her mother, her cousins, weeping for others' woes, letting everything go in her household, and detesting corsets; but so slow of movement, such a bore to listen to, so common in appearance, and of such restricted conversation, that although she was thirty and he only twenty, although they slept in rooms next each other and he spoke to her daily, he never thought that she might be a woman to anyone, or that she possessed anything else of her sex than the gown.

And what else was there? Binet, a few shopkeepers, two or three innkeepers, the curé, and, finally, Monsieur Tuvache, the mayor, with his two sons, rich, haughty, obtuse people, who farmed their own lands and had feasts among themselves, devout Christians at that, but altogether unbearable as companions.

But from the general background of all these human faces the figure of Emma stood out isolated and yet farthest off; for between her and him he seemed to sense a vague abyss.

In the beginning he had called on her several times along with the pharmacist. Charles had not appeared particularly anxious to see him again, and Léon did not know what to do between his fear of being indiscreet and the desire for an intimacy that seemed almost impossible.

IV

When the first cold days set in Emma left her bedroom for the parlour, a long, low-ceilinged room, with on the mantelpiece a large bunch of coral spread out against the looking-glass. Seated in her armchair near the window, she could see the villagers pass along the pavement.

Twice a day Léon went from his office to the Lion d'Or. Emma could watch him coming from afar; she leant forward listening, and the young man glided past the curtain, always dressed in the same way, and without turning his head. But in the twilight, when, her chin resting on her left hand, she let her begun embroidery fall on her knees, she often shuddered at the apparition of this shadow suddenly gliding past. She would get up and order the table to be laid.

Monsieur Homais called at dinner-time. Skull-cap in hand, he came in on tiptoe, in order to disturb no one, always repeating the same phrase, "Good evening, everybody." Then, when he had taken his seat at table between them, he asked the doctor about his patients, and the latter consulted him as to the probability of their payment. Next they talked of "what was in the paper." By this hour of the day, Homais knew it almost by heart, and he repeated from beginning to end, including the comments of the journalist, all the stories of individual catastrophes that had occurred in France or abroad. But the subject becoming exhausted, he was not slow in throwing out some remarks on the dishes before him. Sometimes even, half-rising, he delicately pointed out to madame the tenderest morsel, or turning to the maid, gave her some advice on the manipulation of stews and the hygiene of seasoning. He talked aroma, osmazome, juices, and gelatine in a bewildering manner. Moreover, Homais, with his head fuller of recipes than his shop of jars, excelled in making all kinds of preserves, vinegars, and sweet liqueurs; he knew also all the latest inventions in economic stoves, together with the art of preserving cheeses and of curing sick wines.

At eight o'clock Justin came to fetch him to shut up the shop. Then Monsieur Homais gave him a sly look, especially if Félicité was there, for he had noticed that his apprentice was fond of the doctor's house.

"The young man," he said, "is beginning to have ideas, and the devil take me if I don't believe he's in love with your maid!"

But a more serious fault with which he reproached Justin was his constantly listening to conversation. On Sunday, for example, one could not get him out of the parlor, even when Madame Homais called him to fetch the children, who had fallen asleep in the armchairs, dragging down with their backs the overwide slip-covers.

Not many people came to the pharmacist's evening parties, his scandal-mongering and political opinions having successfully alienated various persons. The clerk never failed to be there. As soon as he heard the bell he ran to meet Madame Bovary, took her shawl, and put away under the shop-counter the heavy overshoes she wore when it snowed.

First they played some hands at trente-et-un; next Monsieur Homais played écarté with Emma; Léon standing behind her, gave advice. Standing up with his hands on the back of her chair, he saw the teeth of her comb that bit into her chignon. With every movement that she made to throw her cards the right side of her dress was drawn up. From her turned-up hair a dark colour fell over her back, and growing gradually paler, lost itself little by little in the shade. Her dress dropped on both sides of her chair, blowing out into many folds before it spread on the floor. When Léon occasionally felt the sole of his boot resting on it, he drew back as if he had trodden on something alive.

When the game of cards was over, the pharmacist and the Doctor played dominoes, and Emma, changing her place, leant her elbow on the table, turning over the pages of "L'Illustration." She had brought her ladies' journal with her. Léon sat down near her; they looked at the engravings together, and waited for one another at the bottom of the pages. She often begged him to read her the verses; Léon declaimed them in a languid voice, to which he carefully gave a dying fall in the love passages. But the noise of the dominoes annoyed him. Monsieur Homais was strong at the game; he could beat Charles and give him a double-six. Then the three hundred finished, they both stretched in front of the fire, and were soon asleep. The fire was dying out in the cinders; the teapot was empty, Léon was still reading. Emma listened to him, mechanically turning round the lampshade, its gauze decorated with painted clowns in carriages, and tightrope dancers with balancing-poles.

Léon stopped, pointing with a gesture to his sleeping audience; then they talked in low tones, and their conversation seemed the sweeter to them because it was unheard.

Thus a kind of bond was established between them, a constant exchange of books and of romances. Little inclined to jealousy, Monsieur Bovary thought nothing of it.

On his birthday he received a beautiful phrenological head, all marked with figures to the thorax and painted blue. This was a gift of the clerk's. He showed him many other attentions, to the point of running errands for him at Rouen: and a novel having made the mania for cactuses fashionable, Léon bought some for Madame Bovary, bringing them back on his knees in the "Hirondelle," pricking his fingers on their hard spikes.

She had a railed shelf suspended against her window to hold the pots. The clerk, too, had his small hanging garden; they saw each other tending their flowers at their windows.

One of the village windows was even more often occupied; for on Sundays from morning to night, and every morning when the weather was bright, one could see at an attic-window the profile of Monsieur Binet bending over his lathe; its monotonous humming could be heard at the Lion d'Or.

One evening on coming home Léon found in his room a rug in velvet and wool with leaves on a pale ground. He called Madame Homais, Monsieur Homais, Justin, the children, the cook; he spoke of it to his employer; every one wanted to see this rug. Why did the doctor's wife give the clerk presents? It looked odd; and they decided that he must be her lover.

He gave plenty of reason for this belief, so ceaselessly did he talk of her charms and of her wit; so much so, that Binet once roughly interrupted him:

"What do I care since I'm not one of her friends?"

He tortured himself to find out how he could make his declaration to her, and always halting between the fear of displeasing her and the shame of being such a coward, he wept with discouragement and desire. Then he took energetic resolutions, wrote letters that he tore up, put it off to times that he again deferred. Often he set out with the determination to dare all; but this resolution soon deserted him in Emma's presence; and when Charles, dropping in, invited him to jump into his carriage to go with him to see some patient in the neighborhood, he at once accepted, bowed to madame, and left. Wasn't the husband also a part of her after all?

As for Emma, she did not ask herself whether she loved him. Love, she thought, must come suddenly, with great outbursts and lightnings,—a hurricane of the skies, which sweeps down on life, upsets everything, uproots the will like a leaf and carries away the heart as in an abyss. She did not know that on the terrace of houses the rain makes lakes when the pipes are choked, and she would thus have remained safe in her ignorance when she suddenly discovered a rent in the wall.

V

It was a Sunday in February, an afternoon when the snow was falling.

Monsieur and Madame Bovary, Homais, and Monsieur Léon had all gone to see a yarn-mill that was being built in the valley a mile and a half from Yonville. The druggist had taken Napoleon and Athalie to give them some exercise, and Justin accompanied them, carrying the umbrellas over his shoulder.

Nothing, however, could be less worth seeing than this sight. A great piece of waste ground, on which, amid a mass of sand and stones, were scattered a few rusty cogwheels, surrounded by a long rectangular building pierced with numerous little windows. The building was unfinished; the sky could be seen through the beams of the roofing. Attached to the ridgepole of the gable a bunch of straw mixed with corn-ears fluttered its tricoloured ribbons in the wind.

Homais was talking. He explained to the company the future importance of this establishment, computed the strength of the floorings, the thickness of the walls, and regretted extremely not having a yard-stick such as Monsieur Binet possessed for his own special use.

Emma, who had taken his arm, bent lightly against his shoulder, and she looked at the sun's disc shining afar through the mist with pale splendour. She turned; there was Charles. His cap was drawn down over his eyebrows, and his two thick lips were trembling, which added a look of stupidity to his face; his very back, his calm back, was irritating to behold, and she saw all his platitude spelled out right there, on his very coat.

While she was considering him thus, savoring her irritation with a sort of depraved pleasure, Léon made a step forward. The cold that made him pale seemed to add a more gentle languor to his face; between his cravat and his neck the somewhat loose collar of his shirt showed the skin; some of his ear was showing beneath a lock of hair, and his large blue eyes, raised to the clouds, seemed to Emma more limpid and more beautiful than those mountain-lakes which mirror the heavens.

"Look out there!" suddenly cried the pharmacist.

And he ran to his son, who had just jumped into a pile of lime in order to whiten his boots. Overcome by his father's reproaches, Napoleon began to howl, while Justin dried his shoes with a wisp of straw. But a knife was needed; Charles offered his.

"Ah!" she said to herself, "he carries a knife in his pocket like a peasant."

It was beginning to snow and they turned back to Yonville.

In the evening Madame Bovary did not go to her neighbor's, and when Charles had left and she felt herself alone, the comparison again forced itself upon her, almost with the clarity of direct sensation, and with that lengthening of perspective which memory gives to things. Looking from her bed at the bright fire that was burning, she still saw, as she had down there, Léon standing up with one hand bending his cane, and with the other holding Athalie, who was quietly sucking a piece of ice. She thought him charming; she could not tear herself away from him; she recalled his other attitudes on other days, the words he had spoken, the sound of his voice, his whole person; and she repeated, pouting out her lips as if for a kiss:

"Yes, charming! charming! Is he not in love?" . . . she asked herself; "but with whom? . . . With me!"

All the evidence asserted itself at once; her heart leapt. The flame of the fire threw a joyous light upon the ceiling; she turned on her back, stretched out her arms.

Then began the eternal lamentation: "Oh, if Heaven had but willed it! And why not? What prevented it?"

When Charles came home at midnight, she seemed to have just awakened, and as he made a noise undressing, she complained of a headache, then asked casually what had happened that evening.

"Monsieur Léon," he said, "went to his room early."

She could not help smiling, and she fell asleep, her soul filled with a new delight.

The next day, at dusk, she received a visit from Monsieur Lheureux, the owner of the local general store.

He was a smart man, this shopkeeper.

Born in Gascony but bred a Norman, he grafted upon his southern volubility the cunning of the Cauchois. His fat, flabby, beardless face seemed dyed by a decoction of liquorice, and his white hair made even more vivid the keen brilliance of his small black eyes. No one knew what he had been formerly; some said he was a peddler, others that he was a banker at Routot. One thing was certain: he could make complex figurings in his head that would have frightened Binet himself. Polite to obsequiousness, he always held himself with his back bent in the attitude of one who bows or who invites.

After leaving at the door his black-bordered hat, he put down a green cardboard box on the table, and began by complaining to madame, with many civilities, that he should have remained till that day without the benefit of her confidence. A poor shop like his was not made to attract a lady of fashion; he stressed the words; yet she had only to command, and he would undertake to provide her with anything she might wish, whether it be lingerie or knitwear, hats or dresses, for he went to town regularly four times a month. He was connected with the best houses. His name could be mentioned at the "Trois Frères," at the "Barbe d'Or," or at the "Grand Sauvage"; all these gentlemen knew him inside out. To-day, then, he had come to show madame, in passing, various articles he happened to have by an unusual stroke of luck. And he pulled out half-a-dozen embroidered collars from the box.

Madame Bovary examined them.

"I don't need anything," she said.

Then Monsieur Lheureux delicately exhibited three Algerian scarves, several packages of English needles, a pair of straw slippers, and, finally, four eggcups in cocoa-nut wood, carved in open work by convicts. Then, with both hands on the table, his neck stretched out, leaning forward with open mouth, he watched Emma's gaze wander undecided over the merchandise. From time to time, as if to remove some dust, he flicked his nail against the silk of the scarves spread out at full length, and they rustled with a little noise, making the gold spangles of the material sparkle like stars in the greenish twilight.

"How much are they?"

"A mere trifle," he replied, "a mere trifle. But there's no hurry; whenever it's convenient. We are no Jews."

She reflected for a few moments, and ended by again declining Monsieur Lheureux's offer. Showing no concern, he replied:

"Very well! Better luck next time. I have always got on with ladies . . . even if I didn't with my own!"

Emma smiled.

"I wanted to tell you," he went on good-naturedly, after his joke, "that it isn't the money I should trouble about. Why, I could give you some, if need be."

She made a gesture of surprise.

"Ah!" he said quickly and in a low voice, "I shouldn't have to go far to find you some, rely on that."

And he began asking after Père Tellier, the owner of the "Café Français," who was being treated by Monsieur Bovary at the time.

"What's the matter with Père Tellier? He makes the whole house shake with his coughing, and I'm afraid he'll soon need a pine coat rather than a flannel jacket. He certainly lived it up when he was young! These people, madame, they never know when to stop! He burned himself up with brandy. Still it's sad, all the same, to see an acquaintance go."

And while he fastened up his box he discoursed about the doctor's patients.

"It's the weather, no doubt," he said, looking frowningly at the floor, "that causes these illnesses. I myself don't feel just right. One of these days I shall even have to consult the doctor for a pain I have in my back. Well, good-bye, Madame Bovary. At your service; your very humble servant."

And he gently closed the door behind him.

Emma had her dinner served in her bedroom on a tray by the fireside; she took a long time eating; everything seemed wonderful.

"How good I was!" she said to herself, thinking of the scarves.

She heard steps on the stairs. It was Léon. She got up and took from the chest of drawers the first pile of dusters to be hemmed. When he came in she seemed very busy.

The conversation languished; Madame Bovary let it drop every few minutes, while he himself seemed quite embarrassed. Seated on a low chair near the fire, he kept turning the ivory thimble case with his fingers. She stitched on, or from time to time turned down the hem of the cloth with her nail. She did not speak; he was silent, captivated by her silence, as he would have been by her speech.

"Poor fellow!" she thought.

"How have I displeased her?" he asked himself.

At last, however, Léon said that one of these days, he had to go to Rouen on business.

"Your music subscription has expired; shall I renew it?"

"No," she replied.

"Why?"

"Because . . ."

And pursing her lips she slowly drew a long stitch of grey thread.

This work irritated Léon. It seemed to roughen the ends of her fingers. A gallant phrase came into his head, but he did not risk it.

"Then you are giving it up?" he went on.

"What?" she asked hurriedly. "Music? Ah! yes! Have I not my house to look after, my husband to attend to, a thousand things, in fact, many duties that must be considered first?"

She looked at the clock. Charles was late. Then she affected anxiety. Two or three times she even repeated, "He is so good!"

The clerk was fond of Monsieur Bovary. But this tenderness on his behalf came as an unpleasant surprise; still, he sang his praise: everyone did, he said, especially the pharmacist.

"Ah! he is a good man," continued Emma.

"Certainly," replied the clerk.

And he began talking of Madame Homais, whose very untidy appearance generally made them laugh.

"What does it matter?" interrupted Emma. "A good housewife does not trouble about her appearance."

Then she relapsed into silence.

It was the same on the following days; her talks, her manners, everything changed. She took interest in the housework, went to church regularly, and looked after her maid with more severity.

She took Berthe away from the nurse. When visitors called, Félicité brought her in, and Madame Bovary undressed her to show off her limbs. She claimed to love children; they were her consolation, her joy, her passion, and she accompanied her caresses with lyrical outbursts that would have reminded any one but the Yonvillians of Sachette[37] in "Notre Dame de Paris."[38]

When Charles came home he found his slippers put to warm near the fire. His waistcoat now never wanted lining, nor his shirt buttons, and it was quite a pleasure to see in the cupboard the night-caps arranged in piles of the same height. She no longer grumbled as before when asked to take a walk in the garden; what he proposed was always done, although she never anticipated the wishes to which she submitted without a murmur; and when Léon saw him sit by his fireside after dinner, his two hands on his stomach, his two feet on the fender, his cheeks flushed with wine, his eyes moist with happiness, the child crawling along the carpet, and this woman with the slender waist who came behind his armchair to kiss his forehead:

"What madness!" he said to himself. "How could I ever hope to reach her?"

She seemed so virtuous and inaccessible to him that he lost all hope, even the faintest. But, by thus renouncing her, he made her ascend to extraordinary heights. She transcended, in his eyes, those sensuous attributes which were forever out of his reach; and in his heart she rose forever, soaring away from him like a winged apotheosis. It was one of those pure feelings that do not interfere with life, that are cultivated for their rarity, and whose loss would afflict more than their fulfilment rejoices.

Emma grew thinner, her cheeks paler, her face longer. With her black hair, her large eyes, her straight nose, her birdlike walk, and always silent now, did she not seem to be passing through life scarcely touching it, bearing on her brow the slight mark of a sublime destiny? She was so sad and so calm, at once so gentle and so reserved, that near her one came under the spell of an icy charm, as we shudder in churches at the perfume of the flowers mingling with the cold of the marble. Even others could not fail to be impressed. The pharmacist said:

"She is a real lady! She would not be out of place in a sous-préfecture!"

---

37. Sachette ("sackcloth"); Paguette la Chantefleurie is the mother of Agnès, the girl abducted by gypsies who takes the name Esmeralda. She worshipped a shoe of her stolen child.

38. *Notre Dame de Paris* (1831) is a historical novel by Victor Hugo (1802–1885).

The housewives admired her thrift, the patients her politeness, the poor her charity.

But she was eaten up with desires, with rage, with hate. The rigid folds of her dress covered a tormented heart of which her chaste lips never spoke. She was in love with Léon, and sought solitude that she might more easily delight in his image. His physical presence troubled the voluptuousness of this meditation. Emma thrilled at the sound of his step; then in his presence the emotion subsided, and afterwards there remained in her only an immense astonishment that ended in sorrow.

Léon did not know that when he left her in despair she rose after he had gone to see him in the street. She concerned herself about his comings and goings; she watched his face; she invented quite a story to find an excuse for going to his room. She envied the pharmacist's wife for sleeping under the same roof, and her thoughts constantly centered upon this house, like the Lion d'Or pigeons who alighted there to dip their pink feet and white wings in the rainpipes. But the more Emma grew conscious of her love, the more she repressed it, hoping thus to hide and to stifle her true feeling. She would have liked Léon to know, and she imagined circumstances, catastrophes that would make this possible. What restrained her was, no doubt, idleness and fear, as well as a sense of shame. She thought she had repulsed him too much, that the time was past, that all was lost. Then, pride, the joy of being able to say to herself, "I am virtuous," and to look at herself in the mirror striking resigned poses, consoled her a little for the sacrifice she thought she was making.

Then the desires of the flesh, the longing for money, and the melancholy of passion all blended into one suffering, and instead of putting it out of her mind, she made her thoughts cling to it, urging herself to pain and seeking everywhere the opportunity to revive it. A poorly served dish, a half open door would aggravate her; she bewailed the clothes she did not have, the happiness she had missed, her overexalted dreams, her too cramped home.

What exasperated her was that Charles did not seem to be aware of her torment. His conviction that he was making her happy looked to her a stupid insult, and his self-assurance on this point sheer ingratitude. For whom, then, was she being virtuous? Was it not for him, the obstacle to all happiness, the cause of all misery, and, as it were, the sharp clasp of that complex strap that buckled her in all sides?

Thus he became the butt of all the hatred resulting from her frustrations; but all efforts to conquer them augmented her suffering— for this useless humiliation still added to her despair and widened the gap between them. His very gentleness would drive her at times to rebellion. Domestic mediocrity urged her on to wild extravagance, matrimonial tenderness to adulterous desires. She would have liked

Charles to beat her, that she might have a better right to hate him, to revenge herself upon him. She was surprised sometimes at the shocking thoughts that came into her head, and she had to go on smiling, to hear repeated to her at all hours that she was happy, to pretend to be happy and let it be believed.

Yet, at moments, she loathed this hypocrisy. She was tempted to flee somewhere with Léon and try a new life; but at once a dark, shapeless chasm would open within her soul.

"Besides, he no longer loves me," she thought. "What is to become of me? What help can I hope for, what consolation, what relief?"

Such thoughts would leave her shattered, exhausted, frozen, sobbing silently, with flowing tears.

"Why don't you tell monsieur?" the maid asked her when she came in during these crises.

"It is nerves," said Emma. "Don't mention it to him, he would worry."

"Ah! yes," Félicité went on, "you are just like La Guérine, the daughter of Père Guérin, the fisherman at le Pollet,[39] that I used to know at Dieppe before I came to see you. She was so sad, so sad, that to see her standing on the threshold of her house, she looked like a winding-sheet spread out before the door. Her illness, it appears, was a kind of fog that she had in the head, and the doctors could do nothing about it, neither could the priest. When she had a bad spell, she went off by herself to the sea-shore, so that the customs officer, going his rounds, often found her flat on her face, crying on the pebbles. Then, after her marriage, it stopped, they say."

"But with me," replied Emma, "it was after marriage that it began."

VI

One evening when she was sitting by the open window, watching Lestiboudois, the sexton, trim the boxwood, she suddenly heard the Angelus ringing.

It was the beginning of April, when the primroses are in bloom, and a warm wind blows over the newly-turned flower beds, and the gardens, like women, seem to be getting ready for the summer dances. Through the bars of the arbour and away beyond, the river could be seen in the fields, meandering through the grass in sinuous curves. The evening vapors rose between the leafless poplars, touching their outlines with a violet tint, paler and more transparent than a subtle gauze caught amidst their branches. Cattle moved around in the distance; neither their steps nor their lowing could be heard; and the bell, still ringing through the air, kept up its peaceful lamentation.

39. Suburb of Dieppe, where the fishermen live.

This repeated tinkling stirred in the young woman distant memories of her youth and school-days. She remembered the great candle-sticks that rose above the vases full of flowers on the altar, and the tabernacle with its small columns. She would have liked to be once more lost in the long line of white veils, marked off here and there by the stiff black hoods of the good sisters bending over their praying-chairs. At mass on Sundays, when she looked up, she saw the gentle face of the Virgin amid the blue smoke of the rising incense. The image awoke a tender emotion in her; she felt limp and helpless, like the down of a bird whirled by the tempest, and it was unconsciously that she went towards the church, ready for any kind of devotion, provided she could humble her soul and lose all sense of selfhood.

On the Square she met Lestiboudois on his way back, for, in order not to lose out on a full day's wages, he preferred to interrupt his gardening-work and go ring the Angelus when it suited him best. Besides, the earlier ringing warned the boys that catechism time had come.

Already a few who had arrived were playing marbles on the stones of the cemetery. Others, astride the wall, swung their legs, trampling with their wooden shoes the large nettles that grew between the little enclosure and the newest graves. This was the only green spot. All the rest was but stones, always covered with a fine dust, in spite of Lestiboudois' broom.

The children played around in their socks, as if they were on their own ground. The shouts of their voices could be heard through the humming of the bell. The noise subsided with the swinging of the great rope that, hanging from the top of the belfry, dragged its end on the ground. Swallows flitted to and fro uttering little cries, cutting the air with the edge of their wings, and swiftly returned to their yellow nests under the eave-tiles of the coping. At the end of the church a lamp was burning, the wick of a night-light hung up in a glass. Seen from a distance, it looked like a white stain trembling in the oil. A long ray of the sun fell across the nave and seemed to darken the lower sides and the corners.

"Where is the priest?" Madame Bovary asked one of the boys, who was entertaining himself by shaking the turnstile in its too loose socket.

"He is coming," he answered.

Indeed, the door of the rectory creaked and the Abbé Bournisien appeared; the children fled in a heap into the church.

"The little brats!" muttered the priest, "always the same!" Then, picking up a ragged catechism on which he had stepped:

"They have respect for nothing!"

But, as soon as he caught sight of Madame Bovary:

"Excuse me," he said; "I did not recognise you."

He thrust the catechism into his pocket, and stopped, balancing the heavy key of the sacristy between his two fingers.

The full light of the setting sun upon his face made the cloth of his cassock, shiny at the elbows and frayed at the hem, seem paler. Grease and tobacco stains ran along his broad chest, following the line of his buttons, growing sparser in the vicinity of his neckcloth, in which rested the massive folds of his red chin; it was dotted with yellow spots that disappeared beneath the coarse hair of his greyish beard. He had just eaten his dinner, and was breathing noisily.

"And how are you?" he added.

"Not well," replied Emma; "I am suffering."

"So do I," answered the priest. "The first heat of the year is hard to bear, isn't it? But, after all, we are born to suffer, as St. Paul says. But, what does Monsieur Bovary think of it?"

"He!" she said with a gesture of contempt.

"What!" he replied, genuinely surprised, "doesn't he prescribe something for you?"

"Ah!" said Emma, "it is no earthly remedy I need."

But the curé time and again was looking into the church, where the kneeling boys were shouldering one another, and tumbling over like packs of cards.

"I should like to know . . ." she went on.

"You look out, Riboudet," the priest cried angrily, "I'll box your ears, you scoundrel!" Then turning to Emma. "He's Boudet the carpenter's son; his parents are well off, and let him do just as he pleases. Yet he could learn quickly if he would, for he is very sharp. And so sometimes for a joke I call him Riboudet (like the road one takes to go to Maromme), and I even say 'Mon Riboudet.' Ha! ha! 'Mont Riboudet.' The other day I repeated this little joke to the bishop, and he laughed. Can you imagine? He deigned to laugh. And how is Monsieur Bovary?"

She seemed not to hear him. And he went on . . .

"Always very busy, no doubt; for he and I are certainly the busiest people in the parish. But he is doctor of the body," he added with a thick laugh, "and I of the soul."

She fixed her pleading eyes upon the priest. "Yes," she said, "you solace all sorrows."

"Ah! don't tell me of it, Madame Bovary. This morning I had to go to Bas-Diauville for a cow was all swollen; they thought it was under a spell. All their cows, I don't know how it is . . . But pardon me! Longuemarre and Boudet! Bless me! Will you stop it?"

And he bounded into the church.

The boys were just then clustering round the large desk, climbing over the cantor's footstool, opening the missal; and others on tiptoe were just about to venture into the confessional. But the priest suddenly distributed a shower of blows among them. Seizing them by the collars of their coats, he lifted them from the ground, and deposited them on their knees on the stones of the choir, firmly, as if he meant to plant them there.

"Yes," said he, when he returned to Emma, unfolding his large cotton handkerchief, one corner of which he put between his teeth, "farmers are much to be pitied."

"Others, too," she replied.

"Certainly. Workingmen in the cities, for instance."

"I wasn't thinking of them . . ."

"Oh, but excuse me! I've known housewives there, virtuous women, I assure you, real saints, who didn't even have bread to eat."

"But those," replied Emma, and the corners of her mouth twitched as she spoke, "those, Monsieur le Curé, who have bread and have no . . ."

"Fire in the winter," said the priest.

"Oh, what does it matter?"

"What! What does it matter? It seems to me that when one has firing and food . . . for, after all . . ."

"My God! my God!" she sighed.

"Do you feel unwell?" he asked, approaching her anxiously. "It is indigestion, no doubt? You must get home, Madame Bovary; drink a little tea, that will strengthen you, or else a glass of fresh water with a little moist sugar."

"Why?"

And she looked like one awaking from a dream.

"Well, you see, you were putting your hand to your forehead. I thought you felt faint."

Then, bethinking himself: "But you were asking me something? What was it? I don't remember."

"I? Oh, nothing . . . nothing," Emma repeated.

And the glance she cast round her slowly fell upon the old man in the cassock. They looked at each other face to face without speaking.

"Well then, Madame Bovary," he said at last, "excuse me, but duty comes first as the saying goes; I must look after my brats. The first communion will soon be upon us, and I fear we shall be behind, as ever. So after Ascension Day I regularly keep them an extra hour every Wednesday. Poor children! One cannot lead them too soon into the path of the Lord . . . he himself advised us to do so, through the mouth of his Divine Son. Good health to you, madame; my respects to your husband."

And he went into the church making a genuflexion as soon as he reached the door.

Emma saw him disappear between the double row of benches, walking with heavy tread, his head a little bent over his shoulder, and with his two half-open hands stretched sidewards.

Then she turned on her heel all of one piece, like a statue on a pivot, and went homewards. But the loud voice of the priest, the clear voices of the boys still reached her ears, and pursued her:

"Are you a Christian?"

"Yes, I am a Christian."

"What is a Christian?"

"He who, being baptized . . . baptized . . . baptized . . ."

She climbed the steps of the staircase holding on to the banisters, and when she was in her room threw herself into an arm-chair.

The whitish light of the window-panes was softly wavering. The pieces of furniture seemed more frozen in their places, about to lose themselves in the shadow as in an ocean of darkness. The fire was out, the clock went on ticking, and Emma vaguely wondered at this calm of all things while within herself there was such tumult. But little Berthe was there, between the window and the work-table, tottering on her knitted shoes, and trying to reach the end of her mother's apron-strings.

"Leave me alone," Emma said, pushing her back with her hand.

The little girl soon came up closer against her knees, and leaning on them with her arms, she looked up with her large blue eyes, while a small thread of clear saliva drooled from her lips on to the silk of her apron.

"Leave me alone," repeated the young woman quite angrily.

Her expression frightened the child, who began to scream.

"Will you leave me alone?" she said, forcing her away with her elbow.

Berthe fell at the foot of the chest of drawers against the brass handle; she cut her cheek, blood appeared. Madame Bovary rushed to lift her up, broke the bell-rope, called for the maid with all her might, and she was just going to curse herself when Charles appeared. It was dinner time; he was coming home.

"Look, dear!" said Emma calmly, "the child fell down while she was playing, and she hurt herself."

Charles reassured her; it was only a slight cut, and he went for some adhesive plaster.

Madame Bovary did not go downstairs to the dining-room; she wished to remain alone to look after the child. Then watching her sleep, the little anxiety she still felt gradually wore off, and she seemed very stupid to herself, and very kind to have been so worried just now at so little. Berthe, in fact, no longer cried. Her breathing now imperceptibly raised the cotton covering. Big tears lay in the corner of the half-closed eyelids, through whose lashes one could see two pale sunken pupils; the adhesive plaster on her cheek pulled the skin aside.

"It is very strange," thought Emma, "how ugly this child is!"

When at eleven o'clock Charles came back from the pharmacist's shop, where he had gone after dinner to return the remainder of the plaster, he found his wife standing by the cradle.

"I assure you it's nothing," he said, kissing her on the forehead. "Don't worry, my poor darling; you will make yourself ill."

He had stayed a long time at the pharmacist's. Although he had not seemed much concerned, Homais, nevertheless, had exerted himself to buoy him up, to "raise his spirits." Then they had talked of the various dangers that threaten childhood, of the carelessness of servants. Madame Homais knew what he meant: she still carried on her chest the scars of a load of charcoal that a cook dropped on her when she was a child. Hence that her kind parents took all sorts of precautions. The knives were not sharpened, nor the floors waxed; there were iron gratings in front of the windows and strong bars across the fireplace. In spite of their spirit, the little Homais could not stir without some one watching them; at the slightest cold their father stuffed them with cough-syrups; and until they turned four they all were mercilessly forced to use padded headwear. This, it is true, was a fancy of Madame Homais'; her husband was secretly afflicted by it. Fearing the possible consequences of such compression to the intellectual organs, he even went so far as to say to her:

"Do you want to make them into Caribs or Botocudos?"

Charles, however, had several times tried to interrupt the conversation.

"I would like a word with you," he whispered, addressing the clerk who preceded him on the stairs.

"Can he suspect anything?" Léon asked himself. His heart beat faster, and all sorts of conjectures occured to him.

At last, Charles, having closed the door behind him, begged him to inquire at Rouen after the price of a fine daguerreotype. It was a sentimental surprise he intended for his wife, a delicate attention: his own portrait in black tail coat. But he wanted first to know how much it would cost. It wouldn't cause Monsieur Léon too much trouble to find out, since he went to town almost every week.

Why? Monsieur Homais suspected some love affair, an intrigue. But he was mistaken. Léon was carrying on no flirtations. He was sadder than ever, as Madame Lefrançois saw from the amount of food he left on his plate. To find out more about it she questioned the tax-collector. Binet answered roughly that he wasn't being paid to spy on him.

All the same, his companion's behavior seemed very strange to him, for Léon often threw himself back in his chair, and stretching out his arms, complained vaguely about life.

"It's because you have no distractions," said the collector.

"What distractions?"

"If I were you I'd have a lathe."

"But I don't know how to turn," answered the clerk.

"Ah! that's true," said the other, rubbing his chin with an air of mingled contempt and satisfaction.

Léon was weary of loving without success; moreover, he was beginning to feel that depression caused by the repetition of the same life, with no interest to inspire and no hope to sustain it. He was so bored with Yonville and the Yonvillers, that the sight of certain persons, of certain houses, irritated him beyond endurance; and the pharmacist, good companion though he was, was becoming absolutely unbearable to him. Yet the prospect of a new condition of life frightened as much as it seduced him.

This apprehension soon changed into impatience, and then Paris beckoned from afar with the music of its masked balls, the laughter of the grisettes. Since he was to go to law-school there anyway, why not set out at once? Who prevented him? And, inwardly, he began making preparations; he arranged his occupations beforehand. In his mind, he decorated an apartment. He would lead an artist's life there! He would take guitar lessons! He would have a dressing-gown, a Basque béret, blue velvet slippers! He already admired two crossed foils over his chimney-piece, with a skull on the guitar above them.

The main difficulty was to obtain his mother's consent, though nothing could seem more reasonable. Even his employer advised him to go to some other law office where he could learn more rapidly. Taking a middle course, then, Léon looked for some position as second clerk in Rouen; found none, and at last wrote his mother a long letter full of details, in which he set forth the reasons for going to live in Paris at once. She consented.

He did not hurry. Every day for a month Hivert carried boxes, valises, parcels for him from Yonville to Rouen and from Rouen to Yonville; and when Léon had rounded out his wardrobe, had his three armchairs restuffed, bought a supply of neckties, in a word, had made more preparations than for a trip round the world, he put it off from week to week, until he received a second letter from his mother urging him to leave, since he wanted to pass his examination before the vacation.

When the moment for the farewells had come, Madame Homais wept, Justin sobbed; Homais, as a strong man, concealed his emotion; he wished to carry his friend's overcoat himself as far as the gate of the notary, who was taking Léon to Rouen in his carriage. The latter had just time to bid farewell to Monsieur Bovary.

When he reached the head of the stairs he stopped, he was so out of breath. When he entered, Madame Bovary rose hurriedly.

"It is I again!" said Léon.

"I was sure of it!"

She bit her lips, and a rush of blood flowing under her skin made her red from the roots of her hair to the top of her collar. She remained standing, leaning with her shoulder against the wainscot.

"The doctor is not here?" he went on.

"He is out."

She repeated:

"He is out."

Then there was silence. They looked one at the other, and their thoughts, united in the same agony, clung together like two hearts in a passionate embrace.

"I would like to kiss little Berthe good-bye," said Léon.

Emma went down a few steps and called Félicité.

He threw one long look around him that took in the walls, the shelves, the fireplace, as if to appropriate everything, to carry it with him.

She returned, and the servant brought Berthe, who was swinging an upside down windmill at the end of a string. Léon kissed her several times on the neck.

"Good-bye poor child! good-bye, dear little one! good-bye!" And he gave her back to her mother.

"Take her away," she said.

They remained alone—Madame Bovary, her back turned, her face pressed against a window-pane; Léon held his cap in his hand, tapping it softly against his thigh.

"It is going to rain," said Emma.

"I have a coat," he answered.

"Ah!"

She turned round, her chin lowered, her forehead bent forward. The light covered it to the curve of the eyebrows, like a single piece of marble, without revealing what Emma was seeing on the horizon or what she was thinking within herself.

"Well, good-bye," he sighed.

She raised her head with a quick movement.

"Yes, good-bye . . . go!"

They faced each other; he held out his hand; she hesitated.

"In the English manner, then," she said, offering him her hand and forcing a laugh.

Léon felt it between his fingers, and the very substance of all his being seemed to pass into that moist palm.

He opened his hand; their eyes met again, and he disappeared. When he reached the market-place, he stopped and hid behind a pillar to look for the last time at this white house with the four green blinds. He thought he saw a shadow behind the window in the room; but the curtain, sliding along the rod as though no one were touching it, slowly opened its long oblique folds, that spread out all at once, and thus hung straight and motionless as a plaster wall. Léon ran away.

From afar he saw his employer's buggy in the road, and by it a man in a coarse apron holding the horse. Homais and Monsieur Guillaumin were talking. They were waiting for him.

"Embrace me," said the pharmacist with tears in his eyes. "Here is your coat, my good friend. Mind the cold; take care of yourself; don't overdo it!"

"Come, Léon, jump in," said the notary.

Homais bent over the splash-board, and in a voice broken by sobs uttered these three sad words:

"A pleasant journey!"

"Good-night," said Monsieur Guillaumin. "Go ahead!"

They departed and Homais went home.

Madame Bovary had opened her window that looked out over the garden and watched the clouds. They were gathering round the sunset in the direction of Rouen, and rolling back swiftly in black swirls, behind which the great rays of the sun looked out like the golden arrows of a suspended trophy, while the rest of the empty heavens was white as porcelain. But a gust of wind bowed the poplars, and suddenly the rain fell; it rattled against the green leaves. Then the sun reappeared, the hens clucked, sparrows shook their wings in the damp thickets, and the pools of water on the gravel as they flowed away carried off the pink flowers of an acacia.

"Ah! how far off he must be already!" she thought.

Monsieur Homais, as usual, came at half-past six during dinner.

"Well," said he, "so we've sent off our young friend!"

"So it seems," replied the doctor.

Then, turning on his chair: "Any news at home?"

"Nothing much. Only my wife was a little out of sorts this afternoon. You know women—a nothing upsets them, especially my wife. And we shouldn't object to that, since their nervous system is much more fragile than ours."

"Poor Léon!" said Charles. "How will he live at Paris? Will he get used to it?"

Madame Bovary sighed.

"Of course!" said the pharmacist, smacking his lips. "The late night suppers! the masked balls, the champagne—he won't be losing his time, I assure you."

"I don't think he'll go wrong," objected Bovary.

"Nor do I," said Monsieur Homais quickly; "although he'll have to do like the rest for fear of passing for a Jesuit. And you don't know what a life those jokers lead in the Latin quarter, actresses and the rest! Besides, students are thought a great deal of in Paris. Provided they have a few accomplishments, they are received in the best society; there are even ladies of the Faubourg Saint-Germain[40] who fall in love with them, which later gives them opportunities for making very good matches."

"But," said the doctor, "I fear for him that . . . down there . . ."

"You are right," interrupted the pharmacist, "that is the other side of the coin. And you are constantly obliged to keep your hand in your pocket there. Let us say, for instance, you are in a public garden. A fellow appears, well dressed, even wearing a decoration, and whom one would take for a diplomat. He addresses you, you chat with him; he forces himself upon you; offers you a pinch of snuff, or picks up your hat. Then you become more intimate; he takes you to a café, invites you to his countryhouse, introduces you, between two drinks, to all sorts of people; and three-fourths of the time it's only to get hold of your money or involve you in some shady deal"

"That is true," said Charles; "but I was thinking specially of illnesses—of typhoid fever, for example, that attacks students from the provinces."

Emma shuddered.

"Because of the change of diet," continued the pharmacist, "and of the resulting upset for the whole system. And then the water at Paris, don't you know! The dishes at restaurants, all the spiced food, end by heating the blood, and are not worth, whatever people may say of them, a good hearty stew. As for me, I have always preferred home cooking; it is healthier. So when I was studying pharmacy at Rouen, I boarded in a boarding-house; and dined with the professors."

And thus he went on, expounding his general opinions and his personal preferences, until Justin came to fetch him for a mulled egg for a customer.

"Not a moment's peace!" he cried; "always at it! I can't go out for a minute! Like a plough-horse, I have always to be sweating blood and water! What drudgery!" Then, when he was at the door, "By the way, do you know the news?"

"What news?"

"It is very likely," Homais went on, raising his eyebrows and assuming one of his gravest expressions, "that the agricultural fair

40. Faubourg Saint-Germain is the aristocratic quarter of Paris.

of the Seine-Inférieure will be held this year at Yonville-l'Abbaye."

The rumor, at all events, is going the round. This morning the paper alluded to it. It would be of the utmost importance for our district. But we'll talk it over later. I can see, thank you; Justin has the lantern."

VII

The next day was a dreary one for Emma. Everything seemed shrouded in an atmosphere of bleakness that hung darkly over the outward aspect of things, and sorrow blew into her soul with gentle moans, as the winter wind makes in ruined castles. Her reverie was that of things gone forever, the exhaustion that seizes you after everything is done; the pain, in short, caused by the interruption of a familiar motion, the sudden halting of a long drawn out vibration.

As on the return from Vaubyessard, when the quadrilles were running in her head, she was full of a gloomy melancholy, of a numb despair. Léon reappeared, taller, handsomer, more charming, more vague. Though separated from her, he had not left her; he was there, and the walls of the house seemed to hold his shadow. She could not detach her eyes from the carpet where he had walked, from those empty chairs where he had sat. The river still flowed on and slowly drove its ripples along the slippery banks. They had often walked there listening to the murmur of the waves over the moss-covered pebbles. How bright the sun had been! What happy afternoons they had known, alone, in the shade at the end of the garden! He read aloud, bare-headed, sitting on a footstool of dry sticks; the fresh wind of the meadow set trembling the leaves of the book and the nasturtiums of the arbour. Ah! he was gone, the only charm of her life, the only possible hope of joy. Why had she not seized this happiness when it came to her? Why did she not keep him from leaving, beg him on her knees, when he was about to flee from her? And she cursed herself for not having loved Léon. She thirsted for his lips. She wanted to run after him, to throw herself into his arms and say to him, "It is I; I am yours." But Emma recoiled beforehand at the difficulties of the enterprise, and her desires, increased by regret, became only the more acute.

Henceforth the memory of Léon was the center of her boredom; it burnt there more brightly than the fires left by travellers on the snow of a Russian steppe. She threw herself at his image, pressed herself against it; she stirred carefully the dying embers, sought all around her anything that could make it flare; and the most distant reminiscences, like the most immediate occasions, what she experienced as well as what she imagined, her wasted voluptuous desires that were unsatisfied, her projects of happiness that crackled in the wind like dead boughs, her sterile virtue, her lost hopes, the yoke of domesticity,—she gathered it all up, took everything, and made it all serve as fuel for her melancholy.

The flames, however, subsided, either because the supply had exhausted itself, or because it had been piled up too much. Love, little by little, was quelled by absence; regret stifled beneath habit; and the bright fire that had empurpled her pale sky was overspread and faded by degrees. In her slumbering conscience, she took her disgust for her husband for aspirations towards her lover, the burning of hate for the warmth of tenderness; but as the tempest still raged, and as passion burnt itself down to the very cinders, and no help came, no sun rose, there was night on all sides, and she was lost in the terrible cold that pierced her through.

Then the evil days of Tostes began again. She thought herself now far more unhappy; for she had the experience of grief, with the certainty that it would not end.

A woman who had consented to such sacrifices could well allow herself certain whims. She bought a gothic prie-Dieu, and in a month spent fourteen francs on lemons for polishing her nails; she wrote to Rouen for a blue cashmere gown; she chose one of Lheureux's finest scarves, and wore it knotted round her waist over her dressing-gown; thus dressed, she lay stretched out on the couch with closed blinds.

She often changed her hairdo; she did her hair *à la Chinoise*, in flowing curls, in plaited coils; she parted it on one side and rolled it under, like a man's.

She wanted to learn Italian; she bought dictionaries, a grammar, and a supply of white paper. She tried serious reading, history, and philosophy. Sometimes in the night Charles woke up with a start, thinking he was being called to a patient:

"I'm coming," he stammered.

It was the noise of a match Emma had struck to relight the lamp. But her reading fared like her pieces of embroidery, all of which, only just begun, filled her cupboard; she took it up, left it, passed on to other books.

She had attacks in which she could easily have been driven to commit any folly. She maintained one day, to contradict her husband, that she could drink off a large glass of brandy, and, as Charles was stupid enough to dare her to, she swallowed the brandy to the last drop.

In spite of her vaporish airs (as the housewives of Yonville called them), Emma, all the same, never seemed gay, and usually she had at the corners of her mouth that immobile contraction that puckers the faces of old maids, and those of men whose ambition has failed. She was pale all over, white as a sheet; the skin of her nose was drawn at the nostrils, her eyes had a vague look. After discovering three grey hairs on her temples, she talked much of her old age.

She often had spells. One day she even spat blood, and, as Charles fussed round her showing his anxiety . . .

"Bah!" she answered, "what does it matter?"

Charles fled to his study and wept there, both his elbows on the table, sitting in his office chair under the phrenological head.

Then he wrote to his mother to beg her to come, and they had many long consultations together on the subject of Emma.

What should they decide? What was to be done since she rejected all medical treatment?

"Do you know what your wife wants?" replied Madame Bovary senior. "She wants to be forced to occupy herself with some manual work. If she were obliged, like so many others, to earn her living, she wouldn't have these vapors, that come to her from a lot of ideas she stuffs into her head, and from the idleness in which she lives."

"Yet she is always busy," said Charles.

"Ah! always busy at what? Reading novels, bad books, works against religion, and in which they mock at priests in speeches taken from Voltaire. But all that leads you far astray, my poor child. A person who has no religion is bound to go astray."

So it was decided to keep Emma from reading novels. The enterprise did not seem easy. The old lady took it upon herself: She was, when she passed through Rouen, to go herself to the lending library and represent that Emma had discontinued her subscription. Would they not have a right to call in the police if the bookseller persisted all the same in his poisonous trade?

The farewells of mother and daughter-in-law were cold. During the three weeks that they had been together they had not exchanged half-a-dozen words except for the usual questions and greetings when they met at table and in the evening before going to bed.

Madame Bovary left on a Wednesday, the market-day at Yonville.

Since morning, the Square had been crowded by end on end of carts, which, with their shafts in the air, spread all along the line of houses from the church to the inn. On the other side there were canvas booths for the sale of cotton goods, blankets, and woolen stockings, together with harness for horses, and packages of blue ribbon, whose ends fluttered in the wind. The coarse hardware was spread out on the ground between pyramids of eggs and hampers of cheeses showing pieces of sticky straw. Near the wheat threshers clucking hens passed their necks through the bars of flat cages. The crowds piled up in one place and refused to budge; they threatened at times to smash the window of the pharmacy. On

Wednesdays his shop was never empty, and the people pushed in less to buy drugs than for consultations, so great was Homais' reputation in the neighboring villages. His unshakable assurance deeply impresssed the country people. They considered him a greater doctor than all the doctors.

Emma was standing in the open window (she often did so: in the provinces, the window takes the place of the theatre and the promenade) and she amused herself with watching the rustic crowd, when she saw a gentleman in a green velvet coat. Although he was wearing heavy boots, he had on yellow gloves; he was coming towards the doctor's house, followed by a worried looking peasant with lowered head and quite a thoughtful air.

"Can I see the doctor?" he asked Justin, who was talking on the doorsteps with Félicité.

And, mistaking him for a servant of the house, he added,

"Tell him that M. Rodolphe Boulanger *de la* Huchette is here."

It was not out of affectation that the new arrival added "*de la* Huchette" to his name, but to make himself the better known. La Huchette, in fact, was an estate near Yonville, where he had just bought the château and two farms that he cultivated himself, without, however, taking too many pains. He lived as a bachelor, and was supposed to have an income of "at least fifteen thousand francs a year."

Charles came into the room. Monsieur Boulanger introduced his man, who wanted to be bled because he felt "as if ants were crawling all over him."

"It will clear me out," was his answer to all reasonable objections.

So Bovary brought a bandage and a basin, and asked Justin to hold it. Then addressing the peasant, who was already turning pale:

"Don't be scared, my friend."

"No, no, sir," said the other; "go ahead!"

And with an air of bravado he held out his heavy arm. At the prick of the lancet the blood spurted out, splashing against the looking-glass.

"Hold the basin nearer," exclaimed Charles.

"Look!" said the peasant, "one would swear it was a little fountain flowing. How red my blood is! That's a good sign, isn't it?"

"Sometimes," answered the officier de santé, "one feels nothing at first, and them they start fainting, especially when they're strong like this one."

At these words the peasant dropped the lancet-case he was holding back of his chair. A shudder of his shoulders made the chair-back creak. His hat fell off.

"I thought as much," said Bovary, pressing his finger on the vein.

The basin was beginning to tremble in Justin's hands; his knees shook, he turned pale.

"My wife! get my wife!" called Charles.

With one bound she rushed down the staircase.

"Vinegar," he cried. "Lord, two at a time!"

And he was so upset he could hardly put on the compress.

"It is nothing," said Monsieur Boulanger quietly, taking Justin in his arms. He seated him on the table with his back resting against the wall.

Madame Bovary opened the collar of his shirt. The strings of his shirt had got into a knot, and she was for some minutes moving her light fingers about the young fellow's neck. Then she poured some vinegar on her cambric handkerchief; she moistened his temples with little dabs, and then blew delicately upon them.

The ploughman revived, but Justin remained unconscious. His eyeballs disappeared in their whites like blue flowers in milk.

"We must hide this from him," said Charles.

Madame Bovary took the basin to put it under the table. With the movement she made in bending down, her dress (it was a summer dress with four flounces, yellow, long in the waist and wide in the skirt) spread out around on the tiles; and as Emma, stooping, staggered a little in stretching out her arms, the pull of her dress made it hug more closely the line of her bosom. Then she went to fetch a bottle of water, and she was melting some pieces of sugar when the pharmacist arrived. The maid had gone for him at the height of the confusion; seeing his pupil with his eyes open he gave a sigh of relief; then going round him he looked at him from head to foot.

"You fool!" he said, "you're a real fool! A capital idiot! And all that for a little blood-letting! and coming from a fellow who isn't afraid of anything! a real squirrel, climbing to incredible heights in order to steal nuts! You can be proud of yourself! showing a fine talent for the pharmaceutical profession; for, later on, you may be called before the courts of justice in serious circumstances, to enlighten the consciences of the magistrates, and you would have to keep your head then, to reason, show yourself a man, or else pass for an imbecile."

Justin did not answer. The pharmacist went on:

"Who asked you to come? You are always pestering the doctor and madame. Anyway, on Wednesday, I need you in the shop. There are over 20 people there now waiting to be served. I left them just out of concern for you. Get going! hurry! Wait for me there and keep an eye on the jars."

When Justin, who was rearranging his clothes, had gone, they talked for a little while about fainting-fits. Madame Bovary had never fainted.

"That is most unusual for a lady," said Monsieur Boulanger; "but some people are very susceptible. Thus in a duel, I have seen a witness faint away at the mere sound of the loading of pistols."

"As for me," said the pharmacist, "the sight of other people's blood doesn't affect me in the least, but the mere thought of my own flowing would make me faint if I reflected upon it too much."

Monsieur Boulanger, however, dismissed his servant and told him to be quiet, now that his whim was satisfied.

"It gave me the opportunity of making your acquaintance," he added, and he looked at Emma as he said this.

Then he put three francs on the corner of the table, bowed casually, and went out.

He soon had crossed to the other bank of the river (this was his way back to La Huchette), and Emma saw him in the meadow, walking under the poplars, slackening his pace now and then as one who reflects.

"She is nice, very nice, that doctor's wife," he said to himself. "Fine teeth, black eyes, a dainty foot, a figure like a Parisienne's. Where the devil does she come from? Where did that boor ever pick her up?"

Monsieur Rodolphe Boulanger was thirty-four; he combined brutality of temperament with a shrewd judgment, having had much experience with women and being something of a connoisseur. This one had seemed pretty to him; so he kept dreaming about her and her husband.

"I think he is very stupid. She must be tired of him, no doubt. He has dirty nails, and hasn't shaven for three days. While he is trotting after his patients, she sits there mending socks. How bored she gets! How she'd want to be in the city and go dancing every night! Poor little woman! She is gaping after love like a carp on the kitchen table after water. Three gallant words and she'd adore me, I'm sure of it. She'd be tender, charming. Yes; but how get rid of her afterwards?"

The prospect of love's involvements brought to mind, by contrast, his present mistress. She was an actress in Rouen whom he kept, and when he had pondered over this image, even in memory he found himself satiated.

"Madame Bovary," he thought, "is much prettier, much fresher too. Virginie is decidedly beginning to grow fat. Her enthusiasms bore me to tears. And that habit of hers of eating prawns all the time . . . !"

The fields were empty; around him Rodolphe only heard the

noise of the grass as it rubbed against his boots, and the chirping of the cricket hidden away among the oats. He again saw Emma in her room, dressed as he had seen her, and he undressed her.

"Oh, I will have her," he cried, smashing, with a blow of his cane, a clod of earth before him.

At once, he began to consider the strategy. He wondered:

"Where shall we meet? And how? We shall always be having the brat on our hands, and the maid, the neighbors, the husband, all sorts of worries. Bah!" he concluded, "it would be too time-consuming!"

Then he started again:

"But she really has eyes that bore into your heart. And that pale complexion! And I, who love pale women!"

When he reached the top of the Argueil hills he had made up his mind.

"All that remains is to create the proper opportunity. Well, I will call in now and then, I'll send game and poultry; I'll have myself bled, if need be. We shall become friends; I'll invite them to my place. Of course!" he added, "the agricultural fair is coming on; she'll be there, I'll see her. We'll begin boldly, for that's the surest way."

VIII

At last it came, the much-awaited agricultural fair. Ever since the morning of the great day, the villagers, on their doorsteps, were discussing the preparations. The facade of the townhall had been hung with garlands of ivy; a tent had been erected in a meadow for the banquet; and in the middle of the Place, in front of the church, a kind of a small cannon was to announce the arrival of the prefect and the names of the fortunate farmers who had won prizes. The National Guard of Buchy (there was none at Yonville) had come to join the corps of firemen, of whom Binet was captain. On that day he wore a collar even higher than usual; and, tightly buttoned in his tunic, his figure was so stiff and motionless that all life seemed to be confined to his legs, which moved in time with the music, with a single motion. As there was some rivalry between the tax-collector and the colonel, both, to show off their talents, drilled their men separately. The red epaulettes and the black breastplates kept parading up and down, one after the other; there was no end to it, and it constantly began again. Never had there been such a display of pomp. Several citizens had washed down their houses the evening before; tricolor flags hung from half-open windows; all the cafés were full; and in the lovely weather the starched caps, the golden crosses, and the colored neckerchiefs seemed whiter than snow, shone in the sun, and relieved with their motley colors the somber monotony of the frock-coats and blue smocks. The neighboring farmers' wives, when they got off their horses, removed the long pin with which they had gathered their dresses tight around them for fear of getting them spattered; while their husbands protected their hats by covering them with handkerchiefs, of which they held one corner in their teeth.

The crowd came into the main street from both ends of the village. People poured in from the lanes, the alleys, the houses; and from time to time one heard the banging of doors closing behind ladies of the town in cotton gloves, who were going out to see the fête. Most admired of all were two long lamp-stands covered with lanterns, that flanked a platform on which the authorities were to sit. Aside from this, a kind of pole had been placed against the four columns of the townhall, each bearing a small standard of greenish cloth, embellished with inscriptions in gold letters. On one was written, "To Commerce"; on the other, "To Agriculture"; on the third, "To Industry"; and on the fourth, "To the Fine Arts".

But the jubilation that brightened all faces seemed to darken that of Madame Lefrançois, the innkeeper. Standing on her kitchen-steps she muttered to herself:

"How stupid! How stupid they are with their canvas booth! Do they think the prefect will be glad to dine down there under a tent like a gipsy? They call all this fussing for the good of the town! As if it helped the town to send to Neufchâtel for the keeper of a cookshop! And for whom? For cowheads! for tramps!"

The pharmacist passed by. He was wearing a frock-coat, nankeen trousers, beaver shoes, and, to everyone's surprise, a hat—a low crowned hat.

"Your servant," he said. "Excuse me, I am in a hurry."

And as the fat widow asked where he was going . . .

"It seems odd to you, doesn't it, I who am always more cooped up in my laboratory than the man's rat in his cheese."

"What cheese?" asked the landlady.

"Oh, nothing, never mind!" Homais continued. "I merely wished to convey to you, Madame Lefrançois, that I usually live at home like a recluse. To-day, however, considering the circumstances, it is necessary . . ."

"Oh, are you going down there?" she said contemptuously.

"Yes, I am going," replied the pharmacist, astonished. "Am I not a member of the Advisory committee?"

Mère Lefrançois looked at him for a few moments, and ended by saying with a smile:

"That's another matter! But is agriculture any of your business? Do you understand anything about it?"

"Certainly I understand it, since I am a pharmacist,—that is to say, a chemist. And the object of chemistry, Madame Lefrançois, being the knowledge of the reciprocal and molecular action of all natural bodies, it follows that agriculture is comprised within its domain. And, in fact, the composition of the manure, the fermentation of liquids, the analyses of gases, and the effects of miasmas, what, I ask you, is all this, if it isn't chemistry, pure and simple?"

The landlady did not answer. Homais went on:

"Do you think that to be an agriculturist it is necessary to have tilled the earth or fattened fowls oneself? It is much more important to know the composition of the substances in question—the geological strata, the atmospheric actions, the quality of the soil, the minerals, the waters, the density of the different bodies, their capillarity, and what not. And one must be master of all the principles of hygiene in order to direct, criticise the construction of buildings, the feeding of animals; the diet of the servants. And, moreover, Madame Lefrançois, one must know botany, be able to distinguish between plants, you understand, which are the wholesome and those that are deleterious, which are unproductive and which nutritive, if it is well to pull them up here and re-sow them there, to propagate some, destroy others; in brief, one must keep pace with science by reading publications and papers, be always on the alert to detect improvements."

The landlady never took her eyes off the "Café Français" and the pharmacist went on:

"Would to God our agriculturists were chemists, or that at least they would pay more attention to the counsels of science. Thus lately I myself wrote a substantial paper, a memoir of over seventy-two pages, entitled, 'Cider, its Manufacture and its Effects, together with some New Reflections on this Subject,' that I sent to the Agricultural Society in Rouen, and which even procured me the honor of being received among its members—Section, Agriculture; Class, Pomology. Well, if my work had been given to the public . . ."

But the pharmacist stopped, so distracted did Madame Lefrançois seem.

"Just look at them!" she said. "It's past comprehension! Such a hash-house!" And with a shrug of the shoulders that stretched out the stitches of her sweater, she pointed with both hands at the rival establishment, from where singing erupted. "Well, it won't last long," she added, "It'll be over before a week."

Homais drew back in surprise. She came down three steps and whispered in his ear:

"What! you didn't know it? They'll foreclose this week. It's Lheureux who does the selling; he killed them off with his notes."

"What a dreadful catastrophe!" exclaimed the pharmacist, who always found expressions that filled all imaginable circumstances.

Then the landlady began telling him this story, that she had heard from Theodore, Monsieur Guillaumin's servant, and although she detested Tellier, she blamed Lheureux. He was "a wheedler, a fawner."

"There!" she said. "Look at him! There he goes down the square; he is greeting Madame Bovary, who's wearing a green hat. And she is on Monsieur Boulanger's arm."

"Madame Bovary!" exclaimed Homais. "I must go at once and pay her my respects. Perhaps she'll be pleased to have a seat in the enclosure under the peristyle." And, without heeding Madame Lefrançois, who was calling him back for more gossip, the pharmacist walked off rapidly with a smile on his face and his walk jauntier than ever, bowing copiously to right and left, and taking up much room with the large tails of his frock-coat that fluttered behind him in the wind.

Rodolphe having caught sight of him from afar, quickened his pace, but Madame Bovary couldn't keep up; so he walked more slowly, and, smiling at her, said roughly:

"It's only to get away from that fat fellow, you know, the pharmacist."

She nudged him with her elbow.

"How shall I understand that?" he asked himself.

And, walking on, he looked at her out of the corner of his eyes.

Her profile was so calm that it revealed nothing. It stood out in the light from the oval of her hat that was tied with pale ribbons like waving rushes. Her eyes with their long curved lashes looked straight before her, and though wide open, they seemed slightly slanted at the cheek-bones, because of the blood pulsing gently under the delicate skin. A rosy light shone through the partition between her nostrils. Her head was bent upon her shoulder, and the tips of her teeth shone through her lips like pearls.

"Is she making fun of me?" thought Rodolphe.

Emma's gesture, however, had only been meant for a warning; for Monsieur Lheureux was accompanying them, and spoke now and again as if to enter into the conversation.

"What a beautiful day! Everybody is outside! The wind is from the east!"

Neither Madame Bovary nor Rodolphe answered him, but their slightest movement made him draw near saying, "I beg your pardon!" and raising his hat.

When they reached the blacksmith's house, instead of following the road up to the fence, Rodolphe suddenly turned down a path, drawing Madame Bovary with him. He called out:

"Good evening, Monsieur Lheureux! We'll see you soon!"

"How you got rid of him!" she said, laughing.

"Why," he went on, "allow oneself to be intruded upon by others? And as to-day I have the happiness of being with you . . ."

Emma blushed. He did not finish his sentence. Then he talked of the fine weather and of the pleasure of walking on the grass. A few daisies had sprung up again.

"Here are some pretty Easter daisies," he said, "and enough to provide oracles for all the lovers in the vicinity."

He added,

"Shall I pick some? What do you think?"

"Are you in love?" she asked, coughing a little.

"H'm, h'm! who knows?" answered Rodolphe.

The meadow was beginning to fill up, and the housewives were hustling about with their great umbrellas, their baskets, and their babies. One often had to make way for a long file of country girls, servant-maids with blue stockings, flat shoes and silver rings, who smelt of milk when one passed close to them. They walked along holding one another by the hand, and thus they spread over the whole field from the row of open trees to the banquet tent. But this was the judging time, and the farmers one after the other entered a kind of enclosure formed by ropes supported on sticks.

The beasts were there, their noses turned toward the rope, and making a confused line with their unequal rumps. Drowsy pigs were burrowing in the earth with their snouts, calves were lowing and bleating; the cows, one leg folded under them stretched their bellies on the grass, slowly chewing their cud, and blinking their heavy eyelids at the gnats that buzzed around them. Ploughmen with bare arms were holding by the halter prancing stallions that neighed with dilated nostrils looking in the direction of the mares. These stood quietly, stretching out their heads and flowing manes, while their foals rested in their shadow, or sucked them from time to time. And above the long undulation of these crowded bodies one saw some white mane rising in the wind like a wave, or some sharp horns sticking out, and the heads of men running about. Apart, outside the enclosure, a hundred paces off, was a large black bull, muzzled, with an iron ring in its nostrils, and who moved no more than if he had been in bronze. A child in rags was holding him by a rope.

Between the two lines the committee-men were walking with heavy steps, examining each animal, then consulting one another in a low voice. One who seemed of more importance now and then took notes in a book as he walked along. This was the president of the jury, Monsieur Derozerays de la Panville. As soon as he recognised Rodolphe he came forward quickly, and smiling amiably, said:

"What! Monsieur Boulanger, you are deserting us?"

Rodolphe protested that he would come. But when the president had disappeared:

"To tell the truth," he said, "I shall not go. Your company is better than his."

And while poking fun at the show, Rodolphe, to move about more easily, showed the gendarme his blue card, and even stopped now and then in front of some fine beast, which Madame Bovary did not at all admire. He noticed this, and began jeering at the Yonville ladies and their dresses; then he apologised for his own casual attire. It had the inconsistency of things at once common-place and refined which enchants or exasperates the ordinary man because he suspects that it reveals an unconventional existence, a dubious morality, the affectations of the artist, and, above all, a certain contempt for established conventions. The wind, blowing up his batiste shirt with pleated cuffs revealed a waistcoat of grey linen, and his broad-striped trousers disclosed at the ankle nankeen boots with patent leather gaiters. These were so polished that they reflected the grass. He trampled on horse's dung, one hand in the pocket of his jacket and his straw hat tilted on one side.

"Anyway," he added, "when one lives in the country. . . . ."

"Nothing is worth while," said Emma.

"That is true," replied Rodolphe. "To think that not one of these people is capable of understanding even the cut of a coat!"

Then they talked about provincial mediocrity, of the lives it stifles, the lost illusions.

"No wonder," said Rodolphe, "that I am more and more sinking in gloom."

"You!" she said in astonishment; "I thought you very light-hearted."

"Oh, yes, it seems that way because I know how to wear a mask of mockery in society, and yet, how many a time at the sight of a cemetery by moonlight have I not asked myself whether it were not better to join those sleeping there!"

"Oh! and your friends?" she said. "How can you forget them."

"My friends! What friends? Have I any? Who cares about me?" And he followed up the last words with a kind of hissing whistle.

They were obliged to separate because of a great pile of chairs that a man was carrying behind them. He was so overladen that one could only see the tips of his wooden shoes and the ends of his two outstretched arms. It was Lestiboudois, the gravedigger, who was carrying the church chairs about amongst the people. Alive to all that concerned his interests, he had hit upon this means of turning the agricultural show to his advantage, and his idea was succeeding, for he no longer knew which way to turn. In fact, the villagers, who were tired and hot, quarrelled for these seats, whose straw smelt of incense, and they leant against the thick backs, stained with the wax of candles, with a certain veneration.

Madame Bovary again took Rodolphe's arm; he went on as if speaking to himself:

"Yes, I have missed so many things. Always alone! Ah! if I had some aim in life, if I had met some love, if I had found some one! Oh, how I would have spent all the energy of which I am capable, surmounted everything, overcome everything!"

"Yet it seems to me," said Emma, "that you are not to be pitied."

"Ah! you think so?" said Rodolphe.

"For, after all," she went on, "you are free . . ."

She hesitated,

"Rich . . ."

"Don't mock me," he replied.

And she protested that she was not mocking him, when the sound of a cannon was heard; immediately all began crowding one another towards the village.

It was a false alarm. The prefect seemed not to be coming, and the members of the jury felt much embarrassed, not knowing if they ought to begin the meeting or wait longer.

At last, at the end of the Place a large hired landau appeared, drawn by two thin horses, generously whipped by a coachman in a white hat. Binet had only just time to shout, "Present arms!" and the colonel to imitate him. There was a rush towards the guns; every one pushed forward. A few even forgot their collars.

But the prefectoral coach seemed to sense the trouble, for the two yoked nags, dawdling in their harness, came at a slow trot in front of the townhall at the very moment when the National Guard and firemen deployed, beating time with their boots.

"Present arms!" shouted Binet.

"Halt!" shouted the colonel. "By the left flank, march!"

And after presenting arms, during which the clang of the band, letting loose, rang out like a brass kettle rolling downstairs, all the guns were lowered.

Then was seen stepping down from the carriage a gentleman in a short coat with silver braiding, with bald brow, and wearing a tuft of hair at the back of his head, of a sallow complexion and the most benign of aspects. His eyes, very large and covered by heavy lids, were half-closed to look at the crowd, while at the same time he raised his sharp nose, and forced a smile upon his sunken mouth. He recognised the mayor by his scarf, and explained to him that the prefect was not able to come. He himself was a councillor at the prefecture; then he added a few apologies. Monsieur Tuvache reciprocated with polite compliments, humbly acknowledged by the other; and they remained thus, face to face, their foreheads almost touching, surrounded by members of the jury, the municipal council, the notable personages, the National Guard and the crowd. The councillor pressing his little cocked hat to his breast repeated his greetings, while Tuvache, bent like a bow, also smiled, stammered, tried to say something, protested his devotion to the monarchy and the honor that was being done to Yonville.

Hippolyte, the groom from the inn, took the head of the horses from the coachman, and, limping along with his clubfoot, led them to the door of the "Lion d'Or" where a number of peasants collected to look at the carriage. The drum beat, the howitzer thundered, and the gentlemen one by one mounted the platform, where they sat down in red utrecht velvet arm-chairs that had been lent by Madame Tuvache.

All these people looked alike. Their fair flabby faces, somewhat tanned by the sun, were the color of sweet cider, and their puffy whiskers emerged from stiff collars, kept up by white cravats with broad bows. All the waistcoats were of velvet, double-breasted; all the watches had, at the end of a long ribbon, an oval seal; all rested their two hands on their thighs, carefully stretching the stride of their trousers, whose unspunged glossy cloth shone more brilliantly than the leather of their heavy boots.

The ladies of the company stood at the back under the porch between the pillars, while the common herd was opposite, standing up or sitting on chairs. Lestiboudois had brought there all the chairs that he had moved from the field, and he even kept running back every minute to fetch others from the church. He caused such confusion with this piece of business that one had great difficulty in getting to the small steps of the platform.

"I think," said Monsieur Lheureux to the pharmacist who was heading for his seat, "that they ought to have put up two Venetian masts with something rather severe and rich for ornaments; it would have been a very pretty sight."

"Certainly," replied Homais; "but what can you expect? The mayor took everything on his own shoulders. He hasn't much taste. Poor Tuvache! he is completely devoid of what is called the genius of art."

Meanwhile, Rodolphe and Madame Bovary had ascended to the first floor of the townhall, to the "council-room," and, as it was empty, he suggested that they could enjoy the sight there more comfortably. He fetched three chairs from the round table under the bust of the monarch, and having carried them to one of the windows, they sat down together.

There was commotion on the platform, long whisperings, much parleying. At last the councillor got up. It was known by now that his name was Lieuvain, and in the crowd the name was now passing from lip to lip. After he had reshuffled a few pages, and bent over them to see better, he began:

"Gentlemen! May I be permitted first of all (before addressing you on the object of our meeting to-day, and this sentiment will, I am sure, be shared by you all), may I be permitted, I say, to pay a tribute to the higher administration, to the government, to the monarch, gentlemen, our sovereign, to that beloved king, to whom no branch of public or private prosperity is a matter of indifference, and who directs with a hand at once so firm and wise the chariot of the state amid the incessant perils of a stormy sea, knowing, more-over, how to make peace respected as well as war, industry, com-merce, agriculture, and the fine arts."

"I ought," said Rodolphe, "to get back a little further."

"Why?" said Emma.

But at this moment the voice of the councillor rose to an extraor-dinary pitch. He declaimed—

"This is no longer the time, gentlemen, when civil discord made blood flow in our market squares, when the landowner, the business-man, the working-man himself, lying down to peaceful sleep, trem-bled lest he should be awakened suddenly by the noise of alarming tocsins, when the most subversive doctrines audaciously sapped foundations . . ."

"Well, some one down there might see me," Rodolphe resumed, "then I should have to invent excuses for a fortnight; and with my bad reputation . . ."

"Oh, you are slandering yourself," said Emma.

"No! It is dreadful, I assure you."

"But, gentlemen," continued the councillor, "if, banishing from my memory the remembrance of these sad pictures, I carry my eyes back to the present situation of our dear country, what do I see there? Everywhere commerce and the arts are flourishing; every-where new means of communication, like so many new arteries in the body politic, establish within it new relations. Our great indus-trial centers have recovered all their activity; religion, more consoli-dated, smiles in all hearts; our ports are full, confidence is born again, and France breathes once more! . . ."

"Besides," added Rodolphe, "perhaps from the world's point of view they are right."

"How so?" she asked.

"What!" said he. "Don't you know that there are souls constantly tormented? They need by turns to dream and to act, the purest passions and the most turbulent joys, and thus they fling themselves into all sorts of fantasies, of follies."

Then she looked at him as one looks at a traveler who has voyaged over strange lands, and went on:

"We have not even this distraction, we poor women!"

"A sad distraction, for happiness isn't found in it."

"But is it ever found?" she asked.

"Yes; one day it comes," he answered.

"And this is what you have understood," said the councillor. "You, farmers, agricultural laborers! you pacific pioneers of a work that belongs wholly to civilisation! you, men of progress and morality, you have understood, I say, that political storms are even more redoubtable than atmospheric disturbances!"

"A day comes," repeated Rodolphe, "one is near despair. Then the horizon expands; it is as if a voice cried, 'It is here!' You feel the need of confiding the whole of your life, of giving everything, sacrificing everything to this person. There is no need for explanations; one understands each other, having met before in dreams!" (And he looked at her.) "At last, here it is, this treasure so sought after, here before you. It glitters, it flashes; yet one still doubts, one does not believe it; one remains dazzled, as if one went out from darkness into light."

And as he ended Rodolphe suited the action to the word. He passed his hand over his face, like a man about to faint. Then he let it fall on Emma's. She drew hers back. But the councillor was still reading.

"And who would be surprised at it, gentlemen? He only who was so blind, so imprisoned (I do not fear to say it), so imprisoned by the prejudices of another age as still to misunderstand the spirit of our rural populations. Where, indeed, is more patriotism to be found than in the country, greater devotion to the public welfare, in a word, more intelligence? And, gentlemen, I do not mean that superficial intelligence, vain ornament of idle minds, but rather that profound and balanced intelligence that applies itself above all else to useful objects, thus contributing to the good of all, to the common amelioration and to the support of the state, born of respect for law and the practice of duty . . ."

"Ah! again!" said Rodolphe. "Always 'duty.' I am sick of the word. They are a lot of old jackasses in woolen vests and old bigots with foot-warmers and rosaries who constantly drone into our ears

'Duty, duty!' Ah! by Jove! as if one's real duty were not to feel what is great, cherish the beautiful, and not accept all the conventions of society with the hypocrisy it forces upon us."

"Yet . . . yet . . ." objected Madame Bovary.

"No, no! Why cry out against the passions? Are they not the one beautiful thing on earth, the source of heroism, of enthusiasm, of poetry, music, the arts, in a word, of everything?"

"But one must," said Emma, "to some extent bow to the opinion of the world and accept its morality."

"Ah, but there are two moralities," he replied, "the petty one, the morality of small men that constantly keeps changing, but yells itself hoarse; crude and loud like the crowd of imbeciles that you see down there. But the other, the eternal, that is about us and above, like the landscape that surrounds us, and the blue heavens that give us light."

Monsieur Lieuvain had just wiped his mouth with a pocket-handkerchief. He continued:

"It would be presumptuous of me, gentlemen, to point out to you the uses of agriculture. Who supplies our wants, who provides our means of subsistence, if not the farmer? It is the farmer, gentlemen, who sows with laborious hand the fertile furrows of the country, brings forth the wheat, which, being ground, is made into a powder by means of ingenious machinery, issues from there under the name of flour, and is then transported to our cities, soon delivered to the baker, who makes it into food for poor and rich alike. Again, is it not the farmer who fattens his flocks in the pastures in order to provide us with warm clothing? For how should we clothe or nourish ourselves without his labor? And, gentlemen, is it even necessary to go so far for examples? Who has not frequently reflected on all the momentous things that we get out of that modest animal, the ornament of poultry-yards, that provides us at once with a soft pillow for our bed, with succulent flesh for our tables, and eggs? But I should never end if I were to enumerate one after the other all the different products which the earth, well cultivated, like a generous mother, lavishes upon her children. Here it is the vine; elsewhere apple trees for cider; there colza; further, cheeses; and flax; gentlemen, let us not forget flax, which has made such great strides forward these last years and to which I call your special attention!"

He had no need to call it, for all the mouths of the multitude were wide open, as if to drink in his words. Tuvache by his side listened to him with staring eyes. Monsieur Derozerays from time to time softly closed his eyelids, and farther on the pharmacist, with his son Napoleon between his knees, put his hand behind his ear in order not to lose a syllable. The chins of the other members of the jury nodded slowly up and down in their waistcoats in sign of approval. The firemen at the foot of the platform rested on their bayonets; and Binet, motionless, stood with out-turned elbows, the point of his sabre in the air. Perhaps he could hear, but he certainly couldn't see a thing, for the visor of his helmet fell down on his nose. His lieutenant, the youngest son of Monsieur Tuvache, had an even bigger one; it was so large that he could hardly keep it on, in spite of the cotton scarf that peeped out from underneath. He wore a smile of childlike innocence, and his thin pale face, dripping with sweat, expressed satisfaction, some exhaustion and sleepiness.

The square was crowded up to the houses. People were leaning on their elbows at all the windows, others were standing on their doorsteps, and Justin, in front of the pharmacy, seemed fascinated by the spectacle. In spite of the silence Monsieur Lieuvain's voice was lost in the air. It reached you in fragments of phrases, interrupted here and there by the creaking of chairs in the crowd; then, the long bellowing of an ox would suddenly burst forth from behind, or else the bleating of the lambs, who answered one another from street to street. Even the cowherds and shepherds had driven their beasts this far, and one could hear their lowing from time to time, while with their tongues they tore down some scrap of foliage that hung over their muzzles.

Rodolphe had drawn nearer to Emma, and was whispering hurriedly in her ear:

"Doesn't this conspiracy of society revolt you? Is there a single sentiment it does not condemn? The noblest instincts, the purest feelings are persecuted, slandered; and if at length two poor souls do meet, all is organized in such a way as to keep them from becoming one. Yet they will try, they will call to each other. Not in vain, for sooner or later, be it in six or ten years, they will come together in love; for fate has decreed it, and they are born for each other."

His arms were folded across his knees, and thus lifting his face at her from close by, he looked fixedly at her. She noticed in his eyes small golden lines radiating from the black pupils; she even smelt the perfume of the pomade that made his hair glossy. Then something gave way in her; she recalled the Viscount who had waltzed with her at Vaubyessard, and whose beard exhaled a similar scent of vanilla and lemon, and mechanically she half-closed her eyes the better to breathe it in. But in making this movement, as she leant back in her chair, she saw in the distance, right on the line of the horizon, the old diligence the "Hirondelle," that was slowly descending the hill of Leux, dragging after it a long trail of dust. It was in this yellow carriage that Léon had so often come back to her, and by this route down there that he had gone for ever. She fancied she saw him opposite at his window; then all grew confused; clouds gathered; it seemed to her that she was again turning in the waltz under the light of the lustres on the arm of the Viscount, and that Léon was not far away, that he was coming . . . and yet all the time she was conscious of Rodolphe's head by her side. The sweetness of this sensation revived her past desires, and like grains of sand under a gust of wind, they swirled around in the subtle breath of the perfume that diffused over her soul. She breathed deeply several times to drink in the freshness of the ivy round the columns. She took off her gloves and wiped her hands; then she fanned her face with her handkerchief while she kept hearing, through the throbbing of her temples, the murmur of the crowd and the voice of the councillor intoning his phrases.

He was saying:

"Persevere! listen neither to the suggestions of routine, nor to the over-hasty councils of a rash empiricism. Apply yourselves, above all, to the amelioration of the soil, to good manures, to the development of the breeds, whether equine, bovine, ovine, or porcine. May these shows be to you pacific arenas, where the victor in leaving will hold forth a hand to the vanquished, and will fraternise with him in the hope of even greater success. And you, aged servants! humble helpers, whose hard labor no Government up to this day has taken into consideration, receive the reward of your silent virtues, and be assured that the state henceforward has its eye upon you; that it encourages you, protects you; that it will accede to your just demands, and alleviate as much as possible the heavy burden of your painful sacrifices."

Monsieur Lieuvain sat down; Monsieur Derozerays got up, beginning another speech. His was not perhaps so florid as that of the councillor, but it stood out by a more direct style, that is to say, by more specific knowledge and more elevated considerations. Thus the praise of the Government took up less space; religion and agriculture more. He showed the relation between both, and how they had always contributed to civilisation. Rodolphe was talking dreams, forebodings, magnetism with Madame Bovary. Going back to the cradle of society, the orator painted those fierce times when men lived on acorns in the heart of woods. Then they had left off the skins of beasts, had put on cloth, tilled the soil, planted the vine. Was this a good, or wasn't there more harm than good in this discovery? That was the problem to which Monsieur Derozerays addressed himself. From magnetism little by little Rodolphe had come to affinities, and while the president was citing Cincinnatus[41] and his plough, Diocletian[42] planting his cabbages, and the Emperors

41. Cincinnatus was a Roman Consul (460 B.C.), who was supposedly called to his office while found plowing.

42. Diocletian (245–313) was Roman emperor from 284 to 305. He resigned in 305 and retired to Salone, (now Split) in Dalmatia, to cultivate his garden.

of China inaugurating the year by the sowing of seed, the young man was explaining to the young woman that these irresistible attractions find their cause in some previous state of existence.

"Take us, for instance," he said, "how did we happen to meet? What chance willed it? It was because across infinite distances, like two streams uniting, our particular inclinations pushed us toward one another."

And he seized her hand; she did not withdraw it.

"First prize for general farming!" announced the president.

"—Just now, for example, when I went to your home . . ."

"To Mr. Bizat of Quincampoix."

"—Did I know I would accompany you?"

"Seventy francs!"

"—A hundred times I tried to leave; yet I followed you and stayed . . ."

"For manures!"

"—As I would stay to-night, to-morrow, all other days, all my life!"

"To Monsieur Caron of Argueil, a gold medal!"

"—For I have never enjoyed anyone's company so much."

"To Monsieur Bain of Givry-Saint-Martin."

"—And I will never forget you."

"For a merino ram . . ."

"—Whereas you will forget me; I'll pass through your life as a mere shadow . . ."

"To Monsieur Belot of Notre-Dame."

"—But no, tell me there can be a place for me in your thoughts, in your life, can't there?"

"Hog! first prize equally divided between Messrs. Lehérissé and Cullembourg, sixty francs!"

Rodolphe was holding her hand on his; it was warm and quivering like a captive dove that wants to fly away; perhaps she was trying to take it away or perhaps she was answering his pressure, at any rate, she moved her fingers; he exclaimed

"Oh, thank you! You do not repulse me! You are kind! You understand that I am yours! Let me see you, let me look at you!"

A gust of wind that blew in at the window ruffled the cloth on the table, and in the square below all the large bonnets rose up like the fluttering wings of white butterflies.

"Use of oil-cakes!" continued the president.

He was hurrying now: "Flemish manure, flax-growing, drainage, long term leases . . . domestic service."

Rodolphe was no longer speaking. They looked at each other. As their desire increased, their dry lips trembled and languidly, effortlessly, their fingers intertwined.

"Catherine Nicaise Elizabeth Leroux, of Sassetot-la-Guerrière, for fifty-four years of service at the same farm, a silver medal—value, twenty-five francs!"

"Where is Catherine Leroux?" repeated the councillor.

She did not appear, and one could hear whispering voices:

"Go ahead!"

"No."

"To the left!"

"Don't be afraid!"

"Oh, how stupid she is!"

"Well, is she there?" cried Tuvache.

"Yes; here she is."

"Then what's she waiting for?"

There came forward on the platform a frightened-looking little old lady who seemed to shrink within her poor clothes. On her feet she wore heavy wooden shoes, and from her hips hung a large blue apron. Her pale face framed in a borderless cap was more wrinkled than a withered russet apple, and from the sleeves of her red jacket looked out two large hands with gnarled joints. The dust from the barns, washing soda and grease from the wool had so encrusted, roughened, hardened them that they seemed dirty, although they had been rinsed in clear water; and by dint of long service they remained half open, as if to bear humble witness of so much suffering endured. Something of monastic rigidity dignified her. No trace of sadness or tenderness weakened her pale face. Having lived so long among animals, she had taken on their silent and tranquil ways. It was the first time that she found herself in the midst of so large a company; and inwardly scared by the flags, the drums, the gentlemen in frock-coats, and the decorations of the councillor, she stood motionless, not knowing whether she should advance or run away, nor why the crowd was cheering and the jury smiling at her. Thus, a half century of servitude confronted these beaming bourgeois.

"Step forward, venerable Catherine Nicaise Elizabeth Leroux!" said the councillor, who had taken the list of prize-winners from the president; and, looking at the piece of paper and the old woman by turns, he repeated in a fatherly tone:

"Step forward, step forward!"

"Are you deaf?" said Tuvache, who was jumping around in his arm-chair; and he began shouting in her ear, "Fifty-four years of service. A silver medal! Twenty-five francs! For you!"

Then, when she had her medal, she looked at it, and a smile of beatitude spread over her face; and as she walked away they could hear her muttering:

"I'll give it to our curé at home, to say some masses for me!"

"What fanaticism!" exclaimed the pharmacist, leaning across to the notary.

The meeting was over, the crowd dispersed, and now that the speeches had been read, everything fell back into place again, and everything into the old grooves; the masters bullied the servants, the servants beat the animals, indolent victors returning to their stables with a green wreath between their horns.

The National Guards, however, had climbed up to the second floor of the townhall; brioches were stuck on their bayonets, and the drummer of the battalion carried a basket with bottles. Madame Bovary took Rodolphe's arm; he saw her home; they separated at her door; then he walked about alone in the meadow while waiting for the banquet to start.

The feast was long, noisy, ill served; the guests were so crowded that they could hardly move their elbows; and the narrow planks that served as benches almost broke under their weight. They ate huge amounts. Each one stuffed himself with all he could lay hands on. Sweat stood on every brow, and a whitish steam, like the vapour of a stream on an autumn morning, floated above the table between the hanging lamps. Rodolphe, leaning against the canvas of the tent, was thinking so intently of Emma that he heard nothing. Behind him on the grass the servants were piling up the dirty plates, his neighbors were talking; he did not answer them; they filled his glass, and there was silence in his thoughts in spite of the noise around him. He was dreaming of what she had said, of the line of her lips; her face, as in a magic mirror, shone on the plates of the shakos, the folds of her gown fell along the walls, and endless days of love unrolled before him in the future.

He saw her again in the evening during the fireworks, but she was with her husband, Madame Homais, and the pharmacist, who was worrying about the danger of stray rockets. Time and again he left the company to give some advice to Binet.

The fireworks sent to Monsieur Tuvache had, through an excess of caution, been locked in his cellar; so the damp powder would not light, and the main piece, that was to represent a dragon biting his tail, failed completely. From time to time, a meagre Roman-candle went off; then the gaping crowd sent up a roar that mingled with the giggling of the women who were being tickled in the darkness. Emma silently nestled against Charles's shoulder; then, raising her chin, she watched the luminous rays of the rockets against the dark sky. Rodolphe gazed at her in the light of the burning lanterns.

One by one, they went out. Stars appeared. A few drops of rain began to fall. She tied her scarf over her bare head.

At this moment the councillor's carriage came out from the inn. His coachman, who was drunk, suddenly fell asleep, and one could see the mass of his body from afar above the hood, framed by the two lanterns, swaying from right to left with the motion of the springs.

"Truly," said the pharmacist, "severe measures should be taken against drunkenness! I should like to see written up weekly at the door of the townhall on a board *ad hoc* the names of all those who during the week got intoxicated on alcohol. Besides, with regard to statistics, one would thus have, as it were, public records that one could refer to if needed . . . But excuse me!"

And he once more ran off to the captain. The latter was returning to see his lathe.

"You might do well," said Homais to him, "to send one of your men, or to go yourself . . ."

"Oh, leave me alone!" answered the tax-collector. "I'm telling you everything is taken care of."

"There is nothing for you to worry about," said the pharmacist, when he returned to his friends. "Monsieur Binet has assured me that all precautions have been taken. No sparks have fallen; the pumps are full. Let's go to bed."

"I can certainly use some sleep," said Madame Homais with a huge yawn. "But never mind; we've had a beautiful day for our fete."

Rodolphe repeated in a low voice, and with a tender look, "Oh, yes! very beautiful!"

And after a final good night, they parted ways.

Two days later, in the "Fanal de Rouen," there was a long article on the show. Homais had composed it on the spur of the moment, the very morning after the banquet.

"Why these festoons, these flowers, these garlands? Whereto was the crowd hurrying, like the waves of a furious sea under the torrents of a tropical sun pouring its heat upon our meadows?"

Then he spoke of the condition of the peasants. Certainly the Government was doing much, but not enough. "Be bold!" he told them; "a thousand reforms are needed; let us carry them out! Then, reporting on the entry of the councillor, he did not forget "the martial spirit of our militia," nor "our dazzling village maidens," nor the "bald-headed elders like patriarchs, some of whom, left over from our immortal phalanxes, still felt their hearts beat at the manly sound of the drums." He cited himself among the first of the members of the jury, and he even called attention in a note to the fact that Monsieur Homais, pharmacist, had sent a memoir on cider to the agricultural society. When he came to the distribution of the prizes, he painted the joy of the prize-winners in dithyrambic strophes. "The father embraced the son, the brother the brother, the husband his wife. More than one showed his humble medal with pride; and no doubt when he got home to his good housewife, he hung it up weeping on the modest walls of his cottage.

"About six o'clock a banquet prepared in the meadow of Monsieur Leigeard brought together the main participants in the festivities. The utmost merriment reigned throughout. Several toasts were proposed: Monsieur Lieuvain, To the king! Monsieur Tuvache, To the prefect! Monsieur Derozerays, To Agriculture! Monsieur Homais, To the twin sisters, Industry and Fine Arts! Monsieur Leplichey, To Improvements! At night some brilliant fireworks suddenly lit up the sky. It was a real kaleidoscope, an operatic scene; and for a moment our little locality might have thought itself transported into the midst of a dream from the 'Thousand and One Nights.'

"Let us state that no untoward event disturbed this family meeting."

And he added: "Only the absence of the clergy was noted. No doubt the priests do not understand progress in the same way. Just as you please, *messieurs de Loyola!*"[43]

IX

Six weeks passed. Rodolphe did not come again. At last one evening he appeared.

The day after the fair he told himself:

"Let's not go back too soon; that would be a mistake."

And at the end of a week he had gone off hunting. After the hunting he first feared that too much time had passed, and then he reasoned thus:

"If she loved me from the first day, impatience must make her love me even more. Let's persist!"

And he knew that his calculation had been right when, on entering the room, he saw Emma turn pale.

She was alone. Night was falling. The small muslin curtain along the windows deepened the twilight, and the gilding of the barometer, on which the rays of the sun fell, shone in the looking-glass between the meshes of the coral.

Rodolphe remained standing, and Emma hardly answered his first conventional phrases.

"I have been busy," he said, "I have been ill."

"Nothing serious?" she cried.

"Well," said Rodolphe, sitting down at her side on a footstool, "no . . . It was because I did not want to come back."

"Why?"

"Can't you guess?"

He looked at her again, but so hard that she lowered her head, blushing. He pursued:

"Emma . . ."

"Monsieur!" she exclaimed, drawing back a little.

"Ah! you see," he replied in a melancholy voice, "that I was right

43. Messieurs de Loyola, or Jesuits. Ignatius Loyola (1491–1556), a Spaniard, founded the Order of the Jesuits in 1534. The Jesuits were expelled from France in 1762.

not to come back; for this name, this name that fills my whole soul, and that escaped me, you forbid me its use! Madame Bovary! . . . why, the whole world calls you thus! Moreover, it is not your name; it is the name of another!"

He repeated,

"Of another!"

And he hid his face in his hands.

"Yes, I think of you constantly! . . . The thought of you drives me to despair. Ah! forgive me! . . . I'll go . . . Adieu . . . I'll go far away, so far that you will never hear of me again; yet . . . today . . . I don't know what force made me come here. For one does not struggle against Heaven; it is impossible to resist the smile of angels; one is carried away by the beautiful, the lovely, the adorable."

It was the first time that Emma had heard such words addressed to her, and her pride unfolded languidly in the warmth of this language, like someone stretching in a hot bath.

"But if I didn't come," he continued, "if I couldn't see you, at least I have gazed long on all that surrounds you. At night, every night, I arose; I came here; I watched your house, the roof glimmering in the moon, the trees in the garden swaying before your window, and the little lamp, a gleam shining through the window-panes in the darkness. Ah! you never knew that there, so near you, so far from you, was a poor wretch . . ."

She turned towards him with a sob.

"Oh, you are kind!" she said.

"No, I love you, that is all! You do not doubt that! Tell me; one word, one single word!"

And Rodolphe imperceptibly glided from the footstool to the ground; but a sound of wooden shoes was heard in the kitchen, and he noticed that the door of the room was not closed.

"You would do an act of charity," he went on, rising, "if you accepted to gratify a whim!" It was to visit her home, he wished to see it, and since Madame Bovary could see no objection to this, they both rose just when Charles came in.

"Good morning, doctor," Rodolphe said to him.

Flattered by this unexpected title, Charles launched into elaborate displays of politeness. Of this the other took advantage to pull himself together.

"Madame was speaking to me," he then said, "about her health."

Charles interrupted; she was indeed giving him thousands of worries; her palpitations were beginning again. Then Rodolphe asked if riding would not be helpful.

"Certainly! excellent, just the thing! What a good idea! You ought to try it."

And as she objected that she had no horse, Monsieur Rodolphe offered one. She refused his offer; he did not insist. Then to explain his visit he said that his ploughman, the man of the blood-letting, still suffered from dizziness.

"I'll drop by," said Bovary.

"No, no! I'll send him to you; we'll come; that will be more convenient for you."

"Ah! very good! I thank you."

And as soon as they were alone, "Why don't you accept Monsieur Boulanger's offer? It was so gracious of him."

She seemed to pout, invented a thousand excuses, and finally declared that perhaps it would look odd.

"That's the least of my worries!" said Charles, turning on his heel. "Health first! You are making a mistake."

"Could I go riding without proper clothes?"

"You must order a riding outfit," he answered.

The riding-habit decided her.

When it was ready, Charles wrote to Monsieur Boulanger that his wife was able to accept his invitation and thanked him in advance for his kindness.

The next day at noon Rodolphe appeared at Charles's door with two saddle-horses. One had pink rosettes at his ears and a deerskin side-saddle.

Rodolphe had put on high soft boots, assuming that she had never seen the likes of them. In fact, Emma was charmed with his appearance as he stood on the landing in his great velvet coat and white corduroy breeches. She was ready; she was waiting for him.

Justin escaped from the store to watch her depart, and the pharmacist himself also came out. He was giving Monsieur Boulanger some good advice.

"An accident happens so easily. Be careful! Your horses may be skittish!"

She heard a noise above her; it was Félicité drumming on the window-panes to amuse little Berthe. The child blew her a kiss; her mother answered with a wave of her whip.

"Have a pleasant ride!" cried Monsieur Homais. "Be careful! above all, be careful!"

And he flourished his newspaper as he saw them disappear.

As soon as he felt the ground, Emma's horse set off at a gallop. Rodolphe galloped by her side. Now and then they exchanged a word. With slightly bent head, her hand well up, and her right arm stretched out, she gave herself up to the cadence of the movement that rocked her in her saddle.

At the bottom of the hill Rodolphe gave his horse its head; they set off together at a bound, then at the top suddenly the horses stopped, and her large blue veil fell about her.

It was early in October. There was fog over the land. Hazy clouds hovered on the horizon between the outlines of the hills; others, rent asunder, floated up and disappeared. Sometimes through a rift in the clouds, beneath a ray of sunshine, gleamed from afar the roofs of Yonville, with the gardens at the water's edge, the yards, the walls and the church steeple. Emma half closed her eyes to pick out her house, and never had this poor village where she lived appeared so small. From the height on which they were the whole valley seemed an immense pale lake sending off its vapour into the air. Clumps of trees here and there stood out like black rocks, and the tall lines of the poplars that rose above the mist were like a beach stirred by the wind.

By the side, on the grass between the pines, a brown light shimmered in the warm atmosphere. The earth, ruddy like the powder of tobacco, deadened the noise of their steps, and as they walked, the horses kicked up fallen pine cones before them.

Rodolphe and Emma thus skirted the woods. She turned away from time to time to avoid his look, and then she saw only the line of pine trunks, whose monotonous succession made her a little giddy. The horses were panting; the leather of the saddles creaked.

Just as they were entering the forest the sun came out.

"God is with us!" said Rodolphe.

"Do you think so?" she said.

"Forward! forward!" he continued.

He clucked with his tongue. The horses set off at a trot.

Long ferns by the roadside caught in Emma's stirrup. Rodolphe leant forward and removed them as they rode along. At other times, to turn aside the branches, he passed close to her, and Emma felt his knee brushing against her leg. The sky was blue now. The leaves no longer stirred. There were spaces full of heather in flower, and patches of purple alternated with the confused tangle of the trees, grey, fawn, or golden colored, according to the nature of their leaves. Often in the thicket one could hear the fluttering of wings, or else the hoarse, soft cry of the ravens flying off amidst the oaks.

They dismounted. Rodolphe fastened up the horses. She walked on in front on the moss between the paths.

But her long dress got in her way, although she held it up by the skirt; and Rodolphe, walking behind her, saw between the black cloth and the black shoe the delicacy of her white stocking, that seemed to him as if it were a part of her nakedness.

She stopped.

"I am tired," she said.

"Come, try some more," he went on. "Courage!"

Some hundred paces further on she stopped again, and through her veil, that fell sideways from her man's hat over her hips, her face appeared in a bluish transparency as if she were floating under azure waves.

"But where are we going?"

He did not answer. She was breathing irregularly. Rodolphe looked round him biting his moustache.

They came to a larger space which had been cleared of undergrowth. They sat down on the trunk of a fallen tree, and Rodolphe began speaking to her of his love.

He did not frighten her at first with compliments. He was calm, serious, melancholy.

Emma listened to him with bowed head, and stirred the bits of wood on the ground with the tip of her foot.

But at the words, "Are not our destinies now forever united?"

"Oh, no!" she replied. "You know they aren't. It is impossible!"

She rose to go. He seized her by the wrist. She stopped. Then, having gazed at him for a few moments with an amorous and moist look, she said hurriedly:

"Well let's not speak of it again! Where are the horses? Let's go back."

He made a gesture of anger and annoyance. She repeated:

"Where are the horses? Where are the horses?"

Then smiling a strange smile, looking straight at her, his teeth set, he advanced with outstretched arms. She recoiled trembling. She stammered:

"Oh, you frighten me! You hurt me! Take me back!"

"If it must be," he went on, his face changing; and he again became respectful, caressing, timid. She gave him her arm. They went back. He said:

"What was the matter with you? Why? I do not understand. You were mistaken, no doubt. In my soul you are as a Madonna on a pedestal, in a place lofty, secure, immaculate. But I cannot live without you! I need your eyes, your voice, your thought! Be my friend, my sister, my angel!"

And he stretched out his arm and caught her by the waist. Gently she tried to disengage herself. He supported her thus as they walked along.

They heard the two horses browsing on the leaves.

"Not quite yet!" said Rodolphe. "Stay a minute longer! Please stay!"

He drew her farther on to a small pool where duckweeds made a greenness on the water. Faded waterlilies lay motionless between the reeds. At the noise of their steps in the grass, frogs jumped away to hide themselves.

"I shouldn't, I shouldn't!" she said. "I am out of my mind listening to you!"

"Why? . . . Emma! Emma!"

"Oh, Rodolphe! . . ." she said slowly and she pressed against his shoulder.

The cloth of her dress clung to the velvet of his coat. She threw back her white neck which swelled in a sigh, and, faltering, weeping, and hiding her face in her hands, with one long shudder, she abandoned herself to him.

The shades of night were falling; the horizontal sun passing between the branches dazzled the eyes. Here and there around her, in the leaves or on the ground, trembled luminous patches, as if humming-birds flying about had scattered their feathers. Silence was everywhere; something sweet seemed to come forth from the trees. She felt her heartbeat return, and the blood coursing through her flesh like a river of milk. Then far away, beyond the wood, on the other hills, she heard a vague prolonged cry, a voice which lingered, and in silence she heard it mingling like music with the last pulsations of her throbbing nerves. Rodolphe, a cigar between his lips, was mending with his penknife one of the two broken bridles.

They returned to Yonville by the same road. On the mud they saw again the traces of their horses side by side, the same thickets, the same stones in the grass; nothing around them seemed changed; and yet for her something had happened more stupendous than if the mountains had moved in their places. Rodolphe now and again bent forward and took her hand to kiss it.

She was charming on horseback—upright, with her slender waist, her knee bent on the mane of her horse, her face somewhat flushed by the fresh air in the red of the evening.

On entering Yonville she made her horse prance in the road.

People looked at her from the windows.

At dinner her husband thought she looked well, but she pretended not to hear him when he inquired about her ride, and she remained sitting there with her elbow at the side of her plate between the two lighted candles.

"Emma!" he said.

"What?"

"Well, I spent the afternoon at Monsieur Alexandre's. He has an old filly, still very fine, just a little broken in the knees, and that could be bought, I am sure, for a hundred crowns." He added, "And thinking it might please you, I have reserved her . . . I bought her . . . Have I done right? Do tell me!"

She nodded her head in assent; then a quarter of an hour later:

"Are you going out to-night?" she asked.

"Yes. Why?"

"Oh, nothing, nothing, dear!"

And as soon as she had got rid of Charles she went and shut herself up in her room.

At first she felt stunned; she saw the trees, the paths, the ditches, Rodolphe, and she again felt the pressure of his arms, while the leaves rustled and the reeds whistled.

But when she saw herself in the mirror she wondered at her face. Never had her eyes been so large, so black, nor so deep. Something subtle about her being transfigured her.

She repeated: "I have a lover! a lover!" delighting at the idea as if a second puberty had come to her. So at last she was to know those joys of love, that fever of happiness of which she had despaired! She was entering upon a marvelous world where all would be passion, ecstasy, delirium. She felt herself surrounded by an endless rapture. A blue space surrounded her and ordinary existence appeared only intermittently between these heights, dark and far away beneath her.

Then she recalled the heroines of the books that she had read, and the lyric legion of these adulterous women began to sing in her memory with the voice of sisters that charmed her. She became herself, as it were, an actual part of these lyrical imaginings; at long last, as she saw herself among those lovers she had so envied, she fulfilled the love-dream of her youth. Besides, Emma felt a satisfaction of revenge. How she had suffered! But she had won out at last, and the love so long pent up erupted in joyous outbursts. She tasted it without remorse, without anxiety, without concern.

The next day brought a new-discovered sweetness. They exchanged vows. She told him of her sorrows. Rodolphe interrupted her with kisses; and she, looking at him through half-closed eyes, asked him to call her again by her name and to say that he loved her. They were in the forest, as yesterday, this time in the hut of some *sabot* makers. The walls were of straw, and the roof so low they had to stoop. They were seated side by side on a bed of dry leaves.

From that day on they wrote to one another regularly every evening. Emma placed her letter at the end of the garden, by the river, in a crack of the wall. Rodolphe came to fetch it, and put another in its place that she always accused of being too short.

One morning, when Charles had gone out before daybreak, she felt the urge to see Rodolphe at once. She would go quickly to La Huchette, stay there an hour, and be back again at Yonville while every one was still asleep. The idea made her breathless with desire, and she soon found herself in the middle of the field, walking with rapid steps, without looking behind her.

Day was just breaking. Emma recognised her lover's house from a distance. Its two dove-tailed weathercocks stood out black against the pale dawn.

Beyond the farmyard there was a separate building that she assumed must be the château. She entered it as if the doors at her approach had opened wide of their own accord. A large straight staircase led up to the corridor. Emma raised the latch of a door, and suddenly at the end of the room she saw a man sleeping. It was Rodolphe. She uttered a cry.

"You here? You here?" he repeated. "How did you manage to come? Ah! your dress is wet."

"I love you!" she answered, winding her arm around his neck.

This first bold attempt having been successful, now every time Charles went out early Emma dressed quickly and slipped on tiptoe down the steps that led to the waterside.

But when the cow plank was taken up, she had to follow the walls alongside the river; the bank was slippery; to keep from falling, she had to catch hold of the tufts of faded wall-flowers. Then she went across ploughed fields, stumbling, her thin shoes sinking in the heavy mud. Her scarf, knotted round her head, fluttered to the wind in the meadows. She was afraid of the oxen; she began to run; she arrived out of breath, with rosy cheeks, and breathing out from her whole person a fresh perfume of sap, of verdure, of the open air. At this hour Rodolphe was still asleep. It was like a spring morning bursting into his room.

The golden curtains along the windows let a heavy, whitish light filter into the room. Emma would find her way gropingly, with blinking eyes, the drops of dew hanging from her hair, making a topaz halo around her face. Rodolphe, laughing, would draw her to him and press her to his breast.

Then she inspected the room, opened the drawers of the tables, combed her hair with his comb, and looked at herself in his shaving mirror. Often she put between her teeth the big pipe that lay on the bedtable, amongst lemons and pieces of sugar near the water bottle.

It took them a good quarter of an hour to say good-bye. Then Emma cried: she would have wished never to leave Rodolphe. Something stronger than herself drew her to him; until, one day, when she arrived unexpectedly, he frowned as one put out.

"What is wrong?" she said. "Are you ill? tell me!"

He ended up declaring earnestly that her visits were too dangerous and that she was compromising herself.

X

Gradually Rodolphe's fears took possession of her. At first, love had intoxicated her, and she had thought of nothing beyond. But now that he was indispensable to her life, she feared losing the smallest part of his love or upsetting him in the least. When she came back from his house, she looked all about her, anxiously watching every form that passed in the horizon, and every village window from which she could be seen. She listened for steps, cries, the noise of the ploughs, and she stopped short, white, and trembling more than the aspen leaves swaying overhead.

One morning as she was thus returning, she suddenly thought she saw the long barrel of a carbine that seemed to be aimed at her. It stuck out sideways from the end of a small barrel half-buried in the grass on the edge of a ditch. Emma, half-fainting with terror, nevertheless walked on, and a man stepped out of the barrel like a Jack-in-the-box jumping out of his cage. He had gaiters buckled up to the knees, his cap pulled down over his eyes; his lips shivered in the cold and his nose was red. It was Captain Binet lying in ambush for wild ducks.

"You ought to have called out long ago!" he exclaimed. "When one sees a gun, one should always give warning."

The tax-collector was thus trying to hide his own fright, for a prefectorial order prohibited duck-hunting except in boats, Monsieur Binet, despite his respect for the laws, was breaking the law and he expected to see the garde champêtre turn up any moment. But this anxiety whetted his pleasure, and, all alone in his barrel, he congratulated himself on his luck and his cleverness.

The sight of Emma seemed to relieve him of a great weight, and he at once opened the conversation.

"Pretty cold, isn't it; it's nippy!"

Emma didn't answer. He pursued:

"You're certainly off to an early start today."

"Yes," she stammered; "I am just coming from the nurse who is keeping my child."

"Ah, yes indeed, yes indeed. As for myself, I am here, just as you see me, since break of day; but the weather is so muggy, that unless one had the bird at the mouth of the gun . . ."

"Good day, Monsieur Binet," she interrupted, turning her back on him.

"Your servant, madame," he replied drily.

And he went back into his barrel.

Emma regretted having left the tax-collector so abruptly. No doubt he would jump to the worst conclusions. The story about the nurse was the weakest possible excuse, for every one at Yonville knew that the Bovary baby had been at home with her parents for a year. Besides, no one was living in this direction; this path led only to La Huchette. Binet, then, could not fail to guess where she came from, and he would not remain silent; he would talk, that was certain. She remained until evening racking her brain with every lie she could think up, but the image of that idiot with his game bag would not leave her.

Seeing her so gloomy, Charles proposed after dinner to take her to the pharmacist by way of distraction, and the first person she caught sight of in the shop was him again, the tax-collector! He was standing in front of the counter, lit up by the gleams of the red jar, saying:

"Could I have half an ounce of vitriol, please?"

"Justin," cried the pharmacist, "bring us the sulphuric acid."

Then to Emma, who was going up to Madame Homais' room, "Don't go up, it's not worth the trouble, she is just coming down. Why not warm yourself by the fire . . . Excuse me . . . Good-day, doctor" (for the pharmacist much enjoyed pronouncing the word "doctor," as if addressing another by it reflected on himself some of the grandeur of the title). "Justin, take care not to upset the mortars! You'd better fetch some chairs from the little room; you know very well that the arm-chairs are not to be taken out of the drawing-room."

And he was just about to put his arm-chair back in its place when Binet asked him for half an ounce of sugar acid.

"Sugar acid!" said the pharmacist contemptuously, "never heard of it! There is no such thing. Perhaps it is Oxalic acid you want. It is Oxalic, isn't it?"

Binet explained that he wanted a corrosive to make himself some copper-water with which to remove rust from his hunting things. Emma shuddered. The pharmacist was saying:

"Indeed, the dampness we're having is certainly not propitious."

"Nevertheless," replied the tax-collector, with a sly look, "some people seem to like it." She was stifling.

"And give me . . ."

"Will he never go?" she thought.

"Half an ounce of resin and turpentine, four ounces of beeswax, and three half ounces of animal charcoal, if you please, to clean the leather of my togs."

The druggist was beginning to cut the wax when Madame Homais appeared with Irma in her arms, Napoleon by her side, and Athalie following. She sat down on the velvet seat by the window, and the boy squatted down on a footstool, while his eldest sister hovered round the jujube box near her papa. The latter was filling funnels and corking phials, sticking on labels, making up parcels. Around him all were silent; only from time to time could one hear the weights jingling in the scales, and a few words of advice from the pharmacist to his apprentice.

"And how is your little girl?" Madame Homais asked suddenly.

"Silence!" exclaimed her husband, who was writing down some

figures on a scratch pad.

"Why didn't you bring her?" she went on in a low voice.

"Hush! hush!" said Emma, pointing a finger at the pharmacist.

But Binet, quite absorbed in checking over his bill, had probably heard nothing. At last he went out. Then Emma, relieved, uttered a deep sigh.

"How heavily you are breathing!" said Madame Homais.

"It is so hot in here," she replied.

So the next day they agreed to arrange their rendezvous. Emma wanted to bribe her servant with a present, but it would be better to find some safe house at Yonville. Rodolphe promised to look for one.

All through the winter, three or four times a week, in the dead of night he came to the garden. Emma had on purpose taken away the key of the gate, letting Charles think it was lost.

To call her, Rodolphe threw a handful of sand at the shutters. She jumped up with a start; but sometimes he had to wait, for Charles had the habit of talking endlessly by the fireside.

She was wild with impatience; if her eyes could have done it, they would have hurled him out of the window. At last she would begin to undress, then take up a book, and go on reading very quietly as if the book amused her. But Charles, who was in bed, would call her to bed.

"Come, now, Emma," he said, "it is time."

"Yes, I am coming," she answered.

Then, as the candles shone in his eyes, he turned to the wall and fell asleep. She escaped, holding her breath, smiling, half undressed.

Rodolphe had a large cloak; he wrapped it around her, and putting his arm round her waist, he drew her without a word to the end of the garden.

It was in the arbour, on the same bench of half rotten sticks where formerly Léon had stared at her so amorously on the summer evenings. She never thought of him now.

The stars shone through the leafless jasmine branches. Behind them they heard the river flowing, and now and again on the bank the rustling of the dry reeds. Masses of deeper darkness stood out here and there in the night and sometimes, shaken with one single motion, they would rise up and sway like immense black waves pressing forward to engulf them. The cold of the nights made them clasp each other more tightly; the sighs of their lips seemed to them deeper; their eyes, that they could hardly see, larger; and in the midst of the silence words softly spoken would fall on their souls with a crystalline sound, that echoed in endless reverberations.

When the night was rainy, they took refuge in the consulting-room between the cart-shed and the stable. She would light one of the kitchen candles that she had hidden behind the books. Rodolphe settled down there as if at home. The sight of the library, of the desk, of the entire room, in fine, would arouse his mirth; and he could not refrain from making jokes at Charles' expense despite Emma's embarrassment. She would have liked to see him more serious, and even on occasions more dramatic; as, for example, when she thought she heard a noise of approaching steps in the alley.

"Some one is coming!" she said.

He blew out the light.

"Have you your pistols?"

"Why?"

"Why, to defend yourself," replied Emma.

"From your husband? Oh, the poor fellow!" And Rodolphe finished his sentence with a gesture that said, "I could crush him with a flip of my finger."

She was awed at his bravery, although she felt in it a sort of indecency and a naïve coarseness that scandalised her.

Rodolphe reflected a good deal on the pistol incident. If she had spoken in earnest, he thought it most ridiculous, even odious; for he had no reason whatever to hate the good Charles, not exactly being devoured by jealousy; and in this same connection, Emma had made him a solemn promise that he did not think in the best of taste.

Besides, she was becoming dreadfully sentimental. She had insisted on exchanging miniatures; handfuls of hair had been cut off, and now she was asking for a ring—a real wedding-ring, in token of eternal union. She often spoke to him of the evening chimes, of the "voices of nature." Then she talked to him of their respective mothers. Rodolphe's had died twenty years ago. Emma none the less consoled him with conventional phrases, like those one would use with a bereaved child; sometimes she even said to him, gazing at the moon:

"I am sure that, from up there, both approve our love."

But she was so pretty! He had possessed so few women of similar ingenuousness. This love without debauchery was a new experience for him, and, drawing him out of his lazy habits, caressed at once his pride and his sensuality. Although his bourgeois common sense disapproved of it, Emma's exaltations, deep down in his heart, enchanted him, since they were directed his way. Then, sure of her love, he no longer made an effort, and insensibly his manner changed.

No longer, did he, as before, find words so tender that they made her cry, nor passionate caresses that drove her into ecstasy; their great love, in which she had lived immersed, seemed to run out beneath her, like the water of a river absorbed by its own bed; and she could see the bottom. She would not believe it; she redoubled in tenderness, and Rodolphe concealed his indifference less and less.

She did not know if she regretted having yielded to him, or whether she did not wish, on the contrary, to love him even more. The humiliation of having given in turned into resentment, tempered by their voluptuous pleasures. It was not tenderness; it was like a continual seduction. He held her fully in his power; she almost feared him.

On the surface, however, things seemed calm enough, Rodolphe having carried out his adultery just as he had wanted; and at the end of six months, when the spring-time came, they were to one another like a married couple, tranquilly keeping up a domestic flame.

It was the time of year when old Rouault sent his turkey in rememberance of the setting of his leg. The present always arrived with a letter. Emma cut the string that tied it to the basket, and read the following lines:

MY DEAR CHILDREN,—I hope this will find you in good health, and that it will be as good as the others, for it seems to me a little more tender, if I may venture to say so, and heavier. But next time, for a change, I'll give you a turkeycock, unless you would prefer a capon; and send me back the hamper, if you please, with the two old ones. I have had an accident with sheds; the coverings flew off one windy night among the trees. The harvest has not been over-good either. Finally, I don't know when I shall come to see you. It is so difficult now to leave the house since I am alone, my poor Emma.

Here there was a break in the lines as if the old fellow had dropped his pen to dream a little while.

"As for myself, I am very well, except for a cold I caught the other day at Yvetot, where I had gone to hire a shepherd, having got rid of mine because no cooking was good enough for his taste. We are to be pitied with rascals like him! Moreover, he was dishonest.

I heard from a peddler who had a tooth pulled out when he passed through your part of the country this winter, that Bovary was as usual working hard. That doesn't surprise me; and he showed me his tooth; we had some coffee together. I asked him if he had seen you, and he said no, but that he had seen two horses in the stables, from which I conclude that business is looking up. So much the better, my dear children, and may God send you every imaginable happiness!

It grieves me not yet to have seen my dear little grand-daughter, Berthe Bovary. I have planted an Orleans plum-tree for her in the garden under your room, and I won't have it touched until we can make jam from it, that I will keep in the cupboard for her when she comes.

Good-bye, my dear children. I kiss you, my girl, you too, my son-in-law, and the little one on both cheeks. I am, with best compliments, your loving father.

THEODORE ROUAULT

She held the coarse paper in her fingers for some minutes. A continuous stream of spelling mistakes ran through the letter, and Emma followed the kindly thought that cackled right through it like a hen half hidden in a hedge of thorns. The writing had been dried with ashes from the hearth, for a little grey powder slipped from the letter on her dress, and she almost thought she saw her father bending over the hearth to take up the tongs. How long since she had been with him, sitting on the footstool in the chimney-corner, where she used to burn the end of a stick in the crackling flame of the sea-sedges! She remembered the summer evenings all full of sunshine. The colts whinnied when one passed by, and galloped, galloped . . . Under her window there was a beehive and at times, the bees wheeling round in the light, struck against her window like rebounding balls of gold. What happiness she had known at that time, what freedom, what hope! What a wealth of illusions! It was all gone now. She had lost them one by one, at every stage in the growth of her soul, in the succession of her conditions; maidenhood, marriage and love—shedding them along her path like a traveller who leaves something of his wealth at every inn along his road.

But who was it, then, who made her so unhappy? What extraordinary catastrophe had destroyed her life? And she raised her head, as if seeking around her for the cause of all that suffering.

An April sunray was dancing on the china in the shelves; the fire burned; beneath her slippers she felt the softness of the carpet; the day was bright, the air warm, and she heard her child shouting with laughter.

In fact, the little girl was just then rolling on the lawn in the new-mown grass. She was lying flat on her stomach at the top of a rick. The maid was holding her by her skirt. Lestiboudois was raking by her side, and every time he came near she bent forward, beating the air with both her arms.

"Bring her to me," said her mother, rushing over to kiss her. "How I love you, my poor child! How I love you!"

Then noticing that the tips of her ears were rather dirty, she rang at once for warm water, and washed her, changed her underwear, her stockings, her shoes, asked a thousand questions about her health, as if on the return from a long journey, and finally, kissing her again and crying a little, she gave her back to the maid, who was dumbfounded at this sudden outburst.

That evening Rodolphe found her more reserved than usual.

"It will blow over," he thought, "a passing whim . . ."

And he missed three successive rendezvous. When he did appear, her attitude was cold, almost contemptuous.

"Ah! you're wasting time, sweetheart!"

And he pretended not to notice her melancholy sighs, nor the handkerchief she pulled out.

Then Emma knew what it was to repent!

She even wondered why she hated Charles; wouldn't it have been better trying to love him? But he offered little hold for these re-awakened sentiments, so she remained rather embarrassed with her sacrificial intentions until the pharmacist provided her with a timely opportunity.

XI

He had recently read a paper praising a new method for curing club-foot, and since he was a partisan of progress, he conceived the patriotic idea that Yonville should show its pioneering spirit by having some club-foot operations performed there.

"Look here," he told Emma, "what do we risk?" and he ticked off on his fingers the advantages of the attempt, "success practically assured, relief and better appearance for the patient, quick fame for the surgeon. Why, for example, should not your husband relieve poor Hippolyte of the 'Lion d'Or'? He is bound to tell all passing travellers about his cure, and then" (Homais lowered his voice and looked round him) "who is to prevent me from sending a short piece on the subject to the paper? And! My God! an article gets around . . . people talk about it . . . it snowballs! And who knows? who knows?"

After all, Bovary might very well succeed. Emma had no reason to suppose he lacked skill, it would be a satisfaction for her to have urged him to a step by which his reputation and fortune would be increased! She only longed to lean on something more solid than love.

Pressed by her and the pharmacist, Charles allowed himself to be persuaded. He sent to Rouen for Dr. Duval's volume, and every evening, with his head between his hands, he embarked on his reading assignment.

While he struggled with the equinus, varus and valgus—that is to say, *katastrephopody, endostrephopody,* and *exostrephopody,* or in other words, the various deviations of the foot, to the inside, outside, or downwards, as well as with *hypostrephopody* and *anastrephopody* or torsion below and contraction above,—Monsieur Homais was trying out all possible arguments on the stable boy in order to persuade him to submit to the operation.

"At the very most you'll feel a slight pain, a small prick, like a little blood letting, less than the extraction of certain corns."

Hippolyte thought it over, rolling his stupid eyes.

"Anyway," continued the pharmacist, "it is none of my business. I am telling you this for your own sake! out of pure humanity! I would like to see you freed from that hideous caudication as well as that swaying in your lumbar region which, whatever you say, must considerably interfere with the proper performance of your work."

Then Homais represented to him how much more dashing and nimble he would feel afterwards, and even hinted that he would be more likely to please the women; and the stable boy broke into a stupid grin. Then he attacked him through his vanity:

"Come on, act like a man! Think what would have happened if you had been called into the army, and had to fight under our national banner! . . . Ah! Hippolyte!"

And Homais left him, declaring that he could not understand such blindness, such obstinacy, in refusing the benefits of science.

The poor wretch finally gave in, for it was like a conspiracy. Binet, who never interfered with other people's business, Madame Lefrançois, Artémise, the neighbors, even the mayor, Monsieur Tuvache—every one tried to convince him by lecture and reproof; but what finally won him over was that it would cost him nothing. Bovary even undertook to provide the machine for the operation. This generosity was an idea of Emma's, and Charles consented to it, thinking in his heart of hearts that his wife was an angel.

So with the advice of the pharmacist, and after three fresh starts, he had a kind of box made by the carpenter, with the assistance of the locksmith; it weighed about eight pounds, for iron, wood, sheet-iron, leather, screws, and nuts had not been spared.

Yet, to know which of Hippolyte's tendons had to be cut, it was necessary first of all to find out what kind of club-foot he had.

His foot almost formed a straight line with the leg, which, how-ever, did not prevent it from being turned in, so that it was an equinus combined with something of a varus, or else a slight varus with a strong tendency to equinus. But on the equine foot, wide indeed as a horse's hoof, with its horny skin, and large toes, whose black nails resembled the nails of a horse shoe, the cripple ran about like a deer from morn til! night. He was constantly to be seen on the Square, jumping round the carts, thrusting his limping foot forwards. He seemed even stronger on that leg than the other. By dint of hard service it had acquired, as it were, moral qualities of patience and energy; and when he was given some heavy work to do, he would support himself on it in preference to the sound one.

Now, as it was an equinus, it was necessary to cut the Achilles tendon first; if need be, the anterior tibial muscle could be seen to afterwards to take care of the varus. For the doctor did not dare to risk both operations at once; he was already sufficiently worried for fear of injuring some important region that he did not know.

Neither Ambroise Paré, applying a ligature to an artery, for the first time since Celsus did it fifteen centuries before; nor Dupuytren, cutting open abscesses through a thick layer of brain; nor Gensoul on first removing the superior maxilla, had hearts that trembled, hands that shook, minds that strained as Monsieur Bovary's when he approached Hippolyte, his tenotomy knife between his fingers. Just as in a hospital, near by on a table lay a heap of lint, with waxed thread, many bandages—a pyramid of bandages— every bandage to be found at the pharmacy. It was Monsieur Homais who since morning had been organising all these preparations, as much to dazzle the multitude as to keep up his illusions. Charles pierced the skin; a dry crackling was heard. The tendon was cut, the operation over. Hippolyte could not believe his eyes: he bent over Bovary's hands to cover them with kisses.

"Come, be calm," said the pharmacist; "later on you will show your gratitude to your benefactor."

And he went down to report the result to five or six bystanders who were waiting in the yard, and who fancied that Hippolyte would reappear walking straight up. Then Charles, having strapped his patient into the machine, went home, where Emma was anxiously waiting for him on the doorstep. She threw herself on his neck; they sat down at the table; he ate much, and at dessert he even wanted to take a cup of coffee, a luxury he only permitted himself on Sundays when there was company.

The evening was charming, full of shared conversation and common dreams. They talked about their future success, of the improvements to be made in their house; with his rising reputation, he saw his comforts increasing, his wife always loving him; and she was happy to refresh herself with a new sentiment, healthier and purer, and to feel at last some tenderness for this poor man who adored her. The thought of Rodolphe for one moment passed through her mind, but her eyes turned again to Charles; she even noticed with surprise that he had rather handsome teeth.

They were in bed when Monsieur Homais, sidestepping the cook, suddenly entered the room, holding in his hand a newly written sheet of paper. It was the article he intended for the "Fanal de Rouen." He brought it them to read.

"You read it," said Bovary.

He read:

" 'Braving the prejudices that still spread over the face of Europe like a net, the light nevertheless begins to penetrate into our country places. Thus on Tuesday our little town of Yonville found itself the scene of a surgical operation which was at the same time an act of loftiest philanthropy. Monsieur Bovary, one of our most distinguished practitioners . . ."

"Oh, that is too much! too much!" said Charles, choking with emotion.

—"But certainly not! far from it! . . . 'operated on a club-foot.' I have not used the scientific term, because you know in newspapers . . . not everyone would understand . . . the masses, after all, must . . ."

"Certainly," said Bovary; "please go on!"

"I proceed," said the pharmacist. " 'Monsieur Bovary, one of our most distinguished practitioners, performed an operation on a club-footed man, one Hippolyte Tautain, stable-man for the last twenty-five years at the hotel of the "Lion d'Or," kept by Widow Lefrancois, at the Place d'Armes. The novelty of the experiment and the general interest in the patient had attracted such a number of people that a crowd gathered on the threshold of the establishment. The operation, moverover, was performed as if by magic, and barely a few drops of blood appeared on the skin, as though to say that the rebellious tendon had at last given way under the efforts of the medical arts. The patient, strangely enough (we affirm it *de visu*) complained of no pain. His condition up to the present time leaves nothing to be desired. Everything tends to show that his convalescence will be brief; and who knows if, at our next village festivity we shall not see our good Hippolyte appear in the midst of a bacchic dance, surrounded by a group of gay companions, and thus bear witness to all assembled, by his spirit and his capers, of his total recovery? Honor, then, to those generous men of science! Honor to those tireless spirits who consecrate their vigils to the improvement and relief of their kind! Honor to them! Hasn't the time come to cry out that the blind shall see, the deaf hear, the lame walk? What fanaticism formerly promised to a few elect, science now accomplishes for all men. We shall keep our readers informed as to the subsequent progression of this remarkable cure.' "

All this did not prevent Mère Lefrançois from coming five days later, scared out of her wits and shouting:

"Help! he is dying! I am going out of my mind!"

Charles rushed to the "Lion d'Or," and the pharmacist, who caught sight of him passing along the Square without a hat, left his shop. He arrived himself breathless, flushed, anxious, and asked from every one who was going up the stairs:

"What can be the matter with our interesting patient?"

The interesting patient was writhing, in dreadful convulsions, so violent that the contraption in which his foot was locked almost beat down the wall.

With many precautions, in order not to disturb the position of the limb, the box was removed, and an awful spectacle came into view. The outlines of the foot disappeared in such a swelling that the entire skin seemed about to burst; moreover, the leg was covered with bruises caused by the famous machine. Hippolyte had abundantly complained, but nobody had paid any attention to him; now they admitted he might have some grounds for protest and he was freed for a few hours. But hardly had the oedema somewhat gone down, that the two specialists thought fit to put back the limb in the machine, strapping it even tighter to speed up matters. At last, three days after, when Hippolyte could not stand it any longer, they once more removed the machine, and were much surprised at the result they saw. A livid tumescence spread over the entire leg, and a black liquid oozed from several blisters. Things had taken a turn for the worse. Hippolyte was getting bored, and Mère Lefrançois had him installed in the little room near the kitchen, so that he might at least have some distraction.

But the tax-collector, who dined there every day, complained bitterly of such companionship. Then Hippolyte was removed to the billiard-room.

He lay there moaning under his heavy blankets, pale and unshaven, with sunken eyes; from time to time he rubbed his sweating head over the fly-covered pillow. Madame Bovary came to see him. She brought him linen for his poultices; she comforted, and encouraged him. Besides, he did not want for company, especially on market days, when farmers around him were hitting the billiard balls around and fencing with the cues while they drank, sang and brawled.

"How are things?" they would say, clapping him on the shoulder. "Ah! not so well from what we hear. But that's your fault. You should do this! do that!"

And then they told him stories of people who had all been cured by other means. Then by way of consolation they added:

"You pamper yourself too much! You should get up; you coddle yourself like a king. Just the same, old boy, you do smell pretty awful!"

Gangrene was indeed spreading higher and higher. It made Bovary ill to think of it. He came every hour, every moment. Hippolyte looked at him with terrified eyes and sobbed:

"When will I be cured?—Oh, please save me! . . . How unhappy I am! . . . How unhappy I am!"

And the doctor left him, prescribing a strict diet.

"Don't listen to him," said Mère Lefrançois. "Haven't they tortured you enough already? You'll grow still weaker. Here! swallow this."

And she gave him some strong broth, a slice of mutton, a piece of bacon, and sometimes small glasses of brandy, that he had not the strength to put to his lips.

The abbé Bournisien, hearing that he was growing worse, asked to see him. He began by pitying his sufferings, declaring at the same time that he ought to rejoice since it was the will of the Lord, and hasten to reconcile himself with Heaven.

"For," said the ecclesiastic in a paternal tone, "you rather neglected your duties; you were rarely seen at divine worship. How many years is it since you approached the holy table? I understand that your work, that the whirl of the world may have distracted you from your salvation. But now the time has come. Yet don't despair. I have known great sinners, who, about to appear before God (you are not yet at this point I know), had implored His mercy, and who certainly died in a truly repenting frame of mind. Let us hope that, like them, you will set us a good example! Thus, as a precaution, what is to prevent you from saying morning and evening a Hail Mary and an Our Father? Yes, do that, for my sake, to oblige me. That won't cost you anything. Will you promise me?"

The poor devil promised. The curé came back day after day. He chatted with the landlady, and even told anecdotes interspersed with jokes and puns that Hippolyte did not understand. Then, as soon as he could, he would return to religious considerations, putting on an appropriate expression.

His zeal seemed to bring results, for the club-foot soon manifested a desire to go on a pilgrimage to Bon-Secours if he were cured; to which Monsieur Bournisien replied that he saw no objection; two precautions were better than one; moreover, it certainly could do no harm.

The pharmacist was incensed by what he called the priest's machinations; they were prejudicial, he said, to Hippolyte's convalescence, and he kept repeating to Madame Lefrançois, "Leave him alone! leave him alone! You're ruining his morale with your mysticism."

But the good woman would no longer listen to him; she blamed him for being the cause of it all. In sheer rebellion, she hung near the patient's bedside a well-filled basin of holy water and a sprig of boxwood.

Religion, however, seemed no more able than surgery to bring relief and the irresistible putrefaction kept spreading from the foot to the groin. It was all very well to vary the potions and change the poultices; the muscles each day rotted more and more; Charles replied by an affirmative nod of the head when Mére Lefrançois asked him if she could not, as a last resort, send for Monsieur Canivet, a famous surgeon from Neufchâtel.

Charles' fifty-year old colleague, a doctor of medicine with a well established practice and a solid self confidence, did not refrain from laughing disdainfully when he had uncovered the leg, gangrened to the knee. Then having flatly declared that it must be amputated, he went off to the pharmacist's to rail at the asses who could have reduced a poor man to such a state. Shaking Monsieur Homais by his coat-button, he shouted for everyone to hear:

"That is what you get from listening to the fads from Paris! What will they come up with next, these gentlemen from the capital! It is like strabismus, chloroform, lithotrity, monstrosities the Government ought to prohibit. But they want to be clever and cram you full of remedies without troubling about the consequences. We are not so clever out here, not we! We are no specialists, no cure-alls, no fancy talkers! We are practitioners; we cure people, and we wouldn't dream of operating on someone who is in perfect health. Straighten club-feet! As if one could straighten club-feet indeed! It is as if one wished to make a hunchback straight!"

Homais suffered as he listened to this discourse, and he concealed his discomfort beneath a courtier's smile; for he needed to humour Monsieur Canivet, whose prescriptions sometimes came as far as Yonville. So he did not take up the defence of Bovary; he did not even make a single remark, and, renouncing his principles, he sacrificed his dignity to the more serious interests of his business.

This thigh amputation by Doctor Canivet was a great event in the village. On that day all the inhabitants got up earlier, and the Grande Rue, crowded as it was, had something lugubrious about it, as though one were preparing for an execution. At the grocers they discussed Hippolyte's illness; the shops did no business, and Madame Tuvache, the mayor's wife, did not stir from her window, such was her impatience to see the surgeon arrive.

He came in his gig, which he drove himself. The springs of the right side had all given way beneath his corpulence and the carriage tilted a little as it rolled along, revealing on the cushion near him a large case covered in red sheep-leather, whose three brass clasps shone grandly.

Like a whirlwind, the doctor entered the porch of the Lion d'Or and, shouting loudly, he ordered to unharness. Then he went into the stable to see that his horse was eating his oats all right; for on arriving at a patient's he first of all looked after his mare and his gig. The habit made people say, "Ah, that Monsieur Canivet, what a character!" but he was the more esteemed for his composure. The universe as a whole might have been blown apart, and he would not have changed the least of his habits.

Homais introduced himself.

"I count on you," said the doctor. "Are you ready? Come along!"

But the pharmacist blushingly confessed that he was too sensitive to witness such an operation.

"When one is a simple spectator," he said, "the imagination, you know, is easily impressed. And then, my nerves are so . . ."

"Bah!" interrupted Canivet; "on the contrary, you seem like the apoplectic type to me. But I am not surprised, for you gentlemen pharmacists are always poking about your kitchens, which must end by spoiling your constitutions. Now just look at me. I get up every day at four o'clock; I shave with cold water (and am never cold). I don't wear flannel underwear, and I never catch cold; my carcass is good enough! I take things in my stride, philosophically, as they come my way. That is why I am not squeamish like you, and it doesn't matter to me whether I carve up a Christian or the first fowl that comes my way. Habit, you'll say . . . mere habit! . . ."

Then, without any consideration for Hippolyte, who was sweating with agony between his sheets, these gentlemen began a conversation, in which the druggist compared the coolness of a surgeon to that of a general; and this comparison was pleasing to Canivet, who held forth on the demands of his art. He looked upon it as a sacred office, although the ordinary practitioners dishonored it. At last, coming back to the patient, he examined the bandages brought by Homais, the same that had appeared for the club-foot, and asked for some one to hold the limb for him. Lestiboudois was sent for, and Monsieur Canivet having turned up his sleeves, passed into the billiard-room, while the druggist stayed with Artémise and the landlady, both whiter than their aprons, and with ears strained towards the door.

Meanwhile, Bovary didn't dare to stir from his house.

He kept downstairs in the sitting-room by the side of the fireless chimney, his chin on his breast, his hands clasped, his eyes staring. "What a misfortune," he thought, "what a disappointment!" Yet, he had taken all possible precautions. Luck must have been against him. All the same, if Hippolyte died later on, he would be considered the murderer. And how would he defend himself against the questions his patients were bound to ask him during his calls? Maybe, after all, he had made some slip. He thought and thought, but nothing came. The most famous surgeons also made mistakes. But no one would ever believe that; on the contrary, people would laugh, jeer! The news would spread as far as Neufchâtel, as Rouen, everywhere! Who could say if his colleagues would not write against him? Polemics would ensue; he would have to answer in the papers. Hippolyte might even prosecute him. He saw himself dishonored, ruined, lost; and his imagination, assailed by numberless hypotheses, tossed amongst them like an empty cask dragged out to sea and pitched about by the waves.

Emma, opposite, watched him; she did not share his humiliation; she felt another—that of having imagined that such a man could have any worth, as if twenty times already she had not sufficiently perceived his mediocrity.

Charles was pacing the room. His boots creaked on the floor.

"Sit down," she said; "you irritate me!"

He sat down again.

How was it that she—she, who was so intelligent—could have allowed herself to be deceived again? Moreover, what madness had driven her to ruin her life by continual sacrifices? She recalled all her instincts of luxury, all the privations of her soul, the sordidness of marriage, of the household, her dreams sinking into the mire like wounded swallows; all that she had longed for, all that she had denied herself, all that she might have had! And for what? for what?

In the midst of the silence that hung over the village a heart-rending cry pierced the air. Bovary turned white as a sheet. She knit her brows with a nervous gesture, then returned to her thought. And it was for him, for this creature, for this man, who understood nothing, who felt nothing! For he sat there as if nothing had happened, not even suspecting that the ridicule of his name would henceforth sully hers as well as his. She had made efforts to love him, and she had repented with tears for having yielded to another!

"But it was perhaps a valgus after all!" exclaimed Bovary suddenly, interrupting his meditations.

At the unexpected shock of this phrase falling on her thought like a leaden bullet on a silver plate, Emma shuddered and raised her head in an effort to find out what he meant to say; and they gazed at one another in silence, almost amazed to see each other, so far sundered were they by their respective states of consciousness. Charles gazed at her with the dull look of a drunken man, while he listened motionless to the last cries of the sufferer, following each other in long-drawn modulations, broken by sharp spasms like the far-off howling of some beast being slaughtered. Emma bit her wan lips, and rolling between her fingers a piece of wood she had peeled from the coral-tree, fixed on Charles the burning glance of her eyes like two arrows of fire about to dart forth. Everything in him irritated her now; his face, his dress, all the things he did not say, his whole person, in short, his existence. She repented of her past virtue as of a crime, and what still remained of it crumbled away beneath the furious blows of her pride. She revelled in all the evil ironies of triumphant adultery. The memory of her lover came back to her with irresistible, dizzying attractions; she threw her whole soul towards this image, carried by renewed passion; and Charles seemed to her as removed from her life, as eternally absent, as incongruous and annihilated, as if he were dying under her very eyes.

There was a sound of steps on the pavement. Charles looked up, and through the lowered blinds he saw Dr. Canivet standing in broad sunshine at the corner of the market, wiping his brow with his handerchief. Homais, behind him, was carrying a large red bag in his hand, and both were going towards the pharmacy.

Then with a feeling of sudden tenderness and discouragement Charles turned to his wife and said:

"Oh, kiss me, my dear!"

"Don't touch me!" she cried, flushed with anger.

"What is it? what is it?" he repeated, in utter bewilderment. "Don't be upset! calm down! You know that I love you . . . come! . . ."

"Stop it!" she cried with a terrible look.

And rushing from the room, Emma closed the door so violently that the barometer fell from the wall and smashed on the floor.

Charles sank back into his arm-chair thoroughly shaken, wondering what could have come over her, imagining it might be some nervous disease, weeping, and vaguely feeling something fatal and incomprehensible was whirling around him.

When Rodolphe came to the garden that evening, he found his mistress waiting for him at the foot of the steps on the lowest stair. They threw their arms round one another, and all their rancor melted like snow beneath the warmth of that kiss.

XII

Their love resumed its course. Often in the middle of the day, Emma would suddenly write to him, then beckon Justin through the window; he quickly untied his apron and flew to La Huchette. Rodolphe would come; she had to tell him again how bored she was, that her husband was odious, her life dreadful.

"What do you expect me to do about it?" he asked one day impatiently.

"Ah, if only you wanted . . ."

She was sitting on the floor between his knees, her hair loosened, staring in a void.

"Wanted what?" said Rodolphe.

She sighed.

"We would go and live elsewhere . . . anywhere . . ."

"Are you out of your mind!" he said laughing. "How could we?"

She mentioned it again; he pretended not to understand, and changed the subject. What he did not understand was all this worry about so simple an affair as love. But she had a motive, a reason that gave added grounds to her attachment.

Her tenderness, in fact, grew daily as her repulsion toward her husband increased. The more she yielded to the one, the more she loathed the other. Never did Charles seem so unattractive, slow-witted, clumsy and vulgar as when she met him after her rendez-vous with Rodolphe. Then while playing the part of the virtuous wife, she would burn with passion at the thought of his head, the black curl falling over the sun-tanned brow; of his figure, both elegant and strong, of the man so experienced in his thought, so impetuous in his desires! It was for him that she filed her nails with a sculptor's care, that there was never enough cold-cream for her skin, nor patchouli for her handkerchiefs. She loaded herself with bracelets, rings, and necklaces. When she expected him, she filled her two large blue glass vases with roses, and prepared herself and her room like a courtesan receiving a prince. The servant was kept busy steadily laundering her linen, and all day Félicité did not stir from the kitchen, where little Justin, who often kept her company, watched her at work.

With his elbows on the long board on which she was ironing, he greedily watched all these women's garments spread out about him, the dimity petticoats, the fichus, the collars, and the drawers with running strings, wide at the hips and narrowing below.

"What is that for?" asked the young boy, passing his hand over the crinoline or the hooks and eyes.

"Why, haven't you ever seen anything?" Félicité answered laughing. "As if your mistress, Madame Homais, didn't wear the same."

"Oh, well, Madame Homais . . ."

And he added thoughtfully,

"Is she a lady like Madame?"

But Félicité grew impatient of seeing him hanging round her. She was six years older than he, and Theodore, Monsieur Guillau-min's servant, was beginning to pay court to her.

"Leave me alone," she said, moving her pot of starch. "You'd better be off and pound almonds; you are always snooping around women. Before you bother with such things, naughty boy, wait till you've got a beard to your chin."

"Oh, don't be cross! I'll go and clean her boots."

And he hurriedly took down Emma's boots from the shelf all coated with mud—the mud of the rendezvous—that crumbled into powder beneath his fingers, and that he watched as it gently rose in a ray of sunlight.

"How scared you are of spoiling them!" said the maid, who wasn't so particular when she cleaned them herself, because if the boots looked slightly worn Madame would give them to her.

Emma kept a number in her cupboard that she squandered one after the other, without Charles allowing himself the slightest observation.

He also spent three hundred francs for a wooden leg that she thought had to be given to Hippolyte. The top was covered with cork, and it had spring joints, a complicated mechanism, covered over by black trowsers ending in a patent-leather boot. But Hippolyte didn't dare use such a handsome leg every day, and he begged Madame Bovary to get him another more convenient one. The doctor, of course, had to pay for this purchase as well.

So little by little the stable-boy returned to work. One saw him running about the village as before, and when Charles heard from afar the tap of the wooden leg on the pavement, he quickly went in another direction.

It was Monsieur Lheureux, the shopkeeper, who had ordered the wooden leg. This provided him with an excuse for visiting Emma. He chatted with her about the new goods from Paris, about a thousand feminine trifles, made himself very obliging and never asked for his money. Emma yielded to this lazy mode of satisfying all her caprices. When she wanted to give Rodolphe a handsome riding-crop from an umbrella store in Rouen, Monsieur Lheureux placed it on her table the very next week.

But the next day he called on her with a bill for two hundred and seventy francs, not counting the centimes. Emma was much embarrassed; all the drawers of the writing-table were empty; they owed over a fortnight's wages to Lestiboudois, six months to the maid, and there were several other bills. Bovary was impatiently waiting to hear from Monsieur Derozeray who was in the habit of settling every year about Midsummer.

She succeeded at first in putting off Lheureux. At last he lost patience; he was being sued; he was short of capital and unless he could collect on some of his accounts, he would be forced to take back all the goods she had received.

"Oh, very well, take them!" said Emma.

"I was only joking," he replied; "the only thing I regret is the riding crop. Well, I'll have to ask Monsieur to return it to me."

"No, no!" she said.

"Ah! I've got you!" thought Lheureux.

And, certain of his discovery, he went out muttering to himself and with his usual low whistle . . .

"Good! we shall see! we shall see!"

She was wondering how to handle the situation when the maid entered and put on the mantelpiece a small roll of blue paper "with the compliments of Monsieur Derozeray." Emma grasped it, tore it open. It contained fifteen napoleons: the account paid in full. Hearing Charles on the stairs, she threw the money to the back of her drawer, and took out the key.

Three days later, Lheureux returned.

"I have a suggestion to make," he said. "If, instead of the sum, agreed on, you would take. . . ."

"Here it is," she said handing him fourteen napoleons.

The shopkeeper was taken aback. Then, to conceal his disappointment, he was profuse in apologies and offers of service, all of which Emma declined; she remained a few moments fingering in the pocket of her apron the two five-franc pieces of change he had returned to her. She told herself she would economise in order to pay back later . . . "Bah!," she thought, "he'll forget all about it."

Besides the riding-crop with its silver-gilt top, Rodolphe had received a signet with the motto *Amor nel cor*, furthermore, a scarf for a muffler, and, finally, a cigar-case exactly like the Viscount's, that Charles had formerly picked up in the road, and that Emma had kept. These presents, however, humiliated him; he refused several; she insisted, and he ended by obeying, thinking her tyrannical and over-exacting.

Then she had strange ideas.

"When midnight strikes," she said, "you must think of me."

And if he confessed that he had not thought of her, there were floods of reproaches that always ended with the eternal question:

"Do you love me?"

"Why, of course I love you," he answered.

"A great deal?"

"Certainly!"

"You haven't loved any others?"

"Did you think you'd got a virgin?" he exclaimed laughing.

Emma cried, and he tried to console her, adorning his protestations with puns.

"Oh," she went on, "I love you! I love you so that I could not live without you, do you see? There are times when I long to see you again, when I am torn by all the anger of love. I ask myself, where is he? Perhaps he is talking to other women. They smile upon him; he approaches. Oh no; no one else pleases you. There are some more beautiful, but I love you best. I know how to love best. I am your servant, your concubine! You are my king, my idol! You are good, you are beautiful, you are clever, you are strong!"

He had so often heard these things said that they did not strike him as original. Emma was like all his mistresses; and the charm of novelty, gradually falling away like a garment, laid bare the eternal monotony of passion, that has always the same shape and the same language. He was unable to see, this man so full of experience, the variety of feelings hidden within the same expressions. Since libertine or venal lips had murmured similar phrases, he only faintly believed in the candor of Emma's; he thought one should beware of exaggerated declarations which only serve to cloak a tepid love; as though the abundance of one's soul did not sometimes overflow with empty metaphors, since no one ever has been able to give the exact measure of his needs, his concepts, or his sorrows. The human tongue is like a cracked cauldron on which we beat out tunes to set a bear dancing when we would make the stars weep with our melodies.

But with the superiority of critical insight of the person who holds back his emotions in any engagement, Rodolphe perceived that there were other pleasures to be exploited in this love. He discarded all modesty as inconvenient. He treated her without consideration. And he made her into something at once malleable and corrupt. It was an idiotic sort of attachment, full of admiration on his side and voluptuousness on hers, a beatitude which left her numb; and her soul sunk deep into this intoxication and drowned in it, all shrivelled up, like the duke of Clarence[44] in his butt of malmsey.

Solely as a result of her amorous practices, Madame Bovary began to change in appearance. Her glances were bolder, her speech freer; she even went as far as to go out walking with Rodolphe, a cigarette in her mouth, "just to scandalize the town"; finally, those who had doubted doubted no longer when they saw her descend one day from the Hirondelle wearing a tight-fitting waistcoat cut like a man's. And Madame Bovary senior who, after a frightful scene with her husband, had come to seek refuge with her son, was not the least scandalized lady in town. Many other things displeased her too: first of all, Charles had not followed her advice in banning novels from the house; then, the "tone" of the house upset her; she allowed herself to make observations, and there were arguments, especially, on one occasion, concerning Felicité.

The previous evening, while crossing the corridor, Madame Bovary senior had come upon her in the company of a man of about forty wearing a brown collar, who on hearing footsteps, had quickly fled from the kitchen. Emma had burst out laughing; but the good woman was furious, declaring that anyone who took morality seriously ought to keep an eye on their servant's behavior.

"What kind of society do you come from?" asked the daughter-in-law, with so impertinent a look that Madame Bovary asked her if

---

44. The duke of Clarence was the younger brother of King Edward IV of England and the elder brother of Richard Duke of Gloucester. He was condemned to death for treason and, according to rumor, drowned in a butt of malmsey (a sweet aromatic wine) in February 1478. See Shakespeare, *Richard III*, Act 1, sc. 4, 1. 155.

she were not perhaps defending her own case.

"Get out!" said the young woman, rising in fury.

"Emma! . . . Mother! . . ." cried Charles, trying to reconcile them.

But both had fled in their exasperation. Emma was stamping her feet as she repeated:

"Oh! what manners! What a peasant!"

He ran to his mother; she was beside herself. She stammered: "How insolent she is! and how flighty! worse perhaps!"

And she was ready to leave at once if the other did not apologise. So Charles went back again to his wife and implored her to give way; he threw himself at her feet; finally, she said:

"Very well! I'll go to her."

And she actually held out her hand to her mother-in-law with the dignity of a marquise as she said:

"Excuse me, madame."

Then, having returned to her room, she threw herself flat on her bed and cried there like a child, her face buried in the pillow.

She and Rodolphe had agreed that in the event of anything extraordinary occurring, she should fasten a small piece of white paper to the blind, so that if by chance he happened to be in Yonville, he could hurry to the lane behind the house. Emma made the signal; she had been waiting three-quarters of an hour when she suddenly caught sight of Rodolphe at the corner of the square. She felt tempted to open the window and call him, but he had already disappeared. She fell back in despair.

Soon, however, it seemed to her that someone was walking on the pavement. It was he, no doubt. She went downstairs, crossed the yard. He was there outside. She threw herself into his arms.

"Watch out!" he said.

"Ah! if only you knew!" she replied.

And she began telling him everything, hurriedly, disjointedly, exaggerating the facts, inventing many, and with so many digressions that he understood nothing at all.

"Come now, my poor angel, be brave, console yourself, be patient!"

"But I have been patient; I have suffered for four years. A love like ours ought to show itself in the face of heaven. They torture me! I can bear it no longer! Save me!"

She clung to Rodolphe. Her eyes, full of tears, flashed like flames beneath a wave; her panting made her breast rise and fall; never had she seemed more lovely, so much so that he lost his head and said:

"What do you want me to do?"

"Take me away," she cried, "carry me off! . . . I beg you!"

She pressed her lips against his mouth, as if to capture the unhoped for consent the moment it was breathed forth in a kiss.

"But . . ." Rodolphe began.

"What?"

"Your little girl!"

She reflected a few moments, then replied:

"We'll take her with us, there is no other way!"

"What a woman!" he said to himself, watching her as she went. For she had run into the garden. Some one was calling her.

On the following days the elder Madame Bovary was much surprised at the change in her daughter-in-law. Emma, in fact, was showing herself more docile, and even carried her deference to the point of asking for a recipe for pickles.

Was it the better to deceive them both? Or did she wish by a sort of voluptuous stoicism to feel the more profoundly the bitterness of the things she was about to leave? But she paid no heed to them; on the contrary, she lived as lost in the anticipated delight of her coming happiness. It was an eternal subject for conversation with Rodolphe. She leant on his shoulder murmuring:

"Think, we will soon be in the mail-coach! Can you imagine? Is it possible? It seems to me that the moment the carriage will start, it will be as if we were rising in a balloon, as if we were setting out for the clouds. Do you know that I count the hours? . . . Don't you?"

Never had Madame Bovary been so beautiful as at this period; she had that indefinable beauty that results from joy, from enthusiasm, from success, and that expresses the harmony between temperament and circumstances. Her cravings, her sorrows, her sensuous pleasures and her ever-young illusions had slowly brought her to full maturity, and she blossomed forth in the fulness of her being, like a flower feeding on manure, on rain, wind and sunshine. Her half-closed eyelids seemed perfectly shaped for the long languid glances that escaped from them; her breathing dilated the fine nostrils and raised the fleshy corners of her mouth, shaded in the light by a slight black down. Some artist skilled in corruption seemed to have devised the shape of her hair as it fell on her neck, coiled in a heavy mass, casually reassembled after being loosened daily in adultery. Her voice now took more mellow inflections, her figure also; something subtle and penetrating escaped even from the folds of her gown and from the line of her foot. Charles thought her exquisite and altogether irresistible, as when they were first married.

When he came home in the middle of the night, he did not dare to wake her. The porcelain night-light threw a round trembling gleam upon the ceiling, and the drawn curtains of the little cot formed as it were a white hut standing out in the shade by the bedside. Charles looked at them. He seemed to hear the light breathing of his child. She would grow big now; every season would bring rapid progress. He already saw her coming from school as the day drew in, laughing, with ink-stains on her jacket, and carrying her basket on her arm. Then she would have to be sent to a boarding-school; that would cost much; how was it to be done? He kept thinking about it. He thought of renting a small farm in the neighborhood, that he would supervise every morning on his way to his patients. He would not spend what he brought in; he would put it in the savings-bank. Then he would invest in some stocks, he didn't know which; besides, his practice would increase; he counted on it, for he wanted Berthe to be well-educated, to be accomplished, to learn to play the piano. Ah! how pretty she would be later on when she was fifteen, when, resembling her mother, she would, like her, wear large straw hats in the summer-time; from a distance they would be taken for two sisters. He pictured her to himself working in the evening by their side beneath the light of the lamp; she would embroider him slippers; she would look after the house; she would fill all the home with her charm and her gaiety. At last, they would think of her marriage; they would find her some good young fellow with a steady business; he would make her happy; this would last for ever.

Emma was not asleep; she pretended to be; and while he dozed off by her side she awakened to other dreams.

To the gallop of four horses she was carried away for a week towards a new land, from where they would never return. They went on and on, their arms entwined, without speaking a word. Often from the top of a mountain there suddenly appeared some splendid city with domes, and bridges, and ships, forests of lemon trees, and cathedrals of white marble, their pointed steeples crowned with storks' nests. The horses slowed down to a walk because of the wide pavement, and on the ground there were bouquets of flowers, offered by women dressed in red. They heard the chiming of bells, the neighing of mules, together with the murmur of guitars and the noise of fountains, whose rising spray refreshed heaps of fruit arranged like a pyramid at the foot of pale statues that smiled beneath playing waters. And then, one night they came to a fishing village, where brown nets were drying in the wind along the cliffs and in front of the huts. It was there that they would stay; they would live in a low, flat-roofed house, shaded by a palm-tree, in the heart of a gulf, by the sea. They would row in gondolas, swing in hammocks, and their existence would be easy and free as their wide silk gowns, warm and star-spangled as the nights they would contemplate. However, in the immensity of this future that she conjured up, nothing specific stood out; the days, all magnificent, resembled each other like waves; and the vision swayed in the horizon, infinite, harmonised, azure, and bathed in sunshine. But the child began to cough in her cot or Bovary snored more loudly, and Emma did not fall asleep till morning, when the dawn whitened the windows, and when little Justin was already in the square taking down the shutters of the pharmacy.

She had sent for Monsieur Lheureux, and had said to him:

"I want a cloak—a large lined cloak with a deep collar."

"You are going on a journey?" he asked.

"No; but . . . never mind. I count on you to get it in a hurry."

He bowed.

"Besides, I shall want," she went on, "a trunk . . . not too heavy . . . a handy size."

"Yes, yes, I understand. About three feet by a foot and a half, as they are being made just now."

"And a travelling bag."

"No question about it," thought Lheureux, "she is up to something."

"And," said Madame Bovary, taking her watch from her belt, "take this; you can pay yourself out of it."

But the shopkeeper protested that it was not necessary; as if he didn't know and trust her. She was being childish!

She insisted, however, on his taking at least the chain, and Lheureux had already put it in his pocket and was going, when she called him back.

"You will leave everything at your place. As to the cloak"—she seemed to be reflecting—"do not bring it either; you can give me the maker's address, and tell him to have it ready for me."

It was the next month that they were to run away. She was to leave Yonville as if she was going on some business to Rouen. Rodolphe would have booked the seats, obtained the passports, and even have written to Paris in order to have the whole mail-coach reserved for them as far as Marseilles, where they would buy a carriage, and go on from there straight by the Genoa road. She would have sent her luggage to Lheureux, from where it would be taken directly to the "Hirondelle," so that no one would have any suspicion. And in all this there never was any allusion to the child. Rodolphe avoided the subject; it may be that he had forgotten about it.

He wished to have two more weeks before him to arrange some affairs; then at the end of a week he wanted two more; then he said he as ill; next he went on a journey. The month of August passed, and, after all these delays, they decided that it was to be irrevocably fixed for the 4th September—a Monday.

At last the Saturday before arrived.

Rodolphe came in the evening earlier than usual.

"Is everything ready?" she asked him.

"Yes."

Then they walked round a garden-bed, and sat down near the terrace on the kerb-stone of the wall.

"You are sad," said Emma.

"No; why?"

And yet he looked at her strangely, though with tenderness.

"Is it because you are going away?" she went on; "because you are leaving behind what is dear to you, your own life? I can understand that . . . But I have nothing in the world! You are everything I have, and I'll be everything to you. I'll be your family, your country; I'll look after you, I'll love you."

"How sweet you are!" he said, taking her in his arms.

"Am I really?" she said with a voluptuous laugh. "Do you love me? Swear it then!"

"Do I love you? Do I? But I adore you, my love!"

The moon, full and purple-colored, was rising right out of the earth at the end of the meadow. It rose quickly between the branches of the poplar trees, partly hidden as by a tattered black curtain. Then it appeared dazzling white, lighting up the empty sky; slowing down, it let fall upon the river a great stain that broke up into an infinity of stars; and the silver sheen seemed to writhe through the very depths like a headless serpent covered with luminous scales; it also resembled some monster candelabra from which sparkling diamonds fell like molten drops. The soft night was about them; masses of shadow filled the branches. Emma, her eyes half closed, breathed in with deep sighs the fresh wind that was blowing. They did not speak, caught as they were in their dream. The tenderness of the old days came back to their hearts, full and silent as the flowing river, with the soft perfume of the syringas, and threw across their memories shadows more immense and more sombre than those of the still willows that lengthened out over the grass. Often some night-animal, hedgehog or weasel, setting out on the hunt, disturbed the lovers, or sometimes they heard a ripe peach fall by itself from the tree.

"Ah! what a lovely night!" said Rodolphe.

"We shall have others," replied Emma.

Then, as if speaking to herself:

"Yes, it will be good to travel. And yet, why should my heart be so heavy? Is it dread of the unknown? The weight of old habits? . . . Or else? No, it is the excess of happiness. How weak I am! You must forgive me!"

"There is still time!" he cried. "Think! You may regret it later!"

"Never!" she cried impetuously.

And, drawing closer to him:

"What ill could come to me? There is no desert, no precipice, no ocean I would not traverse with you. The longer we live together the more it will be like an embrace, every day closer, more complete. There will be nothing to trouble us, no cares, no obstacle. We shall be alone, all to ourselves forever . . . Say something, answer me!"

At regular intervals he answered, "Yes . . . Yes . . ." She had passed her hands through his hair, and she repeated in a childlike voice through her tears:

"Rodolphe! Rodolphe! . . . Sweet little Rodolphe!"

Midnight struck.

"Midnight!" she said. "Come, it is to-morrow. One more day!"

He rose to go; and as if the movement he made had been the signal for their flight, Emma suddenly seemed gay:

"You have the passports?"

"Yes."

"You are forgetting nothing?"

"No."

"Are you sure?"

"Absolutely."

"You'll be waiting for me at the Hotel de Provence, won't you? . . . at noon?"

He nodded.

"Till to-morrow then!" said Emma in a last caress; and she watched him go.

He did not turn round. She ran after him, and, leaning over the water's edge between the bushes:

"Till to-morrow!" she cried.

He was already on the other side of the river and walking fast across the meadow.

After a few moments Rodolphe stopped; and when he saw her with her white gown gradually fade away in the shade like a ghost, his heart beat so wildly that he had to support himself against a tree.

"What a fool I am!" he said, swearing a dreadful oath. "All the same, she was the prettiest mistress ever."

And immediately Emma's beauty, with all the pleasures of their love, came back to him. For a moment he weakened, but then he rebelled against her.

"For, after all," he exclaimed, gesticulating, "I can't exile myself, and with a child on my hands to boot!"

He was saying these things to strengthen his determination.

"And besides, the worries, the cost! No, no, a thousand times no! It would have been too stupid."

XIII

No sooner was Rodolphe at home than he sat down quickly at his desk under the stag's head that hung as a trophy on the wall. But when he had the pen between his fingers, he could think of nothing, so that, resting on his elbows, he began to reflect. Emma seemed to him to have receded into a far-off past, as if the resolution he had taken had suddenly placed an immeasurable distance between them.

In order to recapture something of her presence, he fetched from the cupboard at the bedside an old Rheims cookie-box, in which he usually kept his love letters. An odour of dry dust and withered roses emanated from it. First he saw a handkerchief stained with pale drops. It was a handkerchief of hers. Once when they were walking her nose had bled; he had forgotten it. Near it, almost too large for the box, was Emma's miniature: her dress seemed pretentious to him, and her languishing look in the worst possible taste. Then, from looking at this image and recalling the memory of the original, Emma's features little by little grew confused in his remembrance, as if the living and the painted face, rubbing one against the other, had erased each other. Finally, he read some of her letters; they were full of explanations relating to their journey, short, technical, and urgent, like business notes. He wanted to see the long ones again, those of old times. In order to find them at the bottom of the box, Rodolphe disturbed all the others, and mechanically began rummaging among this mass of papers and things, finding pell-mell bouquets, garters, a black mask, pins, and hair . . . lots of hair! Some dark, some fair, some, catching in the hinges of the box, even broke when he opened it.

Following his memories, he examined the writing and the style of the letters, as varied as their spelling. They were tender or jovial, facetious, melancholy; there were some that asked for love, others that asked for money. A word recalled faces to him, certain gestures, the sound of a voice; sometimes, however, he remembered nothing at all.

All these women, crowding into his consciousness, rather shrank in size, levelled down by the uniformity of his feeling. Seizing the letters at random, he amused himself for a while by letting them cascade from his right into his left hand. At last, bored and weary, Rodolphe took back the box to the cupboard, saying to himself:

"What a lot of nonsense!"

Which summed up his opinion; for pleasures, like schoolboys in a school courtyard, had so trampled upon his heart that no green thing was left; whatever entered there, more heedless than children, did not even, like them, leave a name carved upon the wall.

"Come," he said, "let's go."

He wrote:

> Courage, Emma! you must be brave! I don't want to be the one to ruin your life . . .

"After all, that's true," thought Rodolphe. "I am acting in her interest; I am honest."

> Have you carefully weighed your resolution? Do you know to what an abyss I was dragging you, poor angel? No, you don't, I assure you. You were coming confident and fearless, believing in a future happiness . . . Ah! the wretched creatures we are! We nearly lost our minds!

Rodolphe paused to think of some good excuse.

"If I told her that I lost all my money? No! Besides, that would stop nothing. It would all start again later on. As if one could make women like that listen to reason!"

He thought for a moment, then added:

> I shall not forget you, believe me; and I shall forever have a profound devotion for you; but some day, sooner or later, this ardour (such is the fate of human things) would doubtlessly have diminished. Weariness would have been unavoidable, and who knows if I would not even have had the atrocious pain of witnessing your remorse, of sharing it myself, since I would have been its cause? The mere idea of the grief that would come to you tortures me, Emma. Forget me! Why did I ever know you? Why were you so beautiful? Is it my fault? God, no! only fate is to blame!

"That's a word that always helps," he said to himself.

> Ah, if you had been one of those shallow women of which there are so many, I might, out of selfishness, have tried an experiment, in that case without danger for you. But your exquisite sensitivity, at once your charm and your torment, has prevented you from understanding, adorable woman that you are, the falseness of our future position. I myself had not fully realized this till now; I was living in the bliss of this ideal happiness as under the shade of a poisonous tree, without forseeing the consequences.

"She may suspect that it is out of stinginess that I am giving her up . . . But never mind, let's get this over with!"

> This is a cruel world, Emma. Wherever we might have gone, it would have persecuted us. You would have had to put up with indiscreet questions, calumny, contempt, insult perhaps. Imagine you being insulted! It is unbearable! . . . I who would place you on a throne! I who bear with me your memory as a talisman! For I am going to punish myself by exile for all the ill I have done you. I am going away. I don't know where, I am too close to madness to think. Farewell! Continue to be good! Remember the unfortu-

nate man who caused your undoing. Teach my name to your child; let her repeat it in her prayers.

The wicks of the candles flickered. Rodolphe got up to close the window, and when he sat down again:

"I think that covers it. Ah, let me add this for fear she might pursue me here."

I shall be far away when you read these sad lines, for I have wished to flee as quickly as possible to shun the temptation of seeing you again. No weakness! I shall return, and perhaps later on we shall be able to talk coldly of our past love. Adieu!

And there was a last "adieu" divided into two words: "A Dieu!" which he thought in very excellent taste.

"Now how am I to sign?" he asked himself. " 'Yours devotedly?' No! 'Your friend?' Yes, that's it."

YOUR FRIEND.

He re-read his letter and thought it quite good.

"Poor little woman!" he thought tenderly. "She'll think me harder than a rock. There ought to have been some tears on this; but I can't cry; it isn't my fault." Then, having emptied some water into a glass, Rodolphe dipped his finger into it, and let a big drop fall on the paper, making a pale stain on the ink. Then looking for a seal, he came upon the one "*Amor nel cor.*"

"Hardly the right thing under the circumstances . . . But who cares?"

Whereupon he smoked three pipes and went to bed.

Upon arising the next morning—around two o'clock in the afternoon, for he had slept late—Rodolphe had a basket of apricots picked. He put his letter at the bottom under some vine leaves, and at once ordered Girard, his ploughman, to take it with care to Madame Bovary. They used to correspond this way before and he would send her fruit or game according to season.

"If she asks about me," he said, "tell her that I have gone on a journey. You must give the basket to her herself, into her own hands. Get going now, and be careful!"

Girard put on his new smock, knotted his handkerchief round the apricots, and, walking heavily in his hobnailed boots, quietly made his way to Yonville.

When he got to the house, Madame Bovary was arranging a bundle of linen on the kitchen-table with Félicité.

"Here," said the ploughboy, "is something for you from my master."

She was seized with apprehension, and as she sought in her pocket for some small change, she looked at the peasant with haggard eyes, while he himself stared at her with amazement, not understanding how such a small present could stir up such violent emotions. Finally he left. Félicité stayed. She could bear it no longer; she ran into the sitting room as if to take the apricots there, overturned the basket, tore away the leaves, found the letter, opened it, and, as if pursued by some fearful fire, Emma flew in terror to her room.

Charles was there; she saw him; he spoke to her; she heard nothing, and she ran quickly up the stairs, breathless, distraught, crazed, and ever holding this horrible piece of paper, that crackled between her fingers like a plate of sheet-iron. On the second floor she stopped before the closed attic-door.

Then she tried to calm herself; she recalled the letter; she must finish it but she didn't dare. Where and how was she to read it? She would be seen!

"Here," she thought, "I'll be safe here."

Emma pushed open the door and went in.

The slates projected a heavy heat that gripped her temples, stifled her; she dragged herself to the closed window, drew back the bolt, and the dazzling sunlight burst in.

Opposite, beyond the roofs, the open country stretched as far as the eye could reach. Down below, underneath her, the village square was empty; the stones of the pavement glittered, the weathercocks on the houses stood motionless. At the corner of the street, from a lower story, rose a kind of humming with strident modulations. It was Binet turning.

She leant against the window-frame, and re-read the letter with angry sneers. But the more she concentrated on it, the more confused she grew. She could see him, hear him, feel his embrace; the throbbing of her heart, beating irregularly in her breast like the blows of a battering ram, grew faster and faster. She looked about her wishing that the earth might crumble. Why not end it all? What restrained her? She was free. She advanced, looked at the paving-stones, saying to herself, "Jump! jump!"

The ray of light reflected straight from below drew the weight of her body towards the abyss. The ground of the village square seemed to tilt over and climb up the walls, the floor to pitch forward like in a tossing boat. She was right at the edge, almost hanging, surrounded by vast space. The blue of the sky invaded her, the air was whirling in her hollow head; she had but to yield, to let herself be taken; and the humming of the lathe never ceased, like an angry voice calling her.

"My wife! my wife!" cried Charles.

She stopped.

"Where have you gone? Come here!"

The thought that she had just escaped from death almost made her faint with terror. She closed her eyes; then she started at the touch of a hand on her sleeve; it was Félicité.

"Monsieur is waiting for you, madame; the soup is on the table."

And she had to go down! and sit at the table!

She tried to eat. The food choked her. Then she unfolded her napkin as if to examine the darns, and really tried to concentrate on this work, counting the stitches in the linen. Suddenly she remembered the letter. How had she lost it? Where could it be found? But she felt such weariness of spirit that she could not even invent a pretext for leaving the table. Then she became a coward; she was afraid of Charles; he knew all, that was certain! Just then, he said, in an odd tone:

"We are not likely to see Monsieur Rodolphe soon again, it seems."

"Who told you?" she said, shuddering.

"Who told me!" he replied, rather astonished at her abrupt tone. "Why, Girard, whom I met just now at the door of the Café Français. He has gone on a journey, or is about to go."

She could not suppress a sob.

"What is so surprising about that? He goes away like that from time to time for a change, and I certainly can't blame him. A bachelor, and rich as he is! And from what I hear, he isn't exactly starved for pleasures, our friend! he enjoys life. Monsieur Langlois told me . . ."

He stopped for propriety's sake because the maid had just come in.

She collected the apricots that were strewn over the sideboard and put them back in the basket. Charles, unaware that his wife had turned scarlet, had them brought to him, took one, and bit into it.

"Perfect!" he said; "have a taste!"

And he handed her the basket, which she gently put away from her.

"Smell them! Such perfume!" he insisted, moving it back and forth under her nose.

"I am choking," she exclaimed, leaping up.

By sheer willpower, she succeeded in forcing back the spasm.

"It is nothing," she said, "it is nothing! Just nerves. Sit down and eat."

For she dreaded most of all that he would question her, try to help and not leave her to herself.

Charles, to obey her, sat down again, and he spat the stones of the apricots into his hands, afterwards putting them on his plate.

Suddenly a blue tilbury passed across the square at a rapid trot. Emma uttered a cry and fell back rigid on the floor.

After many hesitations, Rodolphe had finally decided to set out for Rouen. Now, as from La Huchette to Buchy there is no other way than by Yonville, he had to go through the village, and Emma had recognised him by the rays of the lanterns, which like lightning flashed through the twilight.

The general commotion which broke out in the house brought the pharmacist over in a hurry. The table, with all the plates, had been knocked over; sauce, meat, knives, the salt, and cruet-stand were strewn over the room; Charles was calling for help; Berthe, scared, was crying; and Félicité, whose hands trembled, was unlacing her mistress, whose whole body shivered convulsively.

"I'll run to my laboratory for some aromatic vinegar," said the pharmacist.

Then as she opened her eyes on smelling the bottle:

"I thought so," he said, "this thing would resuscitate a corpse!"

"Speak to us," said Charles "try to recover! It is Charles, who loves you . . . Do you know me? Look, here is your little girl; kiss her, darling!"

The child stretched out her arms to cling to her mother's neck. But turning away her head, Emma said in a broken voice:

"No, no . . . I want no one!"

She fainted again. They carried her to her bed.

She lay there stretched at full length, her lips apart, her eyelids closed, her hands open, motionless, and white as a waxen image. Two streams of tears flowed from her eyes and fell slowly upon the pillow.

Charles stood at the back of the alcove, and the pharmacist, near him, maintained the meditative silence that is fitting on the serious occasions of life.

"Don't worry," he said, touching his elbow; "I think the paroxysm is past."

"Yes, she is resting a little now," answered Charles, watching her sleep. "Poor girl! poor girl! She has dropped off now!"

Then Homais asked how the accident had occurred. Charles answered that she had been taken ill suddenly while she was eating some apricots.

"Extraordinary!" continued the pharmacist. "It is quite possible that the apricots caused the syncope. Some natures are so sensitive to certain smells; it would even be a very fine question to study both from a pathological and physiological point of view. The priests know all about it; that's why they use aromatics in all their ceremonies. It is to stupefy the senses and to bring on ecstasies,—a thing, moreover, very easy in persons of the weaker sex, who are more sensitive than we are. Some are reported fainting at the smell of burnt horn, or fresh bread . . ."

"Be careful not to wake her!" warned Bovary.

But the pharmacist was not to be stopped. "Not only," he resumed, "are human beings subject to such anomalies, but animals also. You are of course not ignorant of the singularly aphrodisiac effect produced by the *Nepeta cataria*, vulgarly called catnip, on the feline race; and, on the other hand, to quote an example whose authenticity I can vouch for, Bridaux (one of my old schoolmates, at present established in the Rue Malpalu) owns a dog that falls into convulsions as soon as you hold out a snuff-box to him. He often performs the experiment before his friends at his summerhouse in Bois-Guillaume. Could you believe that a simple sternutative could cause such damage to a quadrupedal organism? Wouldn't you agree that it is extremely curious?"

"Yes," said Charles, who was not listening.

"It just goes to show," pursued the pharmacist, smiling with benign self-satisfaction, "the numberless irregularities of the nervous system. With regard to madame, I must say that she has always seemed extremely susceptible to me. And so I should by no means recommend to you, my dear friend, any of those so-called remedies that, under the pretence of attacking the symptoms, attack the constitution. No, no gratuitous medications! Diet, that is all; sedatives, emollients, dulcifiers. And then, don't you think we ought to stimulate the imagination?"

"In what way? How?" said Bovary.

"Ah, that is the problem. 'That is the question' (he said it in English) as I lately read in a newspaper."

But Emma, awaking, cried out:

"The letter! Where is the letter?"

They thought she was delirious; and she was by midnight. Brainfever had set in.

For forty-three days Charles did not leave her. He gave up all his patients; he no longer went to bed; he was constantly feeling her pulse, applying mustard plasters and cold-water compresses. He sent Justin as far as Neufchâtel for ice; the ice melted on the way; he sent him back again. He called Monsieur Canivet into consultation; he sent for Dr. Larivière, his old master, from Rouen; he was in despair. What alarmed him most was Emma's prostration, for she did not speak, did not listen, did not even seem to suffer—as if both her body and her soul were resting after all their tribulations.

About the middle of October she could sit up in bed supported by pillows. Charles wept when he saw her eat her first piece of bread and jam. Her strength returned; she got up for a few hours of an afternoon, and one day, when she felt better, he tried to take her, leaning on his arm, for a walk round the garden. The sand of the paths was disappearing beneath the dead leaves; she walked slowly, dragging her slippers, and leaning against Charles's shoulder. She smiled all the time.

They went thus to the end of the garden near the terrace. She drew herself up slowly, shading her eyes with her hand. She looked far off, as far as she could, but on the horizon were only great bonfires of grass smoking on the hills.

"You will tire yourself, darling!" said Bovary.

And, pushing her gently to make her enter the arbour: "Sit down on this seat; you'll be comfortable."

"Oh! no; not there!" she said in a faltering voice.

She was seized with giddiness, and that evening, she suffered a relapse, less specific in character, it is true, and with more complex symptoms. At times it was her heart that troubled her, then her head or her limbs; she had vomitings, in which Charles thought he detected the first signs of cancer.

And, on top of all this, the poor fellow had money troubles!

XIV

To begin with, he did not know how to reimburse Monsieur Homais for all the drugs he had supplied and although, as a doctor, he could have forgone paying for them, he blushed at the thought of such an obligation. Then the expenses of the household, now that the maid was in charge, became staggering. Bills flooded the house; the tradesmen grumbled; Monsieur Lheureux especially harassed him. At the height of Emma's illness, he had taken advantage of the situation to increase his bill; he hurriedly brought the cloak, the travelling-bag, two trunks instead of one, and a number of other things. Charles protested in vain; the shopkeeper rudely replied that the merchandise had been ordered and that he had no intention of taking it back. Besides, it would interfere with madame's convalescence; the doctor had better think it over; in short, he was resolved to sue him rather than give up his rights and take it off his hands. Charles subsequently ordered them sent back to the shop. Félicité forgot and, having other things on his mind, Charles thought no more about it. Monsieur Lheureux did not desist and, alternating threats with whines, he finally forced Bovary into signing him a six months' promissory note. But hardly had he signed the note than a bold idea occurred to him: he meant to borrow a thousand francs from Lheureux. So, with an embarrassed air, he asked if he could get them, adding that it would be for a year, at any interest. Lheureux ran off to his shop, brought back the money, and dictated another note, by which Bovary undertook to pay to his order on the 1st of September next the sum of one thousand and seventy francs, which, with the hundred and eighty already agreed to, made just twelve hundred and fifty. He was thus lending at six per cent in addition to one-fourth for commission; and since the merchandise brought him a good third profit at least, he stood to make one hundred and thirty francs in twelve months. He hoped that the business would not stop there; that the notes would not be paid on time and would have to be renewed, and that his puny little investment, thriving in the doctor's care like a patient in a rest home, would return to him one day considerably plumper, fat enough to burst the bag.

All of Lheureux's enterprises were thriving. He got the franchise for supplying the Neufchâtel hospital with cider; Monsieur Guillaumin promised him some shares in the turf-bogs of Gaumesnil, and he dreamt of establishing a new coach service between Argueil and Rouen, which no doubt would not be long in putting the ramshackle van of the "Lion d'Or" out of business. Travelling faster, at a cheaper rate, and carrying more luggage, it would concentrate into his hands all of Yonville's business.

Charles often wondered how he would ever be able to pay back so much money next year. He tried to think of solutions, such as applying to his father or selling something. But his father would be deaf, and he—he had nothing to sell. He foresaw such difficulties that he quickly dismissed so disagreeable a subject of meditation from his mind. He reproached himself with forgetting Emma, as if, all his thoughts belonging to this woman, it was robbing her of something not to be constantly thinking of her.

It was a severe winter. Madame Bovary's convalescence was slow. On good days they wheeled her arm-chair to the window that overlooked the square, for she now disliked the garden, and the blinds on that side were always down. She wanted her horse to be sold; what she formerly liked now displeased her. The limit of her concerns seemed to be her own health. She stayed in bed taking light meals, rang for the maid to inquire about her tea or merely to chat. The snow on the market-roof threw a white, still light into the room; then the rain began to fall; and every day Emma would wait with a kind of anxiety for the inevitable return of some trifling event that was of little or no concern to her. The most important was the arrival of the "Hirondelle" in the evening. Then the innkeeper would shout and other voices answered, while Hippolyte's lantern, as he took down the luggage from the roof, was like a star in the darkness. At noontime, Charles came home; then he left again; next she took some broth, and towards five o'clock, as night fell, the children coming back from school, dragging their wooden shoes along the pavement, beat with their rulers against the clapper of the shutters.

Around this time of day, Monsieur Bournisien came to see her. He inquired after her health, gave her news, exhorted her to religion in a playful, gossipy tone that was not without charm. The mere sight of his cassock comforted her.

Once, at the height of her illness, she thought she was about to die and asked for communion; and while they were making the preparations in her room for the sacrament, while they were clearing the night table of its medicine bottles and turning it into an altar, and while Félicité was strewing dahlia flowers on the floor, Emma felt some power passing over her that freed her from her pains, from all perception, from all feeling. Her body, relieved, no longer thought; another life was beginning; it seemed to her that her being, mounting toward God, would be annihilated in that love like a burning incense that melts into vapour. The bed-clothes were sprinkled with holy water, the priest drew the white host from the holy pyx and she fainted with celestial joy as she advanced her lips to accept the body of the Saviour presented to her. The curtains of the alcove floated gently round her like clouds, and the rays of the two tapers burning on the night table seemed to shine like dazzling halos. Then she let her head fall back, fancying she heard in space the music of seraphic harps, and perceived in an azure sky, on a golden throne in the midst of saints holding green palms, God the Father, resplendent with majesty, who ordered to earth angels with wings of fire to carry her away in their arms.

This splendid vision dwelt in her memory as the most beautiful thing that it was possible to dream, so that now she strove to recall her sensation; it was still with her, albeit in a less overpowering manner, but with the same profound sweetness. Her soul, tortured by pride, at length found rest in Christian humility, and, tasting the joy of weakness, she saw within herself the destruction of her will opening wide the gates for heavenly grace to conquer her. She realised the existence of a bliss that could replace happiness, another love beyond all loves, without pause and without end, that would grow forever! Amid the illusions of her hope, she saw a state of purity floating above the earth, mingling with heaven. She wanted to become a saint. She bought rosaries and wore holy medals; she wished to have in her room, by the side of her bed, a reliquary set in emeralds that she might kiss it every evening.

The priest was delighted with her new state of mind, although he couldn't help worrying that Emma's excessive fervor might lead to heresy, to extravagance. But not being much versed in these matters once they went beyond a certain point he wrote to Monsieur Boulard, the bishop's bookseller, to send him "something first rate for a lady with a very distinguished mind." With as much concern as if he were shipping kitchen ware to savages, the bookseller made a random package of whatever happened to be current in the religious booktrade at the time. It contained little question and answer manuals, pamphlets written in the brusque tone of Joseph de Maistre,[45] pseudo-novels in rose-coloured bindings and a sugary style, manufactured by sentimental seminarists or penitent blue-stockings.

45. Joseph de Maistre (1753–1821) was the main theorist of Catholic conservatism. His books, *Du Pape* (1819) and *Soirées de Saint-Petersbourg* (1821), defended the power of the pope and the sovereign king and argued that the reign of evil on earth has to be curbed by authority.

There were titles such as "Consider carefully: the Man of the World at the Feet of the Virgin Mary, by Monsieur de * * * , decorated with many Orders"; "The Errors of Voltaire, for the Use of the Young," &c.

Madame Bovary's mind was not yet sufficiently clear to apply herself seriously to anything; moreover, she began this reading in too great a hurry. She grew provoked at the doctrines of religion; the arrogance of the polemic writings displeased her by their ferocious attacks on people she did not know; and the secular stories, sprinkled with religious seasoning, seemed to her written in such ignorance of the world, that they rather led her away from the truths she wanted to see confirmed. Nevertheless, she persevered; and when the volume slipped from her hands, she fancied herself seized with the finest Catholic melancholy ever conceived by an ethereal soul.

As for the memory of Rodolphe, she had locked it away in the deepest recesses of her heart, and it remained there solemn and motionless as a pharaoh's mummy in a catacomb. A fragance escaped from this embalmed love, that, penetrating through everything, perfumed with tenderness the immaculate atmosphere in which she longed to live. When she knelt on her Gothic prie-Dieu, she addressed to the Lord the same suave words that she had murmured formerly to her lover in the outpourings of adultery. She was searching for faith; but no delights descended from the heavens, and she arose with aching limbs and the vague feeling that she was being cheated.

Yet she thought this search all the more admirable, and in the pride of her devoutness Emma compared herself to those grand ladies of long ago whose glory she had dreamed of over a portrait of La Vallière, and who, trailing with so much majesty the lace-trimmed trains of their long gowns, retired into solitude to shed at the feet of Christ the tears of hearts that life had wounded.

Then she indulged in excessive charity. She sewed clothes for the poor, she sent wood to women in childbirth; and on coming home one day, Charles found three tramps eating soup in the kitchen. Her little girl, whom her husband had sent back to the nurse during her illness, returned home. She wanted to teach her to read; even Berthe's crying no longer irritated her. She was resigned, universally tolerant. Her speech was full of elevated expressions. She would say:

"Is your stomach-ache any better, my angel?"

The elder Madame Bovary couldn't find fault with anything except perhaps this mania of knitting jackets for orphans instead of mending her own dishtowels; but, harassed with domestic quarrels, the good woman took pleasure in this quiet house, and she even stayed there till after Easter, to escape the sarcasms of old Bovary, who never failed to order a big pork sausage on Good Friday.

Besides the companionship of her mother-in-law, who strengthened her resolutions somewhat by the rigor of her judgment and her stern appearance, Emma almost every day had other visitors: Madame Langlois, Madame Caron, Madame Dubreuil, Madame Tuvache, and regularly from two to five o'clock the sterling Madame Homais who, for her part, had never believed any of the gossip about her neighbor. The Homais children also came to see her, accompanied by Justin. He went up with them to her bedroom, and remained standing near the door without daring to move or to utter a word. Often enough Madame Bovary, taking no heed of him, would start dressing. She began by taking out her comb and tossing her head, in a brusk gesture, and when for the first time the poor boy saw this mass of hair fall in ringlets to her knees, it was as if he entered suddenly into a new and strange world, whose splendour terrified him.

Emma probably did not notice his silent attentions or his timidity. She had no inkling that love, which presumably had left her life forever, was pulsating right there, under that coarse shirt, in that adolescent heart open to the emanations of her beauty. Besides, she now wrapped all things in the same mood of indifference, she combined gentleness of speech with such haughty looks, affected such contradictory ways, that one could no longer distinguish selfishness from charity, or corruption from virtue. One evening, for example, she first got angry with the maid, who had asked to go out, and stammered as she tried to find some pretext; then suddenly:

"So you love him, don't you?" she said.

And without waiting for an answer from Félicité, who was blushing, she added sadly:

"All right! run along, and have a good time!"

In early spring she had the garden all changed around, over Bovary's objections; yet he was pleased to see her at last express some will of her own. She did so more and more as her strength returned. First, she found occasion to expel Mère Rollet, the nurse, who during her convalescence had taken to visiting the kitchen in the company of her two nurslings and her young boarder, whose appetite surpassed that of a cannibal. She cut down on the visits of the Homais family, gradually freed herself from the other visitors, and even went to church less assiduously, to the great approval of the pharmacist, who remarked to her:

"I suspect you were beginning to fall for the priest's sales talk!"

As before, Monsieur Bournisien would drop in every day after catechism class. He preferred to take the air in the "grove," as he called the arbour. This was the time when Charles came home. They were hot; some sweet cider was brought out, and they drank together to madame's complete recovery.

Binet was often there, that is to say, a little lower down against the terrace wall, fishing for crayfish. Bovary invited him to have a drink, and he proved to be a real expert on the uncorking of the stone bottles.

Looking around with utter self-satisfaction, first at his companions, then at the furthest confines of the landscape, he would say:

"You must first hold the bottle perpendicularly on the table, and after the strings are cut, press the cork upwards inch by inch, gently, very gently—the way they handle soda water in restaurants."

But during his demonstration the cider often spurted right into their faces, and the priest, laughing his thick laugh, would never fail to make his little joke:

"Its excellence certainly strikes the eye!"

He was undoubtedly a kindly fellow and one day he was not even scandalised at the pharmacist, who advised Charles to give madame some distraction by taking her to the theatre at Rouen to hear the illustrious tenor, Lagardy. Homais, surprised at this silence, wanted to know his opinion, and the priest declared that he considered music less dangerous for morals than literature.

But the pharmacist took up the defence of letters. The theatre, he contended, served to decry prejudices and, while pretending to amuse, it taught virtue.

"*Castigat ridendo mores,*[46] Monsieur Bournisien! Look at most of Voltaire's tragedies: they contain a wealth of philosophical considerations that make them into a real school of morals and diplomacy for the people."

"I," said Binet, "once saw a play called the 'Gamin de Paris,'[47] in which there is a really fine part of an old general. He settles the account of a rich young fellow who has seduced a working girl, and at the end . . ."

"Of course," pursued Homais, "there is bad literature as there is bad pharmacy, but to condemn in a lump the most important of the fine arts seems to me a stupidity, a Gothic aberration worthy of the abominable times that imprisoned Galileo."[48]

"I know very well," objected the curé, "that there are good works, good authors. Still, the very fact of crowding people of different sexes into the same room, made to look enticing by displays of worldly pomp, these pagan disguises, the makeup, the lights, the effeminate voices, all this must, in the long-run, engender

46. *Castigat ridendo mores:* "It [comedy] reproves the manners, through laughter"—a slogan for comedy invented by the poet Jean de Santeuil (1630–1697), and given to the harlequin Dominique to put it on the curtain of his theater.

47. *Gamin de Paris* is a comedy by Bayard and Vanderbusch performed in 1836 in Paris.

48. Galileo Galilei (1564–1642), the astronomer, was confined to his house in Arcetri (near Florence) after his book propounding the view that the earth circled around the sun was condemned by the Inquisition (in 1633).

a certain mental libertinage, give rise to immodest thoughts and impure temptations. Such, at any rate, is the opinion of all the church fathers. Moreover," he added, suddenly assuming a mystic tone of voice while he rolled a pinch of snuff between his fingers, "if the Church has condemned the theatre, she must be right; we must bow to her decrees."

"Why," asked the druggist, "should she excommunicate actors when formerly they used to take part openly in religious ceremonies? They would play right in the middle of the choir and perform a kind of farce called "mystery plays" that frequently offended against the laws of decency."

The curé merely groaned and the pharmacist persisted:

"It's like in the Bible; you know . . . there are things in it . . . certain details . . . I'd call them downright daring . . . bordering on obscenity!"

And as Monsieur Bournisien signaled his annoyance:

"Ah! you'll admit that it is not a book to place in the hands of a young girl, and I wouldn't at all like it if Athalie . . ."

"But it is the Protestants, and not we," protested the other impatiently, "who recommend the Bible."

"All the same," said Homais. "I am surprised that in our days, in this century of enlightenment, any one should still persist in proscribing an intellectual relaxation that is inoffensive, morally uplifting, and sometimes even good for the health—isn't that right, doctor?"

"Quite," the doctor replied in a non-committal tone, either because, sharing the same ideas, he wished to offend no one, or else because he simply had no ideas on the subject.

The conversation seemed at an end when the pharmacist thought fit to try a parting shot.

"I've known priests who put on civilian clothes to go watch burlesque shows."

"Come, come!" said the curé.

"Ah yes, I've known some!"

And, separating the words, he repeated:

"I—have—known—some!"

"Well, they did wrong," said Bournisien, prepared to listen to anything with resignation.

"And they didn't stop at that, either!" persisted the pharmacist.

"That's enough! . . ." exclaimed the priest, looking so fierce that the other thought safe to retreat.

"I only mean to say," he replied in a much less aggressive tone, "that tolerance is the surest way to draw people to religion."

"That is true! that is true!" conceded the priest, sitting down again.

But he stayed only a few minutes. Hardly had he left that Monsieur Homais said to the doctor:

"That's what I call a good fight! See how I found his weak spot? I didn't give him much of a chance . . . Now take my advice. Take madame to the theatre, if only to get for once the better of one of these rooks! If someone could keep the store in my absence, I'd go with you. But hurry! Lagardy is only going to give one performance; he's going to play in England for a tremendous fee. From what I hear, he's quite a character. He's simply loaded with money! He travels with three mistresses and a cook. All these great artists burn the candle at both ends; they need to lead a dissolute life to stir the imagination of the public. But they die at the poorhouse, because they don't have the sense to save their money when it comes in. Well, enjoy your dinner! See you to-morrow."

This theatre idea quickly grew in Bovary's mind; he at once communicated it to his wife, who at first refused, alleging the fatigue, the worry, the expense; but, for once, Charles did not give in, so sure was he that this occasion would do her good. He saw nothing to prevent it: his mother had sent three hundred francs he no longer counted on, the current bills were far from staggering and Lheureux's notes were not due for such a long time that he could dismiss them from his mind. Besides, imagining that she was refusing out of consideration for him, he insisted all the more, until she finally consented. The next day at eight o'clock they set out in the "Hirondelle."

The pharmacist, who had nothing whatever to keep him at Yonville but fancied himself to be indispensable, sighed with envy as he saw them go.

"Well, a pleasant journey!" he said to them; "happy mortals that you are!"

Then addressing himself to Emma, who was wearing a blue silk gown with four flounces:

"You are prettier than ever. You'll make quite an impression in Rouen."

The diligence stopped at the "Croix-Rouge" on the Place Beavoisine. It was a typical provincial inn, with large stables and small bedrooms and chickens in the courtyard, picking at the oats under the muddy gigs of travelling salesmen;—a fine old place, with worm-eaten balconies that creak in the wind on winter nights, always crowded, noisy and full of food, its black tables stained with coffee and brandy, the thick windows yellowed by flies, the napkins spotted with cheap red wine. Like farmboys dressed in Sunday-clothes, the place still reeks of the country; it has a café on the street and a vegetable-garden on the back. Charles at once set out on his errands. He confused stage-boxes and gallery, orchestra seats and regular boxes, asked for explanations which he did not understand, was sent from the box-office to the manager, came back to the inn, returned to the theatre and ended up by crossing the full length of the town, from theatre to outer boulevard, several times.

Madame bought herself a hat, gloves, and a bouquet. Monsieur worried greatly about missing the beginning, and, without having had time to swallow a plate of soup, they arrived at the gates of the theatre well before opening time.

XV

The crowd was lined up against the wall, evenly distributed on both sides of the entrance rails. At the corner of the neighbouring streets huge bills, printed in Gothic letters, announced "Lucie de Lammermoor-Lagardy-Opera &c."[49] The weather was fine, the people hot; sweat trickled among fancy coiffures and pocket handkerchiefs were mopping red foreheads; now and then a warm wind that blew from the river gently stirred the edges of the canvass awnings hanging from the doors of the cafés. A little lower down, however, one was refreshed by a current of icy air that smelt of tallow, leather, and oil, breathed forth from the Rue des Charrettes with its huge, dark warehouses resounding with the noise of rolling barrels.

For fear of seeming ridiculous, Emma first wanted to take a little stroll in the harbor, and Bovary carefully kept clutching the tickets in his trouser pockets, pressed against his stomach.

Her heart began to beat as soon as she reached the entrance hall. She involuntarily smiled with vanity on seeing the crowd rushing to the right by the other corridor while she went up the staircase to the reserved seats. She was as pleased as a child to push the large tapestried door open with her finger; she breathed deeply the dusty smell of the lobbies, and when she was seated in her box she drew herself up with the self-assurance of a duchess.

The theatre was beginning to fill; opera-glasses were taken from their cases, and the subscribers greeted and bowed as they spotted each other at a distance. They sought relief from the pressures of commerce in the arts, but, unable to take their minds off business matters, they still talked about cotton, spirits of wine, or indigo. The placid and meek heads of the old men, with their pale whitish hair and complexion, resembled silver medals tarnished by lead fumes. The young beaux were strutting about in the orchestra, exhibiting their pink or apple-green cravats under their gaping waistcoats; sitting above them, Madame Bovary admired how they leant the tight-drawn palm of their yellow gloves on the golden knobs of their canes.

49. *Lucia di Lammermoor* is an opera by Gaetano Donizetti (1797–1848) first performed in Naples in 1835 (in Paris in 1837). It is based on Walter Scott's novel, *The Bride of Lammermoor* (1819). See the extended note p. 591.

Now the lights of the orchestra were lit; the chandelier, let down from the ceiling, threw the sudden gaiety of its sparkling crystals over the theatre; then the musicians began to file in; and first there was the protracted hubbub of roaring cellos, squeaking violins, blaring trumpets and piping flutes. But three knocks were heard on the stage, a rolling of drums began, the brass instruments played some chords, and the curtain rose, discovering a country-scene.

It was the cross-roads of a wood, with a fountain on the left, shaded by an oak tree. Peasants and lords with tartans over their shoulders were singing a hunting-song in chorus; a captain suddenly appeared, who evoked the spirit of evil by lifting both his arms to heaven. Another followed; they departed, and the hunters started afresh.

She felt herself carried back to the reading of her youth, into the midst of Walter Scott. She seemed to hear through the mist the sound of the Scotch bagpipes re-echoing over the moors. Her remembrance of the novel helping her to understand the libretto, she followed the story phrase by phrase, while the burst of music dispersed the fleeting thoughts that came back to her. She gave herself up to the flow of the melodies, and felt all her being vibrate as if the violin bows were being drawn over her nerves. Her eyes could hardly take in all the costumes, the scenery, the actors, the painted trees that shook whenever someone walked, and the velvet caps, cloaks, swords—all those imaginary things that vibrated in the music as in the atmosphere of another world. But a young woman stepped forward, throwing a purse to a squire in green. She was left alone on the stage, and the flute was heard like the murmur of a fountain or the warbling of birds. Lucie bravely attacked her cavatina in G major. She begged for love, longed for wings. Emma, too, would have liked to flee away from life, locked in a passionate embrace. Suddenly Edgar Lagardy appeared.

He had that splendid pallor that gives something of the majesty of marble to the ardent races of the South. His vigourous form was tightly clad in a brown-coloured doublet; a small chiselled dagger swung against his left thigh, and he rolled languid eyes while flashing his white teeth. They said that a Polish princess having heard him sing one night on the beach at Biarritz, where he used to be a boatsman, had fallen in love with him. She had lost her entire fortune for his sake. He had deserted her for other women, and this sentimental fame did not fail to enhance his artistic reputation. A skilled ham actor, he never forgot to have a phrase on his seductiveness and his sensitive soul inserted in the accounts about him. He had a fine voice, colossal aplomb, more temperament than intelligence, more pathos than lyric feeling; all this made for an admirable charlatan type, in which there was something of the hairdresser as well as of the bullfighter.

From the first scene he brought down the house. He pressed

Lucie in his arms, he left her, he came back, he seemed desperate; he had outbursts of rage, then elegiac gurglings of infinite sweetness, and tones like sobs and kisses escaped from his bare throat. Emma bent forward to see him, scratching the velvet of the box with her nails. Her heart filled with these melodious lamentations that were accompanied by the lugubrious moanings of the double-basses, like the cries of the drowning in the tumult of a tempest. She recognised all the intoxication and the anguish that had brought her close to death. The voice of the prima donna seemed to echo her own conscience, and the whole fictional story seemed to capture something of her own life. But no one on earth had loved her with such love. He had not wept like Edgar that last moonlit night when they had said "Till tomorrow! Till tomorrow! . . ." The theatre rang with cheers; they repeated the entire stretto; the lovers spoke of the flowers on their tomb, of vows, exile, fate, hopes; and when they uttered the final farewell, Emma gave a sharp cry that mingled with the vibrations of the last chords.

"But why," asked Bovary, "is that lord torturing her like that?"

"No, no!" she answered; "he is her lover!"

"Yet he vows vengeance on her family, while the other one who came on before said, 'I love Lucie and she loves me!' Besides, he went off with her father arm in arm. For he certainly is her father, isn't he—the ugly little man with a cock's feather in his hat?"

Despite Emma's explanations, as soon as the recitative duet began in which Gilbert lays bare his abominable machinations to his master Ashton, Charles, seeing the false engagement ring that is to deceive Lucie, thought it was a love-gift sent by Edgar. He confessed, moreover, that he did not understand the story because of the music, which interfered very much with the words.

"What does it matter?" said Emma. "Do be quiet!"

"Yes, but you know," he went on, leaning against her shoulder, "I like to understand things."

"Be quiet! be quiet!" she cried impatiently.

Lucie came on, half supported by her women, a wreath of orange blossoms in her hair, and paler than the white satin of her gown. Emma dreamed of her marriage day; she saw herself at home again among the fields in the little path as they walked to the church. Why didn't she, like this woman, resist and implore? Instead, she had walked joyously and unwittingly towards the abyss . . . Ah! if in the freshness of her beauty, before the degradation of marriage and the disillusions of adultery, she could have anchored her life upon some great, strong heart! Virtue, affection, sensuous pleasure and duty would have combined to give her eternal bliss. But such happiness, she realized, was a lie, a mockery to taunt desire. She knew now how small the passions were that art magnified. So, striving for detachment, Emma resolved to see in this reproduction of her sorrows a mere formal fiction for the entertainment of the eye, and she smiled inwardly in scornful pity when from behind the velvet curtains at the back of the stage a man appeared in a black cloak.

His large Spanish hat fell at a gesture he made, and immediately the instruments and the singers began the sextet. Edgar, flashing with fury, dominated all the others with his clearer voice; Ashton hurled homicidal provocations at him in deep notes; Lucie uttered her shrill lament; Arthur sang modulated asides in a middle register and the deep basso of the minister pealed forth like an organ, while the female voices re-echoed his words in a delightful chorus. They were lined up in one single gesticulating row, breathing forth anger, vengeance, jealousy, terror, mercy and surprise all at once from their open mouths. The outraged lover brandished his naked sword; his lace ruff rose and fell jerkily with the movements of his chest, and he walked from right to left with long strides, clanking against the boards the silver-gilt spurs of his soft, flaring boots. She thought that he must have inexhaustible supplies of love in him to lavish it upon the crowd with such effusion. All her attempts at critical detachment were swept away by the poetic power of the acting, and, drawn to the man by the illusion of the part, she tried to imagine his life—extraordinary, magnificent, notorious, the life that could have been hers if fate had willed it. If only they had met! He would have loved her, they would have travelled together through all the kingdoms of Europe from capital to capital, sharing in his success and in his hardships, picking up the flowers thrown to him, mending his clothes. Every night, hidden behind the golden lattice of her box, she would have drunk in eagerly the expansions of this soul that would have sung for her alone; from the stage, even as he acted, he would have looked at her. A mad idea took possession of her: he was looking at her right now! She longed to run to his arms, to take refuge in his strength, as in the incarnation of love itself, and to say to him, to cry out, "Take me away! carry me with you! let us leave! All my passion and all my dreams are yours!"

The curtain fell.

The smell of gas mingled with the people's breath and the waving fans made the air even more suffocating. Emma wanted to go out; the crowd filled the corridors, and she fell back in her armchair with palpitations that choked her. Charles, fearing that she would faint, ran to the refreshment-room to get a glass of orgeat.

He had great difficulty in getting back to his seat, for as he was holding the glass in his hands, his elbows bumped into someone at every step; he even spilt three-fourths on the shoulders of a Rouen lady in short sleeves, who feeling the cold liquid running down her back, started to scream like a peacock, as if she were being murdered. Her mill-owner husband lashed out at his clumsiness, and while she used her handkerchief to wipe off the stains from her handsome cherry-coloured taffeta gown, he angrily muttered about indemnity, costs, reimbursement. Charles was quite out of breath when he finally reached his wife:

"I thought I'd never make it. What a crowd! . . . What a crowd!"

And he added:

"Just guess whom I met up there! Monsieur Léon!"

"Léon?"

"Himself! He's coming along to pay his respects."

And as he finished these words the ex-clerk of Yonville entered the box.

He held out his hand with the casual ease of a gentleman; and Madame Bovary extended hers, yielding no doubt to the pressure of a stronger will. She had not felt it since that spring evening when the rain fell upon the green leaves, and they had said good-bye while standing near the window. But soon recalling herself to the necessities of the situation, she managed to shake off the torpor of her memories, and began stammering a few hurried words.

"Ah! good evening . . . What, you here?"

"Silence!" cried a voice from the orchestra, for the third act was beginning.

"So you are at Rouen?"

"Yes."

"And since when?"

"Be quiet! Throw them out!"

People were looking at them; they fell silent.

But from that moment she listened no more; and the chorus of the guests, the scene between Ashton and his servant, the grand duet in D major, all became more distant, as if the instruments had grown less sonorous and the characters more remote. She remembered the card games at the pharmacist, the walk to the nurse, the poetry readings in the arbour, the tête-à-têtes by the fireside—all the sadness of their love, so calm and so protracted, so discreet, so tender, and that she had nevertheless forgotten. And why had he come back? What combination of circumstances had brought him back into her life? He was standing behind her, leaning with his shoulder against the wall of the box; now and again she felt herself shudder as she felt the warmth of his breath on her hair.

"Do you find this amusing?" he said, bending over her so closely that the end of his moustache brushed her cheek.

She replied flippantly:

"Heavens, no! not particularly."

Then he suggested that they leave the theatre and have an ice somewhere.

"Oh, not yet; let us stay," said Bovary. "Her hair's undone; this is going to be tragic."

But the madness scene did not interest Emma, and she thought the singer was overacting.

"She screams too loud," she said, turning to Charles who was listening.

"Yes . . . perhaps . . . a little," he replied, torn between his genuine enjoyment and his respect for his wife's opinion.

Then Léon sighed:

"Don't you find it hot . . ."

"Unbearably so! Yes!"

"Don't you feel well?" Bovary inquired.

"Yes, I am stifling; let's go."

Monsieur Léon draped her long lace shawl carefully about her shoulders, and the three of them left and sat down near the harbor, on the terrace of a café. First they spoke of her illness, although Emma interrupted Charles from time to time, for fear, she said, of boring Monsieur Léon; and the latter told them that he had come to spend two years in a big Rouen law firm, in order to gain some experience of how business is conducted in Normandy—so different from Paris. Then he inquired after Berthe, the Homais, Mère Lefrançois, and as they had, in the husband's presence, nothing more to say to one another, the conversation soon came to an end.

People coming out of the theatre walked along the pavement, humming or shouting at the top of their voices, "*O bel ange, ma Lucie!*" Then Léon, playing the dilettante, began to talk music. He had seen Tamburini, Rubini, Persiani, Grisi,[50] and, compared with them, Lagardy, despite his grand outbursts, was nowhere.

"Yet," interrupted Charles, who was slowly sipping his rum-sherbet, "they say that he is quite admirable in the last act. I regret leaving before the end, just when I was beginning to enjoy myself."

"Why," said the clerk, "he will soon give another performance."

But Charles replied that they had to leave the next day. "Unless," he added, turning to his wife, "you'd like to stay by yourself, my darling?"

And changing his tactics at the unexpected opportunity that presented itself to his hopes, the young man sang the praises of Lagardy in the last aria. It was really superb, sublime. Then Charles insisted:

"You'll come back on Sunday. Come, make up your mind. If you feel that this is doing you the least bit of good, you shouldn't

---

50. Antonio Tamburini (1800–1876), Gian-Battista Rubini (1795–1854), Fanny Facchinardi Persiani (who was the first Lucia), and Ciulia Grisi (1811–1869) were all famous Bel-Canto singers who appeared in Paris in the operas of Rossini and Donizetti.

hesitate to stay."

The adjoining tables, however, were emptying; a waiter came and stood discreetly near them. Charles, who understood, took out his purse; the clerk held back his arm, and made a point of leaving two extra pieces of silver that he made chink on the marble.

"I am really sorry," said Bovary, " for all the money you are . . ."

The other silenced him with a gesture of affable disdain and, taking his hat, said:

"So, we are agreed, to-morrow at six o'clock?"

Charles explained once more that he could not absent himself longer, but that nothing prevented Emma . . .

"But," she stammered, with a strange smile, "I don't know if I ought . . ."

"Well, you must think it over. Sleep over it and we'll see in the morning."

Then, to Léon, who was walking along with them:

"Now that you are in our part of the world, I hope you'll come and have dinner with us from time to time."

The clerk declared he would not fail to do so, being obliged, moreover, to go to Yonville on some business for his office. And they parted before the passage Saint-Herbland just as the cathedral struck half-past eleven.

Part Three

I

Monsieur Léon, while studying law, had been a fairly assiduous customer at the Chaumière, a dance-hall where he was particularly successful with the grisettes who thought him distinguished looking. He was the best-mannered of the students; he wore his hair neither too long nor too short, didn't spend all his quarter's money on the first day of the month, and kept on good terms with his professors. As for excesses, he had always abstained from them, as much from cowardice as from refinement.

Often when he stayed in his room to read, or else when sitting in the evening under the linden-trees of the Luxembourg,[51] he let his law-code fall to the ground, and the memory of Emma came back to him. But gradually this feeling grew weaker, and other desires took the upperhand, although the original passion still acted through them. For Léon did not lose all hope; there was for him, as it were, a vague promise floating in the future, like a golden fruit suspended from some fantastic tree.

51. Luxembourg refers to the gardens of the Palace of Luxembourg (built between 1615 and 1620 for Marie de Me-dici). The gardens are open to the public and much frequented by students, as they are near the Sorbonne.

Then, seeing her again after three years of absence, his passion reawakened. He must, he thought, finally make up his mind to possess her. Moreover, his timidity had worn off in the gay company of his student days, and he returned to the provinces in utter contempt of whoever had not set foot on the asphalt of the boulevards. In the presence of a genuine Parisienne, in the house of some famous physician surrounded by honors and luxury, the poor clerk would no doubt have trembled like a child; but here, on the quais of Rouen, with the wife of a small country-doctor, he felt at his ease, sure to shine. Self-confidence depends on environment: one does not speak in the same tone in the drawing room than in the kitchen; and the wealthy woman seems to have about her, to guard her virtue, all her bank-notes, like an armour, in the lining of her corset.

On leaving the Bovarys the night before, Léon had followed them through the streets at a distance; when he saw them enter the Croix-Rouge, he returned home and spent the night planning his strategy.

So the next afternoon about five o'clock he walked into the kitchen of the inn, pale and apprehensive, driven by a coward's resolution that stops at nothing.

"Monsieur isn't in," a servant told him.

This seemed to him a good omen. He went upstairs.

She didn't seem surprised at his arrival; on the contrary, she apologized for having failed to tell him where they were staying.

"Oh, I guessed it!" said Léon.

He pretended he had found her by chance, guided by instinct. When he saw her smile, he tried to repair his blunder by telling her he had spent the morning looking for her in all the hotels in the town.

"So you have made up your mind to stay?" he added.

"Yes," she said, "and I shouldn't have. One should avoid getting used to inaccessible pleasures when one is burdened by so many responsibilities . . ."

"Oh, I can imagine . . ."

"No, you can't, you are not a woman."

But men too had their trials, and the conversation started off by some philoshical considerations. Emma expatiated on the frailty of earthly affections, and the eternal isolation that stifles the human heart.

To show off, or in a naive imitation of this melancholy which stirred his own, the young man declared that he had been dreadfully despondent. He was bored by the law, attracted by other vocations and his mother had never ceased to harrass him in all her letters. As they talked, they stated the reasons for their respective unhappiness with more precision and they felt a shared exaltation in this growing confidence. But they sometimes stopped short of revealing their thought in full, and then sought to invent a phrase that might nevertheless express it. She did not confess her passion for another; he did not say that he had forgotten her.

Perhaps he no longer remembered the suppers with girls after masked balls; and no doubt she did not recollect the rendezvous of old when she ran across the fields in the morning to her lover's house. The noises of the town hardly reached them, and the room seemed small, as if to bring them even closer together in their solitude. Emma, in a dimity dressing gown, leant her chignon against the back of the old arm-chair; the yellow wall-paper formed, as it were, a golden background behind her, and her bare head was reflected in the mirror with the white parting in the middle, the tip of her ears peeping out from the folds of her hair.

"How bad of me!" she said, "you must forgive me for boring you with my eternal complaints."

"No, never, never!"

"If only you knew," she went on, raising to the ceiling her beautiful eyes, in which a tear was trembling, "if only you knew all I dreamed!"

"So did I! Oh, I too have suffered! Often I went out; I went away. I left, dragging myself along the quays, seeking distraction amid the din of the crowd without being able to banish the heaviness that weighed upon me. In an engraver's shop on the boulevard I found an Italian print of one of the Muses. She is draped in a tunic, and she is looking at the moon, with forget-me-nots in her flowing hair. Something continually drove me there, I would stay for hour after hour."

Then, in a trembling voice:

"She looked a little like you."

Madame Bovary turned away her head that he might not see the irrepressible smile she felt rising to her lips.

"Often," he went on, "I wrote you letters that I tore up."

She did not answer. He continued;

"I sometimes fancied that some chance would bring you. I thought I recognised you at street-corners, and I ran after carriages when I saw a shawl or a veil like yours flutter in the window . . ."

She seemed resolved to let him speak without interruption. With arms crossed and her head lowered, she stared at the rosettes on her slippers, and from time to time moved her toes under the satin.

At last she sighed.

"But what I find worst of all is to drag out, as I do, a useless existence. If our pains could be of use to some one, we should find consolation in the thought of the sacrifice."

He started off in praise of virtue, duty, and silent immolation, having himself an incredible longing for self-sacrifice that he could not satisfy.

"What I would like," she said "is to work in a hospital as a nursing Sister."

"Unfortunately," he replied, "no such holy vocations are open to men, and I can think of no profession . . . except perhaps a doctor's . . ."

With a slight shrug of the shoulders, Emma interrupted him to speak of her illness, which had almost killed her. How she regretted her cure! if she had died, she would not now be suffering. Léon was quick to express his own longing for "the quiet of the tomb"; one night, he had even made his will, asking to be buried in that beautiful coverlet with velvet stripes he had received from her. For this was how they would have wished to be, each setting up an ideal to which they were now trying to adapt their past life. Besides, speech is like a rolling machine that always stretches the sentiment it expresses.

But this made-up story of the coverlet made her ask:

"Why?"

"Why?" He hesitated.

"Because I loved you so!"

And congratulating himself at having surmounted the obstacle, Léon watched her face out of the corner of his eye.

It was like the sky when a gust of wind sweeps the clouds away. The mass of darkening sad thoughts lifted from her blue eyes; her whole face shone.

He waited. At last she replied:

"I always suspected it."

Then they went over all the trifling events of that far-off existence, of which the joys and sorrows had just been conjured up by that one word. He remembered the clematis arbour, the dresses she had worn, the furniture of her room, the entire house.

"And our poor cactuses, where are they?"

"The cold killed them this winter."

"How often did I think of them! I see them again as they looked when on summer mornings the sun shone on your blinds, and I saw your two bare arms among the flowers.

"Poor friend!" she said, holding out her hand.

Léon swiftly pressed his lips to it. Then, when he had taken a deep breath:

"In those days, you were like an incomprehensible power to me which held me captive. Once, for instance, I came to see you, but you probably don't remember."

"I do," she said; "go on."

"You were downstairs in the hall, ready to go out, standing on the last stair; you were wearing a hat with small blue flowers; and without being invited, in spite of myself, I went with you. But I grew more and more conscious of my folly every moment, and I kept walking by your side, not daring to follow you completely but unable to leave. When you went into a shop, I waited in the street, and I watched you through the window taking off your gloves and counting the change on the counter. Then you rang at Madame Tuvache's; you were let in, and I stood like an idiot in front of the great heavy door that had closed after you."

Madame Bovary, as she listened to him, wondered that she was so old. All these things reappearing before her seemed to expand her existence; it was like some sentimental immensity to which she returned; and from time to time she said in a low voice, her eyes half closed:

"Yes, it is true . . . it is true . . ."

They heard eight o'clock strike on the different towers that surround the Place Beauvoisine, a neighborhood of schools, churches, and large empty private dwellings. They no longer spoke, but as they looked upon each other, they felt their heads whirl, as if waves of sound had escaped from their fixed glances. They were hand in hand now, and the past, the future, reminiscences and dreams, all were confounded in the sweetness of this ecstasy. Night was darkening over the walls, leaving visible only, half hidden in the shade, the coarse colours of four bills representing scenes from *La Tour de Nesle*,[52] with Spanish and French captions underneath. Through the sash-window they could see a patch of sky between the pointed roofs.

She rose to light two wax-candles on the chest of drawers, then she sat down again.

"Well . . . ?" said Léon.

"Well . . . ?" she replied.

He was wondering how to resume the interrupted conversation, when she said to him:

"How is it that no one until now has ever expressed such sentiments to me?"

The clerk retorted that idealistic natures rarely found understanding. But he had loved her from the very first moment; the thought of their possible happiness filled him with despair. If only they had met earlier, by some stroke of chance, they would have been forever bound together.

"I have sometimes thought of it," she went on.

"What a dream!" murmured Léon.

And fingering gently the blue border of her long white belt, he

---

52. A melodrama by Alexandre Dumas the elder (1803–1870) and Gaillardet (1832) in which Marie de Bourgogne, famous for her crimes, is the main heroine.

added,

"Who prevents us from starting all over again?"

"No, my friend," she replied; "I am too old . . . You are too young . . . forget me! Others will love you . . . you will love them."

"Not as I love you!"

"What a child you are! Come, let us be sensible, I want it."

She told him again that their love was impossible, that they must remain, as before, like brother and sister to each other.

Was she speaking seriously? No doubt Emma did not herself know, absorbed as she was by the charm of the seduction and the necessity of defending herself; looking tenderly at the young man, she gently repulsed the timid caresses that his trembling hands attempted.

"Ah! forgive me!" he cried, drawing back.

Emma was seized with a vague fear at this shyness, more dangerous to her than the boldness of Rodolphe when he advanced to her open-armed. No man had ever seemed to her so beautiful. His demeanor suggested an exquisite candor. He lowered his long curling eyelashes. The soft skin of his cheek was flushed, she thought, with desire for her, and Emma felt an invincible longing to press her lips to it. Then, leaning towards the clock as if to see the time:

"How late it is!" she exclaimed. "How we have been chattering!"

He understood the hint and took up his hat.

"You made me forget about the opera! And poor Bovary who left me here especially for that! Monsieur Lormeaux, of the Rue Grand-Pont, was to take me and his wife."

And there would be no other opportunity, as she was to leave the next day.

"Really?" said Léon.

"Yes."

"But I must see you again," he went on. "I had something to tell you . . ."

"What?"

"Something . . . important, serious. I cannot possibly let you go like this. If only you knew . . . Listen to me . . . Haven't you understood? Can't you guess?"

"You made yourself very clear" said Emma.

"Ah! you can jest! But you shouldn't. Have mercy, and allow me to see you again . . . only once . . . one single time."

"Well . . ."

She stopped; then, as if changing her mind:

"But not here!"

"Wherever you say."

"Will you . . ."

She seemed to think; then suddenly:

"To-morrow at eleven o'clock in the cathedral."

"I shall be there," he cried, seizing her hands, which she withdrew.

And as they were both standing up, he behind and Emma with lowered head, he stooped over her and pressed long kisses on her neck.

"You are crazy, you are crazy!" she cried between bursts of laughter, as the kisses multiplied.

Then bending his head over her shoulder, he seemed to beg the consent of her eyes, but when they met his, they seemed icy and distant.

Léon took three paces backwards. He stopped on the threshold; then he whispered in a trembling voice:

"Till to-morrow."

She answered with a nod, and vanished like a bird into the next room.

In the evening Emma wrote the clerk an interminable letter, in which she cancelled the rendezvous; all was over between them; they must not, for the sake of their happiness, meet again. But when the letter was finished, as she did not know Léon's address, she was puzzled.

"I'll give it to him myself," she said; "he'll come."

The next morning, humming a tune while he stood on his balcony by the open window, Léon polished his shoes with special care. He put on white trousers, silken socks, a green coat, emptied all the scent he had into his handkerchief, then having had his hair curled, he uncurled it again, in order to give it a more natural elegance.

"It is still too early," he thought, looking at the barber's cuckoo-clock, that pointed to the hour of nine.

He read an old fashion journal, went out, smoked a cigar, walked up three streets, thought the time had come and walked slowly towards the porch of Notre Dame.

It was a beautiful summer morning. Silver sparkled in the window of the jeweler's store and the light, falling obliquely on the cathedral, threw shimmering reflections on the edges of the grey stones; a flock of birds fluttered in the grey sky round the trefoiled turrets; the square, resounding with cries, was fragrant with the flowers that bordered the pavement, roses, jasmines, carnations, narcissus, and tuberoses, unevenly spaced out between moist grasses, catnip, and chickweed for the birds; the fountains gurgled in the center, and under large umbrellas, amidst heaps of piled up mellons, bare-headed flower vendors wrapped bunches of violets in pieces of paper.

The young man took one. It was the first time that he had

bought flowers for a woman, and his breast, as he smelt them, swelled with pride, as if this homage that he meant for another had been reflected upon himself.

But he was afraid of being seen and resolutely entered the church.

The verger was just then standing on the threshold in the middle of the left doorway, under the figure of Salomé dancing, known in Rouen as the "dancing Marianne". He wore a feather cap, a rapier dangled against his leg and he looked more majestic than a cardinal, as shining as a pyx.

He came towards Léon, and, with the bland benign smile of a priest when questioning a child, asked:

"I gather that Monsieur is a visitor in this town? Would Monsieur care to be shown the church?"

"No!" said Léon.

And he first went round the lower aisles. Then he went out to look at the Place. Emma was not coming yet, so he returned as far as the choir.

The nave was reflected in the full fonts together with the base of the arches and some fragments of the stained glass windows. But the reflections of the painted glass, broken by the marble rim, were continued farther on upon the pavement, like a many-coloured carpet. The broad daylight from outside entered the church in three enormous rays through the three opened portals. From time to time a sacristan crossed the far end of the church, making the sidewise genuflection of a hurried worshipper in the direction of the altar. The crystal lustres hung motionless. In the choir a silver lamp was burning, and from the side chapels and dark places of the church sounds like sighs arose, together with the clang of a closing grating that echoed under the lofty vaults.

Léon walked solemnly alongside the walls. Life had never seemed so good to him. She would soon appear, charming and agitated, looking back to see if anyone was watching her—with her flounced dress, her gold eyeglass, her delicate shoes, with all sorts of elegant trifles that he had never been allowed to taste, and with the ineffable seduction of yielding virtue. The church was set around her like a huge boudoir; the arches bent down to shelter in their darkness the avowal of her love; the windows shone resplendent to light up her face, and the censers would burn that she might appear like an angel amid sweet-smelling clouds.

Meanwhile, she did not come. He sat down on a chair, and his eyes fell upon a blue stained window representing boatmen carrying baskets. He looked at it long, attentively, and he counted the scales of the fishes and the button-holes of the doublets, while his thoughts wandered off in search of Emma.

The verger, left to himself, resented the presence of someone who dared to admire the cathedral without his assistance. He considered this a shocking way to behave, robbing him of his due, close to committing sacrilege.

There was a rustle of silk on the pavement, the edge of a hat, a hooded cape—it was she! Léon rose and ran to meet her.

Emma was pale. She walked hurriedly.

"Read this!" she said, holding out a piece of paper to him. "Oh, no!"

And she abruptly withdrew her hand to enter the chapel of the Virgin, where, kneeling on a chair, she began to pray.

The young man was irritated by this display of piety; then he nevertheless felt a certain charm in seeing her thus lost in devotions in the middle of a rendezvous, like an Andalusian marquise; then he grew bored, for she seemed to go on for ever.

Emma prayed, or rather tried to pray, hoping that some sudden resolution might descend to her from heaven; and to draw down divine aid she filled her eyes with the splendors of the tabernacle. She breathed in the perfumes of the full-blown flowers in the large vases, and listened to the stillness of the church—a stillness that only heightened the tumult in her own heart.

She rose, and they were about to leave, when the verger quickly approached:

"Madame is perhaps a stranger here? Madame would like to visit the church?"

"Oh, no!" the clerk cried.

"Why not?" she said.

For, with her expiring virtue, she clung to the Virgin, the sculptures, the tombs—to anything.

Then, in order to do things right, the verger took them to the entrance near the square, where, pointing out with his cane a large circle of black stones, without inscription or carving:

"This," he said majestically, "is the circumference of the beautiful bell of Ambroise. It weighed forty thousand pounds. There was not its equal in all Europe. The workman who cast it died of joy . . ."

"Let's go," said Léon.

The old man started off again; then, having got back to the chapel of the Virgin, he waved his arm in a theatrical gesture of demonstration, and, prouder than a country squire showing his orchard, he announced:

"This simple stone covers Pierre de Brézé, lord of Varenne and of Brissac, grand marshal of Poitou, and governor of Normandy, who died at the battle of Montlhéry on the 16th of July, 1465."

Léon was furiously biting his lips of impatience.

"And on the right, this gentleman in full armour, on the prancing horse, is his grandson, Louis de Brézé, lord of Breval and of Montchauvet, Count de Maulevrier, Baron de Mauny, chamberlain to the king, Knight of the Order, and also governor of Normandy; he died on the 23rd of July, 1531—a Sunday, as the inscription specifies; and below, this figure, about to descend into the tomb, portrays the same person. How could one conceive of a better way to depict the void of human destiny?"

Madame Bovary lifted her eyeglass. Motionless, Léon watched her without even trying to protest, to make a gesture, so discouraged was he by this double display of idle talk and indifference.

Nothing could stop the guide:

"Near him, this kneeling woman who weeps is his spouse, Diane de Poitiers, comtesse de Brézé, duchesse de Valentinois, born in 1499, died in 1566, and to the left, the one with the child is the Holy Virgin. Now if you turn to this side, you will see the tombs of the Ambroise. They were both cardinals and archbishops of Rouen. That one was minister under Louis XII. He did a great deal for the cathedral. In his will he left thirty thousand gold crowns for the poor."

And without ceasing to talk, he pushed them into a chapel crowded with wooden railings; he pushed some aside and discovered a kind of wooden block that looked vaguely like a poorly carved statue.

"It seems hard to believe," he sighed sadly, "but this used to adorn the tomb of Richard Coeur de Lion,[53] King of England and Duke of Normandy. It was the Calvinists, Monsieur, who reduced it to this condition. They were mean enough to bury it in the earth, under the episcopal throne of Monseigneur the bishop. You can see from here the door by which Monseigneur passes to his house. Let's move on to the gargoyle windows."

But Léon hastily extracted some silver coins from his pocket and seized Emma's arm. The verger stood dumbfounded, not able to understand this untimely munificence when there were still so many things for the stranger to see. He called after him:

"Monsieur! The steeple! the steeple!"[54]

"No, thank you!" said Léon.

"You are missing the best! It is four hundred and forty feet high, nine less than the great pyramid of Egypt. It is all cast iron, it . . ."

Léon was fleeing, for it seemed to him that his love, that for nearly two hours had been frozen in the church like the stones, would now vanish like a vapor through that sort of truncated fun-

53. Richard Coeur de Lion, the Lion Hearted (born 1175), was king of England from 1189–1199. He died at the siege of the Castle of Châlus.

54. The Cathedral of Rouen built in the Gothic style in stages from the thir-

teenth century to the early sixteenth, got a high cast iron spire (485 feet), which is generally considered a tasteless disfigurement. Construction was begun in 1824 but not finished until 1876.

nel, rectangular cage or open chimney that rises so grotesquely from the cathedral like the extravagant brainchild of some fantastic roofer.

"But where are we going?" she said.

He pushed on without answering, and Madame Bovary was already dipping her finger in the holy water when behind them they heard a panting breath interrupted by the regular sound of a tapping cane. Léon turned around.

"Monsieur!"

"What is it?"

And he recognised the verger, holding under his arms and bracing against his stomach some twenty large volumes, all of them works on the cathedral.

"Idiot!" muttered Léon, rushing out of the church.

A boy was playing on the sidewalk:

"Go and get me a cab!"

The child bounded off like a ball by the rue des Quatre-Vents; then they were alone a few minutes, face to face, and a little embarrassed.

"Oh Léon! Truly . . . I don't know . . . if I should . . ."

She simpered. Then, in a serious tone:

"It's very improper, you know, it isn't done."

"Everybody does it in Paris!" replied the clerk.

This, like a decisive argument, entirely convinced her. She had made up her mind.

But no cab arrived. Léon shuddered at the thought that she might return into the church. At last the cab appeared.

"At least, you should go out by the northern gate," cried the verger, who was left alone on the threshold, "and look at the Ressurection, the Last Judgment, Paradise, King David, and the damned burning in the flames of Hell!"

"Where to, sir?" asked the coachman.

"Anywhere!" said Léon, pushing Emma into the cab.

And the lumbering machine set out.

It went down the Rue Grand-Pont, crossed the Place des Arts, the Quai Napoleon, the Pont Neuf, and stopped short before the statue of Pierre Corneille.

"Go on," cried a voice that came from within.

The cab went on again, and as soon as it reached the Carrefour Lafayette, set off down-hill, and entered the railroad station at a gallop.

"No, straight on!" cried the same voice.

The cab came out by the gate, and soon having reached the Mall, trotted quietly beneath the elm-trees. The coachman wiped his brow, put his leather hat between his knees, and drove his carriage beyond the side alley by the meadow to the margin of the waters.

It went along by the river, along the towing-path paved with sharp pebbles, and for a long while in the direction of Oyssel, beyond the islands.

But suddenly it turned sideways across Quatremares, Sotteville, La Grande-Chaussée, the Rue d'Elbeuf, and made its third halt in front of the Jardin des Plantes.

"Get on, will you?" cried the voice more furiously.

And at once resuming its course, it passed by Saint Sever, by the Quai des Curandiers, the Quai aux Meules, once more over the bridge, by the Place du Champ de Mars, and behind the hospital gardens, where old men in black coats were walking in the sun along the ivy-covered terraces. It went up the Boulevard Bouvreuil, along the Boulevard Cauchoise, then the whole of Mont-Riboudet to the Deville hills.

It came back; and then, without any fixed plan or direction, wandered about at random. The cab was seen at Saint-Pol, at Lescure, at Mont Gargan, at La Rougue-Marc and Place du Gaillardbois; in the Rue Maladrerie, Rue Dinanderie, before Saint-Romain, Saint-Vivien, Saint-Maclou, Saint-Nicaise—in front of the Customs, at the Basse-Vieille-Tour, the "Trois Pipes," and the Cimetière monumental. From time to time the coachman on his seat cast despairing glances at the passing cafés. He could not understand what furious locomotive urge prevented these people from ever coming to a stop. Time and again he would try, but exclamations of anger would at once burst forth behind him. Then he would whip his two sweating nags, but he no longer bothered dodging bumps in the road; the cab would hook on to things on all sides but he couldn't have cared less, demoralised as he was, almost weeping with thirst, fatigue and despair.

Near the harbor, among the trucks and the barrels, and along the street corners and the sidewalks, bourgeois stared in wonder at this thing unheard of in the provinces: a cab with all blinds drawn that reappeared incessantly, more tightly sealed than a tomb and tossed around like a ship on the waves.

One time, around noon, in the open country, just as the sun beat most fiercely against the old plated lanterns, a bare hand appeared under the yellow canvass curtain, and threw out some scraps of paper that scattered in the wind, alighting further off like white butterflies on a field of red clover all in bloom.

Then, at about six o'clock the carriage stopped in a back street of the Beauvoisine Quarter, and a woman got out, walking with her veil down and without looking back.

II

On reaching the inn, Madame Bovary was surprised not to see

the stage coach. Hivert had waited for her fifty-three minutes, but finally left without her.

Nothing forced her to go, but she had promised to return that same evening. Moreover, Charles expected her, and in her heart she felt already that cowardly docility that is for some women at once the chastisement and atonement of adultery.

She packed her bag quickly, paid her bill, took a cab in the yard, hurrying on the driver, urging him on, every moment inquiring about time and distance traversed. He succeeded in catching up with the Hirondelle as it neared the first houses of Quincampoix.

Hardly was she seated in her corner that she closed her eyes, and opened them at the foot of the hill, when from afar she recognised Félicité, who was on the look-out in front of the blacksmith's. Hivert pulled up his horses, and the maid, reaching up to the window, said in a tone of mystery:

"Madame, you must go at once to Monsieur Homais. It's for something urgent."

The village was silent as usual. At the corner of the streets little pink mounds lay smoking in the air, for this was the time for jam-making, and every one at Yonville prepared his supply on the same day. But in front of the pharmacist's shop one might admire a far larger heap; it surpassed the others with the superiority that a laboratory must have over domestic ovens, a general need over individual fancy.

She went in. The big arm chair had fallen over and even the "Fanal de Rouen" lay on the ground, outspread between two pestles. She pushed open the door of the hall, and in the middle of the kitchen, amid brown jars full of picked currants, powdered and lump sugar, scales on the table and pans on the fire, she saw assembled all the Homais, big and little, with aprons reaching to their chins, and holding forks in their hands. Justin was standing with bowed head, and the pharmacist was screaming:

"Who told you to go fetch it in the *Capharnaum?*"

"What is it? What is the matter?"

"What is it?" replied the pharmacist. "We are making jelly; it is cooking; but it threatens to boil over because there is too much juice, and I ask for another pan. Then this one here, out of laziness, goes to my laboratory, and dares to take the key to the capharnaum from the nail!"

This name had been given to a small room under the eaves, crammed with the tools and the goods of his trade. He often spent long hours there alone, labelling, decanting, and packaging. He looked upon it not as a simple store-room, but as a veritable sanctuary from where the creations of his own hands were to set forth: pills, lotions and potions that would spread far and wide his rising fame. No one in the world was allowed to set foot there, and he revered it to the point of sweeping it himself. If the pharmacy, open to all comers, was the stage where he displayed his pride, the Capharnaum was the refuge where in selfish concentration, Homais indulged in his most relished pursuits. Therefore, Justin's thoughtlessness seemed to him a monstrous piece of irreverence, and, his face redder than the currants, he continued:

"Yes, the key to the Capharnaum! The key that locks up the acids and caustic alkalis! To go and get a spare pan! a pan with a lid! and that I shall perhaps never use! Everything is of importance in the delicate operations of our art! One must maintain the proper distinctions, and not employ for nearly domestic purposes what is destined for pharmaceutical science! It is as if one were to carve a fowl with a scalpel; as if a magistrate . . ."

"Quiet down," Madame Homais was saying.

And Athalie, pulling at his coat, cried:

"Papa! papa!"

"No, leave me alone!" the pharmacist cried, "leave me alone! I tell you, I might as well be running a grocery store. Just keep at it, don't mind me and break everything to pieces! Smash the testtubes, let the leeches loose, burn the marshmallows, put pickles in the medical jars, tear up the bandages!"

"I thought you wanted to . . ."

"In a moment . . . Do you know what risks you took? Didn't you see something in the corner, on the left, on the third shelf? Speak! Answer me! Say something!"

"I . . . don't . . . know . . ." stammered the boy.

"Ah! you don't know! Well, *I* do! You saw a bottle of blue glass sealed with yellow wax, that contains a white powder carefully marked *Dangerous!* And do you know what is in it? Arsenic! And you go and touch it! You take a pan that stands right next to it!"

"Right next to it!" cried Madame Homais, clasping her hands. "Arsenic! You might have poisoned us all."

And the children began to scream as if they already felt dreadful stomach pains.

"Or poison a patient!" continued the pharmacist. "Do you want to see me dragged into court like a common criminal? or taken to the scaffold? As if you didn't know how careful one has to be in handling chemicals, even I who spent my life doing nothing else. Often I am horrified when I think of my responsibility; the Government persecutes us, and the absurd legislation that rules us is a veritable Damocles' sword suspended over our heads."

Emma gave up trying to find out what they wanted her for, and the pharmacist continued without pausing for breath:

"That is how you thank us for the many kindnesses we have shown you! That is how you reward me for the truly paternal care that I lavish on you! Where would you be if I hadn't taken you in hand? What would you be doing? Who provides you with food, education, clothes, and all the means to rise to a respectable level in society? But if you want to get there, you'll have to learn to pull hard at the oars—get callouses on your hands, as they saying goes. *Fabricando fit faber, age quod agis.*" [55]

He was so exasperated he quoted Latin. He would have used Chinese or Greenlandic had he known them, for he was rocked by one of these crises in which the soul reveals all it contains, just as the storm lays bare the ocean from the seaweed on the shore down to the sand on its deepest bottom.

And he went on:

"I am beginning to regret that I ever took you in charge! I would have done a lot better if I'd let you wallow in poverty and filth, where you were born. The best you can hope for is to be a cowhand. You are not fit to be a scientist! You hardly know how to stick on a label! And there you are, dwelling with me snug as a parson, living in clover, taking your ease!"

Emma turned in despair to Madame Homais:

"I was told to come . . . "

"Heavens!" the lady exclaimed in a mournful tone "How am I to tell you? . . . Such a misfortune!"

She could not finish. The pharmacist was thundering:

"Empty it! Clean it! Take it back! And hurry!"

And seizing Justin by the collar of his apron, he shook him so vigorously that a book fell out of his pocket. The boy stooped, but Homais was the quicker, and, having picked up the volume, he stared at it with bulging eyes and open mouth.

"Conjugal . . . love!" he said, slowly separating the two words. "Ah! very good! very good! very pretty! And with illustrations! . . . Truly, this is too much!"

Madame Homais drew near.

"No, don't touch it!"

The children wanted to look at the pictures.

"Leave the room," he said imperiously.

They went out.

First he walked up and down, with the open book in his hand, rolling his eyes, choking, fuming, apoplectic. Then he came straight to his apprentice, and, planting himself in front of him with folded arms:

"So you are blessed with all the vices under the sun, you little wretch? Watch out! you are following a dangerous path! . . . Did

55. *Fabricando fit Faber, age quod agis* ("Do what you do"), the artisan becomes proficient through practice; practice what you are supposed to do.

it never occur to you that this infamous book might fall into the hands of my children, kindle a spark in their minds, tarnish the purity of Athalie, corrupt Napoleon! He is close to being a man. Are you quite sure, at least, that they have not read it? Can you certify to me . . ."

"But, Monsieur," said Emma, "you wished to tell me . . ."

"Oh yes, madame . . . your father-in-law is dead."

Indeed, the elder Bovary had suddenly died from a stroke the evening before, as he got up from the table; overanxious to spare Emma's sensitive nerves, Charles had asked Monsieur Homais to break the horrible news to her as carefully as possible.

Homais had meditated at length over his speech; he had rounded, polished it, given it the proper cadence; it was a masterpiece of prudence and transitions, of subtle turns and delicacy; but anger had got the better of rhetoric.

Emma, abandoning all hope to learn any further details, left the pharmacy; for Monsieur Homais had resumed his vituperations. He was growing calmer, however, and was now grumbling in a paternal tone whilst he fanned himself with his skull-cap.

"It is not that I entirely disapprove of the book. The author was a doctor! It contains scientific information that a man might well want to know; I'd go as far as saying that he ought to know. But later . . . later! You should at least wait till you are yourself full-grown, and your character formed."

When Emma knocked at the door, Charles, who was waiting for her, came forward with open arms and said in a tearful voice:

"Ah! my dear wife. . . ."

And he leant over gently to kiss her. But at the contact of his lips the memory of the other returned; she passed her hand over her face and shuddered.

Yet, she answered:

"Yes, I know . . . I know . . ."

He showed her the letter in which his mother told the event without any sentimental hypocrisy. Her only regret was that her husband had not received the consolation of religion; he had died at Doudeville, in the street, at the door of a café after a patriotic dinner with some ex-officers.

Emma gave him back the letter; then at dinner, for appearance's sake, she affected a lack of appetite. But as he urged her to try, she resolutely began eating, while Charles opposite her sat motionless and dejected.

Now and then he raised his head and gave her a long, distressed look. Once he sighed:

"I'd have liked to see him again!"

She was silent. At last, realizing that she must say something: "How old was your father?" she asked.

"Fifty-eight."

"Ah!"

And that was all.

A quarter of an hour later, he added: "My poor mother! what will become of her now?"

She made a gesture of ignorance.

Seeing her so taciturn, Charles imagined her much affected, and forced himself to say nothing, not to reawaken this sorrow which moved him. And, shaking off his own:

"Did you enjoy yourself yesterday?" he asked.

"Yes."

When the cloth was removed, Bovary did not rise, nor did Emma; and as she looked at him, the monotony of the spectacle drove little by little all pity from her heart. He seemed to her paltry, weak, a nonentity—a sorry creature in every way. How to get rid of him? What an interminable evening! She felt a stupor invading her, as if from opium fumes.

They heard the sharp noise of a wooden leg on the boards of the entrance hall. It was Hippolyte bringing back Emma's luggage.

To put them down, he had to bring around his wooden stump painfully in a quarter circle.

"He doesn't even seem to remember" she thought, looking at the poor devil, whose coarse red hair was wet with perspiration.

Bovary was searching for a coin at the bottom of his purse; he did not seem to realize how humiliating the man's presence was for him, standing there as the living embodiment of his hopeless ineptitude.

"Oh, you have a pretty bouquet," he said, noticing Léon's violets on the mantlepiece.

"Yes," she replied indifferently; "it's a bouquet I bought just now . . . from a beggar-woman."

Charles picked up the flowers and, bathing his tear-stained eyes in their freshness, he delicately sniffed their perfume. She took them quickly from his hand and put them in a glass of water.

The next day the elder Madame Bovary arrived. She and her son spent much time weeping. Pretending to be busy in the house, Emma managed to stay by herself.

The following day, they had to discuss together the arrangements for the period of mourning. They went and sat down with their workboxes by the waterside under the arbor.

Charles was thinking of his father, and was surprised to feel so much affection for this man, whom up till now he thought he cared little about. The older Madame Bovary was thinking of her husband. The worst days of the past seemed enviable to her. All was forgotten beneath the instinctive regret of such a long habit, and from time to time, while sewing, a big tear rolled down her nose and hung suspened there a moment.

Emma was thinking that it was scarcely forty-eight hours since they had been together, far from the world, lost in ecstasy, and not having eyes enough to gaze upon each other. She tried to recall the slightest details of that past day. But the presence of her husband and mother-in-law bothered her. She would have liked to stop hearing and seeing, in order to keep intact the stillness of her love; but, try as she would, the memory would vanish under the impact of outer sensations.

She was removing the lining of a dress, and the strips were scattered around her. Mother Bovary, without looking up, kept her scissors busy, and Charles, in his felt slippers and his old brown coat that he used as a dressing gown, sat in silence with both hands in his pockets; near them Berthe, in a little white apron, was raking the sandwalks with her spade.

Suddenly they saw Monsieur Lheureux, the storekeeper, come in through the gate.

He came to offer his services "on this sad occasion." Emma replied that none were needed, but the shopkeeper wouldn't take no for an answer.

"I beg your pardon," he said, "but I should like to have a word in private."

Then, in a low voice, he added:

"It is about this little matter . . . you know . . ." Charles turned crimson.

"Oh yes . . . of course."

And, in his confusion, he turned to his wife:

"Darling, could you perhaps . . . ?"

She seemed to understand him, for she rose; and Charles said to his mother:

"Nothing important. Some household trifle, I suppose."

Fearing her reproaches, he didn't want her to know about the note.

As soon as they were alone, Monsieur Lheureux began by congratulating Emma outspokenly on the inheritance, then talked of this and that, the fruit trees, the harvest, his own health which had endless ups and downs. He had to work like a devil and, regardless of what people thought, didn't make enough to buy butter for his bread.

Emma let him talk. She had been so dreadfully bored, these last two days!

"And so you're quite well again?" he went on. "Believe me, your husband was in quite a state. He's a good fellow, though we did have a little misunderstanding."

She asked what the misunderstanding was about, for Charles had told her nothing of the dispute about the goods supplied to her.

"As if you didn't know!" exclaimed Lheureux. "It was about your little caprice . . . the trunks."

He had drawn his hat over his eyes, and, with his hands behind his back, smiling and whistling, he looked straight at her in an unbearable manner. Did he suspect anything? She was lost in all kinds of apprehensions. Finally he said:

"We made it up, and I've come to propose still another arrangement."

He offered to renew the note Bovary had signed. The doctor, of course, would do as he pleased; he was not to trouble himself, especially just now, when he would have a lot to attend to.

"It seems to me he'd do well to turn it all over to some one else, —to you for example. With a power of attorney it could be easily managed, and then the two of us could have our little business transactions together . . ."

She did not understand. He did not insist, and brought the conversation back to his trade; it was impossible that Madame didn't need anything. He would send her a black barège, twelve yards, just enough to make a dress.

"The one you've on is good enough for the house, but you want another for calls. I saw that the very moment that I came in. I've got a quick eye for these things!"

He did not send the material, he brought it. Then he came again to take her measurements; he came again on other pretexts, always trying to make himself agreeable, useful, like a vassal serving his master, as Homais might have put it, and never failing to drop a hint about the power of attorney. He never mentioned the note. She didn't think of it; although Charles doubtlessly had mentioned something at the beginning of her convalescence, so many emotions had passed through her head that she no longer remembered it. Besides, she made it a point never to bring up any money questions. Charles' mother seemed surprised at this, and attributed the change in her ways to the religious sentiments she had contracted during her illness.

But as soon as she left, Emma greatly astounded Bovary by her practical good sense. They would have to make inquiries, look into the mortgages, decide whether it would be more advantageous to sell by auction or by other means.

She quoted legal jargon at random, and grand words such as "order", "the future", "foresight". She constantly exaggerated the difficulties of settling his father's affairs; at last, one day she showed him the rough draft of a power of attorney to manage and administer his business, arrange all notes, sign and endorse all bills, pay all sums, etc. She had profited by Lheureux's lessons.

Charles naively asked her where this paper came from.

"From Master Guillaumin."

And with the utmost coolness she added:

"I don't trust him overmuch. Notaries have such a bad reputation. Perhaps we ought to consult . . . But the only person we know . . . There is no one."

"Unless perhaps Léon . . ." replied Charles, who was thinking. But it was difficult to explain matters by letter. Then she offered to make the journey. He refused. She insisted. It was quite a contest of mutual consideration. At last she exclaimed, in a childish tone of mock-rebellion:

"No, enough, I will!"

"How good you are!" he said, kissing her on the forehead.

The next morning she set out in the "Hirondelle" for Rouen to consult Monsieur Léon, and she stayed there three days.

III

They were three full, exquisite, magnificent days—a true honeymoon. They stayed at the Hôtel-de-Boulogne, on the harbor; and they lived there behind drawn blinds and closed doors, with flowers on the floor, and iced fruit syrups that were brought them early in the morning.

Towards evening they took a covered boat and went to dine on one of the islands.

At this time of the day, one could hear the caulking irons sound against the hulls in the dockyard. Tar smoke rose up between the trees and large oily patches floated on the water, undulating unevenly in the purple sunlight like surfaces of Florentine bronze.

They drifted down among moored ships whose long slanting cables grazed lightly the top of their boat.

The sounds of the city gradually fainted in the distance, the rattling of carriages, the tumult of voices, the yelping of dogs on the decks of barges. She loosened her hat and they landed on their island.

They sat down in the low-ceilinged room of a tavern with black fishing-nets hanging across the door. They ate fried smelts, cream and cherries. They lay down upon the grass, kissed behind the poplar trees; like two Robinson Crusoes, they would gladly have lived forever in this spot; in their bliss, it seemed to them the most magnificent place on earth. It was not the first time that they had seen trees, a blue sky, meadows; or heard the water flow and the wind blow in the branches. But they had never really felt any of this; it was as if nature had not existed before, or had only begun to be beautiful since the gratification of their desires.

At nightfall they returned. The boat glided along the shores of the islands. They stayed below, hidden in darkness, without saying a word. The square-tipped oars sounded against the iron oar-locks; in the stillness, they seemed to mark time like the beat of a metronome, while the rope that trailed behind never ceased its gentle splash against the water.

One night the moon rose, and they did not fail to make fine phrases about how melancholical and poetic it appeared to them. She even began to sing:

> One night, do you remember,
> We were sailing . . .

Her thin musical voice died away over the water; Léon could hear the wind-borne trills pass by him like a fluttering of wings.

She faced him, leaning against the wall of the cabin while the moon shone through the open blinds. Her black dress, falling around her like a fan, made her seem more slender, taller. Her head was raised, her hands clapsed, her eyes turned towards heaven. At times the shadow of the willows hid her completely; then she reappeared suddenly, like a vision in the moonlight.

Léon, on the floor by her side, found under his hand a ribbon of scarlet silk.

The boatman looked at it, and said at last:

"Perhaps it belongs to the party I took out the other day. They were a jolly bunch of ladies and gentlemen, with cakes, champagne, trumpets—everything in style! There was one especially, a tall handsome man with small moustaches, who was the life of the party. They kept asking him 'Come on, Adolphe—or Dodolphe, or something like that—tell us a story . . .' "

She shuddered.

"Don't you feel well?" Léon inquired, coming closer.

"Oh, it's nothing! Just a chill from the cold night air."

"He's another one who seems to have no trouble finding women," the old sailor added softly, intending to pay Léon a compliment.

Then, spitting on his hands, he took the oars again.

Yet the time to part had come. The farewells were sad. He was to send his letters to Mère Rollet, and she gave him such precise instructions about a double envelope that he was much impressed with her shrewdness in love matters.

"So you can guarantee me that everything is in order?" she said with her last kiss.

"Yes, certainly."

"But why," he thought afterwards as he came back through the streets alone, "is she so very anxious to get this power of attorney?"

IV

Léon soon put on superior airs with his friends, avoided their company, and completely neglected his work.

He waited for her letters, read and re-read them. He wrote to her. He called her to mind with all the strength of his desires and of his memories. Instead of lessening with absence, his longing to see her kept growing to the point where, one Saturday morning he escaped from his office.

When, from the summit of the hill, he saw in the valley below the church-spire with its metal flag swinging in the wind, he felt that delight mingled with triumphant vanity and selfish benevolence that millionaires must experience when they come back to their native village.

He went prowling around round her house. A light was burning in the kitchen. He watched for her shadow behind the curtains, but nothing appeared.

Mère Lefrançois, on seeing him, uttered many exclamations. She thought he had grown taller and thinner, while Artémise, on the contrary, thought him stouter and darker.

He ate in the little dining-room, as in the past, but alone, without the tax collector; for Binet, tired of waiting for the "Hirondelle," had definitely moved his meal an hour earlier. Now he dined punctually at five, which didn't keep him from complaining that the rickety old carriage was late.

Léon finally made up his mind, and knocked at the doctor's door. Madame was in her room, and did not come down for a quarter of an hour. The doctor seemed delighted to see him, but he never left the house that evening, nor the next day.

He saw her alone in the evening, very late, behind the garden in the lane;—in the lane, as with the other one! It was a stormy night, and they talked under an umbrella by lightning flashes.

They couldn't bear the thought of parting.

"I'd rather die!" said Emma.

She seized his arm convulsively, and wept.

"Good bye! When shall I see you again?"

They came back again to embrace once more, and it was then that she promised him to find soon, no matter how, some assured way of meeting in freedom at least once a week. Emma was certain to find a way. She was generally in a hopeful frame of mind: the inheritance money was bound to come in soon.

On the strength of it she bought a pair of yellow curtains with large stripes for her room; Monsieur Lheureux had recommended them as a particularly good buy. She dreamt of getting a carpet, and Lheureux, declaring that it wasn't that much of an investment after all, politely undertook to supply her with one. She could no longer do without his services. Twenty times a day she sent for him, and he at once interrupted whatever he was doing, without a murmur. Neither could people understand why Mére Rollet ate at her house every day, and even paid her private visits.

It was about this time, in the early part of the Winter, that a sudden urge to make music seemed to come over her.

One evening when Charles was listening to her, she began the same piece four times over, each time with much vexation, while he, totally oblivious to her mistakes, exclaimed:

"Bravo! . . . Very good! . . . Don't stop. Keep going!"

"Oh, no. It's awful! My fingers are much too rusty!"

The next day he begged her to play for him again.

"Very well, if you wish."

And Charles had to confess that she had slipped a little. She played wrong notes and blundered; then, stopping short:

"Ah! it's no use. I ought to take some lessons, but . . . ."

Biting her lip, she added:

"Twenty francs a lesson, that's too expensive!"

"Maybe it is . . . a little," said Charles with a stupid giggle. "But it seems to me that one might be able to do it for less; for there are artists of little reputation, who are often better than the celebrities."

"Find them!" said Emma.

The next day on coming home, he gave her a sly look, and finally could no longer repress what he had to say:

"How stubborn you can be at times! I went to Barfuchéres to-day. Well, Madame Liégard assured me that her three daughters, who go to school at Miséricorde, take lessons at fifty sous apiece, and that from an excellent teacher!"

She shrugged her shoulders and did not open her piano again.

But whenever she passed in front of it (provided Bovary was present), she sighed:

"Ah! my poor piano!"

And whenever someone came to call, she did not fail to inform them that she had given up music, and could not begin again now for important reasons. People would commiserate. What a pity! She had so much talent! They even spoke to Bovary about it. They put him to shame, especially the pharmacist.

"You are wrong. One should never let any natural faculties lie fallow. Besides, just think, my good friend, that by inducing madame to study, you are economising on the subsequent musical education of your child. For my own part, I think that mothers ought themselves to instruct their children. It's an idea of Rousseau's, still rather new perhaps, but bound to win out sooner or later, like vaccination and breast-feeding."

So Charles returned once more to this question of the piano. Emma replied bitterly that it would be better to sell it. Poor piano!

it had given his vanity so many satisfactions that to see it go was for Bovary, in an undefinable manner, like Emma's partial suicide.

"If you really want it . . ." he said, "a lesson from time to time wouldn't ruin us after all."

"But lessons," she replied, "are only of use if one persists."

And this is how she managed to obtain her husband's permission to go to town once a week to see her lover. At the end of a month she was even considered to have made considerable progress.

v

She went on Thursdays. She got up and dressed silently, in order not to awaken Charles, who would have reproached her for getting ready too early. Then she walked up and down, stood at the windows, and looked out over the Square. The early dawn was broadening between the pillars of the market, and the pharmacy, still boarded up, showed in the pale light of the dawn the large letters of the signboard.

When the clock pointed to a quarter past seven, she went to the "Lion d'Or," where a yawning Artémise unlocked the door for her. She would poke the fire in Madame's honor, and Emma remained alone in the kitchen. Now and again she went out. Hivert was leisurely harnessing his horses while listening to the Mère Lefrançois who, sticking her head and night cap through a window, was instructing him on his errands and giving him explanations that would have bewildered any one else. Emma tapped her boots on the cobblestones of the yard.

At last, when he had eaten his soup, put on his cloak, lighted his pipe, and grasped his whip, he calmly took his place on the seat.

The "Hirondelle" started at a slow trot, and for about a mile stopped time and again to pick up waiting passengers along the roadside, before their house-gates. Those who had booked seats the night before kept it waiting; some even were still in bed in their houses. Hivert called, shouted, swore; then he got down from his seat and knocked loudly at the doors. The wind blew through the cracked windows.

Gradually, the four benches filled up. The carriage rolled off; rows of apple-trees followed one upon another, and the road between its two long ditches, full of yellow water, rose, constantly narrowing towards the horizon.

Emma knew every inch of the road: after a certain meadow there was a sign post, then a barn or roadmender's hut. Sometimes, in hope of being surprised, she would close her eyes, but she never lost a clear sense of the distance still to be covered.

At last the brick houses began to follow one another more closely, the earth resounded beneath the wheels, the "Hirondelle" glided between the gardens, revealing through an occasional opening, statues, a summer pavillion, trimmed yew trees, a swing. Then all at once, the city came into sight.

Sloping down like an amphitheatre, and drowned in the fog, it overflowed unevenly beyond its bridges. Then the open country mounted again in a monotonous sweep until it touched in the distance the elusive line of the pale sky. Seen thus from above, the whole landscape seemed frozen, like a picture; the anchored ships were massed in one corner, the river curved round the foot of the green hills, and the oblong islands looked like giant fishes lying motionless on the water. The factory chimneys belched forth immense plumes of brown smoke, their tips carried off in the wind. One heard the rumbling of the foundries, mingled with the clear chimes of the churches, dimly outlined in the fog. The leafless trees on the boulevards seemed violet thickets in the midst of the houses, and the roofs, shining from the rain, threw back unequal reflections, according to the heights of the various districts. From time to time a gust of wind would drive the clouds towards the slopes of Saint Catherine, like aerial waves breaking silently against a cliff.

Something seemed to emanate from this mass of human lives that left her dizzy; her heart swelled as though the hundred and twenty thousand souls palpitating there had all at once wafted to her the passions with which her imagination had endowed them. Her love grew in the presence of this vastness, and filled with the tumult of the vague murmuring which rose from below. She poured it out, onto the squares, the avenues, the streets; and the old Norman city spread out before her like some incredible capital, a Babylon into which she was about to enter. She lifted the window with both hands to lean out, drinking in the breeze; the three horses galloped, the stones grated in the mud, the diligence rocked, and Hivert, from afar, hailed the carts on the road, while the well-to-do residents of Bois Guillaume sedately descended the hill to town in their little family carriages.

The coach made a stop at the city gates; Emma undid her overshoes, put on other gloves, rearranged her shawl, and some twenty paces farther she descended from the "Hirondelle."

The town was beginning to awake. Shop-boys in caps were polishing the front windows of the stores, and women, with baskets balanced on their hips, would stand on the street corners calling out from time to time some sonorous cry. She walked with downcast eyes, close to the walls, and smiling with pleasure beneath her lowered black veil.

For fear of being seen, she did not usually take the most direct road. She would plunge into dark alleys, and emerge, all in a sweat, near the little fountain at the beginning of the Rue Nationale. This was the quarter of the theaters, cabarets, and prostitutes. Often, a cart loaded with shaking scenery passed close by her. Waiters in aprons were sprinkling sand on the flagstones between green shrubs. There was a smell of absinthe, cigars and oysters.

She turned a corner; she recognised him by his curling hair that escaped from beneath his hat.

Léon kept on walking ahead of her along the sidewalk. She followed him into the hotel. He went up, opened the door, entered — What an embrace!

Then, after the kisses, the words rushed forth. They told each other the sorrows of the week, the forebodings, the anxiety for the letters; but now everything was forgotten; they gazed at each other with voluptuous laughs, and tender names.

The bed was a large one, made of mahogany and shaped like a boat. The red silk curtains which hung from the ceiling, were gathered together too low, close to the lyre-shaped headboards;—and nothing in the world was so lovely as her brown hair and white skin set off against that deep crimson color, when with a gesture of modesty, she closed her arms and hid her face in her hands.

The warm room, with its subdued carpet, its frivolous ornaments and its soft light, seemed made for the intimacies of passion. The curtain-rods, ending in arrows, the brass pegs and the great balls of the andirons would suddenly light up if a ray of sunlight entered. On the chimney, between the candelabra there were two of those pink shells in which one hears the murmur of the sea when one holds them against one's ear.

How they loved that room, so full of gaiety, despite its somewhat faded splendour! They always found the furniture arranged the same way, and sometimes hairpins, that she had forgotten the Thursday before, under the pedestal of the clock. They lunched by the fireside on a little round table, inlaid with rosewood. Emma carved, put bits on his plate while playing all sorts of coquettish tricks; she would laugh a ringing libertine laugh when the froth from the champagne overflowed the fragile glass onto the rings of her fingers. They were so completely lost in the possession of each other that they thought themselves in their own house, that they would go on living there until separated by death, like an eternally young married couple. They said "our room," "our carpet," she even said "my slippers," referring to the gift Léon had bought to satisfy a whim of hers. They were rose-colored satin, bordered with swansdown. When she sat on his lap, her leg, which was then too short, hung in the air, and the dainty shoe having no back, was held on only by the toes of her bare foot.

He savoured for the first time the inexpressible delights of feminine refinement. He had never encountered this grace of language, this direction in dress, these poses of a weary dove. He admired the exaltation of her soul and the lace on her petticoat. Besides, was she not a "woman of the world", and a married woman! in short a real mistress!

According to her changing moods, in turn meditative and gay, talkative and silent, passionate and langorous, she awakened in him a thousand desires, called up instincts or memories. She was the mistress of all the novels, the heroine of all the dramas, the vague "she" of all the volumes of verse. On her shoulders, he rediscovered the amber color of the "Odalisque au Bain";[56] her waist was long like the feudal chatelaines; she resembled Musset's "Femme Pâle de Barcelone."[57] Above all, she was his Angel.

It often seemed to him that his soul, fleeing toward her, broke like a wave against the contours of her head, and was drawn irrisistibly down into the whiteness of her breast.

He knelt on the ground before her; and resting his elbows on her lap, he would gaze at her smilingly, his face uplifted.

She bent over him, and murmured, as if choking with intoxication:

"Oh! don't move! don't speak! Look at me! There is something so tender that comes from your eyes. It does me so much good!"

She called him child.

"Do you love me, child?"

And she never heard his reply, his lips always rose so fast to find her mouth.

There was a little bronze cupid on the clock, who simpered as he held up his arms under a golden garland. They had laughed at it many a time, but when they had to part everything seemed serious.

Motionless, they looked at each other and kept repeating:

"Till Thursday! . . . Till Thursday! . . ."

Suddenly she would take his head between her hands and kiss him quickly on the forehead while crying "Adieu" and rush down the stairs.

She went next to a hairdresser in the Rue de la Comédie to have her hair arranged. Night would be falling; they lit the gas in the shop.

She heard the bell in the theatre calling the actors to the performance; and she saw white-faced men and women in faded dresses pass by on the other side of the street and enter in at the stage door.

It was hot in the little low-ceilinged room with its stove humming amidst the wigs and pommades. The smell of the tongs together with the oily hands that were manipulating her hair, would soon stupefy her and she would begin to doze a bit in her dressing gown.

56. Famous painting by Jean Auguste Dominique Ingres.
57. Alfred de Musset frequently incarnates, for Flaubert, the type of stilted romantic sentimentality he despises.

Often, as he did her hair, the man offered her tickets for a masked ball.

Then she left! She remounted the streets; reached the Croix Rouge, retrieved her overshoes which she had hidden under the bench that morning, and settled into her place among the impatient passengers. The other passengers got out at the foot of the hill in order to spare the horses. She remained alone in the carriage.

At every turn, they could see more and more of the city below, forming a luminous mist above the mass of houses. Emma knelt on the cushions, and let her eyes wander over the dazzling light. She sobbed, called to Léon, sent him tender words and kisses which were lost in the wind.

There was a wretched creature on the hillside, who would wander about with his stick right in the midst of the carriages. A mass of rags covered his shoulders, and an old staved-in beaver hat, shaped like a basin, hid his face; but when he took it off he revealed two gaping bloody orbits in the place of eyelids. The flesh hung in red strips; and from them flowed a liquid which congealed into green scales reaching down to his nose with its black nostrils, which kept sniffing convulsively. To speak to you he threw back his head with an idiotic laugh;—then his blueish eyeballs, rolling round and round, would rub against the open wound near the temples.

He sang a little song as he followed the carriages:

> Often the warmth of a summer day
> Makes a young girl dream her heart away.

And all the rest was about birds and sunshine and green leaves.

Sometimes he would appear behind Emma, his head bare. She would draw back with a cry. Hivert liked to tease him. He would advise him to get a booth at the Saint Romain fair, or else ask him, laughing, how his girl friend was.

Often the coach was already in motion when his hat would be thrust violently in at the window, while he clung with his other arm to the footboard, between the spattering of the wheels. His voice, at first weak and quavering, would grow sharp. It lingered into the night like an inarticulate lament of some vague despair; and, heard through the jingling of the horses' bells, the murmuring of the trees, and the rumble of the empty coach, it had something so distant and sad that it filled Emma with dread. It went to the very depths of her soul, like a whirlwind in an abyss, and carried her away to a boundless realm of melancholy. But Hivert, noticing a weight behind, would lash out savagely at the blind man with his whip. The thong lashed his wounds and he fell back into the mud with a shriek.

The passengers in the Hirondelle would all finally drop off to sleep, some with their mouths open, others their chins pressed against their chests, leaning on their neighbor's shoulder, or with their arm passed through the strap, all the time swaying regularly with the jolting of the carriage; and the sight of the lantern, that was swinging back and forth outside and reflecting on the rumps of the shaft horses, penetrated into the coach through the chocolate-colored curtains, throwing blood-red shadows over all those motionless beings within. Emma, drunk with grief, shivered under her coat and felt her feet grow colder and colder, with death in her soul.

Charles at home would be waiting for her; the "Hirondelle" was always late on Thursdays. Madame arrived at last! She scarcely kissed the child. The dinner was not ready, no matter! She excused the cook. The girl now seemed allowed to do just as she liked.

Often her husband, noting her pallor, asked if she were unwell.

"No," said Emma.

"But," he replied, "you seem so strange this evening."

"Oh, it's nothing! nothing!"

There were even days when she had no sooner come in than she went up to her room; and Justin, who would happen to be there, moved about noiselessly, more adroit at helping her than the best of maids. He put the matches ready, the candlestick, a book, arranged her nightgown, turned back the bedclothes.

"All right," she'd say "that's fine, get going!"

For he stood there, his hands hanging down and his eyes wide open, as if enmeshed in the innumerable threads of a sudden reverie.

The following day was frightful, and those that came after still more unbearable, because of her impatience to once again seize her happiness,—this fierce lust, enflamed by recent memories, which on the seventh day would erupt freely within Léon's embraces. His own passion was manifested by continual expressions of wonder and gratitude. Emma tasted this love discreetly, and with all her being, nourished it by every tender device she knew, and trembled a little that some day it might be lost.

She often said to him, with a sweet melancholy in her voice:

"Ah! you too, you will leave me! You will marry! You will be like all the others."

He asked:

"What others?"

"Why, like all men," she replied.

Then added, repulsing him with a languid movement:

"You are all of you wretches!"

One day, as they were talking philosophically of earthly disillusions she happened to mention (in order to provoke his jealousy, or perhaps through some irrisistible urge to confide in him) that in the past, before she knew him, she had loved someone else. "Not like you," she went on quickly, swearing on the head of her child "that nothing had happened."

The young man believed her, but none the less questioned her to find out what kind of a man *He* was.

"He was a ship's captain, my dear."

Was this not preventing any inquiry, and, at the same time, assuming a higher ground because of the aura of fascination which is supposed to surround a man who must have been of warlike nature and accustomed to receive homage?

The clerk then felt the lowliness of his position; he longed for epaulettes, crosses, titles. These things would please her; he suspected as much from her extravagant habits.

However, Emma never mentioned a number of her most extravagant ideas, such as her desire to have a blue tilbury to drive into Rouen, drawn by an English horse and driven by a groom in turned down boots. It was Justin who had inspired her with this whim, by begging her to take him into service as footman; and if the privation of it did not lessen the pleasure of her arrival at each of their weekly rendez-vous, it certainly augmented the bitterness of the return.

Often, when they were talking together of Paris, she would end by murmuring,

"Ah, how happy we could be living there."

"Are we not happy?" the young man would gently ask, passing his hands over her hair.

"Yes, that is true," she said. "I am mad: kiss me!"

To her husband she was more charming than ever. She made him pistachio-creams and played him waltzes after dinner. He thought himself the most fortunate of men, and Emma was without uneasiness, when, suddenly one evening:

"It is Mademoiselle Lempereur, isn't it, who gives you lessons?"

"Yes."

"Well, I saw her just now," Charles went on, "at Madame Liégard's. I spoke to her about you; and she doesn't know you."

This was like a thunderbolt. However, she replied quite naturally: "She must have forgotten my name."

"But perhaps," said the doctor, "there are several Demoiselles Lempereur at Rouen who are music teachers."

"Possibly!"

Then she added quickly:

"Nevertheless, I have her receipts, here! Look."

And she went to the writing-table, ransacked all the drawers, mixed up the papers, and at last lost her head so completely that Charles earnestly begged her not to take so much trouble about those wretched receipts.

"Oh! I will find them," she said.

And, in fact, on the following Friday, as Charles was putting on one of his boots in the dark closet where his clothes were kept, he felt a piece of paper between the leather and his sock. He took it out and read:

"Received, for three months' lessons and several pieces of music, the sum of sixty-three francs.—FELICIE LEMPEREUR, professor of music."

"How the devil did it get into my boots?"

"It must," she replied, "have fallen from the old box of bills that is on the edge of the shelf."

From that moment on, her existence was one long tissue of lies, in which she wrapped her love as under a veil in order to hide it. It became a need, an obsession, a delight, to such a point that, if she claimed to have walked on the right side of the street the previous day, one could be sure she had walked on the left.

One morning, when she had gone, as usual, rather lightly clothed, it suddenly began to snow, and as Charles was watching the weather from the window, he caught sight of Monsieur Bournisien in the chaise of Monsieur Tuvache, who was driving him to Rouen. Then he went down to give the priest a thick shawl that he was to hand over to Emma as soon as he reached the Croix-Rouge. When he got to the inn, Monsieur Bournisien asked for the wife of the Yonville doctor. The landlady replied that she very rarely came to her establishment. So that evening, when he recognised Madame Bovary in the "Hirondelle," the curé told her his dilemma, without, however, appearing to attach much importance to it, for he began praising a preacher who was doing wonders at the Cathedral, and whom all the ladies were rushing to hear.

Still, even if he had not asked for any explanations, others, later on, might prove less discreet. So she thought it would be a good idea to get out of the coach at the Croix Rouge each time she came so that the good folk of her village seeing her on the stairs would not become suspicious.

One day, however, Monsieur Lheureux met her coming out of the Hôtel de Boulogne on Léon's arm; and she was frightened, thinking he would gossip. He was not such a fool.

But three days after he came to her room, shut the door, and said:

"I must have some money."

She declared she could not give him any. Lheureux began to moan, reminding her of all the favors he had done her.

In fact, of the two bills signed by Charles, Emma up to the present had paid only one. As to the second, the shopkeeper, at her request, had consented to replace it by another, which again had been renewed for a long date. Then he drew from his pocket a list of goods not paid for; to wit, the curtains, the carpet, the material for the arm-chairs, several dresses, and diverse articles of dress, totalling in all a sum of about two thousand francs.

She hung her head; he continued:

"But if you haven't any ready money, you do have some property."

And he called to her attention a miserable little shack situated at Barneville, near Aumale, that brought in almost nothing. It had formerly been part of a small farm sold by Monsieur Bovary senior; for Lheureux knew everything, even down to the number of acres and the names of the neighbors.

"If I were in your place," he said, "I'd get it off my hands, and have some money left over."

She pointed out the difficulty of finding a buyer; he said he thought he could find one; but she asked him how she should manage to sell it.

"Haven't you your power of attorney?" he replied.

The phrase came to her like a breath of fresh air. "Leave me the bill," said Emma.

"Oh, it isn't worth while," answered Lheureux.

He came back the following week boasting that after having gone to a great deal of trouble, he had finally tracked down a certain man named Langlois, who had had his eye on the property for a long time but had never mentioned a price.

"Never mind the price!" she cried.

On the contrary, he said, they must take their time and sound the fellow out. The affair was certainly worth the trouble of a trip, and, as she could not undertake it, he offered to go to the place and bargain with Langlois. On his return he announced that the purchaser proposed four thousand francs.

Emma's heart rose at this news.

"Frankly," he added, "that's a good price."

She drew half the sum at once, and when she was about to pay her account the shopkeeper said:

"It grieves me, it really does, to see you give up such a considerable sum of money as that all at once." She stared at the bank notes and began to dream of the countless rendez-vous with Léon that those two thousand francs represented.

"What! What do you mean!" she stammered.

"Oh!" he went on, laughing good-naturedly, "one puts anything one likes on receipts. Don't you think I know what household affairs are?"

And he looked at her fixedly, while in his hand he held two long papers which he kept sliding between his nails. At last, opening his billfold, he spread out on the table four bills to order, each for a thousand francs.

"Sign these," he said, "and keep it all!"

She cried out, scandalised.

"But if I give you the balance," replied Monsieur Lheureux impudently, "isn't that doing you a service?"

And taking a pen he wrote at the bottom of the account, "Received from Madame Bovary four thousand francs."

"What is there to worry about, since in six months you'll draw the arrears for your cottage, and I don't make the last bill due till after you've been paid?"

Emma was becoming somewhat confused in her calculations and her ears rang as though gold pieces were bursting out of their bags and tinkling onto the floor all around her. At last Lheureux explained that he had a very good friend named Vinçart, a banker in Rouen, who would discount these four bills. Then he himself would hand over to madame the remainder after the actual debt was paid.

But instead of two thousand francs he brought her only eighteen hundred, for his friend Vinçart (which was "only fair") had deducted two hundred francs for commission and discount.

Then he carelessly asked for a receipt.

"You understand . . . in business . . . sometimes . . . And with the date, please don't forget the date."

A whole horizon of new possibilities now opened up before Emma. She was wise enough to set aside three thousand francs, with which the first three bills were paid when they fell due; but the fourth happened to arrive at the house on a Thursday, and a stunned Charles patiently awaited his wife's return for an explanation.

If she had not told him about this note, it was only to spare him such domestic worries; she sat on his lap, caressed him, cooed at him, gave a long enumeration of all the indispensable things that had been got on credit.

"Really, you must confess, considering the number of things, it isn't too expensive."

Charles, at his wit's end, soon had recourse to the eternal Lheureux, who promised to arrange everything if Charles would sign two more notes, one of which was for seven hundred francs and would be payable in three months. To take care of this he wrote his mother a pathetic letter. Instead of sending a reply she came herself; and when Emma wanted to know whether he had got anything out of her:

"Yes," he replied; "but she wants to see the account."

The next morning at daybreak Emma ran to Lheureux to beg him to make out another account for not more than a thousand francs: for to show the one for four thousand it would be necessary to say that she had paid two-thirds, and confess, consequently, the sale of the property, for the transaction had been well handled by the shopkeeper and only came to light later on.

Despite the low price of each article, Madame Bovary senior of course thought the expenditure extravagant.

"Couldn't you do without a carpet? Why did you re-cover the arm-chairs? In my time there was a single arm-chair in a house, for elderly persons,—at any rate it was so at my mother's, who was a respectable woman, I assure you.—Everybody can't be rich! No fortune can hold out against waste! I should be ashamed to pamper myself as you do! And yet I am old. I need looking after . . . and look at this! Look at this! alterations! frills and finery! What is that! silk for lining at two francs; . . . when you get jaconet for ten sous, or even for eight which does just as well!"

Emma lying on a lounge, replied as calmly as she could "Ah! Madame, enough! enough! . . ."

The other went on lecturing her, predicting they would end in the workhouse. But it was Bovary's fault. Luckily he had promised to destroy that power of attorney.

"What?"

"Ah! he swore he would," went on the good woman.

Emma opened the window, called Charles, and the poor fellow was obliged to confess the promise torn from him by his mother.

Emma disappeared, then came back quickly, and majestically handed her a large sheet of paper.

"Thank you," said the old woman. And she threw the power of attorney into the fire.

Emma began to laugh, a strident, piercing, continuous laugh; she had an attack of hysterics.

"Oh! my God!" cried Charles. "Ah! You are in the wrong too! You come here and make scenes with her! . . ."

His mother, shrugging her shoulders, declared it was "all put on."

But Charles, rebelling for the first time, took his wife's part, so that Madame Bovary senior said she would leave. She went the very next day, and on the threshold, as he was trying to detain her, she replied:

"No, no! You love her better than me, and you are right. It is natural. Take care of yourself! . . . for I'm not likely to be back again soon to 'make scenes' as you say."

Charles nevertheless was very crestfallen before Emma, who did not hide the resentment she still felt at his want of confidence, and it needed many prayers before she would consent to another power of attorney. He even accompanied her to Monsieur Guillaumin to have a second one, just like the other, drawn up.

"I know how it is," said the notary; "a man of science can't be worried with the practical details of life."

And Charles felt relieved by this comfortable reflection, which gave his weakness the flattering appearance of higher preoccupation.

How exalted she was the following Thursday at the hotel in their room with Léon! She laughed, cried, sang, sent for sherbets, wanted to smoke cigarettes, seemed to him wild and extravagant, but adorable, superb.

He did not know what combination of forces within her was driving her to throw herself so recklessly after the pleasures of life. She became irritable, greedy, voluptuous. She walked boldly through the streets with him, her head high, unconcerned, she said, about being compromised. At times, however, Emma shuddered at the sudden thought of meeting Rodolphe, for it seemed to her that, although they were separated forever, she was not completely free from the power he held over her.

One night she did not return to Yonville at all. Charles lost his head with anxiety, and little Berthe refusing to go to bed without her mamma, sobbed as though her heart would break. Justin had gone out searching the road at random. Monsieur Homais even had left his pharmacy.

At last, at eleven o'clock, able to bear it no longer, Charles harnessed his chaise, jumped in, whipped up his horse, and reached the Croix-Rouge about two o'clock in the morning. No one there! He thought that the clerk had perhaps seen her; but where did he live? Happily, Charles remembered his employer's address, and rushed off there.

Day was breaking, and he could make out some letters over the door; he knocked. Some one, without opening the door, shouted out the required information and added a generous number of insults concerning people who disturb others in the middle of the night.

The house inhabited by the clerk had neither bell, knocker, nor porter. Charles beat on the shutters with his fists. A policeman happened to pass by; he felt nervous and left.

"What a fool I am" he said. "M. Lormeaux must have asked her to stay to dinner."

The Lormeaux no longer lived in Rouen.

"She probably stayed to look after Madame Dubreuil. Oh, but Madame Dubreuil has been dead these ten months . . . Then where can she be?"

An idea occurred to him. At a café he asked for a Directory, and hurriedly looked for the name of Mademoiselle Lempereur, who turned out to live at No. 74 Rue de la Renelle-des-Maroquiniers.

As he was turning into the street, Emma herself appeared at the other end of it; he threw himself upon her rather than embraced her, crying:

"What kept you yesterday?"

"I was not well."

"What! . . . Where! . . . How! . . ."

She passed her hand over her forehead and answered,

"At Mme. Lempereur's."

"I was sure of it! I was just on my way there."

"Oh!" said Emma. "It's not worth while now. She just stepped out a minute ago; don't get so excited. I will never feel free, you understand, if the slightest delay is going to make you lose your head like this."

This was a sort of permission that she gave herself, so as to get perfect freedom in her escapades. And she took full and free advantage of it. Whenever she was seized with the desire to see Léon, she would set out upon any pretext whatever, and if he were not expecting her that day, she would go to fetch him at his office.

It was a great delight at first, but soon he no longer concealed the truth, which was, that his master complained very much about these interruptions.

"Oh, who cares!" she said, "come along."

And he slipped out.

She wanted him to dress all in black, and grow a pointed beard, to look like the portraits of Louis XIII.[58] She asked to see his rooms and found them lacking in taste. This embarrassed him but she paid no attention; she then advised him to buy curtains like hers, and when he objected to the expense:

"Ah! ah! you hold onto your pennies!" she said laughing.

Each time Léon had to tell her everything that he had done since their last meeting. She asked him for some verses—some verses "for herself," a "love poem" in honor of her. But he never succeeded in getting a rhyme for the second verse; and at last ended by copying a sonnet from a Keepsake.

He did this less from vanity, than simply out of a desire to please her. He never questioned her ideas; he accepted all her tastes; he was becoming her mistress rather than she his. She had tender words and kisses that thrilled his soul. Where could she have learnt this corruption so deep and well masked as to be almost unseizable?

VI

On his trips to see her, Léon often dined at the pharmacist's, and he felt obliged out of politeness to invite him in turn.

"With pleasure!" Monsieur Homais had replied; "besides, I must

---

58. Louis XIII (born 1601, king 1610–1643) was the father of Louis XIV.

recharge my mind a bit, for I am getting rusty here. We'll go to the theatre, to the restaurant. We'll do the town."

"Oh, my dear!" tenderly murmured Madame Homais, alarmed at the vague perils he was preparing to brave.

"Well, what? Do you think I'm not sufficiently ruining my health living here amid the continual emanations of the pharmacy? But there! That's just like a woman! They are jealous of science, and then are opposed to our taking the most legitimate distractions. No matter! Count upon me. One of these days I shall turn up at Rouen, and we'll paint the town together."

The pharmacist would formerly have taken good care not to use such an expression, but he was cultivating a flippant Parisian manner which he thought very stylish; and, like his neighbor, Madame Bovary, he questioned the clerk avidly about life in the capital; he even used slang in order to impress . . . the "bourgeois", saying "flip", "cool", "sweet", "neat-o", and "I must break it up", for "I must leave."

So one Thursday Emma was surprised to meet Monsieur Homais in the kitchen of the "Lion d'Or," wearing a traveller's costume, that is to say, wrapped in an old cloak which no one knew he had, while he carried a valise in one hand and the foot-warmer of his establishment in the other. He had confided his intentions to no one, for fear of causing the public anxiety by his absence.

The prospect of seeing again the scenes of his youth no doubt excited him for he never stopped talking during the whole trip; the coach had barely stopped when he leaped out in search of Léon; and in vain the clerk struggled to free himself. M. Homais dragged him off to the flashy Cafe de la Normandie, where he entered majestically, without taking off his hat, for he thought it highly provincial to uncover in any public place.

Emma waited for Léon three quarters of an hour. At last she ran to his office, and, lost in all sorts of conjectures, accusing him of indifference, and reproaching herself for her weakness, she spent the afternoon, her face pressed against the window-panes.

At two o'clock they were still at table opposite each other. The large room was emptying; the stove-pipe, in the shape of a palm-tree, spread its gilt leaves over the white ceiling; and near them, just outside the window, in the full sun, a little fountain gurgled into a white basin, where, among the watercress and asparagus, sluggish lobsters stretched out their claws towards a heap of quail lying on their sides.

Homais relished it all. He was more intoxicated by the luxury than by the fine food and drink, but nevertheless, the Pommard wine began to go to his head, and by the time the "omelette au rhum" appeared, he began expounding scandalous theories on

women. What attracted him above all else, was "chic." He adored
an elegant outfit and hairdo in a well-furnished apartment, and
when it came to their physical proportions, he didn't mind them on
the plump side.

Léon watched the clock in despair. The pharmacist went on
drinking, eating, and talking.

"You must be completely deprived here in Rouen," he said suddenly. "But then the object of your affections doesn't live far
away."

And, when the other blushed:

"Come now, be frank. Can you deny that at Yonville . . ."

The young man began to stammer.

"At Madame Bovary's, can you deny that you were courting . . ."

"Whom do you mean?"

"The maid!"

He was not joking; but vanity getting the better of his judge-
ment, Léon protested indignantly in spite of himself. Besides, he
only liked dark women.

"I approve of your taste," said the pharmacist; "they have more
temperament."

And whispering into his friend's ear, he pointed out the symptoms by which one could detect temperament in a woman. He even
launched into an ethnographic digression: the German was romantic, the French woman licentious, the Italian passionate.

"And negresses?" asked the clerk.

"They are for artistic tastes!" said Homais. "Waiter! Two demi-
tasses!"

"Shall we go?" asked Léon, at last reaching the end of his
patience.

"Yes" said Homais in English.

But before leaving he wanted to see the proprietor of the establishment and made him a few compliments. Then the young man,
to be alone, alleged he had some business engagement.

"Ah! I will escort you," said Homais.

And all the while he was walking through the streets with him he
talked of his wife, his children, of their future, and of his business;
told him in what a dilapidated condition he had found it, and to
what a state of perfection he had now raised it.

When they arrived in front of the Hôtel de Boulogne, Léon left
him abruptly, ran up the stairs, and found his mistress almost
hysterical.

On hearing the name of the pharmacist, she flew into a passion.
Nevertheless, he kept overwhelming her with good reasons; it wasn't
his fault; didn't she know Homais? Could she believe that he would

prefer his company? But she turned away; he held her back, and falling on his knees, he encircled her waist with his arm, in a pose at once langorous, passionate, and imploring.

She stood there looking at him, her large flashing eyes were serious, almost terrible. Then her tears clouded them over, her pink eyelids lowered, and she gave him her hands. Léon was just pressing them to his lips when a servant appeared to say that someone wanted to see the gentleman.

"You will come back?" she said.

"Yes."

"But when?"

"Immediately."

"It's a trick," said the pharmacist, when he saw Léon. "I wanted to interrupt this visit, that seemed to me to annoy you. Let's go and have a glass of *garus*[59] at Bridoux'."

Léon swore that he must get back to his office. Then the pharmacist began making jokes about legal papers and procedure.

"Forget about Cujas[60] and Barthole[61] a bit, what the Devil! Who's going to stop you? Be a man! Let's go to Bridoux'. You'll see his dog. It's very interesting."

And as the clerk still insisted:

"I'll go with you. I'll read a paper while I wait for you, or thumb through a code."

Léon, bewildered by Emma's anger, Monsieur Homais' chatter, and perhaps, by the heaviness of the luncheon, was undecided, and, as though he were under the spell of the pharmacist who kept repeating:

"Let's go to Bridoux'. It's just by here, in the Rue Malpalu."

Then, out of cowardice, out of stupidity, out of that undefinable necessity that leads us towards those actions we are most set against, he allowed himself to be led off to Bridoux'; they found him in his small courtyard overseeing three workmen who panted as they turned the huge wheel of a selza water machine. Homais gave them some advice; he embraced Bridoux; they drank some garus. Twenty times Léon tried to escape, but the other seized him by the arm saying:

"Wait a minute! I'm coming! We'll go to the Fanal de Rouen' to see the fellows there. I'll introduce you to Thomassin."

He finally got rid of him, however, and flew to the hotel. Emma was gone.

She had just left in exasperation. She detested him now. His failure to come as he had promised she took as an insult, and she looked for other reasons for separating from him: he was incapable

---

59. A liqueur named after its inventor, Garus.

60. Jacques Cugar (1522–1590) was a famous jurist who interpreted Roman Law in contemporary terms.

61. Barthole, or Bartole, was an early Italian jurist (1313–1357) in Bologna.

of heroism, weak, banal, more spiritless than a woman, avaricious, and timorous as well.

Later when she was calmer, she realized that she had doubtless been unjust to him. But the picking apart of those we love always alienates us from them. One must not touch one's idols, a little of the gilt always comes off on one's fingers.

They gradually began to talk more frequently of matters outside their love, and in the letters that Emma wrote him she spoke of flowers, poetry, the moon and the stars, naïve resources of a waning passion striving to keep itself alive by all external aids. She was constantly promising herself a profound happiness on her next trip; then she confessed to herself that she had felt nothing extraordinary. This disappointment quickly gave way to a new hope, and Emma returned to him more avid and inflamed than before. She undressed brutally, ripping off the thin laces of her corset so violently that they would whistle round her hips like a gliding snake. She went on tiptoe, barefooted, to see once more that the door was locked, then with one movement, she would let her clothes fall at once to the ground;—then, pale and serious, without a word, she would throw herself against his breast with a long shudder.

Yet there was upon that brow covered with cold drops, on those stammering lips, in those wild eyes, in the grip of those arms, something strange, vague and sinister that seemed to Léon to be subtly gliding between them to force them apart.

He did not dare to question her; but finding how experienced she was, he told himself that she must have passed through all the extremes of both pleasure and pain. What had once charmed now frightened him a little. Furthermore, he revolted against the daily increased absorption of his personality into hers. He resented her, because of this constant victory. He even strove not to love her; then, when he heard the creaking of her boots, he felt his courage desert him, like drunkards at the sight of strong liquor.

It is true, she showered him with every sort of attention, from exotic foods, to little coquettish refinements in her dress and languishing glances. She used to bring roses from Yonville hidden in her bosom which she would toss up into his face; she was worried about his health, advised him how he should behave; and in order to bind him closer to her, hoping perhaps that heaven would take her part, she hung a medal of the Virgin round his neck. She inquired like a virtuous mother about his companions. She said to him:

"Don't see them; don't go out; only think of us; love me!"

She would have liked to be able to watch over his life, and the idea occurred to her of having him followed in the streets. Near the hotel there was always a kind of vagabond who accosted travellers, and who would surely not refuse . . . But her pride revolted at this.

"Ah! So what! What does it matter if he betrays me! What do I care?"

One day, when they had parted early and she was returning alone along the boulevard, she saw the walls of her convent; she sat down on a bench in the shade of the elms. How calm her life had been in those days! How she envied her first undefinable sentiments of love which she had tried to construct from the books she read.

The first months of her marriage, her rides in the forest, the viscount who had waltzed with her, and Lagardy singing, all repassed before her eyes . . . And Léon suddenly appeared to her as far off as the others.

"I do love him!" she said to herself.

No matter! She was not happy, she never had been. Why was her life so unsatisfactory, why did everything she leaned on instantly rot and give way? . . . But suppose there existed somewhere some one strong and beautiful, a man of valor, passionate yet refined, the heart of a poet in the form of an angel, a bronze stringed lyre, playing elegaic epithalamia to the heavens, why might she not someday happen on him? What a vain thought! Besides, nothing was worth the trouble of seeking it; everything was a lie. Every smile concealed a yawn of boredom, every joy a curse, every pleasure its own disgust, and the sweetest kisses left upon your lips only the unattainable desire for a greater delight.

A coarse metallic rattle sounded around her, and the convent bell struck four. And it seemed to her that she had been sitting on that bench since the beginning of time. But an infinity of time can be compressed into a minute like a crowd of people into a small space.

Emma lived all absorbed in her passions and worried no more about money matters than an archduchess.

There came a day, however, when a seedy looking man with a red face and a bald head came to her house, saying he had been sent by Monsieur Vinçart of Rouen. He took out the pins that held together the side-pockets of his long green overcoat, stuck them into his sleeve, and politely handed her a paper.

It was a bill for seven hundred francs, signed by her, and which Lheureux, in spite of all his promises had endorsed to Vinçart.

She sent her servant for him. He could not come.

Then the stranger who had remained standing, casting around him to the right and left curious glances which were hidden behind his blond eyebrows, asked with an innocent air:

"What answer am I to take Vinçart?"

"Well!" said Emma, "tell him . . . that I haven't got it . . . I'll pay him next week . . . He must wait . . . yes, next week."

And the fellow went without another word.

But the next day at twelve o'clock she received a summons, and the sight of the stamped paper, on which appeared several times in large letters, "Maître Hereng, bailiff at Buchy," so frightened her that she rushed in all haste to Lheureux. She found him in his shop, tying up a parcel.

"At your service," he said. "What can I do for you?"

But Lheureux continued what he was doing, aided by a young girl of about thirteen, somewhat hunchbacked, who was both his clerk and his servant.

Then, his sabots clattering on the wooden planks of the shop, he mounted in front of Madame Bovary to the second floor and showed her into a narrow closet, where, in a large pine wood desk, lay some ledgers, protected by an iron bar laid horizontally across them and padlocked down. Against the wall, under some remnants of calico, one caught sight of a safe, but of such dimensions that it must contain something besides promisory notes and cash. Monsieur Lheureux, in fact, went in for pawnbroking, and it was there that he had put Madame Bovary's gold chain, together with the earrings of poor old Tellier, who had been forced, at last, to sell his café, and had bought a small grocery store in Quincampoix, where he was dying of catarrh amongst his candles, that were less yellow than his face.

Lheureux sat down in a large cane arm-chair, saying:

"What's new?"

"Look here!"

"Well, what do you want me to do about it?"

Then she lost her temper, reminding him that he had promised not to endorse her notes away. He admitted it.

"But I was pressed myself; they were holding a knife against my throat too."

"And what will happen now?" she went on.

"Oh, it's very simple; a judgment and then a seizure . . . that's about it!"

Emma kept down a desire to strike him, and asked gently if there was no way of quieting Monsieur Vinçart.

"Oh, sure! appease Vinçart, indeed! You don't know him; he's fiercer than an Arab!"

Nevertheless, Monsieur Lheureux had to help her.

"All right then, listen, it seems to me that I've been pretty good to you so far."

And opening one of his ledgers:

"Look!" he said.

Then moving his finger up the page:

"Let's see . . . let's see . . . ! August 3d, two hundred francs . . . June 17th, a hundred and fifty . . . March 23d, forty-six . . . In April . . ."

He stopped, as if afraid of making some mistake.

"I won't even mention the bills signed by Monsieur Bovary, one for seven hundred francs, and another for three hundred. As to the little payments on your account and the interest, I'd never get to the end of the list, I can't figure that high. I'll have nothing more to do with it."

She wept; she even called him "her good Monsieur Lheureux." But he always fell back upon "that rascal Vinçart." Besides, he hadn't a penny, no one was paying him these days, they were eating his coat off his back, a poor shopkeeper like himself couldn't advance money.

Emma was silent, and Monsieur Lheureux, who was biting the feathers of a quill, no doubt became uneasy at her silence, for he went on:

"Perhaps, if something were paid on this, one of these days . . . I might . . ."

"Well," she said, "as soon as the balance on the Barneville property . . ."

"What? . . ."

And on hearing that Langlois had not yet paid he seemed much surprised. Then in a honied voice:

"Then we'll agree, what do you say to . . . ?"

"Oh! Whatever you say!"

On this he closed his eyes to reflect, wrote down a few figures, and saying that this was really going to hurt him, it was a risky affair, that he was "bleeding" himself for her, he wrote out four bills for two hundred and fifty francs each, to fall due month by month.

"Provided that Vinçart will listen to me! However, it's settled. I don't back down on my word. I'm as square as a brick."

Next he carelessly showed her several new goods; not one of which, however, was in his opinion worthy of madame.

"When I think that there's a dress that costs seven cents a yard and guaranteed color-fast! And they actually swallow it all down! Of course you understand one doesn't tell them what it really is!" He hoped by this confession of chicanery towards others to convince her of his honesty with her.

Then he called her back to show her three yards of guipure that he had lately picked up "at a sale."

"Isn't it lovely?" said Lheureux. "It is very much used now for the backs of arm-chairs. It's quite the rage."

And, quicker than a juggler, he wrapped up the guipure in some blue paper and put it in Emma's hands.

"But at least let me know . . ."

"Yes, some other time," he replied, turning on his heel.

That same evening she urged Bovary to write to his mother, to ask her to send at once the whole of the balance due from the father's estate. The mother-in-law replied that she had nothing more: that the liquidation was complete, and, aside from Barneville, there remained for them an income of six hundred francs, that she would pay them punctually.

Madame Bovary then sent bills to two or three patients, and was soon making great use of this method which turned out to be very successful. She was always careful to add a postscript: "Do not mention this to my husband; you know how proud he is . . . forgive my having to . . . your humble servant. . . ." There were a few complaints; she intercepted them.

To get money she began selling her old gloves, her old hats, all sorts of old odds and ends, and she bargained rapaciously, her peasant blood standing her in good stead. Then on her trips to town she searched the second hand stores for nick-nacks which she was sure, if no one else, Monsieur Lheureux would certainly take off her hands. She bought ostrich feathers, Chinese porcelain, and trunks; she borrowed from Félicité, from Madame Lefrançois, from the landlady at the "Croix Rouge," from everybody, no matter where. With the money she at last received from Barneville she paid two bills; the other fifteen hundred francs fell due. She renewed the notes, and then renewed them again!

Sometimes, it is true, she tried to add up her accounts, but the results were always so staggering, she couldn't believe they were possible. Then she would begin over again, soon get confused, leave everything where it was and forget about it.

The house was a dreary place now! Tradesmen were seen leaving it with angry faces. Handkerchiefs hung drying on the stoves, and little Berthe, to the great scandal of Madame Homais, wore stockings with holes in them. If Charles timidly ventured a remark, she would snap back at him savagely that it certainly wasn't her fault!

What was the meaning of all these fits of temper? He explained everything by her old nervous illness, and reproaching himself with having taken her infirmities for faults, accused himself of egotism, and longed to go and take her in his arms.

"Ah, no!" he said to himself; "I would only annoy her."

And he stayed where he was.

After dinner he would walk about alone in the garden; he took little Berthe on his lap and unfolding his medical journal, tried to teach her to read. But the child, who had never had any schooling at all, would soon open wide her large eyes in bewilderment and begin to cry. Then he would comfort her; he fetched water in her watering can to make rivers on the sand path, or broke off branches from the privet hedges to plant trees in the flower beds. This did not spoil the garden much, which was now overgrown with long weeds. They owed Lestiboudois for so many day's wages. Then the child would grow cold and ask for her mother.

"Go call your nurse," said Charles. "You know, my darling, that mama does not like to be disturbed!"

Autumn was setting in, and the leaves were already falling—as they had two years ago when she was ill!—Where would it all end! . . . And he would continue to pace up and down, his hands behind his back.

Madame was in her room. No one was allowed to enter. There she stayed from morning to night, listless and hardly dressed, from time to time lighting a tablet of Turkish incense she had bought at the shop of an Algerian in Rouen. In order to get rid of this sleeping man stretched out beside her at night, she finally managed by continual badgering to relegate him to a room on the third floor; then she would read until morning, lurid novels where there would be scenes of orgies, violence and bloodshed. Often she would be seized by a sudden terror and cry out. Charles would come running.

"Oh! Leave me alone!" she would say.

Or at other times, when she was burnt more fiercely by that inner flame which her adultery kept feeding, panting and overcome with desire, she would throw open the window breathing in the chill air and letting the wind blow back her hair which hung too heavy on her neck, and, looking up at the stars, she would long for the love of a prince. She thought of him, of Léon. She would then have given anything for a single one of those meetings which would appease her.

These were her gala days. She was determined that they should be magnificent! When he could not pay all the expenses himself, she made up the deficit liberally, which happened pretty well every time. He tried to convince her that they would be just as well off somewhere else, in a more modest hotel, but she always found some objection.

One day she drew six small silver-gilt spoons from her bag (they were old Rouault's wedding present), begging him to pawn them at once for her; Léon obeyed, although the errand annoyed him. He was afraid of compromising himself.

Then, on reflection, he began to think that his mistress was beginning to behave rather strangely, and perhaps they were not wrong in wishing to separate him from her.

In fact, some one had sent his mother a long anonymous letter to warn her that he was "ruining himself with a married woman"; and immediately the good woman had visions of the eternal bug-a-boo of every family, that is to say, that vague and terrible creature, the

siren, the fantastic monster which makes its home in the treacherous depths of love. She wrote to Maître Dubocage, his employer,
who behaved perfectly in the affair. He kept him for three quarters
of an hour trying to open his eyes, to warn him of the abyss into
which he was falling. Such an intrigue would damage him later on
in his career. He implored him to break with her, and, if he would
not make this sacrifice in his own interest, to do it at least for his,
Dubocage's sake.

Léon finally swore he would not see Emma again; and he reproached himself with not having kept his word, considering all
the trouble and reproaches she was likely to bring down on him,
not counting the jokes made by his fellow clerks as they sat around
the stove in the morning. Besides, he was soon to be head clerk;
it was time to settle down. So he gave up his flute, his exalted
sentiments, his poetic imagination; for every bourgeois in the flush
of his youth, were it but for a day, a moment, has believed himself
capable of immense passions, of lofty enterprises. The most mediocre libertine has dreamed of sultanas; every notary bears within
him the débris of a poet.

He was bored now when Emma suddenly began to sob on his
breast; and his heart, like the people who can only stand a certain
amount of music, became drowsy through indifference to the vibrations of a love whose subtleties he could no longer distinguish.

They knew one another too well to experience any of those
sudden surprises which multiply the enjoyment of a possession a
hundredfold. She was as sick of him as he was weary of her. Emma
found again in adultery all the platitudes of marriage.

But how to get rid of him? Then, though she felt humiliated by
the sordidity of such a happiness, she clung to it out of habit, or out
of degeneration; she pursued it more desperately than ever, destroying every pleasure by always wishing for it to be too great. She
blamed Léon for her disappointed hopes, as if he had betrayed her;
and she even longed for some catastrophe that would bring about
their separation, since she had not the courage to do it herself.

She none the less went on writing him love letters, in keeping
with the notion that a woman must write to her lover.

But while writing to him, it was another man she saw, a phantom
fashioned out of her most ardent memories, of her favorite books,
her strongest desires, and at last he became so real, so tangible, that
her heart beat wildly in awe and admiration, though unable to see
him distinctly, for, like a god, he was hidden beneath the abundance of his attributes. He dwelt in that azure land where silken
ladders swung from balconies in the moonlight, beneath a flower-
scented breeze. She felt him near her; he was coming and would
ravish her entire being in a kiss. Then she would fall back to earth

again shattered; for these vague ecstasies of imaginary love, would exhaust her more than the wildest orgies.

She now felt a constant pain throughout her body. Often she even received summonses, stamped paper that she barely looked at. She would have liked not to be alive, or to be always asleep.

On the day of Mid-Lent she did not return to Yonville; that evening she went to a masked ball. She wore velvet breeches, red stockings, a peruke, and a three-cornered hat cocked over one ear. She danced all night to the wild sounds of the trombones; people gathered around her, and in the morning she found herself on the steps of the theatre together with five or six other masked dancers, dressed as stevadores or sailors, friends of Léon's who were talking about going out to find some supper.

The neighboring cafés were full. They found a dreadful looking restaurant at the harbor, where the proprietor showed them to a little room on the fifth floor.

The men were whispering in a corner, no doubt consulting about expenses. There were a clerk, two medical students, and a shop assistant: what company for her! As to the women, Emma soon perceived from the tone of their voices that most of them probably came from the lowest class. This frightened her, she drew back her chair and lowered her eyes.

The others began to eat; she ate nothing. Her head was on fire, her eyes smarted, and her skin was ice-cold. In her head she seemed to feel the floor of the ball-room rebounding again beneath the rhythmical pulsation of thousands of dancing feet. The smell of punch and cigar smoke made her dizzy. She fainted: they carried her to the window.

Day was breaking, and a large purple stain was spreading across the pale sky in the direction of the St. Catherine hills. The ashen river was shivering in the wind; there was no one on the bridges; the street lamps were going out.

She came to herself, however, and began to think of Berthe asleep at home in the maid's room. But just then a cart loaded with long strips of iron passed by, and made a deafening metallic vibration against the walls of the house.

She abruptly slipped out of the room; removed her costume; told Léon she had to return; and found herself alone at last in the Hôtel de Boulogne. Everything, herself included, was now unbearable to her. She would have liked to take wing like a bird, and fly off far away to become young again in the realms of immaculate purity.

She left the hotel, crossed the Boulevard, the Place Cauchoise, and the Faubourg, as far as an open street that overlooked the park. She walked rapidly, the fresh air calmed her; and, little by little, the faces of the crowd, the masks, the quadrilles, the lights, the supper, those women, all, disappeared like rising mists. Then, reaching the "Croix-Rouge," she threw herself on the bed in her little room on the second floor, where there were pictures of the "Tour de Nesle." At four o'clock Hivert awoke her.

When she got home, Félicité showed her a grey paper stuck behind the clock. She read:

"In virtue of the seizure in execution of a judgment."

What judgment . . . ? As a matter of fact, the evening before another paper had been brought that she had not yet seen, and she was stunned by these words:

"By power of the king, the law, and the courts, Mme. Bovary is hereby ordered . . ."

Then, skipping several lines, she read:

"Within twenty-four hours, at the latest . . ." But what? "To pay the sum of eight thousand francs." There was even written at the bottom of the page, "She will be constrained thereto by every form of law, and notably by a writ of distraint on her furniture and effects."

What should she do? . . . In twenty-four hours; tomorrow! Lheureux, she thought, probably wanted to frighten her again, for, all at once, she saw through his manoeuvres, the reason for his favors. The only thing that reassured her was the extraordinary amount of the figure.

Nevertheless, as a result of buying and not paying, of borrowing, signing notes, and renewing these notes which grew ever larger each time they fell due, she had ended by preparing a capital for Monsieur Lheureux which he was impatiently waiting to collect to use in his own financial speculations.

She went over to his place, assuming an air of indifference.

"Do you know what has happened to me? It's a joke, I'm sure!"

"No."

"What do you mean?"

He slowly turned around, and, folding his arms, said to her:

"Did you think, my dear lady, that I was going to go on to the end of time providing you with merchandise and cash, just for the love of God? I certainly have to get back what I laid out, let's be fair."

She objected to the amount of the debt.

"Ah! Too bad! The court has recognised it! There's a judgment. You've been notified. Besides, it isn't my fault. It's Vinçart's."

"But couldn't you . . . ?"

"No! Not a single thing!"

"But . . . Still . . . let's talk it over."

And she began beating about the bush; she had known nothing about it . . . it was a surprise . . .

"Whose fault is that?" said Lheureux, bowing ironically. "While I'm slaving like a nigger, you go gallivanting about."

"Ah! Don't preach to me!"

"It never does any harm," he replied.

She turned coward; she implored him; she even pressed her pretty white and slender hand against the shopkeeper's knee.

"There, that'll do! Any one'd think you wanted to seduce me!"

"You are a wretch!" she cried.

"Oh, oh! What a fuss you are making!"

"I will show you up. I'll tell my husband . . ."

"All right! I too, I'll show your husband something!"

And Lheureux drew from his strong box the receipt for eighteen hundred francs that she had given him when Vinçart had discounted the bills.

"Do you think," he added, "that he won't catch on to your little theft, the poor dear man?"

She collapsed, more overcome than if felled by the blow of a club. He was walking up and down from the window to the bureau, repeating all the while:

"I'll show him all right . . . I'll show him all right . . ."

Then he approached her, and said in a soft voice:

"It's no fun, I know; but after all it hasn't killed anyone, and, since that is the only way that is left for you paying back my money . . ."

"But where am I to get any?" said Emma, wringing her hands.

"Bah! when one has friends like you!"

And he looked at her with such a knowing and terrible stare, that she shuddered to the very core of her heart.

"I promise you," she said, "I'll sign . . ."

"I've enough of your signatures!"

"I will sell something else . . ."

"Oh come!" he said, shrugging his shoulders. "You've nothing left to sell."

And he called through the peep-hole that looked down into the shop:

"Annette, don't forget the three coupons of No. 14."

The servant appeared; Emma caught the hint and asked how much money would be needed to put a stop to the proceedings.

"It is too late."

"But if I were to bring you several thousand francs, a quarter of the sum, a third, almost all?"

"No; it's no use!"

And he pushed her gently towards the staircase.

"I implore you, Monsieur Lheureux, just a few days more!"

She was sobbing.

"Ah that's good! let's have some tears!"

"You'll drive me to do something desperate!"

"Don't make me laugh!" said he, shutting the door.

VII

She was stoical the next day when Maître Hareng, the bailiff, with two assistants arrived at her house to draw up inventory for the seizure.

They began with Bovary's consulting-room, and did not write down the phrenological head, which was considered an "instrument of his profession"; but in the kitchen they counted the plates, the saucepans, the chairs, the candlesticks, and in the bedroom all the nick-nacks on the wall-shelf. They examined her dresses, the linen, the dressing-room; and her whole existence, to its most intimate details, was stretched out like a cadavre in an autopsy before the eyes of these three men.

Maître Hareng, buttoned up in his thin black coat, wearing a white choker and very tight foot-straps, repeated from time to time:

"Allow me madame? Allow me?"

Often he uttered exclamations:

"Charming! very pretty."

Then he began writing again, dipping his pen into the horn inkstand he carried in his left hand.

When they had done with the rooms they went up to the attic.

She kept a desk there in which Rodolphe's letters were locked. It had to be opened.

"Ah! a correspondence!" said Maître Hareng, with a discreet smile. "But allow me! for I must make sure the box contains nothing else." And he tipped up the papers lightly, as if to let the napoleons fall out. This made her furious to see this coarse hand, with red moist fingers like slugs, touching these pages against which her heart had beaten.

They went at last! Félicité came back. Emma had sent her out to watch for Bovary in order to keep him away, and they hastily installed the man set to guard the seizure, in the attic, where he swore he would not stir.

During the evening Charles seemed to her careworn. Emma watched him with a look of anguish, fancying she saw an accusation in every line of his face. Then, when her eyes wandered over the chimney-piece ornamented with Chinese screens, over the large curtains, the arm-chairs, all those things that had softened the bitterness of her life, remorse seized her, or rather an immense regret, that, far from destroying her passion, rather irritated it. Charles placidly poked the fire, both his feet on the andirons.

Once the man, no doubt bored in his hiding-place, made a slight noise.

"Is any one walking upstairs?" said Charles.

"No," she replied; "it is a window that has been left open, and is banging in the wind."

The next day which was Sunday, she went to Rouen to call on all the brokers whose names she knew. They were either in the country, or away on a trip. She was not discouraged; and those whom she did manage to see she asked for money, insisting that she absolutely had to have it, that she would pay it back. Some laughed in her face; all refused.

At two o'clock she ran to Léon's apartment, and knocked at the door. No one answered. At length he appeared.

"What brings you here?"

"Am I disturbing you?"

"No . . . but . . ." And he admitted that his landlord didn't like his having "women" there.

"I must speak to you," she went on.

Then he took down the key, but she stopped him.

"No, no! Over there, in our home!"

And they went to their room at the Hôtel de Boulogne.

On arriving she drank off a large glass of water. She was very pale. She said to him:

"Léon, I have a favor to ask you."

And, shaking him by both hands which she held tightly in hers, she added:

"Listen, I must have eight thousand francs."

"But you are mad!"

"Not yet."

And thereupon, telling him the story of the seizure, she explained her distress to him; for Charles knew nothing of it; her mother-in-law detested her; old Rouault could do nothing; but he, Léon, he would set about finding this indispensable sum . . .

"But what do you want me . . . ?"

"What a coward you are!" she cried.

Then he said stupidly, "You're making things out to be worse than they are. Your fellow there could probably be quieted with three thousand francs."

All the more reason to try and do something; it was inconceivable that they couldn't find three thousand francs. Besides, Léon could sign the notes instead of her.

"Go! try! you must! run! . . . Oh! Try! try! I will love you so!"

He went out, and came back at the end of an hour, saying, with a solemn face:

"I have been to three people . . . with no success!"

Then they sat there facing each other on either side of the

fireplace, motionless, without speaking. Emma shrugged her shoulders as she tapped her foot impatiently. He heard her murmur:

"If I were in your place I'd certainly find some!"

"Where?"

"At your office."

And she looked at him.

A diabolical determination showed in her burning eyes which were half closed in a lascivious and encouraging manner;—so that the young man felt himself growing weak beneath the mute will of this woman who was urging him to commit a crime. Then he was afraid, and to avoid any explanation he smote his forehead crying:

"Morel is coming back tonight! He will not refuse me, I hope" (this was one of his friends, the son of a very rich merchant); "and I will bring it you to-morrow," he added.

Emma did not seem to welcome this new hope with all the joy he had expected. Did she suspect the lie? He went on, blushing:

"However, if you don't see me by three o'clock, do not wait for me, my darling. I must leave now, forgive me. Good-bye!"

He pressed her hand, but it felt quite lifeless. Emma had no strength left for any sentiment whatever.

Four o'clock struck; and she rose to return to Yonville, mechanically obeying the force of old habits.

The weather was beautiful; it was one of those March days, clear and sharp, when the sun shines in a perfectly white sky. The people of Rouen, dressed in their Sunday-clothes, seemed happy as they strolled by. She reached the Place du Parvis. People were coming out of the cathedral after vespers; the crowd flowed out through the three portals like a river through the three arches of a bridge, and in the middle, more immobile than a rock, stood the verger.

Then she remembered the day when, eager and full of hope, she had entered beneath this large nave, that had opened out before her, less profound than her love; and she walked on weeping beneath her veil, dazed, staggering, almost fainting.

"Look out!" cried a voice issuing from behind a carriage gate which was swinging open.

She stopped to let pass a black horse, prancing between the shafts of a tilbury, driven by a gentleman dressed in sables. Who was it? She knew him . . . The carriage sprang forward and disappeared.

Why, it was he, the Viscount! She turned away; the street was empty. She was so crushed, so sad, that she had to lean against a wall to keep herself from falling.

Then she thought she had been mistaken.

How could she tell? Everything, within herself and without, was abandoning her. She felt that she was lost, that she was wandering about at random within undefinable abysses, and she was almost happy, on reaching the "Croix Rouge," to see the good Homais, who was watching a large box full of pharmaceutical stores being hoisted on to the "Hirondelle"; holding in his hand a silk handkerchief containing six "cheminots" for his wife.

Madame Homais was very fond of these small, heavy rolls shaped like turbans which are eaten during Lent with salt butter: a last relic of Gothic fare, going back, perhaps, to the Crusades, and with which the hardy Normans would stuff themselves in times goneby, thinking that they saw, illuminated in the golden light of the torches, between the tankards of Hippocras[62] and the gigantic slabs of meat, the heads of Saracens to be devoured. The druggist's wife crunched them up as they had done, heroically, in spite of her wretched teeth; so whenever Homais made a trip to town, he never failed to bring her home some which he bought at the great baker's in the Rue Massacre.

"Charmed to see you," he said, offering Emma a hand to help her into the "Hirondelle."

Then he tied his "cheminots" to the baggage net and remained with his head bare and his arms folded in an attitude pensive and Napoleonic.

But when the blind man appeared as usual at the foot of the hill he exclaimed indignantly:

"I can't understand why the authorities continue to tolerate such criminal occupations! These unfortunate people should be locked up, forced to do some work. I give you my word, Progress marches at a snail's pace! We are paddling about in a state of total barbarism!"

The blind man held out his hat which flapped about in the window as though it were a pocket in the upholstery which had come loose.

"This," said the pharmacist, "is a scrofulous disease."

And though he knew the poor devil, he pretended to see him for the first time, muttering such words as "cornea," "opaque cornea," "sclerotic," "facies," then asked him in a paternal tone:

"My friend, have you suffered long from this dreadful affliction? Instead of getting drunk in the café you would do better to follow a diet."

He advised him to drink good wine, good beer and to eat good roasts of meat. The blind man went on with his song. He actually seemed almost insane. At last Monsieur Homais opened his purse.

"Now there's a sou; give me back two liards: don't forget what I told you, you'll find it does you good."

Hivert openly cast some doubt on its efficacy. But the druggist said that he would cure the man himself with an antiphlogistic salve of his own composition, and he gave his address: "Monsieur

62. Hippocras (Hippocrates, the Greek physician) was an aromatic, highly spiced   wine of medieval Europe.

Homais, near the market, everyone knows me."

"All right!" said Hivert, "in payment, you can 'put on your act' for us."

The blind man squatted down on his haunches with his head thrown back, and rolling his greenish eyes and sticking out his tongue, he rubbed his stomach with both hands while uttering a sort of low howl like a famished dog. Emma, overcome with disgust, threw him a five franc piece over her shoulder. It was all her fortune. It seemed like a grand thing to her to throw it away like this.

The coach had already started again when Monsieur Homais suddenly leaned out of the window and shouted:

"No farinacious foods or dairy products, wear woolen clothing next to the skin, and expose the diseased areas to the smoke of juniper berries."

The sight of the familiar things that passed before her eyes gradually diverted Emma from her present suffering. An intolerable fatigue overwhelmed her, and she reached home stupefied, discouraged, almost asleep.

"Let come what may!" she told herself.

Besides, anything could happen. Couldn't some extraordinary event occur at any moment? Lheureux might even die.

At nine o'clock in the morning she was awakened by the sound of voices in the square. A crowd around the market was reading a large bill fixed to one of the posts, and she saw Justin climb on a milepost and tear down the bill. The local policeman had just seized him by the collar. Monsieur Homais came out of his shop, and Mère Le-françois, in the midst of the crowd, was talking the loudest of all.

"Madame! madame!" cried Félicité, running in, "it's an outrage!"

And the poor girl, all in tears, handed her a yellow paper that she had just torn off the door. Emma read with a glance that her furniture was for sale.

Then they looked at one another in silence. Servant and master had no secrets from each other. At last Félicité whispered:

"If I were you, madame, I'd go see Monsieur Guillaumin."

"You think so?"

The question meant:

"You who know all about the house from the butler, has the master sometimes spoken of me?"

"Yes, you'd do well to go there."

She dressed, put on her black gown, and her cape with jet beads, and that she might not be seen (there was still a crowd on the Square), she took the path by the river, outside the village.

She was out of breath when she reached the notary's gate. The sky was sombre, and a little snow was falling.

At the sound of the bell, Theodore in a red waistcoat appeared on the steps; he came to open the door with a casual air, as if she were an old acquaintance, and showed her into the dining-room.

A large porcelain stove crackled beneath a cactus that filled up the niche in the wall, and in black wood frames against the oak-stained paper hung Steuben's[63] "Esmeralda" and Schopin's "Putiphar."[64] The ready-laid table, the two silver chafing-dishes, the crystal door-knobs, the parquet and the furniture, all shone with a scrupulous, English cleanliness; the windows were ornamented at each corner with stained glass.

"Now this," thought Emma, "is the kind of dining-room I ought to have."

The notary came in. With his left hand, he pressed his palm-embroidered dressing gown against his body, while with his other hand he quickly took off and replaced his brown velvet skullcap, which he wore jauntily cocked to the right. After circling around his bald cranium, the end of three strains of blond hair stuck out from underneath the cap.

After he had offered her a seat he sat down to breakfast, apologising profusely for his rudeness.

"I have come," she said, "to beg you, sir . . ."

"What, madame? I am listening."

And she began telling him about her situation.

Monsieur Guillaumin knew all about it. He was working in secret partnership with the shopkeeper, who always provided him with the capital for the mortgage loans he was asked to arrange.

So he knew (and better than she herself) the long story of these notes, small at first, bearing the names of several endorsers, made out for long terms and constantly renewed up to the day when, gathering together all the protested notes, the shopkeeper had asked his friend Vinçart to take in his own name all the necessary legal steps to collect the money, not wishing to appear as a shark in the eyes of his fellow-citizens.

She mingled her story with recriminations against Lheureux, to which the notary from time to time gave meaningless replies. Eating his cutlet and drinking his tea, he buried his chin in his sky-blue cravat, into which were thrust two diamond pins, held together by a small gold chain; and he smiled a singular smile, in a sugary, ambiguous fashion. Noticing that her feet were damp:

"Do get closer to the stove," he said, "put your feet up against the porcelain."

She was afraid of dirtying it but the notary replied gallantly:

63. Karl Steuben (1788–1856) was a German history painter. Esmeralda is the gypsy girl in Hugo's *Notre Dame de Paris* (a picture, "Esmeralda et Quasimodo"—the Dwarf—was exhibited in 1839).

64. Schopin was (with a different spelling) the brother of the composer Chopin. Putiphar is the official of the court of Egypt who was Joseph's master—the wife of Putiphar tried to seduce him. The picture represents the seduction scene.

"Pretty things never spoil anything."

Then she tried to appeal to his better feelings and, growing moved herself, she began telling him about the tightness of her household, her worries, her wants. He could understand that—such an elegant woman!—and, without interrupting his lunch, he turned completely round towards her, so that his knee brushed against her boot; the sole was beginning to curl in the heat of the stove.

But when she asked for three thousand francs, his lips drew tight and he said how sorry he was not to have had the management of her capital before, for there were hundreds of ways very convenient, even for a lady, of turning her money to account. In the turf-pits of Gaumesnil or in Le Havre real estate, they could have ventured, with hardly any risk, on some excellent speculations; and he let her consume herself with rage at the thought of the fabulous sums that she would certainly have made.

"How was it," he went on, "that you didn't come to me?"

"I don't know," she said.

"Why not? Did I frighten you so much? It is I, on the contrary, who ought to complain. We hardly know one another; yet I am very devoted to you. You do not doubt that any longer, I hope?"

He held out his hand, took hers, kissed it greedily, then held it on his knee; and he played delicately with her fingers, while muttering thousands of compliments.

His bland voice rustled like a running brook; a light shone in his eyes through the glimmering of his spectacles, and his hand was advancing up Emma's sleeve to press her arm. She felt against her cheek his panting breath. This man was intolerable.

She sprang to her feet and told him:

"Sir, I am waiting."

"For what?" said the notary, who suddenly became very pale.

"This money."

"But . . ."

Then, yielding to an irresistible wave of desire:

"Well then, . . . yes!"

He dragged himself towards her on his knees, regardless of his dressing gown.

"I beg you, stay! I love you!"

He seized her by the waist. Madame Bovary's face flushed purple. She recoiled with a terrible look, exclaiming:

"You shamelessly take advantage of my distress, sir! I am to be pitied—not to be sold."

And she went out.

The notary remained dumbfounded, his eyes fixed on his fine embroidered slippers. They were a love gift, and their sight finally consoled him. Besides, he reflected that such an adventure might have carried him too far.

"The wretch! the scoundrel! . . . what an infamy!" she said to herself, as she fled with nervous steps under the aspens that lined the road. The disappointment of her failure increased the indignation of her outraged modesty; it seemed to her that Providence pursued her implacably, and, strengthening herself in her pride, she had never felt so much esteem for herself nor so much contempt for others. A spirit of warfare transformed her. She would have liked to strike all men, to spit in their faces, to crush them; she kept walking straight on, as quickly as she could, pale, shaking and furious, searching the empty horizon with tear-dimmed eyes, almost rejoicing in the hatred that was choking her.

When she saw her house a numbness came over her. She could not go on; yet she had to. Besides, what escape was there for her?

Félicité was waiting for her at the door.

"Well?"

"No!" said Emma.

And for a quarter of an hour the two of them went over the various persons in Yonville who might perhaps be inclined to help her. But each time that Félicité named some one Emma replied:

"Out of the question! they won't!"

"And the master'll soon be in."

"I know that well enough . . . Now leave me alone."

She had tried everything; there was nothing more to be done now; and when Charles came in she would have to tell him:

"Step aside! This rug on which you are walking is no longer ours. In your own house you don't own a chair, a pin, a straw, and it is I, poor man, who have ruined you."

Then there would be a great sob; next he would weep abundantly, and at last, the surprise past, he would forgive her.

"Yes," she murmured, grinding her teeth, "*he* will forgive me, the man I could never forgive for having known me, even if he had a million to spare! . . . Never! never!"

The thought of Bovary's magnanimity exasperated her. He was bound to find out the catastrophe, whether she confessed or not, now, soon, or to-morrow; so there was no escape from the horrible scene and she would have to bear the weight of his generosity. She wanted to return to Lheureux, but what good would it do? To write to her father—it was too late; and perhaps she began to repent now that she had not yielded to the notary, when she heard the trot of a horse in the alley. It was he; he was opening the gate; he was whiter than the plaster wall. Rushing to the stairs, she fled to the Square; and the wife of the mayor, who was talking to Lestiboudois in front of the church, saw her enter the house of the tax-collector.

She hurried off to tell Madame Caron, and the two ladies went up to the attic; hidden behind a sheet strung up on two poles, they stationed themselves comfortably in full command of Binet's room.

He was alone in his garret, busily copying in wood one of those indescribable bits of ivory, composed of crescents, of spheres hollowed out one within the other, the whole as straight as an obelisk, and of no use whatever; and he was beginning on the last piece—he was nearing his goal! In the twilight of the workshop the white dust was flying from his tools like a shower of sparks under the hoofs of a galloping horse; the two wheels were turning, droning; Binet smiled, his chin lowered, his nostrils distended. He seemed lost in the state of complete bliss that only the most menial tasks can offer: distracting the mind by easily overcome obstacles, they satisfy it completely, leading to a fulfilled achievement that leaves no room for dreams beyond.

"Ah! there she is!" exclaimed Madame Tuvache.

But the noise of the lathe made it impossible to hear what she was saying.

At last the two ladies thought they made out the word "francs," and Madame Tuvache whispered in a low voice:

"She's asking for extra time to pay her taxes."

"Apparently!" replied the other.

They saw her walking up and down, examining the napkin-rings, the candlesticks, the banister rails against the walls, while Binet stroked his beard with satisfaction.

"Do you think she wants to order something from him?" said Madame Tuvache.

"Why, he never sells anything," objected her neighbor.

The tax-collector seemed to be listening with wide-open eyes, as if he did not understand. She went on in a tender, suppliant manner. She came nearer to him, her breast heaving; they no longer spoke.

"Is she making advances to him?" said Madame Tuvache.

Binet was scarlet to his very ears. She took hold of his hands.

"Oh, it's too much!"

And no doubt she was suggesting something abominable to him; for the tax-collector—yet he was brave, had fought at Bautzen[65] and at Lützen,[66] had been through the French campaign,[67] and had even been proposed for the Croix de Guerre—suddenly, as at the sight of a serpent, recoiled as far as he could from her, exclaiming:

"Madame! How dare you? . . ."

"Women like that ought to be whipped," said Madame Tuvache.

"But where did she go?" Madame Caron asked. For while they talked, she had vanished out of sight, till they discovered her running up the Grande Rue and turning right as if making for the graveyard, leaving them lost in wonder.

"Mère Rollet," she cried on reaching the nurse's home, "I am choking; unlace me!" She fell sobbing on the bed. Nurse Rollet

---

65. Bautzen (in Saxony, now in Poland, called Budyszin) was the scene of a battle in 1813 where Napoleon defeated the Prussians and Russians.

66. Lützen, in Saxony, was the scene of another battle of Napoleon.

67. The French campaign refers to the battles in France before the Allies captured Paris and forced the abdication of Napoleon and his banishment to Elba in 1814.

covered her with a petticoat and remained standing by her side.
Then, as she did not answer, the woman withdrew, took her wheel
and began spinning flax.

"Please, stop that!" she murmured, fancying she heard Binet's
lathe.

"What's bothering her?" said the nurse to herself. "Why has she
come here?"

She had come, impelled by a kind of horror that drove her from
her home.

Lying on her back, motionless, and with staring eyes, she saw
things but vaguely, although she tried with idiotic persistence to
focus her attention on them. She looked at the scaling walls, two
logs smoking end to end in the fireplace, and a long spider crawling
over her head in a cracked beam. At last she began to collect her
thoughts. She remembered—one day, with Léon . . . Oh! how
long ago that was—the sun was shining on the river, and the air full
of the scent from the clematis . . . Then, carried by her memories
as by a rushing torrent, she soon remembered what had happened
the day before.

"What time is it?" she asked.

Mère Rollet went out, raised the fingers of her right hand to that
side of the sky that was brightest, and came back slowly, saying:

"Nearly three."

"Ah! thank you, thank you!"

For he would come, he was bound to. He would have found the
money. But he would, perhaps, go down to her house, not guessing
where she was, and she told the nurse to run and fetch him.

"Be quick!"

"I'm going, my dear lady, I'm going!"

She wondered now why she had not thought of him from the
first. Yesterday he had given his word; he would not break it. And
she already saw herself at Lheureux's spreading out her three banknotes on his desk. Then she would have to invent some story to
explain matters to Bovary. What would she tell him?

The nurse, however, was a long time returning. But, as there was
no clock in the cot, Emma feared she was perhaps exaggerating the
length of time. She began walking round the garden, step by step;
she went into the path by the hedge, and returned quickly, hoping
that the woman would have come back by another road. At last,
weary of waiting, assailed by fears that she thrust from her, no
longer conscious whether she had been here a century or a moment,
she sat down in a corner, closed her eyes, and stopped her ears. The
gate grated; she sprang up. Before she could speak, Mère Rollet
told her:

"There is no one at your house!"

"What?"

"He isn't there. And Monsieur is crying. He is calling for you. Everybody is looking for you."

Emma did not answer. She gasped with wild, rolling eyes, while the peasant woman, frightened at her face drew back instinctively, thinking her mad. Suddenly she struck her brow and uttered a cry; for the thought of Rodolphe, like a flash of lightning in a dark night, had struck into her soul. He was so good, so tender, so generous! And besides, should he hesitate to come to her assistance, she would know well enough how one single glance would reawaken their lost love. So she set out towards La Huchette, unaware that she was hastening to offer what had so angered her a while ago, not in the least conscious of her prostitution.

VIII

She asked herself as she walked along, "What am I going to say? How shall I begin?" And as she went on she recognised the thickets, the trees, the sea-rushes on the hill, the château beyond. All the sensations of her first love came back to her, and her poor oppressed heart expanded in the warmth of this tenderness. A warm wind blew in her face; melting snow fell drop by drop from the leave-buds onto the grass.

She entered, as in the past, through the small park-gate, reached the main courtyard, planted with a double row of lindens, their long whispering branches swaying in the wind. The dogs in their kennels barked, but their resounding voices brought no one out.

She went up the large straight staircase with wooden banisters that led to the hallway paved with dusty flagstones, into which a row of doors opened, as in a monastery or an inn. He was at the top, right at the end, on the left. When she placed her fingers on the lock her strength suddenly deserted her. She was afraid, almost wished he would not be there, though this was her only hope, her last chance of salvation. She collected her thoughts for one moment, and, strengthening herself by the feeling of present necessity, went in.

He was sitting in front of the fire, both his feet propped against the mantelpiece, smoking a pipe.

"Oh, it's you!" he said, getting up hurriedly.

"Yes, it is I . . . I have come, Rodolphe, to ask your advice." And, despite all her efforts, it was impossible for her to open her lips.

"You have not changed; you're as charming as ever!"

"Oh," she replied bitterly, "they are poor charms since you disdained them."

Then he began a long justification of his conduct, excusing himself in vague terms, since he was unable to invent better.

She yielded to his words, still more to his voice and the sight of him, so that she pretended to believe, or perhaps believed, in the pretext he gave for their break; it was a secret on which depended the honor, the very life of a third person.

"Never mind," she said, looking at him sadly. "I have suffered much."

He replied philosophically:

"Life is that way!"

"Has life," Emma went on, "been kind to you at least since our separation?"

"Oh, neither good . . . nor bad."

"Perhaps it would have been better never to have parted."

"Yes, perhaps."

"You think so?" she said, drawing nearer.

Then, with a sigh:

"Oh, Rodolphe! if only you knew! . . . I loved you so!"

It was then that she took his hand, and they remained some time, their fingers intertwined, like that first day at the Agricultural Fair. With a gesture of pride he struggled against this emotion. But sinking upon his breast she told him:

"How did you think I could live without you? One cannot lose the habit of happiness. I was desperate, I thought I was going to die! I'll tell you about it . . . But you, you fled from me!"

With the natural cowardice that characterizes the stronger sex, he had carefully avoided her for the last three years; now Emma persisted, with coaxing little motions of the head, playful and feline:

"I know you love others, you may as well admit it. Oh! I don't blame them, I understand! You seduced them just as you seduced me. You're a man, a real man! you have all it takes to make yourself loved. But we'll start all over, won't we? We'll love each other as before! Look, I am laughing, I am happy! . . . Say something!"

She was irresistible, with a tear trembling in her eye, like a raindrop in a blue flower-cup, after the storm.

He had drawn her upon his knees, and with the back of his hand was caressing her smooth hair; a last ray of the sun was mirrored there, like a golden arrow. She lowered her head; at last he kissed her on the eyelids quite gently with the tips of his lips.

"Why, you have been crying! Why?"

She burst into tears. Rodolphe thought this was an outburst of her love. As she did not speak, he took this silence to be a last remnant of resistance, so he exclaimed:

"Oh, forgive me! You are the only one who really pleases me. I was a fool, a wicked fool! I love you, I'll always love you! What is the matter? Tell me . . ."

He knelt before her.

"Well, Rodolphe . . . I am ruined! You must lend me three thousand francs."

"But . . ." he said, as he slowly rose to his feet, "but . . ." His face assumed a grave expression.

"You know," she went on quickly, "that my husband had entrusted his money to a notary to invest, and he absconded. So we borrowed; the patients don't pay us. Moreover, the estate isn't settled yet; we shall have the money later on. But to-day, for want of three thousand francs, we are to be sold out, right now, this very minute. Counting on your friendship, I have come to you for help."

"Ah!" thought Rodolphe, turning very pale, "so that's what she came for."

At last he said, very calmly:

"My dear lady, I haven't got them."

He did not lie. If he had had it, he would probably have given the money, although it is generally unpleasant to do such fine things: a demand for money being, of all the winds that blow upon love, the coldest and most destructive.

She stared at him in silence for minutes.

"You haven't got them!"

She repeated several times:

"You haven't got them! . . . I ought to have spared myself this last shame. You never loved me. You are no better than the others."

She was losing her head, giving herself away.

Rodolphe interrupted her, declaring he was himself "hard up."

"Oh! I feel sorry for you!" said Emma, "exceedingly sorry!"

And fixing her eyes upon an embossed rifle that shone against its panoply:

"But when one is so poor one doesn't have silver on the butt of one's gun. One doesn't buy a clock inlaid with tortoiseshell," she went on, pointing to the Boulle clock, "nor silver-gilt whistles for one's whips," and she touched them, "nor charms for one's watch. Oh, he has all he needs! even a liqueur-stand in his bedroom; for you pamper yourself, you live well. You have a château, farms, woods; you go hunting; you travel to Paris. Why, if it were but that," she cried, taking up two cuff-links from the mantlepiece, "even for the least of these trifles, one could get money . . . Oh, I don't want anything from you; you can keep them!"

And she flung the links away with such force that their gold chain broke as it struck against the wall.

"But I! I would have given you everything. I would have sold all, worked for you with my hands, I would have begged on the high-

roads for a smile, for a look, to hear you say 'Thank you!' And you
sit there quietly in your arm-chair, as if you had not made me suffer
enough already! But for you, and you know it, I might have lived
happily. What made you do it? Was it a bet? Yet you loved
me . . . you said so. And but a moment ago . . . Ah! it would
have been better to have driven me away. My hands are hot with
your kisses, and there is the spot on the carpet where at my knees
you swore an eternity of love! You made me believe you; for two
years you held me in the most magnificent, the sweetest dream!
. . . Our plans for the journey, do you remember? Oh, your letter!
your letter! it tore my heart! And then when I come back to him—
to him, rich, happy, free—to implore the help the first stranger
would give, a suppliant, and bringing back to him all my tenderness,
he repulses me because it could cost him three thousand francs!"

"I haven't got them," replied Rodolphe, with that perfect calm
with which resigned rage covers itself as with a shield.

She went out. The walls trembled, the ceiling was crushing her,
and she passed back through the long alley, stumbling against the
heaps of dead leaves scattered by the wind. At last she reached the
low hedge in front of the gate; she broke her nails against the lock
in her haste to open it. Then a hundred paces beyond, breathless,
almost falling, she stopped. And now turning round, she once more
saw the impassive château, with the park, the gardens, the three
courts, and all the windows of the façade.

She remained lost in stupor, and only conscious of herself
through the beating of her arteries, that seemed to burst forth like a
deafening music filling all the fields. The earth beneath her feet was
more yielding than the sea, and the furrows seemed to her immense
brown waves breaking into foam. All the memories and ideas that
crowded her head seemed to explode at once like a thousand pieces
of fireworks. She saw her father, Lheureux's closet, their room at
home, another landscape. Madness was coming upon her; she grew
afraid, and managed to recover herself, in a confused way, it is true,
for she did not remember the cause of her dreadful confusion,
namely the money. She suffered only in her love, and felt her soul
escaping from her in this memory, as wounded men, dying, feel
their life ebb from their bleeding wounds.

Night was falling, crows were flying about.

Suddenly it seemed to her that fiery spheres were exploding in the
air like bullets when they strike, and were whirling, whirling, to
melt at last upon the snow between the branches of the trees. In the
midst of each of them appeared the face of Rodolphe. They multiplied and drew near, they penetrated her. It all disappeared; she
recognised the lights of the houses that shone through the fog.

Now her plight, like an abyss, loomed before her. She was panting as if her heart would burst. Then in an ecstasy of heroism, that made her almost joyous, she ran down the hill, crossed the cowplank, the footpath, the alley, the market, and reached the pharmacy. She was about to enter, but at the sound of the bell some one might come, and slipping in by the gate, holding her breath, feeling her way along the walls, she went as far as the door of the kitchen, where a candle was burning on the stove. Justin in his shirt-sleeves was carrying out a dish.

"Ah! they're eating; let's wait."

He returned; she tapped at the window. He came out.

"The key! the one for upstairs where he keeps the . . ."

"What?"

And he looked at her, astonished at the pallor of her face, that stood out white against the black background of the night. She seemed to him extraordinarily beautiful and majestic as a phantom. Without understanding what she wanted, he had the presentiment of something terrible.

But she went on quickly in a low voice that was sweet and melting:

"I want it; give it to me."

As the partition wall was thin, they could hear the clatter of the forks on the plates in the dining-room.

She pretended that she wanted to kill the rats that kept her from sleeping.

"I must go ask Monsieur."

"No, stay!"

Then with a casual air:

"Oh, it's not worth bothering him about, I'll tell him myself later. Come, hold the light for me."

She entered the corridor into which the laboratory door opened. Against the wall was a key labelled *Capharnaüm*.

"Justin!" called the pharmacist, growing impatient.

"Let's go up."

And he followed her. The key turned in the lock, and she went straight to the third shelf, so well did her memory guide her, seized the blue jar, tore out the cork, plunged in her hand, and withdrawing it full of white powder, she ate it greedily.

"Stop!" he cried, throwing himself upon her.

"Quiet! They might hear us . . ."

He was in despair, ready to call out.

"Say nothing, or all the blame will fall on your master."

Then she went home, suddenly calmed, with something of the serenity of one that has done his duty.

When Charles, thunderstruck at the news of the execution, rushed home, Emma had just gone out. He cried aloud, wept, fainted, but she did not return. Where could she be? He sent Félicité to Homais, to Monsieur Tuvache, to Lheureux, to the "Lion d'Or," everywhere, and in between the waves of his anxiety he saw his reputation destroyed, their fortune lost, Berthe's future ruined. By what?—Not a word! He waited till six in the evening. At last, unable to bear it any longer, and fancying she had gone to Rouen, he set out along the highroad, walked a mile, met no one, again waited, and returned home.

She had come back.

"What happened? . . . Why did you? . . . Tell me . . ."

She sat down at her writing-table and wrote a letter, which she sealed slowly, adding the date and the hour.

Then she said in a solemn tone:

"You are to read it to-morrow; till then, I beg you, don't ask me a single question. No, not one!"

"But . . ."

"Oh, leave me!"

She lay down full length on her bed.

A bitter taste in her mouth awakened her. She saw Charles, and again closed her eyes.

She was studying herself curiously, to detect the first signs of suffering. But no! nothing as yet. She heard the ticking of the clock, the crackling of the fire, and Charles breathing as he stood upright by her bed.

"Ah! it is but a little thing, death!" she thought. "I shall fall asleep and all will be over."

She drank a mouthful of water and turned her face to the wall. The frightful taste of ink persisted.

"I am thirsty; oh! so thirsty," she sighed.

"What is the matter?" said Charles, who was handing her a glass.

"It's nothing . . . Open the window, I'm choking."

She was seized with a sickness so sudden that she had hardly time to draw out her handkerchief from under the pillow.

"Take it away," she said quickly; "throw it away."

He spoke to her; she did not answer. She lay motionless, afraid that the slightest movement might make her vomit. But she felt an icy cold creeping from her feet to her heart.

"Ah! It's beginning," she murmured.

"What did you say?"

She gently rocked her head to and fro in anguish, opening her jaws as if something very heavy were weighing upon her tongue. At eight o'clock the vomiting began again.

Charles noticed that at the bottom of the basin there was a trace of white sediment sticking to the sides of the porcelain.

"This is extraordinary, very strange!" he repeated.

"No!" she loudly replied, "you are mistaken."

Then gently, almost caressingly, he passed his hand over her stomach. She uttered a sharp cry. He recoiled in terror.

Then she began to moan, faintly at first. Her shoulders were shaken by a strong shudder, and she was growing paler than the sheets in which she buried her clenched fists. Her unequal pulse was now almost imperceptible.

Drops of sweat oozed from her face, that had turned blue and rigid as under the effect of a metallic vapor. Her teeth chattered, her dilated eyes looked vaguely about her, and to all questions she replied only with a shake of the head; she even smiled once or twice. Gradually, her moaning grew louder; she couldn't repress a muffled scream; she pretended she felt better and that she'd soon get up. But she was seized with convulsions and cried out:

"God! It's horrible!"

He threw himself on his knees by her bed.

"Tell me! what have you eaten? Answer, for heaven's sake!"

And he looked at her with a tenderness in his eyes such as she had never seen.

"Well, there . . . there . . ." she said in a faltering voice.

He flew to the writing-table, tore open the seal, and read aloud: "Let no one be blamed . . ." He stopped, passed his hands over his eyes, and read it over again.

"What! . . . Help! Help!"

He could only keep repeating the word: "Poisoned! poisoned!" Félicité ran to Homais, who proclaimed it in the market-place; Madame Lefrançois heard it at the "Lion d'Or;" some got up to go and tell their neighbors, and all night the village was on the alert.

Distracted, stammering, reeling, Charles wandered about the room. He knocked against the furniture, tore his hair, and the pharmacist had never believed that there could be so terrible a sight.

He went home to write to Monsieur Canivet and to Doctor Larivière. His mind kept wandering, he had to start over fifteen times. Hippolyte went to Neufchâtel, and Justin so spurred Bovary's horse that he left it foundered and three parts dead by the hill at Bois-Guillaume.

Charles tried to look up his medical dictionary, but could not read it; the lines were jumping before his eyes.

"Be calm," said the pharmacist; "we must administer a powerful antidote. What is the poison?"

Charles showed him the letter. It was arsenic.

"Very well," said Homais, "we must make an analysis."

For he knew that in cases of poisoning an analysis must be made; and the other, who did not understand, answered:

"Oh, do it! Do anything! Save her . . ."

Then going back to her, he sank upon the carpet, and lay there with his head leaning against the edge of her bed, sobbing.

"Don't cry," she said to him. "Soon I won't trouble you any longer."

"Why did you do it? Who made you?"

She replied:

"There was no other way!"

"Weren't you happy? Is it my fault? But I did the best I could!"

"Yes, that's true . . . you're good, not like the others."

And she slowly passed her hand over his hair. The sweetness of this sensation deepened his sadness; he felt his whole being dissolving in despair at the thought that he must lose her, just when she was confessing more love for him than she ever did. He didn't know what to do, felt paralyzed by fear; the need for an immediate decision took away his last bit of self-control.

Emma thought that, at last, she was through with lying, cheating and with the numberless desires that had tortured her. She hated no one now; a twilight dimness was settling upon her thoughts, and, of all earthly noises, Emma heard none but the intermittent lamentations of this poor heart, sweet and remote like the echo of a symphony dying away.

"Bring me the child," she said, raising herself on her elbow.

"You're not feeling worse, are you?" asked Charles.

"No, no!"

The child, serious, and still half-asleep, was carried in on the maid's arm in her long white nightgown, from which her bare feet peeped out. She looked wonderingly at the disordered room, and half-closed her eyes, dazzled by the burning candles on the table. They reminded her, no doubt, of the morning of New Year's day and Mid-Lent, when thus awakened early by candlelight she came to her mother's bed to fetch her presents.

"But where is it, mamma?" she asked.

And as everybody was silent, "But I can't see my little stocking."

Félicité held her over the bed while she still kept looking towards the mantelpiece.

"Did nurse take it away?" she asked.

At the mention of this name, that carried her back to the memory of her adulteries and her calamities, Madame Bovary turned away her head, as at the loathing of another bitterer poison that rose to her mouth. But Berthe remained perched on the bed.

"Oh, how big your eyes are, mamma! How pale you are! how you sweat!"

Her mother looked at her.

"I'm frightened!" cried the child, recoiling.

Emma took her hand to kiss it; the child struggled.

"Enough! Take her away!" cried Charles, who was sobbing at the foot of the bed.

Then the symptoms ceased for a moment; she seemed less agitated; and at every insignificant word she spoke, every time she drew breath a little easier, his hopes revived. At last, when Canivet came in, he threw himself into his arms.

"Ah; it's you. Thank you! How good of you to come. But she's better. See! look at her."

His colleague was by no means of this opinion, and "never beating about the bush"—as he put it—he prescribed an emetic in order to empty the stomach completely.

She soon began vomiting blood. Her lips became drawn. Her limbs were convulsed, her whole body covered with brown spots, and her pulse slipped beneath the fingers like a stretched thread, like a harp-string about to break.

After this she began to scream horribly. She cursed the poison, railed at it, and implored it to be quick, and thrust away with her stiffened arms everything that Charles, in more agony than herself, tried to make her drink. He stood up, his handkerchief to his lips, moaning, weeping, and choked by sobs that shook his whole body. Félicité was running up and down the room. Homais, motionless, uttered great sighs; and Monsieur Canivet, always retaining his self-command, nevertheless began to feel uneasy.

"The devil! yet she has been purged, and since the cause has been removed . . ."

"The effect must cease," said Homais, "that's obvious."

"Oh, save her!" cried Bovary.

And, without listening to the pharmacist, who was still venturing the hypothesis, "It is perhaps a salutary paroxysm," Canivet was about to administer theriaca, when they heard the cracking of a whip; all the windows rattled, and a postchaise drawn by three horses abreast, up to their ears in mud, drove at a gallop round the corner of market. It was Doctor Larivière.

The apparition of a god would not have caused more commotion. Bovary raised his hands; Canivet stopped short; and Homais pulled off his cap long before the doctor had come in.

He belonged to that great school of surgeons created by Bichat,[68] to that generation, now extinct, of philosophical practitioners, who, cherishing their art with a fanatical love, exercised it with enthusiasm and wisdom. Every one in his hospital trembled when he was angry; and his students so revered him that they tried, as soon

68. Marie-Françoise-Xavier Bichat (1771–1802) was the author of an *Anat-* *omie générale.*

as they were themselves in practice, to imitate him as much as possible. They could be found in all the neighboring towns wearing exactly the same merino overcoat and black frock. The doctor's buttoned cuffs slightly covered his fleshy hands—very beautiful hands, never covered by gloves, as though to be more ready to plunge into suffering. Disdainful of honors, of titles, and of academies, hospitable, generous, fatherly to the poor, and practising virtue without believing in it, he would almost have passed for a saint if the keenness of his intellect had not caused him to be feared as a demon. His glance, more penetrating than his scalpels, looked straight into your soul, and would detect any lie, regardless how well hidden. He went through life with the benign dignity that goes with the assurance of talent and wealth, with forty years of a hard-working, blameless life.

He frowned as soon as he had passed the door when he saw the cadaverous face of Emma stretched out on her back with her mouth open. Then, while apparently listening to Canivet, he rubbed his fingers up and down beneath his nostrils, repeating:

"I see, yes, yes . . ."

But he slowly shrugged his shoulders. Bovary watched him; they looked at one another; and this man, accustomed as he was to the sight of pain, could not keep back a tear that fell on his shirt front.

He tried to take Canivet into the next room. Charles followed him.

"She is sinking, isn't she? If we put on poultices? Anything! Oh, think of something, you who have saved so many!"

Charles put both arms around him, and looked at him in anxious supplication, half-fainting against his breast.

"Come, my poor boy, courage! There is nothing more to be done."

And Doctor Larivière turned away.

"You are leaving?"

"I'll be back."

He went out as if to give an order to the coachman, followed by Canivet, who was equally glad to escape from the spectacle of Emma dying.

The pharmacist caught up with them on the Square. He could not by temperament keep away from celebrities, so he begged Monsieur Larivière to do him the signal honor of staying for lunch.

He sent quickly to the "Lion d'Or" for some pigeons; to the butcher's for all the cutlets that could be found; to Tuvache for cream; and to Lestiboudois for eggs; and Homais himself aided in the preparations, while Madame Homais was saying as she tightened her apron-strings:

"I hope you'll forgive us, sir, for in this village, if one is caught unawares . . ."

"Stemmed glasses!" whispered Homais.

"If only we were in the city, I'd be able to find stuffed pig's feet . . ."

"Be quiet . . . Please doctor, à table!"

He thought fit, after the first few mouthfuls, to supply some details about the catastrophe.

"We first had a feeling of siccity in the pharynx, then intolerable pains at the epigastrium, super-purgation, coma."

"But how did she poison herself?"

"I don't know, doctor, and I don't even know where she can have procured the arsenious acid."

Justin, who was just bringing in a pile of plates, began to tremble.

"What's the matter?" said the pharmacist.

At this question the young man dropped the whole lot on the floor with a dreadful crash.

"Imbecile!" cried Homais, "clumsy lout! blockhead! confounded ass!"

But suddenly controlling himself:

"I wished, doctor, to make an analysis, and *primo* I delicately introduced a tube . . ."

"You would have done better," said the physician, "to introduce your fingers into her throat."

His colleague was silent, having just before privately received a severe lecture about his emetic, so that this good Canivet, so arrogant and so verbose at the time of the club-foot, was to-day very modest. He smiled an incessantly approving smile.

Homais dilated in Amphitryonic pride,[69] and the affecting thought of Bovary vaguely contributed to his pleasure by a kind of selfish comparison with his own lot. Moreover, the presence of the surgeon exalted him. He displayed his erudition, spoke effusively about cantharides, upas, the manchineel, adder bites.

"I have even read that various persons have found themselves under toxicological symptoms, and, as it were, paralyzed by blood sausage that had been too strongly smoked. At least, this was stated in a very fine paper prepared by one of our pharmaceutical authorities, one of our masters, the illustrious Cadet de Gassicourt!"[70]

Madame Homais reappeared, carrying one of those shaky machines that are heated with spirits of wine; for Homais liked to make his coffee at the table, having, moreover, torrefied it, pulverised it, and mixed it himself.

---

69. Amphitryonic pride, a host's pride. *Amphitryon* is a comedy by Molière (1668). The verse:
Le véritable Amphitryon
Est l'Amphitryon où l'on dîne
has become a proverb. It means a man who brings companions to his table, a rich and powerful man whom we flatter.

70. Cadet de Gassicourt (1769–1821) was the pharmacist of Emperor Napoleon I who had considerable trouble under the Restoration because of his liberal ideas.

"*Saccharum*, doctor?" he said, offering sugar.

Then he had all his children brought down, anxious to have the physician's opinion on their constitutions.

At last Monsieur Larivière was about to leave, when Madame Homais asked for a consultation about her husband. He was making his blood too thick by falling asleep every evening after dinner.

"Oh, it isn't his blood I'd call too thick," said the physician.

And, smiling a little at his unnoticed joke, the doctor opened the door. But the shop was full of people; he had the greatest difficulty in getting rid of Monsieur Tuvache, who feared his wife would get pneumonia because she was in the habit of spitting on the ashes; then of Monseiur Binet, who sometimes experienced sudden attacks of great hunger; and of Madame Caron, who suffered from prickling sensations; of Lheureux, who had dizzy spells; of Lestiboudois, who had rheumatism; and of Madame Lefrançois, who had heartburn. At last the three horses started; and it was the general opinion that he had not shown himself at all obliging.

Public attention was distracted by the appearance of Monsieur Bournisien, who was going across the square carrying the holy oil.

Homais, as was due to his principles, compared priests to ravens attracted by the smell of death. The sight of an ecclesiastic was personally disagreeable to him, for the cassock made him think of the shroud, and his dislike of the one matched his fear of the other.

Nevertheless, not shrinking from what he called his "Mission," he returned to Bovary's house with Canivet, who had been strongly urged by Dr. Larivière to make this call; and he would, but for his wife's objections, have taken his two sons with him, in order to accustom them to great occasions; that this might be a lesson, an example, a solemn picture, that should remain in their heads later on.

The room when they went in was full of mournful solemnity. On the work-table, covered over with a white cloth, there were five or six small balls of cotton in a silver dish, near a large crucifix between two lighted candles.

Emma, her chin sunken upon her breast, had her eyes inordinately wide open, and her poor hands wandered over the sheets with that hideous and gentle movement of the dying, that seems as if they already wanted to cover themselves with the shroud. Pale as a statue and with eyes red as fire, Charles, beyond weeping, stood opposite her at the foot of the bed, while the priest, bending one knee, was muttering in a low voice.

She turned her face slowly, and seemed filled with joy on suddenly seeing the violet stole. She was doubtlessly reminded, in this moment of sudden serenity, of the lost bliss of her first mystical flights, mingling with the visions of eternal beatitude that were beginning.

The priest rose to take the crucifix; then she stretched forward her neck like one suffering from thirst, and glueing her lips to the body of the Man-God, she pressed upon it with all her expiring strength the fullest kiss of love that she had ever given. Then he recited the *Misereatur* and the *Indulgentiam*, dipped his right thumb in the oil, and began to give extreme unction. First, upon the eyes, that had so coveted all wordly goods; then upon the nostrils, that had been so greedy of the warm breeze and the scents of love; then upon the mouth, that had spoken lies, moaned in pride and cried out in lust; then upon the hands that had taken delight in the texture of sensuality; and finally upon the soles of the feet, so swift when she had hastened to satisfy her desires, and that would now walk no more.

The curé wiped his fingers, threw the bit of oil-stained cotton into the fire, and came and sat down by the dying woman, to tell her that she must now blend her sufferings with those of Jesus Christ and abandon herself to the divine mercy.

Finishing his exhortations, he tried to place in her hand a blessed candle, symbol of the celestial glory with which she was soon to be surrounded. Emma, too weak, could not close her fingers, and if it hadn't been for Monsieur Bournisien, the taper would have fallen to the ground.

Yet she was no longer quite so pale, and her face had an expression of serenity as if the sacrament had cured her.

The priest did not fail to point this out; he even explained to Bovary that the Lord sometimes prolonged the life of persons when he thought it useful for their salvation; and Charles remembered the day when, so near death, she had received communion. Perhaps there was no need to despair, he thought.

In fact, she looked around her slowly, as one awakening from a dream; then in a distinct voice she asked for her mirror, and remained bent over it for some time, until big tears fell from her eyes. Then she turned away her head with a sigh and fell back upon the pillows.

Her chest soon began heaving rapidly; the whole of her tongue protruded from her mouth; her eyes, as they rolled, grew paler, like the two globes of a lamp that is going out, so that one might have thought her already dead but for the fearful labouring of her ribs, shaken by violent breathing, as if the soul were struggling to free itself. Félicité knelt down before the crucifix, and the pharmacist himself slightly bent his knees, while Monsieur Canivet looked out vaguely at the Square. Bournisien had resumed his praying, his face bowed against the edge of the bed, his long black cassock trailing behind him in the room. Charles was on the other side, on his knees, his arms outstretched towards Emma. He had taken her hands and pressed them, shuddering at every heartbeat, as at the tremors of a falling ruin. As the death-rattle became stronger the priest prayed faster; his prayers mingled with Bovary's stifled sobs, and sometimes all seemed lost in the muffled murmur of the Latin syllables that sounded like a tolling bell.

Suddenly from the pavement outside came the loud noise of wooden shoes and the clattering of a stick; and a voice rose—a raucous voice—that sang

> Often the heat of a summer's day
> Makes a young girl dream her heart away.

Emma raised herself like a galvanised corpse, her hair streaming, her eyes fixed, staring.

> To gather up all the new-cut stalks
> Of wheat left by the scythe's cold swing,
> Nanette bends over as she walks
> Toward the furrows from where they spring.

"The blind man!" she cried.

And Emma began to laugh, an atrocious, frantic, desperate laugh, thinking she saw the hideous face of the poor wretch loom out of the eternal darkness like a menace.

> The wind blew very hard that day
> It blew her petticoat away.

A final spasm threw her back upon the mattress. They all drew near. She had ceased to exist.

IX

Someone's death always causes a kind of stupefaction; so difficult it is to grasp this advent of nothingness and to resign ourselves to the fact that it has actually taken place. But still, when he saw that she did not move, Charles flung himself upon her, crying:

"Farewell! farewell!"

Homais and Canivet dragged him from the room.

"Control yourself!"

"Yes," he said, struggling, "I'll be quiet. I won't do anything. But let me stay. I want to see her. She is my wife!"

And he wept.

"Cry," said the pharmacist; "let nature take its course; that will relieve you."

Weaker than a child, Charles let himself be led downstairs into the sitting-room, and Monsieur Homais soon went home. On the Square he was accosted by the blind man, who, having dragged himself as far as Yonville in the hope of getting the antiphlogistic salve, was asking every passer-by where the pharmacist lived.

"Good heavens, man, as if I didn't have other fish to fry! I can't help it, but you'll have to come back later."

And he hurried into the shop.

He had to write two letters, to prepare a soothing potion for Bovary, to invent some lie that would conceal the poisoning, and work it up into an article for the "Fanal," without counting the people who were waiting to get the news from him; and when the Yonvillers had all heard his story of the arsenic that she had mistaken for sugar in making a vanilla cream, Homais once more returned to Bovary's.

He found him alone (Monsieur Canivet had left), sitting in an arm-chair near the window, staring with a vacant look at the stone floor.

"Well," Homais said, "you ought yourself to fix the hour for the ceremony."

"Why? What ceremony?"

Then, in a stammering, frightened voice:

"Oh, no! not that. No! I want to keep her here."

Homais, to save face, took up a pitcher from the whatnot to water the geraniums.

"Ah! thank you," said Charles; "how kind of you!"

But he did not finish, choked by the flow of memories that Homais' action had released in him.

Then to distract him, Homais thought fit to talk a little about horticulture: plants wanted moisture. Charles bowed his head in approval.

"Besides, we'll soon be having fine weather again."

"Ah!" said Bovary.

The pharmacist, at his wit's end, gently drew aside the small window-curtain.

"Look! there's Monsieur Tuvache passing by."

Charles repeated mechanically:

"Monsieur Tuvache passing by!"

Homais did not dare to bring up the funeral arrangements again; it was the priest who finally convinced him of the necessity to bury Emma.

He shut himself up in his consulting-room, took a pen, and after sobbing for some time, wrote:

"I wish her to be buried in her wedding dress, with white shoes, and a wreath. Her hair is to be spread out over her shoulders. Three coffins, one oak, one mahogany, one of lead. Let no one try to overrule me; I shall have the strength to resist him. She is to be covered with a large piece of green velvet. This is my wish; see that it is done."

The two men were much taken aback by Bovary's romantic ideas. The pharmacist was first to remonstrate with him:

"This velvet seems excessive to me. Besides, think of the expense . . ."

"What's that to you?" cried Charles. "Leave me alone! You didn't love her. Go away!"

The priest took him by the arm for a walk in the garden. He discoursed on the vanity of earthly things. God was very great, very good: one must submit to his decrees without a murmur, even learn to be grateful for one's suffering.

Charles burst into blasphemy:

"I hate your God!"

"The spirit of rebellion is still upon you," sighed the priest.

Bovary was far away. He was striding along by the wall, near the espalier, and he ground his teeth; he raised to heaven looks of malediction, but not so much as a leaf stirred.

A fine rain was falling: Charles, whose chest was bare, at last began to shiver; he went in and sat down in the kitchen.

At six o'clock a noise like a clatter of old iron was heard on the square; it was the "Hirondelle" coming in, and he remained with his forehead pressed against the window-pane, watching all the passengers get out, one after the other. Félicité put down a mattress for him in the drawing-room. He threw himself upon it and fell asleep.

Although a philosopher, Monsieur Homais respected the dead. So bearing poor Charles no grudge, he returned in the evening to sit up with the body, bringing with him three books and a writing-pad for taking notes.

Monsieur Bournisien was there, and two large candles were burning at the head of the bed, which had been taken out of the alcove.

The pharmacist, unable to keep silent, soon began to express some regrets about this "unfortunate young woman," and the priest replied that there was nothing to do now but pray for her.

"Still," Homais insisted, "it is one of two things; either she died in a state of grace (as the Church calls it), and then she doesn't need our prayers; or else she died unrepentant (that is, I believe, the correct technical term), and then . . ."

Bournisien interrupted him, replying testily that it was none the less necessary to pray.

"But," the pharmacist objected, "since God knows all our needs, what can be the good of prayer?"

"What!" the priest exclaimed, "of prayer? Why, aren't you a Christian?"

"I beg your pardon," said Homais; "I admire Christianity. It freed the slaves, brought morality into the world . . ."

"That isn't the point. Look at the texts . . ."

"Oh! oh! As to texts, look at history; everybody knows that the Jesuits have falsified all the texts!"

Charles came in, and advancing towards the bed, slowly drew the curtains.

Emma's head was turned towards her right shoulder, the corner of her mouth, which was open, seemed like a black hole at the lower part of her face; her two thumbs were bent into the palms of her hands; a kind of white dust besprinkled her lashes, and her eyes were beginning to disappear in a viscous pallor, as if covered by a spiderweb. The sheet sunk in from her breast to her knees, and then rose at the tips of her toes, and it seemed to Charles that infinite masses, an enormous load, were weighing upon her.

The church clock struck two. They could hear the loud murmur of the river flowing in the darkness at the foot of the terrace. Monsieur Bournisien noisily blew his nose from time to time, and Homais' pen was scratching over the paper.

"Come, my good friend," he said, "don't stay here; the sight is too much for you."

When Charles had left, the pharmacist and the priest resumed their argument.

"Read Voltaire," said the one, "read D'Holbach, read the *Encyclopédie!*"[71]

"Read the 'Letters of some Portuguese Jews,' "[72] said the other; "read 'The Meaning of Christianity,'[73] by the former magistrate Nicolas."

They grew warm, they grew red, they both talked at once without listening to each other. Bournisien was scandalised at such audacity; Homais marvelled at such stupidity; and they were about to come to blows when Charles suddenly reappeared. He couldn't resist coming upstairs as though he were spellbound.

He stood at the foot of the bed to see her better, and he lost himself in a contemplation so deep that it was no longer painful.

He recalled stories of catalepsy, the marvels of magnetism, and he said to himself that by willing it with all his force he might perhaps succeed in reviving her. Once he even bent towards her, and cried in a low voice, "Emma! Emma!" His strong breathing made the flames of the candles tremble against the wall.

At daybreak the elder Madame Bovary arrived. As he embraced her, Charles burst into another flood of tears. She tried, as the pharmacist had done, to remonstrate with him on the expenses for the funeral. He became so angry that she was silent, and he even

---

71. Paul-Henri Dietrich, baron d' Holbach (1723–1789), friend and disciple of **Diderot, was one of the most outspoken opponents of religion in the French Enlightenment. The *Encyclopédie*, a dictionary of the sciences, arts and letters, edited by Diderot and d'Alembert** (1751–1772) is the intellectual monument of the French Enlightenment, a fountainhead of later secular and agnostic thought.

72. *Letters of Some Portuguese Jews* (1769) refers to a book by the Abbé Antoine Guéné directed against Voltaire.

73. *The Meaning of Christianity* is one of the many books defending Roman Catholicism by Jean-Jacques-Auguste Nicolas (1807–1888).

commissioned her to go to town at once and buy what was necessary.

Charles remained alone the whole afternoon; they had taken Berthe to Madame Homais'; Félicité was in the room upstairs with Madame Lefrançois.

In the evening he had some visitors. He rose and shook hands with them, unable to speak. Then they sat down together, and formed a large semicircle in front of the fire. With lowered head, they crossed and uncrossed their legs, and uttered from time to time a deep sigh. They were bored to tears, yet none would be the first to go.

Homais, when he returned at nine o'clock (for the last two days Homais seemed to have made the public Square his residence), was laden with a supply of camphor, benzoin and aromatic herbs. He also carried a large jar full of chlorine water, to keep off the miasma. Just then the servant, Madame Lefrançois and the elder Madame Bovary were busy getting Emma dressed, and they were drawing down the long stiff veil that covered her to her satin shoes.

Félicité was sobbing:

"Oh, my poor mistress! my poor mistress!"

"Look at her," said the innkeeper, sighing; "how pretty she still is! Now, couldn't you swear she was going to get up in a minute?"

Then they bent over her to put on her wreath. They had to raise the head a little, and a rush of black liquid poured from her mouth, as if she were vomiting.

"Heavens! Watch out for her dress!" cried Madame Lefrançois. "Now, just come and help us," she said to the pharmacist, "or are you afraid?"

"Afraid?" he replied, "I? As if I hadn't seen a lot worse when I was a student at the Hotel-Dieu. We used to make punch in the dissecting room! Nothingness does not frighten a philosopher; I have often said that I intend to leave my body to the hospitals, to serve the cause of science."

On arriving, the curé inquired after Monsieur Bovary and, at Homais' reply, he said:

"Of course, the blow is still too recent."

Then Homais congratulated him on not being exposed, like other people, to the loss of a beloved companion; this lead to a discussion on the celibacy of priests.

"You must admit," said the pharmacist, "that it is against nature for a man to do without women. There have been crimes . . ."

"For Heaven's sake!" exclaimed the priest, "how do you expect an individual who is married to keep the secrets of the confessional, for example?"

Homais attacked confession. Bournisien defended it; he discoursed on the acts of restitution that it brought about. He cited various anecdotes about thieves who had suddenly become honest. Military men on approaching the tribunal of penitence had finally seen the light. At Fribourg there was a minister . . .

His companion had fallen asleep. Then he felt somewhat stifled by the over-heavy atmosphere of the room; he opened the window; this awoke the pharmacist.

"Come, take a pinch of snuff," he told him. "Take it, it'll do you good."

A continual barking was heard in the distance.

"Do you hear that dog howling?" said the pharmacist.

"They smell the dead," replied the priest. "It's like bees; they leave their hives when there is a death in the neighborhood."

Homais failed to object to these prejudices, for he had again dropped asleep. Monsieur Bournisien, stronger than he, went on moving his lips and muttering for some time, then insensibly his chin sank down, he dropped his big black book, and began to snore.

They sat opposite one another, with bulging stomachs, puffed-up faces, and frowning looks, after so much disagreement uniting at last in the same human weakness, and they moved no more than the corpse by their side, that also seemed to be sleeping.

Charles coming in did not wake them. It was the last time; he came to bid her farewell.

The aromatic herbs were still smoking, and spirals of bluish vapour blended at the window with the entering fog. There were few stars, and the night was warm.

The wax of the candles fell in great drops upon the sheets of the bed. Charles watched them burn, straining his eyes in the glare of their yellow flame.

The watered satin of her gown shimmered white as moonlight. Emma was lost beneath it; and it seemed to him that, spreading beyond her own self, she blended confusedly with everything around her—the silence, the night, the passing wind, the damp odors rising from the ground.

Then suddenly he saw her in the garden at Tostes, on a bench against the thorn hedge, or else at Rouen in the streets, on the threshold of their house, in the yard at Bertaux. He again heard the laughter of the happy boys dancing under the appletrees: the room was filled with the perfume of her hair; and her dress rustled in his arms with a crackling noise. It was the same dress she was wearing now!

For a long while he thus recalled all his lost joys, her attitudes, her movements, the sound of her voice. Wave upon wave of despair came over him, like the tides of an overflowing sea.

He was seized by a terrible curiosity. Slowly, with the tips of his fingers, his heart pounding, he lifted her veil. But he uttered a cry of horror that awoke the other two.

They dragged him down into the sitting-room. Then Félicité came up to say that he wanted some of her hair.

"Cut some off," replied the pharmacist.

And as she did not dare to, he himself stepped forward, scissors in hand. He trembled so that he nicked the skin of the temple in several places. At last, stiffening himself against emotion, Homais gave two or three great cuts at random that left white patches amongst that beautiful black hair.

The pharmacist and the curé resumed their original occupations, not without time and again falling asleep—something of which they accused each other whenever they awoke. Monsieur Bournisien sprinkled the room with holy water and Homais threw a little chlorine on the floor.

Félicité had been so considerate as to put on the chest of drawers, for each of them, a bottle of brandy, some cheese, and a large brioche, and about four o'clock in the morning, unable to restrain himself any longer, the pharmacist sighed:

"I must say that I wouldn't mind taking some sustenance."

The priest did not need any persuading; he left to say mass and, upon his return, they ate and drank, chuckling a little without knowing why, stimulated by that vague gaiety that comes upon us after times of sadness. At the last glass the priest said to the pharmacist, as he clapped him on the shoulder:

"We'll end up good friends, you and I."

In the passage downstairs they met the undertaker's men, who were coming in. Then for two hours Charles had to suffer the torture of hearing the hammer resound against the wood. Next day they lowered her into her oak coffin, that was fitted into the other two; but as the bier was too large, they had to fill up the gaps with the wool of a mattress. At last, when the three lids had been planed down, nailed, soldered, it was placed outside in front of the door; the house was thrown open, and the people of Yonville began to flock round.

Old Rouault arrived, and fainted on the square at the sight of the black cloth.

X

He had only received Homais' letter thirty-six hours after the event; and, to cushion the blow, he had worded it in such a manner that it was impossible to make out just what had happened.

First, the old man had been shaken as if struck by apoplexy. Next, he understood that she was not dead, but she might be . . . At last, he had put on his smock, taken his hat, fastened his spurs to his boots, and set out at full speed; and the whole of the way old Rouault, panting, had been devoured by anxiety. He felt so dizzy that he was forced to dismount. He fancied he heard voices around him and thought he was losing his mind.

Day broke. He saw three black hens asleep in a tree. He shuddered, horrified at this omen. Then he promised the Holy Virgin three chasubles for the church, and vowed that he would go barefooted from the cemetery at Bertaux to the chapel of Vassonville.

He entered Maromme calling out ahead at the people of the inn, burst open the door with a thrust of his shoulder, made for a sack of oats and emptied a bottle of sweet cider into the manger; then he remounted his nag, whose feet struck sparks as it galloped along.

He told himself that they would certainly save her; the doctors were bound to discover a remedy. He remembered all the miraculous cures he had been told about.

Then she appeared to him dead: She was there, before his eyes, lying on her back in the middle of the road. He reined in his horse, and the hallucination disappeared.

At Quincampoix, to give himself heart, he drank three cups of coffee one after the other.

He imagined that they had written the wrong name on the letter. He looked for the letter in his pocket, felt it there, but did not dare to open it.

At last he began to think it was all a bad joke, a spiteful farce, somebody's idea of a fine prank; besides, if she were dead, he would have known. It couldn't be! the countryside looked as usual: the sky was blue, the trees swayed; a flock of sheep passed by. He reached the village; they saw him coming, hunched over his horse, whipping it savagely till its saddle-girths dripped with blood.

When he recovered consciousness, he fell, weeping, into Bovary's arms:

"My daughter! Emma! my child! tell me . . ."

The other replied between sobs:

"I don't know! I don't know! It's a curse!"

The pharmacist pulled them apart.

"Spare him the horrible details. I'll tell monsieur all about it. People are coming, show some dignity, for heaven's sake! Let's behave like philosophers."

Poor Charles tried as hard as he could, and repeated several times:

"Yes, be brave . . ."

"Damn it, I'll be brave," cried the old man, "I'll stay with her till the end!"

The bell was tolling. All was ready; they had to start.

Seated together in a stall of the choir, they saw the three chanting choristers continually pass and repass in front of them. The serpent-player was blowing with all his might. Monsieur Bournisien, in full regalia, was singing in a shrill voice. He bowed before the tabernacle, raising his hands, stretched out his arms. Lestiboudois went about the church with his verger's staff. The bier stood near the lectern, between four rows of candles. Charles felt an urge to get up and put them out.

Yet he tried to stir into himself the proper devotional feelings, to throw himself into the hope of a future life in which he would see her again. He tried to convince himself that she had gone on a long journey, far away, for a long time. But when he thought of her lying there, and that it was all over and that they would put her in the earth, he was seized with a fierce, gloomy, desperate rage. It seemed at times that he felt nothing, and he welcomed this lull in his pain, while blaming himself bitterly for being such a scoundrel.

The sharp noise of an iron-tipped stick was heard on the stones, striking them at irregular intervals. It came from the end of the church, and stopped short at the lower aisles. A man in a coarse brown jacket knelt down painfully. It was Hippolyte, the stable-boy at the "Lion d'Or." He had put on his new leg.

One of the choir boys came round the nave taking collection, and the coppers chinked one after the other on the silver plate.

"Oh hurry up!" cried Bovary, angrily throwing him a five-franc piece. "I can't stand it any longer."

The singer thanked him with a deep bow.

They sang, they knelt, they stood up; it was endless! He remembered how once, in the early days of their marriage, they had been to mass together, and they had sat down on the other side, on the right, by the wall. The bell began again. There was a great shuffling of chairs; the pall bearers slipped their three poles under the coffin, and every one left the church.

Then Justin appeared in the doorway of the pharmacy, but retreated suddenly, pale and staggering.

People stood at the windows to see the procession pass by. Charles walked first, as straight as he could. He tried to look brave and nodded to those who joined the crowd, coming from the side streets or from the open doors. The six men, three on either side, walked slowly, panting a little. The priests, the choristers, and the two choir-boys recited the *De profundis*, and their voices echoed over the fields, rising and falling with the shape of the hills. Sometimes they disappeared in the windings of the path; but the great silver cross always remained visible among the trees.

The women followed, wearing black coats with turned-down hoods; each of them carried a large lighted candle, and Charles felt himself grow faint at this continual repetition of prayers and torch-lights, oppressed by the sweetish smell of wax and of cassocks. A fresh breeze was blowing; the rye and colza were turning green and along the roadside, dewdrops hung from the hawthorn hedges. All sorts of joyous sounds filled the air; the jolting of a cart rolling way off in the ruts, the crowing of a cock, repeated again and again, or the gamboling of a foal under the apple-trees. The pure sky was dappled with rosy clouds; a blueish haze hung over the iris-covered cottages. Charles recognized each courtyard as he passed. He remembered mornings like this, when, after visiting a patient, he left one of those houses to return home, to his wife.

The black cloth decorated with silver tears, flapped from time to time in the wind, baring the coffin underneath. The tired bearers walked more slowly, and the bier advanced jerkily, like a boat that pitches with every wave.

They reached the cemetery.

The men went right down to a place in the grass where a grave had been dug. They grouped themselves all round; and while the priest spoke, the red soil thrown up at the sides kept noiselessly slipping down at the corners.

Then, when the four ropes were laid out, the coffin was pushed onto them. He watched it go down; it seemed to go down forever.

At last a thud was heard; the ropes creaked and were drawn up. Then Bournisien took the spade handed to him by Lestiboudois; while his right hand kept sprinkling holy water, he vigorously threw in a spadeful of earth with the left; and the wood of the coffin, struck by the pebbles, gave forth that dread sound that seems to us the reverberation of eternity.

The priest passed the holy water sprinkler to his neighbor, Monsieur Homais. The pharmacist swung it gravely, then handed it to Charles, who sank to his knees and threw in handfuls of earth, crying, "Adieu!" He sent her kisses; he dragged himself towards the grave, as if to engulf himself with her.

They led him away, and he soon grew calmer, feeling perhaps, like the others, a vague satisfaction that it was all over.

Old Rouault on his way back began quietly smoking a pipe, to Homais' silent disapproval. He also noticed that Monsieur Binet had not come, that Tuvache had disappeared after mass, and that Theodore, the notary's servant, wore a blue coat—"as if he couldn't respect customs, and wear a black coat, for Heaven's sake!" And to share his observations with others he went from group to group. They were deploring Emma's death, especially Lheureux, who had not failed to come to the funeral.

"Poor little lady! What a blow for her husband!"

"Can you imagine," the pharmacist replied, "that he would have done away with himself if I hadn't intervened?"

"Such a fine person! To think that I saw her only last Saturday in my store."

"I haven't had leisure," said Homais, "to prepare a few words that I would cast over her tomb."

On getting home, Charles undressed, and old Rouault put on his blue smock. It was new, and as he had repeatedly wiped his eyes on the sleeves during his journey, the dye had stained his face, and traces of tears lined the layer of dust that covered it.

Mother Bovary joined them. All three were silent. At last the old man sighed:

"Do you remember, my friend, I came to Tostes once when you had just lost your first deceased? I consoled you that time. I could think of something to say then, but now . . ."

Then, with a loud groan that shook his whole chest,

"Ah! this is the end for me! I saw my wife go . . . then my son . . . and now today my daughter!"

He wanted to go back at once to Bertaux, saying that he couldn't sleep in this house. He even refused to see his grand-daughter.

"No, no! It would grieve me too much. You'll kiss her many times for me. Good bye . . . You're a good man! And I'll never forget this," he said, slapping his thigh. "Never fear, you shall always have your turkey."

But when he reached the top of the hill he turned back, as he had turned once before on the road of Saint-Victor when he had parted from her. The windows of the village were all ablaze in the slanting rays of the sun that was setting behind the meadow. He put his hand over his eyes, and saw at the horizon a walled enclosure, with black clusters of trees among the white stones; then he went on his way at a gentle trot, for his nag was limping.

Despite their fatigue, Charles and his mother stayed up talking very long that evening. They spoke of the days of the past and of the future. She would come to live at Yonville; she would keep house for him; they would never part again. She was subtly affectionate, rejoicing in her heart at regaining some of the tenderness that had wandered from her for so many years. Midnight struck. The village was silent as usual, and Charles lay awake, never ceasing to think of her.

Rodolphe, who, to distract himself, had been roaming in the woods all day, was quietly asleep in his château; and Léon, away in the city, also slept.

There was another who at that hour was not asleep.

On the grave between the pine-trees a child was on his knees weeping, and his heart, rent by sobs, was panting in the dark under the weight of an immense sorrow, tender as the moon and unfathomable as the night.

The gate suddenly grated. It was Lestiboudois coming to fetch the spade he had forgotten. He recognised Justin climbing over the wall, and knew at last who had been stealing his potatoes.

XI

The next day Charles had the child brought back. She asked for her mamma. They told her she was away; that she would bring her back some toys. Berthe mentioned her again several times, then finally forgot her. The child's gaiety broke Bovary's heart, and he had to put up besides with the intolerable consolations of the pharmacist.

Before long, money troubles started again. Monsieur Lheureux was putting his friend Vinçart back on the warpath, and before long Charles was signing notes for exorbitant amounts. For he would never consent to let the smallest of the things that had belonged to *her* be sold. His mother was exasperated with him; he grew even more angry than she did. He was a changed man. She left the house.

Then every one began to collect what they could. Mademoiselle Lempereur presented a bill for six months' teaching, although Emma had never taken a lesson (despite the receipted bill she had shown Bovary); it was an arrangement between the two women. The lending library demanded three years' subscriptions; Mère Rollet claimed postage for some twenty letters, and when Charles asked for an explanation, she was tactful enough to reply:

"Oh, I know nothing about it. It was her business."

With every debt he paid Charles thought he had reached the end. But others followed ceaselessly.

He tried to collect accounts due him from patients. He was shown the letters his wife had written. Then he had to apologise.

Félicité now wore Madame Bovary's dresses; not all, for he had kept some, and he locked himself up in Emma's room to look at them. Félicité was about her former mistress's height and often, on seeing her from behind, Charles thought she had come back and cried out:

"Oh, stay, don't go away!"

But at Pentecost she ran away from Yonville, carried off by Theodore, stealing all that was left of the wardrobe.

It was about this time that the widow Dupuis had the honor to inform him of the "marriage of Monsieur Léon Dupuis her son, notary at Yvetot, to Mademoiselle Léocadié Lebœuf Bondeville." Charles, among the other congratulations he sent him, wrote this sentence:

"How happy this would have made my poor wife!"

One day when, wandering aimlessly about the house, he had gone up to the attic, he felt a crumpled piece of paper under his slipper. He opened it and read: "Courage, Emma, courage. I would not bring misery into your life." It was Rodolphe's letter, fallen to the ground between the boxes, where it had remained till now, when the wind from the open dormer had blown it toward the door. And Charles stood, motionless and staring, in the very same place where, long ago, Emma, in despair, and paler even than he had thought of dying. At last he discovered a small R at the bottom of the second page. What did this mean? He remembered Rodolphe's attentions, his sudden disappearance, his embarrassed air on two or three subsequent occasions. But the respectful tone of the letter deceived him.

"Perhaps they loved one another platonically," he told himself.

Besides, Charles was not of those who go to the root of things; he shrank from the proofs, and his vague jealousy was lost in the immensity of his sorrow.

Every one, he thought, must have adored her; all men inevitably must have coveted her. This made her seem even more beautiful, and it awoke in him a fierce and persistent desire, which inflamed his despair and grew boundless, since it could never be assuaged.

To please her, as if she were still living, he adopted her taste, her ideas; he bought patent leather boots and took to wearing white cravats. He waxed his moustache and, just like her, signed promissory notes. She corrupted him from beyond the grave.

He was obliged to sell his silver piece by piece; next he sold the drawing-room furniture. All the rooms were stripped; but the bedroom, her own room, remained as before. After his dinner Charles went up there. He pushed the round table in front of the fire, and drew up *her* arm-chair. He sat down facing it. A candle burnt in one of the gilt candlesticks. Berthe, at his side, colored pictures.

He suffered, poor man, at seeing her so badly dressed, with laceless boots, and the arm-holes of her pinafore torn down to the hips; for the cleaning woman took no care of her. But she was so sweet, so pretty, and her little head bent forward so gracefully, letting her fair hair fall over her rosy cheeks, that an infinite joy came upon him, a happiness mingled with bitterness, like those ill-made wines that taste of resin. He mended her toys, made her puppets from cardboard, or sewed up half-torn dolls. Then, if his eyes fell upon the sewing kit, a ribbon lying about, or even a pin left in a crack of the table, he began to dream, and looked so sad that she became as sad as he.

No one now came to see them, for Justin had run away to Rouen, where he worked in a grocery, and the pharmacist's children saw less and less of the child. In view of the difference in their social positions, Monsieur Homais had chosen to discontinue the former intimacy.

The blind man, whom his salve had not cured, had gone back to the hill of Bois-Guillaume, where he told the travellers of his failure, to such an extent, that Homais when he went to town hid himself behind the curtains of the "Hirondelle" to avoid meeting him. He detested him, and wishing, in the interests of his own reputation, to get rid of him at all costs, he directed against him a secret campaign, that betrayed the depth of his intellect and the baseness of his vanity. Thus, for six consecutive months, one could read in the "Fanal de Rouen" editorials such as these:

"Anyone who has ever wended his way towards the fertile plains of Picardy has, no doubt, remarked, by the Bois-Guillaume hill, an unfortunate wretch suffering from a horrible facial wound. He bothers the passers by, pursues them and levies a regular tax on all travellers. Are we still living in the monstrous times of the Middle Ages, when vagabonds were permitted to display in our public places leprosy and scrofulas they had brought back from the Crusades?"

Or:

"In spite of the laws against vagrancy, the approaches to our great towns continue to be infected by bands of beggars. Some are seen going about alone, and these are, by no means, the least dangerous. Why don't our City Authorities intervene?"

Then Homais invented incidents:

"Yesterday, by the Bois-Guillaume hill, a skittish horse . . ." And then followed the story of an accident caused by the presence of the blind man.

He managed so well that the fellow was locked up. But he was released. He began again, and so did Homais. It was a struggle. Homais won out, for his foe was condemned to lifelong confinement in an asylum.

This success emboldened him, and henceforth there was no longer a dog run over, a barn burnt down, a woman beaten in the parish, of which he did not immediately inform the public, guided always by the love of progress and the hatred of priests. He instituted comparisons between the public and parochial schools to the detriment of the latter; called to mind the massacre of St. Bartholomew *à propos* of a grant of one hundred francs to the church; denounced abuses and kept people on their toes. That was his phrase. Homais was digging and delving; he was becoming dangerous.

However, he was stifling in the narrow limits of journalism, and soon a book, a major work, became a necessity. Then he composed "General Statistics of the Canton of Yonville, followed by Climatological Remarks." The statistics drove him to philosophy. He busied himself with great questions: the social problem, the moral plight of the poorer classes, pisciculture, rubber, railways, &c. He even began to blush at being a bourgeois. He affected bohemian manners, he smoked. He bought two *chic* Pompadour statuettes to adorn his drawing-room.

He by no means gave up his store. On the contrary, he kept well abreast of new discoveries. He followed the great trend towards chocolates; he was the first to introduce *Cho-ca* and *Revalenta* into the Seine-Inférieure. He was enthusiastic about the hydro-electric Pulvermacher health-belts; he wore one himself, and when at night he took off his flannel undershirt, Madame Homais was dazzled by the golden spiral that almost hid him from view. Her ardor would redouble for that man, swaddled more than a Scythian and as resplendent as one of the Magi.

He had fine ideas about Emma's tomb. First he proposed a broken column surmounted by a drapery, next a pyramid, then a Temple of Vesta, a sort of rotunda . . . or else a large pile of ruins. And in all his plans Homais always stuck to the weeping willow, which he looked upon as the indispensable symbol of sorrow.

Charles and he made a journey to Rouen together to look at some tombs, accompanied by an artist, one Vaufrylard, a friend of Bridoux's, who never ceased to make puns. At last, after having examined some hundred drawings, having ordered an estimate and made another journey to Rouen, Charles decided in favor of a mausoleum, whose two principal sides were to be decorated with "a spirit bearing an extinguished torch."

As to the inscription, Homais could think of nothing finer than *Sta viator*,[74] and he got no further; he racked his brain in vain; all that he could come up with was *Sta viator*. At last he hit upon *Amabilem conjugem calcas*,[75] which was adopted.

A strange thing was happening to Bovary: while continually thinking of Emma, he was nevertheless forgetting her. He grew desperate as he felt this image fading from his memory in spite of all efforts to retain it. Yet every night he dreamt of her; it was always the same dream. He approached her, but when he was about to embrace her she fell into decay in his arms.

For a week he was seen going to church in the evening. Monsieur Bournisien even paid him two or three visits, then gave him up. Moreover, the old man was growing bigoted and fanatic, according to Homais. He thundered against the spirit of the age, and never failed, every other week, in his sermon, to recount the death agony of Voltaire, who died devouring his excrements, as every one knows.

In spite of Bovary's thrifty life, he was far from being able to pay off his old debts. Lheureux refused to renew any more notes. Execution became imminent. Then he appealed to his mother, who consented to let him take a mortgage on her property, but with a great

74. *Sta viator*, "Stop, traveler." 75. *Amabilem conjugem calcas*, "you are treading upon the beloved spouse."

many recriminations against Emma; and in return for her sacrifice she asked for a shawl that had escaped from Félicité's raids. Charles refused to give it to her; they quarrelled.

She made the first peace overtures by offering to let the little girl, who could help her in the house, live with her. Charles consented to this, but when the time for parting came, all his courage failed him. Then there was a final, complete break between them.

As his affections vanished, he clung more closely to the love of his child. She worried him, however, for she coughed sometimes, and had red patches on her cheeks.

Across the square, facing his house, the prospering family of the pharmacist was more flourishing and thriving than ever. Napoleon helped him in the laboratory, Athalie embroidered him a skullcap, Irma cut out rounds of paper to cover the preserves, and Franklin recited the tables of Pythagoras by rote, without the slightest hesitation. He was the happiest of fathers, the most fortunate of men.

Not quite, however! A secret ambition devoured him. Homais hankered after the cross of the Legion of Honour. He had plenty of claims to it.

"First, having at the time of the cholera distinguished myself by a boundless devotion; second, by having published, at my expense, various works of public usefulness, such as" (and he recalled his pamphlet entitled, *On Cider, its Manufacture and Effects*, besides observations on the wooly aphis that he had sent to the Academy; his volume of statistics, and down to his pharmaceutical thesis); "without counting that I am a member of several learned societies" (he was member of a single one).

"And if this won't do," he said, turning on his heels, "there always is the assistance I give at fires!"

Homais' next step was trying to win over the Government to his cause. He secretly did the prefect several favors during the elections. He sold, in a word, prostituted himself. He even addressed a petition to the sovereign in which he implored him to "do him justice;" he called him "our good king," and compared him to Henri IV.

And every morning the pharmacist rushed for the paper to see if his nomination appeared. It was never there. At last, unable to bear it any longer, he had a grass plot in his garden designed to represent the Star of the Cross of Honour, with two little strips of grass running from the top to imitate the ribbon. He walked round it with folded arms, meditating on the folly of the Government and the ingratitude of men.

Out of respect, or because he took an almost sensuous pleasure in dragging out his investigations, Charles had not yet opened the secret drawer of Emma's rosewood desk. One day, however, he sat down before it, turned the key, and pressed the spring. All Léon's letters were there. There could be no doubt this time. He devoured them to the very last, ransacked every corner, all the furniture, all the drawers, behind the walls, sobbing and shouting in mad distress. He discovered a box and kicked it open. Rodolphe's portrait flew out at him, from among the pile of love-letters.

People wondered at his despondency. He never went out, saw no one, refused even to visit his patients. Then they said "he shut himself up to drink."

At times, however, someone would climb on the garden hedge, moved by curiosity. They would stare in amazement at this long-bearded, shabbily clothed, wild figure of a man, who wept aloud as he walked up and down.

On summer evenings, he would take his little girl with him to visit the cemetery. They came back at nightfall, when the only light left in the village was that in Binet's window.

He was unable, however, to savor his grief to the full, for he had no one to share it with. He paid visits to Madame Lefrançois to be able to speak of *her*. But the innkeeper only listened with half an ear, having troubles of her own. For Monsieur Lheureux had finally set up his own business, *les Favorites du Commerce*, and Hivert, every one's favorite messenger, threatened to go to work for the competition unless he received higher wages.

One day when he had gone to the market at Argueil to sell his horse—his last resource—he met Rodolphe.

They both turned pale when they caught sight of one another. Rodolphe, who had only sent his card for the funeral, first stammered some apologies, then grew bolder, and even invited Charles (it was in the month of August and very hot) to share a bottle of beer with him at the terrace of a café.

Leaning his elbows on the table, he chewed his cigar as he talked, and Charles was lost in reverie at the sight of the face she had loved. He seemed to find back something of her there. It was quite a shock to him. He would have liked to have been this man.

The other went on talking of agriculture, cattle and fertilizers, filling with banalities all the gaps where an allusion might slip in. Charles was not listening to him; Rodolphe noticed it, and he could follow the sequence of memories that crossed his face. This face gradually reddened; Charles's nostrils fluttered, his lips quivered. For a moment, Charles stared at him in somber fury and Rodolphe, startled and terrified, stopped talking. But soon the same look of mournful weariness returned to his face.

"I can't blame you for it," he said.

Rodolphe remained silent. And Charles, his head in his hands, went on in a broken voice, with the resigned accent of infinite grief:

"No, I can't blame you any longer."

He even made a phrase, the only one he'd ever made:

"Fate willed it this way."

Rodolphe, who had been the agent of this fate, thought him very meek for a man in his situation, comic even and slightly despicable.

The next day Charles sat down on the garden seat under the arbor. Rays of light were straying through the trellis, the vine leaves threw their shadows on the sand, jasmines perfumed the blue air, Spanish flies buzzed round the lilies in bloom, and Charles was panting like an adolescent under the vague desires of love that filled his aching heart.

At seven o'clock little Berthe who had not seen him all afternoon, came to fetch him for dinner.

His head was leaning against the wall, with closed eyes and open mouth, and in his hand was a long tress of black hair.

"Papa, come!"

And thinking he wanted to play, she gave him a gentle push. He fell to the ground. He was dead.

Thirty-six hours later, at the pharmacist's request, Monsieur Canivet arrived. He performed an autopsy, but found nothing.

When everything had been sold, there remained twelve francs and seventy-five centimes, just enough to send Mademoiselle Bovary off to her grandmother. The woman died the same year; and since Rouault was paralyzed, it was an aunt who took charge of her. She is poor, and sends her to a cotton-mill to earn a living.

Since Bovary's death three doctors have succeeded one another in Yonville without any success, so effectively did Homais hasten to eradicate them. He has more customers than there are sinners in hell; the authorities treat him kindly and he has the public on his side.

He has just been given the cross of the Legion of Honor.

FYODOR DOSTOEVSKY
(1821–1881)
Notes from Underground* [1]

Part I

UNDERGROUND

I

I am a sick man. . . . I am a spiteful man. I am an unattractive man. I believe my liver is diseased. However, I know nothing at all about my disease, and do not know for certain what ails me. I don't consult a doctor for it, and never have, though I have a respect for medicine and doctors. Besides, I am extremely superstitious, sufficiently so to respect medicine, anyway (I am well-educated enough not to be superstitious, but I am superstitious). No, I refuse to consult a doctor from spite. That you probably will not understand. Well, I understand it, though. Of course I can't explain who it is precisely that I am mortifying in this case by my spite: I am perfectly well aware that I cannot "pay out" the doctors by not consulting them; I know better than any one that by all this I am only injuring myself and no one else. But still, if I don't consult a doctor it is from spite. My liver is bad, well—let it get worse!

I have been going on like that for a long time—twenty years. Now I am forty. I used to be in the government service, but am no longer. I was a spiteful official. I was rude and took pleasure in being so. I did not take bribes, you see, so I was bound to find a recompense in that, at least. (A poor jest, but I will not scratch it out. I wrote it thinking it would sound very witty; but now that I have seen myself that I only wanted to show off in a despicable way, I will not scratch it out on purpose!)

When petitioners used to come for information to the table at which I sat, I used to grind my teeth at them, and felt intense enjoyment when I succeeded in making anybody unhappy. I almost always did succeed. For the most part they were all timid people—

* 1864. Translated by Constance Garnett. Reprinted in full. The punctuation ". . ." does not indicate omissions from this text.

1. The author of the diary and the diary itself are, of course, imaginary. Nevertheless it is clear that such persons as the writer of these notes not only may, but positively must, exist in our society, when we consider the circumstances in the midst of which our society is formed. I have tried to expose to the view of the public more distinctly than is commonly done, one of the characters of the recent past. He is one of the representatives of a generation still living. In this fragment, entitled "Underground," this person introduces himself and his views, and, as it were, tries to explain the causes owing to which he has made his appearance and was bound to make his appearance in our midst. In the second fragment there are added the actual notes of this person concerning certain events in his life. [Author's note.]

of course, they were petitioners. But of the uppish ones there was one officer in particular I could not endure. He simply would not be humble, and clanked his sword in a disgusting way. I carried on a feud with him for eighteen months over that sword. At last I got the better of him. He left off clanking it. That happened in my youth, though.

But do you know, gentlemen, what was the chief point about my spite? Why, the whole point, the real sting of it lay in the fact that continually, even in the moment of the acutest spleen, I was inwardly conscious with shame that I was not only not a spiteful but not even an embittered man, that I was simply scaring sparrows at random and amusing myself by it. I might foam at the mouth, but bring me a doll to play with, give me a cup of tea with sugar in it, and maybe I should be appeased. I might even be genuinely touched, though probably I should grind my teeth at myself afterwards and lie awake at night with shame for months after. That was my way.

I was lying when I said just now that I was a spiteful official. I was lying from spite. I was simply amusing myself with the petitioners and with the officer, and in reality I never could become spiteful. I was conscious every moment in myself of many, very many elements absolutely opposite to that. I felt them positively swarming in me, these opposite elements. I knew that they had been swarming in me all my life and craving some outlet from me, but I would not let them, would not let them, purposely would not let them come out. They tormented me till I was ashamed: they drove me to convulsions and—sickened me, at last, how they sickened me! Now, are not you fancying, gentlemen, that I am expressing remorse for something now, that I am asking your forgiveness for something? I am sure you are fancying that . . . However, I assure you I do not care if you are. . . .

It was not only that I could not become spiteful, I did not know how to become anything: neither spiteful nor kind, neither a rascal nor an honest man, neither a hero nor an insect. Now, I am living out my life in my corner, taunting myself with the spiteful and useless consolation that an intelligent man cannot become anything seriously, and it is only the fool who becomes anything. Yes, a man in the nineteenth century must and morally ought to be pre-eminently a characterless creature; a man of character, an active man is pre-eminently a limited creature. That is my conviction of forty years. I am forty years old now, and you know forty years is a whole lifetime; you know it is extreme old age. To live longer than forty years is bad manners, is vulgar, immoral. Who lives beyond forty? Answer that, sincerely and honestly. I will tell you who do: fools and worthless fellows. I tell all old men that to their face, all these venerable old men, all these silver-haired and reverend seniors! I tell the whole world that to its face! I have a right to say so, for I shall go on living to sixty myself. To seventy! To eighty! . . . Stay, let me take breath. . . .

You imagine no doubt, gentlemen, that I want to amuse you. You are mistaken in that, too. I am by no means such a mirthful person as you imagine, or as you may imagine; however, irritated by all this babble (and I feel that you are irritated) you think fit to ask me who am I—then my answer is, I am a collegiate assessor. I was in the service that I might have something to eat (and solely for that reason), and when last year a distant relation left me six thousand roubles in his will I immediately retired from the service and settled down in my corner. I used to live in this corner before, but now I have settled down in it. My room is a wretched, horrid one in the outskirts of the town. My servant is an old country-woman, ill-natured from stupidity, and, moreover, there is always a nasty smell about her. I am told that the Petersburg climate is bad for me, and that with my small means it is very expensive to live in Petersburg. I know all that better than all these sage and experienced counsellors and monitors. . . . But I am remaining in Petersburg; . . . I am not going away from Petersburg! I am not going away because . . . ech! Why, it is absolutely no matter whether I am going away or not going away.

But what can a decent man speak of with most pleasure?

Answer: Of himself.

Well, so I will talk about myself.

II

I want now to tell you, gentlemen, whether you care to hear it or not, why I could not even become an insect. I tell you solemnly, that I have many times tried to become an insect. But I was not equal even to that. I swear, gentlemen, that to be too conscious is an illness—a real thoroughgoing illness. For man's everyday needs, it would have been quite enough to have the ordinary human consciousness, that is, half or a quarter of the amount which falls to the lot of a cultivated man of our unhappy nineteenth century, especially one who has the fatal ill-luck to inhabit Petersburg, the most theoretical and intentional town on the whole terrestrial globe. (There are intentional and unintentional towns.) It would have been quite enough, for instance, to have the consciousness by which all so-called direct persons and men of action live. I bet you think I am writing all this from affectation, to be witty at the expense of men of action; and what is more, that from ill-bred affectation, I am clanking a sword like my officer. But, gentlemen, whoever can pride himself on his diseases and even swagger over them?

Though, after all, every one does do that; people do pride themselves on their diseases, and I do, may be, more than any one else. We will not dispute it; my contention was absurd. But yet I am firmly persuaded that a great deal of consciousness, every sort of consciousness, in fact, is a disease. I stick to that. Let us leave that, too, for a minute. Tell me this: why does it happen that at the very, yes, at the very moments when I am most capable of feeling every refinement of all that is "good and beautiful," as they used to say at one time, it would, as though of design, happen to me not only to feel but to do such ugly things, such that . . . Well, in short, actions that all, perhaps, commit; but which, as though purposely, occurred to me at the very time when I was most conscious that they ought not to be committed. The more conscious I was of goodness and of all that was "good and beautiful," the more deeply I sank into my mire and the more ready I was to sink in it altogether. But the chief point was that all this was, as it were, not accidental in me, but as though it were bound to be so. It was as though it were my most normal condition, and not in the least disease or depravity, so that at last all desire in me to struggle against this depravity passed. It ended by my almost believing (perhaps actually believing) that this was perhaps my normal condition. But at first, in the beginning, what agonies I endured in that struggle! I did not believe it was the same with other people, and all my life I hid this fact about myself as a secret. I was ashamed (even now, perhaps, I am ashamed): I got to the point of feeling a sort of secret abnormal, despicable enjoyment in returning home to my corner on some disgusting Petersburg night, acutely conscious that that day I had committed a loathsome action again, that what was done could never be undone, and secretly, inwardly gnawing, gnawing at myself for it, tearing and consuming myself till at last the bitterness turned into a sort of shameful accursed sweetness, and at last—into positive real enjoyment! Yes into enjoyment, into enjoyment! I insist upon that. I have spoken of this because I keep wanting to know for a fact whether other people feel such enjoyment? I will explain; the enjoyment was just from the too intense consciousness of one's own degradation; it was from feeling oneself that one had reached the last barrier, that it was horrible, but that it could not be otherwise; that there was no escape for you; that you never could become a different man; that even if time and faith were still left you to change into something different you would most likely not wish to change; or if you did wish to, even then you would do nothing; because perhaps in reality there was nothing for you to change into.

And the worst of it was, and the root of it all, that it was all in accord with the normal fundamental laws of over-acute consciousness, and with the inertia that was the direct result of those laws, and that consequently one was not only unable to change but could do absolutely nothing. Thus it would follow, as the result of acute consciousness, that one is not to blame in being a scoundrel; as though that were any consolation to the scoundrel once he has come to realize that he actually is a scoundrel. But enough. . . . Ech, I have talked a lot of nonsense, but what have I explained? How is enjoyment in this to be explained? But I will explain it. I will get to the bottom of it! That is why I have taken up my pen. . . .

I, for instance, have a great deal of *amour propre*. I am as suspicious and prone to take offence as a hunchback or a dwarf. But upon my word I sometimes have had moments when if I had happened to be slapped in the face I should, perhaps, have been positively glad of it. I say, in earnest, that I should probably have been able to discover even in that a peculiar sort of enjoyment—the enjoyment, of course, of despair; but in despair there are the most intense enjoyments, especially when one is very acutely conscious of the hopelessness of one's position. And when one is slapped in the face—why then the consciousness of being rubbed into a pulp would positively overwhelm one. The worst of it is, look at it which way one will, it still turns out that I was always the most to blame in everything. And what is most humiliating of all, to blame for no fault of my own but, so to say, through the laws of nature. In the first place, to blame because I am cleverer than any of the people surrounding me. (I have always considered myself cleverer than any of the people surrounding me, and sometimes, would you believe it, have been positively ashamed of it. At any rate, I have all my life, as it were, turned my eyes away and never could look people straight in the face.) To blame, finally, because even if I had had magnanimity, I should only have had more suffering from the sense of its uselessness. I should certainly have never been able to do anything from being magnanimous—neither to forgive, for my assailant would perhaps have slapped me from the laws of nature, and one cannot forgive the laws of nature; nor to forget, for even if it were owing to the laws of nature, it is insulting all the same. Finally, even if I had wanted to be anything but magnanimous, had desired on the contrary to revenge myself on my assailant, I could not have revenged myself on any one for anything because I should certainly never have made up my mind to do anything, even if I had been able to. Why should I not have made up my mind? About that in particular I want to say a few words.

III

With people who know how to revenge themselves and to stand up for themselves in general, how is it done? Why, when they are possessed, let us suppose, by the feeling of revenge, then for the time there is nothing else but that feeling left in their whole being. Such a gentleman simply dashes straight for his object like an infuriated bull with its horns down, and nothing but a wall will stop him. (By the way: facing the wall, such gentlemen—that is, the "direct" persons and men of action—are genuinely nonplussed. For them a wall is not an evasion, as for us people who think and consequently do nothing; it is not an excuse for turning aside, an excuse for which we are always very glad, though we scarcely believe in it ourselves, as a rule. No, they are nonplussed in all sincerity. The wall has for them something tranquillizing, morally soothing, final—maybe even something mysterious . . . but of the wall later.)

Well, such a direct person I regard as the real normal man, as his tender mother nature wished to see him when she graciously brought him into being on the earth. I envy such a man till I am green in the face. He is stupid. I am not disputing that, but perhaps the normal man should be stupid, how do you know? Perhaps it is very beautiful, in fact. And I am the more persuaded of that suspicion, if one can call it so, by the fact that if you take, for instance, the antithesis of the normal man, that is, the man of acute consciousness, who has come, of course, not out of the lap of nature but out of a retort (this is almost mysticism, gentlemen, but I suspect this, too), this retort-made man is sometimes so nonplussed in the presence of his antithesis that with all his exaggerated consciousness he genuinely thinks of himself as a mouse and not a man. It may be an acutely conscious mouse, yet it is a mouse, while the other is a man, and therefore, et cætera, et cætera. And the worst of it is, he himself, his very own self, looks on himself as a mouse; no one asks him to do so; and that is an important point. Now let us look at this mouse in action. Let us suppose, for instance, that it feels insulted, too (and it almost always does feel insulted), and wants to revenge itself, too. There may even be a greater accumulation of spite in it than in *l'homme de la nature et de la vérité*.[2] The base and nasty desire to vent that spite on its assailant rankles perhaps even more nastily in it than in *l'homme de la nature et de la vérité*. For through his innate stupidity the latter looks upon his revenge as justice pure and simple; while in consequence of his acute consciousness the mouse does not be-

2. "the man of nature and truth"; Rousseau's description of himself in the *Confessions* (1781–1788), which created an enormous stir because they professed to tell the whole truth about the author and were sometimes self-accusing.

lieve in the justice of it. To come at last to the deed itself, to the very act of revenge. Apart from the one fundamental nastiness the luckless mouse succeeds in creating around it so many other nastinesses in the form of doubts and questions, adds to the one question so many unsettled questions that there inevitably works up around it a sort of fatal brew, a stinking mess, made up of its doubts, emotions, and of the contempt spat upon it by the direct men of action who stand solemnly about it as judges and arbitrators, laughing at it till their healthy sides ache. Of course the only thing left for it is to dismiss all that with a wave of its paw, and, with a smile of assumed contempt in which it does not even itself believe, creep ignominiously into its mouse-hole. There in its nasty, stinking, underground home our insulted, crushed and ridiculed mouse promptly becomes absorbed in cold, malignant and, above all, everlasting spite. For forty years together it will remember its injury down to the smallest, most ignominious details, and every time will add, of itself, details still more ignominious, spitefully teasing and tormenting itself with its own imagination. It will itself be ashamed of its imaginings, but yet it will recall it all, it will go over and over every detail, it will invent unheard of things against itself, pretending that those things might happen, and will forgive nothing. Maybe it will begin to revenge itself, too, but, as it were, piecemeal, in trivial ways, from behind the stove, incognito, without believing either in its own right to vengeance, or in the success of its revenge knowing that from all its efforts at revenge it will suffer a hundred times more than he on whom it revenges itself, while he, I daresay, will not even scratch himself. On its deathbed it will recall it all over again, with interest accumulated over all the years and. . . .

But it is just in that cold, abominable half despair, half belief, in that conscious burying oneself alive for grief in the underworld for forty years, in that acutely recognized and yet partly doubtful hopelessness of one's position, in that hell of unsatisfied desires turned inward, in that fever of oscillations, or resolutions determined for ever and repented of again a minute later—that the savour of that strange enjoyment of which I have spoken lies. It is so subtle, so difficult of analysis, that persons who are a little limited, or even simply persons of strong nerves, will not understand a single atom of it. "Possibly," you will add on your own account with a grin, "people will not understand it either who have never received a slap in the face," and in that way you will politely hint to me that I, too, perhaps, have had the experience of a slap in the face in my life, and so I speak as one who knows. I bet that you are thinking that. But set your minds at rest, gentlemen, I have not received a slap in the face, though it is absolutely a matter of indifference to me what you may think about it. Possibly, I even regret, myself, that I have given so few slaps in the face during my life. But enough . . . not another word on that subject of such extreme interest to you.

I will continue calmly concerning persons with strong nerves who do not understand a certain refinement of enjoyment. Though in certain circumstances these gentlemen bellow their loudest like bulls, though this, let us suppose, does them the greatest credit, yet, as I have said already, confronted with the impossible they subside at once. The impossible means the stone wall! What stone wall? Why, of course, the laws of nature, the deductions of natural science, mathematics. As soon as they prove to you, for instance, that you are descended from a monkey, then it is no use scowling, accept it for a fact. When they prove to you that in reality one drop of your own fat must be dearer to you than a hundred thousand of your fellow-creatures, and that this conclusion is the final solution of all so-called virtues and duties and all such prejudices and fancies, then you have just to accept it, there is no help for it, for twice two is a law of mathematics. Just try refuting it.

"Upon my word," they will shout at you, "it is no use protesting: it is a case of twice two makes four! Nature does not ask your permission, she has nothing to do with your wishes, and whether you like her laws or dislike them, you are bound to accept her as she is, and consequently all her conclusions. A wall, you see, is a wall . . ." and so on, and so on.

Merciful Heavens! but what do I care for the laws of nature and arithmetic, when, for some reason I dislike those laws and the fact that twice two makes four? Of course I cannot break through the wall by battering my head against it if I really have not the strength to knock it down, but I am not going to be reconciled to it simply because it is a stone wall and I have not the strength.

As though such a stone wall really were a consolation, and really did contain some word of conciliation, simply because it is as true as twice two makes four. Oh, absurdity of absurdities! How much better it is to understand it all, to recognize it all, all the impossibilities and the stone wall; not to be reconciled to one of those impossibilities and stone walls if it disgusts you to be reconciled to it; by the way of the most inevitable, logical combinations to reach the most revolting conclusions on the everlasting theme, that even for the stone wall you are yourself somehow to blame, though again it is as clear as day you are not to blame in the least, and therefore grinding your teeth in silent impotence to sink into luxurious inertia, brooding on the fact that there is no one even for you to feel vindictive against, that you have not, and perhaps never will have, an object for your spite, that it is a sleight of hand, a bit of juggling, a card-sharper's trick, that it is simply a mess, no knowing what and no knowing who, but in spite of all these un-certainties and jugglings, still there is an ache in you, and the more you do not know, the worse the ache.

IV

"Ha, ha, ha! You will be finding enjoyment in toothache next," you cry, with a laugh.

"Well? Even in toothache there is enjoyment," I answer. I had toothache for a whole month and I know there is. In that case, of course, people are not spiteful in silence, but moan; but they are not candid moans, they are malignant moans, and the malig-nancy is the whole point. The enjoyment of the sufferer finds expression in those moans; if he did not feel enjoyment in them he would not moan. It is a good example, gentlemen, and I will develop it. Those moans express in the first place all the aimless-ness of your pain, which is so humiliating to your consciousness; the whole legal system of nature on which you spit disdainfully, of course, but from which you suffer all the same while she does not. They express the consciousness that you have no enemy to punish, but that you have pain; the consciousness that in spite of all possible Wagenheims[3] you are in complete slavery to your teeth; that if some one wishes it, your teeth will leave off aching, and if he does not, they will go on aching another three months; and that finally if you are still contumacious and still protest, all that is left you for your own gratification is to thrash yourself or beat your wall with your fist as hard as you can, and absolutely nothing more. Well, these mortal insults, these jeers on the part of some one unknown, end at last in an enjoyment which sometimes reaches the highest degree of voluptuousness. I ask you, gentlemen, listen sometimes to the moans of an educated man of the nineteenth century suffering from toothache, on the second or third day of the attack, when he is beginning to moan, not as he moaned on the first day, that is, not simply because he has toothache, not just as any coarse peasant, but as a man affected by progress and European civilization, a man who is "divorced from the soil and the national elements," as they express it now-a-days. His moans become nasty, disgustingly malignant, and go on for whole days and nights. And of course he knows himself that he is doing himself no sort of good with his moans; he knows better than any one that he is only lacerating and harassing himself and others for nothing; he knows that even the audience before whom he is making his efforts, and his whole family, listen to him with loathing, do not put the

---

3. Wagenheim was apparently a Ger-man who advertised painless dentistry; he may have used hypnosis or auto-suggestion.

least faith in him, and inwardly understand that he might moan differently, more simply, without trills and flourishes, and that he is only amusing himself like that from ill-humour, from malignancy. Well, in all these recognitions and disgraces it is that there lies a voluptuous pleasure. As though he would say: "I am worrying you, I am lacerating your hearts, I am keeping every one in the house awake. Well, stay awake then, you, too, feel every minute that I have toothache. I am not a hero to you now, as I tried to seem before, but simply a nasty person, an impostor. Well, so be it, then! I am very glad that you see through me. It is nasty for you to hear my despicable moans: well, let it be nasty; here I will let you have a nastier flourish in a minute. . . ." You do not understand even now, gentlemen? No, it seems our development and our consciousness must go further to understand all the intricacies of this pleasure. You laugh? Delighted. My jests, gentlemen, are of course in bad taste, jerky, involved, lacking self-confidence. But of course that is because I do not respect myself. Can a man of perception respect himself at all?

V

Come, can a man who attempts to find enjoyment in the very feeling of his own degradation possibly have a spark of respect for himself? I am not saying this now from any mawkish kind of remorse. And, indeed, I could never endure saying, "Forgive me, Papa, I won't do it again," not because I am incapable of saying that—on the contrary, perhaps just because I have been too capable of it, and in what a way, too! As though of design I used to get into trouble in cases when I was not to blame in any way. That was the nastiest part of it. At the same time I was genuinely touched and penitent, I used to shed tears and, of course, deceived myself, though I was not acting in the least and there was a sick feeling in my heart at the time. . . . For that one could not blame even the laws of nature, though the laws of nature have continually all my life offended me more than anything. It is loathsome to remember it all, but it was loathsome even then. Of course, a minute or so later I would realize wrathfully that it was all a lie, a revolting lie, an affected lie, that is, all this penitence, this emotion, these vows of reform. You will ask why did I worry myself with such antics: answer, because it was very dull to sit with one's hands folded, and so one began cutting capers. That is really it. Observe yourselves more carefully, gentlemen, then you will understand that it is so. I invented adventures for myself and made up a life, so as at least to live in some way. How many times it has happened to me—well, for instance, to take offence simply on purpose, for nothing; and one knows oneself, of course, that one is offended at nothing, that one is putting it on, but yet one brings oneself, at last to the point of being really offended. All my life I have had an impulse to play such pranks, so that in the end I could not control it in myself. Another time, twice, in fact, I tried hard to be in love. I suffered, too, gentlemen, I assure you. In the depth of my heart there was no faith in my suffering, only a faint stir of mockery, but yet I did suffer, and in the real, orthodox way; I was jealous, beside myself . . . and it was all from *ennui*, gentlemen, all from *ennui*; inertia overcame me. You know the direct, legitimate fruit of consciousness is inertia, that is, conscious sitting-with-the-hands-folded. I have referred to this already. I repeat, I repeat with emphasis: all "direct" persons and men of action are active just because they are stupid and limited. How explain that? I will tell you: in consequence of their limitation they take immediate and secondary causes for primary ones, and in that way persuade themselves more quickly and easily than other people do that they have found an infallible foundation for their activity, and their minds are at ease and you know that is the chief thing. To begin to act, you know, you must first have your mind completely at ease and no trace of doubt left in it. Why, how am I, for example to set my mind at rest? Where are the primary causes on which I am to build? Where are my foundations? Where am I to get them from? I exercise myself in reflection, and consequently with me every primary cause at once draws after itself another still more primary, and so on to infinity. That is just the essence of every sort of consciousness and reflection. It must be a case of the laws of nature again. What is the result of it in the end? Why, just the same. Remember I spoke just now of vengeance. (I am sure you did not take it in.) I said that a man revenges himself because he sees justice in it. Therefore he has found a primary cause, that is, justice. And so he is at rest on all sides, and consequently he carries out his revenge calmly and successfully, being persuaded that he is doing a just and honest thing. But I see no justice in it, I find no sort of virtue in it either, and consequently if I attempt to revenge myself, it is only out of spite. Spite, of course, might overcome everything, all my doubts, and so might serve quite successfully in place of a primary cause, precisely because it is not a cause. But what is to be done if I have not even spite (I began with that just now, you know). In consequence again of those accursed laws of consciousness, anger in me is subject to chemical disintegration. You look into it, the object flies off into air, your reasons evaporate, the criminal is not to be found, the wrong becomes not a wrong but a phantom, something like the toothache, for which no one is to blame, and consequently there is only the same outlet left again—that is, to beat the wall as hard as you can. So you give it up with a wave of the hand because you have not tound a fundamental cause. And try letting yourself be carried away by your feelings, blindly, without reflection, without a primary cause, repelling consciousness at least for a time; hate or love, if only not to sit with your hands folded. The day after to-morrow, at the latest, you will begin despising yourself for having knowingly deceived yourself. Result: a soap-bubble and inertia. Oh, gentlemen, do you know, perhaps I consider myself an intelligent man, only because all my life I have been able neither to begin nor to finish anything. Granted I am a babbler, a harmless vexatious babbler, like all of us. But what is to be done if the direct and sole vocation of every intelligent man is babble, that is, the intentional pouring of water through a sieve?

VI

Oh, if I had done nothing simply from laziness! Heavens, how I should have respected myself, then. I should have respected myself because I should at least have been capable of being lazy; there would at least have been one quality, as it were, positive in me, in which I could have believed myself. Question: What is he? Answer: A sluggard; how very pleasant it would have been to hear that of oneself! It would mean that I was positively defined, it would mean that there was something to say about me. "Sluggard"—why, it is a calling and vocation, it is a career. Do not jest, it is so. I should then be a member of the best club by right, and should find my occupation in continually respecting myself. I knew a gentlemen who prided himself all his life on being a connoisseur of Lafitte. He considered this as his positive virtue, and never doubted himself. He died, not simply with a tranquil, but with a triumphant, conscience, and he was quite right, too. Then I should have chosen a career for myself, I should have been a sluggard and a glutton, not a simple one, but, for instance, one with sympathies for everything good and beautiful. How do you like that? I have long had visions of it. That "good and beautiful" weighs heavily on my mind at forty. But that is at forty; then—oh, then it would have been different! I should have found for myself a form of activity in keeping with it, to be precise, drinking to the health of everything "good and beautiful." I should have snatched at every opportunity to drop a tear into my glass and then to drain it to all that is "good and beautiful." I should then have turned everything into the good and the beautiful; in the nastiest, unquestionable trash, I should have sought out the good and the beautiful. I should have exuded tears like a wet sponge. An artist, for instance, paints a picture worthy of Gay.[4] At once I drink to the health of the artist who painted the picture worthy of Gay,

4. Nikolay Nikolaevich Gay (1831–1894), Russian painter of historical pictures who then had a great reputation. His father was a French emigrant.

because I love all that is "good and beautiful." An author has written *What you will*:[5] at once I drink to the health of "what you will" because I love all that is "good and beautiful."

I should claim respect for doing so. I should persecute any one who would not show me respect. I should live at ease, I should die with dignity, why, it is charming, perfectly charming! And what a good round belly I should have grown, what a triple chin I should have established, what a ruby nose I should have coloured for myself, so that every one would have said, looking at me: "Here is an asset! Here is something real and solid!" And, say what you like, it is very agreeable to hear such remarks about oneself in this negative age.

VII

But these are all golden dreams. Oh, tell me, who was it first announced, who was it first proclaimed, that man only does nasty things because he does not know his own interests; and that if he were enlightened, if his eyes were opened to his real normal interests, man would at once cease to do nasty things, would at once become good and noble because, being enlightened and understanding his real advantage, he would see his own advantage in the good and nothing else, and we all know that not one man can, consciously, act against his own interests, consequently, so to say, through necessity, he would begin doing good? Oh, the babe! Oh, the pure, innocent child! Why, in the first place, when in all these thousands of years has there been a time when man has acted only from his own interest? What is to be done with the millions of facts that bear witness that men, *consciously*, that is fully understanding their real interests, have left them in the background and have rushed headlong on another path, to meet peril and danger, compelled to this course by nobody and by nothing, but, as it were, simply disliking the beaten track, and have obstinately, wilfully, struck out another difficult, absurd way, seeking it almost in the darkness. So, I suppose, this obstinacy and perversity were pleasanter to them than any advantage. . . . Advantage! What is advantage? And will you take it upon yourself to define with perfect accuracy in what the advantage of man consists? And what if it so happens that a man's advantage, *sometimes*, not only may, but even must, consist in his desiring in certain cases what is harmful to himself and not advantageous. And if so, if there can be such a case, the whole principle falls into dust. What do you think—are there such cases? You laugh; laugh away, gentlemen, but only answer me: have man's advantages been reckoned up with perfect certainty? Are there not some which not only have

5. subtitle of Shakespeare's comedy *Twelfth Night*, generally used on the Continent instead of the main title, which is difficult to translate.

not been included but cannot possibly be included under any classification? You see, you gentlemen have, to the best of my knowledge, taken your whole register of human advantages from the averages of statistical figures and politico-economical formulas. Your advantages are prosperity, wealth, freedom, peace—and so on, and so on. So that the man who should, for instance, go openly and knowingly in opposition to all that list would, to your thinking, and indeed mine, too, of course, be an obscurantist or an absolute madman: would not he? But, you know, this is what is surprising: why does it so happen that all these statisticians, sages and lovers of humanity, when they reckon up human advantages invariably leave out one? They don't even take it into their reckoning in the form in which it should be taken, and the whole reckoning depends upon that. It would be no great matter, they would simply have to take it, this advantage, and add it to the list. But the trouble is, that this strange advantage does not fall under any classification and is not in place in any list. I have a friend for instance . . . Ech! gentlemen, but of course he is your friend, too; and indeed there is no one, no one, to whom he is not a friend! When he prepares for any undertaking this gentleman immediately explains to you, elegantly and clearly, exactly how he must act in accordance with the laws of reason and truth. What is more, he will talk to you with excitement and passion of the true normal interests of man; with irony he will upbraid the shortsighted fools who do not understand their own interests, nor the true significance of virtue; and, within a quarter of an hour, without any sudden outside provocation, but simply through something inside him which is stronger than all his interests, he will go off on quite a different tack—that is, act in direct opposition to what he has just been saying about himself, in opposition to the laws of reason, in opposition to his own advantage, in fact in opposition to everything . . . I warn you that my friend is a compound personality, and therefore it is difficult to blame him as an individual. The fact is, gentlemen, it seems there must really exist something that is dearer to almost every man than his greatest advantages, or (not to be illogical) there is a most advantageous advantage (the very one omitted of which we spoke just now) which is more important and more advantageous than all other advantages, for the sake of which a man if necessary is ready to act in opposition to all laws; that is, in opposition to reason, honour, peace, prosperity—in fact, in opposition to all those excellent and useful things if only he can attain that fundamental, most advantageous advantage which is dearer to him than all. "Yes, but it's advantage all the same" you will retort. But excuse me, I'll make the point clear, and it is not a case of playing upon words. What matters is, that this advantage is remarkable from the very fact that it breaks down all our classifications, and continually shatters every system constructed by lovers of mankind for the benefit of mankind. In fact, it upsets everything. But before I mention this advantage to you, I want to compromise myself personally, and therefore I boldly declare that all these fine systems, all these theories for explaining to mankind their real normal interests, in order that inevitably striving to pursue these interests they may at once become good and noble —are, in my opinion, so far, mere logical exercises! Yes, logical exercises. Why, to maintain this theory of the regeneration of mankind by means of the pursuit of his own advantage is to my mind almost the same thing as . . . as to affirm, for instance, following Buckle,[6] that through civilization mankind becomes softer, and consequently less bloodthirsty and less fitted for warfare. Logically it does seem to follow from his arguments. But man has such a predilection for systems and abstract deductions that he is ready to distort the truth intentionally, he is ready to deny the evidence of his senses only to justify his logic. I take this example because it is the most glaring instance of it. Only look about you: blood is being spilt in streams, and in the merriest way, as though it were champagne. Take the whole of the nineteenth century in which Buckle lived. Take Napoleon—the Great and also the present one. Take North America—the eternal union. Take the farce of Schleswig-Holstein.[7] . . . And what is it that civilization softens in us? The only gain of civilization for mankind is the greater capacity for variety of sensations—and absolutely nothing more. And through the development of this many-sidedness man may come to finding enjoyment in bloodshed. In fact, this has already happened to him. Have you noticed that it is the most civilized gentlemen who have been the subtlest slaughterers, to whom the Attilas[8] and Stenka Razins[9] could not hold a candle, and if they are not so conspicuous as the Attilas and Stenka Razins it is simply because they are so often met with, are so ordinary and have become so familiar to us. In any case civilization has made mankind if not more bloodthirsty, at least more vilely, more loathsomely bloodthirsty. In old days he saw justice in bloodshed and with his conscience at peace exterminated those he thought proper. Now we do think bloodshed abominable and yet we engage in this

6. Henry Thomas Buckle (1821–1862), the author of the *History of Civilization in England* (two volumes, 1857, 1861), which held that all progress is due to the march of mind. There is no moral progress except indirectly, as a result of intellectual enlightenment.

7. Austria and Prussia invaded Denmark and annexed its southernmost part, Schleswig-Holstein, in 1864.

8. Attila (406?–453 A.D.) was king of the Huns (433?–453). In 451 his armies penetrated as far as Orléans, in what today is France. He was defeated in the battle of Châlons on the Catalaunian plains and retired to Hungary. In 452 he led an expedition against Rome.

9. Stenka Razin was a Don Cossack leader who in 1670 conquered many cities along the Volga. He was finally defeated, captured, and executed in 1671.

abomination, and with more energy than ever. Which is worse? Decide that for yourselves. They say that Cleopatra (excuse an instance from Roman history) was fond of sticking gold pins into her slave-girls' breasts and derived gratification from their screams and writhings. You will say that that was in the comparatively barbarous times; that these are barbarous times too, because also, comparatively speaking, pins are stuck in even now; that though man has now learned to see more clearly than in barbarous ages, he is still far from having learnt to act as reason and science would dictate. But yet you are fully convinced that he will be sure to learn when he gets rid of certain old bad habits, and when common sense and science have completely re-educated human nature and turned it in a normal direction. You are confident that then man will cease from *intentional* error and will, so to say, be compelled not to want to set his will against his normal interests. That is not all; then, you say, science itself will teach man (though to my mind it's a superfluous luxury) that he never has really had any caprice or will of his own, and that he himself is something of the nature of a piano-key or the stop of an organ, and that there are, besides, things called the laws of nature; so that everything he does is not done by his willing it, but is done of itself, by the laws of nature. Consequently we have only to discover these laws of nature, and man will no longer have to answer for his actions and life will become exceedingly easy for him. All human actions will then, of course, be tabulated according to these laws, mathematically, like tables of logarithms up to 108,000, and entered in an index; or, better still, there would be published certain edifying works of the nature of encyclopædic lexicons, in which everything will be so clearly calculated and explained that there will be no more incidents or adventures in the world.

Then—this is all what you say—new economic relations will be established, all ready-made and worked out with mathematical exactitude, so that every possible question will vanish in the twinkling of any eye, simply because every possible answer to it will be provided. Then the "Crystal Palace"[10] will be built. Then . . . . In fact, those will be halcyon days. Of course there is no guaranteeing (this is my comment) that it will not be, for instance, frightfully dull then (for what will one have to do when everything will be calculated and tabulated), but on the other hand everything will be extraordinarily rational. Of course boredom may lead you to anything. It is boredom sets one sticking golden pins into people, but all that would not matter. What is bad (this is my

10. Dostoevsky has in mind the London Crystal Palace, a structure of glass and iron built in 1851–1854, and at that time admired as the newest wonder of architecture. The nave was five hundred yards long. The building burned down in 1936.

comment again) is that I dare say people will be thankful for the gold pins then. Man is stupid, you know, phenomenally stupid; or rather he is not at all stupid, but he is so ungrateful that you could not find another like him in all creation. I, for instance, would not be in the least surprised if all of a sudden, *à propos* of nothing, in the midst of general prosperity a gentleman with an ignoble, or rather with a reactionary and ironical, countenance were to arise and, putting his arms akimbo, say to us all: "I say, gentlemen, hadn't we better kick over the whole show and scatter rationalism to the winds, simply to send these logarithms to the devil, and to enable us to live once more at our own sweet foolish will!" That again would not matter, but what is annoying is that he would be sure to find followers—such is the nature of man. And all that for the most foolish reason, which, one would think, was hardly worth mentioning: that is, that man everywhere and at all times, whoever he may be, has preferred to act as he chose and not in the least as his reason and advantage dictated. And one may choose what is contrary to one's own interests, and sometimes one *positively ought* (that is my idea). One's own free unfettered choice, one's own caprice, however wild it may be, one's own fancy worked up at times to frenzy—is that very "most advantageous advantage" which we have overlooked, which comes under no classification and against which all systems and theories are continually being shattered to atoms. And how do these wiseacres know that man wants a normal, a virtuous choice? What has made them conceive that man must want a rationally advantageous choice? What man wants is simply *independent* choice, whatever that independence may cost and wherever it may lead. And choice, of course, the devil only knows what choice.

VIII

"Ha! ha! ha! But you know there is no such thing as choice in reality, say what you like," you will interpose with a chuckle. "Science has succeeded in so far analysing man that we know already that choice and what is called freedom of will is nothing else than——"

Stay, gentlemen, I meant to begin with that myself. I confess, I was rather frightened. I was just going to say that the devil only knows what choice depends on, and that perhaps that was a very good thing, but I remembered the teaching of science . . . and pulled myself up. And here you have begun upon it. Indeed, if there really is some day discovered a formula for all our desires and caprices—that is, an explanation of what they depend upon, by what laws they arise, how they develop, what they are aiming at in one case and in another and so on, that is a real mathematical formula—then, most likely, man will at once cease to feel desire, indeed, he will be certain to. For who would want to choose by rule? Besides, he will at once be transformed from a human being into an organ-stop or something of the sort; for what is a man without desires, without freewill and without choice, if not a stop in an organ? What do you think? Let us reckon the chances—can such a thing happen or not?

"H'm!" you decide. "Our choice is usually mistaken from a false view of our advantage. We sometimes choose absolute nonsense because in our foolishness we see in that nonsense the easiest means for attaining a supposed advantage. But when all that is explained and worked out on paper (which is perfectly possible, for it is contemptible and senseless to suppose that some laws of nature man will never understand), then certainly so-called desires will no longer exist. For if a desire should come into conflict with reason we shall then reason and not desire, because it will be impossible retaining our reason to be *senseless* in our desires, and in that way knowingly act against reason and desire to injure ourselves. And as all choice and reasoning can be really calculated —because there will some day be discovered the laws of our so-called freewill—so, joking apart, there may one day be something like a table constructed of them, so that we really shall choose in accordance with it. If, for instance, some day they calculate and prove to me that I make a long nose at some one because I could not help making a long nose at him and that I had to do it in that particular way, what *freedom* is left me, especially if I am a learned man and have taken my degree somewhere? Then I should be able to calculate my whole life for thirty years beforehand. In short, if this could be arranged there would be nothing left for us to do; anyway, we should have to understand that. And, in fact, we ought unwearyingly to repeat to ourselves that at such and such a time and in such and such circumstances nature does not ask our leave; that we have got to take her as she is and not fashion her to suit our fancy, and if we really aspire to formulas and tables of rules, and well, even . . . to the chemical retort, there's no help for it, we must accept the retort too, or else it will be accepted without our consent. . . ."

Yes, but here I come to a stop! Gentlemen, you must excuse me for being over-philosophical; it's the result of forty years underground! Allow me to indulge my fancy. You see, gentlemen, reason is an excellent thing, there's no disputing that, but reason is nothing but reason and satisfies only the rational side of man's nature, while will is a manifestation of the whole life, that is, of the whole human life including reason and all the impulses. And although our life, in this manifestation of it, is often worthless, yet it is life and not simply extracting square roots. Here I, for instance, quite naturally want to live, in order to satisfy all my capacities for life, and not simply my capacity for reasoning, that is, not simply one twentieth of my capacity for life. What does reason know? Reason only knows what it has succeeded in learning (some things, perhaps, it will never learn; this is a poor comfort, but why not say so frankly?) and human nature acts as a whole, with everything that is in it, consciously or unconsciously, and, even if it goes wrong, it lives. I suspect, gentlemen, that you are looking at me with compassion; you tell me again that an enlightened and developed man, such, in short, as the future man will be, cannot consciously desire anything disadvantageous to himself, that that can be proved mathematically. I thoroughly agree, it can—by mathematics. But I repeat for the hundredth time, there is one case, one only, when man may consciously, purposely, desire what is injurious to himself, what is stupid, very stupid—simply in order to have the right to desire for himself even what is very stupid and not to be bound by an obligation to desire only what is sensible. Of course, this very stupid thing, this caprice of ours, may be in reality, gentlemen, more advantageous for us than anything else on earth, especially in certain cases. And in particular it may be more advantageous than any advantage even when it does us obvious harm, and contradicts the soundest conclusions of our reason concerning our advantage—for in any circumstances it preserves for us what is most precious and most important—that is, our personality, our individuality. Some, you see, maintain that this really is the most precious thing for mankind; choice can, of course, if it chooses, be in agreement with reason; and especially if this be not abused but kept within bounds. It is profitable and sometimes even praiseworthy. But very often, and even most often, choice is utterly and stubbornly opposed to reason . . . and . . . and . . . do you know that that, too, is profitable, sometimes even praiseworthy? Gentlemen, let us suppose that man is not stupid. (Indeed one cannot refuse to suppose that, if only from the one consideration, that, if man is stupid, then who is wise?) But if he is not stupid, he is monstrously ungrateful! Phenomenally ungrateful. In fact, I believe that the best definition of man is the ungrateful biped. But that is not all, that is not his worst defect; his worst defect is his perpetual moral obliquity, perpetual —from the days of the Flood to the Schleswig-Holstein period. Moral obliquity and consequently lack of good sense; for it has long been accepted that lack of good sense is due to no other cause than moral obliquity. Put it to the test and cast your eyes upon the history of mankind. What will you see? Is it a grand spectacle?

Grand, if you like. Take the Colossus of Rhodes,[11] for instance, that's worth something. With good reason Mr. Anaevsky testifies of it that some say that it is the work of man's hands, while others maintain that it has been created by nature herself. Is it many-coloured? May be it is many-coloured, too: if one takes the dress uniforms, military and civilian, of all peoples in all ages—that alone is worth something, and if you take the undress uniforms you will never get to the end of it; no historian would be equal to the job. Is it monotonous? May be it's monotonous too: it's fighting and fighting; they are fighting now, they fought first and they fought last—you will admit, that it is almost too monotonous. In short, one may say anything about the history of the world—anything that might enter the most disordered imagination. The only thing one can't say is that it's rational. The very word sticks in one's throat. And, indeed, this is the odd thing that is continually happening: there are continually turning up in life moral and rational persons, sages and lovers of humanity who make it their object to live all their lives as morally and rationally as possible, to be, so to speak, a light to their neighbours simply in order to show them that it is possible to live morally and rationally in this world. And yet we all know that those very people sooner or later have been false to themselves, playing some queer trick, often a most unseemly one. Now I ask you: what can be expected of man since he is a being endowed with such strange qualities? Shower upon him every earthly blessing, drown him in a sea of happiness, so that nothing but bubbles of bliss can be seen on the surface; give him economic prosperity, such that he should have nothing else to do but sleep, eat cakes and busy himself with the continuation of his species, and even then out of sheer ingratitude, sheer spite, man would play you some nasty trick. He would even risk his cakes and would deliberately desire the most fatal rubbish, the most uneconomical absurdity, simply to introduce into all this positive good sense his fatal fantastic element. It is just his fantastic dreams, his vulgar folly that he will desire to retain, simply in order to prove to himself—as though that were so necessary—that men still are men and not the keys of a piano, which the laws of nature threaten to control so completely that soon one will be able to desire nothing but by the calendar. And that is not all: even if man really were nothing but a piano-key, even if this were proved to him by natural science and mathematics, even then he would not become reasonable, but would purposely do something perverse out of simple ingratitude, simply to gain his point. And if he does not find means he will contrive

11. a statue of Helios (Apollo) at Rhodes (an island in the Aegean Sea), about a hundred feet high, which was considered one of the Seven Wonders of the World. It was erected about 290 B.C.

destruction and chaos, will contrive sufferings of all sorts, only to gain his point! He will launch a curse upon the world, and as only man can curse (it is his privilege, the primary distinction between him and other animals), may be by his curse alone he will attain his object—that is, convince himself that he is a man and not a piano-key! If you say that all this, too, can be calculated and tabulated—chaos and darkness and curses, so that the mere possibility of calculating it all beforehand would stop it all, and reason would reassert itself, then man would purposely go mad in order to be rid of reason and gain his point! I believe in it, I answer for it, for the whole work of man really seems to consist in nothing but proving to himself every minute that he is a man and not a piano-key! It may be at the cost of his skin, it may be by cannibalism! And this being so, can one help being tempted to rejoice that it has not yet come off, and that desire still depends on something we don't know?

You will scream at me (that is, if you condescend to do so) that no one is touching my free will, that all they are concerned with is that my will should of itself, of its own free will, coincide with my own normal interests, with the laws of nature and arithmetic.

Good Heavens, gentlemen, what sort of free will is left when we come to tabulation and arithmetic, when it will all be a case of twice two makes four? Twice two makes four without my will. As if free will meant that!

IX

Gentlemen, I am joking, and I know myself that my jokes are not brilliant, but you know one can't take everything as a joke. I am, perhaps, jesting against the grain. Gentlemen, I am tormented by questions; answer them for me. You, for instance, want to cure men of their old habits and reform their will in accordance with science and good sense. But how do you know, not only that it is possible, but also that it is *desirable*, to reform man in that way? And what leads you to the conclusion that man's inclinations *need* reforming? In short, how do you know that such a reformation will be a benefit to man? And to go to the root of the matter, why are you so positively convinced that not to act against his real normal interests guaranteed by the conclusions of reason and arithmetic is certainly always advantageous for man and must always be a law for mankind? So far, you know, this is only your supposition. It may be the law of logic, but not the law of humanity. You think, gentlemen, perhaps that I am mad? Allow me to defend myself. I agree that man is pre-eminently a creative animal, predestined to strive consciously for an object and to engage in engineering—that is, incessantly and eternally to make new roads, *wherever they may lead*. But the reason why he wants sometimes to go off at a tangent may just be that he is *predestined* to make the road, and perhaps, too, that however stupid the "direct" practical man may be, the thought sometimes will occur to him that the road almost always does lead *somewhere*, and that the destination it leads to is less important than the process of making it, and that the chief thing is to save the well-conducted child from despising engineering, and so giving way to the fatal idleness, which, as we all know, is the mother of all the vices. Man likes to make roads and to create, that is a fact beyond dispute. But why has he such a passionate love for destruction and chaos also? Tell me that! But on that point I want to say a couple of words myself. May it not be that he loves chaos and destruction (there can be no disputing that he does sometimes love it) because he is instinctively afraid of attaining his object and completing the edifice he is constructing? Who knows, perhaps he only loves that edifice from a distance, and is by no means in love with it at close quarters; perhaps he only loves building it and does not want to live in it, but will leave it, when completed, for the use of *les animaux domestiques*—such as the ants, the sheep, and so on. Now the ants have quite a different taste. They have a marvellous edifice of that pattern which endures for ever—the ant-heap.

With the ant-heap the respectable race of ants began and with the ant-heap they will probably end, which does the greatest credit to their perseverance and good sense. But man is a frivolous and incongruous creature, and perhaps, like a chess player, loves the process of the game, not the end of it. And who knows (there is no saying with certainty), perhaps the only goal on earth to which mankind is striving lies in this incessant process of attaining, in other words, in life itself, and not in the thing to be attained, which must always be expressed as a formula, as positive as twice two makes four, and such positiveness is not life, gentlemen, but is the beginning of death. Anyway, man has always been afraid of this mathematical certainty, and I am afraid of it now. Granted that man does nothing but seek that mathematical certainty, he traverses oceans, sacrifices his life in the quest, but to succeed, really to find it, he dreads, I assure you. He feels that when he has found it there will be nothing for him to look for. When workmen have finished their work they do at least receive their pay, they go to the tavern, then they are taken to the police-station—and there is occupation for a week. But where can man go? Anyway, one can observe a certain awkwardness about him when he has attained such objects. He loves the process of attaining, but does not quite like to have attained, and that, of course, is very absurd. In fact, man is a comical creature; there seems to be a kind of jest in it all. But yet mathematical certainty is, after all, something insufferable. Twice two makes four seems to me simply a piece of insolence. Twice two makes four is a pert coxcomb who stands with arms akimbo barring your path and spitting. I admit that twice two makes four is an excellent thing, but if we are to give everything its due, twice two makes five is sometimes a very charming thing too.

And why are you so firmly, so triumphantly, convinced that only the normal and the positive—in other words, only what is conducive to welfare—is for the advantage of man? Is not reason in error as regards advantage? Does not man, perhaps, love something besides well-being? Perhaps he is just as fond of suffering? Perhaps suffering is just as great a benefit to him as well-being? Man is sometimes extraordinarily, passionately, in love with suffering, and that is a fact. There is no need to appeal to universal history to prove that; only ask yourself, if you are a man and have lived at all. As far as my personal opinion is concerned, to care only for well-being seems to me positively ill-bred. Whether it's good or bad, it is sometimes very pleasant, too, to smash things. I hold no brief for suffering nor for well-being either. I am standing for . . . my caprice, and for its being guaranteed to me when necessary. Suffering would be out of place in vaudevilles, for instance; I know that. In the "Crystal Palace" it is unthinkable; suffering means doubt, negation, and what would be the good of a crystal palace if there could be any doubt about it? And yet I think man will never renounce real suffering, that is, destruction and chaos. Why, suffering is the sole origin of consciousness. Though I did lay it down at the beginning that consciousness is the greatest misfortune for man, yet I know man prizes it and would not give it up for any satisfaction. Consciousness, for instance, is infinitely superior to twice two makes four. Once you have mathematical certainty there is nothing left to do or to understand. There will be nothing left but to bottle up your five senses and plunge into contemplation. While if you stick to consciousness, even though the same result is attained, you can at least flog yourself at times, and that will, at any rate, liven you up. Reactionary as it is, corporal punishment is better than nothing.

X[12]

You believe in a crystal palace that can never be destroyed— a palace at which one will not be able to put out one's tongue or make a long nose on the sly. And perhaps that is just why I am afraid of this edifice, that it is of crystal and can never be destroyed and that one cannot put one's tongue out at it even on the sly.

12. Section X was badly mutilated by the censor, as Dostoevsky makes clear in the letter to his brother Mikhail, dated March 26, 1864, which is quoted in our introduction.

You see, if it were not a palace, but a hen-house, I might creep into it to avoid getting wet, and yet I would not call the hen-house a palace out of gratitude to it for keeping me dry. You laugh and say that in such circumstances a hen-house is as good as a mansion. Yes, I answer, if one had to live simply to keep out of the rain.

But what is to be done if I have taken it into my head that that is not the only object in life, and that if one must live one had better live in a mansion. That is my choice, my desire. You will only eradicate it when you have changed my preference. Well, do change it, allure me with something else, give me another ideal. But meanwhile I will not take a hen-house for a mansion. The crystal palace may be an idle dream, it may be that it is inconsistent with the laws of nature and that I have invented it only through my own stupidity, through the old-fashioned irrational habits of my generation. But what does it matter to me that it is inconsistent? That makes no difference since it exists in my desires, or rather exists as long as my desires exist. Perhaps you are laughing again? Laugh away; I will put up with any mockery rather than pretend that I am satisfied when I am hungry. I know, anyway, that I will not be put off with a compromise, with a recurring zero, simply because it is consistent with the laws of nature and actually exists. I will not accept as the crown of my desires a block of slum tenements on a lease of a thousand years, and perhaps with a sign-board of Wagenheim the dentist hanging out. Destroy my desires, eradicate my ideals, show me something better, and I will follow you. You will say, perhaps, that it is not worth your trouble; but in that case I can give you the same answer. We are discussing things seriously; but if you won't deign to give me your attention, I will drop your acquaintance. I can retreat into my underground hole.

But while I am alive and have desires I would rather my hand were withered off than bring one brick to such a building! Don't remind me that I have just rejected the crystal palace for the sole reason that one cannot put out one's tongue at it. I did not say because I am so fond of putting my tongue out. Perhaps the thing I resented was, that of all your edifices there has not been one at which one could not put out one's tongue. On the contrary, I would let my tongue be cut off out of gratitude if things could be so arranged that I should lose all desire to put it out. It is not my fault that things cannot be so arranged, and that one must be satisfied with model flats. Then why am I made with such desires? Can I have been constructed simply in order to come to the conclusion that all my construction is a cheat? Can this be my whole purpose? I do not believe it.

But do you know what: I am convinced that we underground folk ought to be kept on a curb. Though we may sit forty years underground without speaking, when we do come out into the light of day and break out we talk and talk and talk. . . .

XI

The long and the short of it is, gentlemen, that it is better to do nothing! Better conscious inertia! And so hurrah for underground! Though I have said that I envy the normal man to the last drop of my bile, yet I should not care to be in his place such as he is now (though I shall not cease envying him). No, no; anyway the underground life is more advantageous. There, at any rate, one can. . . . Oh, but even now I am lying! I am lying because I know myself that it is not underground that is better, but something different, quite different, for which I am thirsting, but which I cannot find! Damn underground!

I will tell you another thing that would be better, and that is, if I myself believed in anything of what I have just written. I swear to you, gentlemen, there is not one thing, not one word of what I have written that I really believe. That is, I believe it, perhaps, but at the same time I feel and suspect that I am lying like a cobbler.

"Then why have you written all this?" you will say to me. "I ought to put you underground for forty years without anything to do and then come to you in your cellar, to find out what stage you have reached! How can a man be left with nothing to do for forty years?"

"Isn't that shameful, isn't that humiliating?" you will say, perhaps, wagging your heads contemptuously. "You thirst for life and try to settle the problems of life by a logical tangle. And how persistent, how insolent are your sallies, and at the same time what a scare you are in! You talk nonsense and are pleased with it; you say impudent things and are in continual alarm and apologizing for them. You declare that you are afraid of nothing and at the same time try to ingratiate yourself in our good opinion. You declare that you are gnashing your teeth and at the same time you try to be witty so as to amuse us. You know that your witticisms are not witty, but you are evidently well satisfied with their literary value. You may, perhaps, have really suffered, but you have no respect for your own suffering. You may have sincerity, but you have no modesty; out of the pettiest vanity you expose your sincerity to publicity and ignominy. You doubtlessly mean to say something, but hide your last word through fear, because you have not the resolution to utter it, and only have a cowardly impudence. You boast of consciousness, but you are not sure of your ground, for though your mind works, yet your heart is darkened and corrupt, and you cannot have a full, genuine consciousness without a pure heart. And how intrusive you are, how you insist and grimace! Lies, lies, lies!"

Of course I have myself made up all the things you say. That, too, is from underground. I have been for forty years listening to you through a crack under the floor. I have invented them myself, there was nothing else I could invent. It is no wonder that I have learned it by heart and it has taken a literary form. . .

But can you really be so credulous as to think that I will print all this and give it to you to read too? And another problem: why do I call you "gentlemen," why do I address you as though you really were my readers? Such confessions as I intend to make are never printed nor given to other people to read. Anyway, I am not strong-minded enough for that, and I don't see why I should be. But you see a fancy has occurred to me and I want to realize it at all costs. Let me explain.

Every man has reminiscences which he would not tell to every one, but only to his friends. He has other matters in his mind which he would not reveal even to his friends, but only to himself, and that in secret. But there are other things which a man is afraid to tell even to himself, and every decent man has a number of such things stored away in his mind. The more decent he is, the greater the number of such things in his mind. Anyway, I have only lately determined to remember some of my early adventures. Till now I have always avoided them, even with a certain uneasiness. Now, when I am not only recalling them, but have actually decided to write an account of them, I want to try the experiment whether one can, even with oneself, be perfectly open and not take fright at the whole truth. I will observe, in parenthesis, that Heine[13] says that a true autobiography is almost an impossibility, and that man is bound to lie about himself. He considers that Rousseau certainly told lies about himself in his *Confessions*, and even intentionally lied, out of vanity. I am convinced that Heine is right; I quite understand how sometimes one may, out of sheer vanity, attribute regular crimes to oneself, and indeed I can very well conceive that kind of vanity. But Heine judged of people who made their confessions to the public. I write only for myself, and I wish to declare once and for all that if I write as though I were addressing readers, that is simply because it is easier for me to write in that form. It is a form, an empty form—I shall never have readers. I have made this plain already. . .

I don't wish to be hampered by any restrictions in the compilation of my notes. I shall not attempt any system or method. I will jot things down as I remember them.

But here, perhaps, some one will catch at the word and ask me: if you really don't reckon on readers, why do you make such compacts with yourself—and on paper too—that is, that you won't at-

13. Dostoevsky alludes to *Confessions* (*Geständnisse*, 1854), fragmentary memoirs written by the German poet Heinrich Heine (1797–1856), in which on the very first page Heine speaks of Rousseau as lying and inventing disgraceful incidents about himself for his *Confessions*. (See footnote 2.)

tempt any system or method, that you jot things down as you remember them, and so on, and so on? Why are you explaining? Why
do you apologize?

Well, there it is, I answer.

There is a whole psychology in all this, though. Perhaps it is
simply that I am a coward. And perhaps that I purposely imagine
an audience before me in order that I may be more dignified while
I write. There are perhaps thousands of reasons. Again, what is my
object precisely in writing? If it is not for the benefit of the public
why should I not simply recall these incidents in my own mind
without putting them on paper?

Quite so; but yet it is more imposing on paper. There is something more impressive in it; I shall be better able to criticize myself
and improve my style. Besides, I shall perhaps obtain actual relief
from writing. To-day, for instance, I am particularly oppressed by
one memory of a distant past. It came back vividly to my mind a
few days ago, and has remained haunting me like an annoying tune
that one cannot get rid of. And yet I must get rid of it somehow. I
have hundreds of such reminiscences; but at times some one stands
out from the hundred and oppresses me. For some reason I believe
that if I write it down I should get rid of it. Why not try?

Besides, I am bored, and I never have anything to do. Writing
will be a sort of work. They say work makes man kind-hearted and
honest. Well, here is a chance for me, anyway.

Snow is falling to-day, yellow and dingy. It fell yesterday, too, and
a few days ago. I fancy it is the wet snow that has reminded me
of that incident which I cannot shake off now. And so let it be a
story *à propos* of the falling snow.

Part II

À PROPOS OF THE WET SNOW

When from dark error's subjugation
My words of passionate exhortation
    Had wrenched thy fainting spirit free;
And writhing prone in thine affliction
Thou didst recall with malediction
    The vice that had encompassed thee:
And when thy slumbering conscience, fretting
    By recollection's torturing flame,
Thou didst reveal the hideous setting
    Of thy life's current ere I came:
When suddenly I saw thee sicken,
    And weeping, hide thine anguished face,
Revolted, maddened, horror-stricken,
    At memories of foul disgrace, etc., etc., etc. . . . .
                    NEKRASOV[14] (*translated by Juliet Soskice*)

14. Nikolay A. Nekrasov (1821–
1878) was a famous Russian poet and
editor of radical sympathies. The poem
quoted dates from 1845, and is without
title. The poem ends with the lines,
"Into my house come bold and free, /
Its rightful mistress there to be."

I

At that time I was only twenty-four. My life was even then gloomy, ill-regulated, and as solitary as that of a savage. I made friends with no one and positively avoided talking, and buried myself more and more in my hole. At work in the office I never looked at any one, and I was perfectly well aware that my companions looked upon me, not only as a queer fellow, but even looked upon me—I always fancied this—with a sort of loathing. I sometimes wondered why it was that nobody except me fancied that he was looked upon with aversion? One of the clerks had a most repulsive, pock-marked face, which looked positively villainous. I believe I should not have dared to look at any one with such an unsightly countenance. Another had such a very dirty old uniform that there was an unpleasant odor in his proximity. Yet not one of these gentlemen showed the slightest self-consciousness—either about their clothes or their countenance or their character in any way. Neither of them ever imagined that they were looked at with repulsion; if they had imagined it they would not have minded—so long as their superiors did not look at them in that way. It is clear to me now that, owing to my unbounded vanity and to the high standard I set for myself, I often looked at myself with furious discontent, which verged on loathing, and so I inwardly attributed the same feeling to every one. I hated my face, for instance: I thought it disgusting, and even suspected that there was something base in my expression, and so every day when I turned up at the office I tried to behave as independently as possible, and to assume a lofty expression, so that I might not be suspected of being abject. "My face may be ugly," I thought, "but let it be lofty, expressive, and, above all, *extremely* intelligent." But I was positively and painfully certain that it was impossible for my countenance ever to express those qualities. And what was worst of all, I thought it actually stupid looking, and I would have been quite satisfied if I could have looked intelligent. In fact, I would even have put up with looking base if, at the same time, my face could have been thought strikingly intelligent.

Of course, I hated my fellow clerks one and all, and I despised them all, yet at the same time I was, as it were, afraid of them. In fact, it happened at times that I thought more highly of them than of myself. It somehow happened quite suddenly that I alternated between despising them and thinking them superior to myself. A cultivated and decent man cannot be vain without setting a fearfully high standard for himself, and without despising and almost hating himself at certain moments. But whether I despised them or thought them superior I dropped my eyes almost every time I met any one. I even made experiments whether I could face so and so's looking at me, and I was always the first to drop my eyes. This worried me to distraction. I had a sickly dread, too, of being ridiculous, and so had a slavish passion for the conventional in everything external. I loved to fall into the common rut, and had a whole-hearted terror of any kind of eccentricity in myself. But how could I live up to it? I was morbidly sensitive, as a man of our age should be. They were all stupid, and as like one another as so many sheep. Perhaps I was the only one in the office who fancied that I was a coward and a slave, and I fancied it just because I was more highly developed. But it was not only that I fancied it, it really was so. I was a coward and a slave. I say this without the slightest embarrassment. Every decent man of our age must be a coward and a slave. That is his normal condition. Of that I am firmly persuaded. He is made and constructed to that very end. And not only at the present time owing to some casual circumstances, but always, at all times, a decent man is bound to be a coward and a slave. It is the law of nature for all decent people all over the earth. If any one of them happens to be valiant about something, he need not be comforted nor carried away by that; he would show the white feather just the same before something else. That is how it invariably and inevitably ends. Only donkeys and mules are valiant, and they only till they are pushed up to the wall. It is not worth while to pay attention to them for they really are of no consequence.

Another circumstance, too, worried me in those days: that there was no one like me and I was unlike any one else. "I am unique and they are all alike," I thought—and pondered.

From that it is evident that I was still a youngster.

The very opposite sometimes happened. It was loathsome sometimes to go to the office; things reached such a point that I often came home ill. But all at once, *à propos* of nothing, there would come a phase of scepticism and indifference (everything happened in phases to me), and I would laugh myself at my intolerance and fastidiousness, I would reproach myself with being *romantic*. At one time I was unwilling to speak to any one, while at other times I would not only talk, but go to the length of contemplating making friends with them. All my fastidiousness would suddenly, for no rhyme or reason, vanish. Who knows, perhaps I never had really had it, and it had simply been affected, and got out of books. I have not decided that question even now. Once I quite made friends with them, visited their homes, played preference, drank vodka, talked of promotions. . . . But here let me make a digression.

We Russians, speaking generally, have never had those foolish transcendental "romantics"—German, and still more French—on whom nothing produces any effect; if there were an earthquake, if all France perished at the barricades, they would still be the same, they would not even have the decency to affect a change, but would still go on singing their transcendental songs to the hour of their death, because they are fools. We, in Russia, have no fools; that is well known. That is what distinguishes us from foreign lands. Consequently these transcendental natures are not found amongst us in their pure form. The idea that they are is due to our "realistic" journalists and critics of that day, always on the look out for Kostanzhoglos[15] and Uncle Pyotr Ivanichs[16] and foolishly accepting them as our ideal; they have slandered our romantics, taking them for the same transcendental sort as in Germany or France. On the contrary, the characteristics of our "romantics" are absolutely and directly opposed to the transcendental European type, and no European standard can be applied to them. (Allow me to make use of this word "romantic"—an old-fashioned and much respected word which has done good service and is familiar to all). The characteristics of our romantic are to understand everything, *to see everything and to see it often incomparably more clearly than our most realistic minds see it*; to refuse to accept anyone or anything, but at the same time not to despise anything; to give way, to yield, from policy; never to lose sight of a useful practical object (such as rent-free quarters at the government expense, pensions, decorations), to keep their eye on that object through all the enthusiasms and volumes of lyrical poems, and at the same time to preserve "the good and the beautiful" inviolate within them to the hour of their death, and to preserve themselves also, incidentally, like some precious jewel wrapped in cotton wool if only for the benefit of "the good and the beautiful." Our "romantic" is a man of great breadth and the greatest rogue of all our rogues, I assure you. . . . I can assure you from experience, indeed. Of course, that is, if he is intelligent. But what am I saying! The romantic is always intelligent, and I only meant to observe that although we have had foolish romantics they don't count, and they were only so because in the flower of their youth they degenerated into Germans, and to preserve their precious jewel more comfortably, settled somewhere out there—by preference in Weimar or the Black Forest.

I, for instance, genuinely despised my official work and did not openly abuse it simply because I was in it myself and got a salary for it. Anyway, take note, I did not openly abuse it. Our romantic would rather go out of his mind—a thing, however, which very rarely happens—than take to open abuse, unless he had some other

15. Konstanzhoglo is the ideal efficient landowner in the second part of Gogol's novel *Dead Souls* (published posthumously in 1852).

16. Uncle Pyotr Ivanich, a character in Ivan Goncharov's novel *A Common Story* (1847), is a high bureaucrat, a factory owner who teaches lessons of sobriety and good sense to the romantic hero, Alexander Aduyev.

career in view; and he is never kicked out. At most, they would take him to the lunatic asylum as "the King of Spain"[17] if he should go very mad. But it is only the thin, fair people who go out of their minds in Russia. Innumerable "romantics" attain later in life to considerable rank in the service. Their many-sidedness is remarkable! And what a faculty they have for the most contradictory sensations! I was comforted by this thought even in those days, and I am of the same opinion now. That is why there are so many "broad natures" among us who never lose their ideal even in the depths of degradation; and though they never stir a finger for their ideal, though they are arrant thieves and knaves, yet they tearfully cherish their first ideal and are extraordinarily honest at heart. Yes, it is only among us that the most incorrigible rogue can be absolutely and loftily honest at heart without in the least ceasing to be a rogue. I repeat, our romantics, frequently, become such accomplished rascals (I use the term "rascals" affectionately), suddenly display such a sense of reality and practical knowledge that their bewildered superiors and the public generally can only ejaculate in amazement.

Their many-sidedness is really amazing, and goodness knows what it may develop into later on, and what the future has in store for us. It is not a poor material! I do not say this from any foolish or boastful patriotism. But I feel sure that you are again imagining that I am joking. Or perhaps it's just the contrary and you are convinced that I really think so. Anyway, gentlemen, I shall welcome both views as an honour and a special favour. And do forgive my digression.

I did not, of course, maintain friendly relations with my comrades and soon was at loggerheads with them, and in my youth and inexperience I even gave up bowing to them, as though I had cut off all relations. That, however, only happened to me once. As a rule, I was always alone.

In the first place I spent most of my time at home, reading. I tried to stifle all that was continually seething within me by means of external impressions. And the only external means I had was reading. Reading, of course, was a great help—exciting me, giving me pleasure and pain. But at times it bored me fearfully. One longed for movement in spite of everything, and I plunged all at once into dark, underground, loathsome vice of the pettiest kind. My wretched passions were acute, smarting, from my continual, sickly irritability. I had hysterical impulses, with tears and convulsions. I had no resource except reading, that is, there was nothing in my surroundings which I could respect and which attracted me. I was overwhelmed with depression, too; I had a hysterical craving for incongruity and

17. an allusion to Gogol's story "Memoirs of a Madman" (1835). The narrator imagines himself "the King of Spain" and is finally carried off to a lunatic asylum.

for contrast, and so I took to vice. I have not said all this to justify myself. . . . But, no! I am lying. I did want to justify myself. I make that little observation for my own benefit, gentlemen. I don't want to lie. I vowed to myself I would not.

And so, furtively, timidly, in solitude, at night, I indulged in filthy vice, with a feeling of shame which never deserted me, even at the most loathsome moments, and which at such moments nearly made me curse. Already even then I had my underground world in my soul. I was fearfully afraid of being seen, of being met, of being recognized. I visited various obscure haunts.

One night as I was passing a tavern I saw through a lighted window some gentlemen fighting with billiard cues, and saw one of them thrown out of a window. At other times I should have felt very much disgusted, but I was in such a mood at the time, that I actually envied the gentleman thrown out of a window—and I envied him so much that I even went into the tavern and into the billiard-room. "Perhaps," I thought, "I'll have a fight, too, and they'll throw me out of the window."

I was not drunk—but what is one to do—depression will drive a man to such a pitch of hysteria? But nothing happened. It seemed that I was not even equal to being thrown out of the window and I went away without having my fight.

An officer put me in my place from the first moment.

I was standing by the billiard-table and in my ignorance blocking up the way, and he wanted to pass; he took me by the shoulders and without a word—without a warning or explanation—moved me from where I was standing to another spot and passed by as though he had not noticed me. I could have forgiven blows, but I could not forgive his having moved me without noticing me.

Devil knows what I would have given for a real regular quarrel— a more decent, a more *literary* one, so to speak. I had been treated like a fly. This officer was over six foot, while I was a spindly little fellow. But the quarrel was in my hands. I had only to protest and I certainly would have been thrown out of the window. But I changed my mind and preferred to beat a resentful retreat.

I went out of the tavern straight home, confused and troubled, and the next night I went out again with the same lewd intentions, still more furtively, abjectly and miserably than before, as it were, with tears in my eyes—but still I did go out again. Don't imagine, though, it was cowardice made me slink away from the officer: I never have been a coward at heart, though I have always been a coward in action. Don't be in a hurry to laugh—I assure you I can explain it all.

Oh, if only that officer had been one of the sort who would consent to fight a duel! But no, he was one of those gentlemen (alas, long extinct!) who preferred fighting with cues or, like Gogol's Lieutenant Pirogov,[18] appealing to the police. They did not fight duels and would have thought a duel with a civilian like me an utterly unseemly procedure in any case—and they looked upon the duel altogether as something impossible, something free-thinking and French. But they were quite ready to bully, especially when they were over six foot.

I did not slink away through cowardice, but through an un-bounded vanity. I was afraid not of his six foot, not of getting a sound thrashing and being thrown out of the window; I should have had physical courage enough, I assure you; but I had not the moral courage. What I was afraid of was that every one present, from the insolent marker down to the lowest little stinking, pimply clerk in a greasy collar, would jeer at me and fail to understand when I began to protest and to address them in literary language. For of the point of honour—not of honour, but of the point of honour (*point d'honneur*)—one cannot speak among us except in literary language. You can't allude to the "point of honour" in ordinary language. I was fully convinced (the sense of reality, in spite of all my romanticism!) that they would all simply split their sides with laughter, and that the officer would not simply beat me, that is, without insulting me, but would certainly prod me in the back with his knee, kick me round the billiard-table, and only then per-haps have pity and drop me out of the window.

Of course, this trivial incident could not with me end in that. I often met that officer afterwards in the street and noticed him very carefully. I am not quite sure whether he recognized me, I imagine not; I judge from certain signs. But I—I stared at him with spite and hatred and so it went on . . . for several years! My resentment grew even deeper with years. At first I began making stealthy in-quiries about this officer. It was difficult for me to do so, for I knew no one. But one day I heard some one shout his surname in the street as I was following him at a distance, as though I were tied to him—and so I learnt his surname. Another time I followed him to his flat, and for ten kopecks learned from the porter where he lived, on which storey, whether he lived alone or with others, and so on—in fact, everything one could learn from a porter. One morning, though I had never tried my hand with the pen, it suddenly occurred to me to write a satire on this officer in the form of a novel which would unmask his villainy. I wrote the novel with relish. I did unmask his villainy, I even exaggerated it; at first I so altered his surname that it could easily be recognized, but on second thoughts

18. a character in Gogol's story "The Nevsky Prospekt" (1835). He pays violent court to the wife of a German tradesman and is thrown out by him and his friends. He does not actually call the police.

I changed it, and sent the story to the *Otechestvenniye Zapiski*.[19] But at that time such attacks were not the fashion and my story was not printed. That was a great vexation to me.

Sometimes I was positively choked with resentment. At last I determined to challenge my enemy to a duel. I composed a splendid, charming letter to him, imploring him to apologize to me, and hinting rather plainly at a duel in case of refusal. The letter was so composed that if the officer had had the least understanding of the good and the beautiful he would certainly have flung himself on my neck and have offered me his friendship. And how fine that would have been! How we should have got on together! "He could have shielded me with his higher rank, while I could have improved his mind with my culture, and, well . . . my ideas, and all sorts of things might have happened." Only fancy, this was two years after his insult to me, and my challenge would have been a ridiculous anachronism, in spite of all the ingenuity of my letter in disguising and explaining away the anachronism. But, thank God (to this day I thank the Almighty with tears in my eyes) I did not send the letter to him. Cold shivers run down my back when I think of what might have happened if I had sent it.

And all at once I revenged myself in the simplest way, by a stroke of genius! A brilliant thought suddenly dawned upon me. Sometimes on holidays I used to stroll along the sunny side of the Nevsky[20] about four o'clock in the afternoon. Though it was hardly a stroll so much as a series of innumerable miseries, humiliations and resentments; but no doubt that was just what I wanted. I used to wriggle along in a most unseemly fashion, like an eel, continually moving aside to make way for generals, for officers of the guards and the hussars, or for ladies. At such minutes there used to be a convulsive twinge at my heart, and I used to feel hot all down my back at the mere thought of the wretchedness of my attire, of the wretchedness and abjectness of my little scurrying figure. This was a regular martyrdom, a continual, intolerable humiliation at the thought, which passed into an incessant and direct sensation, that I was a mere fly in the eyes of all this world, a nasty, disgusting fly— more intelligent, more highly developed, more refined in feeling than any of them, of course—but a fly that was continually making way for every one, insulted and injured by every one. Why I inflicted this torture upon myself, why I went to the Nevsky, I don't know. I felt simply drawn there at every possible opportunity.

Already then I began to experience a rush of the enjoyment of

19. *Notes of the Fatherland*, the most famous radical Russian journal, founded in 1839.

20. Nevsky Prospekt, the most elegant main street in St. Petersburg, about three miles long; now called "Prospekt of the 25th October."

which I spoke in the first chapter. After my affair with the officer I felt even more drawn there than before: it was on the Nevsky that I met him most frequently, there I could admire him. He, too, went there chiefly on holidays. He, too, turned out of his path for generals and persons of high rank, and he, too, wriggled between them like an eel; but people, like me, or even better dressed like me, he simply walked over; he made straight for them as though there was nothing but empty space before him, and never, under any circumstances, turned aside. I gloated over my resentment watching him and . . . always resentfully made way for him. It exasperated me that even in the street I could not be on an even footing with him.

"Why must you invariably be the first to move aside?" I kept asking myself in hysterical rage, waking up sometimes at three o'clock in the morning. "Why is it you and not he? There's no regulation about it; there's no written law. Let the making way be equal as it usually is when refined people meet: he moves half-way and you move half-way; you pass with mutual respect."

But that never happened, and I always moved aside, while he did not even notice my making way for him. And lo and behold a bright idea dawned upon me! "What," I thought, "if I meet him and don't move on one side? What if I don't move aside on purpose, even if I knock up against him? How would that be?" This audacious idea took such a hold on me that it gave me no peace. I was dreaming of it continually, horribly, and I purposely went more frequently to the Nevsky in order to picture more vividly how I should do it when I did do it. I was delighted. This intention seemed to me more and more practical and possible.

"Of course I shall not really push him," I thought, already more good-natured in my joy. "I will simply not turn aside, will run up against him, not very violently, but just shouldering each other—just as much as decency permits. I will push against him just as much as he pushes against me." At last I made up my mind completely. But my preparations took a great deal of time. To begin with, when I carried out my plan I should need to be looking rather more decent, and so I had to think of my get-up. "In case of emergency, if, for instance, there were any sort of public scandal (and the public there is of the most *recherché*: the Countess walks there; Prince D. walks there; all the literary world is there), I must be well dressed; that inspires respect and of itself puts us on an equal footing in the eyes of society."

With this object I asked for some of my salary in advance, and bought at Churkin's a pair of black gloves and a decent hat. Black gloves seemed to me both more dignified and *bon ton* than the lemon-coloured ones which I had contemplated at first. "The colour is too gaudy, it looks as though one were trying to be conspicuous," and I did not take the lemon-coloured ones. I had got ready long beforehand a good shirt, with white bone studs; my overcoat was the only thing that held me back. The coat in itself was a very good one, it kept me warm; but it was wadded and it had a raccoon collar which was the height of vulgarity. I had to change the collar at any sacrifice, and to have a beaver one like an officer's. For this purpose I began visiting the Gostiny Dvor[21] and after several attempts I pitched upon a piece of cheap German beaver. Though these German beavers soon grow shabby and look wretched, yet at first they look exceedingly well, and I only needed it for one occasion. I asked the price; even so, it was too expensive. After thinking it over thoroughly I decided to sell my raccoon collar. The rest of the money— a considerable sum for me, I decided to borrow from Anton Antonich Syetochkin, my immediate superior, an unassuming person, though grave and judicious. He never lent money to any one, but I had, on entering the service, been specially recommended to him by an important personage who had got me my berth. I was horribly worried. To borrow from Anton Antonich seemed to me monstrous and shameful. I did not sleep for two or three nights. Indeed, I did not sleep well at that time, I was in a fever; I had a vague sinking at my heart or else a sudden throbbing, throbbing, throbbing! Anton Antonich was surprised at first, then he frowned, then he reflected, and did after all lend me the money, receiving from me a written authorization to take from my salary a fortnight later the sum that he had lent me.

In this way everything was at last ready. The handsome beaver replaced the mean-looking raccoon, and I began by degrees to get to work. It would never have done to act off-hand, at random; the plan had to be carried out skilfully, by degrees. But I must confess that after many efforts I began to despair: we simply could not run into each other. I made every preparation, I was quite determined— it seemed as though we should run into one another directly—and before I knew what I was doing I had stepped aside for him again and he had passed without noticing me. I even prayed as I approached him that God would grant me determination. One time I had made up my mind thoroughly, but it ended in my stumbling and falling at his feet because at the very last instant when I was six inches from him my courage failed me. He very calmly stepped over me, while I flew on one side like a ball. That night I was ill again, feverish and delirious.

And suddenly it ended most happily. The night before I had made up my mind not to carry out my fatal plan and to abandon it all, and

21. originally a guesthouse for foreign merchants; later used for displaying their wares.

with that object I went to the Nevsky for the last time, just to see how I would abandon it all. Suddenly, three paces from my enemy, I unexpectedly made up my mind—I closed my eyes, and we ran full tilt, shoulder to shoulder, against one another! I did not budge an inch and passed him on a perfectly equal footing! He did not even look round and pretended not to notice it; but he was only pretending, I am convinced of that. I am convinced of that to this day! Of course, I got the worst of it—he was stronger, but that was not the point. The point was that I had attained my object, I had kept up my dignity, I had not yielded a step, and had put myself publicly on an equal social footing with him. I returned home feeling that I was fully avenged for everything. I was delighted. I was triumphant and sang Italian arias. Of course, I will not describe to you what happened to me three days later; if you have read my first chapter you can guess that for yourself. The officer was afterwards transferred; I have not seen him now for fourteen years. What is the dear fellow doing now? Whom is he walking over?

II

But the period of my dissipation would end and I always felt very sick afterwards. It was followed by remorse—I tried to drive it away: I felt too sick. By degrees, however, I grew used to that too. I grew used to everything, or rather I voluntarily resigned myself to enduring it. But I had a means of escape that reconciled everything— that was to find refuge in "the good and the beautiful," in dreams, of course. I was a terrible dreamer, I would dream for three months on end, tucked away in my corner, and you may believe me that at those moments I had no resemblance to the gentleman who, in the perturbation of his chicken heart, put a collar of German beaver on his great coat. I suddenly became a hero. I would not have admitted my six-foot lieutenant even if he had called on me. I could not even picture him before me then. What were my dreams and how I could satisfy myself with them—it is hard to say now, but at the time I was satisfied with them. Though, indeed, even now, I am to some extent satisfied with them. Dreams were particularly sweet and vivid after a spell of dissipation; they came with remorse and with tears, with curses and transports. There were moments of such positive intoxication, of such happiness, that there was not the faintest trace of irony within me, on my honour. I had faith, hope, love. I believed blindly at such times that by some miracle, by some external circumstance, all this would suddenly open out, expand; that suddenly a vista of suitable activity—beneficent, good, and, above all, *ready made* (what sort of activity I had no idea, but the great thing was that it should be all ready for me)—would rise up before me— and I should come out into the light of day, almost riding a white horse and crowned with laurel. Anything but the foremost place I could not conceive for myself, and for that very reason I quite content-edly occupied the lowest in reality. Either to be a hero or to grovel in the mud—there was nothing between. That was my ruin, for when I was in the mud I comforted myself with the thought that at other times I was a hero, and the hero was a cloak for the mud: for an ordinary man it was shameful to defile himself, but a hero was too lofty to be utterly defiled, and so he might defile himself. It is worth noting that these attacks of the "good and the beautiful" visited me even during the period of dissipation and just at the times when I was touching bottom. They came in separate spurts, as though re-minding me of themselves, but did not banish the dissipation by their appearance. On the contrary, they seemed to add a zest to it by contrast, and were only sufficiently present to serve as an ap-petizing sauce. That sauce was made up of contradictions and suf-ferings, of agonizing inward analysis, and all these pangs and pin-pricks gave a certain piquancy, even a significance to my dissipa-tion—in fact, completely answered the purpose of an appetizing sauce. There was a certain depth of meaning in it. And I could hardly have resigned myself to the simple, vulgar, direct debauchery of a clerk and have endured all the filthiness of it. What could have allured me about it then and have drawn me at night into the street? No, I had a lofty way of getting out of it all.

And what loving-kindness, oh Lord, what loving-kindness I felt at times in those dreams of mine! in those "flights into the good and the beautiful;" though it was fantastic love, though it was never applied to anything human in reality, yet there was so much of this love that one did not feel afterwards even the impulse to apply it in reality; that would have been superfluous. Everything, however, passed satisfactorily by a lazy and fascinating transition into the sphere of art, that is, into the beautiful forms of life, lying ready, largely stolen from the poets and novelists and adapted to all sorts of needs and uses. I, for instance, was triumphant over every one; every one, of course, was in dust and ashes, and was forced spontaneously to recognize my superiority, and I forgave them all. I was a poet and a grand gentleman, I fell in love; I came in for countless millions and immediately devoted them to humanity, and at the same time I confessed before all the people my shameful deeds, which, of course, were not merely shameful, but had in them much that was "good and beautiful" something in the Manfred[22] style. Every one would kiss me and weep (what idiots they would be if they did not), while I should go barefoot and hungry preaching new ideas and fighting a victorious Austerlitz[23] against the obscurantists. Then the

22. the hero of Lord Byron's verse drama *Manfred* (1817), who was op-pressed by a mysterious guilt.

23. a village near Brno, the capital of Moravia, now in Czechoslovakia, where Napoleon defeated the combined Austrian and Russian armies in 1805.

band would play a march, an amnesty would be declared, the Pope would agree to retire from Rome to Brazil; then there would be a ball for the whole of Italy at the Villa Borghese[24] on the shores of the Lake of Como,[25] the Lake of Como being for that purpose transferred to the neighbourhood of Rome; then would come a scene in the bushes, and so on, and so on—as though you did not know all about it? You will say that it is vulgar and contemptible to drag all this into public after all the tears and transports which I have myself confessed. But why is it contemptible? Can you imagine that I am ashamed of it all, and that it was stupider than anything in your life, gentlemen? And I can assure you that some of these fancies were by no means badly composed. . . . It did not all happen on the shores of Lake Como. And yet you are right—it really is vulgar and contemptible. And most contemptible of all it is that now I am attempting to justify myself to you. And even more contemptible than that is my making this remark now. But that's enough, or there will be no end to it: each step will be more contemptible than the last. . . .

I could never stand more than three months of dreaming at a time without feeling an irresistible desire to plunge into society. To plunge into society meant to visit my superior at the office, Anton Antonich Syetochkin. He was the only permanent acquaintance I have had in my life, and wonder at the fact myself now. But I only went to see him when that phase came over me, and when my dreams had reached such a point of bliss that it became essential at once to embrace my fellows and all mankind; and for that purpose I needed, at least, one human being, actually existing. I had to call on Anton Antonich, however, on Tuesday—his at-home day; so I had always to time my passionate desire to embrace humanity so that it might fall on a Tuesday.

This Anton Antonich lived on the fourth storey in a house in Five Corners, in four low-pitched rooms, one smaller than the other, of a particularly frugal and sallow appearance. He had two daughters and their aunt, who used to pour out the tea. Of the daughters one was thirteen and another fourteen, they both had snub noses, and I was awfully shy of them because they were always whispering and giggling together. The master of the house usually sat in his study on a leather couch in front of the table with some grey-headed gentleman, usually a colleague from our office or some other department. I never saw more than two or three visitors there, always the same. They talked about the excise duty; about business in the Senate,[26] about salaries, about promotions, about His Excellency, and the best means of pleasing him, and so on. I had the patience to sit like a fool beside these people for four hours at a stretch, lis-

24. in Rome.
25. on the border of Italy and Switzerland.

26. The Russian Senate was at that time not a parliamentary body, but a high court.

tening to them without knowing what to say to them or venturing to say a word. I became stupefied, several times I felt myself perspiring, I was overcome by a sort of paralysis; but this was pleasant and good for me. On returning home I deferred for a time my desire to embrace all mankind.

I had however one other acquaintance of a sort, Simonov, who was an old schoolfellow. I had a number of schoolfellows, indeed, in Petersburg, but I did not associate with them and had even given up nodding to them in the street. I believe I had transferred into the department I was in simply to avoid their company and to cut off all connection with my hateful childhood. Curses on that school and all those terrible years of penal servitude! In short, I parted from my schoolfellows as soon as I got out into the world. There were two or three left to whom I nodded in the street. One of them was Simonov, who had been in no way distinguished at school, was of a quiet and equable disposition; but I discovered in him a certain independence of character and even honesty. I don't even suppose that he was particularly stupid. I had at one time spent some rather soulful moments with him, but these had not lasted long and had somehow been suddenly clouded over. He was evidently uncomfortable at these reminiscences, and was, I fancy, always afraid that I might take up the same tone again. I suspected that he had an aversion for me, but still I went on going to see him, not being quite certain of it.

And so on one occasion, unable to endure my solitude and knowing that as it was Thursday Anton Antonich's door would be closed, I thought of Simonov. Climbing up to his fourth storey I was thinking that the man disliked me and that it was a mistake to go and see him. But as it always happened that such reflections impelled me, as though purposely, to put myself into a false position, I went in. It was almost a year since I had last seen Simonov.

III

I found two of my old schoolfellows with him. They seemed to be discussing an important matter. All of them took scarcely any notice of my entrance, which was strange, for I had not met them for years. Evidently they looked upon me as something on the level of a common fly. I had not been treated like that even at school, though they all hated me. I knew, of course, that they must despise me now for my lack of success in the service, and for my having let myself sink so low, going about badly dressed and so on—which seemed to them a sign of my incapacity and insignificance. But I had not expected such contempt. Simonov was positively surprised at my turning up. Even in old days he had always seemed surprised at my coming. All this disconcerted me: I sat down, feeling rather miserable, and began listening to what they were saying.

They were engaged in warm and earnest conversation about a farewell dinner which they wanted to arrange for the next day to a comrade of theirs called Zverkov, an officer in the army, who was going away to a distant province. This Zverkov had been all the time at school with me too. I had begun to hate him particularly in the upper grades. In the lower grades he had simply been a pretty, playful boy whom everybody liked. I had hated him, however, even in the lower grades, just because he was a pretty and playful boy. He was always bad at his lessons and got worse and worse as he went on; however, he left with a good certificate, as he had powerful interest. During his last year at school he came in for an estate of two hundred serfs, and as almost all of us were poor he took up a swaggering tone among us. He was vulgar in the extreme, but at the same time he was a good-natured fellow, even in his swaggering. In spite of superficial, fantastic and sham notions of honour and dignity, all but very few of us positively grovelled before Zverkov, and the more so the more he swaggered. And it was not from any interested motive that they grovelled, but simply because he had been favoured by the gifts of nature. Moreover, it was, as it were, an accepted idea among us that Zverkov was a specialist in regard to tact and the social graces. This last fact particularly infuriated me. I hated the abrupt self-confident tone of his voice, his admiration of his own witticisms, which were often frightfully stupid, though he was bold in his language; I hated his handsome, but stupid face (for which I would, however, have gladly exchanged my intelligent one), and the free-and-easy military manners in fashion in the 'forties. I hated the way in which he used to talk of his future conquests of women (he did not venture to begin his attack upon women until he had the epaulettes of an officer, and was looking forward to them with impatience), and boasted of the duels he would constantly be fighting. I remember how I, invariably so taciturn, suddenly fastened upon Zverkov, when one day talking at a leisure moment with his schoolfellows of his future relations with the fair sex, and growing as sportive as a puppy in the sun, he all at once declared that he would not leave a single village girl on his estate unnoticed, that that was his *droit de seigneur*,[27] and that if the peasants dared to protest he would have them all flogged and double the tax on them, the bearded rascals. Our servile rabble applauded, but I attacked him, not from compassion for the girls and their fathers, but simply because they were applauding such an insect. I got the better of him on that occasion, but though Zverkov was stupid he was lively and impudent, and so laughed it off, and in such a way that my victory was not really complete: the laugh was on his side. He got the better of me on several occasions afterwards, but without malice, jestingly,

27. "the right of the master," i.e., to all the women serfs.

casually. I remained angrily and contemptuously silent and would not answer him. When we left school he made advances to me; I did not rebuff them, for I was flattered, but we soon parted and quite naturally. Afterwards I heard of his barrack-room success as a lieutenant, and of the fast life he was leading. Then there came other rumours—of his successes in the service. By then he had taken to cutting me in the street, and I suspected that he was afraid of compromising himself by greeting a personage as insignificant as me. I saw him once in the theatre, in the third tier of boxes. By then he was wearing shoulder-straps. He was twisting and twirling about, ingratiating himself with the daughters of an ancient General. In three years he had gone off considerably, though he was still rather handsome and adroit. One could see that by the time he was thirty he would be corpulent. So it was to this Zverkov that my school-fellows were going to give a dinner on his departure. They had kept up with him for those three years, though privately they did not consider themselves on an equal footing with him, I am convinced of that.

Of Simonov's two visitors, one was Ferfichkin, a Russianized German—a little fellow with the face of a monkey, a blockhead who was always deriding every one, a very bitter enemy of mine from our days in the lower grades—a vulgar, impudent, swaggering fellow, who affected a most sensitive feeling of personal honour, though, of course, he was a wretched little coward at heart. He was one of those worshippers of Zverkov who made up to the latter from interested motives, and often borrowed money from him. Simonov's other visitor, Trudolyubov, was a person in no way remarkable—a tall young fellow, in the army, with a cold face, fairly honest, though he worshipped success of every sort, and was only capable of thinking of promotion. He was some sort of distant relation of Zverkov's, and this, foolish as it seems, gave him a certain importance among us. He always thought me of no consequence whatever; his behaviour to me, though not quite courteous, was tolerable.

"Well, with seven roubles each," said Trudolyubov, "twenty-one roubles between the three of us, we ought to be able to get a good dinner. Zverkov, of course, won't pay."

"Of course not, since we are inviting him," Simonov decided.

"Can you imagine," Ferfichkin interrupted hotly and conceitedly, like some insolent flunkey boasting of his master the General's decorations, "can you imagine that Zverkov will let us pay alone? He will accept from delicacy, but he will order half a dozen bottles of champagne."

"Do we want half a dozen for the four of us?" observed Trudolyubov, taking notice only of the half dozen.

"So the three of us, with Zverkov for the fourth, twenty-one roubles, at the Hôtel de Paris at five o'clock to-morrow," Simonov, who had been asked to make the arrangements, concluded finally.

"How twenty-one roubles?" I asked in some agitation, with a show of being offended; "if you count me it will not be twenty-one, but twenty-eight roubles."

It seemed to me that to invite myself so suddenly and unexpectedly would be positively graceful, and that they would all be conquered at once and would look at me with respect.

"Do you want to join, too?" Simonov observed, with no appearance of pleasure, seeming to avoid looking at me. He knew me through and through.

It infuriated me that he knew me so thoroughly.

"Why not? I am an old schoolfellow of his, too, I believe, and I must own I feel hurt that you have left me out," I said, boiling over again.

"And where were we to find you?" Ferfichkin put in roughly.

"You never were on good terms with Zverkov," Trudolyubov added, frowning.

But I had already clutched at the idea and would not give it up.

"It seems to me that no one has a right to form an opinion upon that," I retorted in a shaking voice, as though something tremendous had happened. "Perhaps that is just my reason for wishing it now, that I have not always been on good terms with him."

"Oh, there's no making you out . . . with these refinements," Trudolyubov jeered.

"We'll put your name down," Simonov decided, addressing me. "To-morrow at five o'clock at the Hôtel de Paris."

"What about the money?" Ferfichkin began in an undertone, indicating me to Simonov, but he broke off, for even Simonov was embarrassed.

"That will do," said Trudolyubov, getting up. "If he wants to come so much, let him."

"But it's a private thing, between us friends," Ferfichkin said crossly, as he, too, picked up his hat. "It's not an official gathering."

"We do not want at all, perhaps . . ."

They went away. Ferfichkin did not greet me in any way as he went out, Trudolyubov barely nodded. Simonov, with whom I was left *tête-à-tête*, was in a state of vexation and perplexity, and looked at me queerly. He did not sit down and did not ask me to.

"H'm . . . yes . . . to-morrow, then. Will you pay your subscription now? I just ask so as to know," he muttered in embarrassment.

I flushed crimson, and as I did so I remembered that I had owed Simonov fifteen roubles for ages—which I had, indeed, never forgotten, though I had not paid it.

"You will understand, Simonov, that I could have no idea when I came here. . . . I am very much vexed that I have forgotten. . . ."

"All right, all right, that doesn't matter. You can pay to-morrow after the dinner. I simply wanted to know. . . . Please don't . . ."

He broke off and began pacing the room still more vexed. As he walked he began to stamp with his heels.

"Am I keeping you?" I asked, after two minutes of silence.

"Oh!" he said, starting, "that is—to be truthful—yes. I have to go and see some one . . . not far from here," he added in an apologetic voice, somewhat abashed.

"My goodness, why didn't you say so?" I cried, seizing my cap, with an astonishingly free-and-easy air, which was the last thing I should have expected of myself.

"It's close by . . . not two paces away," Simonov repeated, accompanying me to the front door with a fussy air which did not suit him at all. "So five o'clock, punctually, to-morrow," he called down the stairs after me. He was very glad to get rid of me. I was in a fury.

"What possessed me, what possessed me to force myself upon them?" I wondered, grinding my teeth as I strode along the street, "for a scoundrel, a pig like that Zverkov! Of course, I had better not go; of course, I must just snap my fingers at them. I am not bound in any way. I'll send Simonov a note by to-morrow's post. . . ."

But what made me furious was that I knew for certain that I should go, that I should make a point of going; and the more tactless, the more unseemly my going would be, the more certainly I would go.

And there was a positive obstacle to my going: I had no money. All I had was nine roubles, I had to give seven of that to my servant, Apollon, for his monthly wages. That was all I paid him—he had to keep himself.

Not to pay him was impossible, considering his character. But I will talk about that fellow, about that plague of mine, another time.

However, I knew I should go and should not pay him his wages.

That night I had the most hideous dreams. No wonder; all the evening I had been oppressed by memories of my miserable days at school, and I could not shake them off. I was sent to the school by distant relations, upon whom I was dependent and of whom I have heard nothing since—they sent me there a forlorn, silent boy, already crushed by their reproaches, already troubled by doubt, and looking with savage distrust at every one. My schoolfellows met me with spiteful and merciless jibes because I was not like any of them. But I could not endure their taunts; I could not give in to them with the ignoble readiness with which they gave in to one another. I hated them from the first, and shut myself away from every one in

timid, wounded and disproportionate pride. Their coarseness revolted me. They laughed cynically at my face, at my clumsy figure;
and yet what stupid faces they had themselves. In our school the
boys' faces seemed in a special way to degenerate and grow stupider.
How many fine-looking boys came to us! In a few years they became
repulsive. Even at sixteen I wondered at them morosely; even then
I was struck by the pettiness of their thoughts, the stupidity of their
pursuits, their games, their conversations. They had no understanding of such essential things, they took no interest in such striking,
impressive subjects, that I could not help considering them inferior
to myself. It was not wounded vanity that drove me to it, and for
God's sake do not thrust upon me your hackneyed remarks, repeated
to nausea, that "I was only a dreamer," while they even then had
an understanding of life. They understood nothing, they had no
idea of real life, and I swear that that was what made me most indignant with them. On the contrary, the most obvious, striking
reality they accepted with fantastic stupidity and even at that time
were accustomed to respect success. Everything that was just, but
oppressed and looked down upon, they laughed at heartlessly and
shamefully. They took rank for intelligence; even at sixteen they
were already talking about a snug berth. Of course, a great deal of
it was due to their stupidity, to the bad examples with which they
had always been surrounded in their childhood and boyhood. They
were monstrously depraved. Of course a great deal of that, too, was
superficial and an assumption of cynicism; of course there were
glimpses of youth and freshness even in their depravity; but even
that freshness was not attractive, and showed itself in a certain rak-
ishness. I hated them horribly, though perhaps I was worse than
any of them. They repaid me in the same way, and did not conceal
their aversion for me. But by then I did not desire their affection:
on the contrary I continually longed for their humiliation. To escape
from their derision I purposely began to make all the progress I
could with my studies and forced my way to the very top. This
impressed them. Moreover, they all began by degrees to grasp that
I had already read books none of them could read, and understood
things (not forming part of our school curriculum) of which they
had not even heard. They took a savage and sarcastic view of it, but
were morally impressed, especially as the teachers began to notice
me on those grounds. The mockery ceased, but the hostility remained, and cold and strained relations became permanent between
us. In the end I could not put up with it: with years a craving for
society, for friends, developed in me. I attempted to get on friendly
terms with some of my schoolfellows; but somehow or other my
intimacy with them was always strained and soon ended of itself.
Once, indeed, I did have a friend. But I was already a tyrant at

heart; I wanted to exercise unbounded sway over him; I tried to instil into him a contempt for his surroundings; I required of him a disdainful and complete break with those surroundings. I frightened him with my passionate affection; I reduced him to tears, to hysterics. He was a simple and devoted soul; but when he devoted himself to me entirely I began to hate him immediately and repulsed him—as though all I needed him for was to win a victory over him, to subjugate him and nothing else. But I could not subjugate all of them; my friend was not at all like them either, he was, in fact, a rare exception. The first thing I did on leaving school was to give up the special job for which I had been destined so as to break all ties, to curse my past and shake the dust from off my feet. . . . And goodness knows why, after all that, I should go trudging off to Simonov's!

Early next morning I roused myself and jumped out of bed with excitement, as though it were all about to happen at once. But I believed that some radical change in my life was coming, and would inevitably come that day. Owing to its rarity, perhaps, any external event, however trivial, always made me feel as though some radical change in my life were at hand. I went to the office, however, as usual, but sneaked away home two hours earlier to get ready. The great thing, I thought, is not to be the first to arrive, or they will think I am overjoyed at coming. But there were thousands of such great points to consider, and they all agitated and overwhelmed me. I polished my boots a second time with my own hands; nothing in the world would have induced Apollon to clean them twice a day, as he considered that it was more than his duties required of him. I stole the brushes to clean them from the passage, being careful he should not detect it, for fear of his contempt. Then I minutely examined my clothes and thought that everything looked old, worn and threadbare. I had let myself get too slovenly. My uniform, perhaps, was tidy, but I could not go out to dinner in my uniform. The worst of it was that on the knee of my trousers was a big yellow stain. I had a foreboding that that stain would deprive me of nine-tenths of my personal dignity. I knew, too, that it was very bad to think so. "But this is no time for thinking: now I am in for the real thing," I thought, and my heart sank. I knew, too, perfectly well even then, that I was monstrously exaggerating the facts. But how could I help it? I could not control myself and was already shaking with fever. With despair I pictured to myself how coldly and disdainfully that "scoundrel" Zverkov would meet me; with what dull-witted, invincible contempt the blockhead Trudolyubov would look at me; with what impudent rudeness the insect Ferfichkin would snigger at me in order to curry favour with Zverkov; how completely Simonov would take it all in, and how he would despise me for the abjectness of my vanity and lack of spirit—and, worst of all, how paltry, *unliterary*, commonplace it would all be. Of course, the best thing would be not to go at all. But that was most impossible of all: if I feel impelled to do anything, I seem to be pitchforked into it. I should have jeered at myself ever afterwards: "So you funked it, you funked it, you funked the *real thing!*" On the contrary, I passionately longed to show all that "rabble" that I was by no means such a spiritless creature as I seemed to myself. What is more, even in the acutest paroxysm of this cowardly fever, I dreamed of getting the upper hand, of dominating them, carrying them away, making them like me—if only for my "elevation of thought and unmistakable wit." They would abandon Zverkov, he would sit on one side, silent and ashamed, while I should crush him. Then, perhaps, we would be reconciled and drink to our everlasting friendship; but what was most bitter and most humiliating for me was that I knew even then, knew fully and for certain, that I needed nothing of all this really, that I did not really want to crush, to subdue, to attract them, and that I did not care a straw really for the result, even if I did achieve it. Oh, how I prayed for the day to pass quickly! In unutterable anguish I went to the window, opened the movable pane and looked out into the troubled darkness of the thickly falling wet snow. At last my wretched little clock hissed out five. I seized my hat and trying not to look at Apollon, who had been all day expecting his month's wages, but in his foolishness was unwilling to be the first to speak about it, I slipt between him and the door and jumping into a high-class sledge, on which I spent my last half rouble, I drove up in grand style to the Hôtel de Paris.

IV

I had been certain the day before that I should be the first to arrive. But it was not a question of being the first to arrive. Not only were they not there, but I had difficulty in finding our room. The table was not laid even. What did it mean? After a good many questions I elicited from the waiters that the dinner had been ordered not for five, but for six o'clock. This was confirmed at the buffet too. I felt really ashamed to go on questioning them. It was only twenty-five minutes past five. If they changed the dinner hour they ought at least to have let me know—that is what the post is for, and not to have put me in an absurd position in my own eyes and . . . and even before the waiters. I sat down; the servant began laying the table; I felt even more humiliated when he was present. Towards six o'clock they brought in candles, though there were lamps burning in the room. It had not occurred to the waiter, however, to bring them in at once when I arrived. In the next room two gloomy, angry-looking persons were eating their dinners in silence at two different tables. There was a great deal of noise, even shouting, in a room further away; one could hear the laughter of a crowd of people, and nasty little shrieks in French: there were ladies at the dinner. It was sickening, in fact. I rarely passed more unpleasant moments, so much so that when they did arrive all together punctually at six I was overjoyed to see them, as though they were my deliverers, and even forgot that it was incumbent upon me to show resentment.

Zverkov walked in at the head of them; evidently he was the leading spirit. He and all of them were laughing; but, seeing me, Zverkov drew himself up a little, walked up to me deliberately with a slight, rather jaunty bend from the waist. He shook hands with me in a friendly, but not over-friendly, fashion, with a sort of circumspect courtesy like that of a General, as though in giving me his hand he were warding off something. I had imagined, on the contrary, that on coming in he would at once break into his habitual thin, shrill laugh and fall to making his insipid jokes and witticisms. I had been preparing for them ever since the previous day, but I had not expected such condescension, such high-official courtesy. So, then, he felt himself ineffably superior to me in every respect! If he only meant to insult me by that high-official tone, it would not matter, I thought—I could pay him back for it one way or another. But what if, in reality, without the least desire to be offensive, that sheepshead had a notion in earnest that he was superior to me and could only look at me in a patronizing way? The very supposition made me gasp.

"I was surprised to hear of your desire to join us," he began, lisping and drawling, which was something new. "You and I seem to have seen nothing of one another. You fight shy of us. You shouldn't. We are not such terrible people as you think. Well, anyway, I am glad to renew our acquaintance."

And he turned carelessly to put down his hat on the window.

"Have you been waiting long?" Trudolyubov inquired.

"I arrived at five o'clock as you told me yesterday," I answered aloud, with an irritability that threatened an explosion.

"Didn't you let him know that we had changed the hour?" said Trudolyubov to Simonov.

"No, I didn't. I forgot," the latter replied, with no sign of regret, and without even apologizing to me he went off to order the *hors d'œuvres*.

"So you've been here a whole hour? Oh, poor fellow!" Zverkov cried ironically, for to his notions this was bound to be extremely funny. That rascal Ferfichkin followed with his nasty little snigger like a puppy yapping. My position struck him, too, as exquisitely ludicrous and embarrassing.

"It isn't funny at all!" I cried to Ferfichkin, more and more irritated. "It wasn't my fault, but other people's. They neglected to let me know. It was . . . it was . . . it was simply absurd."

"It's not only absurd, but something else as well," muttered Trudolyubov, naïvely taking my part. "You are not hard enough upon it. It was simply rudeness—unintentional, of course. And how could Simonov . . . h'm!"

"If a trick like that had been played on me," observed Ferfichkin, "I should . . ."

"But you should have ordered something for yourself," Zverkov interrupted, "or simply asked for dinner without waiting for us."

"You will allow that I might have done that without your permission," I rapped out. "If I waited, it was . . ."

"Let us sit down, gentlemen," cried Simonov, coming in. "Everything is ready; I can answer for the champagne; it is capitally frozen. . . . You see, I did not know your address, where was I to look for you?" he suddenly turned to me, but again he seemed to avoid looking at me. Evidently he had something against me. It must have been what happened yesterday.

All sat down; I did the same. It was a round table. Trudolyubov was on my left, Simonov on my right. Zverkov was sitting opposite, Ferfichkin next to him, between him and Trudolyubov.

"Tell me, are you . . . in a government office?" Zverkov went on attending to me. Seeing that I was embarrassed he seriously thought that he ought to be friendly to me, and, so to speak, cheer me up.

"Does he want me to throw a bottle at his head?" I thought, in a fury. In my novel surroundings I was unnaturally ready to be irritated.

"In the N—— office," I answered jerkily, with my eyes on my plate.

"And ha-ave you a go-od berth? I say, what ma-a-de you leave your original job?"

"What ma-a-de me was that I wanted to leave my original job," I drawled more than he, hardly able to control myself. Ferfichkin went off into a guffaw. Simonov looked at me ironically. Trudolyubov left off eating and began looking at me with curiosity.

Zverkov winced, but he tried not to notice it.

"And the remuneration?"

"What remuneration?"

"I mean, your sa-a-lary?"

"Why are you cross-examining me?" However, I told him at once what my salary was. I turned horribly red.

"It is not very handsome," Zverkov observed majestically.

"Yes, you can't afford to dine at cafés on that," Ferfichkin added insolently.

"To my thinking it's very poor," Trudolyubov observed gravely.

"And how thin you have grown! How you have changed!" added Zverkov, with a shade of venom in his voice, scanning me and my attire with a sort of insolent compassion.

"Oh, spare his blushes," cried Ferfichkin, sniggering.

"My dear sir, allow me to tell you I am not blushing," I broke out at last; "do you hear? I am dining here, at this café, at my own expense, not at other people's—note that, Mr. Ferfichkin."

"Wha-at? Isn't every one here dining at his own expense? You would seem to be . . ." Ferfichkin flew out at me, turning as red as a lobster, and looking me in the face with fury.

"Tha-at," I answered, feeling I had gone too far, "and I imagine it would be better to talk of something more intelligent."

"You intend to show off your intelligence, I suppose?"

"Don't disturb yourself, that would be quite out of place here."

"Why are you clacking away like that, my good sir, eh? Have you gone out of your wits in your office?"

"Enough, gentlemen, enough!" Zverkov cried, authoritatively.

"How stupid it is!" muttered Simonov.

"It really is stupid. We have met here, a company of friends, for a farewell dinner to a comrade and you carry on an altercation," said Trudolyubov, rudely addressing himself to me alone. "You invited yourself to join us, so don't disturb the general harmony."

"Enough, enough!" cried Zverkov. "Give over, gentlemen, it's out of place. Better let me tell you how I nearly got married the day before yesterday. . . ."

And then followed a burlesque narrative of how this gentleman had almost been married two days before. There was not a word about the marriage, however, but the story was adorned with generals, colonels and gentlemen-in-waiting, while Zverkov almost took the lead among them. It was greeted with approving laughter; Ferfichkin positively squealed.

No one paid any attention to me, and I sat crushed and humiliated.

"Good Heavens, these are not the people for me!" I thought. "And what a fool I have made of myself before them! I let Ferfichkin go too far, though. The brutes imagine they are doing me an honour in letting me sit down with them. They don't understand that it's an honour to them and not to me! I've grown thinner! My clothes! Oh, damn my trousers! Zverkov noticed the yellow stain on the knee as soon as he came in. . . . But what's the use! I must get up at once, this very minute, take my hat and simply go without a word . . . with contempt! And to-morrow I can send a challenge. The scoundrels! As though I cared about the seven roubles. They may think. . . . Damn it! I don't care about the seven roubles. I'll go this minute!"

Of course I remained. I drank sherry and Lafitte by the glassful in my discomfiture. Being unaccustomed to it, I was quickly affected. My annoyance increased as the wine went to my head. I longed all at once to insult them all in a most flagrant manner and then go away. To seize the moment and show what I could do, so that they would say, "He's clever, though he is absurd," and . . . and . . . in fact, damn them all!

I scanned them all insolently with my drowsy eyes. But they seemed to have forgotten me altogether. They were noisy, vociferous, cheerful. Zverkov was talking all the time. I began listening. Zverkov was talking of some exuberant lady whom he had at last led on to declaring her love (of course, he was lying like a horse), and how he had been helped in this affair by an intimate friend of his, a Prince Kolya, an officer in the hussars, who had three thousand serfs.

"And yet this Kolya, who has three thousand serfs, has not put in an appearance here to-night to see you off," I cut in suddenly.

For a minute every one was silent. "You are drunk already." Trudolyubov deigned to notice me at last, glancing contemptuously in my direction. Zverkov, without a word, examined me as though I were an insect. I dropped my eyes. Simonov made haste to fill up the glasses with champagne.

Trudolyubov raised his glass, as did every one else but me.

"Your health and good luck on the journey!" he cried to Zverkov. "To old times, to our future, hurrah!"

They all tossed off their glasses, and crowded round Zverkov to kiss him. I did not move; my full glass stood untouched before me.

"Why, aren't you going to drink it?" roared Trudolyubov, losing patience and turning menacingly to me.

"I want to make a speech separately, on my own account . . . and then I'll drink it, Mr. Trudolyubov."

"Spiteful brute!" muttered Simonov. I drew myself up in my chair and feverishly seized my glass, prepared for something extraordinary, though I did not know myself precisely what I was going to say.

"*Silence!*" cried Ferfichkin. "Now for a display of wit!"

Zverkov waited very gravely, knowing what was coming.

"Mr. Lieutenant Zverkov," I began, "let me tell you that I hate phrases, phrasemongers and men in corsets . . . that's the first point, and there is a second one to follow it."

There was a general stir.

"The second point is: I hate ribaldry and ribald talkers. Especially ribald talkers! The third point: I love justice, truth and honesty." I went on almost mechanically, for I was beginning to shiver with horror myself and had no idea how I came to be talking like this. "I love thought, Monsieur Zverkov; I love true comradeship, on an equal footing and not . . . H'm . . . I love. . . . But, however, why not? I will drink your health, too, Mr. Zverkov. Seduce the Circassian girls, shoot the enemies of the fatherland and . . . and . . . to your health, Monsieur Zverkov!"

Zverkov got up from his seat, bowed to me and said:

"I am very much obliged to you." He was frightfully offended and turned pale.

"Damn the fellow!" roared Trudolyubov, bringing his fist down on the table.

"Well, he wants a punch in the face for that," squealed Ferfichkin.

"We ought to turn him out," muttered Simonov.

"Not a word, gentlemen, not a movement!" cried Zverkov solemnly, checking the general indignation. "I thank you all, but I can show him for myself how much value I attach to his words."

"Mr. Ferfichkin, you will give me satisfaction to-morrow for your words just now!" I said aloud, turning with dignity to Ferfichkin.

"A duel, you mean? Certainly," he answered. But probably I was so ridiculous as I challenged him and it was so out of keeping with my appearance that everyone, including Ferfichkin, was prostrate with laughter.

"Yes, let him alone, of course! He is quite drunk," Trudolyubov said with disgust.

"I shall never forgive myself for letting him join us," Simonov muttered again.

"Now is the time to throw a bottle at their heads," I thought to myself. I picked up the bottle . . . and filled my glass. . . . "No, I'd better sit on to the end," I went on thinking; "you would be pleased, my friends if I went away. Nothing will induce me to go. I'll go on sitting here and drinking to the end, on purpose, as a sign that I don't think you of the slightest consequence. I will go on sitting and drinking, because this is a public-house and I paid my entrance money. I'll sit here and drink, for I look upon you as so many pawns, as inanimate pawns. I'll sit here and drink . . . and sing if I want to, yes, sing, for I have the right to . . . to sing . . . H'm!"

But I did not sing. I simply tried not to look at any of them. I assumed most unconcerned attitudes and waited with impatience for them to speak *first*. But alas, they did not address me! And oh, how I wished, how I wished at that moment to be reconciled to them! It struck eight, at last nine. They moved from the table to the sofa. Zverkov stretched himself on a lounge and put one foot on a round table. Wine was brought there. He did, as a fact, order three bottles on his own account. I, of course, was not invited to join them. They all sat round him on the sofa. They listened to him, almost with reverence. It was evident that they were fond of him. "What for? What for?" I wondered. From time to time they were moved to drunken enthusiasm and kissed each other. They talked of the Caucasus, of the nature of true passion, of snug berths in the service, of the income of an hussar called Podkharzhevsky, whom none of them knew personally, and rejoiced in the largeness of it, of the extraordinary grace and beauty of a Princess D., whom none of them had ever seen; then it came to Shakespeare's being immortal.

I smiled contemptuously and walked up and down the other side of the room, opposite the sofa, from the table to the stove and back again. I tried my very utmost to show them that I could do without them, and yet I purposely made a noise with my boots, thumping with my heels. But it was all in vain. They paid no attention. I had the patience to walk up and down in front of them from eight o'clock till eleven, in the same place, from the table to the stove and back again. "I walk up and down to please myself and no one can prevent me." The waiter who came into the room stopped, from time to time, to look at me. I was somewhat giddy from turning round so often; at moments it seemed to me that I was in delirium. During those three hours I was three times soaked with sweat and dry again. At times, with an intense, acute pang I was stabbed to the heart by the thought that ten years, twenty years, forty years would pass, and that even in forty years I would remember with loathing and humiliation those filthiest, most ludicrous, and most awful moments of my life. No one could have gone out of his way to degrade himself more shamelessly, and I fully realized it, fully, and yet I went on pacing up and down from the table to the stove. "Oh, if you only knew what thoughts and feelings I am capable of, how cultured I am!" I thought at moments, mentally addressing the sofa on which my enemies were sitting. But my enemies behaved as though I were not in the room. Once —only once—they turned towards me, just when Zverkov was talking about Shakespeare, and I suddenly gave a contemptuous laugh. I laughed in such an affected and disgusting way that they all at once broke off their conversation, and silently and gravely for two minutes watched me walking up and down from the table to the stove, *taking no notice of them*. But nothing came of it: they said nothing, and two minutes later they ceased to notice me again. It struck eleven.

"Friends," cried Zverkov getting up from the sofa, "let us all be off now, *there!*"

"Of course, of course," the others assented. I turned sharply to Zverkov. I was so harassed, so exhausted, that I would have cut my throat to put an end to it. I was in a fever; my hair, soaked with perspiration, stuck to my forehead and temples.

"Zverkov, I beg your pardon," I said abruptly and resolutely. "Ferfichkin, yours too, and every one's, every one's: I have insulted you all!"

"Aha! A duel is not in your line, old man," Ferfichkin hissed venomously.

It sent a sharp pang to my heart.

"No, it's not the duel I am afraid of, Ferfichkin! I am ready to fight you to-morrow, after we are reconciled. I insist upon it, in fact, and you cannot refuse. I want to show you that I am not afraid of a duel. You shall fire first and I shall fire into the air."

"He is comforting himself," said Simonov.

"He's simply raving," said Trudolyubov.

"But let us pass. Why are you barring our way? What do you want?" Zverkov answered disdainfully.

They were all flushed, their eyes were bright: they had been drinking heavily.

"I ask for your friendship, Zverkov; I insulted you, but . . ."

"Insulted? *You* insulted *me*? Understand, sir, that you never, under any circumstances, could possibly insult *me*."

"And that's enough for you. Out of the way!" concluded Trudolyubov.

"Olympia is mine, friends, that's agreed!" cried Zverkov.

"We won't dispute your right, we won't dispute your right," the others answered, laughing.

I stood as though spat upon. The party went noisily out of the room. Trudolyubov struck up some stupid song. Simonov remained behind for a moment to tip the waiters. I suddenly went up to him.

"Simonov! give me six roubles!" I said, with desperate resolution.

He looked at me in extreme amazement, with vacant eyes. He, too, was drunk.

"You don't mean you are coming with us?"

"Yes."

"I've no money," he snapped out, and with a scornful laugh he went out of the room.

I clutched at his overcoat. It was a nightmare.

"Simonov, I saw you had money. Why do you refuse me? Am I a scoundrel? Beware of refusing me: if you knew, if you knew why I am asking! My whole future, my whole plans depend upon it!"

Simonov pulled out the money and almost flung it at me.

"Take it, if you have no sense of shame!" he pronounced pitilessly, and ran to overtake them.

I was left for a moment alone. Disorder, the remains of dinner, a broken wine-glass on the floor, spilt wine, cigarette ends, fumes of drink and delirium in my brain, an agonizing misery in my heart and finally the waiter, who had seen and heard all and was looking inquisitively into my face.

"I am going there!" I cried. "Either they shall all go down on their knees to beg for my friendship, or I will give Zverkov a slap in the face!"

v

"So this is it, this is it at last—contact with real life," I muttered as I ran headlong downstairs. "This is very different from the Pope's leaving Rome and going to Brazil, very different from the ball on Lake Como!"

"You are a scoundrel," a thought flashed through my mind, "if you laugh at this now."

"No matter!" I cried, answering myself. "Now everything is lost!"

There was no trace to be seen of them, but that made no difference—I knew where they had gone.

At the steps was standing a solitary night sledge-driver in a rough peasant coat, powdered over with the still falling, wet, and as it were warm, snow. It was hot and steamy. The little shaggy piebald horse was also covered with snow and coughing, I remember that very well. I made a rush for the roughly made sledge; but as soon as I raised my foot to get into it, the recollection of how Simonov had just given me six roubles seemed to double me up and I tumbled into the sledge like a sack.

"No, I must do a great deal to make up for all that," I cried. "But I will make up for it or perish on the spot this very night. Start!"

We set off. There was a perfect whirl in my head.

"They won't go down on their knees to beg for my friendship. That is a mirage, cheap mirage, revolting, romantic and fantastical —that's another ball on Lake Como. And so I am bound to slap Zverkov's face! It is my duty to. And so it is settled; I am flying to give him a slap in the face. Hurry up!"

The driver tugged at the reins.

"As soon as I go in I'll give it him. Ought I before giving him the slap to say a few words by way of preface? No. I'll simply go in and give it him. They will all be sitting in the drawing-room, and he with Olympia on the sofa. That damned Olympia! She laughed at my looks on one occasion and refused me. I'll pull Olympia's hair, pull Zverkov's ears! No, better one ear, and pull him by it round the room. Maybe they will all begin beating me and will kick me out. That's most likely, indeed. No matter! Anyway, I shall first slap him; the initiative will be mine; and by the laws of honour that is everything: he will be branded and cannot wipe off the slap by any blows, by nothing but a duel. He will be forced to fight. And let them beat me now. Let them, the ungrateful wretches! Trudolyubov will beat me hardest, he is so strong; Ferfichkin will be sure to catch hold sideways and tug at my hair. But no matter, no matter! That's what I am going for. The blockheads will be forced at last to see the tragedy of it all! When they drag me to the door I shall call out to them that in reality they are not worth my little finger. Get on, driver, get on!" I cried to the driver. He started and flicked his whip, I shouted so savagely.

"We shall fight at daybreak, that's a settled thing. I've done with the office. Ferfichkin made a joke about it just now. But where can I get pistols? Nonsense! I'll get my salary in advance and buy them. And powder, and bullets? That's the second's business. And how can it all be done by daybreak? And where am I to get a second? I have no friends. Nonsense!" I cried, lashing myself up more and more. "It's of no consequence! the first person I meet in the street is bound to be my second, just as he would be bound to pull a drowning man out of water. The most eccentric things may happen. Even if I were to ask the director himself to be my second to-morrow, he would be bound to consent, if only from a feeling of chivalry, and to keep the secret! Anton Antonich. . . ."

The fact is, that at that very minute the disgusting absurdity of my plan and the other side of the question was clearer and more vivid to my imagination than it could be to any one on earth. But. . . .

"Get on, driver, get on, you rascal, get on!"

"Ugh, sir!" said the son of toil.

Cold shivers suddenly ran down me.

Wouldn't it be better . . . to go straight home? My God, my God! Why did I invite myself to this dinner yesterday? But no, it's impossible. And my walking up and down for three hours from the table to the stove? No, they, they and no one else must pay for my walking up and down! They must wipe out this dishonour! Drive on!

And what if they give me into custody? They won't dare! They'll be afraid of the scandal. And what if Zverkov is so contemptuous that he refuses to fight a duel? He is sure to; but in that case I'll show them . . . I will turn up at the posting station when he is setting off to-morrow, I'll catch him by the leg, I'll pull off his coat when he gets into the carriage. I'll get my teeth into his hand, I'll bite him. "See what lengths you can drive a desperate man to!"

He may hit me on the head and they may belabour me from behind. I will shout to the assembled multitude: "Look at this young puppy who is driving off to captivate the Circassian girls after letting me spit in his face!"

Of course, after that everything will be over! The office will have vanished off the face of the earth. I shall be arrested, I shall be tried, I shall be dismissed from the service, thrown in prison, sent to Siberia. Never mind! In fifteen years when they let me out of prison I will trudge off to him, a beggar, in rags. I shall find him in some provincial town. He will be married and happy. He will have a grown-up daughter. . . . I shall say to him: "Look, monster, at my hollow cheeks and my rags! I've lost everything—my career, my happiness, art, science, *the woman I loved,* and all through you. Here are pistols. I have come to discharge my pistol and . . . and I . . . forgive you. Then I shall fire into the air and he will hear nothing more of me. . . ."

I was actually on the point of tears, though I knew perfectly well at that moment that all this was out of Pushkin's *Silvio*[28] and Lermontov's *Masquerade.*[29] And all at once I felt horribly ashamed, so ashamed that I stopped the horse, got out of the sledge, and stood still in the snow in the middle of the street. The driver gazed at me, sighing and astonished.

What was I to do? I could not go on there—it was evidently stupid, and I could not leave things as they were, because that would seem as though . . . Heavens, how could I leave things! And after such insults! "No!" I cried, throwing myself into the sledge again. "It is ordained! It is fate! Drive on, drive on!"

And in my impatience I punched the sledge-driver on the back of the neck.

"What are you up to? What are you hitting me for?" the peasant shouted, but he whipped up his nag so that it began kicking.

The wet snow was falling in big flakes; I unbuttoned myself, regardless of it. I forgot everything else, for I had finally decided on the slap, and felt with horror that it was going to happen *now, at once,* and that *no force could stop it.* The deserted street lamps gleamed sullenly in the snowy darkness like torches at a funeral. The snow drifted under my great-coat, under my coat, under my cravat, and melted there. I did not wrap myself up—all was lost, anyway.

At last we arrived. I jumped out, almost unconscious, ran up the steps and began knocking and kicking at the door. I felt fearfully weak, particularly in my legs and my knees. The door was opened

28. actually "The Shot" (1830), by the Russian Poet Alexander Pushkin (1799–1837), a story in which the hero, Silvio, finally gives up the idea of revenging himself for a slap in the face.
29. a verse play (1835) by the poet Mikhail Y. Lermontov (1814–1841).

quickly as though they knew I was coming. As a fact, Simonov had warned them that perhaps another gentleman would arrive, and this was a place in which one had to give notice and to observe certain precautions. It was one of those "millinery establishments" which were abolished by the police a good time ago. By day it really was a shop; but at night, if one had an introduction, one might visit it for other purposes.

I walked rapidly through the dark shop into the familiar drawing-room, where there was only one candle burning, and stood still in amazement: there was no one there. "Where are they?" I asked somebody. But by now, of course, they had separated. Before me was standing a person with a stupid smile, the "madam" herself, who had seen me before. A minute later a door opened and another person came in.

Taking no notice of anything I strode about the room, and, I believe, I talked to myself. I felt as though I had been saved from death and was conscious of this, joyfully, all over: I should have given that slap, I should certainly, certainly have given it! But now they were not here and . . . everything had vanished and changed! I looked round. I could not realize my condition yet. I looked mechanically at the girl who had come in: and had a glimpse of a fresh, young, rather pale face, with straight, dark eyebrows, and with grave, as it were wondering, eyes that attracted me at once; I should have hated her if she had been smiling. I began looking at her more intently and, as it were, with effort. I had not fully collected my thoughts. There was something simple and good-natured in her face, but something strangely grave. I am sure that this stood in her way here, and no one of those fools had noticed her. She could not, however, have been called a beauty, though she was tall, strong-looking, and well built. She was very simply dressed. Something loathsome stirred within me. I went straight up to her.

I chanced to look into the glass. My harassed face struck me as revolting in the extreme, pale, angry, abject, with dishevelled hair. "No matter, I am glad of it," I thought; "I am glad that I shall seem repulsive to her; I like that."

VI

. . . Somewhere behind a screen a clock began wheezing, as though oppressed by something, as though some one were strangling it. After an unnaturally prolonged wheezing there followed a shrill, nasty, and as it were unexpectedly rapid, chime—as though some one were suddenly jumping forward. It struck two. I woke up, though I had indeed not been asleep but lying half conscious.

It was almost completely dark in the narrow, cramped, low-pitched room, cumbered up with an enormous wardrobe and piles of cardboard boxes and all sorts of frippery and litter. The candle end that had been burning on the table was going out and gave a faint flicker from time to time. In a few minutes there would be complete darkness.

I was not long in coming to myself; everything came back to my mind at once, without an effort, as though it had been in ambush to pounce upon me again. And, indeed, even while I was unconscious a point seemed continually to remain in my memory unforgotten, and round it my dreams moved drearily. But strange to say, everything that had happened to me in that day seemed to me now, on waking, to be in the far, far away past, as though I had long, long ago lived all that down.

My head was full of fumes. Something seemed to be hovering over me, rousing me, exciting me, and making me restless. Misery and spite seemed surging up in me again and seeking an outlet. Suddenly I saw beside me two wide open eyes scrutinizing me curiously and persistently. The look in those eyes was coldly detached, sullen, as it were utterly remote; it weighed upon me.

A grim idea came into my brain and passed all over my body, as a horrible sensation, such as one feels when one goes into a damp and mouldy cellar. There was something unnatural in those two eyes, beginning to look at me only now. I recalled, too, that during those two hours I had not said a single word to this creature, and had, in fact, considered it utterly superfluous; in fact, the silence had for some reason gratified me. Now I suddenly realized vividly the hideous idea—revolting as a spider—of vice, which, without love, grossly and shamelessly begins with that in which true love finds its consummation. For a long time we gazed at each other like that, but she did not drop her eyes before mine and her expression did not change, so that at last I felt uncomfortable.

"What is your name?" I asked abruptly, to put an end to it.

"Liza," she answered almost in a whisper, but somehow far from graciously, and she turned her eyes away.

I was silent.

"What weather! The snow . . . it's disgusting!" I said, almost to myself, putting my arm under my head despondently, and gazing at the ceiling.

She made no answer. This was horrible.

"Have you always lived in Petersburg?" I asked a minute later, almost angrily, turning my head slightly towards her.

"No."

"Where do you come from?"

"From Riga," she answered reluctantly.

"Are you a German?"

"No, Russian."

"Have you been here long?"

"Where?"

"In this house?"

"A fortnight."

She spoke more and more jerkily. The candle went out; I could no longer distinguish her face.

"Have you a father and mother?"

"Yes . . . no . . . I have."

"Where are they?"

"There . . . in Riga."

"What are they?"

"Oh, nothing."

"Nothing? Why, what class are they?"

"Tradespeople."

"Have you always lived with them?"

"Yes."

"How old are you?"

"Twenty."

"Why did you leave them?"

"Oh, for no reason."

That answer meant "Let me alone; I feel sick, sad."

We were silent.

God knows why I did not go away. I felt myself more and more sick and dreary. The images of the previous day began of themselves, apart from my will, flitting through my memory in confusion. I suddenly recalled something I had seen that morning when, full of anxious thoughts, I was hurrying to the office.

"I saw them carrying a coffin out yesterday and they nearly dropped it," I suddenly said aloud, not that I desired to open the conversation, but as it were by accident.

"A coffin?"

"Yes, in the Haymarket; they were bringing it up out of a cellar."

"From a cellar?"

"Not from a cellar, but from a basement. Oh, you know . . . down below . . . from a house of ill-fame. It was filthy all round . . . Egg-shells, litter . . . stench. It was loathsome."

Silence.

"A nasty day to be buried," I began, simply to avoid being silent.

"Nasty, in what way?"

"The snow, the wet." (I yawned.)

"It makes no difference," she said suddenly, after a brief silence.

"No, it's horrid." (I yawned again.) "The gravediggers must have sworn at getting drenched by the snow. And there must have been water in the grave."

"Why water in the grave?" she asked, with a sort of curiosity, but speaking even more harshly and abruptly than before.

I suddenly began to feel provoked.

"Why, there must have been water at the bottom a foot deep. You can't dig a dry grave in Volkovo Cemetery."

"Why?"

"Why? Why, the place is waterlogged. It's a regular marsh. So they bury them in water. I've seen it myself . . . many times."

(I had never seen it once, indeed I had never been in Volkovo, and had only heard stories of it.)

"Do you mean to say, you don't mind how you die?"

"But why should I die?" she answered, as though defending herself.

"Why, some day you will die, and you will die just the same as that dead woman. She was . . . a girl like you. She died of consumption."

"A wench would have died in a hospital . . ." (She knows all about it already: she said "wench," not "girl.")

"She was in debt to her madam," I retorted, more and more provoked by the discussion; "and went on earning money for her up to the end, though she was in consumption. Some sledge-drivers standing by were talking about her to some soldiers and telling them so. No doubt they knew her. They were laughing. They were going to meet in a pot-house to drink to her memory."

A great deal of this was my invention. Silence followed, profound silence. She did not stir.

"And is it better to die in a hospital?"

"Isn't it just the same? Besides, why should I die?" she added irritably.

"If not now, a little later."

"Why a little later?"

"Why, indeed? Now you are young, pretty, fresh, you fetch a high price. But after another year of this life you will be very different—you will go off."

"In a year?"

"Anyway, in a year you will be worth less," I continued malignantly. "You will go from here to something lower, another house; a year later—to a third, lower and lower, and in seven years you will come to a basement in the Haymarket. That will be if you were lucky. But it would be much worse if you got some disease, consumption, say . . . and caught a chill, or something or other. It's not easy to get over an illness in your way of life. If you catch anything you may not get rid of it. And so you would die."

"Oh, well, then I shall die," she answered, quite vindictively, and she made a quick movement.

"But one is sorry."

"Sorry for whom?"

"Sorry for life."

Silence.

"Have you been engaged to be married? Eh?"

"What's that to you?"

"Oh, I am not cross-examining you. It's nothing to me. Why are you so cross? Of course you may have had your own troubles. What is it to me? It's simply that I felt sorry."

"Sorry for whom?"

"Sorry for you."

"No need," she whispered hardly audibly, and again made a faint movement.

That incensed me at once. What! I was so gentle with her, and she. . . .

"Why, do you think that you are on the right path?"

"I don't think anything."

"That's what's wrong, that you don't think. Realize it while there is still time. There still is time. You are still young, good-looking; you might love, be married, be happy. . . ."

"Not all married women are happy," she snapped out in the rude abrupt tone she had used at first.

"Not all, of course, but anyway it is much better than the life here. Infinitely better. Besides, with love one can live even without happiness. Even in sorrow life is sweet; life is sweet, however one lives. But here what is there but . . . filth? Phew!"

I turned away with disgust; I was no longer reasoning coldly. I began to feel myself what I was saying and warmed to the subject. I was already longing to expound the cherished ideas I had brooded over in my corner. Something suddenly flared up in me. An object had appeared before me.

"Never mind my being here, I am not an example for you. I am, perhaps, worse than you are. I was drunk when I came here, though," I hastened, however, to say in self-defence. "Besides, a man is no example for a woman. It's a different thing. I may degrade and defile myself, but I am not any one's slave. I come and go, and that's an end of it. I shake it off, and I am a different man. But you are a slave from the start. Yes, a slave! You give up everything, your whole freedom. If you want to break your chains afterwards, you won't be able to: you will be more and more fast in the snares. It is an accursed bondage. I know it. I won't speak of anything else, maybe you won't understand, but tell me: no doubt you are in debt to your madam? There, you see," I added, though she made no answer, but only listened in silence, entirely absorbed, "that's a bondage for you! You will never buy your freedom. They will see to that. It's like selling your soul to the devil. . . . And besides . . . perhaps I, too, am just as unlucky—how do you know

—and wallow in the mud on purpose, out of misery? You know, men take to drink from grief; well, maybe I am here from grief. Come, tell me, what is there good here? Here you and I . . . came together . . . just now and did not say one word to one another all the time, and it was only afterwards you began staring at me like a wild creature, and I at you. Is that loving? Is that how one human being should meet another? It's hideous, that's what it is!"

"Yes!" she assented sharply and hurriedly.

I was positively astounded by the promptitude of this "Yes." So the same thought may have been straying through her mind when she was staring at me just before. So she, too, was capable of certain thoughts? "Damn it all, this was interesting, this was a point of likeness!" I thought, almost rubbing my hands. And indeed it's easy to turn a young soul like that!

It was the exercise of my power that attracted me most.

She turned her head nearer to me, and it seemed to me in the darkness that she propped herself on her arm. Perhaps she was scrutinizing me. How I regretted that I could not see her eyes. I heard her deep breathing.

"Why have you come here?" I asked her, with a note of authority already in my voice.

"Oh, I don't know."

"But how nice it would be to be living in your father's house! It's warm and free; and you have a home of your own."

"But what if it's worse than this?"

"I must take the right tone," flashed through my mind. "I may not get far with sentimentality." But it was only a momentary thought. I swear she really did interest me. Besides, I was exhausted and moody. And cunning so easily goes hand-in-hand with feeling.

"Who denies it!" I hastened to answer. "Anything may happen. I am convinced that some one has wronged you, and that you are more sinned against than sinning. Of course, I know nothing of your story, but it's not likely a girl like you has come here of her own inclination. . . ."

"A girl like me?" she whispered, hardly audibly; but I heard it.

Damn it all, I was flattering her. That was horrid. But perhaps it was a good thing. . . . She was silent.

"See, Liza, I will tell you about myself. If I had had a home from childhood, I shouldn't be what I am now. I often think that. However bad it may be at home, anyway they are your father and mother, and not enemies, strangers. Once a year at least, they'll show their love of you. Anyway, you know you are at home. I grew up without a home; and perhaps that's why I've turned so . . . unfeeling."

I waited again. "Perhaps she doesn't understand," I thought, "and, indeed, it is absurd—it's moralizing."

"If I were a father and had a daughter, I believe I should love my daughter more than my sons, really," I began indirectly, as though talking of something else, to distract her attention. I must confess I blushed.

"Why so?" she asked.

Ah! so she was listening!

"I don't know, Liza. I knew a father who was a stern, austere man, but used to go down on his knees to his daughter, used to kiss her hands, her feet, he couldn't make enough of her, really. When she danced at parties he used to stand for five hours at a stretch, gazing at her. He was mad over her: I understand that! She would fall asleep tired at night, and he would wake to kiss her in her sleep and make the sign of the cross over her. He would go about in a dirty old coat, he was stingy to every one else, but would spend his last penny for her, giving her expensive presents, and it was his greatest delight when she was pleased with what he gave her. Fathers always love their daughters more than the mothers do. Some girls live happily at home! And I believe I should never let my daughters marry."

"What next?" she said, with a faint smile.

"I should be jealous, I really should. To think that she should kiss any one else! That she should love a stranger more than her father! It's painful to imagine it. Of course, that's all nonsense, of course every father would be reasonable at last. But I believe before I should let her marry, I should worry myself to death; I should find fault with all her suitors. But I should end by letting her marry whom she herself loved. The one whom the daughter loves always seems the worst to the father, you know. That is always so. So many family troubles come from that."

"Some are glad to sell their daughters, rather than marrying them honourably."

Ah, so that was it!

"Such a thing, Liza, happens in those accursed families in which there is neither love nor God," I retorted warmly, "and where there is no love, there is no sense either. There are such families, it's true, but I am not speaking of them. You must have seen wickedness in your own family, if you talk like that. Truly, you must have been unlucky. H'm! . . . that sort of thing mostly comes about through poverty."

"And is it any better with the gentry? Even among the poor, honest people live happily."

"H'm . . . yes. Perhaps. Another thing, Liza, man is fond of reckoning up his troubles, but does not count his joys. If he counted them up as he ought, he would see that every lot has enough happiness provided for it. And what if all goes well with the family, if the blessing of God is upon it, if the husband is a good one, loves you, cherishes you, never leaves you! There is happiness in such a family! Even sometimes there is happiness in the midst of sorrow; and indeed sorrow is everywhere. If you marry *you will find out for yourself*. But think of the first years of married life with one you love: what happiness, what happiness there sometimes is in it! And indeed it's the ordinary thing. In those early days even quarrels with one's husband end happily. Some women get up quarrels with their husbands just because they love them. Indeed, I knew a woman like that: she seemed to say that because she loved him, she would torment him and make him feel it. You know that you may torment a man on purpose through love. Women are particularly given to that, thinking to themselves 'I will love him so, I will make so much of him afterwards, that it's no sin to torment him a little now.' And all in the house rejoice in the sight of you, and you are happy and gay and peaceful and honourable. . . . Then there are some women who are jealous. If he went off anywhere—I knew one such woman, she couldn't restrain herself, but would jump up at night and run off on the sly to find out where he was, whether he was with some other woman. That's a pity. And the woman knows herself it's wrong, and her heart fails her and she suffers, but she loves—it's all through love. And how sweet it is to make it up after quarrels, to own herself in the wrong or to forgive him! And they are both so happy all at once—as though they had met anew, been married over again; as though their love had begun afresh. And no one, no one should know what passes between husband and wife if they love one another. And whatever quarrels there may be between them they ought not to call in their own mother to judge between them and tell tales of one another. They are their own judges. Love is a holy mystery and ought to be hidden from all other eyes, whatever happens. That makes it holier and better. They respect one another more, and much is built on respect. And if once there has been love, if they have been married for love, why should love pass away? Surely one can keep it! It is rare that one cannot keep it. And if the husband is kind and straightforward, why should not love last? The first phase of married love will pass, it is true, but then there will come a love that is better still. Then there will be the union of souls, they will have everything in common, there will be no secrets between them. And once they have children, the most difficult times will seem to them happy, so long as there is love and courage. Even toil will be a joy, you may deny yourself bread for your children and even that will be a joy. They will love you for it afterwards; so you are laying by for your future. As the children grow up you feel that you are an example, a support for them; that even after you die your children will always keep your thoughts and feelings, because they have received them from you, they will take on your semblance and likeness. So you see this is a great duty. How can it fail to draw the father and mother nearer? People say it's a trial to have children. Who says that? It is heavenly happiness! Are you fond of little children, Liza? I am awfully fond of them. You know—a little rosy baby boy at your bosom, and what husband's heart is not touched, seeing his wife nursing his child! A plump little rosy baby, sprawling and snuggling, chubby little hands and feet, clean tiny little nails, so tiny that it makes one laugh to look at them; eyes that look as if they understand everything. And while it sucks it clutches at your bosom with its little hand, plays. When its father comes up, the child tears itself away from the bosom, flings itself back, looks at its father, laughs, as though it were fearfully funny and falls to sucking again. Or it will bite its mother's breast when its little teeth are coming, while it looks sideways at her with its little eyes as though to say, 'Look, I am biting!' Is not all that happiness when they are the three together, husband, wife and child? One can forgive a great deal for the sake of such moments. Yes, Liza, one must first learn to live oneself before one blames others!"

"It's by pictures, pictures like that one must get at you," I thought to myself, though I did speak with real feeling, and all at once I flushed crimson. "What if she were suddenly to burst out laughing, what should I do then?" That idea drove me to fury. Towards the end of my speech I really was excited, and now my vanity was somehow wounded. The silence continued. I almost nudged her.

"Why are you——" she began and stopped. But I understood: there was a quiver of something different in her voice, not abrupt, harsh and unyielding as before, but something soft and shamefaced, so shamefaced that I suddenly felt ashamed and guilty.

"What?" I asked, with tender curiosity.

"Why, you . . ."

"What?"

"Why, you . . . speak somehow like a book," she said, and again there was a note of irony in her voice.

That remark sent a pang to my heart. It was not what I was expecting.

I did not understand that she was hiding her feelings under irony, that this is usually the last refuge of modest and chaste-souled people when the privacy of their soul is coarsely and intrusively invaded, and that their pride makes them refuse to surrender till the last moment and shrink from giving expression to their feelings before you. I ought to have guessed the truth from the timidity with which she had repeatedly approached her sarcasm, only bringing herself to utter it at last with an effort. But I did not guess, and an evil feeling took possession of me.

"Wait a bit!" I thought.

VII

"Oh, hush, Liza! How can you talk about being like a book, when it makes even me, an outsider, feel sick? Though I don't look at it as an outsider, for, indeed, it touches me to the heart. . . . Is it possible, is it possible that you do not feel sick at being here yourself? Evidently habit does wonders! God knows what habit can do with any one. Can you seriously think that you will never grow old, that you will always be good-looking, and that they will keep you here for ever and ever? I say nothing of the loathsomeness of the life here. . . . Though let me tell you this about it—about your present life, I mean; here though you are young now, attractive, nice, with soul and feeling, yet you know as soon as I came to myself just now I felt at once sick at being here with you! One can only come here when one is drunk. But if you were anywhere else, living as good people live, I should perhaps be more than attracted by you, should fall in love with you, should be glad of a look from you, let alone a word; I should hang about your door, should go down on my knees to you, should look upon you as my betrothed and think it an honour to be allowed to. I should not dare to have an impure thought about you. But here, you see, I know that I have only to whistle and you have to come with me whether you like it or not. I don't consult your wishes, but you mine. The lowest labourer hires himself as a workman, but he doesn't make a slave of himself altogether; besides, he knows that he will be free again presently. But when are you free? Only think what you are giving up here? What is it you are making a slave of? It is your soul, together with your body; you are selling your soul which you have no right to dispose of! You give your love to be outraged by every drunkard! Love! But that's everything, you know, it's a priceless diamond, it's a maiden's treasure, love—why, a man would be ready to give his soul, to face death to gain that love. But how much is your love worth now? You are sold, all of you, body and soul, and there is no need to strive for love when you can have everything without love. And you know there is no greater insult to a girl than that, do you understand? To be sure, I have heard that they comfort you, poor fools, they let you have lovers of your own here. But you know that's simply a farce, that's simply a sham, it's just laughing at you, and you are taken in by it! Why, do you suppose he really loves you, that lover of yours? I don't believe it. How can he love you when he knows you may be called away from him any minute?

He would be a low fellow if he did! Will he have a grain of respect
for you? What have you in common with him? He laughs at you
and robs you—that is all his love amounts to! You are lucky if he
does not beat you. Very likely he does beat you, too. Ask him, if
you have got one, whether he will marry you. He will laugh in your
face, if he doesn't spit in it or give you a blow—though maybe he
is not worth a bad halfpenny himself. And for what have you ruined
your life, if you come to think of it? For the coffee they give you to
drink and the plentiful meals? But with what object are they feeding
you up? An honest girl couldn't swallow the food, for she would
know what she was being fed for. You are in debt here, and, of
course, you will always be in debt, and you will go on in debt to the
end, till the visitors here begin to scorn you. And that will soon
happen, don't rely upon your youth—all that flies by express train
here, you know. You will be kicked out. And not simply kicked out;
long before that she'll begin nagging at you, scolding you, abusing
you, as though you had not sacrificed your health for her, had not
thrown away your youth and your soul for her benefit, but as though
you had ruined her, beggared her, robbed her. And don't expect
any one to take your part: the others, your companions, will attack
you, too, to win her favour, for all are in slavery here, and have lost
all conscience and pity here long ago. They have become utterly
vile, and nothing on earth is viler, more loathsome, and more insulting than their abuse. And you are laying down everything here, unconditionally, youth and health and beauty and hope, and at twenty-
two you will look like a woman of five-and-thirty, and you will be
lucky if you are not diseased, pray to God for that! No doubt you
are thinking now that you have a gay time and no work to do! Yet
there is no work harder or more dreadful in the world or ever has
been. One would think that the heart alone would be worn out with
tears. And you won't dare to say a word, not half a word when they
drive you away from here; you will go away as though you were to
blame. You will change to another house, then to a third, then
somewhere else, till you come down at last to the Haymarket. There
you will be beaten at every turn; that is good manners there, the
visitors don't know how to be friendly without beating you. You
don't believe that it is so hateful there? Go and look for yourself
some time, you can see with your own eyes. Once, one New Year's
Day, I saw a woman at a door. They had turned her out as a joke,
to give her a taste of the frost because she had been crying so much,
and they shut the door behind her. At nine o'clock in the morning
she was already quite drunk, dishevelled, half-naked, covered with
bruises, her face was powdered, but she had a black-eye, blood was
trickling from her nose and her teeth; some cabman had just given
her a drubbing. She was sitting on the stone steps, a salt fish of some

sort was in her hand; she was crying, wailing something about her luck and beating with the fish on the steps, and cabmen and drunken soldiers were crowding in the doorway taunting her. You don't believe that you will ever be like that? I should be sorry to believe it, too, but how do you know; maybe ten years, eight years ago that very woman with the salt fish came here fresh as a cherub, innocent, pure, knowing no evil, blushing at every word. Perhaps she was like you, proud, ready to take offence, not like the others; perhaps she looked like a queen, and knew what happiness was in store for the man who should love her and whom she should love. Do you see how it ended? And what if at that very minute when she was beating on the filthy steps with that fish, drunken and dishevelled— what if at that very minute she recalled the pure early days in her father's house, when she used to go to school and the neighbour's son watched for her on the way, declaring that he would love her as long as he lived, that he would devote his life to her, and when they vowed to love one another for ever and be married as soon as they were grown up! No, Liza, it would be happy for you if you were to die soon of consumption in some corner, in some cellar like that woman just now. In the hospital, do you say? You will be lucky if they take you, but what if you are still of use to the madam here? Consumption is a queer disease, it is not like fever. The patient goes on hoping till the last minute and says he is all right. He deludes himself. And that just suits your madam. Don't doubt it, that's how it is; you have sold your soul, and what is more you owe money, so you daren't say a word. But when you are dying, all will abandon you, all will turn away from you, for then there will be nothing to get from you. What's more, they will reproach you for cumbering the place, for being so long over dying. However you beg you won't get a drink of water without abuse: 'Whenever are you going off, you nasty hussy, you won't let us sleep with your moaning, you make the gentlemen sick.' That's true, I have heard such things said myself. They will thrust you dying into the filthiest corner in the cellar—in the damp and darkness; what will your thoughts be, lying there alone? When you die, strange hands will lay you out, with grumbling and impatience; no one will bless you, no one will sigh for you, they only want to get rid of you as soon as may be; they will buy a coffin, take you to the grave as they did that poor woman to-day, and celebrate your memory at the tavern. In the gravest sleet, filth, wet snow—no need to put themselves out for you—'Let her down, Vanyukha; it's just like her luck—even here, she is head-foremost, the hussy. Shorten the cord, you rascal.' 'It's all right as it is.' 'All right, is it? Why, she's on her side! She was a fellow-creature, after all! But, never mind, throw the earth on her.' And they won't care to waste much time quarrelling over you. They will scatter the wet blue clay as quick as they can and go off to the tavern . . . and there your memory on earth will end; other women have children to go to their graves, fathers, husbands. While for you neither tear, nor sigh, nor remembrance; no one in the whole world will ever come to you, your name will vanish from the face of the earth —as though you had never existed, never been born at all! Nothing but filth and mud, however you knock at your coffin lid at night, when the dead arise, however you cry: 'Let me out, kind people, to live in the light of day! My life was no life at all; my life has been thrown away like a dish-clout; it was drunk away in the tavern at the Haymarket; let me out, kind people, to live in the world again.' "

And I worked myself up to such a pitch that I began to have a lump in my throat myself, and . . . and all at once I stopped, sat up in dismay, and bending over apprehensively, began to listen with a beating heart. I had reason to be troubled.

I had felt for some time that I was turning her soul upside down and rending her heart, and—and the more I was convinced of it, the more eagerly I desired to gain my object as quickly and as effectually as possible. It was the exercise of my skill that carried me away; yet it was not merely sport. . . .

I knew I was speaking stiffly, artificially, even bookishly, in fact, I could not speak except "like a book." But that did not trouble me: I knew, I felt that I should be understood and that this very bookishness might be an assistance. But now, having attained my effect, I was suddenly panic-stricken. Never before had I witnessed such despair! She was lying on her face, thrusting her face into the pillow and clutching it in both hands. Her heart was being torn. Her youthful body was shuddering all over as though in convulsions. Suppressed sobs rent her bosom and suddenly burst out in weeping and wailing, then she pressed closer into the pillow: she did not want any one here, not a living soul, to know of her anguish and her tears. She bit the pillow, bit her hand till it bled (I saw that afterwards), or, thrusting her fingers into her dishevelled hair seemed rigid with the effort of restraint, holding her breath and clenching her teeth. I began saying something, begging her to calm herself, but felt that I did not dare; and all at once, in a sort of cold shiver, almost in terror, began fumbling in the dark, trying hurriedly to get dressed to go. It was dark: though I tried my best I could not finish dressing quickly. Suddenly I felt a box of matches and a candlestick with a whole candle in it. As soon as the room was lighted up, Liza sprang up, sat up in bed, and with a contorted face, with a half insane smile, looked at me almost senselessly. I sat down beside her and took her hands; she came to herself, made an impulsive movement towards me, would have caught hold of me, but did not dare, and slowly bowed her head before me.

"Liza, my dear, I was wrong . . . forgive me, my dear," I began, but she squeezed my hand in her fingers so tightly that I felt I was saying the wrong thing and stopped.

"This is my address, Liza, come to me."

"I will come," she answered resolutely, her head still bowed.

"But now I am going, good-bye . . . till we meet again."

I got up; she, too, stood up and suddenly flushed all over, gave a shudder, snatched up a shawl that was lying on a chair and muffled herself in it to her chin. As she did this she gave another sickly smile, blushed and looked at me strangely. I felt wretched; I was in haste to get away—to disappear.

"Wait a minute," she said suddenly, in the passage just at the doorway, stopping me with her hand on my overcoat. She put down the candle in hot haste and ran off; evidently she had thought of something or wanted to show me something. As she ran away she flushed, her eyes shone, and there was a smile on her lips—what was the meaning of it? Against my will I waited: she came back a minute later with an expression that seemed to ask forgiveness for something. In fact, it was not the same face, not the same look as the evening before: sullen, mistrustful and obstinate. Her eyes now were imploring, soft, and at the same time trustful, caressing, timid. The expression with which children look at people they are very fond of, of whom they are asking a favour. Her eyes were a light hazel, they were lovely eyes, full of life, and capable of expressing love as well as sullen hatred.

Making no explanation, as though I, as a sort of higher being, must understand everything without explanations, she held out a piece of paper to me. Her whole face was positively beaming at that instant with naïve, almost childish, triumph. I unfolded it. It was a letter to her from a medical student or some one of that sort—a very high-flown and flowery, but extremely respectful, love-letter. I don't recall the words now, but I remember well that through the high-flown phrases there was apparent a genuine feeling, which cannot be feigned. When I had finished reading it I met her glowing, questioning, and childishly impatient eyes fixed upon me. She fastened her eyes upon my face and waited impatiently for what I should say. In a few words, hurriedly, but with a sort of joy and pride, she explained to me that she had been to a dance somewhere in a private house, a family of "very nice people *who knew nothing*, absolutely nothing, for she had only come here so lately and it had all happened . . . and she hadn't made up her mind to stay and was certainly going away as soon as she had paid her debt . . ."

and at that party there had been the student who had danced with her all the evening. He had talked to her, and it turned out that he had known her in old days at Riga when he was a child, they had played together, but a very long time ago—and he knew her parents, but *about this* he knew nothing, nothing whatever, and had no suspicion! And the day after the dance (three days ago) he had sent her that letter through the friend with whom she had gone to the party . . . and . . . well, that was all.

She dropped her shining eyes with a sort of bashfulness as she finished.

The poor girl was keeping that student's letter as a precious treasure, and had run to fetch it, her only treasure, because she did not want me to go away without knowing that she, too, was honestly and genuinely loved; that she, too, was addressed respectfully. No doubt that letter was destined to lie in her box and lead to nothing. But none the less, I am certain that she would keep it all her life as a precious treasure, as her pride and justification, and now at such a minute she had thought of that letter and brought it with naïve pride to raise herself in my eyes that I might see, that I, too, might think well of her. I said nothing, pressed her hand and went out. I so longed to get away. . . . I walked all the way home, in spite of the fact that the melting snow was still falling in heavy flakes. I was exhausted, shattered, in bewilderment. But behind the bewilderment the truth was already gleaming. The loathsome truth.

VIII

It was some time, however, before I consented to recognize that truth. Waking up in the morning after some hours of heavy, leaden sleep, and immediately realizing all that had happened on the previous day, I was positively amazed at my last night's *sentimentality* with Liza, at all those "outcries of horror and pity." "To think of having such an attack of womanish hysteria, pah!" I concluded. And what did I thrust my address upon her for? What if she comes? Let her come, though; it doesn't matter. . . . But *obviously*, that was not now the chief and the most important matter: I had to make haste and at all costs save my reputation in the eyes of Zverkov and Simonov as quickly as possible; that was the chief business. And I was so taken up that morning that I actually forgot all about Liza.

First of all I had at once to repay what I had borrowed the day before from Simonov. I resolved on a desperate measure: to borrow fifteen roubles straight off from Anton Antonich. As luck would have it he was in the best of humours that morning, and gave it to me at once, on the first asking. I was so delighted at this that, as I signed the I O U with a swaggering air, I told him casually that the night before "I had been keeping it up with some friends at the Hôtel de Paris; we were giving a farewell party to a comrade, in fact,

I might say a friend of my childhood, and you know—a desperate rake, fearfully spoilt—of course, he belongs to a good family, and has considerable means, a brilliant career; he is witty, charming, a regular Lovelace, you understand; we drank an extra 'half-dozen' and . . ."

And it went off all right; all this was uttered very easily, unconstrainedly and complacently.

On reaching home I promptly wrote to Simonov.

To this hour I am lost in admiration when I recall the truly gentlemanly, good-humoured, candid tone of my letter. With tact and good-breeding, and, above all, entirely without superfluous words, I blamed myself for all that had happened. I defended myself, "if I really may be allowed to defend myself," by alleging that being utterly unaccustomed to wine, I had been intoxicated with the first glass, which I said, I had drunk before they arrived, while I was waiting for them at the Hôtel de Paris between five and six o'clock. I begged Simonov's pardon especially; I asked him to convey my explanations to all the others, especially to Zverkov, whom "I seemed to remember as though in a dream" I had insulted. I added that I would have called upon all of them myself, but my head ached, and besides I had not the face to. I was particularly pleased with a certain lightness, almost carelessness (strictly within the bounds of politeness, however), which was apparent in my style, and better than any possible arguments, gave them at once to understand that I took rather an independent view of "all that unpleasantness last night;" that I was by no means so utterly crushed as you, my friends, probably imagine; but on the contrary, looked upon it as a gentleman serenely respecting himself should look upon it. "On a young hero's past no censure is cast!"

"There is actually an aristocratic playfulness about it!" I thought admiringly, as I read over the letter. And it's all because I am an intellectual and cultivated man! Another man in my place would not have known how to extricate himself, but here I have got out of it and am as jolly as ever again, and all because I am "a cultivated and educated man of our day." And, indeed, perhaps, everything was due to the wine yesterday. H'm! . . . no, it was not the wine. I did not drink anything at all between five and six when I was waiting for them. I had lied to Simonov; I had lied shamelessly; and indeed I wasn't ashamed now. . . . Hang it all though, the great thing was that I was rid of it.

I put six roubles in the letter, sealed it up, and asked Apollon to take it to Simonov. When he learned that there was money in the letter, Apollon became more respectful and agreed to take it. Towards evening I went out for a walk. My head was still aching and giddy after yesterday. But as evening came on and the twilight grew denser, my impressions and, following them, my thoughts, grew more and more different and confused. Something was not dead within me, in the depths of my heart and conscience it would not die, and it showed itself in acute depression. For the most part I jostled my way through the most crowded business streets, along Myeshchansky Street, along Sadovy Street and in Yusupov Garden. I always liked particularly sauntering along these streets in the dusk, just when there were crowds of working people of all sorts going home from their daily work, with faces looking cross with anxiety. What I liked was just that cheap bustle, that bare prose. On this occasion the jostling of the streets irritated me more than ever. I could not make out what was wrong with me, I could not find the clue, something seemed rising up continually in my soul, painfully, and refusing to be appeased. I returned home completely upset, it was just as though some crime were lying on my conscience.

The thought that Liza was coming worried me continually. It seemed queer to me that of all my recollections of yesterday this tormented me, as it were, especially, as it were, quite separately. Everything else I had quite succeeded in forgetting by the evening; I dismissed it all and was still perfectly satisfied with my letter to Simonov. But on this point I was not satisfied at all. It was as though I were worried only by Liza. "What if she comes," I thought incessantly, "well, it doesn't matter, let her come! H'm! it's horrid that she should see, for instance, how I live. Yesterday I seemed such a hero to her, while now, h'm! It's horrid, though, that I have let myself go so, the room looks like a beggar's. And I brought myself to go out to dinner in such a suit! And my American leather sofa with the stuffing sticking out. And my dressing-gown, which will not cover me, such tatters, and she will see all this and she will see Apollon. That beast is certain to insult her. He will fasten upon her in order to be rude to me. And I, of course, shall be panic-stricken as usual, I shall begin bowing and scraping before her and pulling my dressing-gown round me, I shall begin smiling, telling lies. Oh, the beastliness! And it isn't the beastliness of it that matters most! There is something more important, more loathsome, viler! Yes, viler! And to put on that dishonest lying mask again!" . . .

When I reached that thought I fired up all at once.

"Why dishonest? How dishonest? I was speaking sincerely last night. I remember there was real feeling in me, too. What I wanted was to excite an honourable feeling in her. . . . Her crying was a good thing, it will have a good effect."

Yet I could not feel at ease. All that evening, even when I had come back home, even after nine o'clock, when I calculated that Liza could not possibly come, she still haunted me, and what was worse, she came back to my mind always in the same position. One moment out of all that had happened last night stood vividly before my imagination; the moment when I struck a match and saw her pale, distorted face, with its look of torture. And what a pitiful, what an unnatural, what a distorted smile she had at that moment! But I did not know then, that fifteen years later I should still in my imagination see Liza, always with the pitiful, distorted, inappropriate smile which was on her face at that minute.

Next day I was ready again to look upon it all as nonsense, due to over-excited nerves, and, above all, as *exaggerated*. I was always conscious of that weak point of mine, and sometimes very much afraid of it. "I exaggerate everything, that is where I go wrong," I repeated to myself every hour. But, however, "Liza will very likely come all the same," was the refrain with which all my reflections ended. I was so uneasy that I sometimes flew into a fury: "She'll come, she is certain to come!" I cried, running about the room, "if not to-day, she will come to-morrow; she'll find me out! The damnable romanticism of these pure hearts! Oh, the vileness—oh, the silliness—oh, the stupidity of these 'wretched sentimental souls!' Why, how fail to understand? How could one fail to understand? . . ."

But at this point I stopped short, and in great confusion, indeed.

And how few, how few words, I thought, in passing, were needed; how little of the idyllic (and affectedly, bookishly, artificially idyllic too) had sufficed to turn a whole human life at once according to my will. That's virginity, to be sure! Freshness of soil!

At times a thought occurred to me, to go to her, "to tell her all," and beg her not to come to me. But this thought stirred such wrath in me that I believed I should have crushed that "damned" Liza if she had chanced to be near me at the time. I should have insulted her, have spat at her, have turned her out, have struck her!

One day passed, however, another and another; she did not come and I began to grow calmer. I felt particularly bold and cheerful after nine o'clock, I even sometimes began dreaming, and rather sweetly: I, for instance, became the salvation of Liza, simply through her coming to me and my talking to her. . . . I develop her, educate her. Finally, I notice that she loves me, loves me passionately. I pretend not to understand (I don't know, however, why I pretend, just for effect, perhaps). At last all confusion, transfigured, trembling and sobbing, she flings herself at my feet and says that I am her saviour, and that she loves me better than anything in the world. I am amazed, but. . . . "Liza," I say, "can you imagine that I have not noticed your love, I saw it all, I divined it, but I did not dare to approach you first, because I had an influence over you and was afraid that you would force yourself, from gratitude, to respond to my love, would try to rouse in your heart a feeling which was perhaps absent, and I did not wish that . . . because it would be tyranny . . . it would be indelicate (in short, I launch off at that point into European, inexplicably lofty subtleties à la George Sand[30]), but now, now you are mine, you are my creation, you are pure, you are good, you are my noble wife.

> 'Into my house come bold and free,
>   Its rightful mistress there to be.' "[31]

Then we begin living together, go abroad and so on, and so on. In fact, in the end it seemed vulgar to me myself, and I began putting out my tongue at myself.

Besides, they won't let her out, "the hussy!" I thought. They don't let them go out very readily, especially in the evening (for some reason I fancied she would come in the evening, and at seven o'clock precisely). Though she did say she was not altogether a slave there yet, and had certain rights; so, h'm! Damn it all, she will come, she is sure to come!

It was a good thing, in fact, that Apollon distracted my attention at that time by his rudeness. He drove me beyond all patience! He was the bane of my life, the curse laid upon me by Providence. We had been squabbling continually for years, and I hated him. My God, how I hated him! I believe I had never hated any one in my life as I hated him, especially at some moments. He was an elderly, dignified man, who worked part of his time as a tailor. But for some unknown reason he despised me beyond all measure, and looked down upon me insufferably. Though, indeed, he looked down upon every one. Simply to glance at that flaxen, smoothly brushed head, at the tuft of hair he combed up on his forehead and oiled with sunflower oil, at that dignified mouth, compressed into the shape of the letter V, made one feel one was confronting a man who never doubted of himself. He was a pedant, to the most extreme point, the greatest pedant I had met on earth, and with that had a vanity only befitting Alexander of Macedon. He was in love with every button on his coat, every nail on his fingers—absolutely in love with them, and he looked it! In his behaviour to me he was a perfect tyrant, he spoke very little to me, and if he chanced to glance at me he gave me a firm, majestically self-confident and invariably ironical look that drove me sometimes to fury. He did his work with the air of doing me the greatest favour. Though he did scarcely anything for me, and did not, indeed, consider himself bound to do anything. There could be no doubt that he looked upon me as the greatest fool on earth, and that "he did not get rid of me" was simply that

30. pseudonym of the French woman novelist Mme. Aurore Dudevant (1804–1876), famous also as a promoter of feminism.

31. the last lines of the poem by Nekrasov used as the epigraph of Part II of this story.

he could get wages from me every month. He consented to do nothing for me for seven roubles a month. Many sins should be forgiven
me for what I suffered from him. My hatred reached such a point
that sometimes his very step almost threw me into convulsions.
What I loathed particularly was his lisp. His tongue must have been
a little too long or something of that sort, for he continually lisped,
and seemed to be very proud of it, imagining that it greatly added
to his dignity. He spoke in a slow, measured tone, with his hands
behind his back and his eyes fixed on the ground. He maddened me
particularly when he read aloud the psalms to himself behind his
partition. Many a battle I waged over that reading! But he was
awfully fond of reading aloud in the evenings, in a slow, even, singsong voice, as though over the dead. It is interesting that that is
how he has ended: he hires himself out to read the psalms over the
dead, and at the same time he kills rats and makes blacking. But at
that time I could not get rid of him, it was as though he were
chemically combined with my existence. Besides, nothing would
have induced him to consent to leave me. I could not live in furnished lodgings: my lodging was my private solitude, my shell, my
cave, in which I concealed myself from all mankind, and Apollon
seemed to me, for some reason, an integral part of that flat, and for
seven years I could not turn him away.

To be two or three days behind with his wages, for instance,
was impossible. He would have made such a fuss, I should not have
known where to hide my head. But I was so exasperated with every
one during those days, that I made up my mind for some reason
and with some object to *punish* Apollon and not to pay him for a
fortnight the wages that were owing him. I had for a long time—
for the last two years—been intending to do this, simply in order to
teach him not to give himself airs with me, and to show him that if
I liked I could withhold his wages. I purposed to say nothing to
him about it, and was purposely silent indeed, in order to score off
his pride and force him to be the first to speak of his wages. Then I
would take the seven roubles out of a drawer, show him I have the
money put aside on purpose, but that I won't, I won't, I simply
won't pay him his wages, I won't just because that is "what I wish,"
because "I am master, and it is for me to decide," because he has
been disrespectful, because he has been rude; but if he were to ask
respectfully I might be softened and give it to him, otherwise he
might wait another fortnight, another three weeks, a whole
month. . . .

But angry as I was, yet he got the better of me. I could not hold
out for four days. He began as he always did begin in such cases, for
there had been such cases already, there had been attempts (and it
may be observed I knew all this beforehand, I knew his nasty tactics

by heart). He would begin by fixing upon me an exceedingly severe stare, keeping it up for several minutes at a time, particularly on meeting me or seeing me out of the house. If I held out and pretended not to notice these stares, he would, still in silence, proceed to further tortures. All at once, *à propos* of nothing, he would walk softly and smoothly into my room, when I was pacing up and down or reading, stand at the door, one hand behind his back and one foot behind the other, and fix upon me a stare more than severe, utterly contemptuous. If I suddenly asked him what he wanted, he would make me no answer, but continue staring at me persistently for some seconds, then, with a peculiar compression of his lips and a most significant air, deliberately turn round and deliberately go back to his room. Two hours later he would come out again and again present himself before me in the same way. It had happened that in my fury I did not even ask him what he wanted, but simply raised my head sharply and imperiously and began staring back at him. So we stared at one another for two minutes; at last he turned with deliberation and dignity and went back again for two hours.

If I were still not brought to reason by all this, but persisted in my revolt, he would suddenly begin sighing while he looked at me, long, deep sighs as though measuring by them the depths of my moral degradation, and, of course, it ended at last by his triumphing completely: I raged and shouted, but still was forced to do what he wanted.

This time the usual staring manœuvres had scarcely begun when I lost my temper and flew at him in a fury. I was irritated beyond endurance apart from him.

"Stay," I cried, in a frenzy, as he was slowly and silently turning, with one hand behind his back, to go to his room, "stay! Come back, come back, I tell you!" and I must have bawled so unnaturally, that he turned round and even looked at me with some wonder. However, he persisted in saying nothing, and that infuriated me.

"How dare you come and look at me like that without being sent for? Answer!"

After looking at me calmly for half a minute, he began turning round again.

"Stay!" I roared, running up to him, "don't stir! There. Answer, now: what did you come in to look at?"

"If you have any order to give me it's my duty to carry it out," he answered, after another silent pause, with a slow, measured lisp, raising his eyebrows and calmly twisting his head from one side to another, all this with exasperating composure.

"That's not what I am asking you about, you torturer!" I shouted, turning crimson with anger. "I'll tell you why you came here myself: you see, I don't give you your wages, you are so proud you don't want to bow down and ask for it, and so you come to punish me with your stupid stares, to worry me and you have no sus . . . pic . . . ion how stupid it is—stupid, stupid, stupid, stupid!" . . .

He would have turned round again without a word, but I seized him.

"Listen," I shouted to him. "Here's the money, do you see, here it is" (I took it out of the table drawer); "here's the seven roubles complete, but you are not going to have it, you . . . are . . . not . . . going . . . to . . . have it until you come respectfully with bowed head to beg my pardon. Do you hear?"

"That cannot be," he answered, with the most unnatural self-confidence.

"It shall be so," I said, "I give you my word of honour, it shall be!"

"And there's nothing for me to beg your pardon for," he went on, as though he had not noticed my exclamations at all. "Why, besides, you called me a 'torturer,' for which I can summon you at the police-station at any time for insulting behaviour."

"Go, summon me," I roared, "go at once, this very minute, this very second! You are a torturer all the same! a torturer!"

But he merely looked at me, then turned, and regardless of my loud calls to him, he walked to his room with an even step and without looking round.

"If it had not been for Liza nothing of this would have happened," I decided inwardly. Then, after waiting a minute, I went myself behind his screen with a dignified and solemn air, though my heart was beating slowly and violently.

"Apollon," I said quietly and emphatically, though I was breathless, "go at once without a minute's delay and fetch the police-officer."

He had meanwhile settled himself at his table, put on his spectacles and taken up some sewing. But, hearing my order, he burst into a guffaw.

"At once, go this minute! Go on, or else you can't imagine what will happen."

"You are certainly out of your mind," he observed, without even raising his head, lisping as deliberately as ever and threading his needle. "Whoever heard of a man sending for the police against himself? And as for being frightened—you are upsetting yourself about nothing, for nothing will come of it."

"Go!" I shrieked, clutching him by the shoulder. I felt I should strike him in a minute.

But I did not notice the door from the passage softly and slowly open at that instant and a figure come in, stop short, and begin staring at us in perplexity. I glanced, nearly swooned with shame, and rushed back to my room. There, clutching at my hair with both hands, I leaned my head against the wall and stood motionless in that position.

Two minutes later I heard Apollon's deliberate footsteps. "There is some woman asking for you," he said, looking at me with peculiar severity. Then he stood aside and let in Liza. He would not go away, but stared at us sarcastically.

"Go away, go away," I commanded in desperation. At that moment my clock began whirring and wheezing and struck seven.

IX

> "Into my house come bold and free,
> Its rightful mistress there to be."
>
> (From the same poem)

I stood before her crushed, crestfallen, revoltingly confused, and I believe I smiled as I did my utmost to wrap myself in the skirts of my ragged wadded dressing-gown—exactly as I had imagined the scene not long before in a fit of depression. After standing over us for a couple of minutes Apollon went away, but that did not make me more at ease. What made it worse was that she, too, was overwhelmed with confusion, more so, in fact, than I should have expected. At the sight of me, of course.

"Sit down," I said mechanically, moving a chair up to the table, and I sat down on the sofa. She obediently sat down at once and gazed at me open-eyed, evidently expecting something from me at once. This naïveté of expectation drove me to fury, but I restrained myself.

She ought to have tried not to notice, as though everything had been as usual, while instead of that, she . . . and I dimly felt that I should make her pay dearly for *all this*.

"You have found me in a strange position, Liza," I began, stammering and knowing that this was the wrong way to begin. "No, no, don't imagine anything," I cried, seeing that she had suddenly flushed. "I am not ashamed of my poverty. . . . On the contrary I look with pride on my poverty. I am poor but honourable. . . . One can be poor and honourable," I muttered. "However . . . would you like tea?". . .

"No," she was beginning.

"Wait a minute."

I leapt up and ran to Apollon. I had to get out of the room somehow.

"Apollon," I whispered in feverish haste, flinging down before him the seven roubles which had remained all the time in my clenched fist, "here are your wages, you see I give them to you; but for that you must come to my rescue: bring me tea and a dozen rusks from the restaurant. If you won't go, you'll make me a miserable man! You don't know what this woman is. . . . This is—everything! You may be imagining something. . . . But you don't know what that woman is!" . . .

Apollon, who had already sat down to his work and put on his spectacles again, at first glanced askance at the money without speaking or putting down his needle; then, without paying the slightest attention to me or making any answer he went on busying himself with his needle, which he had not yet threaded. I waited before him for three minutes with my arms crossed *à la Napoléon*. My temples were moist with sweat. I was pale, I felt it. But, thank God, he must have been moved to pity, looking at me. Having threaded his needle he deliberately got up from his seat, deliberately moved back his chair, deliberately took off his spectacles, deliberately counted the money, and finally asking me over his shoulder: "Shall I get a whole portion?" deliberately walked out of the room. As I was going back to Liza, the thought occurred to me on the way: shouldn't I run away just as I was in my dressing-gown, no matter where, and then let happen what would.

I sat down again. She looked at me uneasily. For some minutes we were silent.

"I will kill him," I shouted suddenly, striking the table with my fist so that the ink spurted out of the inkstand.

"What are you saying!" she cried, starting.

"I will kill him! kill him!" I shrieked, suddenly striking the table in absolute frenzy, and at the same time fully understanding how stupid it was to be in such a frenzy. "You don't know, Liza, what that torturer is to me. He is my torturer. . . . He has gone now to fetch some rusks; he . . ."

And suddenly I burst into tears. It was an hysterical attack. How ashamed I felt in the midst of my sobs; but still I could not restrain them.

She was frightened.

"What is the matter? What is wrong?" she cried, fussing about me.

"Water, give me water, over there!" I muttered in a faint voice, though I was inwardly conscious that I could have got on very well without water and without muttering in a faint voice. But I was, what is called, *putting it on*, to save appearances, though the attack was a genuine one.

She gave me water, looking at me in bewilderment. At that moment Apollon brought in the tea. It suddenly seemed to me that this commonplace, prosaic tea was horribly undignified and paltry after all that had happened, and I blushed crimson. Liza looked at Apollon with positive alarm. He went out without a glance at either of us.

"Liza, do you despise me?" I asked, looking at her fixedly, trembling with impatience to know what she was thinking.

She was confused, and did not know what to answer.

"Drink your tea," I said to her angrily. I was angry with myself, but, of course, it was she who would have to pay for it. A horrible spite against her suddenly surged up in my heart; I believe I could have killed her. To revenge myself on her I swore inwardly not to say a word to her all the time. "She is the cause of it all," I thought. Our silence lasted for five minutes. The tea stood on the table; we did not touch it. I had got to the point of purposely refraining from beginning in order to embarrass her further; it was awkward for her to begin alone. Several times she glanced at me with mournful perplexity. I was obstinately silent. I was, of course, myself the chief sufferer, because I was fully conscious of the disgusting meanness of my spiteful stupidity, and yet at the same time I could not restrain myself.

"I want to . . . get away . . . from there altogether," she began, to break the silence in some way, but, poor girl, that was just what she ought not to have spoken about at such a stupid moment to a man so stupid as I was. My heart positively ached with pity for her tactless and unnecessary straightforwardness. But something hideous at once stifled all compassion in me; it even provoked me to greater venom. I did not care what happened. Another five minutes passed.

"Perhaps I am in your way," she began timidly, hardly audibly, and was getting up.

But as soon as I saw this first impulse of wounded dignity I positively trembled with spite, and at once burst out.

"Why have you come to me, tell me that, please?" I began, gasping for breath and regardless of logical connection in my words. I longed to have it all out at once, at one burst; I did not even trouble how to begin. "Why have you come? Answer, answer," I cried, hardly knowing what I was doing. "I'll tell you, my good girl, why you have come. You've come because I talked sentimental stuff to you then. So now you are soft as butter and longing for fine sentiments again. So you may as well know that I was laughing at you then. And I am laughing at you now. Why are you shuddering? Yes, I was laughing at you! I had been insulted just before, at dinner, by the fellows who came that evening before me. I came to you, meaning to thrash one of them, an officer; but I didn't succeed, I didn't find him; I had to avenge the insult on some one to get back my own again; you turned up, I vented my spleen on you and laughed at you. I had been humiliated, so I wanted to humiliate; I had been treated like a rag, so I wanted to show my power. . . . That's what it was, and you imagined I had come there on purpose to save you. Yes? You imagined that? You imagined that?"

I knew that she would perhaps be muddled and not take it all in exactly, but I knew, too, that she would grasp the gist of it, very well indeed. And so, indeed, she did. She turned white as a handkerchief, tried to say something, and her lips worked painfully; but she sank on a chair as though she had been felled by an axe. And all the time afterwards she listened to me with her lips parted and her eyes wide open, shuddering with awful terror. The cynicism, the cynicism of my words overwhelmed her. . . .

"Save you!" I went on, jumping up from my chair and running up and down the room before her. "Save you from what? But perhaps I am worse than you myself. Why didn't you throw it in my teeth when I was giving you that sermon: 'But what did you come here yourself for? was it to read us a sermon?' Power, power was what I wanted then, sport was what I wanted, I wanted to ring out your tears, your humiliation, your hysteria—that was what I wanted then! Of course, I couldn't keep it up then, because I am a wretched creature, I was frightened, and, the devil knows why, gave you my address in my folly. Afterwards, before I got home, I was cursing and swearing at you because of that address, I hated you already because of the lies I had told you. Because I only like playing with words, only dreaming, but, do you know, what I really want is that you should all go to hell. That is what I want. I want peace; yes, I'd sell the whole world for a farthing, straight off, so long as I was left in peace. Is the world to go to pot, or am I to go without my tea? I say that the world may go to pot for me so long as I always get my tea. Did you know that, or not? Well, anyway, I know that I am a blackguard, a scoundrel, an egoist, a sluggard. Here I have been shuddering for the last three days at the thought of your coming. And do you know what has worried me particularly for these three days? That I posed as such a hero to you, and now you would see me in a wretched torn dressing-gown, beggarly, loathsome. I told you just now that I was not ashamed of my poverty; so you may as well know that I am ashamed of it; I am more ashamed of it than of anything, more afraid of it than of being found out if I were a thief, because I am as vain as though I had been skinned and the very air blowing on me hurts. Surely by now you must realize that I shall never forgive you for having found me in this wretched dressing-gown, just as I was flying at Apollon like a spiteful cur. The saviour, the former hero, was flying like a mangy, unkempt sheep-dog at his lackey, and the lackey was jeering at him! And I shall never forgive you for the tears I could not help shedding before you just now, like some silly woman put to shame! And for what I am confessing to you now, I shall never forgive *you* either! Yes— you must answer for it all because you turned up like this, because

I am a blackguard, because I am the nastiest, stupidest, absurdest and most envious of all the worms on earth, who are not a bit better than I am, but, the devil knows why, are never put to confusion; while I shall always be insulted by every louse, that is my doom! And what is it to me that you don't understand a word of this! And what do I care, what do I care about you, and whether you go to ruin there or not? Do you understand? How I shall hate you now after saying this, for having been here and listening. Why, it's not once in a lifetime a man speaks out like this, and then it is in hysterics! . . . What more do you want? Why do you still stand confronting me, after all this? Why are you worrying me? Why don't you go?"

But at this point a strange thing happened. I was so accustomed to think and imagine everything from books, and to picture everything in the world to myself just as I had made it up in my dreams beforehand, that I could not all at once take in this strange circumstance. What happened was this: Liza, insulted and crushed by me, understood a great deal more than I imagined. She understood from all this what a woman understands first of all, if she feels genuine love, that is, that I was myself unhappy.

The frightened and wounded expression on her face was followed first by a look of sorrowful perplexity. When I began calling myself a scoundrel and a blackguard and my tears flowed (the tirade was accompanied throughout by tears) her whole face worked convulsively. She was on the point of getting up and stopping me; when I finished she took no notice of my shouting: "Why are you here, why don't you go away?" but realized only that it must have been very bitter to me to say all this. Besides, she was so crushed, poor girl; she considered herself infinitely beneath me; how could she feel anger or resentment? She suddenly leapt up from her chair with an irresistible impulse and held out her hands, yearning towards me, though still timid and not daring to stir. . . . At this point there was a revulsion in my heart, too. Then she suddenly rushed to me, threw her arms round me and burst into tears. I, too, could not restrain myself, and sobbed as I never had before.

"They won't let me . . . I can't be good!" I managed to articulate; then I went to the sofa, fell on it face downwards, and sobbed on it for a quarter of an hour in genuine hysterics. She came close to me, put her arms round me and stayed motionless in that position. But the trouble was that the hysterics could not go on for ever, and (I am writing the loathsome truth) lying face downwards on the sofa with my face thrust into my nasty leather pillow, I began by degrees to be aware of a far-away, involuntary but irresistible feeling that it would be awkward now for me to raise my head and look Liza straight in the face. Why was I ashamed? I don't know, but I was ashamed. The thought, too, came into my overwrought brain that our parts now were completely changed, that she was now the heroine, while I was just such a crushed and humiliated creature as she had been before me that night—four days before. . . . And all this came into my mind during the minutes I was lying on my face on the sofa.

My God! surely I was not envious of her then.

I don't know, to this day I cannot decide, and at the time, of course, I was still less able to understand what I was feeling than now. I cannot get on without domineering and tyrannizing over some one, but . . . there is no explaining anything by reasoning and so it is useless to reason.

I conquered myself, however, and raised my head; I had to do so sooner or later . . . and I am convinced to this day that it was just because I was ashamed to look at her that another feeling was suddenly kindled and flamed up in my heart . . . a feeling of mastery and possession. My eyes gleamed with passion, and I gripped her hands tightly. How I hated her and how I was drawn to her at that minute! The one feeling intensified the other. It was almost like an act of vengeance. At first there was a look of amazement, even of terror on her face, but only for one instant. She warmly and rapturously embraced me.

X

A quarter of an hour later I was rushing up and down the room in frenzied impatience, from minute to minute I went up to the screen and peeped through the crack at Liza. She was sitting on the ground with her head leaning against the bed, and must have been crying. But she did not go away, and that irritated me. This time she understood it all. I had insulted her finally, but . . . there's no need to describe it. She realized that my outburst of passion had been simply revenge, a fresh humiliation, and that to my earlier, almost causeless hatred was added a *personal hatred*, born of envy. . . . Though I do not maintain positively that she understood all this distinctly; but she certainly did fully understand that I was a despicable man, and what was worse, incapable of loving her.

I know I shall be told that this is incredible—but it is incredible to be as spiteful and stupid as I was; it may be added that it was strange I should not love her, or at any rate, appreciate her love. Why is it strange? In the first place, by then I was incapable of love, for I repeat, with me loving meant tyrannizing and showing my moral superiority. I have never in my life been able to imagine any other sort of love, and have nowadays come to the point of sometimes thinking that love really consists in the right—freely given by the beloved object—to tyrannize over her.

Even in my underground dreams I did not imagine love except as a struggle. I began it always with hatred and ended it with moral subjugation, and afterwards I never knew what to do with the subjugated object. And what is there to wonder at in that, since I had succeeded in so corrupting myself, since I was so out of touch with "real life," as to have actually thought of reproaching her, and putting her to shame for having come to me to hear "fine sentiments"; and did not even guess that she had come not to hear fine sentiments, but to love me, because to a woman all reformation, all salvation from any sort of ruin, and all moral renewal is included in love and can only show itself in that form.

I did not hate her so much, however, when I was running about the room and peeping through the crack in the screen. I was only insufferably oppressed by her being here. I wanted her to disappear. I wanted "peace," to be left alone in my underground world. Real life oppressed me with its novelty so much that I could hardly breathe.

But several minutes passed and she still remained, without stirring, as though she were unconscious. I had the shamelessness to tap softly at the screen as though to remind her. . . . She started, sprang up, and flew to seek her kerchief, her hat, her coat, as though making her escape from me. . . . Two minutes later she came from behind the screen and looked with heavy eyes at me. I gave a spiteful grin, which was forced, however, to *keep up appearances*, and I turned away from her eyes.

"Good-bye," she said, going towards the door.

I ran up to her, seized her hand, opened it, thrust something in it and closed it again. Then I turned at once and dashed away in haste to the other corner of the room to avoid seeing her, anyway. . . .

I did not mean a moment since to tell a lie—to write that I did this accidentally, not knowing what I was doing through foolishness, through losing my head. But I don't want to lie, and so I will say straight out that I opened her hand and put the money in it . . . from spite. It came into my head to do this while I was running up and down the room and she was sitting behind the screen. But this I can say for certain: though I did that cruel thing purposely, it was not an impulse from the heart, but came from my evil brain. This cruelty was so affected, so purposely made up, so completely a product of the brain, of books, that I could not even keep it up a minute—first I dashed away to avoid seeing her, and then in shame and despair rushed after Liza. I opened the door in the passage and began listening.

"Liza! Liza!" I cried on the stairs, but in a low voice, not boldly.

There was no answer, but I fancied I heard her footsteps, lower down on the stairs.

"Liza!" I cried, more loudly.

No answer. But at that minute I heard the stiff outer glass door open heavily with a creak and slam violently, the sound echoed up the stairs.

She had gone. I went back to my room in hesitation. I felt horribly oppressed.

I stood still at the table, beside the chair on which she had sat and looked aimlessly before me. A minute passed, suddenly I started; straight before me on the table I saw. . . . In short, I saw a crumpled blue five-rouble note, the one I had thrust into her hand a minute before. It was the same note; it could be no other, there was no other in the flat. So she had managed to fling it from her hand on the table at the moment when I had dashed into the further corner.

Well! I might have expected that she would do that. Might I have expected it? No, I was such an egoist, I was so lacking in respect for my fellow-creatures that I could not even imagine she would do so. I could not endure it. A minute later I flew like a madman to dress, flinging on what I could at random and ran headlong after her. She could not have got two hundred paces away when I ran out into the street.

It was a still night and the snow was coming down in masses and falling almost perpendicularly, covering the pavement and the empty street as though with a pillow. There was no one in the street, no sound was to be heard. The street lamps gave a disconsolate and useless glimmer. I ran two hundred paces to the cross-roads and stopped short.

Where had she gone? And why was I running after her?

Why? To fall down before her, to sob with remorse, to kiss her feet, to entreat her forgiveness! I longed for that, my whole breast was being rent to pieces, and never, never shall I recall that minute with indifference. But—what for? I thought. Should I not begin to hate her, perhaps, even to-morrow, just because I had kissed her feet to-day? Should I give her happiness? Had I not recognized that day, for the hundredth time, what I was worth? Should I not torture her?

I stood in the snow, gazing into the troubled darkness and pondered this.

"And will it not be better?" I mused fantastically, afterwards at home, stifling the living pang of my heart with fantastic dreams. "Will it not be better that she should keep the resentment of the insult for ever? Resentment—why, it is purification; it is a most stinging and painful consciousness! To-morrow I should have defiled her soul and have exhausted her heart, while now the feeling of insult will never die in her heart, and however loathsome the filth awaiting her—the feeling of insult will elevate and purify her . . .

by hatred . . . h'm! . . . perhaps, too, by forgiveness. . . . Will all that make things easier for her though? . . ."

And, indeed, I will ask on my own account here, an idle question: which is better—cheap happiness or exalted sufferings? Well, which is better?

So I dreamed as I sat at home that evening, almost dead with the pain in my soul. Never had I endured such suffering and remorse, yet could there have been the faintest doubt when I ran out from my lodging that I should turn back half-way? I never met Liza again and I have heard nothing of her. I will add, too, that I remained for a long time afterwards pleased with the phrase about the benefit from resentment and hatred in spite of the fact that I almost fell ill from misery.

Even now, so many years later, all this is somehow a very evil memory. I have many evil memories now, but . . . hadn't I better end my "Notes" here? I believe I made a mistake in beginning to write them, anyway I have felt ashamed all the time I've been writing this story; so it's hardly literature so much as a corrective punishment. Why, to tell long stories, showing how I have spoiled my life through morally rotting in my corner, through lack of fitting environment, through divorce from real life, and rankling spite in my underground world, would certainly not be interesting; a novel needs a hero, and all the traits for an anti-hero *expressly* gathered together here, and what matters most, it all produces an unpleasant impression, for we are all divorced from life, we are all cripples, every one of us, more or less. We are so divorced from it that we feel at once a sort of loathing for real life, and so cannot bear to be reminded of it. Why, we have come almost to looking upon real life as an effort, almost as hard labour, and we are all privately agreed that it is better in books. And why do we fuss and fume sometimes? Why are we perverse and ask for something else? We don't know what ourselves. It would be the worse for us if our petulant prayers were answered. Come, try, give any one of us, for instance, a little more independence, untie our hands, widen the spheres of our activity, relax the control and we . . . yes, I assure you . . . we should be begging to be under control again at once. I know that you will very likely be angry with me for that, and will begin shouting and stamping. Speak for yourself, you will say, and for your miseries in your underground holes, and don't dare to say "all of us"—excuse me, gentlemen, I am not justifying myself with that "all of us." As for what concerns me in particular I have only in my life carried to an extreme what you have not dared to carry half-way, and what's more, you have taken your cowardice for good sense, and have found comfort in deceiving yourselves. So that perhaps, after all, there is more life in me than in you. Look into it more carefully! Why, we don't even know what living means now, what it is, and what it is called? Leave us alone without books and we shall be lost and in confusion at once. We shall not know what to join on to, what to cling to, what to love and what to hate, what to respect and what to despise. We are oppressed at being men— men with a real individual flesh and blood, we are ashamed of it, we think it a disgrace and try to contrive to be some sort of impossible generalized man. We are stillborn, and for generations past have been begotten, not by living fathers, and that suits us better and better. We are developing a taste for it. Soon we shall contrive to be born somehow from an idea. But enough; I don't want to write more from "Underground."

(*The notes of this paradoxalist do not end here, however. He could not refrain from going on with them, but it seems to us that we may stop here.*)

LEO TOLSTOY
(1828–1910)
The Death of Iván Ilyich[*]

I

During an interval in the Melvínski trial in the large building of the Law Courts the members and public prosecutor met in Iván Egórovich Shébek's private room, where the conversation turned on the celebrated Krasóvski case. Fëdor Vasílievich warmly maintained that it was not subject to their jurisdiction, Iván Egórovich maintained the contrary, while Peter Ivánovich, not having entered into the discussion at the start, took no part in it but looked through the *Gazette* which had just been handed in.

"Gentlemen," he said, "Iván Ilyich has died!"

"You don't say!"

"Here, read it yourself," replied Peter Ivánovich, handing Fëdor Vasílievich the paper still damp from the press. Surrounded by a black border were the words: "Praskóvya Fëdorovna Goloviná, with profound sorrow, informs relatives and friends of the demise of her beloved husband Iván Ilyich Golovín, Member of the Court of Justice, which occurred on February the 4th of this year 1882. The funeral will take place on Friday at one o'clock in the afternoon."

[*] 1886. Translated by Louise and Aylmer Maude.

Iván Ilyich had been a colleague of the gentlemen present and was liked by them all. He had been ill for some weeks with an illness said to be incurable. His post had been kept open for him, but there had been conjectures that in case of his death Alexéev might receive his appointment, and that either Vínnikov or Shtábel would succeed Alexéev. So on receiving the news of Iván Ilyich's death the first thought of each of the gentlemen in that private room was of the changes and promotions it might occasion among themselves or their acquaintances.

"I shall be sure to get Shtábel's place or Vínnikov's," thought Fëdor Vasílievich. "I was promised that long ago, and the promotion means an extra eight hundred rubles a year for me besides the allowance."

"Now I must apply for my brother-in-law's transfer from Kalúga," thought Peter Ivánovich. "My wife will be very glad, and then she won't be able to say that I never do anything for her relations."

"I thought he would never leave his bed again," said Peter Ivánovich aloud. "It's very sad."

"But what really was the matter with him?"

"The doctors couldn't say—at least they could, but each of them said something different. When last I saw him I thought he was getting better."

"And I haven't been to see him since the holidays. I always meant to go."

"Had he any property?"

"I think his wife had a little—but something quite trifling."

"We shall have to go to see her, but they live so terribly far away."

"Far away from you, you mean. Everything's far away from your place."

"You see, he never can forgive my living on the other side of the river," said Peter Ivánovich, smiling at Shébek. Then, still talking of the distances between different parts of the city, they returned to the Court.

Besides considerations as to the possible transfers and promotions likely to result from Iván Ilyich's death, the mere fact of the death of a near acquaintance aroused, as usual, in all who heard of it the complacent feeling that, "it is he who is dead and not I."

Each one thought or felt, "Well, he's dead but I'm alive!" But the more intimate of Iván Ilyich's acquaintances, his so-called friends, could not help thinking also that they would now have to fulfil the very tiresome demands of propriety by attending the funeral service and paying a visit of condolence to the widow.

Fëdor Vasílievich and Peter Ivánovich had been his nearest acquaintances. Peter Ivánovich had studied law with Iván Ilyich and had considered himself to be under obligations to him.

Having told his wife at dinner-time of Iván Ilyich's death, and of his conjecture that it might be possible to get her brother transferred to their circuit, Peter Ivánovich sacrificed his usual nap, put on his evening clothes, and drove to Iván Ilyich's house.

At the entrance stood a carriage and two cabs. Leaning against the wall in the hall downstairs near the cloak-stand was a coffin-lid covered with cloth of gold, ornamented with gold cord and tassels, that had been polished up with metal powder. Two ladies in black were taking off their fur cloaks. Peter Ivánovich recognized one of them as Iván Ilyich's sister, but the other was a stranger to him. His colleague Schwartz was just coming downstairs, but on seeing Peter Ivánovich enter he stopped and winked at him, as if to say: "Iván Ilyich has made a mess of things—not like you and me."

Schwartz's face with his Piccadilly whiskers, and his slim figure in evening dress, had as usual an air of elegant solemnity which contrasted with the playfulness of his character and had a special piquancy here, or so it seemed to Peter Ivánovich.

Peter Ivánovich allowed the ladies to precede him and slowly followed them upstairs. Schwartz did not come down but remained where he was, and Peter Ivánovich understood that he wanted to arrange where they should play bridge that evening. The ladies went upstairs to the widow's room, and Schwartz with seriously compressed lips but a playful look in his eyes, indicated by a twist of his eyebrows the room to the right where the body lay.

Peter Ivánovich, like everyone else on such occasions, entered feeling uncertain what he would have to do. All he knew was that at such times it is always safe to cross oneself. But he was not quite sure whether one should make obeisances while doing so. He therefore adopted a middle course. On entering the room he began crossing himself and made a slight movement resembling a bow. At the same time, as far as the motion of his head and arm allowed, he surveyed the room. Two young men—apparently nephews, one of whom was a high-school pupil—were leaving the room, crossing themselves as they did so. An old woman was standing motionless, and a lady with strangely arched eyebrows was saying something to her in a whisper. A vigorous, resolute Church Reader, in a frock-coat, was reading something in a loud voice with an expression that precluded any contradiction. The butler's assistant, Gerásim, stepping lightly in front of Peter Ivánovich, was strewing something on the floor. Noticing this, Peter Ivánovich was immediately aware of a faint odour of a decomposing body.

The last time he had called on Iván Ilyich, Peter Ivánovich had seen Gerásim in the study. Iván Ilyich had been particularly fond of him and he was performing the duty of a sick nurse.

Peter Ivánovich continued to make the sign of the cross slightly inclining his head in an intermediate direction between the coffin, the Reader, and the icons on the table in a corner of the room. Afterwards, when it seemed to him that this movement of his arm in crossing himself had gone on too long, he stopped and began to look at the corpse.

The dead man lay, as dead men always lie, in a specially heavy way, his rigid limbs sunk in the soft cushions of the coffin, with the head forever bowed on the pillow. His yellow waxen brow with bald patches over his sunken temples was thrust up in the way peculiar to the dead, the protruding nose seeming to press on the upper lip. He was much changed and had grown even thinner since Peter Ivánovich had last seen him, but, as is always the case with the dead, his face was handsomer and above all more dignified than when he was alive. The expression on the face said that what was necessary had been accomplished, and accomplished rightly. Besides this there was in that expression a reproach and a warning to the living. This warning seemed to Peter Ivánovich out of place, or at least not applicable to him. He felt a certain discomfort and so he hurriedly crossed himself once more and turned and went out of the door—too hurriedly and too regardless of propriety, as he himself was aware.

Schwartz was waiting for him in the adjoining room with legs spread wide apart and both hands toying with his top-hat behind his back. The mere sight of that playful, well-groomed, and elegant figure refreshed Peter Ivánovich. He felt that Schwartz was above all these happenings and would not surrender to any depressing influences. His very look said that this incident of a church service for Iván Ilyich could not be a sufficient reason for infringing the order of the session—in other words, that it would certainly not prevent his unwrapping a new pack of cards and shuffling them that evening while a footman placed four fresh candles on the table: in fact, that there was no reason for supposing that this incident would hinder their spending the evening agreeably. Indeed he said this in a whisper as Peter Ivánovich passed him, proposing that they should meet for a game at Fëdor Vasílievich';. But apparently Peter Ivánovich was not destined to play bridge that evening. Praskóvya Fëdorovna (a short, fat woman who despite all efforts to the contrary had continued to broaden steadily from her shoulders downwards and who had the same extraordinary arched eyebrows as the lady who had been standing by the coffin), dressed all in black, her head covered with lace, came out of her own room with some other ladies, conducted them to the room where the dead body lay, and said: "The service will begin immediately. Please go in."

Schwartz, making an indefinite bow, stood still, evidently neither accepting nor declining this invitation. Praskóvya Fëdorovna recognizing Peter Ivánovich, sighed, went close up to him, took his hand, and said: "I know you were a true friend to Iván Ilyich . . ." and looked at him awaiting some suitable response. And Peter Ivánovich knew that, just as it had been the right thing to cross himself in that room, so what he had to do here was to press her hand, sigh, and say, "Believe me . . ." So he did all this and as he did it felt that the desired result had been achieved: that both he and she were touched.

"Come with me. I want to speak to you before it begins," said the widow. "Give me your arm."

Peter Ivánovich gave her his arm and they went to the inner rooms, passing Schwartz who winked at Peter Ivánovich compassionately.

"That does for our bridge! Don't object if we find another player. Perhaps you can cut in when you do escape," said his playful look.

Peter Ivánovich sighed still more deeply and despondently, and Praskóvya Fëdorovna pressed his arm gratefully. When they reached the drawing-room, upholstered in pink cretonne and lighted by a dim lamp, they sat down at the table—she on a sofa and Peter Ivánovich on a low hassock, the springs of which yielded spasmodically under his weight. Praskóvya Fëdorovna had been on the point of warning him to take another seat, but felt that such a warning was out of keeping with her present condition and so changed her mind. As he sat down on the hassock Peter Ivánovich recalled how Iván Ilyich had arranged this room and had consulted him regarding this pink cretonne with green leaves. The whole room was full of furniture and knick-knacks, and on her way to the sofa the lace of the widow's black shawl caught on the carved edge of the table. Peter Ivánovich rose to detach it, and the springs of the hassock, relieved of his weight, rose also and gave him a push. The widow began detaching her shawl herself, and Peter Ivánovich again sat down, suppressing the rebellious springs of the hassock under him. But the widow had not quite freed herself and Peter Ivánovich got up again, and again the hassock rebelled and even creaked. When this was all over she took out a clean cambric handkerchief and began to weep. The episode with the shawl and the struggle with the hassock had cooled Peter Ivánovich's emotions and he sat there with a sullen look on his face. This awkward situation was interrupted by Sokolóv, Iván Ilyich's butler, who came to report that the plot in the cemetery that Praskóvya Fëdorovna had chosen would cost two hundred rubles. She stopped weeping and, looking at Peter Ivánovich with the air of a victim, remarked in French that it was very hard for her. Peter Ivánovich made a silent gesture signifying his full conviction that it must indeed be so.

"Please smoke," she said in a magnanimous yet crushed voice, and turned to discuss with Sokolóv the price of the plot for the grave.

Peter Ivánovich while lighting his cigarette heard her inquiring very circumstantially into the prices of different plots in the cemetery and finally decide which she would take. When that was done she gave instructions about engaging the choir. Sokolóv then left the room.

"I look after everything myself," she told Peter Ivánovich, shifting the albums that lay on the table; and noticing that the table was endangered by his cigarette-ash, she immediately passed him an ash-tray, saying as she did so: "I consider it an affectation to say that my grief prevents my attending to practical affairs. On the contrary, if anything can—I won't say console me, but—distract me, it is seeing to everything concerning him." She again took out her handkerchief as if preparing to cry, but suddenly, as if mastering her feeling, she shook herself and began to speak calmly. "But there is something I want to talk to you about."

Peter Ivánovich bowed, keeping control of the springs of the hassock, which immediately began quivering under him.

"He suffered terribly the last few days."

"Did he?" said Peter Ivánovich.

"Oh, terribly! He screamed unceasingly, not for minutes but for hours. For the last three days he screamed incessantly. It was unendurable. I cannot understand how I bore it; you could hear him three rooms off. Oh, what I have suffered!"

"Is it possible that he was conscious all that time?" asked Peter Ivánovich.

"Yes," she whispered. "To the last moment. He took leave of us a quarter of an hour before he died, and asked us to take Volódya away."

The thought of the sufferings of this man he had known so intimately, first as a merry little boy, then as a school-mate, and later as a grown-up colleague, suddenly struck Peter Ivánovich with horror, despite an unpleasant consciousness of his own and this woman's dissimulation. He again saw that brow, and that nose pressing down on the lip, and felt afraid for himself.

"Three days of frightful suffering and then death! Why, that might suddenly, at any time, happen to me," he thought, and for a moment felt terrified. But—he did not himself know how—the customary reflection at once occurred to him that this had happened to Iván Ilyich and not to him, and that it should not and could not happen to him, and that to think that it could would be yielding to depression which he ought not to do, as Schwartz's expression plainly showed. After which reflection Peter Ivánovich felt reassured, and began to ask with interest about the details of Iván Ilyich's death, as though death was an accident natural to Iván Ilyich but certainly not to himself.

After many details of the really dreadful physical sufferings Iván Ilyich had endured (which details he learnt only from the effect those sufferings had produced on Praskóvya Fëdorovna's nerves) the widow apparently found it necessary to get to business.

"Oh, Peter Ivánovich, how hard it is! How terribly, terribly hard!" and she again began to weep.

Peter Ivánovich sighed and waited for her to finish blowing her nose. When she had done so he said, "Believe me . . ." and she again began talking and brought out what was evidently her chief concern with him—namely, to question him as to how she could obtain a grant of money from the government on the occasion of her husband's death. She made it appear that she was asking Peter Ivánovich's advice about her pension, but he soon saw that she already knew about that to the minutest detail, more even than he did himself. She knew how much could be got out of the government in consequence of her husband's death, but wanted to find out whether she could not possibly extract something more. Peter Ivánovich tried to think of some means of doing so, but after reflecting for a while and, out of propriety, condemning the government for its niggardliness, he said he thought that nothing more could be got. Then she sighed and evidently began to devise means of getting rid of her visitor. Noticing this, he put out his cigarette, rose, pressed her hand, and went out into the anteroom.

In the dining-room where the clock stood that Iván Ilyich had liked so much and had bought at an antique shop, Peter Ivánovich met a priest and a few acquaintances who had come to attend the service, and he recognized Iván Ilyich's daughter, a handsome young woman. She was in black and her slim figure appeared slimmer than ever. She had a gloomy, determined, almost angry expression, and bowed to Peter Ivánovich as though he were in some way to blame. Behind her, with the same offended look, stood a wealthy young man, an examining magistrate, whom Peter Ivánovich also knew and who was her fiancé, as he had heard. He bowed mournfully to them and was about to pass into the death-chamber, when from under the stairs appeared the figure of Iván Ilyich's schoolboy son, who was extremely like his father. He seemed a little Iván Ilyich, such as Peter Ivánovich remembered when they studied law together. His tear-stained eyes had in them the look that is seen in the eyes of boys of thirteen or fourteen who are not pure-minded.

When he saw Peter Ivánovich he scowled morosely and shame-facedly. Peter Ivánovich nodded to him and entered the death-chamber. The service began: candles, groans, incense, tears, and sobs. Peter Ivánovich stood looking gloomily down at his feet. He did not look once at the dead man, did not yield to any depressing influence, and was one of the first to leave the room. There was no one in the anteroom, but Gerásim darted out of the dead man's room, rummaged with his strong hands among the fur coats to find Peter Ivánovich's and helped him on with it.

"Well, friend Gerásim," said Peter Ivánovich, so as to say something. "It's a sad affair, isn't it?"

"It's God's will. We shall all come to it some day," said Gerásim, displaying his teeth—the even, white teeth of a healthy peasant—and, like a man in the thick of urgent work, he briskly opened the front door, called the coachman, helped Peter Ivánovich into the sledge, and sprang back to the porch as if in readiness for what he had to do next.

Peter Ivánovich found the fresh air particularly pleasant after the smell of incense, the dead body, and carbolic acid.

"Where to, sir?" asked the coachman.

"It's not too late even now. . . . I'll call round on Fëdor Vasílievich."

He accordingly drove there and found them just finishing the first rubber, so that it was quite convenient for him to cut in.

II

Iván Ilyich's life had been most simple and most ordinary and therefore most terrible.

He had been a member of the Court of Justice, and died at the age of forty-five. His father had been an official who after serving in various ministries and departments in Petersburg had made the sort of career which brings men to positions from which by reason of their long service they cannot be dismissed, though they are obviously unfit to hold any responsible position, and for whom therefore posts are specially created, which though fictitious, carry salaries of from six to ten thousand rubles that are not fictitious, and in receipt of which they live on to a great age.

Such was the Privy Councillor and superfluous member of various superfluous institutions, Ilya Epímovich Golovín.

He had three sons, of whom Iván Ilyich was the second. The eldest son was following in his father's footsteps only in another department, and was already approaching that stage in the service at which a similar sinecure would be reached. The third son was a failure. He had ruined his prospects in a number of positions and was now serving in the railway department. His father and brothers, and still more their wives, not merely disliked meeting him, but avoided remembering his existence unless compelled to do so. His sister had married Baron Greff, a Petersburg official of her father's type. Iván Ilyich was *le phénix de la famille*[1] as people said. He was neither as cold and formal as his elder brother nor as wild as the younger, but was a happy mean between them—an intelligent, polished, lively and agreeable man. He had studied with his younger brother at the School of Law, but the latter had failed to complete the course and was expelled when he was in the fifth class. Iván Ilyich finished the course well. Even when he was at the School of Law he was just what he remained for the rest of his life: a capable, cheerful, good-natured, and sociable man, though strict in the fulfilment of what he considered to be his duty: and he considered his duty to be what was so considered by those in authority. Neither as a boy nor as a man was he a toady, but from early youth was by nature attracted to people of high station as a fly is drawn to the light, assimilating their ways and views of life and establishing friendly relations with them. All the enthusiasms of childhood and youth passed without leaving much trace on him; he succumbed to sensuality, to vanity, and latterly among the highest classes to liberalism, but always within limits which his instinct unfailingly indicated to him as correct.

At school he had done things which had formerly seemed to him very horrid and made him feel disgusted with himself when he did them; but when later on he saw that such actions were done by people of good position and that they did not regard them as wrong, he was able not exactly to regard them as right, but to forget about them entirely or not be at all troubled at remembering them.

Having graduated from the School of Law and qualified for the tenth rank of the civil service, and having received money from his father for his equipment, Iván Ilyich ordered himself clothes at Scharmer's, the fashionable tailor, hung a medallion inscribed *respice finem*[2] on his watch-chain, took leave of his professor and the prince who was patron of the school, had a farewell dinner with his comrades at Donon's first-class restaurant, and with his new and fashionable portmanteau, linen, clothes, shaving and other toilet appliances, and a travelling rug, all purchased at the best shops, he set off for one of the provinces where, through his father's influence, he had been attached to the governor as an official for special service.

In the province Iván Ilyich soon arranged as easy and agreeable a position for himself as he had had at the School of Law. He performed his official tasks, made his career, and at the same time amused himself pleasantly and decorously. Occasionally he paid

1. "the phoenix of the family." The word "phoenix" is used here to mean "rare bird," "prodigy."
2. "Regard the end" (a Latin motto).

official visits to country districts, where he behaved with dignity both to his superiors and inferiors, and performed the duties entrusted to him, which related chiefly to the sectarians,[3] with an exactness and incorruptible honesty of which he could not but feel proud.

In official matters, despite his youth and taste for frivolous gaiety, he was exceedingly reserved, punctilious, and even severe; but in society he was often amusing and witty, and always good-natured, correct in his manner, and *bon enfant*, as the governor and his wife —with whom he was like one of the family—used to say of him.

In the province he had an affair with a lady who made advances to the elegant young lawyer, and there was also a milliner; and there were carousals with aides-de-camp who visited the district, and after-supper visits to a certain outlying street of doubtful reputation; and there was too some obsequiousness to his chief and even to his chief's wife, but all this was done with such a tone of good breeding that no hard names could be applied to it. It all came under the heading of the French saying: "*Il faut que jeunesse se passe.*"[4] It was all done with clean hands, in clean linen, with French phrases, and above all among people of the best society and consequently with the approval of people of rank.

So Iván Ilyich served for five years and then came a change in his official life. The new and reformed judicial institutions were introduced, and new men were needed. Iván Ilyich became such a new man. He was offered the post of Examining Magistrate, and he accepted it though the post was in another province and obliged him to give up the connexions he had formed and to make new ones. His friends met to give him a send-off; they had a group-photograph taken and presented him with a silver cigarette-case, and he set off to his new post.

As examining magistrate Iván Ilyich was just as *comme il faut* and decorous a man, inspiring general respect and capable of separating his official duties from his private life, as he had been when acting as an official on special service. His duties now as examining magistrate were far more interesting and attractive than before. In his former position it had been pleasant to wear an undress uniform made by Scharmer, and to pass through the crowd of petitioners and officials who were timorously awaiting an audience with the governor, and who envied him as with free and easy gait he went straight into his chief's private room to have a cup of tea and a cigarette with him. But not many people had then been directly dependent on him—only police officials and the sectarians

3. the Old Believers, a large group of Russians (about twenty-five million in 1900), members of a sect which originated in a break with the Orthodox Church in the seventeenth century; they were subject to many legal restrictions.
4. Youth must have its fling. [Translator's note.]

when he went on special missions—and he liked to treat them politely, almost as comrades, as if he were letting them feel that he who had the power to crush them was treating them in this simple, friendly way. There were then but few such people. But now, as an examining magistrate, Iván Ilyich felt that everyone without exception, even the most important and self-satisfied, was in his power, and that he need only write a few words on a sheet of paper with a certain heading, and this or that important, self-satisfied person would be brought before him in the role of an accused person or a witness, and if he did not choose to allow him to sit down, would have to stand before him and answer his questions. Iván Ilyich never abused his power; he tried on the contrary to soften its expression, but the consciousness of it and of the possibility of softening its effect, supplied the chief interest and attraction of his office. In his work itself, especially in his examinations, he very soon acquired a method of eliminating all considerations irrelevant to the legal aspect of the case, and reducing even the most complicated case to a form in which it would be presented on paper only in its externals, completely excluding his personal opinion of the matter, while above all observing every prescribed formality. The work was new and Iván Ilyich was one of the first men to apply the new Code of 1864.[5]

On taking up the post of examining magistrate in a new town, he made new acquaintances and connexions, placed himself on a new footing, and assumed a somewhat different tone. He took up an attitude of rather dignified aloofness towards the provincial authorities, but picked out the best circle of legal gentlemen and wealthy gentry living in the town and assumed a tone of slight dissatisfaction with the government, of moderate liberalism, and of enlightened citizenship. At the same time, without at all altering the elegance of his toilet, he ceased shaving his chin and allowed his beard to grow as it pleased.

Iván Ilyich settled down very pleasantly in this new town. The society there, which inclined towards opposition to the governor, was friendly, his salary was larger, and he began to play *vint* [a form of bridge], which he found added not a little to the pleasure of life, for he had a capacity for cards, played good-humouredly, and calculated rapidly and astutely, so that he usually won.

After living there for two years he met his future wife, Praskóvya Fëdorovna Míkhel, who was the most attractive, clever, and brilliant girl of the set in which he moved, and among other amusements and relaxations from his labours as examining magistrate, Iván Ilyich established light and playful relations with her.

While he had been an official on special service he had been ac-

5. The emancipation of the serfs in 1861 was followed by a thorough all- round reform of judicial proceedings. [Translator's note.]

customed to dance, but now as an examining magistrate it was exceptional for him to do so. If he danced now, he did it as if to show that though he served under the reformed order of things, and had reached the fifth official rank, yet when it came to dancing he could do it better than most people. So at the end of an evening he sometimes danced with Praskóvya Fëdorovna, and it was chiefly during these dances that he captivated her. She fell in love with him. Iván Ilyich had at first no definite intention of marrying, but when the girl fell in love with him he said to himself: "Really, why shouldn't I marry?"

Praskóvya Fëdorovna came of a good family, was not bad looking, and had some little property. Iván Ilyich might have aspired to a more brilliant match, but even this was good. He had his salary, and she, he hoped, would have an equal income. She was well connected, and was a sweet, pretty, and thoroughly correct young woman. To say that Iván Ilyich married because he fell in love with Praskóvya Fëdorovna and found that she sympathized with his views of life would be as incorrect as to say that he married because his social circle approved of the match. He was swayed by both these considerations: the marriage gave him personal satisfaction, and at the same time it was considered the right thing by the most highly placed of his associates.

So Iván Ilyich got married.

The preparations for marriage and the beginning of married life, with its conjugal caresses, the new furniture, new crockery, and new linen, were very pleasant until his wife became pregnant—so that Iván Ilyich had begun to think that marriage would not impair the easy, agreeable, gay, and always decorous character of his life, approved of by society and regarded by himself as natural, but would even improve it. But from the first months of his wife's pregnancy, something new, unpleasant, depressing, and unseemly, and from which there was no way of escape, unexpectedly showed itself.

His wife, without any reason—*de gaieté de coeur* as Iván Ilyich expressed it to himself—began to disturb the pleasure and propriety of their life. She began to be jealous without any cause, expected him to devote his whole attention to her, found fault with everything, and made coarse and ill-mannered scenes.

At first Iván Ilyich hoped to escape from the unpleasantness of this state of affairs by the same easy and decorous relation to life that had served him heretofore: he tried to ignore his wife's disagreeable moods, continued to live in his usual easy and pleasant way, invited friends to his house for a game of cards, and also tried going out to his club or spending his evenings with friends. But one day his wife began upbraiding him so vigorously, using such coarse words, and continued to abuse him every time he did not fulfil her demands, so resolutely and with such evident determination not to give way till he submitted—that is, till he stayed at home and was bored just as she was—that he became alarmed. He now realized that matrimony—at any rate with Praskóvya Fëdorovna—was not always conducive to the pleasures and amenities of life, but on the contrary often infringed both comfort and propriety, and that he must therefore entrench himself against such infringement. And Iván Ilyich began to seek for means of doing so. His official duties were the one thing that imposed upon Praskóvya Fëdorovna, and by means of his official work and the duties attached to it he began struggling with his wife to secure his own independence.

With the birth of their child, the attempts to feed it and the various failures in doing so, and with the real and imaginary ill-nesses of mother and child, in which Iván Ilyich's sympathy was demanded but about which he understood nothing, the need of securing for himself an existence outside his family life became still more imperative.

As his wife grew more irritable and exacting and Iván Ilyich transferred the centre of gravity of his life more and more to his official work, so did he grow to like his work better and became more ambitious than before.

Very soon, within a year of his wedding, Iván Ilyich had realized that marriage, though it may add some comforts to life, is in fact a very intricate and difficult affair towards which in order to perform one's duty, that is, to lead a decorous life approved of by society, one must adopt a definite attitude just as towards one's official duties.

And Iván Ilyich evolved such an attitude towards married life. He only required of it those conveniences—dinner at home, house-wife, and bed—which it could give him, and above all that propriety of external forms required by public opinion. For the rest he looked for light-hearted pleasure and propriety, and was very thankful when he found them, but if he met with antagonism and querulousness he at once retired into his separate fenced-off world of official duties, where he found satisfaction.

Iván Ilyich was esteemed a good official, and after three years was made Assistant Public Prosecutor. His new duties, their importance, the possibility of indicting and imprisoning anyone he chose, the publicity his speeches received, and the success he had in all these things, made his work still more attractive.

More children came. His wife became more and more querulous and ill-tempered, but the attitude Iván Ilyich had adopted towards his home life rendered him almost impervious to her grumbling.

After seven years' service in that town he was transferred to another province as Public Prosecutor. They moved, but were short of money and his wife did not like the place they moved to. Though the salary was higher the cost of living was greater, besides which two of their children died and family life became still more unpleasant for him.

Praskóvya Fëdorovna blamed her husband for every inconvenience they encountered in their new home. Most of the conversations between husband and wife, especially as to the children's education, led to topics which recalled former disputes, and those disputes were apt to flare up again at any moment. There remained only those rare periods of amorousness which still came to them at times but did not last long. These were islets at which they anchored for a while and then again set out upon that ocean of veiled hostility which showed itself in their aloofness from one another. This aloofness might have grieved Iván Ilyich had he considered that it ought not to exist, but he now regarded the position as normal, and even made it the goal at which he aimed in family life. His aim was to free himself more and more from those unpleasantnesses and to give them a semblance of harmlessness and propriety. He attained this by spending less and less time with his family, and when obliged to be at home he tried to safeguard his position by the presence of outsiders. The chief thing however was that he had his official duties. The whole interest of his life now centered in the official world and that interest absorbed him. The consciousness of his power, being able to ruin anybody he wished to ruin, the importance, even the external dignity of his entry into court, or meetings with his subordinates, his success with superiors and inferiors, and above all his masterly handling of cases, of which he was conscious—all this gave him pleasure and filled his life, together with chats with his colleagues, dinners, and bridge. So that on the whole Iván Ilyich's life continued to flow as he considered it should do—pleasantly and properly.

So things continued for another seven years. His eldest daughter was already sixteen, another child had died, and only one son was left, a schoolboy and a subject of dissensions. Iván Ilyich wanted to put him in the School of Law, but to spite him Praskóvya Fëdorovna entered him at the High School. The daughter had been educated at home and had turned out well: the boy did not learn badly either.

III

So Iván Ilyich lived for seventeen years after his marriage. He was already a Public Prosecutor of long standing, and had declined several proposed transfers while awaiting a more desirable post, when an unanticipated and unpleasant occurrence quite upset the peaceful course of his life. He was expecting to be offered the post of presiding judge in a University town, but Hoppe somehow came to the front and obtained the appointment instead. Iván Ilyich became irritable, reproached Hoppe, and quarrelled both with him and with his immediate superiors—who became colder to him and again passed him over when other appointments were made.

This was in 1880, the hardest year of Iván Ilyich's life. It was then that it became evident on the one hand that his salary was insufficient for them to live on, and on the other that he had been forgotten, and not only this, but that what was for him the greatest and most cruel injustice appeared to others a quite ordinary occurrence. Even his father did not consider it his duty to help him. Iván Ilyich felt himself abandoned by everyone, and that they regarded his position with a salary of 3,500 rubles as quite normal and even fortunate. He alone knew that with the consciousness of the injustices done him, with his wife's incessant nagging, and with the debts he had contracted by living beyond his means, his position was far from normal.

In order to save money that summer he obtained leave of absence and went with his wife to live in the country at her brother's place.

In the country, without his work, he experienced *ennui* for the first time in his life, and not only *ennui* but intolerable depression, and he decided that it was impossible to go on living like that, and that it was necessary to take energetic measures.

Having passed a sleepless night pacing up and down the veranda, he decided to go to Petersburg and bestir himself, in order to punish those who had failed to appreciate him and to get transferred to another ministry.

Next day, despite many protests from his wife and her brother, he started for Petersburg with the sole object of obtaining a post with a salary of five thousand rubles a year. He was no longer bent on any particular department, or tendency, or kind of activity. All he now wanted was an appointment to another post with a salary of five thousand rubles, either in the administration, in the banks, with the railways, in one of the Empress Márya's Institutions,[6] or even in the customs—but it had to carry with it a salary of five thousand rubles and be in a ministry other than that in which they had failed to appreciate him.

And this quest of Iván Ilyich's was crowned with remarkable and unexpected success. At Kursk an acquaintance of his, F. I. Ilyín, got into the first-class carriage, sat down beside Iván Ilyich, and told him of a telegram just received by the governor of Kursk announcing that a change was about to take place in the ministry: Peter Ivánovich was to be superseded by Iván Semënovich.

The proposed change, apart from its significance for Russia, had

6. reference to the charitable organization founded by the Empress Márya, wife of Paul I, late in the eighteenth century.

a special significance for Iván Ilyich, because by bringing forward a new man, Peter Petróvich, and consequently his friend Zachár Ivánovich, it was highly favourable for Iván Ilyich, since Zachár Ivánovich was a friend and colleague of his.

In Moscow this news was confirmed, and on reaching Petersburg Iván Ilyich found Zachár Ivánovich and received a definite promise of an appointment in his former department of Justice.

A week later he telegraphed to his wife: "Zachár in Miller's place. I shall receive appointment on presentation of report."

Thanks to this change of personnel, Iván Ilyich had unexpectedly obtained an appointment in his former ministry which placed him two stages above his former colleagues besides giving him five thousand rubles salary and three thousand five hundred rubles for expenses connected with his removal. All his ill humour towards his former enemies and the whole department vanished, and Iván Ilyich was completely happy.

He returned to the country more cheerful and contented than he had been for a long time. Praskóvya Fëdorovna also cheered up and a truce was arranged between them. Iván Ilyich told of how he had been fêted by everybody in Petersburg, how all those who had been his enemies were put to shame and now fawned on him, how envious they were of his appointment, and how much everybody in Petersburg had liked him.

Praskóvya Fëdorovna listened to all this and appeared to believe it. She did not contradict anything, but only made plans for their life in the town to which they were going. Iván Ilyich saw with delight that these plans were his plans, that he and his wife agreed, and that, after a stumble, his life was regaining its due and natural character of pleasant lightheartedness and decorum.

Iván Ilyich had come back for a short time only, for he had to take up his new duties on the 10th of September. Moreover, he needed time to settle into the new place, to move all his belongings from the province, and to buy and order many additional things: in a word, to make such arrangements as he had resolved on, which were almost exactly what Praskóvya Fëdorovna too had decided on.

Now that everything had happened so fortunately, and that he and his wife were at one in their aims and moreover saw so little of one another they got on together better than they had done since the first years of marriage. Iván Ilyich had thought of taking his family away with him at once, but the insistence of his wife's brother and her sister-in-law, who had suddenly become particularly amiable and friendly to him and his family, induced him to depart alone.

So he departed, and the cheerful state of mind induced by his success and by the harmony between his wife and himself, the one intensifying the other, did not leave him. He found a delightful house, just the thing both he and his wife had dreamt of. Spacious, lofty reception rooms in the old style, a convenient and dignified study, rooms for his wife and daughter, a study for his son—it might have been specially built for them. Iván Ilyich himself superintended the arrangements, chose the wallpapers, supplemented the furniture (preferably with antiques which he considered particularly *comme il faut*), and supervised the upholstering. Everything progressed and progressed and approached the ideal he had set himself: even when things were only half completed they exceeded his expectations. He saw what a refined and elegant character, free from vulgarity, it would all have when it was ready. On falling asleep he pictured to himself how the reception-room would look. Looking at the yet unfinished drawing-room he could see the fireplace, the screen, the what-not, the little chairs dotted here and there, the dishes and plates on the walls, and the bronzes, as they would be when everything was in place. He was pleased by the thought of how his wife and daughter, who shared his taste in this matter, would be impressed by it. They were certainly not expecting as much. He had been particularly successful in finding, and buying cheaply, antiques which gave a particularly aristocratic character to the whole place. But in his letters he intentionally understated everything in order to be able to surprise them. All this so absorbed him that his new duties—though he liked his official work—interested him less than he had expected. Sometimes he even had moments of absent-mindedness during the Court Sessions, and would consider whether he should have straight or curved cornices for his curtains. He was so interested in it all that he often did things himself, rearranging the furniture, or rehanging the curtains. Once when mounting a step-ladder to show the upholsterer, who did not understand, how he wanted the hangings draped, he made a false step and slipped, but being a strong and agile man he clung on and only knocked his side against the knob of the window frame. The bruised place was painful but the pain soon passed, and he felt particularly bright and well just then. He wrote: "I feel fifteen years younger." He thought he would have everything ready by September, but it dragged on till mid-October. But the result was charming not only in his eyes but to everyone who saw it.

In reality it was just what is usually seen in the houses of people of moderate means who want to appear rich, and therefore succeed only in resembling others like themselves: there were damasks, dark wood, plants, rugs, and dull and polished bronzes—all the things people of a certain class have in order to resemble other people of that class. His house was so like the others that it would never have been noticed, but to him it all seemed to be quite exceptional. He was very happy when he met his family at the station and brought them to the newly furnished house all lit up, where a footman in a white tie opened the door into the hall decorated with plants, and when they went on into the drawing room and the study uttering exclamations of delight. He conducted them everywhere, drank in their praises eagerly, and beamed with pleasure. At tea that evening, when Praskóvya Fëdorovna among other things asked him about his fall, he laughed, and showed them how he had gone flying and had frightened the upholsterer.

"It's a good thing I'm a bit of an athlete. Another man might have been killed, but I merely knocked myself, just here; it hurts when it's touched, but it's passing off already—it's only a bruise."

So they began living in their new home—in which, as always happens, when they got thoroughly settled in they found they were just one room short—and with the increased income, which as always was just a little (some five hundred rubles) too little, but it was all very nice.

Things went particularly well at first, before everything was finally arranged and while something had still to be done: this thing bought, that thing ordered, another thing moved, and something else adjusted. Though there were some disputes between husband and wife, they were both so well satisfied and had so much to do that it all passed off without any serious quarrels. When nothing was left to arrange it became rather dull and something seemed to be lacking, but they were then making acquaintances, forming habits, and life was growing fuller.

Iván Ilyich spent his mornings at the law court and came home to dinner, and at first he was generally in a good humour, though he occasionally became irritable just on account of his house. (Every spot on the tablecloth or the upholstery, and every broken window-blind string, irritated him. He had devoted so much trouble to arranging it all that every disturbance of it distressed him.) But on the whole his life ran its course as he believed life should do: easily, pleasantly, and decorously.

He got up at nine, drank his coffee, read the paper, and then put on his undress uniform and went to the law courts. There the harness in which he worked had already been stretched to fit him and he donned it without a hitch: petitioners, inquiries at the chancery, the chancery itself, and the sittings public and administrative. In all this the thing was to exclude everything fresh and vital, which always disturbs the regular course of official business, and to admit only official relations with people, and then only on official grounds. A man would come, for instance, wanting some information. Iván Ilyich, as one in whose sphere the matter did not lie, would have nothing to do with him: but if the man had some business with him in his official capacity, something that could be expressed on officially stamped paper, he would do everything, positively everything he could within the limits of such relations, and in doing so would maintain the semblance of friendly human relations, that is, would observe the courtesies of life. As soon as the official relations ended, so did everything else. Iván Ilyich possessed this capacity to separate his real life from the official side of affairs and not mix the two, in the highest degree, and by long practice and natural aptitude had brought it to such a pitch that sometimes, in the manner of a virtuoso, he would even allow himself to let the human and official relations mingle. He let himself do this just because he felt that he could at any time he chose resume the strictly official attitude again and drop the human relation. And he did it all easily, pleasantly, correctly, and even artistically. In the intervals between the sessions he smoked, drank tea, chatted a little about politics, a little about general topics, a little about cards, but most of all about official appointments. Tired, but with the feelings of a virtuoso—one of the first violins who has played his part in an orchestra with precision—he would return home to find that his wife and daughter had been out paying calls, or had a visitor, and that his son had been to school, had done his homework with his tutor, and was duly learning what is taught at High Schools. Everything was as it should be. After dinner, if they had no visitors, Iván Ilyich sometimes read a book that was being much discussed at the time, and in the evening settled down to work, that is, read official papers, compared the depositions of witnesses, and noted paragraphs of the Code applying to them. This was neither dull nor amusing. It was dull when he might have been playing bridge, but if no bridge was available it was at any rate better than doing nothing or sitting with his wife. Iván Ilyich's chief pleasure was giving little dinners to which he invited men and women of good social position, and just as his drawing-room resembled all other drawing-rooms so did his enjoyable little parties resemble all other such parties.

Once they even gave a dance. Iván Ilyich enjoyed it and everything went off well, except that it led to a violent quarrel with his wife about the cakes and sweets. Praskóvya Fëdorovna had made her own plans, but Iván Ilyich insisted on getting everything from an expensive confectioner and ordered too many cakes, and the quarrel occurred because some of those cakes were left over and the confectioner's bill came to forty-five rubles. It was a great and disagreeable quarrel. Praskóvya Fëdorovna called him "a fool and an imbecile," and he clutched at his head and made angry allusions to divorce.

But the dance itself had been enjoyable. The best people were there, and Iván Ilyich had danced with Princess Trúfonova, a sister of the distinguished founder of the Society "Bear my Burden."

The pleasures connected with his work were pleasures of ambition; his social pleasures were those of vanity; but Iván Ilyich's greatest pleasure was playing bridge. He acknowledged that whatever disagreeable incident happened in his life, the pleasure that beamed like a ray of light above everything else was to sit down to bridge with good players, not noisy partners, and of course to four-handed bridge (with five players it was annoying to have to stand out, though one pretended not to mind), to play a clever and serious game (when the cards allowed it) and then to have supper and drink a glass of wine. After a game of bridge, especially if he had won a little (to win a large sum was unpleasant), Iván Ilyich went to bed in specially good humour.

So they lived. They formed a circle of acquaintances among the best people and were visited by people of importance and by young folk. In their views as to their acquaintances, husband, wife, and daughter were entirely agreed, and tacitly and unanimously kept at arm's length and shook off the various shabby friends and relations who, with much show of affection, gushed into the drawing-room with its Japanese plates on the walls. Soon these shabby friends ceased to obtrude themselves and only the best people remained in the Golovíns' set.

Young men made up to Lisa, and Petríshchev, an examining magistrate and Dmítri Ivánovich Petríshchev's son and sole heir, began to be so attentive to her that Iván Ilyich had already spoken to Praskóvya Fëdorovna about it, and considered whether they should not arrange a party for them, or get up some private theatricals.

So they lived, and all went well, without change, and life flowed pleasantly.

IV

They were all in good health. It could not be called ill health if Iván Ilyich sometimes said that he had a queer taste in his mouth and felt some discomfort in his left side.

But this discomfort increased and, though not exactly painful, grew into a sense of pressure in his side accompanied by ill humour. And his irritability became worse and worse and began to mar the agreeable, easy, and correct life that had established itself in the Golovín family. Quarrels between husband and wife became more and more frequent, and soon the ease and amenity disappeared and even the decorum was barely maintained. Scenes again became frequent, and very few of those islets remained on which husband and wife could meet without an explosion. Praskóvya Fëdorovna now had good reason to say that her husband's temper was trying. With characteristic exaggeration she said he had always had a dreadful temper, and that it had needed all her good nature to put up with it for twenty years. It was true that now the quarrels were started by him. His bursts of temper always came just before dinner, often just as he began to eat his soup. Sometimes he noticed that a plate or dish was chipped, or the food was not right, or his son put his elbow on the table, or his daughter's hair was not done as he liked it, and for all this he blamed Praskóvya Fëdorovna. At first she retorted and said disagreeable things to him, but once or twice he fell into such a rage at the beginning of dinner that she realized it was due to some physical derangement brought on by taking food, and so she restrained herself and did not answer, but only hurried to get the dinner over. She regarded this self-restraint as highly praiseworthy. Having come to the conclusion that her husband had a dreadful temper and made her life miserable, she began to feel sorry for herself, and the more she pitied herself the more she hated her husband. She began to wish he would die; yet she did not want him to die because then his salary would cease. And this irritated her against him still more. She considered herself dreadfully unhappy just because not even his death could save her, and though she concealed her exasperation, that hidden exasperation of hers increased his irritation also.

After one scene in which Iván Ilyich had been particularly unfair and after which he had said in explanation that he certainly was irritable but that it was due to his not being well, she said that if he was ill it should be attended to, and insisted on his going to see a celebrated doctor.

He went. Everything took place as he had expected and as it always does. There was the usual waiting and the important air assumed by the doctor, with which he was so familiar (resembling that which he himself assumed in court), and the sounding and listening, and the questions which called for answers that were foregone conclusions and were evidently unnecessary, and the look of importance which implied that "if only you put yourself in our hands we will arrange everything—we know indubitably how it has to be done, always in the same way for everybody alike." It was all just as it was in the law courts. The doctor put on just the same air towards him as he himself put on towards an accused person.

The doctor said that so-and-so indicated that there was so-and-so inside the patient, but if the investigation of so-and-so did not confirm this, then he must assume that and that. If he assumed that and that, then . . . and so on. To Iván Ilyich only one question was important: was his case serious or not? But the doctor ignored that inappropriate question. From his point of view it was not the one under consideration, the real question was to decide between a floating kidney, chronic catarrh, or appendicitis. It was not a question of Iván Ilyich's life or death, but one between a floating kidney and appendicitis. And that question the doctor solved brilliantly, as it seemed to Iván Ilyich, in favour of the appendix, with the reservation that should an examination of the urine give fresh indications the matter would be reconsidered. All this was just what Iván Ilyich had himself brilliantly accomplished a thousand times in dealing with men on trial. The doctor summed up just as brilliantly, looking over his spectacles triumphantly and even gaily at the accused. From the doctor's summing up Iván Ilyich concluded that things were bad, but that for the doctor, and perhaps for everybody else, it was a matter of indifference, though for him it was bad. And this conclusion struck him painfully, arousing in him a great feeling of pity for himself and of bitterness towards the doctor's indifference to a matter of such importance.

He said nothing of this, but rose, placed the doctor's fee on the table, and remarked with a sigh: "We sick people probably often put inappropriate questions. But tell me, in general, is this complaint dangerous, or not? . . ."

The doctor looked at him sternly over his spectacles with one eye, as if to say: "Prisoner, if you will not keep to the questions put to you, I shall be obliged to have you removed from the court."

"I have already told you what I consider necessary and proper. The analysis may show something more." And the doctor bowed.

Iván Ilyich went out slowly, seated himself disconsolately in his sledge, and drove home. All the way home he was going over what the doctor had said, trying to translate those complicated, obscure, scientific phrases into plain language and find in them an answer to the question: "Is my condition bad? Is it very bad? Or is there as yet nothing much wrong?" And it seemed to him that the meaning of what the doctor had said was that it was very bad. Everything in the streets seemed depressing. The cabmen, the houses, the passers-by, and the shops, were dismal. His ache, this dull gnawing ache that never ceased for a moment, seemed to have acquired a new and more serious significance from the doctor's dubious remarks. Iván Ilyich now watched it with a new and oppressive feeling.

He reached home and began to tell his wife about it. She listened, but in the middle of his account his daughter came in with her hat on, ready to go out with her mother. She sat down reluctantly to listen to this tedious story, but could not stand it long, and her mother too did not hear him to the end.

"Well, I am very glad," she said. "Mind now to take your medicine regularly. Give me the prescription and I'll send Gerásim to the chemist's." And she went to get ready to go out.

While she was in the room Iván Ilyich had hardly taken time to breathe, but he sighed deeply when she left it.

"Well," he thought, "perhaps it isn't so bad after all."

He began taking his medicine and following the doctor's directions, which had been altered after the examination of the urine. But then it happened that there was a contradiction between the indications drawn from the examination of the urine and the symptoms that showed themselves. It turned out that what was happening differed from what the doctor had told him, and that he had either forgotten, or blundered, or hidden something from him. He could not, however, be blamed for that, and Iván Ilyich still obeyed his orders implicitly and at first derived some comfort from doing so.

From the time of his visit to the doctor, Iván Ilyich's chief occupation was the exact fulfilment of the doctor's instructions regarding hygiene and the taking of medicine, and the observation of his pain and his excretions. His chief interests came to be people's ailments and people's health. When sickness, deaths, or recoveries were mentioned in his presence, especially when the illness resembled his own, he listened with agitation which he tried to hide, asked questions, and applied what he heard to his own case.

The pain did not grow less, but Iván Ilyich made efforts to force himself to think that he was better. And he could do this so long as nothing agitated him. But as soon as he had any unpleasantness with his wife, any lack of success in his official work, or held bad cards at bridge, he was at once acutely sensible of his disease. He had formerly borne such mischances, hoping soon to adjust what was wrong, to master it and attain success, or make a grand slam. But now every mischance upset him and plunged him into despair. He would say to himself. "There now, just as I was beginning to get better and the medicine had begun to take effect, comes this accursed misfortune, or unpleasantness . . ." And he was furious with the mishap, or with the people who were causing the unpleasantness and killing him, for he felt that this fury was killing him but could not restrain it. One would have thought that it should have been clear to him that this exasperation with circumstances and people aggravated his illness, and that he ought therefore to ignore unpleasant occurrences. But he drew the very opposite conclusion: he said that he needed peace, and he watched for everything that might disturb it and became irritable at the slightest infringement of it. His condition was rendered worse by the fact that he read medical books and consulted doctors. The progress of his disease was so gradual that he could deceive himself when comparing one day with another—the difference was so slight. But when he consulted the doctors it seemed to him that he was getting worse, and even very rapidly. Yet despite this he was continually consulting them.

That month he went to see another celebrity, who told him almost the same as the first had done but put his questions rather differently, and the interview with this celebrity only increased Iván Ilyich's doubts and fears. A friend of a friend of his, a very good doctor, diagnosed his illness again quite differently from the others, and though he predicted recovery, his questions and suppositions bewildered Iván Ilyich still more and increased his doubts. A homeopathist diagnosed the disease in yet another way, and prescribed medicine which Iván Ilyich took secretly for a week. But after a week, not feeling any improvement and having lost confidence both in the former doctor's treatment and in this one's, he became still more despondent. One day a lady acquaintance mentioned a cure effected by a wonder-working icon. Iván Ilyich caught himself listening attentively and beginning to believe that it had occurred. This incident alarmed him. "Has my mind really weakened to such an extent?" he asked himself. "Nonsense! It's all rubbish. I mustn't give way to nervous fears but having chosen a doctor must keep strictly to his treatment. That is what I will do. Now it's all settled. I won't think about it, but will follow the treatment seriously till summer, and then we shall see. From now there must be no more of this wavering!" This was easy to say but impossible to carry out. The pain in his side oppressed him and seemed to grow worse and more incessant, while the taste in his mouth grew stranger and stranger. It seemed to him that his breath had a disgusting smell, and he was conscious of a loss of appetite and strength. There was no deceiving himself: something terrible, new, and more important than anything before in his life, was taking place within him of which he alone was aware. Those about him did not understand or would not understand it, but thought everything in the world was going on as usual. That tormented Iván Ilyich more than anything. He saw that his household, especially his wife and daughter who were in a perfect whirl of visiting, did not understand anything of it and were annoyed that he was so depressed and so exacting, as if he were to blame for it. Though they tried to disguise it he saw that he was an obstacle in their path, and that his wife had adopted a definite line in regard to his illness and kept to it regardless of anything he said or did. Her attitude was this: "You know," she would say to her friends, "Iván Ilyich can't do as other people do, and keep to the treatment prescribed for him. One day he'll take his drops and keep strictly to his diet and go to bed in good time, but the next day unless I watch him he'll suddenly forget his medicine, eat sturgeon—which is forbidden—and sit up playing cards till one o'clock in the morning."

"Oh, come, when was that?" Iván Ilyich would ask in vexation. "Only once at Peter Ivánovich's."

"And yesterday with Shébek."

"Well, even if I hadn't stayed up, this pain would have kept me awake."

"Be that as it may you'll never get well like that, but will always make us wretched."

Praskóvya Fëdorovna's attitude to Iván Ilyich's illness, as she expressed it both to others and to him, was that it was his own fault and was another of the annoyances he caused her. Iván Ilyich felt that this opinion escaped her involuntarily—but that did not make it easier for him.

At the law courts too, Iván Ilyich noticed, or thought he noticed, a strange attitude towards himself. It sometimes seemed to him that people were watching him inquisitively as a man whose place might soon be vacant. Then again, his friends would suddenly begin to chaff him in a friendly way about his low spirits, as if the awful, horrible, and unheard-of thing that was going on within him, incessantly gnawing at him and irresistibly drawing him away, was a very agreeable subject for jests. Schwartz in particular irritated him by his jocularity, vivacity, and *savoir-faire*, which reminded him of what he himself had been ten years ago.

Friends came to make up a set and they sat down to cards. They dealt, bending the new cards to soften them, and he sorted the diamonds in his hand and found he had seven. His partner said "No trumps" and supported him with two diamonds. What more could be wished for? It ought to be jolly and lively. They would make a grand slam. But suddenly Iván Ilyich was conscious of that gnawing pain, that taste in his mouth, and it seemed ridiculous that in such circumstances he should be pleased to make a grand slam.

He looked at his partner Mikháil Mikháylovich, who rapped the table with his strong hand and instead of snatching up the tricks pushed the cards courteously and indulgently towards Iván Ilyich that he might have the pleasure of gathering them up without the trouble of stretching out his hand for them. "Does he think I am too weak to stretch out my arm?" thought Iván Ilyich, and forgetting what he was doing he over-trumped his partner, missing the grand slam by three tricks. And what was most awful of all was that he saw how upset Mikháil Mikháylovich was about it but did not himself care. And it was dreadful to realize why he did not care.

They all saw that he was suffering, and said: "We can stop if you are tired. Take a rest." Lie down? No, he was not at all tired, and he finished the rubber. All were gloomy and silent. Iván Ilyich felt that he had diffused this gloom over them and could not dispel it. They had supper and went away, and Iván Ilyich was left alone with the consciousness that his life was poisoned and was poisoning the lives of others, and that this poison did not weaken but penetrated more and more deeply into his whole being.

With this consciousness, and with physical pain besides the terror, he must go to bed, often to lie awake the greater part of the night. Next morning he had to get up again, dress, go to the law courts, speak, and write; or if he did not go out, spend at home those twenty-four hours a day each of which was a torture. And he had to live thus all alone on the brink of an abyss, with no one who understood or pitied him.

V

So one month passed and then another. Just before the New Year his brother-in-law came to town and stayed at their house. Iván Ilyich was at the law courts and Praskóvya Fëdorovna had gone shopping. When Iván Ilyich came home and entered his study he found his brother-in-law there—a healthy, florid man—unpacking his portmanteau himself. He raised his head on hearing Iván Ilyich's footsteps and looked up at him for a moment without a word. That stare told Iván everything. His brother-in-law opened his mouth to utter an exclamation of surprise but checked himself, and that action confirmed it all.

"I have changed, eh?"

"Yes, there is a change."

And after that, try as he would to get his brother-in-law to return to the subject of his looks, the latter would say nothing about it. Praskóvya Fëdorovna came home and her brother went out to her. Iván Ilyich locked the door and began to examine himself in the glass, first full face, then in profile. He took up a portrait of himself taken with his wife, and compared it with what he saw in the glass. The change in him was immense. Then he bared his arms to the elbow, looked at them, drew the sleeves down again, sat down on an ottoman, and grew blacker than night.

"No, no, this won't do!" he said to himself, and jumped up, went to the table, took up some law papers and began to read them, but could not continue. He unlocked the door and went into the reception-room. The door leading to the drawing-room was shut. He approached it on tiptoe and listened.

"No, you are exaggerating!" Praskóvya Fëdorovna was saying.

"Exaggerating! Don't you see it? Why, he's a dead man! Look at his eyes—there's no light in them. But what is it that is wrong with him?"

"No one knows. Nikoláevich [that was another doctor] said something, but I don't know what. And Leshchetítsky [this was the celebrated specialist] said quite the contrary . . ."

Iván Ilyich walked away, went to his own room, lay down and began musing: "The kidney, a floating kidney." He recalled all the doctors had told him of how it detached itself and swayed about. And by an effort of imagination he tried to catch that kidney and arrest it and support it. So little was needed for this, it seemed to him. "No, I'll go to see Peter Ivánovich again." [That was the friend whose friend was a doctor.] He rang, ordered the carriage, and got ready to go.

"Where are you going, *Jean?*" asked his wife, with a specially sad and exceptionally kind look.

This exceptionally kind look irritated him. He looked morosely at her.

"I must go to see Peter Ivánovich."

He went to see Peter Ivánovich, and together they went to see his friend, the doctor. He was in, and Iván Ilyich had a long talk with him.

Reviewing the anatomical and physiological details of what in the doctor's opinion was going on inside him, he understood it all.

There was something, a small thing, in the vermiform appendix. It might all come right. Only stimulate the energy of one organ and check the activity of another, then absorption would take place and everything would come right. He got home rather late for dinner, ate his dinner, and conversed cheerfully, but could not for a long time bring himself to go back to work in his room. At last, however, he went to his study and did what was necessary, but the consciousness that he had put something aside—an important, intimate matter which he would revert to when his work was done—never left him. When he had finished his work he remembered that this intimate matter was the thought of his vermiform appendix. But he did not give himself up to it, and went to the drawing-room for tea. There were callers there, including the examining magistrate who was a desirable match for his daughter, and they were conversing, playing the piano, and singing. Iván Ilyich, as Praskóvya Fëdorovna remarked, spent that evening more cheerfully than usual, but he never for a moment forgot that he had postponed the important matter of the appendix. At eleven o'clock he said goodnight and went to his bedroom. Since his illness he had slept alone in a small room next to his study. He undressed and took up a novel by Zola,[7] but instead of reading it he fell into thought, and in his imagination that desired improvement in the vermiform appendix occurred. There was the absorption and evacuation and the re-

<hr>

7. Émile Zola (1840–1902), French novelist, author of the *Rougon-Macquart* novels (*Nana, Germinal,* and so on). Tolstoy condemned Zola for his naturalistic theories and considered his novels crude and gross.

establishment of normal activity. "Yes, that's it!" he said to himself. "One need only assist nature, that's all." He remembered his
medicine, rose, took it, and lay down on his back watching for the
beneficent action of the medicine and for it to lessen the pain. "I
need only take it regularly and avoid all injurious influences. I am
already feeling better, much better." He began touching his side:
it was not painful to the touch. "There, I really don't feel it. It's
much better already." He put out the light and turned on his
side . . . "The appendix is getting better, absorption is occurring."
Suddenly he felt the old, familiar, dull, gnawing pain, stubborn and
serious. There was the same familiar loathsome taste in his mouth.
His heart sank and he felt dazed. "My God! My God!" he muttered. "Again, again! And it will never cease." And suddenly the
matter presented itself in a quite different aspect. "Vermiform
appendix! Kidney!" he said to himself. "It's not a question of
appendix or kidney, but of life and . . . death. Yes, life was there
and now it is going, going and I cannot stop it. Yes. Why deceive
myself? Isn't it obvious to everyone but me that I'm dying, and that
it's only a question of weeks, days . . . it may happen this moment.
There was light and now there is darkness. I was here and now
I'm going there! Where?" A chill came over him, his breathing
ceased, and he felt only the throbbing of his heart.

"When I am not, what will there be? There will be nothing.
Then where shall I be when I am no more? Can this be dying? No,
I don't want to!" He jumped up and tried to light the candle, felt
for it with trembling hands, dropped candle and candlestick on the
floor, and fell back on his pillow.

"What's the use? It makes no difference," he said to himself,
staring with wide-open eyes into the darkness. "Death. Yes, death.
And none of them know or wish to know it, and they have no pity
for me. Now they are playing." (He heard through the door the
distant sound of a song and its accompaniment.) "It's all the same
to them, but they will die too! Fools! I first, and they later, but
it will be the same for them. And now they are merry . . . the
beasts!"

Anger choked him and he was agonizingly, unbearably miserable.
"It is impossible that all men have been doomed to suffer this
awful horror!" He raised himself.

"Something must be wrong. I must calm myself—must think it
all over from the beginning." And he again began thinking. "Yes,
the beginning of my illness: I knocked my side, but I was still quite
well that day and the next. It hurt a little, then rather more. I saw
the doctors, then followed despondency and anguish, more doctors,
and I drew nearer to the abyss. My strength grew less and I kept
coming nearer and nearer, and now I have wasted away and there

is no light in my eyes. I think of the appendix—but this is death! I think of mending the appendix, and all the while here is death! Can it really be death?" Again terror seized him and he gasped for breath. He leant down and began feeling for the matches, pressing with his elbow on the stand beside the bed. It was in his way and hurt him, he grew furious with it, pressed on it still harder, and upset it. Breathless and in despair he fell on his back, expecting death to come immediately.

Meanwhile the visitors were leaving. Praskóvya Fëdorovna was seeing them off. She heard something fall and came in.

"What has happened?"

"Nothing. I knocked it over accidentally."

She went out and returned with a candle. He lay there panting heavily, like a man who has run a thousand yards, and stared upwards at her with a fixed look.

"What is it, Jean?"

"No . . . o . . . thing. I upset it." ("Why speak of it? She won't understand," he thought.)

And in truth she did not understand. She picked up the stand, lit his candle, and hurried away to see another visitor off. When she came back he still lay on his back, looking upwards.

"What is it? Do you feel worse?"

"Yes."

She shook her head and sat down.

"Do you know, Jean, I think we must ask Leshchetísky to come and see you here."

This meant calling in the famous specialist, regardless of expense. He smiled malignantly and said "No." She remained a little longer and then went up to him and kissed his forehead.

While she was kissing him he hated her from the bottom of his soul and with difficulty refrained from pushing her away.

"Good-night. Please God you'll sleep."

"Yes."

VI

Iván Ilyich saw that he was dying, and he was in continual despair.

In the depth of his heart he knew he was dying, but not only was he not accustomed to the thought, he simply did not and could not grasp it.

The syllogism he had learned from Kiesewetter's *Logic*:[8] "Caius is a man, men are mortal, therefore Caius is mortal," had always seemed to him correct as applied to Caius, but certainly not as

8. Karl Kiesewetter (1766–1819) was a German popularizer of Kant's philosophy. His *Outline of Logic Ac-* *cording to Kantian Principles* (1796) was widely used in Russian adaptations as a schoolbook.

applied to himself. That Caius—man in the abstract—was mortal, was perfectly correct, but he was not Caius, not an abstract man, but a creature quite, quite separate from all others. He had been little Ványa, with a mamma and a papa, with Mítya and Volódya, with the toys, a coachman and a nurse, afterwards with Kátenka and with all the joys, griefs, and delights of childhood, boyhood, and youth. What did Caius know of the smell of that striped leather ball Ványa had been so fond of? Had Caius kissed his mother's hand like that, and did the silk of her dress rustle so for Caius? Had he rioted like that at school when the pastry was bad? Had Caius been in love like that? Could Caius preside at a session as he did? Caius really was mortal, and it was right for him to die; but for me, little Ványa, Iván Ilyich, with all my thoughts and emotions, it's altogether a different matter. It cannot be that I ought to die. That would be too terrible."

Such was his feeling.

"If I had to die like Caius I should have known it was so. An inner voice would have told me so, but there was nothing of the sort in me and I and all my friends felt that our case was quite different from that of Caius. And now here it is!" he said to himself. "It can't be. It's impossible! But here it is. How is this? How is one to understand it?"

He could not understand it, and tried to drive this false, incorrect, morbid thought away and to replace it by other proper and healthy thoughts. But that thought, and not the thought only but the reality itself, seemed to come and confront him.

And to replace that thought he called up a succession of others, hoping to find in them some support. He tried to get back into the former current of thoughts that had once screened the thought of death from him. But strange to say, all that had formerly shut off, hidden, and destroyed, his consciousness of death, no longer had that effect. Iván Ilyich now spent most of his time in attempting to re-establish that old current. He would say to himself: "I will take up my duties again—after all I used to live by them." And banishing all doubts he would go to the law courts, enter into conversation with his colleagues, and sit carelessly as was his wont, scanning the crowd with a thoughtful look and leaning both his emaciated arms on the arms of his oak chair; bending over as usual to a colleague and drawing his papers nearer he would interchange whispers with him, and then suddenly raising his eyes and sitting erect would pronounce certain words and open the proceedings. But suddenly in the midst of those proceedings the pain in his side, regardless of the stage the proceedings had reached, would begin its own gnawing work. Iván Ilyich would turn his attention to it and try to drive the thought of it away, but without success. *It* would come and stand before him and look at him, and he would be petrified and the light would die out of his eyes, and he would again begin asking himself whether *It* alone was true. And his colleagues and subordinates would see with surprise and distress that he, the brilliant and subtle judge, was becoming confused and making mistakes. He would shake himself, try to pull himself together, manage somehow to bring the sitting to a close, and return home with the sorrowful consciousness that his judicial labours could not as formerly hide from him what he wanted them to hide, and could not deliver him from *It*. And what was worst of all was that *It* drew his attention to itself not in order to make him take some action but only that he should look at *It*, look it straight in the face: look at it without doing anything, suffer inexpressibly.

And to save himself from this condition Iván Ilyich looked for consolations—new screens—and new screens were found and for a while seemed to save him, but then they immediately fell to pieces or rather became transparent, as if *It* penetrated them and nothing could veil *It*.

In these latter days he would go into the drawing-room he had arranged—that drawing-room where he had fallen and for the sake of which (how bitterly ridiculous it seemed) he had sacrificed his life—for he knew that his illness originated with that knock. He would enter and see that something had scratched the polished table. He would look for the cause of this and find that it was the bronze ornamentation of an album, that had got bent. He would take up the expensive album which he had lovingly arranged, and feel vexed with his daughter and her friends for their untidiness—for the album was torn here and there and some of the photographs turned upside down. He would put it carefully in order and bend the ornamentation back into position. Then it would occur to him to place all those things in another corner of the room, near the plants. He would call the footman, but his daughter or wife would come to help him. They would not agree, and his wife would contradict him, and he would dispute and grow angry. But that was all right, for then he did not think about *It. It* was invisible.

But then, when he was moving something himself, his wife would say: "Let the servants do it. You will hurt yourself again." And suddenly *It* would flash through the screen and he would see it. It was just a flash, and he hoped it would disappear, but he would involuntarily pay attention to his side. "It sits there as before, gnawing just the same!" And he could no longer forget *It*, but could distinctly see it looking at him from behind the flowers. "What is it all for?"

"It really is so! I lost my life over that curtain as I might have done when storming a fort. Is that possible? How terrible and how stupid. It can't be true! It can't, but it is."

He would go to his study, lie down, and again be alone with It: face to face with It. And nothing could be done with It except to look at it and shudder.

VII

How it happened it is impossible to say because it came about step by step, unnoticed, but in the third month of Iván Ilyich's illness, his wife, his daughter, his son, his acquaintances, the doctors, the servants, and above all he himself, were aware that the whole interest he had for other people was whether he would soon vacate his place, and at last release the living from the discomfort caused by his presence and be himself released from his sufferings.

He slept less and less. He was given opium and hypodermic injections of morphine, but this did not relieve him. The dull depression he experienced in a somnolent condition at first gave him a little relief, but only as something new, afterwards it became as distressing as the pain itself or even more so.

Special foods were prepared for him by the doctors' orders, but all those foods became increasingly distasteful and disgusting to him.

For his excretions also special arrangements had to be made, and this was a torment to him every time—a torment from the uncleanliness, the unseemliness, and the smell, and from knowing that another person had to take part in it.

But just through this most unpleasant matter, Iván Ilyich obtained comfort. Gerásim, the butler's young assistant, always came in to carry the things out. Gerásim was a clean, fresh peasant lad, grown stout on town food and always cheerful and bright. At first the sight of him, in his clean Russian peasant costume, engaged on that disgusting task embarrassed Iván Ilyich.

Once when he got up from the commode too weak to draw up his trousers, he dropped into a soft armchair and looked with horror at his bare, enfeebled thighs with the muscles so sharply marked on them.

Gerásim with a firm light tread, his heavy boots emitting a pleasant smell of tar and fresh winter air, came in wearing a clean Hessian apron, the sleeves of his print shirt tucked up over his strong bare young arms; and refraining from looking at his sick master out of consideration for his feelings, and restraining the joy of life that beamed from his face, he went up to the commode.

"Gerásim!" said Iván Ilyich in a weak voice.

Gerásim started, evidently afraid he might have committed some blunder, and with a rapid movement turned his fresh, kind, simple young face which just showed the first downy signs of a beard.

"Yes, sir?"

"That must be very unpleasant for you. You must forgive me. I am helpless."

"Oh, why, sir," and Gerásim's eyes beamed and he showed his glistening white teeth, "what's a little trouble? It's a case of illness with you, sir."

And his deft strong hands did their accustomed task, and he went out of the room stepping lightly. Five minutes later he as lightly returned.

Iván Ilyich was still sitting in the same position in the armchair.

"Gerásim," he said when the latter had replaced the freshly-washed utensil. "Please come here and help me." Gerásim went up to him. "Lift me up. It is hard for me to get up, and I have sent Dmítri away."

Gerásim went up to him, grasped his master with his strong arms deftly but gently, in the same way that he stepped—lifted him, supported him with one hand, and with the other drew up his trousers and would have set him down again, but Iván Ilyich asked to be led to the sofa. Gerásim, without an effort and without apparent pressure, led him, almost lifting him, to the sofa and placed him on it.

"Thank you. How easily and well you do it all!"

Gerásim smiled again and turned to leave the room. But Iván Ilyich felt his presence such a comfort that he did not want to let him go.

"One thing more, please move up that chair. No, the other one—under my feet. It is easier for me when my feet are raised."

Gerásim brought the chair, set it down gently in place, and raised Iván Ilyich's legs on to it. It seemed to Iván Ilyich that he felt better while Gerásim was holding up his legs.

"It's better when my legs are higher," he said. "Place that cushion under them."

Gerásim did so. He again lifted the legs and placed them, and again Iván Ilyich felt better while Gerásim held his legs. When he set them down Iván Ilyich fancied he felt worse.

"Gerásim," he said. "Are you busy now?"

"Not at all, sir," said Gerásim, who had learnt from the townsfolk how to speak to gentlefolk.

"What have you still to do?"

"What have I to do? I've done everything except chopping the logs for to-morrow."

"Then hold my legs up a bit higher, can you?"

"Of course I can. Why not?" And Gerásim raised his master's legs higher and Iván Ilyich thought that in that position he did not feel any pain at all.

"And how about the logs?"

"Don't trouble about that, sir. There's plenty of time."

Iván Ilyich told Gerásim to sit down and hold his legs, and began to talk to him. And strange to say it seemed to him that he felt better while Gerásim held his legs up.

After that Iván Ilyich would sometimes call Gerásim and get him to hold his legs on his shoulders, and he liked talking to him. Gerásim did it all easily, willingly, simply, and with a good nature that touched Iván Ilyich. Health, strength, and vitality in other people were offensive to him, but Gerásim's strength and vitality did not mortify but soothed him.

What tormented Iván Ilyich most was the deception, the lie, which for some reason they all accepted, that he was not dying but was simply ill, and that he only need keep quiet and undergo a treatment and then something very good would result. He however knew that do what they would nothing would come of it, only still more agonizing suffering and death. This deception tortured him—their not wishing to admit what they all knew and what he knew, but wanting to lie to him concerning his terrible condition, and wishing and forcing him to participate in that lie. Those lies —lies enacted over him on the eve of his death and destined to degrade this awful, solemn act to the level of their visitings, their curtains, their sturgeon for dinner—were a terrible agony for Iván Ilyich. And strangely enough, many times when they were going through their antics over him he had been within a hairbreadth of calling out to them: "Stop lying! You know and I know that I am dying. Then at least stop lying about it!" But he had never had the spirit to do it. The awful, terrible act of his dying was, he could see, reduced by those about him to the level of a casual, unpleasant, and almost indecorous incident (as if someone entered a drawing-room diffusing an unpleasant odour) and this was done by that very decorum which he had served all his life long. He saw that no one felt for him, because no one even wished to grasp his position. Only Gerásim recognized and pitied him. And so Iván Ilyich felt at ease only with him. He felt comforted when Gerásim supported his legs (sometimes all night long) and refused to go to bed, saying: "Don't you worry, Iván Ilyich. I'll get sleep enough later on," or when he suddenly became familiar and exclaimed: "If you weren't sick it would be another matter, but as it is, why should I grudge a little trouble?" Gerásim alone did not lie; everything showed that he alone understood the facts of the case and did not consider it necessary to disguise them, but simply felt sorry for his emaciated and enfeebled master. Once when Iván Ilyich was sending him away he even said straight out: "We shall all of us die, so why should I grudge a little trouble?"—expressing the fact that he did not think his work burdensome, because he was doing it for a dying man and hoped someone would do the same for him when his time came.

Apart from this lying, or because of it, what most tormented Iván Ilyich was that no one pitied him as he wished to be pitied. At certain moments after prolonged suffering he wished most of all (though he would have been ashamed to confess it) for someone to pity him as a sick child is pitied. He longed to be petted and comforted. He knew he was an important functionary, that he had a beard turning grey, and that therefore what he longed for was impossible, but still he longed for it. And in Gerásim's attitude towards him there was something akin to what he wished for, and so that attitude comforted him. Iván Ilyich wanted to weep, wanted to be petted and cried over, and then his colleague Shébek would come, and instead of weeping and being petted, Iván Ilyich would assume a serious, severe, and profound air, and by force of habit would express his opinion on a decision of the Court of Appeal and would stubbornly insist on that view. This falsity around him and within him did more than anything else to poison his last days.

VIII

It was morning. He knew it was morning because Gerásim had gone, and Peter the footman had come and put out the candles, drawn back one of the curtains, and begun quietly to tidy up. Whether it was morning or evening, Friday or Sunday, made no difference, it was all just the same: the gnawing, unmitigated, agonizing pain, never ceasing for an instant, the consciousness of life inexorably waning but not yet extinguished, the approach of that ever dreaded and hateful Death which was the only reality, and always the same falsity. What were days, weeks, hours, in such a case?

"Will you have some tea, sir?"

"He wants things to be regular, and wishes the gentlefolk to drink tea in the morning," thought Iván Ilyich, and only said "No."

"Wouldn't you like to move onto the sofa, sir?"

"He wants to tidy up the room, and I'm in the way. I am uncleanliness and disorder," he thought, and said only:

"No, leave me alone."

The man went on bustling about. Iván Ilyich stretched out his hand. Peter came up, ready to help.

"What is it, sir?"

"My watch."

Peter took the watch which was close at hand and gave it to his master.

"Half-past eight. Are they up?"

"No sir, except Vladímir Ivánich" (the son) "who has gone to school. Praskóvya Fëdorovna ordered me to wake her if you asked for her. Shall I do so?"

"No, there's no need to." "Perhaps I'd better have some tea," he thought, and added aloud: "Yes, bring me some tea."

Peter went to the door, but Iván Ilyich dreaded being left alone. "How can I keep him here? Oh yes, my medicine." "Peter, give me my medicine." "Why not? Perhaps it may still do me some good." He took a spoonful and swallowed it. "No, it won't help. It's all tomfoolery, all deception," he decided as soon as he became aware of the familiar, sickly, hopeless taste. "No, I can't believe in it any longer. But the pain, why this pain? If it would only cease just for a moment!" And he moaned. Peter turned towards him. "It's all right. Go and fetch me some tea."

Peter went out. Left alone Iván Ilyich groaned not so much with pain, terrible though that was, as from mental anguish. Always and forever the same, always these endless days and nights. If only it would come quicker! If only *what* would come quicker? Death, darkness? . . . No, no! Anything rather than death!

When Peter returned with the tea on a tray, Iván Ilyich stared at him for a time in perplexity, not realizing who and what he was. Peter was disconcerted by that look and his embarrassment brought Iván Ilyich to himself.

"Oh, tea! All right, put it down. Only help me to wash and put on a clean shirt."

And Iván Ilyich began to wash. With pauses for rest, he washed his hands and then his face, cleaned his teeth, brushed his hair, and looked in the glass. He was terrified by what he saw, especially by the limp way in which his hair clung to his pallid forehead.

While his shirt was being changed he knew that he would be still more frightened at the sight of his body, so he avoided looking at it. Finally he was ready. He drew on a dressing-gown, wrapped himself in a plaid, and sat down in the armchair to take his tea. For a moment he felt refreshed, but as soon as he began to drink the tea he was again aware of the same taste, and the pain also returned. He finished it with an effort, and then lay down stretching out his legs, and dismissed Peter.

Always the same. Now a spark of hope flashes up, then a sea of despair rages, and always pain; always pain, always despair, and always the same. When alone he had a dreadful and distressing desire to call someone, but he knew beforehand that with others present it would be still worse. "Another dose of morphine—to lose consciousness. I will tell him, the doctor, that he must think of something else. It's impossible, impossible, to go on like this."

An hour and another pass like that. But now there is a ring at the door bell. Perhaps it's the doctor? It is. He comes in fresh, hearty, plump, and cheerful, with that look on his face that seems to say: "There now, you're in a panic about something, but we'll arrange it all for you directly!" The doctor knows this expression is out of place here, but he has put it on once for all and can't take it off—like a man who has put on a frock-coat in the morning to pay a round of calls.

The doctor rubs his hands vigorously and reassuringly.

"Brr! How cold it is! There's such a sharp frost; just let me warm myself!" he says, as if it were only a matter of waiting till he was warm, and then he would put everything right.

"Well now, how are you?"

Iván Ilyich feels that the doctor would like to say: "Well, how are our affairs?" but that even he feels that this would not do, and says instead: "What sort of a night have you had?"

Iván Ilyich looks at him as much as to say: "Are you really never ashamed of lying?" But the doctor does not wish to understand this question, and Iván Ilyich says: "Just as terrible as ever. The pain never leaves me and never subsides. If only something . . ."

"Yes, you sick people are always like that. . . . There, now I think I'm warm enough. Even Praskóvya Fëdorovna, who is so particular, could find no fault with my temperature. Well, now I can say good-morning," and the doctor presses his patient's hand.

Then, dropping his former playfulness, he begins with a most serious face to examine the patient, feeling his pulse and taking his temperature, and then begins the sounding and auscultation.

Iván Ilyich knows quite well and definitely that all this is nonsense and pure deception, but when the doctor, getting down on his knee, leans over him, putting his ear first higher then lower, and performs various gymnastic movements over him with a significant expression on his face, Iván Ilyich submits to it all as he used to submit to the speeches of the lawyers, though he knew very well that they were all lying and why they were lying.

The doctor, kneeling on the sofa, is still sounding him when Praskóvya Fëdorovna's silk dress rustles at the door and she is heard scolding Peter for not having let her know of the doctor's arrival.

She comes in, kisses her husband, and at once proceeds to prove that she has been up a long time already, and only owing to a misunderstanding failed to be there when the doctor arrived.

Iván Ilyich looks at her, scans her all over, sets against her the whiteness and plumpness and cleanness of her hands and neck, the gloss of her hair, and the sparkle of her vivacious eyes. He hates her with his whole soul. And the thrill of hatred he feels for her makes him suffer from her touch.

Her attitude towards him and his disease is still the same. Just as the doctor had adopted a certain relation to his patient which he could not abandon, so had she formed one towards him—that he was not doing something he ought to do and was himself to blame, and that she reproached him lovingly for this—and she could not now change that attitude.

"You see he doesn't listen to me and doesn't take his medicine at the proper time. And above all he lies in a position that is no doubt bad for him—with his legs up."

She described how he made Gerásim hold his legs up.

The doctor smiled with a contemptuous affability that said: "What's to be done? These sick people do have foolish fancies of that kind, but we must forgive them."

When the examination was over the doctor looked at his watch, and then Praskóvya Fëdorovna announced to Iván Ilyich that it was of course as he pleased, but she had sent to-day for a celebrated specialist who would examine him and have a consultation with Michael Danílovich (their regular doctor).

"Please don't raise any objections. I am doing this for my own sake," she said ironically, letting it be felt that she was doing it all for his sake and only said this to leave him no right to refuse. He remained silent, knitting his brows. He felt that he was so surrounded and involved in a mesh of falsity that it was hard to unravel anything.

Everything she did for him was entirely for her own sake, and she told him she was doing for herself what she actually was doing for herself, as if that was so incredible that he must understand the opposite.

At half-past eleven the celebrated specialist arrived. Again the sounding began and the significant conversations in his presence and in another room, about the kidneys and the appendix, and the questions and answers, with such an air of importance that again, instead of the real question of life and death which now alone confronted him, the question arose of the kidney and the appendix which were not behaving as they ought to and would now be attacked by Michael Danílovich and the specialist and forced to amend their ways.

The celebrated specialist took leave of him with a serious though not hopeless look, and in reply to the timid question Iván Ilyich, with eyes glistening with fear and hope, put to him as to whether there was a chance of recovery, said that he could not vouch for it but there was a possibility. The look of hope with which Iván Ilyich watched the doctor out was so pathetic that Praskóvya Fëdorovna, seeing it, even wept as she left the room to hand the doctor his fee.

The gleam of hope kindled by the doctor's encouragement did not last long. The same room, the same pictures, curtains, wallpaper, medicine bottles, were all there, and the same aching suffering body, and Iván Ilyich began to moan. They gave him a subcutaneous injection and he sank into oblivion.

It was twilight when he came to. They brought him his dinner and he swallowed some beef tea with difficulty, and then everything was the same again and night was coming on.

After dinner, at seven o'clock, Praskóvya Fëdorovna came into the room in evening dress, her full bosom pushed up by her corset, and with traces of powder on her face. She had reminded him in the morning that they were going to the theatre. Sarah Bernhardt was visiting the town and they had a box, which he had insisted on their taking. Now he had forgotten about it and her toilet offended him, but he concealed his vexation when he remembered that he had himself insisted on their securing a box and going because it would be an instructive and aesthetic pleasure for the children.

Praskóvya Fëdorovna came in, self-satisfied but yet with a rather guilty air. She sat down and asked how he was, but, as he saw, only for the sake of asking and not in order to learn about it, knowing that there was nothing to learn—and then went on to what she really wanted to say: that she would not on any account have gone but that the box had been taken and Helen and their daughter were going, as well as Petríshchev (the examining magistrate, their daughter's fiancé) and that it was out of the question to let them go alone; but that she would have much preferred to sit with him for a while; and he must be sure to follow the doctor's orders while she was away.

"Oh, and Fëdor Petróvich" (the fiancé) "would like to come in. May he? And Lisa?"

"All right."

Their daughter came in in full evening dress, her fresh young flesh exposed (making a show of that very flesh which in his own case caused so much suffering), strong, healthy, evidently in love, and impatient with illness, suffering, and death, because they interfered with her happiness.

Fëdor Petróvich came in too, in evening dress, his hair curled *à la Capoul*, a tight stiff collar round his long sinewy neck, an enormous white shirt-front and narrow black trousers tightly stretched over his strong thighs. He had one white glove tightly drawn on, and was holding his opera hat in his hand.

Following him the schoolboy crept in unnoticed, in a new uniform, poor little fellow, and wearing gloves. Terribly dark shadows showed under his eyes, the meaning of which Iván Ilyich knew well.

His son had always seemed pathetic to him, and now it was dreadful to see the boy's frightened look of pity. It seemed to Iván Ilyich that Vásya was the only one besides Gerásim who understood and pitied him.

They all sat down and again asked how he was. A silence followed

Lisa asked her mother about the opera-glasses, and there was an altercation between mother and daughter as to who had taken them and where they had been put. This occasioned some unpleasantness.

Fëdor Petróvich inquired of Iván Ilyich whether he had ever seen Sarah Bernhardt. Iván Ilyich did not at first catch the question, but then replied: "No, have you seen her before?"

"Yes, in *Adrienne Lecouvreur*."[9]

Praskóvya Fëdorovna mentioned some rôles in which Sarah Bernhardt was particularly good. Her daughter disagreed. Conversation sprang up as to the elegance and realism of her acting—the sort of conversation that is always repeated and is always the same.

In the midst of the conversation Fëdor Petróvich glanced at Iván Ilyich and became silent. The others also looked at him and grew silent. Iván Ilyich was staring with glittering eyes straight before him, evidently indignant with them. This had to be rectified, but it was impossible to do so. The silence had to be broken, but for a time no one dared to break it and they all became afraid that the conventional deception would suddenly become obvious and the truth become plain to all. Lisa was the first to pluck up courage and break that silence, but by trying to hide what everybody was feeling, she betrayed it.

"Well, if we are going it's time to start," she said, looking at her watch, a present from her father, and with a faint and significant smile at Fëdor Petróvich relating to something known only to them. She got up with a rustle of her dress.

They all rose, said good-night, and went away.

When they had gone it seemed to Iván Ilyich that he felt better; the falsity had gone with them. But the pain remained—that same pain and that same fear that made everything monotonously alike, nothing harder and nothing easier. Everything was worse.

Again minute followed minute and hour followed hour. Everything remained the same and there was no cessation. And the inevitable end of it all became more and more terrible.

"Yes, send Gerásim here," he replied to a question Peter asked.

IX

His wife returned late at night. She came in on tiptoe, but he heard her, opened his eyes, and made haste to close them again. She wished to send Gerásim away and to sit with him herself, but he opened his eyes and said: "No, go away."

"Are you in great pain?"

"Always the same."

"Take some opium."

9. a play (1849) by the French dramatist Eugène Scribe (1791–1861), in which the heroine was a famous actress of the eighteenth century. Tolstoy considered Scribe, who wrote over four hundred plays, a shoddy, commercial playwright.

He agreed and took some. She went away.

Till about three in the morning he was in a state of stupefied misery. It seemed to him that he and his pain were being thrust into a narrow, deep black sack, but though they were pushed further and further in they could not be pushed to the bottom. And this, terrible enough in itself, was accompanied by suffering. He was frightened yet wanted to fall through the sack, he struggled but yet co-operated. And suddenly he broke through, fell, and regained consciousness. Gerásim was sitting at the foot of the bed dozing quietly and patiently, while he himself lay with his emaciated stockinged legs resting on Gerásim's shoulders; the same shaded candle was there and the same unceasing pain.

"Go away, Gerásim," he whispered.

"It's all right, sir. I'll stay a while."

"No. Go away."

He removed his legs from Gerásim's shoulders, turned sideways onto his arm, and felt sorry for himself. He only waited till Gerásim had gone into the next room and then restrained himself no longer but wept like a child. He wept on account of his helplessness, his terrible loneliness, the cruelty of man, the cruelty of God, and the absence of God.

"Why hast Thou done all this? Why hast Thou brought me here? Why, dost Thou torment me so terribly?"

He did not expect an answer and yet wept because there was no answer and could be none. The pain again grew more acute, but he did not stir and did not call. He said to himself: "Go on! Strike me! But what is it for? What have I done to Thee? What is it for?"

Then he grew quiet and not only ceased weeping but even held his breath and became all attention. It was as though he were listening not to an audible voice but to a voice of his soul, to the current of thoughts arising within him.

"What is it you want?" was the first clear conception capable of expression in words, that he heard.

"What do you want? What do you want?" he repeated to himself.

"What do I want? To live and not to suffer," he answered.

And again he listened with such concentrated attention that even his pain did not distract him.

"To live? How?" asked his inner voice.

"Why, to live as I used to—well and pleasantly."

"As you lived before, well and pleasantly?" the voice repeated.

And in imagination he began to recall the best moments of his pleasant life. But strange to say none of those best moments of his pleasant life now seemed at all what they had then seemed—none of them except the first recollections of childhood. There, in childhood, there had been something really pleasant with which it would be possible to live if it could return. But the child who had experienced that happiness existed no longer, it was like a reminiscence of somebody else.

As soon as the period began which had produced the present Iván Ilyich, all that had then seemed joys now melted before his sight and turned into something trivial and often nasty.

And the further he departed from childhood and the nearer he came to the present the more worthless and doubtful were the joys. This began with the School of Law. A little that was really good was still found there—there was light-heartedness, friendship, and hope. But in the upper classes there had already been fewer of such good moments. Then during the first years of his official career, when he was in the service of the Governor, some pleasant moments again occurred: they were the memories of love for a woman. Then all became confused and there was still less of what was good; later on again there was still less that was good, and the further he went the less there was. His marriage, a mere accident, then the disenchantment that followed it, his wife's bad breath and the sensuality and hypocrisy: then that deadly official life and those preoccupations about money, a year of it, and two, and ten, and twenty, and always the same thing. And the longer it lasted the more deadly it became. "It is as if I had been going downhill while I imagined I was going up. And that is really what it was. I was going up in public opinion, but to the same extent life was ebbing away from me. And now it is all done and there is only death."

"Then what does it mean? Why? It can't be that life is so senseless and horrible. But if it really has been so horrible and senseless, why must I die and die in agony? There is something wrong!"

"Maybe I did not live as I ought to have done," it suddenly occurred to him. "But how could that be, when I did everything properly?" he replied, and immediately dismissed from his mind this, the sole solution of all the riddles of life and death, as something quite impossible.

"Then what do you want now? To live? Live how? Live as you lived in the law courts when the usher proclaimed 'The judge is coming!' The judge is coming, the judge!" he repeated to himself. "Here he is, the judge. But I am not guilty!" he exclaimed angrily. "What is it for?" And he ceased crying, but turning his face to the wall continued to ponder on the same question: Why, and for what purpose, is there all this horror? But however much he pondered he found no answer. And whenever the thought occurred to him, as it often did, that it all resulted from his not having lived as he ought to have done, he at once recalled the correctness of his whole life, and dismissed so strange an idea.

x

Another fortnight passed. Iván Ilyich now no longer left his sofa. He would not lie in bed but lay on the sofa, facing the wall nearly all the time. He suffered ever the same unceasing agonies and in his loneliness pondered always on the same insoluble question: "What is this? Can it be that it is Death?" And the inner voice answered: "Yes, it is Death."

"Why these sufferings?" And the voice answered, "For no reason —they just are so." Beyond and besides this there was nothing.

From the very beginning of his illness, ever since he had first been to see the doctor, Iván Ilyich's life had been divided between two contrary and alternating moods: now it was despair and the expectation of this uncomprehended and terrible death, and now hope and an intently interested observation of the functioning of his organs. Now before his eyes there was only a kidney or an intestine that temporarily evaded its duty, and now only that incomprehensible and dreadful death from which it was impossible to escape.

These two states of mind had alternated from the very beginning of his illness, but the further it progressed the more doubtful and fantastic became the conception of the kidney, and the more real the sense of impending death.

He had but to call to mind what he had been three months before and what he was now, to call to mind with what regularity he had been going downhill, for every possibility of hope to be shattered.

Latterly during that loneliness in which he found himself as he lay facing the back of the sofa, a loneliness in the midst of a populous town and surrounded by numerous acquaintances and relations but that yet could not have been more complete anywhere—either at the bottom of the sea or under the earth—during that terrible loneliness Iván Ilyich had lived only in memories of the past. Pictures of his past rose before him one after another. They always began with what was nearest in time and then went back to what was most remote—to his childhood—and rested there. If he thought of the stewed prunes that had been offered him that day, his mind went back to. the raw shrivelled French plums of his childhood, their peculiar flavour and the flow of saliva when he sucked their stones, and along with the memory of that taste came a whole series of memories of those days: his nurse, his brother, and their toys. "No, I mustn't think of that. . . . It is too painful," Iván Ilyich said to himself, and brought himself back to the present—to the button on the back of the sofa and the creases in its morocco. "Morocco is expensive, but it does not wear well: there had been a quarrel about it. It was a different kind of quarrel and a different kind of morocco that time when we tore father's portfolio and were punished, **and** mamma brought us some tarts. . . ." And again his thoughts dwelt on his childhood, and again it was painful and he tried to banish them and fix his mind on something else.

Then again together with that chain of memories another series passed through his mind—of how his illness had progressed and grown worse. There also the further back he looked the more life there had been. There had been more of what was good in life and more of life itself. The two merged together. "Just as the pain went on getting worse and worse, so my life grew worse and worse," he thought. "There is one bright spot there at the back, at the beginning of life, and afterwards all becomes blacker and blacker and proceeds more and more rapidly—in inverse ratio to the square of the distance from death," thought Iván Ilyich. And the example of a stone falling downwards with increasing velocity entered his mind. Life, a series of increasing sufferings, flies further and further towards its end—the most terrible suffering. "I am flying. . . ." He shuddered, shifted himself, and tried to resist, but was already aware that resistance was impossible, and again with eyes weary of gazing but unable to cease seeing what was before them, he stared at the back of the sofa and waited—awaiting that dreadful fall and shock and destruction.

"Resistance is impossible!" he said to himself. "If I could only understand what it is all for! But that too is impossible. An explanation would be possible if it could be said that I have not lived as I ought to. But it is impossible to say that," and he remembered all the legality, correctitude, and propriety of his life. "That at any rate can certainly not be admitted," he thought, and his lips smiled ironically as if someone could see that smile and be taken in by it. "There is no explanation! Agony, death. . . . What for?"

XI

Another two weeks went by in this way and during that fortnight an event occurred that Iván Ilyich and his wife had desired. Petríshchev formally proposed. It happened in the evening. The next day Praskóvya Fëdorovna came into her husband's room considering how best to inform him of it, but that very night there had been a fresh change for the worse in his condition. She found him still lying on the sofa but in a different position. He lay on his back, groaning and staring fixedly straight in front of him.

She began to remind him of his medicines, but he turned his eyes towards her with such a look that she did not finish what she was saying; so great an animosity, to her in particular, did that look express.

"For Christ's sake let me die in peace!" he said.

She would have gone away, but just then their daughter came in and went up to say good morning. He looked at her as he had done at his wife, and in reply to her inquiry about his health said dryly that he would soon free them all of himself. They were both silent and after sitting with him for a while went away.

"Is it our fault?" Lisa said to her mother. "It's as if we were to blame! I am sorry for papa, but why should we be tortured?"

The doctor came at his usual time. Iván Ilyich answered "Yes" and "No," never taking his angry eyes from him, and at last said: "You know you can do nothing for me, so leave me alone."

"We can ease your sufferings."

"You can't even do that. Let me be."

The doctor went into the drawing-room and told Praskóvya Fëdorovna that the case was very serious and that the only resource left was opium to allay her husband's sufferings, which must be terrible.

It was true, as the doctor said, that Iván Ilyich's physical sufferings were terrible, but worse than the physical sufferings were his mental sufferings which were his chief torture.

His mental sufferings were due to the fact that that night, as he looked at Gerásim's sleepy, good-natured face with its prominent cheek-bones, the question suddenly occurred to him: "What if my whole life has really been wrong?"

It occurred to him that what had appeared perfectly impossible before, namely that he had not spent his life as he should have done, might after all be true. It occurred to him that his scarcely perceptible attempts to struggle against what was considered good by the most highly placed people, those scarcely noticeable impulses which he had immediately suppressed, might have been the real thing, and all the rest false. And his professional duties and the whole arrangement of his life and of his family, and all his social and official interests, might all have been false. He tried to defend all those things to himself and suddenly felt the weakness of what he was defending. There was nothing to defend.

"But if that is so," he said to himself, "and I am leaving this life with the consciousness that I have lost all that was given me and it is impossible to rectify it—what then?"

He lay on his back and began to pass his life in review in quite a new way. In the morning when he saw first his footman, then his wife, then his daughter, and then the doctor, their every word and movement confirmed to him the awful truth that had been revealed to him during the night. In them he saw himself—all that for which he had lived—and saw clearly that it was not real at all, but a terrible and huge deception which had hidden both life and death. This consciousness intensified his physical suffering tenfold. He groaned and tossed about, and pulled at his clothing which choked and stifled him. And he hated them on that account.

He was given a large dose of opium and became unconscious, but at noon his sufferings began again. He drove everybody away and tossed from side to side.

His wife came to him and said:

"*Jean*, my dear, do this for me. It can't do any harm and often helps. Healthy people often do it."

He opened his eyes wide.

"What? Take communion? Why? It's unnecessary! However . . ."

She began to cry.

"Yes, do, my dear. I'll send for our priest. He is such a nice man."

"All right. Very well," he muttered.

When the priest came and heard his confession, Iván Ilyich was softened and seemed to feel a relief from his doubts and consequently from his sufferings, and for a moment there came a ray of hope. He again began to think of the vermiform appendix and the possibility of correcting it. He received the sacrament with tears in his eyes.

When they laid him down again afterwards he felt a moment's ease, and the hope that he might live awoke in him again. He began to think of the operation that had been suggested to him. "To live! I want to live!" he said to himself.

His wife came in to congratulate him after his communion, and when uttering the usual conventional words she added:

"You feel better, don't you?"

Without looking at her he said "Yes."

Her dress, her figure, the expression of her face, the tone of her voice, all revealed the same thing. "This is wrong, it is not as it should be. All you have lived for and still live for is falsehood and deception, hiding life and death from you." And as soon as he admitted that thought, his hatred and his agonizing physical suffering again sprang up, and with that suffering a consciousness of the unavoidable, approaching end. And to this was added a new sensation of grinding shooting pain and a feeling of suffocation.

The expression of his face when he uttered that "yes" was dreadful. Having uttered it, he looked her straight in the eyes, turned on his face with a rapidity extraordinary in his weak state and shouted:

"Go away! Go away and leave me alone!"

XII

From that moment the screaming began that continued for three days, and was so terrible that one could not hear it through two closed doors without horror. At the moment he answered his wife he realized that he was lost, that there was no return, that the end had come, the very end, and his doubts were still unsolved and remained doubts.

"Oh! Oh! Oh!" he cried in various intonations. He had begun by screaming "I won't!" and continued screaming on the letter "o."

For three whole days, during which time did not exist for him, he struggled in that black sack into which he was being thrust by an invisible, resistless force. He struggled as a man condemned to death struggles in the hands of the executioner, knowing that he cannot save himself. And every moment he felt that despite all his efforts he was drawing nearer and nearer to what terrified him. He felt that his agony was due to his being thrust into that black hole and still more to his not being able to get right into it. He was hindered from getting into it by his conviction that his life had been a good one. That very justification of his life held him fast and prevented his moving forward, and it caused him most torment of all.

Suddenly some force struck him in the chest and side, making it still harder to breathe, and he fell through the hole and there at the bottom was a light. What had happened to him was like the sensation one sometimes experiences in a railway carriage when one thinks one is going backwards while one is really going forwards and suddenly becomes aware of the real direction.

"Yes, it was all not the right thing," he said to himself, "but that's no matter. It can be done. But what *is* the right thing?" he asked himself, and suddenly grew quiet.

This occurred at the end of the third day, two hours before his death. Just then his schoolboy son had crept softly in and gone up to the bedside. The dying man was still screaming desperately and waving his arms. His hand fell on the boy's head, and the boy caught it, pressed it to his lips, and began to cry.

At that very moment Iván Ilyich fell through and caught sight of the light, and it was revealed to him that though his life had not been what it should have been, this could still be rectified. He asked himself, "What *is* the right thing?" and grew still, listening. Then he felt that someone was kissing his hand. He opened his eyes, looked at his son, and felt sorry for him. His wife came up to him and he glanced at her. She was gazing at him open-mouthed, with undried tears on her nose and cheek and a despairing look on her face. He felt sorry for her too.

"Yes, I am making them wretched," he thought. "They are sorry, but it will be better for them when I die." He wished to say this but had not the strength to utter it. "Besides, why speak? I must act," he thought. With a look at his wife he indicated his son and said: "Take him away . . . sorry for him . . . sorry for you too. . . ." He tried to add, "forgive me," but said "forego" and waved his hand, knowing that He whose understanding mattered would understand.

And suddenly it grew clear to him that what had been oppressing him and would not leave him was all dropping away at once from two sides, from ten sides, and from all sides. He was sorry for them, he must act so as not to hurt them: release them and free himself from these sufferings. "How good and how simple!" he thought. "And the pain?" he asked himself. "What has become of it? Where are you, pain?"

He turned his attention to it.

"Yes, here it is. Well, what of it? Let the pain be."

"And death . . . where is it?"

He sought his former accustomed fear of death and did not find it. "Where is it? What death?" There was no fear because there was no death.

In place of death there was light.

"So that's what it is!" he suddenly exclaimed aloud. "What joy!"

To him all this happened in a single instant, and the meaning of that instant did not change. For those present his agony continued for another two hours. Something rattled in his throat, his emaciated body twitched, then the gasping and rattle became less and less frequent.

"It is finished!" said someone near him.

He heard these words and repeated them in his soul.

"Death is finished," he said to himself. "It is no more!"

He drew in a breath, stopped in the midst of a sigh, stretched out, and died.

HENRIK IBSEN

(1828–1906)
Hedda Gabler*

Characters

GEORGE TESMAN, *research graduate
in cultural history*
HEDDA, *his wife*
MISS JULIANA TESMAN, *his aunt*

MRS. ELVSTED
JUDGE BRACK
EILERT LOEVBORG
BERTHA, *a maid*

The action takes place in TESMAN'S *villa in the fashionable quarter of town.*

Act I

SCENE—A *large drawing room, handsomely and tastefully furnished; decorated in dark colors. In the rear wall is a broad open doorway, with curtains drawn back to either side. It leads to a*

* Translated by Michael Meyer.

smaller room, decorated in the same style as the drawing room. In the right-hand wall of the drawing room, a folding door leads out to the hall. The opposite wall, on the left, contains french windows,[1] also with curtains drawn back on either side. Through the glass we can see part of a verandah, and trees in autumn colors. Downstage stands an oval table, covered by a cloth and surrounded by chairs. Downstage right, against the wall, is a broad stove tiled with dark porcelain; in front of it stand a high-backed armchair, a cushioned footrest, and two footstools. Upstage right, in an alcove, is a corner sofa, with a small, round table. Downstage left, a little away from the wall, is another sofa. Upstage of the french windows, a piano. On either side of the open doorway in the rear wall stand what-nots holding ornaments of terra cotta and majolica. Against the rear wall of the smaller room can be seen a sofa, a table, and a couple of chairs. Above this sofa hangs the portrait of a handsome old man in general's uniform. Above the table a lamp hangs from the ceiling, with a shade of opalescent, milky glass. All round the drawing room bunches of flowers stand in vases and glasses. More bunches lie on the tables. The floors of both rooms are covered with thick carpets. Morning light. The sun shines in through the french windows.

MISS JULIANA TESMAN, *wearing a hat and carrying a parasol, enters from the hall, followed by* BERTHA, *who is carrying a bunch of flowers wrapped in paper.* MISS TESMAN *is about sixty-five, of pleasant and kindly appearance. She is neatly but simply dressed in grey outdoor clothes.* BERTHA, *the maid, is rather simple and rustic-looking. She is getting on in years.*

MISS TESMAN. [*Stops just inside the door, listens, and says in a hushed voice*] No, bless my soul! They're not up yet.

BERTHA. [*Also in hushed tones*] What did I tell you, miss? The boat didn't get in till midnight. And when they did turn up—Jesus, miss, you should have seen all the things Madam made me unpack before she'd go to bed!

MISS TESMAN. Ah, well. Let them have a good lie in. But let's have some nice fresh air waiting for them when they do come down. [*Goes to the french windows and throws them wide open*]

BERTHA. [*Bewildered at the table, the bunch of flowers in her hand*] I'm blessed if there's a square inch left to put anything. I'll have to let it lie here, miss. [*Puts it on the piano*]

MISS TESMAN. Well, Bertha dear, so now you have a new mistress. Heaven knows it nearly broke my heart to have to part with you.

BERTHA. [*Snivels*] What about me, Miss Juju? How do you suppose I felt? After all the happy years I've spent with you and Miss Rena?

---

1. *French windows:* Door-sized windows through which people may pass, in this case opening to the outdoors.

MISS TESMAN. We must accept it bravely, Bertha. It was the only way. George needs you to take care of him. He could never manage without you. You've looked after him ever since he was a tiny boy.

BERTHA. Oh, but, Miss Juju, I can't help thinking about Miss Rena, lying there all helpless, poor dear. And that new girl! She'll never learn the proper way to handle an invalid.

MISS TESMAN. Oh, I'll manage to train her. I'll do most of the work myself, you know. You needn't worry about my poor sister, Bertha dear.

BERTHA. But Miss Juju, there's another thing. I'm frightened Madam may not find me suitable.

MISS TESMAN. Oh, nonsense, Bertha. There may be one or two little things to begin with——

BERTHA. She's a real lady. Wants everything just so.

MISS TESMAN. But of course she does! General Gabler's daughter! Think of what she was accustomed to when the General was alive. You remember how we used to see her out riding with her father? In that long black skirt? With the feather in her hat?

BERTHA. Oh, yes, miss. As if I could forget! But, Lord! I never dreamed I'd live to see a match between her and Master Georgie.

MISS TESMAN. Neither did I. By the way, Bertha, from now on you must stop calling him Master Georgie. You must say: Dr. Tesman.

BERTHA. Yes, Madam said something about that too. Last night —the moment they'd set foot inside the door. Is it true, then, miss?

MISS TESMAN. Indeed it is. Just imagine, Bertha, some foreigners have made him a doctor. It happened while they were away. I had no idea till he told me when they got off the boat.

BERTHA. Well, I suppose there's no limit to what he won't become. He's that clever. I never thought he'd go in for hospital work, though.

MISS TESMAN. No, he's not that kind of doctor. [*Nods impressively*] In any case, you may soon have to address him by an even grander title.

BERTHA. You don't say! What might that be, miss?

MISS TESMAN. [*Smiles*] Ah! If you only knew! [*Moved*] Dear God, if only poor dear Joachim could rise out of his grave and see what his little son has grown into! [*Looks round*] But Bertha, why have you done this? Taken the chintz covers off all the furniture!

BERTHA. Madam said I was to. Can't stand chintz covers on chairs, she said.

MISS TESMAN. But surely they're not going to use this room as a parlor?

BERTHA. So I gathered, miss. From what Madam said. He didn't say anything. The Doctor.

[GEORGE TESMAN *comes into the rear room, from the right,*

humming, with an open, empty travelling bag in his hand. He is about thirty-three, of medium height and youthful appearance, rather plump, with an open, round, contented face, and fair hair and beard. He wears spectacles, and is dressed in comfortable, indoor clothes.]

MISS TESMAN. Good morning! Good morning, George!

TESMAN. [*In open doorway*] Auntie Juju! Dear Auntie Juju! [*Comes forward and shakes her hand*] You've come all the way out here! And so early! What?

MISS TESMAN. Well, I had to make sure you'd settled in comfortably.

TESMAN. But you can't have had a proper night's sleep.

MISS TESMAN. Oh, never mind that.

TESMAN. We were so sorry we couldn't give you a lift. But you saw how it was—Hedda had so much luggage—and she insisted on having it all with her.

MISS TESMAN. Yes, I've never seen so much luggage.

BERTHA. [*To* TESMAN] Shall I go and ask Madam if there's anything I can lend her a hand with?

TESMAN. Er—thank you, Bertha; no, you needn't bother. She says if she wants you for anything she'll ring.

BERTHA. [*Over to right*] Oh. Very good.

TESMAN. Oh, Bertha—take this bag, will you?

BERTHA. [*Takes it.*] I'll put it in the attic.
[*Goes out into the hall*]

TESMAN. Just fancy, Auntie Juju, I filled that whole bag with notes for my book. You know, it's really incredible what I've managed to find rooting through those archives. By Jove! Wonderful old things no one even knew existed——

MISS TESMAN. I'm sure you didn't waste a single moment of your honeymoon, George dear.

TESMAN. No, I think I can truthfully claim that. But, Auntie Juju, do take your hat off. Here. Let me untie it for you. What?

MISS TESMAN. [*As he does so*] Oh dear, oh dear! It's just as if you were still living at home with us.

TESMAN. [*Turns the hat in his hand and looks at it*] I say! What a splendid new hat!

MISS TESMAN. I bought it for Hedda's sake.

TESMAN. For Hedda's sake? What?

MISS TESMAN. So that Hedda needn't be ashamed of me, in case we ever go for a walk together.

TESMAN. [*Pats her cheek*] You still think of everything, don't you, Auntie Juju? [*Puts the hat down on a chair by the table*] Come on, let's sit down here on the sofa. And have a little chat while we wait for Hedda.
[*They sit. She puts her parasol in the corner of the sofa.*]

MISS TESMAN. [*Clasps both his hands and looks at him*] Oh, George, it's so wonderful to have you back, and be able to see you with my own eyes again! Poor dear Joachim's own son!

TESMAN. What about me! It's wonderful for me to see you again, Auntie Juju. You've been a mother to me. And a father, too.

MISS TESMAN. You'll always keep a soft spot in your heart for your old aunties, won't you. George dear?

TESMAN. I suppose Auntie Rena's no better? What?

MISS TESMAN. Alas, no. I'm afraid she'll never get better, poor dear. She's lying there just as she has for all these years. Please God I may be allowed to keep her for a little longer. If I lost her I don't know what I'd do. Especially now I haven't you to look after.

TESMAN. [*Pats her on the back*] There, there, there!

MISS TESMAN. [*With a sudden change of mood*] Oh but George, fancy you being a married man! And to think it's you who've won Hedda Gabler! The beautiful Hedda Gabler! Fancy! She was always so surrounded by admirers.

TESMAN. [*Hums a little and smiles contentedly*] Yes, I suppose there are quite a few people in this town who wouldn't mind being in my shoes. What?

MISS TESMAN. And what a honeymoon! Five months! Nearly six.

TESMAN. Well, I've done a lot of work, you know. All those archives to go through. And I've had to read lots of books.

MISS TESMAN. Yes, dear, of course. [*Lowers her voice confidentially*] But tell me, George—haven't you any—any extra little piece of news to give me?

TESMAN. You mean, arising out of the honeymoon?

MISS TESMAN. Yes.

TESMAN. No, I don't think there's anything I didn't tell you in my letters. My doctorate, of course—but I told you about that last night, didn't I?

MISS TESMAN. Yes, yes, I didn't mean that kind of thing. I was just wondering—are you—are you expecting——?

TESMAN. Expecting what?

MISS TESMAN. Oh, come on George, I'm your old aunt!

TESMAN. Well actually—yes, I am expecting something.

MISS TESMAN. I knew it!

TESMAN. You'll be happy to hear that before very long I expect to become a professor.

MISS TESMAN. Professor?

TESMAN. I think I may say that the matter has been decided. But, Auntie Juju, you know about this.

MISS TESMAN. [*Gives a little laugh*] Yes, of course. I'd forgotten. [*Changes her tone*] But we were talking about your honeymoon. It must have cost a dreadful amount of money, George?

TESMAN. Oh well, you know, that big research grant I got helped a good deal.

MISS TESMAN. But how on earth did you manage to make it do for two?

TESMAN. Well, to tell the truth it was a bit tricky. What?

MISS TESMAN. Especially when one's traveling with a lady. A little bird tells me that makes things very much more expensive.

TESMAN. Well, yes, of course it does make things a little more expensive. But Hedda has to do things in style, Auntie Juju. I mean, she has to. Anything less grand wouldn't have suited her.

MISS TESMAN. No, no, I suppose not. A honeymoon abroad seems to be the vogue nowadays. But tell me, have you had time to look round the house?

TESMAN. You bet. I've been up since the crack of dawn.

MISS TESMAN. Well, what do you think of it?

TESMAN. Splendid. Absolutely splendid. I'm only wondering what we're going to do with those two empty rooms between that little one and Hedda's bedroom.

MISS TESMAN. [*Laughs slyly*] Ah, George dear, I'm sure you'll manage to find some use for them—in time.

TESMAN. Yes, of course, Auntie Juju, how stupid of me. You're thinking of my books. What?

MISS TESMAN. Yes, yes, dear boy. I was thinking of your books.

TESMAN. You know, I'm so happy for Hedda's sake that we've managed to get this house. Before we became engaged she often used to say this was the only house in town she felt she could really bear to live in. It used to belong to Mrs. Falk—you know, the Prime Minister's widow.

MISS TESMAN. Fancy that! And what a stroke of luck it happened to come into the market. Just as you'd left on your honeymoon.

TESMAN. Yes, Auntie Juju, we've certainly had all the luck with us. What?

MISS TESMAN. But, George dear, the expense! It's going to make a dreadful hole in your pocket, all this.

TESMAN. [*A little downcast*] Yes, I—I suppose it will, won't it?

MISS TESMAN. Oh, George, really!

TESMAN. How much do you think it'll cost? Roughly, I mean? What?

MISS TESMAN. I can't possibly say till I see the bills.

TESMAN. Well, luckily Judge Brack's managed to get it on very favorable terms. He wrote and told Hedda so.

MISS TESMAN. Don't you worry, George dear. Anyway I've stood security for all the furniture and carpets.

TESMAN. Security? But dear, sweet Auntie Juju, how could you possibly stand security?

MISS TESMAN. I've arranged a mortgage on our annuity.

TESMAN. [*Jumps up*] What? On your annuity? And—Auntie Rena's?

MISS TESMAN. Yes. Well, I couldn't think of any other way.

TESMAN. [*Stands in front of her*] Auntie Juju, have you gone completely out of your mind? That annuity's all you and Auntie Rena have.

MISS TESMAN. All right, there's no need to get so excited about it. It's a pure formality, you know. Judge Brack told me so. He was so kind as to arrange it all for me. A pure formality; those were his very words.

TESMAN. I dare say. All the same——

MISS TESMAN. Anyway, you'll have a salary of your own now. And, good heavens, even if we did have to fork out a little—tighten our belts for a week or two—why, we'd be happy to do so for your sake.

TESMAN. Oh, Auntie Juju! Will you never stop sacrificing yourself for me?

MISS TESMAN. [*Gets up and puts her hands on his shoulders*] What else have I to live for but to smooth your road a little, my dear boy? You've never had any mother or father to turn to. And now at last we've achieved our goal. I won't deny we've had our little difficulties now and then. But now, thank the good Lord, George dear, all your worries are past.

TESMAN. Yes, it's wonderful really how everything's gone just right for me.

MISS TESMAN. Yes! And the enemies who tried to bar your way have been struck down. They have been made to bite the dust. The man who was your most dangerous rival has had the mightiest fall. And now he's lying there in the pit he dug for himself, poor misguided creature.

TESMAN. Have you heard any news of Eilert? Since I went away?

MISS TESMAN. Only that he's said to have published a new book.

TESMAN. What! Eilert Loevborg? You mean—just recently? What?

MISS TESMAN. So they say. I don't imagine it can be of any value, do you? When your new book comes out, that'll be another story. What's it going to be about?

TESMAN. The domestic industries of Brabant[2] in the Middle Ages.

MISS TESMAN. Oh, George! The things you know about!

TESMAN. Mind you, it may be some time before I actually get down to writing it. I've made these very extensive notes, and I've got to file and index them first.

MISS TESMAN. Ah, yes! Making notes; filing and indexing; you've always been wonderful at that. Poor dear Joachim was just the same.

TESMAN. I'm looking forward so much to getting down to that. Especially now I've a home of my own to work in.

MISS TESMAN. And above all, now that you have the girl you set your heart on, George dear.

TESMAN. [*Embraces her*] Oh, yes, Auntie Juju, yes! Hedda's the loveliest thing of all! [*Looks towards the doorway*] I think I hear her coming. What?

> [HEDDA *enters the rear room from the left, and comes into the drawing room. She is a woman of twenty-nine. Distinguished, aristocratic face and figure. Her complexion is pale and opalescent. Her eyes are steel-grey, with an expression of cold, calm serenity. Her hair is of a handsome auburn color, but is not especially abundant. She is dressed in an elegant, somewhat loose-fitting morning gown.*]

---

2. *Brabant:* In the Middle Ages, a duchy located in parts of what are now Belgium and the Netherlands.

MISS TESMAN. [*Goes to greet her*] Good morning, Hedda dear! Good morning!

HEDDA. [*Holds out her hand*] Good morning, dear Miss Tesman. What an early hour to call. So kind of you.

MISS TESMAN. [*Seems somewhat embarrassed*] And has the young bride slept well in her new home?

HEDDA. Oh—thank you, yes. Passably well.

TESMAN. [*Laughs*] Passably. I say, Hedda, that's good! When I jumped out of bed, you were sleeping like a top.

HEDDA. Yes. Fortunately. One has to accustom oneself to anything new, Miss Tesman. It takes time. [*Looks left*] Oh, that maid's left the french windows open. This room's flooded with sun.

MISS TESMAN. [*Goes towards the windows*] Oh—let me close them.

HEDDA. No, no, don't do that. Tesman dear, draw the curtains. This light's blinding me.

TESMAN. [*At the windows*] Yes, yes, dear. There, Hedda, now you've got shade and fresh air.

HEDDA. This room needs fresh air. All these flowers——But my dear Miss Tesman, won't you take a seat?

MISS TESMAN. No, really not, thank you. I just wanted to make sure you have everything you need. I must see about getting back home. My poor dear sister will be waiting for me.

TESMAN. Be sure to give her my love, won't you? Tell her I'll run over and see her later today.

MISS TESMAN. Oh yes, I'll tell her that. Oh, George——[*Fumbles in the pocket of her skirt*] I almost forgot. I've brought something for you.

TESMAN. What's that, Auntie Juju? What?

MISS TESMAN. [*Pulls out a flat package wrapped in newspaper and gives it to him*] Open and see, dear boy.

TESMAN. [*Opens the package*] Good heavens! Auntie Juju, you've kept them! Hedda, this is really very touching. What?

HEDDA. [*By the what-nots, on the right*] What is it, Tesman?

TESMAN. My old shoes! My slippers, Hedda!

HEDDA. Oh, them. I remember you kept talking about them on our honeymoon.

TESMAN. Yes, I missed them dreadfully. [*Goes over to her*] Here, Hedda, take a look.

HEDDA. [*Goes away towards the stove*] Thanks, I won't bother.

TESMAN. [*Follows her*] Fancy, Hedda, Auntie Rena's embroidered them for me. Despite her being so ill. Oh, you can't imagine what memories they have for me.

HEDDA. [*By the table*] Not for me.

MISS TESMAN. No, Hedda's right there, George.

TESMAN. Yes, but I thought since she's one of the family now——

HEDDA. [*Interrupts*] Tesman, we really can't go on keeping this maid.

MISS TESMAN. Not keep Bertha?

TESMAN. What makes you say that, dear? What?

HEDDA. [*Points*] Look at that! She's left her old hat lying on the chair.

TESMAN. [*Appalled, drops his slippers on the floor*] But, Hedda——!

HEDDA. Suppose someone came in and saw it?

TESMAN. But Hedda—that's Auntie Juju's hat.

HEDDA. Oh?

MISS TESMAN. [*Picks up the hat*] Indeed it's mine. And it doesn't happen to be old, Hedda dear.

HEDDA. I didn't look at it very closely, Miss Tesman.

MISS TESMAN. [*Tying on the hat*] As a matter of fact, it's the first time I've worn it. As the good Lord is my witness.

TESMAN. It's very pretty, too. Really smart.

MISS TESMAN. Oh, I'm afraid it's nothing much really. [*Looks round*] My parasol? Ah, here it is. [*Takes it*] This is mine, too. [*Murmurs*] Not Bertha's.

TESMAN. A new hat and a new parasol! I say, Hedda, fancy that!

HEDDA. Very pretty and charming.

TESMAN. Yes, isn't it? What? But Auntie Juju, take a good look at Hedda before you go. Isn't she pretty and charming?

MISS TESMAN. Dear boy, there's nothing new in that. Hedda's been a beauty ever since the day she was born.

    [*Nods and goes right.*]

TESMAN. [*Follows her*] Yes, but have you noticed how strong and healthy she's looking? And how she's filled out since we went away?

MISS TESMAN. [*Stops and turns*] Filled out?

HEDDA. [*Walks across the room*] Oh, can't we forget it?

TESMAN. Yes, Auntie Juju—you can't see it so clearly with that dress on. But I've good reason to know——

HEDDA. [*By the french windows, impatiently*] You haven't good reason to know anything.

TESMAN. It must have been the mountain air up there in the Tyrol——

HEDDA. [*Curtly, interrupts him*] I'm exactly the same as when I went away.

TESMAN. You keep on saying so. But you're not. I'm right, aren't I, Auntie Juju?

MISS TESMAN. [*Has folded her hands and is gazing at her*] She's beautiful—beautiful. Hedda is beautiful. [*Goes over to* HEDDA, *takes her head between her hands, draws it down and kisses her hair*] God bless and keep you, Hedda Tesman. For George's sake.

HEDDA. [*Frees herself politely*] Oh—let me go, please.

MISS TESMAN. [*Quietly, emotionally*] I shall come see you both every day.

TESMAN. Yes, Auntie Juju, please do. What?

MISS TESMAN. Good-bye! Good-bye!

    [*She goes out into the hall.* TESMAN *follows her. The door remains open.* TESMAN *is heard sending his love to* AUNT

RENA *and thanking* MISS TESMAN *for his slippers. Meanwhile* HEDDA *walks up and down the room raising her arms and clenching her fists as though in desperation. Then she throws aside the curtains from the french windows and stands there, looking out. A few moments later,* TESMAN *returns and closes the door behind him.*]

TESMAN. [*Picks up his slippers from the floor*] What are you looking at, Hedda?

HEDDA. [*Calm and controlled again*] Only the leaves. They're so golden. And withered.

TESMAN. [*Wraps up the slippers and lays them on the table*] Well, we're in September now.

HEDDA. [*Restless again*] Yes. We're already into September.

TESMAN. Auntie Juju was behaving rather oddly, I thought, didn't you? Almost as though she was in church or something. I wonder what came over her. Any idea?

HEDDA. I hardly know her. Does she often act like that?

TESMAN. Not to the extent she did today.

HEDDA. [*Goes away from the french windows*] Do you think she was hurt by what I said about the hat?

TESMAN. Oh, I don't think so. A little at first, perhaps——

HEDDA. But what a thing to do, throw her hat down in someone's drawing room. People don't do such things.

TESMAN. I'm sure Auntie Juju doesn't do it very often.

HEDDA. Oh well, I'll make it up with her.

TESMAN. Oh Hedda, would you?

HEDDA. When you see them this afternoon invite her to come out here this evening.

TESMAN. You bet I will! I say, there's another thing which would please her enormously.

HEDDA. Oh?

TESMAN. If you could bring yourself to call her Auntie Juju. For my sake, Hedda? What?

HEDDA. Oh no, really Tesman, you mustn't ask me to do that. I've told you so once before. I'll try to call her Aunt Juliana. That's as far as I'll go.

TESMAN. [*After a moment*] I say, Hedda, is anything wrong? What?

HEDDA. I'm just looking at my old piano. It doesn't really go with all this.

TESMAN. As soon as I start getting my salary we'll see about changing it.

HEDDA. No, no, don't let's change it. I don't want to part with it. We can move it into that little room and get another one to put in here.

TESMAN. [*A little downcast*] Yes, we—might do that.

HEDDA. [*Picks up the bunch of flowers from the piano*] These flowers weren't here when we arrived last night.

TESMAN. I expect Auntie Juju brought them.

HEDDA. Here's a card. [*Takes it out and reads*] "Will come back later today." Guess who it's from?

TESMAN. No idea. Who? What?

HEDDA. It says: "Mrs. Elvsted."

TESMAN. No, really? Mrs. Elvsted! She used to be Miss Rysing, didn't she?

HEDDA. Yes. She was the one with that irritating hair she was always showing off. I hear she used to be an old flame of yours.

TESMAN. [*Laughs*] That didn't last long. Anyway, that was before I got to know you, Hedda. By Jove, fancy her being in town!

HEDDA. Strange she should call. I only knew her at school.

TESMAN. Yes, I haven't seen her for—oh, heaven knows how long. I don't know how she manages to stick it out up there in the north. What?

HEDDA. [*Thinks for a moment, then says suddenly*] Tell me, Tesman, doesn't he live somewhere up in those parts? You know—Eilert Loevborg?

TESMAN. Yes, that's right. So he does.

[BERTHA *enters from the hall.*]

BERTHA. She's here again, madam. The lady who came and left the flowers. [*Points*] The ones you're holding.

HEDDA. Oh, is she? Well, show her in.

[BERTHA *opens the door for* MRS. ELVSTED *and goes out.* MRS. ELVSTED *is a delicately built woman with gentle, attractive features. Her eyes are light blue, large, and somewhat prominent, with a frightened, questioning expression. Her hair is extremely fair, almost flaxen, and is exceptionally wavy and abundant. She is two or three years younger than* HEDDA. *She is wearing a dark visiting dress, in good taste but not quite in the latest fashion.*]

HEDDA. [*Goes cordially to greet her*] Dear Mrs. Elvsted, good morning. How delightful to see you again after all this time.

MRS ELVSTED. [*Nervously, trying to control herself*] Yes, it's many years since we met.

TESMAN. And since *we* met. What?

HEDDA. Thank you for your lovely flowers.

MRS. ELVSTED. Oh, please—I wanted to come yesterday afternoon. But they told me you were away——

TESMAN. You've only just arrived in town, then? What?

MRS. ELVSTED. I got here yesterday, around midday. Oh, I became almost desperate when I heard you weren't here.

HEDDA. Desperate? Why?

TESMAN. My dear Mrs. Rysing—Elvsted——

HEDDA. There's nothing wrong, I hope?

MRS ELVSTED. Yes, there is. And I don't know anyone else here whom I can turn to.

HEDDA. [*Puts the flowers down on the table*] Come and sit with me on the sofa——

MRS. ELVSTED. Oh, I feel too restless to sit down.

HEDDA. You **must**. Come along, now.

[*She pulls* MRS. ELVSTED *down on to the sofa and sits beside her.*]

TESMAN. Well? Tell us, Mrs.—er——

HEDDA. Has something happened at home?

MRS. ELVSTED. Yes—that is, yes and no. Oh, I do hope you won't misunderstand me——

HEDDA. Then you'd better tell us the whole story, Mrs. Elvsted.

TESMAN. That's why you've come. What?

MRS. ELVSTED. Yes—yes, it is. Well, then—in case you don't already know—Eilert Loevborg is in town.

HEDDA. Loevborg here?

TESMAN. Eilert back in town? By Jove, Hedda, did you hear that?

HEDDA. Yes, of course I heard.

MRS. ELVSTED. He's been here a week. A whole week! In this city. Alone. With all those dreadful people——

HEDDA. But my dear Mrs. Elvsted, what concern is he of yours?

MRS. ELVSTED. [*Gives her a frightened look and says quickly*] He's been tutoring the children.

HEDDA. Your children?

MRS. ELVSTED. My husband's. I have none.

HEDDA. Oh, you mean your stepchildren.

MRS. ELVSTED. Yes.

TESMAN. [*Gropingly*] But was he sufficiently—I don't know how to put it—sufficiently regular in his habits to be suited to such a post? What?

MRS. ELVSTED. For the past two to three years he has been living irreproachably.

TESMAN. You don't say! By Jove, Hedda, hear that?

HEDDA. I hear.

MRS ELVSTED. Quite irreproachably, I assure you. In every respect. All the same—in this big city—with money in his pockets—I'm so dreadfully frightened something may happen to him.

TESMAN. But why didn't he stay up there with you and your husband?

MRS. ELVSTED. Once his book had come out, he became restless.

TESMAN. Oh, yes—Auntie Juju said he'd brought out a new book.

MRS. ELVSTED. Yes, a big new book about the history of civilization. A kind of general survey. It came out a fortnight ago. Everyone's been buying it and reading it—it's created a tremendous stir——

TESMAN. Has it really? It must be something he's dug up, then.

MRS. ELVSTED. You mean from the old days?

TESMAN. Yes.

MRS. ELVSTED. No, he's written it all since he came to live with us.

TESMAN. Well, that's splendid news, Hedda. Fancy that!

MRS. ELVSTED. Oh, yes! If only he can go on like this!

HEDDA. Have you met him since you came here?

MRS. ELVSTED. No, not yet. I had such dreadful difficulty finding his address. But this morning I managed to track him down at last.

HEDDA. [*Looks searchingly at her*] I must say I find it a little strange that your husband—hm——

MRS. ELVSTED. [*Starts nervously*] My husband! What do you mean?

HEDDA. That he should send you all the way here on an errand of this kind. I'm surprised he didn't come himself to keep an eye on his friend.

MRS. ELVSTED. Oh, no, no—my husband hasn't the time. Besides, I—er—wanted to do some shopping here.

HEDDA. [*With a slight smile*] Ah. Well, that's different.

MRS. ELVSTED. [*Gets up quickly, restlessly*] Please, Mr. Tesman, I beg you—be kind to Eilert Loevborg if he comes here. I'm sure he will. I mean, you used to be such good friends in the old days. And you're both studying the same subject, as far as I can understand. You're in the same field, aren't you?

TESMAN. Well, we used to be, anyway.

MRS. ELVSTED. Yes—so I beg you earnestly, do please, please, keep an eye on him. Oh, Mr. Tesman, do promise me you will.

TESMAN. I shall be only too happy to do so, Mrs. Rysing.

HEDDA. Elvsted.

TESMAN. I'll do everything for Eilert that lies in my power. You can rely on that.

MRS. ELVSTED. Oh, how good and kind you are! [*Presses his hands*] Thank you, thank you, thank you. [*Frightened*] My husband's so fond of him, you see.

HEDDA. [*Gets up*] You'd better send him a note, Tesman. He may not come to you of his own accord.

TESMAN. Yes, that'd probably be the best plan, Hedda. What?

HEDDA. The sooner the better. Why not do it now?

MRS. ELVSTED. [*Pleadingly*] Oh yes, if only you would!

TESMAN. I'll do it this very moment. Do you have his address, Mrs.—er—Elvsted?

MRS. ELVSTED. Yes.

[*Takes a small piece of paper from her pocket and gives it to him.*]

TESMAN. Good, good. Right, well I'll go inside and——[*Looks round*] Where are my slippers? Oh yes, here.

[*Picks up the package and is about to go*]

HEDDA. Try to sound friendly. Make it a nice long letter.

TESMAN. Right, I will.

MRS. ELVSTED. Please don't say anything about my having seen you.

TESMAN. Good heavens no, of course not. What?

[*Goes out through the rear room to the right*]

HEDDA. [*Goes over to* MRS. ELVSTED, *smiles, and says softly*] Well! Now we've killed two birds with one stone.

MRS. ELVSTED. What do you mean?

HEDDA. Didn't you realize I wanted to get him out of the room?

MRS. ELVSTED. So that he could write the letter?

HEDDA. And so that I could talk to you alone.

MRS. ELVSTED. [*Confused*] About this?

HEDDA. Yes, about this.

MRS. ELVSTED. [*In alarm*] But there's nothing more to tell, Mrs. Tesman. Really there isn't.

HEDDA. Oh, yes there is. There's a lot more. I can see that. Come along, let's sit down and have a little chat.

[*She pushes* MRS. ELVSTED *down into the armchair by the stove and seats herself on one of the footstools.*]

MRS. ELVSTED. [*Looks anxiously at her watch*] Really, Mrs. Tesman, I think I ought to be going now.

HEDDA. There's no hurry. Well? How are things at home?

MRS. ELVSTED. I'd rather not speak about that.

HEDDA. But my dear, you can tell me. Good heavens, we were at school together.

MRS. ELVSTED. Yes, but you were a year senior to me. Oh, I used to be terribly frightened of you in those days.

HEDDA. Frightened of me?

MRS. ELVSTED. Yes, terribly frightened. Whenever you met me on the staircase you used to pull my hair.

HEDDA. No, did I?

MRS. ELVSTED. Yes. And once you said you'd burn it all off.

HEDDA. Oh, that was only in fun.

MRS. ELVSTED. Yes, but I was so silly in those days. And then afterwards—I mean, we've drifted so far apart. Our backgrounds were so different.

HEDDA. Well, now we must try to drift together again. Now listen. When we were at school we used to call each other by our Christian names——

MRS. ELVSTED. No, I'm sure you're mistaken.

HEDDA. I'm sure I'm not. I remember it quite clearly. Let's tell each other our secrets, as we used to in the old days. [*Moves closer on her footstool*] There, now. [*Kisses her on the cheek*] You must call me Hedda.

MRS. ELVSTED. [*Squeezes her hands and pats them*] Oh, you're so kind. I'm not used to people being so nice to me.

HEDDA. Now, now, now. And I shall call you Tora, the way I used to.

MRS. ELVSTED. My name is Thea.

HEDDA. Yes, of course. Of course. I meant Thea. [*Looks at her sympathetically*] So you're not used to kindness, Thea? In your own home?

MRS. ELVSTED. Oh, if only I had a home! But I haven't. I've never had one.

HEDDA. [*Looks at her for a moment*] I thought that was it.

MRS. ELVSTED. [*Stares blankly and helplessly*] Yes—yes—yes.

HEDDA. I can't remember exactly now, but didn't you first go to Mr. Elvsted as a housekeeper?

MRS. ELVSTED. Governess, actually. But his wife—at the time, I mean—she was an invalid, and had to spend most of her time in bed. So I had to look after the house too.

HEDDA. But in the end, you became mistress of the house.

MRS. ELVSTED. [*Sadly*] Yes, I did.

HEDDA. Let me see. Roughly how long ago was that?

MRS. ELVSTED. When I got married, you mean?

HEDDA. Yes.

MRS. ELVSTED. About five years.

HEDDA. Yes; it must be about that.

MRS. ELVSTED. Oh, those five years! Especially the last two or three. Oh, Mrs. Tesman, if you only knew——

HEDDA. [*Slaps her hand gently*] Mrs. Tesman? Oh, Thea!

MRS. ELVSTED. I'm sorry, I'll try to remember. Yes—if you had any idea——

HEDDA. [*Casually*] Eilert Loevborg's been up there too, for about three years, hasn't he?

MRS. ELVSTED. [*Looks at her uncertainly*] Eilert Loevborg? Yes, he has.

HEDDA. Did you know him before? When you were here?

MRS. ELVSTED. No, not really. That is—I knew him by name, of course.

HEDDA. But up there, he used to visit you?

MRS. ELVSTED. Yes, he used to come and see us every day. To give the children lessons. I found I couldn't do that as well as manage the house.

HEDDA. I'm sure you couldn't. And your husband——? I suppose being a magistrate he has to be away from home a good deal?

MRS. ELVSTED. Yes. You see, Mrs.——you see, Hedda, he has to cover the whole district.

HEDDA. [*Leans against the arm of* MRS. ELVSTED's *chair*] Poor, pretty little Thea! Now you must tell me the whole story. From beginning to end.

MRS. ELVSTED. Well—what do you want to know?

HEDDA. What kind of a man is your husband, Thea? I mean, as a person. Is he kind to you?

MRS. ELVSTED. [*Evasively*] I'm sure he does his best to be.

HEDDA. I only wonder if he isn't too old for you. There's more than twenty years between you, isn't there?

MRS. ELVSTED. [*Irritably*] Yes, there's that too. Oh, there are so many things. We're different in every way. We've nothing in common. Nothing whatever.

HEDDA. But he loves you, surely? In his own way?

MRS. ELVSTED. Oh, I don't know. I think he just finds me useful. And then I don't cost much to keep. I'm cheap.

HEDDA. Now you're being stupid.

MRS. ELVSTED. [*Shakes her head*] It can't be any different. With him. He doesn't love anyone except himself. And perhaps the children—a little.

HEDDA. He must be fond of Eilert Loevborg, Thea.

MRS. ELVSTED. [*Looks at her*] Eilert Loevborg? What makes you think that?

HEDDA. Well, if he sends you all the way down here to look for him——[*Smiles almost imperceptibly*] Besides, you said so yourself to Tesman.

MRS. ELVSTED. [*With a nervous twitch*] Did I? Oh yes, I suppose I did. [*Impulsively, but keeping her voice low*] Well, I might as well tell you the whole story. It's bound to come out sooner or later.

HEDDA. But my dear Thea——?

MRS. ELVSTED. My husband had no idea I was coming here.

HEDDA. What? Your husband didn't know?

MRS. ELVSTED. No, of course not. As a matter of fact, he wasn't even there. He was away at the assizes. Oh, I couldn't stand it any longer, Hedda! I just couldn't. I'd be so dreadfully lonely up there now.

HEDDA. Go on.

MRS. ELVSTED. So I packed a few things. Secretly. And went.

HEDDA. Without telling anyone?

MRS. ELVSTED. Yes. I caught the train and came straight here.

HEDDA. But my dear Thea! How brave of you!

MRS. ELVSTED. [*Gets up and walks across the room*] Well, what else could I do?

HEDDA. But what do you suppose your husband will say when you get back?

MRS. ELVSTED. [*By the table, looks at her*] Back there? To him?

HEDDA. Yes. Surely——?

MRS. ELVSTED. I shall never go back to him.

HEDDA. [*Gets up and goes closer*] You mean you've left your home for good?

MRS. ELVSTED. Yes. I didn't see what else I could do.

HEDDA. But to do it so openly!

MRS. ELVSTED. Oh, it's no use trying to keep a thing like that secret.

HEDDA. But what do you suppose people will say?

MRS. ELVSTED. They can say what they like. [*Sits sadly, wearily on the sofa*] I had to do it.

HEDDA. [*After a short silence*] What do you intend to do now? How are you going to live?

MRS. ELVSTED. I don't know. I only know that I must live wherever Eilert Loevborg is. If I am to go on living.

HEDDA. [*Moves a chair from the table, sits on it near* MRS. ELVSTED *and strokes her hands*] Tell me, Thea, how did this—friendship between you and Eilert Loevborg begin?

MRS. ELVSTED. Oh, it came about gradually. I developed a kind of—power over him.

HEDDA. Oh?

MRS. ELVSTED. He gave up his old habits. Not because I asked him to. I'd never have dared to do that. I suppose he just noticed I didn't like that kind of thing. So he gave it up.

HEDDA. [*Hides a smile*] So you've made a new man of him. Clever little Thea!

MRS. ELVSTED. Yes—anyway, he says I have. And he's made a—sort of—real person of me. Taught me to think—and to understand all kinds of things.

HEDDA. Did he give you lessons too?

MRS. ELVSTED. Not exactly lessons. But he talked to me. About—oh, you've no idea—so many things! And then he let me work with him. Oh, it was wonderful. I was so happy to be allowed to help him.

HEDDA. Did he allow you to help him!

MRS. ELVSTED. Yes. Whenever he wrote anything we always—did it together.

HEDDA. Like good pals?

MRS. ELVSTED. [*Eagerly*] Pals! Yes—why, Hedda, that's exactly the word he used! Oh, I ought to feel so happy. But I can't. I don't know if it will last.

HEDDA. You don't seem very sure of him.

MRS. ELVSTED. [*Sadly*] Something stands between Eilert Loevborg and me. The shadow of another woman.

HEDDA. Who can that be?

MRS. ELVSTED. I don't know. Someone he used to be friendly with in—in the old days. Someone he's never been able to forget.

HEDDA. What has he told you about her?

MRS. ELVSTED. Oh, he only mentioned her once, casually.

HEDDA. Well! What did he say?

MRS. ELVSTED. He said when he left her she tried to shoot him with a pistol.

HEDDA. [*Cold, controlled*] What nonsense. People don't do such things. The kind of people we know.

MRS. ELVSTED. No. I think it must have been that red-haired singer he used to——

HEDDA. Ah yes, very probably.

MRS. ELVSTED. I remember they used to say she always carried a loaded pistol.

HEDDA. Well then, it must be her.

MRS. ELVSTED. But Hedda, I hear she's come back, and is living here. Oh, I'm so desperate——!

HEDDA. [*Glances toward the rear room*] Ssh! Tesman's coming. [*Gets up and whispers*] Thea, we mustn't breathe a word about this to anyone.

MRS. ELVSTED. [*Jumps up*] Oh, no, no! Please don't!

[GEORGE TESMAN *appears from the right in the rear room with a letter in his hand, and comes into the drawing room.*]

TESMAN. Well, here's my little epistle all signed and sealed.

HEDDA. Good. I think Mrs. Elvsted wants to go now. Wait a moment—I'll see you as far as the garden gate.

TESMAN. Er—Hedda, do you think Bertha could deal with this?

HEDDA. [*Takes the letter*] I'll give her instructions.

[BERTHA *enters from the hall.*]

BERTHA. Judge Brack is here and asks if he may pay his respects to Madam and the Doctor.

HEDDA. Yes, ask him to be so good as to come in. And—wait a moment—drop this letter in the post box.

BERTHA. [*Takes the letter*] Very good, madam.

[*She opens the door for* JUDGE BRACK, *and goes out.* JUDGE BRACK *is forty-five; rather short, but well-built, and elastic in his movements. He has a roundish face with an aristocratic profile. His hair, cut short, is still almost black, and is carefully barbered. Eyes lively and humorous. Thick eyebrows. His moustache is also thick, and is trimmed square at the ends. He is wearing outdoor clothes which are elegant but a little too youthful for him. He has a monocle in one eye; now and then he lets it drop.*]

BRACK. [*Hat in hand, bows*] May one presume to call so early?

HEDDA. One may presume.

TESMAN. [*Shakes his hand*] You're welcome here any time. Judge Brack—Mrs. Rysing.

[HEDDA *sighs.*]

BRACK. [*Bows*] Ah—charmed——

HEDDA. [*Looks at him and laughs*] What fun to be able to see you by daylight for once, Judge.

BRACK. Do I look—different?

HEDDA. Yes. A little younger, I think.

BRACK. Obliged.

TESMAN. Well, what do you think of Hedda? What? Doesn't she look well? Hasn't she filled out——?

HEDDA. Oh, do stop it. You ought to be thanking Judge Brack for all the inconvenience he's put himself to——

BRACK. Nonsense, it was a pleasure——

HEDDA. You're a loyal friend. But my other friend is pining to get away. Au revoir, Judge. I won't be a minute.

[*Mutual salutations.* MRS. ELVSTED *and* HEDDA *go out through the hall.*]

BRACK. Well, is your wife satisfied with everything?

TESMAN. Yes, we can't thank you enough. That is—we may have to shift one or two things around, she tells me. And we're short of one or two little items we'll have to purchase.

BRACK. Oh? Really?

TESMAN. But you musn't worry your head about that. Hedda says she'll get what's needed. I say, why don't we sit down? What?

BRACK. Thanks, just for a moment. [*Sits at the table*] There's something I'd like to talk to you about, my dear Tesman.

TESMAN. Oh? Ah yes, of course. [*Sits*] After the feast comes the reckoning. What?

BRACK. Oh, never mind about the financial side—there's no hurry about that. Though I could wish we'd arranged things a little less palatially.

TESMAN. Good heavens, that'd never have done. Think of Hedda, my dear chap. You know her. I couldn't possibly ask her to live like a suburban housewife.

BRACK. No, no—that's just the problem.

TESMAN. Anyway, it can't be long now before my nomination[3]

3. *Nomination:* For the professorship. Professors at European universities were less numerous and more socially promi- nent than their contemporary American counterparts.

comes through.

BRACK. Well, you know, these things often take time.

TESMAN. Have you heard any more news? What?

BRACK. Nothing definite. [*Changing the subject*] Oh, by the way, I have one piece of news for you.

TESMAN. What?

BRACK. Your old friend Eilert Loevborg is back in town.

TESMAN. I know that already.

BRACK. Oh? How did you hear that?

TESMAN. She told me. That lady who went out with Hedda.

BRACK. I see. What was her name? I didn't catch it.

TESMAN. Mrs. Elvsted.

BRACK. Oh, the magistrate's wife. Yes, Loevborg's been living up near them, hasn't he?

TESMAN. I'm delighted to hear he's become a decent human being again.

BRACK. Yes, so they say.

TESMAN. I gather he's published a new book, too. What?

BRACK. Indeed he has.

TESMAN. I hear it's created rather a stir.

BRACK. Quite an unusual stir.

TESMAN. I say, isn't that splendid news! He's such a gifted chap— and I was afraid he'd gone to the dogs for good.

BRACK. Most people thought he had.

TESMAN. But I can't think what he'll do now. How on earth will he manage to make ends meet? What?

[*As he speaks his last words,* HEDDA *enters from the hall.*]

HEDDA. [*To* BRACK, *laughs slightly scornfully*] Tesman is always worrying about making ends meet.

TESMAN. We were talking about poor Eilert Loevborg, Hedda dear.

HEDDA. [*Gives him a quick look*] Oh, were you? [*Sits in the arm-chair by the stove and asks casually*] Is he in trouble?

TESMAN. Well, he must have run through his inheritance long ago by now. And he can't write a new book every year. What? So I'm wondering what's going to become of him.

BRACK. I may be able to enlighten you there.

TESMAN. Oh?

BRACK. You mustn't forget he has relatives who wield a good deal of influence.

TESMAN. Relatives? Oh, they've quite washed their hands of him, I'm afraid.

BRACK. They used to regard him as the hope of the family.

TESMAN. Used to, yes. But he's put an end to that.

HEDDA. Who knows? [*With a little smile*] I hear the Elvsteds have made a new man of him.

BRACK. And then this book he's just published——

TESMAN. Well, let's hope they find something for him. I've just written him a note. Oh, by the way, Hedda, I asked him to come over and see us this evening.

BRACK. But my dear chap, you're coming to me this evening. My bachelor party.[4] You promised me last night when I met you at the boat.

HEDDA. Had you forgotten, Tesman?

TESMAN. Good heavens, yes, I'd quite forgotten.

BRACK. Anyway, you can be quite sure he won't turn up here.

TESMAN. Why do you think that? What?

BRACK. [*A little unwillingly, gets up and rests his hands on the back of his chair*] My dear Tesman—and you, too, Mrs. Tesman—there's something I feel you ought to know.

TESMAN. Concerning Eilert?

BRACK. Concerning him and you.

TESMAN. Well, my dear Judge, tell us, please!

BRACK. You must be prepared for your nomination not to come through quite as quickly as you hope and expect.

TESMAN. [*Jumps up uneasily*] Is anything wrong? What?

BRACK. There's a possibility that the appointment may be decided by competition——

TESMAN. Competition! By Jove, Hedda, fancy that!

HEDDA. [*Leans further back in her chair*] Ah! How interesting!

TESMAN. But who else——? I say, you don't mean——?

BRACK. Exactly. By competition with Eilert Loevborg.

TESMAN. [*Clasps his hands in alarm*] No, no, but this is inconceivable! It's absolutely impossible! What?

BRACK. Hm. We may find it'll happen, all the same.

TESMAN. No, but—Judge Brack, they couldn't be so inconsiderate toward me! [*Waves his arms*] I mean, by Jove, I—I'm a married man! It was on the strength of this that Hedda and I *got* married! We ran up some pretty hefty debts. And borrowed money from Auntie Juju! I mean, good heavens, they practically promised me the appointment. What?

BRACK. Well, well, I'm sure you'll get it. But you'll have to go through a competition.

HEDDA. [*Motionless in her armchair*] How exciting, Tesman. It'll be a kind of duel, by Jove.

TESMAN. My dear Hedda, how can you take it so lightly?

HEDDA. [*as before*] I'm not. I can't wait to see who's going to win.

BRACK. In any case, Mrs. Tesman, it's best you should know how things stand. I mean before you commit yourself to these little items I hear you're threatening to purchase.

HEDDA. I can't allow this to alter my plans.

BRACK. Indeed? Well, that's your business. Good-bye. [*To* TESMAN] I'll come and collect you on the way home from my afternoon walk.

TESMAN. Oh, yes, yes. I'm sorry, I'm all upside down just now.

HEDDA. [*Lying in her chair, holds out her hand*] Good-bye, Judge. See you this afternoon.

BRACK. Thank you. Good-bye, good-bye.

---

4. *Bachelor party:* A party for men only, whether single or married.

TESMAN. [*Sees him to the door*] Good-bye, my dear Judge. You will excuse me, won't you?

[JUDGE BRACK *goes out through the hall.*]

TESMAN. [*Pacing up and down*] Oh, Hedda! One oughtn't to go plunging off on wild adventures. What?

HEDDA. [*Looks at him and smiles*] Like you're doing?

TESMAN. Yes. I mean, there's no denying it, it was a pretty big adventure to go off and get married and set up house merely on expectation.

HEDDA. Perhaps you're right.

TESMAN. Well, anyway, we have our home, Hedda. By Jove, yes. The home we dreamed of. And set our hearts on. What?

HEDDA. [*Gets up slowly, wearily*] You agreed that we should enter society. And keep open house. That was the bargain.

TESMAN. Yes. Good heavens, I was looking forward to it all so much. To seeing you play hostess to a select circle! By Jove! What? Ah, well, for the time being we shall have to make do with each other's company, Hedda. Perhaps have Auntie Juju in now and then. Oh dear, this wasn't at all what you had in mind——

HEDDA. I won't be able to have a liveried footman.[5] For a start.

TESMAN. Oh no, we couldn't possibly afford a footman.

HEDDA. And that thoroughbred horse you promised me——

TESMAN. [*Fearfully*] Thoroughbred horse!

HEDDA. I mustn't even think of that now.

TESMAN. Heaven forbid!

HEDDA. [*Walks across the room*] Ah, well. I still have one thing left to amuse myself with.

TESMAN. [*Joyfully*] Thank goodness for that. What's that, Hedda? What?

HEDDA. [*In the open doorway, looks at him with concealed scorn*] My pistols, George darling.

TESMAN. [*Alarmed*] Pistols!

HEDDA. [*Her eyes cold*] General Gabler's pistols.

[*She goes into the rear room and disappears.*]

TESMAN. [*Runs to the doorway and calls after her*] For heaven's sake, Hedda dear, don't touch those things. They're dangerous. Hedda—please—for my sake! What?

Act II

SCENE—*The same as in Act I except that the piano has been removed and an elegant little writing table, with a bookcase, stands in its place. By the sofa on the left a smaller table has been placed. Most of the flowers have been removed.* MRS. ELVSTED'S *bouquet stands on the larger table, downstage. It is afternoon.*

HEDDA, *dressed to receive callers, is alone in the room. She is*

5. *Liveried footman*: A uniformed manservant.

standing by the open french windows, loading a revolver. The pair to it is lying in an open pistol case on the writing table.

HEDDA. [*Looks down into the garden and calls*] Good afternoon, Judge.

BRACK. [*In the distance, below*] Afternoon, Mrs. Tesman.

HEDDA. [*Raises the pistol and takes aim*] I'm going to shoot you, Judge Brack.

BRACK. [*Shouts from below*] No no, no! Don't aim that thing at me!

HEDDA. This'll teach you to enter houses by the back door. [*Fires*]

BRACK. [*Below*] Have you gone completely out of your mind?

HEDDA. Oh dear! Did I hit you?

BRACK. [*Still outside*] Stop playing these silly tricks.

HEDDA. All right, Judge. Come along in.

[JUDGE BRACK, *dressed for a bachelor party, enters through the french windows. He has a light overcoat on his arm.*]

BRACK. For God's sake! Haven't you stopped fooling around with those things yet? What are you trying to hit?

HEDDA. Oh, I was just shooting at the sky.

BRACK. [*Takes the pistol gently from her hand*] By your leave, ma'am. [*Looks at it*] Ah, yes—I know this old friend well. [*Looks around*] Where's the case? Oh, yes. [*Puts the pistol in the case and closes it*] That's enough of that little game for today.

HEDDA. Well, what on earth *am* I to do?

BRACK. You haven't had any visitors?

HEDDA. [*Closes the french windows*] Not one. I suppose the best people are all still in the country.

BRACK. Your husband isn't home yet?

HEDDA. [*Locks the pistol case away in a drawer of the writing table*] No. The moment he'd finished eating he ran off to his aunties. He wasn't expecting you so early.

BRACK. Ah, why didn't I think of that? How stupid of me.

HEDDA. [*Turns her head and looks at him*] Why stupid?

BRACK. I'd have come a little sooner.

HEDDA. [*Walks across the room*] There'd have been no one to receive you. I've been in my room since lunch, dressing.

BRACK. You haven't a tiny crack in the door through which we might have negotiated?

HEDDA. You forgot to arrange one.

BRACK. Another stupidity.

HEDDA. Well, we'll have to sit down here. And wait. Tesman won't be back for some time.

BRACK. Sad. Well, I'll be patient.

[HEDDA *sits on the corner of the sofa.* BRACK *puts his coat over the back of the nearest chair and seats himself, keeping his hat in his hand. Short pause. They look at each other.*]

HEDDA. Well?

BRACK. [*In the same tone of voice*] Well?

HEDDA. I asked first.

BRACK. [*Leans forward slightly*] Yes, well, now we can enjoy a nice, cosy little chat—Mrs. Hedda.

HEDDA. [*Leans further back in her chair*] It seems such ages since we had a talk. I don't count last night or this morning.

BRACK. You mean: *à deux?*[6]

HEDDA. Mm—yes. That's roughly what I meant.

BRACK. I've been longing so much for you to come home.

HEDDA. So have I.

BRACK. You? Really, Mrs. Hedda? And I thought you were having such a wonderful honeymoon.

HEDDA. Oh, yes. Wonderful!

BRACK. But your husband wrote such ecstatic letters.

HEDDA. He! Oh, yes! He thinks life has nothing better to offer than rooting around in libraries and copying old pieces of parchment, or whatever it is he does.

BRACK. [*A little maliciously*] Well, that *is* his life. Most of it, anyway.

HEDDA. Yes, I know. Well, it's all right for him. But for me! Oh no, my dear Judge. I've been bored to death.

BRACK. [*Sympathetically*] Do you mean that? Seriously?

HEDDA. Yes. Can you imagine? Six whole months without ever meeting a single person who was one of us, and to whom I could talk about the kind of things we talk about.

BRACK. Yes, I can understand. I'd miss that, too.

HEDDA. That wasn't the worst, though.

BRACK. What was?

HEDDA. Having to spend every minute of one's life with—with the same person.

BRACK. [*Nods*] Yes. What a thought! Morning; noon; and——

HEDDA. [*Coldly*] As I said: every minute of one's life.

BRACK. I stand corrected. But dear Tesman is such a clever fellow, I should have thought one ought to be able——

HEDDA. Tesman is only interested in one thing, my dear Judge. His special subject.

BRACK. True.

HEDDA. And people who are only interested in one thing don't make the most amusing company. Not for long, anyway.

BRACK. Not even when they happen to be the person one loves?

HEDDA. Oh, don't use that sickly, stupid word.

BRACK. [*Starts*] But, Mrs. Hedda——!

HEDDA. [*Half laughing, half annoyed*] You just try it, Judge. Listening to the history of civilization morning, noon and——

BRACK. [*Corrects her*] Every minute of one's life.

HEDDA. All right. Oh, and those domestic industries of Brabant in the Middle Ages! That really is beyond the limit.

BRACK. [*Looks at her searchingly*] But, tell me—if you feel like this why on earth did you—? Ha——

6. *À deux:* Just the two of us.

HEDDA. Why on earth did I marry George Tesman?

BRACK. If you like to put it that way.

HEDDA. Do you think it so very strange?

BRACK. Yes—and no, Mrs. Hedda.

HEDDA. I'd danced myself tired, Judge. I felt my time was up——
[*Gives a slight shudder*] No, I mustn't say that. Or even think it.

BRACK. You've no rational cause to think it.

HEDDA. Oh—cause, cause——[*Looks searchingly at him*] After all, George Tesman—well, I mean, he's a very respectable man.

BRACK. Very respectable, sound as a rock. No denying that.

HEDDA. And there's nothing exactly ridiculous about him. Is there?

BRACK. Ridiculous? N-no, I wouldn't say that.

HEDDA. Mm. He's very clever at collecting material and all that, isn't he? I mean, he may go quite far in time.

BRACK. [*Looks at her a little uncertainly*] I thought you believed, like everyone else, that he would become a very prominent man.

HEDDA. [*Looks tired*] Yes, I did. And when he came and begged me on his bended knees to be allowed to love and to cherish me, I didn't see why I shouldn't let him.

BRACK. No, well—if one looks at it like that——

HEDDA. It was more than my other admirers were prepared to do, Judge dear.

BRACK. [*Laughs*] Well, I can't answer for the others. As far as I myself am concerned, you know I've always had a considerable respect for the institution of marriage. As an institution.

HEDDA. [*Lightly*] Oh, I've never entertained any hopes of you.

BRACK. All I want is to have a circle of friends whom I can trust, whom I can help with advice or—or by any other means, and into whose houses I may come and go as a—trusted friend.

HEDDA. Of the husband?

BRACK. [*Bows*] Preferably, to be frank, of the wife. And of the husband too, of course. Yes, you know, this kind of—triangle is a delightful arrangement for all parties concerned.

HEDDA. Yes, I often longed for a third person while I was away. Oh, those hours we spent alone in railway compartments——

BRACK. Fortunately your honeymoon is now over.

HEDDA. [*Shakes her head*] There's a long, long way still to go. I've only reached a stop on the line.

BRACK. Why not jump out and stretch your legs a little, Mrs. Hedda?

HEDDA. I'm not the jumping sort.

BRACK. Aren't you?

HEDDA. No. There's always someone around who——

BRACK. [*Laughs*] Who looks at one's legs?

HEDDA. Yes. Exactly.

BRACK. Well, but surely——

HEDDA. [*With a gesture of rejection*] I don't like it. I'd rather stay where I am. Sitting in the compartment. À *deux*.

BRACK. But suppose a third person were to step into the compartment?

HEDDA. That would be different.

BRACK. A trusted friend—someone who understood——

HEDDA. And was lively and amusing——

BRACK. And interested in—more subjects than one——

HEDDA. [*Sighs audibly*] Yes, that'd be a relief.

BRACK. [*Hears the front door open and shut*] The triangle is completed.

HEDDA. [*Half under breath*] And the train goes on.

    [GEORGE TESMAN, *in grey walking dress with a soft felt hat, enters from the hall. He has a number of paper-covered books under his arm and in his pockets.*]

TESMAN. [*Goes over to the table by the corner sofa*] Phew! It's too hot to be lugging all this around. [*Puts the books down*] I'm positively sweating, Hedda. Why, hullo, hullo! You here already, Judge? What? Bertha didn't tell me.

BRACK. [*Gets up*] I came in through the garden.

HEDDA. What are all those books you've got there?

TESMAN. [*Stands glancing through them*] Oh, some new publications dealing with my special subject. I had to buy them.

HEDDA. Your special subject?

BRACK. His special subject, Mrs. Tesman.

    [BRACK *and* HEDDA *exchange a smile.*]

HEDDA. Haven't you collected enough material on your special subject?

TESMAN. My dear Hedda, one can never have too much. One must keep abreast of what other people are writing.

HEDDA. Yes. Of course.

TESMAN. [*Rooting among the books*] Look—I bought a copy of Eilert Loevborg's new book, too. [*Holds it out to her*] Perhaps you'd like to have a look at it, Hedda? What?

HEDDA. No, thank you. Er—yes, perhaps I will, later.

TESMAN. I glanced through it on my way home.

BRACK. What's your opinion—as a specialist on the subject?

TESMAN. I'm amazed how sound and balanced it is. He never used to write like that. [*Gathers his books together*] Well, I must get down to these at once. I can hardly wait to cut the pages.[7] Oh, I've got to change, too. [*To* BRACK] We don't have to be off just yet, do we? What?

BRACK. Heavens, no. We've plenty of time yet.

TESMAN. Good, I needn't hurry, then. [*Goes with his books, but stops and turns in the doorway*] Oh, by the way, Hedda, Auntie Juju won't be coming to see you this evening.

HEDDA. Won't she? Oh—the hat, I suppose.

TESMAN. Good heavens, no. How could you think such a thing of

---

7. *Cut the pages:* Books used to be sold with the pages folded but uncut as they came fom the printing press; the owner had to cut the pages in order to read the book.

Auntie Juju? Fancy——! No, Auntie Rena's very ill.

HEDDA. She always is.

TESMAN. Yes, but today she's been taken really bad.

HEDDA. Oh, then it's quite understandable that the other one should want to stay with her. Well, I shall have to swallow my disappointment.

TESMAN. You can't imagine how happy Auntie Juju was in spite of everything. At your looking so well after the honeymoon!

HEDDA. [*Half beneath her breath, as she rises*] Oh, these everlasting aunts!

TESMAN. What?

HEDDA. [*Goes over to the french windows*] Nothing.

TESMAN. Oh. All right.

[*Goes into the rear room and out of sight*]

BRACK. What was that about the hat?

HEDDA. Oh, something that happened with Miss Tesman this morning. She'd put her hat down on a chair. [*Looks at him and smiles*] And I pretended to think it was the servant's.

BRACK. [*Shakes his head*] But my dear Mrs. Hedda, how could you do such a thing? To that poor old lady?

HEDDA. [*Nervously, walking across the room*] Sometimes a mood like that hits me. And I can't stop myself. [*Thows herself down in the armchair by the stove*] Oh, I don't know how to explain it.

BRACK. [*Behind her chair*] You're not really happy. That's the answer.

HEDDA. [*Stares ahead of her*] Why on earth should I be happy? Can you give me a reason?

BRACK. Yes. For one thing you've got the home you always wanted.

HEDDA. [*Looks at him*] You really believe that story?

BRACK. You mean it isn't true?

HEDDA. Oh, yes, it's partly true.

BRACK. Well?

HEDDA. It's true I got Tesman to see me home from parties last summer——

BRACK. It was a pity my home lay in another direction.

HEDDA. Yes. Your interests lay in another direction, too.

BRACK. [*Laughs*] That's naughty of you, Mrs. Hedda. But to return to you and Tesman——

HEDDA. Well, we walked past this house one evening. And poor Tesman was fidgeting in his boots trying to find something to talk about. I felt sorry for the great scholar——

BRACK. [*Smiles incredulously*] Did you? Hm.

HEDDA. Yes, honestly I did. Well, to help him out of his misery, I happened to say quite frivolously how much I'd love to live in this house.

BRACK. Was that all?

HEDDA. That evening, yes.

BRACK. But—afterwards?

HEDDA. Yes. My little frivolity had its consequences, my dear Judge.

BRACK. Our little frivolities do. Much too often, unfortunately.

HEDDA. Thank you. Well, it was our mutual admiration for the late Prime Minister's house that brought George Tesman and me together on common ground. So we got engaged, and we got married, and we went on our honeymoon, and—Ah well, Judge, I've —made my bed and I must lie in it, I was about to say.

BRACK. How utterly fantastic! And you didn't really care in the least about the house?

HEDDA. God knows I didn't.

BRACK. Yes, but now that we've furnished it so beautifully for you?

HEDDA. Ugh—all the rooms smell of lavender and dried roses. But perhaps Auntie Juju brought that in.

BRACK. [*Laughs*] More likely the Prime Minister's widow, rest her soul.

HEDDA. Yes, it's got the odor of death about it. It reminds me of the flowers one has worn at a ball—the morning after. [*Clasps her hands behind her neck, leans back in the chair and looks up at him*] Oh, my dear Judge, you've no idea how hideously bored I'm going to be out here.

BRACK. Couldn't you find some kind of occupation, Mrs. Hedda? Like your husband?

HEDDA. Occupation? That'd interest me?

BRACK. Well—preferably.

HEDDA. God knows what. I've often thought——[*Breaks off*] No, that wouldn't work either.

BRACK. Who knows? Tell me about it.

HEDDA. I was thinking—if I could persuade Tesman to go into politics, for example.

BRACK. [*Laughs*] Tesman! No, honestly, I don't think he's quite cut out to be a politician.

HEDDA. Perhaps not. But if I could persuade him to have a go at it?

BRACK. What satisfaction would that give you? If he turned out to be no good? Why do you want to make him do that?

HEDDA. Because I'm bored. [*After a moment*] You feel there's absolutely no possibility of Tesman becoming Prime Minister, then?

BRACK. Well, you know, Mrs. Hedda, for one thing he'd have to be pretty well off before he could become that.

HEDDA. [*Gets up impatiently*] There you are! [*Walks across the room*] It's this wretched poverty that makes life so hateful. And ludicrous. Well, it is!

BRACK. I don't think that's the real cause.

HEDDA. What is, then?

BRACK. Nothing really exciting has ever happened to you.

HEDDA. Nothing serious, you mean?

BRACK. Call it that if you like. But now perhaps it may.

HEDDA. [*Tosses her head*] Oh, you're thinking of this competition for that wretched professorship? That's Tesman's affair. I'm not going to waste my time worrying about that.

BRACK. Very well, let's forget about that then. But suppose you were to find yourself faced with what people call—to use the conventional phrase—the most solemn of human responsibilities? [*Smiles*] A new responsibility, little Mrs. Hedda.

HEDDA. [*Angrily*] Be quiet! Nothing like that's going to happen.

BRACK. [*Warily*] We'll talk about it again in a year's time. If not earlier.

HEDDA. [*Curtly*] I've no leanings in that direction, Judge. I don't want any—responsibilities.

BRACK. But surely you must feel some inclination to make use of that—natural talent which every woman—

HEDDA. [*Over by the french windows*] Oh, be quiet, I say! I often think there's only one thing for which I have any natural talent.

BRACK. [*Goes closer*] And what is that, if I may be so bold as to ask?

HEDDA. [*Stands looking out*] For boring myself to death. Now you know. [*Turns, looks toward the rear room and laughs*] Talking of boring, here comes the Professor.

BRACK. [*Quietly, warningly*] Now, now, now, Mrs. Hedda!

[GEORGE TESMAN, *in evening dress, with gloves and hat in his hand, enters through the rear room from the right.*]

TESMAN. Hedda, hasn't any message come from Eilert? What?

HEDDA. No.

TESMAN. Ah, then we'll have him here presently. You wait and see.

BRACK. You really think he'll come?

TESMAN. Yes, I'm almost sure he will. What you were saying about him this morning is just gossip.

BRACK. Oh?

TESMAN. Yes. Auntie Juju said she didn't believe he'd ever dare to stand in my way again. Fancy that!

BRACK. Then everything in the garden's lovely.

TESMAN. [*Puts his hat, with his gloves in it, on a chair, right*] Yes, but you really must let me wait for him as long as possible.

BRACK. We've plenty of time. No one'll be turning up at my place before seven or half past.

TESMAN. Ah, then we can keep Hedda company a little longer. And see if he turns up. What?

HEDDA. [*Picks up* BRACK's *coat and hat and carries them over to the corner sofa*] And if the worst comes to the worst, Mr. Loevborg can sit here and talk to me.

BRACK. [*Offering to take his things from her*] No, please. What do you mean by "if the worst comes to the worst"?

HEDDA. If he doesn't want to go with you and Tesman.

TESMAN. [*Looks doubtfully at her*] I say, Hedda, do you think it'll be all right for him to stay here with you? What? Remember Auntie Juju isn't coming.

HEDDA. Yes, but Mrs. Elvsted is. The three of us can have a cup of tea together.

TESMAN. Ah, that'll be all right then.

BRACK. [*Smiles*] It's probably the safest solution as far as he's concerned.

HEDDA. Why?

BRACK. My dear Mrs. Tesman, you always say of my little bachelor parties that they should be attended only by men of the strongest principles.

HEDDA. But Mr. Loevborg is a man of principle now. You know what they say about a reformed sinner——

[BERTHA *enters from the hall.*]

BERTHA. Madam, there's a gentleman here who wants to see you——

HEDDA. Ask him to come in.

TESMAN. [*Quietly*] I'm sure it's him. By Jove. Fancy that!

[EILERT LOEVBORG *enters from the hall. He is slim and lean, of the same age as* TESMAN, *but looks older and somewhat haggard. His hair and beard are of a blackish-brown; his face is long and pale, but with a couple of reddish patches on his cheekbones. He is dressed in an elegant and fairly new black suit, and carries black gloves and a top hat in his hand. He stops just inside the door and bows abruptly. He seems somewhat embarrassed.*]

TESMAN. [*Goes over and shakes his hand*] My dear Eilert! How grand to see you again after all these years!

EILERT LOEVBORG. [*Speaks softly*] It was good of you to write, George. [*Goes nearer to* HEDDA] May I shake hands with you, too, Mrs. Tesman?

HEDDA. [*Accepts his hand*] Delighted to see you, Mr. Loevborg. [*With a gesture*] I don't know if you two gentlemen——

LOEVBORG. [*Bows slightly*] Judge Brack, I believe.

BRACK. [*Also with a slight bow*] Correct. We—met some years ago——

TESMAN. [*Puts his hands on* LOEVBORG'S *shoulders*] Now you're to treat this house just as though it were your own home, Eilert. Isn't that right, Hedda? I hear you've decided to settle here again? What?

LOEVBORG. Yes, I have.

TESMAN. Quite understandable. Oh, by the bye—I've just bought your new book. Though to tell the truth I haven't found time to read it yet.

LOEVBORG. You needn't bother.

TESMAN. Oh? Why?

LOEVBORG. There's nothing much in it.

TESMAN. By Jove, fancy hearing that from you!

BRACK. But everyone's praising it.

LOEVBORG. That was exactly what I wanted to happen. So I only wrote what I knew everyone would agree with.

BRACK. Very sensible.

TESMAN. Yes, but my dear Eilert——

LOEVBORG. I want to try to re-establish myself. To begin again—from the beginning:

TESMAN. [*A little embarrassed*] Yes, I—er—suppose you do. What?

LOEVBORG. [*Smiles, puts down his hat and takes a package wrapped in paper from his coat pocket*] But when this gets published—George Tesman—read it. This is my real book. The one in which I have spoken with my own voice.

TESMAN. Oh, really? What's it about?

LOEVBORG. It's the sequel.

TESMAN. Sequel? To what?

LOEVBORG. To the other book.

TESMAN. The one that's just come out?

LOEVBORG. Yes.

TESMAN. But my dear Eilert, that covers the subject right up to the present day.

LOEVBORG. It does. But this is about the future.

TESMAN. The future! But, I say, we don't know anything about that.

LOEVBORG. No. But there are one or two things that need to be said about it. [*Opens the package*] Here, have a look.

TESMAN. Surely that's not your handwriting?

LOEVBORG. I dictated it. [*Turns the pages*] It's in two parts. The first deals with the forces that will shape our civilization. [*Turns further on towards the end*] And the second indicates the direction in which that civilization may develop.

TESMAN. Amazing! I'd never think of writing about anything like that.

HEDDA. [*By the french windows, drumming on the pane*] No. You wouldn't.

LOEVBORG. [*Puts the pages back into their cover and lays the package on the table*] I brought it because I thought I might possibly read you a few pages this evening.

TESMAN. I say, what a kind idea! Oh, but this evening——? [*Glances at* BRACK] I'm not quite sure whether——

LOEVBORG. Well, some other time, then. There's no hurry.

BRACK. The truth is, Mr. Loevborg, I'm giving a little dinner this evening. In Tesman's honour, you know.

LOEVBORG. [*Looks round for his hat*] Oh—then I mustn't——

BRACK. No, wait a minute. Won't you do me the honor of joining us?

LOEVBORG. [*Curtly, with decision*] No I can't. Thank you so much.

BRACK. Oh, nonsense. Do—please. There'll only be a few of us. And I can promise you we shall have some good sport, as Mrs. Hed—as Mrs. Tesman puts it.

LOEVBORG. I've no doubt. Nevertheless——

BRACK. You could bring your manuscript along and read it to Tesman at my place. I could lend you a room.

TESMAN. By Jove, Eilert, that's an idea. What?

HEDDA. [*Interposes*] But Tesman, Mr. Loevborg doesn't want to go.

I'm sure Mr. Loevborg would much rather sit here and have supper with me.

LOEVBORG. [*Looks at her*] With you, Mrs. Tesman?

HEDDA. And Mrs. Elvsted.

LOEVBORG. Oh. [*Casually*] I ran into her this afternoon.

HEDDA. Did you? Well, she's coming here this evening. So you really must stay, Mr. Loevborg. Otherwise she'll have no one to see her home.

LOEVBORG. That's true. Well—thank you, Mrs. Tesman, I'll stay then.

HEDDA. I'll just tell the servant.

[*She goes to the door which leads into the hall, and rings. BERTHA enters. HEDDA talks softly to her and points towards the rear room. BERTHA nods and goes out.*]

TESMAN. [*To LOEVBORG, as HEDDA does this*] I say, Eilert. This new subject of yours—the—er—future—is that the one you're going to lecture about?

LOEVBORG. Yes.

TESMAN. They told me down at the bookshop that you're going to hold a series of lectures here during the autumn.

LOEVBORG. Yes, I am. I—hope you don't mind, Tesman.

TESMAN. Good heavens, no! But——?

LOEVBORG. I can quite understand it might queer your pitch a little.

TESMAN. [*Dejectedly*] Oh well, I can't expect you to put them off for my sake.

LOEVBORG. I'll wait till your appointment's been announced.

TESMAN. You'll wait! But—but—aren't you going to compete with me for the post? What?

LOEVBORG. No. I only want to defeat you in the eyes of the world.

TESMAN. Good heavens! Then Auntie Juju was right after all! Oh, I knew it, I knew it! Hear that, Hedda? Fancy! Eilert *doesn't* want to stand in our way.

HEDDA. [*Curtly*] Our? Leave me out of it, please.

[*She goes towards the rear room, where BERTHA is setting a tray with decanters and glasses on the table. HEDDA nods approval, and comes back into the drawing room. BERTHA goes out.*]

TESMAN. [*While this is happening*] Judge Brack, what do you think about all this? What?

BRACK. Oh, I think honor and victory can be very splendid things——

TESMAN. Of course they can. Still——

HEDDA. [*Looks at TESMAN with a cold smile*] You look as if you'd been hit by a thunderbolt.

TESMAN. Yes, I feel rather like it.

BRACK. There was a black cloud looming up, Mrs. Tesman. But it seems to have passed over.

HEDDA. [*Points towards the rear room*] Well, gentlemen, won't you go in and take a glass of cold punch?

BRACK. [*Glances at his watch*] A stirrup cup?[8] Yes, why not?

TESMAN. An admirable suggestion, Hedda. Admirable! Oh, I feel so relieved!

HEDDA. Won't you have one, too, Mr. Loevborg?

LOEVBORG. No, thank you. I'd rather not.

BRACK. Great heavens, man, cold punch isn't poison. Take my word for it.

LOEVBORG. Not for everyone, perhaps.

HEDDA. I'll keep Mr. Loevborg company while you drink.

TESMAN. Yes, Hedda dear, would you?

[*He and* BRACK *go into the rear room, sit down, drink punch, smoke cigarettes and talk cheerfully during the following scene.* EILERT LOEVBORG *remains standing by the stove.* HEDDA *goes to the writing table.*]

HEDDA. [*Raising her voice slightly*] I've some photographs I'd like to show you, if you'd care to see them. Tesman and I visited the Tyrol on our way home.

[*She comes back with an album, places it on the table by the sofa and sits in the upstage corner of the sofa.* EILERT LOEVBORG *comes toward her, stops and looks at her. Then he takes a chair and sits down on her left, with his back toward the rear room.*]

HEDDA. [*Opens the album*] You see these mountains, Mr. Loevborg? That's the Ortler group. Tesman has written the name underneath. You see: "The Ortler Group near Meran."[9]

LOEVBORG. [*Has not taken his eyes from her; says softly, slowly*] Hedda—Gabler!

HEDDA. [*Gives him a quick glance*] Ssh!

LOEVBORG. [*Repeats softly*] Hedda Gabler!

HEDDA. [*Looks at the album*] Yes, that used to be my name. When we first knew each other.

LOEVBORG. And from now on—for the rest of my life—I must teach myself never to say: Hedda Gabler.

HEDDA. [*Still turning the pages*] Yes, you must. You'd better start getting into practice. The sooner the better.

LOEVBORG. [*Bitterly*] Hedda Gabler married? And to George Tesman?

HEDDA. Yes. Well—that's life.

LOEVBORG. Oh, Hedda, Hedda! How could you throw yourself away like that?

HEDDA. [*Looks sharply at him*] Stop it.

LOEVBORG. What do you mean?

[TESMAN *comes in and goes toward the sofa.*]

---

8. *Stirrup cup:* A drink before parting. (Originally, it was taken by riders on horseback just before setting forth.)

9. *Meran:* Or Merano, a city in the Austrian Tyrol, since 1918 in Italy. The scenic features mentioned here and later are tourist attractions. The Ortler Group and the Dolomites are ranges of the Alps; the Ampezzo Valley lies beyond the Dolomites to the east; and the Brenner Pass is a major route through the Alps to Austria.

HEDDA. [*Hears him coming and says casually*] And this, Mr. Loevborg, is the view from the Ampezzo valley. Look at those
mountains. [*Glances affectionately up at* TESMAN] What did you
say those curious mountains were called, dear?

TESMAN. Let me have a look. Oh, those are the Dolomites.

HEDDA. Of course. Those are the Dolomites, Mr. Loevborg.

TESMAN. Hedda, I just wanted to ask you, can't we bring some
punch in here? A glass for you, anyway. What?

HEDDA. Thank you, yes. And a biscuit[10] or two, perhaps.

TESMAN. You wouldn't like a cigarette?

HEDDA. No.

TESMAN. Right.

> [*He goes into the rear room and over to the right.* BRACK
> *is sitting there, glancing occasionally at* HEDDA *and* LOEV-
> BORG.]

LOEVBORG. [*Softly, as before*] Answer me, Hedda. How could you
do it?

HEDDA. [*Apparently absorbed in the album*] If you go on calling me
Hedda I won't talk to you any more.

LOEVBORG. Mayn't I even when we're alone?

HEDDA. No. You can think it. But you mustn't say it.

LOEVBORG. Oh, I see. Because you love George Tesman.

HEDDA. [*Glances at him and smiles*] Love? Don't be funny.

LOEVBORG. You don't love him?

HEDDA. I don't intend to be unfaithful to him. That's not what I
want.

LOEVBORG. Hedda—just tell me one thing——

HEDDA. Ssh!

> [TESMAN *enters from the rear room, carrying a tray.*]

TESMAN. Here we are! Here come the goodies!

> [*Puts the tray down on the table*]

HEDDA. Why didn't you ask the servant to bring it in?

TESMAN. [*Fills the glasses*] I like waiting on you, Hedda.

HEDDA. But you've filled both glasses. Mr. Loevborg doesn't want
to drink.

TESMAN. Yes, but Mrs. Elvsted'll be here soon.

HEDDA. Oh yes, that's true. Mrs. Elvsted——

TESMAN. Had you forgotten her? What?

HEDDA. We're so absorbed with these photographs. [*Shows him
one*] You remember this little village?

TESMAN. Oh, that one down by the Brenner Pass. We spent a night
there——

HEDDA. Yes, and met all those amusing people.

TESMAN. Oh yes, it was there, wasn't it? By Jove, if only we could
have had you with us, Eilert! Ah, well.

> [*Goes back into the other room and sits down with* BRACK]

LOEVBORG. Tell me one thing, Hedda.

---

10. *Biscuit:* Or tea biscuit; a cookie.

HEDDA. Yes?

LOEVBORG. Didn't you love me either? Not—just a little?

HEDDA. Well now, I wonder? No, I think we were just good pals— Really good pals who could tell each other anything. [*Smiles*] You certainly poured your heart out to me.

LOEVBORG. You begged me to.

HEDDA. Looking back on it, there was something beautiful and fascinating—and brave—about the way we told each other everything. That secret friendship no one else knew about.

LOEVBORG. Yes, Hedda, yes! Do you remember? How I used to come up to your father's house in the afternoon—and the General sat by the window and read his newspapers—with his back toward us——

HEDDA. And we sat on the sofa in the corner——

LOEVBORG. Always reading the same illustrated magazine——

HEDDA. We hadn't any photograph album.

LOEVBORG. Yes, Hedda. I regarded you as a kind of confessor. Told you things about myself which no one else knew about—then. Those days and nights of drinking and— Oh, Hedda, what power did you have to make me confess such things?

HEDDA. Power? You think I had some power over you?

LOEVBORG. Yes—I don't know how else to explain it. And all those —oblique questions you asked me——

HEDDA. You knew what they meant.

LOEVBORG. But that you could sit there and ask me such questions! So unashamedly——

HEDDA. I thought you said they were oblique.

LOEVBORG. Yes, but you asked them so unashamedly. That you could question me about—about that kind of thing!

HEDDA. You answered willingly enough.

LOEVBORG. Yes—that's what I can't understand—looking back on it. But tell me, Hedda—what you felt for me—wasn't that—love? When you asked me those questions and made me confess my sins to you, wasn't it because you wanted to wash me clean?

HEDDA. No, not exactly.

LOEVBORG. Why did you do it, then?

HEDDA. Do you find it so incredible that a young girl, given the chance to do so without anyone knowing, should want to be allowed a glimpse into a forbidden world of whose existence she is supposed to be ignorant?

LOEVBORG. So that was it?

HEDDA. One reason. One reason—I think.

LOEVBORG. You didn't love me, then. You just wanted—knowledge. But if that was so, why did you break it off?

HEDDA. That was your fault.

LOEVBORG. It was you who put an end to it.

HEDDA. Yes, when I realized that our friendship was threatening to develop into something—something else. Shame on you, Eilert Loevborg! How could you abuse the trust of your dearest friend?

LOEVBORG. [*Clenches his fists*] Oh, why didn't you do it? Why didn't you shoot me dead? As you threatened to?

HEDDA. I was afraid. Of the scandal.

LOEVBORG. Yes, Hedda. You're a coward at heart.

HEDDA. A dreadful coward. [*Changes her tone*] Luckily for you. Well, now you've found consolation with the Elvsteds.

LOEVBORG. I know what Thea's been telling you.

HEDDA. I dare say you told her about us.

LOEVBORG. Not a word. She's too silly to understand that kind of thing.

HEDDA. Silly?

LOEVBORG. She's silly about that kind of thing.

HEDDA. And I am a coward. [*Leans closer to him, without looking him in the eyes, and says quietly*] But let me tell you something. Something you don't know.

LOEVBORG. [*Tensely*] Yes?

HEDDA. My failure to shoot you wasn't my worst act of cowardice that evening.

LOEVBORG. [*Looks at her for a moment, realizes her meaning and whispers passionately*] Oh, Hedda! Hedda Gabler! Now I see what was behind those questions. Yes! It wasn't knowledge you wanted! It was life!

HEDDA. [*Flashes a look at him and says quietly*] Take care! Don't you delude yourself!

[*It has begun to grow dark.* BERTHA, *from outside, opens the door leading into the hall.*]

HEDDA. [*Closes the album with a snap and cries, smiling*] Ah, at last! Come in, Thea dear!

[MRS. ELVSTED *enters from the hall, in evening dress. The door is closed behind her.*]

HEDDA. [*On the sofa, stretches out her arms toward her*] Thea darling, I thought you were never coming!

[MRS. ELVSTED *makes a slight bow to the gentlemen in the rear room as she passes the open doorway, and they to her. Then she goes to the table and holds out her hand to* HEDDA. EILERT LOEVBORG *has risen from his chair. He and* MRS. ELVSTED *nod silently to each other.*]

MRS. ELVSTED. Perhaps I ought to go in and say a few words to your husband?

HEDDA. Oh, there's no need. They're happy by themselves. They'll be going soon.

MRS. ELVSTED. Going?

HEDDA. Yes, they're off on a spree this evening.

MRS. ELVSTED. [*Quickly, to* LOEVBORG] You're not going with them?

LOEVBORG. No.

HEDDA. Mr. Loevborg is staying here with us.

MRS. ELVSTED. [*Takes a chair and is about to sit down beside him*] Oh, how nice it is to be here!

HEDDA. No, Thea darling, not there. Come over here and sit beside me. I want to be in the middle.

MRS. ELVSTED. Yes, just as you wish.

[*She goes round the table and sits on the sofa, on* HEDDA'S
right. LOEVBORG *sits down again in his chair.*]

LOEVBORG. [*After a short pause, to* HEDDA] Isn't she lovely to look
at?

HEDDA. [*Strokes her hair gently*] Only to look at?

LOEVBORG. Yes. We're just good pals. We trust each other implicitly. We can talk to each other quite unashamedly.

HEDDA. No need to be oblique?

MRS. ELVSTED. [*Nestles close to* HEDDA *and says quietly*] Oh,
Hedda I'm so happy. Imagine—he says I've inspired him!

HEDDA. [*Looks at her with a smile*] Dear Thea! Does he really?

LOEVBORG. She has the courage of her convictions, Mrs. Tesman.

MRS. ELVSTED. I? Courage?

LOEVBORG. Absolute courage. Where friendship is concerned.

HEDDA. Yes. Courage. Yes. If only one had that——

LOEVBORG. Yes?

HEDDA. One might be able to live. In spite of everything. [*Changes
her tone suddenly*] Well, Thea darling, now you're going to
drink a nice glass of cold punch.

MRS. ELVSTED. No, thank you. I never drink anything like that.

HEDDA. Oh. You, Mr. Loevborg?

LOEVBORG. Thank you, I don't either.

MRS. ELVSTED. No, he doesn't, either.

HEDDA. [*Looks into his eyes*] But if I want you to?

LOEVBORG. That doesn't make any difference.

HEDDA. [*Laughs*] Have I no power over you at all? Poor me!

LOEVBORG. Not where this is concerned.

HEDDA. Seriously, I think you should. For your own sake.

MRS. ELVSTED. Hedda!

LOEVBORG. Why?

HEDDA. Or perhaps I should say for other people's sake.

LOEVBORG. What do you mean?

HEDDA. People might think you didn't feel absolutely and unashamedly sure of yourself. In your heart of hearts.

MRS. ELVSTED. [*Quietly*] Oh, Hedda, no!

LOEVBORG. People can think what they like. For the present.

MRS. ELVSTED. [*Happily*] Yes, that's true.

HEDDA. I saw it so clearly in Judge Brack a few minutes ago.

LOEVBORG. Oh. What did you see?

HEDDA. He smiled so scornfully when he saw you were afraid to go
in there and drink with them.

LOEVBORG. Afraid! I wanted to stay here and talk to you.

MRS. ELVSTED. That was only natural, Hedda.

HEDDA. But the Judge wasn't to know that. I saw him wink at
Tesman when you showed you didn't dare to join their wretched
little party.

LOEVBORG. Didn't dare! Are you saying I didn't dare?

HEDDA. I'm not saying so. But that was what Judge Brack thought.

LOEVBORG. Well, let him.

HEDDA. You're not going, then?

LOEVBORG. I'm staying here with you and Thea.

MRS. ELVSTED. Yes, Hedda, of course he is.

HEDDA. [*Smiles, and nods approvingly to* LOEVBORG] Firm as a rock! A man of principle! That's how a man should be! [*Turns to* MRS. ELVSTED *and strokes her cheek*] Didn't I tell you so this morning when you came here in such a panic——

LOEVBORG. [*Starts*] Panic?

MRS. ELVSTED. [*Frightened*] Hedda! But—Hedda!

HEDDA. Well, now you can see for yourself. There's no earthly need for you to get scared to death just because——[*Stops*] Well! Let's all three cheer up and enjoy ourselves.

LOEVBORG. Mrs. Tesman, would you mind explaining to me what this is all about?

MRS. ELVSTED. Oh, my God, my God, Hedda, what are you saying? What are you doing?

HEDDA. Keep calm. That horrid Judge has his eye on you.

LOEVBORG. Scared to death, were you? For my sake?

MRS. ELVSTED. [*Quietly, trembling*]Oh, Hedda! You've made me so unhappy!

LOEVBORG. [*Looks coldly at her for a moment. His face is distorted.*] So that was how much you trusted me.

MRS. ELVSTED. Eilert dear, please listen to me——

LOEVBORG. [*Takes one of the glasses of punch, raises it and says quietly, hoarsely*] Skoal, Thea!

[*Empties the glass, puts it down and picks up one of the others.*]

MRS. ELVSTED. [*Quietly*] Hedda, Hedda! Why did you want this to happen?

HEDDA. I—want it? Are you mad?

LOEVBORG. Skoal to you too, Mrs. Tesman. Thanks for telling me the truth. Here's to the truth!

[*Empties his glass and refills it*]

HEDDA. [*Puts her hand on his arm*] Steady. That's enough for now. Don't forget the party.

MRS. ELVSTED. No, no, no!

HEDDA. Ssh! They're looking at you.

LOEVBORG. [*Puts down his glass*] Thea, tell me the truth——

MRS. ELVSTED. Yes!

LOEVBORG. Did your husband know you were following me?

MRS. ELVSTED. Oh, Hedda!

LOEVBORG. Did you and he have an agreement that you should come here and keep an eye on me? Perhaps he gave you the idea? After all, he's a magistrate.[11] I suppose he needed me back in his office. Or did he miss my companionship at the card table?

11. *Magistrate:* Also translated *sheriff*. A civil official with duties associated with the courts.

MRS. ELVSTED. [*Quietly, sobbing*] Eilert, Eilert!

LOEVBORG. [*Seizes a glass and is about to fill it*] Let's drink to him, too.

HEDDA. No more now. Remember you're going to read your book to Tesman.

LOEVBORG. [*Calm again, puts down his glass*] That was silly of me, Thea. To take it like that, I mean. Don't be angry with me, my dear. You'll see—yes, and they'll see, too—that though I fell, I—I have raised myself up again. With your help, Thea.

MRS. ELVSTED. [*Happily*] Oh, thank God!

[BRACK *has meanwhile glanced at his watch. He and* TESMAN *get up and come into the drawing room.*]

BRACK. [*Takes his hat and overcoat*] Well, Mrs. Tesman. It's time for us to go.

HEDDA. Yes, I suppose it must be.

LOEVBORG. [*Gets up*] Time for me too, Judge.

MRS. ELVSTED. [*Quietly, pleadingly*] Eilert, please don't!

HEDDA. [*Pinches her arm*] They can hear you.

MRS. ELVSTED. [*Gives a little cry*] Oh!

LOEVBORG. [*To* BRACK] You were kind enough to ask me to join you.

BRACK. Are you coming?

LOEVBORG. If I may.

BRACK. Delighted.

LOEVBORG. [*Puts the paper package in his pocket and says to* TESMAN] I'd like to show you one or two things before I send it off to the printer.

TESMAN. I say, that'll be fun. Fancy——! Oh, but Hedda, how'll Mrs. Elvsted get home? What?

HEDDA. Oh, we'll manage somehow.

LOEVBORG. [*Glances over toward the ladies*] Mrs. Elvsted? I shall come back and collect her, naturally. [*Goes closer*] About ten o'clock, Mrs. Tesman? Will that suit you?

HEDDA. Yes. That'll suit me admirably.

TESMAN. Good, that's settled. But you mustn't expect me back so early, Hedda.

HEDDA. Stay as long as you c— as long as you like, dear.

MRS. ELVSTED. [*Trying to hide her anxiety*] Well then, Mr. Loevborg, I'll wait here till you come.

LOEVBORG. [*His hat in his hand*] Pray do, Mrs. Elvsted.

BRACK. Well, gentlemen, now the party begins. I trust that, in the words of a certain fair lady, we shall enjoy good sport.

HEDDA. What a pity the fair lady can't be there, invisible.

BRACK. Why invisible?

HEDDA. So as to be able to hear some of your uncensored witticisms, your honor.

BRACK. [*Laughs*] Oh, I shouldn't advise the fair lady to do that.

TESMAN. [*Laughs too*] I say, Hedda, that's good. By Jove! Fancy that!

BRACK. Well, good night, ladies, good night!

LOEVBORG. [*Bows farewell*] About ten o'clock, then.

> [BRACK, LOEVBORG *and* TESMAN *go out through the hall. As they do so* BERTHA *enters from the rear room with a lighted lamp. She puts it on the drawing-room table, then goes out the way she came.*]

MRS. ELVSTED. [*Has got up and is walking uneasily to and fro*] Oh Hedda, Hedda! How is all this going to end?

HEDDA. At ten o'clock, then. He'll be here. I can see him. With a crown of vine-leaves in his hair.[12] Burning and unashamed!

MRS. ELVSTED. Oh, I do hope so!

HEDDA. Can't you see? Then he'll be himself again! He'll be a free man for the rest of his days!

MRS. ELVSTED. Please God you're right.

HEDDA. That's how he'll come! [*Gets up and goes closer*] You can doubt him as much as you like. I believe in him! Now we'll see which of us——

MRS. ELVSTED. You're after something, Hedda.

HEDDA. Yes, I am. For once in my life I want to have the power to shape a man's destiny.

MRS. ELVSTED. Haven't you that power already?

HEDDA. No, I haven't. I've never had it.

MRS. ELVSTED. What about your husband?

HEDDA. Him! Oh, if you could only understand how poor I am. And you're allowed to be so rich, so rich! [*Clasps her passionately*] I think I'll burn your hair off after all!

MRS. ELVSTED. Let me go! Let me go! You frighten me, Hedda!

BERTHA. [*In the open doorway*] I've laid tea in the dining room, madam.

HEDDA. Good, we're coming.

MRS. ELVSTED. No, no, no! I'd rather go home alone! Now—at once!

HEDDA. Rubbish! First you're going to have some tea, you little idiot. And then—at ten o'clock—Eilert Loevborg will come. With a crown of vine-leaves in his hair!

> [*She drags* MRS. ELVSTED *almost forcibly toward the open doorway.*]

Act III

SCENE—*The same. The curtains are drawn across the open doorway, and also across the french windows. The lamp, half turned down, with a shade over it, is burning on the table. In the stove, the door of which is open, a fire has been burning, but it is now almost out.*

MRS. ELVSTED, *wrapped in a large shawl and with her feet resting on a footstool, is sitting near the stove, huddled in the armchair.*

12. *A crown . . . hair:* Like Bacchus, the god of wine, and his followers.

HEDDA *is lying asleep on the sofa, fully dressed, with a blanket over her.*

MRS. ELVSTED. [*After a pause, suddenly sits up in her chair and listens tensely. Then she sinks wearily back again and sighs.*] Not back yet! Oh, God! Oh, God! Not back yet!

> [BERTHA *tiptoes cautiously in from the hall. She has a letter in her hand.*]

MRS. ELVSTED. [*Turns and whispers*] What is it? Has someone come?

BERTHA. [*Quietly*] Yes, a servant's just called with this letter.

MRS. ELVSTED. [*Quickly, holding out her hand*] A letter! Give it to me!

BERTHA. But it's for the Doctor, madam.

MRS. ELVSTED. Oh. I see.

BERTHA. Miss Tesman's maid brought it. I'll leave it here on the table.

MRS. ELVSTED. Yes, do.

BERTHA. [*Puts down the letter*] I'd better put the lamp out. It's starting to smoke.

MRS. ELVSTED. Yes, put it out. It'll soon be daylight.

BERTHA. [*Puts out the lamp*] It's daylight already, madam.

MRS. ELVSTED. Yes. Broad day. And not home yet.

BERTHA. Oh dear, I was afraid this would happen.

MRS. ELVSTED. Were you?

BERTHA. Yes. When I heard that a certain gentleman had returned to town, and saw him go off with them. I've heard all about him.

MRS. ELVSTED. Don't talk so loud. You'll wake your mistress.

BERTHA. [*Looks at the sofa and sighs*] Yes. Let her go on sleeping, poor dear. Shall I put some more wood on the fire?

MRS. ELVSTED. Thank you, don't bother on my account.

BERTHA. Very good.

> [*Goes quietly out through the hall*]

HEDDA. [*Wakes as the door closes and looks up*] What's that?

MRS. ELVSTED. It was only the maid.

HEDDA. [*Looks round*] What am I doing here? Oh, now I remember. [*Sits up on the sofa, stretches herself and rubs her eyes*] What time is it, Thea?

MRS. ELVSTED. It's gone seven.

HEDDA. When did Tesman get back?

MRS. ELVSTED. He's not back yet.

HEDDA. Not home yet?

MRS. ELVSTED. [*Gets up*] No one's come.

HEDDA. And we sat up waiting for them till four o'clock.

MRS. ELVSTED. God! How I waited for him!

HEDDA. [*Yawns and says with her hand in front of her mouth*] Oh, dear. We might have saved ourselves the trouble.

MRS. ELVSTED. Did you manage to sleep?

HEDDA. Oh, yes. Quite well, I think. Didn't you get any?

MRS. ELVSTED. Not a wink. I couldn't, Hedda. I just couldn't.

HEDDA. [*Gets up and comes over to her*] Now, now, now. There's nothing to worry about. I know what's happened.

MRS. ELVSTED. What? Please tell me.

HEDDA. Well, obviously the party went on very late——

MRS. ELVSTED. Oh dear, I suppose it must have. But——

HEDDA. And Tesman didn't want to come home and wake us all up in the middle of the night. [*Laughs*] Probably wasn't too keen to show his face either, after a spree like that.

MRS. ELVSTED. But where could he have gone?

HEDDA. I should think he's probably slept at his aunts'. They keep his old room for him.

MRS. ELVSTED. No, he can't be with them. A letter came for him just now from Miss Tesman. It's over there.

HEDDA. Oh? [*Looks at the envelope*] Yes, it's Auntie Juju's handwriting. Well, he must still be at Judge Brack's, then. And Eilert Loevborg is sitting there, reading to him. With a crown of vine-leaves in his hair.

MRS. ELVSTED. Hedda, you're only saying that. You don't believe it.

HEDDA. Thea, you really are a little fool.

MRS. ELVSTED. Perhaps I am.

HEDDA. You look tired to death.

MRS. ELVSTED. Yes. I am tired to death.

HEDDA. Go to my room and lie down for a little. Do as I say, now; don't argue.

MRS. ELVSTED. No, no. I couldn't possibly sleep.

HEDDA. Of course you can.

MRS. ELVSTED. But your husband'll be home soon. And I must know at once——

HEDDA. I'll tell you when he comes.

MRS. ELVSTED. Promise me, Hedda?

HEDDA. Yes, don't worry. Go and get some sleep.

MRS. ELVSTED. Thank you. All right, I'll try.

[*She goes out through the rear room.* HEDDA *goes to the french windows and draws the curtains. Broad daylight floods into the room. She goes to the writing table, takes a small hand mirror from it and arranges her hair. Then she goes to the door leading into the hall and presses the bell. After a few moments,* BERTHA *enters.*]

BERTHA. Did you want anything, madam?

HEDDA. Yes, put some more wood on the fire. I'm freezing.

BERTHA. Bless you, I'll soon have this room warmed up. [*She rakes the embers together and puts a fresh piece of wood on them. Suddenly she stops and listens.*] There's someone at the front door, madam.

HEDDA. Well, go and open it. I'll see to the fire.

BERTHA. It'll burn up in a moment.

[*She goes out through the hall.* HEDDA *kneels on the footstool and puts more wood in the stove. After a few seconds,*

GEORGE TESMAN *enters from the hall. He looks tired, and rather worried. He tiptoes toward the open doorway and is about to slip through the curtains.*]

HEDDA. [*At the stove, without looking up*] Good morning.

TESMAN. [*Turns*] Hedda! [*Comes nearer*] Good heavens, are you up already? What?

HEDDA. Yes, I got up very early this morning.

TESMAN. I was sure you'd still be sleeping. Fancy that!

HEDDA. Don't talk so loud. Mrs. Elvsted's asleep in my room.

TESMAN. Mrs. Elvsted? Has she stayed the night here?

HEDDA. Yes. No one came to escort her home.

TESMAN. Oh. No, I suppose not.

HEDDA. [*Closes the door of the stove and gets up*] Well. Was it fun?

TESMAN. Have you been anxious about me? What?

HEDDA. Not in the least. I asked if you'd had fun.

TESMAN. Oh yes, rather! Well, I thought, for once in a while—The first part was the best; when Eilert read his book to me. We arrived over an hour too early—what about that, eh? By Jove! Brack had a lot of things to see to, so Eilert read to me.

HEDDA. [*Sits at the right-hand side of the table*] Well? Tell me about it.

TESMAN. [*Sits on a footstool by the stove*] Honestly, Hedda, you've no idea what a book that's going to be. It's really one of the most remarkable things that's ever been written. By Jove!

HEDDA. Oh, never mind about the book——

TESMAN. I'm going to make a confession to you, Hedda. When he'd finished reading a sort of beastly feeling came over me.

HEDDA. Beastly feeling?

TESMAN. I found myself envying Eilert for being able to write like that. Imagine that, Hedda!

HEDDA. Yes. I can imagine.

TESMAN. What a tragedy that with all those gifts he should be so incorrigible.

HEDDA. You mean he's less afraid of life than most men?

TESMAN. Good heavens, no. He just doesn't know the meaning of the word moderation.

HEDDA. What happened afterwards?

TESMAN. Well, looking back on it I suppose you might almost call it an orgy, Hedda.

HEDDA. Had he vine-leaves in his hair?

TESMAN. Vine-leaves? No, I didn't see any of them. He made a long, rambling oration in honor of the woman who'd inspired him to write this book. Yes, those were the words he used.

HEDDA. Did he name her?

TESMAN. No. But I suppose it must be Mrs. Elvsted. You wait and see!

HEDDA. Where did you leave him?

TESMAN. On the way home. We left in a bunch—the last of us, that is—and Brack came with us to get a little fresh air. Well, then, you see, we agreed we ought to see Eilert home. He'd had a drop too much.

HEDDA. You don't say?

TESMAN. But now comes the funny part, Hedda. Or I should really say the tragic part. Oh, I'm almost ashamed to tell you. For Eilert's sake, I mean——

HEDDA. Why, what happened?

TESMAN. Well, you see, as we were walking toward town I happened to drop behind for a minute. Only for a minute—er—you understand——

HEDDA. Yes, yes——?

TESMAN. Well then, when I ran on to catch them up, what do you think I found by the roadside. What?

HEDDA. How on earth should I know?

TESMAN. You mustn't tell anyone, Hedda. What? Promise me that—for Eilert's sake. [*Takes a package wrapped in paper from his coat pocket*] Just fancy! I found this.

HEDDA. Isn't this the one he brought here yesterday?

TESMAN. Yes! The whole of that precious, irreplaceable manuscript! And he went and lost it! Didn't even notice! What about that? By Jove! Tragic.

HEDDA. But why didn't you give it back to him?

TESMAN. I didn't dare to, in the state he was in.

HEDDA. Didn't you tell any of the others?

TESMAN. Good heavens, no. I didn't want to do that. For Eilert's sake, you understand.

HEDDA. Then no one else knows you have his manuscript?

TESMAN. No. And no one must be allowed to know.

HEDDA. Didn't it come up in the conversation later?

TESMAN. I didn't get a chance to talk to him any more. As soon as we got into the outskirts of town, he and one or two of the others gave us the slip. Disappeared, by Jove!

HEDDA. Oh? I suppose they took him home.

TESMAN. Yes, I imagine that was the idea. Brack left us, too.

HEDDA. And what have you been up to since then?

TESMAN. Well, I and one or two of the others—awfully jolly chaps, they were—went back to where one of them lived, and had a cup of morning coffee. Morning-after coffee—what? Ah, well. I'll just lie down for a bit and give Eilert time to sleep it off, poor chap, then I'll run over and give this back to him.

HEDDA. [*Holds out her hand for the package*] No, don't do that. Not just yet. Let me read it first.

TESMAN. Oh no, really, Hedda dear, honestly, I daren't do that.

HEDDA. Daren't?

TESMAN. No—imagine how desperate he'll be when he wakes up and finds his manuscript's missing. He hasn't any copy, you see. He told me so himself.

HEDDA. Can't a thing like that be rewritten?

TESMAN. Oh no, not possibly, I shouldn't think. I mean, the inspiration, you know——

HEDDA. Oh, yes. I'd forgotten that. [*Casually*] By the way, there's a letter for you.

TESMAN. Is there? Fancy that!

HEDDA. [*Holds it out to him*] It came early this morning.

TESMAN. I say, it's from Auntie Juju! What on earth can it be? [*Puts the package on the other footstool, opens the letter, reads it and jumps up*] Oh, Hedda! She says poor Auntie Rena's dying.

HEDDA. Well, we've been expecting that.

TESMAN. She says if I want to see her I must go quickly. I'll run over at once.

HEDDA. [*Hides a smile*] Run?

TESMAN. Hedda dear, I suppose you wouldn't like to come with me? What about that, eh?

HEDDA. [*Gets up and says wearily and with repulsion*] No, no, don't ask me to do anything like that. I can't bear illness or death. I loathe anything ugly.

TESMAN. Yes, yes. Of course. [*In a dither*] My hat? My overcoat? Oh yes, in the hall. I do hope I won't get there too late, Hedda? What?

HEDDA. You'll be all right if you run.

[BERTHA *enters from the hall.*]

BERTHA. Judge Brack's outside and wants to know if he can come in.

TESMAN. At this hour? No, I can't possibly receive him now.

HEDDA. I can. [*To* BERTHA] Ask his honor to come in.

[BERTHA *goes.*]

HEDDA. [*Whispers quickly*] The manuscript, Tesman.

[*She snatches it from the footstool.*]

TESMAN. Yes, give it to me.

HEDDA. No, I'll look after it for now.

[*She goes over to the writing table and puts it in the bookcase.* TESMAN *stands dithering, unable to get his gloves on.* JUDGE BRACK *enters from the hall.*]

HEDDA. [*Nods to him*] Well, you're an early bird.

BRACK. Yes, aren't I? [*To* TESMAN] Are you up and about, too?

TESMAN. Yes, I've got to go and see my aunts. Poor Auntie Rena's dying.

BRACK. Oh dear, is she? Then you mustn't let me detain you. At so tragic a——

TESMAN. Yes, I really must run. Good-bye! Good-bye!

[*Runs out through the hall*]

HEDDA. [*Goes nearer*] You seem to have had excellent sport last night—Judge.

BRACK. Indeed yes, Mrs. Hedda. I haven't even had time to take my clothes off.

HEDDA. *You* haven't either?

BRACK. As you see. What's Tesman told you about last night's escapades?

HEDDA. Oh, only some boring story about having gone and drunk coffee somewhere.

BRACK. Yes, I've heard about that coffee party. Eilert Loevborg wasn't with them, I gather?

HEDDA. No, they took him home first.

BRACK. Did Tesman go with him?

HEDDA. No, one or two of the others, he said.

BRACK. [*Smiles*] George Tesman is a credulous man, Mrs. Hedda.

HEDDA. God knows. But—has something happened?

BRACK. Well, yes, I'm afraid it has.

HEDDA. I see. Sit down and tell me.

[*She sits on the left of the table,* BRACK *at the long side of it, near her.*]

HEDDA. Well?

BRACK. I had a special reason for keeping track of my guests last night. Or perhaps I should say some of my guests.

HEDDA. Including Eilert Loevborg?

BRACK. I must confess—yes.

HEDDA. You're beginning to make me curious.

BRACK. Do you know where he and some of my other guests spent the latter half of last night, Mrs. Hedda?

HEDDA. Tell me. If it won't shock me.

BRACK. Oh, I don't think it'll shock you. They found themselves participating in an exceedingly animated *soirée*.[13]

HEDDA. Of a sporting character?

BRACK. Of a highly sporting character.

HEDDA. Tell me more.

BRACK. Loevborg had received an invitation in advance—as had the others. I knew all about that. But he had refused. As you know, he's become a new man.

HEDDA. Up at the Elvsteds', yes. But he went?

BRACK. Well, you see, Mrs. Hedda, last night at my house, unhappily, the spirit moved him.

HEDDA. Yes, I hear he became inspired.

BRACK. Somewhat violently inspired. And as a result, I suppose, his thoughts strayed. We men, alas, don't always stick to our principles as firmly as we should.

HEDDA. I'm sure you're an exception, Judge Brack. But go on about Loevborg.

BRACK. Well, to cut a long story short, he ended up in the establishment of a certain Mademoiselle Danielle.

HEDDA. Mademoiselle Danielle?

BRACK. She was holding the *soirée*. For a selected circle of friends and admirers.

HEDDA. Has she got red hair?

BRACK. She has.

HEDDA. A singer of some kind?

BRACK. Yes—among other accomplishments. She's also a celebrated

---

13. *Soirée:* Evening party.

huntress—of men, Mrs. Hedda. I'm sure you've heard about her. Eilert Loevborg used to be one of her most ardent patrons. In his salad days.[14]

HEDDA. And how did all this end?

BRACK. Not entirely amicably, from all accounts. Mademoiselle Danielle began by receiving him with the utmost tenderness and ended by resorting to her fists.

HEDDA. Against Loevborg?

BRACK. Yes. He accused her, or her friends, of having robbed him. He claimed his pocketbook had been stolen. Among other things. In short, he seems to have made a bloodthirsty scene.

HEDDA. And what did this lead to?

BRACK. It led to a general free-for-all, in which both sexes participated. Fortunately, in the end the police arrived.

HEDDA. The police too?

BRACK. Yes. I'm afraid it may turn out to be rather an expensive joke for Master Eilert. Crazy fool!

HEDDA. Oh?

BRACK. Apparently he put up a very violent resistance. Hit one of the constables on the ear and tore his uniform. He had to accompany them to the police station.

HEDDA. Where did you learn all this?

BRACK. From the police.

HEDDA. [*To herself*] So that's what happened. He didn't have a crown of vine-leaves in his hair.

BRACK. Vine-leaves, Mrs. Hedda?

HEDDA. [*In her normal voice again*] But, tell me, Judge, why do you take such a close interest in Eilert Loevborg?

BRACK. For one thing it'll hardly be a matter of complete indifference to me if it's revealed in court that he came there straight from my house.

HEDDA. Will it come to court?

BRACK. Of course. Well, I don't regard that as particularly serious. Still, I thought it my duty, as a friend of the family, to give you and your husband a full account of his nocturnal adventures.

HEDDA. Why?

BRACK. Because I've a shrewd suspicion that he's hoping to use you as a kind of screen.

HEDDA. What makes you think that?

BRACK. Oh, for heaven's sake, Mrs. Hedda, we're not blind. You wait and see. This Mrs. Elvsted won't be going back to her husband just yet.

HEDDA. Well, if there were anything between those two there are plenty of other places where they could meet.

BRACK. Not in anyone's home. From now on every respectable house will once again be closed to Eilert Loevborg.

HEDDA. And mine should be too, you mean?

14. *Salad days:* Indiscreet youth.

BRACK. Yes. I confess I should find it more than irksome if this
gentleman were to be granted unrestricted access to this house.
If he were superfluously to intrude into——

HEDDA. The triangle?

BRACK. Precisely. For me it would be like losing a home.

HEDDA. [*Looks at him and smiles*] I see. You want to be the cock
of the walk.

BRACK. [*Nods slowly and lowers his voice*] Yes, that is my aim.
And I shall fight for it with—every weapon at my disposal.

HEDDA. [*As her smile fades*] You're a dangerous man, aren't you?
When you really want something.

BRACK. You think so?

HEDDA. Yes. I'm beginning to think so. I'm deeply thankful you
haven't any kind of hold over me.

BRACK. [*Laughs equivocally*] Well, well, Mrs. Hedda—perhaps
you're right. If I had, who knows what I might not think up?

HEDDA. Come, Judge Brack. That sounds almost like a threat.

BRACK. [*Gets up*] Heaven forbid! In the creation of a triangle—and
its continuance—the question of compulsion should never arise.

HEDDA. Exactly what I was thinking.

BRACK. Well, I've said what I came to say. I must be getting back.
Good-bye, Mrs. Hedda.

　　　[*Goes toward the french windows*]

HEDDA. [*Gets up*] Are you going out through the garden?

BRACK. Yes, it's shorter.

HEDDA. Yes. And it's the back door, isn't it?

BRACK. I've nothing against back doors. They can be quite intriguing—sometimes.

HEDDA. When people fire pistols out of them, for example?

BRACK. [*In the doorway, laughs*] Oh, people don't shoot tame cocks.

HEDDA. [*Laughs too*] I suppose not. When they've only got one.
　　　[*They nod good-bye, laughing. He goes. She closes the french
　　　windows behind him, and stands for a moment, looking out
　　　pensively. Then she walks across the room and glances
　　　through the curtains in the open doorway. Goes to the writ-
　　　ing table, takes* LOEVBORG's *package from the bookcase and
　　　is about to leaf through the pages when* BERTHA *is heard
　　　remonstrating loudly in the hall.* HEDDA *turns and listens.
　　　She hastily puts the package back in the drawer, locks it
　　　and puts the key on the inkstand.* EILBERT LOEVBORG, *with
　　　his overcoat on and his hat in his hand, throws the door
　　　open. He looks somewhat confused and excited.*]

LOEVBORG. [*Shouts as he enters*] I must come in, I tell you! Let me
pass!
　　　[*He closes the door, turns, see* HEDDA, *controls himself im-
　　　mediately and bows.*]

HEDDA. [*At the writing table*] Well, Mr. Loevborg, this is rather a
late hour to be collecting Thea.

LOEVBORG. And an early hour to call on you. Please forgive me.

HEDDA. How do you know she's still here?

LOEVBORG. They told me at her lodgings that she has been out all night.

HEDDA. [*Goes to the table*] Did you notice anything about their behavior when they told you?

LOEVBORG. [*Looks at her, puzzled*] Notice anything?

HEDDA. Did they sound as if they thought it—strange?

LOEVBORG. [*Suddenly understands*] Oh, I see what you mean. I'm dragging her down with me. No, as a matter of fact I didn't notice anything. I suppose Tesman isn't up yet?

HEDDA. No, I don't think so.

LOEVBORG. When did he get home?

HEDDA. Very late.

LOEVBORG. Did he tell you anything?

HEDDA. Yes. I gather you had a merry party at Judge Brack's last night.

LOEVBORG. He didn't tell you anything else?

HEDDA. I don't think so. I was so terribly sleepy——

[MRS. ELVSTED *comes through the curtains in the open doorway.*]

MRS. ELVSTED. [*Runs toward him*] Oh, Eilert! At last!

LOEVBORG. Yes—at last. And too late.

MRS. ELVSTED. What is too late?

LOEVBORG. Everything—now. I'm finished, Thea.

MRS. ELVSTED. Oh, no, no! Don't say that!

LOEVBORG. You'll say it yourself, when you've heard what I——

MRS. ELVSTED. I don't want to hear anything!

HEDDA. Perhaps you'd rather speak to her alone? I'd better go.

LOEVBORG. No, stay.

MRS. ELVSTED. But I don't want to hear anything, I tell you!

LOEVBORG. It's not about last night.

MRS. ELVSTED. Then what——?

LOEVBORG. I want to tell you that from now on we must stop seeing each other.

MRS. ELVSTED. Stop seeing each other!

HEDDA. [*Involuntarily*] I knew it!

LOEVBORG. I have no further use for you, Thea.

MRS. ELVSTED. You can stand there and say that! No further use for me! Surely I can go on helping you? We'll go on working together, won't we?

LOEVBORG. I don't intend to do any more work from now on.

MRS. ELVSTED. [*Desperately*] Then what use have I for my life?

LOEVBORG. You must try to live as if you had never known me.

MRS. ELVSTED. But I can't!

LOEVBORG. Try to, Thea. Go back home——

MRS. ELVSTED. Never! I want to be wherever you are! I won't let myself be driven away like this! I want to stay here—and be with you when the book comes out.

HEDDA. [*Whispers*] Ah, yes! The book!

LOEVBORG. [*Looks at her*] Our book; Thea's and mine. It belongs to both of us.

MRS. ELVSTED. Oh, yes! I feel that, too! And I've a right to be with you when it comes into the world. I want to see people respect and honor you again. And the joy! The joy! I want to share it with you!

LOEVBORG. Thea—our book will never come into the world.

HEDDA. Ah!

MRS. ELVSTED. Not——?

LOEVBORG. It cannot. Ever.

MRS. ELVSTED. Eilert—what have you done with the manuscript? Where is it?

LOEVBORG. Oh Thea, please don't ask me that!

MRS. ELVSTED. Yes, yes—I must know. I've a right to know. Now!

LOEVBORG. The manuscript. I've torn it up.

MRS. ELVSTED. [*Screams*] No, no!

HEDDA. [*Involuntarily*] But that's not——!

LOEVBORG. [*Looks at her*] Not true, you think?

HEDDA. [*Controls herself*] Why—yes, of course it is, if you say so. It just sounded so incredible——

LOEVBORG. It's true, nevertheless.

MRS. ELVSTED. Oh, my God, my God, Hedda—he's destroyed his own book!

LOEVBORG. I have destroyed my life. Why not my life's work, too?

MRS. ELVSTED. And you—did this last night?

LOEVBORG. Yes, Thea. I tore it into a thousand pieces. And scattered them out across the fjord.[15] It's good, clean, salt water. Let it carry them away; let them drift in the current and the wind. And in a little while, they will sink. Deeper and deeper. As I shall, Thea.

MRS. ELVSTED. Do you know, Eilert—this book—all my life I shall feel as though you'd killed a little child?

LOEVBORG. You're right. It is like killing a child.

MRS. ELVSTED. But how could you? It was my child, too!

HEDDA. [*Almost inaudibly*] Oh—the child——!

MRS. ELVSTED. [*Breathes heavily*] It's all over, then. Well—I'll go now, Hedda.

HEDDA. You're not leaving town?

MRS. ELVSTED. I don't know what I'm going to do. I can't see anything except—darkness.

    [*She goes out through the hall.*]

HEDDA. [*Waits a moment*] Aren't you going to escort her home, Mr. Loevborg?

LOEVBORG. I? Through the streets? Do you want me to let people see her with me?

HEDDA. Of course I don't know what else may have happened last night. But is it so utterly beyond redress?

---

15. *Fjord:* An inlet of the sea. [Pronounced *fyord*.]

LOEVBORG. It isn't just last night. It'll go on happening. I know it.
But the curse of it is, I don't want to live that kind of life. I
don't want to start all that again. She's broken my courage. I
can't spit in the eyes of the world any longer.

HEDDA. [*As though to herself*] That pretty little fool's been trying
to shape a man's destiny. [*Looks at him*] But how could you be
so heartless toward her?

LOEVBORG. Don't call me heartless!

HEDDA. To go and destroy the one thing that's made her life worth
living? You don't call that heartless?

LOEVBORG. Do you want to know the truth, Hedda?

HEDDA. The truth?

LOEVBORG. Promise me first—give me your word—that you'll never
let Thea know about this.

HEDDA. I give you my word.

LOEVBORG. Good. Well; what I told her just now was a lie.

HEDDA. About the manuscript?

LOEVBORG. Yes. I didn't tear it up. Or throw it in the fjord.

HEDDA. You didn't? But where is it, then?

LOEVBORG. I destroyed it, all the same. I destroyed it, Hedda!

HEDDA. I don't understand.

LOEVBORG. Thea said that what I had done was like killing a child.

HEDDA. Yes. That's what she said.

LOEVBORG. But to kill a child isn't the worst thing a father can do
to it.

HEDDA. What could be worse than that?

LOEVBORG. Hedda—suppose a man came home one morning, after a
night of debauchery, and said to the mother of his child: "Look
here. I've been wandering round all night. I've been to—such-
and-such a place and such-and-such a place. And I had our child
with me. I took him to—these places. And I've lost him. Just—
lost him. God knows where he is or whose hands he's fallen
into."

HEDDA. I see. But when all's said and done, this was only a book——

LOEVBORG. Thea's heart and soul were in that book. It was her
whole life.

HEDDA. Yes. I understand.

LOEVBORG. Well, then you must also understand that she and I
cannot possibly ever see each other again.

HEDDA. Where will you go?

LOEVBORG. Nowhere. I just want to put an end to it all. As soon
as possible.

HEDDA. [*Takes a step toward him*] Eilert Loevborg, listen to me.
Do it—beautifully!

LOEVBORG. Beautifully? [*Smiles*] With a crown of vine-leaves in my
hair? The way you used to dream of me—in the old days?

HEDDA. No. I don't believe in that crown any longer. But—do it
beautifully, all the same. Just this once. Good-bye. You must go
now. And don't come back.

LOEVBORG. Adieu, madam. Give my love to George Tesman.
[*Turns to go*]
HEDDA. Wait. I want to give you a souvenir to take with you.
[*She goes over to the writing table, opens the drawer and the pistol-case, and comes back to* LOEVBORG *with one of the pistols.*]
LOEVBORG. [*Looks at her*] This? Is this the souvenir?
HEDDA. [*Nods slowly*] You recognize it? You looked down its barrel once.
LOEVBORG. You should have used it then.
HEDDA. Here! Use it now!
LOEVBORG. [*Puts the pistol in his breast pocket*] Thank you.
HEDDA. Do it beautifully, Eilert Loevborg. Only promise me that!
LOEVBORG. Good-bye, Hedda Gabler.
[*He goes out through the hall.* HEDDA *stands by the door for a moment, listening. Then she goes over to the writing table, takes out the package containing the manuscript, glances inside it, pulls some of the pages half out and looks at them. Then she takes it to the armchair by the stove and sits down with the package in her lap. After a moment, she opens the door of the stove; then she opens the packet.*]
HEDDA. [*Throws one of the pages into the stove and whispers to herself*] I'm burning your child, Thea! You with your beautiful wavy hair! [*She throws a few more pages into the stove.*] The child Eilert Loevborg gave you. [*Throws the rest of the manuscript in*] I'm burning it! I'm burning your child!

Act IV

SCENE—*The same. It is evening. The drawing room is in darkness. The small room is illuminated by the hanging lamp over the table. The curtains are drawn across the french windows.* HEDDA, *dressed in black, is walking up and down in the darkened room. Then she goes into the small room and crosses to the left. A few chords are heard from the piano. She comes back into the drawing room.*

BERTHA *comes through the small room from the right with a lighted lamp, which she places on the table in front of the corner sofa in the drawing room. Her eyes are red with crying, and she has black ribbons on her cap. She goes quietly out, right.* HEDDA *goes over to the french windows, draws the curtains slightly to one side and looks out into the darkness.*

A few moments later, MISS TESMAN *enters from the hall. She is dressed in mourning, with a black hat and veil.* HEDDA *goes to meet her and holds out her hand.*

MISS TESMAN. Well, Hedda, here I am in the weeds of sorrow. My poor sister has ended her struggles at last.
HEDDA. I've already heard. Tesman sent me a card.

MISS TESMAN. Yes, he promised me he would. But I thought, no, I must go and break the news of death to Hedda myself—here, in the house of life.

HEDDA. It's very kind of you.

MISS TESMAN. Ah, Rena shouldn't have chosen a time like this to pass away. This is no moment for Hedda's house to be a place of mourning.

HEDDA. [*Changing the subject*] She died peacefully, Miss Tesman?

MISS TESMAN. Oh, it was quite beautiful! The end came so calmly. And she was so happy at being able to see George once again. And say good-bye to him. Hasn't he come home yet?

HEDDA. No. He wrote that I mustn't expect him too soon. But please sit down.

MISS TESMAN. No, thank you, Hedda dear—bless you. I'd like to. But I've so little time. I must dress her and lay her out as well as I can. She shall go to her grave looking really beautiful.

HEDDA. Can't I help with anything?

MISS TESMAN. Why, you mustn't think of such a thing! Hedda Tesman mustn't let her hands be soiled by contact with death. Or her thoughts. Not at this time.

HEDDA. One can't always control one's thoughts.

MISS TESMAN. [*Continues*] Ah, well, that's life. Now we must start to sew poor Rena's shroud. There'll be sewing to be done in this house too before long, I shouldn't wonder. But not for a shroud, praise God.

[GEORGE TESMAN *enters from the hall.*]

HEDDA. You've come at last! Thank heavens!

TESMAN. Are you here, Auntie Juju? With Hedda? Fancy that!

MISS TESMAN. I was just on the point of leaving, dear boy. Well, have you done everything you promised me?

TESMAN. No, I'm afraid I forgot half of it. I'll have to run over again tomorrow. My head's in a complete whirl today. I can't collect my thoughts.

MISS TESMAN. But George dear, you mustn't take it like this.

TESMAN. Oh? Well—er—how should I?

MISS TESMAN. You must be happy in your grief. Happy for what's happened. As I am.

TESMAN. Oh, yes, yes. You're thinking of Aunt Rena.

HEDDA. It'll be lonely for you now, Miss Tesman.

MISS TESMAN. For the first few days, yes. But it won't last long, I hope. Poor dear Rena's little room isn't going to stay empty.

TESMAN. Oh? Whom are you going to move in there? What?

MISS TESMAN. Oh, there's always some poor invalid who needs care and attention.

HEDDA. Do you really want another cross like that to bear?

MISS TESMAN. Cross! God forgive you, child. It's been no cross for me.

HEDDA. But now—if a complete stranger comes to live with you——?

MISS TESMAN. Oh, one soon makes friends with invalids. And I need so much to have someone to live for. Like you, my dear. Well, I expect there'll soon be work in this house too for an old aunt, praise God!

HEDDA. Oh—please!

TESMAN. By Jove, yes! What a splendid time the three of us could have together if——

HEDDA. If?

TESMAN. [*Uneasily*] Oh, never mind. It'll all work out. Let's hope so—what?

MISS TESMAN. Yes, yes. Well, I'm sure you two would like to be alone. [*Smiles*] Perhaps Hedda may have something to tell you, George. Good-bye. I must go home to Rena. [*Turns to the door*] Dear God, how strange! Now Rena is with me and with poor dear Joachim.

TESMAN. Fancy that. Yes, Auntie Juju! What?

[MISS TESMAN *goes out through the hall.*]

HEDDA. [*Follows* TESMAN *coldly and searchingly with her eyes*] I really believe this death distresses you more than it does her.

TESMAN. Oh, it isn't just Auntie Rena. It's Eilert I'm so worried about.

HEDDA. [*Quickly*] Is there any news of him?

TESMAN. I ran over to see him this afternoon. I wanted to tell him his manuscript was in safe hands.

HEDDA. Oh? You didn't find him?

TESMAN. No. He wasn't at home. But later I met Mrs. Elvsted and she told me he'd been here early this morning.

HEDDA. Yes, just after you'd left.

TESMAN. It seems he said he'd torn the manuscript up. What?

HEDDA. Yes, he claimed to have done so.

TESMAN. You told him we had it, of course?

HEDDA. No. [*Quickly*] Did you tell Mrs. Elvsted?

TESMAN. No, I didn't like to. But you ought to have told him. Think if he should go home and do something desperate! Give me the manuscript, Hedda. I'll run over to him with it right away. Where did you put it?

HEDDA. [*Cold and motionless, leaning against the armchair*] I haven't got it any longer.

TESMAN. Haven't got it? What on earth do you mean?

HEDDA. I've burned it.

TESMAN. [*Starts, terrified*] Burned it! Burned Eilert's manuscript!

HEDDA. Don't shout. The servant will hear you.

TESMAN. Burned it! But in heaven's name——! Oh, no, no, no! This is impossible!

HEDDA. Well, it's true.

TESMAN. But Hedda, do you realize what you've done? That's appropriating lost property! It's against the law! By Jove! You ask Judge Brack and see if I'm not right.

HEDDA. You'd be well advised not to talk about it to Judge Brack or anyone else.

TESMAN. But how could you go and do such a dreadful thing? What on earth put the idea into your head? What came over you? Answer me! What?

HEDDA. [*Represses on almost imperceptible smile*] I did it for your sake, George.

TESMAN. For my sake?

HEDDA. When you came home this morning and described how he'd read his book to you——

TESMAN. Yes, yes?

HEDDA. You admitted you were jealous of him.

TESMAN. But, good heavens, I didn't mean it literally!

HEDDA. No matter. I couldn't bear the thought that anyone else should push you into the background.

TESMAN. [*Torn between doubt and joy*] Hedda—is this true? But— but—but I never realized you loved me like that! Fancy——

HEDDA. Well, I suppose you'd better know. I'm going to have—— [*Breaks off and says violently*] No, no—you'd better ask your Auntie Juju. She'll tell you.

TESMAN. Hedda! I think I understand what you mean. [*Clasps his hands*] Good heavens, can it really be true! What?

HEDDA. Don't shout. The servant will hear you.

TESMAN. [*Laughing with joy*] The servant! I say, that's good! The servant! Why, that's Bertha! I'll run out and tell her at once!

HEDDA. [*Clenches her hands in despair*] Oh, it's destroying me, all this—it's destroying me!

TESMAN. I say, Hedda, what's up? What?

HEDDA. [*Cold, controlled*] Oh, it's all so—absurd—George.

TESMAN. Absurd? That I'm so happy? But surely——? Ah, well— perhaps I won't say anything to Bertha.

HEDDA. No, do. She might as well know too.

TESMAN. No, no, I won't tell her yet. But Auntie Juju—I must let her know! And you—you called me George! For the first time! Fancy that! Oh, it'll make Auntie Juju so happy, all this! So very happy!

HEDDA. Will she be happy when she hears I've burned Eilert Loev- borg's manuscript—for your sake?

TESMAN. No, I'd forgotten about that. Of course no one must be allowed to know about the manuscript. But that you're burning with love for me, Hedda, I must certainly let Auntie Juju know that. I say, I wonder if young wives often feel like that toward their husbands? What?

HEDDA. You might ask Auntie Juju about that too.

TESMAN. I will, as soon as I get the chance. [*Looks uneasy and thoughtful again*] But I say, you know, that manuscript. Dread- ful business. Poor Eilert!

[MRS. ELVSTED, *dressed as on her first visit, with hat and overcoat, enters from the hall.*]

MRS. ELVSTED. [*Greets them hastily and tremulously*] Oh, Hedda dear, do please forgive me for coming here again.

HEDDA. Why, Thea, what's happened?

TESMAN. Is it anything to do with Eilert Loevborg? What?

MRS. ELVSTED. Yes—I'm so dreadfully afraid he may have met with an accident.

HEDDA. [*Grips her arm*] You think so?

TESMAN. But, good heavens, Mrs. Elvsted, what makes you think that?

MRS. ELVSTED. I heard them talking about him at the boarding-house, as I went in. Oh, there are the most terrible rumors being spread about him in town today.

TESMAN. Fancy. Yes, I heard about them too. But I can testify that he went straight home to bed. Fancy that!

HEDDA. Well—what did they say in the boarding-house?

MRS. ELVSTED. Oh, I couldn't find out anything. Either they didn't know, or else—— They stopped talking when they saw me. And I didn't dare to ask.

TESMAN. [*Fidgets uneasily*] We must hope—we must hope you misheard them, Mrs. Elvsted.

MRS. ELVSTED. No, no, I'm sure it was he they were talking about. I heard them say something about a hospital——

TESMAN. Hospital!

HEDDA. Oh no, surely that's impossible!

MRS. ELVSTED. Oh, I became so afraid. So I went up to his rooms and asked to see him.

HEDDA. Do you think that was wise, Thea?

MRS. ELVSTED. Well, what else could I do? I couldn't bear the uncertainty any longer.

TESMAN. But *you* didn't manage to find him either? What?

MRS. ELVSTED. No. And they had no idea where he was. They said he hadn't been home since yesterday afternoon.

TESMAN. Since yesterday? Fancy that!

MRS. ELVSTED. I'm sure he must have met with an accident.

TESMAN. Hedda, I wonder if I ought to go into town and make one or two enquiries?

HEDDA. No, no, don't you get mixed up in this.

> [JUDGE BRACK *enters from the hall, hat in hand.* BERTHA, *who has opened the door for him, closes it. He looks serious and greets them silently.*]

TESMAN. Hullo, my dear Judge. Fancy seeing you!

BRACK. I had to come and talk to you.

TESMAN. I can see Auntie Juju's told you the news.

BRACK. Yes, I've heard about that too.

TESMAN. Tragic, isn't it?

BRACK. Well, my dear chap, that depends how you look at it.

TESMAN. [*Looks uncertainly at him*] Has something else happened?

BRACK. Yes.

HEDDA. Another tragedy?

BRACK. That also depends on how you look at it, Mrs. Tesman.

MRS. ELVSTED. Oh, it's something to do with Eilert Loevborg!

BRACK. [*Looks at her for a moment*] How did you guess? Perhaps you've heard already——?

MRS. ELVSTED. [*Confused*] No, no, not at all—I——

TESMAN. For heaven's sake, tell us!

BRACK. [*Shrugs his shoulders*] Well, I'm afraid they've taken him to the hospital. He's dying.

MRS. ELVSTED. [*Screams*] Oh God, God!

TESMAN. The hospital! Dying!

HEDDA. [*Involuntarily*] So quickly!

MRS. ELVSTED. [*Weeping*] Oh, Hedda! And we parted enemies!

HEDDA. [*Whispers*] Thea—Thea!

MRS. ELVSTED. [*Ignoring her*] I must see him! I must see him before he dies!

BRACK. It's no use, Mrs. Elvsted. No one's allowed to see him now.

MRS. ELVSTED. But what's happened to him? You must tell me!

TESMAN. He hasn't tried to do anything to himself? What?

HEDDA. Yes, he has. I'm sure of it.

TESMAN. Hedda, how can you——?

BRACK. [*Who has not taken his eyes from her*] I'm afraid you've guessed correctly, Mrs. Tesman.

MRS. ELVSTED. How dreadful!

TESMAN. Attempted suicide! Fancy that!

HEDDA. Shot himself!

BRACK. Right again, Mrs. Tesman.

MRS. ELVSTED. [*Tries to compose herself*] When did this happen, Judge Brack?

BRACK. This afternoon. Between three and four.

TESMAN. But, good heavens—where? What?

BRACK. [*A little hesitantly*] Where? Why, my dear chap, in his rooms of course.

MRS. ELVSTED. No, that's impossible. I was there soon after six.

BRACK. Well, it must have been somewhere else, then. I don't know exactly. I only know that they found him. He'd shot himself—through the breast.

MRS. ELVSTED. Oh, how horrible! That he should end like that!

HEDDA. [*To* BRACK] Through the breast, you said?

BRACK. That is what I said.

HEDDA. Not through the head?

BRACK. Through the breast, Mrs. Tesman.

HEDDA. The breast. Yes; yes. That's good, too.

BRACK. Why, Mrs. Tesman?

HEDDA. Oh—no, I didn't mean anything.

TESMAN. And the wound's dangerous, you say? What?

BRACK. Mortal. He's probably already dead.

MRS. ELVSTED. Yes, yes—I feel it! It's all over. All over. Oh Hedda——!

TESMAN. But, tell me, how did you manage to learn all this?

BRACK. [*Curtly*] From the police. I spoke to one of them.

HEDDA. [*Loudly, clearly*] At last! Oh, thank God!

TESMAN. [*Appalled*] For God's sake, Hedda, what are you saying?

HEDDA. I am saying there's beauty in what he has done.

BRACK. Mm—Mrs. Tesman——

TESMAN. Beauty! Oh, but I say!

MRS. ELVSTED. Hedda, how can you talk of beauty in connection with a thing like this?

HEDDA. Eilert Loevborg has settled his account with life. He's had the courage to do what—what he had to do.

MRS. ELVSTED. No, that's not why it happened. He did it because he was mad.

TESMAN. He did it because he was desperate.

HEDDA. You're wrong! I know!

MRS. ELVSTED. He must have been mad. The same as when he tore up the manuscript.

BRACK. [*Starts*] Manuscript? Did he tear it up?

MRS. ELVSTED. Yes. Last night.

TESMAN. [*Whispers*] Oh, Hedda, we shall never be able to escape from this.

BRACK. Hm. Strange.

TESMAN. [*Wanders round the room*] To think of Eilert dying like that. And not leaving behind him the thing that would have made his name endure.

MRS. ELVSTED. If only it could be pieced together again!

TESMAN. Yes, fancy! If only it could! I'd give anything——

MRS. ELVSTED. Perhaps it can, Mr. Tesman.

TESMAN. What do you mean?

MRS. ELVSTED. [*Searches in the pocket of her dress*] Look! I kept the notes he dictated it from.

HEDDA. [*Takes a step nearer*] Ah!

TESMAN. You kept them, Mrs. Elvsted! What?

MRS. ELVSTED. Yes, here they are. I brought them with me when I left home. They've been in my pocket ever since.

TESMAN. Let me have a look.

MRS. ELVSTED. [*Hands him a wad of small sheets of paper*] They're in a terrible muddle. All mixed up.

TESMAN. I say, just fancy if we can sort them out! Perhaps if we work on them together——?

MRS. ELVSTED. Oh, yes! Let's try, anyway!

TESMAN. We'll manage it. We must! I shall dedicate my life to this.

HEDDA. *You*, George? Your life?

TESMAN. Yes—well, all the time I can spare. My book'll have to wait. Hedda, you do understand? What? I owe it to Eilert's memory.

HEDDA. Perhaps.

TESMAN. Well, my dear Mrs. Elvsted, you and I'll have to pool our brains. No use crying over spilt milk, what? We must try to approach this matter calmly.

MRS. ELVSTED. Yes, yes, Mr. Tesman. I'll do my best.

TESMAN. Well, come over here and let's start looking at these notes right away. Where shall we sit? Here? No, the other room. You'll excuse us, won't you, Judge? Come along with me, Mrs. Elvsted.

MRS. ELVSTED. Oh, God! If only we can manage to do it!

[TESMAN *and* MRS. ELVSTED *go into the rear room. He takes off his hat and overcoat. They sit at the table beneath the hanging lamp and absorb themselves in the notes.* HEDDA *walks across to the stove and sits in the armchair. After a moment,* BRACK *goes over to her.*]

HEDDA. [*Half aloud*] Oh, Judge! This act of Eilert Loevborg's—doesn't it give one a sense of release!

BRACK. Release, Mrs. Hedda? Well, it's a release for him, of course——

HEDDA. Oh, I don't mean him—I mean me! The release of knowing that someone can do something really brave! Something beautiful!

BRACK. [*Smiles*] Hm—my dear Mrs. Hedda——

HEDDA. Oh, I know what you're going to say. You're a bourgeois at heart too, just like—ah, well!

BRACK. [*Looks at her*] Eilert Loevborg has meant more to you than you're willing to admit to yourself. Or am I wrong?

HEDDA. I'm not answering questions like that from you. I only know that Eilert Loevborg has had the courage to live according to his own principles. And now, at last, he's done something big! Something beautiful! To have the courage and the will to rise from the feast of life so early!

BRACK. It distresses me deeply, Mrs. Hedda, but I'm afraid I must rob you of that charming illusion.

HEDDA. Illusion?

BRACK. You wouldn't have been allowed to keep it for long, anyway.

HEDDA. What do you mean?

BRACK. He didn't shoot himself on purpose.

HEDDA. Not on purpose?

BRACK. No. It didn't happen quite the way I told you.

HEDDA. Have you been hiding something? What is it?

BRACK. In order to spare poor Mrs. Elvsted's feelings, I permitted myself one or two small—equivocations.

HEDDA. What?

BRACK. To begin with, he is already dead.

HEDDA. He died at the hospital?

BRACK. Yes. Without regaining consciousness.

HEDDA. What else haven't you told us?

BRACK. The incident didn't take place at his lodgings.

HEDDA. Well, that's utterly unimportant.

BRACK. Not utterly. The fact is, you see, that Eilert Loevborg was found shot in Mademoiselle Danielle's boudoir.

HEDDA. [*Almost jumps up, but instead sinks back in her chair*]

That's impossible. He can't have been there today.

BRACK. He was there this afternoon. He went to ask for something he claimed they'd taken from him. Talked some crazy nonsense about a child which had got lost——

HEDDA. Oh! So that was the reason!

BRACK. I thought at first he might have been referring to his manuscript. But I hear he destroyed that himself. So he must have meant his pocketbook—I suppose.

HEDDA. Yes, I suppose so. So they found him there?

BRACK. Yes; there. With a discharged pistol in his breast pocket. The shot had wounded him mortally.

HEDDA. Yes. In the breast.

BRACK. No. In the—hm—stomach. The—lower part——

HEDDA. [*Looks at him with an expression of repulsion*] That too! Oh, why does everything I touch become mean and ludicrous? It's like a curse!

BRACK. There's something else, Mrs. Hedda. It's rather disagreeable, too.

HEDDA. What?

BRACK. The pistol he had on him——

HEDDA. Yes? What about it?

BRACK. He must have stolen it.

HEDDA. [*Jumps up*] Stolen it! That isn't true! He didn't!

BRACK. It's the only explanation. He must have stolen it. Ssh!

[TESMAN *and* MRS. ELVSTED *have got up from the table in the rear room and come into the drawing room.*]

TESMAN. [*His hands full of papers*] Hedda, I can't see properly under that lamp. Think!

HEDDA. I am thinking.

TESMAN. Do you think we could possibly use your writing table for a little? What?

HEDDA. Yes, of course. [*Quickly*] No, wait! Let me tidy it up first.

TESMAN. Oh, don't you trouble about that. There's plenty of room.

HEDDA. No, no, let me tidy it up first, I say. I'll take this in and put them on the piano. Here.

[*She pulls an object, covered with sheets of music, out from under the bookcase, puts some more sheets on top and carries it all into the rear room and away to the left.* TESMAN *puts his papers on the writing table and moves the lamp over from the corner table. He and* MRS. ELVSTED *sit down and begin working again.* HEDDA *comes back.*]

HEDDA. [*Behind* MRS. ELVSTED'S *chair, ruffles her hair gently*] Well, my pretty Thea! And how is work progressing on Eilert Loevborg's memorial?

MRS. ELVSTED. [*Looks up at her, dejectedly*] Oh, it's going to be terribly difficult to get these into any order.

TESMAN. We've got to do it. We must! After all, putting other people's papers into order is rather my specialty, what?

[HEDDA *goes over to the stove and sits on one of the foot-*

stools. BRACK *stands over her, leaning against the armchair.*]

HEDDA. [*Whispers*] What was that you were saying about the pistol?

BRACK. [*Softly*] I said he must have stolen it.

HEDDA. Why do you think that?

BRACK. Because any other explanation is unthinkable, Mrs. Hedda, or ought to be.

HEDDA. I see.

BRACK. [*Looks at her for a moment*] Eilert Loevborg was here this morning. Wasn't he?

HEDDA. Yes.

BRACK. Were you alone with him?

HEDDA. For a few moments.

BRACK. You didn't leave the room while he was here?

HEDDA. No.

BRACK. Think again. Are you sure you didn't go out for a moment?

HEDDA. Oh—yes, I might have gone into the hall. Just for a few seconds.

BRACK. And where was your pistol-case during this time?

HEDDA. I'd locked it in that——

BRACK. Er—Mrs. Hedda?

HEDDA. It was lying over there on my writing table.

BRACK. Have you looked to see if both the pistols are still there?

HEDDA. No.

BRACK. You needn't bother. I saw the pistol Loevborg had when they found him. I recognized it at once. From yesterday. And other occasions.

HEDDA. Have you got it?

BRACK. No. The police have it.

HEDDA. What will the police do with this pistol?

BRACK. Try to trace the owner.

HEDDA. Do you think they'll succeed?

BRACK. [*Leans down and whispers*] No, Hedda Gabler. Not as long as I hold my tongue.

HEDDA. [*Looks nervously at him*] And if you don't?

BRACK. [*Shrugs his shoulders*] You could always say he'd stolen it.

HEDDA. I'd rather die!

BRACK. [*Smiles*] People say that. They never do it.

HEDDA. [*Not replying*] And suppose the pistol wasn't stolen? And they trace the owner? What then?

BRACK. There'll be a scandal, Hedda.

HEDDA. A scandal!

BRACK. Yes, a scandal. The thing you're so frightened of. You'll have to appear in court. Together with Mademoiselle Danielle. She'll have to explain how it all happened. Was it an accident, or was it—homicide? Was he about to take the pistol from his pocket to threaten her? And did it go off? Or did she snatch the pistol from his hand, shoot him and then put it back in his pocket? She might quite easily have done it. She's a resourceful lady, is Mademoiselle Danielle.

HEDDA. But I had nothing to do with this repulsive business.

BRACK. No. But you'll have to answer one question. Why did you give Eilert Loevborg this pistol? And what conclusions will people draw when it is proved you did give it to him?

HEDDA. [*Bows her head*] That's true. I hadn't thought of that.

BRACK. Well, luckily there's no danger as long as I hold my tongue.

HEDDA. [*Looks up at him*] In other words, I'm in your power, Judge. From now on, you've got your hold over me.

BRACK. [*Whispers, more slowly*] Hedda, my dearest—believe me—I will not abuse my position.

HEDDA. Nevertheless, I'm in your power. Dependent on your will, and your demands. Not free. Still not free! [*Rises passionately*] No. I couldn't bear that. No.

BRACK. [*Looks half-derisively at her*] Most people resign themselves to the inevitable, sooner or later.

HEDDA. [*Returns his gaze*] Possibly they do.

[*She goes across to the writing table.*]

HEDDA. [*Represses an involuntary smile and says in* TESMAN'S *voice*] Well, George. Think you'll be able to manage? What?

TESMAN. Heaven knows, dear. This is going to take months and months.

HEDDA. [*In the same tone as before*] Fancy that, by Jove! [*Runs her hands gently through* MRS. ELVSTED'S *hair*] Doesn't it feel strange, Thea? Here you are working away with Tesman just the way you used to work with Eilert Loevborg.

MRS. ELVSTED. Oh—if only I can inspire your husband too!

HEDDA. Oh, it'll come. In time.

TESMAN. Yes—do you know, Hedda, I really think I'm beginning to feel a bit—well—that way. But you go back and talk to Judge Brack.

HEDDA. Can't I be of use to you two in any way?

TESMAN. No, none at all. [*Turns his head*] You'll have to keep Hedda company from now on, Judge, and see she doesn't get bored. If you don't mind.

BRACK. [*Glances at* HEDDA] It'll be a pleasure.

HEDDA. Thank you. But I'm tired this evening. I think I'll lie down on the sofa in there for a little while.

TESMAN. Yes, dear—do. What?

[HEDDA *goes into the rear room and draws the curtains behind her. Short pause. Suddenly she begins to play a frenzied dance melody on the piano.*]

MRS. ELVSTED. [*Starts up from her chair*] Oh, what's that?

TESMAN. [*Runs to the doorway*] Hedda dear, please! Don't play dance music tonight! Think of Auntie Rena. And Eilert.

HEDDA. [*Puts her head out through the curtains*] And Auntie Juju. And all the rest of them. From now on I'll be quiet.

[*Closes the curtains behind her*]

TESMAN. [*At the writing table*] It distresses her to watch us doing this. I say, Mrs. Elvsted, I've an idea. Why don't you move in with Auntie Juju? I'll run over each evening, and we can sit and work there. What?

MRS. ELVSTED. Yes, that might be the best plan.

HEDDA. [*From the rear room*] I can hear what you're saying, Tesman. But how shall I spend the evenings out here?

TESMAN. [*Looking through his papers*] Oh, I'm sure Judge Brack'll be kind enough to come over and keep you company. You won't mind my not being here, Judge?

BRACK. [*In the armchair, calls gaily*] I'll be delighted, Mrs. Tesman. I'll be here every evening. We'll have great fun together, you and I.

HEDDA. [*Loud and clear*] Yes, that'll suit you, won't it, Judge? The only cock on the dunghill——!

[*A shot is heard from the rear room.* TESMAN, MRS. ELVSTED *and* JUDGE BRACK *start from their chairs.*]

TESMAN. Oh, she's playing with those pistols again.

[*He pulls the curtains aside and runs in.* MRS. ELVSTED *follows him.* HEDDA *is lying dead on the sofa. Confusion and shouting.* BERTHA *enters in alarm from the right.*]

TESMAN. [*Screams to* BRACK] She's shot herself! Shot herself in the head! By Jove! Fancy that!

BRACK. [*Half paralyzed in the armchair*] But, good God! People don't do such things!

ANTON CHEKHOV

(1860–1904)

The Cherry Orchard[1]

A Comedy in Four Acts

LIST OF CHARACTERS

LYUBOV ANDREEVNA RANEVSKAYA, *a landowner*
ANYA, *her daughter, age seventeen*
VARYA, *her adopted daughter, age twenty-four*
LEONID ANDREEVICH GAEV, *brother of Mrs. Ranevskaya*
YERMOLAY ALEXEEVICH LOPAKHIN, *a merchant*
PYOTR SERGEEVICH TROFIMOV, *a student*
BORIS BORISOVICH SIMEONOV-PISHCHIK, *a landowner*
SHARLOTTA IVANOVNA, *a governess*
SEMYON PANTELEEVICH YEPIKHODOV, *a clerk*
DUNYASHA, *a maidservant*

1. Translated by Eugene K. Bristow.

FIRS, *an old manservant, age eighty-seven*
YASHA, *a young manservant*
A PASSER-BY
A STATIONMASTER
A POST OFFICE CIVIL SERVANT
GUESTS *and* SERVANTS

The action takes place on the estate of MRS. RANEVSKAYA.

Act One

A room that still goes by the name of the nursery. One of the doors leads to ANYA'S *room. It is dawn and the sun will soon come up. It is May. The cherry trees are in flower, but in the orchard it is cold, there is morning frost. The windows in the room are closed. Enter* DUNYASHA *with a candle and* LOPAKHIN *with a book in his hand.*

LOPAKHIN. The train's arrived, thank the Lord. What's the time?

DUNYASHA. Almost two o'clock. [*Extinguishes the candle.*] It's already light.

LOPAKHIN. How late was the train, how many hours? About two, at least. [*Yawns and stretches himself.*] Of all the stupid tricks to pull, damned if I haven't gone and done it again. I came here on purpose so I could meet them at the station, and before you know it, I slept right through it . . . Went dead to sleep sitting up. Annoying, that's what . . . If only you might've awakened me.

DUNYASHA. I thought you'd left. [*Listens.*] There, I think they're coming now.

LOPAKHIN. [*listens*] No . . . they've got luggage to get, and one thing or another . . . [*Pause.*] Lyubov Andreevna has been living five years abroad, and I don't know what she's become now . . . She's a very fine person. An obliging person, simple. I remember when I was a youngster about fifteen, my father—he's dead now but at the time he was a shopkeeper in the village here—hit me in the face with his fist. The blood ran out of my nose . . . We had come to the yard here for some reason, and he'd been drinking. Lyubov Andreevna, as I remember right now, was still very young, such a slim woman she was. She led me over to the washstand here in this very room, the nursery. "Don't cry, little peasant," she says "it will heal before your wedding . . ." [*Pause.*] Little peasant . . . It's true my father was a peasant, and here I am in a white waistcoat and yellow boots. Like a pig's nozzle showing up in a row of wedding cakes . . . It's just that I'm rich, lots of money for sure, but if you really think about it and look into it, you'll know I'm just a peasant through and through . . . [*Turns the pages of the book.*] I read this book and didn't catch on to a single thing. I was reading and fell right to sleep. [*Pause.*]

DUNYASHA. The dogs didn't sleep the whole night. They can sense their masters are coming.

LOPAKHIN. What is it with you, Dunyasha, such . . .

DUNYASHA. My hands are shaking. I'm going to faint.

LOPAKHIN. You're really delicate, Dunyasha, too much so. You dress yourself like a lady, and your hair is fixed up the same way. You can't do things like that. Better remember who you are.

> YEPIKHODOV *enters, carrying a bouquet. He wears a jacket and brightly scrubbed high boots that squeak loudly. Entering, he drops the bouquet.*

YEPIKHODOV. [*picks up the bouquet*] Here's what the gardener sent, he says to put them in the dining room. [*Gives the bouquet to* DUNYASHA.]

LOPAKHIN. And bring me some kvas.[2]

DUNYASHA. Yes, sir. [*Goes out.*]

YEPIKHODOV. There's morning frost right now, three degrees of frost, but the cherry trees are all in bloom. I can't approve of our climate. [*Sighs.*] I can't. Our climate just can't promote the most suitable time. Here, Yermolay Alexeich, be so kind as to let me append to you, I bought myself these boots the day before yesterday, and they, I make bold to assure you, they squeak so it's beyond the realm of possibility. What should I lubricate them with?

LOPAKHIN. Leave me alone. I'm sick and tired of you.

YEPIKHODOV. Every day some catastrophe happens to me. But I don't grumble. I'm used to it, and I even smile. [DUNYASHA *enters and gives* LOPAKHIN *kvas.*] I'm going. [*Stumbles against a chair, which falls.*] There . . . [*As if he is celebrating it.*] There you see, excuse the expression, the kind of circumstance I bump into, by the way . . . It's simply even out of this world! [*Goes out.*]

DUNYASHA. Oh, Yermolay Alexeich, I must confess Yepikhodov made a proposal to me.

LOPAKHIN. Oh!

DUNYASHA. I really don't know how . . . he's a mild sort of person, but those times he starts talking, you can't figure out a thing he says. Oh, it's very fine and there's plenty of feeling in it, only nothing makes a bit of sense. I'm pretty sure I like him. He's madly in love with me. He's an unlucky person, and there's something or other every day. That's why they keep teasing him, calling him "Two-and-Twenty Hard Knocks . . ."

LOPAKHIN. [*listening*] There, I think they're coming . . .

DUNYASHA. They're coming! Oh, what's the matter with me . . . I've gotten colder all over.

LOPAKHIN. They're coming, it's a fact. Let's go and meet them. Will she recognize me, I wonder? It's been five years since we've seen each other.

---

2. A homemade beer with a slightly acid flavor, made by pouring water over a mixture of rye, barley, and other grains and letting it ferment.

DUNYASHA. [*agitated*] I'm going to faint right now . . . Oh, I know I'm going to faint!

> *Two carriages are heard driving up to the house.* LOPAKHIN *and* DUNYASHA *quickly go out. The stage is empty. The sound of hubbub begins in the adjoining rooms. Leaning on a stick,* FIRS *hurriedly goes across the stage. He has been to the station to meet* LYUBOV ANDREEVNA. *He wears old-fashioned livery and a high hat. He keeps saying something to himself, but not a single word can be understood. The noise offstage keeps growing louder. A voice is heard saying: Let's go through here." Enter, all walking through the room,* LYUBOV ANDREEVNA, ANYA, *and* SHARLOTTA IVANOVNA *with a small dog on a chain—all are in traveling clothes—*VARYA, *wearing an overcoat and a scarf over her head,* GAEV, SIMEONOV-PISHCHIK, LOPAKHIN, DUNYASHA *with a bundle and an umbrella, and servants with luggage.*

ANYA. Let's go through here. Mama, do you remember what room this is?

LYUBOV ANDREEVNA. [*jubilantly, through tears*] The nursery!

VARYA. How cold it is, my hands are growing numb. [*To* LYUBOV ANDREEVNA.] Your rooms are the very same as they were, *Mamochka,*[3] white and violet.

LYUBOV ANDREEVNA. The nursery, my dear, beautiful room . . . I slept here when I was a little girl . . . [*Weeps.*] And now I'm like a little girl again . . . [*Kisses her brother and* VARYA, *then her brother again.*] Varya is just the same as she's always been, she still looks like a nun. And I recognized Dunyasha . . . [*Kisses* DUNYASHA.]

GAEV. The train was two hours late. That's something, isn't it? What a way to manage things, wouldn't you say?

SHARLOTTA. [*to* PISHCHIK] My dog eats nuts, too.

PISHCHIK. [*surprised*] What do you think of that!

> *All go out except* ANYA *and* DUNYASHA.

DUNYASHA. We've been waiting and expecting you for so long . . . [*Takes off* ANYA's *overcoat and hat.*]

ANYA. I haven't slept four whole nights on the way . . . now I feel terribly cold.

DUNYASHA. You went away during Lent, it was snowing and there was a frost then, but now? My dear! [*Laughs and kisses her.*] I've been waiting so long for you, my precious darling . . . I must tell you right now, I can't stand it another minute . . .

ANYA. [*listlessly*] Not something again, surely . . .

DUNYASHA. Right after Holy Week the clerk Yepikhodov made a proposal to me.

ANYA. You keep going on about the same thing . . . [*Adjusting her hair.*] I've been losing all my hairpins . . . [*She is very exhausted, she even staggers and sways.*]

3. Intimate nickname for *Mama.*

DUNYASHA. I really don't know what to think. He's in love with me, he loves me so!

ANYA. [*looks through the door into her own room, affectionately*] My own room, my windows, it's just as if I'd never gone away. I'm home, home! Tomorrow morning I'll get up and run out to the orchard . . . Oh, if only I could fall asleep! I didn't get one wink of sleep the whole way coming back, I wore myself out worrying.

DUNYASHA. Pyotr Sergeich arrived the day before yesterday.

ANYA. [*jubilantly*] Petya!

DUNYASHA. He's asleep in the bathhouse, it's where he's living. "I'm afraid," he says, "of getting in their way." [*Having looked at her pocket watch.*] He ought to be wakened, but Varvara Mikhaylovna gave the word not to. "Don't you go and wake him," she says.

VARYA *enters; she has a bunch of keys on her belt.*

VARYA. Dunyasha, bring some coffee quickly . . . *Mamochka* is asking for some.

DUNYASHA. It won't be a minute. [*Goes out.*]

VARYA. Well, thank the Lord, you've all come back. You're home again. [*Adoringly.*] My precious is here, my beautiful darling has come back!

ANYA. I've had a horrible time of it.

VARYA. I can well imagine!

ANYA. I left just before Easter. It was cold at the time. Sharlotta kept on talking and doing her silly conjuring tricks the whole way there. Why you tacked Sharlotta onto me, I'll never know . . .

VARYA. You couldn't have gone all alone, my precious. At seventeen!

ANYA. We finally got to Paris and found it cold and snowing. My French was terrible. Mama was living on the fifth floor, and when I came to her place, some French people were visiting, ladies and an old priest with a little book. It was filled with smoke and not one bit cozy. All of a sudden I felt sorry for Mama, so sorry for her, I took her head in my arms and pressed her close to me and simply couldn't let go. Afterwards Mama tried to make everything up to me, she was gentle and sweet and she kept crying. . .

VARYA. [*through tears*] Don't go on talking about it, don't . . .

ANYA. She'd already sold her dacha[4] near Mentone, and she had nothing left, nothing. I didn't have anything either, not a single kopek. We scarcely had enough to get here. But Mama just can't understand it! Whenever we sit down for dinner at the station, she keeps demanding the most expensive things and tipping the waiters a ruble each. Sharlotta's the same way. Yasha keeps demanding his share, too, it was simply terrible. Yasha is Mama's servant, you know. We brought him here with us . . .

VARYA. I've seen the scoundrel.

---

4. Summer vacation home. Mentone is located on the French Mediterranean coast.

ANYA. Well, then, how are things going here? Have you paid the interest?

VARYA. Not a chance in the world.

ANYA. Dear God in heaven, dear God . . .

VARYA. The estate will be sold in August . . .

ANYA. Dear God in heaven . . .

LOPAKHIN. [*looks in through the door and bleats like a calf*] Meh-meh-meh . . . [*Goes out.*]

VARYA. [*through tears*] Oh, I'd like to give him something . . . [*Threatens with her fist.*]

ANYA. [*embraces* VARYA, *quietly*] Varya, has he proposed to you? [VARYA *shakes her head.*] Surely he loves you . . . Why don't the two of you talk it out, what on earth are you waiting for?

VARYA. I don't think anything will come of it. He has so many things to do he hasn't one bit of time for me . . . and he doesn't pay one bit of attention to me, either. God help him, I've had enough. It bothers me just to see him . . . Everyone is talking about our wedding and offering congratulations, but in fact there's nothing to it. It's all like a dream . . . [*In a different tone of voice.*] You have a brooch that looks something like a little bee.

ANYA. [*sadly*] Mama bought it. [*Goes into her own room and speaks happily like a child.*] You know in Paris I flew up in a balloon!

VARYA. My precious is here, my beautiful darling has come back! [DUNYASHA *has already returned with a coffee pot and is preparing coffee.* VARYA *stands near the door.*] I spend the whole day managing the house, my precious, but I keep dreaming and dreaming. I'd like to see you married to a rich person, and then I wouldn't feel troubled at all. I could start out to a cloister, and then on to Kiev[5] . . . to Moscow, and so I'd keep walking from one holy place to the next . . . I'd keep on walking and walking. What a blessed way to live! . .

ANYA. The birds are singing in the orchard. What time is it now?

VARYA. It must be past two. It's time for you to go to sleep, my precious. [*Going into* ANYA's *room.*] What a blessed way to live!

YASHA *enters with a rug and a traveling bag.*

YASHA. [*goes across the stage, delicately*] Is it possible for one to go through here, Miss?

DUNYASHA. A person wouldn't recognize you, Yasha. You've become something else since you've been abroad.

YASHA. Hmm . . . and who are you?

DUNYASHA. When you left here, I was about as big as this . . . [*Indicates distance from the floor.*] I'm Dunyasha, the daughter of Fyodor Kozoedov. You can't remember me!

YASHA. Hmm . . . Saucy little cucumber! [*Looks around and embraces her. She screams and drops a saucer.* YASHA *quickly goes out.*]

---

5. Ancient city of old Russia, ranked seventh in population at the end of the nineteenth century.

VARYA. [*in a dissatisfied tone of voice, in the doorway*] What's going on now?

DUNYASHA. [*through tears*] I broke a saucer . . .

VARYA. It's a good sign.

ANYA. [*coming out of her room*] Mama ought to be warned in advance that Petya's here . . .

VARYA. I gave word not to wake him.

ANYA. [*deep in thought*] Six years ago father died, and a month later our brother Grisha drowned in the river. He was a beautiful little boy, just seven years old. Mama couldn't stand it anymore, and she went away, she went away without so much as a backward glance . . . [*Shudders.*] How well I can understand her, if she only knew! [*Pause.*] But Petya Trofimov was Grisha's tutor, and he might bring to mind . . .

FIRS *enters, wearing a jacket and white waistcoat.*

FIRS. [*goes to the coffee pot, anxiously*] The mistress will sup in here . . . [*Puts on white gloves.*] Is the coffee prepared? [*To* DUNYASHA, *sternly.*] You there! And the cream?

DUNYASHA. Oh, dear God in heaven . . . [*Goes out quickly.*]

FIRS. [*bustling around the coffee pot*] Oh, you silly galoot, you . . . [*Mumbles to himself.*] She's come back from Paris . . . Once upon a time the master himself used to go to Paris . . . by carriage . . . [*Laughs.*]

VARYA. What is it, Firs?

FIRS. What can I do for you, please? [*Jubilantly.*] My mistress has come back! Home, home at last! I'm even ready to die now . . . [*Weeps from joy.*]

LYUBOV ANDREEVNA, GAEV, *and* SIMEONOV-PISHCHIK *enter.* PISHCHIK *wears a long peasant coat made out of thin cloth and high boots. Entering,* GAEV *moves his arms and body as if he were playing billiards.*

LYUBOV ANDREEVNA. How does it go? Let me remember a bit . . . "Off the yellow into the corner pocket! Bank shot into the middle!"

GAEV. An english shot into the corner! Once upon a time, sister, you and I used to sleep here in this very room, and now I'm fifty-one, fifty-one years old. Strange, isn't it . . .

LOPAKHIN. Yes, time flies.

GAEV. How's that?

LOPAKHIN. Time flies, I was saying.

GAEV. This place reeks of patchouli.[6]

ANYA. I'm going to sleep now. Good night, Mama. [*Kisses her mother.*]

LYUBOV ANDREEVNA. My beloved little girl. [*Kisses her hands.*] You're glad you're home, aren't you? I just can't get hold of myself.

ANYA. Fare you well, Uncle.

6. A perfume made from an East Indian mint.

GAEV. [*kisses her face and hands*] God be with you. Oh, you look so much like your mother! [*To his sister.*] When you were her age, Lyuba, you were exactly like she is.

ANYA *gives her hand to* LOPAKHIN *and* PISHCHIK, *goes out, and shuts the door to her room.*

LYUBOV ANDREEVNA. She's completely exhausted.

PISHCHIK. Most likely it's the long trip.

VARYA. [*to* LOPAKHIN *and* PISHCHIK] Well, hmm, gentlemen? It's after two and time you said your good-byes.

LYUBOV ANDREEVNA. [*laughs*] You're the same as you've always been, Varya. [*Draws* VARYA *to her and kisses her.*] I'll just drink some coffee, then we'll all go away. [FIRS *puts a little cushion under her feet.*] Thank you, my dear. I'm used to coffee now. I drink it day and night. Thank you, my dear old man. [*Kisses* FIRS.]

VARYA. I must go and see if they've brought in all the things . . . [*Goes out.*]

LYUBOV ANDREEVNA. It can't really be me sitting here, can it? [*Laughs.*] I want to jump up, leap around, and wave my arms. [*Covers her face with her hands.*] But suddenly I feel I may only be sleeping! God can see I love my country, I love it warmly. I couldn't even see it from the train—I was crying the whole time. [*Through tears.*] All the same I must drink my coffee. Thank you, Firs, thank you, my dear old man. I'm so glad you're still alive.

FIRS. The day before yesterday.

GAEV. He's hard of hearing.

LOPAKHIN. I must start for Kharkov pretty soon, after four this morning. Damned annoying! I wanted to have more of a look at you, talk awhile . . . You're the same as you've always been, a magnificent person.

PISHCHIK. [*breathes heavily*] Even prettier . . . Wearing Parisian clothes . . . Oh, my, that's something! "Get lost, my cart," as the saying goes, "all four wheels . . ."

LOPAKHIN. Your brother, Leonid Andreich here, keeps talking about me, saying I'm a peasant, a scoundrel grabbing with both hands, but it doesn't matter what he says, not a bit. Let him go on talking. The only thing I want is for you to believe in me as you used to and look at me with your beautiful, gentle eyes as you did in times gone by. Oh, merciful God in heaven! My father was a serf, belonging to your grandfather and after him your father, but you—you personally—did so much for me once I've forgotten all that and I love you as if we were flesh and blood . . . even more than my own flesh and blood.

LYUBOV ANDREEVNA. I can't sit any longer, not the way I feel . . . [*Jumps up and walks in great agitation.*] I'm so happy I can't stand it . . . Go ahead and laugh at me, I know I'm silly . . . My own dear little bookcase . . . [*Kisses the bookcase.*] My own little table . . .

GAEV. Oh, when you were gone *nyanya*[7] died.

LYUBOV ANDREEVNA. [*sits down and drinks her coffee*] Yes, may God in heaven be with her. They wrote me.

GAEV. And Anastasy died. Petrushka—the squint-eyed fellow—left me and now he's with the police chief in town. [*Takes a box of hard candy out of his pocket and sucks one.*]

PISHCHIK. My daughter Dashenka . . . sends her regards to you . . .

LOPAKHIN. I want to tell you something very pleasing and cheerful. [*Having glanced at his watch.*] I'm on my way right now, there's no time to talk . . . Oh, well, I can get to it in two or three words. As you already know, your cherry orchard is being sold to pay off debts. The auction is set for August twenty-second, but you mustn't worry, my dear, you can sleep in peace. There's a way out . . . Here's my plan. I beg your close attention! Your estate is located only twenty versts[8] from town, the railroad goes nearby, and if the cherry orchard and the land by the river were broken up into residential lots and then leased for summer homes, you'll have an income, at the very least, of twenty-five thousand rubles each year.

GAEV. Excuse me, I've never heard such stuff and nonsense.

LYUBOV ANDREEVNA. I don't quite understand you, Yermolay Alexeich.

LOPAKHIN. You will get from the tenants, at the very least, twenty-five rubles a year for every plot of about three acres, and if you advertise right away, I'm willing to bet whatever you like that you won't have a sliver of land left by autumn. Every bit of it will be grabbed up. In short, I congratulate you. You are saved. It's a marvelous place for building, and the river is deep. Only one thing, of course, it must be cleaned up a little, whipped into shape . . . For example, you'll have to pull down all the old buildings, let's say, and this house here, which is no longer of any use, cut down the old cherry orchard . . .

LYUBOV ANDREEVNA. Cut down? My dear, forgive me, but you don't know what you're talking about. If there's anything at all in this whole district that's still exciting, even incredible, that one thing is our cherry orchard.

LOPAKHIN. The only thing incredible about that cherry orchard is that it's damn big. There's only one crop every two years, and when it comes there's plenty of cherries around, but nobody will buy them.

GAEV. This orchard is even mentioned in the *Encyclopedia*.

LOPAKHIN. [*having glanced at his watch*] If we don't think of something or come up with an idea, the cherry orchard and the whole estate will be sold at auction on August twenty-second. You can make up your minds to it! There's no other way out, I swear it to you. None at all, none.

---

7. "Nanny" or nurse.
8. A former Russian unit of measure-   ment, about 3500 feet.

FIRS. In times before, about forty or fifty years ago, the cherries were dried, soaked, marinated, and jam was made, and it used to be . . .

GAEV. Be quiet, Firs.

FIRS. And it used to be they'd send cartloads of dried cherries off to Moscow and to Kharkov.[9] Oh, there was money galore! And dried cherries at that time were soft and juicy, sweet and a good smell to them . . . They knew a way of doing it at that time . . .

LYUBOV ANDREEVNA. And where on earth is that way now?

FIRS. They've forgotten. No one remembers it.

PISHCHIK [*to* LYUBOV ANDREEVNA] What's in Paris? How did it go? Did you eat frogs?

LYUBOV ANDREEVNA. I ate crocodiles.

PISHCHIK. What do you think of that . . .

LOPAKHIN. Until recently you'd find only gentlemen and peasants in town, and now people for the summer are showing up. All the cities, even the very smallest, are surrounded now with summer places. You might even say, in the course of about twenty years, these people will multiply beyond the wildest dreams. Nowadays the summer resident only drinks tea on his balcony, but you know it might happen he'll take up farming his own plot of ground, and then your cherry orchard will become happy, rich, sumptuous . . .

GAEV. [*exasperated*] I've never heard such stuff and nonsense.

VARYA *and* YASHA *enter.*

VARYA. *Mamochka,* there are two telegrams for you. [*Picks out a key and noisily opens an old bookcase.*] Here they are.

LYUBOV ANDREEVNA. They're from Paris. [*Tears up the telegrams without reading them.*] Paris is over and done with . . .

GAEV. Oh, Lyuba, do you know how old this bookcase is? Last week I pulled out the bottom drawer, I looked and saw some figures scorched on it. The bookcase was made exactly one hundred years ago. That's something, isn't it? Ah! We could celebrate its anniversary. It's an inanimate object, but all the same it's a receptacle for books, after all.

PISHCHIK. [*surprised*] One hundred years . . . What do you think of that! . .

GAEV. Yes . . . It's quite a thing . . . [*Having touched all parts of the bookcase.*] Dear, honored bookcase! I hail your existence. For more than one hundred years your very being has been directed to the shining ideals of cardinal good and justice. Your silent appeal to fruitful labor has never lessened in the course of a hundred years, upholding [*through tears*] in generations of our line personal courage and faith in a better future and nurturing in us the ideals of cardinal good and social consciousness. [*Pause.*]

LOPAKHIN. Yes . . .

LYUBOV ANDREEVNA. You're the same as you've always been, Lyonya.

GAEV. [*a little embarrassed*] Off the ball right into the corner

9. Large city in the northeastern Ukraine.

pocket! An english shot into the middle!

LOPAKHIN. [*having glanced at his watch*] Well, time for me to go.

YASHA. [*handing medicine to* LYUBOV ANDREEVNA] Perhaps you'll take your pills now . . .

PISHCHIK. No need to take medicines, my dearest . . . Oh, no damage comes from it, no benefit, either . . . Here, let me have them . . . honored lady. [*Takes the pills, pours them into the palm of his hand, blows on them, puts them in his mouth, and drinks them down with kvas.*] There!

LYUBOV ANDREEVNA. [*frightened*] Why, you've lost your mind!

PISHCHIK. I've taken all the pills.

LOPAKHIN. It's a hog with a hollow leg!

Everyone laughs.

FIRS. The gentleman was visiting us in Holy Week and ate half a bucket of cucumbers . . . [*Mumbles to himself.*]

LYUBOV ANDREEVNA. What is it he's saying?

VARYA. He's been mumbling that way for three years now. We've become used to it.

YASHA. Old as Methuselah, I'd say.

SHARLOTTA IVANOVNA, *in a white dress, walks across the stage. She is very thin and tightly laced, with a lorgnette on her belt.*

LOPAKHIN. Forgive me, Sharlotta Ivanovna, I haven't had time yet to say how do you do to you. [*Wants to kiss her hand.*]

SHARLOTTA. [*taking her hand away*] If you were permitted to kiss my hand, why you'd want to go right to the elbow next, and then the shoulder . . .

LOPAKHIN. It's not my lucky day. [*Everyone laughs.*] Sharlotta Ivanovna, show us a trick or two!

LYUBOV ANDREEVNA. Yes, Sharlotta, show us a trick!

SHARLOTTA. I don't want to. I'd like to go to sleep. [*Goes out.*]

LOPAKHIN. We'll see each other in three weeks. [*Kisses* LYUBOV ANDREEVNA's *hand.*] In the meantime, good-bye. It's time for me. [*To* GAEV.] Until we meet again. [*Kisses* PISHCHIK.] Until we meet again. [*Shakes hands with* VARYA, *then with* FIRS *and* YASHA.] I don't want to leave. [*To* LYUBOV ANDREEVNA.] If you make up your mind about those summer places and decide to go ahead with it, just give me the word and I'll loan you fifty thousand or so. Think about it seriously.

VARYA. [*angrily*] You're on your way, why don't you just leave now!

LOPAKHIN. I'll go, I'll go . . . [*Goes out.*]

GAEV. Grabbing peasant. Nevertheless, I beg your pardon . . . Varya's going to marry him. He's Varya's dear fiancé.

VARYA. You're talking much too much, Uncle dear.

LYUBOV ANDREEVNA. Well, hmm, Varya, I shall be very glad. He's a good person.

PISHCHIK. A person, if the truth were said . . . who's most worthy

... And my Dashenka ... keeps saying also that ... she keeps saying all sorts of words. [*Snores, but immediately wakes up.*] Be that as it may, my honored lady, if you'll oblige me with ... a loan of two hundred and forty rubles ... I can pay the interest due on the mortgage tomorrow ...

VARYA. [*frightened*] We don't have it, we don't!

LYUBOV ANDREEVNA. As a matter of fact, I have nothing.

PISHCHIK. It'll turn up. [*Laughs.*] I never lose one bit of hope. Oh, time and again, I think everything's lost, gone, I've had it, and then—lo and behold—they built a railroad right through my land and ... then went and paid me for it. Wait and see, something or other will happen—if not today, then tomorrow ... Dashenka is going to win two hundred thousand ... She has a lottery ticket.

LYUBOV ANDREEVNA. The coffee is finished, we can get some peace and rest.

FIRS. [*brushes* GAEV's *clothes, reprovingly*] Again you've put on the wrong trousers. Oh, what on earth am I going to do with you!

VARYA. [*quietly*] Anya is sleeping. [*quietly opens the window.*] The sun's come up now, and it isn't cold. Look, *Mamochka*, what marvelous trees! And the air, too, dear God in heaven! The starlings are singing!

GAEV. [*opens another window*] The orchard is all in white. You haven't forgotten, Lyuba, have you? That long avenue over there keeps running straight, straight as a cord stretched tight. It shines brightly on moonlit nights. You remember, you haven't forgotten, have you?

LYUBOV ANDREEVNA. [*looks through the window at the orchard*] Oh, my childhood, days of my innocence! In this very nursery I used to sleep, I used to look out at the orchard from here, and when I woke up each morning I felt happy, so happy. At that time too the orchard was exactly the same, nothing at all has changed. [*Laughs jubilantly.*] All in white, all! Oh, my orchard! After the dreary, rainy autumn and cold winter, I find you young once more, filled with happiness, and I know the angels in heaven have not deserted you ... If only the heaviness I feel in my heart, the millstone I carry now, were suddenly taken away forever, if only I could forget my past!

GAEV. Yes, and the orchard will be sold to pay off debts. Strange, isn't it ...

LYUBOV ANDREEVNA. Just look, our own mama is walking in the orchard ... in a white dress! [*Laughs jubilantly.*] See, it's Mama.

GAEV. Where is she?

VARYA. God be with you, *Mamochka*.

LYUBOV ANDREEVNA. There's no one, it just seemed to me I saw her. To the right, as the path turns to the summerhouse, there's a white small tree bending down—it looks like a woman ... [TRO-FIMOV *enters, wearing spectacles and dressed in a threadbare stu-*

dent's uniform.] What a splendid orchard! Row upon row of white blossoms, the light blue sky . . .

TROFIMOV. Lyubov Andreevna! [*She looks around at him.*] I'll only pay my respects and then go away at once. [*Ardently kisses her hand.*] I was told to wait until morning, but I didn't have the patience . . .

LYUBOV ANDREEVNA *looks at him, bewildered.*

VARYA. [*through tears*] It's Petya Trofimov . . .

TROFIMOV. Petya Trofimov, former tutor of your Grisha . . . Can it be I've changed so much?

LYUBOV ANDREEVNA *embraces him and weeps quietly.*

GAEV. [*embarrassed*] Enough, Lyuba, that'll do.

VARYA. [*weeps*] You see, Petya, I told you to wait until tomorrow.

LYUBOV ANDREEVNA. My Grisha . . . my little boy . . . Grisha . . . my son . . .

VARYA. What could we do, *Mamochka*? It was God's will.

TROFIMOV. [*gently, through tears*] There, there . . .

LYUBOV ANDREEVNA. [*weeps quietly*] My little boy is gone, drowned . . . and for what? Whatever was it for, my friend? [*More quietly.*] Anya is sleeping in there, and I go on talking in a loud voice . . . making so much noise . . . Well, Petya? Why do you look so homely now? Why have you started putting on years?

TROFIMOV. An old peasant woman on the train called me "that used-up old gentleman."

LYUBOV ANDREEVNA. You were no more than a boy then, a sweet young student, but now your hair is getting thin and you're wearing spectacles. Don't tell me you're still a student? [*Walks toward the door.*]

TROFIMOV. No doubt I'll be a student forever and ever.

LYUBOV ANDREEVNA. [*kisses her brother, then* VARYA] Well then, better go to sleep . . . You've started putting on years, too, Leonid.

PISHCHIK. [*follows her*] So now we're going to sleep . . . Oh, my gout! I'll stay the night here . . . Lyubov Andreevna, my darling, if you could help me out tomorrow morning, you know . . . two hundred and forty rubles . . .

GAEV. Oh, he keeps harping on the same old string.

PISHCHIK. Two hundred and forty rubles . . . to pay the interest due on the mortgage.

LYUBOV ANDREEVNA. I have no money, dear.

PISHCHIK. I'll pay it back, my dear . . . a trifling sum . . .

LYUBOV ANDREEVNA. Well, all right, Leonid will give you the amount . . . Leonid, you give it to him.

GAEV. Give it to him, Me? Oh, sure, open your pocket and see what comes!

LYUBOV ANDREEVNA. What on earth can we do? Give him the money . . . he needs it . . . He'll pay it back.

LYUBOV ANDREEVNA, TROFIMOV, PISHCHIK, *and* FIRS *go out*; GAEV, VARYA, *and* YASHA *remain.*

GAEV. My sister still hasn't lost the habit of scattering all her money to the winds. [*To* YASHA.] Step out of the way, dear fellow, you smell like a dunghill biddy.

YASHA. [*with an ironical smile*] You're just the same as you've always been, too, Leonid Andreevich.

GAEV. How's that? [*To* VARYA.] What did he say?

VARYA. [*to* YASHA] Your mother's come from the village. She's been sitting in the servants' lodgings since yesterday. She wants to see you . . .

YASHA. She can go to the devil, for all I care!

VARYA. Oh, you insolent pup, I'd be ashamed!

YASHA. She's a big help, isn't she? She might have come here tomorrow. [*Goes out.*]

VARYA. *Mamochka* is just the same as she was, she hasn't changed one whit. If she were given free rein, she'd give away everything.

GAEV. Yes . . . [*Pause.*] If plenty of remedies are prescribed for some sort of disease, it means the disease can't possibly be cured. I keep on thinking, stewing my brains over it, and I've come up with a lot of remedies, plenty of them. Of course, that means I really don't have a single one that would work. It would be fine to receive some sort of inheritance, it would be nice to marry our Anya off to a rich person, it would be fine to leave for Yaroslavl[10] and try our luck with our dear aunt, the countess. Our auntie is rich, you know, very much so.

VARYA. [*weeps*] If only God would help.

GAEV. Stop blubbering. Our auntie is very rich, but she doesn't care one iota for us. First of all, my sister married a lawyer, not a nobleman . . . [ANYA *appears in the doorway.*] She did not marry into the nobility, and you can't say she's led a particularly upright and godly life. She is kind and good, a glorious person, really, and I love her very much. But whatever excuses you think of to justify what she's gone through, you must still admit she's an immoral woman. You're conscious of it in her slightest movement.

VARYA. [*in a whisper*] Anya is standing in the doorway.

GAEV. How's that? [*Pause.*] You know, it's surprising, but something landed in my right eye . . . I've started to see poorly. And on Thursday when I was at the district court . . .

ANYA *enters.*

VARYA. Why on earth aren't you asleep, Anya?

ANYA. I can't fall aleep. I just can't.

GAEV. My little darling. [*Kisses* ANYA's *face and hands.*] My dear child . . . [*Through tears.*] You're not simply my niece, you're my angel, you mean everything to me. Believe me, believe . . .

ANYA. I believe you, Uncle. Everyone loves and respects you . . . but you must keep quiet, dear Uncle, only keep quiet. What were you saying just now about my mama, about your own sister? Whatever in the world made you say it?

10. An old Russian town on the Volga.

GAEV. Yes, yes . . . [Covers his face with her hand.] It's terrible, really it is! Dear God in heaven! Dear God help me! And the speech I made today—to the bookcase . . . so very foolish! And only when I finished did I realize it was so foolish.

VARYA. It's true, dear Uncle, you ought to keep quiet. Just keep quiet, that's all.

ANYA. If you'll stop talking, you will feel more at peace with yourself.

GAEV. I'll keep quiet. [Kisses ANYA's and VARYA's hands.] I'll keep quiet. Only there is this business matter I should bring up. On Thursday I was at the district court, well, a bunch of us got together and talk started about this thing and that, skipping around from here to there; and it seems we might arrange a loan on promissory notes and pay the interest to the bank.

VARYA. If only God will help!

GAEV. On Tuesday I'll go and talk it over with them once more. [To VARYA.] Stop blubbering. [To ANYA.] Your mother is going to talk with Lopakhin. Of course, he won't turn her down . . . After you've had some peace and rest, you will leave for Yaroslavl to see the countess, your grandmother. In this way we'll be working from three sides—and so our whole business drops nicely into the hat. I'm convinced we'll pay off the interest . . . [Puts a piece of candy into his mouth.] I give you my word of honor, I'll swear by anything you want, this estate will not be sold! [Excitedly.] I swear by my own happiness! Here, take my hand and then you can call me a good-for-nothing rapscallion if I even so much as let the estate come up for auction! I swear it with all my heart and soul!

ANYA. [a peaceful mood having returned to her, she is happy] What a good person you are, Uncle, and so smart too! [Embraces her uncle.] I'm at peace now! At peace and so happy!

FIRS enters.

FIRS. [reproachfully] Leonid Andreich, have you no fear of God? When is it you're going to sleep?

GAEV. At once, at once. You can leave, Firs. I, yes, it's perfectly all right, I can undress myself. Well, my children, time to say byebyes . . . We'll save the details until tomorrow, and now you go off to sleep. [Kisses ANYA and VARYA.] I'm a man of the eighties . . . No one pays tribute to those days, but I still went through plenty in life for my convictions, I can tell you I did. The peasant has reason to love me. You must get to know the peasant, I say. You must know how to . . .

ANYA. You're starting again, Uncle!

VARYA. You better keep quiet, Uncle dear.

FIRS. [angrily] Leonid Andreich!

GAEV. I'm coming, I'm coming . . . Lie down and go to sleep. Off two cushions right into the middle! I pocket the white . . . [Goes out. FIRS quickly toddles after him.]

ANYA. I'm at peace now. I don't want to go to Yaroslavl and I don't love my grandmother, but I still feel at peace. Thanks to Uncle. [*Sits down.*]

VARYA. We must go to sleep. I'm going to. Oh, something unpleasant happened here when you were gone. Only some old servants still live in the old servants' lodgings, as you well know—Yefimyushka, Polya, Yevstigney, and there's Karp, too. They started letting some rascals and passers-by spend the night there. I kept silent. Only then I began hearing a rumor they were spreading that I'd given orders to feed them nothing but dried peas. Out of stinginess, if you can imagine . . . Yevstigney was behind it all . . . All right, I think, if that's the way it is—then just you wait. I call in Yevstigney . . . [*Yawns.*] He shows up . . . "What are you up to," I say, "Yevstigney . . . you're such a fool . . ." [*Having glanced at* ANYA.] Anichka![11] [*Pause.*] She's fallen right to sleep . . . [*Takes* ANYA *by the arm.*] Come to your bed . . . Come along! . . [*Leading her.*] My precious has gone to sleep! Come along . . .

> *They go. A shepherd is heard playing on a reed pipe far beyond the orchard.* TROFIMOV *crosses the stage and, having seen* VARYA *and* ANYA, *stops.*

VARYA. Tsss . . . she's sleeping . . . sleeping . . . Come along, darling.

ANYA. [*quietly, half-asleep*] I'm so tired . . . those bells keep ringing . . . Uncle . . . dear . . . and Mama and Uncle . . .

VARYA. Come, darling, come along . . . [*They go into* ANYA'S *room.*]

TROFIMOV. [*deeply moved*] Light of my life! My springtime!

CURTAIN

Act Two

> *A field. A very small, old chapel—bent out of shape and deserted a long time ago. Near it are an old bench, a well, and large stones that apparently were once used as tombstones. A road to* GAEV'S *estate can be seen. Towering poplar trees loom darkly on one side, where the cherry orchard begins. In the distance is a row of telegraph poles, and far, far away on the horizon—appearing indistinct—is a large town, clearly seen only in very fine, clear weather. It is shortly before sunset.* SHARLOTTA, YASHA, *and* DUNYASHA *are sitting on the bench.* YEPIKHODOV *stands nearby and plays the guitar, as the others sit lost in thought.* SHARLOTTA, *wearing an old peaked cap, has taken a gun from her shoulder and is adjusting the buckle on the sling.*

11. A term of endearment for *Anya.*

SHARLOTTA. [*in a thoughtful mood*] I don't have a genuine passport.[12] I don't know how old I am, but I keep on thinking I'm very young. When I was a small little girl, my father and *mamasha* used to travel from fair to fair and give shows—very good ones too. Oh, I used to jump around, doing *salto-mortale*[13] and all sorts of tricks. And when *papasha* and *mamasha* died, a certain German woman took me into her home and started teaching me. All right. I grew up and then became a governess. But where I come from and who I am—I don't know . . . Who were my parents, maybe they weren't even married . . . I don't know. [*Takes a cucumber out of her pocket and begins eating it.*] I don't know anything. [*Pause.*] I'd really like to start a conversation, but there's no one to start with . . . I don't have anybody at all.

YEPIKHODOV. [*plays the guitar and sings*]

"What care I for the world and its tumult,
  What care I for my friends or my foes . . ."[14]

How pleasant it is to play the mandolin!

DUNYASHA. It's a guitar, not a mandolin. [*Looks at herself in a small mirror and powders herself.*]

YEPIKHODOV. To a man who's lost his mind and fallen in love, this is a mandolin . . . [*Croons.*]

"Oh, how much my heart will burn
  With the heat of your love in return . . ."

YASHA *joins in.*

SHARLOTTA. It's terrible the way these people sound . . . phew! Like jackals.

DUNYASHA. [*to* YASHA] All the same, what luck to go visiting abroad.

YASHA. Yes, of course. I can't possibly disagree with you on that point. [*Yawns, then lights a cigar.*]

YEPIKHODOV. It makes good sense. A long time ago everything abroad shaped up and achieved its full build.

YASHA. Goes without saying.

YEPIKHODOV. I'm a well-developed person, and I read all sorts of wonderful books. But I can't comprehend at all the direction I personally want to take, that is, to go on living or to shoot myself, personally speaking. But nonetheless I always carry a revolver on me. Here it is . . . [*Indicates the revolver.*]

SHARLOTTA. So much for that. Now I'm on my way. [*Slings on her gun.*] Yepikhodov, you are a very intelligent man and dreadfully frightening. Women must fall madly in love with you. Brrr! [*Walks.*] These intellectuals are all so stupid, there's no one to talk to . . . I feel alone all the time, all alone, I don't have anybody at all and . . . and who I am, what on earth I'm here for, is be-

---

12. An "internal" passport, for movement within Russia rather than crossing its borders into foreign lands.

13. A complete somersault.

14. Words from a popular turn-of-the-century ballad.

yond me . . . [*Goes out without hurrying.*]

YEPIKHODOV. Personally speaking, and I'm not going to touch on other topics, I must explain something about myself, by the way. That is, fate treats me without one bit of remorse, like a storm regards a small ship. If, let us assume, I'm mistaken, then why is it I wake up this morning—and I'm saying this by way of illustration —I look, and perched on my chest is a spider of dreadful dimensions . . . That's how big. [*Indicates size with both hands.*] And also if I pick up some kvas so I can have a good drink, what do I see inside? Something or other extremely indecent like a cockroach. [*Pause.*] Have you read Buckle?[15] [*Pause.*] Avdotya Fyodorovna, I wish to bother you for a couple of words or so.

DUNYASHA. Go ahead and talk.

YEPIKHODOV. I'd find it most desirable if it were with you privately . . . [*Sighs.*]

DUNYASHA. [*embarrassed*] Very well . . . Only first of all bring me my cape . . . it's somewhere near the cupboard . . . It's a little damp here . . .

YEPIKHODOV. Very good, miss . . . I'll bring it, miss . . . Now I know what I can do with my revolver . . . [*Takes the guitar and goes out playing.*]

YASHA. Two-and-Twenty Hard Knocks! A stupid man, just between you and me. [*Yawns.*]

DUNYASHA. God forbid he doesn't shoot himself. [*Pause.*] I've grown so uneasy, I'm always in a dither. I was still a little girl when the master and mistress took me into their place, and now I've lost the habit of living the way common people do. Here, you can see my hands, white as white can be, just like a lady's. I've grown fragile, so delicate, refined and ladylike, everything in the world frightens me . . . terribly so. And if you deceive me, Yasha, I just don't know what it will go and do to my nerves.

YASHA. [*kisses her*] Saucy little cucumber! Every girl must remember who she is, to be sure, and there's nothing I dislike more than a girl who doesn't behave herself as she should.

DUNYASHA. I love you so terribly much. You're educated, there's nothing in the world you can't figure out. [*Pause.*]

YASHA. [*yawns*] Yes, miss . . . The way I look at it, if a girl loves anyone, it means she's immoral. [*Pause.*] It's pleasant to smoke a cigar in clean, pure air . . . [*Listens.*] Somebody's coming here . . . It's the ladies and gentlemen . . . [DUNYASHA *impulsively embraces him.*] You go on home as if you've gone to the river to bathe. Take that path, or else you'll meet them and they'll start thinking I made a point of going out with you. I can't take something like that.

DUNYASHA. [*quietly coughs*] I'm starting to get a headache from your cigar . . . [*Goes out.*]

---

15. Henry Thomas Buckle (1821–1862) wrote a *History of Civilization in England* (1857–1861) which was considered daringly materialistic and free-thinking.

YASHA *remains and sits down near the chapel.* LYUBOV AN-
DREEVNA, GAEV, *and* LOPAKHIN *enter.*

LOPAKHIN. You must come to a decision once and for all—time
waits for no one. Surely the question is quite simple. Do you
agree to lease your land for summer cottages or don't you? You
can answer in one word. Is it yes or no? Just one word!

LYUBOV ANDREEVNA. Who's smoking disgusting cigars out here . . .
[*Sits down.*]

GAEV. Things became convenient once they built the railroad. [*Sits
down.*] We made a short trip to town and had lunch . . . Off the
yellow into the middle pocket! I'd like to go to the house first and
play one game . . .

LYUBOV ANDREEVNA. You'll have time.

LOPAKHIN. Just one word! [*Beseechingly.*] Give me an answer,
do!

GAEV. [*yawning*] How's that?

LYUBOV ANDREEVNA. [*looks in her purse*] Yesterday I had plenty
of money, and today there's not much at all. Trying to save money,
my poor Varya feeds all of us milk soup, and the old folks in the
kitchen get nothing but dried peas. And yet I go on spending
money thoughtlessly, somehow. [*Drops her purse, scattering gold
coins.*] Now, they've fallen down . . . [*She is annoyed.*]

YASHA. Allow me, I'll go pick them up at once. [*Gathers up the
coins.*]

LYUBOV ANDREEVNA. Please do, Yasha. Why on earth did I lunch in
town . . . That good-for-nothing restaurant of yours with its music
and tablecloths smelling of soap . . . Why did you drink so much,
Lyonya, or eat so much? And talk so much? Today in the restaurant you were talking too much again, and every bit of it was out
of place—about the seventies and the decadent movement. And to
whom? Talking to the waiters about the decadents![16]

LOPAKHIN. Yes.

GAEV. [*waves his hand*] I'm incorrigible, that's obvious . . . [*Irritably, to* YASHA.] What are you doing, popping up in front of me
all the time . . .

YASHA. [*laughs*] I can't listen to your voice without laughing.

GAEV. [*to his sister*] Either he, or I . . .

LYUBOV ANDREEVNA. You can leave, Yasha, on your way now . . .

YASHA. [*gives* LYUBOV ANDREEVNA *her purse*] I'm going right now.
[*Scarcely able to contain his laughter.*] This very minute . . .
[*Goes out.*]

LOPAKHIN. That rich fellow Deriganov is thinking about buying
your estate. They say he's coming to the auction himself.

LYUBOV ANDREEVNA. Oh, where did you hear that?

LOPAKHIN. They're talking about it in town.

16. A group of French poets (Mallarmé is today the most famous) of the
1880's were labeled "decadents" by their
enemies and sometimes adopted the name
themselves, proud of their refinement and
sensitivity.

GAEV. Our auntie in Yaroslavl promised to send us money, but when, or how much, is beyond me. . . .

LOPAKHIN. How much will she send? A hundred thousand? Two hundred thousand?

LYUBOV ANDREEVNA. Well . . . about ten or fifteen thousand, and we're thankful to get that.

LOPAKHIN. You must forgive me, but I've never met people as rattlebrained as you two are, my friends, or so unbusinesslike and strange, too. You are told in plain language your estate is going to be sold, and it's just as if you don't understand it.

LYUBOV ANDREEVNA. But what is it we can do? You tell us, what?

LOPAKHIN. I keep telling you every day. Every day I keep on saying one and the same thing. Both the cherry orchard and the land must be leased for summer residences. You must do it right now, as soon as possible—the auction is practically under our nose. Try and grasp what I'm saying. When you decide once and for all on the summer cottages, you can raise whatever sum of money you'd like to and then you're safe and sound.

LYUBOV ANDREEVNA. Summer cottages and the people who go with them. Forgive me, but it's all so petty, so vulgar.

GAEV. I agree with you completely.

LOPAKHIN. I'm going to burst into tears, or shout, or fall on the ground and faint. I can't stand it! You've worn me out completely! [*To* GAEV.] You're an old woman!

GAEV. How's that?

LOPAKHIN. An old woman, that's what! [*Wants to leave.*]

LYUBOV ANDREEVNA. [*frightened*] No, don't go away, stay with us, dear. I beg you. Perhaps we'll think of something or other!

LOPAKHIN. What's there to think about?

LYUBOV ANDREEVNA. Don't go away, I beg you. When you're around it's more cheerful . . . [*Pause.*] I keep waiting for something, just as if the house were going to fall down on us.

GAEV. [*deep in thought*] Bank shot into the corner . . . Across into the middle . . .

LYUBOV ANDREEVNA. Oh, how very much we have sinned . . .

LOPAKHIN. What sins could you possibly have . . .

GAEV. [*puts a piece of candy into his mouth*] They say I've eaten up my fortune in candy . . . [*Laughs.*]

LYUBOV ANDREEVNA. Oh, my sins, my sins . . . I've always scattered money to the winds, impulsively, like someone out of her mind, and I married a man who did nothing but build up debts. My husband died of champagne, he reveled in drinking, and then I was unlucky enough to fall in love with someone else. I began living with him. And just at that time—it was my first punishment, a blow that drove me mad with grief—here in this very river . . . My little boy was drowned. I went abroad, left forever, never to return —never to see this river again . . . I just closed my eyes and ran, losing all sense of what I was doing or who I am, and *he* followed me . . . callously, brutally. I bought a dacha near Mentone because it was there he fell sick, and for the next three years I knew neither rest nor peace, nursing him day and night. He wore me out completely, my soul dried up. And last year, when the dacha was sold to pay off debts, I left for Paris. It was there he robbed me, deserted me, and began living with another woman. I tried to poison myself . . . It was all so stupid and degrading . . . And suddenly I felt a longing to come home to Russia, home to my own land and my little girl . . . [*Wipes away her tears.*] Oh, Lord, dear Lord in heaven, be gracious, forgive me my sins! Don't punish me anymore! [*Takes a telegram out of her pocket.*] This came today from Paris . . . He begs forgiveness and implores me to return . . . [*Tears up the telegram.*] That's music coming from somewhere, I think. [*Listens.*]

GAEV. It's our celebrated Jewish orchestra. You remember, don't you, the four violins, flute, and double bass?

LYUBOV ANDREEVNA. It still exists, then? We ought to send for them sometime and arrange an evening party at the house.

LOPAKHIN. [*listens*] I can't hear anything . . . [*Sings quietly.*]

"For the right amount of money, oh, the Germans can
  Change a solid Russian into a Frenchy man."[17] [*Laughs.*]

What a play I saw at the theatre yesterday. Really a lot to laugh at.

LYUBOV ANDREEVNA. And probably there wasn't anything funny in it. Going to see plays isn't what you people should do. Try looking at yourselves a little more often and see what gray lives you all lead. How much of what you say is unnecessary.

LOPAKHIN. That's very true. You can be honest and say we all lead the life of a fool . . . [*Pause.*] My *papasha* was a peasant, an idiot. He didn't understand anything, so he taught me nothing and just beat me when he was drunk, always with a stick, too. As a matter of fact, I'm just as big a lunkhead and idiot myself. I never learned anything, and my handwriting's miserable. The way I write I'm ashamed to let people see it. Just the way a pig might write.

LYUBOV ANDREEVNA. You should get married, my friend.

LOPAKHIN. Yes . . . That's very true.

LYUBOV ANDREEVNA. To our own Varya. She's a fine girl.

LOPAKHIN. Yes.

LYUBOV ANDREEVNA. Her parents are common people. She works the whole day long, but what's really important is that she loves you. And you know you've liked her for a long time.

LOPAKHIN. Well, hmm? I've nothing against it . . . She's a fine girl. [*Pause.*]

GAEV. They offered me a job in a bank. Six thousand rubles a year

17. Critics have been unable to trace the origin of these lines.

. . . Have you heard?

LYUBOV ANDREEVNA. Oh, you're not up to it! You can stay as you are . . .

FIRS *enters, bringing a coat.*

FIRS. [*to* GAEV] Be so good as to put this on, sir, it's damp here.

GAEV. [*puts on coat*] You're bothering me, old man.

FIRS. No use going on . . . This morning you left without saying one word to me. [*Looks him over.*]

LYUBOV ANDREEVNA. Oh, the years you've put on, Firs, the years!

FIRS. What can I do for you?

LOPAKHIN. They're saying you look so much older!

FIRS. I've been living a long time now. They were going to get me married before your *papasha* was even in the world yet . . . [*Laughs.*] When freedom came for the serfs,[18] I was already the head valet. I did not accept freedom at that time, so I kept on with the master and mistress . . . [*Pause.*] Oh, I remember everyone was glad, but what they were glad about, why, they didn't even know themselves.

LOPAKHIN. Oh, it was very good in the old days. At least they used to flog them.

FIRS. [*not having heard him*] Yes, the good old days. The peasants were attached to the master, and the master to the peasants, but nowadays they are all mixed up, and you can't tell one from the other.

GAEV. Keep quiet for a moment, Firs. Tomorrow I must go to town. I was promised an introduction to a certain general who might give us money on a promissory note.

LOPAKHIN. Nothing will come out of it. And you won't pay the interest, either, you can rest assured of that.

LYUBOV ANDREEVNA. He's just ranting and raving again. There aren't any generals, none.

TROFIMOV, ANYA, *and* VARYA *enter.*

GAEV. Oh, here come the children.

ANYA. Mama's sitting down.

LYUBOV ANDREEVNA. [*affectionately*] Come, come along . . . my darlings . . . [*Embraces* ANYA *and* VARYA.] If you both only knew how much I love you. Sit down beside me, that's the way.

All sit down.

LOPAKHIN. Our eternal student always takes good care of the young ladies.

TROFIMOV. It's none of your business.

LOPAKHIN. He's going to be fifty soon, but he's still a student.

TROFIMOV. You can stop your asinine jokes right now.

LOPAKHIN. What's a peculiar fellow like you getting angry about, anyway?

TROFIMOV. Oh, don't keep on pestering me, that's all.

LOPAKHIN. [*laughs*] Permit me, if you will, one question. What do

18. Refers to the emancipation of the serfs in 1861.

you think about me?

TROFIMOV. I, Yermolay Alexeich, this is what I think. You are a rich man, and you're going to be a millionaire soon. In the economy of nature one form of matter is exchanged for another, and so we find indispensable the beast of prey which devours everything that lands on its path. In that way you too are indispensable.

All laugh.

VARYA. Oh, Petya, you'd better tell us about the planets.

LYUBOV ANDREEVNA. No, let's go on with what we were saying yesterday.

TROFIMOV. What was it about?

GAEV. Pride.

TROFIMOV. We talked a long time yesterday, but we didn't get anywhere. The proud person in your sense of the word has something mystical inside. Maybe you're even right the way you see it. But if we reason it out simply and not try to be one bit fancy, then what sort of pride can you possibly take or what's the sense of ever having it, if man is poorly put together as a physiological type and if the enormous majority of the human race is brutal, stupid, and profoundly unhappy? We must stop admiring ourselves. What we ought to do is just keep on working.

GAEV. We're going to die, so it doesn't matter.

TROFIMOV. Who knows for certain? Besides, what does "to die" really mean? It may be that man has a hundred senses and at death only the five known to us are lost, while the remaining ninety-five go on living.

LYUBOV ANDREEVNA. How intelligent you are, Petya!

LOPAKHIN. [*ironically*] Terribly!

TROFIMOV. Humankind strides on, perfecting its strength. All that lies beyond us now will become one day comprehensible and within our grasp. The one thing we must do is to work and do all we can for those who seek the truth. Here in Russia very few people really work now. The educated people I know, the vast majority at any rate, aren't in search of a single thing, and they certainly don't do anything. So far they lack even the ability for real work. They call themselves the intelligentsia, but they speak to their servants as inferiors and treat their peasants as if they were animals. They are poor students, they read absolutely nothing serious, and they do precisely nothing. They only talk about science, and as for art, they understand next to nothing. They are all very serious people with stern expressions on their faces. They discuss nothing but important matters and like to philosophize a great deal, while at the same time everyone can see that the workers are detestably fed, sleep without suitable bedding, thirty to forty in a room with bedbugs everywhere, the stench, the dampness, and the moral corruption . . . Obviously all our fine talk has gone on simply to hoodwink ourselves and other people as well. Show me the day nurseries that they're talking so much about. And where are the libraries? Why, they just write about nurseries and libraries in novels, while in fact not a single one even exists. What does exist is nothing but dirt, vulgarity, and a barbarian way of life . . . I dislike these terribly serious faces, they frighten me, and I'm afraid of serious conversations, too. We'd be better off if we all would just shut up for a while!

LOPAKHIN. You know, I get up before five in the morning, and I work from morning till night. Now, I've always got money on hand—my own and other people's—and so I can see what kind of people are around. You have only to start doing something or other to realize how few honest, decent people there are. Sometimes when I can't get to sleep, I keep thinking, "Dear Lord in heaven, you gave us these enormous forests, boundless fields, broad horizons, and living among them we really ought to be giants ourselves . . ."

LYUBOV ANDREEVNA. Now you find giants indispensable . . . Oh, they are very nice only in fairy stores; anywhere else they can scare you. [YEPIKHODOV *crosses at the depth of the stage, playing his guitar.* LYUBOV ANDREEVNA *is deep in thought.*] There goes Yepikhodov . . .

ANYA. [*deep in thought*] There goes Yepikhodov . . .

GAEV. The sun has set, ladies and gentlemen.

TROFIMOV. Yes.

GAEV. [*in a low voice, as if reciting*] Oh, nature, marvelous nature, shining with eternal radiance, beautiful yet unfeeling, you whom we name as mother, in whom are united both the living and the dead, you give life and you destroy . . .

VARYA. [*beseechingly*] Uncle dear!

ANYA. Uncle, you're starting again!

TROFIMOV. You'd better try a bank shot off the yellow into the middle.

GAEV. I'll keep silent, silent.

All are sitting, deep in thought. Silence. All that can be heard is FIRS, *who mumbles quietly. Suddenly a sound is heard far off in the distance, as if coming from the sky. It is the sound of a string breaking that dies away sadly.*

LYUBOV ANDREEVNA. What was that?

LOPAKHIN. I don't know. Somewhere far off in the mines a bucket must have broken loose. But it's somewhere far, far away.

GAEV. Perhaps it was a bird of some kind . . . like a heron.

TROFIMOV. Or an eagle owl . . .

LYUBOV ANDREEVNA. [*shudders*] It was unpleasant, and I don't know why. [*Pause.*]

FIRS. It was just the same before the troubles—and the owl kept hooting and the samovar humming without stopping.

GAEV. What troubles are you talking about?

FIRS. Just before the serfs were given their freedom. [*Pause.*]

LYUBOV ANDREEVNA. You know, dear friends, evening has come.

Let's go on our way. [*To* ANYA.] You have tears in your eyes . . .
What is it, my little girl? [*Embraces her.*]

ANYA. No reason, Mama, it's nothing.

TROFIMOV. There's someone coming.

> *A passer-by appears, wearing a threadbare white peaked cap
> and an overcoat. He is slightly drunk.*

PASSER-BY. Permit me if you will one question. Can I go from here
straight to the station?

GAEV. You can. Take that road.

PASSER-BY. I thank you from the bottom of my heart. [*Having
coughed.*] Superb weather . . . [*Recites.*] "Oh, my brother, my
suffering brother . . . come out to the Volga, whose moan . . ."[19]
[*To* VARYA.] Mademoiselle, could you allow a starving Russian
thirty kopeks . . .

> VARYA *is frightened and shrieks.*

LOPAKHIN. [*angrily*] Even rascals ought to know how to behave
properly.

LYUBOV ANDREEVNA. [*shocked and confused*] Take it . . . here. . . .
[*Looks in her purse.*] There's no silver here . . . It doesn't
matter, here's a gold coin for you . . .

PASSER-BY. I thank you from the bottom of my heart! [*Goes out.*]

> *There is laughter from those onstage.*

VARYA. [*frightened*] I'm going away . . . I'm going . . . Oh, there's
nothing at home for the servants to eat, *Mamochka*, and you
gave him a gold coin.

LYUBOV ANDREEVNA. I am foolish. What can be done with me,
what! When we get home, I'll give you everything I have. Yermolay Alexeich, lend me something more, do! . .

LOPAKHIN. Yes, ma'am.

LYUBOV ANDREEVNA. Let's go, ladies and gentlemen, it's time. Oh,
Varya, we've just signed, sealed, and absolutely promised you in
marriage. Congratulations.

VARYA. [*through tears*] Mama, this is nothing to joke about.

LOPAKHIN. Oralia, get thee to a nunnery . . .[20]

GAEV. Oh, my hands are shaking. I haven't played a billiard game in
a long time.

LOPAKHIN. Oralia, oh nymph, remember me in thy orisons!

LYUBOV ANDREEVNA. Come along, ladies and gentlemen. We'll sit
down soon for supper.

VARYA. Oh, how he scared me. My heart hasn't stopped pounding
yet.

LOPAKHIN. I'd like to remind you, ladies and gentlemen, the
cherry orchard will be up for sale on the twenty-second of August. Think about it! . . Keep it in mind, do! . .

19. The quotations are from poems by
Syomon Nadson (1862–1887) and Nikolay Nekrasov (1821–1878) respectively.

20. Lopakhin makes comic use of
Hamlet's meeting with Ophelia (in the
Russian distorted to "Okhmelia"). Hamlet, seeing her approaching, says:
"Nymph, in thy orisons / Be all my sins
remembered." (Act III, sc. 1, ll. 89–90),
and later, suspecting her of spying for
her father, sends her off with "Get thee
to a nunnery" (1. 121).

All go out except TROFIMOV *and* ANYA.

ANYA. [*laughing*] Thanks to that man who came by, Varya is scared, and we're alone now.

TROFIMOV. Varya's frightened we might suddenly fall in love, so she hasn't left us alone for days. With her narrow mind she can't possibly understand that we are above love. To give up all that is petty and unreal, which stops our being free and happy—that's the purpose and meaning of our lives. On then, ahead! We stride invincibly on to that bright star burning there in the distance! On then, ahead! Don't fall behind, my friends!

ANYA. [*throwing up her arms*] How wonderfully you speak! [*Pause.*] It's unbelievable here today!

TROFIMOV. Yes, the weather is striking.

ANYA. Whatever have you done to me, Petya? Why is it I no longer love the cherry orchard as I used to? I loved it so tenderly, and I thought no place on earth was better than our own orchard.

TROFIMOV. All Russia is our orchard. The land is vast and beautiful and filled with marvelous places. [*Pause.*] Just think, Anya, your grandfather and your great-grandfather and all your ancestors owned both land and serfs, they owned living souls. Don't you see that from every cherry tree in the orchard, from every leaf and every trunk, generations of human beings are gazing down at you, don't you hear their voices . . . To own human souls—it has transformed every one of you, don't you see, those who lived before and those living today. And so your mother, your uncle, and you no longer notice that you are living in debt, at the expense of other people, at the expense of the very people you will allow no farther than the entrance to your home[21] . . .We are at least two hundred years behind the times, we haven't made any real headway yet, and we still don't have any clear idea about our relation to the past. We just philosophize, complain of boredom, or drink vodka. It's so clear, you see, that if we're to begin living in the present, we must first of all redeem our past and then be done with it forever. And the only way we can redeem our past is by suffering and by giving ourselves over to exceptional labor, to steadfast and endless work. You must realize this, Anya.

ANYA. The house we live in hasn't really been ours for a long time, and I'm going to leave it. I give you my word.

TROFIMOV. If you're given the keys to the household, throw them into the well and walk away, go. Be free like the wind.

ANYA. [*in exaltation*] How wonderfully you said everything!

TROFIMOV. Believe me, Anya, you must believe! I'm not yet thirty, I'm a young man, and I'm still a student, but I have already gone through so much! As soon as winter's come, I find myself hungry,

21. The Russian censors objected to this and the previous sentence, so in his manuscript Chekhov substituted the following: "Your orchard is a fearful place, and when you pass through it in the evening or at night, the old bark on the trees gleams faintly, and the cherry trees seem to be dreaming of things that happened a hundred, two hundred years ago and to be tormented by painful visions." (Translated by Avrahm Yarmolinsky.)

ill, worried, poor as a beggar, and—the places fate has driven me, the places! Where haven't I been, where? And the whole time, every minute of the day and night, I've felt impressions of the future abound in my soul, visions I can't explain. I know happiness is coming, Anya, I can feel it. I already see it on the way . . .

ANYA. [*deep in thought*] The moon is rising.

> YEPIKHODOV *is heard playing the guitar, the same sad song as before. The moon rises. Somewhere near the poplar trees,* VARYA *is looking for* ANYA *and is calling,* "Anya! Where are you?"

TROFIMOV. Yes, the moon is rising. [*Pause.*] There it is, happiness. There it comes, coming nearer, always nearer. I can already hear its footsteps. And if we don't see it, if we don't experience it, what does it matter? Other people will see it.

VARYA'S VOICE. [*offstage*] Anya! Where are you?

TROFIMOV. It's Varya again! [*Angrily.*] Oh, she is exasperating!

ANYA. Well, hmm? Let's go to the river. It's fine there.

TROFIMOV. Yes, let's go. [*They go out.*]

VARYA'S VOICE. [*offstage*] Anya! Anya!

CURTAIN

Act Three

The drawing room. In the distance, through the archway, the ballroom can be seen. The chandelier is lighted. The Jewish orchestra mentioned in the second act is heard playing in the entrance hall. It is evening. In the ballroom they are dancing a grand rond. *The voice of* SIMEONOV-PISHCHIK *is heard,* "Promenade à une paire!" *They enter the drawing room:* PISHCHIK *and* SHARLOTTA IVANOVNA *are the first couple;* TROFIMOV *and* LYUBOV ANDREEVNA *the second;* ANYA *and the* POST OFFICE CIVIL SERVANT, *the third;* VARYA *and the* STATIONMASTER, *the fourth; and so on.* VARYA *is weeping quietly, and as she dances, she wipes her tears away.* DUNYASHA *is in the last couple. They walk around the drawing room, and* PISHCHIK *shouts,* "Grand rond, balancez!" *and* "Les cavaliers à genoux et remerciez vos dames!"[22] FIRS, *wearing a dress coat, brings in a tray with seltzer water.* PISHCHIK *and* TROFIMOV *enter the drawing room.*

PISHCHIK. I'm a pretty full-blooded man. I've had two strokes already so dancing is hard work for me, but, as the saying goes,

---

22. "*Promenade à une paire!*": "Promenade with your partner!" "*Grand Rond, balancez!*": "The great ring dance, get set!" "*Les cavaliers à genoux et remerciez vos dames!*": "Gentlemen, on your knees and thank your ladies!"

"If you run with the pack,
　　　　　you can trail.
Keep silent or bark back,
　　　　　you can't fail.
But you'd better get crack-
　　　　ing to jiggle and jaggle
　　　　and wiggle and waggle
　　　　　　your tail."

I'm as healthy as a horse, however. My departed father was some-thing of a joker—may the kingdom of heaven be his—and he used to explain our origins like this. The ancient line of Simeonov-Pishchik, he'd say, comes down from the very same horse that Caligula had seated in the senate . . . [*Sits down.*] But my trouble is I don't have any money, none! A hungry dog puts his trust only in meat . . . [*Snores and then wakes up immediately.*] That fits me to a . . . the only thing I keep thinking about is money . . .

TROFIMOV. Indeed your build is somehow like a horse.

PISHCHIK. Well, hmm . . . a horse is a fine animal . . . You can sell a horse . . .

　　　The sound of a billiard game being played in an adjoining room is heard. VARYA *appears in the ballroom underneath the archway.*

TROFIMOV. [*teases*] Madame Lopakhina! Madame Lopkhina! . .

VARYA. [*angrily*] You're a used-up old gentleman!

TROFIMOV. Yes, I am a used-up old gentleman, and I'm proud of it!

VARYA. [*meditating bitterly*] Here we've gone and hired musicians, but what are we going to pay them with? [*Goes out.*]

TROFIMOV. [*to* PISHCHIK] Just consider how much energy you've used up in the course of your life trying to find money to pay the interest on your loans. If you'd spent that same energy on some-thing else, there's a good chance, when all's been said and done, you might have turned the world upside down.

PISHCHIK. Nietzsche[23] . . . the philosopher . . . the greatest, very fa-mous . . . a fellow of enormous intellect. Well, he says in his own works that it's all right to forge banknotes.

TROFIMOV. Then you've read Nietzsche?

PISHCHIK. Well . . . Dashenka talked to me about it. Oh, the kind of situation I'm in right now, forging banknotes is about the only thing left for me to do . . . The day after tomorrow I must pay out three hundred and ten rubles . . . and what I've already got is one hundred and thirty . . . [*Feels his pockets, alarmed.*] The money is gone! I've lost my money! [*Through tears.*] Where's my money? [*Jubilantly.*] Here it is, inside the lining . . . You know, I even started to sweat . . .

　　　LYUBOV ANDREEVNA *and* SHARLOTTA IVANOVNA *enter.*

23. Friedrich W. Nietzsche (1844–1900), German philosopher.

LYUBOV ANDREEVNA. [*hums a lezginka*]²⁴ Why is Leonid taking so long? What's he doing in town? [*To* DUNYASHA.] Dunyasha, offer the musicians some tea . . .

TROFIMOV. I'd say the auction probably never took place.

LYUBOV ANDREEVNA. · Oh, what on earth were we thinking of? Of all moments to send for the musicians. Of all moments to give a ball. The most inopportune of all . . . Well, it's nothing, really . . . [*Sits and hums quietly.*]

SHARLOTTA. [*gives a pack of cards to* PISHCHIK] Here's a pack of cards. Think of a card, any card you want.

PISHCHIK. I've thought of one.

SHARLOTTA. Now shuffle the pack. Very good. Now let me have them, oh my dear Mister Pishchik. *Ein, zwei, drei!*²⁵ And now just look. There it is, in your side pocket . . .

PISHCHIK. [*takes a card out of his side pocket*] The eight of spades, you're positively right! [*Surprised.*] What do you think of that!

SHARLOTTA. [*holds the pack of cards on the palm of her hand; to* TROFIMOV] Tell me quickly, what card is on top?

TROFIMOV. Well, hmm? Well, the queen of spades.

SHARLOTTA. And here it is! [*To* PISHCHIK.] Well, what do you say the top card is now?

PISHCHIK. The ace of hearts.

SHARLOTTA. And here it is! [*Claps her hands and the pack of cards disappears.*] Oh, what fine weather today! [*She is answered by a mysterious woman's voice that apparently comes from under the floor,* "Oh, yes, the weather is incredible, dear leady."] Oh, you're so fine, indeed you're my ideal . . .

The voice, "I like you very much, too, dear lady."

THE STATION MASTER. [*applauds*] Bravo, our Miss Ventriloquist, bravo!

PISHCHIK. [*surprised*] What do you think of that! You're charming, Sharlotta Ivanovna, just charming . . . you know I've simply fallen in love . . .

SHARLOTTA. In love? [*Having shrugged her shoulders.*] How could you ever fall in love, really? *Guter Mensch, aber schlechter Musikant.*²⁶

TROFIMOV. [*claps* PISHCHIK *on the shoulder*] Not bad for an old horse . . .

SHARLOTTA. I beg your attention, one last trick, if you please. [*Takes a lap robe from a chair.*] Here you see a very fine lap robe I'd like to sell . . . [*Shakes it.*] Isn't there anyone who'd like to buy it?

PISHCHIK. [*surprised*] What do you think of that!

---

24. Music which in the Caucasus mountains accompanies a courtship dance in which the man dances with abandon around the woman, who moves with grace and ease.
25. "One, two, three" (in German).
26. "A good man, but a bad musician" (in German), usually quoted in the plural: "*Gute Leute, schlechte Musikanten.*" It comes from *Das Buch le Grand* (1826) by the German poet Heinrich Heine (1799–1856). Here it suggests that Pishchik may be a good man but a bad lover.

SHARLOTTA. *Ein, zwei, drei!* [*Quickly raises the lap robe, which she had lowered and held like a curtain, and behind it stands* ANYA, *who curtsies, runs to her mother, embraces her, and runs back into the ballroom amid general excitement.*]

LYUBOV ANDREEVNA. [*applauds*] Bravo, bravo! . .

SHARLOTTA. Now once more! *Ein, zwei, drei!* [*Raises the lap robe and behind it stands* VARYA, *who bows.*]

PISHCHIK. [*surprised*] What do you think of that!

SHARLOTTA. That's all there is—the end! [*Throws the lap robe at* PISHCHIK, *curtsies, and runs off to the ballroom.*]

PISHCHIK. [*hurries after her*] Oh, you little scamp . . . Think you're something, don't you? Really something? [*Goes out.*]

LYUBOV ANDREEVNA. And Leonid still isn't back yet. I can't imagine what he's doing in town all this time! You know the whole thing must be finished by now, either the estate's sold or the auction didn't take place. Then why on earth keep us in the dark all this time!

VANYA. [*trying to comfort her*] Dear Uncle bought it, I'm convinced he did.

TROFIMOV. [*derisively*] Yes.

VARYA. Grandmother sent him the authority to buy it in her name and transfer the mortgage to her. It's for Anya's sake she's doing it. And with God's help I'm convinced dear Uncle will buy it.

LYUBOV ANDREEVNA. Grandmother in Yaroslavl sent fifteen thousand rubles to buy the estate in her name—she didn't trust us— and the money she sent won't even pay the interest. [*Covers her face with her hands.*] My fate is being decided today, my fate . . .

TROFIMOV. [*teases* VARYA] Madame Lopakhina!

VARYA. [*angrily*] Oh, it's the eternal student! He's been thrown out of the university two times so far.

LYUBOV ANDREEVNA. Why are you getting angry, Varya? He's teasing you about Lopakhin, oh well, hmm? If you want to, then go and marry Lopakhin. He's a fine, interesting person. If you don't want to, then don't marry him. No one is forcing you, darling . . .

VARYA. I look on this whole matter seriously, *Mamochka*, I must tell you frankly. He is a fine person and I like him.

LYUBOV ANDREEVNA. Then go and marry him. What is it you're waiting for, I simply don't understand!

VARYA. *Mamochka*, I can't propose to him myself, I can't. For the past two years everyone's been talking to me about him, and they haven't stopped talking yet, but either he doesn't say anything or else he jokes about it. And I can understand why. He's growing rich, he's very busy, and he hasn't one bit of time for me. If only I had the money, even a little, if it were only a hundred rubles, I'd drop everything and walk off. I'd go as far as I could. I'd go into a convent.

TROFIMOV. What a blessed way to live!

VARYA. [*to* TROFIMOV] Our student can't stop proving how smart he is! [*In a gentle tone, in tears.*]. Oh, Petya, you've grown so homely, and you look old, so very old! [*No longer weeping, she speaks to* LYUBOV ANDREEVNA.] I just can't go through life without things to do, *Mamochka*. I must be doing something or other every single minute.

    YASHA *enters*.

YASHA. [*scarcely able to contain his laughter*] Yepikhodov's gone and broken a billiard cue! . . [*Goes out.*]

VARYA. Why on earth is Yepikhodov here? And who gave him permission to play billiards? These people don't make any sense to me . . . [*Goes out.*]

LYUBOV ANDREEVNA. Don't tease her, Petya. You can see, can't you, she's unhappy enough without that.

TROFIMOV. She's much too much the fanatic. Why can't she stick to things that concern her? She's kept on bothering me and Anya the whole summer long, so afraid a love affair might come about. Why should it matter to her, anyway? Not for a single moment did I ever give any semblance of it, I'm far beyond vulgarity like that. We are above love!

LYUBOV ANDREEVNA. And here I am beneath love, I suppose. [*In great apprehension*] Why on earth isn't Leonid back? I'd just like to know if the estate's sold or not. I can't believe this terrible thing has gone as far as it has—it's so incredible I don't even know what to think anymore, somehow I feel lost . . . I could scream right now . . . or do something foolish. Save me, Petya. Say something now, talk to me . . .

TROFIMOV. Does it really matter whether the estate is sold today or not? It's over and done with, there's no turning back now, that path's already overgrown. Get hold of yourself, my dear. And don't go and deceive yourself now. At least for once in your life look the truth right in the eyes.

LYUBOV ANDREEVNA. What truth? You can see, can't you, where the truth is and where it isn't, but it seems I've lost my sight, I see nothing. You confidently find answers for all the important problems, but tell me, my dear, isn't that because you're young, because you're not old enough for a single one of your problems to have brought about any substantial suffering? You look ahead so boldly, and you don't see or expect anything terrible to happen, and isn't that because life is still hidden from your young eyes? You are bolder, more honest, deeper than we are, but try and go into the heart of the matter—be at least halfway generous and have mercy on me. You know I was born here, my father and my mother lived here, my grandfather, too. I love this house. Without the cherry orchard my life would lose its meaning, and if it must really be sold then go and sell me with the orchard . . . [*Embraces* TROFIMOV *and kisses him on the forehead.*] You see my son was drowned here . . . [*Weeps.*] Have pity on me, my fine, kind friend.

TROFIMOV. You know I feel for you with all my heart and soul.

LYUBOV ANDREEVNA. But that isn't the way to say it, it isn't the way at all . . . [*Takes out her handkerchief. A telegram falls on the floor.*] Today I feel I've lost heart and soul, you can't imagine how difficult it is for me. It's too noisy here for me. Every sound cuts deep inside and I feel I'm trembling all over, but I can't go to my room, I can't. All alone in the silence, it's terrifying. Don't condemn me, Petya . . . I love you as if you were one of my very own. I'd willingly let Anya marry you, I swear I would, my dear, only you must study and get your degree. You aren't doing a single thing, you just let fate throw you from one place to another, and that's what is so strange . . . Isn't it the truth? Yes? And you ought to do something or other with that beard to make it grow somehow . . . [*Laughs.*] Oh, you're funny, you really are!

TROFIMOV. [*picks up telegram*] I don't have the slightest desire to be good looking.

LYUBOV ANDREEVNA. That telegram is from Paris. I get one every day. Both yesterday and today. That wild creature has fallen ill again, and he's in trouble again . . . He begs forgiveness and implores me to go to him, and I really should go to Paris and spend some time near him. You disapprove, Petya, I can see from your face, but what else can be done, my dear, what can I really do? He is sick, he is alone and unhappy, and who is there to look after him? Who can stop him from doing the wrong things, and who will give him his medicine at the right time? Then why try to hide it or keep quiet about the way I feel? I love him, that's clear. I love him, I love him . . . That man's a millstone around my neck, I'm being dragged down with him, but I love that stone and I can't live without it. [*Presses* TROFIMOV'S *hand.*] Don't think badly of me, Petya, don't say anything to me, don't say anything . . .

TROFIMOV. [*through tears*] Forgive me for being outspoken, for God's sake, but you know he robbed you!

LYUBOV ANDREEVNA. No, no, no, you mustn't talk that way . . . [*Puts her hands over her ears.*]

TROFIMOV. That man is a good-for-nothing louse, and you're the only one who doesn't know it! He's a little, good-for-nothing louse, a nobody . . .

LYUBOV ANDREEVNA. [*having gotten angry, she controls herself*] You are twenty-six or twenty-seven years old, but you are still a schoolboy!

TROFIMOV. And even if I am!

LYUBOV ANDREEVNA. You ought to be a man—at your age you ought to have some understanding of people in love. And you ought to know what it is to love . . . You should fall in love yourself! [*Angrily.*] Yes, yes! And don't think you're so innocent and pure, you're simply an immaculate prude—that's what you are—a laughable eccentric boy, some kind of freak . . .

TROFIMOV. [*horrified*] What can she be saying!

LYUBOV ANDREEVNA. "I am above love!" You aren't above love, but —as our Firs keeps saying—you are just a silly galoot, that's all. At your age and not to have a mistress! . .

TROFIMOV. [*horrified*] This is terrible! What can she be saying? [*Having clutched his head, he goes into the ballroom.*] This is terrible . . . I can't stand it, I'm going . . . [*Goes out, but returns immediately.*] All is over between us! [*Goes out into the entrance hall.*]

LYUBOV ANDREEVNA. [*shouts after him*] Petya, wait a moment! You ridiculous boy, I was joking! Petya!

> *In the entrance hall there are the sounds of someone quickly running on the stairway and suddenly falling downstairs with a clatter.* ANYA *and* VARYA *scream, which is followed immediately by the sound of laughter.*

LYUBOV ANDREEVNA. What's going on out there?

> ANYA *runs in.*

ANYA. [*laughing*] Petya fell downstairs! [*Runs out.*]

LYUBOV ANDREEVNA. What an eccentric boy Petya is . . . [*Having stopped in the middle of the ballroom, the stationmaster recites "The Sinful Woman" by Aleksey Tolstoy.*[27] *They listen to him, but he has recited only a few lines when the sounds of a waltz come from the entrance hall and the reading is broken off. All dance.* TROFIMOV, ANYA, VARYA, *and* LYUBOV ANDREEVNA *enter from the entrance hall.*] Now, Petya . . . now there, you dear innocent soul . . . Forgive me, I beg you . . . Let's dance . . . [*Dances with* PETYA.]

> ANYA *and* VARYA *dance.* FIRS *enters and puts his walking stick near the side door.* YASHA *has also come in from the drawing room and is watching the dancing.*

YASHA. What do you say, Grandpa?

FIRS. I don't feel too well. In times gone by, why generals, barons, and admirals came to our dances, but now we send for the post office clerk and the stationmaster—and even they come against their will. Somehow I feel I've gotten weaker. My old master, who was their grandfather, used to dose every one of us with powdered sealing wax no matter what sickness we had. I've been taking sealing wax for about twenty years now, but it might even be more. Maybe I'm still alive because of it.

YASHA. Gramps, you make me sick and tired. [*Yawns.*] If only you'd go off and croak—the sooner the better.

FIRS. Oh, you . . . you silly galoot, you! [*Mumbles.*]

> TROFIMOV *and* LYUBOV ANDREEVNA *dance in the ballroom and then into the drawing room.*

LYUBOV ANDREEVNA. *Merci.* I'd like to sit down for a while . . . [*Sits down.*] I'm tired.

---

27. (1817–1875), a distant relative of Leo Tolstoy, popular in his time as a dramatist and poet. The poem begins thus:

A bustling crowd with happy laughter,

With twanging lutes and clashing cymbals
With flowers and foliage all around
The colonnaded portico.

ANYA *enters.*

ANYA. [*excitedly*] In the kitchen just now someone was saying that the cherry orchard was sold today.

LYUBOV ANDREEVNA. Sold? To whom?

ANYA. He didn't say. He's gone now. [*Dances with* TROFIMOV; *they go into the ballroom.*]

YASHA. It was just some old man wagging his tongue out there. We didn't know him.

FIRS. Oh, Leonid Andreich still isn't here, he hasn't come back yet. He's only wearing his lightweight overcoat, his "between-seasons" one, and before you can bat an eye he's going to catch cold. Oh, these green young things—they never learn.

LYUBOV ANDREEVNA. I'm going to die, I know it. Yasha, go and find out whom it was sold to.

YASHA. But he went away a long time back, it was an old man. [*Laughs.*]

LYUBOV ANDREEVNA. [*slightly annoyed*] Well, what are you laughing about? What's making you so happy?

YASHA. Oh, that Yepikhodov is really very funny. The man's so useless. Two-and-Twenty Hard Knocks.

LYUBOV ANDREEVNA. If the estate is sold, Firs, where will you go?

FIRS. Wherever you tell me, that's where I'll go.

LYUBOV ANDREEVNA. Why do you look like that? Aren't you feeling well? You ought to go lie down and sleep, you know . . .

FIRS. Yes . . . [*With an ironic smile.*] I'd go off to sleep, and if I'm not here who will there be to serve and keep things going the way they should? I'm the only one in charge of the whole house.

YASHA. [*to* LYUBOV ANDREEVNA] Lyubov Andreevna! Allow me to ask you something, if you'd be so kind! If you go to Paris again, do me a favor and take me with you, please. I can't stay here, it's absolutely impossible here. [*Looks around, in an undertone.*] I suppose it's needless to say it, you can see for yourself, this country is uncivilized and the people don't have any morals at all. Then there's the boredom, too. In the kitchen they feed you disgusting things, and to make it worse—that man Firs keeps walking around the whole time and mumbling all sorts of words that don't make much sense. Take me with you, if you'd be so kind!

PISHCHIK *enters.*

PISHCHIK. Please do me the favor . . . of this little waltz, oh gorgeous woman . . . [LYUBOV ANDREEVNA *goes with him.*] But I'll still take that one hundred and eighty rubles from you, my charming lady . . . Yes, I will . . . [*Dances.*] One hundred and eighty rubles . . . [*They go into the ballroom.*]

YASHA. [*quietly sings*] "If you could but know the excitement of my soul . . ."

In the ballroom a woman dressed in a gray top hat and checked trousers is seen jumping around and waving her arms. There are shouts of "Bravo, Sharlotta Ivanovna."

DUNYASHA. [*stops to powder*] The young mistress told me to dance.

There are plenty of gentlemen and only a few ladies, but dancing makes my head spin around and my heart is pounding. Just now, Firs Nikolaevich, the clerk from the post office told me something that made me lose my breath.

    The music subsides.

FIRS. What exactly did he tell you?

DUNYASHA. You are like a flower, he said.

YASHA. [*yawns*] Sheer case of ignorance . . . [*Goes out.*]

DUNYASHA. Like a flower . . . I'm such a delicate girl I just love hearing sweet words like that.

FIRS. You'll get swept off your feet before you know it.

    YEPIKHODOV *enters.*

YEPIKHODOV. You don't want to look at me, Avdotya Fyodorovna . . . as if I were an insect of some kind. [*Sighs.*] Oh, that's life!

DUNYASHA. What do you want?

YEPIKHODOV. No doubt you are right, perhaps. [*Sighs.*] But, of course, if you look at it from one point of view—and I will allow myself to express myself this way, please excuse me for being so outspoken—you have completely reduced me to a state of mind. I know what luck I face. Every day some catastrophe or other happens to me, but I got used to that long, long ago, so that I look upon my fate with a smile on my face. You gave me your word, and even though I . . .

DUNYASHA. I beg you, let's talk a little later on, but now just leave me alone. I'm dreaming right now. [*Plays with her fan.*]

YEPIKHODOV. I have a catastrophe every day and—I'll permit myself to express myself this way—I just go on smiling, and sometimes I even laugh.

    VARYA *enters from the ballroom.*

VARYA. Haven't you left yet, Semyon? Who do you think you are, really, don't you have any respect? [*To* DUNYASHA.] Be off, Dunyasha, you can leave. [*To* YEPIKHODOV] First you play billiards and break a cue, and now you walk around the drawing room as if you were a guest.

YEPIKHODOV. You can't make me—if you'll permit me to say—answer for it.

VARYA. I'm not making you answer for it, I'm just telling you. All you know how to do is walk from one place to the next, but you don't do one bit of work. We keep a clerk, but for what—it's beyond me.

YEPIKHODOV. [*offended*] Whether I work or ramble about, whether I eat or play billiards, these are issues up for discussion only by more reasonable and older people.

VARYA. How dare you talk to me that way! [*Having flared up.*] How dare you? Do you mean I'm not reasonable, is that it? Well, you can remove yourself, get out of here! This minute!

YEPIKHODOV. [*having become intimidated*] I beg you to express yourself in a delicate way.

VARYA. [*flying into a rage*] Get out of here this very minute! Out of

here, out! [*He goes to the door and she follows him.*] Two-and-
Twenty Hard Knocks! Out you go and never come in here again!
Don't let me catch sight of you ever again! [YEPIKHODOV *goes
out. Behind the door his voice is heard:* "I'm going to bring a
complaint against you."] So you're coming back in here?
[*Seizes the stick which* FIRS *placed near the door.*] Come on . . .
come on . . . come on, I'll show you. . . . So you're coming back?
You are, are you? Then take that . . . [*Flourishes the stick at the
very moment* LOPAKHIN *enters.*]

LOPAKHIN. Thank you ever so much.

VARYA. [*angrily and derisively*] I'm very sorry!

LOPAKHIN. It's nothing, Miss. Thanks so much for your heartfelt
generosity.

VARYA. Don't mention it. [*Walks away, then looks around and
gently asks.*] I didn't hurt you, did I?

LOPAKHIN. No, it's nothing. There's going to be one whale of a
swelling, though.

    Voices are heard in the ballroom: "Lopakhin's arrived! Yerm-
    olay Alexeich!"

PISHCHIK. Well, squint your eyes and bend your ears—it's him himself . . . [*Kisses* LOPAKHIN.] I caught a whiff of brandy on you,
my dear old soul. We've been kicking up our heels around here
too.

    LYUBOV ANDREEVNA *enters.*

LYUBOV ANDREEVNA. Then it's you, Yermolay Alexeich? What's
taken you so long? Where is Leonid?

LOPAKHIN. Leonid Andreich came with me, he's on his way . . .

LYUBOV ANDREEVNA. [*agitated*] Well, what is it? Did the auction
take place? Talk to me, tell me!

LOPAKHIN. [*embarrassed, fearing to betray his elation*] The auction was over by four . . . We were late for the train, and we had to
wait until half past nine. [*Having sighed heavily.*] Phew! My
head's starting to go round and round . . .

    GAEV *enters. He has his purchases in his right hand and wipes
    away his tears with his left hand.*

LYUBOV ANDREEVNA. Lyonya, what is it? Well, Lyonya? [*Impatiently, in tears.*] Tell me, for God's sake! Quickly . . .

GAEV. [*he can say nothing to her and only waves his hand; to* FIRS,
weeping] Here, take these . . . It's anchovies and Kerch herrings
. . . I've had nothing to eat today . . . How much I've had to go
through! [*The door to the billiard room is open. The cracking of billiard balls is heard, and* YASHA's *voice:* "Seven and eighteen!" GAEV's *expression changes and he no longer weeps.*] I'm
terribly tired. Give me a hand, Firs, I must change my clothes.
[*Goes to his room through the ballroom, followed by* FIRS.]

PISHCHIK. What went on at the auction? Tell us now, do!

LYUBOV ANDREEVNA. Is the cherry orchard sold?

LOPAKHIN. It's sold.

LYUBOV ANDREEVNA. Who bought it?

LOPAKHIN. I bought it. [*Pause.* LYUBOV ANDREEVNA *is crushed. If she were not standing next to the armchair and table, she would have fallen. Varya takes the keys from her belt, throws them on the floor in the middle of the drawing room, and goes out.*] I bought it! Wait, ladies and gentlemen, be kind and wait one moment. My head's going round in circles, I can't talk . . . [*Laughs.*] When we got to the auction, Deriganov was already there. Leonid Andreich had only fifteen thousand rubles, and right away Deriganov bid thirty over and above the arrearage on the mortgage. I saw the shape things were in, so I took him on. I bid forty. He went to forty-five, I made it fifty-five. That's the way it went. He kept raising his offer by five thousand, I kept raising mine by ten . . . Well, it came to a finish at last. I bid ninety thousand rubles on top of the arrears, and I got it. The cherry orchard is mine now! Mine! [*Shouts with laughter.*] God in heaven, dear Lord God, the cherry orchard is mine! Tell me I'm drunk or out of my mind, that it's all a daydream I see before my eyes . . . [*Stamps his feet.*] Don't laugh at me! If only my father and grandfather could rise from their graves and see their Yermolay now—their Yermolay who was forever getting beaten, Yermolay who could scarcely read or write, who ran barefoot in the winter—if they could only see how this very same Yermolay went and bought this estate, the most beautiful spot in the world. I bought the estate where my grandfather and my father were slaves, where they weren't even allowed to go into the kitchen. I'm asleep, it's only a dream, it's only something that seems to be . . . This is the fruit of your imagination, concealed in the shadows of uncertainty . . . [*Picks up the keys, smiling affectionately.*] She threw down the keys—she wants to show she doesn't run this house anymore . . . [*Jingles the keys.*] Well, it doesn't matter anyway. [*The orchestra is heard tuning up.*] Hey there, musicians, start playing. I want to hear you! Come on, all of you, come and see Yermolay Lopakhin slash the cherry orchard with his axe. Watch and see the trees come crashing down! We're going to build summer cottages, and our grandchildren and our great-grandchildren are going to see a new way to live around here . . . Music, start playing! [*The orchestra plays.* LYUBOV ANDREEVNA *has sunk into a chair and is weeping bitterly.* LOPAKHIN *speaks reproachfully.*] Why on earth, why didn't you listen to me before? My poor, fine friend, you can't turn round and go back now. [*In tears.*] Oh, if only this would pass by as quickly as possible, if only we could hurry and change our life somehow, this unhappy, helter-skelter way we live.

PISHCHIK. [*takes him by the arm, in an undertone*] She's crying. Let's go into the ballroom, let her be alone . . . Come, let's go . . . [*Takes him by the arm and leads him into the ballroom.*]

LOPAKHIN. What's going on? Say, you doing the music, play lively and clear! Let's start having things the way I want it. [*Ironi-*

cally.] Here comes the new landlord, the owner of the cherry orchard! [*Accidentally shoves a small table, nearly overturns the candelabra.*] I can pay for everything! [*Goes out with* PISHCHIK.]

There is no one left in the ballroom or the drawing room except LYUBOV ANDREEVNA, *who sits all shrunken and is weeping bitterly. The orchestra plays quietly.* ANYA *and* TROFIMOV *enter quickly.* ANYA *goes to her mother and kneels down in front of her.* TROFIMOV *stays by the entrance to the ballroom.*

ANYA. Mama! . . Mama, are you crying? My dear, kind, beautiful Mama, my precious, I love you, I do . . . I give you my blessing. The cherry orchard is sold, it's gone now, it's true, so true, but don't cry, Mama. Your life is still ahead of you, and you haven't lost your beautiful, innocent soul . . . Come with me, my dear, let's go away from here, let's go! . . We shall plant a new orchard, far more splendid than this one. You shall see it, you shall know and find understanding, and happiness shall descend into your heart and soul—you shall know a quiet and profound joy—like the setting sun at the evening hour, and you shall smile, Mama! Come, my dear, let's go! Let's go! . .

CURTAIN

Act Four

The setting is the same as in the first act. There are no window curtains or pictures. The few remaining pieces of furniture have been piled into one corner, as if for sale. There is a feeling of emptiness. Suitcases, traveling bags, etc., have been piled up near the outer door at the rear of the stage. Through the open door, left, the voices of ANYA *and* VARYA *can be heard.* LOPAKHIN *is standing, waiting.* YASHA *is holding a tray with glasses filled with champagne. In the entrance hall* YEPI-KHODOV *is tying up a box. There is a rumble coming from offstage at the rear, the voices of the peasants who have come to say good-bye.* GAEV'S *voice is heard:* "Thanks, brothers, thank you."

YASHA. The peasants have come to say good-bye. The way I look at it, Yermolay Alexeich, such folks are decent enough, but they don't really know what's what.

The rumble of voices subsides. LYUBOV ANDREEVNA *and* GAEV *come in through the entrance hall. She is not weeping; however, she is pale, her face is quivering, and she is unable to speak.*

GAEV. You gave them your purse, Lyuba. That's something you shouldn't do! You know you shouldn't!

LYUBOV ANDREEVNA. I couldn't help it! I simply couldn't help it! [*Both go out.*]

LOPAKHIN. [*in the doorway, calling after them*] Please, I ask you from the bottom of my heart, let's have one little glass since we must say good-bye. I didn't come up with the idea of bringing it from town, and I could only find one bottle at the station. Please, I beg you! [*Pause.*] Well, hmm, friends! Don't you want some? [*Walks away from the door.*] If I'd known, I wouldn't have bought it. Well, then, I'm not going to drink any, either. [YASHA *carefully puts the tray on a chair.*] You take some, Yasha, at least you.

YASHA. To those who are going away! And good luck to those who stay behind! [*Drinks.*] This champagne isn't the real stuff, you can take my word for it.

LOPAKHIN. Eight rubles a bottle. [*Pause.*] Damn, it's cold in here.

YASHA. They didn't start the fires today. It doesn't matter, we're going away. [*Laughs.*]

LOPAKHIN. What's so funny?

YASHA. I feel pleased, that's all.

LOPAKHIN. October has come, but it's sunny and quiet outside, like in the summer. Good weather for building. [*Having glanced at his watch, calls through the doorway.*] Keep in mind, ladies and gentlemen, forty-six minutes before the train leaves. That means we must start for the station in twenty minutes. Better hurry up.

Trofimov, wearing an overcoat, enters from outside.

TROFIMOV. I think it's time we set off. They've brought the horses to the door. Damned if I know where my galoshes are. They've disappeared. [*Calls through the doorway.*] Anya, my galoshes aren't here! Can't find them at all!

LOPAKHIN. I must go to Kharkov. I'll be going with you on the same train. I'll spend the whole winter in Kharkov. I've been shooting the breeze with you folks all the time, it really bothers me when I don't have things to do. I can't stand going without work, because I don't know what to do with my hands. You can see the peculiar way they dangle, just as if they belonged to someone else.

TROFIMOV. We're going away pretty soon, and you can get down to your useful labor again.

LOPAKHIN. How about it, have a little glass.

TROFIMOV. No, thanks.

LOPAKHIN. So you're going to Moscow, right?

TROFIMOV. Yes, I'll see them off and on their way in town, and tomorrow I'll start for Moscow.

LOPAKHIN. Yes . . . Well, hmm, the professors haven't started their lectures yet, I suppose, they must be waiting for you to show up!

TROFIMOV. It's none of your business.

LOPAKHIN. How many years have you been studying at the university?

TROFIMOV. Think of something new to say. That joke is old and flat. [*Looks for his galoshes.*] You know, don't you, we may not see each other anymore, so let me give you a word or two of advice. Don't wave your arms around! Get rid of that habit of waving your arms. Another thing too. When you count on building those summer homes and say that the owners in time will turn out to be independent farmers, you count so much on it—that's just the same as waving your arms around . . . Well, be that as it may, I still like you very much. You have delicate and gentle fingers like an artist has, and in the same way, you are delicate and gentle too in your soul . . .

LOPAKHIN. [*embraces him*] Good-bye, my friend. Thank you for everything. Let me give you some money for the trip, in case you need it.

TROFIMOV. Whatever for? I don't need it.

LOPAKHIN. You know you have nothing!

TROFIMOV. Yes, I have, and I thank you. I got something for a translation. It's here, in my pocket. [*Anxiously.*] But I still don't have my galoshes!

VARYA. [*from the adjoining room*] Oh, take your filthy things! [*Throws a pair of rubber galoshes out on the stage.*]

TROFIMOV. Why are you so angry, Varya? Hmm . . . Oh, these aren't my galoshes!

LOPAKHIN. In the spring I seeded almost three thousand acres in poppies, and I just earned forty thousand rubles clear and clean. And when my poppies were in flower, what a picture of beauty that was! What I'm saying is this. I made forty thousand, so I'm offering you a loan because I can well afford to. So why stick your nose in the air? I'm a peasant . . . and I call a spade a spade.

TROFIMOV. Your father was a peasant, mine was a druggist, and these simple facts prove—exactly nothing. [LOPAKHIN *takes out his wallet.*] Oh, leave it alone, do . . . Even if you gave me two hundred thousand, I wouldn't take it. I'm a free person. And everything you value so highly and is held so dear by all of you, both rich and poor, not one of these things can sway me one iota. Why, they have as much power as a fluff of eiderdown floating in the air. I can make a go of it without you, I can even pass you by. I'm strong and proud. Humankind is on its way to a higher truth, to the greatest happiness possible on this earth, and I'm in the vanguard!

LOPAKHIN. Will you get there?

TROFIMOV. I will. [*Pause.*] I'll either get there or show others the way to get there.

> *There is heard the sound of an axe striking a tree in the distance.*

LOPAKHIN. Well, good-bye, dear boy. It's time to go. You and I stick our noses in the air and look down on each other, but life goes on without giving a hoot about us. When I work and keep at it steadily for some time, thoughts come more easily, and it seems

to me I too know why I exist. But think how many people there
are in Russia who just exist, brother, and for what—it's beyond
me. Well, it doesn't matter, that isn't what keeps the wheels
greased and spinning. Leonid Andreich has taken a job at the
bank, they say, at six thousand a year . . . He just won't stick to
it, you know, he's much too lazy . . .

ANYA. [*in the doorway*] Mama begs you not to cut down the orchard until after she's gone.

TROFIMOV. Yes, really, don't you have tact enough to see . . . [*Goes
out through the entrance hall.*]

LOPAKHIN. All right, it'll take only a minute . . . Oh, these people,
really. [*Goes out after him.*]

ANYA. Has Firs been sent to the hospital?

YASHA. I told them this morning. They've sent him, it stands to reason they have.

ANYA. [*to* YEPIKHODOV, *who is passing through the room*] Semyon
Panteleich, please ask and find out if they've taken Firs to the
hospital.

YASHA. [*offended*] I told Yegor this morning. Why keep on asking
about it? You've brought it up ten times.

YEPIKHODOV. Firs has lived through so many years, my final and
decisive opinion is that he's gone far beyond repair. It's time for
him to meet his forefathers. And I can only envy him. [*He has
put the suitcase down on a hatbox and has crushed it.*] Well,
that's it, of course. I knew it'd turn out like that. [*Goes out.*]

YASHA. [*derisively*] Two-and-Twenty Hard Knocks . . .

VARYA. [*from behind the door*] Has Firs been taken to the hospital?

ANYA. Yes, he has.

VARYA. Why is it they didn't take the letter to the doctor?

ANYA. Then we must send it on after him . . . [*Goes out.*]

VARYA. [*from the adjoining room*] Where is Yasha? Tell him his
mother's come and wants to say good-bye.

YASHA. [*waves his hand*] That's enough to make you lose your
patience.

> *All this time* DUNYASHA *has been fussing with the luggage.
> Now that* YASHA *is alone, she goes up to him.*

DUNYASHA. Why didn't you even glance at me once, Yasha? You are
going away . . . You're walking out on me . . . [*Weeps and
throws her arms around his neck.*]

YASHA. What are you crying about, hmm? [*Drinks champagne.*]
I'll be in Paris again in six days. Tomorrow we'll take the express
train, off we'll roll, and that's the last you'll see of us. I can't
even believe it, somehow. *Vive la France!* . . It doesn't suit me
here, I really can't stand this sort of life . . . and that's all there
is to it. I've seen enough ignorance, oh, have I had my fill of it.
[*Drinks champagne.*] What are you crying about, hmm? Behave
yourself as you should, and you won't have to cry then.

DUNYASHA. [*looking in the small mirror, powders*] Send me a letter from Paris. You know I loved you, Yasha, I loved you so much! I'm a tenderhearted person, Yasha, through and through!

YASHA. Someone is coming. [*Fusses with a suitcase, quietly hums.*]

    LYUBOV ANDREEVNA, GAEV, ANYA, *and* SHARLOTTA IVANOVNA *enter.*

GAEV. We ought to go. There's just a little time left. [*Looking at* YASHA.] Who is it in here reeks of herring?

LYUBOV ANDREEVNA. In about ten minutes we must be getting into the carriages . . . [*Looks around the room.*] Good-bye, my home. Fare thee well, dear old house of our forefathers. Winter will pass, spring will come in time, and then you won't be here anymore, you will be pulled down. Oh, the sights these walls have seen in days gone by! [*Kisses her daughter fervently.*] My treasure, how radiant you look, your eyes are shining like diamonds. Are you pleased, child? Really pleased?

ANYA. Really! This is the beginning of a new life, Mama!

GAEV. [*cheerfully*] Yes, indeed, everything is fine again. Before the cherry orchard was sold, we were all upset and worried ourselves sick, but afterwards, when the whole thing was settled once and for all, and not one chance of turning back, we all simmered down and even started to feel cheerful . . . I'm an employee of a bank now. I'm a financier . . . Off the yellow right into the middle. And Lyuba, in spite of everything, you are looking better, no doubt about it, none.

LYUBOV ANDREEVNA. Yes. My nerves are much better, that's true. [*Someone helps her put on her hat and coat.*] I'm sleeping fine. Take my things out, Yasha. It's time. [*To* ANYA.] My little girl, we'll see each other again soon . . . I'm going to Paris, and I'll live there on the money your grandmother from Yaroslavl sent to buy the estate—long live Grandmother! That money won't last for long.

ANYA. You'll come back soon, Mama, very soon . . . isn't that so? I'm going to study and pass my school examinations, and then I'll go to work and help you. Mama, we'll read all kinds of books together . . . isn't that so? [*Kisses her mother's hands.*] We shall read during the autumn evenings, we'll read through lots of books, and a new marvelous world will open up before us . . . [*Daydreams.*] Mama, come back . . .

LYUBOV ANDREEVNA. I will, my precious. [*Embraces her daughter.*]

    LOPAKHIN *enters.* SHARLOTTA *quietly hums a song.*

GAEV. Happy Sharlotta, she's singing!

SHARLOTTA. [*picks up a bundle which resembles a baby in swaddling clothes*] Bye, bye, little baby mine . . . [*The crying of a baby is heard,* "Wah, Wah! . ."] Be quiet, my dear, my fine little boy. ["Wah! . . Wah! . ."] I feel sorry for you, so sorry! [*Throws the bundle down.*] Then please find me another job, won't you? I can't go on like this.

LOPAKHIN. We'll find something for you, Sharlotta Ivanovna, don't get upset.

GAEV. Everyone's discarding us. Varya's going away too . . . All of a sudden we're not needed.

SHARLOTTA. I don't have any place to live in town. I must go away . . . [*Hums.*] It doesn't matter . . .

PISHCHIK *enters.*

LOPAKHIN. What do I see? One of nature's miracles! . .

PISHCHIK. [*out of breath*] Phew, give me a chance to get my breath back . . . I'm bushed . . . My dear venerable friends . . . give me some water . . .

GAEV. You're after some money, I suppose? Your humble servant, I'm going to go now and leave my tempter behind me . . . [*Goes out.*]

PISHCHIK. It's been a while since I've been here . . . most beautiful lady . . . [*To* LOPAKHIN.] You're here too . . . I'm glad to see you . . . a fellow of most enormous intellect . . . Here, take it . . . accept it, do . . . [*Gives* LOPAKHIN *money.*] Four hundred rubles . . . I still owe you eight hundred and forty.

LOPAKHIN. [*bewildered, shrugs his shoulders*] It's like a dream . . . Where on earth did you get it?

PISHCHIK. Wait a bit . . . I'm really hot . . . A most extraordinary incident. Some Englishmen arrived at my place and found some kind of white clay in the ground . . . [*To* LYUBOV ANDREEVNA.] And four hundred for you . . . my beautiful stunning woman . . . [*Gives her money.*] I'll give you the rest later on. [*Drinks water.*] Just now a certain young man on the train was saying that some sort of . . . great philosopher advises everybody to run and jump off a roof . . . "Go ahead and jump," he says, and in that lies the whole problem. [*Surprised.*] What do you think of that! Give me some water! . .

LOPAKHIN. What sort of Englishmen were they?

PISHCHIK. I leased them the land with the clay in it for twenty-four years . . . And now, please excuse me, I've no more time . . . Must gallop farther on . . . I'm going to see Znoykov . . . and Kardamonov . . . I'm in debt to everybody . . . [*Drinks.*] I wish you all a good day . . . I'll drop by on Thursday . . .

LYUBOV ANDREEVNA. We're just now moving our things to town, and tomorrow I go abroad . . .

PISHCHIK. What's that? [*Becomes anxious.*] Why to town? Oh, yes, now I see the furniture . . . suitcases . . . Well, it's nothing . . . [*Through tears.*] It's nothing . . . People of mammoth intellect . . . these Englishmen . . . It's nothing . . . all happiness to you . . . God will help you . . . It's nothing . . . Everything in this world must come to an end . . . [*Kisses* LYUBOV ANDREEVNA'S *hand.*] And if the news gets to you that my end has come, just recall this very . . . old horse and say, "Once on this earth there was such-and-such a person . . . Simeonov-Pishchik . . . may the

kingdom of heaven be his . . ." Most remarkable weather today
. . . Yes . . . [*Goes out greatly troubled, but returns immediately to speak from the doorway.*] Dashenka sends her regards
to you! [*Goes out.*]

LYUBOV ANDREEVNA. Well, we can go now. I'm leaving with two
things weighing on my mind. My first worry is Firs and the fact
that he's ill. [*Having glanced at her watch.*] We have about five
minutes left . . .

ANYA. Mama, they've already sent Firs to the hospital. Yasha sent
him this morning.

LYUBOV ANDREEVNA. My other distress is Varya. She's accustomed to
getting up early and working, and now without anything to do—
she's like a fish out of water. She's become so thin and pale, and
she weeps all the time, poor darling . . . [*Pause.*] As you very well
know, Yermolay Alexeich, I've dreamed . . . of giving her in marriage to you. Besides, that's the way things seemed to look—you
were planning to get married. [*Whispers to* ANYA, *who nods to*
SHARLOTTA, *and they both go out.*] She loves you, you like her,
and I don't know—I really don't—why it is you try to avoid each
other. I simply can't understand it!

LOPAKHIN. I don't understand it, either, to tell the truth. Somehow
it's all pretty strange . . . If there's still time, I'm all set to go
ahead right now . . . Let's get it settled, finish it up, and—
basta.[28] But I don't feel I can make a proposal unless you're here
too.

LYUBOV ANDREEVNA. Oh, that's splendid. You know it'll take about a
minute, no more. I'll call her now . . .

LOPAKHIN. By the way, we even have champagne. [*Having glanced
at the glasses.*] Empty, someone's already drunk it all.
[YASHA *coughs.*] That's really called lapping it up . . .

LYUBOV ANDREEVNA. [*vivaciously*] Wonderful. We'll leave you now
. . . Yasha, *allez!*[29] I'll call her. . . [*In the doorway.*] Varya, leave
everything and come here. Come along now! [*Goes out with*
YASHA.]

LOPAKHIN. [*having glanced at his watch*] Yes . . . [*Pause.*]

> *Suppressed laughter and whispering are heard from behind
> the door. Finally* VARYA *enters.*

VARYA. [*examines the luggage for a long time*] It's strange, I
just can't seem to find . . .

LOPAKHIN. What are you searching for?

VARYA. I packed it away myself, and I can't remember. [*Pause.*]

LOPAKHIN. Where is it you're going now, Varvara Mikhaylovna?

VARYA. Me? To Ragulins' . . . I've agreed to look after their
place . . . as the housekeeper. At least that's the impression I get.

LOPAKHIN. That's at Yashnevo, isn't it? About seventy versts away
from here. [*Pause.*] And so life is over and done with in this
house . . .

28. "Enough!" (in Italian).   29. "Let's go!" (in French).

VARYA. [*examining the luggage*] Where on earth could it . . . Or, maybe, I packed it away in the trunk . . . Yes, life in this house is over and done with . . . And it will never come back here anymore . . .

LOPAKHIN. And I'm just now on my way to Kharkov . . . On the next train, you see. I've got plenty to do. I'm leaving Yepikhodov here to look after the work outside . . . I've hired him.

VARYA. Well, hmm!

LOPAKHIN. Last year at this time we had snow on the ground, if you recall, but now it's pretty quiet and plenty of sunshine. It's just cold, that's all . . . About three degrees of frost.

VARYA. I haven't looked. [*Pause.*] Besides, our thermometer's broken . . . [*Pause.*]

> A *voice from outside is heard calling through the door,* "Yermolay Alexeich!"

LOPAKHIN. [*as if he has been waiting a long time for this summons*] This very minute! [*Quickly goes out.*]

> VARYA *sits on the floor, having laid her head on a bundle of clothing, and quietly sobs. The door opens, and* LYUBOV ANDREEVNA *enters warily.*

LYUBOV ANDREEVNA. Well? [*Pause.*] We must go.

VARYA. [*no longer is weeping and has wiped her eyes*] Yes, it's time, *Mamochka.* If I don't miss my train I can get to the Ragulins' today . . .

LYUBOV ANDREEVNA. [*in the doorway*] Anya, bundle up! [ANYA *enters, then* GAEV *and* SHARLOTTA IVANOVNA. GAEV *is wearing a warm overcoat with a hood. A* MAIDSERVANT *and* COACHMEN *enter and begin to fetch and carry.* YEPIKHODOV *bustles about and supervises those who carry the luggage.*] Now we can start on our way.

ANYA. [*jubilantly*] Yes, on our way!

GAEV. My friends, my dear, good friends! Deserting this home forever, how can I be silent, how can I refrain from expressing my feelings in saying good-bye, feelings that now fill my whole being . . .

ANYA. [*beseechingly*] Uncle!

VARYA. Uncle dear, you mustn't!

GAEV. [*despondently*] A bank shot off the yellow into the middle . . . I'll keep quiet . . .

> TROFIMOV *enters, then* LOPAKHIN.

TROFIMOV. What about it, ladies and gentlemen, it's time to go!

LOPAKHIN. Yepikhodov, my overcoat!

LYUBOV ANDREEVNA. I'll just sit down one more minute. It's just as if I'd never noticed what the walls and ceiling of this house look like, and now I see them eagerly, with such a gentle love . . .

GAEV. I remember when I was six years old. I was sitting in this window on Trinity Sunday, and I saw my father going to church . . .

LYUBOV ANDREEVNA. Have they taken out all the things?

LOPAKHIN. Yes, it seems they have, everything. [*Putting on his coat, to* YEPIKHODOV.] Yepikhodov, be sure to look and see that everything's in the right order.

YEPIKHODOV. [*speaks in a hoarse voice*] You can rest assured, Yermolay Alexeich!

LOPAKHIN. What's the trouble with your voice?

YEPIKHODOV. I just now drank some water, I must have swallowed something or other.

YASHA. [*scornfully*] Sheer case of ignorance . . .

LYUBOV ANDREEVNA. We're going away, and not one soul will be left here . . .

LOPAKHIN. Until this coming spring.

VARYA. [*Pulls an umbrella out of a bundle and it looks as if she were going to strike someone.* LOPAKHIN *pretends that he is frightened.*] Oh, you're not serious, you can't be . . . Why, the thought never entered my mind.

TROFIMOV. Ladies and gentlemen, let's go and get in the carriages . . . It's time, time! The train will soon be in!

VARYA. Petya, here they are, your galoshes, next to the suitcase. [*Through tears.*] And how filthy they are, and old . . .

TROFIMOV. [*putting on his galoshes*] On our way, ladies and gentlemen!

GAEV. [*greatly troubled and afraid of breaking into tears*] The train . . . The station . . . Across into the middle, bank shot off the white into the corner . . .

LYOBOV ANDREEVNA. On our way!

LOPAKHIN. Is everyone here? Nobody left behind? [*Locks the side door at left.*] Some things are stored in here, better keep it locked. Let's go! . .

ANYA. Good-bye, house! Fare thee well, old life!

TROFIMOV. Welcome, new life! . .

> He goes out with ANYA. VARYA *looks around the room and goes out without hurrying.* YASHA *and* SHARLOTTA, *with her dog, go out.*

LOPAKHIN. And so, till spring then. Come along, everybody . . . Until we meet again! . . [*Goes out.*]

> LYUBOV ANDREEVNA *and* GAEV *are left alone. They seem to have waited for this moment and throw their arms around each other. They sob quietly, with restraint, afraid they might be overheard.*

GAEV. [*in despair*] My sister, my sister . . .

LYUBOV ANDREEVNA. Oh, my beautiful orchard, my dear sweet orchard! . . My life, my youth, my happiness, good-bye! . . Good-bye! . .

ANYA. [*offstage, cheerfully and appealingly*] Mama! . .

TROFIMOV. [*offstage, cheerfully and excitedly*] Hullo! . .

LYUBOV ANDREEVNA. One last look at the walls and the windows . . . Our dear mother loved to walk in this room . . .

GAEV. My sister, my sister! . .

ANYA. [*offstage*] Mama! . .

TROFIMOV. [*offstage*] Hullo! . .

LYUBOV ANDREEVNA. We're on our way! . .

> *They go out. The stage is empty. The sound of all the doors being locked is heard, then of carriages being driven away. It grows quiet. In the stillness a dull thud is heard, the striking of an axe into a tree. It sounds solitary and dolorous. Footsteps are heard. From the door, right, appears* FIRS. *He is dressed, as always, in a jacket and white waistcoat, and he is wearing slippers. He is ill.*

FIRS. [*goes up to the door and touches the handle*] Locked. They've gone away . . . [*Sits on the sofa.*] They forgot me . . . It's nothing . . . I'll sit here for a while . . . And Leonid Andreich didn't put on his fur coat, I suppose, he must have gone away in his light one . . . [*Sighs anxiously.*] I just didn't look after it . . . Oh, these green young things—they never learn! [*Mumbles something that cannot be understood.*] Life just slipped by as if I'd never even lived . . . [*Lies down.*] I'll lie down for a while . . . You just don't have any strength, none, nothing's left, nothing at all. . . . Oh, you . . . silly galoot, you! . .

> *He lies motionless. A sound is heard far off in the distance, as if coming from the sky. It is the sound of a string breaking that dies away sadly. A stillness falls, and nothing is heard but the sound of an axe striking a tree far away in the orchard.*

CURTAIN

Masterpieces of the
Modern World

EDITED BY

KENNETH DOUGLAS
Late of Yale University

AND

SARAH N. LAWALL
Professor of Comparative Literature
University of Massachusetts, Amherst

Time has cast its definitive vote in favor of most of the earlier works in this anthology. Over the centuries, they have held the attention and aroused the enthusiasm of generations of readers; moreover, at the remove of a century or more, it is possible to see fairly clearly what qualities they have in common, so that such collective terms as "Neoclassicism," "Romanticism," and "Realism" have an agreed-upon meaning in literary history.

But what is "Modernism"? Is there such a thing? In our century, many authors have been widely appreciated, among them those included here, and their works hailed as modern masterpieces; and in some respects they are easier to assess, being close enough to our own time so that their vocabulary, and the

historical and social contexts from which they spring, are reasonably familiar. Yet their very closeness in time puts them all in the foreground, so that it is hard to make out affinities and differences among them with any certainty. We can see them more sharply, in fact, if we look at them first in the light of some features of late nineteenth century writing that they simultaneously incorporate yet rebel against.

i.

The realist-naturalist movement, which dominated literature in the second half of the nineteenth century, claimed to focus on the actual world, viewing it without theological or moral presuppositions, in the manner of empirical science, and giving due weight to the social, political, and psychological forces influencing human behavior. At the same time, however, the introspective and visionary tradition of Romantic poetry was evolving into a new, subjective poetry taking reality only as a point of departure, as something not to be photographically described and scientifically analyzed but to be transformed into an imaginative vision of the "essence" of things. This new poetry was called "symbolist," after its use of symbolic language to evoke hidden meanings.

Of course the literary use of symbols is not new. Medieval literature, for example, alludes constantly to shared religious beliefs through a system of symbols where the rose symbolizes love, the dove the Holy Spirit, and the serpent Satan. Yet the nineteenth century symbolists developed their own approach, which focuses on a more personal, earthly vision and on an extreme self-consciousness in the use of language. A symbol, in their sense, is an image or cluster of images created in a particular poem to suggest another plane of reality, alluding to some idea that cannot be expressed in more direct and rational terms. Each poem offers its own vision or state of mind, and allows the reader to penetrate appearances through its unique transformation of perspective. Such intuitive penetration is held to be a fuller and more meaningful mode of thought and perception than mere objectivity. Its aim is to touch a primitive level of being

where, for example, the five senses fuse: colors have taste, sights have physical texture, sounds have odor, and so on. (This fusion is called *synesthesia*.) Objective reality still exists, but appears transformed. An actual flower described in photographically realistic detail will not do; on the contrary, the poet must suggest the "idea of flower," an essence reflected in all real flowers, yet, as Mallarmé puts it, "absent from all bouquets." As can be seen, symbolist poetry can be very abstract in its implications, but it is also firmly based in concrete images and runs the gamut from the most material objects (a carcass, a deck of cards, a rainspout) to the most unreal: a "musician of silence," "hearses . . . parading in the brain," the "clash of icicles against stars." It is not, therefore, an escape from everyday reality so much as a transformation of it, the creation of a new world reassembled in the mind from pieces of the old.

The other great theme of symbolist poetry is language, especially the process of writing. The writer who must express underlying reality has an awesome responsibility to find the right words, a responsibility that Mallarmé found paralyzing as he faced "the empty paper whose blank whiteness defends it." The symbolist poet uses the same language as all of us, for there is no other, but this language must be purified into "poetic language" through a totally controlled arrangement of all possible levels of form. It is the relationship of words that counts, not just their dictionary definitions, as will be seen in the symbolist poems that follow. In Baudelaire's "Spleen," the combined use of so many words suggesting water (from the squeaky logs to the woman's dropsy) permeates the scene with unhealthy damp. Rimbaud's "Barbarian" introduces startling images, openly denies their reality ("they don't exist"), and then goes deeper into the world of the imagination by using more of the same kind of images. Many poems, like Baudelaire's "Windows," describe the process of writing itself; others, like Mallarmé's "Saint," evoke a focal point of ideal artistic creation which is that of poetry and music alike. The extraordinary self-consciousness of the symbolist poet became an element of the poem itself, focusing attention on its manipulations and distortions of language to assert, once and for all, that the only reality is that of the mind.

Symbolist writers frequently compared their poetry with music, whose characteristics they tried to reproduce. Both poetry and music they felt to be "pure" arts, where line and harmony mattered more than individual notes or words. They saw analogies, too, between their art and painting, whose distinctive new methods of depicting reality were being tried at the same period, as every visitor to a modern art gallery knows. Yet these moves away from the familiar seemed, in the poetic as in the art world, upsetting to the average citizen, whose common sense was outraged. Accused of being wilfully obscure, a num-

ber of these writers retired further into their own private worlds in the face of a hostile and unsympathetic society; the lesser among them lost touch with the very realities they claimed to transform. Yet, at its best, symbolist poetry remains a powerful example of the human imagination shaping its world—a challenge to the empirical observations of the scientist from what Rimbaud called, in his own writing, the "alchemy of the word."

ii.

Charles Baudelaire (1821–1867), the first of these symbolist writers, set out deliberately to startle the bourgeois, and he succeeded. His chief collection of poems bears the provocative title *Flowers of Evil* (*Les Fleurs du mal*) and includes invocations to Satan as well as half a dozen poems that in 1857, the year of the volume's publication (and the year of *Madame Bovary*), were banned as obscene. Yet Baudelaire's intentions reach far beyond sensationalism: the reader was to be started, but into serious involvement with the work. Baudelaire's verse preface involves both poet and reader in an overarching acknowledgment of human weakness and hypocrisy, made worse by an inertia of will causing and overshadowing all other sins. "Hypocritical reader, —my fellow,—my brother!" he ends, in a famous cry of common guilt that was later taken up by T. S. Eliot in *The Waste Land.*

Baudelaire is a master of precise and realistic description

used for effects that go beyond realism. The rhythmic thump of firewood being delivered coordinates images in "Song of Autumn" (*Chant d'automne*). Interruptions by the bill-collector and editor's messenger-boy bring the poet's idealized reverie down to earth in "The Double Room." The decaying, maggoty carcass of "A Carcass" (*Une Charogne*) becomes the source of a strange and ironic beauty, a swarming, vibrating new life covering the outline of the old. A chill revelation of mortality emerges from the description of the city in "Spleen," where the mundane details, from the cat twisting and turning uncomfortably on cold tiles to the smelly deck of cards left behind by an old woman, exist not for themselves but to evoke an atmosphere of lethargy and decay climaxing in the tiny, altogether unrealistic final scene where two face cards talk sinisterly of their past loves.

Baudelaire was also an experimenter with language, founder of the modern prose poem, and a visionary who wrote poetry about the act of writing. In "Windows" (*Les Fenêtres*), a prose poem of 1863, he ends an apparently realistic description of an old woman by saying that her story is not true—only a "legend"—or at least that he does not care whether it is true, so long as it provides a point of departure for his own imagination, letting him know "who he is, and what he is." Two other prose poems reiterate the subjective cast of this poetic imagination. The enigmatic hero of "The Stranger" (*L'Etranger*) refuses all usual human ties to follow the clouds, and the pee-

vish narrator of "The Bad Glazier" (*Le Mauvais vitrier*) throws a flowerpot through the glass-seller's clear panes because they transmit reality too harshly, without the coloring effect of art.

For Baudelaire, artistic beauty is necessary to lighten the burden of human existence. One of his rare contented and even happy poems is the lyrical "Invitation to the Voyage" (*L'Invitation au voyage*), a lover's invitation to an exotic land of peace, beauty, and sensuous harmony: the picture itself evokes the glowing interiors painted by Dutch masters like Vermeer. This peace is not always available. In "A Former Life" (*La Vie antérieure*), another beautiful scene is undermined by a secret sadness, and elsewhere beauty itself is a "stone dream," a cold sphinx-like mistress whose ideal lines fascinate while repelling the poet ("Beauty," *La Beauté*). Frequently Baudelaire is racked by the torment of a divided self ("Heautontimoroumenos") or overwhelmed by a feeling of melancholy inertia or ennui, a "spleen" that prevents any positive action. Even art, at this low point, is governed by ennui, and in the four "Spleen" poems the poet subsides into describing his own lethargy.

Love is a possible way out of lethargy, a way to move from *spleen* to *ideal*—the chief section of *Flowers of Evil* is a series of verse poems titled "Spleen and Ideal." Abandoning oneself to passion, as in "Her Hair" (*La Chevelure*), invites one to another ecstatic voyage, an "oasis of dream" or perhaps to a "world of dazzling stones and of previous metals" ("Jewels," *Les Bijoux*). Yet often love cannot be attained, as in the momentary recognition of "To a Passer-by" (*A une passante*), or is somehow flawed. Either the loved one repulses him ("I adore you as much . . .") or she must be bought with jewels ("Her Hair"). Here again there is a dual or contradictory experience, both aspects of which are accepted by the poet and even welcomed as a perverse heightening of consciousness.

For Baudelaire is an ironic poet, an inheritor of that Romantic irony that wishes to embrace all dualisms of human existence, good and evil, love and hate, dream and reality. His world is complex, a universe of echoes and correspondences. Baudelaire's most influential poem, in fact, is titled "Correspondences," and is a vision of the mystic unity of all nature revealed in the correspondence through synesthesia of our senses. Nature, says the poet, is a system of perpetual analogies; one thing corresponds to another—physical objects to each other (a pillar in a temple, for example, to a tree in the forest), spiritual reality to physical reality, and the senses (taste, smell, touch, sight, and hearing) among themselves to produce such combinations as *bitter green*, a *soft look*, a *harsh sound*. We are not usually aware of the "universal analogy" —the forest of the first stanza observes us without our knowing it—but the poet acts as seer and guide to urge us on toward a state of awareness where both "mind and senses" are transported into another dimension. Even describing a state of ecstasy, however, "Correspondences" is shaped like a logical argument: the thesis is set out in the first stanza, explained in the second, and illustrated with cumulative examples in the third and fourth. Baudelaire's yearning for the infinite does not make him neglect either mundane reality or intellectual rigor, and his combination of all three elements is an example of the visionary imagination and craftsmanlike discipline typical of the best symbolist work.

iii.

Arthur Rimbaud (1854–1891) and Stéphane Mallarmé (1842–1898) developed other aspects of the symbolist transformation of experience into vision. In a short and violent literary career—he wrote all his poetry between the ages of fifteen and twenty—Rimbaud moved from an aggressive, cynical realism to an attempt to transform both self and surroundings into a magically perfect whole. Running away several times from a repressive and disciplinarian home, Rimbaud sought in early poems like "The Seekers of Lice" (*Les Chercheuses de poux*) to transform a sordid scene into new beauty and harmony, or to imagine a successful flight into a world of the liberated imagination. "The Drunken Boat" (*Le Bateau ivre*), written when Rimbaud was still sixteen and had never seen the sea, uses the traditional literary theme of the voyage to express the poet's rebellion against guides and restraints. Speaking as a boat let loose on the high seas, the narrator describes a gradually intensifying series of encounters with a total reality —at once beautiful and terrifying—that goes beyond his individual power to sustain. Faced with the ultimate risk of abandoning his individual subjectivity, of splitting asunder and merging with the sea, he retreats to a Europe of familiar outlines and security. Yet the concluding section is not a resolution of the original need for flight: Rimbaud cannot accept the world of proud commercial shipping, or of prison ships, and envisages only the childhood world of a solitary paper boat set adrift in a small pool. The poem ends in a clearer restatement of its original alienation, and in an attitude which many have interpreted as prefiguring Rimbaud's eventual departure from England and rejection of poetry.

Rimbaud's attempt to become a seer or *voyant*, to transform his everyday reality by means of the re-creating power of poetry, is both summarized and mocked in the bitter autobiographical prose poem *A Season in Hell* (*Une Saison en enfer*, 1873). In an atmosphere of perpetual crisis, alternating between tones of agonized idealism and cynical disbelief, he reviews his quest for perfect truth and love, and vividly describes his effort to reach the unknown by pure hallucination, a "derangement of all the senses." "I saw very plainly a mosque in place of a factory, a school of drummers composed of angels . . . a drawing room at the bottom of the lake . . . I became a fabulous opera." The nadir of *A Season in Hell* is reached in "Night of Hell" (*Nuit d'enfer*), followed immediately by a satire on his erstwhile lover the poet Paul Ver-

laine in "The Foolish Virgin" (*La Vierge folle*) and on his own attempt to write magical verse in "Alchemy of the Word" (*L'Alchimie du verbe*). At the end of *A Season in Hell*, he tells us that he has rejected these earlier illusions and embraced earth and rugged reality; indeed, a good deal of Rimbaud's legend comes from this extraordinary example of a great poet who simply did not find what he sought in literature and therefore ceased to write. The visionary *Illuminations* that were apparently completed after the *Season in Hell* are his last works, and since he never wrote poetry to celebrate his newly rediscovered realism, he remains best known for the passion and beauty of his apocalyptic visions.

These *Illuminations*—almost entirely prose poems—are intricately organized in complex rhythmic and visual patterns. "Tale" (*Conte*) and "Morning of Drunkenness" (*Matinée d'ivresse*) still echo certain autobiographical themes: the fleeting grasp of a perfect union in beauty and love, and the discovery of drugs as a method of hallucinatory vision. In "Tale," a prince who is unsatisfied with earthly limits, especially with the shallowness of accepted ideas of love, violently destroys all he can lay his hands on until he finally encounters his poetic alter ego, the Genie. Their union is brief: poetic genius dies, and the prince is left to live out the rest of his ordinary life. There is still some visible autobiographical basis in "Bridges" (*Les Ponts*), an impressionistic memory of the London Rimbaud knew, but the emphasis is placed on the transformation of the scene itself. "Seascapes" (*Marine*) plays with the juxtaposition of land and sea, ploughed field and broken water, and "Flowers" (*Fleurs*) takes the next step by making it impossible to determine whether the original scene is transposed nature or an allegorized theater. Finally, "Barbarian" ("Barbare") transcends the question of any single source in reality. Set outside normal time and space, "Long after the days and the seasons, and the creatures and the countries," it enacts a withdrawal that moves gradually from echoes of the real world to an elemental core of tenderness and beauty, completely inside the world of imagination.

Clearly the reader cannot approach this poem as if it were by Victor Hugo—or even by Baudelaire. Rimbaud's vision has leaped beyond the picturing of actual scenes, whether a green pastoral landscape or a city room on a rainy day, and beyond the rational core that so often supports even a visionary poem—for example, the argument of Baudelaire's "Correspondences," describing the notion of transcendental vision and explaining how to reach it. Rimbaud, in fact, cuts short all explanations and simply presents the vision for itself. His poem is not, however, a merely impressionistic, unstructured collection of words. It is carefully organized according to an almost musical development of themes and pattern of oppositions. The poet first notifies his reader that this *is* a vision, taking place well apart from the world of real people, established nations, and the normal passage of time. He then proceeds to set out the particular materials with which he is going to build his world of the imagination. It is made of primitive, "barbarian" oppositions: red and white (raw meat and arctic flowers, embers and frost, fire and diamonds, flames and drift ice), heat and cold, subterranean volcanos and starry sky. On a more fundamental level, it is a world that swings between the real and the ideal. Rimbaud moves from a quasi-autobiographical world of "old fanfares . . . old retreats" to an ideal world where there are ultimately no complete images, only "forms, sweats, eyes . . ." as component parts for a new creation. The types of images already symbolize this change. The "banner of bleeding meat" (a distortion of the expected silken banner) and the arctic flowers that do not exist are "hallucinated" from relatively familiar objects. In the second half of the poem, after the pivotal word "Delights!", the chief images are cosmic and unimaginable as real scenes. Now it is the "old retreats" that are set aside, subordinated in parentheses, and the "veering of whirlpools" that becomes a new reality. The poem's second half also introduces the separate themes of delight, world, and music, combining them musically in the final paragraph where everything poises on the edge of new life, with the introduction of a feminine voice reaching into the very heart of this fiery, icy existence. "Barbarian" ends on a note of openness and ambiguity, as the cyclical opposition of reality and imagination seem about to recommence with "The banner . . ." Rimbaud's poem typifies the symbolist doctrine of taking ordinary reality apart in order to assemble a new transcendent vision, employing to this end a subtly non-rational language as close as possible to the patterns of music.

Of all the symbolist writers, Mallarmé is the most thoroughly visionary. He chiefly uses ordinary words and images of ordinary things, but only as raw material for a wholly imaginary product. Like Rimbaud, he seeks a way out of sordid reality through the liberating power of the imagination, but unlike the younger poet he did not turn his back on literature even though his lofty poetic ideals made it increasingly difficult for him to write. Mallarmé works to purify language. Avoiding the direct approach, he finds that he can say more obliquely. So he suggests, rather than names; keeps several levels of meaning alive at the same time; complicates his syntax and even sometimes misleads us, to prolong the pleasure of discovery.

The creative process itself is the central topic of Mallarmé's poetry, from the autobiographical descriptions of the writer at work in "Tired of the Bitter Repose" (*Las de l'amer repos*) and "Seabreeze" (*Brise marine*) to the impersonal speculations of "A Lace Curtain . . ." (*Une dentelle s'abolit . . .*). Mallarmé is haunted by the difficulty of writing; he digs his thoughts like a gravedigger out of the "cold and niggard soil" of his brain, or is paralyzed by the blank whiteness of the paper before him. Escaping into art, he would imitate the spare perfection of Chinese painted porcelain ("Tired of the Bitter Repose") or face the risks of a voyage into the unknown ("Seabreeze"). Even such a banal object as a fan, fluttering open and then lying closed against a bracelet, can evoke the desired realm of absolute beauty in the poet's mind: "sceptre of rose-red shores / Stagnant on evenings of gold" ("Another Fan," *Autre Eventail*). Yet a common characteristic of Mallarmé's evocations of beauty, and one that often distinguishes them from scenes in Baudelaire and Rimbaud, is their emphasis on absence. An early poem, "Saint" (*Sainte*), illustrates the way Mallarmé plays with a sense of loss or absence as part of his poem's positive creation.

The saint of the poem (according to an earlier title, Saint Cecilia, the patron saint of music), is seen as if in a stained-glass window before a cabinet where musical instruments are kept. The concealed cedarwood lute, which no longer gleams with gold as it did when formerly played with accompanying flute and mandola (an early mandolin), and the old book lying open at the Magnificat (a hymn of praise to God), establish the idea of an actual music that is now stilled. The last two stanzas evoke in contrast an ideal, soundless music symbolized by the saint who now plays an imaginary harp. She, the "musician of silence," has her finger poised on a golden harp shaped by the outstretched wing of a sculptured angel, a "feathered instrument" that receives from the evening sun all the gilding that was lost to the real instrument of the first stanza. The presence of the ideal music is felt more strongly by the end of the poem than was the discontinued actual music suggested by the poem's beginning.

The ideal music of this and other poems is created by refining and manipulating ordinary language, "the words of the tribe" as Mallarmé says in "The Tomb of Edgar Poe" (*Le Tombeau d'Edgar Poe*). The poet, for Mallarmé as for the Romantics, is isolated by his genius from a society that refuses to understand him. Poe appears as a Saint George of poetry, confronting the dragon of mediocrity and base slander. In another sonnet, "This Virgin, Beautiful, and Lively Day" (*La vierge, le vivace, et le bel aujourd'hui*), the poet as swan is paralyzed in self-imposed exile, frozen into the dazzling glacier of his chosen purity.

Yet Mallarmé was not without a sense of humor, and even poked fun at the lofty imaginings of his and others' rarefied poetry. Starting from the image of a cigar-smoker blowing rings of smoke, he develops an elaborate comparison with poetry as concentric rings of the "breath" of inspiration, an impalpable "vague literature" that is destroyed at the touch of reality ("All the soul indrawn . . .", *Toute l'âme résumée* . . .). Not that Mallarmé sees unreality as an evil: on the contrary, as his last hermetic poetry shows, he prefers a purified creation that emphasizes ambiguity and

potentiality, the resonant musical void in which a poem "might be born" ("A lace curtain . . ."). He is able, however, to envisage this openness and ambiguity in a number of ways.

Mallarmé's best-known poem, one which inspired music by Claude Debussy which in turn was used as a ballet, is "The Afternoon of a Faun" (*L'Après-midi d'un faune*). Here the familiar themes of artistic creation, dream, and loss mingle with a constant eroticism in the warm and sensuous picture of a faun or woodland satyr recounting his pursuit of two numphs. Was it a dream, he wonders, that he caught the two water nymphs—one passionate, one naïve—only to lose them on the brink of erotic fulfilment? The poem is framed by the faun's initial desire to "perpetuate" these nymphs in memory, or finally to follow them back into dream. It is famous for its vivid and sensuous descriptions, intricate imagery, and for the extraordinary musicality of its classical verse (the French alexandrine, or 12-syllable line). Turning to his pipes and to drunken dreams in order to celebrate a perfect union he could not hold, the faun illustrates once more Mallarmé's theme of poetic creation, describing an ideal beauty that is absent and a love that remains perpetually not just out of reach, but in fact a figment of the imagination.

AUGUST STRINDBERG

August Strindberg responded vibrantly to many significant manifestations in the literary and intellectual life of his day and, since that time, has through his writings exerted an influence on every major movement in literature and the drama. Indebted to him are expressionism, the literary exploitation of Freudian theories, surrealism, existentialism, and the theater of the absurd. Both George Bernard Shaw and Eugene O'Neill made known their intense admiration for his achievements. Among the elements by which Strindberg himself was affected were Shakespeare's historical plays and naturalism, with its emulation of the deterministic outlook of science and a concern for social problems. He moved through a Nietzschean individualism to a renewed interest in religion, especially of a nonconfessional kind, embracing Asian doctrines he did not study in depth and putting together a synthesis of his own. He tried to obtain gold by alchemical means and set out to refute the established scientific concept of the elements. After symbolism had been adapted to stage purposes by the Belgian writer Maurice Maeterlinck (1862–1949), Strindberg acknowledged the Belgian's influence and followed his example.

Since Strindberg's dramatic work totals fifty-eight plays, only the most schematic hints as to its nature are possible here. His first great play was *Master Olof*, situated in Sweden at the time of the Reformation. Written in 1872, it was subjected to a process of revision that lasted into 1881. From 1899 on, Strindberg, encouraged by a successful staging of *Master Olof*, wrote a whole series of historical plays which, in the estimation

of one critic, are unique in meriting consideration alongside Shakespeare's Tudor dramas.

The years 1886–1889 witnessed the writing of naturalistic plays, including those constantly revived works *The Father* (1887) and *Miss Julie* (1888). From the vantage point of our later day, we can see that these two plays, with the pattern-repetitive psychological determinism of the former and the mounting hysteria of Miss Julie, anticipate altogether remarkably the theories later propounded by Sigmund Freud (1856–1939). The next phase of dramatic activity, though it extended only from 1898 to 1902, resulted in no fewer than eighteen plays. These included, in addition to the historical dramas, plays that may be classified as realistic, expressionistic, and allegorical. And, finally, there are the five "chamber plays"— *The Ghost Sonata* among them —that Strindberg wrote in 1907 and 1909 for his own Intimate Theater in Stockholm.

The fifty-eight plays do not nearly fill the fifty-five volumes of Strindberg's collected works —beside which must be set the volumes of a lavish correspondence. For him, living and writing were not watertight compartments but the two faces of one whole, each mirroring and penetrating the other in an unending reflective and refractive barrage. Even he himself had to confess, at times, his inability to distinguish between the real and the fictitious. Nor does the fact that some works are largely autobiographical (*Inferno*, for instance, which recounts the hallucinatory experiences of the 1890's) permit one to assume that fictional embroiderings have been excluded. The fictions, conversely, lead us back to their author's real existence, and on occasion he depicts the blackness of a situation in such scrupulous detail that we suspect a burlesque intention. In any event, the author never permits us to forget him.

All this proliferation and diversity have indeed their center in the Strindbergian ego, an ego of no mean proportions hidden and yet revealed under the voluminous folds of its magician's cloak. Cruel to the pretensions and self-esteem of others, he himself was abnormally sensitive to slights. Impelled to expose himself to attack, he was cowardly in confronting and anticipating it. For instance, while a respected functionary of the Royal Library, he published a highly satirical novel, *The Red Room* (1879), that created a great stir. During the relatively tranquil earlier years of his first marriage, he brought on himself a charge of blasphemy with the first volume of *Married* (1884), and with the second volume, published the following year, he incurred the reputation, which subsequent publications only strengthened, of being a fanatical antifeminist. He saw himself as pursued by, initially, a cabal of "denatured" Swedish women and, later, by a world-wide conspiracy of such creatures. This, however, was but one aspect of his lifelong tendency to look on himself as a figure of heroic proportions but an outcast, an Ishmael, son of the banished Hagar, hand-

maiden of the patriarch Abraham. (His own mother had been a servant.) His situation, self-interpreted, may be said to resemble the bastard's lot: tolerated on the fringes of wealth and power but with no heritage of his own except—like Edmund in Shakespeare's *King Lear*—the capacity to dream of or plan a mighty conquest.

The Ghost Sonata, in view of its allusive nature (Strindberg called it "a world of intimations"), has been provided with a more than usually large number of interpretative footnotes. They signal passages that allude to such major themes or motifs as repetition, viewed as undesirable, stagnation, and vampirism, and call attention to other passages that proclaim free will and individual initiative to be mainly or entirely self-deceptions. Here it is important to stress the title of the work. While authors in some instances, and critics more frequently, allege that a piece of writing owes its structure to some musical form, Strindberg quite convincingly, though simply, justifies the *Sonata* of his title. The musical analogy extends beyond the tripartite form, ABA, of the three scenes, it also substitutes for any psychological link between subscene and subscene a first use, the repeated use, and the dropping of a theme. While this repetition underlines a gloomy interpretation of human existence, a conciliatory note is sounded, indeed is actually sung by the Student at the very end. For this, too, there is a musical parallel.

Nevertheless, the characters

are not musical phrases but the ghosts or the paradigm of human beings. But, just as music is found to utter things too indefinite or too close to ourselves to permit their expression in words (see Proust's treatment of "the little phrase" in the selection from *Swann's Way* reproduced below, pp. 1174–1203), these personages are able to convey things that rarely survive the clear but withering light of consciousness. These characters, too, like the ghosts in the classical Hades or the damned of Dante's *Inferno*, are hampered neither by the polite conventions of everyday life nor by the Freudian "censor" at the service of the superego. The musical analogy still functions, however, as support for the assertion that the level of the individual subconscious or unconscious does not dominate the play. There is the common thread pulling all together, as the Old Man declares, and this has the consequence of placing the accent on a linked destiny in which all share, whether within the confines of this particular work or made universally applicable to human life. So—we may set aside the details of the elaborate cosmic scheme that Strindberg expounded elsewhere—the author has labored successfully to exemplify the "We are members one of another" of Saint Paul and the notion of one-in-all and all-in-one affirmed by so many Asian scriptures.

LUIGI PIRANDELLO

Pirandello at no time shared the extravagant hopes voiced by the youthful Rimbaud. He saw all things as garish, kaleidoscopic, hallucinatory, inextricably entangled, and irremediably ambiguous. An unbeliever, he gives the lie to the notion, dear to the believer, that a basic despair unfits a man for goal-oriented activity. Not only was he a prolific writer, but in his plays specifically he created his own genre, his own theater, and public, beyond Italian shores as well as at home, that was able to appreciate his work.

His success is bound up with a courageous refusal to accept the standard routines of middle-class theater and with the adoption of startling, even bewildering innovations which, to a considerable extent, were also the revival of age-old theatrical devices and situations. Plausibility flies out of the window, and there is no attempt to render the implausible more palatable by a shrewd measuring of the dosage. With the rapid, firecracker-like eruptions of unforeseeable occurrences, of reversals of fortune or behavior, that mark his plays, Pirandello calls into existence something akin to the Italian Renaissance's improvisatory Commedia dell'Arte (he calls one play *Tonight We Improvise*) and to the Roman comedies of Plautus, most familiar to today's audiences in the form of the musical *A Funny Thing Happened on the Way to the Forum.*

Yet this sophisticated, highly educated man did not simply purvey popular theatrical concoctions. He had his own attitude to life. Disabused without being cynical, he saw men as fraudulent not alone in their surface pretensions. What lay behind the surface was no less shoddy, uncertain, and vacillating. One mask, one facet of the personality, was replaced by another. There was no center that could impose a genuine order. Many of his personages are bitterly aware of their own incoherence, and their self-examination is both persistent and fruitless. Or it may occur that one especially lucid character acts as spokesman for the author. Even then, the feverish ratiocination and the eruptions of a multicolored unreality that thrill and amaze the theater public do not hide his sadness.

Pirandello's career proceeded from poetry through novels (seven of them) and short stories (they fill fifteen volumes) to plays. In every genre he began with his native Sicilian settings, and he translated several of his works into Sicilian dialect. But his most distinctive gifts required the greater complexity of thought and feeling associated with personages of less restricted horizons, and to such personages he turned, particularly in the three plays most frequently performed today: *Right You Are (If You Think So)*, *Henry IV*, and *Six Characters in Search of an Author*. The first of these exemplifies his skepticism concerning "truth." A family newly arrived in town shocks the natives and arouses their impertinent curiosity by its unorthodox living arrangements. It is discovered, through much prying, that the family's members cannot even agree on what their relationship to one another is though they are content to live with this ambiguity, or would be, were it not for their neighbors' shamelessness. Properly di-

rected and performed, with brio, with rapierlike thrusts and a compelling drive, this play can transport audiences into a frenzy of intellectual excitement.

The "Six Characters" are, as the play's title declares, looking for an author. Restless, unhappy embryos of an act of literary conception that has never reached fulfillment in a completed work, they invade a stage where a play by Pirandello is being rehearsed and demand to be incarnated by the actors. The actors make the attempt, but their dissatisfaction with the unusually raw material that is offered them, and the characters' own disapproval of the actors' substitution of standardized banalities for the uniqueness of the events that make up the whole of the characters' shadow existence, constitute—in the form of a fiasco —a Pirandellian tour de force. He imprisons his audience in an avowed unreality that nevertheless seems to cast an intense (if fitful) light on the audience's own emotional and ideological world.

Henry IV may be regarded as the most massively successful embodiment of Pirandello's concern with the unanswerable question: What is Truth? Unlike Pilate, he could never wash his hands of it. The hero in this play has fallen from a horse and struck his head while participating in a pageant in the role of the medieval German emperor Henry IV. He emerges from unconsciousness but not from the role, and since he is wealthy he is able, with the connivance of friends and hirelings, to maintain it. This is the basic datum—but, since Pirandello is the author, the play bursts from these bonds. The ultimate sequence of reversals might be summarized as: role seen as role, role become reality, role again seen as role but not abandoned, role abandoned, role seen as role yet—for at this juncture something irremediable occurs—unwillingly reassumed. The hero remains locked forever, and consciously so, within a senseless farce. A similar forced wearing of a mask is performed by the French mime, Marcel Marceau: What had been tried on in jest becomes an inescapable destiny.

Pirandello did not comment on politics or social movements, but his writings make it plain that he looked on society as a burden inflicted upon the individual, with which he has to come to terms. He himself had been the obedient son of a father who derived his income from sulphur mines in Sicily. Never was he more disastrously obedient than in 1894, when he accepted as his wife a young woman he had not previously known, the daughter of his father's business partner. After some years of marriage, and with the collapse of the sulphur mining venture, Signora Pirandello's mind became affected. She raged against her husband with an insane jealousy nothing could assuage—though he handed over to her all his earnings, keeping only enough for streetcar fare. Even when her hostility turned also against their daughter, he decided not to have his wife institutionalized. The situation was terminated only with her death in 1918.

The close relationship between this tortured domesticity and Pirandello's fascination by the polar opposites appearance and reality can hardly be denied. In view of accusations that he took a perverse delight in holding up to mockery the normal and respectable, it is important to point out that he was in fact an ethical and deeply responsible person who metamorphosed his own pain into an impressive body of work that has led to a renewed understanding of theater as theater.

MARCEL PROUST

Marcel Proust is known as the author of one book: an enormous, fifteen-volume exploration of time and consciousness called *Remembrance of Things Past* (*À la Recherche du temps perdu*). Written almost completely in the first person, and based on events in the author's life (though by no means purely autobiographical), the novel is famous as both an evocation of and a meditation on universal human emotions in the closed world of turn-of-the-century Parisian society.

The overall theme of the novel is suggested by a literal translation of its title: "In search of lost time." The narrator, partly the real Proust and partly an imagined "Marcel," is an old man weakened by a long illness who puzzles over the events of his past, trying to find in them a significant pattern. He begins with his childhood, ordered within the comfortable security of accepted manners and ideals in the family home at Combray. In succeeding volumes he goes out into the world, experiences love and disappointment, discovers the disparity between idealized images of places and people and their crude, sometimes banal reality, and is increasingly over-come by disillusionment with himself and society. Until the end of the novel Marcel remains a *grand nerveux*, an extremely sensitive person impelled by the large experiences of his life— love, art, separation, death—to discard early certainties and to seek out an intuited meaning for his life and for his dimly felt vocation as a writer.

In the short ending chapter, things suddenly come into focus as Marcel experiences tantaliz-ing moments of spontaneous memory and recognizes the work of time in the aged and enfeebled figures of his old friends. Facing the approach of death with a joyful sense of existential continuity through memory, he realizes that his vo-cation as an artist lies in giving form to this concrete experience of time. The buried and ap-parently lost past is still alive within us, a part of our being, and memory can recapture it to give coherence to our present identity. "Marcel" has not yet begun to write by the end of the last volume, *Time Regained*, but paradoxically the book that fulfills his aims is already there: Proust's *Remembrance of Things Past*.

Love (both heterosexual and homosexual), art, death, pur-suit of pleasure, isolation of the self in its own subjectivity, the fatal passage of time, the con-tradictions between imagination and reality: all these themes ap-pear in passages of rich, mi-nutely detailed sensuous descrip-tion. For according to Proust, his novel of the human condi-tion is not primarily philosoph-ical, not an "analytical novel" but an "introspective" one; it avoids abstract arguments, ex-pressing instead the texture of experience, a concrete percep-tion of life as it grows and changes through time. (Proust's affirmation of life in its fully ex-pressed wholeness is often com-pared with that of Henri Bergson, the twentieth-century French philosopher, remem-bered especially for his view of time as a reality to be lived rather than merely contem-plated.) Marcel's awareness of his life in time comes about not through rational or "forced" memory but through sponta-neous or "involuntary" memory —the chance recollection that occasionally wells up from his subconscious when he repeats a previous action such as drinking tea, stumbling, or opening a particular book. This memory is more powerful because it draws upon a buried level of experi-ence where the five senses are still linked, where life still comes to us whole. Sounds are connected with color (the name *Brabant* with gold), and emo-tions with the settings in which they were experienced (sorrow with the smell of varnish on the stairway up to bed.) Involuntary memory recreates a whole past world in all its concrete reality —and so does art. When Proust attributes such an absolute value to art, and makes it the focus of his book, he joins the tradition of French moralist writers from Montaigne to Camus who speak directly of universal values.

When Proust's first volume (*Swann's Way*) appeared in 1913, it was immediately seen as a new kind of fiction. Unlike nineteenth century novels such as Flaubert's *Madame Bovary*,

Remembrance of Things Past has no clear and continuous plot line building to a dénouement, nor (until the last volume, published in 1927) can the reader detect a consistent development of the central character, Marcel. Most of the novel sets forth a roughly chronological sequence of events, yet its opening pages swing through recollections of many times and places before settling on the narrator's childhood in Combray, and the second volume (*Swann in Love*) is a story told about another character and in the third person. Thus the novel proceeds by apparently discontinuous blocks of recollection, bound together by the central consciousness of the narrator. This was always Proust's plan—he repeatedly asserted that he had had in mind a fixed structure and goal for the novel when he wrote its first and last chapters in 1909, and that this plan was echoed in the "solidity of the smallest parts"—and his substantial revisions of the first draft enriched the already-existing structure without changing the sequence of scenes and events.

Proust's long sentences and mammoth paragraphs reflect the slow and careful progression of thought among the changing objects of its perception. Characters are remembered in different settings and perspectives: Charles Swann appears first as the visitor who often delays the child Marcel's bedtime kiss from his mother, next as an anxious and disappointed lover, and finally as a tragic, dying man rejected by his friends the Guermantes in their haste to get to a ball. Marcel's grandmother appears throughout the scenes in Combray, later during a visit to the seaside resort of Balbec, still later in her death agonies when Marcel is unable truly to grieve, and finally as a sudden recollection when Marcel has trouble tying his shoelace in Balbec. The little musical phrase which Marcel first hears as part of a sonata by the composer Vinteuil, and which is associated with love in various settings, recurs toward the end of the novel as part of a septet and becomes a revelation of the subtle constructions of art. Places overlap in the memory: the imagined and the real Balbec or Venice confront one another, the church steeples of Vieuvicq and Martinville are juxtaposed. Proust's style is a flexible instrument sensitive to the vagaries of the mind, a quality also seen, although in very different forms, in such younger writers of the period as James Joyce and Virginia Woolf.

The opening chapter of the novel, "Overture," foreshadows the work's themes and methods rather like the overture of an opera. All but one of the main characters appear or are mentioned, and the patterns of future encounters are set. Marcel, waiting anxiously for his beloved mother's response to a note sent down to her during dinner, suffers the same agony of separation as does Swann in his love for the promiscuous Odette, or the older Marcel himself for Albertine. The strange world of half-sleep, half-waking with which the novel begins prefigures later awakenings of memory. Long passages of intricate introspection, and sudden shifts of time and space, introduce us to the style and point of view of the rest of the book. The narrator shares the painful anxiety of little Marcel's desperate wait for his mother's bedtime kiss; for though his observations and judgments are tempered with mature wisdom, he is only at the beginning of his progress to full consciousness. The remembrance of things past is a key to further discovery but not an end in itself.

"Overture" ends with Proust's most famous image, summing up for many readers the world, the style, and the process of discovery of the Proustian vision: nibbling at a madeleine (a small rich pastry) that he has dipped in lime-blossom tea, Marcel suddenly has an overwhelming feeling of happiness. He soon associates this tantalizing, puzzling phenomenon with the memory of earlier times when he sipped tea with his Aunt Leonie. He realizes that there is something valuable about such passive, spontaneous, and sensuous memory, quite different from the abstract operations of reason forcing itself to remember. Although the Marcel of "Combray" does not yet know it, he will pursue the elusive significance of this moment of happiness until, in *Time Regained*, he can as a complete artist bring it to the surface and link past and present time in a fuller and richer identity.

COLETTE

The purity of Colette's style, and her constant focus on daily scenes of French life, has caused her to be called the most French of twentieth-century writers. Her contemporaries also found her a shocking, sensuous, amoral chronicler of human passions on the fringes of society, a major talent who wrote about courtesans and gigolos, or the adulterous careers of unhappily married women, without any sense of large moral issues. Certainly there are no overt lessons, either moral, political, or philosophical, in Colette's work, as she concentrates on enriching the realm of individual experience through a veritable psychology of the senses. Yet her values are clearly defined: this sensuous world sings a joy in life and nature that is opposed to the artificial entanglements of modern society; it seeks a lost purity linked to childhood and recaptured only in the exclusive devotion of love, or the spontaneous existence of animals; and it celebrates a capacity for sacrifice and endurance.

Colette writes about love because it is the source of the most profound human relationships, and her characters reveal their qualities as they experience passion, jealousy, devotion, and betrayal. Nor is love restricted to human beings; her animals, like Saha in *The Cat*, are full characters in their own right and occasionally transcend the weaker human characters in the purity and understanding of their love. Such love is many-sided. It is "pure and impure," according to one of her titles, "pure" in its exclusive and passionate devotion, and "impure" as an irresistible and inevitable sexuality that is part of growing up. It does not matter whether love is heterosexual or homosexual, adulterous or virginal; what matters is the quality of the emotion. Colette's stories often show the ravages of impure love, with Claudine betrayed by her husband and Rézi in *Claudine Married*, the aging courtesan Léa abandoned by her young lover at the end of *Chéri*, Renée afraid of love after an unhappy marriage in *The Vagabond*, or Julie tricked by her ex-husband in *Julie de Carneilhan*. Yet her characters reach their fullest dimension in accepting and enduring their fate, learning to live a new life or adapting themselves to the pain of the old.

For Colette, it is women who have the fullest experience of love and thus of life. Almost *all* her protagonists are women. Constrained by society and by their own role as childbearers, women arer unable to separate the pure and impure aspects of love, and live closer to the earth and life processes. From the early picture of developing sexuality in the Claudine novels and *Ripening Seed*, through the descriptions of adult womanhood in *The Vagabond* and *Julie de Carneilhan*, to Colette's own meditation on aging in *Break of Day*, there is a constant focus on the various stages of a woman's life and developing awareness. The figure of Colette's mother Sido, already important in *My Mother's House* and central in *Break of Day* and *Sido*, permeates the later books as the example of a richly harmonious female personality instinctively attuned to nature. Male characters in Colette lack this inner dimension, and never seem to reach psychological maturity. Chéri, the young gigolo, kills himself at thirty-two because he cannot

adapt to life without Léa, and adult male characters in general —no matter what their wealth or power—serve chiefly as necessary background for the painful development of female character.

If readers found Colette's topics and characters disconcerting, they immediately recognized her as a writer of classic prose in the best French tradition. She could summon up a range of emotions with a single word or gesture—for example, Alain's turning his head away from Camille's chatter to look out in the garden at the beginning of *The Cat*—or employ a longer, rhythmic, and convoluted phrase whose balanced harmony had not been heard since Chateaubriand (pp. 371-392). (The last three sentences of *The Cat* in our translation, for example, form one long sentence in the French original.) The color and immediacy of her descriptions were unmistakable, as was their precision and detail; she was a consummate realist.

In addition, Colette broadens the focus of her prose narratives to incorporate a unique blend of fiction and reality. Stories in *My Mother's House* are linked only by a common narrator, Colette herself, who sometimes speaks in the first person, sometimes appears as a character along with others, and in the latter case occasionally comments on her own portrayal. The most complicated mixture comes in *Break of Day*, which combines actual letters from Sido, Colette's own commentary on them, and both real and imaginary characters, including one fictional suitor who is refused by the narrator "Colette" because she is turning her back on love —at the same apparent time that the real Colette was passionately involved with her third husband. The lines between fiction and reality are blurred, and perhaps not even important; what is important is the imaginative portrayal of character and the networks of emotional relationships. These networks supersede the concern for plot, even though Colette's stories follow a traditional literary pattern of the love story or erotic triangle. They are more profoundly structured as a duel of personalities, seeking their own fulfilment through or in spite of the bonds of love.

Such a story is *The Cat*, a short novel published in 1933 and celebrated not only for its description of Colette's favorite animal but also because the cat triumphs in the struggle for love. Saha and Camille are Alain's "two females" in an unequal competition between a beautiful animal, "blue as the loveliest dreams," and a shrill, greedy, sensuous, and obtrusively modern wife. The plot is relatively simple: over a single summer Alain finds that he cannot abide being married and retreats to his childhood home. We see Saha and Camille through Alain's eyes, or through a perspective that duplicates his sensitivity, so there is no question about the cat's beauty and selfless devotion or about the horror of Camille's attempt to murder her terrified rival. Similarly, it is clear that the natural beauty of the garden in Alain's old home is far more attractive than the chrome and steel, high rise triangular apartment that

Camille prefers. Yet there is an uncomfortable undercurrent in the midst of this dreamlike retreat, and Camille, for all her shallowness and impurity, is right when she calls Alain a monster. The childhood world in which he was king is a lost paradise, and when he tries to return to it he is rejecting his own maturity. Alain's uncharitable descriptions of his wife's appearance, his criticism of her nakedness and sensuality, demonstrate how far he is caught in a "sweet and interminable adolescence" that is more comfortable with Camille's shadow on the wall than with her physical self. Camille more than Alain recognizes what is at stake, and that he has never truly been on her side. Even his mysterious affinity with animals carries with it an inability to mature as a human being, for he clings to Saha as to a pure love distinct from his wife's impure sexuality. Thus there are two equally admirable but opposing aims throughout the story, one associated with each female character. The ambiguity is maintained to the end, and underlined by an inversion of roles in which the cat triumphs on a human plane and Alain reverts to an animal state. Saha, who is often characterized in human terms, watches her rival's departure "as intently as a human being," while Alain lies on the ground and bats at chestnuts with a pawlike hand.

THOMAS MANN

When the German novelist Thomas Mann died in 1955, he had become an international figure to whom people looked for statements on art, modern society, and the human condition. His career spanned a time of great social and cultural change, and his work reflects both the upheavals of two world wars and the predicament of the artist, isolated from ordinary people by his or her special sensitivity. In stories about the role of the artist, or the decay of the great families of the prosperous middle class, Mann analyzes not only the culture of his time but also the universal human conflicts between art and life, sensuality and intellect, the individual and society. His most famous characters explore the limits of awareness, often ending in disease, madness, or death. Many of them symbolize human attitudes, but never abstractly: they are always described realistically, with pertinent attention to detail and with ironic perception and humor. Mann's novels are long and complex, highly organized with subtly interrelated themes and images that build up an increasingly rich association of ideas. In his own words, they constitute an "epic prose composition . . . understood by me as spiritual thematic pattern, as a musical complex of associations."

Mann drew heavily on personal experience for events and characters, and his letters and essays show that he felt deeply involved in the problems facing his fellow artists. But this was not merely a personal involvement, and Mann's protagonists symbolize much more than his own career. His first novel, *Buddenbrooks*, which describes the decline of a prosperous German family through four generations, is to some extent based on the history of the Mann family business; nonetheless, the elements of autobiography are quickly absorbed into the more universal themes of the inner decay of the German burgher tradition, its isolation from other segments of society, and in the portrait in Hanno Buddenbrooks of a developing artistic sensitivity and its relation to death. As artist and craftsman, Mann always insisted on distinguishing the work of art from its raw material, the emotions and experiences of life. He cultivated objectivity, distance, and irony in his own works, from the seemingly autobiographical *Tonio Kröger* to the humorous *Confessions of Felix Krull, Confidence Man*. No character, including the narrator, is immune from the author's critical eye.

Mann's fictional world is governed by a tension or dualism between sensuous experience and intellect or will. A diseased and alienated imaginative soul is set against a healthy, gregarious, somewhat obtuse normal citizen; the erratic and poor artist against the disciplined and prosperous burgher; the dark, brown-eyed Latin against the blond, blue-eyed Nordic; warm, unselfconscious feelings against icy, distant intellect; freedom against authority; immorality and decadence against moral respectability; a longing for the eternal and infinite against active participation in everyday life. There is no recommended resolution of these polarities, for if either overwhelms the other tragedy must follow. The artist, though representing one side of the dualism, is especially sensitive to the claims of both, and growing awareness of their combined importance is a sign of his or her maturation. The artist must live both extremes at once, in constant lucidity and pain, perpetually giving form to an underlying chaos of vital forces.

In a variety of circumstances throughout the novels, an artistic sensibility confronts different aspects of society and the human condition. The aspects are often linked, as in *Tonio Kröger*, where the budding artist Tonio is fascinated by the blond Teutonic normalcy of Hans and Ingeborg, and also in the overall history of the Buddenbrooks family, where the children of self-confident, aggressive, and disciplined Consul Johann Buddenbrooks become increasingly introspective, hesitant, unhealthy, and artistic. The end of the family comes with young Hanno, a musical genius who is completely absorbed in his piano improvisations and fatal temptation to the infinite that music implies. Yet the artist-figure also confronts destiny on a larger scale than the fall of a prosperous merchant family. In *The Magic Mountain*, Hans Castorp has to decide how to live as he listens to the competing dogmas of the humanist Settembrini and the fanatic antirationalist Naphta, and undergoes a double temptation of oblivion through eroticism (Clavdia Chauchat) and death (symbolized by the mountain sanatorium). Mann's artist is not, however, merely a plaything of his environment: Hans Castorp turns to active participation in a world at war,

and the Joseph of the biblical tetralogy *Joseph and His Brethren* controls not simply his destiny but that of others. The final, humorous metamorphosis of the artist-figure comes in the comic *Confessions of Felix Krull*, whose hero uses his skill and ironic insight to manipulate society to his advantage.

A much more somber vision of the artist, which offers something fairly close to a symbolic interpretation of contemporary history, is contained in the late novel *Doctor Faustus*, which Mann called "the novel of my epoch, dressed up in the story of a highly precarious and sinful artistic life." The composer Adrian Leverkühn sells his soul to the devil in order to become aware of the extremes of his own personality, thus enriching his experience and his composition. His music is determined by the patterns derived from the twelve-tone scale, and it opposes —in Leverkühn's composition, "Lamentation of Doctor Faustus"—the freer formal patterns of Beethoven's Ninth Symphony with its episodic choral finale, the "Ode to Joy." A compelling work, *Doctor Faustus* carries out one of the possibilities of the dialectic tension between art and life. It intensifies and pushes to an extreme the authoritarian arguments of Mann's own *Reflections of a Non-Political Man*, and reflects his horror at the negation of life inherent in Hitler's barbarism.

Many of Mann's themes derive, as he was aware, from the nineteenth-century German aesthetic tradition in which he grew up. The philosophers Schopenhauer and Nietzsche, and the composer Wagner had most influence on his development: Arthur Schopenhauer (1788–1860) for his vision of artistic suffering and development; Friedrich Nietzsche (1844–1900) for his portrait of the diseased artist overcoming chaos and decay to produce, through discipline and will, art works that justify existence; and Richard Wagner (1813–1883), for embodying in his own career Nietzsche's "diseased artist." Wagner planned to integrate completely all aspects of the art work, in his case opera, right down to the musical themes or *Leitmotifs* (pronounced "light-moteefs") each of which is associated with a particular person, thing, action, or state of being, and evokes those associations with increasing richness whenever the leitmotif is repeated. Mann's use of an analogous system of verbal leitmotifs is well known.

Tonio Kröger is an early work, written shortly after *Buddenbrooks*, and published in 1903. Since it describes the childhood and development of an artist in a burgher family, it is often taken as thinly veiled autobiography, or as at least a personal statement. Certainly it contains many elements from Mann's own life: the description of the home town, the Nordic father and Latin mother, recollections of particular childhood friends, boredom with school and enthusiasm for the poet Theodor Storm, a trip to Italy, and even the author's mistaken arrest for fraud when he returned home. The long central discussion of art and life also represents the central ten-

sion of Mann's major works. Yet *Tonio Kröger* is at the same time a highly structured novella (or short novel) that does not require any knowledge of its author's life to make clear the protagonist's growth toward self-knowledge.

The story falls roughly into three parts: Tonio Kröger's school years, with his infatuation with blond, blue-eyed Hans Hansen and his later adolescent love for blond, blue-eyed Ingeborg Holm; his early career as a writer, including a discussion on art with the Russian painter Lisabeta Ivanovna; and a visit to Denmark in which he comes to see Hans and Inge as idealized symbols of that "life" which is the counterpart of his own pull toward art. The point of view develops from an initial objectivity, in which Tonio's successive enthusiams, awkwardness, and disappointments are recorded with little overt interpretation, to a final assessment when the protagonist has earned the right to comment on his past life.

Tonio Kröger is in many ways a microcosm of themes and methods found in Mann's work as a whole. The familiar oppositions between bourgeois and artist, North and South, health and sickness, intellect and emotions, are all here, as well as the artist's final acceptance and transcendence of such oppositions. Leitmotifs, evocative phrases repeated almost word for word, link memories throughout the text and provide an overall emotional resonance: Tonio's "dark, fiery mother, who played the piano and mandolin," his father's "thoughtful blue eyes" and "wild flower in his buttonhole." The leitmotifs occur in Tonio's mind sometimes as clusters of associations: "the fountain, the old walnut tree, his fiddle, and away in the distance the North Sea" evoking his attachment to his childhood home, and the "gypsies living in a green wagon" symbolizing and representing an antithesis to Northern bourgeois respectability.

As the story progresses, the leitmotifs change and occasionally blend: on the boat to Denmark, Tonio recalls both the walnut tree and the "creaking of a garden gate" associated with Hans Hansen. The repetition and variation of leitmotifs unifies the tale, and it also reaffirms *Tonio Kröger* as the cumulative record of Tonio's life experience. The end of the story telescopes these fragments of memory in a half-real, half-imaginary encounter between Tonio and a Danish "Hans" and "Inge," an encounter that permits the mature Tonio to recognize the importance of this kind of recall for his role as an artist. Here both Tonio and the style of *Tonio Kröger* reach a level of awareness in which remembered experience becomes the material for art.

RAINER MARIA RILKE

Rilke's life was an immense *task*. Endowed with a morbid sensitivity and a dubious gift of facility that might have led to disaster in life or in art, he conquered both dangers. He lived, someone has said, the aesthetic life to the full. And so he did, but only in the sense that he submitted himself to a rigorous dis-cipline, aiming at no ivory-tower or coterie art, but at the elucidation of man's rôle in the world.

This "aesthete," then, this wanderer, this lifelong accepter of hospitality from the titled and wealthy, this husband too respectful of his wife's individuality to share a hearth with her— how far too easy it is to mock at Rilke!—had the good fortune or the skill to insure himself the proper material conditions for the fulfillment of his task, in spite of his apparent drifting and his slight financial resources. Residing at different periods in Germany, France, and Switzerland, with visits to Scandinavia, Italy, Spain, Russia, and his native Austria-Hungary, he made himself a truly European poet. The first World War, shattering European unity, shattered his peace of mind also, and not until several years after the war's close did he succeed in finding once again release of his poetic powers, which then flooded out to complete the *Duino Elegies* (*Duineser Elegien*, 1923), fragmentarily given him ten years before, and to call into being their pendant, the *Sonnets to Orpheus* (*Die Sonnette an Orpheus,* 1923).

The *Duino Elegies*, as befits the name, form a lament, but of a very special kind. Their slow modulations conjure up a picture of man ill at ease in the universe. "The sick animal," Nietzsche had called man, and the second elegy finds similarly that "Everything is agreed to remain silent concerning us, in part / as shameful perhaps and in part as an unutterable hope." It is in order to throw some light on the latter possibility that the elegiac form has been adopted, for, says one of the Orpheus sonnets, "Rejoicing *knows*, and longing tells its story,— / only lament learns still . . ."

The ninth of the ten elegies represents the climax of Rilke's long search for the meaning of human life; now he is able to glimpse the goal. This *once* that we live on earth will never *not* have been—but we can neither retain it nor bequeath it to another. Yet, possessing language, we are the only beings who can transmute the material thing and the transitory event into an enduring immateriality. Man can fulfill the hope of the earth by allowing the earth to arise once more, "invisible." In his *Elegies* and *Sonnets to Orpheus*, Rilke joins those who voice the poet's confidence in the supreme importance of his strivings. Almost to the word, he concurs with the French symbolist poet Stéphane Mallarmé, for whom literature was "the Orphic explanation of the earth," and who maintained, both humorously and more than humorously, "with an ineradicable, doubtless, writer's prejudice," that all things were destined to lead to a book.

FRANZ KAFKA

It is not unusual to introduce Kafka in such a fashion that all but the boldest are frightened away from his writings. For tactical reasons, therefore, but also because it is true, let us begin by saying that Kafka's works are meticulously detailed accounts of happenings within the three dimensions and the time element of everyday reality. To see in the mind's eye what is represented as occurring presents no problem at all.

The dialogue, also, follows strictly all the normal rules of syntax; the sentences do not even approach those of Thomas Mann in complexity, the vocabulary is much more restricted than his. A great deal of this discourse, however, is of the "he said and she said" variety; that is, it records statements previously made by characters not present, perhaps reporting actions of yet other characters, or of personages who do not appear at all, or even passing on rumors and conflicting rumors. And nothing, and no one, is ever pinned down, a circumstance which is bound to give rise to bafflement and frustration.

The narrative sections, too, quite frequently expend their lucidity on the reporting of highly improbable or extremely curious incidents. Couples sink to the floor in loving embraces whose embarrassing interruption the circumstances make almost inevitable; mysterious agencies, inconclusively discussed by one or more characters, impinge on the hero decisively, yet in a way which leaves the purport of their intervention far from clear.

The result is that the reader tends to oscillate between the bafflement already alluded to and the search for, even the discovery of, a solution. But the very proponent of this solution may come to see that he has been unjustifiably dogmatic, while those who deny that any solution can be found slip all too easily, a little later, into some one-sided dogmatism of their own.

Most trenchantly characterizing this uneasy pendulum movement to which Kafka drives us is a phrase of Sartre's: "Kafka, or the impossibility of transcendence." For Kafka, unlike the positivists and the horizonless men of every age, saw this world of ours as a system incomplete in itself, traversed by fissures through which we glimpse something that for a moment seems to hold out the promise of a transcendent justification of all things and of ourselves. But then the vision disappears, and we fall back on the patchwork of immanence, of mundane reality. According to the religious interpretation of his work made by his biographer and friend Max Brod, Kafka depicts the world as it is—disconcerting, harsh, incurably ambiguous, the site of our logically undemonstrable conviction that God is good, but not of direct acquaintanceship with God—and does not share the view that a spiritual explanation of reality should try to win recruits by depicting the world as it is not. Yet according to another interpreter, Kafka mocks at the claims of the mystics and of religion in general.

Kafka's career as a whole was powerfully affected by the fact that he was a Jew. To be a Jew is to experience the impact of society in a way concerning which too few non-Jews trouble to inform themselves. Sooner or later the Jewish child is impressed, possibly as the result of some jeering remark or abusive epithet, with the sense of his *difference* from others, a difference about which nothing can be done. It does not stop there. The child learns that in the eyes of others the Jews are to blame,

for anything or everything, and that he himself is guilty with the rest. But when such accusations from outside are repeated often enough, they arouse a sense of guilt within, also. Thus are born the conflicting impulses to admit guilt, yet to rebel against the unspecified and unproven accusation, proudly to refuse the assimilation which is denied and yet to long for it and strive toward it.

It should be mentioned, too, that Kafka's sense of guilt derived not only from these social pressures but also from his emotional involvement with his father, of whom he stood in awe and whose magnificent competence (so Franz Kafka saw it) contrasted with his own unreadiness to shoulder the burdens of marriage and a career. His first short story, "The Judgment" ("Das Urteil," 1913) most directly reveals the ambivalence of his attitude toward his father. Rebellion and repentance are intermingled. The story was written without a moment's hesitation in the course of one night, and the writing of the last sentence, very significantly, as Kafka told Brod, was accompanied by a sense of powerful sexual release.

Kafka's work is a great deal more, however, than an ingenious veiled portrayal of what it means to be a Jew in Western society. It does not affect us solely as the reflection of the situation of a minority to which we may not ourselves belong. For the suggestion may be advanced that the Jew, or the Wandering Jew, has come to be the archetype of Western man. The Jewish diaspora, the scattering of a people over the face of the earth, can be taken as the symbol of two things: of the increased uprootedness of individuals and populations all over the world, and of the state of consciousness induced by this separation from old values, old places, and old beloved objects.

"The Metamorphosis" ("Die Verwandlung," 1912) is the masterful and haunting expansion of a term of abuse. A human being is contemptuously called a louse, an insect. And usually that's all there is to it. Except that something remains—the wound, the sense of having been depreciated or degraded. Perhaps even an element of fear lurks in some crevice of the psyche, especially when the psyche is that of a child. Who knows, at what tender age, what dread transformations may sometimes occur!

Transformation is a common literary motif. Sometimes the fanciful and poetic predominated; sometimes the horrible. Here the horrible has the upper hand. It pounds at us all the more relentlessly because of the matter-of-fact tone used and the precise and circumstantial detailing of the embarrassments and physical difficulties that beset the transformed Gregor Samsa. Nor does he enjoy the privilege of suffering in isolation. The family is at once drawn in, and so is Gregor's employer, to whom the family is indebted. Gregor's uncomplaining readiness to support the entire family and the quiet sacrifice of his personal desires—all this goes unrecognized. The faults he attributes to himself and the sense of guilt they have instilled, built up to intolerable proportions by the massive disapproval of society and family —of his father, to be precise—

set a gulf between him and human kind. Step by step, whatever is human recedes from him.

The peak of tension in this quietly told drama is reached when the father begins to pelt Gregor with apples. To this painful dilemma there can be only one solution. It happens, and at once. The family—sister, mother, and father—is bathed in light and joy; they experience a genuine renewal, for the monster is dead.

Few readers will fail to sense the persistent echo that this tale arouses in them. We were all once ten-year-olds; we still are a little. We do not have Kafka's gift for dredging up, in mythical form, the fears that afflicted us then, but we can recognize them when Kafka brings them to the light of day.

ISAK DINESEN

"I am a storyteller," wrote Isak Dinesen, the Danish author whose series of tales celebrates the art of storytelling itself, and whose characters often spin tales within tales. "The divine art is the story," one of them says, "luminous and on a higher plane . . . not quite human" as opposed to the newer, more sympathetic and earthbound art of the novel. Readers of Dinesen's stories, from *Seven Gothic Tales* (1934) to *Anecdotes of Destiny* (1958), are struck by this atmosphere of intricate perfection, and by the way in which individually living characters play out their roles in some larger pattern which is the pattern of destiny, mirrored and humanly expressed in the shape of the tale. Dinesen felt that her tales fell into a "Gothic" or a "winter" type: either fantastic and cosmopolitan, or Danish and close to the earth, but in either type reality is held at a distance—transformed into art by the storyteller so as to express a mysterious order through which, if they accept it, human beings may transcend themselves.

The human voice is important in these stories. Most tales are told by the characters themselves, so that there are stories embedded within stories as well as a great many conversations in which different anecdotes are set off one against the other to compose a larger tale. Like the narrators in Boccaccio's *Decameron*, the storytellers are often isolated by circumstances: a group stranded on a hayloft during the flood of "A Deluge at Norderney," or people who happen to meet in a hotel in "The Roads around Pisa." Emphasis is thus placed on the telling of the tale, and on the way the narrative first hides and then reveals reality: the heroic cardinal of "A Deluge" finally explains that he is the former actor and valet Kasparson, who has killed his master to take his place, and the several narrators of "The Dreamers" describe their affairs with three different women who turn out to be assumed roles of the same woman, Pellegrina Leoni, a famous opera singer who after losing her voice has chosen to live different lives. Even stories such as "Sorrow-Acre," told in the third person, contain layers of anecdote and much conversation. Goske Piil's guilt, which is probable though ambiguous, is brought to light through stories told by a keeper and a wheelwright; the old lord tells Adam about it, and introduces a new element of challenge and sacrifice in the character of Anne-Marie; Adam and the old lord interpret the story in different lights as it draws to its fatal end. Dinesen's characters are marvelous conversationalists, but their eloquence does not so much reveal individual personalities as it casts light on the essential questions of the story: the nature of heroism, of old and new values, of dream and reality, comedy and tragedy, and a sense of order.

The world of these stories has a particular set of values—honor, an aristocratic *noblesse oblige*, artistic sensitivity, a strong moral sense—which the author often associates with an older, semi-feudal culture. Dinesen seeks the purity of an heroic, aristocratic world when social roles were fixed and obligations, hence moral choices, were clearer. Her preferred era is the eighteenth century, the last flowering of traditional nobility before the levelling of values in the modern age. Not that her picture of the eighteenth century is necessarily realistic: indeed, it is frequently extravagant, and seems to have little to do with major historical events. Even "Sorrow-Acre," an apparently realistic story set late in the century, is an adaptation of an earlier folktale, and uses its few historical references as part of a meditation on destiny. But Dinesen uses this distance in time to achieve a certain freedom and idealized perspective that would be lost in a more realistic setting: "I moved my stories back into a really romantic time when people and conditions were different from today.

I would become completely free only by doing this."

In this purified atmosphere, she can create fantastic, often grotesque stories in which her heroes and heroines struggle with love and fate, commit themselves to extreme ideas, sacrifices, and punishments, and work out a very personal sense of destiny. Their ultimate achievement comes when they live to the full their assigned role in the pre-established design: when the coldly virginal Lady Flora of "The Cardinal's Third Tale" accepts the syphilis she contracts from kissing the foot of a religious statue, when Eitel kneels before Linnert who is about to be executed for poaching on Eitel's land and who may well be the real heir to the estate ("Country Tale"), and when Anne-Marie and the lord of "Sorrow-Acre" fulfil opposing roles in their drama of transcendental sacrifice. By understanding and asserting their fated roles they fulfil their individual natures, but they also rise to a level of tragedy that goes beyond impersonal fate. Such transcendence, suggests Dinesen, is reserved for mortals, for only they can suffer and die; tragedy has no real meaning for the all-powerful, so that the gods—lacking human vulnerability—are restricted to a "comic" dimension. They themselves contribute to the grand design, completing a pattern that recalls Dinesen's description of her own stories as a pentagram, a self-contained form in which "there's nothing to add . . . and nothing to take away."

"Sorrow-Acre" is one such complete tale. Written during the war years and published in 1942 as part of the *Winter's Tales*, it is a beautifully designed story that emphasizes universal themes over and above any connection with history. There is, of course, a specific historical setting, for Adam returns to his uncle's estate from a position at the court of King George III of England, and much of the story consists of a debate of old and new values. The mercy and sympathy of Adam's new humanism come into conflict with a sterner view of fate, and the old lord's harsh bargain with Anne-Marie illustrates an older, authoritarian, and tragic sense of life. But as happens so frequently in Dinesen, the particular historical and geographic references that locate the story in the real world— here, in the Danish system of inherited manorial estates during the late eighteenth century—serve only as a point of departure for larger themes that come to be the real focus of the story. The plot itself transcends history, for it is part of Danish folklore. Biblical associations are common, from the hierarchical relationship of Adam and the unnamed "lord" to the pastoral scenes in the Book of Ruth; mythological references abound, and the central ethical questions are seen in terms of two mythologies, Nordic and Greco-Roman, or two genres, tragedy and comedy. Dinesen supplies no dates throughout, and the context appears not so much political as ethical or cultural. Most of the historical references relate to literature (*Balder's Death*, a tragedy by Johannes Ewald written in 1774) or music (the French version of Gluck's opera *Alceste*, first performed in 1776).

Even these specific chronological references direct attention outside history to universal themes, for *Balder's Death*, describing the death of a Nordic demi-god who had loved a mortal, introduces the discussion of mythologies, and *Alceste* retells the Greek myth of a woman sacrificing her life for someone she loves.

"Sorrow-Acre" thus is a grand design with many levels. It correlates a family tale of inheritance and dynasty (and possible cuckoldry), a celebration of the age-old harmony between the Danish soil and those who live by it, a conflict of generations, and a contrast of value systems between a newer, more humane age and one that forces heroic choice: "That with your own life you may buy the life of your son." It is clear that Dinesen's sympathies are with the older, starker order, for the stately elegance of the old lord's ceremonial dress and actions, and the transformation at the end of Anne-Marie's struggle into a "divine procession or rite" when "the meadows and the grasslands became pure gold; the barley field near by . . . a live lake of shining silver," lift not only Anne-Marie but the whole world to a level of transcendent inhuman beauty.

ANNA AKHMATOVA

The shape of Anna Akhmatova's poetic career cannot be understood apart from the influence of the Soviet government policies on the arts during the regime of Joseph Stalin. New works were closely examined for political correctness and social utility; writers who expressed subjective feelings and personal opinions instead of celebrating the heroes and heroic deeds of the masses were simply not published, and in many cases criticized officially in the most harsh and offensive terms. Akhmatova, for instance, though well known in Russian literary circles at the time of the Bolshevik Revolution of 1917, was allowed to publish no original work from Stalin's accession in 1923 until 1956, three years after his death. During the Second World War this ban was temporarily lifted, and she wrote the patriotic poems the times demanded, inspired rather by love of her country than by love of the regime. But in 1946 the Central Committee of the Communist Party again cracked down on "individualistic" writers, and her work was attacked by the Politburo's literary expert, A. A. Zhdanov, as the "poetry of an overwrought upper-class lady who frantically races back and forth between boudoir and chapel." (The allusion is to her aristocratic upbringing, her religious faith, and her poems' explorations of love.)

Akhmatova's early poetry is lyric and personal, experimental only in that it breaks away from the faded sentimentalities of late nineteenth-century Russian poetry to find a new clarity and directness. In a poem of 1910, she registers an intense aesthetic appreciation of a particular configuration of sight and sound: "The crow upon the wing with raucous caw, / And, down the dwindling path, the archway's curve." She also records the small details of behavior that reveal a state of mind, as in a poem where a distraught woman puts her glove on the wrong hand. Her work at this period often has for its theme unhappy love and separation, though expressed with honesty and indeed toughness: "Me, honor and obey? You've lost your mind! . . . Husband spells headsman to me, housed—confined." Though one or another poem may show her aware of the great movements of history around her, she is concerned mainly with personal meanings: "No one will listen now to songs. The tragic, / So long foreshadowed days have come around."

At no point in her long career was Akhmatova able to write the officially promoted socialist poetry that was required to gain acceptance and publication. She therefore suffered continuously from a feeling of internal exile; in "Not with a Loved One's Lyre," she refers to herself as a leper, and describes the painful isolation of one who is shunned not only by officialdom but also by the common people, who look on her as an outcast from their new society. To elude the ideological censor, she began to use historical or Biblical settings to hide contemporary references; thus in "Imitation from the Armenian," a bereaved mother sheep asks the Shah, "But what about my boy, did you enjoy his taste?" During the brief period of World War II when she was allowed to publish again, she seemed to be discovering a new role for herself as a national poet. Her poem "Courage," published in *Pravda* in 1942, rallies the Russian people to defend their homeland (and their language). Even the less "public"

poems have a new tone, as she finds poetry in "An angry cry, the smell of fresh bitumen, / Along some wall a runic lichen sign, / And verses answer, tender, brash, and human, / For your delight and mine." The sharpness of perception is still there, but she now includes her readers with herself rather than setting herself apart. It was during these years that she wrote the cycle of poems called "Requiem," though it could not be published then and has not yet been published in its entirety in Russia.

"Requiem" shows vividly her reconciliation of personal and public voices. Its poems express not only her own grief and anxiety for an imprisoned son, but also the community of grief felt by all the women who had lost or were losing sons and husbands during the Stalinist purges of 1937–1938.

The title of the cycle, alluding to the Roman Catholic mass for the dead, is a protest against the official atheism of the state. The two prefaces establish the historical situation and Akhmatova's own role as speaker for the people. In the dedication and introduction, the scene is set in Leningrad and populated with grieving women who are defined not individually but as those—"The same everywhere" —who wait in fear. Epic in scope, the first poems recall a period when "only the dead smiled" and Russia seemed like an enormous prison camp. Subsequent poems shift to more personal feelings, as she speaks of her own as well as a more universal grief, of any mother's sense of loss and anxiety for a son. References to the arrest of

Akhmatova's third husband Nikoali Punin (poem 1), the execution of her first husband Nikolai Gumilev (poem 2), and her son's imprisonment build rapidly into a picture of both individual and communal bereavement.

The speaker of these poems, the *I*, undergoes a certain dissociation of personality (poems 2 and 3), even the risk of madness (poem 9), and looks back unbelievingly at an earlier self (poem 4) in the struggle to free her son (poem 5). Ultimately, when the point of madness has been reached, the lyrical *I* gives way to a third-person description of the crucifixion (poem 10), and the theme of grieving mother and lost son moves to the transcendental level of Christian symbol. Though the tenth is the last numbered poem, two epilogues then reestablish the framework of memory and reassert the religious and historical motifs that have united the poems throughout. The immensity of the national grief is compared with the grandeur of the Russian landscape, especially its great rivers, yet is simultaneously seen as petrifying the soul and turning faces into tablets incised by suffering. At the very end, the poet herself reaches a stony immobility, metamorphosed by her suffering into the monument that is the traditional memorial to a national poet.

SURREALISM: BRETON, ÉLUARD, PÉRET

Around the same time that Marcel Proust was writing his often realistic novel set in turn-of-the-century France, rebellious writers and artists in Germany, Switzerland, and France ventured into Dadaism, an artistic movement of total revolt expressed in the nonsense word *dada*, and then Surrealism, an anti-realism or super-realism based on total freedom of the creative imagination. Surrealism, coming at the same time as the popularization of Freud's discoveries, also appeals to the subconscious mind; according to its leader André Breton, it aims at the "total recuperation of our psychic force by a means that is nothing else than the dizzy descent into ourselves, the systematic illumination of hidden places and the progressive darkening of other places, the perpetual promenade in the middle of the forbidden zone." Plunging into the subconscious self, the Surrealist expects to communicate with readers on a plane that does not depend on rational thought.

Surrealism recalls Romanticism in many ways, in its emphasis on the individual self, its suspicion of rational discourse (logic solves only "secondary problems," says Breton), its interest in dreams and madness, its belief in love as a means of transcendence, and its consciously revolutionary attitude. In addition, however, the Surrealists were strongly antiesthetic and did not wish to form part of literary tradition. Poetry for them was supremely important as a kind of "mental electricity" but not as style or technique. Perhaps not even the famous Surrealist sense of humor would enable them to accept being part of a literary anthology that purports to contain "masterpieces." Yet the richness of the Surrealist imagination and its liberation of artistic techniques make it an important and influential movement within twentieth century Modernism.

Certain themes and ideals recur constantly: imagination, liberty, and the marvelous. Imagination helps us break out of the framework of previous thought, to see what *might be* instead of only what has been. Complete liberty—political, cultural, and intellectual—is a prerequisite for using the imagination. The marvelous, which the Surrealists carefully refused to define, can appear at any time to who views reality with poetic imagination, who has reached a special *beyond* or *sublime point* where contradictions cease to exist. Surrealist writers found a number of ways to break the hold of rational thought and venture into the realms of the marvelous. They plunged themselves into waking dreams, sometimes by hypnosis, to capture the voice of the unconscious; they refused all terms of logical discourse (*like, therefore*, or any rational sequence) and preferred challenging contradictions such as Breton's "soluble fish"; they employed "automatic writing," the free flow of words unfettered by reason, morals, or esthetic preoccupations; they played party games or signed readymade objects so as to let "objective chance" enter their subjective universe. There is a great deal of variety among these writers. Some are more formally inclined, others less so; some favor free verse mixed with traditional meters, others prose; some remained resolutely uncommitted while others moved out of Surrealism into Communism or the anti-Nazi Resistance. Not all Surrealist writing is "atuomatic," but Surrealist doctrine gives special importance to this untrammeled, associative flow of words and both of our selections happened to be "automatic" texts.

"A Life Full of Interest" (*Une Vie pleine d'intérêt*) is a short story written by Benjamin Péret in 1922, during a period known for surrealist experiments in sleepwriting. Like Péret's other stories, it is an adult wonder tale in which familiar reality is turned topsy-turvy, and the person who tries to proceed along normal, rational, or aggressive lines appears completely out of step. The reader is enticed into this magical world by the appearance of reason: Mrs. Lannor comes out of her house, as usual, and looks at her cherry trees. No sooner is the stage set, however, than it explodes into a series of nonsensical images and impossible happenings which are, in fact, the reality of this surreal world. Mrs. Lannor accepts this reality, much as we accept a dream, but earns only frustration and failure when she mistakenly tries to control it through rational means. Protecting her property and seeking revenge on the impertinent lovers, she throws a stone and digs tunnels in a world whose rapid transformations outstrip her every move, where a flying fish gives her directions and where she herself —committed to orderly concepts of time and space—unexpectedly gives birth to an ornate clock. Humiliated and overcome, she finally dies "as mushrooms die," and is absorbed into a polymorphous life cycle. Yet the tale is not so much the story of Mrs. Lannor as it is the description of the subconscious, irrational world she tried to control, a universe of constant change and metamorphosis, of wonder and chance, and above all of powerful erotic drives.

Péret's text, like any Surrealist text, does not try to explain this universe but rather to present it to the reader's imagination. Many details cannot be explained—the sausage-cloud with fan-like ears, or exactly *how* mushrooms die—while others, the sexual symbolism of the obelisk and tunnel, have fairly obvious references. Just as Péret has given his story texture with details freely associated from his own imagination, so the reader must bring his or her associations to these images and participate in the creation of a personal magic universe. Such is the aim of Surrealist art: it frees the mind to create its own "marvelous" universe, and to discover a fuller vision of life in tune with subconscious experience.

The Immaculate Conception (*L'Immaculée conception*), written jointly by André Breton and Paul Eluard and published in 1930, is a series of prose poems whose "immaculate" nature—free from rationality and tradition—is assured by the process of automatic writing. The title is of course also a parody of the Catholic dogma of the Immaculate Conception according to which the Virgin Mary was conceived and born without original sin; as such, it reflects Surrealist contempt for the rules and constraints of organized religion, and for its promise of salvation through superhuman agency. This *Immaculate Conception* is a new description of the human condition. The first part is a simulation of the chief stages of human life, from conception to death; the second is the famous "Possessions," a simulation of five conditions of mental illness from mental weakness to dementia praecox; the third describes "Mediations," from habit to the idea of becoming; and the last part is "The Original Judgment," another Biblical parody titling a series of commandments that emphasize the immediate (not otherworldly) dimension of Surrealist imagination. "Intra-Uterine Life" is the second section of the first part, and simulates the fetus' experience inside the womb. There is some illogic here in that the vocabulary and references reflect adult experience; however, it is just those rational distinctions that are refused by the Surrealists, for whom all experience was potentially one. The writing in *The Immaculate Conception* is much freer than in "A Life Full of Interest," which is still somewhat governed by the form of the tale. Here, however, there is still a psycho-logic, if not logic, in the associations of words, of physical sensations, of everyday objects. At the beginning, the sunflower turning on its stem to follow the light suggests the pointer on a sundial, or is itself a natural sundial. The sundial's pointer casts a shadow—the opposite of light—which in its negativity may be related to the "nothing" of the first sentence as well as to the absence or "regret" of something felt in the light of the sun. The shape of the pointer may again suggest "crossed bones," words whose *sound* suggests "crosswords": the rhyme is almost identical in French, where "bones"—*os*, pronounced *oh*—rhymes with "words"—*mots*. With crossword puzzles we associate the "volumes of ignorance and knowledge" needed to solve them. Here, as in the rest of the poem, the reader's imagination follows lines suggested by Breton but fills in his or her own associations. These associations are all framed by a movement from nothingness ("To be nothing") to birth ("They are expecting me"), and illustrate an intuitive, prenatal harmony that the child hopes not to forget in "real life" with its categorized perceptions.

BERTOLT BRECHT

Bertolt Brecht is a dominant figure in modern drama not only as the author of half a dozen plays which rank as modern classics, but as the first master of a powerful new concept of theater. Dissatisfied with the traditional notion, derived from Aristotle's *Poetics*, that drama should draw its spectators into identification with and sympathy for the characters, and with the Realist aesthetic of naturalness and psychological credibility, he also believed that the modern stage should break open the closed world established as a dramatic convention by writers like Ibsen and Chekhov, whose audiences were to look at the action as if it were a slice of real life going on behind an invisible "fourth wall" between stage and audience. For Brecht, a radical Marxist, the modern audience must not be allowed to indulge in emotional identification at a safe distance;

it must be educated and moved to political action. The movement called "epic theater," which was born in the twenties, suited his needs well, and through his plays, theoretical writings, and dramatic productions he developed its basic ideas into one of the most powerful theatrical styles of the century.

The name "epic theater" derives from a famous essay "On Epic and Dramatic Poetry" by Goethe and Schiller, who in 1797 described *dramatic* poetry as pulling the audience into emotional identification, in contrast to *epic* poetry, which by being distanced in the time, place, and nature of the action can be absorbed in calm contemplation. The idea of an epic theater is a paradox: how can a play engage an audience that is still held at a distance? Brecht's solution was to employ many "alienation effects" that were genuinely dramatic, but prevented total identification with the characters and forced spectators to think critically about what was taking place. These alienation effects have since become standard production techniques in the modern theater. In spite of Brecht's intentions and frequent revisions, however, the characters and situations of his plays remain emotionally engrossing, especially in his best-known works such as *Mother Courage and Her Children*.

Most of Brecht's plays are didactic, either openly or by implication. After he became a fervent Marxist in the mid-twenties, he wrote a number of plays intended to set forth Communist doctrine, instructing the workers of Germany in the meaning of social revolution.

These plays were condemned as unattractive and "intellectualist" by the Communist press in Berlin and Moscow. In truth, Brecht's mind was too keen and questioning, too attracted by irony and paradox, for him to have a comfortable relation with authority, whether of the left or the right. His new ideas of theater, although he tactfully said that they were elements of a Marxist aesthetic, went directly against the prevailing Party view. After 1934 the Soviet bureaucracy of the arts supported as the official dramatic mode a style called "socialist realism," whose goal was to offer simple messages and foster identification with revolutionary heroes. Though the East German government subsidized Brecht's *Berliner Ensemble*, and refrained from interfering with the style of its productions, it also obliged him to defend some of his plays against charges of political unorthodoxy, and indeed to revise them. After Brecht settled in East Berlin in 1948, he wrote no major new plays but only minor propaganda pieces and adaptations of classical works such as Molière's *Don Juan* and Shakespeare's *Coriolanus*.

Brecht's concept of an epic theater touches on all aspects: dramatic structure, stage setting, music, and the actor's performance. The structure is to be open, episodic, and broken by dramatic or musical interludes. It is a "chronicle" that recounts events in an epic or distanced perspective. Episodes may be performed independently as self-contained dramatic parables, instead of being organically tied to a centrally-developing plot. Skits appear between scenes: in

A Man's a Man, there is a fantastic interlude in which an elephant is accused of having murdered its mother. Sometimes a narrator comments on the action (*Three-Penny Opera*, *A Man's a Man*). The alienation effects are also heightened by setting most of the plays in far-away lands (China in *The Good Person of Setzuan*, India in *A Man's a Man*, England in *The Three-Penny Opera*, Russia in *The Caucasian Chalk Circle*, Chicago in *Saint Joan of the Stockyards* and *The Resistible Rise of Arturo Ui*), or times (the seventeenth century in *Mother Courage*, Renaissance Italy in *Galileo*, or an imagined ghostly afterlife in *The Trial of Lucullus*).

Stagecraft and performance further support Brecht's concept of a critical, intellectualized theater. Events on stage are announced beforehand by signs, or are accompanied by projected films and images during the action itself. Place names are printed on signs and suspended over the actors, and footlights and stage machinery are openly displayed. Songs that interrupt the dramatic action are addressed directly to the audience, and are often heralded by a sign Brecht called a "musical emblem: in *Mother Courage*, 'a trumpet, a drum, a flag, and electric globes that lit up.'" In addition, Brecht described a special kind of acting: actors should "demonstrate" their parts instead of being submerged in them. At rehearsals, Brecht often asked actors to speak their parts in the third person instead of the first. Masks were occasionally used for wicked people, or soldiers' faces chalked white to suggest a stylized fear. Such constant artificiality injected into all aspects of the performance makes it difficult for the audience to identify completely and unselfconsciously with the characters on stage.

Audiences may react emotionally to Brecht's plays and characters, but their reactions are unusually mixed and changing. Brecht's characters are complex and inhabit complex situations. Galileo is both a dedicated scientist who sacrifices his reputation for honesty so as to complete his work, and a weak sensualist who fails to recognize how his recantation will affect others' pursuit of scientific knowledge. In *The Good Person of Setzuan*, the overgenerous Shen Te can survive only by periodically adopting the mask of a harshly practical "cousin," Shui Ta. Mother Courage is both a tragic mother figure and a small-time profiteer who loses her children as she battens on war.

Brecht's work teems with such paradoxes, at all levels. He is a cynic who deflates religious zeal, militant patriotism, and heroic example as delusions that lead the masses on to futile sacrifice; yet an idealistic tone also pervades the plays, with prominent use of Biblical language and imagery and themes of individual sacrifice. Brecht's own zeal is directed toward enlightening the common man, giving him the force and clearsightedness to break out of a manipulative system. In *A Man's a Man*, the timid dock worker Galy Gay is transformed by fright and persuasion into another person, the ferociously successful soldier Jeriah Jip. When Jip turns up at the end of the play, he is given Gay's papers and forced to reassume Gay's identity. The play teaches that human personality can be broken down and reassembled like a machine; the only weapon against such mindless manipulation is awareness, an awareness that enables people to understand and control their destiny. Brecht's theater finds its dimension and purpose in achieving this complex and difficult goal.

Mother Courage was written shortly after Brecht turned forty, in a period of major plays including *Galileo*, *The Trial of Lucullus*, and *The Good Person of Setzuan*. It is set in Germany in the middle years of a war involving all of Europe, believed at the time Brecht was writing to have destroyed half the German population: the Thirty Years' War (1618–1648). But senseless violence, religious intolerance, artificial patriotism, and cynical opportunism were no more characteristic of seventeenth-century Germany than of the Nazi state, and the setting gave Brecht what he needed to write a strongly pacifist play in 1939, the year in which World War II was to begin.

Mother Courage evoked the sympathy of early audiences for her tragic inability to prevent her children's death. Such was not Brecht's intention, and he rewrote several sections of the play to bring out her avarice and blindness, her belief that she can use the war, by profiting from others' misery, without endangering her own family. For to Brecht, the tragedy of her life lay in her failure to relate the general fate of society to that of her own family. In trying to manipulate the system for her personal advantage, she denies the human rights of others: she calls to others to enlist but not to her own children, and she would rather sell shirts to the officers than use them to bind a peasant's wounds. Yet the war that Mother Courage saw as a good provider ends by killing her three children, and even sooner because of their virtues (Eilif's martial zeal, Swisscheese's honesty, Kattrin's pity). Mother Courage is ruined, all the more so since she has learned nothing from the war and does not protest it. Instead, her bitter "Song of the Great Capitulation" presents compromise as inevitable, and at the end of the play she is chasing after a new regiment to continue her peddler's career.

Each of the twelve parable-like scenes of *Mother Courage* presents a particular aspect or lesson of the war. Setting and props encourage the audience to see the action as a "demonstration," by drawing attention to the way the play is put on. Signs or titles are projected onto a screen to announce what is about to happen; a revolving stage and projected backgrounds suggest the wagon's travels in a highly stylized way; a group of musicians sits in full view beside the stage to accompany the songs; realistic but sketchy three-dimensional structures represent buildings. The main piece of stage furniture is Mother Courage's canteen wagon, whose increasingly dilapidated appearance reveals her fall from prosperity into lonely poverty. In the first scene, the whole family appears with the wagon: at the end, Mother Courage pulls it alone.

Brecht hoped that *Mother Courage* would show its audiences "that in wartime the big profits are not made by little people. That war, which is a continuation of business by other means, makes the human virtues fatal even to their possessors. That no sacrifice is too great for the struggle against war." This last point is demonstrated by Kattrin's death, for she is the only one of Mother Courage's family whose virtue is not perverted by the war, and whose death is meant to provide a moral example. Drumming frantically to awaken the endangered city of Halle, she sacrifices her life to save the city's threatened children. Religious and secular themes join at this point, as they do so often in the course of the play, for Kattrin acts immediately after hearing the peasant family bemoan their helplessness and pray to God for miraculous aid. It is action, not passive prayer, that Brecht hopes to evoke with his epic theater. Both the play itself and its self-conscious, "alienated" staging try to move the audience toward a clearer understanding of forces in society, and to a responsible choice of their own roles.

VLADIMIR NABOKOV

"I have never been interested in what is called the literature of social comment," Vladimir Nabokov once remarked; "I am not 'sincere.'" Indeed, his fiction creates intricate, unrealistic mirror-worlds of verbal brilliance, sly and hidden allusions, and surprising shifts in narrative strategy. A devoted chess player, he has compared the plots and counterplots of his novels with those of chess. He is also a composer of chess problems, diagrams of positions to be solved by forcing checkmate within a specified number of moves. In a similar way, he challenges his readers to try to "solve" his novels. Since both the novels and the chess problems afford various solutions, simple as well as complex, the fun of the game is to recognize the several possibilities and seek out the least obvious but most elegant.

A Nabokov work offers puzzles of every kind. In his most famous novel, Lolita, the narrator Humbert Humbert first fears and then pursues his rival for Lolita's love, a mysterious figure whose appearance and other characterictics seem much like Humbert's own. For a moment it seems that the rival may be a figment of his imagination, a phantom double, yet Humbert murders the person after all—or perhaps he doesn't. Humbert's obsession with nymphets such as the twelve-year-old Lolita is on the one hand psychologically grounded in the frustration of his love as a boy for young Annabel Leigh, his subconscious forever scarred by the interruption of their lovemaking on the beach; but on the other hand the girl's name recalls ironically Edgar Allan Poe's sentimental poem of a lost seaside love, "Annabel Lee." (One critic has even observed that Lolita herself is described in terms that apply with remarkable precision to the butterfly Lycaeides sublivens Nabokov, a species which the author was first to identify —for he was also an expert lepidopterist.) A later novel, Pale Fire, begins as a critical edition of a 999-word poem by John Francis Shade carrying pedantic commentary by Charles Kinbote; but it then turns out

to be the mad autobiography of the exiled King of Zembla, or of a man who thinks he is. An earlier "biography," The Real Life of Sebastian Knight, concludes by suggesting that the biography remains unwritten and that perhaps the man himself never existed.

Nabokov's fiction is thus always playful, always resisting single interpretations. Yet it does return to certain images and themes. One recurring image is of an ideal setting or time that lies always just out of reach of the limits of sordid reality and offers a vision of aesthetic perfection. The beautiful and unattainable pastoral scene in "Cloud, Castle, Lake," made all the more poignant by the banality and cruelty of the world from which the unhappy Vasili Ivanovich hopes to find refuge there, is one such vision. Another is the precocious preadolescence that Humbert Humbert seeks in his nymphet lovers—a charmed age, as it seems to him, an "island of entranced time" lifted out of the stream of human mortality. To certain spirits these idealized realms offer a special kind of aesthetic ecstasy, an ecstasy such as Nabokov himself found in solving a particularly complicated chess problem or in finding a rare butterfly. His main characters generally show this kind of artistic sensitivity and the vulnerability that goes with it, while his secondary characters are often caricatures of uncaring, unimaginative people. The police state in Bend Sinister, for example, reduces its citizens to interchangeable personalities, complicated "anagrams" of one another. The tour members of "Cloud, Castle, Lake" cannot permit anyone to eat, read, sing, or think differently from themselves. The interaction of these two kinds of characters—not their development, for they do not change, instead carrying out to the end the roles he has assigned them —implies an important theme, a plea for the individuality of artistic consciousness as against a mechanical, conformist view of the imagination.

Although Nabokov disliked comparisons between his life and the situations in his work, it is often possible to discern echoes of one in the other. "Cloud, Castle, Lake," written in 1937 when the author had lived for several years in Hitler's Berlin, centers on another Russian refugee who is likewise living in Berlin in 1937, and the cruel conformity enforced by the tour guide and the noisy Philistine tourists sharply satirizes Nazi political and social attitudes: "Let us march and sweat together / With the steel-and-leather guys." Yet the story is more than social satire: Vasili at the end insists that he has "not the strength to belong to mankind any longer," and the narrator, suddenly assuming godlike authority, says, "Of course, I let him go." Such a role for the fictional narrator is not at all alien to Nabokov, who believes in total control of his literary universe and describes the narrator of another novel as "an anthropomorphic deity impersonated by me."

ISAAC BASHEVIS SINGER

The Yiddish language, in which I. B. Singer writes his books, is approximately one thousand years old. Basically German (though not standard modern German) in grammatical structure and vocabulary, but containing many Hebrew words and adding, subsequently, others from Russian, Polish and, most recently, English, this language mirrors the circumstances under which Jews lived during that long period.

Originating in the Rhineland and along the Danube, the language traveled eastward as its speakers fled the pogroms that had begun as an accompaniment to the First Crusade (1096). Thus the Jews of Eastern Europe, the Ashkenazi, spoke Yiddish, that is, Jewish German. (The Sephardic Jews, similarly, who were expelled from Spain in the late fifteenth century, have maintained until today, in their "exile" in the eastern Mediterranean, a form of medieval Spanish as their language.)

In English translation, the best-known Yiddish writer is undoubtedly Shalom Aleichem, who died in Brooklyn in 1916— the earlier migrations to the East were matched, in the late nineteenth and twentieth centuries, by migrations to the west. Renewed fame has come to him, throughout the United States and the world, because of the successful musical *Fiddler on the Roof*, which is based on his stories of Tevyeh the dairyman.

Isaac Bashevis Singer, born in 1904, had a briefer experience in the now vanished world of Eastern Jewry. But he nevertheless was deeply immersed in it. His father was a rabbi in a small town near Warsaw and was extremely poor, since he begrudged the time it would have taken him to learn Russian and thus qualify for recognition by the Russian authorities. He preferred to devote his time, when no other demands were made on it, to the study of the Torah (the Pentateuch, the first five books of the Bible). The elder Singer subsequently moved to a poor district in Warsaw. But Isaac spent the later war years with his mother's family in Bilgoray, near Lublin, where the food supplies were better. The boy's grandfather had been a highly esteemed rabbi, whose religious learning was matched by a commanding presence and practical competence. And he often heard tales of the glorious past that had revolved around his grandfather.

I. B. Singer, separated while still quite a young man from the narrow, but also intense and remarkably variegated life of Polish Jewry, still lives intensely in this world in his imagination, and this attitude is the driving force behind his creativity. In his short stories he ranges over every aspect of Jewish life. That the supernatural has a special allure for him is of little wonder, since the boy heard constant talk about "spirits of the dead that possess the bodies of the living, souls reincarnated as animals, houses inhabited by hobgoblins, cellars haunted by demons." Though he will not be pinned down concerning precise details, even today I. B. Singer avows his belief in spiritual entities of which the scientific rationalist knows nothing. His tales, including those he has written for children, make use of the elements of folklore and superstition for which he himself had been so avid. He has also written a number of novels, one of them situated in the seventeenth century, whose aim it is to paint a broad panorama of

Jewish life. More recently he has placed some of his fiction in the United States, but he limits himself to dealing with Jewish immigrants, the people he knows best.

For a direct, nonfictional account of his boyhood years, one may read *A Day of Pleasure* (1969) or the partially overlapping *In My Father's Court* (1966). This does not refer, of course, to a royal or ducal court, or even the busy, populous "court" of a Hasidic rabbi, adulated by his followers and attracting countless hangers-on. It was simply his father the rabbi in his function as judge or conciliator in disputes that arose between members of his congregation, or others, who then came to him and undertook to abide by his decision. The book introduces the reader to well-established patterns of thinking and behavior that are nevertheless quite astounding, on occasion, and which in the main are, no doubt, strategies that tended to preserve individual and group existence during the centuries of compressed and ever-threatened existence in the ghettos. For a more disabused, less fond reflection of the life of this same family, with its ineffectual male head and his more energetic, more skeptical spouse, one can turn to *Of a World That Is No More* (1970), by I. J. Singer, the older-by-eleven-years brother of I. B. Singer. This brother detested his sixty-hour school week, was an unenthusiastic student of the Torah, and loved the open fields, horses, and handicrafts, all inappropriate interests for the son of a Rabbi.

The story reprinted here, "The Gentleman from Cracow," testifies to the Evil One's maleficent powers—which extend far beyond the individual and can wreak havoc on a whole town. The story unfolds in its own picturesque, gripping way; as a piece of fiction it requires no commentary here. It is more important to point out that whole communities of Jews in Eastern Europe sometimes *were* eliminated. The refusal of any individual to conform to the accepted laws and mores was potentially too dangerous to be tolerated, and was looked on as apostasy and treason. Gradually, as the danger lessened, some sought to adapt to the non-Jewish world and hankered after a secular education. What had been the bliss of the Sabbath and the inexhaustible riches of the Torah became an intolerably irksome network of prohibitions and ritual requirements. The worm, if not the serpent Satan, had entered the fruit, and one fateful step led to another: Gentile dress and ways were adopted and, as in this story, cards were played and men and women actually danced together. Disaster on earth, the traditionalists believed, would be the direct expression of the Divine anger. Singer is also sensitive, however, to the psychological problems confronting the innovators, to their irrational fears and guilt feelings at having broken with tradition. He himself had listened to the skeptical remarks of his older brother and had been swayed by them. Consequently, though situated in a shadowy past, this legend reveals something of Singer's own doubts and ambivalences. He is a figure bridging two generations, two continents, and two irreconcilable outlooks on life.

JEAN-PAUL SARTRE

Sartre is one of those rare authors who have been outstandingly successful in a great variety of genres. His publications embrace short stories, novels, plays, essays, psychology, philosophy, and public affairs. It would be misleading, however, not to indicate that, despite his prodigious literary activities and, probably, the many thousands of pages he has written but not published, he has not been equally active in every type of writing all the time. His five short stories all appeared in the 1930's. There was one prewar novel, *Nausea*, and in the 1950's he abandoned a novel, *Roads to Liberty*, after publishing the first three volumes. He has totally repudiated the 728 pages of *Being and Nothingness*, the philosophical work that aroused an extraordinary furor immediately after World War II and which, with the backing of several consistently successful plays, brought him world fame. The one thing that has remained constant, in this flood of words so diversely used, is the flood itself. It is in this sense that Sartre ironically gave the title *The Words* to an early sketch.

No adequate account of this immense production can be given here. It is important to realize, however, that the reader whose interests are purely literary can gain only a fragmentary view of Sartre as writer, publicist, and ideologue. To complete the picture, he would have to plow through many pages that use several technical vocabularies and strange terms coined by Sartre himself. *Existentialism* was not his invention, actually, and it has also been applied, with excessive liberality, to the thinking of the German philosopher Martin Heidegger and of many others whose theories cannot possibly all be reconciled. Sartre's outlook, unlike Heidegger's, was rigidly dualistic. He maintained, in *Being and Nothingness*, that man had been regarded by philosophers and psychologists from the outside as though he were an object, and that previous attempts to deal with man's inwardness had actually smuggled the object inside him, in a disguised form. But the object is simply what it is, knowing no past and hoping for and fearing no future. Man, on the contrary, is divided against himself, looking backward and forward, and imagining how the present could be changed into what it is not (*néantiser*, "to nihilize," is Sartre's word for this procedure). Each man's project, no matter how varied the methods and envisaged goal may be, is fundamentally the endeavor to realize himself fully, like a solid object, but at the same time to realize, or be conscious, that he has become an unconscious object. He would thus have welded into unity the essence of the object and the existence of the subject. But this aim is self-contradictory, hence impossible, and man—to quote the last phrase of *Being and Nothingness*—"is a useless passion."

There are, on the path to this conclusion, many fascinating psychological analyses of great originality and depth. Some commentators have declared a number of the book's individual parts to be more impressive than the whole, and they find Sartre more successful as a psychologist than on the metaphysical level. For Sartre today, existentialism is but a trend, petit bourgeois in origin (since Sartre, its originator, is a petit bourgeois), within the one great ideology of the last hundred years and more: Marxism. Today, even when the psychology of one individual is at the center of his attention, he no longer finds it valid to consider this individual apart from the immediate social group and the wider society in which he has grown up and still lives.

One immense change that has taken place in Sartre's outlook can be simply stated. He had declared, in *Being and Nothingness,* that man was totally free—even though, as he paradoxically put it, man was "condemned to be free" and "free to commit himself." Now Sartre holds that man's freedom is but a nuance within societal patterns, whether these be firmly established, undergoing significant modification, or on the way out. However, freedom is no less precious and essential, because of that.

In this volume we present *No Exit*, one of Sartre's earliest and, almost certainly, the most frequently performed of his plays. The scene is laid in hell, and the play's three characters find themselves there not because one is a deserter and coward, another a Lesbian, and the third utterly frivolous—not even, really, because they have made a false use of their freedom, leading "inauthentic" lives. They are there because of their cruelty to other human beings on earth. They may be considered self-condemned to hell by their own self-centeredness, and by the need they have for other people, whom they nevertheless manipulate and abuse, to massage their egos. Now, in a hell that economizes on demons, instruments of torture, and so forth, they set about torturing each other.

Inès assumed that all was predestined because of her "nature." Garcin made all his actions—that is, those visible to the world at large—conform to his carefully cultivated image of himself as an idealist, intellectual, and courageous liberal. This imposed no restrictions on his private life, nor did it enable him to live up to his self-image and reputation in a moment of crisis. For Estelle, life was shaped exclusively by her inauthentic desire to be admired. To the mask of beauty and innocence, which she offered to the world, she sacrificed every other consideration. Like an actress, she assumed the roles assigned to her. It is because they have never made authentic decisions while alive that the three protagonists cannot decide to depart when the opportunity is offered them. Each becomes hell to the others, yet each needs the others, because none of the three can turn away from the past and confront an unknown future. Sartre has intensified this human drama of squandered human freedom by placing his characters in an Empire drawing room. It is this background of shabby gentility, a clinging to what is not, that symbolizes their outlook.

Many years ago, Sartre announced that he would undertake an "existential psychoanalysis" of Gustave Flaubert, while revealing on a number of occasions that he did not esteem the man behind the novels. In *L'Idiot de la famille* he has recently begun to carry out this promise. Two volumes, two thousand pages, perhaps one million words, lead us to the time when Flaubert published *Madame Bovary*, his first novel. In this connection, too, there has been a radical change in Sartre's outlook. First of all, the book could be written as currently conceived only because there is a huge amount of material available on Flaubert's childhood and the circumstances surrounding it. Reversing the old-fashioned deterministic practice of using an author's works simply as documents that throw light on the man, Sartre maintains that a man's life may enable us to understand better his writings, which realize in fantasy possibilities that the real world denies. But Sartre is not content merely to stand the old practice on its head. Utilizing the abundant materials and allowing himself, too, interpretative leaps that a cautious academic scholar would not even dream of, he works out and concretely exemplifies a method that flows in both directions: from milieu to individual, from individual to milieu. In this way, Sartre believes, it is possible to converge upon the complex truth of a man (a child, first of all) as society molds him, and also to illuminate more powerfully just what the individual has done with the measure of freedom that is his lot.

A study of these crushing dimensions is not going to be thoroughly read by very many people. It is conceivable, however, that the model Sartre has provided will significantly influence writers in the fields of literary history, social and political history, and sociology. In this way it may come to influence, at a considerable number of removes, and perhaps affecting public affairs as well as scholarly fields, the lives of people to whom the very name of Sartre is unknown. At all events, the serious investigator owes it to himself to examine whether he has anything to learn from this extraordinary work.

ALBERT CAMUS

Though Camus was a mature, established writer and recipient of the Nobel Prize for Literature at the time of his death in an automobile crash, it is nevertheless hard to shake off the feeling that his life's work had not been fully rounded out. Perhaps this is due to the shocking suddenness of his death, which was felt as a personal loss by many who had never known him. Perhaps he had arrived at a hiatus in his career, and stood on the verge of deciding, or discovering, in what direction he would next proceed. Or it may be that his writings themselves reveal him as a man dumbfounded, on the one hand, by the beauty of the world: a North African landscape shimmering in the heat, the swimmer's plunge and resurfacing in the sunlight, the unproblematical sensualities of growing up in the popular quarters of a French North African city. But the hideous, too, was a shock whose tremors refused to subside: shock at the callousness of men and at the yet grimmer reality of death and disease, to which even innocent children fall victim. Camus, though a professed unbeliever, nevertheless voiced his sense of outrage in terms that recall the questioning of Job and *The Brothers*

Karamazov of Dostoevsky, along with countless others throughout history: How can unmerited suffering be reconciled with the existence of a God who is both all-powerful and good?

This questioning, or accusation, emerges most clearly at one stage of what is, in terms of length, Camus' most ambitious work, when a priest gives the orthodox Christian answer to this difficulty but fails to convince his hearer. *The Plague*—which, Camus insists, is a chronicle and not a novel—is related in the first person by a doctor who witnesses the outbreak and ravages of pestilence in a town which, because of this, is segregated from the rest of the country. The onset, worsening, and slow ebb of the malady form the setting against which men play their varied parts, which range from selfless dedication to a devil-may-care attitude that might have brought about the deaths of all. Some critics regard the work as that rare literary phenomenon in modern times, a piece of allegorical writing. The plague-bringing rats would then be the Nazis, and the isolated town would represent France or Nazi-occupied Europe. However, it is impossible to demonstrate that Camus' fiction and historical reality coincide in every essential feature. No one in the town, not even the most frivolous individual, was actually on the side of the rats. The situation in France under Nazi domination was distressingly different.

Dostoevskian questions had already been posed by Camus in his first novel, *The Stranger*, published in 1942. As in *The Brothers Karamazov*, a man is shot and an innocent man is absurdly convicted of the deed. Though innocent of his father's murder, Dimitrof was condemned because of a series of events that seemed to point to him as the culprit. Meursault, hero of *The Stranger*, did actually commit murder, but one might say that the deed was done "in all innocence." It was a reflex movement that, in the glaring heat of noon, made him reach for the revolver in his pocket when the Arab's knife flashed menacingly.

On legal grounds Meursault should have been acquitted, since he had acted in self-defense. But what rendered him suspect and intolerable was his general behavior, which threatened to expose the duplicity of accepted mores. The first slip had been his failure to weep during his mother's funeral. Society, acting as judge, could not understand this individual who did not pay homage to the forces of the universal cliché. Condemned to death for his strangeness, the stranger is turned in on himself and forced to reflect as he has never reflected before. He emerges from his anguished pondering still in rebellion against his fate but able to rejoice in the "tender indifference" of the natural world, with its stars, night odors, salty air.

The hero's previous attitude (nothing "made sense," it "didn't matter") is an essential component, and does much to explain the success of the book. The failure of this stranger to understand, to respect, to abide by the conventional petty hypocrisies that keep society moving smoothly in the old grooves, make of him an exemplar of "alienated" or "turned off" youth, just as, within the limits of possibility of time and place, he had become a dropout. The number of Meursaults in circulation was to multiply mightily, after the end of World War II.

The Myth of Sisyphus, also published in 1942, restates in a more theoretical way what *The Stranger* had expressed in novelistic terms. Sisyphus, condemned by the gods to a labor of utter futility, was for Camus the archetype of the "absurd hero." But his Sisyphus, in a sense, escapes his punishment. Knowing that his work is in vain, that the boulder, once he has pushed it to the mountain top, will inevitably roll to the bottom, Sisyphus joyously carries out his repetitive task. "One ought to be Sisyphus, and happy," that is the lesson to be drawn. Camus finds happiness in activity and in a full and sensuous union with the world. Yet one question continues to obtrude itself. In this godless universe, where "everything is permitted," that is, where man is not held back by fear of divine retribution, is everything, indeed, permitted? This Dostoevskian question pursues Camus through novels, essays, and plays until he reaches the conclusion that man, in relation to his fellow man, can sin.

The Fall (1957), which once more takes up this problem of man's guilt and the extent of his freedom, again reminds us of *The Brothers Karamazov*, especially of the chapter on the Grand Inquisitor. The narrator and protagonist identifies himself as a "judge-penitent" and confesses to a life filled with self-love and vanity: "I, I, I is the refrain of my whole life." Vanity has led to duplicity, for the self-created image of self established a role that must be maintained and that must be acknowledged by others. The more virtuous this image, in terms of what society expects, the greater the applause that will be won. Yet the individual, basking in the warmth of this applause, may be situated at a far remove from any reality corresponding to the image. But he continues to live his lie, to play the role assigned to him partly by himself and partly by others, until something occurs that shatters his complacency.

The "I" of this novel is not unique; it is really "we." And this is generally true of Camus' highly stylized characters. They remain lifelike, nevertheless; though we do not expect to meet any individual so generically simplified, like a clown or a personage from the commedia dell' arte, these characters nonetheless possess stark reality.

"The Renegade" is also a narrative in the first person. This is the most savage and the most impressive of the stories that make up *Exile and the Kingdom* (published in 1958). In it Camus has created a masklike living thing that is horrifyingly real. A slave speaks, and the story centers around the problem of man's freedom. In this "renegade," slavery seems to be innate. His changes of allegiance leave him ever both slave and prisoner. It matters little that one of his masters is the god of love and the other a god of hatred. His dedication to the god of love has led him to flee the confines of the seminary and to set himself up as

a missionary among the most cruel savages. Eager to accept suffering and torture in the service of his lord, he believes that the faith radiating from him will conquer his oppressors. The actuality is very different.

In their harsh city of salt, these silent savages, dressed in black, are his undoubted masters, So he abandons the god of love (in actual fact, nothing of the sort but only the means by which he sought to establish his own domination) and pays homage to the Fetish, the god of hatred. Here, he believes, is "the principle of the world." Once more he is disappointed. The god of malice and hatred also turns out to be vulnerable. Soldiers arrive; they punish the worshippers of the Fetish. The missionary-turned-slave can achieve no second apostasy that would place him on the side of the big batallions. His tongueless mouth is stuffed with salt, and he dies a slave. Free men cannot be renegades because they have no masters. He who wanted to enslave others with the power of his word remains tongueless and can express his pain only in animallike grunts and cries.

The technique used by Camus in telling this story is rather extraordinary. It is an interior monologue. There is not even the nameless interlocutor of *The Fall*. Part of the story is a flashback. As he lies in wait for the new missionary, whom he has decided to kill, the renegade recapitulates his life. But though the flashback ends when, seemingly, he shoots the new missionary, the story goes on. Ramblingly, and between grunts of pain, the renegade finally acknowledges that the power of the sorcerer has been vanquished by the power of the soldiers, who are in the service of the god of love. Power replaces power, and the renegade's feeble gesture of aid has changed nothing. He dies, his mouth filled with salt. It is a bleak and despairing tale that Camus relates. We might do well to look back to his Sisyphus, happy in the recognition of the futility of his labor, in no man's service and rewarded by none.

LIVES, WRITINGS, AND CRITICISM
Biographical and critical works are listed only if they are available in English.

CHARLES BAUDELAIRE

LIFE. Born in Paris on April 9, 1821. In 1828 his widowed mother married Jacques Aupick, later to become a general and an ambassador. Throughout his life Baudelaire remained greatly attached to his mother and detested his stepfather. His independent behavior having caused alarm, in 1841 he was dispatched on a voyage to the tropics. The following year saw the beginning of his lifelong liaison with Jeanne Duval, a mulatto woman, and of his frequent changes of residence in Paris. Disturbed by his extravagance, the family in 1844 placed him under a financial tutelage which was never to be lifted. The revolutionary disturbances of 1848 awakened his enthusiasm, though later he expressed reactionary political views. The same year he published the first of his many translations from Edgar Allan Poe. His long-heralded collection of poems *Flowers of Evil (Les Fleurs du mal)*, which at last appeared in 1857, was judged to contain matter offensive to morals: author and publisher were fined, and obliged to omit six poems. Baudelaire, who had probably acquired a venereal infection many years before, noted in 1862 that he had felt on his forehead "the breeze from imbecility's wing." Two years later he left Paris, and his creditors, for Brussels. There, in 1866, he was stricken with aphasia and hemiplegia, and he was brought back to Paris. After prolonged suffering he died in his mother's arms, on August 31, 1867. He was interred beside the body of General Aupick.

CHIEF WRITINGS. *Flowers of Evil (Les Fleurs du mal,* 1857), translated by Lewis Piaget Shanks (1931), George Dillon and Edna St. Vincent Millay (1936), C. F. McIntyre (1947), Geoffrey Wagner (1949), Roy Campbell (1952), and William Aggeler (1954); *Artificial Paradises (Les Paradis artificiels,* 1860); *Aesthetic Curiosities (Curiosités esthétiques,* 1868); *Little Poems in Prose (Petits Poèmes en prose,* 1869) translated by A. Crowley (1928) and James Huneker (1929); *Romantic Art (L'Art romantique,* 1869); *Posthumous Works and Unedited Correspondence (Œuvres posthumes et correspondances inédites,* 1887), including material translated by Christopher Isherwood as *Intimate Journals* (1930); *Baudelaire as a Literary Critic* (1964), translated and edited by Lois B. and Francis E. Hyslop, Jr.; *Painter of Modern Life and Other Writings on Art* (1964), edited by Jonathan Mayne.

BIOGRAPHY AND CRITICISM. François Porché, *Charles Baudelaire* (1928); Peter Quennell, *Baudelaire and the Symbolists* (1929); S. A. Rhodes, *The Cult of Beauty in Charles Baudelaire* (1929); Enid Starkie, *Baudelaire* (1933); Margaret Gilman, *Baudelaire the Critic* (1943); Joseph D. Bennett, *Baudelaire, a Criticism* (1944); Marcel Raymond, *From Baudelaire to Surrealism* (1949); Jean-Paul Sartre, *Baudelaire* (1950); P. M. Jones, *Baudelaire* (1952); Martin Turnell, *Baudelaire* (1954); D. J. Mossop, *Baudelaire's Tragic Hero* (1961); Henri Peyre (ed.), *Baudelaire* (1962); G. Poulet, *Who Was Baudelaire?* (1969); Pierre Emmanuel, *Baudelaire: The Paradox of Redemptive Satanism* (1970); Walter Benjamin, *Charles Baudelaire: A Lyric Poet in the Era of High Capitalism* (1973); Alex de Jonge, *Baudelaire, Prince of Clouds* (1976); Garnet Rees, *Baudelaire, Sartre and Camus: Lectures and Commentaries* (1976); and Alfred E. Carter, *Charles Baudelaire* (1977).

STÉPHANE MALLARMÉ

LIFE. Etienne (called Stéphane) Mallarmé was born in Paris on March 18, 1842, into a settled bourgeois family. His father was Deputy Clerk in the Registry, and ancestors on both sides of the family had been minor government bureaucrats as far back as the French Revolution. Mallarmé's mother died when he was five, and his sister in 1857; the pain of their loss recurs in images of his later poetry. After graduating from boarding school in 1860, he worked for two years in his grandfather's office before deciding to become a teacher of English. In 1863 he received a teaching position in the southeastern provincial town of Tournon and moved there with his new wife, a young German woman named Maria Gerhard. Their daughter, Geneviève, was born in 1864. A son, Anatole, was born in 1871 and died in 1879.

Mallarmé began publishing poems and articles in 1862, although his output was always meager and he did not produce a collection in book form until 1887. Much of his work was published separately in different journals. His first important group of poems was published in 1866 in the new literary magazine *Le Parnasse Contemporain*, and his translations of Edgar Allan Poe appeared in 1872. Mallarmé was eager to move to Paris, the capital of the arts, but as a young teacher in the state educational system he was dependent on governmental assignments. Sent in 1886 to Besançon, and in 1867 to Avignon, he was finally able to move to Paris in 1871 where he taught at the Lycée Fontanes. Mallarmé was not a particularly good language teacher, had little aptitude for drills and discipline, and was often a figure of fun for his students. On the other hand, he was an important and charismatic figure for the young writers, artists, and musicians who heard him talk about the nature of poetry at the "Tuesdays," gatherings held in Mallarmé's home every Tuesday evening from 1880 until shortly before his death. Mallarmé's influence was widespread. In 1876 Edouard Manet illustrated Mallarmé's "L'Après-midi d'un faune" ("Afternoon of a Faun"), and in 1894 Claude Debussy composed his musical "Prelude" to the same text. Verlaine included Mallarmé in his account of the new poets, *Les Poètes maudits* (*The Doomed Poets*, 1883), and after Verlaine's death Mallarmé was elected "Prince of Poets" by his colleagues in 1896. Upon his retirement from teaching in 1894, Mallarmé lectured on poetry and experimented with different kinds of poetic form, including the typographical arrangements of *Un Coup de dès* (*Dice Thrown*, 1897) that foreshadowed modern concrete poetry. For years, he had worked on the notion of a universal "Book," a complicated text that would be performed and not merely read. Yet he himself finally felt that his vision had outstripped technical possibilities, and when he died on September 9, 1898, the work remained incompleted.

CHIEF WRITINGS. *Herodias*, translated by Clark Mills (1940); *Poems*, translated by Roger Fry (1951); *Selected Prose Poems, Essays, and Letters*, translated by Bradford Cook (1956); *Selected Poems*, translated by C. F. MacIntyre (1959); and *Mallarmé*, edited by Anthony Hartley (1965).

BIOGRAPHY AND CRITICISM. Wallace Fowlie, *Mallarmé* (1953); Joseph Chiari, *Symbolisme from Poe to Mallarmé* (1956); A. R. Chisholm, *Mallarmé's "L'Après-midi d'un Faune," An Exegetical and Critical Study* (1958); Haskell Block, *Mallarmé and the Symbolist Drama* (1963); Charles Mauron, *Introduction to the Psychoanalysis of Mallarmé* (1963); Robert G. Cohn, *Toward the Poems of Mallarmé* (1965); Robert G. Cohn, *Mallarmé's Masterwork* (1966); Guy Michaud, *Mallarmé* (1966); Bernard Weinberg, *The Limits of Symbolism* (1966); Norman Paxton, *The Development of Mallarmé's Prose Style* (1968);

Frederic C. St. Aubyn, *Stéphane Mallarmé* (1969); Thomas A. Williams, *Mallarmé and the Language of Mysticism* (1970); Ursula Franklin, *An Anatomy of Poesis: the Prose Poems of Stéphane Mallarmé* (1976); Judy Kravis, *The Prose of Mallarmé: The Evolution of a Literary Language* (1976); and Paula G. Lewis, *The Aesthetics of Stéphane Mallarmé in Relation to His Public* (1976).

ARTHUR RIMBAUD

LIFE. Jean Nicholas Arthur Rimbaud was born on October 20, 1854, in Charleville, a town of northeastern France. He proved to be an unusually gifted student, and was encouraged in his literary tastes and endeavors, and also in his revolutionary ardor, by Georges Izambard, his teacher. In 1870 he made the first of his flights from home, and spent ten days in jail as a vagrant. The following year, the poet Paul Verlaine invited Rimbaud to Paris. It was the beginning of a stormy relationship. Together they visited London and Brussels, where, in 1873, Verlaine shot Rimbaud through the wrist and was sentenced to two years' imprisonment. In the same year, at the age of nineteen, Rimbaud gave up the writing of poetry. He found his way to many parts of Europe, to Cyprus, to Java, and to Aden, where he worked for an exporting firm, later moving to Harar, in Abyssinia. As an independent trader he went on expeditions in Abyssinia, and engaged in gunrunning, but it cannot be definitely established that he trafficked in slaves. Falling ill in 1891, he returned to France, and his leg, which was in horrible condition, was amputated at Marseilles. He died on November 10, 1891.

CHIEF WRITINGS. *A Season in Hell* (*Une Saison en enfer*, 1873), translated by Louise Varèse (1945), Norman Cameron (1950); *Illuminations* (*Les Illuminations*, 1887), partially translated by Louise Varèse in *Prose Poems from The Illuminations* (1946); *Complete Poems* (*Poésies complètes*, 1895); *Complete Works* (*Œuvres complètes*, 1946); *Works* (*Œuvres*, 1950). Other translations are to be found in Lionel Abel, *Some Poems of Rimbaud* (1939); Norman Cameron, *Selected Verse Poems* (1942); *Complete Works with Selected Letters*, translated by Wallace Fowlie (1966).

BIOGRAPHY AND CRITICISM. Peter Quennell, *Baudelaire and the Symbolists* (1929); Konrad Bercovici, *Savage Prodigal* (1948); Marcel Raymond, *From Baudelaire to Surrealism* (1949); W. M. Frohock, *Rimbaud's Poetic Practice* (1963); Gwendolyn Bays, *The Orphic Vision* (1964); Wallace Fowlie, *Rimbaud* (1966); Enid Starkie, *Arthur Rimbaud* (revised edition, 1968); Yves Bonnefoy, *Rimbaud* (1973); Robert G. Cohn, *The Poetry of Rimbaud* (1973); Nathaniel Wing, *Present Appearances: Aspects of Poetic Structure in Rimbaud's*

Illuminations (1974); and F. C. St. Aubyn, *Arthur Rimbaud* (1975).

AUGUST STRINDBERG

LIFE. Strindberg was born in Stockholm in 1849 to a father of upper-class origins who was then living in financially distressed circumstances with a former domestic servant. He had married her only a short while before the birth of this child, the fourth of eleven children. Though the boy was highly intelligent and did well at school, he dropped out of the university, repelled by the milieu and embarrassed by his poverty. He began to write for the theater, and at the age of twenty-one was awarded a prize by the Swedish Academy. For eight years (1874–1882) a post in the Royal Library gave him social status and a livelihood. However, an underlying compulsion to brand himself an outsider was revealed in his bitingly sarcastic novel *The Red Room* (1879).

In the 1880's he proclaimed his left-wing sympathies, his atheism, and his adherence to naturalistic doctrines in literature. Toward the end of that decade, having become acquainted with the works of Friedrich Nietzsche (1844–1901), he moved toward a heroic individualism. During the 1890's, while living in Paris, he spent a great deal of time endeavoring to transmute "baser" substances into gold and in trying to prove that the so-called elements were actually compounds. He was hospitalized with severe injuries to his hands. During this period he was beset by frightening hallucinations. A record of this phase of his life is found in his *Inferno* (1898).

Although Strindberg moved in the direction of religious belief, he stopped short of adherence to Catholicism, or to any other creed. But it was a natural extension of his occult concerns that he should incorporate the Eastern doctrine of reincarnation into his view of things.

The last years of his life were spent in Sweden, and were marked by a renewal of the sensitivity to social ills that he had expressed in the 1880s. He died in 1912 of cancer of the stomach.

A significant source of turmoil in Strindberg's chaotic yet astonishingly productive existence was his difficulty in living either with or without a wife. Each of his three marriages ended in divorce—predictably, one might say, since he insisted that all three, ambitious and career-minded women, should content themselves with the roles of wife and mother. He gave vent to a fascination with and dread of women in much of his writing; e.g., in the plays *The Father* (1887) and *Dance of Death* (1901). In the 1890's he even came to believe that an international cabal of women was conspiring against him.

CHIEF WRITINGS. Plays: *Six Plays* (1955); *Selected History Plays*, 5 vols. (1955–59); *Three Plays* (1958); *Miss Julie and Other Plays* (1960); *Five Plays* (1960); *The Road to Damascus: A Trilogy* (1960); *Seven Plays* (1960); *The Chamber Plays* (1962); *The Plays of Strindberg*, vol. I (1964); *Selected Plays* (1964); *World Historical Plays* (1970). Other Works: *Legends: Autobiographical Sketches* (1912); *The People of Hemsö* (1959), also translated as *The Natives of Hemsö* (1965); *Letters of Strindberg to Harriet Bosse* (1959); *A. Madman's Defense* (1967), also translated as *A Madman's Manifesto* (1971); *Inferno* (1962), also translated in *Inferno, Alone, and Other Writings* (1968); *From an Occult Diary, Marriage with Harriet* (1965); *The Son of a Servant* (1966); *The Red Room* (1967); *The Scapegoat* (1967); *The Strindberg Reader* (1968).

BIOGRAPHY AND CRITICISM. Joan Bulman, *Strindberg and Shakespeare* (1933); G. A. Campbell, *Strindberg* (1933); Frida Strindberg (Frieda Uhl), *Marriage with Genius* (2d ed., 1940); Eric Bentley, *The Playwright as Thinker* (1946, 1955); Brita M. E. Mortensen and B. W. Downs, *Strindberg: An Introduction to His Life and Work* (1949); Elizabeth Sprigge, *The Strange Life of August Strindberg* (1949); Martin Lamm, *Modern Drama* (1952); Otto Heller, *Prophets of Dissent* (1960); Harry Levin, *The Power of Darkness* (1960); Alrik Gustafson, *A History of Swedish Literature* (1961); John Stewart Collis, *Marriage and Genius* (1963); Maurice Valency, *The Flower and the Castle* (1963); C. E. Dahlström, *Strindberg's Dramatic Expressionism* (2d ed., 1965); Robert Brustein, *The Theatre of Revolt* (1966); Carl Reinhold Smedmark (ed.) *Essays on Strindberg* (1966); Eric O. Johannesson, *The Novels of August Strindberg* (1968); Martin Lamm, *August Strindberg* (1971).

LUIGI PIRANDELLO

LIFE. Pirandello was born in Girgenti, Sicily, in 1867. Having convinced his father that he had no head for business, he went off to study at the University of Rome, later transferring to the University of Bonn, in Germany. He wrote his Ph.D. dissertation on the dialect of his native town. He married in 1894 and settled in Rome. For ten years he was able to write without having to earn a livelihood, since his father gave him a generous allowance. The failure of the family business put an end to that, and for many years Pirandello taught in Rome at the equivalent of a normal school for women. His home life was made burdensome by his wife's increasingly serious mental derangement. She died in 1918. Pirandello achieved fame as a playwright about 1920, and thereupon gave up his teaching position. He traveled in Italy and elsewhere in Europe, and in America, with a theatrical troupe that performed his own plays. In 1934 he was awarded the Nobel Prize for Literature. He died in 1936.

CHIEF WRITINGS. *Naked Masks: Five Plays* (1922, 1952); *Each in His Own Way, and Two Other Plays* (1923); *The One-Act Plays* (1928); *The Old and the Young*, 2 volumes (1928); *As You Desire Me* (1931); *Horse in the Moon, Twelve Short Stories* (1932); *Tonight We Improvise* (1932); *One, None and a Hundred Thousand: A Novel* (1933); *The Naked Truth, and Eleven Other Stories* (1934); *Better Think Twice About It and Twelve Other Stories* (1935); *Six Characters in Search of an Author* (1935); *The Outcast: A Novel* (1935); *The Medals and Other Stories* (1939); *Right You Are* (1954); *When Someone Is Somebody* (1956); *The Mountain Giants* (1958); *Short Stories* (1959); *To Clothe the Naked, and Two Other Plays* (1962); *Pirandello's One-Act Plays* (1964); *The Late Mattia Pascal* (1923, 1964); *Short Stories* (1965).

BIOGRAPHY AND CRITICISM. John Palmer, *Studies in the Contemporary Theater* (1927); Stark Young, *Immortal Shadows* (1948); Francis Fergusson, *The Idea of a Theater* (1949); Lander MacClintock, *The Age of Pirandello* (1951); Thomas Bishop, *Pirandello and the French Theater* (1960); Walter Starkie, *Luigi Pirandello, 1867–1936*, third revised edition (1965); Oscar Büdel, *Pirandello* (1966); Glauco Cambon (ed.), *Pirandello: A Collection of Essays* (1967); Domenico Vittorini, *The Drama of Luigi Pirandello* (1957, 1969); Jörn Moestrup, *The Structural Patterns of Pirandello's Work* (1972); Anne Paolucci, *Pirandello's Theater* (1974); and Gaspare Giudice, *Pirandello: a Biography* (1975).

MARCEL PROUST

LIFE. Proust was born on July 10, 1871, to a wealthy middle-class Parisian family. His father was a well-known doctor and professor of medicine, a Catholic of provincial background; his mother was a sensitive, intelligent woman of urban Jewish background who had much influence on her son. Proust fell ill with an asthma attack when he was nine, and thereafter spent his childhood holidays at a seaside resort, the model for Balbec, instead of in the country. In spite of his illness, Proust studied in Paris where he met many young writers and composers, and did a year of military service at Orleans. In 1890, he began to frequent the salons of the wealthy bourgeoisie and the aristocracy of the Faubourg Saint Germain, from which he drew much of the material for his portraits of society. He wrote for symbolist magazines like *Le Banquet* and *La Revue Blanche*, and published an elegant book, *Pleasures and Days* (1896), with drawings by Madeleine Lemaire and music by Reynaldo Hahn. In 1899 he also began to translate the English moralist and art critic, John Ruskin.

Proust's health started seriously to decline in 1902, and in addition he had lost both parents by 1905. The following year, his asthma worsening, he moved into a cork-lined, fumigated room at 102 Boulevard Haussmann, from which he emerged rarely and then only late at night for dinners with friends. There he wrote most of *Remembrance of Things Past*. Its first part (*Swann's Way*) was published at his own expense in 1913; World War I delayed publication of subsequent volumes, and Proust then began the painstaking revision and enlargement of the whole, from 1500 to 4000 pages, that was to occupy him until his death on November 18, 1922.

CHIEF WRITINGS. *Pleasures and Days* (*Les Plaisirs et les jours*, 1896); *Remembrance of Things Past* (*À la Recherche du temps perdu*, 1913–1927); *Sketches and Miscellanies* (*Pastiches et mélanges*, 1919); *Letters* (*Correspondance*, 6 vols. 1930–1936); *Jean Santeuil* (1952); *Contre Sainte-Beuve* (1954). Other volumes of translations: *Marcel Proust: A Selection from His Miscellaneous Writings*, edited by Gerard Hopkins (1948); *Marcel Proust on Art and Literature*, edited by Sylvia T. Warner (1958); *Letters of Marcel Proust*, edited by Mina Curtiss (1949); and *Letters to his Mother*, edited by George Painter (1957).

BIOGRAPHY AND CRITICISM. Samuel Beckett, *Proust* (1931); Harold March, *The Two Worlds of Marcel Proust* (1948); F. C. Green, *The Mind of Proust* (1949); André Maurois, *Proust, Portrait of a Genius* (1950); Charlotte Haldane, *Proust* (1951); Walter Strauss, *Proust and Literature: The Novelist as Critic* (1957); Richard Barker, *Marcel Proust, A Biography* (1958); George Painter, *Proust, The Early Years* (1959); *Proust: A Collection of Critical Essays*, edited by René Girard (1962); Milton Hindus, *A Reader's Guide to Marcel Proust* (1962); Howard Moss, *The Magic Lantern of Marcel Proust* (1962); William Bell, *Proust's Nocturnal Muse* (1963); Roger Shattuck, *Proust's Binoculars* (1963); Leo Bersani, *Marcel Proust: The Fictions of Life and Art* (1965); George Painter, *Proust: The Later Years* (1965); Germaine Brée, *Marcel Proust and Deliverance from Time* (revised edition 1969); George Stambolian, *Marcel Proust and The Creative Encounter* (1972); *In Search of Marcel Proust*, edited by Monique

Chefdor (1973); P. A. Spalding and R. H. Cortie, *A Reader's Handbook to Proust* (1974); Wallace Fowlie, *A Reading of Proust* (revised 1975); and Céleste Albaret, *Monsieur Proust*, translated by B. Bray (1977).

COLETTE

LIFE AND WRITINGS. Sidonie-Gabrielle Colette was born on January 28, 1873, to a prosperous family in Saint-Sauveur-en-Puisaye, a small town in Burgundy. Her father was an adventurous career officer from Toulon who was crippled by war wounds and pensioned off as tax collector to the provincial town; her mother was raised in Paris and in Brussels, where she lived among an artistic intelligentsia before a first marriage brought her to Saint-Sauveur. Her mother's directness, love of nature, and respect for life enormously influenced Colette, many of whose works recall her childhood home and the character of "Sido." In 1890, the family lost its money and was forced to move in with Colette's half-brother, a doctor in nearby Châtillon-Coligny.

Colette as a child was given much freedom: she roamed the woods, observed nature, and read voraciously (especially Balzac). She finished her formal education at sixteen, at the local schools, and at nineteen she married the Parisian music critic and man about town, Henry Gauthier-Villars, known as "Willy" and fifteen years her elder. "Willy," known for his many love affairs, his collection of pornography, and a literary reputation gained by publishing others' commissioned work under his own name, introduced her to Bohemian life. In need of money, he suggested to Colette that she write a story about her schoolgirl experiences, and signed himself the four novels that she wrote about "Claudine." After the success of the first novel Willy locked her in her room to write four hours a day, and under his supervision, she quickly acquired a discipline maintained for the rest of her life.

Colette's first work in her own name, as Colette Willy, was *Creatures Great and Small* (*Dialogues de bêtes*, 1904), imaginary dialogues between her dog Toby-Chien and cat Kiki-la-Doucette. In 1906 the couple separated, and were formally divorced in 1910. Colette supported herself until 1911 by dancing and acting in mime-dramas, one of which provoked a scandal in 1907; recollections of this period appear in *Music-Hall Sidelights* (*L'Envers du music-hall*, 1913). She went on tour as Claudine in a theatrical version of "Claudine à Paris," wrote novels, short stories, plays, and began writing columns for the Paris newspaper *Le Matin*. In 1912 she married *Le Matin*'s editor, Henry de Jouvenel; their daughter Colette was born in 1913. Her first important novel, *Chéri*, was published in 1920, and she was

named Chevalier de la Légion d'honneur in the same year.

In 1923 she separated from de Jouvenel, and also used the single name "Colette" to sign *Ripening Seed* (*Le Blé en herbe*), a novel whose serialization in *Le Matin* was terminated when readers protested its immorality. From then on Colette became increasingly well known, playing the character Léa in a dramatization of *Chéri*, writing further novels, and composing a libretto *The Boy and the Magic* (*L'Enfant et les sortilèges* 1925) for an opera by Maurice Ravel. In 1925 she met Maurice Goudeket, beginning a lifelong companionship that included marriage in 1935. Colette and Goudeket lived summers in a villa at St. Tropez in the south of France, with her cherished Russian blue cat, bulldog, and other animals. Here she produced some of her major works: *The Last of Chéri* (*La Fin de Chéri*, 1926), the autobiographical *Break of Day* (*La Naissance du jour*, 1928), *Sido* (1930), and the story of her first marriage, *My Apprenticeship* (*Mes Apprentissages*, 1936). In 1932 she opened a beauty salon in Paris, but it was not a financial success and closed a year later. From 1933 to 1938 she wrote drama criticism for Parisian weeklies, and in 1936 the Royal Academy of Belgium elected her to the chair of French literature and language previously held by the poetess Anna de Noailles.

When World War II came, Colette broadcast to America until the occupation of Paris, and then fled temporarily to the south of France. She and Goudeket soon returned to her cherished Paris, where Goudeket was arrested by the Nazis in 1941 and scheduled for deportation to Germany. After two months of appeals, he was freed and went into hiding for the rest of the war. Colette remained in Paris, still writing but kept more and more to her bed by a painful arthritis. Her lighthearted novel *Gigi* (1944), was followed by the autobiographical *Evening Star* (*L'Etoile vesper*, 1948) and *The Blue Lantern* (*Le Fanal bleu*, 1949). She was elected to the Académie Goncourt in 1945, becoming president in 1949; in 1953 she was made Grand Officer of la Légion d'honneur. She died on August 3, 1954, and was given a State funeral on August 7, the only woman in France to be so honored, and in spite of the fact that the Archbishop of Paris refused to allow Christian rites at her burial.

BIOGRAPHY AND CRITICISM. *Colette, Music-Hall Sidelights* (*L'Envers du music-hall*, 1913, tr. Anne-Marie Callimachi 1958); Colette, *My Apprenticeship* (*Mes Apprentissages*, 1936, tr. Helen Beauclerk 1957); Margaret Crosland, *Madame Colette, A Provincial in Paris* (1953); Maurice Goudeket, *Close to Colette* (*Près de Colette*, 1956, tr. Enid McLeod 1957); Elaine Marks, *Colette*

(1960); Margaret Davies, *Colette* (1961); Margaret Crosland, *Colette: The Difficulty of Loving* (1973); Robert D. Cottrell, *Colette* (1974); Colette, *Looking Backwards* (*Journal à rebours*, 1941, and *De ma fenêtre*, 1942, tr. David Le Vay, 1975); Yvonne Mitchell, *Colette: A Taste for Life* (1975). (See also by Colette: *My Mother's House, The Pure and the Impure, Sido, The Evening Star, The Blue Lantern*.)

THOMAS MANN

LIFE. Thomas Mann was born in the north German town of Lübeck on June 6, 1875. His father was a grain merchant and head of the family firm; his mother came from a German-Brazilian family and was known for her beauty and musical talent. Mann disliked the scientific emphasis of his secondary education and left school in 1894 after repeating two years. Rejoining his family in Munich, where they had moved after his father's death in 1891, he worked as an unpaid apprentice in a fire insurance business, but found more interest in university lectures in history, political economy, literature, and art. From 1896 to 1898 he lived and wrote in Italy, returning to Munich in 1898 for a two-year stint as manuscript reader for the satiric weekly *Simplicissimus*. He served less than three months in the Royal Bavarian Infantry, and after his discharge for poor health devoted himself to writing. In 1905 he married Katia Pringsheim; they had six children.

Through his writings up to and during World War I, Mann established himself as an important spokesman for modern Germany. His early conservatism and defense of authoritarian government later gave way to outspoken criticism of Nazi aims and methods. Mann went into voluntary exile on Hitler's becoming Chancellor in 1933. He had received the Nobel Prize in 1929, and was already an international figure. From 1933 to 1938 he lived in Switzerland, where he cofounded and edited the periodical *Measure and Worth*. In 1938 he came to America where he wrote, lectured, broadcast attacks on Hitlerism, and helped other exiles. Mann was Consultant in Germanic Literature to the Library of Congress in 1942 and became an American citizen in 1944. After the war, he visited Germany but refused to live there. He remained in America until 1952, when he moved to Switzerland. He died in Zurich on August 12, 1955.

CHIEF WRITINGS. *Buddenbrooks* (1900); "Tonio Kröger" (1903); *Royal Highness* (*Königliche Hoheit*, 1909); *Death in Venice* (*Der Tod in Venedig*, 1913); *Of the German Republic* (*Von deutscher Republik*, 1923); *The Magic Mountain* (*Der Zauberberg*, 1924); *Mario and the Magician* (*Mario und der Zauberer*, 1929); *Joseph and His Brethren* (*Joseph und seine Brüder*, 4 vols., 1933–

1944); *Lotte in Weimar* (1939), translated as *The Beloved Returns* (1940); *Doctor Faustus* (*Doktor Faustus*, 1947); *The Holy Sinner* (*Der Erwählte*, 1951); *Confessions of Felix Krull, Confidence Man* (*Bekenntnisse des Hochstaplers Felix Krull*, 1954). Other volumes of translations are *Stories of Three Decades* (1936); *Selected Essays* (1941); *Order of the Day* (1942); *Essays of Three Decades* (1946); *The Thomas Mann Reader*, edited by J. W. Angell (1950); and *Letters of Thomas Mann*, edited by Richard and Clara Winston (1970).

BIOGRAPHY AND CRITICISM. H. J. Weigand, *Thomas Mann's Novel Der Zauberberg* (1933); J. G. Brennan, *Thomas Mann's World* (1942); G. Lukacs, *Essays on Thomas Mann* (1949, revised and translated 1964); H. Hatfield, *Thomas Mann* (1951); K. W. Jonas, *Fifty Years of Thomas Mann Studies, A Bibliography of Criticism* (1955; new volumes forthcoming); R. H. Thomas, *Thomas Mann: The Meditation of Art* (1956); F. Kaufmann, *Thomas Mann: The World as Will and Representation* (1957); E. Heller, *The Ironic German* (1958); Thomas Mann, *A Sketch of My Life* (rev. ed. 1960); *Thomas Mann: A Collection of Critical Essays*, edited by H. Hatfield, (1964); H. Bürgin and H. O. Mayer, *Thomas Mann: A Chronicle of His Life* (1969); E. Kahler, *The Orbit of Thomas Mann* (1969); R. Hollingdale, *Thomas Mann: A Critical Study* (1971); W. A. Berendsohn, *Thomas Mann: Artist and Partisan in Troubled Times* (1973); and T. J. Reed, *Thomas Mann: The Uses of Tradition* (1974).

RAINER MARIA RILKE

LIFE. Born in Prague, Austria-Hungary, on December 4, 1875, of Bohemian and Alsatian stock. The family had strong military traditions, and between 1886 and 1891 the sensitive boy spent utterly wretched years in the military academies of Sankt Pölten and Weisskirchen. Abandoning the prospect of a military career, he attended the commercial school at Linz for a year, and then was allowed to study the humanities at the universities of Prague and Munich. From 1899 on, he traveled extensively. He made two trips to Russia, in 1899 and 1900, meeting Tolstoy and acquiring a lively interest in Russian language and literature. He next spent two years in an artists' colony at Worpswede, near Bremen, Germany, and there met Clara Westhoff, a sculptress, whom he married in 1901. A daughter was born in 1902, but henceforth Rilke and his wife never again lived for any long period together. Rilke was frequently a guest at the houses of titled and wealthy people, and for a while, in 1905–1906, he acted as secretary to the sculptor Rodin, whom he revered. In 1912, at the castle of Duino, which is situated overlooking the Adriatic not far from Trieste (then Austrian territory), Rilke first conceived his *Duino Elegies (Duineser Elegien)*. But inspiration deserted him, the war of 1914–1918 numbed his spirit, and not until 1922, at Muzot, his residence in French Switzerland, did the *Elegies* "write themselves" in the space of eight days, preceded and followed by the totally unexpected gift of the *Sonnets to Orpheus (Die Sonnette an Orpheus)*, first and second parts. On December 29, 1926, the poet died, after considerable suffering, of myeloid leukemia. Its first symptom was the improper healing of the scratch of a rose thorn. He had been plucking roses to give to a young girl whose visit he expected.

CHIEF WRITINGS. *Stories of God (Geschichten vom lieben Gott*, 1900), translated by M. D. Herter Norton and Nora Purtscher-Wydenbruck (1932); *The Book of Pictures (Das Buch der Bilder*, 1902, and enlarged edition, 1906); *Auguste Rodin* (1903); *The Book of Hours (Das Stundenbuch*, 1905), translated in part by Babette Deutsch in *Poems from the Book of Hours* (1941); *The Tale of the Love and Death of Cornet Christopher Rilke (Die Weise von Liebe und Tod des Cornets Christoph Rilke*, 1906), translated by M. D. Herter Norton (1932); *New Poems (Neue Gedichte)*, 2 vols., 1907–1908; *The Notebooks of Malte Laurids Brigge (Die Aufzeichnungen des Malte Laurids Brigge*, 1910), translated by M. D. Herter Norton (1949); *Duino Elegies (Duineser Elegien*, 1923), translated by J. B. Leishman and Stephen Spender (1939); *Sonnets to Orpheus (Die Sonnette an Orpheus*, 1923), translated by M. D. Herter Norton (1942). See also *Sonnets to Orpheus* [and] *Duino Elegies*, translated by Jessie Lemont (1945). For other translations see Richard von Mises, *Rilke in English: A Tentative Bibliography* (1947).

BIOGRAPHY AND CRITICISM. F. Olivero, *Rainer Maria Rilke* (1931); E. C. Mason, *Rilke's Apotheosis* (1938); W. Rose and C. G. Houston (eds.), *Rainer Maria Rilke: Aspects of His Mind and Poetry* (1938); E. M. Butler, *Rainer Maria Rilke* (1941); C. M. Bowra, *The Heritage of Symbolism* (1943); Nora Purtscher, *Rilke, Man and Poet* (1949); F. W. van Heerikhuizen, *Rainer Maria Rilke* (1952); H. E. Holthusen, *Rainer Maria Rilke* (1952); H. W. Belmore, *Rilke's Craftsmanship* (1954); Geoffrey H. Hartman, *The Unmediated Vision* (1954); H. W. Belmore, *Rilke's Craftsmanship* (1955); W. L. Graff, *Rainer Maria Rilke* (1956); H. Frederic Peters, *Rainer Maria Rilke* (1960); Romano Guardini, *Rilke's Duino Elegies* (1961); Eudo C. Mason, *Rilke, Europe and the English-speaking World* (1961); J. R. von Salis, *Rainer Maria Rilke: The Years in Swit-*

zerland (1964); and Priscilla Shaw, *Rilke, Valéry and Yeats* (1964).

FRANZ KAFKA

LIFE. Born on July 3, 1883, in Prague, then an important town of the Austro-Hungarian Empire. The son of a well-to-do middle-class Jewish merchant, he studied at the German University in Prague, obtaining his law degree in 1906. He then worked for many years in the workmen's insurance division of an insurance company that had official state backing. He was much impressed by his father and his father's satisfactory adjustment to life in the role of breadwinner and head of a family, and was troubled by a sense of his own contrasting inadequacy. For several years he entertained the idea of marriage, and he became engaged, but the projected marriage did not take place. In 1923 he met Dora Dymant, descendant of a prominent Eastern Jewish family, an excellent Hebrew scholar and a gifted actress. At the end of July he left Prague and established himself with her in Berlin. "I found an idyll," writes Max Brod of his visits to him there. "At last I saw my friend in a happy frame of mind; his physical condition however had grown worse." He had had several attacks of tuberculosis, and died, after considerable suffering, on June 3, 1924.

CHIEF WRITINGS. "The Judgment" ("Das Urteil," 1913), and "In the Penal Colony" ("In der Strafkolonie," 1919), translated in *The Penal Colony* (1948); *The Trial (Der Prozess*, 1925); *The Castle (Das Schloss*, 1926); *America (Amerika*, 1927); *Collected Works (Gesammelte Schriften*, 1935–1937); *The Diaries (Tagebücher*, 1951), translated (from the unpublished manuscript) by Joseph Kresh, 2 vols. (1948–1949); *Letters to Milena (Briefe an Milena*, 1952). Other translations are available in *Parables in German and English* (1947); *Selected Short Stories*, translated by Willa and Edwin Muir (1952); *Wedding Preparations in the Country, and Other Posthumous Writings*, translated by Ernest Kaiser and Eithne Wilkins (1954); and *I Am a Memory Come Alive; Autobiographical Writings*, edited by Nahum Glatzer (1974).

BIOGRAPHY AND CRITICISM. For biography see Max Brod, *Franz Kafka* (1947); G. Janouch, *Conversations with Kafka* (1953, 1971). For criticism see Paul Goodman, *Kafka's Prayer* (1947); Charles Neider, *Kafka: His Mind and Art* (1949); Antel Flores and Homer Swanda (eds.), *Franz Kafka Today* (1958); Ronald D. Gray (ed.), *Kafka* (1963); Mark Spilka, *Dickens and Kafka* (1963); Angel Flores (ed.), *The Kafka Problem* (1946, 1963); Margarete Buber-Neumann, *Mistress to Kafka: The Life and Death* of Milena (1966); Heinz Politzer, *Franz Kafka: Parable and Paradox* (1962, revised and enlarged edition, 1967); Martin Greenberg, *The Terror of Art: Kafka and Modern Literature* (1968); Herbert Tauber, *Franz Kafka: An Interpretation of His Works* (1968); Johann Bauer, *Kafka and Prague* (1971); Franz Baumer, *Franz Kafka* (1971); Anthony Thorlby, *Kafka: A Study* (1972); Deborah Crawford, *Franz Kafka: Man Out of Step* (1973); Patrick Bridgwater, *Kafka and Nietzsche* (1974); *Franz Kafka: A Collection of Criticism*, edited by Leo Hamalian (1974); Franz Kuna, *Kafka: Literature as Corrective Punishment* (1974); and John Hibberd, *Kafka in Context* (1975).

ISAK DINESEN

LIFE. Karen Dinesen was born on April 17, 1885, at Rungstedlund, a small estate about fifteen miles north of Copenhagen. As a child, she was very close to her father, an adventurous man who served in several European wars, was a French officer in the Franco-Prussian War, and spent two years among Indian tribes in the United States; he committed suicide in 1895. Dinesen, her two brothers, and two sisters were all raised by their mother, an intelligent, politically liberal, somewhat authoritarian woman, with the close assistance of a grandmother and an aunt who was a determined champion of women's rights and Unitarianism. The children were all tutored by the grandmother and a retired schoolteacher instead of being sent to school in the city, and Dinesen rebelled against the strict Victorian atmosphere of her home. She much preferred to visit her father's brother at Katholm, enjoying their freer life and associations with Danish aristocracy. It was at this time that she discovered Shakespeare, whose poetic imagination and verbal artistry had a great influence on her own writing.

Dinesen studied at the school of design in Copenhagen, enrolled in 1902 in the Danish Royal Academy of Art, and in 1910 spent some time in Paris ostensibly to study painting but actually enjoying the cosmopolitan life of that international city. She maintained her interest in drawing and painting throughout life, but realized it would not be a career for her. Though in 1908–09, under the pen name Osceola, she published two stories in the Danish periodical *Tilskueren*, she did not consider writing to be her career at this time.

In January 1912 Dinesen married a Swedish cousin, the Baron Bror von Blixen-Finecke, and moved to Africa to take up farming on a coffee plantation near Nairobi. The marriage was not a success, as her husband preferred big-game hunting to farming or literature, and long before the formal separation in 1921, and the divorce in 1925, she had been left alone in charge of the Kenya plantation. A narrative of this period, including her wartime experience and love for the Englishman Denys Finch-Hatton, is recorded in the autobiographical *Out of Africa* (1937).

In 1920, when her health began to deteriorate, Dinesen traveled to Denmark for treatment of a condition (probably venereal disease) that she blamed on her husband, hid from her mother, and—insufficiently treated—was to cause her recurrent and severe pain for the rest of her life. On her return to Kenya, the farm became increasingly unprofitable and had to be sold. In 1931 she returned to Denmark, settled permanently in Rungstedlund, and with her brother's encouragement began to compose her first collection of stories. *Seven Gothic Tales*, published in America in 1934 under the pen name Isak Dinesen, met with an enthusiastic reception. She rewrote the book in Danish for publication in Denmark in 1935, still using the name Isak Dinesen; later she used Isak Dinesen only for works appearing in English, and Karen Blixen for the same works in Danish. Dinesen wrote most of her work first in English, but always counted on writing a Danish version; the notes for her books are written both in Danish and in English.

As World War II approached, Dinesen, concerned by Mussolini's plans to invade Africa, tried in vain to become a war correspondent. When this failed, she resumed her writing with *Out of Africa* (1937, 1938 in English). She was able to visit Berlin briefly as a correspondent in March 1940, and returned home just before the German invasion of Denmark on April 9. Dinesen's house was part of a Resistance network that enabled 7000 Jews to escape to Sweden. During the war years she wrote the *Winter's Tales* (1942) and had the English version smuggled out to America via Sweden. She also wrote a light novel, *The Angelic Avengers* (1944, English version 1946) under the name of Pierre Andrézel.

After the war, as Dinesen's reputation increased, she became the focus of a new literary group associated with the 1948–53 magazine *Heretica*, a group of young writers who rebelled against the current socialist-realist mode and tried to create a more Romantic literature with fantasy, wit, and daring. She continued to write her tales (*Last Tales*, 1957; *Anecdotes of Destiny*, 1958) and memories of Africa (*Shadows on the Grass*, 1961), but was often in great pain as her health became worse and she underwent a series of spinal operations. A novel composed of related stories, *Albondocani*, was never finished and appears only as the first section in the *Last Tales*. She died on September 7, 1962.

BIOGRAPHY AND CRITICISM. Eric O. Johannesson, *The World of Isak Dinesen*

(1961); Robert W. Langbaum, *The Gayety of Vision* (1965); Parmenia Migel, *Titania: The Biography of Isak Dinesen* (1967); Donald Hannah, *Isak Dinesen and Karen Blixen: the mask and the reality* (1971); Thomas R. Whissen, *Isak Dinesen's Aesthetics* (1973); Thomas Dinesen, *My Sister, Isak Dinesen* (1975, transl. Joan Tate).

ANNA AKHMATOVA

LIFE. Anna Andreevna Gorenko was born June 11, 1889, in a suburb of Odessa in Russia. Her father was a maritime engineer and mathematics professor; her mother was a strong-willed woman of populist sympathies who belonged to an early revolutionary group. (The *nom de plume* Akhmatova is the name of the poet's maternal great-grandmother.) The family was well off, and soon moved to Tsarskoe Selo, a small town outside St. Petersburg (now Leningrad) which had also been the summer residence of the tsars for more than a century.

Akhmatova turned to poetry after reading the work of Innokenti Annesky, a poet who had also been principal of the Tsarskoe Selo school. In 1910 she married a young poet Nikolai Gumilev; she visited Paris in 1910 and again in 1911, meeting many writers and artists, including Modigliani, who sketched her several times and read aloud with her the Symbolist poetry of Paul Verlaine. In 1912 she traveled with Gumilev in Northern Italy; in the same year, she published her first collection of poems, *Evening*, and gave birth to her only child, a son, Lev. Spending their winters in the literary society of St. Petersburg, Akhmatova, Gumilev, and Osip Mandelshtam were the leading figures of a small new literary movement, Acmeism, joining forces to reject the romantic quasi-religious aims of Russian Symbolism and to promote their own work.

Akhmatova's second volume of poetry, *The Rosary*, brought her wide fame and was quickly sold out; her third collection, *The White Flock*, published a month before the 1917 revolution, received little attention outside St. Petersburg. During the civil war that followed the execution of the Royal Family, Akhmatova refused to flee abroad, and her political difficulties began. Though she and Gumilev had been divorced in 1918, his arrest and execution for counter-revolutionary activities in 1921 put her own status into question, and after *Anno Domini MCMXXI* appeared in 1922 she was no longer able to publish, and was forced into the unwilling withdrawal from public activity that Russians of the time called "the internal emigration." Political harassment continued, however, aimed now at her son, who was arrested in 1934 and imprisoned again from 1937 to 1941, and yet again from 1949 to 1956. During the Second World War her patriotic activities and resistance poems earned her a brief rehabilitation; she was even allowed in 1940 to publish a new collection, *From Six Books*. But the edition was recalled by officials within six months, and in 1946 she was expelled from the Writer's Union. Unable to publish, Akhmatova supported herself between 1946 and 1958 by translating poetry from other languages; in 1950, hoping to obtain her son's release, Akhmatova wrote some peace poems in the approved Soviet style, but to no effect.

During the slow thaw that followed Stalin's death, Akhmatova was rehabilitated. In 1958 she was even elected to an honorary position on the executive council of the Writer's Union. She published a new collection called *Poems* in that same year, and in 1964 was allowed to travel to Italy to receive the Taormina poetry prize. She died on March 5, 1966.

CHIEF WRITINGS. *Evening* (1912); *Rosary* (1914); *White Flock* (1917); *Anno Domini MCMXXI* · (1922); *From Six Books* (1940); *Poems* (1958); *A Poem Without a Hero* (1960); *Requiem* (1963); *The Course of Time* (1965). Translations: in *Modern Russian Poetry*, edited by Vladimir Markov and Merrill Sparks (1967), *Anna Akhmatova, Selected Poems*, translated by Richard McKane, essay by Andrei Sinyavsky (1969); *Poems of Akhmatova*, translated by Stanley Kunitz with Max Hayward (1973); and *Anna Akhmatova, Selected Poems*, translated by Walter Arndt, Robin Kemball, Carl Proffer (1976). The last three volumes also contain introductory material.

BIOGRAPHY AND CRITICISM. Sam Driver, *Anna Akhmatova* (1972); Jeanne van der Eng-Liedmeier and Kees Verheul, *Tale Without a Hero and Twenty-Two Poems by Anna Akhmatova* (1973); and Amanda Haight, *Anna. Akhmatova: A Poetic Pilgrimage* (1977).

PAUL ÉLUARD

LIFE. Eugene-Emile-Paul Grindel, who later took his great-grandmother's name and became Paul Éluard, was born on December 14, 1895, in the north Paris suburb of Saint-Denis. His father was a bookkeeper and his mother a seamstress. Although the family was relatively well off, when Éluard was thirteen he was sent to school for a practical education, rather than the more literary education of the lycée which his fellow surrealist André Breton received. In 1912, on summer vacation in Switzerland, he was struck with lung disease and had to spend two years in the Swiss sanatorium of Clavadel, where he read a great deal, especially Symbolist and modern poetry. Here also he met a young Russian student Helen Dimitrovnie Diakonova ("Gala"), and the two became unofficially engaged.

In 1914 both father and son were drafted. Éluard began in the health services but later was moved, at his own request, into the infantry. In 1916 Gala arrived in Paris, and they were married in February 1917; Éluard had previously converted (like his wife) to Roman Catholicism, to the great displeasure of his freethinking socialist father. A daughter, Cécile, was born in 1918.

Éluard published his first poems in 1917 ("Duty and Anxiety," *Le Devoir et l'inquiétude*) and 1918 ("Poems for Peace," *Poèmes pour la paix*.) In 1918 he also met André Breton, beginning a friendship that lasted for many years. Éluard, Breton, and others collaborated in the first Surrealist review, titled ironically (*Literature*, 1919–24), and in 1924—perhaps inspired by Breton's poem "Let Everything Go!" (*Lâchez-tout!*), perhaps by Gala's departure with a friend—Éluard set off on a trip around the world. Gala found him in Singapore and they returned home, but themes of love and anguished separation dominate the poetry of this period ("Dying of Not Dying," *Mourir de ne pas mourir*, 1925, "Capital of Pain," *Capitale de la douleur*, 1926 and "Love, Poetry," *L'Amour, la poésie*, 1929) until Gala finally left him to marry the painter Salvador Dali in 1929. In the same year, however, he met Nusch (Maria Benz) who was to become in 1934 his second wife and the inspiration for his next books of love poetry.

Éluard collaborated regularly with Breton in Surrealist manifestoes, reviews, and other publications. In the Second Manifesto of Surrealists (1930), he and Breton broke with a number of former Surrealists who were no longer willing to accept Breton's leadership. In the same year, Éluard, Breton, and René Char published "Slow, Men Working," (*Ralentir travaux*), a series of poems written collectively by the three poets, and Éluard and Breton published "The Immaculate Conception (*L'Immaculée Conception*). In 1927 he joined the Communist Party, only to break with it again—like Breton—when the Party proved suspicious of Surrealist methods. There is political poetry in "The Public Rose" (*La Rose publique* 1934) and in "Fertile Eyes" (*Les Yeux Fertiles*, 1936) as Éluard like many other artists and intellectuals was shocked by the wanton destruction of the Spanish Civil War. A break with Breton came in 1938 over the issue of commitment; during World War II, when Breton and Péret fled to the United States and Mexico, Éluard abandoned any uncommitted Surrealist attitude, re-entered the Party, and joined the Resistance. He now wrote poetry to sustain and encourage the French, books like "Poetry and Truth (*Poésie et vérité*, 1942) and individual poems like the famous "Liberté," passed out in leaflets or memorized. By the end of the war, Éluard had become a national poet.

Nusch died in 1946, and Éluard remarried in 1950. He kept writing steadily almost until his death: love poems, political poems, longer and more didactic poetry—even, in 1952, the first volume of an anthology of writings on art. On November 18, 1952, he died of a heart attack in Paris.

BIOGRAPHY AND CRITICISM. J. H. Matthews, *Surrealist Poetry in France* (1969); Mary Ann Caws, *The Poetry of Dada and Surrealism* (1970); Robert Nugent, *Paul Éluard* (1974).

ANDRÉ BRETON

LIFE AND WRITINGS. André Breton was born in Tinchebray, Normandy, on February 19, 1896. He was an only child, the son of a small businessman to whom he was quite close and a straightlaced, puritanical mother whom he resented. The family moved soon to Lorient, a fishing port in Brittany, where Breton received his early schooling. From 1907 to 1912 he studied at the Lycée Chaptal in Paris; in 1913, he enrolled at his parents' urging in medical studies at the University of Paris (Sorbonne), but preferred reading the Symbolist poets, Apollinaire, and Lautréamont. Early poems published in a neo-Symbolist review, "The Phalanx" (*La Phalange*), in 1941 show the influence of Mallarmé.

Breton was drafted in 1915, and became a medical assistant. In 1917 he was assigned to the neuropsychiatric center at Saint-Dizier, where he found that there was a nightmare coherence to the hallucinations of shell-shocked soldiers. This belief in the consistency of the unconscious mind was confirmed by his reading of Pierre Janet, a professor of psychiatric medicine and former teacher of Jung whose interest in automatic writing and the notion of a collective self is echoed in Breton's later work. Breton later read Freud and met him in Vienna, but the chief influence seems to be that of Janet.

In 1916–17 he read Jarry and Lautréamont, and began to reject the aesthetic and intellectual poetry of the Symbolists. A first volume of poetry, Mount of Piety (*Mont de Piété*, a term also used for a pawnshop) collected his earlier poems up to the Dada experiments. From 1919 to 1921, Breton participated in the Dada Movement with Pierre Soupault, Louis Aragon, Paul Eluard, and Benjamin Péret. Breton, Soupault, and Aragon founded the first Surrealist review, *Literature* (1919–24), and in 1920 he wrote with Philippe Soupault the first "automatic" text, Magnetic Fields (*Les Champs magnétiques*). He married Simone Kahn in 1921; they were divorced in 1931. In 1922 he took part in experiments in hypnotic sleepwriting, and in 1924 issued the first *Manifesto of*

Surrealism, followed by the automatic texts of Soluble Fish (*Poisson soluble*). The first exposition of Surrealist art took place in 1925, and Breton and Robert Desnos wrote the preface for a catalogue of works by Arp, Chirico, Ernst, Klee, Masson, Miro, Picasso, and Man Ray. In the same year, he took over direction of the chief Surrealist review, *La Révolution surréaliste.*

Breton entered the Communist Party in 1926, but it was an uneasy alliance since from the beginning he could not accept political control of Surrealist expression (see *Legitimate Defense/Légitime Défense,* 1926). In 1929 he founded and edited the journal *Le Surréalisme au service de la révolution).* (*Surrealism in the Service of the Revolution*). Breton put Surrealist freedom above everything, however, and—with Eluard—left the Party after the "Aragon affair" in which his former friend proclaimed his willingness to accept political direction. It was a time of bitter quarrels. The *Second Manifesto of Surrealism* in 1930 denounced Artaud, Desnos, and other early friends and brought into the open the factionalism that has typically marked the Surrealist movement.

Breton was writing both prose and poetry at this time: the joint poems of "Slow, Men Working" (*Ralentir Travaux*) with René Char and Paul Eluard in 1930, and simulated states of mind in the lyrical prose of "The Immaculate Conception" (*L'Immaculée Conception*) with Paul Eluard, the same year; *Nadja,* an autobiographical "novel" in 1928; and his own poems in "Free Union" (*L'Union libre,* 1931), "The White-haired Revolver" (*Le Revolver à cheveux blancs*) and "Communicating Vessels" (*Les Vases communicants*) in 1932. "Air of Water" (*L'air de l'eau*) and "Daybreak" (*Point du jour*) in 1934. In 1934 also he met his second wife, Jacqueline Lamba, who was to be the mother of his cherished daughter Aube. Breton, whom his detractors called the "Pope" of Surrealism and who was certainly its spokesman, was busy publicizing the movement. In 1934 he wrote *What is Surrealism?* and in 1938, with Eluard, an *Abridged Dictionary of Surrealism.* In 1936 and 1938 he organized International Surrealist Exhibitions in London and Paris, and in 1938 visited Mexico to collaborate with the exiled Russian revolutionary leader Leon Trotsky in setting up and writing a manifesto for an "International Federation of Independent Revolutionary Art."

When World War II came and the Germans occupied France, Breton fled to the United States where he was an announcer for the Voice of America, and tried to keep the idea of Surrealism alive. He founded the review *VVV* in New York with Marcel Duchamp, David Hare, and Max Ernst in 1941, wrote the *Prolegomenon to a Third Manifesto of Surrealism* (or not), and directed an International Exhibit of Surrealism in New York in 1942. In 1945, divorced again, he married Elisa Bindhoff; in the same year he visited the American Southwest and Haiti, where his lectures set off a student riot and general strike. He returned to Paris in 1946, where he organized another International Exhibit of Surrealism the next year. At this time, however, Eluard was being hailed as a national poet, following his wartime commitment to political poetry, and the Surrealists were accused of irrelevance and self-indulgence. Breton did not change his attitude: he actively supported the "Citizens of the World" movement from 1948 to 1950, refused the Key to the City of Paris in 1950 as he had refused all honors, and helped found a series of Surrealist reviews: *Néon, Medium, Le Surréalisme même,* and *La Brêche.* Breton remained the key figure in a movement that was no longer the same as the 1924 revolt, but continued to attract new adherents. He died in Paris on September 28, 1966.

BIOGRAPHY AND CRITICISM. Michel Carrouges, *André Breton and the Basic Concepts of Surrealism* (*André Breton et les données fondamentales du surréalisme,* 1959, transl. Maura Prendergast 1974); J. H. Matthew, *An Introduction to Surrealism* (1965); J. H. Matthews, *André Breton* (1967); Clifford Browder, *André Breton, Arbiter of Surrealism* (1968); Mary Ann Caws, *The Poetry of Dada and Surrealism* (1970); Anna Balakian, *André Breton, Magus of Surrealism* (1971); Mary Ann Caws, *André Breton* (1971); J. H. Matthews, *Towards the Poetics of Surrealism* (1976); Franklin Rosemont, ed. *André Breton and the First Principles of Surrealism* (1978).

BERTOLT BRECHT

LIFE. Eugen Berthold Brecht was born on February 10, 1898, in the medieval town of Augsburg, Bavaria. His father was a respected town citizen, director of a paper mill, and a Catholic. His mother, the daughter of a civil servant from the Black Forest, was a Protestant who raised young Berthold in her own faith (The spelling *Bertolt* was adopted later.) Brecht attended local schools until 1917, when he enrolled in Munich University to study natural sciences and medicine. He continued his studies while writing his first plays and acting as drama critic for an Augsburg newspaper, and in 1918 was mobilized as an orderly in a military hospital. In 1929 he married Helene Weigel, an actress who worked closely with him and for whom he wrote many leading roles. Together, they directed and made famous the theater group founded in 1949 for them in East Berlin: the *Berliner Ensemble.*

Brecht's unorthodoxy, his pacifism, his enthusiasm for Marx (whom he read in 1926), and his desire to create an activist popular theater that would embody a Marxist view of art, all put him at odds with the rising power of Hitler's National Socialism. He fled Germany for Denmark in 1933, before the Nazis could include him in their purge of left-wing intellectuals; in 1935, he was deprived of his German citizenship. Brecht was to flee several more times before the Nazi invasions: in 1939 to Sweden, in 1940 to Finland, and finally in 1941 to America, where he joined a colony of German exiles in Santa Monica, California, working for the film industry. Brecht continued to write and to arrange for translations of his work into English: *Galileo*, with Charles Laughton in the title role, was produced in 1947. In the same year, Brecht was questioned by the House Un-American Activities Committee. No charges were brought, but he left the United States the day after testifying before the Committee. A stateless man, Brecht lived in Switzerland until 1949, when the *Berliner Ensemble* was founded and he settled in East Berlin. He received Austrian citizenship (through his wife's nationality) in 1950. He died on August 14, 1956.

CHIEF WRITINGS. Plays: *Baal* (1918); *Drums in the Night (Trommeln in der Nacht*, 1918); *In the Jungle of the Cities (Im Dickicht der Städte*, 1921–23); *Life of Edward II of England (Leben Eduards des Zweiten von England*, with Lion Feuchtwanger, 1923–24); *A Man's a Man (Mann ist Mann*, 1924–25); *The Threepenny Opera (Die Dreigroschenoper*, 1928); *Rise and Fall of the City of Mahoganny (Aufstieg und Fall der Stadt Mahagonny*, 1928–29); *The Didactic Play of Baden: On Consent (Das Badener Lehrstück vom Einverständnis*, 1928–29); *St. Joan of the Stockyards (Die Heilige Johanna der Schlachthöfe*, 1929–30); *The Measures Taken (Die Massnahme*, 1930); *The Mother (Die Mutter*, 1930–32); *Fear and Misery of the Third Reich (Furcht und Elend des Dritten Reiches*, 1935–38); *Mother Courage and Her Children (Mutter Courage und ihre Kinder*, 1939); *The Trial of Lucullus (Das Verhör des Lukullus*, 1939); *Galileo (Leben des Galilei*, 1938–39); *The Good Person of Setzuan (Der gute Mensch von Sezuan*, 1938–40); *Mr. Puntila and His Hired Man, Matti (Herr Puntila und sein knecht Matti*, 1940–41); *The Resistible Rise of Arturo Ui (Der aufhaltsame Aufstieg des Arturo Ui*, 1941); *Schweik in the Second World War (Schweik im Zweiten Weltkrieg*, 1941–44); *The Caucasian Chalk Circle (Der Kaukasische Kreidedreis*, 1944–45). Poetry: *Manual of Piety (Die Hauspostille*, 1927); *Selected Poems* (1959). Prose: *Tales from The Calendar (Kalendergeschichten*, 1948); *Threepenny Novel (Dreigroschenroman*, 1934);

Brecht on Theatre (collection, 1964); and *The Messingkauf Dialogues* (Der Messingkauf, 1937–51).

BIOGRAPHY AND CRITICISM. M. Esslin, *Brecht, The Man and His Work* (1959, revised 1974); J. Willett, *The Theatre of Bertolt Brecht* (1950, revised 1968); P. Demetz, *Brecht, A Collection of Critical Essays* (1962); W. Weideli, *The Art of Bertolt Brecht* (translation 1963); F. Ewen, *Bertolt Brecht, His Life, His Art, and His Times* (1967); C. Lyons, *Bertolt Brecht; the Despair and the Polemic* (1968); J. Fuegi, *The Essential Brecht* (1972); D. Suvin, "Brecht—An Essay at a Dramaturgic Bibliography" in *Brecht*, edited by E. Munk (1972); *Essays on Brecht: Theater and Politics*, edited by H. Knust and S. Mews (1974); *Brecht As They Knew Him*, edited by H. Witt and translated by J. Peet (1974); C. Hill, *Bertolt Brecht Chronicle* (translated in 1975); and R. Gray, *Brecht the Dramatist* (1976).

VLADIMIR NABOKOV

LIFE. Vladimir Vladimirovich Nabokov was born on April 23, 1899, in St. Petersburg (now Leningrad), Russia. He was the oldest of five children in a wealthy aristocratic family with strong liberal, artistic, and professional traditions. At first educated at home by tutors, he learned several languages, reading English before Russian, and traveled with his family often to Berlin, Paris, and resorts in the South of France and on the Adriatic. When he was seven Nabokov took up the study of butterflies, a field in which he was eventually to become a recognized authority. From 1911 to 1917 he attended the liberal Prince Tenishev School in St. Petersburg, but at the Bolshevik Revolution in 1917 the family fled to the Crimea and then again in 1919 to Germany; three years later Nabokov's father was shot and killed at a political rally in Berlin. Nabokov studied at Cambridge University from 1919 to 1922 before moving to Berlin. There he wrote his first published works (in Russian) and tutored students in English and French. He married Véra Evseevna Slonim in 1925; their one child, Dmitri, was born in 1934.

Nabokov used the pen name Vladimir Sirin for his Russian works: three volumes of poetry, many articles for the emigré press, and eight novels published between 1926 (*Mary*) and 1938 (*The Gift*). In 1937 he and his family fled Hitler's Germany for Paris, where he wrote his first novel in English, *The Real Life of Sebastian Knight* (published in 1941). The Nazi invasion of France in 1940 forced him to emigrate to America, where he became a citizen in 1945.

Once in America, Nabokov taught at several institutions before accepting a professorship at Cornell University from 1948 to 1959. He received Guggenheim Fellowships in 1943 and 1953, and a grant from the National Institute of Arts and Letters in 1951, continuing to publish novels, short stories, a critical biography of Gogol, and English translations of his earlier works in Russian. He first reached wide recognition, or perhaps notoriety, with the publication in Paris of *Lolita* (1955), the story of a middle-aged man and his twelve-year-old "nymphet" lover, Lolita. *Lolita's* success enabled Nabokov to retire from teaching in 1959 and devote all his time to writing. He then took up residence in Montreux, Switzerland, where he lived in the Palace Hotel overlooking Lake Geneva until his death. Among his new publications were a controversial four-volume translation of and commentary on Pushkin's *Eugene Onegin* (1964), a revision of his autobiography (*Speak, Memory*, 1966), several anthologies (including one that combines poetry and chess problems), and three new novels in English. Nabokov died in Switzerland on July 2, 1977.

CHIEF WRITINGS. *Mary* (*Mashen'ka*, 1926), translated in 1970; *King, Queen, Knave* (*Korol', Dama, Valet*, 1928), translated in 1968; *The Luzhin Defense* (*Zashchita Luzhina*, 1930,) translated in 1964; *Glory* (*Podvig'*, 1932), translated in 1971; *Camera Obscura* (*Kamera Obskura*, 1933), translated in 1937, revised and translated as *Laughter in the Dark*, 1938; *Despair* (*Otchayanie*, 1936), translated in 1937, revised 1966; *Invitation to a Beheading* (*Priglashenie na Kazn'*, 1938), translated in 1959; *The Real Life of Sebastian Knight* (1941); *Nine Stories* (1947); *Bend Sinister* (1947); *The Gift* (*Dar*, 1952), translated in 1963; *Conclusive Evidence: A Memoir* (1951, revised in 1966 as *Speak, Memory: An Autobiography Revisited*); *Lolita* (1955), *Pnin* (1957); *Nabokov's Dozen* (1958); *Pale Fire* (1962); *Nabokov's Quartet* (1967); *Nabokov's Congeries* (1968); *Ada; or, Ardor* (1969); *Poems and Problems* (1971); *A Russian Beauty and Other Stories* (1973); *Transparent Things* (1973); *Strong Opinions* (1974); *Look at the Harlequins!* (1974); and *Tyrants Destroyed and Other Stories* (1975). See also translation of and commentary on Alexander Pushkin, *Eugene Onegin* (1964).

BIOGRAPHY AND CRITICISM. Page Stegner, *The Art of Vladimir Nabokov: Escape into Aesthetics* (1966); Andrew Field, *Nabokov: His Life in Art* (1967); *Nabokov: The Man and His Work*, edited by L. S. Dembo (1967); Carl Proffer, *Keys to Lolita* (1968); *Nabokov: Criticisms, Reminiscences, Translations and Tributes*, edited by Alfred Appel, Jr. and Charles Newman (1970); Julian Moynahan, *Vladimir Nabokov* (1971); W. Woodlin Rowe, *Nabokov's Deceptive World* (1971); Julia Bader, *Crystal Land* (1972); Andrew Field, *Nabokov: A Bibliography* (1973); Donald Morton, *Vladimir Nabokov* (1974); Alfred Appel, Jr.,

Nabokov's Dark Cinema (1974); Douglas Fowler, *Reading Nabokov* (1974); *A Book of Things about Vladimir Nabokov*, edited by Carl R. Proffer (1974); and Andrew Field, *Nabokov: His Life in Part* (1977).

BENJAMIN PÉRET

LIFE AND WRITINGS. Benjamin Péret was born on July 4, 1899, at Rezé, close to Nantes. His father was a civil servant. In 1901 the parents separated, and Péret was raised by his mother in Nantes. He did not like school and was a constant truant described in school records as obstinate, unmotivated, and uncooperative. After an escapade in 1917 his mother obliged him to enlist in the army; sent to Salonika in Greece, he caught amoebic dysentery and was returned to France until the end of World War I. His discovery of a book of Mallarmé's poems while waiting for a train launched his interest in literature, and after his discharge from the army in 1920 he made the acquaintance of André Breton, Paul Éluard, Louis Aragon, and other young intellectuals in Paris just as the Dada movement came into being. Péret supported himself then and later by proofreading, and he was often in poverty. In 1922 he broke with Dadaism over what he considered its sterile negativity. With Breton, Eluard, Aragon, and Robert Desnos he founded the Surrealist movement, editing *The Surrealist Revolution* with Pierre Naville in 1924–25, and participating actively in all Surrealist activities until his death.

Péret published collections of poems and tales in 1923–25, and collaborated with Paul Éluard in 1925 on a comic series of *152 Proverbs Updated for Modern Taste*. He joined the Communist Party in 1926 and worked for a while on the newspaper *L'Humanité*, but soon rejected the orthodox Party to work for the Trotskyite left with other intellectuals. In 1927 he married the Brazilian singer Elsie Houston, and after 1929 they lived in Brazil until 1931, when their son Geyser was born, and when Péret was expelled from the country for his revolutionary activities. He continued to write poetry and tales, and devoted himself to the Surrealist movement with its demonstrations and tracts. In 1935 he and Breton broke with the Communist party over its authoritarian politics, and in August of 1936, a few days after the military rebellion in Spain, he arrived in Barcelona to fight on the side of the Republic.

In Barcelona Péret fell in love with the painter Remedios Varo, who became his constant companion and whom he married in 1943 after the death of his first wife. He was depressed by the factionalism and bureaucracy of the army and especially by the struggle between Stalinist and anarchist wings of the left.

He fought with the anarchist militia on the Aragon front in 1937, but later returned to France where he tried unsuccessfully to get passports for himself and Remedios to travel to Mexico before the outbreak of World War II. Drafted in February 1940, he continued his revolutionary activities and was arrested and imprisoned at Rennes in May; freed (for a price) by the German invaders, he made his way to Mexico where he stayed for the rest of the war.

Returning to Paris in 1948, Péret continued to write and to collaborate on Surrealist reviews and experimental films such as *The Invention of the World* (1952). He supported himself again through a heavy schedule of proofreading, but his health deteriorated and in June 1952 he gave up his job and went to live with friends. In 1955–56 he traveled to Brazil again and made a trip down the Amazon River to visit Indian tribes and collect photographs of Precolumbian and primitive art for a book. The next three years brought more political activity, during which Péret spoke out both against the conservative regime of Charles de Gaulle and against Soviet policy in Hungary and Eastern Europe. His health, however, was increasingly fragile, and after several operations he died in Paris on September 18, 1959.

CHIEF WRITINGS. *125 Boulevard Saint-Germain* (*Au 125 du boulevard Saint-Germain*, 1923); *Immortal Illness* (*Immortelle maladie*, 1924); *Once There was a Baker's Wife* (*Il était une boulangere*, 1925); *152 Proverbs Updated for Modern Taste* (with Paul Éluard, *152 Proverbes mis au goût du jour*, 1925); *The Great Game* (*Le Grand Jeu*, 1928); *From In Back* (*De Derrière les fagots*, 1934); *I Don't Eat That Kind of Bread* (*Je ne mange pas de ce pain-là*, 1936); *Péret Speaks* (*La Parole est à Péret*, 1943); *The Dishonor of Poets* (*Le Déshonneur des poètes*, 1945); *Proper Assistance* (*Main-forte*, 1946); *Central Fire* (*Feu central*, 1947); *The Gallant Sheep* (*La Brebis galante*, 1949); *Death to Cops and the Field of Honor* (*Mort aux vaches et au champ d'honneur*, 1953); *The Leg of Mutton, its Life and Works* (*Le Gigot, sa vie et son oeuvre*, 1957); *Natural History* (*Histoire naturelle*, 1958); *Anthology of Myths, Legends, and Popular Tales of America* (*Anthologie des mythes, légendes et contes populaires d'Amérique*, 1960). A few translations are available in Péret, *Remove Your Hat*, twenty poems selected and transl. by Humphrey Jennings and David Gascoyne (1936); *Péret's Score*, ed. J. H. Matthews (1965), and three stories in *The Custom-House of Desire*, ed. and transl. J. H. Matthews (1975).

BIOGRAPHY AND CRITICISM. J. H. Matthews, *Benjamin Péret* (1975). See also J. H. Matthews, *An Introduction to Surrealism* (1965); Herbert Gershman, *The Surrealismt Revolution in France* (1969); and J. H. Matthews, *Surrealist Poetry in France* (1969).

ISAAC BASHEVIS SINGER

LIFE. Singer was born in Russian Poland in 1904, the son of a poor rabbi. The family moved to Warsaw while he was still a very small boy. In 1917 his mother took him and her other young children to live with relatives in the small town of Bilgoray, returning with them to Warsaw when the war ended. The older brother, I. J. Singer, left the strict confines of orthodox Judaism to establish himself as a writer, and in the early twenties Isaac Bashevis Singer followed him. At first he wrote in Hebrew, but soon changed to Yiddish. In 1935 he emigrated to the United States, separating from his first wife—who, with their son, found her way to Russia and later to Israel. Singer was married again in 1940, to a former resident of Munich. While he continues to write in Yiddish, he pays very close attention to the translation of his works into English.

CHIEF WRITINGS. *The Family Moskat* (1950); *Gimpel the Fool and Other Stories* (1957); *The Magician of Lublin* (1960); *The Spinoza of Market Street* (1961); *The Slave* (1962); *Short Friday and Other Stories* (1964); *In My Father's Court* (1966); *The Manor* (1967); *The Estate* (1969); *A Day of Pleasure: Stories of a Boy Growing Up in Warsaw* (1969); *Enemies: A Love Story* (1972).

BIOGRAPHY AND CRITICISM. Marcia Allentuck (ed.), *The Achievement of Isaac Bashevis Singer* (1969); Irving Malin, *Isaac Bashevis Singer* (1972); Irving Malin (ed.), *Critical Views of Isaac Bashevis Singer* (1972).

JEAN-PAUL SARTRE

LIFE. Sartre was born in Paris on June 21, 1905. His father, an officer in the French Navy, died while Sartre was still an infant, and his mother took him to live with her family. Sartre's mother remarried in 1916. After two years in a provincial secondary school, Sartre spent the rest of his schooldays in Paris, going on to study at the University of Paris. He became a secondary-school teacher. He was able to spend one year's leave of absence in Berlin. Made prisoner by the Germans after the French collapse of 1940, Sartre was released fairly soon and returned to teaching. He took part in the Resistance as a writer, though not as an activist, and became famous in 1943 with the performance of *The Flies* (*Les Mouches*) and the extraordinary success of his massive philosophical work *Being and Nothingness* (*L'Être et le Néant*). He gave up teaching the following year, and in 1945 founded the periodical *Les Temps Modernes*. Since then he has continued to write on philosophical, psychological, political, and topical matters, and has written many plays. His one postwar novel, *Roads to Freedom* (*Les Chemins de la Liberté*, 1945 and following years) remains unfinished. In 1962 he published the first volume of his autobiography, *The Words* (*Les Mots*), which deals with his childhood in grandfather Schweitzer's household. In 1964 he was awarded but refused to accept the Nobel Prize.

CHIEF WRITINGS. *Nausea* (*La Nausée*, 1938), translated by Lloyd Alexander (1949); *The Wall* (*Le Mur*, 1939), translated also as *Intimacy and Other Stories* by Lloyd Alexander (1948); *Outline of a Theory of the Emotions* (*Esquisse d'une Théorie des Émotions*, 1940), translated by Bernard Frechtman (1948); *The Flies* (*Les Mouches*, 1942), translated by Stuart Gilbert (1947); *Being and Nothingness* (*L'Être et le Néant*, 1943), translated by Hazel E. Barnes (1956); *No Exit* (*Huis-Clos*, 1944), translated by Stuart Gilbert (1947); *The Age of Reason, The Reprieve*, and *Troubled Sleep* (*L'Âge du Raison, Le Sursis*, and *La Mort dans l'Âme*, constituting three parts of *Les Chemins de la Liberté*, 1945–1949), translated by Eric Sutton (1947) and by Gerard Hopkins (1950); *Existentialism* (*L'Existentialisme est un Humanisme*, 1946), translated by Bernard Frechtman (1947); *Baudelaire* (1947), translated by Martin Turnell (1950); *Saint Genet, Actor and Martyr* (1952), translated by Bernard Frechtman (1962); *Literary Essays* (1957); *The Devil and the Good Lord, and Two Other Plays* (1960); *The Condemned of Altona* (1961); *Sartre on Cuba* (1961); *The Words* (*Les Mots*, 1962), translated by Bernard Frechtman (1964); *The Problem of Method* (1963); *Saint Genet, Actor and Martyr* (1968); *Situations* (1965); *Literary and Philosophical Essays* (1966); *The Communists and Peace* (1968); *The Ghost of Stalin* (1968); *On Genocide* (1968); *Sartre on Theater*, edited by Michel Contat and Michel Rybalka (*Un Théâtre de situations*, 1973), translated by Frank Jellinek (1976); and *Life/Situations* (*Situations, X*), translated by Paul Auster and Lydia Davis (1977).

BIOGRAPHY AND CRITICISM. Peter J. Dempsey, *The Psychology of Sartre* (1950); Hazel Barnes, *The Literature of Possibility* (1959); Robert Champigny, *Stages on Sartre's Way, 1938–1952* (1959); Wilfrid Desan, *The Tragic Finale: An Essay on the Philosophy of Jean-Paul Sartre* (revised edition, 1960); Norman H. Greene, *Jean-Paul Sartre: The Existentialist Ethic* (1960); Iris Murdoch, *Sartre: Romantic Rationalist* (1960); Philip Thody, *Jean-Paul Sartre: A Literary and Political Study* (1960); Fredric Jameson, *Sartre: The Origin of a Style* (1961); Edith Kern (ed.), *Sartre: A Collection of Critical Essays* (1962); René Marill-Albérès, *Jean-Paul Sartre, Philosopher without Faith* (1964); Mary Warnock, *The Philosophy of Sartre* (1965); Eugene H. Falk, *Types of Thematic Structure* (1967); George H. Bauer, *Sartre and the Artist* (1969); Dorothy McCall, *The Theatre of Jean-Paul Sartre* (1969); James F. Sheridan, *Sartre: The Radical Conversion* (1969); Edith Kern, *Existential Thought and Fictional Technique* (1970); Benjamin Suhl, *Jean-Paul Sartre: The Philosopher as Literary Critic* (1970); George Bauer, *Sartre and the Artist* (1969); Joseph H. McMahon, *Human Beings: The World of Jean-Paul Sartre* (1971); Philip M. W. Thody, *Sartre: A Biographical Introduction* (1971); *Sartre: A Collection of Critical Essays*, edited by Mary Warnock (1971); Germaine Brée, *Camus and Sartre: Crisis and Commitment* (1972); Hazel Barnes, *Sartre* (1973); Marjorie Grene, *Sartre* (1973); Michel Contat and M. Rybalka, *The Writings of Jean-Paul Sartre* (1974); Thomas M. King, *Sartre and the Sacred* (1974); Arthur C. Danto, *Jean-Paul Sartre* (1975); and Ian Craib, *Existentialism and Sociology: A Study of Jean-Paul Sartre* (1976).

ALBERT CAMUS

LIFE. Camus was born in Mondovi, Algeria, on November 7, 1913, to a working-class family. The father was killed early in World War I, and the mother, who was Spanish, moved to the city of Algiers. The boy grew up talking the mixed dialect—French, Spanish, Arabic—of the streets. A schoolteacher who took a special interest in Camus arranged for a scholarship to secondary school. After several years of university work, Camus turned to journalism, joined the Communist Party but stayed a member less than three years, and became very active in the theater. He moved to Paris in 1940. He first attracted wide attention as a writer in 1942 for the underground newspaper *Combat*, and after the war he continued to write editorials for it. His total work brought him the Nobel prize in 1957. He died on January 4, 1960, in a car accident.

CHIEF WRITINGS. *The Stranger* (*L'Étranger*, 1942); *The Myth of Sisyphus* (*Le mythe de Sisyphe*, 1942); *The Plague* (*La Peste*, 1948); *The Rebel* (*L'homme révolté*, 1954); *The Fall* (*La chute*, 1957); *Exile and the Kingdom* (*L'exil et la royaume*, 1958); *Caligula and Other Plays* (1958); *Possessed* (1960); *Resistance, Rebellion, and Death* (1960); *Notebook 1935–1942*; *Notebook, 1942–1951* (1965); *Lyrical and Critical Essays* (1968); *A Happy Death* (previously unpublished earlier version of *The Stranger*) (1972).

BIOGRAPHY AND CRITICISM. Albert Maquet, *Albert Camus: An Invincible*

Summer (1958); John Cruickshank, *Albert Camus and the Literature of Revolt* (1959); Philip Thody, *Albert Camus* (1959); Thomas Hanna, *The Thought and Art of Albert Camus* (1959); and *Lyrical Existentialists* (1962); Germaine Brée, *Albert Camus* (1961) and *Camus: A Collection of Critical Essays* (1961); Adele King, *Albert Camus* (1964); Phillip H. Rhein, *Albert Camus* (1969); Maurice Friedman, *The Problematic Rebel* (revised edition, 1970); Conor C. O'Brien, *Albert Camus: Of Europe and Africa* (1970); Jean Onimus, *Albert Camus*

and Christianity (1970); Morvan Lebesque, *Portrait of Camus: An Illustrated Biography* (1971); Paul Archambault, *Camus' Hellenic Sources* (1972); Germaine Brée, *Camus and Sartre* (1972); Donald Lazere, *The Unique Creation of Albert Camus* (1973); Lev Braun, *Witness of Decline: Albert Camus: Moralist of the Absurd* (1974); Irina Kirk, *Dostoevskij and Camus: The Themes of Unconsciousness, Isolation, Freedom and Love* (1974); Brian Masters, *Camus: A Study* (1974); and *Albert Camus' Literary Milieu: Arid Lands*, edited by W. T. Zyla (1976).

CHARLES BAUDELAIRE
(1821–1867)

THE FLOWERS OF EVIL

Correspondences[a]

Nature is a temple where living pillars
Sometimes allow confused words to escape;
Man passes there through forests of symbols
That watch him with familiar glances.

Like long-drawn-out echoes mingled far away   5
Into a deep and shadowy unity,
Vast as darkness and light,
Scents, colors, and sounds answer one another.

There are some scents cool as the flesh of children,
Sweet as oboes and green as meadows,   10
—And others corrupt, rich, and triumphant

Having the expansion of things infinite.
Like amber, musk, benzoin, and incense,
Singing the raptures of the mind and senses.

Former Life[b]

I've lived beneath huge portals where marine
Suns colored, with a myriad fires, the waves;
At eve majestic pillars made the scene
Resemble those of vast basaltic caves.

The breakers, rolling the reflected skies,   5
Mixed, in a solemn, enigmatic way,
The powerful symphonies they seem to play
With colors of the sunset in my eyes.

There did I live in a voluptuous calm
Where breezes, waves, and splendors roved as vagrants; 10
And naked slaves, impregnated with fragrance,

---

a. Translated by Anthony Hartley.
13. *amber:* Or ambergris, a substance secreted by whales. Ambergris, musk (a secretion of the musk deer) and ben- zoin (an aromatic resin) are used in making perfume.
b. Translated by Roy Campbell.

Would fan my forehead with their fronds of palm:
Their only charge was to increase the anguish
Of secret grief in which I loved to languish.

Beauty[a]

I am beautiful, O mortals! like a dream of stone.
And my breast, where each one in turn has bruised himself,
Is made to inspire in the poet a dream
As eternal and silent as matter.

I sit enthroned in the azure sky like an undeciphered sphinx;   5
I join a heart of snow to the whiteness of swans;
I hate motion which displaces lines;
And never do I weep and never do I laugh.

Poets, before my grand poses,
Which I seem to borrow from the proudest monuments,   10
Will consume their days in austere studies;

For I have, to fascinate those submissive lovers,
Pure mirrors that make all things more beautiful:
My eyes, my wide eyes, eternally bright.

Jewels[b]

The darling one was naked and, knowing my wish,
Had kept only the regalia of her jewelry
Whose resonant charms can lure and vanquish
Like a Moorish slave-girl's in her moment of glory.

A world of dazzling stones and of precious metals   5
Flinging, in its quick rhythm, glints of mockery
Ravishes me into ecstasy, I love to madness
The mingling of sounds and lights in one intricacy.

Naked, then, she was to all of my worship,
Smiling in triumph from the heights of her couch   10
At my desire advancing, as gentle and deep
As the sea sending its waves to the warm beach.

---

a. Translated by Elaine Marks.
5. *sphinx*: Baudelaire fuses the monumental Egyptian sculpture, with its
human head and winged lion's body,
with the old story of the "riddle of the
sphinx" solved by Oedipus.

b. Translated by David Paul.
4. *Moorish*: The Moors or Saracens
were a Moslem people that invaded
Spain in the eighth century A.D.; Baudelaire evokes exotic overtones of another
culture.

Her eyes fixed as a tiger's in the tamer's trance,
Absent, unthinking, she varied her poses
With an audacity and wild innocence   15
That gave a strange pang to each metamorphosis.

Her long legs, her hips, shining smooth as oil,
Her arms and her thighs, undulant as a swan,
Lured my serene, clairvoyant gaze to travel
To her belly and breasts, the grapes of my vine.   20

With a charm as powerful as an evil angel
To trouble the calm where my soul had retreated,
They advanced slowly to dislodge it from its crystal
Rock, where its loneliness meditated.

With the hips of Antiope, the torso of a boy,   25
So deeply was the one form sprung into the other
It seemed as if desire had fashioned a new toy.
Her farded, fawn-brown skin was perfection to either!

—And the lamp having at last resigned itself to death,
There was nothing now but firelight in the room,   30
And every time a flame uttered a gasp for breath
It flushed her amber skin with the blood of its bloom.

Her Hair[a]

O fleece, that down the neck waves to the nape!
O curls! O perfume nonchalant and rare!
O ecstacy! To fill this alcove shape
With memories that in these tresses sleep,
I would shake them like pennons in the air!   5

Languorous Asia, burning Africa,
And a far world, defunct almost, absent,
Within your aromatic forest stay!
As other souls on music drift away,
Mine, o my love! still floats upon your scent.   10

I shall go there where, full of sap, both tree
And man swoon in the heat of southern climes;
Strong tresses, be the swell that carries me!
I dream upon your sea of ebony
Of dazzling sails, of oarsmen, masts and flames: 15

25. *Antiope*: An Amazon, mother of
Hippolytus.
28. *Farded*: Painted as with cosmetics.

a. Translated by Doreen Bell.
3. *alcove*: Bedroom.

A sun-drenched and reverberating port,
Where I imbibe color and sound and scent;
Where vessels, gliding through the gold and moire,
Open their vast arms as they leave the shore
To clasp the pure and shimmering firmament.   20

I'll plunge my head, enamored of its pleasure,
In this black ocean where the other hides;
My subtle spirit then will know a measure
Of fertile idleness and fragrant leisure,
Lulled by the infinite rhythm of its tides!   25

Pavilion, of blue-shadowed tresses spun,
You give me back the azure from afar;
And where the twisted locks are fringed with down
Lurk mingled odors I grow drunk upon
Of oil of coconut, of musk and tar.   30

A long time! always! my hand in your hair
Will sow the stars of sapphire, pearl, ruby,
That you be never deaf to my desire,
My oasis and gourd whence I aspire
To drink deep of the wine of memory!   35

I Adore You as Much . . .[a]

I adore you as much as the vault of night,
O vessel of sorrow, O tall, silent woman,
And I love you the more, my beauty, the more you flee me,
And seem, O ornament of my nights,
To pile up ironically the leagues   5
That separate my arms from the blue spaces.

I advance to the attack and I climb to the assault
Like a band of worms on a corpse,
And I hold dear, O mercilessly cruel beast!
Even that coldness through which you appear more beautiful to
    me!   10

Invitation to the Voyage[b]

My child, my sister, dream
How sweet all things would seem

18. *moire*: Watered silk.   b. Translated by Richard Wilbur.
a. Translated by Anthony Hartley.

Were we in that kind land to live together,
  And there love slow and long,
  There love and die among   5
Those scenes that image you, that sumptuous weather.

    Drowned suns that glimmer there
    Through cloud-dishevelled air
Move me with such a mystery as appears
    Within those other skies   10
    Of your treacherous eyes
When I behold them shining through their tears.

There, there is nothing else but grace and measure,
Richness, quietness, and pleasure.

    Furniture that wears   15
    The lustre of the years
Softly would glow within our glowing chamber,
    Flowers of rarest bloom
    Proffering their perfume
Mixed with the vague fragrances of amber;   20
    Gold ceilings would there be,
    Mirrors deep as the sea,
The walls all in an Eastern splendor hung—
    Nothing but should address
    The soul's loneliness,   25
Speaking her sweet and secret native tongue.

There, there is nothing else but grace and measure,
Richness, quietness, and pleasure.

    See, sheltered from the swells
    There in the still canals   30
Those drowsy ships that dream of sailing forth;
    It is to satisfy
    Your least desire, they ply
Hither through all the waters of the earth.
    The sun at close of day   35
    Clothes the fields of hay,
Then the canals, at last the town entire
    In hyacinth and gold:
    Slowly the land is rolled
Sleepward under a sea of gentle fire.   40

There, there is nothing else but grace and measure,
Richness, quietness, and pleasure.

Song of Autumn I[a]

Soon we shall plunge into the chilly fogs;
Farewell, swift light! our summers are too short!
I hear already the mournful fall of logs
Re-echoing from the pavement of the court.

All of winter will gather in my soul: 5
Hate, anger, horror, chills, the hard forced work;
And, like the sun in his hell by the north pole,
My heart will be only a red and frozen block.

I shudder, hearing every log that falls;
No scaffold could be built with hollower sounds.   10
My spirit is like a tower whose crumbling walls
The tireless battering-ram brings to the ground.

It seems to me, lulled by monotonous shocks,
As if they were hastily nailing a coffin today.
For whom?—Yesterday was summer. Now autumn knocks.   15
That mysterious sound is like someone's going away.

Heautontimoroumenos[b]

I shall beat you without rage
Or hate, as Moses struck the rock,
As a butcher strikes his block.
I shall make your tears assuage

My drought, my desert in their tide.   5
You shall weep for my relief,
And on the salt waves of your grief
My longings swollen with hope shall ride,

Like a ship that puts to sea.
My heart, delirious with the sound,   10
Shall hear your sobs rebound, rebound—
Like a drum that's summoning me.

Am I not a jarring note
In the heavenly symphony

---

a. Translated by C. F. McIntyre.
12. *battering-ram*: A heavy beam often mounted on wheels, used to batter down the enemy's fortifications; here associated with the sound of firewood being delivered.
b. Translated by Naomi Lewis. The title, in Greek, means "The Self-Tormentor," and applies also to a play by the Roman dramatist Terence (185–159 B.C).
2. *Moses*: Moses struck a rock in the desert and brought forth water for his people to drink (Exodus 17,6).

Since devouring Irony   15
Gnaws me, shakes me by the throat?

Hers is the shrillness in my voice;
Through my blood her poisons race.
I am the unholy mirror
Where the shrew can watch her face.   20

I am the ulcer and the lance;
I am the bruise; I am the blow;
I am the rack, the limbs also,
Hangman and hanged at once.

I am my own heart's vampire—   25
One of the vast abandoned host;
Laughter's the doom of those who've lost
The power to smile forever.

Spleen LXXV^a

Old Pluvius, month of rains, in peevish mood
Pours from his urn chill winter's sodden gloom
On corpses fading in the near graveyard,
On foggy suburbs pours life's tedium.

My cat seeks out a litter on the stones,   5
Her mangy body turning without rest.
An ancient poet's soul in monotones
Whines in the rain-spouts like a chilblained ghost.

A great bell mourns, a wet log wrapped in smoke
Sings in falsetto to the wheezing clock,   10
While from a rankly perfumed deck of cards

(A dropsical old crone's fatal bequest)
The Queen of Spades, the dapper Jack of Hearts
Speak darkly of dead loves, how they were lost.

Spleen LXXVI^b

I have more memories than if I had lived a thousand years.

15. *Irony*: Irony, Baudelaire's self-crit-
ical dual vision, is here personified.
28. *smile*: According to legend, vampires cannot smile.
a. Translated by Kenneth O. Hanson.
1. *Pluvius*: Pluvius is literally "the

rainy time" (Latin), a period extending
from January 20 to February 18 as the
fifth month of the French Revolutionary
calendar.
b. Translated by Anthony Hecht.

Even a bureau crammed with souvenirs,
Old bills, love letters, photographs, receipts,
Court depositions, locks of hair in plaits,
Hides fewer secrets than my brain could yield.   5
It's like a tomb, a corpse-filled Potter's Field,
A pyramid where the dead lie down by scores.
I am a graveyard that the moon abhors:
Like guilty qualms, the worms burrow and nest
Thickly in bodies that I loved the best.   10
I'm a stale boudoir where old-fashioned clothes
Lie scattered among wilted fern and rose,
Where only the Boucher girls in pale pastels
Can breathe the uncorked scents and faded smells.

Nothing can equal those days for endlessness   15
When in the winter's blizzardy caress
Indifference expanding to Ennui
Takes on the feel of Immortality.
O living matter, henceforth you're no more
Than a cold stone encompassed by vague fear   20
And by the desert, and the mist and sun;
An ancient Sphinx ignored by everyone,
Left off the map, whose bitter irony
Is to sing as the sun sets in that dry sea.

Spleen LXXVII[a]

I'm like the king of a rain-country, rich
but sterile, young but with an old wolf's itch,
one who escapes his tutor's monologues,
and kills the day in boredom with his dogs;
nothing cheers him, darts, tennis, falconry,   5
his people dying by the balcony;
the bawdry of the pet hermaphrodite
no longer gets him through a single night;
his bed of fleur-de-lys becomes a tomb;
even the ladies of the court, for whom   10
all kings are beautiful, cannot put on

---

6. *Potter's Field*: A general term describing the common cemetery for those buried at public expense.

13. *Boucher girls*: François Boucher (1703–1770), court painter for Louis XV of France, drew many pictures of young women clothed and nude.

17. *Ennui*: A melancholy, paralyzing boredom.

23–25. Baudelaire combines two references to ancient Egypt, the sphinx and the legendary statue of Memnon at Thebes, which was supposed to sing at sunset.

a. Translated by Robert Lowell.

9. *fleur-de-lys*: Literally lily-flower, the emblem of French royalty, which is embroidered on the linen.

shameful enough dresses for this skeleton;
the scholar who makes his gold cannot invent
washes to cleanse the poisoned element;
even in baths of blood, Rome's legacy, 15
our tyrants' solace in senility,
he cannot warm up his shot corpse, whose food
is syrup-green Lethean ooze, not blood.

Spleen LXXVIII[a]

When the low heavy sky weighs like a lid
Upon the spirit aching for the light
And all the wide horizon's line is hid
By a black day sadder than any night;

When the changed earth is but a dungeon dank 5
Where batlike Hope goes blindly fluttering
And, striking wall and roof and mouldered plank,
Bruises his tender head and timid wing;

When like grim prison bars stretch down the thin,
Straight, rigid pillars of the endless rain, 10
And the dumb throngs of infamous spiders spin
Their meshes in the caverns of the brain,

Suddenly, bells leap forth into the air,
Hurling a hideous uproar to the sky
As 'twere a band of homeless spirits who fare 15
Through the strange heavens, wailing stubbornly.

And hearses, without drum or instrument,
File slowly through my soul; crushed, sorrowful,
Weeps Hope, and Grief, fierce and omnipotent,
Plants his black banner on my drooping skull. 20

To a Passer-By[b]

Amid the deafening traffic of the town,
Tall, slender, in deep mourning, with majesty,
A woman passed, raising, with dignity
In her poised hand, the flounces of her gown;

13. *the scholar who makes his gold*:
The alchemist, who can transmute and
purify elements, but who cannot cure the
king.
18. *Lethean*: Refers to Lethe, the

mythical underworld river of forgetfulness and oblivion.
a. Translated by Sir John Squire.
b. Translated by C. F. McIntyre.

Graceful, noble, with a statue's form.   5
And I drank, trembling as a madman thrills,
From her eyes, ashen sky where brooded storm,
The softness that fascinates, the pleasure that kills.

A flash . . . then night!—O lovely fugitive,
I am suddenly reborn from your swift glance;   10
Shall I never see you till eternity?

Somewhere, far off! too late! *never*, perchance!
Neither knows where the other goes or lives;
We might have loved, and you knew this might be!

Meditation[a]

Calm down, my Sorrow, we must move with care.
You called for evening; it descends, it's here.
The town is coffined in its atmosphere,
bringing relief to some, to others care.

Now while the common multitude strips bare,   5
feels pleasure's cat o' nine tails on its back,
and fights off anguish at the great bazaar,
give me your hand, my Sorrow. Let's stand back;

back from these people! Look, the dead years dressed
in old clothes crowd the balconies of the sky.   10
Regret emerges smiling from the sea,

the sick sun slumbers underneath an arch,
and like a shroud strung out from east to west,
listen, my Dearest, hear the sweet night march!

PARIS SPLEEN[b]

The Stranger

Tell me, enigmatical man, whom do you love best, your father, your
mother, your sister, or your brother?
I have neither father, nor mother, nor sister, nor brother.
Your friends?
Now you use a word whose meaning I have never known.
Your country?
I do not know in what latitude it lies.
Beauty?
I could indeed love her, Goddess and Immortal.

a. Translated by Robert Lowell.   b. Translated by Louise Varèse.

Gold?

I hate it as you hate God.

Then, what do you love, extraordinary stranger?

I love the clouds . . . the clouds that pass . . . up there . . . up there . . . the wonderful clouds!

The Double Room

A room that is like a dream, a truly *spiritual* room, where the stagnant atmosphere is nebulously tinted pink and blue.

Here the soul takes a bath of indolence, scented with all the aromatic perfumes of desire and regret. There is about it something crepuscular, bluish shot with rose; a voluptuous dream in an eclipse.

Every piece of furniture is of an elongated form, languid and prostrate, and seems to be dreaming; endowed, one would say, with a somnambular existence like minerals and vegetables. The hangings speak a silent language like flowers, skies, and setting suns.

No artistic abominations on the walls. Definite, positive art is blasphemy compared to dream and the unanalyzed impression. Here all is bathed in harmony's own adequate and delicious obscurity.

An infinitesimal scent of the most exquisite choosing, mingled with the merest breath of humidity, floats through this atmosphere where hot-house sensations cradle the drowsy spirit.

Muslin in diaphanous masses rains over the window and over the bed, spreads in snowy cataracts. And on this bed lies the Idol, the sovereign queen of my dreams. But why is she here? Who has brought her? What magic power has installed her on this throne of revery and of pleasure? No matter. She is here. I recognize her.

Yes, those are her eyes whose flame pierces the gloaming; those subtle and terrible eyes that I recognize by their dread mockery! They attract, they subjugate, they devour the imprudent gaze. Often I have studied them—black stars compelling curiosity and wonder.

To what good demon am I indebted for this encompassing atmosphere of mystery, silence, perfume, and peace? O bliss! What we are wont to call life, even in its happiest moments of expansion, has nothing in common with this supreme life which I am now experiencing, and which I relish minute by minute, second by second.

No! there are no more minutes, there are no more seconds! Time has disappeared; it is Eternity that reigns, an eternity of bliss!

But a knock falls on the door, an awful, a resounding knock, and I feel, as in my dreams of hell, a pitchfork being stuck into my stomach.

Then a Spectre enters. It is a bailiff come to torture me in the name of the law; it is an infamous concubine come with her complaints to add the trivialities of her life to the sorrows of mine; it is a messenger boy from a newspaper editor clamoring for the last installment of a manuscript.

The paradisiac room and the idol, the sovereign of dreams, the *Sylphid*,[1] as the great René used to say, the whole enchantment has vanished at the Spectre's brutal knock.

Horrors! I remember! Yes, I remember! this filthy hole, this abode of eternal boredom is truly mine. Look at the stupid, dusty, dilapidated furniture; the hearth without fire, without embers, disgusting with spittle; the sad windows where rain has traced furrows through the dust; manuscripts covered with erasures or unfinished, the calendar where a pencil has marked all the direst dates!

And that perfume out of another world which in my state of exquisite sensibility was so intoxicating? Alas, another odor has taken its place, of stale tobacco mixed with nauseating mustiness. The rancid smell of desolation.

In this narrow world, but with plenty of room for disgust, there is one object alone that delights me: the vial of opium: an old and dreadful love; and like all mistresses, alas! prolific in caresses and betrayals.

Oh! yes! Time has reappeared; Time is sovereign ruler now, and with that hideous old man the entire retinue of Memories, Regrets, Spasms, Fears, Agonies, Nightmares, Nerves, and Rages have returned.

I can assure you that the seconds are now strongly accepted, and rush out of the clock crying: "I am Life, unbearable and implacable Life!"

There is only one Second in human life whose mission it is to bring good news, *the good news*[2] that causes every one such inexplicable terror.

Yes, Time reigns; he has resumed his brutal tyranny. And he pokes me with his double goad as if I were an ox. "Then hoi, donkey! Sweat, slave! Man, be damned and live!"

The Bad Glazier*

There are certain natures, purely contemplative and totally unfit for action, which nevertheless, moved by some mysterious and unaccountable impulse, act at times with a rapidity of which they would never have dreamed themselves capable.

1. Probably a reference to the 1832 ballet, "La Sylphide," the story of a forest sprite (or "sylph") loved by a Scottish youth. *the great René*: François René de Chateaubriand (1768–1848), French novelist and essayist, author of *René*.

2. Reference to the Biblical four gospels, also called the Evangels (Greek for *good news*).

* Someone who sells window-glass.

Like the man who, dreading some painful news, instead of going for his mail as usual, cravenly prowls around his concierge's[1] door without daring to go in; or the one who keeps a letter for two weeks without opening it; or the man who only makes up his mind at the end of six months to do something that has urgently needed doing for a year; then, all of a sudden, they feel themselves hurled into action by an irresistible force, like an arrow out of a bow. The moralist and the doctor, who pretend to know everything, are unable to explain how these voluptuous, indolent souls suddenly acquire such a mad energy, or how it is that, although incapable of doing the simplest and most necessary things, they yet discover in themselves at a given moment a lavish courage for performing the most absurd and the most dangerous act.

One of my friends, the most inoffensive dreamer that ever lived, once set fire to a forest to see, he explained, if it were really as easy to start a fire as people said. Ten times in succession the experiment failed; but the eleventh time it succeeded only too well.

Another will light a cigar standing beside a keg of gunpowder, just *to see*, *to find out*, *to test* his luck, to prove to himself he has enough energy to play the gambler, to taste the pleasures of fear, or for no reason at all, through caprice, through idleness.

It is the kind of energy that springs from boredom and daydreaming; and those who display it so unexpectedly are, in general, as I have said, the most indolent and dreamiest of mortals.

And another man I know, who is so shy that he lowers his eyes even when *men* look at him, so shy that it takes all the poor courage he can muster to enter a café or, at the theatre, to approach the ticket *controlleurs* who seem to him invested with all the majesty of Minos, Iacchus, and Radamanthus,[2] will suddenly throw his arms around an old man in the street and kiss him impetuously before the astonished eyes of the passers-by.

Why? Because . . . because suddenly that particular physiognomy seemed irresistibly appealing? Perhaps; but it would probably be nearer the truth to suppose that he himself has no idea why.

I, too, have more than once been the victim of these outbursts of energy which justify our concluding that some malicious Demon gets into us, forcing us, in spite of ourselves, to carry out his most absurd whims.

One morning I got up feeling out of sorts, sad, and worn out with idleness, and with what seemed to me a compelling urge to do something extraordinary, to perform some brilliant deed. And I opened the window—alas!

(I should like to point out that with certain persons playing practical jokes is not the result of planning or scheming, but a fortui-

---

1. A concierge is a doorkeeper or building attendant, in whose office tenants' mail would be kept for them.

2. The three judges of the underworld in Greek mythology, who impose sentence on each entrant.

tous inspiration akin, if only because of the compelling force of the impulse, to that humor called hysterical by doctors, satanic by those with more insight than doctors, that drives us toward a multitude of dangerous or improper actions.)

The first person I noticed in the street was a glazier whose piercing and discordant cry floated up to me through the heavy, filthy Paris air. It would be impossible for me to say why I was suddenly seized by an arbitrary loathing for this poor man.

"Hey! Hey!" I shouted, motioning him to come up. And the thought that my room was up six flights of stairs, and that the man must be having a terrible time getting up them with his fragile wares, added not a little to my hilarity.

Finally he appeared. After looking curiously over his panes of glass one by one, I exclaimed: "What! You have no colored glass, no pink, no red, no blue! No magic panes, no panes of Paradise? Scoundrel, what do you mean by going into poor neighborhoods without a single glass to make life beautiful!" And I pushed him, stumbling and grumbling, toward the stairs.

Going out on my balcony I picked up a little flower pot, and when the glazier appeared at the entrance below, I let my engine of war fall down perpendicularly on the edge of his pack. The shock knocked him over and, falling on his back, he succeeded in breaking the rest of his poor ambulatory stock with a shattering noise as of lightning striking a crystal palace.

And drunk with my madness, I shouted down at him furiously: "Make life beautiful! Make life beautiful!"

Such erratic pranks are not without danger and one often has to pay dearly for them. But what is an eternity of damnation compared to an infinity of pleasure in a single second?

L'Invitation au voyage*

There is a wonderful country, a country of Cocaigne,[1] they say, that I dream of visiting with an old love. A strange country lost in the mists of the North and that might be called the East of the West, the China of Europe, so freely has a warm and capricious fancy been allowed to run riot there, illustrating it patiently and persistently with an artful and delicate vegetation.

A real country of Cocaigne where everything is beautiful, rich, honest, and calm; where order is luxury's mirror; where life is unctuous and sweet to breathe; where disorder, tumult, and the unexpected are shut out; where happiness is wedded to silence; where

* The Invitation to the Voyage (French); compare the poem of that title on page 1158.

1. An imaginary country of abundance, a never-never land.

even the cooking is poetic, rich, and yet stimulating as well; where everything, dear love, resembles you.

You know that feverish sickness which comes over us in our cold despairs, that nostalgia for countries we have never known, that anguish of curiosity? There is a country that resembles you, where everything is beautiful, rich, honest, and calm, where fancy has built and decorated an Occidental China, where life is sweet to breathe, where happiness is wedded to silence. It is there we must live, it is there we must die.

Yes, it is there we must go to breathe, to dream, and to prolong the hours in an infinity of sensations. A musician[2] has written *l'Invitation à la valse*; who will write *l'Invitation au voyage* that may be offered to the beloved, to the chosen sister?

Yes, in such an atmosphere it would be good to live—where there are more thoughts in slower hours, where clocks strike happiness with a deeper, a more significant solemnity.

On shining panels or on darkly rich and gilded leathers, discreet paintings repose, as deep, calm, and devout as the souls of the painters who depicted them. Sunsets throw their glowing colors on the walls of dining-room and drawing-room, sifting softly through lovely hangings or intricate high windows with mullioned panes. All the furniture is immense, fantastic, strange, armed with locks and secrets like all civilized souls. Mirrors, metals, fabrics, pottery, and works of the goldsmith's art play a mute mysterious symphony for the eye, and every corner, every crack, every drawer, and curtain's fold breathes forth a curious perfume, a perfume of Sumatra[3] whispering *come back*, which is the soul of the abode.

A true country of Cocaigne, I assure you, where everything is rich, shining, and clean like a good conscience or well-scoured kitchen pots, like chiseled gold or variegated gems! All the treasures of the world abound there, as in the house of a laborious man who has put the whole world in his debt. A singular country and superior to all others, as art is superior to Nature who is there transformed by dream, corrected, remodeled, and adorned.[4]

Let them seek and seek again, let them endlessly push back the limits of their happiness, those horticultural Alchemists.[5] Let them offer prizes of sixty, a hundred thousand florins for the solution of their ambitious problems! As for me, I have found my *black tulip*, I have found my *blue dahlia*![6]

---

2. Carl Maria von Weber (1786–1826), composer of "Invitation to the Dance" in waltz tempo.

3. Sumatra is the second largest island of Indonesia, famed for its spices and perfume.

4. The superiority of art and the poet's dream to mere nature is a recurrent Baudelairean theme.

5. As the medieval alchemists tried to transmute base elements into gold, so the horticultural alchemists try to produce an ideal flower from existing varieties.

6. Ideal flowers, especially in the German Romantic tradition. In the novel by Novalis (1772–1801), *Heinrich von Ofterdingen*, the hero's dream of a blue dahlia initiates a long quest for the ideal country.

Incomparable flower, rediscovered tulip, allegorical dahlia, it is there, is it not, in that beautiful country, so calm, so full of dream, that you must live, that you must bloom? Would you not there be framed within your own analogy, would you not see yourself reflected there in your own *correspondence*, as the mystics say?

Dreams! Always dreams! And the more ambitious and delicate the soul, all the more impossible the dreams. Every man possesses his own dose of natural opium, ceaselessly secreted and renewed, and from birth to death how many hours can we reckon of positive pleasure, of successful and decided action? Shall we ever live in, be part of, that picture my imagination has painted, and that resembles you?

These treasures, these furnishings, this luxury, this order, these perfumes, and these miraculous flowers, they are you! And you are the great rivers too, and the calm canals. And those great ships that they bear along laden with riches and from which rise the sailors' rhythmic chants, they are my thoughts that sleep or that rise on the swells of your breast. You lead them gently toward the sea which is the Infinite, as you mirror the sky's depth in the crystalline purity of your soul;—and when, weary with rolling waters and surfeited with the spoils of the Orient, they return to their port of call, still they are my thoughts coming back, enriched, from the Infinite to you.

Windows

Looking from outside into an open window one never sees as much as when one looks through a closed window. There is nothing more profound, more mysterious, more pregnant, more insidious, more dazzling than a window lighted by a single candle. What one can see out in the sunlight is always less interesting than what goes on behind a window pane. In that black or luminous square life lives, life dreams, life suffers.

Across the ocean of roofs I can see a middle-aged woman, her face already lined, who is forever bending over something and who never goes out. Out of her face, her dress, and her gestures, out of practically nothing at all, I have made up this woman's story, or rather legend, and sometimes I tell it to myself and weep.

If it had been an old man I could have made up his just as well.

And I go to bed proud to have lived and to have suffered in some one besides myself.

Perhaps you will say "Are you sure that your story is the real one?" But what does it matter what reality is outside myself, so long as it has helped me to live, to feel that I am, and what I am?

STÉPHANE MALLARMÉ
(1842–1898)

Tired of the Bitter Repose . . .*

Tired of the bitter repose where my idleness hurts
A glory for which I once fled the adorable
Childhood of roses and woods beneath nature's
Azure, and seven times more tired of the harsh
Pact to scoop out every night a fresh grave   5

In the cold and niggard soil of my brain,
Pitiless sexton of sterility,
—What, my Dreams, can I, rose visited, say
To that Dawn when fearful of its livid roses
The vast cemetery joins its hollow graves?—   10

I would leave the voracious Art of a cruel
Country and smiling at worn-out reproaches
Which my friends and my past and my genius make
And my lamp which natheless my agony knows,
Imitate the Chinese of clear delicate heart   15
Whose ecstasy pure lies in painting the end,
On his cups as white as moon-ravished snow,
Of a bizarre flower that perfumed his transparent
Life, the flower which he felt as a child
On the filigrane blue of his soul engrafted.   20
And, my death such with the sage's sole dream,
Some youthful landscape serenely I'll choose
That too will I paint on my cups, abstracted.
A pale and thin line of azure should be
A lake 'mid the heaven of nude porcelain,   25
A clear crescent moon in a white cloud lost
Dips its calm horn in the icy waters,
Near three great emerald eyelashes, reeds.

Sea Breeze

The flesh is sad alas! and all books I have read.
To fly far away! I know that the sea-birds are drunk
With being amid the unknown foam and the skies!

---

* This, and the other poems by
Mallarmé collected here, are translated
by Roger Fry.

  21. *such . . . dream*: Similar to the
dream of the sage.

  23. *abstracted*: Refers to the poet; distracted.

Nothing, not old gardens reflected in eyes
Will keep back this heart that is plunged in the sea   5
Oh nights! nor the deserted light of the lamp
On the empty paper which its whiteness protects
Nor even the young woman suckling her child.
I will start! Steamer balancing your masts,
Heave anchor to reach a nature exotic!   10

Ennui, devastated by my cruel hopes,
Still believes in the handkerchief's final adieu!
And perhaps the masts, inviting tempests,
Are of those which a wind bends over shipwrecks
Lost, without masts, without masts or fertile isles . . .   15
But oh my heart listen to the sailors' song!

Another Fan*

Dear dreamer, that I may plunge
Into pure trackless delight,
Know, by a subtle deceit,
How to hold my wing in your hand.

A freshness of twilight comes   5
Upon you at each wing-beat
Whose prisoned strokes defer
The horizon delicately.

Vastness! See how thrills
Space like an immense kiss   10
Which, mad to be born for no one
Neither can flow nor be still.

Do you feel the wild paradise
Which like laughter entombed
Flows from the lips' last curve   15
Down the unanimous fold!

---

11. *Ennui*: Boredom or melancholy.

* Written for the poet's daughter. This poem, and an earlier "Fan" for the poet's wife, were actually written on fans, thus uniting the statement to its illustration.

1–4. The fan speaks to the "dreamer" holding it. Manipulated in the air, it appears to be a wing—hence the "deceit."

5–8. Imprisoned in the hand, and held before the face, the fan's strokes seem to push back the horizon, or actually to hide it from the eyes.

9–10. *thrills space*: Space is agitated by the fan's motion.

15–16. The laugh would flow directly down from her mouth along the fold of the closed fan, held next to her lips.

The sceptre of rose-red shores
Stagnant on evenings of gold is
This white flight which you place
Against a bracelet's fire.   20

The Afternoon of a Faun
Eclogue*

The Faun

These nymphs I would perpetuate.

                            So clear
Their light carnation, that it floats in the air
Heavy with tufted slumbers.

                      Was it a dream I loved?
My doubt, a heap of ancient night, is finishing
In many a subtle branch, which, left the true   5
Wood itself, proves, alas! that all alone I gave
Myself for triumph the ideal sin of roses.
Let me reflect. . . .

                      if the girls of which you tell
Figure a wish of your fabulous senses!
Faun, the illusion escapes from the blue eyes   10
And cold, like a spring in tears, of the chaster one:
But, the other, all sighs, do you say she contrasts
Like a breeze of hot day in your fleece!
But no! through the still, weary faintness
Choking with heat the fresh morn if it strives,   15
No water murmurs but what my flute pours
On the chord sprinkled thicket; and the sole wind
Prompt to exhale from my two pipes, before
It scatters the sound in a waterless shower,
Is, on the horizon's unwrinkled space,   20
The visible serene artificial breath
Of th'inspiration, which regains the sky.

17–20. The fan's "wing" or "flight" is now closed, and takes on the appearance of a scepter placed next to her sparkling bracelet.

* A faun is a Greek woodland satyr with goat-like horns. An eclogue is a bucolic poem, usually in dialogue form, originating in Greek and Latin poetry.

2. *carnation*: Flesh pink.

4–7. As the faun awakens, he finds that only woods surround him and that he has therefore dreamed about nymphs ("roses," the symbol of love and female beauty) yielding to him.

9. *fabulous*: Both "wonderful" and "storytelling."

18–22. The only water here is the dry rain of music from the faun's flute, liquid chords produced by his "inspiration" (breathing) that return to the sky as part of a natural cycle.

Oh you, Sicilian shores of a calm marsh
That more than the suns my vanity havocs,
Silent beneath the flowers of sparks, RELATE   25
'That here I was cutting the hollow reeds tamed
By talent, when on the dull gold of the distant
Verdures dedicating their vines to the springs,
There waves an animal whiteness at rest:
And that to the prelude where the pipes first stir   30
This flight of swans, no! Naiads, flies
Or plunges . . .'

                  Inert, all burns in the fierce hour
Nor marks by what art all at once bolted
Too much hymen desired by who seeks the *la*:
Then shall I awake to the primitive fervor,   35
Straight and alone, 'neath antique floods of light,
Lilies! and one of you all through my ingenuousness.

As well as this sweet nothing their lips purr,
The kiss, which a hush assures of the perfid ones,
My breast, though proofless, still attests a bite   40
Mysterious, due to some august tooth;
But enough! for confidant such mystery chose
The great double reed which one plays 'neath the blue:
Which, the cheek's trouble turning to itself
Dreams, in a solo long, we might amuse   45
Surrounding beauties by confusions false
Between themselves and our credulous song;
And to make, just as high as love modulates,
Die out of the everyday dream of a back
Or a pure flank followed by my curtained eyes,   50
An empty, sonorous, monotonous line.

Try then, instrument of flights, oh malign
Syrinx, to reflower by the lakes where you wait for me!
I, proud of my rumor, for long I will talk
Of goddesses; and by picturings idolatrous,   55
From their shades unloose yet more of their girdles:
So when of grapes the clearness I've sucked,

23. The invocation to the countryside recalls the openings of ancient poems, such as the *Iliad* and the *Aeneid*, which invoke divine inspiration.
26. The faun's pipes were made from cut reeds.
31. *Naiads*: Water nymphs.
34. *Hymen*: Marriage or sexual union. *La*: Both a musical note and the feminine article *the* in French.

45–47. The faun turns his frustration and guilt into song, blending nature and music and transforming the nymphs' remembered silhouette into lines of music.
53. *Syrinx*: In Greek mythology, a nymph who fled from Pan and was turned into reeds, which then became the "panpipes" or faun's flute.
54. *Rumor*: The sounds he makes.

To banish regret by my ruse disavowed,
Laughing, I lift the empty bunch to the sky,
Blowing into its luminous skins and athirst   60
To be drunk, till the evening I keep looking through.

Oh nymphs, we diverse MEMORIES refill.
'My eye, piercing the reeds, shot at each immortal
Neck, which drowned its burning in the wave
With a cry of rage to the forest sky;   65
And the splendid bath of their hair disappears
In the shimmer and shuddering, oh diamonds!
I run, when, there at my feet, enlaced, lie
(Hurt by the languor they taste to be two)
Girls sleeping amid their own casual arms;   70
Them I seize, and not disentangling them, fly
To this thicket, hated by the frivolous shade,
Of roses drying up their scent in the sun
Where our delight may be like the day sun-consumed.'
I adore it, the anger of virgins, the wild   75
Delight of the sacred nude burden which slips
To escape from my hot lips drinking, as lightning
Flashes! the secret terror of the flesh:
From the feet of the cruel one to the heart of the timid
Who together lose an innocence, humid   80
With wild tears or less sorrowful vapors.
'My crime is that I, gay at conquering the treacherous
Fears, the dishevelled tangle divided
Of kisses, the gods kept so well commingled;
For before I could stifle my fiery laughter   85
In the happy recesses of one (while I kept
With a finger alone, that her feathery whiteness
Should be dyed by her sister's kindling desire,
The younger one, naive and without a blush)
When from my arms, undone by vague failing,   90
This prey without gratitude sets herself free
Nor pities the sob wherewith I was still drunk.'

Ah well, towards happiness others will lead me
With their tresses knotted to the horns of my brow:
You know, my passion, that purple and just ripe,   95
The pomegranates burst and murmur with bees;

58. *my ruse*: To indulge in further lascivious dreams in order to forget his
loss.
62. In order to continue the story.
83–84. The two nymphs were entwined
in sleep, and the faun's crime is to have
separated them in his attempted rape; it
is also his mistake, since they are able
to escape.
95–98. As pomegranates burst and
scatter seeds in their ripeness, so the
faun, bursting with passion, becomes
himself a fruit to be consumed—perhaps
by Venus, the goddess of love.

And our blood, aflame for her who will take it,
Flows for all the eternal swarm of desire.
At the hour when this wood's dyed with gold and with ashes
A festival glows in the leafage extinguished: 100
Etna! 'tis amid you, visited by Venus
On your lava fields placing her candid feet,
When a sad stillness thunders wherein the flame dies.
I hold the queen!

             O penalty sure . . .

                       No, but the soul
Void of word and my body weighed down   105
Succumb in the end to midday's proud silence:
No more, I must sleep, forgetting the outrage,
On the thirsty sand lying, and as I delight
Open my mouth to wine's potent star!

Adieu, both! I shall see the shade you became.   110

Saint

      At the window holding
      The old cedarwood disgilt
      Of her lute shining
      Once with flute or mandola,

      Stands the pale saint spreading   5
      The old book which unfolds
      On the Magnificat glistening
      Once for vespers and compline:

      At this monstrance window
      Brushed by the harp that an angel   10
      Makes in his evening flight
      For the delicate tip

      Of the finger that without cedar
      Or old book she balances
      On the feathered instrument,   15
      Musician of silence.

101. *Etna*: A volcano in Sicily.
104–107. The faun's heightened desire lets him imagine seizing Venus herself, a blasphemy (literal translation of "outrage") quickly punished as he falls back into sleep.
2. *disgilt*: Having lost its gilding, or gold decoration.
8. *vespers and compline*: Evening church services.
9. *monstrance*: An altar receptacle in which the Host is held; it has a small glass window in front.

Sonnet

This virgin, beautiful and lively day
Will it tear with a stroke of its drunken wing
The hard, forgotten lake which haunts 'neath the frost
The transparent glacier of flights unflown!

A swan of past days recalls it is he   5
Magnificent but without hope who is freed
For not having sung the realm where to live
When sterile winter's ennui has shone forth.

All his neck will shake off this white agony
By space inflicted on the bird who denies it,   10
But not the horror of the soil where his plumage is caught.

Fantom that to this place his brightness assigns him,
He is stilled in the icy dream of contempt
Which clothes in his useless exile the Swan.

The Tomb of Edgar Poe*

Such as to himself eternity's changed him,
The Poet arouses with his naked sword
His age fright-stricken for not having known
That Death was triumphing in that strange voice!

They, with a Hydra's vile spasm at hearing the angel   5
Giving a sense more pure to the words of their tribe
Proclaimed aloud the sortilege drunk
In the dishonored flow of some black brew.

2. *Drunken wing*: A wild, impulsive gesture; also in the original French, an astonishing extended rhyme with *is freed* (1. 6: *d'aile ivre* / *délivre*).

4. The accumulation of refusals to fly has frozen the swan into immobility.

13–14. The swan's contempt for mundane reality exiles him from life and warmth, and still leads nowhere. This poem has been called a "sonnet in i" (pronounced *ee*): in the original French, all 14 end-rhymes are based on *ee* and the last line contains the sound 5 times. The grafting effect of the repeated *ee* sound, combined with images of chill whiteness, suggests harshness and sterility.

* Written for a ceremony commemorating the American writer Edgar Allan Poe in 1875 or 1876.

1–4. The poet is truly known only when he is dead.

4. *Death*: As absolute truth; also, Poe's work emphasized themes of death.

5. *Hydra*: A mythical many-headed serpent, here compared with those who slandered Poe when he was alive. *the angel*: The transformed Poet of the first stanza, now seen as battling with the hydra.

7. *sortilege*: Spell. *Drunk*: Poe's critics claimed that he wrote drunken fantasies.

Oh, Grief! From soil and from the hostile cloud,
If thence our idea cannot carve a relief   10
Wherewith to adorn Poe's shining tomb

Calm block fallen down here from some dark disaster
May this granite at least show forever their bourn
To the black flights of Blasphemy sparse in the future.

The Tomb of Edgar Poe*

Such as unto himself at last Eternity changes him,
The Poet arouses with a naked hymn
His century overawed not to have known
That death extolled itself in this strange voice:

But, in a vile writing of an hydra (they) once hearing the Angel   5
To give too pure a meaning to the words of the tribe,
They (between themselves) thought (by him) the spell drunk
In the honorless flood of some dark mixture.

Of the soil and the ether (which are) enemies, o struggle!
If with it my idea does not carve a bas-relief   10
Of which Poe's dazzling tomb be adorned,

(A) Stern block here fallen from a mysterious disaster,
Let this granite at least show forever their bound
To the old flights of Blasphemy (still) spread in the future.

All the Soul Indrawn . . .

All the soul indrawn
When slowly we exhale it
In many rounds of smoke
Lost in other rounds

11–12. The tomb ("granite") seen as a
meteorite fallen from the sky. *Disaster*:
In another play on words, dark or negative *star* (*aster*).

13. *Bourn*: Or boundary, also the
word for the milestone along French
roads. The stone tomb is to mark the
end of the bat-like flights of slander.

* Mallarmé himself made this translation of an earlier version of the poem
(the main difference is the word *hymn*
for *sword* as the poet's weapon, line 2),
and supplied the following notes.

2. *naked hymn*: When the words take
in death in their absolute value.

4. *this*: His own.
5. *the Angel*: The above-said poet.
6. *to give*: Giving.
7. In plain prose: Charged him with
always being drunk.
11. *dazzling*: With the idea of such a
bas-relief.
14. *Blasphemy*: Against poets, such as
the charge of Poe being drunk.
1. *indrawn*: A pun—*drawn in*, also
summed up. *Soul* traditionally implies
breath (of life).
2. The French word used for *exhale*
also means *expire*.

Proves that some cigar   5
Burns skilfully how-so little
Its ash withdraws itself
From the clear kiss of fire

So the choir of songs
Flies it to your lip   10
Exclude if you begin
The real as being base

Its too sharp sense will overscrawl
Your vague literature.

A Lace Curtain . . .

A lace curtain stands effaced
In doubt of the supreme Game
Unfolding like a blasphemy
On eternal bedlessness.

This unanimous white conflict   5
Of a garland with its like
Vanishing on the pallid glass
Is floating more than burying.

But with him where dreams are gilt
Sadly sleeps a mandola   10
Whose hollow void is musical

Such that towards some window pane
According to no womb but its,
Filial one might be born.

5–8. However much or little the cigar burns, it separates ash from the fire and smoke.

9–12. As you compose poetry (smoke rings), exclude base reality.

13. *overscrawl*: Also *cross out*, as in a faulty composition.

1. *Stands effaced*: Also *abolishes itself*. The curtain is barely visible against the window in the pale light of dawn of line 8.

2. The Game of love and creativty, suggested by the absent bed of line 4, or the Game of random chance governing the universe, or the "futile game of writing" that Mallarmé describees elsewhere: a number of possibilities, all contained in the one image.

3–4. The lace curtain suggests bed curtains, but there is no bed.

5–6. The entwined garlands of the lace.

7–8. Emphasis on the quivering curtain, the play of possibilities, rather than on anything it hides.

9–11. With the visionary poet there is the possibility of musical or poetic creation, symbolized by the belly of the mandolin.

11–13. The child (person, poem, or song) born from the mandolin's womb tends toward a windowpane—often, in Mallarmé, an image of art through which one looks at nothingness or pure reality.

ARTHUR RIMBAUD
(1854–1891)
The Seekers of Lice[a]

When the child's forehead, full of red torments,
Implores the white swarm of indistinct dreams,
There come near his bed two tall charming sisters
With slim fingers that have silvery nails.

They seat the child in front of a wide open   5
Window where the blue air bathes a mass of flowers,
And in his heavy hair where the dew falls,
Move their delicate, fearful and enticing fingers.

He listens to the singing of their apprehensive breath
Which smells of long rosy plant honey,   10
And which at times a hiss interrupts, saliva
Caught on the lip or desire for kisses.

He hears their black eyelashes beating in the perfumed
Silence; and their gentle electric fingers
Make in his half-drunken indolence the death of the little lice
Crackle under their royal nails.

Then the wine of Sloth rises in him,
The sigh of an harmonica which could bring on delirium;
The child feels, according to the slowness of the caresses,
Surging in him and dying continuously a desire to cry.   20

Les Chercheuses de poux[b]

Quand le front de l'enfant, plein de rouges tourmentes,
Implore l 'essaim blanc des rêves indistincts,
Il vient près de son lit deux grandes soeurs charmantes
Avec de frêles doights aux ongles argentins.

---

a. Translated by Wallace Fowlie. Compare the original, and the translations by Pound and Lowell. The lice-seekers are two Mlles. Gindre (aunts of Georges Izambard, Rimbaud's former teacher and friend), to whose house the 15-year-old poet came after a week spent in prison for traveling by railroad without a ticket; he had run away from home to Paris.

15. *half-drunken*: The French word for drunken (*gris*) also means *gray*, recalling the "white swarm" of line 2.

b. For comparison with Wallace Fowlie's close translation, the poem is given here in French, and following in two quite different translations.

Elles assoient l'enfant devant une croisée 5
Grande ouverte où l'air bleu baigne un fouillis de fleurs,
Et dans ses lourds cheveux où tombe la rosée
Promènent leurs doigts fins, terribles et charmeurs.

Il écoute chanter leurs haleines craintives
Qui fleurent de longs miels végétaux et rosés, 10
Et qu'interrompt parfois un sifflement, salives
Reprises sur la lèvre ou désirs de baisers.

Il entend leurs cils noirs battant sous les silences
Parfumés; et leurs doigts électriques et doux
Font crépiter parmi ses grises indolences 15
Sous leurs ongles royaux la mort des petits poux.

Voilà que monte en lui le vin de la Paresse,
Soupir d'harmonica qui pourrait délirer;
L'enfant se sent, selon la lenteur des caresses,
Sourdre et mourir sans cesse un désir de pleurer. 20

Lice-Hunters[a]

When the kid's forehead is full of red torments
Imploring swarms of dreams with vague contents,
Two large and charming sisters come
With wafty fingers and silvery nails, to his bedroom.

They set the kid by a wide-open window where 5
A tangle of flowers bathes in the blue air
And run fine, alluring, terrible
Fingers through his thick dew-matted hair.

He hears the rustling of their timid breath
Flowerd with the long pinkish vegetable honies underneath 10
Or broken anon, sibilant, the saliva's hiss
Drawn from a lip, or a desire to kiss.

He hears their black eyelashes beat in that quietude
and "Crack!" to break his inebriated indolences
Neath their electric and so soft fingers death assails 15
The little lice beneath their regal nails.

a. Translated by Ezra Pound.

And Lo! there mounts within him Wine of Laziness—
  a squiffer's sigh
Might bring delirium—and the kid feels
Neath the slowness of their caresses, constantly
Wane and fade a desire to cry.   20

The Lice-Hunters[a]

The child, feverish, frowning, only saw red
finally, and begged the fairies for his life;
the royal sisters sat beside his bed;
each long and silver finger was a knife.

They laid the child beside the window's arch,   5
half-open. A glass of violets drank the blue;
he felt their wicked razor fingers march
through his thick hair to comb away the dew.

He heard their singing breath, and tried to breathe
the scent of rose and almond honey, hissed   10
and whistled through the fissures of their teeth,
sucking saliva from the lips he kissed.

He heard their eyebeows beating in the dark
whenever an electric finger struck to crush
a bloated louse, and blood would pop and mark   15
the indolence of their disdainful touch.

Wine of idleness had flushed his eyes;
somewhere a child's harmonica pushed its sigh
insanely through the wearied lungs—the rise
and dying of his ceaseless wish to cry.   20

The Drunken Boat[b]

As I descended black, impassive Rivers,
I sensed that haulers were no longer guiding me:
Screaming Redskins took them for their targets,
Nailed nude to colored stakes: barbaric trees.

a. Translated by Robert Lowell.
b. Translated by Stepan Stepanchev.
Written as an introductory piece to present to the poet Verlaine and his friends
when Rimbaud ran away to Paris in
September 1871. The French original is
written in alexandrines, the 12-syllable
line as traditional in French poetry as
pentameter is in English.
  2. The image is of a barge being
towed along a canal.

I was indifferent to all my crews;
I carried English cottons, Flemish wheat.
When the disturbing din of haulers ceased,
The Rivers let me ramble where I willed.

Through the furious ripping of the sea's mad tides,
Last winter, deafer than an infant's mind,
I ran! And drifting, green Peninsulas
Did not know roar more gleefully unkind.

A tempest blessed my vigils on the sea.
Lighter than a cork I danced on the waves,
Those endless rollers, as they say, of graves:
Ten nights beyond a lantern's silly eye!

Sweeter than sourest apple-flesh to children,
Green water seeped into my pine-wood hull
And washed away blue wine stains, vomitings,
Scattering rudder, anchor, man's lost rule.

And then I, trembling, plunged into the Poem
Of the Sea, infused with stars, milk-white,
Devouring azure greens; where remnants, pale
And gnawed, of pensive corpses fell from light;

Where, staining suddenly the blueness, delirium.
The slow rhythms of the pulsing glow of day,
Stronger than alcohol and vaster than our lyres,
The bitter reds of love ferment the way!

I know skies splitting into light, whirled spouts
Of water, surfs, and currents: I know the night,
The dawn exalted like a flock of doves, pure wing,
And I have seen what men imagine they have seen.

I saw the low sun stained with mystic horrors,
Lighting long, curdled clouds of violet,
Like actors in a very ancient play,
Waves rolling distant thrills like lattice light!

5

10

15

20

25

30

35

15. A famous poem by Victor Hugo, "Oceano nox," refers to the sea as a graveyard where sailors' corpses roll eternally.

16. *lanterns*: The port beacons that show boats where they are.

19. *blue wine*: A cheap, ordinary, bitter wine.

21–22. The French word for sea sounds the same as the word for mother (*mer*/*mère*); for the Symbolists, the word *poem* always recalls its etymological sense of *creation*. Rimbaud combines these associations in the image of a return to primal creativity, the sea as womb of all life.

34–35. Rimbaud imagines the set poses of ancient actors robed in purple.

36. The regular rhythm of the waves looks like the quivering of lattices or Venetian blinds.

I dreamed of green night, stirred by dazzling snows,
Of kisses rising to the sea's eyes, slowly,
The sap-like coursing of surprising currents,
And singing phosphors, flaring blue and gold!   40

I followed, for whole months, a surge like herds
Of insane cattle in assault on the reefs,
Unhopeful that three Marys, come on luminous feet,
Could force a muzzle on the panting seas!

Yes, I struck incredible Floridas   45
That mingled flowers and the eyes of panthers
In skins of men! And rainbows bridled green
Herds beneath the horizon of the seas.

I saw the ferment of enormous marshes, weirs
Where a whole Leviathan lies rotting in the weeds!   50
Collapse of waters within calms at sea,
And distances in cataract toward chasms!

Glaciers, silver suns, pearl waves, and skies like coals,
Hideous wrecks at the bottom of brown gulfs
Where giant serpents eaten by red bugs   55
Drop from twisted trees and shed a black perfume!

I should have liked to show the young those dolphins
In blue waves, those golden fish, those fish that sing.
—Foam like flowers rocked my sleepy drifting,
And, now and then, fine winds supplied me wings.   60

When, feeling like a martyr, I tired of poles and zones,
The sea, whose sobbing made my tossing sweet,
Raised me its dark flowers, deep and yellow whirled,
And, like a woman, I fell on my knees . . .

Peninsula, I tossed upon my shores   65
The quarrels and droppings of clamorous, blond-eyed birds.
I sailed until, across my rotting cords,
Drowned men, spinning backwards, fell asleep! . . .

40. *Phosphors*: Tiny marine animals, *noctiluca*.
41–44. Refers to a tradition that the three Biblical Marys crossed the sea during a storm to land in Camargue, a region in southern France famous for its wild horses and bulls.
45. *Floridas* [plural]: a name given to any exotic country.
50. *Leviathan*: Vast Biblical sea monster (Job 41:1–10).
64. The ellipsis indicates the passage of time; nothing is left out.
65. *Peninsula*: Two words in the French text (*Presque île*), reading literally "Almost an island"; the combined word *Presqu'île* means peninsula. The boat sails on, isolated in the middle of the sea.

Now I, a lost boat in the hair of coves,
Hurled by tempest into a birdless air, 70
I, whose drunken carcass neither Monitors
Nor Hansa ships would fish back for men's care;

Free, smoking, rigged with violet fogs,
I, who pierced the red sky like a wall
That carries exquisite mixtures for good poets, 75
Lichens of sun and azure mucus veils;

Who, spotted with electric crescents, ran
Like a mad plank, escorted by seahorses,
When cudgel blows of hot Julys struck down
The sea-blue skies upon wild water spouts; 80

I, who trembled, feeling the moan at fifty leagues
Of rutting Behemoths and thick Maelstroms, I,
Eternal weaver of blue .immobilities,
I long for Europe with its ancient quays!

I saw sidereal archipelagoes! and isles 85
Whose delirious skies are open to the voyager:
—Is it in depthless nights you sleep your exile,
A million golden birds, O future Vigor?—

But, truly, I have wept too much! The dawns disturb.
All moons are painful, and all suns break bitterly: 90
Love has swollen me with drunken torpors.
Oh, that my keel might break and spend me in the sea!

Of European waters I desire
Only the black, cold puddle in a scented twilight
Where a child of sorrows squats and sets the sails 95
Of a boat as frail as a butterfly in May.

I can no longer, bathed in languors, O waves,
Cross the wake of cotton-bearers on long trips,
Nor ramble in a pride of flags and flares,
Nor swim beneath the horrible eyes of prison ships. 100

---

69. *Hair of coves*: Seaweed.
71–72. *Monitors*: Armored coast-guard ships. *Hansa ships*: Vessels belonging to the German Hanseatic League of commercial maritime cities.
82. *Behemoth* is a large animal resembling a hippopotamus (Job 40,15).

84. *Quays*: Literally *parapets*, the fixed and familiar forms of older European architecture. Rimbaud is tired of fluidity, insecurity, and lack of form.
100. *Horrible eyes of prison ships*: Portholes of ships tied at anchor and used as prisons.

A Season in Hell*

Night of Hell[1]

I have swallowed a first-rate draught of poison.—Thrice blessed be the counsel that came to me!—My entrails are on fire. The violence of the venom wrings my limbs, deforms me, fells me. I am dying of thirst, I am suffocating, I cannot cry out. This is hell, the everlasting punishment! Mark how the fire surges up again! I am burning properly. There you are, demon!

I had caught a glimpse of conversion to righteousness and happiness, salvation. May I describe the vision; the atmosphere of hell does not permit hymns! It consisted of millions of charming creatures, a sweet sacred concert, power and peace, noble ambitions, and goodness knows what else.

Noble ambitions![2]

And yet this is life!—What if damnation is eternal! A man who chooses to mutilate himself is rightly damned, isn't he? I believe that I am in hell, consequently I am there.[3] This is the effect of the catechism. I am the slave of my baptism.[4] Parents, you have caused my affliction and you have caused your own. Poor innocent!—Hell cannot assail pagans.—This is life, nevertheless! Later, the delights of damnation will be deeper. A crime, quickly, that I may sink to nothingness, in accordance with human law.

Be silent, do be silent! . . . There is shame, reproof, in this place: Satan who says that the fire is disgraceful, that my wrath is frightfully foolish.—Enough! . . . The errors that are whispered to me, enchantments, false perfumes, childish melodies.[5]—And to say that I possess truth, that I understand justice: I have a sound and steady judgment, I am prepared for perfection . . . Pride.—The skin of my head is drying up. Pity! Lord, I am terrified. I am thirsty, so thirsty! Ah! childhood, the grass, the rain, the lake upon the stones, *the moonlight when the bell tower was striking twelve*[6] . . . the devil is in the bell tower, at that hour. Mary! Blessed Virgin! . . .—The horror of my stupidity.

---

* Translated by Enid Rhodes Peschel.
1. After the preface, the second section of the autobiographical *A Season in Hell.* The first section, "Bad Blood," refers to his solitary childhood and his sense of being condemned and belonging to an "inferior race": weak, cowardly, opportunist. "I get from my Gallic ancestors my pale blue eye, my small brain, and my awkwardness in fighting. . . . I cannot understand revolt. My race never rose in rebellion except to plunder: like wolves with the beast they have not killed." It also establishes the major contrast between European Christianity, allied to an authoritarian and hypocritical colonialist society, and African paganism seen as a freer, more natural and spontaneous existence.

2. Self-mockery as Rimbaud recalls, in hell, his earlier idealism and the temptations of conversion—of becoming a practicing Catholic.
3. A parody of the well-known phrase, "I think, therefore I am," of the seventeenth-century French rationalist philosopher René Descartes, a phrase which had become a symbol of French respect for well-ordered thought.
4. Rimbaud suggests that Christian baptism establishes the context of heaven and hell, and therefore the possibility of being damned.
5. The poetic visions and harmonies that Rimbaud explored with Verlaine.
6. A collection of romanticized childhood memories.

Over there, are they not honest souls, who wish me well? . . . Come . . . I have a pillow over my mouth, they don't hear me, they are phantoms. Besides, no one ever thinks of others. Let no one approach. I reek of burning, that's certain.

The hallucinations are countless. It's exactly what I've always had: no more faith in history, neglect of principles. I shall be silent about this: poets and visionaries would be jealous. I am a thousand times the richest, let us be avaricious like the sea.

Now then! the clock of life has just stopped. I am no longer in the world.—Theology is serious, hell is certainly *below*—and heaven above.—Ecstasy, nightmare, sleep in a nest of flames.

What pranks during my vigilance in the country . . . Satan, Ferdinand,[7] races with the wild seeds . . . Jesus walks on the purplish briers, without bending them . . . Jesus used to walk on the troubled waters. The lantern revealed him to us, a figure standing, pale and with brown tresses, beside a wave of emerald. . . .[8]

I am going to unveil all the mysteries: mysteries religious or natural, death, birth, futurity, antiquity, cosmogony, nothingness. I am a master of phantasmagories.

Listen! . . .

I have all the talents!—There is nobody here and there is somebody: I would not wish to scatter my treasure.—Do you wish for Negro chants, dances of houris?[9] Do you wish me to vanish, to dive in search of the *ring*?[10] Do you? I shall produce gold, cures.

Rely, then, upon me: faith comforts, guides, heals. All of you, come,—even the little children,[11]—that I may console you, that one may pour out his heart for you,—the marvelous heart!—Poor men, laborers! I do not ask for prayers; with your confidence alone, I shall be happy.

—And let's think of me.[12] This makes me miss the world very little. I have the good fortune not to suffer any longer. My life was nothing but sweet follies, regrettably.

Bah! let's make all the grimaces imaginable.

Decidedly, we are out of the world. No more sound. My sense of touch has disappeared. Ah! my castle, my Saxony,[13] my forest of willows. The evenings, the mornings, the nights, the days . . . Am I weary!

I ought to have my hell for wrath, my hell for pride,—and the

---

7. Name given to the devil by the peasants at Vouziers, where Rimbaud wrote *A Season in Hell*.

8. In John 6, 16–21, Jesus' disciples see him walking on the sea at night.

9. Beautiful virgins in the Koranic paradise.

10. At the end of Wagner's four-part operatic cycle, "The Ring of the Nibelung," Hagen plunges into the river Rhine to recapture the golden ring of world power.

11. Parody of Jesus' words: "Suffer little children, and forbid them not, to come unto me" (Matthew 19,14).

12. Abrupt change to a conversational tone that contrasts sharply with the preceding Luciferian ambition to resemble God.

13. Germanic duchy, part of Rimbaud's visionary memories.

hell of the caress; a concert of hells.

I am dying of weariness. This is the tomb, I am going to the worms, horror of horrors! Satan, jester, you wish to undo me, with your spells. I protest. I protest! one jab of the pitchfork, one lick of fire.

Ah! to rise again to life! To cast eyes upon our deformities. And that poison, that kiss a thousand times accursed! My weakness, the cruelty of the world! Dear God, your mercy, hide me, I regard myself too poorly!—I am hidden and I am not.

It is the fire that rises again with the soul condemned to it.

Morning[1]

Did I not *once* have a lovely youth, heroic, fabulous, to be inscribed on leaves of gold,—too much luck! Through what crime, through what error, have I deserved my present weakness? You who maintain that animals heave sobs of grief, that the sick despair, that the dead have bad dreams, try to recount my fall and my sleep. As for me, I can no more explain myself than the beggar with his perpetual *Paters* and *Ave Marias*. *I no longer know how to speak!*

Today, however, I think I have finished the account of my hell. It surely was hell; the old one, the one whose gates the son of man opened.[2]

From the same wilderness, in the same night, always my tired eyes waken to the silver star, always, although the Kings of life, the three magi,[3] the heart, the soul, the mind, are not moved. When shall we go, beyond the shores and the mountains, to acclaim the birth of the new work, the new wisdom, the flight of tyrants and of demons, the end of superstition, to adore—the first worshipers!— Christmas on earth!

The song of the heavens, the procession of peoples! Slaves, let us not blaspheme life.

Farewell

Autumn already!—But why yearn for an eternal sun, if we are committed to the discovery of divine light,—far from the people who die by the seasons.

Autumn. Our boat lifted up through the motionless mists turns

---

1. After "Night of Hell," Rimbaud describes his affair with Verlaine and mocks the frustrated ambitions of his own early poetry. He contrasts Western society with an imaginary, Edenic Eastern civilization, and rejects once more any solution through work or religious faith. In "Morning" and "Farewell," the concluding sections, he summarizes and rejects his previous career and its nostalgia for religious explanations, and enters

a new era of hope, absolute modernity, and the continuing quest for truth.

2. Reference to the belief that Christ descended into Hell after death, in order to free the souls of Old Testament saints from Limbo.

3. Another reworking of a Biblical motif, this time of the Nativity scene and the visit of the Magi (Matthew 2, 1–11).

toward the port of poverty, the enormous city[1] with its sky stained
by fire and mud. Ah! the putrid rags, the rain-drenched bread, the
drunkenness, the thousand loves that have crucified me! Will she
not stop at all, then, this ghoul queen of millions of souls and of
dead bodies *which be judged!* I see myself again, my skin pitted by
mud and pestilence, my hair and my armpits full of worms, and
even bigger worms in my heart; lying among strangers without age,
without feeling . . . I could have died there . . . Frightful recollection! I abhor poverty.

And I dread winter because it is the season of comfort![2]

—Sometimes I see in the sky endless beaches covered with joyful
white nations. A great golden ship, above me, waves its multicolored pennants in the morning breezes. I have created all festivals,
all triumphs, all dramas. I have tried to invent new flowers, new
stars, new flesh, new tongues. I believed I acquired supernatural
powers. Well! I must bury my imagination and my memories! A
great glory as an artist and storyteller swept away![3]

I! I who called myself a seer or an angel, exempt from all morality, I am restored to the earth, with a duty to seek, and rugged reality to embrace![4] Peasant!

Am I deceived? would charity be the sister of death, for me?

Finally, I shall beg pardon for having nourished myself on
falsehood.[5] Then let's go.

But not one friendly hand! and where am I to draw help?

Yes, the new hour is at the least very harsh.

For I can say that victory is won for me: the gnashings of teeth,
the hissing of fire, the reeking sighs are subsiding. All the foul memories are fading away. My last regrets are scampering off—jealousies
for beggars, brigands,[6] friends of death, backward characters of all
sorts.—Damned creatures, if I avenged myself!

One must be absolutely modern.

No hymns: keep the stride made. Hard night! dried blood
smokes on my face, and I have nothing behind me, but that horrible bush![7] . . . Spiritual combat is as brutal as the battle of men;
but the vision of justice is the delight of God alone.

Meanwhile this is the eve. Let us receive all influxes of vigor and

1. Probably London, where Rimbaud and Verlaine lived for a time in poverty.

2. Rimbaud uses this English spelling (not French *confort*) in the French text, recalling his months in London and the model of bourgeois comfort from which he felt so alienated.

3. Rimbaud speaks of his earlier at-tempt to write visionary poetry, criticized in "Alchemy of the Word," a preceding section.

4. The season in hell has passed, along with the temptation to accept a Christian belief that damns the sinner.

5. The whole attempt to deny reality and create a transfigured vision.

6. In a preceding section, "The Flash of Lightning," Rimbaud has associated beggars and bandits with priests.

7. Probably the Tree of Good and Evil in Paradise (Genesis 2, 17); see a similar image in "Morning of Drunken-ness." Possibly also a reference to the burning bush of the Old Testament, from which Moses heard the voice of God (Exodus 3, 2–4).

of real tenderness. And at dawn, armed with an ardent patience, we shall enter the splendid cities.[8]

What was I saying about a friendly hand! One great advantage is that I can laugh at the old false loves, and smite with shame those deceitful couples,—I have seen the hell of women down there;— and it will be permissible for me to *possess truth in one soul and one body*.

April-August 1873

The Illuminations[*]

III. Tale

A Prince was vexed at never having occupied himself with anything but the perfection of ordinary generosities. He foresaw astonishing revolutions in love, and suspected his wives of being capable of something better than that complaisance adorned by heaven and by luxury. He demanded to see the truth, the hour of essential desire and satisfaction. Whether or not this was an aberration of piety, he demanded it. He possessed at least a rather large human power.

All the women who had known him were assassinated. What havoc in the garden of beauty! Under the sword, they blessed him. He did not order any new ones.—The women reappeared.

He killed all those who followed him, after the hunt or the libations.—All followed him.

He amused himself by butchering beasts of luxury. He made palaces burn. He hurled himself at people and hacked them to pieces. —The crowd, the golden roofs, the beautiful beasts still subsisted.

Can one go into ecstasies over destruction, be rejuvenated by cruelty! The people did not murmur. No one offered the assistance of his own views.

One evening he was galloping proudly. A Genie appeared, of a beauty ineffable, undeclarable even. From his physiognomy and from his bearing issued the promise of a love manifold and complex! of a happiness inexpressible, insupportable even! The Prince and the Genie destroyed one another probably in essential health.[1] How could they not have died of it? Together, then, they died.

But this Prince expired, in his palace, at a normal age. The Prince was the Genie. The Genie was the Prince.

Masterly music disappoints our desire.

8. Optimistic vision of the modern world and cities, contrasting with misery in London at the beginning of "Farewell"; a comparison recalling the contrast, in St. Augustine, of the new Jerusalem or "city of God" and the sinful worldly city of Babylon.

* A series of prose poems (with 2 exceptions) probably written between 1872 and 1875: intense condensed visions expressed in highly organized and rhythmic prose. Translated by Enid Rhodes Peschel.

1. Not mere physical fitness, but the essence of all forms of health.

XI. *Morning of Drunkenness*[1]

O *my* Good! O *my* Beautiful! Excruciating fanfare in which I do not stumble! Magical rack![2] Hurrah for the unheard-of work and for the marvelous body, for the first time! It began with the laughter of children, it will end with it. This poison will remain in all our veins even when, with the changing fanfare, we shall be surrendered to our former disharmony. O now let us, so deserving of these tortures! fervently summon up this superhuman promise made to our created body and soul: this promise, this madness! Elegance, knowledge, violence! We were promised that they would bury in darkness the tree of good and evil, that they would banish tyrannical proprieties, so that we might bring here our very pure love. It began with some repugnance, and it ends—since we cannot at once grasp this eternity—ends with a stampede of perfumes.

Laughter of children, circumspection of slaves, austerity of virgins, horror of the countenances and objects of this place, may you be consecrated by the memory of this vigil. It began with all loutishness, behold that it ends with angels of fire and of ice.

Little vigil of drunkenness, sanctified! were it only for the mask you have conferred on us. We affirm you, method![3] We don't forget that yesterday you glorified each of our ages. We have faith in the poison. We know how to give up your entire life day after day.

This is the time of the Assassins.[4]

XIV. *The Bridges*[1]

Crystalline gray skies. A strange pattern of bridges, these straight, those arched, others descending obliquely at angels to the first, and these configurations repeating themselves in the other illuminated circuits of the canal,[2] but all so long and light that the shores, laden with domes, sink and diminish. Some of these bridges are still encumbered with hovels.[3] Others support masts, signals, frail parapets. Minor chords interweave, and flow smoothly; ropes rise from the steep banks. One detects a red jacket, perhaps other costumes and musical instruments. Are these popular tunes, fragments of manorial concerts, remnants of public anthems? The water is gray

1. Apparently written after Rimbaud's first experience with hashish.
2. The medieval torture rack on which the victims' bodies were stretched.
3. In his letter to Paul Demeny (May 15, 1871), Rimbaud writes of a "long, gigantic, and rational *derangement* of *all the senses*" as a method for becoming a seer (*voyant*) and "reaching the *unknown.*"
4. Word derived from "Hashish-eaters," an eleventh-century Persian sect of murderers whose members' drugged dreams of an exotic afterlife inspired them to extreme bravery and disregard for life.

1. An impressionistic memory of London.
2. The river Thames as it undulates and winds through the city.
3. Houses were once built on London Bridge.

and blue, ample as an arm of the sea.

A white ray, falling.from the summit of the sky, reduces to nothingness this theatrical performance.

XXIII. *Flowers*

From a step of gold—among cords of silk, gray gauzes, green velvets and crystal disks that darken like bronze in the sun—I see the foxglove open on a carpet of silver filigree, of eyes and of hair.[1]

Bits of yellow gold seeded in agate, pillars of mahogany supporting a dome of emeralds, bouquets of white satin and of fine rods of ruby surround the water rose.

Like a god with enormous blue eyes and configurations of snow,[2] the sea and the sky attract to the marble terraces the multitude of young and hardy roses.

XXV. *Seascape*[1]

Chariots of silver and of copper—
Prows of steel and of silver—
Beat the foam—
Uproot the stubs of the briers.
The currents of the heath,
And the huge ruts of the reflux,
Veer in a circle toward the east,
Toward the pillars of the forest,
Toward the shafts[2] of the pier,
Whose corner is struck by whirlwinds of light.

XXIX. *Barbarian*

Long after the days and the seasons, and the creatures and the countries,

The banner of bleeding meat[1] on the silk of the seas and of the arctic flowers; (they do not exist.)

Delivered from the old fanfares of heroism—that still attack our heart and our head—far from the former assassins.

—Oh! the banner of bleeding meat on the silk of the seas and of the arctic flowers; (they do not exist.)

Delights!

1. Possibly a visionary transformation of the theater, with its stage setting, décor, and audience.

2. Mythic personification (through echoed colors of blue and white) of the scene itself: terrace, water, and sky.

1. "Seascape" and "Movement," both published in 1886, are the first French poems in free verse. They still reveal ties to traditional versification, and half of the lines in "Seascape" are in classical meter.

2. The French word for shafts also means *saplings*, thus continuing the juxtaposition of sea and land images.

1. According to some, a description of the Danish flag (white cross on red field) which Rimbaud would have seen on a visit to Iceland, then a Danish possession.

Blazing coals, raining in squalls of hoarfrost—Delights!—fires in the rain of the wind of diamonds, rain hurled down by the earthly heart eternally carbonized for us—O world!—

(Far from the old retreats and the old flames, that are known, that are felt,)

Blazing coals and froths. Music, veering of whirlpools and collisions of drift ice with the stars.

O Delights, oh world, oh music! And there, the forms, the sweats, the heads of hair and the eyes, floating.[2] And the white tears, boiling—oh delights!—and the feminine voice borne down to the bottom of the volcanoes and the arctic grottoes.

The banner . . .

2. Recalls the period when Rimbaud (see "Morning of Drunkenness"). smoked hashish with his Paris friends

AUGUST STRINDBERG

1849–1912

The Ghost Sonata (Spöksonaten) *

Characters

THE OLD MAN, *Hummel, a company director*
THE STUDENT, *Arkenholtz*
THE MILKMAID, *an apparition*
THE CARETAKER'S WIFE
THE CARETAKER
THE LADY IN BLACK, *the daughter of the Caretaker's Wife and the Dead Man. Also referred to as the Dark Lady*
THE COLONEL
THE MUMMY, *the Colonel's wife*
THE GIRL, *the Colonel's daughter, actually the daughter of the Old Man*
THE ARISTOCRAT, *Baron Skanskorg. Engaged to the Lady in Black*
JOHANSSON, *the Old Man's servant*
BENGTSSON, *the Colonel's servant*
THE FIANCÉE, *a white-haired old woman, once betrothed to the Old Man*
THE COOK
A MAIDSERVANT
BEGGARS

* From *Six Plays by Strindberg.* Translated by Elizabeth Sprigge.

Strindberg first thought of calling the play *Kama-Loka*, a term he had happened upon in some theosophical work. It signifies the realm occupied by spirits who are a prey to their own passions.

The actual title reflects the author's conscious choice of a musical structure for his play, whose three scenes represent the sonata structure ABA, followed by a "coda." The underlying piece of music was conceived as being Beethoven's sonata opus 31, no. 2 in D major.

Scene I

Outside the house. The corner of the façade of a modern house, showing the ground floor above, and the street in front. The ground floor terminates on the right in the Round Room, above which, on the first floor, is a balcony with a flagstaff. The windows of the Round Room face the street in front of the house, and at the corner look onto the suggestion of a side-street running towards the back. At the beginning of the scene the blinds of the Round Room are down. When, later, they are raised, the white marble statue of a young woman can be seen, surrounded with palms and brightly lighted by rays of sunshine.

To the left of the Round Room is the Hyacinth Room; its window filled with pots of hyacinths, blue, white and pink. Further left, at the back, is an imposing double front door with laurels in tubs on either side of it. The doors are wide open, showing a staircase of white marble with a banister of mahogany and brass. To the left of the front door is another ground-floor window, with a window-mirror.[1] On the balcony rail in the corner above the Round Room are a blue silk quilt and two white pillows. The windows to the left of this are hung with white sheets.[2]

In the foreground, in front of the house, is a green bench; to the right a street drinking-fountain, to the left an advertisement column.

It is a bright Sunday morning, and as the curtain rises the bells of several churches, some near, some far away, are ringing.

On the staircase the LADY IN BLACK *stands motionless.*

The CARETAKER'S WIFE *sweeps the doorstep, then polishes the brass on the door and waters the laurels.*

In a wheel-chair by the advertisement column sits the OLD MAN, *reading a newspaper. His hair and beard are white and he wears spectacles.*

The MILKMAID[3] *comes round the corner on the right, carrying milk bottles in a wire basket. She is wearing a summer dress with brown shoes, black stockings and a white cap. She takes off her cap and hangs it on the fountain, wipes the perspiration from her forehead, washes her hands and arranges her hair, using the water as a mirror.*

A steamship bell is heard, and now and then the silence is broken by the deep notes of an organ in a nearby church.

After a few moments, when all is silent and the MILKMAID *has finished her toilet, the* STUDENT *enters from the left. He has had a sleepless night and is unshaven. He goes straight up to the fountain. There is a pause before he speaks.*

STUDENT. May I have the cup? [*The* MILKMAID *clutches the cup to her.*] Haven't you finished yet? [*The* MILKMAID *looks at him with horror.*]

OLD MAN [*to himself*] Who's he talking to? I don't see anybody. Is

---

1. "Set at an angle inside the window, so as to show what is going on in the street" [translator's note].

2. "Sign of mourning" [translator's note].

3. She is described as an "apparition" in the list of characters.

he crazy? [*He goes on watching them in great astonishment.*]

STUDENT [*to the* MILKMAID]. What are you staring at? Do I look so terrible? Well, I've had no sleep, and of course you think I've been making a night of it. . . . [*The* MILKMAID *stays just as she is.*] You think I've been drinking, eh? Do I smell of liquor? [*The* MILKMAID *does not change.*] I haven't shaved, I know. Give me a drink of water, girl. I've earned it. [*Pause.*] Oh well, I suppose I'll have to tell you. I spent the whole night dressing wounds and looking after the injured. You see, I was there when that house collapsed[4] last night. Now you know. [*The* MILKMAID *rinses the cup and gives him a drink.*] Thanks. [*The* MILKMAID *stands motionless. Slowly.*] Will you do me a great favor? [*Pause.*] The thing is, my eyes, as you can see, are inflamed, but my hands have been touching wounds and corpses, so it would be danger-ous to put them near my eyes. Will you take my handkerchief—it's quite clean—and dip it in the fresh water and bathe my eyes? Will you do this? Will you play the good Samaritan? [*The* MILK-MAID *hesitates, but does as he bids.*] Thank you, my dear. [*He takes out his purse. She makes a gesture of refusal.*] Forgive my stupidity, but I'm only half-awake. . . . [*The* MILKMAID *disappears.*]

OLD MAN [*to the* STUDENT]. Excuse me speaking to you, but I heard you say you were at the scene of the accident last night. I was just reading about it in the paper.

STUDENT. Is it in the paper already?

OLD MAN. The whole thing, including your portrait. But they regret that they have been unable to find out the name of the splendid young student. . . .

STUDENT. Really? [*Glances at the paper.*] Yes, that's me. Well I never!

OLD MAN. Who was it you were talking to just now?

STUDENT. Didn't you see? [*Pause.*]

OLD MAN. Would it be impertinent to inquire—what in fact your name is?

STUDENT. What would be the point? I don't care for publicity. If you get any praise, there's always disapproval too. The art of run-ning people down has been developed to such a pitch. . . . Besides, I don't want any reward.

OLD MAN. You're well off, perhaps.

STUDENT. No, indeed. On the contrary, I'm very poor.

OLD MAN. Do you know, it seems to me I've heard your voice before. When I was young I had a friend who pronounced cer-tain words just as you do. I've never met anyone else with quite that pronunciation. Only him—and you. Are you by any chance related to Mr. Arkenholtz,[5] the merchant?

---

4. This is the first of many evocations of houses under construction, enduring, decaying, and collapsing or being wrecked—and this first mention refers to a collapse.

5. Not long before there has been a biblical reference, to the "good Samar-itan" of the New Testament parable. The name Arkenholtz may be intended to sug-gest the Ark in which Noah preserved mankind from destruction, or the Ark of the Covenant constructed by the Israelites at the command of the Almighty and carried by them everywhere in their wan-derings.

STUDENT. He was my father.

OLD MAN. Strange are the paths of fate. I saw you when you were an infant, under very painful circumstances.

STUDENT. Yes, I understand I came into the world in the middle of a bankruptcy.[6]

OLD MAN. Just that.

STUDENT. Perhaps I might ask your name.

OLD MAN. I am Mr. Hummel.[7]

STUDENT. Are you the? . . . I remember that . . .

OLD MAN. Have you often heard my name mentioned in your family?

STUDENT. Yes.

OLD MAN. And mentioned perhaps with a certain aversion? [*The* STUDENT *is silent.*] Yes, I can imagine it. You were told, I suppose, that I was the man who ruined your father? All who ruin themselves through foolish speculations consider they were ruined by those they couldn't fool. [*Pause.*] Now these are the facts. Your father robbed me of seventeen thousand crowns—the whole of my savings at that time.

STUDENT. It's queer that the same story can be told in two such different ways.

OLD MAN. You surely don't believe I'm telling you what isn't true?

STUDENT. What am I to believe? My father didn't lie.

OLD MAN. That is so true. A father never lies.[8] But I too am a father, and so it follows . . .

STUDENT. What are you driving at?

OLD MAN. I saved your father from disaster, and he repaid me with all the frightful hatred that is born of an obligation to be grateful.[9] He taught his family to speak ill of me.

STUDENT. Perhaps you made him ungrateful by poisoning your help with unnecessary humiliation.

OLD MAN. All help is humiliating, sir.

STUDENT. What do you want[10] from me?

OLD MAN. I'm not asking for the money, but if you will render me a few small services, I shall consider myself well paid. You see that I am a cripple. Some say it is my own fault; others lay the blame on my parents. I prefer to blame life itself, with its pitfalls. For if you escape one snare, you fall headlong into another. In any case, I am unable to climb stairs or ring doorbells, and that is why I am asking you to help me.

STUDENT. What can I do?

OLD MAN. To begin with, push my chair so that I can read those playbills. I want to see what is on tonight.

6. Strindberg's own birth occurred at a time of great financial stringency for the family.

7. The German word for bumblebee. Like this insect, Mr. Hummel wandered widely and found sustenance in every flower.

8. This sly dig at conventional pieties precedes the unmasking of other shams that constitute the so-called real world.

9. Strindberg himself found this obligation irksome. On one occasion he even complained, in writing, that people from whom he had borrowed money had been sponging on him. And he was humiliated and resentful when friends launched a public appeal for funds for his support.

10. The Student's question shows that he has accepted the truth of the Old Man's story and that he now admits an obligation to him.

STUDENT [*pushing the chair*]. Haven't you got an attendant?

OLD MAN. Yes, but he has gone on an errand. He'll be back soon. Are you a medical student?

STUDENT. No, I am studying languages, but I don't know at all what I'm going to do.

OLD MAN. Aha! Are you good at mathematics?

STUDENT. Yes, fairly.

OLD MAN. Good. Perhaps you would like a job.

STUDENT. Yes, why not?

OLD MAN. Splendid. [*He studies the playbills.*] They are doing *The Valkyrie* for the matinée. That means the Colonel will be there[11] with his daughter, and as he always sits at the end of the sixth row, I'll put you next to him. Go to that telephone kiosk please and order a ticket for seat eighty-two in the sixth row.

STUDENT. Am I to go to the Opera in the middle of the day?

OLD MAN. Yes. Do as I tell you and things will go well with you. I want to see you happy, rich and honored. Your début last night as the brave rescuer will make you famous by tomorrow and then your name will be worth something.

STUDENT [*going to the telephone kiosk*]. What an odd adventure!

OLD MAN. Are you a gambler?[12]

STUDENT. Yes, unfortunately.

OLD MAN. We'll make it fortunately. Go on now, telephone. [*The* STUDENT *goes. The* OLD MAN *reads his paper. The* LADY IN BLACK *comes out on to the pavement and talks to the* CARETAKER'S WIFE. *The* OLD MAN *listens, but the audience hears nothing. The* STUDENT *returns.*] Did you fix it up?

STUDENT. It's done.

OLD MAN. You see that house?

STUDENT. Yes, I've been looking at it a lot. I passed it yesterday when the sun was shining on the windowpanes, and I imagined all the beauty and elegance there must be inside. I said to my companion: "Think of living up there in the top flat, with a beautiful young wife, two pretty little children and an income of twenty thousand crowns a year."

OLD MAN. So that's what you said. That's what you said. Well, well! I too am very fond of this house.

STUDENT. Do you speculate in houses?

OLD MAN. Mm—yes. But not in the way you mean.

STUDENT. Do you know the people who live here?

OLD MAN. Every one of them. At my age one knows everybody, and their parents and grandparents too, and one's always related[13] to them in some way or other. I am just eighty, but no one knows me—not really. I take an interest in human destiny.[14] [*The*

---

11. The first direct revelation of the Old Man's apparent omniscience and of his power drive.

12. Strindberg, though he did not gamble, was greatly addicted to the search for "hidden meanings" in any casual occurrence.

13. This enunciates another important factor in the play. There are multiple blood ties, some not generally known,

that link the characters, and some of these ties were created by secret liaisons. Later there is a reference to a homosexual attraction, and there are also bonds of one sort or another arising from criminal activities.

14. Another hint that the Old Man is far more than the decrepit figure he appears to be.

blinds of the Round Room are drawn up. The COLONEL *is seen, wearing mufti. He looks at the thermometer outside one of the windows, then turns back into the room and stands in front of the marble statue.*] Look, that's the Colonel, whom you will sit next to this afternoon.

STUDENT. Is he—the Colonel? I don't understand any of this, but it's like a fairy story.

OLD MAN. My whole life's like a book of fairy stories,[15] sir. And although the stories are different, they are held together by one thread, and the main theme constantly recurs.

STUDENT. Who is that marble statue of?

OLD MAN. That, naturally, is his wife.

STUDENT. Was she such a wonderful person?

OLD MAN. Er . . . yes.

STUDENT. Tell me.

OLD MAN. We can't judge people, young man. If I were to tell you that she left him, that he beat her, that she returned to him and married him a second time,[16] and that now she is sitting inside there like a mummy, worshipping her own statue—then you would think me crazy.

STUDENT. I don't understand.

OLD MAN. I didn't think you would. Well, then we have the window with the hyacinths.[17] His daughter lives there. She has gone out for a ride, but she will be home soon.

STUDENT. And who is the dark lady talking to the caretaker?

OLD MAN. Well, that's a bit complicated, but it is connected with the dead man,[18] up there where you see the white sheets.

STUDENT. Why, who was he?

OLD MAN. A human being like you or me, but the most conspicuous thing about him was his vanity. If you were a Sunday child,[19] you would see him presently come out of that door to look at the Consulate flag flying at half-mast. He was, you understand, a Consul, and he reveled in coronets and lions and plumed hats and colored ribbons.

STUDENT. Sunday child, you say? I'm told I was born on a Sunday.

OLD MAN. No, were you really? I might have known it. I saw it from the color of your eyes. Then you can see what others can't. Have you noticed that?

STUDENT. I don't know what others do see, but at times. . . . Oh, but one doesn't talk of such things!

OLD MAN. I was almost sure of it. But you can talk to me, because I understand such things.

STUDENT. Yesterday, for instance . . . I was drawn to that obscure little street where later on the house collapsed. I went there and stopped in front of that building which I had never seen before.

---

15. The Old Man voices Strindberg's own conviction that life has the qualities of fiction, and that seemingly unrelated matters are actually closely connected.

16. Recurrence, or repetition, is a theme built into the structure of the play. Another theme touched on here is that of stagnation.

17. The symbolism of these flowers is explained in Scene 3.

18. Though not listed in the cast of characters, he appears later in this scene.

19. Children born on Sunday were credited with possessing the gift of second sight, the ability to see apparitions.

Then I noticed a crack in the wall. . . . I heard the floor-boards snapping. . . . I dashed over and picked up a child that was passing under the wall. . . . The next moment the house collapsed. I was saved, but in my arms, which I thought held the child, was nothing at all.

OLD MAN. Yes, yes, just as I thought. Tell me something. Why were you gesticulating that way just now by the fountain? And why were you talking to yourself?

STUDENT. Didn't you see the milkmaid I was talking to?

OLD MAN [*in horror*]. Milkmaid?

STUDENT. Surely. The girl who handed me the cup.

OLD MAN. Really? So that's what was going on. Ah well, I haven't second sight, but there are things I can do. [THE FIANCÉE *is now seen to sit down by the window which has the window-mirror.*] Look at that old woman in the window. Do you see her? Well, she was my fiancée once, sixty years ago. I was twenty. Don't be alarmed. She doesn't recognize me. We see one another every day, and it makes no impression on me, although once we vowed to love one another eternally. Eternally!

STUDENT. How foolish you were in those days! We never talk to our girls like that.

OLD MAN. Forgive us, young man. We didn't know any better. But can you see that that old woman was once young and beautiful?

STUDENT. It doesn't show. And yet there's some charm in her looks. I can't see her eyes.

[*The* CARETAKER'S WIFE *comes out with a basket of chopped fir branches.*[20]]

OLD MAN. Ah, the caretaker's wife! That dark lady is her daughter by the dead man. That's why her husband was given the job of caretaker. But the dark lady has a suitor, who is an aristocrat with great expectations. He is in the process of getting a divorce—from his present wife, you understand. She's presenting him with a stone mansion in order to be rid of him. This aristocratic suitor is the son-in-law of the dead man, and you can see his bedclothes being aired on the balcony upstairs. It is complicated, I must say.

STUDENT. It's fearfully complicated.

OLD MAN. Yes, that it is, internally and externally, although it looks quite simple.

STUDENT. But then who was the dead man?

OLD MAN. You asked me that just now, and I answered. If you were to look round the corner, where the tradesmen's entrance is, you would see a lot of poor people whom he used to help—when it suited him.

STUDENT. He was a kind man then.

OLD MAN. Yes—sometimes.

STUDENT. Not always?

OLD MAN. No-o. That's the way of people. Now, sir, will you push my chair a little, so that it gets into the sun. I'm horribly cold. When you're never able to move about, the blood congeals. I'm

---

20. "It was customary in Sweden to strew the ground with these for a funeral" [translator's note].

going to die soon, I know that, but I have a few things to do first. Take my hand and feel how cold I am.

STUDENT [*taking it*]. Yes, inconceivably. [*He shrinks back, trying in vain to free his hand.*]

OLD MAN. Don't leave me. I am tired now and lonely, but I haven't always been like this, you know. I have an enormously long life behind me, enormously long. I have made people unhappy and people have made me unhappy—the one cancels out the other—but before I die I want to see you happy. Our fates are entwined through your father—and other things.

STUDENT. Let go of my hand. You are taking all my strength. You are freezing me. What do you want with me?

OLD MAN. [*letting go*]. Be patient and you shall see and understand. Here comes the young lady. [*They watch the* GIRL *approaching, though the audience cannot yet see her.*]

STUDENT. The Colonel's daughter?

OLD MAN. His daughter—yes. Look at her. Have you ever seen such a masterpiece?

STUDENT. She is like the marble statue in there.

OLD MAN. That's her mother, you know.

STUDENT. You are right. Never have I seen such a woman of woman born. Happy the man who may lead her to the altar and his home.

OLD MAN. You can see it. Not everyone recognizes her beauty. So, then, it is written.[21]

[*The* GIRL *enters, wearing an English riding habit. Without noticing anyone she walks slowly to the door, where she stops to say a few words to the* CARETAKER'S WIFE. *Then she goes into the house. The* STUDENT *covers his eyes with his hand.*]

OLD MAN. Are you weeping?

STUDENT. In the face of what's hopeless there can be nothing but despair.

OLD MAN. I can open doors and hearts, if only I find an arm to do my will. Serve me and you shall have power.

STUDENT. Is it a bargain? Am I to sell my soul?

OLD MAN. Sell nothing. Listen. All my life I have *taken*. Now I have a craving to give—give. But no one will accept. I am rich, very rich, but I have no heirs, except for a good-for-nothing who torments the life out of me. Become my son. Inherit me while I am still alive. Enjoy life so that I can watch, at least from a distance.

STUDENT. What am I to do?

OLD MAN. First go to *The Valkyrie*.

STUDENT. That's settled. What else?

OLD MAN. This evening you must be in there—in the Round Room.

STUDENT. How am I to get there?

OLD MAN. By way of *The Valkyrie*.

STUDENT. Why have you chosen me as your medium? Did you know me before?

21. It is foreordained. The following interchange underlines this sense of being a pawn in a far-ranging plan conceived by some invisible, irresistible power.

OLD MAN. Yes, of course. I have had my eye on you for a long time. But now look up there at the balcony. The maid is hoisting the flag to half-mast for the Consul. And now she is turning the bed-clothes. Do you see that blue quilt? It was made for two to sleep under, but now it covers only one. [*The* GIRL, *having changed her dress, appears in the window and waters the hyacinths.*] There is my little girl. Look at her, look! She is talking to the flowers. Is she not like that blue hyacinth herself? She gives them drink—nothing but pure water, and they transform the water into color and fragrance. Now here comes the Colonel with the newspaper. He is showing her the bit about the house that collapsed. Now he's pointing to your portrait. She's not indifferent. She's reading of your brave deed. . . .

I believe it's clouding over. If it turns to rain I shall be in a pretty fix, unless Johansson comes back soon. [*It grows cloudy and dark. The* FIANCÉE *at the window-mirror closes her window.*] Now my fiancée is closing the window. Seventy-nine years old. The window-mirror is the only mirror she uses, because in it she sees not herself, but the world outside—in two directions. But the world can see her; she hasn't thought of that. Anyhow she's a handsome old woman.

[*Now the* DEAD MAN, *wrapped in a winding sheet, comes out of the door.*]

STUDENT. Good God, what do I see?

OLD MAN. What do you see?

STUDENT. Don't *you* see? There, in the doorway, the dead man?

OLD MAN. I see nothing, but I expected this. Tell me.

STUDENT. He is coming out into the street. [*Pause.*] Now he is turning his head and looking up at the flag.

OLD MAN. What did I tell you? You may be sure he'll count the wreaths and read the visiting cards. Woe to him who's missing.

STUDENT. Now he's turning the corner.

OLD MAN. He's gone to count the poor at the back door. The poor are in the nature of a decoration, you see. "Followed by the blessings of many." Well, he's not going to have my blessing. Between ourselves he was a great scoundrel.

STUDENT. But charitable.

OLD MAN. A charitable scoundrel, always thinking of his grand funeral. When he knew his end was near, he cheated the State out of fifty thousand crowns. Now his daughter has relations with another woman's husband and is wondering about the Will. Yes, the scoundrel can hear every word we're saying, and he's welcome to it. Ah, here comes Johansson! [JOHANSSON *enters.*] Report! [JOHANSSON *speaks, but the audience does not hear.*] Not at home, eh? You are an ass. And the telegram? Nothing? Go on. . . . At six this evening? That's good. Special edition, you say? With his name in full. Arkenholtz, a student, born . . . parents . . . That's splendid. . . . I think it's beginning to rain. . . . What did he say about it? So—so. He wouldn't? Well, he must. Here comes the aristocrat. Push me round the corner, Johansson, so I can hear what the poor are saying. And, Arkenholtz, you wait for me here. Understand? [*To* JOHANSSON.] Hurry up now, hurry up.

[JOHANSSON *wheels the chair round the corner. The* STUDENT *remains watching the* GIRL, *who is now loosening the earth round the hyacinths. The* ARISTOCRAT, *wearing mourning, comes in and speaks to the* DARK LADY, *who has been walking to and fro on the pavement.*]

ARISTOCRAT. But what can we do about it? We shall have to wait.

LADY. I can't wait.

ARISTOCRAT. You can't? Well then, go into the country.[22]

LADY. I don't want to do that.

ARISTOCRAT. Come over here or they will hear what we are saying. [*They move towards the advertisement column and continue their conversation inaudibly.* JOHANSSON *returns.*]

JOHANSSON [*to the* STUDENT.] My master asks you not to forget that other thing, sir.

STUDENT [*hesitating.*] Look here . . . first of all tell me . . . who is your master?

JOHANSSON. Well, he's so many things, and he has been everything.

STUDENT. Is he a wise man?

JOHANSSON. Depends what that is. He says all his life he's been looking for a Sunday child, but that may not be true.

STUDENT. What does he want? He's grasping, isn't he?

JOHANSSON. It's power he wants. The whole day long he rides round in his chariot like the god Thor[23] himself. He looks at houses, pulls them down, opens up new streets, builds squares. . . But he breaks into houses too, sneaks through windows, plays havoc with human destinies, kills his enemies—and never forgives. Can you imagine it, sir? This miserable cripple was once a Don Juan—although he always lost his women.

STUDENT. How do you account for that?

JOHANSSON. You see he's so cunning he makes the women leave him when he's tired of them. But what he's most like now is a horse-thief in the human market. He steals human beings in all sorts of different ways. He literally stole me out of the hands of the law. Well, as a matter of fact I'd made a slip—hm, yes—and only he knew about it. Instead of getting me put in gaol, he turned me into a slave. I slave—for my food alone, and that's none of the best.

STUDENT. Then what is it he means to do in this house?

JOHANSSON. I'm not going to talk about that. It's too complicated.

STUDENT. I think I'd better get away[24] from it all.

[*The* GIRL *drops a bracelet out the window.*]

JOHANSSON. Look! The young lady has dropped her bracelet out of the window. [*The* STUDENT *goes slowly over, picks up the bracelet and returns it to the* GIRL, *who thanks him stiffly. The* STUDENT *goes back to* JOHANSSON.] So you mean to get away.

22. This suggests that the Lady is pregnant.

23. The Scandinavian god of thunder, who carried a hammer.

24. The Student dismisses this prudent notion because of what he takes to be a sign of encouragement from the girl.

That's not so easy as you think, once he's got you in his net. And he's afraid of nothing between heaven and earth—yes, of one thing he is—of one person rather. . . .

STUDENT. Don't tell me. I think perhaps I know.

JOHANSSON. How can you know?

STUDENT. I'm guessing. Is it a little milkmaid he's afraid of?

JOHANSSON. He turns his head the other way whenever he meets a milk cart. Besides, he talks in his sleep. It seems he was once in Hamburg. . . .

STUDENT. Can one trust this man?

JOHANSSON. You can trust him—to do anything.

STUDENT. What's he doing now round the corner?

JOHANSSON. Listening to the poor. Sowing a little word, loosening one stone at a time, till the house falls down—[25]metaphorically speaking. You see I'm an educated man. I was once a book-seller. . . . Do you still mean to go away?

STUDENT. I don't like to be ungrateful. He saved my father once, and now he only asks a small service in return.

JOHANSSON. What is that?

STUDENT. I am to go to *The Valkyrie*.

JOHANSSON. That's beyond me. But he's always up to new tricks. Look at him now, talking to that policeman. He is always thick with the police. He uses them, gets them involved in his interests, holds them with false promises and expectations, while all the time he's pumping them. You'll see that before the day is over he'll be received in the Round Room.

STUDENT. What does he want there? What connection has he[26] with the Colonel?

JOHANSSON. I think I can guess, but I'm not sure. You'll see for yourself once you're in there.

STUDENT. I shall never be in there.

JOHANSSON. That depends on yourself. Go to *The Valkyrie*.

STUDENT. Is that the way?

JOHANSSON. Yes, if he said so. Look. Look at him in his war chariot, drawn in triumph by the beggars, who get nothing for their pains but the hint of a treat at his funeral.

[*The* OLD MAN *appears standing up in his wheel-chair, drawn by one of the beggars and followed by the rest.*]

OLD MAN. Hail the noble youth who, at the risk of his own life, saved so many others in yesterday's accident. Three cheers for Arkenholtz! [*The* BEGGARS *bare their heads but do not cheer. The* GIRL *at the window waves her handkerchief. The* COLONEL *gazes from the window of the Round Room. The* OLD WOMAN *rises at her window. The* MAID *on the balcony hoists the flag to the top.*] Clap your hands, citizens. True, it is Sunday, but the

---

25. Destruction, together with Creation and Preservation, form a divine trinity in Hindu thought.

26. Notice the number of connections mentioned but left unexplained or only partly explained. As in a detective novel, tension is built up by arousing our curiosity but deferring its satisfaction. Again, as in a detective novel, this is a sealed-off house, or world. Nothing exists outside it or unconnected with it.

ass in the pit[27] and the ear in the corn field[28] will absolve us. And although I am not a Sunday child, I have the gift of prophecy and also that of healing. Once I brought a drowned person back to life. That was in Hamburg on a Sunday morning just like this. . . .

The MILKMAID *enters, seen only by the* STUDENT *and the* OLD MAN. *She raises her arms like one who is drowning and gazes fixedly at the* OLD MAN. *He sits down, then crumples up, stricken with horror.]*

Johansson! Take me away! Quick! . . . Arkenholtz, don't forget *The Valkyrie.*

STUDENT. What is all this?

JOHANSSON. We shall see. We shall see.

Scene II

Inside the Round Room. At the back is a white porcelain stove. On either side of it are a mirror, a pendulum clock and candelabra. On the right of the stove is the entrance to the hall beyond which is a glimpse of a room furnished in green and mahogany. On the left of the stove is the door to a cupboard, papered like the wall. The statue, shaded by palms, has a curtain which can be drawn to conceal it.

A door on the left leads into the Hyacinth Room, where the GIRL *sits reading.*

The back of the COLONEL *can be seen, as he sits in the Green Room, writing.*

BENGTSSON, *the Colonel's servant, comes in from the hall. He is wearing livery, and is followed by* JOHANSSON, *dressed as a waiter.*

BENGTSSON. Now you'll have to serve the tea, Johansson, while I take the coats. Have you ever done it before?

JOHANSSON. It's true I push a war chariot in the daytime, as you know, but in the evenings I go as a waiter to receptions and so forth. It's always been my dream to get into this house. They're queer people here, aren't they?

BENGTSSON. Ye-es. A bit out of the ordinary anyhow.

JOHANSSON. Is it to be a musical party or what?

BENGTSSON. The usual ghost supper, as we call it. They drink tea and don't say a word—or else the Colonel does all the talking. And they crunch their biscuits, all at the same time. It sounds like rats in an attic.

JOHANSSON. Why do you call it the ghost supper?

BENGTSSON. They look like ghosts. And they've kept this up for twenty years, always the same people saying the same things or saying nothing at all for fear of being found out.

JOHANSSON. Isn't there a mistress of the house?

---

27. Jesus defended his disciples' right to pick ears of corn on the sabbath by saying that even a sheep (not an ass) may be rescued from a pit on the Sabbath (Matthew 12:11).

28. See Mark 2:25–28; Matthew 12:1–8; Luke 6:1–5.

BENGTSSON. Oh yes, but she's crazy. She sits in a cupboard because her eyes can't bear the light. [*He points to the papered door.*] She sits in there.

JOHANSSON. In there?

BENGTSSON. Well, I told you they were a bit out of the ordinary.

JOHANSSON. But then—what does she look like?

BENGTSSON. Like a mummy. Do you want to have a look at her? [*He opens the door.*] There she is.

The figure of the COLONEL'S WIFE *is seen, white and shrivelled into a* MUMMY.]

JOHANSSON. Oh my God!

MUMMY. [*babbling*]. Why do you open the door? Haven't I told you to keep it closed?

BENGTSSON [*in a wheedling tone.*] Ta, ta, ta, ta. Be a good girl now, then you'll get something nice. Pretty Polly.[29]

MUMMY [*parrot-like.*] Pretty Polly. Are you there, Jacob? Currrrr!

BENGTSSON. She thinks she's a parrot, and maybe she's right. [*To the* MUMMY.] Whistle for us, Polly. [*The* MUMMY *whistles.*]

JOHANSSON. Well, I've seen a few things in my day, but this beats everything.

BENGTSSON. You see, when a house gets old, it grows moldy, and when people stay a long time together and torment each other they go mad. The mistress of the house—shut up, Polly!—that mummy there, has been living here for forty years—same husband, same furniture, same relatives, same friends. [*He closes the papered door.*] And the goings-on in this house—well, they're beyond me. Look at that statue—that's her when she was young.

JOHANSSON. Good Lord! Is that the mummy?

BENGTSSON. Yes. It's enough to make you weep. And somehow, carried away by her own imagination or something, she's got to be a bit like a parrot—the way she talks and the way she can't stand cripples or sick people. She can't stand the sight of her own daughter, because she's sick.

JOHANSSON. Is the young lady sick?

BENGTSSON. Didn't you know that?

JOHANSSON. No. And the Colonel, who is he?

BENGTSSON. You'll see.

JOHANSSON [*looking at the statue.*] It's horrible to think that . . . How old is she now?

BENGTSSON. Nobody knows. But it's said that when she was thirty-five she looked nineteen, and that's what she made the Colonel believe[30] she was—here in this very house. Do you know what that black Japanese screen by the couch is for? They call it the death-screen, and when someone's going to die, they put it round —same as in a hospital.

JOHANSSON. What a horrible house! And the student was longing to get in, as if it were paradise.

---

29. She identifies herself with a parrot, that is, is reduced to repeating lifelessly what has already been said.

30. This element of deception is at the very origin of the situation.

BENGTSSON. What student? Oh, I know. The one who's coming here this evening. The Colonel and the young lady happened to meet him at the Opera, and both of them took a fancy to him. Hm. Now it's my turn to ask questions. Who is your master—the man in the wheelchair?

JOHANSSON. Well, he er . . . Is he coming here too?

BENGTSSON. He hasn't been invited.

JOHANSSON. He'll come uninvited—if need be.

[*The* OLD MAN *appears in the hall on crutches, wearing a frock-coat and top-hat. He steals forward and listens.*]

BENGTSSON. He's a regular old devil, isn't he?

JOHANSSON. Up to the ears.

BENGTSSON. He looks like old Nick himself.

JOHANSSON. And he must be a wizard too, for he goes through locked doors.[31]

[*The* OLD MAN *comes forward and takes hold of* JOHANSSON *by the ear.*]

OLD MAN. Rascal—take care! [*To* BENGTSSON.] Tell the Colonel I am here.

BENGTSSON. But we are expecting guests.

OLD MAN. I know. But my visit is as good as expected, if not exactly looked forward to.

BENGTSSON. I see. What name shall I say? Mr. Hummel?

OLD MAN. Exactly. Yes. [BENGTSSON *crosses the hall to the Green Room, the door of which he closes behind him. To* JOHANSSON.] Get out! [JOHANSSON *hesitates.*] Get out! [JOHANSSON *disappears into the hall. The* OLD MAN *inspects the room and stops in front of the statue in much astonishment.*] Amelia! It is she—she!

MUMMY. [*from the cupboard*]. Prrr-etty Polly. [*The* OLD MAN *starts.*]

OLD MAN. What was that? Is there a parrot in the room? I don't see it.

MUMMY Are you there, Jacob?

OLD MAN. The house is haunted.

MUMMY. Jacob!

OLD MAN. I'm scared. So these are the kind of secrets they guard in this house. [*With his back turned to the cupboard he stands looking at a portrait.*] There he is—he!

[*The* MUMMY *comes out behind the* OLD MAN *and gives a pull at his wig.*]

MUMMY. Currrrr! Is it . . . ? Currrrr!

OLD MAN [*jumping out of his skin.*] God in heaven! Who is it?

MUMMY [*in a natural voice.*] Is it Jacob?

OLD MAN. Yes, my name is Jacob.

MUMMY [*with emotion.*] And my name is Amelia.

OLD MAN. No, no, no . . . Oh my God!

MUMMY. That's how I look. Yes. [*Pointing to the statue.*] And that's how I *did* look. Life opens one's eyes, does it not? I live

---

31. Another hint that the Old Man has supernatural powers.

mostly in the cupboard to avoid seeing and being seen. . . . But, Jacob, what do you want here?

OLD MAN. My child. Our child.

MUMMY There she is.

OLD MAN. Where?

MUMMY. There—in the Hyacinth Room.

OLD MAN [*looking at the* GIRL]. Yes, that is she. [*Pause.*] And what about her father—the Colonel, I mean—your husband?

MUMMY. Once, when I was angry with him, I told him everything.

OLD MAN. Well . . .?

MUMMY. He didn't believe me. He just said: "That's what all wives say when they want to murder their husbands."[32] It was a terrible crime none the less. It has falsified his whole life—his family tree too. Sometimes I take a look in the Peerage, and then I say to myself: Here she is, going about with a false birth certificate like some servant girl, and for such things people are sent to the reformatory.

OLD MAN. Many do it. I seem to remember your own date of birth was given incorrectly.

MUMMY. My mother made me do that. I was not to blame. And in our crime, *you* played the biggest part.

OLD MAN. No. Your husband caused that crime, when he took my fiancée from me. I was born one who cannot forgive until he has punished. That was to me an imperative duty—and is so still.

MUMMY. What are you expecting to find in this house? What do you want? How did you get in? Is it to do with my daughter? If you touch her, you shall die.

OLD MAN. I mean well by her.

MUMMY. Then you must spare her father.

OLD MAN. No.

MUMMY. Then you shall die. In this room, behind that screen.

OLD MAN. That may be. But I can't let go once I've got my teeth into a thing.

MUMMY. You want to marry her to that student. Why? He is nothing and has nothing.

OLD MAN. He will be rich, through me.

MUMMY Have you been invited here tonight?

OLD MAN. No, but I propose to get myself an invitation to this ghost supper.

MUMMY. Do you know who is coming?

OLD MAN. Not exactly.

MUMMY. The Baron. The man who lives up above—whose father-in-law was buried this afternoon.

OLD MAN. The man who is getting a divorce in order to marry the daughter of the Caretaker's Wife . . . The man who used to be —your lover.

MUMMY. Another guest will be your former fiancée, who was seduced by my husband.

32. This device was used by the wife in Strindberg's play *The Father* to drive her husband insane. Strindberg had tortured himself by surmising that his children by his first wife might be the offspring of another man.

OLD MAN. A select gathering.

MUMMY. Oh God, if only we might die, might die!

OLD MAN. Then why have you stayed together?

MUMMY. Crime and secrets and guilt bind us together. We have broken our bonds and gone our own ways, times without number, but we are always drawn together again.

OLD MAN. I think the Colonel is coming.

MUMMY. Then I will go in to Adèle. [*Pause.*] Jacob, mind what you do. Spare him. [*Pause. She goes into the Hyacinth Room and disappears.*]

[*The* COLONEL *enters, cold and reserved, with a letter in his hand.*]

COLONEL. Be seated, please. [*Slowly the* OLD MAN *sits down. Pause. The* COLONEL *stares at him.*] You wrote this letter, sir?

OLD MAN. I did.

COLONEL. Your name is Hummel?

OLD MAN. It is. [*Pause.*]

COLONEL. As I understand, you have bought in all my unpaid promissory notes. I can only conclude that I am in your hands. What do you want?

OLD MAN. I want payment, in one way or another.

COLONEL. In what way?

OLD MAN. A very simple one. Let us not mention the money. Just bear with me in your house as a guest.

COLONEL. If so little will satisfy you . . .

OLD MAN. Thank you.

COLONEL. What else?

OLD MAN. Dismiss Bengtsson.

COLONEL. Why should I do that? My devoted servant, who has been with me a lifetime, who has the national medal for long and faithful service—why should I do that?

OLD MAN. That's how you see him—full of excellent qualities. He is not the man he appears to be.

COLONEL. Who is?

OLD MAN. [*taken aback.*] True. But Bengtsson must go.

COLONEL. Are you going to run my house?

OLD MAN. Yes. Since everything here belongs to me—furniture, curtains, dinner service, linen . . . and more too.

COLONEL. How do you mean—more?

OLD MAN. Everything. I own everything here. It is mine.

COLONEL. Very well, it is yours. But my family escutcheon[33] and my good name remain my own.

OLD MAN. No, not even those. [*Pause.*] You are not a nobleman.

COLONEL. How dare you!

OLD MAN. [*producing a document.*] If you read this extract from *The Armorial Gazette,* you will see that the family whose name you are using has been extinct for a hundred years.

COLONEL. I have heard rumors to this effect, but I inherited the

---

33. Shield on which armorial bearings are depicted. Here the term is used fig- uratively for the noble family itself.

name from my father. [*Reads.*] It is true. You are right. I am
not a nobleman. Then I must take off my signet ring. It is true,
it belongs to you. [*Gives it to him.*] There you are.

OLD MAN. [*pocketing the ring.*] Now we will continue. You are not
a Colonel either.

COLONEL. I am not . . .?

OLD MAN. No. You once held the temporary rank of Colonel in the
American Volunteer Force, but after the war in Cuba and the
reorganization of the Army, all such titles were abolished.

COLONEL. Is this true?

OLD MAN [*indicating his pocket.*] Do you want to read it?

COLONEL. No, that's not necessary. Who are you, and what right
have you to sit there stripping me in this fashion?

OLD MAN. You will see. But as far as stripping you goes . . . do you
know who you are?

COLONEL. How dare you?

OLD MAN. Take off that wig and have a look at yourself in the
mirror. But take your teeth out at the same time and shave off
your moustache. Let Bengtsson unlace your metal stays and perhaps a certain X.Y.Z. a lackey, will recognize himself. The fellow
who was a cupboard lover in a certain kitchen . ... [*The* COLONEL
reaches for the bell on the table, but HUMMEL *checks him.*]
Don't touch that bell, and don't call Bengtsson. If you do, I'll
have him arrested. [*Pause.*] And now the guests are beginning to
arrive. Keep your composure and we will continue to play our old
parts for a while.

COLONEL. Who are you? I recognize your voice and eyes.

OLD MAN. Don't try to find out. Keep silent and obey.

[*The* STUDENT *enters and bows to the* COLONEL.]

STUDENT. How do you do, sir.

COLONEL. Welcome to my house, young man. Your splendid behavior at that great disaster has brought your name to everybody's
lips, and I count it an honor to receive you in my home.

STUDENT. My humble descent, sir . . . your illustrious name and
noble birth. . . .

COLONEL. May I introduce Mr. Arkenholtz—Mr. Hummel. If you
will join the ladies in here, Mr. Arkenholtz—I must conclude my
conversation with Mr. Hummel. [*He shows the* STUDENT *into
the Hyacinth Room, where he remains visible, talking shyly to
the* GIRL.] A splendid young man, musical, sings, writes poetry. If
he only had blue blood in him, if he were of the same station, I
don't think I should object . . .

OLD MAN. To what?

COLONEL. To my daughter . . .

OLD MAN. Your daughter! But apropos of that, why does she spend
all her time in there?

COLONEL. She insists on being in the Hyacinth Room except when
she is out-of-doors. It's a peculiarity of hers. Ah, here comes Miss
Beatrice von Holsteinkrona—a charming woman, a pillar of the
Church, with just enough money of her own to suit her birth and
position.

OLD MAN [*to himself.*] My fiancée.

[*The* FIANCÉE *enters, looking a little crazy.*]

COLONEL. Miss Holsteinkrona—Mr. Hummel. [*The* FIANCÉE *curt-
seys and takes a seat. The* ARISTOCRAT *enters and seats himself.
He wears mourning and looks mysterious.*] Baron Skanskorg . . .

OLD MAN [*aside, without rising.*] That's the jewel-thief, I think.
[*To the* COLONEL.] If you bring in the Mummy, the party will
be complete.

COLONEL [*at the door of the Hyacinth Room.*] Polly!

MUMMY [*entering*] Currrrr . . . !

COLONEL. Are the young people to come in too?

OLD MAN. No, not the young people. They shall be spared. [*They
all sit silent in a circle.*]

COLONEL. Shall we have the tea brought in?

OLD MAN. What's the use? No one wants tea. Why should we pretend about it?

COLONEL. Then shall we talk?

OLD MAN. Talk of the weather, which we know? Inquire about each
other's health, which we know just as well. I prefer silence—then
one can hear thoughts and see the past. Silence cannot hide anything—but words can. I read the other day that differences of
language originated among savages for the purpose of keeping
one tribe's secrets hidden from another. Every language therefore
is a code, and he who finds the key can understand every language in the world. But this does not prevent secrets from being
exposed without a key, specially when there is a question of
paternity to be proved. Proof in a Court of Law is another matter.
Two false witnesses suffice to prove anything about which they
are agreed, but one does not take witnesses along on the kind of
explorations I have in mind. Nature herself has instilled in
human beings a sense of modesty which tries to hide what should
be hidden, but we slip into situations unintentionally, and by
chance sometimes the deepest secret is divulged—the mask torn
from the impostor, the villain exposed. . . . [*Pause. All look at
each other in silence.*] What a silence there is now! [*Long
silence.*] Here, for instance, in this honorable house, in this elegant home, where beauty, wealth and culture are united. . . .
[*Long silence.*] All of us now sitting here know who we are—do
we not? There's no need for me to tell you. And you know me,
although you pretend ignorance. [*He indicates the Hyacinth
Room.*] In there is my daughter. *Mine*—you know that too. She
had lost the desire to live, without knowing why. The fact is she
was withering away in this air charged with crime and deceit and
falseness of every kind. That is why I looked for a friend for her
in whose company she might enjoy the light and warmth of
noble deeds. [*Long silence.*] That was my mission in this house:
to pull up the weeds, to expose the crimes, to settle all accounts
so that those young people might start afresh in this home, which
is my gift to them. [*Long silence.*] Now I am going to grant
safe-conduct, to each of you in his and her proper time and turn.
Whoever stays I shall have arrested. [*Long silence.*] Do you hear

the clock ticking like a death-watch beetle in the wall? Do you hear what it says? "It's time, it's time, it's time." When it strikes, in a few moments, your time will be up. Then you can go, but not before. It's raising its arm against you before it strikes. Listen! It is warning you. "The clock can strike." And I can strike too. [*He strikes the table with one of his crutches.*] Do you hear? [*Silence. The* MUMMY *goes up to the clock and stops it, then speaks in a normal and serious voice.*]

MUMMY. But I can stop time in its course. I can wipe out the past and undo what is done. But not with bribes, not with threats—only through suffering and repentance. [*She goes up to the* OLD MAN.] We are miserable human beings, that we know. We have erred and we have sinned, we like all the rest. We are not what we seem, because at bottom we are better than ourselves, since we detest our sins. But when you, Jacob Hummel, with your false name, choose to sit in judgment over us, you prove yourself worse than us miserable sinners. For you are not the one you appear to be. You are a thief of human souls. You stole me once with false promises. You murdered the Consul who was buried today; you strangled him with debts. You have stolen the student, binding him by the pretence of a claim on his father, who never owed you a farthing. [*Having tried to rise and speak, the* OLD MAN *sinks back in his chair and crumples up more and more as she goes on.*] But there is one dark spot in your life which I am not quite sure about, although I have my suspicions. I think Bengtsson knows. [*She rings the bell on the table.*]

OLD MAN. No, not Bengtsson, not him.

MUMMY. So he does know. [*She rings again. The* MILKMAID *appears in the hallway door, unseen by all but the* OLD MAN, *who shrinks back in horror. The* MILKMAID *vanishes as* BENGTSSON *enters.*] Do you know this man, Bengtsson?

BENGTSSON. Yes, I know him and he knows me. Life, as you are aware, has its ups and downs. I have been in his service; another time he was in mine. For two whole years he was a sponger in my kitchen. As he had to be away by three, the dinner was got ready at two, and the family had to eat the warmed-up leavings of that brute. He drank the soup stock, which the cook then filled up with water. He sat out there like a vampire,[34] sucking the marrow out of the house, so that we became like skeletons. And he nearly got us put in prison when we called the cook a thief. Later I met the man in Hamburg under another name. He was a usurer then, a blood-sucker. But while he was there he was charged with having lured a young girl out on to the ice so as to drown her, because she had seen him commit a crime he was afraid would be discovered. . . . [*The* MUMMY *passes her hand over the* OLD MAN's *face.*]

MUMMY. *This* is you. Now give up the notes and the Will. [JOHANSSON *appears in the hallway door and watches the scene*

---

34. This replaces the less offensive bumblebee image suggested by the name Hummel.

with great interest, knowing he is now to be freed from slavery. The OLD MAN *produces a bundle of papers and throws it on the table. The* MUMMY *goes over and strokes his back.*] Parrot. Are you there, Jacob?

OLD MAN [*like a parrot.*] Jacob is here. Pretty Polly.[35] Currrrr!

MUMMY. May the clock strike?

OLD MAN [*with a clucking sound.*] The clock may strike. [*Imitating a cuckoo clock.*] Cuckoo, cuckoo, cuckoo. . . . [*The* MUMMY *opens the cupboard door.*]

MUMMY. Now the clock has struck. Rise, and enter the cupboard where I have spent twenty years repenting our crime. A rope is hanging there, which you can take as the one with which you strangled the Consul, and with which you meant to strangle your benefactor. . . . Go! [*The* OLD MAN *goes in to the cupboard. The* MUMMY *closes the door.*] Bengtsson! Put up the screen—the death-screen. [BENGTSSON *places the screen in front of the door.*] It is finished. God have mercy on his soul.

ALL. Amen. [*Long silence.*]

[*The* GIRL *and the* STUDENT *appear in the Hyacinth Room. She has a harp, on which she plays a prelude, and then accompanies the* STUDENT's *recitation.*]

STUDENT. *I saw the sun. To me it seemed*
that I beheld the Hidden.
Men must reap what they have sown;
blest is he whose deeds are good.
Deeds which you have wrought in fury,
cannot in evil find redress.
Comfort him you have distressed
with loving-kindness—this will heal.
No fear has he who does no ill.
Sweet is innocence.

Scene III

Inside the Hyacinth Room. The general effect of the room is exotic and oriental. There are hyacinths everywhere, of every color, some in pots, some with the bulbs in glass vases and the roots going down into the water.

On top of the tiled stove is a large seated Buddha, in whose lap rests a bulb from which rises the stem of a shallot (Allium ascalonicum), bearing its globular cluster of white, starlike flowers.

On the right is an open door, leading into the Round Room, where the COLONEL *and the* MUMMY *are seated, inactive and silent. A part of the death-screen is also visible.*

On the left is a door to the pantry and kitchen.

The STUDENT *and the* GIRL *(Adèle) are beside the table; he standing, she seated with her harp.*

---

35. The Old Man, on the point of attaining final victory, is now defeated and entangled in his own past. Therefore he takes over the repetitive role of the Mummy, who has escaped by seeing the possibility of salvation "through suffering and repentance."

GIRL. Now sing to my flowers.

STUDENT. Is this the flower of your soul?

GIRL. The one and only. Do you too love the hyacinth?

STUDENT. I love it above all other flowers—its virginal shape rising straight and slender out of the bulb, resting on the water and sending its pure white roots down into the colorless fluid. I love its colors; the snow-white, pure as innocence, the yellow honey-sweet, the youthful pink, the ripe red, but best of all the blue—the dewy blue, deep-eyed and full of faith. I love them all, more than gold or pearls. I have loved them ever since I was a child, have worshipped them because they have all the fine qualities I lack. ... And yet ...

GIRL. Go on.

STUDENT. My love is not returned, for these beautiful blossoms hate me.

GIRL. How do you mean?

STUDENT. Their fragrance, strong and pure as the early winds of spring which have passed over melting snows, confuses my senses, deafens me, blinds me, thrusts me out of the room, bombards me with poisoned arrows that wound my heart and set my head on fire. Do you know the legend of that flower?

GIRL. Tell it to me.

STUDENT. First its meaning. The bulb is the earth, resting on the water or buried in the soil. Then the stalk rises, straight as the axis of the world, and at the top are the six-pointed star-flowers.

GIRL. Above the earth—the stars. Oh, that is wonderful! Where did you learn this? How did you find it out?

STUDENT. Let me think. ... In your eyes. And so, you see, it is an image of the Cosmos. This is why Buddha[36] sits holding the earth-bulb, his eyes brooding as he watches it grow, outward and upward, transforming itself into a heaven. This poor earth will become a heaven. It is for this that Buddha waits.

GIRL. I see it now. Is not the snowflake six-pointed too like the hyacinth flower?

STUDENT. You are right. The snowflakes must be falling stars.

GIRL. And the snowdrop is a snow-star, grown out of snow.

STUDENT. But the largest and most beautiful of all the stars in the firmament, the golden-red Sirius, is the narcissus with its gold and red chalice and its six white rays.

GIRL. Have you seen the shallot in bloom?

STUDENT. Indeed I have. It bears its blossoms within a ball, a globe like the celestial one, strewn with white stars.

GIRL. Oh how glorious! Whose thought was that?

STUDENT. Yours.

GIRL. Yours.

STUDENT. Ours. We have given birth to it together. We are wedded.

GIRL. Not yet.

STUDENT. What's still to do?

36. The flower traditionally associated with Buddha is the lotus, which also grows on the surface of the water.

GIRL. Waiting, ordeals, patience.

STUDENT. Very well. Put me to the test. [*Pause.*] Tell me. Why do your parents sit in there so silently, not saying a single word?

GIRL. Because they have nothing to say to each other, and because neither believes what the other says. This is how my father puts it: What's the point of talking, when neither of us can fool the other?[37]

STUDENT. What a horrible thing to hear!

GIRL. Here comes the Cook. Look at her, how big and fat she is. [*They watch the* COOK, *although the audience cannot yet see her.*]

STUDENT. What does she want?

GIRL. To ask me about the dinner. I have to do the housekeeping as my mother's ill.

STUDENT. What have we to do with the kitchen?

GIRL. We must eat. Look at the Cook. I can't bear the sight of her.

STUDENT. Who is that ogress?

GIRL. She belongs to the Hummel family of vampires. She is eating us.

STUDENT. Why don't you dismiss her?

GIRL. She won't go. We have no control over her. We've got her for our sins. Can't you see that we are pining and wasting away?[38]

STUDENT. Don't you get enough to eat?

GIRL. Yes, we get many dishes, but all the strength has gone. She boils the nourishment out of the meat and gives us the fibre and water, while she drinks the stock herself. And when there's a roast, she first boils out the marrow, eats the gravy and drinks the juices herself. Everything she touches loses its savor. It's as if she sucked with her eyes. We get the grounds when she has drunk the coffee. She drinks the wine and fills the bottles up with water.

STUDENT. Send her packing.

GIRL. We can't.

STUDENT. Why not?

GIRL. We don't know. She won't go. No one has any control over her. She has taken all our strength from us.

STUDENT. May I get rid of her?

GIRL. No. It must be as it is. Here she is. She will ask me what is to be for dinner. I shall tell her. She will make objections and get her own way.

STUDENT. Let her do the ordering herself then.

GIRL. She won't do that.

STUDENT. What an extraordinary house! It is bewitched.

---

37. Reciprocal deceit and pretense are presented as the base that makes conversation possible.

38. Strindberg sometimes complained that the food set before him did not nourish him properly. The Cook is, among other things, his highly personal version of the class struggle—with victory, it would seem, lying inevitably within the grasp of the "underclass," as he called it.

GIRL. Yes. But now she is turning back, because she has seen you.

THE COOK [*in the doorway.*] No, that wasn't the reason. [*She grins, showing all her teeth.*]

STUDENT. Get out!

COOK. When it suits me. [*Pause.*] It does suit me now. [*She disappears.*]

GIRL. Don't lose your temper. Practise patience. She is one of the ordeals we have to go through in this house. You see, we have a housemaid too, whom we have to clean up after.

STUDENT. I am done for. *Cor in æthere.*[39] Music!

GIRL. Wait.

STUDENT. Music!

GIRL. Patience. This room is called the room of ordeals. It looks beautiful, but it is full of defects.

STUDENT. Really? Well, such things must be seen to. It is very beautiful, but a little cold. Why don't you have a fire?

GIRL. Because it smokes.

STUDENT. Can't you have the chimney swept?

GIRL. It doesn't help. You see that writing-desk there?

STUDENT. An unusually fine piece.

GIRL. But it wobbles.[40] Every day I put a piece of cork under that leg and every day the housemaid takes it away when she sweeps and I have to cut a new piece. The penholder is covered with ink every morning and so is the inkstand. I have to clean them up every morning after that woman, as sure as the sun rises. [*Pause.*] What's the worst job you can think of?

STUDENT. To count the washing. Ugh!

GIRL. That I have to do. Ugh!

STUDENT. What else?

GIRL. To be waked in the middle of the night and have to get up and see to the window, which the housemaid has left banging.

STUDENT. What else?

GIRL. To get up on a ladder and tie the cord on the damper[41] which the housemaid has torn off.

STUDENT. What else?

GIRL. To sweep after her, to dust after her, to light the fire in the stove when all she's done is throw in some wood. To see to the damper, to wipe the glasses, to lay the table over again, to open the bottles, to see that the rooms are aired, to remake my bed, to rinse the water-bottle when it's green with sediment, to buy matches and soap which are always lacking, to wipe the chimneys and trim the wicks to keep the lamps from smoking—and so that they don't go out when we have company, I have to fill them myself. . . .

STUDENT. Music!

39. Latin for "A horn is heard in the air."

40. Strindberg was abnormally sensitive to the least flaw in everyday domestic arrangements.

41. "Damper to the big stove" [translator's note].

GIRL. Wait. The labor comes first. The labor of keeping the dirt of life at a distance.

STUDENT. But you are wealthy and have two servants.

GIRL. It doesn't help. Even if we had three. Living is hard work, and sometimes I grow tired. [*Pause.*] Think then if there were a nursery as well.

STUDENT. The greatest of joys.

GIRL. And the costliest. Is life worth so much hardship?

STUDENT. That must depend on the reward you expect for your labors. I would not shrink from anything to win your hand.

GIRL. Don't say that. You can never have me.

STUDENT. Why not?

GIRL. You mustn't ask. [*Pause.*]

STUDENT. You dropped your bracelet out of the window. . . .

GIRL. Because my hand has grown so thin. [*Pause. The* COOK *appears with a Japanese bottle in her hand.*] There she is—the one who devours me and all of us.

STUDENT. What has she in her hand?

GIRL. It is the bottle of coloring matter that has letters like scorpions on it. It is the soy which turns water into soup and takes the place of gravy. She makes cabbage soup with it—and mock-turtle soup too.

STUDENT [*to* COOK.] Get out!

COOK. You drain us of sap, and we drain you. We take the blood and leave you the water, but colored . . . colored. I am going now, but all the same I shall stay, as long as I please. [*She goes out.*]

STUDENT. Why did Bengtsson get a medal?

GIRL. For his great merits.

STUDENT. Has he no defects?

GIRL. Yes, great ones. But you don't get a medal for them. [*They smile.*]

STUDENT. You have many secrets in this house.

GIRL. As in all others. Permit us to keep ours.

STUDENT. Don't you approve of candor?

GIRL. Yes—within reason.

STUDENT. Sometimes I'm seized with a raging desire to say all I think. But I know the world would go to pieces if one were completely candid. [*Pause.*] I went to a funeral the other day . . . in church. It was very solemn and beautiful.

GIRL. Was it Mr. Hummel's?

STUDENT. My false benefactor's—yes. At the head of the coffin stood an old friend of the deceased. He carried the mace. I was deeply impressed by the dignified manner and moving words of the clergyman. I cried. We all cried. Afterwards we went to a tavern, and there I learned that the man with the mace had been in love with the dead man's son. . . . [*The* GIRL *stares at him,*

42. What the Student had taken as a sign of encouragement was a trivial mis- hap—and a hook baited by Destiny.

trying to understand.] And that the dead man had borrowed money from his son's admirer. [*Pause.*] Next day the clergyman was arrested for embezzling the church funds. A pretty story.

GIRL. Oh . . . ! [*Pause.*]

STUDENT. Do you know how I am thinking about you now?

GIRL. Don't tell me, or I shall die.

STUDENT. I must, or I shall die.

GIRL. It is in asylums that people say everything they think.

STUDENT. Exactly. My father finished up in an asylum.

GIRL. Was he ill?

STUDENT. No, he was well, but he was mad. You see, he broke out once—in these circumstances. Like all of us, he was surrounded with a circle of acquaintances; he called them friends for short. They were a lot of rotters, of course, as most people are, but he had to have some society—he couldn't get on all alone. Well, as you know, in everyday life no one tells people what he thinks of them, and he didn't either. He knew perfectly well what frauds they were—he'd sounded the depths of their deceit—but as he was a wise and well-bred man, he was always courteous to them. Then one day he gave a big party. It was in the evening and he was tired by the day's work and by the strain of holding his tongue and at the same time talking rubbish with his guests. . . . [*The* GIRL *is frightened.*] Well, at the dinner table he rapped for silence, raised his glass, and began to speak. Then something loosed the trigger. He made an enormous speech in which he stripped the whole company naked, one after the other, and told them of all their treachery. Then, tired out, he sat down on the table and told them all to go to hell.

GIRL. Oh!

STUDENT. I was there, and I shall never forget what happened then. Father and Mother came to blows, the guests rushed for the door . . . and my father was taken to a madhouse, where he died. [*Pause.*] Water that is still too long stagnates, and so it is in this house too. There is something stagnating here. And yet I thought it was paradise itself that first time I saw you coming in here. There I stood that Sunday morning, gazing in. I saw a Colonel who was no Colonel. I had a benefactor who was a thief and had to hang himself. I saw a mummy who was not a mummy and an old maid—what of the maidenhood, by the way? Where is beauty to be found? In nature, and in my own mind, when it is in its Sunday clothes. Where are honor and faith? In fairy-tales and children's fancies. Where is anything that fulfills its promise? In my imagination. Now your flowers have poisoned me and I have given the poison back to you. I asked you to become my wife in a home full of poetry and song and music. Then the Cook came. . . . *Sursum Corda!*[43] Try once more to strike fire

43. Latin for "Lift up your hearts" or "Be of good cheer." They are the first words in the Preface of the Mass.

and glory out of the golden harp. Try, I beg you, I implore you on my knees. [*Pause.*] Then I will do it myself. [*He picks up the harp, but the strings give no sound.*] It is dumb and deaf. To think that the most beautiful flowers are so poisonous, are the most poisonous. The curse lies over the whole of creation, over life itself. Why will you not be my bride? Because the very life-spring within you is sick . . . now I can feel that vampire in the kitchen beginning to suck me. I believe she is a Lamia,[44] one of those that suck the blood of children. It is always in the kitchen quarters that the seed-leaves of the children are nipped, if it has not already happened in the bedroom. There are poisons that destroy the sight and poisons that open the eyes. I seem to have been born with the latter kind, for I cannot see what is ugly as beautiful, nor call evil good. I cannot. Jesus Christ descended into hell. That was His pilgrimage on earth[45]—to this mad-house, this prison, this charnel-house, this earth. And the madmen killed Him when He wanted to set them free; but the robber they let go. The robber[46] always gets the sympathy. Woe! Woe to us all. Saviour of the world, save us! We perish. [*And now the* GIRL *has drooped, and it is seen that she is dying. She rings.* BENGTSSON *enters.*]

GIRL. Bring the screen. Quick, I am dying. [BENGTSSON *comes back with the screen, opens it and arranges it in front of the* GIRL.]

STUDENT. The Liberator is coming. Welcome, pale and gentle one. Sleep, you lovely, innocent, doomed creature, suffering for no fault of your own. Sleep without dreaming, and when you wake again . . . may you be greeted by a sun that does not burn, in a home without dust, by friends without stain, by a love without flaw. You wise and gentle Buddha, sitting there waiting for a Heaven to sprout from the earth, grant us patience in our ordeal and purity of will, so that this hope may not be confounded. [*The strings of the harp hum softly and a white light fills the room.*]

I saw the sun. To me it seemed
that I beheld the Hidden.
Men must reap what they have sown,
blest is he whose deeds are good.
Deeds which you have wrought in fury,
cannot in evil find redress.
Comfort him you have distressed
with loving-kindness—this will heal.
No fear has he who does no ill.
Sweet is innocence.

[*A faint moaning is heard behind the screen.*] You poor little child, child of this world of illusion, guilt, suffering and death,

---

44. A vampirelike creature of classical antiquity, having the head and breast of a woman and the body of a serpent.

45. Elsewhere Strindberg has presented earth as purgatory, here he sees it as hell.

46. Barabbas, released by Pilate, whereas Jesus was scourged and taken away to be crucified (Mark 15:7–15).

this world of endless change, disappointment, and pain. May the Lord of Heaven be merciful to you upon your journey.

[*The room disappears. Böcklin's picture* The Island of the Dead[47] *is seen in the distance, and from the island comes music, soft, sweet, and melancholy.*]

47. The Swiss-German painter Arnold Böcklin (1827–1901) is remembered today above all for this picture, which represents, in somber tones, the vessel conveying the dead on its passage to the island. Copies of this picture and of its companion piece, *The Island of the Living*, flanked the proscenium arch of Strindberg's Intimate Theater.

LUIGI PIRANDELLO

(1867–1936)

Henry IV*

A Tragedy in Three Acts

Characters

HENRY IV[1]
THE MARCHIONESS MATILDA SPINA
FRIDA, *her daughter*
CHARLES DI NOLLI, *the young Marquis*
BARON TITO BELCREDI
DOCTOR DIONYSIUS GENONI
HAROLD (FRANK)
LANDOLPH (LOLO)
ORDULPH (MOMO)
BERTHOLD (FINO)
JOHN, *the old waiter*
THE TWO VALETS IN COSTUME

} *The four private counsellors (The names in brackets are nicknames)*

A Solitary Villa in Italy in Our Own Time

Act I

Salon in the villa, furnished and decorated so as to look exactly like the throne room of Henry IV in the royal residence at Goslar.[2] Among the antique decorations there are two modern life-size portraits in oil

* From *Naked Masks: Five Plays* by Luigi Pirandello. Translated by Edward Storer. Edited by Eric Bentley.

1. German emperor, 1065–1106. During a reign filled with conflict, his greatest antagonist was Gregory VII, pope from 1073 to 1085. Twice excommunicated, Henry had on one occasion, at Canossa, to wait three days in the snow before Gregory received and pardoned him.

2. The permanent capital of Henry IV.

painting. They are placed against the back wall, and mounted in a wooden stand that runs the whole length of the wall. (It is wide and protrudes, so that it is like a large bench.) One of the paintings is on the right; the other on the left of the throne, which is in the middle of the wall and divides the stand.

The Imperial chair and Baldachin.[3]

The two portraits represent a lady and a gentleman, both young, dressed up in carnival costumes: one as "Henry IV," the other as the "Marchioness Matilda of Tuscany."[4] Exits to right and left.

When the curtain goes up, the two valets jump down, as if surprised, from the stand on which they have been lying, and go and take their positions, as rigid as statues, on either side below the throne with their halberds in their hands. Soon after, from the second exit, right, enter HAROLD, LANDOLPH, ORDULPH *and* BERTHOLD, *young men employed by the* MARQUIS CHARLES DI NOLLI *to play the part of "Secret Counsellors" at the court of "Henry IV." They are, therefore, dressed like German knights of the XIth century.* BERTHOLD, *nicknamed Fino, is just entering on his duties for the first time. His companions are telling him what he has to do and amusing themselves at his expense. The scene is to be played rapidly and vivaciously.*

LANDOLPH [*to* BERTHOLD *as if explaining*]. And this is the throne room.

HAROLD. At Goslar.

ORDULPH. Or at the castle in the Hartz, if you prefer.

HAROLD. Or at Wurms.

LANDOLPH. According as to what's doing, it jumps about with us, now here, now there.

ORDULPH. In Saxony.

HAROLD. In Lombardy.

LANDOLPH. On the Rhine.

ONE OF THE VALETS [*without moving, just opening his lips*]. I say . . .

HAROLD [*turning round*]. What is it?

FIRST VALET [*like a statue*]. Is he coming in or not? [*He alludes to* HENRY IV.]

ORDULPH. No, no, he's asleep. You needn't worry.

SECOND VALET [*releasing his pose, taking a long breath and going to lie down again on the stand*]. You might have told us at once.

FIRST VALET [*going over to* HAROLD]. Have you got a match, please?

LANDOLPH. What? You can't smoke a pipe here, you know.

FIRST VALET [*while* HAROLD *offers him a light*]. No; a cigarette. [*Lights his cigarette and lies down again on the stand.*]

BERTHOLD [*who has been looking on in amazement, walking round the room, regarding the costumes of the others*]. I say . . . this

---

3. A fixed canopy. the castle at Canossa.
4. Henry's lifelong enemy, she owned

room . . . these costumes . . . Which Henry IV is it? I don't quite get it. Is he Henry IV of France or not? [*At this* LANDOLPH, HAROLD, *and* ORDULPH, *burst out laughing.*]

LANDOLPH [*still laughing; and pointing to* BERTHOLD *as if inviting the others to make fun of him*]. Henry of France he says: ha! ha!

ORDULPH. He thought it was the king of France!

HAROLD. Henry IV of Germany, my boy: the Salian dynasty![5]

ORDULPH. The great and tragic Emperor!

LANDOLPH. He of Canossa. Every day we carry on here the terrible war between Church and State, by Jove.

ORDULPH. The Empire against the Papacy!

HAROLD. Anti-popes against the Pope!

LANDOLPH. Kings against anti-kings!

ORDULPH. War on the Saxons!

HAROLD. And all the rebels Princes!

LANDOLPH. Against the Emperor's own sons!

BERTHOLD [*covering his head with his hands to protect himself against this avalanche of information*]. I understand! I understand! Naturally, I didn't get the idea at first. I'm right then: these aren't costumes of the XVIth century?

HAROLD. XVIth century be hanged!

ORDULPH. We're somewhere between a thousand and eleven hundred.

LANDOLPH. Work it out for yourself: if we are before Canossa on the 25th of January, 1071 . . .[6]

BERTHOLD [*more confused than ever*]. Oh my God! What a mess I've made of it!

ORDULPH. Well, just slightly, if you supposed you were at the French court.

BERTHOLD. All that historical stuff I've swotted up!

LANDOLPH. My dear boy, it's four hundred years earlier.

BERTHOLD [*getting angry*]. Good Heavens! You ought to have told me it was Germany and not France. I can't tell you how many books I've read in the last fifteen days.

HAROLD. But I say, surely you knew that poor Tito was Adalbert of Bremen,[7] here?

BERTHOLD. Not a damned bit!

LANDOLPH. Well, don't you see how it is? When Tito died, the Marquis Di Nolli . . .

BERTHOLD. Oh, it was he, was it? He might have told me.

HAROLD. Perhaps he thought you knew.

LANDOLPH. He didn't want to engage anyone else in substitution. He thought the remaining three of us would do. But *he* began to cry out: "With Adalbert driven away . . .":[8] because, you see, he

---

5. Line of German emperors, in power from 1024 to 1125.

6. 1077 is the correct date.

7. Archbishop, appointed by Henry III,

and regent until Henry IV came of age in 1066.

8. On acceding to the throne in 1066, Henry had been obliged to dismiss him.

didn't imagine poor Tito was dead; but that, as Bishop Adalbert, the rival bishops of Cologne and Mayence had driven him off . . .

BERTHOLD [*taking his head in his hand*]. But I don't know a word of what you're talking about.

ORDULPH. So much the worse for you, my boy!

HAROLD. But the trouble is that not even we know who you are.

BERTHOLD. What? Not even you? You don't know who I'm supposed to be?

ORDULPH. Hum! "Berthold."

BERTHOLD. But which Berthold? And why Berthold?

LANDOLPH [*solemnly imitating* HENRY IV]. "They've driven Adalbert away from me. Well then, I want Berthold! I want Berthold!" That's what he said.

HAROLD. We three looked one another in the eyes: who's got to be Berthold?

ORDULPH. And so here you are, "Berthold," my dear fellow!

LANDOLPH. I'm afraid you will make a bit of a mess of it.

BERTHOLD [*indignant, getting ready to go*]. Ah, no! Thanks very much, but I'm off! I'm out of this!

HAROLD [*restraining him with the other two, amid laughter*]. Steady now! Don't get excited!

LANDOLPH. Cheer up, my dear fellow! We don't any of us know who we are really. He's Harold; he's Ordulph! I'm Landolph! That's the way he calls us. We've got used to it. But who are we? Names of the period! Yours, too, is a name of the period: Berthold! Only one of us, poor Tito, had got a really decent part, as you can read in history: that of the Bishop of Bremen. He was just like a real bishop. Tito did it awfully well, poor chap!

HAROLD. Look at the study he put into it!

LANDOLPH. Why, he even ordered his Majesty about, opposed his views, guided and counselled him. We're "secret counsellors"—in a manner of speaking only; because it is written in history that Henry IV was hated by the upper aristocracy for surrounding himself at court with young men of the bourgeoisie.

ORDULPH. Us, that is.

LANDOLPH. Yes, small devoted vassals, a bit dissolute and very gay . . .

BERTHOLD. So I've got to be gay as well?

HAROLD. I should say so! Same as we are!

ORDULPH. And it isn't too easy, you know.

LANDOLPH. It's a pity; because the way we're got up, we could do a fine historical reconstruction. There's any amount of material in the story of Henry IV. But, as a matter of fact, we do nothing. We have the form without the content. We're worse than the real secret counsellors of Henry IV; because certainly no one had given them a part to play—at any rate, they didn't feel they had a part to play. It was their life. They looked after their own interests at the expense of others, sold investitures and—what not! We stop here in this magnificent court—for what?—Just doing nothing. We're like so many puppets hung on the wall, waiting for someone to come and move us or make us talk.

HAROLD. Ah, no, old sport, not quite that! We've got to give the proper answer, you know. There's trouble if he asks you something and you don't chip in with the cue.

LANDOLPH. Yes. that's true.

BERTHOLD. Don't rub it in too hard! How the devil am I to give him the proper answer, if I've swatted up Henry IV of France, and now he turns out to be Henry IV of Germany? [*The other three laugh.*]

HAROLD. You'd better start and prepare yourself at once.

ORDULPH. We'll help you out.

HAROLD. We've got any amount of books on the subject. A brief run through the main points will do to begin with.

ORDULPH. At any rate, you must have got some sort of general idea.

HAROLD. Look here! [*Turns him around and shows him the portrait of the Marchioness Matilda on the wall.*] Who's that?

BERTHOLD [*looking at it*]. That? Well, the thing seems to me somewhat out of place, anyway: two modern paintings in the midst of all this respectable antiquity!

HAROLD. You're right! They weren't there in the beginning. There are two niches there behind the pictures. They were going to put up two statues in the style of the period. Then the places were covered with those canvases there.

LANDOLPH [*interrupting and continuing*]. They would certainly be out of place if they really were paintings!

BERTHOLD. What are they, if they aren't paintings?

LANDOLPH. Go and touch them! Pictures all right . . . but for him! [*Makes a mysterious gesture to the right, alluding to* HENRY IV.] . . . who never touches them! . . .

BERTHOLD. No? What are they for him?

LANDOLPH. Well, I'm only supposing, you know; but I imagine I'm about right. They're images such as . . . well—such as a mirror might throw back. Do you understand? That one there represents himself, as he is in this throne room, which is all in the style of the period. What's there to marvel at? If we put you before a mirror, won't you see yourself, alive, but dressed up in ancient costume? Well, it's as if there were two mirrors there, which cast back living images in the midst of a world which, as you well see, when you have lived with us, comes to life too.

BERTHOLD. I say, look here . . . I've no particular desire to go mad here.

HAROLD. Go mad, be hanged! You'll have a fine time!

BERTHOLD. Tell me this: how have you all managed to become so learned?

LANDOLPH. My dear fellow, you can't go back over 800 years of history without picking up a bit of experience.

HAROLD. Come on! Come on! You'll see how quickly you get into it!

ORDULPH. You'll learn wisdom, too, at this school.

BERTHOLD. Well, for Heaven's sake, help me a bit! Give me the main lines, anyway.

HAROLD. Leave it to us. We'll do it all between us.

LANDOLPH. We'll put your wires on you and fix you up like a first-class marionette. Come along! [THEY *take him by the arm to lead him away.*]

BERTHOLD [*stopping and looking at the portrait on the wall*]. Wait a minute! You haven't told me who that is. The Emperor's wife?

HAROLD. No! The Emperor's wife is Bertha of Susa, the sister of Amadeus II of Savoy.

ORDULPH. And the Emperor, who wants to be young with us, can't stand her, and wants to put her away.

LANDOLPH. That is his most ferocious enemy: Matilda, Marchioness of Tuscany.

BERTHOLD. Ah, I've got it: the one who gave hospitality to the Pope!

LANDOLPH. Exactly: at Canossa!

ORDULPH. Pope Gregory VII!

HAROLD. Our *bête noir*! Come on! come on! [*All four move toward the right to go out, when, from the left, the old servant* JOHN *enters in evening dress.*]

JOHN [*quickly, anxiously*]. Hss! Hss! Frank! Lolo!

HAROLD [*turning round*]. What is it?

BERTHOLD [*marvelling at seeing a man in modern clothes enter the throne room*]. Oh! I say, this is a bit too much, this chap here!

LANDOLPH. A man of the XXth century, here! Oh, go away! [THEY *run over to him, pretending to menace him and throw him out.*]

ORDULPH [*heroically*]. Messenger of Gregory VII, away!

HAROLD. Away! Away!

JOHN [*annoyed, defending himself*]. Oh, stop it! Stop it, I tell you!

ORDULPH. No, you can't set foot here!

HAROLD. Out with him!

LANDOLPH [*to* BERTHOLD]. Magic, you know! He's a demon conjured up by the Wizard of Rome! Out with your swords! [*Makes as if to draw a sword.*]

JOHN [*shouting*]. Stop it, will you? Don't play the fool with me! The Marquis has arrived with some friends . . .

LANDOLPH. Good! Good! Are there ladies too?

ORDULPH. Old or young?

JOHN. There are two gentlemen.

HAROLD. But the ladies, the ladies, who are they?

JOHN. The Marchioness and her daughter.

LANDOLPH [*surprised*]. What do you say?

ORDULPH. The Marchioness?

JOHN. The Marchioness! The Marchioness!

HAROLD. Who are the gentlemen?

JOHN. I don't know.

HAROLD [*to* BERTHOLD]. They're coming to bring us a message from the Pope, do you see?

ORDULPH. All messengers of Gregory VII! What fun!

JOHN. Will you let me speak, or not?

ORDULPH. Come on then!

JOHN. One of the two gentlemen is a doctor, I fancy.

LANDOLPH. Oh, I see, one of the usual doctors.

HAROLD. Bravo Berthold, you'll bring us luck!

LANDOLPH. You wait and see how we'll manage this doctor!

BERTHOLD. It looks as if I were going to get into a nice mess right away.

JOHN. If the gentlemen would allow me to speak . . . they want to come here into the throne room.

LANDOLPH [*surprised*]. What? She? The Marchioness here?

HAROLD. Then this is something quite different! No play-acting this time!

LANDOLPH. We'll have a real tragedy: that's what!

BERTHOLD [*curious*]. Why? Why?

ORDULPH [*pointing to the portrait*]. She is that person there, don't you understand?

LANDOLPH. The daughter is the fiancée of the Marquis. But what have they come for, I should like to know?

ORDULPH. If he sees her, there'll be trouble.

LANDOLPH. Perhaps he won't recognize her any more.

JOHN. You must keep him there, if he should wake up . . .

ORDULPH. Easier said than done, by Jove!

HAROLD. You know what he's like!

JOHN. —even by force, if necessary! Those are my orders. Go on! Go on!

HAROLD. Yes, because who knows if he hasn't already wakened up?

ORDULPH. Come on then!

LANDOLPH [*going towards* JOHN *with the others*]. You'll tell us later what it all means.

JOHN [*shouting after them*]. Close the door there, and hide the key! That other door too. [*Pointing to the other door on right.*]

JOHN [*to the* TWO VALETS]. Be off, you two! There! [*Pointing to exit right.*] Close the door after you, and hide the key!

[*The* TWO VALETS *go out by the first door on right.* JOHN *moves over to the left to show in:* DONNA MATILDA SPINA, *the young* MARCHIONESS FRIDA, DR. DIONYSIUS GENONI, *the* BARON TITO BELCREDI *and the young* MARQUIS CHARLES DI NOLLI, *who, as master of the house, enters last.*

DONNA MATILDA SPINA *is about 45, still handsome, although there are too patent signs of her attempts to remedy the ravages of time with make-up. Her head is thus rather like a Walkyrie.[9] This facial make-up contrasts with her beautiful sad mouth. A widow for many years, she now has as her friend the* BARON TITO BELCREDI, *whom neither she nor anyone else takes seriously—at least so it would appear.*

What TITO BELCREDI *really is for her at bottom, he alone knows; and he is, therefore, entitled to laugh, if his friend feels the need of pretending not to know. He can always laugh at the jests which the beautiful Marchioness makes with the others at his expense. He is slim, prematurely gray, and younger than she is. His head is bird-like in shape. He would be a*

---

9. In Germanic mythology, female creature who rode over battlefields and gath-ered up spirits of dead warriors.

very vivacious person, if his ductile agility (which among other things makes him a redoubtable swordsman) were not enclosed in a sheath of Arab-like laziness, which is revealed in his strange, nasal drawn-out voice.

FRIDA, *the daughter of the Marchioness is* 19. *She is sad; because her imperious and too beautiful mother puts her in the shade, and provokes facile gossip against her daughter as well as against herself. Fortunately for her, she is engaged to the* MARQUIS CHARLES DI NOLLI.

CHARLES DI NOLLI *is a stiff young man, very indulgent towards others, but sure of himself for what he amounts to in the world. He is worried about all the responsibilities which he believes weigh on him. He is dressed in deep mourning for the recent death of his mother.*

DR. DIONYSIUS GENONI *has a bold rubicund Satyr-like face, prominent eyes, a pointed beard (which is silvery and shiny) and elegant manners. He is nearly bald. All enter in a state of perturbation, almost as if afraid, and all (except* DI NOLLI*) looking curiously about the room. At first, they speak sotto voce.*]

DI NOLLI [*to* JOHN]. Have you given the orders properly?

JOHN. Yes, my Lord; don't be anxious about that.

BELCREDI. Ah, magnificent! magnificent!

DOCTOR. How extremely interesting! Even in the surroundings his raving madness—is perfectly taken into account!

DONNA MATILDA [*glancing round for her portrait, discovers it, and goes up close to it*]. Ah! Here it is! [*Going back to admire it, while mixed emotions stir within her.*] Yes . . . yes . . . [*Calls her daughter* FRIDA.]

FRIDA. Ah, your portrait!

DONNA MATILDA. No, no . . . look again; it's you, not I, there!

DI NOLLI. Yes, it's quite true. I told you so. I . . .

DONNA MATILDA. But I would never have believed it! [*Shaking as if with a chill.*] What a strange feeling it gives one! [*Then looking at her daughter.*] Frida, what's the matter? [*She pulls her to her side, and slips an arm round her waist.*] Come: don't you see yourself in me there?

FRIDA. Well, I really . . .

DONNA MATILDA. Don't you think so? Don't you, really? [*Turning to* BELCREDI.] Look at it, Tito! Speak up, man!

BELCREDI [*without looking*]. Ah, no! I shan't look at it. For me, *a priori*, certainly not!

DONNA MATILDA. Stupid! You think you are paying me a compliment! [*Turning to* DOCTOR GENONI.] What do you say, Doctor? Do say something, please!

DOCTOR [*makes a movement to go near to the picture*].

BELCREDI [*with his back turned, pretending to attract his attention secretly*].—Hss! No, Doctor! For the love of Heaven, have nothing to do with it!

DOCTOR [*getting bewildered and smiling*]. And why shouldn't I?

DONNA MATILDA. Don't listen to him! Come here! He's insufferable!

FRIDA. He acts the fool by profession, didn't you know that?

BELCREDI [*to the* DOCTOR, *seeing him go over*]. Look at your feet, Doctor! Mind where you're going!

DOCTOR. Why?

BELCREDI. Be careful you don't put your foot in it!

DOCTOR [*laughing feebly*]. No, no. After all, it seems to me there's no reason to be astonished at the fact that a daughter should resemble her mother!

BELCREDI. Hullo! Hullo! He's done it now; he's said it.

DONNA MATILDA [*with exaggerated anger, advancing towards* BELCREDI]. What's the matter? What has he said? What has he done?

DOCTOR [*candidly*]. Well, isn't it so?

BELCREDI [*answering the* MARCHIONESS]. I said there was nothing to be astounded at—and you are astounded! And why so, then, if the thing is so simple and natural for you now?

DONNA MATILDA [*still more angry*]. Fool! fool! It's just because it is so natural! Just because it isn't my daughter who is there. [*Pointing to the canvas.*] That is my portrait; and to find my daughter there instead of me fills me with astonishment, an astonishment which, I beg you to believe, is sincere. I forbid you to cast doubts on it.

FRIDA [*slowly and wearily*]. My God! It's always like this . . . rows over nothing . . .

BELCREDI [*also slowly, looking dejected, in accents of apology*]. I cast no doubt on anything! I noticed from the beginning that you haven't shared your mother's astonishment; or, if something did astonish you, it was because the likeness between you and the portrait seemed so strong.

DONNA MATILDA. Naturally! She cannot recognize herself in me as I was at her age; while I, there, can very well recognize myself in her as she is now!

DOCTOR. Quite right! Because a portrait is always there fixed in the twinkling of an eye: for the young lady something far away and without memories, while, for the Marchioness, it can bring back everything: movements, gestures, looks, smiles, a whole heap of things . . .

DONNA MATILDA. Exactly!

DOCTOR [*continuing, turning towards her*]. Naturally enough, you can live all these old sensations again in your daughter.

DONNA MATILDA. He always spoils every innocent pleasure for me, every touch I have of spontaneous sentiment! He does it merely to annoy me.

DOCTOR [*frightened at the disturbance he has caused, adopts a professorial tone*]. Likeness, dear Baron, is often the result of imponderable things. So one explains that . . .

BELCREDI [*interrupting the discourse*]. Somebody will soon be finding a likeness between you and me, my dear Professor!

DI NOLLI. Oh! let's finish with this, please! [*Points to the two doors on the right, as a warning that there is someone there who may be listening.*] We've wasted too much time as it is!

FRIDA. As one might expect when *he's* present. [*Alludes to* BELCREDI.]

DI NOLLI. Enough! The Doctor is here; and we have come for a very serious purpose which you all know is important for me.

DOCTOR. Yes, that is so! But now, first of all, let's try to get some points down exactly. Excuse me, Marchioness, will you tell me why your portrait is here? Did you present it to him then?

DONNA MATILDA. No, not at all. How could I have given it to him? I was just like Frida then—and not even engaged. I gave it to him three or four years after the accident. I gave it to him because his mother wished it so much . . . [*Points to* DI NOLLI.]

DOCTOR. She was his sister? [*Alludes to* HENRY IV.]

DI NOLLI. Yes, Doctor; and our coming here is a debt we pay to my mother who has been dead for more than a month. Instead of being here, she and I [*Indicating Frida.*] ought to be traveling together . . .

DOCTOR. . . . . taking a cure of quite a different kind!

DI NOLLI. —Hum! Mother died in the firm conviction that her adored brother was just about to be cured.

DOCTOR. And can't you tell me, if you please, how she inferred this?

DI NOLLI. The conviction would appear to have derived from certain strange remarks which he made, a little before mother died.

DOCTOR. Oh, remarks! . . . Ah! . . . It would be extremely useful for me to have those remarks, word for word, if possible.

DI NOLLI. I can't remember them. I know that mother returned awfully upset from her last visit with him. On her death-bed, she made me promise that I would never neglect him, that I would have doctors see him, and examine him.

DOCTOR. Um! Um! Let me see! let me see! Sometimes very small reasons determine . . . and this portrait here then? . . .

DONNA MATILDA. For Heaven's sake, Doctor, don't attach excessive importance to this. It made an impression on me because I had not seen it for so many years!

DOCTOR. If you please, quietly, quietly . . .

DI NOLLI. —Well, yes, it must be about fifteen years ago.

DONNA MATILDA. More, more: eighteen!

DOCTOR. Forgive me, but you don't quite know what I'm trying to get at. I attach a very great importance to these two portraits . . . They were painted, naturally, prior to the famous—and most regrettable pageant, weren't they?

DONNA MATILDA. Of course!

DOCTOR. That is . . . when he was quite in his right mind—that's what I've been trying to say. Was it his suggestion that they should be painted?

DONNA MATILDA. Lots of the people who took part in the pageant had theirs done as a souvenir . . .

BELCREDI. I had mine done—as "Charles of Anjou!"[10]

10. (1246–85). Founder of the line of Anjou.

DONNA MATILDA. . . . as soon as the costumes were ready.

BELCREDI. As a matter of fact, it was proposed that the whole lot of us should be hung together in a gallery of the villa where the pageant took place. But in the end, everybody wanted to keep his own portrait.

DONNA MATILDA. And I gave him this portrait of me without very much regret . . . since his mother . . . [*Indicates* DI NOLLI.]

DOCTOR. You don't remember if it was he who asked for it?

DONNA MATILDA. Ah, that I don't remember . . . Maybe it was his sister, wanting to help out . . .

DOCTOR. One other thing: was it his idea, this pageant?

BELCREDI [*at once*]. No, no, it was mine!

DOCTOR. If you please . . .

DONNA MATILDA. Don't listen to him! It was poor Belassi's idea.

BELCREDI. Belassi! What had he got to do with it?

DONNA MATILDA. Count Belassi, who died, poor fellow, two or three months after . . .

BELCREDI. But if Belasi wasn't there when . . .

DI NOLLI. Excuse me, Doctor; but is it really necessary to establish whose the original idea was?

DOCTOR. It would help me, certainly!

BELCREDI. I tell you the idea was mine? There's nothing to be proud of in it, seeing what the result's been. Look here, Doctor, it was like this. One evening, in the first days of November, I was looking at an illustrated German review in the club. I was merely glancing at the pictures, because I can't read German. There was a picture of the Kaiser, at some University town where he had been a student . . . I don't remember which.

DOCTOR. Bonn, Bonn!

BELCREDI. —You are right: Bonn! He was on horseback, dressed up in one of those ancient German student guild-costumes, followed by a procession of noble students, also in costume. The picture gave me the idea. Already someone at the club had spoken of a pageant for the forthcoming carnival. So I had the notion that each of us should choose for this Tower of Babel pageant to represent some character: a king, an emperor, a prince, with his queen, empress, or lady, alongside of him—and all on horseback. The suggestion was at once accepted.

DONNA MATILDA. I had my invitation from Belassi.

BELCREDI. Well, he wasn't speaking the truth! That's all I can say, if he told you the idea was his. He wasn't even at the club the evening I made the suggestion, just as he [*Meaning* HENRY IV.] wasn't there either.

DOCTOR. So he chose the character of Henry IV?

DONNA MATILDA. Because I . . . thinking of my name, and not giving the choice any importance, said I would be the Marchioness Matilda of Tuscany.

DOCTOR. I . . . don't understand the relation between the two.

DONNA MATILDA. —Neither did I, to begin with, when he said that in that case he would be at my feet like Henry IV at Canossa. I had heard of Canossa of course; but to tell the truth, I'd forgotten most of the story; and I remember I received a curious impression when I had to get up my part, and found that I was the faithful and zealous friend of Pope Gregory VII in deadly enmity with the Emperor of Germany. Then I understood why, since I had chosen to represent his implacable enemy, he wanted to be near me in the pageant as Henry IV.

DOCTOR. Ah, perhaps because . . .

BELCREDI. —Good Heavens, Doctor, because he was then paying furious court to her! [*Indicates the* MARCHIONESS.] And she, naturally . . .

DONNA MATILDA. Naturally? Not naturally at all . . .

BELCREDI [*pointing to her*]. She shouldn't stand him . . .

DONNA MATILDA. —No, that isn't true! I didn't dislike him. Not at all! But for me, when a man begins to want to be taken seriously, well . . .

BELCREDI [*continuing for her*]. He gives you the clearest proof of his stupidity.

DONNA MATILDA. No, dear; not in this case; because he was never a fool like you.

BELCREDI. Anyway, I've never asked you to take me seriously.

DONNA MATILDA. Yes, I know. But with him one couldn't joke. [*Changing her tone and speaking to the* DOCTOR.] One of the many misfortunes which happen to us women, Doctor, is to see before us every now and again a pair of eyes glaring at us with a contained intense promise of eternal devotion. [*Bursts out laughing.*] There is nothing quite so funny. If men could only see themselves with that eternal look of fidelity in their faces! I've always thought it comic; then more even than now. But I want to make a confession—I can do so after twenty years or more. When I laughed at him then, it was partly out of fear. One might have almost believed a promise from those eyes of his. But it would have been very dangerous.

DOCTOR [*with lively interest*]. Ah! ah! This is most interesting! Very dangerous, you say?

DONNA MATILDA. Yes, because he was very different from the others. And then, I am . . . well . . . what shall I say? . . . a little impatient of all that is pondered, or tedious. But I was too young then, and a woman. I had the bit between my teeth. It would have required more courage than I felt I possessed. So I laughed at him too—with remorse, to spite myself, indeed; since I saw that my own laugh mingled with those of all the others—the other fools—who made fun of him.

BELCREDI. My own case, more or less!

DONNA MATILDA. You make people laugh at you, my dear, with your trick of always humiliating yourself. It was quite a different affair with him. There's a vast difference. And you—you know—people laugh in your face!

BELCREDI. Well, that's better than behind one's back!

DOCTOR. Let's get to the facts. He was then already somewhat exalted, if I understand rightly.

BELCREDI. Yes, but in a curious fashion, Doctor.

DOCTOR. How?

BELCREDI. Well, cold-bloodedly so to speak.

DONNA MATILDA. Not at all! It was like this, Doctor! He was a bit strange, certainly; but only because he was fond of life: eccentric, there!

BELCREDI. I don't say he simulated exaltation. On the contrary, he was often genuinely exalted. But I could swear, Doctor, that he saw himself at once in his own exaltation. Moreover, I'm certain it made him suffer. Sometimes he had the most comical fits of rage against himself.

DOCTOR. Yes?

DONNA MATILDA. That is true.

BELCREDI [to DONNA MATILDA]. And why? [To the DOCTOR.] Evidently, because that immediate lucidity that comes from acting, assuming a part, at once put him out of key with his own feelings, which seemed to him not exactly false, but like something he was obliged to give the value there and then of—what shall I say—of an act of intelligence, to make up for that sincere cordial warmth he felt lacking. So he improvised, exaggerated, let himself go, so as to distract and forget himself. He appeared inconstant, fatuous, and —yes—even ridiculous, sometimes.

DOCTOR. And may we say unsociable?

BELCREDI. No, not at all. He was famous for getting up things: *tableaux vivants*,[11] dances, theatrical performances for charity: all for the fun of the thing, of course. He was a jolly good actor, you know!

DI NOLLI. Madness has made a superb actor of him.

BELCREDI. —Why, so he was even in the old days. When the accident happened, after the horse fell . . .

DOCTOR. Hit the back of his head, didn't he?

DONNA MATILDA. Oh, it was horrible! He was beside me! I saw him between the horse's hoofs! It was rearing!

BELCREDI. None of us thought it was anything serious at first. There was a stop in the pageant, a bit of disorder. People wanted to know what had happened. But they'd already taken him off to the villa.

DONNA MATILDA. There wasn't the least sign of a wound, not a drop of blood.

BELCREDI. We thought he had merely fainted.

DONNA MATILDA. But two hours afterwards . . .

BELCREDI. He reappeared in the drawing-room of the villa . . . that is what I wanted to say . . .

DONNA MATILDA. My God! What a face he had. I saw the whole thing at once!

11. People in costume, grouped to resemble a famous painting.

BELCREDI. No, no! that isn't true. Nobody saw it, Doctor, believe me!

DONNA MATILDA. Doubtless, because you were all like mad folk.

BELCREDI. Everybody was pretending to act his part for a joke. It was a regular Babel.

DONNA MATILDA. And you can imagine, Doctor, what terror struck into us when we understood that he, on the contrary, was playing his part in deadly earnest . . .

DOCTOR. Oh, he was there too, was he?

BELCREDI. Of course! He came straight into the midst of us. We thought he'd quite recovered, and was pretending, fooling, like all the rest of us . . . only doing it rather better; because, as I say, he knew how to act.

DONNA MATILDA. Some of them began to hit him with their whips and fans and sticks.

BELCREDI. And then—as a king, he was armed, of course—he drew out his sword and menaced two or three of us . . . It was a terrible moment, I can assure you!

DONNA MATILDA. I shall never forget that scene—all our masked faces hideous and terrified gazing at him, at that terrible mask of his face, which was no longer a mask, but madness, madness personified.

BELCREDI. He was Henry IV, Henry IV in person, in a moment of fury.

DONNA MATILDA. He'd got into it all the detail and minute preparation of a month's careful study. And it all burned and blazed there in the terrible obsession which lit his face.

DOCTOR. Yes, that is quite natural, of course. The momentary obsession of a dilettante became fixed, owing to the fall and the damage to the brain.

BELCREDI [*to* FRIDA *and* DI NOLLI]. You see the kind of jokes life can play on us. [*To* DI NOLLI.] You were four or five years old. [*To* FRIDA.] Your mother imagines you've taken her place there in that portrait; when, at the time, she had not the remotest idea that she would bring you into the world. My hair is already grey; and he—look at him—[*Points to portrait*]—ha! A smack on the head, and he never moves again: Henry IV for ever!

DOCTOR [*seeking to draw the attention of the others, looking learned and imposing*]. —Well, well, then it comes, we may say, to this . . .
[*Suddenly the first exit to right, the one nearest footlights, opens, and* BERTHOLD *enters all excited.*]

BERTHOLD [*rushing in*]. I say! I say! [*Stops for a moment, arrested by the astonishment which his appearance has caused in the others.*]

FRIDA [*running away terrified*]. Oh dear! oh dear! it's he, it's . . .

DONNA MATILDA [*covering her face with her hands so as not to see*]. Is it, is it he?

DI NOLLI. No, no, what are you talking about? Be calm!

DOCTOR. Who is it then?

BELCREDI. One of our masqueraders.

DI NOLLI. He is one of the four youths we keep here to help him out in his madness . . .

BERTHOLD. I beg your pardon, Marquis . . .

DI NOLLI. Pardon be damned! I gave orders that the doors were to be closed, and that nobody should be allowed to enter.

BERTHOLD. Yes, sir, but I can't stand it any longer, and I ask you to let me go away this very minute.

DI NOLLI. Oh, you're the new valet, are you? You were supposed to begin this morning, weren't you?

BERTHOLD. Yes, sir, and I can't stand it, I can't bear it.

DONNA MATILDA [*to* DI NOLLI *excitedly*]. What? Then he's not so calm as you said?

BERTHOLD [*quickly*]. —No, no, my lady, it isn't he; it's my companions. You say "help him out with his madness," Marquis; but they don't do anything of the kind. They're the real madmen. I come here for the first time, and instead of helping me . . .

[LANDOLPH *and* HAROLD *come in from the same door, but hesitate on the threshold.*]

LANDOLPH. Excuse me?

HAROLD. May I come in, my Lord?

DI NOLLI. Come in! What's the matter? What are you all doing?

FRIDA. Oh God! I'm frightened! I'm going to run away. [*Makes towards exit at left.*]

DI NOLLI [*restraining her at once*]. No, no, Frida!

LANDOLPH. My Lord, this fool here . . . [*Indicates* BERTHOLD.]

BERTHOLD [*protesting*]. Ah, no thanks, my friends, no thanks! I'm not stopping here! I'm off!

LANDOLPH. What do you mean—you're not stopping here?

HAROLD. He's ruined everything, my Lord, running away in here!

LANDOLPH. He's made him quite mad. We can't keep him in there any longer. He's given orders that he's to be arrested; and he wants to "judge" him at once from the throne: What is to be done?

DI NOLLI. Shut the door, man! Shut the door! Go and close that door! [LANDOLPH *goes over to close it.*]

HAROLD. Ordulph, alone, won't be able to keep him there.

LANDOLPH. —My Lord, perhaps if we could announce the visitors at once, it would turn his thoughts. Have the gentlemen thought under what pretext they will present themselves to him?

DI NOLLI. —It's all been arranged! [*To the* DOCTOR.] If you, Doctor, think it well to see him at once. . . .

FRIDA. I'm not coming! I'm not coming! I'll keep out of this. You too, mother, for Heaven's sake, come away with me!

DOCTOR. —I say . . . I suppose he's not armed, is he?

DI NOLLI. —Nonsense! Of course not. [*To* FRIDA.] Frida, you know this is childish of you. You wanted to come!

FRIDA. I didn't at all. It was mother's idea.

DONNA MATILDA. And I'm quite ready to see him. What are we going to do?

BELCREDI. Must we absolutely dress up in some fashion or other?

LANDOLPH. —Absolutely essential, indispensable, sir. Alas! as you
see . . . [*Shows his costume*], there'd be awful trouble if he saw
you gentlemen in modern dress.

HAROLD. He would think it was some diabolical masquerade.

DI NOLLI. As these men seem to be in costume to you, so we appear
to be in costume to him, in these modern clothes of ours.

LANDOLPH. It wouldn't matter so much if he wouldn't suppose it to
be the work of his mortal enemy.

BELCREDI. Pope Gregory VII?

LANDOLPH. Precisely. He calls him "a pagan."

BELCREDI. The Pope a pagan? Not bad that!

LANDOLPH. —Yes, sir,—and a man who calls up the dead! He accuses him of all the diabolical arts. He's terribly afraid of him.

DOCTOR. Persecution mania!

HAROLD. He'd be simply furious.

DI NOLLI [*to* BELCREDI]. But there's no need for you to be there,
you know. It's sufficient for the Doctor to see him.

DOCTOR. —What do you mean? . . . I? Alone?

DI NOLLI. —But they are there. [*Indicates the three young men.*]

DOCTOR. I don't mean that . . , I mean if the Marchioness . . .

DONNA MATILDA. Of course. I mean to see him too, naturally. I want
to see him again.

FRIDA. Oh, why, mother, why? Do come away with me, I implore you!

DONNA MATILDA [*imperiously*]. Let me do as I wish! I came here for
this purpose! [*To* LANDOLPH.] I shall be "Adelaide," the mother.

LANDOLPH. Excellent! The mother of the Empress Bertha. Good!
It will be enough if her Ladyship wears the ducal crown and puts
on a mantel that will hide her other clothes entirely. [*To* HAROLD.]
Off you go, Harold!

HAROLD. Wait a moment! And this gentleman here? . . . [*Alludes
to the* DOCTOR.]

DOCTOR. —Ah yes . . . we decided I was to be . . . the Bishop of
Cluny, Hugh of Cluny!

HAROLD. The gentleman means the Abbot. Very good! Hugh of
Cluny.[12]

LANDOLPH. —He's often been here before!

DOCTOR [*amazed*]. —What? Been here before?

LANDOLPH. —Don't be alarmed! I mean that it's an easily prepared
disguise . . .

HAROLD. We've made use of it on other occasions, you see!

DOCTOR. But . . .

LANDOLPH. Oh, no there's no risk of his remembering. He pays more
attention to the dress than to the person.

DONNA MATILDA. That's fortunate for me too then.

DI NOLLI. Frida, you and I'll get along. Come on, Tito!

BELCREDI. Ah no. If she [*Indicates the* MARCHIONESS.] stops here,
so do I!

DONNA MATILDA. But I don't need you at all.

12. Godfather of Henry IV.

BELCREDI. You may not need me, but I should like to see him again myself. Mayn't I?

LANDOLPH. Well, perhaps it would be better if there were three.

HAROLD. How is the gentleman to be dressed then?

BELCREDI. Oh, try and find some easy costume for me.

LANDOLPH [*to* HAROLD]. Hum! Yes . . . he'd better be from Cluny too.

BELCREDI. What do you mean—from Cluny?

LANDOLPH. A Benedictine's habit of the Abbey of Cluny. He can be in attendance on Monsignor. [*To* HAROLD.] Off you go! [*To* BERTHOLD.] And you too get away and keep out of sight all today. No, wait a bit! [*To* BERTHOLD.] You bring here the costumes he will give you. [*To* HAROLD.] You go at once and announce the visit of the "Duchess Adelaide" and "Monsignor Hugh of Cluny." Do you understand? [HAROLD *and* BERTHOLD *go off by the first door on the right.*]

DI NOLLI. We'll retire now. [*Goes off with* FRIDA, *left.*]

DOCTOR. Shall I be a *persona grata*[13] to him, as Hugh of Cluny?

LANDOLPH. Oh, rather! Don't worry about that! Monsignor has always been received here with great respect. You too, my Lady, he will be glad to see. He never forgets that it was owing to the intercession of you two that he was admitted to the Castle of Canossa and the presence of Gregory VII, who didn't want to receive him.

BELCREDI. And what do I do?

LANDOLPH. You stand a little apart, respectfully: that's all.

DONNA MATILDA [*irritated, nervous*]. You would do well to go away, you know.

BELCREDI [*slowly, spitefully*]. How upset you seem! . . .

DONNA MATILDA [*proudly*]. I am as I am. Leave me alone!
      [BERTHOLD *comes in with the costumes.*]

LANDOLPH [*seeing him enter*]. Ah, the costumes: here they are. This mantle is for the Marchioness . . .

DONNA MATILDA. Wait a minute! I'll take off my hat. [*Does so and gives it to* BERTHOLD.]

LANDOLPH. Put it down there! [*Then to the* MARCHIONESS, *while he offers to put the ducal crown on her head.*] Allow me!

DONNA MATILDA. Dear, dear! Isn't there a mirror here?

LANDOLPH. Yes, there's one there [*Points to the door on the left.*] If the Marchioness would rather put it on herself . . .

DONNA MATILDA. Yes, yes, that will be better. Give it to me! [*Takes up her hat and goes off with* BERTHOLD, *who carries the cloak and the crown.*]

BELCREDI. Well, I must say, I never thought I should be a Benedictine monk! By the way, this business must cost an awful lot of money.

THE DOCTOR. Like any other fantasy, naturally!

BELCREDI. Well, there's a fortune to go upon.

LANDOLPH. We have got there a whole wardrobe of costumes of the

13. Person declared to be officially acceptable.

period, copied to perfection from old models. This is my special
job. I get them from the best theatrical costumers. They cost lots
of money. [DONNA MATILDA *re-enters, wearing mantle and crown.*]

BELCREDI [*at once, in admiration*]. Oh magnificent! Oh, truly regal!

DONNA MATILDA [*looking at* BELCREDI *and bursting out into laughter*].
Oh no, no! Take it off! You're impossible. You look like an ostrich
dressed up as a monk.

BELCREDI. Well, how about the Doctor?

THE DOCTOR. I don't think I looked so bad, do I?

DONNA MATILDA. No; the Doctor's all right . . . but you are too funny
for words.

THE DOCTOR. Do you have many receptions here then?

LANDOLPH. It depends. He often gives orders that such and such a
person appear before him. Then we have to find someone who will
take the part. Women too . . .

DONNA MATILDA [*hurt, but trying to hide the fact*]. Ah, women too?

LANDOLPH. Oh, yes; many at first.

BELCREDI [*laughing*]. Oh, that's great! In costume, like the Marchioness?

LANDOLPH. Oh well, you know, women of the kind that lend themselves to . . .

BELCREDI. Ah, I see! [*Perfidiously to the* MARCHIONESS.] Look out,
you know he's becoming dangerous for you.

[*The second door on the right opens, and* HAROLD *appears
making first of all a discreet sign that all conversation should
cease.*]

HAROLD. His Majesty, the Emperor!

[*The* TWO VALETS *enter first, and go and stand on either side
of the throne. Then* HENRY IV *comes in between* ORDULPH
and HAROLD, *who keep a little in the rear respectfully.*

HENRY IV *is about 50 and very pale. The hair on the back of
his head is already grey; over the temples and forehead it
appears blond, owing to its having been tinted in an evident
and puerile fashion. On his cheek bones he has two small,
doll-like dabs of color, that stand out prominently against the
rest of his tragic pallor. He is wearing a penitent's sack over
his regal habit, as at Canossa. His eyes have a fixed look which
is dreadful to see, and this expression is in strained contrast
with the sackcloth.* ORDULPH *carries the Imperial crown;* HAR-
OLD, *the sceptre with eagle, and the globe with the cross.*]

HENRY IV [*bowing first to* DONNA MATILDA *and afterwards to the* DOC-
TOR]. My lady . . . Monsignor . . . [*Then he looks at* BELCREDI *and
seems about to greet him too; when, suddenly, he turns to* LAN-
DOLPH, *who has approached him, and asks him sotto voce and with
diffidence.*] Is that Peter Damiani?[14]

LANDOLPH. No, Sire. He is a monk from Cluny who is accompanying

---

14, Cardinal-bishop of Ostia. He had tried to compel Henry IV to take back his first
wife.

the Abbot.

HENRY IV [*looks again at* BELCREDI *with increasing mistrust, and then noticing that he appears embarrassed and keeps glancing at* DONNA MATILDA *and the* DOCTOR, *stands upright and cries out*]. No, it's Peter Damiani! It's no use, father, your looking at the Duchess. [*Then turning quickly to* DONNA MATILDA *and the* DOCTOR *as though to ward off a danger.*] I swear it! I swear that my heart is changed towards your daughter. I confess that if he [*Indicates* BELCREDI.] hadn't come to forbid it in the name of Pope Alexander, I'd have repudiated her. Yes, yes, there were people ready to favour the repudiation: the Bishop of Mayence would have done it for a matter of one hundred and twenty farms. [*Looks at* LANDOLPH *a little perplexed and adds.*] But I mustn't speak ill of the bishops at this moment! [*More humbly to* BELCREDI.] I am grateful to you, believe me, I am grateful to you for the hindrance you put in my way!—God knows, my life's been all made of humiliations: my mother,[15] Adalbert, Tribur,[16] Goslar! And now this sackcloth you see me wearing! [*Changes tone suddenly and speaks like one who goes over his part in a parenthesis of astuteness.*] It doesn't matter: clarity of ideas, perspicacity, firmness and patience under adversity that's the thing. [*Then turning to all and speaking solemnly.*] I know how to make amends for the mistakes I have made; and I can humiliate myself even before you, Peter Damiani. [*Bows profoundly to him and remains curved. Then a suspicion is born in him which he is obliged to utter in menacing tones, almost against his will.*] Was it not perhaps you who started that obscene rumor that my holy mother had illicit relations with the Bishop of Augusta?

BELCREDI [*since* HENRY IV *has his finger pointed at him*]. No, no, it wasn't I . . .

HENRY IV [*straightening up*]. Not true, not true? Infamy! [*Looks at him and then adds.*] I didn't think you capable of it! [*Goes to the* DOCTOR *and plucks his sleeve, while winking at him knowingly.*] Always the same, Monsignor, those bishops, always the same!

HAROLD [*softly, whispering as if to help out the doctor*]. Yes, yes, the rapacious bishops!

THE DOCTOR [*to* HAROLD, *trying to keep it up*]. Ah, yes, those fellows . . . ah yes . . .

HENRY IV. Nothing satisfies them! I was a little boy, Monsignor . . . One passes the time, playing even, when, without knowing it, one is a king.—I was six years old; and they tore me away from my mother, and made use of me against her without my knowing anything about it . . . always profaning, always stealing, stealing! . . . One greedier than the other . . . Hanno[17] worse than Stephen![18] Stephen worse than Hanno!

---

15. She had served as his first regent.

16. There Henry had been forced by the nobles and clergy of Saxony to seek Pope Gregory's pardon.

17. Archbishop of Cologne, Henry's second regent.

18. Probably Pope Stephen IX.

LANDOLPH [*sotto voce, persuasively, to call his attention*]. Majesty!

HENRY IV [*turning round quickly*]. Ah yes . . . this isn't the moment to speak ill of the bishops. But this infamy against my mother, Monsignor, is too much. [*Looks at the* MARCHIONESS *and grows tender.*] And I can't even weep for her, Lady . . . I appeal to you who have a mother's heart! She came here to see me from her convent a month ago . . . They had told me she was dead! [*Sustained pause full of feeling. Then smiling sadly.*] I can't weep for her; because if you are here now, and I am like this [*Shows the sackcloth he is wearing.*] it means I am twenty-six years old!

HAROLD. And that she is therefore alive, Majesty! . . .

ORDULPH. Still in her convent!

HENRY IV [*looking at them*]. Ah yes! And I can postpone my grief to another time. [*Shows the* MARCHIONESS *almost with coquetry the tint he has given to his hair.*] Look! I am still fair . . . [*Then slowly as if in confidence.*] For you . . . there's no need! But little exterior details do help! A matter of time, Monsignor, do you understand me? [*Turns to the* MARCHIONESS *and notices her hair.*] Ah, but I see that you too, Duchess . . . Italian, eh? [*As much as to say "false"; but without any indignation, indeed rather with malicious admiration.*] Heaven forbid that I should show disgust or surprise! Nobody cares to recognize that obscure and fatal power which sets limits to our will. But I say, if one is born and one dies . . . Did you want to be born, Monsignor? I didn't! And in both cases, independently of our wills, so many things happen we would wish didn't happen, and to which we resign ourselves as best we can! . . .

DOCTOR [*merely to make a remark, while studying* HENRY IV *carefully*]. Alas! Yes, alas!

HENRY IV. It's like this: When we are not resigned, out come our desires. A woman wants to be a man . . . an old man would be young again. Desires, ridiculous fixed ideas of course—But reflect! Monsignor, those other desires are not less ridiculous: I mean, those desires where the will is kept within the limits of the possible. Not one of us can lie or pretend. We're all fixed in good faith in a certain concept of ourselves. However, Monsignor, while you keep yourself in order, holding on with both your hands to your holy habit, there slips down from your sleeves, there peels off from you like . . . like a serpent . . . something you don't notice: life, Monsignor! [*Turns to the* MARCHIONESS.] Has it never happened to you, my Lady, to find a different self in yourself? Have you always been the same? My God! One day . . . how was it, how was it you were able to commit this or that action? [*Fixes her so intently in the eyes as almost to make her blanch.*] Yes, that particular action, that very one: we understand each other! But don't be afraid: I shall reveal it to none. And you, Peter Damiani, how could you be a friend of that man? . . .

LANDOLPH. Majesty!

HENRY IV [*at once*]. No, I won't name him! [*Turning to* BELCREDI.] What did you think of him? But we all of us cling tight to our conceptions of ourselves, just as he who is growing old dyes his hair. What does it matter that this dyed hair of mine isn't a reality for you, if it *is*, to some extent, for me?—you, you, my Lady, certainly don't dye your hair to deceive the others, nor even yourself; but only to cheat your own image a little before the looking-glass. I do it for a joke! You do it seriously! But I assure you that you too, Madam, are in masquerade, though it be in all seriousness; and I am not speaking of the venerable crown on your brows or the ducal mantle. I am speaking only of the memory you wish to fix in yourself of your fair complexion one day when it pleased you—or of your dark complexion, if you were dark: the fading image of your youth! For you, Peter Damiani, on the contrary, the memory of what you have been, of what you have done, seems to you a recognition of past realities that remain within you like a dream. I'm in the same case too: with so many inexplicable memories—like dreams! Ah! . . . There's nothing to marvel at in it, Peter Damiani! Tomorrow it will be the same thing with our life of today! [*Suddenly getting excited and taking hold of his sackcloth.*] This sackcloth here . . . [*Beginning to take it off with a gesture of almost ferocious joy while the* THREE VALETS *run over to him, frightened, as if to prevent his doing so.*] Ah, my God! [*Draws back and throws off sackcloth.*] Tomorrow, at Bressanone, twenty-seven German and Lombard bishops will sign with me the act of deposition of Gregory VII! No Pope at all! Just a false monk!

ORDULPH [*with the other three*]. Majesty! Majesty! In God's name! . . .

HAROLD [*inviting him to put on the sackcloth again*]. Listen to what he says, Majesty!

LANDOLPH. Monsignor is here with the Duchess to intercede in your favor. [*Makes secret signs to the* DOCTOR *to say something at once.*]

DOCTOR [*foolishly*]. Ah yes . . . yes . . . we are here to intercede . . .

HENRY IV [*repenting at once, almost terrified, allowing the three to put on the sackcloth again, and pulling it down over him with his own hands*]. Pardon . . . yes . . . yes . . . pardon, Monsignor: forgive me, my Lady . . . I swear to you I feel the whole weight of the anathema. [*Bends himself, takes his face between his hands, as though waiting for something to crush him. Then changing tone, but without moving, says softly to* LANDOLPH, HAROLD *and* ORDULPH.] But I don't know why I cannot be humble before that man there! [*Indicates* BELCREDI.]

LANDOLPH [*sotto voce*]. But why, Majesty, do you insist on believing he is Peter Damiani, when he isn't, at all?

HENRY IV [*looking at him timorously*]. He isn't Peter Damiani?

HAROLD. No, no, he is a poor monk, Majesty.

HENRY IV [*sadly with a touch of exasperation*]. Ah! None of us can estimate what we do when we do it from instinct . . . You perhaps, Madam, can understand me better than the others, since you are a woman and a Duchess. This is a solemn and decisive moment. I could, you know, accept the assistance of the Lombard bishops, arrest the Pope, lock him up here in the castle, run to Rome and elect an anti-Pope; offer alliance to Robert Guiscard[19]—and Gregory VII would be lost! I resist the temptation; and, believe me, I am wise in doing so. I feel the atmosphere of our times and the majesty of one who knows how to be what he ought to be! a Pope! Do you feel inclined to laugh at me, seeing me like this? You would be foolish to do so; for you don't understand the political wisdom which makes this penitent's sack advisable. The parts may be changed tomorrow. What would you do then? Would you laugh to see the Pope a prisoner? No! It would come to the same thing: I dressed as a penitent, today; he, as prisoner tomorrow! But woe to him who doesn't know how to wear his mask, be he king or Pope!—Perhaps he is a bit too cruel! No! Yes, yes, maybe!— You remember, my Lady, how your daughter Bertha, for whom, I repeat, my feelings have changed [*Turns to* BELCREDI *and shouts to his face as if he were being contradicted by him.*]—Yes, changed on account of the affection and devotion she showed me in that terrible moment . . . [*Then once again to the* MARCHIONESS.] . . . you remember how she came with me, my Lady, followed me like a beggar and passed two nights out in the open, in the snow?[20] You are her mother! Doesn't this touch your mother's heart? Doesn't this urge you to pity, so that you will beg His Holiness for pardon, beg him to receive us?

DONNA MATILDA [*trembling, with feeble voice*]. Yes, yes, at once . . .

DOCTOR. It shall be done!

HENRY IV. And one thing more! [*Draws them in to listen to him.*] It isn't enough that he should receive me! You know he can do *everything—everything.* I tell you! He can even call up the dead. [*Touches his chest.*] Behold me! Do you see me? There is no magic art unknown to him. Well, Monsignor, my Lady, my torment is really this: that whether here or there [*Pointing to his portrait almost in fear.*] I can't free myself from this magic. I am a penitent now, you see; and I swear to you I shall remain so until he receives me. But you two, when the excommunication is taken off, must ask the Pope to do this thing he can so easily do: to take me away from that; [*Indicating the portrait again.*] and let me live wholly and freely my miserable life. A man can't always be twenty-six, my Lady. I ask this of you for your daughter's sake too; that I may love her as she deserves to be loved, well disposed as I am now, all tender towards her for her pity. There: it's all there! I am in your hands! [*Bows.*] My Lady! Monsignor!

[*He goes off, bowing grandly, through the door by which he entered, leaving everyone stupefied, and the* MARCHIONESS *so profoundly touched, that no sooner has he gone than she breaks out into sobs and sits down almost fainting.*]

CURTAIN

19. A Norman prince, allied with Gregory VII.   20. Outside the castle of Canossa, in 1077.

Act II

Another room of the villa, adjoining the throne room. Its furniture is antique and severe. Principal exit at rear in the background. To the left, two windows looking on the garden. To the right, a door opening into the throne room.

Late afternoon of the same day.

DONNA MATILDA, *the* DOCTOR *and* BELCREDI *are on the stage engaged in conversation; but* DONNA MATILDA *stands to one side, evidently annoyed at what the other two are saying; although she cannot help listening, because, in her agitated state, everything interests her in spite of herself. The talk of the other two attracts her attention, because she instinctively feels the need for calm at the moment.*

BELCREDI. It may be as you say, Doctor, but that was my impression.

DOCTOR. I won't contradict you; but, believe me, it is only . . . an impression.

BELCREDI. Pardon me, but he even said so, and quite clearly [*Turning to the* MARCHIONESS.] Didn't he, Marchioness?

DONNA MATILDA [*turning round*]. What did he say? . . . [*Then not agreeing.*] Oh yes . . . but not for the reason you think!

DOCTOR. He was alluding to the costumes we had slipped on . . . Your cloak [*Indicating the* MARCHIONESS.] our Benedictine habits . . . But all this is childish!

DONNA MATILDA [*turning quickly, indignant*]. Childish? What do you mean, Doctor?

DOCTOR. From one point of view, it is—I beg you to let me say so, Marchioness! Yet, on the other hand, it is much more complicated than you can imagine.

DONNA MATILDA. To me, on the contrary, it is perfectly clear!

DOCTOR [*with a smile of pity of the competent person towards those who do not understand*]. We must take into account the peculiar psychology of madmen; which, you must know, enables us to be certain that they observe things and can, for instance, easily detect people who are disguised; can in fact recognize the disguise and yet believe in it; just as children do, for whom disguise is both play and reality. That is why I used the word childish. But the thing is extremely complicated, inasmuch as he must be perfectly aware of being an image to himself and for himself—that image there, in fact! [*Alluding to the portrait in the throne room, and pointing to the left.*]

BELCREDI. That's what he said!

DOCTOR. Very well then— An image before which other images, ours, have appeared: understand? Now he, in his acute and perfectly lucid delirium, was able to detect at once a difference between his image and ours: that is, he saw that ours were make-believes. So he suspected us; because all madmen are armed with a special diffidence. But that's all there is to it! Our make-believe, built up all round his, did not seem pitiful to him. While his seemed all the more tragic to us, in that he, as if in defiance—understand?—and induced by his suspicion, wanted to show us up merely as a joke. That was also partly the case with him, in coming before us with painted cheeks and hair, and saying he had done it on purpose for a jest.

DONNA MATILDA [*impatiently*]. No, it's not that, Doctor. It's not like that! It's not like that!

DOCTOR. Why isn't it, may I ask?

DONNA MATILDA [*with decision but trembling*]. I am perfectly certain he recognized me!

DOCTOR. It's not possible . . . it's not possible!

BELCREDI [*at the same time*]. Of course not!

DONNA MATILDA [*more than ever determined, almost convulsively*]. I tell you, he recognized me! When he came close up to speak to me—looking in my eyes, right into my eyes—he recognized me!

BELCREDI. But he was talking of your daughter!

DONNA MATILDA. That's not true! He was talking of me! Of me!

BELCREDI. Yes, perhaps, when he said . . .

DONNA MATILDA [*letting herself go*]. About my dyed hair! But didn't you notice that he added at once: "or the memory of your dark hair, if you were dark"? He remembered perfectly well that I was dark—then!

BELCREDI. Nonsense! nonsense!

DONNA MATILDA [*not listeng to him, turning to the* DOCTOR]. My hair, Doctor, is really dark—like my daughter's! That's why he spoke of her.

BELCREDI. But he doesn't even know your daughter! He's never seen her!

DONNA MATILDA. Exactly! Oh, you never understand anything! By my daughter, stupid, he meant me—as I was then!

BELCREDI. Oh, this is catching! This is catching, this madness!

DONNA MATILDA [*softly, with contempt*]. Fool!

BELCREDI. Excuse me, were you ever his wife? Your daughter is his wife—in his delirium: Bertha of Susa.

DONNA MATILDA. Exactly! Because I, no longer dark—as he remembered me—but *fair*, introduced myself as "Adelaide," the mother. My daughter doesn't exist for him: he's never seen her—you said so yourself! So how can he know whether she's fair or dark?

BELCREDI. But he said dark, speaking generally, just as anyone who wants to recall, whether fair or dark, a memory of youth in the color of the hair! And you, as usual, begin to imagine things! Doctor, you said I ought not to have come! It's she who ought not to have come!

DONNA MATILDA [*upset for a moment by* BELCREDI'S *remark, recovers herself. Then with a touch of anger, because doubtful*]. No, no . . . he spoke of me . . . He spoke all the time to me, with me, of me . . .

BELCREDI. That's not bad! He didn't leave me a moment's breathing space and you say he was talking all the time to you? Unless you think he was alluding to you too, when he was talking to Peter Damiani!

DONNA MATILDA [*defiantly, almost exceeding the limits of courteous discussion*]. Who knows? Can you tell me why, from the outset, he showed a strong dislike for you, for you alone? [*From the tone of the question, the expected answer must almost explicitly be: "because he understands you are my lover."* BELCREDI *feels this so well that he remains silent and can say nothing.*]

DOCTOR. The reason may also be found in the fact that only the visit of the Duchess Adelaide and the Abbot of Cluny was announced to him. Finding a third person present, who had not been announced, at once his suspicions . . .

BELCREDI. Yes, exactly! His suspicion made him see an enemy in me: Peter Damiani! But she's got it into her head, that he recognized her . . .

DONNA MATILDA. There's no doubt about it! I could see it from his eyes, doctor. You know, there's a way of looking that leaves no doubt whatever . . . Perhaps it was only for an instant, but I am sure!

DOCTOR. It is not impossible: a lucid moment . . .

DONNA MATILDA. Yes, perhaps . . . And then his speech seemed to me full of regret for his and my youth—for the horrible thing that happened to him, that has held him in that disguise from which he has never been able to free himself, and from which he longs to be free—he said so himself!

BELCREDI. Yes, so as to be able to make love to your daughter, or you, as you believe—having been touched by your pity.

DONNA MATILDA. Which is very great, I would ask you to believe.

BELCREDI. As one can see, Marchioness; so much so that a miracle-worker might expect a miracle from it!

DOCTOR. Will you let me speak? I don't work miracles, because I am a doctor and not a miracle-worker. I listened very intently to all he said; and I repeat that that certain analogical elasticity, common to all systematized delirium, is evidently with him much . . . what shall I say?—much relaxed! The elements, that is, of his delirium no longer hold together. It seems to me he has lost the equilibrium of his second personality and sudden recollections drag him—and this is very comforting—not from a state of incipient apathy, but rather from a morbid inclination to reflective melancholy, which shows a . . . a very considerable cerebral activity. Very comforting, I repeat! Now if, by this violent trick we've planned . . .

DONNA MATILDA [*turning to the window, in the tone of a sick person complaining*]. But how is it that the motor has not returned? It's three hours and a half since . . .

DOCTOR. What do you say?

DONNA MATILDA. The motor, Doctor! It's more than three hours and a half . . .

DOCTOR [*taking out his watch and looking at it*]. Yes, more than four hours, by this!

DONNA MATILDA. It could have reached here an hour ago at least! But, as usual . . .

BELCREDI. Perhaps they can't find the dress . . .

DONNA MATILDA. But I explained exactly where it was! [*Impatiently.*] And Frida . . . where is Frida?

BELCREDI [*looking out of the window*]. Perhaps she is in the garden with Charles . . .

DOCTOR. He'll talk her out of her fright.

BELCREDI. She's not afraid, Doctor; don't you believe it: the thing bores her rather . . .

DONNA MATILDA. Just don't ask anything of her! I know what she's like.

DOCTOR. Let's wait patiently. Anyhow, it will soon be over, and it has to be in the evening . . . It will only be the matter of a moment! If we can succeed in rousing him, as I was saying, and in breaking at one go the threads—already slack—which still bind him to this fiction of his, giving him back what he himself asks for—you remember, he said: "one cannot always be twenty-six years old, madam!" if we can give him freedom from this torment, which even *he* feels is a torment, then if he is able to recover at one bound the sensation of the distance of time . . .

BELCREDI [*quickly*]. He'll be cured! [*Then emphatically with irony.*] We'll pull him out of it all!

DOCTOR. Yes, we may hope to set him going again, like a watch which has stopped at a certain hour . . . just as if we had our watches in our hands and were waiting for that other watch to go again.—A shake—so—and let's hope it'll tell the time again after its long stop. [*At this point the* MARQUIS CHARLES DI NOLLI *enters from the principal entrance.*]

DONNA MATILDA. Oh, Charles! . . . And Frida? Where is she?

DI NOLLI. She'll be here in a moment.

DOCTOR. Has the motor arrived?

DI NOLLI. Yes.

DONNA MATILDA. Yes? Has the dress come?

DI NOLLI. It's been here some time.

DOCTOR. Good! Good!

DONNA MATILDA [*trembling*]. Where is she? Where's Frida?

DI NOLLI [*shrugging his shoulders and smiling sadly, like one lending himself unwillingly to an untimely joke*]. You'll see, you'll see! . . . [*Pointing towards the hall.*] Here she is! . . . [BERTHOLD *appears at the threshold of the hall, and announces with solemnity.*]

BERTHOLD. Her Highness the Countess Matilda of Canossa! [FRIDA *enters, magnificent and beautiful, arrayed in the robes of her mother as "Countless Matilda of Tuscany," so that she is a living copy of the portrait in the throne room.*]

FRIDA [*passing* BERTHOLD, *who is bowing, says to him with disdain*]. Of Tuscany, of Tuscany! Canossa is just one of my castles!

BELCREDI [*in admiration*]. Look! Look! She seems another person . . .

DONNA MATILDA. One would say it were I! Look!—Why, Frida, look! She's exactly my portrait, alive!

DOCTOR. Yes, yes . . . Perfect! Perfect! The portrait, to the life.

BELCREDI. Yes, there's no question about it. She *is* the portrait! Magnificent!

FRIDA. Don't make me laugh, or I shall burst! I say, mother, what a tiny waist you had? I had to squeeze so to get into this!

DONNA MATILDA [*arranging her dress a little*]. Wait! . . . Keep still! . . . These pleats . . . is it really so tight?

FRIDA. I'm suffocating! I implore you, to be quick! . . .

DOCTOR. But we must wait till it's evening!

FRIDA. No, no, I can't hold out till evening!

DONNA MATILDA. Why did you put it on so soon?

FRIDA. The moment I saw it, the temptation was irresistible . . .

DONNA MATILDA. At least you could have called me, or have had someone help you! It's still all crumpled.

FRIDA. So I saw, mother; but they are old creases; they won't come out.

DOCTOR. It doesn't matter, Marchioness! The illusion is perfect. [*Then coming nearer and asking her to come in front of her daughter, without hiding her.*] If you please, stay there, there . . . at a certain distance . . . now a little more forward . . .

BELCREDI. For the feeling of the distance of time . . .

DONNA MATILDA [*slightly turning to him*]. Twenty years after! A disaster! A tragedy!

BELCREDI. Now don't let's exaggerate!

DOCTOR [*embarrassed, trying to save the situation*]. No, no! I meant the dress . . . so as to see . . . You know . . .

BELCREDI [*laughing*]. Oh, as for the dress, Doctor, it isn't a matter of twenty years! It's eight hundred! An abyss! Do you really want to shove him across it [*Pointing first to* FRIDA *and then to* MARCHIONESS.] from there to here? But you'll have to pick him up in pieces with a basket! Just think now: for us it is a matter of twenty years, a couple of dresses, and a masquerade. But, if, as you say, Doctor, time has stopped for and around him: if he lives there [*Pointing to* FRIDA.] with her, eight hundred years ago . . . I repeat: the giddiness of the jump will be such, that finding himself suddenly among us . . . [*The* DOCTOR *shakes his head in dissent.*] You don't think so?

DOCTOR. No, because life, my dear baron, can take up its rhythms. This—our life—will at once become real also to him; and will pull him up directly, wresting from him suddenly the illusion, and showing him that the eight hundred years, as you say, are only twenty! It will be like one of those tricks, such as the leap into space, for instance, of the Masonic rite, which appears to be heaven knows how far, and is only a step down the stairs.

BELCREDI. Ah! An idea! Yes! Look at Frida and the Marchioness, doctor! Which is more advanced in time? We old people, Doctor! The young ones think they are more ahead; but it isn't true: we are more ahead, because time belongs to us more than to them.

DOCTOR. If the past didn't alienate us . . .

BELCREDI. It doesn't matter at all! How does it alienate us? They [*Pointing to* FRIDA *and* DI NOLLI.] have still to do what we have accomplished, Doctor: to grow old, doing the same foolish things, more or less, as we did . . . This is the illusion: that one comes forward through a door to life. It isn't so! As soon as one is born, one starts dying; therefore, he who started first is the most advanced of all. The youngest of us is father Adam! Look there: [*Pointing to* FRIDA.] eight hundred years younger than all of us— the Countess Matilda of Tuscany. [*He makes her a deep bow.*]

DI NOLLI. I say, Tito, don't start joking.

BELCREDI. Oh, you think I am joking? . . .

DI NOLLI. Of course, of course . . . all the time.

BELCREDI. Impossible! I've even dressed up as a Benedictine . . .

DI NOLLI. Yes, but for a serious purpose.

BELCREDI. Well, exactly. If it has been serious for the others . . . for Frida, now, for instance. [*Then turning to the* DOCTOR.] I swear, Doctor, I don't yet understand what you want to do.

DOCTOR [*annoyed*]. You'll see! Let me do as I wish . . . At present you see the Marchioness still dressed as . . .

BELCREDI. Oh, she also . . . has to masquerade?

DOCTOR. Of course! of course! In another dress that's in there ready to be used when it comes into his head he sees the Countess Matilda of Canossa before him.

FRIDA [*while talking quietly to* DI NOLLI *notices the doctor's mistake*]. Of Tuscany, of Tuscany!

DOCTOR. It's all the same!

BELCREDI. Oh, I see! He'll be faced by two of them . . .

DOCTOR. Two, precisely! And then . . .

FRIDA [*calling him aside*]. Come here, doctor! Listen!

DOCTOR. Here I am! [*Goes near the two young people and pretends to give some explanations to them.*]

BELCREDI [*softly to* DONNA MATILDA]. I say, this is getting rather strong, you know!

DONNA MATILDA [*looking him firmly in the face*]. What?

BELCREDI. Does it really interest you as much as all that—to make you willing to take part in . . . ? For a woman this is simply enormous! . . .

DONNA MATILDA. Yes, for an ordinary woman.

BELCREDI. Oh, no, my dear, for all women,—in a question like this! It's an abnegation.

DONNA MATILDA. I owe it to him.

BELCREDI. Don't lie! You know well enough it's not hurting you!

DONNA MATILDA. Well, then, where does the abnegation come in?

BELCREDI. Just enough to prevent you losing caste in other people's eyes—and just enough to offend me! . . .

DONNA MATILDA. But who is worrying about you now?

DI NOLLI [*coming forward*]. It's all right. It's all right. That's what we'll do! [*Turning toward* BERTHOLD.] Here you, go and call one of those fellows!

BERTHOLD. At once! [*Exit.*]

DONNA MATILDA. But first of all we've got to pretend that we are going away.

DI NOLLI. Exactly! I'll see to that . . . [*To* BELCREDI.] you don't mind staying here?

BELCREDI [*ironically*]. Oh, no, I don't mind, I don't mind! . . .

DI NOLLI. We must look out not to make him suspicious again, you know.

BELCREDI. Oh, Lord! *He* doesn't amount to anything!

DOCTOR. He must believe absolutely that we've gone away. [LANDOLPH *followed by* BERTHOLD *enters from the right.*]

LANDOLPH. May I come in?

DI NOLLI. Come in! Come in! I say—your name's Lolo, isn't it?

LANDOLPH. Lolo, or Landolph, just as you like!

DI NOLLI. Well, look here: the Doctor and the Marchioness are leaving, at once.

LANDOLPH. Very well. All we've got to say is that they have been able to obtain the permission for the reception from His Holiness. He's in there in his own apartments repenting of all he said—and in an awful state to have the pardon! Would you mind coming a minute? . . . If you would, just for a minute . . . put on the dress again . . .

DOCTOR. Why, of course, with pleasure . . .

LANDOLPH. Might I be allowed to make a suggestion? Why not add that the Marchioness of Tuscany has interceded with the Pope that he should be received?

DONNA MATILDA. You see, he has recognized me!

LANDOLPH. Forgive me . . . I don't know my history very well. I am sure you gentlemen know it much better! But I thought it was believed that Henry IV had a secret passion for the Marchioness of Tuscany.

DONNA MATILDA [*at once*]. Nothing of the kind! Nothing of the kind!

LANDOLPH. That's what I thought! But he says he's loved her . . . he's always saying it . . . And now he fears that her indignation for this secret love of his will work him harm with the Pope.

BELCREDI. We must let him understand that this aversion no longer exists.

LANDOLPH. Exactly! Of course!

DONNA MATILDA [*to* BELCREDI]. History says—I don't know whether you know it or not—that the Pope gave way to the supplications of the Marchioness Matilda and the Abbot of Cluny. And I may say, my dear Belcredi, that I intended to take advantage of this fact—at the time of the pageant—to show him my feelings were not so hostile to him as he supposed.

BELCREDI. You are most faithful to history, Marchioness . . .

LANDOLPH. Well then, the Marchioness could spare herself a double disguise and present herself with Monsignor [*Indicating the* DOCTOR.] as the Marchioness of Tuscany.

DOCTOR [*quickly, energetically*]. No, no! That won't do at all. It would ruin everything. The impression from the conformation must be a sudden one, give a shock! No, no, Marchioness, you will appear again as the Duchess Adelaide, the mother of the Empress. And then we'll go away. This is most necessary: that he should know we've gone away. Come on! Don't let's waste any more time! There's a lot to prepare.

[*Exeunt the* DOCTOR, DONNA MATILDA, *and* LANDOLPH, *right.*]

FRIDA. I am beginning to feel afraid again.

DI NOLLI. Again, Frida?

FRIDA. It would have been better if I had seen him before.

DI NOLLI. There's nothing to be frightened of, really.

FRIDA. He isn't furious, is he?

DI NOLLI. Of course not! he's quite calm.

BELCREDI [*with ironic sentimental affectation*]. Melancholy! Didn't you hear that he loves you?

FRIDA. Thanks! That's just why I am afraid.

BELCREDI. He won't do you any harm.

DI NOLLI. It'll only last a minute . . .

FRIDA. Yes, but there in the dark with him . . .

DI NOLLI. Only for a moment; and I will be near you, and all the others behind the door ready to run in. As soon as you see your mother, your part will be finished . . .

BELCREDI. I'm afraid of a different thing: that we're wasting our time . . .

DI NOLLI. Don't begin again! The remedy seems a sound one to me.

FRIDA. I think so too! I feel it! I'm all trembling!

BELCREDI. But, mad people, my dear friends—though they don't know it, alas—have this felicity which we don't take into account . . .

DI NOLLI [*interrupting, annoyed*]. What felicity? Nonsense!

BELCREDI [*forcefully*]. They don't reason!

DI NOLLI. What's reasoning got to do with it, anyway?

BELCREDI. Don't you call it reasoning that he will have to do—according to us—when he sees her [*Indicates* FRIDA.] and her mother? We've reasoned it all out, surely!

DI NOLLI. Nothing of the kind: no reasoning at all! We put before him a double image of his own fantasy, or fiction, as the doctor says.

BELCREDI [*suddenly*]. I say, I've never understood why they take degrees in medicine.

DI NOLLI [*amazed*]. Who?

BELCREDI. The alienists!

DI NOLLI. What ought they to take degrees in, then?

FRIDA. If they are alienists, in what else should they take degrees?

BELCREDI. In law, of course! All a matter of talk! The more they talk, the more highly they are considered. "Analogous elasticity," "the sensation of distance in time!" And the first thing they tell you is that they don't work miracles—when a miracle's just what is wanted! But they know that the more they say they are not miracle-workers, the more folk believe in their seriousness!

BERTHOLD [*who has been looking through the keyhole of the door on right*]. There they are! There they are! They're coming in here.

DI NOLLI. Are they?

BERTHOLD. He wants to come with them . . . Yes! . . . He's coming too!

DI NOLLI. Let's get away, then! Let's get away, at once! [*To* BER-THOLD.] You stop here!

BERTHOLD. Must I?

> [*Without answering him,* DI NOLLI, FRIDA, *and* BELCREDI *go out by the main exit, leaving* BERTHOLD *surprised. The door on the right opens, and* LANDOLPH *enters first, bowing. Then* DONNA MATILDA *comes in, with mantle and ducal crown as in the first act; also the* DOCTOR *as the* ABBOT OF CLUNY. HENRY IV *is among them in royal dress.* ORDULPH *and* HAROLD *enter last of all.*]

HENRY IV [*following up what he has been saying in the other room*]. And now I will ask you a question: how can I be astute, if you think me obstinate?

DOCTOR. No, no, not obstinate!

HENRY IV [*smiling, pleased*]. Then you think me really astute?

DOCTOR. No, no, neither obstinate, nor astute.

HENRY IV [*with benevolent irony*]. Monsignor, if obstinacy is not a vice which can go with astuteness, I hoped that in denying me the former, you would at least allow me a little of the latter. I can assure you I have great need of it. But if you want to keep it all for yourself . . .

DOCTOR. I? I? Do I seem astute to you?

HENRY IV. No. Monsignor! What do you say? Not in the least! Perhaps in this case, I may seem a little obstinate to you [*Cutting short to speak to* DONNA MATILDA.] With your permission: a word in confidence to the Duchess. [*Leads her aside and asks her very earnestly.*] Is your daughter really dear to you?

DONNA MATILDA [*dismayed*]. Why, yes, certainly . . .

HENRY IV. Do you wish me to compensate her with all my love, with all my devotion, for the grave wrongs I have done her—though you must not believe all the stories my enemies tell about my dissoluteness!

DONNA MATILDA. No, no, I don't believe them. I never have believed such stories.

HENRY IV. Well, then are you willing?

DONNA MATILDA [*confused*]. What?

HENRY IV. That I return to love your daughter again? [*Looks at her and adds, in a mysterious tone of warning.*] You mustn't be a friend of the Marchioness of Tuscany!

DONNA MATILDA. I tell you again that she has begged and tried not less than ourselves to obtain your pardon . . .

HENRY IV [*softly, but excitedly*]. Don't tell me that! Don't say that to me! Don't you see the effect it has on me, my Lady?

DONNA MATILDA [*looks a him; then very softly as if in confidence*]. You love her still?

HENRY IV [*puzzled*]. Still? Still, you say? You know, then? But nobody knows! Nobody must know!

DONNA MATILDA. But perhaps she knows, if she has begged so hard for you!

HENRY IV [*looks at her and says*]. And you love your daughter? [*Brief pause. He turns to the* DOCTOR *with laughing accents.*] Ah, Monsignor, it's strange how little I think of my wife! It may be a sin, but I swear to you that I hardly feel her at all in my heart. What is stranger is that her own mother scarcely feels her in her heart. Confess, my Lady, that she amounts to very little for you. [*Turning to* DOCTOR.] She talks to me of that other woman, insistently, insistently, I don't know why! . . .

LANDOLPH [*humbly*]. Maybe, Majesty, it is to disabuse you of some ideas you have had about the Marchioness of Tuscany. [*Then, dismayed at having allowed himself this observation, adds.*] I mean just now, of course . . .

HENRY IV. You too maintain that she has been friendly to me?

LANDOLPH. Yes, at the moment, Majesty.

DONNA MATILDA. Exactly! Exactly! . . .

HENRY IV. I understand. That is to say, you don't believe I love her. I see! I see! Nobody's ever believed it, nobody's ever thought it. Better so, then! But enough, enough! [*Turns to the* DOCTOR *with changed expression.*] Monsignor, you see? The reasons the Pope has had for revoking the excommunication have got nothing at all to do with the reasons for which he excommunicated me originally. Tell Pope Gregory we shall meet again at Brixen. And you, Madame, should you chance to meet your daughter in the courtyard of the castle of your friend the Marchioness, ask her to visit me. We shall see if I succeed in keeping her close beside me as wife and Empress. Many women have presented themselves here already assuring me that they were she. And I thought to have her—yes, I tried sometimes—there's no shame in it, with one's wife!—But when they said they were Bertha, and they were from Susa, all of them—I can't think why—started laughing! [*Confidentially.*] Understand?—in bed—I undressed—so did she—yes, by God, undressed—a man and a woman—it's natural after all! Like that, we don't bother much about who we are. And one's dress is like a phantom that hovers always near one. Oh, Monsignor, phantoms in general are nothing more than trifling disorders of the spirit: images we cannot contain within the bounds of sleep. They reveal themselves even when we are awake, and they frighten us. I . . . ah . . . I am always afraid when, at night time, I see disordered images before me. Sometimes I am even afraid of my own blood pulsing loudly in my arteries in the silence of night, like the sound of a distant step in a lonely corridor! . . . But, forgive me! I have kept you standing too long already. I thank you, my Lady, I thank you, Monsignor. [DONNA MATILDA *and the* DOCTOR *go off bowing. As soon as they have gone,* HENRY IV *suddenly changes his tone.*] Buffoons, buffoons! One can play any tune on them! And that other fellow . . . Pietro Damiani! . . . Caught him out perfectly! He's afraid to appear before me again. [*Moves up and down excitedly while saying this; then sees* BER-

THOLD, *and points him out to the other three valets.*] Oh, look at this imbecile watching me with his mouth wide open! [*Shakes him.*] Don't you understand? Don't you see, idiot, how I treat them, how I play the fool with them, make them appear before me just as I wish? Miserable, frightened clowns that they are! And you [*Addressing the* VALETS.] are amazed that I tear off their ridiculous masks now, just as if it wasn't I who had made them mask themselves to satisfy this taste of mine for playing the madman!

LANDOLPH — HAROLD — ORDULPH [*bewildered, looking at one another*]. What? What does he say? What?

HENRY IV [*answers them imperiously*]. Enough! enough! Let's stop it. I'm tired of it. [*Then as if the thought left him no peace.*] By God! The impudence! To come here along with her lover! . . . And pretending to do it out of pity? So as not to infuriate a poor devil already out of the world, out of time, out of life! If it hadn't been supposed to be done out of pity, one can well imagine that fellow wouldn't have allowed it. Those people expect others to behave as they wish all the time. And, of course, there's nothing arrogant in that! Oh, no! Oh, no! It's merely their way of thinking, of feeling, of seeing. Everybody has his own way of thinking; you fellows, too. Yours is that of a flock of sheep—miserable, feeble, uncertain . . . But those others take advantage of this and make you accept their way of thinking; or, at least, they suppose they do; because, after all, what do they succeed in imposing on you? Words, words which anyone can interpret in his own manner! That's the way public opinion is formed! And it's a bad look out for a man who finds himself labelled one day with one of these words which everyone repeats; for example "madman," or "imbecile." Don't you think it is rather hard for a man to keep quiet, when he knows that there is a fellow going about trying to persuade everybody that he is as he sees him, trying to fix him in other people's opinion as a "madman"—according to him? Now I am talking seriously! Before I hurt my head, falling from my horse . . . [*Stops suddenly, noticing the dismay of the four young men.*] What's the matter with you? [*Imitates their amazed looks.*] What? Am I, or am I not, mad? Oh, yes! I'm mad all right! [*He becomes terrible.*] Well, then, by God, down on your knees, down on your knees! [*Makes them go down on their knees one by one.*] I order you to go down on your knees before me! And touch the ground three times with your foreheads! Down, down! That's the way you've got to be before madmen! [*Then annoyed with their facile humiliation.*] Get up, sheep! You obeyed me, didn't you? You might have put the strait jacket on me! . . . Crush a man with the weight of a word—it's nothing—a fly! all our life is crushed by the weight of words: the weight of the dead. Look at me here: can you really suppose that Henry IV is still alive? All the same, I speak, and order you live men about! Do you think it's a joke that the dead continue to live?—Yes, *here* it's a joke! But get out into the live world!—Ah, you say: what a beautiful sunrise—for us! All time is before us!—Dawn! We will do what we like with this day—.

Ah, yes! To Hell with tradition, the old conventions! Well, go on! You will do nothing but repeat the old, old words, while you imagine you are living! [*Goes up to* BERTHOLD *who has now become quite stupid*] You don't understand a word of this do you? What's your name?

BERTHOLD. I? . . . What? . . . Berthold . . .

HENRY IV. Poor Berthold! What's your name here?

BERTHOLD. I . . . I . . . my name is Fino.

HENRY IV [*feeling the warning and critical glances of the others, turns to them to reduce them to silence*]. Fino?

BERTHOLD. Fino Pagliuca, sire.

HENRY IV [*turning to* LANDOLPH]. I've heard you call each other by your nick-names often enough! Your name is Lolo isn't it?

LANDOLPH. Yes, sire . . . [*Then with a sense of immense joy.*] Oh Lord! Oh Lord! Then he is not mad . . .

HENRY IV [*brusquely*]. What?

LANDOLPH [*hesitating*]. No . . . I said . . .

HENRY IV. Not mad, any more. No. Don't you see? We're having a joke on those that think I am mad! [*To* HAROLD.] I say, boy, your name's Franco . . . [*To* ORDULPH] And yours . . .

ORDULPH. Momo.

HENRY IV. Momo, Momo . . . A nice name that!

LANDOLPH. So he isn't . . .

HENRY IV. What are you talking about? Of course not! Let's have a jolly, good laugh! . . . [*Laughs.*] Ah! . . . Ah! . . . Ah! . . .

LANDOLPH — HAROLD — ORDULPH [*looking at each other half happy and half dismayed*]. Then he's cured! . . . he's all right! . . .

HENRY IV. Silence! Silence! . . . [*To* BERTHOLD.] Why don't you laugh? Are you offended? I didn't mean it especially for you. It's convenient for everybody to insist that certain people are mad, so they can be shut up. Do you know why? Because it's impossible to hear them speak! What shall I say of these people who've just gone away? That one is a whore, another a libertine, another a swindler . . . don't you think so? You can't believe a word he says . . . don't you think so?—By the way, they all listen to me terrified. And why are they terrified, if what I say isn't true? Of course, you can't believe what madmen say—yet, at the same time, they stand there with their eyes wide open with terror!—Why? Tell me, tell me, why?—You see I'm quite calm now!

BERTHOLD. But perhaps, they think that . . .

HENRY IV. No, no, my dear fellow! Look me well in the eyes! . . . I don't say that it's true—nothing is true, Berthold! But . . . look me in the eyes!

BERTHOLD. Well . . .

HENRY IV. You see? You see? . . . You have terror in your own eyes now because I seem mad to you! There's the proof of it! [*Laughs.*]

LANDOLPH [*coming forward in the name of the others, exasperated*]. What proof?

HENRY IV. Your being so dismayed because now I seem again mad to you. You have thought me mad up to now, haven't you? You feel that this dismay of yours can become terror too—something to dash away the ground from under your feet and deprive you of the air you breathe! Do you know what it means to find yourselves face to face with a madman—with one who shakes the foundations of all you have built up in yourselves, your logic, the logic of all your constructions? Madmen, lucky folk! construct without logic, or rather with a logic that flies like a feather. Voluble! Voluble! Today like this and tomorrow—who knows? You say: "This cannot be"; but for them everything can be. You say: "This isn't true!" And why? Because it doesn't seem true to you, or you, or you . . . [*Indicates the three of them in succession.*] . . . and to a hundred thousand others! One must see what seems true to these hundred thousand others who are not supposed to be mad! What a magnificent spectacle they afford, when they reason! What flowers of logic they scatter! I know that when I was a child, I thought the moon in the pond was real. How many things I thought real! I believed everything I was told—and I was happy! Because it's a terrible thing if you don't hold on to that which seems true to you today—to that which will seem true to you tomorrow, even if it is the opposite of that which seemed true to you yesterday. I would never wish you to think, as I have done, on this horrible thing which really drives one mad: that if you were beside another and looking into his eyes—as I one day looked into somebody's eyes—you might as well be a beggar before a door never to be opened to you; for he who does enter there will never be you, but someone unknown to you with his own different and impenetrable world . . . [*Long pause. Darkness gathers in the room, increasing the sense of strangeness and consternation in which the four young men are involved.* HENRY IV *remains aloof, pondering on the misery which is not only his, but everybody's. Then he pulls himself up, and says in an ordinary tone.*] It's getting dark here . . .

ORDULPH. Shall I go for a lamp?

HENRY IV [*ironically*]. The lamp, yes the lamp! . . . Do you suppose I don't know that as soon as I turn my back with my oil lamp to go to bed, you turn on the electric light for yourselves, here, and even there, in the throne room? I pretend not to see it!

ORDULPH. Well, then, shall I turn it on now?

HENRY IV. No, it would blind me! I want my lamp!

ORDULPH. It's ready here behind the door. [*Goes to the main exit, opens the door, goes out for a moment, and returns with an ancient lamp which is held by a ring at the top.*]

HENRY IV. Ah, a little light! Sit there around the table, no, not like that; in an elegant, easy, manner! . . . [*To* HAROLD.] Yes, you, like that! [*Poses him.*] [*Then to* BERTHOLD.] You, so! . . . and I, here! [*Sits opposite them.*] We could do with a little decorative moonlight. It's very useful for us, the moonlight. I feel a real necessity for it, and pass a lot of time looking up at the moon from my window. Who would think, to look at her that she knows that eight hundred years have passed, and that I, seated at the window, cannot really be Henry IV gazing at the moon like any poor devil? But, look, look! See what a magnificent night scene we have here: the emperor surrounded by his faithful counsellors! . . . How do you like it?

LANDOLPH [*softly to* HAROLD, *so as not to break the enchantment*]. And to think it wasn't true!

HENRY IV. True? What wasn't true?

LANDOLPH [*timidly as if to excuse himself*]. No . . . I mean . . . I was saying this morning to him [*Indicates* BERTHOLD.]—he has just entered on service here—I was saying: what a pity that dressed like this and with so many beautiful costumes in the wardrobe . . . and with a room like that . . . [*Indicates the throne room.*]

HENRY IV. Well? what's the pity?

LANDOLPH. Well . . . that we didn't know . . .

HENRY IV. That it was all done in jest, this comedy?

LANDOLPH. Because we thought that . . .

HAROLD [*coming to his assistance*]. Yes . . . that it was done seriously!

HENRY IV. What do you say? Doesn't it seem serious to you?

LANDOLPH. But if you say that . . .

HENRY IV. I say that—you are fools! You ought to have known how to create a fantasy for yourselves, not to act it for me, or anyone coming to see me; but naturally, simply, day by day, before nobody, feeling yourselves alive in the history of the eleventh century, here at the court of your emperor, Henry IV! You, Ordulph [*Taking him by the arm.*], alive in the castle of Goslar, waking up in the morning, getting out of bed, and entering straightway into the dream, clothing yourself in the dream that would be no more a dream, because you would have lived it, felt it all alive in you. You would have drunk it in with the air you breathed; yet knowing all the time that it was a dream, so you could better enjoy the privilege afforded you of having to do nothing else but live this dream, this far off and yet actual dream! And to think that at a distance of eight centuries from this remote age of ours, so colored and so sepulchral, the men of the twentieth century are torturing themselves in ceaseless anxiety to know how their fates and fortunes will work out! Whereas you are already in history with me . . .

LANDOLPH. Yes, yes, very good!

HENRY IV. . . . . Everything determined, everything settled!

ORDULPH. Yes, yes!

HENRY IV. And sad as is my lot, hideous as some of the events are, bitter the struggles and troublous the time—still all history! All history that cannot change, understand? All fixed for ever! And you could have admired at your ease how every effect followed obediently its cause with perfect logic, how every event took place precisely and coherently in each minute particular! The pleasure, the pleasure of history, in fact, which is so great, was yours.

LANDOLPH. Beautiful, beautiful!

HENRY IV. Beautiful, but it's finished! Now that you know, I could not do it any more! [*Takes his lamp to go to bed.*] Neither could you, if up to now you haven't understood the reason of it! I am sick of it now. [*Almost to himself with violent contained rage.*] By God, I'll make her sorry she came here! Dressed herself up as a mother-in-law for me . . . ! And he as an abbot . . . ! And they bring a doctor with them to study me . . . ! Who knows if they don't hope to cure me? . . . Clowns . . . ! I'd like to smack one of them at least in the face: yes, that one—a famous swordsman, they say! . . . He'll kill me . . . Well, we'll see, we'll see! . . . [*A knock at the door.*] Who is it?

THE VOICE OF JOHN. Deo Gratias!

HAROLD [*very pleased at the chance for another joke*]. Oh, it's John, it's old John, who comes every night to play the monk.

ORDULPH [*rubbing his hands*]. Yes, yes! Let's make him do it!

HENRY IV [*at once, severely*]. Fool, why? Just to play a joke on a poor old man who does it for love of me?

LANDOLPH [*to* ORDULPH]. It has to be as if it were true.

HENRY IV. Exactly, as if true! Because, only so, truth is not a jest [*Opens the door and admits* JOHN *dressed as a humble friar with a roll of parchment under his arm.*] Come in, come in, father! [*Then assuming a tone of tragic gravity and deep resentment.*] All the documents of my life and reign favorable to me were destroyed deliberately by my enemies. One only has escaped destruction, this, my life, written by a humble monk who is devoted to me. And you would laugh at him! [*Turns affectionately to* JOHN, *and invites him to sit down at the table.*] Sit down, father, sit down! Have the lamp near you! [*Puts the lamp near him.*] Write! Write!

JOHN [*opens the parchment and prepares to write from dictation*]. I am ready, your Majesty!

HENRY IV [*dictating*]. "The decree of peace proclaimed at Mayence helped the poor and the good, while it damaged the powerful and the bad. [*Curtain begins to fall.*] It brought wealth to the former, hunger and misery to the latter . . ."

CURTAIN

Act III

The throne room so dark that the wall at the bottom is hardly seen. The canvases of the two portraits have been taken away; and, within their frames, FRIDA, *dressed as the "Marchioness of Tuscany" and* CHARLES DI NOLLI, *as "Henry IV," have taken the exact positions of the portraits.*

For a moment, after the raising of curtain, the stage is empty. Then the door on the left opens; and HENRY IV, *holding the lamp by the ring on top of it, enters. He looks back to speak to the four young men, who, with* JOHN, *are presumedly in the adjoining hall, as at the end of the second act.*

HENRY IV. No, stay where you are, stay where you are. I shall manage all right by myself. Good night! [*Closes the door and walks, very sad and tired, across the hall towards the second door on the right, which leads into his apartments.*]

FRIDA [*as soon as she sees that he has just passed the throne, whispers from the niche like one who is on the point of fainting away with fright*]. Henry . . .

HENRY IV [*stopping at the voice, as if someone had stabbed him traitorously in the back, turns a terror-stricken face towards the wall at the bottom of the room; raising an arm instinctively, as if to defend himself and ward·off a blow*]. Who is calling me? [*It is not a question, but an exclamation vibrating with terror, which does not expect a reply from the darkness and the terrible silence of the hall, which suddenly fills him with the suspicion that he is really mad.*]

FRIDA [*at his shudder of terror, is herself not less frightened at the part she is playing, and repeats a little more loudly*]. Henry! . . . [*But, although she wishes to act the part as they have given it to her, she stretches her head a little out of frame towards the other frame.*]

HENRY IV [*gives a dreadful cry; lets the lamp fall from his hands to cover his head with his arms, and makes a movement as if to run away*].

FRIDA [*jumping from the frame on to the stand and shouting like a mad woman*]. Henry! . . . Henry! . . . I'm afraid! . . . I'm terrified! . . .

[*And while* DI NOLLI *jumps in turn on to the stand and thence to the floor and runs to* FRIDA *who, on the verge of fainting, continues to cry out, the* DOCTOR, DONNA MATILDA, *also dressed as "Matilda of Tuscany,"* TITO BELCREDI. LANDOLPH, BERTHOLD *and* JOHN *enter the hall from the doors on the right and on the left. One of them turns on the light: a strange light coming from lamps hidden in the ceiling so that only the upper part of the stage is well lighted. The others without taking notice of* HENRY IV, *who looks on astonished by the unexpected inrush, after the moment of terror which still causes him to tremble, run anxiously to support and comfort the still shaking* FRIDA, *who is moaning in the arms of her fiancé. All are speaking at the same time.*]

DI NOLLI. No, no, Frida . . . Here I am . . . I am beside you!

DOCTOR [*coming with the others*]. Enough! Enough! There's nothing more to be done! . . .

DONNA MATILDA. He is cured, Frida. Look! He is cured! Don't you see?

DI NOLLI [*astonished*]. Cured?

BELCREDI. It was only for fun! Be calm!

FRIDA. No! I am afraid! I am afraid!

DONNA MATILDA. Afraid of what? Look at him! He was never mad at all! . . .

DI NOLLI. That isn't true! What are you saying? Cured?

DOCTOR. It appears so. I should say so . . .

BELCREDI. Yes, yes! They have told us so. [*Pointing to the four young men.*]

DONNA MATILDA. Yes, for a long time! He has confided in them, told them the truth!

DI NOLLI [*now more indignant than astonished*]. But what does it mean? If, up to a short time ago . . . ?

BELCREDI. Hum! He was acting, to take you in and also us, who in good faith . . .

DI NOLLI. Is it possible? To deceive his sister, also, right up to the time of her death?

HENRY IV [*remains apart, peering at one and now at the other under the accusation and the mockery of what all believe to be a cruel joke of his, which is now revealed. He has shown by the flashing of his eyes that he is meditating a revenge, which his violent contempt prevents him from defining clearly, as yet. Stung to the quick and with a clear idea of accepting the fiction they have insidiously worked up as true, he bursts forth at this point*]. Go on, I say! Go on!

DI NOLLI [*astonished at the cry*]. Go on! What do you mean?

HENRY IV. It isn't *your* sister only that is dead!

DI NOLLI. My sister? Yours, I say, whom you compelled up to the last moment, to present herself here as your mother Agnes!

HENRY IV. And was she not *your* mother?

DI NOLLI. My mother? Certainly my mother!

HENRY IV. But your mother is dead for me, *old and far away!* You have just got down now from there. [*Pointing to the frame from which he jumped down.*] And how do you know whether I have not wept her long in secret, dressed even as I am?

DONNA MATILDA [*dismayed, looking at the others*]. What does he say? [*Much impressed, observing him.*] Quietly! quietly, for Heaven's sake!

HENRY IV. What do I say? I ask all of you if Agnes was not the mother of Henry IV? [*Turns to* FRIDA *as if she were really the "Marchioness of Tuscany."*] You, Marchioness, it seems to me, ought to know.

FRIDA [*still frightened, draws closer to* DI NOLLI]. No, no, I don't know. Not I!

DOCTOR. It's the madness returning. . . . Quiet now, everybody!

BELCREDI [*indignant*]. Madness indeed, Doctor! He's acting again! . . .

HENRY IV [*suddenly*]. I? You have emptied those two frames over there, and he stands before my eyes as Henry IV . . .

BELCREDI. We've had enough of this joke now.

HENRY IV. Who said joke?

DOCTOR [*loudly to* BELCREDI]. Don't excite him, for the love of God!

BELCREDI [*without lending an ear to him, but speaking louder*]. But they have said so [*Pointing again to the four young men.*], they, they!

HENRY IV [*turning around and looking at them*]. You? Did you say it was all a joke?

LANDOLPH [*timid and embarrassed*]. No . . . really we said that you were cured.

BELCREDI. Look here! Enough of this! [*To* DONNA MATILDA.] Doesn't it seem to you that the sight of him, [*Pointing to* DI NOLLI.] Marchioness, and that of your daughter dressed so, is becoming an intolerable puerility?

DONNA MATILDA. Oh, be quiet! What does the dress matter, if he is cured?

HENRY IV. Cured, yes! I am cured! [*To* BELCREDI.] ah, but not to let it end this way all at once, as you suppose! [*Attacks him.*] Do you know that for twenty years nobody has ever dared to appear before me here like you and that gentleman? [*Pointing to the* DOCTOR.]

BELCREDI. Of course I know it. As a matter of fact, I too appeared before you this morning dressed . . .

HENRY IV. As a monk, yes!

BELCREDI. And you took me for Peter Damiani! And I didn't even laugh, believing, in fact, that . . .

HENRY IV. That I was mad! Does it make you laugh seeing her like that, now that I am cured? And yet you might have remembered that in my eyes her appearance now . . . [*Interrupts himself with a gesture of contempt.*] Ah! [*Suddenly turns to the* DOCTOR.] You are a doctor, aren't you?

DOCTOR. Yes.

HENRY IV. And you also took part in dressing her up as the Marchioness of Tuscany? To prepare a counterjoke for me here, eh?

DONNA MATILDA [*impetuously*]. No, no! What do you say? It was done for you! I did it for your sake.

DOCTOR [*quickly*]. To attempt, to try, not knowing . . .

HENRY IV [*cutting him short.* I understand. I say counter-joke, in his case [*Indicates* BELCREDI.] because he believes that I have been carrying on a jest . . .

BELCREDI. But excuse me, what do you mean? You say yourself you are cured.

HENRY IV. Let me speak! [*To the* DOCTOR.] Do you know, Doctor, that for a moment you ran the risk of making me mad again? By God, to make the portraits speak; to make them jump alive out of their frames . . .

DOCTOR. But you saw that all of us ran in at once, as soon as they told us . . .

HENRY IV. Certainly! [*Contemplates* FRIDA *and* DI NOLLI, *and then looks at the* MARCHIONESS, *and finally at his own costume.*] The combination is very beautiful . . . Two couples . . . Very good, very good, Doctor! For a madman, not bad! . . . [*With a slight wave of his hand to* BELCREDI.] It seems to him now to be a carnival out of season, eh? [*Turns to look at him.*] We'll get rid now of this masquerade costume of mine, so that I may come away with you. What do you say?

BELCREDI. With me? With us?

HENRY IV. Where shall we go? To the Club? In dress coats and with white ties? Or shall both of us go to the Marchioness' house?

BELCREDI. Wherever you like! Do you want to remain here still, to

continue—alone—what was nothing but the unfortunate joke of
a day of carnival? It is really incredible, incredible how you have
been able to do all this, freed from the disaster that befell you!

HENRY IV. Yes, you see how it was! The fact is that falling from my
horse and striking my head as I did, I was really mad for I know
not how long . . .

DOCTOR. Ah! Did it last long?

HENRY IV [*very quickly to the* DOCTOR]. Yes, Doctor, a long time! I
think it must have been about twelve years. [*Then suddenly
turning to speak to* BELCREDI.] Thus I saw nothing, my dear fellow,
of all that, after that day of carnival, happened for you but not
for me: how things changed, how my friends deceived me, how
my place was taken by another, and all the rest of it! And suppose
my place had been taken in the heart of the woman I loved? . . .
And how should I know who was dead or who had disappeared? . . .
All this, you know, wasn't exactly a jest for me, as it seems to
you . . .

BELCREDI. No, no! I don't mean that if you please. I mean after . . .

HENRY IV. Ah, yes? After? One day [*Stops and addresses the* DOC-
TOR.]—A most interesting case, Doctor! Study me well! Study me
carefully! [*Trembles while speaking.*] All by itself, who knows how,
one day the trouble here [*Touches his forehead.*] mended. Little
by little, I open my eyes, and at first I don't know whether I am
asleep or awake. Then I know I am awake. I touch this thing and
that; I see clearly again . . . Ah!—then, as *he* says [*Alludes to* BEL-
CREDI.] away, away with this masquerade, this incubus! Let's open
the windows, breathe life once again! Away! Away! Let's run out!
[*Suddenly pulling himself up.*] But where? And to do what? To
show myself to all, secretly, as Henry IV, not like this, but arm
in arm with you, among my dear friends?

BELCREDI. What are you saying?

DONNA MATILDA. Who could think it? It's not to be imagined. It
was an accident.

HENRY IV. They all said I was mad before. [*To* BELCREDI.] And you
know it! You were more ferocious than any one against those who
tried to defend me.

BELCREDI. Oh, that was only a joke!

HENRY IV. Look at my hair! [*Shows him the hair on the nape of his
neck.*]

BELCREDI. But mine is grey too!

HENRY IV. Yes, with this difference: that mine went grey here, as
Henry IV, do you understand? And I never knew it! I perceived it
all of a sudden, one day, when I opened my eyes; and I was terrified because I understood at once that not only had my hair gone
grey, but that I was all grey, inside; that everything had fallen to
pieces, that everything was finished; and I was going to arrive
hungry as a wolf, at a banquet which had already been cleared
away . . .

BELCREDI. Yes, but, what about the others? . . .

HENRY IV [*quickly*]. Ah, yes, I know! They couldn't wait until I was

cured, not even those, who, behind my back, pricked my saddled
horse till it bled. . . .

DI NOLLI [*agitated*]. What, what?

HENRY IV. Yes, treacherously, to make it rear and cause me to fall.

DONNA MATILDA [*quickly, in horror*]. This is the first time I knew that.

HENRY IV. That was also a joke, probably!

DONNA MATILDA. But who did it? Who was behind us, then?

HENRY IV. It doesn't matter who it was. All those that went on feast-
ing and were ready to leave me their scrapings, Marchioness, of
miserable pity, or some dirty remnant of remorse in the filthy
plate! Thanks! [*Turning quickly to the* DOCTOR.] Now, Doctor,
the case must be absolutely new in the history of madness; I preferred to remain mad—since I found everything ready and at my
disposal for this new exquisite fantasy. I would live it—this madness of mine—with the most lucid consciousness; and thus revenge myself on the brutality of a stone which had dented my
head. The solitude—this solitude—squalid and empty as it appeared to me when I opened my eyes again— I determined to
deck it out with all the colors and splendors of that far off day of
carnival, when you [*Looks at* DONNA MATILDA *and points* FRIDA *out
to her.*]—when you, Marchioness, triumphed. So I would oblige
all those who were around me to follow, by God, at my orders that
famous pageant which had been—for you and not for me—the
jest of a day. I would make it become—for ever—no more a joke
but a reality, the reality of a real madness: here, all in masquerade,
with throne room, and these my four secret counsellors: secret
and, of course, traitors. [*He turns quickly towards them.*] I should
like to know what you have gained by revealing the fact that I
was cured! If I am cured, there's no longer any need of you, and
you will be discharged! To give anyone one's confidence . . . that
is really the act of a madman. But now I accuse you in my turn.
[*Turning to othe others.*] Do you know? They thought [*Alludes
to the* VALETS.] they could make fun of me too with you. [*Bursts
out laughing. The others laugh, but shamefacedly, except* DONNA
MATILDA.]

BELCREDI [*to* DI NOLLI]. Well, imagine that . . . That's not bad . . .

DI NOLLI [*to the* FOUR YOUNG MEN]. You?

HENRY IV. We must pardon them. This dress [*Plucking his dress*].
which is for me the evident, involuntary caricature of that other
continuous, everlasting masquerade, of which we are the involuntary puppets [*Indicates* BELCREDI.], when, without knowing it, we
mask ourselves with that which we appear to be . . . ah, that dress
of theirs, this masquerade of theirs, of course, we must forgive it
them, since they do not yet see it is identical with themselves . . .
[*Turning again to* BELCREDI.] You know, it is quite easy to get
accustomed to it. One walks about as a tragic character, just as if
it were nothing . . . [*Imitates the tragic manner.*] in a room like
this . . . Look here, doctor! I remember a priest, certainly Irish, a
nice-looking priest, who was sleeping in the sun one November
day, with his arm on the corner of the bench of a public garden.

He was lost in the golden delight of the mild sunny air which must have seemed for him almost summery. One may be sure that in that moment he did not know any more that he was a priest, or even where he was. He was dreaming . . . A little boy passed with a flower in his hand. He touched the priest with it here on the neck. I saw him open his laughing eyes, while all his mouth smiled with the beauty of his dream. He was forgetful of everything . . . But all at once, he pulled himself together, and stretched out his priest's cassock; and there came back to his eyes the same seriousness which you have seen in mine; because the Irish priests defend the seriousness of their Catholic faith with the same zeal with which I defend the sacred rights of hereditary monarchy! I am cured, gentlemen: because I can act the madman to perfection, here; and I do it very quietly, I'm only sorry for you that have to live your madness so agitatedly, without knowing it or seeing it.

BELCREDI. It comes to this, then, that it is we who are mad. That's what it is!

HENRY IV [*containing his irritation*]. But if you weren't mad, both you and she [*Indicating the* MARCHIONESS.] would you have come here to see me?

BELCREDI. To tell the truth, I came here believing that you were the madman.

HENRY IV [*suddenly indicating the* MARCHIONESS]. And she?

BELCREDI. Ah, as for her . . . I can't say. I see she is all fascinated by your words, by this *conscious* madness of yours. [*Turns to her.*] Dressed as you are [*Speaking to her.*], you could even remain here to live it out, Marchioness.

DONNA MATILDA. You are insolent!

HENRY IV [*conciliatingly*]. No, Marchioness, what he means to say is that the miracle would be complete, according to him, with you here, who—as the Marchioness of Tuscany, you well know,—could not be my friend, save, as at Canossa, to give me a little pity . . .

BELCREDI. Or even more than a little! She said so herself!

HENRY IV [*to the* MARCHIONESS, *continuing*]. And even, shall we say, a little remorse! . . .

BELCREDI. Yes, that too she has admitted.

DONNA MATILDA [*angry*]. Now look here . . .

HENRY IV [*quickly, to placate her*]. Don't bother about him! Don't mind him! Let him go on infuriating me—though the Doctor's told him not to. [*Turns to* BELCREDI.] But do you suppose I am going to trouble myself any more about what happened between us—the share you had in my misfortune with her [*Indicates the* MARCHIONESS *to him and pointing* BELCREDI *out to her.*] the part he has now in your life? This is my life! Quite a different thing from your life! Your life, the life in which you have grown old—I have not lived that life. [*To* DONNA MATILDA.] Was this what you wanted to show me with this sacrifice of yours, dressing yourself up like this, according to the Doctor's idea? Excellently done, Doctor! Oh, an excellent idea:—"As we were then, eh? and as we are now?" But I am not a madman according to your way of think-

ing, Doctor. I know very well that that man there [*Indicates* DI
NOLLI.] cannot be me; because I am Henry IV, and have been,
these twenty years, cast in this eternal masquerade. She has lived
these years! [*Indicates the* MARCHIONESS.] She has enjoyed them
and has become—look at her!—a woman I can no longer recognize. It is so that I knew her! [*Points to* FRIDA *and draws near
her.*] This is the Marchioness I know, always this one! . . . You
seem a lot of children to be so easily frightened by me . . . [*To*
FRIDA.] And you're frightened too, little girl, aren't you, by the
jest that they made you take part in—though they didn't understand it wouldn't be the jest they meant it to be, for me? Oh
miracle of miracles! Prodigy of prodigies! The dream alive in you!
More than alive in you! It was an image that wavered there and
they've made you come to life! Oh, mine! You're mine, mine,
mine, in my own right! [HE *holds her in his arms, laughing like a
madman, while all stand still terrified. Then as they advance to
tear* FRIDA *from his arms, he becomes furious, terrible and cries imperiously to his* VALETS.] Hold them! Hold them! I order you to
hold them!

> [*The* FOUR YOUNG MEN *amazed, yet fascinated, move to ex-
> ecute his orders, automatically, and seize* DI NOLLI, *the* DOC-
> TOR, *and* BELCREDI.]

BELCREDI [*freeing himself*]. Leave her alone! Leave her alone! You're
no madman!

HENRY IV [*in a flash draws the sword from the side of* LANDOLPH, *who
is close to him*]. I'm not mad, eh! Take that, you! . . . [*Drives
sword into him. A cry of horror goes up. All rush over to assist*
BELCREDI, *crying out together.*]

DI NOLLI. Has he wounded you?

BERTHOLD. Yes, yes, seriously!

DOCTOR. I told you so!

FRIDA. Oh God, oh God!

DI NOLLI. Frida, come here!

DONNA MATILDA. He's mad, mad!

DI NOLLI. Hold him!

BELCREDI [*while* THEY *take him away by the left exit,* HE *protests as
he is borne out*]. No, no, you're not mad! You're not mad. He's
not mad!

> [THEY *go out by the left amid cries and excitement. After a
> moment, one hears a still sharper, more piercing cry from*
> DONNA MATILDA, *and then, silence.*]

HENRY IV [*who has remained on the stage between* LANDOLPH, HAROLD
and ORDULPH, *with his eyes almost starting out of his head, terrified by the life of his own masquerade which has driven him to
crime.*] Now, yes . . . we'll have to [*Calls his* VALETS *around him as
if to protect him.*] here we are . . . together . . . for ever!

CURTAIN

MARCEL PROUST

(1871–1922)

Remembrance of Things Past*[1]

(À la Recherche du temps perdu)

For a long time I used to go to bed early. Sometimes, when I had put out my candle, my eyes would close so quickly that I had not even time to say "I'm going to sleep." And half an hour later the thought that it was time to go to sleep would awaken me; I would try to put away the book which, I imagined, was still in my hands, and to blow out the light; I had been thinking all the time, while I was asleep, of what I had just been reading, but my thoughts had run into a channel of their own, until I myself seemed actually to have become the subject of my book: a church, a quartet, the rivalry between François I and Charles V.[2] This impression would persist for some moments after I was awake; it did not disturb my mind, but it lay like scales upon my eyes and prevented them from registering the fact that the candle was no longer burning. Then it would begin to seem unintelligible, as the thoughts of a former existence must be to a reincarnate spirit; the subject of my book would separate itself from me, leaving me free to choose whether I would form part of it or no; and at the same time my sight would return and I would be astonished to find myself in a state of darkness, pleasant and restful enough for the eyes, and even more, perhaps, for my mind, to which it appeared incomprehensible, without a cause, a matter dark indeed.

I would ask myself what o'clock it could be; I could hear the whistling of trains, which, now nearer and now farther off, punctuating the distance like the note of a bird in a forest, showed me in perspective the deserted countryside through which a traveler

---

* Published 1913–1927. Translated by C. K. Scott Moncrieff.

1. This selction, "Overture," is the opening section of Combray, the first volume of *Swann's Way* (*Du Côté de chez Swann*, 1913), itself the first full volume of Proust's novel. "Swann's way" is one of the two directions in wʰⁱch Marcel's family used to take walks from their home in Combray, toward Tansonville, home of Charles Swann, and is associated with various scenes and anecdotes of love and private life. The longer walk toward the estate of the Guermantes (*Guermantes Way*, 1921, the novel's third volume), a fic-

tional family of the highest aristocracy appearing frequently in the novel, evokes an aura of high society and French history, a more public sphere. The narrator is Marcel as an old man. The verb tense of the French original through all but the final volume of the novel is typically the imperfect, a tense of uncompleted action. Fictional people and places mingle with the real; where a name is not annotated, it is Proust's invention.

2. Francis I (1496–1567), King of France, and Charles V (1500–1558), Holy Roman Emperor and King of Spain, fought four wars over the Empire's expansion in Europe.

would be hurrying toward the nearest station: the path that he followed being fixed for ever in his memory by the general excitement due to being in a strange place, to doing unusual things, to the last words of conversation, to farewells exchanged beneath an unfamiliar lamp which echoed still in his ears amid the silence of the night; and to the delightful prospect of being once again at home.

I would lay my cheeks gently against the comfortable cheeks of my pillow, as plump and blooming as the cheeks of babyhood. Or I would strike a match to look at my watch. Nearly midnight. The hour when an invalid, who has been obliged to start on a journey and to sleep in a strange hotel, awakens in a moment of illness and sees with glad relief a streak of daylight showing under his bedroom door.[3] Oh, joy of joys! it is morning. The servants will be about in a minute: he can ring, and some one will come to look after him. The thought of being made comfortable gives him strength to endure his pain. He is certain he heard footsteps: they come nearer, and then die away. The ray of light beneath his door is extinguished. It is midnight; some one has turned out the gas; the last servant has gone to bed, and he must lie all night in agony with no one to bring him any help.

I would fall asleep,[4] and often I would be awake again for short snatches only, just long enough to hear the regular creaking of the wainscot,[5] or to open my eyes to settle the shifting kaleidoscope of the darkness, to savor, in an instantaneous flash of perception, the sleep which lay heavy upon the furniture, the room, the whole surroundings of which I formed but an insignificant part and whose unconsciousness I should very soon return to share. Or, perhaps, while I was asleep I had returned without the least effort to an earlier stage in my life, now for ever outgrown; and had come under the thrall of one of my childish terrors, such as that old terror of my great-uncle's pulling my curls, which was effectually dispelled on the day—the dawn of a new era to me—on which they were finally cropped from my head. I had forgotten that event during my sleep; I remembered it again immediately I had succeeded in making myself wake up to escape my great uncle's fingers; still, as a measure of precaution, I would bury the whole of my head in the pillow before returning to the world of dreams.

Sometimes, too, just as Eve was created from a rib of Adam, so a woman would come into existence while I was sleeping, conceived from some strain in the position of my limbs. Formed by the

3. The point of view is no longer the child's, nor yet that of the old man, but reflects Marcel's adult experience as an invalid traveler.

4. The narrator returns to the child's perspective in a typical alternation of two narrative views, two layers of the same existence.

5. The wooden paneling of the walls.

appetite that I was on the point of gratifying, she it was, I imagined, who offered me that gratification. My body, conscious that its own warmth was permeating hers, would strive to become one with her, and I would awake. The rest of humanity seemed very remote in comparison with this woman whose company I had left but a moment ago: my cheek was still warm with her kiss, my body bent beneath the weight of hers. If, as would sometimes happen, she had the appearance of some woman whom I had known in waking hours, I would abandon myself altogether to the sole quest of her, like people who set out on a journey to see with their own eyes some city that they have always longed to visit, and imagine that they can taste in reality what has charmed their fancy. And then, gradually, the memory of her would dissolve and vanish, until I had forgotten the maiden of my dream.

When a man is asleep, he has in a circle round him the chain of the hours, the sequence of the years, the order of the heavenly host.[6] Instinctively, when he awakes, he looks to these, and in an instant reads off his own position on the earth's surface and the amount of time that has elapsed during his slumbers; but this ordered procession is apt to grow confused, and to break its ranks. Suppose that, toward morning, after a night of insomnia, sleep descends upon him while he is reading, in quite a different position from that in which he normally goes to sleep, he has only to lift his arm to arrest the sun and turn it back in its course,[7] and, at the moment of waking, he will have no idea of the time, but will conclude that he has just gone to bed. Or suppose that he gets drowsy in some even more abnormal position; sitting in an armchair, say, after dinner: then the world will fall topsy-turvy from its orbit, the magic chair will carry him at full speed through time and space, and when he opens his eyes again he will imagine that he went to sleep months earlier and in some far distant country. But for me it was enough if, in my own bed, my sleep was so heavy as completely to relax my consciousness; for then I lost all sense of the place in which I had gone to sleep, and when I awoke at midnight, not knowing where I was, I could not be sure at first who I was; I had only the most rudimentary sense of existence, such as may lurk and flicker in the depths of an animal's consciousness; I was more destitute of human qualities than the cave-dweller; but then the memory, not yet of the place in which I was, but of various other places where I had lived, and might now very possibly be, would come like a rope let down from heaven to draw me up out of the

6. Theologians divide the angels into nine ranks or choirs of precedence.
7. If his uplifted arm prevents him from seeing the sunlight, he will think it is still night.

abyss of not-being, from which I could never have escaped by myself: in a flash I would traverse and surmount centuries of civilization, and out of a half-visualized succession of oil-lamps, followed by shirts with turned-down collars,[8] would put together by degrees the component parts of my ego.

Perhaps the immobility of the things that surround us is forced upon them by our conviction that they are themselves, and not anything else, and by the immobility of our conceptions of them. For it always happened that when I awoke like this, and my mind struggled in an unsuccessful attempt to discover where I was, everything would be moving round me through the darkness: things, places, years. My body, still too heavy with sleep to move, would make an effort to construe the form which its tiredness took as an orientation of its various members, so as to induce from that where the wall lay and the furniture stood, to piece together and to give a name to the house in which it must be living. Its memory, the composite memory of its ribs, knees, and shoulder blades offered it a whole series of rooms in which it had at one time or another slept; while the unseen walls kept changing, adapting themselves to the shape of each successive room that it remembered, whirling madly through the darkness. And even before my brain, lingering in consideration of when things had happened and of what they had looked like, had collected sufficient impressions to enable it to identify the room, it, my body, would recall from each room in succession what the bed was like, where the doors were, how daylight came in at the windows, whether there was a passage outside, what I had had in my mind when I went to sleep, and had found there when I awoke. The stiffened side underneath my body would, for instance, in trying to fix its position, imagine itself to be lying, face to the wall, in a big bed with a canopy; and at once I would say to myself, "Why, I must have gone to sleep after all, and Mamma never came to say good night!" for I was in the country with my grandfather, who died years ago; and my body, the side upon which I was lying, loyally preserving from the past an impression which my mind should never have forgotten, brought back before my eyes the glimmering flame of the night light in its bowl of Bohemian glass,[9] shaped like an urn and hung by chains from the ceiling, and the chimney piece of Siena marble[10] in my bedroom at Combray, in my great-aunt's house, in those far distant days which, at the moment of waking, seemed present without being clearly defined,

<hr />

8. The narrator's memory links successive segments of the past to recreate his personal identity, just as evolution links stages in the growth from caveman to the modern Parisian, with his reading lamps and fashionable shirts.

9. Likely to have been ornately engraved. (Bohemia, the western part of Czechoslovakia, was a major center of the glass industry).

10. The marble from Siena, in central Italy, mottled and reddish in color.

but would become plainer in a little while when I was properly awake.

Then would come up the memory of a fresh position; the wall slid away in another direction; I was in my room in Mme. de Saint-Loup's[11] house in the country; good heavens, it must be ten o'clock, they will have finished dinner! I must have overslept myself, in the little nap which I always take when I come in from my walk with Mme. de Saint-Loup, before dressing for the evening. For many years have now elapsed since the Combray days, when, coming in from the longest and latest walks, I would still be in time to see the reflection of the sunset glowing in the panes of my bedroom window. It is a very different kind of existence at Tansonville now with Mme. de Saint-Loup, and a different kind of pleasure that I now derive from taking walks only in the evenings, from visiting by moonlight the roads on which I used to play, as a child, in the sunshine; while the bedroom, in which I shall presently fall asleep instead of dressing for dinner, from afar off I can see it, as we return from our walk, with its lamp shining through the window, a solitary beacon in the night.

These shifting and confused gusts of memory never lasted for more than a few seconds; it often happened that, in my spell of uncertainty as to where I was, I did not distinguish the successive theories of which that uncertainty was composed any more than, when we watch a horse running, we isolate the successive positions of its body as they appear upon a bioscope.[12] But I had seen first one and then another of the rooms in which I had slept during my life, and in the end I would revisit them all in the long course of my waking dream: rooms in winter, where on going to bed I would at once bury my head in a nest, built up out of the most diverse materials, the corner of my pillow, the top of my blankets, a piece of a shawl, the edge of my bed, and a copy of an evening paper, all of which things I would contrive, with the infinite patience of birds building their nests, to cement into one whole; rooms where, in a keen frost, I would feel the satisfaction of being shut in from the outer world (like the sea-swallow which builds at the end of a dark tunnel and is kept warm by the surrounding earth), and where, the fire keeping in all night, I would sleep wrapped up, as it were, in a great cloak of snug and savory air, shot with the glow of the logs which would break out again in flame: in a sort of alcove without walls, a cave of warmth dug out of the heart of the room itself, a zone of heat whose boundaries were constantly shifting and altering in temperature as gusts of air ran across them to strike freshly upon

11. Charles Swann's daughter, Gilberte, who has married Robert de Saint-Loup, a nephew of the Guermantes.

12. An early moving-picture machine that showed photographs in rapid succession.

my face, from the corners of the room, or from parts near the window or far from the fireplace which had therefore remained cold —or rooms in summer, where I would delight to feel myself a part of the warm evening, where the moonlight striking upon the half-opened shutters would throw down to the foot of my bed its enchanted ladder; where I would fall asleep, as it might be in the open air, like a titmouse[13] which the breeze keeps poised in the focus of a sunbeam—or sometimes the Louis XVI room,[14] so cheerful that I could never feel really unhappy, even on my first night in it: that room where the slender columns which lightly supported its ceiling would part, ever so gracefully, to indicate where the bed was and to keep it separate; sometimes again that little room with the high ceiling, hollowed in the form of a pyramid out of two separate stories, and partly walled with mahogany, in which from the first moment my mind was drugged by the unfamiliar scent of flowering grasses,[15] convinced of the hostility of the violet curtains and of the insolent indifference of a clock that chattered on at the top of its voice as though I were not there; while a strange and pitiless mirror with square feet, which stood across one corner of the room, cleared for itself a site I had not looked to find tenanted in the quiet surroundings of my normal field of vision:[16] that room in which my mind, forcing itself for hours on end to leave its moorings, to elongate itself upward so as to take on the exact shape of the room, and to reach to the summit of that monstrous funnel, had passed so many anxious nights while my body lay stretched out in bed, my eyes staring upward, my ears straining, my nostrils sniffing uneasily, and my heart beating; until custom[17] had changed the color of the curtains, made the clock keep quiet, brought an expression of pity to the cruel, slanting face of the glass, disguised or even completely dispelled the scent of flowering grasses, and distinctly reduced the apparent loftiness of the ceiling. Custom! that skillful but unhurrying manager who begins by torturing the mind for weeks on end with her provisional arrangements; whom the mind, for all that, is fortunate in discovering, for without the help of custom it would never contrive, by its own efforts, to make any room seem habitable.

Certainly I was now well awake; my body had turned about for the last time and the good angel of certainty had made all the surrounding objects stand still, had set me down under my bedclothes,

13. Small, sparrow-like bird.

14. Furnished in late-18th-century style, named for the French monarch of the time, and marked by great elegance. The room is that in which Marcel visits Robert de Saint-Loup in *Guermantes Way*.

15. *Vetiver*, the aromatic root of a

tropical grass packaged as a moth-preventive.

16. The narrator's room at the fictional seaside resort of Balbec, a setting in *Within a Budding Grove* (1918, the novel's second volume).

17. Literally, "habit."

in my bedroom, and had fixed, approximately in their right places in the uncertain light, my chest of drawers, my writing-table, my fireplace, the window overlooking the street, and both the doors. But it was no good my knowing that I was not in any of those houses of which, in the stupid moment of waking, if I had not caught sight exactly, I could still believe in their possible presence; for memory was now set in motion; as a rule I did not attempt to go to sleep again at once, but used to spend the greater part of the night recalling our life in the old days at Combray with my great-aunt, at Balbec, Paris, Doncières, Venice,[18] and the rest; remembering again all the places and people that I had known, what I had actually seen of them, and what others had told me.

At Combray, as every afternoon ended, long before the time when I should have to go up to bed, and to lie there, unsleeping, far from my mother and grandmother, my bedroom became the fixed point on which my melancholy and anxious thoughts were centered. Someone had had the happy idea of giving me, to distract me on evenings when I seemed abnormally wretched, a magic lantern,[19] which used to be set on top of my lamp while we waited for dinner time to come: in the manner of the master-builders and glass-painters of gothic days it substituted for the opaqueness of my walls an impalpable iridescence, supernatural phenomena of many colors, in which legends were depicted, as on a shifting and transitory window. But my sorrows were only increased, because this change of lighting destroyed, as nothing else could have done, the customary impression I had formed of my room, thanks to which the room itself, but for the torture of having to go to bed in it, had become quite endurable. For now I no longer recognized it, and I became uneasy, as though I were in a room in some hotel or furnished lodging, in a place where I had just arrived, by train, for the first time.

Riding at a jerky trot, Golo,[20] his mind filled with an infamous design, issued from the little three-cornered forest which dyed dark-green the slope of a convenient hill, and advanced by leaps and bounds toward the castle of poor Geneviève de Brabant. This castle was cut off short by a curved line which was in fact the circumference of one of the transparent ovals in the slides which were pushed into position through a slot in the lantern. It was only the wing of a castle, and in front of it stretched a moor on which Geneviève stood, lost in contemplation, wearing a blue girdle.[21] The castle and the moor were yellow, but I could tell their color without wait-

---

18. Main settings for the rest of the novel. Doncières, like Balbec, is a fictional locale.
19. A kind of slide projector.
20. Villain of a fifth-century legend.

He falsely accuses Geneviève de Brabant of adultery. (Brabant was a principality in what is now Belgium)
21. Belt.

ing to see them, for before the slides made their appearance the old-gold sonorous name of Brabant had given me an unmistakable clue. Golo stopped for a moment and listened sadly to the little speech read aloud by my great-aunt,[22] which he seemed perfectly to understand, for he modified his attitude with a docility not devoid of a degree of majesty, so as to conform to the indications given in the text; then he rode away at the same jerky trot. And nothing could arrest his slow progress. If the lantern were moved I could still distinguish Golo's horse advancing across the window-curtains, swelling out with their curves and diving into their folds. The body of Golo himself, being of the same supernatural substance as his steed's, overcame all material obstacles—everything that seemed to bar his way—by taking each as it might be a skeleton and embodying it in himself: the door-handle, for instance, over which, adapting itself at once, would float invincibly his red cloak or his pale face, never losing its nobility or its melancholy, never showing any sign of trouble at such a transubstantiation.

And, indeed, I found plenty of charm in these bright projections, which seemed to have come straight out of a Merovingian[23] past, and to shed around me the reflections of such ancient history. But I cannot express the discomfort I felt at such an intrusion of mystery and beauty into a room which I had succeeded in filling with my own personality until I thought no more of the room than of myself. The anesthetic effect of custom being destroyed, I would begin to think and to feel very melancholy things. The door handle of my room, which was different to me from all the other door handles in the world, inasmuch as it seemed to open of its own accord and without my having to turn it, so unconscious had its manipulation become; lo and behold, it was now an astral body[24] for Golo. And as soon as the dinner bell rang I would run down to the dining room, where the big hanging lamp, ignorant of Golo and Bluebeard[25] but well acquainted with my family and the dish of stewed beef, shed the same light as on every other evening; and I would fall into the arms of my mother, whom the misfortunes of Geneviève de Brabant had made all the dearer to me, just as the crimes of Golo had driven me to a more than ordinarily scrupulous examination of my own conscience.

But after dinner, alas, I was soon obliged to leave Mamma, who stayed talking with the others, in the garden if it was fine, or in the

22. Marcel's great-aunt is reading the story to him as they wait for dinner.
23. The first dynasty of French kings, 500-751 A.D.
24. Spiritual counterpart of the physical body; according to the doctrine of Theosophy (a spiritualist movement originating in 1875), the astral body survives the death of the physical body.
25. The legendary wife-murderer, presumably depicted on another set of slides.

little parlor where everyone took shelter when it was wet. Everyone except my grandmother, who held that "It is a pity to shut oneself indoors in the country," and used to carry on endless discussions with my father on the very wettest days, because he would send me up to my room with a book instead of letting me stay out of doors. "That is not the way to make him strong and active," she would say sadly, "especially this little man, who needs all the strength and character that he can get." My father would shrug his shoulders and study the barometer, for he took an interest in meteorology, while my mother, keeping very quiet so as not to disturb him, looked at him with tender respect, but not too hard, not wishing to penetrate the mysteries of his superior mind. But my grandmother, in all weathers, even when the rain was coming down in torrents and Françoise had rushed indoors with the precious wicker armchairs, so that they should not get soaked—you would see my grandmother pacing the deserted garden, lashed by the storm, pushing back her grey hair in disorder so that her brows might be more free to imbibe the life-giving drafts of wind and rain. She would say, "At last one can breathe!" and would run up and down the soaking paths— too straight and symmetrical for her liking, owing to the want of any feeling for nature in the new gardener, whom my father had been asking all morning if the weather were going to improve— with her keen, jerky little step regulated by the various effects wrought upon her soul by the intoxication of the storm, the force of hygiene, the stupidity of my education and of symmetry in gardens, rather than by any anxiety (for that was quite unknown to her) to save her plum-colored skirt from the spots of mud under which it would gradually disappear to a depth which always provided her maid with a fresh problem and filled her with fresh despair.

When these walks of my grandmother's took place after dinner there was one thing which never failed to bring her back to the house: that was if (at one of those points when the revolutions of her course brought her, moth-like, in sight of the lamp in the little parlor where the liqueurs were set out on the card table) my great-aunt called out to her: "Bathilde! Come in and stop your husband from drinking brandy!" For, simply to tease her (she had brought so foreign a type of mind into my father's family that everyone made a joke of it), my great-aunt used to make my grandfather, who was forbidden liqueurs, take just a few drops. My poor grandmother would come in and beg and implore her husband not to taste the brandy; and he would become annoyed and swallow his few drops all the same, and she would go out again sad and discouraged, but still smiling, for she was so humble and so sweet that her

gentleness toward others, and her continual subordination of herself
and of her own troubles, appeared on her face blended in a smile
which, unlike those seen on the majority of human faces, had no
trace in it of irony, save for herself, while for all of us kisses seemed
to spring from her eyes, which could not look upon those she loved
without yearning to bestow upon them passionate caresses. The torments inflicted on her by my great-aunt, the sight of my grandmother's vain entreaties, of her in her weakness conquered before
she began, but still making the futile endeavor to wean my grandfather from his liqueur glass—all these were things of the sort to
which, in later years, one can grow so well accustomed as to smile at
them, to take the tormentor's side with a happy determination
which deludes one into the belief that it is not, really, tormenting;
but in those days they filled me with such horror that I longed to
strike my great-aunt. And yet, as soon as I heard her "Bathilde!
Come in and stop your husband from drinking brandy!" in my
cowardice I became at once a man, and did what all we grown
men do when face to face with suffering and injustice; I preferred not to see them; I ran up to the top of the house to cry by
myself in a little room beside the schoolroom and beneath the
roof which smelt of orris root,[26] and was scented also by a wild
currant bush which had climbed up between the stones of the outer
wall and thrust a flowering branch in through the half-opened window. Intended for a more special and a baser use,[27] this room,
from which, in the daytime, I could see as far as the keep of
Roussainville-le-Pin,[28] was for a long time my place of refuge,
doubtless because it was the only room whose door I was allowed to
lock, whenever my occupation was such as required an inviolable
solitude; reading or dreaming, secret tears or paroxysms of desire.
Alas! I little knew that my own lack of will power, my delicate
health, and the consequent uncertainty as to my future weighed far
more heavily on my grandmother's mind than any little breach of
the rules by her husband, during those endless perambulations,
afternoon and evening, in which we used to see passing up and
down, obliquely raised toward the heavens, her handsome face with
its brown and wrinkled cheeks, which with age had acquired almost
the purple hue of tilled fields in autumn, covered, if she were walking abroad, by a half-lifted veil, while upon them either the cold or
some sad reflection invariably left the drying traces of an involuntary tear.

My sole consolation when I went upstairs for the night was that
Mamma would come in and kiss me after I was in bed. But this

---

26. A powder then used as a deodor-
izer for rooms.
27. As a toilet.

28. The *keep* is the best-fortified tower
of a medieval castle.

good night lasted for so short a time: she went down again so soon that the moment in which I heard her climb the stairs, and then caught the sound of her garden dress of blue muslin, from which hung little tassels of plaited straw, rustling along the double-doored corridor, was for me a moment of the keenest sorrow. So much did I love that good night that I reached the stage of hoping that it would come as late as possible, so as to prolong the time of respite during which Mamma would not yet have appeared. Sometimes when, after kissing me, she opened the door to go, I longed to call her back, to say to her "Kiss me just once again," but I knew that then she would at once look displeased, for the concession which she made to my wretchedness and agitation in coming up to me with this kiss of peace always annoyed my father, who thought such ceremonies absurd, and she would have liked to try to induce me to outgrow the need, the custom of having her there at all, which was a very different thing from letting the custom grow up of my asking her for an additional kiss when she was already crossing the threshold. And to see her look displeased destroyed all the sense of tranquillity she had brought me a moment before, when she bent her loving face down over my bed, and held it out to me like a Host,[29] for an act of Communion in which my lips might drink deeply the sense of her real presence, and with it the power to sleep. But those evenings on which Mamma stayed so short a time in my room were sweet indeed compared to those on which we had guests to dinner, and therefore she did not come at all. Our "guests" were practically limited to M. Swann, who, apart from a few passing strangers, was almost the only person who ever came to the house at Combray, sometimes to a neighborly dinner (but less frequently since his unfortunate marriage,[30] as my family did not care to receive his wife) and sometimes after dinner, uninvited. On those evenings when, as we sat in front of the house beneath the big chestnut tree and round the iron table, we heard, from the far end of the garden, not the large and noisy rattle which heralded and deafened as he approached with its ferruginous,[31] interminable, frozen sound any member of the household who had put it out of action by coming in "without ringing," but the double peal—timid, oval, gilded—of the visitors' bell, everyone would at once exclaim, "A visitor! Who in the world can it be?" but they knew quite well that it could only be M. Swann. My great-aunt, speaking in a loud voice, to set an example, in a tone which she endeavored to make sound natural, would tell the others not to whisper so; that nothing could be more unpleasant for a stranger coming in, who would be led to think that

29. Communion wafer.
30. To his mistress, Odette de Crécy, whose reputation for promiscuity would

continue.
31. Iron-like

people were saying things about him which he was not meant to hear; and then my grandmother would be sent out as a scout, always happy to find an excuse for an additional turn in the garden, which she would utilize to remove surreptitiously, as she passed, the stakes of a rose-tree or two, so as to make the roses look a little more natural, as a mother might run her hand through her boy's hair, after the barber had smoothed it down, to make it stick out properly round his head.

And there we would all stay, hanging on the words which would fall from my grandmother's lips when she brought us back her report of the enemy, as though there had been some uncertainty among a vast number of possible invaders, and then, soon after, my grandfather would say: "I can hear Swann's voice." And, indeed, one could tell him only by his voice, for it was difficult to make out his face with its arched nose and green eyes, under a high forehead fringed with fair, almost red hair, dressed in the Bressant style,[32] because in the garden we used as little light as possible, so as not to attract mosquitoes: and I would slip away as though not going for anything in particular, to tell them to bring out the syrups;[33] for my grandmother made a great point, thinking it "nicer," of their not being allowed to seem anything out of the ordinary, which we kept for visitors only. Although a far younger man, M. Swann was very much attached to my grandfather, who had been an intimate friend, in his time, of Swann's father, an excellent but an eccentric man in whom the least little thing would, it seemed, often check the flow of his spirits and divert the current of his thoughts. Several times in the course of a year I would hear my grandfather tell at table the story, which never varied, of the behavior of M. Swann the elder upon the death of his wife, by whose bedside he had watched day and night. My grandfather, who had not seen him for a long time, hastened to join him at the Swanns' family property on the outskirts of Combray, and managed to entice him for a moment, weeping profusely, out of the death chamber, so that he should not be present when the body was laid in its coffin. They took a turn or two in the park, where there was a little sunshine. Suddenly M. Swann seized my grandfather by the arm and cried, "Oh, my dear old friend, how fortunate we are to be walking here together on such a charming day! Don't you see how pretty they are, all these trees—my hawthorns, and my new pond, on which you have never congratulated me? You look as glum as a nightcap. Don't you feel this little breeze? Ah! whatever you may say, it's good to be alive all the same, my dear Amédée!" And then,

32. Close-cropped, like a crew cut; named after a French actor.

33. Such as Grenadine, a sweet, nonalcoholic drink served as a cordial.

abruptly, the memory of his dead wife returned to him, and probably thinking it too complicated to inquire into how, at such a time, he could have allowed himself to be carried away by an impulse of happiness, he confined himself to a gesture which he habitually employed whenever any perplexing question came into his mind: that is, he passed his hand across his forehead, dried his eyes, and wiped his glasses. And he could never be consoled for the loss of his wife, but used to say to my grandfather, during the two years for which he survived her, "It's a funny thing, now; I very often think of my poor wife, but I cannot think of her very much at any one time." "Often, but a little at a time, like poor old Swann," became one of my grandfather's favorite phrases, which he would apply to all kinds of things. And I should have assumed that this father of Swann's had been a monster if my grandfather, whom I regarded as a better judge than myself, and whose word was my law and often led me in the long run to pardon offences which I should have been inclined to condemn, had not gone on to exclaim, "But after all, he had a heart of gold."

For many years, albeit—and especially before his marriage—M. Swann the younger came often to see them at Combray, my great-aunt and grandparents never suspected that he had entirely ceased to live in the kind of society which his family had frequented, or that, under the sort of incognito which the name of Swann gave him among us, they were harboring—with the complete innocence of a family of honest innkeepers who have in their midst some distinguished highwayman and never know it—one of the smartest[34] members of the Jockey Club, a particular friend of the Comte de Paris and of the Prince of Wales, and one of the men most sought after in the aristocratic world of the Faubourg Saint-Germain.[35]

Our utter ignorance of the brilliant part which Swann was playing in the world of fashion was, of course, due in part to his own reserve and discretion, but also to the fact that middle-class people in those days took what was almost a Hindu view of society,[36] which they held to consist of sharply defined castes, so that everyone at his birth found himself called to that station in life which his parents already occupied, and nothing, except the chance of a

34. Most stylish.
35. The Faubourg Saint-Germain is a fashionable area of Paris on the left bank of the Seine; many of the French aristocracy lived there. The Jockey Club was an exclusive men's club devoted not only to horseracing but to other diversions (such as the Opera). The Comte de Paris (1838–1894) was heir apparent to the French throne, in the unlikely chance that the monarchy were rein-

stated, and the Prince of Wales became in 1901 King Edward VII of England. The implication is that Swann's social connections were not merely of the highest but of an idle and somewhat hedonistic sort.
36. Which divides all of its members into four distinct hereditary castes, with relative restrictions on occupations and marriage.

brilliant career or of a "good" marriage, could extract you from that station or admit you to a superior caste. M. Swann, the father, had been a stockbroker; and so "young Swann" found himself immured for life in a caste where one's fortune, as in a list of taxpayers, varied between such and such limits of income. We knew the people with whom his father had associated, and so we knew his own associates, the people with whom he was "in a position to mix." If he knew other people besides, those were youthful acquaintances on whom the old friends of the family, like my relatives, shut their eyes all the more good-naturedly that Swann himself, after he was left an orphan, still came most faithfully to see us; but we would have been ready to wager that the people outside our acquaintance whom Swann knew were of the sort to whom he would not have dared to raise his hat, had he met them while he was walking with ourselves. Had there been such a thing as a determination to apply to Swann a social coefficient peculiar to himself, as distinct from all the other sons of other stockbrokers in his father's position, his coefficient would have been rather lower than theirs, because, leading a very simple life, and having always had a craze for "antiques" and pictures, he now lived and piled up his collections in an old house which my grandmother longed to visit, but which stood on the Quai d'Orléans,[37] a neighborhood in which my great-aunt thought it most degrading to be quartered. "Are you really a connoisseur, now?" she would say to him; "I ask for your own sake, as you are likely to have 'fakes' palmed off on you by the dealers," for she did not, in fact, endow him with any critical faculty, and had no great opinion of the intelligence of a man who, in conversation, would avoid serious topics and showed a very dull preciseness, not only when he gave us kitchen recipes, going into the most minute details, but even when my grandmother's sisters were talking to him about art. When challenged by them to give an opinion, or to express his admiration for some picture, he would remain almost impolitely silent, and would then make amends by furnishing (if he could) some fact or other about the gallery in which the picture was hung, or the date at which it had been painted. But as a rule he would content himself with trying to amuse us by telling us the story of his latest adventure—and he would have a fresh story for us on every occasion—with someone whom we ourselves knew, such as the Combray chemist,[38] or our cook, or our coachman. These stories certainly used to make my great-aunt laugh, but she could never tell whether that was on account of the absurd parts which Swann invariabley made himself play in the adventures, or of the wit that he showed in telling us of

37. A beautiful though less fashionable section in the heart of Paris, along the Seine.
38. Pharmacist.

them. "It is easy to see that you are a regular 'character,' M. Swann!"

As she was the only member of our family who could be described as a trifle "common," she would always take care to remark to strangers, when Swann was mentioned, that he could easily, if he had wished to, have lived in the Boulevard Haussmann or the Avenue de l'Opéra,[39] and that he was the son of old M. Swann who must have left four or five million francs, but that it was a fad of his A fad which, moreover, she thought was bound to amuse other people so much that in Paris, when M. Swann called on New Year's Day bringing her a little pack of *marrons glacés*,[40] she never failed, if there were strangers in the room, to say to him: "Well, M. Swann, and do you still live next door to the Bonded Vaults,[41] so as to be sure of not missing your train when you go to Lyons?" and she would peep out of the corner of her eye, over her glasses, at the other visitors.

But if anyone had suggested to my aunt that this Swann, who, in his capacity as the son of old M. Swann, was "fully qualified" to be received by any of the "upper middle class," the most respected barristers and solicitors[42] of Paris (though he was perhaps a trifle inclined to let this hereditary privilege go into abeyance), had another almost secret existence of a wholly different kind: that when he left our house in Paris, saying that he must go home to bed, he would no sooner have turned the corner than he would stop, retrace his steps, and be off to some drawing room on whose like no stockbroker or associate of stockbrokers had ever set eyes— that would have seemed to my aunt as extraordinary as, to a woman of wider reading, the thought of being herself on terms of intimacy with Aristaeus,[43] of knowing that he would, when he had finished his conversation with her, plunge deep into the realms of Thetis, into an empire veiled from mortal eyes, in which Virgil depicts him as being received with open arms; or—to be content with an image more likely to have occurred to her, for she had seen it painted on the plates we used for biscuits at Combray—as the thought of having had to dinner Ali Baba,[44] who, as soon as he found himself alone and unobserved, would make his way into the cave, resplendent with its unsuspected treasures.

One day when he had come to see us after dinner in Paris, and

---

39. Two large modern avenues where the wealthy *bourgeoisie* (or middle class) liked to live.

40. Candied chestnuts, a traditional gift on New Year's Day, then a more common day for exchanging gifts than Christmas.

41. A wine warehouse in southeastern Paris, close to the *Gare de Lyon*, the terminal from which trains depart for the industrial city of Lyon and other destinations in southeastern France.

42. Trial lawyers and lawyers of other kinds.

43. Son of the Greek god Apollo. In Virgil's *Fourth Georgic*, Aristaeus seeks help from the sea nymph Thetis.

44. Hero of an *Arabian Nights* tale, a poor youth who discovers a robber's cave filled with treasure.

had begged pardon for being in evening clothes, Françoise, when he had gone, told us that she had got it from his coachman that he had been dining "with a princess." "A pretty sort of princess,"[45] drawled my aunt; "I know them," and she shrugged her shoulders without raising her eyes from her knitting, serenely ironical.

Altogether, my aunt used to treat him with scant ceremony. Since she was of the opinion that he ought to feel flattered by our invitations, she thought it only right and proper that he should never come to see us in summer without a basket of peaches or raspberries from his garden, and that from each of his visits to Italy he should bring back some photographs of old masters for me.

It seemed quite natural, therefore, to send to him whenever we wanted a recipe for some special sauce or for a pineapple salad for one of our big dinner parties, to which he himself would not be invited, not seeming of sufficient importance to be served up to new friends who might be in our house for the first time. If the conversation turned upon the Princes of the House of France,[46] "Gentlemen you and I will never know, will we, and don't want to, do we?" my great-aunt would say tartly to Swann, who had, perhaps, a letter from Twickenham[47] in his pocket; she would make him play accompaniments and turn over music on evenings when my grandmother's sister sang; manipulating this creature, so rare and refined at other times and in other places, with the rough simplicity of a child who will play with some curio from the cabinet no more carefully than if it were a penny toy. Certainly the Swann who was a familiar figure in all the clubs of those days differed hugely from the Swann created in my great-aunt's mind when, of an evening, in our little garden at Combray, after the two shy peals had sounded from the gate, she would vitalize, by injecting into it everything she had ever heard about the Swann family, the vague and unrecognizable shape which began to appear, with my grandmother in its wake, against a background of shadows, and could at last be identified by the sound of its voice. But then, even in the most insignificant details of our daily life, none of us can be said to constitute a material whole, which is identical for everyone, and need only be turned up like a page in an account-book or the record of a will; our social personality is created by the thoughts of other people. Even the simple act which we describe as "seeing someone we know" is, to some extent, an intellectual process. We pack the physical outline of the creature we see with all the ideas we have already formed about him, and in the complete picture of him which we compose in our minds those ideas have certainly the prin-

45. That is, a "princess" of some shady level of society.
46. The male members of the French royal family, such as the Comte de Paris. The spirit of the times was anti-Royalist, and in fact all claimants to the French throne and their heirs were banished from France by law in 1886.
47. Fashionable London suburb. The French royal family had a house there.

cipal place. In the end they come to fill out so completely the curve of his cheeks, to follow so exactly the line of his nose, they blend so harmoniously in the sound of his voice that these seem to be no more than a transparent envelope, so that each time we see the face or hear the voice it is our own ideas of him which we recognize and to which we listen. And so, no doubt, from the Swann they had built up for their own purposes my family had left out, in their ignorance, a whole crowd of the details of his daily life in the world of fashion, details by means of which other people, when they met him, saw all the Graces[48] enthroned in his face and stopping at the line of his arched nose as at a natural frontier; but they contrived also to put into a face from which its distinction had been evicted, a face vacant and roomy as an untenanted house, to plant in the depths of its unvalued eyes a lingering sense, uncertain but not unpleasing, half memory and half oblivion, of idle hours spent together after our weekly dinners, round the card table or in the garden, during our companionable country life. Our friend's bodily frame had been so well lined with this sense, and with various earlier memories of his family, that their own special Swann had become to my people a complete and living creature; so that even now I have the feeling of leaving someone I know for another quite different person when, going back in memory, I pass from the Swann whom I knew later and more intimately to this early Swann —this early Swann in whom I can distinguish the charming mistakes of my childhood, and who, incidentally, is less like his successor than he is like the other people I knew at that time, as though one's life were a series of galleries in which all the portraits of any one period had a marked family likeness, the same (so to speak) tonality—this early Swann abounding in leisure, fragrant with the scent of the great chestnut tree, of baskets of raspberries and of a sprig of tarragon.

And yet one day, when my grandmother had gone to ask some favor of a lady whom she had known at the Sacré Coeur[49] (and with whom, because of our caste theory, she had not cared to keep up any degree of intimacy in spite of several common interests), the Marquise de Villeparisis,[50] of the famous house of Bouillon, this lady had said to her:

"I think you know M. Swann very well; he is a great friend of my nephews, the des Laumes."

My grandmother had returned from the call full of praise for the house, which overlooked some gardens, and in which Mme. de Villeparisis had advised her to rent a flat; and also for a repairing tailor and his daughter, who kept a little shop in the courtyard, into

---

48. Greek divinities, young women who personified beauty and grace.
49. A convent school in Paris, at-tended by daughters of the aristocracy and the wealthy *bourgeoisie*.

which she had gone to ask them to put a stitch in her skirt, which she had torn on the staircase. My grandmother had found these people perfectly charming: the girl, she said, was a jewel, and the tailor a most distinguished man, the finest she had ever seen. For in her eyes distinction was a thing wholly independent of social position. She was in ecstasies over some answer the tailor had made, saying to Mamma:

"Sévigné[51] would not have said it better!" and, by the way of contrast, of a nephew of Mme. de Villeparisis whom she had met at the house:

"My dear, he is so common!"

Now, the effect of that remark about Swann had been, not to raise him in my great-aunt's estimation, but to lower Mme. de Villeparisis. It appeared that the deference which, on my grandmother's authority, we owed to Mme. de Villeparisis imposed on her the reciprocal obligation to do nothing that would render her less worthy of our regard, and that she had failed in her duty in becoming aware of Swann's existence and in allowing members of her family to associate with him. "How should she know Swann? A lady who, you always made out, was related to Marshal MacMahon!"[52] This view of Swann's social atmosphere which prevailed in my family seemed to be confirmed later on by his marriage with a woman of the worst class, you might almost say a "fast" woman, whom, to do him justice, he never attempted to introduce to us, for he continued to come to us alone, though he came more and more seldom; but from whom they thought they could establish, on the assumption that he had found her there, the circle, unknown to them, in which he ordinarily moved.

But on one occasion my grandfather read in a newspaper that M. Swann was one of the most faithful attendants at the Sunday luncheons given by the Duc de X———, whose father and uncle had been among our most prominent statesmen in the reign of Louis Philippe.[53] Now my grandfather was curious to learn all the little details which might help him to take a mental share in the private lives of men like Molé, the Duc Pasquier, or the Duc de Broglie.[54] He was delighted to find that Swann associated with people who had known them. My great-aunt, however, interpreted

50. Member of the Guermantes family. Proust enhances the apparent reality of the Guermantes by relating them to the historical house of Bouillon, a famous aristocratic family tracing its descent from the Middle Ages. The des Laumes, on the other hand, are fictional.

51. The Marquise de Sévigné (1626–1696), known for the lively style of her letters.

52. (1808–1893), Marshal of France, elected President of the French Republic in 1873.

53. King of France from 1830 to 1848, father of the Comte de Paris.

54. Comte Louis Mathieu Molé (1781–1855) held various cabinet positions before becoming premier of France in 1836; Duc Etienne Denis de Pasquier (1767–1862) also held important public positions up to 1837; and Duc Achille Charles Leonce Victor de Broglie (1785–1870) had a busy public career that ended in 1851. All were active during the reign of Louis Philippe.

this piece of news in a sense discreditable to Swann; for anyone who chose his associates outside the caste in which he had been born and bred, outside his "proper station," was condemned to utter degradation in her eyes. It seemed to her that such a one abdicated all claim to enjoy the fruits of those friendly relations with people of good position which prudent parents cultivate and store up for their children's benefit, for my great-aunt had actually ceased to "see" the son of a lawyer we had known because he had married a "Highness" and had thereby stepped down—in her eyes—from the respectable position of a lawyer's son to that of those adventurers, upstart footmen or stable-boys mostly, to whom we read that queens have sometimes shown their favors. She objected, therefore, to my grandfather's plan of questioning Swann, when next he came to dine with us, about these people whose friendship with him we had discovered. On the other hand, my grandmother's two sisters, elderly spinsters who shared her nobility of character but lacked her intelligence, declared that they could not conceive what pleasure their brother-in-law could find in talking about such trifles. They were ladies of lofty ambition, who for that reason were incapable of taking the least interest in what might be called the "pinchbeck"[55] things of life, even when they had an historic value, or, generally speaking, in anything that was not directly associated with some object esthetically precious. So complete was their negation of interest in anything which seemed directly or indirectly a part of our everyday life that their sense of hearing—which had gradually come to understand its own futility when the tone of the conversation, at the dinner table, became frivolous or merely mundane, without the two old ladies' being able to guide it back to the topic dear to themselves—would leave its receptive channels unemployed, so effectively that they were actually becoming atrophied. So that if my grandfather wished to attract the attention of the two sisters, he would have to make use of some such alarm signals as mad-doctors adopt in dealing with their distracted patients; as by beating several times on a glass with the blade of a knife, fixing them at the same time with a sharp word and a compelling glance, violent methods which the said doctors are apt to bring with them into their everyday life among the sane, either from force of professional habit or because they think the whole world a trifle mad.

Their interest grew, however, when, the day before Swann was to dine with us, and when he had made them a special present of a case of Asti,[56] my great-aunt, who had in her hand a copy of the *Figaro*[57] in which to the name of a picture then on view in a Corot[58] exhibition were added the words, "from the collection of

55. Petty or spurious; here, gossip or small talk.
56. An Italian white wine.
57. Leading Parisian newspaper.
58. (1796–1875), French landscape painter, very popular at the time.

M. Charles Swann," asked: "Did you see that Swann is 'mentioned' in the *Figaro*?"

"But I have always told you," said my grandmother, "that he had plenty of taste."

"You would, of course," retorted my great-aunt, "say anything just to seem different from *us*." For, knowing that my grandmother never agreed with her, and not being quite confident that it was her own opinion which the rest of us invariably endorsed, she wished to extort from us a wholesale condemnation of my grandmother's views, against which she hoped to force us into solidarity with her own.

But we sat silent. My grandmother's sisters having expressed a desire to mention to Swann this reference to him in the *Figaro*, my great-aunt dissuaded them. Whenever she saw in others an advantage, however trivial, which she herself lacked, she would persuade herself that it was no advantage at all, but a drawback, and would pity so as not to have to envy them.

"I don't think that would please him at all; I know very well, I should hate to see my name printed like that, as large as life, in the paper, and I shouldn't feel at all flattered if anyone spoke to me about it."

She did not, however, put any very great pressure upon my grandmother's sisters, for they, in their horror of vulgarity, had brought to such a fine art the concealment of a personal allusion in a wealth of ingenious circumlocution, that it would often pass unnoticed even by the person to whom it was addressed. As for my mother, her only thought was of managing to induce my father to consent to speak to Swann, not of his wife, but of his daughter, whom he worshipped, and for whose sake it was understood that he had ultimately made his unfortunate marriage.

"You need only say a word; just ask him how she is. It must be so very hard for him."

My father, however, was annoyed: "No, no; you have the most absurd ideas. It would be utterly ridiculous."

But the only one of us in whom the prospect of Swann's arrival gave rise to an unhappy foreboding was myself. And that was because on the evenings when there were visitors, or just M. Swann in the house, Mamma did not come up to my room. I did not, at that time, have dinner with the family: I came out to the garden after dinner, and at nine I said good night and went to bed. But on these evenings I used to dine earlier than the others, and to come in afterwards and sit at table until eight o'clock, when it was understood that I must go upstairs; that frail and precious kiss which Mamma used always to leave upon my lips when I was in bed and just going to sleep I had to take with me from the dining room to my own, and to keep inviolate all the time that it took me to undress, without letting its sweet charm be broken, without letting its volatile essence diffuse itself and evaporate; and just on those very evenings when I must needs take most pains to receive it with due formality, I had to snatch it, to seize it instantly and in public, without even having the time or being properly free to apply to what I was doing the punctiliousness which madmen use who compel themselves to exclude all other thoughts from their minds while they are shutting a door, so that when the sickness of uncertainty sweeps over them again they can triumphantly face and overcome it with the recollection of the precise moment in which the door was shut.

We were all in the garden when the double peal of the gatebell sounded shyly. Everyone knew that it must be Swann, and yet they looked at one another inquiringly and sent my grandmother scouting.

"See that you thank him intelligibly for the wine," my grandfather warned his two sisters-in-law; "you know how good it is, and it is a huge case."

"Now, don't start whispering!" said my great-aunt. "How would you like to come into a house and find everyone muttering to themselves?"

"Ah! there's M. Swann," cried my father. "Let's ask him if he thinks it will be fine tomorrow."

My mother fancied that a word from her would wipe out all the unpleasantness which my family had contrived to make Swann feel since his marriage. She found an opportunity to draw him aside for a moment. But I followed her: I could not bring myself to let her go out of reach of me while I felt that in a few minutes I should have to leave her in the dining room and go up to my bed without the consoling thought, as on ordinary evenings, that she would come up, later, to kiss me.

"Now, M. Swann," she said, "do tell me about your daughter; I am sure she shows a taste already for nice things, like her papa."

"Come along and sit down there with us all on the verandah," said my grandfather, coming up to him. My mother had to abandon the quest, but managed to extract from the restriction itself a further refinement of thought, as great poets do when the tyranny of rhyme forces them into the discovery of their finest lines.

"We can talk about her again when we are by ourselves," she said, or rather whispered to Swann. "It is only a mother who can understand. I am sure that hers would agree with me."

And so we all sat down round the iron table. I should have liked not to think of the hours of anguish which I should have to spend, that evening, alone in my room, without the possibility of going to sleep: I tried to convince myself that they were of no importance, really, since I should have forgotten them next morning, and to fix my mind on thoughts of the future which would carry me, as on a bridge, across the terrifying abyss that yawned at my feet. But my mind, strained by this foreboding, distended like the look which I shot at my mother, would now allow any other impression to enter. Thoughts did, indeed, enter it, but only on the condition that they left behind them every element of beauty, or even of quaintness, by which I might have been distracted or beguiled. As a surgical patient, by means of a local anesthetic, can look on with a clear consciousness while an operation is being performed upon him and yet feel nothing, I could repeat to myself some favorite lines, or watch my grandfather attempting to talk to Swann about the Duc d'Audriffet-Pasquier,[59] without being able to kindle any emotion from one or amusement from the other. Hardly had my grandfather begun to question Swann about that orator when one of my grandmother's sisters, in whose ears the question echoed like a solemn but untimely silence which her natural politeness bade her interrupt, addressed the other with:

"Just fancy, Flora, I met a young Swedish governess today who told me some most interesting things about the cooperative movement in Scandinavia. We really must have her to dine here one evening."

"To be sure!" said her sister Flora, "but I haven't wasted my time either. I met such a clever old gentleman at M. Vinteuil's[60] who knows Maubant[61] quite well, and Maubant has told him every little thing about how he gets up his parts. It is the most interesting thing I ever heard. He is a neighbor of M. Vinteuil's, and I never knew; and he is so nice besides."

"M. Vinteuil is not the only one who has nice neighbors," cried my aunt Céline in a voice which seemed loud because she was so timid, and seemed forced because she had been planning the little speech for so long; darting, as she spoke, what she called a "significant glance" at Swann. And my aunt Flora, who realized that this veiled utterance was Céline's way of thanking Swann intelligibly for the Asti, looked at him with a blend of congratulation and irony, either just because she wished to underline her sister's little epigram, or because she envied Swann his having inspired it, or merely because she imagined that he was embarrassed, and could not help having a little fun at his expense.

"I think it would be worth while," Flora went on, "to have this old gentleman to dinner. When you get him upon Maubant or Mme. Materna[62] he will talk for hours on end."

---

59. A fictitious nobleman.
60. A fictitious composer and neighbor of the family.
61. Actor at the Comédie Francaise, the French national theater.
62. Austrian soprano, who took part in the premiere of Wagner's *Ring* cycle at Bayreuth in 1876.

"That must be delightful," sighed my grandfather, in whose mind nature had unfortunately forgotten to include any capacity whatsoever for becoming passionately interested in the cooperative movement among the ladies of Sweden or in the methods employed by Maubant to get up his parts, just as it had forgotten to endow my grandmother's two sisters with a grain of that precious salt which one has oneself to "add to taste" in order to extract any savor from a narrative of the private life of Molé or of the Comte de Paris.

"I say!" exclaimed Swann to my grandfather, "what I was going to tell you has more to do than you might think with what you were asking me just now, for in some respects there has been very little change. I came across a passage in Saint-Simon[63] this morning which would have amused you. It is in the volume which covers his mission to Spain; not one of the best, little more in fact than a journal, but at least it is a journal wonderfully well written, which fairly distinguishes it from the devastating journalism that we feel bound to read in these days, morning, noon and night."

"I do not agree with you: there are some days when I find reading the papers very pleasant indeed!" my aunt Flora broke in, to show Swann that she had read the note about his Corot in the *Figaro*.

"Yes," aunt Céline went one better. "When they write about things or people in whom we are interested."

"I don't deny it," answered Swann in some bewilderment. "The fault I find with our journalism is that it forces us to take an interest in some fresh triviality or other every day, whereas only three or four books in a lifetime give us anything that is of real importance. Suppose that, every morning, when we tore the wrapper off our paper with fevered hands, a transmutation were to take place, and we were to find inside it—oh! I don't know; shall we say Pascal's *Pensées*?"[64] He articulated the title with an ironic emphasis so as not to appear pedantic. "And then, in the gilt and tooled volumes which we open once in ten years," he went on, showing that contempt for the things of this world which some men of the world like to affect, "we should read that the Queen of the Hellenes had arrived at Cannes, or that the Princesse de Léon had given a fancy dress ball. In that way we should arrive at the right proportion between 'information' and 'publicity.'" But at once regretting that he had allowed himself to speak, even in jest, of serious matters, he added ironically: "We are having a most entertaining conversation; I cannot think why we climb to these lofty summits," and then, turning to my grandfather: "Well, Saint-Simon tells how Maule-

---

63. The memoirs of the Duc de Saint-Simon (1675–1755) describe court life and intrigue during the reigns of Louis XIV and Louis XV. He was sent to Spain in 1721 to arrange the marriage of Louis XV and the daughter of the King of Spain.

64. The *Thoughts* of the French mathematician and religious philosopher Blaise Pascal (1623–1662) are comments on the human condition, and one of the triumphant works of French classicism.

vrier had had the audacity to offer his hand to his sons. You remember how he says of Maulevrier, 'Never did I find in that coarse bottle anything but ill-humor, boorishness, and folly.' "[65]

"Coarse or not, I know bottles in which there is something very different!" said Flora briskly, feeling bound to thank Swann as well as her sister, since the present of Asti had been addressed to them both. Céline began to laugh.

Swann was puzzled, but went on: " 'I cannot say whether it was his ignorance or a trap,' writes Saint-Simon; 'he wished to give his hand to my children. I noticed it in time to prevent him.' "

My grandfather was already in ecstasies over "ignorance or a trap," but Miss Céline—the name of Saint-Simon, a "man of letters," having arrested the complete paralysis of her sense of hearing—had grown angry.

"What! You admire that, do you? Well, it is clever enough! But what is the point of it? Does he mean that one man isn't as good as another? What difference can it make whether he is a duke or a groom so long as he is intelligent and good? He had a fine way of bringing up his children, your Saint-Simon, if he didn't teach them to shake hands with all honest men. Really and truly, it's abominable. And you dare to quote it!"

And my grandfather, utterly depressed, realizing how futile it would be for him, against this opposition, to attempt to get Swann to tell him the stories which would have amused him, murmured to my mother: "Just tell me again that line of yours which always comforts me so much on these occasions. Oh, yes:

What virtues, Lord, Thou makest us abhor![66]

Good, that is, very good."

I never took my eyes off my mother. I knew that when they were at table I should not be permitted to stay there for the whole of dinner time, and that Mamma, for fear of annoying my father, would not allow me to give her in public the series of kisses that she would have had in my room. And so I promised myself that in the dining room, as they began to eat and drink and as I felt the hour approach, I would put beforehand into this kiss, which was bound to be so brief and stealthy in execution, everything that my own efforts could put into it; would look out very carefully first the exact spot on her cheek where I would imprint it, and would so prepare my thoughts that If might be able, thanks to these mental preliminaries, to consecrate the whole of the minute Mamma would allow me to the sensation of her cheek against my lips, as a painter who

---

65. Maulevrier was the French ambassador to Spain. Saint-Simon considered him of inferior birth, and refused to let his own children shake Maulevrier's hand. (*Memoirs*, vol. **XXXIX.**)

66. From *Pompey's Death* (line 1072), a tragedy by the French dramatist Pierre Corneille (1606–1684).

can have his subject for short sittings only prepares his palette, and from what he remembers and from rough notes does in advance everything which he possibly can do in the sitter's absence. But tonight, before the dinner bell had sounded, my grandfather said with unconscious cruelty: "The little man looks tired; he'd better go up to bed. Besides, we are dining late tonight."

And my father, who was less scrupulous than my grandmother or mother in observing the letter of a treaty, went on: "Yes, run along; to bed with you."

I would have kissed Mamma then and there, but at that moment the dinner bell rang.

"No, no, leave your mother alone. You've said good night quite enough. These exhibitions are absurd. Go on upstairs."

And so I must set forth without viaticum;[67] must climb each step of the staircase "against my heart," as the saying is, climbing in opposition to my heart's desire, which was to return to my mother, since she had not, by her kiss, given my heart leave to accompany me forth. That hateful staircase, up which I always passed with such dismay, gave out a smell of varnish which had to some extent absorbed, made definite and fixed the special quality of sorrow that I felt each evening, and made it perhaps even more cruel to my sensibility because, when it assumed this olfactory guise, my intellect was powerless to resist it. When we have gone to sleep with a maddening toothache and are conscious of it only as a little girl whom we attempt, time after time, to pull out of the water, or as a line of Molière[68] which we repeat incessantly to ourselves, it is a great relief to wake up, so that our intelligence can disentangle the idea of toothache from any artificial semblance of heroism or rhythmic cadence. It was the precise converse of this relief which I felt when my anguish at having to go up to my room invaded my consciousness in a manner infinitely more rapid, instantaneous almost, a manner at once insidious and brutal as I breathed in—a far more poisonous thing than any moral penetration—the peculiar smell of the varnish upon that staircase.

Once in my room I had to stop every loophole, to close the shutters, to dig my own grave as I turned down the bedclothes, to wrap myself in the shroud of my nightshirt. But before burying myself in the iron bed which had been placed there because, on summer nights, I was too hot among the rep curtains of the four-poster,[69] I was stirred to revolt, and attempted the desperate stratagem of a condemned prisoner. I wrote to my mother begging her to come upstairs for an important reason which I could not put in writing.

67. The communion wafer and wine given to the dying in Catholic rites.
68. (1622–1673), French dramatist.

69. Bed with corner pillars to support a canopy and curtains. *rep*: a heavy, ribbed fabric.

My fear was the Françoise, my aunt's cook who used to be put in charge of me when I was at Combray, might refuse to take my note. I had a suspicion that, in her eyes, to carry a message to my mother when there was a stranger in the room would appear flatly inconceivable, just as it would be for the door keeper of a theatre to hand a letter to an actor upon the stage. For things which might or might not be done she possessed a code at once imperious, abundant, subtle, and uncompromising on points themselves imperceptible or irrelevant, which gave it a resemblance to those ancient laws which combine such cruel ordinances as the massacre of infants at the breast with prohibitions, of exaggerated refinement, against "seething the kid in his mother's milk," or "eating of the sinew which is upon the hollow of the thigh."[70] This code, if one could judge it by the sudden obstinacy which she would put into her refusal to carry out certain of our instructions, seemed to have foreseen such social complications and refinements of fashion as nothing in Françoise's surroundings or in her career as a servant in a village household could have put into her head; and we were obliged to assume that there was latent in her some past existence in the ancient history of France, noble and little understood, just as there is in those manufacturing towns where old mansions still testify to their former courtly days, and chemical workers toil among delicately sculptured scenes of the Miracle of Theophilus or the Quatre Fils Aymon.[71]

In this particular instance, the article of her code which made it highly improbable that—barring an outbreak of fire—Françoise would go down and disturb Mamma when M. Swann was there for so unimportant a person as myself was one embodying the respect she showed not only for the family (as for the dead, for the clergy, or for royalty), but also for the stranger within our gates; a respect which I should perhaps have found touching in a book, but which never failed to irritate me on her lips, because of the solemn and gentle tones in which she would utter it, and which irritated me more than usual this evening when the sacred character in which she invested the dinner party might have the effect of making her decline to disturb its ceremonial. But to give myself one chance of success I lied without hesitation, telling her that it was not in the least myself who had wanted to write to Mamma, but Mamma who, on saying good night to me, had begged me not to forget to send her an answer about something she had asked me to find, and that she would certainly be very angry if this note were not taken to

70. Refers to the strict dietary laws of *Deuteronomy* 14:21 (the kid) and *Genesis* 32:32 the thigh).

71. Theophile was saved from damnation by the Virgin Mary after having signed a pact with the devil, and the four sons of Aymon were heroic knights who together rode the magic horse Bayard.

her. I think that Françoise disbelieved me, for, like those primitive men whose senses weres so much keener than our own, she could immediately detect, by signs imperceptible to the rest of us, the truth or falsehood of anything that we might wish to conceal from her. She studied the envelope for five minutes as though an examination of the paper itself and the look of my handwriting could enlighten her as to the nature of the contents, or tell her to which article of her code she ought to refer the matter. Then she went out with a air of resignation which seemed to imply: "What a dreadful thing for parents to have a child like this!"

A moment later she returned to say that they were still at the ice stage and that it was impossible for the butler to deliver the note at once, in front of everybody; but that when the finger bowls were put round he would find a way of slipping it into Mamma's hand. At once my anxiety subsided; it was now no longer (as it had been a moment ago) until tomorrow that I had lost my mother, for my little line was going—to annoy her, no doubt, and doubly so because this contrivance would make me ridiculous in Swann's eyes —but was going all the same to admit me, invisibly and by stealth, into the same room as herself, was going to whisper from me into her ear; for that forbidden and unfriendly dining room, where but a moment ago the ice itself—with burned nuts in it—and the finger bowls seemed to me to be concealing pleasures that were mischievous and of a mortal sadness because Mamma was tasting of them and I was far away, had opened its doors to me and, like a ripe fruit which bursts through its skin, was going to pour out into my intoxicated heart the gushing sweetness of Mamma's attention while she was reading what I had written. Now I was no longer separated from her; the barriers were down; an exquisite thread was binding us. Besides, that was not all, for surely Mamma would come.

As for the agony through which I had just passed, I imagined that Swann would have laughed heartily at it if he had read my letter and had guessed its purpose; whereas, on the contrary, as I was to learn in due course, a similar anguish[72] had been the bane of his life for many years, and no one perhaps could have understood my feelings at that moment so well as himself; to him, that anguish which lies in knowing that the creature one adores is in some place of enjoyment where oneself is not and cannot follow— to him that anguish came through Love, to which it is in a sense predestined, by which it must be equipped and adapted; but when, as had befallen me, such an anguish possesses one's soul before Love has yet entered into one's life, then it must drift, awaiting Love's coming, vague and free, without precise attachment, at the

---

72. That is, his unhappy love for Odette de Crécy, described in *Swann in Love*.

disposal of one sentiment today, of another tomorrow, of filial piety or affection for a comrade. And the joy with which I first bound myself apprentice, when Françoise returned to tell me that my letter would be delivered; Swann, too, had known well that false joy which a friend can give us, or some relative of the woman we love, when on his arrival at the house or theatre where she is to be found, for some ball or party or "first night" at which he is to meet her, he sees us wandering outside, desperately awaiting some opportunity of communicating with her. He recognizes us, greets us familiarly, and asks what we are doing there. And when we invent a story of having some urgent message to give to his relative or friend, he assures us that nothing could be more simple, takes us in at the door, and promises to send her down to us in five minutes. How much we love him—as at that moment I loved Françoise—the good-natured intermediary who by a single word has made supportable, human, almost propitious the inconceivable, infernal scene of gaiety in the thick of which we have been imagining swarms of enemies, perverse and seductive, beguiling away from us, even making laugh at us, the woman whom we love. If we are to judge of them by him, this relative who has accosted us and who is himself an initiate in those cruel mysteries, then the other guests cannot be so very demoniacal. Those inaccessible and torturing hours into which she had gone to taste of unknown pleasures—behold, a breach in the wall, and we are through it. Behold, one of the moments whose series will go to make up their sum, a moment as genuine as the rest, if not actually more important to ourself because our mistress is more intensely a part of it; we picture it to ourselves, we possess it, we intervene upon it, almost we have created it: namely, the moment in which he goes to tell her that we are waiting there below. And very probably the other moments of the party will not be essentially different, will contain nothing else so exquisite or so well able to make us suffer, since this kind friend has assured us that "Of course, she will be delighted to come down! It will be far more amusing for her to talk to you than to be bored up there." Alas! Swann had learned by experience that the good intentions of a third party are powerless to control a woman who is annoyed to find herself pursued even into a ballroom by a man whom she does not love. Too often, the kind friend comes down again alone.

My mother did not appear, but with no attempt to safeguard my self-respect (which depended upon her keeping up the fiction that she had asked me to let her know the result of my search for something or other) made Françoise tell me, in so many words "There is no answer"—words I have so often, since then, heard the hall-porters in "minions" and the flunkeys in gambling clubs and the like, repeat to some poor girl, who replies in bewilderment: "What! he's said nothing? It's not possible. You did give him my letter, didn't you? Very well, I shall wait a little longer." And just as she invariably protests that she does not need the extra gas which the porter offers to light for her, and sits on there, hearing nothing further, except an occasional remark on the weather which the porter exchanges with a messenger whom he will send off suddenly, when he notices the time, to put some customer's wine on the ice; so, having declined Françoise's offer to make me some tea or to stay beside me, I let her go off again to the servants' hall, and lay down and shut my eyes, and tried not to hear the voices of my family who were drinking their coffee in the garden.

But after a few seconds I realized that, by writing that line to Mamma, by approaching—at the risk of making her angry—so near to her that I felt I could reach out and grasp the moment in which I should see her again, I had cut myself off from the possibility of going to sleep until I actually had seen her, and my heart began to beat more and more painfully as I increased my agitation by ordering myself to keep calm and to acquiesce in my ill-fortune. Then, suddenly, my anxiety subsided, a feeling of intense happiness coursed through me, as when a strong medicine begins to take effect and one's pain vanishes: I had formed a resolution to abandon all attempts to go to sleep without seeing Mamma, and had decided to kiss her at all costs, even with the certainty of being in disgrace with her for long afterward, when she herself came up to bed. The tranquillity which followed my anguish made me extremely alert, no less than my sense of expectation, my thirst for and my fear of danger.

Noiselessly I opened the window and sat down on the foot of my bed; hardly daring to move in case they should hear me from below. Things outside seemed also fixed in mute expectation, so as not to disturb the moonlight which, duplicating each of them and throwing it back by the extension, forward, of a shadow denser and more concrete than its substance, had made the whole landscape seem at once thinner and longer, like a map which, after being folded up, is spread out upon the ground. What had to move—a leaf of the chestnut tree, for instance—moved. But its minute shuddering, complete, finished to the least detail and with utmost delicacy of gesture, made no discord with the rest of the scene, and yet was not merged on it, remaining clearly outlined. Exposed upon this surface of silence, which absorbed nothing from them, the most distant sounds, those which must have come from gardens at the far end of the town, could be distinguished with such exact "finish" that the impression they gave of coming from a distance seemed due only to their "pianissimo" execution, like those movements on muted strings so well performed by the orchestra of the Conservatoire[73]

---

73. The national music conservatory in Paris.

that, although one does not lose a single note, one thinks all the same that they are being played somewhere outside, a long way from the concert hall, so that all the old subscribers, and my grandmother's sisters too, when Swann had given them his seats, used to strain their ears as if they had caught the distant approach of an army on the march, which had not yet rounded the corner of the Rue de Trévise.[74]

I was well aware that I had placed myself in a position than which none could be counted upon to involve me in graver consequences at my parents' hands; consequences far graver, indeed, than a stranger would have imagined, and such as (he would have thought) could follow only some really shameful fault. But in the system of education which they had given me faults were not classified in the same order as in that of other children, and I had been taught to place at the head of the list (doubtless because there was no other class of faults from which I needed to be more carefully protected) those in which I can now distinguish the common feature that one succumbs to them by yielding to a nervous impulse. But such words as these last had never been uttered in my hearing; no one had yet accounted for my temptations in a way which might have led me to believe that there was some excuse for my giving in to them, or that I was actually incapable of holding out against them. Yet I could easily recognize this class of transgressions by the anguish of mind which preceded, as well as by the rigor of the punishment which followed them; and I knew that what I had just done was in the same category as certain other sins for which I had been severely chastised, though infinitely more serious than they. When I went out to meet my mother as she herself came up to bed, and when she saw that I had remained up so as to say good night to her again in the passage, I should not be allowed to stay in the house a day longer, I should be packed off to school[75] next morning; so much was certain. Very good: had I been obliged, the next moment, to hurl myself out of the window, I should still have preferred such a fate. For what I wanted now was Mamma, and to say good night to her; I had gone too far along the road which led to the realization of this desire to be able to retrace my steps.

I could hear my parents' footsteps as they went with Swann; and, when the rattle of the gate assured me that he had really gone, I crept to the window. Mamma was asking my father if he had thought the lobster good, and whether M. Swann had had some of the coffee-and-pistachio ice. "I thought it rather so-so," she was saying; "next time we shall have to try another flavor."

"I can't tell you," said my great-aunt, "what a change I find in Swann. He is quite antiquated!" She had grown so accustomed to

---

74. A street in Combray. 75. Boarding school.

seeing Swann always in the same stage of adolescence that it was a shock to her to find him suddenly less young than the age she still attributed to him. And the others too were beginning to remark in Swann that abnormal, excessive, scandalous senescence, meet only in a celibate, is one of that class for whom it seems that the great day which knows no morrow must be longer than for other men, since for such a one it is void of promise, and from its dawn the moments steadily accumulate without any subsequent partition[76] among his offspring.

"I fancy he has a lot of trouble with that wretched wife of his, who 'lives' with a certain Monsieur de Charlus,[77] as all Combray knows. It's the talk of the town."

My mother observed that, in spite of this, he had looked much less unhappy of late. "And he doesn't nearly so often do that trick of his, so like his father, of wiping his eyes and passing his hand across his forehead. I think myself that in his heart of hearts he doesn't love his wife any more."

"Why, of course he doesn't," answered my grandfather. "He wrote me a letter about it, ages ago, to which I took care to pay no attention, but it left no doubt as to his feelings, let alone his love for his wife. Hullo! you two; you never thanked him for the Asti!" he went on, turning to his sisters-in-law.

"What! we never thanked him? I think, between you and me, that I put it to him quite neatly," replied my aunt Flora.

"Yes, you managed it very well; I admired you for it," said my aunt Céline.

"But you did it very prettily, too."

"Yes; I liked my expression about 'nice neighbors.' "

"What! Do you call that thanking him?" shouted my grandfather. "I heard that all right, but devil take me if I guessed it was meant for Swann. You may be quite sure he never noticed it."

"Come, come; Swann is not a fool. I am positive he appreciated the compliment. You didn't expect me to tell him the number of bottles, or to guess what he paid for them."

My father and mother were left alone and sat down for a moment; then my father said: "Well, shall we go up to bed?"

"As you wish, dear, though I don't feel in the least like sleeping. I don't know why; it can't be the coffee ice—it wasn't strong enough to keep me awake like this. But I see a light in the servants' hall: poor Françoise has been sitting up for me, so I will get her to unhook me while you go and undress."

My mother opened the latticed door which led from the hall to the staircase. Presently I heard her coming upstairs to close her

---

76. Sharing, as under a will.
77. Brother of the Duc de Guer-   mantes.

window. I went quietly into the passage; my heart was beating so violently that I could hardly move, but at least it was throbbing no longer with anxiety, but with terror and with joy. I saw in the well of the stair a light coming upward, from Mamma's candle. Then I saw Mamma herself: I threw myself upon her. For an instant she looked at me in astonishment, not realizing what could have happened. Then her face assumed an expression of anger. She said not a single word to me; and, for that matter, I used to go for days on end without being spoken to, for far less offences than this. A single word from Mamma would have been an admission that further intercourse with me was within the bounds of possibility, and that might perhaps have appeared to me more terrible still, as indicating that, with such a punishment as was in store for me, mere silence, and even anger, were relatively puerile.

A word from her then would have implied the false calm in which one converses with a servant to whom one has just decided to give notice: the kiss one bestows on a son who is being packed off to enlist, which would have been denied him if it had merely been a matter of being angry with him for a few days. But she heard my father coming from the dressing room, where he had gone to take off his clothes, and, to avoid the "scene" which he would make if he saw me, she said, in a voice half stifled by her anger; "Run away at once. Don't let your father see you standing there like a crazy jane!"[78]

But I begged her again to "Come and say good night to me!" terrified as I saw the light from my father's candle already creeping up the wall, but also making use of his approach as a means of blackmail, in the hope that my mother, not wishing him to find me there, as find me he must if she continued to hold out, would give in to me, and say: "Go back to your room. I will come."

Too late: my father was upon us. Instinctively I murmured, though no one heard me, "I am done for!"

I was not, however. My father used constantly to refuse to let me do things which were quite clearly allowed by the more liberal charters granted me by my mother and grandmother, because he paid no heed to "Principles," and because in his sight there were no such things as "Rights of Man."[79] For some quite irrelevant reason, or for no reason at all, he would at the last moment prevent me from taking some particular walk, one so regular and so consecrated to my use that to deprive me of it was a clear breach of faith; or again, as he had done this evening, long before the

78. Lunatic.
79. Reference to the "Declaration of the Rights of Man" in the preamble to the French Constitution of 1791, and to Thomas Paine's *Rights of Man* (1791–1792), a passionate defense of republi-canism. Marcel sees the relationship between himself and his mother and grandmother as somehow democratic; his father plays the role of tyrant in their small society.

appointed hour he would snap out: "Run along up to bed now; no excuses!" But then again, simply because he was devoid of principles (in my grandmother's sense), so he could not, properly speaking, be called inexorable. He looked at me for a moment with an air of annoyance and surprise, and then when Mamma had told him, not without some embarrassment, what had happened, said to her: "Go along with him, then; you said just now that you didn't feel like sleep, so stay in his room for a little. I don't need anything."

"But dear," my mother answered timidly, "whether or not I feel like sleep is not the point; we must not make the child accustomed ..."

"There's no question of making him accustomed," said my father, with a shrug of the shoulders; "you can see quite well that the child is unhappy. After all, we aren't jailers. You'll end by making him ill, and a lot of good that will do. There are two beds in his room; tell Françoise to make up the big one for you, and stay beside him for the rest of the night. I'm off to bed, anyhow; I'm not nervous like you. Good night."

It was impossible for me to thank my father; what he called my sentimentality would have exasperated him. I stood there, not daring to move; he was still confronting us, an immense figure in his white nightshirt, crowned with the pink and violet scarf of Indian cashmere in which, since he had begun to suffer from neuralgia,[80] he used to tie up his head, standing like Abraham in the engraving after Benozzo Gozzoli[81] which M. Swann had given me, telling Sarah that she must tear herself away from Isaac. Many years have passed since that night. The wall of the staircase, up which I had watched the light of his candle gradually climb, was long ago demolished. And in myself, too, many things have perished which, I imagined, would last for ever, and new structures have arisen, giving birth to new sorrows and new joys which in those days I could not have foreseen, just as now the old are difficult of comprehension. It is a long time, too, since my father has been able to tell Mamma to "Go with the child." Never again will such hours be possible for me. But of late I have been increasingly able to catch, if I listen attentively, the sound of the sobs which I had the strength to control in my father's presence, and which broke out only when I found myself alone with Mamma. Actually, their echo has never ceased: it is only because life is now growing more and more quiet round about me that I hear them afresh, like those convent bells which are so effectively drowned during the day by the noises of the streets that one would suppose them to have been stopped forever, until they sound out again through the silent evening air.

80. neuralgia: Headache.
81. (1420–1497). Florentine painter whose frescoes at Pisa contain scenes from the life of the Hebrew patriarch Abraham.

Mamma spent that night in my room: when I had just committed a sin so deadly that I was waiting to be banished from the
household, my parents gave me a far greater concession than I
should ever have won as the reward of a good action. Even at the
moment when it manifested itself in this crowning mercy, my
father's conduct toward me was still somewhat arbitrary, and regardless of my deserts, as was characteristic of him and due to the fact
that his actions were generally dictated by chance expediencies
rather than based on any formal plan. And perhaps even what I
called his strictness, when he sent me off to bed, deserved that title
less, really, than my mother's or grandmother's attitude, for his
nature, which in some respects differed more than theirs from my
own, had probably prevented him from guessing, until then, how
wretched I was every evening, a thing which my mother and grandmother knew well; but they loved me enough to be unwilling to
spare me that suffering, which they hoped to teach me to overcome,
so as to reduce my nervous sensibility and to strengthen my will. As
for my father, whose affection for me was of another kind, I doubt
if he would have shown so much courage, for as soon as he had
grasped the fact that I was unhappy he had said to my mother:
"Go and comfort him."

Mamma stayed all night in my room, and it seemed that she did
not wish to mar by recrimination those hours, so different from anything that I had had a right to expect; for when Françoise (who
guessed that something extraordinary must have happened when she
saw Mamma sitting by my side, holding my hand and letting me cry
unchecked) said to her: "But, Madame, what is little Master crying
for?" she replied: "Why, Françoise, he doesn't know himself: it is
his nerves. Make up the big bed for me quickly and then go off to
your own." And thus for the first time my unhappiness was
regarded no longer as a fault for which I must be punished, but as
an involuntary evil which had been officially recognized a nervous
condition for which I was in no way responsible: I had the consolation that I need no longer mingle apprehensive scruples with the
bitterness of my tears; I could weep henceforward without sin. I felt
no small degree of pride, either, in Françoise's presence at this
return to humane conditions which, not an hour after Mamma
had refused to come up to my room and had sent the snubbing
message that I was to go to sleep, raised me to the dignity of a
grown-up person, brought me of a sudden to a sort of puberty of
sorrow, to emancipation from tears. I ought then to have been
happy; I was not. It struck me that my mother had just made a first
concession which must have been painful to her, that it was a first
step down from the ideal she had formed for me, and that for the
first time she, with all her courage, had to confess herself beaten. It

struck me that if I had just scored a victory it was over her; that I had succeeded, as sickness or sorrow or age might have succeeded, in relaxing her will, in altering her judgment; that this evening opened a new era, must remain a black date in the calendar. And if I had dared now, I should have said to Mamma; "No, I don't want you; you mustn't sleep here." But I was conscious of the practical wisdom, of what would be called nowadays the realism with which she tempered the ardent idealism of my grandmother's nature, and I knew that now the mischief was done she would prefer to let me enjoy the soothing pleasure of her company, and not to disturb my father again. Certainly my mother's beautiful features seemed to shine again with youth that evening, as she sat gently holding my hands and trying to check my tears; but, just for that reason, it seemed to me that this should not have happened; her anger would have been less difficult to endure than this new kindness which my childhood had not known; I felt that I had with an impious and secret finger traced a first wrinkle upon her soul and made the first white hair show upon her head. This thought redoubled my sobs, and then I saw that Mamma, who had never allowed herself to go to any length of tenderness with me, was suddenly overcome by my tears and had to struggle to keep back her own. Then, as she saw that I had noticed this, she said to me, with a smile: "Why, my little buttercup, my little canary boy, he's going to make Mamma as silly as himself if this goes on. Look, since you can't sleep, and Mamma can't either, we mustn't go on in this stupid way; we must do something; I'll get one of your books." But I had none there. "Would you like me to get out the books now that your grandmother is going to give you for your birthday? Just think it over first, and don't be disappointed if there is nothing new for you then."

I was only too delighted, and Mamma went to find a parcel of books in which I could not distinguish, through the paper in which it was wrapped, any more than its squareness and size, but which, even at this first glimpse, brief and obscure as it was, bade fair to eclipse already the paint box of last New Year's Day and the silk-worms of the year before. It contained *La Mare au Diable*, *Françoise le Champi*, *La Petite Fadette*, and *Les Maîtres Sonneurs*.[82] My grandmother, as I learned afterward, had at first chosen Musset's poems, a volume of Rousseau, and *Indiana*; for while she considered light reading as unwholesome as sweets and cakes, she did not reflect that the strong breath of genius must have upon the very soul of a child an influence at once more dangerous

---

82. *The Devil's Pool, François the Foundling Discovered in the Fields, Little Fadette*, and *The Master Bellringers*, novels of idealized country life by the French woman writer George Sand (1806–1876).

and less quickening than those of fresh air and country breezes upon his body. But when my father had seemed almost to regard her as insane on learning the names of the books she proposed to give me,[83] she had journeyed back by herself to Jouy-le-Viccomte to the bookseller's, so that there should be no fear of my not having my present in time (it was a burning hot day, and she had come home so unwell that the doctor had warned my mother not to allow her again to tire herself in that way), and had there fallen back upon the four pastoral novels of George Sand.

"My dear," she had said to Mamma, "I could not allow myself to give the child anything that was not well written."

The truth was that she could never make up her mind to purchase anything from which no intellectual profit was to be derived, and, above all, that profit which good things bestowed on us by teaching us to seek our pleasures elsewhere than in the barren satisfaction of worldly wealth. Even when she had to make someone a present of the kind called "useful," when she had to give an armchair or some table silver or a walking-stick, she would choose "antiques," as though their long desuetude had effaced from them any semblance of utility and fitted them rather to instruct us in the lives of the men of other days than to serve the common requirements of our own. She would have liked me to have in my room photographs of ancient buildings or of beautiful places. But at the moment of buying them, and for all that the subject of the picture had an esthetic value of its own, she would find that vulgarity and utility had too prominent a part in them, through the mechanical nature of their reproduction by photography. She attempted by a subterfuge, if not to eliminate altogether their commercial banality, at least to minimize it, to substitute for the bulk of it what was art still, to introduce, as it might be, several "thicknesses" of art; instead of photographs of Chartres Cathedral, of the Fountains of Saint-Cloud, or of Vesuvius she would inquire of Swann whether some great painter had not made pictures of them, and preferred to give me photographs of "Chartres Cathedral" after Corot, of the "Fountains of Saint-Cloud" after Hubert Robert, and of 'Vesuvius" after Turner,[84] which were a stage higher in the scale of art. But although the photographer had been prevented from reproducing directly the masterpieces or the beauties of nature, and had there been replaced by a great artist, he resumed his odious position when it came to reproducing the artist's interpretation. Accordingly,

83. The works of Alfred de Musset (1810–1857) and Jean-Jacques Rousseau (1712–1778), often romantic and sometimes confessional, and some by Sand (*Indiana* was a novel of free love), would be thought unsuitable reading for a young child.

84. The Cathedral of Chartres, painted in 1830 by Corot; the fountains in the old park at Saint-Cloud, outside Paris, painted by Hubert Robert (1733–1809), and Vesuvius, the famous volcano near Naples, painted by W. M. J. Turner (1775–1851).

having to reckon again with vulgarity, my grandmother would endeavor to postpone the moment of contact still further. She would ask Swann if the picture had not been engraved, preferring, when possible, old engravings with some interest of association apart from themselves, such, for example, as show us a masterpiece in a state in which we can no longer see it today, as Morghen's print of the "Cenacolo" of Leonardo before it was spoiled by restoration.[85] It must be admitted that the results of this method of interpreting the art of making presents were not always happy. The idea which I formed of Venice, from a drawing by Titian[86] which is supposed to have the lagoon in the background, was certainly far less accurate than what I have since derived from ordinary photographs. We could no longer keep count in the family (when my great-aunt tried to frame an indictment of my grandmother) of all the armchairs she had presented to married couples, young and old, which on a first attempt to sit down upon them had at once collapsed beneath the weight of their recipient. But my grandmother would have thought it sordid to concern herself too closely with the solidity of any piece of furniture in which could still be discerned a flourish, a smile, a brave conceit of the past. And even what in such pieces supplied a material need, since it did so in a manner to which we are no longer accustomed, was as charming to her as one of those old forms of speech in which we can still see traces of a metaphor whose fine point has been worn away by the rough usage of our modern tongue. In precisely the same way the pastoral novels of George Sand, which she was giving me for my birthday, were regular lumber rooms of antique furniture, full of expressions that have fallen out of use and returned as imagery, such as one finds now only in country dialects. And my grandmother had bought them in preference to other books, just as she would have preferred to take a house that had a gothic dovecot, or some other such piece of antiquity as would have a pleasant effect on the mind, filling it with a nostalgic longing for impossible journeys through the realms of time.

Mamma sat down by my bed; she had chosen *François le Champi*, whose reddish cover and incomprehensible title[87] gave it a distinct personality in my eyes and a mysterious attraction. I had not then read any real novels. I had heard it said that George Sand was a typical novelist. That prepared me in advance to imagine that *François le Champi* contained something inexpressibly delicious. The course of the narrative, where it tended to arouse curiosity or

---

85. Leonardo da Vinci's *Last Supper* was the subject of a famous engraving by Morghen, a late eighteenth-century engraver. The paints in the original fresco had deteriorated rapidly, and a major restoration took place in the nine-

teenth century.
86. Venetian painter (1477–1576).
87. *Champi* (see note 82) is an old French word the child Marcel would not have known.

melt to pity, certain modes of expression which disturb or sadden the reader, and which, with a little experience, he may recognize as "common form" in novels, seemed to me then distinctive—for to me a new book was not one of a number of similar objects, but was like an individual man, unmatched, and with no cause of existence beyond himself—an intoxicating whiff of the peculiar essence of *François le Champi*. Beneath the everyday incidents, the common-place thoughts and hackneyed words, I could hear, or overhear, an intonation, a rhythmic utterance fine and strange. The "action" began: to me it seemed all the more obscure because in those days, when I read to myself, I used often, while I turned the pages, to dream of something quite different. And to the gaps which this habit made in my knowledge of the story more were added by the fact that when it was Mamma who was reading to me aloud she left all the love scenes out. And so all the odd changes which take place in the relations between the miller's wife and the boy, changes which only the birth and growth of love can explain, seemed to me plunged and steeped in a mystery, the key to which (as I could readily believe) lay in that strange and pleasant-sounding name of *Champi*, which draped the boy who bore it, I knew not why, in its own bright color, purpurate and charming. If my mother was not a faithful reader, she was, none the less, admirable when reading a work in which she found the note of true feeling by the respectful simplicity of her interpretation and by the sound of her sweet and gentle voice. It was the same in her daily life, when it was not works of art but men and women whom she was moved to pity or admire: it was touching to observe with what deference she would banish from her voice, her gestures, from her whole conversation, now the note of joy which might have distressed some mother who had long ago lost a child, now the recollection of an event or anni-versary which might have reminded some old gentleman of the burden of his years, now the household topic which might have bored some young man of letters. And so, when she read aloud the prose of George Sand, prose which is everywhere redolent of that generosity and moral distinction which Mamma had learned from my grandmother to place above all other qualities in life, and which I was not to teach her until much later to refrain from placing, in the same way, above all other qualities in literature; taking pains to banish from her voice any weakness or affectation which might have blocked its channel for that powerful stream of language, she sup-plied all the natural tenderness, all the lavish sweetness which they demanded to phrases which seemed to have been composed for her voice, and which were all, so to speak, within her compass. She came to them with the tone that they required, with the cordial accent which existed before they were, which dictated them, but which is not to be found in the words themselves, and by these means she smoothed away, as she read on, any harshness there might be or disordance in the tenses of verbs, endowing the imperfect and preterite[88] with all the sweetness which there is in generosity, all the melancholy which there is in love; guided the sentence that was drawing to an end toward that which was waiting to begin, now hastening, now slackening the pace of the syllables so as to bring them, despite their difference of quantity, into a uniform rhythm, and breathed into this quite ordinary prose a kind of life, continuous and full of feeling.

My agony was soothed; I let myself be borne upon the current of this gentle night on which I had my mother by my side. I knew that such a night could not be repeated; that the strongest desire I had in the world, namely, to keep my mother in my room through the sad hours of darkness, ran too much counter to general requirements and to the wishes of others for such a concession as had been granted me this evening to be anything but a rare and casual exception. Tomorrow night I should again be the victim of anguish and Mamma would not stay by my side. But when these storms of anguish grew calm I could no longer realize their existence; besides, tomorrow evening was still a long way off; I reminded myself that I should still have time to think about things, albeit that remission of time could bring me no access of power, albeit the coming event was in no way dependent upon the exercise of my will, and seemed not quite inevitable only because it was still separated from me by this short interval.

And so it was that, for a long time afterwards, when I lay awake at night and revived old memories of Combray, I saw no more of it than this sort of luminous panel, sharply defined against a vague and shadowy background, like the panels which a Bengal fire[89] or some electric sign will illuminate and dissect from the front of a building the other parts of which remain plunged in darkness: broad enough at its base, the little parlor, the dining room, the alluring shadows of the path along which would come M. Swann, the unconscious author of my sufferings, the hall through which I would journey to the first step of that staircase, so hard to climb, which constituted, all by itself, the tapering "elevation" of an irregular pyramid; and, at the summit, my bedroom, with the little passage through whose glazed[90] door Mamma would enter; in a word,

88. The imperfect is the tense of continued and incomplete action in the past, while the preterite describes a single completed action. The mother's gentle voice renders harmonious Sand's occasional awkwardness in the use of these tenses.

89. Fireworks.

90. I.e., with glass panes.

seen always at the same evening hour, isolated from all its possible surroundings, detached and solitary against its shadowy background, the bare minimum of scenery necessary (like the setting one sees printed at the head of an old play, for its performance in the provinces) to the drama of my undressing, as though all Combray had consisted of but two floors joined by a slender staircase, and as though there had been no time there but seven o'clock at night. I must own[91] that I could have assured any questioner that Combray did include other scenes and did exist at other hours than these. But since the facts which I should then have recalled would have been prompted only by an exercise of the will, by my intellectual memory, and since the pictures which that kind of memory shows us of the past preserve nothing of the past itself, I should never have had any wish to ponder over this residue of Combray. To me it was in reality all dead.

Permanently dead? Very possibly.

There is a large element of hazard in these matters, and a second hazard, that of our own death, often prevents us from awaiting for any length of time the favors of the first.

I feel that there is much to be said for the Celtic belief that the souls of those whom we have lost are held captive in some inferior being, in an animal, in a plant, in some inanimate object, and so effectively lost to us until the day (which to many never comes) when we happen to pass by the tree or to obtain possession of the object which forms their prison.[92] Then they start and tremble, they call us by our name, and as soon as we have recognized their voice the spell is broken. We have delivered them: they have overcome death and return to share our life.

And so it is with our own past. It is a labor in vain to attempt to recapture it: all the efforts of our intellect must prove futile. The past is hidden somewhere outside the realm, beyond the reach of intellect, in some material object (in the sensation which that material object will give us) which we do not suspect. And as for that object, it depends on chance whether we come upon it or not before we ourselves must die.

Many years had elapsed during which nothing of Combray, save what was comprised in the theatre and the drama of my going to bed there, had any existence for me, when one day in winter, as I came home, my mother, seeing that I was cold, offered me some tea, a thing I did not ordinarily take. I declined at first, and then, for no particular reason, changed my mind. She sent out for one of those short, plump little cakes called "petites madeleines," which look as though they had been molded in the fluted scallop of a pil-

grim's shell.[93] And soon, mechanically, weary after a dull day with
the prospect of a depressing morrow, I raised to my lips a spoonful
of the tea in which I had soaked a morsel of the cake. No sooner
had the warm liquid, and the crumbs with it, touched my palate
than a shudder ran through my whole body, and I stopped, intent
upon the extraordinary changes that were taking place. An exquisite
pleasure had invaded my senses, but individual, detached, with no
suggestion of its origin. And at once the vicissitudes of life had
become indifferent to me, its disasters innocuous, its brevity illusory
—this new sensation having had on me the effect which love has of
filling me with a precious essence; or rather this essence was not in
me, it was myself. I had ceased now to feel mediocre, accidental,
mortal. Whence could it have come to me, this all-powerful joy? I
was conscious that it was connected with the taste of tea and cake,
but that it infinitely transcended those savors, could not, indeed, be
of the same nature as theirs. Whence did it come? What did it signify? How could I seize upon and define it?

I drink a second mouthful, in which I find nothing more than in
the first, a third, which gives me rather less than the second. It is
time to stop; the potion is losing its magic. It is plain that the
object of my quest, the truth, lies not in the cup but in myself. The
tea has called up in me, but does not itself understand, and can only
repeat indefinitely with a gradual loss of strength, the same testimony; which I, too, cannot interpret, though I hope at least to be
able to call upon the tea for it again and to find it there presently,
intact and at my disposal, for my final enlightenment. I put down
my cup and examine my own mind. It is for it to discover the
truth. But how? What an abyss of uncertainty whenever the mind
feels that some part of it has strayed beyond its own borders; when
it, the seeker, is at once the dark region through which it must go
seeking, where all its equipment will avail it nothing. Seek? More
than that: create. It is face to face with somthing which does not so
far exist, to which it alone can give reality and substance, which it
alone can bring into the light of day.

And I begin again to ask myself what it could have been, this
unremembered state which brought with it no logical proof of its
existence, but only the sense that it was a happy, that it was a real
state in whose presence other states of consciousness melted and
vanished. I decide to attempt to make it reappear. I retrace my
thoughts to the moment at which I drank the first spoonful of tea.
I find again the same state, illumined by no fresh light. I compel
my mind to make one further effort, to follow and recapture once
again the fleeting sensation. And that nothing may interrupt it in

93. The scallop shell was a badge worn by Christian pilgrims to holy places.

its course I shut out every obstacle, every extraneous idea, I stop my ears and inhibit all attention to the sounds which come from the next room. And then, feeling that my mind is growing fatigued without having any success to report, I compel it for a change to enjoy that distraction which I have just denied it, to think of other things, to rest and refresh itself before the supreme attempt. And then for the second time I clear an empty space in front of it. I place in position before my mind's eye the still recent taste of that first mouthful, and I feel something start within me, something that leaves its resting place and attempts to rise, something that has been embedded like an anchor at a great depth; I do not know yet what it is, but I can feel it mounting slowly; I can measure the resistance, I can hear the echo of great spaces traversed.

Undoubtedly what is thus palpitating in the depths of my being must be the image, the visual memory which, being linked to that taste, has tried to follow it into my conscious mind. But its struggles are too far off, too much confused; scarcely can I perceive the colorless reflection in which are blended the uncapturable whirling medley of radiant hues, and I cannot distinguish its form, cannot invite it, as the one possible interpreter, to translate to me the evidence of its contemporary, its inseparable paramour, the taste of cake soaked in tea; cannot ask it to inform me what special circumstance is in question, of what period in my past life.

Will it ultimately reach the clear surface of my consciousness, this memory, this old, dead moment which the magnetism of an identical moment has traveled so far to importune, to disturb, to raise up out of the very depths of my being? I cannot tell. Now that I feel nothing, it has stopped, has perhaps gone down again into its darkness, from which who can say whether it will ever rise? Ten times over I must essay the task, must lean down over the abyss. And each time the natural laziness which deters us from every difficult enterprise, every work of importance, has urged me to leave the thing alone, to drink my tea and to think merely of the worries of today and of my hopes for tomorrow, which let themselves be pondered over without effort or distress of mind.

And suddenly the memory returns. The taste was that of the little crumb of madeleine which on Sunday mornings at Combray (because on those mornings I did not go out before church time), when I went to say good day to her in her bedroom, my aunt Léonie used to give me, dipping it first in her own cup of real or of lime-flower tea. The sight of the little madeleine had recalled nothing to my mind before I tasted it; perhaps because I had so often seen such things in the interval, without tasting them, on the trays in pastry-cooks' windows, that their image had dissociated itself from those Combray days to take its place among others more recent; perhaps because of those memories, so long abandoned and put out of mind, nothing now survived, everything was scattered; the forms of things, including that of the little scallop shell of pastry, so richly sensual under its severe, religious folds, were either obliterated or had been so long dormant as to have lost the power of expansion which would have allowed them to resume their place in my consciousness. But when from a long-distant past nothing subsists, after the people are dead, after the things are broken and scattered, still, alone, more fragile, but with more vitality, more unsubstantial, more persistent, more faithful, the smell and taste of things remain poised a long time, like souls, ready to remind us, waiting and hoping for their moment, amid the ruins of all the rest; and bear unfaltering, in the tiny and almost impalpable drop of their essence, the vast structure of recollection.

And once I had recognized the taste of the crumb of madeleine soaked in her decoction of lime flowers which my aunt used to give me (although I did not yet know and must long postpone the discovery of why this memory made me so happy) immediately the old grey house upon the street, where her room was, rose up like the scenery of a theatre to attach itself to the little pavilion, opening on to the garden, which had been built out behind it for my parents (the isolated panel which until that moment had been all that I could see); and with the house the town, from morning to night and in all weathers, the Square where I was sent before luncheon, the streets along which I used to run errands, the country roads we took when it was fine. And just as the Japanese amuse themselves by filling a porcelain bowl with water and steeping in it little crumbs of paper which until then are without character or form, but, the moment they become wet, stretch themselves and bend, take on color and distinctive shape, become flowers or houses or people, permanent and recognizable, so in that moment all the flowers in our garden and in M. Swann's park, and the water lilies on the Vivonne[94] and the good folk of the village and their little dwellings and the parish church and the whole of Combray and of its surroundings, taking their proper shapes and growing solid, sprang into being, town and gardens alike, from my cup of tea.

94. The local river.

SIDONIE-GABRIELLE COLETTE
(1873–1954)
The Cat*

ONE

Towards ten o'clock, the family poker-players began to show signs of weariness. Camille was fighting against sleepiness as one does at nineteen. By starts she would become fresh and clear-eyed again; then she would yawn behind her clasped hands and reappear pale, her chin white and her cheeks a little black under their ochre-tinted powder, with two tiny tears in the corners of her eyes.

"Camille, you ought to be in bed!"

"At ten o'clock, Mummy, at ten o'clock! Who on earth goes to bed at ten o'clock?"

Her eyes appealed to her fiancé, who lay back, overcome, in the depths of an armchair.

"Leave them alone," said another maternal voice. "They've still seven days to wait for each other. They're a bit dazed at the moment. It's very natural."

"Exactly. One hour more or less . . . Camille, you ought to go home to bed. So ought we."

"Seven days!" cried Camille. "But it's Monday today! And I hadn't given it a thought! Alain! Wake up! Alain!"

She threw her cigarette into the garden and lit a fresh one. Then she sorted out the scattered cards, shuffled them and laid them out as fortune-tellers do.

"To know whether we'll get the car, that marvellous baby roadster, before the ceremony! Look, Alain! I'm not cheating! It's coming out with a journey and an important piece of news!"

"What's that?"

"The roadster, of course!"

Without raising the nape of his neck from the chair, Alain turned his head towards the open french window,[1] through which came the sweet smell of fresh spinach and new-mown hay. The grass had been shorn during the day, and the honeysuckle, which draped a tall dead tree, added the nectar of its first flowers to the scent of the cut grass. A crystalline tinkle announced the entrance of the ten o'clock tray of soft drinks and iced water, carried by old Émile's tremulous hands, and Camille got up to fill the glasses.

She served her fiancé last, offering him the misted tumbler with a smile of secret understanding. She watched him drink and felt a

* Written in 1933; translated by Antonia White.

1. Doorlike windows opening outwards, usually hung in pairs.

1302

sudden pang of desire at the sight of his mouth pressing against the rim of the glass. But he felt so weary that he refused to share that pang and merely touched the white fingers with the red nails as they removed his empty tumbler.

"Are you coming to lunch tomorrow?" she asked him under her breath.

"Ask the cards."

Camille drew back quickly, and began to act the clown a little over her fortune-telling.

"Never, never joke about twenty-four-hours! Doesn't matter so much about crossed knives, or pennies with holes in them, or the talkies,[2] or God the Father . . ."

"Camille!"

"Sorry, Mummy. But one mustn't joke about Twenty-four-hours! He's a good little chap, the knave of spades. A nice black express messenger, always in a hurry."

"In a hurry to do what?"

"Why, to talk, of course! Just think, he brings the news of the next twenty-four hours, even of the next two days. If you put two more cards on his right and left, he foretells the coming week."

She was talking fast, scratching at two little smudges of lipstick at the corners of her mouth with a pointed nail. Alain listened to her, not bored, but not indulgent either. He had known her for several years and classified her as a typical modern girl. He knew the way she drove a car, a little too fast and a little too well; her eye alert and her scarlet mouth always ready to swear violently at a taxi-driver. He knew that she lied unblushingly, as children and adolescents do; that she was capable of deceiving her parents so as to get out after dinner and meet him at a night-club. There they danced together, but they drank only orange-juice because Alain disliked alcohol.

Before their official engagement, she had yielded her discreetly-wiped lips to him both by daylight and in the dark. She had also yielded her impersonal breasts, always imprisoned in a lace brassière, and her very lovely legs in the flawless stockings she bought in secret; stockings "like Mistinguett's,[3] you know. Mind my stockings, Alain!" Her stockings and her legs were the best things about her.

"She's pretty," Alain thought dispassionately, "because not one of her features is ugly, because she's an out-and-out brunette. Those lustrous eyes perfectly match that sleek, glossy, frequently-washed hair that's the color of a new piano." He was also perfectly aware that she could be as violent and capricious as a mountain stream.

---

2. Movies with sound; the first extended use of recorded dialogue came in 1927). *Crossed knives . . . pennies with*

holes in them: Objects of superstition.
3. A Parisian music hall performer, famous for her beautiful legs.

She was still talking about the roadster.

"No, Daddy, *no*! Absolutely no question of my letting Alain take the wheel while we're driving through Switzerland! He's too absent-minded. And besides, he doesn't really like driving. I know him!"

"She knows me," Alain echoes in his mind. "Perhaps she really thinks she does. Over and over again, I've said to her too: 'I know you my girl.' Saha knows her too. Where is that Saha?"

His eyes searched round for the cat. Then, starting limb by limb, first one shoulder, then the other, he unglued himself from the armchair and went lazily down the five steps into the garden.

The garden was very large and surrounded by other gardens. It breathed out into the night the heavy smell of well-manured earth given over to producing flowers and constantly forced into fertility. Since Alain's birth, the house had hardly changed at all. "An only son's house," Camille said jeeringly. She did not hide her contempt for the high-pitched roof with the top-storey windows set in the slates and for certain modest mouldings which framed the french windows on the ground floor.

The garden, like Camille, also seemed to despise the house. Huge trees, which showered down the black, calcined twigs which fall from elms in their old age, protected it from neighbors and passersby. A little farther on, in a property for sale and in the playground of a school, stood isolated pairs of similar old elms, relics of a princely avenue which had formed part of a park which the new Neuilly[4] was fast destroying.

"Where are you, Alain?"

Camille was calling him from the top of the steps but, on an impulse, he refused to answer. Deliberately, he made for the safer refuge of the shadows, feeling his way along the edge of the shaven lawn with his foot. High in the sky a hazy moon held court, looking larger than usual through the mist of the first warm days. A single tree—a poplar with newly opened glossy leaves—caught the moonlight and trickled with as many sparkles as a waterfall. A silver shadow leapt out of a clump of bushes and glided like a fish against Alain's ankles.

"Ah! There you are, Saha! I was looking for you. Why didn't you appear at table tonight?"

"Merrouwa," answered the cat, "me-rrou-wa."

"What, me-rrou-wa? And why me-rrou-wa? Do you really mean it?"

"Me-rrou-wa," insisted the cat, "me-rrou-wa."

He stroked her, tenderly groping his way down the long spine that was softer than a hare's fur. Then he felt under his hand the small, cold nostrils dilated by her violent purring. "She's my cat.

4. A residential suburb of Paris.

My very own cat."

"M—rrou-wa," said the cat very softly. "R . . . rrou-wa."

Camille called once more from the house and Saha vanished under a clipped euonymus hedge, black-green like the night.

"Alain! We're going!"

He ran to the steps, while Camille watched him with a welcoming smile.

"I can see your hair running," she called out. "It's crazy to be as fair as all that!"

He ran quicker still, strode up the five steps in one bound, and found Camille alone in the drawing-room.

"Where are the others?" he asked under his breath.

"Cloakroom," she whispered back. "Cloakroom and visit to 'work in progress.' General gloom. 'It's not getting on! It'll never be finished!' What the hell do we care! If one was smart, one could hold on to Patrick's studio for keeps. Patrick could find himself another. I'll fix it, if you like."

"But Patrick would only leave the 'Wedge' as a special favor to please *you*."

"Of course. One will take advantage of that."

Her face sparkled with that peculiarly feminine unscrupulousness which Alain could not bring himself to accept as a matter of course. But he remonstrated only on her habit of saying "one" for "we," and she took this as a reproach.

"I'll soon get into the way of saying 'we.' "

So that he should want to kiss her, she turned out the ceiling light as if by accident. The one lamp left alight on a table threw a tall, sharply defined shadow behind the girl.

With her arms raised and her hands clapsed on the nape of her neck, Camille gave him an inviting look. But he had eyes only for the shadow. "How beautiful she is on the wall! Just fine-drawn enough, just as I should like her to be."

He sat down to compare the one with the other. Flattered, Camille arched herself, thrusting her breasts and her hips like a nautch-girl,[5] but the shadow was better at that game than she was. Unclasping her hands, the girl walked across the room, preceded by the ideal shadow. Arrived at the open french window, the shadow leapt on one side and fled out into the garden along the pink gravel of a path, embracing the moon-spangled poplar between its two long arms as it went. "What a pity!" sighed Alain. Then he feebly reproached himself for his inclination to love in Camille herself some perfect or motionless image of Camille. This shadow, for example, or a portrait or the vivid memory she left him of certain moments, certain dresses.

"What's the matter with you tonight? Come and help me put on

5. An Indian dancing-girl.

my cape, at least."

He was shocked at what that "at least" secretly implied and also because Camille, as she passed before him through the door leading to the cloakroom and pantry, had almost imperceptibly shrugged her shoulders. "She doesn't need to shrug her shoulders. Nature and habit do that for her anyway. When she's not careful, her neck makes her look dumpy. Ever, ever so slightly dumpy."

In the cloakroom they found Alain's mother and Camille's parents stamping as if with cold and leaving footmarks the color of dirty snow on the matting. The cat, seated on the window-sill outside, watched them inhospitably but with no animosity. Alain imitated her patience and endured the ritual of pessimistic lamentations.

"It's the same old thing."

"It's hardly any farther on than it was a week ago."

"My dear, if you want to know what *I* think, it won't be a fortnight, it'll be a month. What am I talking about, a month? More likely two months before their nest . . ."

At the word "nest," Camille flung herself into the peaceful fray so shrilly that Alain and Saha closed their eyes.

"But since we've already decided what to do! And since we're actually frightfully *pleased* at having Patrick's place! And since it suits Patrick down to the ground because he hasn't a bean—hasn't any money—sorry Mummy. We'll just take our suitcases and—Alley Oop!—straight up to heaven on the ninth floor! Won't we, Alain?"

He opened his eyes again, smiled into the void, and put her light cape around her shoulders. In the mirror opposite them he met Camille's black, reproachful look but it did not soften his heart. "I didn't kiss her on the lips when we were alone. All right, very well then, I didn't kiss her on the lips. She hasn't had her full ration of kisses-on-the-lips today. She had the quarter-to-twelve one in the Bois,[6] she had the two o'clock one after coffee, she had the half-past-six one in the garden, but she's missed tonight's. Well, if she's not satisfied, she's only got to put it down on the account . . . What's the matter with me? I'm so sleepy, I'm going mad. This life's idiotic; we're seeing far too much of each other and yet we never see each other properly. On Monday I'll definitely go down to the shop and . . ."

In imagination, the chemical acidity of the bales of new silk assailed his nostrils. But the inscrutable smile of M. Veuillet appeared to him as in a dream and, as in a dream, he heard words which, at twenty-four, he had still not learnt to hear without dread. "No, no, my young friend. Will a new adding-machine that costs seventeen thousand francs pay back its initial outlay within the

---

6. The Bois de Boulogne, a large park in Paris.

year? It all depends on that. Allow your poor father's oldest partner
. . ." Catching sight again in the looking-glass of the vindictive
image and handsome dark eyes which were watching him, he folded
Camille in both his arms.

"Well, Alain?"

"Oh, my dear, let him alone! These poor infants . . ."

Camille blushed and disengaged herself. Then she held up her
cheek to Alain in such a boyish brotherly grace that he nearly put
his head on her shoulder. "Oh, to lie down and go to sleep! Oh,
good Lord! Just to lie down and sleep!"

From the garden came the voice of the cat.

"Me-rrou-wa . . . Rrr-rrouwa."

"Hark at the cat! She must be hunting," said Camille calmly.
"Saha! Saha!"

The cat was silent.

"Hunting?" protested Alain. "Whatever makes you think that?
To begin with, we're in May. And then she's saying: 'Me-rrou-
wa!'"

"So what?"

"She wouldn't be saying 'Me-rrou-wa' if she were hunting! What
she's saying there—and it's really rather strange—means a warning.
It's almost the cry calling her little ones together."

"Good Lord!" cried Camille, flinging up her arms. "If Alain's
going to start interpreting the cat, we shall be here all night!"

She ran down the steps and, at the touch of old Émile's shaking
hand, two old-fashioned gas-globes,[7] like huge mauve planets, illuminated the garden.

Alain walked ahead with Camille. At the entrance gate, he kissed
her under the ear, breathed in, under a perfume too old for her, a
good smell of bread and dark hair, and squeezed the girl's bare
elbows under her cape. When she seated herself at the steering-
wheel, with her parents in the back, he felt suddenly wide awake
and gay.

"Saha! Saha!"

The cat sprang out of the shadow, almost under his feet. When
he began to run, she ran too, leaping ahead of him with long
bounds. He guessed she was there without seeing her; she burst
before him into the hall and came back to wait for him at the top
of the steps. With her frill standing out and her ears low, she
watched him running towards her, urging him on with her yellow
eyes. Those deep-set eyes were proud and suspicious, completely
masters of themselves.

"Saha! Saha!"

Pronounced in a certain way, under his breath, with the "h"
strongly aspirated, her name sent her crazy. She lashed her tail,

7. Gaslights in spherical lanterns.

bounded into the middle of the poker table and, with her two cat's hands spread wide open, she scattered the playing-cards.

"That cat, that cat!" said his mother's voice. "She hasn't the faintest notion of hospitality! Look how delighted she is that our friends have gone!"

Alain let out a spurt of childish laughter, the laugh he kept for home and the close intimacy which did not extend beyond the screen of elms or the black, wrought-iron gate. Then he gave a frantic yawn.

"Good heavens, how tired you look! Is it possible to look as tired as that when one's happy! There's still some orangeade. No? We can go up then. Don't bother, Émile will turn out the lights."

"Mother's talking to me as if I were getting over an illness or as if I were starting up paratyphoid again."

"Saha! Saha! What a demon! Alain, you couldn't persuade that cat? . . ."

By a vertical path known to herself, marked on the worn brocade, the cat had almost reached the ceiling. One moment she imitated a gray lizard, flattening against the wall with her paws spread out; then she pretended to be giddy and tried an affected little cry of appeal. Alain obediently came and stood below and Saha slid down, glued to the wall like a raindrop sliding down a pane. She came to rest on Alain's shoulder and the two of them went up together to their bedroom.

A long hanging cluster of laburnum,[8] black outside the open window, became a long pale yellow cluster when Alain turned on the ceiling light and the bedside lamp. He poured the cat off on to the bed by inclining his shoulder, then wandered aimlessly to and fro between his room and the bathroom like a man who is too tired to go to bed.

He leaned out over the garden, looked with a hostile eye for the white mass of the "alterations."[9] Then he opened and shut several drawers and boxes in which reposed his real secrets: a gold dollar, a signet ring, an agate charm attached to his father's watch chain, some red and black seeds from an exotic canna plant,[10] a First Communicant's mother-of-pearl rosary and a thin broken bracelet, the souvenir of a tempestuous young mistress who had passed swiftly and noisily out of his life. The rest of his worldly goods consisted merely of some paper-covered books he had had rebound and some letters and autographs.

Dreamily he turned over these little scraps of wreckage, bright

---

8. A flowering tree or shrub often called "golden chain."
9. The apartment being constructed for Alain and Camille on the west side of the house, in the garden.
10. A tropical plant with bright red or yellow flowers.

and worthless as the colored stones one finds in the nests of pilfering birds. "Should I throw all this away . . . or leave it here? It means nothing to me. Or does it mean something?" Being an only child, he was attached to everything which he had never shared with anyone else and for whose possession he had never had to fight.

He saw his face in the glass and became suddenly irritated with himself. "Why can't you go to bed? You look a wreck. Positively disgraceful!" he said to the handsome fair young man. "People only think me handsome because I'm fair. If I were dark, I'd be hideous." For the hundredth time, he criticized his long cheeks and his slightly equine nose. But, for the hundredth time, he smiled so as to display his teeth to himself and admiringly touched the natural wave in his fair, over-thick hair. Once again he was pleased with the color of his eyes, greenish-gray between dark lashes. Two dints hollowed his cheeks on either side of the smile, his eyes receded, circled with mauve shadows. He had shaved this morning but already a pale, stubbly bristle coarsened his upper lip. "What a mug! I pity myself. No, I repel myself. Is *that* a face for a wedding night?" In the depths of the mirror, Saha gravely watched him from the distance.

"I'm coming. I'm coming."

He flung himself on the cool expanse of the sheets, humoring the cat. Rapidly, he went through certain ritual litanies dedicated to the particular graces and virtues of a small, perfect, pure-bred Russian Blue.[11]

"My little bear with the big cheeks. Exquisite, exquisite, exquisite cat. My blue pigeon. Pearl-colored demon."

As soon as he turned out the light, the cat began to trample delicately on her friend's chest. Each time she pressed down her feet, one single claw pierced the silk of the pajamas, catching the skin just enough for Alain to feel an uneasy pleasure.

"Seven more days, Saha," he sighed.

In seven days and seven nights he would begin a new life in new surroundings with an amorous and untamed young woman. He stroked the cat's fur, warm and cool at the same time and smelling of clipped-box, thuya,[12] and lush grass. She was purring full-throatedly and, in the darkness, she gave him a cat's kiss, laying her damp nose for a second under Alain's nose between his nostrils and his lip. A swift, immaterial kiss which she rarely accorded him.

"Ah! Saha. Our nights . . ."

The headlights of a car in the nearest avenue pierced the leaves with two revolving white beams. Over the wall of the room passed the enlarged shadow of the laburnum and of a tulip-tree which stood alone in the middle of a lawn. Above his own face Alain saw

11. A rare breed of cat with thick short grayish-blue fur.   12. Arbor vitae.

Saha's face illuminated for a moment. Before it was eclipsed again, he had seen that her eyes were hard.

"Don't frighten me!" he implored.

For, when Alain was sleepy, he became once more weak and fanciful, caught in the mesh of a sweet and interminable adolescence.

He shut his eyes while Saha kept vigil, watching all the invisible signs which hover over sleeping human beings when the light is put out.

He always dreamed a great deal and descended into his dreams by definite stages. When he woke up, he did not talk about his adventures of the night. He was jealous of a realm which had been enlarged by a delicate and ill-governed childhood; by long sojourns in bed during his swift growth into a tall frail slender boy.

He loved his dreams and cultivated them. Not for anything in the world would he have revealed the successive stages which awaited him. At the first stopping-place, while he could still hear the motor-horns in the avenue, he met an eddy of faces, familiar yet distorted, which he passed through as he might have passed through a friendly crowd, greeting one here and there. Eddying, bulbous, the faces approached Alain, growing larger and larger. Light against a dark background, they became lighter still as if they received their illumination from the sleeper himself. Each was furnished with one great eye and they circled round in an effortless giration. But a submerged electric current shot them far away as soon as they touched an invisible barrier. In the humid gaze of a circular monster, in the eye of a plump moon or that of a wild archangel with rays of light for hair, Alain could recognize the same expression, the same intention which none of them had put into words and which Alain of the dream noted with a sense of security: "They'll tell it me tomorrow."

Sometimes they disappeared by exploding into scattered, faintly luminous fragments. At other times, they only continued as a hand, an arm, a forehead, an eyeball full of thoughts or as a starry dust of chins and noses. But always there remained that prominent, convex eye which, just at the moment of making itself clear, turned round and exposed only its other, black surface.

The sleeping Alain pursued, under Saha's watchful care, his nightly shipwreck. He passed beyond the world of convex faces and eyes and descended through a zone of darkness where he was conscious of nothing but a powerful, positive blackness, indescribably varied and, as it were, composed of submerged colors. On the confines of this, he launched into the real, complete, fully-formed dream.

He came up violently against a barrier which gave a great clang like the prolonged, splintering clash of a cymbal. And then he found himself in the dream city, among the passers-by, the inhabitants standing in their doorways, the gold-crowned guardians of the square and the stage crowd posted along the path of an Alain who was completely naked and armed with a walking-stick. This Alain was extremely lucid and sagacious: "If I walk rather fast, after tying my tie in a special way, and particularly if I whistle, there's every chance that no one will notice I am naked." So he tied his tie in a heart-shaped knot and whistled. "That's not whistling, what I'm doing. It's purring. Whistling's like this . . ." But he still continued to purr. "I'm not at the end of my tether yet. All I've got to do . . . it's perfectly simple . . . is to cross this sun-drenched open space and go round the bandstand where the military band is playing. Child's play. I run, making perilous jumps to distract attention, and I come out in the zone of shadow . . ."

But he was paralysed by the warm, dangerous look of a dark man in the stage crowd; a young man with a Greek profile perforated by a great eye like a carp's. "The zone of shadow . . . the zone of *the* shadow . . ." Two long shadowy arms, graceful and rustling with poplar leaves appeared at the word "shadow" and carried Alain away. During the most ambiguous hour of the short night, he rested in that provisional tomb where the living exile sighs, weeps, fights, and succumbs, and from which he rises, unremembering, with the day.

TWO

The high sun was edging the window when Alain awoke. The newly-opened cluster of laburnum hung, translucid, above the head of Saha; a blue, diurnal Saha, innocently engaged in washing herself.

"Saha!"

"Me-rrang!" answered the cat aggressively.

"Is it my fault if you're hungry? You only had to go downstairs and ask for your milk if you're in a hurry."

She softened at her friend's voice and repeated the same word less emphatically, showing her red mouth planted with white teeth. The look of loyal and exclusive love alarmed Alain: "Oh heavens, this cat! What to do with this cat? I'd forgotten I was getting married. And that we've got to live in Patrick's place."

He turned towards the photograph in the chromium frame where Camille gleamed as if covered in oil; a great splash of reflected light on her hair, painted mouth vitrified in inky black, her eyes enormous between two palisades of eyelashes.

"Fine piece of studio portraiture," muttered Alain.

He had quite forgotten that he himself had chosen this photograph for his room; a photograph which bore no resemblance to Camille or to anyone at all. "That eye . . . I've seen that eye."

He took a pencil and lightly retouched the eye, toning down the excess of white. All he succeeded in doing was to spoil the print.

"Mouck, mouck, mouck. Ma-a-a-a . . . M-a-a-a-a," said Saha, addressing a little moth imprisoned between the window-pane and the net curtain.

Her leonine chin was trembling; she coveted it so much that she stammered. Alain caught the moth with two fingers and offered it to the cat.

"*Hors-d'oeuvre*, Saha!"

In the garden, a rake was lazily combing the gravel. Alain could see in his mind the hand that guided the rake; the hand of an aging woman; a mechanical, obstinate hand in a huge white glove like a policeman's.

"Good morning, Mother!" he called.

A distant voice answered him, a voice whose words he did not try to catch; the affectionate, insignificant murmur was all that he needed. He ran downstairs, the cat at his heels. In broad daylight, she knew how to change herself into a kind of blustering dog. She would hurtle noisily down the stairs and rush into the garden with tomboyish jumps that had no magic about them. She seated herself on the little breakfast table, among the medallions of sunlight, beside Alain's plate. The rake, which had stopped, slowly resumed its task.

Alain poured out Saha's milk, stirred a pinch of salt and a pinch of sugar into it, then gravely helped himself. When he breakfasted alone, he did not have to blush for certain gestures elaborated by the unconscious wishes of the maniac age between six and seven. He was free to blind all the "eyes" in his bread with butter and to frown when the coffee in his cup rose above the water-line marked by a certain gilt arabesque. A second thin slice had to follow the first thick slice, whereas the second cup demanded an extra lump of sugar. In fact a very small Alain, hidden in the depths of a tall, fair, handsome young man, was impatiently waiting for breakfast to be over so that he could lick both sides of the honey spoon; an old ivory spoon, blackened and flexible with age.

"Camille, at this moment, is eating her breakfast standing up. She's biting at one and the same time into a slice of lean ham squeezed between two rusks[13] and into an American apple. And she keeps putting down a cup of tea without sugar in it on various bits of furniture and forgetting it."

He raised his eyes and contemplated his domain; the domain of a privileged child which he cherished and whose every inch he knew. Over his head the old, severely pollarded[14] elms stirred only the tips of their young leaves. A cushiony mass of pink silene, fringed with forget-me-nots, dominated one lawn. Dangling liker a scarf

13. Dry bread or biscuit.
14. Trees whose top branches are reg- ularly cut back to the trunk to produce thick new growth below.

from the dead tree's scraggy elbow, a trail of polygonum[15] intertwined with the four-petalled purple clematis fluttered in every breath of wind. One of the standard sprinklers spread a white peacock tail shot with a shifting rainbow as it revolved over the turf.

"Such a beautiful garden . . . such a beautiful garden," said Alain under his breath. He stared disgustedly at the silent heaps of rubbish, timber, and bags of plaster which defaced the west side of the house. "Ah! It's Sunday, so they're not working. It's been Sunday all the week for me." Though young and capricious, and pampered, he now lived according to the commercial rhythm of a six-day week and felt Sunday in his bones.

A white pigeon moved furtively behind the weigela and the pink clusters of the deutzias.[16] "It's not a pigeon; it's mother's hand in her gardening glove." The big white glove moved just above ground, raising a drooping stalk, weeding out the blades of grass that sprang up overnight. Two greenfinches came hopping along the gravel path to pick up the breakfast crumbs, and Saha followed them with her eye without getting excited. But a tomtit, hanging upside down in an elm above the table, chirped at the cat out of bravado. Sitting there with her paws folded, her head thrown back, and the frill of fur under her chin displayed liked a pretty woman's jabot,[17] Saha tried hard to restrain herself; but her cheeks swelled with fury and her little nostrils moistened.

"As beautiful as a fiend! More beautiful than a fiend!" Alain told her.

He wanted to stroke the broad skull in which lodged ferocious thoughts, and the cat bit him sharply to relieve her anger. He looked at the two little beads of blood on his palm with the irascibility of a man whose woman has bitten him at the height of her pleasure.

"Bad girl! Bad girl! Look what you've done to me!"

She lowered her head, sniffed the blood, and timidly questioned her friend's face. She knew how to amuse him and charm him back to good humor. She scooped up a rusk from the table and held it between her paws like a squirrel.

The May breeze passed over them, bending a yellow rose-bush which smelt of flowering reeds. Between the cat, the rose-bush, the pairs of tomtits, and the last cockchafers,[18] Alain had one of those moments when he slipped out of time and felt the anguished illusion of being once more back in his childhood. The elms suddenly became enormous, the path grew wider and longer and vanished under the arches of a pergola[19] that no longer existed. Like the

15. Silene is "catchfly," polygonum a plant with knotlike stems.
16. Weigela and deutzia are shrubs with pink, white, or red flowers.

17. Frills on a shirt front.
18. Large beetles.
19. An arbor or arched trellis on which plants are trained to grow.

hag-ridden dreamer who falls off a tower, Alain returned violently to the consciousness of being nearly twenty-four.

"I ought to have slept another hour. It's only half-past nine. It's Sunday. Yesterday was Sunday for me too. Too many Sundays. But tomorrow . . ."

He smiled at Saha as though she were an accomplice. "Tomorrow, Saha, there's the final trying-on of the white dress. Without me. It's a surprise. Camille's dark enough to look her best in white. During that time, I'll go and look at the car. It's a bit cheese-paring, a bit mingy,[20] as Camille would say, a roadster. That's what you get for being 'such a young married couple.'"

With a vertical bound, rising in the air like a fish leaping to the surface of the water, the cat caught a black-veined cabbage-white.[21] She ate it, coughed, spat out one wing, and licked herself affectionately. The sun played on her fur, mauve and bluish like the breast of a woodpigeon.

"Saha!"

She turned her head and smiled at him.

"My little puma! Beloved cat! Creature of the tree-tops! How will you live if we're separated? Would you like us to enter an Order?[22] Would you like? . . . oh, I don't know what . . ."

She listened to him, watching him with a tender, absent expression. But when the friendly voice began to tremble, she looked away.

"To begin with, you'll come with us. You don't hate cars. If we take the saloon[23] instead of the roadster, behind the seats there's a ledge . . ."

He broke off and became gloomy at the recent memory of a girl's vigorous voice, ideally pitched for shouting in the open air, trumpeting the numerous merits of the roadster. "And then, when you put down the windscreen, Alain, its *marvellous*. When she's all out, you can feel the skin of your cheeks shrinking right back to your *ears*."

"Shrinking right back to your ears. Can you imagine anything more frightful, Saha?"

He compressed his lips and made a long face like an obstinate child planning to get its own way by guile.

"It's not settled yet. Suppose I prefer the saloon? I suppose I've got *some* say in the matter?"

He glared at the yellow rose-bush as if it were the young girl with the resonant voice. Promptly the path widened, the elms grew taller, and the non-existent pergola reappeared. Cowering among the skirts of two or three female relatives, a childish Alain surveyed another compact family among whose opaque block gleamed a very dark little girl whose big eyes and black ringlets rivalled each other

20. Stingy.
21. A butterfly.
22. A monastic order.
23. A sedan.

in a hostile, jetty brilliance. "Say 'How d'you do. . . .' Why don't you want to say 'How d'you do?'" It was a faint voice from other days, preserved through years of childhood, adolescence, college, the boredom of military service, false seriousness, false business competence. Camille did not want to say "How d'you do?" She sucked the inside of her cheek and stiffly sketched the brief curtsy expected of little girls. "Now she calls that a 'twist-your-ankle' curtsy. But when she's in a temper, she still bites the inside of her cheek. It's a funny thing, but at those moments she doesn't look ugly."

He smiled and felt an honest glow of warmth for his fiancée. After all, he was quite glad that she should be healthy and slightly commonplace in her sensuality. Defying the innocent morning, he called up images designed now to excite her vanity and impatience, now to engender anxiety, even confusion. Emerging from these disturbing fancies, he found the sun too white and the wind dry. The cat had disappeared but, as soon as he stood up, she was at his side and accompanied him, walking with a long, deerlike step and avoiding the round pebbles in the pinkish gravel. They went together as far as the "alterations" and inspected with equal hostility the pile of rubbish, a new french window, devoid of panes, inserted in a wall, various bathroom appliances, and some porcelain tiles.

Equally offended, they calculated the damage done to their past and their present. An old yew had been torn up and was very slowly dying upside down, with its roots in the air. "I ought never, never to have allowed that," muttered Alain. "It's a disgrace. You've only known it for three years, Saha, that yew. But I . . ."

At the bottom of the hole left by the yew, Saha sensed a mole whose image, or rather whose smell went to her head. For a minute she forgot herself to the point of frenzy, scratching like a fox-terrier and rolling over like a lizard. She jumped on all four paws like a frog, clutched a ball of earth between her thighs as a fieldmouse does with the egg it has stolen; escaped from the hole by a series of miracles, and found herself sitting on the grass, cold and prudish and recovering her breath.

Alain stood gravely by, not moving. He knew how to keep a straight face when Saha's demons possessed her beyond her control. The admiration and understanding of cats was innate in him. Those inborn rudiments made it easy for him, later on, to read Saha's thoughts. He had read her like some masterpiece from the day, when on his return from a cat-show, Alain had put down a little five-months old she-cat on the smooth lawn at Neuilly. He had brought her because of her perfect face, her precocious dignity, and her modesty that hoped for nothing behind the bars of a cage.

"Why didn't you buy a Persian instead?" asked Camille.

"That was long before we were engaged," thought Alain. "It wasn't only a little she-cat I bought. It was the nobility of all cats, their infinite disinterestedness, their knowledge of how to live, their affinities with the highest type of humans." He blushed and mentally excused himself. "The highest, Saha, is the one that understands *you* best."

He had not yet got to the point of thinking "likeness" instead of "understanding" because he belonged to that class of human beings which refuses to recognize or even to imagine its animal affinities. But at the age when he might have coveted a car, a journey abroad, a rare binding, a pair of skis, Alain nevertheless remained the young-man-who-has-bought-a-little-cat. His narrow world resounded with it. The staff of Amparat et Fils[24] in the Rue des Petits Champs were astonished and M. Veuillet inquired after the "little beastie."

"Before I chose you, Saha, I don't believe I'd ever realized that one *could* choose. As for all the rest . . . My marriage pleases everyone, including Camille. There are moments when it pleases me too, but . . ."

He got up from the green bench and assumed the important smile of the heir of Amparat Silks who is condescendingly marrying the daughter of Malmert Mangles,[25] "a girl who's not *quite* our type," as Mme. Amparat said. But Alain was well aware that, when Malmert Mangles spoke about Amparat Silks among themselves, they did not forget to mention, sticking up their chins: "The Amparats aren't in silk any more. The mother and son have only kept their shares in the business and the son's not the real director, only a figurehead."

Cured of her madness, her eyes gentle and golden, the cat seemed to be waiting for the return of mental trust, of that telepathic murmur for which her silver-fringed ears were straining.

"You're not just a pure and sparkling spirit of a cat either," went on Alain. "What about your first seducer, the white tom without a tail? Do you remember that, my ugly one, my trollop in the rain, my shameless one?"

"What a bad mother your cat is!" exclaimed Camille indignantly. "She doesn't even give a thought to her kittens, now they've been taken away from her."

"But that was just what a young girl would say," Alain went on defiantly. "Young girls are always admirable mothers before they're married."

The full, deep note of a bell sounded on the tranquil air. Alain leapt up with a guilty start at the sound of wheels crushing the gravel.

"Camille! It's half-past eleven . . . Good Heavens!"

He pulled his pajama jacket together and retied the cord so hastily and nervously that he scolded himself. "Come, come, what's the

---

24. Amparat and Son.   25. Laundry machines.

matter with me? I shall be seeing plenty more of them in a week. Saha, are you coming to meet them?"

But Saha had vanished and Camille was already stamping across the lawn with reckless heels. "Ah! She really does look attractive." His blood pulsed pleasurably in his throat and flushed his cheeks. He was entirely absorbed in the spectacle of Camille in white, with a little lock of well-tapered hair on either temple and a tiny red scarf which matched her lipstick. Made-up with skill and restraint, her youth was not obvious at first glance. Then it revealed itself in the cheek that was white under the ochre powder; in the smooth, unwrinkled eyelids under the light dusting of beige powder round the great eyes that were almost black. The brand-new diamond on her left hand broke the light into a thousand colored splinters.

"Oh!" she cried. "You're not ready! On a lovely day like this!"

But she stopped at the sight of the rough, dishevelled fair hair, of the naked chest under the pajamas and Alain's flushed confusion. Her young girl's face so clearly expressed a woman's warm indulgence that Alain no longer dared to give her the quarter-to-twelve kiss of the Bois.

"Kiss me," she implored, very low, as if she were asking him for help.

Gauche, uneasy and ill-protected by his thin pajamas, he made a gesture towards the pink flowering shrubs from whence came the sound of the shears and the rake. Camille did not dare throw herself on his neck. She lowered her eyes, plucked a leaf, and pulled her shining locks of hair forward on her cheeks. But, from the movement of her nostrils, Alain saw she was searching in the air, with a certain primitive wildness, for the fragrance of a fair-skinned, barely-covered body. In his heart he secretly condemned her for not being sufficiently afraid of it.

THREE

When he woke up, he did not sit up in bed at one bound. Haunted in his sleep by the unfamiliar room, he half-opened his eyes and realized that cunning and constraint had not entirely left him during his sleep, for his left arm, flung out across a desert of linen sheet, lay ready to recognize, but ready, also, to repel . . . But all the wide expanse of bed to his left was empty and cool once more. If there had been nothing in front of the bed but the barely rounded corner of the triangular room and the unaccustomed green gloom, split by a rod of bright yellow light which separated two curtains of solid shadow, Alain would have gone to sleep again lulled by the sound of someone humming a little Negro song.

He turned his head cautiously and opened his eyes a trifle wider. He saw someone moving about, now white, now pale blue according to whether she was in the narrow strip of sunlight or the shadow. It was a naked young woman with a comb in her hand and a cigarette between her lips, wandering about the room and humming. "What impudence," he thought. "Completely naked! Where does she think she is?"

He recognized the lovely legs with which he had long been familiar, but the stomach, shortened by a navel placed rather low, surprised him. An impersonal youthfulness justified the muscular buttocks and the breasts were small above the visible ribs. "Has she got thinner, then?" The solidity of her back, which was as wide as her chest, shocked Alain. "She's got a common back." At that moment, Camille leaned her elbow on one of the window-sills, arched her back, and hunched up her shoulders. "She's got a back like a charwoman." But suddenly she stood upright again, took a couple of dancing steps and made a charming gesture of embracing the empty air. "No, I'm wrong. She's beautiful. But what a . . . what brazenness. Does she think I'm dead? Or does it seem perfectly natural to her to wander about stark naked? Oh, but that will change!"

As she turned towards the bed, he closed his eyes again. When he opened them, Camille had seated herself at the dressing-table they called the "invisible dressing-table," a transparent sheet of beautiful thick glass laid on a black metal frame. She powdered her face, touched her cheeks and chin with the tips of her fingers, and suddenly smiled, turning her eyes from the glass with a gravity and a weariness which disarmed Alain. "Is she happy then? Happy about what? *I* certainly don't deserve it. But why is she naked?"

"Camille," he called out.

He thought she would rush towards the bathroom, hastily covering herself with some hastily snatched-up undergarment. Instead, she ran to the bed and bent over the young man who lay there, overwhelming him with her strong brunette's smell.

"Darling! Have you slept well?"

"Stark naked!" he scolded.

She opened her big eyes comically.

"What about you?"

Bare to his waist, he did not know what to reply. She paraded for him, so proudly and so completely devoid of modesty that he rather rudely flung her the crumpled pajama-jacket which lay on the bed.

"Quick, put that on. Personally, I'm hungry."

"Old mother Buque's at her post. Everything's in working order and functioning."

She disappeared and Alain wanted to get up and dress and smooth his rumpled hair. But Camille returned, girded in a big bathrobe that was new and too long for her, and gaily carrying a loaded tray.

"What a mess, my dears! There's a kitchen bowl and a pyrex cup and the sugar's in the lid of a tin. I'll get it all straightened out in a day or two. My ham's dry. These anemic peaches are left-overs from lunch. Mother Buque's a bit lost in her electric kitchen. I'll teach her how to manage the various switches. Then I've put some water in the ice compartments of the 'fridge. It's a good thing I'm here! Monsieur has his coffee very hot and his milk boiling and his butter hard. No, that's my tea, don't touch! What are you looking for?"

"Nothing."

Because of the smell of coffee, he was looking for Saha.

"What's the time?"

"At last a tender word!" cried Camille. "Very early, my husband. It was a quarter-past eight by the kitchen alarm-clock."

As they ate, they laughed a good deal and spoke little. By the increasing smell of the green oilcloth curtains, Alain could guess the strength of the sun which warmed them. He could not take his mind off that sun outside, the unfamiliar horizon, the nine vertiginous storeys, and the bizarre architecture of the "Wedge" which was their temporary home.

He listened to Camille as attentively as he could, touched at her pretending to have forgotten what had passed between them in the night. He was touched, too, by her pretending to be perfectly at home in their haphazard lodging and by her unselfconsciousness, as if she had been married at least a week. Now that she had something on, he tried to find a way of showing his gratitude. "She doesn't resent either what I've done to her or what I haven't, poor child. After all, the most tiresome part is over. Is it always like this the first night? This bruised, unsatisfactory feeling? This half-success, half-disaster?"

He threw his arm cordially round her neck and kissed her.

"Oh! You're nice!"

She had said it so loud and with so much feeling that she blushed and he saw her eyes fill with tears. But she bravely fought down her emotion and jumped off the bed on the pretext of removing the tray. She ran towards the windows, tripped over her long bathrobe, let out a great oath, and hauled on a ship's rope. The oilcloth curtains slid back. Paris, with its suburbs, bluish and unbounded like the desert, dotted with still-fresh verdure and flashes of shining panes, entered at one bound into the triangular room which had only one cement wall, the other two being half glass.

"It's beautiful," said Alain softly.

But he was half lying and his head sought the support of a young shoulder from which the bathrobe had slipped. "It's not a place for human beings to live. All this horizon right on top of one, right in one's bed. And what about stormy days. Abandoned on the top of a lighthouse among the albatrosses."

Camille was lying beside him on the bed now. Her arm was

round his neck and she looked fearlessly, now at the giddy horizons of Paris, now at the fair, dishevelled head. This new pride of hers which seemed to draw strength ahead from the coming night and the days that would follow, was no doubt satisfied with her newly-acquired rights. She was licensed to share his bed, to prop up a young man's naked body against her thigh and shoulder, to become acquainted with its color and curves and defects. She was free to contemplate boldly and at length the small dry nipples, the loins she envied, and the strange design of the capricious sex.

They bit into the same tasteless peach and laughed, showing each other their splendid, glistening teeth and the gums which were a little pale, like tired children's.

"That day yesterday!" signed Camille. "When you think that there are people who get married so often!"

Her vanity returned and she added: "All the same, it went off very well. Not a single hitch. It did go off well, didn't it?"

"Yes," said Alain feebly.

"Oh *you* . . . You're just like your mother, I mean, as long as your lawn isn't ruined and people don't throw cigarette-ends on your gravel, you think everything's fine. Isn't that a fact? All the same, our wedding would have been prettier at Neuilly. Only that would have disturbed the sacred cat! Tell me, you bad boy, what do you keep looking at all round you?"

"Nothing," he said sincerely, "because there's nothing to look at. I've seen the dressing-table. I've seen the chair—we've seen the bed . . ."

"Couldn't you live here? I'd love to. Just think . . . three rooms and three balconies! If only one could stay here!"

"Doesn't one say: 'If only *we* could stay here'?"

"Then why do *you* say: 'One says'? Yes, if only one could stay here, as *we* say."

"But Patrick will be back from his cruise in three months."

"Who cares? He'll come back. And we'll explain that we want to stay on. And we'll chuck him out."

"Oh! You'd actually do that?"

She shook her black mop affirmatively, with a radiant, feminine assurance in dishonesty. Alain wanted to give her a severe look but, under his eyes, Camille changed and became as nervous as he felt himself. Hastily he kissed her on the mouth.

Silent and eager, she returned his kiss, feeling for the hollow of the bed with a movement of her loins. At the same time her free hand, which was holding a peach-stone, groped in the air for an empty cup or ashtray.

Leaning over her, he caressed her lightly, waiting for her to open her eyes again.

She was pressing her eyelashes down over two small, glittering tears which she was trying to stop from flowing. He respected this restraint and this pride. They had done their best, the two of them, aided by the morning warmth and their two odorous, facile bodies.

Alain remembered Camille's quickened breathing and her warm docility. She had shown an untimely eagerness which was very charming. She reminded him of no other woman; in possessing her for the second time, he had thought only of the careful handling she deserved. She lay against him, her legs and arms relaxed, her hands half-closed, catlike for the first time, "Where is Saha?"

Mechanically he gave Camille the ghost of a caress "for Saha," drawing his nails slowly and delicately all the way down her stomach. She cried out with shock and stiffened her arms. One of them hit Alain who nearly hit her back. She sat up, with her hair on end and her eyes hostile and threatening.

"Are you vicious, by any chance?"

He had expected nothing like this and burst out laughing.

"There's nothing to laugh about!" cried Camille. "I've always been told that men who tickle women are vicious. They may even be sadists!"

He got off the bed so as to be able to laugh more freely, quite forgetting he was naked. Camille stopped talking so suddenly that he turned round and surprised her lit-up, dazed face staring at the body of the young man whom one night of marriage had made hers.

"D'you mind if I steal the bathroom for ten minutes?"

He opened the glass door set into one end of the longest wall which they called the hypotenuse.

"And then I'll go over to my mother's for a moment."

"Yes . . . Don't you want me to come with you?"

He looked shocked and she blushed for the first time that day.

"I'll see if the alterations . . ."

"Oh! the alterations! Don't tell me you're interested in those alterations! Admit"—she folded her arms like a tragic actress—"admit that you're going to see my rival!"

"Saha's not your rival," said Alain simply.

"How can she be your rival," he went on to himself. "You can only have rivals in what's impure."

"I don't need *such* a serious protestation, darling. Hurry up! You haven't forgotten that we're lunching together on our own at Père Léopold's? On our own at last, just the two of us! You'll come back soon? You haven't forgotten we're going for a drive? Are you taking in what I'm saying?"

What he took in very clearly was that the words "come back" had acquired a new and preposterous significance and he looked at Camille askance. She was flaunting her newly-married bride's tiredness, drawing his attention to the faint swelling of her lower lids under the corners of her great eyes. "Will you always have such enormous eyes the moment you wake up, whatever time of day or night? Don't you know how to keep your eyes half-closed? It gives me a headache to see eyes as wide open as all that."

He felt a dishonest pleasure, an evasive comfort in calling her to account in his mind. "After all, it's less ungracious then being frank." He hurried to reach the square bathroom, the hot water, and a solitude propitious to thought. But, as the glass door inserted in the hypotenuse reflected him from head to foot, Alain opened it with complacent slowness and was in no haste to shut it again.

When he was leaving the flat an hour later, he opened the wrong door on one of the balconies which ran along every side of the Wedge. Like the sharp down-stroke of a fan, the east wind which was turning Paris blue, blowing away the smoke and scouring the distant Sacré Coeur,[26] caught him full in the face. On the cement parapet, five or six pots, put there by well-meaning hands, contained white roses and hydrangeas and lilies sullied by their pollen. "Last night's dessert is never attractive." Nevertheless, before he went down, he sheltered the ill-treated flowers from the wind.

FOUR

He stole into the garden like a boy in his teens who has stayed out all night. The air was full of the heady scent of beds being watered, of the secret exhalation of the filth which nourishes fleshy, expensive flowers and of spray blown on the breeze. In the very act of drawing a deep breath to inhale it all, he suddenly discovered he needed comforting.

"Saha! Saha!"

She did not come for a moment or two, and at first he did not recognize that bewildered, incredulous face which seemed clouded by a bad dream.

"Saha darling!"

He took her on his chest, smoothing the soft flanks which seemed to him a trifle hollow, and removed cobwebs, pine needles, and elm twigs from the neglected fur. She pulled herself together quickly and resumed her familiar expression and her cat's dignity. He face, her pure golden eyes looked again as he had known them. Under his thumb, Alain could feel the palpitations of a hard, irregular little heart and also the beginnings of a faint, uncertain purr. He put her down on an iron table and stroked her head. But at the moment of thrusting her head into Alain's hand, wildly and as if for life in the way she had, she sniffed that hand and stepped back a pace.

His eyes sought the white pigeon, the gloved hand behind the

---

26. Or Sacred Heart, the great white church on the heights of the Montmartre district.

pink flowering shrubs, behind the flaming rhododendrons. He rejoiced that yesterday's "ceremony" had respected the beautiful garden and only ravaged Camille's home.

"Imagine those people here! And those four bridesmaids in pink paper! And the flowers they'd have picked, and the deutzias[27] sacrificed to adorn fat women's bosoms! And Saha!"

He called in the direction of the house: "Has Saha had anything to eat or drink? She looks awfully queer. I'm here, Mother."

A heavy white shape appeared in the doorway of the hall and answered from the distance: "No. Just fancy, she had no supper and wouldn't drink her milk this morning. I think she was waiting for you. Are you all right, dear?"

He stood at the foot of the steps, deferential in his mother's presence. He noticed that she did not offer him her cheek as usual and that she kept her hands clasped together at her waist. He understood and shared this motherly sense of decency with a mixture of embarrassment and gratitude. "Saha hasn't kissed me either."

"After all, the cat's often seen you go away. She made allowances for your going off sometimes."

"But I didn't go so far," he thought.

Near him, on the iron table, Saha drank her milk avidly like an animal that has walked far and slept little.

"Alain, wouldn't you like a cup of warm milk too? Some bread and butter?"

"I've had breakfast, Mother. *We've* had breakfast."

"Not much of a breakfast, I imagine. In such a glory-hole!"

With the eye of an exile, Alain contemplated the cup with the gilt arabesque beside Saha's saucer; then his mother's heavy face, amiable under the mass of wavy, prematurely white hair.

"I haven't asked you whether my new daughter is satisfied." She was frightened he would misunderstand her and added hurriedly: "I mean, whether she's in good health."

"Excellent, Mother. We're going out to Rambouillet for lunch in the forest. I've got to run the car in."[28] He corrected himself: "*We've* got to run the car in, I mean."

They remained alone together in the garden, he and Saha, both torpid with silence and weariness and overcome with longing to sleep.

The cat fell asleep suddenly on her side, her chin up and her teeth bared like a dead animal. Feathery panicles from the Venetian sumac and clematis petals rained down on her without her so much as twitching in the depths of the dream in which, no doubt, she was enjoying the security of her friend's inalienable presence. Her defeated attitude, the pale, drawn corners of her periwinkle-gray lips gave evidence of a night of miserable watching.

27. Shrubs with white or pink flowers.   by driving it at first at fairly low speeds.
28. That is, break it in—in those days

Above the withered stump draped with climbing plants, a flight of bees over the ivy-flowers gave out a solemn cymbal note, the identical note of so many summers. "To go to sleep out here, on the grass, between the yellow rosebush and the cat. Camille won't come till dinner-time, that will be very pleasant. And the cat, good heavens, the cat . . ." Over by the "alterations" could be heard the rasp of a plane shaving a beam, the clang of an iron hammer on a metal girder, and Alain promptly embarked on a dream about a village peopled with mysterious blacksmiths. As eleven sounded from the belfry of the school near by, he got up and fled without daring to wake the cat.

FIVE

June came with its longer days, its night skies devoid of mystery which the late glow of the sunset and the early glimmer of dawn over the east of Paris kept from being wholly dark. But June is cruel only to city-dwellers who have no car and are caged up in hot stone and forced to live elbow to elbow. A never-still breeze played round the Wedge, rippling the yellow awnings. It blew through the triangular room and the studio, broke against the prow of the building, and dried up the little hedges of privet that stood in boxes on the balconies. With the help of their daily drives, Alain and Camille lived pleasantly enough. The warm weather and their sensual life combined to make them drowsy and less exacting with each other.

"Why did I call her an untamed girl?" Alain asked himself in surprise. Camille swore less when she was driving the car and had lost certain crudities of speech. She had also lost her passion for night-clubs with female gipsy singers who had nostrils like horses.

She spent much time eating and sleeping, opened her now much gentler eyes very wide, gave up a dozen summer projects, and became interested in the "alterations" which she visited daily. Often she lingered long in the garden at Neuilly, where Alain, when he came back from the dark offices of Amparat et Fils in the Rue des Petits-Champs, would find her idle, ready to prolong the afternoon and drive along the hot roads.

Then his mood would darken. He would listen to her giving orders to the singing painters and the distant electricians. She would question him in a general, peremptory way as if, as soon as he was there, it was her duty to renounce her new gentleness.

"Business going all right? Crisis still expected? Have you managed to put over the spotted foulard[29] on the big dress-houses?"

She did not even respect old Émile, whom she shook until he let fall certain formulas pregnant with oracular imbecility.

"What do you think of our shanty, Émile? Have you ever seen the house looking so nice?"

29. A light silk fabric.

Between his whiskers, the old butler muttered answers as shallow and colorless as himself.

"You wouldn't know the place any more. Had anyone told me, in the old days, that this house would be divided up into little compartments . . . There's certainly a difference. It will be very nice being so near each other, very gay."

Or else, drop by drop, he poured a stream of blessings over Alain, blessings in which there was an under-current of hostility.

"Monsieur Alain's young lady is beginning to look ever so well. What a fine voice she has. When she's speaking loud, the neighbors can hear every word. You can't deny she has a splendid voice but . . . The young lady speaks her mind all right. She told the gardener that the bed of pink silene and forget-me-not looked cuckoo. I still have to laugh when I think of it."

And he raised his pale, oyster-colored eyes, which had never laughed in their life, to the pure sky. Alain did not laugh either. He was worried about Saha. She was getting thinner and seemed to have given up a hope; undoubtedly the hope of seeing Alain every day again—and alone. She no longer ran away when Camille arrived. But she did not escort Alain to the gate and, when he sat by her, she looked at him with a profound and bitter wisdom. "Her look when she was a little cat behind the bars. The same, same look." He called her very softly: "Saha . . . Saha . . ." strongly aspirating the "H's." But she did not jump or flatten her ears and it was days since she had given her insistent. "Me-rrang"! or the "Mouck-mouck-mouck" of good humor and greed.

One day, when he and Camille had been summoned to Neuilly to be informed that the enormous, heavy, new sunk bath would cave in the tiled platform supporting it, he heard his wife sigh: "It'll never be finished!"

"But," he said, surprised, "I thought you really much preferred the Wedge with its petrels and cormorants."[30]

"Yes. But all the same . . . And after all it's your house here, your real house. *Our* house."

She leaned on his arm, rather limp and unusually hesitant. The bluish whites of her eyes, amost as blue as her light summer dress; the unnecessary but admirable make-up of her cheeks and mouth and eyelids did not move him in the least.

Nevertheless, it seemed to him that, for the first time, she was asking his advice without speaking. "Camille here with me. So soon! Camille in pajamas under the rose trellis." One of the oldest climbing roses carried its load of flowers, which faded as soon as they opened, as high as his head and their oriental scent dominated the garden in the evening; he could smell it where they stood by the steps. "Camille in a bathrobe under the screen of elms.

30. Sea birds.

Wouldn't it be better, all things considered, to keep her shut away in the little gazebo[31] of the Wedge? Not here, not here . . . not yet."

The June evening, drenched with light, was reluctant to give way to darkness. Some empty glasses on a wicker table were still attracting the big orange bumble-bees but, under all the trees except the pines, an area of impalpable damp was growing, bringing a promise of coolness. Neither the rose geraniums, so prodigal of their southern scent upon the air, nor the fiery poppies suffered from the fierce onslaught of summer. "Not here, not here." Alain repeated to the rhythm of his own footsteps. He was looking for Saha and did not want to call her out loud. He found her lying on the little low wall which buttressed a blue knoll covered with lobelias.[32] She was asleep, or appeared to be asleep, curled up in a ball. "Curled up in a ball? At this time and in this weather? Sleeping curled up like this is a winter position!"

"Saha darling!"

She did not quiver as he picked her up and held her in the air. She only opened two hollow eyes, very beautiful and almost indifferent.

"Heavens, how light you are! But you're ill, my little puma!"

He carried her off and ran back to his mother and Camille.

"But Mother, Saha's ill! Her coat's shocking—she weighs next to nothing—and you never told me!"

"It's because she eats nothing," said Mme. Amparat. "She refuses to eat."

"She doesn't eat? And what else?"

He cradled the cat against his chest and Saha abandoned herself to him. Her breathing was shallow and her nostrils dry. Mme. Amparat's eyes, under the thick, white waves, glanced intelligently at Camille.

"Nothing else," she said.

"She's bored with you," said Camille. "After all she's your cat, isn't she?"

He thought she was laughing at him and raised his head defiantly. But Camille's face had not changed and she was seriously examining Saha, who shut her eyes again as soon as touched by her.

"Feel her ears," said Alain sharply. "They're burning."

In an instant, his mind was made up.

"Right. I'm taking her with me. Mother, get them to fetch me her basket, will you? And a sack of sand for the tray. We've got everything else she needs. You understand I simply couldn't bear . . . This cat believes . . ."

He broke off and turned belatedly to his wife.

31. A pavilion with a view.   flowers.
32. A low plant with small blue

"It won't worry you, Camille, if I take Saha while we're waiting to come back here?"

"What a question! But where do you propose to put her at night?" she added so naïvely that Alain blushed because of his mother's presence and answered acridly: "That's for her to decide."

They left in a little procession; Alain carrying Saha, mute in her traveling-basket. Old Émile was bowed under the sack full of sand and Camille brought up the rear, bearing an old frayed kasha traveling rug which Alain called the Kashasaha.

SIX

"No, I never thought a cat would get acclimatized so quickly."

"A cat's merely a cat. But Saha's Saha."

Alain was proudly doing the honors of Saha. He himself had never kept her so close at hand, imprisoned in twenty-five square meters and visible at all hours. For her feline meditation, for her craving for solitude and shadow, she was reduced to withdrawing under the giant armchairs scattered about the studio or into the miniature hall or into one of the built-in wardrobes camouflaged with mirrors.

But Saha was determined to triumph over all obstacles. She accepted the uncertain times of meals and of getting up and going to bed. She chose the bathroom with its cork-topped stool to sleep in and she explored the Wedge with no affectation of wildness or disgust. In the kitchen, she condescended to listen to the lazy voice of Mme. Buque summoning "the pussy" to raw liver. When Alain and Camille went out, she installed herself on the giddy parapet and gazed into the abysses of air, following the flying backs of swallows and sparrows below her with a calm, untroubled eye. Her impassiveness on the edge of a sheer drop of nine storeys and the habit she had of washing herself at length on the parapet, terrified Camille.

"Stop her," she yelled to Alain. "She makes my heart turn over and gives me cramp in my calves."

Alain gave an unperturbed smile and admired his cat who had recovered her taste for food and life.

It was not that she was blooming or particularly gay. She did not recover the iridescence of her fur that had gleamed like a pigeon's mauve plumage. But she was more alive; she waited for the dull "poom" of the lift which brought up Alain and accepted extra attentions from Camille, such as a tiny saucer of milk at five o'clock or a small chicken bone offered high up, as if to a dog who was expected to jump for it.

"Not like that! Not like that!" scolded Alain.

And he would lay the bone on a bathmat or simply on the thick-piled beige carpet.

"Really . . . on Patrick's carpet!" Camille scolded in turn.

"But a cat can't eat a bone or any solid food on a polished surface. When a cat takes a bone off a plate and puts it down on the carpet before eating it, she's told she's dirty. But the cat needs to hold it down with her paw while she crunches and tears it and she can only do it on bare earth or on a carpet. People don't know that."

Amazed, Camille broke in: "And how do *you* know?"

He had never asked himself that and got out of it by a joke: "Hush! It's because I'm extremely intelligent. Don't tell a soul. M. Veuillet hasn't a notion of it."

He taught her all the ways and habits of the cat, like a foreign language over-rich in subtle shades of meaning. In spite of himself, he spoke with emphatic authority as he taught. Camille observed him narrowly and asked him any number of questions which he answered unreservedly.

"Why does the cat play with a piece of string when she's frightened of the big ship's rope?"

"Because the ship's rope is the snake. It's the thickness of a snake. She's afraid of snakes."

"Has she ever seen a snake?"

Alain looked at his wife with the gray-green, black-lashed eyes she found so beautiful . . . "So treacherous" she said.

"No . . . certainly not. Where could she have seen one?"

"Well, then?"

"Well, then she invents one. She creates one. You'd be frightened of snakes too, even if you'd never seen one."

"Yes, but I've been told about them. I've seen them in pictures. I know they exist."

"So does Saha."

"But how?"

He gave her a haughty smile.

"How? But by her birth, like persons of quality."

"So I'm not a person of quality?"

He softened, but only out of compassion.

"Good Heavens, no. Console yourself: I'm not either. Don't you believe what I tell you?"

Camille, sitting at her husband's feet, contemplated him with her wildest eyes, the eyes of the little girl of other days who did not want to say "How d'you do?"

"I'd better believe it," she said gravely.

They took to dining at home nearly every night, because of the heat, said Alain, "and because of Saha" insinuated Camille. One evening after dinner, Saha was sitting on her friend's knee.

"What about me?" said Camille.

"I've two knees," Alain retorted.

Nevertheless, the cat did not use her privilege for long. Some mysterious warning made her return to the polished ebony table where she seated herself on her own bluish reflection immersed in a dusky pool. There was nothing unusual about her behavior except the fixed attention she gave to the invisible things straight in front of her in the air.

"What's she looking at?" asked Camille.

She was pretty every evening at that particular hour; wearing white pajamas, her hair half loosened on her forehead and her cheeks very brown under the layers of powder she had been super-imposing since the morning. Alain sometimes kept on his summer suit, without a waistcoat, but Camille laid impatient hands on him, taking off his jacket and tie, opening his collar and rolling up his shirt-sleeves, seeking and displaying the bare skin. He treated her as a hussy, letting her do as she wished. She laughed a little unhappily as she contained her feelings. And it was he who lowered his eyes with an anxiety that was not entirely voluptuous. "What ravages of desire on that face! Her mouth is quite distorted with it. A young wife who's so *very* young. Who taught her to forestall me like that?"

The round table, flanked by a little trolley on rubber wheels, gathered the three of them together at the entrance to the studio, near the open bay window. Three tall old poplars, relics of a beauti-ful garden that had been destroyed, waved their tops at the height of the balcony and the great setting sun of Paris, dark red and smothered in mists, was going down behind their lean heads from which the sap was retreating.

Mme. Buque's dinner—she cooked food well and served it badly—enlivened the hour. Refreshed, Alain forgot his day and the Amparat office and the tutelage of M. Veuillet. His two captives in the glass tower made a fuss of him. "Were you waiting for me?" he murmured in Saha's ear.

"I heard you coming!" cried Camille. "One can hear every sound from here!"

"Have you been bored?" he asked her one evening, fearing that she was going to complain. But she shook her black mop in denial.

"Not the least bit in the world. I went over to Mummy's. She's presented me with the treasure."

"What treasure?"

"The little woman who'll be my maid over there. Provided old Émile doesn't give her a baby. She's quite attractive."

She laughed as she rolled up her white crêpe sleeves over her bare arms before she cut open the red-fleshed melon round which Saha was tiptoeing. But Alain did not laugh: he was too taken up with the horror of imagining a new maid in his house.

"Yes? But do you remember," he brought out, "my mother's

never changed her servants since I was a child."

"That's obvious," said Camille trenchantly. "What a museum of old crocks!"

She was biting into a crescent of melon as she spoke and laughing, with her face to the setting sun. Alain admired, in a detached way, how vivid a certain cannibal radiance could be in those glittering eyes and on the glittering teeth in the narrow mouth. There was something Italian about her regular features. He made one more effort to be considerate.

"You never see your girl friends nowadays, it seems to me. Mightn't you perhaps . . ."

She took him up fiercely.

"And what girl friends, may I ask? Is this your way of telling me I'm a burden on you? So that I shall give you a little breathing space. That's it, isn't it?"

He raised his eyebrows and clicked his tongue "tst . . . tst." She yielded at once with a plebeian respect for the man's disdain.

"It's quite true. I never had any friends when I was a little girl. And now . . . can you see me with a girl who's not married. Either I'd have to treat her as a child or I'd have to answer all her dirty questions: 'And what does one do *here* and how does he do *that* to you!' Girls," she explained with some bitterness, "girls don't stick together decently. There's no solidarity. It's not like all you men."

"Forgive me! I'm not one of 'all-you-men'!"

"Oh, I know that all right," she said sadly. "Sometimes I wonder if I wouldn't rather . . ."

She was very rarely sad and, when she was, it was because of some secret reticence or some doubt that she did not express.

"*You* haven't any friends either," she went on. "Except Patrick and he's away. And even Patrick, you don't really care a damn about him."

She broke off at a gesture from Alain.

"Don't let's talk about these things," she said intelligently. "There'll only be a quarrel."

The long-drawn-out cries of children rose from the ground level and blended with the airy whistling of the swallows. Saha's beautiful yellow eyes, in which the great nocturnal pupil was slowly invading the iris, stared into space, picking out moving, floating, invisible points.

"Tell me, whatever's the cat looking at? Are you sure there's nothing, over there where she's staring?"

"Nothing . . . for us."

Alain evoked with regret the faint shiver, the seductive fear that his cat friend used to communicate to him in the days when she slept on his chest at night.

"She doesn't make you frightened, I hope?" he said condescendingly.

Camille burst out laughing, as if the insulting word were just what she had been waiting for.

"Frightened? There aren't many things that frighten *me*, you know!"

"That's the statement of a silly little fool," said Alain angrily.

"Let's say you're feeling the storm coming, shall we?" said Camille, shrugging her shoulders.

She pointed to the wall, purpled with clouds which were coming up with the night.

"And you're like Saha," she added. "You don't like storms."

"No one likes storms."

"I don't hate them," said Camille judicially. "Anyway, I'm not the slightest bit afraid of them."

"The whole world is afraid of storms," said Alain, hostile.

"All right, I'm not the whole world, that's all."

"You are for me," he said with a sudden, artificial grace which did not deceive her.

"Oh!" she scolded under her breath. "I shall hit you."

He bent his fair head towards her over the table and showed his white teeth.

"All right, hit me!"

But she deprived herself of the pleasure of rumpling that golden hair and offering her bare arm to those shining teeth.

"You've got a crooked nose," she flung at him fiercely.

"It's the storm," he said, laughing.

This subtlety was not at all to Camille's taste, but the first low rumblings of the thunder distracted her attention. She threw down her napkin to run out on the balcony.

"Come along! There'll be some marvellous lightning."

"No," said Alain, without moving. "Come along, yourself."

"Where to?"

He jerked his chin in the direction of their room. Camille's face assumed the obstinate expression, the dull-witted greed he knew so well. Nevertheless, she hesitated.

"But couldn't we look at the lightning first?"

He made a sign of refusal.

"Why not, horrid?"

"Because *I'm* frightened of storms. Choose. The storm or . . . me."

"What do you think!"

She ran to their room with an eagerness which flattered Alain's vanity. But, when he joined her there, he found she had deliberately lighted a luminous glass cube near the vast bed. He deliberately turned it out.

The rain came in through the open bay-windows as they lay calm again, warm and tingling, breathing in the ozone that filled the room with freshness. Lying in Alain's arms, Camille made him understand that, while the storm raged, she would have liked him once gain to forget his terror of it with her. But he was nervously counting the great sheets of lightning and the tall dazzling trees silhouetted against the cloud and he moved away from Camille. She resigned herself, raised herself on her elbow and combed her husband's crackling hair with one hand. In the pulsations of the lightning-flashes their two blue plaster faces rose out of the night and were swallowed up in it again.

"We'll wait till the storm's over," she consented.

"And *that*," said Alain to himself, "*that*'s what she finds to say after an encounter that really means something. She might at least have kept quiet. As Emile says, the young lady speaks her mind straight out."

A flickering flash, long as a dream, was reflected in a blade of fire in the thick slab of glass on the invisible dressing-table. Camille clutched Alain against her bare leg.

"Is that to reassure me? We know you're not frightened of lightning."

He raised his voice so as to be heard above the hollow rumbling and the rain cascading on the flat roof. He felt tired and on edge, tempted to be unjust yet frightened to say openly that nowadays he was never alone. In his mind he returned violently to his old room with its white wallpaper patterned with stiff conventional flowers, a room which no one had ever tried to make prettier or uglier. His longing for it was so fierce that the murmur of the inefficient old radiator came back with the memory of the pale flowers on the wallpaper. The wheezy mutter that came from the hollow space below its copper pipes seemed to be part of the murmurs of the whole house; of the whispering of the worn old servants, half-buried in their basement, who no longer cared to go out even into the garden. . . . "They used to say 'She' when they talked about my mother but I've been 'Monsieur Alain' since I first went into knickerbockers."[33]

A dry crackle of thunder roused him from the brief doze into which he had fallen. His young wife, leaning over him, propped on her elbow, had not stirred.

"I like you so much when you're asleep," she said. "The storm's going off."

He took this as a demand and sat up.

"I'm following its example," he said. "How hot and sticky it is! I'm going to sleep on the waiting-room bench."

33. Knee-length pants, a boy's costume.

The "waiting-room bench" was their name for the narrow divan which was the solitary piece of furniture in a tiny room, a mere strip of glass-walled passage which Patrick used for sunbathing.

"Oh, no! Oh, no!" implored Camille. "Do stay."

But he had already slipped out of the bed. The great flashes in the clouds revealed Camille's hard, offended face.

"Pooh! Baby boy!"

At this, which he was not expecting, she pulled his nose. With an instinctive reflex of his arm, which he could not control and did not regret, he beat down the disrespectful hand. A sudden lull in the wind and rain left them alone in the silence, as if struck dumb. Camille massaged her hand.

"But . . ." she said at last, "But . . . you're a brute."

"Possibly," said Alain. "I don't like having my face touched. Isn't the rest of me enough for you! Never touch my face."

"But you *are* . . . you really *are* a brute," Camille repeated slowly.

"Don't keep on saying it. Apart from that, I've nothing against you. Just mind you don't do it again."

He lifted his bare leg back on to the bed.

"You see that big gray square on the carpet? It's nearly daybreak. Shall we go to sleep?"

"Yes. . . let's . . ." said the same, hesitant voice.

"Come on, then!"

He stretched out his left arm so that she could rest her head on it. She did so submissively and with a circumspect politeness. Pleased with himself, Alain gave her a friendly jostle and pulled her towards him by her shoulder. But he bent his knees a little to keep her at a safe distance and fell asleep almost at once. Camille lay awake, breathing carefully, and watched the gray patch on the carpet growing lighter. She listened to the sparrows celebrating the end of the storm in the three poplars whose rustling sounded like the faint continuation of the rain. When Alain, changing his position, withdrew his arm, he gave her an unconscious caress. Three times his hand slid lightly over her head as if accustomed to stroking fur that was even softer than her soft black hair.

SEVEN

It was towards the end of June that incompatibility became established between them like a new season of the year. Like a season, it had its surprises and even its pleasures. To Alain, it was like a harsh, chilly spring inserted in the heart of summer. He was incessantly and increasingly aware of his repugnance at the idea of making a place for this young woman, this outsider, in his own home. He nursed this resentment and fed it with secret soliloquies and the sullen contemplation of their new dwelling. Camille, exhausted with the heat, called out from the high and now windless balcony: "Oh, let's chuck everything. Let's take the old scooter and go somewhere where we can bathe. Shall we, Alain?"

"All right by me," he answered with wily promptitude. "Where shall we go?"

There was a peaceful interlude while Camille enumerated beaches and names of hotels. With his eye on Saha who lay flat and prostrated, Alain had the leisure to think and to conclude: "I don't want to go away with her I . . . I daren't. I'm quite willing to go for a drive, as we used to, and come back in the evening or late at night. But that's all. I don't want evenings in hotels and nights in a casino, evenings of . . ." He shuddered: "I need time. I realize that I take a long time to get used to things, that I'm a difficult character, that . . . But I don't want to go off with *her*." He felt a pang of shame as he realized that he had mentally said *"her"* just like Emile and Adele when they were discussing "Madame" in undertones.

Camille bought road maps and they played at traveling through a France spread in quarters over the polished ebony table which reflected their two blurred, inverted faces.

They added up the mileage, ran down their car, cursed each other affably and felt revived, even rehabilitated by a comradeship they had forgotten. But tropical showers, unaccompanied by gales, drowned the last days of June and the balconies of the Wedge. Sheltering behind the closed panes, Saha watched the level rivulets, which Camille mopped up by stamping on table-napkins, winding across the inlaid tiles. The horizon; the city; the shower itself; all took on the color of clouds loaded with inexhaustible rain.

"Would you rather we took the train?" suggested Alain suavely.

He had foreseen that Camille would fly out at the detested word. Fly out she did indeed—and blasphemously.

"I'm afraid," he went on, "that you're getting bored. All those trips we'd promised ourselves."

"All those summer hotels. All those restaurants full of flies. All those seas full of people bathing; she railed plaintively. "Look here, you and I are quite used to driving around. But what we're good at is just going for drives. We're quite lost when it comes to a real journey."

He saw that she was slightly depressed and gave her a brotherly kiss. But she turned round and bit him on his mouth and under his ear. Once again, they fell into the diversion which shortens the hours and makes the body attain its pleasure easily. It was beginning to make Alain tired. When he dined at his mother's with Camille and had to stifle his yawns, Mme. Amparat lowered her eyes and Camille invariably gave a little, swaggering laugh. For she was proudly conscious of the habit Alain had acquired of making love to her hurriedly and almost peevishly, flinging her away the moment it was over to return to the cool side of the uncovered bed.

Ingenuously, she would rejoin him there and he did not forgive her for that although, silently, he would yield again. After that he felt at liberty to probe at leisure into the sources of what he called their incompatibility. He was wise enough to put these outside their frequent lovemaking. Clear-headed, helped by the very fact of his sexual exhaustion, he returned to those retreats where the hostility of man to woman keeps its unaging freshness. Sometimes she revealed herself to him in some commonplace realm where she slept in broad sunshine, like an innocent creature. Sometimes he was astonished, even scandalized, that she should be so dark. Lying in bed behind her, he surveyed the short hairs on her shaved neck, ranged like the prickles of a sea-urchin and drawn on the skin like the hatching on a map. The shortest of them were blue and visible under the fine skin before each one emerged through a small blackened pore.

"Have I never really had a dark woman?" he wondered. "Two or three little black-haired things haven't left me any impression of *such* darkness." And he held his own arm up to the light. It was yellowish-white; a typical fair man's arm with green-gold down and jade-colored veins. His own hair seemed to him like a forest with violet shadows, whereas Camille's showed the strange whiteness of the skin between the exotic abundance of those ranks of black, slightly crinkled stalks.

The sight of a fine, very black hair stuck to the side of a basin made him feel sick. Then the little neurosis changed and, abandoning the detail, he concentrated on her whole body. Holding that young, appeased body in his arms in the night which hid its contours he began to be annoyed that a creative spirit, in moulding Camille, had shown a strict reasonableness like that of his English nurse. "Not more prunes than rice, my boy," she used to say. "Not more rice than chicken." That spirit had modelled Camille adequately but with no concessions to lavishness or fantasy. He carried his annoyances and regrets into the antechamber of his dreams during that incalculable moment reserved for the black landscape peopled with bulbous eyes, fish with Greek noses, moons and chins. There he desired a big-hipped charmer of the 1900 type, liberally developed above a tiny waist, to compensate for the acid smallness of Camille's breasts. At other times, half asleep, he compromised and preferred a top-heavy bosom; two quivering, monstrous hillocks of flesh with sensitive tips. Such feverish desires, which were born of the sexual act and survived it, never affronted the light of day nor even complete wakefulness. They merely peopled a narrow isthmus between nightmare and voluptuous dream.

When her flesh was warm, the "foreigner" smelt of wood licked by tongues of flame; birch, violets . . . a whole bouquet of sweet, dark, tenacious scents which clung long to the palms. These fragrances produced in Alain a kind of perverse excitement but did not always arouse his desire.

"You're like the smell of roses," he said one day to Camille, "you take away one's appetite."

She looked at him dubiously and assumed the slightly gauche, downcast expression with which she received double-edged compliments.

"How awfully eighteen-thirty you are," she murmured.

"You're much more so," replied Alain. "Oh, ever so much more so. I know who you're like."

"Marie Dubas,[34] the actress. I've been told that before."

"Hopelessly wrong, my girl! Minus the bandeaux,[35] you're like all those girls who weep on the tops of towers in the works of Loïsa Puget.[36] You can see them weeping on the cover of his romantic songs, with *your* great, prominent Greek eyes and those thick rims to the lower lid that makes the tears jump down on to the cheeks . . ."

One after another, Alain's senses took advantage of him to condemn Camille. He had to admit, at least, that she stood up admirably to certain remarks he fired at her point-blank. They were provocative rather than grateful remarks that burst out of him at the times when, lying on the floor, he measured her with narrowed eyes and appraised her new merits without indulgence or regard for her feelings. He judged her particular aptitudes; he noted how that sensual ardor of hers, that slightly monotonous passion, had already developed an enlightened self-interest remarkable in so young a married woman. Those were moments of frankness and certainty and Camille did all she could to prolong their half silent atmosphere of conflict; their tension like that of a tight-rope on which balance was precarious and dangerous.

Having no deep-seated malice in herself, Camille never suspected that Alain was only half taken in by deliberate challenges, pathetic appeals and even by a cool Polynesian cynicism, and that each time he possessed his wife, he meant it to be the last. He mastered her as he might have put a hand on her mouth to stop her from screaming or as he might have murdered her.

When she was dressed again and sitting upright beside him in their roadster, he could look at her closely without rediscovering what it was that had made her his worst enemy. As soon as he regained his breath, listening to his decreasing heartbeats, he ceased to be the dramatic young man who stripped himself naked before wrestling with his companion and overthrowing her. The brief rou-

34. French singer popular in the 1920s; she sang in the principal music halls like the Olympia or the Casino de Paris.

35. Headbands.

36. French composer (1810–1889) of two comic operas and a number of romances that she sang in salons around 1830.

tine of pleasure; the controlled expert movements, the real or simulated gratitude were relegated to the ranks of what is over, of what will probably never happen again. Then his greatest preoccupation would return, the one which he accepted as natural and honorable, the question which reassumed the first place it had so long deserved: "How to stop Camille from living in MY house?"

Once this period of hostility towards the "alterations" had passed, he had genuinely put his faith in the return to the home of his childhood, in the tranquilizing influence of a life on ground level; a life in contact with the earth and everything the earth brings forth. "Here, I'm suffering from living up in the air. Oh, to see branches and birds from *underneath* again!" he sighed. But he concluded severely "Pastoral life is no solution," and once more had recourse to his indispensable ally, the lie.

On a blazing afternoon which melted the asphalt he went to his domain. All about it, Neuilly was a desert of the empty roads and empty tramways[37] of July; the gardens were abandoned except for a few yawning dogs. Before leaving Camille, he had installed Saha on the coolest balcony of the Wedge. He was vaguely worried every time he left his two females alone together.

The garden and the house were asleep and the little iron gate did not creak as he opened it. Overblown roses, red poppies, the first ruby-throated Canna lilies and dark snap-dragons burned in isolated clumps on the lawns. At the side of the house gaped the new doorway and two new windows in a freshly painted little one-storey building. "It's all finished," Alain realized. He walked carefully, as he did in his dreams, and trod only on the grass.

Hearing the murmur of a voice rising from the basement, he stopped and absent-mindedly listened. It was only the old well-known voices of servility and ritual grumbling, the old voices which used to say "She" and "Monsieur Alain." Once upon a time they had flattered the fragile, fair-haired little boy and his childish pride . . . "I was a king, once," Alain said to himself, smiling sadly.

"Well, so *she'll* soon be coming to sleep here, I suppose?" one of the old voices asked audibly.

"That's Adèle," thought Alain. Leaning against the wall, he listened without the least scruple.

"Of course she will," bleated Émile. "That flat's shockingly badly built."

The housemaid, a graying Basque[38] woman with a hairy face, broke in: "You're right there. From their bathroom you can hear everything that goes on in the water-closet.[39] Monsieur Alain won't like *that*."

37. Streetcar tracks.
38. Of a people inhabiting the western Pyrenée mountains between France and Spain.
39. Toilet room—not necessarily including a bath.

"*She* said, the last time *she* came that *she* didn't need curtains in her little drawing-room because there are no neighbors on the garden side."

"No neighbors? What about us when we go to the wash-house? What's one going to see when *she's* with Monsieur Alain?"

Alain could guess the smothered laughter and the ancient Émile continued: "Oh, perhaps one won't see as much as all *that*. *She*'ll be put in her place, all right. Monsieur Alain's not the sort to let himself go on a sofa at any time of day or night."

There was a silence during which Alain could hear nothing but the sound of a knife on the grindstone. But he stayed listening, with his back against the hot wall and his eyes vaguely searching between a flaming geranium and the acid green of the turf as if he half-expected to see Saha's moonstone-colored fur.

"As for me," said Adèle, "I think it's oppressive, that scent *she* puts on."

"And her frocks," supplemented Juliette, the Basque woman. "The way she dresses isn't really good style. *She* looks more like an actress. Behaves like one too, with that brazen way of hers. And now what's she going to land us with in the way of a lady's maid? Some creature out of an orphanage, I believe, or worse."

A fanlight[40] slammed and the voices were cut off. Alain felt weak and trembling. He breathed like a man who has just been spared by a gang of murderers. He was neither surprised nor indignant. There was not much difference between his own opinion of Camille and that of the harsh judges in the basement. But his heart was beating fast because he had meanly eavesdropped without being punished for it and because he had been listening to prejudiced witnesses and unsought accomplices. He wiped his face and took a deep breath as if inhaling this gust of misogyny, this pagan incense offered exclusively to the male principle, had anesthetized him. His mother, who had just wakened from her siesta and was putting back the shutters of her room, saw him standing there, with his cheek still leant against the wall.

She called softly, like a wise mother.

"Ah! my boy . . . . Is anything the matter?"

He took her hands over the window-sill, like a lover.

"Nothing at all. I was out for a walk and just thought I'd look in."

"A very good idea."

She did not believe him but they smiled at each other, perfectly aware that neither was telling the truth.

"Mother, could I ask you to do me a little favor?"

"A little favor in the way of money, isn't that it? I know you're none too well off this year, my poor children."

40. Transom window.

"No, Mother. Please, would you mind not telling Camille that I came here today? As I didn't come here for any special reason, I mean with no special reason except just to look in and give you a kiss. I'd rather . . . Actually, that's not all. I want you to give me some advice. Strictly between the two of us, you know."

Mme. Amparat lowered her eyes, ran her hand through her wavy white hair, and tried to avert the confidence.

"I'm not much of a talker, as you know. You've caught me all untidy. I look like an old gipsy. Won't you come inside into the cool?"

"No, Mother. Do you think there's any way . . . it's an idea I can't get out of my head . . . a polite way, of course . . . something that wouldn't offend anyone . . . but some way of stopping Camille from living here?"

He seized his mother's hands, expecting them to tremble or to draw away. But they stayed, cold and soft, between his own.

"These are just a young husband's ideas," she said, embarrassed. "What do you mean?"

"With young married couples, things go too well or they go too badly. I don't know which works out best in the end. But they never go straightforwardly, just for their own accord."

"But, Mother, that's not what I'm asking you. I'm asking you whether there isn't any way . . ."

For the first time, he was unable to look his mother in the face. She gave him no help and he turned away irritably.

"You're talking like a child. You run about the streets in this frightful heat and you come to me after a quarrel and ask me impossible questions. I don't know. Questions whose only answer is divorce. Or moving house. Or heaven knows what."

She got breathless whenever she talked and Alain only reproached himself for making her flush and pant even at saying so little. "That's enough for today," he thought prudently.

"We haven't had a quarrel, Mother. It's only I who can't get used to the idea . . . who doesn't want to see . . ."

With a wide, embarrassed gesture, he indicated the garden that surrounded them: the green lake of the lawn; the bed of fallen petals under the rose arches; a swarm of bees over the flowering ivy; the ugly, revered house.

The hand he had kept in one of his clenched and hardened into a little fist and he suddenly kissed that sensitive hand: "Enough, that's enough for today."

"I'm off now, Mother. Monsieur Veuillet's telephoning you at eight tomorrow about this business of the shares going down. Do I look better now, Mother?"

He raised his eyes that looked greener in the shade of the tulip-tree and threw back his face which from habit, affection, and diplomacy he had forced into his old childish expression. A flutter of the lids to brighten the eye, the seductive smile, a little pout of the lips. His mother's hand unclenched again and reached over the sill to feel Alain's well-known weak spots; his shoulder-blades, his Adam's apple, the top of his arm. She did all this before replying.

"A little better. Yes, really, quite a lot better."

"I've pleased her by asking her to keep something secret from Camille." At the remembrance of his mother's last caress, he tightened his belt under his jacket. "I've got thinner, I'm getting thinner. No more physical culture—no physical culture other than making love."

He went off with a light step, in his summer clothes, and the cooling breeze dried his sweat and blew the acrid smell of it ahead of him. He left his native castle inviolate, his subterranean cohort intact, and the rest of the day would pass easily enough. Until midnight, no doubt, sitting in the car beside an inoffensive Camille, he would drink in the evening air, now sylvan as they drove between oak plantations edged with muddy ditches, now dry and smelling of wheatstraw. "And I'll bring back some fresh couch-grass for Saha."

Vehemently, he reproached himself for the lot of his cat who lived so soundlessly at the top of their glass tower. "She's like her own chrysalis, and it's my fault." At the hour of their conjugal games she banished herself so rigorously that Alain had never seen her in the triangular room. She ate just sufficient to keep alive; she had lost her varied language and given up all her demands, seeming to prefer her long waiting to everything else. "Once again, she's waiting behind bars. She's waiting for me."

Camille's shattering voice came through the closed door as he reached the landing.

"It's that filthy bloody swine of an animal! I wish it were dead! What? No, Madame Buque, I don't care what you say. To hell with it! To hell with it!"

He made out a few more violent expressions. Very softly he turned the key in the lock but, once over his own threshold, he could not consent to listen without being seen. "A filthy bloody swine of an animal? But what animal? An animal in the house?"

In the studio Camille, wearing a little sleeveless pullover and a knitted béret miraculously balanced on her skull, was furiously pulling a pair of gauntlet gloves over her bare hands. She seemed stupefied at the sight of her husband.

"It's you! Where have you sprung from?"

"I haven't sprung from anywhere. I've simply arrived home. Who are you so furious with?"

She avoided the trap and neatly turned the attack on Alain.

"You're very cutting, the first time you get home punctually. *I'm* ready. I've been waiting for you."

"You haven't been waiting for me since I'm punctual to the minute. Who were you so angry with? I heard 'filthy bloody swine of an animal?' What animal?"

She squinted very slightly but sustained Alain's look.

"The dog!" she cried. "That damned dog downstairs, the dog that barks morning, noon, and night. It's started again! Can't you hear it barking? Listen!"

She raised her finger to make him keep quiet and Alain had time to notice that the gloved finger was shaking. He yielded to a naïve need to make sure.

"Just fancy, I thought you were talking about Saha."

"Me?" cried Camille. "Me speak about Saha in that tone? Why I wouldn't dare! The heavens would fall if I did! For goodness' sake, are you coming?"

"Go and get the car out. I'll join you down below. I've just got to get a handkerchief and a pullover."

His first thought was to find the cat. On the coolest balcony, near the deck-chair in which Camille occasionally slept in the afternoon, he could see nothing but some fragments of broken glass. He stared at them blankly.

"The cat's with me, Monsieur," came the fluting voice of Mme. Buque. "She's very fond of my wicker stool. She sharpens her claws on it."

"In the kitchen," thought Alain painfully. "My little puma, my cat of the garden, my cat of the lilacs and the butterflies, in the kitchen! Ah! All that's going to change!"

He kissed Saha on the forehead and chanted some ritual praises, very low. He promised her couch-grass and sweet acacia flowers. But he found both the cat and Mme. Buque artificial and constrained; Mme. Buque in particular.

"We may be back to dinner and we may not, Madame Buque. Has the cat everything she needs?"

"Yes, Monsieur. Oh yes, indeed, Monsieur," said Mme. Buque hurriedly. "I do everything I possibly can, really I do, Monsieur!"

The big, fat woman was red in the face and seemed on the verge of tears. She ran a friendly, clumsy hand over the cat's back. Saha arched her back and proffered a little "m'hain," the mew of a poor timid cat which made her friend's heart swell with sadness.

The drive was more peaceful than he had hoped. Sitting at the wheel, her eyes alert, her feet and hands perfectly synchronized, Camille drove him as far as the slope of Montfort-l'Amaurey.[41]

"Shall we have dinner out-of-doors, Alain? Shall we, Alain, darling?"

---

41. A small medieval town in the northern part of the great forest of Rambouillet, southwest of Paris.

She smiled at him in profile, beautiful as she always was in the twilight; her cheek brown and transparent, her teeth and the corner of her eye the same glittering white. In the forest of Rambouillet, she put down the windscreen and the wind filled Alain's ears with a sound of leaves and running water.

"A little rabbit! . . ." cried Camille. "A pheasant!"

"It's still a rabbit . . . One moment more and I . . ."

"He doesn't know his luck, that chap!"

"You've got a dimple in your cheek like you have in your photos as a child," said Alain, beginning to come to life.

"Don't talk about it! I'm getting enormous!" she said, shaking her shoulders.

He watched for the return of the laugh and the dimple, and his eyes wandered down to the robust neck, free of any trace of the "girdle of Venus," the round, inflexible neck of a handsome white Negress. "Yes, she really has got fatter. And in the most seductive way. For her breasts, those too . . ." He withdrew into himself once more and came up, morosely, against the age-old male grievance. "She's getting fat from making love. She's battening on *me*." He slipped a jealous hand under his jacket, felt his ribs, and ceased to admire the childish dimple in her cheeks.

But he felt a certain gratified vanity when they sat down a little later at a famous inn and the neighboring diners stopped talking and eating to stare at Camille. And he exchanged with his wife the smiles, the movements of the chin and all the rituals of coquetry suitable to a "handsome couple."

However, it was only for him that Camille lowered her voice and displayed a certain languor and certain charming attentions which were not in the least for show. In revenge, Alain snatched out of her hand the dish of raw tomatoes and the basket of strawberries, insisted that she ate chicken with a cream sauce, and poured her out a wine which she did not care for but which she drank fast.

"You know perfectly well I don't like wine," she repeated each time she emptied her glass.

The sun had set but the sky was still almost white, dappled with small deep-pink clouds. But night and coolness seemed to be rising as one from the forest which loomed, massive beyond the tables of the inn. Camille laid her hand on Alain's.

"What is it? What is it? What's the matter?" he said in terror.

Astonished, she withdrew her hand. The little wine she had drunk gleamed gaily in her eyes in which shone the tiny, quivering image of the pink balloons hung from the pergola.

"Nothing's the matter, silly. You're as nervous as a cat! Is it forbidden for me to put my hand on yours?"

"I thought," he admitted weakly, "I thought you wanted to tell me something . . . something serious . . . I thought," he burst out with it, "you were going to tell me you were pregnant."

Camille's shrill little laugh attracted the attention of the men at the near-by tables.

"And you were as overcome as all that? With joy or . . . fed-up-ness?"

"I don't exactly know. What about you? Would you be pleased or not pleased? We've hardly thought about it . . . at least, *I* haven't. But what are you laughing at?"

"Your face! All of a sudden, a face as if you were just going to be hanged. It's too funny. You'll make my eye-black come unstuck."

With her two forefingers, she lifted up either eyelid.

"It isn't funny, it's serious," said Alain, glad to put her in the wrong. "But why was I so terrified?" he thought.

"It's only serious," said Camille, "for people who've got nowhere to live or who've only got two rooms. But people like us . . ."

Serene, lulled into optimism by the treacherous wine, she smoked and talked as if she were by herself, her thigh against the table and her legs crossed.

"Pull down your skirt, Camille."

She did not hear him and went on: "We've got all the essentials a child needs. A garden—and what a garden! And a dream of a room with its own bathroom."

"A room?"

"Your old room. We'd have it repainted. And it would be very nice of you not to insist on a frieze of little ducks and fir trees on a sky-blue background. That would ruin the taste of our offspring."

He restrained himself from stopping her. She was talking at random, her cheeks flushed, as she stared into the distance, seeing all she was building up. He had never seen her so beautiful. He was fascinated by the base of her neck, like the smooth unwrinkled bole of a tree, and by the nostrils which were blowing out smoke. "When I give her pleasure and she tightens her lips, she opens her nostrils like a little horse as she breathes."

He heard such crazy predictions fall from the reddened scornful lips that they ceased to alarm him: Camille was calmly proceeding with her woman's life among the wreckage of Alain's past. "Good Lord," he thought. "How she's got it all organized. I'm certainly learning something!" A tennis-court was to replace the great, useless lawn. The kitchen and the pantries . . .

"Haven't you ever realized how inconvenient they are? And think of all that wasted space. It's like the garage. I'm only saying all this, darling, so as you should know I think a lot about our real setting up house. Above all, we must be tactful with your mother. She's so awfully sweet . . . we mustn't do anything she wouldn't approve of. Must we?"

He put in haphazard "Yesses" and "Noes" as he picked up some wild strawberries scattered on the cloth. After hearing her say "your old room," he had been immunized by a provisional calm, a fore-taste of indifference.

"Only one thing may make things awkward for us," Camille went on. "Patrick's last postcard dated from the Balearic Isles.[42] Do pay attention! It'll take less time for Patrick to get back from the Balearics than for our decorator to get everything finished. I hope he comes to a violent end, that son of Penelope by a male tor-toise! But I shall put on my siren[43] voice: 'Patrick, my pet . . .' You know my siren voice makes a tremendous impression on Patrick."

"From the Balearic Isles . . ." broke in Alain thoughtfully. "From the Balearic Isles."

"Otherwise practically from next door. Where are you off to? Do you want us to go? It was so nice here."

Her brief intoxication was over. She stood up shivering and yawn-ing with sleepiness.

"I'll drive." said Alain. "Put on the old coat that's under the cushion. And go to sleep."

A flak of flying insects, bright silver moths and stag-beetles hard as pebbles, whirled in front of the headlights and the car drove back the wing-laden air like a wave. Camille did indeed go to sleep, sit-ting perfectly upright. She was trained not to encumber the driver's arm and shoulder, even in her sleep. She merely gave a little for-ward jerk of her head at every jolt in the road.

"From the Balearic Isles," Alain kept repeating to himself. The dark air, the white fires which caught and repulsed and decimated the flying creatures took him back to the populous threshold of his dreams; the sky with its stardust of exploded faces, the great hostile eyes which put off till tomorrow a reckoning, a password or a signif-icant figure. He was so deep in that world that he forgot to take the short cut between Pontchartrain and the Versailles[44] toll-gate and Camille scolded him in her sleep. "Bravo!" applauded Alain. "Good reflex action! Good little faithful, vigilant senses. Ah, how much I like you, how well we get on, when you're asleep and I'm awake."

Their sleeves and their unprotected hair were wet with dew when they set foot in their newly-built street, empty in the moon-light. Alain looked up; nine storeys up, in the middle of the almost round moon, the little horned shadow of a cat was leaning forward, waiting.

"Look! Look how she's waiting!"

"You've got good eyes," said Camille, yawning.

---

42. Mediterranean islands east of Spain, including Majorca and Minorca.
43. Temptress.
44. Pontchartrain, famous for its cha-teau by Mansart, and Versailles, the pa-latial home of French royalty and now a national museum, lie between Ram-bouillet and Paris.

"If she were to fall! Whatever you do, don't call her!"

"You needn't worry," said Camille. "If I did call her, she wouldn't come."

"For good reason," said Alain unpleasantly.

As soon as he had said it, he was angry with himself. "Too soon, too soon! And what a bad moment to choose!" Camille dropped the hand that was just about to push the bell.

"For good reason? For what good reason? Come on, out with it. I've been lacking in respect to the sacred animal again? The cat's complained of me?"

"I've gone too far," thought Alain, as he closed the garage door. He crossed the street again and rejoined his wife who was waiting for him in battle order. "Either I give in for the sake of a quiet night, or I stop the discussion by giving her a good, hard slap . . . or . . . It's too soon."

"Well! I'm talking to you!"

"Let's go up first," said Alain.

They did not speak as they went up, squeezed side by side in the narrow lift. As soon as they reached the studio, Camille tore off her béret and gloves and threw them across the room as if to show she had not given up the quarrel. Alain busied himself with Saha, inviting her to quit her perilous post. Patient, determined not to displease him, the cat followed him into the bathroom.

"If it's because of what you heard before dinner, when you came in," began Camille shrilly the moment he reappeared.

Alain had decided on his line and interrupted her wearily: "My dear, what are we going to say to each other? Nothing that we don't know already. That you can't bear the cat, that you blew up at Mother Buque because the cat broke a vase—or a glass—I saw the pieces. I shall answer that I'm extremely fond of Saha and that you'd be just as jealous if I'd kept a warm affection for some friend of my childhood. And so it'll go on all night. I'd prefer to sleep, thanks very much. Look here, the next time, I advise you to take the initiative and have a little dog."

Startled, embarrassed by having nothing for her temper to fasten on, Camille stared at him with raised eyebrows.

"The next time? What next time? What do you mean? What initiative?"

As Alain merely shrugged his shoulders, she flushed, her face suddenly became very young again and the extreme brightness of her eyes presaged tears. "Oh, how bored I am!" groaned Alain inwardly. "She's going to admit it. She's going to tell me I was right. How boring!"

"Listen, Alain."

With an effort, he feigned anger and assumed a false air of authority.

"No, my dear. No, no, no! You're not going to force me to finish off this charming evening with a barren discussion. You're not going to make a drama out of a piece of childish nonsense any more than you're going to stop me being fond of animals."

A kind of bitter gaiety came into Camille's eyes but she said nothing. "Perhaps I was a little hard. 'Childish nonsense,' was unnecessary. And as to being fond of animals, what do I know about that?" A small, shadowy blue shape, outlined like a cloud with a hem of silver, sitting on the dizzy edge of the night, absorbed his thoughts and removed him from that soulless place where, inch by inch, he was defending his chance of solitude, his egotism, his poetry . . .

"Come along, my little enemy," he said with disloyal charm. "let's go and rest."

She opened the door of the bathroom where Saha, installed for the night on the cork-seated stool, appeared to take only the faintest notice of her.

"But why, but why? Why did you say 'the next time'?"

The noise of running water drowned Camille's voice. Alain did not attempt to answer. When he rejoined her in the huge bed, he wished her good-night and kissed her carelessly on her unpowdered nose, while Camille's mouth clung to his chin with a small greedy sound.

Waking early, he went off quietly to lie down on the "waiting-room bench," the narrow divan squeezed between two walls of glass panes.

It was there that, during the following nights, he finished off his sleep. He closed the opaque oilcloth curtains on either side; they were almost new but already half destroyed by the sun. He breathed on his body the very perfume of his solitude, the sharp feline smell of restharrow[45] and flowering box. One arm extended, the other folded on his chest, he resumed the relaxed, lordly attitude of his childhood sleep. Suspended from the narrow top of the three-cornered house, he encouraged with all his might the return of his old dreams which the lover's exhaustion had dispersed.

He escaped more easily than Camille could have wished, constrained as he was to fly on the very spot. Escape no longer meant a staircase descended on tiptoe, the slamming of a taxi door, a brief farewell note. None of his mistresses had prepared him for Camille and her young girl's eagerness; Camille and her reckless desire. Neither had they prepared him for Camille's stoical behavior as an offended partner. She made it a point of honor not to complain.

Having escaped and lain down again on the waiting-room bench, Alain strained an uneasy ear toward the room he had just left, as his head felt for the hard little cushion he preferred to all the others.

45. A plant with pink or purplish flowers.

But Camille never reopened the door. Left alone, she pulled the crumpled sheet and the silk eiderdown over her, gnawed her bent finger in resentful regret, and snapped off the chromium strip-light which threw a narrow white beam across the bed. Alain never knew whether she had slept in the empty bed or whether she was learning so young that a solitary night imposes an armed vigil. It was impossible to tell, since she reappeared fresh and rather carefully dressed instead of in the bathrobe and pajamas of the night before. But she could not understand that a man's sensuality is brief and seasonal and that its unpredictable return is never a new beginning.

Lying alone, bathed in the night air, measuring the height and the silence of his tower-top by the faintness of the hoots from the boats on the near-by Seine,[46] the unfaithful husband delayed going to sleep till the apparition of Saha. She came to him, a shadow bluer than the shadows, along the ledge outside the open glass pane. There she stayed on the watch and would not come down on to Alain's chest although he implored her with the words that she knew: "Come, my little puma, come along . . . My cat of the tree-tops, my cat of the lilacs. Saha, Saha, Saha."

She resisted, sitting there above him on the window-sill. He could see nothing of her but her cat's shape against the sky, her chin down and her ears passionately oriented towards him. He could never catch the expression of her look.

Sometimes the dry dawn, the dawn before the wind got up, found the two of them sitting on the east side balcony. Cheek by cheek they watched the sky pale and the flight of white pigeons leaving the beautiful cedar of the Folie-Saint-James[47] one by one. Together they felt the same surprise at being so high above the earth, so alone and so far from being happy. With the ardent, sinuous movement of a huntress, Saha followed the pigeons' flight and uttered an occasional "ck . . . ck . . ." the faint echo of the "mouck . . . mouck . . ." of excitement, greed, and violent games.

"Our room," Alain said in her ear. "Our garden, our house."

She was getting thin again and Alain found her light and enchanting. But he suffered at seeing her so gentle and patient. Her patience was that of all those who are wearied out and sustained by a promise.

Sleep overcame Alain again as soon as daylight had begun to shorten the shadows. Rayless at first and looming larger through the mist of Paris, the sun swiftly shrank and lightened. As it rose, already burning hot, it awoke a twittering of sparrows in the gardens. The growing light revealed all the untidiness of a hot night on balconies and window-sills and in little yards where captive

46. The river that flows through Paris.
47. "Saint James's Folly": one of several "follies," or pleasure houses built as a costly whim of the owner in the Parisian suburbs during the 18th century.

shrubs languished—a garment forgotten on a deck-chair, empty glasses on a metal table, a pair of sandals. Alain hated the indecency of small dwellings oppressed by summer and regained his bed with one bound through a yawning panel in the glass. At the foot of the nine-storeyed building, a gardener lifted his head and saw this white young man leap through the transparent wall like a burglar.

Saha did not follow him. Sometimes she strained her ears in the direction of the triangular room; sometimes she dispassionately watched the awakening of the distant world on ground level. Someone let out a dog from a small decrepit house. The dog leapt forward without a bark, rushed round and round the tiny garden, and did not recover its voice until it had finished its aimless run. Women appeared at the windows; a maid furiously slammed doors and shook out orange cushions on a flat roof; men, waking regretfully, lit the first bitter cigarette. At last, in the fireless kitchen of the Wedge, the automatic, whistling coffeepot and the electric teapot clashed against each other; through the porthole window of the bathroom there emerged Camille's perfume and her noisy yawning. Saha resignedly folded her paws beneath her and pretended to sleep.

EIGHT

One evening in July, when the two of them were waiting for Alain's return, Camille and the cat were resting on the same parapet; the cat crouched on all four paws, Camille leaning on her folded arms. Camille did not like this balcony-terrace, reserved for the cat and shut in by two cement partitions which cut off both the wind and all communication with the balcony on the prow.

They exchanged a glance of sheer mutual investigation and Camille did not say a word to Saha. Propped on her elbows, she leant over as if to count the storeys by the orange awnings that flapped from top to bottom of the dizzy façade, she brushed against the cat who got up to make room for her, stretched, and lay down a little farther off.

When Camille was alone, she looked very much like the little girl who did not want to say "how d'you do?" Her face returned to childhood because it wore the expression of inhuman innocence, of angelic hardness which ennobles children's faces. Her gaze wandered over Paris, over the sky from which the light drained a little earlier each day, with an impartial severity which possibly condemned nothing. She yawned nervously, stood upright, and took a few absent-minded steps. Then she leant over again, forcing the cat to jump down. Saha stalked away with dignity and would have preferred to go back into the room. But the door in the hypotenuse had been shut and Saha patiently sat down. The next moment she had to get out of Camille's way for she was pacing from one parti-tion to the other with long, jerky strides. The cat jumped back on to the parapet. As if in play, Camille dislodged her as she leant on her elbows and once again Saha took refuge against the closed door.

Motionless, her eyes far away, Camille stood with her back to her. Nevertheless the cat was looking at Camille's back and her breath came faster. She got up, turned two or three times on her own axis and looked questioningly at the closed door. Camille had not moved. Saha inflated her nostrils and showed a distress which was almost like nausea. A long, desolate mew escaped from her, the wretched reply to a silent imminent threat. Camille faced round abruptly.

She was a trifle pale; that is to say, her rouge stood out in two oval moons on her cheeks. She affected an air of absent-mindedness as she would if a human eye had been staring at her. She even began to sing under her breath and resumed her pacing from one partition to the other, pacing to the rhythm of her song, but her voice failed her. She forced the cat, whom her foot was about to kick, to regain her narrow observation post with one bound, then to flatten herself against the door.

Saha had regained her self-control and would have died rather than utter a second cry. Tracking the cat down, without appearing to see her, Camille paced to and fro in silence. Saha did not jump on the parapet till Camille's feet were right on top of her and she only leapt down again on to the floor of the balcony to avoid the outstretched arm which would have hurled her from the height of the nine storeys.

She fled methodically and jumped carefully, keeping her eyes fixed on her adversary and condescending neither to fury nor to sup-plication. The most violent emotion of all, the terror of dying, soaked the sensitive soles of her paws with sweat so that they left flower-like prints on the stucco balcony.

Camille seemed the first to weaken and to lose her criminal strength. She made the mistake of noticing that the sun was going down, gave a glance at her wrist watch, and was aware of the clink of glasses inside. A moment or two more and her resolution would have deserted her as sleep deserts the somnambulist, leaving her guiltless and exhausted. Saha felt her enemy's firmness waver, hesi-tated on the parapet and Camille, stretching out both arms, pushed her into space.

She had time to hear the grating of claws on the rough-cast wall, to see Saha's blue body, twisted into an S, clutching the air with the force of a rising trout; then she shrank away, with her back to the wall.

She felt no temptation to look down into the little kitchen garden edged with new rubble. Back in the room, she put her hands over her ears, withdrew them, and shook her head as if she could hear the hum of a mosquito. Then she sat down and nearly fell asleep. But the oncoming night brought her to her feet again. She drove away the twilight by lighting up glass bricks, luminous tubes, and blinding mushrooms of lamps. She also lit up the long chromium eye which poured the opaline beam of its glance across the bed.

She walked about with supple movements, handling objects with light, adroit, dreaming hands.

"It's as if I'd got thinner," she said out loud.

She changed her clothes and dressed herself in white.

"My fly in the milk," she said, imitating Alain's voice. Her cheeks regained their color at a sudden sensual memory which brought her back to reality and she waited for Alain's arrival.

She bent her head in the direction of the buzzing lift and shivered at every noise; those dull knockings, those metallic clangs, those sounds as of a boat grinding at anchor, those muffled bursts of music which echo the discordant life of a new block of flats. But she was not surprised when the hollow tinkle of the bell in the hall replaced the fumbling of a key in the lock. She ran and opened the door herself.

"Shut the door," Alain ordered. "I must see first of all whether she hasn't hurt herself. Come and hold the lamp for me."

He carried Saha alive in his arms. He went straight to the bedroom, pushed aside the things on the invisible dressing-table, and gently put the cat on the slab of glass. She held herself upright and firm on her paws but her deep-set eyes wandered all about her as they would have done in a strange house.

"Saha!" called Alain in a whisper. "If there's nothing the matter with her, it's a miracle. Saha!"

She raised her head, as if to reassure her friend, and leant her cheek against his hand.

"Walk a little, Saha. Look, she's walking! Good Lord! Falling six storeys. It was the awning of the chap on the second floor that broke the fall. From there she bounced off on to the concierge's little lawn—the concierge saw her pass in the air. He said: 'I thought it was an umbrella falling.' What's she got on her ear? No, it's some white off the wall. Wait till I listen to her heart."

He laid the cat on her side and listened to the beating ribs, the tiny disordered mechanism. With his fair hair spread out and his eyes closed, he seemed to be sleeping on Saha's flank and to wake with a sigh only to see Camille standing there silent and apart, watching the close-knit group they made.

"Can you believe it? There's nothing wrong. At least I can't find anything wrong with her except a terribly agitated heart. But a cat's heart is usually agitated. But however could it have happened! I'm asking you as if you could possibly know, my poor pet! She fell from this side," he said, looking at the open french window. "Jump down on the ground, Saha, if you can."

After hesitating, she jumped but lay down again on the carpet. She was breathing fast and went on looking all round the room with the same uncertain look.

"I think I'll phone Chéron. Still, look, she's washing herself. She wouldn't wash herself if she'd been injured internally. Oh, good Lord!"

He stretched, threw his jacket on the bed, and came over to Camille.

"What a fright. How pretty you look, all in white. Kiss me, my fly in the milk!"

She let herself fall into the arms which had remembered her at last and could not hold back some broken sobs.

"No? You're actually crying?"

He was upset himself and hid his forehead in the soft, black hair.

"I . . . I didn't know that you were kind."

She had the courage not to draw away from him at that. However, Alain quickly returned to Saha whom he wanted to take out on the balcony because of the heat. But the cat resisted and contented herself with lying near the open door, turned towards the evening, blue as herself. From time to time, she gave a brief shudder and looked anxiously into the triangular room behind her.

"It's the shock," explained Alain. "I wanted her to go and sit outside."

"Leave her alone," said Camille faintly, "since she doesn't want to."

"Her wishes are orders. Today, of all days! Is there likely to be anything eatable left over at this hour? It's half-past nine!"

Mother Buque wheeled the table out on to the balcony and they dined looking over the east side of Paris where the most lights glimmered. Alain talked a lot, drank water with a little wine in it, and accused Saha of clumsiness, impudence, and "cat's sins."

" 'Cat's sins' are the kind of playful mistakes and lapses of judgment which can be put down to their having been civilized and domesticated. They've nothing in common with the clumsiness and carelessness that are almost deliberate."

But Camille no longer asked him: "How do you know that?" After dinner, he carried Saha and drew Camille into the studio where the cat consented to drink the milk she had refused. As she drank, she shivered all over as cats do when they are given something too cold to drink.

"It's the shock," Alain repeated. "All the same, I shall ask Chéron to look in and see her tomorrow morning. Oh, I'm forgetting everything!" he cried gaily. "Will you phone the concierge?

I've left that roll of plans down in his lodge. The one that Massart, our precious furnishing chap, deposited there."

Camille obeyed while Alain, tired and relaxed after the strain, dropped into one of the scattered armchairs and closed his eyes.

"Hallo!" said Camille at the telephone. "Yes . . . That must be it. A big roll . . . Thanks so much."

He laughed with his eyes still closed. She had returned to his side and stood there, watching him laugh.

"That absurd little voice you put on! What is this new little voice? 'A big roll . . . Thanks so much,'" he mimicked. "Do you keep that extremely small voice for the concierge? Come here, it needs the two of us to face Massart's latest creations."

He unrolled a sheet of thick drawing-paper, on the ebony table. Saha, who loved all kinds of paper, promptly leapt on the tinted drawing.

"Isn't she sweet!" exclaimed Alain. "It's to show me she's not in the least hurt. O my miraculously escaped one! Hasn't she a bump on her head? Camille, feel her head. No, she hasn't a bump. Feel her head all the same, Camille."

A poor little murderess meekly tried to emerge from her banishment, stretched out her hand, and touched the cat's head with humble hatred.

Her gesture was received with the most savage snarl, a scream, and an epileptic leap. Camille shrieked "Ha!" as if she had been burned. Standing on the unrolled drawing the cat covered the young woman with a flaming stare of accusation, the fur on her back erect, her teeth bared, and the dry red of her open jaw showing.

Alain had sprang up, ready to protect Saha and Camille from each other.

"Take care! She's . . . perhaps she's mad . . . Saha!"

She stared at him angrily but with a lucidity that proved she had not lost her reason.

"What happened? Where did you touch her?"

"I didn't touch her at all."

They were both speaking low, hardly moving their lips.

"Then, why this?" said Alain. "I don't understand. Put your hand out again."

"No, I don't want to!" protested Camille. "Perhaps she's gone wild," she added.

Alain took the risk of stroking Saha. She flattened her erect fur and yielded to the friendly palm but glared once more at Camille with brilliant, accusing eyes.

"Why *this*?" Alain repeated slowly. "Look, she's got a scratch on her nose. I hadn't seen it. It's dried blood. Saha, Saha, good now," he said, seeing the fury growing in the yellow eyes.

Because her cheeks were swelled out and her whiskers stiffly thrust forward as if she were hunting, the furious cat seemed to be laughing. The joy of battle stretched the mauve corners of her mouth and tautened the mobile, muscular chin. The whole of her feline face was striving towards a universal language, towards a word forgotten by men.

"Whatever's *that*?" said Alain suddenly.

"Whatever's *what*?"

Under the cat's stare Camille was recovering her courage and the instinct of self-defense. Leaning over the drawing, Alain could make out damp prints in groups of four little spots round a central, irregular patch.

"Her paws . . . wet?" muttered Alain.

"She must have walked in some water," said Camille. "You're making a fuss about nothing."

Alain raised her head towards the dry blue night.

"In water? What water?"

He turned again to his wife. He looked at her with round eyes which made him look suddenly extraordinarily ugly.

"Don't you know what those footprints mean?" he said harshly. "No, *you* wouldn't know. Fear, d'you understand, *fear*. The sweat of fear. Cat's sweat, the only time cats *do* sweat. So she was frightened."

Delicately, he lifted one of Saha's front paws and dried the sweat on the fleshy pad. Then he pulled back the living white sheath into which the claws had been drawn back.

"She's got all her claws broken," he said, talking to himself. "She must have held on . . . clutching. She scratched the stone trying to save herself. She . . ."

He broke off his monologue and, without another word, took the cat under his arm and carried her off to the bathroom.

Alone, unmoving, Camille strained her ears. She kept her hands knotted together; free as she was, she seemed to be loaded with fetters.

"Madame Buque," said Alain's voice, "have you any milk?"

"Yes, Monsieur. In the 'fridge."

"Then it's ice-cold?"

"But I can warm it on the stove. It won't take a second. It is for the cat? She's not ill, is she?"

"No, she's . . ."

Alain's voice stopped short and changed its tone: "She's a little off meat in this heat. Thank you, Madame Buque. Yes, you can go now. See you in the morning."

Camille heard her husband moving to and fro and turning on a tap. She knew that he was giving the cat food and fresh water. A diffused shadow, above the metal lampshade, came up as high as her face which was as still as a mask except for the slow movement of the great eyes.

Alain returned, carelessly tightening his leather belt, and sat down again at the ebony table. But he did not summon Camille back to sit beside him and she was forced to speak first.

"You've sent old Mother Buque off?"

"Yes. Shouldn't I have?"

He lit a cigarette and squinted at the flame of the lighter.

"I wanted her to bring something tomorrow morning."

"Oh, it doesn't matter a bit . . . don't apologize."

"But I'm not apologizing. Though, actually, I ought to."

He went over to the open bay window, drawn by the blue of the night. He was studying a certain tremor in himself, a tremor which did not come from his recent emotion, but which was more like the tremolo of an orchestra, muffled and foreboding. From the Folie-Saint-James a rocket shot up, burst into luminous petals that withered one by one as they fell, and the blue of the night recovered its peace and its powdery depth. In the amusement park, a grotto, a colonnade, and a waterfall were suddenly lit up with incandescent white; Camille came nearer to him.

"Are they having a gala night? Let's wait for the fireworks. Do you hear the guitars?"

Absorbed in his inner tremor, he did not answer her. His wrists and hands were tingling, his loins were weak and felt as if a thousand insects were crawling over them. His state reminded him of the hateful lassitude, the fatigue he used to feel after the school sports. After running and rowing he would emerge vindictive, throbbing and exhausted and equally contemptuous of his victory or defeat. Now, he was at peace only in that part of himself which was no longer anxious about Saha. For several minutes—or perhaps for very few—ever since the discovery of the broken claws, ever since Saha's furious terror, he had lost all sense of time.

"It's not fireworks," he said. "Probably just some dances."

From the movement Camille made beside him in the shadow, he realized that she had given up expecting him to answer her. He felt her coming closer without apprehension. He saw the outline of the white dress; a bare arm; a half face lit by the yellow light from the lamps indoors and a half face that shadowed blue in the clear night. The two halves were divided by the small straight nose and each was provided with a large, almost unblinking eye.

"Yes, of course, it's dances," she agreed. "They're mandolins, not guitars. Listen . . . 'Les donneurs . . . de sé-é-réna . . . des, Et les bel-les é-écou-teu . . .'"[48]

Her voice cracked on the highest note and she coughed to excuse her failure.

48. "The singers of serenades, And the beautiful listeners . . ."

"But what a tiny voice . . ." thought Alain, astonished. "What has she done with her voice that's as big and open as her eyes? She's singing in a little girl's voice. Hoarse, too."

The mandolins stopped and the breeze brought a faint human noise of clapping and applause. A moment later, a rocket shot up, burst into an umbrella of mauve rays in which hung tears of living fire.

"Oh!" cried Camille.

Both of them had emerged from the darkness like two statues; Camille in lilac marble; Alain whiter, with his hair greenish and his eyes almost colorless. When the rocket had gone out, Camille sighed.

"It never lasts long enough," she said plaintively.

The distant music started again. But the capricious wind deadened the sound of the stringed instruments into a vague shrill buzzing and carried the blasts of the accompanying brass, on two notes, loudly and insistently right into their ears.

"What a shame," said Camille. "They've probably got a frightfully good jazz band. That's *Love in the Night* they're playing."

She hummed the tune in a high, shaky, almost inaudible voice, as if she had just been crying. This new voice of hers acutely increased Alain's disquiet. It induced in him a need for revelation, a desire to break down whatever it was that—a long time ago or only a moment ago?—had risen between himself and Camille. It was something to which he could not yet give a name but which was growing fast; something which prevented him from putting his arm round her neck like a boy; something which kept him motionless at her side, alert and expectant, against the wall still warm from the heat of the day. Turning impatient, he said, "Go on singing."

A long red, white, and blue shower, falling like the branches of a weeping willow, streaked the sky over the park and showed Alain a Camille startled and already defiant: "Singing what?"

"*Love in the Night* or anything else. It doesn't matter what."

She hesitated, then refused.

"Let me listen to the jazz . . . even from here you can hear it's simply marvellous."

He did not insist. He restrained his impatience and mastered the tingling which had now spread over his entire body.

A swarm of gay little suns, revolving brightly against the darkness, took flight. Alain secretly confronted them with the constellations of his favorite dreams.

"Those are the ones to remember. I'll try and take them with me down there," he noted gravely. "I've neglected my dreams too much." At last, in the sky over the Folie, there rose and expanded a kind of straying pink and yellow dawn which burst into vermilion discs and fiery ferns and ribbons of blinding metal.

The shouts of children on the lower balconies greeted this miraculous display. By its light, Alain saw Camille absent and remote, absorbed in other lights in her own mind.

As soon as the night closed in again, his hesitation vanished and he slipped his own bare arm under Camille's. As he touched that bare arm, he fancied he could see it; its whiteness hardly tinged by the summer and clothed in a fine down that lay flat on the skin, reddish-brown on the forearm, paler near the shoulder.

"You're cold," he murmured. "You're not feeling ill?"

She began to cry very quietly and so promptly that Alain suspected she had been preparing her tears.

"No. It's you. It's you who . . . who don't love me."

He leant back against the wall and drew Camille against his hip. He could feel her trembling, and cold from her shoulders to her knees, bare above her rolled stockings. She clung to him faithfully, leaning all her weight on him.

"Aha, so I don't love you. Right! Is this another jealousy scene on account of Saha?"

He felt a muscular tremor run through the whole of the body he was supporting, a renewal of energy and self-defense. Encouraged by the moment, by a kind of indescribable opportunism, he insisted: "Instead of adopting this charming animal, like me. Are we the only young couple who have a cat or a dog? Would you like a parrot or a marmoset—a pair of doves—a dog, to make me very jealous in my turn?"

She shook her shoulders, protesting with annoyance through closed lips. With his head high, Alain carefully controlled his own voice and egged himself on. "Go on, a few more bits of nonsense; fill her up and we'll get somewhere. She's like a jar that I've got to turn upside down to empty. Go on. Go on."

"Would you like a little lion . . . or a baby crocodile of barely fifty? No? Come on, you'd much better adopt Saha. If you'd just take the least bit of trouble, you'd soon see . . ."

Camille wrenched herself out of his arms so violently that he staggered.

"No!" she cried. "*That*, never! Do you hear me? *Never!*"

"Ah, now we've got it!" Alain said to himself with delight. He pushed Camille into the room, pulled down the outer blind, lit up the rectangle of glass in the ceiling, and shut the window. With an animal movement, Camille rushed over to the window and Alain opened it again.

"On condition you don't scream," he said.

He wheeled the only armchair up to Camille and sat astride on the solitary chair at the foot of the wide, turned-down bed with its new, clean sheets. The oilcloth curtains, drawn for the night, gave a greenish cast to Camille's pale face and her creased white dress.

"Well?" begain Alain. "No compromise possible? Appalling story? Either her or me?"

She answered with a brief nod and Alain realized that he must drop his bantering tone.

"What do you want me to say?" he went on, after a silence. "The only thing I don't want to say to you? You know very well I'll never give up this cat. I should be ashamed to. Ashamed in myself and ashamed before her."

"I know," said Camille.

"And before you," Alain finished.

"Oh, *me!*" said Camille, raising her hand.

"You count too," said Alain hardly. "Tell me. Is it only me you've anything against? You've no reproach against Saha except her affection for me?"

She answered only with a troubled, hesitant look and he was irritated at having to go on questioning her. He had thought that a short violent scene would force all the issues; he had relied on this easy way out. But, after her one cry, Camille had stiffened defensively and was furnishing no fuel for a quarrel. He resorted to patience: "Tell me, my dear. What is it? Mustn't I call you my dear? Tell me, if it were a question of another cat and not Saha, would you be so intolerant?"

"Of course I wouldn't," she said very quickly. "You wouldn't love it as much as that one."

"Quite true," said Alain with loyal accuracy.

"Even a woman," went on Camille, beginning to get heated, "you probably wouldn't love a *woman* as much as that."

"Quite true," said Alain.

"You're not like most people who are fond of animals. No, you're *not*. Patrick's fond of animals. He takes big dogs by the scruff of their necks and rolls them over. He imitates cats to see the faces they make—he whistles to the birds."

"Quite. In other words, he's not difficult," said Alain.

"But you're quite different. You *love* Saha."

"I've never pretended not to. But I wasn't lying to you, either, when I said to you: 'Saha's not your rival.' "

He broke off and lowered his eyelids over his secret which was a secret of purity.

"There are rivals *and* rivals," said Camille sarcastically.

Suddenly she reddened. Flushed with sudden intoxication, she advanced to Alain.

"I saw the two of you!" she almost shrieked. "In the morning, when you spend the night on your little divan. Before daybreak. I've seen you, both of you."

She pointed a shaking hand towards the balcony.

"Sitting there, the two of you . . . you didn't even hear me! You were like that, cheek to cheek."

She went over to the window, recovered her breath and marched down on Alain again.

"It's for you to say honestly whether I'm wrong in being jealous of this cat and wrong in suffering."

He kept silence so long that she became angry again.

"Do speak! Do *say* something! At the point we've got to . . . What are you waiting for?"

"The sequel," said Alain. "The rest."

He stood up quietly, bent over his wife, and lowered his voice as he indicated the french window: "It was you, wasn't it? You threw her over?"

With a swift movement she put the bed between herself and him but she did not deny it. He watched her escape with a kind of smile: "You threw her over," he said dreamily. "I felt very definitely that you'd changed everything between us. You threw her over . . . she broke her claws trying to clutch on to the wall."

He lowered his head, imagining the attempted murder.

"But *how* did you throw her over? By holding her by the skin of her neck? By taking advantage of her being asleep on the parapet? Had you been planning this for a long time? You hadn't had a fight with each other first?"

He raised his head and stared at Camille's hands and arms.

"No, you've no marks. She accused you well and truly, didn't she, when I made you touch her. She was magnificent."

His eyes left Camille and embraced the night, the dust of stars, the tops of the three poplars which the lights in the room lit up.

"Very well," he said simply, "I'm going away."

"Oh listen . . . do *listen* . . ." Camille implored wildly, almost in a whisper.

Nevertheless, she let him go out of the room. He opened cupboards, talked to the cat in the bathroom. The sound of his footsteps warned Camille that he had changed into his outdoor shoes and she looked, automatically, at the time. He came in again, carrying Saha in a bulging basket which Mme. Buque used for shopping. Hurriedly dressed, with his hair dishevelled and a scarf round his neck, his untidiness so much suggested that of a lover that Camille's eyelids pricked. But she heard Saha moving in the basket and tightened her lips.

"As you see, I'm going away," repeated Alain. He lowered his eyes, lifted the basket a trifle, and corrected himself with calculated cruelty. "*We're* going away."

He secured the wicker lid, explaining as he did so: "This was all I could find in the kitchen."

"You're going to your home?" inquired Camille, forcing herself to imitate Alain's calm.

"But of course."

"Are you . . . can I count on seeing you during the next few days?"

"Why, certainly."

Surprise made her weaken again. She had to make an immense effort not to plead, not to weep.

"What about you?" said Alain. "Will you stay here alone tonight? You won't be frightened? If you insisted, I'd stay, but . . ."

He turned his head towards the balcony.

"But, frankly, I'm not keen on it. What do you propose to say to your family?"

Hurt at his sending her, by implication, home to her people, Camille pulled herself together.

"I've nothing to say to them. These are things which only concern *me*, I presume. I've no inclination for family councils."

"I entirely agree with you . . . provisionally."

"Anyway, we can decide as from tomorrow."

He raised his free hand to ward off this threat of a future.

"No. Not tomorrow. Today there isn't any tomorrow."

In the doorway, he turned back.

"In the bathroom, you'll find my key and all the money we've got here."

She interrupted with irony: "Why not a hamper of provisions and a compass?"

She was putting on a brave act and surveyed him with one hand on her hip and her head erect on her handsome neck. "She's building up my exit," thought Alain. He wanted to reply with some similar last-minute coquetry, to toss his hair over his forehead and give her that narrowed look between his lashes which seemed to disdain what it rested on. But he renounced a pantomime which would look absurd when he was carrying a shopping-basket and confined himself to a vague bow in Camille's direction.

She kept up her expression of bravado and her theatrical stance. But before he went out, he could see more clearly, at a distance, the dark circles round her eyes and the moisture which covered her temples and her smooth, unlined neck.

Downstairs, he crossed the street automatically, the key of the garage in his hand. "I can't do that," he thought and he retraced his steps towards the avenue some way off where cruising taxis could be picked up at night. Saha mewed two or three times and he calmed her with his voice. "I can't do that. But it really would be much pleasanter to take the car. Neuilly is impossible at night." He was surprised, having counted on a blessed sense of release, to find himself losing his composure as soon as he was alone. Walking did not restore his calm. When, at last, he found a stray taxi, the five-minute drive seemed almost interminable.

He shivered in the warm night under the gas-jet, waiting for the gate to be opened. Saha, who had recognized the smell of the garden, was giving short sharp mews in the basket which he had put down on the pavement.

The scent of the wistarias in their second flowering came across the air and Alain shivered more violently, stamping from one foot to the other as if it were bitterly cold. He rang again but the house gave no sign of life in spite of the solemn, scandalous clamor of the big bell. At last a light appeared in the little buildings by the garage and he heard old Émile's dragging feet on the gravel.

"It's me, Émile," he said when the colorless face of the old valet peered through the bars.

"Monsieur Alain?" said Émile, exaggerating his quavering voice. "Monsieur Alain's young lady isn't indisposed? The summer is so treacherous. Monsieur Alain has some luggage, I see."

"No, it's Saha. Leave her, I'll carry her. No, don't turn up the gas-lamps, the light might wake Madame. Just open the front door for me and go back to bed."

"Madame is awake—it was she who rang for me. I hadn't heard the big bell. In my first sleep, you see."

Alain hurried ahead to escape Émile's chatter and the sound of his shaky footsteps following him. He did not stumble at the turnings of the paths though there was no moon that night. The great lawn, paler than the flowerbeds, guided him. The dead, draped tree in the middle of the grass looked like a huge standing man with his coat over his arm. The smell of watered geraniums made Alain's throat tighten and he stopped. He bent down, opened the basket with groping fingers, and released the cat.

"Saha, our garden."

He felt her glide out of the basket and, from pure tenderness, took no more notice of her. Like an offering, he gave her back the night, her liberty, the soft spongy earth, the wakeful insects, and the sleeping birds.

Behind the shutters on the ground floor, a lighted lamp was waiting and Alain's spirits fell again. "To have to talk again, to have to explain to my mother . . . explain what? It's so simple. It's so difficult."

All he longed for was silence, the room with the faded flowers on the wallpaper, his bed, and, above all, for vehement tears; great sobs as raucous as coughs that would be his secret, guilty compensation.

"Come in, darling, come in."

He seldom went into his mother's room. His selfish aversion to medicine bottles and droppers, boxes of digitalis pills and homeopathic remedies dated from childhood and was as acute as ever. But he could not resist the sight of the narrow, unadorned bed and of the woman with the thick white hair who was heaving herself up on her wrists.

"You know, Mother, there's nothing extraordinary about all this."

He accompanied this idiotic statement with a smile of which he was promptly ashamed; a horizontal, stiff-cheeked smile. His tiredness had overwhelmed him in the sudden rush, making him do and say the exact opposite of what he meant to. He sat down by his mother's bedside and loosened his scarf.

"Forgive my appearance. I came just as I was. I arrive at preposterous times without giving you warning."

"But you did give me warning," said Mme. Amparat.

She glanced at Alain's dusty shoes.

"Your shoes look like a tramp's."

"I've only come from my place, Mother. But it was a long time before I could find a taxi. I was carrying the cat."

"Ah," said Mme. Amparat, with an understanding look. "You've brought back the cat?"

"Yes, of course. If you knew . . ."

He stopped, restrained by an odd discretion. "These are things one doesn't tell. These stories aren't for parents."

"Camille's not very fond of Saha, Mother."

"I know," said Mme. Amparat.

She forced herself to smile and shook her wavy hair.

"That's extremely serious!"

"Yes. For Camille," said Alain spitefully.

He got up and paced about among the furniture. It had white covers on it for the summer like the furniture in houses in the provinces. Having made up his mind not to denounce Camille, he could find nothing more to say.

"You know, Mother, there haven't been any screams or smashing of crockery. The glass dressing-table's still intact and the neighbors haven't come rushing up. Only I just need a little . . . a little time to be by myself . . . to rest. I won't hide it from you. I'm at the end of my tether," he said, seating himself on the bed.

"No. You don't hide it from me," said Mme. Amparat. She laid a hand on Alain's forehead, turning up the young face, on which the pale stubble was beginning to show, towards the light. He complained, turning his changeable eyes away, and succeeded in holding off a little longer the storm of tears he had promised himself.

"If there aren't any sheets on my old bed, Mother, I'll wrap myself up in any old thing."

"There are sheets on your bed," said Mme. Amparat.

At that, he threw his arms round his mother and kissed her blindly on her eyes and cheeks and hair. He thrust his face into her neck, stammered "Good-night" and went out of the room, sniffing.

In the hall, he pulled himself together and did not go upstairs at once. The night which was ending called to him and so did Saha. But he did not go far. The steps down into the garden were far enough. He sat down on one of them in the darkness and his outstretched hand encountered the fur, the sensitive antennae-like whiskers, and the cool nostrils of Saha.

She turned round and round on one spot according to the ritual of wild creatures when they caress. She seemed very small to him and light as a kitten. Because he was hungry himself, he thought she must be needing food.

"We'll eat tomorrow . . . quite soon now . . . it's almost daylight."

Already she smelt of mint and geranium and box. He held her there, trusting and perishable, promised, perhaps, ten years of life. And he suffered at the thought of the briefness of so great a love.

"After you, probably anyone can have me who wants me. A woman, many women. But never another cat."

A blackbird whistled four notes that rang through the whole garden. But the sparrows had heard it and answered. On the lawn and the massed flowerbeds, faint ghosts of color began to appear. Alain could make out a sickly white, a dull red more melancholy than black itself, a yellow smeared on the surrounding green, a round yellow flower which began to revolve and become more yellow and was followed by eyes and moons. Staggering, dropping with sleep, Alain reached his room, threw off his clothes, uncovered the bed, and was unconscious almost as soon as he had slipped between the cool sheets.

Lying on his back with one arm flung out and the cat, silent and concentrated, kneading his shoulder, he was falling straight like a plummet into the very depths of sleep when a start brought him back to the daylight, the swaying of the awakened trees, and the blessed clanging of the distant trams.

"What's the matter with me? I wanted . . . Ah, yes! I wanted to cry." He smiled and fell asleep again.

His sleep was feverish and crowded with dreams. Two or three times he thought he had woken up and was becoming conscious of where he was, but each time he was undeceived by the expression of the walls of his room. They were angrily watching the fluttering of a winged eye.

"But I'm asleep . . . of course, I'm asleep."

"I'm asleep . . ." he answered again to the crunching gravel. "I'm asleep, I tell you," he called to two dragging feet that brushed against the door. The feet went away and the sleeper congratulated himself in his dream. But the dream had come to a head under the repeated solicitings and Alain opened his eyes.

The sun he had left on the window-sill in May had become an

August sun and reached no farther than the satiny trunk of the tulip-tree opposite the house. "How the summer has aged," Alain said to himself. He got up, naked, looked for something to wear and found some pajamas, too short and too tight in the sleeves and a faded dressing-gown which he joyfully pulled on. The window summoned him but he was stopped by Camille's photograph which he had left, forgotten, by his bed. Curiously, he examined the inaccurate, retouched little portrait; whitened here, blackened there. "It's more like her than I supposed," he thought. "How was it I didn't notice it? Four months ago I used to say 'Oh, she's entirely different from that. Much more subtle, not nearly so hard.' But I was wrong."

The long, steady breeze ran through the trees with a murmur like a river's. Dazed and quite painfully hungry, Alain lay back on his pillows. "How delightful it is, a convalescene." To complete the illusion a knuckle tapped on the door and the bearded Basque woman entered, carrying a tray.

"But I'd have had breakfast in the garden, Juliette!"

A kind of smile appeared among the gray hairs on her face.

"I thought as much. Would Monsieur Alain like me to take the tray down?"

"No, no, I'm too hungry. Leave that there. Saha'll come in by the window."

He called the cat who rose from some invisible retreat as if she had come into existence at his call. She bounded up the vertical path of climbing plants and fell back again—she had forgotten her broken claws.

"Wait, I'm coming!"

He brought her back in his arms and they gorged themselves, she on milk and rusks, he on slices of bread and butter and scalding hot coffee. On one corner of the tray, a little rose adorned the lid of the honey-pot.

"It's not one of my mother's roses," Alain decided. It was an ill-made, stunted little rose, picked from a low branch, that gave out the queer smell of a yellow rose. "It's a little homage from the Basque."

Saha, radiant, seemed to have grown plumper overnight. Her shirt-frill erect, her four darker stripes well marked between her ears, she stared at the garden with the eyes of a happy despot.

"How simple it all is, isn't it, Saha? For you, at any rate."

Old Émile entered in his turn and insisted on removing Alain's shoes.

"There's one of the laces got very worn. Monsieur Alain hasn't another? It doesn't matter, I'll put one of my own laces in," he bleated with emotion.

"Decidedly, it's my gala-day," said Alain to himself. The word drove him back by contrast to all the things that only yesterday had been daily bothers; time to get up and dress, time to go to the Amparat office, time to come back to lunch with Camille.

"But I've nothing on earth to put on!" he cried.

In the bathroom he recognized the slightly rusty razor, the worn cake of pink soap, and the old toothbrush and used them with a delight of a man who has got shipwrecked for fun. But he had to come down in the outgrown pajamas as the Basque woman had carried off his clothes.

"Come Saha, Saha."

She went ahead and he ran after her uncertainly in a pair of frayed raffia sandals that kept threatening to slip off. He stretched out his shoulders to feel the cape of the mild sun fall on them and half closed his eyes that had grown unaccustomed to the green reverberations of the lawns and the hot colors which blazed above a serried block of crimson love-lies-bleeding and a tuft of red salvias bordered with heliotrope.

"Oh, the same, the very same salvias!"

Alain had always known that little heart-shaped bed as red and invariably bordered with heliotropes. It was shaded by a lean, ancient cherry-tree which occasionally produced a few cherries in September.

"I can see six . . . seven. Seven green cherries!"

He was talking to the cat who, with empty, golden eyes, had her mouth half open, almost overcome by the excessive scent of the heliotropes. Her face had the look of almost sickened ecstasy animals assume when confronted with an overpowering smell.

She ate a blade of grass to recover herself, listened to various voices, and rubbed her nose against the hard twigs of the privet hedge. But she did not display any exuberance, any irresponsible gaiety and she walked nobly, surrounded by the tiny silver halo which outlined all her body.

"Thrown, from a height of nine storeys," Alain thought as he watched her. "Grabbed . . . or pushed. Perhaps she defended herself . . . perhaps she escaped to be caught again and thrown over. Assassinated."

He tried by such conjectures to arouse his just anger, but he did not succeed. "If I truly, deeply loved Camille, how furious I should be." Around him shone his kingdom, threatened like all kingdoms. "My mother assures me that in less than twenty years no one will be able to keep on houses and gardens like this. She's probably right. I'm quite willing to lose them. I don't want to let *them* come into them."

He was shaken by the sound of a telephone ringing in the house. "Come, come now! I'm not frightened, am I? Camille's not so stupid as to telephone me. To do her justice, I've never known a young woman so restrained in using that instrument."

But he could not stop himself from running awkwardly towards the house, losing his sandals and tripping over pebbles, and calling out: Mother! Who's that on the phone?"

The thick white dressing-gown appeared on the steps and Alain felt ashamed of having called out.

"How I love your big white dressing-gown, Mother! Always the same, always the same."

"Thank you very much on behalf of my dressing-gown," said Mme. Amparat.

She kept Alain waiting a moment before she said: "It was Monsieur Veuillet. It's half-past nine. Have you forgotten the ways of the house?"

She combed her son's hair with her fingers and buttoned up the too-tight pajamas jacket.

"You're a pretty sight. I suppose you don't intend to spend the rest of your life as a ragamuffin?"

Alain was grateful to her for questioning him so adroitly.

"No question of that, Mother. In a moment, I'll get busy about all that."

Mme. Amparat tenderly interrupted his vague, wide gesture.

"Tonight . . . where will you be?"

"Here!" he cried, and the tears welled up in his eyes.

"Good gracious, what a child!" said Mme. Amparat and he took up the word with the earnestness of a boy scout.

"Perhaps I am a child, Mother. That's why I want to think over what I ought to do to get out of this childishness."

"Get out of it how? By a divorce? That's a door that makes a lot of noise."

"But which lets in some air," he dared to retort sharply.

"Wouldn't a separation . . . a temporary one, give just as good results? What about a thorough rest or a little travel, perhaps?"

He threw up his arms indignantly.

"My poor dear Mother, you've no idea. You're a thousand miles from imagining."

He was going to bring it all out and tell her about the attempted murder.

"Very well then, leave me a thousand miles! Such things don't concern me. Have a little . . . a little reserve," said Mme. Amparat hastily and Alain took advantage of a misunderstanding which was due to her innate modesty.

"Now, Mother, there's still all the tiresome side to be thought of. I mean the family point of view which is all mixed up with the business side. From the Malmerts' point of view, my divorce will be quite indefensible, no matter how much Camille may be partly responsible. A bride of three and a half months! I can hear it all."

"Where do you get the idea that there's a business side involved? You and the little Malmert girl aren't running a firm together. A married couple is not a pair of business partners."

"I know, Mother. But if things turn out as I expect, there's bound to be a horrible period of formalities and interviews and so on. It's never as simple as everyone says, a divorce."

She listened to her son with gentle forbearance. She knew that certain causes produce unexpected results and that, all through his life, a man has to be born many times with no other assistance than that of chance, of bruises, of mistakes.

"It's never simple to leave anything we've wanted to attach to ourselves," said Mme. Amparat. "She's not so bad, that little Malmert. A little . . . coarse, a little lacking in manners. No, not so bad. At least, that's my way of seeing it. I don't want to impose it on you. We've plenty of time to think it over."

"I've taken care of that," said Alain with harsh politeness. "And, at the moment, I prefer to keep a certain story to myself."

His face suddenly lit up in a laugh that restored it to childhood. Standing up on her hind legs, Saha, using her paw as a spoon, was fishing drowned ants out of a brimming watering-can.

"Look at her, Mother! Isn't she a miraculous cat?"

"Yes," sighed Mme. Amparat. "She's your chimera."[49]

He was always surprised when his mother employed an unusual word. He greeted this one with a kiss on her prematurely aged hand with its swollen veins and the little brown flecks which Juliette lugubriously called "earthstains."

At the sound of the bell ringing at the gate, he jerked himself upright.

"Run and hide," said Mme. Amparat. "We're right in the way of the tradesmen. Go and dress yourself. Do you want the butcher's little boy to catch you in that extraordinary get-up?"

But they both knew perfectly well that it was not the butcher's little boy ringing at the visitor's gate. Mme. Amparat had already turned her back and was hurrying up the steps, holding up her dressing-gown in both hands. Behind the clipped hedge Alain could see the Basque woman retreating in disorder, her black silk apron flying in the wind, while a slither of slippers on the gravel announced the flight of old Emile. Alain cut off his escape.

"You have at least opened the gate?"

"Yes, Monsieur Alain. The young lady's behind her car."

He lifted terrified eyes to the sky, hunched up his shoulders, as if he were in a hailstorm, and vanished.

"Well, that's certainly something like a picnic! I wish I'd had time to get dressed. Gracious, she's got a new suit!"

Camille had seen him and came straight up to him without over-

49. Mythical monster; also, an illusion or foolish fancy.

much haste. In one of those moments of almost hilarious anxiety that crop up on dramatic occasions, he thought confusedly: "Perhaps she's come to lunch."

"Carefully and lightly made-up as she was, armed with black lashes and beautiful parted lips and shining teeth, she seemed all the same to lose her self-assurance when Alain came forward to meet her. For he was approaching without breaking away from the shelter of his protective atmosphere. He was treading his native lawn under the rich patronage of the trees, and Camille looked at him with the eyes of a poor person.

"Forgive me, I look like a schoolboy who's suddenly shot up out of all knowledge. We didn't arrange to meet this morning, did we?"

"No. I've brought you your big suitcase. It's packed full."

"But you shouldn't have done that!" he expostulated. "I'd have sent Émile around today to fetch it."

"Don't talk to me about Émile. I wanted to give him your case but the old idiot rushed off as if I'd got the plague. The case is down there by the gate."

She flushed with humiliation, biting the inside of her cheek. "It's beginning well," said Alain to himself.

"I'm terribly sorry. You know what Émile's like. Listen," he decided, "let's go on the lawn inside the yew hedges. It'll be quieter there than in the house."

He promptly repented his choice for that clearing, enclosed in clipped yews and furnished with wicker chairs, had been the scene of their secret kisses in the old days.

"Wait while I dust the twigs off. You mustn't spoil the pretty suit. Incidentally, I don't know it, do I?"

"It's new," said Camille in a tone of profound sadness, as if she had said: "It's dead."

She sat sideways, looking about her. Two arched arcades, one opposite the other, broke the circle of greenery. Alain remembered something Camille had once confided to him: "You've no idea how your beautiful garden used to frighten me. I used to come here like the little girl from the village who comes to play with the son of the grand people at the château, in their park. And yet, when you come to think of it . . ." She had spoiled everything by that last remark. That "when you come to think of it" implied the prosperity of Malmert Mangles compared with the declining house of Amparat.

He observed that Camille kept her gloves on. "That's a precaution that defeats its own ends. Without those gloves it's possible I mightn't have thought about her hands, about what they've done. Ah, at last a little . . . just a little anger," he said to himself, listening to his heartbeats. "I've taken enough time about it."

"Well," said Camille sadly, "well, what are you going to do? Perhaps you haven't decided yet."

"Oh yes. I've decided," said Alain.

"Ah!"

"Yes. I can't come back."

"I quite understand that there's no question of your coming back today."

"I don't want to come back."

"Not at all? Ever?"

He shrugged his shoulders:

"What does that mean, ever? I don't want to come back. Not now, I don't want to."

She watched him closely, trying to distinguish the false from the true, the deliberate irritation from the authentic shudder. He returned her suspicion for suspicion. "She's small, this morning. She looks rather like a pretty shopgirl. She's lost in all this green. We've already exchanged a fair number of useless remarks."

In the distance, through one of the arched arcades, Camille caught sight of traces of the "alterations" on one side of the face of the house; a new window, some freshly-painted shutters. Bravely she threw herself into the path of danger: "Suppose I'd said nothing yesterday?" she suggested abruptly. "Suppose you'd known nothing?"

"What a superb woman's idea," he sneered. "It does you honor."

"Oh," said Camille, shaking her head. "Honor, honor. It wouldn't be the first time that the happiness of two married people depended on something that couldn't be owned up to . . . or wasn't owned up to. But I've got the idea that by *not* telling you, I'd only have made things worse than ever for myself. I didn't feel you were . . . I don't know how to put it."

Hunting for the word, she mimed it by clenching her hands together. "She's wrong to draw attention to her hands," thought Alain vindictively. "Those hands that have sent someone to their death."

"After all, you're so awfully little on my side," said Camille. "That's true, isn't it?"

That struck him. He had to admit, mentally, that she was right. He said nothing and Camille insisted plaintively in a voice he knew all too well.

"Isn't it true, you hateful man?"

"But, good God!" he burst out. "That's not the question. The only thing that can possibly interest me—interest me in *you*—is to know whether you regret what you've done, whether you can't stop thinking about it, whether it makes you sick to think of it. Remorse, good heavens, remorse! There does exist such a thing as remorse!"

Carried away he got up and strode round the circular lawn, wiping his brow on his sleeve.

"Ah!" said Camille with a contrite, affected expression. "Naturally, of course. I'd a million times rather *not* have done it. I must have lost my head."

"You're lying," he cried, trying not to shout. "All you regret is that you didn't bring it off! One's only got to listen to you, to look at you with your little hat on one side and your gloves and your new suit—everything you've so carefully arranged to charm me. If you really had any regret, I'd see it in your face. I'd feel it!"

He was shouting now, in a low grating voice, and was no longer quite master of the rage he had fostered. The worn stuff of his pajamas burst at the elbow and he tore off nearly the whole sleeve and flung it on a bush.

At first Camille had eyes only for the gesticulating arm, extraordinarily white against the dark block of the yew hedge.

He put his hands over his eyes and forced himself to speak lower.

"A little blameless creature, blue as the loveliest dreams. A little soul. Faithful, capable of quietly, delicately dying if what she has chosen fails her. You held *that* in your hands, over empty space . . . and you opened your hands. You're a monster. I don't wish to live with a monster."

He uncovered his damp face and came nearer to Camille, trying to find words which would overwhelm her. Her breath came short and her eyes went from the white naked arm to the bloodless face which was no less white.

"An animal!" she cried indignantly. "You're sacrificing me to an animal. I'm your wife, all the same! You're leaving me for an animal!"

"An animal? Yes, an animal."

Apparently calm now, he hid behind a mysteriously informed smile. "I'm perfectly willing to admit that Saha's an animal. If she's really one, what is there higher than this animal and how can I make Camille understand that? She makes me laugh, this barefaced little criminal, all virtue and indignation, who pretends to know what an animal is." He was prevented from going further by the sound of Camille's voice.

"*You're* the monster!"

"Pardon?"

"Yes, you. Unfortunately I can't exactly explain why. But I assure you I'm right. *I* wanted to get rid of Saha. That wasn't at all admirable. But to kill something that gets in her way, that makes her suffer—it's the first idea that comes into a woman's head, especially a jealous woman's. It's perfectly normal. What's abnormal, what's monstrous, is you. It's . . ."

She was struggling to make herself understood and, at the same time, pointing to certain accidental things about Alain which did indeed suggest a kind of delirium: the torn-off sleeve; the trembling, insulting mouth; the cheek from which all the blood had retreated; the wild crest of dishevelled fair hair. He made no protest and did not deign to defend himself. He seemed lost in some exploration from which there was no return.

"If I'd killed . . . or wanted to kill . . . a woman out of jealousy, you'd probably forgive me. But since I raised my hand against the cat, you're through with me. And yet you don't want me to treat you as a monster."

"Have I said I didn't want you to?" he broke in haughtily.

She looked at him with terrified eyes and made a gesture of impotence. Sombre and detached, he watched the young, execrable gloved hand every time it moved.

"Now for the future, what are we going to do? What's going to happen to us, Alain?"

He was so brimming over with intolerance that he nearly groaned. He wanted to cry out: "We separate, we keep silent, we sleep, we breathe without the other always there! I'll withdraw far, far away—under this cherry-tree for example, under the wing of that magpie. Or into the peacock's tail of the hose-jet. Or into my cold room under the protection of a little golden dollar, a handful of relics, and a Russian Blue cat."

He mastered himself and deliberately lied:

"But nothing, at the moment. It's too soon to make a . . . a decision. Later on, we'll see."

This final effort to be reasonable and sociable exhausted him. He tottered as soon as he took the first steps when he got up to accompany Camille. She accepted this vague conciliation with hungry hope.

"Yes, of course. It's much too soon. A little later on. Stay where you are, don't bother to come with me to the gate. With your sleeve, people will think we've been fighting. Listen, perhaps I'll go and get a little swimming at Ploumanach[50] with Patrick's brother and sister-in-law. Because the mere idea of living with my family at this moment . . ."

"Yes, do that. Take the roadster," proposed Alain.

She flushed and thanked him too effusively.

"I'll give it you back, you know, the minute I get back to Paris. You may need it. Don't hesitate to ask me for it back. Anyway, I'll let you know when I'm going and when I get back."

"Already she's organizing it all. Already she's throwing out the strands of her web, throwing out bridges. Already she's picking up the fabric, darning it, weaving the threads together again. It's horrifying. Is that what my mother admires in her? Perhaps, after all, it's very fine. I don't feel any more capable of understanding her than of making things up with her. How completely at ease she is in

50. Fishing village and bathing beach in Brittany.

everything I find insupportable. If she'd only go now, if she'd only go away!"

She was going away, carefully avoiding holding out her hand to him. But, under the arcade of clipped trees, she dared vainly to brush against him with her ripening breasts. Left alone, he collapsed into a chair and near him, on the wicker table, suddenly, like a miracle, appeared the cat.

A bend in the path and a gap in the leaves allowed Camille to see Alain and the cat once more from the distance. She stopped short and made a movement as if to retrace her steps. But she swayed only for an instant and then walked away faster than ever. For a while Saha, on guard, was following Camille's departure as intently as a human being. Alain was half-lying on his side, ignoring it. With one hand hollowed into a paw, he was playing deftly with the first green, prickly August chestnuts.

THOMAS MANN*

1875–1955

Tonio Kröger

The winter sun, poor ghost of itself, hung milky and wan behind layers of cloud above the huddled roofs of the town. In the gabled streets it was wet and windy and there came in gusts a sort of soft hail, not ice, not snow.

School was out. The hosts of the released streamed over the paved court and out at the wrought-iron gate, where they broke up and hastened off right and left. Elder pupils held their books in a strap high on the left shoulder and rowed, right arm against the wind, toward dinner. Small people trotted gaily off, splashing the slush with their feet, the tools of learning rattling amain in their walrus-skin satchels. But one and all pulled off their caps and cast down their eyes in awe before the Olympian hat and ambrosial beard[1] of a master moving homeward with measured stride. . . .

"Ah, there you are at last, Hans," said Tonio Kröger. He had been waiting a long time in the street and went up with a smile to the friend he saw coming out of the gate in talk with other boys and about to go off with them. . . . "What?" said Hans, and looked at Tonio. "Right-oh! We'll take a little walk, then."

Tonio said nothing and his eyes were clouded. Did Hans forget, had he only just remembered that they were to take a walk together

---

* Published in 1903. Translated by H. T. Lowe-Porter.   1. That is, divine-seeming attributes.

today? And he himself had looked forward to it with almost incessant joy.

"Well, good-bye, fellows," said Hans Hansen to his comrades.
"I'm taking a walk with Kröger." And the two turned to their left,
while the others sauntered off in the opposite direction.

Hans and Tonio had time to take a walk after school because in
neither of their families was dinner served before four o'clock. Their
fathers were prominent business men, who held public office and
were of consequence in the town. Hans' people had owned for
some generations the big wood yards down by the river, where powerful machine saws hissed and spat and cut up timber; while Tonio
was the son of Consul Kröger,[2] whose grain sacks with the firm
name in great black letters you might see any day driven through
the streets; his large, old ancestral home was the finest house in all
the town. The two friends had to keep taking off their hats to their
many acquaintances; some folk did not even wait for the fourteen-
year-old lads to speak first, as by rights they should.

Both of them carried their satchels across their shoulders and
both were well and warmly dressed: Hans in a short sailor jacket,
with the wide blue collar of his sailor suit turned out over shoulders
and back, and Tonio in a belted grey overcoat. Hans wore a Danish
sailor cap with black ribbons, beneath which streamed a shock of
straw-colored hair. He was uncommonly handsome and well built,
broad in the shoulders and narrow in the hips, with keen, far-apart,
steel-blue eyes; while beneath Tonio's round fur cap was a brunette
face with the finely chiseled features of the south; the dark eyes,
with delicate shadows and too heavy lids, looked dreamily and a
little timorously on the world. Tonio's walk was idle and uneven,
whereas the other's slim legs in their black stockings moved with an
elastic, rhythmic tread.

Tonio did not speak. He suffered. His rather oblique brows were
drawn together in a frown, his lips were rounded to whistle, he
gazed into space with his head on one side. Posture and manner
were habitual.

Suddenly Hans shoved his arm into Tonio's, with a sideways look
—he knew very well what the trouble was. And Tonio, though he
was silent for the next few steps, felt his heart soften.

"I hadn't forgotten, you see, Tonio," Hans said, gazing at the
pavement, "I only thought it wouldn't come off today because it
was so wet and windy. But I don't mind that at all, and it's jolly of
you to have waited. I thought you had gone home, and I was
cross. . . ."

Everything in Tonio leaped and jumped for joy at the words.

"All right; let's go over the wall," he said with a quaver in his

---

2. Title given to a member of the City
Council, the main governing body of independent city-states such as Lübeck, on
the north coast of Germany.

voice. "Over the Millwall and the Holstenwall,[3] and I'll go as far as your house with you, Hans. Then I'll have to walk back alone, but that doesn't matter; next time you can go round my way."

At bottom he was not really convinced by what Hans said; he quite knew the other attached less importance to this walk than he did himself. Yet he saw Hans was sorry for his remissness and willing to be put in a position to ask pardon, a pardon that Tonio was far indeed from withholding.

The truth was, Tonio loved Hans Hansen, and had already suffered much on his account. He who loves the more is the inferior and must suffer; in this hard and simple fact his fourteen-year-old soul had already been instructed by life; and he was so organized that he received such experiences consciously, wrote them down as it were inwardly, and even, in a certain way, took pleasure in them, though without ever letting them mold his conduct, indeed, or drawing any practical advantage from them. Being what he was, he found this knowledge far more important and far more interesting than the sort they made him learn in schools; yes, during his lesson hours in the vaulted Gothic classrooms he was mainly occupied in feeling his way about among these intuitions of his and penetrating them. The process gave him the same kind of satisfaction as that he felt when he moved about in his room with his violin—for he played the violin—and made the tones, brought out as softly as ever he knew how, mingle with the plashing of the fountain that leaped and danced down there in the garden beneath the branches of the old walnut tree.

The fountain, the old walnut tree, his fiddle, and away in the distance the North Sea, within sound of whose summer murmurings he spent his holidays—these were the things he loved, within these he enfolded his spirit, among these things his inner life took its course. And they were all things whose names were effective in verse and occurred pretty frequently in the lines Tonio Kröger sometimes wrote.

The fact that he had a notebook full of such things, written by himself, leaked out through his own carelessness and injured him no little with the masters as well as among his fellows. On the one hand, Consul Kröger's son found their attitude both cheap and silly, and despised his schoolmates and his masters as well, and in his turn (with extraordinary penetration) saw through and disliked their personal weaknesses and bad breeding. But then, on the other hand, he himself felt his verse-making extravagant and out of place and to a certain extent agreed with those who considered it an unpleasing occupation. But that did not enable him to leave off.

As he wasted his time at home, was slow and absent-minded at school, and always had bad marks from the masters, he was in the

3. Park-like walks built on the top of the old city walls.

habit of bringing home pitifully poor reports, which troubled and angered his father, a tall, fastidiously dressed man, with thoughtful blue eyes, and always a wild flower in his buttonhole. But for his mother, she cared nothing about the reports—Tonio's beautiful black-haired mother, whose name was Consuelo, and who was so absolutely different from the other ladies in the town, because father had brought her long ago from some place far down on the map.

Tonio loved his dark, fiery mother, who played the piano and mandolin so wonderfully, and he was glad his doubtful standing among men did not distress her. Though at the same time he found his father's annoyance a more dignified and respectable attitude and despite his scoldings understood him very well, whereas his mother's blithe indifference always seemed just a little wanton. His thoughts at times would run something like this: "It is true enough that I am what I am and will not and cannot alter: heedless, self-willed, with my mind on things nobody else thinks of. And so it is right they should scold and punish me and not smother things all up with kisses and music. After all, we are not gypsies living in a green wagon; we're respectable people, the family of Consul Kröger." And not seldom he would think: "Why is it I am different, why do I fight everything, why am I at odds with the masters and like a stranger among the other boys? The good scholars, and the solid majority—they don't find the masters funny, they don't write verses, their thoughts are all about things that people do think about and can talk about out loud. How regular and comfortable they must feel, knowing that everybody knows just where they stand! It must be nice! But what is the matter with me, and what will be the end of it all?"

These thoughts about himself and his relation to life played an important part in Tonio's love for Hans Hansen. He loved him in the first place because he was handsome; but in the next because he was in every respect his own opposite and foil. Hans Hansen was a capital scholar, and a jolly chap to boot, who was head at drill,[4] rode and swam to perfection, and lived in the sunshine of popularity. The masters were almost tender with him, they called him Hans and were partial to him in every way; the other pupils curried favor with him; even grown people stopped him on the street, twitched the shock of hair beneath his Danish sailor cap, and said; "Ah, here you are, Hans Hansen, with your pretty blond hair! Still head of the school? Remember me to your father and mother, that's a fine lad!"

Such was Hans Hansen; and ever since Tonio Kröger had known him, from the very minute he set eyes on him, he had burned inwardly with a heavy, envious longing. "Who else has blue eyes

4. Gymnastics.

like yours, or lives in such friendliness and harmony with all the world? You are always spending your time with some right and proper occupation. When you have done your prep[5] you take your riding lesson, or make things with a fret-saw; even in the holidays, at the seashore, you row and sail and swim all the time, while I wander off somewhere and lie down in the sand and stare at the strange and mysterious changes that whisk over the face of the sea. And all that is why your eyes are so clear. To be like you . . ."

He made no attempt to be like Hans Hansen, and perhaps hardly even seriously wanted to. What he did ardently, painfully want was that just as he was, Hans Hansen should love him; and he wooed Hans Hansen in his own way, deeply, lingeringly, devotedly, with a melancholy that gnawed and burned more terribly than all the sudden passion one might have expected from his exotic looks.

And he wooed not in vain. Hans respected Tonio's superior power of putting certain difficult matters into words; moreover, he felt the lively presence of an uncommonly strong and tender feeling for himself; he was grateful for it, and his response gave Tonio much happiness—though also many pangs of jealousy and disillusion over his futile efforts to establish a communion of spirit between them. For the queer thing was that Tonio, who after all envied Hans Hansen for being what he was, still kept on trying to draw him over to his own side; though of course he could succeed in this at most only at moments and superficially. . . .

I have just been reading something so wonderful and splendid . . ." he said. They were walking and eating together out of a bag of fruit toffees they had bought at Iverson's sweet shop in Mill Street for ten pfennigs.[6] "You must read it, Hans, it is Schiller's *Don Carlos*[7] . . . I'll lend it to you if you like; . . ."

"Oh, no," said Hans Hansen, "you needn't, Tonio, that's not anything for me. I'll stick to my horse books. There are wonderful cuts in them, let me tell you. I'll show them to you when you come to see me. They are instantaneous photography—the horse in motion; you can see him trot and canter and jump, in all positions, that you never can get to see in life, because they happen so fast. . . ."

"In all positions?" asked Tonio politely. "Yes, that must be great. But about *Don Carlos*—it is beyond anything you could possibly dream of. There are places in it that are so lovely they make you jump . . . as though it were an explosion—"

"An explosion?" asked Hans Hansen. "What sort of an explosion?"

"For instance, the place where the king has been crying because

---

5. Homework. *Fret-saw*: A coping-saw or jigsaw.
6. Pennies. 100 pfennigs equal 1 mark.
7. An historical drama by the German Romantic author Friedrich von Schiller (1759–1805). In the passage mentioned later, the king has just learned, by reading captured letters destined for rebels in Brabant and Flanders, that the Marquis of Posa has betrayed him.

the marquis betrayed him . . . but the marquis did it only out of love for the prince, you see, he sacrifices himself for his sake. And the word comes out of the cabinet[8] into the antechamber that the king has been weeping. 'Weeping? The king been weeping?' All the courtiers are fearfully upset, it goes through and through you, for the king has always been so frightfully stiff and stern. But it is so easy to understand why he cried, and I feel sorrier for him than for the prince and the marquis put together. He is always so alone, nobody loves him, and then he thinks he has found one man, and then *he* betrays him. . . ."

Hans Hansen looked sideways into Tonio's face, and something in it must have won him to the subject, for suddenly he shoved his arm once more into Tonio's and said;

"How had he betrayed him, Tonio?"

Tonio went on.

"Well," he said, "you see all the letters for Brabant and Flanders—"

"There comes Irwin Immerthal," said Hans.

Tonio stopped talking. If only the earth would open and swallow Immerthal up! "Why does he have to come disturbing us? If he only doesn't go with us all the way and talk about the riding lessons!" For Irwin Immerthal had riding lessons too. He was the son of the bank president and lived close by, outside the city wall. He had already been home and left his bag, and now he walked toward them through the avenue. His legs were crooked and his eyes like slits.

" 'lo, Immerthal," said Hans. "I'm taking a little walk with Kröger. . . ."

"I have to go into town on an errand," said Immerthal. "But I'll walk a little way with you. Are those fruit toffees you've got? Thanks, I'll have a couple. Tomorrow we have our next lesson, Hans." He meant the riding lesson.

"What larks!" said Hans. "I'm going to get the leather gaiters for a present, because I was top lately in our papers."

"You don't take riding lessons, I suppose, Kröger?" asked Immerthal, and his eyes were only two gleaming cracks.

"No . . ." answered Tonio, uncertainly.

"You ought to ask your father," Hans Hansen remarked, "so you could have lessons too, Kröger."

"Yes . . ." said Tonio. He spoke hastily and without interest; his throat had suddenly contracted, because Hans had called him by his last name. Hans seemed conscious of it too, for he said by way of explanation: "I call you Kröger because your first name is so crazy. Don't mind my saying so, I can't do with it all. Tonio—why, what sort of name is that? Though of course I know it's not your fault in the least."

8. Private chamber, study.

"No, they probably called you that because it sounds so foreign and sort of something special," said Immerthal, obviously with intent to say just the right thing.

Tonio's mouth twitched. He pulled himself together and said:

"Yes, it's a silly name—Lord knows I'd rather be called Heinrich or Wilhelm. It's all because I'm named after my mother's brother Antonio. She comes from down there,[9] you know. . . ."

There he stopped and let the others have their say about horses and saddles. Hans had taken Immerthal's arm; he talked with a fluency that *Don Carlos* could never have roused in him. . . . Tonio felt a mounting desire to weep pricking his nose from time to time; he had hard work to control the trembling of his lips.

Hans could not stand his name—what was to be done? He himself was called Hans, and Immerthal was called Irwin; two good, sound, familiar names, offensive to nobody. And Tonio was foreign and queer. Yes, there was always something queer about him, whether he would or no, and he was alone, the regular and usual would none of him; although after all he was no gypsy in a green wagon, but the son of Consul Kröger, a member of the Kröger family. But why did Hans call him Tonio as long as they were alone and then feel ashamed as soon as anybody else was by? Just now he had won him over, they had been close together, he was sure. "How had he betrayed him, Tonio?" Hans asked, and took his arm. But he had breathed easier directly Immerthal came up, he had dropped him like a shot, even gratuitously taunted him with his outlandish name. How it hurt to have to see through all this! . . . Hans Hansen did like him a little, when they were alone, that he knew. But let a third person come, he was ashamed, and offered up his friend. And again he was alone. He thought of King Philip. The king had wept. . . .

"Goodness, I have to go," said Irwin Immerthal. "Good-bye, and thanks for the toffee." He jumped upon a bench that stood by the way, ran along it with his crooked legs, jumped down, and trotted off.

"I like Immerthal," said Hans, with emphasis. He had a spoilt and arbitrary way of announcing his likes and dislikes, as though graciously pleased to confer them like an order on this person and that. . . . He went on talking about the riding lessons where he had left off. Anyhow, it was not very much farther to his house; the walk over the walls was not a long one. They held their caps and bent their heads before the strong, damp wind that rattled and groaned in the leafless trees. And Hans Hansen went on talking, Tonio throwing in a forced yes or no from time to time. Hans talked eagerly, had taken his arm again; but the contact gave Tonio no pleasure. The nearness was only apparent, not real; it meant nothing. . . .

9. Italy.

They struck away from the walls close to the station, where they saw a train puff busily past, idly counted the coaches, and waved to the man who was perched on top of the last one bundled in a leather coat. They stopped in front of the Hansen villa on the Lindenplatz, and Hans went into detail about what fun it was to stand on the bottom rail of the garden gate and let it swing on its creaking hinges. After that they said good-bye.

"I must go in now," said Hans. "Good-bye, Tonio. Next time I'll take you home, see if I don't."

"Good-bye, Hans," said Tonio. "It was a nice walk."

They put out their hands, all wet and rusty from the garden gate. But as Hans looked into Tonio's eyes, he bethought himself, a look of remorse came over his charming face.

"And I'll read *Don Carlos* pretty soon, too," he said quickly. "That bit about the king in his cabinet must be nuts." Then he took his bag under his arm and ran off through the front garden. Before he disappeared he turned and nodded once more.

And Tonio went off as though on wings. The wind was at his back; but it was not the wind alone that bore him along so lightly.

Hans would read *Don Carlos*, and then they would have something to talk about, and neither Irwin Immerthal nor another could join in. How well they understood each other! Perhaps—who knew? —some day he might even get Hans to write poetry! . . . No, no, that he did not ask. Hans must not become like Tonio, he must stop just as he was, so strong and bright, everybody loved him as he was, and Tonio most of all. But it would do him no harm to read *Don Carlos*. . . . Tonio passed under the squat old city gate, along by the harbor, and up the steep, wet, windy, gabled street to his parents' house. His heart beat richly: longing was awake in it, and a gentle envy; a faint contempt, and no little innocent bliss.

Ingeborg Holm, blonde little Inge, the daugher of Dr. Holm, who lived on Market Square opposite the tall old Gothic fountain with its manifold spires—she it was Tonio Kröger loved when he was sixteen years old.

Strange how things come about! He had seen her a thousand times; then one evening he saw her again; saw her in a certain light, talking with a friend in a certain saucy way, laughing and tossing her head; saw her lift her arm and smooth her back hair with her schoolgirl hand, that was by no means particularly fine or slender, in such a way that the thin white sleeve slipped down from her elbow; heard her speak a word or two, a quite indifferent phrase, but with a certain intonation, with a warm ring in her voice; and his heart throbbed with ecstasy, far stronger than that he had once felt when he looked at Hans Hansen long ago, when he was still a little, stupid boy.

That evening he carried away her picture in his eye: the thick blond plait, the longish, laughing blue eyes, the saddle of pale freck-les across the nose. He could not go to sleep for hearing that ring in her voice; he tried in a whisper to imitate the tone in which she had uttered the commonplace phrase, and felt a shiver run through and through him. He knew by experience that this was love. And he was accurately aware that love would surely bring him much pain, affliction, and sadness, that it would certainly destroy his peace, filling his heart to overflowing with melodies which would be no good to him because he would never have the time or tranquill-ity to give them permanent form. Yet he received this love with joy, surrendered himself to it, and cherished it with all the strength of his being; for he knew that love made one vital and rich, and he longed to be vital and rich, far more than he did to work tranquilly on anything to give it permanent form.

Tonio Kröger fell in love with merry Ingeborg Holm in Frau Consul[10] Hustede's drawing room on the evening when it was emp-tied of furniture for the weekly dancing class. It was a private class, attended only by members of the first families; it met by turns in the various parental houses to receive instruction from Knaak, the dancing-master, who came from Hamburg expressly for the purpose.

François Knaak was his name, and what a man he was! "*J'ai l'honneur de me vous représenter*," he would say, "*mon nom est Knaak*. . . .[11] This is not said during the bowing, but after you have finished and are standing up straight again. In a low voice, but dis-tinctly. Of course one does not need to introduce oneself in French every day in the week, but if you can do it correctly and faultlessly in French you are not likely to make a mistake when you do it in German." How marvelously the silky black frock coat fitted his chubby hips! His trouser legs fell down in soft folds upon his patent leather pumps with their wide satin bows, and his brown eyes glanced about him with languid pleasure in their own beauty.

All this excess of self-confidence and good form was positively overpowering. He went trippingly—and nobody tripped like him, so elastically, so weavingly, rockingly, royally—up to the mistress of the house, made a bow, waited for a hand to be put forth. This vouchsafed, he gave murmurous voice to his gratitude, stepped buoyantly back, turned on his left foot, swiftly drawing the right one backwards on its toe-tip, and moved away, with his hips shak-ing.

When you took leave of a company you must go backward out at the door; when you fetched a chair, you were not to shove it along the floor or clutch it by one leg; but gently, by the back, and set it

10. "Mrs. Consul"; the wife of a dig-nitary would be formally addressed using her husband's title.
11. "I am honored to represent myself to you . . . my name is Knaak." French was the accepted language for elegant society at that time, particularly in the ballroom. *Represent* rather than *present* is bad French, and undermines Knaak's claim to faultless elegance.

down without a sound. When you stood, you were not to fold your hands on your tummy or seek with your tongue the corners of your mouth. If you did, Herr Knaak had a way of showing you how it looked that filled you with disgust for the particular gesture all the rest of your life.

This was deportment. As for dancing, Herr Knaak was, if possible, even more of a master at that. The salon was emptied of furniture and lighted by a gas chandelier in the middle of the ceiling and candles on the mantel shelf. The floor was strewn with talc, and the pupils stood about in a dumb semicircle. But in the next room, behind the portières,[12] mothers and aunts sat on plush-upholstered chairs and watched Herr Knaak through their lorgnettes,[13] as in little springs and hops, curtsying slightly, the hem of his frock coat held up on each side by two fingers, he demonstrated the single steps of the mazurka.[14] When he wanted to dazzle his audience completely he would suddenly and unexpectedly spring from the ground, whirling his two legs about each other with bewildering swiftness in the air, as it were trilling with them, and then, with a subdued bump, which nevertheless shook everything within him to its depths, return to earth.

"What an unmentionable monkey!" thought Tonio Kröger to himself. But he saw the absorbed smile on jolly little Inge's face as she followed Herr Knaak's movements; and that, though not that alone, roused in him something like admiration of all this wonderfully controlled corporeality How tranquil, how imperturbable was Herr Knaak's gaze! His eyes did not plumb the depth of things to the place where life becomes complex and melancholy; they knew nothing save that they were beautiful brown eyes. But that was just why his bearing was so proud. To be able to walk like that, one must be stupid; then one was loved, then one was lovable. He could so well understand how it was that Inge, blonde, sweet little Inge, looked at Herr Knaak as she did. But would never a girl look at him like that?

Oh, yes, there would, and did. For instance, Magdalena Vermehren, Attorney Vermehren's daughter, with the gentle mouth and the great, dark, brilliant eyes, so serious and adoring. She often fell down in the dance; but when it was "ladies' choice" she came up to him; she knew he wrote verses and twice she had asked him to show them to her. She often sat at a distance, with drooping head, and gazed at him. He did not care. It was Inge he loved, blonde, jolly Inge, who most assuredly despised him for his poetic effusions . . . he looked at her, looked at her narrow blue eyes full of fun and mockery, and felt an envious longing; to be shut away from her like

12. Curtains hung as a screen across the doorway.
13. Eyeglasses with a short handle.
14. The mazurka, the quadrille, and the polonaise—all used by Mann in this story—are ballroom dances involving patterns performed by a series of couples.

this, to be forever strange—he felt it in his breast, like a heavy, burning weight.

"First couple *en avant*,"[15] said Herr Knaak; and no words can tell how marvelously he pronounced the nasal. They were to practice the quadrille, and to Tonio Kröger's profound alarm he found himself in the same set with Inge Holm. He avoided her where he could, yet somehow was forever near her; kept his eyes away from her person and yet found his gaze ever on her. There she came, tripping up hand-in-hand with red-headed Ferdinand Matthiessen; she flung back her braid, drew a deep breath, and took her place opposite Tonio. Herr Heinzelmann, at the piano, laid bony hands upon the keys, Herr Knaak waved his arm, the quadrille began.

She moved to and fro before his eyes, forward and back, pacing and swinging; he seemed to catch a fragrance from her hair or the folds of her thin white frock, and his eyes grew sadder and sadder. "I love you, dear, sweet Inge," he said to himself, and put into his worlds all the pain he felt to see her so intent upon the dance with not a thought of him. Some lines of an exquisite poem by Storm came into his mind: "I would sleep, but thou must dance."[16] It seemed against all sense, and most depressing, that he must be dancing when he was in love. . . .

"First couple *en avant*," said Herr Knaak; it was the next figure. "*Compliment! Moulinet des dames! Tour de main!*"[17] and he swallowed the silent *e* in the "*de*," with quite indescribable ease and grace.

"Second couple *en avant!*" This was Tonio Kröger and his partner. "*Compliment!*" And Tonio Kröger bowed. "*Moulinet des dames!*" And Tonio Kröger, with bent head and gloomy brows, laid his hand on those of the four ladies, on Ingeborg Holm's hand, and danced the *moulinet*.

Roundabout rose a tittering and laughing. Herr Knaak took a ballet pose conventionally expressive of horror. "Oh, dear! Oh, dear!" he cried. "Stop! Stop! Kröger among the ladies! *En arrière*, Fräulein Kröger, step back, *fi donc!*[18] Everybody else understood it but you. Shoo! Get out! Get away!" He drew out his yellow silk handkerchief and flapped Tonio Kröger back to his place.

Everyone laughed, the girls and the boys and the ladies beyond the portières; Herr Knaak had made something too utterly funny out of the little episode, it was as amusing as a play. But Herr Hein-

15. Forward.
16. From the poem "Hyacinth" by Theodor Storm (1817–1888), German poet and novella writer noted for his poetic realism. His lyrics and early stories (such as *Immensee*, whose theme is the lost happiness of childhood) express a tone of melancholy resignation, and were much read by the young Thomas Mann.
17. "Bow and curtsey! Windmill for the ladies! Change hands;" Instructions for ballroom dancing would normally be given in French. The dance figure described here is a "windmill" in which the women join right hands and walk around the center.
18. "Back, Miss Kröger . . . shame on you!" (Tonio is mockingly called Fräulein, i.e., "Miss.")

zelmann at the piano sat and waited, with a dry, business-like air, for a sign to go on; he was hardened against Herr Knaak's effects.

Then the quadrille went on. And the intermission followed. The parlormaid came clinking in with a tray of wine-jelly[19] glasses, the cook followed in her wake with a load of plum cake. But Tonio Kröger stole away. He stole out into the corridor and stood there, his hands behind his back, in front of a window with the blind down. He never thought that one could not see through the blind and that it was absurd to stand there as though one were looking out.

For he was looking within, into himself, the theatre of so much pain and longing. Why, why was he here? Why was he not sitting by the window in his own room, reading Storm's *Immensee* and lifting his eyes to the twilight garden outside, where the old walnut tree moaned? That was the place for him! Others might dance, others bend their fresh and lively minds upon the pleasure in hand! . . . But no, no, after all, his place was here, where he could feel near Inge even though he stood lonely and aloof, seeking to distinguish the warm notes of her voice amid the buzzing, clattering, and laughter within. Oh, lovely Inge, blonde Inge of the narrow, laughing blue eyes! So lovely and laughing as you are one can only be if one does not read *Immensee* and never tries to write things like it. And that was just the tragedy!

Ah, she *must* come! She *must* notice where he had gone, must feel how he suffered! She must slip out to him, even pity must bring her, to lay her hand on his shoulder and say: "Do come back to us, ah, don't be sad—I love you, Tonio." He listened behind him and waited in frantic suspense. But not in the least. Such things did not happen on this earth.

Had she laughed at him too like all the others? Yes, she had, however gladly he would have denied it for both their sakes. And yet it was only because he had been so taken up with her that he had danced the *moulinet des dames*. Suppose he had—what did that matter? Had not a magazine accepted a poem of his a little while ago—even though the magazine had failed before his poem could be printed? The day was coming when he would be famous, when they would print everything he wrote; and *then* he would see if that made any impression on Inge Holm! No, it would make no impression at all; that was just it. Magdalena Vermehren, who was always falling down in the dances, yes, she would be impressed. But never Ingeborg Holm, never blue-eyed, laughing Inge. So what was the good of it?

Tonio Kröger's heart contracted painfully at the thought. To feel stirring within you the wonderful and melancholy play of strange forces and to be aware that those others you yearn for are blithely

19. A gelatin dessert made with wine.

inaccessible to all that moves you—what a pain is this! And yet! He stood there aloof and alone, staring hopelessly at a drawn blind and making, in his distraction, as though he could look out. But yet he was happy. For he lived. His heart was full; hotly and sadly it beat for thee, Ingeborg Holm, and his soul embraced thy blonde, simple, pert, commonplace little personality in blissful self-abnegation.

Often after that he stood thus, with burning cheeks, in lonely corners, whither the sound of music, the tinkling of glasses and fragrance of flowers came but faintly, and tried to distinguish the ringing tones of thy voice amid the distant happy din; stood suffering for thee—and still was happy! Often it angered him to think that he might talk with Magdalena Vermehren, who always fell down in the dance. She understood him, she laughed or was serious in the right places; while Inge the fair, let him sit never so near her, seemed remote and estranged, his speech not being her speech. And still—he was happy. For happiness, he told himself, is not in being loved—which is a satisfaction of the vanity and mingled with disgust. Happiness is in loving, and perhaps in snatching fugitive little approaches to the beloved object. And he took inward note of this thought, wrote it down in his mind; followed out all its implications and felt it to the depths of his soul.

"Faithfulness," thought Tonio Kröger. "Yes, I will be faithful, I will love thee, Ingeborg, as long as I live!" He said this in the honesty of his intentions. And yet a still small voice whispered misgivings in his ear: after all, he had forgotten Hans Hansen utterly, even though he saw him every day! And the hateful, the pitiable fact was that this still, small, rather spiteful voice was right: time passed and the day came when Tonio Kröger was no longer so unconditionally ready as once he had been to die for the lively Inge, because he felt in himself desires and powers to accomplish in his own way a host of wonderful things in this world.

And he circled with watchful eye the sacrificial altar, where flickered the pure, chaste flame of his love; knelt before it and tended and cherished it in every way, because he so wanted to be faithful. And in a little while, unobservably, without sensation or stir, it went out after all.

But Tonio Kröger still stood before the cold altar, full of regret and dismay at the fact that faithfulness was impossible upon this earth. Then he shrugged his shoulders and went away.

He went the way that go he must, a little idly, a little irregularly, whistling to himself, gazing into space with his head on one side; and if he went wrong it was because for some people there is no such thing as a right way. Asked what in the world he meant to become, he gave various answers, for he was used to say (and had even already written it) that he bore within himself the possibility of a thousand ways of life, together with the private conviction that they were all sheer impossibilities.

Even before he left the narrow streets of his native city, the threads that bound him to it had gently loosened. The old Kröger family gradually declined, and some people quite rightly considered Tonio Kröger's own existence and way of life as one of the signs of decay. His father's mother, the head of the family, had died, and not long after his own father followed, the tall, thoughtful, carefully dressed gentleman with the field flower in his buttonhole. The great Kröger house, with all its stately tradition, came up for sale, and the firm was dissolved. Tonio's mother, his beautiful, fiery mother, who played the piano and mandolin so wonderfully and to whom nothing mattered at all, she married again after a year's time; married a musician, moreover, a virtuoso with an Italian name, and went away with him into remote blue distances. Tonio Kröger found this a little irregular, but who was he to call her to order, who wrote poetry himself and could not even give an answer when asked what he meant to do in life?

And so he left his native town and its tortuous, gabled streets with the damp wind whistling through them; left the fountain in the garden and the ancient walnut tree, familiar friends of his youth; left the sea too, that he loved so much, and felt no pain to go. For he was grown up and sensible and had come to realize how things stood with him; he looked down on the lowly and vulgar life he had led so long in these surroundings.

He surrendered utterly to the power that to him seemed the highest on earth, to whose service he felt called, which promised him elevation and honors: the power of intellect, the power of the Word, that lords it with a smile over the unconscious and inarticulate. To this power he surrendered with all the passion of youth, and it rewarded him with all it had to give, taking from him inexorably, in return, all that it is wont to take.

It sharpened his eyes and made him see through the large words which puff out of the bosoms of mankind; it opened for him men's souls and his own, made him clairvoyant, showed him the inwardness of the world and the ultimate behind men's words and deeds. And all that he saw could be put in two words: the comedy and the tragedy of life.

And then, with knowledge, its torment and its arrogance, came solitude; because he could not endure the blithe and innocent with their darkened understanding, while they in turn were troubled by the sign on his brow.[20] But his love of the world kept growing

---

20. In the Old Testament, Cain, who had killed his brother Abel, is set apart from the rest of mankind by a mark which God puts on his forehead. [*Genesis* 4:15.]

sweeter and sweeter, and his love of form; for he used to say (and had already said it in writing) that knowledge of the soul would unfailingly make us melancholy if the pleasures of expression did not keep us alert and of good cheer.

He lived in large cities and in the south, promising himself a luxuriant ripening of his art by southern suns; perhaps it was the blood of his mother's race that drew him thither. But his heart being dead and loveless, he fell into adventures of the flesh, descended into the depths of lust and searing sin, and suffering unspeakably thereby. It might have been his father in him, that tall, thoughtful, fastidiously dressed man with the wild flower in his buttonhole, that made him suffer so down there in the south; now and again he would feel a faint, yearning memory of a certain joy that was of the soul; once it had been his own, but now, in all his joys, he could not find it again.

Then he would be seized with disgust and hatred of the senses; pant after purity and seemly peace, while still he breathed the air of art, the tepid, sweet air of permanent spring, heavy with fragrance where it breeds and brews and burgeons in the mysterious bliss of creation. So for all result he was flung to and fro forever between two crass extremes: between icy intellect and scorching sense, and what with his pangs of conscience led an exhausting life, rare, extraordinary, excessive, which at bottom he, Tonio Kröger, despised. "What a labyrinth!" he sometimes thought. "How could I possibly have got into all these fantastic adventures? As though I had a wagonful of traveling gypsies for my ancestors!"

But as his health suffered from these excesses, so his artistry was sharpened; it grew fastidious, precious, *raffiné*,[21] morbidly sensitive in questions of tact and taste, rasped by the banal. His first appearance in print elicited much applause; there was joy among the elect, for it was a good and workmanlike performance, full of humor and acquaintance with pain. In no long time his name—the same by which his masters had reproached him, the same he had signed to his earliest verses on the walnut tree and the fountain and the sea, those syllables compact of the north and the south, that good middle-class name with the exotic twist to it—became a synonym for excellence; for the painful thoroughness of the experiences he had gone through, combined with a tenacious ambition and a persistent industry, joined battle with the irritable fastidiousness of his taste and under grinding torments issued in work of a quality quite uncommon.

He worked, not like a man who works that he may live; but as one who is bent on doing nothing but work; having no regard for himself as a human being but only as a creator; moving about grey

21. Refined, exquisite.

and unobtrusive among his fellows like an actor without his make-up, who counts for nothing as soon as he stops representing something else. He worked withdrawn out of sight and sound of the small fry, for whom he felt nothing but contempt, because to them a talent was a social asset like another; who, whether they were poor or not, went about ostentatiously shabby or else flaunted startling cravats,[22] all the time taking jolly good care to amuse themselves, to be artistic and charming without the smallest notion of the fact that good work only comes out under pressure of a bad life; that he who lives does not work; that one must die to life in order to be utterly a creator.

———————

"Shall I disturb you?" asked Tonio Kröger on the threshold of the atelier.[23] He held his hat in his hand and bowed with some ceremony, although Lisabeta Ivanovna was a good friend of his, to whom he told all his troubles.

"Mercy on you, Tonio Kröger! Don't be so formal," answered she, with her lilting intonation. "Everybody knows you were taught good manners in your nursery." She transferred her brush to her left hand, that held the palette, reached him her right, and looked him in the face, smiling and shaking her head.

"Yes, but you are working," he said. "Let's see. Oh, you've been getting on," and he looked at the color sketches leaning against chairs at both sides of the easel and from them to the large canvas covered with a square linen mesh, where the first patches of color were beginning to appear among the confused and schematic lines of the charcoal sketch.

This was in Munich, in a back building in Schellingstrasse, several stories up. Beyond the wide window facing the north were blue sky, sunshine, birds twittering; the young sweet breath of spring streaming through an open pane mingled with the smells of paint and fixative.[24] The afternoon light, bright golden, flooded the spacious emptiness of the atelier; it made no secret of the bad flooring or the rough table under the window, covered with little bottles, tubes, and brushes; it illumined the unframed studies on the unpapered walls, the torn silk screen that shut off a charmingly furnished little living-corner near the door; it shone upon the inchoate work on the easel, upon the artist and the poet there before it.

She was about the same age as himself—slightly past thirty. She sat there on a low stool, in her dark blue apron, and leant her chin in her hand. Her brown hair, compactly dressed, already a little grey at the sides, was parted in the middle and waved over the temples, framing a sensitive, sympathetic, dark-skinned face, which was Slavic in its facial structure, with flat nose, strongly accentuated cheek bones, and little bright black eyes. She sat there measuring

---

22. Neckties.
23. Artist's studio.

24. Liquid preservative applied to water color paintings or charcoal drawings.

her work with her head on one side and her eyes screwed up; her features were drawn with a look of misgiving, almost of vexation.

He stood beside her, his right hand on his hip, with the other furiously twirling his brown moustache. His dress, reserved in cut and a soothing shade of grey, was punctilious and dignified to the last degree. He was whistling softly to himself, in the way he had, and his slanting brows were gathered in a frown. The dark brown hair was parted with severe correctness, but the labored forehead beneath showed a nervous twitching, and the chiseled southern features were sharpened as though they had been gone over again with a graver's tool. And yet the mouth—how gently curved it was, the chin how softly formed! . . . After a little he drew his hand across his brow and eyes and turned away.

"I ought not to have come," he said.

"And why not, Tonio Kröger?"

"I've just got up from my desk, Lisabeta, and inside my head it looks just the way it does on this canvas. A scaffolding, a faint first draft smeared with corrections and a few splotches of color; yes, and I come up here and see the same thing. And the same conflict and contradiction in the air," he went on, sniffing, "that has been torturing me at home. It's extraordinary. If you are possessed by an idea, you find it expressed everywhere, you even *smell* it. Fixative and the breath of spring; art and—what? Don't say nature, Lisabeta, 'nature' isn't exhausting. Ah, no, I ought to have gone for a walk, though it's doubtful if it would have made me feel better. Five minutes ago, not far from here, I met a man I know, Adalbert, the novelist. 'God damn the spring!' says he in the aggressive way he has. 'It is and always has been the most ghastly time of the year. Can you get hold of a single sensible idea, Kröger? Can you sit still and work out even the smallest effect, when your blood tickles till it's positively indecent and you are teased by a whole host of irrelevant sensations that when you look at them turn out to be unworkable trash? For my part, I am going to a café. A café is neutral territory, the change of the seasons doesn't affect it; it represents, so to speak, the detached and elevated sphere of the literary man, in which one is only capable of refined ideas.' And he went into the café . . . and perhaps I ought to have gone with him."

Lisabeta was highly entertained.

"I like that, Tonio Kröger. That part about the indecent tickling is good. And he is right too, in a way, for spring is really not very conducive to work. But now listen. Spring or no spring, I will just finish this little place—work out this little effect, as your friend Adalbert would say. Then we'll go into the 'salon' and have tea, and you can talk yourself out, for I can perfectly well see you are too full for utterance. Will you just compose yourself somewhere—on that chest, for instance, if you are not afraid for your aristocratic garments—"

"Oh, leave my clothes alone, Lisabeta Ivanovna! Do you want me to go about in a ragged velveteen jacket or a red waistcoat? Every artist is as bohemian as the deuce, inside! Let him at least wear proper clothes and behave outwardly like a respectable being. No, I am not too full for utterance," he said as he watched her mixing her paints. "I've told you, it is only that I have a problem and a conflict, that sticks in my mind and disturbs me at my work. . . . Yes, what was it we were just saying? We were talking about Adalbert, the novelist, that stout and forthright man. 'Spring is the most ghastly time of the year,' says he, and goes into a café. A man has to know what he needs, eh? Well, you see he's not the only one; the spring makes me nervous, too; I get dazed with the triflingness and sacredness of the memories and feelings it evokes; only that I don't succeed in looking down on it; for the truth is it makes me ashamed; I quail before its sheer naturalness and triumphant youth. And I don't know whether I should envy Adalbert or despise him for his ignorance. . . .

"Yes, it is true; spring is a bad time for work; and why? Because we are feeling too much. Nobody but a beginner imagines that he who creates must feel. Every real and genuine artist smiles at such naïve blunders as that. A melancholy enough smile, perhaps, but still a smile. For what an artist talks about is never the main point; it is the raw material, in and for itself indifferent, out of which, with bland and serene mastery, he creates the work of art. If you care too much about what you have to say, if your heart is too much in it, you can be pretty sure of making a mess. You get pathetic, you wax sentimental; something dull and doddering, without roots or outlines, with no sense of humor—something tiresome and banal grows under your hand, and you get nothing out of it but apathy in your audience and disappointment and misery in yourself. For so it is, Lisabeta; feeling, warm, heartfelt feeling, is always banal and futile; only the irritations and icy ecstasies of the artist's corrupted nervous system are artistic. The artist must be unhuman, extra-human; he must stand in a queer aloof relationship to our humanity; only so is he in a position, I ought to say only so would he be tempted, to represent it, to present it, to portray it to good effect. The very gift of style, of form and expression, is nothing else than this cool and fastidious attitude toward humanity; you might say there has to be this impoverishment and devastation as a preliminary condition. For sound natural feeling, say what you like, has no taste. It is all up with the artist as soon as he becomes a man and begins to feel. Adalbert knows that; that's why he betook himself to the café, the neutral territory—God help him!"

"Yes, God help him, Batushka,"[25] said Lisabeta, as she washed

25. Literally, "Little Father," an affectionate Russian diminutive.

her hands in a tin basin. "You don't need to follow his example."

"No, Lisabeta, I am not going to; and the only reason is that I am now and again in a position to feel a little ashamed of the springtime of my art. You see sometimes I get letters from strangers, full of praise and thanks and admiration from people whose feelings I have touched. I read them and feel touched myself at these warm if ungainly emotions I have called up; a sort of pity steals over me at this naïve enthusiasm; and I positively blush at the thought of how these good people would freeze up if they were to get a look behind the scenes. What they, in their innocence, cannot comprehend is that a properly constituted, healthy, decent man never writes, acts, or composes—all of which does not hinder me from using his admiration for my genius to goad myself on; nor from taking it in deadly earnest and aping the airs of a great man. Oh, don't talk to me, Lisabeta. I tell you I am sick to death of depicting humanity without having any part or lot in it. . . . Is an artist a male, anyhow? Ask the females! It seems to me we artists are all of us something like those unsexed papal singers[26] . . . we sing like angels; but—"

"Shame on you, Tonio Kröger. But come to tea. The water is just on the boil, and here are some *papyros*.[27] You were talking about singing soprano, do go on. But really you ought to be ashamed of yourself. If I did not know your passionate devotion to your calling and how proud you are of it—"

"Don't talk about 'calling,' Lisabeta Ivanovna. Literature is not a calling, it is a curse, believe me! When does one begin to feel the curse? Early, horribly early. At a time when one ought by rights still to be living in peace and harmony with God and the world. It begins by your feeling yourself set apart, in a curious sort of opposition to the nice, regular people; there is a gulf of ironic sensibility, of knowledge, scepticism, disagreement between you and the others; it grows deeper and deeper, you realize that you are alone; and from then on any *rapprochement*[28] is simply hopeless! What a fate! That is, if you still have enough heart, enough warmth of affections, to feel how frightful it is! . . . Your self-consciousness is kindled, because you among thousands feel the sign on your brow and know that everyone else sees it. I once knew an actor, a man of genius, who had to struggle with a morbid self-consciousness and instability. When he had no role to play, nothing to represent, this man, consummate artist but impoverished human being, was overcome by an exaggerated consciousness of his ego. A genuine artist

---

26. *Castrati* were singers castrated as young boys to preserve their soprano voices. The practice stopped in 1878, but the pope's chapel employed them as late as 1903 because women were not permitted to become part of the papal establishment.

27. Cigarettes.

28. Reconciliation.

—not one who has taken up àrt as a profession like another, but artist foreordained and damned—you can pick out, without boasting very sharp perceptions, out of a group of men. The sense of being set apart and not belonging, of being known and observed, something both regal and incongruous shows in his face. You might see something of the same sort on the features of a prince walking through a crowd in ordinary clothes. But no civilian clothes are any good here, Lisabeta. You can disguise yourself, you can dress up like an attaché or a lieutenant of the guard on leave; you hardly need to give a glance or speak a word before everyone knows you are not a human being, but something else: something queer, different, inimical.

"But what is it, to be an artist? Nothing shows up the general human dislike of thinking, and man's innate craving to be comfortable, better than his attitude to this question. When these worthy people are affected by a work of art, they say humbly that that sort of thing is a 'gift.' And because in their innocence they assume that beautiful and uplifting results must have beautiful and uplifting causes, they never dream that the 'gift' in question is a very dubious affair and rests upon extremely sinister foundations. Everybody knows that artists are 'sensitive' and easily wounded; just as everybody knows that ordinary people, with a normal bump of self-confidence, are not. Now you see, Lisabeta, I cherish at the bottom of my soul all the scorn and suspicion of the artist gentry—translated into terms of the intellectual—that my upright old forebears there on the Baltic would have felt for any juggler or mountebank that entered their houses. Listen to this. I know a banker, grey-haired business man, who has a gift for writing stories. He employs this gift in his idle hours, and some of his stories are of the first rank. But despite—I say despite—this excellent gift his withers are by no means unwrung:[29] on the contrary, he has had to serve a prison sentence, on anything but trifling grounds. Yes, it was actually first *in prison* that he became conscious of his gift, and his experiences as a convict are the main theme in all his works. One might be rash enough to conclude that a man has to be at home in some kind of jail in order to become a poet. But can you escape the suspicion that the source and essence of his being an artist had less to do with his life in prison than they had with the reasons that *brought him there?* A banker who writes—that is a rarity, isn't it? But a banker who isn't a criminal, who is irreproachably respectable, and yet writes—he doesn't exist. Yes, you are laughing, and yet I am more than half serious. No problem, none in the world, is more tormenting than this of the artist and his human aspect. Take the most

29. I.e., he is by no means untroubled.

miraculous case of all, take the most typical and therefore the most powerful of artists, take such a morbid and profoundly equivocal work as *Tristan and Isolde*,[30] and look at the effect it has on a healthy young man of thoroughly normal feelings. Exaltation, encouragement, warm, downright enthusiasm, perhaps incitement to 'artistic' creation of his own. Poor young dilettante![31] In us artists it looks fundamentally different from what he wots[32] of, with his 'warm heart' and 'honest enthusiasm.' I've seen women and youths go mad over artists . . . and I *knew* about them . . . ! The origin, the accompanying phenomena, and the conditions of the artist life—good Lord, what I haven't observed about them, over and over!"

"Observed, Tonio Kröger? If I may ask, only 'observed'?"

He was silent, knitting his oblique brown brows and whistling softly to himself.

"Let me have your cup, Tonio. The tea is weak. And take another cigarette. Now, you perfectly know that you are looking at things as they do not necessarily have to be looked at. . . ."

"That is Horatio's answer, dear Lisabeta. ' 'Twere to consider too curiously,[33] to consider so.' "

"I mean, Tonio Kröger, that one can consider them just exactly as well from another side. I am only a silly painting female, and if I can contradict you at all, if I can defend your own profession a little against you, it is not by saying anything new, but simply by reminding you of some things you very well know yourself: of the purifying and healing influence of letters, the subduing of the passions by knowledge and eloquence; literature as the guide to understanding, forgiveness, and love, the redeeming power of the Word, literary art as the noblest manifestation of the human mind, the poet as the most highly developed of human beings, the poet as saint. Is it to consider things not curiously enough, to consider them so?"

"You may talk like that, Lisabeta Ivanovna, you have a perfect right. And with reference to Russian literature, and the words of your poets, one can really worship them; they really come close to being that elevated literature you are talking about. But I am not ignoring your objections, they are part of the things I have in my mind today. . . . Look at me, Lisabeta. I don't look any too cheerful, do I? A little old and tired and pinched, eh? Well, now to

---

30. Opera by Richard Wagner on the legendary doomed love of the knight Tristan and his uncle's wife, Queen Isolde. The sensuous appeal of the lovers' longing for night, death, and erotic transcendence, and the revolutionary example of Wagner's new musical forms, overwhelmed young artists and amateurs in the late 19th and early 20th centuries.

31. A dabbler or amateur of the arts.

32. Knows (consciously archaic language).

33. I.e., "too closely"—the words with which Horatio reproaches Hamlet (V,i, 106) for adopting a morbid perspective.

come back to the 'knowledge.' Can't you imagine a man, born orthodox, mild-mannered, well-meaning, a bit sentimental, just simply over-stimulated by his psychological clairvoyance, and going to the dogs? Not to let the sadness of the world unman you; to read, mark, learn, and put to account even the most torturing things and to be of perpetual good cheer, in the sublime conscious-ness of moral superiority over the horrible invention of existence— yes, thank you! But despite all the joys of expression once in a while the thing gets on your nerves. *'Tout comprendre c'est tout pardonner.'*[34] I don't know about that. There is something I call being sick of knowledge, Lisabeta; when it is enough for you to see through a thing in order to be sick to death of it, and not in the least in a forgiving mood. Such was the case of Hamlet the Dane, that typical literary man. He knew what it meant to be called to knowledge without being born to it. To see things clear, if even through your tears, to recognize, notice, observe—and have to put it all down with a smile, at the very moment when hands are cling-ing, and lips meeting, and the human gaze is blinded with feeling —it is infamous, Lisabeta, it is indecent, outrageous—but what good does it do to be outraged?

"Then another and no less charming side of the thing, of course, is your ennui,[35] your indifferent and ironic attitude toward truth. It is a fact that there is no society in the world so dumb and hopeless as a circle of literary people who are hounded to death as it is. All knowledge is old and tedious to them. Utter some truth that it gave you considerable youthful joy to conquer and possess—and they will all chortle at you for your naïveté. Oh, yes, Lisabeta, literature is a wearing job. In human society, I do assure you, a reserved and skeptical man can be taken for stupid, whereas he is really only arro-gant and perhaps lacks courage. So much for 'knowledge.' Now for the 'Word.' It isn't so much a matter of the 'redeeming power' as it is of putting your emotions on ice and serving them up chilled! Honestly, don't you think there's a good deal of cool cheek in the prompt and superficial way a writer can get rid of his feelings by turning them into literature? If your heart is too full, if you are overpowered with the emotions of some sweet or exalted moment —nothing simpler! Go to the literary man, he will put it all straight for you instanter.[36] He will analyze and formulate your affair, label it and express it and discuss it and polish it off and make you indif-ferent to it for time and eternity—and not charge you a farthing.[37] You will go home quite relieved, cooled off, enlight-ened; and wonder what it was all about and why you were so might-ily moved. And will you seriously enter the lists in behalf of this

34. "To understand everything is to forgive everything." [Voltaire.]
35. Boredom.

36. Right away.
37. A quarter of a penny.

vain and frigid charlatan? What is uttered, so runs this *credo*,[38] is
finished and done with. If the whole world could be expressed, it
would be saved, finished and done. . . . Well and good. But I am
not a nihilist—"

"You are not a—" said Lisabeta. . . . She was lifting a teaspoon-
ful of tea to her mouth and paused in the act to stare at him.

"Come, come, Lisabeta, what's the matter? I say I am not a
nihilist,[39] with respect, that is, to lively feeling. You see, the literary man does not understand that life may go on living, unashamed,
even after it has been expressed and therewith finished. No matter
how much it has been redeemed by becoming literature, it keeps
right on sinning—for all action is sin in the mind's eye—

"I'm nearly done, Lisabeta. Please listen. I love life—this is an
admission. I present it to you, you may have it. I have never made
it to anyone else. People say—people have even written and printed
—that I hate life, or fear or despise or abominate it. I liked to hear
this, it has always flattered me; but that does not make it true. I
love life. You smile; and I know why, Lisabeta. But I implore you
not to take what I am saying for literature. Don't think of Caesar
Borgia[40] or any drunken philosophy that has him for a standard-
bearer. He is nothing to me, your Caesar Borgia. I have no opinion
of him, and I shall never comprehend how one can honor the
extraordinary and demonic[41] as an ideal. No, life as the eternal
antinomy of mind and art does not represent itself to us as a vision
of savage greatness and ruthless beauty; we who are set apart and
different do not conceive it as, like us, unusual; it is the normal,
respectable, and admirable that is the kingdom of our longing: life,
in all its seducitve banality! That man is very far from being an
artist, my dear, whose last and deepest enthusiasm is the *raffiné*, the
eccentric and satanic; who does not know a longing for the innocent, the simple, and the living, for a little friendship, devotion,
familiar human happiness—the gnawing, surreptitious hankering,
Lisabeta, for the bliss of the commonplace. . . .

"A genuine human friend. Believe me, I should be proud and
happy to possess a friend among men. But up to now all the friends
I have had have been demons, kobolds,[42] impious monsters, and
specters dumb with excess of knowledge—that is to say, literary
men.

"I may be standing upon some platform, in some hall in front of
people who have come to listen to me. And I find myself looking

38. Statement of faith (Latin, *I be-*
lieve).

39. One who denies all social order
and collective values.

40. Caesar (Cesare) Borgia (1467–
1507), ruthless ruler and patron of the
arts in Renaissance Italy, taken by
Machiavelli as the model for his essay on
government, *The Prince*.

41. Possessed of supernatural genius.

42. Mischievous elves in German folklore.

round among my hearers, I catch myself secretly peering about the auditorium, and all the while I am thinking who it is that has come here to listen to me, whose grateful applause is in my ears, with whom my art is making me one. . . . I do not find what I seek, Lisabeta, I find the herd. The same old community, the same old gathering of early Christians, so to speak: people with fine souls in uncouth bodies, people who are always falling down in the dance, if you know what I mean; the kind to whom poetry serves as a sort of mild revenge on life. Always and only the poor and suffering, never any of the others, the blue-eyed ones, Lisabeta—they do not need mind. . . .

"And, after all, would it not be a lamentable lack of logic to want it otherwise? It is against all sense to love life and yet bend all the powers you have to draw it over to your own side, to the side of finesse and melancholy and the whole sickly aristocracy of letters. The kingdom of art increases and that of health and innocence declines on this earth. What there is left of it ought to be carefully preserved; one ought not to tempt people to read poetry who would much rather read books about the instantaneous photography of horses.

"For, after all, what more pitiable sight is there than life led astray by art? We artists have a consummate contempt for the dilettante, the man who is leading a living life and yet thinks he can be an artist too if he gets the chance. I am speaking from personal experience, I do assure you. Suppose I am in a company in a good house, with eating and drinking going on, and plenty of conversation and good feeling: I am glad and grateful to be able to lose myself among good regular people for a while. Then all of a sudden —I am thinking of something that actually happened—an officer gets up, a lieutenant, a stout, good-looking chap, whom I could never have believed guilty of any conduct unbecoming his uniform, and actually in good set terms asks the company's permission to read some verses of his own composition. Everybody looks disconcerted, they laugh and tell him to go on, and he takes them at their word and reads from a sheet of paper he has up to now been hiding in his coat-tail pocket—something about love and music, as deeply felt as it is inept. But I ask you: a lieutenant! A man of the world! He surely did not need to. . . . Well, the inevitable result is long faces, silence, a little artificial applause, everybody thoroughly uncomfortable. The first sensation I am conscious of is guilt—I feel partly responsible for the disturbance this rash youth has brought upon the company; and no wonder, for I, as a member of the same guild, am a target for some of the unfriendly glances. But next minute I realize something else: this man for whom just now I felt the greatest respect has suddenly sunk in my eyes. I feel a benevolent pity. Along with some other brave and good-natured gentlemen

I go up and speak to him. 'Congratulations, Herr Lieutenant,' I say, 'that is a very pretty talent you have. It was charming.' And I am within an ace of clapping him on the shoulder. But is that the way one is supposed to feel toward a lieutenant—benevolent? . . . It was his own fault. There he stood, suffering embarrassment for the mistake of thinking that one may pluck a single leaf from the laurel tree of art[43] without paying for it with his life. No, there I go with my colleague, the convict banker—but don't you find, Lisabeta, that I have quite a Hamlet-like flow of oratory today?"

"Are you done, Tonio Kröger?"

"No. But there won't be any more."

"And quite enough too. Are you expecting a reply?"

"Have you one ready?"

"I should say. I have listened to you faithfully, Tonio, from beginning to end, and I will give you the answer to everything you have said this afternoon and the solution of the problem that has been upsetting you. Now: the solution is that you, as you sit there, are, quite simply, a bourgeois."

"Am I?" he asked a little crestfallen.

"Yes, that hits you hard, it must. So I will soften the judgment just a little. You are a bourgeois on the wrong path, a bourgeois *manqué*."[44]

Silence. Then he got up resolutely and took his hat and stick.

"Thank you, Lisabeta Ivanovna; now I can go home in peace. I am expressed."[45]

Toward autumn Tonio Kröger said to Lisabeta Ivanovna:

"Well, Lisabeta, I think I'll be off. I need a change of air. I must get away, out into the open."

"Well, well, well, little Father! Does it please your Highness to go down to Italy again?"

"Oh, get along with your Italy, Lisabeta. I'm fed up with Italy, I spew it out of my mouth. It's a long time since I imagined I could belong down there. Art, eh? Blue-velvet sky, ardent wine, the sweets of sensuality. In short, I don't want it—I decline with thanks. The whole *bellezza*[46] business makes me nervous. All those frightfully animated people down there with their black animal-like eyes; I don't like them either. These Romance peoples have no soul in their eyes. No, I'm going to take a trip to Denmark."

"To Denmark?"

---

43. The laurel tree was sacred to Apollo, the Greek god of poetry and prophecy.

44. The German says literally, a *bourgeois gone astray*. Tonio is caught between two worlds; he can neither reject nor live up to his bourgeois heritage.

45. In recognizing and accepting Lisabeta's description of himself, Tonio uses the same word (*erledigt*) that was earlier translated as "get rid of," "polished off," and "finished" in the discussion of the fixative role of art.

46. "Beauty" (Italian).

"Yes. I'm quite sanguine of the results. I happen never to have been there, though I lived all my youth so close to it. Still I have always known and loved the country. I suppose I must have this northern tendency from my father, for my mother was really more for the *bellezza*, in so far, that is, as she cared very much one way or the other. But just take the books that are written up there, that clean, meaty, whimsical Scandinavian literature. Lisabeta, there's nothing like it, I love it. Or take the Scandinavian meals, those incomparable meals, which can only be digested in strong sea air (I don't know whether I can digest them in any sort of air); I know them from my home too, because we ate that way up there. Take even the names, the given names that people rejoice in up north; we have a good many of them in my part of the country too: Inge-borg, for instance, isn't it the purest poetry—like a harp-tone? And then the sea—up there it's the Baltic! . . . In a word, I am going, Lisabeta, I want to see the Baltic again and read the books and hear the names on their native heath; I want to stand on the terrace at Kronberg,[47] where the ghost appeared to Hamlet, bringing despair and death to that poor, noble-souled youth. . . ."

"How are you going, Tonio, if I may ask? What route are you taking?"

"The usual one," he said, shrugging his shoulders, and blushed perceptibly. "Yes, I shall touch my—my point of departure, Lisa-beta, after thirteen years, and that may turn out rather funny."

She smiled.

"That is what I wanted to hear, Tonio Kröger. Well, be off, then, in God's name. Be sure to write to me, do you hear? I shall expect a letter full of your experiences in—Denmark."

And Tonio Kröger traveled north. He traveled in comfort (for he was wont to say that anyone who suffered inwardly more than other people had a right to a little outward ease); and he did not stay until the towers of the little town he had left rose up in the grey air. Among them he made a short and singular stay.

The dreary afternoon was merging into evening when the train pulled into the narrow, reeking shed, so marvelously familiar. The volumes of thick smoke rolled up to the dirty glass roof and wreathed to and fro there in long tatters, just as they had, long ago, on the day when Tonio Kröger, with nothing but derision in his heart, had left his native town.—He arranged to have his luggage sent to his hotel and walked out of the station.

There were the cabs, those enormously high, enormously wide black cabs drawn by two horses, standing in a rank. He did not take one, he only looked at them, as he looked at everything: the narrow

47. Castle in Helsingör (Elsinore), the supposed setting of Shakespeare's *Hamlet.*

gables, and the pointed towers peering above the roofs close at hand; the plump, fair, easy-going populace, with their broad yet rapid speech. And a nervous laugh mounted in him, mysteriously akin to a sob.—He walked on, slowly, with the damp wind constantly in his face, across the bridge, with the mythological statues on the railings, and some distance along the harbor.

Good Lord, how tiny and close it all seemed! The comical little gabled streets were climbing up just as of yore from the port to the town! And on the ruffled waters the smokestacks and masts of the ships dipped gently in the wind and twilight. Should he go up that next street, leading, he knew, to a certain house? No, tomorrow. He was too sleepy. His head was heavy from the journey, and slow, vague trains of thought passed through his mind.

Sometimes in the past thirteen years, when he was suffering from indigestion, he had dreamed of being back home in the echoing old house in the steep, narrow street. His father had been there too, and reproached him bitterly for his dissolute manner of life, and this, each time, he had found quite as it should be. And now the present refused to distinguish itself in any way from one of those tantalizing dream fabrications in which the dreamer asks himself if this be delusion or reality and is driven to decide for the latter, only to wake up after all in the end. . . . He paced through the half-empty streets with his head inclined against the wind, moving as though in his sleep in the direction of the hotel, the first hotel in the town, where he meant to sleep. A bow-legged man, with a pole at the end of which burned a tiny fire, walked before him with a rolling, seafaring gait and lighted the gas lamps.

What was at the bottom of this? What was it burning darkly beneath the ashes of his fatigue, refusing to burst out into a clear blaze? Hush, hush, only no talk. Only don't make words! He would have liked to go on so, for a long time, in the wind, through the dusky, dreamily familiar streets—but everything was so little and close together here. You reached your goal at once.

In the upper town there were arc-lamps,[48] just lighted. There was the hotel with the two black lions in front of it; he had been afraid of them as a child. And there they were, still looking at each other as though they were about to sneeze; only they seemed to have grown much smaller. Tonio Kröger passed between them into the hotel.

As he came on foot, he was received with no great ceremony. There was a porter, and a lordly gentleman dressed in black, to do the honors; the latter, shoving back his cuffs with his little fingers, measured him from the crown of his head to the soles of his boots, obviously with intent to place him, to assign him to his proper cate-

48. Electrical street lights.

gory socially and hierarchically speaking and then mete out the suitable degree of courtesy. He seemed not to come to any clear decision and compromised on a moderate display of politeness. A mild-mannered waiter with yellow-white side whiskers, in a dress suit shiny with age, and rosettes on his soundless shoes, led him up two flights into a clean old room furnished in patriarchal style. Its windows gave on a twilight view of courts and gables, very medieval and picturesque, with the fantastic bulk of the old church close by. Tonio Kröger stood awhile before this window; then he sat down on the wide sofa, crossed his arms, drew down his brows, and whistled to himself.

Lights were brought and his luggage came up. The mild-mannered waiter laid the hotel register on the table, and Tonio Kröger, his head on one side, scrawled something on it that might be taken for a name, a station, and a place of origin. Then he ordered supper and went on gazing into space from his sofa-corner. When it stood before him he let it wait long untouched, then took a few bites and walked up and down an hour in his room, stopping from time to time and closing his eyes. Then he very slowly undressed and went to bed. He slept long and had curiously confused and ardent dreams.

It was broad day when he woke. Hastily he recalled where he was and got up to draw the curtains; the pale-blue sky, already with a hint of autumn, was streaked with frayed and tattered cloud; still, above his native city the sun was shining.

He spent more care than usual upon his toilette,[49] washed and shaved and made himself fresh and immaculate as though about to call upon some smart family where a well-dressed and flawless appearance was *de rigueur*;[50] and while occupied in this wise he listened to the anxious beating of his heart.

How bright it was outside! He would have liked better a twilight air like yesterday's, instead of passing through the streets in the broad sunlight, under everybody's eye. Would he meet people he knew, be stopped and questioned and have to submit to be asked how he had spent the last thirteen years? No, thank goodness, he was known to nobody here; even if anybody remembered him, it was unlikely he would be recognized—for certainly he had changed in the meantime! He surveyed himself in the glass and felt a sudden sense of security behind his mask, behind his work-worn face, that was older than his years. . . . He sent for breakfast, and after that he went out; he passed under the disdainful eye of the porter and the gentleman in black, through the vestibule and between the two lions, and so into the street.

Where was he going? He scarcely knew. It was the same as yesterday. Hardly was he in the midst of this long-familiar scene, this stately conglomeration of gables, turrets, arcades, and fountains, hardly did he feel once more the wind in his face, that strong current wafting a faint and pungent aroma from far-off dreams, when the same mistiness laid itself like a veil about his senses. . . . The muscles of his face relaxed, and he looked at men and things with a look grown suddenly calm. Perhaps right there, on that street corner, he might wake up after all. . . .

Where was he going? It seemed to him the direction he took had a connection with his sad and strangely rueful dreams of the night. . . . He went to Market Square, under the vaulted arches of the Rathaus,[51] where the butchers were weighing out their wares red-handed, where the tall old Gothic fountain stood with its manifold spires. He paused in front of a house, a plain narrow building, like many another, with a fretted[52] baroque gable; stood there lost in contemplation. He read the plate on the door, his eyes rested a little while on each of the windows. Then slowly he turned away.

Where did he go? Toward home. But he took a round-about way outside the walls—for he had plenty of time. He went over the Millwall and over the Holstenwall, clutching his hat, for the wind was rushing and moaning through the trees. He left the wall near the station, where he saw a train puffing busily past, idly counted the coaches, and looked after the man who sat perched upon the last. In the Lindenplatz he stopped at one of the pretty villas, peered long into the garden and up at the windows, lastly conceived the idea of swinging the gate to and fro upon its hinges till it creaked. Then he looked awhile at his moist, rust-stained hand and went on, went through the squat old gate, along the harbor, and up the steep, windy street to his parents' house.

It stood aloof from its neighbors, its gable towering above them; grey and somber, as it had stood these three hundred years; and Tonio Kröger read the pious, half-illegible motto above the entrance. Then he drew a long breath and went in.

His heart gave a throb of fear, lest his father might come out of one of the doors on the ground floor, in his office coat, with the pen behind his ear, and take him to task for his excesses. He would have found the reproach quite in order; but he got past unchidden. The inner door was ajar, which appeared to him reprehensible though at the same time he felt as one does in certain broken dreams, where obstacles melt away of themselves, and one presses onward in marvelous favor with fortune. The wide entry, paved with great square flags, echoed to his tread. Opposite the silent kitchen was the curious projecting structure, of rough boards, but cleanly varnished, that had been the servants' quarters. It was quite high up and could

51. Town hall.
52. Decorated with elaborately carved ornaments.

only be reached by a sort of ladder from the entry. But the great cupboards and carven presses were gone. The son of the house climbed the majestic staircase, with his hand on the white-enameled, fret-work balustrade. At each step he lifted his hand, and put it down again with the next as though testing whether he could call back his ancient familiarity with the stout old railing. . . . But at the landing of the entresol[53] he stopped. For on the entrance door was a white plate; and on it in black letters he read; "Public Library."

"Public Library?" thought Tonio Kröger. What were either literature or the public doing here? He knocked . . . heard a "come in," and obeying it with gloomy suspense gazed upon a scene of most unhappy alteration.

The story was three rooms deep, and all the doors stood open. The walls were covered nearly all the way up with long rows of books in uniform bindings, standing in dark-colored bookcases. In each room a poor creature of a man sat writing behind a sort of counter. The farthest two just turned their heads, but the nearest got up in haste and, leaning with both hands on the table, stuck out his head, pursed his lips, lifted his brows, and looked at the visitor with eagerly blinking eyes.

"I beg pardon," said Tonio Kröger without turning his eyes from the bookshelves. "I am a stranger here, seeing the sights. So this is your Public Library? May I examine your collection a little?"

"Certainly, with pleasure," said the official, blinking still more violently. "It is open to everybody. . . . Pray look about you. Should you care for a catalogue?"

"No, thanks," answered Tonio Kröger, "I shall soon find my way about." And he began to move slowly along the walls, with the appearance of studying the rows of books. After a while he took down a volume, opened it, and posted himself at the window.

This was the breakfast room. They had eaten here in the morning instead of in the big dining room upstairs, with its white statues of gods and goddesses standing out against the blue walls. . . . Beyond there had been a bedroom, where his father's mother had died—only after a long struggle, old as she was, for she had been of a pleasure-loving nature and clung to life. And his father too had drawn his last breath in the same room; tht tall, correct, slightly melancholy and pensive gentleman with the wild flower in his button-hole. . . . Tonio had sat at the foot of his death bed, quite given over to unutterable feelings of love and grief. His mother had knelt at the bedside, his lovely, fiery mother, dissolved in hot tears, and after that she had withdrawn with her artist into the far blue south. . . . And beyond still, the small third room, likewise full of books

53. Mezzanine.

and presided over by a shabby man—that had been for years on end his own. Thither he had come after school and a walk—like today's; against that wall his table had stood with the drawer where he had kept his first clumsy, heartfelt attempts at verse. . . . The walnut tree . . . a pang went through him. He gave a sidewise glance out at the window. The garden lay desolate, but there stood the old walnut tree where it used to stand, groaning and creaking heavily in the wind. And Tonio Kröger let his gaze fall upon the book he had in his hands, an excellent piece of work, and very familiar. He followed the black lines of print, the paragraphs, the flow of words that flowed with so much art, mounting in the ardor of creation to a certain climax and effect and then as artfully breaking off.

"Yes, that was well done," he said; put back the book and turned away. Then he saw that the fuctionary still stood bolt-upright, blinking with a mingled expression of zeal and misgiving. "A capital collection, I see," said Tonio Kröger. "I have already quite a good idea of it. Much obliged to you. Good-bye." He went out; but it was a poor exit, and he felt sure the official would stand there perturbed and blinking for several minutes.

He felt no desire for further researches. He had been home. Strangers were living upstairs in the large rooms behind the pillared hall; the top of the stairs was shut off by a glass door which used not to be there, and on the door was a plate. He went away, down the steps, across the echoing corridor, and left his parental home. He sought a restaurant, sat down in a corner, and brooded over a heavy, greasy meal. Then he returned to his hotel.

"I am leaving," he said to the fine gentleman in black. "This afternoon." And he asked for his bill, and for a carriage to take him down to the harbor where he should take the boat for Copenhagen. Then he went up to his room and sat there stiff and still, with his cheek on his hand, looking down on the table before him with absent eyes. Later he paid his bill and packed his things. At the appointed hour the carriage was announced and Tonio Kröger went down in travel array.

At the foot of the stairs the gentleman in black was waiting.

"Beg pardon," he said, shoving back his cuffs with his little fingers. . . . "Beg pardon, but we must detain you just a moment. Herr Seehaase, the proprietor, would like to exchange two words with you. A matter of form. . . . He is back there. . . . If you will have the goodness to step this way. . . . It is *only* Herr Seehaase, the proprietor."

And he ushered Tonio Kröger into the background of the vestibule. . . . There, in fact, stood Herr Seehaase. Tonio Kröger recognized him from old time. He was small, fat, and bow-legged. His shaven sidewhisker was white, but he wore the same old low-cut dress coat and little velvet cap embroidered in green. He was not alone. Beside him, at a little high desk fastened into the wall, stood a policeman in a helmet, his gloved right hand resting on a document in colored inks; he turned towards Tonio Kröger with his honest, soldierly face as though he expected Tonio to sink into the earth at his glance.

Tonio Kröger looked at the two and confined himself to waiting.

"You came from Munich?" the policeman asked at length in a heavy, good-natured voice.

Tonio Kröger said he had.

"You are going to Copenhagen?"

"Yes, I am on the way to a Danish seashore resort."

"Seashore resort? Well, you must produce your papers," said the policeman. He uttered the last word with great satisfaction.

"Papers . . . ?" He had no papers. He drew out his pocketbook and looked into it; but aside from notes there was nothing there but some proof-sheets of a story which he had taken along to finish reading. He hated relations with officials and had never got himself a passport. . . . .

"I am sorry," he said, "but I don't travel with papers."

"Ah!" said the policeman. "And what might be your name?"

Tonio replied.

"Is that a fact?" asked the policeman, suddenly erect, and expanding his nostrils as wide as he could. . . .

"Yes, that is a fact," answered Tonio Kröger.

"And what are you, anyhow?"

Tonio Kröger gulped and gave the name of his trade in a firm voice. Herr Seehaase lifted his head and looked him curiously in the face.

"H'm," said the policeman. "And you give out that you are not identical with an individdle named"—he said "individdle" and then, referring to his document in colored inks, spelled out an involved, fantastic name which mingled all the sounds of all the races—Tonio Kröger forgot it next minute—"of unknown parentage and unspecified means," he went on, "wanted by the Munich police for various shady transactions, and probably in flight toward Denmark?"

"Yes, I give out all that, and more," said Tonio Kröger, wriggling his shoulders. The gesture made a certain impression.

"What? Oh, yes, of course," said the policeman. "You say you can't show any papers—"

Herr Seehaase threw himself into the breach.

"It is only a formality," he said pacifically, "nothing else. You must bear in mind the official is only doing his duty. If you could only identify yourself somehow—some document . . ."

They were all silent. Should he make an end of the business, by revealing to Herr Seehaase that he was no swindler without specified means, no gypsy in a green wagon, but the son of the late Consul Kröger, a member of the Kröger family? No, he felt no desire to do that. After all, were not these guardians of civic order within their right? He even agreed with them—up to a point. He shrugged his shoulders and kept quiet.

"What have you got, then?" asked the policeman. "In your portfoly, I mean?"

"Here? Nothing. Just a proof-sheet," answered Tonio Kröger.

"Proof-sheet? What's that? Let's see it."

And Tonio Kröger handed over his work. The policeman spread it out on the shelf and began reading. Herr Seehaase drew up and shared it with him. Tonio Kröger looked over their shoulders to see what they read. It was a good moment, a little effect he had worked out to a perfection. He had a sense of self-satisfaction.

"You see," he said, "there is my name. I wrote it, and it is going to be published, you understand."

"All right, that will answer," said Herr Seehaase with decision, gathered up the sheets and gave them back. "That will have to answer, Petersen," he repeated crisply, shutting his eyes and shaking his head as though to see and hear no more. "We must not keep the gentleman any longer. The carriage is waiting. I implore you to pardon the little inconvenience, sir. The officer has only done his duty, but I told him at once he was on the wrong track. . . ."

"Indeed!" thought Tonio Kröger.

The officer seemed still to have his doubts; he muttered something else about individdle and document. But Herr Seehaase, overflowing with regrets, led his guest through the vestibule, accompanied him past the two lions to the carriage, and himself, with many respectful bows, closed the door upon him. And then the funny, high, wide old cab rolled and rattled and bumped down the steep, narrow street to the quay.

And such was the manner of Tonio Kröger's visit to his ancestral home.

Night fell and the moon swam up with silver gleam as Tonio Kröger's boat reached the open sea. He stood at the prow wrapped in his cloak against a mounting wind, and looked beneath into the dark going and coming of the waves as they hovered and swayed and came on, to meet with a clap and shoot erratically away in a bright gush of foam.

He was lulled in a mood of still enchantment. The episode at the hotel, their wanting to arrest him for a swindler in his own home, had cast him down a little, even though he found it quite in order

—in a certain way. But after he came on board he had watched, as he used to do as a boy with his father, the lading of goods into the deep bowels of the boat, amid shouts of mingled Danish and Plattdeutsch;[54] not only boxes and bales, but also a Bengal tiger and a polar bear were lowered in cages with stout iron bars. They had probably come from Hamburg and were destined for a Danish menagerie. He had enjoyed these distractions. And as the boat glided along between flat riverbanks he quite forgot Officer Petersen's inquisition; while all the rest—his sweet, sad, rueful dreams of the night before, the walk he had taken, the walnut tree—had welled up again in his soul. The sea opened out and he saw in the distance the beach where he as a lad had been let to listen to the ocean's summer dreams; saw the flashing of the lighthouse tower and the lights of the Kurhaus[55] where he and his parents had lived. . . . The Baltic! He bent his head to the strong salt wind; it came sweeping on, it enfolded him, made him faintly giddy and a little deaf; and in that mild confusion of the senses all memory of evil, of anguish and error, effort and exertion of the will, sank away into joyous oblivion and were gone. The roaring, foaming, flapping, and slapping all about him came to his ears like the groan and rustle of an old walnut tree, the creaking of a garden gate. . . . More and more the darkness came on.

"The stars! Oh, by Lord, look at the stars!" a voice suddenly said, with a heavy singsong accent that seemed to come out of the inside of a tun.[56] He recognized it. It belonged to a young man with red-blond hair who had been Tonio Kröger's neighbor at dinner in the salon. His dress was very simple, his eyes were red, and he had the moist and chilly look of a person who has just bathed. With nervous and self-conscious movements he had taken unto himself an astonishing quantity of lobster omelet. Now he leaned on the rail beside Tonio Kröger and looked up at the skies, holding his chin between thumb and forefinger. Beyond a doubt he was in one of those rare and festal and edifying moods that cause the barriers between man and man to fall; when the heart opens even to the stranger, and the mouth utters that which otherwise it would blush to speak. . . .

"Look, by dear sir, just look at the stars. There they stahd and glitter; by goodness, the whole sky is full of theb! And I ask you, when you stahd ahd look up at theb, ahd realize that bany of theb are a huddred tibes larger thad the earth, how does it bake you feel? Yes, we have idvehted the telegraph and the telephode and all the triuphs of our bodern tibes. But whed we look up there, after all we have to recogdize and uhderstad that we are worbs, biserable worbs,

54. A northern German dialect.
55. Boarding house (at a health resort or spa).
56. Large barrel or vat.

ahd dothing else. Ab I right, sir, or ab I wrog? Yes, we are worbs,"
he answered himself, and nodded meekly and abjectly in the direction of the firmament.

"Ah, no, he has no literature in his belly," thought Tonio Kröger.
And he recalled something he had lately read, an essay by a famous
French writer on cosmological and psychological philosophies, a
very delightful *causerie*.[57]

He made some sort of reply to the young man's feeling remarks,
and they went on talking, leaning over the rail, and looking into the
night with its movement and fitful lights. The young man, it
seemed, was a Hamburg merchant on his holiday.

"Y'ought to travel to Copedhagen on the boat, thigks I, and so
here I ab, and so far it's been fide. But they shouldn't have given us
the lobster obelet, sir, for it's going to be storby—the captain said
so hibself—and that's do joke with indigestible food like that in
your stobach. . . ."

Tonio Kröger listened to all this engaging artlessness and was privately drawn to it.

"Yes," he said, "all the food up here is too heavy. It makes one
lazy and melancholy."

"Belancholy?" repeated the young man, and looked at him, taken
aback. Then he asked, suddenly: "You are a stradger up here, sir?"

"Yes, I come from a long way off," answered Tonio Kröger
vaguely, waving his arm.

"But you're right," said the youth; "Lord knows you are right
about the belancholy. I am dearly always belancholy, but specially
on evedings like this when there are stars in the sky." And he supported his chin again with thumb and forefinger.

"Surely this man writes verses," thought Tonio Kröger; "business
man's verses, full of deep feeling and single-mindedness."

Evening drew on. The wind had grown so violent as to prevent
them from talking. So they thought they would sleep a bit, and
wished each other good-night.

Tonio Kröger stretched himself out on the narrow cabin bed, but
he found no repose. The strong wind with its sharp tang had power
to rouse him; he was strangely restless with sweet anticipations. Also
he was violently sick with the motion of the ship as she glided
down a steep mountain of wave and her screw[58] vibrated as in
agony, free of the water. He put on all his clothes again and went
up to the deck.

Clouds raced across the moon. The sea danced. It did not come
on in full-bodied, regular waves; but far out in the pale and flickering light the water was lashed, torn, and tumbled; leaped upward

57. Chat. According to a letter of July
21, 1954, the reference is to an essay on
the "cosmological and psychological

perspective" by the French novelist and
essayist, Paul Bourget (1852–1935).
58. Propeller.

like great licking flames; hung in jagged and fantastic shapes above dizzy abysses, where the foam seemed to be tossed by the playful strength of colossal arms and flung upward in all directions. The ship had a heavy passage; she lurched and stamped and groaned through the welter; and far down in her bowels the tiger and the polar bear voiced their acute discomfort. A man in an oilskin, with the hood drawn over his head and a lantern strapped to his chest, went straddling painfully up and down the deck. And at the stern, leaning far out, stood the young man from Hamburg suffering the worst. "Lord!" he said, in a hollow, quavering voice, when he saw Tonio Kröger. "Look at the uproar of the elebents, sir!" But he could say no more—he was obliged to turn hastily away.

Tonio Kröger clutched at a taut rope and looked abroad into the arrogance of the elements. His exultation outvied storm and wave; within himself he chanted a song to the sea, instinct with love of her: "O thou wild friend of my youth, Once more I behold thee—" But it got no further, he did not finish it. It was not fated to receive a final form nor in tranquillity to be welded to a perfect whole. For his heart was too full. . . .

Long he stood; then stretched himself out on a bench by the pilot-house and looked up at the sky, where stars were flickering. He even slept a little. And when the cold foam splashed his face it seemed in his half-dreams like a caress.

Perpendicular chalk-cliffs, ghostly in the moonlight, came in sight. They were nearing the island of Möen.[59] Then sleep came again, broken by salty showers of spray that bit into his face and made it stiff. . . . When he really roused, it was broad day, fresh and palest grey, and the sea had gone down. At breakfast he saw the young man from Hamburg again, who blushed rosy-red for shame of the poetic indiscretions he had been betrayed into by the dark, ruffled up his little red-blond moustache with all five fingers, and called out a brisk and soldierly good-morning—after that he studiously avoided him.

And Tonio Kröger landed in Denmark. He arrived in Copenhagen, gave tips to everybody who laid claim to them, took a room at a hotel, and roamed the city for three days with a open guidebook and the air of an intelligent foreigner bent on improving his mind. He looked at the King's New Market and the "Horse" in the middle of it, gazed respectfully up the columns of the Frauenkirch, stood long before Thorwaldsen's noble and beautiful statuary, climbed the round tower, visited castles, and spent two lively evenings in the Tivoli.[60] But all this was not exactly what he saw.

59. Danish island in the Baltic Sea.
60. Scenic spots and monuments in Copenhagen, the capital of Denmark. The King's New Market is a large square with a statue of King Christian V on a horse; the Frauenkirch (or Vor Frue Kirke, in Danish) is the Cathedral of Our Lady; Bertel Thorwaldsen (1770–1844) was a famous Danish sculptor; Tivoli is a large recreation park with lake, restaurants, theatre and concert halls, and an amusement midway.

The doors of the houses—so like those in his native town, with open-work gables of baroque shape—bore names known to him of old; names that had a tender and precious quality, and withal in their syllables an accent of plaintive reproach, of repining after the lost and gone. He walked, he gazed, drawing deep, lingering drafts of moist sea air; and everywhere he saw eyes as blue, hair as blond, faces as familiar, as those that had visited his rueful dreams the night he had spent in his native town. There in the open street it befell him that a glance, a ringing word, a sudden laugh would pierce him to his marrow.

He could not stand the bustling city for long. A restlessness, half memory and half hope, half foolish and half sweet, possessed him; he was moved to drop this role of ardently inquiring tourist and lie somewhere, quite quietly, on a beach. So he took ship once more and traveled under a cloudy sky, over a black water, northward along the coast of Seeland[61] toward Helsingör. Thence he drove, at once, by carriage, for three-quarters of an hour, along and above the sea, reaching at length his ultimate goal, the little white "bath-hotel" with green blinds. It stood surrounded by a settlement of cottages, and its shingled turret tower looked out on the beach and the Swedish coast. Here he left the carriage, took possession of the light room they had ready for him, filled shelves and presses with his kit, and prepared to stop awhile.

It was well on in September; not many guests were left in Aalsgaard.[62] Meals were served on the ground floor, in the great beamed dining room, whose lofty windows led out upon the veranda and the sea. The landlady presided, an elderly spinster with white hair and faded eyes, a faint color in her cheek and a feeble twittering voice. She was forever arranging her red hands to look well upon the tablecloth. There was a short-necked old gentleman, quite blue in the face, with a grey sailor beard; a fish-dealer he was, from the capital, and strong at the German. He seemed entirely congested and inclined to apoplexy; breathed in short gasps, kept putting his beringed first finger to one nostril, and snorting violently to get a passage of air through the other. Notwithstanding, he addressed himself constantly to the whisky bottle, which stood at his place at luncheon and dinner, and breakfast as well. Besides him the company consisted only of three tall American youths with their governor or tutor, who kept adjusting his glasses in unbroken silence. All day long he played football with his charges, who had narrow, taciturn faces and reddish-yellow hair parted in the middle. "Please pass the *wurst*," said one. "That's not *wurst*, it's

---

61. Seeland or Zealand is the largest of the Danish islands; Copenhagen is located on Seeland.

62. A fishing village close to Elsinore; the seaside here is directly opposite the Swedish coast.

schinken,"[63] said the other, and this was the extent of their conversation, as the rest of the time they sat there dumb, drinking hot water.

Tonio Kröger could have wished himself no better table companions. He reveled in the peace and quiet, listened to the Danish palatals,[64] the clear and the clouded vowels in which the fish-dealer and the landlady desultorily conversed; modestly exchanged views with the fish-dealer on the state of the barometer, and then left the table to go through the veranda and onto the beach once more, where he had already spent long, long morning hours.

Sometimes it was still and summery there. The sea lay idle and smooth, in stripes of blue and russet and bottle-green, played all across with glittering silvery lights. The seaweed shriveled in the sun and the jellyfish lay steaming. There was a faintly stagnant smell and a whiff of tar from the fishing boat against which Tonio Kröger leaned, so standing that he had before his eyes not the Swedish coast but the open horizon, and in his face the pure, fresh breath of the softly breathing sea.

Then grey, stormy days would come. The waves lowered their heads like bulls and charged against the beach; they ran and ramped high up the sands and left them strewn with shining wet sea grass, driftwood, and mussels. All abroad beneath an overcast sky extended ranges of billows, and between them foaming valleys palely green; but above the spot where the sun hung behind the cloud a patch like white velvet lay on the sea.

Tonio Kröger stood wrapped in wind and tumult, sunk in the continual dull, drowsy uproar that he loved. When he turned away it seemed suddenly warm and silent all about him. But he was never unconscious of the sea at his back; it called, it lured, it beckoned him. And he smiled.

He went landward, by lonely meadow paths, and was swallowed up in the beech groves that clothed the rolling landscape near and far. Here he sat down on the moss, against a tree, and gazed at the strip of water he could see between the trunks. Sometimes the sound of surf came on the wind—a noise like boards collapsing at a distance. And from the treetops over his head a cawing—hoarse, desolate, forlorn. He held a book on his knee, but did not read a line. He enjoyed profound forgetfulness, hovered disembodied above space and time; only now and again his heart would contract with a fugitive pain, a stab of longing and regret, into whose origin he was too lazy to inquire.

Thus passed some days. He could not have said how many and had no desire to know. But then came one on which something happened; happened while the sun stood in the sky and people were about; and Tonio Kröger, even, felt no vast surprise.

---

63. *Wurst*: sausage; *schinken*: ham.   pronunciation of Copenhagen: *T*yubben-
64. For example, in the Danish   haven.

The very opening of the day had been rare and festal. Tonio Kröger woke early and suddenly from his sleep, with a vague and exquisite alarm; he seemed to be looking at a miracle, a magic illumination. His room had a glass door and balcony facing the sound; a thin white gauze curtain divided it into living- and sleeping-quarters, both hung with delicately tinted paper and furnished with an airy good taste that gave them a sunny and friendly look. But now to his sleep-drunken eyes it lay bathed in a serene and roseate light, an unearthly brightness that gilded walls and furniture and turned the gauze curtain to radiant pink cloud. Tonio Kröger did not at once understand. Not until he stood at the glass door and looked out did he realize that this was the sunrise.

For several days there had been clouds and rain; but now the sky was like a piece of pale-blue silk, spanned shimmering above sea and land, and shot with light from red and golden clouds. The sun's disk rose in splendor from a crisply glittering sea that seemed to quiver and burn beneath it. So began the day. In a joyous daze Tonio Kröger flung on his clothes, and breakfasting in the veranda before everybody else, swam from the little wooden bathhouse some distance out into the sound, then walked for an hour along the beach. When he came back, several omnibuses[65] were before the door, and from the dining room he could see people in the parlor next door where the piano was, in the veranda, and on the terrace in front; quantities of people sitting at little tables enjoying beer and sandwiches amid lively discourse. There were whole families, there were old and young, there were even a few children.

At second breakfast—the table was heavily laden with cold viands,[66] roast, pickled, and smoked—Tonio Kröger inquired what was going on.

"Guests," said the fish-dealer. "Tourists and ball-guests from Helsingör. Lord help us, we shall get no sleep this night! There will be dancing and music, and I fear me it will keep up till late. It is a family reunion, a sort of celebration and excursion combined; they all subscribe to it and take advantage of the good weather. They came by boat and bus and they are having breakfast. After that they go on with their drive, but at night they will all come back for a dance here in the hall. Yes, damn it, you'll see we shan't get a wink of sleep."

"Oh, it will be a pleasant change," said Tonio Kröger.

After that there was nothing more said for some time. The landlady arranged her red fingers on the cloth, the fish-dealer blew through his nostril, the Americans drank hot water and made long faces.

Then all at once a thing came to pass: *Hans Hansen and Ingeborg Holm walked through the room.*

Tonio Kröger, pleasantly fatigued after his swim and rapid walk,

65. Buses.   66. Meats.

was leaning back in his chair and eating smoked salmon on toast; he sat facing the veranda and the ocean. All at once the door opened and the two entered hand-in-hand—calmly and unhurried. Inge-borg, blonde Inge, was dressed just as she used to be at Herr Knaak's dancing class. The light flowered frock reached down to her ankles and it had a tulle fichu[67] draped with a pointed opening that left her soft throat free. Her hat hung by its ribbons over her arm. She, perhaps, was a little more grown up than she used to be, and her wonderful plait of hair was wound round her head; but Hans Hansen was the same as ever. He wore his sailor overcoat with gilt buttons, and his wide blue sailor collar lay across his shoulders and back; the sailor cap with its short ribbons he was dangling carelessly in his hand. Ingeborg's narrow eyes were turned away; perhaps she felt shy before the company at table. But Hans Hansen turned his head straight toward them, and measured one after another defiantly with his steel-blue eyes; challengingly, with a sort of con-tempt. He even dropped Ingeborg's hand and swung his cap harder than ever, to show what manner of man he was. Thus the two, against the silent, blue-dyed sea, measured the length of the room and passed through the opposite door into the parlor.

This was at half past eleven in the moning. While the guests of the house were still at table the company in the veranda broke up and went away by the side door. No one else came into the dining room. The guests could hear them laughing and joking as they got into the omnibuses, which rumbled away one by one. . . . "So they are coming back?" asked Tonio Kröger.

"That they are," said the fish-dealer. "More's the pity. They have ordered music, let me tell you—and my room is right above the dining room."

"Oh, well, it's a pleasant change," repeated Tonio Kröger. Then he got up and went away.

The day he spent as he had the others, on the beach and in the wood, holding a book on his knee and blinking in the sun. He had but one thought; they were coming back to have a dance in the hall, the fish-dealer had promised they would; and he did nothing but glad of this, with a sweet and timorous gladness such as he had not felt through all these long dead years. Once he happened, by some chance association, to think of his friend Adalbert, the novelist, the man who had known what he wanted and betaken himself to the café to get away from the spring. Tonio Kröger shrugged his shoulders at the thought of him.

Luncheon was served earlier than usual, also supper, which they ate in the parlor because the dining room was being got ready for the ball, and the whole house flung in disorder for the occasion. It grew dark; Tonio Kröger sitting in his room heard on the road and in the house the sounds of approaching festivity. The picknickers were

---

67. A cloak or shawl made of lacy, netlike fabric.

coming back; from Helsingör, by bicycle and carriage, new guests were arriving; a fiddle and a nasal clarinet might be heard practicing down in the dining room. Everything promised a brilliant ball. . . .

Now the little orchestra struck up a march; he could hear the notes, faint but lively. The dancing opened with a polonaise. Tonio Kröger sat for a while and listened. But when he heard the march time go over into a waltz he got up and slipped noiselessly out of his room.

From his corridor it was possible to go by the side stairs to the side entrance of the hotel and thence to the veranda without passing through a room. He took this route, softly and stealthily as though on forbidden paths, feeling along through the dark, relentlessly drawn by this stupid jigging music that now came up to him loud and clear.

The veranda was empty and dim, but the glass door stood open into the hall, where shone two large oil lamps, furnished with bright reflectors. Thither he stole on soft feet; and his skin prickled with the thievish pleasure of standing unseen in the dark and spying on the dancers there in the brightly lighted room. Quickly and eagerly he glanced about for the two whom he sought. . . .

Even though the ball was only half an hour old, the merriment seemed in full swing; however, the guests had come hither already warm and merry, after a whole day of carefree, happy companionship. By bending forward a little, Tonio Kröger could see into the parlor from where he was. Several old gentlemen sat there smoking, drinking, and playing cards; others were with their wives on the plush-upholstered chairs in the foreground watching the dance. They sat with their knees apart and their hands resting on them, puffing out their cheeks with a prosperous air; the mothers, with bonnets perched on their parted hair, with their hands folded over their stomachs and their heads on one side, gazed into the whirl of dancers. A platform had been erected on the long side of the hall, and on it the musicians were doing their utmost. There was even a trumpet, that blew with a certain caution, as though afraid of its own voice, and yet after all kept breaking and cracking. Couples were dipping and circling about, others walked arm-in-arm up and down the room. No one wore ballroom clothes; they were dressed as for an outing in the summertime: the men in countrified suits which were obviously their Sunday wear; the girls in light-colored frocks with bunches of field flowers in their bodices. Even a few children were there, dancing with each other in their own way, even after the music stopped. There was a long-legged man in a coat with a little swallow-tail, a provincial lion with an eyeglass and frizzed hair, a post office clerk or some such thing; he was like a comic figure stepped bodily out of a Danish novel; and he seemed to be the leader and manager of the ball. He was everywhere at once, bustling, perspiring, officious, utterly absorbed; setting down his feet, in shiny, pointed, military half-boots, in a very artificial and involved manner, toes first; waving his arms to issue an order, clapping his hands for the music to begin; here, there, and everywhere, and glancing over his shoulder in pride at his great bow of office, the streamers of which fluttered grandly in his rear.

Yes, there they were, those two, who had gone by Tonio Kröger in the broad light of day; he saw them again—with a joyful start he recognized them almost at the same moment. Here was Hans Hansen by the door, quite close; his legs apart, a little bent over, he was eating with circumspection a large piece of sponge cake, holding his hand cupwise under his chin to catch the crumbs. And there by the wall sat Ingeborg Holm, Inge the fair; the post office clerk was just mincing up to her with an exaggerated bow and asking her to dance. He laid one hand on his back and gracefully shoved the other into his bosom. But she was shaking her head in token that she was a little out of breath and must rest awhile, whereat the post office clerk sat down by her side.

Tonio Kröger looked at them both, these two for whom he had in time past suffered love—at Hans and Ingeborg. They were Hans and Ingeborg not so much by virtue of individual traits and similarity of costume as by similarity of race and type. This was the blonde, fair-haired breed of the steel-blue eyes, which stood to him for the pure, the blithe, the untroubled in life; for a virginal aloofness that was at once both simple and full of pride. . . . He looked at them. Hans Hansen was standing there in his sailor suit, lively and well built as ever, broad in the shoulders and narrow in the hips; Ingeborg was laughing and tossing her head in a certain high-spirited way she had; she carried her hand, a schoolgirl hand, not at all slender, not at all particularly aristocratic, to the back of her head in a certain manner so that the thin sleeve fell away from her elbow—and suddenly such a pang of homesickness shook his breast that involuntarily he drew farther back into the darkness lest someone might see his features twitch.

"Had I forgotten you?" he asked. "No, never. Not thee, Hans, not thee, Inge the fair! It was always you I worked for; when I heard applause I always stole a look to see if you were there. . . . Did you read *Don Carlos*, Hans Hansen, as you promised me at the garden gate? No, don't read it! I do not ask it any more. What have you to do with a king who weeps for loneliness? You must not cloud your clear eyes or make them dreamy and dim by peering into melancholy poetry. . . . To be like you! To begin again, to grow up like you, regular like you, simple and normal and cheerful, in conformity and understanding with God and man, beloved of the innocent and happy. To take you, Ingeborg Holm, to wife, and have a son like you, Hans Hansen—to live free from the curse of knowledge and the torment of creation, live and praise God in blessed mediocrity! Begin again? But it would do no good. It would turn out the same—everything would turn out the same as it did before. For some go of necessity astray, because for them there is no such thing as a right path."

The music ceased; there was a pause in which refreshments were handed round. The post office assistant tripped about in person with a trayful of herring salad and served the ladies; but before Ingeborg Holm he even went down on one knee as he passed her the dish, and she blushed for pleasure.

But now those within began to be aware of a spectator behind the glass door; some of the flushed and pretty faces turned to measure him with hostile glances; but he stood his ground. Ingeborg and Hans looked at him too, at almost the same time, both with that utter indifference in their eyes that looks so like contempt. And he was conscious too of a gaze resting on him from a different quarter; turned his head and met with his own the eyes that had sought him out. A girl stood not far off, with a fine, pale little face—he had already noticed her. She had not danced much, she had few partners, and he had seen her sitting there against the wall, her lips closed in a bitter line. She was standing alone now too; her dress was a thin light stuff, like the others, but beneath the transparent frock her shoulders showed angular and poor, and the thin neck was thrust down so deep between those meager shoulders that as she stood there motionless she might almost be thought a little deformed. She was holding her hands in their thin mitts across her flat breast, with the finger tips touching; her head was drooped, yet she was looking up at Tonio Kröger with black swimming eyes. He turned away. . . .

Here, quite close to him, were Ingeborg and Hans. He had sat down beside her—she was perhaps his sister—and they ate and drank together surrounded by other rosy-cheeked folk; they chattered and made merry, called to each other in ringing voices, and laughed aloud. Why could he not go up and speak to them? Make some trivial remark to him or her, to which they might at least answer with a smile? It would make him happy—he longed to do it; he would go back more satisfied to his room if he might feel he had established a little contact with them. He thought out what he might say; but he had not the courage to say it. Yes, this too was just as it had been: they would not understand him, they would listen like strangers to anything he was able to say. For their speech was not his speech.

It seemed the dance was about to begin again. The leader developed a comprehensive activity. He dashed hither and thither, adjuring everybody to get partners; helped the waiters to push chairs and glasses out of the way, gave orders to the musicians, even took some awkward people by the shoulders and shoved them aside. . . . What was coming? They formed squares of four couples each. . . . A frightful memory brought the color to Tonio Kröger's cheeks. They were forming for a quadrille.

The music struck up, the couples bowed and crossed over. The leader called off; he called off—Heaven save us—in French! And pronounced the nasals with great distinction. Ingeborg Holm danced close by, in the set nearest the glass door. She moved to and fro before him, forward and back, pacing and turning; he caught a waft from her hair or the thin stuff of her frock, and it made him close his eyes with the old, familiar feeling, the fragrance and bitter-sweet enchantment he had faintly felt in all these days, that now filled him utterly with irresistible sweetness. And what was the feeling? Longing, tenderness? Envy? Self-contempt? . . . *Moulinet des dames!* "Did you laugh, Ingeborg the blonde, did you laugh at me when I disgraced myself by dancing the *moulinet*? And would you still laugh today even after I have become something like a famous man? Yes, that you would, and you would be right to laugh. Even if I in my own person had written the nine symphonies and *The World as Will and Idea* and painted the Last Judgment,[68] you would still be eternally right to laugh. . . ." As he looked at her he thought of a line of verse once so familiar to him, now long forgotten: "I would sleep, but thou must dance." How well he knew it, that melancholy northern mood it evoked—its heavy inarticulateness. To sleep. . . . To long to be allowed to live the life of simple feeling, to rest sweetly and passively in feeling alone, without compulsion to act and achieve—and yet to be forced to dance, dance the cruel and perilous sword dance of art; without even being allowed to forget the melancholy conflict within oneself; to be forced to dance, the while one loved. . . .

A sudden wild extravagance had come over the scene. The sets had broken up, the quadrille was being succeeded by a galop, and all the couples were leaping and gliding about. They flew past Tonio Kröger to a maddeningly quick tempo, crossing, advancing, retreating, with quick, breathless laughter. A couple came rushing and circling toward Tonio Kröger; the girl had a pale, refined face and lean, high shoulders. Suddenly, directly in front of him, they tripped and slipped and stumbled. . . . The pale girl fell, so hard and violently it almost looked dangerous; and her partner with her. He must have hurt himself badly, for he quite forgot her, and, half rising, began to rub his knee and grimace; while she, quite dazed, it seemed, still lay on the floor. Then Tonio Kröger came forward, took her gently by the arms, and lifted her up. She looked dazed, bewildered, wretched; then suddenly her delicate face flushed pink.

"*Tak, O, mange tak!*"[69] she said, and gazed up at him with dark, swimming eyes.

<hr>

68. The nine symphonies of Beethoven, Schopenhauer's philosophical work *The World as Will and Idea*, and Michelangelo's Last Judgment, painted in the Sistine Chapel, were regarded as the greatest achievements of mind and art.
69. "Thanks, oh many thanks" (Danish).

"You should not dance any more, Fräulein,"[70] he said gently. Once more he looked round at *them*, at Ingeborg and Hans, and then he went out, left the ball and the veranda and returned to his own room.

He was exhausted with jealousy, worn out with the gaiety in which he had had no part. Just the same, just the same as it had always been. Always with burning cheeks he had stood in his dark corner and suffered for you, you blond, you living, you happy ones! And then quite simply gone away. Somebody *must* come now! Ingeborg *must* notice he had gone, must slip after him, lay a hand on his shoulder and say: "Come back and be happy. I love you!" But she came not at all. No, such things did not happen. Yes, all was as it had been, and he too was happy, just as he had been. For his heart was alive. But between that past and this present what had happened to make him become that which he now was? Icy desolation, solitude: mind, and art, forsooth!

He undressed, lay down, put out the light. Two names he whispered into his pillow, the few chaste northern syllables that meant for him his true and native way of love, of longing and happiness; that meant to him life and home, meant simple and heartfelt feeling. He looked back on the years that had passed. He thought of the dreamy adventures of the senses, nerves, and mind in which he had been involved; saw himself eaten up with intellect and introspection, ravaged and paralyzed by insight, half worn out by the fevers and frosts of creation, helpless and in anguish of conscience between two extremes, flung to and fro between austerity and lust; *raffiné*, impoverished, exhausted by frigid and artificially heightened ecstasies; erring, forsaken, martyred, and ill—and sobbed with nostalgia and remorse.

Here in his room it was still and dark. But from below life's lulling, trivial waltz-rhythm came faintly to his ears.

Tonio Kröger sat up in the north, composing his promised letter to his friend Lisabeta Ivanovna.

"Dear Lisabeta down there in Arcady,[71] whither I shall shortly return," he wrote: "Here is something like a letter, but it will probably disappoint you, for I mean to keep it rather general. Not that I have nothing to tell; for indeed, in my way, I have had experiences; for instance, in my native town they were even going to arrest me. . . . but of that by word of mouth. Sometimes now I have days when I would rather state things in general terms than go on telling stories.

"You probably still remember, Lisabeta, that you called me a *bourgeois, a bourgeois manqué?* You called me that in an hour when, led on by other confessions I had previously let slip, I confessed to you my love of life, or what I call life. I ask myself if you were aware how very close you came to the truth, how much my love of 'life' is one and the same thing as my being a *bourgeois*. This journey of mine has given me much occasion to ponder the subject.

"My father, you know, had the temperament of the north: solid, reflective, puritanically correct, with a tendency to melancholia. My mother, of indeterminate foreign blood, was beautiful, sensuous, naïve, passionate, and careless at once, and, I think, irregular by instinct. The mixture was no doubt extraordinary and bore with it extraordinary dangers. The issue of it, a *bourgeois* who strayed off into art, a bohemian who feels nostalgic yearnings for respectability, an artist with a bad conscience. For surely it is my *bourgeois* conscience makes me see in the artist life, in all irregularity and all genius, something profoundly suspect, profoundly disreputable; that fills me with this lovelorn *faiblesse*[72] for the simple and good, the comfortably normal, the average unendowed respectable human being.

"I stand between two worlds. I am at home in neither, and I suffer in consequence. You artists call me a *bourgeois*, and the *bourgeois* try to arrest me. . . . I don't know which makes me feel worse. The *bourgeois* are stupid; but you adorers of the beautiful, who call me phlegmatic and without aspirations, you ought to realize that there is a way of being an artist that goes so deep and is so much a matter of origins and destinies that no longing seems to it sweeter and more worth knowing than longing after the bliss of the commonplace.

"I admire those proud, cold beings who adventure upon the paths of great and demonic beauty and despise 'mankind'; but I do not envy them. For if anything is capable of making a poet of a literary man, it is my *bourgeois* love of the human, the living and usual. It is the source of all warmth, goodness, and humor; I even almost think it is itself that love of which it stands written that one may speak with the tongues of men and of angels and yet having it not is as sounding brass and tinkling cymbals.[73]

"The work I have so far done is nothing or not much—as good as nothing. I will do better, Lisabeta—this is a promise. As I write, the sea whispers to me and I close my eyes. I am looking into a world unborn and formless, that needs to be ordered and shaped; I see into a whirl of shadows of human figures who beckon to me to weave spells to redeem them: tragic and laughable figures and some that are both together—and to these I am drawn. But my deepest

---

72. Weakness (French).

73. Luther's translation from the Bible, *I Corinthians* 13:1. The Bible goes on to define this kind of love as "patient and kind . . . not jealous or boastful . . . not arrogant or rude; [it]

does not insist on its own way, . . . is not irritable or resentful . . . does not rejoice at wrong, but rejoices in the right. Love bears all things, believes all things, hopes all things, endures all things [and] never ends."

and secretest love belongs to the blond and blue-eyed, the fair and living, the happy, lovely, and commonplace.

"Do not chide this love, Lisabeta; it is good and fruitful. There is longing in it, and a gentle envy; a touch of contempt and no little innocent bliss."

1903

RAINER MARIA RILKE
(1875–1926)
Duino Elegies

Third Elegy*

It's one thing
        to sing the beloved.
                That hidden
guilty river-god
        of the blood   5
                is something else.
What does her young lover
        whom she can recognize
                at a distance
understand of that   10
        lord of desire, who often
                out of this lonely young man
(before the girl soothed him
        and often as if
                she didn't exist)   15
raised his godhead
        dripping with what
                unrecognizable stuff
rousing the night
        to a continuous   20
                tumult.
Oh Neptune of the blood
        his terrible trident.
                Oh the dark wind
sounding from his chest   25
        through the spiral conch!
                Listen to the night
scooping and hollowing out . . .
        You stars
                doesn't the lover's   30

* Translated by David Young.
  22. *Neptune*: Ancient sea god, here presented with his trident (three-pointed spear) and horn made from a conch shell.

delight in his
loved one's countenance
come from you?
Doesn't his secret insight
into her pure face   35
come from the pure constellations?

It wasn't you
oh no
and it wasn't his mother
who bent his brows   40
to this expectant arch.
Not from your mouth
girl so aware of him
not from that contact
did his lips curve   45
into this fruitful expression.
Do you really think
your soft approach
could shake him that way
you who walk   50
like the wind at dawn?
Oh yes you startled
his heart
but more ancient fears
crashed down inside him   55
at the shock of your touch.
Call him . . .
you can't free him
completely from
those dark companions.   60
Of course he *wants* to escape
and he does
and relieved he gets used to
your heart's seclusion
and takes hold   65
and begins to be himself.
But did he
ever really
begin himself?
Mother   70
you made him little
you started him
he was new to you
and you arched
the friendly world   75

over his new eyes
            and shut out
                        the strange one.
Where, where
            are the years   80
                        when your slender shape
was simply enough
            to block out
                        waves of approaching chaos?
You hid so much from him this way   85
            rendering harmless
                        the room that grew
suspicious at night
            and from the full
                        sanctuary of your heart   90
you mixed something human
            into his nightspace
                        And you set the night-light
not in the darkness
            but in your nearness   95
                        your presence
and it shone
            out of friendship.
                        There wasn't a creak
you couldn't explain   100
            smiling
                        as if you had known
for a long time
            exactly when
                        the floor would assert itself . . .   105
And he listened
            and he was soothed.
                        That's what your
getting up
            so tenderly   110
                        achieved: his tall
cloaked fate went back
            behind the wardrobe
                        and his unruly future
(so easily mussed)   115
            conformed to the folds
                        of the curtain.

                                                                    5

And while he lay there
            relieved
                        with your image   120

dissolving sweetly
     under his drowsy lids
         as he sank towards sleep
he *seemed* protected . . .
     but *within*   125
         who could divert
or contain
     the floods
         of his origin?
Ah, there *were*   130
     no precautions in the sleeper
         . . . sleeping
but dreaming, but
     running a fever
         how he let himself go!   135
He, the new one
     the shy one
         how he was tangled
in the spreading
     roots and tendrils   140
         of inner event
twisting in primitive patterns
     in choking growths
         in the shapes
of killer animals.   145
     How he submitted.
         Made love.
Loved his own
     inwardness
         his inner wilderness   150
the primeval forest
     where his heart stood
         like a green shoot
among huge fallen trees.
     Made love.   155
         Let it go, went on
down through his own
     roots and out
         to the monstrous beginning
where his little birth   160
     had happened so long ago.
         Loving it
he waded downward
     into more ancient blood
         into canyons   165

where Horror itself
         lay gorged from eating
              his fathers
and every Terror
         knew him   170
              and winked in complicity.
Yes, Atrocity smiled . . .
         seldom had you
              smiled that tenderly, mother.
Why shouldn't he love it   175
         since it had smiled.
              He loved it
before he loved you
         because when you carried him
              it was already   180
dissolved
         in the water that makes
              the embryo float.

You see
         we don't love   185
              a single season
like the flowers.
         When we love
              a sap
older than time   190
         rises through our arms.
              My dear
it's like this:
         that we love *inside* ourselves
              not one person   195
not some future being
         but seething multitudes
              not a particular child
but the fathers
         who lie at rest   200
              in our depths
like ruined mountains
         and the dry riverbeds
              of earlier mothers
and the whole   205
         soundless landscape
              under the clouded

or clear sky
  of its destiny .
    this, my dear   210
came before you.

And you yourself
  what do you know?
    You stirred up
prehistory   215
  in your lover.
    What passions
welled up
  from those long dead beings?
    What women   220
hated you
  what kind of men
    lost in darkness
did you waken within
  his youthful veins?   225
    Dead children
strained to touch you . . .
  Oh gently, gently
    do a loving day's work
for his sake   230
  lead him
    toward the garden
let him have
  more than enough of the night . . . .

    Hold him back . . .   235

FRANZ KAFKA

(1883–1924)

The Metamorphosis (Die Verwandlung) *

As Gregor Samsa awoke one morning from uneasy dreams he found himself transformed in his bed into a gigantic insect. He was lying on his hard, as it were armor-plated, back and when he lifted his head a little he could see his dome-like brown belly divided into stiff arched segments on top of which the bed quilt could hardly

* 1916. Reprinted from *The Penal Colony* by Franz Kafka. Translated by Willa and Edwin Muir.

keep in position and was about to slide off completely. His numerous legs, which were pitifully thin compared to the rest of his bulk, waved helplessly before his eyes.

What has happened to me? he thought. It was no dream. His room, a regular human bedroom, only rather too small, lay quiet between the four familiar walls. Above the table on which a collection of cloth samples was unpacked and spread out—Samsa was a commercial traveler—hung the picture which he had recently cut out of an illustrated magazine and put into a pretty gilt frame. It showed a lady, with a fur cap on and a fur stole, sitting upright and holding out to the spectator a huge fur muff into which the whole of her forearm had vanished!

Gregor's eyes turned next to the window, and the overcast sky—one could hear rain drops beating on the window gutter—made him quite melancholy. What about sleeping a little longer and forgetting all this nonsense, he thought, but it could not be done, for he was accustomed to sleep on his right side and in his present condition he could not turn himself over. However violently he forced himself towards his right side he always rolled on to his back again. He tried it at least a hundred times, shutting his eyes to keep from seeing his struggling legs, and only desisted when he began to feel in his side a faint dull ache he had never experienced before.

Oh God, he thought, what an exhausting job I've picked on! Traveling about day in, day out. It's much more irritating work than doing the actual business in the office, and on top of that there's the trouble of constant traveling, of worrying about train connections, the bed and irregular meals, casual acquaintances that are always new and never become intimate friends. The devil take it all! He felt a slight itching up on his belly; slowly pushed himself on his back nearer to the top of the bed so that he could lift his head more easily; identified the itching place which was surrounded by many small white spots the nature of which he could not understand and made to touch it with a leg, but drew the leg back immediately, for the contact made a cold shiver run through him.

He slid down again into his former position. This getting up early, he thought, makes one quite stupid. A man needs his sleep. Other commercials live like harem women. For instance, when I come back to the hotel of a morning to write up the orders I've got, these others are only sitting down to breakfast. Let me just try that with my chief; I'd be sacked on the spot. Anyhow, that might be quite a good thing for me, who can tell? If I didn't have to hold my hand because of my parents I'd have given notice long ago, I'd have gone to the chief and told him exactly what I think of him. That would knock him endways from his desk! It's a queer way of doing, too, this sitting on high at a desk and talking down to employees, especially when they have to come quite near because the chief is hard of hearing. Well, there's still hope; once I've saved enough money to pay back my parents' debts to him—that should take another five or six years—I'll do it without fail. I'll cut myself completely loose then. For the moment, though, I'd better get up, since my train goes at five.

He looked at the alarm clock ticking on the chest. Heavenly Father! he thought. It was half-past six o'clock and the hands were quietly moving on, it was even past the half-hour, it was getting on toward a quarter to seven. Had the alarm clock not gone off? From the bed one could see that it had been properly set for four o'clock; of course it must have gone off. Yes, but was it possible to sleep quietly through that ear-splitting noise? Well, he had not slept quietly, yet apparently all the more soundly for that. But what was he to do now? The next train went at seven o'clock; to catch that he would need to hurry like mad and his samples weren't even packed up, and he himself wasn't feeling particularly fresh and active. And even if he did catch the train he wouldn't avoid a row with the chief, since the firm's porter would have been waiting for the five o'clock train and would have long since reported his failure to turn up. The porter was a creature of the chief's, spineless and stupid. Well, supposing he were to say he was sick? But that would be most unpleasant and would look suspicious, since during his five years' employment he had not been ill once. The chief himself would be sure to come with the sick-insurance doctor, would reproach his parents with their son's laziness and would cut all excuses short by referring to the insurance doctor, who of course regarded all mankind as perfectly healthy malingerers. And would he be so far wrong on this occasion? Gregor really felt quite well, apart from a drowsiness that was utterly superfluous after such a long sleep, and he was even unusually hungry.

As all this was running through his mind at top speed without his being able to decide to leave his bed—the alarm clock had just struck a quarter to seven—there came a cautious tap at the door behind the head of his bed. "Gregor," said a voice—it was his mother's—"it's a quarter to seven. Hadn't you a train to catch?" That gentle voice! Gregor had a shock as he heard his own voice answering hers, unmistakably his own voice, it was true, but with a persistent horrible twittering squeak behind it like an undertone, that left the words in their clear shape only for the first moment and then rose up reverberating round them to destroy their sense, so that one could not be sure one had heard them rightly. Gregor wanted to answer at length and explain everything, but in the circumstances he confined himself to saying: "Yes, yes, thank you, Mother, I'm getting up now." The wooden door between them must have kept the change in his voice from being noticeable outside, for his mother contented herself with this statement and shuffled away.

Yet this brief exchange of words had made the other members of the family aware that Gregor was still in the house, as they had not expected, and at one of the side doors his father was already knocking, gently, yet with his fist. "Gregor, Gregor," he called, "what's the matter with you?" And after a little while he called again in a deeper voice: "Gregor! Gregor!" At the other side door his sister was saying in a low, plaintive tone: "Gregor? Aren't you well? Are you needing anything?" He answered them both at once: "I'm just ready," and did his best to make his voice sound as normal as possible by enunciating the words very clearly and leaving long pauses between them. So his father went back to his breakfast, but his sister whispered: "Gregor, open the door, do." However, he was not thinking of opening the door, and felt thankful for the prudent habit he had acquired in traveling of locking all doors during the night, even at home.

His immediate intention was to get up quietly without being disturbed, to put on his clothes and above all eat his breakfast, and only then to consider what else was to be done, since in bed, he was well aware, his meditations would come to no sensible conclusion. He remembered that often enough in bed he had felt small aches and pains, probably caused by awkward postures, which had proved purely imaginary once he got up, and he looked forward eagerly to seeing this morning's delusions gradually fall away. That the change in his voice was nothing but the precursor of a severe chill, a standing ailment of commercial travelers, he had not the least possible doubt.

To get rid of the quilt was quite easy; he had only to inflate himself a little and it fell off by itself. But the next move was difficult, especially because he was so uncommonly broad. He would have needed arms and hands to hoist himself up; instead he had only the numerous little legs which never stopped waving in all directions and which he could not control in the least. When he tried to bend one of them it was the first to stretch itself straight; and did he succeed at last in making it do what he wanted, all the other legs meanwhile waved the more wildly in a high degree of unpleasant agitation. "But what's the use of lying idle in bed," said Gregor to himself.

He thought that he might get out of bed with the lower part of his body first, but this lower part, which he had not yet seen and of which he could form no clear conception, proved too difficult to move; it shifted so slowly; and when finally, almost wild with annoyance, he gathered his forces together and thrust out recklessly, he had miscalculated the direction and bumped heavily against the lower end of the bed, and the stinging pain he felt informed him that precisely this lower part of his body was at the moment probably the most sensitive.

So he tried to get the top part of himself out first, and cautiously moved his head towards the edge of the bed. That proved easy enough, and despite its breadth and mass the bulk of his body at last slowly followed the movement of his head. Still, when he finally got his head free over the edge of the bed he felt too scared to go on advancing, for after all if he let himself fall in this way it would take a miracle to keep his head from being injured. And at all costs he must not lose consciousness now, precisely now; he would rather stay in bed.

But when after a repetition of the same efforts he lay in his former position again, sighing, and watched his little legs struggling against each other more wildly than ever, if that were possible, and saw no way of bringing any order into this arbitrary confusion, he told himself again that it was impossible to stay in bed and that the most sensible course was to risk everything for the smallest hope of getting away from it. At the same time he did not forget meanwhile to remind himself that cool reflection, the coolest possible, was much better than desperate resolves. In such moments he focused his eyes as sharply as possible on the window, but, unfortunately, the prospect of the morning fog, which muffled even the other side of the narrow street, brought him little encouragement and comfort. "Seven o'clock already," he said to himself when the alarm clock chimed again, "seven o'clock already and still such a thick fog." And for a little while he lay quiet, breathing lightly, as if perhaps expecting such complete repose to restore all things to their real and normal condition.

But then he said to himself: "Before it strikes a quarter past seven I must be quite out of this bed, without fail. Anyhow, by that time someone will have come from the office to ask for me, since it opens before seven." And he set himself to rocking his whole body at once in a regular rhythm, with the idea of swinging it out of the bed. If he tipped himself out in that way he could keep his head from injury by lifting it at an acute angle when he fell. His back seemed to be hard and was not likely to suffer from a fall on the carpet. His biggest worry was the loud crash he would not be able to help making, which would probably cause anxiety, if not terror, behind all the doors. Still, he must take the risk.

When he was already half out of the bed—the new method was more a game than an effort, for he needed only to hitch himself across by rocking to and fro—it struck him how simple it would be if he could get help. Two strong people—he thought of his father and the servant girl—would be amply sufficient; they would only have to thrust their arms under his convex back, lever him out of the bed, bend down with their burden and then be patient enough to let him turn himself right over on the the floor, where it was to be hoped his legs would then find their proper function. Well, ignoring the fact that the doors were all locked, ought he really to call for help? In spite of his misery he could not suppress a smile at the very idea of it.

He had got so far that he could barely keep his equilibrium when he rocked himself strongly, and he would have to nerve himself very soon for the final decision since in five minutes' time it would be a quarter past seven—when the front door bell rang. "That's someone from the office," he said to himself, and grew almost rigid, while his little legs only jigged about all the faster. For a moment everything stayed quiet. "They're not going to open the door," said Gregor to himself, catching at some kind of irrational hope. But then of course the servant girl went as usual to the door with her heavy tread and opened it. Gregor needed only to hear the first good morning of the visitor to know immediately who it was—the chief clerk himself. What a fate, to be condemned to work for a firm where the smallest omission at once gave rise to the gravest suspicion! Were all employees in a body nothing but scoundrels, was there not among them one single loyal devoted man who, had he wasted only an hour or so of the firm's time in a morning, was so tormented by conscience as to be driven out of his mind and actually incapable of leaving his bed? Wouldn't it really have been sufficient to send an apprentice to inquire—if any inquiry were necessary at all—did the chief clerk himself have to come and thus indicate to the entire family, an innocent family, that this suspicious circumstance could be investigated by no one less versed in affairs than himself? And more through the agitation caused by these reflections than through any act of will Gregor swung himself out of bed with all his strength. There was a loud thump, but it was not really a crash. His fall was broken to some extent by the carpet, his back, too, was less stiff than he thought, and so there was merely a dull thud, not so very startling. Only he had not lifted his head carefully enough and had hit it; he turned it and rubbed it on the carpet in pain and irritation.

"That was something falling down in there," said the chief clerk in the next room to the left. Gregor tried to suppose to himself that something like what had happened to him today might some day happen to the chief clerk; one really could not deny that it was possible. But as if in brusque reply to this supposition the chief clerk took a couple of firm steps in the next-door room and his patent leather boots creaked. From the right-hand room his sister was whispering to inform him of the situation: "Gregor, the chief clerk's here." "I know," muttered Gregor to himself; but he didn't dare to make his voice loud enough for his sister to hear it.

"Gregor," said his father now from the left-hand room, "the chief clerk has come and wants to know why you didn't catch the early train. We don't know what to say to him. Besides, he wants to talk to you in person. So open the door, please. He will be good enough to excuse the untidiness of your room." "Good morning, Mr. Samsa," the chief clerk was calling amiably meanwhile. "He's not well," said his mother to the visitor, while his father was still speaking through the door, "he's not well, sir, believe me. What else would make him miss a train! The boy thinks about nothing but his work. It makes me almost cross the way he never goes out in the evenings; he's been here the last eight days and has stayed at home every single evening. He just sits there quietly at the table reading a newspaper or looking through railway timetables. The only amusement he gets is doing fretwork. For instance, he spent two or three evenings cutting out a little picture frame; you would be surprised to see how pretty it is; it's hanging in his room; you'll see it in a minute when Gregor opens the door. I must say I'm glad you've come, sir; we should never have got him to unlock the door by ourselves; he's so obstinate; and I'm sure he's unwell, though he wouldn't have it to be so this morning." "I'm just coming," said Gregor slowly and carefully, not moving an inch for fear of losing one word of the conversation. "I can't think of any other explanation, madam," said the chief clerk, "I hope it's nothing serious. Although on the other hand I must say that we men of business— fortunately or unfortunately—very often simply have to ignore any slight indisposition, since business must be attended to." "Well, can the chief clerk come in now?" asked Gregor's father impatiently, again knocking on the door. "No," said Gregor. In the left-hand room a painful silence followed this refusal, in the right-hand room his sister began to sob.

Why didn't his sister join the others? She was probably newly out of bed and hadn't even begun to put on her clothes yet. Well, why was she crying? Because he wouldn't get up and let the chief clerk in, because he was in danger of losing his job, and because the chief would begin dunning his parents again for the old debts? Surely these were things one didn't need to worry about for the present. Gregor was still at home and not in the least thinking of deserting the family. At the moment, true, he was lying on the carpet and no one who knew the condition he was in could seriously expect him to admit the chief clerk. But for such a small discourtesy, which could plausibly be explained away somehow later on, Gregor could hardly be dismissed on the spot. And it seemed to Gregor that it would be much more sensible to leave him in peace for the present than to trouble him with tears and entreaties. Still, of course, their uncertainty bewildered them all and excused their behavior.

"Mr. Samsa," the chief clerk called now in a louder voice, "what's the matter with you? Here you are, barricading yourself in your room, giving only 'yes' and 'no' for answers, causing your parents a lot of unnecessary trouble and neglecting—I mention this only in passing—neglecting your business duties in an incredible fashion. I am speaking here in the name of your parents and of your chief, and I beg you quite seriously to give me an immediate and precise explanation. You amaze me, you amaze me. I thought you were a quiet, dependable person, and now all at once you seem bent on making a disgraceful exhibition of yourself. The chief did hint to me early this morning a possible explanation for your disappearance —with reference to the cash payments that were entrusted to you recently—but I almost pledged my solemn word of honor that this could not be so. But now that I see how incredibly obstinate you are, I no longer have the slightest desire to take your part at all. And your position in the firm is not so unassailable. I came with the intention of telling you all this in private, but since you are wasting my time so needlessly I don't see why your parents shouldn't hear it too. For some time past your work has been most unsatisfactory; this is not the season of the year for a business boom, of course, we admit that, but a season of the year for doing no business at all, that does not exist, Mr. Samsa, must not exist."

"But, sir," cried Gregor, beside himself and in his agitation forgetting everything else, "I'm just going to open the door this very minute. A slight illness, an attack of giddiness, has kept me from getting up. I'm still lying in bed. But I feel all right again. I'm getting out of bed now. Just give me a moment or two longer! I'm not quite so well as I thought. But I'm all right, really. How a thing like that can suddenly strike one down! Only last night I was quite well, my parents can tell you, or rather I did have a slight presentiment. I must have showed some sign of it. Why didn't I report it at the office! But one always thinks that an indisposition can be got over without staying in the house. Oh sir, do spare my parents! All that you're reproaching me with now has no foundation; no one has ever said a word to me about it. Perhaps you haven't looked at the last orders I sent in. Anyhow, I can still catch the eight o'clock train, I'm much the better for my few hours' rest. Don't let me detain you here, sir; I'll be attending to business very soon, and do be good enough to tell the chief so and to make my excuses to him!"

And while all this was tumbling out pell-mell and Gregor hardly knew what he was saying, he had reached the chest quite easily, perhaps because of the practice he had had in bed, and was now trying to lever himself upright by means of it. He meant actually to open the door, actually to show himself and speak to the chief clerk; he was eager to find out what the others, after all their insistence, would say at the sight of him. If they were horrified then the responsibility was no longer his and he could stay quiet. But if they took it calmly, then he had no reason either to be upset, and could really get to the station for the eight o'clock train if he hurried. At first he slipped down a few times from the polished surface of the chest, but at length with a last heave he stood upright; he paid no more attention to the pains in the lower part of his body, however they smarted. Then he let himself fall against the back of a near-by chair, and clung with his little legs to the edges of it. That brought him into control of himself again and he stopped speaking, for now he could listen to what the chief clerk was saying.

"Did you understand a word of it?" the chief clerk was asking; "surely he can't be trying to make fools of us?" "Oh dear," cried his mother, in tears, "perhaps he's terribly ill and we're tormenting him. Grete! Grete!" she called out then. "Yes Mother?" called his sister from the other side. They were calling to each other across Gregor's room. "You must go this minute for the doctor. Gregor is ill. Go for the doctor, quick. Did you hear how he was speaking?" "That was no human voice," said the chief clerk in a voice noticeably low beside the shrillness of the mother's. "Anna! Anna!" his father was calling through the hall to the kitchen, clapping his hands, "get a locksmith at once!" And the two girls were already running through the hall with a swish of skirts—how could his sister have got dressed so quickly?—and were tearing the front door open. There was no sound of its closing again; they had evidently left it open, as one does in houses where some great misfortune has happened.

But Gregor was now much calmer. The words he uttered were no longer understandable, apparently, although they seemed clear enough to him, even clearer than before, perhaps because his ear had grown accustomed to the sound of them. Yet at any rate people now believed that something was wrong with him, and were ready to help him. The positive certainty with which these first measures had been taken comforted him. He felt himself drawn once more into the human circle and hoped for great and remarkable results from both the doctor and the locksmith, without really distinguishing precisely between them. To make his voice as clear as possible for the decisive conversation that was now imminent he coughed a little, as quietly as he could, of course, since this noise too might not sound like a human cough for all he was able to judge. In the next room meanwhile there was complete silence. Perhaps his parents were sitting at the table with the chief clerk, whispering, perhaps they were all leaning against the door and listening.

Slowly Gregor pushed the chair towards the door, then let go of it, caught hold of the door for support—the soles at the end of his little legs were somewhat sticky—and rested against it for a moment after his efforts. Then he set himself to turning the key in the lock with his mouth. It seemed, unhappily, that he hadn't really any teeth—what could he grip the key with?—but on the other hand his jaws were certainly very strong; with their help he did manage to set the key in motion, heedless of the fact that he was undoubtedly damaging them somewhere, since a brown fluid issued from his mouth, flowed over the key and dripped on the floor. "Just listen to that," said the chief clerk next door; "he's turning the key." That was a great encouragement to Gregor; but they should all have shouted encouragement to him, his father and mother too: "Go on, Gregor," they should have called out, "keep going, hold on to that key!" And in the belief that they were all following his efforts intently, he clenched his jaws recklessly on the key with all the force at his command. As the turning of the key progressed he circled round the lock, holding on now only with his mouth, pushing on the key, as required, or pulling it down again with all the weight of his body. The louder click of the finally yielding lock literally quickened Gregor. With a deep breath of relief he said to himself: "So I didn't need the locksmith," and laid his head on the handle to open the door wide.

Since he had to pull the door towards him, he was still invisible when it was really wide open. He had to edge himself slowly round the near half of the double door, and to do it very carefully if he was not to fall plump upon his back just on the threshold. He was still carrying out this difficult manoeuvre, with no time to observe anything else, when he heard the chief clerk utter a loud "Oh!"— it sounded like a gust of wind—and now he could see the man, standing as he was nearest to the door, clapping one hand before his open mouth and slowly backing away as if driven by some invisible steady pressure. His mother—in spite of the chief clerk's being there her hair was still undone and sticking up in all directions— first clasped her hands and looked at his father, then took two steps towards Gregor and fell on the floor among her outspread skirts, her face quite hidden on her breast. His father knotted his fist with a fierce expression on his face as if he meant to knock Gregor back into his room, then looked uncertainly round the living room, covered his eyes with his hands and wept till his great chest heaved.

Gregor did not go now into the living room, but leaned against the inside of the firmly shut wing of the door, so that only half his body was visible and his head above it bending sideways to look at the others. The light had meanwhile strengthened; on the other side of the street one could see clearly a section of the endlessly long, dark gray building opposite—it was a hospital—abruptly punctuated by its row of regular windows; the rain was still falling, but only in large singly discernible and literally singly splashing drops. The breakfast dishes were set out on the table lavishly, for breakfast was the most important meal of the day to Gregor's father, who lingered it out for hours over various newspapers. Right opposite Gregor on the wall hung a photograph of himself on military service, as a lieutenant, hand on sword, a carefree smile on his face, inviting one to respect his uniform and military bearing. The door leading to the hall was open, and one could see that the front door stood open too, showing the landing beyond and the beginning of the stairs going down.

"Well," said Gregor, knowing perfectly that he was the only one who had retained any composure, "I'll put my clothes on at once, pack up my samples and start off. Will you only let me go? You see, sir, I'm not obstinate, and I'm willing to work; traveling is a hard life, but I couldn't live without it. Where are you going, sir? To the office? Yes? Will you give a true account of all this? One can be temporarily incapacitated, but that's just the moment for remembering former services and bearing in mind that later on, when the incapacity has been got over, one will certainly work with all the more industry and concentration. I'm loyally bound to serve the chief, you know that very well. Besides, I have to provide for my parents and my sister. I'm in great difficulties, but I'll get out of them again. Don't make things any worse for me than they are. Stand up for me in the firm. Travelers are not popular there, I know. People think they earn sacks of money and just have a good time. A prejudice there's no particular reason for revising. But you, sir, have a more comprehensive view of affairs than the rest of the staff, yes, let me tell you in confidence, a more comprehensive view than the chief himself, who, being the owner, lets his judgment easily be swayed against one of his employees. And you know very well that the traveler, who is never seen in the office almost the whole year round, can so easily fall a victim to gossip and ill luck and unfounded complaints, which he mostly knows nothing about, except when he comes back exhausted from his rounds, and only then suffers in person from their evil consequences, which he can no longer trace back to the original causes. Sir, sir, don't go away without a word to me to show that you think me in the right at least to some extent!"

But at Gregor's very first words the chief clerk had already backed away and only stared at him with parted lips over one twitching shoulder. And while Gregor was speaking he did not stand still one moment but stole away towards the door, without taking his eyes off Gregor, yet only an inch at a time, as if obeying some secret injunction to leave the room. He was already at the hall, and the suddenness with which he took his last step out of the living room would have made one believe he had burned the sole of his foot. Once in the hall he stretched his right arm before him towards the staircase, as if some supernatural power were waiting there to deliver him.

Gregor perceived that the chief clerk must on no account be allowed to go away in this frame of mind if his position in the firm were not to be endangered to the utmost. His parents did not understand this so well; they had convinced themselves in the course of years that Gregor was settled for life in this firm, and besides they were so preoccupied with their immediate troubles that all foresight had forsaken them. Yet Gregor had this foresight. The chief clerk must be detained, soothed, persuaded and finally won over; the whole future of Gregor and his family depended on it! If only his sister had been there! She was intelligent; she had begun to cry while Gregor was still lying quietly on his back. And no doubt the chief clerk, so partial to ladies, would have been guided by her; she would have shut the door of the flat and in the hall talked him out of his horror. But she was not there, and Gregor would have to handle the situation himself. And without remembering that he was still unaware what powers of movement he possessed, without even remembering that his words in all possibility, indeed in all likelihood, would again be unintelligible, he let go the wing of the door, pushed himself through the opening, started to walk towards the chief clerk, who was already ridiculously clinging with both hands to the railing on the landing; but immediately, as he was feeling for a support, he fell down with a little cry upon all his numerous legs. Hardly was he down when he experienced for the first time this morning a sense of physical comfort; his legs had firm ground under them; they were completely obedient, as he noted with joy; they even strove to carry him forward in whatever direction he chose; and he was inclined to believe that a final relief from all his sufferings was at hand. But in the same moment as he found himself on the floor, rocking with suppressed eagerness to move, not far from his mother, indeed just in front of her, she, who had seemed so completely crushed, sprang all at once to her feet, her arms and fingers outspread, cried: "Help, for God's sake, help!" bent her head down as if to see Gregor better, yet on the contrary kept backing senselessly away; had quite forgotten that the laden table stood behind her; sat upon it hastily, as if in absence of mind, when she bumped into it; and seemed altogether unaware that the big coffee pot beside her was upset and pouring coffee in a flood over the carpet.

"Mother, Mother," said Gregor in a low voice, and looked up at her. The chief clerk, for the moment, had quite slipped from his mind; instead, he could not resist snapping his jaws together at the sight of the streaming coffee. That made his mother scream again, she fled from the table and fell into the arms of his father, who hastened to catch her. But Gregor had now no time to spare for his parents; the chief clerk was already on the stairs; with his chin on the banisters he was taking one last backward look. Gregor made a spring, to be as sure as possible of overtaking him; the chief clerk must have divined his intention, for he leaped down several steps and vanished; he was still yelling "Ugh!" and it echoed through the whole staircase.

Unfortunately, the flight of the chief clerk seemed completely to upset Gregor's father, who had remained relatively calm until now, for instead of running after the man himself, or at least not hindering Gregor in his pursuit, he seized in his right hand the walking stick which the chief clerk had left behind on a chair, together with a hat and greatcoat, snatched in his left hand a large newspaper from the table and began stamping his feet and flourishing the stick and the newspaper to drive Gregor back into his room. No entreaty of Gregor's availed, indeed no entreaty was even understood, however humbly he bent his head his father only stamped on the floor the more loudly. Behind his father his mother had torn open a window, despite the cold weather, and was leaning far out of it with her face in her hands. A strong draught set in from the street to the staircase, the window curtains blew in, the newspapers on the table fluttered, stray pages whisked over the floor. Pitilessly Gregor's father drove him back, hissing and crying "Shoo!" like a savage. But Gregor was quite unpracticed in walking backwards, it really was a slow business. If he only had a chance to turn round he could get back to his room at once, but he was afraid of exasperating his father by the slowness of such a rotation and at any moment the stick in his father's hand might hit him a fatal blow on the back or on the head. In the end, however, nothing else was left for him to do since to his horror he observed that in moving backwards he could not even control the direction he took; and so, keeping an anxious eye on his father all the time over his shoulder, he began to turn round as quickly as he could, which was in reality very slowly. Perhaps his father noted his good intentions, for he did not interfere except every now and then to help him in the manoeuvre from a distance with the point of the stick. If only he would have stopped making that unbearable hissing noise! It made Gregor quite lose his head. He had turned almost completely round when the hissing noise so distracted him that he even turned a little the wrong way again. But when at last his head was fortunately right in front of the doorway, it appeared that his body was too broad simply to get through the opening. His father, of course, in his present mood was far from thinking of such a thing as opening the other half of the door, to let Gregor have enough space. He had merely the fixed idea of driving Gregor back into his room as quickly as possible. He would never have suffered Gregor to make the circumstantial preparations for standing up on end and perhaps slipping his way through the door. Maybe he was now making more noise than ever to urge Gregor forward, as if no obstacle impeded him; to Gregor, anyhow, the noise in his rear sounded no longer like the voice of one single father; this was really no joke, and Gregor thrust himself —come what might—into the doorway. One side of his body rose up, he was tilted at an angle in the doorway, his flank was quite bruised, horrid blotches stained the white door, soon he was stuck fast and, left to himself, could not have moved at all, his legs on one side fluttered trembling in the air, those on the other were crushed painfully to the floor—when from behind his father gave him a strong push which was literally a deliverance and he flew far into the room, bleeding freely. The door was slammed behind him with the stick, and then at last there was silence.

II

Not until it was twilight did Gregor awake out of a deep sleep, more like a swoon than a sleep. He would certainly have waked up of his own accord not much later, for he felt himself sufficiently rested and well-slept, but it seemed to him as if a fleeting step and a cautious shutting of the door leading into the hall had aroused him. The electric lights in the street cast a pale sheen here and there on the ceiling and the upper surfaces of the furniture, but down below, where he lay, it was dark. Slowly, awkwardly trying out his feelers, which he now first learned to appreciate, he pushed his way to the door to see what had been happening there. His left side felt like one single long, unpleasantly tense scar, and he had actually to limp on his two rows of legs. One little leg, moreover, had been severely damaged in the course of that morning's events— it was almost a miracle that only one had been damaged—and trailed uselessly behind him.

He had reached the door before he discovered what had really drawn him to it: the smell of food. For there stood a basin filled with fresh milk in which floated little sops of white bread. He could almost have laughed with joy, since he was now still hungrier than in the morning, and he dipped his head almost over the eyes straight into the milk. But soon in disappointment he withdrew it again; not only did he find it difficult to feed because of his tender left side—and he could only feed with the palpitating collaboration of his whole body—he did not like the milk either, although milk had been his favorite drink and that was certainly why his sister had set it there for him, indeed it was almost with repulsion that he turned away from the basin and crawled back to the middle of the room.

He could see through the crack of the door that the gas was turned on in the living room, but while usually at this time his father made a habit of reading the afternoon newspaper in a loud voice to his mother and occasionally to his sister as well, not a sound was now to be heard. Well, perhaps his father had recently given up this habit of reading aloud, which his sister had mentioned so often in conversation and in her letters. But there was the same silence all around, although the flat was certainly not empty of occupants. "What a quiet life our family has been leading," said Gregor to himself, and as he sat there motionless staring into the darkness he felt great pride in the fact that he had been able to provide such a life for his parents and sister in such a fine flat. But what if all the quiet, the comfort, the contentment were now to end in horror? To keep himself from being lost in such thoughts Gregor took refuge in movement and crawled up and down the room.

Once during the long evening one of the side doors was opened a little and quickly shut again, later the other side door too; someone had apparently wanted to come in and then thought better of it. Gregor now stationed himself immediately before the living room door, determined to persuade any hesitating visitor to come in or at least to discover who it might be; but the door was not opened again and he waited in vain. In the early morning, when the doors were locked, they had all wanted to come in, now that he had opened one door and the other had apparently been opened during the day, no one came in and even the keys were on the other side of the doors.

It was late at night before the gas went out in the living room, and Gregor could easily tell that his parents and his sister had all stayed awake until then, for he could clearly hear the three of them stealing away on tiptoe. No one was likely to visit him, not until the morning, that was certain; so he had plenty of time to meditate at his leisure on how he was to arrange his life afresh. But the lofty, empty room in which he had to lie flat on the floor filled him with an apprehension he could not account for, since it had been his very own room for the past five years—and with a half-unconscious action, not without a slight feeling of shame, he scuttled under the sofa, where he felt comfortable at once, although his back was a little cramped and he could not lift his head up, and his only regret was that his body was too broad to get the whole of it under the sofa.

He stayed there all night, spending the time partly in a light slumber, from which his hunger kept waking him up with a start, and partly in worrying and sketching vague hopes, which all led to the same conclusion, that he must lie low for the present and, by exercising patience and the utmost consideration, help the family to bear the inconvenience he was bound to cause them in his present condition.

Very early in the morning, it was still almost night, Gregor had the chance to test the strength of his new resolutions, for his sister, nearly fully dressed, opened the door from the hall and peered in. She did not see him at once, yet when she caught sight of him under the sofa—well, he had to be somewhere, he couldn't have flown away, could he?—she was so startled that without being able to help it she slammed the door shut again. But as if regretting her behavior she opened the door again immediately and came in on tiptoe, as if she were visiting an invalid or even a stranger. Gregor had pushed his head forward to the very edge of the sofa and watched her. Would she notice that he had left the milk standing, and not for lack of hunger, and would she bring in some other kind of food more to his taste? If she did not do it of her own accord, he would rather starve than draw her attention to the fact, although he felt a wild impulse to dart out from under the sofa, throw himself at her feet and beg her for something to eat. But his sister at once noticed, with surprise, that the basin was still full, except for a little milk that had been spilt all around it, she lifted it immediately, not with her bare hands, true, but with a cloth and carried it away. Gregor was wildly curious to know what she would bring instead, and made various speculations about it. Yet what she actually did next, in the goodness of her heart, he could never have guessed at. To find out what he liked she brought him a whole selection of food, all set out on an old newspaper. There were old, half-decayed vegetables, bones from last night's supper covered with a white sauce that had thickened; some raisins and almonds; a piece of cheese that Gregor would have called uneatable two days ago; a dry roll of bread, a buttered roll, and a roll both buttered and salted. Besides all that, she set down again the same basin, into which she had poured some water, and which was apparently to be reserved for his exclusive use. And with fine tact, knowing that Gregor would not eat in her presence, she withdrew quickly and even turned the key, to let him understand that he could take his ease as much as he liked. Gregor's legs all whizzed towards the food. His wounds must have healed completely, moreover, for he felt no disability, which amazed him and made him reflect how more than a month ago he had cut one finger a little with a knife and had still suffered pain from the wound only the day before yesterday. Am I less sensitive now? he thought, and sucked greedily at the cheese, which above all the other edibles attracted him at once and strongly. One after another and with tears of satisfaction in his eyes he quickly devoured the cheese, the vegetables and the sauce; the fresh food, on the other hand, had no charms for him, he could not even stand the smell of it and actually dragged away to some little distance the things he could eat. He had long finished his meal and was only lying lazily on the same spot when his sister turned the key slowly as a sign for him to retreat. That roused him at once, although he was nearly asleep, and he hurried under the sofa again. But it took considerable self-control for him to stay under the sofa, even for the short time his sister was in the room, since the large meal had swollen his body somewhat and he was so cramped he could hardly breathe. Slight attacks of breathlessness afflicted him and his eyes were starting a little out of his head as he watched his unsuspecting sister sweeping together with a broom not only the remains of what he had eaten but even the things he had not touched, as if these were now of no use to anyone, and hastily shoveling it all into a bucket, which she covered with a wooden lid and carried away. Hardly had she turned her back when Gregor came from under the sofa and stretched and puffed himself out.

In this manner Gregor was fed, once in the early morning while his parents and the servant girl were still asleep, and a second time after they had all had their midday dinner, for then his parents took a short nap and the servant girl could be sent out on some errand or other by his sister. Not that they would have wanted him to starve, of course, but perhaps they could not have borne to know more about his feeding than from hearsay, perhaps too his sister wanted to spare them such little anxieties wherever possible, since they had quite enough to bear as it was.

Under what pretext the doctor and the locksmith had been got rid of on that first morning Gregor could not discover, for since what he said was not understood by the others it never struck any of them, not even his sister, that he could understand what they said, and so whenever his sister came into his room he had to content himself with hearing her utter only a sigh now and then and an occasional appeal to the saints. Later on, when she had got a little used to the situation—of course she could never get completely used to it—she sometimes threw out a remark which was kindly meant or could be so interpreted. "Well, he liked his dinner today," she would say when Gregor had made a good clearance of his food; and when he had not eaten, which gradually happened more and more often, she would say almost sadly: "Everything's been left standing again."

But although Gregor could get no news directly, he overheard a lot from the neighboring rooms, and as soon as voices were audible, he would run to the door of the room concerned and press his whole body against it. In the first few days especially there was no conversation that did not refer to him somehow, even if only indirectly. For two whole days there were family consultations at every meal-time about what should be done; but also between meals the same subject was discussed, for there were always at least two members of the family at home, since no one wanted to be alone in the flat and to leave it quite empty was unthinkable. And on the very first of these days the household cook—it was not quite clear what and how much she knew of the situation—went down on her knees to his mother and begged leave to go, and when she departed, a quarter of an hour later, gave thanks for her dismissal with tears in her eyes as if for the greatest benefit that could have been conferred on her, and without any prompting swore a solemn oath that she would never say a single word to anyone about what had happened.

Now Gregor's sister had to cook too, helping her mother; true, the cooking did not amount to much, for they ate scarcely anything. Gregor was always hearing one of the family vainly urging another to eat and getting no answer but: "Thanks, I've had all I want," or something similar. Perhaps they drank nothing either. Time and again his sister kept asking his father if he wouldn't like some beer and offered kindly to go and fetch it herself, and when he made no answer suggested that she could ask the concierge to fetch it, so that he need feel no sense of obligation, but then a round "No" came from his father and no more was said about it.

In the course of that very first day Gregor's father explained the family's financial position and prospects to both his mother and his sister. Now and then he rose from the table to get some voucher or memorandum out of the small safe he had rescued from the collapse of his business five years earlier. One could hear him opening the complicated lock and rustling papers out and shutting it again. This statement made by his father was the first cheerful information Gregor had heard since his imprisonment. He had been of the opinion that nothing at all was left over from his father's business, at least his father had never said anything to the contrary, and of course he had not asked him directly. At that time Gregor's sole desire was to do his utmost to help the family to forget as soon as possible the catastrophe which had overwhelmed the business and thrown them all into a state of complete despair. And so he had set to work with unusual ardor and almost overnight had become a commercial traveler instead of a little clerk, with of course much greater chances of earning money, and his success was immediately translated into good round coin which he could lay on the table for his amazed and happy family. These had been fine times, and they had never recurred, at least not with the same sense of glory, although later on Gregor had earned so much money that he was able to meet the expenses of the whole household and did so. They had simply got used to it, both the family and Gregor; the money was gratefully accepted and gladly given, but there was no special uprush of warm feeling. With his sister alone had he remained intimate, and it was a secret plan of his that she, who loved music, unlike himself, and could play movingly on the violin, should be sent next year to study at the Conservatorium, despite the great expense that would entail, which must be made up in some other way. During his brief visits home the Conservatorium was often mentioned in the talks he had with his sister, but always merely as a beautiful dream which could never come true, and his parents discouraged even these inno-cent references to it; yet Gregor had made up his mind firmly about it and meant to announce the fact with due solemnity on Christmas Day.

Such were the thoughts, completely futile in his present condi-tion, that went through his head as he stood clinging upright to the door and listening. Sometimes out of sheer weariness he had to give up listening and let his head fall negligently against the door, but he always had to pull himself together again at once, for even the slight sound his head made was audible next door and brought all conversation to a stop. "What can he be doing now?" his father would say after a while, obviously turning towards the door, and only then would the interrupted conversation gradually be set going again.

Gregor was now informed as amply as he could wish—for his father tended to repeat himself in his explanations, partly because it was a long time since he had handled such matters and partly because his mother could not always grasp things at once—that a certain amount of investments, a very small amount it was true, had sur-vived the wreck of their fortunes and had even increased a little because the dividends had not been touched meanwhile. And be-sides that, the money Gregor brought home every month—he had kept only a few dollars for himself—had never been quite used up and now amounted to a small capital sum. Behind the door Gregor nodded his head eagerly, rejoiced at this evidence of unexpected thrift and foresight. True, he could really have paid off some more of his father's debts to the chief with this extra money, and so brought much nearer the day on which he could quit his job, but doubtless it was better the way his father had arranged it.

Yet this capital was by no means sufficient to let the family live on the interest of it; for one year, perhaps, or at the most two, they could live on the principal, that was all. It was simply a sum that ought not to be touched and should be kept for a rainy day; money for living expenses would have to be earned. Now his father was still hale enough but an old man, and he had done no work for the past five years and could not be expected to do much; during these five years, the first years of leisure in his laborious though unsuccessful life, he had grown rather fat and become sluggish. And Gregor's old mother, how was she to earn a living with her asthma, which troubled her even when she walked through the flat and kept her lying on a sofa every other day panting for breath beside an open window? And was his sister to earn her bread, she who was still a child of seventeen and whose life hitherto had been so pleasant, consisting as it did in dressing herself nicely, sleeping long, helping in the housekeeping, going out to a few modest entertainments and above all playing the violin? At first whenever the need for earning money was mentioned Gregor let go his hold on the door and threw himself down on the cool leather sofa beside it, he felt so hot with shame and grief.

Often he just lay there the long nights through without sleeping at all, scrabbling for hours on the leather. Or he nerved himself to the great effort of pushing an armchair to the window, then crawled up over the window sill and, braced against the chair, leaned against the window panes, obviously in some recollection of the sense of freedom that looking out of a window always used to give him. For in reality day by day things that were even a little way off were growing dimmer to his sight; the hospital across the street, which he used to execrate for being all too often before his eyes, was now quite beyond his range of vision, and if he had not known that he lived in Charlotte Street, a quiet street but still a city street, he might have believed that his window gave on a desert waste where gray sky and gray land blended indistinguishably into each other. His quick-witted sister only needed to observe twice that the armchair stood by the window; after that whenever she had tidied the room she always pushed the chair back to the same place at the window and even left the inner casements open.

If he could have spoken to her and thanked her for all she had to do for him, he could have borne her ministrations better; as it was, they oppressed him. She certainly tried to make as light as possible of whatever was disagreeable in her task, and as time went on she succeeded, of course, more and more, but time brought more enlightenment to Gregor too. The very way she came in distressed him. Hardly was she in the room when she rushed to the window, without even taking time to shut the door, careful as she was usually to shield the sight of Gregor's room from the others, and as if she were almost suffocating tore the casements open with hasty fingers, standing then in the open draught for a while even in the bitterest cold and drawing deep breaths. This noisy scurry of hers upset Gregor twice a day; he would crouch trembling under the sofa all the time, knowing quite well that she would certainly have spared him such a disturbance had she found it at all possible to stay in his presence without opening the window.

On one occasion, about a month after Gregor's metamorphosis, when there was surely no reason for her to be still startled at his appearance, she came a little earlier than usual and found him gazing out of the window, quite motionless, and thus well placed to look like a bogey. Gregor would not have been surprised had she not come in at all, for she could not immediately open the window while he was there, but not only did she retreat, she jumped back as if in alarm and banged the door shut; a stranger might well have thought that he had been lying in wait for her there meaning to bite her. Of course he hid himself under the sofa at once, but he had to wait until midday before she came again, and she seemed more ill at ease than usual. This made him realize how repulsive the sight of him still was to her, and that it was bound to go on being repulsive, and what an effort it must cost her not to run away even from the sight of the small portion of his body that stuck out from under the sofa. In order to spare her that, therefore, one day he carried a sheet on his back to the sofa—it cost him four hours' labor—and arranged it there in such a way as to hide him completely, so that even if she were to bend down she could not see him. Had she considered the sheet unnecessary, she would certainly have stripped it off the sofa again, for it was clear enough that this curtaining and confining of himself was not likely to conduce to Gregor's comfort, but she left it where it was, and Gregor even fancied that he caught a thankful glance from her eye when he lifted the sheet carefully a very little with his head to see how she was taking the new arrangement.

For the first fortnight his parents could not bring themselves to the point of entering his room, and he often heard them expressing their appreciation of his sister's activities, whereas formerly they had frequently scolded her for being as they thought a somewhat useless daughter. But now, both of them often waited outside the door, his father and his mother, while his sister tidied his room, and as soon as she came out she had to tell them exactly how things were in the room, what Gregor had eaten, how he had conducted himself this time and whether there was not perhaps some slight improvement in his condition. His mother, moreover, began relatively soon to want to visit him, but his father and sister dissuaded her at first with arguments which Gregor listened to very attentively and altogether approved. Later, however, she had to be held back by main force, and when she cried out: "Do let me in to Gregor, he is my unfortunate son! Can't you understand that I must go to him?" Gregor thought that it might be well to have her come in, not every day, of course, but perhaps once a week; she understood things, after all, much better than his sister, who was only a child despite the efforts she was making and had perhaps taken on so difficult a task merely out of childish thoughtlessness.

Gregor's desire to see his mother was soon fulfilled. During the daytime he did not want to show himself at the window, out of consideration for his parents, but he could not crawl very far around the few square yards of floor space he had, nor could he bear lying quietly at rest all during the night, while he was fast losing any interest he had ever taken in food, so that for mere recreation he had formed the habit of crawling crisscross over the walls and ceiling. He especially enjoyed hanging suspended from the ceiling; it was much better than lying on the floor; one could breathe more freely; one's body swung and rocked lightly; and in the almost blissful absorption induced by this suspension it could happen to his own surprise that he let go and fell plump on the floor. Yet he now had his body much better under control than formerly, and even such a big fall did him no harm. His sister at once remarked the new distraction Gregor had found for himself—he left traces behind him of the sticky stuff on his soles wherever he crawled—and she got the idea in her head of giving him as wide a field as possible to crawl in and of removing the pieces of furniture that hindered him, above all the chest of drawers and the writing desk. But that was more than she could manage all by herself; she did not dare ask her father to help her; and as for the servant girl, a young creature of sixteen who had had the courage to stay on after the cook's departure, she could not be asked to help, for she had begged as an especial favor that she might keep the kitchen door locked and open it only on a definite summons; so there was nothing left but to apply to her mother at an hour when her father was out. And the old lady did come, with exclamations of joyful eagerness, which, however, died away at the door of Gregor's room. Gregor's sister, of course, went in first, to see that everything was in order before letting his mother enter. In great haste Gregor pulled the sheet lower and rucked it more in folds so that it really looked as if it had been thrown accidentally over the sofa. And this time he did not peer out from under it; he renounced the pleasure of seeing his mother on this occasion and was only glad that she had come at all. "Come in, he's out of sight," said his sister, obviously leading her mother in by the hand. Gregor could now hear the two women struggling to shift the heavy old chest from its place, and his sister claiming the greater part of the labor for herself, without listening to the admonitions of her mother who feared she might overstrain herself. It took a long time. After at least a quarter of an hour's tugging his mother objected that the chest had better be left where it was, for in the first place it was too heavy and could never be got out before his father came home, and standing in the middle of the room like that it would only hamper Gregor's movements, while in the second place it was not at all certain that removing the furniture would be doing a service to Gregor. She was inclined to think to the contrary; the sight of the naked walls made her own heart heavy, and why shouldn't Gregor have the same feeling, considering that he had been used to his furniture for so long and might feel forlorn without it. "And doesn't it look," she concluded in a low voice—in fact she had been almost whispering all the time as if to avoid letting Gregor, whose exact whereabouts she did not know, hear even the tones of her voice, for she was convinced that he could not understand her words—"doesn't it look as if we were showing him, by taking away his furniture, that we have given up hope of his ever getting better and are just leaving him coldly to himself? I think it would be best to keep his room exactly as it has always been, so that when he comes back to us he will find everything unchanged and be able all the more easily to forget what has happened in between."

On hearing these words from his mother Gregor realized that the lack of all direct human speech for the past two months together with the monotony of family life must have confused his mind, otherwise he could not account for the fact that he had quite earnestly looked forward to having his room emptied of furnishing. Did he really want his warm room, so comfortably fitted with old family furniture, to be turned into a naked den in which he would certainly be able to crawl unhampered in all directions but at the price of shedding simultaneously all recollection of his human background? He had indeed been so near the brink of forgetfulness that only the voice of his mother, which he had not heard for so long, had drawn him back from it. Nothing should be taken out of his room; everything must stay as it was; he could not dispense with the good influence of the furniture on his state of mind; and even if the furniture did hamper him in his senseless crawling round and round, that was no drawback but a great advantage.

Unfortunately his sister was of the contrary opinion; she had grown accustomed, and not without reason, to consider herself an expert in Gregor's affairs as against her parents, and so her mother's advice was now enough to make her determined on the removal not only of the chest and the writing desk, which had been her first intention, but of all the furniture except the indispensable sofa. This determination was not, of course, merely the outcome of childish recalcitrance and of the self-confidence she had recently developed so unexpectedly and at such cost; she had in fact perceived that Gregor needed a lot of space to crawl about in, while on the other hand he never used the furniture at all, so far as could be seen. Another factor might have been also the enthusiastic temperament of an adolescent girl, which seeks to indulge itself on every opportunity and which now tempted Grete to exaggerate the horror of her brother's circumstances in order that she might do all the more for him. In a room where Gregor lorded it all alone over empty walls no one save herself was likely ever to set foot.

And so she was not to be moved from her resolve by her mother, who seemed moreover to be ill at ease in Gregor's room and therefore unsure of herself, was soon reduced to silence and helped her daughter as best she could to push the chest outside. Now, Gregor could do without the chest, if need be, but the writing desk he must retain. As soon as the two women had got the chest out of his room, groaning as they pushed it, Gregor stuck his head out from under the sofa to see how he might intervene as kindly and cautiously as possible. But as bad luck would have it, his mother was the first to return, leaving Grete clasping the chest in the room next door where she was trying to shift it all by herself, without of course moving it from the spot. His mother however was not accustomed to the sight of him, it might sicken her and so in alarm Gregor backed quickly to the other end of the sofa, yet could not prevent the sheet from swaying a little in front. That was enough to put her on the alert. She paused, stood still for a moment and then went back to Grete.

Although Gregor kept reassuring himself that nothing out of the way was happening, but only a few bits of furniture were being changed round, he soon had to admit that all this trotting to and fro of the two women, their little ejaculations and the scraping of furniture along the floor affected him like a vast disturbance coming from all sides at once, and however much he tucked in his head and legs and cowered to the very floor he was bound to confess that he would not be able to stand it for long. They were clearing his room out; taking away everything he loved; the chest in which he kept his fret saw and other tools was already dragged off; they were now loosening the writing desk which had almost sunk into the floor, the desk at which he had done all his homework when he was at the commercial academy, at the grammar school before that, and, yes, even at the primary school—he had no more time to waste in weighing the good intentions of the two women, whose existence he had by now almost forgotten, for they were so exhausted that they were laboring in silence and nothing could be heard but the heavy scuffling of their feet.

And so he rushed out—the women were just leaning against the writing desk in the next room to give themselves a breather—and four times changed his direction, since he really did not know what to rescue first, then on the wall opposite, which was already otherwise cleared, he was struck by the picture of the lady muffled in so much fur and quickly crawled up to it and pressed himself to the glass, which was a good surface to hold on to and comforted his hot belly

This picture at least, which was entirely hidden beneath him, was going to be removed by nobody. He turned his head towards the door of the living room so as to observe the women when they came back.

They had not allowed themselves much of a rest and were already coming; Grete had twined her arm round her mother and was almost supporting her. "Well, what shall we take now?" said Grete, looking round. Her eyes met Gregor's from the wall. She kept her composure, presumably because of her mother, bent her head down to her mother, to keep her from looking up, and said, although in a fluttering, unpremeditated voice: "Come, hadn't we better go back to the living room for a moment?" Her intentions were clear enough to Gregor, she wanted to bestow her mother in safety and then chase him down from the wall. Well, just let her try it! He clung to his picture and would not give it up. He would rather fly in Grete's face.

But Grete's words had succeeded in disquieting her mother, who took a step to one side, caught sight of the huge brown mass on the flowered wallpaper, and before she was really conscious that what she saw was Gregor screamed in a loud, hoarse voice: "Oh God, oh God!" fell with outspread arms over the sofa as if giving up and did not move. "Gregor!" cried his sister, shaking her fist and glaring at him. This was the first time she had directly addressed him since his metamorphosis. She ran into the next room for some aromatic essence with which to rouse her mother from her fainting fit. Gregor wanted to help too—there was still time to rescue the picture—but he was stuck fast to the glass and had to tear himself loose; he then ran after his sister into the next room as if he could advise her, as he used to do; but then had to stand helplessly behind her; she meanwhile searched among various small bottles and when she turned round started in alarm at the sight of him; one bottle fell on the floor and broke; a splinter of glass cut Gregor's face and some kind of corrosive medicine splashed him; without pausing a moment longer Grete gathered up all the bottles she could carry and ran to her mother with them; she banged the door shut with her foot. Gregor was now cut off from his mother, who was perhaps nearly dying because of him; he dared not open the door for fear of frightening away his sister, who had to stay with her mother; there was nothing he could do but wait; and harassed by self-reproach and worry he began now to crawl to and fro, over everything, walls, furniture and ceiling, and finally in his despair, when the whole room seemed to be reeling round him, fell down on to the middle of the big table.

A little while elapsed, Gregor was still lying there feebly and all around was quiet, perhaps that was a good omen. Then the doorbell rang. The servant girl was of course locked in her kitchen, and Grete would have to open the door. It was his father. "What's been happening?" were his first words; Grete's face must have told him everything. Grete answered in a muffled voice, apparently hiding her head on his breast: "Mother has been fainting, but she's better now. Gregor's broken loose." "Just what I expected," said his father, "just what I've been telling you, but you women would never listen." It was clear to Gregor that his father had taken the worst interpretation of Grete's all too brief statement and was assuming that Gregor had been guilty of some violent act. Therefore Gregor must now try to propitiate his father, since he had neither time nor means for an explanation. And so he fled to the door of his own room and crouched against it, to let his father see as soon as he came in from the hall that his son had the good intention of getting back into his room immediately and that it was not necessary to drive him there, but that if only the door were opened he would disappear at once.

Yet his father was not in the mood to perceive such fine distinctions. "Ah!" he cried as soon as he appeared, in a tone which sounded at once angry and exultant. Gregor drew his head back from the door and lifted it to look at his father. Truly, this was not the father he had imagined to himself; admittedly he had been too absorbed of late in his new recreation of crawling over the ceiling to take the same interest as before in what was happening elsewhere in the flat, and he ought really to be prepared for some changes. And yet, and yet, could that be his father? The man who used to lie wearily sunk in bed whenever Gregor set out on a business journey; who welcomed him back of an evening lying in a long chair in a dressing gown; who could not really rise to his feet but only lifted his arms in greeting, and on the rare occasions when he did go out with his family, on one or two Sundays a year and on high holidays, walked between Gregor and his mother, who were slow walkers anyhow, even more slowly than they did, muffled in his old greatcoat, shuffling laboriously forward with the help of his crook-handled stick which he set down most cautiously at every step and, whenever he wanted to say anything, nearly always came to a full stop and gathered his escort around him? Now he was standing there in fine shape; dressed in a smart blue uniform with gold buttons, such as bank messengers wear; his strong double chin bulged over the stiff high collar of his jacket; from under his bushy eyebrows his black eyes darted fresh and penetrating glances; his onetime tangled white hair had been combed flat on either side of a shining and carefully exact parting. He pitched his cap, which bore a gold monogram, probably the badge of some bank, in a wide sweep across the whole room on to a sofa and with the tail-ends of his jacket thrown back, his hands in his trouser pockets, advanced with a grim visage towards Gregor. Likely enough he did not himself know what he meant to do, at any rate he lifted his feet uncommonly high, and Gregor was dumbfounded at the enormous size of his shoe soles. But Gregor could not risk standing up to him, aware as he had been from the very first day of his new life that his father believed only the severest measures suitable for dealing with him. And so he ran before his father, stopping when he stopped and scuttling forward again when his father made any kind of move. In this way they circled the room several times without anything decisive happening, indeed the whole operation did not even look like a pursuit because it was carried out so slowly. And so Gregor did not leave the floor, for he feared that his father might take as a piece of peculiar wickedness any excursion of his over the walls or the ceiling. All the same, he could not stay this course much longer, for while his father took one step he had to carry out a whole series of movements. He was already beginning to feel breathless, just as in his former life his lungs had not been very dependable. As he was staggering along, trying to concentrate his energy on running, hardly keeping his eyes open; in his dazed state never even thinking of any other escape than simply going forward; and having almost forgotten that the walls were free to him, which in this room were well provided with finely carved pieces of furniture full of knobs and crevices—suddenly something lightly flung landed close behind him and rolled before him. It was an apple; a second apple followed immediately; Gregor came to a stop in alarm; there was no point in running on, for his father was determined to bombard him. He had filled his pockets with fruit from the dish on the sideboard and was now shying apple after apple, without taking particularly good aim for the moment. The small red apples rolled about the floor as if magnetized and cannoned into each other. An apple thrown without much force grazed Gregor's back and glanced off harmlessly. But another following immediately landed right on his back and sank in; Gregor wanted to drag himself forward, as if this startling, incredible pain could be left behind him; but he felt as if nailed to the spot and flattened himself out in a complete derangement of all his senses. With his last conscious look he saw the door of his room being torn open and his mother rushing out ahead of his screaming sister, in her underbodice, for her daughter had loosened her clothing to let her breathe more freely and recover from her swoon, he saw his mother rushing towards his father, leaving one after another behind her on the floor her loosened petticoats, stumbling over her petticoats straight to his father and embracing him, in complete union with him—but here Gregor's sight began to fail—with her hands clasped round his father's neck as she begged for her son's life.

III

The serious injury done to Gregor, which disabled him for more than a month—the apple went on sticking in his body as a visible reminder, since no one ventured to remove it—seemed to have made even his father recollect that Gregor was a member of the family, despite his present unfortunate and repulsive shape, and ought not to be treated as an enemy, that, on the contrary, family duty required the suppression of disgust and the exercise of patience, nothing but patience.

And although his injury had impaired, probably for ever, his powers of movement, and for the time being it took him long, long minutes to creep across his room like an old invalid—there was no question now of crawling up the wall—yet in his own opinion he was sufficiently compensated for this worsening of his condition by the fact that towards evening the living-room door, which he used to watch intently for an hour or two beforehand, was always thrown open, so that lying in the darkness of his room, invisible to the family, he could see them all at the lamp-lit table and listen to their talk, by general consent as it were, very different from his earlier eavesdropping.

True, their intercourse lacked the lively character of former times, which he had always called to mind with a certain wistfulness in the small hotel bedrooms where he had been wont to throw himself down, tired out, on damp bedding. They were now mostly very silent. Soon after supper his father would fall asleep in his armchair; his mother and sister would admonish each other to be silent; his mother, bending low over the lamp, stitched at fine sewing for an underwear firm; his sister, who had taken a job as a salesgirl, was learning shorthand and French in the evenings on the chance of bettering herself. Sometimes his father woke up, and as if quite unaware that he had been sleeping said to his mother: "What a lot of sewing you're doing today!" and at once fell asleep again, while the two women exchanged a tired smile.

With a kind of mulishness his father persisted in keeping his uniform on even in the house; his dressing gown hung uselessly on its peg and he slept fully dressed where he sat, as if he were ready for service at any moment and even here only at the beck and call of his superior. As a result, his uniform, which was not brand-new to start with, began to look dirty, despite all the loving care of the mother and sister to keep it clean, and Gregor often spent whole evenings gazing at the many greasy spots on the garment, gleaming with gold buttons always in a high state of polish, in which the old man sat sleeping in extreme discomfort and yet quite peacefully.

As soon as the clock struck ten his mother tried to rouse his father with gentle words and to persuade him after that to get into bed, for sitting there he could not have a proper sleep and that was what he needed most, since he had to go on duty at six. But with the mulishness that had obsessed him since he became a bank messenger he always insisted on staying longer at the table, although he regularly fell asleep again and in the end only with the greatest trouble could be got out of his armchair and into his bed. However insistently Gregor's mother and sister kept urging him with gentle reminders, he would go on slowly shaking his head for a quarter of an hour, keeping his eyes shut, and refuse to get to his feet. The mother plucked at his sleeve, whispering endearments in his ear, the sister left her lessons to come to her mother's help, but Gregor's father was not to be caught. He would only sink down deeper in his chair. Not until the two women hoisted him up by the armpits did he open his eyes and look at them both, one after the other, usually with the remark: "This is a life. This is the peace and quiet of my old age." And leaning on the two of them he would heave himself up, with difficulty, as if he were a great burden to himself, suffer them to lead him as far as the door and then wave them off and go on alone, while the mother abandoned her needlework and the sister her pen in order to run after him and help him farther.

Who could find time, in this overworked and tired-out family, to bother about Gregor more than was absolutely needful? The household was reduced more and more; the servant girl was turned off; a gigantic bony charwoman with white hair flying round her head came in morning and evening to do the rough work; everything else was done by Gregor's mother, as well as great piles of sewing. Even various family ornaments, which his mother and sister used to wear with pride at parties and celebrations, had to be sold, as Gregor discovered of an evening from hearing them all discuss the prices obtained. But what they lamented most was the fact that they could not leave the flat which was much too big for their present circumstances, because they could not think of any way to shift Gregor. Yet Gregor saw well enough that consideration for him was not the main difficulty preventing the removal, for they could have easily shifted him in some suitable box with a few air holes in it; what really kept them from moving into another flat was rather their own complete hopelessness and the belief that they had been singled out for a misfortune such as had never happened to any of their relations or acquaintances. They fulfilled to the uttermost all that the world demands of poor people, the father fetched breakfast for the small clerks in the bank, the mother devoted her energy to making underwear for strangers, the sister trotted to and fro behind the counter at the behest of customers, but more than this they had not the strength to do. And the wound in Gregor's back began to nag at him afresh when his mother and sister, after getting his father into bed, came back again, left their work lying, drew close to each other and sat cheek to cheek; when his mother, pointing towards his room, said: "Shut that door now, Grete," and he was left again in darkness, while next door the women mingled their tears or perhaps sat dry-eyed staring at the table.

Gregor hardly slept at all by night or by day. He was often haunted by the idea that next time the door opened he would take the family's affairs in hand again just as he used to do; once more, after this long interval, there appeared in his thoughts the figures of the chief and the chief clerk, the commercial travelers and the apprentices, the porter who was so dull-witted, two or three friends in other firms, a chambermaid in one of the rural hotels, a sweet and fleeting memory, a cashier in a milliner's shop, whom he had wooed earnestly but too slowly—they all appeared, together with strangers or people he had quite forgotten, but instead of helping him and his family they were one and all unapproachable and he was glad when they vanished. At other times he would not be in the mood to bother about his family, he was only filled with rage at the way they were neglecting him, and although he had no clear idea of what he might care to eat he would make plans for getting into the larder to take the food that was after all his due, even if he were not hungry. His sister no longer took thought to bring him what might especially please him, but in the morning and at noon before she went to business hurriedly pushed into his room with her foot any food that was available, and in the evening cleared it out again with one sweep of the broom, heedless of whether it had been merely tasted, or—as most frequently happened—left untouched. The cleaning of his room, which she now did always in the evenings, could not have been more hastily done. Streaks of dirt stretched along the walls, here and there lay balls of dust and filth. At first Gregor used to station himself in some particularly filthy corner when his sister arrived, in order to reproach her with it, so to speak. But he could have sat there for weeks without getting her to make any improvement; she could see the dirt as well as he did, but she had simply made up her mind to leave it alone. And yet, with a touchiness that was new to her, which seemed anyhow to have infected the whole family, she jealously guarded her claim to be the sole caretaker of Gregor's room. His mother once subjected his room to a thorough cleaning, which was achieved only by means of several buckets of water—all this dampness of course upset Gregor too and he lay widespread, sulky and motionless on the sofa—but she was well punished for it. Hardly had his sister noticed the changed aspect of his room that evening than she rushed in high dudgeon into the living room and, despite the imploringly raised hands of her mother, burst into a storm of weeping, while her parents—her father had of course been startled out of his chair—looked on at first in helpless amazement; then they too began to go into action; the father reproached the mother on his right for not having left the cleaning of Gregor's room to his sister; shrieked at the sister on his left that never again was she to be allowed to clean Gregor's room; while the mother tried to pull the father into his bedroom, since he was beyond himself with agitation; the sister, shaken with sobs, then beat upon the table with her small fists; and Gregor hissed loudly with rage because not one of them thought of shutting the door to spare him such a spectacle and so much noise.

Still, even if the sister, exhausted by her daily work, had grown tired of looking after Gregor as she did formerly, there was no need for his mother's intervention or for Gregor's being neglected at all. The charwoman was there. This old widow, whose strong bony frame had enabled her to survive the worst a long life could offer, by no means recoiled from Gregor. Without being in the least curious she had once by chance opened the door of his room and at the sight of Gregor, who, taken by surprise, began to rush to and fro although no one was chasing him, merely stood there with her arms folded. From that time she never failed to open his door a little for a moment, morning and evening, to have a look at him. At first she even used to call him to her, with words which apparently she took to be friendly, such as: "Come along, then, you old dung beetle!" or "Look at the old dung beetle, then!" To such allocutions Gregor made no answer, but stayed motionless where he was, as if the door had never been opened. Instead of being allowed to disturb him so senselessly whenever the whim took her, she should rather have been ordered to clean out his room daily, that charwoman! Once, early in the morning—heavy rain was lashing on the windowpanes, perhaps a sign that spring was on the way—Gregor was so exasperated when she began addressing him again that he ran at her, as if to attack her, although slowly and feebly enough. But the charwoman instead of showing fright merely lifted high a chair that happened to be beside the door, and as she stood there with her mouth wide open it was clear that she meant to shut it only when she brought the chair down on Gregor's back. "So you're not coming any nearer?" she asked, as Gregor turned away again, and quietly put the chair back into the corner.

Gregor was now eating hardly anything. Only when he happened to pass the food laid out for him did he take a bit of something in his mouth as a pastime, kept it there for an hour at a time and usually spat it out again. At first he thought it was chagrin over the state of his room that prevented him from eating, yet he soon got used to the various changes in his room. It had become a habit in the family to push into his room things there was no room for elsewhere, and there were plenty of these now, since one of the rooms had been let to three lodgers. These serious gentlemen—all three of them with full beards, as Gregor once observed through a crack in the door—had a passion for order, not only in their own room but, since they were now members of the household, in all its arrangements, especially in the kitchen. Superfluous, not to say dirty, objects they could not bear. Besides, they had brought with them most of the furnishings they needed. For this reason many things could be dispensed with that it was no use trying to sell but that should not be thrown away either. All of them found their way into Gregor's room. The ash can likewise and the kitchen garbage can. Anything that was not needed for the moment was simply flung into Gregor's room by the charwoman, who did everything in a hurry; fortunately Gregor usually saw only the object, whatever it was, and the hand that held it. Perhaps she intended to take the things away again as time and opportunity offered, or to collect them until she could throw them all out in a heap, but in fact they just lay wherever she happened to throw them, except when Gregor pushed his way through the junk heap and shifted it somewhat, at first out of necessity, because he had not room enough to crawl, but later with increasing enjoyment, although after such excursions, being sad and weary to death, he would lie motionless for hours. And since the lodgers often ate their supper at home in the common living room, the living-room door stayed shut many an evening, yet Gregor reconciled himself quite easily to the shutting of the door, for often enough on evenings when it was opened he had disregarded it entirely and lain in the darkest corner of his room, quite unnoticed by the family. But on one occasion the charwoman left the door open a little and it stayed ajar even when the lodgers came in for supper and the lamp was lit. They set themselves at the top end of the table where formerly Gregor and his father and mother had eaten their meals, unfolded their napkins and took knife and fork in hand. At once his mother appeared in the other doorway with a dish of meat and close behind her his sister with a dish of potatoes piled high. The food steamed with a thick vapor. The lodgers bent over the food set before them as if to scrutinize it before eating, in fact the man in the middle, who seemed to pass for an authority with the other two, cut a piece of meat as it lay on the dish, obviously to discover if it were tender or should be sent back to the kitchen. He showed satisfaction, and Gregor's mother and sister, who had been watching anxiously, breathed freely and began to smile.

The family itself took its meals in the kitchen. None the less, Gregor's father came into the living room before going into the kitchen and with one prolonged bow, cap in hand, made a round of the table. The lodgers all stood up and murmured something in their beards. When they were alone again they ate their food in almost complete silence. It seemed remarkable to Gregor that among the various noises coming from the table he could always distinguish the sound of their masticating teeth, as if this were a sign to Gregor that one needed teeth in order to eat, and that with toothless jaws even of the finest make one could do nothing. "I'm hungry enough," said Gregor sadly to himself, "but not for that kind of food. How these lodgers are stuffing themselves, and here am I dying of starvation!"

On that very evening—during the whole of his time there Gregor could not remember ever having heard the violin—the sound of violin-playing came from the kitchen. The lodgers had already finished their supper, the one in the middle had brought out a newspaper and given the other two a page apiece, and now they were leaning back at ease reading and smoking. When the violin began to play they pricked up their ears, got to their feet, and went on tiptoe to the hall door where they stood huddled together. Their movements must have been heard in the kitchen, for Gregor's father called out: "Is the violin-playing disturbing you, gentlemen? It can be stopped at once." "On the contrary," said the middle lodger, "could not Fräulein Samsa come and play in this room, beside us, where it is much more convenient and comfortable?" "Oh certainly," cried Gregor's father, as if he were the violin-player. The lodgers came back into the living room and waited. Presently Gregor's father arrived with the music stand, his mother carrying the music and his sister with the violin. His sister quietly made everything ready to start playing; his parents, who had never let rooms before and so had an exaggerated idea of the courtesy due to lodgers, did not venture to sit down on their own chairs; his father leaned against the door, the right hand thrust between two buttons of his livery coat, which was formally buttoned up; but his mother was offered a chair by one of the lodgers and, since she left the chair just where he had happened to put it, sat down in a corner to one side.

Gregor's sister began to play; the father and mother, from either side, intently watched the movements of her hands. Gregor, attracted by the playing, ventured to move forward a little until his head was actually inside the living room. He felt hardly any surprise at his growing lack of consideration for the others; there had been a time when he prided himself on being considerate. And yet just on this occasion he had more reason than ever to hide himself, since owing to the amount of dust which lay thick in his room and rose into the air at the slightest movement, he too was covered with dust; fluff and hair and remnants of food trailed with him, caught on his back and along his sides; his indifference to everything was much too great for him to turn on his back and scrape himself clean on the carpet, as once he had done several times a day. And in spite of his condition, no shame deterred him from advancing a little over the spotless floor of the living room.

To be sure, no one was aware of him. The family was entirely absorbed in the violin-playing; the lodgers, however, who first of all had stationed themselves, hands in pockets, much too close behind the music stand so that they could all have read the music, which must have bothered his sister, had soon retreated to the window, half-whispering with downbent heads, and stayed there while his father turned an anxious eye on them. Indeed, they were making it more than obvious that they had been disappointed in their expectation of hearing good or enjoyable violin-playing, that they had had more than enough of the performance and only out of courtesy suffered a continued disturbance of their peace. From the way they all kept blowing the smoke of their cigars high in the air through nose and mouth one could divine their irritation. And yet Gregor's sister was playing so beautifully. Her face leaned sideways, intently and sadly her eyes followed the notes of music. Gregor crawled a little farther forward and lowered his head to the ground so that it might be possible for his eyes to meet hers. Was he an animal, that music had such an effect upon him? He felt as if the way were opening before him to the unknown nourishment he craved. He was determined to push forward till he reached his sister, to pull at her skirt and so let her know that she was to come into his room with her violin, for no one here appreciated her playing as he would appreciate it. He would never let her out of his room, at least, not so long as he lived; his frightful appearance would become, for the first time, useful to him; he would watch all the doors of his room at once and spit at intruders; but his sister should need no constraint, she should stay with him of her own free will; she should sit beside him on the sofa, bend down her ear to him and hear him confide that he had had the firm intention of sending her to the Conservatorium, and that, but for his mishap, last Christmas—surely Christmas was long past?—he would have announced it to everybody without allowing a single objection. After this confession his sister would be so touched that she would burst into tears, and Gregor would then raise himself to her shoulder and kiss her on the neck, which, now that she went to business, she kept free of any ribbon or collar.

"Mr. Samsa!" cried the middle lodger, to Gregor's father, and pointed, without wasting any more words, at Gregor, now working himself slowly forwards. The violin fell silent, the middle lodger first smiled to his friends with a shake of the head and then looked at Gregor again. Instead of driving Gregor out, his father seemed to think it more needful to begin by soothing down the lodgers, although they were not at all agitated and apparently found Gregor more entertaining than the violin-playing. He hurried towards them and spreading out his arms, tried to urge them back into their own room and at the same time to block their view of Gregor. They now began to be really a little angry, one could not tell whether because of the old man's behavior or because it had just dawned on them that all unwittingly they had such a neighbor as Gregor next door. They demanded explanations of his father, they waved their arms like him, tugged uneasily at their beards, and only with reluctance backed towards their room. Meanwhile Gregor's sister, who stood there as if lost when her playing was so abruptly broken off, came to life again, pulled herself together all at once after standing for a while holding violin and bow in nervelessly hanging hands and staring at her music, pushed her violin into the lap of her mother, who was still sitting in her chair fighting asthmatically for breath, and ran into the lodgers' room to which they were now being shepherded by her father rather more quickly than before. One could see the pillows and blankets on the beds flying under her accustomed fingers and being laid in order. Before the lodgers had actually reached their room she had finished making the beds and slipped out.

The old man seemed once more to be so possessed by his mulish self-assertiveness that he was forgetting all the respect he should show to his lodgers. He kept driving them on and driving them on until in the very door of the bedroom the middle lodger stamped his foot loudly on the floor and so brought him to a halt. "I beg to announce," said the lodger, lifting one hand and looking also at Gregor's mother and sister, "that because of the disgusting conditions prevailing in this household and family"—here he spat on the floor with emphatic brevity—"I give you notice on the spot. Naturally I won't pay you a penny for the days I have lived here, on the contrary I shall consider bringing an action for damages against you, based on claims—believe me—that will be easily susceptible of proof." He ceased and stared straight in front of him, as if he expected something. In fact his two friends at once rushed into the breach with these words: "And we too give notice on the spot." On that he seized the door-handle and shut the door with a slam.

Gregor's father, groping with his hands, staggered forward and fell into his chair; it looked as if he were stretching himself there for his ordinary evening nap, but the marked jerkings of his head, which was as if uncontrollable, showed that he was far from asleep. Gregor had simply stayed quietly all the time on the spot where the lodgers had espied him. Disappointment at the failure of his plan, perhaps also the weakness arising from extreme hunger, made it impossible for him to move. He feared, with a fair degree of certainty, that at any moment the general tension would discharge itself in a combined attack upon him, and he lay waiting. He did not react even to the noise made by the violin as it fell off his mother's lap from under her trembling fingers and gave out a resonant note.

"My dear parents," said his sister, slapping her hand on the table by way of introduction, "things can't go on like this. Perhaps you don't realize that, but I do. I won't utter my brother's name in the presence of this creature, and so all I say is: we must try to get rid of it. We've tried to look after it and to put up with it as far as is humanly possible, and I don't think anyone could reproach us in the slightest."

"She is more than right," said Gregor's father to himself. His mother, who was still choking for lack of breath, began to cough hollowly into her hand with a wild look in her eyes.

His sister rushed over to her and held her forehead. His father's thoughts seemed to have lost their vagueness at Grete's words, he sat more upright, fingering his service cap that lay among the plates still lying on the table from the lodgers' supper, and from time to time looked at the still form of Gregor.

"We must try to get rid of it," his sister now said explicitly to her father, since her mother was coughing too much to hear a word, "it will be the death of both of you, I can see that coming. When one has to work as hard as we do, all of us, one can't stand this continual torment at home on top of it. At least I can't stand it any longer." And she burst into such a passion of sobbing that her tears dropped on her mother's face, where she wiped them off mechanically.

"My dear," said the old man sympathetically, and with evident understanding, "but what can we do?"

Gregor's sister merely shrugged her shoulders to indicate the feeling of helplessness that had now overmastered her during her weeping fit, in contrast to her former confidence.

"If he could understand us," said her father, half questioningly; Grete, still sobbing, vehemently waved a hand to show how unthinkable that was.

"If he could understand us," repeated the old man, shutting his eyes to consider his daughter's conviction that understanding was impossible, "then perhaps we might come to some agreement with him. But as it is—"

"He must go," cried Gregor's sister, "that's the only solution, Father. You must just try to get rid of the idea that this is Gregor. The fact that we've believed it for so long is the root of all our trouble. But how can it be Gregor? If this were Gregor, he would have realized long ago that human beings can't live with such a creature, and he'd have gone away on his own accord. Then we wouldn't have any brother, but we'd be able to go on living and keep his memory in honor. As it is, this creature persecutes us, drives away our lodgers, obviously wants the whole apartment to himself and would have us all sleep in the gutter. Just look, Father," she shrieked all at once, "he's at it again!" And in an access of panic that was quite incomprehensible to Gregor she even quitted her mother, literally thrusting the chair from her as if she would rather sacrifice her mother than stay so near to Gregor, and rushed behind her father, who also rose up, being simply upset by her agitation, and half-spread his arms out as if to protect her.

Yet Gregor had not the slightest intention of frightening anyone, far less his sister. He had only begun to turn round in order to crawl back to his room, but it was certainly a startling operation to watch, since because of his disabled condition he could not execute the difficult turning movements except by lifting his head and then bracing it against the floor over and over again. He paused and looked round. His good intentions seemed to have been recognized; the alarm had only been momentary. Now they were all watching him in melancholy silence. His mother lay in her chair, her legs stiffly outstretched and pressed together, her eyes almost closing for sheer weariness; his father and his sister were sitting beside each other, his sister's arm around the old man's neck.

Perhaps I can go on turning round now, thought Gregor, and began his labors again. He could not stop himself from panting with the effort, and had to pause now and then to take breath. Nor did anyone harass him, he was left entirely to himself. When he had completed the turn-round he began at once to crawl straight back. He was amazed at the distance separating him from his room and could not understand how in his weak state he had managed to accomplish the same journey so recently, almost without remarking it. Intent on crawling as fast as possible, he barely noticed that not a single word, not an ejaculation from his family, interfered with his progress. Only when he was already in the doorway did he turn his head round, not completely, for his neck muscles were getting stiff, but enough to see that nothing had changed behind him except that his sister had risen to her feet. His last glance fell on his mother, who was not quite overcome by sleep.

Hardly was he well inside his room when the door was hastily pushed shut, bolted and locked. The sudden noise in his rear startled him so much that his little legs gave beneath him. It was his sister who had shown such haste. She had been standing ready waiting and had made a light spring forward, Gregor had not even heard her coming, and she cried "At last!" to her parents as she turned the key in the lock.

"And what now?" said Gregor to himself, looking round in the darkness. Soon he made the discovery that he was now unable to stir a limb. This did not surprise him, rather it seemed unnatural that he should ever actually have been able to move on these feeble little legs. Otherwise he felt relatively comfortable. True, his whole body was aching, but it seemed that the pain was gradually growing less and would finally pass away. The rotting apple in his back and the inflamed area around it, all covered with soft dust, already hardly troubled him. He thought of his family with tenderness and love. The decision that he must disappear was one that he held to even more strongly than his sister, if that were possible. In this state of vacant and peaceful meditation he remained until the tower clock struck three in the morning. The first broadening of light in the world outside the window entered his consciousness once more. Then his head sank to the floor of its own accord and from his nostrils came the last faint flicker of his breath.

When the charwoman arrived early in the morning—what between her strength and her impatience she slammed all the doors so loudly, never mind how often she had been begged not to do so, that no one in the whole apartment could enjoy any quiet sleep after her arrival—she noticed nothing unusual as she took her customary peep into Gregor's room. She thought he was lying motionless on purpose, pretending to be in the sulks; she credited him with every kind of intelligence. Since she happened to have the long-handled broom in her hand she tried to tickle him up with it from the doorway. When that too produced no reaction she felt provoked and poked at him a little harder, and only when she had pushed him along the floor without meeting any resistance was her attention aroused. It did not take her long to establish the truth of the matter, and her eyes widened, she let out a whistle, yet did not waste much time over it but tore open the door of the Samsas' bedroom and yelled into the darkness at the top of her voice: "Just look at this, it's dead; it's lying here dead and done for!"

Mr. and Mrs. Samsa started up in their double bed and before they realized the nature of the charwoman's announcement had some difficulty in overcoming the shock of it. But then they got out of bed quickly, one on either side, Mr. Samsa throwing a blanket over his shoulders, Mrs. Samsa in nothing but her nightgown; in this array they entered Gregor's room. Meanwhile the door of the living room opened, too, where Grete had been sleeping since the advent of the lodgers; she was completely dressed as if she had not been to bed, which seemed to be confirmed also by the paleness of her face. "Dead?" said Mrs. Samsa, looking questioningly at the charwoman, although she could have investigated for herself, and the fact was obvious enough without investigation. "I should say so," said the charwoman, proving her words by pushing Gregor's corpse a long way to one side with her broomstick. Mrs. Samsa made a movement as if to stop her, but checked it. "Well," said Mr. Samsa, "now thanks be to God." He crossed himself, and the three women followed his example. Grete, whose eyes never left the corpse, said: "Just see how thin he was. It's such a long time since he's eaten anything. The food came out again just as it went in." Indeed, Gregor's body was completely flat and dry, as could only now be seen when it was no longer supported by the legs and nothing prevented one from looking closely at it.

"Come in beside us, Grete, for a little while." said Mrs. Samsa with a tremulous smile, and Grete, not without looking back at the corpse, followed her parents into their bedroom. The charwoman shut the door and opened the window wide. Although it was so early in the morning a certain softness was perceptible in the fresh air. After all, it was already the end of March.

The three lodgers emerged from their room and were surprised to see no breakfast; they had been forgotten. "Where's our breakfast?" said the middle lodger peevishly to the charwoman. But she put her finger to her lips and hastily, without a word, indicated by gestures that they should go into Gregor's room. They did so and stood, their hands in the pockets of their somewhat shabby coats, around Gregor's corpse in the room where it was now fully light.

At that the door of the Samsas' bedroom opened and Mr. Samsa appeared in his uniform, his wife on one arm, his daughter on the other. They all looked a little as if they had been crying; from time to time Grete hid her face on her father's arm.

"Leave my house at once!" said Mr. Samsa, and pointed to the door without disengaging himself from the women. "What do you mean by that?" said the middle lodger, taken somewhat aback, with a feeble smile. The two others put their hands behind them and kept rubbing them together, as if in gleeful expectation of a fine set-to in which they were bound to come off the winners. "I mean just what I say," answered Mr. Samsa, and advanced in a straight line with his two companions towards the lodger. He stood his ground at first quietly, looking at the floor as if his thoughts were taking a new pattern in his head. "Then let us go, by all means," he said, and looked up at Mr. Samsa as if in a sudden access of humility he were expecting some renewed sanction for this decision. Mr. Samsa merely nodded briefly once or twice with meaning eyes. Upon that the lodger really did go with long strides into the hall, his two friends had been listening and had quite stopped rubbing their hands for some moments and now went scuttling after him as if afraid that Mr. Samsa might get into the hall before them and cut them off from their leader. In the hall they all three took their hats from the rack, their sticks from the umbrella stand, bowed in silence and quitted the apartment. With a suspiciousness which proved quite unfounded Mr. Samsa and the two women followed them out to the landing; leaning over the banister they watched the three figures slowly but surely going down the long stairs, vanishing from sight at a certain turn of the staircase on every floor and coming into view again after a moment or so; the more they dwindled, the more the Samsa family's interest in them dwindled, and when a butcher's boy met them and passed them on the stairs coming up proudly with a tray on his head, Mr. Samsa and the two women soon left the landing and as if a burden had been lifted from them went back into their apartment.

They decided to spend this day in resting and going for a stroll; they had not only deserved such a respite from work, but absolutely needed it. And so they sat down at the table and wrote three notes of excuse, Mr. Samsa to his board of management, Mrs. Samsa to her employer and Grete to the head of her firm. While they were writing, the charwoman came in to say that she was going now, since her morning's work was finished. At first they only nodded without looking up, but as she kept hovering there they eyed her irritably. "Well?" said Mr. Samsa. The charwoman stood grinning in the doorway as if she had good news to impart to the family but meant not to say a word unless properly questioned. The small ostrich feather standing upright on her hat, which had annoyed Mr. Samsa ever since she was engaged, was waving gaily in all directions. "Well, what is it then?" asked Mrs. Samsa, who obtained more respect from the charwoman than the others. "Oh," said the charwoman, giggling so amiably that she could not at once continue, "just this, you don't need to bother about how to get rid of the thing next door. It's been seen to already." Mrs. Samsa and Grete bent over their letters again, as if preoccupied; Mr. Samsa, who perceived that she was eager to begin describing it all in detail, stopped her with a decisive hand. But since she was not allowed to tell her story, she remembered the great hurry she was in, being obviously deeply huffed: "Bye, everybody," she said, whirling off violently, and departed with a frightful slamming of doors.

"She'll be given notice tonight," said Mr. Samsa, but neither from his wife nor his daughter did he get any answer, for the charwoman seemed to have shattered again the composure they had barely achieved. They rose, went to the window and stayed there, clasping each other tight. Mr. Samsa turned in his chair to look at them and quietly observed them for a little. Then he called out: "Come along, now, do. Let bygones by bygones. And you might have some consideration for me." The two of them complied at once, hastened to him, caressed him and quickly finished their letters.

Then they all three left the apartment together, which was more than they had done for months, and went by tram into the open country outside the town. The tram, in which they were the only passengers, was filled with warm sunshine. Leaning comfortably back in their seats they canvassed their prospects for the future, and it appeared on closer inspection that these were not at all bad, for the jobs they had got, which so far they had never really discussed with each other, were all three admirable and likely to lead to better things later on. The greatest immediate improvement in their condition would of course arise from moving to another house; they wanted to take a smaller and cheaper but also better situated and more easily run apartment than the one they had, which Gregor had selected. While they were thus conversing, it struck both Mr. and Mrs. Samsa, almost at the same moment, as they became aware of their daughter's increasing vivacity, that in spite of all the sorrow of recent times, which had made her cheeks pale, she had bloomed into a pretty girl with a good figure. They grew quieter and half unconsciously exchanged glances of complete agreement, having come to the conclusion that it would soon be time to find a good husband for her. And it was like a confirmation of their new dreams and excellent intentions that at the end of their journey their daughter sprang to her feet first and stretched her young body.

ISAK DINESEN
(1885–1962)
Sorrow-Acre

The low, undulating Danish landscape was silent and serene, mysteriously wide-awake in the hour before sunrise. There was not a cloud in the pale sky, not a shadow along the dim, pearly fields, hills and woods. The mist was lifting from the valleys and hollows, the air was cool, the grass and the foliage dripping wet with morning-dew. Unwatched by the eyes of man, and undisturbed by his activity, the country breathed a timeless life, to which language was inadequate.

All the same, a human race had lived on this land for a thousand years, had been formed by its soil and weather, and had marked it with its thoughts, so that now no one could tell where the existence of the one ceased and the other began. The thin grey line of a road, winding across the plain and up and down hills, was the fixed materialisation of human longing, and of the human notion that it is better to be in one place than another.

A child of the country would read this open landscape like a book. The irregular mosaic of meadows and cornlands was a picture, in timid green and yellow, of the people's struggle for its daily bread; the centuries had taught it to plough and sow in this way. On a distant hill the immovable wings of a windmill, in a small blue cross against the sky, delineated a later stage in the career of bread. The blurred outline of thatched roofs—a low, brown growth of the earth—where the huts of the village thronged together, told the history, from his cradle to his grave, of the peasant, the creature nearest to the soil and dependent on it, prospering in a fertile year and dying in years of drought and pests.

A little higher up, with the faint horizontal line of the white cemetery wall round it, and the vertical contour of tall poplars by its side, the red-tiled church bore witness, as far as the eye reached, that this was a Christian country. The child of the land knew it as a strange house, inhabited only for a few hours every seventh day, but with a strong, clear voice in it to give out the joys and sorrows of the land: a plain, square embodiment of the nation's trust in the justice and mercy of heaven. But where, amongst cupular[1] woods and groves, the lordly, pyramidal silhouette of the cut lime avenues rose in the air, there a big country house lay.

The child of the land would reach much within these elegant, geometrical ciphers[2] on the hazy blue. They spoke of power, the lime trees paraded round a stronghold. Up here was decided the destiny of the surrounding land and of the men and beasts upon it, and the peasant lifted his eyes to the green pyramids with awe. They spoke of dignity, decorum and taste. Danish soil grew no finer flower than the mansion to which the long avenue led. In its lofty rooms life and death bore themselves with stately grace. The country house did not gaze upward, like the church, nor down to the ground like the huts; it had a wider earthly horizon than they, and was related to much noble architecture all over Europe. Foreign artisans had been called in to panel and stucco it, and its own inhabitants travelled and brought back ideas, fashions and things of beauty. Paintings, tapestries, silver and glass from distant countries had been made to feel at home here, and now formed part of Danish country life.

The big house stood as firmly rooted in the soil of Denmark as the peasants' huts, and was as faithfully allied to her four winds and her changing seasons, to her animal life, trees and flowers. Only its interests lay in a higher plane. Within the domain of the lime trees it was no longer cows, goats and pigs on which the minds and the talk ran, but horses and dogs. The wild fauna, the game of the land, that the peasant shook his fist at, when he saw it on his young green rye or in his ripening wheat field, to the residents of the country houses were the main pursuit and the joy of existence.

The writing in the sky solemnly proclaimed continuance, a worldly immortality. The great country houses had held their ground through many generations. The families who lived in them revered the past as they honoured themselves, for the history of Denmark was their own history.

A Rosenkrantz had sat at Rosenholm, a Juel at Hverringe, a Skeel at Gammel-Estrup[3] as long as people remembered. They had seen kings and schools of style succeed one another and, proudly and humbly, had made over their personal existence to that of their

1. Cup-shaped.
2. The outlines of cup and pyramid, here viewed as symbols in a code.

3. Noble Danish families and their ancestral homes.

land, so that amongst their equals and with the peasants they passed by its name: Rosenholm, Hverringe, Gammel-Estrup. To the King and the country, to his family and to the individual lord of the manor himself it was a matter of minor consequence which particular Rosenkrantz, Juel or Skeel, out of a long row of fathers and sons, at the moment in his person incarnated the fields and woods, the peasants, cattle and game of the estate. Many duties rested on the shoulders of the big landowners—towards God in heaven, towards the King, his neighbour and himself—and they were all harmoniously consolidated into the idea of his duties towards his land. Highest amongst these ranked his obligation to uphold the sacred continuance, and to produce a new Rosenkrantz, Juel or Skeel for the service of Rosenholm, Hverringe and Gammel-Estrup.

Female grace was prized in the manors. Together with good hunting and fine wine it was the flower and emblem of the higher existence led there, and in many ways the families prided themselves more on their daughters than on their sons.

The ladies who promenaded in the lime avenues, or drove through them in heavy coaches with four horses, carried the future of the name in their laps and were, like dignified and debonair caryatides,[4] holding up the houses. They were themselves conscious of their value, kept up their price, and moved in a sphere of pretty worship and self-worship. They might even be thought to add to it, on their own, a graceful, arch, paradoxical haughtiness. For how free were they, how powerful! Their lords might rule the country, and allow themselves many liberties, but when it came to that supreme matter of legitimacy which was the vital principle of their world, the centre of gravity lay with them.

The lime trees were in bloom. But in the early morning only a faint fragrance drifted through the garden, an airy message, an aromatic echo of the dreams during the short summer night.

In a long avenue that led from the house all the way to the end of the garden, where, from a small white pavilion in the classic style, there was a great view over the fields, a young man walked. He was plainly dressed in brown, with pretty linen and lace, bare-headed, with his hair tied by a ribbon. He was dark, a strong and sturdy figure with fine eyes and hands; he limped a little on one leg.

The big house at the top of the avenue, the garden and the fields had been his childhood's paradise. But he had travelled and lived out of Denmark, in Rome and Paris, and he was at present appointed to the Danish Legation to the Court of King George,[5] the brother of the late, unfortunate young Danish Queen. He had not

---

4. In Greek architecture, a supporting column shaped like a woman.

5. King George III of England (1738–1820); he was actually the nephew of George II's daughter Louise (1724–51), who married King Frederick V of Denmark.

seen his ancestral home for nine years. It made him laugh to find, now, everything so much smaller than he remembered it, and at the same time he was strangely moved by meeting it again. Dead people came towards him and smiled at him; a small boy in a ruff ran past him with his hoop and kite, in passing gave him a clear glance and laughingly asked: "Do you mean to tell me that you are I?" He tried to catch him in the flight, and to answer him: "Yes, I assure you that I am you," but the light figure did not wait for a reply.

The young man, whose name was Adam, stood in a particular relation to the house and the land. For six months he had been heir to it all; nominally he was so even at this moment. It was this circumstance which had brought him from England, and on which his mind was dwelling, as he walked along slowly.

The old lord up at the manor, his father's brother, had had much misfortune in his domestic life. His wife had died young, and two of his children in infancy. The one son then left to him, his cousin's playmate, was a sickly and morose boy. For ten years the father travelled with him from one watering place to another, in Germany and Italy, hardly ever in other company than that of his silent, dying child, sheltering the faint flame of life with both hands, until such time as it could be passed over to a new bearer of the name. At the same time another misfortune had struck him: he fell into disfavour at Court, where till now he had held a fine position. He was about to rehabilitate his family's prestige through the marriage which he had arranged for his son, when before it could take place the bridegroom died, not yet twenty years old.

Adam learned of his cousin's death, and his own changed fortune, in England, through his ambitious and triumphant mother. He sat with her letter in his hand and did not know what to think about it.

If this, he reflected, had happened to him while he was still a boy, in Denmark, it would have meant all the world to him. It would be so now with his friends and schoolfellows, if they were in his place, and they would, at this moment, be congratulating or envying him. But he was neither covetous nor vain by nature; he had faith in his own talents and had been content to know that his success in life depended on his personal ability. His slight infirmity had always set him a little apart from other boys; it had, perhaps, given him a keener sensibility of many things in life, and he did not, now, deem it quite right that the head of the family should limp on one leg. He did not even see his prospects in the same light as his people at home. In England he had met with greater wealth and magnificence than they dreamed of; he had been in love with, and made happy by, an English lady of such rank and fortune that to her, he felt, the finest estate of Denmark would look but like a child's toy farm.

And in England, too, he had come in touch with the great new ideas of the age: of nature, of the right and freedom of man, of justice and beauty. The universe, through them, had become infinitely wider to him; he wanted to find out still more about it and was planning to travel to America, to the new world. For a moment he felt trapped and imprisoned, as if the dead people of his name, from the family vault at home, were stretching out their parched arms for him.

But at the same time he began to dream at night of the old house and garden. He had walked in these avenues in dream, and had smelled the scent of the flowering limes. When at Ranelagh[6] an old gypsy woman looked at his hand and told him that a son of his was to sit in the seat of his father, he felt a sudden, deep satisfaction, queer in a young man who till now had never given his sons a thought.

Then, six months later, his mother again wrote to tell him that his uncle had himself married the girl intended for his dead son. The head of the family was still in his best age, not over sixty, and although Adam remembered him as a small, slight man, he was a vigorous person; it was likely that his young wife would bear him sons.

Adam's mother in her disappointment lay the blame on him. If he had returned to Denmark, she told him, his uncle might have come to look upon him as a son, and would not have married; nay, he might have handed the bride over to him. Adam knew better. The family estate, differing from the neighbouring properties, had gone down from father to son ever since a man of their name first sat there. The tradition of direct succession was the pride of the clan and a sacred dogma to his uncle; he would surely call for a son of his own flesh and bone.

But at the news the young man was seized by a strange, deep, aching remorse towards his old home in Denmark. It was as if he had been making light of a friendly and generous gesture, and disloyal to someone unfailingly loyal to him. It would be but just, he thought, if from now the place should disown and forget him. Nostalgia, which before he had never known, caught hold of him; for the first time he walked in the streets and parks of London as a stranger.

He wrote to his uncle and asked if he might come and stay with him, begged leave from the Legation and took ship for Denmark. He had come to the house to make his peace with it; he had slept little in the night, and was up so early and walking in the garden, to explain himself, and to be forgiven.

While he walked, the still garden slowly took up its day's work. A big snail, of the kind that his grandfather had brought back from France, and which he remembered eating in the house as a child,

6. A then fashionable English resort bordering the River Thames.

was already, with dignity, dragging a silver train down the avenue. The birds began to sing; in an old tree under which he stopped a number of them were worrying an owl; the rule of the night was over.

He stood at the end of the avenue and saw the sky lightening. An ecstatic clarity filled the world; in half an hour the sun would rise. A rye field here ran along the garden; two roe-deer were moving in it and looked roseate in the dawn. He gazed out over the fields, where as a small boy he had ridden his pony, and towards the wood where he had killed his first stag. He remembered the old servants who had taught him; some of them were now in their graves.

The ties which bound him to this place, he reflected, were of a mystic nature. He might never again come back to it, and it would make no difference. As long as a man of his own blood and name should sit in the house, hunt in the fields and be obeyed by the people in the huts, wherever he travelled on earth, in England or amongst the red Indians of America, he himself would still be safe, would still have a home, and would carry weight in the world.

His eyes rested on the church. In old days, before the time of Martin Luther,[7] younger sons of great families, he knew, had entered the Church of Rome, and had given up individual wealth and happiness to serve the greater ideals. They, too, had bestowed honour upon their homes and were remembered in its registers.[8] In the solitude of the morning half in jest he let his mind run as it listed; it seemed to him that he might speak to the land as to a person, as to the mother of his race. "Is it only my body that you want," he asked her, "while you reject my imagination, energy and emotions? If the world might be brought to acknowledge that the virtue of our name does not belong to the past only, will it give you no satisfaction?" The landscape was so still that he could not tell whether it answered him yes or no.

After a while he walked on, and came to the new French rose garden laid out for the young mistress of the house. In England he had acquired a freer taste in gardening,[9] and he wondered if he could liberate these blushing captives, and make them thrive outside their cut hedges. Perhaps, he meditated, the elegantly conventional garden would be a floral portrait of his young aunt from Court, whom he had not yet seen.

As once more he came to the pavilion at the end of the avenue his eyes were caught by a bouquet of delicate colours which could not possibly belong to the Danish summer morning. It was in fact his uncle himself, powdered and silk-stockinged, but still in a brocade dressing-gown, and obviously sunk in deep thought. "And

7. German monk (1483–1546), founder of Protestantism. *The Church of Rome*: Roman Catholicism.
8. Parish records.

9. English gardeners had turned away from the extremely formal French tradition and favored a more natural style.

what business, or what meditations," Adam asked himself, "drags a connoisseur of the beautiful, but three months married to a wife of seventeen, from his bed into his garden before sunrise?" He walked up to the small, slim, straight figure.

His uncle on his side showed no surprise at seeing him, but then he rarely seemed surprised at anything. He greeted him, with a compliment on his matunality,[10] as kindly as he had done on his arrival last evening. After a moment he looked to the sky, and solemnly proclaimed: "It will be a hot day." Adam, as a child, had often been impressed by the grand, ceremonial manner in which the old lord would state the common happenings of existence; it looked as if nothing had changed here, but all was what it used to be.

The uncle offered the nephew a pinch of snuff. "No, thank you, Uncle," said Adam, "it would ruin my nose to the scent of your garden, which is as fresh as the Garden of Eden, newly created." "From every tree of which," said his uncle, smiling, "thou, my Adam, mayest freely eat." They slowly walked up the avenue together.

The hidden sun was now already gilding the top of the tallest trees. Adam talked of the beauties of nature, and of the greatness of Nordic scenery, less marked by the hand of man than that of Italy. His uncle took the praise of the landscape as a personal compliment, and congratulated him because he had not, in likeness to many young travellers in foreign countries, learned to despise his native land. No, said Adam, he had lately in England longed for the fields and woods of his Danish home. And he had there become acquainted with a new piece of Danish poetry which had enchanted him more than any English or French work. He named the author, Johannes Ewald,[11] and quoted a few of the mighty, turbulent verses.

"And I have wondered, while I read," he went on after a pause, still moved by the lines he himself had declaimed, "that we have not till now understood how much our Nordic mythology in moral greatness surpasses that of Greece and Rome. If it had not been for the physical beauty of the ancient gods, which has come down to us in marble, no modern mind could hold them worthy of worship. They were mean, capricious and treacherous. The gods of our Danish forefathers are as much more divine than they as the Druid is nobler than the Augur.[12] For the fair gods of Asgaard did possess the sublime human virtues; they were righteous, trustworthy, benevolent and even, within a barbaric age, chivalrous." His uncle here for the first time appeared to take any real interest in the

10. Early rising.
11. Danish poet (1743–1781), author of a verse tragedy ("Balder's Death," 1774) that helped revive interest in Scandinavian mythology.
12. Druids were ancient Celtic priests,

skilled as prophets and sorcerers, seen here as counterparts of the Roman augurs, who were also readers of omens. Asgaard, home of the gods and dead heroes, is a Nordic version of the Greek Olympus.

conversation. He stopped, his majestic nose a little in the air. "Ah, it was easier to them," he said.

"What do you mean, Uncle?" Adam asked. "It was a great deal easier," said his uncle, "to the northern gods than to those of Greece to be, as you will have it, righteous and benevolent. To my mind it even reveals a weakness in the souls of our ancient Danes that they should consent to adore such divinities." "My dear uncle," said Adam, smiling, "I have always felt that you would be familiar with the modes of Olympus. Now please let me share your insight, and tell me why virtue should come easier to our Danish gods than to those of milder climates." "They were not as powerful," said his uncle.

"And does power," Adam again asked, "stand in the way of virtue?" "Nay," said his uncle gravely. "Nay, power is in itself the supreme virtue. But the gods of which you speak were never all-powerful. They had, at all times, by their side those darker powers which they named the Jotuns,[13] and who worked the suffering, the disasters, the ruin of our world. They might safely give themselves up to temperance and kindness. The omnipotent gods," he went on, "have no such facilitation. With their omnipotence they take over the woe of the universe."

They had walked up the avenue till they were in view of the house. The old lord stopped and ran his eyes over it. The stately building was the same as ever; behind the two tall front windows, Adam knew, was now his young aunt's room. His uncle turned and walked back.

"Chivalry," he said, "chivalry, of which you were speaking, is not a virtue of the omnipotent. It must needs imply mighty rival powers for the knight to defy. With a dragon inferior to him in strength, what figure will St. George[14] cut? The knight who finds no superior forces ready to hand must invent them, and combat wind-mills; his knighthood itself stipulates dangers, vileness, darkness on all sides of him. Nay, believe me, my nephew, in spite of his moral worth, your chivalrous Odin of Asgaard as a Regent must take rank below that of Jove[15] who avowed his sovereignty, and accepted the world which he ruled. But you are young," he added, "and the experience of the aged to you will sound pedantic."

He stood immovable for a moment and then with deep gravity proclaimed: "The sun is up."

The sun did indeed rise above the horizon. The wide landscape was suddenly animated by its splendour, and the dewy grass shone in a thousand gleams.

13. Mischievous giants in Norse mythology.
14. Patron saint of England and slayer of a fierce dragon. *combat windmills*: A reference to Cervantes' *Don Quixote*.
15. Jove was the ruler of the Roman gods, Odin of the Nordic gods.

"I have listened to you, Uncle," said Adam, "with great interest. But while we have talked you yourself have seemed to me preoccupied; your eyes have rested on the field outside the garden, as if something of great moment, a matter of life and death, was going on there. Now that the sun is up, I see the mowers in the rye and hear them whetting their sickles. It is, I remember you telling me, the first day of the harvest. That is a great day to a landowner and enough to take his mind away from the gods. It is very fine weather, and I wish you a full barn."

The elder man stood still, his hands on his walking-stick. "There is indeed," he said at last, "something going on in that field, a matter of life and death. Come, let us sit down here, and I will tell you the whole story." They sat down on the seat that ran all along the pavilion, and while he spoke the old lord of the land did not take his eyes off the rye field.

"A week ago, on Thursday night," he said, "someone set fire to my barn at Rødmosegaard—you know the place, close to the moor —and burned it all down. For two or three days we could not lay hands on the offender. Then on Monday morning the keeper at Rødmose, with the wheelwright over there, came up to the house; they dragged with them a boy, Goske Piil, a widow's son, and they made their Bible oath that he had done it; they had themselves seen him sneaking round the barn by nightfall on Thursday. Goske had no good name on the farm; the keeper bore him a grudge upon an old matter of poaching, and the wheelwright did not like him either, for he did, I believe, suspect him with his young wife. The boy, when I talked to him, swore to his innocence, but he could not hold his own against the two old men. So I had him locked up, and meant to send him in to our judge of the district, with a letter.

"The judge is a fool, and would naturally do nothing but what he thought I wished him to do. He might have the boy sent to the convict prison for arson, or put amongst the soldiers as a bad character and a poacher. Or again, if he thought that that was what I wanted, he could let him off.

"I was out riding in the fields, looking at the corn that was soon ripe to be mowed, when a woman, the widow, Goske's mother, was brought up before me, and begged to speak to me. Anne-Marie is her name. You will remember her; she lives in the small house east of the village. She has not got a good name in the place either. They tell as a girl she had a child and did away with it.

"From five days' weeping her voice was so cracked that it was difficult for me to understand what she said. Her son, she told me at last, had indeed been over at Rødmose on Thursday, but for no ill purpose; he had gone to see someone. He was her only son, she called the Lord God to witness on his innocence, and she wrung her hands to me that I should save the boy for her.

"We were in the rye field that you and I are looking at now. That gave me an idea. I said to the widow: 'If in one day, between sunrise and sunset, with your own hands you can mow this field, and it be well done, I will let the case drop and you shall keep your son. But if you cannot do it, he must go, and it is not likely that you will then ever see him again.'

"She stood up then and gazed over the field. She kissed my riding boot in gratitude for the favour shown to her."

The old lord here made a pause, and Adam said: "Her son meant much to her?" "He is her only child," said his uncle. "He means to her her daily bread and support in old age. It may be said that she holds him as dear as her own life. As," he added, "within a higher order of life, a son to his father means the name and the race, and he holds him as dear as life everlasting. Yes, her son means much to her. For the mowing of that field is a day's work to three men, or three days' work to one man. Today, as the sun rose, she set to her task. And down there, by the end of the field, you will see her now, in a blue head-cloth, with the man I have set to follow her and to ascertain that she does the work unassisted, and with two or three friends by her, who are comforting her."

Adam looked down, and did indeed see a woman in a blue head-cloth, and a few other figures in the corn.

They sat for a while in silence. "Do you yourself," Adam then said, "believe the boy to be innocent?" "I cannot tell," said his uncle. "There is no proof. The word of the keeper and the wheel-wright stand against the boy's word. If indeed I did believe the one thing or the other, it would be merely a matter of chance, or maybe of sympathy. The boy," he said after a moment, "was my son's playmate, the only other child that I ever knew him to like or to get on with." "Do you," Adam again asked, "hold it possible to her to fulfill your condition?" "Nay, I cannot tell," said the old lord. "To an ordinary person it would not be possible. No ordinary person would ever have taken it on at all. I chose it so. We are not quibbling with the law, Anne-Marie and I."

Adam for a few minutes followed the movement of the small group in the rye. "Will you walk back?" he asked. "No," said his uncle, "I think that I shall stay here till I have seen the end of the thing." "Until sunset?" Adam asked with surprise. "Yes," said the old lord. Adam said: "It will be a long day." "Yes," said his uncle, "a long day. But," he added, as Adam rose to walk away, "if, as you said, you have got that tragedy of which you spoke in your pocket, be as kind as to leave it here, to keep me company." Adam handed him the book.

In the avenue he met two footmen who carried the old lord's morning chocolate down to the pavilion on large silver trays.

As now the sun rose in the sky, and the day grew hot, the lime trees gave forth their exuberance of scent, and the garden was filled with unsurpassed, unbelievable sweetness. Towards the still hour of midday the long avenue reverberated like a soundboard with a low, incessant murmur: the humming of a million bees that clung to the pendulous, thronging clusters of blossoms and were drunk with bliss.

In all the short lifetime of Danish summer there is no richer or more luscious moment than that week wherein the lime trees flower. The heavenly scent goes to the head and to the heart; it seems to unite the fields of Denmark with those of Elysium;[16] it contains both hay, honey and holy incense, and is half fairy-land and half apothecary's locker. The avenue was changed into a mystic edifice, a dryad's[17] cathedral, outward from summit to base lavishly adorned, set with multitudinous ornaments, and golden in the sun. But behind the walls the vaults were benignly cool and sombre, like ambrosial[18] sanctuaries in a dazzling and burning world, and in here the ground was still moist.

Up in the house, behind the silk curtains of the two front windows, the young mistress of the estate from the wide bed stuck her feet into two little high-heeled slippers. Her lace-trimmed nightgown had slid up above her knee and down from the shoulder; her hair, done up in curling-pins for the night, was still frosty with the powder of yesterday, her round face flushed with sleep. She stepped out to the middle of the floor and stood there, looking extremely grave and thoughtful, yet she did not think at all. But through her head a long procession of pictures marched, and she was unconsciously endeavouring to put them in order, as the pictures of her existence had used to be.

She had grown up at Court; it was her world, and there was probably not in the whole country a small creature more exquisitely and innocently drilled to the stately measure of a palace. By favour of the old Dowager Queen[19] she bore her name and that of the King's sister, the Queen of Sweden: Sophie Magdalena. It was with a view to these things that her husband, when he wished to restore his status in high places, had chosen her as a bride, first for his son and then for himself. But her own father, who held an Office in the Royal Household and belonged to the new Court aristocracy, in his day had done the same thing the other way round, and had married a country lady, to get a foothold within the old nobility of Denmark. The little girl had her mother's blood in her veins. The country to her had been an immense surprise and delight.

To get into her castle-court she must drive through the farm yard, through the heavy stone gateway in the barn itself, wherein

16. The home, after death, of heroes and others favored by the Greek gods.
17. A tree-nymph.
18. Ambrosia was the food of the Greek and Roman gods.
19. Name given to the widowed Queen Mother.

the rolling of her coach for a few seconds re-echoed like thunder. She must drive past the stables and the timber-mare,[20] from which sometimes a miscreant would follow her with sad eyes, and might here startle a long string of squalling geese, or pass the heavy, scowling bull, led on by a ring in his nose and kneading the earth in dumb fury. At first this had been to her, every time, a slight shock and a jest. But after a while all these creatures and things, which belonged to her, seemed to become part of herself. Her mothers, the old Danish country ladies, were robust persons, undismayed by any kind of weather; now she herself had walked in the rain and had laughed and glowed in it like a green tree.

She had taken her great new home in possession at a time when all the world was unfolding, mating and propagating. Flowers, which she had known only in bouquets and festoons, sprung from the earth round her; birds sang in all the trees. The new-born lambs seemed to her daintier than her dolls had been. From her husband's Hanoverian stud,[21] foals were brought to her to give names; she stood and watched as they poked their soft noses into their mothers' bellies to drink. Of this strange process she had till now only vaguely heard. She had happened to witness, from a path in the park, the rearing and screeching stallion on the mare. All this luxuriance, lust and fecundity was displayed before her eyes, as for her pleasure.

And for her own part, in the midst of it, she was given an old husband who treated her with punctilious respect because she was to bear him a son. Such was the compact; she had known of it from the beginning. Her husband, she found, was doing his best to fulfill his part of it, and she herself was loyal by nature and strictly brought up. She would not shirk her obligation. Only she was vaguely aware of a discord or an incompatibility within her majestic existence, which prevented her from being as happy as she had expected to be.

After a time her chagrin took a strange form: as the consciousness of an absence. Someone ought to have been with her who was not. She had no experience in analysing her feelings; there had not been time for that at Court. Now, as she was more often left to herself, she vaguely probed her own mind. She tried to set her father in that void place, her sisters, her music master, an Italian singer whom she had admired; but none of them would fill it for her. At times she felt lighter at heart, and believed the misfortune to have left her. And then again it would happen, if she were alone, or in her husband's company, and even within his embrace, that everything round her would cry out: Where? Where? so that she let her wild eyes run about the room in search for the being who should

20. A high wooden beam which public offenders were forced to ride with weights attached to their legs.

21. A stallion bred in Hanover, Germany, then the family seat of English royalty.

have been there, and who had not come.

When, six months ago, she was informed that her first young bridegroom had died and that she was to marry his father in his place, she had not been sorry. Her youthful suitor, the one time she had seen him, had appeared to her infantile and insipid; the father would make a statelier consort. Now she had sometimes thought of the dead boy, and wondered whether with him life would have been more joyful. But she soon again dismissed the picture, and that was the sad youth's last recall to the stage of this world.

Upon one wall of her room there hung a long mirror. As she gazed into it new images came along. The day before, driving with her husband, she had seen, at a distance, a party of village girls bathing in the river, and the sun shining on them. All her life she had moved amongst naked marble deities, but it had till now never occurred to her that the people she knew should themselves be naked under their bodices and trains, waistcoats and satin breeches, that indeed she herself felt naked within her clothes. Now, in front of the looking-glass, she tardily untied the ribbons of her night-gown, and let it drop to the floor.

The room was dim behind the drawn curtains. In the mirror her body was silvery like a white rose; only her cheeks and mouth, and the tips of her fingers and breasts had a faint carmine. Her slender torso was formed by the whalebones that had clasped it tightly from her childhood; above the slim, dimpled knee a gentle narrowness marked the place of the garter. Her limbs were rounded as if, at whatever place they might be cut through with a sharp knife, a perfectly circular transverse incision would be obtained. The side and belly were so smooth that her own gaze slipped and glided, and grasped for a hold. She was not altogether like a statue, she found, and lifted her arms above her head. She turned to get a view of her back, the curves below the waistline were still blushing from the pressure of the bed. She called to mind a few tales about nymphs and goddesses, but they all seemed a long way off, so her mind returned to the peasant girls in the river. They were, for a few minutes, idealized into playmates, or sisters even, since they belonged to her as did the meadow and the blue river itself. And within the next moment the sense of forlornness once more came upon her, a *horror vacui*[22] like a physical pain. Surely, surely someone should have been with her now, her other self, like the image in the glass, but nearer, stronger, alive. There was no one, the universe was empty round her.

A sudden, keen itching under her knee took her out of her reveries, and awoke in her the hunting instincts of her breed. She wetted a finger on her tongue, slowly brought it down and quickly slapped it to the spot. She felt the diminutive, sharp body of the

22. A sense of emptiness; literally, "horror of the void" (Latin).

insect against the silky skin, pressed the thumb to it, and triumphantly lifted up the small prisoner between her fingertips. She stood quite still, as if meditating upon the fact that a flea was the only creature risking its life for her smoothness and sweet blood.

Her maid opened the door and came in, loaded with the attire of the day—shift, stays, hoop and petticoats. She remembered that she had a guest in the house, the new nephew arrived from England. Her husband had instructed her to be kind to their young kinsman, disinherited, so to say, by her presence in the house. They would ride out on the land together.

In the afternoon the sky was no longer blue as in the morning. Large clouds slowly towered up on it, and the great vault itself was colourless, as if diffused into vapours round the white-hot sun in zenith. A low thunder ran along the western horizon; once or twice the dust of the roads rose in tall spirals. But the fields, the hills and the woods were as still as a painted landscape.

Adam walked down the avenue to the pavilion, and found his uncle there, fully dressed, his hands upon his walking-stick and his eyes on the rye field. The book that Adam had given him lay by his side. The field now seemed alive with people. Small groups stood here and there in it, and a long row of men and women were slowly advancing towards the garden in the line of the swath.

The old lord nodded to his nephew, but did not speak or change his position. Adam stood by him as still as himself.

The day to him had been strangely disquieting. At the meeting again with old places the sweet melodies of the past had filled his senses and his mind, and had mingled with new, bewitching tunes of the present. He was back in Denmark, no longer a child but a youth, with a keener sense of the beautiful, with tales of other countries to tell, and still a true son of his own land and enchanted by its loveliness as he had never been before.

But through all these ha.monies the tragic and cruel tale which the old lord had told him in the morning, and the sad contest which he knew to be going on so near by, in the corn field, had re-echoed, like the recurrent, hollow throbbing of a muffled drum, a redoubtable sound. It came back time after time, so that he had felt himself to change colour and to answer absently. It brought with it a deeper sense of pity with all that lived than he had ever known. When he had been riding with his young aunt, and their road ran along the scene of the drama, he had taken care to ride between her and the field, so that she should not see what was going on there, or question him about it. He had chosen the way home through the deep, green wood for the same reason.

More dominantly even than the figure of the woman struggling with her sickle for her son's life, the old man's figure, as he had seen it at sunrise, kept him company through the day. He came to ponder on the part which that lonely, determinate form had played in his own life. From the time when his father died, it had impersonated to the boy law and order, wisdom of life and kind guardianship. What was he to do, he thought, if after eighteen years these filial feelings must change, and his second father's figure take on to him a horrible aspect, as a symbol of the tyranny and oppression of the world? What was he to do if ever the two should come to stand in opposition to each other as adversaries?

At the same time an unaccountable, a sinister alarm and dread on behalf of the old man himself took hold of him. For surely here the Goddess Nemesis[23] could not be far away. This man had ruled the world round him for a longer period than Adam's own lifetime and had never been gainsaid by anyone. During the years when he had wandered through Europe with a sick boy of his own blood as his sole companion he had learned to set himself apart from his surroundings, and to close himself up to all outer life, and he had become insusceptible to the ideas and feelings of other human beings. Strange fancies might there have run in his mind, so that in the end he had seen himself as the only person really existing, and the world as a poor and vain shadow-play, which had no substance to it.

Now, in senile wilfullness, he would take in his hand the life of those simpler and weaker than himself, of a woman, using it to his own ends, and he feared of no retributive justice. Did he not know, the young man thought, that there were powers in the world, different from and more formidable than the short-lived might of a despot?

With the sultry heat of the day this foreboding of impending disaster grew upon him, until he felt ruin threatening not the old lord only, but the house, the name and himself with him. It seemed to him that he must cry out a warning to the man he had loved, before it was too late.

But as now he was once more in his uncle's company, the green calm of the garden was so deep that he did not find his voice to cry out. Instead a little French air which his aunt had sung to him up in the house kept running in his mind.—"*C'est un trop doux effort* . . ."[24] He had good knowledge of music; he had heard the air before, in Paris, but not so sweetly sung.

After a time he asked: "Will the woman fulfill her bargain?" His uncle unfolded his hands. "It is an extraordinary thing," he said animatedly, "that it looks as if she might fulfill it. If you count the hours from sunrise till now, and from now till sunset, you will find the time left her to be half of that already gone. And see! She has now mowed two-thirds of the field. But then we will naturally have to reckon with her strength declining as she works on. All in all, it

---

23. Greek goddess of vengeance.   24. "It's too sweet a task."

is an idle pursuit in you or me to bet on the issue of the matter; we must wait and see. Sit down, and keep me company in my watch." In two minds Adam sat down.

"And here," said his uncle, and took up the book from the seat, "is your book, which has passed the time finely. It is great poetry, ambrosia to the ear and the heart. And it has, with our discourse on divinity this morning, given me stuff for thought. I have been reflecting upon the law of retributive justice." He took a pinch of snuff, and went on. "A new age," he said, "has made to itself a god in its own image, an emotional god. And now you are already writing a tragedy on your god."

Adam had no wish to begin a debate on poetry with his uncle, but he also somehow dreaded a silence, and said: "It may be, then, that we hold tragedy to be, in the scheme of life, a noble, a divine phenomenon."

"Aye," said his uncle solemnly, "a noble phenomenon, the noblest on earth. But of the earth only, and never divine. Tragedy is the privilege of man, his highest privilege. The God of the Christian Church Himself, when He wished to experience tragedy, had to assume human form. And even at that," he added thoughtfully, "the tragedy was not wholly valid, as it would have become had the hero of it been, in very truth, a man. The divinity of Christ conveyed to it a divine note, the moment of comedy. The real tragic part, by the nature of things, fell to the executors, not to the victim. Nay, my nephew, we should not adulterate the pure elements of the cosmos. Tragedy should remain the right of human beings, subject, in their conditions or in their own nature, to the dire law of necessity. To them it is salvation and beatification. But the gods, whom we must believe to be unacquainted with and incomprehensive of necessity, can have no knowledge of the tragic. When they are brought face to face with it they will, according to my experience, have the good taste and decorum to keep still, and not interfere.

"No," he said after a pause, "the true art of the gods is the comic. The comic is a condescension of the divine to the world of man; it is the sublime vision, which cannot be studied, but must ever be celestially granted. In the comic the gods see their own being reflected as in a mirror, and while the tragic poet is bound by strict laws, they will allow the comic artist a freedom as unlimited as their own. They do not even withhold their own existence from his sports. Jove may favour Lucianos of Samosata.[25] As long as your mockery is in true godly taste you may mock at the gods and still remain a sound devotee. But in pitying, or condoling with your god, you deny and annihilate him, and such is the most horrible of atheisms.

---

25. Greek prose writer (*c.* 125–180 A.D.) who wrote satirical *Dialogues of the Gods.*

"And here on earth, too," he went on, "we, who stand in lieu of the gods and have emancipated ourselves from the tyranny of necessity, should leave to our vassals their monopoly of tragedy, and for ourselves accept the comic with grace. Only a boorish and cruel master—a parvenu, in fact—will make a jest of his servants' necessity, or force the comic upon them. Only a timid and pedantic ruler, a *petit-maître*,[26] will fear the ludicrous on his own behalf. Indeed," he finished his long speech, "the very same fatality, which, in striking the burgher or peasant, will become tragedy, with the aristocrat is exalted to the comic. By the grace and wit of our acceptance hereof our aristocracy is known."

Adam could not help smiling a little as he heard the apotheosis of the comic on the lips of the erect, ceremonious prophet. In this ironic smile he was, for the first time, estranging himself from the head of his house.

A shadow fell across the landscape. A cloud had crept over the sun; the country changed colour beneath it, faded and bleached, and even all sounds for a minute seemed to die out of it.

"Ah, now," said the old lord, "if it is going to rain, and the rye gets wet, Anne-Marie will not be able to finish in time. And who comes there?" he added, and turned his head a little.

Preceded by a lackey a man in riding boots and a striped waistcoat with silver buttons, and with his hat in his hand, came down the avenue. He bowed deeply, first to the old lord and then to Adam.

"My bailiff,"[27] said the old lord. "Good afternoon, Bailiff. What news have you to bring?" The bailiff made a sad gesture. "Poor news only, my lord," he said. "And how poor news?" asked his master. "There is," said the bailiff with weight, "not a soul at work on the land, and not a sickle going except that of Anne-Marie in this rye field. The mowing has stopped; they are all at her heels. It is a poor day for a first day of the harvest." "Yes, I see," said the old lord. The bailiff went on. "I have spoken kindly to them," he said, "and I have sworn at them; it is all one. They might as well all be deaf."

"Good bailiff," said the old lord, "leave them in peace; let them do as they like. This day may, all the same, do them more good than many others. Where is Goske, the boy, Anne-Marie's son?" "We have set him in the small room by the barn," said the bailiff. "Nay, let him be brought down," said the old lord; "let him see his mother at work. But what do you say—will she get the field mowed in time?" "If you ask me, my lord," said the bailiff, "I believe that she will. Who would have thought so? She is only a small woman. It is as hot a day today as, well, as I do ever remember. I myself, you

26. A silly, vain person.   27. A steward or overseer of an estate.

yourself, my lord, could not have done what Anne-Marie has done today." "Nay, nay, we could not, Bailiff," said the old lord.

The bailiff pulled out a red handkerchief and wiped his brow, somewhat calmed by venting his wrath. "If," he remarked with bitterness, "they would all work as the widow works now, we would make a profit on the land." "Yes," said the old lord, and fell into thought, as if calculating the profit it might make. "Still," he said, "as to the question of profit and loss, that is more intricate than it looks. I will tell you something that you may not know: The most famous tissue ever woven was ravelled out again every night.[28] But come," he added, "she is close by now. We will go and have a look at her work ourselves." With these words he rose and set his hat on.

The cloud had drawn away again; the rays of the sun once more burned the wide landscape, and as the small party walked out from under the shade of the trees the dead-still heat was heavy as lead; the sweat sprang out on their faces and their eyelids smarted. On the narrow path they had to go one by one, the old lord stepping along first, all black, and the footman, in his bright livery, bringing up the rear.

The field was indeed filled with people like a marketplace; there were probably a hundred or more men and women in it. To Adam the scene recalled pictures from his Bible: the meeting between Esau and Jacob in Edom, or Boas' reapers in his barley field near Bethlehem.[29] Some were standing by the side of the field, others pressed in small groups close to the mowing woman, and a few followed in her wake, binding up sheaves where she had cut the corn, as if thereby they thought to help her, or as if by all means they meant to have part in her work. A younger woman with a pail on her head kept close to her side, and with her a number of half-grown children. One of these first caught sight of the lord of the estate and his suite, and pointed to him. The binders let their sheaves drop, and as the old man stood still many of the onlookers drew close round him.

The woman on whom till now the eyes of the whole field had rested—a small figure on the large stage—was advancing slowly and unevenly, bent double as if she were walking on her knees, and stumbling as she walked. Her blue head-cloth had slipped back from her head; the grey hair was plastered to the skull with sweat, dusty and stuck with straw. She was obviously totally unaware of the

28. In Homer's *Odyssey* (Book 19), Odysseus' wife Penelope unraveled at night the cloth she had woven during the day, because she had promised her suitors to choose from among them a second husband when her weaving was finished.

29. Esau and Jacob were Biblical twin brothers (Genesis 25–33); Esau sold his birthright to Jacob and later settled in Edom. Boas was a rich farmer who told his reapers to let Ruth, a widow, collect fallen sheaves in his fields (Ruth 2–4).

multitude round her; neither did she now once turn her head or her gaze towards the new arrivals.

Absorbed in her work she again and again stretched out her left hand to grasp a handful of corn, and her right hand with the sickle in it to cut it off close to the soil, in wavering, groping pulls, like a tired swimmer's strokes. Her course took her so close to the feet of the old lord that his shadow fell on her. Just then she staggered and swayed sideways, and the woman who followed her lifted the pail from her head and held it to her lips. Anne-Marie drank without leaving her hold on her sickle, and the water ran from the corners of her mouth. A boy, close to her, quickly bent one knee, seized her hands in his own and, steadying and guiding them, cut off a gripe[30] of rye. "No, no," said the old lord, "you must not do that, boy. Leave Anne-Marie in peace to her work." At the sound of his voice the woman, falteringly, lifted her face in his direction.

The bony and tanned face was streaked with sweat and dust; the eyes were dimmed. But there was not in its expression the slightest trace of fear or pain. Indeed amongst all the grave and concerned faces of the field hers was the only one perfectly calm, peaceful and mild. The mouth was drawn together in a thin line, a prim, keen, patient little smile, such as will be seen in the face of an old woman at her spinning-wheel or her knitting, eager on her work, and happy in it. And as the younger woman lifted back the pail, she immediately again fell to her mowing, with an ardent, tender craving, like that of a mother who lays a baby to the nipple. Like an insect that bustles along in high grass, or like a small vessel in a heavy sea, she butted her way on, her quiet face once more bent upon her task.

The whole throng of onlookers, and with them the small group from the pavilion, advanced as she advanced, slowly and as if drawn by a string. The bailiff, who felt the intense silence of the field heavy on him, said to the old lord: "The rye will yield better this year than last," and got no reply. He repeated his remark to Adam, and at last to the footman, who felt himself above a discussion on agriculture, and only cleared his throat in answer. In a while the bailiff again broke the silence. "There is the boy," he said and pointed with his thumb. "They have brought him down." At that moment the woman fell forward on her face and was lifted up by those nearest to her.

Adam suddenly stopped on the path, and covered his eyes with his hand. The old lord without turning asked him if he felt incommoded by the heat. "No," said Adam, "but stay. Let me speak to you." His uncle stopped, with his hand on the stick and looking ahead, as if regretful of being held back.

"In the name of God," cried the young man in French, "force not

30. Handful.

this woman to continue." There was a short pause. "But I force her not, my friend," said his uncle in the same language. "She is free to finish at any moment." "At the cost of her child only," again cried Adam. "Do you not see that she is dying? You know not what you are doing, or what it may bring upon you."

The old lord, perplexed by this unexpected animadversion, after a second turned all round, and his pale, clear eyes sought his nephew's face with stately surprise. His long, waxen face, with two symmetrical curls at the sides, had something of the mien of an idealized and ennobled old sheep or ram. He made sign to the bailiff to go on. The footman also withdrew a little, and the uncle and nephew were, so to say, alone on the path. For a minute neither of them spoke.

"In this very place where we now stand," said the old lord, then, with hauteur, "I gave Anne-Marie my word."

"My uncle!" said Adam. "A life is a greater thing even than a word. Recall that word, I beseech you, which was given in caprice, as a whim. I am praying you more for your sake than for my own, yet I shall be grateful to you all my life if you will grant me my prayer."

"You will have learned in school," said his uncle, "that in the beginning was the word.[31] It may have been pronounced in caprice, as a whim, the Scripture tells us nothing about it. It is still the principle of our world, its law of gravitation. My own humble word has been the principle of the land on which we stand, for an age of man. My father's word was the same, before my day."

"You are mistaken," cried Adam. "The word is creative—it is imagination, daring and passion. By it the world was made. How much greater are these powers which bring into being than any restricting or controlling law! You wish the land on which we look to produce and propagate; you should not banish from it the forces which cause, and which keep up life, nor turn it into a desert by dominance of law. And when you look at the people, simpler than we and nearer to the heart of nature, who do not analyse their feelings, whose life is one with the life of the earth, do they not inspire in you a tenderness, respect, reverence even? This woman is ready to die for her son; will it ever happen to you or me that a woman willingly gives up her life for us? And if it did indeed come to pass, should we make so light of it as not to give up a dogma in return?"

"You are young," said the old lord. "A new age will undoubtedly applaud you. I am old-fashioned, I have been quoting to you texts a thousand years old. We do not, perhaps, quite understand one another. But with my own people I am, I believe, in good understand-

31. The opening of the Gospel According to Saint John.

ing. Anne-Marie might well feel that I am making light of her exploit, if now, at the eleventh hour, I did nullify it by a second word. I myself should feel so in her place. Yes, my nephew, it is possible, did I grant you your prayer and pronounce such an amnesty, that I should find it void against her faithfulness, and that we would still see her at her work, unable to give it up, as a shuttle in the rye field, until she had it all mowed. But she would then be a shocking, a horrible sight, a figure of unseemly fun, like a small planet running wild in the sky, when the law of gravitation had been done away with."

"And if she dies at her task," Adam exclaimed, "her death, and its consequences will come upon your head."

The old lord took off his hat and gently ran his hand over his powdered head. "Upon my head?" he said. "I have kept up my head in many weathers. Even," he added proudly, "against the cold wind from high places. In what shape will it come upon my head, my nephew?" "I cannot tell," cried Adam in despair. "I have spoken to warn you. God only knows." "Amen," said the old lord with a little delicate smile. "Come, we will walk on." Adam drew in his breath deeply.

"No," he said in Danish. "I cannot come with you. This field is yours; things will happen here as you decide. But I myself must go away. I beg you to let me have, this evening, a coach as far as town. For I could not sleep another night under your roof, which I have honoured beyond any on earth." So many conflicting feelings at his own speech thronged in his breast that it would have been impossible for him to give them words.

The old lord, who had already begun to walk on, stood still, and with him the lackey. He did not speak for a minute, as if to give Adam time to collect his mind. But the young man's mind was in uproar and would not be collected.

"Must we," the old man asked, in Danish, "take leave here, in the rye field? I have held you dear, next to my own son. I have followed your career in life from year to year, and have been proud of you. I was happy when you wrote to say that you were coming back. If now you will go away, I wish you well." He shifted his walking-stick from the right hand to the left and gravely looked his nephew in the face.

Adam did not meet his eyes. He was gazing out over the landscape. In the late mellow afternoon it was resuming its colours, like a painting brought into proper light; in the meadows the little black stacks of peat stood gravely distinct upon the green sward. On this same morning he had greeted it all, like a child running laughingly to its mother's bosom; now already he must tear himself from it, in discordance, and forever. And at the moment of parting it seemed infinitely dearer than any time before, so much beautified and solemnized by the coming separation that it looked like the place in a dream, a landscape out of paradise, and he wondered if it was really the same. But, yes—there before him was, once more, the hunting-ground of long ago. And there was the road on which he had ridden today.

"But tell me where you mean to go from here," said the old lord slowly. "I myself have travelled a good deal in my days. I know the word of leaving, the wish to go away. But I have learned by experience that, in reality, the word has a meaning only to the place and the people which one leaves. When you have left my house—although it will see you go with sadness—as far as it is concerned the matter is finished and done with. But to the person who goes away it is a different thing, and not so simple. At the moment that he leaves one place he will be already, by the laws of life, on his way to another, upon this earth. Let me know, then, for the sake of our old acquaintance, to which place you are going when you leave here. To England?"

"No," said Adam. He felt in his heart that he could never again go back to England or to his easy and carefree life there. It was not far enough away; deeper waters than the North Sea must now be laid between him and Denmark. "No, not to England," he said. "I shall go to America, to the new world." For a moment he shut his eyes, trying to form to himself a picture of existence in America, with the grey Atlantic Ocean between him and these fields and woods.

"To America?" said his uncle and drew up his eyebrows. "Yes, I have heard of America. They have got freedom there, a big waterfall, savage red men. They shoot turkeys, I have read, as we shoot partridges. Well, if it be your wish, go to America, Adam, and be happy in the new world."

He stood for some time, sunk in thought, as if he had already sent off the young man to America, and had done with him. When at last he spoke, his words had the character of a monologue, enunciated by the person who watches things come and go, and himself stays on.

"Take service, there," he said, "with the power which will give you an easier bargain than this: That with your own life you may buy the life of your son."

Adam had not listened to his uncle's remarks about America, but the conclusive, solemn words caught his ear. He looked up. As if for the first time in his life, he saw the old man's figure as a whole, and conceived how small it was, so much smaller than himself, pale, a thin black anchorite upon his own land. A thought ran through his head: "How terrible to be old!" The abhorrence of the tyrant, and the sinister dread on his behalf, which had followed him all day, seemed to die out of him, and his pity with all creation to extend even to the sombre form before him.

His whole being had cried out for harmony. Now, with the possibility of forgiving, of a reconciliation, a sense of relief went through him; confusedly he bethought himself of Anne-Marie drinking the water held to her lips. He took off his hat, as his uncle had done a moment ago, so that to a beholder at a distance it would seem that the two dark-clad gentlemen on the path were repeatedly and respectfully saluting one another, and brushed the hair from his forehead. Once more the tune of the garden-room rang in his mind:

> *"Mourir pour ce qu'on aime*
> *C'est un trop doux effort . . ."*[32]

He stood for a long time immobile and dumb. He broke off a few ears of rye, kept them in his hand and looked at them.

He saw the ways of life, he thought, as a twined and tangled design, complicated and mazy; it was not given him or any mortal to command or control it. Life and death, happiness and woe, the past and the present, were interlaced within the pattern. Yet to the initiated it might be read as easily as our ciphers—which to the savage must seem confused and incomprehensible—will be read by the schoolboy. And out of the contrasting elements concord rose. All that lived must suffer; the old man, whom he had judged hardly, had suffered, as he had watched his son die, and had dreaded the obliteration of his being. He himself would come to know ache, tears and remorse, and, even through these, the fullness of life. So might now, to the woman in the rye field, her ordeal be a triumphant procession. For to die for the one you loved was an effort too sweet for words.

As now he thought of it, he knew that all his life he had sought the unity of things, the secret which connects the phenomena of existence. It was this strife, this dim presage, which had sometimes made him stand still and inert in the midst of the games of his playfellows, or which had, at other moments—on moonlight nights, or in his little boat on the sea—lifted the boy to ecstatic happiness. Where other young people, in their pleasures or their amours, had searched for contrast and variety, he himself had yearned only to comprehend in full the oneness of the world. If things had come differently to him, if his young cousin had not died, and the events that followed his death had not brought him to Denmark, his search for understanding and harmony might have taken him to America, and he might have found them there, in the virgin forests of a new world. Now they have been disclosed to him today, in the place

---

32. "Dying for what one loves / Is too sweet a task . . ."; lines from an aria in *Alceste* (1767), an opera written in 1767 by Christoph Willibald von Gluck (1714–1787), based on Euripides' *Alcestis*; it was produced in Paris in 1776. The protagonist, wife to Admetus, agrees to die in place of her husband.

where he had played as a child. As the song is one with the voice that sings it, as the road is one with the goal, as lovers are made one in their embrace, so is man one with his destiny, and he shall love it as himself.

He looked up again, towards the horizon. If he wished to, he felt, he might find out what it was that had brought to him, here, the sudden conception of the unity of the universe. When this same morning he had philosophized, lightly and for his own sake, on his feeling of belonging to this land and soil, it had been the beginning of it. But since then it had grown; it had become a mightier thing, a revelation to his soul. Some time he would look into it, for the law of cause and effect was a wonderful and fascinating study. But not now. This hour was consecrated to greater emotions, to a surrender to fate and to the will of life.

"No," he said at last. "If you wish it I shall not go. I shall stay here."

At that moment a long, loud roll of thunder broke the stillness of the afternoon. It re-echoed for a while amongst the low hills, and it reverberated within the young man's breast as powerfully as if he had been seized and shaken by hands. The landscape had spoken. He remembered that twelve hours ago he had put a question to it, half in jest, and not knowing what he did. Here it gave him its answer.

What it contained he did not know; neither did he inquire. In his promise to his uncle he had given himself over to the mightier powers of the world. Now what must come must come.

"I thank you," said the old lord, and made a little stiff gesture with his hand. "I am happy to hear you say so. We should not let the difference in our ages, or of our views, separate us. In our family we have been wont to keep peace and faith with one another. You have made my heart lighter."

Something within his uncle's speech faintly recalled to Adam the misgivings of the afternoon. He rejected them; he would not let them trouble the new, sweet felicity which his resolution to stay had brought him.

"I shall go on now," said the old lord. "But there is no need for you to follow me. I will tell you tomorrow how the matter has ended." "No," said Adam, "I shall come back by sunset, to see the end of it myself."

All the same he did not come back. He kept the hour in his mind, and all through the evening the consciousness of the drama, and the profound concern and compassion with which, in his thoughts, he followed it, gave to his speech, glance and movements a grave and pathetic substance. But he felt that he was, in the rooms of the manor, and even by the harpsichord on which he accompanied his aunt to her air from *Alceste*, as much in the centre of things as if he had stood in the rye field itself, and as near to those human beings whose fate was now decided there. Anne-Marie and he were both in the hands of destiny, and destiny would, by different ways, bring each to the designated end.

Later on he remembered what he had thought that evening.

But the old lord stayed on. Late in the afternoon he even had an idea; he called down his valet to the pavilion and made him shift his clothes on him and dress him up in a brocaded suit that he had worn at Court. He let a lace-trimmed shirt be drawn over his head and stuck out his slim legs to have them put into thin silk stockings and buckled shoes. In this majestic attire he dined alone, of a frugal meal, but took a bottle of Rhenish wine with it, to keep up his strength. He sat on for a while, a little sunk in his seat; then, as the sun neared the earth, he straightened himself, and took the way down to the field.

The shadows were now lengthening, azure blue along all the eastern slopes. The lonely trees in the corn marked their site by narrow blue pools running out from their feet, and as the old man walked a thin, immensely elongated reflection stirred behind him on the path. Once he stood still; he thought he heard a lark singing over his head, a spring-like sound; his tired head held no clear perception of the season; he seemed to be walking, and standing, in a kind of eternity.

The people in the field were no longer silent, as they had been in the afternoon. Many of them talked loudly among themselves, and a little farther away a woman was weeping.

When the bailiff saw his master, he came up to him. He told him, in great agitation, that the widow would, in all likelihood, finish the mowing of the field within a quarter of an hour.

"Are the keeper and the wheelwright here?" the old lord asked him. "They have been here," said the bailiff, "and have gone away, five times. Each time they have said that they would not come back. But they have come back again, all the same, and they are here now." "And where is the boy?" the old lord asked again. "He is with her," said the bailiff. "I have given him leave to follow her. He has walked close to his mother all the afternoon, and you will see him now by her side, down there."

Anne-Marie was now working her way up towards them more evenly than before, but with extreme slowness, as if at any moment she might come to a standstill. This excessive tardiness, the old lord reflected, if it had been purposely performed, would have been an inimitable, dignified exhibition of skilled art; one might fancy the Emperor of China advancing in like manner on a divine procession or rite. He shaded his eyes with his hand, for the sun was now just beyond the horizon, and its last rays made light, wild, many-coloured specks dance before his sight. With such splendour did the sunset emblazon the earth and the air that the landscape was turned into a melting-pot of glorious metals. The meadows and the grass-lands became pure gold; the barley field near by, with its long ears, was a live lake of shining silver.

There was only a small patch of straw standing in the rye field, when the woman, alarmed by the change in the light, turned her head a little to get a look at the sun. The while she did not stop her work, but grasped one handful of corn and cut it off, then another, and another. A great stir, and a sound like a manifold, deep sigh, ran through the crowd. The field was now mowed from one end to the other. Only the mower herself did not realize the fact; she stretched out her hand anew, and when she found nothing in it, she seemed puzzled or disappointed. The she let her arms drop, and slowly sank to her knees.

Many of the women burst out weeping, and the swarm drew close round her, leaving only a small open space at the side where the old lord stood. Their sudden nearness frightened Anne-Marie; she made a slight, uneasy movement, as if terrified that they should put their hands on her.

The boy, who had kept by her all day, now fell on his knees beside her. Even he dared not touch her, but held one arm low behind her back and the other before her, level with her collar-bone, to catch hold of her if she should fall, and all the time he cried aloud. At that moment the sun went down.

The old lord stepped forward and solemnly took off his hat. The crowd became silent, waiting for him to speak. But for a minute or two he said nothing. Then he addressed her, very slowly.

"Your son is free, Anne-Marie," he said. He again waited a little, and added: "You have done a good day's work, which will long be remembered."

Anne-Marie raised her gaze only as high as his knees, and he understood that she had not heard what he said. He turned to the boy. "You tell your mother, Goske," he said, gently, "what I have told her."

The boy had been sobbing wildly, in raucous, broken moans. It took him some time to collect and control himself. But when at last he spoke, straight into his mother's face, his voice was low, a little impatient, as if he were conveying an everyday message to her. "I am free, Mother," he said. "You have done a good day's work that will long be remembered."

At the sound of his voice she lifted her face to him. A faint, bland shadow of surprise ran over it, but still she gave no sign of having heard what he said, so that the people round them began to wonder if the exhaustion had turned her deaf. But after a moment she slowly and waveringly raised her hand, fumbling in the air as she aimed at his face, and with her fingers touched his cheek. The cheek was wet with tears, so that at the contact her fingertips lightly stuck to it, and she seemed unable to overcome the infinitely slight resistance, or to withdraw her hand. For a minute the two looked each other in the face. Then, softly and lingeringly, like a sheaf of corn that falls to the ground, she sank forward onto the boy's shoulder, and he closed his arms round her.

He held her thus, pressed against him, his own face buried in her hair and head-cloth, for such a long time that those nearest to them, frightened because her body looked so small in his embrace, drew closer, bent down and loosened his grip. The boy let them do so without a word or a movement. But the woman who held Anne-Marie, in her arms to lift her up, turned her face to the old lord. "She is dead," she said.

The people who had followed Anne-Marie all through the day kept standing and stirring in the field for many hours, as long as the evening light lasted, and longer. Long after some of them had made a stretcher from branches of the trees and had carried away the dead woman, others wandered on, up and down the stubble, imitating and measuring her course from one end of the rye field to the other, and binding up the last sheaves, where she had finished her mowing.

The old lord stayed with them for a long time, stepping along a little, and again standing still.

In the place where the woman had died the old lord later on had a stone set up, with a sickle engraved in it. The peasants on the land then named the rye field "Sorrow-Acre." By this name it was known a long time after the story of the woman and her son had itself been forgotten.

ANNA AKHMATOVA

(1889–1966)

Requiem[*]

No, not far beneath some foreign sky then,
Not with foreign wings to shelter me,—
I was with my people then, close by them
Where my luckless people chanced to be.

1916

[*]*Title*: A lament for the poet's son, arrested in 1937 and then imprisoned in Leningrad. A *Requiem* is a mass sung for the dead. Typically, Akhmatova's experience is blended with that of others— here, the women mourning relatives taken during the Stalinist purges of 1937–1938. The sections of "Requiem" were composed at different times, and the verse and prose prefaces were written later than the body of the poem. The complete work was first published in Munich in 1963. Only excerpts have appeared in the Soviet Union. The translation is by Robin Kemble.

By Way of a Preface

In the terrible years of the Yezhovshchina, I spent seventeen months in the prison queues in Leningrad. Somehow, one day, someone "identified" me. Then a woman standing behind me, whose lips were blue with cold, and who, naturally enough, had never even heard of my name, emerged from that state of torpor common to us all and, putting her lips close to my ear (there, everyone spoke in whispers), asked me:

—And could you describe *this*?

And I answered her:

—I can.

Then something vaguely like a smile flashed across what once had been her face.

1 April 1957
Leningrad

Dedication

Mountains bow beneath that boundless sorrow,
And the mighty river stops its flow.
But those prison bolts are tried and thorough,
And beyond them, every "convict's burrow"
Tells a tale of mortal woe.   5
Someone, somewhere, feels the cool wind, bracing,
Sees the sun go nestling down to rest—
We know nothing, we, together facing
Still the sickening clank of keys, the pacing
Of the sentries with their heavy steps.   10
We'd rise, as for early Mass, each morning,
Cross the callous city, wend our way,
Meet, more lifeless than the dead, half mourning,
Watch the sun sink, the Neva mist forming,
But with hope still singing far away.   15
Sentenced . . . And at once the tears come rolling,
Cut off from the world, quite on her own,
Heart reduced to shreds, and almost falling,
Just as if some lout had sent her sprawling,
Still . . . She staggers on her way . . . Alone . . .   20
Where are now the friends of my misfortune,
Those that shared my own two years of hell?
What do the Siberian snow-winds caution,
What bodes the moon circle for their fortunes?
Theirs be this, my greeting and farewell.   25

March, 1940

By Way of a Preface: In 1937–1938, mass arrests were carried out by the secret police. *Yezhovshchina* means "Yezhov's tricks," referring to the head of the secret police, Nicolai Yezhov.

8. *We*: Women waiting before prison gates.

14. *Neva*: The large river that flows through Leningrad.

21. *friends of my misfortune*: The women the poet met while waiting before the prison.

23. *Siberian*: Victims of the purges who were not executed were condemned to prison camps in Siberia.

24. *moon circle*: A ring around the moon, seen refracted through the snow.

Prelude

It was when no one smiled any longer
Save the dead, who were glad of release.
And when Leningrad dangled, incongruous,
By its prisons—a needless caprice.
And when, out of their minds with sheer suffering,   30
The long lines of the newly condemned
Heard the engines' shrill whistles go sputtering
A brief song of farewell to their friends.
Stars of death stood above us, and Russia,
In her innocence, twisted in pain   35
Under blood-spattered boots, and the shudder
Of the Black Marias in their train.

1

It was dawn when they took you. I followed,
As a widow walks after the bier.
By the icons—a candle, burnt hollow;   40
In the bed-room—the children, in tears.
Your lips—cool from the kiss of the icon,
Still to think—the cold sweat on your brow . . .
Like the wives of the Streltsy, now I come
To wait under the Kremlin's gaunt towers.   45

1935

2

Silent flows the silent Don,
Yellow moon looks quietly on,

Cap askew, looks in the room,
Sees a shadow in the gloom.

Sees this woman, sick, at home,   50
Sees this woman, all alone,

Husband buried, then to see
Son arrested . . . Pray for me.

3

No, this is not me, this is somebody else that suffers.
I could never face that, and all that has happened: 55

34. *stars of death*: Stars in the sky, and perhaps also the stars on soldiers' caps and uniforms.
37. *Black Marias*: Police cars for conveying those arrested.
38. Akhmatova's third husband, the art historian Nikolai Punin, was arrested at dawn.
42. *Icon*: Small religious painting. He has kissed it before being taken away.
44. *Streltsy*: Household troops of the Tsar, who revolted in the time of Peter I. A thousand were executed in 1698 before the Kremlin, in the sight of their wives and mothers.
46. *Don*: The great Russian river. The first four lines of this section resemble a Russian lullabye.
52. *Husband buried*: Akhmatova's first husband, the poet Nikolai Gumilev, was shot in 1921.

Let sackcloth and ashes enshroud it,
And see all the lamps are removed . . .
  Night.

4

You, my mocking one, pet of society,
And gay sinner of Tsarskoe Selo: 60
Had you dreamt, in your sweet notoriety,
Of the future that lay in store—
How you'd stand at the Crosses, three-hundredth
In the queue, each bleak New Year,
Hug your precious parcel of comforts,   65
Melt the ice with your hot bright tears.
There the poplar, used to imprisonment,
Sways aloft. Not a sound. But think
Of the numbers rotting there, innocent . . .

5

For seventeen long months my pleas,   70
My cries have called you home.
I've begged the hangman on my knees,
My son, my dread, my own.
My mind's mixed up for good, and I'm
No longer even clear   75
Who's man, who's beast, nor how much time
Before the end draws near.
And only flowers decked with dust,
And censers ringing, footprints thrust
Somewhere-nowhere, afar.   80
And, staring me straight in the eye
And warning me that death is nigh—
One monumental star.

             1939

6

Weeks fly past in light profusion,
How to fathom what's been done;   85
How those long white nights, dear son,
Watched you in your cell's seclusion.

How once more they watch you there,
Eyes like hawks' that burn right through you,
Speak to you of death, speak to you   90
Of the lofty cross you bear.

             1939

60. *Tsarskoe Selo*: Or "The Tsar's Village," a town near Leningrad where Akhmatova spent her childhood, built around the Tsar's Summer Palace.
63. A prison in Leningrad whose buildings form a cross.

72. *the hangman*: Stalin. Akhmatova wrote a letter to him pleading unsuccessfully for the release of her son.
79. *censers*: Incense holders used during religious rites.

7

Sentence

And the word in stone has fallen heavy
On my breast, which was alive till now.
Never mind—for, mark you, I was ready,
I shall get along somehow.   95

So much to be done before tomorrow:
Crush the memory till no thoughts remain,
Carve a heart in stone, immune to sorrow,
Teach myself to face life once again,—

And if not . . . The rustling heat of summer   100
Fills my window with its festive tone.
I long since foresensed that there would come a
Sunny day like this—and empty home.

                                                    1939, Summer

8

To Death

You'll come in any case—then why not right away?
I'm waiting—life has dragged me under.   105
I've put the lamp out, left the door to show the way
When you come in your simple wonder.
For that, choose any guise you like: Burst in on me,
A shell with poison-gas container,
Or bandit with a heavy weight, creep up on me,   110
Or poison me with typhus vapor,
Or be a fable, known *ad nauseam*
To everyone denounced in error,
So I may see the top of that blue cap, and scan
The face of the house-porter, white with terror.   115
But nothing matters now. The Yenisey swirls by,
The Pole star shines above the torrent.
And the glint of those beloved eyes
Conceals the last, the final horror.

                                                    19 August 1939
                                                    Fontanny Dom

9

So madness now has wrapped its wings   120
Round half my soul and plies me, heartless,

---

112. *ad nauseam*: To the point of
nausea. Denunciations for "counterre-
volutionary" activity were common.
114. *blue cap*: Worn by the secret police.
116. *Yenisey*: River in Siberia along
which there were many prison camps.

With drafts of fiery wine, begins
To lure me toward the vale of darkness.

And I can see that I must now
Concede the victory—as I listen,   125
The dream that dogged my fevered brow
Already seems an outside vision.

And though I go on bended knee
To plead, implore its intercession,
There's nothing I may take with me,   130
It countenances no concession:

Nor yet my son's distracted eyes—
The rock-like suffering rooted in them,
The day the storm broke from clear skies,
The hour spent visiting the prison,   135

Nor yet the kind, cool clasp of hands,
The lime-tree shadows' fitful darting,
The far light call across the land—
The soothing words exchanged on parting.

4 May 1940
Fontanny Dom

10

Crucifixion

*Weep not for Me, Mother,
that I am in the grave.*

I

The angels hailed that solemn hour and stately,   140
the heavens dissolved in tongues of fire. And He
Said to the Father; "Why didst Thou forsake Me!"
And to His Mother: "Weep thou not for Me . . ."

II

Magdalena sobbed, and the disciple,
He whom Jesus loved, stood petrified.   145
But there, where His Mother stood in silence,
No one durst so much as lift their eyes.

1940–43

142. *"Why . . . Me!"*: Christ's last words from the Cross. [*Matthew* 27:46.]
143. *"Weep . . Me"*: These words and the epigraph refer to a line from the Russian Orthodox prayer sung at services on Easter Saturday: "Weep not for Me, Mother, when thou lookest in the grave." Christ is comforting Mary with the promise of his resurrection.

Epilogue

I

I've learned how faces droop and then grow hollow,
How fear looks out from underneath the lids,
How cheeks, carved out of suffering and of sorrow,   150
Take on the lines of rough cuneiform scripts.
How heads of curls, but lately black or ashen,
Turn suddenly to silver overnight,
Smiles fade on lips reduced to dread submission,
A hoarse dry laugh stands in for trembling fright.   155
I pray, not for myself alone, my cry
Goes up for all those with me there—for all,
In heart of winter, heat-wave of July,
Who stood beneath that blind, deep-crimson wall.

II

The hour of remembrance is with us again.   160
I see you, I hear you, I feel you as then:

There's one they scarce dragged to the window, and one
Whose days in the land of her forebears are done,

And one tossed her beautiful head back when shown
Her corner, and said; "It's like being back home!"   165

I'd like to remember each one by her name,
But they took the list, and there's no more remain.

I've worked them a funeral shroud from each word
Of pain that escaped them, and I overheard.

I'll think of them everywhere, always, each one.   170
I shall not forget them in dark days to come.

And should they once silence my mortified lips,
Let one hundred millions for whom my voice speaks—

Let *them* take my place, and remember each year
Whenever my day of remembrance draws near.   175

And should they one day, in this country, agree
To raise a memorial somewhere to me,

I'd willingly give my consent to their plan,
But on one condition, which is—that it stand,

---

151. *cuneiform*: Ancient Babylonian writing, carved on tablets.
168. *funeral shroud*: Distant reference to a tenth-century appearance of the Vir-
gin in a church, where she extended her veil over the people in protection—the occasion of a religious festival celebrated on October 1.

Not down by the sea, where I entered this world   180
(I've cut the last links that once bound us of old),

Nor yet by the tree-stump in old Tsarsky Sad,
Whose shade seeks me still with disconsolate love,

But here, where they let me stand three hundred hours,
And never so much as unbolted the doors.   185

For even in death I still fear to forget
The grim Black Marias, their thundering tread,

The sickening slam of that loathsome cell-door,
The old woman's howl, like a wounded beast's roar.

And may the snow, melting, well forth clear and strong,   190
Like tears from my eyelids, unmoving, like bronze,

And may the lone prison-dove coo from afar,
And boats travel silently down the Neva.

                                                        1940, March

182. *Tsarsky Sad*: The park and garden surrounding the Tsar's Summer Palace. The "shade" in the garden is a
ghost, either the restless spirit of Akhmatova's executed husband Gumilev or
the Russian poet Pushkin (1799–1837),
who once lived in Tsarskoe Selo. In
other poems, Akhmatova writes of a favorite willow, later only a stump, and of
Pushkin whom she describes as walking
in the park.
   191. Akhmatova imagines herself me-
morialized as a national poet, and demands that her statue be placed here
where she has experienced both public
and private tragedy.

ANDRÉ BRETON
(1896–1966)
and
PAUL ÉLUARD
(1895–1952)

THE IMMACULATE CONCEPTION

Intra-Uterine Life*

To be nothing. Of all the ways the sunflower has of loving the
light, regret is the most beautiful shadow on the sundial. Cross-
bones, crossword puzzles, volumes and volumes of ignorance and
knowledge. Where is one to begin? The fish is born from a thorn,
the monkey from a walnut.[1] The shadow of Christopher Columbus

* Translated by John Ashbery.
1. May also be read: The fish is born
from a spine, and the old hag from an
old bean.

itself turns on Tierra del Fuego: it is no more difficult than the egg.[2]

A great self-assurance—and great without term of comparison—enables the ghost to deny the reality of the forms that enchain it. But we have not yet reached that point. The disconcerted gestures of statues in their moulds produced those imperfect, ghostly figures: the Venuses whose absent hands[3] caress the poets' hair.

From one bank of the river to the other, washerwomen shout at each other the name of a fantastic personage who wanders over the earth feigning hatred for everything he embraces. Their songs are everything that carries me away and is nevertheless carried itself, as carrier pigeons photograph the enemy camp without wanting to. Their eyes are less far from me than the vulture from its prey. I understand now that a woman's face is visible only during sleep. It is in vertigo,[4] among the even grasses of heaven. Seen from within or without, it is the pearl a thousand times more valuable than the diver's death. From without, it is the admirable slingshot; from within, it is the bird. The brambles tear it and the mulberries stain it black, but it bestows on the bushes the strange source of its seething light.[5] Impossible to find out what has become of it since I discovered it.

The doe between two leaps likes to look at me. I keep her company in the clearing. I fall slowly from the heights, I still weigh only the weight you lose at thirty thousand feet. The extinguished chandelier that lights me bares its teeth when I caress the breasts I didn't choose. Great dead branches pierce them. The valves that open and close in a heart which is not mine and which is my heart are everything useless that will be sung in two-four time: I cry, no one hears me, I dream.

This desert is false. The shadows I dig enable the colors to appear like so many useless secrets.

I shall, they say, see. I shall, they see, hear. Silence as far as the eye can see is the keyboard that begins with those twenty fingers that are not. My mother is a spinning top whose whip is my father.

For seducing the weather I have shivers for adornment, and the return of my body back into itself. Ah, to take a bath, a bath of the Romans,[6] a sand bath, an ass's milk sand bath. *To live* as one must

2. According to legend, Columbus (1451–1506) responded to those who were belittling his discovery of America by asking if they could balance an egg on its end. When they failed, he crushed the end slightly and balanced the egg, commenting that the most difficult part was always finding out how to do it. Tierra del Fuego is an archipelago off the southern tip of South America, discovered in 1520 by Magellan; Columbus never traveled so far south.

3. Venus is the Roman goddess of

love. Many classical statues of Venus have lost their arms.

4. Literally, *dazzle* (a noun).

5. Characteristic theme of the priceless value of love. The dazzling face or pearl contains the contradictions of death and life (slingshot and bird), and illuminates the bushes—a surrealist version of the Old Testament burning bush from which God spoke to Moses (Exodus 3:2).

6. An elaborate experience of washing and massage at one of the Romans' large public baths.

know how to knot one's veins in a bath! To travel on the back of a jellyfish, on the surface of the water, then to sink into the depths to get the appetite of blind fish,[7] of blind fish that have the appetite of the birds that howl at life. Has anyone ever seen[8] birds sing around four in the afternoon in April? Those birds are mad. It is I. Has anyone ever before seen the sun cover the night with its dead weight, as the fire covers the ashes? For suns I have flame becoming smoke, the wild moan of a hunted animal, and the first waterdrop of a shower.

Be careful! They are expecting me.[9] Day and night are going to be at the station. I shall never recognize them if I burden myself with the suitcases of justice.[10]

7. Fish from the deepest waters, where there is no light.
8. Literally, *heard*. The birds, like the fish—and like the speaker—have a mad appetite for life.
9. The child is about to be born.

10. The child's intuitive sense of day and night, light and dark, of a vital harmony in nature, will be lost if he is weighed down by the baggage of logic and morality.

BERTOLT BRECHT
(1898–1956)
Mother Courage and Her Children*

A Chronicle of the Thirty Years' War[1]

Characters

MOTHER COURAGE	A CLERK
KATTRIN, *her mute daughter*	A YOUNG SOLDIER
EILIF, *her elder son*	AN OLDER SOLDIER
SWISS CHEESE, *her younger son*	A PEASANT
THE RECRUITER	THE PEASANT'S WIFE
THE SERGEANT	THE YOUNG MAN
THE COOK	THE OLD WOMAN
THE GENERAL	ANOTHER PEASANT
THE CHAPLAIN	THE PEASANT WOMAN
THE ORDNANCE OFFICER	A YOUNG PEASANT
YVETTE POTTIER	THE LIEUTENANT
THE MAN WITH THE PATCH OVER HIS EYE	SOLDIERS
THE OTHER SERGEANT	A VOICE
THE OLD COLONEL	

* Written in 1939; first performed in Zurich in 1941. Translated by Ralph Manheim.
1. The Thirty Years' War, actually a series of wars fought in central Europe from 1618 to 1648, began with a Protestant revolt in Bohemia (now western Czechoslovakia) that deposed King Ferdinand, then head of the Catholic Habsburg dynasty that ruled Austria from 1282 to 1919. He immediately was elected Holy Roman Emperor and, as chief of a loose confederation of Catholic European princes, organized a confederation that put down the Bohemian revolt, but the war spread quickly into

1

Spring, 1624. General Oxenstjerna recruits troops in Dalarna for the Polish campaign. The canteen woman, Anna Fierling, known as Mother Courage, loses a son.[2]

Highway near a city.

A sergeant and a recruiter stand shivering.

THE RECRUITER. How can anybody get a company together in a place like this? Sergeant, sometimes I feel like committing suicide. The general wants me to recruit four platoons by the twelfth, and the people around here are so depraved I can't sleep at night. I finally get hold of a man, I close my eyes and pretend not to see that he's chicken-breasted and he's got varicose veins, I get him good and drunk and he signs up. While I'm paying for the drinks, he steps out, I follow him to the door because I smell a rat: Sure enough, he's gone, like a fart out of a goose. A man's word doesn't mean a thing, there's no honor, no loyalty. This place has undermined my faith in humanity, sergeant.

THE SERGEANT. It's easy to see these people have gone too long without a war. How can you have morality without a war, I ask you? Peace is a mess, it takes a war to put things in order. In peacetime the human race goes to the dogs. Man and beast are treated like so much dirt. Everybody eats what they like, a big piece of cheese on white bread, with a slice of meat on top of the cheese. Nobody knows how many young men or good horses there are in that town up ahead, they've never been counted. I've been in places where they hadn't had a war in as much as seventy years, the people had no names, they didn't even know who they were. It takes a war before you get decent lists and records; then

Germany. The Protestant side drew first Denmark and then, after the Danes' quick defeat, Sweden into the conflict.

At the time *Mother Courage* opens, in 1624, a Swedish army has been fighting in Poland for three years. After winning the coastal province of Livonia (now part of the U.S.S.R.), it invades Germany in 1630 under the command of King Gustavus Adolphus. The king however fails to relieve the siege of Magdeburg by the imperial general Johan Tserclaes, Count of Tilly, and the Protestant bishopric is burned to the ground. Gustavus Adolphus later defeats Tilly in two major battles, but in 1632 both are killed, and two years later the Swedish force is destroyed by the Imperial army. The ensuing peace is brief, for in 1635 a new Swedish army, joined by troops from Catholic France, renews the fighting. (Religious justifications for the war early lost their strength, and were overshadowed by territorial and dynastic ambitions.) This last phase of the war has just begun at the end of *Mother Courage*, and lasting peace will come only

twelve years later.

Brecht is true to history as he knew it; only recently have historians disputed the traditional belief that the war devastated Germany and halved its population. He does not mention the most famous Imperial general, Wallenstein, a swashbuckling and romantic figure who was the subject of plays and stories Brecht's German audience knew; such an adventurer has no place in an allegory against war, as Brecht is concerned not with the exploits of heroes but with the plight of common people trampled by forces they can neither control nor understand.

2. The heading for this and each new scene is projected on a screen on stage; it situates the action and tells what will happen. *General Oxenstjerna*: One of the Swedish generals. *Dalarna*: a rural province in central Sweden. A canteen woman sells provisions to soldiers; Mother Courage's wagon is "a cross between a military vehicle and a general store." [Brecht's note.]

your boots are done up in bales and your grain in sacks, man and beast are properly counted and marched away, because people realize that without order they can't have a war.

THE RECRUITER. How right you are!

THE SERGEANT. Like all good things, a war is hard to get started. But once it takes root, it's vigorous; then people are as scared of peace as dice players are of laying off, because they'll have to reckon up their losses. But at first they're scared of war. It's the novelty.

THE RECRUITER. Say, there comes a wagon. Two women and two young fellows. Keep the old woman busy, sergeant. If this is another flop, you won't catch me standing out in this April wind any more.

[*A Jew's harp*[3] *is heard. Drawn by two young men, a covered wagon approaches. In the wagon sit Mother Courage and her mute daughter Kattrin*]

MOTHER COURAGE. Good morning, sergeant.

SERGEANT. [*Barring the way*] Good morning, friends. Who are you?

MOTHER COURAGE. Business people. [*Sings*]

Hey, Captains, make the drum stop drumming
And let your soldiers take a seat.
Here's Mother Courage, with boots she's coming
To help along their aching feet.
How can they march off to the slaughter
With baggage, cannon, lice and fleas
Across the rocks and through the water
Unless their boots are in one piece?
  The spring is come. Christian, revive![4]
  The snowdrifts melt. The dead lie dead.
  And if by chance you're still alive
  It's time to rise and shake a leg.

O Captains, don't expect to send them
To death with nothing in their crops.
First you must let Mother Courage mend them
In mind and body with her schnapps.[5]
On empty bellies it's distressing
To stand up under shot and shell.
But once they're full, you have my blessing
To lead them to the jaws of hell.
  The spring is come. Christian, revive!
  The snowdrifts melt, the dead lie dead.
  And if by chance you're still alive
  It's time to rise and shake a leg.

THE SERGEANT. Halt, you scum. Where do you belong?

THE ELDER SON. Second Finnish Regiment.

---

3. A small, twangy instrument held against the teeth, associated with country music.

4. The phrase in German parodies re-ligious announcements of Easter and Christ's resurrection.

5. Liquor, especially gin. (The original says *wein*, or wine.)

THE SERGEANT. Where are your papers?

MOTHER COURAGE. Papers?

THE YOUNGER SON. But she's Mother Courage!

THE SERGEANT. Never heard of her. Why Courage?

MOTHER COURAGE. They call me Courage, sergeant, because when I saw ruin staring me in the face I drove out of Riga through cannon fire with fifty loaves of bread in my wagon. They were getting moldy, it was high time, I had no choice.

THE SERGEANT. No wisecracks. Where are your papers?

MOTHER COURAGE. [*Fishing a pile of papers out of a tin box and climbing down*] Here are my papers sergeant. There's a whole missal, picked it up in Alt-Ötting[6] to wrap cucumbers in, and a map of Moravia, God knows if I'll ever get there, if I don't it's total loss. And this here certifies that my horse hasn't got hoof-and-mouth disease, too bad, he croaked on us, he cost fifteen guilders,[7] but not out of my pocket, glory be. Is that enough paper?

THE SERGEANT. Are you trying to pull my leg? I'll teach you to get smart. You know you need a license.

MOTHER COURAGE. You mind your manners and don't go telling my innocent children that I'd go anywhere near your leg, it's indecent. I want no truck with you. My license in the Second Regiment is my honest face, and if you can't read it, that's not my fault. I'm not letting anybody put his seal on it.

THE RECRUITER. Sergeant, I detect a spirit of insubordination in this woman. In our camp we need respect for authority.

MOTHER COURAGE. Wouldn't sausage be better?

THE SERGEANT. Name.

MOTHER COURAGE. Anna Fierling.

THE SERGEANT. Then you're all Fierlings?

MOTHER COURAGE. What do you mean? Fierling is my name. Not theirs.

THE SERGEANT. Aren't they all your children?

MOTHER COURAGE. That they are, but why should they all have the same name? [*Pointing at the elder son*] This one, for instance. His name is Eilif Nojocki. How come? Because his father always claimed to be called Kojocki or Mojocki. The boy remembers him well, except the one he remembers was somebody else, a Frenchman with a goatee. But aside from that, he inherited his father's intelligence; that man could strip the pants off a peasant's ass without his knowing it. So, you see, we've each got our own name.

THE SERGEANT. Each different, you mean?

MOTHER COURAGE. Don't act so innocent.

THE SERGEANT. I suppose that one's a Chinaman? [*Indicating the younger son*]

MOTHER COURAGE. Wrong. He's Swiss.

---

6. A place of pilgrimage fifty miles east of Munich in the south German kingdom of Bavaria. *Missal*: Prayer book.

7. The basic unit of Dutch money, also called a *florin*. When Brecht was writing; one guilder was worth about twenty-five cents.

THE SERGEANT. After the Frenchman?

MOTHER COURAGE. What Frenchman? I never heard of any French-man. Don't get everything balled up or we'll be here all day. He's Swiss, but his name is Fejos, the name has nothing to do with his father. He had an entirely different name, he was an engineer, built fortifications, but he drank.

[*Swiss Cheese nods, beaming; the mute Kattrin is also tickled*]

THE SERGEANT. Then how can his name be Fejos?

MOTHER COURAGE. I wouldn't want to offend you, but you haven't got much imagination. Naturally his name is Fejos because when he came I was with a Hungarian, it was all the same to him, he was dying of kidney trouble though he never touched a drop, a very decent man. The boy takes after him

THE SERGEANT. But you said he wasn't his father?

MOTHER COURAGE. He takes after him all the same. I call him Swiss Cheese, how come, because he's good at pulling the wagon. [*Pointing at her daughter*] Her name is Kattrin Haupt, she's half German.

THE SERGEANT. A fine family, I must say.

MOTHER COURAGE. Yes, I've been all over the world with my wagon.

THE SERGEANT. It's all being taken down. [*He takes it down*] You're from Bamberg,[8] Bavaria. What brings you here?

MOTHER COURAGE. I couldn't wait for the war to kindly come to Bamberg.

THE RECRUITER. You wagon pullers ought to be called Jacob Ox and Esau Ox.[9] Do you ever get out of harness?

EILIF. Mother, can I clout him one on the kisser? I'd like to.

MOTHER COURAGE. And I forbid you. You stay put. And now, gen-tlemen, wouldn't you need a nice pistol, or a belt buckle, yours is all worn out, sergeant.

THE SERGEANT. I need something else. I'm not blind. Those young fellows are built like tree trunks, big broad chests, sturdy legs. Why aren't they in the army? That's what I'd like to know.

MOTHER COURAGE. [*Quickly*] Nothing doing, sergeant. My chil-dren aren't cut out for soldiers.

THE RECRUITER. Why not? There's profit in it, and glory. Peddling shoes is woman's work. [*To Eilif*] Step up; let's feel if you've got muscles or if you're a sissy.

MOTHER COURAGE. He's a sissy. Give him a mean look and he'll fall flat on his face.

THE RECRUITER. And kill a calf if it happens to be standing in the way. [*Tries to lead him away*]

MOTHER COURAGE. Leave him alone, He's not for you.

THE RECRUITER. He insulted me. He referred to my face as a kisser. Him and me will now step out in the field and discuss this thing as man to man.

EILIF. Don't worry, mother. I'll take care of him.

8. German city of northern Bavaria.   25-7.]
9. Biblical twin brothers. [*Genesis*

MOTHER COURAGE. You stay put. You no-good! I know you, always fighting. He's got a knife in his boot, he's a knifer.

THE RECRUITER. I'll pull it out of him like a milk tooth. Come on, boy.

MOTHER COURAGE. Sergeant, I'll report you to the colonel. He'll throw you in the lock-up. The lieutenant is courting my daughter.

THE SERGEANT. No rough stuff, brother. [*To Mother Courage*] What have you got against the army? Wasn't his father a soldier? Didn't he die fair and square? You said so yourself.

MOTHER COURAGE. He's only a child. You want to lead him off to slaughter, I know you. You'll get five guilders for him.

THE RECRUITER. He'll get a beautiful cap and top boots.

EILIF. Not from you.

MOTHER COURAGE. Oh, won't you come fishing with me? said the fisherman to the worm. [*To Swiss Cheese*] Run and yell that the they're trying to steal your brother. [*She pulls a knife*] Just try to steal him. I'll cut you down, you dogs. I'll teach you to put him in your war! We do an honest business in ham and shirts, we're peaceful folk.

THE SERGEANT. I can see by the knife how peaceful you are. You ought to be ashamed of yourself, put that knife away, you bitch. A minute ago you admitted you lived off war, how else would you live, on what? How can you have a war without soldiers?

MOTHER COURAGE. It doesn't have to be my children.

THE SERGEANT. I see. You'd like the war to eat the core and spit out the apple. You want your brood to batten on war, tax-free. The war can look out for itself, is that it? You call yourself Courage, eh? And you're afraid of the war that feeds you. Your sons aren't afraid of it, I can see that.

EILIF. I'm not afraid of any war.

THE SERGEANT. Why should you be? Look at me: Has the soldier's life disagreed with me? I was seventeen when I joined up.

MOTHER COURAGE. You're not seventy yet.

THE SERGEANT. I can wait.

MOTHER COURAGE. Sure. Under ground.

THE SERGEANT. Are you trying to insult me? Telling me I'm going to die?

MOTHER COURAGE. But suppose it's the truth? I can see the mark on you. You look like a corpse on leave.

SWISS CHEESE. She's got second sight. Everybody says so. She can tell the future.

THE RECRUITER. Then tell the sergeant his future. It might amuse him.

THE SERGEANT. I don't believe in that stuff.

MOTHER COURAGE. Give me your helmet. [*He gives it to her*]

THE SERGEANT. It doesn't mean any more than taking a shit in the grass. But go ahead for the laugh.

MOTHER COURAGE. [*Takes a sheet of parchment and tears it in two*] Eilif, Swiss Cheese, Kattrin: That's how we'd all be torn apart if we got mixed up too deep in the war. [*To the sergeant*]

Seeing it's you, I'll do it for nothing. I make a black cross on this piece. Black is death.

SWISS CHEESE. She leaves the other one blank. Get it?

MOTHER COURAGE. Now I fold them, and now I shake them up together. Same as we're all mixed up together from the cradle to the grave. And now you draw, and you'll know the answer.

[*The sergeant hesitates*]

THE RECRUITER. [*To Eilif*] I don't take everybody, I'm known to be picky and choosey, but you've got spirit, I like that.

THE SERGEANT. [*Fishing in the helmet*] Damn foolishness! Hocus-pocus!

SWISS CHEESE. He's pulled a black cross. He's through.

THE RECRUITER. Don't let them scare you, there's not enough bullets for everybody.

THE SERGEANT. [*Hoarsely*] You've fouled me up.

MOTHER COURAGE. You fouled yourself up the day you joined the army. And now we'll be going, there isn't a war every day, I've got to take advantage.

THE SERGEANT. Hell and damnation! Don't try to hornswoggle me. We're taking your bastard to be a soldier.

EILIF. I'd like to be a soldier, mother.

MOTHER COURAGE. You shut your trap, you Finnish devil.

EILIF. Swiss Cheese wants to be a soldier too.

MOTHER COURAGE. That's news to me. I'd better let you draw too, all three of you. [*She goes to the rear to mark crosses on slips of parchment*]

THE RECRUITER. [*To Eilif*] It's been said to our discredit that a lot of religion goes on in the Swedish camp, but that's slander to blacken our reputation. Hymn singing only on Sunday, one verse! And only if you've got a voice.

MOTHER COURAGE. [*Comes back with the slips in the sergeant's helmet*] Want to sneak away from their mother, the devils, and run off to war like calves to a salt lick. But we'll draw lots on it, then they'll see that the world is no vale of smiles[10] with a "Come along, son, we're short on generals." Sergeant, I'm very much afraid they won't come through the war. They've got terrible characters, all three of them. [*She holds out the helmet to Eilif*] There. Pick a slip. [*He picks one and unfolds it. She snatches it away from him*] There you have it. A cross! Oh, unhappy mother that I am, Oh, mother of sorrows. Has he got to die? Doomed to perish in the springtime of his life? If he joins the army, he'll bite the dust, that's sure. He's too brave, just like his father. If he's not smart, he'll go the way of all flesh, the slip proves it. [*She roars at him*] Are you going to be smart?

EILIF. Why not?

MOTHER COURAGE. The smart thing to do is to stay with your mother, and if they make fun of you and call you a sissy, just laugh.

THE RECRUITER. If you're shitting in your pants, we'll take your brother.

---

10. Parodying the traditional description of this world as a "vale of tears."

MOTHER COURAGE. I told you to laugh. Laugh! And now you pick, Swiss Cheese. I'm not so worried about you, you're honest. [*He picks a slip*] Oh! Why, have you got that strange look? It's got to be blank. There can't be a cross on it. No, I can't lose you. [*She takes the slip*] A cross? Him too? Maybe it's because he's so stupid. Oh, Swiss Cheese, you'll die too, unless you're very honest the whole time, the way I've taught you since you were a baby, always bringing back the change when I sent you to buy bread. That's the only way you can save yourself. Look sergeant, isn't that a black cross?

THE SERGEANT. It's a cross all right. I don't see how I could have pulled one. I always stay in the rear. [*To the recruiter*] It's on the up and up. Her own get it too.

SWISS CHEESE. I get it too. But I can take a hint.

MOTHER COURAGE. [*To Kattrin*] Now you're the only one I'm sure of, you're a cross yourself[11] because you've got a good heart. [*She holds up the helmet to Kattrin in the wagon, but she herself takes out the slip*] It's driving me to despair. It can't be right, maybe I mixed them wrong. Don't be too good-natured, Kattrin, don't, there's a cross on your path too. Always keep very quiet, that ought to be easy seeing you're dumb. Well, now you know. Be careful, all of you, you'll need to be. And now we'll climb up and drive on. [*She returns the sergeant's helmet and climbs up into the wagon*]

THE RECRUITER. [*To the sergeant*] Do something!

THE SERGEANT. I'm not feeling so good.

THE RECRUITER. Maybe you caught cold when you took your helmet off in the wind. Tell her you want to buy something. Keep her busy. [*Aloud*] You could at least take a look at that buckle, sergeant. After all, selling things is these good people's living. Hey, you, the sergeant wants to buy that belt buckle.

MOTHER COURAGE. Half a guilder. A buckle like that is worth two guilders. [*She climbs down*]

THE SERGEANT. It's not new. This wind! I can't examine it here. Let's go where it's quiet. [*He goes behind the wagon with the buckle*]

MOTHER COURAGE. I haven't noticed any wind.,

THE SERGEANT. Maybe it is worth half a guilder. It's silver.

MOTHER COURAGE. [*Joins him behind the wagon*] Six solid ounces.

THE RECRUITER. [*To Eilif*] And then we'll have a drink, just you and me. I've got your enlistment bonus right here. Come on.

[*Eilif stands undecided*]

MOTHER COURAGE. All right. Half a guilder.

THE SERGEANT. I don't get it. I always stay in the rear. There's no safer place for a sergeant. You can send the men up forward to win glory. You've spoiled my dinner. It won't go down, I know it, not a bite.

MOTHER COURAGE. Don't take it to heart. Don't let it spoil your appetite. Just keep behind the lines. Here, take a drink of schnapps, man. [*She hands him the bottle*]

11. I.e., a heavy burden.

THE RECRUITER. [*Has taken Eilif's arm and is pulling him away toward the rear*] A bonus of ten guilders, and you'll be a brave man and you'll fight for the king, and the women will tear each other's hair out over you. And you can clout me one on the kisser for insulting you. [*Both go out*]

[*Mute Kattrin jumps down from the wagon and emits raucous sounds*]

MOTHER COURAGE. Just a minute, Kattrin, Just a minute. The sergeant's paying up. [*Bites the half guilder*] I'm always suspicious of money. I'm a burnt child, sergeant. But your coin is good. And now we'll be going. Where's Eilif?

SWISS CHEESE. He's gone with the recruiter.

MOTHER COURAGE. [*Stands motionless, then*] You simple soul. [*To Kattrin*] I know. You can't talk, you couldn't help it.

THE SERGEANT. You could do with a drink yourself, mother. That's the way it goes. Soldiering isn't the worst thing in the world. You want to live off the war, but you want to keep you and yours out of it. Is that it?

MOTHER COURAGE. Now you'll have to pull with your brother, Kattrin.

[*Brother and sister harness themselves to the wagon and start pulling. Mother Courage walks beside them. The wagon rolls off*]

THE SERGEANT. [*Looking after them*]
If you want the war to work for you
You've got to give the war its due.

2

In 1625 and 1626 Mother Courage crosses Poland in the train of the Swedish armies. Outside the fortress of Wallhof[1] she meets her son again.—A capon is successfully sold, the brave son's fortunes are at their zenith.

The general's tent.

Beside it the kitchen. The thunder of cannon. The cook is arguing with Mother Courage, who is trying to sell him a capon.

THE COOK. Sixty hellers[2] for that pathetic bird?

MOTHER COURAGE. Pathetic bird? You mean this plump beauty? Are you trying to tell me that a general who's the biggest eater for miles around—God help you if you haven't got anything for his dinner—can't afford a measly sixty hellers?

THE COOK. I can get a dozen like it for ten hellers right around the corner.

MOTHER COURAGE. What, you'll find a capon like this right around the corner? With a siege on and everybody so starved you can see right through them. Maybe you'll scare up a rat, maybe, I say, 'cause they've all been eaten, I've seen five men chasing a

1. *in the train*: I.e., with the supplies and baggage at the end of the line of march. Wallhof: Fictional city.

2. A small coin formerly used in Austria and Germany.

starved rat for hours. Fifty hellers for a giant capon in the middle of a siege.

THE COOK. We're not besieged; they are. We're the besiegers, can't you get that through your head?

MOTHER COURAGE. But we haven't got anything to eat either, in fact we've got less than the people in the city. They've hauled it all inside. I hear their life is one big orgy. And look at us. I've been around to the peasants, they haven't got a thing.

THE COOK. They've got plenty. They hide it.

MOTHER COURAGE. [*Triumphantly*] Oh, no! They're ruined, that's what they are. They're starving. I've seen them. They're so hungry they're digging up roots. They lick their fingers when they've eaten a boiled strap. That's the situation. And here I've got a capon and I'm supposed to let it go for forty hellers.

THE COOK. Thirty, not forty. Thirty, I said.

MOTHER COURAGE. It's no common capon. They tell me this bird was so talented that he wouldn't eat unless they played music, he had his own favorite march. He could add and subtract, that's how intelligent he was. And you're trying to tell me forty hellers is too much. The general will bite your head off if there's nothing to eat.

THE COOK. You know what I'm going to do? [*He takes a piece of beef and sets his knife to it*] Here I've got a piece of beef. I'll roast it. Think it over. This is your last chance.

MOTHER COURAGE. Roast and be damned. It's a year old.

THE COOK. A day old. That ox was running around only yesterday afternoon, I saw him with my own eyes.

MOTHER COURAGE. Then he must have stunk on the hoof.

THE COOK. I'll cook it five hours if I have to. We'll see if it's still tough. [*He cuts it*]

MOTHER COURAGE. Use plenty of pepper, maybe the general won't notice the stink.

[*The general, a chaplain and Eilif enter the tent*]

THE GENERAL. [*Slapping Eilif on the back*] All right, son, into your general's tent you go, you'll sit at my right hand. You've done a heroic deed and you're a pious trooper, because this is a war of religion and what you did was done for God, that's what counts with me. I'll reward you with a gold bracelet when I take the city. We come here to save their souls and what do those filthy, shameless peasants do? They drive their cattle away. And they stuff their priests with meat, front and back. But you taught them a lesson. Here's a tankard of red wine for you. [*He pours*] We'll down it in one gulp. [*They do so*] None for the chaplain, he's got his religion. What would you like for dinner, sweetheart?

EILIF. A scrap of meat. Why not?

THE GENERAL. Cook! Meat!

THE COOK. And now he brings company when there's nothing to eat.

[*Wanting to listen, Mother Courage makes him stop talking*]

EILIF. Cutting down peasants whets the appetite.

MOTHER COURAGE. God, it's my Eilif.

THE COOK. Who?

MOTHER COURAGE. My eldest. I haven't seen hide nor hair of him in two years, he was stolen from me on the highway. He must be in good if the general invites him to dinner, and what have you got to offer? Nothing. Did you hear what the general's guest wants for dinner? Meat! Take my advice, snap up this capon. The price is one guilder.

THE GENERAL. [*Has sat down with Eilif. Bellows*] Food, Lamb, you lousy, no-good cook, or I'll kill you.

THE COOK. All right, hand it over. This is extortion.

MOTHER COURAGE. I thought it was a pathetic bird.

THE COOK. Pathetic is the word. Hand it over. Fifty hellers! It's highway robbery

MOTHER COURAGE. One guilder, I say. For my eldest son, the general's honored guest, I spare no expense.

THE COOK. [*Gives her the money*] Then pluck it at least while I make the fire.

MOTHER COURAGE. [*Sits down to pluck the capon*] Won't he be glad to see me! He's my brave, intelligent son. I've got a stupid one too, but he's honest. The girl's a total loss. But at least she doesn't talk, that's something.

THE GENERAL. Take another drink, son, it's my best Falerno,[3] I've only got another barrel or two at the most, but it's worth it to see that there's still some true faith in my army. The good shepherd here just looks on, all he knows how to do is preach. Can he do anything? No. And now, Eilif my son, tell us all about it, how cleverly you hoodwinked those peasants and captured those twenty head of cattle. I hope they'll be here soon.

EILIF. Tomorrow. Maybe the day after.

MOTHER COURAGE. Isn't my Eilif considerate, not bringing those oxen in until tomorrow, or you wouldn't have even said hello to my capon.

EILIF. Well, it was like this: I heard the peasants were secretly— mostly at night—rounding up the oxen they'd hidden in a certain forest. The city people had arranged to come and get them. I let them round the oxen up, I figured they'd find them easier than I would. I made my men ravenous for meat, put them on short rations for two days until their mouths watered if they even heard a word beginning with *me* . . . like measles.

THE GENERAL. That was clever of you.

EILIF. Maybe. The rest was a pushover. Except the peasants had clubs and there were three times more of them and they fell on us like bloody murder. Four of them drove me into a clump of bushes, they knocked my sword out of my hand and yelled: Surrender! Now what'll I do, I says to myself, they'll make hash out of me.

3. A famous wine made from grapes grown in Falerno in Italy.

THE GENERAL. What did you do?

EILIF. I laughed.

THE GENERAL. You laughed?

EILIF. I laughed. Which led to a conversation. The first thing you know, I'm bargaining. Twenty guilders is too much for that ox, I say, how about fifteen? Like I'm meaning to pay. They're flummoxed, they scratch their heads. Quick, I reach for my sword and mow them down. Necessity knows no law. See what I mean?

THE GENERAL. What do you say to that, shepherd?

CHAPLAIN. Strictly speaking, that maxim is not in the Bible. But our Lord was able to turn five loaves into five hundred.[4] So there was no question of poverty; he could tell people to love their neighbors because their bellies were full. Nowadays it's different.

THE GENERAL. [*Laughs*] Very different. All right, you Pharisee,[5] take a swig. [*To Eilif*] You mowed them down, splendid, so my fine troops could have a decent bite to eat. Doesn't the Good Book say: "Whatsoever thou doest for the least of my brethren, thou doest for me"?[6] And what have you done for them? You've got them a good chunk of beef for their dinner. They're not used to moldy crusts; in the old days they had a helmetful of white bread and wine before they went out to fight for God.

EILIF. Yes, I reached for my sword and I mowed them down.

THE GENERAL. You're a young Caesar. You deserve to see the king.

EILIF. I have, in the distance. He shines like a light. He's my ideal.

THE GENERAL. You're something like him already, Eilif. I know the worth of a brave soldier like you. When I find one, I treat him like my own son. [*He leads him to the map*] Take a look at the situation, Eilif; we've still got a long way to go.

MOTHER COURAGE. [*Who has been listening starts plucking her capon furiously*] He must be a rotten general.

THE COOK. Eats like a pig, but why rotten?

MOTHER COURAGE. Because he needs brave soldiers, that's why. If he planned his campaigns right, what would he need brave soldiers for? The run-of-the-mill would do. Take it from me, whenever you find a lot of virtues, it shows that something's wrong.

THE COOK. I'd say it proves that something is all right.

MOTHER COURAGE. No, that something's wrong. See, when a general or a king is real stupid and leads his men up shit creek, his troops need courage, that's a virtue. If he's stingy and doesn't hire enough soldiers, they've all got to be Herculeses. And if he's a slob and lets everything go to pot, they've got to be as sly as serpents or they're done for. And if he's always expecting too much of them, they need an extra dose of loyalty. A country that's run right, or a good king or a good general, doesn't need any of these virtues. You don't need virtues in a decent country, the people

4. Reference to the episode in the Gospels when Jesus fed five thousand people with five loaves and two fishes. [See *Matthew* 15:33 ff.]

5. Biblical: Religious hyprocrite, quibbler on religious doctrine.

6. Spoken by Jesus in the Gospels. [See *Matthew* 25:40 ff.]

can all be perfectly ordinary, medium-bright, and cowards too for my money.

THE GENERAL. I bet your father was a soldier.

EILIF. A great soldier, I'm told. My mother warned me about it. Makes me think of a song.

THE GENERAL. Sing it! [*Bellowing*] Where's that food!

EILIF. It is called: The Song of the Old Wife and the Soldier.
[*He sings, doing a war dance with his saber*]

A gun or a pike[7] they can kill who they like
And the torrent will swallow a wader
You had better think twice before battling with ice
Said the old wife to the soldier.
Cocking his rifle he leapt to his feet
Laughing for joy as he heard the drum beat
The wars cannot hurt me, he told her.
He shouldered his gun and he picked up his knife
To see the wide world. That's the soldier's life.
Those were the words of the soldier.

Ah, deep will they lie who wise counsel defy
Learn wisdom from those that are older
Oh, don't venture too high or you'll fall from the sky
Said the old wife to the soldier.
But the young soldier with knife and with gun
Only laughed a cold laugh and stepped into the run.
The water can't hurt me, he told her.
And when the moon on the rooftop shines white
We'll be coming back. You can pray for that night.
Those were the words of the soldier.

MOTHER COURAGE. [*In the kitchen, continues the song, beating a pot with a spoon*]

Like the smoke you'll be gone and no warmth linger on
And your deeds only leave me the colder!
Oh, see the smoke race. Oh, dear God keep him safe!
That's what she said of the soldier.

EILIF. What's that?

MOTHER COURAGE. [*Goes on singing*]

And the young soldier with knife and with gun
Was swept from his feet till he sank in the run
And the torrent swallowed the waders.
Cold shone the moon on the rooftop white
But the soldier was carried away with the ice
And what was it she heard from the soldiers?

7. Long spear used by the infantry.

> Like the smoke he was gone and no warmth lingered on
> And his deeds only left her the colder.
> Ah, deep will they lie who wise counsel defy!
> That's what she said to the soldiers.

THE GENERAL. What do they think they're doing in my kitchen?

EILIF. [*Has gone into the kitchen. He embraces his mother*] Mother! It's you! Where are the others?

MOTHER COURAGE. [*In his arms*] Snug as a bug in a rug. Swiss Cheese is paymaster of the Second Regiment; at least he won't be fighting, I couldn't keep him out altogether.

EILIF. And how about your feet?

MOTHER COURAGE. Well, it's hard getting my shoes on in the morning.

THE GENERAL. [*Has joined them*] Ah, so you're his mother. I hope you've got more sons for me like this fellow here.

EILIF. Am I lucky! There you're sitting in the kitchen hearing your son being praised.

MOTHER COURAGE. I heard it all right! [*She gives him a slap in the face*]

EILIF. [*Holding his cheek*] For capturing the oxen?

MOTHER COURAGE. No. For not surrendering when the four of them were threatening to make hash out of you! Didn't I teach you to take care of yourself? You Finnish devil!

[*The general and the chaplain laugh*]

3

Three years later Mother Courage and parts of a Finnish[1] regiment are taken prisoner. She is able to save her daughter and her wagon, but her honest son dies.

Army camp.

Afternoon. On a pole the regimental flag. Mother Courage has stretched a clothesline between her wagon, on which all sorts of merchandise is hung in display, and a large cannon. She and Kattrin are folding washing and piling it on the cannon. At the same time she is negotiating with an ordnance officer[2] over a sack of bullets. Swiss Cheese, now in the uniform of a paymaster, is looking on. A pretty woman, Yvette Pottier, is sitting with a glass of brandy in front of her, sewing a gaudy-colored hat. She is in her stocking feet, her red high-heeled shoes are on the ground beside her.

THE ORDNANCE OFFICER. I'll let you have these bullets for two guilders. It's cheap, I need the money, because the colonel's been drinking with the officers for two days and we're out of liquor.

MOTHER COURAGE. That's ammunition for the troops. If it's found

---

1. Finland was under Swedish rule at this time.

2. Officer in charge of weapons, particularly explosives.

here, I'll be court-martialed. You punks sell their bullets and the men have nothing to shoot at the enemy.

THE ORDNANCE OFFICER. Don't be hard-hearted, you scratch my back, I'll scratch yours.

MOTHER COURAGE. I'm not taking any army property. Not at that price.

THE ORDNANCE OFFICER. You can sell it for five guilders, maybe eight, to the ordnance officer of the Fourth before the day is out, if you're quiet about it and give him a receipt for twelve. He hasn't an ounce of ammunition left.

MOTHER COURAGE. Why don't you do it yourself?

THE ORDNANCE OFFICER. Because I don't trust him, he's a friend of mine.

MOTHER COURAGE. [*Takes the sack*] Hand it over. [*To Kattrin*] Take it back there and pay him one and a half guilders. [*In response to the ordnance officer's protest*] One and a half guilders, I say. [*Kattrin drags the sack behind the wagon, the ordnance officer follows her. Mother Courage to Swiss Cheese*] Here's your underdrawers, take good care of them, this is October, might be coming on fall, I don't say it will be, because I've learned that nothing is sure to happen the way we think, not even the seasons. But whatever happens, your regimental funds have to be in order. Are your funds in order?

SWISS CHEESE. Yes, mother.

MOTHER COURAGE. Never forget that they made you paymaster because you're honest and not brave like your brother, and especially because you're too simple-minded to get the idea of making off with the money. That's a comfort to me. And don't go mislaying your drawers.

SWISS CHEESE. No, mother. I'll put them under my mattress.
        [*Starts to go*]

ORDNANCE OFFICER. I'll go with you, paymaster.

MOTHER COURAGE. Just don't teach him any of your tricks.
        [*Without saying good-bye the ordnance officer goes out with Swiss Cheese*]

YVETTE. [*Waves her hand after the ordnance officer*] You might say good-bye officer.

MOTHER COURAGE. [*To Yvette*] I don't like to see those two together. He's not the right kind of company for my Swiss Cheese. But the war's getting along pretty well. More countries are joining in all the time, it can go on for another four, five years, easy. With a little planning ahead, I can do good business if I'm careful. Don't you know you shouldn't drink in the morning with your sickness?.

YVETTE. Who says I'm sick, it's slander.

MOTHER COURAGE. Everybody says so.

YVETTE. Because they're all liars. Mother Courage, I'm desperate. They all keep out of my way like I'm a rotten fish on account of those lies. What's the good of fixing my hat? [*She throws it down*] That's why I drink in the morning, I never used to, I'm getting crow's-feet, but it doesn't matter now. In the Second Finnish Regiment they all know me. I should have stayed home when my first love walked out on me. Pride isn't for the likes of us. If we can't put up with shit, we're through.

MOTHER COURAGE. Just don't start in on your Pieter and how it all happened in front of my innocent daughter.

YVETTE. She's just the one to hear it, it'll harden her against love.

MOTHER COURAGE. Nothing can harden them.

YVETTE. Then I'll talk about it because it makes me feel better. It begins with my growing up in fair Flanders, because if I hadn't I'd never have laid eyes on him and I wouldn't be here in Poland now, because he was an army cook, blond, a Dutchman, but skinny. Kattrin, watch out for the skinny ones, but I didn't know that then, and another thing I didn't know is that he had another girl even then, and they all called him Pete the Pipe, because he didn't even take his pipe out of his mouth when he was doing it, that's all it meant to him. [*She sings the Song of Fraternization*]

When I was only sixteen
The foe came into our land.
He laid aside his saber
And with a smile he took my hand.
  After the May parade
  The May light starts to fade.
  The regiment dressed by the right[3]
  Then drums were beaten, that's the drill.[4]
  The foe took us behind the hill
  And fraternized all night.

There were so many foes came
And mine worked in the mess.[5]
I loathed him in the daytime.
At night I loved him none the less.
  After the May parade
  The May light starts to fade.
  The regiment dressed by the right
  Then drums were beaten, that's the drill.
  The foe took us behind the hill
  And fraternized all night.

The love which came upon me
Was wished on me by fate.
My friends could never grasp why
I found it hard to share their hate.

---

3. I.e., each man aligned himself with the man on his right to form straight ranks for the parade.

4. I.e., that's the usual thing.

5. The kitchen.

The fields were wet with dew
When sorrow first I knew.
The regiment dressed by the right
Then drums were beaten, that's the drill.
And then the foe, my lover still
Went marching from our sight.

Well, I followed him, but I never found him. That was five years ago. [*She goes behind the wagon with an unsteady gait*]

MOTHER COURAGE. You've left your hat.

YVETTE. Anybody that wants it can have it.

MOTHER COURAGE. Let that be a lesson to you, Kattrin. Have no truck with soldiers. It's love that makes the world go round, so you'd better watch out. Even with a civilian it's no picnic. He says he'd kiss the ground you put your little feet on, talking of feet, did you wash yours yesterday, and then you're his slave. Be glad you're dumb, that way you'll never contradict yourself or want to bite your tongue off because you've told the truth, it's a gift of God to be dumb. Here comes the general's cook, I wonder what he wants.

[*The cook and the chaplain enter*]

THE CHAPLAIN. I've got a message for you from your son Eilif. The cook here thought he'd come along, he's taken a shine to you.

THE COOK. I only came to get a breath of air.

MOTHER COURAGE. You can always do that here if you behave, and if you don't, I can handle you. Well, what does he want? I've got no money to spare.

THE CHAPLAIN. Actually he wanted me to see his brother, the paymaster.

MOTHER COURAGE. He's not here any more, or anywhere else either. He's not his brother's paymaster. I don't want him leading him into temptation and being smart at his expense [*Gives him money from the bag slung around her waist*] Give him this, it's a sin, he's speculating on mother love and he ought to be ashamed.

THE COOK. He won't do it much longer, then he'll be marching off with his regiment, maybe to his death, you never can tell. Better make it a little more, you'll be sorry later. You women are hard-hearted, but afterwards you're sorry. A drop of brandy wouldn't have cost much when it was wanted, but it wasn't given, and later, for all you know, he'll be lying in the cold ground and you can't dig him up again.

THE CHAPLAIN. Don't be sentimental, cook. There's nothing wrong with dying in battle, it's a blessing, and I'll tell you why. This is a war of religion. Not a common war, but a war for the faith, and therefore pleasing to God.

THE COOK. That's a fact. In a way you could call it a war, because of the extortion and killing and looting, not to mention a bit of rape, but it's a war of religion, which makes it different from all other wars, that's obvious. But it makes a man thirsty all the same, you've got to admit that.

THE CHAPLAIN. [*To Mother Courage, pointing at the cook*] I tried to discourage him, but he says you've turned his head, he sees you in his dreams.

THE COOK. [*Lights a short-stemmed pipe*] All I want is a glass of brandy from your fair hand, nothing more sinful. I'm already so shocked by the jokes the chaplain's been telling me, I bet I'm still red in the face.

MOTHER COURAGE. And him a clergyman! I'd better give you fellows something to drink or you'll be making me immoral propositions just to pass the time.

THE CHAPLAIN. This is temptation, said the deacon, and succumbed to it. [*Turning toward Kattrin as he leaves*] And who is this delightful young lady?

MOTHER COURAGE. She's not delightful, she's a respectable young lady.

> [*The chaplain and the cook go behind the wagon with Mother Courage. Kattrin looks after them, then she walks away from the washing and approaches the hat. She picks it up, sits down and puts on the red shoes. From the rear Mother Courage is heard talking politics with the chaplain and the cook*]

MOTHER COURAGE. The Poles here in Poland shouldn't have butted in. All right, our king marched his army into their country. But instead of keeping the peace, the Poles start butting into their own affairs and attack the king while he's marching quietly through the landscape. That was a breach of the peace and the blood is on their head.

THE CHAPLAIN. Our king had only one thing in mind; freedom. The emperor had everybody under his yoke, the Poles as much as the Germans; the king had to set them free.

THE COOK. I see it this way, your brandy's first-rate, I can see why I liked your face, but we were talking about the king. This freedom he was trying to introduce into Germany cost him a fortune, he had to levy a salt tax in Sweden, which, as I said, cost the poor people a fortune. Then he had to put the Germans in jail and break them on the rack because they liked being the emperor's slaves. Oh yes, the king made short shrift of anybody that didn't want to be free. In the beginning he only wanted to protect Poland against wicked people, especially the emperor, but the more he ate the more he wanted, and pretty soon he was protecting all of Germany.[6] But the Germans didn't take it lying down and the king got nothing but trouble for all his kindness and expense, which he naturally had to defray from taxes, which made for bad blood, but that didn't discourage him. He had one

---

6. Allusion to Hitler's expansion of German territory allegedly to protect German-speaking peoples, first in Bo- hemia and then, in 1938, through the annexation of Austria.

thing in his favor, the word of God, which was lucky, because otherwise people would have said he was doing it all for himself and what he hoped to get out of it. As it was, he always had a clear conscience and that was all he really cared about.

MOTHER COURAGE. It's easy to see you're not a Swede, or you wouldn't talk like that about the Hero-King.

THE CHAPLAIN. You're eating his bread, aren't you?

THE COOK. I don't eat his bread, I bake it.

MOTHER COURAGE. He can't be defeated because his men believe in him. [*Earnestly*] When you listen to the big wheels talk, they're making war for reasons of piety, in the name of everything that's fine and noble. But when you take another look, you see that they're not so dumb; they're making war for profit. If they weren't, the small fry like me wouldn't have anything to do with it.[7]

THE COOK. That's a fact.

THE CHAPLAIN. And it wouldn't hurt you as a Dutchman to take a look at that flag up there before you express opinions in Poland.

MOTHER COURAGE. We're all good Protestants here! Prosit![8] [*Kattrin has started strutting about with Yvette's hat on, imitating Yvette's gait.*]

> [*Suddenly cannon fire and shots are heard. Drums. Mother Courage, the cook and the chaplain run out from behind the wagon, the two men still with glasses in hand. The ordnance officer and a soldier rush up to the cannon and try to push it away*]

MOTHER COURAGE. What's going on? Let me get my washing first, you lugs. [*She tries to rescue her washing*]

THE ORDNANCE OFFICER. The Catholics. They're attacking. I don't know as we'll get away. [*To the soldier*] Get rid of the gun! [*Runs off*]

THE COOK. Christ, I've got to find the general. Courage, I'll be back for a little chat in a day or two. [*Rushes out*]

MOTHER COURAGE. Stop, you've forgotten your pipe.

THE COOK. [*From the distance*] Keep it for me! I'll need it.

MOTHER COURAGE. Just when we were making a little money!

THE CHAPLAIN. Well, I guess I'll be going too. It might be dangerous though, with the enemy so close. Blessed are the peaceful[9] is the best motto in wartime. If only I had a cloak to cover up with.

MOTHER COURAGE. I'm not lending any cloaks, not on your life. I've had bitter experience in that line.

THE CHAPLAIN. But my religion puts me in special danger.

MOTHER COURAGE. [*Bringing him a cloak*] It's against my better conscience. And now run along.

---

7. The German expression can also be translated, "Wouldn't be doing the same thing."

8. Cheers!

9. A parody of Jesus' Sermon on the Mount: "Blessed are the peacemakers, for they shall be called sons of God." [*Matthew* 5:9.]

THE CHAPLAIN. Thank you kindly, you've got a good heart. But maybe I'd better sit here a while. The enemy might get suspicious if they see me running.

MOTHER COURAGE. [*To the soldier*] Leave it lay, you fool, you won't get paid extra. I'll take care of it for you, you'd only get killed.

THE SOLDIER. [*Running away*] I tried. You're my witness.

MOTHER COURAGE. I'll swear it on the Bible. [*Sees her daughter with the hat*] What are you doing with that floozy hat? Take it off, have you gone out of your mind? Now of all times, with the enemy on top of us? [*She tears the hat off Kattrin's head*] You want them to find you and make a whore out of you? And those shoes! Take them off, you woman of Babylon![10] [*She tries to pull them off*] Jesus Christ, chaplain, make her take those shoes off! I'll be right back. [*She runs to the wagon*]

YVETTE. [*Enters, powdering her face*] What's this I hear? The Catholics are coming? Where is my hat? Who's been stamping on it? I can't be seen like this if the Catholics are coming. What'll they think of me? I haven't even got a mirror. [*To the chaplain*] How do I look? Too much powder?

THE CHAPLAIN. Just right.

YVETTE. And where are my red shoes? [*She doesn't see them because Kattrin hides her feet under her skirt*] I left them here. I've got to get back to my tent. In my bare feet. It's disgraceful! [*Goes out*]

[*Swiss Cheese runs in carrying a small box*]

MOTHER COURAGE. [*Comes out with her hands full of ashes. To Kattrin*] Ashes. [*To Swiss Cheese*] What you got there?

SWISS CHEESE. The regimental funds.

MOTHER COURAGE. Throw it away! No more paymastering for you.

SWISS CHEESE. I'm responsible for it. [*He goes rear*]

MOTHER COURAGE. [*To the chaplain*] Take your clergyman's coat off, chaplain, or they'll recognize you, cloak or no cloak. [*She rubs Kattrin's face with ashes*] Hold still! There. With a little dirt you'll be safe. What a mess! The sentries were drunk. Hide your light under a bushel,[11] as the Good Book says. When a soldier, especially a Catholic, sees a clean face, she's a whore before she knows it. Nobody feeds them for weeks. When they finally loot some provisions, the next thing they want is women. That'll do it. Let me look at you. Not bad. Like you'd been wallowing in a pigsty. Stop shaking. You're safe now. [*To Swiss Cheese*] What did you do with the cashbox?

SWISS CHEESE. I thought I'd put it in the wagon.

MOTHER COURAGE. [*Horrified*] What! In my wagon? Of all the sinful stupidity! If my back is turned for half a second! They'll hang us all!

10. Sinful woman. The ancient Asian city of Babylon is a Biblical locus for sin and decadence: "Babylon the great, mother of harlots and of earth's abominations. [*Revelations* 17:5.]

11. Also parodies the Sermon on the Mount: "Nor do men light a lamp and put it under a bushel [basket] but on a stand, and it gives light to all in the house." [*Matthew* 5:15.]

SWISS CHEESE. Then I'll put it somewhere else, or I'll run away with it.

MOTHER COURAGE. You'll stay right here. It's too late.

THE CHAPLAIN. [*Still changing, comes forward*] Heavens, the flag!

MOTHER COURAGE. [*Takes down the regimental flag*] Bozhe moi![12] I'm so used to it I don't see it. Twenty-five years I've had it.

[*The cannon fire grows louder*]

[*Morning, three days later. The cannon is gone. Mother Courage, Kattrin, the chaplain and Swiss Cheese are sitting dejectedly over a meal*]

SWISS CHEESE. This is the third day I've been sitting here doing nothing; the sergeant has always been easy on me, but now he must be starting to wonder: where can Swiss Cheese be with the cashbox?

MOTHER COURAGE. Be glad they haven't tracked you down.

THE CHAPLAIN. What about me? I can't hold a service here either. The Good Book says: "Whosoever hath a full heart, his tongue runneth over."[13] Heaven help me if mine runneth over.

MOTHER COURAGE. That's the way it is. Look what I've got on my hands: one with a religion and one with a cashbox. I don't know which is worse.

THE CHAPLAIN. Tell yourself that we're in the hands of God.

MOTHER COURAGE. I don't think we're that bad off, but all the same I can't sleep at night. If it weren't for you, Swiss Cheese, it'd be easier. I think I've put myself in the clear. I told them I was against the antichrist;[14] he's a Swede with horns, I told them, and I'd noticed the left horn was kind of worn down. I interrupted the questioning to ask where I could buy holy candles cheap. I knew what to say because Swiss Cheese's father was a Catholic and he used to make jokes about it. They didn't really believe me, but their regiment had no provisioner, so they looked the other way. Maybe we stand to gain. We're prisoners, but so are lice on a dog.

THE CHAPLAIN. This milk is good. Though there's not very much of it or of anything else. Maybe we'll have to cut down on our Swedish appetites. But such is the lot of the vanquished.

MOTHER COURAGE. Who's vanquished? Victory and defeat don't always mean the same thing to the big wheels up top and the small fry underneath. Not by a long shot. In some cases defeat is a blessing to the small fry. Honor's lost, but nothing else. One time in Livonia[15] our general got such a shellacking from the

12. My God! [Polish and Russian expression.]
13. "Out of the abundance of the heart the mouth speaketh," Biblical proverb meaning that one's words reflect the good or evil in one's heart. [Jesus to the Pharisees, *Matthew* 12:34.]
14. Figure of evil, whose appearance on earth is supposed to prefigure the end of the world and the coming of the Last Judgment.
15. Region of the east Baltic, now part of the U.S.S.R.

enemy that in the confusion I laid hands on a beautiful white horse from the baggage train. That horse pulled my wagon for seven months, until we had a victory and they checked up. On the whole, you can say that victory and defeat cost us plain people plenty. The best thing for us is when politics gets bogged down. [*To Swiss Cheese*] Eat!

SWISS CHEESE. I've lost my appetite. How's the sergeant going to pay the men?

MOTHER COURAGE. Troops never get paid when they're running away.

SWISS CHEESE. But they've got it coming to them. If they're not paid, they don't need to run. Not a step.

MOTHER COURAGE. Swiss Cheese, you're too conscientious, it almost frightens me. I brought you up to be honest, because you're not bright, but somewhere it's got to stop. And now me and the chaplain are going to buy a Catholic flag and some meat. Nobody can buy meat like the chaplain, he goes into a trance and heads straight for the best piece, I guess it makes his mouth water and that shows him the way. At least they let me carry on my business. Nobody cares about a shopkeeper's religion, all they want to know is the price. Protestant pants are as warm as any other kind.

THE CHAPLAIN. Like the friar[16] said when somebody told him the Lutherans were going to stand the whole country on its head. They'll always need beggars, he says. [*Mother Courage disappears into the wagon*] But she's worried about that cashbox. They've taken no notice of us so far, they think we're all part of the wagon, but how long can that go on?

SWISS CHEESE. I can take it away.

THE CHAPLAIN. That would be almost more dangerous. What if somebody sees you? They've got spies. Yesterday morning, just as I'm relieving myself, one of them jumps out of the ditch. I was so scared I almost let out a prayer. That would have given me away. I suppose they think they can tell a Protestant by the smell of his shit. He was a little runt with a patch over one eye.

MOTHER COURAGE. [*Climbing down from the wagon with a basket*] Look what I've found. You shameless slut! [*She hold up the red shoes triumphantly*] Yvette's red shoes! She's swiped them in cold blood. It's your fault. Who told her she was a delightful young lady? [*She puts them into the basket*] I'm giving them back. Stealing Yvette's shoes! She ruins herself for money, that I can understand. But you'd like to do it free of charge, for pleasure. I've told you, you'll have to wait for peace. No soldiers! Just wait for peace with your worldly ways.

THE CHAPLAIN. She doesn't seem very worldly to me.

MOTHER COURAGE. Too worldly for me. In Dalarna she was like a stone, which is all they've got around there. The people used to say: We don't see the cripple. That's the way I like it. That way

16. A mendicant or beggar monk.

she's safe. [*To Swiss Cheese*] You leave that box where it is, hear? And keep an eye on your sister, she needs it. The two of you will be the death of me. I'd sooner take care of a bag of fleas. [*She goes off with the chaplain. Kattrin starts clearing away the dishes*]

SWISS CHEESE. Won't be many more days when I can sit in the sun in my shirtsleeves. [*Kattrin points to a tree*] Yes, the leaves are all yellow. [*Kattrin asks him, by means of gestures, whether he wants a drink*] Not now. I'm thinking. [*Pause*] She says she can't sleep. I'd better get the cashbox out of here, I've found a hiding place. All right, get me a drink. [*Kattrin goes behind the wagon*] I'll hide it in the rabbit hole down by the river until I can take it away. Maybe late tonight. I'll go get it and take it to the regiment. I wonder how far they've run in three days? Won't the sergeant be surprised! Well, Swiss Cheese, this is a pleasant disappointment, that's what he'll say. I trust you with the regimental cashbox and you bring it back.

[*As Kattrin comes out from behind the wagon with a glass of brandy, she comes face to face with two men. One is a sergeant. The other removes his hat and swings it through the air in a ceremonious greeting. He has a patch over one eye*]

THE MAN WITH THE PATCH. Good morning, my dear. Have you by any chance seen a man from the headquarters of the Second Finnish Regiment?

[*Scared out of her wits, Kattrin runs front, spilling the brandy. The two exchange looks and withdraw after seeing Swiss Cheese sitting there*]

SWISS CHEESE. [*Starting up from his thoughts*] You've spilled half of it. What's the fuss about? Poke yourself in the eye? I don't understand you. I'm getting out of here, I've made up my mind, it's best. [*He stands up. She does everything she can think of to call his attention to the danger. He only evades her*] I wish I could understand you. Poor thing, I know you're trying to tell me something, you just can't say it. Don't worry about spilling the brandy, I'll be drinking plenty more. What's one glass? [*He takes the cashbox out of the wagon and hides it under his jacket*] I'll be right back. Let me go, you're making me angry. I know you mean well. If only you could talk.

[*When she tries to hold him back, he kisses her and tears himself away. He goes out. She is desperate, she races back and forth, uttering short inarticulate sounds. The chaplain and Mother Courage come back. Kattrin gesticulates wildly at her mother*]

MOTHER COURAGE. What's the matter? You're all upset. Has somebody hurt you? Where's Swiss Cheese? Tell it to me in order, Kattrin. Your mother understands you. What, the no-good's taken the cashbox? I'll hit him over the head with it, the sneak. Take your time, don't talk nonsense, use your hands, I don't like it when you howl like a dog, what will the chaplain think? It gives him the creeps. A one-eyed man?

THE CHAPLAIN. The one-eyed man is a spy. Did they arrest Swiss Cheese? [*Kattrin shakes her head and shrugs her shoulders*] We're done for.

MOTHER COURAGE. [*Takes a Catholic flag out of her basket. The chaplain fastens it to the flagpole*] Hoist the new flag!

THE CHAPLAIN. [*Bitterly*] All good Catholics here.

[*Voices are heard from the rear. The two men bring in Swiss Cheese*]

SWISS CHEESE. Let me go, I haven't got anything. Stop twisting my shoulder, I'm innocent.

THE SERGEANT. He belongs here. You know each other.

MOTHER COURAGE. What makes you think that?

SWISS CHEESE. I don't know them. I don't even know who they are. I had a meal here, it cost me ten hellers. Maybe you saw me sitting here, it was too salty.

THE SERGEANT. Who are you anyway?

MOTHER COURAGE. We're respectable people. And it's true. He had a meal here. He said it was too salty.

THE SERGEANT. Are you trying to tell me you don't know each other?

MOTHER COURAGE. Why should I know him? I don't know everybody. I don't ask people what their name is or if they're heathens; if they pay, they're not heathens. Are you a heathen?

SWISS CHEESE. Of course not.

THE CHAPLAIN. He ate his meal and he behaved himself. He didn't open his mouth except when he was eating. Then you have to.

THE SERGEANT. And who are you?

MOTHER COURAGE. He's only my bartender. You gentlemen must be thirsty, I'll get you a drink of brandy, you must be hot and tired.

THE SERGEANT. We don't drink on duty. [*To Swiss Cheese*] You were carrying something. You must have hidden it by the river. You had something under your jacket when you left here.

MOTHER COURAGE. Was it really him?

SWISS CHEESE. I think you must have seen somebody else. I saw a man running with something under his jacket. You've got the wrong man.

MOTHER COURAGE. That's what I think too, it's a misunderstanding. These things happen. I'm a good judge of people. I'm Mother Courage, you've heard of me, everybody knows me. Take it from me, this man has an honest face.

THE SERGEANT. We're looking for the cashbox of the Second Finnish Regiment. We know what the man in charge of it looks like. We've been after him for two days. You're him.

SWISS CHEESE. I'm not.

THE SERGEANT. Hand it over. If you don't you're a goner, you know that. Where is it?

MOTHER COURAGE. [*With urgency*] He'd hand it over, wouldn't he, knowing he was a goner if he didn't? I've got it, he'd say, take it, you're stronger. He's not that stupid. Speak up, you stupid idiot, the sergeant's giving you a chance.

SWISS CHEESE. But I haven't got it.

THE SERGEANT. In that case come along. We'll get it out of you. [*They lead him away*]

MOTHER COURAGE. [*Shouts after them*] He'd tell you. He's not that stupid. And don't twist his shoulder off! [*Runs after them*] [*The same evening. The chaplain and mute Kattrin are washing dishes and scouring knives*]

THE CHAPLAIN. That boy's in trouble. There are cases like that in the Bible. Take the Passion of our Lord and Savior. There's an old song about it. [*He sings the Song of the Hours*]

In the first hour Jesus mild
Who had prayed since even[17]
Was betrayed and led before
Pontius[18] the heathen.

Pilate found him innocent
Free from fault and error.
Therefore, having washed his hands
Sent him to King Herod.

In the third hour he was scourged
Stripped and clad in scarlet
And a plaited crown of thorns
Set upon his forehead.

On the Son of Man they spat
Mocked him and made merry.
Then the cross of death was brought
Given him to carry.

At the sixth hour with two thieves
To the cross they nailed him
And the people and the thieves
Mocked him and reviled him.

This is Jesus King of Jews
Cried they in derision
Till the sun withdrew its light
From that awful vision.

At the ninth hour Jesus wailed
Why hast thou me forsaken?

17. Evening.
18. Pontius Pilate: Roman judge be- fore whom Jesus was arraigned by the Scribes. [*Matthew* 27:1–24.]

Soldiers brought him vinegar
Which he left untaken.

Then he yielded up the ghost
And the earth was shaken.
Rended was the temple's veil[19]
And the saints were wakened.

Soldiers broke the two thieves' legs
As the night descended
Thrust a spear in Jesus' side
When his life had ended.

Still they mocked, as from his wound
Flowed the blood and water
Thus blasphemed the Son of Man
With their cruel laughter.

MOTHER COURAGE. [*Enters in a state of agitation*] His life's at
stake. But they say the sergeant will listen to reason. Only it
mustn't come out that he's our Swiss Cheese, or they'll say we've
been giving him aid and comfort. All they want is money. But
where will we get the money? Hasn't Yvette been here? I met her
just now, she's latched onto a colonel, he's thinking of buying her
a provisioner's business.

THE CHAPLAIN. Are you really thinking of selling?

MOTHER COURAGE. How else can I get the money for the sergeant?

THE CHAPLAIN. But what will you live on?

MOTHER COURAGE. That's the hitch.

[*Yvette Pottier comes in with a doddering colonel*]

YVETTE. [*Embracing Mother Courage*] My dear Mother Courage. Here we are again! [*Whispering*] He's willing. [*Aloud*]
This is my dear friend who advises me on business matters. I just
chanced to hear that you wish to sell your wagon, due to circumstances. I might be interested.

MOTHER COURAGE. Mortgage it, not sell it, let's not be hasty. It's
not so easy to buy a wagon like this in wartime.

YVETTE. [*Disappointed*] Only mortgage it? I thought you wanted
to sell it. In that case, I don't know if I'm interested. [*To the
colonel*] What do you think?

THE COLONEL. Just as you say, my dear.

MOTHER COURAGE. It's only being mortgaged.

YVETTE. I thought you needed money.

MOTHER COURAGE. [*Firmly*] I need the money, but I'd rather run
myself ragged looking for an offer than sell now. The wagon is
our livelihood. It's an opportunity for you, Yvette, God knows

19. Matthew reports that at the moment of Jesus' death, the veil or curtain in the temple ·which set off the sanc-
tuary was torn from top to bottom; the
earth shook, and dead men rose from
their graves. [*Matthew* 27:51–3.]

when you'll find another like it and have such a good friend to advise you. See what I mean?

YVETTE. My friend thinks I should snap it up, but I don't know. If it's only being mortgaged . . . Don't you agree that we ought to buy?

THE COLONEL. Yes, my dear.

MOTHER COURAGE. Then you'll have to look for something that's for sale, maybe you'll find something if you take your time and your friend goes around with you. Maybe in a week or two you'll find the right thing.

YVETTE. Then we'll go looking, I love to go looking for things, and I love to go around with you, Poldi,[20] it's a real pleasure. Even if it takes two weeks. When would you pay the money back if you get it?

MOTHER COURAGE. I can pay it back in two weeks, maybe one.

YVETTE. I can't make up my mind, Poldi, chéri,[21] tell me what to do. [*She takes the colonel aside*] I know she's got to sell, that's definite. The lieutenant, you know who I mean, the blond one, he'd be glad to lend me the money. He's mad about me, he says I remind him of somebody. What do you think?

THE COLONEL. Keep away from that lieutenant. He's no good. He'll take advantage. Haven't I told you I'd buy you something, pussy-kins?

YVETTE. I can't accept it from you. But then if you think the lieutenant might take advantage . . . Poldi, I'll accept it from you.

THE COLONEL. I hope so.

YVETTE. Your advice is to take it?

THE COLONEL. That's my advice.

YVETTE. [*Goes back to Mother Courage*] My friend advises me to do it. Write me out a receipt, say the wagon belongs to me complete with stock and furnishings when the two weeks are up. We'll take inventory right now, then I'll bring you the two hundred guilders. [*To the colonel*] You go back to camp, I'll join you in a little while, I've got to take inventory, I don't want anything missing from my wagon. [*She kisses him. He leaves. She climbs up in the wagon*] I don't see very many boots.

MOTHER COURAGE. Yvette. This is no time to inspect your wagon if it is yours. You promised to see the sergeant about my Swiss Cheese, you've got to hurry. They say he's to be court-martialed in an hour.

YVETTE. Just let me count the shirts.

MOTHER COURAGE. [*Pulls her down by the skirt*] You hyena, it's Swiss Cheese, his life's at stake. And don't tell anybody where the offer comes from, in heaven's name say it's your gentleman friend, or we'll all get it, they'll say we helped him.

YVETTE. I've arranged to meet One-Eye in the woods, he must be there already.

20. Pet name for Leopold.　　　21. Darling.

THE CHAPLAIN. And there's no need to start out with the whole two hundred, offer a hundred and fifty, that's plenty.

MOTHER COURAGE. Is it your money? You just keep out of this. Don't worry, you'll get your bread and soup. Go on now and don't haggle. It's his life. [*She gives Yvette a push to start her on her way*]

THE CHAPLAIN. I didn't mean to butt in, but what are we going to live on? You've got an unemployable daughter on your hands.

MOTHER COURAGE. You muddlehead, I'm counting on the regimental cashbox. They'll allow for his expenses, won't they?

THE CHAPLAIN. But will she handle it right?

MOTHER COURAGE. It's in her own interest. If I spend her two hundred, she gets the wagon. She's mighty keen on it, how long can she expect to hold on to her colonel? Kattrin, you scour the knives, use pumice. And you, don't stand around like Jesus on the Mount of Olives,[22] bestir yourself, wash those glasses, we're expecting at least fifty for dinner, and then it'll be the same old story: "Oh my feet, I'm not used to running around, I don't run around in the pulpit." I think they'll set him free. Thank God they're open to bribery. They're not wolves, they're human and out for money. Bribe-taking in humans is the same as mercy in God. It's our only hope. As long as people take bribes, you'll have mild sentences and even the innocent will get off once in a while.

YVETTE. [*Comes in panting*] They want two hundred. And we've got to be quick. Or it'll be out of their hands. I'd better take One-Eye to see my colonel right away. He confessed that he'd had the cashbox, they put the thumb screws on him. But he threw it in the river when he saw they were after him. The box is gone. Should I run and get the money from my colonel?

MOTHER COURAGE. The box is gone? How will I get my two hundred back?

YVETTE. Ah, so you thought you could take it out of the cashbox? You thought you'd put one over on me. Forget it. If you want to save Swiss Cheese, you'll just have to pay, or maybe you'd like me to drop the whole thing and let you keep your wagon?

MOTHER COURAGE. This is something I hadn't reckoned with. But don't rush me, you'll get the wagon, I know it's down the drain, I've had it for seventeen years. Just let me think a second, it's all so sudden. What'll I do, I can't give them two hundred, I guess you should have bargained. If I haven't got a few guilders to fall back on, I'll be at the mercy of the first Tom, Dick, or Harry. Say I'll give them a hundred and twenty, I'll lose my wagon anyway.

YVETTE. They won't go along. One-Eye's in a hurry, he's so keyed-up he keeps looking behind him. Hadn't I better give them the whole two hundred?

MOTHER COURAGE. [*In despair*] I can't do it. Thirty years I've worked. She's twenty-five and no husband. I've got her to keep too. Don't needle me, I know what I'm doing. Say a hundred

---

22. The ridge of hills outside Jerusalem where Jesus waited after the Last Supper to be captured and taken before the high priest.

and twenty or nothing doing.

YVETTE. It's up to you. [*Goes out quickly*]

    [*Mother Courage looks neither at the chaplain nor at her daughter. She sits down to help Kattrin scour the knives*]

MOTHER COURAGE. Don't break the glasses. They're not ours any more. Watch what you're doing, you'll cut yourself. Swiss Cheese will be back, I'll pay two hundred if I have to. You'll have your brother. With eighty guilders we can buy a peddler's pack and start all over. Worse things have happened.

THE CHAPLAIN. The Lord will provide.

MOTHER COURAGE. Rub them dry. [*They scour the knives in silence. Suddenly Kattrin runs sobbing behind the wagon*]

YVETTE. [*Comes running*] They won't go along. I warned you. One-Eye wanted to run out on me, he said it was no use. He said we'd hear the drums any minute, meaning he'd been sentenced. I offered a hundred and fifty. He didn't even bother to shrug his shoulders. When I begged and pleaded, he promised to wait till I'd spoken to you again.

MOTHER COURAGE. Say I'll give him the two hundred. Run. [*Yvette runs off. They sit in silence. The chaplain has stopped washing the glasses*]

Maybe I bargained too long. [*Drums are heard in the distance. The chaplain stands up and goes to the rear. Mother Courage remains seated. It grows dark. The drums stop. It grows light again. Mother Courage has not moved*]

YVETTE. [*Enters, very pale*] Now you've done it with your haggling and wanting to keep your wagon. Eleven bullets he got, that's all. I don't know why I bother with you any more, you don't deserve it. But I've picked up a little information. They don't believe the cashbox is really in the river. They suspect it's here and they think you were connected with him. They're going to bring him here, they think maybe you'll give yourself away when you see him. I'm warning you: You don't know him, or you're all dead ducks. I may as well tell you, they're right behind me. Should I keep Kattrin out of the way? [*Mother Courage shakes her head*] Does she know? Maybe she didn't hear the drums or maybe she didn't understand.

MOTHER COURAGE. She knows. Get her.

    [*Yvette brings Kattrin, who goes to her mother and stands beside her. Mother Courage takes her by the hand. Two soldiers come in with a stretcher on which something is lying under a sheet. The sergeant walks beside them. They set the stretcher down*]

THE SERGEANT. We've got a man here and we don't know his name. We need it for the records. He had a meal with you. Take a look, see if you know him. [*He removes the sheet*] Do you know him? [*Mother Courage shakes her head*] What? You'd never seen him before he came here for a meal? [*Mother Courage shakes her head*] Pick him up. Throw him on the dump. Nobody knows him. [*They carry him away*]

Mother Courage sings the Song of the Great Capitula-
tion.⁴

Outside an officer's tent.

Mother Courage is waiting. A clerk looks out of the tent.

THE CLERK. I know you. You had a Protestant paymaster at your
place, he was hiding. I wouldn't put in any complaints if I were
you.

MOTHER COURAGE. I'm putting in a complaint. I'm innocent. If I
take this lying down, it'll look as if I had a guilty conscience.
First they ripped up my whole wagon with their sabers, then they
wanted me to pay a fine of five talers¹ for no reason at all.

THE CLERK. I'm advising you for your own good: Keep your trap
shut. We haven't got many provisioners and we'll let you keep on
with your business, especially if you've got a guilty conscience
and pay a fine now and then.

MOTHER COURAGE. I'm putting in a complaint.

THE CLERK. Have it your way. But you'll have to wait till the captain can see you. [*Disappears into the tent*]

A YOUNG SOLDIER. [*Enters in a rage*] Bouque la Madonne!² Where's
that stinking captain? He embezzled my reward and now he's
drinking it up with his whores. I'm going to get him!

AN OLDER SOLDIER. [*Comes running after him*] Shut up. They'll
put you in the stocks!

THE YOUNG SOLDIER. Come on out, you crook! I'll make chops out
of you. Embezzling my reward! Who jumps in the river? Not
another man in the whole squad, only me. And I can't even buy
myself a beer. I won't stand for it. Come on out and let me cut
you to pieces!

THE OLDER SOLDIER. Holy Mary! He'll ruin himself.

MOTHER COURAGE. They didn't give him a reward?

THE YOUNG SOLDIER. Let me go. I'll run you through too, the more
the merrier.

THE OLDER SOLDIER. He saved the colonel's horse and they didn't
give him a reward. He's young, he hasn't been around long.

MOTHER COURAGE. Let him go, he's not a dog, you don't have to tie
him up. Wanting a reward is perfectly reasonable. Why else
would he distinguish himself?

THE YOUNG SOLDIER. And him drinking in there! You're all a lot of
yellowbellies. I distinguished myself and I want my reward.

MOTHER COURAGE. Young man, don't shout at me. I've got my own
worries and besides, go easy on your voice, you may need it.
You'll be hoarse when the captain comes out, you won't be able
to say boo and he won't be able to put you in the stocks till
you're blue in the face. People that yell like that don't last long,
maybe half an hour, then they're so exhausted you have to sing

---

1. German silver coins.　　　　2. Screw the Virgin!

them to sleep.

THE YOUNG SOLDIER. I'm not exhausted and who wants to sleep? I'm hungry. They make our bread out of acorns and hemp seed, and they skimp on that. He's whoring away my reward and I'm hungry. I'll murder him.

MOTHER COURAGE. I see. You're hungry. Last year your general made you cut across the fields to trample down the grain. I could have sold a pair of boots for ten guilders if anybody'd had ten guilders and if I'd had any boots. He thought he'd be someplace else this year, but now he's still here and everybody's starving. I can see that you might be good and mad.

THE YOUNG SOLDIER. He can't do this to me, save your breath, I won't put up with injustice.

MOTHER COURAGE. You're right, but for how long? How long won't you put up with injustice? An hour? Two hours? You see, you never thought of that, though it's very important, because it's miserable in the stocks when it suddenly dawns on you that you *can* put up with injustice.

THE YOUNG SOLDIER. I don't know why I listen to you. Bouque la Madonne! Where's the captain?

MOTHER COURAGE. You listen to me because I'm not telling you anything new. You know your temper has gone up in smoke, it was a short temper and you need a long one, but that's a hard thing to come by.

THE YOUNG SOLDIER. Are you trying to say I've no right to claim my reward?

MOTHER COURAGE. Not at all. I'm only saying your temper isn't long enough, it won't get you anywhere. Too bad. If you had a long temper, I'd even egg you on. Chop the bastard up, that's what I'd say, but suppose you don't chop him up, because your tail's drooping and you know it. I'm left standing there like a fool and the captain takes it out on me.

THE OLDER SOLDIER. You're right. He's only blowing off steam.

THE YOUNG SOLDIER. We'll see about that. I'll cut him to pieces. [*He draws his sword*] When he comes, I'll cut him to pieces.

THE CLERK. [*Looks out*] The captain will be here in a moment. Sit down

[*The young soldier sits down*]

MOTHER COURAGE. There he sits. What did I tell you? Sitting, aren't you? Oh, they know us like a book, they know how to handle us. Sit down! And down we sit. You can't start a riot sitting down. Better not stand up again, you won't be able to stand the way you were standing before. Don't be embarrassed on my account, I'm no better, not a bit of it. We were full of piss and vinegar, but they've bought it off. Look at me. No back talk, it's bad for business. Let me tell you about the great capitulation. [*She sings the Song of the Great Capitulation*][3]

3. Mother Courage punctuates the story of her own gradual disillusionment with proverbs and common sayings that represent a folk wisdom of successful adjustment.

When I was young, no more than a spring chicken
I too thought that I was really quite the cheese
(No common peddler's daughter, not I with my looks and my
    talent and striving for higher things!)
One little hair in the soup would make me sicken
And at me no man would dare to sneeze.
(It's all or nothing, no second best for me. I've got what it
    takes, the rules are for somebody else!)
But a chickadee
Sang wait and see!
    And you go marching with the show
    In step, however fast or slow
    And rattle off your little song:
    It won't be long.
    And then the whole thing slides.
    You think God provides—
    But you've got it wrong.

And before one single year had wasted
I had learned to swallow down the bitter brew
(Two kinds on my hands and the price of bread and who do they
    take me for anyway!)
Man, the double-edged shellacking that I tasted
On my ass and knees I was when they were through.
(You've got to get along with people, one good turn deserves
    another, no use trying to ram your head through the wall!)
And the chickadee
Sang wait and see!
    And she goes marching with the show
    In step, however fast or slow
    And rattles off her little song:
    It won't be long.
    And then the whole thing slides
    You think God provides—
    But you've got it wrong.

I've seen many fired by high ambition
No star's big or high enough to reach out for.
(It's ability that counts, where there's a will there's a way, one
    way or another, we'll swing it!)
Then while moving mountains they get a suspicion
That to wear a straw hat is too big a chore.
(No use being too big for your britches!)
And the chickadee
Sings wait and see!
    And they go marching with the show
    In step, however fast or slow
    And rattle off their little song:
    It won't be long.

And then the whole thing slides!
You think God provides—
But you've got it wrong!

MOTHER COURAGE. [*To the young soldier*] So here's what I think:
Stay here with your sword if your anger's big enough, I know
you have good reason, but if it's a short quick anger, better make
tracks!

THE YOUNG SOLDIER. Kiss my ass! [*He staggers off, the older soldier
after him*]

THE CLERK. [*Sticking his head out*] The captain is here. You can
put in your complaint now.

MOTHER COURAGE. I've changed my mind. No complaint. [*She
goes out*]

5

Two years have passed. The war has spread far and wide.
With scarcely a pause Mother Courage's little wagon rolls
through Poland, Moravia, Bavaria, Italy, and back again to
Bavaria in 1631. Tilly's victory at Magdeburg[1] costs Mother
Courage four officers' shirts.

Mother Courage's wagon has stopped in a devastated village.

*Thin military music is heard from the distance. Two soldiers at
the bar are being waited on by Kattrin and Mother Courage. One
of them is wearing a lady's fur coat over his shoulders.*

MOTHER COURAGE. What's that? You can't pay? No money, no
schnapps. Plenty of victory marches for the Lord but no pay for
the men.

THE SOLDIER. I want my schnapps. I came too late for the looting.
The general skunked us: permission to loot the city for exactly
one hour. Says he's not a monster; the mayor must have paid
him.

THE CHAPLAIN. [*Staggers in*] There's still some wounded in the
house. The peasant and his family. Help me, somebody, I need
linen.

[*The second soldier goes out with him. Kattrin gets very
excited and tries to persuade her mother to hand out
linen*

MOTHER COURAGE. I haven't got any. The regiment's bought up all
my bandages. You think I'm going to rip up my officers' shirts for
the likes of them?

THE CHAPLAIN. [*Calling back*] I need linen, I tell you.

MOTHER COURAGE. [*Sitting down on the wagon steps to keep Kat-*

1. City eighty miles west of Berlin, besieged by the Imperial Army in 1630.

trin out] Nothing doing. They don't pay, they got nothing to
pay with.

THE CHAPLAIN. [*Bending over a woman whom he has carried out*]
Why did you stay here in all that gunfire?

THE PEASANT WOMAN. [*Feebly*] Farm.

MOTHER COURAGE. You won't catch them leaving their property.
And I'm expected to foot the bill. I won't do it.

THE FIRST SOLDIER. They're Protestants. Why do they have to be
Protestants?

MOTHER COURAGE. Religion is the least of their worries. They've
lost their farm.

THE SECOND SOLDIER. They're no Protestants. They're Catholics like
us.

THE FIRST SOLDIER. How do we know who we're shooting at?

A PEASANT. [*Whom the Chaplain brings in*] They got my arm.

THE CHAPLAIN. Where's the linen?

> [*All look at Mother Courage, who does not move*]

MOTHER COURAGE. I can't give you a thing. What with all my
taxes, duties, fees and bribes! [*Making guttural sounds, Kattrin
picks up a board and threatens her mother with it*] Are you
crazy? Put that board down, you slut, or I'll smack you. I'm not
giving anything, you can't make me, I've got to think of myself.
[*The chaplain picks her up from the step and puts her down on
the ground. Then he fishes out some shirts and tears them into
strips*]
My shirts! Half a guilder apiece! I'm ruined!

> [*The anguished cry of a baby is heard from the house*]

THE PEASANT. The baby's still in there!

> [*Kattrin runs in*]

THE CHAPLAIN. [*To the woman*] Don't move. They're bringing
him out.

MOTHER COURAGE. Get her out of there. The roof'll cave in.

THE CHAPLAIN. I'm not going in there again.

MOTHER COURAGE. [*Torn*] Don't run hog-wild with my expensive linen.

> [*Kattrin emerges from the ruins carrying an infant*]

MOTHER COURAGE. Oh, so you've found another baby to carry
around with you? Give that baby back to its mother this minute,
or it'll take me all day to get it away from you. Do you hear me?
[*To the second soldier*] Don't stand there gaping, go back and
tell them to stop that music, I can see right here that they've
won a victory. Your victory's costing me a pretty penny.

> [*Kattrin rocks the baby in her arms, humming a lullaby*]

MOTHER COURAGE. There she sits, happy in all this misery; give it
back this minute, the mother's coming to. [*She pounces on the
first soldier who has been helping himself to the drinks and is
now making off with the bottle*] Pshagreff![2] Beast! Haven't
you had enough victories for today? Pay up.

2. Son of a bitch! (Polish)

FIRST SOLDIER. I'm broke.

MOTHER COURAGE. [*Tears the fur coat off him*] Then leave the coat here, it's stolen anyway.

THE CHAPLAIN. There's still somebody in there.

6

Outside Ingolstadt[1] in Bavaria Mother Courage attends the funeral of Tilly, the imperial field marshal. Conversations about heroes and the longevity of the war. The chaplain deplores the waste of his talents. Mute Kattrin gets the red shoes. 1632.

Inside Mother Courage's tent.

A bar open to the rear. Rain. In the distance drum rolls and funeral music. The chaplain and the regimental clerk are playing a board game. Mother Courage and her daughter are taking inventory.

THE CHAPLAIN. The procession's starting.

MOTHER COURAGE. It's a shame about the general—socks: twenty-two pairs—I hear he was killed by accident. On account of the fog in the fields. He's up front encouraging the troops. "Fight to the death, boys," he sings out. Then he rides back, but he gets lost in the fog and rides back forward. Before you know it he's in the middle of the battle and stops a bullet—lanterns: we're down to four. [*A whistle from the rear. She goes to the bar*] You men ought to be ashamed, running out on your late general's funeral! [*She pours drinks*]

THE CLERK. They shouldn't have been paid before the funeral. Now they're getting drunk instead.

THE CHAPLAIN. [*To the clerk*] Shouldn't you be at the funeral?

THE CLERK. In this rain?

MOTHER COURAGE. With you it's different, the rain might spoil your uniform. It seems they wanted to ring the bells, naturally, but it turned out the churches had all been shot to pieces by his orders, so the poor general won't hear any bells when they lower him into his grave. They're going to fire a three-gun salute instead, so it won't be too dull—seventeen sword belts.

CRIES. [*From the bar*] Hey! Brandy!

MOTHER COURAGE. Money first! No, you can't come into my tent with your muddy boots! You can drink outside, rain or no rain. [*To the clerk*] I'm only letting officers in. It seems the general had been having his troubles. Mutiny in the Second Regiment because he hadn't paid them. It's a war of religion, he says, should they profit by their faith?

[*Funeral march. All look to the rear*]

1. City forty miles north of Munich.

THE CHAPLAIN. Now they're marching past the body.

MOTHER COURAGE. I feel sorry when a general or an emperor passes away like this, maybe he thought he'd do something big, that posterity would still be talking about and maybe put up a statue in his honor, conquer the world, for instance, that's a nice ambition for a general, he doesn't know any better. So he knocks himself out, and then the common people come and spoil it all, because what do they care about greatness, all they care about is a mug of beer and maybe a little company. The most beautiful plans have been wrecked by the smallness of the people that are supposed to carry them out. Even an emperor can't do anything by himself, he needs the support of his soldiers and his people. Am I right?

THE CHAPLAIN. [*Laughing*] Courage, you're right, except about the soldiers. They do their best. With those fellows out there, for instance, drinking their brandy in the rain. I'll undertake to carry on one war after another for a hundred years, two at once if I have to, and I'm not a general by trade.

MOTHER COURAGE. Then you don't think the war might stop?

THE CHAPLAIN. Because the general's dead? Don't be childish. They grow by the dozen, there'll always be plenty of heroes.

MOTHER COURAGE. Look here, I'm not asking you for the hell of it. I've been wondering whether to lay in supplies while they're cheap, but if the war stops, I can throw them out the window.

THE CHAPLAIN. I understand. You want a serious answer. There have always been people who say: "The war will be over some day." I say there's no guarantee the war will ever be over. Naturally a brief intermission is conceivable. Maybe the war needs a breather, a war can even break its neck, so to speak. There's always a chance of that, nothing is perfect here below. Maybe there never will be a perfect war, one that lives up to all our expectations. Suddenly, for some unforeseen reason, a war can bog down, you can't think of everything. Some little oversight and your war's in trouble. And then you've got to pull it out of the mud. But the kings and emperors, not to mention the pope, will always come to its help in adversity. On the whole, I'd say this war has very little to worry about, it'll live to a ripe old age.

A SOLDIER. [*Sings at the bar*]

A drink, and don't be slow!
A soldier's got to go
And fight for his religion.

Make it double, this is a holiday.

MOTHER COURAGE. If I could only be sure . . .

THE CHAPLAIN. Figure it out for yourself. What's to stop the war?

THE SOLDIER. [*Sings*]

Your breasts, girl, don't be slow!
A soldier's got to go
And ride away to Pilsen.[2]

THE CLERK. [*Suddenly*] But why can't we have peace? I'm from
Bohemia, I'd like to go home when the time comes.
THE CHAPLAIN. Oh, you'd like to go home? Ah, peace! What
becomes of the hole when the cheese has been eaten?
THE SOLDIER. [*Sings*]

Play cards, friends, don't be slow!
A soldier's got to go
No matter if it's Sunday.

A prayer, priest, don't be slow!
A soldier's got to go
And die for king and country.

THE CLERK. In the long run nobody can live without peace.
THE CHAPLAIN. The way I see it, war gives you plenty of peace. It
has its peaceful moments. War meets every need, including the
peaceful ones, everything's taken care of, or your war couldn't
hold its own. In a war you can shit the same as in the dead of
peace, you can stop for a beer between battles, and even on the
march you can always lie down on your elbows and take a little
nap by the roadside. You can't play cards when you're fighting;
but then you can't when you're plowing in the dead of peace
either, but after a victory the sky's the limit. Maybe you've had a
leg shot off, at first you raise a howl; you make a big thing of it.
But then you calm down or they give you schnapps, and in the
end you're hopping around again and the war's no worse off than
before. And what's to prevent you from multiplying in the thick
of the slaughter, behind a barn or someplace, in the long run
how can they stop you, and then the war has your progeny to
help it along. Take it from me, the war will always find an
answer. Why would it have to stop?
    [*Kattrin has stopped working and is staring at the chap-
lain*]
MOTHER COURAGE. Then I'll buy the merchandise. You've convinced me. [*Kattrin suddenly throws down a basket full of bottles and runs out*] Kattrin! [*Laughs*] My goodness, the poor
thing's been hoping for peace. I promised her she'd get a husband when peace comes. [*She runs after her*]
THE CLERK. [*Getting up*] I win, you've been too busy talking. Pay
up.
MOTHER COURAGE. [*Comes back with Kattrin*] Be reasonable, the
war'll go on a little longer and we'll make a little more money,

2. A city in Bohemia, near the German border.

then peace will be even better. Run along to town now, it won't take you ten minutes, and get the stuff from the Golden Lion, only the expensive things, we'll pick up the rest in the wagon later, it's all arranged, the regimental clerk here will go with you. They've almost all gone to the general's funeral, nothing can happen to you. Look sharp, don't let them take anything away from you, think of your dowry.

[*Kattrin puts a kerchief over her head and goes with the clerk*]

THE CHAPLAIN. Is it all right letting her go with the clerk?

MOTHER COURAGE. Who'd want to ruin her? She's not pretty enough.

THE CHAPLAIN. I've come to admire the way you handle your business and pull through every time. I can see why they call you Mother Courage.

MOTHER COURAGE. Poor people need courage. Why? Because they're sunk. In their situation it takes gumption just to get up in the morning. Or to plow a field in the middle of a war. They even show courage by bringing children into the world, because look at the prospects. The way they butcher and execute each other, think of the courage they need to look each other in the face. And putting up with an emperor and a pope takes a whale of a lot of courage, because those two are the death of the poor. [*She sits down, takes a small pipe from her pocket and smokes*] You could be making some kindling.

THE CHAPLAIN. [*Reluctantly takes his jacket off and prepares to chop*] Chopping wood isn't really my trade, you know, I'm a shepherd of souls.

MOTHER COURAGE. Sure. But I have no soul and I need firewood.

THE CHAPLAIN. What's that pipe?

MOTHER COURAGE. Just a pipe.

THE CHAPLAIN. No, it's not "just a pipe," it's a very particular pipe.

MOTHER COURAGE. Really?

THE CHAPLAIN. It's the cook's pipe from the Oxenstjerna regiment.

MOTHER COURAGE. If you know it all, why the mealy-mouthed questions?

THE CHAPLAIN. I didn't know if *you* knew. You could have been rummaging through your belongings and laid hands on some pipe and picked it up without thinking.

MOTHER COURAGE. Yes. Maybe that's how it was.

THE CHAPLAIN. Except it wasn't. You knew who that pipe belongs to.

MOTHER COURAGE. What of it?

THE CHAPLAIN. Courage, I'm warning you. It's my duty. I doubt if you ever lay eyes on the man again, but that's no calamity, in fact you're lucky. If you ask me, he wasn't steady. Not at all.

MOTHER COURAGE. What makes you say that? He was a nice man.

THE CHAPLAIN. Oh, you think he was nice? I differ. Far be it from me to wish him any harm, but I can't say he was nice. I'd say he was a scheming Don Juan.[3] If you don't believe me, take a look at his pipe. You'll have to admit that it shows up his character.

MOTHER COURAGE. I don't see anything. It's beat up.

THE CHAPLAIN. It's half bitten through. A violent man. That is the pipe of a ruthless, violent man, you must see that if you've still got an ounce of good sense.

MOTHER COURAGE. Don't wreck my chopping block.

THE CHAPLAIN. I've told you I wasn't trained to chop wood. I studied theology. My gifts and abilities are being wasted on muscular effort. The talents that God gave me are lying fallow. That's a sin. You've never heard me preach. With one sermon I can whip a regiment into such a state that they take the enemy for a flock of sheep. Then men care no more about their lives than they would about a smelly old sock that they're ready to throw away in hopes of final victory. God has made me eloquent. You'll swoon when you hear me preach.

MOTHER COURAGE. I don't want to swoon. What good would that do me?

THE CHAPLAIN. Courage, I've often wondered if maybe you didn't conceal a warm heart under that hard-bitten talk of yours. You too are human, you need warmth.

MOTHER COURAGE. The best way to keep this tent warm is with plenty of firewood.

THE CHAPLAIN. Don't try to put me off. Seriously, Courage, I sometimes wonder if we couldn't make our relationship a little closer. I mean, seeing that the whirlwind of war has whirled us so strangely together.

MOTHER COURAGE. Seems to me it's close enough. I cook your meals and you do chores, such as chopping wood, for instance.

THE CHAPLAIN. [*Goes toward her*] You know what I mean by "closer"; it has nothing to do with meals and chopping wood and such mundane needs. Don't harden your heart, let it speak.

MOTHER COURAGE. Don't come at me with that ax. That's too close a relationship.

THE CHAPLAIN. Don't turn it to ridicule. I'm serious. I've given it careful thought.

MOTHER COURAGE. Chaplain, don't be silly. I like you, I don't want to have to scold you. My aim in life is to get through, me and my children and my wagon. I don't think of it as mine and besides I'm not in the mood for private affairs. Right now I'm taking a big risk, buying up merchandise with the general dead and everybody talking peace. What'll you do if I'm ruined? See? You don't know. Chop that wood, then we'll be warm in the evening, which is a good thing in times like these. Now what? [*She stands up*]

> [*Enter Kattrin out of breath, with a wound across her forehead and over one eye. She is carrying all sort of things, packages, leather goods, a drum, etc.*]

3. Philanderer.

MOTHER COURAGE. What's this? Assaulted? On the way back? She
was assulted on the way back. Must have been that soldier that
got drunk here! I shouldn't have let you go! Throw the stuff
down! It's not bad, only a flesh wound. I'll bandage it, it'll heal
in a week. They're worse than wild beasts. [*She bandages the
wound*]

THE CHAPLAIN. I can't find fault with them. At home they never
raped anybody. I blame the people that start wars, they're the
ones that dredge up man's lowest instincts.

MOTHER COURAGE. Didn't the clerk bring you back? That's because
you're respectable, they don't give a damn. It's not a deep
wound, it won't leave a mark. There, all bandaged. Don't fret,
I've got something for you. I've been keeping it for you on the
sly, it'll be a surprise. [*She fishes Yvette's red shoes out of a
sack*] See? You've always wanted them. Now you've got them.
Put them on quick before I regret it. It won't leave a mark,
though I wouldn't mind if it did. The girls that attract them get
the worst of it. They drag them around till there's nothing left of
them. If you don't appeal to them, they won't harm you. I've
seen girls with pretty faces, a few years later they'd have given a
wolf the creeps. They can't step behind a bush without fearing
the worst. It's like trees. The straight tall ones get chopped down
for ridgepoles, the crooked ones enjoy life. In other words, it's a
lucky break. The shoes are still in good condition, I've kept them
nicely polished.

[*Kattrin leaves the shoes where they are and crawls into the
wagon*]

THE CHAPLAIN. I hope she won't be disfigured.

MOTHER COURAGE. There'll be a scar. She can stop waiting for
peace.

THE CHAPLAIN. She didn't let them take anything.

MOTHER COURAGE. Maybe I shouldn't have drummed it into her. If
I only knew what went on in her head. One night she stayed out,
the only time in all these years. Afterwards she traipsed around as
usual, except she worked harder. I never could find out what happened. I racked my brains for quite some time. [*She picks up
the articles brought by Kattrin and sorts them angrily*] That's
war for you! A fine way to make a living!

[*Cannon salutes are heard*]

THE CHAPLAIN. Now they're burying the general. This is a historic
moment.

MOTHER COURAGE. To me it's a historic moment when they hit my
daughter over the eye. She's a wreck, she'll never get a husband
now, and she's so crazy about children. It's the war that made
her dumb too, a soldier stuffed something in her mouth when she
was little. I'll never see Swiss Cheese again and where Eilif is,
God knows. God damn the war.

7

Mother Courage at the height of her business career.

Highway.

The chaplain, Mother Courage and her daughter Kattrin are pulling the wagon. New wares are hanging on it. Mother Courage is wearing a necklace of silver talers.

MOTHER COURAGE. Stop running down the war. I won't have it. I know it destroys the weak, but the weak haven't a chance in peacetime either. And war is a better provider. [*Sings*]

If you're not strong enough to take it
The victory will find you dead.
A war is only what you make it.
It's business, not with cheese but lead.

And what good is it staying in one place? The stay-at-homes are the first to get it. [*Sings*]

Some people think they'd like to ride out
The war, leave danger to the brave
And dig themselves a cozy hideout—
They'll dig themselves an early grave.
I've seen them running from the thunder
To find a refuge from the war
But once they're resting six feet under
They wonder what they hurried for.

[*They plod on*]

8

In the same year Gustavus Adolphus, King of Sweden, is killed at the battle of Lützen.[1] Peace threatens to ruin Mother Courage's business. Her brave son performs one heroic deed too many and dies an ignominious death.

A camp.

A summer morning. An old woman and her son are standing by the wagon. The son is carrying a large sack of bedding.

MOTHER COURAGE'S VOICE. [*From the wagon*] Does it have to be at this unearthly hour?
THE YOUNG MAN. We've walked all night, twenty miles, and we've got to go back today.
MOTHER COURAGE'S VOICE. What can I do with bedding? The people haven't any houses.

1. Town a few miles from the great Protestant city of Leipzig.

THE YOUNG MAN. Wait till you've seen it.

THE OLD WOMAN. She won't take it either. Come on.

THE YOUNG MAN. They'll sell the roof from over our heads for taxes. Maybe she'll give us three guilders if you throw in the cross. [*Bells start ringing*] Listen, mother!

VOICES. [*From the rear*] Peace! The king of Sweden is dead!

MOTHER COURAGE. [*Sticks her head out of the wagon. She has not yet done her hair*] Why are the bells ringing in the middle of the week?

THE CHAPLAIN. [*Crawls out from under the wagon*] What are they shouting?

MOTHER COURAGE. Don't tell me peace has broken out when I've just taken in more supplies.

THE CHAPLAIN. [*Shouting toward the rear*] Is it true? Peace?

VOICE. Three weeks ago, they say. But we just found out.

THE CHAPLAIN. [*To Mother Courage*] What else would they ring the bells for?

VOICE. There's a whole crowd of Lutherans, they've driven their carts into town. They brought the news.

THE YOUNG MAN. Mother, it's peace. What's the matter?

[*The old woman has collapsed*]

MOTHER COURAGE. [*Going back into the wagon*] Heavenly saints! Kattrin, peace! Put your black dress on! We're going to church. We owe it to Swiss Cheese. Can it be true?

THE YOUNG MAN. The people here say the same thing. They've made peace. Can you get up? [*The old woman stands up, still stunned*] I'll get the saddle shop started again. I promise. Everything will be all right. Father will get his bed back. Can you walk? [*To the chaplain*] She fainted. It was the news. She thought peace would never come again. Father said it would. We'll go straight home. [*Both go out*]

MOTHER COURAGE'S VOICE. Give her some brandy.

THE CHAPLAIN. They're gone.

MOTHER COURAGE'S VOICE. What's going on in camp?

THE CHAPLAIN. A big crowd. I'll go see. Shouldn't I put on my clericals?

MOTHER COURAGE'S VOICE. Better make sure before you step out in your antichrist costume. I'm glad to see peace, even if I'm ruined. At least I've brought two of my children through the war. Now I'll see my Eilif again.

THE CHAPLAIN. Look who's coming down the road. If it isn't the general's cook!

THE COOK. [*Rather bedraggled, carrying a bundle*] Can I believe my eyes? The chaplain!

THE CHAPLAIN. Courage! A visitor!

[*Mother Courage climbs down*]

THE COOK. Didn't I promise to come over for a little chat as soon as I had time? I've never forgotten your brandy, Mrs. Fierling.

MOTHER COURAGE. Mercy, the general's cook! After all these years! Where's Eilif, my eldest?

THE COOK. Isn't he here yet? He left ahead of me, he was coming to see you too.

THE CHAPLAIN. I'll put on my clericals, wait for me. [*Goes out behind the wagon*]

MOTHER COURAGE. Then he'll be here any minute. [*Calls into the wagon*] Kattrin, Eilif's coming! Bring the cook a glass of brandy! [*Kattrin does not appear*] Put a lock of hair over it, and forget it! Mr. Lamb is no stranger. [*Gets the brandy herself*] She won't come out. Peace doesn't mean a thing to her, it's come too late. They hit her over the eye, there's hardly any mark, but she thinks people are staring at her.

THE COOK. Ech, war! [*He and Mother Courage sit down*]

MOTHER COURAGE. Cook, you find me in trouble. I'm ruined.

THE COOK. What? Say, that's a shame.

MOTHER COURAGE. Peace has done me in. Only the other day I stocked up. The chaplain's advice. And now they'll all demobilize and leave me sitting on my merchandise.

THE COOK. How could you listen to the chaplain? If I'd had time, I'd have warned you against him, but the Catholics came too soon. He's a fly-by-night. So now he's the boss here?

MOTHER COURAGE. He washed my dishes and helped me pull the wagon.

THE COOK. Him? Pulling? I guess he's told you a few of his jokes too, I wouldn't put it past him, he has an unsavory attitude toward women, I tried to reform him, it was hopeless. He's not steady.

MOTHER COURAGE. Are you steady?

THE COOK. If nothing else, I'm steady. Prosit!

MOTHER COURAGE. Steady is no good. I've only lived with one steady man, thank the Lord. I never had to work so hard, he sold the children's blankets when spring came, and he thought my harmonica was unchristian. In my opinion you're not doing yourself any good by admitting you're steady.

THE COOK. You've still got your old bite, but I respect you for it.

MOTHER COURAGE. Don't tell me you've been dreaming about my old bite.

THE COOK. Well, here we sit, with the bells of peace and your world-famous brandy, that hasn't its equal.

MOTHER COURAGE. The bells of peace don't strike my fancy right now. I don't see them paying the men, they're behindhand already. Where does that leave me with my famous brandy? Have you been paid?

THE COOK. [*Hesitantly*] Not really. That's why we demobilized ourselves. Under the circumstances, I says to myself, why should I stay on? I'll go see my friends in the meantime. So here we are.

MOTHER COURAGE. You mean you're out of funds?

THE COOK. If only they'd stop those damn bells! I'd be glad to go into some kind of business. I'm sick of being a cook. They give me roots and shoe leather to work with, and then they throw the hot soup in my face. A cook's got a dog's life these days. I'd rather be in combat, but now we've got peace. [*The chaplain appears in his original dress*] We'll discuss it later.

THE CHAPLAIN. It's still in good condition. There were only a few moths in it.

THE COOK. I don't see why you bother. They won't take you back. Who are you going to inspire now to be an honest soldier and earn his pay at the risk of his life? Besides, I've got a bone to pick with you. Advising this lady to buy useless merchandise on the ground that the war would last forever.

THE CHAPLIN. [*Heatedly*] And why, I'd like to know, is it any of your business?

THE COOK. Because it's unscrupulous. How can you meddle in other people's business and give unsolicited advice?

THE CHAPLAIN. Who's meddling? [*To Mother Courage*] I didn't know you were accountable to this gentleman, I didn't know you were so intimate with him.

MOTHER COURAGE. Don't get excited, the cook is only giving his private opinion. And you can't deny that your war was a dud.

THE CHAPLAIN. Courage, don't blaspheme against peace. You're a battlefield hyena.

MOTHER COURAGE. What am I?

THE COOK. If you insult this lady, you'll hear from me.

THE CHAPLAIN. I'm not talking to you. Your intentions are too obvious. [*To Mother Courage*] But when I see you picking up peace with thumb and forefinger like a snotty handkerchief, it revolts my humanity; you don't want peace, you want war, because you profit by it, but don't forget the old saying: "He hath need of a long spoon that eateth with the devil."

MOTHER COURAGE. I've no use for war and war hasn't much use for me. Anyway, I'm not letting anybody call me a hyena, you and me are through.

THE CHAPLAIN. How can you complain about peace when it's such a relief to everybody else? On account of the old rags in your wagon?

MOTHER COURAGE. My merchandise isn't old rags, it's what I live off, and so did you.

THE CHAPLAIN. Off war, you mean. Aha!

THE COOK. [*To the chaplain*] You're a grown man, you ought to know there's no sense in giving advice. [*To Mother Courage*] The best thing you can do now is to sell off certain articles quick, before the prices hit the floor. Dress yourself and get started, there's no time to lose.

MOTHER COURAGE. That's very sensible advice. I think I'll do it.

THE CHAPLAIN. Because the cook says so!

MOTHER COURAGE. Why didn't *you* say so? He's right, I'd better run over to the market. [*She goes into the wagon*]

THE COOK. My round, chaplain. No presence of mind. Here's what you should have said: me give you advice? All I ever did was talk politics! Don't try to take me on. Cockfighting is undignified in a clergyman.

THE CHAPLAIN. If you don't shut up, I'll murder you, undignified or not.

THE COOK. [*Taking off his shoe and unwinding the wrappings from his feet*] If the war hadn't made a godless bum out of you, you could easily come by a parsonage now that peace is here. They won't need cooks, there's nothing to cook, but people still do a lot of believing, that hasn't changed.

THE CHAPLAIN. See here, Mr. Lamb. Don't try squeeze me out. Being a bum has made me a better man. I couldn't preach to them any more.

[*Yvette Pottier enters, elaborately dressed in black, with a cane. She is much older and fatter and heavily powdered. Behind her a servant*]

YVETTE. Hello there! Is this the residence of Mother Courage?

THE CHAPLAIN. Right you are. With whom have we the pleasure?

YVETTE. The Countess Starhemberg, my good people. Where is Mother Courage.

THE CHAPLAIN. [*Calls into the wagon*] Countess Starhemberg wishes to speak to you!

MOTHER COURAGE. I'm coming.

YVETTE. It's Yvette!

MOTHER COURAGE'S VOICE. My goodness! It's Yvette!

YVETTE. Just dropped in to see how you're doing. [*The cook has turned around in horror*] Pieter!

THE COOK. Yvette!

YVETTE. Blow me down! How did you get here?

THE COOK. In a cart.

THE CHAPLAIN. Oh, you know each other? Intimately?

YVETTE. I should think so. [*She looks the cook over*] Fat!

THE COOK. You're not exactly willowy yourself.

YVETTE. All the same I'm glad I ran into you, you bum. Now I can tell you what I think of you.

THE CHAPLAIN. Go right ahead, spare no details, but wait until Courage comes out.

MOTHER COURAGE. [*Comes out with all sorts of merchandise*] Yvette! [*They embrace*] But what are you in mourning for?

YVETTE. Isn't it becoming? My husband the colonel died a few years ago.

MOTHER COURAGE. The old geezer that almost bought my wagon?

YVETTE. His elder brother.

MOTHER COURAGE. You must be pretty well fixed. It's nice to find somebody that's made a good thing out of the war.

YVETTE. Oh well, it's been up and down and back up again.

MOTHER COURAGE. Let's not say anything bad about colonels. They make money by the bushel.

THE CHAPLAIN. If I were you, I'd put my shoes back on again. [*To Yvette*] Countess Starhemberg, you promised to tell us what you think of this gentleman.

THE COOK. Don't make a scene here.

MOTHER COURAGE. He's a friend of mine, Yvette.

YVETTE. He's Pete the Pipe, that's who he is.

THE COOK. Forget the nicknames, my name is Lamb.

MOTHER COURAGE. [*Laughs*] Pete the Pipe! That drove the women crazy! Say, I've saved your pipe.

THE CHAPLAIN. And smoked it.

YVETTE. It's lucky I'm here to warn you. He's the worst rotter that ever infested the coast of Flanders. He ruined more girls than he's got fingers.

THE COOK. That was a long time ago. I've changed.

YVETTE. Stand up when a lady draws you into a conversation! How I loved this man! And all the while he was seeing a little bandy-legged brunette, ruined her too, naturally.

THE COOK. Seems to me I started you off on a prosperous career.

YVETTE. Shut up, you depressing wreck! Watch your step with him, his kind are dangerous even when they've gone to seed.

MOTHER COURAGE. [*To Yvette*] Come along, I've got to sell my stuff before the prices drop. Maybe you can help me, with your army connections. [*Calls into the wagon*] Kattrin, forget about church, I'm running over to the market. When Eilif comes, give him a drink. [*Goes out with Yvette*]

YVETTE. [*In leaving*] To think that such a man could lead me astray! I can thank my lucky stars that I was able to rise in the world after that. I've put a spoke in your wheel, Pete the Pipe, and they'll give me credit for it in heaven when my time comes.

THE CHAPLAIN. Our conversation seems to illustrate the old adage: The mills of God grind slowly.[2] What do you think of my jokes now?

THE COOK. I'm just unlucky. I'll come clean: I was hoping for a hot meal. I'm starving. And now they're talking about me, and she'll get the wrong idea. I think I'll beat it before she comes back.

THE CHAPLAIN. I think so too.

THE COOK. Chaplain, I'm fed up on peace already. Men are sinners from the cradle, fire and sword are their natural lot. I wish I were cooking for the general again. God knows where he is, I'd roast a fine fat capon, with mustard sauce and a few carrots.

THE CHAPLAIN. Red cabbage. Red cabbage with capon.

THE COOK. That's right, but he wanted carrots.

THE CHAPLAIN. He was ignorant.

THE COOK. That didn't prevent you from gorging yourself.

THE CHAPLAIN. With repugnance.

THE COOK. Anyway you'll have to admit those were good times.

THE CHAPLAIN. I might admit that.

THE COOK. Now you've called her a hyena, your good times here are over. What are you staring at?

THE CHAPLAIN. Eilif? [*Eilif enters, followed by soldiers with pikes. His hands are fettered. He is deathly pale*] What's wrong?

2. From a saying by Friedrich von Logan (1605–1655), as translated by Longfellow: "Though the mills of God grind slowly, / Yet they grind exceeding small."

EILIF. Where's mother?

THE CHAPLAIN. Gone to town.

EILIF. I heard she was here. They let me come and see her.

THE COOK. [*To the soldiers*] Where are you taking him?

A SOLDIER. No good place.

THGE CHAPLAIN. What has he done?

THE SOILDIER. Broke into a farm. The peasant's wife is dead.

THE CHAPLAIN. How could you do such a thing?

EILIF. It's what I've been doing all along.

THE COOK. But in peacetime!

EILIF. Shut your trap. Can I sit down till she comes?

THE SOLDIER. We haven't time.

THE CHAPLAIN. During the war they honored him for it, he sat at the general's right hand. Then it was bravery. Couldn't we speak to the officer?

THE SOLDIER. No use. What's brave about taking a peasant's cattle?

THE COOK. It was stupid.

EILIF. If I'd been stupid. I'd have starved, wise guy.

THE COOK. And for being smart your head comes off.

THE CHAPLAIN. Let's get Kattrin at least.

EILIF. Leave her be. Get me a drink of schnapps.

THE SOLDIER. No time. Let's go!

THE CHAPLAIN. And what should we tell your mother?

EILIF. Tell her it wasn't any different, tell her it was the same. Or don't tell her anything.

[*The soldiers drive him away*]

THE CHAPLAIN. I'll go with you on your hard journey.

EILIF. I don't need any sky pilot.

THE CHAPLAIN. You don't know yet. [*He follows him*]

THE COOK. [*Calls after them*] I'll have to tell her, she'll want to see him.

THE CHAPLAIN. Better not tell her anything. Or say he was here and he'll come again, maybe tomorrow. I'll break it to her when I get back. [*Hurries out*]

[*The cook looks after them, shaking his head, then he walks anxiously about. Finally he approaches the wagon*]

THE COOK. Hey! Come on out! I can see why you'd hide from peace. I wish I could do it myself. I'm the general's cook, remember? Wouldn't you have a bite to eat, to do me till your mother gets back? A slice of ham or just a piece of bread while I'm waiting. [*He looks in*] She's buried her head in a blanket.

[*The sound of gunfire in the rear*]

MOTHER COURAGE. [*Runs in. She is out of breath and still has her merchandise*] Cook, the peace is over, the war started up again three days ago. I hadn't sold my stuff yet when I found out. Heaven be praised! They're shooting each other up in town, the Catholics and Lutherans. We've got to get out of here. Kattrin, start packing. What have *you* got such a long face about? What's wrong?

THE COOK. Nothing.

MOTHER COURAGE. Something's wrong, I can tell by your expression.

THE COOK. Maybe it's the war starting up again. Now I probably won't get anything hot to eat before tomorrow night.

MOTHER COURAGE. That's a lie, cook.

THE COOK. Eilif was here. He couldn't stay.

MOTHER COURAGE. He was here? Then we'll see him on the march. I'm going with our troops this time. How does he look?

THE COOK. The same.

MOTHER COURAGE. He'll never change. The war couldn't take him away from me. He's smart. Could you help me pack? [*She starts packing*] Did he tell you anything? Is he in good with the general? Did he say anything about his heroic deeds?

THE COOK. [*Gloomily*] They say he's been at one of them again.

MOTHER COURAGE. Tell me later, we've got to be going. [*Kattrin emerges*] Kattrin, peace is over. We're moving. [*To the cook*] What's the matter with you?

THE COOK. I'm going to enlist.

MOTHER COURAGE. I've got a suggestion. Why don't . . .? Where's the chaplain?

THE COOK. Gone to town with Eilif.

MOTHER COURAGE. Then come a little way with me, Lamb. I need help.

THE COOK. That incident with Yvette . . .

MOTHER COURAGE. It hasn't lowered you in my estimation. Far from it. Where there's smoke there's fire. Coming?

THE COOK. I won't say no.

MOTHER COURAGE. The Twelfth Regiment has shoved off. Take the shaft. Here's a chunk of bread. We'll have to circle around to meet the Lutherans. Maybe I'll see Eilif tonight. He's my favorite. It's been a short peace. And we're on the move again. [*She sings, while the cook and Kattrin harness themselves to the wagon*]

From Ulm to Metz, from Metz to Pilsen[3]
Courage is right there in the van.
The war both in and out of season
With shot and shell will feed its man.
But lead alone is not sufficient
The war needs soldiers to subsist!
Its diet elseways is deficient.
The war is hungry! So enlist!

3. Ulm is about eighty miles west of Munich. Metz, in the province of Lorraine (ceded to France at the end of the Thirty Years' War), is about two hundred miles west of Ulm; to travel from Metz to Pilsen one must cross the whole of Germany.

9

The great war of religion has been going on for sixteen years. Germany has lost more than half its population. Those whom the slaughter has spared have been laid low by epidemics. Once-flourishing countrysides are ravaged by famine. Wolves prowl through the charred ruins of the cities. In the fall of 1634 we find Mother Courage in Germany, in the Fichtelgebirge[1] at some distance from the road followed by the Swedish armies. Winter comes early and is exceptionally severe. Business is bad, begging is the only resort. The cook receives a letter from Utrecht[2] and is dismissed.

Outside a half-demolished presbytery.

Gray morning in early winter. Gusts of wind. Mother Courage and the cook in shabby sheepskins by the wagon.

THE COOK. No light. Nobody's up yet.

MOTHER COURAGE. But it's a priest. He'll have to crawl out of bed to ring the bells. Then he'll get himself a nice bowl of hot soup.

THE COOK. Go on, you saw the village, everything's been burned to a crisp.

MOTHER COURAGE. But somebody's here, I heard a dog bark.

THE COOK. If the priest's got anything, he won't give it away.

MOTHER COURAGE. Maybe if we sing . . .

THE COOK. I've had it up to here. [*Suddenly*] I got a letter from Utrecht. My mother's died of cholera and the tavern belongs to me. Here's the letter if you don't believe me. It's no business of yours what my aunt says about my evil ways, but never mind, read it.

MOTHER COURAGE[3] [*Reads the letter*] Lamb, I'm sick of roaming around, myself. I feel like a butcher's dog that pulls the meat cart but doesn't get any for himself. I've nothing left to sell and the people have no money to pay for it. In Saxony a man in rags tried to foist a cord[4] of books on me for two eggs, and in Württemberg they'd have let their plow go for a little bag of salt. What's the good of plowing? Nothing grows but brambles. In Pomerania[5] they say the villagers have eaten up all the babies, and that nuns have been caught at highway robbery.

THE COOK. It's the end of the world.

MOTHER COURAGE. Sometimes I have visions of myself driving

---

1. A range of mountains in Germany near the Bohemian border.
2. City in the south of Holland.
3. In this scene, Mother Courage and the Cook for the first time use *du*, the familiar form of *you* in German. (The familiar form is used between lovers, close friends and family, and young people; the formal *sie* is used otherwise.)
4. A large quantity; the same volume as a cord of wood.
5. Saxony, Württemberg, and Pomerania are German principalities.

through hell, selling sulfur and brimstone, or through heaven peddling refreshments to the roaming souls. If me and the children I've got left could find a place where there's no shooting, I wouldn't mind a few years of peace and quiet.

THE COOK. We could open up the tavern again. Think it over. Anna. I made up my mind last night; with or without you, I'm going back to Utrecht. In fact I'm leaving today.

MOTHER COURAGE. I'll have to talk to Kattrin. It's kind of sudden, and I don't like to make decisions in the cold with nothing in my stomach. Kattrin! [*Kattrin climbs out of the wagon*] Kattrin, I've got something to tell you. The cook and me are thinking of going to Utrecht. They've left him a tavern there. You'd be living in one place, you'd meet people. A lot of men would be glad to get a nice, well-behaved girl, looks aren't everything. I'm all for it. I get along fine with the cook. I've got to hand it to him: He's got a head for business. We'd eat regular meals, wouldn't that be nice? And you'd have your own bed, wouldn't you like that? It's no life on the road, year in year out. You'll go to rack and ruin. You're crawling with lice already. We've got to decide, you see, we could go north with the Swedes, they must be over there. [*She points to the left*] I think we'll do it, Kattrin.

THE COOK. Anna, could I have a word with you alone?

MOTHER COURAGE. Get back in the wagon, Kattrin.

[*Kattrin climbs back in*]

THE COOK. I interrupted you because I see there's been a misunderstanding, I thought it was too obvious to need saying. But if it isn't, I'll just have to say it. You can't take her, it's out of the question. Is that plain enough for you?

[*Kattrin sticks her head out of the wagon and listens*]

MOTHER COURAGE. You want me to leave Kattrin?

THE COOK. Look at it this way. There's no room in the tavern. It's not one of those places with three taprooms. If the two of us put our shoulder to the wheel, we can make a living, but not three, it can't be done. Kattrin can keep the wagon.

MOTHER COURAGE. I'd been thinking she could find a husband in Utrecht.

THE COOK. Don't make me laugh! How's she going to find a husband? At her age? And dumb! And with that scar!

MOTHER COURAGE. Not so loud.

THE COOK. Shout or whisper, the truth's the truth. And that's another reason why I can't have her in the tavern. The customers won't want a sight like that staring them in the face. Can you blame them?

MOTHER COURAGE. Shut up. Not so loud, I say.

THE COOK. There's a light in the presbytery.[6] Let's sing.

MOTHER COURAGE. How could she pull the wagon by herself? She's afraid of the war. She couldn't stand it. The dreams she must have! I hear her groaning at night. Especially after battles. What

---

6. That part of a church in which the bishop and clergy sit.

she sees in her dreams, God knows. It's pity that makes her suffer so. The other day the wagon hit a hedgehog, I found it hidden in her blanket.

THE COOK. The tavern's too small. [*He calls*] Worthy gentleman and members of the household! We shall now sing the Song of Solomon, Julius Caesar, and other great men, whose greatness didn't help them any. Just to show you that we're God-fearing people ourselves, which makes it hard for us, especially in the winter. [*They sing*]

You saw the wise King Solomon[7]
You know what came of him.
To him all hidden things were plain.
He cursed the hour gave birth to him
And saw that everything was vain.
How great and wise was Solomon!
Now think about his case. Alas
A useful lesson can be won.
It's wisdom that had brought him to that pass!
How happy is the man with none!

Our beautiful song proves that virtues are dangerous things, better steer clear of them, enjoy life, eat a good breakfast, a bowl of hot soup, for instance. Take me, I haven't got any soup and wish I had, I'm a soldier, but what has my bravery in all those battles got me, nothing, I'm starving, I'd be better off if I'd stayed home like a yellowbelly. And I'll tell you why.

You saw the daring Caesar[8] next
You know what he became.
They deified him in his life
But then they killed him just the same.
And as they raised the fatal knife
How loud he cried: "You too, my son!"
Now think about his case. Alas
A useful lesson can be won.
It's daring that had brought him to that pass!
How happy is the man with none!

[*In an undertone*] They're not even looking out. Worthy gentleman and members of the household! Maybe you'll say, all right, if bravery won't keep body and soul together, try honesty. That may fill your belly or at least get you a drop to drink. Let's look into it.

You've heard of honest Socrates[9]
Who never told a lie.
They weren't so grateful as you'd think

7. Old Testament ruler celebrated for his wisdom. In line 4 of the stanza, the cook confuses Solomon with the Biblical Job, who does curse the day he was born. [*Job* 3:1.]

8. [100–44 B.C.], Roman general and dictator, assassinated by a republican clique including his young friend Brutus when suspected of imperial ambitions.

9. Greek philosopher, condemned to death in 399 B.C. for teaching the young to question accepted beliefs.

Instead they sentenced him to die
And handed him the poisoned drink.
How honest was the people's noble son!
Now think about his case. Alas
A useful lesson can be won.
His honesty had brought him to that pass.
How happy is the man with none!

Yes, they tell us to be charitable and to share what we have, but
what if we haven't got anything? Maybe philanthropists have a
rough time of it too, it stands to reason, they need a little something for themselves. Yes, charity is a rare virtue, because it
doesn't pay.

St. Martin[10] couldn't bear to see
His fellows in distress.
He saw a poor man in the snow.
"Take half my cloak!" He did, and lo!
They both of them froze none the less.
He thought his heavenly reward was won.
Now think about his case. Alas
A useful lesson can be won.
Unselfishness had brought him to that pass.
How happy is the man with none!

That's our situation. We're God-fearing folk, we stick together,
we don't steal, we don't murder, we don't set fire to anything!
You could say that we set an example which bears out the song,
we sink lower and lower, we seldom see any soup, but if we were
different, if we were thieves and murderers, maybe our bellies
would be full. Because virtue isn't rewarded, only wickedness, the
world needn't be like this, but it is.

And here you see God-fearing folk
Observing God's ten laws.
So far He hasn't taken heed.
You people sitting warm indoors
Help to relieve our bitter need!
Our virtue can be counted on.
Now think about our case. Alas
A useful lesson can be won.
The fear of God has brought us to this pass.
How happy is the man with none!

VOICE. [*From above*] Hey, down there! Come on up! We've got
some good thick soup.

MOTHER COURAGE. Lamb, I couldn't get anything down. I know
what you say makes sense, but is it your last word? We've always
been good friends.

THE COOK. My last word. Think it over.

10. (330–397 A.D.) As a young soldier
in the Roman army, Martin divided his
military cloak with a beggar. He
dreamed of Christ that night and was
baptized thereafter, later becoming
Bishop of Tours.

MOTHER COURAGE. I don't need to think it over. I won't leave her.

THE COOK. It wouldn't be wise, but there's nothing I can do. I'm not inhuman, but it's a small tavern. We'd better go in now, or there won't be anything left, we'll have been singing in the cold for nothing.

MOTHER COURAGE. I'll get Kattrin.

THE COOK. Better bring it down for her. They'll get a fright if the three of us barge in. [*They go out*]

[*Kattrin climbs out of the wagon. She is carrying a bundle. She looks around to make sure the others are gone. Then she spreads out an old pair of the cook's trousers and a skirt belonging to her mother side by side on a wheel of the wagon so they can easily be seen. She is about to leave with her bundle when Mother Courage comes out of the house*]

MOTHER COURAGE. [*With a dish of soup*] Kattrin! Stop! Kattrin! Where do you think you're going with that bundle? Have you taken leave of your wits? [*She examines the bundle*] She's packed her things. Were you listening? I've told him it's no go with Utrecht and his lousy tavern, what would we do there? A tavern's no place for you and me. The war still has a thing or two up its sleeve for us. [*She sees the trousers and skirt*] You're stupid. Suppose I'd seen that and you'd been gone? [*Kattrin tries to leave, Mother Courage holds her back*] And don't go thinking I've given him the gate on your account. It's the wagon. I won't part with the wagon, I'm used to it, it's not you, it's the wagon. We'll go in the other direction, we'll put the cook's stuff out here where he'll find it, the fool. [*She climbs up and throws down a few odds and ends to join the trousers*] There. Now we're shut of him, you won't see me taking anyone else into the business. From now on it's you and me. This winter will go by like all the rest. Harness up, it looks like snow.

[*They harness themselves to the wagon, turn it around and pull it away. When the cook comes out he sees his things and stands dumbfounded*]

10

Throughout 1635 Mother Courage and her daughter Kattrin pull the wagon over the roads of central Germany in the wake of the increasingly bedraggled armies.

Highway.

Mother Courage and Kattrin are pulling the wagon. They come to a peasant's house. A voice is heard singing from within.

THE VOICE.

The rose bush in our garden
Rejoiced our hearts in spring
It bore such lovely flowers.

We planted it last season
Before the April showers.
A garden is a blessèd thing
It bore such lovely flowers.

When winter comes a-stalking
And gales great snow storms bring
They trouble us but little.
We've lately finished caulking
The roof with moss and wattle.[1]
A sheltering roof's a blessèd thing
When winter comes a-stalking.

[*Mother Courage and Kattrin have stopped to listen. Then they move on*]

1. Sticks and branches.

11

January 1636. The imperial troops threaten the Protestant city of Halle.[1] The stone speaks. Mother Courage loses her daughter and goes on alone. The end of the war is not in sight.

The wagon, much the worse for wear, is standing beside a peasant house with an enormous thatch roof. The house is built against the side of a stony hill. Night.

A lieutenant and three soldiers in heavy armor step out of the woods.

THE LIEUTENANT. I don't want any noise. If anybody yells, run him through with your pikes.

FIRST SOLDIER. But we need a guide. We'll have to knock if we want them to come out.

THE LIEUTENANT. Knocking sounds natural. It could be a cow bumping against the barn wall.

[*The soldiers knock on the door. A peasant woman opens. They hold their hands over her mouth. Two soldiers go in*]

A MAN'S VOICE. [*Inside*] Who's there?

[*The soldiers bring out a peasant and his son*]

THE LIEUTENANT. [*Points to the wagon, in which Kattrin has appeared*] There's another one. [*A soldier pulls her out*] Anybody else live here?

THE PEASANT COUPLE. This is our son.—That's a dumb girl.—Her mother's gone into the town on business—Buying up people's belongings, they're selling cheap because they're getting out.—They're provisioners.

THE LIEUTENANT. I'm warning you to keep quiet, one squawk and

1. Protestant city twenty miles northwest of Leipzig.

you'll get a pike over the head. All right. I need somebody who can show us the path to the city. [*Points to the young peasant*] You. Come here!

THE YOUNG PEASANT. I don't know no path.

THE SECOND SOLDIER. [*Grinning*] He don't know no path.

THE YOUNG PEASANT. I'm not helping the Catholics.

THE LIEUTENANT. [*To the second soldier*] Give him a feel of your pike!

THE YOUNG PEASANT. [*Forced down on his knees and threatened with the pike*] You can kill me. I won't do it.

THE FIRST SOLDIER. I know what'll make him think twice. [*He goes over to the barn*] Two cows and an ox. Get this: If you don't help us, I'll cut them down.

THE YOUNG PEASANT. Not the animals!

THE PEASANT WOMAN. [*In tears*] Captain, spare our animals or we'll starve.

THE LIEUTENANT. If he insists on being stubborn, they're done for.

THE FIRST SOLDIER. I'll start with the ox.

THE YOUNG PEASANT. [*To the old man*] Do I have to? [*The old woman nods*] I'll do it.

THE PEASANT WOMAN. And thank you kindly for your forbearance, Captain, for ever and ever, amen.

[*The peasant stops her from giving further thanks*]

THE FIRST SOLDIER. Didn't I tell you? With them it's the animals that come first.

[*Led by the young peasant, the lieutenant and the soldiers continue on their way*]

THE PEASANT. I wish I knew what they're up to. Nothing good.

THE PEASANT WOMAN. Maybe they're only scouts.—What are you doing?

THE PEASANT. [*Putting a ladder against the roof and climbing up*] See if they're alone. [*On the roof*] Men moving in the woods. All the way to the quarry. Armor in the clearing. And a cannon. It's more than a regiment. God have mercy on the city and everybody in it.

THE PEASANT WOMAN. See any light in the city?

THE PEASANT. No. They're all asleep. [*He climbs down*] If they get in, they'll kill everybody.

THE PEASANT WOMAN. The sentry will see them in time.

THE PEASANT. They must have killed the sentry in the tower on the hill, or he'd have blown his horn.

THE PEASANT WOMAN. If there were more of us . . .

THE PEASANT. All by ourselves up here with a cripple . . .

THE PEASANT WOMAN. We can't do a thing. Do you think . . .

THE PEASANT. Not a thing.

THE PEASANT WOMAN. We couldn't get down there in the dark.

THE PEASANT. The whole hillside is full of them. We can't even give a signal.

THE PEASANT WOMAN. They'd kill us.

THE PEASANT. No, we can't do a thing.

THE PEASANT WOMAN. [*To Kattrin*] Pray, poor thing, pray! We can't stop the bloodshed. If you can't talk, at least you can pray. He'll hear you if nobody else does. I'll help you. [*All kneel, Kattrin behind the peasants*] Our Father which art in heaven, hear our prayer. Don't let the town perish with everybody in it, all asleep and unsuspecting. Wake them, make them get up and climb the walls and see the enemy coming through the night with cannon and pikes, through the fields and down the hillside. [*Back to Kattrin*] Protect our mother and don't let the watchman sleep, wake him before it's too late. And succor our brother-in-law, he's in there with his four children, let them not perish, they're innocent and don't know a thing. [*To Kattrin, who groans*] The littlest is less than two, the oldest is seven. [*Horrified, Kattrin stands up*] Our Father, hear us, for Thou alone canst help, we'll all be killed, we're weak, we haven't any pikes or anything, we are powerless and in Thine hands, we and our animals and the whole farm, and the city too, it's in Thine hands, and the enemy is under the walls with great might.

> [*Kattrin has crept unnoticed to the wagon, taken something out of it, put it under her apron and climbed up the ladder to the roof of the barn*]

THE PEASANT WOMAN. Think upon the children in peril, especially the babes in arms and the old people that can't help themselves and all God's creatures.

THE PEASANT. And forgive us our trespasses as we forgive them that trespass against us. Amen.

> [*Kattrin, sitting on the roof, starts beating the drum that she has taken out from under her apron*]

THE PEASANT WOMAN. Jesus! What's she doing?

THE PEASANT. She's gone crazy.

THE PEASANT WOMAN. Get her down, quick!

> [*The peasant runs toward the ladder, but Kattrin pulls it up on the roof*]

THE PEASANT WOMAN. She'll be the death of us all.

THE PEASANT. Stop that, you cripple!

THE PEASANT WOMAN. She'll have the Catholics down on us.

THE PEASANT. [*Looking around for stones*] I'll throw rocks at you.

THE PEASANT WOMAN. Have you no pity? Have you no heart? We're dead if they find out it's us! They'll run us through!

> [*Kattrin stares in the direction of the city, and goes on drumming*]

THE PEASANT WOMAN. [*To the peasant*] I told you not to let those tramps stop here. What do they care if the soldiers drive our last animals away?

THE LIEUTENANT. [*Rushes in with his soldiers and the young peasant*] I'll cut you to pieces!

THE PEASANT WOMAN. We're innocent, captain. We couldn't help it. She sneaked up there. We don't know her.

THE LIEUTENANT. Where's the ladder?

THE PEASANT. Up top.

THE LIEUTENANT. [*To Kattrin*] Throw down that drum. It's an order!

    [*Kattrin goes on drumming*]

THE LIEUTENANT. You're all in this together! This'll be the end of you!

THE PEASANT. They've felled some pine trees in the woods over there. We could get one and knock her down . . .

THE FIRST SOLDIER. [*To the Lieutenant*] Request permission to make a suggestion. [*He whispers something in the lieutenant's ear. He nods*] Listen. We've got a friendly proposition. Come down, we'll take you into town with us. Show us your mother and we won't touch a hair of her head.

    [*Kattrin goes on drumming*]

THE LIEUTENANT. [*Pushes him roughly aside*] She doesn't trust you. No wonder with your mug. [*He calls up*] If I give you my word? I'm an officer, you can trust my word of honor.

    [*She drums still louder*]

THE LIEUTENANT. Nothing is sacred to her.

THE YOUNG PEASANT. It's not just her mother, lieutenant!

THE FIRST SOLDIER. We can't let this go on. They'll hear it in the city.

THE LIEUTENANT. We'll have to make some kind of noise that's louder than the drums. What could we make noise with?

THE FIRST SOLDIER. But we're not supposed to make noise.

THE LIEUTENANT. An innocent noise, stupid. A peaceable noise.

THE PEASANT. I could chop wood.

THE LIEUTENANT. That's it, chop! [*The peasant gets an ax and chops at a log*] Harder! Harder! You're chopping for your life.

    [*Listening, Kattrin has been drumming more softly. Now she looks anxiously around and goes on drumming as before*]

THE LIEUTENANT. [*To the peasant*] Not loud enough. [*To the first soldier*] You chop too.

THE PEASANT. There's only one ax. [*Stops chopping*]

THE LIEUTENANT. We'll have to set the house on fire. Smoke her out.

THE PEASANT. That won't do any good, Captain. If the city people see fire up here, they'll know what's afoot.

    [*Still drumming, Kattrin has been listening again. Now she laughs*]

THE LIEUTENANT. Look, she's laughing at us. I'll shoot her down, regardless. Get the musket!

    [*Two soldiers run out. Kattrin goes on drumming*]

THE PEASANT WOMAN. I've got it, captain. That's their wagon over there. If we start smashing it up, she'll stop. The wagon's all they've got.

THE LIEUTENANT. [*To the young peasant*] Smash away. [*To Kattrin*] We'll smash your wagon if you don't stop.

    [*The young peasant strikes a few feeble blows at the wagon*]

THE PEASANT WOMAN. Stop it, you beast!

> [*Kattrin strares· despairingly at the wagon and emits pitiful sounds. But she goes on drumming*]

THE LIEUTENANT. Where are those stinkers with the musket?

THE FIRST SOLDIER. They haven't heard anything in the city yet, or we'd hear their guns.

THE LIEUTENANT. [*To Kattrin*] They don't hear you. And now we're going to shoot you down. For the last time: Drop that drum!

THE YOUNG PEASANT. [*Suddenly throws the plank away*] Keep on drumming! Or they'll all be killed! Keep on drumming, keep on drumming . . .

> [*The soldier throws him down and hits him with his pike. Kattrin starts crying, but goes on drumming*]

THE PEASANT WOMAN. Don't hit him in the back! My God, you're killing him.

> [*The soldiers run in with the musket*]

THE SECOND SOLDIER. The colonel's foaming at the mouth. We'll be court-martialed.

THE LIEUTENANT. Set it up! Set it up! [*To Kattrin, while the musket is being set up on its stand*] For the last time: Stop that drumming! [*Kattrin in tears drums as loud as she can*] Fire!

> [*The soldiers fire, Kattrin is hit. She beats the drum for a few times more and then slowly collapses*]

THE LIEUTENANT. Now we'll have some quiet.

> [*But Kattrin's last drumbeats are answered by the city's cannon. A confused hubbub of alarm bells and cannon is heard in the distance*]

THE FIRST SOLDIER. She's done it.

12

Night, toward morning. The fifes and drums of troops marching away.

Outside the wagon Mother Courage sits huddled over her daughter. The peasant couple are standing beside them.

THE PEASANT. [*Hostile*] You'll have to be going, woman. There's only one more regiment to come. You can't go alone.[1]

MOTHER COURAGE. Maybe I can get her to sleep. [*She sings*]

> Lullaby baby
> What stirs in the hay?
> The neighbor brats whimper
> Mine are happy and gay.
> They go in tatters
> And you in silk down
> Cut from an angel's
> Best party gown.

---

1. I.e., for protection and for custom- army.
ers Mother Courage must travel with the

They've nothing to munch on
And you will have pie
Just tell your mother
In case it's too dry.
Lullaby baby
What stirs in the hay?
That one lies in Poland
The other—who can say?

Now she's asleep. You shouldn't have told her about your brother-in-law's children.

THE PEASANT. Maybe it wouldn't have happened if you hadn't gone to town to swindle people.

MOTHER COURAGE. I'm glad she's sleeping now.

THE PEASANT WOMAN. She's not sleeping, you'll have to face it, she's dead.

THE PEASANT. And it's time you got started. There are wolves around here, and what's worse, marauders.

MOTHER COURAGE. Yes. [*She goes to the wagon and takes out a sheet of canvas to cover the body with*]

THE PEASANT WOMAN. Haven't you anybody else? Somebody you can go to?

MOTHER COURAGE. Yes, there's one of them left. Eilif.

THE PEASANT. [*While Mother Courage covers the body*] Go find him. We'll attend to this one, give her a decent burial. Set your mind at rest.

MOTHER COURAGE. Here's money for your expenses. [*She gives the peasant money*]
    [*The peasant and his son shake hands with her and carry Kattrin away*]

THE PEASANT WOMAN. [*On the way out*] Hurry up!

MOTHER COURAGE. [*Harnesses herself to the wagon*] I hope I can pull the wagon alone. I'll manage, there isn't much in it. I've got to get back in business.
    [*Another regiment marches by with fifes and drums in the rear*]

MOTHER COURAGE. Hey, take me with you! [*She starts to pull*]
    [*Singing is heard in the rear:*]

With all the killing and recruiting
The war will worry on a while.
In ninety years they'll still be shooting.
It's hardest on the rank-and-file.
Our food is swill, our pants all patches
The higher-ups steal half our pay
And still we dream of God-sent riches.
Tomorrow is another day!
    The spring is come! Christian, revive!
    The snowdrifts melt, the dead lie dead!
    And if by chance you're still alive
    It's time to rise and shake a leg.

VLADIMIR NABOKOV

(1899–1977)

Cloud, Castle, Lake*

One of my representatives—a modest, mild bachelor, very efficient—happened to win a pleasure trip at a charity ball given by Russian refugees.[1] That was in 1936 or 1937. The Berlin summer was in full flood (it was the second week of damp and cold, so that it was a pity to look at everything which had turned green in vain, and only the sparrows kept cheerful); he did not care to go anywhere, but when he tried to sell his ticket at the office of the Bureau of Pleasantrips he was told that to do so he would have to have special permission from the Ministry of Transportation; when he tried them, it turned out that first he would have to draw up a complicated petition at a notary's on stamped paper; and besides, a so-called "certificate of non-absence from the city for the summer-time" had to be obtained from the police.[2]

So he sighed a little, and decided to go. He borrowed an aluminum flask from friends, repaired his soles, bought a belt and a fancy-style flannel shirt—one of those cowardly things which shrink in the first wash. Incidentally, it was too large for that likable little man, his hair always neatly trimmed, his eyes so intelligent and kind. I cannot remember his name at the moment. I think it was Vasili Ivanovich.

He slept badly the night before the departure. And why? Because he had to get up unusually early, and hence took along into his dreams the delicate face of the watch ticking on his night table; but mainly because that very night, for no reason at all, he began to imagine that this trip, thrust upon him by a feminine Fate in a low-cut gown,[3] this trip which he had accepted so reluctantly, would bring him some wonderful, tremulous happiness. This happiness would have something in common with his childhood, and with the excitement aroused in him by Russian lyrical poetry, and with some evening sky line once seen in a dream, and with that lady, another man's wife, whom he had hopelessly loved for seven

* Written in Russian and published in 1937; translated into English by the author and Peter Pertzov in 1941.

1. Those who fled Russia after the 1917 Revolution. Berlin and Paris were the main centers for the refugee "White Russian" communities.

2. "Our utter physical dependence on this or that nation, which had coldly granted us political refuge, became pain-fully evident when some trashy 'visa,' some diabolical 'identity card' had to be obtained or prolonged, for then an avid bureaucratic hell would attempt to close upon the petitioner and he might wilt while his dossier waxed fatter and fatter." (*Speak, Memory*)

3. The woman who presented him with his prize at the ball, as Fate personified.

years—but it would be even fuller and more significant than all that. And besides, he felt that the really good life must be oriented toward something or someone.

The morning was dull, but steam-warm and close, with an inner sun, and it was quite pleasant to rattle in a streetcar to the distant railway station where the gathering place was: several people, alas, were taking part in the excursion. Who would they be, these drowsy beings, drowsy as seem all creatures still unknown to us? By Window No. 6, at 7 A.M., as was indicated in the directions appended to the ticket, he saw them (they were already waiting; he had managed to be late by about three minutes).

A lanky blond young man in Tyrolese garb[4] stood out at once. He was burned the color of a cockscomb, had huge brick-red knees with golden hairs, and his nose looked lacquered. He was the leader furnished by the Bureau, and as soon as the newcomer had joined the group (which consisted of four women and as many men) he led it off toward a train lurking behind other trains, carrying his monstrous knapsack with terrifying ease, and firmly clanking with his hob-nailed boots.

Everyone found a place in an empty car, unmistakably third-class,[5] and Vasili Ivanovich, having sat down by himself and put a peppermint into his mouth, opened a little volume of Tyutchev,[6] whom he had long intended to re-read; but he was requested to put the book aside and join the group. An elderly bespectacled post-office clerk, with skull, chin, and upper lip a· bristly blue as if he had shaved off some extraordinarily luxuriant and tough growth especially for this trip, immediately announced that he had been to Russia and knew some Russian—for instance, *patzlui*[7]—and, recalling philanderings in Tsaritsyn, winked in such a manner that his fat wife sketched out in the air the outline of a backhand box on the ear. The company was getting noisy. Four employees of the same building firm were tossing each other heavyweight jokes: a middle-aged man, Schultz; a younger man, Schultz also, and two fidgety young women with big mouths and big rumps. The red-headed, rather burlesque widow in a sport skirt knew something too about Russia (the Riga[8] beaches). There was also a dark young man by the name of Schramm, with lusterless eyes and a vague velvety vileness about his person and manners, who constantly switched the conversation to this or that attractive aspect of the excursion, and

4. From the Austrian or Italian Tyrol, Alpine country popular with hikers and mountain-climbers. Tyrolese garb includes leather shorts, hiking boots, a mountaineer's stick (or Alpenstock), and a cap with a feather in it.

5. The cheapest and most spartan accommodations on the train.

6. Fedor Ivanovich Tyutchev, Russian poet and diplomat (1803–1873). Tyutchev lived twenty-two years in Western Europe, and was known for poetry that sang the praises of his native land.

7. A garbled version of the Russian word for *kiss*. *Tsaritsyn*: Former name for Stalingrad, now Volgograd, a city on the Volga in southwestern Russia.

8. Major seaport on the Baltic.

who gave the first signal for rapturous appreciation; he was, as it turned out later, a special stimulator from the Bureau of Pleasan-trips.

The locomotive, working rapidly with its elbows, hurried through a pine forest, then—with relief—among fields. Only dimly realizing as yet all the absurdity and horror of the situation, and perhaps attempting to persuade himself that everything was very nice, Vasili Ivanovich contrived to enjoy the fleeting gifts of the road. And indeed, how enticing it all is, what charm the world acquires when it is wound up and moving like a merry-go-round! The sun crept toward a corner of the window and suddenly spilled over the yellow bench. The badly pressed shadow of the car sped madly along the grassy bank, where flowers blended into colored streaks. A crossing: a cyclist was waiting, one foot resting on the ground. Trees appeared in groups and singly, revolving coolly and blandly, display-ing the latest fashions. The blue dampness of a ravine. A memory of love, disguised as a meadow. Wispy clouds—greyhounds of heaven.

We both, Vasili Ivanovich and I, have always been impressed by the anonymity of all the parts of a landscape, so dangerous for the soul, the impossibility of ever finding out where that path you see leads—and look, what a tempting thicket! It happened that on a distant slope or in a gap in the trees there would appear and, as it were, stop for an instant, like air retained in the lungs, a spot so enchanting—a lawn, a terrace—such perfect expression of tender well-meaning beauty—that it seemed that if one could stop the train and go thither, forever, to you, my love . . . But a thousand beech trunks were already madly leaping by, whirling in a sizzling sun pool, and again the chance for happiness was gone.

At the stations, Vasili Ivanovich would look at the configuration of some entirely insignificant objects—a smear on the platform, a cherry stone, a cigarette butt—and would say to himself that never, never would he remember these three little things here in that par-ticular interrelation, this pattern, which he now could see with such deathless precision; or again, looking at a group of children waiting for a train, he would try with all his might to single out at least one remarkable destiny—in the form of a violin or a crown, a propeller or a lyre[9]—and would gaze until the whole party of village school-boys appeared as on an old photograph, now reproduced with a little white cross above the face of the last boy on the right: the hero's childhood.

But one could look out of the window only by snatches. All had been given sheet music with verses from the Bureau:

9. Stringed instrument resembling a harp, emblematic of musical and poetic inspira-tion.

Stop that worrying and moping,
Take a knotted stick and rise,
Come a-tramping in the open
With the good, the hearty guys!

Tramp your country's grass and stubble,
With the good, the hearty guys,
Kill the hermit and his trouble
And to hell with doubts and sighs!

In a paradise of heather
Where the field mouse screams and dies,
Let us march and sweat together
With the steel-and-leather guys!

This was to be sung in chorus: Vasili Ivanovich, who not only could not sing but could not even pronounce German words clearly, took advantage of the drowning roar of mingling voices and merely opened his mouth while swaying slightly, as if he were really singing —but the leader, at a sign from the subtle Schramm, suddenly stopped the general singing and, squinting askance at Vasili Ivanovich, demanded that he sing solo. Vasili Ivanovich cleared his throat, timidly began, and after a minute of solitary torment all joined in; but he did not dare thereafter to drop out.

He had with him his favorite cucumber from the Russian store, a loaf of bread, and three eggs. When evening came, and the low crimson sun entered wholly the soiled seasick car, stunned by its own din, all were invited to hand over their provisions, in order to divide them evenly—this was particularly easy, as all except Vasili Ivanovich had the same things. The cucumber amused everybody, was pronounced inedible, and was thrown out of the window. In view of the insufficiency of his contribution, Vasili Ivanovich got a smaller portion of sausage.

He was made to play cards. They pulled him about, questioned him, verified whether he could show the route of the trip on a map —in a word, all busied themselves with him, at first good-naturedly, then with malevolence, which grew with the approach of night. Both girls were called Greta; the red-headed widow somehow resembled the rooster-leader; Schramm, Schultz, and the other Schultz, the post-office clerk and his wife, all gradually melted together, merged together, forming one collective, wobbly, many-handed being, from which one could not escape. It pressed upon him from all sides. But suddenly at some station all climbed out, and it was already dark, although in the west there still hung a very long, very pink cloud, and farther along the track, with a soul-piercing light, the star of a lamp trembled through the slow smoke of the engine, and crickets chirped in the dark, and from somewhere there came the odor of jasmine and hay, my love.

They spent the night in a tumble-down inn. A mature bedbug is awful, but there is a certain grace in the motions of silky silverfish.[10] The post-office clerk was separated from his wife, who was put with the widow; he was given to Vasili Ivanovich for the night. The two beds took up the whole room. Quilt on top, chamber pot below. The clerk said that somehow he did not feel sleepy, and began to talk of his Russian adventures, rather more circumstantially than in the train. He was a great bully of a man, thorough and obstinate, clad in long cotton drawers, with mother-of-pearl claws on his dirty toes, and bear's fur between fat breasts. A moth dashed about the ceiling, hobnobbing with its shadow. "In Tsaritsyn," the clerk was saying, "there are now three schools, a German, a Czech, and a Chinese one. At any rate, that is what my brother-in-law says; he went there to build tractors."

Next day, from early morning to five o'clock in the afternoon, they raised dust along a highway, which undulated from hill to hill; then they took a green road through a dense fir wood. Vasili Ivanovich, as the least burdened, was given an enormous round loaf of bread to carry under his arm. How I hate you, our daily! But still his precious, experienced eyes noted what was necessary. Against the background of fir-tree gloom a dry needle was hanging vertically on an invisible thread.

Again they piled into a train, and again the small partitionless car was empty. The other Schultz began to teach Vasili Ivanovich how to play the mandolin. There was much laughter. When they got tired of that, they thought up a capital game, which was supervised by Schramm. It consisted of the following: the women would lie down on the benches they chose, under which the men were already hidden, and when from under one of the benches there would emerge a ruddy face with ears, or a big outspread hand, with a skirt-lifting curve of the fingers (which would provoke much squealing), then it would be revealed who was paired off with whom. Three times Vasili Ivanovich lay down in filthy darkness, and three times it turned out that there was no one on the bench when he crawled out from under. He was acknowledged the loser and was forced to eat a cigarette butt.

They spent the night on straw mattresses in a barn, and early in the morning set out again on foot. Firs, ravines, foamy streams. From the heat, from the songs which one had constantly to bawl, Vasili Ivanovich became so exhausted that during the midday halt he fell asleep at once, and awoke only when they began to slap at imaginary horseflies on him. But after another hour of marching, that very happiness of which he had once half dreamt was suddenly discovered.

10. A wingless household pest.

It was a pure, blue lake, with an unusual expression of its water. In the middle, a large cloud was reflected in its entirety. On the other side, on a hill thickly covered with verdure (and the darker the verdure, the more poetic it is), towered, arising from dactyl to dactyl,[11] an ancient black castle. Of course, there are plenty of such views in Central Europe, but just this one—in the inexpressible and unique harmoniousness of its three principal parts, in its smile, in some mysterious innocence it had, my love! my obedient one!—was something so unique, and so familiar, and so long-promised, and it so *understood* the beholder that Vasili Ivanovich even pressed his hand to his heart, as if to see whether his heart was there in order to give it away.

At some distance, Schramm, poking into the air with the leader's alpenstock, was calling the attention of the excursionists to something or other; they had settled themselves around on the grass in poses seen in amateur snapshots, while the leader sat on a stump, his behind to the lake, and was having a snack. Quietly, concealing himself in his own shadow, Vasili Ivanovich followed the shore, and came to a kind of inn. A dog still quite young greeted him; it crept on its belly; its jaws laughing, its tail fervently beating the ground. Vasili Ivanovich accompanied the dog into the house, a piebald two-storied dwelling with a winking window beneath a convex tiled eyelid; and he found the owner, a tall old man vaguely resembling a Russian war veteran, who spoke German so poorly and with such a soft drawl that Vasili Ivanovich changed to his own tongue, but the man understood as in a dream and continued in the language of his environment, his family.

Upstairs was a room for travelers. "You know, I shall take it for the rest of my life," Vasili Ivanovich is reported to have said as soon as he had entered it. The room itself had nothing remarkable about it. On the contrary, it was a most ordinary room, with a red floor, daisies daubed on the white walls, and a small mirror half filled with the yellow infusion of the reflected flowers—but from the window one could clearly see the lake with its cloud and its castle, in a motionless and perfect correlation of happiness. Without reasoning, without considering, only entirely surrendering to an attraction the truth of which consisted in its own strength, a strength which he had never experienced before, Vasili Ivanovich in one radiant second realized that here in this little room with that view, beautiful to the verge of tears, life would at last be what he had always wished it to be. What exactly it would be like, what would take place here, that of course he did not know, but all around him were help, promise, and consolation—so that there could not be any doubt that he must live here. In a moment he

11. Digit or joint: segments of the castle walls. Also echoes "poetic," since a dactyl is a rhythmic unit of a poetic meter.

figured out how he would manage it so as not to have to return to Berlin again, how to get the few possessions that he had—books, the blue suit, her photograph. How simple it was turning out! As my representative, he was earning enough for the modest life of a refugee Russian.

"My friends," he cried, having run down again to the meadow by the shore, "my friends, good-by. I shall remain for good in that house over there. We can't travel together any longer. I shall go no farther. I am not going anywhere. Good-by!"

"How is that?" said the leader in a queer voice, after a short pause, during which the smile on the lips of Vasili Ivanovich slowly faded, while the people who had been sitting on the grass half rose and stared at him with stony eyes.

"But why?" he faltered. "It is here that . . ."

"Silence!" the post-office clerk suddenly bellowed with extraordinary force. "Come to your senses, you drunken swine!"

"Wait a moment, gentlemen," said the leader, and, having passed his tongue over his lips, he turned to Vasili Ivanovich.

"You probably have been drinking," he said quietly. "Or have gone out of your mind. You are taking a pleasure trip with us. Tomorrow, according to the appointed itinerary—look at your ticket—we are all returning to Berlin. There can be no question of anyone—in this case you—refusing to continue this communal journey. We were singing today a certain song—try and remember what it said. That's enough now! Come, children, we are going on."

"There will be beer at Ewald," said Schramm in a caressing voice. "Five hours by train. Hikes. A hunting lodge. Coal mines. Lots of interesting things."

"I shall complain," wailed Vasili Ivanovich. "Give me back my bag. I have the right to remain where I want. Oh, but this is nothing less than an invitation to a beheading"[12]—he told me he cried when they seized him by the arms.

"If necessary we shall carry you," said the leader grimly, "but that is not likely to be pleasant. I am responsible for each of you, and shall bring back each of you, alive or dead."

Swept along a forest road as in a hideous fairy tale, squeezed, twisted, Vasili Ivanovich could not even turn around, and only felt how the radiance behind his back receded, fractured by trees, and then it was no longer there, and all around the dark firs fretted but could not interfere. As soon as everyone had got into the car and the train had pulled off, they began to beat him—they beat him a long time, and with a good deal of inventiveness. It occurred to them, among other things, to use a corkscrew on his palms; then on his feet. The post-office clerk, who had been to Russia, fashioned a knout[13] out of a stick and a belt, and began to use it with devilish

---

12. *Invitation to a Beheading*, title of a book by Nabokov first published in 1938.

13. A leather whip used to flog criminals in Russia.

dexterity. Atta boy! The other men relied more on their iron heels, whereas the women were satisfied to pinch and slap. All had a wonderful time.

After returning to Berlin, he called on me, was much changed, sat down quietly, putting his hands on his knees, told his story; kept on repeating that he must resign his position, begged me to let him go, insisted that he could not continue, that he had not the strength to belong to mankind any longer. Of course, I let him go.[14]

Marienbad, 1937

14. In an interview, Nabokov later added this comment about Vasili: "He will never find it again. If I let him go, it is in the hope that he might find a less dangerous job than that of my agent."

BENJAMIN PÉRET
(1899–1959)

A Life Full of Interest[1]

Coming out of her house early in the morning, as usual, Mrs. Lannor saw that her cherry tress, still covered with fine red fruit the day before, had been replaced during the night by stuffed giraffes. A silly joke! Why did Mrs. Lannor think to accuse a couple of lovers who, the evening before, at nightfall, had come to sit at the foot of one of those trees? To leave there a souvenir of their love, they had engraved their entwined initials in the bark. But Mrs. Lannor had spotted them and, seizing a sucking pig,[2] she had thrown it at the couple, shouting, "What are you doing there, artichoke children! Would you like a begonia, by any chance?"

To her great astonishment the two lovers slid along the trunk of the cherry tree as if a pulley were hoisting them above ground. When they had reached the top, they flew off like swallows, describing ever-widening circles in soaring flight, then they fell into a neighboring pond. At once there was a terrifying racket comparable to that of 3,000 trombones, cornets, saxophones, bass drums, bugles, etc., playing all at once. Mrs. Lannor was, with every right, stupefied at this, but did not want to show, and said, "I've been making pocket mirrors for a long time."

And she had stopped thinking of that incident. But this morning, seeing stuffed giraffes in place of her cherry trees, she could not refrain from making a connection between the event of the evening before and that of today.

To clear the matter up, she decided to go to the pond where the lovers had disappeared. The pond was empty and on the mud car-

1. Parodies newspaper titles of human interest stories. 2. A baby pig.
Translated by J. H. Matthews.

peting the bottom—mud already dried—she saw hundreds of dead marmoset bodies laid out, holding hunting horns. In the middle of the pond rose an obelisk more than ninety feet high, surmounted by a hat in musketeer style.[3] At the foot of the monument, holding hands, were the two lovers from the evening before. His head bent toward her, he was saying, "Gertrude!" and, she, in the same attitude, replied, "Francis!" And so on, indefinitely.

Seeing this spectacle, Mrs. Lannor did not doubt she was in the presence of the guilty parties. Already she was rejoicing at having guessed so quickly and so well. She was rejoicing too soon, even, for one of the marmosets sat up and shouted to her with the purest Provençal accent, "Cast the first stone."[4] An excellent idea. Mrs. Lannor seized an enormous stone and threw it in the direction of the lovers, but, having come within a yard of Francis' head, the stone stopped in flight, a spark shot from the stone to Francis' head, while a formidable sound of broken glass could be heard. The sound had scarcely subsided when from the base of the obelisk emerged a band of naked girls holding hands and linked together by an ivy stalk wrapped around their bodies like alpinists on a rope. They went off singing the *Brabançonne*,[5] to dance around the obelisk. One by one the monkeys got up to dance with them, some singing, others accompanying these on their hunting horns. Mrs. Lannor felt herself become very light indeed, and danced like everyone else. If that poor Mrs. Lannor, instead of dancing, had looked at what was happening at the top of the obelisk, she would have no doubt died of terror.

The obelisk had opened like the two points of a pair of scissors. Between the two points separated in this way rose a thin column of smoke in which all the colors of the spectrum were represented. Above the column of smoke hovered a bicycle on which a couple like Gertrude and Francis were making love. At the very moment when the smoke was starting to form spirals, the front wheel of the bicycle came away from the machine and slowly ran all along down one of the sides of the obelisk, coming to rest delicately on the head of one of the girls. The effect was immediate. All of a sudden every one of the girls burst into flame and in their place a little blue flame could be seen for a few seconds, a few centimeters high, then the girls were replaced by a cherry tree, half of which was in blossom while the other half was covered with ripe cherries.

Mrs. Lannor was so excited by this she forgot her age, so dis-

---

3. A wide-brimmed hat, probably with large feathers; musketeers were royal bodyguards in seventeenth- and eighteenth-century France, and the dashing heroes of romantic historical novels like Alexander Dumas' *The Three Musketeers* (1844).
4. Echo of the Biblical passage in which Jesus rebukes those who would stone an adulteress according to Mosaic Law: "He that is without sin among you, let him first cast a stone at her." (John 8:7). *Provençal:* From the south of France: a heavy accent.
5. The Belgian national hymn; literally, "the woman from Brabant."

turbed she forgot the imminent arrival of her nephew who so advantageously took the place of an eiderdown.[6] "My cherry trees," she said. "So they were the ones!"

She ran toward the obelisk at the foot of which Francis and Gertrude were still kneeling and repeating their names endlessly. She was about to pass the line of cherry trees that formed a circle about the obelisk when she saw with stupefaction two of those trees between which she wanted to pass move closer together and block her way. She wanted to go around them, but if she edged to the right a cherry tree placed itself in front of her and the same was true on the left. She wanted to run: the cherry trees did so too. All that was left to do was fly. She did this. Alas! the cherry trees followed her example. This game of catch could have gone on for a long time if suddenly Mrs. Lannor had not had an idea: "I'm going to dig an underground tunnel that will end up at the obelisk."

At once she alighted on the ground and strode home to fetch a pick and shovel. A moment later, she was at work. The cherry trees, to show her that her mettle did not impress them, dropped a rotten cherry on her head, from minute to minute. Mrs. Lannor raved and worked with increasing rage. Came the moment when the hole was deep enough for her to disappear into. Satisfied, she felt like a moment's rest and stretched out on the grass, her face to the sky. Scarcely had she stretched out when she saw a strange cloud assuming the form of a sausage equipped at each end with an enormous ear moving slowly like a fan.

"There they are again," grumbled Mrs. Lannor.

She was getting ready to go back to work when she saw that sausage was splitting longitudinally and something was being released from it: a cherry ten time bigger than a pumpkin that fell on the obelisk and remained stuck on it. Mrs. Lannor saw in this an act of defiance and got up.

"Oh! the gangsters! We shall see!"

And she seized her pick which she brandished above her head, but remained frozen in that position. She had just seen in the hole she had dug 7 or 8 jaws, opening and closing regularly. That was not enough though to frighten Mrs. Lannor. She pulled a carrot that she threw into one of the jaws, and this made a stream of yellow smoke come from all the jaws, spreading a sickening odor of incense. All the jaws disappeared and when the smoke had cleared away, Mrs. Lannor saw, seated at the bottom of a hole, a little girl holding a leek between her legs. The leek was growing visibly, so rapidly even that the little girl was ashamed and her stomach, soon followed by her heart and liver, left her body and went off with slow steps as though regretfully, while the little girl discovered that her back was covered with scales.

6. Quilt stuffed with down from the eider duck.

"And yet I'm not a mermaid," she whispered.

When she wanted to withdraw the leek, what was not her fright at seeing that henceforth it formed part of her body. After efforts long and painful, she succeeded however in uprooting it, but beneath the leek lay an iris bulb which was only waiting for that moment to blossom. Scarcely had the flower opened up when the little girl felt labor pains and vomited a prayer book that opened on its own to the page with the invocation to Joan of Arc.[7] The little girl saw in this an order from heaven and at once vowed to take the veil. She got up and left the hole without bothering any more with Mrs. Lannor who, in her turn, was feeling labor pains and bringing into the world a ridiculous Louis XV clock[8] that struck the hour ceaselessly. This time, Mrs. Lannor did not feel reassured. Her uneasiness gave way to distress beyond measure, when she felt invisible hands putting on her feet sewerman's boots that were soon full of sweat, Mrs. Lannor fainted.

She came to herself again hearing the sea breaking close by. She opened her eyes and saw herself in an immense metallic box with holes pierced in all its sides. She was in the company of shoals of sardines which, when she sat up, rose on their tails and, politely, bade her welcome, then disappeared all in the same direction as if they had been sucked up by a gigantic pump. Mrs. Lannor moistened her finger with a little saliva and raised it above her head to find the direction of the wind.

"East-north-east," said a flying fish who had approached without her noticing. And she set about undressing, but she was to take off only her boots, for, scarcely had she reached this decision when a human spinal column was coming down from the ceiling to upbraid her over her attitude and abuse her. Conscious of her humiliation, Mrs. Lannor kept silent. The spinal column covered itself in pink phosphorescence and disappeared with the loud noise of a slammed door.

Mrs. Lannor was in despair, for she had understood she would never see her cherry trees again and she was about to make up her mind to go home, sick at heart, when she was taken with violent pains in the feet.

"It's nothing," her limbs told her, "It's springtime."

Mrs. Lannor's feet become covered with cherry tree leaves and blossoms appeared a few seconds later. From each of these fell a wax vesta[9] which burst into flames upon contact with the ground. The blossoms disappeared, replaced immediately by cherries. A current of air passed, laden with sulphurous vapors, the cherries lost their color and their stones appeared. In the time it took her to

---

7. Patron saint of France (1412?–1431).

8. An antique clock from the time of King Louis XV of France (1710–1774).

9. A match.

reach out an arm the stones became shrubs. Mrs. Lannor saw lightning followed immediately by a dreadful roll of thunder. When she
opened her eyes again she was suspended by the feet from the top
of the obelisk on the Place de la Concorde and all around her head
floated thousands of cherries, bursting like puffballs. Then Mrs.
Lannor realized her final hour had come and died as mushrooms
die.

ISAAC BASHEVIS SINGER
(1904–)

The Gentleman from Cracow*

I

Amid thick forests and deep swamps, on the slope of a hill, level
at the summit, lay the village of Frampol. Nobody knew who had
founded it, or why just there. Goats grazed among the tombstones
which were already sunk in the ground of the cemetery. In the community house there was a parchment with a chronicle on it, but the
first page was missing and the writing had faded. Legends were current among the people, tales of wicked intrigue concerning a mad
nobleman, a lascivious lady, a Jewish scholar, and a wild dog. But
their true origin was lost in the past.

Peasants who tilled the surrounding countryside were poor; the
land was stubborn. In the village, the Jews were impoverished; their
roofs were straw, their floors dirt. In summer many of them wore no
shoes, and in cold weather they wrapped their feet in rags or wore
sandals made of straw.

Rabbi Ozer, although renowned for his erudition, received a
salary of only eighteen groszy a week. The assistant rabbi, besides
being ritual slaughterer, was teacher, matchmaker, bath attendant,
and poorhouse nurse as well. Even those villagers who were considered wealthy knew little of luxury. They wore cotton gabardines,
tied about their waists with string, and tasted meat only on the Sabbath. Gold coin was rarely seen in Frampol.

But the inhabitants of Frampol had been blessed with fine children. The boys grew tall and strong, the girls handsome. It was a
mixed blessing, however, for the young men left to marry girls from
other towns, while their sisters, who had no dowries, remained
unwed. Yet despite everything, inexplicably, though the food was

* From *Gimpel the Fool*, translated by Martha Glicklich and Elaine Gottlieb.

scarce and the water foul, the children continued to thrive.

Then, one summer, there was a drought. Even the oldest peasants could not recall a calamity such as this one. No rain fell. The corn was parched and stunted. There was scarcely anything worth harvesting. Not until the few sheaves of wheat had been cut and gathered did the rain come, and with it hail which destroyed whatever grain the drought had spared. Locusts huge as birds came in the wake of the storm; human voices were said to issue from their throats. They flew at the eyes of the peasants who tried to drive them away. That year there was no fair, for everything had been lost. Neither the peasants nor the Jews of Frampol had food. Although there was grain in the large towns, no one could buy it.

Just when all hope had been abandoned and the entire town was about to go begging, a miracle occurred. A carriage, drawn by eight spirited horses, came into Frampol. The villagers expected its occupant to be a Christian gentleman, but it was a Jew, a young man between the ages of twenty and thirty, who alighted. Tall and pale, with a round black beard and fiery dark eyes, he wore a sable hat, silver-buckled shoes, and a beaver-trimmed caftan.[1] Around his waist was a green silk sash. Aroused, the entire town rushed to get a glimpse of the stranger. This is the story he told: He was a doctor, a widower from Cracow. His wife, the daughter of a wealthy merchant, had died with their baby in childbirth.

Overwhelmed, the villagers asked why he had come to Frampol. It was on the advice of a Wonder Rabbi, he told them. The melancholy he had known after his wife's death, would, the rabbi assured him, disappear in Frampol. From the poorhouse the beggars came, crowding about him as he distributed alms—three groszy, six grozy, half-gulden pieces. The stranger was clearly a gift from Heaven, and Frampol was not destined to vanish. The beggars hurried to the baker for bread, and the baker sent to Zamosc for a sack of flour.

"One sack?" the young doctor asked. "Why that won't last a single day. I will order a wagonload, and not only flour, but corn-meal also."

"But we have no money," the village elders explained.

"God willing, you will repay me when times are good," and saying this, the stranger produced a purse crammed with golden ducats. Frampol rejoiced as he counted out the coins.

The next day, wagons filled with flour, buckwheat, barley, millet, and beans, drove into Frampol. News of the village's good fortune reached the ears of the peasants, and they came to the Jews, to buy goods, as the Egyptians had once come to Joseph. Being without money, they paid in kind; as a result, there was meat in town. Now the ovens burned once more; the pots were full. Smoke rose from the chimneys, sending the odors of roast chicken and goose, onion

[1] A long garment with long sleeves and a girdle.

and garlic, fresh bread and pastry, into the evening air. The villagers returned to their occupations; shoemakers mended shoes; tailors picked up their rusted shears and irons.

The evenings were warm and the sky clear, though the Feast of the Tabernacles had already passed. The stars seemed unusually large. Even the birds were awake, and they chirped and warbled as though in mid-summer. The stranger from Cracow had taken the best room at the inn, and his dinner consisted of broiled duck, marchpane,[2] and twisted bread. Apricots and Hungarian wine were his dessert. Six candles adorned the table. One evening after dinner, the doctor from Cracow entered the large public room where some of the more inquisitive townspeople had gathered and asked, "Would anyone care for a game of cards?"

"But it isn't Chanukah[3] yet," they answered in surprise.

"Why wait for Chanukah? I'll put up a gulden for every groszy."

A few of the more frivolous men were willing to try their luck, and it turned out to be good. A groszy meant a gulden, and one gulden became thirty. Anyone played who wished to do so. Everybody won. But the stranger did not seem distressed. Banknotes and coins of silver and gold covered the table. Women and girls crowded into the room, and it seemed as though the gleam of the gold before them was reflected in their eyes. They gasped in wonderment. Never before in Frampol had such things happened. Mothers cautioned their daughters to take pains with their hair, and allowed them to dress in holiday clothes. The girl who found favor in the eyes of the young doctor would be fortunate; he was not one to require a dowry.

II

The next morning, matchmakers called on him, each extolling the virtues of the girl he represented. The doctor invited them to be seated, served them honey cake, macaroons, nuts, and mead, and announced, "From each of you I get exactly the same story: Your client is beautiful and clever and possesses every possible distinction. But how can I know which of you is telling the truth? I want the finest of them all as my wife. Here is what I suggest: Let there be a ball to which all the eligible young women are invited. By observing their appearance and behavior, I shall be able to choose among them. Then the marriage contract will be drawn and the wedding arranged."

The matchmakers were astounded. Old Mendel was the first to find words. "A ball? That sort of thing is all right for rich Gentiles,

2. Marzipan.

3. The Jewish "Feast of Lights," commemorating the rededication of the Temple in Jerusalem by Judas Maccabaeus and his brothers in 165 B.C.

but we Jews have not indulged in such festivities since the destruction of the Temple—except when the Law prescribes it for certain holidays."

"Isn't every Jew obliged to marry off his daughters?" asked the doctor.

"But the girls have no appropriate clothes," another matchmaker protested. "Because of the drought they would have to go in rags."

"I will see that they all have clothes. I'll order enough silk, wool, velvet, and linen from Zamosc to outfit every girl. Let the ball take place. Let it be one that Frampol will never forget."

"But where can we hold it?" another matchmaker interjected. "The hall where we used to hold weddings has burned down, and our cottages are too small."

"There's the market place," the gentleman from Cracow suggested.

"But it is already the month of Heshvan. Any day now, it will turn cold."

"We'll choose a warm night when the moon is out. Don't worry about it."

To all the numerous objections of the matchmakers, the stranger had an answer ready. Finally they agreed to consult the elders. The doctor said he was in no hurry, he would await their decision. During the entire discussion, he had been carrying on a game of chess with one of the town's cleverest young men, while munching raisins.

The elders were incredulous when they heard what had been proposed. But the young girls were excited. The young men approved also. The mothers pretended to hesitate, but finally gave their consent. When a delegation of the older men sought out Rabbi Ozer for his approval, he was outraged.

"What kind of charlatan is this?" he shouted. "Frampol is not Cracow. All we need is a ball! Heaven forbid that we bring down a plague, and innocent infants be made to pay for our frivolity!"

But the more practical of the men reasoned with the rabbi, saying, "Our daughters walk around barefoot and in tatters now. He will provide them with shoes and clothing. If one of them should please him he would marry her and settle here. Certainly that is to our advantage. The synagogue needs a new roof. The windowpanes of the house of study are broken, the bathhouse is badly in need of repairs. In the poorhouse the sick lie on bundles of rotting straw."

"All this is true. But suppose we sin?"

"Everything will be done according to the Law, Rabbi. You can trust us."

Taking down the book of the Law, Rabbi Ozer leafed through it. Occasionally he stopped to study a page, and then, finally, after sighing and hesitating, he consented. Was there any choice? He himself had received no salary for six months.

As soon as the rabbi had given his consent there was a great display of activity. The dry goods merchants traveled immediately to Zamosc and Yanev, returning with cloth and leather paid for by the gentleman from Cracow. The tailors and seamstresses worked day and night; the cobblers left their benches only to pray. The young women, all anticipation, were in a feverish state. Vaguely remembered dance steps were tried out. They baked cakes and other pastries, and used up their stores of jams and preserves which they had been keeping in readiness for illness. The Frampol musicians were equally active. Cymbals, fiddles, and bagpipes, long forgotten and neglected, had to be dusted off and tuned. Gaiety infected even the very old, for it was rumored that the elegant doctor planned a banquet for the poor where alms would be distributed.

The eligible girls were wholly concerned wth self-improvement. They scrubbed their skin and arranged their hair, a few even visited the ritual bath to bathe among the married women. In the evenings, faces flushed, eyes sparkling, they met at each other's houses, to tell stories and ask riddles. It was difficult for them, and for their mothers as well, to sleep at night. Fathers sighed as they slept. And suddenly the young girls of Frampol seemed so attractive that the young men who had contemplated marrying outside of town fell in love with them. Although the young men still sat in the studyhouse poring over the Talmud,[4] its wisdom no longer penetrated to them. It was the ball alone that they spoke of now, only the ball that occupied their thoughts.

The doctor from Cracow also enjoyed himself. He changed his clothes several times daily. First it was a silk coat worn with pompommed slippers, then a woolen caftan with high boots. At one meal he wore a pelerine[5] trimmed with beaver tails, and at the next a cape embroidered with flowers and leaves. He breakfasted on roast pigeon which he washed down with dry wine. For lunch he ordered egg noodles and blintzes, and he was audacious enough to eat Sabbath pudding on weekdays. He never attended prayer, but instead played all sorts of games: cards, goats and wolves, coin-pitching. Having finished lunch, he would drive through the neighborhood with his coachman. The peasants would lift their hats as he passed, and bow almost to the ground. One day he strolled through Frampol with a gold-headed cane. Women crowded to the windows to observe him, and boys, following after him, picked up the rock candy he tossed them. In the evenings he and his companions, gay young men, drank wine until all hours. Rabbi Ozer constantly warned his flock that they walked a downhill path led by the Evil One, but they paid no attention to him. Their minds and hearts

4. The collection of commentaries on oral laws dating from postbiblical times.

5. Cloak.

were completely possessed by the ball, which would be held at the market place in the middle of that month, at the time of the full moon.

III

At the edge of town, in a small valley close to a swamp, stood a hut no larger than a chicken coop. Its floor was dirt, its window was boarded; and the roof, because it was covered with green and yellow moss, made one think of a bird's nest that had been forsaken. Heaps of garbage were strewn before the hut, and lime ditches furrowed the soggy earth. Amidst the refuse there was an occasional chair without a seat, a jug missing an ear, a table without legs. Every type of broom, bone, and rag seemed to be rotting there. This was where Lipa the Ragpicker lived with his daughter, Hodle. While his first wife was alive, Lipa had been a respected merchant in Frampol where he occupied a pew at the east wall of the synagogue. But after his wife had drowned herself in the river, his condition declined rapidly. He took to drink, associated with the town's worst element, and soon ended up bankrupt.

His second wife, a beggar woman from Yanev, bore him a daughter whom she left behind when she deserted him for non-support. Unconcerned about his wife's departure, Lipa allowed the child to shift for herself. Each week he spent a few days collecting rags from the garbage. The rest of the time he was in the tavern. Although the innkeeper's wife scolded him, she received only abusive answers in reply. Lipa had his success among the men as a tale-spinner. He attracted business to the place with his fantastic yarns about witches and windmills and devils and goblins. He could also recite Polish and Ukrainian rhymes and had a knack for telling jokes. The innkeeper allowed him to occupy a place near the stove, and from time to time he was given a bowl of soup and a piece of bread. Old friends, remembering Lipa's former affluence, occasionally presented him with a pair of pants, a threadbare coat, or a shirt. He accepted everything ungraciously. He even stuck out his tongue at his benefactors as they turned away from him.

As in the saying, "Like father, like son," Hodle inherited the vices of both parents—her drunken father, her begging mother. By the time she was six, she had won a reputation as a glutton and thief. Barefoot and half-naked, she roamed the town, entering houses and raiding the larders of those who were not home. She preyed on chickens and ducks, cut their throats with glass, and ate them. Although the inhabitants of Frampol had often warned her father that he was rearing a wanton, the information did not seem to bother him. He seldom spoke to her and she did not even call him father. When she was twelve, her lasciviousness became a matter of discussion among the women. Gypsies visited her shack, and it was rumored that she devoured the meat of cats and dogs, in fact, every kind of carcass. Tall and lean, with red hair and green eyes, she went barefoot summer and winter, and her skirts were made of colored scraps discarded by the seamstresses. She was feared by mothers who said she wove spells that blighted the young. The village elders who admonished her received brazen answers. She had the shrewdness of a bastard, the quick tongue of an adder, and when attacked by street urchins, did not hesitate to strike back. Particularly skilled in swearing, she had an unlimited repertoire. It was like her to call out, "Pox on your tongue and gangrene in your eyes," or, possibly, "May you rot till the skunks run from your smell."

Occasionally her curses were effective, and the town grew wary of incurring her anger. But as she matured she tended to avoid the town proper, and the time came when she was almost forgotten. But on the day that the Frampol merchants, in preparation for the ball, distributed cloth and leather among the town's young women, Hodle reappeared. She was now about seventeen, fully grown, though still in short skirts; her face was freckled, and her hair disheveled. Beads, such as those worn by gypsies, encircled her throat, and on her wrists were bracelets made from wolves' teeth. Pushing her way through the crowd, she demanded her share. There was nothing left but a few odds and ends, which were given to her. Furious with her allotment, she hastened home with it. Those who had seen what had happened laughed, "Look who's going to the ball! What a pretty picture she'll make!"

At last the shoemakers and tailors were done; every dress fit, every shoe was right. The days were miraculously warm, and the nights as luminous as the evenings of Pentecost. It was the morning star that, on the day of the ball, woke the entire town. Tables and benches lined one side of the market. The cooks had already roasted calves, sheep, goats, geese, ducks, and chicken, and had baked sponge and raisin cakes, braided bread and rolls, onion biscuits, and ginger bread. There were mead and beer and a barrel of Hungarian wine that had been brought by the wine dealer. When the children arrived they brought the bows and arrows with which they were accustomed to play at the Omer feast, as well as their Purim rattles and Torah flags. Even the doctor's horses were decorated with willow branches and autumn flowers, and the coachmen paraded them through the town. Apprentices left their work, and yeshiva[6] students their volumes of the Talmud. And despite Rabbi Ozer's injunction against the young matrons' attending the ball, they dressed in their wedding gowns and went, arriving with the young girls, who also came in white, each bearing a candle in her hand as

6. School for advanced studies.

though she were a bridesmaid. The band had already begun to play, and the music was lively. Rabbi Ozer alone was not present, having locked himself in his study. His maidservant had gone to the ball, leaving him to himself. He knew no good could come of such behavior, but there was nothing he could do to prevent it.

By late afternoon all the girls had gathered in the market place, surrounded by the townspeople. Drums were beaten. Jesters performed. The girls danced; first a quadrille, then a scissor dance. Next it was Kozack, and finally the Dance of Anger. Now the moon appeared, although the sun had not yet set. It was time for the gentleman from Cracow. He entered on a white mare, flanked by bodyguards and his best man. He wore a large-plumed hat, and silver buttons flashed on his green coat. A sword hung at his side, and his shiny boots rested in the stirrups. He resembled a gentleman off to war with his entourage. Silently he sat in his saddle, watching the girls as they danced. How graceful they were, how charmingly they moved! But one who did not dance was the daughter of Lipa the Ragpicker. She stood to one side, ignored by them all.

IV

The setting sun, remarkably large, stared down angrily like a heavenly eye upon the Frampol market place. Never before had Frampol seen such a sunset. Like rivers of burning sulphur, fiery clouds streamed across the heavens, assuming the shapes of elephants, lions, snakes, and monsters. They seemed to be waging a battle in the sky, devouring one another, spitting, breathing fire. It almost seemed to be the River of Fire they watched, where demons tortured the evil-doers amidst glowing coals and heaps of ashes. The moon swelled, became vast, blood-red, spotted, scarred, and gave off little light. The evening grew very dark, dissolving even the stars. The young men fetched torches, and a barrel of burning pitch was prepared. Shadows danced back and forth as though attending a ball of their own. Around the market place the houses seemed to vibrate; roofs quivered, chimneys shook. Such gaiety and intoxication had never before been known in Frampol. Everyone, for the first time in months, had eaten and drunk sufficiently. Even the animals participated in the merry-making. Horses neighed, cows mooed, and the few roosters that had survived the slaughter of the fowl crowed. Flocks of crows and strange birds flew in to pick at the leavings. Fireflies illumined the darkness, and lightning flashed on the horizon. But there was no thunder. A weird circular light glowed in the sky for a few moments and then suddenly plummeted toward the horizon, a crimson tail behind it, resembling a burning rod. Then, as everyone stared in wonder at the sky, the gentleman from

Cracow spoke: "Listen to me. I have wonderful things to tell you, but let no one be overcome by joy. Men, take hold of your wives. Young men, look to your girls. You see in me the wealthiest man in the entire world. Money is sand to me, and diamonds are pebbles. I come from the land of Ophir, where King Solomon found the gold for his temple. I dwell in the palace of the Queen of Sheba. My coach is solid gold, its wheels inlaid with sapphires, with axles of ivory, its lamps studded with rubies and emeralds, opals and amethysts. The Ruler of the Ten Lost Tribes of Israel knows of your miseries, and he has sent me to be your benefactor. But there is one condition. Tonight, every virgin must marry. I will provide a dowry of ten thousand ducats for each maiden, as well as a string of pearls that will hang to her knees. But make haste. Every girl must have a husband before the clocks strike twelve."

The crowd was hushed. It was as quiet as New Year's Day before the blowing of the ram's horn. One could hear the buzzing of a fly.

Then one old man called out, "But that's impossible. The girls are not even engaged!"

"Let them become engaged."

"To whom?"

"We can draw lots," the gentleman from Cracow replied. "Whoever is to be married will have his or her name written on a card. Mine also. And then we shall draw to see who is meant for whom."

"But a girl must wait seven days. She must have the prescribed ablutions."

"Let the sin be on me. She needn't wait."

Despite the protestations of the old men and their wives, a sheet of paper was torn into pieces, and on each piece the name of a young man or young woman was written by a scribe. The town's beadle, now in the service of the gentleman from Cracow, drew from one skullcap the names of the young men, and from another those of the young women, chanting their names to the same tune with which he called up members of the congregation for the reading of the Torah.

"Nahum, son of Katriel, betrothed to Yentel, daughter of Nathan. Solomon, son of Cov Baer, betrothed to Tryna, daughter of Jonah Lieb." The assortment was a strange one, but since in the night all sheep are black, the matches seemed reasonable enough. After each drawing, the newly engaged couple, hand in hand, approached the doctor to collect the dowry and wedding gift. As he had promised, the gentleman from Cracow gave each the stipulated sum of ducats, and on the neck of each bride he hung a strand of pearls. Now the mothers, unable to restrain their joy, began to dance and shout. The fathers stood by, bewildered. When the girls lifted their dresses to catch the gold coins given by the doctor, their legs and underclothing were exposed, which sent the men into paroxysms of lust. Fiddles screeched, drums pounded, trumpets blared. The uproar was deafening. Twelve-year-old boys were mated with "spinsters" of nineteen. The sons of substantial citizens took the daughters of paupers as brides; midgets were coupled with giants, beauties with cripples. On the last two slips appeared the names of the gentleman from Cracow and Hodle, the daughter of Lipa the Ragpicker.

The same old man who had called out previously said, "Woe unto us, the girl is a harlot."

"Come to me, Hodle, come to your bridegroom," the doctor bade.

Hodle, her hair in two long braids, dressed in a calico skirt, and with sandals on her feet, did not wait to be asked twice. As soon as she had been called she walked to where the gentleman from Cracow sat on his mare, and fell to her knees. She prostrated herself seven times before him.

"Is it true, what that old fool says?" her prospective husband asked her.

"Yes, my lord, it is so."

"Have you sinned only with Jews or with Gentiles as well?"

"With both."

"Was it for bread?"

"No. For the sheer pleasure."

"How old were you when you started?"

"Not quite ten."

"Are you sorry for what you have done?"

"No."

"Why not?"

"Why should I be?" she answered shamelessly.

"You don't fear the tortures of hell?"

"I fear nothing—not even God. There is no God."

Once more the old man began to scream, "Woe to us, woe to us, Jews! A fire is upon us, burning, Jews, Satan's fire. Save your souls. Jews. Flee, before it is too late!"

"Gag him," the gentleman from Cracow commanded.

The guards seized the old man and gagged him. The doctor leading Hodle by the hand, began to dance. Now, as though the powers of darkness had been summoned, the rain and hail began to fall; flashes of lightning were accompanied by mighty thunderclaps. But, heedless of the storm, pious men and women embraced without shame, dancing and shouting as though possessed. Even the old were affected. In the furor, dresses were ripped, shoes shaken off, hats, wigs and skullcaps trampled in the mud. Sashes, slipping to the ground, twisted there like snakes. Suddenly there was a terrific crash. A huge bolt of lightning had simultaneously struck the synagogue, the study house, and the ritual bath. The whole town was on fire.

Now at last the deluded people realized that there was no natural origin to these occurrences. Although the rain continued to fall and even increased in intensity, the fire was not extinguished. An eerie light glowed in the market place. Those few prudent individuals who tried to disengage themselves from the demented crowd were crushed to earth and trampled.

And then the gentleman from Cracow revealed his true identity. He was no longer the young man the villagers had welcomed, but a creature covered with scales, with an eye in his chest, and on his forehead a horn that rotated at great speed. His arms were covered with hair, thorns, and elflocks, and his tail was a mass of live serpents, for he was none other than Ketev Mriri, Chief of the Devils.

Witches, werewolves, imps, demons, and hobgoblins plummeted from the sky, some on brooms, others on hoops, still others on spiders. Osnath, the daughter of Machlath, her fiery hair loosened in the wind, her breasts bare and thighs exposed, leaped from chimney to chimney, and skated along the eaves. Namah, Hurmizah the daughter of Aff, and many other she-devils did all sorts of somersaults. Satan himself gave away the bridegroom, while four evil spirits held the poles of the canopy, which had turned into writhing pythons. Four dogs escorted the groom. Hodle's dress fell from her and she stood naked. Her breasts hung down to her navel and her feet were webbed. Her hair was a wilderness of worms and caterpillars. The groom held out a triangular ring and, instead of saying, "With this ring be thou consecrated to me according to the laws of Moses and Israel," he said, "With this ring, be thou desecrated to me according to the blasphemy of Korah and Ishmael." And instead of wishing the pair good luck, the evil spirits called out, "Bad luck," and they began to chant:

> "The curse of Eve, the Mark of Cain,
> the cunning of the snake, unite the twain."

Screaming for the last time, the old man clutched at his head and died. Ketev Mriri began his eulogy:

> "Devil's dung and Satan's spell
> Bring his ghost to roast in hell."

v

In the middle of the night, old Rabbi Ozer awoke. Since he was a holy man, the fire which was consuming the town had no power over his house. Sitting up in bed he looked about, wondering if dawn were already breaking. But it was neither day nor night without. The sky was a fiery red, and from the distance came a clamor of shouts and songs that resembled the howling of wild beasts. At first, recalling nothing, the old man wondered what was going on. "Has the world come to an end? Or have I failed to hear the ram's horn heralding the Messiah? Has He arrived?" Washing his hands, he put on his slippers and overcoat and went out.

The town was unrecognizable. Where houses had been, only chimneys stood. Mounds of coal smoldered here and there. He called the beadle, but there was no answer. With his cane, the rabbi went searching for his flock.

"Where are you, Jews, where are you?" he called piteously.

The earth scorched his feet, but he did not slacken his pace. Mad dogs and strange beings attacked him, but he wielded his cane against them. His sorrow was so great that he felt no fear. Where the market place used to be, a terrible sight met him. There was nothing but one great swamp, full of mud, slime, and ashes. Floundering in mud up to their waists, a crowd of naked people went through the movements of dance. At first, the rabbi mistook the weirdly moving figures for devils, and was about to recite the chapter, "Let there be contentment," and other passages dealing with exorcism, when he recognized the men of his town. Only then did he remember the doctor from Cracow, and the rabbi cried out bitterly, "Jews, for the sake of God, save your souls! You are in the hands of Satan!"

But the townspeople, too entranced to heed his cries, continued their frenzied movements for a long time, jumping like frogs, shaking as though with fever. With hair uncovered and breasts bare, the women laughed, cried and swayed. Catching a yeshiva boy by the sidelocks, a girl pulled him to her lap. A woman tugged at the beard of a strange man. Old men and women were immersed in slime up to their loins. They scarcely looked alive.

Relentlessly, the rabbi urged the people to resist evil. Reciting the Torah and other holy books, as well as incantations and the several names of God, he succeeded in rousing some of them. Soon others responded. The rabbi had helped the first man from the mire, then that one assisted the next, and so on. Most of them had recovered by the time the morning star appeared. Perhaps the spirits of their forebears had interceded, for although many had sinned, only one man had died this night in the market place square.

Now the men were appalled, realizing that the devil had bewitched them, had dragged them through muck; and they wept.

"Where is our money?" the girls wailed, "And our gold and our jewelry? Where is our clothing? What happened to the wine, the mead, the wedding gifts?"

But everything had turned to mud; the town of Frampol, stripped and ruined, had become a swamp. Its inhabitants were mud-splashed, denuded, monstrous. For a moment, forgetting their grief, they laughed at each other. The hair of the girls had turned into elflocks, and bats were entangled there. The young men had grown gray and wrinkled; the old were yellow as corpses. In their midst lay the old man who had died. Crimson with shame, the sun rose.

"Let us rend our clothes in mourning," one man called, but his words evoked laughter, for all were naked.

"We are doomed, my sisters," lamented a woman.

"Let us drown ourselves in the river," a girl shrieked. "Why go on living?"

One of the yeshiva boys said, "Let us strangle ourselves with our sashes."

"Brothers, we are lost. Let us blaspheme God," said a horse dealer.

"Have you lost your minds, Jews?" cried Rabbi Ozer, "Repent, before it is too late. You have fallen into Satan's snare, but it is my fault, I take the sin upon myself. I am the guilty one. I will be your scapegoat, and you shall remain clean."

"This is madness!" one of the scholars protested, "God forbid that there be so many sins on your holy head!"

"Do not worry abut that. My shoulders are broad. I should have had more foresight. I was blind not to realize that the Cracow doctor was the Evil One. And when the shepherd is blind, the flock goes astray. It is I who deserve the punishment, the curses."

"Rabbi, what shall we do? We have no homes, no bed clothes, nothing. Woe to us, to our bodies and to our souls."

"Our babies!" cried the young matrons. "Let us hurry to them!"

But it was the infants who had been the real victims of the passion for gold that had caused the inhabitants of Frampol to transgress. The infants' cribs were burned, their little bones were charred. The mothers stooped to pick up little hands, feet, skulls. The wailing and crying lasted long, but how long can a whole town weep? The gravedigger gathered the bones and carried them to the cemetery. Half the town began the prescribed seven days of mourning. But all fasted, for there was no food anywhere.

But the compassion of the Jews is well known, and when the neighboring town of Yanev learned what had happened, clothing, bed linen, bread, cheese, and dishes were collected and sent to Frampol. Timber merchants brought logs for building. A rich man offered credit. The next day the reconstruction of the town was begun. Although work is forbidden to those in mourning, Rabbi Ozer issued a verdict that this was an exceptional case: the lives of the people were in danger. Miraculously, the weather remained mild; no snow fell. Never before had there been such diligence in Frampol. The inhabitants built and prayed, mixed lime with sand, and recited psalms. The women worked with the men, while girls, forgetting their fastidiousness, helped also. Scholars and men of high position assisted. Peasants from the surrounding villages, hearing of the catastrophe, took the old and infirm into their homes. They also brought wood, potatoes, cabbages, onions and other food. Priests and bishops from Lublin, hearing of events that suggested witchcraft, came to examine witnesses. As the scribe recorded the names of those living in Frampol, Hodle, the daughter of Lipa the Ragpicker, was suddenly remembered. But when the townspeople went to where her hut had been, they found the hill covered with weeds and bramble, silent save for the cries of crows and cats; there was no indication that human beings had ever dwelt there.

Then it was understood that Hodle was in truth Lilith,[7] and that the host of the netherworld had come to Frampol because of her. After their investigations, the clergymen from Lublin, greatly astonished at what they had seen and heard, returned home. A few days later, the day before the Sabbath, Rabbi Ozer died. The entire town attended his funeral, and the town preacher said a eulogy for him.

In time, a new rabbi came to the community, and a new town arose. The old people died, the mounds in the cemetery sifted down, and the monuments slowly sank. But the story, signed by trustworthy witnesses, can still be read in the parchment chronicle.

And the events in the story brought their epilogue: the lust for gold had been stifled in Frampol; it was never rekindled. From generation to generation the people remained paupers. A gold coin became an abomination in Frampol, and even silver was looked at askance. Whenever a shoemaker or tailor asked too high a price for his work he was told, "Go to the gentleman from Cracow and he will give you buckets of gold."

And on the grave of Rabbi Ozer, in the memorial chapel, there burns an eternal light. A white pigeon is often seen on the roof: the sainted spirit of Rabbi Ozer.

---

7. In Talmudic legend, a female demon, or Adam's first wife who, having refused to recognize his superior position, abandoned him and was transformed into a demon.

JEAN-PAUL SARTRE
(born 1905)
No Exit (Huis Clos) *
A Play in One Act

Characters in the Play

VALET	ESTELLE
GARCIN	INEZ

Huis Clos (No Exit) was presented for the first time at the Théâtre du Vieux-Colombier, Paris, in May 1944.

SCENE—*A drawing-room in Second Empire style. A massive bronze ornament stands on the mantelpiece.*

GARCIN. [*Enters accompanied by the* ROOM-VALET, *and glances around him*] Hm! So here we are?

VALET. Yes, Mr. Garcin.

GARCIN. And this is what it looks like?

VALET. Yes.

GARCIN. Second Empire furniture, I observe. . . . Well, well, I dare say one gets used to it in time.

VALET. Some do. Some don't.

GARCIN. Are all the other rooms like this one?

VALET. How could they be? We cater for all sorts: Chinamen and Indians, for instance. What use would they have for a Second Empire chair?

GARCIN. And what use do you suppose *I* have for one? Do you know who I was? . . . Oh, well, it's no great matter. And, to tell the truth, I had quite a habit of living among furniture that I didn't relish, and in false positions. I'd even come to like it. A false position in a Louis-Philippe dining-room—you know the style?—well, that had its points, you know. Bogus in bogus, so to speak.

VALET. And you'll find that living in a Second Empire drawing-room has its points.

GARCIN. Really? . . . Yes, yes, I dare say. . . . [*He takes another look around.*] Still, I certainly didn't expect—this! You know what they tell us down there?

VALET. What about?

GARCIN. About [*Makes a sweeping gesture*] this—er—residence.

VALET. Really, sir, how could you belive such cock-and-bull stories? Told by people who'd never set foot here. For, of course, if they had—

* 1945. Reprinted from *No Exit and The Flies* by Jean-Paul Sartre, translated by Stuart Gilbert, by permission of Alfred A. Knopf. The punctuation "..." does not indicate omissions from this text.

GARCIN. Quite so. [*Both laugh. Abruptly the laugh dies from* GARCIN'S *face.*] But, I say, where are the instruments of torture?

VALET. The what?

GARCIN. The racks and red-hot pincers and all the other paraphernalia?

VALET. Ah, you must have your little joke, sir!

GARCIN. My little joke? Oh, I see. No, I wasn't joking. [*A short silence. He strolls around the room.*] No mirrors, I notice. No windows. Only to be expected. And nothing breakable. [*Bursts out angrily.*] But, damn it all, they might have left me my toothbrush!

VALET. That's good! So you haven't yet got over your—what-do-you-call-it?—sense of human dignity? Excuse me smiling.

GARCIN. [*Thumping ragefully the arm of an armchair*] I'll ask you to be more polite. I quite realize the position I'm in, but I won't tolerate . . .

VALET. Sorry, sir. No offense meant. But all our guests ask me the same questions. Silly questions, if you'll pardon me saying so. Where's the torture-chamber? That's the first thing they ask, all of them. They don't bother their heads about the bathroom requisites, that I can assure you. But after a bit, when they've got their nerve back, they start in about their toothbrushes and whatnot. Good heavens, Mr. Garcin, can't you use your brains? What, I ask you, would be the point of brushing your teeth?

GARCIN. [*More calmly*] Yes, of course you're right. [*He looks around again.*] And why should one want to see oneself in a looking-glass? But that bronze contraption on the mantelpiece, that's another story. I suppose there will be times when I stare my eyes out at it. Stare my eyes out—see what I mean? . . . All right, let's put our cards on the table. I assure you I'm quite conscious of my position. Shall I tell you what it feels like? A man's drowning, choking, sinking by inches, till only his eyes are just above water. And what does he see? A bronze atrocity by—what's the fellow's name? —Barbedienne. A collector's piece. As in a nightmare. That's their idea, isn't it? . . . No, I suppose you're under orders not to answer questions; and I won't insist. But don't forget, my man, I've a good notion of what's coming to me, so don't you boast you've caught me off my guard. I'm facing the situation, facing it. [*He starts pacing the room again.*] So that's that; no toothbrush. And no bed, either. One never sleeps, I take it?

VALET. That's so.

GARCIN. Just as I expected. Why should one sleep? A sort of drowsiness steals on you, tickles you behind the ears, and you feel your eyes closing—but why sleep? You lie down on the sofa and—in a flash, sleep flies away. Miles and miles away. So you rub your eyes, get up, and it starts all over again.

VALET. Romantic, that's what you are.

GARCIN. Will you keep quiet, please! . . . I won't make a scene, I shan't be sorry for myself, I'll face the situation, as I said just now. Face it fairly and squarely. I won't have it springing at me from behind, before I've time to size it up. And you call that being "romantic"! . . . So it comes to this; one doesn't need rest. Why bother about sleep if one isn't sleepy? That stands to reason, doesn't it? Wait a minute, there's a snag somewhere; something disagreeable. Why, now, should it be disagreeable? . . . Ah, I see; it's life without a break.

VALET. What do you mean by that?

GARCIN. What do I mean? [*Eyes the* VALET *suspiciously.*] I thought as much. That's why there's something so beastly, so damn bad-mannered, in the way you stare at me. They're paralyzed.

VALET. What are you talking about?

GARCIN. Your eyelids. We move ours up and down. Blinking, we call it. It's like a small black shutter that clicks down and makes a break. Everything goes black; one's eyes are moistened. You can't imagine how restful, refreshing, it is. Four thousand little rests per hour. Four thousand little respites—just think! . . . So that's the idea. I'm to live without eyelids. Don't act the fool, you know what I mean. No eyelids, no sleep; it follows, doesn't it? I shall never sleep again. But then—how shall I endure my own company? Try to understand. You see, I'm fond of teasing, it's a second nature with me—and I'm used to teasing myself. Plaguing myself, if you prefer; I don't tease nicely. But I can't go on doing that without a break. Down there I had my nights. I slept. I always had good nights. By way of compensation, I suppose. And happy little dreams. There was a green field. Just an ordinary field. I used to stroll in it. . . . Is it daytime now?

VALET. Can't you see? The lights are on.

GARCIN. Ah yes, I've got it. It's *your* daytime. And outside?

VALET. Outside?

GARCIN. Damn it, you know what I mean. Beyond that wall.

VALET. There's a passage.

GARCIN. And at the end of the passage?

VALET. There's more rooms, more passages, and stairs.

GARCIN. And what lies beyond them?

VALET. That's all.

GARCIN. But surely you have a day off sometimes. Where do you go?

VALET. To my uncle's place. He's the head valet here. He has a room on the third floor.

GARCIN. I should have guessed as much. Where's the light-switch?

VALET. There isn't any.

GARCIN. What? Can't one turn off the light?

VALET. Oh, the management can cut off the current if they want to. But I can't remember their having done so on this floor. We have all the electricity we want.

GARCIN. So one has to live with one's eyes open all the time?

VALET. To *live*, did you say?

GARCIN. Don't let's quibble over words. With one's eyes open. Forever. Always broad daylight in my eyes—and in my head. [*Short silence.*] And suppose I took that contraption on the mantelpiece and dropped it on the lamp—wouldn't it go out?

VALET. You can't move it. It's too heavy.

GARCIN. [*Seizing the bronze ornament and trying to lift it*] You're right. It's too heavy.

[*A short silence follows.*]

VALET. Very well, sir, if you don't need me any more, I'll be off.

GARCIN. What? You're going? [*The* VALET *goes up to the door.*] Wait. [VALET *looks round.*] That's a bell, isn't it? [VALET *nods.*] And if I ring, you're bound to come?

VALET. Well, yes, that's so—in a way. But you can never be sure about that bell. There's something wrong with the wiring, and it doesn't always work. [GARCIN *goes to the bell-push and presses the button. A bell purrs outside.*]

GARCIN. It's working all right.

VALET. [*Looking surprised*] So it is. [*He, too, presses the button.*] But I shouldn't count on it too much if I were you. It's—capricious. Well, I really must go now. [GARCIN *makes a gesture to detain him.*] Yes, sir?

GARCIN. No, never mind. [*He goes to the mantelpiece and picks up a paper-knife.*] What's this?

VALET. Can't you see? An ordinary paper-knife.

GARCIN. Are there books here?

VALET. No.

GARCIN. Then what's the use of this? [VALET *shrugs his shoulders.*] Very well. You can go. [VALET *goes out.*]

[GARCIN *is by himself. He goes to the bronze ornament and strokes it reflectively. He sits down; then gets up, goes to the bell-push, and presses the button. The bell remains silent. He tries two or three times, without success. Then he tries to open the door, also without success. He calls the* VALET *several times, but gets no result. He beats the door with his fists, still calling. Suddenly he grows calm and sits down again. At the moment the door opens and* INEZ *enters, followed by the* VALET.]

VALET. Did you call sir?

GARCIN. [*On the point of answering "Yes"—but then his eyes fall on* INEZ.] No.

VALET. [*Turning to* INEZ] This is your room, madam, [INEZ *says nothing.*] If there's any information you require—? [INEZ *still keeps silent, and the* VALET *looks slightly huffed.*] Most of our guests have quite a lot to ask me. But I won't insist. Anyhow, as regards the toothbrush, and the electric bell, and that thing on the mantel-shelf, this gentleman can tell you anything you want to know as well as I could. We've had a little chat, him and me. [VALET *goes out.*]

[GARCIN *refrains from looking at* INEZ, *who is inspecting the room. Abruptly she turns to* GARCIN.]

INEZ. Where's Florence? [*Garcin does not reply.*] Didn't you hear? I asked you about Florence. Where is she?

GARCIN. I haven't an idea.

INEZ. Ah, that's the way it works, is it? Torture by separation. Well, as far as I'm concerned, you won't get anywhere. Florence was a tiresome little fool, and I shan't miss her in the least.

GARCIN. I beg your pardon. Who do you suppose I am?

INEZ. You? Why, the torturer, of course.

GARCIN. [*Looks startled, then bursts out laughing*] Well, that's a good one! Too comic for words. I the torturer! So you came in, had a look at me, and thought I was—er—one of the staff. Of course, it's that silly fellow's fault; he should have introduced us. A tor-turer indeed! I'm Joseph Garcin, journalist and man of letters by profession. And as we're both in the same boat, so to speak, might I ask you, Mrs.—?

INEZ. [*Testily*] Not "Mrs." I'm unmarried.

GARCIN. Right. That's a start, anyway. Well, now that we've broken the ice, do you *really* think I look like a torturer? And, by the way, how does one recognize torturers when one sees them? Evi-dently you've ideas on the subject.

INEZ. They look frightened.

GARCIN. Frightened! But how ridiculous! Of whom should they be frightened? Of their victims?

INEZ. Laugh away, but I know what I'm talking about. I've often watched my face in the glass.

GARCIN. In the glass? [*He looks around him.*] How beastly of them! They've removed everything in the least resembling a glass. [*Short silence*] Anyhow, I can assure you I'm not frightened. Not that I take my position lightly; I realize its gravity only too well. But I'm not afraid.

INEZ. [*Shrugging her shoulders*] That's your affair. [*Silence*] Must you be here all the time, or do you take a stroll outside, now and then?

GARCIN. The door's locked.

INEZ. Oh! . . . That's too bad.

GARCIN. I can quite understand that it bores you having me here. And I, too—well, quite frankly, I'd rather be alone. I want to think things out, you know; to set my life in order, and one does that better by oneself. But I'm sure we'll manage to pull along together somehow. I'm no talker, I don't move much; in fact I'm a peaceful sort of fellow. Only, if I may venture on a suggestion, we should make a point of being extremely courteous to each other. That will ease the situation for us both.

INEZ. I'm not polite.

GARCIN. Then I must be polite for two.

[*A longish silence.* GARCIN *is sitting on a sofa, while* INEZ *paces up and down the room.*]

INEZ. [*Fixing her eyes on him*] Your mouth!

GARCIN. [*As if waking from a dream*] I beg your pardon.

INEZ. Can't you keep your mouth still? You keep twisting it about all the time. It's grotesque.

GARCIN. So sorry. I wasn't aware of it.

INEZ. That's just what I reproach you with. [GARCIN's *mouth twitches.*] There you are! You talk about politeness, and you don't even try to control your face. Remember you're not alone; you've no right to inflict the sight of your fear on me.

GARCIN. [*Getting up and going towards her*] How about you? Aren't you afraid?

INEZ. What would be the use? There was some point in being afraid *before*; while one still had hope.

GARCIN. [*In a low voice*] There's no more hope—but it's still "before." We haven't yet begun to suffer.

INEZ. That's so. [*A short silence*] Well? What's going to happen?

GARCIN. I don't know. I'm waiting.

[*Silence again.* GARCIN *sits down and* INEZ *resumes her pacing up and down the room.* GARCIN's *mouth twitches; after a glance at* INEZ *he buries his face in his hands. Enter* ESTELLE *with the* VALET. ESTELLE *looks at* GARCIN, *whose face is still hidden by his hands.*]

ESTELLE. [*To* GARCIN] No! Don't look up. I know what you're hiding with your hands. I know you've no face left. [GARCIN *removes his hands.*] What! [*A short pause. Then, in a tone of surprise*] But I don't know you!

GARCIN. I'm not the torturer, madam.

ESTELLE. I never thought you were. I—I thought someone was trying to play a rather nasty trick on me. [*To the* VALET] Is anyone else coming?

VALET. No, madam. No one else is coming.

ESTELLE. Oh! Then we're to stay by ourselves, the three of us, this gentleman, this lady, and myself. [*She starts laughing.*]

GARCIN. [*Angrily*] There's nothing to laugh about.

ESTELLE. [*Still laughing*] It's those sofas. They're so hideous. And just look how they've been arranged. It makes me think of New Year's Day—when I used to visit that boring old aunt of mine, Aunt Mary. Her house is full of horrors like that. . . . I suppose each of us has a sofa of his own. Is that one mine? [*To the* VALET] But you can't expect me to sit on that one. It would be too horrible for words. I'm in pale blue and it's vivid green.

INEZ. Would you prefer mine?

ESTELLE. That claret-colored one, you mean? That's very sweet of you, but really—no, I don't think it'd be so much better. What's the good of worrying, anyhow? We've got to take what comes to us, and I'll stick to the green one. [*Pauses*] The only one which might do, at a pinch, is that gentleman's. [*Another pause*]

INEZ. Did you hear, Mr. Garcin?

GARCIN. [*With a slight start*] Oh—the sofa, you mean. So sorry. [*He rises.*] Please take it, madam.

ESTELLE. Thanks. [*She takes off her coat and drops it on the sofa. A short silence.*] Well, as we're to live together, I suppose we'd better introduce ourselves. My name's Rigault. Estelle Rigault. [GARCIN *bows and is going to announce his name, but* INEZ *steps in front of him.*]

INEZ. And I'm Inez Serrano. Very pleased to meet you.

GARCIN. [*Bowing again*] Joseph Garcin.

VALET. Do you require me any longer?

ESTELLE. No, you can go. I'll ring when I want you.

[*Exit* VALET, *with polite bows to everyone.*]

INEZ. You're very pretty. I wish we'd had some flowers to welcome you with.

ESTELLE. Flowers? Yes, I loved flowers. Only they'd fade so quickly here, wouldn't they? It's so stuffy. Oh, well, the great thing is to keep as cheerful as we can, don't you agree? Of course, you, too, are—[1]

INEZ. Yes. Last week. What about you?

ESTELLE. I'm—quite recent. Yesterday. As a matter of fact, the ceremony's not quite over. [*Her tone is natural enough, but she seems to be seeing what she describes.*] The wind's blowing my sister's veil all over the place. She's trying her best to cry. Come, dear! Make another effort. That's better. Two tears, two little tears are twinkling under the black veil. Oh dear! What a sight Olga looks this morning! She's holding my sister's arm, helping her along. She's not crying, and I don't blame her; tears always mess one's face up, don't they? Olga was my bosom friend, you know.

INEZ. Did you suffer much?

ESTELLE. No. I was only half conscious, mostly.

INEZ. What was it?

ESTELLE. Pneumonia. [*In the same tone as before*] It's over now, they're leaving the cemetery. Good-by. Good-by. Quite a crowd they are. My husband's stayed at home. Prostrated with grief, poor man. [*To* INEZ] How about you?

1. The word left unuttered is "dead."

INEZ. The gas stove.

ESTELLE. And you, Mr. Garcin?

GARCIN. Twelve bullets through my chest. [ESTELLE *makes a horrified gesture.*] Sorry! I fear I'm not good company among the dead.

ESTELLE. Please, please don't use that word. It's so—so crude. In terribly bad taste, really. It doesn't mean much anyhow. Somehow I feel we've never been so much alive as now. If we've absolutely got to mention this—this state of things, I suggest we call ourselves—wait!—absentees. Have you been—been absent for long?

GARCIN. About a month.

ESTELLE. Where do you come from?

GARCIN. From Rio.

ESTELLE. I'm from Paris. Have you anyone left down there?

GARCIN. Yes, my wife. [*In the same tone as* ESTELLE *has been using*] She's waiting at the entrance of the barracks. She comes there every day. But they won't let her in. Now she's trying to peep between the bars. She doesn't yet know I'm—absent, but she suspects it. Now she's going away. She's wearing her black dress. So much the better, she won't need to change. She isn't crying, but she never did cry, anyhow. It's a bright sunny day and she's like a black shadow creeping down the empty street. Those big tragic eyes of hers—with that martyred look they always had. Oh, how she got on my nerves!

[*A short silence.* GARCIN *sits on the central sofa and buries his head in his hands.*]

INEZ. Estelle!

ESTELLE. Please, Mr. Garcin!

GARCIN. What is it?

ESTELLE. You're sitting on my sofa.

GARCIN. I beg your pardon. [*He gets up.*]

ESTELLE. You looked so—so far away. Sorry I disturbed you.

GARCIN. I was setting my life in order. [INEZ *starts laughing.*] You may laugh, but you'd do better to follow my example.

INEZ. No need. My life's in perfect order. It tidied itself up nicely of its own accord. So I needn't bother about it now.

GARCIN. Really? You imagine it's so simple as that. [*He runs his hand over his forehead.*] Whew! How hot it is here! Do you mind if—? [*He begins taking off his coat.*]

ESTELLE. How dare you! [*More gently*] No, please don't. I loathe men in their shirt sleeves.

GARCIN. [*Putting on his coat again*] All right. [*A short pause*] Of course, I used to spend my nights in the newspaper office, and it was a regular Black Hole, so we never kept our coats on. Stiflingly hot it could be. [*Short pause. In the same tone as previously*] Stifling, that it *is*. It's night now.

ESTELLE. That's so. Olga's undressing; it must be after midnight.

How quickly the time passes, on earth!

INEZ. Yes, after midnight. They've sealed up my room. It's dark, pitch-dark, and empty.

GARCIN. They've slung their coats on the backs of the chairs and rolled up their shirt-sleeves above the elbow. The air stinks of men and cigar-smoke. [*A short silence*] I used to like living among men in their shirt-sleeves.

ESTELLE. [*Aggressively*] Well, in that case our tastes differ. That's all it proves. [*Turning to* INEZ] What about you? Do you like men in their shirt-sleeves?

INEZ. Oh, I don't care much for men any way.

ESTELLE. [*Looking at the other two with a puzzled air*] Really I can't imagine why they put us three together. It doesn't make sense.

INEZ. [*Stifling a laugh*] What's that you said?

ESTELLE. I'm looking at you two and thinking that we're going to live together. . . . It's so absurd. I expected to meet old friends, or relatives.

INEZ. Yes, a charming old friend—with a hole in the middle of his face.

ESTELLE. Yes, him too. He danced the tango so divinely. Like a professional. . . . But why, why should we of all people be put together?

GARCIN. A pure fluke, I should say. They lodge folks as they can, in the order of their coming. [*To* INEZ] Why are you laughing?

INEZ. Because you amuse me, with your "flukes." As if they left anything to chance! But I suppose you've got to reassure yourself somehow.

ESTELLE. [*Hesitantly*] I wonder, now. Don't you think we may have met each other at some time in our lives?

INEZ. Never. I shouldn't have forgotten you.

ESTELLE. Or perhaps we have friends in common. I wonder if you know the Dubois-Seymours?

INEZ. Not likely.

ESTELLE. But *everyone* went to their parties.

INEZ. What's their job?

ESTELLE. Oh, they don't do anything. But they have a lovely house in the country, and hosts of people visit them.

INEZ. I didn't. I was a post-office clerk.

ESTELLE. [*Recoiling a little*] Ah. yes. . . . Of course, in that case— [*A pause*] And you, Mr. Garcin?

GARCIN. We've never met. I always lived in Rio.

ESTELLE. Then you must be right. It's mere chance that has brought us together.

INEZ. Mere chance? Then it's by chance this room is furnished as we see it. It's an accident that the sofa on the right is a livid green, and that one on the left's wine-red. Mere chance? Well, just try to shift the sofas and you'll see the difference quick enough. And that statue on the mantelpiece, do you think it's there by accident? And what about the heat here? How about that? [*A short silence*] I tell you they've thought it all out. Down to the last detail. Nothing was left to chance. This room was all set for us.

ESTELLE. But really! Everything here's so hideous; all in angles, so uncomfortable. I always loathed angles.

INEZ. [*Shrugging her shoulders*] And do you think I lived in a Second Empire drawing-room?

ESTELLE. So it was all fixed up beforehand?

INEZ. Yes. And they've put us together deliberately.

ESTELLE. Then it's not mere chance that *you* precisely are sitting opposite *me*? But what can be the idea behind it?

INEZ. Ask me another! I only know they're waiting.

ESTELLE. I never could bear the idea of anyone's expecting something from me. It always made me want to do just the opposite.

INEZ. Well, do it. Do it if you can. You don't even know what they expect.

ESTELLE. [*Stamping her foot*] It's outrageous! So something's coming to me from you two? [*She eyes each in turn.*] Something nasty, I suppose. There are some faces that tell me everything at once. Yours don't convey anything.

GARCIN. [*Turning abruptly towards* INEZ] Look here! Why are we together? You've given us quite enough hints, you may as well come out with it.

INEZ. [*In a surprised tone*] But I know nothing, absolutely nothing about it. I'm as much in the dark as you are.

GARCIN. We've got to know. [*Ponders for a while*]

INEZ. If only each of us had the guts to tell—

GARCIN. Tell what?

INEZ. Estelle!

ESTELLE. Yes?

INEZ. What have you done? I mean, why have they sent you here?

ESTELLE. [*Quickly*] That's just it. I haven't a notion, not the foggiest. In fact, I'm wondering if there hasn't been some ghastly mistake. [*To* INEZ] Don't smile. Just think of the number of people who—who become absentees every day. There must be thousands and thousands, and probably they're sorted out by—by understrappers, you know what I mean. Stupid employees who don't know their job. So they're bound to make mistakes sometimes. . . . Do stop smiling. [*To* GARCIN] Why don't you speak? If they made a mistake in my case, they may have done the same about you. [*To* INEZ] And you, too. Anyhow, isn't it better to think we've got here by mistake?

INEZ. Is that all you have to tell us?

ESTELLE. What else should I tell? I've nothing to hide. I lost my parents when I was a kid, and I had my young brother to bring up. We were terribly poor and when an old friend of my people asked me to marry him I said yes. He was very well off, and quite nice. My brother was a very delicate child and needed all sorts of attention, so really that was the right thing for me to do, don't you agree? My husband was old enough to be my father, but for six years we had a happy married life. Then two years ago I met the man I was fated to love. We knew it the moment we set eyes on each other. He asked me to run away with him, and I refused. Then I got pneumonia and it finished me. That's the whole story. No doubt, by certain standards, I did wrong to sacrifice my youth to a man nearly three times my age. [To GARCIN] Do *you* think that could be called a sin?

GARCIN. Certainly not. [A *short silence*] And now, tell me, do you think it's a crime to stand by one's principles?

ESTELLE. Of course not. Surely no one could blame a man for that!

GARCIN. Wait a bit! I ran a pacifist newspaper. Then war broke out. What was I to do? Everyone was watching me, wondering: "Will he dare?" Well, I dared. I folded my arms and they shot me. Had I done anything wrong?

ESTELLE. [*Laying her hand on his arm*] Wrong? On the contrary. You were—

INEZ. [*Breaks in ironically*]—a hero! And how about your wife, Mr. Garcin?

GARCIN. That's simple. I'd rescued her from—from the gutter.

ESTELLE. [*To* INEZ] You see! You see!

INEZ. Yes, I see. [A *pause*] Look here! What's the point of play-acting, trying to throw dust in each other's eyes? We're all tarred with the same brush.

ESTELLE. [*Indignantly*] How dare you!

INEZ. Yes, we are criminals—murderers—all three of us. We're in hell, my pets; they never make mistakes, and people aren't damned for nothing.

ESTELLE. Stop! For heaven's sake—

INEZ. In hell! Damned souls—that's us, all three!

ESTELLE. Keep quiet! I forbid you to use such disgusting words.

INEZ. A damned soul—that's you, my little plaster saint. And ditto our friend there, the noble pacifist. We've had our hour of pleasure, haven't we? There have been people who burned their lives out for our sakes—and we chuckled over it. So now we have to pay the reckoning.

GARCIN. [*Raising his fist*] Will you keep your mouth shut, damn it!

INEZ. [*Confronting him fearlessly, but with a look of vast surprise*] Well, well! [*A pause*] Ah, I understand now. I know why they've put us three together.

GARCIN. I advise you to—to think twice before you say any more.

INEZ. Wait! You'll see how simple it is. Childishly simple. Obviously there aren't any physical torments—you agree, don't you? And yet we're in hell. And no one else will come here. We'll stay in this room together, the three of us, for ever and ever. . . . In short, there's someone absent here, the official torturer.

GARCIN. [*Sotto voce*] I'd noticed that.

INEZ. It's obvious what they're after—an economy of man-power—or devil-power, if you prefer. The same idea as in the cafeteria, where customers serve themselves.

ESTELLE. What ever do you mean?

INEZ. I mean that each of us will act as torturer of the two others.

[*There is a short silence while they digest this information.*]

GARCIN. [*Gently*] No, I shall never be your torturer. I wish neither of you any harm, and I've no concern with you. None at all. So the solution's easy enough, each of us stays put in his or her corner and takes no notice of the others. You here, you here, and I there. Like soldiers at our posts. Also, we mustn't speak. Not one word. That won't be difficult; each of us has plenty of material for self-communings. I think I could stay ten thousand years with only my thoughts for company.

ESTELLE. Have *I* got to keep silent, too?

GARCIN. Yes. And that way we—we'll work out our salvation. Looking into ourselves, never raising our heads. Agreed?

INEZ. Agreed.

ESTELLE. [*After some hesitation*] I agree.

GARCIN. Then—good-by.

[*He goes to his sofa and buries his head in his hands. There is a long silence; then* INEZ *begins singing to herself.*]

INEZ. [*Singing*]

> What a crowd in Whitefriars Lane!
> They've set trestles in a row,
> With a scaffold and the knife,
> And a pail of bran below.
> Come, good folks, to Whitefriars Lane,
> Come to see the merry show!
>
> The headsman rose at crack of dawn,
> He'd a long day's work in hand,
> Chopping heads off generals,
> Priests and peers and admirals,
> All the highest in the land.
> What a crowd in Whitefriars Lane!

> See them standing in a line,
> Ladies all dressed up so fine.
> But their heads have got to go,
> Heads and hats roll down below.
> Come, good folks, to Whitefriars Lane,
> Come to see the merry show!

[*Meanwhile* ESTELLE *has been plying her powder-puff and lipstick. She looks round for a mirror, fumbles in her bag, then turns towards* GARCIN.]

ESTELLE. Excuse me, have you a glass? [GARCIN *does not answer.*] Any sort of glass, a pocket-mirror will do. [GARCIN *remains silent.*] Even if you won't speak to me, you might lend me a glass.

[*His head still buried in his hands,* GARCIN *ignores her.*]

INEZ. [*Eagerly*] Don't worry. I've a glass in my bag. [*She opens her bag. Angrily*] It's gone! They must have taken it from me at the entrance.

ESTELLE. How tiresome!

[*A short silence.* ESTELLE *shuts her eyes and sways, as if about to faint.* INEZ *turns forward and holds her up.*]

INEZ. What's the matter?

ESTELLE. [*Opens her eyes and smiles*] I feel so queer. [*She pats herself.*] Don't you ever get taken that way? When I can't see myself I begin to wonder if I really and truly exist. I pat myself just to make sure, but it doesn't help much.

INEZ. You're lucky. I'm always conscious of myself—in my mind. Painfully conscious.

ESTELLE. Ah yes, in your mind. But everything that goes on in one's head is so vague, isn't it? It makes one want to sleep. [*She is silent for a while.*] I've six big mirrors in my bedroom. There they are. I can see them. But they don't see me. They're reflecting the carpet, the settee, the window—but how empty it is, a glass in which I'm absent! When I talked to people I always made sure there was one near by in which I could see myself. I watched myself talking. And somehow it kept me alert, seeing myself as the others saw me. . . . Oh dear! My lipstick! I'm sure I've put it on all crooked. No, I can't do without a looking-glass for ever and ever, I simply can't.

INEZ. Suppose I try to be your glass? Come and pay me a visit, dear. Here's a place for you on my sofa.

ESTELLE. But—[*Points to* GARCIN]

INEZ. Oh, he doesn't count.

ESTELLE. But we're going to—to hurt each other. You said it youself.

INEZ. Do I look as if I wanted to hurt you?

ESTELLE. One never can tell.

INEZ. Much more likely *you'll* hurt *me*. Still, what does it matter?

If I've got to suffer, it may as well be at your hands, your pretty hands. Sit down. Come closer. Closer. Look into my eyes. What do you see?

ESTELLE. Oh, I'm there! But so tiny I can't see myself properly.

INEZ. But *I* can. Every inch of you. Now ask me questions. I'll be as candid as any looking-glass.

[ESTELLE *seems rather embarrassed and turns to* GARCIN, *as if appealing to him for help.*]

ESTELLE. Please, Mr. Garcin. Sure our chatter isn't boring you?

[GARCIN *makes no reply.*]

INEZ. Don't worry about him. As I said, he doesn't count. We're by ourselves. . . . Ask away.

ESTELLE. Are my lips all right?

INEZ. Show! No, they're a bit smudgy.

ESTELLE. I thought as much. Luckily [*Throws a quick glance at* GAR-CIN] no one's seen me. I'll try again.

INEZ. That's better. No. Follow the line of your lips. Wait! I'll guide your hand. There. That's quite good.

ESTELLE. As good as when I came in?

INEZ. Far better. Crueler. Your mouth looks quite diabolical that way.

ESTELLE. Good gracious! And you say you like it! How maddening, not being able to see for myself! You're quite sure, Miss Serrano, that it's all right now?

INEZ. Won't you call me Inez?

ESTELLE. Are you sure it looks all right?

INEZ. You're lovely, Estelle.

ESTELLE. But how can I rely upon your taste? Is it the same as *my* taste? Oh, how sickening it all is, enough to drive one crazy!

INEZ. I *have* your taste, my dear, because I like you so much. Look at me. No, straight. Now smile. I'm not so ugly, either. Am I not nicer than your glass?

ESTELLE. Oh, I don't know. You scare me rather. My reflection in the glass never did that; of course, I knew it so well. Like something I had tamed. . . . I'm going to smile, and my smile will sink down into your pupils, and heaven knows what it will become.

INEZ. And why shouldn't you "tame" *me*? [*The women gaze at each other,* ESTELLE *with a sort of fearful fascination.*] Listen! I want you to call me Inez. We must be great friends.

ESTELLE. I don't make friends with women very easily.

INEZ. Not with postal clerks, you mean? Hullo, what's that—that nasty red spot at the bottom of your cheek? A pimple?

ESTELLE. A pimple? Oh, how simply foul! Where?

INEZ. There. . . . You know the way they catch larks—with a mirror? I'm your lark-mirror, my dear, and you can't escape me. . . . There isn't any pimple, not a trace of one. So what about it?

Suppose the mirror started telling lies? Or suppose I covered my eyes—as he is doing—and refused to look at you, all that loveliness of yours would be wasted on the desert air. No, don't be afraid, I can't help looking at you, I shan't turn my eyes away. And I'll be nice to you, ever so nice. Only you must be nice to me, too.

[*A short silence*]

ESTELLE. Are you really—attracted by me?

INEZ. Very much indeed.

[*Another short silence*]

ESTELLE. [*Indicating* GARCIN *by a slight movement of her head*] But I wish he'd notice me, too.

INEZ. Of course! Because he's a Man! [*To* GARCIN] You've won. [GARCIN *says nothing.*] But look at her, damn it! [*Still no reply from* GARCIN] Don't pretend. You haven't missed a word of what we've said.

GARCIN. Quite so; not a word. I stuck my fingers in my ears, but your voices thudded in my brain. Silly chatter. Now will you leave me in peace, you two? I'm not interested in you.

INEZ. Not in me, perhaps—but how about this child? Aren't you interested in her? Oh, I saw through your game; you got on your high horse just to impress her.

GARCIN. I asked you to leave me in peace. There's someone talking about me in the newspaper office and I want to listen. And, if it'll make you any happier, let me tell you that I've no use for the "child," as you call her.

ESTELLE. Thanks.

GARCIN. Oh, I didn't mean it rudely.

ESTELLE. You cad!

[*They confront each other in silence for some moments.*]

GARCIN. So's that's that. [*Pause*] You know I begged you not to speak.

ESTELLE. It's *her* fault; she started. I didn't ask anything of her and she came and offered me her—her glass.

INEZ. So you say. But all the time you were making up to him, trying every trick to catch his attention.

ESTELLE. Well, why shouldn't I?

GARCIN. You're crazy, both of you. Don't you see where this is leading us? For pity's sake, keep your mouths shut. [*Pause*] Now let's all sit down again quite quietly; we'll look at the floor and each must try to forget the others are there.

[*A longish silence.* GARCIN *sits down. The women return hesitantly to their places. Suddenly* INEZ *swings round on him.*]

INEZ. To forget about the others? How utterly absurd! I *feel* you there, in every pore. Your silence clamors in my ears. You can nail up your mouth, cut your tongue out—but you can't prevent your *being there.* Can you stop your thoughts? I hear them ticking away like a clock, tick-tock, tick-tock, and I'm certain you hear mine. It's all very well skulking on your sofa, but you're every-where, and every sound comes to me soiled, because you've inter-cepted it on its way. Why, you've even stolen my face; you know it and I don't! And what about her, about Estelle? You've stolen her from me, too; if she and I were alone do you suppose she'd treat me as she does? No, take your hands from your face, I won't leave you in peace—that would suit your book too well. You'd go on sitting there, in a sort of trance, like a yogi, and even if I didn't see her I'd feel it in my bones—that she was making every sound, even the rustle of her dress, for your benefit, throwing you smiles you didn't see. . . . Well, I won't stand for that, I prefer to choose my hell; I prefer to look you in the eyes and fight it out face to face.

GARCIN. Have it your own way. I suppose we were bound to come to this; they knew what they were about, and we're easy game. If they'd put me in a room with men—men can keep their mouths shut. But it's no use wanting the impossible. [*He goes to* ESTELLE *and lightly fondles her neck.*] So I attract you, little girl? It seems you were making eyes at me?

ESTELLE. Don't touch me.

GARCIN. Why not? We might, anyhow, be natural. . . . Do you know, I used to be mad about women? And some were fond of me. So we may as well stop posing, we've nothing to lose. Why trouble about politeness, and decorum, and the rest of it? We're between ourselves. And presently we shall be naked as—as new-born babes.

ESTELLE. Oh, let me be!

GARCIN. As new-born babes. Well, I'd warned you, anyhow. I asked so little of you, nothing but peace and a little silence. I'd put my fingers in my ears. Gomez was spouting away as usual, stand-ing in the center of the room, with all the pressmen listening. In their shirtsleeves. I tried to hear, but it wasn't too easy. Things on earth move so quickly, you know. Couldn't you have held your tongues? Now it's over, he's stopped talking, and what he thinks of me has gone back into his head. Well, we've got to see it through somehow. . . . Naked as we were born. So much the better; I want to know whom I have to deal with.

INEZ. You know already. There's nothing more to learn.

GARCIN. You're wrong. So long as each of us hasn't made a clean breast of it—why they've damned him or her—we know nothing. Nothing that counts. You, young lady, you shall begin. Why? Tell us why. If you are frank, if we bring our specters into the open, it may save us from disaster. So—out with it! Why?

ESTELLE. I tell you I haven't a notion. They wouldn't tell me why.

GARCIN. That's so. They wouldn't tell me, either. But I've a pretty good idea. . . . Perhaps you're shy of speaking first? Right. I'll lead off. [*A short silence*] I'm not a very estimable person.

INEZ. No need to tell us that. We know you were a deserter.

GARCIN. Let that be. It's only a side-issue. I'm here because I treated my wife abominably. That's all. For five years. Naturally, she's suffering still. There she is: the moment I mention her, I see her. It's Gomez who interests me, and it's she I see. Where's Gomez got to? For five years. There! They've given her back my things; she's sitting by the window, with my coat on her knees. The coat with the twelve bullet-holes. The blood's like rust; a brown ring round each hole. It's quite a museum-piece, that coat; scarred with history. And I used to wear it, fancy! . . . Now, can't you shed a tear, my love? Surely you'll squeeze one out—at last? No? You can't manage it? . . . Night after night I came home blind drunk, stinking of wine and women. She'd sat up for me, of course. But she never cried, never uttered a word of reproach. Only her eyes spoke. Big, tragic eyes. I don't regret anything. I must pay the price, but I shan't whine. . . . It's snowing in the street. Won't you cry, confound you? That woman was a born martyr, you know; a victim by vocation.

INEZ. [*Almost tenderly*] Why did you hurt her like that?

GARCIN. It was so easy. A word was enough to make her flinch. Like a sensitive-plant. But never, never a reproach. I'm fond of teasing. I watched and waited. But no, not a tear, not a protest. I'd picked her up out of the gutter, you understand. . . . Now she's stroking the coat. Her eyes are shut and she's feeling with her fingers for the bullet-holes. What are you after? What do you expect? I tell you I regret nothing. The truth is, she admired me too much. Does that mean anything to you?

INEZ. No. Nobody admired *me*.

GARCIN. So much the better. So much the better for you. I suppose all this strikes you as very vague. Well, here's something you can get your teeth into. I brought a half-caste girl to stay in our house. My wife slept upstairs; she must have heard—everything. She was an early riser and, as I and the girl stayed in bed late, she served us our morning coffee.

INEZ. You brute!

GARCIN. Yes, a brute, if you like. But a well-beloved brute. [*A faraway look comes to his eyes*] No, it's nothing. Only Gomez, and he's not talking about *me*. . . . What were you saying? Yes, a brute. Certainly. Else why should I be here? [*To* INEZ] Your turn.

INEZ. Well, I was what some people down there called "a damned bitch." Damned already. So it's no surprise, being here.

GARCIN. Is that all you have to say?

INEZ. No. There was that affair with Florence. A dead men's tale.

With three corpses to it. He to start with; then she and I. So
there's no one left, I've nothing to worry about; it was a clean
sweep. Only that room. I see it now and then. Empty, with the
doors locked. . . . No, they've just unlocked them. "To Let." It's
to let; there's a notice on the door. That's—too ridiculous.

GARCIN. Three. Three deaths, you said?

INEZ. Three.

GARCIN. One man and two women?

INEZ. Yes.

GARCIN. Well, well. [*A pause*] Did he kill himself?

INEZ. He? No, he hadn't the guts for that. Still, he'd every reason;
we led him a dog's life. As a matter of fact, he was run over by
a tram. A silly sort of end. . . . I was living with them; he was my
cousin.

GARCIN. Was Florence fair?

INEZ. Fair? [*Glances at* ESTELLE] You know, I don't regret a thing;
still, I'm not so very keen on telling you the story.

GARCIN. That's all right. . . . So you got sick of him?

INEZ. Quite gradually. All sorts of little things got on my nerves.
For instance, he made a noise when he was drinking—a sort of
gurgle. Trifles like that. He was rather pathetic really. Vulnerable.
Why are you smiling?

GARCIN. Because I, anyhow, am *not* vulnerable.

INEZ. Don't be too sure. . . . I crept inside her skin, she saw the
world through my eyes. When she left him, I had her on my
hands. We shared a bed-sitting-room at the other end of the town.

GARCIN. And then?

INEZ. Then that tram did its job. I used to remind her every day:
"Yes, my pet, we killed him between us." [*A pause*] I'm rather
cruel, really.

GARCIN. So am I.

INEZ. No, you're not cruel. It's something else.

GARCIN. What?

INEZ. I'll tell you later. When I say I'm cruel, I mean I can't get on
without making people suffer. Like a live coal. A live coal in
others' hearts. When I'm alone I flicker out. For six months I
flamed away in her heart, till there was nothing but a cinder.
One night she got up and turned on the gas while I was asleep.
Then she crept back into bed. So now you know.

GARCIN. Well! Well!

INEZ. Yes? What's in your mind?

GARCIN. Nothing. Only that it's not a pretty story.

INEZ. Obviously. But what matter?

GARCIN. As you say, what matter? [*To* ESTELLE] Your turn. What have
you done?

ESTELLE. As I told you, I haven't a notion. I rack my brain, but it's no use.

GARCIN. Right. Then we'll give you a hand. That fellow with the smashed face, who was he?

ESTELLE. Who—who do you mean?

INEZ. You know quite well. The man you were so scared of seeing when you came in.

ESTELLE. Oh, him! A friend of mine.

GARCIN. Why were you afraid of him?

ESTELLE. That's my business, Mr. Garcin.

INEZ. Did he shoot himself on your account?

ESTELLE. Of course not. How absurd you are!

GARCIN. Then why should you have been so scared? He blew his brains out, didn't he? That's how his face got smashed.

ESTELLE. Don't! Please don't go on.

GARCIN. Because of you. Because of you.

INEZ. He shot himself because of you.

ESTELLE. Leave me alone! It's—it's not fair, bullying me like that. I want to go! I want to go!

[*She runs to the door and shakes it.*]

GARCIN. Go if you can. Personally, I ask for nothing better. Unfortunately, the door's locked.

[ESTELLE *presses the bell-push, but the bell does not ring.* INEZ *and* GARCIN *laugh.* ESTELLE *swings round on them, her back to the door.*]

ESTELLE. [*In a muffled voice*] You're hateful, both of you.

INEZ. Hateful? Yes, that's the word. Now get on with it. That fellow who killed himself on your account—you were his mistress, eh?

GARCIN. Of course she was. And he wanted her to have her to himself alone. That's so, isn't it?

INEZ. He danced the tango like a professional, but he was poor as a church mouse—that's right, isn't it?

[*A short silence*]

GARCIN. Was he poor or not? Give a straight answer.

ESTELLE. Yes, he was poor.

GARCIN. And then you had your reputation to keep up. One day he came and implored you to run away with him, and you laughed in his face.

INEZ. That's it. You laughed at him. And so he killed himself.

ESTELLE. Did you use to look at Florence in that way?

INEZ. Yes.

[*A short pause, then* ESTELLE *bursts out laughing.*]

ESTELLE. You've got it all wrong, you two. [*She stiffens her shoulders, still leaning against the door, and faces them. Her voice grows shrill, truculent.*] He wanted me to have a baby. So there!

GARCIN. And you didn't want one?

ESTELLE. I certainly didn't. But the baby came, worse luck. I went to Switzerland for five months. No one knew anything. It was a girl. Roger was with me when she was born. It pleased him no end, having a daughter. It didn't please *me!*

GARCIN. And then?

ESTELLE. There was a balcony overlooking the lake. I brought a big stone. He could see what I was up to and he kept on shouting: "Estelle, for God's sake, don't!" I hated him then. He saw it all. He was leaning over the balcony and he saw the rings spreading on the water—

GARCIN. Yes? And then?

ESTELLE. That's all. I came back to Paris—and he did as he wished.

GARCIN. You mean he blew his brains out?

ESTELLE. It was absurd of him, really, my husband never suspected anything. [*A pause*] Oh, how I loathe you! [*She sobs tearlessly.*]

GARCIN. Nothing doing. Tears don't flow in this place.

ESTELLE. I'm a coward. A coward! [*Pause*] If you knew how I hate you!

INEZ. [*Taking her in her arms*] Poor child! [*To* GARCIN] So the hearing's over. But there's no need to look like a hanging judge.

GARCIN. A hanging judge? [*He glances around him.*] I'd give a lot to be able to see myself in a glass. [*Pause*] How hot it is! [*Unthinkingly he takes off his coat.*] Oh, sorry! [*He starts putting it on again.*]

ESTELLE. Don't bother. You can stay in your shirt-sleeves. As things are—

GARCIN. Just so. [*He drops his coat on the sofa.*] You mustn't be angry with me, Estelle.

ESTELLE. I'm not angry with you.

INEZ. And what about me? Are you angry with me?

ESTELLE. Yes.

[*A short silence*]

INEZ. Well, Mr. Garcin, now you have us in the nude all right. Do you understand things any better for that?

GARCIN. I wonder. Yes, perhaps a trifle better. [*Timidly*] And now suppose we start trying to help each other.

INEZ. I don't need help.

GARCIN. Inez, they've laid their snare damned cunningly—like a cobweb. If you make any movement, if you raise your hand to fan yourself, Estelle and I feel a little tug. Alone, none of us can save himself or herself; we're linked together inextricably. So you can take your choice. [*A pause*] Hullo? What's happening?

INEZ. They've let it. The windows are wide open, a man is sitting on my bed. *My* bed, if you please! They've let it, let it! Step in, step in, make yourself at home, you brute! Ah, there's a woman, too. She's going up to him, putting her hands on his shoulders. . . . Damn it, why don't they turn the lights on? It's getting dark. Now he's going to kiss her. But that's my room, *my* room. Pitch-dark now. I can't see anything, but I hear them whispering, whispering. Is he going to make love to her on *my* bed? What's that she said? That it's noon and the sun is shining? I must be going blind. [*A pause*] Blacked out. I can't see or hear a thing. So I'm done with the earth, it seems. No more alibis for me! [*She shudders*] I feel so empty, desiccated—really dead at last. All of me's here in this room. [*A pause*] What were you saying? Something about helping me, wasn't it?

GARCIN. Yes.

INEZ. Helping me to do what?

GARCIN. To defeat their devilish tricks.

INEZ. And what do you expect me to do, in return?

GARCIN. To help *me*. It only needs a little effort, Inez; just a spark of human feeling.

INEZ. Human feeling. That's beyond my range. I'm rotten to the core.

GARCIN. And how about me? [*A pause*] All the same, suppose we try?

INEZ. It's no use. I'm all dried up. I can't give and I can't receive. How could *I* help you? A dead twig, ready for the burning. [*She falls silent, gazing at* ESTELLE, *who has buried her head in her hands.*] Florence was fair, a natural blonde.

GARCIN. Do you realize that this young woman's fated to be your torturer?

INEZ. Perhaps I've guessed it.

GARCIN. It's through her they'll get you. I, of course, I'm different— aloof. I take no notice of her. Suppose you had a try—

INEZ. Yes?

GARCIN. It's a trap. They're watching you, to see if you'll fall into it.

INEZ. I know. And you're another trap. Do you think they haven't foreknown every word you say? And of course there's a whole nest of pitfalls that we can't see. Everything here's a booby-trap. But what do I care? I'm a pitfall, too. For her, obviously. And perhaps I'll catch her.

GARCIN. You won't catch anything. We're chasing after each other, round and round in a vicious circle, like the horses on a roundabout. That's part of their plan, of course. . . . Drop it, Inez. Open your hands and let go of everything. Or else you'll bring disaster on all three of us.

INEZ. Do I look the sort of person who lets go? I know what's coming to me. I'm going to burn, and it's to last forever. Yes, I *know* everything. But do you think I'll let go? I'll catch her, she'll see you through my eyes, as Florence saw that other man. What's the good of trying to enlist my sympathy? I assure you I know everything, and I can't feel sorry even for myself. A trap! Don't I know it, and that I'm in a trap myself, up to the neck, and there's nothing to be done about it? And if it suits their book, so much the better!

GARCIN. [*Gripping her shoulders*] Well, I, anyhow, can feel sorry for you, too. Look at me, we're naked, naked right through, and I can see into your heart. That's one link between us. Do you think I'd want to hurt you? I don't regret anything, I'm dried up, too. But for you I can still feel pity.

INEZ. [*Who has let him keep his hands on her shoulders until now, shakes herself loose*] Don't. I hate being pawed about. And keep your pity for yourself. Don't forget, Garcin, that there are traps for you, too, in this room. All nicely set for you. You'd do better to watch your own interests. [*A pause.*] But, if you will leave us in peace, this child and me, I'll see I don't do you any harm.

GARCIN. [*Gazes at her for a moment, then shrugs his shoulders*] Very well.

ESTELLE. [*Raising her head*] Please, Garcin.

GARCIN. What do you want of me?

ESTELLE. [*Rises and goes up to him*] You can help *me*, anyhow.

GARCIN. If you want help, apply to her.

[INEZ *has come up and is standing behind* ESTELLE, *but without touching her. During the dialogue that follows she speaks almost in her ear. But* ESTELLE *keeps her eyes on* GARCIN, *who observes her without speaking, and she addresses her answers to him, as if it were he who is questioning her.*]

ESTELLE. I implore you, Garcin—you gave me your promise, didn't you? Help me quick. I don't want to be left alone. Olga's taken him to a cabaret.

INEZ. Taken whom?

ESTELLE. Peter. . . . Oh, now they're dancing together.

INEZ. Who's Peter?

ESTELLE. Such a silly boy. He called me his glancing stream—just fancy! He was terribly in love with me. . . . She's persuaded him to come out with her tonight.

INEZ. Do you love him?

ESTELLE. They're sitting down now. She's puffing like a grampus. What a fool the girl is to insist on dancing! But I dare say she does it to reduce. . . . No, of course I don't love him; he's only eighteen, and I'm not a baby-snatcher.

INEZ. Then why bother about them? What difference can it make?

ESTELLE. He belonged to me.

INEZ. Nothing on earth belongs to you any more.

ESTELLE. I tell you he was mine. All mine.

INEZ. Yes, he was yours—once. But now— Try to make him hear, try to touch him. Olga can touch him, talk to him as much as she likes. That's so, isn't it? She can squeeze his hands, rub herself against him—

ESTELLE. Yes, look! She's pressing her great fat chest against him, puffing and blowing in his face. But, my poor little lamb, can't you see how ridiculous she is? Why don't you laugh at her? Oh, once I'd have only had to glance at them and she'd have slunk away. Is there really nothing, nothing left of me?

INEZ. Nothing whatever. Nothing of you's left on earth—not even a shadow. All you own is here. Would you like that paper-knife? Or that ornament on the mantelpiece? That blue sofa's yours. And I, my dear, am yours forever.

ESTELLE. You mine! That's good! Well, which of you two would dare to call me his glancing stream, his crystal girl? You know too much about me, you know I'm rotten through and through. . . . Peter dear, think of me, fix your thoughts on me, and save me. All the time you're thinking "my glancing stream, my crystal girl," I'm only half here, I'm only half wicked, and half of me is down there with you, clean and bright and crystal-clear as running water. . . . Oh, just look at her face, all scarlet, like a tomato. No, it's absurd, we've laughed at her together, you and I, often and often. . . . What's that tune?—I always loved it. Yes, the *St. Louis Blues*. . . . All right, dance away, dance away. Garcin, I wish you could see her, you'd die of laughing. Only—she'll never know I see her. Yes, I see you Olga, with your hair all anyhow, and you do look a dope, my dear. Oh, now you're treading on his toes. It's a scream! Hurry up! Quicker! Quicker! He's dragging her along, bundling her round and round—it's too ghastly! He always said I was so light, he loved to dance with me. [*She is dancing as she speaks.*] I tell you, Olga, I can see you. No, she doesn't care, she's dancing through my gaze. What's that? What's that you said? "Our poor dear Estelle"? Oh, don't be such a humbug! You didn't even shed a tear at the funeral. . . . And she has the nerve to talk to him about her poor dear friend Estelle! How dare she discuss me with Peter? Now then, keep time. She never could dance and talk at once. Oh, what's that? No, no. Don't tell him. Please, please don't tell him. You can keep him, do what you like with him, but please don't tell him about—that! [*She has stopped dancing.*] All right. You can have him now. Isn't it *foul*, Garcin? She's told him everything, about Roger, my trip to Switzerland, the baby. "Poor Estelle wasn't exactly—" No, I wasn't exactly— True enough. He's looking grave, shaking his head, but he doesn't seem so very much surprised, not what one would expect. Keep him, then—I won't haggle with you over his long eyelashes, his pretty girlish face. They're yours for the asking. His glancing stream, his crystal. Well, the crystal's shattered into bits. "Poor Estelle!" Dance, dance, dance. On with it. But do keep time. One, two. One, two. How I'd love to go down to earth for just a moment, and dance with him again. [*She dances again for some moments.*] The music's growing fainter. They've turned down the lights, as they do for a tango. Why are they playing so softly? Louder, please. I can't hear. It's so far away, so far away. I—I can't hear a sound. [*She stops dancing.*] All over. It's the end. The earth has left me. [*To* GARCIN] Don't turn from me—please. Take me in your arms. [*Behind* ESTELLE's *back,* INEZ *signs to* GARCIN *to move away.*]

INEZ. [*Commandingly*] Now then, Garcin!

[GARCIN *moves back a step, and, glancing at* ESTELLE, *points to* INEZ.]

GARCIN. It's to her you should say that.

ESTELLE. [*Clinging to him*] Don't turn away. You're a man, aren't you, and surely I'm not such a fright as all that! Everyone says I've lovely hair and, after all, a man killed himself on my account. You have to look at something, and there's nothing here to see except the sofas and that awful ornament and the table. Surely I'm better to look at than a lot of stupid furniture. Listen! I've dropped out of their hearts like a little sparrow fallen from its nest. So gather me up, dear, fold me to your heart—and you'll see how nice I can be.

GARCIN. [*Freeing himself from her, after a short struggle*] I tell you it's to that lady you should speak.

ESTELLE. To her? But she doesn't count, she's a woman.

INEZ. Oh, I don't count? Is that what you think? But, my poor little fallen nestling, you've been sheltering in my heart for ages, though you didn't realize it. Don't be afraid; I'll keep looking at you for ever and ever, without a flutter of my eyelids, and you'll live in my gaze like a mote in a sunbeam.

ESTELLE. A sunbeam indeed! Don't talk such rubbish! You've tried that trick already, and you should know it doesn't work.

INEZ. Estelle! My glancing stream! My crystal!

ESTELLE. *Your* crystal? It's grotesque. Do you think you can fool me with that sort of talk? Everyone knows by now what I did to my baby. The crystal's shattered, but I don't care. I'm just a hollow dummy, all that's left of me is the outside—but it's not for you.

INEZ. Come to me, Estelle. You shall be whatever you like: a glancing stream, a muddy stream. And deep down in my eyes you'll see yourself just as you want to be.

ESTELLE. Oh, leave me in peace. You haven't any eyes. Oh, damn it, isn't there anything I can do to get rid of you? I've an idea. [*She spits in* INEZ's *face.*] There!

INEZ. Garcin, you shall pay for this.

    [*A pause,* GARCIN *shrugs his shoulders and goes to* ESTELLE.]

GARCIN. So it's a man you need?

ESTELLE. Not *any* man. You.

GARCIN. No humbug now. Any man would do your business. As I happen to be here, you want me. Right!—[*He grips her shoulders.*] Mind, I'm not your sort at all, really; I'm not a young nincompoop and I don't dance the tango.

ESTELLE. I'll take you as you are. And perhaps I shall change you.

GARCIN. I doubt it. I shan't pay much attention; I've other things to think about.

ESTELLE. What things?

GARCIN. They wouldn't interest you.

ESTELLE. I'll sit on your sofa and wait for you to take some notice of me. I promise not to bother you at all.

INEZ. [*With a shrill laugh*] That's right, fawn on him, like the silly bitch you are. Grovel and cringe! And he hasn't even good looks to commend him!

ESTELLE. [*To* GARCIN] Don't listen to her. She has no eyes, no ears. She's—nothing.

GARCIN. I'll give you what I can. It doesn't amount to much. I shan't love you; I know you too well.

ESTELLE. Do you want me, anyhow?

GARCIN. Yes.

ESTELLE. I ask no more.

GARCIN. In that case—[*He bends over her.*]

INEZ. Estelle! Garcin! You must be going crazy. You're not alone. I'm here too.

GARCIN. Of course—but what does it matter?

INEZ. Under my eyes? You couldn't—couldn't do it.

ESTELLE. Why not? I often undressed with my maid looking on.

INEZ. [*Gripping* GARCIN's *arm*] Let her alone. Don't paw her with your dirty man's hands.

GARCIN. [*Thrusting her away roughly*] Take care. I'm no gentleman, and I'd have no compunction about striking a woman.

INEZ. But you promised me; you promised. I'm only asking you to keep your word.

GARCIN. Why should I, considering you were the first to break our agreement?

    [INEZ *turns her back on him and retreats to the far end of the room.*]

INEZ. Very well, have it your own way. I'm the weaker party, one against two. But don't forget I'm here, and watching. I shan't take my eyes off you, Garcin; when you're kissing her, you'll feel them boring into you. Yes, have it your own way, make love and get it over. We're in hell; my turn will come.

[*During the following scene she watches them without speaking.*]

GARCIN. [*Coming back to* ESTELLE *and grasping her shoulders*] Now then. Your lips. Give me your lips.

[*A pause. He bends to kiss her, then abruptly straightens up.*]

ESTELLE. [*Indignantly*] Really! [*A pause*] Didn't I tell you not to pay any attention to her?

GARCIN. You've got it wrong. [*Short silence*] It's Gomez; he's back in the press-room. They've shut the windows; it must be winter down there. Six months since I—Well, I warned you I'd be absent-minded sometimes, didn't I? They're shivering, they've kept their coats on. Funny they should feel the cold like that, when I'm feeling so hot. Ah, this time he's talking about me.

ESTELLE. Is it going to last long? [*Short silence*] You might at least tell me what he's saying.

GARCIN. Nothing. Nothing worth repeating. He's a swine, that's all. [*He listens attentively.*] A god-damned bloody swine. [*He turns to* ESTELLE.] Let's come back to—to ourselves. Are you going to love me?

ESTELLE. [*Smiling*] I wonder now !

GARCIN. Will you trust me?

ESTELLE. What a quaint thing to ask! Considering you'll be under my eyes all the time, and I don't think I've much to fear from Inez, so far as you're concerned.

GARCIN. Obviously. [*A pause. He takes his hands off* ESTELLE'S *shoulders.*] I was thinking of another kind of trust. [*Listens*] Talk away, talk away, you swine. I'm not there to defend myself. [*To* ESTELLE] Estelle, you must give me your trust.

ESTELLE. Oh, what a nuisance you are! I'm giving you my mouth, my arms, my whole body—and everything could be so simple. . . . My trust! I haven't any to give, I'm afraid, and you're making me terribly embarrassed. You must have something pretty ghastly on your conscience to make such a fuss about my trusting you.

GARCIN. They shot me.

ESTELLE. I know. Because you refused to fight. Well, why shouldn't you?

GARCIN. I—I didn't exactly refuse. [*In a far-away voice*] I must say he talks well, he makes out a good case against me, but he never says what I should have done instead. Should I have gone to the general and said: "General, I decline to fight"? A mug's game; they'd have promptly locked me up. But I wanted to show my colors, my true colors, do you understand? I wasn't going to be silenced. [*To* ESTELLE] So I—I took the train. . . . They caught me at the frontier.

ESTELLE. Where were you trying to go?

GARCIN. To Mexico. I meant to launch a pacifist newspaper down there. [*A short silence*] Well, why don't you speak?

ESTELLE. What could I say? You acted quite rightly, as you didn't want to fight. [GARCIN *makes a fretful gesture.*] But, darling, how on earth can I guess what you want me to answer?

INEZ. Can't you guess? Well, *I* can. He wants you to tell him that he bolted like a lion. For "bolt" he did, and that's what's biting him.

GARCIN. "Bolted," "went away"—we won't quarrel over words.

ESTELLE. But you *had* to run away. If you'd stayed they'd have sent you to jail, wouldn't they?

GARCIN. Of course. [*A pause*] Well, Estelle, am I a coward?

ESTELLE. How can I say? Don't be so unreasonable, darling. I can't put myself in your skin. You must decide that for yourself.

GARCIN. [*Wearily*] I can't decide.

ESTELLE. Anyhow, you must remember. You must have had reasons for acting as you did.

GARCIN. I had.

ESTELLE. Well?

GARCIN. But were they the real reasons?

ESTELLE. You've a twisted mind, that's your trouble. Plaguing yourself over such trifles!

GARCIN. I'd thought it all out, and I wanted to make a stand. But was that my real motive?

INEZ. Exactly. That's the question. Was that your real motive? No doubt you argued it out with yourself, you weighed the pros and cons, you found good reasons for what you did. But fear and hatred and all the dirty little instincts one keeps dark—they're motives too. So carry on, Mr. Garcin, and try to be honest with yourself— for once.

GARCIN. Do I need you to tell me that? Day and night I paced my cell, from the window to the door, from the door to the window. I pried into my heart, I sleuthed myself like a detective. By the end of it I felt as if I'd given my whole life to introspection. But always I harked back to the one thing certain—that I had acted as I did, I'd taken that train to the frontier. But why? Why? Finally I thought: My death will settle it. If I face death courageously, I'll prove I am no coward.

INEZ. And how did you face death?

GARCIN. Miserably. Rottenly. [INEZ *laughs.*] Oh, it was only a physical lapse—that might happen to anyone; I'm not ashamed of it.

Only everything's been left in suspense, forever. [*To* ESTELLE] Come here, Estelle. Look at me. I want to feel someone looking at me while they're talking about me on earth. . . . I like green eyes.

INEZ. Green eyes! Just hark to him! And you, Estelle, do you like cowards?

ESTELLE. If you knew how little I care! Coward or hero, it's all one—provided he kisses well.

GARCIN. There they are, slumped in their chairs, sucking at their cigars. Bored they look. Half-asleep. They're thinking: "Garcin's a coward." But only vaguely, dreamily. One's got to think of something. "That chap Garcin was a coward." That's what they've decided, those dear friends of mine. In six months' time they'll be saying: "Cowardly as that skunk Garcin." You're lucky, you two; no one on earth is giving you another thought. But I—I'm long in dying.

INEZ. What about your wife, Garcin?

GARCIN. Oh, didn't I tell you? She's dead.

INEZ. Dead?

GARCIN. Yes, she died just now. About two months ago.

INEZ. Of grief?

GARCIN. What else should she die of? So all is for the best, you see; the war's over, my wife's dead, and I've carved out my place in history.

[*He gives a choking sob and passes his hand over his face.* ESTELLE *catches his arm.*]

ESTELLE. My poor darling! Look at me. Please look. Touch me. Touch me. [*She takes his hand and puts it on her neck.*] There! Keep your hand there. [GARCIN *makes a fretful movement.*] No, don't move. Why trouble what those men are thinking? They'll die off one by one. Forget them. There's only me, now.

GARCIN. But *they* won't forget *me*, not they! They'll die, but others will come after them to carry on the legend. I've left my fate in their hands.

ESTELLE. You think too much, that's your trouble.

GARCIN. What else is there to do now? I was a man of action once. . . . Oh, if only I could be with them again, for just one day— I'd fling their lie in their teeth. But I'm locked out; they're passing judgment on my life without troubling about me, and they're right, because I'm dead. Dead and done with. [*Laughs*] A back number.

[*A short pause*]

ESTELLE. [*Gently*] GARCIN.

GARCIN. Still there? Now listen! I want you to do me a service. No, don't shrink away. I know it must seem strange to you, having someone asking you for help; you're not used to that. But if you'll make the effort, if you'll only *will* it hard enough, I dare say we can really love each other. Look at it this way. A thousand of them are proclaiming I'm a coward; but what do numbers matter? If there's someone, just one person, to say quite positively I did not run away, that I'm not the sort who runs away, that I'm brave and decent and the rest of it—well, that one person's faith would save me. Will you have that faith in me? Then I shall love you and cherish you for ever. Estelle—will you?

ESTELLE. [*Laughing*] Oh, you dear silly man, do you think I could love a coward?

GARCIN. But just now you said—

ESTELLE. I was only teasing you. I like men, my dear, who're real men, with tough skin and strong hands. You haven't a coward's chin, or a coward's mouth, or a coward's voice, or a coward's hair. And it's for your mouth, your hair, your voice, I love you.

GARCIN. Do you mean this? *Really* mean it?

ESTELLE. Shall I swear it?

GARCIN. Then I snap my fingers at them all, those below and those in here. Estelle, we shall climb out of hell. [INEZ *gives a shrill laugh. He breaks off and stares at her.*] What's that?

INEZ. [*Still laughing*] But she doesn't mean a word of what she says. How can you be such a simpleton? "Estelle, am I a coward?" As if she cared a damn either way.

ESTELLE. Inez, how dare you? [*To* GARCIN] Don't listen to her. If you want me to have faith in you, you must begin by trusting me.

INEZ. That's right! That's right! Trust away! She wants a man—that far you can trust her—she wants a man's arm round her waist, a man's smell, a man's eyes glowing with desire. And that's all she wants. She'd assure you you were God Almighty if she thought it would give you pleasure.

GARCIN. Estelle, is this true? Answer me. Is it true?

ESTELLE. What do you expect me to say? Don't you realize how maddening it is to have to answer questions one can't make head or tail of? [*She stamps her foot.*] You do make things difficult. . . . Anyhow, I'd love you just the same, even if you were a coward. Isn't that enough?

[*A short pause*]

GARCIN. [*To the two women*] You disgust me, both of you. [*He goes towards the door.*]

ESTELLE. What are you up to?

GARCIN. I'm going.

INEZ. [*Quickly*] You won't get far. The door is locked.

GARCIN. I'll make them open it. [*He presses the bell-push. The bell does not ring.*]

ESTELLE. Please! Please!

INEZ. [*To* ESTELLE] Don't worry, my pet. The bell doesn't work.

GARCIN. I tell you they shall open. [*Drums on the door*] I can't endure
it any longer, I'm through with you both. [ESTELLE *runs to him;
he pushes her away.*] Go away. You're even fouler than she. I won't
let myself get bogged in your eyes. You're soft and slimy. Ugh!
[*Bangs on the door again*] Like an octopus. Like a quagmire.

ESTELLE. I beg you, oh, I beg you not to leave me. I'll promise not
to speak again, I won't trouble you in any way—but don't go.
I daren't be left alone with Inez, now she's shown her claws.

GARCIN. Look after yourself. I never asked you to come here.

ESTELLE. Oh, how mean you are! Yes, it's quite true you're a coward.

INEZ. [*Going up to* ESTELLE] Well, my little sparrow fallen from the
nest, I hope you're satisfied now. You spat in my face—playing
up to him, of course—and we had a tiff on his account. But he's
going, and a good riddance it will be. We two women will have the
place to ourselves.

ESTELLE. You won't gain anything. If that door opens, I'm going,
too.

INEZ. Where?

ESTELLE. I don't care where. As far from you as I can.

[GARCIN *has been drumming on the door while they talk.*]

GARCIN. Open the door! Open, blast you! I'll endure anything, your
red-hot tongs and molten lead, your racks and prongs and gar-
rotes—all your fiendish gadgets, everything that burns and flays
and tears—I'll put up with any torture you impose. Anything, anything would be better than this agony of mind, this creeping
pain that gnaws and fumbles and caresses one and never hurts
quite enough. [*He grips the door-knob and rattles it.*] Now will
you open? [*The door flies open with a jerk, and he just avoids
falling.*] Ah! [*A long silence*]

INEZ. Well, Garcin? You're free to go.

GARCIN. [*Meditatively*] Now I wonder why that door opened.

INEZ. What are you waiting for? Hurry up and go.

GARCIN. I shall not go.

INEZ. And you, Estelle? [ESTELLE *does not move.* INEZ *bursts out
laughing.*] So what? Which shall it be? Which of the three of us
will leave? The barrier's down, why are we waiting? . . . But what
a situation! It's a scream! We're—inseparables!

[ESTELLE *springs at her from behind.*]

ESTELLE. Inseparables? Garcin, come and lend a hand. Quickly.
We'll push her out and slam the door on her. That'll teach her a
lesson.

INEZ. [*Struggling with* ESTELLE] Estelle! I beg you, let me stay. I
won't go, I won't go! Not into the passage.

GARCIN. Let go of her.

ESTELLE. You're crazy. She hates you.

GARCIN. It's because of her I'm staying here.

[ESTELLE *releases* INEZ *and stares dumbfoundedly at* GARCIN.]

INEZ. Because of me? [*Pause*] All right, shut the door. It's ten times hotter here since it opened. [GARCIN *goes to the door and shuts it.*] Because of me, you said?

GARCIN. Yes. *You*, anyhow, know what it means to be a coward.

INEZ. Yes, I know.

GARCIN. And you know what wickedness is, and shame, and fear. There were days when you peered into yourself, into the secret places of your heart, and what you saw there made you faint with horror. And then, next day, you didn't know what to make of it, you couldn't interpret the horror you had glimpsed the day before. Yes, you know what evil *costs*. And when you say I'm a coward, you know from experience what that means. Is that so?

INEZ. Yes.

GARCIN. So it's you whom I have to convince; you are of my kind. Did you suppose I meant to go? No, I couldn't leave you here, gloating over my defeat, with all those thoughts about me running in your head.

INEZ. Do you really wish to convince me?

GARCIN. That's the one and only thing I wish for now. I can't hear them any longer, you know. Probably that means they're through with me. For good and all. The curtain's down, nothing of me is left on earth—not even the name of coward. So, Inez, we're alone. Only you two remain to give a thought to me. She—she doesn't count. It's you who matter; you who hate me. If you'll have faith in me I'm saved.

INEZ. It won't be easy. Have a look at me. I'm a hard-headed woman.

GARCIN. I'll give you all the time that's needed.

INEZ. Yes, we've lots of time in hand. *All* time.

GARCIN. [*Putting his hands on her shoulders*] Listen! Each man has an aim in life, a leading motive; that's so, isn't it? Well, I didn't give a damn for wealth, or for love. I aimed at being a real man. A tough, as they say. I staked everything on the same horse. . . . Can one possibly be a coward when one's deliberately courted danger at every turn? And can one judge a life by a single action?

INEZ. Why not? For thirty years you dreamt you were a hero, and condoned a thousand petty lapses—because a hero, of course, can do no wrong. An easy method, obviously. Then a day came when you were up against it, the red light of real danger—and you took the train to Mexico.

GARCIN. I "dreamt," you say. It was no dream. When I chose the hardest path, I made my choice deliberately. A man is what he wills himself to be.

INEZ. Prove it. Prove it was no dream. It's what one does, and nothing else, that shows the stuff one's made of.

GARCIN. I died too soon. I wasn't allowed time to—to do my deeds.

INEZ. One always dies too soon—or too late. And yet one's whole life is complete at that moment, with a line drawn neatly under it, ready for the summing up. You are—your life, and nothing else.

GARCIN. What a poisonous woman you are! With an answer for everything.

INEZ. Now then! Don't lose heart. It shouldn't be so hard, convincing me. Pull yourself together, man, rake up some arguments. [GARCIN *shrugs his shoulders.*] Ah, wasn't I right when I said you were vulnerable? Now you're going to pay the price, and what a price! You're a coward, Garcin, because I wish it. I wish it—do you hear? —I wish it. And yet, just look at me, see how weak I am, a mere breath on the air, a gaze observing you, a formless thought that thinks you. [*He walks towards her, opening his hands.*] Ah, they're open now, those big hands, those coarse, man's hands! But what do you hope to do? You can't throttle thoughts with hands. So you've no choice, you must convince me, and you're at my mercy.

ESTELLE. Garcin!

GARCIN. What?

ESTELLE. Revenge yourself.

GARCIN. How?

ESTELLE. Kiss me, darling—then you'll hear her squeal.

GARCIN. That's true, Inez. I'm at your mercy, but you're at mine as well. [*He bends over* ESTELLE. INEZ *gives a little cry.*]

INEZ. Oh, you coward, you weakling, running to women to console you!

ESTELLE. That's right, Inez. Squeal away.

INEZ. What a lovely pair you make! If you could see his big paw splayed out on your back, rucking up your skin and creasing the silk. Be careful, though! He's perspiring, his hand will leave a blue stain on your dress.

ESTELLE. Squeal away, Inez, squeal away! . . . Hug me tight, darling; tighter still—that'll finish her off, and a good thing too!

INEZ. Yes, Garcin, she's right. Carry on with it, press her to you till you feel your bodies melting into each other; a lump of warm, throbbing flesh. . . . Love's a grand solace, isn't it, my friend? Deep and dark as sleep. But I'll see you don't sleep.

[GARCIN *makes a slight movement.*]

ESTELLE. Don't listen to her. Press your lips to my mouth. Oh, I'm yours, yours, yours.

INEZ. Well, what are you waiting for? Do as you're told. What a lovely scene: coward Garcin holding baby-killer Estelle in his man-

ly arms! Make your stakes, everyone. Will coward Garcin kiss
the lady, or won't he dare? What's the betting? I'm watching you,
everybody's watching, I'm a crowd all by myself. Do you hear
the crowd? Do you hear them muttering, Garcin? Mumbling and
muttering. "Coward! Coward! Coward! Coward!"—that's what
they're saying. . . . It's no use trying to escape, I'll never let you
go. What do you hope to get from her silly lips? Forgetfulness?
But I shan't forget you, not I! "It's I you must convince." So
come to me. I'm waiting. Come along, now. . . . Look how obedient he is, like a well-trained dog who comes when his mistress
calls. You can't hold him, and you never will.

GARCIN. Will night never come?

INEZ. Never.

GARCIN. You will always see me?

INEZ. Always.

> [GARCIN *moves away from* ESTELLE *and takes some steps across
> the room. He goes to the bronze ornament.*]

GARCIN. This bronze. [*Strokes it thoughtfully*] Yes, now's the moment; I'm looking at this thing on the mantelpiece, and I understand that I'm in hell. I tell you, everything's been thought out
beforehand. They knew I'd stand at the fireplace stroking this
thing of bronze, with all those eyes intent on me. Devouring me.
[*He swings round abruptly.*] What? Only two of you? I thought
there were more; many more. [*Laughs*] So this is hell. I'd never
have believed it. You remember all we were told about the torture-
chambers, the fire and brimstone, the "burning marl."[2] Old wives
tales! There's no need for red-hot pokers. Hell is—other people!

ESTELLE. My darling! Please—

GARCIN. [*Thrusting her away*] No, let me be. She is between us. I
cannot love you when she's watching.

ESTELLE. Right! In that case, I'll stop her watching. [*She picks up
the paper-knife from the table, rushes at* INEZ, *and stabs her several
times.*]

INEZ. [*Struggling and laughing*] But, you crazy creature, what do
you think you're doing? You know quite well I'm dead.

ESTELLE. Dead?

> [*She drops the knife. A pause.* INEZ *picks up the knife and
> jabs herself with it regretfully.*]

INEZ. Dead! Dead! Dead! Knives, poison, ropes—all useless. It has
happened already, do you understand? Once and for all. So here
we are, forever. [*Laughs*]

ESTELLE. [*With a peal of laughter*] Forever. My God, how funny!
Forever.

---

2. earth.

GARCIN. [*Looks at the two women, and joins in the laughter*] For
ever, and ever, and ever.

> [*They slump onto their respective sofas. A long silence. Their
> laughter dies away and they gaze at each other.*]

GARCIN. Well, well, let's get on with it. . . .

CURTAIN

ALBERT CAMUS
(1913–1960)
The Renegade (Le Renégat)*

"What a jumble! What a jumble! I must tidy up my mind. Since
they cut out my tongue, another tongue, it seems, has been constantly wagging somewhere in my skull, something has been talking,
or someone, that suddenly falls silent and then it all begins again—
oh, I hear too many things I never utter, what a jumble, and if I
open my mouth it's like pebbles rattling together. Order and method, the tongue says, and then goes on talking of other matters
simultaneously—yes, I always longed for order. At least one thing
is certain, I am waiting for the missionary who is to come and take
my place. Here I am on the trail, an hour away from Taghâsa,
hidden in a pile of rocks, sitting on my old rifle. Day is breaking over
the desert, it's still very cold, soon it will be too hot, this country
drives men mad and I've been here I don't know how many years.
. . . No, just a little longer. The missionary is to come this morning,
or this evening. I've heard he'll come with a guide, perhaps they'll
have but one camel between them. I'll wait. I am waiting, it's only
the cold making me shiver. Just be patient a little longer, lousy
slave!

But I have been patient for so long. When I was home on that
high plateau of the Massif Central,[1] my coarse father, my boorish
mother, the wine, the pork soup every day, the wine above all, sour
and cold, and the long winter, the frigid wind, the snowdrifts, the
revolting bracken—oh, I wanted to get away, leave them all at once
and begin to live at last, in the sunlight, with fresh water. I believed
the priest, he spoke to me of the seminary, he tutored me daily, he
had plenty of time in that Protestant region, where he used to hug
the walls as he crossed the village. He told me of the future and of
the sun, Catholicism is the sun, he used to say, and he would get

* 1957. Reprinted from *Exile and the
Kingdom* by Albert Camus, translated
by Justin O'Brien.

1. the mountainous region that covers
one fifth of the area of France.

me to read, he beat Latin into my hard head ('The kid's bright but he's pig-headed'), my head was so hard that, despite all my falls, it has never once bled in my life: 'Bull-headed,' my pig of a father used to say. At the seminary they were proud as punch, a recruit from the Protestant region was a victory, they greeted me like the sun at Austerlitz.[2] The sun was pale and feeble, to be sure, because of the alcohol, they have drunk sour wine and the children's teeth are set on edge, *gra gra*,[3] one really ought to kill one's father, but after all there's no danger that *he*'ll hurl himself into missionary work since he's now long dead, the tart wine eventually cut through his stomach, so there's nothing left but to kill the missionary.

I have something to settle with him and with his teachers, with my teachers who deceived me, with the whole of lousy Europe, everybody deceived me. Missionary work, that's all they could say, go out to the savages and tell them: 'Here is my Lord, just look at him, he never strikes or kills, he issues his orders in a low voice, he turns the other cheek, he's the greatest of masters, choose him, just see how much better he's made me, offend me and you will see.' Yes, I believed, *gra gra*, and I felt better, I had put on weight, I was almost handsome, I wanted to be offended. When we would walk out in tight black rows, in summer, under Grenoble's hot sun and would meet girls in cotton dresses, I didn't look away, I despised them, I waited for them to offend me, and sometimes they would laugh. At such times I would think: 'Let them strike me and spit in my face,' but their laughter, to tell the truth, came to the same thing, bristling with teeth and quips that tore me to shreds, the offense and the suffering were sweet to me! My confessor couldn't understand when I used to heap accusations on myself: 'No, no, there's good in you!' Good! There was nothing but sour wine in me, and that was all for the best, how can a man become better if he's not bad, I had grasped that in everything they taught me. That's the only thing I did grasp, a single idea, and, pig-headed bright boy, I carried it to its logical conclusion, I went out of my way for punishments, I groused at the normal, in short I too wanted to be an example in order to be noticed and so that after noticing me people would give credit to what had made me better, through me praise my Lord.

Fierce sun! It's rising, the desert is changing, it has lost its mountain-cyclamen color, O my mountain, and the snow, the soft enveloping snow, no, it's a rather grayish yellow, the ugly moment before the great resplendence. Nothing, still nothing from here to the horizon over yonder where the plateau disappears in a circle of still soft colors. Behind me, the trail climbs to the dune hiding Taghâsa, whose iron name has been beating in my head for so many years. The first to mention it to me was the half-blind old

2. Here, in 1805, Napoleon defeated 3. an inarticulate sound.
the Austrians and Russians.

priest who had retired to our monastery, but why do I say the first, he was the only one, and it wasn't the city of salt, the white walls under the blinding sun, that struck me in his account but the cruelty of the savage inhabitants and the town closed to all outsiders, only one of those who had tried to get in, one alone, to his knowledge, had lived to relate what he had seen. They had whipped him and driven him out into the desert after having put salt on his wounds and in his mouth, he had met nomads who for once were compassionate, a stroke of luck, and since then I had been dreaming about his tale, about the fire of the salt and the sky, about the House of the Fetish and his slaves, could anything more barbarous, more exciting be imagined, yes, that was my mission and I had to go and reveal to them my Lord.

They all expatiated on the subject at the seminary to discourage me, pointing out the necessity of waiting, that it was not missionary country, that I wasn't ready yet, I had to prepare myself specially, know who I was, and even then I had to go through tests, then they would see! But go on waiting, ah, no!—yes, if they insisted, for the special preparation and the tryouts because they took place at Algiers and brought me closer, but for all the rest I shook my pig-head and repeated the same thing, to get among the most barbarous and live as they did, to show them at home, and even in the House of the Fetish, through example, that my Lord's truth would prevail. They would offend me, of course, but I was not afraid of offenses, they were essential to the demonstration, and as a result of the way I endured them I'd get the upper hand of those savages like a strong sun. Strong, yes, that was the word I constantly had on the tip of my tongue, I dreamed of absolute power, the kind that makes people kneel down, that forces the adversary to capitulate, converts him in short, and the blinder, the crueler he is, the more he's sure of himself, mired in his own conviction, the more his consent establishes the royalty of whoever brought about his collapse. Converting good folk who had strayed somewhat was the shabby ideal of our priests, I despised them for daring so little when they could do so much, they lacked faith and I had it, I wanted to be acknowledged by the torturers themselves, to fling them on their knees and make them say: 'O Lord, here is thy victory,' to rule in short by the sheer force of words over an army of the wicked. Oh, I was sure of reasoning logically on that subject, never quite sure of myself otherwise, but once I get an idea I don't let go of it, that's my strong point, yes the strong point of the fellow they all pitied!

The sun has risen higher, my forehead is beginning to burn. Around me the stones are beginning to crack open with a dull sound, the only cool thing is the rifle's barrel, cool as the fields, as the evening rain long ago when the soup was simmering, they would wait for me, my father and mother who would occasionally smile at me, perhaps I loved them. But that's all in the past, a film of heat

is beginning to rise from the trail, come on, missionary, I
for you, now I know how to answer the message, my new
taught me, and I know they are right, you have to settle acco
with that question of love. When I fled the seminary in Algiers I ha
a different idea of the savages and only one detail of my imaginings
was true, they are cruel. I had robbed the treasurer's office, cast off
my habit, crossed the Atlas,[4] the upper plateaus and the desert, the
bus-driver of the Trans-Sahara line made fun of me: 'Don't go there,'
he too, what had got into them all, and the gusts of sand for
hundreds of wind-blown kilometers, progressing and backing in the
face of the wind, then the mountains again made up of black peaks
and ridges sharp as steel, and after them it took a guide to go out on
the endless sea of brown pebbles, screaming with heat, burning
with the fires of a thousand mirrors, to the spot on the confines of
the white country and the land of the blacks where stands the city of
salt. And the money the guide stole from me, ever naïve I had shown
it to him, but he left me on the trail—just about here, it so happens
—after having struck me: 'Dog, there's the way, the honor's all
mine, go ahead, go on, they'll show you,' and they did show me, oh
yes, they're like the sun that never stops, except at night, beating
sharply and proudly, that is beating me hard at this moment, too
hard, with a multitude of lances burst from the ground, oh shelter,
yes shelter, under the big rock, before everything gets muddled.

The shade here is good. How can anyone live in the city of salt,
in the hollow of that basin full of dazzling heat? On each of the
sharp right-angle walls cut out with a pickax and coarsely planed,
the gashes left by the pickax bristle with blinding scales, pale scattered sand yellows them somewhat except when the wind dusts the
upright walls and terraces, then everything shines with dazzling
whiteness under a sky likewise dusted even to its blue rind. I was
going blind during those days when the stationary fire would crackle
for hours on the surface of the white terraces that all seemed to
meet as if, in the remote past, they had all together tackled a
mountain of salt, flattened it first, and then had hollowed out
streets, the insides of houses and windows directly in the mass, or as
if—yes, this is more like it, they had cut out their white, burning
hell with a powerful jet of boiling water just to show that they could
live where no one ever could, thirty days' travel from any living
thing, in this hollow in the middle of the desert where the heat of
day prevents any contact among creatures, separates them by a
portcullis of invisible flames and of searing crystals, where without
transition the cold of night congeals them individually in their
rock-salt shells, nocturnal dwellers in a dried-up icefloe, black Eski-
moes suddenly shivering in their cubical igloos. Black because they
wear long black garments, and the salt that collects even under their

---

4. a range of mountains in Morocco, Algeria, and Tunisia.

nue tasting bitterly and swallowing during the
nights, the salt they drink in the water from
e hollow of a dazzling groove, often spots their
something like the trail of snails after a rain.
t one real rain, long and hard, rain from your
t the hideous city, gradually eaten away, would
y cave in and, utterly melted in a slimy torrent,
savage inhabitants toward the sands. Just one
rain, Lord! But what do I mean, what Lord, they are the lords and
masters! They rule over their sterile homes, over their black slaves
that they work to death in the mines and each slab of salt that is cut
out is worth a man in the region to the south, they pass by, silent,
wearing their mourning veils in the mineral whiteness of the streets,
and at night, when the whole town looks like a milky phantom, they
stoop down and enter the shade of their homes, where the salt walls
shine dimly. They sleep with a weightless sleep and, as soon as they
wake, they give orders, they strike, they say they are a united people,
that their god is the true god, and that one must obey. They are my
masters, they are ignorant of pity and, like masters, they want to be
alone, to progress alone, to rule alone, because they alone had the
daring to build in the salt and the sands a cold torrid city. And I . . .

What a jumble when the heat rises, I'm sweating, they never do,
now the shade itself is heating up, I feel the sun on the stone above
me, it's striking, striking like a hammer on all the stones and it's the
music, the vast music of noon, air and stones vibrating over hundreds
of kilometers, *gra*, I hear the silence as I did once before. Yes, it was
the same silence, years ago, that greeted me when the guards led me
to them, in the sunlight, in the center of the square, whence the
concentric terraces rose gradually toward the lid of hard blue sky
sitting on the edge of the basin. There I was, thrown on my knees in
the hollow of that white shield, my eyes corroded by the swords of
salt and fire issuing from all the walls, pale with fatigue, my ear
bleeding from the blow given by my guide, and they, tall and black,
looked at me without saying a word. The day was at its midcourse.
Under the blows of the iron sun the sky resounded at length, a sheet
of white-hot tin, it was the same silence, and they stared at me,
time passed, they kept on staring at me, and I couldn't face their
stares, I panted more and more violently, eventually I wept, and
suddenly they turned their backs on me in silence and all together
went off in the same direction. On my knees, all I could see, in the
red-and-black sandals, was their feet sparkling with salt as they
raised the long black gowns, the tip rising somewhat, the heel
striking the ground lightly, and when the square was empty I was
dragged to the House of the Fetish.

Squatting, as I am today in the shelter of the rock and the fire
above my head pierces the rock's thickness, I spent several days
within the dark of the House of the Fetish, somewhat higher than

the others, surrounded by a wall of salt, but without windows, full of a sparkling night. Several days, and I was given a basin of brackish water and some grain that was thrown before me the way chickens are fed, I picked it up. By day the door remained closed and yet the darkness became less oppressive, as if the irresistible sun managed to flow through the masses of salt. No lamp, but by feeling my way along the walls I touched garlands of dried palms decorating the walls and, at the end, a small door, coarsely fitted, of which I could make out the bolt with my fingertips. Several days, long after—I couldn't count the days or the hours, but my handful of grain had been thrown me some ten times and I had dug out a hole for my excrements that I covered up in vain, the stench of an animal den hung on anyway—long after, yes, the door opened wide and they came in.

One of them came toward me where I was squatting in a corner. I felt the burning salt against my cheek, I smelled the dusty scent of the palms, I watched him approach. He stopped a yard away from me, he stared at me in silence, a signal, and I stood up, he stared at me with his metallic eyes that shone without expression in his brown horse-face, then he raised his hand. Still impassive, he seized me by the lower lip, which he twisted slowly until he tore my flesh and, without letting go, made me turn around and back up to the center of the room, he pulled on my lip to make me fall on my knees there, mad with pain and my mouth bleeding, then he turned away to join the others standing against the walls. They watched me moaning in the unbearable heat of the unbroken daylight that came in the wide-open door, and in that light suddenly appeared the Sorcerer with his raffia hair, his chest covered with a breastplate of pearls, his legs bare under a straw skirt, wearing a mask of reeds and wire with two square openings for the eyes. He was followed by musicians and women wearing heavy motley gowns that revealed nothing of their bodies. They danced in front of the door at the end, but a coarse, scarcely rhythmical dance, they just barely moved, and finally the Sorcerer opened the little door behind me, the masters did not stir, they were watching me, I turned around and saw the Fetish, his double ax-head, his iron nose twisted like a snake.

I was carried before him, to the foot of the pedestal, I was made to drink a black, bitter, bitter water, and at once my head began to burn, I was laughing, that's the offense, I have been offended. They undressed me, shaved my head and body, washed me in oil, beat my face with cords dipped in water and salt, and I laughed and turned my head away, but each time two women would take me by the ears and offer my face to the Sorcerer's blows while I could see only his square eyes, I was still laughing, covered with blood. They stopped, no one spoke but me, the jumble was beginning in my head, then they lifted me up and forced me to raise my eyes toward the Fetish, I had ceased laughing. I knew that I was now consecrated to him to serve him, adore him, no, I was not laughing any more, fear and pain stifled me. And there, in that white house, between those walls that the sun was assiduously burning on the outside, my face taut, my memory exhausted, yes, I tried to pray to the Fetish, he was all there was and even his horrible face was less horrible than the rest of the world. Then it was that my ankles were tied with a cord that permitted just one step, they danced again, but this time in front of the Fetish, the masters went out one by one.

The door once closed behind them, the music again, and the Sorcerer lighted a bark fire around which he pranced, his long silhouette broke on the angles of the white walls, fluttered on the flat surfaces, filled the room with dancing shadows. He traced a rectangle in a corner to which the women dragged me, I felt their dry and gentle hands, they set before me a bowl of water and a little pile of grain and pointed to the Fetish, I grasped that I was to keep my eyes fixed on him. Then the Sorcerer called them one after the other over to the fire, he beat some of them who moaned and who then went and prostrated themselves before the Fetish my god, while the Sorcerer kept on dancing and he made them all leave the room until only one was left, quite young, squatting near the musicians and not yet beaten. He held her by a shock of hair which he kept twisting around his wrist, she dropped backward with eyes popping until she finally fell on her back. Dropping her, the Sorcerer screamed, the musicians turned to the wall, while behind the square-eyed mask the scream rose to an impossible pitch, and the woman rolled on the ground in a sort of fit and, at last on all fours, her head hidden in her locked arms, she too screamed, but with a hollow, muffled sound, and in this position, without ceasing to scream and to look at the Fetish, the Sorcerer took her nimbly and nastily, without the woman's face being visible, for it was covered with the heavy folds of her garment. And, wild as a result of the solitude, I screamed too, yes, howled with fright toward the Fetish until a kick hurled me against the wall, biting the salt as I am biting this rock today with my tongueless mouth, while waiting for the man I must kill.

Now the sun has gone a little beyond the middle of the sky. Through the breaks in the rock I can see the hole it makes in the white-hot metal of the sky, a mouth voluble as mine, constantly vomiting rivers of flame over the colorless desert. On the trail in front of me, nothing, no cloud of dust on the horizon, behind me they must be looking for me, no, not yet, it's only in the late afternoon that they opened the door and I could go out a little, after having spent the day cleaning the House of the Fetish, set out fresh offerings, and in the evening the ceremony would begin, in which I was sometimes beaten, at others not, but always I served the Fetish, the Fetish whose image is engraved in iron in my memory and now in my hope also. Never had a god so possessed or enslaved me, my whole life day and night was devoted to him, and pain and the absence of pain, wasn't that joy, were due him and even, yes, desire, as a result of being present, almost every day, at that impersonal and nasty act which I heard without seeing it inasmuch as I now had to face the wall or else be beaten. But, my face up against the salt, obsessed by the bestial shadows moving on the wall, I listened to the long scream, my throat was dry, a burning sexless desire squeezed my temples and my belly as in a vise. Thus the days followed one another, I barely distinguished them as if they had liquefied in the torrid heat and the treacherous reverberation from the walls of salt, time had become merely a vague lapping of waves in which there would burst out, at regular intervals, screams of pain or possession, a long ageless day in which the Fetish ruled as this fierce sun does over my house of rocks, and now, as I did then, I weep with unhappiness and longing, a wicked hope consumes me, I want to betray, I lick the barrel of my gun and its soul inside, its soul, only guns have souls—oh, yes! the day they cut out my tongue, I learned to adore the immortal soul of hatred!

What a jumble, what a rage, *gra gra*, drunk with heat and wrath, lying prostrate on my gun. Who's panting here? I can't endure this endless heat, this waiting, I must kill him. Not a bird, not a blade of grass, stone, an arid desire, their screams, this tongue within me talking, and since they mutilated me, the long, flat, deserted suffering deprived even of the water of night, the night of which I would dream, when locked in with the god, in my den of salt. Night alone with its cool stars and dark fountains could save me, carry me off at last from the wicked gods of mankind, but ever locked up I could not contemplate it. If the newcomer tarries more, I shall see it at least rise from the desert and sweep over the sky, a cold golden vine that will hang from the dark zenith and from which I can drink at length, moisten this black dried hole that no muscle of live flexible flesh revives now, forget at last that day when madness took away my tongue.

How hot it was, really hot, the salt was melting or so it seemed to me, the air was corroding my eyes, and the Sorcerer came in without his mask. Almost naked under grayish tatters, a new woman followed him and her face, covered with a tattoo reproducing the mask of the Fetish, expressed only an idol's ugly stupor. The only thing alive about her was her thin flat body that flopped at the foot of the god when the Sorcerer opened the door of the niche. Then he went out without looking at me, the heat rose, I didn't stir, the Fetish looked at me over that motionless body whose muscles stirred gently and the woman's idol-face didn't change when I approached. Only her eyes enlarged as she stared at me, my feet touched hers, the heat then began to shriek, and the idol, without a word, still staring at me with her dilated eyes, gradually slipped onto her back, slowly drew her legs up and raised them as she gently spread her knees. But, immediately afterward, *gra*, the Sorcerer was lying in wait for me, they all entered and tore me from the woman, beat me dreadfully on the sinful place, what sin, I'm laughing, where is it and where is virtue, they clapped me against a wall, a hand of steel gripped my jaws, another opened my mouth, pulled on my tongue until it bled, was it I screaming with that bestial scream, a cool cutting caress, yes cool at last, went over my tongue. When I came to, I was alone in the night, glued to the wall, covered with hardened blood, a gag of strange-smelling dry grasses filled my mouth, it had stopped bleeding, but it was vacant and in that absence the only living thing was a tormenting pain. I wanted to rise, I fell back, happy, desperately happy to die at last, death too is cool and its shadow hides no god.

I did not die, a new feeling of hatred stood up one day, at the same time I did, walked toward the door of the niche, opened it, closed it behind me, I hated my people, the Fetish was there and from the depth of the hole in which I was I did more than pray to him, I believed in him and denied all I had believed up to then. Hail! he was strength and power, he could be destroyed but not converted, he stared over my head with his empty, rusty eyes. Hail! he was the master, the only lord, whose indisputable attribute was malice, there are no good masters. For the first time, as a result of offenses, my whole body crying out a single pain, I surrendered to him and approved his maleficent order, I adored in him the evil principle of the world. A prisoner of his kingdom—the sterile city carved out of a mountain of salt, divorced from nature, deprived of those rare and fleeting flowerings of the desert, preserved from those strokes of chance or marks of affection such as an unexpected cloud or a brief violent downpour that are familiar even to the sun or the sands, the city of order in short, right angles, square rooms, rigid men—I freely became its tortured, hate-filled citizen, I repudiated the long history that had been taught me. I had been misled, solely the reign of malice was devoid of defects, I had been misled, truth is square, heavy, thick, it does not admit distinctions, gold is an idle dream, an intention constantly postponed and pursued with exhausting effort, a limit never reached, its reign is impossible. Only evil can reach its limits and reign absolutely, it must be served to establish its visible kingdom, then we shall see, but what does 'then' mean, only evil is present, down with Europe, reason, honor, and the cross. Yes, I was to be converted to the religion of my masters, yes indeed, I was a slave, but if I too become vicious I cease to be a slave, despite my shackled feet and my mute mouth. Oh, this heat is driving me crazy, the desert cries out everywhere under the unbearable light, and he, the Lord of kindness, whose very name revolts me, I disown him, for I know him now. He dreamed and wanted to lie, his tongue was cut out so that his word would no longer be able to deceive the world, he was pierced with nails even in his head, his poor head, like mine now, what a jumble, how weak I am, and the earth didn't tremble, I am sure, it was not a righteous man they had killed, I refuse to believe it, there are no righteous men but only evil masters who bring about the reign of relentless truth. Yes, the Fetish alone has power, he is the sole god of this world, hatred is his commandment, the source of all life, the cool water, cool like mint that chills the mouth and burns the stomach.

Then it was that I changed, they realized it, I would kiss their hands when I met them, I was on their side, never wearying of admiring them, I trusted them, I hoped they would mutilate my people as they had mutilated me. And when I learned that the missionary was to come, I knew what I was to do. That day like all the others, the same blinding daylight that had been going on so long! Late in the afternoon a guard was suddenly seen running along the edge of the basin, and, a few minutes later, I was dragged to the House of the Fetish and the door closed. One of them held me on the ground in the dark, under threat of his cross-shaped sword, and the silence lasted for a long time until a strange sound filled the ordinarily peaceful town, voices that it took me some time to recognize because they were speaking my language, but as soon as they rang out the point of the sword was lowered toward my eyes, my guard stared at me in silence. Then two voices came closer and I can still hear them, one asking why that house was guarded and whether they should break in the door, Lieutenant, the other said: 'No' sharply, then added, after a moment, that an agreement had been reached, that the town accepted a garrison of twenty men on condition that they would camp outside the walls and respect the customs. The private laughed, 'They're knuckling under,' but the officer didn't know, for the first time in any case they were willing to receive someone to take care of the children and that would be the chaplain, later on they would see about the territory. The other said they would cut off the chaplain's you know what if the soldiers were not there. 'Oh, no!' the officer answered. 'In fact, Father Beffort will come before the garrison; he'll be here in two days.' That was all I heard, motionless, lying under the sword, I was in pain, a wheel of needles and knives was whirling in me. They were crazy, they were crazy, they were allowing a hand to be laid on the city, on their invincible power, on the true god, and the fellow who was to come would not have his tongue cut out, he would show off his insolent goodness without paying for it, without enduring any offense. The reign of evil would be postponed, there would be doubt again, again time would be wasted dreaming of the impossible good, wearing oneself out in fruitless efforts instead of hastening the realization of the only possible kingdom and I looked at the sword threatening me, O sole power to rule over the world! O power, and the city gradually emptied of its sounds, the door finally opened, I remained alone, burned and bitter, with the Fetish, and I swore to him to save my new faith, my true masters, my despotic God, to betray well, whatever it might cost me.

Gra, the heat is abating a little, the stone has ceased to vibrate, I can go out of my hole, watch the desert gradually take on yellow and ocher tints that will soon be mauve. Last night I waited until they were asleep, I had blocked the lock on the door, I went out with the same step as usual, measured by the cord, I knew the streets, I knew where to get the old rifle, what gate wasn't guarded, and I reached here just as the night was beginning to fade around a handful of stars while the desert was getting a little darker. And now it seems days and days that I have been crouching in these rocks. Soon, soon, I hope he comes soon! In a moment they'll begin to look for me, they'll speed over the trails in all directions, they won't know that I left for them and to serve them better, my legs are weak, drunk with hunger and hate. Oh! over there, *gra*, at the end of the trail, two camels are growing bigger, ambling along, already multiplied by short shadows, they are running with that lively and dreamy gait they always have. Here they are, here at last!

Quick, the rifle, and I load it quickly. O Fetish, my god over yonder, may your power be preserved, may the offense be multipled, may hate rule pitilessly over a world of the damned, may the wicked forever be masters, may the kingdom come, where in a single city of salt and iron black tyrants will enslave and possess without pity! And now, *gra gra*, fire on pity, fire on impotence and its charity, fire on all that postpones the coming of evil, fire twice, and there they are toppling over, falling, and the camels flee toward the horizon, where a geyser of black birds has just risen in the unchanged sky. I laugh, I laugh, the fellow is writhing in his detested habit, he is raising his head a little, he sees me—me his all-powerful shackled master, why does he smile at me, I'll crush that smile! How pleasant is the sound of a rifle butt on the face of goodness, today, today at last, all is consummated and everywhere in the desert, even hours away from here, jackals sniff the nonexistent wind, then set out in a patient trot toward the feast of carrion awaiting them. Victory! I raise my arms to a heaven moved to pity, a lavender shadow is just barely suggested on the opposite side, O nights of Europe, home, childhood, why must I weep in the moment of triumph?

He stirred, no the sound comes from somewhere else, and from the other direction here they come rushing like a flight of of dark birds, my masters, who fall upon me, seize me, ah yes! strike, they fear their city sacked and howling, they fear the avenging soldiers I called forth, and this is only right, upon the sacred city. Defend yourselves now, strike! strike me first, you possess the truth! O my masters, they will then conquer the soldiers, they'll conquer the word and love, they'll spread over the deserts, cross the seas, fill the light of Europe with their black veils—strike the belly, yes, strike the eyes —sow their salt on the continent, all vegetation, all youth will die out, and dumb crowds with shackled feet will plod beside me in the world-wide desert under the cruel sun of the true faith, I'll not be alone. Ah! the pain, the pain they cause me, their rage is good and on this cross-shaped war-saddle where they are now quartering me, pity! I'm laughing, I love the blow that nails me down crucified.

* * *

How silent the desert is! Already night and I am alone, I'm thirsty. Still waiting, where is the city, those sounds in the distance, and the soldiers perhaps the victors, no, it can't be, even if the soldiers are victorious, they're not wicked enough, they won't be able to rule, they'll still say one must become better, and still millions of men between evil and good, torn, bewildered, O Fetish, why hast thou forsaken me? All is over, I'm thirsty, my body is burning, a darker night fills my eyes.

This long, this long dream, I'm awaking, no, I'm going to die, dawn is breaking, the first light, daylight for the living, and for me the inexorable sun, the flies. Who is speaking, no one, the sky is not opening up, no, no, God doesn't speak in the desert, yet whence comes that voice saying: 'If you consent to die for hate and power, who will forgive us?' Is it another tongue in me or still that other fellow refusing to die, at my feet, and repeating: 'Courage! courage! courage!'? Ah! supposing I were wrong again! Once fraternal men, sole recourse, O solitude, forsake me not! Here, here who are you, torn, with bleeding mouth, is it you, Sorcerer, the soldiers defeated you, the salt is burning over there, it's you my beloved master! Cast off that hate-ridden face, be good now, we were mistaken, we'll begin all over again, we'll rebuild the city of mercy, I want to go back home. Yes, help me, that's right, give me your hand. . . .

A handful of salt fills the mouth of the garrulous slave.

A Note on Translation

Reading literature in translation is a pleasure on which it is fruitless to frown. The purist may insist that we ought always read in the original languages, and we know ideally that he is right. But his counsel is a counsel of perfection, quite impractical even for him, since no man in one lifetime can master all the languages whose literatures he might wish to explore. Master languages as fast as we may, we shall always have to read to some extent in translation, and this means we must be alert to what we are about: if in reading a work of literature in translation we are not reading the "original," what precisely are we reading? This is a question of great complexity, to which justice cannot be done in a brief note. Nevertheless, the following sketch of some of the considerations that a mature answer would involve may be helpful to those who are coming into a self-conscious relation with literature in translation for the first time.

One of the memorable scenes of ancient literature is the meeting of Hector and Andromache in Book VI of Homer's *Iliad*. Hector, leader and mainstay of the armies defending Troy, is implored by his wife Andromache to withdraw within the city walls and carry on the defense from there, where his life will not be constantly at hazard. In Homer's text her opening words to him are these: δαιμόνιε, φθίσει σε τὸ σὸν μένος (daimonie, phthisei se to son menos). How should they be translated into English?

Here is how they have actually been translated into English by capable translators, at various periods, in verse and prose.

1. George Chapman, 1598

> O noblest in desire,
> Thy mind, inflamed with others' good, will set thy self on fire.

2. John Dryden, 1693

> Thy dauntless heart (which I foresee too late),
> Too daring man, will urge thee to thy fate.

3. Alexander Pope, 1715

> Too daring Prince! ...
> For sure such courage length of life denies,
> And thou must fall, thy virtue's sacrifice.

1627

4. William Cowper, 1791

> Thy own great courage will cut short thy days,
> My noble Hector....

5. Lang, Leaf, and Myers, 1883 (prose)

> Dear my lord, this thy hardihood will undo thee....

6. A. T. Murray, 1924 (prose, Loeb Library)

> Ah, my husband, this prowess of thine will be thy doom....

7. E. V. Rieu, 1950 (prose)

> "Hector," she said, "you are possessed. This bravery of yours will be your end."

8. I.A. Richards, 1950 (prose)

> "Strange man," she said, "your courage will be your destruction."

9. Robert Fitzgerald, 1976

> Oh, my wild one, your bravery will be
> your own undoing!

From these strikingly different renderings of the same six words, certain facts about the nature of translation begin to emerge. We notice, for one thing, that Homer's word μένος (menos) is diversified by the translators into "mind," "dauntless heart," "such courage," "great courage," "hardihood," "prowess," "bravery," "courage," and again "bravery." The word has in fact all these possibilities. Used of things, it normally means "force"; of animals, "fierceness" or "brute strength" or (in the case of horses) "mettle"; of men, "passion" or "spirit" or even "purpose." Homer's application of it in the present case points our attention equally—whatever particular sense we may imagine Andromache to have uppermost—to Hector's force, strength, fierceness in battle, spirited heart and mind. But since English has no matching term of like inclusiveness, the passage as the translators give it to us reflects this lack and we find one attribute singled out to the exclusion of the rest.

Here then is the first and most crucial fact about any work of literature read in translation. It cannot escape the linguistic characteristics of the language into which it is turned: the grammatical, syntactical, lexical, and phonetic boundaries which constitute collectively the individuality or "genius" of that language. A Greek play or a Russian novel in English will be governed first of all by the resources of the English language, resources which are certain to be in every instance very different, as the efforts with μένος show, from those of the original.

Turning from μένος to δαιμόνιε (daimonie) in Homer's clause, we encounter a second crucial fact about translations. Nobody knows exactly what shade of meaning δαιμόνιε had for Homer. In later writers the word normally suggests divinity, something miraculous, wondrous; but in Homer it appears as a vocative of address for both chieftain and commoner, man and wife. The coloring one gives it must therefore be determined either by the way one thinks a Greek wife of Homer's era might actually address her husband (a subject on which we have no information whatever), or in the way one thinks it suitable for a hero's wife to address her husband in an epic poem, that is to say, a highly stylized and formal work. In general, the translators of our century will be seen to have eschewed formality in order to stress the intimacy, the wifeliness, and, especially in Fitzgerald's case, a certain motherliness, in Andromache's appeal: (6) "Ah, my husband," (7) "Hector" (with perhaps a hint, in "you are possessed," of the alarmed distaste with which wives have so often viewed their husbands' bellicose moods), (8) "Strange man," (9) "Oh, my wild one." On the other hand, the older translators have obviously removed Andromache to an epic or heroic distance from her beloved, whence she sees and kindles to his selfless courage, acknowledging, even in the moment of pleading with him to be otherwise, his moral grandeur and the tragic destiny this too certainly implies: (1) "On noblest in desire, . . . inflamed by others' good"; (2) "Thy dauntless heart (which I foresee too late), / Too daring man"; (3) "Too daring Prince! . . . / And thou must fall, thy virtue's sacrifice"; (4) "My noble Hector." Even the less specific "Dear my lord" of Lang, Leaf, and Myers looks in the same direction because of its echo of the speech of countless Shakespearean men and women who have shared this powerful moral sense: "Dear my lord, make me acquainted with your cause of grief"; "Perseverance, dear my lord, keeps honor bright"; etc.

The fact about translation which emerges from all this is that just as the translated work reflects the individuality of the language it is turned into, so it reflects the individuality of the age in which it is done, and the age will permeate it everywhere like yeast in dough. We think of one kind of permeation when we think of the governing verse forms and attitudes toward verse at a given epoch. In Chapman's time, experiments seeking an "heroic" verse form for English were widespread, and accordingly he tries a "fourteener" couplet (two rhymed lines of seven stresses each) in his *Iliad* and a pentameter couplet in his *Odyssey*. When Dryden and Pope wrote, a closed pentameter couplet had become established as the heroic form *par excellence*. By Cowper's day, thanks largely to the prestige of *Paradise Lost*, the couplet had gone out of fashion for narrative poetry in favor of blank verse. Our age, inclining to prose and in verse to proselike informalities and relaxations, has, predictably, produced half a dozen excellent prose translations of the *Iliad*, but only two in verse (Fitzgerald's and that of Richmond Lattimore), both relying on rhythms that are much of the time closer to the verse of William Carlos Williams and some of the prose of novelists like Faulkner than to the swift firm tread of Homer's Greek. For if it is true that what we translate from a given work is what, wearing the spectacles of our time, we see in it, it is also true that we see in it what we have the power to translate.

Of course there are other effects of the translator's epoch on his translation besides those exercised by contemporary taste in verse and verse forms. Chapman writes in a great age of poetic metaphor and therefore almost instinctively translates his understanding of Homer's verb φθίσει (phthisei, "to cause to wane, consume, waste, pine") into metaphorical terms of flame, presenting his Hector to us as a man of burning generosity who will be consumed by his very ardor. This is a conception rooted in large part in the psychology of the Elizabethans, who had the habit of speaking of the soul as "fire," of one of the four temperaments as "fiery," of even the more material bodily processes, like digestion, as if they were carried on by the heat of fire ("concoction," "decoction"). It is rooted too in that characteristic Renaissance élan so unforgettably expressed in characters like Tamburlaine and Dr. Faustus, the former of whom exclaims to the stars above:

> ... I, the chiefest lamp of all the earth,
> First rising in the East with mild aspect,
> But fixèd now in the meridian line,
> Will send up fire to your turning spheres,
> And cause the sun to borrow light of you....

Pope and Dryden, by contrast, write to audiences for whom strong metaphor has become suspect. They therefore reject the fire image (which we must recall is not present in the Greek) in favor of a form of speech more congenial to their age, the *sententia* or aphorism, and give it extra vitality by making it the scene of a miniature drama: in Dryden's case, the hero's dauntless heart "urges" him (in the double sense of physical as well as moral pressure) to his fate; in Pope's, the hero's courage, like a judge, "denies" continuance of life, with the consequence that he "falls"—and here Pope's second line suggests analogy to the sacrificial animal—the victim of his own essential nature, of what he is.

To pose even more graphically the pressures that a translator's period brings, consider the following lines from Hector's reply to Andromache's appeal that he withdraw, first in Chapman's Elizabethan version, then in Fitzgerald's twentieth-century one:

Chapman, 1598:
> The spirit I did first breathe
> Did never teach me that—much less since the contempt of death
> Was settled in me, and my mind knew what a Worthy was,
> Whose office is to lead in fight and give no danger pass
> Without improvement. In this fire must Hector's trial shine.
> Here must his country, father, friends be in him made divine.

Fitzgerald, 1976:

> ... Long ago I learned
> how to be brave, how to go forward always
> and to contend for honor, Father's and mine.

If one may exaggerate to make a necessary point, the world of Henry V and Othello suddenly gives way here to our own, a world so embarrassed by heroic language that "to lead in fight" reshapes itself to the much more neutral "to go forward always," while terms of really large implication like "brave" and "honor" are left to jostle uncomfortably against a phrase banal enough to refer easily to a piece of real estate or the family car: "Father's and mine."

Besides the two factors so far mentioned, language and period, as affecting the character of a translation, there is inevitably a third—the translator himself, with his particular degree of talent, his personal way of regarding the work to be translated, his own special hierarchy of values, moral, esthetic, metaphysical (which may or may not be summed up in a "world view"), his unique style or lack of it. But this influence all readers are likely to bear in mind, and it needs no laboring here. That, for example, two translators of Hamlet, one a Freudian, the other an Existentialist, will produce impressively different translations is obvious from the fact that when Freudian and Existentialist argue about the play in English they often seem to have different plays in mind.

We can now return to the question from which we started. After all allowances have been made for language, age, and individual translator, is anything of the original left? What, in short, does the reader of translations read? Let it be said at once that in utility prose —prose whose function is mainly referential—he reads everything that matters. "*Nicht Rauchen*," "*Défense de Fumer*," and "*No Smoking*," posted in a railway car, make their point, and the differences between them in sound and form have no significance for us in that context. Since the prose of a treatise and of most fiction is preponderantly referential, we rightly feel, when we have paid close attention to Cervantes or Montaigne or Machiavelli or Tolstoy in a good English translation, that we have had roughly the same experience as a native Spaniard, Frenchman, Italian, or Russian. But "roughly" is the correct word; for good prose points iconically *to* itself as well as referentially beyond itself, and everything that it points to in itself in the original (rhythms, sounds, idioms, word play, etc.) must alter radically in being translated. The best analogy is to imagine a Van Gogh painting reproduced in the medium of tempera, etching, or engraving: the "picture" remains, but the intricate interanimation of volumes with colorings with brushstrokes has disappeared.

When we move on to poetry, even in its longer narrative and dramatic forms—plays like *Oedipus*, poems like the *Iliad* or the *Divine Comedy*—our situation as English readers worsens appreciably, as the many unlike versions of Andromache's appeal to Hector make very clear. But, again, only appreciably. True, this is the point at which the fact that a translation is *always* an interpretation explodes irresistibly on our attention; but if it is a good translation, the result will be a sensitive interpretation and also a work with intrinsic interest in its own right—at very best, a true work of art, a new poem. It is only when the shorter, primarily lyrical forms of poetry are presented that the reader of translations faces insuperable disadvantage. In these forms, the referential aspect of language has a tendency to disappear into, or, more often, draw its real meaning and accreditation from, the iconic aspect. Let us look for just a moment at a brief poem by Federico García Lorca and its English translation (by Stephen Spender and J. L. Gili):

> *Alto pinar!*
> *Cuatro palomas por el aire van.*
>
> *Cuatro palomas*
> *vuelan y tornan.*
> *Llevan heridas*
> *sus cuatro sombras.*
>
> *Bajo pinar!*
> *Cuatro palomas en la tierra están.*

> Above the pine trees:
> Four pigeons go through the air.
>
> Four pigeons
> fly and turn round.
> They carry wounded
> their four shadows.
>
> Below the pine trees:
> Four pigeons lie on the earth.

In this translation the referential sense of the English words follows with remarkable exactness the referential sense of the Spanish words they replace. But the life of Lorca's poem does not lie in that sense. It lies in such matters as the abruptness, like an intake of breath at a sudden revelation, of the two exclamatory lines (1 and 7), which then exhale musically in images of flight and death; or as the echoings of *palomas* in *heridas* and *sombras*, bringing together (as in fact the hunter's gun has done) these unrelated nouns and the unrelated experiences they stand for in a sequence that seems, momentarily, to have all the logic of a tragic action, in which *doves* become *wounds* become *shadows*; or as the external and internal rhyming among the five verbs, as though all motion must (as in fact it must) end with *están*.

Since none of this can be brought over into another tongue (least of all Lorca's rhythms), the translator must decide between leaving his reader to wonder why Lorca is a poet to be bothered about at all, and making a new but true poem of his own, whose merit will almost certainly be in inverse ratio to its likeness to the original. Samuel Johnson made such a poem in translating Horace's famous *Diffugere nives,* and so did A. E. Housman. If we juxtapose the last two stanzas of each translation, and the corresponding Latin, we can see at a glance that each has the consistency and inner life of a genuine poem, and that neither of them (even if we consider only what is obvious to the eye, the line-lengths) is very close to Horace.

> *Cum semel occideris, et de te splendida Minos*
> *fecerit arbitria,*
> *non, Torquate, genus, non te facundia, non te*
> *restituet pietas.*
>
> *Infernis neque enim tenebris Diana pudicum*
> *liberat Hippolytum*
> *nec Lethaea valet Theseus abrumpere caro*
> *vincula Pirithoo.*

Johnson:

> Not you, Torquatus, boast of Rome,
> When Minos once has fixed your doom,
> Or eloquence, or splendid birth,
> Or virtue, shall restore to earth.
> Hippolytus, unjustly slain,
> Diana calls to life in vain;
> Nor can the might of Theseus rend
> The chains of hell that hold his friend.

Housman:

> When thou descendest once the shades among,
>   The stern assize and equal judgment o'er,
> Not thy long lineage nor thy golden tongue,
>   No, nor thy righteousness, shall friend thee more.
>
> Night holds Hippolytus the pure of stain,
>   Diana steads him nothing, he must stay;
> And Theseus leaves Pirithous in the chain
>   The love of comrades cannot take away.

We may assure ourselves, then, that the reading of literature in translation is not the disaster it has sometimes been represented. It is true that, however good the translation, we remain at a remove from the original, the remove becoming closest to impassable in the genre of the lyric poem. But with this exception, it is obvious that translation brings us closer by far to the work than we could be if we did not read it at all, or read it with a defective knowledge of the language. "To a thousand cavils," said Samuel Johnson, "one answer is sufficient; the purpose of a writer is to be read, and the criticism which would destroy the power of pleasing must be blown aside." Johnson was defending Pope's Homer for those marks of its own time and place that make it the great interpretation it is; but Johnson's exhilarating common sense applies equally to the problem we are considering here. Literature is to be read, and the criticism that would destroy the reader's power to make some form of contact with much of the world's great writing must indeed be blown aside.

MAYNARD MACK

Copyright Notices

Akhmatova: "Requiem," translated by Robin Kemball, copyright 1976 by Ardis, in Anna Akhmatova, *Selected Poems*, edited by Walter Arndt, Ann Arbor: Ardis, 1976.

Baudelaire: "Correspondences" and "I Adore You as Much as the Vault of Night," by Charles Baudelaire, translated by Anthony Hartley, from Brian Woledge, Geoffrey Brereton and Anthony Hartley (eds): *The Penguin Book of French Verse* (Penguin Poets, 1975) © Anthony Hartley, 1957. Reprinted by permission of Penguin Books Ltd. "Jewels," translated by David Paul, Copyright © 1974 by David Paul, reprinted with the permission of David Paul. "Her Hair," translated by Doreen Bell, reprinted with the permission of Michael Bell. "Charles Baudelaire: L'Invitation au voyage," from *Things of This World*, © 1956 by Richard Wilbur. Reprinted by permission of Harcourt Brace Jovanovich, Inc. "Song of Autumn I" and "To a Passer-By" reprinted by permission from *One Hundred Poems from Les Fleurs du mal* by Charles Baudelaire, translated by C. F. MacIntyre, University of California Press, 1947. "Heautontimorou-menos," translated by Naomi Lewis, reprinted with the permission of Naomi Lewis. "Spleen ('I have more memories')" translated by Anthony Hecht, © 1955, 1962 by New Directions; reprinted with the permission of Anthony Hecht. Robert Lowell's English language translation of "Spleen" and "Meditation" by Charles Baudelaire. From *Imitations* by Robert Lowell. Copyright © 1958, 1959, 1960, 1961 by Robert Lowell. reprinted with the permission of Farrar, Straus and Giroux, Inc. "Spleen ('When the low heavy sky')" translated by Sir John Squire, reprinted with the permission of Raglan Squire, sole executor of Sir John Squire. Selections from Charles Baudelaire, *Paris Spleen*, translated by Louise Varese. Copyright © 1947, 1955, 1962, 1970 by New Directions Publishing Corporation. Reprinted by permission of New Directions. "Former Life," from *Poems of Baudelaire*, translated by Roy Campbell. Reprinted courtesy of Hughes Massie Limited. "Spleen ('Old Pluvius')" translated by Kenneth O. Hanson, copyright by Kenneth O. Hanson and reprinted with his permission.

Brecht: "Mother Courage and Her Children," translated by Ralph Manheim. Copyright © 1972 by Stefan S. Brecht. Reprinted from *Collected Plays by Bertolt Brecht, Volume V*, by Bertolt Brecht, by permission of Pantheon Books and Eyre Methuen Ltd.

Breton & Eluard: "Intra-uterine Life," from *The Immaculate Conception*, by André Breton and Paul Eluard. Copyright © 1961 by Pierre Seghers. English translation by John Ashbery, first published in Locus Solus, #2 (Summer 1961). English translation copyright © 1961 by John Ashbery. Reprinted by permission of the translator and Georges Borchardt, Inc.

Büchner: *Woyzeck* from *Georg Büchner: Complete Plays and Prose* translated and with an Introduction by Carl Richard Mueller. Copyright © 1963 by Carl Richard Mueller. Reprinted with the permission of Hill and Wang (now a division of Farrar, Straus & Giroux, Inc.).

Camus: "The Renegade" From *Exile and the Kingdom*, by Albert Camus, translated by Justin O'Brien. Copyright © 1957, 1958 by Alfred A. Knopf, Inc. Reprinted by permission of Alfred A. Knopf, Inc.

Chateaubriand: "René" from *Atala and René*, translated by Irving Putter. Reprinted by permission of the University of California Press.

Chekov: *The Cherry Orchard* from *Anton Chekhov's Plays*, translated and edited by Eugene K. Bristow. Copyright © 1977 by W. W. Norton & Company Inc. and reprinted with their permission.

Colette: "The Cat," from *7 by Colette*, translated by Antonia White. Copyright 1955 by Farrar, Straus and Cudahy, Inc. (now Farrar, Straus and Giroux, Inc.). Reprinted with the permission of Farrar, Straus and Giroux, Inc.

Diderot: "Rameau's Nephew" from *Diderot: Rameau's Nephew and Other Works*, translated by Jacques Barzun and Ralph H. Bowen. Reprinted by permission of Doubleday & Company, Inc.

Dinesen: "Sorrow-Acre" Copyright 1942 by Random House, Inc., and renewed 1970 by Johan Philip Thomas Ingersley. Reprinted from *Winter's Tale*, by Isak Dinesen, by permission of Random House, Inc., The University of Chicago Press, and the Rungstedlund Foundation.

Dostoevsky: "Notes from Underground," from *White Nights and Other Stories* by Fyodor Dostoevsky, translated by Constance Garnett. Reprinted by permission of the publisher, William Heinemann Ltd.

Flaubert: *Madame Bovary* translated by Paul De Man. Copyright © 1965 by W. W. Norton & Company, Inc. Reprinted by permission of the publisher.

Goethe: From Goethe's *Faust*, translated by Louis MacNeice. Copyright 1951 by Louis MacNeice. Reprinted by permission of Oxford University Press, Inc. and Faber and Faber Ltd.

Heine: From *The Poetry and Prose of Heinrich Heine*, selected and edited by Frederic Ewen: "Die Rose, die Lilie, die Taube, die Sonne" translated by Webb, and "Die schlesischen Weber" and "Babylonische Sorgen" translated by Kramer. Published by Citadel Press and reprinted with permission. "Du sollst mich liebend umschliessen" from *Heine* by Meno Spann, published by Bowes & Bowes; reprinted by permission of The Bodley Head. "At Parting" by Heinrich Heine from *An Anthology of German Poetry from Holderlin to Rilke in English Translation*, edited by Angel Flores; reprinted with the permission of Angel Flores. "Ein Jüngling liebt ein Mädchen," "Ich weiss nicht, was soll es bedeuten," "Der Asra," "Wie langsam kriechet sie dahin," "Die Wanderratten," and "Morphine." Reprinted from *Heinrich Heine—Lyric Poems and Ballads*, translated by Ernst Feise, by permission of the University of Pittsburgh Press, © 1961 by the University of Pittsburgh Press. "A Spruce Is Standing Lonely", translated by Max Knight & Joseph Fabry, from *Heinrich Heine: Selected Works*, edited by Helen Mustard. Copyright © 1973 by Random House, Inc. Reprinted by permission of Random House, Inc.

Ibsen: *Hedda Gabler* reprinted by permission of Harold Ober Associates Incorporated.

1636 · Copyright Notices

Copyright © 1961 by Michael Meyer. This translation of *Hedda Gabler* is the sole property of the translator and is fully protected by copyright. It may not be acted by professionals or amateurs without formal permission and the payment of a royalty. All rights including professional, amateur, stock, radio and television broadcasting, motion picture, recitation, lecturing, public reading, and the rights of translation in foreign languages are reserved. All enquiries should be addressed to the translator's agent: Margaret Ramsay, Ltd., 14A Goodwin's Court, St. Martin's Lane, London W.C. 2, England.

Kafka: "The Metamorphosis" Reprinted by permission of Schocken Books Inc. from *The Penal Colony* by Franz Kafka. Copyright © 1948, 1975 by Schocken Books Inc.

La Fontaine: From *The Fables of La Fontaine*, translated by Marianne Moore. Copyright 1954 by Marianne Moore. Reprinted by permission of Viking Penguin Inc.

Lermontov: "Princess Mary" from *A Hero of Our Time* by Mikhail Lermontov, translated by Vladimir Nabokov in collaboration with Dimitri Nabokov. Copyright © 1958 by Vladimir & Dimitri Nabokov. Reprinted by permission of Doubleday & Company, Inc.

Mallarmé: Selections from *Poems* by Stephane Mallarmé, translated by Roger Fry. Reprinted with the permission of Pamela Diamond and Chatto & Windus.

Mann: "Tonio Kröger" Copyright 1936 and renewed 1964 by Alfred A. Knopf, Inc. Reprinted from *Stories of Three Decades*, by Thomas Mann, translated by H. T. Lowe Porter, by permission of Alfred A. Knopf, Inc.

Molière: *Tartuffe*, translated by Richard Wilbur, © 1961, 1962, 1963 by Richard Wilbur. Reprinted by permission of Harcourt Brace Jovanovich, Inc. CAUTION: Professionals and amateurs are hereby warned that this translation, being fully protected under the copyright laws of the United States of America, the British Empire, including the Dominion of Canada, and all other countries which are signatories to the Universal Copyright Convention and the International Copyright Union, is subject to royalty. All rights, including professional, amateur, motion picture, recitation, lecturing, public reading, radio broadcasting, and television, are strictly reserved. Inquiries on professional rights should be addressed to Mr. Gilbert Parker, Curtis Brown Brown Ltd., 575 Madison Avenue, New York, New York 10022. Inquiries on translation rights should be addressed to Harcourt Brace Jovanovich, Inc., 757 Third Avenue, New York, New York 10017.

Nabokov: "Cloud, Castle, Lake" copyright © 1941 by The Atlantic Monthly Company from *Nabokov's Dozen* by Vladimir Nabokov. Reprinted by permission of Doubleday & Company, Inc.

Péret: "A Life Full of Interest" by Benjamin Péret, from *The Custom House of Desire*, edited by J. H. Matthews. Reprinted by permission of the University of California Press.

Pirandello: *Henry IV* from *Naked Masks: Five Plays*, edited by Eric Bentley. Copyright, 1922, by E. P. Dutton & Co., Inc. Renewal, 1950, in the names of Stefano, Fausto, & Lisetta Pirandello. Reprinted by permission of the publisher, E. P. Dutton.

Proust: "Swann's Way: Overture" from *Remembrance of Things Past*, by Marcel Proust, translated by C. K. Scott Moncrieff. Copyright 1934 and renewed 1952 by Random House, Inc. Reprinted by permission of Random House, Inc., the Estate of C. K. Scott Moncrieff and Chatto & Windus Ltd.

Pushkin: From *Eugene Onegin* by Alexander Pushkin, translated by Walter Arndt. Copyright © 1953 by Walter Arndt. Reprinted by permission of the publisher, E. P. Dutton.

Racine: *Phaedra* by Jean Racine from *Phaedra and Figaro* translated by Robert Lowell. Copyright © 1960, 1961 by Robert Lowell. Reprinted by permission of Farrar, Straus & Giroux, Inc.

Rilke: "Duino Elegy III" from *Duino Elegies* by Rainer Maria Rilke, translated by David Young. Copyright © 1978 by W. W. Norton & Company, Inc. Reprinted by permission of W. W. Norton & Company, Inc., the author's literary estate, and The Hogarth Press.

Rimbaud: "Night of Hell," "Morning," "Farewell" from *A Season in Hell*, "III, Tale," "XI, Morning of Drunkenness," "XIV, The Bridges," "XXIII, Flowers," "XXV, Seascape," "XXIX, Barbarian" from *The Illuminations*. From *A Season in Hell: The Illuminations* by Arthur Rimbaud; a new translation by Enid Rhodes Peschel. Copyright © 1973 by Oxford University Press, Inc. Reprinted by permission. "The Lice-Hunters" by Arthur Rimbaud from *Imitations* by Robert Lowell. Copyright © 1958, 1959, 1960, 1961 by Robert Lowell. Reprinted by permission of Farrar, Straus & Giroux, Inc. "Lice-Hunters" by Arthur Rimbaud, from Ezra Pound, *Translations*. Copyright © 1963 by Ezra Pound. Reprinted by permission of New Directions. "The Seekers of Lice" from *Complete Works of Arthur Rimbauld*, translated by Wallace Fowlie, published by The University of Chicago Press; reprinted with the permission of the publisher.

Sartre: "No Exit" from *No Exit and the Flies*, by Jean-Paul Sartre, translated by Stuart Gilbert. Copyright 1946 by Stuart Gilbert. Reprinted by permission of Alfred A. Knopf, Inc.

Singer: "The Gentleman from Cracow" from *Gimpel the Fool and Other Stories* by Isaac Bashevis Singer. Copyright © 1957 by Isaac Bashevis Singer. Reprinted with the permission of Farrar, Straus & Giroux, Inc.

Strindberg: *The Ghost Sonata* from *Six Plays by Strindberg*, translated by Elizabeth Sprigge. Reprinted by permission of Curtis Brown, Ltd. Copyright © 1955 by Elizabeth Sprigge.

Tolstoy: From *The Death of Ivan Ilych* by Leo Tolstoy, translated by Louise and Aylmer Maude and published by Oxford University Press (1935). Reprinted by permission of the publisher.

Voltaire: *Candide, or Optimism* translated with notes by Robert A. Adams. Copyright © 1966 by W. W. Norton & Company, Inc. Reprinted by permission of Robert M. Adams.

Index

Afternoon of a Faun, The: Eclogue (Mallarmé), 1169

Akhmatova, Anna (1889–1966), 1117, 1143, 1488

All the Soul Indrawn . . . (Mallarmé), 1174

Another Fan (Mallarmé), 1168

Asra, The (Heine), 419

At Parting (Heine), 423

Babylonian Sorrows (Heine), 420

Bad Glazier, The (Baudelaire), 1162

Barbarian (Rimbaud), 1188

Baudelaire, Charles (1821–1867), 1091, 1135, 1151

Beauty (Baudelaire), 1152

Brecht, Bertolt (1898–1956), 1122, 1146, 1497

Breton, André (1896–1966), 1119, 1145, 1495

Bridges, The (Rimbaud), 1187

Büchner, Georg (1813–1837), 261, 270, 469

Camus, Albert (1913–1960), 1132, 1150, 1614

Candide, or Optimism (Voltaire), 133

Cat, The (Colette), 1302

Chateaubriand, François René de (1768–1848), 250, 267, 371

Chekhov, Anton (1860–1904), 583, 590, 1042

Chercheuses de poux, Les (Rimbaud), 1176

Cherry Orchard, The (Chekhov), 1042

Cloud, Castle, Lake (Nabokov), 1156

Colette, Sidonie-Gabrielle (1873–1954), 1105, 1139, 1302

Confessions (Rousseau), 273

Correspondences (Baudelaire), 1151

Death of Iván Ilyich, The (Tolstoy), 934

Diderot, Denis (1713–1784), 13, 18, 210

Dinesen, Isak (1885–1962), 1114, 1142, 1462

Dostoevsky, Fyodor (1821–1881), 569, 587, 846

Double Room, The (Baudelaire), 1161

Drunken Boat, The (Rimbaud), 1178

Duino Elegy III (Rilke), 1417

Éluard, Paul (1895–1952), 1119, 1144, 1495

Et nox facta est (Hugo), 462

Eugene Onegin (Pushkin), 424

Fables (La Fontaine), 128

Farewell (Rimbaud), 1184

Faust (Goethe), 283

Flaubert, Gustave (1821–1880), 564, 587, 591

Flowers (Rimbaud), 1188

Flowers of Evil, The (Baudelaire), 1151

Former Life (Baudelaire), 1151

Gentleman from Cracow, The (Singer), 1567

Ghost Sonata, The (Strindberg), 1189

Goethe, Johann Wolfgang von (1749–1832), 246, 266, 283

Heautontimoroumenos (Baudelaire), 1156

Hedda Gabler (Ibsen), 981

Heine, Heinrich (1797–1856), 254, 268, 416

Henry IV (Pirandello), 1215

Her Hair (Baudelaire), 1153

Hoffman, E. T. A. (1776–1822), 252, 267, 393

How Slowly Time, the Loathsome Snail (Heine), 421

Hugo, Victor-Marie (1802–1885), 258, 269, 459

I Adore You as Much ... (Baudelaire), 1154

Ibsen, Henrik (1828–1906), 578, 589, 981

Illuminations, The (Rimbaud), 1190

Immaculate Conception, The (Breton and Éluard), 1495

Intra-Uterine Life (Breton and Éluard), 1495

Invitation au Voyage, L' (Baudelaire), 1164

Invitation to the Voyage (Baudelaire), 1154

Jewels (Baudelaire), 1152

Kafka, Franz (1883–1924), 1112, 1142, 1422

La Fontaine, Jean de (1621–1695) 8, 17, 128

Lace Curtain, A ... (Mallarmé) 1175

Lermontov, Mikhail Yurievich (1814–1841), 264, 271, 492

Lice-Hunters (Rimbaud/Pound), 1177

Lice-Hunters, The (Rimbaud/Lowell), 1178

Life Full of Interest, A (Péret), 1563

Loreley (Heine), 417

Madame Bovary (Flaubert), 591

Mallarmé, Stéphane (1848–1898), 1093, 1135, 1167

Mann, Thomas (1875–1955), 1107, 1140, 1371

Maxims (Rochefoucauld), 124

Meditation (Baudelaire), 1160

Memory of the Night of the Fourth (Hugo), 460

Metamorphosis, The (Kafka), 1422

Migratory Rats, The (Heine), 421

Molière, Jean-Baptiste Poquelin (1622–1673), 5, 15, 19

Morning (Rimbaud), 1184

Morning of Drunkenness (Rimbaud), 1187

Morphine (Heine), 423

Mother Courage and Her Children (Brecht), 1497

My Beauty, My Love, You Have Bound Me (Heine), 418

Nabokov, Vladimir (1899–1977), 1125, 1147, 1566

New Year's Eve Adventure, A (Hoffmann), 393

Night of Hell (Rimbaud), 1182

No Exit (Sartre), 1581

Notes from Underground (Dostoevsky), 846

Paris Spleen (Baudelaire), 1164

Péret, Benjamin (1899–1959), 1119, 1147, 1563

Phaedra (Racine), 80

Pirandello, Luigi (1867–1936), 1100, 1138, 1215

Princess Mary (Lermontov), 492

Proust, Marcel (1871–1922), 1102, 1138, 1259

Pushkin Alexander Sergeyevich (1799–1837), 257, 269, 424

Racine, Jean (1639–1680), 6, 16, 80

Rameau's Nephew (Diderot), 210

Remembrance of Things Past (Proust), 1259

René (Chateaubriand), 371

Renegade, The (Camus), 1614

Requiem (Akhmatova), 1488

Reverie (Hugo), 459

Rilke, Rainer Maria (1875–1926), 1111, 1141, 1417

Rimbaud, Arthur (1854–1891), 1093, 1136, 1176

Rochefoucauld, François, Duc de la (1613–1680), 7, 17, 124

Rose, the Lily, the Sun and the Dove, The (Heine), 416

Rousseau, Jean-Jacques (1712–1778), 239, 266, 273

Saint (Mallarmé), 1172
Sartre, Jean-Paul (1905–   ), 1129, 1149, 1581
Sea Breeze (Mallarmé), 1167
Seascape (Rimbaud), 1188
Season in Hell, A (Rimbaud), 1182
Seekers of Lice, The (Rimbaud), 1176
Silesian Weavers, The (Heine), 418
Singer, Isaac Bashevis (1904–   ), 1127, 1148, 1567
Song of Autumn I (Baudelaire), 1156
Sonnet ("This virgin, beautiful and lively day") (Mallarmé), 1173
Sorrow-Acre (Dinesen), 1462
Sowing Season. Evening (Hugo), 468
Spleen ("I have more memories") (Baudelaire), 1157
Spleen ("I'm like the king of a rain-country") (Baudelaire), 1158
Spleen ("Old Pluvius, month of rains") (Baudelaire), 1157
Spleen ("When the low heavy sky weighs like a lid") (Baudelaire), 1159
Spruce Is Standing Lonely, A (Heine), 417

Stranger, The (Baudelaire), 1160
Strindberg, August (1849–1912), 1097, 1137, 1189
Swann's Way: Overture (Proust), 1277

Tale (Rimbaud), 1186
Tartuffe, or The Imposter (Molière), 19
This virgin, beautiful and lively day (Mallarmé), 1177
Tired of the Bitter Repose (Mallarmé), 1167
To a Passer-By (Baudelaire), 1159
Tolstoy, Leo (1828–1910), 575, 588, 934
Tomb of Edgar Poe, The (Mallarmé), 1173, 1174
Tomorrow, at Daybreak (Hugo), 460
Tonio Kröger (Mann), 1371

Voltaire, François-Marie Arouet de (1694–1778), 11, 17, 133

Windows (Baudelaire), 1166
Woyzeck (Büchner), 469

Young Man Loves a Maiden, A (Heine), 417